UNIVERSAL ACCLAIM FOR OLD SCHOOL BOOKS

"The latest selections soar on deft prose, wicked plots, hell-bent characters, and wry insight . . . just the kind of iconoclastic fiction we can now count on from Old School Books."

—*Kirkus Reviews*

"[The editors] have unearthed a motherload of revelation; a shadow tradition of hot-wired prose playing its own variations on noir with bebop abandon and rhythm-and-blues momentum." —*Newsday*

"One of the most exciting literary revival series since the rediscovery of Jim Thompson novels." —*Playboy*

"With any luck, the legacy of the Old School Books will not be lost again." —*USA Today*

"[Old School Books] is subtly transforming the landscape of post-War black fiction . . . proving idiosyncratic and essential."

—*Bomb*

"These novels are hard-core, not to be sensational, but in an attempt to examine issues of real concern and substance in our communities that were not being addressed in mainstream literature."

—*Emerge*

"Issues of race, though fundamental, do not cloud the humanity of these Old School Books. Rays of genius flow from their pages . . . and without exception, the Old School will give the modern

reader a wake-up slap, alerting them to a subversive canon too long ignored."
—*Detour Magazine*

"They take the brutality and ruin of the urban black landscape and transform them into art."
—*The Source*

"The missing link between Richard Wright agitprop and Donald Goines pimp-lit, these late 50s/early 60s novels offset cultural moments, rejecting the early civil rights movement's optimism, but also refusing the Black Panther's romanticism of gunplay-as-revolution. Which isn't to say they're no fun—every author stirs in enough sex, drugs, and violence to keep you turning the pages."
—*Spin*

"Unflinching biographies of the streets . . . a bloodsoaked landmark of crime fiction."
—*Time Out London*

S.R.O.

OLD SCHOOL BOOKS

edited by Marc Gerald and Samuel Blumenfeld

Black! CLARENCE COOPER, JR.

The Scene CLARENCE COOPER, JR.

Daddy Cool DONALD GOINES

The End of a Primitive CHESTER HIMES

Yesterday Will Make You Cry CHESTER HIMES

The School on 103rd Street ROLAND S. JEFFERSON

Portrait of a Young Man Drowning CHARLES PERRY

Giveadamn Brown ROBERT DEANE PHARR

S.R.O. ROBERT DEANE PHARR

Corner Boy HERBERT SIMMONS

Man Walking on Eggshells HERBERT SIMMONS

The Jones Men VERN E. SMITH

Dead Piano HENRY VAN DYKE

The Angry Ones JOHN A. WILLIAMS

ROBERT DEANE PHARR

S.R.O.

Old School Books

W · W · Norton & Company

New York · London

Printed in the United States of America

The text of this book is composed in Sabon
with the display set in Stacatto 555 and Futura.
Composition by Crane Typesetting Service, Inc.
Manufacturing by Courier Companies, Inc.
Book design by Jack Meserole.

Library of Congress Cataloging-in-Publication Data
Pharr, Robert Deane.
S.R.O. / Robert Deane Pharr.
p. cm.—(Old school books)
ISBN 0-393-31706-4 (pbk.)
I. Title. II. Series.
PS3566.H33S7 1998
813′.54—dc21 97-32047
CIP

W. W. Norton & Company, Inc., 500 Fifth Avenue, New York, N.Y. 10110
http://www.wwnorton.com

W. W. Norton & Company Ltd., 10 Coptic Street, London WC1A 1PU

1 2 3 4 5 6 7 8 9 0

ROBERT DEANE PHARR

It is easy to envision the conversation Robert Deane Pharr must have had with his original editor when he proposed *S.R.O.,* a novel that gamely follows the gloomy lives of a half-dozen residents in a rat trap of a Harlem, single room occupancy hotel.

Just a few years earlier, Pharr had struck literary gold with his first novel, *The Book of Numbers,* a work that chronicled the bloody rise of a small-town gambling kingpin. Brutal but breezy, *Numbers* was the kind of book that managed to keep its integrity while appealing to a mass audience.

"What are you, crazy? How are we going to sell this thing?"

"That's your problem."

There is evidence that Pharr (and Doubleday Books) paid a high price for his Kamikaze approach to his literary career—but from the little we've been able to find out about the author, it appears he didn't give a damn.

A career waiter, Pharr was fifty-three when he published *The Book of Numbers,* and he would go on to do three more books—*The Welfare Bitch, The Soul Murder Case,* and *Giveadamn Brown*—in the years after *S.R.O.* Each cast light on a black America invisible to all but its inhabitants; each were demanding works, characterized by their hell-bent prose, wicked humor, and brass-knuckled plots. In retrospect, it is easy to see his mission as crazy and self-defeating, the kind of retreat from success that leaves you shaking your head and wondering why.

We don't have the answers, but thanks to the good folks at W. W. Norton, we are pleased to give you *S.R.O.* in its unblemished entirety. Will it do any better the second time around? God knows, we'd like to think so. But commercial prospects aside, it's safe to say you may read a lot of books this year but you won't read anything like this one.

S.R.O.

Let Him Drink, and Forget His Poverty, and Remember His Misery No More.

PROVERBS 31:7

CHAPTER 1

THE SUBWAY LURCHED into 125th Street and Broadway and I got off and made it over to Amsterdam Avenue. As soon as I turned left and headed up, the damn hill began to get me. Too weak to curse out loud, I plodded on, each step a separate agony. My dizziness increased; it was only moments before I'd get the blind staggers. At the curb of 121st Street I missed my step and almost fell. I paused a minute to get myself together, wondering if I could make the rest of the way on nerve alone.

At 119th Street I looked up and, yeah, there it was. The Hotel Logan. I was so goddam twisted I hadn't been sure, but there it was. And it didn't look any worse than it had four years ago. Maybe better even. And there weren't any Black or Spanish winos loitering about. So maybe that meant peace and quiet inside. But just maybe.

All these managers believe in putting a prospective tenant on the defensive. "Why'd you leave the place you was living at?"

"I work late nights," I told him, trying hard to hang in there for just a few more minutes. "And I don't go for this coming home and finding that some bastard has broken in and stole all I got including the toothbrush."

Realizing he was now sort of on the defensive, the elderly guy took time out to reassess me—a middle-aged Black, obviously at the tail end of a monstrous drunk. I stood my ground while he was looking me over, and thought a prayer of thanks for my suit and raincoat, both saying they were too good for a Welfare drunkard. And I *did* have a job. He could check that out on the phone.

"I got a room you'd be crazy for," he finally said. "It's one of the C rooms. All the C rooms is alike, but on the fifth floor you gotta unlock the foyer door before you can get in the hallway where the rooms are at. Ya see?"

I didn't see anything. But the old man rambled on as a hot, sticky sweat began to ooze from every pore in my body. Even my scalp itched. And what the devil kind of game was this slick old bird trying to run on me anyway? Sales talks don't go with rooms in "hotels" like this, even if the place was still mostly white.

But I knew I had to stand there and take it. This was the end of the rope. With the money I had left in my pocket and the condition I was in, there weren't many rooms I could get except maybe in the roughest part of Harlem, or a rathole like the Duane or Cambridge House, and my nerves just couldn't stand all that noise, blood and stickups.

The manager finally took a bunch of keys off the wall and unlocked the door of his barred office. After he emerged he relocked the door and beckoned for me to follow as he led the way to the elevator.

When we stepped off into the foyer on the fifth floor I was reminded that the Logan had once been a rather fine apartment house with five spacious apartments on each of its six floors. The front doors of the former apartments still hung like badges of shame. And I knew that behind each door was a warren of six hotel rooms plus a community kitchen and bath. The place had long since been cut up into a single-room-occupancy hotel. There are specific laws governing the operation of these makeshift hotels. But no hotel operator in his right mind has ever heeded the meaning or the letter of these laws for S.R.O.s.

Actually it was simply impossible, but maybe the Logan had escaped its own fate. For now, at the middle of the sixties, all S.R.O.s were turning into Welfare joints, catering in the main to the male and female tramps who suckled at the giant teats of the Welfare Department. Yet I hadn't seen a boot or a spic. Of course I knew that some were around. There'd been a few four years ago. So there had to be some now, but at least it would seem that this wasn't a bucket of blood . . . yet.

A dull-witted woman came out of one of the doors to my left and buttonholed the manager. She began to blather about somebody had puked all over the toilet seat in 5-B. And wanted to know what anybody was going to do about it this time.

I had no choice but to ignore the warning. This Logan had to be it for now. Yeah. It was the Logan now for better or worse. So while the manager and the old woman rapped on, I forced myself to contemplate the five doors that faced onto the foyer. Those doors were lettered from A to E, and the number of the floor preceded the letter. Thus the two doors to my left were 5-A and 5-B. I stood facing 5-C, which was directly in front of the elevator, and to my right were 5-D and 5-E. There was an extension phone on the wall next to 5-C and I recalled that the office summoned you for your phone calls by sounding a buzzer in your room.

The woman went away, and the manager waved at the doors to both sides of him. "Them doors can't be locked no more," he sneered. "You just heard what can happen when anybody can come walking down your hall and use the can. Now these here rooms are different." He unlocked the 5-C door and we stepped into a dim-lit hallway.

Directly facing us was the community kitchen, so named because all who lived in this 5-C sector had an equal right to its use. The first door to the right of the kitchen was the bath, and past that were the doors of rooms 5-C-5 and 5-C-6. The manager led the way to the first door on the other side of the kitchen, 5-C-4, and unlocking this door, proudly showed me the room. It was a bigger room than I'd had the last time around.

"Thirteen ninety-five a week and you don't hafta pay no city tax," the old man said. "And I know I don't have to tell you you got as much right as the next to use that box in the kitchen, but I can see that you're the type of man that likes his own things. Now, if you want, I can put a refrigerator right here in your room. Five bucks a month. And you don't hafta pay in advance like the rent."

"I eat on the job," I told him, "but I always got to have my ice water. And I'm not intending to risk drinking out of a bottle some psycho went and pissed in just for kicks. So put one in."

We went back down and straightened things out. Once back in the room I went to the dresser and emptied my pockets—a comb and stocking cap, a toothbrush and all the other sundry things a man stuffs in his pockets when he knows he is going to be locked out of his hotel room. There were four dollar bills and some change.

I went to the bed and stretched out, and again I was bathed in sweat. I remember reaching in my pocket for a handkerchief, and then remembering that I'd put it on the dresser. I turned over and rubbed my face in the pillow instead. And that's when the pictures started.

Inside my head, right behind my eyeballs, was the whirr of a motion picture projector gone mad. It was the form of delirium tremens that I was prone to. Every time I began to come off a drunk like this one, an unholy imagery would dance before my every gaze. And you simply can't explain the torture of having to look at a movie of receiving a wicked massage from a nurse who had poisonous snakes for arms. Or a coal-black dog, bigger than a pony, grinning at you sweetly before going rabid and attacking you. Or Black Panthers shooting at you because you are an educated pussy. And those bullets were for real.

It's not exactly like hallucinations or bad dreams. I am always fully conscious and aware of the fact that the pictures are just pictures. That's what makes them so ungodly.

And I had to stare at them. Nothing would make them go away. With my eyes wide open they were there. I could stare at any object in the room and see it clearly, but superimposed over that object would be these delirious photos.

With all my might I stared at a crack in the ceiling, but I couldn't outstare the pictures of Alise's rachitic legs with calves thrown back. That's how Alise stood. Then I saw her face. Her smile of triumph. It is the most humiliating thing in the world to be told by a razor-legged woman that your services are no longer required.

I turned on my side and saw a woman with hideously white skin, milking her breasts. It was just like she was jerking off, only it was green pus coming out of those tiny teats and splattering on my face. I rolled over on my back and used every muscle in my head to bulge my eyes and outstare those pictures, but they still came.

A chilling moment of peace came. As I thought of Kim, the wonderful kid I'd knocked up in college. But she'd given me an annulment like she'd promised soon after the baby was born. It was because she knew I was on my way to becoming a periodic drunk that she'd given me that annulment so willingly.

The hot sweats turned cold. I shivered. One of these days I was going to go stark raving mad from drinking gin. Twenty-four hours without a single drink and I was still woozy, still half drunk, and the worst was yet to come. Another day without a drink and I would sink into a three-day siege of nervous prostration, coupled with crapulence, colitis and fear.

Then I began to worry: how long would that goddam Hotel Rex hold my things? It would take a taxi and a good-sized tip in advance to get all my stuff hauled way uptown here. And I'd already hocked my watch and overcoat to be able to pay for this room. Somehow I was going to have to make it until Sunday with only four lousy dollars and change. And out of that I still had to buy two bottles of Kaopectate.

Now the pictures in my head became a grotesque review of every foolish thing I had done during my three-week binge. I was made to look at photos of every Bowery stray I had drunk with on Sixth Avenue, from Fifteenth Street to Forty-second. Hell. I'd even gone over on Eighth Avenue. I'd forgotten all about that, but there were the goddam pictures of me standing in a bar on Eighth, telling a damn lie about I was a writer looking for local color. Every time I got blotto I told that one.

Then the crazy machine in my head took me back to the Rex, and I relived the puking on top of puking every night until I fell into an exhausted coma of sleep. Only to wake up in a few hours, craving more gin, and the bars wouldn't be open yet.

I trembled as my eyes filled with tears. But what goddam right did Sid Bailey have to cry? Wasn't it his goddam money that bought the goddam ignorant-oil? And nobody'd put a gun to my head and told me to drink it.

And it'd been that goddam oil that made me curse out the manager of the Rex, a damned nice Greek who never pushed a workingman too hard for the rent. I must have raised all kinds of hell to have made the guy so disgusted he wouldn't accept any more rent. Wouldn't take rent from a man he knew from experience was going to be too sick to raise any more hell for days.

Whiskey and a no-good woman had been the cause of it all. Hell. Whiskey and a no-good woman was the story of my life ever since that annulment I thought I wanted and had received. And these last five years since I'd loosed and been loosed by Alise had been the living end. Whiskey, no-good women and Lundy's.

Nothing but whores and barflies. There's no torture on earth worse than that feeling of loneliness you get after laying up with one of those. And you've got to be over thirty-five to know what loneliness really is in New York City. And you got to be a guy who likes to drink in bars. Hell. Lots of crimes are committed by barflies who are just too lonely not to.

Suddenly I realized that the pictures had stopped, and no sooner had I realized this than they started up all over again. I had to step over raging gila monsters to get to the desk to cuss out the night clerk in the Rex. The guy had been trying to do me a favor when he told that beat-up junky broad that she couldn't go up to my room at three in the morning. He knew that she was only interested in my watch and wallet. But you couldn't tell *me* that. Hell no.

But it wasn't all exactly like it looked. Hell. Actually I'd only played my part of being a Lundy's waiter, trying to break out of my prison. Yeah. Each and every Lundy's waiter lived in a prison cell and you had to take your kicks where you found them. And when a guy's job demands that you work from five in the afternoon until after midnight, and you've got to make time every weekend and holiday, where the hell are you going to find your sport except in the gutter? And in a damn bottle? That's why it's no accident that over half the apes who work at Lundy's are self-made queers and/or part-time junkies to boot.

And for why?

Why do so many black-assed healthy men like to work at Lundy's?

And how come all the real faggots who worked at Lundy's had good wives or steady boy friends while we so-called normal men lived in one dreary hotel room after another?

I saw Alise's legs again. How could I have married a woman with legs like that? And how could a woman built like that find so many different men? Alise wasn't ever lonely. Not for a goddam minute was *she* ever lonely.

Alise's legs went away, and now I was looking down at my own stinking corpse. Nobody would bury me, and the stench rose from my dead body in visible waves.

The real DTs were getting ready to set in now. And I knew that only a thin blue line separated me from Bellevue, and that I ought to crawl out of bed and take the blade out of my razor and toss it out the window, but I was getting more feeble by the minute. I might even fall out the window.

However, I did try to summon my strength to get up and then suddenly collapsed in a shivering heap of fear because for the first time I realized all the activity going on right outside my door. People on top of people had knocked at that foyer door, only a few paces from my own. And every one had been admitted.

And those voices! Loud, profane, Black and country. What the hell was 5-C anyhow? Some kind of nip joint? But—hell!—the bars and liquor stores were still open. I tried to tell myself that all that coming and going was just one more phase of my DTs. And to prove it I got out of bed and crept to my door and listened. It was real. Those Black folks and their voices were for real!

And worst of all was the knowledge that not every voice was loud. Lots of times the person who was admitted was led close to my door. Then there were whispers. And the whispers were more sinister than the loudness. Those whispers were evil. And their evilness crept under my doorsill. Evil encompassed the room. Its fingers grabbed at my throat. Hardly able to breathe, and crying now that I knew my time had come, I fell to my knees and crawled back to bed and waited.

SCENE I

DIRECTLY OVER SID a man was eating cookies as he wandered about his room. The cookies were small chocolate-covered morsels, but the man opened his mouth as wide as possible before taking each sharklike bite, and he chomped many times on every mouthful. His chomping was like the warning of a dog's growl. Even after the last of a cookie had been swallowed the man continued to chew as if it gave him a sensual satisfaction. His lips smacked with a loud plopping sound.

When the cookies were gone he took out a cigarette. He inspected it and then rolled it between the palms of his hands. After that he meticulously tapped both ends, one after the other. He waited until the match was flaming evenly before touching it to the cigarette. Men have learned to kill time like this in Elmira, Sing Sing and Dannemora.

He smoked as he had eaten the cookies, sucking in each lungful and holding it for a long time before exhaling through his flat nose. Now and then he would stop his pacing to inspect his heavy black face in the mirror, and with evident satisfaction he would purse his lips as he delicately fingered his conked hair with his left hand. The one that bore the outsize zircon.

Sometimes, after looking in the mirror, he would go to the closet and gently stroke the suits hanging there. A look of genuine sorrow seemed to come to his eyes as he noted the tiny cigarette burns here and there on his clothes. Although they had all been bought hot, every one of the suits would have retailed for more than a hundred and fifty dollars. But like the clothes of all junkies, who are the world's most careless smokers, they were not pawnable in an emergency.

He took off his shirt and smelled it. It was soiled, but he hung it carefully in the closet. There was another shirt on a hanger that was just as dirty as the one he had taken off, but dingy as it was, he put it on with the air of a man who is fastidiously dressing for the evening.

It was an essentially empty room, but it was this man's home. This is where his clothes were. The closet bulged with suits he changed several times a day.

He glanced at his wrist and swore under his breath; his watch was in pawn. As if to reassure himself of his worth, he pulled a small bundle of glassine packets from his pocket. The packets looked like those that contain proprietary headache powders, and in them was a white crystalline substance. Heroin.

He raised his left leg like a urinating dog and scratched his crotch. His thick lips formed a soundless Aaah of pleasure. Suddenly he frowned. Where the hell were those two stupid kids? Those two dumb diddy-bop punks! Sometimes it didn't pay to have a great brain if you had to waste it on little punks who had to have two sticks of pot before they had sense enough to follow the simplest instructions on how to make a sting. Even a small sting like this one.

It would be easy, he'd told them. Just walk in and announce their business, and tell the refugee and his wife to stand still. The refugee was smart. Those German camps had taught him his smarts, and that chick he'd just married was pretty as hell. Too much of a fox to want to get hurt. But the bitch had looked freakish as hell, and he wondered if the kids might take the notion to try it out in the back room. He swore aloud even as he told himself that the punks were not that dumb. They would stick to business because this was their first chance to work with a guy like himself, an all-round fast cat.

One of the boys came into the room without knocking. He was greasy with sweat and out of breath. His lips were twisted like a man who is crying, but his eyes were dry and didn't seem afraid.

"Well?"

"It was easy. And then that sonofabitching Ronnie started shooting."

The man's mouth opened in disbelief. His hand went to the pocket that held the bundle of heroin, as all he could think of right now was that his habit was in danger. Later on he would have to think about the Sinman's gun. No. He would have to think about the Sinman now because he was probably going to need that whitey to beat the frame the pigs were sure to try. Yeah. He had to get to the Sinman right away; the very thought of having to spend time in the lockup without any narco terrified him. He was too strung out to have to take any long questioning from the pigs.

He turned to the boy. "Both of them?"

"I don't know. My back was turned; I was at the cash register. When Ronnie started blasting, I took off."

"And you left the bread?"

The youth took some money from out of his coat pocket. About fifty dollars. "I wasn't that scared. He wasn't shooting at me. Jesus. That dumb Ronnie."

"But you come right here to the Logan, didn't you? You didn't take the D train to Fifty-ninth Street like I tole you, and then come back up Broadway?"

"Yes, I did. I got off at 125th and walked. Ain't I been gone long enough for that?"

The door opened and Ronnie came in. He was still dazed. "Jesus," he whispered.

"I never tole you to waste that Jew bastard," the man said to the boy.

"Jesus. Are you crazy? Why would I shoot the motherfucker?"

Blinded in a rage of terror, the man flashed a knife and drove it into the boy's stomach two times. The boy grunted and stepped back, but the man closed in and began to wrestle him for the gun in his waistband.

"I didn't shoot him, man," the boy gasped. "His wife did."

CHAPTER 2

I'LL NEVER KNOW HOW I made it through those seventy-two hours of pure unadulterated hell, but I made it. And on Sunday morning I was feeling pretty good and hungry enough to eat a Christmas dinner. And believe it or not it was great to get back to the normalcy of slaving over tables in the world's largest restaurant. Yeah. It was great because at least for eight hours a day I was free of loneliness and hate for Alise.

So in two days time I was also back in my old rut of sobriety, which is so bitterly boring for a part-time alcoholic.

Each morning I got up around ten and soon after made it out to the bar on the corner of Columbus and Ninety-seventh Street to put in my numbers. After that I'd go over to the Duane Hotel or the Cambridge House on Ninety-ninth to pass the time with Lundy's waiters until about three-thirty when we would all troop to the subway station for the dreary ride to Sheepshead Bay.

Every time I entered those two beat-up hotels I'd ruefully recall that I'd put them down as too ratty when I was hard up for a room. Actually, I still wouldn't want to live in either of them, but the first night I returned from work I learned that the Logan was far worse. That night and every night thereafter the Logan's lobby was crowded with nodding junkies. A few were whiteys, but most were Black. And it was an eerie business to thread your way past them to the elevator.

And in the morning things were not much better. I never got on or off the elevator that I wasn't approached by a wino, trying to cop a beg. One morning I was put down by the obscene and desperate proposals of a lard tub of a Jewish woman. She had to be older than I am and was obviously an addict. A middle-aged Jewish junky whore! The one thing I firmly believed could not exist in New York City.

And that locked foyer door was just one big laugh. People trooped in and out of 5-C like it was a five-and-ten-cent store. Since the bars and liquor stores were always open when I was around in the mornings I knew folks couldn't be running a nip joint, but in the room next to mine *something* alcoholic and crooked was constantly going on. There were just too many drunks coming and going.

So I considered myself to be adequately forewarned and didn't even think of going down to the Rex to get my clothes and things. With a whole passel of drunks and/or junkies trooping past my door at all hours it was easy to figure the score. What I mean is that these kind of people had to steal to make it. There was no way in hell these rats could hold a job, and Welfare could never foot the bill for all the juice they evidently drank. I expected any night to come home to find my door had been jimmied.

So, with things being what they seemed to be, I avoided contact with every living soul in 5-C. And the lobby too. When I went to the bathroom I first waited until it was all quiet in the hall. Then I would make a dash for it. Out of the corner of my eye I would sometimes see someone in the kitchen, but I'd keep going just like I hadn't seen them.

The only person in the whole hotel who I could actually say I knew was Paula. Paula was the fifth-floor maid. The first morning she knocked on my door and called out she was the maid I was so twisted with the DTs I was too petrified to answer her. Besides, I thought it was some kind of ruse. And when she put her key in the lock I put my head under the covers. And when I heard her walk in I nearly blew it all.

But when I heard her soft and gentle "Excuse me" I came out from under. And I must have looked like hell because she went straight to the refrigerator and got me a glass of water. I don't think she said another word, but there was a look about her I sort of savored and loved. Like she refused to judge. No. Not exactly. It was more as if she thought she had no right to judge.

The next morning she talked a little and ended up asking me if there was anything she could get for me. I asked her to get me two bottles of Kaopectate. I had to.

Paula was a proud, arrogant girl. Twenty-five maybe, and beautiful. Her age alone put her out of my class, but that air of sort of refusing to judge plus the strangeness of the fact that she worked in the Logan made me hit on her. Not too hard. But I did let her know that I was unattached and could get off any week night and take her to the movies. You know. Stuff like that.

I can't remember exactly what she said, and it's not important anyhow because it was all in her eyes. But I got the message that she was in love with some character she was ashamed of and I knew it had to be one of those junkies down in the lobby. So in a way Paula was another reason I didn't break my neck to go get the rest of my things. Yeah, man. I wasn't long for the Logan.

But two weeks passed before I took a day off. Since it was now spring we could work as many days as we wanted to and I chose to work them all. A day off with nothing to do in this Logan and I just might take a drink, and then another, and another. You know. And I'd be pushing the hell out of my luck because even if I didn't get fired I'd surely be relegated to one of those slow no-money stations out at Lundy's that only pimps and hustlers were willing to work so that they could prove to their parole officers that they were gainfully employed.

However, on this particular morning it was raining and it looked like it was going to pour all day. That meant that Lundy's would operate with a skeleton crew. I couldn't have worked if I wanted to. It was early for me, but I went out and played my numbers and got back soaking wet.

I unlocked the foyer door and stepped into the hall just as a rotund little Irishman jauntily bounced out of the kitchen.

"I'm Joey. Right next door to you in 5-C-3," he said, pumping my hand.

I was shook. Not only was Joey's hand soft and girlish, but this guy who looked like a toy bulldog had the voice of a woman—although it was rough and coarse. I tried not to show my disgust; still, eight hours a day of the proposals of the would-be girls who worked at Lundy's was enough of a cross to bear without having a faggot in the next room to me.

"And I want you should meet the wife," Joey said. Then he bellowed, "Jinny!"

"And what the hell are you yelling like that for?" a voice answered.

"C'mere. I want you should meet the new guy next door."

Jinny came out of her room and down the hall. She was the color of well-burnt toast with some of the nappiest hair this side of Borneo. It was hair that had been straightened with a hot comb some time ago, but I don't think this broad's hair had even looked like much then. However, Jinny was small with a mischievous, disarming grin. Ugly as hell but in a cute sort of Afric way. And I had not one doubt that I was now staring at the most gruesomely matched couple in America today. These two really inspired awe.

Here was a happily married pair who absolutely had no right to be. And I didn't for a moment question the legality of their marriage. They were too weird not to be for real. But there they stood. A Black boogie gal, married to an Irisher, and both of them as delightful as dirty-faced toddlers. But this Irish pug was a fairy! Now why the hell would a Black gal go to the trouble of marrying a white faggot? And just to make it real crazy, Jinny was one of those Black gals who have a pervasive aura of sex about them at all times. Very often men will mistake this sensuality for beauty. It went without saying that Jinny was the kind of woman who would never have to look long for a man.

Now some of the pansy cooks out at Lundy's have wives whom they not only live with but by whom they have four and five children, but this was different. Big different! And I continued to question it all as Jinny sort of faded back against the foyer door and Joey chattered on and on.

"Everybody in this hotel knows me and Jinny," he informed me. "Whenever you hear somebody talking about J&J they're talking about us. And all of us up here in this 5-C try to make it a happy home. No rough stuff. No bums or winos. We wants it peaceful at all times. That's why everybody goes to the trouble to see that this foyer door stays locked at all times. Ya see?"

Of course I could not see. In fact, I was wondering how best to end this stupid conversation before some drunk came banging on this locked foyer door.

Joey pointed down the hall like he was showing me the Grand Canyon. "Now right there, next to the bathroom, is Mrs. Moriarty. She don't ever stay here more than a couple of nights a week at most. She's a private nurse. Been here for years since when all this part of Amsterdam Avener was all Irish. Back there then those micks would stone the hell outa niggers if they dared to walk through this neighborhood. And she's tough. These damn junkies don't scare her at all.

"And in that last room is Mr. Grimm. He worked for Columbia for forty years before he retired. Engineer. And he'll never bother you. He's stone deaf and a loner. Just him and his pissing goddam cat. He and Mrs. Moriarty are the only whiteys up here."

I was amazed by the many inconsistencies of Joey. This would-be male had not only a woman's voice but a Southern Negro accent as well. However, it was not until Joey began to preface his remarks with such phrases as: "We Negroes . . ." and "All us colored people . . ." that I began to feel cordially uptight.

And it was while Joey was rambling along that I noticed that Jinny was a pretty sick little woman. She had repeatedly gone into the bathroom, and I thought I'd heard her coughing or choking but the last time I distinctly heard her vomiting. That shook me more than Joey had been able to do. Now when a grown normal woman takes ill she goes to bed. Only a junky stands around puking. I wasn't any prissy, better-than-thou punk, but just the same I knew it was time to cut loose from these two.

Just then Jinny came out of the bathroom.

"You getting sicker, huh, hon?" Joey said in a voice that caressed.

Jinny inclined her head, too nauseated to speak.

"You think a little drink might help?" I knew it was a stupid question, but I've always been stupid like that.

"It's a Silver Spur she needs," Joey said anxiously just as if he expected me to do something about it.

"A silver spur, eh?" I said, trying not to sound self-righteous.

"You wouldn't mind going and getting her one, would you?" Joey said, taking little dancing steps back and forth. It was really obscene. Joey was devoid of all manhood now, yet I felt pity for this little fellow in the bulging jacket that had surely been stolen from some Columbia athlete. But how could the most depraved man on earth beg for a needle for his wife like this?

"Silver Spur is what she's gotta have," Joey said again. "It only costs fifty cents," he added.

Jinny forced a grin. "We owe the lady so we can't go in ourselves and get it."

"Yeah," Joey said in the same anxious way as before. "We can't go in, but all you gotta do is ask for a pint of Silver Spur. She don't *have* to know it's for us. Silver Spur is the only kind Jinny can keep down first thing in the morning, or else I wouldn't ask you to buy that particular brand."

Man, I was so damned glad to hear that Jinny wasn't a junky I flew out of there to the liquor store. I came back to their room and handed Jinny the pint bottle of the strong yellow wine. In one uninterrupted flow of motion she opened it, poured a drink and downed it. I figured she had broke some kind of record doing it.

"She's needed that ever since five-thirty," Joey said. There was a touch of pride in his voice.

Two more drinks later and Jinny became the smoothly beguiling confidence woman I had presumed her to be from the beginning.

"First off, buddee, you are too smooth with your shit to be nothing but a waiter," she was soon telling me. "Now I don't want to know what it is you're really putting down because I myself am now a scared and retired old lady. But I like to see other folks making it. If you know what I mean. And whatever you do, it keeps you well dressed and not too skinny. So righteous!"

"You're in with the Sinman, ain'tcha?" Joey said confidentially.

"Sinman?" I asked. "Who and what is the Sinman?"

"Sinman is a faggot," Jinny said sullenly.

"Shut up, Jinny," Joey yelled. "You don't know nothing about the guy. And why you gotta be always saying things you don't know a goddam thing about?"

"There was no Sinman around here four years ago," I said.

"You lived here four years ago?" Joey asked.

"Yeah," I said kind of ruefully. "But it was nothing like it is now."

"This place stinks," Joey said. "Nothing but ratty-assed winos and junkies."

"It's not half bad if you stay out of the lobby and off the sixth floor," Jinny said.

"That lobby looks like a movie set at night," I said. "A regular court of thieves. And it's not too hot in the daytime, if you ask me."

"You ain't seen nothing yet," Jinny said. "Wait until Checkday."

"The only thing I don't understand is where were all the lobby lice the day I registered," I said. "If that lobby had looked like it does every day now I'd never have asked for a room. It'd of been never no Logan for me."

"I remember the day you came," Jinny said. "And the lobby was clean because this joint was hotter than one of them Columbia kid's pussies. Three detectives are up in 6-D in this junky's room. See? Waiting for him to show so they can bust him for that killing over on Park Avenue. You know. The doctor's wife. The one who got stabbed so many times."

"How could that oily old bastard been so calm and talkative with the hotel full of cops?" I asked them.

"The manager? The old one? We got two, you know. One old, and one just about thirty," Jinny said.

"What's a fleabag like this need with two?" I said. "But that bastard sure didn't give a damn about those cops."

"The young one owns it," Jinny said, "but he tells everybody he's the bookkeeper. The old guy might have money in here too, but I don't know."

"He owns it!" Joey said excitedly. "Old man Epstein owns it. Ginsburg is only the bookkeeper like he says."

"Okay, hon. Okay," Jinny said soothingly. "Don't lose your cool. It's really not that important. The refugees only own the operating company anyhow. Columbia owns the property for real."

"Columbia owns every inch of land from here to 137th Street," Joey hollered at the top of his lungs. "The greedy bastids!"

"But I still don't see how this Epstein could've been so cool that day," I said again.

Jinny chuckled. "The only time those refugees get uptight is Checkday. The day Welfare checks arrive. That's when they draw a couple or more thousand out of the bank so they can cash everybody's Welfare check. And that lobby is the Devil's own on Checkday. Women fighting more than the men, but the men ain't no slouch either. Everybody full of wine or heroin. Nobody able to get their debts straight 'cause they're too high. Fighting on top of fighting. And there's all these assorted pimps, junkies and meatballs who don't even live here, standing around waiting and watching to see what they can cut out of the action. Why, if anybody waved a gun those refugees would shit in their pants."

"So why leave themselves open like that?" I asked. "Why don't they make the bums go to the bank and cash their checks?"

"Jesus Christ, Sid! Where you been?" Jinny exclaimed. "Goddam! You sound like a rich whitey. You think any S.R.O. manager is going to let these Welfare cases take their checks out of this hotel and then get drunk and rolled before they get back?"

"If they don't get back the hell with them," I said. "Rent's in advance. So why they got to worry? More Welfare bums will come along to take the rooms."

"Listen, take it easy on people on Welfare because my husband is on it himself," Jinny said lightly. "But for Chrissakes, Sid, a manager like this one has to loan out money between checks to keep folks from starving around here. So how's he ever going to collect if he don't cash their checks for them? And this manager is a square. A beautiful cat. Ginsburg, I mean. He don't shylock like the other landlords. Like on Ninety-ninth Street for instance. Those bastids charge a quarter on a dollar. When they get through cashing a check you only got maybe two dollars coming to last you two weeks till the next Checkday.

"One time on Ninety-ninth Street they kept a dead wino for forty-eight hours so they could cash his check when Checkday came. Then they called the police and said they'd just found him. Those dumb greedy refugees. Just as if there's no such thing as autopsies any more. Just the same, not a damn soul ever asked how a dead man could cash a check."

"Dead or alive, us niggers don't have no win!" Joey yelled.

"You really colored, Joey?" I asked. I had to; this cat had me going out of my head.

Jinny laughed. "All depends on how the bastid feels," she said cheerfully. "When things go swimmingly we are both Black, but when he gets one of his Irish fits on I'm the only damn nigger in our house."

"That's another one of your goddam lies," Joey yelled.

"Cool your role, hon," Jinny said. "When we first met I agreed to let you be a nigger, didn't I? Fourteen years ago." Then she turned to me with a knowing smile. "And you keep some lovely hours, buddee. Gorgeous ones. Sometimes we are getting up when you make it in here."

"Me?" I exclaimed. "Well, what about yourselves? In fact, when the devil do you two sleep? All night long you got visitors. Every few minutes someone knocks on that foyer door until I go to sleep at least."

"You got us all wrong," Jinny said. "J&J lock their door at eight every night and don't open it for anybody until five or maybe after in the morning. Not in this Logan do we open our room door after 8 P.M. Those are the junkies you hear knocking. Those bastids never sleep."

"It's that goddam Leah and Ray," Joey snarled.

"Leah's got the big room up in front: 5-C-1," Jinny said.

Joey came close to me and, in that confidential whisper only an Irish tosspot can affect, said, "Leah and her ole lady sell dope, see?"

The many knockings at that foyer door, the frenetic exclamations, entreaties, oaths of anger and disappointment all spelled one word: d-o-p-e! And any dumb lame would have known it already. All, that is, except me. Sid Bailey, man about town.

"But those whiteys," I argued. "Who would sell dope around them? And that goddam Epstein told me that this was the most respectable sector in the whole hotel. You mean to say the fool don't know when dope is being sold on his premises?"

"He knows," Jinny said. "And Ginsburg even buzzes all the pushers time the fuzz steps foot on the elevator. We got six pushers in here, you know. One on each floor."

"And I'll bet they're all just fronting for him." I was so goddam bitter I was ready to put in a call to the Narco Squad myself.

"Nope," Jinny said. "You got everything in the Logan all wrong, Sid. Like I told you before: Ginsburg is a square. But you know how some respectable people are; they just love to rub shoulders with anybody who is really down with it. Well, this young Jewboy thinks it's real cool to be in with these cutthroats. I talk to him a lot. He likes me as a friend. He's young and dap, but he's a very religious cat. He even wears one of those skullcaps around his house, he told me. Yet and still the bastid risks his neck and his hotel to tip off the dope peddlers when the fuzz comes to call. Now you go ahead and figure that one out."

"I didn't know a Jewboy could be so stupid," I said.

"Not exactly stupid," Jinny said. "Remember, he owns this joint. We don't."

"He is dumb. And so is that goddam Leah," Joey yelled excitedly. "And why she gotta pick 5-C to sell her shit in anyhow? The only hallway in the whole building that's kept locked all the time. When you sell dope you wants it quiet. You don't want no sick junkies standing out in the foyer banging away on the door for all to see and hear. And I tole Leah that, too."

So this J&J had me uptight again: what were they really trying to do or say? Jinny had already gone on record as believing I wasn't a waiter. So was I being put to some kind of test? Did they think I was some kind of undercover man? And did they have some kind of grudge on for this Leah and Ray and want them busted? Or were they simply telling me to pack up and git?

A weirdly attractive woman strolled into the room. She looked to be in her late twenties or early thirties, but that might have been because she was so tiny and wore slacks that bagged in the seat. She could have been older. Much older. I immediately took a dislike to her while admitting to her freakish attractiveness. I was at once revolted and made curious by her lips, which were loose and rubbery. They boldly announced to the world that they had tasted all that was evil and liked it. Her color was an ashy light brown. Her hair was good and her nose was cute. If it were not for those heavy lips she would have been pretty. She tried to stare at me, but her eyes did not seem to focus too well.

"You the new stud next door?" The woman's words were couched in the whispery soft and faraway tones of a junky who has just had a fix.

"Yes," I said before it dawned upon me that this woman had not actually asked me a question. She had only conveyed her opinion of me.

And I had no doubt that this was Leah, the dope pusher. I watched her walk to the dresser and help herself to a cigarette. J&J were silent, and I thought that theirs was a subservient silence. It was just like they were standing at attention.

"I don't like it," Leah said. "What kinda shit these managers think they're putting down? That room was supposed to be reserved for Doris when she gets loosed. So what's this man doing in it?" She turned to focus on Joey. "You know him?" she asked.

It was not quite a smile that played around the corners of Jinny's mouth as she answered for her husband. "Why the hell don't you call up the precinct, Leah? Yeah. And ask them if they sent Sid over here to bust you."

"That's not funny!" Leah snapped.

"So what you going to do? Dispossess him?"

Leah puffed ferociously on her cigarette but said nothing.

There was a knock on the foyer door and Jinny went to answer it.

"Tell them we're out," Leah called down the hall to Jinny.

"Okay," Jinny said.

I took this opportunity to wander out of the room.

CHAPTER 3

TIME I GOT BACK to my room I realized that I had used no smarts at all. So what if I didn't like Leah? She would probably have left in a few minutes anyhow. And with this rain, what else was there to do but to sit around and talk to J&J? And now I couldn't go back. I'd look like some kind of nut for real then.

I went to the window. It was still pouring. Across the areaway, in the next building, I could see two girls fighting. One was white, the other Chinese. They fought savagely and, from what I could see, silently. The Caucasian girl was battering the little oriental girl's face with her fists, but that China gal was holding her own by kicking as well as sometimes punching. Never once did they grapple. Still fighting, they passed from my view.

I turned from the window and looked at my disheveled bed. It made me think of Paula. Which reminded me that I had not been to bed with a woman for over a month.

I went back to the window and saw that the China gal's face was bloody. Strange; I had never seen a Chinese bleed before. Somehow it made me very sad and lonely while at the same time a funky kind of restlessness overcame me. And I thought of how New York was filled with women who fought each other over other women and yet a sober Sid Bailey could not find a single breast to call his own.

For a moment Alise crossed my mind. Damn Alise. And damn the Logan. But the Logan was where I was at. And wasn't this hole jammed with junky and wino broads? And that didn't have to be all either. Suppose there was an unattached Paula around. A square working chick who, like me, had checked in without thoroughly casing the joint and had not as yet checked out. Or maybe they couldn't afford to move just yet, and were dying to meet a guy like Sid Bailey. Filled with an emotion that can only be described as angry intent, I left my room and headed for the elevator.

A real cool-looking babe got on at the fourth floor. She smiled. Her lips were an offering, but this chick was just a little bit too cool for me. I wanted an amateur if possible. I let her get off ahead of me without even bothering to hit on her.

The lobby of the Logan is amber limestone. Amber. Like it had been aged in cheap sherry wine. It is big, about twenty feet by twenty feet. A huge mausoleum with at least ten semi-erect bodies in it at all times. It is not quite as denuded as the foyers above it because there is a cigarette machine, a soft drink machine and two telephone booths.

I looked around. There was a complete assortment of disappointing females present, and I began to regret not having tried to start something going with the pretty girl on the elevator. With a grunt of disgust I turned to go back upstairs and almost collided with James Ronald Person.

"Ah, yes. Ah, yes. I remember. I remember."

I didn't even hear the words. I only heard those whispery tones of vocal cords made tight by heroin and a block of ice racketed around in my gut. I tried to summon anger to combat the nausea that was smothering me, but I couldn't. No more than I could have fled, hid or even tried to pray. No. None of these; I could only stand and gawk at the shell of a boy who had once been a brilliant Juilliard student.

Person had lost weight. Much weight, it seemed. But it was with a sort of horror that I also noted the carefully combed wavy blond hair and the costly silk suit that fitted too well. Too goddam well for a junky. It was like the embalmer's assistant had done a masterful job.

"I remember. I remember," Jimmy Person repeated. "Was it not without spontaneity and compassion that you once befriended me?"

Time reeled back and once more I saw the nineteen-year-old

student begging the manager to tell him how best to go about regaining his most cherished possessions.

"We can't be responsible for valuables left in the rooms," the woman who was then the manager said. Just as if the boy could have checked at the desk his violin and saxophone, his stereo equipment and all the other paraphernalia so indispensable to a student of music.

I had been standing behind Jimmy at the office window,waiting to see if I had any mail. After the woman had turned away without giving Jimmy satisfaction, I had apologized as a Black man who was thoroughly ashamed of the way three reefer-high Black punks had plundered Jimmy's room. What they had not taken they had smashed.

Young Person had blinked and tried to smile, but it was evident that the robbery had taken away all sense of his belonging anywhere. "I—I got a bottle of wine they missed," the boy said. It was a desperate plea for companionship.

And the two of us had shared his bottle of chianti. It was then that Jimmy Person had told me of his love for music and I even confided that ever since college I had wanted to be a playwright. But that Jimmy was not the same boy who stood before me now.

A too brilliant smile crossed his thin face. "And now it behooves us to rekindle that friendship that was so unseemly quenched before its prime."

There it was again. The first time I only sort of sensed it, but here it was again and this time for real. Nineteenth-century drawing-room speech. I was bitter as hell. Jimmy had not talked or been like this four years ago.

"I have always dug you the most," Person said as he took me by the arm and steered me toward the door marked 1-C. "And just to think! We met on that fateful day of my baptism by theft, love's fire and the *Word.*"

With a shudder I remembered that all the junkies I had ever known had been egocentrics. In my book, all junkies are unable to bestow their friendship or even their casual interest upon anyone or anything that does not return instant gratification in some form.

We entered Jimmy's room, which was 1-C-1, and the man was still talking. It came to me that Jimmy didn't converse. He pattered. His was the monologue of a clever MC, and in no time my horror was gone and I was grinning appreciatively although every now and then I would wonder what had happened to this man who looked at least four years older than his twenty-three years.

How, I wanted to know, could being robbed change a naïve college kid into this? And furthermore, what is the intrinsic value of the hobby things of a millionaire's nineteen-year-old son. Only one thing was certain to me: those weed-high Black bastards had stolen this boy's spirit that day and left him with a dead soul.

". . . and you must always call me the Sinman," Person was blithely pattering on.

"Sinman?" I echoed. "*The* Sinman?"

Person nodded happily. "It is something of a misnomer, but I abide it. And I *am* a student of sin. I study it constantly, and I have found that sin is never what man professes it to be. You religionists are convinced that all that is best and good in this world is either sinful or unhealthy. Don't you think Oscar put it well when he said that all things man loves he kills?"

I couldn't imagine what Person was talking about for real, but he didn't wait for answers anyhow. It was like he couldn't stop talking. His pattering was a sickness that was making me sick even as I grinned at him.

As Jimmy, this so-called Sinman, pattered away I recalled how in his college days he had maintained what was tantamount to an open house for the Logan's Black tenants. They had always been welcome to come listen to his records and drink his wine and whiskey. It had seemed to me that Jimmy shunned the company of the other white students who lived in the hotel at the time. However, I really didn't know Jimmy well; for it was not until the day of the robbery that I ever spoke more than a casual greeting to him. And I never saw him again after that day.

But as this evident nut pattered on, I grew realistic. Like it was a matter of self-preservation, I had to coldly suspicion that Jimmy, like so many other whiteys who liked to live in close proximity to

Black people, did so out of a subtle contempt for the Black man; they had no genuine feelings of brotherhood. I have always lumped these Negrophiles collectively, thinking that they all conceived of themselves as being Great-white-fathers-whom-the-savages-simply-had-to-love. And in my book the Living-God-the-father-of-them-all was Dr. Albert Schweitzer.

And so while this addict pattered on I came to the abrupt conclusion that the real trauma inflicted on Jimmy by that robbery was the curt delivery of the message to him that Negroes didn't *love* him, nor could he use his beautiful blondness and hospitality to inflict his good will upon the hapless Blacks in his world.

Like a harmless madman, Sinman was saying, "Man is prone to murder his own spirit. Also his gods. And then, like swine, men root in the ground today in search of a God Who is dead."

"Dead?" I asked.

"Yes, dead. Murdered by His own hand. And I, for one, insist upon a living God . . ."

"Are you trying to tell me you sell dope?"

Sinman bowed. "And I am quite a success."

That did it. I put my hand on the doorknob, but the Sinman's chatter had a strangely detaining effect. He never paused long enough for me to put in a decent good-by. And then things got real weird as I gradually came to feel sorry for the nut; I grew quite sure that this guy, even if he was a dope peddler, did not have many opportunities to talk to other people. For I have always been convinced that all normal people tend to use the speech patterns of their associates. A guy would have to be damned near a hermit to be able to toss around words and phrases that are a hundred years behind the times. This kid was blighted from way back.

Since this Sinman had not invited me to sit down, we both were still standing just a step or two inside his room. And my mind was pretty much on the restless side; I gave the room a casual once-over. It was easily the largest and most expensive-looking room I had seen so far in the Logan. Spang in the middle of the room was an electric organ and for some ungodly reason I was of the unshakable opinion that the thing would not play. Don't ask me why. Another thing I noted was that Sinman had a washbasin and running water.

I was completely ignorant of the value of the many paintings that covered the walls, but I liked them. I thought that most of them were surrealistic attempts to depict ecstatic enjoyment of music. Some of the paintings, I decided, could be classified as cartoons. All of the musicians in them were Black and appeared to be slightly mad. There was an ancient typewriter and a carton of eggs on the dresser. And there must have been at least six hassocks on the floor as well as a dirty white bearskin rug.

There was also a grandfather clock that had the right time, a decrepit console radio piled high with junk, a magnificent stereo, but no TV. Several ebony African carvings were here and there about the room, and a huge pink refrigerator stood against one wall. Further inspection revealed an ornate bed in a far corner of the room. The bed made me think of orgies; it could have held three couples easily.

I froze, and then ceased to breathe at all when I looked in the dark corner opposite the bed. A giant was sitting there. A coal-black monster enthroned on a morris chair. The giant wore dark glasses and in his hands was a heavy cane that had been crudely painted an off-white color. It was like violence, even murder, hovered in a smoking cloud about his head. Like this blind man held in the palm of his hand all that was black and mighty in this world.

The monster's bitter thin, un-negroid lips were curled with a harsh air of superiority and disgust. The expression was one of arrogant invincibility. His head, an ebony carving, was huge, round and close-shaven. There was a thrust to the features that had the impact on the eye of an iron fist. This man's face *projected.* He was Blackest Africa's answer to Caesar and he scared me witless.

"Now tell me about Pal Joey and her wife," Sinman was saying. "How does the old fraud and Jinny treat you in that profane bower of love?"

I glanced away from the blind man. "So Joey really is a little faggot," I murmured. "I thought so."

"No. Joey is a woman. She gave birth to a son several years my senior. No man could have wrought that miracle even here in the Logan."

"You sure?" I said stupidly. "I mean, are you sure Joey had a baby once?"

Sinman nodded. "Her son comes to me. Cocaine. Joey is a transvestite and a lesbian, but nevertheless a woman. She also was a topflight hijacker in her day until love bade her and Jinny renounce crime to live in serenity on Welfare."

"Jinny was a hijacker too?"

"No. A confidence woman. Clever, too." Sinman smiled and lit a cigarette. "That 5-C hall intrigues me. All of you tend to be freaks. Not quite normal. If I remember correctly you are enamored of the bottle. And you look too lonely not to be. Leah in 5-C-1 is in love with a huge cow of a woman named Ray. This Ray is so lazy that Leah has to come to the bedside to hit her during the day although Ray does answer the door and sells the heroin after midnight when business is brisk."

"What do you mean, Leah has to hit her? What for?"

"Hit: to inject with heroin. Every junky's dream of heaven is to be the one to hit Ray Charles."

"Why?"

"With his income, and you ask such a question? But getting back to the loves of 5-C: we have Mrs. Moriarty, who is enamored of any and all novenas. There is sixty-five-year-old Dick Smith up there in 5-C-2, who is madly in love with his junky mistress. She is twenty-two years old and that romance has been going on for fourteen years. I shall not speak of Mr. Grimm and his unspeakable cat."

I was taking all of this in, but it was only for brief moments that I could take my eyes away from the blind ogre in the corner. When finally Sinman noticed my fascination he said, "That is Blind Charlie, my friend and confidant. It is a shame, but we must forgo introductions; Charlie simply refuses to meet strangers; and he is a stubborn man. Adamant unto death—anybody's death. He is insane too. Charlie can come up with ideas that would put an impotent evangelist to shame. But he is my dearest friend and cross to bear."

I simply did not believe the Sinman's inanities. Blind Charlie could never have silly ideas. The man was a gorilla, but it was so evident that this was a gargantua possessed of superhuman intellect. I even thought I could read some of the minor thoughts that surged behind that broad black brow. This man had to be brooding upon what pestiferousness his gnat-sized enemies would be trying next. And I felt sorry for those enemies, who had to be legion. But I felt sorry for them just the same.

". . . but when Charlie comes to like your voice, or rather, comes to like what your voice denotes you to be, he will assail you with endless conversation and friendship. And I must warn you: Charlie's devotion to his friends can be devilishly unbounded."

Naturally I didn't believe that either. That arrogant ape in the corner could not possibly become engaged in aimless chatter with anyone on earth.

A character who had to be from 125th Street bustled into the room. He was short, dark, conk-headed. His eyes bulged with a seeming need to steal everything he saw. Although the man's skin was very black, it seemed to me that here was a man who lived around soot. A gray dinginess covered him from head to foot. His mouth was a juicy red gash with lips that put Leah's rubbery lips to shame. How a woman could ever bring herself to kiss this guy was more than I could understand. I lazily wondered if he might not be one of those mannish homos. Maybe even a latent one.

Sinman looked at the guy but said nothing. He moved to the organ and flicked it on but did not play it.

"Well, I come like I said," the man said to Sinman and then exhaled a big cloud of cigarette smoke.

"Ah, my friend Cuestick. And with money?" the Sinman purred.

And so help me, I actually wondered if there was not some exotic snake that purred instead of hissed at its intended victims.

Surprisingly, the man did not answer. Instead he walked over to Blind Charlie and, taking what can only be described as a dramatic stance, said, "Nobody ever beat the breaks all the time, now did they, Blind Charlie?"

Charlie remained silent, his chin resting atop the crook of that heavy cane. I was awed. Charlie's was a mighty silence; it was as overwhelming as the man.

But Cuestick still insisted upon making a formal speech to Blind Charlie. "What's with the Sinman?" he cried. "He's gonna put me down like I'm a cat what don't never keep his word just because the breaks weren't for me last night?"

The silent room was filled with a furious kind of savagery. These three men were kinetic. My nerves could not have been more on edge if they had drawn knives on each other.

And when Cuestick spoke again I was sure he was not the least bit frightened, and yet there was an urgency to what he said. Like a ravening need to be believed. The entire scene was strange and way out to me, this argument that was no argument at all.

"Last night I got me this chump, what is a freak, see?" Cuestick declaimed to Charlie. "And all I gotta do for him is get the girl. Dig it? He's had my old lady before so I can't bring her in no more, dig? But he wants that I should bring this new chick up to his pad over on the east side where he's got this coffin. Dig it?" Cuestick peered anxiously at Blind Charlie. "You dig the play, don't you, Charlie? He's just gonna be laying up there nekkid in his box when I walks in with this here chick on my arm . . ." Here he paused to let everyone digest this much of his story.

"Now I ain't supposed to tell this chick nothing, but what the hell kinda dumb bastid would I be to do that?" Cuestick demanded. "Sure. I goes ahead and explains in front what's happening so that the chick don't have to faint for real. She just makes out like she faints from walking in on this john what's already dead. See what I mean? And then this nut will jump outa his box and snatch hisself a little pussy, thinking that the bitch is out cold and don't know from nothing, but she does, dig it?"

Cuestick's greasy eyes bulged with wrath, and he suddenly advanced toward me with that pigeon-toed gait of a street fighter.

"Now who in hell can beat breaks like I got last night?" he yelled directly into my mouth. "Not one lousy bitch on 125th will go for the okey-doke! And this chump is gonna give me a yard for my trouble!"

Cuestick whirled around and went back to Blind Charlie. His movements were just like a jackleg minister's; in fact I've always thought that there is a strong personality link between a pimp and an ignorant preacher.

"And it's all mine!" Cuestick howled. "I'm supposed to be bringing a square chick with no smarts about her at all. He gives me because he don't want no repercussions, but the damn fool figgers we don't have to deal the chick nothing because she's gonna be out cold and don't even know she's getting screwed! I tole ya the chump motherfucker had freakish nuts for brains, didn't I?" Then he crouched down and whispered, "I offers bitches twenty-five bucks to turn the trick for me, which leaves me holding a cool six bits, dig? But not one single whore I see will help me."

Cuestick strolled back to me and I saw that he was trembling. "They all claims they's scared! They calls him crazy!" Cuestick shouted. "He ain't crazy! He just likes to get his cakes that way!"

Finally he turned to Sinman with a sigh. "So there goes your fifty like I promised. I walks 125th till I'm late for my connection so I blows that too. I ain't got a dose of anything to my name. But don't you worry none; you'll get yours like I promised. Only a little later. Dig?"

Sinman sighed too. "I suppose Charlie believes you," he said.

"Well, all right then," Cuestick said gruffly. He was relaxed now and spoke in his natural voice, which was rough and coarse. "Let me have one bag," he said to the Sinman, producing a five-dollar bill. He turned to me. "See that?" he said. "You dig it, don't you? I ain't one of them cats what takes their business somewheres else just because they owes a honest debt."

"Allah be praised," Sinman murmured. His eyes brightened, and for the first time he showed real interest. "Tell me," he said to Cuestick, "why didn't you come to me for a lady with the vapors?"

The popeyes angrily tried to leave their sockets. "Jesus Gawd!" Cuestick gasped. "I never even thought! Them dumb bitches had me so goddam mad I couldn't even think no more. Jesus to Jesus! How could I do it?"

"You never forget anything," Sinman said dreamily. "And you

remembered that it would have been a forty-sixty split with you getting the forty dollars."

Cuestick did not even bother to argue. With an odd sort of deprecatory wave of his hand, and then picking up the packet of heroin the Sinman had placed on the organ, he hurried out of the room.

"That was the greediest-looking little bastard I ever saw!" I said as soon as Cuestick was gone. "He had 'rat' written all over him. Especially his mouth. Did you ever see a mouth like that before?"

Sinman nodded. "Most men have their price, but not our Cuestick. There is nothing dishonest he would not do for nothing if necessary. What a pill-boy. He is a lower than an ethical M.D.—and only God knows how low they can get."

Sinman saw my look of bewilderment. "Cuestick has many sources and connections and is able to obtain Dolophine, Doriden, paraldehyde, Darvon, Demerol and the like. Even methadone. All of these medications—perhaps I should say nostrums—are thought by addicts to ease the agony of withdrawal symptoms. This puts Cuestick in the same category as a doctor."

I grunted. "Anyhow, selling pills is a lot better than selling heroin," I said. "But how the devil can a man support a habit waiting for sick junkies to come along? Sounds penny ante. And you say his stuff don't even work?"

Sinman smiled a gracious apology. "Forgive me. I talk too fast and too much at times. Methadone is the most miraculous thing to hit New York since that one-legged Dutchman. Nothing can be compared to meth. Not even penicillin. Why, in two hours' time methadone could eradicate the entire heroin problem in New York City."

"For crying out loud," I exclaimed almost hysterically. "Even a child knows better than that. Don't you realize if that were true Rockefeller, Lindsay and Adam Powell would have machines dispensing the stuff for free on every street corner in Harlem?"

"Like all squares, you are unaware of our supra-government. The Heroin Establishment would never think of letting our duly elected officials flood this town with meth. And neither will your high-salaried psychiatrists for that matter. They claim it is addictive . . ."

"I *thought* so!" I said meaningfully.

"That can't be proved. Your heroin addict is an addictive person. If your shrinks would be honest they would have to admit that all they know is that addicts *like* to take methadone just as many people like to drink coffee. Coffee is addictive?"

"I don't know enough about it to argue sensibly," I said. "But for the time being I'm not going to believe Rockefeller and the rest are yellow-bellied idiots, if you know what I mean." Then I added, "But you still haven't told me how Cuestick can make it, looking for sick junkies to sell to."

"Cuestick does a land-office business. Girls especially seek him out. All addicts intend to reduce their intake tomorrow. And so they'll need Cuestick's other nostrums to tide them over the rough spells. Girls buy his wares with the same intentions in mind that a fat lady has when she buys reducing pills. Mañana."

"But junkies never think of tomorrow, do they?"

"A gross exaggeration. If the square has tomorrow to dwell upon, the junky has tonight and every night. But never worry about our man's making it. Cuestick gets his pills for twenty cents apiece and sells them for a dollar. He buys meth at two dollars a bottle and never sells it for less than eight. Sometimes ten and twelve. Whereas one has not only got to beg the M.D., but he must also pay for the script. So who is more dishonest, the doctor or Cuestick?"

This was getting so stupid that I changed the subject. "How come Cuestick owes you fifty dollars?"

Sinman grimaced girlishly. "He is squarely in love with one of those lesbians who have a fixation on flimflamming males. Apparently it is the only way they can obtain complete sexual satisfaction from a man. And although this girl is a stud, she hustles, and is always alert to make that sting. She prefers to pick up a john and entice him to take her to a hotel. But once in the room she will suddenly crave a drink. And she always waits until the john is almost completely disrobed before she makes her wants known.

But, being a wonderful sport, she will offer to run out and get a bottle herself."

Sinman's thin face was etched with cynicism. "Any and all marks will go for this particular type of murphy because it immediately casts them in the role of being waited upon by a fair lady. And since the girl has already been promised fifteen or twenty dollars for the use of her body, they never doubt that the girl will return with the bottle and the change from a five- or ten-dollar bill. But Barbra just has to steal. She has to prove her mental superiority over men. She doesn't come back."

"Well, that's a safe enough hustle," I said. "What kind of man is going to the police with a complaint like that?"

"She pulled it on a policeman's brother. And since Barbra regularly prowls the Times Square district it was not hard for him to find her. The fellow just rode around in his car every night until he spotted her. His brother was with him at the time and quite naturally the policeman-brother deigned to arrest her. He only wished her to cough up one hundred dollars or have her neck broken. She took them to Cuestick, but he did not have a yard at the time. Therefore he came to me for the balance, which I gladly loaned to him."

I was so upset I was whispering. "You mean to tell me that a white cop puts a Black girl in his private car and brings her up to Harlem for a deal like that? Cuestick lied to you. No cop would ever do that."

"Why not?"

"Why not? You ask *me* why not? He could have caused a riot for one thing! And he was guilty of kidnapping. Extortion! And I thought that damned Cuestick was so goddam hepped!"

"And just what did you have in mind for Cuestick to have done?"

"Anything and everything! He could have had that cop and his brother arrested."

"And just who do you suppose is going to arrest one of New York's Finest for trying to turn an honest penny after work is done? Justice Motley? Adam?" And it was just as silly the way the Sinman abruptly changed the subject. "Oh yes. I forgot to ask if those sacred cows have forgiven you. I take it that you are the well-dressed stranger who moved into 5-C and frightened poor Leah so that she ingested an overdose. You must be the man. There are no other vacant rooms up there. How many weeks have you been here anyhow?"

"Leah took an overdose?"

"During the first twenty-four hours of your stay Leah was afraid to deal. She fumed and fretted herself into a tizzy. And then absently hit herself twice within the hour. Ray and J&J had quite a time of it, I hear. But we digress. Have the cows since made you welcome?"

"I just met J&J and Leah for the first time a few minutes ago. This Ray I haven't even seen yet."

"I hope there'll be no friction. You know, that is a lovely room you have. An ideal location for a square who goes out to labor. You'll never need worry about being robbed."

I looked at him. "With drunks and junkies trooping in and out all day and all night?"

The Sinman's smile was a warm baby bath. "Don't fret. I give you my word for it that no junky would dare steal anything that lies behind the foyer door of 5-C. They are afraid of having their connection with Leah cut off. Actually Leah wouldn't care what they stole as long as it wasn't her property, but not many addicts would know that. And no addict willingly jeopardizes his source of supply."

I really didn't know enough about it to comment so I didn't say anything.

Sinman asked, "You realize that no junky trusts another?"

"Why should they?"

He laughed. "Precisely. And so there will be many who will believe that Leah's professed disquietude over your appearing on the scene is some kind of camouflage. They will think that Leah is lying about you. Many will even suspect that you are Leah's silent partner or boss. And Leah doesn't have a man, you know. Therefore, you may rest assured that each and every junky who deals with Leah will not believe what Leah says you are. It is the way of the junky mind. Junkies are unteachable."

To be respected by the meatball junkies in the Logan! That was what the Sinman was saying. Already I was feeling better. In fact, since my first night at work I had been mildly concerned that sooner or later the junkies in the lobby would find out that I was a waiter who returned home late each night with tips in his pocket. If the Sinman was right, I would be able to walk in the lobby at all times in relative safety.

The lush fox with whom I had ridden down on the elevator walked in. "Hello, everybody," she said. "How's it going, Charlie?"

I looked at Charlie, practically holding my breath, waiting for him to speak at last. But the blind giant simply raised his chin and moved his cane in a tight little circle.

Sinman was beaming. "Gloria, my love. And at such a propitious moment," he exclaimed. Then he lowered his voice and he and the girl spoke to each other in voices I could not hear.

I took the opportunity to study this beauty more closely and saw that there were several things about her I had overlooked on the elevator. This Gloria was much more than just lushly attractive. In her own way she was just as kinetic a personality as Sinman and Blind Charlie. This Juno personified sexual capability. And I knew that here was one girl who had no hangup, no frustrations. She was the absolute master of her sex life. And she was so godawfully pretty! Her complexion was a mellow sort of beige. Like a ridiculously healthy Lena Horne. And her hair was longer than Lena's with plenty of waves.

Gloria suddenly turned and caught me looking at her, but she smiled, and this time her smile was not a coy fishnet. It was the artless friendliness of a country girl. "You're new, huh?"

I instantly fell in love with that open smile, but Gloria's beauty tied my tongue in knots although I did manage to say, "Yeah. Kinda. I'm Sid."

I guess those clumsy words turned her off because she turned back to Sinman and continued their low-keyed conversation. And now my heart was a lump in my throat. I was in love for real at last. And I knew that her connection with the likes of the Sinman and Blind Charlie could easily be explained if I just kept my cool and waited for an explanation. In fact, this girl just might be one of the few innocents left around Harlem.

Then Gloria punctured all of the lovely bubbles my mind was blowing. "I met the nicest john last night," she chortled. "He was celebrating because he'd just had this fine apartment redecorated. And was it boss! That apartment. And he wants to gimme everything. Dig it? A real gone john. So help me. He wants me to shack up with him. So I came to tell you, Sinman."

And Sinman really looked unhappy. "Oh dear," he said. "And I was just going to give you to Sid."

Gloria's eyes glistened as she turned to realistically inspect me for the first time. And for some strange reason she *liked* what she saw. Her moist eyes held no secrets. They were almost confessing. Naturally, you know how I felt after five years of emptiness and hate.

"But first things first," the Sinman said with the weirdest kind of sanctimoniousness I ever heard. Then cajolingly, like a quizmaster, he began to prompt Gloria. "Now exactly what does this wonderful john have to offer us?"

"All that fabulous pad on West End Avenue. And I can tell good furniture. It never came from 125th Street or Fourteenth either."

"You are taking it for granted that the gentleman is a pussy?"

"All johns are pussies, aren't they? Anyhow, he's scared of us. He practically admitted it."

"But some pussies are cop-callers," Sinman said. "Is he Jewish?"

"No, he's colored. I thought I told you. I wouldn't even have mentioned it if he was a Jewboy."

Sinman nodded. "Jews are notorious cop-callers. And they are a determined lot as a rule. But whom does this gentleman of color have in his corner? Who among his connections would thwart us?"

"Nobody," Gloria said promptly. "His kind don't ever have no real friends. And like I said: he's afraid of us. He said he wouldn't have picked me up if I hadn't been so light-skin. He even tried to make out like he's not a boot himself, but he's just as much nigger as I am. More so. He talks foreign like. Dig it? He's Haitian or from that country that that big-time playboy came from. You know. The one that married all them rich bitches."

"Ah, yes. And so you will answer his call of love," Sinman said. "Then in a few days Sid and Charlie will arrive for a short visit."

It was unbelievable. This damn fool dope fiend actually believed that Sid Bailey was going to help murder a man for a few sticks of furniture?

"All I'll need is Charlie," Gloria said meditatively. "I'll say he's my uncle."

The big black giant emitted an animal sound which was supposed to be a guffaw. But that noise made terror shriek down my spine.

But Gloria went on unperturbed. "This john thinks he's a big thing, ya know. Like he's in society even if he don't have no friends. And he'd be ashamed to go to the pigs or anybody else."

Since they evidently did not intend to kill their victim I was able to breathe a little easier. Sinman went to the huge pink refrigerator and took out a bottle of Cutty Sark. He poured two large drinks and handed one to me and one to Gloria. Gloria took hers over to Blind Charlie, who tossed it off immediately. Then she brought her glass back and Sinman filled it again.

As for me, I absolutely did not want a drink. One drink and I might blow it all, but it seemed so very faggotish to refuse a drink from a heroin addict.

"Suppose the furniture is not paid for?" Sinman asked Gloria.

"So what?" she said lightly. "And anyhow that's what he was celebrating. Last night was what he called a mortgage-burning and housewarming. Me and him. He picked me up outside his door and he never put me down until he laid me on the bed." Gloria's smile was still an innocent, happy thing. "Gee, it was cute, Sinman. I sort of went for him. I liked his style even if all foreigners are crazy. But since I dug him a little it was easy to stroke him, and in no time at all he was begging me to move in with him."

"And what is our turkey's profession?" Sinman asked.

"He's got a job like a whitey. For an airplane company he works.

It flies all over the world, I guess. But he's not a pilot. I asked him and he said no. He's downtown in an office somewheres."

And then that one lousy drink of Cutty Sark made me get in the conversation. "You mean he works for an airline," I told Gloria.

"Like I said." Gloria seemed to be soothing me. "They fly all over."

"What should we say the furnishings are worth?" Sinman mused.

Gloria shrugged. "Like any other white stud's. That stuff is fabulous, Sinman." Suddenly she smiled with a child's heart-fetching directness. "Couldn't me and Sid *keep* the apartment, Sinman?"

Absolute proof that I am an alcoholic is the fact that I went and poured another drink instead of going to Gloria and putting my arm around her waist.

"Of course not!" Sinman said severely. "In time the yellowest rat will stop running and look back over his shoulder. Sometime after Charlie has sent him packing, this chump will return to spy upon you. He will write anonymous letters to the police." Sinman sighed. "He will be most dishonest and unfair. No. We must sell that apartment to the highest bidder." He sighed again. "So you must go ahead with your project as we first planned, Gloria darling." The Sinman smiled a benediction that closed the conference.

Gloria and I looked at each other and sort of let the air out of our lungs. Then we both went to the organ where the scotch was and had another drink.

As I put my glass down Gloria impulsively took my hand and led me to the big, sinful-looking bed. There we sat, still holding hands, directly facing Blind Charlie, which didn't seem to faze Gloria at all. However, I sincerely believed that I could never relax in this giant's presence.

At close range the man looked to be more murderous than ever. But this alone could never explain the stark terror he aroused in me. And after all, this was a *blind* man. Actually he was harmless. He couldn't hurt a flea unless that flea was handed to him.

Then, from out of the blue, the truth came to me. Blind Charlie's terrorizing strength was not important at all. The thing that made

Charlie so fearsome was an aura of intellect about him. And I could only think of this aura as "pent-up intellect." Blind Charlie possessed a giant brain encased in ignorance. Without a doubt Charlie, practically speaking, was ignorant. And I presumed that it was but another act of God. For if that genius had been honed with knowledge and fired with ambition this man would have been one of the true monsters of the ages. Blind Charlie would have been more than a Caesar, a Genghis Khan, an Attila or a Hannibal. This Black Reaper would have surpassed them all.

To free myself of these awful thoughts I whispered to Gloria, "Let's take a powder. Want to go up to my room?"

Gloria's quick and agreeable nod did not entirely free me from my mesmerized feeling, but a few moments later we left the Sinman and Charlie. We walked through the lobby hand in hand.

CHAPTER 4

WHEN WE CAME THROUGH the foyer door J&J broke off what sounded like a lovely argument to rush out of the kitchen.

"Not for days!" Jinny cried to Gloria. "You living here now? What room you got? You look swell, and I can see you've got that damned monkey off your back. How'd you do it?"

"House of D," Gloria said.

"So how you feel now?" Joey asked.

"It's been a kinda drag. I was getting restless as hell until I walked in the Sinman's room and met Sid here. But I gotta get out of this Logan," Gloria said with a sigh. "Too many sources and too many addicts. Know what I mean?"

"I dig," Jinny said. "But if you don't want the shit you can lay right down beside it and never give a damn. Heroin is only a substitute. It tries like hell to take the place of something you know you got to have. Now I was a cokey pure and simple when Joey got loosed last time, but I haven't had a snort since she came home." Her eyes danced wickedly. "You and Sid just wait and see."

"All I know is that I was sick and tired of leading a junky life when I got busted," Gloria said. "So if I gotta be a slave to something it might as well be a man."

Those few words did it. I looked at Gloria with hungry appreciation. And I saw that this lovely creature had gone through changes galore since she'd left the Sinman's and Blind Charlie's presence. She was even more than just a complete personality. She was an unveiled enigma. There was a purposefulness about her now. It formed a miasma like that around the big cats in the zoo. It tensed you, even tensed the air you breathed.

J&J were still happily cackling away when Gloria made her move: she firmly ended the chitchat by again taking my hand and leading me out of the kitchen. As soon as we crossed the threshold of 5-C-4 Gloria snorted like a race horse, and with a backward kick slammed the door shut. Then she emitted a low moan and proceeded to go absolutely ape.

Her beautiful face contorted in a rage of passion, she squirmed in my arms; soon, instead of kissing me she was sucking and nibbling at my lips as if she was both angry and hungry. All at once she loosed her death lock about my neck and grabbed my ears. "Make me love you," she grated.

It was a long time before I came to realize that there had been nothing false or theatrical in that command. In fact, it hadn't even been a command. It was only a prayer from the damned. But at the moment I never guessed this. I thought Gloria *was* being phony and my passion vanished. And I thought to myself that this was the dirtiest trick fate had played upon me yet.

Woodenly, with eyes wide open, I tried to see what I could of Gloria's face. To fathom her. I couldn't. And there was nothing else to do so I sincerely tried to return her furor, but it was like I had the detachment of a clinician watching a wholly improbable reaction in a test tube which I would have to report to my dubious colleagues in the morning.

After a while in angry defiance I tried again, closing my eyes and trying to prove to myself that the impossible was not happening. But the cold indifference would not leave me. I just wasn't for it as I kept thinking that this was one lousy trick.

Meanwhile, Gloria was lost in a hellishly private turmoil of her own, and I sensed that she neither knew nor cared about my small problems at the moment. Moaning and sobbing, she would now and then tear her lips from mine to mutter in an unknown tongue like a Holy Roller.

I have never been really down with anything. At least I don't think I have unless it was with my classwork in college. Yet and still I had always thought of myself as being capable. And it is true that I can take charge in most situations—provided they are square situations. But this was all from another country, another life, a world I never dreamed existed. I was helpless and lonely. More lonely than I'd ever been before.

Gloria abruptly released me, stepped back, glared and said, "You motherfucker." All the while her moist eyes were glinting with a hunger that belonged to no human thing.

Then, with the grimaces of a wrestler, she grabbed me by the arm and threw me on the bed. She executed a sort of high dive and landed on top of me. As all the wind gushed out of my lungs I wondered indifferently whether I was losing my mind too. For, after all, I really didn't go for a damn bit of this and yet I kept telling myself that this was better than loneliness without Gloria.

Wickedly, with a steady grind, Gloria's body beat at me while she valiantly tried to bury her tongue in my throat. It was the unleashing of her turbulence and not the ecstasy that would suddenly convulse her body into a grotesque knot. Her grunts and snorts beat those of a rutting megalomaniac; and actually it was all becoming slightly hilarious to me, but in the caves of my mind I heard the knell, the warning about women scorned, and I figured that this went double for madwomen scoffed at.

While suffering the brunt of this attack it came to me that I was not Gloria's sexual partner at all. This mad passion of hers did not necessarily embrace me. Her rage demanded a body for fuel, but in reality I was no more a part of her experience than the mattress although I took far more punishment.

This marathon cohabitation spanned three days and before it was ended I almost succeeded in making myself enjoy every rugged minute of it, knowing that when it was over I would be more celibate, more melancholy than ever before. Maybe even insane.

On the morning of the fourth day I woke up first. Sometime during the night we had kicked the covers off. And so I looked at the nude form of Gloria. And damned if a tear didn't come in the corner of my eye. For I realized that I would always have to cherish this lovely body. This body had destroyed all desire in me to get drunk; I owed it a debt. It might even have saved my job—something no other woman's body had been able to do. I had been pleasantly high when we left the Sinman's room, but on any other occasion those few drinks would have triggered a three-week period of compulsive drinking. Today I was cold sober and ready to go back in for the weekend.

And Gloria's was an exceedingly fine body to look at in the morning sunlight. There was a fire of youthfulness in every line of it, and I wondered how it was that heroin had not exacted its toll. I could only guess that Gloria's habit had not been of long duration.

Then one thought crashed down into the middle of my reverie: Gloria and I were born mates! Fate had united us through physical—or were they psychosomatic?—handicaps. I was crippled with alcoholism, Gloria was hobbled with nymphomania. It was sad, but it was ours.

I looked at Gloria's body again, this time with a subtle feeling of possession. The only flaw was her stomach. Flat-bellied girls have always held a truly mystical allure for me; I'd much rather contemplate a flat abdomen than a pert rump any day. But Gloria's stomach protruded slightly and I knew that this was only temporary, coming from her recently acquired "chuck habit," the phrase which is descriptive of both the alcoholic's and the narcotics addict's ravenous appetite that follows the halting of addiction.

Suddenly my mind wanted to do gymnastics. Like some half-witted god, I essayed to write Gloria's biography from out of the past into the future. All in all I was being masochistic, yet it gave me some pleasure to deem Gloria one of the beautiful people; she had been born with the face and figure augmented with the brains to succeed. She was a natural-born world beater. But her passions, coupled with a weakness for letting evil men guide her, would always thwart her. I was convinced that it was the Sinman who had taught her the art of prostitution, and I was almost as certain that he had hooked her on heroin. Later I found out how wrong this bathetic biography of Gloria's was, but I did hit on one truth. Which was that Gloria was not a known nympho. I guessed correctly that her frenetic sexuality was so painful to her that she kept her passions on a short leash, never baring her torture save to a few men whom she trusted and whom she believed she could somehow love. You'll never know how sorry I felt for this poor child of damnation.

And in my sorrow I turned to Gloria's future. Surely it would have to embrace me also, and it was frightening to think that we faced so great a love without love. I could foresee all the many beds Gloria would wander into. So in all her loveliness she was but a crown of thorns the playful gods had tossed upon my lonely head. Still, this crown was all I'd been given since my breakup with Alise.

I did not know it, but Gloria had been awake and studying my face for some time. With a derisive smile at the corners of her mouth she said tonelessly, "Don't worry about it. I'm going to let you go back to work today. You won't miss the weekend and get put in the street for a week."

"What makes you think I'm worrying about it?"

The passionate girl was drained of hope and her voice was a measuring rod of her despair. "I know I get—well, greedy, when I let myself go." It was a stark and lonely admission, but it meshed my being with hers. This made it forever. I could never forget my love for Gloria after hearing the heartbreak that had surged through those few words.

She reached for my hand and placed it on her breast. "But I would never have hurt you. I mean I would never have put on the jealousy act. Been phony. Nothing like that."

In all the world I don't think there was a man better suited to truly understand what Gloria meant. She would never hide her indiscretions behind accusations like Alise had done.

And it was so strange. Gloria had spoken in the past tense, she was releasing me, and I knew that she knew I could never be released. And so to let her know that I knew, I asked, "What are you going to do while I'm at work?"

She shrugged her shoulders as if there was a cramp in them. "I don't know . . ." she said in a high voice like a child's. "I never thought about it until you just mentioned it. What do you want me to do?"

Then it was my turn to shrug. "I don't know," I said. "You understand you don't have to hustle any more, don't you?"

"Yeah . . ."

"You sound like you still want to be turning tricks."

Gloria gazed at the ceiling, and I was immediately conscious of her total relaxation. That we were discussing her future, her life to be, was of no moment to her. She was as blandly inscrutable and detached as a Zen Buddhist.

She broke the silence. "I like men," she said defiantly. "I get a pain in the ass every time I hear some broad talking all dainty about she don't like sex much. Sounds like they were talking about spinach or something." She turned to face me. "How the hell can you dislike having sex with a man like you? If you go for a guy you've had it. Know what I mean? Even a stone freak got a natural need to get screwed by a man every now and then. Even when I was strung out I still liked to have my men around once in a while."

This dame had a stiletto and she was twisting it around in all the stupid loneliness of my past. Right in my gut. But I gave a silly grin and said, "Cool baby. You know what's happening. You and I could have a good thing going."

"You really think so? You want that we really get tight? No fooling around? The real thing?"

I looked at her and saw it all: her lovely thighs, her berserk womanhood that might even in time banish alcoholism. There could never be but one answer. I took her in my arms and kissed her for a long time.

"But you don't want me to hustle for you, do you?"

"I just told you you don't have to hustle any more. I make enough. What we need that kind of money for?"

"I don't guess you're the jealous type," Gloria said as if she seriously doubted her words.

"A cat who's been around don't even know what jealousy is," I said, hoping against hope she would not detect my fear and desperation.

Gloria's answering smile was filled with the protectiveness that only a woman who has been a junky whore can know or give. "You ain't been around, Sid. But I'd never hold that against you. . . ." She looked at the ceiling and thought for a moment and then said, "It's only that I don't like to get beat up. I hate fighting, Sid. You know, lots of hustling girls give up tricking after they fall in love with a square man, but I've never seen it work out. Every time the chump will suddenly start accusing the girl of giving away what she was selling before. What makes him figger like that I don't know, but I guess there's no use trying to figger out what goes on inside a square's mind anyhow."

This kid really knew the art of knifing a chump. "You say all that to say what?" I said, verging on hysteria.

Again she faced me. "I'm a screwing woman, Sid," she said softly, gently.

"I know. We'll work it out."

"But there's more. What I mean is if you say don't hustle, well, crazy! But I don't ever want to hear any crap about you saved me from something. Dig it?"

"I *dig* it," I said.

"Maybe a hustling girl should only try to make it with a hustling man," Gloria mused aloud.

"So why'd you bother with me?"

"I want you. You've got brains. Not scrounging brains like a pimp, but real brains."

That didn't soothe me one bit. She'd simply increased my jealousy of that other world she and the Sinman and Blind Charlie inhabited. I had to hurt her, to destroy her other world.

"Don't you have to ask the Sinman's permission to be my woman?" I asked.

"Sinman's not my pimp!" Gloria said sharply. "He's just a good friend. And who needs a pimp anyhow? Do I look like some dumb bitch that'll give her hard-earned bread to some cat who's too dumb and lazy to get out and make his own? There's bread enough in the life for everybody. All you got to do is get out and git it. Dig?" And Gloria talked on. It was an old recording I had heard many times since the ending of my last marriage, and I'd always wondered why every whore had to repeat it so vociferously. The more Gloria preached the less I believed and she finally must have dug that because she finally wound down, saying, "I asked Sinman if he wanted to be once, but he wouldn't. Just the same, he said that he and Blind Charlie would always be in my corner—so I don't need a pimp like other girls do."

I couldn't help it; I was caught in a web of desolate inferiority. "How stupid can you get?" I sneered. "You too dumb to remember that I was in his room when you came in? Who gave you permission to move in on that guy on West End Avenue? And how the hell was he going to give you to me if you weren't his bitch?"

Gloria absolutely refused to lose her cool. "Anybody can give a girl away to anybody they want to," she said. "Besides, the Sinman didn't really mean it the way you think. What he was saying was that he was going to encourage us to get tight with each other. And what's so wrong about that? You just said you were all for it."

"Well, he said he was giving you to me and I can only go by what I hear."

"So what if he did say so? Sid, you don't even have to know a girl to give her away, especially in Harlem. Girls get given away every day. It's no big thing."

"How many girls have *you* given to somebody else?"

"I don't know, but I know I gave a cousin of mine to a pimp once. A low-down, mean and dirty pimp."

"Yeah. I'll bet."

"When she came to New York it was just supposed to be a visit. But when she got in with a bunch of whores and it got so good to her she decides to stay. She was one of those chicks who never feel secure unless they're downing somebody who's already made it. Know what I mean? So she starts going around saying things like 'I had to leave home because of bad blood, the syph.' That was the lyingest bitch ever to hit Harlem—or Brooklyn either."

"So what happened?"

"Nothing at first. At that time I had a boss hustle. And I was boss. She couldn't get next to the johns I was tricking. No class. See? But I got sick of the shit when after she gets busted she's got the nerve to come lay up on me. Catting. No place to stay. Well, I lets her stay temporarily, but she keeps on with her jive and so I decides to teach her something. One night she comes in drunk and flops across the bed. Dead to the world. So I just go down to the telephone and calls this no-'count pimp and tells him he can have her if he comes gets her. So he comes and I lets him in. And then he goes and gets in bed with her." Gloria spread her hands in a gesture of finality. "After that she was his. It ain't hard to give a young kid or a dumb broad away, Sid."

"How's she doing now?"

"She's dead. OD."

I laid back and closed my eyes. Actually I was scared until it came to me that I had joined a world of Zen Negroes; after that I no longer thought of Gloria as being a cold-blooded murderess.

Yeah. There was no getting away from it. As long as I lived in an S.R.O., as long as I loved Gloria, I would be a Zen Negro too. You see, each and every S.R.O. tenant has got to transcend himself into a state of absolute nothingness. Everyone I had come in contact with had reached so perfect a state of nonbeing that they were nothing at all: mindless, ambitionless and essentially homeless. Since they changed race at will, they were raceless and, by the same token, sexless. To add to their nothingness, S.R.O. inmates were colorlessly unimaginative and ultraconservative in all their anti-social thoughts and behavior.

"You act like you never heard of people giving other people

away before," Gloria said. I wondered why she wouldn't drop it, but it was like a hangup with her. "Where you been, Sid? It's been done since Bible times, and I guess folks always will. Whiteys especially. Don't you remember the stories about rich white men and their wards?" She reached over and began to massage my chest. "All women like to be given away. Honest. Deep down inside they do."

I grunted noncommittally.

"The way you usually do it," Gloria said, "is to tell the chick you are going to try to get her a nice little break. And that she's never going to have to worry about anything no more in life. Dig it? Like she's gonna go to heaven without having to die."

"What you mean is that all whores need a manager, a pimp," I said.

Gloria must have thought I was referring to all women when I said that. "Dig," she said. "Women don't really like to think. They always want to be tole what to do in a nice way. Even smart girls in college like to have the professor tell them when to go pee."

"What do you know about girls in college?"

"I was in college until I got pregnant. Then they made me leave. Bennett College."

"In North Carolina?" I groaned. "You went and got yourself knocked up in an all-girls' school?"

"It was during the summer it happened, and it wasn't any professor like you think. It was my boy friend. Isn't it time for you to go put your numbers in?"

If putty can be jelly too, then that's what I was. It had been so awfully long since a woman had shown the slightest interest in my comings in and goings out that I actually had to bite my tongue to keep from thanking Gloria.

I got up and went in the bathroom to shave. After I was dressed I decided not to come back before going on to work. Sure. I was in love now, but there was no sense in killing myself. Just before I left I tossed a ten-dollar bill on the bed and told Gloria to take good care of herself until I got back.

"Make us lots of money, honey," she replied with a smile.

That Friday was one of the roughest I've ever seen at Lundy's. I personally waited on more crazy Jews than they got in the loony bin in Israel. And if anybody thinks a Jewish mother only drives her son nuts they ain't seen nothing at all until they see what one of those bitches can do to a Lundy's waiter.

Sure. Being with Gloria had been rough, but it was like an exaggeration. It hadn't all been tough. There had been lots of beautiful conversation. In fact it was Gloria's conversation that gave me to think that she might be the best girl I'd ever met. And kindness was there. Yeah. After the sex there had been lots of soul, if you know what I mean. So by the time the dining room closed I was renewed.

I unlocked the door and came bounding in to those lovely thighs. But the thighs weren't there. After three nights and days of intermittent conversation Gloria knew exactly what my hours were. In fact she knew my whole daily schedule. So I figured I'd be a fool to run around the Logan looking for her. After an hour of lying in bed wasting cigarettes I changed my mind and went up to her room. She wasn't there. Neither was she in Sinman's room. I told Sinman good night and came back to my room.

About ten the next morning there was a knock on the door and I jumped out of bed to let Gloria in and maybe cuss her out a little. But it was Ginsburg, the youngest of the two managers, standing there grinning at me.

"You know Gloria Bascomb?"

I don't know how it is, but everything that went on in the Logan has to be described in contradictions. Ginsburg was grinning at me with a perfectly blended attitude of respect and insolent familiarity. So even though I was already mad that grin made me madder.

"You woke me up to ask me who I know and don't know?"

The grin did not fade. "Gloria's in jail. House of D. She says she thinks she's gonna have to do sixty days, but not to worry." Then the bastard paused to catch my reaction, but I felt too ornery to react. I knew he was waiting for me to ask something square. Like could I get in her room for her belongings. But I was hepped enough to know that S.R.O. managers put all the belongings of locked-up prostitutes in the storeroom until their release. So Ginsburg could go to hell. I didn't even thank him.

"That's a good girl, that Gloria," Ginsburg said.

I lit a cigarette. The thing was beginning to get next to me now and was starting to hurt. I wished the bastard would go away.

"Well . . . I gotta get back to the office."

After another pause Ginsburg went away. I pulled on my pants and went down to the Sinman's, but nobody was there. I had to talk to somebody so I went into J&J's room.

"Sid, you know all about what kind of woman Gloria is by now, don't you?" Jinny said slowly.

"Yeah, Sid," Joey said. "Gloria's not like other girls. She's different so you can't never be no square with her. See what I mean? Now I like Gloria. She's a swell kid, but people like Gloria should be treated nice only when they come to *visit you.* You don't never visit them, if you know what I mean. Don't let her phone call fool you. You understand that, don't you? You got to go ahead and forget her. She's got sixty days to cool her butt, and when she gets out she mightn' even remember your name."

"And don't write," Jinny said. "If she ever wants anything she'll let you know."

Of course J&J were right. Right as rain. But there was one thing they did not know: that Gloria and I were crippled lovers and that I must dwell in my blighted woman forever. But just the same, they were right.

CHAPTER 5

NOW IT WAS A brand-new kind of loneliness, silent and exquisite torment. The only thing that kept me from calling it quits forever was the certain knowledge that my day would come. That Gloria had rushed from my bed to go hustle in the streets was unimportant.

I knew that the thing between us was what we had been doomed to; it was truly immutable.

One hour after I heard of Gloria's arrest I began to drink. This time whiskey didn't do me like it had been doing for the last six years. It was like old times when I tippled through every waking hour. Never quite sober, but always in full possession of my faculties. I worked practically every day although I stopped going by the other S.R.O.s to visit. Instead I always came back to the Logan after playing my numbers. Most of the time I would go in J&J's to drink and talk. Me whiskey, they had their wine. Once in a while I would switch to gin, but it was only when I was feeling very condescending and *very* democratic that I would drink Silver Spur.

My life was almost as drab as ever, but not quite. Some nights I would luck up on a chick and bring her home. In a way I wanted to punish Gloria, and I figured the best way to do that was to lay up with a chick, whaling away while Gloria was rotting in jail. But that was not like it was. Every time the chick of the evening cut out I was left feeling worse than before I ever laid eyes on Gloria. So when you came right down to it, I was just as much in a prison as Gloria was.

The one cheerful interlude in my dreary day was what I came to think of as the morning newscast. These newscasts were delivered at my bedside by either Jinny or Joey—usually Jinny—about ten every morning. And just like police reporters, they told me of all that had transpired in the Logan while I was at work. Being natural-born historians, J&J also interspersed their news bulletins with many little biographical sketches of the newsworthy souls in the Logan.

However, it was not exactly free on board that these broadcasts were delivered. At some point Jinny or Joey, whichever one, would offhandedly mention the need of a fifty-cent loan until Check-day. Or would I go to the store for them? I never failed the pair.

All this would seem to indicate that we were now close friends and cohorts. This was not quite the case. Half of the time I was all messed up in the damnedest arguments and situations with J&J. They violently denounced any and all of the female company I occasionally had. And actually came right out and accused me of being untrue to Gloria! They even gave me hell for drinking. Finally I stopped letting that precious pair bug me and steadfastly thought of myself as a changeling who had been snatched up and flung into the care of a tumultuous family. Yeah, I was a full-time nut in their nutty family. Both J&J would rush to me with complaints of the other's perfidy. Like Solomon, I always told them to do nothing until I had thought things over. I think that was the only answer they expected or wanted.

But if I now thought myself a member of the family, it was all too evident that J&J also considered me to be a very willful black sheep in their lovely ménage. But since they were so critical of all I did there was no use to try to change my black-sheep image. Actually I couldn't because J&J were absolutely unpredictable. It was totally impossible to guess what either Jinny or Joey would do next. If I'd let them I would have been bananas long ago.

Every day was a thing unto itself. One morning, after the newscast, Jinny would brush past my door, viciously muttering that "Mister Bastid" was too lazy to take his turn at answering the door like everybody else. And the very next morning Joey would arrogantly inform me that since I was a square and a stranger it was not seemly for me to answer the foyer door with all these unprotected females about. But always was I a member of the family.

In many ways all of the tenants in 5-C comprised a family of sorts. Even Mrs. Moriarty, the ancient nurse, was a recalcitrant member of the clan. The old woman brewed her tea in the kitchen and always stood over the sink to drink it. Some days when she was home she would stand there for hours, sipping her tea. J&J would fly into whispered high dudgeon whenever the old lady did this. They always had imaginary pots to cook when Mrs. Moriarty chose to drink her tea.

Pointless arguments were the order of the day every day in 5-C, and I soon decided that everyone who lived in there was a damn fool Irish comedian. And I was just as convinced that Mrs. Moriarty was the least Irish of them all. Every single one of the others simply loved disputes. This went for Mr. Grimm as well as Dick and both of them were almost deaf.

J&J, like true Irishmen, were able to forget the most violent argument immediately, and I believe that the mercurial Joey could forget an argument right in the middle of one.

Leah and Ray feared and hated Mr. Grimm's cat and cursed and screamed like maniacs whenever it wandered into their room. They would run to Mr. Grimm to threaten him with bodily harm while calling him seven different kinds of motherfucker. Yet within an hour of cursing out Mr. Grimm and his cat they would knock at his door and coquettishly inquire if they could use his private telephone.

Dick was forever putting a pot on the stove and then going to his room and falling asleep. When the place filled with smoke and fumes Joey always had to have a violent asthma attack and Jinny would threaten not only to sue Dick but to have him evicted.

It didn't take but so long for me to find out that J&J's unpredictability was caused mostly by Leah's changing attitude toward them. After an exceptionally good night Leah would munificently give Joey a dollar or two to act as official door-keeper (these were the mornings when Mister Bastid was requested not to answer the door), but when Leah moodily announced that she could admit her customers herself, J&J would be chagrined into picking an argument with me—after they had delivered the newscast and borrowed fifty cents.

J&J's come-and-go attitude notwithstanding, I did take my turns at the foyer door while I was not at work. And I learned a whole lot from answering that door.

Like most pushers, Leah did most of her business at night, but there was a regular and constant dribble of daytime customers and visitors whom I got to know fairly well. And I don't have the slightest idea of why it was so, but the daytime customers were a far cry from Leah's night trade. Those in the day had different voices from the night visitors, who spoke in the most coarse and profane tones.

Every morning at ten a handsome young couple knocked on the front door. Very likely I was on my way to or from the bathroom at this time of the morning and so it was I who usually admitted them.

Until I found out from Joey that both of them were addicts I held this couple in the greatest esteem. They were Black America's answer to whitey's boy and girl next door. Lonnie was tall, lightly bronzed and certainly no more than twenty years old. Margo, his wife, was younger, with a tiny shape that was sheer perfection. I don't think she was more than five foot two and probably weighed in at less than a hundred and five but what there was of her was fabulous. Both of them had low, well-modulated voices and cheerful smiles. Neither of them ever appeared to be sick for want of a fix, but then none of Leah's morning callers ever seemed to be uptight.

Naturally, so well-groomed and handsome a couple in the Logan aroused my curiosity. One day I asked Jinny how Lonnie and Margo supported their habits.

"Pretty-boy Lonnie is a fence and a pill-boy," Jinny said.

"A fence? He looks so young."

"What the hell has age got to do with it?"

"How could he get up a bankroll so young? And with a habit? And a fence has to have ready cash. Lots of cash."

"For heaven's sake, Sid. A sting is a sting. It don't matter how young you are, if you make it you got it. A sting don't care how old you are. Dig it?"

"Yeah," I said doubtfully.

"And why you always got to know where from Black people get their bread? Whitey's law says that a nigger can't make a decent living unless he steals, sells narco or banks numbers. And you go to jail for long periods of time for doing any one of those things. Now will you please dig that? And do you realize that in this man's town you get more time for having a list of numbers in your pocket than for a bag of heroin? So you don't ever ask how a Black man made it; you just congratulate him and hope that you get that lucky too. Now how about loaning me the price of a pint?"

I still wasn't satisfied, but I never learned any more about Lonnie and Margo than that.

Another of Leah's regulars was a nervous little wreck named Frances. She was a comedienne without knowing it. She was the only nervous addict I've ever seen. She actually fluttered, and most junkies are relaxed even when sick. I think that they are too lazy to be nervous; junkies are a pretty stolid bunch of people anyhow. But when Frances came to the door she would rap incessantly until admitted. Then she would gush a greeting and put out her hand as if to shove you out of her way. "I gotta see Leah right away," she would gasp. "Wait. I'll be right back." Then she'd fly down the hall and stay in Leah's room no less than fifteen minutes.

Another morning fixture was a young white man named Joe, who usually brought his wife and tiny baby with him. Why he always brought his entire family was another Logan mystery. Furthermore, he stayed less than five minutes.

"Joe runs a call-girl service," Jinny told me. "He's really making it. He buys four bags every morning. Three for him to start the day and one for his wife. He's got to have his three every morning or he can't make it. His wife doesn't do anything. He loves that black ugly gal."

I had to agree that Jean, Joe's wife, was most black, but she wasn't ugly by a long shot, and she had that lean belly and well-rounded hips that were exactly my dish.

Joe and Jean lived on the first floor, and since Joe was a whitey I often wondered why he never dealt with the Sinman. But then, junkies tend to pick their pushers in a way that borders on the superstitious.

Mary was one of the most superstitious. She was convinced that Leah sold the most potent bags in New York City, and no one could tell her different. She lived way over across the park on Eighth Avenue, but she didn't mind the cab fare to come deal with Leah. And Eighth Avenue from 110th Street on up is the heroin center of the world, but every morning she came way over to Leah. After I became a confirmed wino I was always on the lookout for Mary because from the beginning she would often ask me to let her take off in my room. Leah allowed no one to use dope in her room. And Mary always gave me a dollar for the privilege. After taking off, Mary was a wonderful conversationalist. She was a brilliant girl. Although she was a high school dropout I think she was one of the most intelligent women in all Harlem. Certainly in and around the Logan.

Bald-headed Nappy was a round-the-clock customer. He looked middle-aged, about fifty, although there's no telling the age of most male junkies because the men have twice as hard a life to live as the women. A junky girl, no matter how far strung out, can always find some man who'll let her sleep with him for the night, but many male addicts have to go for days sometimes before they ever lie in a bed.

No matter who admitted Nappy, we never bothered to say any more than hello because Nappy always made a beeline into the kitchen where he would sit at the table and count his money over and over. There would be some bills but most of his money was silver. After being in the kitchen as long as an hour Nappy would go into Leah's room and make his purchases. And complicated purchases they were. Since nobody but Mrs. Moriarty kept their door closed during the day, I could hear Nappy arguing, begging and wheedling.

"Nappy gets shit from Leah at four-fifty a bag most times," Joey explained. "Then he goes out on 125th and peddles it for all the traffic will bear. He's in here day and night. The bastid never sleeps."

But Kingfish was Leah's stellar attraction. Kingfish was not a bad-looking guy, but he was so crooked he could actually make you think he was ugly. And Kingfish always had something to sell. He was a supersalesman and his main hustles was lemons. A lemon is a packet of milk sugar or some other substance that looks like heroin. Lemons are palmed off on the unwary. Usually women who are unable to beat up the Kingfish and his type and take their money back. Of course Kingfish was an excellent thief like all junkies, male or female. And he always came to me first with his loot. I considered this to be an insult because he was tacitly saying that I was dumber than Leah and would give him a higher price than Leah would. I refused to take some beautiful bargains from him out of pure meanness. And Kingfish peddled everything. He was a truly catholic thief. He went in bookstores and came out with three or four best sellers. Two or three times a week he offered me Kuppenheimer or Hammonton Park suits. And the next day it might be playing cards or women's panties. Anything that could be picked up and carried was sold by Kingfish sooner or later. After I turned the Kingfish down he would go in to Leah and the subsequent haggling and arguing was straight out of Amos 'n' Andy, but Kingfish always got what he came for in the end.

I also got to know Butch and Joan, who came to visit every day. These young girls were reputed to be lovers, but to my way of thinking they only lived for the next fix. They were pushers and lived in the room directly beneath Leah. Butch at least had an Afro hairdo, but neither one ever bothered to comb her hair and they dressed worse than any of the male junkies down in the lobby. They looked like hell at all times; and were so strung out I simply did not believe they were able to be lovers even if they wanted to be.

Most times Bill and Reba would drop by before Joan and Butch left. Bill and Reba were middle-aged, I guess, but like I said, you simply cannot tell a junky's age after they become strung out. Bill's room was on the third floor and he was reputed to have the largest trade in the Logan. Bill wasn't much taller than me, but he was a formidable guy. His arms were almost as thick as Blind Charlie's. And although his arms were covered with tracks from needles he never wore a shirt. He was that proud of his physique.

I liked Bill. He simply was not self-centered like the average junky. Every time he came he would stop at my door and ask how I felt and how was the job going. And I believe he was sincerely interested. Now if any other addicted man in the Logan asked how my job was going I would have been sure that thoughts of robbery were dancing in his head. But Bill was really interested even if he was a pusher and strung way, way out.

And it was when Reba and Bill, Butch and Joan, and Ray and Leah were congregated together with the door open that I learned the ins and outs of the heroin business. The first startling thing I learned was that these six were far more than furtive pushers, in the glib journalistic sense. These people were dedicated merchants, just as purposeful and serious about their trade and image as any member of the Junior Chamber of Commerce. Why, those people really were conducting a seminar in Leah's room. They discussed ethical questions like whether to let a sick junky have a bag for less than five dollars. Butch and Joan insisted that even a sick junky should be made to go back in the street and hustle up the full price of a fix. On the other hand, Bill and Reba believed that a sick junky is a menace to all junkies, and especially the pushers. A sick junky should be fixed up before he does something that will arouse the community and/or the police.

I also found out that pushers are accused of doing many things that a really professional pusher simply does not have time to do. No bona fide pusher has the time to hang around schoolyards. Heroin turns over fast. And it is also true that the more narco found on a prisoner the stiffer the sentence. So the pusher stays put and lets the customers come to him, dealing as fast as he can. Only a stone idiot would wander around the streets, hawking his wares to the uninitiated. Sure, there is heroin in our schools, but the pushers don't take it there. Never.

And the wonder is that anyone is ever caught peddling heroin. After a week or two in business a pusher will have more addicted customers than he can supply. It is only the dumbest of lames who sell to some unknown, some undercover police agent, who apparently doesn't even have a habit. If a pusher is not greedy he can operate forever until the police make a formal raid on his premises and find his cache.

And the pusher's only real enemies are his closest friends. No one can harm a pusher unless they possess some kind of information. I believe this solves part of the riddle of the Sinman. He not only didn't want any junky friends, but he developed a way of talking that would irritate most people and keep them at arm's length at all times.

All six were generally agreed that the greatest pitfall was to let yourself become a fence, taking in stolen goods for the price of heroin. I've already told you about Leah and the Kingfish, but in these seminars she staunchly denied ever being so foolish as to accept stolen goods.

I overheard enough from these six to be able to go into the heroin business tomorrow.

Another discovery I made during Gloria's prison term was the fact that Leah just might have been the only addicted pusher in New York who went on periodic binges. During these three- or four-day drinking sprees Leah was the friendliest and funniest female drunk imaginable. She was downright cute and it was utterly impossible to dislike her while she was drinking. In fact, I loved for her to come in my room with her foolishness.

Leah's binges presaged good times for J&J. Leah never trusted herself to deal while she drank, and since Ray slept all day, she would entrust Jinny with five bags at a time to sell for her. These bags, as the junkies called the glassine packets of heroin, contained one dosage and sold for five dollars. Jinny received fifty cents commission on every bag she sold.

But when Leah was not drinking, J&J's finances were a mystery. Common sense told me that Joey's Welfare check could not possibly take care of all the wine they consumed daily, but it was very slowly that I learned of the dozens of different ways the pair came by their food and drink money. And each of those different ways was touched by pure genius.

Every morning after the newscast Jinny took a stroll through the halls of the Logan. In an hour or so she would return with at least a dollar and often two or three. I didn't have the slightest idea of what she did to get hold of this money, but I was sure she didn't borrow it. She couldn't. At least not to my way of thinking, because J&J never paid any debts.

After a few days off I learned that J&J were all things to all people in the Logan. Most afternoons they held what was tantamount to a Chatauqua in their room with Joey leading the meeting.

In her role as leader of the Chatauqua, Joey was an amazing

personality. She dispensed all kinds of advice, especially legal and criminal advice, plus theatrical history and lore, and some pure entertainment as well. J&J were both excellent comediennes. Those two did not know the meaning of the words "boredom" or "loneliness." People would be drinking in other rooms in the Logan and all of a sudden they would pick up their glasses to come to J&J. Sometimes to have the weirdest arguments settled. Joey answered all these questions with little sermonettes and parables. And Joey *was* entertaining. So it was no longer a mystery why people thronged in and out of J&J's room all day long, especially when you consider the fact that there was only one television set in the whole hotel and it was owned by cantankerous Joe Ash, the Logan's shylocking bootlegger.

J&J were the final arbiters, the givers of the last word in the Logan. But when the pair graciously admitted they were stumped, it was Jinny who flew to the telephone in the lobby to call the *Daily News,* the inmates' Bible.

Nothing about J&J was ever certain, but I believe that Joey's efforts brought in the most drinks while it was Jinny who raised the most actual cash. She was the official five percenter. And in this capacity she introduced new tenants to Joe Ash and vouched for their dependability. She also acted as an intermediary between the managers and those tenants who had somehow incurred their wrath.

And Jinny could tell to the penny what any article would bring in the pawnshop. Also Jinny could always find reliable runners to go to the pawnshop for ladies who were either too sick or too shy to go themselves. And it was this mischievous little lady who manufactured all the tall tales of distress the Loganites told their Welfare investigators.

Most of the people who frequented J&J's room were winos who usually brought bottles or small change to chip in on bottles, but there were others who never touched wine, but were unable to stay away from J&J for long. One of these was a very handsome girl named Suzie. She was a beer drinker, but her beer just did not taste right unless drunk to the accompaniment of J&J's chatter.

J&J were not by any means hardrock hustlers or vultures. Many was the shaking wino who came to them for an early morning pick-me-up. And he was never refused unless he came too early.

One morning J&J came to my room about seven-thirty. I sat up in bed. Only the most earth-shattering news was delivered in duet and never had either of them come this early before.

Jackie, they said, was sick. Their concerned faces and solicitude surprised me since they had never shown any interest in the girl before. I thought they hardly knew her. The Sinman once told me that Jackie and old Dick had been sweethearts ever since Jackie was eight years old, but all I really knew was that Jackie did not have a key to either the foyer door or to Dick's door. I had gone to the door to admit Jackie several mornings, and twice, when Dick was not home, she asked if she could sit with me until he returned. That's all I knew about Jackie.

"Dick got his clothing check from Welfare yesterday and you know what that means," Jinny said.

"How the hell do I know what it means?"

"It means that Dick's gone out to gamble. And he's not coming home until he breaks everybody on 116th or they break him. He's one of the originals. One of the biggest numbers bankers we had, and he thinks he can still get up another bankroll and go back in business," Jinny said.

"A former Harlem numbers king now on Welfare and living in the Logan," I mused aloud. "But, anyhow, what part do you all expect me to play?"

"What we got to say is this," Joey said. "Jackie bought a fix with her last money—only money. She turned a trick and the john ends up mugging her, the bastid. But she managed a five-dollar trick after that—"

"Get to the point, will you?" Jinny said. Then she turned to me. "Jackie needs a five-dollar loan. Leah's all out and so we can't get no credit there. . . ."

"Well, what's wrong with the fix you said she bought?" I asked.

"Goddamit, Sid! Can't you dig nothing?" Joey hollered. "They laid a lemon on her!"

"Oh," I said.

"So will you loan Jackie a pound?" Jinny asked.

I took my time to answer. Getting yourself involved in the purchase of heroin for a young girl is something else again. My reputation here in the Logan was not too hot as it was. More and more I was becoming known as an easy mark to the winos; now I was being asked to take the junkies on my back too. Any way you looked at it, this was a bad show.

"I don't really have it," I said. "I stayed in the bar until it closed last night. So now I've only got enough dough for a few drinks and my numbers until I go to work."

"Don't worry, Sid," Joey said. "You'll get your money back in plenty of time to play your numbers. You'll have it back before half past nine. Jackie's so sick now she can't turn a trick, but as soon's she cops and gets her stomach settled, she can turn one with the old man who runs the grocery. He hates colored, but he's a stone john for Black women. And you know for yourself that Jackie is one *black* child."

"You mean to stand and tell me that that KKK pig is a sucker for *my women?*"

"How you think so many of these bitches can blow all their checks on Checkday and still eat?" Joey demanded.

Jackie walked in and J&J left immediately. She was a slightly built girl who had probably never been nice-looking. And she certainly looked like hell now. Her kinky hair looked as wild as her eyes. I think maybe she had been pulling it. And her lips were trembling before she spoke. When she did speak I could see that the saliva in her mouth was like cotton, hanging in many fine threads from her top incisors to her bottom ones.

"Sid, please loan me five dollars," Jackie said. It really was a moan. "I'll pay you back in an hour, as soon as the grocer comes. In less than an hour maybe, I'll pay you back; that's all right, isn't it?"

I shifted uncomfortably, knowing that I was going to have to do some smooth lying to get this poor chick off my back. "I was drunk yesterday and cussed out both the managers," I said. "And now my rent is due today. If I don't pay on time, they just might start some shit. You know how it is. I only wish I could do something for you, but I just can't take that chance."

Strange, the way Jackie wandered out of the room. It was just as if she hadn't asked for anything or heard my reply. I sighed with relief. Jackie was sick as hell, and I felt as sorry for her as J&J did, but I had to maintain what little bit of rep I had left in this crumby hotel. If a square is dumb enough to loan a junky five bucks he's had it. Those junkies would never get up off me.

I got up and began to dress. Now that I was awake I'd never be able to go back to sleep without a whole fistful of drinks, and I couldn't do that. I decided to go play my numbers and then go by and visit some of the boys. Jackie walked back in as I was combing my hair.

"Sid, loan me five dollars on this watch," she moaned.

It was an old watch of foreign make, but it was gold. I looked at the thing out of politeness. It was a lady's watch, designed to be worn around the neck.

"It's valuable, Sid. Like an heirloom. And you don't have to worry about me coming back for it because it was my sister's. It's the only thing I got to remember her by. She was wearing it when she lay dying. She told me I should always keep it. So now you know exactly what's what."

I sighed and pulled a five-dollar bill out of my pocket.

"You won't sell it on me, will you, Sid? It's real valuable. But I'm going to get it back in an hour anyway. And please don't tell anybody I had to do this, Sid. *Please.* So help me. I'm so ashamed I could die."

"Don't worry about a thing," I said, kind of choked up. It was a real pitiful scene. Not just Jackie. But I didn't have the heart to tell her that the watch wasn't worth one buck as old gold.

Jackie went back in J&J's room and then those two skipped into mine. "You're a sweetheart," Jinny trilled, and kissed me. Joey stood behind her, grinning manfully.

"Want some Spur?" I asked to cover my embarrassment.

When I came back from the store with their wine I passed Mrs. Moriarty, who was coming out of the kitchen.

"Did you see that bad gurl?" Mrs. Moriarty's brogue was thick with anger and dismay.

"Girl? Which girl?"

"That sneaky little one they call Jackie. She came in my room and wanted to borrow five dollars, but I didna have it to lend. I had a watch on the dresser, and we talked about it. I told her how my dying sister gave it to me. I brought it from Ireland forty years ago. Why did she take it? She could never sell it. We were never rich; the watch didna cost much when it was new years ago."

"Jackie stole your watch?" I said slowly.

"It had to be that Jackie," the nurse said. "It was right there on the dresser when she came in. I didna move it. I'm going to have that bad gurl arrested. She's got no business in here anyhow. I heard Mr. Ginsburg telling Dick he'd have to pay extra for that gurl sleeping in his room every day. But Dick hollered and said he wasn't paying nobody's rent but his own. And I'm also going to tell that Dick that she can't come in here any more."

Honestly. I was more heartbroken than the old nurse. And on top of it I felt dirty. Dirty as hell. Dirtier than the whole goddam Logan put together. But what was I to do? Go get the watch and give it to her? It just wasn't as simple as that. In the first place, the watch Jackie had pawned to me did not have to be the watch she stole from Mrs. Moriarty. Jackie even might be planning to pawn Mrs. Moriarty's watch to redeem the watch she had me holding. Any way you looked at it, I would be stupid to hand over that watch. I would be courting not only ostracism but maybe even physical harm if I dared do such a thing here in the Logan. I would immediately become not just a square but an out-and-out pussy. And all junkies have a way with pussies. Nor was the old nurse to be trusted completely. Having once regained her watch, she might still go to the police, and I could wind up being held as an accessory or receiver of stolen goods.

"You sure?" I asked, sparring for a solution.

"Shure! It was right there in plain sight and nobody else has been in my room. 'Tis a dirty shame."

"If she stole it, I will see that you get it back," I said. It was an easy enough promise to make under the circumstances. I knew for certain that Jackie would have no further use for the watch I was holding—provided it was the stolen watch. So I'd tell Jackie to keep her five dollars and I'd be the only loser. Of course there was the chance that Jackie would remain true to the junkies' way of doing things. In that case she would soon come to me with only a fraction of the five dollars and ask me to let her have the watch—and she would lay some kind of off-the-wall jive on me about the balance due. This would give me the opportunity to refuse her and to keep the watch; then in a few days I would tell Jackie that I'd been strapped for cash and had to sell it. Thus I would be gaining a rep among the junkies as being a tough man to deal with. At the same time I would be playing a sort of Black Robin Hood to Mrs. Moriarty.

Back in my room I still felt all the dirt in the Logan seeping into my pores. After all, nobody had really been hurt permanently and yet it was one of the most vicious little crimes I'd ever heard about. Something told me not to discuss this thing with J&J. Intuitively I knew that somehow the Sinman would be the only person in the entire hotel who would agree with me and my plans.

SCENE II

G*INSBURG WAVED HIS HAND in futility and frowned. "But why do those motherfuckers always have to call me a refugee? My grandfather came over here in 1882. You colored people had just got out of slavery yourselves."*

"You've got a hotel full of Southern country Negroes," Paula said slowly. "Most of them never saw a Jew until they came north to Harlem. Some of them are so dumb that they think a Jew is something Hitler invented."

"Bullshit. They had Bibles down there."

"No kidding. I mean what I say." She turned her head on the pillow and smiled at him. "And the Negro just does not believe in democracy anyhow. They like the American system exactly the way it is now except for one thing: they don't like the idea of being low man on the totem pole. They can think of a lot more deserving people to take their place. Refugees, for instance."

"Bullshit."

"Do you have to swear? You sound just like one of your tenants."

"You work there, Miss High-and-Mighty. And if you work there you should be used to strong language by now. You forget that, don't you?"

"No," Paula said wearily. "I know. I know that I am a black-assed maid in the Logan, and you are the refugee manager, and that you furnish this apartment for me, and I accept it, and therefore I am a damn sight lower than anyone in the Logan, including the junkies who committed murder last night."

"Those goddam junkies!"

"They're your *tenants, not mine. You're the one who gives them rooms."*

"Everybody on earth needs a room, someplace to live. You ever hear of fair housing laws? What you want me to do? Tell a junky he ain't got no right to lie down?"

"Yes. And take your hands off my titties. They're sore. I'm going to be sick tomorrow."

"Is that what's the matter with you tonight?"

"No. It's you and that damned Logan."

"So why do you insist on working there? You don't have to."

"The boss ain't mean."

"You said that like you hate me, and I'll be damned if I don't think you do."

"You think I'd be laying here with you if I did? Slavery's over. You just said so."

"Sometimes I think you hate me." He began to kiss her, but she lay beneath his embrace like a prisoner. He stopped kissing her and studied her face. "Would you feel any different about me if I was the manager of the Waldorf-Astoria?"

"You know better. I go with you because I can't help myself. Now shut up."

"Don't tell me to shut up. You know I don't like it when people tell me to shut up. I got a right to talk."

"Well, go talk to your tenants and tell them you don't like being called a refugee. And tell them to stop selling dope on your premises. And tell them to stop cutting each other up with broken wine bottles and knives. There's lots of things you don't have to shut up about."

He raised up on one elbow. "You know," he began, "I don't think you like to face facts. Now I don't sell dope. I don't hustle whores. I don't run around stabbing people. See what I mean?"

"Sure. You mean you're better than Black people. Better than me."

"I mean that I am better than some colored people. And I mean I wish I was only half as fine a person as you are. You know that."

"Leave my tits alone, I told you." She shrugged herself farther away from him.

"You got a damned good high school education. You got dignity. You're pretty. Why don't you get a job as a salesgirl?"

"You've asked me that a dozen times."

"And you never answered it and now I think I know the answer: you're ashamed of me so you punish yourself by working at the Logan. You're ashamed of yourself for loving a white man."

"You're no white man. You're a goddam refugee."

"Why the hell can't you say kike? Or sheeny? Or Jew bastard?"

" 'Refugee' hurts you more."

"Well, why you got to hurt me more?"

"I don't know. Maybe I am ashamed of myself for loving you. But, honest to God, there's something wrong with a man running an S.R.O. like you do. It's like being a slave trader. . . ."

"Then, like I say: why do you insist on working for me?"

"I can't work no place else," Paula yelled. "I'm too independent to work any place else. At least you leave me alone. I mean, you don't come following me around, checking on what I'm doing."

"You do good work."

"I know it, but I can't stand white people standing over me, giving me orders. I hate white people, can't you see that?"

"I always thought you did. But when I think of you and me it just don't make sense."

"Nothing connected with the Logan makes sense."

"We aren't connected with the Logan. The thing we got the Logan don't touch. When we met you didn't even know what the Logan was."

"So what? I came there, didn't I? I was spiritually headed for the Logan. You know that."

"You didn't even know the name of the place when you came in and asked for a room."

Her smile was soft and kind. "I don't know what got into me that day. Everything you said was just right, I guess."

"It had to be just right. I was desperate. I took one look at you. And that was it. Funny, huh?"

"Yeah," Paula said disgustedly.

"I showed you a room and told you you didn't have to take it; I would find you a better one, an apartment."

"And I took it like a damn whore."

"Don't say that."

"It's true, isn't it?"

"Not like that, it isn't true."

"Why isn't it?"

"We looked at each other and fell in love. All of a sudden we had this thing. That's how it was. We met in the Logan is true, but the Logan don't touch us."

"Yes, it does. You know it does. Some days I think we are lower than anybody in the Logan."

"No, we're not."

"Why don't you ask your wife about that?"

"My wife ain't interested and you know it."

"No, I don't know it, Mr. Ginsburg."

"Well, I'm telling you."

"Save it."

"I'm going to leave and go home if you're gonna keep on acting this way."

"And how am I acting, please?"

"Like you hate my guts. Like you wish I'd never been born. How you think I feel?"

"I'm not interested in how you feel."

"That's just what I mean. Every once in a while you let the Logan come between us. Can't you realize that it's just another hotel? And that I just happen to be the manager? I don't like being manager of the place, but somebody has to be. And sometimes I hate those people. Sometimes when they rob a room or a girl gets busted, or a pusher gets busted, it hurts. Don't you think that I think that it gives all of us a bad name? Don't you know I know you hurt?"

"It took you a hell of a long time to get around to saying that, didn't it?"

"Now what the hell does that mean?"

"It means that you've happily got a bunch of underprivileged

Black people all bundled up in one building, but unfortunately you find that you're not completely happy unless you are screwing one of them. Me."

"For Chrissakes, Paula, come off it, will ya? I provide shelter for a group of unlucky people like you say is true. But leave me and you out of it, can't you?"

"I can't."

"Sometimes I think that you think the Logan wouldn't exist if I wasn't managing it."

"Well, why can't heroin be sold on street corners, or in vacant lots? Why have you got to rent out rooms for it to be sold in?"

"Goddamit. Everybody's got to have a roof, I tell ya."

"But not from you."

"You think I'm proud of it?"

"No. You don't even care that much."

"The hell I don't. You think I like it when my friends call me up and say they read about the Logan in the newspaper? But even so, the people who really give the Logan its reputation don't even live there. They hang out in the lobby is all. Like the Kingfish. Like—"

"You could bar them off the premises."

"You work there. You know better."

"Yeah, I guess I do."

"Then what are you chewing me out for then?"

"I don't know. I guess I'm mad because you're just a little nobody, all fucked up in a system that can't be beat. You know, you ain't no refugee. You're just another damn nigger."

A little later Ginsburg said, "You ever realize that the Logan is a house of people without a God?"

"Now what brought that on?"

"Most of the people in the Logan are harmless. Winos and stuff, but harmless. But the thing is they got no sources, no connections, just me. I'm the only connection they got. Me and Welfare. I loan them money to keep them from starving between checks. I call Welfare for them when they don't have a dime. I take them to the hospital. I bring them their checks to the hospital. I lie to their

investigators for them; say they ain't been drunk, and that they've paid their rent when sometimes they ain't. I'm the only thing them people got to have faith in. You ever realize that?"

"You dirty Jew bastid."

"I don't mean it that way, Paula. Not the way you think."

"Great-white-refugee-God-the-bastid-Father!"

"Paula, give me a break and listen for a minute, would ya? I mean that those people are like children without parents. Delinquents with nothing to go by. Nothing on this earth but me. And who am I? A young Jew that ain't even really dry behind the ears yet, if you know what I mean."

"And you are just as delinquent as they are. Who grabs the phone and warns all the pushers time a detective walks in?"

"I'm against dope just as much as anybody, but if the police really want to wipe out heroin addiction in New York they gotta do a damn sight more than put a 'raided premises' sign on the front of the Logan. New York's a jungle and I'm in this jungle, protecting my investment."

"Oh, for Chrissakes. Come on and do it if you're going to."

CHAPTER 6

A CURIOUS GLADNESS FILLED me when I saw that the door of 1-C-1 was open, for I hadn't seen the Sinman since Gloria had been in the Women's House of Detention. Even though the door was ajar, I knocked.

"Come on in!" It was a command filled with disgust, and I realized that I shouldn't have bothered to knock. I entered and saw that Blind Charlie was the only person in the room. The same terror I'd had before seized me, but I was even too scared to turn my butt and haul it.

"It's me. Sid, Charlie," I piped, wondering if a foolish virgin could have sounded any sillier.

The blind man snorted like a big black whale. "I knows it."

Since he had deigned to speak to me I took heart. "You want a drink of wine, Charlie?" That question gushed from my lips without ever having been touched by my brains. Just one look at Blind Charlie would tell the biggest fool that here was a man who never touched sneaky pete and never would, come what may. I stood and trembled, waiting for Charlie's scornful rebuff.

I must have even closed my eyes as I trembled there because it was like seeing an old photo. Charlie was sitting in the same place, in the same chair and in the same position as the first time I'd seen him. So with my fool's imagination I just knew that this was not only a blind man but a hopelessly crippled one as well. But even so I was afraid.

Just then Kingfish burst into the room. "Where's Sinman?" he screamed.

I darted a look at Blind Charlie, but Charlie sat quietly in his chair. Of course Charlie could not see the insanity burning in the Kingfish's eyes, but certainly he could hear the madness in that one scream. "He's not here," I said at last, knowing that somehow I had to get this insane dope fiend away from the room and poor Blind Charlie.

Kingfish gave a sudden shriek of terror and pain and collapsed at my feet. His body was racked by convulsions, but the mad eyes were now closed as if in death. I knew the only smart thing to do when a junky approaches death is to go someplace else because in no time at all the place can be filled with police and questions. I was debating whether or not to lead Charlie out with me when Kingfish grabbed my ankles, and using my legs for support, pulled himself up to a kneeling position.

Now his arms were about my flanks as he moaned, "Gawd hab mercy!"

I swear I thought I could hear what writers call a death rattle in his throat.

"Please call the cops. Please! Can't you see I'm dying?"

Kingfish suddenly dived backwards and his head hit the floor with a chilling plop. That settled it. This was no act. I reluctantly decided to call the police. I had to; city ambulances do not come to the Logan or any other S.R.O. unless summoned by a policeman on the beat. It was a sticky situation any way you looked at it. But I was a square! I was not a pusher. I was not a junky. And I was the only able-bodied person in the room!

I looked at the crippled Blind Charlie. He moved. It was so fast I was reminded of a black snake.

Khuhh—lokkk! It was the sound of Charlie's heavy cane striking Kingfish squarely in the forehead. Its crook had caught the prostrate man just above the bridge of his nose. It was so eerie I shivered. This able-bodied blind man could strike with accuracy at the source of a sound. Then, to my surprise, Kingfish scrabbled to his feet and scurried out of the room.

"Why that junky bastid want to make me kill him?" Charlie's voice was high, almost effeminate with indignation. "He know we don't 'low none of that in here."

I didn't know exactly what Charlie meant, but I heartily agreed. "Damn right," I said. "You really handled that guy. Do you know who it was? It was the Kingfish."

"I know that!" Charlie roared. "You must think I'm deef and dumb too. Don't you, boy?"

"Nonh-no, Charlie. I only thought maybe you didn't know him. He comes up Leah's every day. I thought maybe he only did business with her."

Charlie made an angry sound. "Junkies gotta keep more'n one source open. What'd they do effen their only connection got busted? He buys here too, but only for cash. Leah gives him breaks the Sinman won't. He's a low one, that boy."

"J&J told me a long time ago that he sold lemons."

"Lemons? He's lower than that mosta the time."

"There's not much lower a man can get than selling lemons," I said, thinking of Jackie and the agony she had been through.

"What I hate about the Kingfish is that he don't try his lemon crap on nobody but women and pussies," Charlie said. "But that don't give no woman no excuse not to have a man in her corner at all times."

I realized that Charlie and I were having a conversation. Just like that I'd been accepted. I got a glow on like the most successful social climber. I had joined the church without even having to pay my dues. "I wonder why he came in here and tried his murphy on us?" I mused grandly.

"He don't know hisself. Junkies can't never plan nothing through. That's why the jails is always overcrowded. And them junkies ain't never in jail for using junk either. They is there because they do everything dumber than everybody else. They is even dumber than the pigs."

"But he really did put on a good act. He sure had me fooled—in the beginning. I wonder what I should have done if he really was sick?"

"Nothing! Effen he really was dying he wouldn't have come in here in the first place. When a junky is getting ready to kick the bucket for want of a fix he is too weak to walk even much less carry on like that bastid was doing." Charlie's voice grew surprisingly gentle. "You is a square, boy. Ain't no need to be ashamed of that. Don't have to wear no hip boots effen you ain't breaking the man's law. So what a junky does is never none of your business. Now you just go ahead and believe that."

"Sure. I'm square," I said without conviction. "But even so, Kingfish should have known better than to try to con you and me."

"He wasn't trying to con *me,*" Charlie said succinctly. "He comes in and takes one look at you and decides it ain't no harm to try."

"But the way he rushed in," I said. "And he didn't even know I was in here."

"Mebbe he did. And anyways he comes in like that all the time. Always in a rush. Especially when he don't have the full price of a bag. Like four seventy-five mebbe. He figgers somebody'll see him go for a quarter. But when he sees your stupid ass in here he decides to go for the whole hog. And the bastid thinks I won't say a goddam word while he's scaring a damn fool chump inta buying a whole bag!"

I wanted to cry. I knew the junkies all put me down as a square who worked, but I never dreamed they considered me a downright fool.

"But that dumb sonofabitch oughta know that effen he ever dies in here it's gonna be 'cause Blind Charlie done kilt him."

The cold, bald statement of fact sent chills all over my body. For a while Charlie did not speak until I said, "I *hate* that damn Kingfish. I can understand a man making it under any and all circumstances, but nobody got to be crooked with everybody they meet every second out of the day. And that damned Leah's not much better. Those two even look alike!"

"You on the right track now, boy. And no sense in ever having truck with the enemy and all junkies is your natural-born enemies. They all comes outa the same shithouse. And they hates the world cause that shit don't never come offen them. Now once in a while you meets a man like the Sinman that *uses* drugs, but drugs don't never use him. Sinman ain't no junky."

I had plenty of thoughts on that subject, but Charlie was never going to hear them. Not from me he wasn't!

Charlie actually looked to be less murderous as he said meditatively, "Folks always talking about a junky'll kill his mother for a fix, but effen you asks me, them mothers is the only ones them junkies got a right to kill. Them mothers shoulda killed them junkies the day they was born." Then his face contorted with rage and he jumped up from the morris chair. "Where the hell's that wine you was talking about, boy?"

I was palsied. I'd never seen such rage. "I—I gotta go get it, Blind Charlie," I managed to say. "What kind you want? Silver Spur?"

"What the hell do I care?" Charlie shouted.

"Guess I'll get Spur then," I mumbled, sidling toward the door. "Anything else I can get you, Charlie?"

"Hell no! I don't need nothing."

A girl named Sandy was sprawled across the bed when I got back from the store. I liked Sandy, and every time I thought about her I grew sad because she was an addict. The first time I'd ever paid much attention to her was one day I let her in the foyer door. She only said hello then, but after she came out of Leah's room she'd stopped at my door and asked if I'd let her take off in my room.

Of course I said yes. You know; a damsel in distress and all that jive. You think I was going to say no?

I tried to look all calm and sophisticated as Sandy took her works out of her bra. Her works being the usual Harlem homemade affair of a medicine dropper which the junky attaches to his needle. I put on a bored look as she cooked her stuff in the cap from a whiskey bottle. All this I'd never seen before, and I knew I was going to get queasy when she stuck that hypo in her arm so I walked over to J&J.

"Sid, when the hell are you ever going to learn?" Jinny had said in a fine blending of anger and disgust. "You know she can die before she pulls that damned spike out of her arm, don't you? And who's to pull it out before the pigs come to take you in for running a shooting gallery? You?"

"And she stinks!" Joey yelled with downright happiness. "Maybe she's even lousy. Supposing she leaves lice in your bed?"

I was wondering if all junkies sat on the edge of a bed to take a fix as I went back in my room. Sandy had shed that drawn gray look for the bright shell of a rather handsome twenty-year-old kid.

She smiled. "You're aces with me, Sid. Boss. I won't forget this."

I had to play it as cool as the next square. "Any time," I said offhandedly.

"You really live alone, Sid?"

"Don't it look like it?"

She laughed. "I'm too down with it to go by looks anymore."

"Well, I'm a bachelor. So you don't have to ever worry about any dames messing over you in here."

"Good," Sandy said with a complacent little sigh. "I kinda dig you, Sid. You don't think you're Gawd's little helper just because you don't use shit."

Maybe I didn't know then, but I've learned since that all junkies have a genius for saying the right thing at the right time. And Sandy had said the right words to turn me on. Even if she was an addict she'd make a good girl friend to have on the side.

"And any time you got five bucks to spend on some fun, let me know," Sandy said. "And I'm not one of those hit-and-run broads. I know a man don't stay ready all the time." She was very sober-faced now. "Everything takes time. See what I mean? And I don't never rush guys that are okay. We're all Black together and got to look out for each other. Right? And dig this: we all gotta live and keep our men relaxed. Am I right?"

"Well, I sure could use some company every now and then," I said. It was not only that Sandy was in the fox class, but I figured to be saving all those taxi fares and drinks over the bar. "But how do I get in touch with you? Leah?"

"Hell no! Leave Leah out of everything you do," Sandy warned me. "I live up in 6-B-5 with my old man. That's why I asked to take off in here. I was damned if I was going to give that lazy bastid any of that bag. If I'd had to share I'd of hardly got my sickness off. And you know I wasn't going for that. First thing after I get up I gotta have my own bag to myself."

Gloria had not crossed my mind until Sandy mentioned her old man. In fact, I'd been forming some masterfully illogical plans until the mention of her pimp. "So what do I do if I want to see you?" I asked again.

"Come get me," Sandy said flatly. "No boy friend of mine is ever going to get between me and a buck. Dig? And if I'm not there, tell him. What the hell good is a man if he can't give his old lady a message like that?"

And Sandy had left nothing to be desired. She was a professional through and through. I even thought that maybe she liked her work. And Sandy had brains; she could carry on a conversation just as well as Mary from Eighth Avenue. Another thing that made Sandy rate so high with me is that she rated high with the winos. Every single one of them often said that Sandy was the only junky they knew who did not steal. But Joey had been right: Sandy did stink to high heaven.

"Hi, Sid," she greeted me. "What's new?"

"Nothing much." I grinned. "Charlie tell you about the Kingfish?"

"Naw." Sandy pouted. "Blind Charlie don't talk to me. But there ain't a goddam thing I want to hear about the Kingfish unless you gonna tell me he's dead. I had to cut his throat once."

"You? You cut that big ox's throat?"

"Yeah," Sandy said carelessly. "He finds this john for me, see? And after I turns the trick and the john's split, Kingfish comes in my room and tries to gorilla me. He's running a game, see? Dig it: he goes straight to Hollywood, yelling about the john gimme a five-buck tip to give to him—the Kingfish. Can you dig that? And the john only gimme eight for the whole trick." Sandy snorted cigarette smoke through her nostrils like she'd never be known in the Logan for being pussy. "But anyhow this Kingfish is screaming all over the place that tough, see? He says he's gonna get his five dollars or go to jail trying. So when he slaps me I tried to pull his goddam head off his neck." Like magic she produced a hook-bladed knife from somewhere. It was one of those wicked things like you cut linoleum with. She waved it."It went deep in the back of his neck but only sliced his throat a little. I wish I *had* killed him."

"Pour that wine, boy!" Blind Charlie's shout was filled with fury.

I jumped straight up in the air. What was most terrifying about Charlie was that I was never sure why he was in a particular rage. His rages were blind things I did not know how to cope with. Sandy had said that she was one of the people Charlie refused to talk to. And I wondered if Charlie forbade others to talk to those people also. I clumsily opened the bottle and took it to Charlie without a glass.

"Where's the Sinman?" Sandy asked. "Blind Charlie won't even answer a civilized question."

"I don't know. He wasn't here when I came in and then the Kingfish comes and puts on his act and I forgot to ask."

"Well, ask Charlie now, will you?"

I had my doubts about Charlie accepting questions relayed from those he didn't speak to, but I had no choice in the matter. I'd rather for Charlie to kill me than to admit to a fearless kid like Sandy that I was a pussy.

"Did I ask you where the Sinman was, Charlie?" I ventured.

Charlie came over loud and clear. "Tell that little stinking skunk that the Sinman ain't coming home soon and when he does he ain't gonna have no time to be answering no simple-assed questions from a simple-assed broad."

Sandy jumped to her feet in a fury that was just as inexplicable as Charlie's had been. "My IQ is 138!" she yelled. Charlie said nothing. Sandy bent from the waist to emphasize her words. "I got more brains in my left titty than you got in your whole blind-assed body. And I'm tired of a stupid blind bastid calling me simple-assed. Every time I come in here you got insults. But from now on you can kiss my ass! You hear me? I said kiss my ass!"

This time Charlie flowed out of his chair and was at Sandy's throat quicker than any blacksnake could have bit her. Even while he was choking her Charlie was gently laying her out on her deathbed like a little rag doll.

My knees simply dissolved although they seemed to be still banging against each other. My head was a big balloon of fear. And I numbly stared at the blind giant throttling Sandy with one hand while slapping her face with the other. The horror of it all was etched in the ineffectual waves Sandy was making with her knife at Charlie's wrist.

I put out my hands in entreaty, but my lips were frozen so I couldn't utter a sound. I began to feel my tongue hanging out in sympathy with Sandy's tongue, which was beginning to loll out of her mouth in a crazy fashion. And I felt my eyes popping just like hers.

Suddenly, from a distance, I heard my voice, but I knew it was all too late now. "Charlie, don't do it!" I was screaming. "She ain't worth it. Jail ain't worth it!"

I touched Charlie's arm. It was as hard and immovable as a mountainside, so there was nothing to do but scream louder. And all the time I was scared to death that he would stop killing Sandy and turn on me.

Sandy's hand, the one that held the knife, collapsed on the pillow. I knew she was going fast. "She's only a junky whore, Charlie," I pleaded. "What you want to go to jail for a junky whore for? Please listen to me, Charlie. Please! Please don't kill her." And as I heard my voice with its high girlish notes I was wild with shame and anger. Anger for this dying girl who was the cause of my shame for not being able to do anything to save her life.

The limp body of Sandy grew deader. And in my hysteria I knew I'd be a raving maniac if I had to stand here and watch this blind man continue to strangle a dead woman.

"She's dead!" I screamed. "Goddamit, she's dead. You don't have to kill her no more!"

Charlie released Sandy and stepped back, arms loosely held at his side. His voice was a hoarse, spent rasp. "She really dead, boy?"

"I don't know. Move." In my supreme terror of being involved in a murder I was no longer too afraid of Blind Charlie. Maybe I even figured that he was going to kill me too as soon as he got himself back together again. I bent toward Sandy. I couldn't tell if she was breathing or not.

Charlie began to cry, and I thought about what my grandfather used to say: "A crying nigger's so bent on killing he'll even kill hisself."

"But she tole me to kiss her ass, and don't no woman tell me that," Charlie was blubbering. "Why she hafta go make me kill her anyhow? 'Twarn't my fault. I ain't done nothing. She's the one that done it!"

Sandy came off the bed to a sitting position on its side and let her head hang down between her knees. She hawked to clear her throat and then spat a bright red glob of blood on the floor. I stared at the blood with a prayer on my lips. Charlie was still blubbering and waving his arms now. I went to the dresser and picked up the wine. I didn't know I'd drained the bottle until I suddenly realized that I was offering Sandy an empty bottle. But Sandy shook her head anyhow. She wanted no drink.

I watched her raise her eyes to look at Charlie, who still stood over the bed, waving his arms and shouting pleas and admonitions to heaven. All the high had been choked out of Sandy, but she was so scared I figured she didn't even know she needed a fix. Her eyeballs kept swiveling recklessly, reduced to animal terror. Suddenly she bolted for the door and was gone.

With a frightful kind of clarity I saw that the human body can do anything impossible if it is sufficiently frightened. Sandy had jetted from the bed, crouched to duck Charlie's flailing arms and run out of the room. She had never become erect again after passing under Charlie's arms, or had her kneecaps ever touched the floor, but somehow she had run on her knees all the way out of the room.

"She ain't daid! Ain't that her just run outa here?" Charlie bent over and felt about on the bed. Then he straightened up and whirled on me. "Why you let me stand here and cry like a fool for?"

"She just this minute scooted out of here, Charlie," I said. "Honest. I thought she was dead myself."

"And why you let me do that poor little girl up like that?"

Charlie placed his hands on his hips. "Here I went and took you for a fren' and now look what you went and did. Why, I never heard of such a thing in my life. Why, dammit to hell, you make the sorriest fren' a man ever had! I coulda been sitting in jail right this minute just on account of what you went and did. You should have taken time and *reasoned* with me!" Charlie shouted at the top of his lungs.

And I began to wonder if they'd even trust me with scissors to cut out those paper dolls. The Sinman had intimated that Blind Charlie was not all there, but I never dreamed he meant the man was a goddam maniac. Right then and there I promised myself that if I ever got out of this room alive I'd never come near it again or near *any* blind man as long as I lived.

But all at once Blind Charlie turned into a big black pudding of motherliness; only his voice was gently reproving. "Now effen you don't want to be my fren' all you gotta do is say so, Sid. I ain't never forced my fren'ship on nobody and I ain't gonna start now." Somehow, it was the meek and doleful plea of a Salvation Army lady, but it scared the hell out of me.

"I—I gonna be your fren'—friend, Charlie," I chattered like an idiot. "Nobody's gonna be better fren's than you and me. You can bet your life on that, Charlie."

"Tha's better," Charlie mumbled. I looked down at his right hand. All this time, parallel to his arm, he had been holding what was left of some chef's french knife. It had been honed down until it was a razor-edged triangle of not more than four inches.

"Don't you want another drink, Charlie?" I asked to get his mind off that knife.

"Of course I do," Charlie said genially. He walked straight to the organ; gently as a butterfly's wing his hands swept the top until they came in contact with the empty bottle. He picked it up and put it to his lips. "What the hell you think you're doing now?" he roared and walked right up to me. "Don't nobody play over Blind Charlie! Why you want to make me kill you too, boy?" And then he primly added, "And I ain't even had but one drink."

I made a dash for it, and when I reached the door I turned and said, "What I meant was, did you want me to go to the store right away, Charlie. I'm going now. But I'll be right back. You just wait and see."

I came back from the store and handed Charlie the quart. The brute unscrewed the top and took a long, gurgling drink. "Aaah," he sighed. "That one hit the spot. Now what's the name of this wine?"

It tickled me. Like all the other brutal men I have ever known, Charlie now spoke in a mincing falsetto. It was their idea of conversing courteously.

"It's Silver Spur, Charlie," I said. A couple of drinks later I asked, "Do you know a young girl named Jackie who's supposed to be going with an old guy named Dick up in 5-C-2?"

"I knows every junky in this place, plus. Why you ask?"

I told him all about the watch and then ended up asking him what he thought I should do about it, just as if my mind wasn't already made up.

"She's white, ain't she?"

"Mrs. Moriarty? Yes, but . . ."

"Ain't no buts about it. She's white."

"You make it as simple as that?"

Charlie went to the organ for another drink. "Simpler."

"Supposing you liked her even if she is white?"

"She said she was going to the police, didn't she?"

"She was only bluffing. She didn't mean it."

"Pigs is hired to protect whitey. Even the Black ones work only for whitey. So effen the pigs can't find that watch, then it's whitey's fault, not your'n. Not mine."

The blinding kernel of pathological truth in that statement chilled me. That death knell in Charlie's words made me feel cheated. Harlem had took and not given. So had America.

I felt so bad I had to talk about something else. "How long you've been blind, Charlie?" I asked.

"Four years, just about."

"Only four years? You act like you've been blind all your life almost. I mean you get around so good it's sometimes hard to remember you can't see."

"When I woke up in Harlem Hospital I was scared shitless. And I cried so bad the doctor had to stop working on my eyes. And I laid there and cried for two whole days." He laughed softly as if at a happy memory. "And I'm one of the few guys in the world who shouldn't have been that way. Hell, boy, I worked in the dark I don't know how many times. I robbed many a house in complete blackness, but this here was different. Whoooeee!"

"You went blind suddenly? Not gradually?"

"Yeah," Charlie said, remembering with something like surprise. "I come to and this here doctor has got a pair of tweezers, felt like, and he was picking the skin offen my eyeballs, felt like."

"What for?"

"I dunno!" Charlie snarled. "How the hell should I know?"

Some questions amused Charlie while others threw him into a frenzy for no apparent reason at all. You courted death to engage in conversation with Blind Charlie. But wine and Charlie's professed "fren'ship" gave me a fool's courage. I probed on. "So what happened anyway? A woman throw lye or acid on you?"

"Naw. It was a nigger threw a glass of water in my face," Charlie said.

"Water? It couldn't have been just plain water. There had to be something in that water, Charlie."

Charlie jumped up. "I said that that nigger threw water in my face and that's what he threw! Don't you thinks I knows water when I sees it? Feels it? What the hell is wrong with you anyhow?" Charlie's hand went toward his pocket.

But I was so upset by Charlie's apparent unconcern about the cause of his blindness that I didn't care about his knife. "Well, what made you unconscious when you got to the hospital?" I retorted.

"He hit me nine times in the head with a hatchet."

"*Nine times?* With a hatchet?"

"Yeah," Charlie said. Then he swelled with pride. "But in a week's time I could walk just as good as I can now. There was this old man in the bed next to mine what had been blind for years, see? One morning he says to me: 'You need to go pee, boy?' And so I tole him yes. Then he says: 'You just put your left hand on my right shoulder and stay in back of me. Just keep walking like Gawd wants us to. And keep in step now. Ain't nothing to be scared of. You is going where I'm goin' and I ain't gonna walk inta no wall or down no stairs long as I got this stick in my hand. So come on, boy, and walk!' And we walked. I can walk from here to hell and gone effen I got me a good shoulder to grab hold of and lead me."

Charlie smiled reminiscently. "One time me and the Sinman goes out to pick up some heroin. After we cops, Sinman says that there's some real queer-looking studs following us. Now you know damn well that you can't be starting no rumble with nobody if you got almost a hundred bags of shit in your pocket, even effen these cats ain't pigs, see? So I yelled: 'Run, boy, run!' And the Sinman lit out with me hanging on his shoulder every step of the way. We run and run all through them side streets until we gets to the subway."

"What did you do for a living before you lost your sight, Charlie?"

"Mostly I stole. That was down home in Florida. But them judges loved to gimme too much time. Got so them wardens had picked out a gang for me before I even reached the joint. I was big and strong then so I was a natural boss. In Florida they only beats the leader of the gang effen the work ain't done. And they knew I'd kick the living shit outa every man in the gang effen I got a strapping." Charlie glowered. "I've cleared off more land and snakes for whitey to enjoy than this here New York sits on. That's why I left Florida."

"Huh?" It seemed to me that I'd missed a part of Charlie's story.

"Well, effen I hada go to jail all the time, I figgered I might as well be in one of these New York jails where they don't beat you half to death and wants to shoot you besides."

"Well, I'll be goddam!" I exclaimed. "Now we got niggers that come to Harlem because they don't like their home-town jails." I couldn't help it; the wine was going to my head.

But Charlie roared. "You sure said a mouthful, boy. Sinman

ain't never said nothing no keener than that." He laughed louder. "And that's why I'm taking up my time with you. I don't never take up with no fools that don't know nothing but talking about fighting and killing and stealing. You got a good head on you, boy." He walked unerringly to the organ and took another drink.

"And you don't fool me none neither," he said. "I tole the Sinman you talks all slurred like to get along with these here corn-bread niggers we got, but you was born up North here somewheres, weren't you, boy? And I'll bet you went to college just like me and Sinman did. . . ."

My jaw sagged.

"Now ain't you been to college, boy?"

I nodded my head, too shocked to realize that Blind Charlie could not see, but he must have took my silence for assent because he smiled and said, "That's good. Now I never bothered to learn nothing even before I went. Looks like I wasn't born to no book learning. But I had my chances. I been to four good colleges . . ."

"Four?" I squeaked. "What four?"

Charlie named them. Two were obscure church schools, but the other two were pretty good Black colleges. All of them were way down South.

"Of course they all kicked me out before Thanksgiving."

"Thanksgiving? Why Thanksgiving?"

Charlie was on his feet again. "How the hell do I know?" he shouted. "There ain't no goddam reason for kicking a man outa college before Thanksgiving!" And just as suddenly Charlie sat back down and was politely carrying on the conversation. ". . . but don't never know when a little college education's gonna come in handy," he was saying. "Why, I knows personally of some college cats that got some of the nicest little breaks from the screws up at Elmira and Sing Sing. Soft jobs. Like in the library and stuff like that. Education is a good thing at all times, boy. You is lucky."

I wondered if I was the only man on earth who had been congratulated for graduating from college because it would stand him in good stead when he got to prison.

"I'm going for another bottle," I said.

"What in hell you take me for?" Charlie bellowed. He came at me with his fists clenched. "You think you gonna come in here and buy all the something to drink? That ain't no way to treat a fren'. You ain't got no right to call me no chiseler!"

I tried to laugh him out of his rage. And I was now pretty high and getting an esoteric kick out of being with so murderously vacillating a man as Charlie.

Anyhow I must have sounded like some kind of fag when I merrily burbled, "I am the world's champion pain in the ass when I go for drunk. So today it is only fitting and proper that I pay for all the ignorant-oil."

"That ain't no way to talk," Charlie said as if I'd cheated him out of a lovely opportunity to break my neck. He fished a withered dollar bill out of his watch pocket. "Get the same kind as before," he said. "What you call it? Golden Boots?"

"No. Spur, Charlie. Silver Spur."

"I knew it had something to do with feets. I don't forget nothing, boy."

My entire life to date has been shaped by one thing: my father's razor strop. That bastard used to cover my body with welts that would today put his Baptist preaching butt in prison for a long, long time.

All through my childhood I lived in fear of that strop; and today that fear has changed, but it is still with me. Today it is as if I am afraid of fear. Never in my adult life have I ever done anything just because I wanted to or because it was logical and right. What made me act was the question of: am I afraid to do this or that?

I don't think I would have ever smoked or taken my first drink if it had not been necessary to prove that I was no longer afraid of that strop.

And as I walked to the liquor store for the third time I tried to be honest with myself: was I having a good time or was I ashamed to admit that I was afraid to walk away from Blind Charlie? I just didn't know, and so I figured that I certainly wasn't having a good time. Therefore, it was my duty not to go back. I would buy the bottle and then give it to one of the lobby lice to take to Blind Charlie. Then I would go to my bar on Ninety-seventh Street and hang around until time to go to work. Then I turned right around and decided that that would be cowardly also; I had to go back and fraternize with that blind murderer to prove I wasn't scared to. But I did promise myself to never visit the Sinman's room again.

The Sinman had returned while I was gone, and looking at him this time, I was once again struck by his handsomeness. Sinman was two inches taller than I am. I'm barely five eight. And the guy was not half as thin as I'd first thought him to be. It was just that his face had lost every bit of the baby fat he used to have. It really was a handsome face now; one that both lesbians and almost normal women would think groovy. His eyes were gray, but nobody ever noticed Sinman's eyes. They were not expressive like the rest of his features.

Sinman was wearing a white shirt open at the collar. His gray slacks fitted perfectly, especially about his flat buttocks. He wore no belt and his shoes gleamed. They were alligator shoes and I suspected that the Sinman wore them in a kind of defiance of whitey's establishment and in deference to the ways of Harlem. After all, more Harlem hustlers believe in ninety-dollar alligator shoes than in Cadillacs.

"Greetings," the Sinman cried. "Charlie tells me you are a fabulous companion. But of course I always knew that."

I grinned. "Did he tell you about the Kingfish? Man, was I dumb. I was getting ready to call the ambulance. I was dumb to be confidenced. I never dreamed that all he was after was a free fix from me."

"Oh. Junkies are some of our finest Black thespians. You should see some of the performances the female of the species can give."

"If they can do better than the Kingfish I want to see it."

"No, I don't think you would. It is not very pleasant to see so much talent and brains buried beneath heroin." Sinman went to the hutch cabinet and took out a bottle of Cutty Sark. I did not know if it was a silent reproof for the cheap wine or not. "Tell me, how goes it up there in that profane bower of love? I trust that J&J are still valiantly trying to annihilate each other?"

"They're still holding their own."

"I hear that you are implicated in the theft of a watch. My stars, Sid. Didn't you know that all you had to do was give Jackie a token and tell her to go to the hospital of her choice?"

"How'd you find out about the watch?" I asked.

Charlie snorted a jeer of a laugh but said nothing as he came to the organ for a drink.

Sinman grimaced. "The lobby lice are still standing about relishing Jackie's daring exploit. Those children are actually hypnotized by these minuscule victories over whitey. As for the watch, I command you to give it to me. You would be courting all kinds of distress if you do the square thing with it that I am afraid you will do. Give it to me and the case will be closed."

"You can have it," I muttered and pulled the damned thing out of my pocket and handed it to him. "But you're exaggerating. They'd call me stupid, but I don't think . . ."

"That's it exactly. I do not want the lice to call you stupid." Sinman paused a moment and then said, " 'Tis a pity about Gloria."

"Oversexed?" I asked, and then saw the look on Sinman's face. "Oh. You mean jail?"

"You really have a churchly outlook on life, haven't you?" he said. "But Gloria is not oversexed. She is woefully lacking in that respect. It is impossible for her to achieve climax, and when she meets someone she likes, she literally tears herself to pieces trying to reach that forbidden plateau. Our Gloria is a cripple. Treat her gently."

God. Prejudice is more deadly than heroin. It not only can blind but can make you hallucinate things that are not present. Just because the Sinman's vocal cords had been tight from dope I had seen a depraved dope fiend. I had reacted like a proper old maid on her initial encounter with a beautiful playboy. The Sinman himself was now forcing me to meet a moment of truth: James Ronald Person was no spiritual cadaver. He was alive and well, and still possessing a cleanly analytical mind which drugs probably could never destroy. There was even a driving spirit of intelligence about that lean frame as if he carried no excess baggage. He was free to go when and where his agile mind cared to take him.

"Is that all that I can do?" I asked. "Treat her gently?"

"It is most important that you impress upon Gloria that you are a rock. More so than other Harlem girls. She must believe that no matter how much the fates deny her, or make her search hysterically after the denied, she can always return home to you. You must be her home. Gloria, like you, suffers illusions of loneliness. She thinks of herself as being an outcast . . ."

"Which ain't right," Charlie said coldly.

"Charlie, I do not wish to hear any ideas of yours about the need of brutality to cure a bodily ill. Please be sane."

The thin, bitter lips curled and Charlie said, "She ain't been conquered is all. Women want to be bested. They gotta be bested for their own good. They ain't no good to nobody effen they ain't. I could make Gloria drop her oyster in five minutes effen I put my mind to it."

Sinman sighed but refused to answer. I asked him, "Why so much kindness for Gloria and nothing but ridicule for J&J? All three were born uptight, weren't they?"

"J&J are an entirely different matter. I depise that husband-and-wife game they play. And since they are both in their forties they are rather immature, are they not?"

"It's more than that," I said. "I think you actually hate J&J."

Sinman did a disguised double-take as if he'd thought it impossible for anyone to fathom anything about him which he did not want known. Then he replied, "Homosexuality today is for the birds. And it is doubly degrading because mankind has corrupted a form of love which God himself gave to man when He was still alive. Do I make myself clear?"

"No."

"Search your books of ancient history. And you will find that the purely platonic love of one man for another has had a far greater impact upon the world than any heterosexual love affair you might be able to mention. Do you happen to know how many women were present at the Last Supper?"

A blonde beauty walked into the room without knocking, like everybody else who came to the Sinman's door.

"Hello, fellas," she said. I winced. She was a cracker broad. Way-down-South broad and probably poor white trash at that. She went to the Sinman. "What are you holding, honey?"

"My darling Margo," Sinman cried. "I am delighted to hear you ask that. It means that I will be able to do you and Black Bob a good turn."

Margo laughed merrily at me. It was a very plain invitation to laugh with her, but I was uptight. Margo and the Sinman were too beautiful a pair. Too white at the moment. A crazy jealousy of their skin practically nauseated me. And I knew I shouldn't have mixed that Spur with Cutty Sark. Yeah. The two were too damn young. Too blond and too victorious. I was getting sicker with a jealousy that was almost strong enough to kill. I hated them only a little bit less than I hated my own shriveled Black soul.

As they chattered on my uptightness increased. And I hated the nigger in me that made me begin to wonder what it'd be like to lay a good job on Margo. The more I thought about it and the more I stared at her the more beautiful she got. She might have been twenty-five. No more. With wicked curves but just fair to middling breasts. Since she evidently was a junky I knew I could get to those cookies. And maybe I'd just try it one time. Yeah, man. Hate 'em and screw 'em. Black Power!

"I can't take any favors this time," Margo was saying. "I came by to give *you* a play."

"What's wrong?" Sinman asked quickly. "Is Bob all right?"

"Don't get worried. Bob's fine. It's just that business is so great we can't keep all our friends supplied. Four girls asked me to save out a bag for them for this afternoon when they get up and we're out already. And they are four of my favorite people. I've just got to take care of them. And so Black Bob said to come and give you our business. You know how Bob is."

"I most certainly do," Sinman said. "So business is booming away?"

Margo sighed her contentment. "Selling narco in Harlem is the life. There's nothing finer. In fact the living's so great I'm not going to mind taking the fall when the bust comes. Why, I haven't raised a sweat since I met Black Bob. And I don't intend to either."

"I thought you knew Bob in Alabama. You mean to say you two met here in Harlem? How could I have been so mistaken? I was under the romantic impression that you two outwitted a lynch mob and escaped to New York and peace and safety."

"No. I was a cracker bitch in good standing when I left home. It was at a party on Sutton Place. You know the kind of mixed-up parties. And I was so ashamed of myself because I couldn't keep my eyes off this big Black nigger." Margo laughed. "Well, I hurried up and learned where it's at, didn't I?"

"You are of the beautiful people, Margo. Now tell me what I can deal for you?"

"Make it twelve bags, honey. Bob and I need a little until way late tonight." Margo took a sheaf of bills out of her bra.

Charlie got up and went to the console radio. He pulled it out from the wall and went in the back to extract a tube. After he had somehow separated the glass bulb from the base of the tube he took out some packets of heroin and counted them. Margo handed her money to Sinman and then went to Charlie. She kissed him and took the heroin.

"I just love Blind Charlie," she said. "But I guess every single woman in the life does too. There's not too many ace warriors left in Harlem now. Now you all take care now."

As she walked out of the room I returned to normal.

"What were we talking about when she walked in?" Sinman asked.

"*You* were talking about the Last Supper." I tried my damnedest to let him know there was supposed to be a sneer in my words.

"Correct."

"Correct," I said.

"Perhaps now I should explain that I am called the Sinman in very much the same way that one who studies bacteria is called a bacteriologist. In the beginning I was intrigued by the fact that God always seemed to be out to lunch with a whitey whenever a Black man came to call. But it did not take long before I reached the inescapable conclusion that God was not out to lunch. The poor chap had been dead for ages."

"Don't you think maybe you got to make up this stuff to sort of neutralize the fact of your heroin habit?" Like it was my duty to talk as sensible as I could to this guy who I really liked, but I was getting higher and higher.

"But for the present I am much more interested in the phenomena of sin than in why your silly God kicked the bucket. Very few people know how to sin. Take yourself for example. You don't even know what sin is. While at the same time you are convinced that all that is good and pleasurable is sinful. At this very moment you fret about the life of sin you and Gloria face. But where is the sin? Can't you open your mind and see that you and that wonderful girl have the unique opportunity to attain the ultimate form of intelligent intercourse known to man? Not since Adam and Eve blew it. You and Gloria must not fail."

If I understood the Sinman right he was talking about stuff that could blow the strongest mind. I got almost maudlin there for a moment. There were tears in me when I almost snarled, "What's so ultimate about restraining yourself from going upside a chick's head because she lets her nuts rule her?"

"Don't be childish, Sid. You can actually *make* a life. Gloria's life."

Sometimes when your stomach is queasy you can settle it with one more drink. It sort of paralyzes your gut. I tried one more Cutty Sark. I gagged but kept it down. I didn't dare to light a cigarette.

I must not have showed anything because Sinman went right on talking. "Why is it that every time you get drunk you end up filled with remorse? And don't you know that remorse is only your inability to communicate with your gods? And why do you insist upon running around, trying to bury the shame of an adulterous wife between the legs of every passable whore you meet? Why didn't you seek to celebrate your freedom with a fine square girl?"

"At least I didn't turn into a goddam junky."

Maybe I struck pay dirt because the Sinman ran off on a tangent. "Yes," he almost purred. "Into this good right arm I have shot five houses, enough money to buy ten Lincoln Continentals. You have been clean all your life. How many Continentals have you driven? In whose house do you live? In truth, your life is more of a confession that God is dead than mine is. I *use* drugs. I do not *take* drugs like a junky. I am heroin's master. I have attained the supreme freedom!"

Charlie laughed in his corner. It was a kind of amen laugh.

"Which came first? The drugs or your crazy ideas?" I asked.

"Knowledge came first. After that I was free to do all things until a new god is come."

"Do you also know *how* God died?"

"God was like a junky with too much money. He overindulged Himself. He assumed a human form and took an alias—Jesus. And for no reason at all, mind you. God committed suicide just like a stupid junky who takes an OD."

"*Like* a junky," I repeated with all the disgust I could summon. This nut was only one step away from a Black Mass.

"The stupid junky with money to spare will kill himself with an overdose if he gets half a chance," Sinman said. "And didn't our God with His last breath here on earth admit that He had been a fool?"

"Do you carry on like this every day?"

"Was it not God the Father and God the Son who cried out on the cross: *'My God! My God! Why hast Thou forsaken Me?'* That was God rebuking God. And how do you think the silly junky feels when he knows he is dying from an overdose that he himself administered to himself?"

I gagged. The puke was right in my throat. I circled the room to find something to let it out in, but I couldn't find anything. Sinman didn't have a wastebasket. I made a dash out of the room to the toilet, but when I stood over the stool nothing would come up. Just being away from that goddam Sinman had settled my stomach. But I was still drunk enough to want to be polite. I had to go back and say I'd had a nice time, etc. I didn't creep or tiptoe. I just sort of made it back to the Sinman's real slow with my hand on the wall. I almost made it to the door when I heard Sinman say, "What do you think of him now, Charlie?"

I didn't move.

"It ain't right to tell wishy-washy men like that there ain't no God," Charlie said. "People like Sid gotta have some kind of God or they'll think they ain't gonna have no luck atall and go kill themselves. They don't know that you can make it on your own effen you only puts your mind to it." Charlie paused to laugh softly. "Still, Sid ain't no pussy for real. Not no Baptist or Catholic pussy. But he's *stupid.* He got his books maybe, but when it comes to being for real he might as well get his hat. But me and him's gonna be real good fren's. He needs me to pull his coat."

"Yes, Charlie," Sinman said. "I remember one cruel day when I just knew all gods were against me. If Sid had known who had robbed me he would have told me and they might have killed him. Sid is a morally brave coward, Charlie. I wonder why the fates have brought him back to the Logan?"

I turned and scurried out of 1-C.

CHAPTER 7

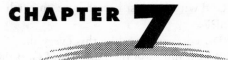

I WENT STRAIGHT to my room and laid down. I knew I'd never be able to make it to Lundy's with my stomach acting up like this. My stomach, my frame of mind, plus all the pervasive evil in the Logan, all added up to another drunk that I knew I could not let happen. Not with the only woman I loved locked up in jail. I'd never get sober again until *after* I'd died of acute alcoholism. So I laid still and fought all the silly urges in me. And my thoughts were not any less silly than the urges. Like I even wondered if the Sinman had been deliberately trying to drive me crazy. And just what part did he play in Blind Charlie's madness? After all, Sinman had taken one look at me that first day and known how lonely I was. He had given me Gloria. Had he also snatched her away? *Somebody had.*

A wish for just one more drink to sober me up became a craving. I almost started to get up and go in J&J's room, but they'd been arguing on and off all day and still were at it. And I had to have peace and quiet even more than I had to have that one more drink.

Someone knocked at the foyer door. Leah was sold out, and evidently J&J couldn't hear the knocking over their yelling at each other so that left me to go. Dick, Mr. Grimm and Mrs. Moriarty never went to the door.

It was Suzie, the girl whose beer tasted best with J&J's chatter. I liked to open up for Suzie because she could give you a crazy kind of lift. Suzie was not only a hot-natured-looking piece of womanhood, she managed to always seem interested in sex.

Suzie was a mellow yellowish brown. As light as Gloria, and had a generous mouth. Nice though, but really generous. Her forehead was high and deceptively intelligent-looking and her gray-green eyes could flash imperiously at times. She usually wore a housecoat or slacks, and in slacks her five nine figure was out of sight by any man's standards. Suzie was a fox.

The first time I ever saw Suzie she was sitting astride the bully of the Logan, a two-hundred-pound woman. And Suzie's fists had been really fitting the bully for a pair of round heels when five or six lobby lice pulled her off. I'll never forget the glorious sight that was Suzie, breathing heavily, head proudly thrown back and smiling like some movie starlet, as she received the plaudits of men and women alike who had at one time or another been bullied by the big woman whose butt she had just whipped. I remember that the woman had to borrow a man's jacket; Suzie had damn near stripped her naked while beating her.

About a week after that Jinny introduced us, and from the beginning I had a feeling that it would be easy to make it with Suzie, but I never made any moves. One reason being that Suzie was loud.

As soon as I got to know Suzie well I asked her how she happened to be fighting the bully that day in the lobby.

"I don't know," Suzie had replied with a shrug. "She just wanted to fight me and so I fit her."

And I believe that that was exactly how it was; for as I had often told J&J, Suzie was the sort of person trouble just followed. In some ways Suzie did not belong in the Logan. Her good clothes and the fact that she was legally married were two of the reasons. Therefore many of the less fortunate inmates of the Logan went out of their way to needle Suzie even if it was not safe; their jealousy overrode their discretion. As far as I knew, Suzie never picked on anyone, but I guess it is also true that Suzie always welcomed the conflict once it came.

"Hiya, Sid?" she trilled. Suzie's big toothy smile went well with her sexy torso, and it always seemed to me that her "hiyas?" were not so much an asking about my general well-being, but a question as to how rapacious I felt at the time. "The young marrieds in?" she asked.

"Yeah. Fighting," I said, and wondered why the middle-aged J&J were always referred to as young by everyone in the hotel. It must have been because they petted each other so much in public.

Suzie went on down the hall to J&J's room and I laid back down.

"Three goddam rooming houses! Two bars on Third Avener! And this hopheaded bitch signs them all away on me," Joey was yelling at the top of her lungs.

"Now, Joey, you should always try to carry yourself nice," Suzie said smugly. "Ah allus carries myself nice, don't I, Jinny? So let's all have a nice little drink and forget it."

"I don' wan nothing tuh drink," Joey hollered. "This cokey bitch has drunk me broke and onta Welfare already! And whadda I got to show for it? Nothing. That's what. Nothin! Even the law come and took away my little Black baby even. Whaaa!"

Joey had a Black baby too? Sinman had evidently missed a beat in the rhythm of J&J's life. Now I was sober as a judge and I got up to go stand in J&J's doorway. I sure in hell wasn't going to miss any of this.

Joey was walking back and forth, swinging her arms in the accepted Harlem fashion of argument. "Here I was, trying to make me a nest egg for this cokey whore, and whadda I get for my trouble? A Black bastid baby," she yelled.

"What you want, Mr. Seditty?"

I blinked at Suzie, who was glaring at me. "Seditty?" I asked her. "What does that mean?"

"You's a seditty bastid," Suzie contended.

I glanced at Jinny, who looked as if her nerves could not stand much more of Joey's ranting and raving. "You know, Sid," she said wearily. "Like slow. Real respectable."

"Sedate?"

"Tha's whut ah said you wuz. You seditty bastid," Suzie said. "And ah heard whut you been goin' around saying about me and from now on you can jest keep my goddam name outa your mouth!"

"I've never said anything bad about you," I protested. "Ask J&J."

"Them's who tole me."

"Oh," I said. "You mean about trouble following you? Well, that's not your fault. The women around here are just naturally jealous of you and pick on you. And you don't take no picking on. You're a fox with a jock shape, but you don't take low from nobody and I don't blame you." I wondered why I was going out of my way to explain myself so energetically. Anyhow, all I'd said was the truth.

Suzie forgot her rage to do battle and preened. Her eyelids drooped idiotically and when she spoke honey dribbled all over her words. "Now be sweet, Sid baby. And go to the store for me. Ah wants me a Miller's and J&J needs a Spur."

"I'm too damned seditty to be seen in a whiskey store," I told her and marched back to my room.

Suzie followed me. First she grinned like a beautiful devil. Then she stretched her torrid-looking body like a dancer. After that she laid that wonderful body right on top of mine and moaned deliciously. She started doing a wicked grind. "Good?" she asked. Her voice was warm, promising. "See how nice Ah am to you and you won't do nothin' for me." She jumped up grinning wider than before.

This fine chick had actually gotten my motor started even though I knew this wasn't going anywhere. "Okay," I said. "I'll go, but that little bit of dry-fucking isn't what's making me go. I'm just a damn nice guy to you women. That's all."

"Someday me and you'll be doing it up right, honey baby."

"Yeah. Someday far away."

"Oh, Lawdee!" Suzie screamed.

My back was to her. I jumped around. "What the hell is wrong now?" I yelped.

"Ah forgets mah pus."

"Damn," I said softly, knowing I had absolutely no right to let any screams of Suzie's startle me. After all, it was Suzie's big mouth that kept us from getting on some righteous time from the very beginning. Suzie always screamed her discoveries to the world and women with loud voices were non-existent in my sex life. It didn't matter how fine a chick was, if she talked loud I just couldn't go for her. On the other hand I am a freak for soft-voiced women. A real cool chick can whisper me out of anything.

In a minute Suzie came back with her "pus," which was a billfold, and handed me a dollar. "And get us a pack of Pall Malls too."

"A dollar's not enough."

"Whut ain't a dollah enuff for? Now don't go getting all seditty again. Ah knows whut a dollah will buy."

But the sad and awful truth was that this lovely twenty-six-year-old girl did not know what a dollar would buy. Suzie could neither read, write nor count money although she liked to tell how she'd played hooky to go sell corn whiskey for a bootlegger in her home down near Wilson, North Carolina. However, I had no intention of reminding Suzie of her ignorance. And Suzie's ignorance was secondary anyhow; she was dumb too. Jinny had to accompany her whenever she left the hotel. Suzie couldn't even tell an A train from a D train, much less the numbered streets of Manhattan. And to make her life all the more Hotel Loganish, Suzie's husband was a forty-seven-year-old caddy who read the *New York Times* on his way to work every morning.

When I got back with Suzie's stuff I figured that I was out twenty-five cents. At first I started to get even by drinking some of the Spur, but I was pretty sober now and I just might be able to make it to work at three o'clock, so I laid back down again.

J&J continued their argument. Or, more truthfully, Joey continued picking on the silent Jinny. I grew both cynical and philosophical; Joey's ranting was but an extension of the husband-and-wife game the two were forever playing. Joey was only doing what she thought to be her duty as the man of the house. Then I thought about how everything in the Logan was nothing but a game. This hotel was a temple of mass ignorance and game. Nothing was real; even sickness and death was a time for charades. In fact, the inmates of the Logan loved sickness. Anybody's sickness. It made a wonderful excuse to get in the act. It was like recreational therapy. Even the patient enjoyed it.

One had only to announce that they felt under the weather and in no time at all their room would be filled with nurses, doctors and would-be mourners. Ambulances were never called except for knifing victims; taxis wouldn't haul them. And medical supplies were always in abundance in the Logan because the junkies were constantly breaking into the doctors' cars that were parked all around St. Luke's Hospital.

Yeah, man. A Loganite is a compulsive nurse. J&J used to religiously empty the bag of a bedridden female colostomy patient in 5-A-1, never using drunkenness as an excuse not to do so. And J&J despised that whitey woman, who cordially despised any and all Blacks.

Then it dawned on me that poverty and disease were never victorious in the Logan for the simple reason that the Logan never allowed sad hearts to remain sad for long. The inmates derived some kind of satisfaction and enjoyment from every little thing that transpired about them. Just like Suzie was enjoying the hell out of Joey's bickering.

"Three goddam bars and two rooming houses fulla roomers in Washington Heights. And this bitch loses them all! The goddam coke-sniffing whore," Joey was yelling.

I noted that Joey had changed her count on her bars and rooming houses and wondered if there was any truth at all in what she was saying. It seemed impossible that a woman nearing fifty years of age would make up lies and then pick fights over them. And Joey wasn't *really* crazy.

"Now be nice, Joey. Be a nice boy," Suzie chimed in. I snorted. It always got my goat how the women around J&J had to call Joey a male if they wanted to stay in with the crowd. Games. Games. Games.

"Goddam you and your bars!" Jinny suddenly shouted. "The lawyer gimme eleven hundred dollars to live on. He said not to do anything until you was loosed, he said you said. What the hell did you expect me to eat for five years? And we ain't legally married, bitch. Yeah, I was supposed to eat nothing but grits, eh?" She paused and I knew she was pouring another drink. Then she said, "I wish to hell he had gimme eleven hundred thousand dollars and I'd of had triplets for you to come home to, you bastid!"

Whock! And I knew that was the sound of Joey going upside Jinny's jawbone. And 5-C was filled with curses, crashes and bangs. And the crashes and bangs coming from J&J's room would not have been half so bad if they hadn't been punctuated by Suzie's screams. She was underlining everything as it happened just as if she'd never seen two women fighting before.

The ruckus continued. Finally I got up. J&J couldn't ever pay for the furniture they evidently were breaking up. I didn't want them evicted so that meant that I just might have to pay for this fight and so it was to save money that I went to break it up. But when I reached their door I froze. Jinny was bobbing and weaving like a tiny Sugar Ray, and the punches she was throwing had accuracy and lots of sting.

At the same time, Joey was petulantly trying to hit back at her wifely adversary with all the elegance of the Queen of Sheba swatting at a gnat. The toy bulldog was a fake. I burst out laughing. I couldn't help it.

"Whut's so funny, motherfucker?" Suzie had rushed up to me. Her face was working with excitement. She was so caught up in the spirit of battle that she was now ready to take on anybody in the Logan. It was like a sister getting the spirit at a revival meeting. Suzie was all for it.

"Hit me! Hit me," she panted. She bent her knees so her chin was on a level with my shoulders. "Jest hit me one time so Ah kin kill you," Suzie pleaded.

When she saw I had no intention of hitting her she actually went out of her cotton-picking head and flew across the room to the table drawer and took out a paring knife. Joey snatched the knife out of her hand and slashed at Jinny with it.

"The bastid's cut my arm off!" Jinny shrieked.

"Thought I wouldn't do it, didn'tcha?" Joey sneered. But her fright-blanched face told another story.

Jinny ran to the kitchen to run water on her arm. When she passed me I saw that she had a superficial cut, but I didn't think it was any business of mine to tell Joey.

When Jinny came back she had a majestic bandage made of toilet paper on her arm. She faced Suzie. "Now just where the hell do you get off at, coming in here and giving my old man a knife to cut me with, Miss Bitch? That why you bought him that wine? Wanted to make sure he'd use the knife you gave him, didn't you? You tired of *your* old man and want mine? Get the hell out of here, you conniving bitch. Go and be Black. Go and never come back. I mean that, bitch!"

Suzie's face screwed up into a howling mask of tears. "Lawd, Jin, ah wuz gonna cut *Sid* with that knife. Ah nevah dreamed Joey wuz gonna take it. You knows Ah allus carries myself nice. Ah doan nevah approves of no violence lessen somebody like Sid starts somethin'. If he hadna come in here all grinnin' like a fool and all the whole thing would nevah of happent."

"Sid's the best friend we got," Jinny yelled. "And who the hell are you to be saying who can come to my door and who can't? He can laugh if he wants. The first day I met him he damn near saved my life with a drink when I was broke and sick. You and that beer don't do me no good. Git! Go! Don't never come back!"

"It wuz Sid's fault," Suzie sobbed. "That bastid starts everything that goes on in 5-C. Don't he, Joey?"

Joey was still too out of breath to speak, but she continued trying to look ferocious and only succeeding in looking like an aggrieved baby.

Suzie began to bawl. "Ah ain' goin' nowheres till my two bestest fren's say Ah ain' tried to make 'em kill one anudder . . ."

I walked away from it all. Games. Games. Games. Ten minutes later I could hear them gossiping away like at a coffee klatsch.

CHAPTER 8

JUST AS I DECIDED that I would make it on out to Sheepshead Bay, someone knocked on the foyer door. I went. It was Sandy, smiling self-consciously.

"Leah's out," I told her.

"I don't want anything from Leah. I came to thank you, Sid. You saved my life and no doubt about it. All these cats around here who go for bad would have stood right there and let Blind Charlie do me in, and never said a mumbling word. They'd of let me get wasted every time before they opened their mouths."

I turned and walked to the room so she wouldn't see how embarrassed I was. She followed. "So thanks," she said again.

"I guess I was scared *not* to try and do something. You know, sometimes it takes a whole lot of cool to be a real coward. I guess I don't have it. So you really shouldn't be thanking me. I didn't do anything anyhow. Not for real. Charlie just stopped."

"Yes, you did. I was almost gone, but I could still hear you pleading with Blind Charlie. It was like you were in another room, but I could hear you plain as day. And that's what made Charlie stop. I know it was. Thanks, Sid."

"But whatinell made you talk to Charlie like that? You've been around the Logan long enough to've heard how dangerous that man can be, haven't you?"

Sandy shrugged carelessly. "I dunno. That damn H will make you do some funny things sometimes. And I was pretty high." Then she smiled like a bashful schoolgirl. "I went back in the Sinman's and talked to Charlie."

I gasped in admiration more than anything else. "You did? What'd he say?"

"Nothing. Only I told him he could sleep in my room from now on. I never sleep at night anyhow."

"What about your old man?"

"He can get *hat*. I'm tired of that damn junky laying up on me. I don't need a monkey *and* some man both on my back at the same time. You dig it? Welfare pays my rent. Why I need him?"

"You're on Welfare? How the hell could anybody like you be on Welfare? Don't they know you got a habit?"

"What's my habit bugging you for?"

"Every damn thing. Why should anybody who can afford to shoot ten and twenty dollars' worth of shit a day up their arm be given free room and board?"

"Any girl that gets busted is automatically put on Welfare when she gets out of the House of D—if she's broke. The same thing goes when you get out of Manhattan General for the cure. Of course you got to go down to Avenue B every month to see if they got a job for you, but they never do. Who's going to hire an addict?"

"So they've actually got you on Welfare *because* you are an addict?"

"What's wrong with that, Sid? It's not my fault no one will hire me, is it?"

"But they know you *earn* money to pay for your habit, why can't you earn a few dollars more and support yourself entirely?"

"If I was a diabetic and my insulin cost as much as my heroin habit and I couldn't earn one more cent than my insulin cost, would you mind if I was on Welfare? And living off *your* taxes?"

"You ain't nuts. Welfare is! I ought to get on it myself."

She gently shoved me toward the bed. "I wish my life was worth more than this, Sid. But this is all I got to give you right now."

I twisted out of her embrace. "A few moments ago I was laying up here with a hard on. I wanted some trim in a bad way. But I'll be damned if I'm going to let you give me some like this."

Sandy was hurt. "You've bought it plenty of times, what's wrong with it when it's free? And it's not free. I owe you."

"Goddamit, Sandy. Your life is worth more than a piece of tail. I'd be less than a man if I accepted your offer. Can't you see that?"

"I'm not so sure about what my life is worth any more, Sid. But is it all right if I stay around awhile?"

"Sure. You know it is."

She measured me with her eyes. A kind of maternal gleam was in them. "I can't get over you, Sid. In a way, you're a little man. You're no taller than me hardly, especially if I put on heels. But you stood right there and yelled at that crazy bastard just as if you could have done something about it if he suddenly changed his mind and started to waste you instead of me."

"And don't you think I was thinking about that? Woman, I was scared as hell. But I still wasn't smart enough to play it cool like I should have."

"Yeah. And that's why you gotta take me. Sid, if you don't screw me right this minute I'll never let you even for money as long as I live. I wouldn't be able to. It'd be like family. Dig?"

"So you need a big brother in this goddam Logan."

"You want it that way?"

"Well, we'd each have someone to talk to and relax with without worrying about things. You know what I mean."

"Oh, Sid." The dame was nearly knocked out with some mystical kind of joy. And even if some nut will someday announce that all the inmates of any S.R.O. comprise one big family, there's lots of lonely people in that family as they call it.

"What's the name of that slop you and Charlie were drinking?

I'm going to the store myself and buy you a quart of the piss, and you better not give a damn soul a sip of it. Not even Blind Charlie."

When Sandy got back from the store we talked and talked, laying side by side on my bed. Somehow I got to raving about how ignorance was so goddam rampant in the Logan. Especially the Logan. And that led us into a general discussion of education; and then Sandy happened to mention that she'd been to business college. Gradually, since I'd returned to the Logan, I'd learned that you just don't believe an addict right off the bat. So I didn't know whether to believe Sandy or not.

Sandy must have seen disbelief on my face. "What's so unbelievable about that, Sid? I know you think this place is the personification of ignorance, but at the same time you've got to admit that there's a whole lot of educated people in here too. Or is it that you think that it's *me* that's too dumb to have been in business college?"

"No, Sandy. I've not said anything about you being dumb."

"My IQ is 138. No kidding. The shrink at Bedford told me."

"What the devil did you do to get sent to Bedford?"

"I took a fall for a guy once."

"And *you've* got a 138 IQ?"

"He would've got fifteen years. I did eighteen months. I don't regret it."

"And what'd he ever do for you, before or since? Where's he now?"

"He died. OD. But I loved him. God, he was beautiful man."

I got jealous. Not love-affair jealous, but jealous because no woman had ever cared that much about me. "Do you think you could take a bust for me?" I asked.

"I wouldn't even have to love you to do that, Sid. And don't you ever forget that this brother and sister idea is your idea, not mine. If you ever want me you got me. I mean that, Sid. All I've ever asked of a man is to be one. Not no pussy. If you didn't play pussy while Blind Charlie was out of his mind this morning you'll never play one. But you think I'm dumb, too dumb for you, huh? Why you think that anyway?"

"I don't think you're too dumb for *me*. But you got to admit that no smart person uses shit."

"You never used skag and so you don't know, Sid. You'll never understand until after you've used it once."

"Doesn't it make you feel kind of worthless?"

"I feel worthless without it."

Our talk drifted on until I thought to ask her, "Just how many inmates around here *have* been to college?"

"Well, there's Pop Brown, first of all. He taught at Tuskegee. He's on Welfare now, but that's what he says. And there's Jinny. She says she went to Morgan for a while. Sinman went to Juilliard and the New School. And did you know that Kingfish was a track star at Hampton? And there's College Joe. He goes to Columbia. All honors. And has a full-time job driving an ambulance. He majors in pyschology, but to look at him you wouldn't think he had sense enough to pour piss outa a boot. I take him to the movies sometimes when my bread is kinda long."

"I keep hearing about this College Joe. He moved in here before I left last time I lived here. He should be graduating in a few more months. Several times I started to look him up, but why would a psychology major at Columbia want to meet a college graduate who's only a Lundy's waiter?"

"Joe would be glad to meet you," Sandy said warmly. "And he'd drink with you. *Wine.*"

"Get out of here," I said, scoffing.

"Oh yes, he would. Joe is hell on wheels when it comes to his studies, but he's more regular than a dollar bill. You should get Blind Charlie to take you up his room sometime. Joe's wife is a drag, but Joe makes up for her; he's an okay guy. Ace."

Sandy left about eleven o'clock to go hustle. The quart was empty, but I wasn't even high. Instead, I was nervously wide awake, and every molecule in my body cried for Gloria. And when I tried to tell myself to be cool, that Gloria would be back soon enough, it seemed as if my body angrily retorted with a demand for any woman. Naturally, I began to have second thoughts and wondered why I'd had to be so damned quixotic with a professional harlot.

At least her finely tooled body would have put me to sleep by now. But here I was, wide awake and needing one more drink. I left my room to go roam the halls of the Logan for the first time.

Nobody was in the Sinman's room so I went up to Sandy's room, hoping Blind Charlie might be there, but no one was there either. Then all the wine I had drunk this day told me to go back to the lobby and fraternize with the lobby lice—the ones who drank wine, that is. And they were glad for me to join them because I had a few bills on me. Later on that night I found myself drinking in a strange room on the third floor. The stranger I was drinking with suddenly stretched out on his bed and went sound asleep. I left and went to the elevator, deciding to try Sandy's room again.

While I was waiting for the elevator Tony Scott, an ex-boxer, came out of the 3-D hallway. Tony and I had been the most casual of acquaintances when I was around before, but suddenly we were long-lost buddies.

"Let's go down to Pop Brown's room," Tony said. "Everybody on this third floor is either drunk or doped to the gills. I want some action even if it's only sitting around and talking some."

"Okay," I said. "I've got lots of friends who know Pop Brown, but I never met the guy and I want to. In fact, I was talking about him with Sandy early tonight. But let's go buy a couple of bottles first. I got money."

Pop Brown was a rotund, seventy-year-old cripple. He had a barrel chest and a fearless-sounding voice. The very kind you need to teach a Black class or a white football team, if you know what I mean. When Tony introduced me and told Pop I had bought the wine, I was immediately established as the guest of honor. Then Pop informed me that he was an authority on brickmaking and Black history.

"I come up under Booker T. and I knows what I am talking about at all times or I shuts up. That's something the young folks today just ain't learned yet. Sometimes I thinks young'uns today don't know nothing."

"Well, I don't know nothing but women," Tony said.

"Oh, hush, boy," Pop exclaimed. "You knows as much about

prize fighting as the next. They got a prize-fighting play opened downtown last week. I bet you could have wrote it better than that James Earl Jones what did. And you could write about how them refugee managers brought you along wrong. Be a lesson to our youth. Yessir."

Altogether there were six men in the room. No women. And every one of these men with the possible exception of Pop Brown was in the same state of nervous intoxication that I was. Without asking I could tell that we all suffered from the same disease: we had all been deserted by our women. We had female trouble.

The talk was loud and sometimes funny, but actually none of us listened to the other. We were like clanging cymbals. We tried to outtalk our thoughts. I tried to think about Gloria, but it was no good. Alise kept walking onto the stage of my mind. I couldn't understand it, but she would not go away. So I was the sickest guy in the room.

I did all the buying; everybody else was broke because this was the day before Checkday and everyone's last check was long since spent. We were drinking strong sherry now, but after six quarts were gone not a single man was any drunker than he was when Tony and I first arrived. These were true S.R.O. inmates. Even strong wine failed them in their times of need.

I was still conjuring up these stupid thoughts about Alise. Gloria just would not stay with me. And I wondered just how crazy I was going to get this night. Finally my hateful thoughts became pleasurable. I wanted to be alone with them and so I left.

Back in my room I laid on the bed fully dressed. Not that I was too drunk to take them off, but my night wasn't finished yet, even if I did want to be alone now.

And then it all came back in a narcotic rush.

It had been like whiskey mixed with love. Long legs. Sweeter than honey and the color of honey. We'd been closer than twins . . . a warm cocoon . . . but those legs . . . long giving legs . . . rachitic ugliness hidden in slacks . . . beautiful in bed beneath the sheets . . . but always free . . . free . . . married in Knoxville, just for the fun of it . . . slender hips slashed by love . . . whiskey . . .

always whiskey . . . drinking partners who were lovers . . . long slender legs . . . big tits that never held milk.

Roanoke . . . Richmond . . . Atlantic City . . . Hot Springs . . . Saratoga . . . jobs on top of jobs . . . laughing at jobs . . . laughing at towns . . . laughing at landladies . . . laughing at God . . . and God laughing back . . . laughing at Alise and Sid . . . that was the best part of it.

A drunken excursion . . . ending up in a room in the Dawn Hotel . . . so it was New York and a drunken vow to conquer the hick town . . . bringing home her tips like a sacrificial offering . . . but oh, those tits . . . those great big tits . . . on that slim body . . . so slim from giving . . . night moans that only a gal with long legs can sing . . . a fountain of love and peaceful surrender. AND THEN IT WAS ALL OVER BECAUSE I COULDN'T HOLD MY LIQUOR ANY MORE AND I'D FORGOTTEN HOW TO LAUGH.

I came out of those pieces of memory writhing like an epileptic and then all the ugly times began to crowd in on me. I wanted to puke as I recalled how I'd come home from AA meetings three nights in a row and found Alise lying in a stupor on the floor.

I was still high—and a little mighty—from all that rhetoric at the meeting. So I said, "Tomorrow morning I'm going to the bank. And then I'm putting you on the train. You're going to live with your mother until you dry out. And I mean for you not to come back until you're sober. Good and sober. You've had it. And so have I. Understand?"

Alise came from a small town in Virginia, and although she was groggy she said, "I don't have any clothes to wear."

"I don't want you to wear nothing," I shouted. "I want you to stay right in your mother's house until you're ready to come back here. I don't even want you to let any of your friends to know you are there. Can't you understand what's happening?"

"And let you stay here in this apartment full of women? You must think I'm crazy for real, don't you? I know what kind of AA meetings you're going to every night almost. I don't like Suffolk. I've outgrown it. I'm a New Yorker, why should I go back down there? And you're just as drunk as I am. And you've got a nerve to tell me to go someplace and get sober. So you can have your women in here."

"Yeah. You're a New Yorker all right. And wait until they snatch you for Kings County and you'll really be a bona fide one. You're so drunk now you can't even remember I've been on the wagon for five months." I decided to cool it. "Look, Alise," I said patiently. "We can't drink any more. I don't know why, but we can't. Neither of us. We've got to quit it. Our whole life style has got to be different. I even realize that it just might be boring as hell, but alcohol will kill us if we don't want to be bored."

"Who's the woman you want to move in here?"

"I'll go stay at a hotel until you return. When you get back we'll both walk into this apartment together."

The next morning I got the money and gave it to her. But for some idiotic reason I didn't wait around to help her pack or even see her to the railroad station. I just had to get away from her. I don't really know if it was that I was sick of her or sick of living in Brooklyn. All I know is that I had to get out of that apartment. And so that's when I handed Alise over to "Shorty" on a silver platter.

Two weeks passed without a word from Alise. Her mother didn't have a phone, but I wrote. No answer. I knew it was stupid, but I called the apartment. I got a recording about "Not a working number. Please check, etc." I didn't push the panic button, but the button was there if I ever got around to pushing it. I called her job at the fish and chip joint. And whoever it was who answered the phone said that Alise had just left to go home. She'd gotten sick on the job.

At first I was filled with a cold anger and told myself that I was now a divorced man. The only thing was that I started going to the bar on Ninety-seventh Street which was only a block down the street from the Park West Hotel where I had a room. And the few drinks I was having daily began to create what I can only call a false conscience. I didn't call the fish and chip joint again. After all, there was really nothing to say. But like I said: I got this false feeling of responsibility. Just how sick was Alise? She was stupid; was she on narcotics? Finally my intermittent drinking began to tell and my imagination ran wild. Alise needed me.

I took the A train to Brooklyn. I went to our apartment. Strangers were living in it; they'd never heard of Alise and me. I went to the fish and chip joint. Alise was there, perfectly sober and perfectly at ease among the fish and chips and the customers, who looked and smelled like fish and chips.

I sat at the counter like I always had the few times I'd come around and waited for Alise to bring me a cup of coffee as usual. "Where've you been and what's happening?" I said when Alise finally got around to bringing me the coffee.

"I've been sick, but they called me up and begged me to come in today," Alise said with a wicked lisp. I knew she was lying because Alise only lisps when she is lying or getting ready to do something stupid—probably illegal.

"What time you get off?" I asked.

"Late. Why?"

"I'm sitting right here until you do. And then we're going someplace and talk."

"I gave up the apartment."

"That's one of the things I want to talk about. And about my clothes and money too."

"What money?"

"All that security I had to put up on that apartment. You got it back, didn't you? And you sold it, didn't you? I know you didn't just *give* it up. And what about that three hundred I gave you to go to Suffolk with and you didn't go?"

"I didn't know you could sell an apartment. Why didn't you tell me?"

"Bitch! I didn't even know you were going to give it up. Don't you think I might have wanted to keep it even if you do leave me? And is that what you call yourself doing, leaving me?"

More customers came in and Alise had to go peddle her fish and chips. Business got pretty steady, but Alise did keep my coffee cup filled until closing time. About eleven o'clock the joint was empty and it was time to close, but Alise stalled changing her clothes.

I even began to get the idea that she was hanging around for someone to show up. And I didn't like that a bit. You know. If a stud starts going with a married woman and makes the scene right in front of the bitch's husband that stud is a killer. Then I told myself that nobody was going to risk jail or getting hurt in a rumble over a razor-legged woman who was a stone alcoholic. And after that summation I realized just how sorry a position I was in myself. But finally Alise was ready to leave.

"I live with a funny old woman now," she lisped without being asked. "And she doesn't allow any of us girls to have company."

I told you Alise was from a hick Southern town and so she probably believed that I believed her. "So even though I'm your husband I can't come in and have a strictly business conference with you?"

"I just told you you couldn't."

"Well, let's go in that bar," I said and took her arm to guide her toward the neon sign across the street. The next thing I know I was holding an empty coat by one sleeve and Alise was hightailing it down the street like hound dogs were after her.

I can't say what my reactions were. I guess I was too surprised to think anything. And maybe I didn't care. All I know is I tossed the coat over my arm and went in the bar alone.

I stayed until the bar closed, pretty sure that Alise would walk in the next minute and at least demand her coat. But when the barkeep started yelling last call I got mad—and then worried. It was quickly becoming evident that Alise was not only an alcoholic but a mental case as well. Or was she on narcotics? I didn't know the first thing about narco at the time. I only knew that heroin was something pimps hooked women on so the women would go out and peddle their flesh for the pimps. Yeah. I was really uptight then. And after all, Alise was not a bad-looking woman even if she did have lousy legs. And anyhow they didn't look ugly in bed. Only in dresses. In fact she looked damn nice in slacks. And Alise was weak-minded even when she did have good sense and who was there to say she was acting sanely now? What really bugged me was the knowledge that if Alise was truly insane I was too much of a Baptist pussy to divorce her as long as she remained in the insane asylum. I got hat and left the bar.

I took a taxi back to Manhattan, still toting Alise's coat. The next day I didn't even think about going to work, and was well into a three-week binge by noon. It was the binge of an alcoholic. It wasn't anything to do with Alise. I was secretly glad to be rid of her. AA might be a success to some people, but to me it is a colossal failure and the reason why is because alcoholics simply don't like each other. Sober alcoholics, I mean. AA gets . . . and loses . . . more members than any other organization of any kind whatsoever in the world. Furthermore, I didn't think I'd ever loved Alise; how can you love a woman you're ashamed of? In bed? Okay. But I didn't like to walk down the street with those legs beside me.

One night about ten a man knocked at my door at the hotel and when I answered he asked me if I was Sidney Bailey. Talk about scared? My legs were so weak I told the man to come inside so I could sit down. Something terrible had happened to Alise or this whitey wouldn't be here asking my name. And just like that the old love came down. All I could remember were the happy times. My eyes were full of tears and I loved Alise very much.

Then the man handed me a summons charging me with unlawful possession of property. It had been sworn out by Alise. As soon as the guy left I went out to the bar, but I'd only had two drinks when I realized that now was the time to get sober. The summons in my pocket was certainly no proof that Alise was well and sane. Maybe I faced all kinds of things and didn't even know what was coming next.

It so happened that the courtroom was crowded when I got there. I saw Alise standing about three feet away from me. As usual, Alise wore a dress; it was like she was afraid to dress in slacks around white people. And today she looked unusually country. She had on a new coat, and I was more ashamed than ever. Alise was a broad with absolutely no taste. I had always picked out her clothes for her and had been secretly proud of all the compliments she used to get. But today this cheap rag of a black coat was already so wrinkled that I guess everybody thought she hadn't bothered to take it off the last time she jumped into bed. So I stood in that court and despised Alise and my carnality that had made me her husband.

Alise turned her head and saw me but didn't speak, so I had to go over to her. "Do you know what you're doing?" I asked.

"What do *you* think?"

"I wouldn't of asked if I had an opinion. And you know damn well I don't have anything belonging to you except that coat and you left me holding that. But you've got my property! You know that, don't you?"

She sniffed but did not answer, so I moved away and concentrated on what I'd say to the judge. It would be simple and to the point. I wanted my wife committed to Kings County Hospital until such time as she was sane and sober. Right now she is hallucinating. And the proof of that is that I'm standing right here in this court being charged with withholding her property. That's all. It'd be enough. I began to fret over how long it would take to sign the papers. I didn't want to miss another day at work.

The case was called.

"Your honor," Alise said. "I was standing on the corner of Fulton and Saratoga when this man came up and snatched my coat and pocketbook."

I made a strangling sound. The judge looked at me and said, "You keep quiet. I'll tell you when to talk." Then he looked at Alise.

"You don't have the correct charge here. How much money was in your pocketbook?"

"About fifty dollars."

"Well, you have the wrong thing here, young lady." The judge waved a paper he had picked up from the bench. "We don't have a case of unlawful withholding here. You go in the clerk's office and tell them exactly what you've just told me and they'll give you the correct warrant." He glared at me. "And you go stand over there to the side. And don't move!"

When Alise came back she had a warrant, charging one Sidney

Bailey with purse snatching. And it carried a penalty of up to fifteen years.

"Both of you be back here a week from today and I'll try to round up a jury to hear this charge," the judge said. I opened my mouth, but he said, "One word out of you and you'll be held for bail. The only reason I haven't is because you showed up here this morning."

Alise had already walked away. I hurried to catch up with her. She was standing on the steps of the courthouse. And the one thing that was outstanding about her was her evident sanity. She looked like she had more sense now than she'd ever had before.

"C'mon," I said. "We're going to have this out right now."

The country clown actually managed to look haughty. "You were in front of the judge," she said. "Why didn't you have something to talk about then?"

"After you told that goddam lie I was speechless and you know it. And where the hell did you get that story from? You're too goddam dumb to have made it up by yourself." Then I cooled it just like that. I was going about it all wrong. I started over again: "I realize that I was too harsh on you . . ."

"It's too late now." She walked on down the steps. I let her go. I really was in no mood to stroke her, especially since she had a dumpy-looking little guy with her. He looked like one of her fish and chip customers, and I imagined that he had volunteered—for a pint of wine—to act as her bodyguard. But the twerp was so harmless-looking the whole thing seemed like a farce.

But things weren't too bad, I reflected. Alise was sane; she just wanted me back. All of this court business was a dumb country chick's way of getting her man back on her terms. And if I wasn't careful I might have to go back to her. That purse-snatching bit could cost me fifteen years of my life. But actually I knew that no intelligent judge was going to let a jury do that, especially after he found out that Alise and I were husband and wife.

But I woke up too drunk to make it to court that Monday. And as usual my whiskey told me to do it all wrong. I took a train to Harrisburg, Pennsylvania, and managed to get locked up there for ten days. When I got out I sent a telegram to a headwaiter friend in Florida who sent me the fare to come work the season in Fort Myers.

When the season was over in Florida I went up to Lake Delavan in Wisconsin. In the fall I returned to New York and the Park West Hotel. There was no chance of me getting my job back in the Village and so I went out to try the job of last resort as far as a Black waiter in New York is concerned. That means I went to work at Lundy's. It took me about two weeks to learn that huge kitchen, but after you worked out your own private system of picking up your orders things weren't too tough. Lundy's isn't a bad hustle at all, but you got to be in damn good health, and strong. After about two weeks at Lundy's that old false conscience went back to work and in no time at all Alise was constantly on my mind. On top of that Lundy's precludes any respectable social life. I had never dealt with a whore before, but pretty soon I was a regular in and out of the St. Louis Grill.

Being a john is the most degrading thing on earth. You are a damn sight lower than the whore's pimp. And if you don't believe me, ask any whore. The only solace I had was that thing in the Bible about it's better to cast your seed in the belly of a whore. In fact I got so uptight about being a john I wanted to read the whole chapter that passage came from. So one night I picked up my Gideon and began to leaf around in it. I couldn't find anything like that and so I got mad and started reading the whole thing, chapter by chapter. Every night I read myself to sleep. When I finished the Good Book I still hadn't found it. And when I found out that the one solace I had had was not even in the Bible I was really zapped. It was then that the periodic three-week binges became a regular thing in my life.

Since life was one big dissatisfaction I finally decided that I had punished Alise enough and I'd go take her back. I went to her job; I figured she'd still be working there.

I walked in. And the old woman who owned the restaurant took one look at me and screamed. She screamed bloody murder; all about I had come to kill everybody in the joint. I was so unnerved

I hustled right out of there, but once outside I just stood there, trying to make sense out of what the old woman was screaming. Then the big Black scar-faced cook ran out with a cleaver in his hand and came straight for me. I hauled ass. And that was wrong because every junky and wino in the restaurant suddenly got a whole lot of heart and chased me. The cops got in the act and I ended up in Raymond Street jail, held on the old purse-snatching charge. I spent the next ten days in jail because I didn't know a damn thing about making bail. It was only five hundred dollars, but I didn't have it, and who was there to call? I spent Christmas and New Year's in jail, but the day after New Year's the joint was so packed they took a bunch of us prisoners to some kind of court and the judge paroled us. He told me to come back to court on January 16.

When I showed up for the trial I looked around the courtroom for Alise. I spotted her with the same guy as before. He looked dumpier and dumber than ever. During a recess I went over to Alise, kidding myself that it was now time to stop fooling around and tell her that I was willing to take her back.

"Okay, you win," I told her.

"I know *that.*"

"Well, let's go then," I said. After all, I did have to take the clown back if I didn't want to risk a trial, but there was no law saying I had to be a Prince Charming about it.

"Go where? Where do you think I'd go with you?" Alise asked.

There'd been a note of triumph and contempt in her voice I didn't quite dig, but she'd won, so what difference did it make? "We've got to go tell the clerk or somebody that you're dropping the charges," I said irritably.

"I'm not dropping any charges. I want you to be handled."

"Handle me for what?" It was almost a scream. "You got everything you wanted, haven't you?"

"Not yet, but I will."

"What the hell more you want?"

"I want you to stay away from me," Alise lisped. I knew it was on then. She took Shorty's hand. "I love him," she told me, still lisping. "You killed my love for you."

I walked away and out of the courtroom to a nearby bar. And it was not until I'd had two drinks that it really hit me. What Alise had said. I damn near flipped for real: all this damn foolishness in jail and court over a half-wit wino whom he was welcome to.

And then the cold reality of Alise's being willing to send me to jail just so she'd be able to screw this wino without let or hindrance blew my mind completely. I hightailed it out of that bar and went back to the court.

"Don't you know that if you send me to prison for fifteen years you're dead?" I asked her. "Don't you realize that even if I didn't want to I'd still have to kill you?" I got hysterical and began to wander. "And what about my clothes?" I demanded. "You gonna give this punk my pajamas to screw you in even?"

Both Shorty and Alise laughed merrily. I swear I don't remember throwing the punch, but Alise was lying out cold on the floor, Shorty had fled and I felt so good I thought I was going to come in my pants until everybody in uniform in the courtroom rushed me. But all they did was to give me a bum's rush out of the courtroom.

I went back to the bar, feeling good as hell. My drink tasted like heaven. Hitting Alise and seeing her stretched out there on the floor with her dirty panties showing had been beautiful. Then I got mad all over again: I was Alise's superior, but she had ignored that truth and fucked over me. She'd pay.

I marched back to court, but it was over. One clerk was still there. I asked him what I should do now.

"You've had a ball, haven't you?" he asked me.

"Ball? How could I be having a ball?"

"A drink. Don't you know what it means to have a ball or two?"

"I had a couple of drinks, but I'm not drunk."

"Well, don't you remember the judge letting you go?" He was looking at a paper in his hand.

"Huh?" I said. "I haven't been tried yet."

Well, it turned out that somehow the judge had signed a paper dismissing my case. How, I don't know. All I know is that this clerk told me to get the hell out of there and don't come back.

"I'm not going anywhere," I said. "I don't want this case closed. I want it reopened. I want my wife charged with giving false information and false arrest . . ."

"That was your wife? I didn't know that. But any time a man cold-cocks a woman like you did right in front of the judge he's innocent. Now will you please get the hell outa here? You've won this time, but mebbe not next time."

I went.

And so now I laid in the Logan suffering it all over again!

THE BITCH HAD RUINED ME FOR LIFE. DEEP DOWN INSIDE I WAS AFRAID OF ALL WOMEN. I'M THE GUY WHO ONCE HATED WHORES, BUT NOW I'M AFRAID OF ALL WOMEN WHO AREN'T WHORES. THE BORN BITCHES WHO CANNOT POSSIBLY LOVE ANY MAN. THEM I'M NOT AFRAID OF. I SHOULD WRITE A BOOK: *CAN A SOBER MAN FIND PEACE AND PUSSY IN HARLEM?*

I began to pace the floor and brokenly reminded myself that at one time I'd been so lonely I'd even considered going with one of the faggots out at Lundy's, but Alise had twisted me so that I wouldn't even make a decent boy friend for a fairy.

So that's the real truth why I didn't blow my top over Gloria. I didn't deserve her; those four days with her had been all I deserved. More. A man as fucked up as I am didn't have a right to the love of even a hopheaded nymphomaniac.

So when you can't kill nothing and nothing won't die, you just don't fit in nobody's world . . . especially whitey's. I felt in my pockets knowing full well I was broke. I'd have to wake J&J. They had to loan me the dough so I could buy a pint from Joe Ash.

SCENE III

"BUT IT'S LIKE DEFILING *your own nest," the girl said.*

"But here I know exactly what I'll be taking out. You mug a drunk out in the street and what're you sure of? Twenty cents? A subway token?"

"But even you said I'm bringing in good money every night."

"Sure. You're a fast little hustler, but I gotta make me a real sting. You can hardly support our habits. I wanna be big time. I gotta be big time, can't you understand that? And if you got busted tonight, where'd we be? I got me a dream too. I dream of a Caddy, and a white dog. A big white dog . . . and a white whore to bring in the dough when you're tired. Don't you realize what it's all about in Harlem today? I want clothes like a motherfucker. Real bad. I want everyone who looks at me to wonder who I am."

"It don't seem right to just sit here and plan killing an old woman in cold blood. This is a meatball thing. . . ." The girl's eyes were frightened.

"You mean it's a sure thing," the boy retorted. "The old woman takes in almost two hundred bucks every Thursday. Mostly she takes it in after the bank's closed. I gotta make it plainer than that?"

"No." She paused, not knowing how to say what she felt. "Couldn't you wait until next week, Lonnie? Meanwhile I'll hustle twice as hard. You'll see. I'll cut down on my habit . . ."

"You don't have any habit now to speak of."

"I'll cut down on that, Lonnie. I'll just take one little joy-pop before I go out every night. I do need a little pop before I hit the street, but that's all, Lonnie." She clasped her tiny hands in entreaty. "Supposing tonight I make a two-hundred-dollar string? Tomorrow

morning you could buy two, three bundles and be in business. Just think of it, Lonnie."

"Sure," he sneered. "And how many stings like two yards have you made so far? You'll never pick up two hundred in the street; chumps don't carry that kind of bread around with them any more. And after you make your sting you're not sure there'll be no bust. You know that, don't you?"

"A john might just give me the money."

"Don't make me laugh. We know that money's downstairs, waiting for us, what we waiting for?"

"Lonnie, if you promise not to kill her I'll take the fall if anything goes wrong. Honest. And she don't know who we really are. Just two young kids, that's all. And we're younger than even she thinks. You could even go back to your parents . . . and school. We haven't got any marriage license to be traced. Nothing. We've got no record. Nothing, Lonnie. So let her live. I'll take the bust."

"You might get three to five. But like you say: we're clean. We make a clean getaway; and she won't be able to talk."

"I don't care. Right is smart at times, Lonnie. If we let her live we'll never get caught. I know. I feel it in my bones."

"That's your trouble; you don't have heart. Me? I got enough heart for both of us. That's why I'm the boss. Dig it?"

"I dig, Lonnie. Only . . ."

The widowed Mrs. Bertha Brothers now lived in the basement apartment of her 137th Street home. Since the death of her husband, Dr. Brothers, the Harlem socialite had found it expedient to let out eight rooms of her residence at an average price of eighteen dollars a week. She insisted that all rents be paid before eight o'clock on Thursday night. Why? Nobody knew.

Mrs. Brothers was very strict about references and always asked permission to call the employers of prospective tenants. But this young couple had looked so very young and clean-cut that Mrs. Brothers had thought it actually indecent to ask for any references.

Since Mrs. Brothers turned off her TV before eleven each night and retired to a sound sleep, there was no way that she could know that the attractive little Mrs. Margo Jones was a streetwalker on

125th Street. Neither did she know that Mr. Lonnie Jones was unemployed but daily supported a twenty-dollar-a-day heroin habit.

Nor did Mrs. Brothers know that she was going to die in five minutes. "My little lovebirds," she cooed. "Come to pay their rent. Isn't that nice? I just love the way you two young ones do everything together. I was just telling my sister on the phone what a nice couple you are."

It was eight-fifteen. Lonnie figured that all the other roomers had already paid their rent and he was now free to make this little sting in peace. He handed Mrs. Brothers a twenty-dollar bill. Then he was taken aback to see her take two dollars from her dress pocket and hand it to him. He had intended to kill her while she went into her day's receipts for the change. It was almost in anger that he punched her on the chin, and when she fell, he quickly jumped up and down on her head three times.

One hour later they had not found the money.

"Go upstairs and pack," Lonnie panted.

"For what? We can go out in the street and prove that we were not home all night, Lonnie."

"We ain't got no rent receipt."

"I'll come down first thing in the morning, since we were out all night. And it'll be me who finds the body . . ."

"Goddamit! I said to go pack."

"That would be a giveaway, Lonnie. Can't you see that?"

"Don't argue with me, woman."

"Well, okay. But what you going to stay here for? Come on. If you haven't found that bread by now you'll never find it. Maybe it isn't even in here."

"It's got to be here somewheres."

"I'm tired. And I'm sick of looking at her there."

"Three lousy rooms and we can't even find the bread."

"Let's go for a walk and think it over, Lonnie."

"C'mon. We're going to pack like I said."

"Why don't you take a fix, Lonnie?"

"You think I'm panicking?"

"Only there's no need to run, honey. We didn't do it and that's

all there is to it. Dig it? And we can prove we didn't cause we don't have the bread. The meatball who did it is carrying over a yard and a half at least. And we're broke except for the twenty and her two bucks."

"Yeah," Lonnie said. "Yeah. Maybe I do need a fix. Tomorrow we come down to tell her we're moving."

The police found the money in a waterproof packet on the bottom of the toilet tank. They'd found it less than an hour after Margo called them and told them she'd found the body when she came to tell Mrs. Brothers they were moving to the Hotel Logan. And they never made the same mistake again.

CHAPTER 9

THE NEXT MORNING I got up with the kind of hangover that makes you want to talk. And what I wanted to talk about was the Sinman. I picked up the remains of my bottle and went in J&J's room.

As usual, I circled my target. "You two ever remember hearing about the Sinman being robbed? His room, I mean?"

"Nobody's ever been that dumb around here," Jinny said flatly.

"Sinman hasn't always been the Sinman, you know. He used to be a fresh-faced college kid."

Jinny fluttered her eyes. "How you sound," she murmured.

I smiled sheepishly. "Well, there's no other way to describe how he used to be."

"I don't care," Joey said. "Sinman's never been robbed around here. That man is an armorer, Sid. And I've even heard rumors that he and Blind Charlie will accept a contract. I'm not sure about that, but I do know that you can get any kind of killing instrument from him for a price. And you better hurry up and believe it, mister. And I said *any* kind of instrument. Not just a knife or gun. And I've told you dozens of times that nobody in the life fucks over their sources. You just don't mess over your connections, Sid. Don't you ever want to understand these things?"

"Well, Sinman got robbed once; before he was the Sinman. I lived here then. In fact it was the same day that we really got to be friends."

"Have it your way, buddee," Jinny said. "But I think you're drunk already. And since you want to get down with it, how come you and that faggot stay so tight?"

"I tole ya, Jinny," Joey hollered.

"Sinman's no faggot," I said. "I don't know why he insists on talking the way he does. He didn't used to. But he's nobody's sissy. I know. He's got women."

"Sid, you are drunk," Jinny exclaimed. "Didn't Gloria tell you that he didn't fool with women?"

"He refused to be her pimp," I said. "A man's a faggot because he won't pimp?"

And then I decided that J&J were not the right people with whom to discuss the Sinman. "Say," I said suddenly on my way out, "I keep seeing a girl. A woman rather. In the lobby or on the elevator. And she has the cutest little baby-doll face you ever want to see, and she's got a shape, too. She's really cute, and the way she dresses you can tell she doesn't really belong in here. I can't figure her out at all, but she sure is nice-looking."

Jinny assumed that phony air of boredom she put on whenever she was about to dispense some of her more cabalistic knowledge of what was current in the Logan. "She always have a rag doll with her?"

"Damn," I said. "I think so. Once or twice anyhow, I think. What's the matter with her? She afraid somebody's going to steal her kid's doll?"

"No, it's hers. She always carries it," Jinny said.

"Gee. And she looks so intelligent and pretty."

"She was intelligent, Sid. But now she's only got one tit. It made her like that. She's nothing but a child now."

"What they cut it off for? Cancer?"

"No. Her husband cut it off."

"What for?"

"He walks in 6-A-1 to find Shorty sucking it. He's doing time now and Shorty lives up there with her."

"Don't the people in this goddam hotel do anything besides fuck and fight, drink wine and take dope?" I shouted.

"You can always move," Jinny said, not smiling.

"Now what the hell does that mean?"

"You figger it," Jinny said.

"One damn thing," I said, "I don't have to beg for no drinking partners in this rathole. You and Joey don't want my company, just say so. And I'll take my wine someplace else every time."

"Do what you want with your goddam wine," Joey yelled. "You must think you're the only person in this goddam hotel that can buy wine. And I been watching you lately, Sid Bailey, but you think I don't see. You think you're better'n anybody else just because you got a piece of a job you go to sometimes when you ain't drunk. But you ain't better'n anybody else."

"Now what the hell brought this one on?"

"And you been treating that poor Gloria worsert'n a dog," Joey added.

"Me? Can't you remember that she's in jail? And I'm not supposed to write? I'm not supposed to know her unless she's in my bed with me?"

"Where you get that kinda crap from?" Joey screamed. She looked at me as if I was some kind of murderer.

Jinny said: "And last night you come knocking on our door way past midnight. And you know we never open up for nobody after eight. We thought you were sick, but all you wanted was money to get drunk on. You're getting to be a ballbreaker, buddee. A real pain in the ass."

After that kick in the head I walked out. It seemed to me that Pop Brown was the proper person with whom to discuss the Sinman. It was pretty evident that he was a laborer brought in to teach labor like brickmaking or farming, but I felt that a former faculty member had to have some sense even if he was now on Welfare. I also felt that it would be nice to take my last fifty cents and go for a bottle before I went by Pop's room.

"I came to discuss the Sinman," I said as I walked in his room with my bottle.

"Then git out. And don't bother to open that bottle in my room."

"What's the matter with you?" I said. "I ain't saying I agree with him. I came to you because you are the only man in this building I know who should have enough insight to discuss the man intelligently."

Pop rose up in his bed. "And I was meaning to tell you about coming in here last night and talking all your ignorant-sounding talk. You wasn't brought up to speak no broken-down talk like that. You do it so's to get along with the likes of us what ain't got as much book learning. But I've taught niggers what's got more learning than you got. And talking about the Sinman is nothing but ignorance. He ain't got no understanding. Blind Charlie got more sense in his blind eyes than Sinman got in that pretty head of his. Now git out."

Then it came to me: the thronged lobby with its curses and hysterical gaiety and bottles of wine. And I felt just like somebody had thrown a slop jar in my face. It was Checkday. Yeah, Checkday, New York's day of atonement. J&J had accepted that drink from me because they didn't feel like standing in line at the office window just yet. And cripples such as Pop had their checks brought to their rooms by the super to be endorsed, then cashed on the spot. Pop had his money already and was now waiting for a runner to bring him a bottle from the store.

I walked out the door. "Hey! Ain't you gonna leave the old man a little drink?" Pop had suddenly realized that his errand boy might be a long time in returning since this was Checkday.

"Everybody can buy their own wine today," I said, and kept on going; thinking about how J&J had gladly loaned me two dollars last night. But today was Checkday, a disease that turned everyone on Welfare into mean, cantankerous, nigger-rich, arrogant fools.

As if it would punish the world for making me so unwanted on this day I went down to the Sinman's room; fully prepared to agree with any crazy thing he might say. And it was a precious sight I walked in on. The Sinman was playing a jumping little bit on his organ; Blind Charlie was doing a soft shoe. Charlie must have weighed over two hundred and fifty pounds, but he was shuffling and breaking like a ten-year-old Florida street arab. And all the while he was chanting blues doggerel to the Sinman's improvisations.

They didn't stop for me, but Sinman cordially pointed at the bottle of scotch on top of the organ. I put my pint of Spur beside it, preferring to drink the Cutty Sark. Then I just stood and watched Charlie and the Sinman.

Precipitately ending with a flourish of chords, the Sinman smiled. "Greetings, my lonely-hearted one. How now is the drunkard?" He tch-tched and then said, "I have pondered your predicament and have reached the conclusion that grass is your only salvation. It is a wonderful tranquilizer, and you must not let the fool lawmakers of this land deceive you. It is not nearly so deleterious as alcohol."

"Reefers are for the birds," I said. "Alcohol is my thing and I'm going to stick to it."

"It is all too evident that alcohol is not your thing, my man. It is your damnation. And you most certainly were not born to the spike, so what are we going to do with you? You are a slob and a mark when you're in your cups. Overnight your insane proclivity for drinking with anyone and anything has become a legend among the lobby lice. Charlie, what shall we do to be saved of our friend?"

"Nuthin'. He don't harm nobody but hisself. So lettum drink. And ain't nobody gonna mess over him around here nohow. Not as long as I'm around."

"But I cannot bear to have men around me who are uncool. And we are both enamored of Sid. We will be derelict in our duty if we allow Sid to continue in his slobbery."

It seemed to me that Charlie was unnecessarily compassionate today. "I like that boy," he declared. "He sure can talk in circles, but actually he got good sense even effen he don't know how to keep outa trouble. It's a damn good thing he got me for a fren'."

I shivered even as the scotch warmed me.

"Yes," the Sinman said. "And that is all very well, but you cannot watch over him every hour of the day. And that raging do-right complex of his. He is positively berserk with it at times. We must do something."

How warm and comfortable it was to listen to the two madmen calling me insane.

Charlie laughed softly. "Funny," he said. "With all his brains he still ain't got nuthin' to do but be running around making fren's with everybody."

"Well, what's so wrong with that?" I demanded.

"Bet you ain't got a real enemy to your name," Charlie said accusingly.

"You're wrong," I said. "I'm a Baptist minister's son. I was born with enemies."

"How so?" Sinman asked.

"I don't know. It's just that most Negroes react violently to preachers' children. They either love 'em or hate 'em."

"Them ain't true blue enemies," Charlie said severely. "And you know what that means? It means you play with people too much. Now I carries myself nice. I always do, but don't nobody ever make the mistake of messing over Blind Charlie like they fucks over you."

"I wouldn't say all that," I replied.

Sandy came in and after smiling cheerily at Sinman and me she went over to sit on the arm of Charlie's chair. And I immediately began to wonder about how tight they were now, if they were lovers. I could easily picture Charlie being the sexual partner of almost any woman on earth, but the lover of none.

"What are you men talking about?" Sandy asked.

"I am telling Sid that he should take time out to cultivate a few foes now and then," Sinman said. He looked at me. "You must do that if you don't wish to remain a square forever and a day."

"And what is a square?"

"A square is a negative quantity. To refuse to be a square is the dynamic thing to do."

"And?"

"Not to be a square is to be able to keep in mind at all times just who and what you are, and never to lower your banner. You, for instance, must always remember that you are a stranger in an alien land, a man doomed to walk among serpents; and that you are always and totally without the protection of the law or anyone else, except perhaps Charlie. That is your key to survival in the Logan."

"That's cute," Sandy said.

"You ever think about all the friendships that are formed over fifty-cent pints of wine?" I said. "People in the Logan are not hostile or strangers to each other. There's plenty people actually love J&J."

"Poppycock and old roosters," Sinman exclaimed. "The estimable inmates of this well of original sin hate each other unto perpetuity. They are mad dogs, finding happiness only when their victims succumb to their bites. Have you ever observed a sad eye when the gendarmes dragged a screaming black sacrifice through the lobby? Who is there to mourn when some lucky devil dies of an overdose? What man wept and gnashed his teeth upon hearing that his neighbor was robbed? And just whom would you turn to in this warren of lost souls for the donation of a pint of blood for last night's stabbing victim? We are all alone in here. And I would hurry up and believe it if I were you."

"You don't have to tear your clothes and weep in the street to feel compassion for your neighbor," I said.

"That's a goddam lie!" Charlie thundered. "Even Jesus wept."

I thought it best to make believe I hadn't heard this revelation, but I did muse: "Maybe everyone is afraid. Maybe no one wants a Logan inmate for a friend."

"That is why I stay here. When brotherhood comes to the Logan we will have the answers to all that besets the world."

I was not sure of what the Sinman was talking about, but at the same time I felt that I should remind him of what seemed very important to me. "This place was created by a lack of brotherhood, you know," I said. "This was a fairly decent hotel four or five years ago before the white tenants made their exodus. Not a single junky. Only a few reefer heads perhaps."

"You're saying that whitey had no right to move out when the junkies moved in?"

"They moved out *before* the junkies came," I said. "They fled from nice respectable Afro-Americans. If they'd stayed and showed their brotherhood, and insisted upon this hotel remaining a moral place to live, there'd be no rathole here today. But they fled and there were so many empty rooms the management had to take in a few undesirables. Then more, until the junkies ruled the roost. Whiteys create slums, not Black people."

"I dig that," Sandy said. "Don't you, Blind Charlie?"

Charlie only grunted.

I turned to the Sinman. "You white people . . ."

"I am not white," Sinman said crisply.

"Didn't you know the Sinman is Black?" Sandy asked. Blind Charlie laughed.

But I didn't see anything funny. "What's your angle?" I asked Sinman.

"I am the Sinman."

"You couldn't like sin that much. Or the Black man either."

"I hate niggers."

"So why the hell claim to be one then?"

"We Blacks are closer to the coming creation. It is to us a new god will be born and . . ."

"Real gone talk, ain't it? Way, way out. But what the hell does it mean . . . if anything?" I snapped because something was making me see again James Person, the kid who was making a name for himself at Juilliard. And I didn't like it one bit. It was too much like a faggot's depraved cherishment for a dead lover.

I marched to the organ, poured a drink and then went back to sit on a hassock. Sinman began to play a mad thing that was part Wagner, part Tchaikovsky with the added blue rumble of Duke Ellington's "Black and Tan Fantasy." It was a madman's prayer of exultation, and I knew that it had to be the Sinman's own work.

And the crazy thing got next to you. Sandy began to laugh almost hysterically. She slipped over into Charlie's lap and began to squirm in time to the music. She was really working out, and I wondered how Charlie could sit there with all that heat in his lap and look so unconcerned.

Suddenly the Sinman jumped up. A picture of masculinity and intelligence. "I have told you that I study Sin. Sin: that is, with a capital *S*. Now let me tell you what I have discovered. Sin is positive.

Your Christianity is but a negation of Sin. Sin is immutable. It cannot die. God is dead and . . ."

Sandy gave a little yelp of a scream. "I believe that God's a whitey, but you shouldn't say He's dead. It don't sound right, Sinman."

Sinman smiled as if at a child, but otherwise ignored her. "Even the Manicheans are wrong. Sin is the source of all; therefore we must evolve a creed out of Sin," he said. "That is why the American Black man is the center of the new cosmos to come. For he is sprung from a lewd blackamoor and a degenerate white man . . ."

"That's a goddam lie!" Sandy shouted. "Our Black women always got raped. How can a raped woman be lewd?" And Sandy never stopped talking after that, but the Sinman kept on just the same.

"So the American Blacks are what's happening today," Sinman said over Sandy's babble. "So it behooves any Sinman to be Black."

"Raped. Raped. Raped," Sandy chanted.

"And the Black inmates of the Logan are the fountainhead of what must come. Do you realize how un-American this hotel is?" Sinman asked me. "Women rule this place. They sell the bulk of the narcotics. Their bodies are the only thing of value in this place. Who complains to the managers when complaints are necessary? Women and Sin. It is only here in this pit of the purely profane, this holiest of profanities, that we can ever hope to find any need or love of the sacred."

"Winos and junkies are going to create a new god, eh?" I said.

"No god at any time, or of any creed, ever forbade wine or narcotics to be used in worship. I despise junkies, but do not tell me that the judicious use of narcotics is wrong because of them and their stupid acts."

"Oh, shit," I said softly.

"I am telling you that Sin is imperishable, that it can destroy the weak at will. It takes the strong heart, the S.R.O. heart, the female heart to survive with your soul at peace. Today is for the moral loner. All fools are cultists. Junkies and your religionists of all persuasions are cultists."

Sandy hooted. I said, "We got more female junkies than male around here."

"I am coming to that," Sinman said equably. Too equably for me. "Junkies are born. They are a breed apart. And your female junky is a would-be male, and vice versa."

"And that's another goddam lie," Sandy said.

"All junkies are cut from the same cloth," Sinman went on. "Economic circumstance has nothing to do with the birth of a junky. There is a mix of traits that one must have when born to become a junky. Without those congenital traits there is no junky . . ."

All I could think to say was, "Nerts."

Like some messiah on a Harlem street corner, Sinman paid me no never mind. "First and foremost," he said, "your junky is a cabalistic wretch. That is why no psychiatrist can communicate with him. There is a general misconception that junkies have evolved a jargon to befuddle the forces of law and order. That is not true. The born junky insists upon isolation from the entire community. He desires to associate only with his ilk."

"I got more square friends in here than Sid and Charlie combined," Sandy yelled.

Sinman bowed politely but evidently was undaunted. "When the born cultist seeks to commune with kindred spirits he goes to the cult. The cult never *has* to seek him out. Does this not prove that your true junky is born?"

"No," I said. "You're trying to make all junkies a part of a herd. There's no herd instinct out there." I pointed toward the door and the lobby. "As far as I'm concerned, a junky is the last of the rugged individualists. Junkies thrive on any dog-eat-dog situation. They live for the big sting that's coming their way tomorrow. It's the Great American Dream . . . if you know what I mean."

Sinman's smile was pitying. "You are as unteachable as a junky at times," he said.

"And every junky in the world will turn his sister on if he can gain from it," I said. "How much more selfish can you get? That's rugged individualism. And nothing but."

"A junky cannot turn his sister on unless his sister is a born junky," Sinman replied. "In the first place a junky would be reluctant to let his sister know he is a junky. And if some overzealous junky should succeed in hooking a born square, that square will eventually kick the habit cold turkey, if necessary, rather than go through all the changes required to live a junky life, especially in Harlem. And it is when these born squares kick the habit that quack psychiatrists rejoice and ask the mayor for more funds to 'combat drug abuse in our community.' And the charlatans know perfectly well that death is the only cure for heroin addiction."

I thought of Gloria and got scared as hell. "Who the hell are you to give opinions?" I said bitterly. "And no two junkies are alike," I added desperately.

"It is as if they came off a production line," Sinman said firmly. "Tell me: when have you met a junky who did not claim to be an intellectual even if he was illiterate? Have you ever talked to a junky of either sex who did not inform you of their IQ within ten minutes? And wasn't that IQ 138? Why 138? And why is it that not a single square knows his IQ?"

"Junkies are persecuted," Sandy yelled. "They get sent to prison on phony charges and the prison shrink tells 'em what their IQ is. And it's not always just 138 either!"

"There has to be certain sexual and social deviations present before a junky can be produced," Sinman said. "I call it the junky syndrome. Here are your symptoms: selfish unto sickness; congenitally unable to relate to anyone else's hopes, problems or aspirations; an unholy inability to concentrate. Certainly you are aware by now that every single junky has more than just one sexual aberration. And that both the male and female junky of the species prefer to give and receive their sexual kicks orally. And that every single one is bisexual. All born addicts have indulged in subnormal or abnormal sex relations long before they came to plunge the deadly spike in their flesh."

"Charlie!" Sandy screamed. "This dirty-mouthed white-Black-bastard just called me a cocksucker!" She came off Charlie's lap and advanced on Sinman. "I never gave a head job in my life!"

And I believed Sandy. Sinman had to be wrong. Sandy was a

real pro. It was like she was committed to give beyond the line of duty; like she was able to actually tear off a piece of her very being and give it to you for a few moments. She made you think that she cared about you and what you needed. It was like Sandy had parceled all her love in equal little packages and sold them. But like Sandy said: she did not give any head. On the other hand, all other junky prostitutes I knew preferred to french their dates. In fact, getting on their back was the last thing they ever wanted to do.

"When a junky speaks of having normal sexual relations, heterosexual relations, he will invariably speak of it as 'freaking off,'" Sinman said.

This madman could be so goddam right in all his insanity. It was more than eerie.

"If all the known narcotics were somehow to vanish from this earth we would still have the junky syndrome. Their personalities would not vanish or change," Sinman said. "Their innate selfishness would be just as apparent as now. Their instability and lack of direction would still set them apart as a group. And the junky cult would re-emerge because of the born junky's inability to communicate with people unlike himself. And that regenerated cult would in no time find a new river Lethe from which to drink so that they may dream of what they could have been if the squares of this world had not been so jealous of them."

Sandy turned to Charlie. "Why don't you say something to that whitey bastard? Don't you realize what he called over one hundred thousand Black men and women in Harlem? How dirty can the motherfucker get?"

"And so we find that, given a thief and a born liar who is possessed of the weirdest sexual desires, who is vain and vainglorious and selfish beyond bestiality, you are going to have a junky on your hands come hell or high water. This is the junky syndrome and you must face it."

"Don't tell me," I sneered. "I know. I know you are going to say that you are the living proof of your theory. You are not a born junky. Therefore you can use heroin without becoming an addict." I was actually snarling.

"I am the Sinman and the master. Your junky is the willing slave of everything he likes, including meth!"

"Bullshit," Sandy said.

"Which came first, Sinman," I asked, "heroin or your crazy ideas?"

Sinman smiled mystically. "It all came at the same time. A few days after I met you and Sharlee. Sharlee was living proof that God had died. After that I was free to do all things until our new creed is come."

"And who the hell is Sharlee?" I screamed. I don't know why that name I'd never heard before should make me so furious.

"Sharlee is the most beautiful creature on this earth," Sinman said.

"That she is," Charlie said. His voice was low but certain.

"How the hell would you know?" I shouted.

"I felt her." After that hoarse whisper Charlie said no more.

And it was that silence that got next to me even more. "Well? Well?" I said impatiently.

"I felt her all over and she's beautiful. Her hair is soft like you want to wipe tears away with it. Her tits are tiny like you want to kiss them to make them grow some more. Like a little child's they are, and you know it ain't right to touch them, but you gotta. You gotta kiss them . . . you gotta. And there's no flesh like Sharlee's. You touch her hips and you know . . ." Charlie's voice drifted on in a messianic rumble that was so low it was as if he were praying. I was mesmerized but at the same time I could not keep my eyes away from Sandy, who was cuddling Blind Charlie in a way that was so feverish I could almost hear her cooing to him.

And I was like some unholy and lonely well that Charlie was refilling as the little whore cuddled him. Weak all over, with a frenzied prickling up and down my legs, I still could not make myself sit down. I also needed to go to the bathroom, but I knew that I would just have to pee on myself before I'd interrupt Charlie. For something was now turned on in this room, something more important than life itself.

I glanced at the Sinman, who was fingering the keys of the silent organ, and then again at Blind Charlie, still reciting his litany. All of us, even Sandy, seemed to breathe with a cautious politeness, as if we dared not draw in more than our rightful share of that which was loose in this room.

While Charlie continued to rumble on, describing a girl he never had seen and would never see, I forlornly wished for a gift of cynicism so that I could accuse Charlie and the Sinman of trying to run a game on me. But both my heart and my mind told me that what was permeating this room was a thing of truth. Already Charlie had created a blood-and-flesh chimera with whom I had fallen in love. Crude and cruel as he was, Charlie was the ultimate pimp; I lusted for this woman, and I had no choice but to listen greedily to the end.

"Sharlee is our priestess," Sinman said when Charlie had finished. "Many men worship her and her time is really not her own; but it is only through her body that you will ever regain your soul and banish your loneliness. No man can ever be whole until he knows Sharlee. I shall see that you do."

"No," I muttered. "You gave me Gloria and I've been fucked up ever since."

"But I am not giving Sharlee to you. How could I? I am only going to introduce you."

Like some kind of man possessed, I felt superior to everyone in the room. Sharlee now belonged to me even though I wasn't sure she even existed. There came a desperate demand to leave these three—the whore, the dope fiend and the blind killer. I could not let them defile this thing that had seized my heart. So I said, "I'll be seeing you." And moved abruptly toward the door.

From out of nowhere Charlie's cane was about my neck. The crook was almost choking me. Horror and anger were one, and for the first time I realized that it is not only stupid, but it is no fun to associate with maniacs. I stood and sobbed for breath.

"I must tell you about Sharlee," Sinman said when Charlie had released me and gone back to his chair. "Her birth was contrived by a fate far more imaginative than the one that brought about that episode at Bethlehem."

"Now ain't that a kick in the head," Sandy said. Once more her old self.

"Perhaps," Sinman said, "but I must give Sid a brief sketch of Sharlee's progenitors if he would appreciate all the coincidences that led up to the birth of our priestess. Therefore I shall begin with the Peabodys. The Boston Peabodys. America's finest family. We have it on the best authority that it was the Peabodys who first introduced the Lowells and the Cabots to God.

"Now Mr. and Mrs. Branch Peabody suffered a rage to do good long before do-gooding was the in thing to do. Ah. What was this mad urge that made this stodgy pair of newlyweds from the moneyed clan of Peabody suddenly dash off to Asia Minor to hurl the Word of God at the unwary natives? Why not China? Or Africa? Don't you see the capricious hand of fate at work here?"

I shrugged noncommittally. So far, Sinman was running a poor second to Blind Charlie.

"Now this churchly couple were sterile (or perhaps they did not know how), so when their five-year tour of duty was up in Iran they adopted a Black child and brought her back to America in swaddling clothes."

Sinman paused and then continued. "Once home, the Peabodys did not shirk in their care of the tiny infant they had impetuously adopted. They called her Prudence, and she grew comely as well as intelligent. But little Prudence did cause gnawing doubts to lodge in the heavenly breasts of her foster parents. From the very beginning the little girl was amazingly independent and impulsive. She did not conform to the docile pattern of the Negro as the Boston Peabodys knew the American Negro.

"I suppose it is immaterial to add that Prudence is not a Negro . . . no African lineage . . . although she is darker than most of the Black people one meets in Harlem today. But I suppose that these Branch Peabodys were very catholic in their ideas of what constitutes a Negro in America anyway.

"But be that as it may, Prudence early showed signs of becoming a very improper Bostonian. Oddly enough, the child refused to do anything the Peabodys could actually put their finger on. Perhaps it should be said that Prudence merely showed intimations of willfulness that disturbed her foster parents, but never did those parents regret their adoption of the child.

"Blindly given to faith, hope and charity, Prudence's guardians somehow managed to maintain a sophisticated realism toward their ward in that they did not delude themselves that this was not America or that Prudence could ever be fully integrated among the Brahmins, or the Peabody clan as a whole for that matter."

Still upset by Charlie's totally unnecessary latching me around the neck, I grew more and more restless and nervous as the Sinman continued his pointless tale. Charlie's appreciative murmurs were no help either.

"In kindness, not selfishness, the young couple refused to insist that Prudence bear the name of Peabody. They named her after Boston's Black Revolutionary hero and called her Prudence Attucks. When the child was fifteen years of age they enrolled her in Mrs. Simpson's Boarding School, which was a very proper depository for the children of divorced parents, alcoholics and the like. The school is very ultra as everyone from Boston knows, but this did constitute a very grievous error on the part of the young Peabodys. Perhaps they were not bright anyway. Probably why the corporation-holding clan of Peabody was glad to see them go off on their missionary kick in the first place.

"Please pour Sid a drink, Charlie," Sinman said with idiotic courtliness. I glanced down at my almost full glass as Charlie rose and lumbered toward me. I quickly drained the glass and handed it to him.

"Within two years the child become convinced that whatever the world had in store for her would never be found within the confines of Mrs. Simpson's snobbish school. Prudence fled, making her way to Harlem. The Peabodys set out in worried pursuit of the girl's soul, one might say, but they were killed in a collision on the Milford Turnpike. It was years later when Prudence learned of their demise.

"And although the New York police had been alerted to search out a teenager from Iran, it never occurred to them to seek a dusky miss with a Boston accent in Harlem. They were looking for some exotic sort of Egyptian."

I guess the Sinman paused to catch my reactions. But I registered nothing. I felt nothing.

"Don't you see the shadowy hand of a greater circumstance than usually attends?" he asked.

"No," I said. "Not for real. When I was in school, every Black college or boarding school had at least two African students who had been adopted or sponsored by missionaries. Prudence only got a little better treatment. Ate higher on the hog is all."

"But none were from Iran. None of them were Mandeans. So here we have an altogether unique occurrence, and a uniquely continuing event," Sinman said. "But let us proceed. . . . New York did not have much to offer an Iranian miss who looked and talked like a New England Negro. The depression was still on in Harlem, and if the truth be known, I seriously doubt if Prudence had anything to offer New York."

Then the fool actually looked wistful. "The life of Prudence for the next two years is rather vague. I wish I knew it all. I only know that she was nineteen when she married Wilhelm Black. Now Wilhelm was, of all things, the love child of a Javanese serving girl and a Dutch planter."

Again Sinman paused to check my reaction and again he found none. He sighed and continued: "I believe that each married the other for gain. It was not a love match, but I believe that love was there. It had to be. But they did marry each other under false pretenses. Prudence thought that Will was a naturalized American or, if not that, at least a citizen of Java or Holland. On the other hand, Will thought his bride was a native of America.

"I see Wilhelm occasionally. He looks every inch the United States senator. Long bob . . . no oriental aspects at all. But anyhow . . . things went from bad to worse when Will finally confessed to Prudence that he had jumped a freighter to marry her.

"We have, then, two young foreigners abroad in Harlem, filled with fear lest they be caught up with and deported. Will did have a native land, but Prudence was a child without a country. She knew neither who her parents were nor what their language was. Now just what fate was it that decreed that these two torn souls should bring forth the most beautiful child in the world?"

Then I got it. I gasped. "Sharlee is their child?"

"Yes."

"Dutch, Javanese, Iranian Mandean out of Boston!" I exclaimed. "There couldn't be another bloodline like that in the world. I can't believe it."

"Above all else, Sharlee is a living truth. How in the world can you say she doesn't exist?"

"Well . . . in the beginning . . . I thought you and Charlie said she was a Negro. A Black American."

"We did not. But she is."

"No, she's not. You know better."

"Sharlee told me that she is a Black woman, and I prefer to take her word for it."

I happened to have the whiskey bottle in my hand and I waved it like a battle flag. "Why does every goddam fool who moves into the Logan want to pass for a nigger?"

"Sharlee never lived here!" Charlie roared.

That cooled me right there, and I subsided into a trembling calm.

"Sharlee loathes the Logan and all it stands for," Sinman explained. "She seldom comes here when she is free."

"What do you mean, free? She married?"

"Free from prison."

"How could a young girl of her background ever go to jail?"

"For over ten years Sharlee held the record for being the youngest heroin addict ever treated by the state of New York."

In my blindness I forgot that the Sinman had not known Sharlee for ten years. "You dirty no-good sonofabitch," I said coldly.

Sinman showed no anger. Only sadness. "I only wish I had been there," he said softly.

Charlie got up and went to the hutch cabinet and took out three clean glasses. He came to the organ and filled them. "You gotta take your own," he said tonelessly.

Sinman tossed off his drink, went to the closet for a sport jacket and then said, "Come, my friends, let us go visit Sharlee."

I did and I did not want to go. I was not ready to meet this girl just yet. But both the Sinman and Blind Charlie had been so way out all morning I was actually afraid to demur. But I wasn't ready. Not by a long shot. You were supposed to be calm, cool and collected when you met up with a unique person like this Sharlee had to be. And I was like, well . . .

Sandy was dismissed like a galley slave and five minutes later we were in a taxi headed for Brooklyn and MacDonald Street.

Charlie was up front with the driver and Sinman and I were in the back. Sinman leaned toward me and spoke in a low murmur. "After you left for work that day I was robbed, I went to sit in Morningside Park. But when I got there I couldn't remain still. I walked. You know those paths that are almost level that lead to the steps down the mountain? The park *is* a mountain, you know. Well, I've read of widows' walks and the path seemed just like one that afternoon because there was Sharlee, pacing back and forth, waiting for her connection.

"Her diamond-black hair tumbled to her shoulders and flowed out slightly as she walked. Sharlee is tall, about five seven or more, and unconsciously beautiful at all times. I stopped, stared and silently offered my soul. I could not move. She turned and saw me staring at her; she was sick, extremely sick. But I knew nothing about heroin then. But sick as she was, she must have known me to be her slave because she smiled. And only the fates know why because Charlotte Black is not a friendly girl. She is kind, but not friendly. You will know what I mean when you meet her.

"Her connection came in a moment and then I took her home with me. She thought I was a john; but I immediately made it clear that I would gladly die before I ever became a john for her. I also gave her my vow that only death would ever really part us. And I shall keep that vow. There is no possible life for me after Sharlee passes. I can only hope to die first."

I looked at Sinman and wished there was some way I could gauge just how crazy he really was . . . if at all.

"Sharlee hated the very smell of the Logan. She took a fix as soon as we got in the room, but it seemed to do her very little good. In five minutes she was a caged animal . . . nothing vicious, but caged. In less than an hour I had packed what few things the thieves had left and departed the Logan for a room on 112th Street.

"Sharlee became my all. Her habit had to be a part of me. That very night I plunged the first needle into my arm.

"Sharlee's habit was oooh-long. And got longer. So in time even with extraordinary help from my mother I could not support both our habits. But we remained one until she was arrested again. We have never lived together since, what with parole and all, but we are still friends and lovers."

Sinman jerked at his left earlobe and then said, "Sharlee told me on the phone this morning that the screws have broken her spirit. They must have beaten her almost to death; I hate the very name of Bedford. Sharlee is built like a junior grade amazon, an Astarte who can fight any three men, but she said she has given up the life. No more jail cells for her and I am glad; she is not a born junky anyhow."

The taxi stopped in front of a two-family house, Brooklyn's foretaste of its version of the S.R.O. I gave my shoulder to Charlie and the three of us went up on the porch. Charlie still grasped my shoulder as we waited after Sinman rang the bell. His great paw felt good; it was as if a part of his monstrous strength was also a part of me. And I knew I needed it.

Sharlee answered the door. I was numb, dumb; helpless as all the air billowed out of my lungs. She was an indescribable girl. Like a raindrop and as perfect. It was a liquid sort of beauty. It drowned you pleasantly.

True beauty seldom soothes. And sometimes there is a hidden hideousness in great allure that makes you quickly glance away to spare the mind and eye. But Sharlee was different from all other women. Your eyes were smoothly washed by her being and you felt good within yourself. I never dreamed that a girl could be so pretty.

And there was nothing equivocal about her looks. Her beauty

was there and it had to be faced like a moment of truth. And, like truth, it had to be humbly acknowledged. And her face was so other-worldly; it had never been here before. She was a person with no look-alikes. It was not only her features, but her rich red-brown coloring and amazing hair.

Sharlee gave a glorious smile to the one man who could not see it and nodded rather stiffly to the Sinman. The look she gave me mingled curiosity with displeasure. She did not speak as she stepped back and opened the door wider.

She led the way into her tiny two-room apartment and nodded for us to be seated. Then she began to pace the floor before I had even led Charlie to a chair.

Not a single word was spoken as the lovely girl continued to pace. She wore a long oriental-style housecoat that heightened her Polynesian good looks and her other-worldly complexion. Her hair did seem to flow back when she walked. There was a bottle of expensive sherry on the coffee table and every now and then Sharlee would stop her pacing to pour herself a drink, but she never offered us any.

As far as I was concerned, this was the most way-out scene the Sinman and Blind Charlie had yet produced. It was very evident that the Sinman had come only to gaze and worship in silence. Blind Charlie must have come to act as some kind of deacon in the rites. What part I was supposed to play was not told to me.

So there was absolutely nothing to do but look at Sharlee. I soon noted that her eyes were slanted but only slightly, her only oriental aspect. And she was tall, almost an amazon, as the Sinman had said, but not quite. She was too willowy. I guessed that she was probably leggy, but the flowing housecoat covered her legs and body completely.

One of the times Sharlee poured a drink Sinman said, "Wine kick, my dear?"

Sharlee only nodded, but Charlie said, "Wine is good for her and it ain't no sweet lucy. Leave her have it."

After that the room was silent again. Sharlee's swishing housecoat made the only sounds. And I thought that this was how she must have looked the day Sinman first saw her, and there was no question in my mind how much more beautiful she must have looked four years ago before the screws had broken her. Perhaps then her beauty had been hideous.

But Sharlee did not have the rounded, doll-like features of the average Asian beauty. Her Dutch heritage showed in the strong character planes in her face and also in her height, but the way she drank and smoked was American as hell.

"Mother at work?" Sinman asked her.

"Yes."

It was the first word Sharlee had spoken and it told me all I had to know. That one syllable was triumphant proof that Sharlee was the greatest. It was low and melodious, restrained as if out of kindness to her tortured beholder.

It was sheer insanity, but somehow I was suddenly filled with only one desire, and that was to take Sharlee to dinner at Lundy's. It made no kind of sense at all, of course. Although sex was simply out of the question anyway—God certainly did not intend for a chronic lonelyheart like me to ever make love to a creature like Sharlee—I could want something more appropriate for her than dining at Lundy's and having a silly faggot waiting on us. But there I sat with my crazy wish.

Sharlee walked the floor for the whole hour we stayed, and during that time she gave no further clues as to her personality. But in the hallway when we were leaving she suddenly took the Sinman's arm and squeezed it.

"I'm sorry you caught me like this, James," she said softly.

"It was to be expected, my dear. You must come visit me soon. A little Cutty Sark with me will do wonders for you."

Sharlee hugged her arms beneath her tiny breasts. "Damn right it will," she said in a soul-like, pensive yet toneless voice. Then she smiled that wonderful smile. I thought it had to hold some special message for the Sinman, but already I knew that nothing was sure about Sharlee except her beauty.

CHAPTER 10

WE WERE ALL SILENT in the cab back to the Logan. I was bursting with pent-up everything, but Sinman was meditative and aloof, while Blind Charlie seemed almost belligerently keeping the silence for the Sinman. Vindictively, and somehow triumphantly, I pondered the possibility that Sinman was suffering pangs of remorse now that Sharlee was free of heroin and he was not.

When the cab stopped in front of the Logan, Sinman quickly paid the fare and disappeared into the hotel. I gave Charlie my shoulder and we entered the lobby. I was somewhat shocked to see the pretty-faced little woman with the rag doll in a nearly drunken condition. Even in this state, however, there was some odd and gentle quality about her that S.R.O. women simply do not have. And my fantastic imagination carried me off into immediate conjectures: if a man showered this woman with love, kindness and trust, would it be possible to restore her mind? I was so carried away with the idea that I walked unevenly and Charlie tripped over my heels but didn't fall.

"What the hell is wrong with you now?" Charlie yelled. "You walk like you's drunk and can't see a goddam thing. Look and see where you's going at, can't you?"

"Sorry, man," I murmured. "I was looking at a fine chick and thinking kinda. She's a fox, but Jinny says she doesn't have good sense."

"She wouldn't be standing here in this lobby effen she had good sense. What she look like and what she doing?"

"Well, she was muttering something about somebody stealing her coat. She's a little bit drunk. Like a child."

"Then she ain't no fox! Only decent-looking women in this hotel is them stinking junkies. Wino bitches is all broke, ugly and on Welfare, and most times smell worser than the junkies."

"Well, this one is different. She's what you call a fetching sort of beauty. And she got long shiny hair with waves in it, almost as nice as Sharlee's. And pretty skin and eyes like a baby. She's got a pretty little face all right."

"Whoooee! Whyn't you stop and say something? You said she was drinking, didn't you?"

"Yeah, she's practically drunk, I guess, but just the same she's no S.R.O. babe. Nice silk dress. And it's no charity deal either; that dress was bought for *her*. Fits just right. And she's kinda small."

"Well, whyn't you stop, I tole ya?"

"I did almost. That's how you tripped."

Charlie's laughter boomed. "Breaking my goddam neck over a piece of ass, is you, boy? Anyhow you's on the right track. That's how come I lets you be my fren'."

We went to the cigarette machine and bought Pall Malls. When we entered 1-C-1, Sinman was at his organ, still pensive and withdrawn. He might have needed a fix, but I was not sure. "Why don't you go visit Mr. Johnson?" he asked Charlie.

There had to be something arcane in that question and I immediately got the funky idea that Sinman was expecting a visit from Sharlee in a little while. Yeah. It was a funky idea, but not exactly a jealous one.

I also wondered why the Sinman had suggested Mr. Johnson's room to us. The old man lived on the sixth floor, but I had never been in his room. However, I did know who he was because Mr. Johnson believed that he and I had met and been buddies years ago. Whenever he was drinking, and happened to meet me in the lobby, he would stop and renew this imaginary friendship. He could never remember the town we had met in or the year, but he could vividly recall the drinking we had done together.

With Charlie holding onto my shoulder I led the way into Mr. Johnson's room, and once more realized that it was Checkday. Quarts of wine were jumping from every angle, and a whole slew of girls were present and nearly half of them were flirting with Mr. Johnson, who was a handsome old codger of maybe sixty-five years old. And not a single girl in the room appeared to be over twenty-two or twenty-three.

"Blind Charlie!" It was a fervent gasp that rose from the girls circled about Mr. Johnson. And then they rushed us.

"Ooooh, Charlie," many of them moaned as they all tried to make over Charlie at the same time.

"Git back. Git back thar, I say!" Blind Charlie roared. "How'm I gonna feel all you pretty gals at oncet? Stop it now and go slow. You is crowding the ole sugar daddy."

But the girls just crowded closer. And I felt funkier than ever as I realized that I had never really been a part of the Logan. Even in this ratty bucket of blood I was unwanted, and I told myself that you have to be real brutal to make it with any and all chicks. Blindness had nothing to do with the way these chicks had rushed to Charlie. Charlie was a warrior, I was a pussy. And that's where it was at.

Meanwhile the giant was trying to kiss and identify each girl by touch. Every once in a while he would bellow at a girl: "Stop all that wrigglin' and twistin' so's I can feel who you is!"

I looked around; I wanted to see it all. This was one of those Checkday affairs which our sociological journalists like to hint about. But, save for a few loud voices, it was a pretty innocuous gathering. There was no music or dancing, and as far as I could see, the only activities going on were kissing and propositioning. At first glance this thing could have been called a sort of Whores' Exchange. Only I knew by word of mouth through the years that these girls were not whores by a long shot. And that most of them were housewives who all had the same quirk that made them want to visit and drink with the poorest of the poor twice a month. None of the girls were on Welfare, all having hardworking men. Neither were they chiselers; they could and would chip in for more wine when the occasion demanded.

And this type of girl was not peculiar to the Logan. Their breed is to be seen in any S.R.O. on Checkday. As for the girls in Mr. Johnson's room, I knew without being told that not a single one lived in the Logan, and to the best of my knowledge seldom if ever entered the place except on Checkday. I also knew the rep these chicks had as fighting women; they loved to do battle and were absolutely fearless. Jinny once said that every single one of these girls would fight a striped-ass ape if the spirit so moved them. Much of the Checkday havoc wrought in New York's S.R.O.s is done by this pugnacious flock.

All of the male revelers were residents of the Logan, ranging in age from Charlie's and my early forties to the seventies. All were either pensioned or on Welfare; hence paupers or near paupers, and yet the girls seemed to be carrying on extramarital affairs with these ancient has-beens.

Mr. Johnson shoved through the pack of admiring girls to shake Charlie's hand. "And welcome to you too, Sid," he said after greeting Charlie. "You know me and you been drinking buddies from way back and I was beginning to think kinda bad of you, boy. Thought maybe you had the idee that us sixth-floor folks was too low down for you 5-C high-society folks, but I sees you're finally here although it had to take ole Blind Charlie to get you up here. Now these sixth-floor people got their ways, just like everybody else, but they ain't no worse on the sixth floor than anywheres else. Believe me. And even if we has got a pusher or two up here they is smooth with it and don't have nobody taking off, and OD'ing or sleeping in the kitchen and toilets. In fact, nobody dares to sleep in our kitchens."

And then Mr. Johnson went through his ritual of renewing our acquaintance. "Damn if I can remember the name of that town but we sure had fun, didn't we, son? Boy! Them was the days. Yessiree. Whiskey flowed like water and our pockets was big, weren't they, boy? Didn't have to drink no sneaky pete wine then. Why, we'd never even heard of sweet lucy."

A cute little girl who was so short she had to throw her head back to look at Mr. Johnson interrupted him. "Mr. Johnson, that Obie took and put a bottle of sherry in his pocket. I saw him do it."

The handsome old man smiled benignly. "Oh, pshaw, gal, what you care? He done bought four, five or more bottles. It's probably his'n anyways."

"Mr. Johnson, you know it ain't correct to take a bottle you brought in a friend's room back out again. You are supposed to leave what you bring. That's etiquette, Mr. Johnson. That Obie ain't right and ain't got no smarts at all, trying to make trouble."

Mr. Johnson scowled. "Now see here, gal," he bawled. "I don't want no fighting in here today. You just mind your own affairs and leave other folks' mannus alone. You hear me, gal? I don't need no fighting in here today!"

The little girl looked like she had been spanked. "Yessir, Mr. Johnson."

The girl walked away and Mr. Johnson said, "That there little mite ain't big as a minute yet she come up here and start a fight on the sixth floor every Checkday. Seem like she don't get her kicks right lessen there be a ruckus up here. But the little bitch can fight," he added with a touch of pride.

"So why invite her?" I asked.

"Oh, c'mon, boy," Mr. Johnson exclaimed. "I ain't gonna let her do that much fighting." He paused for a little introspection. "But she did cut a gal for nothing last Checkday . . ."

Charlie had long since wandered off. However, we separately joined in the active drinking. And I was very actively feeling no pain when I first took notice of the little mahogany chick sitting on Mr. Johnson's bed. I guess you know by now that I go for dark little chicks with soft voices and ways but almost always end up with the exact opposites. But this time I was in luck because this little frail seemed to be unable to keep her eyes off of me. Maybe she was nobody's fox in the strictest sense of the word, but she had a small nose and a well-shaped mouth, and maybe I didn't want to inspect her too hard since her glances already denoted that she was all for it; and didn't give a damn what "it" was. Yeah, man.

Naturally I flipped . . . in a drunken sort of way. I really didn't try to guess her age either, but she had to be about the same age as the rest of the girls, maybe younger, if she drank a lot; and she had a glass in her hand at the moment.

"How you making it, little girl?" I said.

She showed all her teeth, but it was only because of the wine and her dusky hue that I thought her smile was flashing white. In reality her teeth were stained amber from too much cheap wine and cigarette smoking.

"Jes' fine, suh. Jes' fine," she said, and I knew she'd had a cornfield education, but what difference would that make in bed? Besides, Sharlee's amazing allure was still upon me, making me magnanimous toward all members of the female race.

Other beautiful women always made me critical of girls of lesser beauty, but Sharlee was so different; she made you search out the good points in other women. Like everyone seemed lovely after you have gazed at Sharlee.

"But Ah is mos' suttingly hot," the girl added. "Wish Ah had me a nice cool place to lay down. Ah jest got back from the horspital and Ah needs mah rest."

"I've got a nice cool room right here in the hotel," I said. No, I didn't even consider the stupidity of taking up with a potential walking drugstore.

"Ah kin?" She stood up, ready and thankful.

"Sure. C'mon."

The little thing leaned toward me and whispered with childlike seriousness, "Aw right, but don' let Mr. Johnson see."

It pricked my vanity to be in competition with a sixty-odd-year-old man, but just the same I muttered darkly, "Nobody's going to mess over you in 5-C. We don't let everybody come wandering down our hall like they do up here."

"Sho 'nuff?" And then the frail whispered: "You go stand outside de do'. Ah gonna tell Mr. Johnson Ah gotta go pee."

"Okay," I said, "but don't take all day." Then I went over to Blind Charlie and said, "I'm cruising a little chick out of here. I don't know the exact score, but anyhow, if I don't come back you'll know where I am."

"Whoooee! Git it while it's hot!" Charlie roared in a voice that could be heard as far as St. Paul's Chapel on the campus. The whole room looked at us and then burst out laughing. I was so uptight that I had to do something with my hands and so it was for no other reason that I reached into Charlie's breast pocket for one of his cigarettes I had just bought in the lobby. Like always the last one to take a cigarette usually put them in his own pocket. Charlie had smoked last, but when I extracted those cigarettes all hell broke loose.

Charlie stood up and daintily cupped his hands about my jawbones. Just as daintily he lifted me up and tossed me about five feet away. My head went upside the radiator, but I was still halfway conscious. Charlie moved in like a big black cat and proceeded to beat my brains out with that heavy cane of his.

"Sid! Whar you at, Sid?" Charlie roared. "Come tell me who's this thieving bastid sonofabitch went in my pockets!" And he whaled me across the forehead and face. Then I didn't hear any more because I had mercifully faded away.

Lina and Mr. Johnson later told me that two of the girls jerked the cane out of Charlie's hands and ran out of the room with it. Charlie roared and went for his knife. And began turning in complete circles while making vicious swipes through the air. All of the girls were screaming by now and trying to edge their way out the door at the same time. The old men looked and trembled before the deadly windmill and didn't know what to do or say or even where to run to.

Someone screamed for the police. That really got to Charlie. "Don't need no titty-sucking pigs in here. I'm gonna kill this here thieving bastid all by my lonesome. Where the hell is he, Sid? I got him? Sid? Sid, c'mere, you lil sonofabitch, and tell me so's I kin git my hands on him good. Tell me who I'm gonna kill, I say!"

Yeah. That's the way they told it and that's the way it had to have been. Charlie had smashed my eyeglasses, and everyone was sure that he was pounding the shards into my eyeballs. But luckily Charlie struck me everywhere but directly in the eyes. Then two old men, both lamed with arthritis, stealthily dragged my body out of the room by the feet. And those two brave souls more than likely saved my life because it was only a few moments later that Blind Charlie hurled his knife into the exact same spot where I had been laying.

Out in the hall I began to come to, but I hurt so bad I wanted to be unconscious again and I tried. Oh, how I tried. It was just like the beating had made me drunker. I had no smarts at all. None. Like a zombie. And I was bleeding like a stuck pig. And the looks on the faces of the girls who crowded around me with their handkerchiefs all said that I was not long for this world.

Finally the little girl I had intended taking to my room grabbed my arm and hustled me out of that 6-D hallway. She asked where my room was, but I was so incoherent she couldn't understand me. However, some junky told her to take me to 5-C.

Jinny opened the foyer door and screamed. Joey grabbed a knife and came running. Leah and Ray came with a baseball bat they were actually fighting over. My Good Samaritan girl friend dug the scene and split, but Jinny caught her before she reached the staircase.

"Ah jes' brung him. Ah ain't done it," the little girl whimpered.

Joey was first in command. "Take Sid and lay him in his room," she told Leah and Ray. To the girl she said, "And you better have a damn good story."

"Mistah Blind Charlie done did it," the girl said.

Thereupon Jinny turned into a little black carrier pigeon and took wing. She flew all over the fifth floor bearing her fierce and bloody tidings with great joy.

I lay on the bed, trying my damnedest to again lose consciousness, and dimly heard the girl tell Joey that her name was Lina. Then Lina proceeded to tell a most incomprehensible story, but somehow Joey was able to divine that Lina was in no way responsible for my condition. So she manfully anointed Lina, granting her permission to stay with me.

Then Joey went someplace and came back with a pint of Spur. I drained it with only a little bit of help from Lina. After that I either fell out, went to sleep or lapsed into a coma. I guess Lina didn't have anything else to do and so she crawled into bed beside me. Anyways, we were both laying there asleep when a furious pounding came at the foyer door. My clock said 4 A.M. I didn't know what was happening, but it had to all be bad. I wasn't too drunk to know that.

Ray went to the door. "Who is it?" she quavered. Like me, I guess she figured it was a narcotics raid.

"Blind Charlie! Who else got a cane to knock with? Goddamit! Open this damn door!"

"Well, you don't have to knock the door down just because you got a cane. You know what time of morning this is?" Now that her fright was over, Ray was madder than a fairy who has managed to get himself locked up in a women's jail, but she opened the door.

"Git outen my way, you goddam junky! I ain't got no time to waste in arguing with you! I wants me that Sid!" Charlie roared. "I'm gonna kill that boy!"

Hung over; half dead; you'll never know how scared I was.

"Ain't you about done that already?" Ray snarled.

"I got me more important things to do than stand here talking to a simple-assed hopheaded woman. Sid! Sid! Goddamit, answer me, Sid!"

Drunk as he was, Charlie made his way straight to my open door and walked in. "Sid, you drunken fool. Where you at, Sid? Don't hide from me, boy. It's just poor ole Blind Charlie come to visit. Lemme in, Sid!"

I began to mumble to my God. I told God it was a lousy trick to let me die right after I'd met Sharlee. And there were several other things I meant to tell God, but Charlie was making such a racket I couldn't hear myself pray.

Charlie advanced further into the room, slashing his cane about like a berserk duelist. "First off, I wants to know why you run off and leaves your bes' fren' to fight off them pocket-picking sonofbitches all by my lonesome? You knows that ain't no way to do. Now *I'm* gonna show how good a fren' I am to *you.* I'm gonna make believe you ain't ever done it. But that ain't no kind of a way to treat a fren'? But like I say: I already done forgot it. And all I'm gonna ast you to do is tell me the name of the dirty bastids that went in my pockets. And where the hell is something to drink for poor ole Blind Charlie?"

I didn't say one word. I just turned my battered butt over and went back to sleep.

I opened one sad eye and examined one of the longest and narrowest heads that ever adorned a human neck. Sick as I was, it was with profound admiration that I observed this watermelon-headed woman who was sleeping beside me. I groaned and closed my eye as I sank back on the pillow to ponder where the hell this woman had come from.

But I had a memory block. Try as hard as I could to recall, my brain strove mightier to forget yesterday. It was that kind of morning for real and I figured I must be guilty. I couldn't imagine what I had done, but it must have been awful and I was guilty as hell or this watermelon head wouldn't be lying beside me now.

Sleep almost reclaimed me when I suddenly became aware of all the infernal racket going on in my room. Like a vacuum cleaner with a busted gasket. I opened both eyes and saw that the noise was coming from a black heap on the floor. Even without my glasses that big black heap looked a lot like Blind Charlie. I leaned over the side of the bed to make sure and saw the white cane still in his hands.

And I remembered Charlie!!!!!!!!!

I remembered Charlie so well that thoughts of homicide pleasantly ran 'round my head. But sober reason soon came to counsel me: some fine upstanding Christian soldier had already smote this maniac upon the head nine times with a hatchet and the menace had not only refused to die, but there's no proof the upstanding Christian soldier is yet alive. So what the hell was Sid Bailey supposed to bash him with, a sweet bunch of violets? I snarled like a dog and laid back with a gurgle of an oath searing my throat. This oath was more or less directed at my Lord and Maker Who at one time seemed to think rather well of me . . . before Blind Charlie and the Sinman killed Him.

"Whoooeee thar." Charlie bolted up in a sitting position. "Who that, I say? And whar the hell am I?"

I changed horses and hysterically began to mutter the Lord's Prayer.

It was plain that Charlie was still drunk, but he got on all fours and began to crawl about. Finally he reached the bed, and with those great paws of his he felt all over Lina's body. He seemed slightly terrorized. "Lawd have mercy. Who the hell is this?" he screamed. "I ain't never felt nothing like this before in the morning. Who dis?"

I decided to repeat the Lord's Prayer.

"Goddamit! I ain't playing. Whar the hell am I?"

Lina woke up and I guess that gentle touching of those great black hands over her body had felt very good. "I'se Lina, Mistah Blind Charlie," she cooed.

"Lina? Who the hell is skinny-assed Lina?" Charlie demanded. "Ain't you never had nothing to eat in your life?"

"Ah eats right good when Ah ain't drinking, Mist' Blind Charlie," Lina said genially. "Ah jes come from the horspital, and Ah felt right tired, and so Sid said Ah could come lay down with him."

"This that goddam Sid's room?"

"What you mad for now, Mist' Blind Charlie?"

"Now? Mad now? Where the hell was you when they went in my pockets and tried to steal all my money? And that no-good Sid run off to leave me fight all them thieving bastids all by my lonesome. He ain't no good atall, that boy. And I oughta kill him dead. That's what I should do, but I ain't. I forgives him. He's stupid, you know."

"You awready done aboot kilt him, Mist' Blind Charlie."

And to me she sounded mighty proud of the fact.

"I ain't never touched that lil stupid bastid in my life," Charlie shouted. "Why you want to tell a lie on me like that?"

"Yass, you did," Lina said flatly.

"When I hurt that boy?" Charlie demanded. "I ain't even seen him since before them guys jumped me up in 6-D-3."

"That was Sid went in your pocket for a cigarette. And you went and tried your mightiest to kill him and . . ."

"OOOWaaah!" Charlie howled. Tears jumped out of his sightless eyes. "I done went and almos' kilt my bes' fren'. Whar he at? Whar's the hospital he in? I gotta go be with my bestes' fren'!"

Charlie's sincere blathering gave me some slight balm but I still didn't know whether to pray some more or not.

"There weren't no need to take Sid to duh horspital, Mist' Blind Charlie," Lina said.

"Poleeese!" Charlie bellowed. "Here I is! Come take me, poleese.

I did it. I done kilt my bes' fren'. He done died and I done done it. Oh, Lawd have mercy!"

Suddenly Charlie stopped howling, and with one careless swipe of his hand swept Lina off the bed to the floor. With amazing tenderness his hands felt over the bed until they touched me. A drop of water splattered on my chest, and with hysterical dispassion I divined that even Charlie's tears were bigger than anybody else's.

"Sid? Sid? Ain't this you, Sid? Ain't she lying? You ain't daid, is you, Sid?"

I expelled my pent-up breath as Charlie fingered the clotted blood in my eyebrows, but even though the butterfly touching was excruciating I did not dare to brush the madman's hands away.

"Wake up, boy," Charlie ordered. "You ain't dead. What you need is a good stiff drink. How much money we got? I ain't got none."

I didn't even bother to feign that I was just waking up. "None," I said shortly. "And you gave your Welfare check to the Sinman to hold."

"Well, we can't go see the Sinman with your head all split open like that," Charlie said indignantly.

Lina, who must have deemed it safer to remain on the floor, made gurgling sounds that mystified me. Did she need a drink too, or had Charlie's attitude surprised that noise out of her?

"Why can't you go down the Sinman's by yourself?" I asked.

"Them goddam junkies done tole him what happened by now. And I don't want to hear no more about it. Not from Sinman especially."

"Oh."

"But we can always get money . . ." Charlie began and stopped. But when I didn't say anything he got mad. "Well, I can!" he yelled. "Put your clothes on, boy. I'll show you that Charlie Jones don't ever be broke unlessen he want to."

I clenched my teeth, refusing to groan, and got out of bed. My glasses were nowhere in sight, and I didn't have the heart to ask Lina about them.

"What you taking your time for?" Charlie demanded. "You want a drink or don't you?"

"Hell yes," I snarled.

"Well, shake it up then. I ain't got all day."

As soon as I was dressed Charlie clapped his hand on my shoulder and we left the room without a word to Lina. She was still on the floor, but actually, I don't even think we realized that she was down there.

On the sidewalk, Charlie told me to lead him to a small confectionery six blocks away. When we reached the store Charlie asked, "Who the hell is in there?"

"How the hell do I know?" I shouted. "You went and broke my goddam glasses."

"Well, goddamit, go near and look and see."

"You mean customers or behind the counter?"

"What the hell do I care how many customers he got?"

I went to the show window and peered in. There was a man and woman behind the counter. I came back to the curb and told Charlie.

"What the bitch look like?"

"I can't see that well. All I know's she got a dress on."

"That's her," Charlie muttered. "Well, I can't go in," he grumbled as if it was my fault. "When that ole bag is busy you go in and tell Benny that poor ole Blind Charlie got robbed last night and needs five dollars to pay on his rent or he'll hafta sleep in the street. Now tell him just like I said. Don't go adding nothing to it."

I had reached a point of psychological no return; without another word I marched in that store. I didn't mind at all because I wanted to see and talk to the man who could believe that poor ole Blind Charlie could be robbed.

Benny was a nervously wrong-looking character. He tried to smile but it didn't quite come off. "He's not drunk, is he?" he whispered. I shook my head, resolved to obey Charlie's instructions explicitly. "Wait right here. Don't move," Benny said, still whispering. He went to where the cigarettes were stacked and took a pack of Pall Malls. He dropped them and bent down to pick them up.

When he handed them to me there was a folded bill with the matches. I thanked him and walked out. I went over to Charlie. He grabbed my shoulder and we headed back to the hotel.

"G'wan past the liquor store and stop," Charlie said. And when I did just that he said, "I can't go in the goddam place. I owes them too much." He sounded like the owners of the store had played a dirty trick on him.

"I'll go in. What do you want, Spur?"

"You goddam right I wants Silver Spur. And don't go thinking I punks that Jew faggot neither!"

"I haven't said a goddam word about you and no damn faggot," I shouted back. And right then and there I was no longer afraid of Blind Charlie. This business of being scared to death all the time was getting to be boring as hell. Besides, it was pretty evident that Blind Charlie was going to kill me anyway unless I checked out of the Logan within the next few minutes. So what was there to be scared of?

"What you want, a pint or a quart?" I snapped.

"You go get me five of them Spurs! What you think I borrowed all that money for, to give to that scrawny-butted woman you got laying up there in your bed? And hurry up!"

In the lobby Charlie tugged on my shoulder. "We oughta go up to Mr. Johnson's room. We owes him a drink," he said peevishly.

"Git on in heah," Mr. Johnson greeted us just as if yesterday had never happened.

There was a barely perceptible tic in the oldster's right cheek which I had come to recognize as one of the nervous reactions of the confirmed wino who cannot beg, borrow or steal a morning drink. I wondered if Mr. Johnson was stone broke the day after Checkday. Anyhow, I promptly opened a bottle and we all had a drink. There was a woman in the room who also needed a drink. Her name was Rosy. I had seen her dozens of times in the lobby; always arguing about nothing at all.

We were sipping our drinks when someone knocked. Mr. Johnson yelled a "Come in," and in walked Sally, the Logan's most ignorant man and its most knife-happy freak. Sally was not only a disputatious knife wielder but a chiseler as well. Sometimes he came by J&J's to mooch a drink. And I was sure that they gave it to him only because they were afraid of him and his knife.

Charlie and I were sitting apart on the bed. Sally plumped himself down between us, and no sooner had Mr. Johnson poured him a drink then the fool began talking off the wall. "I wuz reading yesterday," began this man who could not read, "about this woman who kilt six husbin's . . ."

Charlie snorted.

"All at one time?" I asked.

Sally glared at me but didn't answer. Instead he said, "Now every one of them wuz declared legally dead by a professional certified doctor." His voice rose. "Legally dead from a heart attack."

"Well," Charlie said, "that's the end of that lie."

"Whut lie?" Sally demanded. "Ah jes tole you Ah read it in the paper. Black and white don't lie. I got the newspaper downstairs whut say so. I got it right downstairs in reading. Now how you gonna say black and white's a lie?"

"A person can write a lie as well as they can tell one," I said.

I guess Sally ignored me because he had heard that I was crazy anyhow.

"And nobody would have been the wiser effen she hadn't of got drunk this time and started mumbling about them husbin's in this bar. And this cat whut's sitting next her hears all her mumbling and he goes out and calls up the law. And this detectoff goes and digs up all them husbin's . . ."

"Batshit!" I said, and I was so angry I meant every syllable of it. It drives me up the wall every time a dumb boot attributes some magical rights to a whitey. White people have enough going for them as it is without boots granting them absolute supremacy. But I knew that Sally was congenitally incapable of understanding that even a white man cannot go out and dig up six bodies without a court order, among other things.

"How come you got to make me out a liar?" Sally demanded as his red eyes looked me over.

Lina walked in and I was shook. She was a cripple. Mr. Johnson jumped up and gave her a drink and his chair.

Then Sally said, "So when they digs up these six cats they finds that all this woman done to them is . . ."

"All she done," I muttered.

Rosy jumped up and stood over me. "Why can't you leave Sally tell it like it is? Was you there? You done read it yourself? So why you got to have so much more opinion than everybody else?" She turned to Sally. "Now you go ahead and tell us what wants to hear what happent, Sally."

Sally nodded with all the aplomb of a college president who has been rudely interrupted and then apologized to.

"And all she'd done was put one teeny-weeny drop of hot lead in each one's ear whilst he was sleeping." Sally's eyes widened and his voice dropped to a melodramatic whisper. "And that one itty-bitty drop of lead settles in the back of their brain and kills them without no trace. The coroner couldn't tell nothing by looking at 'em. But when this detectoff holds a total and complete autotopsy he goes in dem brains and way back he finds these little balls of lead whut kilt 'em. And they hung that woman."

"She was lucky as hell to find six hollow-headed husbands," I said.

Rosy daintily dropped her eyelids and said, "You just can't guess science these days. Now who'da thought science could tell there was them little balls of lead in the back of them heads?"

"Everybody who believes Sally's lie, stand on their heads," Charlie said.

"Six goddam niggers that won't even wake up when their old lady pours hot lead in their ears," I said to Charlie. "Bet I could kill half the drunken fools in the Logan like that. We ain't got nothing but hollow-headed niggers around here."

"Now see here, Sid, or whatever your half-assed name is. I don't go for being called no liar all the time," Sally said. "Now *you* is the goddam liar, bastid. Now you see effen you wants to make something outa *that*. And effen you says you do Ah'm gonna take this blade and pull your motherfucking head off."

"Sally," Charlie rumbled.

"You ain't in this, Charlie. Ah'm talking to this here Sid."

"You ain't gonna pull no fren' of mine's head offen in here or no place else, Sally."

Since he was sitting between Charlie and me, I guess Sally thought he could mess me all up before Blind Charlie ever got the message.

So he said, "You jes' stay outen this, Charlie. Ah ain't got no fuss with nobuddy but this Sid here. And effen he say Ah'm a liar once more . . ."

"But you *is* a liar, Sally," Charlie said. "Don't make no difference who call you one."

Sally chose to ignore Charlie. He took out his knife and flicked it open. "Now you jes' call me a liar one more time, mother," he said to me.

Buh-lappp!

The palm of Charlie's right hand covered Sally's nose and mouth with one whopping smack. I looked down at the blood that had squirted in my lap. Sally went over backward on the bed with Charlie atop him. The deadly snub of a french knife flashed as Charlie plunged it where he calculated Sally's throat to be. The knife must have struck Sally's clenched teeth and glanced off, but it left a wicked gash from the corner of Sally's mouth to his left ear.

"*Now* try and say you gonna pull somebody's head off," Charlie said coldly.

When I came out of shock Lina and Charlie were the only people in the room.

Out in the hall Mr. Johnson was yelling, "Call de cops. Call de law! Sally done went and got his throat cut!"

"What's that ole fool calling the pigs for?" Charlie demanded.

"You cain't get no ambulances lessen you calls the cops first, Mistah Blind Charlie," Lina said. Then she hobbled past Charlie to come sit on the bed beside me. She put her arms around my neck and buried her face in my neck. Her tongue felt like an eel.

Sometimes a woman can do the damnedest things. Now that

this little cripple had seen a murder damn near committed she felt like screwing.

"C'mon, boy," Charlie rumbled. "We gotta git outa here. Them pigs is gonna come and swear poor ole Charlie done done this thing for nothing."

I got up and went to him and gave him my shoulder. We forgot all about Lina again.

"Go down the steps," Charlie urged. "We ain't got no time to be waiting for no elevator." And on the steps he asked, "Where we gonna hide, boy?"

"In my room," I said. I seriously doubted if the police would search the hotel for Charlie, and if they did come to 5-C looking for him, they would first have to knock on that foyer door. When and if they did, I planned to take Charlie up the fire escape that ran past the kitchen window, and go right back to Mr. Johnson's room. And so, just like that, I became a true inmate of the Logan. I had passed all tests in criminal aptitude, moral turpitude and just plain anti-social oneriness. It hadn't been hard at all.

When we got to my room I led Charlie to the one easy chair by the window. Then I stretched out on the bed. Lina hobbled in and sat beside me. The room was filled with the sounds of our breathing.

Suddenly Charlie jumped to his feet. "That goddam Sally done went and made me forget my Spurs!" he yelled.

"Ah brung a bottle with me, Mist' Blind Charlie."

I gawked at the crazy girl. Why had she bothered to tell this lie? Then, as my very eyelids faltered, she raised her dress as shamelessly as a child. I gasped. Not because of her totally fleshless legs, but because she was wearing red snuggies when it was actually pretty hot weather. Lina partly lowered the snuggies and extracted a quart of Spur.

Seeing my shocked look, she leaned over and whispered, "It aw right. He blind. He cain't see mah nooky."

"Well, whar is it? And what you all kissing and whispering for? And you even got your hand up her dress, ain't you?" Charlie cried sternly. "Can't even wait till we gits a drink?"

"No!" I shouted. I was delirious with anger at both of them.

Charlie for accusing me of this impossible little broad and Lina for having had more presence of mind than I did.

Lina innocently raised my temperature. "Ah jes' knowed we wuz gonna need a little somepin' and so Ah took us some. Ah didn't know it wuz yours, Mistah Blind Charlie, or Ah'd brought anudder."

"Well, bless your scrawny little butt, gal," Charlie said. "You might be skinny but you sure got more sense than Sid. Can't nobody beat that boy in stupidity when he puts his mind to it. Now pour me a drink there."

"Yassuh, Mist' Blind Charlie. Ah'm opening it now."

I took a long sober look at this girl who could and would filch a quart of wine while a murder was in process. After that I thought only in terms of dismissal. "Where do you live?" I began my campaign.

" 'Round yonder, but Ah doan' like it," she said sullenly.

"How old are you?" I asked because she had answered so much like a child.

"Forty-foah."

"How much?"

"Forty-foah next month."

"This is the same bag of bones as this morning, ain't it?" Charlie asked.

"Yeah," I said. "Hasn't got a line in her face and don't weigh in at more than seventy-five pounds soaking wet."

"Ah weighs eighty pounds now. Ah done right good in the horspital this time."

"You sounds like you goes to the hospital any time you takes the notion," Charlie said. "You crazy or you got TB?"

"Ah ain't got none of that," Lina said sharply. "And ain't nothing wrong with mah blood neither. So there!"

"I ain't asking you for no trim," Charlie protested. "What you telling me about your blood for?"

"Ah doan' never sell mah body."

"You ain't got no body to *sell,*" Charlie hollered. "Anybody wants a bag of bones they goes to the butcher shop. Not no nappy-headed gal like you."

"Ah'm jes as good-looking 'neath mah clothes as the next un!"

"Lawd have mercy," Charlie gasped. "Ain't you a Black gal?"

"Ah ain't no darker than you."

"Tha's it. I know your kind and you gotta be Black 'cause you just like all these other Sapphires what thinks they can put a bag over they head and make like Madame X in the bed. But I got news for you and I'm gonna pull your coat with it. And pour me another drink of that Spur."

"Ain't got no mo'," Lina said triumphantly. "Ain't but foah good drinks in a quart and we's all had two. And Ah ain't *got* no TB. Ah goes to the horspital 'cause Ah won't eat. So there."

"Whatin'ell you talking about, woman?"

"Ah doan' eats when Ah drinks," Lina grumbled almost inaudibly. "Ah doan' like to." She turned to me with a sudden fetching smile. "Ah got fifty cents if you'll go to the store for me." Her soft pleading voice made me realize that Lina positively looked like an underdeveloped nineteen-year-old kid.

"Goddamit to hell, Sid," Charlie shouted. "You warn't doing nothing. You could've brought them Spurs. Can't you do nothing right without me telling you?"

"You want me to go back up there and get them?" I knew that bit of sarcasm would not be lost on him.

"Yes!" Charlie jumped to his feet. "Go and get my Spurs right this minute!"

"Okay. Okay," I said hastily. "But what do you expect me to say to the cops if they're still up there?"

"Don't say nothing! That's all. Don't say nothing."

"Yeah. And suppose they decide to follow me back down here?"

"Don't come back."

"Don't come back. Don't come back," I kept mumbling as I got up and went out of the room.

It was so easy I laughed all the way coming back. Mr. Johnson had been standing in the hall, talking to two cops. I simply went in his room, picked up the bag of wine and walked out. Mr. Johnson didn't say a word and neither did I. The Logan Hotel does everything real cool when the fuzz is around.

Leah was just letting one of her customers out when I got back and so I didn't have to use my key. Neither did Charlie or Lina notice me as I came and stood in the doorway.

"Lina?" Charlie said.

"Yassuh, Mist' Blind Charlie?"

"That your name, eh? Lina?"

"Yassuh."

"No, it ain't," Charlie said angrily. "Ain't nobody named Lina."

"Wal . . . it's Paulina, but Ah doan' like that. Nobody better call me Paulina."

"Folks around here don't like nothing they got. Don't like their race no more. Don't like what sex they got. Now they don't even want they names."

Their ensuing silence was an uneasy truce. Lina broke it first. "You sleep here all the time, Mist' Blind Charlie?"

"Hell no! What'm I gonna sleep in here for all the time?"

"Ah jes' wondered."

"Why you wonder that? You aiming on moving in?"

"Yassuh."

"What makes you think Sid's *that* dumb?"

"Ah might be crip-legged, but Ah got as much to offer as the next."

"You sure must be one *black* gal. Ain't nobody but the blackest of Black women ever talk like that."

"Sid got hisself a girl friend?"

"What you care? You done already moved in, ain't you?"

"Ah doan' like no foolishment," Lina muttered.

Charlie gasped. "You mean to say you ain't gonna let Sid even look at all these *normal*-looking women we got in this hotel?"

"Doan' make no never mind. Ah doan' play."

"The reason you don't eat is because you're crazy! And you crazy because you is *black*. Ain't no pretty yaller woman talk like you in they life. You is *crazy black!* But I bet that Sid don't have no better sense than to let you lay up in here. Where you live anyhow? And how come you's scared to go there? I knows damn well you ain't got no man with that scrawny butt you got."

"Ah done tole you Ah lives 'round there." She moved her enormous head in a vague circle of a motion.

"Can't you talk no English atall? I wants to know what street you lives on. What hotel? I can tell by your talk you ain't nothing but a Welfare bitch, so's you got to be living in one of these kind of hotels."

"Ah doan' remember the name, but it's 'round the corner like. And Ah ain't gonna stay there no more neither. And ain't nobody gonna make me." Lina was in a complete sulk now.

Charlie looked crafty. "Supposing Sid don't let you stay in here? What you gonna do then?"

"Ain't you got a room?"

"Hell no!" Charlie sputtered. "Do I look like some kind of fool to you? Welfare and the Blind Folks don't give me enough to hardly *eat* on much less pay these refugees their crazy rent."

"You is lying, Mist' Blind Charlie. You got to show your rent receet to your investigator."

"Just because your ass is little don't mean I won't kick it for calling Blind Charlie a liar!" Charlie shouted. "The Sinman gives me a receipt to show the fool Welfare bastids. But I don't pay him or nobody else no goddam rent. How you expect me to enjoy myself effen I gotta pay rent?"

"You kin have mah room if you want it 'cause Ah doan ever sleep by mahself. Ah'm scared. And Ah ain't gonna sleep there neither," she added, muttering.

"Bitch! You just tole me you don't know where you room is. How you gonna let me stay in it? You don't talk with no more sense than Sid do. And he don't talk with no sense atall."

"Ah knows how to git there when Ah want to. Ah gotta go get mah check too," Lina said like an afterthought. Her voice grew cunning. "Make Sid take me home, Mist' Blind Charlie? When Ah gets mah checks we'll have lots of wine to drink. Please, Mist' Blind Charlie?"

"I ain't gonna make my fren' do nothing. And somehow you is lying anyhow."

I decided to let them know I was back. I walked in and put the bag of wine in Charlie's lap. Three bottles. "The cops were still up there," I said, "but Mr. Johnson wasn't telling them anything. And Sally *can't* talk right now."

"Now why don't they take that poor man to the hospital like they oughta?" Charlie exclaimed. "Them fool cops know full and well they got all day to look for me and you afterwards without detaining a poor dying man like that."

"Me? *Me* and you?"

Charlie was a picture of practicality. "You was the cause of me cutting Sally, wasn't you? Did I tell you to argue with him?"

I dropped it and said, "Don't worry about Sally. They've taken him to the hospital. What I meant was that his mouth is in no shape to do any talking for a while. And maybe he'll think twice before he does. After all, he had his knife open. But those bulls act like they'd like to arrest Mr. Johnson if only somebody would give them an excuse."

"They oughta arrest the damn fool!" Charlie said. "He ain't got no better sense than let somebody like Sally come in his room and start a whole lot of bullshit like that. I only wish I was a no-good sonofabitching pig. I'd shove his gray tail so far under the jail it'd take *two* sticks of dynamite to blast him out."

I took the bag from Charlie, opened a bottle, poured three drinks and refused to comment.

All this time Lina had been grumbling to herself. After she took a few swigs of wine she talked louder. ". . . and when Ah wuz in the horspital he never come see me one time. And she tole him he better not, but he did. All them nasty hoahs staying in mah room every night like a hoahhouse!"

"Whatinell is that woman talking about?" Charlie yelled. "That poor Sally is a family man. Least he got a wife he stay with every night even effen he's a no-good bastid with a knife. Now why that gal gotta go make up lies on him? Ain't he bad enough off already?"

"Ah ain't talking aboot no Sally," Lina muttered. "Ah'm talking aboot how he done and everything. Ain't no Sally got nothing to do wid it."

"He? Who the hell is *HE?*" Charlie thundered.

"Dat's mah friend boy Ah useta have before Ah went to the horspital. And she even tole him not to do it. He sho better not. But he went and did it jes' the same anyhow until the rent due. And then he went and tole her to hold mah room until Ah gits outen the horspital. And so she takes mah clothes and pots and pans and say Ah owe rent and won't gimme nothing back. And Ah has tuh git this new room Ah doan' like . . ."

"Jesus Gawd," Charlie whispered.

"Lina," I said as gently as I could, "who are all these people you are talking about? Can't you call anybody by their names? How do you expect Charlie and me to understand you?"

"Doan' make no difference what they name is. They do dirt. And she claim Ah owe foah weeks' rent, and so Ah have to move 'round the corner. And he comes and tries, but Ah doan' let him."

"Sid!" Charlie shouted.

"What?"

"Take this she-he-did bitch home!"

Such situations are my Waterloo. I rode right into this she-he-did windmill. "Are you saying that you used to have a boy friend who carried a stick in your room while you were in the hospital?" I asked Lina.

"Whut dat mean?"

"You live in Welfare hotels and you don't know what it means to carry a stick?" I exclaimed.

"Now I carry a stick," Charlie said. "Anybody that don't have a room of their own and bunks in with somebody else for free is carrying a stick, just like a tramp. You is catting, in other words. Now was this man of yours carrying a stick or not? Tha's all we want to know to start with."

Lina shook her head affirmatively. "And he nasty too," she muttered. "He doan' do it like a man should. Ah doan' like it."

"And so after he got you put out of your room while you

were sick in the hospital he starts coming around your new room, pestering you and trying to get tight again, is that right?"

"YASSUH!"

"And he never came to visit all the while you were sick although he was living in your room for nothing?"

"Not even a cigarette."

"And he kept women in your room too?"

"And she tole him he better not."

"Now who the hell is *SHE?*" I exclaimed.

"Mah sistah."

"Let's go kill that nigger!" Charlie said. "Tha's just what we oughta do today: kill us a nigger!"

"And when mah check come she beat me up and take it."

"Who you talking about now?" Charlie demanded in contemplation of two separate killings.

"Mah sistah. She do it all the time."

"Your sister beats you up and takes your check, but you can't even remember her name?" I asked.

"All charcoal gals lie," Charlie said as if that explained it all.

Lina nodded. "She say Ah ain't got 'nuff sense to spend wisely so she take it and spend it on herself. Sometimes Ah doan' have no wine for a whole week."

"Tole you about them women," Charlie said. "Sid, effen you lets her stay here you gotta buy some bleach cream or she'll lie you outa house and home."

"Ah wants me some money of mah own," Lina whined.

"Don't look at me," Charlie said.

"Not you, Mist' Blind Charlie." She turned to me with her most childlike expression and voice. "Please take me home, Sid. Ah got me a clothes check, and a pots and pans check and mah reg'lar check coming. Please take me, Sid."

Charlie stood up. "C'mon, boy. Seems right fitting we should go see why this cat won't leave Lina alone after he been begged to. 'Sides, I want to see these checks she been lying about."

"The guy's at work now," I said. "Let's just sit and enjoy the wine we got. Since I went to so much trouble to get it."

"He jes' a Welfare pimp," Lina said. "He doan' work."

"Now I know I gotta get me a little piece of his butt," Charlie said. "Welfare pimp. I should kill me every one I see. Getting so you can't walk through the lobby on account of them going upside some simple bitch's head."

I looked at Lina; this emaciated woman needed every cent she could get for milk and nourishing food. "Welfare pimps are murderers," I said.

"I been around hustling broads all my life, but even then I never pimped offen none," Charlie said. "Sure. Lots of 'em come up to me and brings me money, but nobody ever said Charlie Jones was a pimp."

I smiled. "What else were you? You accepted proceeds which the girls had gained from prostitution, didn't you?"

" 'Tain't that way at all! Like I'd be standing in some bar around 116th and the gal'ud come up and gimme money. Sometimes I never even saw the gal before. They would do it in front of everybody—especially *everybody*. And I'd *hafta* accept it. But that don't make me no pimp!"

"Yeah. Yeah. Yeah."

"But I still ain't made them prostitute," Charlie said excitedly. "I was the bully of the block, see? And them whores wanted the cats around the neighborhood to *think* they was mine. Can't you see that effen a gal can make a john think that they is tight with the bully of the block she ain't *never* gonna have no trouble outen that john? And even effen I ain't around, lesser men than me is gonna take up for the bully's woman. Can't you even see that? Them whores gimme money just like a barkeep gives a bully pig free drinks and money. If I was a pimp, so was them free-loading pigs. More so!"

"You don't make no logic at all," I said. More to reaffirm the fact that I was no more in terror of Charlie than Lina was than of anything else.

"Why I could do a hell of a lot more for them broads than any pussy cop coulda done for her," Charlie declared. "What cop's gonna make a john give back the money he done took back from a whore 'cause he claim the pussy warn't no good? And take this crazy fool here." Charlie pointed at Lina. "I bets I gets that titty pimp up offen her back *today.* And she ain't gonna have to go down on Centre Street to get cussed at and asked questions and then get a warrant what costs her money. And she won't hafta do no trucking back and forth to court neither. Now who does the most goodness: me or the pigs?"

I thought back on all the mayhem Charlie had wreaked in the last twenty hours and gave a dry brittle laugh. "Okay. C'mon," I said picking up the remaining bottles of wine. "Let's go and get it over with."

On the way to Lina's place I did not know how high we all were until I happened to look back over my shoulder. We really were Logan inmates. I was in front, Charlie was behind me with his hand on my shoulder. I was walking pretty fast like Charlie likes to walk. And poor Lina couldn't hold onto Charlie's other arm because he swings his cane so savagely. Therefore the crippled girl grabbed Charlie's coattail and sort of let him pull her along. Yeah. Just like three drunk ducks.

Lina's hotel was another Hotel Logan but tried to hide the fact.

"I was getting ready to call the police," the manager said happily. "You haven't been in your room since last Checkday, and I've mail. Where you been? Sick?"

"Ah been 'round," Lina muttered sulkily. "Ah ain't been nowheres."

I could see that her manner had nonplused this happy clown when he handed her her mail and did not wait for her to open it and give him her checks to cash and take out rent. And when Lina didn't ask him to cash her checks, I knew the clown didn't care, thinking that Lina belonged with Charlie and me in the Logan. Neither did I care at the moment, and I guess Charlie hadn't had time to think about it yet.

We took the elevator to the third floor. The totally mean bareness of Lina's room was shocking. The dusty dresser was void of any personal articles whatsoever. The open closet was empty. The single personal possession in the entire room was a dirty pot, encrusted with a layer of weeks-old food. It was on the floor in the middle of the room.

I immediately pondered that pot. I had to. Lina was erratic to say the least, but why was this pot left in the middle of the floor? Where were the eating utensils? And seasonings, and everything else that went into the preparing of a pot of food? That manager had been right when he said that Lina had not been in her room since last Checkday. In fact, it was pretty evident that Lina had not spent a night in this room since she had got it. So where had she been staying?

"Where's the bed? I needs me a nap," Charlie said.

Lina guided him to the bed; Charlie flopped on his back and was soon snoring gently. Lina and I drank and talked aimlessly. Or rather, Lina talked inanely and I listened aimlessly. Like my mind wandered, but I did gather that Lina averaged a good four months out of twelve in a hospital or sanitarium although she kept reiterating that she was not tubercular. She also confirmed my suspicions that she was a practicing alcoholic, but I never did learn where she had been staying since being discharged from the hospital.

We had left the door open, 5-C style. Suddenly the weirdest-looking man I've ever seen poked his head in the door. The creature gave me pause, and I had to face up to the fact that Lina did not have a true watermelon head. Actually her head was shaped like a large family-size loaf of bread, but the man in the doorway really did have a watermelon head. Like one of God's less noble experiments.

He pointed his finger like a fresh child. "D-duh W-Welfare done gonna cut you off t-tomorrow," he stuttered.

"Git out!" Lina yelled and grabbed up the pot and flung it at him. It was a puny toss.

"D-duh-dat's aw right. Ah done called and t-told dem you a-ain't been here none atall. And n-now W-Welfare is gone."

"Mistah Blind Charlie!" Lina screamed. "Mist' Charlie, here he is now."

Charlie flowed up off the bed, reached and grabbed Lina and held her aloft like a rag doll. But her weight told him that he had the wrong culprit and so he dropped her and began to yell for me.

The outsize-headed man walked bravely up to the helpless blind man. "D-duh-dis here's muh woman's room. And Ah doan' w-want tu-tuh see you in it n-no mo!"

He didn't.

Charlie grabbed him and lifted him way up before dashing him to the floor. I knew the man's jaw and nose and probably his mouth were smashed.

"C'mon, boy. We ain't gonna be bothered with him no more," Charlie said with strange dispassion.

On the way out Lina stopped to cash her regular check and pay her rent for two more weeks. Then our unearthly trio filed out, still like three drunk ducks.

SCENE IV

JINNY WAS COUGHING in her sleep. The sounds woke Joey up, and she grunted several times before she hoisted her bulk out of the easy chair that was her bed. She padded to the window to do what she called her West Point breathing exercises. Her head didn't feel too good and her mouth tasted like she had been eating Harlem chinches, but she continued the exercises until she was positive that she had breathed all of yesterday's wine out of her system. Joey did this every morning; she was afraid not to.

She looked at the clock. Five-fifteen. Mentally she patted herself on the back: Life on Welfare wasn't keeping her from getting up early and staying on the ball. At the same time she felt a tug of something like compassion for Jinny; Jinny wasn't letting anything get her down either, but Joey did wish the kid didn't need a whole pint to wake up on. That damned Spur was killing them both, and neither one of them had enough smarts to loose the stuff.

She walked over to the narrow cot and gazed at Jinny. Just looking at that cocky little black face made Joey feel so warm and good her eyes misted. There was no denying she loved the little fool. Jinny had been a wild one, a fast cat, even in Bedford where they'd first met. But scared? Wild and scared. Jinny had pulled so many fast ones on so many different people she lived in fear that the head screw was going to walk up someday and tell her she had to go to trial some more. More trials, more time to do. But Joey had stroked Jinny in every way imaginable, and Jinny had done her six years like a champ.

Jinny had loved cocaine, but when Joey got out the last time she had actually stroked Jinny out of the habit. And coke was habit-

forming. Anything that costs money is a habit. And anything that costs more than you got is murder. Once Joey and Jinny and a whole lot of other people in the life had given a three-day weekend party in an after-hours joint. Eddy's. And at that party, in those three days, Joey had watched a stud sniff up two thousand dollars' worth of coke. The sonofabitch had never left the kitchen table except to go to the crapper. That's all: sitting at a kitchen table until he'd sniffed away two grand. No whiskey. No pussy. No nothing. Just coke. And you gonna say that ain't no habit?

Jinny was coughing more often now, a sure sign it was five-thirty. One thing: prison taught you regular hours. You could set your clock by J&J.

Joey went back to the cot to stand over her love. And just like that, her love came down all over again and she touched Jinny's forehead. And as she did she knew her moment of truth: all her fussing, all her bluffing was so much horseshit under the bridge; if Jinny even said, "It's quits," Joey knew she'd go out of her head for keeps. And Joey needed Jinny a damn sight more than Jinny needed Joey. Jinny was self-sufficient. She was the fast cat of the team always. The little rascal could scare up a few bucks to make ends meet every day and it didn't even seem like she was trying. But more important, Jinny was Joey's entree among Black people. Nobody could break the ice for her like Jinny could. And that meant everything because for some weird reason Joey hated white people. She just didn't feel at home around them. So without Jinny she was dead.

When Joey was eight years old her parents died and she was sent to a Catholic home for little girls. It was almost but not quite a reform school, situated in an old renovated apartment building. So the playground was on the roof.

One day Joey stood watching some older girls playing a ball-game. A girl missed the ball and it rolled through the picket fence that encircled the roof. Without a thought the then tiny Joey squeezed between the iron pickets after the ball. The sisters went wild. They thought Joey was bent on suicide. Joey's facile tongue had not yet developed, and even if it had the emotionally unstable sisters would still have preferred to think suicide and to label Joey emotionally disturbed. And so Joey's life was molded when she went through that picket fence. Even in Bedford the shrink had questioned her at length about that episode. It seemed like every damned whitey in New York City thought it was their duty to shield Joey from herself. That is, all except the hoods she later met. So all in all it was only the niggers who thought Joey was for real.

When Jinny's cough began once more Joey went to the refrigerator and poured a glass of water for her.

"Thanks, hon," Jinny said. She reached under the cot and pulled out a plastic washbasin. In a moment she was sick.

Joey opened a pint of wine and handed it to Jinny as the heaves diminished a little. Still with her face over the basin, Jinny began to drink from the bottle, chasing each sip with the cold water.

Joey padded out into the hall to the bathroom. When she came back Jinny got up and went. It was a ritual: Joey first, then Jinny. They never really spoke to each other until after both had visited the toilet.

"Champ killed Earnest last night," Joey said. "Ray knocked on the door way late and yelled it. I don't know what time, but late."

"The Champ? Get out of here! And that lard butt ought to save some of her lies. How can a man who has two withered hands and can't even feed himself kill an able-bodied man like Earnest?"

"Well, Ray said he did it and I believe her. Junkies don't much lie about murder. That is, unless they are personally involved."

"And Ray might be involved someway. She and Leah. You know Champ and Earnest joy-pop sometimes. But Champ couldn't have done it unless he fell on Earnest while Earnest was sleeping."

"Well, don't make me lie none. All I know is what Ray tole me."

"Well, you can bet your bottom dollar that Champ won't get any time. How in hell is a judge going to sentence a man that can't even wash his face hardly?"

"Not only can everybody in the Logan die faster than everybody else; everybody in the Logan can kill *you and you better hurry up and believe it."*

"Yeah. Next thing we'll probably hear is that Pop Brown went out and mugged one of them Columbia cats." Jinny thought a moment and then said, "But I know for a fact that Earnest has been shooting at Champ's old lady."

Joey's face suddenly purpled. "And I never did like that cute little bitch. And what the hell she see in a man with no hands practically? The bitch meant him no good, but what the hell good was he to her? *And him on Welfare. And she's only maybe twenty-one or -two."*

"Well, all right, hon. Don't blow your stack at me. I wonder how soon that drunken Sid is going to wake up? And does the gentleman have any money? Or do I have to go out and hustle for all three of us?"

"Today's Thursday. And he hasn't been to work since Sunday. He must be broke. But at least he can work the weekend."

"You notice the posters in the subway? You know: 'If you don't come in Sunday, then don't come in Monday.' Now those posters are making fun of something that happened in the 1800s, but Sid's boss means it today. That's what I call the racial gap—if you know what I mean."

"You mean only the goddam niggers have to work every Sunday out there?"

"I dunno, but what you think Sid is? You ever hear him say they got some white waiters out there too?"

"It's them goddam refugees ruining the American Capitalistic System!" Joey raged. "Look at this here hotel. Look out on Amsterdam; everybody selling something got a foreign accent."

"Hon, slavery is a part of the American System. You don't belive me, ask President Johnson."

"Why, that dirty bastid got Kennedy kilt!" Joey screamed apoplectically.

"Cool it, hon. If he had we would have known it by now. A whitey can't do but so much dirt to another whitey. Now if John Kennedy had been a Black man I would believe you in a minute. But LBJ didn't have a damn thing to do with that business."

"Well, how come every time Sid starts talking about Lundy's he starts cussing out the refugees? Never mind LBJ for a minute."

"You got the nerve to ask me to explain Sid?" But Jinny softened immediately. "Damn him. He gets under your skin. He's so damned naked—if you know what I mean. Sometimes I even think the junkies pity him a little bit. You ever notice that most everybody that comes to see Leah asks about him? The women, I mean. Especially if his door's not open."

"Because he's a trick!" Joey shouted. "A lousy stupid john. That's why."

"You know better. Sid isn't even a john in the exact meaning of the word. There's certain types of men that whores go for. Not for pimps and maybe not for love. But they like to be around men like Sid. But I wonder what kind of wife he had to make him like he is? So goddam naked."

"How you know his wife had anything to do with it? Every time you see a fucked-up man you want to say some woman did it. Never no faggot, eh? And didja ever stop to figger that maybe a lot of men is born fucked up? No! You never think of downing nobody but us women."

"Oratorical this morning, aren't we?"

"The hell with how oratorical I am. I asked you one lousy question and you can't even answer it. In fact, Jin, that's your trouble. You always gotta try and explain these here bastids in the Logan when all you gotta say is they was born to be here."

"Born to live in the Logan? Now ain't that a kick in the head. You got a hell of a lot of nerve, hon."

Joey was shaking with imaginary anger. "We wasn't, huh? You and me? We was born to be living somewheres else? Don't make me laugh. So why ain't we in the Waldorf? Know why? Bedford made me fat. *I can't run no more, or else I'd still be taking off them trucks with the boys. And at least we'd be living in the Crown Hotel. You realize this?"*

"Yes. Maybe no. If you were still able to run you'd be a boss hijacker is not exactly true. . . . We gave all that shit up. We said we didn't need nothing but each other. We didn't need to steal and

run the murphy. And we made it even if it's only in the Logan. Do you realize we can walk into any goddam courtroom in America and don't feel nothing but curiosity? Know what that means?" Then she smiled as her thoughts changed. "But, yeah, you got a hell of a question. Yeah. How'd we get here?"

Joey went to Jinny and kissed her. "Because I asked you to, hon," she said. "Because I was the man and I brought you here. And . . ."

Russel, one of the new porters, walked in. He grinned. "What you folks putting down this morning?"

"What the hell is this?" Jinny said, laughing. "Don't you damn handy men knock any more? Or is you that *kind of handy man now, buddee?"*

"You got the door wide open, why I got to knock?"

"Well, we're putting down most anything that's halfway legal this morning," Jinny said. She handed Russel the nearly empty bottle and a glass. "So what's your story so bright and early?"

Russel grinned impishly and drained the bottle. But before J&J could complain he said, "Today is payday, and I've got me three whole dollars in my pocket that just don't belong there. Yeah. I just don't need 'em. So you know what I'm gonna do? I'm gonna go get me six pints of sherry. You all want to let me stash it in here so's the boss won't know where I'm getting it from even if he does smell it? You know: do me like you do Fletcher the painter?"

Jinny's eyes became bland masks of nothing. "And how do we treat Fletcher the painter?"

Russel looked sheepish while he grinned ingratiatingly. "I'm not trying to put your business in the street, Jinny. But some days, every time he finishes a wall he walks off and comes in here. And when he leaves he's revived. Dig it? I dug it. So I asked him the score and he told me. So gimme a break too. There's not another person in this whole hotel I can trust with six pints of wine and you know it."

"Okay, lover. You can stash your juice in here and Joey and I won't give all of it away—maybe."

"I'm going for it at eight sharp; long before Ginsburg gets here.

And I got me a little suitcase I'm gonna carry it in so's nobody in the lobby'll get hepped and follow me back up here." Russel rubbed his hands with self-satisfaction.

"What'd you do time for, Russel?" Jinny asked out of the blue.

Russel gaped momentarily. First his face hardened, but then he grinned. "I had me a whole acre of grass in the back seat on 132nd Street. If I'd been able to down that load I'd been sitting pretty today instead of scrubbing halls. But how you know I been in the joint? I never tole nobody except Ginsburg and he ain't tole you, I know."

Jinny grinned. "We got lots of kooks in the Logan, but you gotta admit that damn near every one is a divine. But for starters, there's the simple fact that you work here. On top of that, you're a little bit too intelligent to be swinging a mop, especially in the Logan. And only a nut or a man on parole would take a job in this hellhole."

"You're wrong, Jin. I'm on parole, it's true. And Ginsburg promised a job and got me loosed, but I could leave him now for a nicer gig. But it's something about the Logan. It grabs you. Look at Sinman, for instance. Look at Paula. She—"

"Paula's okay! Leave Paula outa this," Joey shouted angrily.

"Hon, Russel hasn't said anything about Paula," Jinny said.

"Well, he better not," Joey grumbled. "And you started it anyway, talking about nobody works here but jailbirds. You always got to put shit in the game. Why? Why, I ast ya?"

It was eight o'clock and Russel had been warned by Fletcher not to get near any arguments between J&J, so he left for the store.

"I wish we'd had a couple of rocks to give him for us," Jinny said when he left.

"For what?" Joey said, her voice rising. "Ain't we going to be drinking Russel's wine all day? And when he gets off don't you think he'll buy us a nightcap since today is his payday? Now why couldn't you have thought of that? And that's what's wrong with you, Jinny. You never thinks about tomorra."

"Yes, sahib," Jinny said carelessly.

Russel came back carrying a battered suitcase that some former tenant had left behind. "Well, I got it," he said and opened the suitcase. There were six pints of sherry in it. "I'm going to take one little drink now and then get back to my mopping. Okay?"

"Sure. And you know best, Russel," Joey said in a fatherly tone. "And don't worry about nothing. One of us is in this room all day long. What with all these junkies parading in and out all the time, what'd you expect?"

When Russel left Joey took her first drink. It was a generous one and she had not finished it when someone knocked at the foyer door. Jinny went to answer. It was Suzie, red-eyed, looking piteously like some lynch victim's widow. There was nothing about her now that suggested the conquering amazon.

"What happened?" Jinny asked quickly.

Suzie's only answer was to raise her housecoat above her hips. Jinny stared at Suzie's thighs. They were not blue, but coal black and swollen twice their normal size.

"Who the hell did that?" Jinny demanded, but Suzie did not answer. She hobbled past Jinny to go in to Joey.

Joey took one look at Suzie's face and also asked what was wrong. And again Suzie wordlessly raised her housecoat. Just as wordlessly Joey reached for a bottle of witch hazel, got to her knees and began to gently pat the lotion on Suzie's thighs.

"Now look here, Suzie," Jinny said. "Enough is enough. Now talk!"

"We gotta know what happened so we'll know how to go about helping you," Joey said.

"Harold did it," Suzie said tonelessly.

"For what? With what?" Jinny demanded.

"An iron pipe he keeps for me."

"These sonofabitching men!" Joey shouted. "You don't go nowheres by yourself! You couldn't be cutting out on him behind his back! You got his meals ready whenever he shows. What right a bastid got to do that to a good woman? Why the hell you women always gotta marry men I don't know."

"You want us to go to the precinct with you?" Jinny asked doubtfully.

Suzie clenched her teeth and shook her head. "He won't ever do it again," she said and then began to cry. Her bitter sobs racked her entire body.

"Why?" Joey asked, alarmed. "You didn't kill him, did you?"

Suzie shook her head. When she finally stopped sobbing she said no. Without another word she hobbled out of the room.

They heard the foyer door close behind Suzie, but before Jinny went to turn the latch she murmured, "I'm beginning to question that bitch all the way. . . ."

"You goddam fool you!" Joey hollered. "Ain't she black and blue? Ain't her legs swollen bigger'n mine? How goddam dumb can you get?"

"I believe that bitch made *Harold do it," Jinny said slowly. "Yep. Now I know she did. And when Harold saw how her legs looked this morning he said he wasn't going to do it for her again. That's why she's crying; she's crying because Harold's not coming on that kind of freaking off no more. So she'll have to find a new cat. And that's dangerous. The kind she got to ask might let it get good to him and kill her. You know that, don't you? And I thought that bitch was really married!"*

"Jinny, you ain't no freak," Joey said. "I'll say that much for you. But you sure in hell got one freakish mind. You're freakish as hell in the head."

"What say, let's drop it, hon?"

"Damn right, let's drop it if you're gonna go all off like that and accuse our best friend of being a sex deviate."

"Suzie is not our best friend. Sid is."

"That drunken bastid? You realize he don't never go to work except weekends no more?"

"Now what the hell has that got to do with anything? And who else we know works at all?"

"I thought you said let's drop it?"

"And I am. See you later."

"Well, keep off that sixth floor. I'm telling you."

"You're telling me everything this morning."

"Well, I'm tellin' ya."

"Okay. See you later."

"Whyn't you take Pop Brown a little drink? Russel oughta like that. The old man deserves a drink, don't you think?"

Pop Brown was lying in the bed and moaning as if in great pain. Jinny had hardly stepped into the room when Pop groaned and said, "They tole me I could do it and I done it."

Jinny handed him the bottle which contained one good-sized drink. "Shame on you," she said cheerfully. "Aren't you old enough to know never to do what the denizens of the Logan tell you you should do? And what did you do anyhow? Get married? You sound like it."

"Worse," Pop said. "Checkday a month ago I tole the refugees to let me hold five dollars back on my rent and I'd make it right the next Checkday. But when the next Checkday comes I tole 'em I couldn't afford it."

"Don't tell me the rest; I know. I know it by heart. You let it get good to you and you went and borrowed five more dollars. Or was it ten?"

Pop nodded his head. "I was figgering on a clothes check or something. . . ." He shook his head as if that would clear it of his thoughts. "I was drinking when I got that last money. . . . I don't know exactly what I figgered, Jin."

"So now you're on Ginsburg's hook for fifteen dollars. Now I'm not going to say it outright, but lots of times folks gets into their landlords for fifteen bucks when they're planning to move out in the middle of the night leaving said refugees holding the bag. What's up, Pop?"

Pop sighed. "That old refugee woman that runs that S.R.O. on 104th Street sent me word that she'd gimme a room for only eleven dollars a week, but would always gimme a receipt showing I'd paid fourteen. But her place is so full of rats and violations that Welfare is making all their cases move outa there. Nobody on Welfare can move in no more."

"And you'll never have the fifteen to pay Ginsburg unless you starve and die of thirst too. And there's no use going to Joe Ash.

Fifteen dollars at a quarter a week on the dollar? Hell, you couldn't even keep up the interest. And nobody who's on Welfare can get more than three bucks out of him between checks." All at once Jinny shed her airy attitude and became all business. "I'm going to straighten this out for you, Pop, but don't ever do it again. You hear? Now how much money have you got now?"

"I got four dollars and a half, but I needs me another little drink, Jin. Yesterday was rough. Oh. I appreciates what you brought me, but I needs me just a drop or two more."

"I understand. Don't let it get you down. Just give me the four."

"What you gonna do, Jinny? Checkday is over a week away."

"Don't worry about food. J&J always have food. I'll bring you a plate every day. And maybe a little wine. But right now I'm going down and talk to the Jew and make him agree to let you pay a few bucks every Checkday until you're straightened out. Don't worry. If he doesn't agree I'll bring your four back, and tell you how to stay until Checkday and then move out without laying one red cent on him. Give, Daddy-O."

Jinny went down to the office and beckoned to Ginsburg. "Why you keep fucking over Pop Brown?" she demanded.

"Whadya mean, I'm messing over Pop Brown?" Ginsburg yelled. "I tole him already he's the next one gets his room painted, and his don't really need it. And Fletcher's no whizz kid either, you know. He drinks on the job, but what kind of help does anybody have these days? So whadya mean, I'm trying to screw the old man? I let him have fifteen dollars. Right this minute he owes me fifteen bucks, and have I asked for it? I never mentioned it yet. Ask him if you don't believe me."

"There's some kinds of people can say an awful lot without opening their mouths," Jinny said darkly. "That old man is like a father to me and I don't want him being fucked over."

"Jinny, what's the matter with you? We're friends. Me and you are friends from way back, why you do this to me? You ain't got no right to be mad at me for something I ain't even done. And you got it all wrong anyhow."

Jinny shoved the four dollar bills toward him. "Here's three-

fifty. Give me my change and a receipt. You're satisfied now, aren't you? Taking my last bread."

"Satisfied? Fifteen bucks he owes me and you gimme three-fifty and ask me if I'm satisfied?"

"Every Checkday from now on I'll bring you three-fifty until the books are straight. Okay?"

Ginsburg blew out his breath in resignation. "Okay."

On her way back to Pop's room Jinny pondered the fifty cents change Ginsburg had given to her. The fact that she had not had to give all of the four dollars had constituted a major victory over whitey. On the other hand Pop should be made to pay for his foolishness. Besides, she and Joey had to feed him until next Checkday; so why shouldn't she keep the fifty cents for her trouble?

"The Jew bastid had the nerve to charge me fifty cents interest," she told Pop as she handed him the receipt. "But you won't have to pay any more until Checkday after next. Dig it? And if he should happen to say anything to you, tell him to see me. Lord. I don't know what you folks would do without me around to go to bat in the twelfth inning."

"I thank you kindly, Jinny. You is all I got in this here hotel. You is the onliest friend I got. All others is just folks that comes around to drink. And that's for sure. Whilst you were gone I sent for a pint of muscatel. Here it is. Want some?"

Jinny laughed. "This sweet stuff is the junkies' drink. Since when did you start drinking this?"

"I buys it when I'm broke 'cause if you drink it too fast it'll make you sick. I knows that and so I makes myself sip real slow."

"Well, dig the professor," Jinny murmured.

"And, Jin, you is the nicest woman that lives in this hotel. And the smartest. And I don't mind telling you to your face neither. I know *there ain't another soul in here could have gone down there and settled this thing with that refugee the way you did. And I knows you did it like a lady. In fact, that's the onliest way it could of been done. Ladylike. Them Jews don't really like us niggers, but I will say this for them: they treats respectable niggers with respect. They don't never do they dirt to a gentle-bred lady like you. Yessir.*

It was only because you went down and acted the part of a lady that this thing was settled so nice. You just don't never act like some of these . . . pardon me . . . whores around here. You is a true blue lady and nobody can tell me different."

Jinny's mouth opened in surprise. "Shove it to me gently, Daddy-O," she murmured. A little later she left.

Jinny went down to the third floor to drop in on Oney Harris. The good-looking woman was called Oney because she only had one leg. Oney was about thirty-seven but looked ten years younger. She had lost her leg as the result of being shot six times in the leg by one of two jealous suitors. It had been a barroom brawl which Oney herself had instigated with her drunken arrogance. But to look at Oney one would never believe that this was how she lost her leg. Oney's voice was soft and gentle, and warm like her eyes, and like Suzie, she looked very intelligent but was unlearned.

She smiled gently as she opened the door for Jinny. "Jinny, I'm so glad you've come," she exclaimed. "I need a hand to back some letters for me."

"Well, I'm the best letter backer in the business."

Oney got out pencil and paper and cleared off a space on her table so Jinny could write.

It was a long laborious job to write three letters for Oney, but Jinny did it as if she enjoyed it. When she had finished the last letter Jinny said, "Well, I see you still keep the cleanest room in the Logan, Oney."

"Oh, shucks, Jin. I don't do nothing like I should with it." But Oney's room was not only neat and clean, it contained the only living plants in the Logan. And on the walls were pictures of flowers and there were flower decals on the spotless windows. "How much you going to charge me, Jinny?"

"You know I can't charge a person for doing something that they're not able to do themselves, Oney."

For a moment there flashed in Oney's eyes a hint of the hellion she must have once been. "Suppose I asked you to change a tire on my Cadillac?" she asked.

Jinny joined her in laughter. "But you can let me buy you and Joey a little drink then," Oney insisted.

"Oh well. There's no use denying I'm a bottle baby," Jinny said and accepted Oney's proffered dollar bill.

After leaving Oney's room Jinny decided to see what else was going on on the third floor and so she strolled down the B corridor and met Ann Davis.

Ann was about Jinny's age, light-skinned, and if she had ever been nice-looking she was horrifically ugly and dissipated-looking now. "Lawd, girl. Am I glad to see you," Ann said. "Come on back to my room a minute; I want to tell you something," she added in a fierce whisper.

"Must be good if you got to whisper it in the Logan."

"Well, I just don't want everybody in my business." When they reached Ann's room Ann put on an alcoholically doleful expression and said, "My oldest is in the Tombs and I don't know what to do."

"Well, hell," Jinny said. "There's not too much you can do. He went there on his own, didn't he? And he knew you were on Welfare before he went, didn't he? So what does he want from you? Bail? A lawyer? Don't make me laugh. You don't know what to do? What the hell could anybody in your position do? And what he get busted for anyhow?"

"Dope."

"He use it? How old is he?"

"Twenty-two, I think. It's been years since."

"You didn't raise him?"

"No, my husband's mother did, but I helped out when I could. She just called me and told me he'd been arrested."

"Well, if he don't use shit he better hurry up and tell the law he does, or else he might be an old man when he gets out of the pen. And the first thing you got to do in a case like this is to find you a real young gal who's pregnant and take her down to court with you. And you make it a point to let the judge know she loves your son and that the two of them want to get married. And this girl is going to dedicate her life from now on to curing your son's

habit. And your son is all for it. Some of these fool judges think they're running a matrimonial bureau instead of a criminal court."

"You don't mean for real, do you? I mean: let my son marry some fresh girl who's pregnant and he don't even know? I couldn't do that."

"It's a little bit late in the ball game for you to start worrying over things like that, isn't it?"

"Well—I don't guess I been the best mother, but I don't want my son to marry a tramp."

"He won't be; he'll be marrying somebody who ain't in the Tombs."

Ann nodded doubtfully, but with acceptance."And what else can I do?"

"You can go to court and tell the truth. Like you were a bitch of a mother, and it's not the boy's fault he found himself hooked and in the gutter."

"You think that would do any good?"

"What have you to lose? Your good reputation? At least you won't have to go to prison for it."

"You say things so funny I don't know whether to take you at your word or not, Jinny. I know I've been a tramp, but it hurts now that my oldest is going to prison for I don't know how long."

"Well, what do *you want me to tell you? I've told you the two things that any poor person can do to help a guilty man. You aren't foxy enough to go to bed with the judge or the prosecutor or anybody else who's in power. And besides, going to prison isn't the living end. Jail's not bad at all sometimes . . . if you learn how to roll with the punches. And just where do you happen to think you're at? Where do you think anybody's at when they live in the Logan? You think you can really get out of here? This is your prison just as much as the Tombs is his."*

"You say that because you've never been in jail."

"I've been from the House of D to Westfield to Bedford. Now where else is there for a bright Harlem chick to finish her schooling? But I had sense enough to learn, and to make it. Even with the

screws. And I had someone to love and who loved me. I ate good. I almost got fat. Now tell me what more the Logan got to offer?"

"I—I din't ever dream you were so hard, Jinny. Had it so hard."

"I didn't have it hard, and I don't consider myself hard. I'm a Black chick who was on the ball and wanted to make it even if she didn't have a pretty yaller face."

Ann was animated. "I'm gonna take your advice, Jin. All of it. And like you say: I can't go to jail for it."

"That's the way to do it, keed. And don't forget to always wear a black dress in court."

"Why, Jinny?"

"Jesus, woman! I gotta tell you everything?"

Ann took a dollar out of her bra and shyly put it in Jinny's hand. "I want to buy you and Joey a drink, Jin. Is it okay?"

"All donations, large or small, gladly received." She left then and took the elevator back up to the fifth floor. "Paula!" she yelled at the top of her lungs.

"Here I am, Jinny!" Paula yelled back. In another moment she walked out of the A corridor and met Jinny in the foyer.

"What you want for lunch, hon?" Jinny asked.

Paula took a dollar out of her bra and gave it to Jinny. "Get anything, Jinny. Anything. Why don't you surprise me?"

Jinny grinned impudently. "Look. What I fix for you I want you to eat and enjoy. You is well rounded and I want you to stay that way. Curvaceous, as Sid would say. Ya know, he's always talking about how pretty you are?"

Paula's face almost froze, but not quite. "Beauty is as beauty does," she said in a voice that could not be described.

When Jinny left Paula she went back down and out to the A&P store and bought a pound of liver for forty-nine cents. It would be enough for Paula and Joey and her too if she felt like eating, which she probably wouldn't, she figured.

Coming back, she got off the elevator and her eyes widened to see a group of boys. Whiteys. And she didn't even have to think twice to know they were from Columbia. Neither did she have to guess who the leader was. He looked like a fullback and he was mad. Mad clear through.

"Say, lady," he said to Jinny, "we're looking for somebody."

"Didn't you inquire at the desk?" Jinny asked.

"We didn't see anybody in the office," the smallest youth said. He was out of place all the way around the clock as far as Jinny was concerned. White, Jewish and intelligent. He didn't belong in the Logan, but he didn't belong with these other students either. The fullback was from Texas even if Texas fullbacks never came to Columbia. And the other two were Wasps from way back.

And Jinny knew she was going to have to make an ally of this bright Jewboy, but she had to go about it backwards. Not from the front by no means.

Jinny already had the picture. Someone from in or around the Logan had run a game on these kids. But the Logan was Jinny's, her land, her home. And these four whiteys were the enemy.

"This guy we're looking for has funny lips," the fullback said.

"You mean he's got big lips?" Jinny said dryly.

"Yeah, lady," the little Jewboy said.

"He's a thief!" the fullback blurted.

"He stick you up?"

The Jewish boy laughed, and Jinny knew she was beginning to win. But she told herself that it had to be slow all the way.

"What makes you think he's in this building?" she asked.

"We saw him come in here. That's why," the leader said. "And this hotel hasn't got any connecting roof on it. And he even told us he was coming in here."

"And with your money, I suppose?"

The Jewish boy laughed again. This time almost reminiscently.

"He was so sincere. *He comes up and asks us to do this old man a favor. It wouldn't really be costing us anything and we'd be doing the old guy a big favor. But the guy was so sincere," the boy repeated. "It was like he was doing* us *a favor."*

"How much?" Jinny asked.

"Thirty-five dollars he got," the fullback said.

"Well now," Jinny murmured, wondering how much of a cut

she should demand from the Kingfish . . . if it had been Kingfish. It wasn't absolutely certain because the Kingfish only took off pussies. And at least the Texas cracker was no pussy. In fact, he looked to be a little too dumb to even know when it would be wise to play a little pussy.

"He told us this old man's son had given his father a portable color TV set, but the old man had cataracts. And the old man was willing to take thirty-five because he could get a good AM and FM radio for that. And that everybody in this hotel was too poor to do the old man a favor like that and so . . ."

"You offered to take a three-hundred-dollar set off the old man's hands for thirty-five dollars," Jinny put in for him. "Don't you fellows go to Columbia?"

"Now you listen here—" the Texan began.

"No. Let me finish," Jinny said. "Now haven't you all learned enough arithmetic to know you aren't doing anybody a favor when you give them thirty-five dollars for three hundred?"

"Well, you people . . ."

". . . know that only a greedy person can be conned out of money," Jinny put in again for him. "So why don't you put that bread down as added tuition and call yourselves fortunate? You think that con man, whoever he was, is still in this building? He's over on Eighth Avenue by now, buying heroin. He probably never came up past the second floor. All he had to do is take the steps up to the first bend and wait for you suckers to get on the elevator. Then he walks back down the steps and out the front door before the elevator has carried you past the third floor. He's gone. Your money's gone. Now what more do you want to know?"

"She's right," the Jewish boy said. "Let's get out of this place."

"I got a great mind to kick down every door on this floor until I find that nigger," the fullback said.

"You know how many doors we got on this fifth floor?" Jinny asked.

"I got plenty of time," the fullback retorted.

"There's thirty-six," Jinny said, thinking that she might as well tell this cracker where it was at. "That mean's there's going to be

thirty-six knives chopping at your ass while you're doing all this great kicking. How many knives did Princeton have last fall and what was the score?"

"Come on, Bruce," one of the Wasps said. "She's only telling you right." He went and pushed the button for the elevator.

When the elevator door opened the fullback was still pouting, but he got on with the others. Jinny mentally chided herself for not having the presence of mind to have at least bummed a cigarette from the Texan. She must be slipping, she figured.

"I been thinking since you left," Joey said soon after Jinny walked in the room. "And maybe you might be right. Now Suzie didn't cry until after she said Roger wasn't gonna do it any more. Yeah. I been thinking."

"And I'm not going to tell her not to come visiting when more often than not she buys us a drink. No. If she's dumb enough to buy the wine I'm going to drink it. But I don't need no close friends who are freaks. Freaks are supposed to stay to themselves. Has Russel been back? How many times?"

"Twice."

"Good. I want him to feel he's getting his full share. I only hope he knows how to hold it. Pour me a drink, will you, hon?"

Joey poured the drink and said, "That simple-assed Sid came in and took one little drink and said he was going for a walk. He never come back. I wonder where he went?"

"Probably someplace with Blind Charlie." Jinny took a sip and chuckled. "And isn't that one hell of a combination? A cold-blooded murderer who's got a volcano for a temper and a college-bred pussy who don't know where nothing's at."

"Sid's no pussy. He's got guts, plenty of heart, but he don't see no reason why he should die to prove it."

"I know," Jinny said resignedly. "But he and that blind maniac still make a hell of a pair."

"Maybe that's what makes them so thick. Like one complements the other. You know."

Jinny grinned. "Yeah. Like you and me."

"Yeah," Joey said doggedly. "Like you and me. Me and you is a team; being lovers is extra. And let me tell you another thing—"

"Now. Now. Now. Don't lose your cool, hon. Because I feel good. All morning, I've been feeling good. I been going over all the ins and outs about this place and it made me feel good."

"How can thinking about the Logan make anybody feel good unless they're crazy or the owner of the place?"

"You realize how easy it is to make it in here? And you don't have to risk going to jail to make it either."

"When you gonna start making sense?"

"We made sense when we came here. Think it over, hon. Think it over."

CHAPTER 11

IT WAS WHAT I call one of my Gloria mornings. I was in a funk over her and just didn't feel like talking, but Sinman and Charlie did. Since the Sinman was present I guess I don't have to tell you we were in his room.

"I get sick and tired sometimes of having to go upside these Black bastid's heads," Charlie was saying.

"Then why do you do it?" Sinman asked him. "After all, they are no longer malleable. Every time you punch one out you are actually going upside your own head."

"No, I ain't. People in here is different. I know you can't tell 'em nothing, but you can make 'em *feel.* With this wine and dope in them all the time you can't do nothing to make 'em understand except to make 'em feel it."

"But why should you appoint yourself as the avenging angel of the Logan? The Logan is its own correction officer."

"That ain't it," Charlie said excitedly. "I ain't trying to correct nothing. I just makes folks get up offen my back is all. Or Sid's back. And my other fren's'. These Logan niggers is back-riders, they always got to be bugging you or they don't feel natural. Why, this here Logan would be one hell of a place to live in effen I didn't stand up for folks around here. You know that."

"I do not know that. In fact, I've often wondered how necessary you are to the peace of mind of the Logan."

"I didn't say I was *necessary* to anybody. All I said was that these here people get on my nerves with all their unnecessary bullshit. And that it's not right for a whole group of folks to be as dumb as folks in the Logan. Now that's all I said for real."

"We are a living proof that God is dead, I suppose. That is the one and only reason I remain here as I've told you and Sid many times. Any god who would be God must start here in the Logan; I must be here when He comes."

"You got the wrong foot out, like," Charlie said. "There ain't that much unusual about the Logan. Of course there ain't too many Logans around; but just the same there's enough. They's gotta be. You gotta remember there's lots of home folks around with no place to go but to a S.R.O. It was a sin for them to come to New York in the first place."

"And it is a sin to keep them here off the farm. All of these potentially useful lives lying fallow . . ."

"Well, my life ain't fallow. Logan or no Logan."

"No?"

"No, it ain't. You don't see me begging on no subways. And I don't owe nobody . . ."

"No?"

"Wal, mebbe a dollar here and fifty cents there, but it ain't no big thing. And effen I should die tomorra ain't nobody gonna be saying I went off owing them. And there's lots of folks around here gonna be sorry to hear I'm dead and gone. They gonna miss me. And to prove it, all I gotta say is that you and Sid here is the only fren's I got in the Logan—Miss Fronnie don't count. So it's just you and Sid. Everybody else got their hand out, depending on me to do it."

"Depending on you for *what?* To *do* what?"

Charlie nodded complacently. "Now this little Sid Bailey is the first person offered me they fren'ship pure and simple in a long time. Everybody else wants Blind Charlie's muscle. Even the women. They don't fool me none. They either wants me for to make their old man to police up on hisself or to get rid of him."

"How do you figure that?"

"They can tell their man that Blind Charlie will kick the shit outa them effen they fucks over them again. And the men around here ain't no better. Lotsa times they invites me to have a drink 'cause they figger no one will come around chiseling or mebbe trying to gorilla a drink; and so they saves. Everybody in this hotel is a pussy before Gawd. Even scared to tell a moocher he can't have a drink. And that's the real reason why they're here; life sent 'em here. And because they is the kind of people life sent here they is *supposed* to have their asses kicked reg'lar. All except Sid and the like and how Sid happened to get screwed up in here I don't know. Whiskey probably."

"Whiskey?" I exclaimed. "Who drinks more than you?"

"Whiskey ain't the point exactly," Charlie said.

Sinman smiled reminiscently. "Sid offered his friendship to me one bitter day. And I know there were no reservations." I guess he figured that any more on that subject would be kind of gooey and so he asked, "And I suppose you are important to Sandy in the same way you are to the others?"

"Now Sandy is all woman," Charlie said thoughtfully. "Mighty dumb, but she is a woman through and through. Yet and still, Sandy don't play pussy for no man, including me. And she know I can kill her without half trying, but she's never played pussy yet. I'm proud of her. But just the same that don't mean I don't make things a lot easier for her. I made it easy for her to get that junky offen her back what she was keeping in her room, didn't I? And Sandy is what I call the house whore around here. Every single man knows her and her room number. And they knows she's in and out of that room all night. And they knows she can't call the cops to put them outa that room, but do any studs ever try to gorilla her for anything? Only a raving maniac would want to hafta answer to both Sandy *and* me! Why, there's even some women in this hotel not only won't trick around here, but makes believe they ain't even whores, they's so scared of this place, but not Sandy. And you know that a working stiff can get mighty nasty when they get drunk payday. Just like a Welfare bitch on Checkday. But effen they comes in offen the street Sandy'll trick with them effen she thinks there's any chance they can come. Sure. They break bad, Sandy can handle them, but she risks going back to the House of D again. While at the same time the stud only got to hear my name mentioned and he'll back off."

"All very true. But as for me, I feel very unnecessary this morning. It has been a long wait, and I am getting just a little fed up with all the godlessness around here. Even a godless people have no right to wreak so much havoc upon one another. And it is depressing to know that there is very little violence in S.R.O.s that refuse to cater to Blacks. Your whitey simply is not a violent man."

"Ain't you ever heard of war?" Charlie asked.

"Touché."

"And there ain't no sense in your hinting that mebbe whiteys are smarter than niggers 'cause they ain't. It's only that whitey don't segregate hisself like niggers. You ain't never seen a whole bunch of whitey's and every one is as stupid as the next."

Pure amazement showed in the Sinman's eyes. "Charlie, what is this you are talking about?"

"Whiteys stay all jumbled up together," Charlie said doggedly. "Every last one of them got equal rights. A stupid whitey got just as much right to be president of General Motors as the next."

"You believe this?"

"You remember the Hudson?"

"The car? Yes. Why?"

"When I was a kid the Hudson was known as the bootleggers' getaway car. Good. Fast. Dependable. And then when they come out with that step-down model it was better yet, but they went bankrupt! Now how you gonna get to them cookies?"

"I simply do not follow you, Charlie."

"Effen Black people owned that company, they'd of never thought of letting them kind of people run that company."

"I take it that it is a mystery to you how white people can pick as head of a corporation a man who is capable of letting that company go bankrupt?"

"That's about the size of it. First, niggers don't trust niggers. And second, niggers make all dumb niggers hang out together. Now you go join a high-society country club and I bet you gonna find members with IQs from zero to five hundred. Whitey don't believe in segregating his own. We do. So we got S.R.O.s."

"You bring me to another question: what would you say the average IQ of the Logan inmate is?"

Charlie rubbed his chin. "I had no business bringing IQs into this conversation. 'Cause IQ don't mean nothing. I believe them psychiatrists when they say most junkies got high ones, but IQ don't mean nothing if you can't make it work to your advantage. Hell, a cat might be born the best drummer the world will ever know, but what's it mean if the cat ain't able to get to a drum one single time before he dies? If he ain't got sense to get to a drum, what damn difference does his high drumming IQ make?"

"Umm . . ."

"And dumb as the niggers is in here, I bet there ain't a single one in here woulda let Pierce-Arrow get any bankrupteder than it got. So don't nobody tell me that whitey is born smarter than niggers."

"Charlie," I said, "you're always calling me stupid, but I don't talk out of both sides of my mouth at the same time like you do. You know yourself you said that these junkies in here go to jail just because they are stupid and not because they are junkies; and that they are even stupider than the pigs and God knows a pig is stupid. Now didn't you?"

"Now wait a minute, Sid," Charlie said. "Junkies is dumb, but you're forgetting that niggers is smarter'n most white people when you come right down to it. You ever see a picture in the *Daily News* of a Black family what's actually starving? We got white trash, you ever heard anyone talk about Black trash? If you ain't got it to survive, your IQ can't help you. You is just a smart dead nigger. See what I mean?"

"The privilege of being expelled from four colleges has left a fine imprint on you, Charlie," Sinman said.

"And there's a third thing somewheres in the cards," Charlie said meditatively. "I think it's in this thing when Sinman says all junkies is born slaves. Now there's a girl been catting on Sandy for two weeks while she bought up five bottles of bootleg methadone and kept them in the refrigerator. When she got five she started taking it and kicked her habit complete, but do you know that almost every day she'll be sitting around with Sandy and me and she'll kinda shake herself and say: 'Sure wish I had me a little meth.' Now she ain't hooked on meth or nothing. She just *likes* to take meth. And later on it's gonna be Coca-Cola, or coffee. She's a born slave like Sinman says. Maybe one day she'll even be a slave to somebody's dick since Sinman says all junkies is freaks anyways."

I laughed. "It's all way out," I said. "But if a shrink was really on the ball these addictive people could all be made addictive to learning, achieving."

"Most certainly," Sinman said. "But New York is blessed with more quack psychologists and sociologists than the rest of the world combined. No reputable psychiatrist will touch a junky because he knows that as yet there is no way to reach a born junky. Someday a new chemical, a new shock treatment or the like, will come along and then the reputable psychiatrist will come to the forefront and save your addict. But not until then."

"Yeah," I said. "Maybe this new God you're waiting for will bring it with Him."

"That is exactly what I am waiting for."

Charlie went to the door. "C'mon, boy," he said. "Let's go take a walk somewheres."

I rose.

Sinman asked, "Need anything?"

"Naw," Charlie said. "I wants to be as broke as everybody else around here."

"One moment, Charlie," Sinman said. "I forgot to tell you that Cuestick was by and propositioned me last night."

"What kinda proposition that rat got to make?"

"Two dozen .38s for one thousand dollars. Would you take them?"

"New?"

"Yes, but scalding hot. So hot, in fact, that I was tempted to give Cuestick five hundred dollars not to mention them again."

"Being hot don't make too much difference in Harlem or any place else in New York. You use a gun to try and get up in the world, you is going to jail, and effen the gun is stolen or not don't make no difference. But it's hard as hell to down twenty-four pistols even in Harlem."

"Yes. We would have to hold onto them a long time if we are to get a decent price for each and every one. Even at a cut rate of seventy-five dollars apiece we would have to hang onto them a long time. And we should get a hundred and twenty-five for a brand-new virgin pistol."

"I'd take them though," Charlie said thoughtfully. "You can make some wonderful connections, selling guns. It's like doing folks a great big favor, effen you know what I mean."

"Yes, I suppose so. But we have five now, haven't we?"

"Four. The last one you hired out, the kid got busted. That one's gone forever."

"I think I'll buy those guns for moral reasons. Black men should have those arms, not whitey. It was an abject lack of firepower that made the Italian and Irish Mafias supreme among us."

I actually winced at the Sinman's truth. Cops and robbers had made Harlem what it is today.

But Charlie's laughter boomed. "You gonna donate 'em to the Black Panthers so's they can blow your brains out?"

"If only I had a black skin," the Sinman mused wistfully.

"Mine's for sale any time you're ready," Charlie said. With a vague wave of his cane he went out the door.

I didn't follow immediately; Charlie didn't need my shoulder inside the Logan anyhow. "Do you really know why you want to be Black?" I asked Sinman.

"It is the only supreme challenge the world has to offer. And please don't start talking about how we will be soon landing on the moon."

"Challenge is nothing but one of whitey's empty words. Like positive thinking, and egghead, and democracy. To be Black is murder, and there's nothing to challenge—if you're Black!"

"To live in Harlem and be Black is a supreme challenge, Sid. It is a keen game to refuse to do the job whitey has picked out for you and still survive; to stay in bed as long as you please and still enjoy the comforts of life although whitey's lips are hanging low.

Like an idiot, whitey has handed all of the challenges to Blackie. It's no accident that Blackie laughs more than whitey. And the Jew more than the other whiteys. Whitey will spend millions trying to get back and forth to the moon . . . a dead world. Why? And have you ever met a Black man who even has the time to think about the moon?"

I left the Sinman and went out in the lobby. Blind Charlie was standing in front of the elevator. A tiny addict named Pablo came up to Charlie at the same time. Pablo had been born in Puerto Rico and certainly did not weigh more than a hundred pounds.

"Hello, Charlie," Pablo said, "I want to cop from the Sinman but I'm fifty cents short, will you see me go?"

"You know I don't loan no junkies money. What the hell you come to me for?" Charlie's voice had dropped to an ominous rumble. "You trying to mess over me?"

"You know I'd never do that, Blind Charlie. But, so help me, I'm sick. *Mucho* sick. But I got me a boss AM and FM radio stashed. I found it in a car last night, and I'm gonna down it in a bar later on this afternoon, but right now I can hardly walk. After a fix I'll be with it and be able to hold out for a good price. Dig it? Right now somebody'll take it off me for just one bag, and what sense that make. But I'll give you a dollar back this afternoon."

"Go tell the Sinman I'm seeing you go for fifty cents. And I don't want to hafta come looking for you this afternoon, do you dig *that?*"

"I dig. I dig, Charlie," Pablo said with profuse thanks and then hurried into 1-C.

"Whoooeee!" Charlie bellowed as we got off the elevator on the sixth floor. "Who's got a drink for poor ole Blind Charlie this morning?" No one answered his bellow and so he tapped his way to Mr. Johnson's door and walked right in. "Who's in here?" he yelled.

"Come on in here, you ole warhorse," Mr. Johnson exclaimed. "I'm the onliest one in here and don't need no more company than you and Sid 'cause I just got a little piece in this here bottle." He poured three equal drinks of the wine.

"Where's everybody?" I asked Mr. Johnson.

"Dunno. Been mighty quiet up here this morning 'cepting that crazy Bob Whitfield was up here yelling and carrying on at Obie a while back. I'm scared to death of that Bob Whitfield. He really is an old man, over fifty, but he used to be a professional boxer and they tell me he got a punch worser than a mule's kick. I seen him take over men in their twenties that's twice as big as him."

Charlie chuckled in a reflective sort of way. "I've slapped that Bob a dozen times for messing over people."

"That Bob's a bad one," Mr. Johnson said.

"I'm gonna kill that man effen he don't stop fucking over everybody. What he picking on Obie for? Could you hear?"

"Couldn't hear nobody but Bob's voice. He was yelling his head off. But it was something about wine. Now Obie had a whole case of wine Saturday night, Sunday morning. Seems like he and Bob went in and bought that case to sell after hours. But Obie drank it all. Leastways that the way Bob was yelling it. But I dunno."

"Well, let's me and you go talk to Obie," Charlie said.

"All right," Mr. Johnson said doubtfully. "Guess you know what you're doing."

"Of course I knows what I'm doing, don't I always? I just wants to make sure that Bob Whitfield ain't fucking too tough over my drinking buddies."

The three of us went to Obie's room, which was a few doors down the hall from Mr. Johnson. Obie, who looked to be about fifty-five, was sitting dejectedly on his bed. Obie didn't rise or really say anything. We all stood. I guess it never occurred to either Mr. Johnson or myself to sit down because Obie kept a singularly unkempt room. Obie was on Welfare, but he supplemented his checks by collecting junk and bottles in a little cart he had fashioned out of a baby carriage. Obie had a ragpicker's room, and that's why nobody wanted to sit down.

"What's Bob Whitfield been doing to you, Obie?" Charlie demanded.

Obie let out a sigh. "I went and borrowed four dollars from him Saturday night. Leastways I lets him make me take four dollars from him. He was drinking and insisted I take it. I just wasn't thinking. I was drunk too. And I forget he was crazy."

"Even effen you're drunk you ain't suppose' to borrow from no crazy man," Charlie said.

"But I could've paid him back, Charlie. I got it in my pocket right now. You see, my boy come by Saturday afternoon. He's something, that boy. Won't work for nobody, but he'd got money from somewheres and he gimme five dollars and bought me a pint of gin too. So I got drunk off that gin. You know how it is when you're used to drinking sweet lucy. Well, Bob comes down the hall about eleven o'clock and my door's open. So he comes in. He got a bottle and me and him starts in working on it. Meanwhile I tells him that I got five dollars and has got a great mind to go to Joe Ash and borrow four more. Then I could go to the store before it closes and buy a whole case for nine dollars. And I'm gonna sell most of it between midnight and Monday morning when the store opens back up. You see, I'm only paying nine dollars and when I sell twenty-four pints times seventy-five cents I'm gonna be doing all right. Now I didn't actually figger on selling the whole twenty-four pints, but I did mean to sell until I got nine dollars back in my pocket and then me and my friends would drink the rest."

"I see," Charlie said. "So why didn't you?"

"I did!" Obie exclaimed. "I sole ten pints right off the bat Sunday morning. That makes seven-fifty. Then Fletcher stops by and I tells him I only got to sell two more pints and the rest is our'n. So Fletcher goes in his pocket and hands me a dollar and a half. And then we gets drunk for real."

"So?" Charlie prodded.

"Well, I knocks myself out and I don't wake up until about eleven last night and it's this crazy Bob Whitfield. Drunk crazy! Talking all out his head. He works out at that Lundy's Restaurant weekends and makes good money and I guess he went in a bar after he got off."

I was not at all surprised to hear that all this time they had been talking about a fellow waiter. On Sundays during good weather Lundy's has as many as two hundred waiters on the floor during the peak of the rush. There were lots of weekend waiters whom I didn't know by name and there were lots whom I'd never even seen because they worked upstairs and we simply never ran across each other in that huge place. However, I did wonder if I'd ever met up with this man who apparently was crazier than Blind Charlie.

"So Bob is raising all kinds of hell," Obie says. "He's got his old lady with him. She's as old as he is, but she go for bad too. Bob sez that he went in half and half with me and that I now owes him twelve times seventy-five cents, nine dollars. I reminds him that I borrowed that four dollars and that I was going to go to Joe Ash for it but he wouldn't let me. Then Bob slaps me and sez that Joe Ash wouldn't ever loan a man money to buy wine and go into competition with him. You oughta seen him act up. He was jumping around almost like he's doing some kind of dance strut. But scared as I was, I just couldn't give him all of my nine dollars. And then too I figgered this morning he'd be sober and I'd be able to straighten him out for the four like I was suppose' to do. But this morning he comes back up here, still drunk, and sez that since I tried to fuck over him he's gonna show me how to really fuck over people, and tells me that he wants every cent of the wine money. The whole eighteen dollars. Or else he's gonna kill me. And I think he's gonna."

"No, he ain't," Charlie said quietly. "And he's just trying to run a game on you anyhow."

"I don't know, Charlie. That man was simply wild. Crazy. Frothing in the corners of his mouth and all. And you know how bad he goes for."

"Just a game," Charlie said. "He knows how much you drink and so he knows you didn't intend to sell all them pints from the git go. So I'm gonna tell you what to do: when he comes back you tell him that I'm loaning you the money to pay him, but I don't trust your drunken ass with the money and so he got to come see me. You understand that? You tell him to come see Blind Charlie. And effen he hems and haws you just pull him down to see me."

"But what good's that gonna do me?" Obie cried. "Lessen you kills him for real, he's gonna come right back and kill *me*."

"I ain't gonna touch him. I'm just gonna tell him. You know?

I'm mad. Don't make no sense at all when one man can't borrow four dollars from another without there got to be misunderstanding and bloodshed. And you is telling the truth, Obie. Couldn't have been no other way for you to have allowed yourself to have taken that money from Bob Whitfield. How much money you got now? Buy us some wine."

"I got five dollars, not counting the four I owes Bob."

"Wal—we needs us three pints," Charlie said judiciously. "Give Sid the money. He'll go." Obie handed me the money for the wine. Charlie said, "I got me a better idea. I was gonna give Bob Whitfield that four dollars, but I wants to prove something to Sid here. Instead of telling Bob to see me, you tell him to go to the Sinman. I'm gonna prove to Sid and to Bob himself that he's a pussy before Gawd. When that white man tells Bob to get lost and to get off your back Bob is gonna do just that. Yeah. These niggers go for bad and take off a whitey now and then when they is sure the whitey don't know them or where they lives. But when an established white man like the Sinman tells a bad nigger to get lost that nigger is gonna get lost. And I'm talking about right here in Harlem, not no goddam downtown east side."

"That's the Gawd's honest truth," Mr. Johnson exclaimed. "I seen Ginsburg unlock that door and come outa that office many a time after he's been called too many motherfuckers by those real bad junkies and winos."

For some reason I couldn't fathom, Charlie clapped his hand on my shoulder as I passed him to leave for the store. In the hall he said, "We're going by 6-A-5 first."

"Okay," I said and led the way.

Before we reached the room Charlie said, "I'm taking you someplace you never been before. Ain't no men been in this room before 'cepting me and Fletcher. So act like it. You *better* act like it."

"For Chrissakes," I snorted.

And therefore I wasn't too surprised when a handsome old lady answered Charlie's knock on 6-A-5. This had to be the Logan's fabled Miss Fronnie. Not only had J&J talked of her, but Sandy too. Miss Fronnie was more beautiful and regal than I had expected.

Her hair was snow white and so was her face. It was an aristocratic snow whiteness. She had to be seventy, according to J&J and Sandy, but she looked to be a well-preserved fifty-five or so. Like Lina's, her face was totally without lines and I remembered someone once told me that people who seldom smiled seldom had wrinkles. Then I thought how many of the prettiest women in and around the Logan were not exactly what you might call joyous people. All, that is, except possibly Suzie and Gloria. Gloria smiled beautifully and often, but she seldom laughed when you came to think about it.

Miss Fronnie looked at me just like Sharlee had, but in Miss Fronnie's stare there was anger. She seemed to bridle that anger and resolve to be polite because Blind Charlie must have brought me along for some yet to be explained reason which would most certainly be valid.

Her room was spotless; evidently Miss Fronnie had paid Fletcher to paint her walls a pleasant peach color instead of the standard Logan pukish green. She had five pictures of elephants on the wall and there were statuettes all about the room; there actually was a small-size herd of them on the floor beneath her window.

"I can see your shirt better now, Charlie. Take it off. It's not too clean," Miss Fronnie said. So Charlie didn't have to explain my presence right away, and I also thought that Charlie couldn't explain my presence even if he wanted to.

Charlie just grunted and peeled off his T-shirt. "Guess I might as well put on a clean one," he said. "How much I owe you for laundry, Miss Fronnie?"

"You ask that every time you come in here, and you know I *like* to do your things, Charlie. You're like a son. But sometimes I think you don't like the idea of being a son to me."

"A son can pay his mama for doing his laundry, can't he? And it ain't like I was broke. You know I get two different checks. One from the Blind Folks and one from Welfare. And I can get anything I want from Sinman, especially for things like laundry."

"Well, you just keep Sinman's money in your pocket for spending change. I know how you can run through money in this Logan.

The place is jammed with cheap girls who want you to spend on them twenty-five hours a day. But I wish you wouldn't drink so much with them. You drink enough yourself. You don't need a drinking woman too."

"I know I don't. And I ain't got none," Charlie said dryly. "I'm saving myself until a Sunday school teacher moves in here. Then I'm gonna make my play."

"You're teasing me, but I'm serious. It hurts me to hear you associate with the cheap wine-drinking women in this building, Charlie. You don't fool around with nothing but tramps."

"What about Sandy? I thought you liked her?"

"I *do* like Sandy. I love her. She's a darling. My copper-colored little darling. I only wish she'd leave that awful heroin alone. She doesn't need it and it will only ruin her beauty and everything else in the end. And I know I don't have to tell you how she comes by every day to see what I need from the store. And she simply does not swear. All the rest of these girls I can hear all up and down the halls and every other word that comes out of their mouth is 'motherfucker.' And I detest that word. But thank God, Sandy never curses."

"Who tole you Sandy don't swear?"

"Well, she doesn't around me. And don't you forget. If a person is given to swearing they will forget once in a while if they are putting on an act and a curse word will drop from them."

"Is Sandy really pretty?"

"Shame on you, Charlie. How could you ask such a question even if you can't see?"

"She feels good-looking," Charlie admitted. "But she seems to have such a hard time of it—effen you know what I mean."

"I most certainly do know what you mean. Sandy is a high-principled woman. I know because I was in show business and many was the time we were stranded and had to find some nice man to help us get back to New York. But Sandy not only has principles, she won't venture out of the Logan much at all. I don't know why; she certainly is not afraid, but she won't. Yet in a way I don't blame her. I've done everything a girl can do in life except walk the streets. It just isn't right! Walking the streets, I mean. It's a reflection on the Black man. Any time a man can't at least provide a roof and a bed for his woman he is lower than a dead snake at the bottom of the sea."

"A bed and a roof don't mean too much to a hustling girl nowadays," Charlie said. "Any john that's got any sense atall ain't gonna go to a girl's house with her or any place else *she* suggests. Johns know there's danger in following a woman into her own territory."

"And that is just another reflection on the Black man. The pimps should have gotten together long ago and set aside certain streets in Harlem where a white man would be safe at all hours of the day or night. They could have gotten together and forbidden muggers and holdup men to operate on those special streets. Harlem is losing thousands upon thousands of dollars every week just because white people are afraid to come to Harlem. Harlem is like a foreign country. Every other foreign country in the world is begging for American tourists, but not Harlem. Business is business and a Black man just doesn't know how to take care of business."

Charlie grinned. "You must have been something special in your day, Miss Fronnie."

Miss Fronnie smiled in return. "Oh, I could write a book or two. When I was a little girl my mother made me promise that I would never, *never* work in Miss Whitefolk's kitchen or nurse her ugly babies. So you know I must have done a bit of living to get along."

"You never worked in your life?"

"Only in show business. Before I left the South I traveled with Silas Green, Butterbeans and Susie and shows like that. But in the end I had to face it that I was too white-looking. Like when the comedians would put their hands on me the silly crackers wouldn't like it. And they all knew I was just as colored as the comedians, but they'd get mad and start grumbling out there in the audience. There was almost a lynching one time, and so after that I came to New York. I got work in *Hot Chocolates*. Now that was a show."

"What about *Blackbirds*? Was you in that too?"

"No. I tried out for it, but you can see I'm no Blackbird. But after *Hot Chocolates* I started to pass for white on the stage."

"You ever become big time?"

"No, but I was the only white girl who could really do the snakehips. The theater people knew I was colored, but they would bill me like a white girl. I mean they just didn't bother to announce that I was Black."

"People your age don't much like to say they is Black. How come you do?"

"Sandy. She's a little rebel, that girl."

"You ever have a white man, Miss Fronnie?"

Miss Fronnie looked balefully at me. "Why are you asking so many questions today, Charlie? You don't usually."

"I'm getting ready to write a book," Charlie said. And it didn't seem like a joke at all.

"Well," Miss Fronnie said, "I only had one, but he was of the finest. He came from Georgia and made his fortune right here in New York. And when he died—I mean before he died—he made his son promise to take care of me as long as I lived."

"So that's why you ain't on Welfare," Charlie mused aloud.

"It most certainly is. That was a wonderful white man from Georgia even if I have to say so myself."

"But you still don't have any reason not to be on Welfare," Charlie said, musing again. "Nobody could prove you got a secret income. You should be getting checks from both the son and Welfare too."

Miss Fronnie frowned. "Do I sound like one of these Welfare bitches like run all through these halls, Charlie Jones?"

"Now. Now. Don't go getting all excited, Miss Fronnie. I just meant that it's like your *duty* to take from Welfare. Like it's *ours,* and Black folks is suppose' to be getting it by hook or crook. Why, you could even give it away. But it's your'n and you're suppose' to make 'em give it to you."

"Well, I don't want it!"

"But you should think about it. Suppose that son should die tomorra?"

"I won't take that dirty money."

After that Charlie seemed to be discreetly silent for a time to let Miss Fronnie cool off. Or he might have imagined that I might want to take up the conversational bit, but I didn't. I wasn't too sure if I liked Miss Fronnie anyhow. When you come down to it, Miss Fronnie was nothing but Uncle Tom's woman.

In a few moments Charlie and Miss Fronnie resumed their conversation, but now it was the old woman who asked most of the questions. And at one point Miss Fronnie exclaimed, "My goodness, Charlie, how do you know so much about what's happening all the time?"

"With all these junkies trooping in and outa the Sinman's room I could write a newspaper every day. A junky likes to think he's a tight-lipped hood right out of a story about the FBI, but he ain't. Junkies always got to *prove* everything. Now a real smart man will tell you something and if you don't believe it, well, that's your fault. But no junky is like that; he just got to prove it. He boast about a sting and effen you don't believe it, he just might go to the police and confess just to prove it. So all junkies got to prove they is down with it by telling you all they know even while he's thinking he's the close-mouthedest character in Harlem. And then there's Sandy. She ain't like most junkies, but what she don't know about the Logan ain't worth telling."

"Sandy does seem to be into everything, doesn't she?"

"Yeah. You can say that again."

"She must be a lovely girl to live with."

"Yeah, but she stinks."

"Charlie! How can you let those words out of your mouth? Sandy is in here every day. I stand close to her sometimes. I *know* she doesn't smell offensive."

"Underneath her clothes she does. What she needs is a douche bag, but I guess she's too trifling."

"Why don't you buy her one, Charlie? It'd be a lovely gesture and you'd be teaching her in a nice gentle way."

"Why should I spend my hard-earned money on a junky?" Charlie asked indignantly, but I noticed he didn't curse.

"Because you sleep in her room is why. Sandy is a lady before she is a junky and man is supposed to furnish what he thinks his lady needs."

"Sleep with or no sleep with, I ain't wasting good money on no junky." Charlie paused, and then in an almost crafty voice asked, "How much one of them bags cost?"

"You can get a cheap one for two or three dollars, Charlie. But you should get one to last if you are going to get one. Are you?"

"Mebbe not. All I know is she sure needs one." And suddenly the crude giant was as shy as a schoolboy. "You got a pair of shears, Miss Fronnie?"

"Of course I have a pair of shears, Charlie. Why do you ask?"

"I want you to cut off these pants I got on so I'll have me a pair of walking shorts. Sinman's got a pair."

"Why don't you ask Sinman to buy you a pair?"

"I don't want the store kind. Seems like they'd make me feel funny. Just cut these here off, Miss Fronnie."

"I most certainly will not."

"It's all right. Somebody's always giving me a pair of extra pants. I got more pants than Sinman. And my legs sweat something turble in the summer, and it's beginning to get hot already. So take your shears and cut 'em off."

"But they'll have to be basted. I can't baste them with you in them."

"I don't want no basting. Them Columbia gals ain't got no basting."

"How do you know?" I broke my silence to ask. I had to know.

"How you think I know? I felt 'em."

"Where?"

"In Sinman's room. Where you think?"

I shut up.

And clucking like the old maid she was, Miss Fronnie got to her knees and began to cut off the legs of Charlie's pants just above the knee. The two made a vivid picture. A Logan tableau. Charlie, a warrior giant, with a beautiful old handmaiden at his knees.

CHAPTER 12

IT WAS A HOT Monday morning and I had put in a whole weekend at Lundy's. I was carrying plenty of money and felt like drinking with Charlie so I went down to the Sinman's room.

"No, the Blind Gladiator is not with us for the nonce," Sinman said. "Ever so often a wealthy matron drives up in her Continental and whisks him away. I am afraid the 'buck nigra' will always be with us as well as the other more obvious aspects of slavery."

"Damn if I don't miss the maniac already," I said.

"I know you do. Charlie to you is very much like a toddler's blanket. And Charlie has a penchant for toying with death; it hypnotizes you. You can never stay away from Charlie for long. You are afraid to miss his demise so to speak. Even though you think it cannot come. But I must admit that Charlie's death most certainly will be called unexpected."

"Are you saying that Charlie won't be killed?"

"Oh no. But in some ways Charlie's death is foreordained. He is to die a warrior's death. He has extracted that promise from life. Fate promises nothing to squares."

I sighed and wondered if this was going to be one of *those* kinds of bull sessions. It was only like a puny rebellion, but I did attempt to ward off the Sinman by saying, "I see where we might have a strike by the Welfare workers. Sounds bad to me."

"The Logan will survive. Winos and junkies receive only a tiny portion of their daily needs from Welfare. It is more appropriate that you worry about the investigators. *They* are the true recipients of Welfare."

"Why go to the trouble to say that foolishness about college-trained sociologists?"

"They are neither college trained nor sociologists. It is true that an investigator must at some time have received a degree from an accredited college, but it can be in anything. Music, agriculture, shoemaking even—if nigra colleges still teach it. I was an investigator for a while. We were not allowed to do any social work; and we did not know how anyway. A social investigator's work involves only clerking, filing and spying."

"Why did you quit? Drugs?"

"I was asked to leave. My supervisor said I identified too closely with my clients."

"You probably did too. Hell. I bet you wanted to tell the commissioner how to do it."

"I wanted to tell the commissioner of Welfare how not to do it. You see, we have a national problem. I like to call it the college Mafia. We have a surfeit of college graduates who are actually murderous in their vicious muscling in on everyone else's problems."

"Here we go again," I said.

"But what right does a twenty-year-old child from a well-to-do white family have to tell a poor Black woman of forty how to manage her home? What right has an alcoholic psychologist to tell a junky how to kick his habit? In the beginning, the depression was on, and so it might have been right to reserve the soft jobs for college graduates. But this is today. A college graduate no longer has a right to live off Welfare. Every Welfare investigator should be hired directly from our relief rolls. Junkies should administer all drug abuse programs. You are just as intelligent as Rockefeller, do you think you know enough about drugs to help a junky? And you most certainly know more about drugs than Rocky.

"We have building inspectors who don't know what a building is. We have health inspectors who don't know what health is. You'd be surprised to know how many people make their living by *serving* the poor. And these college-trained muscle men will kill off all the junkies, all unwed mothers, all the poverty-stricken, before they'll give up their lush jobs. I've told you time and again that meth is kept from junkies simply and only because a lot of college-trained fools will lose their jobs if meth is made available to the general public."

"Have you got the nerve to tell me that a dope-crazed fiend can straighten out another dope-crazed fiend better than a drunken psychiatrist can?" I asked with all the sarcasm I could summon.

"A junky simply cannot tell the truth. Truth does not exist in a junky's world. To him, truth is slag from the smelting furnace. In the burning crucible of his world of hustling only two things are important when you tell anybody anything. He either tells a person what that person *wants* to believe or he tells that person what *he* wants that person to believe. So what need does your junky have for truth? A psychiatrist cannot work with a person like that. A shrink must have truth. Facts. And psychiatrists know this; that is why I hate your quack shrinks."

"You can throw chicken shit in the fan all day long, can't you?" I said.

"What occurs first in your mind when you enter that building with nothing but employment offices in it down on Warren Street?"

"I don't know. I guess I wonder why they have so many jobs available and we still have so many men out of work. I dunno."

"Yes. And if you were the Welfare commissioner you would immediately realize that all those job openings are not filled because the men swarming in and out of those employment offices do not have the money to buy those jobs, or they do not have the chefs' knives or the plumbers' tools, et cetera. So as commissioner you would set up a fund to loan temporarily indigent persons all the money necessary to gain suitable employment. Why can't the present Welfare commissioner think of that too?"

I could only grunt and I most certainly cannot tell you what that grunt denoted.

But the Sinman was now in high gear. "As Blind Charlie says: we have a vast army in our midst. It is an unemployed army, a conquered army. They are our prisoners of war. We only think in terms of food and shelter when it is our true moral obligation to repatriate these people. Why not a thousand-dollar bonus to everyone who will return to his original home town?"

"Well, the trouble with that is that most of those you wish to repatriate cannot go back to their homes. They are junkies and they cannot go very far away from their sources of heroin."

Sinman nodded. "And that brings me to New York's need for an internal possession law. The so-called Christian penalty for having heroin in the bloodstream should rightly be death. Every accused felon should be given a blood test within two hours after his apprehension. If that test shows heroin in his system he should be executed forthwith. That is the only sane and moral way to fight drug addiction. But America is still in the lynching stage."

Then, just like a crazy old woman, Sinman reached into a brand-new bag. "What is your excuse for staying involved with Lina?"

"Who says I'm involved?"

"You have allowed yourself to be made a complete fool. For two months now you have allowed yourself to be covered with her droppings."

"I only let her hang around. I don't go with her or anything. Half the time I forget she's even around. But Lina needs me."

"No, she doesn't."

"She does. And I don't care what anybody thinks. It's important as hell to be needed. Did Gloria need me? Who else but Lina needs me? So I'm supposed to kick her out to gain the approval of that passel of junkies and winos out there in the lobby?"

"This is not the time for melodramatics. Gloria will be out in a day or two. Gloria is a wonderful, kind and generous woman, but do you think for one minute that she is going to allow herself to compete with the likes of Lina for your affections?"

"Okay. Okay," I said resignedly. It never occurred to me that Gloria might not even return to the Logan. I only knew that the Sinman was right: I had to get rid of Lina. But how? You just don't toss seventy-pound cripples out by the scruff of their necks.

Sinman accurately read my thoughts. "I don't think you realize that I now know much more about Lina than you do," he began. "She is a psychosomatic who will not go abroad without a companion. Neither will she sleep without one. It is also true that arthritis has given Lina a peculiar gait, but she can walk anywhere she chooses unassisted. But since she will not, all you have to do is to take her to her room and leave her there. She will find a sleeping companion before night falls."

"I only let her sleep with me," I mumbled like an ass.

"Why bother to lie? We both know the truth."

"Well, goddamit! Everybody's got a right to their kicks, haven't they? Did I ever tell you not to use heroin? Why should I deny her a little bit of pleasure?"

"Yes, but not from you. I am a strict segregationist. Let Lina return to her own kind."

"I hear rumblings of a race riot all around," I said, deliberately ending all talk about Lina. "I hear a fool cop shot a kid for nothing. Why don't they give those psychos an examination before giving them a gun and a uniform?"

"This riot talk will pass. But you should never speak of them as being riots. Here in New York we have Black-Irish incidents which the Jew inevitably pays for."

"For Chrissakes," I muttered.

"But can you tell me why a Georgia sharecropper always comes North to take part in these incidents? I resent this business of a farmless farmer streaking through the streets yelling that he is come to burn things down for me. If he must burn, let him burn Georgia and Alabama."

"So who's to protest for us? You?"

"With all due conceit, I believe that I can offer better leadership than those plowless fools who have traded in their overalls for dashikis. You Northern Black intellectuals are just a little bit too reluctant for me. If there is to be an incident you should create it. And if you don't want a rebellion you should prevent it."

"You don't think I'm crazy enough to go out and tell those knife freaks to stop looting, do you?"

"Our Black intelligentsia likes to yell home rule, community control, self-government, the Black vote. To rule is to lay down the law to your inferiors. But the Black man lets his inferiors do all the talking to whitey."

"You're really working out of a fruit and nuts bag today, aren't you?" I said.

"I am just sick and tired of Blackie's excuses. In fact, I am getting very tired of Blackie. Slavery ended a century ago but it is still the

Black man's crutch. How many Jews are on Welfare just because Hitler happened to enslave some of their relatives twenty some years ago? Black is Beautiful is just another excuse for failure. Now we are too Black and Beautiful to sweep our sidewalks, to arrest our junkies, even to teach ourselves our *own* history. What right has a Black student to ask a white college to let him study Black history? The clowns should know what their forefathers did before they ever even heard what a college was!"

"You ain't funny."

"I know it. And there is nothing funny in this rage to negate."

"Huh?"

"The Black man and woman refuse to exert their personalities in their own right. They have a rage to negate. This is the age of Black negation. Look at our women. The Black woman thinks that whitey's eyes are upon her at all times. Even in bed. So her sex life is nothing but an attempt to negate what she thinks the white man thinks of her. The Black woman lives a daily lie, trying to disprove a lie. She has totally renounced her male as a sexual partner. Every Black woman I have gone to bed with in the last three years has crawled into bed murmuring, 'I don't really like sex'! Now this is a *race* problem that only we Black men can solve. Whitey is certainly not going to solve it for us."

"Yeah," I said wearily, bitterly, "I know. And if you are right—and maybe this time you are—what we need is for a cracker senator to get up in the Senate and state that all Black women are lesbians. Then Black gals would stop all this foolishness."

"The ingestion of heroin and cocaine is a sexual experience, you know," Sinman said. "Is it any wonder that so many of our women are drug addicts?"

Soon after this I began to tire of the Sinman's tirades. That's what they were—tirades, even if they were couched in his genteel and old-fashioned rhetoric.

I decided to go up and lie down after I left the Sinman's room.

"Sid?" Jinny called as soon as I entered 5-C.

"Yeah?"

"C'mere. I want you to see." And she burst out laughing. I went to her door and looked in. She was really cracked up and couldn't stop laughing. At last she stopped a moment and gasped, "Look in the frig. These goddam junkies just won't quit with their beautiful shit. S'help me, only the junkies are really cool around here. And where were you when all the excitement was going on?"

"I've been down to the Sinman's. What excitement?"

"*Our* junkies, the Logan's junkies, stole a side of beef off the grocer's delivery truck. He goes down and picks up his own meat, you know. So he and the cops come busting in the hotel. And naturally they makes a beeline to the sixth floor because that's where the action naturally is at. Even the pigs *and* the grocer know that. But the junkies are down in the basement. They've got the super's ax and are chopping up that meat. And then the nervy bastids come up and follow the cops through the building until all the meat is sold."

"What the hell are you talking about?"

"I mean the cops start working down from the sixth floor. They go from room to room, asking who's seen anything of a side of beef. They figure that nobody can hide a side of beef in a hotel room so all they do is stand in the doorway and dig each room. See? But it's those nervy goddam junkies I can't get over. Why, just as soon as the cops finish looking on one floor the junkies come right along behind them selling the meat."

I went to the refrigerator and looked. There was a huge chunk of crudely hacked meat in it. Jinny had had to remove one of the shelves to make room for it.

"It cost two dollars," Jinny said, still chuckling. "You, me and Joey and Paula can eat off that for two weeks and still have some left for hash. Lawd. If it wasn't for the junkies we squares would be uptight for real in this man's Logan."

CHAPTER 13

WHEN BLIND CHARLIE returned from his tour of duty all hell broke loose in the Logan. Wine flowed in all his "fren's'" rooms, and Charlie personally saw to it that two junkies had to go to St. Luke's emergency ward to be treated for cuts and contusions. But neither died. Several winos had to go as well because of the deleterious effects of too much wine without food. Lina did not have to go.

On the fourth night junkies robbed him. That night Charlie's wine told him to stretch out on the foyer floor in front of 5-C. Naturally the junkies had to step over him to make their purchases from Leah. And I guess you know by now that it would have been a violation of the Logan's code of conduct for either Leah or Ray to wake me so I could wake Charlie.

And those junkies who did the job took no chances, I heard. First they went to the basement and got the super's ax. Then one of them stood over the sleeping Charlie, ready to split his head open if he so much as moved, while the other two junkies rifled his pockets.

Charlie was fit to be strait-jacketed. "Goddam you, Sid! What the hell you go and let me get robbed for?" he demanded over and over again.

"I didn't even know you were out there," I kept repeating.

"You could have *looked*. I had me over a hundred dollars when I got back here and five days later I'm broke just on account of you. You're supposed to be my fren'. And what good's a fren' what won't even watch over you whilst you is sleeping?"

"We still your friends, Mistah Blind Charlie," Lina said. "You jes' sit and wait. Ah'm gonna go borrow a dollah from Leah." And she hobbled out of the room.

"How come she's so tight with Leah?" Charlie wanted to know.

"She's got everybody in 5-C buffaloed," I grumbled. "Last night

I finally got around to telling her that I wasn't going to let her sleep in here any more. I told her to go home. So she went and got J&J and Leah and Ray and all four of them starts giving me hell. Those bulldikers called me everything but a child of God for wanting to kick a cripple out in the middle of the night. And it wasn't even eight o'clock because J&J were still up. And that damn Joey kept yelling something about 'after doing his dirt!' I wanted to go through the floor after that. Hell. If they're so crazy about her, why don't they take care of her? Gloria is coming home soon, and I can't have Lina following me all over the building after that." I didn't like the look on Charlie's face and so I turned hypocrite for his benefit. "And she even wants me to screw her," I added.

"Well, why don't you?"

"I can't. She's crippled. And she's leeched onto me enough as it is."

"What's that got to do with it?"

"What's what got to do with it?"

"Everything you said. What difference it make effen she is crippled?"

"Goddamit, I don't know. What the hell are you asking me for?"

"You the one that said it, that's why. Ain't no woman gonna ask me twice for a little favor like that. What's the matter with you anyhow? You ain't trying to run no beauty contest in the Logan, is you?"

"That's not the point," I said wearily. "I've got to get rid of her and screwing her isn't going to help."

"Don't be too sure of that. Lots of men can get a gal in a bed oncet, but let 'em try the next time," Charlie said. He paused and rubbed his chin. "Effen she wasn't such a bag of bones I'd try a little of that myself."

"Who's running a beauty contest now?"

"But I could use her bed," Charlie said obliquely. "I can't find Sandy nowhere. She must be dead or in the House of D."

"Well, why don't you call up and find out?"

"What the hell I'm gonna spend a whole dime on a junky for?"

Charlie roared indignantly. "Is you crazy for real? It ain't none of my business effen she jumped off the Empire State Building. Sandy ain't none of my business. All I ever did was sleep in her funky room."

"So what the hell were you going to buy her a douche for?"

"Wal—you said you never screwed Lina, didn't you?"

I was still muttering to myself when Lina came back. She handed me a dollar and said, "Git half and half this time, honey. That ole Spur makes you git drunk too quick sometimes."

"That's the truth," Charlie said. "We needs something different for a change."

For the first time since I had been in the Logan I felt resentment. Always the runner. But who else was there to go? Charlie owed the liquor store owner too much, and Lina simply refused to go outside the hotel by herself. For one brief moment I thought of insisting that Lina go, but that idea vanished in a flash of disgust. But this time I was glad I went because I picked up a few juicy morsels in the lobby.

"They say that Kingfish was one of the guys who robbed you," I told Charlie time I got back.

"Take me to the sonofabitch! I'm gonna collect back every cent and kill him too!"

"Somebody tried that already," I told him. "There were four junkies in on it. I don't know if it was before or after they divvied up the money, but anyhow, they sent Kingfish up to the sixth floor for some heroin and do you know that that damn fool comes back and palms some of his lemons off on his own partners in crime?"

"I tell you junkies ain't never got no smarts," Charlie said.

"And on top of that Kingfish breaks bad when the guys brace him. So one of them goes out and gets his crazy brother, who immediately shoots Kingfish in the stomach. And that Kingfish is still so dumb and greedy that he won't let anybody hold the good heroin he's got on him. So when they undress him in the hospital they finds this narco and so now he's got to go to court if he ever gets out of the hospital."

"Hope he dies," Charlie said. "Running 'round robbing poor

ole blind folks like that. Why don't them bastids rob somebody what ain't helpless like I am?"

"So it looks like your money is gone forever," I said. "And the rest of those junkies aren't thinking about coming around here until that shooting business cools a bit."

"You don't know your junkies," Charlie grumbled. "I bet they never even left the building. And ain't no pigs interested in who shot a junky. Of course when they get the bullet from the hospital and find out it came out of the same gun that killed a whitey some time back, *then* they'll get on the ball. Then they'll even be asking me and you questions."

All of a sudden Lina jumped to her feet. "Ah'm gonna buy me some lye!" she shouted.

"Whoa thar. Whoooee. Hold that fool gal, Sid. What the hell's the matter with her anyhow?"

Lina had quietly sat back down and looked as if she had not done a single thing out of the way.

"You got her, Sid?" Charlie asked anxiously.

"Yeah. She isn't doing anything now."

"Well, what's the matter with her? Who she gonna hit in the face with lye?"

It was like that business with the elephant and the mouse. As far as I was concerned Charlie was scared to death. "Who you going to buy lye for?" I asked Lina.

"Nobuddy." Her face was a mask of secrecy.

"Nobuddy, eh?" I mimicked her.

"Ah wants mah money," Lina muttered.

"What goddam money? Haven't you been spending yourself broke every Checkday?"

"Ah gives him mah money," Lina said in that meek and childlike voice she could affect whenever she wanted to. "And he takes it and doan' gimme nuthin'. And now him whut down there claim he doan' know nuthin' about it. But Ah'm gonna git me some lye dough."

Trying hard to keep my cool, I asked, "Lina, what in the world are you talking about?"

"Aboot mah money Ah give him."

"Who the hell is *him?*" I yelled.

"Him down in de office."

"What goddam office?"

"Dis orfice."

"Don't you hit that gal!" Charlie said.

After I had muttered a string of curses I tried to unravel the "hims." "You sound like you gave somebody downstairs in the office some money," I said. "But you know damn well that you haven't had any money to give anybody to hold for you. So what are you talking about?"

"Nemmine," Lina said.

And it was the secretive look on Lina's face that suddenly made me wonder just how much I really knew about Lina and her affairs. For weeks now I had treated her more like a pet, a little puppy, rather than a real human being. Sure, I had been very nice to her. Or maybe you would want to call it charitable, but be it as it may, I actually had paid no attention to her at all.

And Lina had done nothing to make me pay much attention to her. I had been working fairly regularly. Some mornings she dogged my footsteps, but more often she spent her time with the coterie of wine drinkers up in Mr. Johnson's room. And of late she had begun to get pretty thick with not only J&J but Leah and Ray as well. Why those two lesbian dope pushers allowed her to sit around in their room I'll never know.

Furthermore, whenever wine mellowed Lina she would prattle like a baby, and I paid no more attention to her than I would to a baby. I took it for granted that she had been sending her rent over to her hotel, but now the look on her face made me wonder.

"Don't you still pay rent over 'yonder'?" I asked sarcastically.

"No. Yes. Ah live heah." That was three separate and distinct answers and for a moment I believed all three. Then she added, "He took mah money, but he ain't never gimme no room."

"What damn *he?*"

"He downstairs."

"Where did you get the money to give this *him-he?*"

"He cash' mah check last time."

"No *he* didn't either," I said wearily. "*He* only cashes HE tenants' checks. He is very strict about that."

"He cash' mines."

"Anybody that can borrow a dollar from Leah can do anything," Charlie said like a warning.

I grunted. "So you cashed your check downstairs and gave one of the managers some money down on a room whenever one became available. Right?"

Lina inclined that loaf of dark bread she had for a head. So I pressed on. "How much did you give him and did you pay your rent 'round yonder?"

"Ah ain't gonna live there no mo'," Lina grumbled.

"Don't you know you can get put off Welfare if you don't have a rent receipt to show your investigator?"

"Nemmine," Lina said and it seemed to me she was dropping the matter.

But I didn't want to drop it; I saw a way out of it all. "You don't sleep in this room one more night," I said righteously. "You're not going to have folks around here blaming me for getting you kicked off Welfare. You go right this minute and see if they've got a room for you in here."

"Him whut's down there say he doan' know nuthin' aboot it."

"Come on. I'm going down with you."

"Ah ain't goin' no mo'. You go 'head."

"How the hell can I get the room or your money back if you aren't with me?" I yelled. "And I'm not even going to ask if you demanded a receipt."

"Ah didun't want no receet. Ah jes' lose it."

"Well, come on then."

Without another word Lina got off the bed and stood ready to follow me, but from the expression on her face you would have thought I was about to lead her to the gallows.

"We'll be back in a couple of minutes, Charlie," I said. "The wine is on the dresser."

"Yeah. Go ahead and get that fool gal straightened out. Don't worry about me."

When we got down to the office window Lina pointed to old man Epstein. He saw her pointing and came to the window.

"You never came back for your room," he admonished her. "And now I don't have a single thing to give you."

"Ah doan' want no room," Lina mumbled. "Ah wants mah money back."

He looked at her queerly but said, "Certainly." And then, "That was a deposit. You know that, don't you? If I wanted I could keep that money." Then the fool looked at me. "You've gotta pay an overcharge for her sleeping in your room."

"Like hell I will!" I shouted. "She don't live with me. She's got a room around the corner and you know it. And don't you ever ask me for no rent for nobody but me as long as you live, you hear me?" I was trembling with anger because this man knew my shame.

I turned away and a whirlwind rushed into my arms and it was at least one full second before I realized that it was Gloria. She was hugging and kissing me as greedily as the first time she'd ever done so. But this time it was really beautiful, only Lina was hanging onto me like a toothache.

"I gotta go by a friend's house and get some fresh things to put on," Gloria said rapidly. "I know how they pack your things in here when they put them in storage. I'll be back in an hour."

Five more kisses and she was gone. I wondered if she'd noticed Lina.

"Who dat?" Lina asked.

"My woman."

"Nossuh."

"Nossuh? How do you know?"

"Ah ast Mist' Blind Charlie and he say no."

"How the devil could you ask him questions about a woman you didn't even know existed until this very minute?"

"Nemmine."

"Well, I'm telling you like it is for the last time. You got to stop hanging around in my room like you have been doing. That was

Gloria and she's my woman. So you've got to go sleep where you live from now on. Understand?"

"Ah'm gonna go to mah sistah's."

"I thought she beat you up and took your check?"

"Nemmine."

Upstairs again, Charlie hollered, "You get that money back?"

"Yeah, she got it back, but no fault of hers."

"What you get this time?"

"Nothing," I told him. "Gloria rushed into the lobby while we were at the window. But she ran right back out again to go get some clean clothes from somewhere. She'll be right back, though, she said. And with all that I forgot about going to the store."

"So ole Gloria got herself loosed, eh?"

"That's right. And I know you know how I feel."

"Lina?"

"Yassuh, Mist' Blind Charlie?"

"What you gonna do now?"

"Nemmine. Mah sistah's gonna take care of me."

"I said you was lying when you first showed up around here," Charlie said.

Then Lina had an afterthought. "You want to live with me, 'round yonder, Mist' Blind Charlie?"

"Ah ain't lived with nothing like you in my life!" And Charlie's voice was loud and fearful.

I jeered. "Thought you could use her room so fast?"

"Yeah. But not her," Charlie said emphatically. "Besides, I don't mess with these women with black tongues. I'm scared of them. I just don't have no use for a liar."

Jinny came to the door. "When the devil have you been to work, Sid?" I guess she asked because I blew the weekend, drinking with Charlie.

"I can go in Sunday," I said. "Don't worry." I didn't tell her about Gloria; I thought it would be a nice little surprise for her and Joey.

"So that means I've got to do some extra hustling," Jinny said cheerfully. "You're getting to be a boss pimp, junior."

When she walked away Lina got up and followed her. Charlie and I sat and talked about Gloria and things until Lina came back in and sat on the bed beside me. It was pretty quiet for a while.

Then Lina shouted, "No sich thing!" in a voice that was as deep as Bessie Smith's.

"*Now* what are you yelling about?" I exclaimed.

She looked at me as if I was crazy. After a few moments of staring at me like that she said, "Wal—Ah ain't gonna do it."

"You're not going to what?"

"Ah ain't gonna sleep with you no mo'. So there!" She got up and hobbled out of the room.

"Wonder effen that little fool thought Gloria was gonna let her be catting around forever?" Charlie mused.

In a minute Jinny came in. "Since you got your ass way up on your back, Mister Bastid, you can at least give us cab fare," she said coldly.

"Cab fare for what?" I yelled. "I don't have any money and you know it. Cab fare for what?"

"I've got to take Lina to her sister's since Mister Gawd Almighty has put her out."

"Well, why the hell don't you take her there and stop bugging me? She just got ten bucks from Epstein. So why you got to get on me?"

"I just wanted to see if you had the decency to at least pay her fare after making a fool out of her."

"Get the hell out of my face, will you, please?" I yelled.

With cold hauteur Jinny turned and stalked away. Lina followed her.

"Wonder where that sister lives?" Charlie murmured. "Bet she lives around the corner somewheres. Black sure can lie beautifully."

"Damn right. And she got the nerve to ask for cab fare."

We both sort of relaxed, and Charlie was almost dozing off when Ray came and stood in the doorway. From the little I had seen of Ray, I had formed pretty much the same kind of dislike I formerly had for Leah. In many ways you could say that Leah functioned normally. Ray didn't. Late at night when I got in from work Ray would always be standing in the kitchen, waiting for customers to knock. Always reading the same tattered paperback, nodding and doped to the gills. As time went by that dog-eared book began to fascinate me, and I eventually found out that it was not only the same book she was reading but the same page. The page had a burn on it where she'd laid a cigarette at some time when she went back to her room for more bags. Now a junky woman who can stand up for eight hours, reading the same page over and over again for weeks on end, is a little bit more than I can stand.

And Ray was so very lazy she didn't even come out of her room to go to the bathroom during the day. I was on the verge of asking her what she was doing up and what the hell she wanted when she said, "Gimme a drink of wine, Sid."

Ray was even uglier than Leah. Both had those loose rubbery lips that seem to be the hallmark of so many junkies, but Ray was fat in a most obscene way. She was sloppy whereas Leah was neat as a pin.

So when a repulsive woman like Ray, whom you really don't know, demands a drink in the tone of voice she used you are very happy to tell her that you don't have one. And so I told her. But I did have to ask, "Since when did you start drinking wine?"

"I haven't started yet, but I am," she said. "There's a panic on, and what little bit of stuff we got left is weak as hell. I figger a little wine will help give me a better buzz. Those addicts down on Eighth Avenue drink sneaky pete all the time to boost their high."

I knew what a panic was. Ever so often there comes a shortage of heroin in Harlem as the result of the Mafia holding out for higher prices from their Black flunkies in the racket. Prices shoot up overnight, but they do not skyrocket for long because in a day or two there is no heroin to be had at any price. This is when all but a few foresighted junkies go through agonizing periods of withdrawal symptoms.

During these panics junkies commit their most atrocious crimes. Most of them are sadistic sex crimes because after the first three or four days of torture the junky's ragged nervous system starts to bedevil him with truly maniacal sex drives and urges. Many are capable of raping and killing their own sisters during a prolonged panic. Alcoholics sometimes have the same sex thing after a few days of drying out, but I know it must be mild compared to the junky's excruciation.

"Leah's connection is out," Ray said, "and so I'm gonna stretch my fixes with wine from now on."

"Well, we is broke," Charlie said. "Why don't you spring with one of those big fat dollars you got in your titties there?"

"I'd like to loan you, but I'm scared until after this panic's over. Leah ain't holding very much and there's no telling." She turned to go and then turned back. "You remember that little light girl named Frances from the third floor? Real skinny and dumb? She lived in 3-B-6, and whenever you answered the door she'd tell you to hold it open until she got back or something stupid like that."

"Yeah, I know her. Why?"

"She's dead. OD."

"All junkies oughta die!" Charlie bellowed. "In fact, they *is* dead. Only folks takes too long to get around to burying them."

"Who the hell asked you anything?" Ray snapped. "When I want information I call the *Daily News.* I don't need no advice from a lazy blind bastid like you."

"Nobody got to give me permission to tell a damn fool dead person they is dead," Charlie retorted. "Now will you please get the hell outa here with your stinking Black ass full of dope?"

"Wherever I go to in this world and the next it won't be where a blind meatball told me to go."

"You right. I shouldn't-a tole you to go nowheres. How can you tell a dead person to go somewheres?"

"Go fuck yourself."

"I will before I fucks a junky bitch."

"Why, you blind motherfucker!"

"Now is that any way to talk to a poor ole blind man?"

"You ain't old. And the only reason you are broke is because you're too damn lazy to get out and hustle. You got a natural-born beg to put down. We got a blind customer that works the subway.

He's got a twenty-dollar habit he takes care of with ease. And you, you blind meatball, you can't even support a sneaky pete habit. And you realize he got to pay for someone to hit him? You blind bastids got it made. I can't get on no subway and beg my way through the whole train and get off in half an hour with enough bread to buy two fixes. And the pigs leave you alone even if you do have to occasionally lay something on them. But every damn thing I do the bastids want to put me in jail for."

"I got pride!" Charlie shouted.

"Pride didn't stop you from asking me, did it? And shut up now. I'm not going to get all upset and lose what little bit of high I got."

"Pour poor ole Blind Charlie a drink, Sid," Charlie said mournfully. "This here junky woman got me so shook up I done already lost *my* high."

"Yeah, but my high don't cost no goddam little fifty cents," Ray said.

"You know we don't have any money or wine," I said to Charlie.

"I'll loan you fifty cents if you'll make this meatball shut up," Ray said.

"Charlie?" I said. "Will you get off Ray's back if she loans us fifty cents?"

"Hell, yes. And get Spur this time."

For some reason Ray was gone when I got back, and if she thought I was going to bring her a drink she had another thought coming.

"Johnnie-Lee owes me a dollar," Charlie said after the pint was gone. "She and her old man are both bad pay, but mebbe we can get fifty cents outa her."

"Isn't she that real ugly old woman from the sixth floor that gets drunk and cusses out everybody in the lobby every Saturday night?"

"There's lots around here that fits that description, but mebbe we is talking about the same ole bag. She's got a damn nice husband though. Young boy. He came up from Georgia about four years ago and he been making a name for hisself ever since. They got married right here in the lobby. I was best man."

"Yeah?" After that bit about getting married in the lobby of the Logan you know I wasn't much interested, although I did wonder for a minute what Charlie considered a young man. Johnnie-Lee was well over sixty, so how could she be married to a young boy? Even if the Logan did go in for May-December alliances. Furthermore, Johnnie-Lee was a Welfare bitch if there ever was one. And she was married to a young boy who was making it?

Johnnie-Lee apologized for being broke time we got there. She guided Charlie to her easy chair with a sort of flourish. Uninvited, I sat down at the rickety table piled high with books. But what books. Many of them were "vanity books" or pseudo-scientific titles; all were so much garbage. There was even a copy of the *Bobbsey Twins*. And I just knew they had all been bought from a Salvation Army thrift shop for a dime apiece. Three for a quarter.

"Don't sit thar!"

I looked up from reading the book titles to see Johnnie-Lee glaring at me.

"Doan' nobuddy but my husbin' sit at that thar desk." Her voice was a fine mélange of anger at me and pride in her husband. "Them's all textbooks. Ah doan' 'low nobuddy to interfere with his school things."

"Yeah," Charlie said. "Don't nobody in this whole hotel interfere with College Joe's schooling."

I was all choked up with surprised horror, but I managed to gasp, "Is College Joe your husband?"

The old woman drew herself up huffily. "Everybuddy know who *I* am."

"But he's supposed to be going to Columbia," I said.

"He be," Johnnie-Lee said.

I said no more. Charlie and Johnnie-Lee gossiped away and I stared again at those books that even a Holy Roller church school could not use. It had never occurred to me that all this College Joe business was some kind of running joke in the Logan. But why had everybody put me on? And what the hell was the joke?

Then College Joe walked in and Charlie introduced us. Naturally I flipped and started up the wall. College Joe was barely more than twenty years old although he was well over six feet. And stupid-looking? This Georgia boy would have caught hell getting out of a nursery school for retarded toddlers in Waycross, Georgia. I flipped over and over as I stared at him.

"How's school, boy?" Charlie asked in a hearty voice.

"Fine, Charlie. Fine as wine," College Joe said. "Seems like those whitey professors can't understand a Black man who got brains. I ain't boasting but sometimes they act like they never seen nobody like me before. But anyways I always got my homework done and so they can't flunk me."

"What do you major in?" I asked as if his answer would somehow end this insanity.

"Psychology. I made my fraternity last week." And Joe rightly grinned with pride. "You know, folks around here claimed I couldn't make one of them whitey frats, but I showed them. How could those crackers blackball me with the grades I get? And that initiation was something else. They tried to wear my Black butt out, but I took it."

Between the wine I had drunk and Joe's sincerity I began to waver. I have never seen one of these so-called mad geniuses. So it was possible. In fact, it had to be possible. No man would dare tell a lie that could be so easily disproved.

"What frat did you make?" I asked.

"Cum Laudee."

"Huh?"

"Cum Laudee. That's practically the best. Next year I'm gonna make the best."

"Which one is that?" I was insane with fear.

"I already been nominated. It's Magna Cum Laudee."

I walked to the door; if I had to puke at least I'd be out in the hall. "Let's go cop a beg from the Sinman," I said to Charlie. He got up and we left.

"How could anybody and everybody be so goddam motherfucking ignorant?" I yelled as soon as we got out of earshot.

"Who's ignorant?" Charlie demanded.

"College Joe! Everybody in this goddam hotel!" I shouted. I was so angry my knees were knocking. "How in hell could every so-called intelligent person in the rathole believe that that fool could ever enter an Ivy League school? Tell me. Goddamit, will you please tell?"

"All I can tell you is that he goes," Charlie said in a voice intended to end the discussion.

"That Georgia farm boy don't have enough sense to be stupid," I yelled. "And those books on that table are trash! Do you hear me? I said *trash*. And I know what I'm talking about."

"Don't tell me they ain't," Charlie thundered, angrily agitated. "When that boy opens them books everybody on this sixth floor quiets down. Don't nobody dare disturb him and his studies. That's how much folks around here appreciate somebody who's trying to make something of themselves. But you. You and your stupid little ass gotta go making little of the wisest scholar the Logan ever had. I thought you was a better man than *that*. But now I knows: you just can't ever educate a damn fool. And you is all the proof I need."

"And people talk about Black Power," I muttered.

"What the hell has Black Power got to do with that boy going to college?" Charlie practically screamed.

"Nothing."

No sooner had we got back to the room than Jinny strutted in with a magnificent sneer on her lips. "Lina and her sister said to thank you for all your kind hospitality."

"So you did take her to her sister's, eh?" I said, ignoring that sneer.

"And her sister's got more sense than you'll ever have."

"Oh yeah? What she do?"

"Welfare. Welfare, Mister Bastid."

"She's on Welfare and got more brains than I got, eh?"

"She's a receptionist down there."

"How come she's not at work then?"

"It's none of my business, but I'll go ask if you insist."

"So what she look like?"

"What do you care? Haven't you done Lina dirty enough? Or you want to run through the whole family?"

More to remind Jinny that she and Joey were heavily in my debt and that people she owed money to shouldn't be insulted, I said, "I need a dollar."

"Okay if you pay me back Sunday night when you come from work."

"How many times have I asked you clowns to repay me?" I hollered.

"You got a job. At least you got a job when you're sober."

I was so mad at everything and everybody I marched two blocks past the liquor store before I realized what I was doing.

CHAPTER 14

I BOUGHT A QUART with the dollar and just for meanness Jinny snatched it from me, filled my iced-tea glass to the brim, and then marched out. There was not much more than a pint left so Charlie and I polished that off in no time. When the pint was gone Charlie left.

A little later there was a knock at the foyer door. Jinny answered. It was Gloria. She didn't waste any time on Jinny and came right to my room, but dear little Jin trotted right behind her with profuse greetings just as if she had not been raising hell about Lina less than an hour ago.

But Gloria was the same smart chick as before and soon got rid of Jinny.

"Aren't you going to ask if I'm mad at you?" I asked almost before Jinny closed the door.

"Well, are you?"

"No, but it seems like you should be more worried about it than you look."

She smiled complacently. "I don't think you are." Then her smile became slightly shamefaced. "No. You're really not."

"But what made you do it?"

"I had to, Sid. I was going for you in a big way and I couldn't make any mistakes. You were just that important to me."

"Do you know you're not making any sense?"

"I was going to come back and give the money to you and see if you hit me."

"Will you please tell me what that would prove?"

"You don't know, Sid, but it's like this: when I took my first shot of heroin and this pimp, who called himself schooling me, found out, he beat me something awful. He tore me up. I got a real Harlem whipping. One of those fancy jobs. Both my eyes were closed tight. I had busted ribs on both sides and there were knots on my forehead as big as his fist."

Gloria took a deep breath. "And I was not only sick from the beating, I was sick from that damn heroin. Sick as a bitch. But nobody had a kind word for me; nobody offered to let me stay with them except the junkies. They were all I had to turn to. That man drove me to the junkies. I don't think I'd ever have become a junky if Georgie had talked to me that night and been kind. I'd have never stuck another spike in my arm again. I got beat into being a junky, Sid. So I *had* to find out if you'd beat me or talk to me if I ever did wrong. I couldn't let things get out of control before I knew exactly what kind of man you were. And I had to know right away."

"So what have you found out?"

"I don't know, Sid," Gloria said wearily. "Something's always got to put shit in the game. You didn't write and so I *knew* where it was at. Honest, Sid, I prayed, but you never wrote and said not to worry. I knew I am and was unreasonable. After what you and I put down, what I did was pure dirt but I'm not an ordinary woman, Sid. You know that, don't you?"

"So what are you trying to tell me? You fell in love in jail?"

"Yes. I don't really know, Sid. I don't really know. I know you're going to say I'm fruity as hell for bringing jailhouse love out in the street with me, but for a moment there I loved you so much it hurt. And I was scared, Sid. It's almost like I'm afraid of you, Sid. What do you really want me to do? Say to you?"

I wasn't sore. I wasn't jealous. It didn't really even hurt. All I knew was that I loved this beautiful girl and that someday she would realize that we were long since doomed to each other. There was no rush so what was there to say?

"I want something, Sid. I don't know what it is. I've had narco, whiskey, a thousand men, what else is there for me to try but a goddam bulldiker?"

I remembered the Sinman's advice. "You'll be back. You really can't go away. We are all we've got," I said.

Gloria's eyes glistened. "That's why I love you, Sid. Like when we first hit it off; I knew I could say anything I wanted to you and you'd never make me feel ashamed." She put her arms around my neck and buried her face. Her voice was full of some kind of tears. "I tell you what, Sid. I need you; I've got to have you to talk to. And you want trim, don't you? So we both get what we want and no arguments."

"Anything you say. But did you have to state the facts so baldly?"

She began to undress. "Another reason I think I stayed on drugs as long as I did is because I've been ashamed of my body for a long time now. I'm through apologizing. Just give me this last chance, Sid. I've got to prove to myself that jailhouse love is nowhere. Then I'll be ready to be your woman." She was nude now, and lovelier than God ever intended, I'm sure.

"Maybe we shouldn't," I said. "I don't think you understand exactly how much you mean to me, Gloria. I've been drunk as hell pretty often since you've been away. And now I'm thinking that it's being so moody over you that caused those drunks. I don't know how cool I can keep if I allow myself to screw you, knowing you're going to run from my bed to a stud. I'll be uptight all the time. Maybe we better not."

"Bullshit! I'm a whore that needs you. You're a man. You can take me in your stride. You've *got* to. Dig?"

"Who are you going to live with? Me or her?"

"In the Village. She's got an apartment. She gets out a week from this Thursday. I'm going to stay with you until then."

"What's the matter? Don't she trust you with the keys?"

"She hasn't got 'em. They take everything away from you in the House of D, Sid. Until you get loosed. She can't even send me there to cut the air conditioning off. The super has no key and he probably wouldn't take my word for it anyhow if he did have a key."

"What's she in for?"

"Hustling. Call girl. They set a trap. But she looks like a little doll. Female as hell looking. Blonde. But the hell with her now. I'm with *you.* And I really haven't made up my mind at all, Sid. See what I mean?"

"No. Not exactly. She can satisfy you, can't she? And that's what it's all about. My love has reached the point where I don't even matter any more. The only thing that counts now is that you stop running from pillar to post. Want a drink?" I knew I could borrow some money from the Sinman.

"Yes, Sid. I want a whole lot of drinks, and in between we'll make love." She smiled oddly. "Maybe I forgot just how good a man can do that thing. And maybe I really won't want Butch after all when she gets loosed. How do you like that?"

I loved her for a long time and after that I went down to the Sinman's for a loan.

"I don't know," Gloria said the next morning. "I don't know at all. In the House of D everything seemed so simple, but now everything is mixed up."

"Don't try to tell me that a square like me can turn a chick on and take her away from a dike," I said, trying for the light touch.

"That's a bunch of superstitious crap men made up all by themselves," Gloria said. "If a lesbian could take a woman away from a man whenever she chose there wouldn't be any women living with men at all. Dig? And there's lots of square broads that go for jailhouse love while they're locked up but won't even speak to a stud once they're back in the street."

"How can a square broad get herself locked up?"

"Fucking with Welfare. You'd be surprised at all the church women in the House of D who thought they could cheat Welfare.

And there's lots of broads that killed their husbands; they had to most of the time. But when I used the word 'square' that time I meant girls who don't use heroin. Like right now I'm a square broad to the junkies. I thought you dug that. I mean, I thought you knew all junky broads go top and bottom and all around. In fact, a stone junky never knows what she is, a boy or girl, she's so fucked up. Ask Sinman if you don't believe me."

"You really believe that every stone junky is a freak?"

"I *know* it, Sid. That's why I'm going to take on Butch. I don't believe I'm a freak, not for real. And I know I'm not when I'm in your arms. But this is git-ready time. If I'm a freak I might as well forget you and everybody else and go back to heroin.

"But I just know I'm really straight, Sid. And I'm gonna prove it to myself once and for all." She smiled triumphantly. And then that hidden tigress in her showed. "When I come to you for real, Sid, I'm gonna be clean. So help me God, I'm gonna be the cleanest bitch that ever came to you and you'll never regret it!"

"Yeah," I said. A little choked up.

She gave a little pout. "The proof of what I'm saying is that I just can't relate with a woman. I don't believe any two women can relate. Not with each other. Me? I've got to have a man; a man's mind is always best to go by. I've got to have the use of your brains, Sid. Dig it? So I'm always your woman, but I'm not going to ask you to be my man. I've got no strings on you. Dig? But I'll live with this stud until I get me a bankroll together. Okay?"

There was no use kidding myself. A lonely-assed square like me was a fool to even think about quibbling over terms. Morals are fine, if you can afford them. I couldn't. At least I thought I couldn't. Besides, almost four months in the Logan had made me a realist.

"Let's go down to the Sinman's," Gloria suggested. "I'm going to borrow ten dollars and I'll give you what's left after we buy another fifth of scotch."

We hadn't been in the Sinman's room very long when he abruptly turned to Gloria and asked, "Have you ever run across a girl named Mildred Rowley in your travels?"

For some reason Gloria released my hand before she answered.

"Sure, Sinman. She's a nice kid, but she goes with Red Mike. I thought everybody knew she was one of his girls. In fact, she's his main whore."

Sinman frowned. "Red Mike is going to be hit in a few hours and so is Millie, I suppose. Don't go near her until funeral arrangements have been completed." He went to the hutch cabinet and took out a bottle of Cutty Sark and brought it to the organ. "What was she like? Have you ever done any business with her?"

Gloria made a little sound of defeat in her throat. "What do you want me to say? She's just another kid in the street, trying to make it. Sure. Me and her have double-dated a couple of johns now and then. She's down with it, got the rhythm and all. Once in a while when I was working the Village and thought I needed a fix and didn't want to come all the way back to Harlem I'd buy a bag from her. Red Mike always gave her a few bags to deal to the girls she knew. She never really pushed it or nothing, and she didn't sell lemons, if that's what you mean. Her stuff always took my sickness off."

Sinman said nothing so Gloria continued. "And she won't trick with nothing but white johns, but I don't guess you can really hold that against her; lots of girls do downtown. But why is Red Mike gonna get his now? He's been doing dirt all along and nobody's ever tried to kill him before."

"Mike owes his connection ten thousand dollars."

Gloria stared severely at the Sinman. "As dirty as Red Mike is, his own mother wouldn't trust him with ten cents, Sinman. And you know it. Now how in the world could anybody be dumb enough to trust him with ten Gs worth of narco? You've got it all wrong, Sinman. That can't be so."

Sinman turned from the window. "How he managed to get into his connection for that much I do not know, but it is true. Red Mike and Millie have not only done this stupid thing but they have told this connection to go to the devil. They won't pay, can't pay. In other words, they switched. Found a new source. And the idiots thought their new connection would furnish them protection. How could two grownups be so silly in concert?"

Gloria's lips protruded in disagreement. "It's not hard to get caught up in a bind like that, Sinman. Practically every night some cat I never even seen before comes up to me and wants to talk me into selling doogie for him on consignment. 'It's easy,' he says; 'don't deal to anybody you don't know personally.' And they stroke you and tell you you don't have to worry about some meatball coming up to you and threatening you because you're working his territory. That they'll protect you. They talk real smooth, Sinman."

"But you never went for the okey-doke," Sinman pointed out. "You knew that if what they said was true they would be so down with it that they wouldn't need your unskilled services. So how is it that Red Mike and Millie were so much more stupid? And they are not babes in Harlem, you know. Even the square knows that we in the life must honor our debts and promptly. The underworld has only one way to collect unpaid debts. There is no alternative. If this were not so, all junkies would be getting narcotics on consignment and then refusing to pay for them."

"But, gee, Sinman. Anybody can make a mistake once."

"For ten thousand dollars? Stop rationalizing the acts of those two fools. They were scum who had no right to be born. Even now some worthy person may have to go to prison for ridding the world of them. No hit is perfect, you know."

"I can't help it, Sinman," Gloria wailed. "Millie was pretty straight. And now that she's gonna die I can't think nothing but good of her. She goes to mass every Sunday before she goes in. Rain or shine. She's real religious, Sinman. Can't you help her? Only her, not Red Mike?"

"Death, when it comes, is always a natural phenomenon. No. Time has run out for those two."

"You ain't making no sense at all now," Gloria said succinctly.

I wondered how the Sinman's face could be so stormy-looking and still not look angry. It came to me that I had never seen him angry.

"Why do fools think they have been created by God?" Sinman demanded. "And they think they can do anything with impunity just as long as they go to church on Sunday and praise God for His handiwork."

"I'm not going to leave this hotel today," Gloria said heavily. "Loan me ten dollars, please, Sinman. Sid and I are going to stay put and just drink."

"Certainly," Sinman said, "but you must have a little more Cutty Sark with me before you leave."

Back in the room Gloria asked, "Do you believe like the Sinman that God is dead?"

"No. Why should I?"

"Well . . . it seems like God should have told Millie that you can't go owing a whitey gangster ten grand and tell him to go to hell. Looks like God owed her that much brains."

"It don't have to be that way exactly," I said, thinking. "If this Red Mike is such a tough hustler and pimp maybe Millie wasn't ever given a chance to do her own thinking. Maybe he wouldn't let her talk to him. You know, sometimes those girls are nothing but driven cattle."

"God, Sid," Gloria said fervently. "I'm so damn glad you're a square I don't know what to do. Come here and kiss me, and don't ever want to stop kissing me, honey, honey, honey."

Getting to know Gloria all over again was beautiful. Everything was beautiful. Her intelligence was beautiful, and so was the way she faced life without cringing. In a way Gloria was a split personality. She was a finished college woman and she was a Harlem moll. Tough and honest. Even her speech was equally split between the campus and the gutter. She was two in one and I loved both of her. But by far the most important thing was that I was *important* to her. And it was a so much better and nicer feeling than being important to Lina although in a way I am ashamed to admit that.

Sometimes as Gloria lay in my arms my mind would steal away to Lina and I would wonder who the child-woman had found to sleep with now. It was stone guilt that made me think about Lina, for it was not until I was so very happy that I thought about her probable unhappiness. And I had been unfair in so many ways.

First there was the incontrovertible fact that I only liked foxes. I had to be pretty high to make it with a girl with Lina's looks. To some men pussy is pussy and the kind of package it comes in doesn't matter a bit, but not with me. Even Alise had had a pretty face.

And so now I knew that once again the Sinman had been right. He told me that there is no such thing as charity; it can't be given. But, like a fool, I had not listened and thought that doing Lina a favor in bed was charity. It was not; both Lina and myself were poorer. I had wasted her time while inflating my foolish ego for a few fleeting moments like a junky with his heroin.

When those honeymoon days ended Gloria sighed and said, "Well, I'm going to meet my stud this morning so wish me luck."

"I'm beginning to hate that little boy of a bitch," I said.

"I know damn well it isn't going to work out, but I'm going to keep my word and meet her out front of the House of D when she walks out," Gloria said. "Already I know it's wrong but I've got to *prove* it. So don't be surprised to see me back here to stay any time. And I'll be visiting you every day before you go to work. That I promise you."

"I should go out and have a set of keys made for you."

"No. I ain't got no strings on you. And as long as I'm stroking Butch I don't have any right to be walking in here unless you open the door for me."

"Gloria," I said. "We both got hangups, but way off in the future we're going to make it. We're going to get home. Understand? So I'm yours too. It'll take time, but we'll reach where we want to be. You just wait and see."

"I know."

CHAPTER 15

When Gloria walked out the door I lay back and relived all the wonderful things our weird relationship really was. Sinman had advanced his theory as to what was the cause of Gloria's problems, but I still was not sure she wasn't a nympho. But I must say that this last time she had not been anybody's sex maniac; she had constantly remained the master of her body, responding to me only when I was the aggressor. And she had insisted that I go to work every other day. And I don't have to tell you that her insistence was something I needed badly. It was like nobody cared but Gloria.

As she had promised, Gloria came by every day and I worked ten days in succession. Then one morning I got up feeling wonderful, but when I went to the dresser to comb my hair I couldn't raise my arms. Just to try to lift them was excruciating. The pain actually nauseated me. I went in J&J's room and told them about it.

"You've got alcoholic neuritis," Jinny said. "I know because I had it myself something awful. And it took me over a month to get rid of it. Vitamin B shots. Those bastid shots hurt, too."

I sat on their bed and cursed methodically while J&J nodded their sympathy.

"You know, Sid," Joey said, "Jinny had her attack almost ten years ago. Maybe now they got a wonder drug that can knock that pain out in no time. Why don't you finish getting dressed and go to St. Luke's? You got money, ain'tcha?"

"Sure. I've been working ten days straight," I said.

"Well, you go down St. Luke's like I tole ya."

I walked in St. Luke's emergency ward and immediately felt worse when I saw all the Black and Spanish Welfare cases ahead of me. But I went to the desk and registered or whatever you call it and then sat down to wait and I waited three hours. Then I was put on a production line. During the morning all patients to the emergency ward are screened by a young resident who then sends the patients to the clinic he thinks best for them. So when I say I finally was put on the production line my name was called to sit on one of the two benches just outside the resident's little office. Now St. Luke's has a very good system in every respect. But no system is any better than the people in it, and the young doc on duty in the screening office was no Angel of Mercy, or even the near relative of any angel unless it be the Angel of Death.

The man was a medical pol rather than a healer. And he was captivated by his telephone. He couldn't leave it alone. During one interval, between patients, he made five calls to colleagues in the hospital. The two benches outside his office could accommodate maybe ten or fifteen patients, and they were full. And we all could hear every word this medical glad-hander said on the phone. In a way, the fool was fishing for thank yous and compliments.

"I've got a lovely liver on the way up to you," he said during one of his calls. "I know you'll be wanting to see it. There are the damnedest signs of . . ." Then he went into a mumbo-jumbo of medical terms I don't think even he understood.

The woman sitting next to me moaned and fell off the bench in a faint. It seemed pretty evident that she had also brought in a lovely liver. My arms hurt so bad that I was no help, but four other men picked her up, brushed past the screen that hid the screening office so that the telephone fiend could have a look at her.

"What's going on here?" the little fool demanded in a clear boyish voice.

"She just keeled over out there, Doc," I heard one of the men say.

"Well, why did you bring her in here?"

"She's sick, Doc. Like I said, she just keeled over outside there."

The young idiot must have had a burst of inspiration. "Where's her chart?" he demanded excitedly. "Go get her medical records."

"We don't work here, Doc. We're patients too."

"Irregardless, she ought to have a chart," the medic snapped, now in full command of the situation.

Miraculously a nurse scurried into the office with what must have been the woman's chart. At the time I thought it was a true miracle, but I later learned that it wasn't. One of the reasons they keep you waiting so long is because as soon as they take your name they send up to the records office for your chart.

There was quiet in the office as the doctor was evidently reading the lady's medical history. Finally he announced in triumph that the woman had once been a patient in St. Luke's psychiatric ward. He picked up his phone and asked to be connected with some doctor.

"Hello there," he began. "I think I have one of your patients down here. Perhaps I should say former patient, but she seems to be pretty sick. How would you like to come down and take a look at her? In an hour? Fine. And, oh yes, I want to tell you about the schizo we had in here yesterday . . ."

I was real cool. I got up, walked in the office and snatched the telephone wires loose from the wall. Then I walked back to the Logan.

"It takes a bastid from the Logan to tell the doctors how to run their hospital," Jinny observed.

"I'm telling you I did it for his own good," I insisted. "He was a psycho. Afraid to diagnose those patients. He was so scared he'd send somebody to the wrong clinic he had to spend all his time stroking the other docs so maybe they wouldn't tell the whole hospital he was a fool when he did diagnose wrong. He didn't have a damn thing important to say to a single person he called on that telephone."

"So what you gonna do now?" Joey asked. "Take a shot at running Harlem Hospital too?"

"Hell no," I growled. "I'm not ready to die yet. I guess I'll try Metropolitan."

I went by bus to Metropolitan Hospital and was told that the doctors suspected bursitis. They also took X rays and told me that they wouldn't have the results until the following Tuesday. When I asked one doctor how soon it would be before I would be able to work again he played crazy and got all indefinite. *If* the little white pills and aspirin worked I might be able to work in a week or so, but if the pills didn't work, then they would have to operate to remove the calcium deposits.

I left Metropolitan filled with a cold black fire. The pain was partly to blame for the way I felt, but there was something else at work in me that I've never been able to describe. I walked toward Third Avenue and a bar, while my mind coldly decided that somehow both New York City and the Logan were to blame for my condition. It was like my mind was a thing of its own; I had nothing to do with its operation. And my mind also decided that if I was not able to work I was entitled to Welfare just like the rest of the inmates of the Logan. It was a vindictive resolution and yet I somehow did not really have anything to do with it, if you get what I mean.

I left the bar and took a taxi to the Welfare Center on 124th Street. When it was my turn to speak to the receptionist I told her that I was in great pain and the doctors at Metropolitan Hospital had been unable to do anything about it. I also said I was out of work, my rent was due and I was hungry. The receptionist gave me a numbered card and told me to have a seat until my number was called.

It was a three-hour wait, but I didn't mind one bit. Like in a poker game and you're way ahead and suddenly you start getting bad cards, but you don't flip; you keep passing, real cool like, because you know you got good cards coming eventually and you can afford to wait. Yeah. I was cool. Cool as hell.

I never did learn the exact title of the young Jewish fellow that finally called me into his cubicle for the interview, but it was all very simple. And it made me wonder why everyone in Harlem bothered to lie about how tough Welfare workers are and how hard it is to get on Welfare. This man I talked to was primarily interested in how long I had lived and worked in New York and if I had any relatives living in New York who could be forced by law to support me. Of course I told him I had no near relatives in the city, which was the truth.

At the end of the interview the guy asked me if I had any money and if I was hungry. I told him I was broke and hungry so he got up and went out of the office. When he came back he gave me a dollar and twenty cents and had me sign a receipt for it. After that he told me that if everything I said was true I would be put on Welfare, but first an investigator would have to come by the hotel to check up on me. I thanked him and left.

I was still vindictive. I made a beeline to the nearest store and bought two pints of Spur with the dollar bill the Welfare guy had given me. I hailed a cab and went back to the Logan.

"Congratulations," the Sinman cried when I told him what I had done.

His obvious joy caused my first misgivings. "Congratulations, eh?"

"Yes. You see, we Blacks always wait not only until starvation has debilitated us, but also until we are in debt, in hock and all credit gone before we make the first effort to secure what New York owes us. After all, you *are* sick. You most certainly cannot work and in all probability you will be broke before you receive your first check. You acted most intelligently. I don't believe you would have been able to handle things so well if you had never met Blind Charlie. Yes. I congratulate you once more."

I laughed almost giddily. "I don't know why," I said, "but I feel like I've just begun to live. I'm down with it for the first time. And it really wasn't me who went in that Welfare Center. It was like a devil outside of me pushing. It was funny as hell the way I felt."

"It was your subconscious that liberated you. Your subconscious knew that you were dying in your prison of waiting on tables. You are a writer, Sid. Do you remember the day you told me you had won a national contest for a one-act play? True, only college students could enter that contest, but you won it! That is the point. And you can win again when the going is lots more heavy. So now that you have nothing to do but eat and sleep I command you to write. You must pour out all that anguish that has been accumulating since the day we met. I only hope you finish your play before I complete my 'Black Mass.' I simply cannot conclude the blasted thing."

"That was years ago when I won that contest. Now I am over forty. I don't believe I can write any more now. It's too late."

"Nonsense. Some of your best writers never got started until they had reached the age of retirement. You are now retired at the ripe old age of forty-two. And you have no hobbies save drinking with Charlie and J&J. You must write or you will actually perish."

"Yeah, I do need a hobby now," I said with doubt. Suddenly I had to get away from Sinman's enthusiasm. It was obscene in a way. "Well, so long. I guess I'll go upstairs and tell J&J all about the Welfare bit."

"Stick around. Those two old frauds probably had the news before you left 124th Street. Especially Jinny, she's a marvel. But today I must talk to you about higher education as we know it here in the Logan. I hear that you have maligned our greatest scholar. And that is tut-tut."

"You mean that damn fool College Joe? How can an ignorant fool like that bamboozle a whole hotel full of people? It's enough to make you ashamed of the whole Black race."

"The white tenants believe Joe also."

"They couldn't. You know that. And what kind of kick does he get out of his lies?"

"I imagine that it does give him some sort of esoteric pleasure, but there are also many advantages in being a college student. Every little prostie in this place has a soft spot in her granite heart for College Joe. You can't imagine how they will cherish the memory of being escorted to the Apollo by a college man and especially if they are allowed to pay the freight."

"Aaahck." I made a puking sound in my throat.

"Your derision does not change Joe's stature one bit," Sinman said severely. "But it is your welfare that is my immediate concern so I must dwell on this matter for a while even though I know it is painful to you. You risk life and limb when you malign Joe in the Logan. We tenants have not sought the truth from you and you must not insist upon preaching it to us."

"The hell with the Logan and everybody in it."

"Very few of these inmates can read or write to any great extent.

So Joe has become the one bright horizon in their lives. Joe is their alter ego. Do you follow me? They all look forward to the day they can point to Joe, the college graduate, and say that they shared in aiding him to gain that education at Columbia."

"But Joe is so exquisitely ignorant."

"Joe is a success. Niggers go for that. Even the junkies. You will never be forgiven for destroying Joe's image. So be it."

"I wish to hell somebody had the guts to blow up the Logan and everybody in it."

"Including you? Me? Blind Charlie?"

"And what good are we?"

That question was rhetorical, but somehow it flipped the Sinman. "Come to me for all you need in this jungle called Harlem," he pattered in a silkily effeminate voice that was somehow virile as hell. "I have pistols, whores who know their french, male prostitutes who will not beat and rob little boy-girls, powders for your soul and reefers too. All these I have to make it easy for the poor. I am the great Sinman. Selah!"

"You and College Joe should be the first ones to get blown up," I mumbled. "And me next for even letting folks like you bug me." I poured a drink of Cutty, drank it, and walked out of the room leaving the Sinman happily babbling about God being dead and all that jazz.

"It just goes to show you got a good head on you, Sid," Joey exclaimed. "Now all the rest of these fools around here would've waited until they was starving and evicted before they took and went to Welfare, but you went and tole 'em that you was in bad shape before you even got broke. That's what I call using your head. And you ain't done nothing crooked neither. You just let 'em know ahead of time is all."

"I still don't know how I did it," I said, and damned if I wasn't stupid enough to feel bashful. "But I wonder what Gloria's going to say."

"It's none of your business what anybody says or thinks. You went and took care of number one. And that's all you're ever supposed to do. And everybody who matters is gonna be behind you one hundred per cent. You got a right to live decent until your arms get better."

"Every sonofabitch and his brother can get on Welfare except me," Jinny said morosely.

"How come you're not on it and Joey is?" I asked her.

"The little bitch tricked Welfare so tough that she ain't even allowed to walk on the same side of the street a Welfare office is on," Joey said proudly.

"Yeah. I took 'em when I had 'em," Jinny said philosophically. "I cheated them out of so much money they were ashamed to have me arrested, I guess. They didn't want it in the papers."

Joey was still swelled up with pride. "One day she gets drunk and goes to the Welfare office and starts bawling about her husband come up here from Florida and moves in on her. And he's crippled, but mean. And that he beat her up and took her check and got drunk. And she's starving," she said.

Jinny sighed happily. "I was so drunk I didn't even remember having done it."

"We each had our own places then," Joey said. "And when the investigator comes by Jinny's place to talk to her about this husband she ain't got, Jinny don't even know what he's talking about. Can you beat that?"

"But I was nobody's fool, buddee. When I finally caught the rhythm and realized what I had done, I went and got this old man who lived in the building but wasn't on Welfare. And I passed him off as my old man. And lie? You should have heard me and that old man fill in my investigator," Jinny said. She rolled on the bed, laughing.

I took the two pints of Spur out of my pocket and grinned. "Welfare bought this for us," I said.

"Damn right. We *should* celebrate," Joey yelled.

And we drank for the remainder of the day. It was J&J's bedtime, about eight o'clock, when I staggered off to be by myself. For a while I could not go to sleep. I just lay there and thought about it all. Like a reluctant harlot, I toyed all around the idea of remaining on Welfare until I had written the great Black American play. But

I doubted myself so. I knew I didn't have the true S.R.O. intelligence and know-how to keep my investigator always in the dark. And I knew I was not a great playwright. I knew I was nothing. Nothing at all.

A little after eleven I was awakened by a racket at the foyer door and I knew it could only be Blind Charlie and his cane.

"Stop beating on this door like a maniac, you blind fat bastid," Ray yelled. "One of these days I'm gonna take that cane and shove it up your rear."

"You know I ain't never got no time to listen to no junky's foolishness, woman. Git outen my way. Me and Sid's got business to attend to."

Charlie staggered into the room. He made me think of a drunken elephant. His cane was swinging like a trunk from his sausage of an index finger.

And Charlie came right to his drunken point. "We is gonna rob a whiskey store tonight. So hurry up and get outa that bed."

"We? Who's we?"

"Me and you, goddamit! What you think we gonna do? Invite the whole goddam hotel?" the blind man shouted.

"B-b-but how? Just me and you? You're still blind, ain't you?" And, so help me, I was afraid of Charlie's answer to that question.

"What the hell has that got to do with it? I can hold up a whiskey store just as good as the next when I puts my mind to it."

"But how?" I squeaked. "How? And when?"

"Right this minute. C'mon. You got your clothes on yet? Hurry up. They'll be closing in a minute and don't nobody go robbing a whiskey store after they is closed and locked up all the money."

I sat up in bed. I needed a drink so bad I was feverish. "How, Charlie?" I repeated. "How can just the two of us hold up a liquor store?"

"You is the dumbest fren' I ever had," Charlie declared. It was a fine blending of exasperation and pride. "All you gotta do is let me go in first. You leads me up to the store, but way out near the curb. See? Then you turns me to face the door so's I only gotta walk a straight line to get in. See? Then it's your turn to come in and say that this is a stickup. That's all. I'll do the rest."

"What goddam rest?" I shouted, angry with the fear I might not have enough sense to tell Charlie to go to hell.

Charlie heaved a grunt of disgust. "All you gotta do is tie a rag around your face. And you waits until I'm talking face to face with the clerk, and then you comes in and says what I already tole you. And I'm gonna say that you is a dirty criminal. I'm a real pussy, see? And then you tells me to shut up and you calls me a string of motherfuckers. Naturally I resents that and so I goes to work. I swings my cane. You duck. But don't worry. This ole cane is gonna knock the living shit outa that clerk by mistake, see. He's chilled. It's all an accident. I'm innocent and the clerk'll have to swear I was. And if there's any questions I'll say that you sapped me and I don't remember nothing. See? You never dreamed I know my trade, but I does. You ain't got nothing to worry about when you works with Blind Charlie. Now you understand everything?"

"Yes," I said quietly, digesting the enormous insanity of the whole thing. "But I'm sick," I added. "Didn't Sinman tell you?"

"That was this morning. You're okay now, ain't you?"

"Heck no. I can't even raise my arm to take a drink hardly."

"Now ain't that a sonofabitching thing," Charlie said despondently. Then he brightened. "But you ain't got nothing to do. The liquor store man's gonna be dead to the world. All you gotta do is hand me a few bottles and empty the cash register. A man with no arms could do that."

"Ever since I been a man I promised myself I would never go in on a gig if I wasn't able to hold up my end of it," I said, thinking fast. "When I'm not in the physical condition to do something like that I ain't gonna make my buddies take no risks on me. You understand me, don't you?"

"Now ain't that something? Now I gotta go and get somebody what ain't my fren'. And how the hell I know they won't cheat me outen my honest share? I can't see to count it. And the world is fulla folks what thinks nothing of robbing poor ole Blind Charlie."

I feverishly began to mutter to myself and he turned and staggered out of the room without another word. I heaved a sigh of relief and tried to go back to sleep and I almost had when here comes all this banging at the foyer door again. I knew it was Charlie so I went to let him in before Ray started in on him again.

I opened the door and gawked. Charlie's shirt and pants were tattered. Blood was pouring from all over his head like he had been dumped in a cement mixer full of rocks.

"Ooowhaw!" Charlie howled. "Oooowheee. They done tried to kill poor ole Blind Charlie. Sid! Where are you at, Sid? Outen my way, woman. Wake up, Sid!"

"I'm standing right here, holding the door open for you, Charlie," I whispered. "Don't make so much noise. Who you been fighting? Are the cops looking for you? You know Leah and Ray don't want no cops poking around here that they haven't sent for. Come on in and shut up."

"*Damn* Leah and Ray. Looka here what they done did to poor ole Blind Charlie, boy. Yessuh. To poor ole Blind Charlie they did it."

"Who did you up like this, Charlie?"

"Where's Gloria? Wake her up, tell her to come nurse me."

"You know damn well Gloria's not here. You just left here a little over an hour ago. Sit down and tell me what happened."

"Don't call no ambulances, please. Oh, Lawdee!"

"You know damn well we got to call the cops first for an ambulance at the Logan. You don't want no cops, do you? First, let me look at your head and see how bad off you are."

He let me look at his head. There were plenty of cuts and bumps, but actually nothing serious. "You want me to wash these cuts or you want to let the blood clot first?"

"Oh, Lawdee. I don't know."

"Well, what the devil happened?"

"It was them goddam pussies of Puerto Ricans I went and got to help."

"You really went out of here and tried to rob that liquor store as drunk as you were?" I shouted.

"What you think? I ain't no sick pussy like you."

"Damn," was all I could mutter. Charlie finally sat down, but he still kept on moaning. I decided to make him talk because I was sick of the moaning. "All right. C'mon and tell me what happened. Why did they beat you up?"

"Ain't nobody beat me up!" Charlie shouted.

"Well, goddamit, I'm sick and tired of asking you what happened!"

"They went and let me fall down a hole."

"A hole? What damn hole?"

"A super's hole. I fell down the basement steps. They leads poor ole Blind Charlie to a hole and lets him tumble down the steps. And I near broke my goddam neck."

"What you need is a good hot bath."

"What?" Charlie boomed. "Why, I never tooken a bath in my life and I ain't gonna start now that I'm dying and damn near kilt."

I took another look at Charlie's head and decided that there was nothing to do about it. So I got back in bed and closed my eyes and ears to Charlie and his Oooowhaaas.

The next morning I left Charlie asleep on the floor to go see the Sinman.

"Well, the maniac has succeeded this time," Sinman said. "He has managed to infuriate every junky on Morningside Heights."

"What did he really do anyhow?" I asked.

Sinman grimaced. "He enlisted a tiny junky named Pablo who hangs out around here to help him rob that store down near 113th Street," he said. "The scheme was harebrained enough without a sky-high junky and a drunken blind man trying to execute it."

"There was only one Puerto Rican?"

Sinman nodded. "Only Pablo. But when he and Charlie arrived at the liquor store there was already a delegation from the Oxford Hotel there. Pablo informs Charlie of this fact and Charlie is wild with fury to hear that others are about to steal that which he considers to be rightfully his. Against Pablo's warning and advice, Charlie insists upon being led into the store. The leader of the Oxford group knows Charlie by both sight and reputation, and so he wisely fired a shot from his gun in the direction of Charlie's feet."

Sinman took a deep drag and continued. "Charlie lit out with Pablo leading him, but no sooner had they got outside the store than Charlie decides that Pablo is not running fast enough. So he actually lifts Pablo up by the shoulder he is holding onto. I can see it all," Sinman said sadly. "Here is Charlie running down the street with Pablo. And you see, Pablo's feet are no longer on the ground and so he cannot lead Charlie. But he did yell, 'Turn,' and Charlie turned. He made a U turn and went down a flight of cellar stairs that led off the sidewalk. The next thing he is tumbling down those steps with Pablo beneath him. Pablo is now in the hospital with six broken ribs. The delegation from the Oxford was apprehended. Since Charlie and Pablo were at the foot of those basement stairs they were not caught. And that Oxford group is going to get ooh-long time because of the gun and so forth. Only Blind Charlie got off scot-free. It's a pity, don't you think?"

CHAPTER 16

ONE TIME JINNY had just finished her newscast and simply out of idle curiosity I asked, "Are Leah and Ray really partners?"

"For Chrissakes, Sid. When are you going to learn? They're *lovers.* Where do you get that partnership crap from?"

"Ray takes all the chances. She does all the selling at night when things are jumping. Leah just sells to her personal friends like during the daytime. How come she never risks *her* butt at night, when it's dangerous?"

"Ray loves Leah, Sid. Ray took a bust for Leah once. She did three years for Leah."

"Are you for real?"

"What's there to lie about? Ray went into court and told the judge that Leah wasn't guilty, that she was. She went to Bedford for three years. And you talk about they got to worry about divvies?"

So after that little conversation I was totally unprepared for the morning when Joey shook me awake and blurted, "It's a low-down dirty shame!" Her face was the color of an angry beet. "The dirty Black bastid."

"What's eating you?" I asked testily, not liking the tone of voice Joey used to say "Black bastard."

Joey's eyes scalded me with pure loathing. She pointed in the direction of Leah's room. "Right in there he comes and tries to kill his greedy self. We was up all night, walking him up and down the hall and putting ice packs on him. Ray had to go all the way over to Broadway to an all-night joint for milk for him even."

"What guy? Do I know him?" I said to let her know she wasn't making any sense at all.

Joey snorted contemptuously. "No. And Leah and Ray been living here, happily married, for two years. And all of a sudden this bastid gets outa the pen and walks right in here to lay up on Leah. Ain't that some shit?"

I laughed.

"It ain't funny, Sid. The bastid could see they don't need him no more. They got their own little business and happy home. What they need him for?"

In the beginning the relationship between J&J and between Leah and Ray had titillated me, but in time their phony love affairs had become a boring nothingness as far as I was concerned. "Are they legally married?" I asked.

"What difference does that make?" Joey nearly screamed. Just as suddenly she calmed down, and like I was sick in the head she patiently re-explained the situation with Leah. "Here is a bastid that just got outa Dannemora. Six years. And what does he do but come to his wife, trying to fuck up her love affair with a good woman, and takes two whole bags of shit, all the time knowing he ain't had a fix in six years. He knew he was taking an overdose, Sid. But the bastid is a pig. He didn't even care."

"You mean he was trying to commit suicide?"

"No. I mean he's a pig. He keels over, practically dead, and me and Jin and Leah and Ray hadda do everything in the book to try to revive him. That hog had a hell of a nerve. He knows Leah's on record downtown for having three different persons die from ODs in places that was rented in her name."

"Why did Leah and Ray let him take it?" I asked. "They're pros. They are more to blame than he is. Maybe they wanted him to die."

"He sneaked it while they wasn't looking. He's a pig, I tell ya."

Joey stormed out of the room, and as I lay and thought I became angry: why the hell was Sid Bailey expected to side with these queers in their views on life and love? They must think that I'm some kind of freak myself. And Joey with her mad act was phony too because how the hell could this husband have found out Leah's address unless she had written him in prison and given it to him?

Joey's diatribe had left a nasty taste in my mouth. Alise was certainly having the last laugh. What kind of a future did a man have who was just a black-assed sounding board for some lesbians in the Logan?

Leah came to my open door, but stood there and knocked politely. "You awake, Sid? I don't want to disturb you."

"I'm awake," I said. "Come on in."

Leah came in followed by a tall dark stranger. He was in his underwear and I could see that he was a finely built light heavyweight. He was really built, but the most striking thing about him was his face. It was a black blank upon which greed and privation had etched at will—and yet that face was a blank.

"I want you to meet my husband Jimmy," Leah said in a ladylike gush. Then she turned lovingly to Jimmy and said, "This is Sid. He's the man of the house. He takes good care of all us girls. He don't mind going to the store night or day. And he's a cat who's down with it. Sid's no square. But he's clean. We're all in love with Sid. And so now there won't be any mixup when you knock at the door and Sid answers." And she yattered on about how nice I was.

And as she gushed I didn't listen because I was thinking about just how stupid Leah really was. Here was a professional criminal who was too tight to have a twenty-five-cent key made for her husband. I looked at Jimmy again. How stone-faced he was. Inside and out. I don't believe he listened to a single word Leah said. This guy was all alone in a world of his own. A world in which he needed no friends and wanted none.

J&J stayed angry about Jimmy all day long. In fact they stayed angry all week. Even when Jimmy was not around and that was a lot, because Jimmy was on parole and had to work. He worked on a produce truck and left for work around four in the morning. But Jimmy's presence was felt all day. Leah and Ray became two different people in no time at all.

Ray and Leah used to leave the Logan about ten every night to meet their connection. They usually bought three bundles if they could. Sometimes four. And then they would come back and start dealing around eleven. Ray sold all night until they just had enough bags left for themselves and their regular morning customers. By early afternoon they were clean. But now Jimmy had changed all that. Every afternoon he made Leah and Ray go out and meet a new connection and then sell through the afternoon until ten when they went to meet their old connection. Jimmy was a greedy sonofabitch.

When this was explained to me, I said, "I don't blame the guy. If you're going to break the law you might as well do it big. Why sell three bundles when you can sell six?"

"But that ain't all he's done," Joey said excitedly. "He's made Ray squeeze her fat ass inta a pair of slacks and go out on 125th Street and hustle. So now Leah has to be up, selling day and night all by herself almost."

"How can he make a bulldiking broad hustle the streets for him?" I asked.

Jinny laughed bitterly. "Source and connection are the only two real things in a junky's life," she said. "Jimmy is now both the connection and the source as far as Leah and Ray are concerned. And if Ray didn't come back home Jimmy would go out on 125th and find her and break her leg. Besides, one source is as good as another. I mean Ray is strung out, her habit is oooh-long. Right?

When she gets through hustling she's got to go somewhere for a fix. So why not come back to Jimmy?"

"She could go someplace else just out of spite. She should."

"Who could she go to? Another pimp? Jimmy just got out of Dannemora for murder. He's a killer. And no pimp in his right mind is going to get in a gunfight with Jimmy over two forty-year-old women."

"So just because Jimmy is a willing murderer Leah and Ray are his slaves," I said.

"That's about the size of it, Sid. Harlem is mastered by men who don't think nothing of killing people and Jimmy is one of them."

Joey had come in a few minutes before and now she said, "Poor Ray gets in here after four in the morning and has to cook Jimmy's breakfast soon after. Then she got to deal the doogie while Leah sleeps till noon. Only then does that Black bastid say she can sleep."

"That still gives her about ten hours' sleep," I said.

"Jesus to Jesus. You're worse than Jimmy," Joey yelled.

Jimmy ate his two meals in the kitchen, and so I saw him often, but we seldom spoke. However, one day while he was eating I went to the kitchen to fill my water bottle. He had just come from work, but he was already nodding.

"J&J your women?" he asked abruptly.

"No," I said, really peeved at the idea of anybody thinking those two pug-uglies could be anything to me.

"The bitches need to be took, what you waiting for? Especially that Jinny. If I was around here all day like you I'd have her hustling in no time."

"I don't need any woman hustling for me."

The dope-dulled eyes brightened with awed respect. "You got it made, eh? What was your racket? I knew you was smart time I looked at you."

I wanted to tell this bully of a punk that I was not a junky or a pimp and had never been. For one of the few times in my life I wanted to shout out that I was a decent man and a square. But I couldn't. I was so charged that I couldn't give out the words. It was like the Sinman was always saying: Sin and sinning were dynamic. Goodness and decency can only be told in the silent tongue of a pussy.

Finally I did say, "I'm on Welfare." I knew it was the wrong thing to say to a man like Jimmy, but it was the only thing that would issue from my tongue.

Jimmy's lips curled not only with contempt but with actual loathing. I was from another country. "You mean you just sit on your ass, waiting for your little check? Now ain't that a bitch?"

And I realized that a Welfare bum is actually lower than a pimp. At least in some eyes, mine included.

"What the hell Leah put me on like that for?" Jimmy asked more to himself than to me.

"I don't know," I said, filled my bottle and got out of the kitchen.

Jimmy didn't even bother to speak to me after that except one time he came in my room and ordered me to go to the store for him.

"Yeah," he said, "run over the stationery and get me two Viceroys."

I went. I felt like I deserved it.

A few days later Jimmy came to my door. It was open but he knocked and asked if he could come in.

"Leah's goddam sister is in there and that bitch and I can't get along five minutes," he said.

"Sure. Come on in," I said. I got up from the easy chair and sat on the bed. Jimmy ignored the chair and sat on the bed beside me. He began a long story of how Leah's sister, who was some kind of supervisor in the federal government, refused to go his bond one time years ago.

As Jimmy went on with his interminable and vindictive tale he took out a bundle of heroin and a bottle cap. A bundle is twenty-five bags of heroin held together by a rubber band. As he talked Jimmy patiently opened a bag at a time and dropped a few crystals of heroin into the bottle cap. Then he would reseal each bag. After he had done this to the twenty-five bags Jimmy had mulcted a fix for himself.

"Mind if I take off in here?"

Jimmy was already in the nodding stage; that was one reason his story had rambled on so. But I really didn't give a damn. If Jimmy OD'd on me I was simply going to drag his body out in the hall and let Leah and Ray do what they wanted to do with him. No. I didn't care one damn bit.

After Jimmy took off he began to talk in a low monotone. "I got two of the dumbest and laziest whores in Harlem," he said. "That fat bitch don't want to do nothing and Leah ain't much better. I damn near have to kick Ray's fat ass every night."

"You mean she don't know how to hustle?"

"She better not come in here with less than forty dollars. At least that will pay for the shit she shoots up every twenty-four hours."

"She's so fat I didn't think she had much of a chance out in the street," I said, not knowing why.

"Them square cats likes them fat-assed bitches. They likes to back scuttle 'em. And it don't make no difference how a woman looks, any whore can make it out in the street if she knows what she's doing. Now that no-good fat bitch had the nerve to tell me she had female trouble. Hell. I knew that. All bulldikers got female trouble, but what the hell's that got to do with a motherfucking thing?"

And Jimmy went on angrily to list and detail seventeen ways a woman can make a man achieve orgasm without spreading her legs. When Leah's sister departed Jimmy left and I immediately opened the windows wide. I needed airing, not the room. I also felt that Jimmy was the first and only man I truly hated.

A few days later Jimmy stopped in my doorway and announced that he had to go to the hospital. I wanted with all my heart to ask him if he had female trouble too, but Jimmy was a light heavyweight. Later that morning he and Leah left for the hospital. Both of them had dressed meticulously. They returned late that afternoon and said that the hospital had no beds available. Three mornings in a row they dressed up and went out to the hospital and every afternoon they returned with the same story. Then Leah returned without

Jimmy one afternoon and announced that the hospital had finally found a bed for Jimmy.

For a week Leah would go out every afternoon, saying that she was going to visit Jimmy, but after a week went by she ceased to go.

"You notice all of a sudden Leah isn't visiting Jimmy any more?" I said to Joey. "Don't she know he's going to kick asses when he gets out? And Ray's stopped going out nights too."

Joey snorted. "That lying-assed Leah! She would lie about her own mother's funeral. They weren't going to no hospital. They been going to federal court. Jimmy had this case hanging while he did that murder rap. Federal court found him guilty and sent him to Lewis-something, Pennsylvania. You're dumb as hell, thinking someone could go out of here every day to the hospital and come back home every night, talking about ain't no beds ready for them. When you gonna wake up, Sid?"

CHAPTER 17

My conscience became a sometime thing as the days sped into weeks and I remained on Welfare. The little white pills had done their job and my arms were fine, but something inside me would not let me go back to work. Some days I wallowed in shame while at other times, usually when I was drinking with either J&J or Charlie, I would feel for the first time in my life that I now belonged, that I had at last found a home in a world that liked and approved of me. And I hadn't paid my dues, but I daily risked jail in defrauding Welfare so in a way my dues were in my pocket if the damn fool Welfare people ever got around to asking for them.

But the times when I was choked up with my insane remorse were pure hell. Not only for me but for Gloria as well. In a fit of irascibility I would drink the wine she brought me and then heckle her about all she had to say. I even went so far as to make fun of her clothes, and although I never struck her I did push her around a couple of times.

To make things worse, Gloria seemed unable to comprehend that it was the shame of being on Welfare that was making me act crazy. She blamed herself for everything I did. Sometimes she practically groveled with guilt. And so this lovely creature, who was doomed to love me, unwittingly goaded me to seek oblivion in wine, to say the ugliest things, to try my best to murder the thing we had between us. Welfare had taken me prisoner and jailed me in a wine cellar.

One day I went down to the Sinman's room to borrow a dollar. I could have wakened Gloria, who had spent the night with me, but she would have given it to me gladly and I felt that somehow I had to earn my first drink this morning. So I went down to suffer the Sinman's casual contempt.

I walked in and right off Sinman said, "How many times have you spoken to Sharlee on the telephone lately?"

"None. Why?"

"I was speaking to her a few minutes ago and she gave me the impression that you had been calling every day and then suddenly stopped."

"No," I said, "that's not the way it was at all. I called her like you said and asked her to go out with me, but she always had an excuse. That was when I was working. But I haven't called her since I got on Welfare."

"I think now that I have misadvised you. I told you to keep in touch, but I think you have titillated her by not calling any more. Well, Sharlee will pay us a visit tonight, and I suspect you just might be her prime target."

"Well, she's a few weeks too late now," I muttered, realizing that Blind Charlie's ability to shun all blame at all times is a lovely thing to have. "When I was working regular and staying halfway sober she wasn't interested," I continued. "Now she's blown it. Not me, her."

"When do you ever intend to start in on that play of yours?"

Now that question was not really off the wall. It was relevant as hell because the only way I could ever make any time with a goddess such as Sharlee was to become a rich and successful playwright.

"I don't think I ever will," I said. It was my obituary and Sharlee's too, I thought. "I've formally retired from striving at the ripe old age of forty-two. Remember?"

"That was a particularly putrid sort of thing to say. And do you know that you are striving in the most putrid sort of way to impair Gloria's almost congenital respect for you? Why must you squares always feel it necessary to beat up on your women?"

"I never beat Gloria. And what if I did? Pimps do it all the time."

"A whore knows exactly why she is being beaten and that she deserves it. Are you by any chance attempting to become a pimp?"

"No. Hell no! I don't know why I've been trying to play like a gorilla around Gloria. Not exactly, I don't. But I already promised her I wouldn't any more. Didn't she tell you? Seems like she would."

"She hasn't."

"Well, it's been like this: I've been weak, I let Gloria's stone womanhood bug me. I mean she's been too contented about me being on Welfare. If she'd only complain a little or even . . ."

"So you shift to her the beating you know you well deserve. But it's not being on Welfare that has you up against the wall; it is your failure to renounce mental pussyhood. You are afraid to face a piece of paper and write on it.

"Therefore, it is most necessary to experience the intricacies of experiencing Sharlee. I am not mad. Sharlee is not only a gift but a test of your sanity and humanity. She is a crucible. You will succeed or die. Let me tell you how you must be. Play her by ear, and gently. You must allow her all the rein she wants and still remain her master. Sharlee gets drunk, very drunk, but she still will not stand for any man to get drunk in her presence. Warning enough?

"You have complained of the women in the Logan changing sex at will. Well, Sharlee changes sex in the middle of the night.

Sometimes several times. That will be the supreme test; you must not let her."

"Anybody can look at Sharlee and tell she's not a freak!"

"Sharlee was handed over to the penal system of the state of New York at the mature age of thirteen. The penal system taught her all those little sexual proclivities it abhors."

I braced myself and looked him in the eye. "Does it ever occur to you that you judge me pretty harshly in view of the two women in my life? Three, if you count Lina."

"I believe not only in the powers of Sharlee but in the power of being able to father a printed page. So be it."

"I get the impression you've got a pretty stiff hard on for the whole world this morning."

"I have. I am so utterly useless. And only my fellow men are more so."

"What's the matter? Blind Charlie again?"

"No, it was a minion of the 26th Precinct who earned his red badge of courage right in here before my blushing eyes."

"You got busted?" It was a purely selfish question. It would be improper to borrow a dollar if he had.

"Certainly not. My connections rule everyone except Lindsay. And only because he just assumed office. Wait a little while. But this off-duty pig in civilian clothes came and searched this room without benefit of a warrant or my permission. Of course I was too sensible to complain. Anyhow if I am not intelligent enough to hide my wares where a junior grade moron cannot find them I deserve to be arrested."

I nodded my agreement.

Sinman's face was stormy. "A poor damsel entered. The door was closed, but she was too sick to take precaution, for she was in a state beyond all understanding by a square. She was very ill and all her junk had long since run out. Therefore she was clean as a newborn babe, but the porcine minion immediately placed her under arrest."

"He was a lot of bullshit. What the hell could he charge her with?"

"He could not arrest her? Well, he did. And to gain her release he insisted that she fall to her knees and satisfy his desires. Fellatio, I think they call it. However, the darling girl was so in need of a fix she was unable to prevent herself from regurgitating. And the vile stuff spewed all down his pants leg."

"Good!"

"In a raging snit, this member of New York's Finest drew back his foot and kicked the damsel in the pit of her stomach while I bravely stood by and watched."

For a moment the Sinman was just another damn whitey. "I bet that pig would never have done that in front of any living soul except you," I told him.

"As a scholar of sin I take that to be a great compliment. Left-handed perhaps but still an accolade. And by the way: where was your living God? But I have rewarded that little miss for her bravery; I don't believe she *had* to throw up on his pants, she could have turned her head. So now she may come to me thrice a day for a free fix."

"Oh no. No. You couldn't have footed her bill at Freedmens Hospital so she could kick it painlessly. As the Sinman, you had to help dig her pit deeper. Do you actually know why?"

"Because she has a soul. Because she too awaits a new day. A new god. Perhaps not the same god whom I expect. I rather think her god will be Black."

It might be hard for you to understand this, but the Sinman had summed up all my emptiness with superb totality. He and Sandy, two heroin fiends with a vengeance, were blessed with an ability to hope. I was not. I was not equipped to cope with the present and these people not only took their todays in their strides but *knew* what tomorrow would bring.

For how can a man be able to cope with anything on earth if he is so ridiculously square as to succumb to a love for two of the world's most beautiful women at the same time? Other men had looked, worshiped and gone on to a better life. I was on the skids. But all of a sudden these thoughts and feelings changed. I became coldly realistic. Perhaps Sharlee was far more beautiful than Gloria, who was a glorious woman in her own right. And I loved both of them with a love that was not primarily sexual. I loved them sublimely. And when I admitted this I saved my sanity. I no longer apologize to any man or his god for having loved two women simultaneously. After all, God loves us all, doesn't He?

Gloria was dressing to leave when I got back to the room.

"I know I've been screwing up left and right," I said, "but after tonight things are going to be different. Don't ask me to explain it because you would think that I'm really crazy, but I've got to do a crazy thing. It's my only out. But if you'll loan me twenty dollars I promise to go back to work Sunday and to never take another drink of cheap wine as long as I live. In fact I won't ever drink again."

Gloria's smile was a sunburst. "You really mean business, don't you!" Then her smile faded. "But I only have nineteen dollars to my name, Sid."

"You mean you can't loan me any of it?"

"You can have it all, but it's only nineteen."

"I don't want to break you."

"All I need is a token and I've got one. Don't ever worry about me and money, Sid. I got Butch. You're the only worry I have. And I really don't want you to stop drinking. That would be like admitting you're not with it. I only want you to be what I think you deserve, Sid. I want to see you take a drink whenever you feel like it, but I hate to see you when your mouth gets all loose and everything. You get real ugly-looking when you're drunk, Sid. And, honey, you're not a bad-looking man at all. If you didn't drink so hard and get so moody I would have left Butch already." She smiled confidentially. "I don't think I like white people any more. Kinda dumb, considering, but sometimes I think that me and Butch just stop hating each other's color just long enough to do business in bed. Would you think I'm crazy if I told you that I want to go to one of those Black Nationalist meetings?"

"Yeah."

"Why?"

"They forbid liquor and tobacco. But they look the other way about dope. Reefers, at least. I know some who smoke a whole lot of pot."

"Oh. I didn't know that. How come?"

"They don't know what's happening. At least I don't think they do. They lack brain power. After all, they are ex-junkies and ex-convicts, but that don't make them ex-dumbbells."

"See why I always got to talk to you?" Gloria exclaimed. "I need you, Sid. Now I had intended to go to one of those mosques and sort of become affiliated." She kissed me. "Well, it's time for me to be getting back to my stud. Here's the money. You want me to try and get more?"

"No. No, thanks. I'll make it with this, baby. But you just wait and see what happens after tonight."

"I can see it already, honey. You are really cool. Cooler than you've been since I came back."

I took Gloria over to Broadway to catch the train and after that I walked along Riverside Drive for hours. I didn't get back until around three o'clock, got in bed and stayed there, catnapping until after seven. Then I woke and took a bath and shaved. I was cold sober and relaxed. Rested. The way I ought to be to see Sharlee . . . if she showed. And then I was frightened; if Sharlee did not come, I would surely go on a nineteen-dollar drunk at fifty cents a pint. It would mean losing Gloria and, after that, inevitable death. I was actually facing death at the whim of a beautiful ex-junky whom I didn't even know.

I went out to a Chinese restaurant, but with the feelings I had running all over me and through me I hardly touched the food. And to aid and abet my fright I kept telling myself that I was too old. A fool. That I was more than lucky to have Gloria; what right did I have to expect more? But the fact remained: I loved Sharlee . . . and Gloria. It was like they were in reality but one and the same girl. It took the two of them to make a whole for my beleaguered soul. . . .

At about nine o'clock I got to the Sinman's room. Sharlee was sitting on the bench beside the Sinman, who was playing beautifully.

Sharlee was not the caged beauty who paced the floor, smoking and evidencing some kind of odd dislike for the Sinman. She was still fantastically pretty, but now she was a laughing girl whose fabulous hair was done up in high style.

Sinman looked my way and waved to the Cutty Sark on the organ. And Sharlee gave me a wonderful smile. I did not go to the organ immediately; I stood and studied Sharlee. She was still indescribable, a woman who filled me with heavenly sensations and wisps of thoughts. And I wondered again why there was such liquidity to her looks. Tonight I could only think of tears of joy falling into a lovely pool. I thought of all the beautiful bodies of water I had ever seen, but none had touched me like this.

I went over to the corner and patted Blind Charlie on the shoulder. "Get ole Charlie a drink, boy," he said softly.

I poured two drinks and came back to sit on the arm of Charlie's chair. Sinman played on. Although I was neither restless nor bored I began to wonder if the whole evening was going to go like this without any conversation. More than an hour had gone by when Sharlee got up from her seat at the organ and came over.

She pouted slightly. "I want to dance."

I stood up and Sharlee floated into my arms. We took one step and Sharlee abruptly ceased to float. She simply did not know how to dance. And it banged across my mind that this girl had learned to dance in a women's penitentiary. Sharlee couldn't be led. She was aggressive about that. Once she smiled mischievously. It was as if she was telling me that no man could ever hope to lead her anywhere in this life, anywhere she did not wish to be led.

But poorly as Sharlee danced, she looked happy and satisfied. On the other hand I was beginning to feel unhappy. I wanted to hear Sharlee's soft voice in my ear.

"I meant to bring a bottle of Cutty Sark, but I guess the idea of seeing you again was so exciting I just forgot." It was the only thing that came to my mind.

"Don't worry about that. Sinman has plenty for us. And don't believe him either. I don't have to have just one brand."

"He never actually said you insisted on Cutty Sark."

"He usually does. He tells everyone that I'll only drink Cutty. Actually, I like all good scotch. I just order that brand when I'm in a bar. You see, I love scotch. I like the taste of it. I like it cool, but I hate to have the taste destroyed. That's why I only let the bartender put one cube of ice in it. What kind of work do you do, Sid?"

My mind was an instant whirlpool of fearful do's and don'ts: what kind of man did Sharlee respect? I finally decided that a square could not possibly rate high in her books. "I don't work," I said.

"I don't like men who don't work."

"I mean that I've been sick. I'm a waiter."

"Do you make much money?" She pronounced it "monn-nee."

"Yeah. I guess."

"Did Sinman tell you what I am?"

"No." And that was the truth. Neither Charlie nor the Sinman had ever mentioned Sharlee's livelihood. It was an odds-on certainty that she had been a prostitute during her junky days, but I knew she wasn't now. She was so purely beautiful that I didn't believe New York's army of lonely men would let her be. And then she had a mother living who was not much more than forty and who worked, but . . .

"I used to be a junky. I hate junkies. They should all be dead! I used to be a stickup girl, but the last time they broke my spirit."

"Who did?"

"The screws."

"Oh. You're talking about in jail. Were the guards men or women?"

"Bedford and Westfield are for women only. And there's only supposed to be women screws, but they've got men stationed outside and they'll call them in in a minute if a girl gets too tough. They called them in, and they really broke me this time. I used to be able to fight, but no more."

I chuckled indulgently. Sharlee was tall and straight and probably weighed about one hundred and thirty pounds. She was a picture of health, but her paralyzing good looks made me think of her as dainty, even delicate. What she and Sinman probably meant was that Sharlee was both stubborn and had a temper. Sharlee couldn't beat up anybody unless it was another ravishing beauty like herself.

"You think I can't fight, don't you?" Sharlee's eyes flashed a challenge.

"Well . . ." I let the one word hang.

"I beat up two screws at one time. I mean I really whipped them. I hurt them bad. And that's when every single screw on duty jumped me and damn near killed me. They would have except the head screw liked me. She wouldn't let them. I bet you never met a girl before that could beat up two strong men at the same time."

"No. I guess not." My mind wandered to Suzie. I imagined Sharlee and Suzie in a knock-down-drag-out fight and Suzie came off the victor all the way. But at the same time I could not imagine Suzie conquering two prison guards in a fight and I was sure that Sharlee was not lying.

"Sinman is afraid I'll go back to drugs, but he don't know," Sharlee said. "I've been to prison for the last time."

"The very idea of you being locked up in a cell makes me sick to the stomach," I said, wondering if this was the time to go on and tell her just how much I loved her and always would. But the awesomeness of Sharlee would only permit me to say, "You know you've got a tough fight on your hands, don't you?"

"Not for real. I was too young to be a junky for real. I mean my personality had not even been formed when I got hooked. I was too young to have a junky personality as the Sinman calls it. When are you going to take me to your room?"

I faltered. "What do you want to see my room for?" I asked.

Sharlee sort of chuckled. "What kind of chick do you take me for?" she replied.

I had no answer and so I said nothing. Sharlee abruptly stopped dancing and led me to the organ for a drink. She poured three and took one to Charlie. Sinman and I looked at the bottle at the same time and saw that it was empty. Sinman went to the hutch cabinet and got another bottle. I was wondering if Sharlee and Charlie had shared the whole fifth when Sinman dropped the empty bottle in the wastebasket. The clink meant there was another empty bottle in the basket.

Those two empty bottles increased my interest in Sharlee's drinking. Sinman had said Sharlee was not the master of alcohol but, as usual, the Sinman seemed to be wrong. She never let her glass get empty and she was always sipping, but she continued to appear perfectly sober and at ease.

Later in the evening, when the level of the fresh bottle was way down, Sharlee said, "Why are you taking so long to take me to your room?"

"I thought you were just making conversation," I mumbled, but I didn't falter this time. I took her by the hand and led her from the room without even saying so long to the Sinman and Charlie.

When Sharlee got to my room she showed some of that aimless restlessness that had been so apparent the first time we met. "Where's your TV?" she asked. "I like TV. Don't you even have a set?" I shook my head. No. "Then I'm going to sleep." She pulled off her skirt and sweater and jumped in bed. As soon as she got comfortable, she began to snore gently. I was sure she was faking and wondered why. Perhaps she was testing me; to see if I was too much of a pussy to openly resent her going to sleep on me.

I sat beside her on the bed and tried to figure my next move. She looked so lovely that I was actually afraid to touch her. She might resent that. Then fear of her anger gave way to a pounding need. I *had* to fondle her. She did not move. I bent over her and kissed her. Her lips responded slightly. So it had to be some kind of game she was playing and I was more than willing to play. I took off her slip while her supple body moved obligingly. I stared at those long, beautifully shaped legs and wondered if I was being smart. Sharlee could not possibly love me, and although she was willing, all she could really give me was a dissatisfaction with Gloria. And God knows I didn't want that, but I couldn't stop. I unhooked her bra. Her breasts were exactly as Charlie had described them. I kissed them. I didn't want to ever stop, but I did, to remove her panties. When I ran my hands all over her flawless hips and thighs,

I saw that her elbows and knees were not dark and ashy like most other girls'.

I stretched myself over her. She moaned slightly and then sucked at my lips. But even if she had not been awake I would have taken her.

When it was over I laid beside her and wondered when she was going to stop faking sleep. She never did. I sighed, realizing that this was her way out. In the morning she could claim that tonight was just a lost interlude. Then too, I suspected that for some perverse reason she wanted to take some of the joy out of it for me. I went to sleep holding her.

Sharlee woke at about 5 A.M. "I'm hungry," she announced. I was not so sleepy that I could not hear the vindictiveness in her voice.

I also knew that she had been up and inspected my bare refrigerator. "Okay, I'll feed you," I said.

"How?" she demanded.

"There's two bulldikers in the next room that'll be up in half an hour. If I promise them a pint of wine when the store opens they'll fix you a seven-course dinner."

Sharlee looked at me with a suppressed spitefulness. Then her expression changed to pure loathing. "I hate sex!" she said.

"Yeah. So I see," I growled. Now would come the act of innocence.

"Why'd you take my things off?"

"Why do you think?"

"You'd have done it if I was dead!"

I damned near loved Sharlee that much. Her unfair truth hurt! And I was so hopelessly ensnared. I guess when you are brutally frank and come right out and say a girl has good pussy you mean she has a combination of things working for her. Like her health, face, mind, and the amount of fat deposits in her vagina; and maybe a lot more things yet. But whatever the case Sharlee had it and plus. We had been a perfect fit. And it only makes sense to love what your body really goes for. So if I couldn't do or say something to wipe that look of loathing from Sharlee's face I knew I would surely flip for good.

"Sinman told me you were a real special sort of john. I didn't exactly dig the score . . ." Sharlee said almost pensively. "Twenty dollars." Not angrily. Nothing rueful.

"That was a dirty trick! He didn't know if I had one red cent."

"It's not your fault," she said carelessly. "I'm not mad. I shouldn't have been drunk. If I hadn't of been drunk I'd never even thought of trying to turn a trick with you." A little of the hardness returned. "And you thought I came up here for kicks!"

"I loved you so much I didn't take time to even think about it," I said in a rush. She stared. "You came up here. Your body was here in my bed. Goddammit. I love you. What'd you expect me to do? Go ahead. Send me to jail, but you think for one minute I'll ever say I'm sorry? I didn't ask or want love. You're too beautiful to give me that. I only thought you pitied me."

"That's only because you don't know me. You wouldn't spit on me if you knew the truth."

"I know all there is to know about you," I said doggedly. "What kind of a habit did you have anyway?"

"Horse. Forty dollars a day at least, at the end. Did Sinman tell you that I was the youngest junky ever treated by the state of New York?"

"Yes. So I know all about you and what I don't know I can guess at. But how did you support your habit in the beginning? I mean at thirteen?"

The sound she made in her throat was not quite a laugh. "Easy, keed. Real easy if you've got heart. You don't have heart, do you?" She looked at me levelly.

"Don't you think it takes heart to love you and all the time knowing you never will give a damn about me? And how'd you get hold of forty dollars a day?" I didn't want to talk about fruitless love any more. I wanted to talk about her.

"I hate sex, but sometimes if I was uptight I would turn a trick. But not often."

"What else did you do?"

"Stickups mostly. I had a couple of guys for partners. I was the lookout most of the time. And then I had my own little racket." Pride crept into her voice. "I kept a rock in my purse or my pocket." She pointed to my tiny alarm clock. "It was smooth and just fitted into the palm of my hand. Small as that there. I'd pick up a john and insist that it had to be in my own apartment or nothing shaking. Hotels weren't nice, I'd say. I had a couple of favorite houses on Forty-ninth Street. Right off Broadway. I picked up most of my dates in all-night restaurants and drugstores. I can't stand drunks. Well, my favorite houses had nice dark front doors. So when I got in the vestibule I would do the trying-to-unlock-the-door bit. Then I'd turn to the greasy john and smile bravely and ask him to unlock the door for me because I was so nervous, and tell him that the reason I let him pick me up was because I'd just got to New York and couldn't seem to do anything right. And so when the chump turns his back to me and starts fumbling in the lock with the key I'd hit him in the ear with my rock. Then I'd roll him for his ring and watch and wallet. I killed a man once. I read it in the paper the next day."

"What did you do when you read it?"

"I was a junky then," she replied. "What did you expect me to do?"

"I mean, didn't it bother you?"

"Huh," Sharlee said. "In a hotel on 116th Street my best friend got both her breasts cut off by a freak. And I had another friend . . . we used to call each other cousins . . . that had to jump out of an eighth-floor window on 125th. Both of them dead for nothing. I took my chances and the johns took theirs. It wasn't my fault the guy had a thin skull."

I thought of Gloria and how she had laid right here and practically boasted of having caused her cousin's death.

"You think you're in love now?" Sharlee asked.

"I ain't got nothing you can turn off and on like a faucet," I said angrily. "I don't care if you murdered *me*. I'd still have to love you. I ain't got no choice in the matter."

Sharlee turned her face on the pillow and searched my face. Her eyes searched thoroughly. I don't know what she hoped to find, but I knew she hadn't found it.

My only solace was that she wasn't going to find it in any other man's face either.

"How old are you, Sid?"

"Forty-two. Why?"

"I'm twenty-two, but I like older men. Young boys are a nuisance. They always got to be proving something."

An imperious knocking at the foyer door. It wasn't Blind Charlie, but something was up. Sharlee and I listened as we heard Leah open the door and say something cheery, but whoever was at the door wanted no cheer. It was a man and he immediately began to curse Leah.

"Don't bring me that goddam lie," Leah shrieked over the man's cursing. "I never sold a lemon in my life. And how come nobody's complaining but you? All my bags are the same."

"I bought the shit to wake up on and when I hit myself: nothing. It didn't do a goddam thing."

"You're high now," Leah shouted. Then we heard her footsteps followed by the man's going back toward Leah's room. "Ray," Leah yelled. "C'mere and listen to the shit this bastid is putting down."

I went and cracked the door. I didn't have the slightest idea of what part I intended to play. I guess I wanted to show Sharlee that I wasn't a pussy.

Sharlee was bored. "All junkies ought to be dead," she said.

From down the hall came sounds as if the man was putting on a convulsion act like the one Kingfish had pitched in the Sinman's room. Leah came running back down the hall to knock at Mr. Grimm's door. I heard her ask for permission to use his telephone.

When she came out of Mr. Grimm's room she passed my door muttering, "Now we'll see how sick you are, motherfucker."

Ten minutes went by. Leah, Ray and the man argued. He insisted he wasn't going to leave until he got another bag.

There came another knock on the foyer door and Leah came running to answer it. "Come in," she said, cheerful again.

"What's the matter, lady?" a voice said.

"I got this goddam junky in my room who won't get out, see? And he's been going to Hollywood with his fits and things like that, and making out like I sold him a lemon. I'm Leah Benson, and I never sold a lemon in my life. I got a record oooh-long down at headquarters, but I ain't no thief. You remember me, don't you? I've seen you lots of times. I used to be around 116th and Eighth Avenue all the time. C'mon and take a look at this motherfucker. I just want you to dig what he's putting down."

I got back out of bed and went to the door just in time to see this Black policeman clumping past behind Leah.

"Get up off that floor and get the hell outa here before I break this stick over your head," I heard him say.

Leah's tormentor came scurrying by. He was a tiny Chinese cat I knew by sight.

The door to Leah's room slammed shut and Sharlee said harshly, "Now she pays off."

"Pays off?" I said. The payoff for what I had just witnessed would be so enormous that all parties concerned would just have to forget it. There couldn't be any sensible payoff.

Sharlee laughed. "Sinman said you were a hopeless square. Do you actually think a pusher can call the cops like this and not pay off?"

"But what's the price? Do you realize Leah confessed to a crime that could get her five years? She could have got out of this whole thing for a five-dollar bag of shit. But what has she got to pay now? All you can say is the favor that cop did her is priceless."

Sharlee shrugged. "Nothing is priceless to a pig. I know. I've been where it's at and I know. Pigs and junkies were born out of the same bag and when they grow up they all find the same bag to work out of. That girl and the pig are brother and sister. And she'll take care of him."

"Like what?"

"Whatever he wants. Some like monn-nee. Some are junkies and want narco. Some have a cunt-collar and want pussy. Some are stone freaks and maybe Leah might only have to whip him or some other silly thing. And some might want all three or four of those things. Anyhow, she won't have any trouble even if she did let her anger do a silly thing. But even so, when you're dealing you got to be a stone hustler; you let somebody mess over you just once and you've had it. You know a pusher can do a pig a whole lot of favors, don't you?"

"Will you please tell me what kind of a favor a hopheaded pusher can do a cop unless it's stooling?"

"All kinds," Sharlee said patiently. "Suppose they shake down a kid who's just starting out and they find, say, ten bags on him. What else is there to do with that heroin but to bring it to somebody like that woman in there? And they'll make her pay thirty-five, maybe even forty dollars for those ten bags she could get from her connection for three dollars apiece. And neither she nor the pigs knows whether those bags are lemons or not."

Sharlee's cool recital of the facts of life left me feeling so damn alienated I was damn near crazy. In this Logan I was still not only an ignorant fool but useless. And above all else I was useless to Sharlee. And Sinman talked to me about writing about the Logan. What the hell can a blind virgin write about a whorehouse?

Sharlee must have read in my face all I was thinking because she said, "Come here, Sid."

I went to the bed because in a real sense I had no other place to go. She cupped her hands around my face and kissed me in the mouth. It was a long, ravening kiss. In a moment I was on fire. I started to lay with her, but then she uncupped her hands with a motion as if she was tossing my face away, and jumped out of bed. I sank in the spot she had vacated, breathing heavily.

Sharlee went to her big shoulder bag on the dresser and took a bottle of Cutty out of it.

"Did you steal that from the Sinman?" I asked.

"Yes. He won't need it."

"What about Charlie?"

"Charlie understands me." She filled a water glass to the brim and drank a little of it. She put the glass down and stretched out on top of me. Her tiny breasts were pushed against my lips.

"A girl likes to have her whole body made love to," she said softly. After a moment Sharlee twisted her breast away from my lips. "Here! Put your hand there." Her speech was guttural now, choked, as she guided my hand to her clitoris. I never dreamed a girl could go so wild from manipulation. As I continued I looked at her face. It was beautiful, tortured by the exquisite agony of orgasm. And when it was past she did not tire. "Now you," she said, almost sobbing and turned over. She was the most satisfying creature in the whole world. Then we were lying side by side. Spent. Thinking of nothing.

Joey knocked on the door and pushed her way in. Sharlee stared at me with consternation and awe: she simply could not comprehend how dumb I was. But her disgust at my not locking the door vanished as she eyed Joey. A current of something far more burning than electricity passed through their glances at each other. Each gave a short, barely perceptible nod.

After that nod I was literally dismissed. They were soon rapping about mutual acquaintances in Bedford. They knew each other by reputation and each was glad to meet the other in person.

After a while I rebelled. It had not been sex in that look they gave each other. It had been an acknowledgment of their mutual anti-social understanding. One look and each had known that Bedford had been their second home. Why had God made me fall in love with this? Wasn't Gloria enough for me? I got out of bed and grew angier because they didn't even look at buck-naked me. When I was dressed I went down to the Sinman's room without even saying so long.

"Top of the morning," Sinman cried. "And don't tell me." He raised his hand. "I can look and see that you are now one of our mystical sect."

"Sharlee is not like any other woman," I said. "You drown yourself in her and you come up a new man. I'm different now. It's like I've conquered all there is in the world to conquer, been everywhere there is in the world to go. I'm together. I'm at peace, if you know what I mean. Where's Charlie?"

"Prowling the building. Sharlee makes him restless. His personality does not readily lend itself to loving pagan goddesses who refuse to be dominated. But I have heard him cry out in his sleep for her. And just think: he has never seen Sharlee. Only her brain and body have communicated with him, but he is her slave. More so than you and I."

"I'm not so sure about that," I said, reflecting. After all, Blind Charlie and Sid Bailey were not dedicated dope fiends because of Sharlee.

"By the way, your Welfare investigator dropped by and paid her respects. She promises not to annoy you."

I smiled with condescending disbelief. "I don't even have an investigator yet," I said. "The one who came by and put me on Welfare and gave me my ID card said he was quitting and that another one would be assigned to me in the near future, but nobody else has ever showed up."

Sinman was mildly exasperated. "You don't have to be formally introduced to your investigator to have been assigned one. I tell you I have talked to her about you. She is the one who has nearly half the cases in this building. I also told her that you are in dire need of clothing. That check will come in handy. And I can promise you that she will personally see to it that you receive all the little extras."

"Yeah. I bet."

"She loves me and I always try to find time to bed her down whenever she gets a chance to sneak by."

"Sneak by?"

"The darling child is afraid to go above the lobby in this consecrated pesthole. Her husband visits all of her clients for her."

"Now how the hell could she get away with that?"

"She gives him her ID card to flash on these unsuspecting souls who can barely read or write. He asks them questions, takes down their answers and gives them to her. He has been doing it for years."

I laughed. "So I'm not the only one who's taking Welfare for a ride. But suppose one of her clients calls up Welfare and asks to speak to Mr. So-and-so?"

"It would only seem natural to those who work for Welfare. Everybody on Welfare is mentally deficient, to their way of thinking."

"But just because this dame has hot pants for you is no proof she or her husband won't investigate me."

"You can stand a close investigation. Besides, I have told her that you are privy to our little affair."

"You show her a lot of respect, don't you?"

"I hate the clown. She is disgustingly *nouveau riche;* not really *riche,* but absolutely *nouveau,* a degenerate in every sense of the word. But I happen to be interested in her species. Welfare investigators intrigue me. Do you know that they all suffer from the junky syndrome? But since their duties give them autocracy over the lives of several dozen people's health, wealth, prosperity and peace of mind they do not need heroin. Their right to destroy people is a hefty enough narcotic. But they are far less resilient than the user of heroin. All are susceptible to emotional upsets. More social workers need psychiatric care and treatment than any other professional group. But each and every one of them attributes his nervous breakups to the hazards of the profession."

"Why do you go out of your way to screw a chick you hate? What color is she anyhow?"

"Coal black. But you should see her grovel before my so-called lily-white skin. As for your other question, I shall say that pure hatred is a powerful aphrodisiac; it is very easy to make her think I lust for her too."

"Why do so many Black bitches love to be despised by whitey?"

"The human mind and body comprise an intricate maze that only a madman can truly divine. And that brings me to Sharlee: did you leave that child in the clutches of J&J?"

I started. Impossible as it might seem, I had momentarily forgotten Sharlee. "I left her in my room talking to Joey," I said. "They got on my nerves so I left."

"Go get her!" the Sinman ordered. "It would be better if you beat her all the way down here than to have her bed down with a female at this time. I can only hope that the presence of Jinny will serve as a deterrent."

He might just as well have come right out and said I was impotent or at least not enough of a man for Sharlee. "Sharlee's not an animal!" I snapped.

"Don't you know that Charlie will have a fit? He doesn't approve of sexual aberrations anyhow. Neither does he like J&J's style too much. And Leah and Ray might try to get into the act. Scoot and get that child."

And I did. My room was empty and so I went in J&J's. Sharlee was sitting on the bed, Indian fashion. She was nude except for her panties. She was laughing, her face turned up to Joey's. It was a cruelly perfect portrait that Sharlee offered there on the bed. Once more I thought of teardrops to describe her wonderful and exotic face. And she seemed so unself-conscious, so composed in her realm.

I went to her and muttered, "You gotta get out of here."

"Don't whisper," she said sharply.

But I continued to whisper. "Charlie might come by any minute and I don't want him to find you in here."

She looked at me with distaste. "So you're afraid of Charlie, eh? You should've thought of that when you were raping me."

"I didn't rape you."

"Liar."

"You are a dirty sonofabitch," Jinny yelled at me.

"No, he ain't," Joey roared, and proceeded to tell me that I had a raging Oedipus complex.

Suzie arrived and grinned at everybody.

"How'd you get in?" Jinny said eagerly.

"The front door was open," Suzie said.

"You dumb bastid," Joey yelled at me. "You gonna leave the house wide open for anybody to walk in on this kid here and she ain't even dressed yet? What the hell kind of a man are you anyway? You can't even protect yourself, much less a lady like Sharlee here."

"Suppose a junky should have come by, looking for Leah?" Jinny stormed.

"All junkies should be dead," Sharlee said. She remained in her cross-legged position while reaching down between the bed and the wall. She brought up her bottle of scotch and put it to her lips.

"Don't drink out of the bottle, honey," Joey said. "Let me get you a glass."

"Leave her alone, can't you?" Jinny snapped, and put a protective arm around Sharlee's bare shoulders. Joey snorted and glared.

"Now you two shouldn't fight before company," Suzie mewled.

"Keep outa this," Jinny said to her.

Suzie's eyes widened with innocence. "Ah ain't said nothing."

"When me and my old lady is discussing something we don't need you butting in," Joey said loudly. "That's the trouble with the people in this goddam hotel anyhow. If they'd learn to keep their mouths shut there wouldn't never be no fights."

I seized the chance to sit down beside Sharlee. "Please come and put your clothes on."

"You got any monn-nee?"

"Yes," I said desperately.

"Have you got twenty dollars?"

"Almost."

Sharlee sprang off the bed and marched out of the room. I tailed behind her, staring at her long legs. The gleaming black panties were only a wisp but they set those thighs off to perfection.

Sharlee went to my mirror and started putting on make-up. I sat on the bed, admiring that perfect shape once more. "You play basketball in school?" I asked. "Didn't you go in for athletics?"

"No," Sharlee said disinterestedly.

"Your body is so perfectly muscled that it seems impossible. I bet you would have been a star athlete in any sport. Better than Althea Gibson." In her exquisitely female way Sharlee was as finely chiseled as Sugar Ray.

"Oh. That? Lots of men have told me about my body. I'm not so bad-looking either, according to them, but what good has it done me?" She turned from the mirror and smiled. "It even gets me raped in my sleep."

"I'm going to make it up to you for that," I said quickly. "I honestly thought you were awake. I swear it, Sharlee."

She stopped putting on lipstick to stare at me. "How can you keep saying that?" She seemed honestly bewildered.

And that bewilderment was the sword that ripped my guts. "But you moved," I said weakly. "You moved your body like you knew."

"I—I don't know whether to believe you or not," Sharlee said softly as if to herself. Then she shook her head as if to clear it of a painful thought. Her eyes blazed. "I suppose you're going to tell everybody that I got drunk and flipped for you."

"What happened in this room is between me and you only." My voice was gruff with anger, directed not at Sharlee but at anyone who would intrude upon this thing of ours . . . whatever it was.

"It's been a long time since I messed with a square," Sharlee said reflectively. It was as if she was giving a logical explanation of all her acts and words so far.

I took the sixteen dollars I had left out of my pocket. "Here, Sharlee," I said, offering it to her.

"I don't want it," she said, putting on her skirt.

"But I promised it to you."

She stopped and stared at me again. "You had me, isn't that enough?"

"You think I'm trying to make a whore out of you?" I exclaimed. "I love you." And like a frustrated dramatist, I walked out.

"I knew you would not let me down," Sinman said as soon as I got back.

And it wasn't long before Sharlee appeared to astound me with her young virginal appearance. Dewy was the word for her. And I was forced to recall Jinny's repeated assertions that heroin is a preservative. And doggone it, maybe it is. However, social psychologists have long been aware that very anti-social people are very often baby-faced. Like they're always citing Baby Face Nelson, Pretty Boy Floyd, and the like as prime examples. As for me, I can give you all the handsome Black pimps in Manhattan *and* their women. Maybe the real answer might lie in the fact that it would seem that narco is a physical preservative which baby-faced people are prone to use.

The dewy Sharlee had not bothered with last night's intricate hairdo. Now she wore two long braids that nearly reached her childlike breasts.

"Cutty Sark for breakfast, my dear?" Sinman asked her.

"Yes, and don't forget just one ice cube." Without another word she began to pace back and forth. After Sinman had handed her the glass he went to his organ and began to play softly. "Where's Charlie?" Sharlee demanded. "I want to dance with Charlie."

"Sid, please go about the premises and find him," Sinman said.

I decided to try the sixth floor first and work my way down. As soon as I got off the elevator I yelled for Charlie.

"Who dat using my name in vain?" the blind man's voice boomed in return. "Where you at? The elevator?"

"Yeah, it's me, Sid. Sinman and Sharlee want you."

"Well, why didn't you say so?" Charlie came out of the 6-A door. I saw that he was pretty high already.

I brought Charlie over in front of the elevator. As we stood waiting Charlie said, "You is a lucky boy. Sharlee couldn't wait to get you up to your room last night."

I didn't like it, but I wasn't going to tell Charlie that. So I muttered, "There really wasn't anything happening. She just flopped across my bed and went to sleep."

"WHAT? YOU DIDN'T GET NONE OF THAT NOOKY?"

Charlie was so infuriated I was afraid to say yes or no.

"You ain't got the sense you was born with," Charlie said bitterly. "What you think she leaves us for and goes upstairs with you for, to read one of your goddam *Time* magazines? Reading sure must take a man's nature!"

Realizing that I had to admit to something no matter how much I hated to, I said, "I made out all right." I felt like a Judas but, after all, I was dealing with a madman who had the strength of a dozen Samsons.

"You goddam fool you. Why didn't you say so at first? What you trying to upset me for, boy?" Then Charlie grew suspicious. "Ain't you lying, boy?"

"No. Hell no!"

"I'm gonna ast Sharlee and she's gonna tell me the truth. Sharlee don't bother to lie to nobody. I just hope you ain't lying. I don't like to see no good pussy go to waste."

I shivered, not so much because of Charlie's threat as because any way things turned out Sharlee wasn't going to have much respect for me.

In the short time I had been gone the Sinman's room had mysteriously filled with people. I looked in dismay at the ten or twelve people, half of whom were dancing to the Sinman's tunes. The others, both the men and the women, were all flirting with Sharlee. Now she was the gay and laughing princess again and I saw angrily that she did not seem to mind everyone trying to touch her. Yeah. Even the women did not seem to be able to keep their hands off Sharlee.

Charlie had tapped his way over to the morris chair, but I remained rooted inside the door, glaring at the scene. Sharlee was swept from one pair of pawing hands to another. And Sharlee's breasts seemed so tiny, so defenseless.

I was so disgusted that I did not even bother to feel surprise at seeing J&J there. But with a touch of malice I wondered how Joey would react if I went over and asked her for a dance. Before I could fit action to surmise, Joey stopped dancing with Suzie to dance with Jinny. I was doubly galled to see that the two danced well together. Almost like pros.

I went over and sat beside the Sinman. For some time I watched the beautiful hands of the addict as they moved across the keyboard.

"Sharlee is not going to approve of your moping," he said.

"Why does everybody have to put their hands on her?" I exclaimed in a fresh burst of anger.

"I understand how you feel," Sinman said softly. "Her face and figure are something of a curse. Sharlee is by no means stupid, but she does not have the emotional stamina or the level-headed thought processes that a beauty such as hers demands. It is both a strain and a drain upon her to have everyone constantly touching her; she resents it very much when she is not drinking. But every once in a while she gets drunk like this, she sort of resigns herself, as if she is exhausted from fending off the world. Like now, her drinking is murderous. She probably doesn't have the slightest notion of what is going on and if she knew she surely wouldn't care. But she looks far soberer than anyone else, doesn't she?"

"You mean she's ossified? I don't believe it. She couldn't be. Look at her, man. Look at her."

"Yes. It must be a part of her oriental heritage. She never looked like a junky either."

"Can she get any drunker than this? I mean does she ever stagger or get nasty? Want to fight?"

"She used to brawl quite a bit, but she says she has given that up too."

The more I looked at Sharlee the more I was convinced that she knew exactly what was going on. To prove it to myself I asked her to dance with me. She was even more difficult to lead than last night and I had a sudden suspicion that Sharlee purposely danced this way. Like a favor to me, the Sinman began to play a slow blues, and I decided to stay in one spot, just swaying back and forth to the music.

"That bulldiking Joey thinks she's so damned slick!" She really barked her words. "I don't like for some broke-assed broad to take me for granted." She drew back and glared at me. "And you: Why didn't you kick her ass, you pussy?"

"Me? For what?"

"Upstairs in her room. I was *your* company. She and Jinny weren't supposed to be telling you how to take care of me. As far as they're concerned, I'm *yours*." She held me a little tighter and grumbled, "And if those two don't watch it I'll be screwing both of them."

"You'll *what?*"

"You heard what I said. I've been in the life just as tough as they have." She drew back and stared pugnaciously. "I can make any broad I want. Any stud, too."

"That's nothing to boast about. Do you realize how you sound?"

"Don't make like the Sinman now. And I only made a passing remark. But don't you think I can get tired of everybody hitting on me?"

"That's why you should take your time and pick carefully—"

"Oh, shut up and keep in step."

"I'm in step. You keep making it hard for me to lead you. I think you can't stand the idea of a man leading."

"If you don't shut up I'm going to stop dancing with you."

"Okay. So you do the talking. Tell me when you're going to come see me again. And don't forget, I promised to give you twenty dollars."

"I can stay with any man for an hour and make twenty dollars."

Gloria had said the same thing although there seemed to be a psychological variation in the two statements. But the girls were not variations. Each had only distilled the meaning of her life. They had told what was in store for them unless this world suddenly changed for the better. And for the very first time I felt some sympathy for Sinman's futile wish that God was dead and that a new god was on his way.

So once more I thought of Gloria and Sharlee as being components of a whole. They spiritually interlocked. Were viable and without rancor. And both were goddesses. It didn't make sense not to love them. In fact, how could you adore one without adoring the other?

Joey came up with a kind of swinging hop and skip and extended her hand like an impudent schoolboy. And before I knew it Sharlee had been whisked away by Joey. I didn't look at them; I preferred to caricature in my mind those two trying to lead each other. I even had them coming to blows.

When Sharlee and Joey stopped dancing there came an interlude when everyone in that damn room attempted to ravish Sharlee. Sure. They were discreet, but they ravished her just the same. Everyone in the room had maggot hands and each person in the room seemed to be greedily awaiting his or her turn to touch the goddess. And they were all so furtive: why the hell didn't they throw her down and do a gang job? That's what they wanted to do!

When I couldn't stand it any more I quietly left. I was upset. Sure. But I really wasn't angry or even jealous. These were sick people. Sharlee's beauty had made them ill. And Sharlee had seemed so defenseless against those marauding hands. And I believe now that Sharlee was the only person on earth who had a *right* to use narcotics, alcohol or anything else she chose. Like I said before, I really don't think God intended to make Sharlee so lovely. She was one of His mistakes.

I crossed the lobby to the office window. Old man Epstein was on duty. "I want to borrow twenty dollars," I said.

"Ain't you on Welfare?" Epstein squealed. He was frightened.

"Naw," I said sternly. All business. "I've got to go back on the job tomorrow and I need a new pair of tux pants to work in. I'm a waiter and one day's tips will pay you back." I must have sounded pretty good because he went to the cash box and took out the twenty and gave it to me.

"Don't ever tell anybody I did this," he said.

"Thanks. Don't worry, I won't." I took the elevator to the sixth floor and went to Mr. Johnson's room.

"Come in here, boy, and shake my hand," Mr. Johnson cried.

"How's every little thing, Mr. Johnson? Where's all the pretty women today?" I said.

"Aw shucks, boy. Them ole gals just comes around when I got big pockets."

I grinned. "That ain't the way I heard it."

"Don't let 'em fool you, boy. Where's that Lina? I ain't been seeing her lately."

"She cut out when my girl friend got out." And I silently marveled at the short length of time it had taken me to be able to make that statement so casually.

"Good. I hated like all get-out to see a smart man like you get hisself all messed up with the likes of Lina. Now mind you, Lina is my friend, and a good one too. And one time when we lived in the same hotel and I got sick she fed me and nursed me, but that don't keep me from telling the truth and saying that Lina can be low-down. She'll tell a lie on anybody, including herself. And if you ever saw the kind of men she's been sleeping with you'd be ashamed to say you ever had. But you is a Christian boy. People like Lina always can use you, seems like. And lie? Bet she tole you she just come from the hospital, didn't she?"

"Yeah, when I first met her. Didn't she?"

"Lina's a goddam liar!" Mr. Johnson yelled furiously. "That lying little minx had been out three weeks or more and was staying downstairs with that nut!" I absently wondered why all the Logan's tenants get so worked up discussing things that are absolutely none of their business. "You heard about the police taking a damn fool outa here to Bellevue?" Mr. Johnson demanded. "Down on the second floor. He pulled all the plumbing out of the toilet in 2-A and then began to cut hisself all in the head with his own knife?"

Yeah, the Sinman was right and I had been a charitable ass. But charity is what makes a square, I rationalized. I was born to be what I am. And so was Lina for that matter.

"But somebody has to be a friend of Lina's," I said. "And that's all I tried to be. And she's not quite Mary Magdalene." A sudden thought struck me: "She lie about her sister too? Lina said she would beat her up and take her check."

"Lina is a bum and a liar and a beggar, I tell you. She got two sisters. One is married and is a housewife with no children and a good husband. The other works for Welfare. Now which one got a reason to take Lina's few pennies? Did one ever come looking for her all them weeks she laid up on you?"

"And this boy friend who was pestering her, what about him?"

"A watermelon-headed nigger with bugeyes that stammers?"

"That's him."

"Ain't worth flushing down the toilet. I seen him take and throw all Lina's pots and pans outa the window and then turn right around and get in bed with her. And she let him. Both of them is rotten. Yessir."

Now I was silent but my mind was at work; it had to work and somehow save some of my ego. So gradually I worked myself into a righteous indignation at all the healthy people in the Logan who had nothing to do but castigate a seventy-pound cripple who was absolutely harmless. As far as I was concerned, they might as well have been picking on a newborn babe.

I immediately cooled it though when this lovely Black girl walked slowly into the room. She had a jock shape, fairly nice hair and a wonderful mahogany complexion. "How do you do, Mr. Johnson?" she said politely.

"How do you do yourself, stranger?" Mr. Johnson cried. "Have a chair and I got me a little drink here I was saving back from Sid here. It's half and half. You'll like it."

"No, thanks. I stopped drinking wine, Mr. Johnson," she said in the same polite voice as before. "Wine can drive you crazy." She turned to me with interest. "So your name's Sid? Don't you know Lina Davis?"

"Yeah." I grinned. "I know her pretty well."

Her eyes became cat slits just before she flashed a straight razor and slashed at me with all her might. I gave a little scream and jumped back, throwing up my hands to protect my face. And I felt the sting of the razor as it cut into the palms of both my hands.

I figured I had fainted while still standing up because I could hear Mr. Johnson's voice in the distance yelling, "You no-good dirty skunk! What you cut that boy for? Git out! Git out, I say. This here is a can of lye and it's going in your face in a minute!"

The girl fled. I stared at the two fountains of blood spurting from my hands. Mr. Johnson grabbed the sheet off his bed and made a bundle of it for me to hold.

"Crazy bitch. . . . That crazy bitch," he kept muttering.

My lips were trembling so that I could hardly speak. "Who was that?" I quavered.

"Bessie Smith, Lina's sister. The one that works on Welfare, and she still ain't got no better sense than to run 'round stabbing innocent people. That Lina done tole her some dirty lie on you. Might even have said you took her check or worse. And you gotta get to the hospital right away. You gonna need stitches."

When we reached the lobby I began to weaken. "I gotta have a drink, Mr. Johnson," I said. "Let's go in the Sinman's room and get one."

But old man Epstein ran out of the office and started searching my pockets. I couldn't stop him because I had to keep clutching the bundled sheet to quench the flow of blood.

"Leave that boy alone!" Mr. Johnson roared and began to jab warningly at Epstein with his switchblade.

"He's got twenty dollars on him," Epstein squawked. "And he's been fighting and ain't gonna go to work tomorra."

But Mr. Johnson managed to hustle me out of the hotel before the old man could get his twenty back. Lots of cabs passed us by, but finally a Black cabby picked us up and took us to St. Luke's. They took me into the emergency and sewed me up right away. We got back to the Logan in less than an hour.

It was like a concentrated scream the folks let out when Mr. Johnson and I walked into the Sinman's room for a drink. But it was left for Jinny to put on the truly righteous act. First she made believe she had fainted. Then she sat up on the floor and screamed at the top of her lungs.

"Who dat been trying to kill my fren'?" Blind Charlie yelled and came barging over to me, knocking all in his way right and left. "C'mere, boy, and tell me exactly what happent!"

But before he reached me Sharlee put her arms around my neck. "Get me out of here!" she said in a fierce whisper.

CHAPTER 18

"I BET THAT GIRL was a junky," Sharlee said next morning.

"Why?" I asked, wondering if anybody in the whole hotel was ever going to get around to asking me exactly *who* it was who cut me and why.

It was odd, but Mr. Johnson had been very uninformative in the Sinman's room.

"You know it was a junky," Sharlee said mildly, not expecting an answer. "All junkies should be dead."

"Why do you keep saying that? Isn't the Sinman a junky and isn't he your best friend?" I watched her closely for a reaction.

She frowned. "Of course he is. I mean, of course he is an addict. I don't know whether to call him a friend or not sometimes. He makes out like he has to be nice to me whether he wants to or not. I know that sounds very off the wall, but that's the way it is for real. And in lots of ways the Sinman isn't an addict. It's more like he tries to be an addict. Honestly, there's lots of things about him that the average addict can't do. You know, it's funny. Like he *tries* to be a Negro." She sighed. "He's the world's worst failure, that guy."

"Well, that guy happens to be one of the most self-sufficient people I know. He and Blind Charlie. I don't see where he's failed in anything unless it is as a composer."

Sharlee shrugged helplessly. "It's the Logan maybe. It gets me down," she confessed. "And it seems like this morning the Sinman has a lot to do with it. And he used to be so different."

I laughed to lighten her mood. "Somehow I thought you were impervious to his philosophy and things." A sudden thought sobered me. "Do you think if you and he got real tight again he would return to some kind of sanity?"

"No. I tried, but it didn't work at all. I even offered to get a divorce and marry him once." Her laugh was flat and hollow. "He turned me down."

"No!" I exclaimed.

"You know, you've got the wrong idea about me and the Sinman. There's no sex in the way he likes me. Not for real there isn't. If you really want to know the truth, he treats me like a half-witted daughter even though he don't have enough sense to know I'm half-witted. That sounds off the wall too, I guess, but that's the way it is."

"Somehow I had the idea that the Sinman only needed you to marry him and he'd cut out all this dope and God-is-dead business."

"I don't know," Sharlee said uncertainly. "Sometimes I get the idea that there is something I can give the Sinman, but I don't know what it is. It's not love or marriage though. Gee, that guy can get on my nerves sometimes."

"He insinuates that you twisted his life. In fact, he puts it the other way around and says that he found truth the day he met you."

"He didn't find nothing the day he met me."

"Don't say that. What do you mean, nothing? You're only the most beautiful girl in the world. You've got brains. You've got more possibilities than any other girl in New York City. You could make it as a model, in show business, TV announcer, anything!"

"You ever hear of a cabaret card? I can't even get permission to be a hatcheck girl. When I got real tight with Sinman it was because I had no place to live. At least no place where I wanted to live. And he was swell to me, but I never appreciated it. I was a bitch. Just that: a bitch! I made believe my habit was oooh-long. Actually I let my habit get bigger and bigger so that he would have to scuffle harder. It was like freaking off when I would demand more and more heroin. But it was me who got tricked in the end when he couldn't get up the bread any more—while I still had that ooh-long habit for real. I get so ashamed of myself at times. Let's talk about something else."

"I only want to talk about you when I'm with you."

Sharlee actually grunted. "Okay," she said, "but I'm going to leave you."

"I'll follow you."

"I won't talk to you."

"Why aren't you married?"

"I've been married. I told you I offered to get a divorce and marry the Sinman. I was married when I met the Sinman."

"You married now?"

"I guess."

"If I go back to work will you marry me?"

"No."

"Why?"

"Because I don't want to be married to you, that's why. And stop talking about marriage. I've had enough of it. My husband kept beating me up and then he'd get ashamed and go out and get drunk and pick fights, hoping somebody would kill him, but nobody would. Finally he gave it up and ran away. I'm glad. I think he was losing his mind."

"You're so beautiful I can see how a young guy would act that way, but you give me peace. I'm together for the first time since I don't know when. I swear I'm not jealous of you. But maybe it is best for a girl like you to have a career and no special man until you're sure. Real sure. You don't need a permit to model, why don't you try that?"

"Every man that's got a job I can do wants to be my boy friend too. Especially when they find out I'm not real tight with anyone. They think I'm dumb or something . . . I don't know."

"You don't know about what? Modeling or being dumb?"

"Men thinking I'm dumb because I don't have a man to beat my brains out all the time."

"I see what you mean."

"There's lots of white girls better-looking than me, why do I have to screw everybody just because I'm Black?"

"Sinman said you're not a Negro, but you talk like you're only better-looking than Black girls. How come?"

"I don't mean I'm better-looking than anybody. What I mean is that white men have all the jobs. I never finished high school. I got a certificate from prison, but you think I'm going to take that around with me, asking for a job? That certificate is only a license for every man to grab a titty."

"I think you make a big mistake in insisting that you are Black."

"All of my mother's friends are Black. Who would I invite to the wedding?"

"I didn't mean it exactly that way."

"You think I'm going to write my mother out of my life to get a job?"

"Was your mother born in America?" I suddenly doubted what the Sinman had told me.

Sharlee shook her head. "She was brought here by missionaries.

She says she was born in Asia Minor. A place called Mindina or something like that."

"You mean to say you don't know for sure?"

"She only mentioned it one time. It makes no difference."

"You mean you're not interested?"

"Why should I be?"

"Everybody should be interested in where their parents came from."

"We are American Negroes," Sharlee said sharply. "That's the way it was from the beginning until . . . Well, Mom used to drill it into me at first."

"You sound as if she stopped."

"She did. She stopped raising me."

"What does that mean?"

"What I said. Mom is always sick. She still works hard, but she's always sick. After I was twelve she was too sick to raise me. I raised myself. I even raised her . . . I guess."

"She just turned you out in this jungle to survive?"

"No. After I came out of Westfield the first time she even sent me to Bishop Lawson's School down in South Carolina, but they kicked me out. I didn't like it anyway. It was a damn sight worse than Westfield."

"Kicked you out for what?"

"None of your damn business."

"Well, do you think your mother's really sick?"

"She's got a right to be sick! She's not a citizen. She ran away from the people who brought her here and she's been running ever since until last year. Last year the immigration men finally caught up with her, but when they looked up her record and saw where she'd never been arrested and had always worked for rich white people out on Long Island they let her go. I mean that they didn't make her go back home where she came from, but she's still not a citizen. Neither is my father, but they haven't caught up with him yet."

"What's your father like?"

"My father's father was a Dutchman who lived in Java with a

Javanese woman. He's part Dutch and part Javanese. He can't speak much English at all. He jumped ship to marry my mother, but they've been separated ever since I was a baby." Her lovely face was stormy. "Mom's too Black for him. He lives with a white woman now. He's a Welfare pimp! And Mom's got nobody but me. And what the hell good am I to anybody?"

"What kind of hair has your mother got?"

"I don't know," she snapped. "She has to straighten it, but it's nice. She's pretty when she comes from the hairdresser's. What difference does it make?" She jumped from the bed and began to walk the floor. "It makes me mad every time somebody wants to know what complexion Mom is. She's the same color she was when she married my father!"

Sharlee was angry now, but I had to feed my curiosity. I had to know all. Sharlee was a part of Sid Bailey now. Her anger really didn't matter any more. But I didn't ask any more questions for a few minutes.

Sharlee continued to pace back and forth. There was a fiercely impatient air about her. In fact she acted as if she was now my prisoner. I had a fleeting sense of both guilt and defeat and was on the verge of asking her if she wanted to go down to the Sinman's room when she flung the door open and stalked out in the hall.

I listened to her footsteps going toward the foyer door, but she went on past the door and so I knew she was going to the bathroom. I murmured a prayer of thanksgiving. At least she hadn't walked out on me. But when she came out of the bathroom she went out the foyer door.

After that sound of the closing foyer door I began to curse. I felt truly like a maniac. I wanted to be a maniac. What the hell was the use of living in a life that gave only to retract? Fate was mindless: why did the idiot give me a girl who would walk out in the morning? Why give me a girl whom I couldn't keep interested? I was sick of a life that always screwed you without ever bothering to give you a kiss.

Pure masochism made me get out of bed and lock the foyer door. No sooner had I returned to bed than somebody knocked. I went back and opened it. It was Sharlee, carrying a bottle of Cutty Sark.

"Your hands are going to start throbbing in a little while so I made the Sinman give me another bottle of scotch," she said.

I did not smile. I refused to believe that life had relented. The worst was yet to come. And what it would be, only the Devil in hell knew.

"What's the matter, Sid?"

"Nothing. Why?"

"You look funny. Like maybe somebody's been bothering you. Scared like."

"Naw," I said hastily. "I guess maybe my hands are beginning to hurt a little."

"Well, what is the matter besides your hands? You don't look right to me. Aren't you glad I brought you a drink? Aren't you going to thank me?"

"Thanks."

"No kiss?"

"I thought you didn't like to get mushy?"

"I don't like to be pawed is really all. But you keep your hands to yourself; that's why I don't mind being around you. When a man keeps his hands to himself most of the time I don't mind necking once in a while."

It was the first real break I had got in my dealings with Sharlee. I am a stone freak for breasts and can't keep my hands off of a girl who *has* tits. Like Gloria, for instance. But Sharlee's were so small it seemed almost immoral to touch them.

And, like the imaginative fool I am, I let my mind wander further on the matter of Sharlee's breasts. It seemed to me that if Sharlee had been blessed with a bust and an un-negroid-looking mother she would have been the reigning beauty in the whole wide world. And then I suddenly realized that I was alone with this fabulous creature in a room in the most notorious hotel in New York.

"Don't you work for real, Sid?"

Sharlee's tone and the abruptness of her question gave me to think that she was trying to raise me up in her own eyesight.

"I'm a Lundy's waiter," I said.

"I know *them,*" she scoffed. "I used to be a barmaid in Brooklyn. They're all crazy. They smoke reefers and then come in the bar and order doubles. Ordering doubles will make anybody drunk without first smoking pot. I bet your IQ is just as high as mine almost. You should try to make something of yourself besides a Lundy's waiter." Now she spoke with all the sincerity of a W.C.T.U. worker.

Sincere uplift from a pretty girl makes my back ache. "What happened to the barmaid job?" I asked, cutting her off. "A girl with your looks should have made fabulous tips."

Sharlee shrugged and the resigned look on her face hurt. "There was this cop who would come in every night and pick fights with all the men who talked to me. So the owner said I better quit before he killed somebody for nothing."

"Did you go with him?"

"I didn't even know the meatball's name. He was crazy. All cops are crazy, didn't you know that?"

"I'm learning fast."

"I like Jewish men best. They are never meatballs."

"You do?" I don't know why the hell I was so shocked to hear this non-Negro girl say that she preferred non-Negro men.

"Sure. They all got good sense, Sid. Something like you. They don't start fights. They've got wandering hands, but they'll behave if you tell them to. I thought I was in love with a Jewish numbers banker once, but I was on heroin then, and he kept worrying me to kick the habit. I wouldn't. Not then, I couldn't kick it."

"And you thought you loved him? You kicked it in jail, didn't you?"

"Yes, but I wasn't ready to kick it then. You've got to be ready. I loved heroin more than him. And his money didn't mean anything either in a way. We were holding up stores, and everything was too good to be listening to a square even if he was in the money. But one of the guys in our gang was a cornball. Georgia. He loused us up with his big spending. He was a square, never touched heroin. We should have known better. And so the fuzz got the wire and came for us. I only did eighteen months, but the guys got five years."

"How long ago was all this?"

"A long time. I spent my eighteenth birthday in jail before the trial."

"This gang of yours, were you friends or did you just work together?"

"We were pretty good friends. All but the Georgia cornball had big habits. We had to stick together kind of, but we aren't any good friends now."

"Why?"

"After we got time we practically became enemies. At least their old ladies and me became enemies. They think I owe them and their men something because I got off light. Time I did my bit the bitches came to me, threatening about if I didn't send their old men cigarettes and things they were going to beat me up, have me busted. You should have heard them. I sent five dollars a couple of times, but nobody was satisfied. Those three women got so bad I had to start going with a detective in Brooklyn. That scared them. Before, they had threatened to tell the cops about every job I ever helped to pull and more, but then they got scared that I would tell my boy friend on their old men and that they'd have to do more time."

"Everybody seems to enter your life only to spoil it, don't they?"

"When you've been a junky you're always wide open for the rest of your life. When I got out of jail this last time those girls thought I was going straight back on heroin, but I fooled them. In fact, they just took it for granted that I was back on the shit. They told me they were going to blackmail me like. You know, tell my parole officer."

"These were all colored people?"

"Of course! You don't think I'm dumb enough to go holding up joints with some whiteys, do you?"

"What difference would it make?"

"You don't know how dirty a whitey can be."

"It's a wonder you don't hate the world," I said. "I would if I were you."

Sharlee nodded her head like a little girl. "That's why I try to stay in the house when I'm not working. Only sometimes I have to get out and drink like this."

"You're not really drunk, are you?"

"Yes. I'm drunker than I look. I can't stand for people to look drunk, especially men. Do you ever look drunk?"

"Yeah. I get ossified ever so often and don't care how I look."

"You won't get drunk today, will you?" She really looked disturbed.

"Naw. I don't even feel like drinking today. I just want to lay here and get to know you."

"Good. And I'm going to stay with you all day long."

I simply refused to believe that Sharlee could stay in the company of a dull square that long. "Aren't you going down to the Sinman's room at all?" Then I realized that I *wanted* her to go back and forth during the day. Whenever it got monotonous with me she could go down and be entertained by the Sinman's patter. "Don't you want to go talk to the Sinman and Charlie some?"

"I said what I said, didn't I?" Sharlee said sharply.

"I never dreamed I'd ever be in the company of a girl as pretty as you," I said with a kind of groveling inanity. "Do you think you would have ever touched heroin if you hadn't been so pretty?"

Sharlee laughed dryly. "I was a boy, Sid. I mean a real tomboy. I hated girls. I couldn't stand them. I had to be with boys as long as I can remember. When I was around ten or eleven I cut off practically all my hair. And I had no breasts. I don't think the boys I ran with even thought of me as a girl. And it just so happened that I never lived in Harlem. Mom and I always lived in the West Nineties. It was interracial like. None of us were poor or underprivileged. Some of those Irish kids' fathers owned bars and storage companies and things like that. And Mom saw to it that I never wanted."

"Are you trying to tell me that you're a born junky?"

"Don't give me that Sinman jive. Sure. He's right: there are born junkies, but not as many as he says. Anybody can become an addict. It's the time and the place that counts. Nothing else. After that comes a whole lot of things."

"But the first time, didn't you know you'd get a habit? Didn't you care?"

"I don't know! I was an eleven-year-old baby, how the hell could I be thinking of anything? And what are you trying to do, psychoanalyze me? Well, if you are you can cut it out right now. I don't like it."

"No, no, no. Nothing like that. I was just sort of wondering out loud."

"Well, cut out wondering. Don't make me hot now, see?"

"Okay, Sharlee. Let's change the subject completely."

"You better!"

"Let's talk about you and me. When are we going to see each other again?"

"Probably never. I'll probably never get drunk again."

"I love you, Sharlee. I want to help take care of you. Please try to understand me."

She was at the dresser pouring a drink. "That's what they all say until I start taking their monn-nee."

"I'm no goddam *all,*" I yelled, blind with fury. "I'm Sid Bailey. Don't you ever include me in your goddam all as long as you live! You hear me?"

I was not so blind with rage that I did not note that Sharlee had turned around and was regarding me with respect for the first time. Her mouth was slightly open and her eyes shone brighter. I forgot my anger to ponder this new thing. It was plain that only willful and angrily determined people piqued Sharlee's interest. There were no pussies in her life. And realizing this, I knew that Sharlee would despise the real Sid Bailey once she got to know him. But for the moment I had her going.

J&J barged in without knocking.

"How do you do?" Jinny said with exaggerated politeness. "How are you lovebirds making out?"

"This is no love nest, keed," Sharlee said. "This is St. James Infirmary, but we ain't got those blues yet." Joey started over to the dresser and the bottle of scotch, but Sharlee was quicker. "Wait a minute, keed. I'm going to buy you two your own bottle. What's the name of that blood you were drinking yesterday morning?" She went to her big pocketbook and took out her wallet. When she opened it I saw that it was well filled. That Sharlee had plenty of money increased my doubts about myself. She had defeated me again even though she had promised to stay with me all day.

"We drink Silver Spur," Jinny said, catching Sharlee's rhythm. "And that's what I want. It don't carry you so fast like that damn scotch." She turned to me. "Do you know for real who cut you? I got an idea you never saw the gal before."

"Why?" I asked.

"After all, this is the Logan where cutting by mistake is a way of life," Jinny said. "And you have never messed over anybody. So why cut *you?*"

I faked a wince and said, "I don't even want to talk about it." And I made up my mind right then to get up to Mr. Johnson's as soon as possible and ask him not to mention the fact to anyone that I had been knifed by Lina's sister. So I got out of bed and pulled on my pants.

"Where you going, Sid?" Sharlee asked. "I don't think you should walk around too much. After all, you don't know how much blood you lost yesterday."

"Don't worry about me," I said absently. Then I glanced at her, just in time to catch a fleeting look of admiration on her face. So I added, "You stay put, I'm going for the wine."

"His head is hard, Sharlee," Joey said. "Don't try to tell him anything. Just let the fool go outa here and faint."

"No," Sharlee said. "I'm Sid's nurse. I know what's best for him."

But I walked out over her protests and took the elevator up to the sixth floor. When I entered Mr. Johnson's room, who should I see but Lina sitting on the bed.

"You no-good lying little bitch," I said.

"Ah ain't done nuthin', Sid honey. What you calling me names for?"

"Don't she know what her sister did?" I asked Mr. Johnson.

"Bessie went and made all that up in her own mind," Lina

whined. "Ah ain't said nuthin' 'cept you wouldn't let me sleep with you no more."

I looked at Mr. Johnson again. He shrugged, so I decided to let the whole thing drop. "Do me a favor?" I asked Mr. Johnson. "Don't tell anybody who cut me or why, will you?"

"Sure, boy. Sure," Mr. Johnson said. "I don't blame you none. Ain't nobody's business but yours anyhow."

"I'm on my way to the store; you want me to bring you back a pint?"

"If you can afford it, boy. If you can afford it."

"Sid honey, Ah doan' hate you or nuthin'," Lina said suddenly. "Ah ain't even jealous. Ah got mah room back in the Orin Hall and you is welcome to come stay any time you likes. Ah doan' mean you no harm atall. You ain't done nuthin' but treat me good, and mah sister Bessie knows it now. Ah done tole her, but she's scared to come apologize."

"Does she really work for the Welfare Department?" I had to ask her.

"Yes, Sid. She's a receptionist down 'round Thirtieth Street. Her psychiatrist got her the job."

"What's she doing with a psychiatrist? She crazy for real?"

"When her boy friend started taking dope and went and got hisself arrested she had a nervous breakdown and had to go to the horspital. When she got out she couldn't get no easy job and so her doctor got her a job working for Welfare."

I left the room, wondering if everybody who worked for Welfare was crazy. The pretty little woman who always carried a rag doll was at the elevator. I nodded politely, but she ignored me while we waited. We started down, the car stopped at the fourth floor, and a Black girl got on with a white man. I had seen them many times, but I didn't know them to speak to, and I had not been interested enough to ask J&J about them. Neither was a junky and I wondered where the whitey got the courage to frequent the Logan—or was he just plain dumb?

The woman with the rag doll let out a shriek that curdled my blood. The other two passengers turned to stare at the woman with both horror and anger blended in their looks. And then everybody saw the blood. It trickled in a steady stream from the top of the car, through the crevices around the trap door. It had splattered all over the little woman's dress.

The Black gal began to scream in unison with the lady with the doll and I began to get scared. I'd never seen blood flow like this before.

When the elevator reached the lobby the super came running with a hammer in his hand. "What's all the screaming about?" he demanded, looking at me. Although I was just as hysterical as everybody else my anger flared. The Black bastard just knew it had to be me molesting the women; it couldn't possibly have been the whitey.

"Look and see for yourself," I said and got off the elevator.

The woman with the doll pointed at the blood, making an ever widening pool on the floor.

"Well, come on and get out!" the super yelled and began to shift from one foot to the other as if he had to go make water.

Ginsburg ran up. "What's going on? Does everybody hafta be screaming at the same time?" Then he saw the blood and shut up.

"Why the hell don't you call the police?" I asked him.

"The police been here once this morning," the super said. "It's them goddam junkies again," he added. "They've kilt somebody and threw them on top of that car."

"Why the hell would they do that after they killed him?" I demanded. I even sounded cool to myself, but I didn't really know what I was saying.

"You wanna bet they didn't?" the super growled. He took out a special key that would allow the elevator to move without the doors being closed. He got in and lowered the car a few feet and then the crowd of lobby lice gasped. The man on top of the car wasn't really a man, only about eighteen years old, and he was conscious although the elevator had sheared off the front of his left foot.

"What you doing up there?" Ginsburg roared.

The boy grinned stupidly and fainted.

After a moment or two of hesitation the lobby lice lifted the boy from off the car and laid him out on the lobby floor. In a daze I reached out and picked up the toe of the shoe that had been sliced off. I looked at it and saw that the junky's toes were still in it. After I had looked I flipped. It was all like a dream now. I was outside my skin, watching myself. In a trance of horror I walked out of the lobby, still carrying the bloody toe of the shoe. I saw and heard people yelling at me, but I kept right on walking.

I walked into the liquor store with the shoe, which looked like a cup of blood. The proprietor took one look and ran out of the store. I ran out behind her. Two cops were passing in a squad car and, hearing the woman's screams, stopped to have a look. She pointed at me.

"Look what he's got! Look what he's got!" the woman shrieked.

The cops jumped me without bothering to look at what I was holding. All the lobby lice had followed and they stood around watching. One of the cops must have thought he had a little riot on his hands and so he got off me and pulled his gun. This gave the other cop a better chance to choke me. Ginsburg ran up and started yelling for the shoe. I guess he was worried abut lawsuits and wanted those toes back so they could be sewn on the junky. Then the cop saw the toes for the first time and forgot to strangle me any more. He began to turn different colors and got off me.

I scrambled to my feet and lit out for the Logan. I burst through the lobby and took the steps two at a time to the fifth floor. I couldn't get my key out because of the bandages on my hands and so I banged on the foyer door.

Jinny opened it. "What's the matter, hon? Where's our wine?"

I was too out of breath to say anything. But Jinny then saw my bloodstained shirt and the fresh blood on my bandages. "That bitch's cut Sid again!" she screeched.

I walked past her to my room. Jinny let out some more screeches and then went to the extension to call the office. I must have looked like a sleepwalker to Sharlee and Joey. They just stared as if they were afraid to wake me. I got in bed and pulled the covers over my head.

I heard Jinny flit back in the room. "I called the office," she said. "All hell must have have busted loose this time. Somebody must have did up the bitch that cut Sid because they're waiting for an ambulance. I'm going down."

"No, you ain't!" Joey boomed. "What the hell makes you think you got something to do with it?"

"Do with what?" Jinny asked innocently.

"What you said. That's what."

"I didn't say what was going on," Jinny said. "How could I tell you what's going on down in the lobby and I've been up here with you all the time while all hell is bursting loose in the lobby?"

The wail of a siren made them forfeit the argument and everybody but me rushed to Leah's room to look out the front window. I guess they got there just in time to see the young junky being hustled into the ambulance.

"I need a drink," Sharlee said firmly as she marched back in my room. I heard her pour a drink and then she said, "Are you cut again or not?"

"It ain't my blood," I said. "A junky cut his foot off in the elevator."

"A junky cut whose foot off in the elevator? How?"

"It was his own foot. The elevator cut it off."

"That's impossible. They don't make elevators like that any more. Why don't you stop lying and tell me about this chick that keeps cutting you?"

"Why don't you stop asking me crazy questions?"

She sighed and J&J came back in. "He says the elevator cut a junky's foot off, but I don't believe him," Sharlee told J&J.

Leah came in followed by Ray. Ray was hopping mad. "All night long I gotta stay up and sell shit and now you nervous bitches won't let me sleep. Why don't you all go downstairs somewheres?"

"We had a terrible accident," Jinny said haughtily. "We had to come in your room to look. Sid says the elevator sliced off a junky's foot and they had to take him to the hospital."

"Where do you think they'd take him, Yankee Stadium?" Ray snarled.

I heard Jinny leave the room.

Sharlee said, "I'll be good and damned if I can see why anybody in their right mind would want to live in here. Blood flows twenty-four hours a day. It's the Devil's own."

"I know worse," Leah said.

"For Chrissakes, Leah, come off it," Sharlee said.

"You ever hear of the Bryn Mawr or the Oxford?" Leah replied. "Or any of those joints on Ninety-ninth Street? And the Marseillaise is no house of Gawd."

"Yeah," Sharlee admitted. "I guess they're just as bad, but these Logan maniacs do their stuff much more colorfully."

"Welfare is the blame for that," Joey said excitedly. "Every time somebody gets loosed from the nuthouse they give them an emergency check and tell them to come to the Logan. The same goes for junky women fresh outa jail or the hospital. Ginsburg and Epstein don't pay off them Welfare bigshits like they oughta. There's got to be a reason why Welfare drops their worst cases on the Logan and not some other hotels. I know Welfare hotels that don't see a cop once a month, but the damn fuzz *lives* in here."

"The stupid Black bastids that run Welfare don't have sense enough to pour piss outa a boot," Leah said. "They probably don't even know they're filling this place up with undesirables."

"You ever realize how low-down the people are who work for the city?" Sharlee said angrily. "Look at the House of D. A ten-year-old moron could run it a lot better than it's being run now. When those studs get through with a young kid the only place the kid is fit for is the street. I know. I spent plenty of time there."

Jinny burst into the room. "That little Chico up in 6-E somewheres was stashing dope or something on top of the elevator shaft when he lost his balance and fell. And now the cops got the damn thing cut off while they wait for the detectives to come to search the shaft with a fine-tooth comb. Just on account of that dumb little junky I got to walk five flights of stairs!"

"Sid needs his rest," Sharlee said in a voice just like a nurse. "And quiet. Let's give him a break and leave. I promised the Sinman I'd be down there about this time anyhow."

J&J filed out. I poked my head out from under the covers. Sharlee was staring at me fixedly. I couldn't imagine what was going on in her head, but it was the damnedest stare anybody ever gave anybody. Suddenly she began to undress.

"What're you doing?" I said. "You just got dressed a little while ago."

"Shut up," Sharlee said. . . .

CHAPTER 19

SHARLEE STAYED TWO MORE DAYS. Even now I still think of it as Sharlee's having given me two more whole days out of her allotted span. And she gave those days without stint. She was both nursemaid and mistress, and it was boss the way she did both jobs. I even began to think that she might one day take me seriously, but that was pure stupidity. It wasn't even wishful thinking.

In the days that followed Sharlee's departure I tried to unravel the thing that made Sharlee stay with me, and I grew convinced that Sharlee was motivated by two things and only two things in her relationships with others. One was respect and the other was pity. When I first discovered that Sharlee looked up to willful and determined people I had solved only half the riddle. This lovely girl was also equally aroused by the weak. She was essentially a kind person. She hated pussies while at the same time she was defenseless if they sought charity from her. But Sharlee's was a gruff sort of charitable kindness. She had been self-consciously kind to me in all my weakness.

On the last day of Sharlee's stay Gloria stopped by, and the genuine esteem and friendliness the two girls showed toward each other was a strange and beautiful thing.

Gloria had only been in the room a short while when Jinny called Sharlee and as soon as Sharlee left the room Gloria exclaimed,

"It's just like an angel took a bucket of all the beauty in the world and drenched that girl with it. Where'd she ever come from, Sid? My God, she's beautiful. She makes me feel like I wouldn't mind being a bulldiker for her, and you know that ain't like me at all. Not Gloria Bascomb being the stud."

"You mean you've never seen or heard of the Sinman's goddess before?" I asked. "You two took to talking like you knew each other. You sure you never saw her? And hasn't the Sinman talked to you about Sharlee Black?"

"Dammit! I should have known. So that's Sharlee." Then after a moment she said, "She must feel awful inside."

"Now what the hell does that mean? What in the world has Sharlee got to feel awful about?"

"I don't mean it the way you think. I mean she must be like a color-blind person. You know, can see only gray. She couldn't possibly be able to see beauty. I bet she could kiss the ugliest man in the world and think nothing of it."

"Why? And what of it?"

"She just doesn't know what beauty is. If she did, she would take one look in the mirror and nobody on earth would be able to get along with her. See what I mean? She's soaking wet with beauty and she don't even know what it is. See how regular she is? And she's in the life, too. It's a wonder some freak hasn't killed her."

"How do you know she's in the life?"

Gloria shrugged. "In her eyes. It's like I talked to her in a jail cell somewheres." Her eyes flashed. "Can you imagine a judge sending her to prison? I bet he kept a hard on every minute that she was away. The bastard."

"You really think you can tell that Sharlee's been to prison? How? I don't believe you can."

"She has. I know. Prison marks a woman, Sid. But it only marks you to another woman who's been there too. You can believe it or not, but a girl who's been to jail don't look guilty like other people. They look you in the eyes with an even sort of look. They look at you with nothing to hide, nothing to fear. Like they already been baptized in cat shit and there ain't a damn thing more you can do to hurt them."

That made me think. There was something unafraid in both Sharlee and Gloria. J&J, too, for that matter, and even Leah and Ray. Yet I wasn't quite ready to swallow Gloria's dictum in one gulp. There was more to it than that. Because all the female tenants in the Logan were essentially unafraid. They had to be. And it might even be that only the unafraid go to prison. After all, not many crimes are committed by pussies.

Gloria's beautiful twisted smile brought my thoughts back. "I must really be in love with that girl, Sid," she told me. "Why, she don't even make me jealous. I do believe that if I'd walked in here and found you two taking care of business in the bed I would only be able to say I'm proud of you. Proud as hell. See what I mean, Sid?"

And in a like manner Gloria apparently raised Sharlee's estimation of me. Sharlee might even have been a little jealous. "She just comes once in a while like you want me to do, doesn't she?" Sharlee asked me, and that's all she asked. However, she used such a strange tone of voice that it made me think she might have been a little jealous or something.

The day after Sharlee left found me in a blue funk far worse than I had ever been in before. It had evidently come to live with me. J&J and even Charlie could do nothing to dispel it although I am not sure if they were aware of how I felt. I didn't get drunk; I just tippled from the time I got out of bed in the morning until I went to sleep at night. Just what caused the funk is hard to say. I was in love with both Sharlee and Gloria. Or perhaps I should say that I worshiped Sharlee and loved Gloria, and never separated the two. But the very fact that these two lovely girls had met in my room and tacitly admitted that they both liked me was a defeating sort of memory. I really possessed neither one. Somehow they had both given the other Sid Bailey. And this odd circumstance seemed to highlight my ineffectual personality perfectly.

As the weeks sped by Gloria's visits seemed less frequent, but I am not actually sure about that. Maybe the loneliness was more acute when she wasn't around and so I thought she was coming by less often. At any rate I stayed so high that all my days ran into one another. Not one single day during this period stands out in my memory.

I was a confirmed wino, but I can't say I learned to hustle for my wine. It is more like I was born knowing how, although I hadn't used that know-how until now. Leah and Ray supplied what I called my basic wine. By that I mean that they provided at least my morning wine and sometimes more. The first thing I did each day was to go to Leah's room and ask what they wanted from the store. They would always want the *Daily News* and cigarettes and sometimes beer and groceries, and they always told me to buy myself a pint of wine while I was about it. Suzie was also good for at least a pint a day. Since Suzie was too ignorant and dumb to go shopping she came to rely on me more and more as I declined into a permanent sottishness.

Another strange thing that began during this period was that the Logan's winos as a whole got on my nerves very easily. I couldn't stand the conversation in either Mr. Johnson's room or Pop Brown's for more than five minutes. On the other hand Blind Charlie acted like he couldn't stand my company for too long. He dropped by most days but never stayed very long. J&J became my sole conversational pals. I liked to sit in their room and drink, but they had so many wino visitors who got on my nerves that I could only stay when there was no one else there.

I never even considered going to the Sinman's room any more because he now showed open disgust at my steady drinking. And J&J were not above reproaching me from time to time about my drinking although I am sure I never ever drank more than either one of them. Nor did they approve of my allowing Leah's female customers to take off in my room. In fact, I don't believe Leah approved of it, but what could she say? And the girls usually gave me a dollar for the use of the room. Anyway J&J certainly were all too happy to help me drink up the quarts of wine I was able to buy this way. Yeah, sneaky pete had me and wouldn't let me go.

"Sid, if you promise me not to touch another drop of wine I

will see to it that there is a pint of whiskey in this room every day," Gloria said one night after I had unsuccessfully tried to have intercourse with her.

I was so ruined I don't know what I mumbled for an answer. Other pimps were offered money, but I was now reduced to being offered whiskey, that's one thing that ran through my mind.

"That sweet lucy is gonna kill you, Sid. It kills everybody. You can actually see it kill them. First their legs and faces swell up and next thing you know somebody's taken them to the hospital, and they don't come back. That is, the lucky ones don't come back. Some of them come back and have to suffer longer before they die. Please stop drinking wine, Sid," Gloria pleaded. But like I say, I was too ruined to listen or even to say anything.

So every day was a drunken fog of getting up, running errands, and sitting around J&J's room until time to go back to bed. I ate little and what I did eat I usually vomited.

One afternoon I answered the foyer door to stare in amazement at an old friend: Roy Watkins.

"I am soaking wet from head to toe," Roy said. He was a slightly built Lundy's waiter who had an odd way of speaking. Roy could make the most emphatic assertion sound tentative and bemused. But Roy *was* soaking wet from head to toe.

"What in the devil's happened to you?" I exclaimed. I grasped Roy's hand and pulled him into the hallway. "You look like you've been standing under a shower. It's not raining either."

"I jumped in the lake in Central Park."

"What for?"

"My wife."

"Where is your wife now? St. Luke's? You just come from there? How is she?"

"My wife did not jump in the lake," Roy said in his bemused fashion. "I did."

"Why?"

"She made me mad."

From one alcoholic to another, that statement made sense. So

I took Roy in the room and made him take off his jacket and shirt. "Take off your pants too," I said. "I got a pair I'll loan you."

"This is a wash-and-wear suit," Roy said complacently. "I'm all right."

"Are you drunk or crazy or just trying to drive me crazy?" I said. "It'll be hours before your suit dries out and you know it."

"Don't worry about it. And I am not crazy, I'm mad. That woman has been nagging at me for a week. I earn the money I drink with. She works, it's true, but she pays no household expenses. I do. But I like to drink. I like to wake up and go to a bar first thing in the morning. And when I get off from work I like to stop in a bar and have several nightcaps."

"You still working at Lundy's?"

"Yes," Roy said. "Where else can I work just when I feel like it and still make enough money to support my drinking?"

"Well, tell me what you were doing in Central Park this afternoon."

"We live on 110th Street facing the park. Today is her day off and I didn't feel like working. But she got up this morning squawking about the smell of whiskey, how it is not only on my breath all the time, but now it is even coming out of my pores too. Finally I had heard enough so I went to take a walk in the park to be away from her. But she followed me out of the house, still going yackety-yak. So I told her when I could get a word in edgewise that the next word she said to me I was going to jump in the lake and drown myself. And she said I ought to drown myself so I went over and jumped in the lake."

"You're lucky as hell there were no cops around."

"My wife screamed bloody murder and the cops did come," Roy said as if he didn't believe it. "They threw me a rope. The water came up to my neck, but they pulled me out."

I laughed. "Well, how come they didn't take you to Bellevue?"

"For what? I did it with presence of mind and forethought!" Roy said loudly. Then he meekly added, "She said I slipped."

"Well, take off your pants, and I'll take them to the cleaner's. You look like hell."

"I did not come by here to discuss my appearance. I came to see if you would like to go on one of those old-fashioned drunks like we used to pull."

I had to grin as I remembered those drunks. Wild three-day affairs. After three days Roy would go back to work even though he was high as a kite, but I remained stewed for my usual three weeks. "Heck yes," I said. "Only I'm broke. But I certainly do wish we had the dough to pitch one. Almost every day I wish I was back at Lundy's so I could afford to drink whiskey instead of sitting on my ass all day, mooching drinks of wine."

"Don't worry about finances. All you have to do is keep me company. And this is a lovely room to pitch a drunk in," Roy said. "I shall not return to my wife until I am stone broke and in debt to every bartender who'll let me owe him."

"Well, I've been so bored lately that I'd get drunk with a rattlesnake if he'd only talk intelligent. Just before you knocked I was sitting here thinking that winos in this hotel carry on the dumbest conversations known to man. Stupidity and lies! That's all they got to say. Pretty soon I'm going to be just as bad as they are."

"You do have a rather unique-looking clientele in this hotel," Roy said. "The ones in the lobby scared me. They not only seemed to be counting the money in my pockets but planning on how they would spend it. I'm not sure I would have come up here if a smiling Jewish fellow had not been waiting for the elevator too. I deduced that he must be the manager because everybody was kowtowing to him like their rent was due and they didn't have the money."

"Not all those niggers down there live in this hotel," I said. "That's why they kowtow to him but some who live here also kiss his ass because they know they're undesirables and would have a hard time getting a room anywhere else. Did you give your wife your watch and money before you jumped in the lake?"

"Are you crazy? Suppose I'd drowned? She'd be left with all my money. But the damnedest thing did happen."

"What's that?"

"My hat never came off."

There was a terrific pounding on the foyer door that could be nothing but Blind Charlie's cane so I went to let him in.

"What you got for poor ole Blind Charlie to drink?" Charlie roared, and I knew he was pretty high already.

"Come on in the room," I said. "I got some company who is just getting ready to buy a drink."

"You got drinking company? Where the hell they come from and do they know poor ole Blind Charlie?"

"No, but I want you to meet this guy."

"Now you know I don't meet no strangers, Sid."

"Roy isn't a stranger. He's a brother waiter. An okay guy. You'll like him."

"Hadn't oughta do it. Strangers can get you in a awful lot of trouble sometimes." But Charlie came in and allowed me to introduce Roy.

"Do you drink scotch, Charlie?" Roy asked.

"I drink anything that pours," Charlie said.

J&J came to the door. Those two could smell fresh money better than a bloodhound can smell a Black fugitive. "What's going to go on in here?" Jinny asked brightly.

"Come on in and meet one of my best old drinking pals from Lundy's," I said and then introduced them to Roy.

"What will you ladies have to drink?" Roy asked. "We're going to drink scotch."

"We rather have wine," Jinny said. "Scotch is too rich for our blood."

"I love an honest girl," Roy said. "Come on, Sid. Let's go."

The clerk in the whiskey store looked distastefully at the wet and crumpled ten-dollar bill that Roy gave him but said nothing.

"Perhaps we should dry our money before we try to spend any more of it," Roy murmured on the way back to the hotel.

First we went to J&J's room and gave them their bottle of wine, then we got Charlie and went in the kitchen with our glasses. I lit the oven and Roy put his money in it.

"What the hell are you all doing?" Charlie demanded. "And what the hell is you lighting the oven for?"

"Roy's got some money that's soaking wet," I told him. "We're trying to get it dry."

"Wet? How the hell you get it wet? Jump in the lake in Central Park?"

"Yes, I did," Roy answered.

"Don't mess over me, boy," Charlie growled. "I don't even allow Sid to do that."

Joey came in the kitchen. "Why you come in the kitchen to drink for?"

I opened the oven door and showed her.

"Ye gods! That's no way to do it," Joey exclaimed. "What you need to do is to iron it. Bring it in the room and me and Jinny'll iron it for you."

"My room is bigger than yours," I pointed out. "Bring your ironing board in my room and we can all be comfortable while you iron it."

"Okay," Joey said. "How the hell did it get wet in the first place?"

"I jumped in the lake in Central Park," Roy said.

"Yeah. I bet," Joey said.

Jinny came in the kitchen. "What's everybody congregated in here for?" she asked. "Reminds me of home boys. They either got to drink that whiskey in the kitchen or behind the outhouse."

"The bastids are trying to cook money," Joey said. "They got about three hundred dollars in that oven and Sid is so drunk he thinks he can cook it dry, but I tole him us women would iron it for them."

"To get your hands on a couple of hundred you're even willing to call yourself a woman," I said as Blind Charlie hooted.

"I ain't never denied being a woman!" Joey shouted. "Who the hell wants to be a sorry-assed man? Always doing his dirt?"

"I do," Roy said in that voice of his. "I wouldn't ever want to be my wife."

"I'm not speaking of you, Roy," Joey said. "I'm just letting this Sid bastid know what the score is, if you know what I mean. All day long he sits around drinking wine with us women, and still he ain't never got nothing good to say about us."

"The only woman I have evil to say about is my wife," Roy said, "and I guess I even love her some of the time. I wish she didn't know how to argue so well."

"Where'd you guys get all this bread from?" Jinny asked.

"Out of the lake," I told her.

"You can go to hell," Jinny said cheerfully. "And just for that you can buy us another bottle of Spur with one of your wet old dollars."

"How much does a case of that wine cost?" Roy asked.

"Don't ask us," Joey said. "We can hardly get together the price of a pint most times."

"I can get it for eight-fifty," Jinny said.

"Well, call up the store and tell them to deliver a case of that Spur and a quart of scotch," Roy told her.

"Why not a case of scotch too?" she asked.

"We men are going to start making the rounds pretty soon," Roy said. "It's no fun to get drunk if you can't go in strange bars and have the bartender refuse to serve you."

"Damn if I don't believe you're crazier than Sid," Jinny said before she went down to call the whiskey store. The stuff was delivered in fifteen minutes and we all set to to do some serious drinking while J&J ironed Roy's money dry. Charlie, who had been feeling very good when he came, got roaring drunk, to Roy's delight.

"Let's go visit Sharlee," Charlie suggested.

"You know Sharlee can't stand drunk men," I said.

"We don't have to let her know we're drunk," Charlie said indignantly. "Damn effen you can't say some of the dumbest things sometimes."

Jinny said to Roy, "Did you come by to get Sid to go back to work? Somebody ought to do something with him before he drinks himself to death."

"Sid ain't crazy," Joey yelled at her. "He ain't never gonna give up Welfare. Why should he go and give up a good thing?"

"No," Roy said judiciously if vaguely. "Now that fall is here

Sid might just as well remain on Welfare until things bust open again next spring."

"Sid's got a friend named the Sinman who says that Sid is a wonderful writer and should be writing," Joey said, "but Sid's too lazy."

Roy jumped to his feet and came over to shake my hand. "I never had an author for a friend before," he exclaimed. "Why, man, you've got it made. All you have to do is sit in here and write while Welfare pays your room and board. And I promise you that you'll never be out of cigarettes. Now how's that?"

I was just high enough to be indulgent with all of them. "Okay," I said. "As soon as we get over this drunk I'll buckle down and dash off a Pulitzer Prize winner."

"And I'm gonna tell you exactly what to write and how to write it," Charlie said like he was making a promise to a half-witted child. "Just write what I tell you about them Florida work gangs. All you got to do is put it down word for word in highfalutin English."

"Naw," Jinny said. "Sid's a romantic. All he'll ever be able to write is love stories. And I like that because I can't stand to read filth and all this profanity these authors write now'days. All these new authors are pussies who think they can make the public think they're not. I can't stand all that cursing. So don't write nothing about jail or the Logan either, Sid. Write about what you dream or about two women in love. And write something nice so young folks can read it and understand."

"What every child should know about lesbians," I muttered.

"And why the hell not?" Joey demanded. "The world is fulla us, ain't it?"

"There is a whore bar up on 145th Street near St. Nicholas Avenue," Roy said dreamily. "And there is a little girl named Lorraine that works out of there. I've got to go get her right away."

Joey ran up to him as if she would punch him. "We ain't got nothing but whores in the Logan," she shouted indignantly. "Winos and junkies. Junkies and winos. For as little as a pint of wine you can get trim in this joint. Practically every damn woman in here is for sale except me and Jinny. Just produce enough to satisfy their habit and you got your choice."

"Every female you see passing this door is for sale," Jinny said. "They're on their way to buy dope. And their price is going to be right, too. I'll see to that. No damn junky is gonna take you while you are our guest."

"I am not in the market for flesh," Roy said. "I wish only to commune with Lorraine. I met her years ago in the St. Louis Bar and we got to talking. I found out that she is my soul mate. My sister."

"Ain't she a junky?" Joey asked. "How in hell can a junky whore be the soul sister of a man what don't use shit?"

Roy threw his head back and yelled at the top of his lungs, "Lorraine listens!" J&J immediately looked at him with the respect the Logan always accords a maniac. "She is the only person in the world who understands all the problems I have with my wife," Roy said calmly. "Come on. All of us shall go get Lorraine."

Believe it or not, J&J were the first ones to agree to go. "And we'll need you for a bodyguard," I said to Charlie. "Don't you want to come too?"

"Damn effen I ain't drunk enough to come along," Charlie said. "I ain't been in that St. Louis Bar since I went blind. Used to be some pretty whores in there."

We stood out on Amsterdam Avenue until one of those big Checker cabs came along and then we were on our way. There was a pretty good crowd in the St. Louis, but no Lorraine. Roy was undaunted and so was I in a way because we both knew that Lorraine would show eventually. At the bar Roy, J&J and I got into a four-way conversation and forgot all about Blind Charlie until we heard him shouting, "Get the hell outen my face, bitch! I ain't never bought no tail from a junky whore in my life and I ain't gonna start now! Git outen my face, I say."

We all turned and saw that Charlie was addressing a nice-looking girl who evidently had sidled up to him.

"You go to hell, you blind bastard," the girl said.

"I *will* rot in hell before I buys any of your stinking pussy,"

Charlie retorted, and I held my breath, hoping the junky would not tell Charlie to kiss her ass.

"That's what's wrong with this bar now," the girl said bitterly. "All you cornball niggers come in here just to cuss out us girls. That the way you get your kicks? I bet you're creaming all over yourself this minute, you blind freak."

Jinny went to the girl and put her arm around her shoulder and led her over to the juke box. There they held a whispered conversation and when Jinny finally rejoined us she said, "I sent for Lorraine. She should be here in a few minutes."

And in a few minutes Lorraine did walk in. J&J were overjoyed. They knew Lorraine from the House of D, but she had gone by the name of Claire in the women's prison.

Since Lorraine knew that both Roy and I were fools with a dollar when we were drinking, and she didn't know that I wasn't working any more, she quickly agreed to come back to the Logan with us. She even wanted to recruit two more girls for Charlie and me, but I said that Charlie and I had our own women.

Back in the hotel it was a more or less innocuous drinking party although the conversation between Roy and Lorraine never took place. However, Roy did treat Lorraine like a bride. Every six hours he would solicitously inquire if she needed another fix and Lorraine always needed one, or so she said. So even Leah and Ray were glad to have Roy as a visitor.

Roy's treatment of Lorraine taught me one new thing. Of course money is the thing that matters to a girl with a habit, yet and still heroin is more important. If a man wants to have a girl keep him company for a long period of time the way to do it is to keep the girl well supplied with heroin. Lorraine stayed three days and never once mentioned money. She was perfectly happy, contented and a member of the party. She was absolutely no different in her attitudes and moods than anyone else who joined us on our spree. She was damned good fun.

One morning Roy woke up first, quietly dressed, and went out. He returned with two dozen pads of paper, a package of pencils and a fifth of scotch.

"Your last excuse is gone," he said. He handed me the paper and pencils.

"We are trying to get Sid sober enough to write," Jinny explained to Lorraine.

"My God!" Lorraine screamed. "I know Sid from way back. He never comes in the St. Louis that he isn't at least half drunk. He stays drunk. I don't know how he manages to keep a job, but he does. He'd drop dead if he didn't have a drink every day. Now please tell me how you people expect a dead man to write a book."

"It's only when I'm half drunk I ever think about coming in that whore bar," I snapped. "Who the hell wants any junky company except when they're high?"

"Lay off us junkies," Lorraine said good-naturedly. "If it wasn't for us junkies you alcoholics would never get any pussy. And give me a drink. I want to get higher. But when you write your book be sure to put in about how us junkies would all be respected and productive citizens if we lived in England. Dig it? And tell how junkies never bother anybody unless it's some fool that gets between us and our fix. And tell how they keep methadone off the market just to please the pushers. And all that kinda jazz."

"Naw," I said. "When I write there's not going to be a junky or a lesbian in the whole damn story. I'm going to write about men screwing women and not each other. And they are all going to drink whiskey like most colored people do. Besides, if I write anything it's going to be a play and not a book."

"Nobody will go see it," Lorraine said. "Junkies are in. Dope fascinates the squares. You listen to TV or read the papers and all you hear about is the terrible life we junkies live, but every square in the world wants to live a junky's life if only in print. Dig? You got to debunk TV and all and drill it into the squares' heads that we never commit crimes except when we're pushed, like."

"G'wan," Joey said. "Junkies got to get high before you can make the simplest sting. You can't think, in fact most of you can't even walk when your stuff starts running out."

"Which just goes to prove that addicts don't commit crimes because they are in desperate need of a fix," Lorraine replied. "I never met an addict yet who was a stone killer. It's winos who commit all the crimes in Harlem. Take a look at the next junk-junk junky you see. Do you ever see any scars on him? On us? Then take a look at the average wino. A wino looks like somebody walked on his face and then smashed wine bottles in it. I wish somebody did have the guts to tell it like it is. And addicts are intelligent. Educated. They read all the good books; winos are ignorant."

"We ain't got nothing but educated winos in this here hotel," Joey called out. "Even College Joe is a wino, but he's a honor student at Columbia. How many junky students get honors at Columbia?"

Later that morning Lorraine left and Blind Charlie wandered off somewhere. Roy and I continued to drink. Eventually the talk got around to Lundy's. And as Roy talked I wished almost fervently that I had taken psychology in school. If I had, I believed that I could write one of the most compelling studies of a weird strata of Black life. A play about a Lundy's waiter would be a play to end all plays. For he is a breed apart. He is like no other Black man. In some ways, it was a sexual experience to work at Lundy's. This had nothing to do with the homos who worked there. It was something else. All the waiters complained about the BOSS as if he was a white slattern of a wife whom they had to love and cherish even though she was a sadist. I've never yet met a waiter from Lundy's who complained about Lundy's in tones that were not covertly sexual.

"Ray Pierce came to work so high on pot one Sunday that when those Jews started giving him their crazy mixed-up orders with all their wild substitutions he just walked to the window and jumped out," Roy said.

"The second-floor window?" I asked, knowing Ray worked upstairs.

"Yes, the awning broke his fall. And when we all ran and looked out all we could see was his little green jacket, turning the corner just flying."

"Where'd he run to?" I asked.

"Nobody knows. Some of the fellows went by his house, but

his landlady says he never came home. That was a month ago. Old man Grant got fired. He started a lobster-eating school."

"A what?"

"That crazy West Indian saw that a lot of the women out at Lundy's didn't know how to eat a lobster, and so he got these cards printed up announcing a lobster-eating school for them. It takes a West Indian to figure out how to make money."

"And Lundy fired him?"

"Of course. He thought old man Grant was trying to get women to his house to seduce them or something, but that crazy Indian was serious. He was really going to teach these dumb Jews how to eat a lobster in public and make himself some money besides."

"While I think of it, Roy," I said, "please don't tell anyone out there that I'm on Welfare now, will you?"

"Why should I put your business in the street?" Roy said. "But you have no right to feel ashamed of what you are doing. America owes the progeny of all ex-slaves an indemnity. I'm glad to see that you are collecting yours. But you don't look sick to me. What is supposed to be wrong with you?"

"Bursitis."

"You sure? The people I know who have bursitis can't move their arms like you can. I believe you could wait tables if you wanted to. That leads me to a proposition: you should go around to the Faculty Club and get on as an extra waiter. You only work two or three hours on the private parties. It's easy. And I am sure that no one connected with the Welfare Department ever goes there."

There was a knock on the foyer door. It was Lorraine.

"Roy still here?" she asked.

"Yeah," I said, leading the way back to the room.

"I came to get you," Lorraine said to Roy.

"What for?" Roy said. He was drunk but not so drunk he didn't know better than to follow Lorraine into the 145th Street jungle. "Are you of the opinion that I might want to go to your house?"

"We need more privacy than we got here," Lorraine said. "I like Sid and all, but sometimes a woman has to be alone with her man."

"No," Roy said flatly.

Lorraine stayed around the rest of the day, biding her time, and finally she got her way. Roy got so drunk he didn't know what was happening and she firmly took him in hand and led him out of 5-C. J&J were fit to be tied, but since Roy had given me a twenty-dollar bill a little earlier I really didn't care. I went to bed.

The next day I began to drink wine and it seemed like that twenty dollars lasted forever. I drank with a purpose. I had to drink those twenty-four pads of foolscap and those pencils out of my existence. I really got blotto. When the twenty was gone I crawled into bed with one of my best old-fashioned hangovers. The kind I hadn't had since I first came back to the Logan.

I drank like some kind of brand-new fool. In the last stages of that drunk I seldom got out of bed. Actually I was in an intermittent drunken coma. I would sleep approximately three or four hours and then wake up and drink a water glass of wine and in a short time I would be back in my stupor of sleep; I guess you call it sleep.

Then came the DTs and then came ten days and nights on end of sleeplessness. During my days of stupor Charlie had sort of given up on me since I wouldn't get out of bed and roam around with him.

And during the first five days of insomnia Charlie went off on one of his tours of duty. It was then that I believe I crossed the line and was actually insane. I was insanely lonely and yet I was unable to stand the conversation of anyone. Not even J&J or the Sinman. I was a recluse who *had* to be a recluse. The Logan had finally overwhelmed me. And for a while there I actually hated all tenants in the Logan.

Sometimes I would snap out of this lethargy of hate, loneliness and boredom to plunge into a whirlpool of fear. I feared the inevitable climax of this ever growing mania. And I would wonder if Sharlee had put a curse on me. Gloria simply disappeared out of my life the second week of my drunk and I made no attempt to contact her now because I was afraid that she would politely tell me to get lost. And I didn't really want her around anyhow.

I did not go to the extent of locking my door but I kept it closed at all times now. And when Charlie returned to the Logan I told J&J and Leah to always tell him I was out when he came to the foyer door.

CHAPTER 20

JACKIE ABRUPTLY ENDED THIS MORASS of seclusion when she knocked on my door around five o'clock one morning and called my name. I didn't say anything; I was broke, and just before the liquor store closed I had gone out and bought a pint of Spur. But the stuff had not brightened and mellowed me like I had hoped. Instead it had given me indigestion. I had the exact same symptoms of the twenty-four-hour bug. Only I had puked off and on all the rest of the night. So I needed Jackie's company like I needed leprosy.

And if it was money she wanted I simply wasn't coming. Not after that business with Mrs. Moriarty's watch.

Jackie turned the knob and walked in. "Sid, wake up a minute," she whispered.

"I'm not asleep. I just don't feel like being bothered." I wanted my message to get across right off the bat.

"That goddam man won't open the door. Can I stay in here for the rest of the night? I could go home up in the Bronx, but I'm beat. So help me, Sid, I'm beat. I can't stand that subway out there right this minute. But in the morning I'll go."

I had steeled myself to withstand Jackie's promises and importunings for a loan. I wasn't prepared for this. But I didn't say yes; I didn't say anything. So Jackie naturally thought I had consented. That's the junky's way of thinking.

The effort of saying the few words to Jackie had nauseated me again. I turned on my stomach and went into a troubled sleep.

I woke about noon and the first thing I saw was Jackie, down on her knees, scrubbing the floor. I looked around. She had already cleaned the rest of the room. Even the walls and windows had been washed. I got a sinking feeling, but I had no idea why. I watched her.

When Jackie finished the floor she went in the kitchen and I could hear her in there, still working. Jinny came in and said, "I see Jackie's on one of her cleaning kicks again."

I swallowed and grinned weakly. "Yeah. So I see. Don't she know the maid cleans the kitchen?"

Jinny's eyes twinkled. "When Jackie decides to clean she cleans. I thought you knew that."

"You know I don't know anything about her except she's a damn thief."

"You don't look too chipper. You think a little drink might help?"

"Heck no," I muttered. "I don't want to see or smell anything with alcohol in it."

When Jinny walked away I got up and went to the refrigerator. There were two cans of tomato juice inside. I didn't even bother to wonder where they came from. I opened one and drank from the can. No sooner had it hit my stomach than I was sorry. I went back to bed, hoping the juice would stay down if I stayed down—and perfectly still. But in a few minutes I had to jump up and run for the bathroom. I pushed open the door. There was Jackie scrubbing out the tub.

"Get out of here a minute. I got to use the toilet," I said.

"I'm not finished yet," Jackie said dreamily.

I brushed by her and made it just in time.

"You shouldn't do that in my nice clean toilet," Jackie said in the same dreamy voice. "I want everything around here to be clean and shiny and look what you're doing."

I gave an agonized heave and gasped, "Go to hell." Then I went back to bed and vainly tried to go to sleep. I not only had this sense of impending doom which can accompany the slightest hangover, but Leah and J&J were standing out in the hall making wisecracks about Jackie. I went to the door to see what Jackie was up to now. She was standing on a chair, washing walls in the hall.

"Why the hell don't you go to that home you got in the Bronx and scrub?" I asked her.

Just then Dick came out of his room and said, "The bitch is crazy."

"Don't you men like things nice and clean?" Jackie said. "I wouldn't think about doing this if I thought you wouldn't appreciate it."

Dick went out the foyer door without another word and I went back in my room, but I decided that I better get Jackie straightened out. I went back to the hall.

"Do you remember that you and Dick are on the outs?" I began. "Do you realize that I said you could only sleep with me for one night? Why're you cleaning someplace where you don't stay any more? You think Dick's going to appreciate it and let you back in?"

Jackie not only refused to answer, but by the hunch of her shoulders I could tell that she thought I was talking off the wall. And on top of that J&J and Leah were laughing their heads off.

"Now what the hell's the big joke?" I demanded.

Jinny giggled. "What're you beefing about? You got a nice clean room, haven't you?"

I got angrier. "What's with this cleaning kick anyhow? Is Jackie really off her rocker?"

"No," Jinny said, still laughing. "She must have shot up more than one bag. I guess she was mad at Dick. When she gets sky high like this she gets a cleaning fit on. She's going to clean until that shit wears off."

Jinny spoke as if Jackie wasn't even present and as far as Jackie was concerned nobody was there.

"You mean a perfectly sane person can take more than one bag of dope and nobody can make them stop cleaning? Why?"

"All junkies do something freakish or crazy when they shoot up more than their normal amount," Joey said. "Jackie cleans. One time she took Russel's mop and bucket and mopped every hall from here down to the second floor before Russel finally got her to quit.

But don't worry; that skag is gonna be wearing off soon now. She's been at it since seven this morning."

"I'm not worried," I said. "It's not my headache, but why doesn't she go where her cleaning is appreciated? Does she have a home to go to up in the Bronx?"

"Have you?" Jinny said.

"All right, Jinny," Jackie said.

"You mean she hasn't?" I asked.

"That's about the size of it, buddee boy."

"What'd she do?" Joey asked. "Move in on you last night?"

"I dunno," I said. "She came in about five o'clock, but she was supposed to go home later this morning."

"Well, you just tell her that you're a pussy and afraid of Dick," Joey said flatly. "Don't start nothing and there won't be nothing, if you know what I mean."

Sure I knew what Joey meant. I also knew that I was afraid as hell of Dick, but I would rather be killed than have to admit that to anybody. Jinny had told me that Dick had bashed his mother in the head with a hammer soon after he went broke as a numbers banker. He had been put in Manhattan State Hospital for the insane and after his release had been sent to the Logan by the Welfare Department. But since that damn strop of Daddy's ruled my sanity I forgot that I had promised never to have anything to do with Jackie after that watch episode. I forgot that she was a junky. I even forgot that I was supposed to have good sense.

When J&J stopped talking I went back to bed. Jackie came in soon afterward. "At least you could thank me for getting rid of some of the filth that's around here," she said.

"It's none of my goddam filth," I snarled. "Go down the office and ask that Jew to thank you."

Jackie began to take her clothes off. She stripped slowly, dreamily, until she was nude. "Where's a clean bathrobe? I need a bathrobe."

"Don't you have things in Dick's room? And when do you two intend to make up? What is this anyhow? Gloria might show up any minute. What do you expect me to do then?"

The look on Jackie's face was both pitying and maternal. "Gloria and I are good friends. She wouldn't say anything. What in the world could she say to her best friend? Don't let that bother you."

"I'm not going to let that bother me, if you know what I mean."

"What ever gave you the idea that Gloria would complain? Everybody knows Gloria and me are buddies from way back. We used to live together. So where's your bathrobe?"

"Put your clothes back on if you don't have one in Dick's room."

"I can't take a bath with my clothes on. And you don't think I'm not going to take a bath after all the dirty work I've been doing, do you? I'm a clean girl. I don't care how dirty all other addicts get, I stay clean!"

I sat up. "Look here, stupid!" I shouted. "I'm sick as hell. I damn near got the DTs. But I don't mind you hanging around here. That is, I don't mind it as long as you don't think I'm going to play any part in the crazy ideas that shit puts in your head. Get me?"

"I dig," Jackie said meekly and with a strange air of satisfaction. It was as if she had been waiting for my outburst. She put her slip back on and went to the bathroom. When she came back from her bath she fell across the bed at my feet and went to sleep—for six hours. As soon as she woke, she picked up her bra, which she had rolled up, and went to the bathroom. I didn't have to be told that in that rolled-up bra were her works and some heroin. After Jackie had been in the bathroom for half and hour I began to worry. I went to the bathroom door and knocked.

"Just a minute," Jackie said.

At least I knew she wasn't dead from an overdose. To cover my relief I grumbled, "Hurry up. You don't own this john, you know."

Fifteen minutes later Jinny went to the bathroom door and knocked. Again Jackie called, "Just a minute."

Jinny came in. "I heard you telling that dizzy bitch to come out of the toilet," she said. "What's she doing in there? Taking swimming lessons?"

"She took a bath six hours ago," I said. "All I know is that she belongs in an asylum."

"Jackie don't usually act like this," Jinny said.

"How soon you think it'll be before they make up?" I asked.

Jinny shrugged. "She's got to go out around midnight and hustle for that habit. When she comes back she might not even speak to you. Gratitude is something junkies don't have. Probably she'll just walk in Dick's room and the whole thing'll be over."

But Jackie did not go to Dick's door when she returned in the morning. To make matters worse she brought me a pack of Pall Malls. After she handed me the cigarettes she opened the refrigerator.

"It's empty," she said reproachfully.

"Are you expecting a full-course dinner for your lousy pack of cigarettes?" I said. "I chip in with J&J most of the time. I don't do any cooking."

"You're around here all day doing nothing. Why don't you do your own cooking and save? Why should an intelligent man like you want to be eating with those dirty bulldikers?"

"Get off my back. I want no more 'dirt' crap."

Jackie's eyes widened with surprise. "What dirt are you talking about? I don't know anything about any dirt."

"You mean to tell me you don't remember scrubbing your ass off yesterday?"

Jackie grinned. "Was I very high? I know when I get really groovy I start cleaning, but I didn't know about yesterday. I don't know why, but I'm freakish that way. Got to clean. Did I get on your nerves? If I did I'm sorry, Sid."

Jackie had said all that could be said intelligently about the matter. Dick had spoken pleasantly to me last night, and so if Jackie was going to cat on me for another day I might as well stop complaining about it. I felt okay now and she would probably sleep all day so I couldn't say she would be a bother. Furthermore, since she and Gloria were such stone buddies I thought I better wait until I talked to Gloria before doing anything definite anyhow.

In a matter of days it seemed as if Jackie had been living in my room all the time. She was just as lazy as any other junky broad I knew, but since we had maid service there wasn't much I could complain about. And when she was awake Jackie was good company. Every morning after she had taken off she would wake me and tell me what was happening on 125th Street or downtown, and I began to look forward to our little chats just as much as I did the newscasts which J&J still brought later in the morning.

But Jackie's insistence upon going in the bathroom to hit herself was embarrassing as hell. Jackie came in off the streets a little before five every morning. Ray usually let her in. Most of the time she would toss some Pall Malls on the bed and then go to the bathroom for her fix. That meant she was in the bathroom when J&J got up. Each morning Joey would bang on the bathroom door and curse Jackie out, but Jackie would silently ignore her. Later Jinny would come and curse Jackie out too, but Jackie stayed in that bathroom for one full hour every morning. And the strangest part of all was that when she stayed with Dick Jackie did not use the bathroom to take her fixes.

"Why the hell do you purposely make those two bitches mad?" I asked one day. "You've been around 5-C long enough to know that time J&J get up they make a beeline to the can, one right after the other. Why don't you wait until they're finished—or take off in here? Why the hell you got to hog the bathroom to take a fix?"

Jackie evidently was sailing. High and reserved. "If those two cows got anything to say they can say it to me."

"They knock on that door and scream their heads off every morning. What more you want them to do? Kick your ass?"

Jackie laughed. "They wouldn't dare. They know better than to mess over Jackie."

But what was even more bewildering than Jackie's attitude was the fact that although J&J cursed outside the bathroom door they never complained outright to Jackie.

Early one morning, just before Jackie was due to come in, voices in the kitchen woke me. I could tell Leah and Ray were in there and at least two more women and two men. I was still half asleep and wasn't interested anyway, but without even listening I could tell that it was no pleasant conversation being held. I drifted back to sleep and was wakened again, this time by a sharp cry from Leah. It wasn't a cry of pain, more of surprise, as if someone had pinched her. Then someone scurried back to Leah's room and soon scurried back. The foyer door slammed closed and I went back to sleep again with Leah's hysterical profanity shrilling in my ears.

When Jackie came home she had to knock until I went to the foyer door. Jackie needed a fix pretty badly and so she didn't even speak as she brushed by me, almost running to Leah's door. It was closed for the first time since I had been living in 5-C. Neither Leah nor Ray would answer Jackie's knocks.

"Something funny went on last night in the kitchen," I told Jackie when she came in the room. "And I bet that's why they won't answer you. They are in there and I know damn well they're not that sound asleep already."

"Now I got to go around to Broadway," Jackie said.

"Why there?" I asked. "There's five more pushers in here besides Leah."

"Six pushers with the weakest bags in Harlem," Jackie said bitterly. "They might as well be lemons. What happened in the kitchen?"

"There were two couples, I think. And it seemed like they were cussing out Leah and Ray. I don't know why. Then somebody runs back to Leah's room and runs right back and then the visitors leave and Leah starts cussing like a maniac and then she and Ray go back and lock themselves in. There's something funny going on around here."

"I bet she was robbed!" Jackie's was a happy exclamation. "I *knew* something had happened when I came through the lobby, but I didn't see anybody I wanted to rap with and so I didn't stop." She went to the dresser and took a bottle of medicine out of a drawer. I don't know when she'd put it there.

"What's that?" I asked.

"Codeine," she said and put the bottle to her lips and took a long drink. "I need something until I get back."

"You say the lobby is still full?" I said. "It's almost six, don't those junkies ever go to sleep?"

"Don't ask me. I'm never through until after five in the morning but they're there then. But between five and six is get-with-it time.

The men have just finished mugging the drunks, the girls are just coming in, and everybody's got money and had their fix. If anybody owes you money, now is the time to collect it. And there's all kinds of loot for sale. If the cops weren't so dumb they could walk in the lobby any morning this time and get a line on damn near every crime committed last night."

"How many junkies are standing around down there now?"

"Only twenty, but they know what's happening. They can tell you everything you want to know about anything if they want to."

"Yeah, if they want to."

"They'll tell anything for a bag."

"You know," I said, thinking, "I don't think Leah and Ray got robbed. If I remember correctly Leah went back and forth to her room a couple of times. Holdup men wouldn't let her do that. She and Ray have a shotgun, but maybe it won't shoot. I don't know. Although it might have been just a shakedown. She sure was mad after those people left."

Jackie went out and copped and then returned to go through her hour-long ritual in the bathroom. When she came out she was smiling. "I just know somebody's held up that Leah," she said.

"Something told me to get up and see what was going on."

"Are you crazy? What the hell did you have to do with it?" Jackie exclaimed. "They could have been arguing over anything. It could have been Leah's connection wanting his money. Then how'd you sound? And no matter what it was, Leah is no friend of yours. She told me she hates your wino guts. And now you gonna risk your tail for her? Nobody gets involved in nothing Leah does, Sid. She is just that crooked."

Jackie was right as rain, but I still protested feebly. "I could have walked by the kitchen like I was going to the bathroom and let them know somebody else was awake in this apartment."

"You damn squares don't ever want to learn to mind your own business, do you? And then when you get messed up you want to blame somebody in the life for it." Jackie suddenly dropped her angry tone and spoke more softly, seriously. "People in the life—

people who hustle for a living—don't need or want any help, Sid. Try to understand that."

Joey walked in with a long face. "Leah's ruint," she said. "Butch and Joan, those studs that sell stuff downstairs right underneath Leah, brought two strange men up here this morning. Took all Leah's shit and every goddam cent she had. How dirty can two motherfuckers get? Butch and Joan come up here every day visiting Leah."

"Leah got money in the bank?" I asked.

"Have you?" Joey said disgustedly. "Leah's laying in there right now hurting for a fix and no money to buy one."

"In other words she's bankrupt," I said.

Joey purpled. "That ain't funny. How the hell would you like it if somebody robbed you of everything you had and then one of your friends comes up and tells you you're bankrupt?"

"I wasn't being funny," I said. "I was just stating the facts like they are. Leah is not only broke, she is out of business. Right?"

"Yeah," Joey said mournfully. "Leah's got such a bad rep I know damn well her connection is not going to let her have any stuff on credit." Then she swelled self-righteously. "It don't pay to be crooked all the time."

Jackie was high and nodding. She began to laugh in that eerily hollow chuckle of the addict. "She's got a peehole like everybody else and if she ain't she got a head on her. Let her get out and make it like I do," she said.

"Leah ain't no tricking woman!" Joey cried. "Leah ain't turned a trick in ten, maybe fifteen years."

"So she can tell the johns she's a virgin," Jackie said.

Leah walked in. It must have been just about time for her fix when the studs beat her for everything, because she was looking pretty sick now.

"I'm not trying to collect on all the favors I've done for you since you moved in here, Sid," she began.

I recoiled in anger, but I guess nobody noticed. Leah hadn't done me one favor when you came right down to it. When I first moved in I went to the store for her for nothing. And when I started in on wine it was like I was feeding her ego to run errands. It did her a hell of a lot more good than me, if you know what I mean.

"I'm broke," I said. "I'm sorry, but I can't help you."

"But you can talk to the Sinman for me."

I wanted to ask her what was wrong with her going to Bill and Reba, but I didn't. Instead I said, "Don't be too sure. Sinman and I aren't as tight as we used to be." Which was all too true, but the real truth of the matter was that I was recalling the Sinman's cordial dislike for Leah.

Then, just like that, my freak do-goodness grabbed me. I would go down and ask the Sinman to make me a personal loan of a bag of heroin. I also was prompted in this decision by my absolute faith in Leah's ability to do evil. This meant it would be only a matter of days before Leah would somehow be back on her feet again. Probably as soon as she got herself a fix and got her thoughts together. Leah was evil and evil always triumphed in the Logan.

Like an afterthought I said, "Butch and Joan are your best friends, aren't they? They didn't move out, did they?"

Leah saw what I was driving at. Her face contorted, but she spoke patiently with an effort. "The two men were strangers. One pulled a pistol on Ray. The other slapped me. So what the hell difference does it make if Butch and Joan are still in here? They told me when it was happening that the studs had robbed them first and then made them come up here and knock on my door so we'd let them in when we recognized Butch and Joan. Whether or not they're telling the truth, they gotta make out like they're broke and sick now. Don't tell me," Leah said wearily. "I would tell the same damn story if I was in on a sting like that."

"Well, why don't you try them anyhow?" I asked.

"I just tole you they supposed to be broke and sick just like I am!" Leah yelled. "Are you going down the Sinman's or are you going to drag your square balls all day?"

"I'm going," I said heatedly, "but one bag isn't going to do a damn thing. What about Ray?"

"Ray's dressing now. She's going to go live with her sister," Leah snapped.

* * *

"I am going to *give* you a bag," the Sinman said coldly. "You may give it to Leah or do anything else you wish to do with it. But if and when you do give it to Leah you will be saving her from a fate worse than death for the time being. And I want you to remember for the rest of your life just how much gratitude she will show you. I also want you to promise never to attempt to do another junky a favor until Leah repays you for this bag. Tell Leah you had to pay for it and that she owes you the money for it."

I made that promise while thinking how great a void had come between the Sinman and me since I had become a wino. It hurt. "Remember that day you got robbed?" I said, desperately grabbing at a straw.

Sinman must have read all my thoughts. "We are still friends, but I do not intend to condone your idiocies any longer."

"Charlie gets drunk too."

"Can you imagine Blind Charlie standing there in your shoes and begging me for a bag of heroin for Leah?"

Three days later Leah's rent came due. She moved in on me.

"I won't be any trouble," she said. "We've always got along without no trouble. And J&J are going to keep my clothes so I'll dress in there. And I'll be gone all night just like Jackie. And after Jackie gets herself a room you'll need me around to cook and things. You'll appreciate a woman being around."

It was one of those days when my conscience was pricking me. Some days it was so bad that I punished myself by thinking that I had no right to bar anyone from my room because I wasn't paying the rent anyway. Welfare was. Leah had just as much right to use my room as I did. Yeah, I had mush for brains that day.

But Leah and Jackie really weren't any trouble. Time they came in in the morning they took their fixes and then sat nodding until I got out of bed and let them have it. The only thing that did keep me upset was the nagging feeling of guilt about not having been a man about the whole thing.

Sometime that week Gloria came by. Leah and Jackie were sound asleep and so we talked freely. "It's not that I'm a pussy for real," I said at one point. "I'm not scared of either one of them, and yet it's just like I'm afraid to tell them to get the hell out. Can you figure it?"

"I think so, Sid. But I'm not going to say right now. And I think that if I'm right these two bitches will cure what ails you. Now just for openers dig this: I don't know that black-assed bitch lying there." Gloria pointed at Jackie. "I don't know her from a hole in the ground. And she comes in here and tells you that we're the best of friends. Dig it? This chick don't know what's going on between me and you, but narco tells her that I won't chop her damn head off while she's laying there asleep. Dig what I'm getting at?

"And dig this," Gloria went on. "J&J aren't bothered with Leah. Why? Can't you figger that out? Honestly, Sid. It's just like God is giving you a chance to go to the college of life. You got a chance to get yourself a graduate degree without being no junky. You're broke, what clothes you got can't be pawned. You got a radio, but I know it's one of those six ninety-nine jobs from Fourteenth Street. You don't keep food in the refrigerator. So what have you got to lose? These whores can't take you for anything. So you just sit tight and let them school you. And I'm gonna stay out of it. I'm gonna let you make it on your own. If you stay sober you got the chance to become the smartest clean guy in Harlem. Dig it?"

The very next morning around eleven o'clock Sandy came in. Her appearance was like a shot of adrenalin. All those little tired lines of resignation that are in all junkies' faces were gone. Her hair was done up in a boss style. She was a real beauty now and no doubts about it.

"Come on in here and make yourself at home," I cried when I found my tongue. Then I woke up Jackie and Leah. They grumbled like dogs, but I didn't care, I wanted them to get the message clear and even. "This is your bed, you know," I said rapidly as Leah and Jackie slowly piled out of it. "Goddam. You sure look good to me. That House of D is a beauty farm. Every six months you girls should go back there and register."

"So you didn't know I was pretty, eh, Sid?" Sandy said airily.

"All us addicts look great after we get the shit out of our veins. I was walking up Greenwich Avenue to the subway—on my way from jail, mind you—and this Black john hits on me. Just for the hell of it I tells him that I'm no tricking woman, that it's my day off, and I got to go to Harlem to get my hair done before I go back to Long Island."

I grinned like the happy nut I was. "So you're a sleep-in maid now, eh?"

"The chump brings me up to Harlem in a taxi, rents a room for the day and then gives me bread to go and have my hair done. I stayed with him until a little while ago. He was a nice country boy. I liked him a little." She pulled a small roll of bills out of her slacks pocket. "I'm fabulous, keed. And I want you to know it."

"You and Gloria could turn tricks at a faggots' convention," I said. "But I never realized just how good-looking you are until today."

"I just copped from the Sinman, but the fairy bastid won't let me take off in his room. Mind if I hit myself in here, Sid?"

I hesitated. After all, the Sinman had said no, why should I play the fool? "I dunno," I said slowly. "You've been clean for months. You might OD on me . . ."

"I'm only going to joy-pop," Sandy said quickly. "And only half of it. A skin-pop can't hurt nobody. You know that. I'm not stupid enough to start to mainline time I hit the street. You know me, Sid. When I ever do anything stupid?"

Leah probably envisioned Sandy giving her the rest of the bag and so she said, "Let her skin-pop a little of it, Sid. What the hell. As long as she don't hit a vein she can't OD on you. And I'm telling you like a woman who knows. I got a record. Three goddam people died on my premises."

"Okay," I said. "I only hope you two know what you're talking about because I'm a square and I'm not supposed to know. But Sinman wouldn't, why should I?"

"No taking off in the room is Sinman's house rule. Leah was the same way, Sid. Don't you even remember how I met you?"

Leah solicitously lent her works and damn if Sandy not only

shot the whole bag but in a vein. I was madder at myself than I was with Sandy because she had *made* me play pussy. She had known that I wouldn't knock the needle out of her hand and then proceed to also knock her brains out. It's a little frightening for a girl to prove you stupid so easily.

About two minutes after taking that fix Sandy, who was sitting on the bed, sort of snapped back and just as her head was about to touch the bed itself she somehow caught herself. But in the two seconds it took for her to catch herself I died a thousand deaths. I'd never seen anyone OD, but I knew that Sandy had come within a thousandth of a fraction of a minute of OD'ing on me.

After that awful moment Sandy began to talk in a narcotic monotone. "I'm gonna get right back on Welfare, Sid," she said. "But damn if I feel like sitting around that office all day today, waiting for one of those bitches to write up my case. In fact, tomorrow I'm going to have you call 'em and tell 'em I'm too sick to come to the office. That way the bitches'll have to come see *me*. Dig?"

Junkies are not only peculiar persons, but somehow they are blessed. I don't believe I've ever known a junky who somehow didn't have the ability to make you forget that you were angry with them. In less than five minutes Sandy told the girls to go back to bed and she and I were engaged in one of our long rambling conversations, and for the life of me I cannot remember at what point I forgot that I was supposed to be angry with Sandy.

Just before the A&P closed Sandy went out and came back with a whole bag of groceries, cooked up a mess of liver and onions with rice, real soul style. Sandy had been born in Corona, Long Island, and had never been South in her life, but her mother must have come from there and taught her. Anyhow, Sandy was a boss cook.

Just before eleven o'clock each of the girls took a fix and began to get ready to hit the streets. And for the first time I considered how nice it was to have women around the house like this. In fact, I felt a little let down when they trooped out, but the fifth of Spur, although it hadn't made me drunk, had made me pleasantly sleepy. I went to bed.

At five in the morning someone began to knock on the foyer door. I went to answer it, wondering which of the girls was getting in first. I opened the door and in came Lorraine followed by a country girl. She had no business off the farm although she was very good-looking.

"It's colder than a whore's pussy out there this morning," Lorraine exclaimed, all buddy-buddy. "We could only hustle up enough bread for our habits with nothing left over for rent. Suddenly I thought about my baby, Sid Bailey, the bachelor. How'd you like for two red-hot mommas to sleep with you?"

"You took Roy out of here with over seventy-five dollars in his pocket, and I know you didn't let go until you'd bled him dry. Why didn't you take some of that loot and get yourself a pad?"

I was going to say more, but Lorraine and her friend had left me standing in the hall. I followed them into the room. Lorraine had already taken the works out of her bra and was preparing a fix with water from my bottle in the refrigerator.

I stood silent, thinking like a square that my silence would be felt more acutely than any voiced disapproval, but Lorraine was too busy cooking heroin in a bottle cap to give a damn about me and my feelings.

Like every other junky broad I knew, Lorraine's works were the same crude outfit consisting of a medicine dropper and a hypodermic needle. After she had cooked the heroin she drew up half the solution in the needle. All the while the two girls were sitting close together on the bed, talking to each other in low voices. As far as they were concerned I wasn't even present.

Lorraine hit Selma—that was the name of the country girl—in the back of the right thigh. It was in a vein that Selma could not have reached by herself. Then Selma took what was left of the heroin in the cap and hit Lorraine in a vein in the back of Lorraine's right arm.

When an addict is said to mainline it is meant that he injects heroin directly into a vein as opposed to joy-popping or skin-popping, when heroin is injected into a muscle. Injecting the drug into the vein is far more satisfying, but very dangerous. The mainliner can OD, but seldom if ever can one die from using a muscle. However, the mainliner cannot use the same vein for long; it collapses and the addict then must use another vein. In time the mainliner's accessible veins are all collapsed and he must find someone to inject the heroin in the veins he is not able to reach himself. This is when an addict is strung out as far as he can go.

And as I watched Selma and Lorraine going through their act I knew that both had just about reached the end of the road. That Lorraine was strung out did not surprise me. She had been an addict long before I met her in the St. Louis five or more years ago, but Selma looked as if she had not been more than a month or two off the farm.

As soon as the girls had finished and Lorraine had rinsed out her works they undressed and got in bed. In five minutes they were snoring.

I sat down in the easy chair. "Five whores," I muttered.

"Five goddam whores . . ." And I continued to mutter it over and over.

CHAPTER 21

GLORIA HAD SAID THAT I WOULD BE EDUCATED, but even she had not dreamed that I would end up with five professionals. Girls who had written their dissertations in the blood that dripped from their veins. And in the end it was not so much that I was educated: I evolved.

True to her word, Gloria literally disappeared from the scene. I knew that she still loved me and I her. We were doomed to that. But I knew that Gloria could only believe what the frailties of her own body had taught her.

The first most revealing aspect of the whole thing is the essential sexlessness of a junky woman. They were asexual and yet these girls were at all times acutely conscious of their sex, for it was the only coin of their realm. It was unreal how these girls, as sex-conscious as virgins, paraded about the room in various stages of nudity all the time. And it seemed to me that the girls more and more came to think of me as being without sex.

Not long before I would have sold my soul for the pleasure of having five promiscuous women prancing through my room nude or semi-nude, but now that they were present and available I learned that all my frustrations, all that lonely funkiness since leaving Alise, had been mental. In no time at all I became as cool as any pimp, knowing that sex is a chimera that is never allowed to interfere with business.

Yet even if I did not have sex with any of the girls, all of our relations were sexual. In the first place, each of them had moved in on the assumption that if she made her body available to me she would be welcome forever. And when each of the girls in turn found out that the others had come with the same idea they did not relinquish their objective. They all waged warfare for my attention and favors. If one of them wanted some of my instant coffee she would come close to me and place her hand on the fly of my pants, caressing me for all to see.

In fact, that they even asked permission to use anything of mine was a phenomenon because junkies seldom ask permission to do anything.

So it was not only I who evolved. The rules of conduct for all of us slowly but surely changed. In the beginning the girls all acted as if I was the debtor, as if it was the duty of each to get more out of me than the others. It was downright insane how they would smoke my cigarettes in lieu of their own. And every single one of them insinuated at least once a day that she wasn't eating regularly since she had come to live with me.

The girls slept all day until about five or six o'clock in the afternoon. From then until just before midnight, when they left to go hustle, they kept a three-ring circus going in the room. Always there was controversy; a junky woman's politest conversation is actually a veiled argument. In public places all junkies are more or less soft-voiced, but in the privacy of my room the girls were loud and raucous. Since I never have been able to abide loud-mouthed women the most nerve-racking aspect of the girls' stay was their "conversations." In the most mundane talks the girls spoke in controlled shouts.

Either because of life in reform schools and jail or by nature, the girls had no desire or need for privacy. Nor was anything sacred to them. They seemed to cherish no memories. Their sex lives were open books, as were their parents' and everyone else's. I learned that sex is valueless to a junky. They don't enjoy it. They are sexually feeble, and what passes for love with them is no more than a desire to possess, to be able to lay claim upon another. And it doesn't make any difference if it's a man or a woman. Even today I am convinced that junky whores are not whores because they are junkies, but because they are unable to refuse cash for what they consider to be of no importance. When they sold their bodies they were certain that they had outwitted a fool who offered good money for something that was absolutely worthless. I began to understand how these girls could respect pimps, who also think that sex is a thing of no consequence.

And as I evolved I realized that there was a good deal to the Sinman's contention that there is a junky syndrome. In time I went further than the Sinman had gone. There was the greed which was evident in each and every act. It was this self-centered greed that made them thieves. Or better yet, they did not steal in the strictest sense of the word. These girls saw an object and decided that they could make better use of it than the object's owner and so they appropriated it. They were forever stealing from each other, but seldom did one of the girls make an outcry over any missing possession. She would patiently bide her time until it was opportune to steal it back.

Each of the girls had a streak of meanness that she must have been born with. They all used plastic needles, and if ever one of those needles happened to drop to the floor one of the girls was sure to crush it underfoot before it could be retrieved. They threw each other's clothes to the floor every chance they got. Even in their sleep the girls were mean. I used to watch them in bed. When crowded they would beat on the girl who was crowding them until the girl moved over. They actually struck each other in their sleep. They definitely were not awake. I believe that, asleep, a junky can be differentiated from a non-user of heroin. Junkies push out their lips while they are asleep, as if ready to snarl at anyone who would disturb their purchased slumber.

All five of the girls were economically moronic. They were incapable of spending money intelligently and I doubt if heroin had anything to do with it. It was the dead of winter and none of the girls made much more money than would support their habits, plus odds and ends like cigarettes and things, and it seemed to me that the laws of self-preservation would prevail. But not with these addicts. At night they had only subway fare with which to reach their destinations, but in the morning they always returned in taxis, complaining of how much they had tipped the cabby. When one of them had a better than average night it never occurred to her to buy an extra bag of heroin for a rainy day. Neither did they ask me to hold any money for them. All surplus money was spent the same day, usually for comic books which they never got around to reading, or for candy, or was otherwise thrown away.

And, like the Sinman, I soon learned that all junkies are liars, but only in the sense a square thinks of a liar. The Sinman had said that junkies have no need for the truth in their scheme of things and this is absolutely true. But the most appalling thing about this phenomenon is that not one single shrink in America who makes his living from treating addicts has ever admitted this and resigned his lush position.

In view of the fact that truth never prevailed in my room I soon evolved into a man who refused to ask questions. What I didn't see I practically never believed.

Neither did it take long to learn that one never, but never, listens to a junky's first request. You ignore her the first time. For instance, if one asks for a cigarette just act like you didn't hear her. And in a moment she will ask for a drag. If she asks for a dollar, wait. She'll end up asking for a subway token.

I seldom saw the Sinman during this period but my respect for him grew daily. The man had been so absolutely right in all he had said about junkies. And daily his theory of the junky syndrome was proved before my eyes. At least it goes for female junkies; I really don't know many men who are addicts, but I do know my women addicts. And I took the Sinman's syndrome theory a step further and toyed with the obvious fact that nearly all female addicts are physical replicas. At least all the females in the Logan were almost physically alike, Ray and Leah being the exceptions that might prove the rule. All female addicts of my acquaintance are finely chiseled physical specimens. They come in all heights, but every one is shaped more or less like a Juno, with wonderful legs that have well-developed muscles. In other words they all have jock shapes of which they are very proud. All have square, unfemale shoulders and all have medium small to tiny breasts. Certainly there must be a full-breasted female junky somewhere in this world, but I have never seen one. Nor have I ever known a junky girl for long who did not soon profess to be either in love with a female or the mistress of a female.

Junkies do claim to have love affairs, but what passes with them for love is a torturous thing. The junky's maniacal greed breeds possessiveness and jealousy. Junkies do not love, they covet certain persons. This is why the so-called love affairs of the junky so often end in bloodshed and/or the stooling to the police on one another.

Under the bludgeoning tutoring of these girls I grew hardened and cynical. So cynical that I told myself that I for one would never see a sick-sick junky. For I reasoned that if a junky is very sick and you refuse to help, then that junky is going someplace else before he gets so sick he can't even walk. A semi-paralyzed junky is a sick-sick junky. And like I say: I don't intend to ever see one.

At first blush it might sound strange for me to say that these five prostitutes brought out some of the best qualities in me. Before they arrived I was a well-read and perhaps not too bright fellow who thought he was something of a playboy. But actually I had no sense of judgment. I was equipped only for survival among effete snobs. But after a dose of those five junky whores I think I can make it in anybody's world.

Jinny, who should know, said one day, "Damn if you don't have those feather merchants under control, buddee. I didn't think you had it in you. Lots of studs more hip than you would have thrown up their hands and split that scene. Just moved on out and left those five bitches to have the room. You don't have to tell me about their fighting and stealing. I got ears. But yet and still you are the boss. How do you do it? Joey couldn't have done it, and he has actually pimped in his day. He was scared to death by the very thought of Leah moving in on us. How do you do it?"

"I don't really know," I said. "But I think part of the secret is that I haven't screwed a single one of them. That keeps them off balance. Like they're always worried that I'll suddenly get tight with one and kick the others out. And I guess they don't get too tough with each other for the same reason. They don't know who might get to be queen bee tomorrow." I knew this sounded silly and so I grinned and sort of apologized. "Yeah, I know how I sound, but that's the way it is, Jinny."

"Boy, it did me good to hear you yell at them the other night. Joey said they probably heard you down in the lobby."

"I don't remember yelling at them," I said. "They're the ones who do all the yelling. Even when they're whispering they whisper at the top of their lungs."

"You don't remember yelling that you didn't want a goddam one of them asking for more than two cigarettes in any twenty-four-hour period? Me and Joey cracked up. You're on the ball, champ."

"What the hell," I muttered. "They were beginning to hurt me where I lived. From the very beginning they all acted like it was my duty to supply them with cigarettes. They only smoked theirs out in the street. They all acted like I had extended them a personal invitation to move in for my personal pleasure. In fact, a couple of them still try to make me feed them. They come in and announce they're starved, and just stand there like I'm supposed to go out and get them something to eat. Then later on they produce a dollar and ask me to go get them some comic books or some other trash like that. You simply don't pay a junky any mind."

"Well, you keep right on coming in and eating with us. Damn those whores. That Leah thought she was going to be catting on us, but I had news for her. And I don't ever intend to get that close to a junky again. But, so help me, you've gotten to be real smooth now, keed. At first Joey and I thought you were getting dumber and dumber, but you fooled us. And the way you were living, I guess you couldn't help it that those five whores moved in the way they did. But I don't have to tell you now to let that be a lesson to you: always have a woman from now on. It don't make no difference how old or beat she is as long as you're able to tell people that your old lady won't stand for such-and-such. Dig it?"

"How did you really get Leah off your backs?" I asked. "What did you say that kept her from moving in? I know she didn't come to me first."

"I told her that I don't pay rent, which is true. But I also told her that only Joey pays rent because I stoolie for Ginsburg. I tell him who's doubling up so he can charge them extra."

"Do you?"

"Hell, no! But any time you want to get a boot off your back all you have to do is bring a whitey into the act. I don't care how bad or hepped these characters around here claim to be, they still won't lock horns with a whitey. Don't you know that?"

"Winos, yes, but not junkies."

"Whitey can have a junky arrested in a minute and the goddam junky knows it. You can walk in a precinct and tell the desk sergeant that a junky just murdered your mother and the sergeant will tell you it's your fault and just might not even take your name. But all a whitey has to do is call up and say that a junky scared him and that junky is going to jail!"

"And a junky knows you don't get your fix on time in jail, eh?"

"That's about the size of it."

"Well, you sure dumped a heap of nothing in my lap when you passed that damned Leah on to me."

"I didn't pass her on to you. I thought when I nixed her she would go find Ray. They're supposed to be so much in love and all."

"I can't stand to touch Leah," I said.

"Well, don't touch her."

"I have to."

"For what?"

"Her veins are all collapsed and she has to hit herself in the shoulder."

"No!" Jinny exclaimed in disbelief. "You really know what you're talking about, Sid?"

"Yeah. Skinny as she is, her flesh is so flabby that a needle won't go straight in. I have to take her flesh and pinch it into a lump so she can jab her dull-assed needle into it. It gives me the creeps every time."

"Lawd have mercy. Wait till I tell Joey. But why the hell don't you make one of the women do it?"

"She don't want them to know, I guess. She waits until they're all asleep in the morning and tries to get up ahead of them in the evening. If she don't, she asks me to go in the john with her."

"Oh," Jinny murmured. Then she said, "You know that Leah's going to be dead pretty soon, don't you?"

"No. Why you say that?"

"When you have to shoot it in a muscle you're damn near at the end of the line anyhow. When you use a muscle you always get abscesses. Pretty soon your whole body turns into one big abscess and you die."

I knew Jinny was telling the truth. "Already her legs are covered with weeping sores," I said. "That's why she always wears slacks. And skinny as she is, her legs are swollen twice as big as mine. I don't see how any man in the world would want to turn a trick with her. How the devil could a man mess with a chick whose legs are covered with bandages?"

"Don't be dumb, Sid," Jinny said dryly.

I realized what Jinny meant and I got uptight for the first time since the girls had laid up on me. I went to my room and stood looking down on them. I had an angry desire to rape all five of them. Not to ask them, you understand, but to brutally kick their asses and take it. For a moment as I stood over them I could almost hear them begging for mercy. And then like some kind of revelation it came to me that I was a human being and these five women were not. And from this moment on it was up to me to prove it at all times.

I guess I was being melodramatic, but I went to the closet and took down the package of pads that Roy had bought. Then I went to the table that was supposed to be a writing desk and sat down. I began to map out a thesis for a play. I honestly began with a sense of failure; I was putting down the outline of a plot to prove to myself that the thing would never make a play. But in no time at all I was scribbling about the crazy numbers banker I had met when I was in college. The man had inflicted his friendship on me in much the same way Blind Charlie had, but with many differences. I wrote and wrote. The stuff came easily, just like writing a letter to an old friend. I don't know when it happened, but all at once I wasn't writing a thesis any more, or a play, I was writing a novel. In less than three hours I had completed a chapter and a half.

I heard one of the girls stirring on the bed and I quickly stuffed the pads into the drawer of the table. Then I turned and saw that it was Sandy. She must have been watching me for a long time because she said, "Who you writing to, Sid?"

"Myself."

"You that lonely?" She began to laugh but ended up coughing.

All junkies have a cough. I went to the refrigerator and got her a drink of water.

"You want a little loving, Sid?"

"Remember our deal? Right after Blind Charlie choked you?"

Sandy nodded. "But I owe you a little trim for letting me lay around on you like this. I would have contacted Welfare weeks ago, but I can't seem to make my lazy ass do it. Honest. I can't get myself straight before they're closed. They know they got to register us addicts so why don't they stay open hours that suit us? Welfare is run stupid as hell if you ask me."

"I thought you were going to call in too sick to go?"

She wriggled her shoulders restlessly. "With all these goddam whores laying around half naked all day? The investigator would take one look and call the cops."

"For what? You musta got stir crazy in that House of D. Cops can't arrest anybody for sleeping."

"You got five women in here that use skag. And there are five—no, four sets of works in this room plus five doses of heroin for everybody to wake up on. You think the fuzz wouldn't be interested?" She reached in her bra for her works. "No kidding, Sid, what are you writing? A book?"

Sandy was like that, she never gave up. "I told you I was writing to myself, didn't I?"

"Well, why *don't* you write a book? You got a good brain and a college education, and this sorry excuse for a hotel has got a million plots."

"And who the hell would believe them?" I asked. "I don't believe half the things that go on around here myself. Who'd believe that five junky women all catted on a man at one time? And only whiteys buy books and there isn't a single whitey in the world's gonna believe I haven't screwed one of you. And who'd believe that a man could live with five women and not know the last name of any of you?"

"Carrol. Sandra Carrol. That's my name, Sid."

"Glad to meet you."

Sandy laughed in an oddly maternal way. "We all had you down for a sucker, Sid. But we could do this to any other square too, Sid," she added quickly. "And just because the sucker'd think it couldn't be done."

"So why didn't a couple of you pick another sucker? You sure in hell would be a lot more comfortable. Why just me?"

Sandy laughed again. "We're too lazy. And I guess each one of us thinks that the others are going to leave any day now. But it ain't nothing for five addicts to sleep together in one bed, Sid. That's the life. Especially men addicts, they all carry sticks."

"I don't mean you personally, Sandy. In fact, I like to have you around. Maybe I even need you around, but will you tell me what is wrong with me that makes the rest of these women know that I'm too soft to put them out? How did they know I'd be such a damn pussy?"

"You're not looking at it like it is, Sid. Now a cat always moves in on a person without even thinking about it. Then you just sit and wait to see if they'll put you out. None of these babes knew for sure if you'd kick them out or not. And to tell the truth, none of them gave a damn if you did put them out. You think if you got mad or drunk and ran us all outa here that we wouldn't find another pad right here in the Logan to shack up in?" She looked at me, musing. "Ain't it funny, Sid? Five goddam whores, and they don't really hafta."

I went to the bed and stretched out in the narrow space Sandy had occupied.

"Do you realize that four of us, including myself, moved in on you because we actually preferred to live with you, Sid?" Sandy said suddenly. "I mean that they *chose* you. That means you're a wonderful person, Sid. Really beautiful. If you would just leave that damn juice alone you'd be boss, Sid. Really."

"You say four. That means one of you doesn't prefer to live with me. Which one? Selma?"

Sandy giggled. "You're schooling yourself real fast, Sid. But you got a long way to go yet. You know, it's funny how a square won't sit down and figure a junky. And it's so easy. A junky don't have no secrets. They ain't hard to read. But you just won't take the time. Now why you think Jackie always goes in the bathroom to hit herself and then stays for an hour?"

Just thinking about Jackie and her foolishness made me peevish. "How the hell would I know!" I exclaimed. "She's just mean and stubborn, is the real reason."

Sandy shook her head. "Different addicts react in different ways to a fix. Jackie is the damnedest. She'll commit rape right after a fix, and it don't make no difference if it's a man or a woman. But right now it's on account of you she goes in the bathroom and stays."

"How could she be so sure I wouldn't give her a hump if she wanted it so bad?"

"You got it backwards, Sid. She don't want *you*."

"The bitch."

"Jackie is supposed to have the best tail around, didn't you know that?"

I believed that Sandy was joking, but I decided to play it straight like a square would. "How would I know what kind of trim she's got?" I said disgustedly. "In the first place I hang out with winos, they don't know nothing about junky girls. Besides, Jackie is so ugly she don't have much chance to show her wares anyhow, if you know what I mean."

"Jackie is one of the most beautiful Black women there is," Sandy said. "Don't ever let the effects of heroin fool you, Sid. You should see Jackie when she comes out of the House of D. She's lovely. It's that damn shit that makes all Black women look like her sometimes. It loosens their lips and puts those mean-looking weary lines in your face."

"She looks so ugly to me I thought she couldn't do any better than old Dick."

Sandy shook her head. "Jackie's gone with Dick off and on for years, but in the meantime she's taken some awful beatings from cats that don't believe in sharing the wealth. Dig it? Jackie's afraid of you. She don't intend to lay any of that fine pussy on you and then you start thinking that only you is going to have some from now on. She stays in that toilet and masturbates."

I was so angry I was tongue-tied. "Why the hell is everything a junky does unprintable?" I sputtered. "No, I'll change that: A Black junky whore. If five white bitches were laying up on a white guy like this I bet he'd be able to write a charming little tale that *Esquire* or *Playboy* would grab in a minute."

Lorraine and Selma began to stir. Those two did every damn thing in unison. They didn't even speak as they both went out to the bathroom together, but Lorraine came back first.

She went to the closet and went in her overcoat pocket. "Here's a pack of L&Ms I bought you, Sid." She tossed them on the bed.

"Sid smokes Pall Malls. You know damn well he does," Sandy said.

Lorraine glared. "So why the hell didn't you think to buy him some then? Me and Selma is the only ones who appreciate what Sid is doing for us. So we ain't trying to make him poorer. Dig?"

Sandy got up from her chair and strutted over to the bed and picked up the cigarettes. She opened them and lit one, inhaled, and then snorted the smoke out contemptuously. "I'm an invited guest here, you ain't," she said to Lorraine. "And also dig the fact that if I was carrying a stick it'd be just me. I wouldn't be dragging my bitch along too."

"You only wish you had a woman to drag along with you!" Lorraine shouted.

"Even in the House of D I never went for that stuff," Sandy said calmly. "Sure, I might let some dizzy stud kiss around a little bit, but I don't see no sense in wasting myself out here in the street on no jailhouse love. Sandy Carrol is nobody's freak, Miss Bitch."

"Save it, baby," Lorraine snapped. "Didn't your husband knife you because you wouldn't stay away from that stud bitch on Ninety-sixth Street? Now say that's a lie!"

"That was before I started using drugs!" Sandy yelled. "I wasn't in the life then. I was a kid, I didn't know any better."

"And you ain't no smarter now, bitch. You was ready. You was ready for dog-eat-dog. If you know what I mean."

"I'm going to kick your ass, Lorraine."

"You gotta bring ass to get ass! Dig it? And if you don't dig it you better hurry up and ask somebody. Just bring yours when you come to kick mine, and you might as well bring your lunch because we're gonna be fighting all day!"

Jinny came to the door and tried to grin cheerfully. "How come you girls never bring Sid a drink?" she said. "Used to be when I didn't have he had, but not since you bitches arrived. And am I broke this afternoon."

"We don't want Sid to drink," Sandy said.

"That don't mean you got to stop him from buying for his

friends," Jinny said. "Ain't you got a corner in a bottle hid around here somewheres, Sid? I need me another drink bad."

From out of nowhere Lorraine produced a dollar bill and tossed it to me. "Selma and me picked up the fruitiest john last night," she said rapidly as if determined to hold the spotlight. "All he wants is for us to ride the subway with him. He would sit facing us and we had to have our legs crossed real high so he could look up our dresses. Wasn't that a bitch though? He gives us twelve bucks apiece."

"The damn freak knew he was picking up two freaks," Sandy said. "He wanted you to ride the subway to his pad instead of a taxi, and it was in his freakish house you earned your bread. Don't tell me any of your lies."

I gave the dollar to Jinny and she disappeared. There was plenty of room on the bed now so I rolled over and took a nap. I drifted off, thinking about how long it had been since I had taken a drink compulsively, and how I never thought about loneliness, and my being unable to attract woman sexually.

As the days passed the girls had become less and less of a problem; they were no more than five frisky kittens underfoot for a few hours each afternoon and night before they got ready for the street.

Ten days passed and I had completed twelve chapters. Sure they were rough, but they also had something. I was working out of a bog no other writer had yet used. I often wondered why no other Black writer had gone to the numbers racket for a locale or milieu. For numbers are as Black and American as jazz, the Renny, Small's and sweet potato pie. And it didn't take long for me to become afraid that a book would soon appear that would make my stuff obsolete old hat.

But the one thing that kept me at the writing and did not let me be too afraid of being capped by another book on the numbers was that writing creatively can put you together better than anything on earth. Writing can fill all the lonely wells and desolate pits in your soul. You become a god, granting to this character life, this one death, that one riches, another cancer. You cure or condemn. And your characters all belong to you.

But more than that, the manuscript becomes human. In no time at all, not only was I referring to my manuscript as my bitch or My Ole Gal, J&J and the girls all referred to it as a living woman.

And she did live. Of course I could never expect to have an orgasm, but writing is just as much a sexual experience as the Sinman claims the ingestion of narcotics to be.

Now that I had My Ole Woman to caress with a pencil each night and day my life had meaning. Sure, I wanted success and wealth, but that manuscript was mine. *I* liked it and that was all that really mattered even if I did hope the critics would like it too. But always that manuscript was my bitch and nobody else's bitch but mine. I believe I could kill a man who molested my woman in any way whatsoever.

However, My Old Woman could not entirely blot out the all too evident existence of the five whores in my room. Sandy alone took care of that.

I liked Sandy. She was a boss companion, but it is strange how much more troublesome she was. In truth, it was Sandy alone who presented problems. With her 138 IQ, she was the dumbest. Stupidly and determinedly dumb. From the outset I had told all the girls to keep their business out in the street where they found it and where it belonged. I told them the room was crowded to begin with and I didn't even want to meet their friends much less their johns. I thought all this would spike any ideas they had of using my room to turn their tricks because I had no intentions of ever being their muscle man if a john happened to jump salty.

But Sandy simply ignored me. It was like she didn't believe I could tell the truth either. Almost every night she brought some stranger in the room and introduced him. I would barely acknowledge the introduction and pretty soon Sandy would take the man into the kitchen. But Sandy never gave up. Every night she tried the same thing again. I fumed and fussed with her time after time, but as I said: Sandy didn't believe what *anybody* said. So in a way she won out; a few times I wearily consented for her and her company to take off in the room.

So it was through Sandy's intransigence that I found out that there are many part-time addicts in New York. In the main these part-timers are hard-working, law-abiding people, and as far as I could see, they had no steady habit, but an occasional yen came over them for a fix. Perhaps this only occurred two or three times a year, but the part-timer caught far more hell than the hardened addict. For one thing, the part-time users had no regular sources or connections. They had to depend on conniving junkies to get them their occasional bag.

It seemed to me that Sandy had special talent for getting next to these people. One night she brought a tall youth to the room. Without a second thought I believed them to have been former schoolmates. They were about the same age and made a handsome couple. Like some romantic old maid, I was both amused and glad to hear them speak flirtatiously to each other, and I was a little let down when after repeated whispered proddings from Sandy the young man asked for permission to take a fix. They had only one bag between them. Sandy used her works. The man told Sandy to hit herself first and then asked her to hit him. I knew there was something funny because the guy had veins that were in excellent condition, but what was there to say? Ten seconds after Sandy had hit him the boy made a gurgling sound and collapsed on the floor.

"What the hell's wrong with him?" I yelled.

Sandy said nothing. She went to the refrigerator, took out a tray of ice cubes, opened the guy's fly and reached for his testicles. She shoved the tray in his pants so that his privates rested on it. Then she grabbed his legs and began to exercise them, a sort of bicycle-riding movement. By now she was soaking wet with perspiration, but she still had not uttered a word.

"What the hell is going on?" I kept repeating.

"Go get J&J," Sandy said at last.

"Isn't that sonofabitch OD'ing?" Joey yelled after taking one look at the prostrate youth. "What the hell you got him on the floor for? Walk the sonofabitch! Walk! Walk!" She and Sandy grabbed hold of the guy and dragged his lifeless form up and down the hall for more than an hour. After the hour the youth began to take faltering steps of his own. Then Jinny and I took over and walked him. One time when we passed my door I looked in and saw that Sandy was preparing another fix. I let the guy fall and rushed in and punched Sandy in the jaw. She hit the floor.

"Nobody ever takes another fix in this room!" I shrieked.

"I'm only cooking salt and water to hit him with," Sandy said, slowly getting to her feet. "You always hit them with salt and water after an OD. But first you got to cook the iodine out of it, Sid. You shouldn't hit me like that without first asking, Sid."

"Bitch! I ought to kill you," I gritted. "But I'm not. I'm not even going to put you out. But the next stupid goddam thing you do I'm gonna stomp your motherfucking asshole out. You hear me?"

"Honest, Sid. I won't never do nothing like this again. I swear."

J&J now had the man. They paused in front of the door. "Do you know who you are?" Joey asked him.

He nodded affirmatively but could not yet speak.

"Are you really down with it?" Jinny asked.

This time the youth shook his head to say no.

"I thought so," Jinny said and looked knowingly at Joey and me.

About ten minutes later the boy said, "I want to go home."

"Well, go the hell home," Joey cried. All of us were in the hallway now.

"I'm never going to touch heroin again as long as I live," the boy said. And when none of us said anything he said, "I can't afford it anyhow. I can't hardly pay to stay in school now."

"School?" Joey bellowed. "What damn school?"

"Barnard."

"Barnard's a girls' school," Joey yelled.

"Not any more," the boy said. Suddenly he bolted for the foyer door and was gone.

"Goddam! I need me another fix after that," Sandy said.

"Fix?" Joey yelled. "Another fix? Why, you simple-assed bitch, you brought that school kid in here and gave him his first shot of heroin. How much damn dumber can you get than that?"

"How was I to know he was a square?" Sandy shrieked back. "He comes to me and asks if I can get him a fix. What the hell was I supposed to say?"

"No!" Jinny snapped.

Joey turned to me. "This is the dumbest whore in the Logan, Sid. She is too dumb to get out and hustle. All she can do is make wisecracks. Most johns want no part of her. If a john walks up and offers seven dollars she tells him to shove it, she only dates for ten. If he offers twenty dollars she thinks he's crazy and holds out for thirty. The only time she ever gets to turn a trick is when some junky in the lobby brings her a trick on a platter, and the price's already been settled before the junky brings the john to her.

"All she does all night is hang out down in that lobby, cadging a half bag here and a half bag there. She would bring the police commissioner up to this room if the guy promised to share a bag with her. That schoolboy that just walked outa here probably had an argument with his girl friend and wanted to do something real bad to hurt her. And I bet he tole Sandy so. Now if, after what I tole you, you go ahead and let this stupid tramp sleep in your room again I'm never gonna speak to you again in life, Sid Bailey!"

"I meant what I said," I said heavily. "I'm gonna let her stay because I want her to fuck up. And the least single thing she does I'm gonna kill the bitch. And I'm gonna enjoy doing it. Tonight I've had it. Junkies are not gonna fuck over me again in life. Any time one of them does anything I don't like I'm gonna do exactly like Blind Charlie would do, I'm gonna crucify them."

"He means it, Joey," Jinny said. "Leave him be. It's the best thing ever happened to him . . . or Sandy."

I grabbed Sandy by the hair and yanked her into the room. "And don't you say a goddam word about this to them other bitches," I told her. She nodded obediently. Her eyes were filled with a peaceful look of thanksgiving. It was like she felt free at last.

That look in her eyes chased all my anger. Suddenly I could only feel love and pity for this valiant girl whose essence demanded that she always be a slave. In my mind's eye she was a piece of wood, an excellent piece, finely grained. A block of wood which the least talented could work into a masterpiece, and yet . . . she was driftwood.

And if Sandy insisted upon being the dumbest of the lot, Jackie was the most ill equipped. She was the ugliest while using drugs. She looked worse than Leah. Once she told me that she was a skilled shoplifter and proved it by walking around the room with a suit of mine beneath her skirt with not a trace showing. But Jackie's appearance was so startlingly Black and ugly that she did not have time in the shops that sold goods worth stealing. Salespeople would come to her quickly out of curiosity to see what she wanted in a fine shop.

However, Jackie was more of a call girl than the others. She had many regular customers. She only averaged about two seven-dollar tricks a night, I imagine. And these she got by going by the rooms or apartments of older men who expected her. Just why she remained out on 125th Street after turning her two average dates I do not know. But then, a junky never gives up.

Jackie was usually the first girl to come back in the morning, but one morning she came in last. It was after ten o'clock.

"I blew it all," she moaned. And she was in bad shape.

All of the girls were awake, but nodding.

Jackie came close and said, "I starts out *bam!*" She feinted a punch. "It was downtown and a twenty-dollar trick. Then I gets a nine-dollar john after that. Then comes along a guy that hits on me, promising fifteen. This is the Times Square district, mind you. I don't know from nothing down there, but last night I decided to change my style a little. See? Anyhow, this fifteen-buck guy goes in a hotel and rents a room while I'm standing out in front. He comes back and takes me up the room. And time he locks the door, what you think he does?"

I shook my head.

"He hauls off and tags me one," Jackie exclaimed. "I pulls my blade and slashes at him. But damn if this whitey don't get his *kicks* outa me slashing at him. He kept saying: 'Not in my face,' over and over again. But I was after his throat! He musta saw I wasn't playing so he starts in swinging for real. He rips my dress and bra."

She opened her coat and showed me. "Out comes my works and my bread, but I'm too mad to notice. He turns around one time and I jabs this blade up his ass to the hilt and splits outa there. And I don't know I've left my works and my bra until I'm out in the street and a mile away.

"But I don't give up," Jackie continued. "I'm so mad I swear I'm not leaving Broadway until I got my usual bread. I stayed down there until dawn, but nothing was shaking. So I came back to Harlem and turned an eight-dollar trick. I bought a five-dollar bag and one of those three-dollar bags the Puerto Ricans sell and walked home. Now I gotta borrow a spike. My God, I'm sicker'n hell."

Sandy giggled, Leah stared at the wall, Selma and Lorraine continued to whisper.

"Can I borrow your works, Sandy?" Jackie said in a weak voice.

"You could have bought works with the three bucks you spent on the half bag," Sandy said. "So now you got a bag and a half, why don't you make somebody an offer?"

"I need it all," Jackie said. "A bag now and the half to wake up on. And I'm gonna be sick tonight unless I'm lucky. A half bag before you hit the street ain't nothing. It won't even carry you."

"Lorraine and Selma do it," Sandy retorted.

"If you were sick enough you'd offer somebody fifty cents at least," Leah said in a faraway voice. "And why don't you go see Bill and Reba?" I was tempted to ask Leah why she hadn't gone to them the morning after she had been stuck up, but I suddenly decided to keep out of this.

"Ain't no missionaries in here," Sandy said.

"You girls know I don't buy in this hotel," Jackie said tearfully. "And if I was to ask one of those bastids in the lobby they'd probably punch me out and take both bags."

"There's always the Sinman," Leah said.

Selma and Lorraine began to laugh out loud.

I saw that the saliva was beginning to thread in Jackie's mouth. "You're worse than a pack of mad dogs," I said bitterly.

"I told her to go to the Sinman," Leah said, obviously relishing her wit.

When she mentioned the Sinman this time I thought of Blind Charlie and how he would react in a situation such as this. I could not imagine what he would do, but in every circumstance Charlie did not like he made a demonic attempt to destroy it.

"Put your goddam works on this bed!" I screamed. "Every goddam one of you whores put your works on this goddam bed before I kill you!" I leaped to the closet and grabbed a hammer up off the floor.

"Okay. Okay," Lorraine said hastily. "You don't have to let the whole hotel know we got works, do you?"

She reached in her bra and got her works and tossed them on the bed. So did Leah and Sandy. I was truly sorry, I wanted to bash heads. I needed to bash heads. It was the only way I could get unwound.

"Someone might hear you," Leah murmured as she complied. "We're doing like you said, Daddy."

"I ought to break up every one of these things and then keep you all under lock and key for twenty-four hours!" I yelled. And then tears jumped to my eyes because I wasn't quite mad enough to do that.

Leah lit a cigarette and came and put it in my mouth. Sandy slipped out of the room and came back in a few minutes with a drink of J&J's Spur.

"Here, Daddy," she said softly, handing it to me.

But you had to see that light of peace, contentment and even of thanksgiving that was in Leah's and Sandy's eyes. It was as if they were happy that I had released them from a dark something that had demanded they must always show cruelty no matter what their hearts felt. And I realized that in that one flash of murderous desire I had become their master, their pimp. It was like I had brought them captive into my world and they liked it a lot better than their own.

From that morning on things were different in 5-C-4. The girls' attitude changed completely. They brought me not only cigarettes but hamburgers and jars of instant coffee. Soon they were chipping in to buy groceries and Sandy became the chef as we began to eat two good meals a day. Leah even gave me money once a week to buy more pads. Whenever a john had a bottle on him the girls would beg him for it and bring it to me. My writing really had me going now and so I was drinking very little. The closet became loaded with partially filled bottles.

Right after this incident about their works I stopped working on my novel long enough to try a psychological short story about how I had caused all the girls to change, but after I had delineated the facts there seemed no more to tell. I mean I had a climax to start out with, but nothing else. I couldn't make a salable thing out of it, especially since everyone concerned was Black. At least that's what I told myself and so went back to My Old Woman, my novel.

One morning Lorraine and Selma came in first and acted more secretive than ever. Both wore snide smiles of self-satisfaction. At nine o'clock they went out and returned a half hour later. Then they hit each other for the second time that morning and, although each was high and nodding, neither of them went to bed.

Lorraine was in the easy chair and Selma sat near her on the window sill. The other girls were asleep. Suddenly Selma began to laugh hollowly.

"What's the joke?" I asked her.

As usual Lorraine answered for Selma. "We had Steak-eating Johnny last night," she said.

Selma doubled over, laughing.

"Who the hell is Steak-eating Johnny?" I demanded.

"One of our regular tricks. That's the name we gave him. He's a whitey and a big politician and a weirdo if there ever was one. We got a standing date with him once a month," Lorraine said.

"So that's all there is to laugh about?" I asked.

"Well, it was like this," Lorraine said. "When we get there he always makes like he never met us before, see? And after we introduce ourselves he invites us into his kitchen to show us a great big porterhouse steak. So help me, that steak always weighs four or five pounds. Big, dig? And then he stands there like a fool while we oh and ah over the beautiful steak. Goddam. He swells all up like we're admiring his Congressional Medal or something. Then he gets all cute and bashful and says he don't know how to cook. Then me and Selma says we will cook it for him. And we chase him outa the kitchen and make a big to-do about fixing the steak."

"But first he wants us to take our clothes off so we won't get them soiled," Selma said and I realized that this was the most she had ever said to me since she arrived. "And then he says he'll take his off too so we won't feel embarrassed. Dig it?"

"And all he wants is for the steak to be singed on both sides," Lorraine said. "You know, just three or four minutes on each side. Raw and still cold in the middle. And all the time he is strutting around with his gray-assed self, patting us on the can and talking about what nice girls we are. Then we all go in the front room and he sets up a card table. And we bring him his steak. My God, Sid. You ought to see how he eats it. Just like a dog. Like a goddam wild beast he eats it. Blood all running down his chin, and tears out his eyes, and he's growling and sobbing like a goddam crazy man. And when he gets up from the table he's come. Goddam. These whiteys sure know how to freak off."

Selma shrugged her shoulders. "After that he gives us ten bucks apiece and we leaves. No screwing, no kissing around, no nothing but watching him gobble up that damn steak. God. I wish all whiteys was like him." Then she giggled.

"But last night Selma suddenly had to take a leak while he was eating," Lorraine said. "When she goes through his bedroom she spots his watch and wallet. And so she clips the chump."

I was nauseated. "And he's a rich politician?" I said. "And you call him a chump?"

"Sure he's a chump," Lorraine said. "We clipped him, didn't we?"

"And what you gonna do now?" I yelled. "Don't you stupid bitches know that the fuzz don't do nothing but serve politicians? So you went out of here this morning and pawned his watch. And you two dummies don't think you got something to worry about?"

"All he knows is Selina and Terry. Those are the names we go by in the street," Lorraine said.

"And what was in the wallet?" I said bitterly. "No more than twenty, twenty-five bucks, I bet."

"Thirty-five," Selma said. "And we got thirty on the watch."

"For sixty-five dollars you blow a regular thing," I said. "Can't you junkies ever look further than your next fix? And don't you know that guy's gonna have the detectives looking for you without having to swear out a warrant?"

Selma sniffed. "You think he's gonna let us tell the cops he's a steak-eating freak?"

"The cops'll know it's just a damn lie two nigger bitches made up to embarrass a respectable white citizen. Don't you fools realize that you don't even have a change of overcoats? I bet every cop on Times Square got your description and is looking for you right this minute."

Both seemed to think that over. Finally Lorraine retorted, "You don't know what it's all about. You think Selma was going to pass up that money and watch? What the hell do you think a girl goes out in the street for, to get a motherfucking dick shoved in her for kicks? With this bread we might have time to go in a bar and meet a big-time pusher who goes for one of us. And you realize we might have missed a chance to make a grand while we was watching that gray-assed freak eat his steak? Time is valuable. And where the hell would a girl be if all she thought about was staying in good with a john for next time? Hell, that old fart might be dead tomorrow."

"Or we might," Selma said.

To punctuate the end of the conversation Lorraine held a five-dollar bill out to me. I hesitated only briefly. What the hell, I figured the screwballs would throw it away anyhow. And I could always use more pads.

When I took that five Lorraine pronounced the doxology. "Sid, you forget that the fuzz's job is to keep us in jail. So the idea is to do as much as you can before you get busted. It ain't no sweeter in the House of D if you tell the chaplain about all the lovely breaks you gave the stupid johns."

I walked out of the room and went up to see how Mr. Johnson was doing. Blind Charlie was there.

"When you gonna be a man and toss them whores outa there?" Charlie demanded.

"Sid ain't no fool," Mr. Johnson said. "He knows what's what."

"No, he don't," Charlie said. "I knows every single one of them. Nary a one can make enough bread to keep her in heroin even. I bet this dumb boy gotta supply them cigarettes."

Charlie talked on and pretty soon I tired of listening to him so I went back down to my room. Selma and Lorraine had fallen asleep. Selma in the window, Lorraine in the chair. Leah woke up and lit a cigarette. She blew out the smoke and cursed.

"What's with you?" I asked her.

"Bread."

"Bread?"

"I want seventy-five dollars so bad I can't even sleep from thinking about it. With seventy-five dollars I could be back in business. I could down a bundle in less than eight hours for a fifty-buck profit and have my room back and in no time I'd be sitting on top of the heap with that damned Ray begging to come back."

"Joey and I could put you back in business next Checkday," I said. "My check is for forty-eight bucks and so is Joey's, I think. We don't have to pay rent the minute the checks come. If Joey is willing to gamble you could have your seventy-five bucks."

"You think Jinny would let that bastid do me a favor like that? But thanks anyway. You're boss, Sid. Boss friend every time."

"Maybe I don't even like you, Leah," I said, "but you're no dumb chick. And maybe it's wrong the way I believe in you, but you can make it in the world you junkies live in and that's all I'm thinking about right now. You've got to show Joey that she's doing herself a favor. Show her that you will give her two or three dollars a day royalties . . . or whatever you want to call it, after you pay her back. J&J and me too would be living in style and you'd be making it. Just ask Joey what's she got to lose."

"Everything, Sid. Joey'd have everything to lose. Suppose I got picked up bringing that shit back here to sell? Where'd you and Joey's rent money be then? Suppose I got robbed? You don't pay your rent, you get kicked off Welfare. Joey's not like you, Welfare's all Joey's got. Besides, J&J've been in the life, they think they can tell when somebody's washed up. But I'll show 'em. I'm gonna steal me some money even if I've gotta kill for it, so help me."

"Leah, how the hell is it possible that you didn't have any money in the bank? You must have sold three bundles a night. And that gives you a hundred and fifty dollars a day income. You couldn't have blown it all."

Leah laughed bitterly until she began to cough. "You're adding it up wrong, Sid. Me and Ray had what you call a pusher's habit. We took a fix when we felt like it, know what I mean? We must have used fifteen bags a day ourselves. We gave credit and now we're outa business I'll never collect. And I spent. I got clothes mammy, but what good are they to me? I spent more than five bucks a day on J&J. I'm not talking about their damn wine. I mean, I gave. They don't never talk about that. Hell. They haven't offered me a meal since I've been broke.

"And you forget that we didn't have *any*thing to sell mebbe one, two nights a week," Leah went on. "But we still had our big habits. And what about the panics when we didn't have nothing to deal for a whole week sometimes?"

"Came fast and went fast, eh?"

"Yeah. I had mebbe three hundred dollars, but the bastid with the gun said he was going to shoot Ray in the belly if I didn't go back in my room and bring him five hundred bucks and all my stuff."

"Why didn't you bring him just half? You say you didn't have five hundred anyhow."

"I couldn't risk it. He was high as hell and you could see he was a killer. I was scared. I was scared he would shoot both of us if I brought him less than three hundred. After all, three hundred wasn't much for me to be holding. And nobody was playing in that kitchen that night, Sid; we was going for blows."

"Can't you find some john to loan you the money?"

"That's a big order, Sid," Leah said slowly as if thinking about it for the first time. "You see, I don't like men. I been married four times and I told everyone of those husbands that I liked to screw women."

"So what did you get married four times for?"

Leah shrugged. "I'm a hustling woman, Sid. I've been selling narco for thirty years. For thirty years I been making it good. Now a man in the life don't ever think about sex. Not like a square anyhow. I was useful to him and he was useful to me. I had damn good husbands who helped me a whole lot. If I'd not got soft in the head with Ray I'd of had a man here in the Logan and I wouldn't be broke now."

It's funny how your moral values can disappear because you get an idea, but all of a sudden it was important to me to put Leah back in business. It was a challenge. "Supposing I am willing to risk my check even if Joey isn't?" I asked Leah. "All you would have to do is scrounge up thirty more dollars. And I got a plan. It's foolproof. This time you only sell to women. Your personal friends. You get the same room back and I'll answer the door half the time, and we only let women in."

"It won't work, Sid. The idea is to down the stuff as soon as you can. You don't sit on heroin, waiting to pick your customers. You can't turn a sick junky with money down. He'll call the cops and I wouldn't blame him. You got to sell fast in the life. If you sell out in two hours, then that's twenty-two hours out of the day the fuzz can't touch you, see what I mean?"

I gave up because it came to me that Leah didn't really want to make a comeback. She was perfectly satisfied to cat on me and go out each night and scrounge up a twenty-four-hour supply. Leah was no smart hustling woman, she was a *junky.*

And as if to punish her, I asked, "If your habit was half of fifteen bags a day, how come you can make it on two or three now?"

Leah's laugh was as brittle and cruel as she was. "Don't ever let an addict tell you they got to have a certain amount a day, Sid. When all is said and done the main idea is to take your sickness off. That's all and only all. I might not feel too tough now, but I ain't never sick. You ever see me sick in here? Look at Lorraine and Selma sharing a bag between them most times. If they had the bread they would shoot up two bags apiece at a time. Don't ever take no junky's word about how big his habit is. He don't know himself."

That night the five girls all went out. None of them returned. Selma and Lorraine simply vanished. Leah was arrested for attempting to pick a guy's pocket on the E train. Jackie picked up a john in front of the Logan and took him to a friend's room in the Warren Hall where she robbed him, but somehow the john knifed her and she was in Knickerbocker Hospital for over a month. When she came out she went back to Dick.

But it was Sandy, with her 138 IQ, who did it worst. She got busted along with three teenagers, trying to jimmy open parking meters in Long Island, and so she was hit with everything from a dope charge to contributing to the delinquency of minors.

CHAPTER 22

ONE NIGHT SOMEONE PUSHED MY DOOR OPEN without knocking.

"Hello, Sid." It was Sharlee, arrayed in a smile of beauty, and I was filled with an inexplicable foreboding. For one thing, Sharlee never smiled. She laughed at satirical things and at other people sometimes, but Sharlee was essentially a humorless girl. And so I even had a premonition that Sharlee had come to run some kind of game on me.

"Come on in," I said, pointedly not returning her smile.

"Aren't you glad to see me or are you jealous because I've been away so long? I've been all over Pennsylvania. And the only reason I came back was to bury my mother. At least you could say you're glad to see me."

"You don't act like you just buried your mother. Why didn't you let Sinman and me know?"

"You and the Sinman were not a part of my mother's life."

"Well, don't stand out there like that, come on in. Did you stop by the Sinman's on the way up?"

Sharlee frowned as she stepped into the inner hall. "I don't want to see him. This visit is just between me and you."

It sounded like some kind of threat. The feeling of foreboding became a nauseous reality in the pit of my stomach. Blind Charlie was always saying that Sharlee never lied, but I certainly had no reason to believe him. After all, Sharlee had been a junky, and a girl in the life had to tell lies. The Black netherworld in New York is nothing but deceit and lies.

Sharlee walked ahead of me into the room and the first thing she did was to take a bottle of Cutty Sark out of her shoulder bag and put it on the dresser. Again she smiled, and this time so emptily that I *knew* something was wrong. For a second I wondered if the shock of her mother's death had driven Sharlee back on narco, but I quickly told myself that the bottle of scotch proved that couldn't be true. And then, just as quickly, I wondered if she had brought the bottle along as camouflage.

"You need a drink and I'm drinking," Sharlee said.

"I don't need one, but I'll take one with you," I mumbled.

Sharlee poured a half water glass of scotch and began to sip it. Her eyes studied me speculatively like she was trying to make up her mind about me, wondering if I could really be trusted. I no longer had any doubts that she had committed a crime in Pennsylvania. And her mother was not dead; Sharlee had said that to soften me up. I got angry: Why must all women come to me with the dregs of their lives?

"What have you done now?"

Sharlee smiled again. "Why'd you ask that?"

"You're in trouble."

"Trouble? What gives you that silly idea?"

"You keep grinning like you're guilty of something."

"I'm guilty of wanting to be with you, is that such a crime?"

I downed my drink. I figured I'd need it before Sharlee was through.

Sharlee took off her clothes. She did it quickly, almost magically, with a hint of anger. That lovely shape, the glossy pubic hairs, the open arms, were firebrands, and it no longer mattered what the girl had done. We swam on to the bed together and stayed there for a long time.

Later, when we were catching our breath, Sharlee asked, "Did you ever think about having to fight for me?"

"Why?"

"Nothing." She sounded disgusted and she filled me once more with forebodings.

Sharlee went to the dresser for more scotch and for the first time I realized that she was drunk or as drunk as she ever got in her strange way. And I told myself that Sharlee had grinned so guiltily because she was drunk.

Sharlee came back and began to talk. She rambled on and on. It came to me while she talked that for all her apparent intelligence Sharlee was a rote person. She conversed from memory. It was a horrible discovery.

"Ever since I was ten Mom was sick. It was just as if she ran away and hid on me," she said at one point. I was ashamed for her. I wanted to tell her that I had already heard every damn thing she had said. "I don't feel sorry for her at all. She didn't have to be sick so much. I'm glad she died."

"What kind of thing is that to say about your mother?"

Sharlee ignored my angry question. ". . . we weren't bad off. We lived in the Nineties and Mom worked in service. She had lovely manners and talked real proper and so we always had. We weren't rich, understand? But we weren't on Welfare either."

"Yeah. I know."

"But all the big-shot hustlers hung out on the corner in front of the bar on the corner of Columbus Avenue and Ninety-seventh Street. And I was kind of fat—"

"I know that bar," I exclaimed. "I go there now even to play numbers sometimes. I used to go in there every morning to play my numbers and get drunk in there every night."

"Well, every day, on my way to school, those hustlers would

try to get me to come in the bar and have a drink. I was fat, I guess. Big and dumb-looking because I wear smaller sizes now than then."

A black kind of scoff slid from my lips. "Hustlers asking a ten-year-old school kid to have a drink in a bar? Come off it, Sharlee."

"They thought I was a big dumb foreigner, I guess. I keep telling you I was bigger than I am now and just as tall."

I arranged a look of mild disbelief on my face and lay back to listen. At least this was something new.

"So one day I went in that bar with those pimps and hustlers and what not. The kids had all dared me, see? They were mostly boys. I told you I never ran around with girls, didn't I? Well, I said I wanted a lemonade. I really didn't know nothing about liquor anyhow. Mom was so damn religious-acting around the house. She and my father had separated, but I didn't even know it was on account of his drinking then. He used to visit us, but he was never drunk. I thought he and Mom separated on account of our not being citizens."

"So big-shot hustlers had nothing to do but entice this ten-year-old kid to have a lemonade at the bar, eh? There ain't no laws about serving minors?"

Again Sharlee ignored me. In fact, I didn't even have to be there. Sharlee was telling this tale to herself.

"Yes," she said. "You see, I was real hipped on sex, but not about alcohol. I guess they ordered me a tom collins. I didn't even know or care. I was showing off for the kids outside, waiting on me outside. They had dared me, see? I was only going to drink the lemonade and then walk out and show the fellows I wasn't chicken."

"How come you were so hipped on sex?"

"Mom told me. But let me finish. You won't let me finish."

"I'm sorry. Go ahead."

"My mother came in the bar for a drink. Don't ask me if she came in every morning because I don't know. She stopped drinking after she joined the Baptist Church anyhow. But since she looked like any other dark-skinned colored lady on her way to work, I guess the pimps never thought she could be my mother.

"Two sips and I was high and so when my mother walked up

to me, all perched up on that bar stool, and says to get out and go to school, I told her to make me. Gee. I was high, Sid. I can hardly remember . . .

"So she slapped me," Sharlee said, "and I slapped her back. Then I ran home. And Mom came home. All day long we shuffled around that house, peeking at each other, and our eyes were wet and burned like hell. At least mine did, but we never said nothing about that bar even till this day. And after that I was like Mom's nurse or something. She still went to work, but from that day on she was always sick. I had to prepare her to go to work every day. . . ."

Suddenly the lovely nude creature was on all fours almost on top of me, and she stared down with an ancient, knowing look on her face. "Mom was *yellow,* Sid. I loved my mother, but she didn't have heart. Me? I got plenty of heart. I'll fight Blind Charlie in a minute. You don't believe me? Ask him!"

It was so ridiculous I had to laugh, but Sharlee sobered me up quickly.

"And you are just like Mom, Sid. You're a pussy. And I love you because you are a pussy. I love you because you think you need me. But if I needed you like I needed my mother when I was eleven, thirteen, *fourteen,* you wouldn't be any good to me, see what I mean?"

I started to tell Sharlee that I was a different man. I even started to tell her that I now knew the jungle as well as she did. And that I was a damn sight smarter than the jungle. But I knew that I had learned things twenty years too late. So right then and there I decided to stop kidding myself about Sharlee and me.

"Well, what about the Sinman?" I asked. "Don't you have confidence in him?"

Sharlee's smile was a wistful thing. "Don't you know that James is crazy?" she said. "What good is he to anybody? And he used to be such a swell kid once. I'd hate for his mother to have to see him now, but maybe it wouldn't matter too tough. His mother is a nut. You know, my mother was bad enough, but his is worse. When he came East to school he was really running away from home. And his sister's no bargain; she goes in and out of sanitariums like that couple on a clock. You know, those Swiss things."

She got out of bed for another drink. This time she went to the refrigerator and took out one ice cube and put it in her glass. "You ever see a girl like me before that really likes scotch? I mean the taste? I get so mad when I see a person put more than one ice cube in it. I like it cool, but not cold with no taste."

Then she put my bathrobe on and went to the bathroom. She stayed a long time and while she was gone I thought of many things, especially about why Sharlee tried to like me. Maybe even to love me. Perhaps, I thought, Sharlee's exotic face and figure had not carried her to all the places I thought she had been. Like that Jewish numbers banker she had spoken of. I was sure he had taken her to fabulous places on the east side, but maybe she hadn't got to know any of the people in those places. What I mean is that maybe I was the only civilized person Sharlee knew. Me and the Sinman. And Sinman was a junky. Then my thoughts got practical as hell. I was in love with Sharlee, but damn if I could stay married long to a woman who talked by rote. . . .

When Sharlee came back she was that old restless tigress, with anger smoldering under the surface. And I was sure she was angry with herself for having allowed herself to come see me and make love. She poured a short drink and tossed it down. Then she began to pace the floor.

Suddenly she halted and said, "I'm through letting my life be spoiled loving pussies! Mom was one. You are one. Sinman is so scared that he believes God even went and copped out on him."

She took off the robe and flung it to the floor. Then she came to the bed and stood over me. "I'm not a lesbian, but I feel a damn sight safer in a woman's arms than in yours. Than in any man's. A woman thinks in terms of preservation, me and her. Men destroyed my mother; they made me destroy her. If men are for real, why do they destroy ten-year-old schoolgirls?"

She turned away and went to the dresser again for another drink. She sipped it, then said, "I met you and told myself that you are not destructive. I tried to go way out for you, but you confused me. I need you so that I can take care of you, but I hate you because you can't take care of *me*. You're afraid of me just like Mom was."

"That's a damn lie!"

"I could piss in your face, Sid, and all you'd say is don't do it again."

"Are you trying to tell me that from now on you're only going to go in for bulldiking?" I said angrily. "If so, say it and get the hell out!"

She came and knelt beside the bed. I could tell I had hit her where she was living. "Sid," she said uncertainly, "if you were in a wreck and you got all mangled up . . . you know where . . . and the doctors had to cut it off . . . well, I'd love you for real then. And I'd be true. I wouldn't cheat. You believe that, don't you?"

I squirmed uncomfortably on the bed. "I don't want you to love me out of pity."

"I'm not talking about that," Sharlee said harshly. Then her eyes grew large and wild with a weird despair. "I mean that if you only loved me with your hands when I'm sober I might be able to make it."

"Only my hands?"

"Yes, honey. All I need. The other way is nasty. I hate it!"

And then she moved into the bed and kissed me greedily, as if to refute her words. We made love, every kind of love, before we fell, exhausted, to sleep.

The next morning I woke with a sluggish headache from the two drinks I had taken, but Sharlee leaped out of bed as if she'd never had a drink in her life.

The first thing she did was to pick up the bottle and shake it. It was almost empty. She put it down and picked up the bathrobe from off the floor. I hated to see her cover that lovely torso. Absently I instructed myself: Sharlee was not truly a copper-colored girl. She was a ruby brown; blood pulsing beneath a creamy layer of transparent tan. The area between her tiny breasts was very light, almost yellow cream, not like her face at all.

"Come here," I said.

"No." Her back was still to me.

"I want to talk to you about last night."

She turned to face me. Her lips quivered. "What about last night?"

"Nothing," I snapped.

"So you think I was drunk last night, don't you?" And she threw the full glare of her loathing on me. It was like an old movie I had seen before. Was everything Sharlee said and did an unending rerun?

"Well, were you drunk or not?" I asked curiously.

She grunted. "You know damn well I was. I was out cold. You undressed me. Why don't you give up all this jive and get yourself a job working for an undertaker?"

Then the hard cold fact became plain. It didn't seem to come from my head but from my stomach. And the fact was that, as sober as she appeared while drunk, Sharlee was actually blacked out. She had no recollection of what she had said or done. In the morning she accused you of the lowest acts, hoping that they were not as degraded as the truth. I realized that I had never reassured her. And I also realized that an evil man could tell Sharlee she had committed murder and was now a fugitive from justice. He could tell her that and keep her holed up in some room at his disposal forever. It was because she was drunk that Sharlee came to me. It was because she believed that I was a square and a pussy that she had come. And then my heart wrenched my body as I realized that Sharlee was just another slave in the Logan.

I sprang out of bed to fall at her feet. I put my arms around her buttocks and held her tightly. "You were safe with me. You'll always be safe with me."

She threw herself on the floor. "Take me while I'm sober!" she whispered in a guttural voice.

Later, when Sharlee was dressing, she said, "The real reason I came by last night was to tell you good-by. I'm going back to Pennsylvania to live."

"I should have known," I said. "Last night I knew it. I knew you were going away. I thought you were in trouble, but it's only that you're washing your hands of everybody in New York."

"You're the only one I'm saying good-by to, Sid. That means something."

"Yeah."

"Anyway, you couldn't support me, Sid, even if you went back to Lundy's," Sharlee said in a reasonable tone. "You wouldn't stay sober that much and I probably wouldn't want you to."

I thought of Gloria and fought like hell to make her go away. "Your only out is to marry me, you know that," I said.

Sharlee didn't even bother to reply. "I'll be seeing you every time I come to town, so don't move unless you have to. I can't write. I mean you can't write me."

"This person you're going to be living with in Pennsylvania—did they bury your mother?"

Sharlee nodded. "Mom didn't have any money. Neither did I."

"Neither have I," I said helplessly.

"I know."

"That's what you meant when you said I'd never be any good to you when you needed me, isn't it?"

"Did I say that last night? I don't remember saying that last night. Why would I?"

"Well, you did. What did your mother die from? How did she die?"

"Softening of the brain. The women in our house sent her to the hospital in an ambulance."

"Did you get here before she died?"

"No. When I got to the hospital she was gone."

"So she died while you were carousing in Pennsylvania." I don't know why I had to say it.

"I wasn't balling 'em back in Pennsylvania. I was taking care of business."

"What business?"

"The business of living, Sid. What is the matter with you anyway? I took a trip to Pennsylvania and my mother took sick and died. That's all there is to it. Don't make me hot now."

"What difference does it make if I make you mad or not? You're not coming back."

"I'll be back," Sharlee said wearily. "I have to, I guess."

"Oh yeah? Why?"

"Because you're a square and a pussy!" Sharlee flared. "Do you have any money? I want a drink."

I had two dollars that Gloria had given me night before last, but since it wouldn't buy any scotch I shook my head. Sharlee took out her billfold, which was just as well filled as the last time I had glimpsed it.

She handed me a ten-dollar bill. "Get a bottle of Cutty," she said.

Since I knew it was the last time I'd ever see Sharlee, I hoped cravenly that she would get drunk all over again. After all, I was human and Sharlee could make love like no other woman. But she took two small drinks and left.

After she was gone I sat and drank as I mulled things over. And as I drank and wondered I finally began to feel some of that jazz Black people like to say about having been to the mountaintop. And I decided that if Sharlee and I had had a love affair it was the queerest known to man. And yet she had taken me to the top. And on the way up she had given me freedom. I was free of hate, jealousy and fear. I no longer thought about Alise; that wound was healed. And it was like when we got to that mountaintop Sharlee had pointed out Gloria. So help me, it sounds crazy, but that's like it is. I closed my eyes then and prayed thanks for everything. And when I got through praying I got out my pads and began to write like a madman. . . .

SCENE V

GLORIA ALWAYS ADMITTED that Sid was a big thing in her life, especially after he began to write that novel. Sid's writing became both a talisman and a symbol of resurrection after Gloria's past failures. She never thought of Sid's book in terms of either critical or financial success. What it really meant was that at last she and Sid had found the right door.

Gloria not only worshiped Sid, she was thankful for him. He was a gift, a kind mentor and a broad-minded lover. And if Sid was this much to her she had to be all to Sid, whatever he wanted. Until she met Sid, Gloria had been given many chances but had lost them all because of her unwise body. But this time she did not intend to lose Sid because of her body. Therefore she thought it imperative to keep their relationship as loose as possible. This explained the presence of Butch in her life.

One of Gloria's many chances had been the opportunity to be one of the few Black call girls in New York City. And being a topflight prostitute in Manhattan is the most. Gloria could attest to that.

Gloria had come to New York four years before and checked into the Picket Arms Hotel on the upper west side. The third day she was in town she went to the state employment office and got a job working the eleven-to-seven shift in an all-night restaurant on 125th Street. Gloria slept mornings, but she was free in the afternoons. Within three weeks she was friendly with all the pimps and hustlers who hung out in the Watts Bar, two blocks from her hotel on the corner of Eighty-third Street and Columbus Avenue. It hadn't been hard to do. She was friendly, liked her scotch, and was a fabulous fox even if she had just left her small Southern home town.

It was in the Watts Bar that Gloria met Georgie, a middle-aged man with connections. He was a bellhop. For years Georgie had worked on Twenty-third Street, and his largest tips had always come from catering to white pimps and hustlers. He supplied them with colored girls for their own wants. In recent months he had made an arrangement to supply a white pimp with Negro call girls. The pimp was a member of a syndicate that operated a ring of white girls, but every now and then there was a demand for a Black one. Georgie supplied the colored girls. But from the beginning of the arrangement Georgie had died a thousand deaths every time he sent a girl on a call. In his experience all Black prostitutes were kleptomaniacs, junkies who were more interested in making a sting than building up a clientele. And so he was overjoyed when he managed to get Gloria in bed one afternoon and found out that here was a girl who didn't mind screwing.

But Georgie did not proposition Gloria. He took his time and stroked her. Gloria's thing for older men smoothed the situation and soon they became real tight. Georgie lost no opportunity to remind Gloria that she was not making enough money to buy all the things she wanted and that a pretty girl should have. She was soon taken in by Georgie's gentle persuasion that in reality she was a poor girl. And, in fact, all her earnings that did not go for the bare necessities were cheerfully spent across the bar of the Watts.

After Gloria and Georgie got tight it was easy. Georgie found a friend to seduce Gloria and then Georgie simply walked in on the scene and went to Hollywood. He was hurt and bitter and told Gloria petulantly that since she couldn't be true she might as well be selling what she insisted upon giving away. In a delirium of shame and despair Gloria agreed. And so Georgie became her pimp; and a good one. He taught Gloria how to dress and how to walk better and how to use make-up.

It was a complicated financial agreement that Georgie had with the operators of the ring, but he paid Gloria a flat ninety dollars a week for her services and Gloria never thought to question how much Georgie made out of the deal. He was satisfied and in the beginning that was all that mattered.

Like most pimps, Georgie was a bisexual who got his kicks orally, the first of this type Gloria had known. But Georgie did not look or act queer. He was a rather light-skinned Negro—almost the same complexion as Gloria—who would easily be mistaken for a Puerto Rican. He was short for a man, about as tall as Gloria, and slender. Most girls said he had soulful eyes. Most men thought them crafty. His only friends and confidants were men in the life although Georgie was not considered to be a hustler since he reported to work every night at the hotel.

Gloria was at once revolted and titillated by Georgie's manner of making love. She thought it was wrong, but she vainly hoped that this new thing would make her a whole woman someday. It didn't. And since the men who could afford her services were inept oldsters Gloria now felt that her sexual problems were greater than ever. However, she was an instant success and was repeatedly requested by the same johns because she didn't mind giving them their money's worth.

One night Georgie sent Gloria out on a date that was a police trap. She got sixty days, but in the course of events she met Red Rederick, a big Irish detective, whose lusts almost approximated Gloria's.

Heretofore, Gloria had been kept under virtual house arrest by Georgie. He only allowed her to leave the house during the early afternoon. Evenings she had to stay close to her telephone and await his call. Red changed all that. He told Georgie what was happening although he did allow Georgie to continue pimping for Gloria.

Gloria usually completed her nightly trick before four in the morning. Then she would meet Red in a downtown bar and they would make the rounds of after-hours joints all over Manhattan. Their favorite hangout was Eddy's. Eddy lived in the 700 block of St. Nicholas Avenue. He had a small walkup apartment with a good-sized living room and one small bedroom which he rented out by the hour to the girls who frequented the St. Louis Bar. But

Eddy's main income came from selling liquor by the drink after the bars had closed.

Eddy operated his house like an all-night rent party except that there was no dancing allowed. Pimps, prostitutes and hustlers, along with a few Lundy's waiters, made up the bulk of Eddy's clientele. They talked shop over their drinks and whiled away their off hours. Red and Gloria became fixtures in Eddy's.

Red, of course, was catered to because he was the law, but Gloria was popular in her own right. Moreover, she was something of a celebrity, for she was the only bona fide Black call girl in New York at the time. At least she was the only one that the demimonde in Eddy's knew of. Even the junky whores liked her, this girl who was in reality a square broad.

To save time Gloria began to come directly to Eddy's to meet Red after her nightly work. She usually arrived first. This gave her the opportunity to become acquainted with Eddy and his wife Gladys. Gloria often made a ten- or twenty-dollar tip and she always spent this, setting up the house, until Red arrived. Gloria did so not only because she was generous and gregarious, but because she was vaguely ashamed of Red's not paying for their drinks. It was in this way that Gloria met a character who called himself the Sinman. She soon became convinced that the Sinman was the most charming man she had ever met.

And so, too, Gloria became familiar with the many girls who hung out in the St. Louis Bar. Even then the St. Louis was the most notorious bar in Harlem. At night it was jammed with junkies, male and female. The junky women openly solicited the square men who patronized the dive because of them. The male junkies were there in search of a heavy drinker to follow home and rob.

St. Louis prostitutes are a breed apart and it makes no difference if they are white or Black. They are all heroin addicts and contentious knife freaks who must earn at least fifteen dollars a day to support their habits. They are thieves who consider themselves part-time prostitutes at most, living from hand to mouth till the day they make that big sting, but the big sting never comes along for them because the johns who frequent the St. Louis only bring enough money for a few drinks, a girl and a room. These girls seldom make more than seven or eight dollars a trick. It is a windfall for them to catch a ten-dollar john, and they never turn more than three or four tricks a night because there are so many of them competing.

Gloria instantly picked up the jargon of the St. Louis girls, most of who were themselves from Southern rural areas, but who now spoke Harlemese with a vengeance. Since Gloria slept a good part of each day, the St. Louis girls became her main conversational partners. Gloria had a junky vocabulary long before she ever stuck a spike in her arm.

Red's and Gloria's thing lasted over a year. Then Red suddenly resigned from the force. It was more or less hush-hush but Red admitted to Gloria that he had attempted to extort a thousand dollars from a Puerto Rican wholesaler of heroin who he did not know had the best of connections.

It came as a shock to Gloria to find out that Red was a pussy in his own home; his wife put him out within a week after he left the force. He staggered into the Picket Arms to cat on Gloria and never again drew a sober breath. But Red not only became a drunkard, he took to beating Gloria, who hated beatings, physical or verbal. Several times Gloria was not able to work because Red had beaten her so badly. Things finally reached the stage where Georgie had to hire three meatballs to work Red over and break his leg.

Soon after he came out of the hospital Red got drunk, toppled over the third-floor banister in the Picket Arms and fell down the stairwell, breaking his neck. Red did not have a funeral. Gloria would not have gone to it anyhow. It was only because no man she knew had been willing to take Red on singly that she had not dumped Red months ago. And after he was dead Gloria reviled herself for not having openly resented Red's Irish-bred superciliousness toward all Black people, including herself, but at the same time she missed the sex—because Red at least left her exhausted if not fulfilled. Once more Gloria grew dissatisfied and disturbed.

One day she was feeling so restive that she jumped in a cab and rode up to Eddy's house. "Well, well, well," Eddy exclaimed when he opened the door. "What brings the glorious Gloria up on the hill this time of day?"

"The heebie-jeebies," Gloria replied. "I feel like if I had to stare at those four walls of mine any longer I'd blow my top. Can I stay awhile and talk to you and Gladys? You sell whiskey in the daytime too, don't you?"

"Sure, Gloria. Sure." Eddy went in the kitchen to call his wife and mix three scotch and sodas. Gladys came out of the bedroom and chatted for a while, but soon left for the hairdresser's. "What's really happening, Gloria?" Eddy asked after Gladys had left. "It can't be Red. You and Red never had a real thing going, if you ask me. He was the fuzz, he liked you, and so you had to take him on whether you liked him or not. And since you both liked to make the rounds it was no big thing. But I know you were never in love with him so what gives?"

Still restless, Gloria looked around her. Eddy's pad looked shabby in the daylight. And she suddenly felt cheated. "I got the heebie-jeebies, I tell you," she said. "I never realized how small you are, Eddy. And Gladys is smaller than you. How do you manage to keep order among all the thugs you got for customers?"

Eddy smiled. He realized that Gloria had changed the subject. "People in the life aren't roughnecks, Gloria. People who try to be in the life and ain't got the brains get killed or go to jail. A real pro never goes for bad unless you make 'em. People come up here to relax. You don't have to go for bad to keep order with my people." Then he came back to the topic. "You say you got the heebie-jeebies, eh? What's that?"

Gloria shrugged irritably. "I don't know. I could scream. I even feel like fighting, and you know that ain't me."

"You ever try grass?"

"Never! And I don't want to either."

"A reefer never hurt nobody, Gloria. It don't even make you sick after, and everybody except the clowns knows it can't give you a habit. But grass will relax you. It really is a tranquilizer—although tea can make you feel like you want to make love to the whole world sometimes." Eddy's voice grew soft and paternal. "I think I

know how you feel, Gloria. I've seen girls take their first fix when they were uptight like you are now, and I don't want to see that happen to you. You are a beautiful sex goddess to me, baby. And I want you to stay like that. But once you start fooling around with shit you got no sex urges. You know that, don't you?"

"No. What does it do?"

"It freezes your nuts like."

Gloria smiled inwardly, bitterly, but said nothing.

"You're not made for narco, Gloria," Eddy said, breaking the silence. "You're just a different kind than most the girls you meet up here."

"Yeah," Gloria said listlessly. But whenever she looked back on this conversation she was positive that she knew then that she must try heroin.

It was Frankie who introduced Gloria to narcotics. Francine was the girl's name, but everyone in the Watts Bar called her Frankie. She was a tiny girl, about five feet two, who barely weighed a hundred pounds. She had a lovely light brown complexion and a little square chin with a dimple. She was very attractive, almost pretty. Frankie had no breasts, but her little figure had sex appeal, especially when she wore slacks.

Gloria and Frankie met casually, like two women of the world, over drinks in the Watts. Frankie invited Gloria to visit her, but it was not fear that kept Gloria from calling on the girl, who lived in the next building to her, although Gloria was certain that Frankie was an addict. Several weeks passed and after repeated invitations Gloria went to Frankie's. There were four other girls in Frankie's room and they all seemed to be living there. It was also apparent that they were strung out on heroin, but not once did any of the girls suggest that Gloria try it. However, they did include Gloria in their conversations in a way that seemed to make Gloria one of them.

One day Gloria was so restless that she asked Frankie if she could get her some cocaine. Frankie could. Gloria loved that first eight-minute thrill of the drug. Within a week she was sniffing it steadily, but cocaine dries up the sinuses and causes all sorts of headaches even if it is not habit-forming. Gloria began to have nosebleeds. After a while the blood would come out of her nostrils in clots.

"It's time for you to try doogie, Gloria," Frankie said several times. "There's no sense in drying up your brain with coke. And what good is a kick that lasts only three minutes once you get used to using it regular?"

Gloria would never forget her first needle. Frankie gave it to her in the buttock. "Just lean over on the table and bend your right knee a little bit."

The instant the heroin hit Gloria she began to puke. Many people never try their second needle because of the agony that comes after the first, but when the nausea passed Gloria was high. Her body was absolutely free of torment and urges; it was light as seed down. She relaxed in a sea of careless clouds and didn't give a damn about anything. If the sky had dropped on her head Gloria would not have cared. Everything was fuzzy and unimportant; the heebie-jeebies were gone forever. The girls in the room seemed to be farther away from her now, but their voices warmed her. She felt thankful toward them and loved them. She stayed a long time in Frankie's room and was still high when she left.

The effects of that first fix lasted eight hours. Then Gloria got sick. Not sick for want of a fix; just plain sick. It was like a hangover only a thousand times worse. Georgie stopped by and Gloria told him what she had done. Without saying a word he began to hit her. He punched her with his fists until he was exhausted. A weaker girl would have died, but Gloria, who had fallen across the bed from the first blow, took it all without ever losing consciousness. When Georgie was too tired to beat her any more he tore all her clothes to shreds, then ransacked the room, looking for money. He found it all. Then he left.

When Gloria was finally able to drag herself off the bed she made it back to Frankie's room. She didn't have to tell Frankie what had happened. Frankie gave Gloria another shot in the but-

tock. Maybe it saved Gloria's life. The next day Frankie took Gloria to see the Sinman.

"The die is cast?" he asked.

Gloria just was able to purse her swollen lips, but she was a picture of practicality. "Yesterday I was free for the first time since my body got grown up," she said. "I'm young and not bad-looking. I like men and I know now that they are willing to pay me for my body so I will be able to support a habit. What more's there to ask for?"

Sinman smiled gently. "That you don't become a junky with unkempt hair and clothes. That you don't lose your face and figure. That you continue to be life's master. And you must not only ask these things of yourself, you must demand them. Now, I have a friend who is down with it. He lives on Seventy-second Street. His family gives him over a thousand dollars a month to stay away from them. He will eventually die of an OD, but you would make him a lovely mistress until he does. Would you like to meet him?"

Byron Ainsbury was a chilling surprise, and yet, knowing she was doing it all wrong, Gloria allowed herself to really care for this man who talked of murder as the supreme cohabitation. She had thought it impossible for anyone to fall in love with a madman, but she did. Byron was the gentlest and kindest man she had ever met, even if he was crazy. He would talk for hours about the superb agony of having blood on his hands, and even after she began to mainline Gloria still got upset by some of the things Byron enjoyed during her menstrual periods. But Gloria loved this remittance man from Long Island, and with his big monthly allowance he became her source and her connection.

It was not difficult for Gloria to become a mainliner under Byron's gentle prodding because both of Gloria's buttocks had become so infected that she couldn't sit down. She feared that continued skin-popping would soon turn her entire body into one festering sore. Subsequently it was she who asked Byron to inject heroin directly into her vein.

One day through sheer whimsy Byron decided that they should double the amount of heroin they used in their fixes. Gloria survived,

Byron did not. His family brought pressure to bear in the right places and Gloria was given sixty days for possession of a hypodermic needle.

After her release from the Women's House of Detention Gloria moved into the Logan and renewed her acquaintance with the Sinman. Although Gloria never became truly strung out she remained an addict and lived the life of the average female addict around Harlem. Some nights she worked out of the St. Louis Bar. Other nights she worked the Times Square district. Because of her extraordinary good looks she did not have too hard a time making it. Her next to last bust came in the downtown area and this time she resolved never to use heroin again. Soon afterward she met Sid.

Gloria got up and took a shower. She carefully dressed for the street. Going into the front room, she stared for a while at Butch's back. Butch turned abruptly from the window to return Gloria's stare.

Her beautiful lips curled. "I suppose you're headed for that damned Logan and that Sid-bastid."

Gloria shrugged. "What else is there to do?"

"You could stay home and keep me company. That's what you could do."

"I been in for two days and nights already."

"And I was out nights, working like a dog."

"And you slept daytimes."

"I sure would like to know what you see in that gray-assed bastid."

"Sid's not old. He's in the prime of life."

"Get out of here."

"Honest. He's only about forty."

"And you're twenty-three. You're the one who's in the prime of life, not him. You and me are prime, bitch. And don't you ever forget it."

"Well, I'm not going to argue about it."

"Who's arguing? I'm not arguing. And you're the one who's going out. I'm staying right here where I belong."

"And I'm going to visit Sid like I'm supposed to do."

"Well, go!"

After that outburst Butch's irritation dissolved into craftiness. "You need any money?"

"I always need money."

"You can say that again." Butch ran her fingers through her pageboy hairdo. She was a true blonde of Italian ancestry. Her coloring was flawless, and everything about her was exquisitely feminine. She was much smaller than Gloria, who was almost strapping in appearance. Both girls were eye-catching, but if one had to guess which was the aggressive lesbian one would have to pick Gloria.

Butch's lips twisted in a sneer as she exhaled cigarette smoke through her mouth. "Do you realize I took you out of the Logan because I thought you had no business in a dump like that?"

"There's nothing wrong with the Logan. A few junkies might hang out in the lobby is all. But the people who actually live in there are just like the people in any other cheap hotel. Take Sid. He's an okay guy. I oughta be living with him instead of carrying on this jailhouse love."

"Jailhouse love? Where the hell do you get that shit, jailhouse love?"

"Forget it. Forget I ever said it."

"No, I'm not gonna forget it. You said jailhouse love, and I don't like it."

Gloria was a study in calm. "So what're you gonna do, sue me? Call the cops? Or do you want to call it quits?"

Butch's face was a furious red. "And don't think I won't. You think I got nothing else to do but take care of your black ass?"

Gloria smiled thinly. "This black ass has always been able to take care of itself. And whenever you get tired of supporting it you can just loose it 'cause that's where it's at. Like you ain't no big thing. Dig it?"

"Oh, get lost! Go and see your goddam Sid. I only hope he makes you pregnant. And if he does, don't come to me. You dig that?"

"Sid's a man. He'd get off Welfare and go back to work."

"That's what I hate!" Butch yelled. "How you think it feels to be sharing your woman with a bastid what's on Welfare?"

"When we met I tole you what was happening. You gonna go through changes now? Because I don't care, you know. I don't argue. I don't fight. And I can take it to Splitsville in a minute."

Butch dropped into a chair. It was a luxurious chair, like everything else in the apartment, and Butch sat in the chair luxuriously. In a way, she looked about her with an exquisite air of possession that was somehow luxurious. And her possessions included Gloria. Many things ran through her mind. Mostly things about niggers, whom she hated and fruitlessly loved.

Butch had been a call girl for five years. Ever since she was eighteen. Her income was large, but what she did not spend on this apartment and clothes she squandered on nigger women. Only Black girls could give Butch the kind of charge she needed and she had long since given up fighting it. But the hell of it was that Butch disliked everything about colored women. Butch liked to fight; she mauled her women with her fists, but she was deathly afraid of knives. Most of her women eventually pulled a knife on her before the breakup. Twice she had been cut, although not badly.

But Gloria was different. Gloria was not really a nigger when you came right down to it. Colored girls lived for TV; they watched it morning, noon and night. You had to make love to them during the commercials. But all Gloria looked at were a few specials and variety shows once in a while. She would just as soon read as look at TV. And in a whole lot of other ways Gloria was not like the other girls Butch had kept.

Butch sighed with the desperate realization that she would rather give up breathing than give up Gloria. Gloria was the only woman she had ever truly loved. And Gloria was the only girl who could satisfy her for real even if she wouldn't fight. But there was this damn Sid and another guy named the Sinman.

Butch grunted, got up and went to the bar. She mixed two drinks. "You think you own me, don't you?" she said bitterly.

"I don't own nothing," Gloria said.

"You realize if it wasn't for you I wouldn't have to be going outa here every night and turning my ass up to some man for a lousy hundred bucks or so every night?"

"You're lucky. You're white. I'd have to screw twenty men in Harlem for a lousy hundred bucks or so."

Butch let that pass. A little later she said, "I been thinking—you want a fur coat?"

"You got three. I wear 'em when I want, what I want one for?"

"It'd be your own."

"I rather wear yours."

Butch had intended to say something about Sid not being able to buy a fur coat, but Gloria had spoiled the opportunity. "I'm gonna buy a car," she said. "A Jaguar."

"You gotta have money in the bank to buy a Jaguar."

"Who says I don't have money in the bank?" Butch said furiously. "You don't know everything. A smart girl like me ain't supposed to let her woman know how much money's in the bank."

Gloria laughed dryly. "Well, I do know."

Butch sighed again. "Geez. What're we fighting for? I know you love me and I love the hell outa you. What we keep trying to hurt each other for?"

"I don't know."

Butch moved from behind the bar to Gloria and tried to kiss her. "You know I need you," she said, pleading. "I'd kill myself if you ever left. You know that!"

"Then why you keeping picking on me and my friends? When I said I was going out all you had to say was, 'Have a good time, Gloria.' But no. You gotta run Sid in the ground. You gotta talk big because he's on Welfare. Sid could get off Welfare if he wanted, but he's writing a book. Sid's got brains. But just because you don't like him too tough I'm gonna take some of your money and buy him some more paper pads and I hope you don't like it."

Butch went to her quickly. "I like it, honey. I don't really care what you do as long as you're mine. And I know you're not screwing Sid. He's too old."

Gloria didn't say anything, but she was angry, many times angry, and in many different ways. But above all else she was angry with herself. Living with Butch was turning her into some damn fool kind of pussy. Why hadn't she come right out and told Butch that she loved Sid? Would never love anyone but Sid. And that she loved him because he was mature and Black. And she should have told Butch to shove it and walk out, and live with Sid and sell ass to support him until he sold his novel. But then Gloria remembered that her very life depended on her keeping it loose with Sid. She must not smother this last flame.

Gloria finished her drink, sighed, and set the glass on the bar.

"C'mon, darling. Kiss me so long and go visit your damn Sid," Butch said, trying to smile brightly.

CHAPTER 23

"YOU'RE GETTING AS REGULAR AS THAT OLD WATERBURY WATCH Joey used to have," Jinny said from the doorway. "Five A.M. to nine and five to nine at night. You put in an eight-hour day, fucking with that Old Lady of yours."

I did my best to grin sheepishly and not proudly, but I also had to be honest. "This writing business must be exactly the same as an oooh-long heroin habit. So help me, this manuscript is the only thing that counts in my life now. It is my only boss. Ever since I started on Ole Gal here"—I patted the manuscript—"women have only been women. Interesting but nothing you lose your cool over. You understand, don't you? And wine is something you relax with once in a while."

"I believe you really love that damned script," Jinny said. "But don't get me wrong, Sid. I love the damn thing too. It's like a monument we are all building to the Logan. We'll show these uppity niggers in Long Island and New Rochelle that S.R.O. folks can produce too. See what I mean?"

"Honestly, Jinny, I am actually mystified; how did I live, love, even breathe and also keep my sanity without this damn bitch of a script to turn to and return to whenever I needed her?"

"And you're gonna make it, Sid. Make it big. And you deserve it because any man who can walk out of this house of low-lifed motherfuckers with a script under his belt is really what it's all about, you know what I mean?"

Jinny's words were just too rich for my blood. I had to change the subject. "Who was it took Leah's old room last night?" I asked her. "You know them? At the price they charge for that room I know it's another damn pusher."

"Nobody took it. Some junkies came down the kitchen fire escape, forced the lock on the door and went in. But Joey went down and told Archie that they were carrying a stick in there. And he came up and threw them out."

"I thought I heard Archie putting someone in there, not tossing them out. And what the hell were you and Joey doing up after midnight?"

"We woke up."

"Well, why didn't you just stay asleep? I mean, just stay put with your door locked?"

"Joey had one of his Irish fits on. Why, the bastid acted like he owned the joint and the junkies were robbing him out of a night's rent. He even made me get up and go downstairs with him. The dizzy bastid."

Joey walked in and pecked at Jinny's cheek. "How's the great author doing?" she asked. "When you gonna let me and Jin start to read your book?"

"When and if it's ever published and not until," I said. "And then you and Jinny can buy a copy like everybody else. Just go without that damned Spur for a couple of days and you can buy a copy apiece."

There was a racket at the foyer door and all three of us grinned at each other. "I'll go let the maniac in," I said.

"I got me five whole dollars," Blind Charlie crowed as I brought him back to the room. "And I ain't going nowhere until it's spent."

"Well, you came to the right place and the right people," I said.

"How's that crazy Sinman doing?" Joey asked.

"Never saw a man get so much fun outa nothing as that Sinman," Charlie said. "Last night he went and got Sandy outa jail, and he was so happy doing it you'd thought he of died and went to heaven."

"How'd he get her out?" I said. "Didn't she get time for prying open those meters, contributing to the delinquency of minors, and assorted hell? How could the Sinman get her out?"

"She ain't had no trial yet," Charlie said. "Sinman said that if she was guilty they would have tried her by now and sent her up. So he went and got her."

"You mean to tell me she's been locked up all this time and never got a trial?" I asked.

J&J made clucking sounds. "Don't lose your cool, Sid," Jinny said. "The law don't function for real like it does in the books you read, and you ought to hurry up and and learn that." She turned to Charlie. "Did 'God is dead' have anything to do with Sandy getting out? I mean, was the Sinman trying to prove something?"

Charlie grunted. "I don't understand the Sinman and that Sandy anyhow," he said. "He gives her breaks he never oughta do. Like one time he give her three free fixes a day for three months. He never would say why and neither would she. Sometimes I think they got a thing."

"Well, do you believe that God is dead?" Jinny asked.

"Since Gawd is a whitey it don't make no difference to me effen He's dead or not," Charlie said. "Now I believe in fate. It was only fate that didn't keep me in college."

J&J registered the same shock I had when Charlie first told me that he had once attended college.

"Why did you go to college anyway?" I asked. "What'd you take up?"

"Nothing! I didn't like none of them courses they had," Charlie said. "They didn't teach a damn thing a nigger could use out in the street. But I had this opportunity to go to any college I wanted, but I thought I was in love with this ole yaller chick from Key West and when she took off for this sad-assed school in Louisiana I just tagged along. I only stayed the football season, and then I went to jail for fighting a cop and got put out."

"A fullback," I shouted. "Why, goddamit, I just realized it, but you're the perfect fullback. I guess I just can't get it through my head that you haven't always been blind."

"Yeah," Charlie said. "I was pretty good at the rough stuff. I even made some money playing professional ball. You ever hear of the Brown Trojans? I had me plenty of opportunities, but fate always stepped in and messed things up. Why, I could be sitting here writing me a good book instead of you."

"Then that means you're one of the Sinman's disciples," Jinny said mischievously.

Charlie scowled. "What in hell I gotta believe in anything for?" he yelled. "I ain't getting ready to die. And what the hell we sitting here trying to philosophize for when I got me five dollars in my pocket?"

"Give it here," I said. "I'll be the runner. What do you want and how much?"

"Get five quarts of that Spur," Charlie said. "And I hope you got cigarettes because I don't."

"I only got a half pack," I said. "Why don't you get four quarts and three packs of cigarettes?"

"Got more sense than I thought you had," Charlie grumbled.

When I walked back into the room Jinny was asking, "Did you know the Sinman before you went blind, Charlie?"

"Naw. I was already blind."

"What'd the Sinman do?" I asked. "Just walk up to you and start being your friend?"

"Damn near. I was standing in front of the Bryn Mawr over on 121st Street and this white boy comes up to me and sez—"

"How'd you know he was white?" I asked.

"How the hell you think?" Charlie roared. "Any damn fool can tell a white boy from a nigger boy's way of talking without half trying!"

"That was a real dumb question, Sid," Joey said in her blackest Southern accent. "White people and colored people got different vocal cords. Everybody knows that."

"So what did the Sinman do, Charlie?" Jinny asked.

"He comes up to me and asks effen I'd like to take a walk in the park with him."

"No kidding?" Jinny said.

"Yup," Charlie said. "And so I just knows that this is one of them real dangerous junkies that can't do no better than to mug some blind man or some girl or old woman. And so I outpussies him, and I says that I would dearly love to take a walk in the park, but I'm scared to death some ole mean junkies might rob me of the little bit of bread I got on me that I'm saving up to buy me a pair of shoes with."

J&J laughed uproariously until Joey yelled, "I bet you was already planning on how to spend the bread you was gonna take from *him*."

"Just about," Charlie said.

"How were you going to do it, Charlie?" Jinny asked. "Just knock him out when he goes to roll you?"

Charlie shook his head. "No," he said softly. "I wuz gonna stick my knife in him for good. But that white boy fooled me. Made me a little bit mad, too," he reflected with a note of surprise. "That there Sinman started talking in that funny way of his and in no time at all we was both laughing and talking like crazy. And we been fren's ever since."

"So he wasn't the Sinman then?" I asked.

"Sinman always been the Sinman, he tole me. Only thing is he never tole nobody he wuz the Sinman until after that day he met you and Sharlee. I guess I would have gone and flipped too if I met the prettiest girl in the world and the first thing she tells me is that they turned her on before she got through playing with dolls."

Paula rushed into the room. "Every damn one of you might as well start packing," she said breathlessly, bitterly.

"Packing what?" Charlie roared. "I ain't even got no room in this sonofabitch! And who the hell is you anyways?"

"You know me well enough, I'm Paula. And you got things down in the Sinman's room and you can just go down there and pack them because Columbia is going to shut this place up tight tomorrow morning."

J&J cried out as if in pain, and I was just as dismayed. I wanted to stay in the Logan until I finished my book. It was only fitting. Besides that, the place was home. My land. And in terms of the book it was my birthplace. "What's happening?" I asked Paula.

"There's an OD at the table in the kitchen right under you. In the 4-C kitchen."

Jinny laughed her relief. "Columbia wouldn't give a damn if every damn nigger in Harlem died of an overdose. Why, them bastids would be so happy they'd send to Chicago for some black-assed professor to come here and write a thesis on it," she chortled. "Goddam, Paula, where you been all this time?"

"It's a Columbia student," Paula said.

"You've flipped," Jinny said calmly. She stared at Paula. "The management *and* the cops both have warned these pushers never to sell to Columbia students. Now I'm not so dumb as to say a Columbia kid can't buy in here, but nobody or his mammy is going to let them take off in here."

"They tell the pushers that, do they?" I said. "But it's all right to poison niggers, eh?"

"Come off it, Sid," Jinny said. "You want all the cops from the 26th Precinct to lose their lovely homes? But if there is a dead student downstairs I guess we might as well start packing."

"He died in somebody's room and was dragged to the kitchen after he died," Paula said. "He's got expensive clothes on. White and rich. The detectives are down there now trying to figure out which room he was dragged out of."

Jinny flew out of the room.

Joey snarled, "There goes that black-ass bitch, sticking her nose inta some shit she don't have nothing to do with. I swear, I don't understand Jinny sometimes."

"Well, I gotta be going," Paula said. On her way out she must have let Gloria in because there she was standing, grinning at us with a bottle of scotch under her arm.

She kissed me like old times. "How's everybody?" she said. Then she hugged me again. "I almost brought my clothes with me."

"Why didn't you?" I asked.

"If I had a job I would," Gloria said. "But right now's not the time. If I was here and hustling you wouldn't do your best. But Butch and I are in the final act. She's the last whitey I'm ever gonna mess around with, man or woman, and I ain't lying."

There was a knock on the foyer door and I went to answer it. It was one of the lobby lice. "Sinman wants Blind Charlie," he said. "It's important."

"I'll tell him," I said and closed the door.

"Wal," said Charlie, rising, "you all go ahead and drink. I might not be back for days."

As soon as Charlie left, Jinny turned to needle me. "Say," she said, "since you're writing now, don't you need a better high? All writers are crazy, you know. Look at Edgar Allan Poe, don't you maybe want to be like him?"

"Hell no," Gloria said. "Sid don't need *nothing*. He was born with his jive like all Black cats who're for real. He don't even need me for inspiration. Dig it?"

Then she and Jinny got into a jive argument about jive and Black cats who had made it until she turned to me and said, "I'm going down and visit the Sinman. I'll be back pretty soon. You want to come too?"

"Why go now?" I asked. "Maybe he and Charlie got something private to talk over."

"Don't worry. I'm a member in good standing down there," Gloria said and left.

No sooner was she gone than Charlie came back. "I got me five more dollars and five white shirts," he said. "White women knows how to treat poor ole Blind Charlie. Damn your nigger women. White bitches bring presents."

"Then how come you're back so soon?" I said. "Didn't you have to stay and thank her?"

"All in good time. All in good time, I always say." Charlie made his way to the easy chair and sat down. "Pour me a drink of that blood, boy. Always need me a drink after talking to a white woman."

"Why?" I asked. "They scare you or something? Bashful?"

"Naw. But it takes something outa you, having to stroke them just so. It's like play-acting. They expect you to say certain things just like they already been written in a book somewheres. Damn effen a white woman don't expect the damnedest things to come outa a nigger's mouth."

"What you mean, Charlie?" Jinny asked.

"I don't know," Charlie said impatiently. "It's like they always want you to have a hard on, but don't want you to shove it inta them right away. It's more like they want you to tell 'em certain things and they goes ahead and strokes themselves." He chuckled. "White women is the damnedest whores. They're crazy, but I goes for 'em. They'll do."

"You know," I said reflectively, "I've never been around white women too much. On some jobs I've worked they had white waitresses and Black waiters. I got to know some of them a little bit. White waitresses are like whores. I mean, they all got no-good boy friends or husbands that are nothing but pimps. In fact, if you ask me, a smart white boy just might be able to do better with a stable of white waitresses than he could with whores. And he wouldn't have to worry about going to jail."

"I don't talk to no poor white women like waitresses," Charlie said indignantly. "The women I fools with are rich society women. I ain't never had no working bitch. Work makes women evil and I can't stand no grouchy woman. I like *ladies*. I'm a ladies' man."

"Charlie, where'd you meet all these rich bitches that come around here looking for you?" Jinny asked curiously.

"Most I meet through Sinman now," Charlie said. "But I used to know a lot of them when I played football for money."

"Well," Jinny said, "I can't say much about white people either. I don't know many. And there's no way in hell you can call Joey white. That bastid is more of a nigger than I am."

"She sure in hell is," I said with feeling.

Jinny poured herself a drink. "Well, you cats have a good time," she said. "I'm taking this drink and then go take a walk."

"It's nice to come in here and there's no five junky whores laying around," Charlie said soon after Jinny left. "I just can't get over you letting five damn whores cat on you."

"You've told me that a dozen times since they left," I said wearily. "I learned and I didn't mind the little bit I had to pay to learn."

"What'd you learn?"

"Everything. Like there's nothing you can do for a junky but give them dope, and only a damn fool would do that. And I can spot a junky. I can damn near spot a junky woman by her shape. Sinman was right about that junky syndrome business."

"What shape they got?"

"They all got square shoulders and big legs and no tits."

"You're fulla shit!"

"Honest, Charlie. Think back at all the junky women you know and see if I'm not right. And all junkies carry on the same conversation."

"Mebbe but you're just in kindergarten, boy. Gloria and Sharlee could fool you any day."

"In the first place, they aren't born junkies like I'm talking about," I said patiently.

"Wal . . ." Charlie began and then stopped.

"What were Gloria and Sharlee like when they were junkies?" I asked after a pause. "Sinman said Sharlee never looked like a junky, but I guess you wouldn't know about that."

"When Sharlee was a junky she *was* a junky. Not one bit different from any other strung-out broad. And I don't care what the Sinman says," Charlie said definitely. "Now Gloria was different. She kept her own money. Never chiseled. Sharlee was a pig. Beautiful maybe, but a pig, although she never talked like a junk-junk junky. She was no lady, mind you, but she didn't have that junky, wise-guy lingo. On the other hand, Gloria's some kind of mimic. She talked junky talk before she ever saw a spike, I bet."

I smiled ruefully. "Gloria talks like a junky whore now at times," I said. "Everything is dig this. And all those other words in the junkies' lingo like you said. Yeah, any way you figure it, those two dames are perennial question marks. Nobody can figure them for real."

"Yeah," Charlie said doubtfully. "I guess mebbe Gloria's expressions is junky, but she don't say the things a junky broad usually says. She don't carry on the same conversation. You talk to the average strung-out broad five minutes and she's gonna start telling you about her asshole, her pussy or her IQ. Them three things is all a junky broad knows to talk about. I'm so goddam sick and tired of junky women coming running up to me and telling me they is constipated I feel like opening a free castor oil stand in the lobby. Junky women talk beneath their clothes all the time. Like children. Babies almost. Gloria never did."

"And Sharlee?"

"What's the name of that thing you can't tell what it is?"

"Enigma?"

"Yeah, that's it. Now Sharlee could cloak her habit pretty good. But if you gonna tell the truth you gotta say that mebbe Sharlee had a cold, cold heart. That's the thing about Sharlee. Gloria's as pretty as Sharlee, but anybody can read Gloria. Sharlee is like muddy water. Sharlee ain't human for real. Know what I mean?"

"I've always thought of Sharlee in terms of water, but they were beautiful bodies of water."

"You know, you make me think a lot about squares. I'm beginning to think that a square is a guy who wants everything simple. And in apple-pie order. In fact, mebbe a square ain't nothing but apple pie."

"Funny you never screwed Gloria," I said reflectively. "I can even imagine *her* seducing you in her search."

"Mebbe I woulda after she came outa jail the last time and stopped using shit, but you come along and broke that up. Gloria ain't coming back here for an hour or more. Let's go take a walk under the bridge."

"Where the devil is under the bridge?" I asked.

"Goddam," Charlie said disgustedly. "You claim you is a Harlem cat what five junkies done schooled, a man about town, and you don't even know where the bridge is at. Suppose you was starving and only had a dollar to last you a week, where would you go?"

"I don't know. Father Divine's?"

"C'mon and see." Charlie stood up with his arm outstretched for my shoulder. As we left the hotel Charlie said, "Go through Morningside Park to 116th Street."

While we were walking through the park he said, "I don't like this damn park no more. It belongs to that white-assed Columbia."

"No, it doesn't."

"No, it doesn't," Charlie mimicked in a high falsetto. Then he yelled, "Ain't you got no goddam sense atall today? Here I am, taking you for the first time to show you where a bastid what's on Welfare should go to buy his daily bread, and you got the nerve to try and tell me what Columbia don't own? Columbia owns every inch of ground you walks on every day. And don't tell me it don't! You ain't been more'n five, ten blocks away from the Logan in months. And Columbia owns all the land for twenty blocks in any direction!"

"Okay. Okay," I said. "But is that any reason to hate Columbia? They didn't make us either Black or broke and them's the only two things wrong with us. Dig it?"

"The hell they didn't have something to do with it!" Charlie roared. I was glad we were in the middle of the park.

"And damn you having a hard on for Columbia today," I said. "I'm not interested. What I want to know is, where is under the bridge?"

"Every time I goes under the bridge I gets a hard on for whitey."

"Well, why you got to keep this bridge a secret?"

"I ain't making no secret of it. Life done kept it a secret from you all these years you been in New York, why you got to go accusing me of keeping you stupid? And it's the city market on 116th Street." Charlie said it all in a primly mean voice that was almost effeminate.

"You going to walk all the way there?" I asked. "And whereabout on 116th is it? I've walked 116th Street lots of times and never saw any bridge."

"How you think trains get to 125th Street Station if they ain't no bridge?"

"That's a goddam viaduct! A trestle!"

"You college-educated fools can call it what you want to, but the folks what's got enough sense to do their buying there calls it the bridge."

"So I keep walking to the bridge," I said sarcastically. "You can't say Park Avenue or whatever avenue it's on?"

"I done said all I got to say."

"Do you ever show your ass to the Sinman?" I exclaimed. "How come you don't ever get mad at him?"

"I gets mad with the Sinman lots," Charlie said. "I can't call him stupid as often as I call you stupid 'cause he ain't. But lotsa times he used to get on my nerves. Like he's got so many more chances than others."

"Selling dope is chances?"

"I mean he's like a real yaller nigger. He can go white or colored, whichever he chooses. I used to hate them yaller niggers, but since I got hepped to myself I don't care any longer. Shucks, boy, I just as soon be Black and blind than be the Sinman."

"Yeah, because the Sinman's either going to die or go to jail eventually," I said reflectively.

"And everybody gotta die, ain't they? Sinman ain't gonna go to no pen."

"Now, who's being stupid?"

"When a white boy breaks the law like he does he ain't no criminal."

"Jesus Christ! What's got into you today?"

"As long as the Sinman don't sell to no white kids he ain't gonna be arrested," Charlie said. "Not in the Logan anyhow."

"You believe that?" I sneered.

"Certainly. When a white boy don't do nothing to harm his own kind he's just a nice guy trying to get along. And Sinman is. A white man can do anything as long as he does it in Harlem."

"What do you think the Sinman's income is?" I asked, thinking of several different things at one time.

"I dunno. He makes fifty dollars on a bundle and he sells four to five bundles a night. Six or more on Saturdays and Sundays."

"You sound like junkies use more dope on weekends."

"There is more junkies on weekends and you know damn well there is. And you know there's part-time junkies just like we got part-time faggots and whores, who works out just on their days off. People that works like on Wall Street can do some funny things over the weekend."

"So Sinman is going to make his pile in the Logan, eh? And then he's going to die of an OD, I suppose?"

"Naw," Charlie said thoughtfully. "I think he'll check himself into some private hospital and take the cure." Charlie's voice saddened. "Then he won't be Black no more."

"You believe all this?"

"Hell yes. After all, you forgets that Sinman is a white boy. And no matter how hard a man tries not to be what he is born, sooner or later his whiteness gonna come out. Sinman is white and smart with it. So he's having hisself a ball while making his money. Most whiteys don't."

"I doubt if the Sinman could ever be white again," I said slowly. "There's Sharlee for one factor."

"You sure can start out at the wrong end of the stick, can't you? Now Sinman could take Sharlee for his wife and no whitey's gonna high-hat him much. And even if she *was* a nigger, there's lots of whiteys don't think they's men unless they got a hot-assed Black bitch on the side."

"Besides, what about Sinman's sex life? Before and after his cure? I mean, I like the guy, but I bet he's no whizz kid in bed." Actually I believe I was jealous because this most strung-out junky could manipulate Sharlee.

"Boy, you just don't know the Sinman. I *tole* you time and again that Sinman ain't no junky. Now that's one man who uses heroin and can still enjoy hisself with women. And he's no freak either!"

"You sure about that?"

"That's what all his women say and he got plenty. He's one of the exceptions. You know there's maybe one outa every couple of hundred junkies who can raise a hard on whenever they takes the notion, don't you?"

"Man, you hear so much different crap from junkies about junkies you don't ever know what to believe. Sinman says all junkies are deviates of some kind or the other. He says using heroin or cocaine is a sexual experience. And I've even heard that a junky can experience an orgasm seconds after taking off. Before he can pull the spike out of his arm. I've heard junkies are impotent. That most were impotent before they knew what heroin was. So what the hell am I supposed to believe?"

"You believe me. 'Cause when I tells you something I knows what I'm talking about."

"Charlie, suppose we segregated junkies?"

"Huh?"

"I mean, since junkies are born and can't be cured, why not create junky villages? Like reservations?"

"There's no way to solve the junky's problem. None at all. Because people won't sit down and face it. Folks don't want to know the truth about heroin and cocaine. Sure. A rich whitey will even get on TV and apologize for his son getting busted and ask for America's prayers. I think mebbe a lot of whiteys with clean kids secretly wish the kid would start messing with narco so he'd get a chance to be on television and ask for the nation's prayers. See what I mean? But you think any whitey's gonna get on TV and say, 'My son uses heroin because he's a sexual ding-a-ling'?"

I was thinking over that one when we reached the entrance of the market. Inside the huge, barnlike building that ran the length of the block and beyond there was a country fair going on. No kidding. Right in the middle of Manhattan we have a city market that can outdo any country thing I know of. Maybe no acts and stuff like that but it is a way-out bazaar. I have been to the markets in lots of towns, like Harrisburg, Pennsylvania, and so forth, but this one had a vim and vigor all its own. There were stalls everywhere you looked although most of them seemed to be selling the same thing.

"This looks like a little Fulton Fish Market," I murmured.

"They got four more buildings just like this one," Charlie said. "They sell everything from soup to nuts and ladies' drawers besides, but I wants me some porgies. I might let them lazy J&J's cook 'em for me."

"Okay. How many pounds you want?"

"Let me do the buying. You ain't got no sense for this market," Charlie said almost kindly. "Take me to that last stall."

There were so many fish stalls doing business that I was slightly confused, but I led Charlie to the stall I figured was nearest to 115th Street. As we passed along I had noted that all the stalls had unbelievably low prices, but the stall Charlie wanted had prices so low I just knew these fish had already gone bad. And I was about to tell this to Charlie when a white man, evidently a Jew, came up to us and said, "Where the hell you been, Blind Charlie? You ain't eating fish no more?"

"Ain't had me a good shoulder to lead me lately," Charlie said.

"Looks like a good man you got with you now, Charlie."

"He's okay," Charlie said, "but he don't know nothing lessen it come outa *Time* magazine or something. I had to tell him every inch of the way to get here. He's too rich to know where us poor folks comes to get our fresh feesh."

"Oh yeah? Wish I was too rich to know where this place is at. What you gonna have, Charlie? Ten pounds of porgies?"

"Is they fresh?"

The man grinned broadly. "Every time the same old question. What you keep coming back for if they ain't fresh?"

" 'Cause you my fren' even effen you cheats me. So gimme ten pounds of the freshest and don't do nothing to 'em. I'll clean 'em myself."

The man weighed and wrapped the fish. They cost less than half of what they would have cost in the neighborhood of the Logan.

"Do you want to get something?" Charlie asked me.

"Yeah," I said. "Do any of these stalls sell ripe tomatoes? I got a thing for sliced tomatoes, but damn if I can afford them around where we live."

"The next building," Charlie said. "Let's take a walk all the way through the market. It's only five blocks long."

I led Charlie through the whole market to 111th Street. I was fascinated: and once again I realized that everything in New York that is strictly New Yorker is also strictly countrified. I spent the dollar and a half I was holding and considered it more than well spent. And as long as I live I'll never forget the lovely taste of those day-old doughnuts that only cost a dime a dozen.

"So this is under the bridge?" I said as we were leaving. "I'm glad you pulled my coat to this. Why, as long as I'm on Welfare I'm coming down here every Checkday. Why, ten bucks in this place would feed me and J&J until next Checkday. And look at all we'll have left over for wine and cigarettes."

"How them bulldikers cook?" Charlie asked abruptly and almost petulantly.

"Jinny can burn awhile when she wants to. I never knew Joey to cook anything except spaghetti, but she can really cook that. But that Jinny can burn. Real soul."

"I ain't never ate no bulldiker's cooking," Charlie said. "You think it's safe?"

"Now what you ever do to them they gonna put ground glass in your food for?"

"Wal . . . Lots of things ain't safe no more. But we'll take 'em up there. They's gonna be drinking our wine anyhow. Might as well make 'em show their appreciation."

CHAPTER 24

IN JUST TWO DAYS Rosey Posey blew J&J's collective mind. So help me, those two nuts simply could not dig Rosey. They knew she could not be on Welfare and be living by herself in such an expensive room as 5-C-1, Leah's old room. Furthermore, Rosey was old, with a grandmotherly aspect that spoke of Southern fried chicken, country church revivals and maybe a little cotton picking thrown in on the side. If she had been the widow of some old-time Harlem racketeer they would have known about her if not been personally acquainted with her. And no big-shot racketeer's widow is going to live in the Logan anyhow. So naturally J&J flipped.

On the third day after Rosey's arrival Jinny and I were in the kitchen rapping kind of vaguely about Rosey when there came a furious pounding at the foyer door. When Jinny opened the door there stood a coal-black thing that evidently had to be human, but even so I don't know if I'd have bet on it. The lips were hideous in a modern Ubangi sort of way. The hair was butch more than Afro. So all in all it had to be a human male. He was wiry with the implied strength of a gorilla, he looked mad. Not mad at somebody, but mad at everybody because he looked so ugly.

"I want Suzie Bowens," the apparition announced. The harsh voice indicated he was ready to fight.

Jinny was scared. But she managed to say, "You've got the wrong place, honey. Nobody by that name lives in here."

"I oughta know where my grandmaw lives," the thing shouted and shoved Jinny out of the way to go stomping down the hall toward Leah's old room. "I'm here, Suzie Bowens!" he yelled as he went.

"I'm going to call the office," Jinny said. "That poor old woman is going to be scared to death." And Jinny was actually trembling.

"Wait a minute," I said. "Maybe I can handle him." After all, the guy was not as big as I am even if he was a whole lot younger.

Just then Rosey came to her door and hugged and kissed the thing. Then she said to Jinny and me, "This here is my youngest grandchile. Say hello to Jinny, Liza."

Liza lit a cigarette and stared insolently at Jinny, who tried to smile.

"What the hell was all that, hon?" Joey said when we went in the room.

"You heard Rosey Posey talking to us," Jinny said angrily. "This door was open; you saw what passed by, so how the hell can you ask me what that is?"

"But didn't Rosey say there was a girl too?" Joey said. "I only got a glimpse of the man. And don't you think I know a man when I see one? So what did the girl look like?"

"Oh shit," Jinny muttered.

"That woman is a man. I mean that man is a woman," I said to Joey. "And did you dig that walk on her? She looked like a gorilla trying to lead a band and salute the king of the jungle at the same time."

"I never saw such arms," Joey said, just beginning to digest it all. "They came all the way down to her knees. And the way she was swinging them, it did look like she was trying to salute somebody."

Suddenly we all stopped talking to listen to Liza calling her grandmother every kind of bitch in the book.

"I'm a good Catholic and all," Jinny said with slow deliberation, "but if I ever gave birth to something like that I'd kill it. The goddam priest would have to go; he couldn't tell me shit about keeping something like that alive. And I'm telling you like it is now."

"That's no woman," I said suddenly. "That's a faggot who's so fucked up he gorillas his grandmother into saying he's a girl." I darted a look at Joey to see how she would react but she didn't even consider herself in a like category.

"I don't know," Jinny said. "No little fairy would choose Liza for a name. No. Never no Liza."

"Mebbe the bastid's gonna live here," Joey muttered. "Thirty-two fifty is a lot of bread for just one old lady to be paying."

"Goddam," Jinny said softly.

"Lawd, Liza, don't throw my meat out the window!" Rosey cried and we all stared at each other.

"Don't you never call me Black!" we heard Liza snarl.

"I ain't said you wuz Black, chile. I only asked you how you got that dark spot on your face. You didn't have it last week. Please, Liza. Please don't throw my meat out the window. I'll be hongry and I ain't got nothing coming in till Checkday."

"Well I'll be," Joey murmured.

"Checkday," Jinny muttered.

"Liza!" Rosey shrieked. Then we heard the plop as something hit the ground below the window, and we all knew Rosey's meat had gone out the window.

Joey flew to the window to look. Then she turned and said, "Jinny, go get that poor woman's meat. Looks like pork chops. How in 'ell could a bastid be so low as to do a thing like that? Go, Jinny."

Jinny grunted and left.

"Liza baby, why you and Mary keep doing this to me?" Joey

and I heard Rosey wail a little bit later. "You all has got me putten out of eight places already. I can't be moving every week like this. I'm too old."

"Stop your motherfucking crying," Liza snarled. "I'm gonna go out and get you some wine. What kind you want?"

"Any kind, honey. I kin drink any kind. Get what *you* likes."

"Goddamit! I'm buying for you, can't you even open your mouth and say what you want?" Liza shouted.

"Git some half and half then," Rosey sighed.

"You know goddam well I don't drink no half and half."

"That's why I tole you to get what you likes, honey."

"Your goddam brains ain't right," Liza raged and came stalking past the door. Her cowboy boots beat a rugged tattoo.

I took my time following Liza to lock the door. Just as Liza got to the door, Jinny came back. Liza reached out and grabbed Jinny's titty. "Hiya, sweet kid?" she said. "Want a taste of wine? Sure you do. C'mon. I got plenty of money."

"No, thanks," Jinny said weakly. "I'm afraid my old man might start some crap. You know how it is."

"Goddamit!" Liza yelled furiously. "I don't want none of your beat-up pussy. I just wanted to make some friends for my grandmaw. I don't ever beg no bitches as black as you is to drink with me. Get it?" Then she stomped across the foyer for the elevator.

Jinny's refusal of a drink put Liza in a worse temper than before she went to the store. She stayed in her grandmother's room a little over an hour and then stomped out, still cursing at the top of her lungs.

"I never saw anyone I was afraid of just by looking at them," Jinny said. "Blind Charlie never did that to me."

"All I gotta say is that that Black bastid better not come in my room," Joey growled like a little boy. "And calling his grandmaw all them names. That's one bastid ain't never gonna have no luck."

Rosey came and stood outside the door, and for the first time I was truly impressed as to how nice-looking she was. She was old, of course, but she had clean-cut features and looked to be more than half Indian. Her glossy hair didn't seem to have any gray in it. And her shape was small and neat. Perhaps the reason I was so impressed was that it seemed impossible that something like Liza could be related to Rosey.

"I'm so ashamed," Rosey said. "It's just I can't do nothing with that girl since she and her boy friend busted up."

"Do," Jinny murmured.

Joey handed Rosey her pork chops. "We got no criticism to make," she said.

"I don't know what gets into her sometimes, but don't you all worry none, she don't pick on nobody but me."

"Why does Liza call you Suzie Bowens?" Jinny asked.

Rosey smiled bashfully. "I'm on Welfare just like everybody else, but I does days' work by Rosey Posey, which is my real name. And that's what everybody calls me, but Liza."

"Wait! Wait a minute." Jinny held up her hand like a traffic cop. "You are on relief under a phony name?"

"Suzie Bowens is my name too. That's the name my husbin' gave me when he brought me up here in '28. But I wuz born Rosey Posey."

"Well, how do you expect to get your checks if you're registered here under the name of Rosey Posey?" Jinny asked her.

"I get my checks at my other granddaughter's house. The married one."

"Well, Jesus to Jesus!" Jinny exclaimed. "Don't you know they can make your kin pay for you?"

"They don't know she's my granddaughter. They thinks I just rooms and boards there."

Jinny gave up with a sigh. "Everybody in this hotel can outdo Welfare except me. It's a low-down dirty rotten shame. I could write a book and send everybody in this damn building to jail, including the managers, but what the hell good would it do me?"

"You'd get royalties," Joey said. "Plus a cut throat." Then she asked curiously, "How you gonna get the ones what ain't on Welfare arrested?"

"Shylocking, embezzlement of public funds, aiding and abetting pie-in-the-sky schemes. And just plain thievery. You want more?"

"Liza and Mary! I don't know which is the worst," Rosey said tearfully. "They makes me lose every room I get. I ain't been able to keep a room since they made me lose my apartment I had for over eighteen years."

"How do they make you lose them?" Jinny asked. "Fighting?"

"They does everything, but mostly the managers say they make too much noise. They scares people."

"Mary's Liza's sister, eh?" Joey asked. "Where's the mother?"

"Mary is my only chile. She's Liza's mother. Mary got another daughter that's married. She's real pretty and quiet like. She don't ever go no place. A real homebody. And she's got a daughter, my great-grandchile. She'll be dropping by after school some days. You'll see her and she's real sweet too."

"So you've been kicked out of eight hotels and finally had to come here?" I said bitterly. "You were forced to come here."

"They put us outa the Whiterock at five in the morning. And Mary acted up so turble the police took her to Bellevue. She's still there. But I'm too old to be having to move 'fore day in the morning."

There was a racket at the foyer door and this time I knew it was Charlie and his cane. I went and brought him back to my room because I didn't want to hear any more about a grandmother raising so much hell that the great-grandmother had to be put out of her room eight times.

"Whatcha got in the bottle?" Charlie said.

"You're lucky there is a bottle," I replied. "Here's a drop of Spur." I handed him the bottle.

"How's the writing coming?" Then Charlie scowled. "When the hell you gonna finish that goddam book and get it printed?" he shouted. "What the hell you think I keep encouraging you for?"

"It's a slow process, Charlie," I said. "I got to write slow so my writing will be legible. But I'm almost finished now. Then I'll send it to a publisher and wait maybe six weeks to see if they like it."

"Me and you is gonna take that book down to the publisher *personally,*" Charlie said.

"We can't do that," I said quickly. For already I could see

Charlie choking the life out of some editor. "Writers take care of business by mail. It's the thing to do. It's like maybe status."

"Well, goddamit, you just tell 'em you don't know no better. You ain't got no sense noways so what you care about some goddam status?"

"Okay, Charlie. I'll think it over."

"You just finish it and I'll do the rest," Charlie said.

Someone unlocked the foyer door and came running. It was Paula. "Now we got a DOA in 5-D-4," she said.

"DOA?" Charlie roared. "Who's the goddam junky in 5-D-4?"

"He's no junky," Paula said. "He's an epileptic. There's no light in there and he's lying on the floor."

"Let's go and make that goddam epileptic get up offen the floor," Charlie said to me. I wanted none of it. I had never seen a corpse except in a casket and I wanted it to stay like that.

"What you say, Paula? Who you found dead?" It was Joey speaking from the doorway. Jinny was right behind her.

"I was on my way to tell you and Jin," Paula said. "It's Mr. Washington in 5-D-4. And I'm sure he's dead. And he owes me fifty cents from yesterday. I loaned him to get some sherry."

"These winos sure can die," Charlie roared in righteous indignation. Then he became practical. "He got a good radio?" he demanded.

"I think so, Charlie," Paula said.

Charlie turned to me. "Go get my radio," he said.

"Your radio?" I squawked.

"How the hell can a dead man own a radio?" Charlie shouted. "And I thought of it first, didn't I? And don't bring back no wine what's already been opened."

Believe it or not, but it suddenly occurred to me that everything Charlie had said was perfectly right and logical in the Logan. I asked Paula for her passkey and went to get the radio.

I unlocked the door and there was Archie on his knees going through the dead man's pockets. A pretty good portable radio was beside Archie.

Archie scowled. "What you want in here?"

"What you're taking," I said. "That radio belongs to Blind Charlie." Archie was big and went for bad. And he religiously slapped the face of any wino foolish enough to cross him. That is why he was the night watchman in the Logan. But if Archie slapped me today he was going to have to keep on slapping me and Blind Charlie both.

"Where you get that key from?" Archie growled.

"This is daytime, what you doing here?" I said and stooped to pick up the radio. Archie grabbed my wrist.

"The police is gonna want this radio," he said. "And anyways I think you been lying."

I let go of the radio and Archie let go of my wrist. I went back and told Charlie.

"I'm gonna kill that sonofabitch," Charlie said with a mild firmness that was chilling. "Is he still there?"

"I left him there."

"Well, what we waiting for?"

I led Charlie from the room. Archie was standing just outside our foyer door, waiting for the elevator. "Here he is," I told Charlie.

"Archie," Charlie said, "I don't want to have to kick your ass over no little radio."

"Who says it's your radio?" Archie said in a petulant, childish voice.

"I do," Paula said, coming out the foyer door. "Give it to him."

"I'm taking this radio down to the office like I'm supposed to," Archie said.

"And I'm going with you to hear you explain how you got in that room," Paula said.

Archie shoved the radio at Paula. "I knows the kind of Black gal you is," he said.

I looked at Paula. She was a proud haughty princess. She caught me looking at her and irritably shoved the radio at me and then went back in 5-C.

"Come here, Archie," Charlie said absently.

"What you want now, Charlie?" Archie came a little closer.

Bock!

Blind Charlie hit Archie so hard in the mouth that Archie couldn't even fall down. He staggered around in a circle two or three times and then fell against the wall. After that he slowly slid down the wall to the floor.

"Now what the hell did you do that for?" I asked.

"I got me several reasons," Charlie rumbled. "Which one you want?"

We went back in J&J's room and Charlie gave the radio to Jinny to go sell. She came back with five dollars and we all got high.

After that day things got more than just quiet in 5-C. So for three solid weeks I plugged away at My Woman. Yeah. There's no use denying that creative writing can surpass the finest piece of pussy on earth. In fact, I loved that damn script so much that at times I not only didn't want to discuss it with anyone, I also began to regret the day I would have to hand it over to a publisher.

Late one night I put the Ole Gal away and soon conked off to sleep. I don't know how long I'd been asleep when a furious pounding on the foyer door woke me. I dragged my butt out of bed to go curse out the stupid junkies who didn't even know that Leah was long gone. By all the voices and curses outside the door I knew that it wasn't Blind Charlie. Anyway I could tell the sound of his cane from that of a fist. Before cursing out the junky fools I went to the bathroom. I looked at my wrist watch; it was a little after three on this Sunday morning.

When I came out of the bathroom I heard a loud "Psst!" It was Mrs. Moriarty. She was ironing and drinking her tea in the kitchen. Actually there was nothing odd about this. People in 5-C do anything at any time of the day or night. We weren't night people, we were twenty-four-hour people.

"Don't open it," Mrs. Moriarty whispered. "They're drunk and want to fight somebody. I been listening to them I don't know how long. They never called any names and everybody's asleep now anyhow."

The old nurse made sense. Now why should I open that door

to curse out what sounded like a half dozen people? And they're junkies and drunk too?

I left Mrs. Moriarty and went back to bed. I woke about eight and heard unfamiliar voices cussing up a blue streak in J&J's room.

"You *couldn't* of knocked very hard," I heard Jinny saying. "Sid's a light sleeper. He'd have heard you."

"Yass, we did. We banged and banged and that bastid got up and used the toilet, and we heard him come out and say something to somebody in the kitchen, but you think that low-down nigger would open that door?"

I was shocked. Rosey's voice was so thick with profanity, liquor and anger, she sounded like the worst of S.R.O. sluts. Then I recognized the other voice. It was Liza's and even she sounded different.

"I oughta go in there and kick that book-writing motherfucker's ass," Liza snarled. I wondered if she ever said anything without a snarl except when she was going to plead with me to stop kicking *her* butt.

I decided to close my door; if there was going to be a rumble at least I could say they came into my room and started it.

Just as I got to the door, Jinny walked in. "Did you hear anybody trying to get in here last night, Sid?"

"Mrs. Moriarty said they were strangers and drunk as hell and wanted to fight," I said in a low voice. "Hell. Nobody in their right mind would make all that racket trying to get someone to let them in their own house. All Rosey had to do is say who she was and that she'd lost her key. That's what happened, wasn't it? But Mrs. Moriarty wasn't coming and she told me not to. So what was I supposed to do?"

"Nothing," Jinny said. "Nothing at all."

"Who let them in? You?"

"Yeah. Joey let them in when he got up. We got a night watchman who comes in the kitchen every hour to punch his clock, where were they when he came around? Those country clowns aren't telling all the truth, you know."

"Well, they made enough racket for Archie to have called the police," I said. "But everything else in this hotel is so crooked, maybe Archie got some new way to fool that clock. But what I don't like is those women talk like they want to start something with me. I don't want to go to jail, but I'm not going to take much stuff from them if their wine tells them to come in here."

"Don't worry about nothing. J&J live in 5-C too, buddee."

"But I still thought they were drunk junkies looking for Leah. How can a person be so dumb as to make people leery of letting them into their own damn room?"

"Sid, you got one change of mind coming. Don't you know that six junkies could hardly be found drunk together? One of them would have surely dropped dead when that skag and alcohol started to fuse in their hearts. Alcohol causes most ODs, Sid. Furthermore, let me get you entirely straight about that door. There were six strangers out there. Three women and three men. All drunk. And one of those strange men had to be mighty strange because he was with Liza. So that one had to be not only a stone murderer but a freak. You better not of opened that door and let them in this hall while me and Joey was sleeping."

"Who was the third woman?"

"I don't know yet. She's still asleep."

"Maybe the third woman was for Liza," I said. "And what the hell kind of man is going to pick up a seventy-year-old great-grandmother in a bar on Saturday night?"

"Some stiff dicks have no conscience," Jinny said solemnly.

Suddenly Rosey and Liza stopped their cursing in tandem and in a moment the silence was broken by a cultured voice saying, "You two have said enough now. That foyer door was locked and it's supposed to stay locked all the time. The landlord told you that, Rosey. Now if you want a room where they don't keep the outside door closed at all times all you have to do is go down tomorrow morning and tell the landlord. Now it makes no sense at all for you and Liza to stand here dominizing folks for not getting out of their beds to let you in before day in the morning."

Jinny and I looked at each other. If that cultured lady had not used the Southern illiterate verb "dominize," meaning to slander, I would have bet any money that she was a college graduate.

Jinny shrugged sort of helplessly. "That's got to be the third woman," she said.

Then the speaker came to my door and looked in. "I want to apologize to everybody up here," she said. "Rosey and Liza were drunk and so were the men with them. I told them not to let those drunkards follow us home, but they wouldn't listen."

"Are you Mary?" Jinny asked weakly.

"Yes, I'm Mary. And I don't know what Rosey and Liza would do without me to go around making amends for what they do when they're drinking."

I ogled this cultured woman. She certainly didn't look like she'd just come out of Bellevue. She appeared to be about thirty-five, but since she was the mother of Liza, who was at least thirty, I figured this Mary had to be about fifty. And Mary was not exactly a bad-looking woman although her hair was not pretty like Rosey's. In fact, this Mary was nearly bald. The hair at her forehead was still thick and she had combed it back to cover her pate, but you could see through the strands that she was bald. Otherwise Mary was quite a dish in a rather plain sort of way. She was tastefully dressed and had well-shaped legs and feet. It was only after I finished admiring Mary's legs that my gaze returned to her head. She had a hole in it. It was healed, but that gaping hole was hypnotic: a scarred indentation about the size of an orange on the upper left side of Mary's head. I was immediately convinced that she had been born with this hole in her head because I couldn't see how anyone could have been hit in the head that hard and survived.

Mary was still talking to Jinny in her cultured tones and I divined that here was another home girl, who like Gloria, had a genius for mimicry. These Southern girls could parrot the accents and jargon of any and all types of native New Yorkers.

Joey swaggered into the room, followed by Liza and Rosey Posey, who were still puffed up. "You never gimme a chance to introduce myself," Joey said to Mary. "I'm Joey and this is Jinny, my old lady. We're the famous J&J you hear folks always talking about around here. And this is Sid. He's gonna be a famous author one day. And that's not bullshit."

"I had a boy friend who was a writer," Mary exclaimed. "We lived on Seventy-second Street. And was he mean when he was composing. I had to leave him. Who knows where we can get some whiskey? I'm a stranger here myself. But I don't drink wine. Never."

Mary certainly was not crazy, I decided. And I just had to know all about this woman who had had a love affair with an honest-to-goodness writer. I put on my suavest honey-dripper smile. "This hotel has a combination bootlegger and shylock," I said. "He sees us through our Sundays."

"Good. I thought so," Mary said. "Here. Take this five-dollar bill and try to bring me back some change. Get one pint of wine and one pint of whiskey."

I went down to Joe Ash's and when I ordered the pint of whiskey too his eyes widened. "You ain't got that Crazy Mary up there drinking with you, has you?" he asked.

"Crazy Mary? Why do you call her Crazy Mary?"

"I got a feeling she give you this here bill. She and the others come in here twice for wine early this morning. Her mother lost her keys and was cussing the hell outa you. Said they could hear you walking around inside but wouldn't open the door for them. They come in here twice. Musta been drinking out in the hall or kitchen someplace. But you never can tell when that Crazy Mary's gonna flip, so you better watch yourself around her. Her son-in-law had to bash her in the head with a ball-peen hammer. She was trying to cut his heart out of him. The bitch was jealous. In love with her own daughter's husband."

Since he had falsely accused Mary of drinking wine, I figured Joe to be lying about everything else. Certainly Mary wouldn't lie about not drinking wine in front of winos and her own family.

And when I got back to my room I was served the most deadly concoction known to a would-be writer. That concoction is whiskey and praise and Mary mixed and served it to my hungry ego. I never thought twice before downing every bit of it.

J&J, Rosey and Liza killed the wine, leaving all the whiskey to Mary and me. Soon after the wine was gone Liza left; she had to go baby-sit on Long Island, *she* said. Rosey left soon after, very drunk again, to serve a dinner party in the Bronx. Jinny's mother had invited the two over for Sunday dinner, and so that left me alone with Mary.

"Now that those folks are all gone we can drink some wine," Mary said.

I remembered Joe's words with horror. "But you don't drink it," I said in desperation.

"I tell that to everybody," Mary said as she took off her dress. I was doubly tongue-tied. How in hell do you tell a woman who just got out of Bellevue to put her dress back on? "I can't stand wrinkles," Mary said, and I felt a little better—until she started to peel off her underthings. Mary was some kind of nudist. She was totally unself-conscious, but she made no amorous moves.

"You got a quarter?" she asked. "If you have we can get two pints of wine. I won't have any more money until after I go back to work tomorrow."

I dearly wanted to ask how she knew she still had a job after being in Bellevue for almost three weeks, but not only was I scared, I didn't know how to ask her. But with Joe Ash's words ringing in my ears I thought it best to say, "I got a girl friend named Gloria. What are you going to do if she walks in here and catches you laying around naked?"

Mary was picking at her toenails. "If she don't start nothing, won't be nothing."

"She doesn't go for bad, but I want you to know I got a woman."

Mary laughed. "You're on Welfare."

"Who told you that? And what difference does that make anyhow?"

"No man in New York City who's on Welfare has a woman," Mary said absently. "And you're so all by yourself you have to sit all day and night and write letters to yourself. I got the wire when you went for the wine and whiskey. J&J told me. They said you even call those letters your Ole Gal. They said your book is your whore. I'm going to change all that for you."

Was Mary telling the truth? What I mean was, just how uptight was I for real? Was my script for real? Or was it a fetish? Hell.

This crazy woman had me uptight for real. But any way you looked at it I was damned in this nut's eyesight. "Give me that dollar and a quarter," I said. "I'll get the man to trust me for a quarter."

"First it's whiskey and wine. Now it's only wine, and that Crazy Mary ain't left, has she?" Joe said.

"Is it any crime to run an errand for a crazy woman?"

"You been drinking," Joe said.

"So what?"

"You forget already what I tole you, or maybe you got some reason to think I'd lie about that woman?"

"It's neither," I said. "Only thing is that she's the only person left up there. Everybody else is out visiting or at work. I don't even know if she can get into her mother's room. The door might be locked. And what do you expect me to do anyhow, tell her she's too crazy for me to drink with?"

"Wal . . . I guess maybe you got a point there. But you take a fool's advice and don't let that bitch make you screw her. Ain't you got some friends you could get to help you drink this wine? Where's Blind Charlie?"

"He hasn't been around for a couple of days," I mumbled. But the truth of the matter was that, with all that education I had received here in the Logan, I was still the stupid Sid Bailey of old. It was no longer a matter of right or wrong, intelligent or stupid. The only question that dogged me was: Are you afraid to get drunk with Crazy Mary?

After that it was easy. Wasn't I a writer? Wasn't a realistic writer supposed to descend into the very pits of all that was not quite normal so that he could inform his readers? And hadn't this madwoman served one writer? The fates had sent me this archetype, this protagonist, just like they had sent me all the characters in My Woman. And the Ole Bitch was almost finished. I had completed it all except I had to polish up the last three chapters, and to finally put them down in my best handwriting.

Yeah. Sid Bailey had earned a little toot. And why the hell should he fret because he had been granted a new source of material to get high with?

But when I got back to the room it was just as if Mary had overheard Joe Ash's words and was determined to make a liar of him. She talked pleasantly and certainly did not drink any more than I did. She was a total lady—if a naked woman can be a lady. So we got very mellow together. I went back down to Joe's and got two more pints; this time on credit.

Never once did we do any necking or even what one might call flirting. When the room got dark we both stretched out and took a nap.

Our nap turned out to be a night's sleep, and when I woke up in the morning Mary was gone. I immediately began to congratulate myself on my ability to drink with a nut and not get too involved. I reached under the bed and found what was left of the last pint. It was only a corner in the bottle and so after I finished it I went in to talk to J&J.

Jinny poured me a drink and then proceeded to climb all over my back. "You *knew* she was crazy, Sid. Why did you do it?"

"You heard Rosey say that Mary and Liza have made her get put out of eight different rooms," Joey said. "What you want now? That she should get *you* put outa the Logan?"

"What is all this crap about anyhow?" I demanded.

"Yesterday we didn't know that Mary was *the* Crazy Mary," Jinny said. "But we stopped by Joe Ash's when we came home last night and he pulled our coat who she really is. We've known all about Crazy Mary for years, Sid. She's a notorious character all over Harlem. But especially in those bars between 145th and 148th on Amsterdam. We never met her before, but even so we could write you a book on her."

"Well, there was nothing shaking between us," I said to close the discussion.

"You'll never learn," Joey said mournfully.

"Now just what the hell do you mean by that remark?" I snapped. "I'm no goddam babe in the woods. I handled five whores which you yourselves admitted you couldn't of handled. And now all of a sudden: I'll never learn! Where the hell do you all get all this sorry-assed bull?"

"Sid. Sid. Please," Jinny said.

"Mary and I both relaxed a little bit yesterday," I said, trying to regain my cool. "We lounged around with a few pleasant drinks and enjoyed each other's company. I knew what I was doing and still do."

"Sid," Joey said, still unmoved. "We know all about Crazy Mary. She's got a rep, just like Jinny says. Uptown. Crosstown. Wherever you go, you can find someone to tell you to stay away from her. And even in the Logan here. She lied when she said she was a stranger around this hotel."

"Have either of you got any actual proof that she's a maniac?"

"It took Bellevue damn near three weeks to decide she wasn't nuts," Jinny said. "So let's put it this way: it took almost three weeks before they were convinced it was safe to turn her loose on society again. Took them pretty long, didn't it, buddee boy?"

"And Joe Ash is a liar anyway," I said doggedly. "Mary told me how she got that hole in her head and I believe her version, not his. Mary was trying to save her daughter's life."

"And I've heard a dozen different versions," Jinny retorted. "But they all are the same in that it's the truth that Crazy Mary got a hole in the head. And it looks like the truth lies in the fact that Mary, her son-in-law, and her daughter were all so drunk that the police never charged anybody with anything."

"You can't admit that Mary was too kind and too dumb to send her son-in-law to prison, can you?" I said bitterly.

"And you can't even admit to yourself that that woman has a bad rep even in the Logan," Joey said.

"And you two can't admit that all this garbage is over a woman coming to my room and having a drink and laying down on my bed and sleeping for a while," I retorted. "Anybody'd think I was shacking up with the chick already."

"But you should never have got drunk with her," Jinny insisted. "You should have gone for a walk. I told Joey you were going to take it on yourself to entertain Mary. You should have told her you had something important to do. You asked for trouble, buddee, and you're going to get it if you're not careful."

"I would like to speak to you, Mister Bailey." All three of us turned to look at Crazy Mary, standing in the doorway.

"I thought you'd gone to work," I said because I couldn't think of anything else to say.

Mary's eyes were stony. "I would like to speak to you," she repeated.

I knew there was a scene coming, and that J&J had talked so hard and long that they had more or less conjured it up out of the blue. I shrugged. "Go ahead and talk," I said. "There's nothing to be secret about."

"What I have to say is private." And Mary turned on her heel and walked toward my room. I shrugged again and followed her. In the room Mary looked at me with blazing eyes. "What do you mean by laying up with me all night, then time I turn my back you go running to those bitches? Which one are you screwing anyhow?"

"Cut it out," I said wanly. Bored already. "J&J have been tight for fourteen years, why you start something as silly as this?"

"You're a liar. I knew that Joey six years ago and she didn't even know Jinny was alive then. Don't you try to tell me anything about Josephine Hendricks. She likes Black meat is all. She don't care if it's a man or woman."

"Isn't it bad enough for them to be lovers for fourteen years without you making up lies about them?" I exclaimed bitterly.

"I'm not lying. How you think I know Joey's name?"

"I don't know and I don't care," I said. "But they met fourteen years ago in prison. Even Jinny's mother says so, and no woman on earth is going to say her daughter's been in love with a bulldiker for that long unless it's true. So shut the hell up about J&J and say what you've got to say."

Mary screwed up her face into a simpering drool. "I love you so much, honey, that I can't bear to see you talking to another woman, and especially after last night."

"Last night was just like any other night as far as you and I are concerned," I said. "So what the hell was that crack supposed to mean?"

"Kiss me good-by," Mary said hurriedly, "and let me go to work. I'll have ten dollars when I get back."

Talk about catching the rhythm fast! I was the whole damn rhythm section as I got the whole picture in a flash. Mary, Rosey and Liza were all slaves who reported daily to the state slave market on Broadway to shape up for a day's work from middle-class Jewish women on the west side and the Bronx. And it was also quite plain that Mary was a veteran S.R.O. inmate who had lost her room while sojourning in Bellevue. Now she was blessed with the wonderful idea that it would be mighty nice to cat on Sid Bailey instead of Rosey Posey. And the crazy bitch didn't even know she had another thought coming!

"I won't be home when you get back, I promised my old lady to spend a couple of nights with her," I said and walked out of the room. While Jinny was pouring me another drink I heard Mary leave my room and go out the foyer door.

The first smart thing I decided after Mary was gone was not to drink any more. Consequently it was a long tiresome day. I couldn't make myself take out the Ole Gal and even J&J's conversation can be boring when you're not drinking.

I was sitting in my room doing nothing when Mary returned from work. I was the one who went to let her in, but she did not speak as she held her head high and marched past me to go knock on J&J's door. I knew she was wasting her time because there is never any need to knock on their door. If the door is open J&J are "in." If the door is closed they are "out." Never did they open their door to admit someone who had to knock.

Mary cursed softly when J&J refused to answer her knock and came back to me. "I need to have a letter backed," she said. "Come on in my room. But I want you to read something for me first," she added over her shoulder.

I followed her down the hall. What else was there to do? After all, how could an author refuse to "back" a letter for someone who evidently did not know how to read and write?

Mary took a pint of half and half from her pocketbook and, after opening it, poured me a drink which I told her I didn't want.

"What's this?" Mary asked, and handed me a business postcard from a storage company. I read it over. The company was notifying its customers that it was closing down one of its warehouses and that customers with property in the warehouse to be closed could have their choice of having their goods moved to either one of their other two warehouses free of charge. One warehouse was on the east side, the other on the west side.

"It's very simple," I told Mary. "The warehouse where they've got your things stored is going to be closed down, but they're going to put your things in another warehouse and want to know whether you want them stored on the east side or the west side. When they deliver your things they charge you by the hour and so you want to pick the warehouse on the side of town you think you're likely to get your new apartment. So do you have any idea of which side of town you'll get your new apartment?"

"They just want an excuse to sell my things, and I want you to write them and say they better not," Mary said. Her manner suggested that I couldn't read as well as she could.

"This card doesn't say a word about selling your things," I said.

"Well, what does it say?"

"I just told you."

"But you haven't told me what they said about selling my furniture. They got a three-hundred-dollar TV set of Rosey's that she wants. That set don't belong to me, it belongs to Rosey. Write and tell them to deliver that TV set here to Rosey."

"I can't. Not unless you've got the money to have everything delivered here. I mean, you can't get one piece out of storage at a time. You've got to get it all out. How many rooms of furniture you got anyhow?"

"Four. But you ain't reading that thing right. I know they're trying to get away with selling my furniture. They always try that on colored people. I don't even owe them anything and here they are writing to *me*."

"Now how in hell would a clerk in that office know whether

you were colored or not? And the average Negro's furniture isn't worth going to the trouble to sell anyhow," I said.

"I got white folks' furniture!" Mary said sharply. "I bought all my things from Caine's Warehouse, and they got the best. They charge enough for it, don't they? And all you niggers make me sick. Always making out like nobody else can own anything that's worth while just because they're colored."

"You want your things moved to the east side or the west side? That's all I want to know!"

Mary became an idiotic dove. "What you think I should do, honey?" she simpered.

I was slightly nauseated. Mary was too ignorant to ever understand what the postcard was all about but, like her kind, she had discussed it with someone (a stranger) and now she was going to let that someone make the decision for her. This Mary and hundreds of dozens of other Marys had to depend only upon their animal instincts and complete strangers to guide them through the Harlem jungle. I wrote the company to send Mary's things to the west side warehouse.

Mary pointedly did not thank me when I finished and I was glad. I didn't care how she felt toward me as long as it wasn't romantic. I went back to my room and sat and wondered what to do with myself since I still was in a no-writing mood. I was thinking about going down to see the Sinman when Mary came to the door with a five-dollar bill in her hand.

"I need a new uniform," she said brusquely. "And don't get no cheap one. Get one for three ninety-five. Get what color you want," she added.

I gaped, but then I thought quickly that it might be better for Mary to use me as an errand boy than something else. Yeah, I decided, let her think I'm too stupid to be her man. I took the money and asked, "What size you wear?"

"Fourteen. And get white."

When I returned from 125th Street Mary gave me a preoccupied thank you which I was again glad to receive. I went back to the room and took out My Ole Gal, which I reread until about ten-thirty when I got sleepy and went to bed.

It must have been almost midnight when Mary woke me up; she was getting into my bed. "That drunk bitch won't let me sleep," she muttered.

"What drunk bitch?" I asked.

"Rosey."

"She's drunk again? Where's she been?"

"My daughter's house. Are you on Welfare for real?"

"Yes. I told you that before."

"I'm going to get me an apartment and you can live with me. I won't charge you much. How much is your check?"

"Less than fifty dollars, but I can't live with anyone. I've tried, and it's never worked out. I'm too moody."

"Don't worry about that, I'll give you a little trim whenever you want it. That's all you men think about anyhow. So you just give me your check next Checkday . . ."

"You must be kidding!" I said. I was so angry that was all I could think of to say. How in the world could this woman—no matter how crazy she was—think that I would ever live in an apartment with the likes of Rosey Posey and Liza, not to mention herself?

"So that's all taken care of," Mary was saying. "You just give me your check so I can rent an apartment and then you won't have to pay me any more money for four weeks. The next Checkday you'd have your whole check for yourself, see?"

"I like it here in the Logan and I'm staying right here in the Logan," I said. "And my girl friend likes for me to live in the Logan. Can't you get it through your head that I'm real right with Gloria?"

"You better not have a woman," Mary said, laughing pleasantly.

I raised my voice. "I tell you I already got a woman. How thickheaded can you get?"

Mary got out of bed and left the room, and for the first time I realized that she was buck naked. I had hardly let out a sigh of relief when Mary came back in, carrying a quart of Spur.

"I bought this for you before the store closed," she said.

"I don't want anything to drink," I said. "I told you that this afternoon."

Mary smiled cozily. "I'm going to be drinking with you," she told me. "I know how you are, you're afraid of getting drunk. But I'm your woman now and you won't want to any more. You'll see."

"Will you please get out of here and take that bottle with you!" I yelled.

Mary's head was like a stone; nothing I said got through to her. In fact, she was so busy telling me about how her boss was going to help her get this apartment she couldn't have heard me even if she was sane. And her story was so full of flaws I got angrier and angrier. Here she was a day worker and yet she had a boss who was going to see that she got an apartment *if* Sid Bailey was crazy enough to chip in his Welfare check! I drifted off to sleep with Mary chattering as inanely as Lina used to do.

I don't know what time it was, but I woke up to find Mary clumsily trying to have intercourse with me. "Stop that!" I yelped and jumped out of bed.

Mary stared at me and sneered. "You'd rather have that Joey, wouldn't you?"

"Joey is as much a man as I am," I snarled. "And furthermore, it's none of your goddam business who I want to be screwing just as long as it's not *you*. Now I don't want to have to tell you again that I got an old lady and I like what I got. So you don't have a chance. Now get out of here."

Mary got up and left the room and for the first time in I don't know when I locked my door. Just as I was getting back to sleep Mary knocked on my door and called my name. I didn't answer. I heard her mutter a curse and then walk off toward the kitchen. She came back and began to beat on the door with what must have been one of the kitchen chairs.

She flailed away with all her might and the louder the racket she made the madder I got. Finally I jumped up and flung open the door. "You hit on this door one more time and I'm gonna kick you a brand-new asshole!" I shouted. I was mad through and through, but not so mad I couldn't see that Mary was now cross-eyed.

"I thought you didn't go with Joey?" she said.

"Don't come trying to change the subject," I shouted. "I said get away from this door and I mean it."

"It was her. She sneaked out after I went in the kitchen for this chair. That's why you're not afraid to open your door now."

"You crazy bitch, the day I'm scared of you everybody in hell will be eating ice cream cones for breakfast."

"That's it. After you've drank up all my money you gotta show your ass."

"Look here, fool," I said tightly. "I don't *owe* you nothing, but if you think so, well, tomorrow's Checkday. I'll pay you back then."

Still nude, Mary sedately sat down in the chair she had been holding. "You can't ever repay me," she said. "You took my body. That's a woman's whole life you took. How you gonna pay me for taking my life?"

"Bitch! You got two grown daughters, how the hell you gonna say you never been screwed before? And I ain't screwed you anyhow!"

Joey came out of her room and stationed herself beside Mary. "What's the matter, hon?" she asked Mary. "Something wrong?"

Mary nodded and pointed at me. "He went and snuck me in my sleep and now that he's got money coming in the morning he wants to throw me out," she said.

Joey shook her head. "All men are the same," she said. "They all likes to do their dirt and when they're finished they got no more use for you. I know."

"You take your bulldiking ass and get away from this door," I yelled. "And I never did any more dirt to a girl than you have. And you know goddam well this woman is crazy and yet you stand up there and side with her."

"See that?" Joey said to Mary. "Sid ain't got respect for nobody when he gets drunk. That's why Jinny and me are the only friends he's got in this hotel."

"I am not drunk!" I shrieked. "You know better!"

Joey's voice was very kind. "You can't fool me, Sid. And I don't even care. But I *know* when you've had too much to drink. You raise your voice and you don't have no more respect for us women."

"Get away from this goddam door."

"And I guess that goes for me too, eh, Mister Bastid?" Jinny said, coming into the room and pouring herself a drink of Mary's wine.

"Yass! Hell yass! I want some sleep and I don't need three fruity dames standing at my door going yackety-yack."

"See that?" Joey said to Jinny and Mary. "After he's used a poor defenseless woman he don't even want no more company. I'm telling you like it is: there ain't one single man on earth knows what common decency is."

Then the three crazies sort of looked at each other and formally agreed to retire to J&J's room. I went in the hall and picked up the chair and took it back to the kitchen. I didn't think I could go back to sleep, I was so riled up. But it was too early to go visiting any of my wino buddies. I could hear J&J consoling Mary so I got in bed and pulled the sheet over my head.

And I went to sleep in no time at all. At about ten o'clock I woke and after washing up and dressing I made a beeline to Mr. Johnson's room. There was the usual Checkday crowd present and one of the first women I spied was Lina. Believe it or not, I was glad to see her.

"How you doing?"

"Ah'm doing jes' fine, Sid. But Ah ain't eating nothing like I did when I was with you. How's Mist' Blind Charlie?"

"Fine, I guess. He hasn't been around for a couple of days. He disappears like that sometimes. But I sure wish you and he had been around these last few days. I tell you I've been catching hell. Pure D. Hell."

Lina grinned. "You still mah bestest boy friend. What's the matter? Somebody been bothering you?"

"Yes," I said, and then suddenly remembered that most all of these minor tragedies that had come my way in the Logan had all been caused by people's lack of respect for me. Therefore, it would be very smart *not* to tell Lina about Crazy Mary. And so I said, "But it's all over now. Everything's okay."

"Walk me over to my room, Sid?" Lina asked. "I want to go and cash mah check."

There wasn't anything else to do so I took Lina over to her hotel. After she cashed her check she took me to the room of Orin Hall's counterpart of Mr. Johnson. I drank a good bit and actually had a good time. Lina and I didn't leave the man's room until after nine that night. Lina was knocked out and went to sleep as soon as she got back to her room. I took her shoes off, pulled the covers over her, and then walked back to the Logan. I went to sleep wondering how I had managed to forget to get my check from the office.

"You been screwing Liza and I'm gonna cut your throat." It was Mary's insane voice in my ear and I knew I wasn't dreaming. I opened my eyes. The light was on and I looked downward to the knife pressed to my throat. It was my own knife and it had a ten-inch blade which I knew was sharp because I kept it that way to slice my tomatoes whenever I could afford them.

I drew a breath and tried to think of something to say. Mary continued to mutter about me and Liza. Her mouth was twitching like a rabbit's nose and once again she looked cross-eyed.

"Liza likes pussy better than I do," I said at last.

Mary seemed to think that over. Finally she said, "Well, if you're not screwing Liza you're doing it to old Rosey."

"I'm not screwing anybody you know," I said.

"You screwed me."

"I did not." And I realized that my fear was waning. Mainly because I figured that I should have been dead by now. "Look in the icebox," I said wearily, "and hand me that pint of wine."

Like a stupid child, Mary turned away from me and went to the refrigerator. "And you're not going to get *any* of it," she gloated.

I grabbed a pillow and sprang from the bed and ran out the door. Mary screamed her rage at finding no wine and at my escape. As I was fumbling with the lock on the foyer door, she lunged viciously at me with the knife. I turned and parried the blow with the pillow. Then she began slashing like a true maniac, but I was really working out with that pillow. Again Mary lunged, almost losing her balance, so I shoved her further off balance and she fell. I flew to the extension phone. It looked like the office never would answer, but for some strange reason Mary did not come out in the foyer after me.

Finally the office did answer. "Blanche?" I said. "This is Sid Bailey up in 5-C-4. Now don't bother to come up, just call the police and tell them a crazy woman is trying to kill me up here. Please hurry, Blanche." I said it all in a clipped and cool voice so that Blanche would get the message and act accordingly.

But I forgot that Blanche, who worked the three to eleven shift, took nobody's word for anything. Not in the Logan she didn't. So here I am standing in the foyer in my shorts when Blanche steps off the elevator with nobody with her but herself.

If Blanche was that stupid I decided that it was none of my business and so I pointed and said, "She's in my room, I think."

She went into 5-C. I don't know why, but I followed her. Mary was lying on my bed, but she had put my bathrobe on. Blanche looked at Mary, lying quietly on the bed, and then at me in my underwear. I read it all in her eyes so I picked up my pants off the chair, but Mary was out of the bed before I could raise a leg. And she had been holding the knife underneath the bathrobe. She crouched and came at me like some farmer with his small scythe, feinting at my legs every time I would try to put on the pants.

Blanche was finally getting it. "I'm the night manager," she said, "and I want to know what the trouble is up here. And where is your room?"

"She doesn't have one," I said, still trying to put my pants on.

"This is my man," Mary said from her crouch. She looked up at Blanche. "And what the hell do you want? You been screwing him too?"

"Do you have a room in this hotel?" Blanche repeated.

"Her mother lives in Leah's old room," I explained. "That's where she came from. I mean that's where her clothes are. She sure in hell don't live with me. You know that."

"Well, the police will be here in a few minutes," Blanche said to Mary. "And I would advise you to put your clothes on."

"Goddam the police and you too," Mary said offhandedly. "Now get the hell out of here." And she came at me with the knife for real.

But even so Blanche still didn't seem able to get a clear picture of the situation. So she said to me, "Do you really want me to have her arrested?"

"I sure in hell don't want to get killed," I exclaimed. "Can't you see by now she's crazy?"

I looked around and J&J and Rosey were all standing in the doorway, looking.

"After he's gone and done his dirt," Joey announced.

And Jinny murmured, "I told him and told him."

Rosey moaned, "Bellevue will never let her go this time."

Not a damned one of them was interested in the fact that sooner or later I was going to fail to dodge that knife and probably die. Blanche left, presumably to call the police. I grabbed the other pillow off the bed and danced away from Crazy Mary. She had jabbed the pillow full of holes and feathers were flying all over the room when the police arrived. One policeman was Black, the other was white.

"Who sent for the cops?" the Black one asked.

"I told you that I did," Blanche said.

"And I'm the one who asked her to call you," I said, and pointed at Mary. She had stopped slashing away, but she still held the knife. "I want her out of this room." Whereupon Mary ran at me and started jabbing again.

Over her shoulder she said, "This is my man and I ain't going nowhere and neither is he. Now get out of here."

"Why do you want her to leave?" the Black cop asked me.

"Can't you see she's crazy?" I shouted. "What you think I want a crazy woman out of my room for?"

The Black pig cleared his throat. "We are policemen," he said, "and we're not in the eviction business. If you want this woman out you'll have to go down to Centre Street and get an eviction notice."

I stood stock-still and stared at him as I got the message of what it means to be a nigger in New York City. But even as I realized it I fought against it.

"You don't understand," I pleaded. "This is no lovers' quarrel. This woman is sick. She wandered in here out of the hall and picked up my knife and attacked me. You should take her to the hospital. She doesn't live in this hotel and I don't even know her last name. You understand now, don't you?" I pointed to Blanche. "Ask her what's happening."

"You just gonna insist on putting us in the eviction business," the Black one said.

"Look here," I said, desperately fighting for my own sanity now. "That's my bathrobe she's got on. She came in this room stark naked. Take a look in my closet, and if you find one single female article in there I'll apologize. I am a bachelor. I live alone. And I want protection from this crazy woman. You're standing right there looking at her cut at me with that knife. You can arrest her for that!"

The Black one still did all the talking. "Well, we've told you what to do. And that's all we can do." Suddenly his eyes narrowed piggishly. "What's your name?"

"Sid Bailey."

"Bailey, eh? You ever been arrested? Where you work?"

"What's that got to do with me getting killed or not?" I screamed.

"It might have a whole lot to do with it," the pig said.

I was pretty near delirious now. And although I knew I shouldn't say it I just didn't give a damn any longer. If I couldn't save my sanity at least I would be preserving my manhood in front of the Black pig. "You mean to stand there and tell me that if I want to I can go over on Park Avenue and see a pretty white gal I go for, follow her home, force my way into her apartment, take off every stitch and tell her she's got to make love to me or I'll kill and there is not a single thing she can do but wait until the next morning to go down to Centre Street and get a notice to evict me?"

That big Black pig's hand tightened on his stick. It was as chilling as the rattle of a snake.

"Wait a minute," I said hastily. "Will you just hold this woman so I can get my pants on? If you can't make her leave at least you can do that, can't you?"

The white policeman went over to Mary, who was yelling, "You better take this cop-calling sonofabitch out of here because if you don't I'm going to kill him dead time you leave!"

"Give me the knife," the white cop said gently. It was the first time he had said anything.

"Hell no! I'm going to kill that bastard with this knife, I said."

All the time the cop was slowly crowding Mary away from me toward the other side of the room. "Go ahead," he said over his shoulder. "Put your pants on."

I scrambled into my things and flew out the room. As I was closing the foyer door I could hear Joey saying, ". . . and after he went and did all his dirt . . ."

Once in the street I realized that I was broke and cursed myself for not having cashed my check, but I headed for the bar at Ninety-seventh Street anyhow. As I walked I went through my pockets and found eighty cents. Probably some change I had forgotten to give back to Lina.

Petey, the bartender, was the only person in the bar. "What's the matter, Seashore? You look like a striped-ass ape just turned you loose." Petey called all Lundy's waiters Seashore.

"Gimme a drink of gin," I said. "And loan me a dollar too, will you?"

I never picked up the dollar bill Petey placed on the bar. I had three drinks in succession and then Petey poured me one on the house. I sipped the house drink slowly, trying to build an edge, as I tried to figure out the exact thing I had done wrong to start this crazy chain of events. I finally figured that if I had opened the door for Mary and her mother I would probably never have been introduced to Mary. And I also reminded myself that everything that had happened to me this night was because and only because I was a poor Black man.

Since the first day I had renewed my acquaintance with the Sinman he had tried to drill into my stupid head that New York's Finest were the most despicable creatures on earth, but I had been too square. It was like I just loved to be deaf, dumb and square.

But the Sinman had forgotten one important thing: Sid Bailey was no moral coward. I would talk to Ginsburg in the morning. And if he was afraid to make a complaint I would go see Jesse Walker and have the whole thing written up in the *Amsterdam News.* And if Jesse wouldn't listen then I'd go down to the NAACP office and contact Borough President Motley. Yeah. The Sinman was wrong. And those cops were wrong; they were taking it for granted that an S.R.O. inmate was a wino who wouldn't dare lodge a complaint against them.

When I finished my drink I was nice and mellow for about three seconds and then I really got mad. Before, I had been hurt and ashamed, maybe bewildered: now I was in a rage. And the Sinman had been actually telling the truth when he had said that there is no law to protect the nigger. But from now on I was not going to be a nigger. Not a live one anyhow. I might become a dead nigger, but as long as I lived I was going to be a MAN!

Sid Bailey had no one to protect him from insane criminals. So that made it necessary for Sid Bailey to become a law unto himself! I abruptly left the bar and headed back to the Logan. Still seething, I marched into my room. Mary lay naked on the bed, sound asleep. I pulled her up by her hair, but her hair was so sparse and greasy it slid through my fingers. I grabbed an arm and pulled her further up from the bed and smashed her in the mouth. Then I started to be ill. . . . Mary lay there on the floor writhing uncontrollably in orgasm. Then I lost all control and began to kick her. Mary could have gotten to her feet, but she preferred to stay on her knees and crawl around the room like a dog. Each kick brought a soulful "Ooh" or "Ah" out of her. I was maniacally determined to kick her so hard she would no longer get any gratification, but the harder I kicked the more she seemed to enjoy it. I ran in the kitchen and got one of the heavy chairs, and came back to whale her all across her back and head as she crawled out in the hall. And I laid it on her all the way back to Rosey Posey's room. Just as she crossed the doorsill I broke the chair over her rump. I tossed it away and tried for the last time to fit the toe of my shoe all the way up her rectum. Mary let out a last "Ah" of gratification and I went back to my room, nauseated and ashamed.

I inspected the toe of my shoe to see if there was any blood on it and got angry again when I could not see any. I didn't bother to close my door. Mary wouldn't be able to walk too tough any time soon.

I woke up to daylight and Mary was standing over me, slapping me in the face. I jumped out of bed, but before I threw that punch I realized that this was what she wanted. When Mary sensed that I wasn't going to hit her again she ran to my closet, picked up my best shoes and went to the window and tossed them out. Now I forgot all about not wanting to give her any more kicks; Mary was going to die from being stomped. She must have seen her end coming because she dropped to her knees and began to plead. I picked her up and tossed her bodily out of the room. Her head banged upside the wall in the hallway. She got up and staggered toward her mother's room.

In a sheer mean rage I stalked into J&J's room, poured a drink, drank it without saying a word, and then went downstairs for my shoes. I came back with the shoes and tossed them in the closet, then left immediately for Lina's hotel. Lina seemed like a very sane and sober person to be around after a spell of Crazy Mary. But Lina was not in her room and so I came back to the Logan and went in the Sinman's room.

"Why didn't you come to us?" Sinman asked me time I walked in.

"Man, that crazy woman had *me* crazy. I couldn't even think. Anyway I took good care of her and for the last time too."

"Anybody who won't kill a fool when they begs you to can't take care of nothing," Charlie said heavily from his corner. He stood up. "C'mon. I want you to finish that book without no let nor hindrance from that sore-butted freak getting on your nerves. You don't deserve this, but I already took you for a fren' and so I gotta."

"Maybe in the beginning you guys had me down right, but that's not like it is any longer," I said. "You told me that I was in this world naked and alone. But I've got *me!* And *me* is not going to take any more shit from nobody. You hear me? Nobody! And I got me a law; it says when a person just won't stop fucking over you, you gotta kill. And from now on I'm just as much a killer as anybody else in this goddam hotel. I didn't know until last night that a Black man *has* to kill to keep his sanity. I'm keeping mine!"

"I have always thought you were malleable," Sinman said. "The Logan has taught you viability. I could even go so far as to say that you have at last found your personal god. May both of you have a long and happy life."

Charlie grunted something, but I'll never know what it was.

"Charlie and I have to go away for a little while," Sinman said. "Why don't you go stay with Lina for a while? You know that it is quite likely that some man will cut Mary's throat one day soon, don't you?"

"You got the nerve to advise me to get involved with Lina again?" I exclaimed. And even though I had just come from looking for her I was shocked.

Sinman smiled. "Didn't I just say you were now a viable creature of the Logan? Furthermore, you should stay away from Gloria until you are totally and forever annealed."

I didn't know what the hell he meant, but I have to admit even now that he *sounded* very sensible. After I said so long to Sinman and Charlie I went back to check if I had locked my door. I locked it so seldom I wasn't sure. Then I went to Morningside Drive and sat on a bench. Of course I could have gone through Lina's hotel, yelling her name, but it just wasn't necessary. The park bench was good enough for the time being.

Nappy, who had been Leah's most constant customer, came along and sat down beside me. Somehow his presence took my mind off myself. I looked sidelong at Nappy and began to wonder what the guy had looked like as a young man. He most certainly had been tall and handsome, but now he was a bent old man with bad feet.

"I just saw Lina," Nappy said. "She was asking about you and I told her that I don't see you much now that Leah's gone."

"She in her room?"

"Naw, she's in Calypso's room. You know him, don't you? He's always got plenty of wine around. Damn if I know where he gets his bread, but he keeps his stash of wine. He's something like you; never broke for real. Now I don't hate winos like most cats do. Least I don't hate the ones who keeps their own bread. I can't stand no beggars. Tell the truth now, has a junky ever begged you for bread to buy a fix? I mean, begged, not just asked?"

"Damn," I said softly to myself. Then I said, "No junky has ever begged me for anything now that I think of it. Like you say: they ask but never beg. Even that damned Kingfish never really begged me."

"See there?" Nappy looked triumphant. "I'll never understand why all squares gotta lie on an addict like they do. You know. Every addict I know can get himself a fix—if his main source is dealing. I've seen more sick junkies with money and no one to deal with than sick ones that could get if they weren't broke."

"How'd you happen to get hooked, Nappy?" I asked, not really caring to know.

"My mother *and* my father used it and sold it. I had a narco record before I got outa my baby carriage. They used to hide their shit in my diapers."

I laughed and it piqued Nappy. "You square motherfuckers knows it all," he said bitterly. "But you won't let nobody tell you a goddam thing so how the hell can you know *anything?*" He stood up over me. "Opinions! Always you got opinions. But nobody can be around heroin and stay clean. Jesus Christ woulda got hooked if he'd had to be around it and no one to tell him different."

I idly wondered why Nappy should go to all this trouble to claim his parents sold heroin. After all, he should know by now that I knew my heroin facts. Nappy spoke with a Southern accent like most all Black junkies in Harlem. Even the junkies who had been born in Harlem had Southern accents because to a man they had all been born of displaced cotton pickers. They had been raised in ghetto blocks where nothing was heard but Southern accents. And people old enough to be Nappy's parents would have known absolutely nothing about heroin. In other words, Nappy was trying to make me believe that his pickaninny parents had come North with a habit already acquired.

"How old are you, Nappy?" I asked, sure that his reply would prove that he had been born long before heroin became prevalent in Harlem.

"I was born in Harlem Hospital thirty-four years ago. Don't go by looks," Nappy said with a half sneer. "You're almost old enough to be my father."

I didn't want any more of that conversation and so I grew quiet. Nappy tried a couple of times to renew it, but I acted so absent-minded he finally gave up and shuffled off toward the Logan. I got up and walked over to see if Lina was back in her room yet. I met her in front of the elevator on the third floor.

She had a big smile for me. "Hi, Mister Author," she said. "Ah jes' come from telling mah fren's what a nice author Ah has for a fren'."

"Thought I'd come over and have a few drinks with you today," I said, and then remembered that I hadn't stopped at the office for my check and to pay my rent.

Lina squeezed my hand. "C'mon in mah room. Ah got me a fifth of half and half ain't even been opened yet."

We had not been in her room five minutes when a man walked in with a paper bag in his arms. "Lookee what I got for my little Lina," he chortled.

Lina ran to him and put her arm around his waist. "This here's Bilbo, Sid," she said. "And he's the bestest fren'boy Bessie ever had."

I looked his hands and face over thoroughly. He had no knife scars. From that thought I wandered along to dwell upon Crazy Mary's attack on me with my own knife, and from there I went on to think of how every S.R.O. inmate's life is filled and shaped by knives, and the horror and grief that knives can bring. I don't know if a day had ever passed when I had not seen at least one knife flashed if only in jest. Junkies stood in the lobby twenty-four hours a day, and they were often so high on heroin that they could hardly stand erect, but every other one would invariably be practicing how to flick his blade open instantly. And then there was Sally with his ignorant knife. And Sandy and her hook-bladed dagger. And then came the thought of Blind Charlie and his knife to end all knives.

So suddenly I was very glad that Bessie had cut me. It seemed preordained that at some point in their lives each and every S.R.O. inmate must be stabbed, and I was glad that I had already received the slashing that life held in store for me. And I was neither hideously scarred nor dead. How lucky can you get?

While I had been engrossed in my thoughts Lina's room had quietly filled. Several of the newcomers had brought their wine with them, and now it was just like being in Mr. Johnson's room. Only the nice-looking girls were missing.

"I keep on forgetting that yesterday was Checkday," I remarked to Lina at one point. "In fact, I've been so twisted lately I even went in the Sinman's room with the intentions of borrowing five dollars and then I forgot to ask him before I left. I'm really in bad shape."

Lina smiled genially. "Ah thought you come to collect on all them nice times you and Mist' Blind Charlie useta show me." She moved over on the bed and motioned for me to sit beside her. "Ah bets you nevah knew Ah wuz a church organist," she said. "Ah useta could play beautifully till Ah got this arthritis. You nevah dreamed that, did you?"

"No," I said gently, knowing full well that it was all a fable the child-woman had made up more to amuse herself than me. But it was this little bit of whimsy of Lina's that made me suddenly know exactly what I needed. I needed to get away from life. I had been fighting too hard and too long to remain realistic in the S.R.O. world of non-realism. S.R.O. inmates had been granted wine, heroin, cocaine, homosexuality and many other God-given remedies to be used against the obvious facts of life. I had even been granted a woman like no other woman: my manuscript. But not only had I been playing loose with her, but I had still fought to be realistic while annectent to her. Yeah. Realism means death to a fool.

Yeah. You rolled with the punches. Life in an S.R.O. is ugly and it will make you just as ugly if you let it. Every S.R.O. inmate I knew had long ago learned to evade life with a skill I had not even tried to master. Even the Sinman and Blind Charlie were never so foolish as to face life head on. With his brute strength Blind Charlie knocked life out of his way, never once attempting to deal intelligently with this something that was never intelligent. Maybe I was the only damned fool in or around Harlem who tried to reason with fate.

So for the next ten days I gently succumbed to another world. A world that is serene with nothing to regret.

Since Lina had begun to occupy her room in the hotel she had become some kind of talisman to the male winos in the neighborhood. Quite a few went so far as to believe it would bring bad luck to open a bottle of wine in the morning without first coming to see if Lina wanted a drink. So every morning I woke to an offer of a drink. And the inmates in this hotel bought much of their wine on credit from the super at a fifty per cent markup. Ordinarily a Welfare recipient has about twenty-six dollars left after paying two weeks' rent. But many of Lina's friends owed the super as much as twenty-five dollars each Checkday.

And so it was that I laid up on Lina without a care in the world, with even Gloria a vague truism which I might have to deal with in the future—if I ever got around to it. It was a vacation that I needed. Having a manuscript for your woman takes a hell of a lot out of a man without his knowing it.

One night about eleven o'clock Lina scrounged up fifty cents from somewhere and asked me to go to the store for a pint. As I was returning I was stopped by a short dark little man who looked vaguely familiar.

"I like you but you ain't got no sense at all," the little man said cheerfully. And then proceeded to knock the hell out of me. I was half drunk and couldn't have fought anybody, but this was some kind of champ who punched like a heavyweight. It was only because the super and the night clerk saw my predicament and ran out yelling that I didn't wind up in St. Luke's.

"Who de sonabitch that done it?" Lina demanded.

"He didn't tell me his name," I said wearily.

"He ain't got no right to," Lina said indignantly. I don't know what she meant, but I guess she meant well.

The next morning life came back and snatched me out of my never-never world. The manic little man who had tried to assassinate me walked into the room, his face suffused with ninety-proof tears.

"Whut you crying for, Bob Whitfield?" Lina cried.

This Bob turned to me and sobbed, "Sid, I'm so sorry I can't help but cry." And Bob continued to blubber apologies as he handed me a five-dollar bill. Lina took it from me and gave it to a hanger-on who promptly made for the liquor store.

This crazy Whitfield, still blubbering, put his arm around my shoulder and led me out in the hall. In the hall he said, "I've been noticing you for a long time out at Lundy's. I only work weekends and then I'm upstairs. Not downstairs on the first floor with you aces, but I always liked the way you carry yourself nice like you expect life to make something out of you. And so it bugs me now to see you making a fool out of yourself with that Welfare bitch in there." He pointed to Lina's door. "Day in, day out you is in there wining and dining her and who are you doing it for? A no-good whore is all. Don't you know that every single man in this hotel has slept with her?"

"But Lina's a sick kid," I interjected.

Blap! And my head snapped back from Bob Whitfield's slap.

"See that?" he shouted. "I'm trying to school you and what do you do? You try to school *me*. Every time you go to the store for that little bitch my best friend goes in the room and diddles her before you get back with your wine for her."

Blap! My brains rocketed around in my head. But I was still able to recall that business between Obie and this Bob Whitfield. I dashed to the stairs and lit out of that hotel with Bob in pursuit. When I reached 117th Street I looked back and saw that he had run out of steam, but I hardly slackened my pace until I got to the Logan. As soon as I got in 5-C I took a hot bath, got into bed and stayed there for three days.

I really did not have a hangover, but I sort of wanted to dry out a bit. On the third evening that wonderful Ole Woman of mine beckoned. I decided to do the methodical thing this time and so I went down to the office, received my check and cashed it. Then I went around to the A&P store and bought a quart of milk, a loaf of bread and some cold cuts. After putting my things in the frig I opened the bureau drawer to take out the only woman who had ever been true to me. The drawer was empty. I screamed like a woman.

J&J rushed in. "What's the matter, Sid?" Joey asked.

"It's gone. My lovely script is gone," I sobbed, knowing now that it had been an incestuous relationship I'd had with my script. That script was of my own flesh and blood. And I had made all kinds of love and promises to her.

"I bet that Crazy Mary did it," Jinny said.

I didn't see how she got in the room to do it. But Jinny had to be right. No one else in the world could have done this thing. I turned in slow circles in the same spot. "Someone would have to throw your newborn baby out that window for you two to know how I feel," I said.

"What about all those notes and things you had, Sid?" Jinny asked.

"I tore all that stuff up as I went along," I said. "They weren't notes anyhow. Not an outline. Just random thoughts. Ideas."

Joey went to her room and came back with a pint of Spur. She poured me a drink. I downed it, and without saying another word, I went out to the store and bought three quarts, but that wine had no effect on me whatsoever. Later that evening I went down to the Sinman's room, but he and Charlie were evidently away on another expedition.

The days maundered by and I sat and drank, only once in a while going either to the bathroom or in J&J's room. My grief multiplied. My baby was dead. But she had never been alive. She had not gone out to white homes, Black homes to entertain and to teach. She hadn't even been born yet and a crazy bitch had tossed her out the window.

Another Checkday came and went and I was broke again. But somehow I managed to keep enough wine in me to at least dull the sharper pains. And every waking moment was filled with a nameless dread. God was exacting His vengeance, but what had been my crime? And what would be His final act?

Actually I had flipped.

One day Joey said, "Sid, do you realize you don't even know what you're talking about any more?"

"No," I said, not really interested.

"Why, you'll stop in the middle of a sentence and ask me and Jin what you were talking about. Geez. You ain't got no memory at all no more."

"And all that rage in you," Jinny said. "Joey says he can feel it when you walk around your room even. Do you know you walked the floor all night long last night? And you kept picking up that hammer and then throwing it down. Joey didn't sleep a wink either. So you got to do something, Sid. Look at your fingers. They're black with nicotine. So what you gonna do, hon?"

"Well, I'm not going to go out of here and kill Crazy Mary, if that's what you think," I said. "There's no way in hell she can be blamed for a damn bit of this. I hold the police responsible for it all. I know you're thinking that I'm being too damn sensible about it, but it is not Mary's fault at all. She's insane, those motherfucking pigs were not." I stopped walking to stare at them and saw them sort of shrink back. "What I want is to kill me a pig," I said tightly. "Any single one of them. I want to take this hammer and beat his brains out of his head until blood is running all over him and me. And when I'm sure he's dead I want to take down my pants and shit on those brains. You hear me?

"You know? The trouble with me is I *am* a pussy. If I had the heart to go out and kill a cop I could sleep like a dead man. They'd even have to wake me up to walk to the electric chair. You know,

I always thought cop killers were nuts, but they are the only men who are truly brave enough to preserve their sanity."

Joey nodded almost tearfully. "You know, Sid, for a long time before you came back Jinny and I were scared for your novel. Russel come up one day and wants to know who threw all the sheets of yellow writing paper out the window and Jinny said right then: 'You think Crazy Mary's been in Sid's room?' But I tole her to shut up and not to think like that because the sanitation truck had already been by."

I swallowed hard. "I don't know why I'm going to Hollywood like this," I said. "If God really wanted me to be a writer He would have protected that baby. Crazy Mary would never have touched it unless He wanted her to. And when the hell did she throw it out anyhow?"

"She must have waited until you came out of the alley after getting your shoes and then tossed them out while you were coming through the lobby or on the elevator back up," Jinny said.

"I must have been real crazy to think that God would give me a better break than anybody else in here," I said.

"Don't, Sid. Don't say that," Jinny moaned.

"Well, it's true, isn't it?" I smiled. "It's funny how you and Joey think I led Mary on, but I didn't. Maybe my mother and father trained me too much in politeness. I don't know. But we only lazed around and drank."

"Sid," Joey said, "that's just it. You can't let people like you too much if you don't want them to. People like Crazy Mary especially. You gotta let her kind hate you and the more they hate you the better. Mary and people like Mary can't stand to have a good time. It's like they think it's a sin to have a good time. Like God or the whiteys don't approve. So right in the middle of something nice they will spoil it. They have to; they're scared not to. You seen niggers at dances having a ball and then all of a sudden they'll pull a blade and start cutting someone for nothing. I'll bet Mary's eating her heart out now, but what good is that to anybody? I'm telling you, Sid, some niggers will kill you if you let them enjoy being around you too much."

This offbeat white woman's words were so scary I shivered.

"But that ain't what I come to talk about," Joey said. "I'm gonna take you down to St. Luke's Psychiatry Clinic so you can get an appointment. Jinny called and you have to come down and sign up two weeks ahead of time. If you sign today you won't see a doctor until two weeks. Now mebbe in two weeks you'll be okay, but just in case, you'll have that appointment in your pocket. Will you go now if Jin and I take you?"

"Yeah," I said. "There's nothing else to do."

So J&J went with me to make the appointment. And when the time came, they didn't want me to go by myself, but I had to.

The psychiatrist was a lady. She told me her name was Dr. Balsam. She asked what my problem was and I told her everything. You see, I was real hepped on this psychoanalyzing bit because I used to read about it all the time. Hell, at one time I couldn't stand a book or a movie that didn't have some character on a couch. So I started in from the day I returned to live at the Logan until Crazy Mary threw my baby out the window. And I told her just how much I had loved that script and just how much I believed that script loved me. Then Dr. Balsam scared the hell out of me.

"If I can get you a bed today, will you take it?" she asked.

I trembled. This woman was calling me insane right off the bat. But if I *was* insane, wouldn't it be better to let this woman put me away before I went berserk and maybe killed J&J. I'd always heard that crazy people turn on the very people they love best. I numbly nodded my head.

Then I straightened up and made a last-ditch stand for my sanity. Tomorrow was Checkday. I had fifty-six dollars coming my way. I would cash the check but pay no rent. Then I could enter the insane asylum with money in my pockets. And if this Dr. Balsam thought I was going to the nuthouse she had selected for me without even cigarette money, then she was just as crazy as I was.

"Can't I check in tomorrow?" I asked.

"Our beds seldom stay vacant for twenty-four hours."

"You mean you want to put me to bed in here? St. Luke's?"

She laughed. "Where else? You're *our* patient and nobody else's."

"But do you really think I should be put away?"

"I think you should undergo treatment until we can get you back to writing. . . . Your Ole Gal was helpful . . . you must find her."

SCENE VI

KINGFISH WAS HIGH BACK. His knees would buckle every now and then and almost touch the floor before he would snap up to an erect position. "It was truly beautiful last night," he said to Jinny. His vocal cords were so tight he could barely breathe.

Jinny patted his shoulder. "Glad to hear it, Kingfish. If anybody ever needed a break, it's you. Nobody's long for this world when they're selling lemons."

"You is so right." Kingfish nodded somberly. "But I was doing what I had to do. That's all changed now. Beginning from now on I'm gonna be the most righteous dealer around. S'help me. Righteous."

"What was this big sting anyhow?"

Kingfish grinned proudly. "Right at Forty-seventh and Broadway this beautiful chump walks up to me. Straight outa High Point, North Carolina, Gawd sends this lame and you'd never believe it. This fool wants him a Black college gal. Don't ask me why, but that's what he insists on."

"White?"

"Now when you ever hear of a boot being that dumb or that particular?" Kingfish asked. He was indignant.

Jinny smiled sheepishly. "Excuse me for asking. Okay. So he wasn't a blood. But who the hell did you get for him?"

Kingfish swelled with an exaggerated mock importance. "You knows I tell him that a Columbia chick is best. I asks him to take a cab with me to Morningside Heights and then I takes him in a couple of college bars to let him get a whiff of what he's gonna get. But you knows he's coming right here to the Logan in the end. But when I finally cruises him here ain't nobody around. Every bitch and her mother is out in the street. All I can find is Sandy."

"Didn't Sandy cut your throat once?"

"A little misunderstanding," Kingfish said quickly. Then he smiled. "I stood right here in this lobby and showed that chick that bygones is supposed to be bygones. Especially when I got me a High Point chump waiting outside in a taxi. I really stroked that little babe. Cool. You know. Ya understand me?"

"So you went partners in crime, eh?"

"It was beautiful the way we decides to put it down. So we gets in the cab and heads back downtown. And would you believe the mark goes to sleep?"

Slim, Pete and Willy, three junkies, walked into the lobby. It was easy to see that they and the Kingfish were one. All four men were well built, five ten or more, slender, loose mouthed, and dark complexioned. All wore tacky clothes that didn't fit. But it was their feet that marked them as brothers. Four pairs of swollen, misshapen feet; four pairs of run-over shoes, slashed with razor blades for comfort.

Jinny swore she could tell a strung-out junky because he always seemed to be standing on his ankles rather than the soles of his feet. There are many reasons why a junky's feet are a giveaway, and Jinny knew them all. When a junky's habit begins to get ooh-long, the feet are the first thing to swell. For the guy with a long habit seldom finds the time or the place to lie down. They are always hustling, never resting, always looking to make that sting. Another reason the feet get so bad is that often the strung-out junky ends up hitting himself in his feet.

"We hear you was with it last night, Kingfish," Willy said.

"Yeah. Tell us all about this fabulous sting everybody is talking about," Slim added.

"I'm running it down to Jinny here now," Kingfish said. "Like me and Sandy's got this lame who wants a Harlem coed. Can you imagine the nerve of the whitey motherfucker?"

"Why the hell didn't he ask you for a Black Panther bitch and be through with it?" Slim said. "How much bread the fool have?"

"Only about four pounds for taxi fare. I tell him the broad ain't gonna trust him too tough so we all goes down to his pad together. The Sheraton."

"How you expect to make that dressed like you is? You gotta have fine threads to make that scene."

"Ain't nothing too wrong with these," Kingfish said, indignant again. "But anyhow we wakes the chump up when we gets to his pad and he finally acts like he got good sense. He walks right in and lays some righteous jive on the clerk. My mother's worked for him for years, he says. And he's come to New York to find me and straighten me out and bring me back home. Squares can lay some shit sometimes. Believe me. I was getting ready to believe the chump myself. And Sandy is my wife, he says." Kingfish bulged his eyes for emphasis. "And this cat was really drunk!"

"You're a game mother," Pete said. "Everything was so phony I'd have split that scene from the beginning. How you know he wasn't a pig? And you ringing a kid like Sandy in it too?"

"We had plenty of time in the taxi. I went in his pockets and he had the papers to prove he was a bona fide chump from Dixie. And drunk, I tell you. I knew everything was straight from the git go."

Slim grimaced, showing his contempt for all drunks. "But I bet he don't cash a check for much," he said.

"That ain't the way it was," Pete said excitedly. "I know my man Kingfish, and when he says he made a sting I knows he's made a sting."

"Let me tell it, will you?" Kingfish said. "He don't ask to cash no check and so that's a natural giveaway. See?"

Slim's lips curled. "In the room he's got it. And you don't have to tell me another motherfucking word. I can see it all. A born cracker juicehead. And time he gets to the room he starts lapping up more juice like there's no tomorrow. A Black bitch will scare that kind into getting drunk every time."

"Well, that's about the size of it," Kingfish admitted. "Finally he's really stupid and he starts to pawing Sandy. But I don't get pissed off. I gets indignant."

Jinny and the three junkies laughed. "You thought he only wanted to talk to your baby sister, eh?" she said.

Kingfish nodded. "At first I'm all for running the game on him, but what sense that make? I simply takes and punches him out. And when he goes down I kicks him in the mouth so hard Sandy grunts like she's coming. It really did that little bitch good to see me split that cocksucker's mouth open with my feet. Then we takes the room apart. Seven hundred bucks all told. And right then and there I starts using my smarts." He pointed to his forehead. "I wants nothing but his bread. No watch or any of that traceable stuff. But Sandy don't want to leave him nothing. I lets her take his watch and ring, but I tells her she ain't touching his luggage. Sandy ain't all bright at times, you know. How'd we look coming through the lobby with the Dixie's suitcases?"

"You was thinking like the hippest of white boys," Pete said. "Good thinking, man."

Kingfish nodded and his voice grew painfully honest. "You know," he said, "I'm gonna come right out and tell you: I ain't had me no real bread since I been in the life. Not once has I ever had me three yards. So this afternoon I'm gonna buy me four bundles and start to deal. And I want you guys to pass the word along that the Kingfish has stopped the bullshit. From now on I'm gonna be the straightest dealing motherfucker in Harlem, U.S.A. Tell everybody that."

Slim smiled. "Well, that leaves you a nice little piece left. Ain't you gonna see your friends go?"

Kingfish pulled out a bankroll and peeled off four five-dollar bills. Gravely, he handed one to each. Jinny tucked hers in her bra and immediately left the lobby for the A&P.

"Wait here a second," Kingfish said to the others. He walked over to the office window. Ginsburg came to the enclosure. "What you want?" he said.

"Gimme a room." Kingfish's voice was a fine blending of contempt and nigger-richness.

The manager's handsome face contorted. "After the trick you pulled last week I wouldn't rent you a room if I was bankrupt tomorrow."

"What trick, man? How you sound."

"Selling the goddam lemon to that little girl who'd just moved in 4-C-6. To sell heroin is bad enough, but you guys who palm off this milk sugar and quinine for the real thing are lower than snakeshit. You know how low that is, don't you? And just because she was new and got no man to make you give her money back. She like to died. I wish I was her man. I'd of kicked your ass so hard you'd have shit a bag of genuine dynamite. I felt so sorry for that kid I went in my own pocket and give her five dollars. How you can do a woman your own color like that I don't know, you goddam faggot."

"Yeah. You whiteys want to go for bad when you're locked up behind that cage, don't you?"

"You want that I should come outa here?"

Kingfish walked away. That damnfool white boy was for real today. "Let's blow," he said to Slim, Pete and Willy. On the sidewalk he said: "I'm gonna lay fifteen bucks on one of you motherfuckers and I want you to go back in that motherfucking dump and get me a room."

"What you mad about? And what's so terrific about a room in the Logan?" Pete asked. "You act like it's the last word in something. What's so bad about the Hotel Morningside? Damn sight better deal than this here Logan. You ain't being hipped at all now."

"This whole matter is a thing of being hipped," Kingfish said grimly. "That big square refugee motherfucker just tole me I wasn't good enough to get a room from him. Ya understand what I'm talking about? Ya wanta know how I feel? I'm gonna live in the Logan if I have to kill that mother."

"I dig you now," Pete said. "Like you're turning over a new leaf and all the mothers are gonna respect you for it and treat you boss. I dig you, Kingfish. I'll go in and get the room and Ginsburg won't even know you is living with him. Dig it?"

"And you won't have no trouble downing your stuff in the

Logan," Willy added. "There's six dealers in there now, but lots of times you can't get a fix. Everybody's sold out."

"And all you cats can live with me," Kingfish said.

"I dig that!" Pete shouted. "I can't wait to lay me down in your bed. Jesus to Jesus. When have I laid in a bed!"

"I'll be around plenty," Willy said, "but you know I got me this old lady I'm schooling. Boss fox, but dumb."

"Well, I gotta keep on punking my old faggot until I gets on my feet," Slim said. There was a fiery tone of jealousy and hate in the statement.

"Okay then, Pete," Kingfish said. "You take this bread and get the room."

"Sure, Kingfish. I'll get it easy."

The four walked to Morningside Drive and crossed over to the benches. "I know a source," Kingfish said when they were all seated. "A good one. They handles pure dynamite, and I'm gonna connect. I'm coming back to the Logan with either three or four bundles. Pete—you be waiting for us in the lobby. You other guys want to go with me?"

Slim and Willy nodded.

"I'll have the room and be standing in the lobby when you makes it back," Pete said. "How long's it gonna take you to cop?"

"I dunno," Kingfish said. "I gotta go borrow five pounds from Sandy if I'm gonna cop four. I been oversporting myself. I took and shot up three bags already this morning."

"So let's all go up Sandy's room," Pete said. "And in the meantime I can be getting the room."

"Naw," Kingfish said. "You go get her and bring her here. That Blind Charlie stays up in her room sometimes and I don't want nothing to do with that big dumb meatball."

"I'm scared of that blind bastid myself," Pete said.

Slim snorted. "How come everybody is scared shitless of a blind man? How the hell can a blind man do anything to you? No matter how big and bad he is, he gotta get his hands on you first, don't he?"

"You don't know," Kingfish said.

"Yeah. You don't know," Pete said.

"But what you gonna let him get his hands on you for?" Slim yelled. "You cats been taking dumb pills or something?"

"We ain't dumb," Pete said. "And that blind man cannot only fuck you up but he's mean. That cocksucker is mean enough to kill a dead tree and don't you ever forget it." He turned to Kingfish. "You want me to go now?"

"Yeah. And make it snappy. And tell Sandy to make it snappy."

"Say. You want me to get that room now, too? And then I can go with you guys?"

"Yeah. Do that," Kingfish said, pulling out his money again.

Pete started toward the Logan while the three remaining junkies continued to talk. Kingfish did most of the talking. And he was almost messianic in his description of the new life. His friends soon realized that Kingfish was no longer an ordinary punk. From now on he was going to be big time.

In less than ten minutes Pete returned. Sandy looked as bright and honest as a new penny. She had just come from the hairdresser's and her sandy curls clung close to her well-shaped head, setting off her copper complexion, which was darker than her hair. In new slacks her shape was outrageously perfect. "What you want, Kingfish?" she asked. "I'm in a hurry. I'm going down Macy's." She stood facing the four men on the bench.

"Let me hold five pounds," Kingfish said. "Just until tonight when I start dealing."

"With your rep?" Sandy exclaimed. "Who you think is gonna buy from you, Kingfish? Everybody knows you're a freak for selling lemons."

"My men here are gonna pass the word that I'm a new man," Kingfish said. "And I am. From now on I'm straight."

"Yeah," Sandy said thoughtfully. "Yeah. Maybe you can make it, Kingfish. All the cats who're really down with it just might trust you. 'Cause they know that you know that they'll cut your goddam throat if you sell them a lemon. You're gonna make it, Kingfish."

"And I got me the best of connections. What I'm gonna be selling is gonna be pure dynamite compared to the shit they got

around that Logan. Everybody's gonna come to me first to cop. And I'm gonna deal right in the lobby at night. We not only gets the first crack at everybody, but lots of broads is gonna buy because, why should they bother to take the elevator upstairs and maybe get taken off before they cops?"

"Cheesus, Kingfish. I really think you're gonna make it big. You got a head on those shoulders. Like I say: all us addicts need is just one chance." She took money from her bra and gave it to him. "I paid the refugees ten weeks in advance so's I can have my Welfare check to myself for a while, but I can stand twenty-five. And don't bother about money. Just bring me five bags when you start dealing."

Kingfish turned to Pete. "You get the room?"

"No. There was nobody in the office."

"Whyn't you wait? Ginsburg probably just went to take a leak."

"I thought you was in a hurry to see Sandy."

"So what's that gotta do with you?"

"I'm sorry, Kingfish. I wasn't thinking too tough. What I need is some narco."

"Not now. Wait until I meets my connection. I'm gonna give each one of you one bag apiece. And that's gonna be the first and last. Dig it? After that the Kingfish is gonna be dealing. And I mean no credit when I say no credit. You hear me?"

Pete grinned. "Everybody digs you, Kingfish."

Sandy left first. Then the men hailed a taxi and rode up to Lenox Avenue and 132nd, where they went in a bar. Kingfish gave Pete five singles and said, "Stay here until I cop."

He walked up the Avenue until he came to Lenox Terrace, that fine new apartment complex. He went in and told the doorman what apartment he wanted to visit. After the doorman made a call he said that Kingfish could go up. Kingfish took the elevator to the fifth floor.

The number he wanted was a long way from the elevator. A tiny brown-skinned woman with a hunched back and soulful black eyes opened the door for him. The most eye-catching thing in the luxurious suite was a combination television-high fidelity rig that must have been eight feet long.

Kingfish, without being invited, took a seat in a huge overstuffed chair. "Where you been keeping yourself, Kingfish?" the woman said. "If you want to see Harold he isn't here." Almost as an afterthought, she asked, "What you want?"

"I made a big sting and I'm gonna start dealing. No more lemons for the Kingfish. Dig it?"

The bent little lady had a beautiful smile. "Fabulous, Kingfish. I declare I'm glad to hear that. All that education you got and you've been around just scratching out a living like some country boy. I always knew you had it in you. Kingfish, I do declare. How many bundles you want?"

"Gimme four."

The woman, without moving, held out her hand. Kingfish stood up and dug in his pocket for his roll. He began to count. When he got to three hundred dollars he had one five left. The woman slowly recounted the bills, then left the room. She was gone three minutes. When she came back she gave Kingfish four bundles. He told the woman to say hello to Harold and then he was ready to leave.

Before she closed the door the woman said. "We're downing it twenty-four hours a day. Come back any time."

Kingfish picked up his buddies. When they got back to the Logan, Pete went in first to rent a room. After a while he came back out and said, "C'mon. It's on the third floor—3-C. It's not bad at all. But that refugee musta thought I wasn't gonna like it. Had to take me up to see it first and then gimme a sales talk."

"The dirty Jew motherfucker," Kingfish muttered. "Can't stand to see a Black man make it. That's what. But he's so goddam dumb he'll never know where it's at and I'm never gonna tell 'im. But you just wait and see. I'm gonna be dealing so goddam tough the cats is gonna think I got a shit factory upstairs somewheres."

Room 3-C-3 was done in the same bilious, squashed-caterpillar green, favorite color of the Logan's management.

Kingfish took one of the bundles of heroin from his pocket and extracted three bags. "You cats go ahead and take off," he said. "I'm gonna take it easy for now. I've had me enough for the time being." He went to the bed and lay down. "And Pete?"

"Yeah, Kingfish?"

"I want you to go down in that damn lobby and begin to pass the word around. Understand?"

"Soon's I take off, Kingfish," Pete said. After all three had hit they left the room. Kingfish got up to make sure the slam lock on the door was working. Then, after taking off his clothes, he went back to bed. He was soon sound asleep.

A knock wakened him. It was Pete. He had a stranger along. "This guy wants to see you bad, man," Pete said.

Kingfish frowned. "I don't know this cat."

"I know all about you, Kingfish," the stranger said. He tried to sound jocular, but failed. There was a slight twitching in his cheek and his nose was running.

Kingfish knew he was in need of a fix, but he decided to string the strange addict along for a while. "So what you want with me, baby?"

"Sandy's a boss friend of mine. I just saw her on 125th and she told me to come give you a play. She says you is dealing dynamite now. And I'm willing to take Sandy's word for it. I want eight bags. I cops eight a day."

"And you're lying, baby," Kingfish said, smelling a trap. "Sandy is downtown shopping."

"That was five hours ago, Kingfish," Pete said. "You had yourself a four-hour nod. She's back. I saw her myself on Twenty-fifth."

"I really copped some shut-eye?" Kingfish cried. His eyes widened expressively. "I ain't been asleep in a bed in months. No motherfucking place to sleep but these goddam kitchens. If it wasn't for these S.R.O. kitchens we addicts would be uptight for real. But now I've done it I'm gonna keep on doing it. Kingfish is for real. You hear what I say?" Then he ran his hand in his pocket and brought out a bundle, counted off eight bags, and handed them to the stranger, who gave him forty dollars. The man wasted no time leaving.

"You think that stud cops eight a day?" Pete asked.

"Simple fact he come to me proves it," Kingfish said. "With an eight-bag habit you owes everybody. That stud was tickled to death to make a new connection. I only hope Sandy tole him I'm no

credit-giving pussy. But, don't worry, I'll pull his coat when the time comes."

"He just don't look like an eight-bag cat," Pete said. "A cat fast enough to make eight bags looks different from him."

"And I'll betcha he is an eight bagger. I can tell by the way he said it. And that's what I'm gonna be from now on. Two bags at a whop, four times a day. No more and no less. I'm gonna keep an even high on at all times. Never no splurging. But neither am I gonna know what sickness is no more. Dig it?"

"I dig it most much, baby," Pete said enthusiastically.

"Now if we down four bundles a day we gonna be rich in no time. See what I mean?"

"I tole ya already I dig. And if a bust comes I'm gonna take it for you if it's anyway possible. You my man from now on. Dig?"

Kingfish beamed. "Yeah. Yeah, you take the fall and until it comes I'm gonna see you go each and every day. You be my right hand man and I'm your boss, baby. Gawd, it feels good to be dealing on the level. I don't want to see no lemons again as long as I live."

"You's really down with it now, King. Baby, I likes to hear you talk that way."

"And I likes that!" Kingfish exclaimed. "You called me King. And that's what I'm gonna be from now on. Yeah. Call me King from now on."

"You're the boss, King."

"And I just got me a bright little idea."

"Yeah? Tell me."

"You take five bags out and walk 125th with them. You oughta be able to down five bags in an hour with all the studs you know."

"Give 'em here! If I can't down five bags in an hour my name ain't Pete James."

As soon as he left Kingfish went back to sleep. He had slept two hours when there was another knock on the door.

King just knew it was Pete with the money from the bags, but he yelled, "Who is it?"

A man's deep voice said: "I'm looking for the Kingfish."

"Well, that's me," Kingfish said. He went to the door and unlocked it. For a fraction of a moment he turned to chipped ice; he knew the man.

The young stud shoved his way in. "I been knocking on doors all through this hotel, Kingfish. Something tole me you lived in here. Remember me?"

Kingfish nodded. Sure. He knew the chump . . . and a lot more like him. Country boy, stone in love with a little junky whore. You could look at his work shoes and tell this cat risked his life every day on some tough job, making that bread to keep the little bitch in heroin. And when that brick wall or something on the job collapsed on this fool's head the little whore would cut out. Yeah. King knew him. But what the hell: give him a couple of good bags now and the big country ass would go back to the bitch and tell her he scared the daylights out of ole King. What made it so really groovy was that this chump would be a steady customer from now on.

King grinned crookedly and dug in his pocket for the bags to give the young cat. But when the cat saw King's hand go to his pocket he took no chances and laid one on the Kingfish's jaw. As soon as Kingfish hit the floor the guy stomped him unconscious. Then he took a glass from the window sill and went out to the community kitchen. When he came back there was about an inch of water in the glass. He set the glass on the dresser and took a Baggie from his pocket. He emptied the powder from the plastic bag into the water. Then he took out a set of homemade works and filled the hypo with the mixture of water and lye.

After that he got down astride Kingfish. With one hand he opened the lid of Kingfish's left eye and with the other plunged the needle all the way in. Then he refilled the hypo and did the same thing to the King's other eye.

He got up and went to lean back against the dresser, panting. After a while his breath came easier; once he started to go to King and pull out the needle. But he changed his mind. Instead he put out the light and left the room. "Now do it again," he said softly, "you lemon-selling motherfucker."

CHAPTER 25

DR. BALSAM COULD TALK ALL SHE WANTED to about the resurrection of My Baby Girl, but the only message she had conveyed to me was that I was nuts and should be put away. Okay then. But like I said: tomorrow was Checkday.

"Don't worry about your check, Sid," Jinny said. "I'll just go down and tell the Jew that you're sick in bed and want your check. Which will be true. And I won't even bother to bring the check to the hospital; I'll simply sign it and take it back down to Ginsburg and tell him to take out the rent and give me the change. Twenty-six, isn't it?"

"You won't be in the hospital any two weeks anyhow," Joey pointed out. "So this way you'll have your same room to come back to."

I nodded silently, knowing full well that J&J were wrong and that they probably knew it. It would take a hell of a lot more than two weeks to cleanse me of all the anger pent up in me. The only reason I didn't argue with them and ask them to let me put my things in their room was because they were already overcrowded with Leah's things. And there was no telling when she was going to get out of jail. She hadn't even gone to trial yet.

"You need money now, Sid? Joey and I have five dollars saved back. Mad money, kinda. . . ."

Until Jinny asked me that my mind had been pretty blank. I came out of my fog and said, "Yeah. The doctor told me to bring pajamas and a bathrobe. I sleep in my underwear and Crazy Mary took my bathrobe."

"I don't know what kind of bathrobe and things you're going to get with just five dollars," Jinny said. "But here it is."

"Don't worry. I'll make it," I said and I did. Like a very sane person, I went to a Salvation Army secondhand store and bought two pairs of pajamas and a red plaid bathrobe that was heavy enough to serve as a topcoat. They were secondhand but immaculately laundered. My total purchases came to a dollar and thirty-five cents. So I then went to John's Bargain Store and bought a pair of shower scuffs for thirty-nine cents. Since I still had money I bought a pack of razor blades and a new toothbrush. Then I stopped by the stationery and bought four packs of Pall Malls.

When I walked out of the stationery a curious dullness came over me, as if I no longer needed a mind. And since I had done all I was supposed to do before turning myself over to the nut ward of St. Luke's, I guess I didn't need a mind any more anyhow. There seemed to be a lot of things I should remember to think about, but I couldn't remember and really didn't care. I continued on to the hotel like a robot. Back in my room I sat down on the side of the bed, facing my writing table, staring at the spot where my clock should be. Mary must have thrown that out too.

Jinny came in and looked at me anxiously. "You'll be all right, Sid. I swear before God you'll be all right."

In my state of dull uncaring I heard but did not even care enough to wonder if I believed. At the same time I felt good because what I felt now—or rather what I wasn't feeling now—was a damn sight better than all the intensifying hate that had been consuming me these last few weeks. I think I even began to wonder if this uncaring was true insanity. I felt nothing, was perfectly relaxed and had no desire to do anything, and I think I was now decided that insanity was preferable for any and all S.R.O. inmates. Insanity was not a bad state of mind at all.

Yet there had to be a hell of a lot more in the picture, or Dr. Balsam wouldn't have been so eager to get me committed. So the worst must be yet to come. Perhaps what I was feeling now was shock induced by fear; I didn't know for sure. But it seemed to me that I was not actually frightened by this prospect of entering a crazy ward. In fact, the truth of the thing was that since I no longer had a memory and could not produce another Girl of my own I might as well lay up in somebody's crazy asylum. There is absolutely nothing on earth that a man without a memory wants; he doesn't even want his memory back. At least I didn't.

While I sat on the bed it ran through my mind that I should be worrying about what I would do with all the spare time I would have on my hands now that I could no longer write. For a time there, I had thought life without My Woman would be as unbearable as life without a penis. Right now I didn't really give a damn about the book or my dick.

I also had a feeling that I should be sad. But I wasn't. If I was really crazy I was sorry because it would worry and embarrass what family I had left. My sister, my aunts and cousins. I shrugged: it was up to them to explain that insanity didn't run in the family, that I was the only nut.

Then it sort of flashed through my mind that I had no friends to sorrow for me. J&J were not friends, they were only drinking companions. No, that was all wrong. I didn't have friends. I had a family. I was a member in good standing in this S.R.O. clan. Blind Charlie and Sinman were closer than brothers to me. Sandy. Gloria. J&J. Mr. Johnson shouting, "C'mon in here, boy." The complete and happy family with no generation gaps and all relationships were normal.

But then, wasn't this family an intellectual one? Each and every intimate of mine in this hotel had taken pains to remind me of that many times. Now my brain was gone. I felt I was dead as far as they were concerned.

The uncaring dullness left me and in its place came a bone-weary tiredness. I was tired of living, tired of relating realistically, tired of making love to pads and pads of vain scribblings. And even if I'd finished that book, and become rich and famous, Sharlee probably would still have refused to marry me. My relationship with Sharlee was both born and held together by a whim on her part. In fact, all my relationships had been just whims on the part of other people.

And now that I could meditate in this tired and released way I realized that Sharlee and I had never been friends. We had been brief lovers, but never friends.

Somehow, because I was so tired, it became important that I should call someone to let them know where I'd be from now on. I racked my brain but could think of no one to call. It was symbolic of my life here in the Logan.

I looked into the plain face of Jinny, ugly now with grief, as she slowly paced the floor. Jinny wore the same dogged look that people wear in railroad stations, waiting for loved ones to leave on the next train, which is running late. But I knew there was nothing I could do, nothing to say that would make her leave my side.

I thought of Joey, the transvestite, who was too mannish to come in my room and show her tears. Then the reason I had no one to call came over me in a great wave: J&J and Sharlee were the only persons I *loved* and who loved me. No matter how much I cared for Gloria there remained the fact that Gloria had loved my brain, not me. Now that my intelligence was gone she was released from loving me. I began to feel good again about being crazy while at the same time I faced the fact that I loved three deviates. They were all I had to love and all I wanted to love. So who else in this mixed-up world was crazier than Sid Bailey?

I got up from the bed and went to J&J's door to look at their clock. It was three-thirty. Fifteen minutes to wait. Joey was sitting by the window. She tried to smile but did not try to speak. I went back to Jinny. I didn't feel like sitting down any more and so I stood just inside the doorway and looked at Jinny. And I wondered if this was going to be the final form of my insanity. Was I to be one of those nuts who just stood around staring at everything, at nothing?

The fifteen minutes passed. Jinny got up with a sigh. Then she came and put her arms about my neck and pressed her head to my cheek. Her breath was awful and I thought about how I had never kissed a woman who drank wine. Not even Lina. We certainly must stink all the time, I thought, and wondered how Gloria had put up with me.

And Jinny did not release me. Her thighs were pressed to mine like a lover's. Joey came in and said, "Now don't you be worrying about nothing. Sid. We'll be there every visiting day and see you got smokes and things. So you ain't got nothing to worry about but getting yourself straightened out, and that won't take no time at all.

"And if you gotta stay longer than two weeks, then me and Jinny will clean out your room and put your stuff in ours. Won't we, hon?" she said to Jinny, who was still writhing against me in a strangely sexual way. "Naw, Sid," Joey repeated. "You ain't got nothing to worry about."

But it was all too evident that I did have something to worry about because J&J were worried. They were so damned worried that they had stepped out of character. Forgotten their accustomed roles. Now they were both stone women, worried about their man. And when I realized the true enormity of this I also realized the enormity of my sickness; no matter what I wished, I could no longer suffer alone. What happened to me would also tear at the vitals of these two beloved bulldikers.

And after all, insanity is more than just the doctor and loved ones saying you're crazy: you *are* crazy! And furthermore, this being crazy without feeling crazy was beginning to tell on my nerves. I wished the screaming and gnashing-of-teeth bit would hurry up and come on; sadly I realized that I had never bothered to find out what a person does when he gnashes his teeth.

A red-hot sweat of rage swelled in me and burst into my brains: the goddam pigs were responsible for all this. I began to tremble again. Jinny clung tighter. I was delirious with fury and for the first time I felt totally crazy and glad to be crazy.

My mind seemed to suddenly shift back to normal and I resolved not to go to St. Luke's. Why should I give up my freedom, my wine, and be forced to lie in a bed all the time for a crime perpetrated by some pigs I didn't even know? And it wasn't any crime to be crazy. Whoever I had passing for friends here in the Logan had all been crazy, hadn't they? Blind Charlie, Sinman, Gloria, Sharlee, Lina, my five whores and J&J were all crazy as hell—and they didn't need any bed in a hospital!

So that was that. I wasn't going to say anything and give J&J a chance to ladle out some well-meaning advice. I would say goodby, go down to the lobby and sell the pajamas and bathrobe. Probably I could borrow five dollars from the Sinman if he was in. Then I would go and cat on Lina for the rest of my life. And I would stay full of wine until I died of acute alcoholism. No. I was not going to St. Luke's.

Jinny, the confidence woman supreme, stepped back and looked up in my face. "You don't want to go to the hospital, do you, Sid?" she asked.

I inclined my head.

"Want me to go with you? Joey and I will walk you there if you want."

"If you don't take me I ain't going," I said.

"You said that plain enough," Jinny said with a little grunt. "You ready, Joey?"

"Yeah," Joey said, "but it's so damn hot. I wish we could afford a taxi."

Jinny sniffed cheerfully. "Four of the shortest blocks in New York City and he's got to have a taxi. C'mon," she said to Joey. "We can stop at Charlie's liquor store on the way back and buy us a pint." She grinned at me. "Just imagine! A whiskey store we aren't ashamed to go into."

"It's you makes all the credit," Joey grumbled.

"Why you call it Charlie's whiskey store?" I asked.

"Goddamit, Sid. Can't you even remember how he was going to stick it up that time and damn near broke his neck?" Jinny said.

"See, Sid?" Joey said. "You need help."

Jinny chattered all the way to the hospital, but I don't remember a word she said because I was back beneath that tired dullness again. I only wanted to be alone and be able to brood over My Woman of a script who had never lived.

When we got to the receiving desk Jinny made me take a seat while she took over. It was an excellent production she put on until a good-looking Black man in a white uniform came down and called my name. J&J ran up to him to put on another big deal, but this guy knew how to handle nuts from way back and soon got rid of them.

This guy—he was an attendant, I found out later—was a paragon of politeness. He reminded me more of a bellhop in a high-class hotel than a hospital worker. And Miss Chew, the head nurse who signed me in, was even more polite. In no time at all the abject politeness of everyone stationed on this hospital ward called Clark #8 began to upset me. And since no one had addressed me as Mr. Bailey in so long, I was soon wondering if the entire staff had not been forewarned by Dr. Balsam that I was potentially dangerous. Several times I mumbled, "Sid," in correction, but neither the aides, nurses nor attendants heeded me. I still was Mr. Bailey.

And I was frantic with fear when an attendant took my pajamas and bathrobe away, saying that all the male patients in Clark #8 had to wear hospital-issue night things. Was Dr. Balsam a nut, or had I hallucinated?

We went down a hall to my room. As I passed the open doors of the other rooms I could see that St. Luke's Clark #8 is laid out like the floor of an expensive hotel. The ward itself is quartered by two bisecting corridors that needed only carpeting to look like we were in a resort. The room I was ushered into held three beds. They were as unlike hospital beds as beds can be. And the room contained not one stick of sickroom furniture.

A young fellow in white, who looked like an intern, came in and introduced himself as Dr. Lincoln. "I am going to be in charge of you while you are here, Mr. Bailey," he said. "I know it won't be for long, but we always start out by learning all we possibly can about each patient's general health. Now if you'll just take off your clothes we can get down to an examination."

From then on he went about his examination in silence. Even when he finally got around to asking what diseases and operations I'd ever had it seemed as if he was maintaining a pointed silence. Finally I could stand it no longer and blurted, "The reason I came here so willingly was because I can't sleep. It's like I got to kill a policeman before I'll ever go to sleep again."

Dr. Lincoln smiled. "That's why Dr. Balsam was determined to have you come in immediately," he said. "You might have hurt someone—or gotten hurt, which is just as important."

That made me feel good. I reasoned that I could not be very crazy since I had wisely refrained from doing what every molecule in my body had been demanding of me to do ever since I discovered my manuscript was gone. But then I realized that I had nothing to brag about because what had kept me from doing what was right was only a fear of being unsuccessful. I now hated cops so violently that I knew my mind could not stand the hurt of being caught murdering one of them. To kill a lousy cop you must get away clean or else you haven't done anything. If I had been in possession of a bomb I would gladly have tossed it into a precinct window at midnight when the patrols were mustering. Or if I had a pistol I would have shot one in the back in the dark and taken my chances of escaping. But when you hate like I do you can't afford to take chances because if you lose you lose all your cookies as well.

Dr. Lincoln finished his examination and went away. The other two beds were empty and I figured they would stay that way until another Black man came to the ward. But since the attendant had taken away my pajamas and had not given me any others I got in bed in my underwear. I didn't know whether to close the door or not so I left it open.

"Now what do you think you're doing, Mr. Bailey?" a nurse exclaimed from the doorway. "Get right out of that bed and put your clothes back on. It's nowhere near bedtime yet."

I both wanly and fearfully recalled all the jokes about the staff of an insane asylum being nuttier than the patients. "You want me to get up and get dressed and sit beside this bed all day?" I asked slowly.

"Of course not. This isn't a sick ward. The doctors want you to be up and about. You are supposed to mingle. Come with me and I'll show you around Clark #8. We have a lovely solarium with lots and lots of comfortable chairs and TV, a record player and radio, a ping-pong table, books galore, puzzles and games."

She was still standing in the doorway, but she turned her back so I could scramble out of bed and into the private bathroom to put my clothes on. Then the nurse—her name was Miss Pierce—walked with me to the solarium, and on the way the medication they had given me when I arrived began to take over. At least I think it was the medicine; it couldn't have been anything else. I was on a wonderfully pink cloud of uncaring. And I forgot! I forgot everything: why I was in Clark #8, about Crazy Mary, Gloria, Sharlee, or that I'd ever been lonely and diffident in a world that wasn't mine. Now I was in a glorious nest of my own with no worries or woes.

Miss Pierce introduced me to several young white men and women and, to tell the truth, I didn't even think very much about them. I thought they too were patients, but I'm not at all sure. However, they were all gracious and intelligent and to my surprise I found myself talking to them with ease. I don't know when I ever felt so confident among complete strangers.

I was in such a state of euphoria that I didn't think about it at the time, but after I left St. Luke's I did, and I am convinced that the wonderful combination of pills that Dr. Balsam or Dr. Lincoln prescribed for me produced the same effect upon me that heroin produces on an addict.

While in my euphoria I lost all track of time, but I think it lasted five days, and then Dr. Lincoln either changed my medication or those little pills no longer had the same effect on me.

At the end of those lovely five days I was suddenly down, naked and alone. In the same old way. Now I could distinguish the faces of the people around me, and they still came up to me with their pleasant conversation, but I felt tongue-tied and self-conscious before them now. The weather was warm, and in my embarrassment I stayed bathed in sweat. All in all I was pretty miserable; and as yet had not had any conversations with my doctor. So I guess I don't need to tell you that I was ready to check out and go over to Lina's to get drunk.

The first conversation I clearly remembered was with a small wiry chap named Noel. Small as Noel was, he looked a great deal like Gary Cooper, but Noel was as cheerily impudent as Gary was reticent in the roles he played.

"For a time there I thought you were the sickest person in this ward," Noel came up to me and said on the sixth day.

"Me? How can you say that? I don't remember anything too clearly until this morning, but I was feeling great. Just great. In fact, I thought I was playing it all very cool. What did I do? I wasn't violent or anything, was I?"

"Oh, you were okay that way," Noel said with a grin, "but you were like a zombie. Nobody could get a conversation out of you. And you were incoherent as hell when you did say something. I hear you are a writer. Am I supposed to have read anything you wrote?"

"I—I thought I was talking to everybody okay," I muttered. Was Noel the nut or was I? "I thought I was carrying on pleasant conversations with everybody."

"Boy, were you fuzzy."

"Well, I've got to admit I felt fuzzy," I said. "It was like I had a nice smooth high on, but I can hardly remember anything. But so help me, nothing fazed me at all. Although right now I'm beginning to feel a little uptight. Didn't that medicine they gave you when you first came in make you feel the same way? I mean, don't they give all the patients the same thing when they arrive? They almost have to because those little pills have got to be the last word for anyone who is emotionally disturbed."

"I'm not exactly the same kind of case as you," Noel said. "My medication is different. I'm an epileptic and I was drinking too much."

"Is epilepsy a nervous ailment?"

Noel grinned. "I guess so, but they would have put me in here anyhow because I told them that I was drinking too much. Beer. All day and night. I had to have a beer every five minutes, looked like. So I just drove over here in my car and signed myself into this damn ward."

"You drive a car?"

"Yeah. I don't have fits any more."

This was the first conversation that I remembered. But the ones that followed really opened my eyes. In two days I knew that I was a Black man somehow adrift in a snow-white world, and I wondered why the hell Dr. Balsam had been so all-fired determined to get me in with this bunch of crazy whiteys. And it is a fact that none of the paients had anything wrong with them that resembled my case.

Clark #8 contains about twenty patients, I would say, divided roughly half and half between males and females. Everybody but me was either senile or of college age. There were only two old women there, and no old men. So that made it about seventeen or eighteen white youngsters. And I give you my word that every single one of these young whiteys suffered from a form of insanity that niggers just don't have. Sure there are plenty of crazy niggers, but not like the kids I knew in St. Luke's. This business about "Who am I?" is not a joke to lots of young white kids; they absolutely do not know.

In many different ways I was jealous of the young patients in Clark #8, and I guess I still am. Welfare was footing my bill, but one day an attendant told me that it cost over fifty dollars a day to stay in Clark #8 and that didn't include medicine. So I immediately figured that all the other patients in the ward were rich. Rich as hell. I could tell just by looking at them and talking to them that none of them were on Welfare. So that made everyone in Clark #8 above my sympathy.

And believe it or not, these young whiteys made me think a lot about the Sinman's junky syndrome idea. I kept toying with the idea that perhaps it was true: when the Black youth of Harlem is emotionally uptight they turn to heroin and keep their sanity after a fashion while the well-to-do white kids with similar hangups are unable to make heroin connections and so they flip and come to St. Luke's or similar places.

All of the boys except two were actually in college and over half of the girls were. The girls who weren't in college had whitey jobs, glamor jobs on Madison and Park avenues. You don't have to believe it unless you want to, but as far as I could tell from all the conversations I heard and overheard practically every damn one of these kids was a virgin and scared to death of the fact that they were soon expected to make a change.

And all the kids had those wonderfully impossible dreams of the kind that haunt junkies. Each and every one of them wanted to do some type of missionary work, but at the same time they all lacked that inner fire so necessary to teachers and persuaders. In this respect also they were like the Black kid who is born to be a junky. For even the stupidest Black junky dreams of teaching and leading others, and this is why the Phoenix House idea is so successful. You got fools lecturing to each other. Dig it? Every one of these kids hoped to get out of Clark #8 and back to finishing school so they could become Peace Corps workers or Harlem teachers. Molders of public opinion to the left, or even politicians.

So every day I came to think more and more of these patients as latent drug addicts. Their cloistered lives had prevented them from meeting their sources and connections. I felt contempt for these insecure ones who weren't even hip enough to seek out the cult of the insecure.

Finally Dr. Lincoln must have figured that I was sane enough to talk to, because after about a week he instituted private conferences with me. And I was let down again. This psychiatrist never asked me a single question that I can remember. Nothing about my childhood, nothing about my parents. He asked me to tell him why I came to the clinic and that's about all. Sure, he let me talk, but as far as I could see all he wanted to know was what I thought about the other nuts in the ward. And I was the guy who was looking forward to that psychiatric couch. Hell, they didn't even have one up there in St. Luke's!

One day in our conference Dr. Lincoln said, "You demand perfection from everyone, Mr. Bailey. You are not perfect and so why should you always demand it of others? You must learn to remember that life is not meant to be perfect. Once you realize this, I think your drinking problems will be solved."

In a flash of exquisite insight I saw that this medicine man was simply parroting the Sinman and the Sinman could say it a damn sight better than he could. So just like that I decided to sign out of Clark #8.

"Why can't you think of it as being your misfortune that two of the most inefficient policemen in the city responded to your call for assistance in dealing with Crazy Mary?" Dr. Lincoln asked.

He made me so angry I forgot to tell him I was leaving. "Those two cops responded and used routine operating procedure, you mean," I exclaimed. "And furthermore, every man in the world has a right to expect the law to obey the law. That's not seeking perfection."

"Well, do you realize that you even expected perfection from Crazy Mary?" Dr. Lincoln asked. "Why should you have thought her to be the perfect lay for a night? What made you think that she would just disappear after you allowed her to stay the night? You are neat, clean, and a good-looking man. Why didn't Mary have a right to think she had fallen in love with you?"

"But she was only playing a game," I shouted. "She wanted to con me into helping her get an apartment. That's all."

"You gave her reason to think the two of you could share an apartment amicably."

Well, I didn't sign myself out for several reasons. One being that J&J brought me another Welfare check and I endorsed it and gave it back to them to pay another two weeks' rent and bring my change.

The days passed slower and slower. Each day I awoke promising myself to loose Clark #8, but every afternoon something made me put it off for another day.

One morning I picked up a newspaper and read an account of a young woman who had been attacked and killed on a residential street while countless persons heard her screams for help but did nothing. Her name was Kitty Genovese. But when I read the police commissioner's scathing denunciation of all those people who would not come to her aid I flipped. I couldn't wait until my conference with Dr. Lincoln that afternoon.

"Well, what do you want to do about it?" Dr. Lincoln asked after I finished blowing my top.

"I want to write that simple-assed commissioner and tell him where it's at," I said. "I want to tell him about two of his own men who just stood by while a woman slashed at me with a ten-inch kitchen knife. If I had persisted in putting my pants on she would have cut me sure. If cops won't do their duty, what the hell does he expect unarmed civilians to do?"

"I want you to write that letter," Dr. Lincoln said. "And you must give me the letter to mail for you. I think you already know that the nurses screen addresses on all outgoing mail. After all, we can't have some of our more disturbed patients writing to our city officials, but I will see to it that your letter is mailed."

And I wrote it! I was polite as hell, but I told the commissioner exactly what the score was. And to show you that I wasn't quite ready to get back in the street I got scared after I gave that letter to Dr. Lincoln. You see, I thought that the Police Department functioned something like Police Departments in the movies and in books; that they would have a record of the call made from the Logan that night, and that they would have the names of the officers who responded and their written report. Therefore I became slightly paranoid. I had a dark fear that maybe those two cops might come up to Clark #8 and kill me just to save their jobs. It was only after I realized that they would have to kill Blanche, the clerk, J&J, Rosey Posey and a couple of other witnesses that I began to cool it.

However, an assistant of the commissioner's answered my letter, saying that my complaint was being investigated and that I would be contacted soon. In a perverse way I was chagrined: I had been secretly hoping that the commissioner wouldn't even answer my letter.

The next day J&J rushed into the ward during visiting hours.

"Crazy Mary murdered a man, Sid!" Jinny gasped. "And they've got her in jail."

"She stabbed this man for nothing," Joey said. "She didn't even know him."

"And Liza went in Pop Brown's room and robbed him last Checkday," Jinny added. "She took his cane and beat him over the head so bad they had to take him to Knickerbocker Hospital."

Joey said: "It's a new record for the Logan—the first time in the history of the Police Department that a mother and daughter were both being man-hunted at the same time for different felonies."

"Russel was in Rosey Posey's room when the detectives came looking for Mary and Liza," Jinny said. "Neither of them were there, but one of the detectives said to Russel: 'Man, can't you find some other room to visit in? This woman has a daughter and a granddaughter that are wanted for murder and attempted murder!' "

"So now they're both in jail," Joey said.

"And a detective's been by looking for you, Sid," Jinny said.

"How come they know I know Crazy Mary?" I asked.

"We don't know," Jinny said. "But did you or the doctor write to the Police Department? I don't think they wanted to talk about the murder. This detective knew you were in the hospital, but he thought you had been discharged. Ginsburg told me about it, but he don't know nothing except you're supposed to call a Sergeant Keppel at the 26th Precinct as soon as you get out of the hospital."

"I'm going to get permission to call him right now," I snapped stupidly. "I'm going to tell that bastid that if those two cops had done their duty up in my room that poor guy would never have been killed by Crazy Mary."

The next day I told Dr. Lincoln. "I'll call him for you," Dr. Lincoln said.

A few days later Dr. Lincoln came to me in the solarium and said, "Sergeant Keppel is here to see you, Mr. Bailey. Do you still wish to talk to him? You see, I have to ask you this because if you have changed your mind in any way and do not wish to be bothered with him I cannot let him see you."

"I want to talk to him," I said.

Sergeant Keppel was an intelligent man and I thought he was Jewish and so I immediately took it for granted that now I would really see some action.

"Tell me what happened," the sergeant said. I told him exactly how things had gone down. When I was finished he said, "Now this Crazy Mary, as you call her, is a pretty savage character. And she has committed a crime against you, and we want to see that she is punished. As soon as you are discharged, will you come to the precinct to swear out a complaint so we can have her picked up?"

A high crazy laugh broke out of me. "All the law I know is what I read in detective stories," I said. "And so I've been under the impression that people do not commit felonies against each other. I thought they were guilty of breaking the city and state and federal laws. You cops don't need me to make any formal complaint. Your men were there and saw what happened. And when a man is murdered, how is he going to come to you and sign a complaint?" I stood up. "Oh, I forgot to tell you," I said as casually as I could, "Crazy Mary is already in jail. She murdered a man the other day." Then I walked out.

I went back to the solarium and sat down and it was only then that I realized that I was trembling from head to toe. And I couldn't stop trembling. And my mind was trembling too. It was shaking so that I couldn't think straight, but I did keep asking myself if it could be possible that this sergeant had already known that Crazy Mary was in custody. Perhaps that was why he had come to me: he had to somehow get this thing hushed up. That the police had refused to detain a murderess when she first began to show homicidal tendencies would look bad in print. I began to get scared again.

Dr. Lincoln came and sat beside me. "Well, what do you think now, Mr. Bailey?" he asked.

"Look, Doc. There was nothing but whitewash on that guy's mind. He wasn't even interested in punishing those two cops for refusing to do their duty. The whole thing makes me want to puke."

My psychiatrist nodded. "But I am not going to let you forget that you alone precipitated all your misfortune," he said. "I'm not condoning the police by any means, but you erred when you moved into the Logan to live. You went there because you thought no one else would take you in in your hungover state. You erred when you continued to remain in the Logan. You erred when you went on Welfare. You erred and continue to err when you don't go out and find a job that utilizes your intelligence and education. Why, you even did wrong when you went out and left your door unlocked."

"I thought I locked my door," I said weakly.

"Well, all that is said and done. What I want you to do now is to start taking civil service exams. Try anything. City, state and federal. Anything. And I want you to keep on trying until you get a decent job."

I damn near flipped again. "Now how do you expect a man who's lost his memory to pass a civil service exam?" I exclaimed.

"You haven't lost your memory. You just did not feel up to the gigantic task of rewriting that book."

"You really think so?"

"I know so."

"How do you know?"

"We'll find out. There is a typewriter in the conference room as you know. I'm going to leave instructions that you are to be allowed to use the conference room to work whenever a doctor is not using it."

"I can't type," I said.

Dr. Lincoln gave me a funny look. "Very well then. You can write anywhere in the ward. I will tell the nurses to furnish you with all the writing materials you need. Now I don't want you to have any excuses, Mr. Bailey. You can write here in the solarium, in your room, in the dining room or in the consultation room."

"Do you really think I can still write or do you just want me to get back to my hobby?"

"You are intelligent. You say things well. We on the staff think that there is a very good chance of your becoming a writer."

Dr. Lincoln got up and left. I remained seated and pondered the toe of my shoe.

"You don't look crazy to me."

I looked up at the beautiful sight of Gloria. She bent down and kissed me and then sat down. As always, when we sat like this I had the feeling that she was in my lap. Gloria's personality is forever that warm.

"Hiya, stranger," I said weakly. Her beauty and the surprise of it all left me both breathless and tongue-tied. "I guess I don't have to ask you who told you I was here. J&J told you, didn't they?"

Gloria blew out a little sigh of exasperation. "The bitches! At first they wouldn't. Just like two children with a secret. I almost got hysterical. I thought you were in jail or dead," she said with an exclamation of pain and put her hand on my thigh. "I came to see you two nights in a row, but nobody would answer the door. J&J were asleep, Dick is too deaf, and the whiteys won't. God, was I scared. I thought maybe that damned wine had killed you. I'm not kidding. You can drop dead in a hurry from that sneaky pete, honey. People that don't drink it can see what it does to you better than those who drink it. That rotgut makes your head swell up like your ankles, and the next thing they know you're dead. . . ."

"Now wait a minute. Wait a minute," I said. "I'm not in here for drinking wine. What the hell did J&J tell you anyhow?"

"They said you were drinking wine with a woman they called Crazy Mary. And that you should have known better. They said you made love to her one night and then kicked her out and so she tried to kill you. And they said the cops came and neither one of you had any clothes on, and that Crazy Mary threw your manuscript out the window." Gloria's light beige skin looked kind of bluish gray with anger. "The bitch," she cried.

"That's enough. I should have known those two drunks couldn't tell anything straight. Yeah, I'm in here on account of the manuscript, but not for drinking. I'm not here for any drunk cure. So get that straight, will you?"

"Well, anyhow, it's all my fault," Gloria said bitterly.

"Now how the hell could one damn bit of it be your fault?"

"I really love you, Sid," Gloria said slowly. "And I've been jealous in a way. It's kind of hard to explain, Sid. But when those five whores had you by the nuts I guess I hoped you'd end up yelling for momma, me." She smiled crookedly. "I was jealous of you being hipper than I gave you credit for or even wanted you to be. You see, you brought so much intelligence to our thing and I wanted to bring some too, but you didn't give me the chance. You didn't need me, see what I mean? But I was wrong. Man always needs his woman. I'll never let you down again."

And right then and there I made up my mind to quit all this brainwashing I was doing to myself with this Sharlee thing. "Well, anyhow, I'm glad J&J let you know I was here even if they did tell it wrong," I said. "When I first came in I was so ashamed and mixed up I didn't want anyone to know. I told J&J not to tell. Does the Sinman know now? What'd he say?"

"Nothing. It's funny. I went and told him time I left J&J, but he didn't say anything. But Charlie said right out that you weren't crazy and that he was coming to get you. And I'm afraid."

I scoffed. "Don't worry, I'll handle him if he comes up here."

"No. I mean that's he's going to kill that Crazy Mary."

"He can't. She's in jail and's going to be there for some time."

"Are you kidding?" Disdain was all over Gloria's face. "Why that bitch will never even go to trial, honey. The pigs aren't dumb, you know. Not for real are they dumb. They'll never give her lawyer a chance to put you on the stand and say that she's been crazy and long ago you called the cops and begged them to take her away but the pigs wouldn't."

"How come you know all that?"

"I'm a woman who's been in the street, Sid."

The next time J&J showed up they brought me another check. "You know you're supposed to send this one back to Welfare, don't you?" Jinny said, slowly building up to something. "Now do you want the refugee to cash it or do you intend to send it back? If I were you I would send it back, but I ain't you, Mr. Bailey."

"It's his'n!" Joey shouted. "What the hell can Welfare do about it if he does cash it? Cut him off Welfare? And he's in the hospital? And don't he need a room to come home to whenever he does get out? The check is to pay his rent with, ain't it?" Then she changed tones just like Charlie. "Only he don't hafta pay it," she pointed out. "He could put down a deposit for when he gets out and we could keep his clothes and things."

Jinny made like she was ignoring Joey. "It's like this, Sid. Welfare pays your hospital bills so you are not entitled to any rent or food money until you leave here. Dig it? Now when your bitch of an investigator checks up and finds out that you was in the hospital and still cashing your checks at the same time, she's going to make a big deal of things. By rights they could send you to jail. You really ought to send this check back."

What the heck. Jinny was showing me the time of day. "Give me that check," I said. "The bastids who call themselves New York's Finest caused me to come here crazy as a loon. Now if they want to send me to jail for acting like a crazy man just let them go ahead and do it."

Jinny caught the rhythm. "But you need us to cash this little check for you, keed," she said.

"That's what you think," I said. "All I got to do is find somebody who works in here and has a bank account. They can deposit it in their account. Dig?"

Jinny grinned. "Okay, let's cut the bullshit and come down to facts," she said. "Joey wants to borrow twenty dollars."

"Yeah, Sid," Joey said. "You won't be needing any fifty-six dollars in here. And you know me. I don't never mess with other people's money. I might not pay off a fifty-cent loan right away or something like that, but you know I wouldn't mess over you with twenty dollars."

I sighed. It really wasn't blackmail, but what the hell else do you want to call it? I went to Miss Chew and asked her for ten dollars out of my account I had in the office.

"You know patients are not allowed to have money in the ward, Mr. Bailey," she said. "And anything you need from outside you know you may order and we deduct it from your account. I'm surprised at you for asking, Mr. Bailey. After all, you are not one of our *sick* patients."

"I know," I said, "but I've got some visitors and I owe someone ten dollars and I want them to take it to them for me."

"Oh. Why didn't you say so? Why, that'll be perfectly all right." And she went into the other office and brought back the ten. "Dr. Lincoln wants to know when you have visitors," she said as she handed me the money. "He wants to speak to them. I must have him paged right away."

"They aren't family," I said quickly. "Just neighbors."

"I think that's what the doctor wants. Someone who lived in that hotel with you."

Of course I didn't like it. J&J had misinformed Gloria and now they would probably do worse with Dr. Lincoln. However, I didn't see any sense in telling Miss Chew this and so I went back in the solarium and tried to give J&J a bum's rush. "Here's ten," I said. "It's all I got."

Jinny took it. "That's all we expected, Mister Cheap Black Bastid. But anyhow we told Ginsburg you didn't want the room any more and moved all your stuff in our room."

Dr. Lincoln came in. After he nodded to J&J he said, "May I speak to you just a minute, Mr. Bailey?"

I took a few steps away from J&J, who were all ears, and muttered, "I know. I know what you want, but it won't do you any good. They really don't know what happened."

"Oh, don't worry about that, Mr. Bailey. It is something else altogether I want to talk to one of them about."

"Well, you better talk to Joey, the one who looks like a man," I said. "Jinny, the other one, is damn near drunk."

But it was Jinny who jumped to her feet, grinning like a nigger, when Dr. Lincoln told them he would like to speak to one of them in the conference room.

I sat down beside Joey, mumbling about everything being wrong.

"Whadya mean, all wrong?" Joey said. "You're better, Sid. I can tell, you know. When you came in here you looked like a crazy man. You looked even worse than you talked. You ain't sick no more now, Sid. And I bet that's what Jinny's gonna tell that doc. What's his name anyhow? He looks young as hell. I don't want me no young docs. They likes to experiment too much for me."

Jinny returned by herself in less than fifteen minutes. She and Joey had to leave immediately since visiting hours were over. So I never learned what it was that Dr. Lincoln wanted to know or what Jinny told him. But soon after that I sensed that the doctor-patient relationship had changed. After having talked to Jinny, it seemed to me, Dr. Lincoln was no longer treating a despondent writer but an alcoholic. I never could fathom if Dr. Lincoln changed his tactics because of what Jinny said or if he came to that conclusion by himself.

The next visiting day my mouth flew wide open. I saw the Sinman leading Blind Charlie into the solarium. Charlie was subdued, and I imagine that he might be thinking of himself as sort of attending a funeral. But the Sinman was his old pattering self.

"This is your moment of truth," he was soon saying. "You have been granted all the knowledge the fates ever intend to let you know. Now use it. And why did you not let us know you were coming in here? That priceless Gloria saved the day so to speak."

"I didn't let you know because I didn't know if I was really crazy or not," I said matter-of-factly. "After all, you are outside the law. You can't afford to have insane friends . . . and I didn't want to be your friend again until I was sure just what I was. Like, how do you know I wouldn't decide to write the chief of police about you? I was a potential danger to you, you know that. And I'm surprised you even came to see me. If I was you and you were me, I'd be damned if I'd come to see you."

Sinman sighed. "Still a square with a horrendous imagination. Until this happened I did not know just how dangerous it is for a man to insist upon being a square, but you have opened my eyes. And I have done some soul-searching. I find that I have been playing quite the fool. I now believe that each man must find his own god in his own time and in his own place. You found a god you could live with in the Logan. So, too, has Gloria. Even College Joe. I no longer expect to find my god in the Logan.

"Furthermore, the Logan is no longer a cesspit. It is fast becoming a charnel house. The management has now started to take in whole families, charging so much a head and not by the bed. I will not make the narco scene in a place that caters to children."

"Then a lot of my friends must be moving out," I said.

"Yes," Sinman said. "I will not go so far as to say that all have discovered their gods. But the Logan has made the single persons more viable. They are finding one- and two-room apartments while people with families move their families into single rooms. It would seem as though only the stupid and unfit have large families. And so I must leave the Logan."

"Where will you go?"

"Either to the Times Square district off Broadway or to one of those virtually Black communities on Long Island." Then Sinman looked queer and said, "I only wish I knew how to contact Sharlee. She would be a great help to you now."

"I'm not sure I want to see Sharlee again," I said, remembering Gloria's visit.

"But Sharlee actually *needs* you now," Sinman said. "Remember we spoke of dreams once and how Black men had to have them? Even false dreams like College Joe? Well, Sharlee needs to share a dream like yours. Do you know that a creative artist has a social responsibility? You two must have each other for a while. Sharlee has given so much to so many that it is now time for her to receive. I just know Sharlee would love to sit by your side as you go about re-creating that book of yours."

"It'll never be re-created," I said.

"You are being silly now. A manuscript must be written over and over again before it can pass muster. Surely you know that. You have lost your first draft. That is all."

"It was the last draft," I exclaimed. "I rewrote some chapters time after time as I went along. That book was damn near ready for the editor."

"Be that as it may, I refuse to grieve with you or for you. Hurry up and get out of here and you'll find out that you are a better writer than before. Have you tried to write anything in here?"

"I can't concentrate in here. It might be the medicine, I'm not sure. But once I'm out I'm going to try. My doctor thinks I still have talent, but I don't know about that. All I know is that I've got to try before I give up completely."

"Confidence is all that is needed now."

"Yeah. I was scared when I came in here. I thought my memory was gone forever. And my memory is all I had. People like to say that I'm an intelligent man, but that's not exactly the way it is. I've got a phenomenal memory and it passes for intelligence. Why you think Charlie is always calling me stupid? But when I was in school all I had to do was take notes. After that I could give them to some foxy chick because I didn't need them; I never forgot anything I had written. So you see how scared I was."

"Mae West is dead," Blind Charlie said abruptly.

"A taxi," Sinman said. "Hit and run. Right in front of the hotel. Can you imagine? That taxi had to slow down to turn the corner and yet she was killed instantly. The driver had to veer from side to side to shake her body off his fender, and then he was gone."

"Mae West?" I said, remembering. "Wasn't she that real old white woman who didn't look so old until you got right up close to her? Lots and lots of make-up?"

"That's her," Sinman said. "Had a young blood for a man. He is a wino, but not in J&J's clique. He has almost lost his mind."

"And I suppose New York's Finest were able to do nothing?"

Sinman nodded. "It was a simple case of murder. I think one of the denizens of the Logan had previously robbed that cabby. He killed her purposely. I saw the last of it from my window."

"But Mae West was a harmless old woman," I said.

"She was probably staggering and she was white. And whiteys hate whiteys who live with us."

"But there's always someone loafing out in front. Was everybody too drunk to take his number?"

"More likely they were too old to see well at night. But as I say: I've been playing the square. I shall move. The Logan is no longer a dynamic thing. Our inmates are dying like flies."

"Who else has died?"

"Nappy took a dive out the fourth-floor toilet window," Charlie said.

"For what? And did he die?"

Sinman nodded somberly. "Nappy jumped to escape the gendarmes and broke both legs in the process, but that didn't stop the pigs from whipping his head until the ambulance arrived. I think that's what killed him."

"But why did he jump out of the window in the first place? Why didn't he let himself be arrested?"

"When visions of withdrawal symptoms loom before the eyes, you are apt to do most anything," Sinman said.

"Yeah," Charlie said. "Remember that chick that grabbed the wheel of that patrol car and wrecked it? A cop got killed that time."

"The truth in that case will never be known," Sinman said quietly.

And then we were all silent for a while.

"Kingfish blinded himself," Charlie said suddenly.

"He did what?" I shouted.

"Nobody knows for sure," Sinman said. "But it is a certainty that he is now blind. He was in a room in the Logan which they tell me none of his enemies knew he was in. And you know, there is a thing which I have always believed to be one of the junkies' old wives' fables, but it goes that a junky can get so ecstatically high that he wants to attain the supreme high and madly hits himself in the eyeball. This might have been what happened to the Kingfish. All we know is that he's in Bellevue and will be out soon."

"Tell him about the gal with the rag doll," Charlie said.

"Don't tell me she's dead too."

"She died," Sinman said. "However, she died of natural causes, but her husband did not report her death for twelve hours. The poor man simply could not face the fact of them taking the pretty little thing away. But your depraved friend Joey wanted to have the man arrested. That cow simply despises heterosexual love. I tell you the people in the Logan are dying like flies. I don't understand it."

"It's the Ides of March," Charlie said solemnly.

Sinman turned to him. "What in the world are you talking about, Charlie? This is August."

"I don't care," Charlie said doggedly. "Time's run out for the Logan and everybody in it. Look at Sid here. That's why I'm moving with you. I wants out. I might even go to live with Lina until you makes up your mind where you're gonna move to."

"You seen Lina lately?" I asked him. "How's she doing, and does she know I'm crazy too?"

"Ain't seen her," Charlie growled, "but I knows I'm welcome."

"Gloria tells me that she is going to prepare a place for you," Sinman said.

"Well, that's the first I heard of that," I said. "She's only been here once, you know. And she didn't say anything about it then." Then I spoke a sudden thought: "I got this record of emotional instability now. I'm never going to live with anybody again. Suppose I should get violent and hurt them?"

"You ain't crazy," Charlie said. "Just dumb."

"What do you think about Crazy Mary and her daughter?" I asked the Sinman.

"I think that she is going to be a very lucky woman," Sinman replied. "Especially if you were to be so silly as to tell the court that the woman could have been incarcerated long before she did her murder. And I am sure that that is what you intend to do although Gloria has already told me that she has tried to sow the seeds of reason in you."

"So you think I would only be helping to turn her loose in a little while to do more murder?" I said slowly.

"I do. I do. And so does Charlie."

"But on the other hand I would be turning the police loose. Do you follow me?"

"The pigs are not your problem, Sid," Sinman said. "They have been unleashed against the Black man and the Black man can do nothing until the pigs finally turn on whitey himself. What in the world can you, a Black serf, do against a hydrophobic pig?"

"You know what makes me really think I'm crazy sometimes?" I exclaimed.

"No. Tell me."

"I keep thinking that everybody is always wrong," I said. "I know that can't be so, but I just don't agree with all the things everybody else around me seems to be agreed upon. But what can I do?"

"I've told you a dozen times," Sinman said gently.

"Well, I'm not talking like a real square now, am I?"

"No, not at all. But when you completely stop being a square you will note that the world is wrong most of the time, but you must never tell the world that. Survival is mostly a point of being right against the world while at the same time agreeing with the world. God couldn't do it and He died."

Blind Charlie took a ten-dollar bill out of his watch pocket and handed it to me. "I don't need it," I mumbled. I was really choked up.

"Nobuddy ast you what you need," Charlie rumbled. "Here. Take it."

"Why don't you just keep it and get good and drunk for old times' sake?" I said.

"You are hurting my friend's feelings," Sinman said.

I took the money, wondering where Charlie had got it. I just knew that Sinman hadn't given it to him to give to me, and I was more convinced of this when the Sinman rose to leave and handed me a twenty-dollar bill. . . .

CHAPTER 26

"I SIMPLY DO NOT INTEND TO discharge you until you find a decent place to live," Dr. Lincoln told me on the first Tuesday in September. "If all goes well, I'll let you go this Thursday; but you must first let me know where you are going to be living and I am going to have to okay it."

"No decent hotel is going to give a man on Welfare a room," I said.

"Don't tell them you're on Welfare. Once you are settled in a room no one would dare to ask you to move because you are on Welfare."

"So you are letting me go . . ." I mused. "Does that mean I'm no longer crazy?"

"You never were crazy, Mr. Bailey. Insane people are never admitted to Clark #8; if we can't help you, we don't take you. And there were never any doubts about you, although you were a very sick man when you came to us. You were sicker than you've ever been." He cleared his throat. "Now about that place to live: I walk through 112th Street every day and I see that there are several nice-looking hotels between Riverside Drive and Amsterdam Avenue. I don't know why, but I like the looks of the St. Marc Arms the best. Why don't you try that one first? It is less than five minutes' walk from here, and I want you to live within walking distance of the hospital for the next year or so."

"Why?"

"I want you to be able to walk into our psychiatric clinic whenever you feel depressed or upset. We are not giving you a full discharge, you see. You will be an outpatient, and every week I will see you in our clinic. We call it Clinic K."

"I've been to K," I said. "That's how I got in here in the first place."

"Yes, of course. I forgot. But we must have a talk once a week or until you have rewritten that manuscript. I also want you to seriously think about removing yourself from the Welfare rolls. You *must* work, but not as a waiter. Waiting on tables does not require brain power. It is no job for a college man. Have you been thinking about my suggestion?"

"Civil service? Yeah, but I figure I'm dead once they read my application and see where I spent three years in a TB sanitarium."

"That was true at one time, but not any longer. You cannot be turned down now because of an arrested case of tuberculosis. You are in perfect health and whatever physical examination anyone might give you will prove it. I also think that you are in a very unique position: it is only logical to assume that the city will be interested in helping you to get off the relief rolls and going to work."

And just like that a memory exploded in my head: Sinman had been a Welfare investigator. How he had managed it I did not remember, but it was a sure bet that he hadn't majored in either sociology or social work. To get a job as a Welfare investigator was something worth looking into.

"I am going to give you a permanent pass," Dr. Lincoln was saying.

"What's that?"

"It means that every day you may leave the hospital and stay out as long as you wish. This will give you a chance to find a good room. You will have plenty of time between now and Thursday."

Early the next morning I was at the St. Nicholas Welfare Center, asking to speak to my investigator. During the year three different investigators had been assigned to me. It seemed as if Welfare workers in New York City come and go almost as fast as waiters, and nobody can change jobs faster than they can. My current investigator was a pimply-faced intellectual-type Jewboy who I didn't like from the git go. And I didn't get to like him any better when I had to sit and wait for him to see me for two hours. His name was Kallan and when he finally got around to seeing me I found that his breath stank as usual.

"You have to bring us your discharge papers from the hospital before we can make any arrangements about a room for you," he said after I had explained what Dr. Lincoln had told me. "Once you are discharged from the hospital you come back and see me and I will give you some funds to keep you going until we send you an emergency check in the mail—"

"But my doctor won't discharge me until I have a room, and he insists that it be a decent room, and no respectable hotel is going to let me owe them until I hear from you," I protested. "Besides, they won't even take me if they know I'm on Welfare. That's why I came to see you today. Now my idea is to walk into a nice place and plank down two weeks' rent on the desk. Can't you advance me that much? And I figger that once I have the room they'll be ashamed to ask me out just because I'm on Welfare. You understand that, don't you?"

"No, I don't," Kallan said. "Why should your doctor insist that you live where you are not wanted? We have a list of rooms that are available to our clients. Some of them are nice quiet rooms, and all of them will be willing to wait a few days until you receive your emergency check from us. All you have to do is tell them to call me." He paused as if to make up his mind about something. Then he said, "What is your doctor's name?"

"Lincoln. Edward Lincoln."

I waited another hour until Kallan came back downstairs and handed me a mimeographed form which he had filled out. This form was to introduce me to the management of the Alexander Hotel on Ninety-ninth Street.

"Why, this is across the street from the Cambridge House," I exclaimed. "And I know for a fact that the manager of the joint spit in a girl's face one time and nearly set off a race riot on Ninety-ninth Street. I'm in the hospital now for a nervous breakdown."

Kallan was unmoved. "The Alexander has never taken Welfare cases before, but we have just persuaded them to take a few on a trial basis," he said. "I have called them and they are expecting you today. They told me they would hold a room for you until Thursday if you come by today and make arrangements."

"You are a stupid no good sonofabitch," I said as politely as I could and walked out of the joint. I was still fuming when I reached the Logan.

"West Ninety-ninth Street is only three blocks long now that they have built Park West Village, and there have been four murders on those three blocks in the past year," Sinman remarked after I had told him about Kallan.

"Don't you think I know it?" I exclaimed. "One of my best friends lives in the Cambridge House and that place is rougher than the Logan almost. All those joints on Ninety-ninth street are the same."

Sinman shrugged. "And so now you are in possession of absolute proof that some Welfare investigators accept monies from S.R.O. slum lords. Only for money would a college graduate send a nervous wreck to live on Ninety-ninth Street. But this St. Marc Arms you mentioned is always filled with Columbia people. You haven't a chance of getting in there. I have a friend named Max who operates the Hotel Roy further down the street, but the Roy has no cooking facilities and Welfare demands that you have some. I suggest that you go to the sedate little Arvia House and get a room. It is on 112th between Broadway and Riverside Drive.

"I will lend you the money to pay two weeks' rent in advance," Sinman continued, "and after you get the room you can call Welfare and tell them your new address and to send you money, you can't come to get it. Be firm with them. Your investigator will balk at the eighteen- or twenty-dollar rent. He has been trained to lie and tell his clients that Welfare simply won't pay more than fifteen dollars a week rent for anyone. But you remain firm and tell your psychiatrist to remain firm and everything will work out."

"Damn!" I muttered aloud at myself. It was on the tip of my tongue to ask the Sinman how he knew so much about Welfare when I realized that I had come to ask him how he had managed to become a Welfare worker. "Didn't you tell me that you only needed to graduate from college to be a Welfare investigator?" I asked.

"You are correct. All you have to do is walk in off the street and take the exam. If you pass you will be sent an application blank to be filled out and presented when you go in to get your job. A passing grade and proof that you have graduated from an accredited college and you are in. And any drooling idiot with a high school background can pass that exam. It is only an intelligence test."

"But what about sociology and social work? I never took any in college."

Sinman waved his hand. "All you need is a college degree. You could have earned it in shoemaking at Waycross Institute."

"Sounds too good to be true," I murmured. Then I grinned. "Suppose they assign me some cases right here in this hotel when I get appointed," I said. "Boy, would I have a ball."

"As a graduate of Virginia Union University you are eligible to take the exam. It is given on the first and third Tuesdays of each month."

"That often? You mean they need investigators that bad?"

"The Personnel Department and the Welfare Department have worked out a system whereby only the most unfit are allowed to become Welfare investigators," Sinman said. "However, something just occurred to me: you have no more chance of becoming a Welfare worker than you have of becoming a kleagle in the KKK, and for very much the same reasons."

"Are you nuts?" I cried.

Sinman smiled sadly. "Your medical history is against you. You have had TB, and you are even now being treated for a nervous disorder. Please don't set your heart on that job, Sid. I know it is the most wonderful opportunity you ever dreamed of, and that working there a year would give you your second novel, but you must not dream. The mad dogs in the city's Personnel Department can and will cheerfully murder your soul . . . and your spirit. Please believe me."

"Where's Charlie?" I asked with all the contempt I could bring into my voice to let the Sinman know the subject was closed.

"He's upstairs somewhere. But I don't think you should go looking for him. You must not return to the ward with alcohol on your breath. And you know he will insist that you have a drink with him if only to prove you are sane."

I smiled a rueful acknowledgment that the Sinman was always right. Right, that is, except when he tried to tell me I couldn't get a job in the Welfare Department. Why, they would be overjoyed to take me off Welfare and put me to work. And when Lina's sister had flipped, hadn't her psychologist got her a job as a receptionist at Welfare? How damn silly could the Sinman get?

And so because I knew that the Sinman was so dead wrong I put in words my agreement with him about seeing Charlie today. "Yeah, you're right," I said. "Tell Charlie I stopped by on the run and couldn't stay although I would like to see the big maniac."

Sinman beamed his approval. "Now go ahead and tell me exactly what you plan to do when you leave the hospital for good."

"I don't know," I confessed. "I've made a lot of plans and resolutions, but I'm not sure just how I am going to go about putting them in effect. But for starters: I'll never live in a Logan again!"

Sinman nodded approvingly. "You are now a graduate of this college. And now that you have your degree you have outgrown us. Once a graduate, you become a misfit in here. I suppose the doctors have spoken to you of this?"

My lips twisted, but I tried to smile. "According to them, I'm too dumb to continue to live in an S.R.O. They say what Charlie has been saying all the time. They tell me I did everything wrong. They have never told *how* I should have treated Crazy Mary; they just insist upon saying I did it all wrong. And my main doctor even blames me for not locking my door all the time. If I'd of listened to you and Charlie I'd never had to go to Clark #8."

"Have you told your psychiatrist about your innate loneliness?"

"Why should I? I haven't been lonely in months. Not since I started meeting people in here have I been lonely. Who the hell could be lonely around J&J and Blind Charlie . . . and you, too, for that matter?"

"Well, there is one bitter pill I want you to swallow so that the taste will forever be in your mouth," Sinman said. "I want you to always remember that you are the only person whom the Logan has sent to St. Luke's Clark #8."

"Dozens have left here for Bellevue. And hundreds have come here from state institutions. Why is Clark #8 such a big deal?"

"All the others were sent away for the safety of the community, but not you. Think about that for a long time."

"Okay," I sighed, neither knowing nor caring what the Sinman was driving at. "Now tell me, what's with Gloria? That chick certainly disappointed me when she never came back to visit again."

"Gloria is working."

"For what?" I asked angrily. But don't ask me why I was angry.

"Do you wish her to remain a prostitute for the rest of her days? She is now the nurse-companion of a very old and wealthy man."

For a moment I could see only gain for Sinman and danger for Gloria. I even started to threaten the Sinman and then thought better of that. I'd find Gloria and talk to her first.

"She was by the night before last," Sinman said. "Gloria is becoming quite a bit of a Black Nationalist. 'Perfervid' is the word. She lives in Arvia House; that is why I told you to go there."

"Well, why didn't you say so? And has this got something to

do with this going-to-prepare-a-place-for-me bit you went into last time I talked to you?"

"No. I told her that you said you wished to live alone for the time being. Did I do wrong?"

"No. And besides, I'm still on Welfare even if it won't be for long. So I've got to have a room in my name no matter what goes on between us."

"Well, here is the money to get a room in the Arvia."

"Thanks, but I've got plenty of money. I just didn't want those Welfare bastards to know. I got the thirty bucks you and Charlie gave me plus fifteen Gloria gave me plus what I've been saving out of my checks. You know, Welfare made a mistake and sent me two checks I wasn't supposed to get, don't you?"

Sinman stood up from the organ and put out his hand. "Don't forget to let me know where you are living. You'll stop by often, won't you?"

"Sure. Every day. And don't forget to tell Charlie what I said."

The next morning I went to Arvia House, but the manager told me he didn't have any vacancies and didn't think he would have one by Thursday. As I expected, Gloria was not in, so I went back across the street to the Belvedere Hotel and got a room. Then I returned to the Arvia and left word for Gloria to contact me Thursday night at the Belvedere, but it was not until that Sunday night that she knocked on my door and I let her in.

She grabbed me like old times and I grinned from ear to ear. "You been hiding from me?" I asked.

"I work from ten in the morning until after ten at night," she said. "But anyhow, I wanted you to be all settled before I came to bother you. But now you're straight I'll change my hours if you want me to."

"What kind of man would ask somebody to work for twelve hours a day in this day and age?" I asked. "Damn if it don't sound like some nigger you're working for only Sinman already told me he was rich."

Gloria pursed her lips, and I knew I had said something wrong.

"This nigger, as you call him, happens to have made it just like a whitey. And the reason I work twelve hours is because I want to, not because he asked me to or even wants me to."

"Yeah, babee. Run it down to me," I said, scoffing.

"I work for a numbers banker who is rich as hell. But he's real old. One of the originals. He's just taking it easy now, almost sorta waiting to die. And I just do what has to be done and keep him company. He's not sick though. Just real old."

I felt so good, so relieved that I really ate Gloria up when I kissed her.

But Gloria wanted to talk. "The money's good, Sid. And I meet a lot of guys who are for real. The men who work for my boss I mean. They're all brothers who don't take no stuff. They absolutely refuse to work for whitey."

"Brothers!" I said, scoffing again. "You sound like a Muslim. Why can't you say Negro? That's what you were born and that's what you'll die being. In the beginning I went for some of that brotherhood crap, but it's worse than Communism. Just because a man is Black he's my equal? Some shit if you ask me." I didn't say it as tough as it might sound, but at the same time I wanted Gloria to know I wasn't one of these recently arrived Black men. I have liked Black girls all my life. Even when it was hard for a guy to make a fraternity at a Black college if he fooled around too much with dark-skinned girls.

This time Gloria was hell-bent to give me a course in the new Black etymology. "Because 'Negro' is a white word," she said. "The beasts made it up. We prefer to say brothers and sisters whenever we speak of each other. And besides, whitey doesn't like it. The beasts want no unity among the brothers and sisters. You know: divide and rule. That's what they've been doing to Black Nations for years and that's why there aren't gonna be no Negroes any more."

I looked at her closely. "What are you anyway?" I asked. "Muslim, Panther or what?"

"I am a Black Nationalist. And you'll be too as soon as you give me a chance to run it down to you."

"Well," I said at last, "we're not going to debate anything tonight. You realize how long it's been since you and I . . . ?"

"Don't worry about that. You're gonna get plenty tonight."

Funny, but Gloria's promise made me realize that she was not only all woman, but helplessly all woman. And now that she wasn't a hustler or a woman kept by a freak, I was jealous of her, just as Gloria had once intimated I might be some day. And the Devil himself grabbed my tongue and wagged it. "What have you been doing with yourself besides working?" I said. "Giving it away to those real-gone studs you meet at your boss's?"

Gloria stopped taking off her clothes to look me dead in the eye. "Yes. But you didn't have to put it that way, did you? You know I love you. I don't know why my body is untrue to you, but I swear my heart loves you and only you, Sid. Can't you accept me like I am?" She came to me and I saw that she was trembling. "We never went through this before. I've always promised I wouldn't do you dirt."

I felt like dirt, but I couldn't let it go. "I just don't cotton to these real down brothers you talk about," I muttered. "They're criminals. You know that, don't you?"

"No, they're not. They're Black warriors."

"Come off it. You know better than that."

"Oh yeah? Well, they have the guts to work in one of the only real industries the Black man can call his own. And the beasts not only don't want them to work in numbers, but the goddam beasts also want to take over the numbers. And have. Except for my boss and a few other old Black men with heart. And do you think my cats are afraid of the six months to two years whitey hands down for writing numbers? You get less time for peddling heroin to children." Gloria was pacing now, talking with all the evangelical fervor of a Baptist sister. "Those men are martyrs, not criminals. And you know it better than I do, Sid Bailey. Didn't you say a numbers banker was one of your best friends once? Aren't you writing a book about the numbers racket?"

I had to get her off that. So I said, "Would you talk to a psychiatrist if I could arrange it?"

She was enraged. "What for?" she stormed. "Just because I think Black people are better than beasts?"

"No. Sex," I said weakly.

"I don't believe in psychiatrists!"

"That's a hell of a statement to make. How can you say you don't believe in them? They aren't a religion. What do you mean anyhow?"

"Just what I say. Psychiatrists are dangerous. I wouldn't let one come near me."

"Yah," I said, somehow jealous because she felt she was above needing a psychiatrist. "But look how you act. You don't *have* to sleep with those numbers men."

"You were in the hospital, and I was busted up with Butch. I had a right to sleep with who I wanted. And I'm not ashamed. I respect those men. I'm proud to say I slept with them. Supposing you were still in the hospital, what am I supposed to do?"

"An ordinary woman would have waited."

"I'm not so sure about that any more. I'm beginning to think that maybe an ordinary woman would have made you *think* that she waited. Oh hell, Sid—what are we going on like this for?" She threw herself back on the bed and raised her arms to me.

It had been almost two months. I went to her like a stallion, but those goddam tranquilizers had made me impotent.

I was so damned mad I wanted to cut the damn thing off and throw it out the window. I even cried; but then Gloria took me in her arms and soon we made love anyhow. It was good, and then we both cried over each other and confessed that this was the first time we had ever really loved. And it was no jive; I meant what I said and so did Gloria. I knew she meant it and she proved it. And when I say I meant it I mean that I stood still and told myself that all I did was adore Sharlee, but I loved Gloria. I had to; she was the staff of my life. . . .

With Gloria away more than twelve hours a day, I had plenty of time to write. And my memory was a greased pig. The stuff just flowed from my ballpoint. Sometimes I re-created three whole chapters in a day. In six weeks I had rewritten *Pace of Asses.* Yeah. That was the title of the thing. Now *you* figure it out.

One night Gloria came in and looked at the pads of paper I had filled that day. "Gee, Sid. You're coming right along. Is it just the same as before?"

"Better," I admitted. "It's funny, but I can remember faster than I can write. I don't have to stop to think back. All I've got to do is write it down, only it's more refined this time around."

"Well, while I was around the house today with nothing to do I got a bug up my rear and called Grove Press."

"You did?" I was scared to death, scared happily, like when a girl says yes and you never did it before and now you've got to. "What did you say to them?" I said cautiously.

"I told them I had written a novel about the numbers racket."

"I'm not writing a novel about the numbers racket," I told her for the thousandth time. "It's about some characters who just happen to be in the numbers racket. There's a big difference."

"What's the difference?"

"Why don't you read some of my stuff and find out?"

"I try. After you fall asleep I do, but I can't read your writing. I mean, I can't read all of it. I think that when the story starts getting good to you, you start to scribble. But aren't you gonna ask what the Grove Press had to say?"

"Hell yes! Gimme time. What *did* they say?"

"Well, the girl I talked to didn't come right out and say it, but she put across the message that they might be interested. What she said was to send it in and the editors would look it over." She paused. "But she did say the manuscript had to be typed—"

"I don't believe it!" I snapped. Now I was seeing the funny look on Dr. Lincoln's face when I told him I didn't know how to type. "Look, Gloria," I said patiently. "Greenwich Village is full of starving writers who can't buy a hot dog, much less a typewriter. And do you believe that they don't send their stuff to editors? My God, woman, don't you realize that the publishing business would go bankrupt tomorrow if all they did was read only typewritten manuscripts? That broad was pulling your leg."

"I don't think so, Sid." I didn't know how worked up I was until I realized how gently Gloria had spoken. "And there are a million typing services around the neighborhood on account of Columbia," she said. "I'm gonna take your manuscript to one of them."

"Oh no, you're not!"

"Why not, honey?"

"I've had enough bad luck with this manuscript already. It's like God has taken my own creation and is using it to punish me with. Now if God ever intends to stop punishing me and let this book see light, He certainly isn't going to do it after I let myself be a pimp to get it typed."

"I understand you exactly, honey. But you can pay me back out of your royalties. Or you could go out and work some and pay me back when you can. You're not supposed to slap your woman down when she's *got* to help you, Sid. That's what a woman's for. That's what *I'm* for. I've *got* to. It's part of me. Like my body."

The next day I walked over to Columbia University's Men's Faculty Club. The headwaiter told me that he needed extra waiters to work banquets pretty often. In fact, he had one that night and could use me. I worked that banquet and began to average two and three parties a week at the club. In no time at all I had a nice little bankroll. So one morning I called a typing service and asked about their charges.

"Our rate is seventy-five cents a page," the girl told me. "Is your manuscript legible?"

I gave a light laugh. "Well, I can read my own writing," I assured her. "No one has ever complained about the way I wrote until I started on this novel. But you all are experts at reading other people's writing, aren't you?"

"Oh, we don't take manuscripts written in longhand. Nobody does."

"Nobody does?" I echoed. "That's downright silly. You can't be for real. You mean you want to tell me that every published writer is also an expert typist? And so what do they need you for?"

"Neat appearance, editing. Lots of things."

"Well, you asked if the manuscript was legible, didn't you? Well, will you now tell me how a person can type illegibly?"

She was a nice girl and she laughed. "I don't know, but they do. Some of the papers we get in here simply cannot be read."

Since she was nice and I couldn't think of anything else to say I thanked her and hung up. But this time I didn't react like in the old days, the days when I reached for a bottle because I was uptight. This time I walked around the corner to Gordon's Typewriter Service on Broadway and bought one of those booklets, *How to Learn to Type in Eight Hours*. And while there I looked at a couple of used typewriters and ended up putting twenty dollars down on a secondhand portable that looked good to me and was more or less guaranteed.

On her next day off, Gloria was rummaging around in my drawers and found the receipt and like a little angel went right out and got the typewriter. I saw no sense in arguing with her about it; God knows exactly how it was and so what else was there to say?

Furthermore, I wasn't quite so prissy scared of God any more because I was working almost steadily at the Faculty Club now, using Roy Watkins' name and social security number. I salved my conscience by convincing myself that all great writers had been scoundrels.

Every Wednesday afternoon I had to go to Clinic K to see Dr. Lincoln, and I saw no reason to tell him that I was picking up a few extra bucks at the club. And it was because of the doc's incessant prodding that I finally went down and took the social investigator exam. I guess it sounds kind of vain, but I had to finish my book first.

Everything was simpler than picking up a chick in a 145th Street bar. First they take your thumbprint and then give you the exam papers and tell you to take a seat. But not to look at the test until the signal is given and then to start in and go on until you finish, and when you finish to come up, hand in your papers and leave. There were about fifty of us taking the exam and I was the first to finish. I looked around me and all this roomful of college graduates, supposedly, who were frowning and scribbling and erasing like mad. I went up to the guy who was proctoring the exam and told him he must not have given me all of my papers because I was through. The guy looked over my papers, said I had been given all I was supposed to get, and that I was finished. I left the building and went into the nearest drugstore to call Gloria and then the Sinman to tell them I had taken the exam. I knew I had passed because, as the Sinman had said, any high school kid could pass it. Sinman told me to come on up to the Logan.

"But you'll never get the job," is the first thing the Sinman told me after I entered the room.

"You're nuts," I said cheerfully. "I was the first one through. You whiteys can low-rate nigger colleges if you want to, but those white kids in that room were uptight over that exam and I just took it in my stride. Hell, there was nothing tricky about the questions. All you had to do was answer them and even you said a fool could do it."

"You are still Black, my friend."

"Goddamit! It's *civil service!* Can't you remember that?"

"Everyone of importance in the city personnel office is white. You will not see a single Black face when you go down there. You have a medical history they'll eat up. Welfare footed your bills at St. Luke's so you can't hide your record. If you were white you would be accepted, but no Black man with a psychiatric history is ever going to get a job working for the City of New York."

"Save it!" I snapped. "I know what you're trying to do. You're trying to snow me with some of your God-is-dead bullshit. But I happen to know that God is very much alive—and doing well for Sid Bailey. He saved my memory. He rewrote my book; He gave me Gloria. And He's going to prove He's alive by giving me this job He knows I've just got to have."

"Sid?" Sinman said softly. "Will you wager that God is not dead? If you do get this job I will not only apologize to the Personnel Department, but I will go about this hotel testifying to everyone who will listen that God is not dead and has proved Himself. What will you wager?"

I snorted my contempt. "Then I'll admit that God is not only dead, but even if He was alive He wouldn't be worth a damn to any Black man!"

"You'll get it," Dr. Lincoln said Wednesday. "I know you passed that exam. You remember that we also tested your intelligence, don't you? You really impressed us and so you simply have to be acceptable to them. And since you have passed the test, we will take care of the rest."

I smiled and relaxed. The Sinman had gotten me so worked up that I had walked into this conference boiling and doubting, all at the same time. "Yeah," I said like I had a nice mellow high on. "You were right as rain. You said that my weird drinking stemmed from not having a job that utilized my brains and education. But when I came out of the sanitarium after the war I took exams and things, but they always had some excuse not to hire me. Maybe I could have taught in a country school, but I wasn't going to admit to anybody that I was a lunger. And if it wasn't for you, alcohol would still have me licked. Now I got a book, a woman and my sobriety; nothing can lick me now."

"We've got you on the right track now," Dr. Lincoln said. " 'Life begins at forty' is going to have a real meaning for you. And I know that book of yours is going to be a success. How many chapters have you done?"

"I've finished it," I said, "but I was kind of ashamed to bring it up because I've been so dumb. I didn't know a manuscript had to be typed before it could be submitted."

"Finished?" Dr. Lincoln said. "You mean you've put that whole book back together again?"

"Yeah, Doc. It was the easiest job I've had to do in a long time."

"Well then. That means that we can space out your visits. How about making them once every three weeks?"

After that day everything was roses. Gloria was the most. And I never got so stupid again as to ride her about the guys she had fooled with while I was in the hospital. Gloria was my woman and I knew it.

My learn-to-type booklet had been bought with an idea in the back of my mind, the sort of idea that had screwed me up when I began to write. I had bought the thing to prove to myself that I couldn't learn to type. But in five quick weeks I was doing pretty good. I have never learned to touch-type, but with my memory I can look at a whole paragraph of handwriting and then turn back to the typewriter and dash it off, doing about a page every fifteen minutes.

So after those weeks of teaching myself I began on *Pace of Asses.* And I was well into the thing when I received a postal card saying I had passed the social investigator exam. Gloria and I pitched a celebration in the Gay Way Bar that night, and I mean we really tied one on. The next morning I awoke with a headache but not the slightest desire to continue drinking. Headache and all, I got right back to that typewriter and went to work. It's funny, the script was no longer my lover, the typewriter was.

It was about ten days later when I received my application form and a notice to appear for the job interview. When I got to the building downtown I was shown into a roomful of other people all there to be interviewed for investigators. And I was soon aware of how things were going. One person at a time was called in. Each stayed less than ten minutes and then came back in the room and had his picture taken by a pretty little Black girl.

I asked the girl if taking your picture meant that you were hired, and she said that anyone who had their picture taken for an ID card was officially on the city's payroll. Boy, did I wish the Sinman was here to see me now!

Pretty soon it was my turn to go in the inner office, and in a way I was almost bored. I knew I had the job, and I wanted to get the formalities over with so I could call Gloria and the Sinman. There was one little old woman in the office and she merely glanced at my application form and then said, "We will have to defer your appointment until after you've had your physical, Mr. Bailey."

"Everybody else who came out of this office got their picture taken and was placed on the payroll," I said, trying not to get excited. "You mean I don't get my picture taken today?"

"No."

"Why me? What's wrong with me?"

"Well, it says here"—she pointed at my application—"that you've had tuberculosis. You will have to take a thorough medical examination before you can be hired."

"Why can't I have my physical after I'm hired like everybody else?"

"But, Mr. Bailey, it also says here that you have been treated for a nervous disorder. The psychiatrists will have to check on that too."

"I was treated at St. Luke's Hospital and they are the ones who sent me down to take this exam in the first place. I have already been mentally and physically okayed by St. Luke's. You've got to take their word for it in the end so why not now?"

"I'm sorry, sir, but this is how we do things. I just can't make a special case of you. I know how you feel, but I have quite a few more to interview this morning. Now if you'll . . ."

"Well, is there someone else I can talk to?"

"Not that I know of, but since it will only be a matter of days, why bother?"

So the Sinman had been right. But only half right. With St. Luke's medical and psychiatric staff behind me the Devil in hell couldn't keep me from getting this job with Welfare. And I had God on my side to prove it. And thinking about God, I stopped dead still in that corridor on the way out and closed my eyes and prayed. I told God exactly how it was with the Sinman and me, and how He'd simply have to go all out because this job was now almost a matter of life and death to me. I honestly believed that without that Welfare job I was nothing, nothing at all. After I finished praying I felt better. Almost as if I'd already been accepted.

But month followed month and there was no word from the city personnel office. I called several times and each time the same female voice answered, telling me that my application was still being processed.

Six months went by and still no word. And after the ninth month I stopped typing and began to hit the bottle.

"You need a rabbi," Sinman said.

"Eh?" I was half drunk and wasn't really listening to him anyway.

"A rabbi, my square friend, is the title given to any important politician. I can assure you that your application has now been pigeonholed and will never be processed unless you get a rabbi to light a fire under someone downtown. There is also some kind of mark on your application that denotes that you are Black. Without a rabbi, you are dead."

That night I wrote to Adam Powell, an old friend of my father's. In fact, Adam's father left the church in Connecticut to come to Abyssinia Baptist Church while my father took over the church in New Haven. In his capacity as a New York congressman, Dr. Powell wrote to the Personnel Department, demanding to know why I had not been given a job since I had passed the social investigator examination. It was a beautiful letter, polite as hell, but at the same time telling those whiteys downtown to either shit or get off the pot. I still have the copy of the letter Adam sent to me.

So with his letter under my belt I wrote to the highest-ranking Black man in the Welfare setup. The guy wrote and congratulated me for wanting to get off Welfare but told me how hard and arduous the work of a Welfare investigator is and the Personnel Department was simply waiting for a chance to give me a physical examination before giving me its final okay. And since the man could not be a complete ass I believed I had the job sewed up.

Two weeks after I heard from the Welfare big shot a woman called on the phone and asked me why I had stated in my application that I had never been a party to a divorce action.

"For the very simple reason that I've never been a party to a divorce action."

"Oh, we have ways of finding out these things, Mr. Bailey," said the woman. She had identified herself as Miss Goode. "And you should have told the truth."

"Didn't I just *tell* you that I've never been divorced?" I said. "I have an annulment but no divorce."

"Your last wife divorced you, Mr. Bailey, and we think you know it."

"When and where was this divorce granted?" I asked.

"In Virginia."

"Well, since you know something that I don't know, I think that you also know that I am *not* aware of the fact that I'm divorced."

"You are going to have to furnish us with proof of your divorce, Mr. Bailey."

"You've already said you've got it," I shouted.

"We will give you ten days to furnish us with a copy of your divorce decree. Good-by, Mr. Bailey."

As soon as I finished talking to this Miss Goode the Bad I called a former college chum of mine in Richmond who is now practicing law and asked him to try and get me a copy of the decree . . . if Alise had gotten one. He got it for me and charged me ten dollars. I considered it money well spent: Shorty was now screwing his own wife, not mine.

A week later Miss Goode called again. "I'm marking your case closed," she said.

"What for?"

"Lack of cooperation. We asked you a week ago for a copy of your birth certificate and we haven't received it."

"*Who* asked me? You didn't. And you know damn well you didn't."

"Someone from this office called you and asked for it, but since you claim you weren't notified I will give you five days to get a birth certificate to us. Good-by."

That was the first time that I even suspicioned that the Personnel Department was trying to run a game on me. But I wasn't giving up; how could they win? I wrote to the State of Virginia's Bureau of Vital Statistics and asked for a copy of my birth certificate. I knew they wouldn't charge five dollars, but I wasn't taking any chances. I sent a money order with the request.

A week later Miss Goode called and asked me to send her a copy of my marriage certificate. "Which one?" I asked.

"Oh, that's right. Both of them."

This time I had to write to the vital statistics people in two different states, but everything worked out okay and I sent those copies to Miss Goode.

"For goodness' sake, Sid, haven't you woke up to that murphy yet?" Sinman said one night.

"Does that bitch think you want to marry her daughter or does she think you wants a job being a sad-assed investigator?" Charlie said. "But nemmine. Something tells me I'm gonna enjoy going down and having a little piece of Miss Goode."

"Oh no, you won't," I said patiently. "She is simply trying me out. Just why she is I don't know. Maybe they really think I'm sickly or a milksop or something. But no matter how much they give me the runaround the law says they've got to give me that job."

"The *law* says," the Sinman murmured.

"There's nothing in my record that says I am not able to handle the job."

"True," Sinman said. "But I don't think you realized that the Personnel Department is not fighting a legal battle. Now will you please pause a moment and assimilate that fact?"

"So?" I said. "But even if they are being dishonest, I can't give up now. What damned future would I have to look forward to? You think I really want to stay drunk for the rest of my life?"

"I dig," Sinman said wearily.

And Charlie must have dug all the resignation in Sinman's voice because he said, "C'mon. Let's go up and see what Mr. Johnson's talking about."

"Come in here, you old warhorse," Mr. Johnson cried to me. "I hear tell that you gonna be a Welfare investigator one of these days soon. And that's the way it should be. Welfare should investigate Welfare, if you know what I mean. It's like these young folks say about everybody should do their own thing. Us Welfare folks should do our own thing and not be having some educated fools telling us how to be poor."

I stayed up in Mr. Johnson's room all night, drinking it up and laughing and promising everybody they would get an extra clothing check as soon as I was appointed.

A week later I was called and told to go down to the city's public health center for an X ray. A week later I went back for the report and I had passed with flying colors. Then I was finally called down to see a psychiatrist. At least he said he was a psychiatrist. And all he asked me was did I have any problem with my drinking. I played it cool, knowing he couldn't know anything about my drinking.

"No," I said. "Lots of times I've been despondent, but I never have lost a job because of drinking."

"Despondent? What do you mean?"

"Well, right after I got out of school Pearl Harbor came along and I volunteered. They turned me down for TB. I stayed in a sanitarium during the war and when I got out there seemed to be no decent jobs available for tuberculars. I became a traveling waiter. I can honestly say I've never had a decent job in my life, and that's why I'm looking forward so much to this one."

"Now tell me how you happened to go to St. Luke's Hospital."

I cut that one short and sweet. "An insane woman broke into my room while I was out and tossed a manuscript of mine out the window. It was a novel I had worked hard on and when she destroyed every page of it I needed help to calm the anger I felt."

"Are you still taking medicine?"

"Yes, my doctor thinks that I should remain on tranquilizers until I get my job. I don't know why, but he does. And to tell the truth I don't take them often because I actually forget to take them."

"I see."

"So is this the last test I'll have to take?" I asked.

"Yes."

"Then about how soon do you think it'll be before I hear from Personnel?"

"About a week."

Two weeks later I received a letter telling me that I was ineligible for my job because of medical reasons. A few days later I got another letter saying that the exact medical reasons were psychiatric but that I could appeal this ruling. I wrote requesting an appeal. And that letter was answered by return mail and I was informed by the

Personnel Department that I had lost my right to appeal because I had waited until after the termination date of the eligible list I was on. The list on which I was eligible was terminated on October 20. The day I received this letter was December 24. Like Jesus Christ, I wept.

"You must try now for a state job," Dr. Lincoln said. "I am told that they are not as stringent as the city."

"The City of New York has declared me too goddam crazy to be a Welfare worker," I said. "And so I am now going to remain on Welfare the rest of my life. Do you realize that those fatherless bastards had me getting records for them two months after my eligibility expired? Do you think they gave a damn about me being on Welfare and paying to get copies of all those certificates?" Dr. Lincoln didn't say anything. I guess he was waiting for me to get wound down. So into his silence I shouted, "According to the Personnel Department of the City of New York, I have an open-and-shut case against the city!"

"A lawsuit?" Dr. Lincoln asked.

"Hell yes! The cops of this city refused to do their duty and because of their negligence a madwoman not only drove me insane but made me ineligible to work at a decent profession for the rest of my life. Just because of those stupid bastards I've gotta remain on Welfare the rest of my life. Don't you think that's worth a million dollars' damages? You got all my records, my case history. You were present when I notified the Police Department of their dereliction. You'll testify, won't you?"

"I don't think I could. The city would demand expert testimony."

"You're not a psychiatrist?" I asked softly.

"We are on the staff, but we are not psychiatrists yet."

"You mean I didn't even have to put down on that application that I had been treated for a nervous disorder? How could I have been when I haven't ever been treated by a psychiatrist?"

Dr. Lincoln smiled tiredly. I think it was the first time this white boy realized what it is like to be a Black boy. "You are in an unfortunate predicament, Sid."

I went home and got soused. And then went to sleep. Sinman and Charlie woke me up.

"We are moving to West Forty-ninth Street in the morning," Sinman said and gave me a slip of paper with his new address on it.

"Why the sudden rush?" I asked.

"Reasons within reasons. Wheels within wheels. And Columbia is going to close the Logan in a few weeks anyhow. Another student OD'd in there last night. Do you know that fifteen bodies have been taken out of the Logan in the last two months?"

"But the body of no new god has shown up yet, eh?" I asked. "Surely it is now his time. Why don't you wait for the new coming?"

Sinman's smile matched mine, twist for twist. "I see that you are not a very happy convert, are you?"

"Well, I guess I do have to admit that, even if He's not dead, whitey has crippled God. But you know, a sensible man can't just make a bet and then write God off because he loses that bet."

"That goddam Sandy went and OD'd on me!" Charlie roared in anger.

"She died?" I asked the Sinman. He nodded his head.

" 'Sfunny," Charlie said in a strange voice. "Not in her room. They found her in the kitchen on the third floor. Deader'n hell. I went up and felt her. I don't understand it."

Gloria walked in. "My God. You all look like you're sitting around talking about the dead."

"We are," I said. "Sandy's dead."

Gloria collapsed on the bed in tears.

"Well, one thing," I said. "Sandy said dozens of times that if you gotta go the best way is an OD."

"But she had so much heart in her," Gloria sobbed. "You just didn't know Sandy, Sid. I loved that girl."

"Sandy?" I said. "You must be kidding. You're the one who hardly knew her."

Gloria came off that bed like a madwoman. "I knew Sandy as well as anybody in the Logan!" she shrieked. "You never knew her at all! How could you? I didn't run around with her too tough because I didn't have the guts then. But Sandy had the principles I didn't have."

"Gloria," I said, speaking down to her like a fool, "are you high or something? Sure, Sandy and I were tight as hell. And maybe if I didn't love you I'd of been tighter than that, but Sandy was a junky and she died a junky's death. Now what are you getting all excited for, please tell me?"

Gloria stamped a tattoo on the floor with her feet. "You don't know, Sid; you just don't know. Sandy *hated* beasts and was willing to prove it. She almost rather be sick than trick with a white john. That's why she hung around the hotel so close and just took on bloods that came by or lived there."

I figured Gloria was going nuts. Even as I remembered more and more about Sandy.

"Sandy hated the blue-eyed devils so much she didn't even talk to them except Sinman here," Gloria said. "She hated them so much she wouldn't even talk about hating them. But I wanted whitey's money, and although I didn't like beasts I went out in the street looking for them. But not Sandy. That girl stood by her ideals as long as she could. And that monkey on her back had to be riding her like hell before she took on a beast."

"I thought you knew all this," Sinman said quietly.

I looked at him and my eyes were dim. I shook my head.

"I didn't know nothing," Charlie grunted.

"Only the man who is very gentle can ever get to know what drives a lady," Sinman said almost in a whisper.

"And I thought Sandy was trifling," I said wearily, filled with self-loathing.

"You see?" Gloria said. "Sid, you're letting yourself get so far from where it's at that you can't even tell a real sister when you see one. How can you call a normal human being who refuses to traffic with beasts trifling?"

"Let's not get into that brother-and-sister crap tonight," I said. I didn't mean that like it sounded. What I really was doing was making a sort of last-ditch stand for my own self-respect. But Gloria raised her eyes and looked at me in a way no woman has ever looked at me before.

"Sid," she said slowly, "the shit has just hit the fan and it's all over you. You think that you're too good, too intelligent to be Black. And maybe that's the truth because I'm beginning to think you're pussy. Right this minute you should be planning how you're gonna go downtown and put some scars on that bitch's face, that Miss Goode. How long do you think beasts would act the way they do if they knew they'd get scarred for fucking around over us niggers? That woman played you for pussy and you proved you were pussy. She gave you what she knew you would take and what you deserved. And now, before you get any drunker, you can make one decision: you are either gonna stand up and pay your dues like a Black man or you and I are through."

I played it like I thought Blind Charlie would play it. "Gimme six dollars," I said. "Me and Charlie need a drink after that one . . . and maybe you should go and get a fix."

Gloria went to her pocketbook and dug into it. "I'm gonna give it to you," she said. "But if you're really so down with it you oughta get six quarts of Spur because it's the last money I loan you until you show some heart and join the Black Nationalists, the Panthers, or any group that's not crying about some more goddam integrating like you NAACP motherfucker."

Sure. It was on my lips to tell her that I wasn't the bitch who'd turned up her ass for Red and Byron and Butch and maybe a couple of other so-called beasts, but I figured that Gloria would never be anybody's fool forever and pretty soon she would be telling herself that. So I went to the door to go out to the whiskey store. I looked back and Charlie was reaching for the Sinman's shoulder. They were leaving. . . .

CHAPTER 27

GLORIA WAS FAR FROM STUPID. And Gloria could not only cope, she could fight. Not just defensively; Gloria knew how to attack. Any other woman I know would have moved out after she delivered an ultimatum. We weren't married, we had no mutual possessions, nothing to keep Gloria from living in her room at the Arvia. But she didn't move out. She stayed to fight.

It was a war of nerves. I do not know if she realized that she was actually attacking my sanity. I don't think so; Gloria is too kind to purposefully wage such a murderous action, but all the same she had me in bad shape. We just hung around the room at night—Gloria refusing to really talk to me. I guess as far as she was concerned everything had already been said. And I was not only swilling the juice, I was popping tranquilizers into my mouth like salted peanuts.

Once more my days were a dark alcoholic pattern of nothingness. Gloria kept a bottle of scotch on my dresser, out of which she invariably poured at least one drink every night. She never offered me any of it, and I just as stubbornly refused to touch it. Some mornings my tongue was burning for a drink, but I wouldn't even look at that damned bottle. And just as masochistically I refused to bring any Spur home with me. I made myself get out of bed and walk up to J&J's room for my first drink every morning. So it was natural for Gloria and me to leave the Belvedere together each day. I would accompany her as far as Morningside Drive and the 116th Street entrance to the park. There Gloria would leave me to go through the park and on to work. I kept on up the drive to 119th and then to the Logan. There I would sit around J&J's room, drinking Spur and talking until they went to bed for the night.

"That goddam Jinny don't stay in this room five minutes no more," Joey constantly complained. "She stays down in that office more than Ginsburg."

"What for?" I asked the first time Joey said it.

"Now she's the head of the house committee and all she can talk about is petitions and meetings. She only dashes in here to get a drink and dash right back out. Goddam a nigger woman anyhow. I'm sick and tired of this. I'm gonna quit that gal, you hear me?"

"What good are petitions? And who do they send them to?" I asked. "Columbia owns this building, don't they? And with students dying in here like flies they got a right to protect themselves. And don't even try to bother to tell me that these junkies from out of here don't mug the profs and their wives whenever they get the chance."

"Them profs oughta get mugged!" Joey shouted. "What they ever do for us?"

"Christ. That's no excuse to break a man's neck."

Joey was standing over me, angry and red. "Does Columbia care where we hafta move to? This is our *home,* Sid. Goddam Columbia, is all I gotta say. And look at the dirty way they're doing the refugee!"

"Who are you talking about now? Ginsburg?"

Joey nodded vigorously. "I'm talking about Ginsburg is right. That man has a legal lease on this place for ooh-long years, but these Columbia bastids is trying to break it because they say he's operating a public nuisance."

That brought me over on Ginsburg's side. "There is no such thing as a public nuisance," I said. "We got wonderful police to break up any situation before it ever reaches the stage of being a public nuisance. If Columbia thinks the Logan is a nuisance and a danger they should demand that the police clean up the Logan, not close it. Yeah. If you really want to come down to facts, maybe it was Columbia who gently egged the cops into letting the Logan become a menace in the first place. The only public nuisances we got in New York City is cops."

Joey was shaking her head in agreement. "And Jinny is getting up a petition for that too. The poor kid is working her fingers to the bone for these bastids in here, and do you think a single one of them is gonna appreciate it when we don't hafta move?"

One day Jinny rushed in the room. "Ginsburg's finally opened 6-D for a recreation hall," she cried.

"The fool," I muttered. "Now that he's got his back up against that wall he decides we need a recreation room."

"Well, it's a step in the right direction," Jinny said. "C'mon up. It's open now."

"This room is good enough for me," Joey growled. "What's he got up there anyhow? Ping-pong? How in hell could any of these winos hit a ping-pong ball?"

"A TV and card tables," Jinny said.

"Somebody's gonna steal the TV," I said. "We might as well go up and steal it first."

Jinny walked up to me, arms akimbo. "Now see here, Mister Bastid," she yelled. "The tenants we got now is respectable. Don't get us confused with the junkies who used to take over our lobby. Your goddam Sinman had to move, didn't he? Ginsburg put a private detective in that lobby down there and those junkies split. Sinman's business got so bad he had to go too. There isn't a single damn pusher living in the Logan now, and don't you ever forget it!"

"Okay. Okay," I said. "Don't blow your top with me. I don't live here any more and I'm not a Columbia big shot so don't ride me." A little later I laughed and said, "Maybe you're glad to see the Sinman gone, but you got to admit this place isn't the same without Blind Charlie around."

"Blind Charlie and all his mayhem can go and stay gone," Jinny said. "We don't want his kind of bloodshed around here any more, Sid. Can't you get that through your head?"

"How many junkies are left now?" I asked like a sociologist, to get Jinny up off me.

"Only a few down on the first floor," Jinny said, giving me the annual report. "The Kingfish is down there. He's blind now, but he's still got his habit."

"How can he support a habit if he's blind?" I asked.

"Selling shit. How the hell else you expect a blind man to keep a habit?" Jinny barked.

"You just said Ginsburg had put all the pushers out," I said.

"Ginsburg's got a heart! Jesus to Jesus. You gonna make a big deal over one blind man selling a little bit?"

"We, in the Logan, salute you," I said.

"We ain't no worser than nobody else," Joey yelled.

"That's a goddam lie," I said wearily and stood up. "Let's go up and observe this recreation room the Jew gave you nigras."

That day, and every day after, the recreation room was my hangout. Ginsburg had unplastered the connecting doors of 6-D and now it was a pretty nice suite of rooms. There was a television set and card tables and I lived at those tables. We would chip in to buy a pint of wine and then four of us would play bid whist for drink or smell. Tony Scott, the ex-boxer, and I would team up as partners and practically never lost. I stayed good and high up in that rec room.

And it's a funny thing how adversity can bring people together. Like out at Lundy's during the strike of '57. There were two hundred waiters out there that hardly knew each other and to a great extent despised each other, each thinking to himself that if the other was worth a damn as a human being he wouldn't be working for Lundy's. But that strike made everybody drinking partners and brothers. And that feeling has lasted ever since even though we lost the strike.

The Logan tenants walked around that room all day and half the night shaking hands with each other and downing Columbia. Sometimes it looked like a fellowship meeting at a Southern Baptist church. Why, some of the old sisters would even gather in a corner and sing spirituals. Naturally Mr. Johnson was the elected official greeter and host.

Every morning he greeted me with "Hi there, boy. C'mon in here."

But one morning—it must have been a Monday because the tenants of the Logan barred card playing on Sundays and closed the rec room—Lina was standing beside Mr. Johnson, aiding him in his greeting chores. Lina looked pretty good because Lina wasn't a bad-looking Black gal anyhow. It was only her head and her walk that held her back, when you came right down to it. And she looked cold sober. But then Lina never looked very drunk.

"Hello, Mister Author," she said with a big smile.

"What're you doing up here?" I asked. "You come over by yourself?"

"J&J were at my place yesterday and tole me to move in heah. They wants to fill the hotel up with all respectable tenants so that damned Columbia won't have no case when we gits 'em in court."

"Yessirree, bub," Mr. Johnson said. "That lil Jinny got us all organized now. She done made us all brothers and sisters and we gonna fight that mighty college with all our might. Can you imagine the nerve of them educated bastids calling us a public nuisance? Yessirree, Jinny done showed the way. And us old folks is just gonna do our duty. Them wild rapscallion ones done left us in peace to fight our battle. We gonna show Columbia. Mebbe we didn't keep the ground swept too clean in front of the cabin, but we gonna show 'em and make them white folks give us another chance."

I got almost a feeling of being maudlin as I felt for these poor Black souls fighting for their piece of land. And hell, I was a writer, wasn't I? I'd write to the *Times* and the *Amsterdam News* for them. What the hell good was a black-assed newspaper if it wouldn't argue to let people keep their homes in a community?

"Ain't been a knife fight in here since Columbia tried to take over," Mr. Johnson was saying.

"What about lye throwers?" I asked. "They gone too?"

"Oh pshaw, boy. Tossing lye ain't nothing. It's a sensible and respectable way to fight, if you ask me. It's better than going at it with knives and razors, ain't it?"

I wandered over to a corner of the room where Obie was orating. "I got fren's that'll give me two, three hundred thousand dollars to give to that refugee downstairs to buy this place for keeps," he said. "I got me some good white fren's and they ain't gonna let no poor white trash like Columbia put out a bunch of good Black folks like we is." Obie's eyes flashed almost maniacal fires of belief. "I mean exactly what I say. And I knows gangsters too, whut my boy knows, and they'll set up machine guns down in that lobby if I tells 'em to and blow Columbia's ass to high hell." All of his listeners nodded righteously. It was the kind of fairy tale they loved to hear. Several pint bottles were pushed at Obie.

I sat down at an empty card table and wondered if God won't help these outcasts any more than He had helped me. I didn't have enough nerve to tell myself that God didn't give a damn, but I became blue as hell. And what made me so damn down was that these people were not in just an American racial battle. This battle was age old. It was the elite swallowing up the little ones. It was slum clearance in its highest ideals. It was to the victor belong the spoils. So finally I guess it was just as American as Spiro was Greek.

I remember that once the Sinman had called Columbia a brainless dreadnaught of higher education. Maybe he was exactly right. Columbia not only did not know what it was doing, but at bottom it also had no brain that could be dealt with, no feelings to work on. Yeah, the Sinman was always right. Like there was no room in New York for his defeated Black army.

The next morning I walked into J&J's room and was instantly made sick to my stomach. I never saw anybody look like these two looked. Neither spoke, only nodding a good morning. Jinny poured me a drink, but she was still silent and I was filled with a futile anger. It was just as if some power had come into this room and destroyed both of J&J's spirits. The fear and defeat on their faces was total. Then Suzie came in from the bathroom. She actually looked wasted, the picture of death, but it wasn't exactly her death. It was somebody else who had died. Not Suzie, not quite.

Suzie didn't speak either, but she stared at me. It was a funny stare, full of fear and a rage at me for having showed up in this room. Maybe that stare would have fazed me more if the once beautiful amazon had not looked so suddenly shriveled and stooped.

"What the hell is going on here?" I exclaimed.

"Nothing," Jinny said. And then there was more silence.

"You all look like you've seen a ghost and that ghost spoke to you," I said at last. "Now there ain't nothing in the world to be this scared of. Why, the goddam atom bomb don't call for the way you all are acting."

A little scream broke loose from Suzie's lips and she flung herself face downward on the bed, sobs racking her body.

Joey got up from her chair by the window and poured some more Spur in our glasses. "I don't see no harm in telling Sid," she said slowly.

"No!" Suzie shrieked.

Joey sat on the bed beside her and put a hand on her shoulder. "After all, Suzie," she said, "Sid's no dummy. Mebbe he can think of something we ain't thought of."

"No," Suzie sobbed. I figured maybe she had killed Harold, but J&J and the Logan didn't treat murder with all this fuss.

"You can't go on this way," Jinny said in a voice that pleaded. "Please let us tell Sid what happened, Suzie. And like Joey said: Sid's no dummy. Maybe he *can* help us."

Suzie said nothing, but she did nod her head in the pillow.

"Well, it's like this, Sid," Jinny said. "Suzie had to go to the bathroom late last night, and the toilet seat in 1-D where she lives was all messed up so she had to come out in the lobby and cross over to 1-A's toilet. You know. Well, when she comes out again here comes some of the Kingfish's men, dragging a man who is bleeding like a stuck pig. And right behind them comes two girls, down on their knees with rags, wiping up all the blood the man is spilling. They all goes on out the front door, with the women still mopping up while Suzie just stands there like a dumb cluck. Then the women come back and tells Suzie that if they hears one day word about this from anybody they are going to kill Suzie and Harold too. Dig it?"

Yeah, I dug. It was one of the old games Logan tenants had to play. Gangsters. You know, it's not that they should take violence off TV because of what it'll do to little white kids or Black ones but it should be taken off because of what it does to grown black-assed niggers. Junkies, high as a kite, threatening an innocent young woman, just like on TV. And the black-assed woman has to play her part and be scared to death.

Then I brought my anger and contempt down out of the air and back to reality. Maybe the acting was false, but the fear in this room was real. It was a damned sight more real than the fear of a cracker that a black dick is gonna get his daughter's cherry. And who's gonna say that his fear isn't as real as they come?

Yeah, J&J and Suzie were taking their roles seriously, and while I was thinking about it, how could anybody tell that some simple-assed junkies wouldn't play their roles for real too?

So I went ahead and played my role. I was supposed to be the cool and calming brain. "But she and Harold don't have anything to worry about," I said. "She's not going to tell the cops. In fact, if she's smart, she won't even tell Harold. And the cops aren't going to ask questions too tough. Was the guy Black or white?"

"White and deader than hell," Jinny said. "I went down and looked at him where they had laid him out in front of the hotel. It was after five in the morning when Suzie woke us up."

"This Black pig gotta go investigate everything!" Joey yelled.

"What was there to be ascared of?" Jinny asked. "You don't think the junkies would be standing around inspecting their handiwork, do you?"

"So?"

"If the sonofabitch got up and walked away we wouldn't be in here worrying our heads off now," Jinny said.

"As far as I can see, there is nothing to do but to forget it," I said. "This is the Logan and nobody asks many tough questions around the Logan. All Suzie has to do is go about her business as usual."

"No," Jinny said. "Columbia's got the heat on us. Ginsburg, the junkies, everybody. They're going to eat this up. And those police are going to find out who did this one, if you know what I mean. This one is for real."

"So, all the more reason why those junkies are not going to risk killing another person," I said, but I knew that these three women were mesmerized. Deep down inside they even wanted it this way. Even if it meant dying they still wanted it this way because dying was more vital than living in the Logan.

"But Suzie is hysterical," Jinny said. "Right now she thinks that the junkies didn't kill her because they want her to lead them back to her room so they can kill Harold too."

"Just like the junkies don't know which room everybody lives in and the exact value of everything in it," I said.

"But, Sid . . ." Jinny began.

"She don't lead them to Harold, but she leads them up to you, eh?" I said.

Only Jinny got the message. But her eyes twinkled and I knew that she had suddenly realized that it was all a game . . . maybe.

"Gloria's got a room she never sleeps in," I said slowly.

"No!" Suzie shrieked.

"She'd never stay there alone," Jinny said.

"Well, Suzie's having a nervous breakdown," I said. "This is an emergency. Let's take her to the emergency ward. You know, if we play it right they'll ship her right up to Clark #8. And that joint stays locked. Just like a jail. The junkies couldn't get in there at her."

"Go out on Amsterdam Avenue and get us a taxi, Sid," Jinny commanded. "Get him to wait there. We'll leave this room in exactly ten minutes. Ten minutes is long enough for you to hail a cab this time of day."

I got the cab, and while J&J and Suzie sat in the waiting room of the emergency ward I went up to Clark #8 and asked to speak to Dr. Balsam. Now maybe I haven't told you this, but Maria Balsam is all woman. And you've got to be a woman to be a good psychiatrist. I don't think she ever gave a thought to a Harlem S.R.O. and the games that go on in them, but she was a woman and immediately got the picture I tried to draw for her. She came down to emergency with me and pulled a few ropes and in no time at all she had Suzie safely upstairs in Clark #8.

We went directly back to the Logan to see Harold.

"Suzie can stay gone," Harold growled after J&J had told their story.

"What's the matter, Harold?" Jinny asked.

"Any time a woman don't show no more respect for her man

than that bitch did, then she don't deserve no man," Harold said. "She must think I'm a pussy for real."

"It was her woman's instinct, Harold," Joey said. "She was protecting you the only way she knew how."

"The poor thing was so scared she couldn't think straight at all," Jinny said. "Animal instinct told her what to do."

"The hell with Suzie," Harold said.

I studied Harold's face. It was the first time I had ever seen him. He was big and looked to be as much a man as Suzie was a woman. He looked mean, but what I saw in his face was fear. Pure fear like only a Black coward knows it. The junkies had already been in to talk with Harold, I thought, and all Harold wants to do is to wash his hands of Suzie. He probably wanted to blame Suzie for having to take a leak late at night.

But J&J worked on Harold in relays, and in about an hour they did manage to get him to promise to see Suzie.

I was certain that Harold had only agreed to go to get rid of J&J. That man wasn't going near St. Luke's.

And so I was not able to keep myself from saying, "There's no need to talk to him any more. Once he gets up to Clark #8 and finds out he don't have to be scared no more he'll be wanting Suzie back so he can kick her ass as usual."

I didn't give a damn. Harold glared, but big as he was I was going to do my best to kill him if he made one move. Because it's like Blind Charlie says, it's not how you live in this world, it's how you die. And that's where it's at right now.

After that we went up to the rec room. Everyone present had long faces and were as angry as a crowd of lynchers.

"Why somebody got to go kill somebody right in front of our doorstep?" Mr. Johnson kept saying.

"Yeah," Joey said. "The cops is gonna swear somebody in here did it."

"And them cops already said they didn't like it," somebody said. "That man was in a fight and there was supposed to be blood all over the sidewalk and things, but there was only this little bit of blood in one little spot. Next thing you know, they's gonna be claiming he was kilt inside the Logan and then was drugged out there in the street."

"I bet that Kingfish had something to do with it," a little old woman said, but somebody slapped her and she shut up. . . .

CHAPTER 28

TO SLEEP BESIDE A WOMAN as lushly taunting as Gloria is one thing. And to know that she'll immediately turn to an iceberg in your arms is another. But to know that even if this was not so you still are too full of wine and tranquilizers to do the job is pure murder.

I was going to flip soon and for real; but what could I do about it? Sure, I had received an ultimatum. But this was an ultimatum that defeated you in all respects. If I turned pussy and joined up with some group of wild-eyed Blacks, who I didn't even think were sane, Gloria would eventually despise me for being pussy. And both the keystone and touchstone of Gloria's love for me were built on her respect for me. There was absolutely no out for me.

Impossible as it seems, one day I really brooded more than usual over my plight. I drank a lot that day; it was either Checkday or the day after, I'm not sure. But anyhow, when I came in that night Gloria was already home. Serene, aloof, impregnable. But I was nearing the end of the line. Gloria had to talk to me tonight. She was going to converse with me even if I had to choke words out of her by the syllable.

"Have you started screwing your Black warriors again?" I asked just for starters.

"What do you think?"

"You're not screwing me so what else is there to think?"

"Imagine that."

"Can't you say more than two goddam words at a time?"

"From the very first time you came out of St. Luke's I promised myself that I'd never let my body betray you again. Is that enough?"

"No. And I suppose you're gonna get real slick now and tell me that I went and betrayed myself."

"It *is* the truth."

"Well, why do you keep on sleeping with me? You're not broke. You got a room. Why stay here and taunt me?"

You know, something came into Gloria's eyes then, and so help me I could read them like the Bible. She was ready to capitulate. Right there in her eyes she was ready to give up. From now on she was ready to be my whore. Yeah. I don't know what it really meant she intended to do for me. But the war was over.

"One of these days you're gonna need me, Sid. You're gonna need the heart a Black Nationalist's got. And I'll never forgive myself if I let you down again. You needed me when Crazy Mary had you by the nuts, and I was off somewheres where I didn't have to be. But next time it'll be different. Why don't you take your tranquilizers and go to sleep?"

"I take my pills when I'm supposed to. What's the matter? I seem crazier than usual tonight to you?"

"Forget it, Sid. Just forget I said it. It's been so long since we really talked I guess I don't know what to say."

"It's you won't talk. Not me."

"I know."

I was a drowning man. Once I had been the brother, father and lover of this god-awfully beautiful girl, and now here I was, drowning in her slime of total uncaring. This girl had had three separate and distinct loves for me, and look at me now. Then just like that I got sick and tired of all that drowning crap. I swam to shore and climbed up on the beach.

"Gloria," I said. "I want to get in this bed with you and hold you in my arms and we talk and talk until every single little thing is all smoothed out between us. I don't want to live another minute like we've been doing to each other. I need you the old way. You say—at least you used to say—that you needed me around to ask me questions. Well, Gloria, I need for you to *ask* me questions a damned sight more than you need me around. I need you. I need your love and interest. It's like you're cutting my balls off when you don't ask my advice any more." For the first time since hearing of Sandy's death I poured a drink of Gloria's scotch and drank it. And it was like the blood of life that flowed down my throat. Everything was all right. I put out my hand. "Let's both get down on our knees and beg each other's pardon for what we've done and said to each other."

Gloria had her back to me, but she turned and stared and then smiled. She dropped to her knees and crawled over to my feet. I stooped to get down. The extension phone in the hallway rang three times. It was the signal from the office that I had a phone call.

I don't know why I got up off my knees. That ringing phone was like a whirlpool that sucked me in and away from Gloria. In my whole life I don't think I ever received a phone call that I can really now say was important, but yet something took me away from the girl of my life and had me answering a stupid telephone.

"This is the Sinman, Sid. How are you? I have a visitor who is anxious to see you."

"Sharlee?" I asked.

"Yes."

"Is it too late to come down there now?"

"No, but she wants to come to your place."

"I don't want her to come to my place," I said. "Gloria's here. I just can't ask her to leave right now, but I can come to your place for a few minutes."

"Sharlee is despondent. A tragic blow. Can't you possibly come down right away?"

He made me kind of irritable. "I already said I could come down," I told him. "I've been tossing them back all day pretty strong, but I'm dead sober now. Give me your address again so I won't have to go looking through my things to find it."

Sinman gave me his address and then hung up. I went back in the room and there was Gloria still on her knees. And those eyes of hers which are always moist-looking were now wet. I sat down beside her on the floor.

"Was that Sharlee?"

"No," I said. "What made you think so?"

"I got her on my mind, I guess. I been thinking maybe she could help me to make you leave that damned wine alone. I wish she would show up."

"It was the Sinman. He gave me a message from Sharlee. He said she needs me. Do you mind?"

Gloria took my hand and kissed it, then she rubbed it over her breasts and then down below. "You can never hurt me again, Sid. My love for you won't let you. I'm not worried."

And as if to prove it she got up and got her pocketbook and took a twenty-dollar bill out of it. She held it out to me, smiling proudly.

Since I had a twenty-dollar bill and had forgot to ask the Sinman which block he lived in I took a taxi instead of a subway. The cab pulled in front of a house that had a high front porch. I had often passed it when I lived on Forty-seventh Street at the Rex. I got out and paid the driver and started up the steps, feeling good as hell because I knew that Gloria and I had finally made it and this visit of Sharlee's was going to act as some kind of clincher to the deal.

Blind Charlie was sitting on the top step. His face was buried in his arms and by the way his shoulders sagged I could tell that he was crying. I laughed out loud. "Goddam, man. It's cold out here and you ain't got nothing better to do than get a crying jag on and sit out here?"

Blind Charlie only shook his head. I would have spent a couple of more seconds with him, but Sharlee was waiting and I could hear the strains of the Sinman's organ coming through the open front door of the house. I went in and followed the organ notes. On the first-floor hallway there was another door ajar and I pushed it open and saw the Sinman. It was only then that I realized that the Sinman was playing his unfinished symphony. But suddenly it sounded finished to me. I don't know why, but it was different. And though it seemed entirely inappropriate for the arrival of Sharlee, the thing did have the vigor of a new day as every now and then a blue note of truth came across.

Sinman's face was drawn as if he might have needed a fix. Then I saw Sharlee. She was lying on the couch. Her eyes were closed and I wondered if it was another one of her little acts. She looked unbelievably virginal in a gray tweed skirt and a pink cashmere sweater. Yeah. "Virginal" was the only word for Sharlee. Like her tits barely showed through the sweater even if there was a whole lot of hidden sex in her pose.

I turned to the Sinman. "She asleep when you called?" I asked.

"No. She was awake when I left her, but she is dead now. An OD while I was out to the phone. I wiped the foam from her lips. I think she committed suicide. I'm almost sure she did."

I sank to the floor in a sitting position halfway between the Sinman and Sharlee. Then I braced myself and tried to get up to go to Sharlee, but there was something besides the weakness in my legs that would not let me go. Like I was not wanted. After all, Sharlee had made a decision and done what she thought best. She had decided that further talk with Sid Bailey would not release her from the jail of her beauty. In her final moments she had known that I was nothing.

In a few moments my voice came back to me and I said, "You should have called the police. Did you?" Then I remembered that the Sinman was an addict who sold heroin. "I'll call them," I said, scrambling to my feet. "I will say that Sharlee was with me. I'll say, like you did, that I went out to make a phone call and when I came back Sharlee was dead. You go out and sit with Blind Charlie. Which way do I go to a telephone?"

Sinman began to play and then he began to talk. It was strange how he spoke in the rhythm of his music. "Sharlee found a woman to love. She looked like Aunt Jemima, but Sharlee found in her all the things she could not find in us men. They lived happily together in western Pennsylvania. The woman's name was Dorthula.

"Dorthula was a successful businesswoman. Beauty parlor, restaurant and real estate. And she was a devout churchwoman. Baptist. She died four days ago. Dorthula's family was ashamed of Sharlee. And they could not bear the thought of how depraved it would make Dorthula look if her beautiful mistress was to weep at the funeral. So they gave Sharlee the money to come to New York. Sharlee had to take it, or thought she had to. She had never asked Dorthula for any money and so she had none. She went by the funeral parlor to bid Dorthula farewell and then came to New York in search of us. . . ."

"How did she find you?"

"She went to my connections. She followed the grapevine. It was not hard for a girl like Sharlee to do."

Sinman suddenly pressed down on the keyboard with all his strength and the room was filled with the blasts of discordant notes. I waved my hands hysterically. What was he trying to do, make his neighbors send for the police before I could call them?

Sinman got up from the organ and went over to sit beside Sharlee. "I want you to take care of things," he said. He bent over and kissed her. After that he went to the hutch cabinet and took out a thick sheaf of money. "There is enough here to pay for a dozen funerals," he said, "but Sharlee and I want no funerals. We simply wish to be buried side by side." From his pocket he took a business card and handed it to me. "My lawyer," he said. "But he's white. After we are buried in that cemetery on Staten Island I want you to notify him. He will know what else to do. Only after we are buried side by side are you to contact him."

The paralyzing horror of it was surpassed by the realization that the Sinman was one of the truly indomitable ones. More so than Blind Charlie. But in my own weakness I cried out, "She screwed me! She screwed Blind Charlie! And she died over a goddam stud bitch. Can't you understand that?"

Sinman smiled and sighed. "Where Sharlee led, I followed; it was never a matter of choice. But I was happy. I am happy now."

"You're high! That goddam heroin has you so fucked up you don't know nothing. How could you know anything?"

Sinman put out his hand, but I would not take it. Never.

"Strangely enough, you are the only person to whom I can turn to do exactly as Sharlee and I wish," Sinman said. "I tried to shape you another way, but it is you I must kneel to now.

"And when you and Charlie get sober, finish that book of yours.

It will be the only victory over the Logan. Kiss Gloria good-by, and take care of her gently; she is the only woman in the world for you."

On the organ was a leather case. The Sinman opened it. I saw the hypodermic and the little packets of heroin, and there was some Doriden too. I ran out of the room. On the porch I stopped and grasped Charlie's arm. He stood up and let me guide him down the steps. On the sidewalk I gave him my shoulder. And we walked toward Broadway.

And as we went I silently preached Sharlee's eulogy. The world had sinned against her; we called her a goddess, something a whole lot less than God; we had trampled her in a rage to destroy her otherworldliness. And yet she had risen from beneath our feet to lead us with an eerie dispassion; personally guiding me through my maze, through my own hell to reach Gloria's side. Sharlee's body and soul had been a kind of beacon that had picked out and illumined the eternal Black femininity of Gloria in the bleak landscape.

That Knowledge gave me the strength to look deeper into the dark glass: I saw that Sinman and Sharlee had *always* been God's untouchables—His beautiful ones, succored by a beautiful narcotic. While I, and my ugliness, enmeshed in my mean wine, was of no consequence in their world. Irrelevant. The key was to remember that God had taken them and not me and Charlie. So I would bury them. Now if only God knew how to bury His dead. . . .

Charlie's strong left arm was pushing me implacably ahead. I felt a rush of fear. I was almost sprinting now, as if the world was hurtling me into a void.

"Where the hell you running so fast?" Charlie roared. His sound was a thing of beauty. And once more I knew where it was at.

"I promised a fox I'd be there . . ."

My fears were gone and I hurried on into the sudden comfort of the night; away from our dead loved ones. Ahead of me loomed the vision of my newborn child, who would grow to be my constant whore of a manuscript; the relentess womanhood of Gloria; and the pulsing harbor of more life which is God's sole reality.

"Now you walking, boy. Keep on, boy. Keep right on . . ."

Webster's New World™ Dictionary

Fourth Edition

MICHAEL AGNES
Editor in Chief

POCKET BOOKS
New York London Toronto Sydney

POCKET BOOKS, a division of Simon & Schuster, Inc.
1230 Avenue of the Americas, New York, NY 10020

Webster's New World™ Dictionary, Pocket Books Paperback Edition

Published by arrangement with Wiley Publishing, Inc.

ISBN: 0-7434-7069-9

First Pocket Books printing of this revised edition July 2003

10 9 8 7 6 5

Dictionary Editorial offices:
New World Dictionaries
850 Euclid Avenue
Cleveland, OH 44114

Manufactured in the United States of America

FOREWORD

This new Pocket Books paperback dictionary is based on the acclaimed *Webster's New World College Dictionary, Fourth Edition*, published in 1999. It is a completely new work: the previous paperback edition was published in 1990 and revised in 1995. As were all previous editions, it has been edited for readers who need a reliable, up-to-date, portable dictionary for use in the home, at school, or in the office.

The dictionary offers broad coverage of idiomatic expressions, supplements definitions with many helpful illustrative phrases, and provides brief but helpful usage labels and etymologies. Every entry has been designed to enhance the reader's understanding of current meanings and connotations. This dictionary reflects the expertise of Webster's New World staff lexicographers, who have a combined 150 years of experience in editing dictionaries.

This latest edition includes comprehensive coverage of changes in the political structure of Europe and Africa during the past decade and thousands of new terms in the rapidly changing vocabulary of American English. These terms range from technical terminology to slang and include *anti-lock*, *bandwidth*, *balsamic vinegar*, *bipolar*, *broadband*, *HTML*, *microbrewery*, *no-brainer*, *reboot*, *sport utility vehicle*, *up to speed*, *warp speed*, *World Wide Web*, and many others.

Every reader is encouraged to read the Guide to the Use of the Dictionary, which begins on page *v*. It gives a clear explanation of how to access the wealth of information stored within the dictionary's entries.

MICHAEL AGNES
Editor in Chief

JONATHAN L. GOLDMAN
ANDREW N. SPARKS
Project Editors

WEBSTER'S NEW WORLD DICTIONARY STAFF

GUIDE TO THE USE OF THE DICTIONARY

I. GUIDE WORDS

The two GUIDE WORDS at the top of each page indicate the alphabetical range of entries on that page. The first and last main entry words on a page serve as the GUIDE WORDS.

II. THE MAIN ENTRY WORD

A. Arrangement of Entries—All main entries, including single words, hyphenated and unhyphenated compounds, proper names, prefixes, suffixes, combining forms, and abbreviations, are listed in strict alphabetical order and are set in large boldface type.

a[2] (ə; *stressed,* ā) ***adj.*** ...
a[3] *abbrev.* **1** about **2** ...
a-[2] *prefix* ...
aard·vark (ärd′värk′) ***n.*** ...
Aar·on (er′ən) ***n.*** *Bible* ...
AB[1] (ā′bē′) ***n.*** a blood type
AB[2] *abbrev.* **1** Alberta (Canada) **2** ...
ab- ⟦L⟧ *prefix* ...
a·back (ə bak′) ***adv.*** [Archaic] backward; back — **taken aback** ...

In biographical entries only the last, or family, name is used in alphabetization; but when two or more persons have the same family name, they appear within the entry block in alphabetical order by first names.

John·son (jän′sən) **1 An·drew** ... **2 Lyn·don Baines** ...**3 Samuel** ...

Biographical and geographical names that are spelled the same way are given separate entry blocks.

Idiomatic phrases after a main entry are also listed alphabetically within each group.

fly[1] (flī) ***vi.*** ... —**let fly (at)** ... —**on the fly** ...

B. Alternative Spellings and Variant Forms—When different spellings of a word are some distance apart alphabetically, the definition appears with the spelling most frequently used, and the other spellings are cross-referred to this entry. If two commonly used alternative spellings are alphabetically close to each other, they appear as a joint boldface entry, but the order of entry does not necessarily indicate that the form entered first is "more correct" or is preferred.

the·a·ter or **the·a·tre** (thē′ə tər) ***n.*** ...

If an alternative spelling is alphabetically close to the prevailing spelling, it is given at the end of the entry block in small boldface.

cook′ie ***n.*** ...: also **cook′y,** *pl.* **–ies** ...

C. Cross-references—When an entry is cross-referred to another term that has the same meaning but is more frequently used, the entry cross-referred to is usually set in small capitals.

an·aes·the·sia ... ***n.*** ANESTHESIA ...

D. Homographs—Main entries that are spelled alike but are different in meaning and origin, such as **bat** (a club), **bat** (the animal), and **bat** (to wink), have separate entry blocks and are marked by superscript numbers following the boldface spelling.

bat[1] ... ***n.*** ...
bat[2] ... ***n.*** ...
bat[3] ... ***vt.*** ...

E. Foreign Terms—Foreign words and phrases occurring with some frequency in English, but not completely naturalized, are set in boldface italic type. This is a signal to the user of the dictionary to print these terms in italics or underline them in writing.

bon·jour (bōn zhōōr′) ***interj., n.*** [[Fr]] ...

F. Prefixes, Suffixes, & Combining Forms—Prefixes and initial combining forms have a hyphen at the end.

hemi- ... *prefix* half ...

Suffixes and terminal combining forms have a hyphen at the beginning.

-a·ble ... *suffix* **1** that can or will ...

The abundance of these forms, whose syllabification and pronunciation can be determined from the words containing them, makes it possible for the reader to understand and pronounce many complex terms not entered in the dictionary but formed with affixes and words that are entered.

G. Word Division—Boldface entry words are divided into syllables that are separated by either a center dot or a stress mark.

gen′er·a′tor
in′ter·me′di·ar′y

For information regarding stress marks, see the GUIDE TO PRONUNCIATION.

III. PRONUNCIATION

The handling of pronunciations in this dictionary is explained in the GUIDE TO PRONUNCIATION, which follows this general guide.

IV. PART-OF-SPEECH LABELS

This dictionary gives part-of-speech labels, in boldface italic type, for most main entry words that are solid or hyphenated forms. Labels are not given to prefixes, suffixes, combining forms, trademarks and service marks, abbreviations, and biographical and geographical entries.

Here are the part-of-speech labels used in this dictionary:

n.	noun
pl.n.	plural noun
sing.n.	singular noun
fem.n.	feminine noun
masc.n.	masculine noun
pron.	pronoun
v.	verb
vt.	transitive verb
vi.	intransitive verb
v.aux.	auxiliary verb
v.impersonal	impersonal verb
adj.	adjective
adv.	adverb
prep.	preposition
conj.	conjunction
interj.	interjection
definite article	
indefinite article	
possessive pronominal adj.	

When an entry word is used as more than one part of speech, long dashes introduce each separate part-of-speech label.

round ... ***adj.*** ... —***n.*** ... —***vt.*** ... —***vi.*** ... —***adv.*** ... —***prep.*** ...

Sometimes an entry has two or more part-of-speech labels separated by commas, with a definition or cross-reference that is understood to apply to all parts of speech.

des·patch ... ***vt., n.*** DISPATCH

V. INFLECTED FORMS

This dictionary shows three types of inflected forms: plurals of nouns, principal parts of verbs, and comparative and superlative forms of adjectives and adverbs.

Only inflected forms regarded as irregular or offering difficulty in spelling are entered. They appear in boldface immediately after the part-of-speech label. They are shortened where possible, and syllabified and pronounced where necessary.

cit·y ... ***n.,*** *pl.* **-ies** ...
hap·py ... ***adj.*** **-pi·er, -pi·est** ...
an'a·lyze' ... ***vt.*** **-lyzed', -lyz'ing** ...

Plurals: This dictionary does not show regular plurals:

1) formed by adding *-s* to the singular (**cats**)
2) formed by adding *-es* to a singular that ends with *s, x, z,* and *sh* (**boxes** or **bushes**)
3) formed by adding *-es* to a singular that ends with *ch* when *ch* is pronounced [ch] (**churches**) and by adding *-s* when *ch* is pronounced [k] (**stomachs**)

Principal Parts: This dictionary does not show principal parts when:

1) the past tense and past participle are formed by simply adding *-ed* to the infinitive (**search/searched, talk/talked**)
2) the present participle is formed by simply adding *-ing* to the infinitive (**search/searching, talk/talking**)

If only two principal parts are shown, as at **love,** the first is both the past tense and the past participle (**loved**) and the second is the present participle (**loving**). If three principal parts are shown, as at **go,** the first is the past tense (**went**), the second is the past participle (**gone**), and the third is the present participle (**going**).

Comparatives & Superlatives: This dictionary does not show comparatives and superlatives formed by the simple addition of *-er* or *-est* to the base form (**tall/taller/tallest**).

VI. ETYMOLOGY

The etymology, or word history, appears inside open double brackets immediately before the definitions. The symbols and abbreviations used in the etymologies are found in the list immediately preceding page 1 of the dictionary proper.

di·shev·el ... ⟦< OFr *des-,* DIS- + *chevel,* hair⟧ ...

If the parts making up an entry word are obvious to the reader, no etymology appears at that entry.

VII. THE DEFINITIONS

A. ***Order of Senses***—In general, each entry lists meanings in historical order; the standard, general senses of a word appear first. Informal, slang, etc. senses come next. Technical senses preceded by field labels, such as *Astron.* or *Chem.,* follow in alphabetical order.

B. ***Numbering & Grouping of Senses***—Senses are numbered consecutively within a part of speech in boldface numerals. Where a primary sense of a word is subdivided into several closely related meanings, those meanings are preceded by italicized letters.

flat[1] ... ***adj.*** ... **1** having ... **2** lying ... **10** *Music a*) lower ... *b*) below —***adv.*** ... —***n.*** **1** anything ... **2** ... **3** *Music a*) a note ... *b*) the symbol ... —***vt.*** ... —***vi.*** ...

C. ***Capitalization***—If a main entry word is capitalized in all its senses, the entry word itself begins with a capital letter. If a capitalized main entry word has a sense or senses that are not capitalized, these are marked with the corresponding small-boldface, lowercase letter followed by a short dash and enclosed in brackets.

Pu·ri·tan ... ***n.*** ... **1** ... **2** [**p-**] ...

If a lowercase main entry word has a meaning or meanings that are capitalized, they are marked with the corresponding small-boldface, uppercase letter followed by a short dash and enclosed in brackets.

left[1] ... —*n.* **1** ... **2** [*often* **L-**] ...

In some of these usage notes, a self-explanatory qualifying word may be added.

D. Plural Forms—In a singular noun entry, the designation "[*pl.*]" (or "[*often pl.*]," "[*usually pl.*]," etc.) before a definition indicates that it is (or *often, usually,* etc. is) the plural form of the entry word that has the meaning given in the definition.

look ... *vi.* ... —*n.* **1** ... **2** ... **3** [Inf.] *a*) [*usually pl.*] appearance *b*) [*pl.*] personal appearance ...

If a plural is used as a singular with a singular verb, the designation [*with sing. v.*] is added.

E. Verbs Followed by Prepositions or Objects—In many cases, one or more specific prepositions follow a particular verb in general use. This dictionary shows this either by including the preposition in the definition, italicized and usually enclosed in parentheses, or by adding a note after the definition giving the particular prepositions associated with that definition of the verb.

In definitions of transitive verbs, the specific or generalized object of the verb, where given, is enclosed in parentheses, since the object is not grammatically part of the definition of the verb.

F. Illustrative Examples—Phrases or sentences containing the entry word and showing how it is used in context are enclosed in italic brackets. The word being illustrated is set in italics within its phrase or sentence.

a·cross ... *adv.* ... —*prep.* **1**... **2** ... **3** into contact with by chance *[*to come *across* an old friend*]*

VIII. USAGE LABELS

People use language in different ways depending on differences in geographic location, age, education, and employment; people's individual language usage varies also according to the situation they are in or their purpose in speaking or writing. The usage labels used in this dictionary are listed below, with an explanation of each.

Informal: The word or meaning is widely used in everyday talk, personal letters, etc., but not in formal speaking or writing. Abbreviated *Inf.*

Slang: The word or meaning is not generally considered standard usage but is used, even by the best speakers and writers, in very informal situations or for creating special effects. People belonging to a certain group often use their own slang terms.

Old Informal, Old Slang: The word or meaning was informal or slang when regularly used in the recent past and is not used much today.

Obsolete: The word or meaning is no longer used but occurs in earlier writings. Abbreviated *Obs.*

Archaic: The word or meaning is not used in ordinary speech or writing today but occurs in certain special situations such as church ritual and in older books.

Old-fashioned: The word or meaning is not yet considered archaic but seems out-of-date.

Rare: The word or meaning has never been in general use.

Now Rare: The word or meaning is not used much today but was in general use in the past.

Historical: The word or meaning refers to something that no longer exists and for which there is not a modern term.

Old Poetic: The word or meaning was often used in the past, especially in poetry, but is used today only in certain kinds of traditional or somewhat old-fashioned poetry. Abbreviated *Old Poet.*

Literary: The word or meaning is regarded as having an elevated, polished, highly formal quality.

Dialect: The word or meaning is used regularly only in certain geographical areas. When a word or meaning is used mainly in some specific area of the U.S., a more specific label, such as *South* or *Northwest,* appears. Abbreviated *Dial.*

British: The word or meaning is used mainly in Great Britain and also, usually, in the other English-speaking regions of the world outside the U.S. Abbreviated *Brit.*

Canadian (or *Irish,* etc.)*:* The word or meaning is used mainly in Canada (or Ireland, etc.). Abbreviated *Cdn.*, etc.

In addition to the above usage labels, supplementary information often appears in a short note after the definition, indicating that a word or meaning is used in an insulting, familiar, ironic, humorous, or other way.

IX. RUN-IN DERIVED ENTRIES

It is possible in English to create an almost infinite number of derived forms simply by adding certain prefixes and suffixes to the base word. The editors have included as many of these common derived words as space permitted, as run-in entries in boldface type—but only when the meaning of such words is immediately clear from the meanings of the base words and the affixes.

Thus, **greatness** and **liveliness** are run in at the end of the entries for **great** and **lively;** the suffix **-ness** is found as a separate entry meaning "state, quality, or instance of being." Many words formed with common suffixes, such as **-able**, **-er**, **-less**, **-like**, **-ly**, and **-tion**, are similarly treated as run-in entries with the base word from which they are derived. All such entries are syllabified and either accented to show stress in pronunciation or, where necessary, pronounced in full or in part.

When a derived word has a meaning or meanings different from those that can be deduced from the sum of its parts, it has been entered separately, pronounced, and fully defined (see **folder**).

GUIDE TO PRONUNCIATION

I. PRONUNCIATION STYLE

Pronunciations are provided as needed. Pronunciations are given in parentheses immediately after the boldface entry word:

mil·len·ni·um (mi len′ē əm)

Pronunciations have sometimes been shortened so as to cover only a particular part of the entry word, generally the part most likely to cause confusion or difficulty. Hyphens are used to indicate which part of the pronunciation is not shown.

home′stead′ (-sted′)

More than one pronunciation is sometimes given. Each variant pronunciation may be regarded as having wide currency in American English unless a qualifying note has been added to a particular variant indicating that it is less common. Variants may be also qualified with respect to particular grammatical usage.

av·o·ca·do (av′ə kä′dō, ä′və-)

ex·cuse (ek skyo͞oz′; *for n.*, -skyo͞os′)

This dictionary does not attempt to cover all pronunciations of a given word and does not indicate differences arising out of various regional dialects.

II.. PRONUNCIATION KEY

The Pronunciation Key lists the pronunciation symbols used in this dictionary along with several Key Words. Key Words are short, familiar words that illustrate each of the various sounds represented by the symbols.

PRONUNCIATION KEY

Vowel Sounds

Symbol	Key Words
a	at, cap, parrot
ā	ape, play, sail
ä	cot, father, heart
e	ten, wealth, merry
ē	even, feet, money
i	is, stick, mirror
ī	ice, high, sky
ō	go, open, tone
ô	all, law, horn
oo	could, look, pull
yoo	cure, furious
o͞o	boot, crew, tune
yo͞o	cute, few, use
oi	boy, oil, royal
ou	cow, out, sour
u	mud, ton, blood, trouble
ʉ	her, sir, word
ə	ago, agent, collect, focus
′l	cattle, paddle
′n	sudden, sweeten

Consonant Sounds

Symbol	Key Words
b	bed, table, rob
d	dog, middle, sad
f	for, phone, cough
g	get, wiggle, dog
h	hat, hope, ahead
hw	which, white
j	joy, badge, agent
k	kill, cat, quiet
l	let, yellow, ball
m	meet, number, time
n	net, candle, ton
p	put, sample, escape
r	red, wrong, born
s	sit, castle, office
t	top, letter, cat
v	voice, every, love
w	wet, always, quart
y	yes, canyon, onion
z	zoo, misery, rise
ch	chew, nature, punch
sh	shell, machine, bush
th	thin, nothing, truth
th	then, other, bathe
zh	beige, measure, seizure
ŋ	ring, anger, drink

III.. FOREIGN SOUNDS

A number of foreign words are entered in the dictionary. An approximation of the native pronunciation—typically French or Spanish in this dictionary—has been provided. Foreign pronunciations use sounds not generally found in English, and, therefore, some additional pronunciation symbols are required. Below is a short explanation of these symbols.

à — Used in French; a sound between [a] as in *cat* and [ä] as in *cot*.

ë — Used in French; round the lips as though to say *oh* while pronouncing [e] as in *get*.

ö — Used chiefly in French; round the lips as though to say *oh* while pronouncing the sound [ā] as in *ate*.

ô Used in French, German, Spanish, etc.; round the lips loosely as though to say *aw* while pronouncing [u] as in *cut*.

ü Used in French and German; round the lips as though to say *oh* while pronouncing [ē] as in *meet*.

kh Used in German and Scots English; pronounce [k] while allowing the breath to escape in a stream, as in saying [h].

H Used in German; pronounce [sh] while keeping the tip of the tongue pointed downward.

n Used chiefly in French; this symbol indicates that the vowel sound preceding it is pronounced with air expelled through both the mouth and the nose.

r Pronounce [r] with a vibrating of the tip of the tongue in Spanish or Italian, or with a trilling of the uvula in French or German.

' Used in French to indicate that a final consonant is short and unvoiced or that a letter *e* is silent or nearly so.

y' Used in Russian; pronounce an unvoiced [y] immediately after pronouncing the preceding consonant.

IV. STRESS MARKS

Stress marks appear in the pronunciations and in boldface entry words that are not given full pronunciation. A heavy mark [′] after a syllable indicates that the syllable is spoken with the most force. A light mark [′] after a syllable indicates that the syllable is spoken with relatively less force. Syllables with no marking are given the least force.

dic·tion·ar·y (dik′shə ner′ē)

ABBREVIATIONS AND SYMBOLS USED IN THIS DICTIONARY

abbrev.	abbreviated, abbreviation	Ex.	example
adj.	adjective	exc.	except
adv.	adverb	F	Fahrenheit
Afr	African	fem.	feminine
Afrik	Afrikaans	Fl	Flemish
alt.	alternative	fol.	following entry
Am	American	Fr	French
AmInd	American Indian	ft.	foot, feet
AmSp	American Spanish	Gael	Gaelic
Anat.	Anatomy	Geol.	Geology
Anglo-Fr	Anglo-French	Geom.	Geometry
Ar	Arabic	Ger	German
Aram	Aramaic	Gmc	Germanic
Archit.	Architecture	Gr	Classical Greek
Austral.	Australian	Gram.	Grammar
Biol.	Biology	Haw	Hawaiian
Bot.	Botany	Heb	Hebrew
Brit	British	Hung	Hungarian
C	Celsius	IE	Indo-European
c.	century	i.e.	that is
c.	circa	in.	inch(es)
cap.	capital city	indic.	indicative
Cdn	Canadian	Inf., inf.	informal
Celt	Celtic	infl.	influenced
cf.	compare	intens.	intensive
Ch.	Church	interj.	interjection
Chem.	Chemistry	Ir	Irish
Chin	Chinese	It	Italian
compar.	comparative	Jpn	Japanese
Comput.	Computer Science	km	kilometer(s)
conj.	conjunction	L	Classical Latin
contr.	contraction (grammar)	lb.	pound(s)
Dan	Danish	lit.	literally
Dial., dial.	dialectal	LL	Late Latin
dim.	diminutive	LowG	Low German
Du	Dutch	m	meter(s)
E	eastern, English	masc.	masculine
EC	east central	Math.	Mathematics
Eccles.	Ecclesiastical	MDu	Middle Dutch
Educ.	Education	ME	Middle English
e.g.	for example	Mech.	Mechanics
Egypt	Egyptian	Med.	Medicine
Elec.	Electricity	met.	metropolitan
Eng	English	Mex	Mexican
Esk	Eskimo	MHG	Middle High German
esp.	especially	mi.	mile(s)
etc.	and the like	Mil.	Military

ML	Middle Latin
ModGr	Modern Greek
ModL	modern scientific Latin
Myth	Mythology
N	northern
n.	noun
Naut.	nautical usage
NC	north central
NE	northeastern
NormFr	Norman French
Norw	Norwegian
NW	northwestern
Obs., obs.	obsolete
occas.	occasionally
OE	Old English
OFr	Old French
OHG	Old High German
ON	Old Norse
orig.	origin, originally
OS	Old Saxon
OSlav	Old Church Slavonic
oz.	ounce(s)
pers.	person (grammar)
Pers	Persian
Photog.	Photography
pl.	plural
pl.n.	plural noun
Poet.	Poetic
Pol	Polish
pop.	population
Port	Portuguese
poss.	possessive
pp.	past participle
prec.	preceding entry
prep.	preposition
pres.	present tense
prob.	probably
pron.	pronoun
Prov	Provençal
prp.	present participle
pseud.	pseudonym
Psychol.	Psychology
pt.	past tense
R.C.Ch.	Roman Catholic Church
Rom.	Roman
Russ	Russian
S	southern
Sans	Sanskrit
SC	south central
Scand	Scandinavian
Scot	Scottish
SE	southeastern
sing.	singular
sing.n.	singular noun
Sp	Spanish
sp.	spelling, spelled
specif.	specifically
sq.	square
superl.	superlative
SW	southwestern
Swed	Swedish
Theol.	Theology
transl.	translated, translation
Turk	Turkish
ult.	ultimately
v.	verb
var.	variant
v.aux.	auxiliary verb
vi.	intransitive verb
VL	Vulgar Latin
vt.	transitive verb
W	western
WC	west central
WInd	West Indian
WWI	World War I
WWII	World War II

Symbols

<	derived from
?	uncertain or unknown
+	plus
&	and
°	degree

A

a[1] or **A** (ā) ***n.***, *pl.* **a's, A's** (āz) the first letter of the English alphabet

a[2] (ə; *stressed,* ā) ***adj., indefinite article*** ⟦< AN⟧ **1** one; one sort of **2** each; any one —***prep.*** per *[once a day]* Before words beginning with a consonant sound, *a* is used *[a child, a home, a uniform]* See AN

a[3] *abbrev.* **1** about **2** adjective **3** alto **4** answer

A[1] (ā) ***n.*** **1** a blood type **2** a grade indicating excellence **3** *Music* the sixth tone in the scale of C major

A[2] *abbrev.* **1** answer **2** April **3** *Baseball, Basketball* assist(s) **4** August

a-[1] ⟦< OE⟧ *prefix* **1** in, into, on, at, to *[ashore]* **2** in the act or state of *[asleep]*

a-[2] *prefix* **1** ⟦< OE⟧ up, out *[arise]* **2** ⟦< OE⟧ off, of *[akin]* **3** ⟦< Gr⟧ not, without *[amoral]*

AA *abbrev.* **1** Alcoholics Anonymous **2** Associate in (or of) Arts

aard·vark (ärd′värk′) ***n.*** ⟦Du, earth pig⟧ a nocturnal, ant-eating S African mammal

Aar·on (er′ən) ***n.*** *Bible* the first high priest of the Hebrews

AB[1] (ā′bē′) ***n.*** a blood type

AB[2] *abbrev.* **1** Alberta (Canada) **2** Bachelor of Arts: also **A.B.**

ab- ⟦L⟧ *prefix* away, from, from off, down *[abdicate]*

ABA *abbrev.* American Bar Association

a·back (ə bak′) ***adv.*** [Archaic] backward; back —**taken aback** startled and confused; surprised

ABACUS

ab·a·cus (ab′ə kəs) ***n.***, *pl.* **-cus·es** or **-ci′** (-sī′) ⟦< Gr *abax*⟧ a frame with sliding beads for doing arithmetic

a·baft (ə baft′) ***adv.*** ⟦< OE *on,* on + *be,* by + *æftan,* aft⟧ aft —***prep.*** *Naut.* behind

ab·a·lo·ne (ab′ə lō′nē) ***n.*** ⟦< AmInd⟧ an edible sea mollusk with an oval, somewhat spiral shell

a·ban·don (ə ban′dən) ***vt.*** ⟦< OFr *mettre a bandon,* to put under (another's) ban⟧ **1** to give up completely **2** to desert —***n.*** unrestrained activity; exuberance —**a·ban′don·ment** ***n.***

a·ban′doned ***adj.*** **1** deserted **2** shamefully wicked **3** unrestrained

a·base (ə bās′) ***vt.*** **a·based′, a·bas′ing** ⟦< ML *abassare,* to lower⟧ to humble —**a·base′ment** ***n.***

a·bash (ə bash′) ***vt.*** ⟦< OFr *es-,* intens. + *baer,* gape⟧ to make ashamed and uneasy; disconcert —**a·bash′ed·ly** ***adv.***

a·bate (ə bāt′) ***vt., vi.*** **a·bat′ed, a·bat′ing** ⟦< OFr *abattre,* beat down⟧ **1** to make or become less **2** *Law* to end —**a·bate′ment** ***n.***

ab·at·toir (ab′ə twär′) ***n.*** ⟦Fr: see prec.⟧ a slaughterhouse

ab·bé (a′bā) ***n.*** ⟦Fr: see ABBOT⟧ a French priest's title

ab·bess (ab′əs) ***n.*** ⟦see ABBOT⟧ a woman who heads a convent of nuns

ab·bey (ab′ē) ***n.*** **1** a monastery or convent **2** a church belonging to an abbey

ab·bot (ab′ət) ***n.*** ⟦< Aram *abbā,* father⟧ a man who heads a monastery

abbr or **abbrev** *abbrev.* **1** abbreviated **2** abbreviation

ab·bre·vi·ate (ə brē′vē āt′) ***vt.*** **-at′ed, -at′ing** ⟦< L *ad-,* to + *brevis,* brief⟧ to make shorter; esp., to shorten (a word) by omitting letters

ab·bre′vi·a′tion (-ā′shən) ***n.*** **1** a shortening **2** a shortened form of a word or phrase, as *Mr.* for *Mister*

ABC (ā′bē′sē′) ***n.***, *pl.* **ABC's** [*usually pl.*] **1** the alphabet **2** the basic elements (of a subject)

ab·di·cate (ab′di kāt′) ***vt., vi.*** **-cat′ed, -cat′ing** ⟦< L *ab-,* off + *dicare,* to proclaim⟧ **1** to give up formally (a throne, etc.) **2** to surrender (a right, responsibility, etc.) —**ab′di·ca′tion** ***n.***

ab·do·men (ab′də mən, ab dō′-) ***n.*** ⟦L⟧ the part of the body between the diaphragm and the pelvis; belly —**ab·dom′i·nal** (-däm′ə nəl) ***adj.***

ab·duct (ab dukt′) ***vt.*** ⟦< L *ab-,* away + *ducere,* to lead⟧ to kidnap —**ab·duc′tion** ***n.*** —**ab·duc′tor** ***n.***

a·beam (ə bēm′) ***adv., adj.*** at right angles to a ship's length or keel

a·bed (ə bed′) ***adv., adj.*** in bed

A·bel (ā′bəl) ***n.*** *Bible* the second son of Adam and Eve: see CAIN

a·be·li·a (ə bēl′yə, ə bē′lē ə) ***n.*** an ornamental shrub with clusters of fragrant flowers

ab·er·ra·tion (ab′ər ā′shən) ***n.*** ⟦< L *ab-,* from + *errare,* wander⟧ **1** a deviation from what is right, true, normal, etc. **2** mental derangement or lapse **3** *Optics* the failure of light rays from one point to converge at a single focus —**ab·er′rant** (-ənt) ***adj.*** —**ab′er·ra′tion·al** ***adj.***

a·bet (ə bet′) ***vt.*** **a·bet′ted, a·bet′ting** ⟦< OFr *a-,* to + *beter,* to bait⟧ to urge on or help, esp. in crime —**a·bet′tor** or **a·bet′ter** ***n.***

a·bey·ance (ə bā′əns) ***n.*** ⟦< OFr *a-,* to, at + *bayer,* wait expectantly⟧ temporary suspension, as of an activity or ruling

ab·hor (ab hôr′) ***vt.*** **-horred′, -hor′ring**

⟦< L *ab-*, from + *horrere*, to shudder⟧ to shrink from in disgust, hatred, etc.; detest —**ab·hor'rence** ***n.***

ab·hor'rent (-ənt) ***adj.*** causing disgust, hatred, etc.; detestable —**ab·hor'rent·ly** ***adv.***

a·bide (ə bīd') ***vi.*** **a·bode'** or **a·bid'ed, a·bid'ing** ⟦< OE *ā-*, intens. + *bīdan*, bide⟧ **1** to remain **2** [Archaic] to reside —***vt.*** **1** to await **2** to put up with —**abide by 1** to live up to (a promise, etc.) **2** to submit to and carry out —**a·bid'ance** ***n.***

a·bid'ing ***adj.*** enduring; lasting

a·bil·i·ty (ə bil'ə tē) ***n.***, *pl.* **-ties** ⟦< L *habilitas*⟧ **1** a being able; power to do **2** talent or skill

-a·bil·i·ty (ə bil'ə tē) ⟦L *-abilitas*⟧ *suffix* a (specified) ability, capacity, or tendency

ab·ject (ab'jekt', ab jekt') ***adj.*** ⟦< L *ab-*, from + *jacere*, to throw⟧ **1** miserable; wretched **2** lacking self-respect; degraded —**ab'ject'ly** ***adv.*** —**ab·jec'tion** or **ab'ject'ness** ***n.***

ab·jure (ab jo͝or', əb-) ***vt.*** **-jured', -jur'ing** ⟦< L *ab-*, away + *jurare*, swear⟧ **1** to give up (rights, allegiance, etc.) on oath; renounce **2** to recant —**ab·ju·ra·tion** (ab'jə rā'shən) ***n.*** —**ab·jur'a·to'ry** (-ə tôr'ē) ***adj.*** —**ab·jur'er** ***n.***

ab·late (ab lāt') ***vt.*** **-lat'ed, -lat'ing** ⟦see fol.⟧ **1** to remove, as by surgery **2** to wear away, burn away, or vaporize —***vi.*** to be ablated, as a rocket shield in reentry —**ab·la'tion** ***n.***

ab·la·tive (ab'lə tiv) ***n.*** ⟦< L *ab-*, away + *ferre*, to bear⟧ *Gram.* the case expressing removal, cause, agency, etc., as in Latin

a·blaze (ə blāz') ***adj.*** **1** burning brightly **2** greatly excited

a·ble (ā'bəl) ***adj.*** **a'bler, a'blest** ⟦< L *habere*, have⟧ **1** having enough power, skill, etc. to do something **2** skilled; talented **3** *Law* competent —**a'bly** ***adv.***

-a·ble (ə bəl) ⟦< L⟧ *suffix* **1** that can or will *[perishable]* **2** capable of being ___ed *[manageable]* **3** worthy of being ___ed *[lovable]* **4** having qualities of *[comfortable]* **5** inclined to *[peaceable]*

a'ble-bod'ied ***adj.*** healthy and strong

able-bodied seaman a trained or skilled seaman: also **able seaman**

a·bloom (ə blo͞om') ***adj.*** in bloom

ab·lu·tion (ab lo͞o'shən) ***n.*** ⟦< L *ab-*, off + *luere*, to wash⟧ [*usually pl.*] a washing of the body, esp. as a religious ceremony

-a·bly (ə blē) *suffix* in a way indicating a (specified) ability, tendency, etc.

ABM *abbrev.* anti-ballistic missile

ab·ne·gate (ab'nə gāt') ***vt.*** **-gat'ed, -gat'ing** ⟦< L *ab-*, from + *negare*, deny⟧ to give up (rights, claims, etc.); renounce —**ab'ne·ga'tion** ***n.***

ab·nor·mal (ab nôr'məl) ***adj.*** not normal, average, or typical; irregular —**ab·nor'mal·ly** ***adv.***

ab'nor·mal'i·ty (-mal'ə tē) ***n.*** **1** an abnormal condition **2** *pl.* **-ties** an abnormal thing

a·board (ə bôrd') ***adv., prep.*** on or in (a train, ship, etc.)

a·bode (ə bōd') ***vi., vt.*** *alt. pt. & pp. of* ABIDE —***n.*** a home; residence

a·bol·ish (ə bäl'ish) ***vt.*** ⟦< L *abolere*, destroy⟧ to do away with; void —**a·bol'ish·ment** ***n.***

ab·o·li·tion (ab'ə lish'ən) ***n.*** **1** complete destruction; annulment **2** [*occas.* **A-**] the abolishing of slavery in the U.S. —**ab'o·li'tion·ist** ***n.***

a·bom·i·na·ble (ə bäm'ə nə bəl) ***adj.*** ⟦see fol.⟧ **1** disgusting; vile **2** very bad —**a·bom'i·na·bly** ***adv.***

a·bom'i·nate' (-nāt') ***vt.*** **-nat'ed, -nat'ing** ⟦< L *abominari*, regard as an ill omen⟧ **1** to hate; loathe **2** to dislike very much —**a·bom'i·na'tion** ***n.***

ab·o·rig·i·nal (ab'ə rij'ə nəl) ***adj.*** **1** existing (in a region) from the beginning; first; indigenous **2** of aborigines —***n.*** an aborigine

ab'o·rig'i·ne' (-nē') ***n.***, *pl.* **-nes'** ⟦L < *ab-*, from + *origine*, origin⟧ **1** any of the first known inhabitants of a region **2** [**A-**] a member of the aboriginal people of Australia

a·born·ing (ə bôr'niŋ) ***adv.*** while being born or created *[the plan died aborning]*

a·bort (ə bôrt') ***vi.*** ⟦< L *aboriri*, miscarry⟧ to have a miscarriage —***vt.*** **1** to cause to have an abortion **2** to cut short (a flight, etc.), as because of an equipment failure

a·bor·tion (ə bôr'shən) ***n.*** any expulsion of a fetus before it is able to survive, esp. if induced on purpose —**a·bor'tion·ist** ***n.***

a·bor·tive (ə bôrt'iv) ***adj.*** **1** unsuccessful; fruitless **2** *Biol.* arrested in development

a·bound (ə bound') ***vi.*** ⟦< L *ab-*, away + *undare*, rise in waves⟧ **1** to be plentiful **2** to be rich (*in*) or teem (*with*)

a·bout (ə bout') ***adv.*** ⟦< OE *onbūtan*, around⟧ **1** all around **2** near **3** in an opposite direction **4** approximately **5** [Inf.] nearly *[about ready]* —***adj.*** **1** astir *[he is up and about]* **2** likely immediately *[about to leave]* —***prep.*** **1** on all sides of **2** near to **3** with **4** concerning

a·bout'-face' ***n.*** a reversal of position or opinion —***vi.*** **-faced', -fac'ing** to turn or face in the opposite direction

a·bove (ə buv') ***adv.*** ⟦OE *abūfan*⟧ **1** in a higher place; up **2** earlier (in a book, etc.) **3** higher in rank, etc. —***prep.*** **1** over; on top of **2** better or more than *[above the average]* —***adj.*** mentioned earlier —***n.*** something that is above —**above all** most of all; mainly

a·bove'board' ***adv., adj.*** without dishonesty or concealment

a·bove'ground' ***adj., adv.*** **1** above or on the surface of the earth **2** not secret(ly); open(ly)

a·brade (ə brād') ***vt., vi.*** **a·brad'ed, a·brad'ing** ⟦< L *ab-*, away + *radere*, to scrape⟧ to rub off; scrape away

A·bra·ham (ā'brə ham') ***n.*** *Bible* the first patriarch of the Hebrews

a·bra·sion (ə brā'zhən) ***n.*** **1** an abrading **2** an abraded spot

a·bra'sive (-siv) ***adj.*** **1** causing abrasion **2** aggressively annoying; irritating —***n.***

a substance, as sandpaper, used for grinding, polishing, etc.

a·breast (ə brest′) ***adv., adj.*** **1** side by side **2** informed (*of*) recent happenings

a·bridge (ə brij′) ***vt.*** **a·bridged′, a·bridg′ing** ⟦< LL *abbreviare*, abbreviate⟧ **1** to shorten, lessen, or curtail **2** to shorten (a piece of writing) while keeping the substance —**a·bridg′ment** or **a·bridge′ment** ***n.***

a·broad (ə brôd′) ***adv.*** **1** far and wide **2** in circulation; current **3** outdoors **4** to or in foreign lands —**from abroad** from a foreign land

ab·ro·gate (ab′rə gāt′) ***vt.*** **-gat′ed, -gat′ing** ⟦< L *ab-*, away + *rogare*, ask⟧ to cancel or repeal by authority —**ab′ro·ga′tion** ***n.*** —**ab′ro·ga′tor** ***n.***

a·brupt (ə brupt′) ***adj.*** ⟦< L *ab-*, off + *rumpere*, to break⟧ **1** sudden; unexpected **2** brusque **3** very steep **4** disconnected, as some writing —**a·brupt′ly** ***adv.*** —**a·brupt′ness** ***n.***

ABS *abbrev.* anti-lock braking system

Ab·sa·lom (ab′sə ləm) ***n.*** *Bible* David's son who rebelled against him

ab·scess (ab′ses′) ***n.*** ⟦< L *ab(s)-*, from + *cedere*, go⟧ a swollen area in body tissues, containing pus —***vi.*** to form an abscess —**ab′scessed′** ***adj.***

ab·scis·sa (ab sis′ə) ***n.***, *pl.* **-sas** or **-sae** (-ē) ⟦L < *ab-*, from + *scindere*, to cut⟧ *Math.* the horizontal distance of a point from a vertical axis

ab·scond (ab skänd′, əb-) ***vi.*** ⟦< L *ab(s)-*, from + *condere*, hide⟧ to leave hastily and secretly, esp. to escape the law —**ab·scond′er** ***n.***

ab·sence (ab′səns) ***n.*** **1** a being absent **2** the time of this **3** a lack

ab·sent (ab′sənt; *for v.*, ab sent′) ***adj.*** ⟦< L *ab-*, away + *esse*, be⟧ **1** not present **2** not existing; lacking **3** not attentive —***vt.*** to keep (oneself) away —***prep.*** in the absence of [*absent* her testimony, our case is weak] —**ab′sent·ly** ***adv.***

ab·sen·tee (ab′sən tē′) ***n.*** one who is absent, as from work —***adj.*** designating, of, or from one who is absent —**ab′sen·tee′ism′** ***n.***

absentee ballot a ballot to be marked and sent to a board of elections by a person (**absentee voter**) unable to be at the polls at election time

ab′sent-mind′ed or **ab′sent·mind′ed** ***adj.*** **1** not attentive; preoccupied **2** habitually forgetful —**ab′sent-mind′ed·ly** ***adv.*** —**ab′sent-mind′ed·ness** ***n.***

absent without leave *Mil.* absent from duty without official permission

ab·sinthe or **ab·sinth** (ab′sinth′) ***n.*** ⟦< Gr⟧ a green, bitter, toxic liqueur

ab·so·lute (ab′sə lo͞ot′) ***adj.*** ⟦see ABSOLVE⟧ **1** perfect; complete **2** not mixed; pure **3** not limited [*absolute* power] **4** positive **5** not doubted; real [*absolute* truth] **6** not relative —**ab′so·lute′ly** ***adv.***

absolute value the value of a real number, disregarding its positive or negative sign [the *absolute value* of -4 or +4 is 4]

absolute zero the lower limit on physically obtainable temperatures: equal to -273.16°C or -459.69°F

ab·so·lu·tion (ab′sə lo͞o′shən) ***n.*** **1** a freeing (*from* guilt) **2** remission (*of* sin or penalty for it)

ab·so·lut·ism (ab′sə lo͞o tiz′əm) ***n.*** government by absolute rule; despotism —**ab′so·lut′ist** ***n., adj.***

ab·solve (ab zälv′, əb-) ***vt.*** **-solved′, -solv′ing** ⟦< L *ab-*, from + *solvere*, loosen⟧ **1** to free from guilt, a duty, etc. **2** to give religious absolution to

ab·sorb (ab sôrb′, -zôrb′; əb-) ***vt.*** ⟦< L *ab-*, from + *sorbere*, drink in⟧ **1** to suck up **2** to interest greatly; engross **3** to assimilate **4** to pay for (costs, etc.) **5** to take in (a shock, etc.) without recoil **6** to take in and not reflect (light or sound) —**ab·sorb′ing** ***adj.***

ab·sorb′ent ***adj.*** capable of absorbing moisture, etc. —***n.*** a thing that absorbs —**ab·sorb′en·cy** ***n.***

ab·sorp·tion (ab sôrp′shən, -zôrp′-; əb-) ***n.*** **1** an absorbing or being absorbed **2** great interest —**ab·sorp′tive** ***adj.***

ab·stain (ab stān′, əb-) ***vi.*** ⟦< L *ab(s)-*, from + *tenere*, to hold⟧ to voluntarily do without; refrain (*from*) —**ab·stain′er** ***n.*** —**ab·sten′tion** (-sten′shən) ***n.***

ab·ste·mi·ous (ab stē′mē əs, əb-) ***adj.*** ⟦< L *ab(s)-*, from + *temetum*, strong drink⟧ moderate in eating and drinking; temperate

ab·sti·nence (ab′stə nəns) ***n.*** an abstaining from some or all food, liquor, etc. —**ab′sti·nent** ***adj.***

ab·stract (*for adj.*, ab strakt′, ab′strakt′; *for n. & vt. 2*, ab′strakt′; *for vt. 1*, ab strakt′) ***adj.*** ⟦< L *ab(s)-*, from + *trahere*, to draw⟧ **1** thought of apart from material objects **2** expressing a quality so thought of **3** theoretical **4** *Art* not representing things realistically —***n.*** a summary —***vt.*** **1** to take away **2** to summarize —**ab·stract′ly** ***adv.*** —**ab·stract′ness** ***n.***

ab·stract′ed ***adj.*** preoccupied

ab·strac·tion (ab strak′shən) ***n.*** **1** an abstracting; removal **2** an abstract idea, thing, etc. **3** mental withdrawal **4** an abstract painting, sculpture, etc.

ab·struse (ab stro͞os′) ***adj.*** ⟦< L *ab(s)-*, away + *trudere*, to thrust⟧ hard to understand —**ab·struse′ly** ***adv.*** —**ab·struse′ness** ***n.***

ab·surd (ab surd′, -zurd′; əb-) ***adj.*** ⟦< L *ab-*, intens. + *surdus*, dull, insensible⟧ so unreasonable as to be ridiculous —**ab·surd′i·ty** ***n.*** —**ab·surd′ly** ***adv.***

a·bun·dance (ə bun′dəns) ***n.*** ⟦see ABOUND⟧ a great supply; more than enough —**a·bun′dant** ***adj.*** —**a·bun′dant·ly** ***adv.***

a·buse (ə byo͞oz′; *for n.*, ə byo͞os′) ***vt.*** **a·bused′, a·bus′ing** ⟦< L *ab-*, away + *uti*, to use⟧ **1** to use wrongly **2** to mistreat, esp. by inflicting physical or sexual harm on **3** to insult; revile —***n.*** **1** wrong use **2** mistreatment, esp. by the infliction of physical or sexual harm **3** a corrupt practice **4** insulting language —**a·bu·sive** (ə byo͞o′siv) ***adj.*** —**a·bu′sive·ly** ***adv.***

a·but (ə but′) ***vi., vt.*** **a·but′ted, a·**

but′ting ⟦< OFr *a-*, to + *bout*, end⟧ to border (*on* or *upon*)

a·but′ment *n.* **1** an abutting **2** a part supporting an arch, bridge, etc.

a·bys·mal (ə biz′məl) *adj.* **1** of or like an abyss; not measurable **2** very bad; wretched —**a·bys′mal·ly** *adv.*

a·byss (ə bis′) *n.* ⟦< Gr *a-*, without + *byssos*, bottom⟧ **1** a bottomless gulf **2** anything too deep for measurement *[an abyss of shame]*

Ab·ys·sin·i·a (ab′ə sin′ē ə) *former name for* ETHIOPIA —**Ab′ys·sin′i·an** *adj., n.*

ac *abbrev.* acre(s)

Ac *Chem. symbol for* actinium

AC *abbrev.* **1** air conditioning **2** alternating current

-ac (ak, ək) ⟦< Gr⟧ *suffix* **1** characteristic of *[elegiac]* **2** relating to *[cardiac]* **3** affected by *[maniac]*

a·ca·cia (ə kā′shə) *n.* ⟦< Gr *akē*, thorn⟧ **1** a tree or shrub with yellow or white flower clusters **2** the locust tree

ac·a·dem·ic (ak′ə dem′ik) *adj.* **1** of colleges, universities, etc.; scholastic **2** having to do with the liberal arts rather than technical education **3** formal; pedantic **4** merely theoretical —**ac′a·dem′i·cal·ly** *adv.*

a·cad·e·mi·cian (ə kad′ə mish′ən, ak′ə də-) *n.* a member of an ACADEMY (sense 3)

a·cad·e·my (ə kad′ə mē) *n., pl.* **-mies** ⟦< Gr *akadēmeia*, place where Plato taught⟧ **1** a private secondary school **2** a school for special instruction **3** an association of scholars, writers, etc., for advancing an art or science

a·can·thus (ə kan′thəs) *n., pl.* **-thus·es** or **-thi′** (-thī′, -thē′) ⟦< Gr *akē*, a point⟧ **1** a plant with lobed, often spiny leaves **2** *Archit.* a representation of these leaves

a cap·pel·la (ä′ kə pel′ə) ⟦It, in chapel style⟧ without instrumental accompaniment: said of vocalists or vocal groups: also sp. **a ca·pel′la**

A·ca·pul·co (ä′kə po͞ol′kō, ak′ə-) city & seaport in S Mexico, on the Pacific: a winter resort: pop. 593,000

ac·cede (ak sēd′) *vi.* **-ced′ed, -ced′ing** ⟦< L *ad-*, to + *cedere*, go, yield⟧ **1** to enter upon the duties (of an office); attain (*to*) **2** to assent; agree (*to*)

ac·cel·er·ate (ak sel′ər āt′, ək-) *vt.* **-at′ed, -at′ing** ⟦< L *ad-*, to + *celerare*, hasten⟧ **1** to increase the speed of **2** to cause to happen sooner —*vi.* to go faster —**ac·cel′er·a′tion** *n.*

ac·cel′er·a′tor *n.* that which accelerates something; esp., the foot throttle of a motor vehicle

ac·cent (ak′sent′; *for v., also* ak sent′) *n.* ⟦< L *ad-*, to + *canere*, sing⟧ **1** emphasis given a spoken syllable or word **2** a mark showing such emphasis or indicating pronunciation **3** a distinguishing manner of pronunciation *[an Irish accent]* **4** special emphasis or attention **5** *Music, Prosody* rhythmic stress —*vt.* **1** to mark with an accent **2** to emphasize; stress

ac·cen·tu·ate (ak sen′cho͞o āt′, ək-) *vt.* **-at′ed, -at′ing** to accent; emphasize —**ac·cen′tu·a′tion** *n.*

ac·cept (ak sept′, ək-) *vt.* ⟦< L *ad-*, to + *capere*, take⟧ **1** to receive, esp. willingly **2** to approve **3** to agree or consent to **4** to believe in **5** to reply "yes" to **6** to agree to pay

ac·cept′a·ble *adj.* worth accepting; satisfactory —**ac·cept′a·bil′i·ty** or **ac·cept′a·ble·ness** *n.* —**ac·cept′a·bly** *adv.*

ac·cept′ance *n.* **1** an accepting **2** approval **3** belief in; assent **4** a promise to pay

ac·cept′ed *adj.* generally regarded as true, proper, etc.; conventional; approved

ac·cess (ak′ses′) *n.* ⟦see ACCEDE⟧ **1** approach or means of approach **2** the right to enter, use, etc. **3** an outburst; fit *[an access of anger]* —*vt.* to get data from, or add data to, a database

ac·ces·si·ble (ak ses′ə bəl, ək-) *adj.* **1** that can be approached or entered, esp. easily **2** obtainable **3** easily understood —**ac·ces′si·bil′i·ty** *n.* —**ac·ces′si·bly** *adv.*

ac·ces·sion (ak sesh′ən, ək-) *n.* **1** the act of attaining (a throne, power, etc.) **2** assent **3** *a)* increase by addition *b)* an addition

ac·ces·so·ry (ak ses′ər ē, ək-) *adj.* ⟦see ACCEDE⟧ **1** additional; extra **2** helping in an unlawful act —*n., pl.* **-ries 1** something extra or complementary **2** one who, though absent, helps another to break the law

ac·ci·dent (ak′sə dənt) *n.* ⟦< L *ad-*, to + *cadere*, to fall⟧ **1** an unexpected or unintended happening, as one resulting in injury, loss, etc. **2** chance

ac′ci·den′tal (-dent′'l) *adj.* happening by chance —**ac′ci·den′tal·ly** *adv.*

ac′ci·dent-prone′ *adj.* seemingly inclined to become involved in accidents

ac·claim (ə klām′) *vt.* ⟦< L *ad-*, to + *clamare*, to cry out⟧ to greet or announce with loud approval or applause; hail —*n.* loud approval

ac·cla·ma·tion (ak′lə mā′shən) *n.* **1** loud applause or approval **2** an approving vote by voice

ac·cli·mate (ak′lə māt′, ə klī′mət) *vt., vi.* **-mat·ed, -mat·ing** ⟦< L *ad-*, to + Gr *klima*, region⟧ to accustom or become accustomed to a new climate or environment —**ac′cli·ma′tion** *n.*

ac·cli·ma·tize (ə klī′mə tīz′) *vt., vi.* **-tized′, -tiz′ing** ACCLIMATE —**ac·cli′ma·ti·za′tion** *n.*

ac·cliv·i·ty (ə kliv′ə tē) *n., pl.* **-ties** ⟦< L *ad-*, up + *clivus*, hill⟧ an upward slope

ac·co·lade (ak′ə lād′) *n.* ⟦< L *ad*, to + *collum*, neck⟧ anything done or given to show great respect, appreciation, etc.

ac·com·mo·date (ə käm′ə dāt′) *vt.* **-dat′ed, -dat′ing** ⟦< L *ad-*, to + *commodare*, to fit⟧ **1** to adapt **2** to do a favor for **3** to have space for

ac·com′mo·dat′ing *adj.* obliging

ac·com′mo·da′tion *n.* **1** adjustment **2** willingness to do favors **3** a help; convenience **4** [*pl.*] *a)* lodgings *b)* traveling space, as in a train

ac·com·pa·ni·ment (ə kum′pə nə mənt,

-nē-; *often* ə kump′nə-, -nē-) ***n.*** anything that accompanies something else, as an instrumental part supporting a solo voice, etc.

ac·com·pa·ny (ə kum′pə nē; *often* ə kump′nē) ***vt.*** **-nied, -ny·ing** ⟦see AD- & COMPANION⟧ **1** to go with **2** to supplement **3** to play or sing an accompaniment for or to —**ac·com′pa·nist** ***n.***

ac·com·plice (ə käm′plis) ***n.*** ⟦< ME *a* (the article) + LL *complex*, a confederate⟧ a partner in crime

ac·com·plish (ə käm′plish) ***vt.*** ⟦< L *ad-*, intens. + *complere*, fill up⟧ to succeed in doing; complete

ac·com′plished ***adj.*** **1** done; completed **2** skilled; expert

ac·com′plish·ment ***n.*** **1** completion **2** work completed; an achievement **3** a social art or skill: *usually used in pl.*

ac·cord (ə kôrd′) ***vt.*** ⟦< L *ad-*, to + *cor*, heart⟧ **1** to make agree **2** to grant —***vi.*** to agree; harmonize (*with*) —***n.*** mutual agreement; harmony —**of one's own accord** willingly —**with one accord** all agreeing

ac·cord′ance ***n.*** agreement; conformity —**ac·cord′ant** ***adj.***

ac·cord′ing ***adj.*** in harmony —**according to** **1** in agreement with **2** as stated by

ac·cord′ing·ly ***adv.*** **1** in a fitting and proper way **2** therefore

ACCORDION

ac·cor·di·on (ə kôr′dē ən) ***n.*** ⟦prob. < It *accordare*, to be in tune⟧ a musical instrument with keys and a bellows, which is pressed to force air through reeds

ac·cost (ə kôst′) ***vt.*** ⟦< L *ad-*, to + *costa*, side⟧ to approach and speak to, esp. in a bold way

ac·count (ə kount′) ***vt.*** ⟦< OFr *a-*, to + *conter*, tell⟧ to judge to be —***vi.*** **1** to give a financial reckoning (*to*) **2** to give reasons (*for*) **3** to be the reason (*for*) —***n.*** **1** [*often pl.*] a record of business transactions **2** *a*) BANK ACCOUNT *b*) CHARGE ACCOUNT **3** a credit customer or client **4** worth; importance **5** an explanation **6** a report —**on account** as partial payment —**on account of** because of —**on no account** under no circumstances —**take into account** to consider

ac·count′a·ble ***adj.*** responsible; liable —**ac·count′a·bil′i·ty** ***n.***

ac·count′ant ***n.*** one whose work is

accounting

ac·count′ing ***n.*** the figuring and recording of financial accounts

ac·cou·ter (ə ko͞ot′ər) ***vt.*** ⟦prob. < L *consuere*, to sew⟧ to outfit; equip

ac·cou·ter·ments or **ac·cou·tre·ments** (ə ko͞ot′ər mənts, -ko͞o′trə-) ***pl.n.*** **1** clothes **2** equipment

ac·cred·it (ə kred′it) ***vt.*** ⟦see CREDIT⟧ **1** to authorize; certify **2** to believe in **3** to attribute —**ac·cred′i·ta′tion** ***n.***

ac·cre·tion (ə krē′shən) ***n.*** ⟦< L *ad-*, to + *crescere*, to grow⟧ **1** growth in size, esp. by addition **2** accumulated matter **3** a growing together of parts **4** a part added separately; addition

ac·crue (ə kro͞o′) ***vi.*** **-crued′, -cru′ing** ⟦see prec.⟧ to come as a natural growth or periodic increase, as interest on money —**ac·cru′al** ***n.***

acct *abbrev.* account

ac·cul·tur·ate (ə kul′chər āt′) ***vi.***, ***vt.*** **-at′ed, -at′ing** to undergo, or change by, acculturation

ac·cul′tur·a′tion ***n.*** **1** adaptation to a culture, esp. a new or different one **2** mutual influence of different cultures

ac·cu·mu·late (ə kyo͞o′myə lāt′) ***vt.***, ***vi.*** **-lat′ed, -lat′ing** ⟦< L *ad-*, to + *cumulare*, to heap⟧ to pile up or collect —**ac·cu′mu·la′tion** ***n.*** —**ac·cu′mu·la′tive** (-lāt′iv, -lə tiv) ***adj.***

ac·cu·ra·cy (ak′yoor ə sē, -yər-) ***n.*** the quality or state of being accurate; precision

ac′cu·rate (-it) ***adj.*** ⟦< L *ad-*, to + *cura*, care⟧ **1** careful and exact **2** free from errors; precise —**ac′cu·rate·ly** ***adv.*** —**ac′cu·rate·ness** ***n.***

ac·curs·ed (ə kur′sid, -kurst′) ***adj.*** **1** under a curse **2** damnable Also **ac·curst′** —**ac·curs′ed·ness** ***n.***

ac·cu·sa·tion (ak′yo͞o zā′shən, -yə-) ***n.*** **1** an accusing or being accused **2** what one is accused of —**ac·cu·sa·to·ry** (ə kyo͞o′zə tôr′ē) ***adj.***

ac·cu·sa·tive (ə kyo͞o′zə tiv) ***n.*** ⟦see fol.⟧ *Gram.* the case of the direct object of a verb; also, the objective case in English

ac·cuse (ə kyo͞oz′) ***vt.*** **-cused′, -cus′ing** ⟦< L *ad-*, to + *causa*, a cause⟧ **1** to blame **2** to bring charges against —**ac·cus′er** ***n.***

ac·cus·tom (ə kus′təm) ***vt.*** to make familiar with something by custom, habit, or use; habituate (*to*)

ac·cus′tomed ***adj.*** **1** customary; usual **2** habituated (*to*)

AC/DC or **A.C./D.C.** (ā′sē′dē′sē′) ***adj.*** ⟦< *a*(*lternating*) *c*(*urrent or*) *d*(*irect*) *c*(*urrent*)⟧ [Slang] bisexual

ace (ās) ***n.*** ⟦< L *as*, unit⟧ **1** a playing card, etc. with one spot **2** a point, as in tennis, made by a serve one's opponent cannot return **3** an expert, esp. in combat flying —***adj.*** [Inf.] first-rate —***vt.*** **aced, ac′ing** **1** [Slang] to defeat completely: often with *out* **2** [Inf.] to earn a grade of A in, on, etc.

Ace bandage ⟦< *Ace*, trademark for such a bandage⟧ an elasticized cloth bandage used to provide support, as for a sprain

ace in the hole [Slang] any advantage held in reserve

a·cer·bi·ty (ə sur′bə tē) ***n.***, *pl.* **-ties** ⟦< L *acerbus*, bitter⟧ **1** sourness **2** sharpness of temper, words, etc. —**a·cer′bic** ***adj.***

a·ce·ta·min·o·phen (ə sēt′ə min′ə fən, as′ə tə-) ***n.*** a crystalline powder used to lessen fever and pain

ac·et·an·i·lide (as′ət an′ə līd′) ***n.*** ⟦< ACETIC + ANILINE⟧ a drug used to lessen pain and fever

ac·e·tate (as′i tāt′) ***n.*** **1** a salt or ester of acetic acid **2** something, esp. a fabric, made with an acetate of cellulose

a·ce·tic (ə sēt′ik) ***adj.*** ⟦< L *acetum*, vinegar⟧ of the sharp, sour liquid (**acetic acid**) found in vinegar

ac·e·tone (as′i tōn′) ***n.*** ⟦see prec.⟧ a colorless, flammable liquid used as a solvent, esp. in making rayon —**ac′e·ton′ic** (-tän′ik) ***adj.***

a·cet·y·lene (ə set′′l ēn′) ***n.*** a gas used for lighting and, with oxygen, in welding

a·ce·tyl·sal·i·cyl·ic acid (ə sēt′′l sal′ə sil′ik) ASPIRIN

ache (āk) ***vi.*** **ached, ach′ing** ⟦< OE *acan*⟧ **1** to have or give dull, steady pain **2** [Inf.] to yearn —***n.*** a dull, continuous pain

a·chene (ā kēn′, ə-) ***n.*** ⟦< Gr *a-*, not + *chainein*, to gape⟧ any small, dry fruit with one seed

a·chieve (ə chēv′) ***vt.*** **a·chieved′, a·chiev′ing** ⟦< OFr < *a-*, to + L *caput*, head⟧ **1** to do; accomplish **2** to get by effort —**a·chiev′a·ble** ***adj.*** —**a·chiev′er** ***n.***

a·chieve′ment ***n.*** **1** an achieving **2** a thing achieved; feat

achievement test a test for measuring a student's mastery of a given subject or skill

A·chil·les (ə kil′ēz′) ***n.*** a Greek hero killed in the Trojan War

Achilles' heel (one's) vulnerable spot

Achilles tendon the tendon connecting the heel to the calf muscles

a·choo (ä cho͞o′) ***interj.*** used to suggest a sneeze

ach·ro·mat·ic (ak′rə mat′ik; ā′krə-) ***adj.*** ⟦< Gr *a-*, without + *chrōma*, color⟧ refracting white light without breaking it up into its component colors

ach·y (āk′ē) ***adj.*** **-i·er, -i·est** having an ache

ac·id (as′id) ***adj.*** ⟦L *acidus*, sour⟧ **1** sour; sharp; tart **2** of an acid —***n.*** **1** a sour substance **2** [Slang] LSD **3** *Chem.* any compound that reacts with a base to form a salt —**a·cid·i·ty** (ə sid′ə tē), *pl.* **-ties**, ***n.*** —**ac′id·ly** ***adv.***

a·cid·i·fy (ə sid′ə fī′) ***vt.***, ***vi.*** **-fied′, -fy′ing** **1** to make or become sour **2** to change into an acid

ac·i·do·sis (as′ə dō′sis) ***n.*** a condition in which there is an abnormal retention of acid or loss of alkali in the body

acid rain rain with a high concentration of acids produced by the gases from burning fossil fuels

acid test a crucial, final test

a·cid·u·lous (ə sij′o͞o ləs) ***adj.*** **1** somewhat acid or sour **2** sarcastic

-a·cious (ā′shəs) ⟦< L⟧ *suffix* inclined to, full of *[tenacious]*

-ac·i·ty (as′ə tē) ⟦< L⟧ *suffix* a (specified) characteristic, quality, or tendency *[tenacity]*

ac·knowl·edge (ak näl′ij, ək-) ***vt.*** **-edged, -edg·ing** ⟦see KNOWLEDGE⟧ **1** to admit as true **2** to recognize the authority or claims of **3** to respond to **4** to express thanks for **5** to state that one has received (a letter, etc.) —**ac·knowl′edg·ment** or **ac·knowl′edge·ment** ***n.***

ACLU *abbrev.* American Civil Liberties Union

ac·me (ak′mē) ***n.*** ⟦Gr *akmē*, a point, top⟧ the highest point; peak

ac·ne (ak′nē) ***n.*** ⟦see prec.⟧ a skin disorder usually causing pimples on the face, etc.

ac·o·lyte (ak′ə līt′) ***n.*** ⟦< Gr *akolouthos*, follower⟧ **1** one who helps a priest at services, esp. at Mass **2** an attendant; helper

ac·o·nite (ak′ə nīt′) ***n.*** ⟦< Gr⟧ a plant with hoodlike flowers

a·corn (ā′kôrn′) ***n.*** ⟦< OE *æcern*, nut⟧ the nut of the oak tree

acorn squash a kind of winter squash, acorn-shaped with dark-green skin and yellow flesh

a·cous·tic (ə ko͞os′tik) ***adj.*** ⟦< Gr *akouein*, to hear⟧ **1** having to do with hearing or acoustics **2** of or using a musical instrument that is not amplified Also **a·cous′ti·cal** —**a·cous′ti·cal·ly** ***adv.***

a·cous′tics (-tiks) ***pl.n.*** the qualities of a room, etc. that determine how clearly sounds can be heard in it —***n.*** the branch of physics dealing with sound

ac·quaint (ə kwānt′) ***vt.*** ⟦< L *ad-*, to + *cognoscere*, know⟧ **1** to inform **2** to make familiar (*with*)

ac·quaint′ance ***n.*** **1** knowledge gotten from personal experience **2** a person whom one knows slightly

ac·qui·esce (ak′wē es′) ***vi.*** **-esced′, -esc′ing** ⟦< L *ad-*, to + *quiescere*, grow quiet⟧ to consent without enthusiasm: often with *in* —**ac′qui·es′cence** ***n.*** —**ac′qui·es′cent** ***adj.***

ac·quire (ə kwīr′) ***vt.*** **-quired′, -quir′ing** ⟦< L *ad-*, to + *quaerere*, to seek⟧ **1** to gain by one's own efforts **2** to get as one's own —**ac·quire′ment** ***n.***

ac·qui·si·tion (ak′wə zish′ən) ***n.*** **1** an acquiring **2** something acquired

ac·quis·i·tive (ə kwiz′ə tiv) ***adj.*** eager to acquire (money, etc.); grasping —**ac·quis′i·tive·ness** ***n.***

ac·quit (ə kwit′) ***vt.*** **-quit′ted, -quit′ting** ⟦< L *ad-*, to + *quietare*, to quiet⟧ **1** to release from an obligation, etc. **2** to clear (a person) of a charge **3** to conduct (oneself); behave —**ac·quit′tal** ***n.***

a·cre (ā′kər) ***n.*** ⟦OE *æcer*, field⟧ a measure of land, 4,840 sq. yards

a′cre·age ***n.*** acres collectively

ac·rid (ak′rid) ***adj.*** ⟦< L *acris*, sharp⟧ **1** sharp or bitter to the taste or smell **2**

sharp in speech, etc. —**a·crid·i·ty** (ə krid'ə tē) ***n.*** —**ac'rid·ly** ***adv.***

ac·ri·mo·ny (ak'ri mō'nē) ***n.***, *pl.* **-nies** ⟦< L *acer*, sharp⟧ bitterness or harshness of manner or speech —**ac'ri·mo'ni·ous** ***adj.***

ac·ro·bat (ak'rə bat') ***n.*** ⟦< Gr *akrobatos*, walking on tiptoe⟧ a performer on the trapeze, tightrope, etc.; gymnast —**ac'ro·bat'ic** ***adj.***

ac'ro·bat'ics ***pl.n.*** [*also with sing. v.*] **1** an acrobat's tricks **2** any tricks requiring great skill

ac·ro·nym (ak'rə nim') ***n.*** ⟦< Gr *akros*, at the end + *onyma*, name⟧ a word formed from the first (or first few) letters of several words, as *radar*

ac·ro·pho·bi·a (ak'rō fō'bē ə) ***n.*** ⟦< Gr *akros*, at the top + PHOBIA⟧ an abnormal fear of being in high places

A·crop·o·lis (ə kräp'ə lis) ⟦< Gr *akros*, at the top + *polis*, city⟧ the fortified hill in Athens on which the Parthenon was built

a·cross (ə krôs') ***adv.*** **1** crosswise **2** from one side to the other —***prep.*** **1** from one side to the other of **2** on or to the other side of **3** into contact with by chance [to come *across* an old friend]

a·cross'-the-board' ***adj.*** **1** combining win, place, and show, as a bet **2** including or affecting all classes or groups

a·cros·tic (ə krôs'tik) ***n.*** ⟦Gr *akrostichos* < *akros*, at the end + *stichos*, line of verse⟧ a poem, etc. in which certain letters in each line, as the first or last, spell out a word, motto, etc.

a·cryl·ic (ə kril'ik) ***adj.*** **1** designating any of a group of synthetic fibers used to make fabrics **2** designating any of a group of clear, synthetic resins used to make paints, plastics, etc.

act (akt) ***n.*** ⟦< L *agere*, to do⟧ **1** a thing done **2** an action **3** a law **4** a main division of a drama or opera **5** a short performance, as on a variety show **6** something done merely for show —***vt.*** to perform in (a play or part) —***vi.*** **1** to perform in a play, movie, etc. **2** to behave **3** to function **4** to have an effect (*on*) **5** to appear to be —**act up** [Inf.] to misbehave

ACTH ***n.*** ⟦*a*(*dreno*)*c*(*ortico*)*t*(*ropic*) *h*(*ormone*)⟧ a pituitary hormone that acts on the adrenal cortex

act'ing ***adj.*** temporarily doing the duties of another —***n.*** the art of an actor

ac·ti·nide series (ak'tə nīd') a group of radioactive chemical elements from element 89 (actinium) through element 103 (lawrencium)

ac·tin·i·um (ak tin'ē əm) ***n.*** ⟦< Gr *aktis*, ray⟧ a white, radioactive, metallic chemical element

ac·tion (ak'shən) ***n.*** **1** the doing of something **2** a thing done **3** [*pl.*] behavior **4** the way of working, as of a machine **5** the moving parts, as of a gun **6** the sequence of events, as in a story **7** a lawsuit **8** military combat **9** [Slang] activity

ac·ti·vate (ak'tə vāt') ***vt.*** **-vat'ed**, **-vat'ing** **1** to make active **2** to put (a military unit) on active status —**ac'ti·va'tion** ***n.*** —**ac'ti·va'tor** ***n.***

activated carbon a form of highly porous carbon that can adsorb gases, vapors, and colloidal particles: also **activated charcoal**

ac·tive (ak'tiv) ***adj.*** **1** acting; working **2** causing motion or change **3** lively; agile **4** *Gram.* indicating the voice of a verb whose subject performs the action —**ac'tive·ly** ***adv.***

ac'tiv·ism' (-tə viz'əm) ***n.*** the taking of direct action to achieve a political or social end —**ac'tiv·ist** ***adj.***, ***n.***

ac·tiv·i·ty (ak tiv'ə tē) ***n.***, *pl.* **-ties** **1** a being active **2** liveliness **3** a specific action or function [student *activities*]

ac·tor (ak'tər) ***n.*** **1** one who does a thing **2** one who acts in plays, movies, etc. —**ac'tress** (-tris) ***fem.n.***

ac·tu·al (ak'chōō əl) ***adj.*** ⟦< L *agere*, to do⟧ **1** existing in reality **2** existing at the time —**ac'tu·al·ly** ***adv.***

ac'tu·al'i·ty (-al'ə tē) ***n.*** **1** reality **2** *pl.* **-ties** an actual thing; fact

ac'tu·al·ize' (-əl īz') ***vt.*** **-ized'**, **-iz'ing** **1** to make actual or real **2** to make realistic

ac·tu·ar·y (ak'chōō er'ē) ***n.***, *pl.* **-ies** ⟦L *actuarius*, clerk⟧ one who figures insurance risks, premiums, etc. —**ac'tu·ar'i·al** ***adj.***

ac·tu·ate (ak'chōō āt') ***vt.*** **-at'ed**, **-at'ing** **1** to put into action **2** to cause to take action —**ac'tu·a'tor** ***n.***

a·cu·i·ty (ə kyōō'ə tē) ***n.*** ⟦< L *acus*, needle⟧ keenness of thought or vision

a·cu·men (ə kyōō'mən, ak'yə mən) ***n.*** ⟦< L *acuere*, sharpen⟧ keenness of mind; shrewdness

ac·u·punc·ture (ak'yōō puŋk'chər) ***n.*** ⟦< L *acus*, needle + PUNCTURE⟧ the ancient practice, esp. among the Chinese, of piercing parts of the body with needles to treat disease or relieve pain —**ac'u·punc'tur·ist** ***n.***

a·cute (ə kyōōt') ***adj.*** ⟦< L *acuere*, sharpen⟧ **1** sharp-pointed **2** keen of mind **3** sensitive [*acute* hearing] **4** severe, as pain **5** severe but not chronic [an *acute* disease] **6** very serious **7** less than 90° [an *acute* angle] —**a·cute'ly** ***adv.*** —**a·cute'ness** ***n.***

acute accent a mark (´) showing primary stress, the quality of a vowel, etc.

-a·cy (ə sē) ⟦ult. < Gr⟧ *suffix* quality, condition, etc. [*supremacy*]

a·cy·clo·vir (ā sī'klō vir') ***n.*** a synthetic powder used in the treatment of certain viral infections, as herpes

ad (ad) ***n.*** [Inf.] an advertisement

AD or **A.D.** *abbrev.* ⟦L *Anno Domini*, in the year of the Lord⟧ of the Christian era: used with dates

ad- ⟦L⟧ *prefix* motion toward, addition to, nearness to: becomes *a-*, *ac-*, *af-*, *ag-*, *al-*, *an-*, etc. before certain consonants

ad·age (ad'ij) ***n.*** ⟦< L *ad-*, to + *aio*, I say⟧ an old saying; proverb

a·da·gio (ə dä'jō, -zhō) ***adv.*** ⟦It *ad agio*, at ease⟧ *Music* slowly —***adj.*** slow —***n.***, *pl.* **-gios** **1** a slow movement in music **2** a slow ballet dance Also written ***a·da'gio***, *pl.* ***-gios***

Ad·am (ad′əm) ***n.*** ⟦Heb < *adam,* a human being⟧ *Bible* the first man

ad·a·mant (ad′ə mənt) ***adj.*** ⟦< Gr *a-,* not + *daman,* subdue⟧ inflexible; unyielding

Ad·ams (ad′əmz) **1 John** 1735-1826; 2d president of the U.S. (1797-1801) **2 John Quin·cy** (kwin′zē, -sē) 1767-1848; 6th president of the U.S. (1825-29): son of John

Adam's apple the projection of cartilage in the front of the throat: seen chiefly in men

ADAM'S APPLE

a·dapt (ə dapt′) ***vt.*** ⟦< L *ad-,* to + *aptare,* to fit⟧ **1** to make suitable, esp. by changing **2** to adjust (oneself) to new circumstances —***vi.*** to adjust oneself —**ad·ap·ta·tion** (ad′əp tā′shən) ***n.*** —**a·dapt′er** or **a·dap′tor** ***n.***

a·dapt′a·ble ***adj.*** able to adjust or be adjusted —**a·dapt′a·bil′i·ty** ***n.***

add (ad) ***vt.*** ⟦< L *ad-,* to + *dare,* to give⟧ **1** to join (*to*) so as to increase **2** to state further **3** to combine (numbers) into a sum —***vi.*** **1** to cause an increase (*to*) **2** to find a sum —**add up** to seem reasonable —**add up to** to mean; signify

ADD *abbrev.* attention-deficit disorder

ad·dend (ad′end′) ***n.*** ⟦< fol.⟧ *Math.* a number or quantity to be added to another

ad·den·dum (ə den′dəm) ***n.,*** *pl.* **-da** (-də) ⟦L⟧ a thing added, as an appendix

ad·der (ad′ər) ***n.*** ⟦< OE *nædre*⟧ **1** a poisonous snake of Europe **2** any of various other snakes, some harmless

ad·dict (ə dikt′; *for n.,* ad′ikt) ***vt.*** ⟦< L *addicere,* give assent⟧ **1** to give (oneself) up *to* a strong habit: usually in the passive voice *[addicted* to heroin*]* **2** to make an addict of —***n.*** one addicted to a habit, as to using drugs —**ad·dic′tion** ***n.*** —**ad·dic′tive** ***adj.***

Ad·dis A·ba·ba (ad′is ab′ə bə) capital of Ethiopia: pop. 1,700,000

ad·di·tion (ə dish′ən) ***n.*** **1** an adding of numbers to get a sum **2** a joining of one thing to another **3** a part added —**in addition (to)** besides

ad·di′tion·al ***adj.*** added; more; extra —**ad·di′tion·al·ly** ***adv.***

ad·di·tive (ad′ə tiv) ***adj.*** of addition —***n.*** a substance added in small quantities

ad·dle (ad′'l) ***vi., vt.*** **-dled, -dling** ⟦< OE *adela,* mud⟧ to make or become confused

ad·dress (ə dres′; *for n. 2, 3, & 4, also* a′dres′) ***vt.*** ⟦< L *dirigere,* to direct⟧ **1** to direct (words) *to* **2** to speak or write to **3** to write the destination on (a letter, etc.) **4** to apply (oneself) *to* **5** to deal or cope with —***n.*** **1** a speech **2** the place where one lives or receives mail **3** the destination indicated on an envelope, etc. **4** *Comput. a)* a code identifying the location of an item of information *b)* a string of characters serving as an e-mail destination or Web location

ad·dress·ee (a′dres ē′) ***n.*** the person to whom mail, etc. is addressed

ad·duce (ə do͞os′) ***vt.*** **-duced′, -duc′ing** ⟦< L *ad-,* to + *ducere,* to lead⟧ to give as a reason or proof

-ade (ād) ⟦ult. < L⟧ *suffix* **1** the act of ___ing *[blockade]* **2** participant(s) in an action *[brigade]* **3** ⟦after LEMONADE⟧ drink made from *[limeade]*

Ad·e·laide (ad′ə lād′) seaport in S Australia: pop. 1,076,000

A·den (äd′'n, ād′'n), **Gulf of** gulf of the Arabian Sea, south of Arabia

ad·e·nine (ad′ə nēn′) ***n.*** a purine base contained in the DNA, RNA, and ADP of all tissue

ad·e·noids (ad′'n oidz′, ad′noidz′) ***pl.n.*** ⟦< Gr *adēn,* gland + -OID⟧ lymphoid growths in the throat behind the nose: they can obstruct nasal breathing

a·dept (ə dept′; *for n.* ad′ept′) ***adj.*** ⟦< L *ad-,* to + *apisci,* attain⟧ highly skilled —***n.*** **ad′ept′** an expert —**a·dept′ly** ***adv.*** —**a·dept′ness** ***n.***

ad·e·quate (ad′i kwət) ***adj.*** ⟦< L *ad-,* to + *aequus,* equal⟧ enough for what is required; sufficient; suitable —**ad′e·qua·cy** (-kwə sē) ***n.*** —**ad′e·quate·ly** ***adv.***

ad·here (ad hir′, əd-) ***vi.*** **-hered′, -her′ing** ⟦< L *ad-,* to + *haerere,* to stick⟧ **1** to stick fast; stay attached **2** to give allegiance or support (*to*) —**ad·her′ence** ***n.***

ad·her′ent ***n.*** a supporter or follower (*of* a person, cause, etc.)

ad·he·sion (ad hē′zhən, əd-) ***n.*** **1** a being stuck together **2** body tissues abnormally joined

ad·he′sive (-siv) ***adj.*** **1** sticking **2** sticky —***n.*** an adhesive substance

ad hoc (ad häk′) ⟦L, to this⟧ for a specific purpose *[*an *ad hoc* committee*]*

a·dieu (ə dyo͞o′, -do͞o′; *Fr* à dyö′) ***interj., n.,*** *pl.* **a·dieus′** or **a·dieux** (ə dyo͞o′, -do͞o′; *Fr* à dyö′) ⟦Fr⟧ goodbye

ad in·fi·ni·tum (ad in′fə nīt′əm) ⟦L⟧ endlessly; without limit

a·di·os (a′dē ōs′, ä′-; *Sp* ä dyôs′) ***interj.*** ⟦Sp⟧ goodbye

ad·i·pose (ad′ə pōs′) ***adj.*** ⟦ult. < Gr *aleipha,* fat⟧ of animal fat; fatty

Ad·i·ron·dack Mountains (ad′ə rän′dak′) mountain range in NE New York: also **Adirondacks**

adj *abbrev.* **1** adjective **2** adjustment

ad·ja·cent (ə jā′sənt) ***adj.*** ⟦< L *ad-,* to + *jacere,* to lie⟧ near or close (*to*); adjoining —**ad·ja′cen·cy** (-sən sē) ***n.*** —**ad·ja′cent·ly** ***adv.***

ad·jec·tive (aj′ik tiv) ***n.*** ⟦< L *adjacere,* lie near⟧ a word used to modify a noun or other substantive —**ad′jec·ti′val** (-tī′vəl) ***adj.*** —**ad′jec·ti′val·ly** ***adv.***

ad·join (ə join′) ***vt.*** ⟦< L *ad-,* to + *jungere,* to join⟧ to be next to —***vi.*** to be in contact —**ad·join′ing** ***adj.***

ad·journ (ə jurn′) ***vt.*** ⟦< OFr *a,* at + *jorn,* day⟧ to suspend (a meeting, session, etc.) for a time —***vi.*** **1** to close a meeting, etc. for a time **2** [Inf.] to retire (*to* another room, etc.) —**ad·journ′ment** ***n.***

ad·judge (ə juj′) ***vt.*** **-judged′, -judg′ing** ⟦< L *ad-*, to + *judicare*, to judge⟧ **1** to decide by law **2** to declare, order, or award by law

ad·ju·di·cate (ə jo͞o′di kāt′) ***vt.*** **-cat′ed, -cat′ing** to hear and decide (a case) —***vi.*** to serve as a judge (*in* or *on*) —**ad·ju′di·ca′tion** ***n.*** —**ad·ju′di·ca′tor** ***n.*** —**ad·ju′di·ca·to′ry** (-kə tôr′ē) ***adj.***

ad·junct (a′juŋkt′) ***n.*** ⟦see ADJOIN⟧ a secondary or nonessential addition —***adj.*** in a temporary or part-time position

ad·jure (ə joor′) ***vt.*** **-jured′, -jur′ing** ⟦< L *ad-*, to + *jurare*, to swear⟧ **1** to charge solemnly under oath **2** to ask earnestly —**ad·ju·ra·tion** (aj′oo rā′shən) ***n.***

ad·just (ə just′) ***vt.*** ⟦< OFr *a-*, to + *joster*, to tilt⟧ **1** to change so as to fit **2** to regulate or set (a watch, etc.) **3** to settle rightly **4** to decide the amount to be paid in settling (an insurance claim) —***vi.*** to adapt oneself —**ad·just′a·ble** ***adj.*** —**ad·just′er** or **ad·jus′tor** ***n.*** —**ad·just′ment** ***n.***

ad·ju·tant (aj′ə tənt) ***n.*** ⟦< L *ad-*, to + *juvare*, to help⟧ **1** an assistant **2** a military staff officer who assists the commanding officer

ad-lib (ad′lib′) [Inf.] ***vt.***, ***vi.*** **-libbed′, -lib′bing** ⟦< L *ad libitum*, at pleasure⟧ to improvise (words, etc. not in a prepared script, etc.) —***n.*** an ad-libbed remark: also **ad lib** —***adj.*** spoken or done extemporaneously —***adv.*** extemporaneously: also **ad lib**

adm or **admin** *abbrev.* **1** administration **2** administrative

Adm *abbrev.* admiral

ad′man′ ***n.***, *pl.* **-men′** a man whose work is advertising

ad·min·is·ter (ad min′is tər, əd-) ***vt.*** ⟦< L *ad-*, to + *ministrare*, to serve⟧ **1** to manage; direct **2** to give out, as punishment **3** to apply (medicine, etc.) **4** to direct the taking of (an oath, etc.)

ad·min′is·trate′ (-trāt′) ***vt.*** **-trat′ed, -trat′ing** to administer; manage

ad·min′is·tra′tion (-trā′shən) ***n.*** **1** management **2** [*often* **A-**] the executive officials of a government, etc. and their policies **3** their term of office **4** the administering (*of* punishment, medicine, etc.) —**ad·min′is·tra′tive** (-trāt′iv, -trə tiv) ***adj.***

ad·min′is·tra′tor ***n.*** **1** a person who administers **2** *Law* one appointed to settle an estate

ad·mi·ra·ble (ad′mə rə bəl) ***adj.*** deserving admiration; excellent —**ad′mi·ra·bly** ***adv.***

ad·mi·ral (ad′mə rəl) ***n.*** ⟦< Ar *'amīr*, leader + *'ālī*, high⟧ **1** the commanding officer of a fleet **2** a naval officer of the highest rank

ad′mi·ral·ty ***n.***, *pl.* **-ties** [*often* **A-**] the governmental department in charge of naval affairs, as in England

ad·mi·ra·tion (ad′mə rā′shən) ***n.*** **1** an admiring **2** pleased approval

ad·mire (ad mīr′, əd-) ***vt.*** **-mired′, -mir′ing** ⟦< L *ad-*, at + *mirari*, to wonder⟧ **1** to regard with wonder and delight **2** to esteem highly —**ad·mir′er** ***n.***

ad·mis·si·ble (ad mis′ə bəl, əd-) ***adj.*** that can be accepted or admitted —**ad·mis′si·bil′i·ty** ***n.***

ad·mis·sion (ad mish′ən, əd-) ***n.*** **1** an admitting or being admitted **2** an entrance fee **3** a conceding, confessing, etc. **4** a thing conceded, confessed, etc.

ad·mit (ad mit′, əd-) ***vt.*** **-mit′ted, -mit′ting** ⟦< L *ad-*, to + *mittere*, to send⟧ **1** to permit or entitle to enter or use **2** to allow; leave room for **3** to concede or confess —***vi.*** **1** to allow: with *of* **2** to concede or confess (*to*) —**ad·mit′tance** ***n.***

ad·mit′ted·ly ***adv.*** by admission or general agreement

ad·mix·ture (ad miks′chər) ***n.*** ⟦< L *ad-*, to + *miscere*, to mix⟧ **1** a mixture **2** a thing added in mixing

ad·mon·ish (ad män′ish, əd-) ***vt.*** ⟦< L *ad-*, to + *monere*, to warn⟧ **1** to warn **2** to reprove mildly **3** to exhort —**ad·mo·ni·tion** (ad′mə nish′ən) ***n.*** —**ad·mon′i·to′ry** (-i tôr′ē) ***adj.***

ad nau·se·am (ad nô′zē əm) ⟦L⟧ to the point of disgust

a·do (ə do͞o′) ***n.*** fuss; trouble

a·do·be (ə dō′bē) ***n.*** ⟦Sp⟧ **1** unburnt, sun-dried brick **2** clay for making this brick **3** a building of adobe

ad·o·les·cence (ad′ə les′əns) ***n.*** the time of life between puberty and maturity

ad′o·les′cent ***adj.*** ⟦< L *ad-*, to + *alescere*, grow up⟧ of or in adolescence —***n.*** a person during adolescence

A·don·is (ə dän′is) ***n.*** **1** *Gr. Myth.* a young man loved by Aphrodite **2** a handsome young man

a·dopt (ə däpt′) ***vt.*** ⟦< L *ad-*, to + *optare*, to choose⟧ **1** to take legally into one's own family and raise as one's own child **2** to take as one's own **3** to choose or accept —**a·dop′tion** ***n.***

a·dop·tive (ə däp′tiv) ***adj.*** that has become so by adoption

a·dor·a·ble (ə dôr′ə bəl) ***adj.*** [Inf.] delightful; charming —**a·dor′a·bly** ***adv.***

ad·o·ra·tion (ad′ə rā′shən) ***n.*** **1** a worshiping **2** great love or devotion

a·dore (ə dôr′) ***vt.*** **-dored′, -dor′ing** ⟦< L *ad-*, to + *orare*, to speak⟧ **1** to worship as divine **2** to love greatly **3** [Inf.] to like very much

a·dorn (ə dôrn′) ***vt.*** ⟦< L *ad-*, to + *ornare*, fit out⟧ **1** to be an ornament to **2** to put decorations on —**a·dorn′ment** ***n.***

ADP (ā′dē′pē′) ***n.*** ⟦*a*(*denosine*) *d*(*i*)*p*(*hosphate*)⟧ a basic unit of nucleic acids vital to the energy processes of all living cells

a·dre·nal (ə drē′nəl) ***adj.*** ⟦AD- + RENAL⟧ **1** near the kidneys **2** of two ductless glands (**adrenal glands**) just above the kidneys

a·dren·a·line (ə dren′ə lin) ***n.*** ⟦< *Adrenalin*, a trademark⟧ a hormone secreted by the adrenal glands, which increases endurance, strength, etc.

A·dri·at·ic (Sea) (ā′drē at′ik) sea between Italy and the Balkan Peninsula

a·drift (ə drift′) ***adv.***, ***adj.*** floating without mooring or direction

a·droit (ə droit′) ***adj.*** ⟦< Fr *à*, to + L *dirigere*, lay straight⟧ skillful and clever —**a·droit′ly *adv.*** —**a·droit′ness *n.***

ad·sorb (ad sôrb′, -zôrb′) ***vt.*** ⟦< AD- + L *sorbere*, drink in⟧ to collect (a gas, etc.) in condensed form on a surface —**ad·sorb′ent *adj.*** —**ad·sorp′tion** (-sôrp′ shən, -zôrp′-) ***n.***

ad·u·late (a′jo͞o lāt′, -jə-) ***vt.* -lat′ed, -lat′ing** ⟦< L *adulari*, fawn upon⟧ to admire intensely —**ad′u·la′tion *n.*** —**ad′u·la·to′ry** (-lə tôr′ē) ***adj.***

a·dult (ə dult′, ad′ult′) ***adj.*** ⟦see ADOLESCENT⟧ **1** grown up; mature **2** for adult people —***n.*** a mature person, animal, or plant —**a·dult′hood *n.***

a·dul·ter·ate (ə dul′tər āt′) ***vt.* -at′ed, -at′ing** ⟦< L *ad-*, to + *alter*, other⟧ to make inferior, impure, etc. by adding an improper substance —**a·dul′ter·a′tion *n.***

a·dul·ter·y (ə dul′tər ē) ***n.***, *pl.* **-ies** sexual intercourse between a married person and another who is not that person's spouse —**a·dul′ter·er *n.*** —**a·dul′ter·ess *fem.n.*** —**a·dul′ter·ous *adj.***

ad·um·brate (ad um′brāt′, ad′əm brāt′) ***vt.* -brat′ed, -brat′ing** ⟦< L *ad-*, to + *umbra*, shade⟧ **1** to outline vaguely **2** to foreshadow —**ad′um·bra′tion *n.***

adv *abbrev.* **1** adverb **2** advertisement

ad·vance (ad vans′, əd-) ***vt.* -vanced′, -vanc′ing** ⟦< L *ab-*, from + *ante*, before⟧ **1** to bring forward **2** to promote **3** to suggest **4** to raise the rate of **5** to lend —***vi.*** **1** to go forward **2** to improve; progress **3** to rise in rank, price, etc. —***n.*** **1** a moving forward **2** an improvement **3** a rise in value **4** [*pl.*] approaches to get favor **5** a payment made before it is due —***adj.*** **1** in front [*advance* guard] **2** beforehand —**in advance 1** in front **2** ahead of time —**ad·vance′ment *n.***

ad·vanced′ *adj.* **1** in front **2** far on in life; old **3** ahead or higher in progress, price, etc.

advance man a person hired to travel in advance of a theatrical company, political candidate, etc. to arrange for publicity, appearances, etc.

ad·van·tage (ad vant′ij, əd-) ***n.*** ⟦< L *ab-* + *ante*: see ADVANCE⟧ **1** superiority **2** a favorable circumstance, event, etc. **3** gain or benefit —***vt.* -taged, -tag·ing** to be a benefit or aid to —**take advantage of 1** to use for one's own benefit **2** to impose upon —**ad·van·ta·geous** (ad′van tā′jəs) ***adj.***

Ad·vent (ad′vent′) ***n.*** ⟦< L *ad-*, to + *venire*, to come⟧ **1** *Christianity* the period including the four Sundays just before Christmas **2** [**a-**] a coming or arrival

ad·ven·ti·tious (ad′ven tish′əs) ***adj.*** ⟦see prec.⟧ not inherent; accidental

ad·ven·ture (ad ven′chər, əd-) ***n.*** ⟦see ADVENT⟧ **1** a daring, hazardous undertaking **2** an unusual, stirring, often romantic experience —***vi.* -tured, -tur·ing** to engage in adventure —**ad·ven′tur·ous** or **ad·ven′ture·some *adj.*** —**ad·ven′tur·ous·ly *adv.***

ad·ven′tur·er *n.* **1** one who has or looks for adventures **2** one who seeks to become rich, etc. by dubious schemes —**ad·ven′tur·ess *fem.n.***

ad·verb (ad′vurb′) ***n.*** ⟦< L *ad-*, to + *verbum*, word⟧ a word used to modify a verb, an adjective, or another adverb, by expressing time, place, manner, degree, etc. —**ad·ver′bi·al *adj.*** —**ad·ver′bi·al·ly *adv.***

ad·ver·sar·i·al (ad′vər ser′ē əl) ***adj.*** of or relating to adversaries, as in a lawsuit

ad′ver·sar′y *n.*, *pl.* **-ies** ⟦see ADVERT⟧ an opponent; foe

ad·verse (ad vurs′, ad′vurs′) ***adj.*** ⟦see ADVERT⟧ **1** opposed **2** unfavorable —**ad·verse′ly *adv.***

ad·ver·si·ty (ad vur′sə tē) ***n.*** **1** misfortune; wretched or troubled state **2** *pl.* **-ties** a calamity; disaster

ad·vert (ad vurt′) ***vi.*** ⟦< L *ad*, to + *vertere*, to turn⟧ to call attention (*to*)

ad·ver·tise (ad′vər tīz′) ***vt.* -tised′, -tis′ing** ⟦see prec.⟧ to describe or praise publicly, usually so as to promote sales —***vi.*** **1** to call public attention to things for sale **2** to ask (*for*) by public notice —**ad′ver·tis′er *n.*** —**ad′ver·tis′ing *n.***

ad·ver·tise·ment (ad′vər tīz′mənt, əd vur′tiz-) ***n.*** a public notice, usually paid for

ad·ver·to·ri·al (ad′vər tôr′ē əl) ***n.*** ⟦ADVER(TISE) + (EDI)TORIAL⟧ an advertisement, as in a magazine, made to resemble an article or editorial

ad·vice (ad vīs′, əd-) ***n.*** ⟦< L *ad-*, at + *videre*, to look⟧ opinion given as to what to do; counsel

ad·vis·a·ble (ad vīz′ə bəl, əd-) ***adj.*** wise; sensible —**ad·vis′a·bil′i·ty *n.***

ad·vise (ad vīz′, əd-) ***vt.* -vised′, -vis′ing** ⟦< ML *advisum*, advice⟧ **1** to give advice to; counsel **2** to offer as advice **3** to notify; inform —**ad·vi′sor** or **ad·vis′er *n.***

ad·vis′ed·ly (-id lē) ***adv.*** deliberately

ad·vise′ment *n.* careful consideration —**take under advisement** to consider carefully

ad·vi·so·ry (ad vī′zə rē, əd-) ***adj.*** advising or empowered to advise —***n.***, *pl.* **-ries** a report, esp. about weather conditions

ad·vo·cate (ad′və kit; *for v.*, -kāt′) ***n.*** ⟦< L *ad-*, to + *vocare*, to call⟧ one who speaks or writes in support of another or a cause —***vt.* -cat′ed, -cat′ing** to be an advocate of —**ad′vo·ca·cy** (-kə sē) ***n.***

advt. *abbrev.* advertisement

adz or **adze** (adz) ***n.*** ⟦< OE *adesa*⟧ an axlike tool for trimming and smoothing wood

Ae·ge·an (Sea) (ē jē′ən) sea between Greece and Turkey

ae·gis (ē′jis) ***n.*** ⟦< Gr *aigis*, shield of Zeus⟧ **1** protection **2** sponsorship

Ae·ne·as (i nē′əs) ***n.*** *Gr. & Rom. Myth.* a Trojan whose adventures are told in a poem (the **Ae·ne′id**) by Virgil

ae·on (ē′ən, ē′än′) ***n.*** *alt. sp. of* EON

aer·ate (er′āt′, ā′ər āt′) ***vt.* -at′ed, -at′ing** ⟦AER(O)- + -ATE[1]⟧ **1** to expose to air **2** to charge (liquid) with gas, as to make soda water —**aer·a'tion** *n.* —**aer'a'tor** *n.*

aer·i·al (er'ē əl) *adj.* ⟦< Gr *aēr,* air + -AL⟧ 1 of, in, or by air 2 unreal; imaginary 3 of aircraft or flying —*n.* a radio or TV antenna

aer'i·al·ist *n.* an acrobat on a trapeze, high wire, etc.

a·er·ie (ā'ər ē, ē'rē, er'ē, ir'ē) *n.* ⟦prob. < L *ager,* field⟧ 1 the high nest of an eagle or other bird of prey 2 a house or stronghold on a high place

aero- ⟦< Gr *aēr,* air⟧ *combining form* 1 air 2 aircraft or flying 3 gas, gases Also **aer-** or **aeri-**

aer·o·bat·ics (er'ō bat'iks) *pl.n.* ⟦prec. + (ACRO)BATICS⟧ stunts done while flying an aircraft

aer·o·bic (er ō'bik) *adj.* ⟦< Gr *aēr,* air + *bios,* life⟧ 1 able to live or grow only where free oxygen is present 2 of exercise, as running, that conditions the heart and lungs by increasing efficient intake of oxygen by the body —*n.* [*pl., with sing. or pl. v.*] aerobic exercises

aer·o·dy·nam·ics (er'ō dī nam'iks) *n.* the branch of mechanics dealing with forces exerted by air or other gases in motion —*pl.n.* the characteristics of a vehicle's body that affect its efficient movement through the air —**aer'o·dy·nam'ic** *adj.* —**aer'o·dy·nam'i·cal·ly** *adv.*

aer·o·nau·tics (er'ə nôt'iks) *n.* the science of making and flying aircraft —**aer'o·nau'ti·cal** *adj.*

aer·o·sol (er'ə sôl', -säl') *n.* ⟦AERO- + SOL(UTION)⟧ a suspension of insoluble particles in a gas —*adj.* of or from a container in which gas under pressure dispenses liquid spray

aer·o·space (er'ō spās') *n.* the earth's atmosphere and the space outside it —*adj.* of aerospace, or of missiles, etc. for flight in aerospace

Aes·chy·lus (es'ki ləs) 525?-456 B.C.; Gr. writer of tragedies

Ae·sop (ē'səp, -säp') Gr. fable writer: supposedly lived 6th c. B.C.

aes·thete (es'thēt') *n.* ⟦Gr *aisthētēs,* one who perceives⟧ a person who is or pretends to be highly sensitive to art and beauty

aes·thet·ic (es thet'ik) *adj.* 1 of aesthetics 2 of beauty 3 sensitive to art and beauty

aes·thet'ics *n.* the philosophy of art and beauty

a·far (ə fär') *adv.* [Archaic] at or to a distance —**from afar** from a distance

af·fa·ble (af'ə bəl) *adj.* ⟦< L *ad-,* to + *fari,* to speak⟧ pleasant; friendly —**af'fa·bil'i·ty** *n.* —**af'fa·bly** *adv.*

af·fair (ə fer') *n.* ⟦< L *ad-,* to + *facere,* to do⟧ 1 any matter, event, etc. 2 [*pl.*] matters of business 3 an event arousing public controversy 4 a social gathering 5 a sexual relationship outside of marriage

af·fect (ə fekt'; *for vt. 3 & 4, usually* a fekt'; *for n.,* af'ekt') *vt.* ⟦< L *ad-,* to + *facere,* to do⟧ 1 to have an effect on; influence 2 to stir the emotions of 3 to like to use, wear, etc. 4 to make a pretense of being, feeling, etc. —*n.* an emotion or emotional response

af·fec·ta·tion (af'ek tā'shən) *n.* 1 a pretending to like, have, etc. 2 artificial behavior meant to impress others

af·fect·ed (ə fekt'id; *for 4 & 5, usually* a-) *adj.* 1 afflicted 2 influenced 3 emotionally moved 4 assumed for effect 5 full of affectation

af·fect·ing (ə fekt'iŋ) *adj.* emotionally moving

af·fec·tion (ə fek'shən) *n.* fond or tender feeling

af·fec'tion·ate *adj.* tender and loving —**af·fec'tion·ate·ly** *adv.*

af·fect·less (af'ekt'lis) *adj.* lacking emotion

af·fer·ent (af'ər ənt) *adj.* ⟦< L *ad-,* to + *ferre,* to carry⟧ bringing inward to a central part, as nerves

af·fi·da·vit (af'ə dā'vit) *n.* ⟦ML, he has made oath⟧ a written statement made under oath

af·fil·i·ate (ə fil'ē āt'; *for n., usually,* -it) *vt.* **-at'ed, -at'ing** ⟦< ML *affiliare,* adopt as a son⟧ 1 to take in as a member 2 to associate (oneself) *with* a group, etc. —*vi.* to join —*n.* an affiliated person, club, etc. —**af·fil'i·a'tion** *n.*

af·fin·i·ty (ə fin'i tē) *n., pl.* **-ties** ⟦< L *affinis,* adjacent⟧ 1 relationship by marriage 2 close relationship 3 a likeness implying common origin 4 a natural liking or sympathy

af·firm (ə furm') *vt.* ⟦< L *ad-,* to + *firmare,* make firm⟧ 1 to declare positively; assert 2 to confirm; ratify —*vi.* *Law* to make a formal statement, but not under oath —**af·fir·ma·tion** (af'ər mā'shən) *n.*

af·firm·a·tive (ə furm'ə tiv) *adj.* affirming; answering "yes" —*n.* 1 an expression of assent 2 the side upholding the proposition being debated

affirmative action a plan to offset past discrimination in employing or educating women, blacks, etc.

af·fix (ə fiks'; *for n.* af'iks') *vt.* ⟦< L *ad-,* to + *figere,* fasten⟧ 1 to fasten; attach 2 to add at the end —*n.* 1 a thing affixed 2 a prefix or suffix

af·flict (ə flikt') *vt.* ⟦< L *ad-,* to + *fligere,* to strike⟧ to cause pain or suffering to; distress greatly

af·flic·tion (ə flik'shən) *n.* 1 pain; suffering 2 any cause of suffering

af·flu·ence (af'lo͞o əns) *n.* ⟦< L *ad-,* to + *fluere,* to flow⟧ riches; wealth

af'flu·ent *adj.* wealthy; rich —**af'flu·ent·ly** *adv.*

af·ford (ə fôrd') *vt.* ⟦< OE *geforthian,* to advance⟧ 1 to spare (money, time, etc.) without much inconvenience 2 to give; yield [*it affords pleasure*] —**af·ford'a·bil'i·ty** *n.* —**af·ford'a·ble** *adj.*

af·fray (ə frā') *n.* ⟦< OFr *esfraer,* frighten⟧ a noisy brawl

af·front (ə frunt') *vt.* ⟦< ML *ad-,* to + *frons,* forehead⟧ to insult openly —*n.* an open insult

Af·ghan (af'gan', -gən) *n.* 1 a native of Afghanistan 2 [a-] a soft blanket or shawl, crocheted or knitted

Af·ghan·i·stan (af gan'i stan') country

in SC Asia, east of Iran: 251,773 sq. mi.; pop. 15,551,000

a·fi·cio·na·do (ə fish′ə nä′dō) ***n.*** ⟦Sp⟧ a devotee of some sport, art, etc.

a·field (ə fēld′) ***adv.*** **1** in or to the field **2** away (from home); astray

a·fire (ə fīr′) ***adv., adj.*** on fire

a·flame (ə flām′) ***adv., adj.*** **1** in flames **2** glowing

AFL-CIO *abbrev.* American Federation of Labor and Congress of Industrial Organizations

a·float (ə flōt′) ***adj., adv.*** **1** floating **2** at sea **3** flooded **4** current **5** free of debt, etc.

a·flut·ter (ə flut′ər) ***adv., adj.*** in a flutter

a·foot (ə foot′) ***adv.*** **1** on foot **2** in progress

a·fore·men·tioned (ə fôr′men′chənd) ***adj.*** mentioned before

a·fore′said′ ***adj.*** spoken of before

a·fore′thought′ ***adj.*** thought out beforehand; premeditated

a·foul (ə foul′) ***adv., adj.*** in a collision or a tangle —**run** (or **fall**) **afoul of** to get into trouble with

a·fraid (ə frād′) ***adj.*** ⟦see AFFRAY⟧ feeling frightened: followed by *of, that*, or an infinitive: often used informally to indicate regret *[I'm afraid I must go]*

Af·ri·ca (af′ri kə) second largest continent, south of Europe: *c.* 11,700,000 sq. mi.; pop. *c.* 705,000,000 —**Af′ri·can** ***adj., n.***

Af′ri·can-A·mer′i·can ***n.*** a black American of African ancestry —***adj.*** of African-Americans, their culture, etc.

Af·ri·can·ized bee (af′ri kən īzd′) a hybrid of African and European bees, known for superior honey production; killer bee

African violet a tropical African plant with violet, white, or pinkish flowers and hairy leaves, often grown as a houseplant

Af·ri·kaans (af′ri käns′, -känz′) ***n.*** ⟦Afrik < *Afrika*, Africa⟧ an official language of South Africa, based on Dutch

Af·ro (af′rō′) ***n.***, *pl.* **-ros′** a full, bushy hair style, as worn by some African-Americans

Afro- ⟦< L *Afer*, an African⟧ *combining form* African, African and

Af′ro-A·mer′i·can ***n., adj.*** AFRICAN-AMERICAN

aft (aft) ***adv.*** ⟦< OE *æftan*⟧ at, near, or toward the stern of a ship or rear of an aircraft

af·ter (af′tər) ***adv.*** ⟦OE *æfter*⟧ **1** behind **2** later —***prep.*** **1** behind **2** later than **3** in search of **4** as a result of **5** in spite of *[after* all I've said, he's still going*]* **6** lower in rank or order than **7** in imitation of **8** for *[named after* Lincoln*]* —***conj.*** following the time when —***adj.*** **1** next; later **2** nearer the rear

af′ter·birth′ ***n.*** the placenta and membranes expelled after the birth of offspring

af′ter·burn′er ***n.*** a device attached to some engines for burning or utilizing exhaust gases

af′ter·ef·fect′ ***n.*** an effect coming later, or as a secondary result

af′ter·life′ ***n.*** a life after death

af′ter·math′ (-math′) ***n.*** ⟦< AFTER + OE *mæth*, cutting of grass⟧ a result, esp. an unpleasant one

af·ter·noon (af′tər no͞on′; *for adj., also* af′tər no͞on′) ***n.*** the time from noon to evening —***adj.*** in the afternoon

af′ter-tax′ ***n.*** occurring or remaining after the payment of taxes

af′ter·thought′ ***n.*** **1** an idea, explanation, part, etc. coming or added later **2** a thought coming too late to be apt

af′ter·ward ***adv.*** later; subsequently: also **af′ter·wards**

Ag ⟦L *argentum*⟧ *Chem. symbol for* silver

a·gain (ə gen′) ***adv.*** ⟦< OE *on-*, up to + *gegn*, direct⟧ **1** back into a former condition **2** once more **3** besides **4** on the other hand —**again and again** often; repeatedly —**as much again** twice as much

a·gainst (ə genst′) ***prep.*** ⟦see prec.⟧ **1** in opposition to **2** toward so as to strike *[thrown against* the wall*]* **3** in contact with **4** in preparation for **5** as a charge on

Ag·a·mem·non (ag′ə mem′nän′) ***n.*** *Gr. Myth.* commander of the Greek army in the Trojan War

a·gape (ə gāp′) ***adv., adj.*** ⟦A-[1] + GAPE⟧ wide open

a·gar (ä′gər) ***n.*** ⟦Malay⟧ a gelatinous product made from seaweed, used in bacterial cultures: also **a′gar-a′gar**

ag·ate (ag′it) ***n.*** ⟦< Gr *achatēs*⟧ a hard, semiprecious stone with striped or clouded coloring

a·ga·ve (ə gä′vē) ***n.*** ⟦< proper name in Gr. myth⟧ a desert plant with thick, fleshy leaves

agcy *abbrev.* agency

age (āj) ***n.*** ⟦< L *aetas*⟧ **1** the length of time that a person or thing has existed **2** a stage of life **3** old age **4** a historical or geological period **5** [*often pl.*] [Inf.] a long time —***vi., vt.*** **aged, ag′ing** or **age′ing** to grow or make old, ripe, mature, etc. —**of age** having reached the age when one is qualified for full legal rights

-age (ij) ⟦< LL *-aticum*⟧ *suffix* **1** act, state, or result of *[usage]* **2** amount or number of *[acreage]* **3** cost of *[postage]* **4** place of *[steerage]*

a·ged (ā′jid; *for 2* ājd) ***adj.*** **1** old **2** of the age of —**the aged** old people

age·ism (āj′iz′əm) ***n.*** ⟦AGE + (RAC)ISM⟧ discrimination against older people

age′less ***adj.*** **1** seemingly not growing older **2** eternal

a·gen·cy (ā′jən sē) ***n.***, *pl.* **-cies** ⟦< L *agere*, to act⟧ **1** action; power **2** means **3** a firm, etc. empowered to act for another **4** an administrative government division **5** an organization that offers assistance *[a social agency]*

a·gen·da (ə jen′də) ***n.***, *pl.* **-das** ⟦< L *agere*, to do⟧ a list of things to be dealt with, as at a meeting

a·gent (ā′jənt) ***n.*** ⟦< L *agere*, to do⟧ **1** an active force or substance producing an effect **2** a person, firm, etc. empowered to act for another **3** a representative of a government agency

Agent Orange ⟦military code name, from *orange*-colored containers⟧ a highly toxic defoliant

age'-old' ***adj.*** ancient

ag·er·a·tum (aj'ər āt'əm) ***n.*** ⟦< Gr *agēratos*, not growing old⟧ a plant of the composite family with small, thick heads of bluish flowers

ag·glom·er·ate (ə gläm'ər āt'; *for adj. & n.*, -it) ***vt., vi.*** **-at'ed, -at'ing** ⟦< L *ad-*, to + *glomerare*, form into a ball⟧ to gather into a mass or ball —***adj.*** gathered into a mass or ball —***n.*** a jumbled heap, mass, etc.

ag·glu·ti·nate (ə glōōt''n it; *for v.*, -āt') ***adj.*** ⟦< L *ad-*, to + *gluten*, glue⟧ stuck together —***vt., vi.*** **-nat'ed, -nat'ing** to stick together, as with glue —**ag·glu'ti·na'tion** ***n.***

ag·gran·dize (ə gran'dīz'; *also*, ag'rən-) ***vt.*** **-dized', -diz'ing** ⟦< Fr *a-*, to + *grandir*, to increase⟧ to make greater, more powerful, richer, etc. —**ag·gran·dize·ment** (ə gran'diz mənt, ag'rən dīz'-) ***n.***

ag·gra·vate (ag'rə vāt') ***vt.*** **-vat'ed, -vat'ing** ⟦< L *ad-*, to + *gravis*, heavy⟧ **1** to make worse **2** [Inf.] to annoy; vex —**ag'gra·va'tion** ***n.***

ag'gra·vat'ed ***adj.*** *Law* designating a grave form of a specified offense

ag·gre·gate (ag'rə git; *for v.*, -gāt') ***adj.*** ⟦< L *ad-*, to + *grex*, a herd⟧ total —***n.*** a mass of distinct things gathered into a total or whole —***vt.*** **-gat'ed, -gat'ing** **1** to gather into a mass **2** to total —**ag'gre·ga'tion** ***n.***

ag·gres·sion (ə gresh'ən) ***n.*** ⟦< L *aggredi*, to attack⟧ **1** an unprovoked attack or warlike act **2** a being aggressive —**ag·gres'sor** ***n.***

ag·gres·sive (ə gres'iv) ***adj.*** **1** boldly hostile; quarrelsome **2** bold and active; enterprising —**ag·gres'sive·ly** ***adv.*** —**ag·gres'sive·ness** ***n.***

ag·grieve (ə grēv') ***vt.*** **-grieved', -griev'ing** ⟦see AGGRAVATE⟧ to cause grief or injury to; offend

a·ghast (ə gast') ***adj.*** ⟦< OE *gast*, ghost⟧ feeling great horror or dismay

ag·ile (aj'əl) ***adj.*** ⟦< L *agere*, to act⟧ quick and easy of movement —**ag'ile·ly** ***adv.*** —**a·gil·i·ty** (ə jil'ə tē) ***n.***

ag·i·tate (aj'i tāt') ***vt.*** **-tat'ed, -tat'ing** ⟦< L *agere*, to act⟧ **1** to stir up or shake up **2** to excite the feelings of —***vi.*** to stir up people so as to produce changes —**ag'i·ta'tion** ***n.*** —**ag'i·ta'tor** ***n.***

a·gleam (ə glēm') ***adv., adj.*** gleaming

a·glit·ter (ə glit'ər) ***adv., adj.*** glittering

a·glow (ə glō') ***adv., adj.*** in a glow (of color or emotion)

ag·nos·tic (ag näs'tik) ***n.*** ⟦< Gr *a-*, not + base of *gignōskein*, know⟧ one who believes it impossible to know if God exists —***adj.*** of an agnostic —**ag·nos'ti·cism'** (-ti siz'əm) ***n.***

a·go (ə gō') ***adj.*** ⟦< OE *agan*, pass away⟧ gone by; past *[years ago]* —***adv.*** in the past *[long ago]*

a·gog (ə gäg') ***adv., adj.*** ⟦< OFr *en*, in + *gogue*, joke⟧ with eager anticipation or excitement

ag·o·nize (ag'ə nīz') ***vi.*** **-nized', -niz'ing** **1** to struggle **2** to be in agony —***vt.*** to torture

ag·o·ny (ag'ə nē) ***n., pl.*** **-nies** ⟦< Gr *agōn*, a contest⟧ **1** great mental or physical pain **2** death pangs **3** a strong outburst (*of* emotion)

ag·o·ra·pho·bi·a (ag'ər ə fō'bē ə) ***n.*** ⟦< Gr *agora*, marketplace + -PHOBIA⟧ an abnormal fear of being in public places —**ag'o·ra·pho'bic** ***adj., n.***

a·grar·i·an (ə grer'ē ən) ***adj.*** ⟦< L *ager*, field⟧ **1** of land or the ownership of land **2** of agriculture

a·gree (ə grē') ***vi.*** **-greed', -gree'ing** ⟦< L *ad*, to + *gratus*, pleasing⟧ **1** to consent (*to*) **2** to be in accord **3** to be of the same opinion (*with*) **4** to arrive at an understanding (*about* prices, etc.) **5** to be suitable, healthful, etc.: followed by *with* —***vt.*** to grant *[I agree that it's true]*

a·gree'a·ble ***adj.*** **1** pleasing or pleasant **2** willing to consent **3** conformable **4** acceptable —**a·gree'a·bly** ***adv.***

a·gree'ment ***n.*** **1** an agreeing **2** an understanding between people, countries, etc. **3** a contract

agri- *combining form* agriculture: also **agro-**

ag·ri·busi·ness (ag'rə biz'nis) ***n.*** ⟦see fol. + BUSINESS⟧ farming and associated businesses and industries

ag·ri·cul·ture (ag'ri kul'chər) ***n.*** ⟦< L *ager*, field + *cultura*, cultivation⟧ the work of producing crops and raising livestock; farming —**ag'ri·cul'tur·al** ***adj.*** —**ag'ri·cul'tur·al·ly** ***adv.*** —**ag'ri·cul'tur·ist** ***n.***

a·gron·o·my (ə grän'ə mē) ***n.*** ⟦< Gr *agros*, field + *nemein*, govern⟧ the science and economics of crop production —**a·gron'o·mist** ***n.***

a·ground (ə ground') ***adv., adj.*** on or onto the shore, a reef, etc.

a·gue (ā'gyōō') ***n.*** ⟦< ML (*febris*) *acuta*, violent (fever)⟧ a fever, usually malarial, marked by chills

ah (ä, ô) ***interj.*** used to express delight, surprise, pain, etc.

a·ha (ä hä') ***interj.*** used to express triumph, surprise, satisfaction, etc.

a·head (ə hed') ***adv., adj.*** **1** in or to the front **2** forward; onward **3** in advance **4** winning or profiting —**get ahead** to advance financially, etc.

a·hem (ə hem') ***interj.*** used to get someone's attention, etc.

-a·hol·ic (ə hôl'ik, -häl'-) *combining form* one preoccupied with (something specified)

a·hoy (ə hoi') ***interj.*** used in hailing *[ship ahoy!]*

AI *abbrev.* artificial intelligence

aid (ād) ***vt., vi.*** ⟦< L *ad-*, to + *juvare*, to help⟧ to help; assist —***n.*** **1** help or assistance **2** a helper

aide (ād) ***n.*** ⟦Fr⟧ **1** an assistant **2** an aide-de-camp

aide-de-camp or **aid-de-camp** (ād'də

kamp′) *n.*, *pl.* **aides′-** or **aids′-** ⟦Fr⟧ a military officer serving as an assistant to a superior

AIDS (ādz) ***n.*** ⟦*A*(*cquired*) *I*(*mmune*) *D*(*eficiency*) *S*(*yndrome*)⟧ a condition of deficiency of certain leukocytes, resulting in infections, cancer, neural degeneration, etc.: see HIV

ai·grette or **ai·gret** (ā gret′, ā′gret′) ***n.*** ⟦see EGRET⟧ a bunch of the long, white, showy plumes of the egret

ail (āl) ***vt.*** ⟦OE *eglian*, to trouble⟧ to cause pain and trouble to **—*vi.*** to be in poor health

ai·le·ron (ā′lə rän′) ***n.*** ⟦Fr < L *ala*, wing⟧ a pilot-controlled airfoil at the trailing edge of an airplane wing, for controlling rolling

ail·ment (āl′mənt) ***n.*** a mild illness

aim (ām) ***vi.*, *vt.*** ⟦< L *ad-*, to + *aestimare*, to estimate⟧ **1** to direct (a weapon, blow, etc.) so as to hit **2** to direct (one's efforts) **3** to intend **—*n.*** **1** an aiming **2** the ability to hit a target **3** intention **—take aim** to aim a weapon, etc.

aim′less ***adj.*** having no purpose **—aim′less·ly *adv.* —aim′less·ness *n.***

ain't (ānt) ⟦< *amn't*, contr. of *am not*⟧ *contr.* [Inf.] am not: also a dialectal or nonstandard contraction for *is not, are not, has not*, and *have not*

ai·o·li or **aï·o·li** (ī ō′lē) ***n.*** ⟦ult. < L *allium*, garlic + *oleum*, oil⟧ a mayonnaise containing crushed raw garlic

air (er) ***n.*** ⟦< Gr *aēr*⟧ **1** the invisible mixture of gases surrounding the earth **2** *a*) a breeze; wind *b*) fresh air **3** an outward appearance *[an air of dignity]* **4** general mood **5** [*pl.*] affected, superior manners **6** public expression **7** AIR CONDITIONING **8** a song or tune **—*adj.*** of or by aircraft **—*vt.*** **1** to let air into **2** to publicize **3** to broadcast **—*vi.*** to be broadcast **—in the air** current or prevalent **—on** (or **off**) **the air** that is (or is not) broadcasting **—up in the air** not settled

air bag a bag that inflates instantly within an automobile in a collision, to protect riders from being thrown forward

air base a base for military aircraft

air′borne′ ***adj.*** **1** carried by or through the air **2** aloft or flying

air brake a brake operated by the action of compressed air on a piston

air′brush′ ***n.*** an atomizer worked by compressed air and used for spraying on paint, etc.: also **air brush —*vt.*** to spray or modify with an airbrush

air′bus′ ***n.*** an extremely large passenger airplane, esp. for short trips

air conditioning a method of keeping air humidity and temperature at desired levels in buildings, cars, etc. **—air′-con·di′tion *vt.* —air conditioner**

air′-cooled′ ***adj.*** cooled by having air passed over, into, or through it

air′craft′ ***n.***, *pl.* **-craft′** any machine for traveling through the air

aircraft carrier a warship with a large, flat deck, for carrying aircraft

air′drop′ ***n.*** the dropping of supplies, troops, etc. from an aircraft in flight **—air′drop′ *vt.***

Aire·dale (er′dāl′) ***n.*** ⟦after *Airedale*, valley in England⟧ a large terrier with a wiry coat

air′fare′ ***n.*** fare for transportation on a commercial airplane

air′field′ ***n.*** a field where aircraft can take off and land

air′foil′ ***n.*** a wing, rudder, etc. of an aircraft

air force the aviation branch of a country's armed forces

air′freight′ ***n.*** cargo transported by air **—*vt.*** to transport or send by airfreight

air guitar the imagined guitar of someone pretending to play music, using movements typical of actual playing

air gun a gun or gunlike device operated by compressed air

air′head′ ***n.*** [Slang] a silly, ignorant person

air lane a route for travel by air; airway

air′lift′ ***n.*** a system of transporting troops, supplies, etc. by aircraft **—*vt.*** to transport by airlift

air′line′ ***n.*** a system or company for moving freight and passengers by aircraft **—*adj.*** of or on an airline

air′lin′er ***n.*** a large airline-operated aircraft for carrying passengers

air lock an airtight compartment, with adjustable air pressure, between places of unequal air pressure

air′mail′ ***n.*** mail transported by air; esp., in the U.S., mail going overseas by air: also sp. **air mail —*adj.*** of or for mail sent by air **—*vt.*** to send (mail) by air

air′man (-mən) ***n.***, *pl.* **-men** (-mən) **1** an aviator **2** an enlisted person in the U.S. Air Force

air mass *Meteorol.* a huge, uniform body of air having the properties of its place of origin

air mattress a pad filled with air, used as a mattress for camping, etc.

air′plane′ ***n.*** a motor-driven or jet-propelled aircraft kept aloft by the forces of air upon its wings

air′play′ ***n.*** the playing of a recording over radio or TV

air pocket an atmospheric condition that causes an aircraft to make a sudden, short drop while in flight

air′port′ ***n.*** a place where aircraft can land and take off, usually with facilities for repair, etc.

air power the total capacity of a nation for air war

air pressure the pressure of the atmosphere or of compressed air

air raid an attack by aircraft, esp. bombers

air rifle a rifle operated by compressed air

air′ship′ ***n.*** a self-propelled, steerable aircraft that is lighter than air

air′sick′ ***adj.*** nauseated because of air travel **—air′sick′ness *n.***

air′space′ ***n.*** the space above a nation over which it can claim jurisdiction

air′strike′ ***n.*** an attack made by aircraft

air′strip′ *n.* a temporary airfield

air′tight′ *adj.* **1** too tight for air or gas to enter or escape **2** having no weaknesses *[*an *airtight* alibi*]*

air′time′ *n. Radio & TV* the period of time during which a program, commercial, etc. may be broadcast: also **air time**

air′waves′ *pl.n.* the medium through which radio signals are transmitted

air′way′ *n.* AIR LANE

air·y (er′ē) *adj.* **-i·er, -i·est 1** of air **2** open to the air; breezy **3** unsubstantial as air **4** light as air; graceful **5** lighthearted **6** affectedly nonchalant **—air′i·ly** *adv.* **—air′i·ness** *n.*

aisle (īl) *n.* ⟦< L *ala*, wing⟧ a passageway, as between sections of seats in rows

a·jar (ə jär′) *adv., adj.* ⟦OE *cier*, a turn⟧ slightly open, as a door

AK Alaska

aka (ā′kā′ā′) *abbrev.* also known as: used before an alias: also **a.k.a.**, **a k a**

a·kim·bo (ə kim′bō) *adv., adj.* ⟦< ON *keng*, bent + *bogi*, a bow⟧ with hands on hips and elbows bent outward *[*with arms *akimbo]*

a·kin (ə kin′) *adj.* **1** of one kin; related **2** similar

Ak·ron (ak′rən) city in N Ohio: pop. 223,000

Al *Chem. symbol for* aluminum

-al (əl, ′l) ⟦< L⟧ *suffix* **1** of, like, or suitable for *[theatrical]* **2** the act or process of ___ing *[rehearsal]*

à la or **a la** (ä′lə, -lä) ⟦Fr⟧ in the manner or style of

Al·a·bam·a (al′ə bam′ə) Southern state of the SE U.S.: 50,750 sq. mi.; pop. 4,041,000; cap. Montgomery: abbrev. **AL** **—Al′a·bam′i·an** or **Al′a·bam′an** *adj., n.*

al·a·bas·ter (al′ə bas′tər) *n.* ⟦< Gr *alabastros*, perfume vase⟧ a translucent, whitish variety of gypsum, used for statues, vases, etc.

a la carte (ä′lə kärt′) ⟦Fr⟧ with a separate price for each item on the menu

a·lac·ri·ty (ə lak′rə tē) *n.* ⟦< L *alacer*, lively⟧ eager willingness, often with quick, lively action

A·lad·din (ə lad′′n) *n.* a boy in *The Arabian Nights* who finds a magic lamp

à la king (ä′lə kiŋ′) in a cream sauce containing mushrooms, pimentos, etc.

Al·a·mo (al′ə mō′) Franciscan mission at San Antonio, Texas: scene of a massacre of Texans by Mexican troops (1836)

a la mode (al′ə mōd′) ⟦< Fr⟧ **1** in fashion **2** served in a certain style, as pie with ice cream Also **à la mode**

a·lar (ā′lər) *adj.* ⟦< L *ala*, a wing⟧ **1** of a wing **2** having wings

a·larm (ə lärm′) *n.* ⟦< It *all′arme*, to arms⟧ **1** [Archaic] a sudden call to arms **2** a warning of danger **3** a mechanism that warns of danger, arouses from sleep, etc. **4** fear caused by danger **—*vt.* 1** to warn of danger **2** to frighten

alarm clock a clock that can be set to buzz, flash a light, etc. at a given time, as to awaken a person

a·larm′ing *adj.* frightening

a·larm′ist *n.* one who spreads alarming rumors, exaggerated reports of danger, etc. **—*adj.*** of an alarmist

a·las (ə las′) *interj.* an exclamation of sorrow, pity, etc.

A·las·ka (ə las′kə) state of the U.S. in NW North America: 570,374 sq. mi.; pop. 550,000; cap. Juneau: abbrev. *AK* **—A·las′kan** *adj., n.*

alb (alb) *n.* ⟦< L *albus*, white⟧ a white robe worn by a priest at Mass

al·ba·core (al′bə kôr′) *n.* ⟦< Ar *al*, the + *buko*, young camel⟧ a tuna with unusually long pectoral fins

Al·ba·ni·a (al bā′nē ə) country in the W Balkan Peninsula: 11,101 sq. mi.; pop. 3,185,000 **—Al·ba′ni·an** *adj., n.*

Al·ba·ny (ôl′bə nē) capital of New York, on the Hudson: pop. 101,000

al·ba·tross (al′bə trôs′) *n.* ⟦< Sp < Ar *al qādūs*, a scoop⟧ **1** a large, web-footed sea bird **2** a burden

al·be·it (ôl bē′it) *conj.* ⟦ME *al be it*, al(though) it be⟧ although

Al·ber·ta (al burt′ə) province of SW Canada: 255,285 sq. mi.; pop. 2,697,000; cap. Edmonton: abbrev. *AB*

al·bi·no (al bī′nō) *n., pl.* **-nos** ⟦< L *albus*, white⟧ a person, animal, or plant lacking normal coloration: human albinos have white skin, whitish hair, and pink eyes

al·bum (al′bəm) *n.* ⟦< L *albus*, white⟧ **1** a book with blank pages for mounting pictures, stamps, etc. **2** one or more compact discs, LPs, etc. packaged in a holder

al·bu·men (al byo͞o′mən) *n.* ⟦L < *albus*, white⟧ **1** the white of an egg **2** the nutritive protein in seeds, etc. **3** ALBUMIN

al·bu·min (al byo͞o′min) *n.* ⟦see prec.⟧ a water-soluble protein found in milk, egg, blood, vegetable tissues, etc. **—al·bu′mi·nous** *adj.*

Al·bu·quer·que (al′bə kur′kē) city in central New Mexico: pop. 385,000

al·che·my (al′kə mē) *n.* ⟦< Ar < Gr *chēmeia*; infl. by Gr *cheein*, pour⟧ the chemistry of the Middle Ages, the chief aim of which was to change base metals into gold **—al′che·mist** *n.*

al·co·hol (al′kə hôl′) *n.* ⟦< Ar *alkuḥl*, antimony powder⟧ **1** a colorless, volatile, pungent liquid, used in various forms as a fuel, as an intoxicating ingredient in fermented liquors, etc. **2** any such intoxicating liquor

al′co·hol′ic *adj.* **1** of alcohol **2** suffering from alcoholism **—*n.*** one who has chronic alcoholism

al′co·hol′ism′ *n.* the habitual excessive drinking of alcoholic liquor, or a resulting diseased condition

al·cove (al′kōv′) *n.* ⟦< Ar *al*, the + *qubba*, an arch⟧ a recessed section of a room

al·der (ôl′dər) *n.* ⟦OE *alor*⟧ a small tree or shrub of the birch family

al·der·man (ôl′dər mən) *n., pl.* **-men** (-mən) ⟦< OE *eald*, old + *man*⟧ in some U.S. cities, a municipal officer representing a certain district or ward —

al′der·man′ic (-man′ik) ***adj.***

ale (āl) ***n.*** ⟦OE *ealu*⟧ a fermented drink of malt and hops, like beer

a·le·a·to·ry (ā′lē ə tôr′ē) ***adj.*** ⟦< L *aleatorius*, of gambling < *alea*, chance⟧ depending on chance or luck

a·lem·bic (ə lem′bik) ***n.*** ⟦< Ar *al-anbīq* < Gr *ambix*, a cup⟧ **1** an apparatus formerly used for distilling **2** anything that purifies

a·lert (ə lurt′) ***adj.*** ⟦< L *erigere*, to erect⟧ **1** watchful; vigilant **2** active; nimble —***n.*** a warning signal; alarm —***vt.*** **1** to warn to be ready, etc. **2** to make aware of *[alert* them to their duties*]* —**on the alert** vigilant —**a·lert′ly** ***adv.*** —**a·lert′ness** ***n.***

A·leu·tian Islands (ə lo͞o′shən) chain of U.S. islands off the SW tip of Alaska —**A·leu′tian** ***adj., n.***

ale·wife (āl′wīf′) ***n.***, *pl.* **-wives′** ⟦< ?⟧ a NW Atlantic fish resembling the herring, used for food and in fertilizers

Al·ex·an·der the Great (al′ig zan′dər) 356-323 B.C.; military conqueror: king of Macedonia (336-323)

Al′ex·an′dri·a (-drē ə) seaport in N Egypt: pop. 2,319,000

al·fal·fa (al fal′fə) ***n.*** ⟦Sp < Ar *al-fiṣfiṣa*, fodder⟧ a plant of the pea family, used for fodder and pasture and as a cover crop

Al·fred the Great (al′frəd) A.D. 849-899; Anglo-Saxon king (871-899)

al·fres·co (al fres′kō, äl-) ***adv.*** ⟦It < *al*, in the + *fresco*, cool⟧ outdoors —***adj.*** outdoor Also **al fresco**

al·gae (al′jē′) ***pl.n.***, *sing.* **al′ga** (-gə) ⟦pl. of L *alga*, seaweed⟧ a group of simple organisms, one-celled or many-celled, containing chlorophyll and found in water or damp places

al·ge·bra (al′jə brə) ***n.*** ⟦< Ar *al*, the + *jabara*, to reunite⟧ a mathematical system using symbols, esp. letters, to generalize certain arithmetical operations and relationships —**al′ge·bra′ic** (-brā′ik) ***adj.*** —**al′ge·bra′i·cal·ly** ***adv.***

Al·ge·ri·a (al jir′ē ə) country in N Africa: 919,595 sq. mi.; pop. 22,972,000 —**Al·ge′ri·an** ***adj., n.***

-al·gia (al′jə) ⟦< Gr *algos*⟧ *combining form* pain *[neuralgia]*

Al·giers (al jirz′) seaport & capital of Algeria: pop. 1,688,000

Al·gon·qui·an (al gäŋ′kē ən, -kwē-) ***adj.*** designating or of a widespread family of North American Indian languages —***n.*** this family of languages

al·go·rithm (al′gə rith′əm) ***n.*** ⟦ult. < Ar⟧ **1** any systematic method of solving a certain kind of mathematical problem **2** *Comput.* a set of instructions with a limited number of steps for solving a problem

a·li·as (ā′lē əs) ***n.***, *pl.* **-as·es** ⟦L < *alius*, other⟧ an assumed name —***adv.*** otherwise named *[*Bell *alias* Jones*]*

A·li Ba·ba (ä′lē bä′bə, al′ə bab′ə) in *The Arabian Nights*, a poor man who finds the treasure of forty thieves

al·i·bi (al′ə bī′) ***n.***, *pl.* **-bis′** ⟦L < *alius ibi*, elsewhere⟧ **1** *Law* the plea or fact that an accused person was elsewhere than at the scene of the crime **2** [Inf.] an excuse —***vi.***, ***vt.*** **-bied′**, **-bi′ing** [Inf.] to offer an excuse (for)

al·ien (āl′yən, āl′ē ən) ***adj.*** ⟦< L *alius*, other⟧ **1** foreign **2** not natural; strange **3** opposed or repugnant *[*beliefs *alien* to mine*]* **4** of aliens —***n.*** **1** a foreigner **2** a foreign-born resident who is not naturalized **3** a hypothetical being from outer space

al′ien·a·ble (-ə bəl) ***adj.*** capable of being transferred to a new owner

al′ien·ate′ (-āt′) ***vt.*** **-at′ed**, **-at′ing** **1** to transfer the ownership of (property) to another **2** to make unfriendly or withdrawn **3** to cause a transference of (affection) —**al′ien·a′tion** ***n.***

a·light[1] (ə līt′) ***vi.*** **a·light′ed** or **a·lit′**, **a·light′ing** ⟦ME *alihtan*⟧ **1** to get down or off; dismount **2** to come down after flight

a·light[2] (ə līt′) ***adj.*** lighted up; burning

a·lign (ə līn′) ***vt.*** ⟦< Fr *a-*, to + *ligne*, LINE[1]⟧ **1** to bring into a straight line **2** to bring (components or parts) into adjustment **3** to bring into agreement, etc. —***vi.*** to line up —**a·lign′ment** ***n.***

a·like (ə līk′) ***adj.*** ⟦< OE *gelic*⟧ like one another —***adv.*** **1** similarly **2** equally

al·i·ment (al′ə mənt) ***n.*** ⟦< L *alere*, nourish⟧ nourishment; food

al′i·men′ta·ry (-men′tə rē, -men′trē) ***adj.*** **1** of food or nutrition **2** nourishing

alimentary canal (or **tract**) the passage in the body (from the mouth to the anus) that food goes through

al·i·mo·ny (al′ə mō′nē) ***n.*** ⟦< L *alere*, nourish⟧ money a court orders paid to a person by that person's legally separated or divorced spouse

a·line (ə līn′) ***vt.***, ***vi.*** **a·lined′**, **a·lin′ing** ALIGN —**a·line′ment** ***n.***

a·lit (ə lit′) ***vi.*** *alt. pt. & pp. of* ALIGHT[1]

a·live (ə līv′) ***adj.*** ⟦< OE *on*, in + *līfe*, life⟧ **1** having life; living **2** in existence, operation, etc. **3** lively; alert —**alive to** aware of —**alive with** teeming with

a·li·yah or **a·li·ya** (ä′lē yä′) ***n.*** ⟦< Heb, lit., ascent⟧ immigration by Jews to Israel

al·ka·li (al′kə lī′) ***n.***, *pl.* **-lies′** or **-lis′** ⟦< Ar *al-qili*, the ashes of a certain plant⟧ **1** any base, as soda, that is soluble in water and gives off ions in solution **2** a mineral salt, etc. that can neutralize acids

al′ka·line (-lin, -līn′) ***adj.*** of or like an alkali —**al′ka·lin′i·ty** (-lin′ə tē) ***n.***

al′ka·lize′ (-līz′) ***vt.*** **-lized′**, **-liz′ing** to make alkaline —**al′ka·li·za′tion** ***n.***

al′ka·loid′ (-loid′) ***n.*** a bitter, alkaline substance, such as caffeine, morphine, etc., containing nitrogen

al·kyd (al′kid) ***n.*** ⟦ult. < ALKALI + (ACI)D⟧ a synthetic resin used in paints, varnishes, etc.: also **alkyd resin**

all (ôl) ***adj.*** ⟦OE *eal*⟧ **1** the whole quantity of *[all* the gold*]* **2** every one of *[all* men*]* **3** the greatest possible *[*in *all* sincerity*]* **4** any *[*beyond *all* doubt*]* **5** alone; only *[all* work and no play*]* —

pron. 1 [*with pl. v.*] everyone 2 everything 3 every part or bit —*n.* 1 one's whole property, effort, etc. [*gave his all*] 2 a totality; whole —*adv.* 1 wholly; entirely [*all* worn out] 2 apiece [*a score of two all*] —**after all** nevertheless —**all in** [Inf.] very tired —**all in all** 1 considering everything 2 as a whole —**all out** completely —**all the better** (or **worse**) so much the better (or worse) —**all the same** 1 nevertheless 2 unimportant —**at all** 1 in the least 2 in any way 3 under any considerations —**in all** altogether

all- *combining form* 1 wholly, entirely [*all*-American] 2 for every [*all*-purpose] 3 of everything [*all*-inclusive]

Al·lah (al'ə, ä'lə) *n.* ⟦< Ar *al*, the + *ilāh*, god⟧ *the Muslim name for* God

all'-A·mer'i·can *adj.* representative of the U.S. as a whole, or chosen as the best in the U.S. —*n.* 1 a hypothetical football team, etc. made up of U.S. college players voted the best of the year 2 a player on such a team

all'-a·round' *adj.* having many abilities, talents, or uses; versatile

al·lay (a lā', ə-) *vt.* **-layed'**, **-lay'ing** ⟦< OE *a-*, down + *lecgan*, lay⟧ 1 to calm; quiet 2 to relieve (pain, etc.)

all'-clear' *n.* a siren or other signal that an air raid or alert is over

al·le·ga·tion (al'ə gā'shən) *n.* an assertion, esp. one without proof or to be proved

al·lege (ə lej') *vt.* **-leged'**, **-leg'ing** ⟦< L *ex-*, out of + *litigare*, to dispute⟧ 1 to declare or assert, esp. without proof 2 to offer as an excuse

al·leged (ə lejd', ə lej'id) *adj.* 1 declared, but without proof 2 so-called [*alleged* friends] —**al·leg'ed·ly** *adv.*

Al·le·ghe·ny Mountains (al'ə gā'nē) mountain range in Pennsylvania, Maryland, West Virginia, & Virginia: also **Al'le·ghe'nies**

al·le·giance (ə lē'jəns) *n.* ⟦< OFr *liege*, liege⟧ 1 the duty of being loyal to one's ruler, country, etc. 2 loyalty; devotion, as to a cause

al·le·go·ry (al'ə gôr'ē) *n.*, *pl.* **-ries** ⟦< Gr *allos*, other + *agoreuein*, speak in assembly⟧ a story in which people, things, and events have a symbolic meaning, often instructive —**al'le·gor'i·cal** *adj.* —**al'le·gor'i·cal·ly** *adv.* —**al'le·go'rist** *n.*

al·le·gret·to (al'ə gret'ō) *adj.*, *adv.* ⟦It, dim. of *allegro*⟧ *Music* moderately fast: also written ***al'le·gret'to***

al·le·gro (ə le'grō', -lā'-) *adj.*, *adv.* ⟦It⟧ *Music* fast: also written ***al'le'gro'***

al·lele (ə lēl') *n.* ⟦< Gr *allēlōn*, of one another⟧ a gene transferring inherited characteristics

al·le·lu·ia (al'ə lo͞o'yə, ä'lə-) *interj.*, *n.* ⟦LL(Eccles.)⟧ HALLELUJAH

al·ler·gen (al'ər jən) *n.* ⟦Ger⟧ a substance inducing an allergic reaction —**al'ler·gen'ic** (-jen'ik) *adj.*

al·ler·gic (ə lur'jik) *adj.* 1 of, caused by, or having an allergy 2 [Inf.] averse (*to*)

al·ler·gist (al'ər jist) *n.* a doctor who specializes in treating allergies

al·ler·gy (al'ər jē) *n.*, *pl.* **-gies** ⟦Ger < Gr *allos*, other + *ergon*, work⟧ 1 a hypersensitivity to a specific substance (as a food, pollen, dust, etc.) or condition (as heat or cold) 2 an aversion

al·le·vi·ate (ə lē'vē āt') *vt.* **-at'ed**, **-at'ing** ⟦< L *ad-*, to + *levis*, light⟧ 1 to lessen or relieve (pain, etc.) 2 to decrease (poverty, etc.) —**al·le'vi·a'tion** *n.*

al·ley (al'ē) *n.*, *pl.* **-leys** ⟦< OFr *aler*, go⟧ 1 a narrow street between or behind buildings 2 a bowling lane

alley cat a homeless, mongrel cat

al'ley·way' *n.* an alley between buildings

all'-fired' *adj.*, *adv.* ⟦< *hell-fired*⟧ [Slang] extreme(ly)

al·li·ance (ə lī'əns) *n.* ⟦see ALLY⟧ 1 an allying or close association, as of nations for a common objective, families by marriage, etc. 2 an agreement for this 3 the countries, groups, etc. in such association

al·lied (ə līd', al'īd') *adj.* 1 united by kinship, treaty, etc. 2 closely related

al·li·ga·tor (al'ə gāt'ər) *n.* ⟦< Sp *el*, the + L *lacerta*, lizard⟧ a large reptile of the U.S. and China, like the crocodile but with a shorter, broader snout

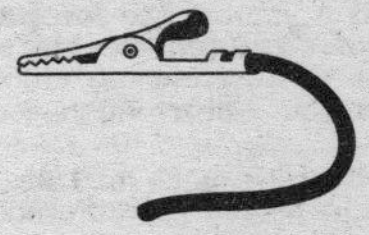

ALLIGATOR CLIP

alligator clip a fastening device with spring-loaded jaws for making an electrical connection

alligator pear AVOCADO

all'-im·por'tant *adj.* highly important; necessary; essential

all'-in·clu'sive *adj.* including everything; comprehensive

al·lit·er·a·tion (ə lit'ər ā'shən) *n.* ⟦< L *ad-*, to + *littera*, letter⟧ repetition of an initial sound in two or more words of a phrase —**al·lit'er·a'tive** (-āt'iv, -ə tiv) *adj.*

al·lo·cate (al'ə kāt') *vt.* **-cat'ed**, **-cat'ing** ⟦< L *ad-*, to + *locus*, a place⟧ 1 to set apart for a specific purpose 2 to distribute or allot —**al'lo·ca'tion** *n.*

al·lot (ə lät') *vt.* **-lot'ted**, **-lot'ting** ⟦< OFr *a-*, to + *lot*, lot⟧ 1 to distribute in arbitrary shares; apportion 2 to assign as one's share —**al·lot'ment** *n.*

all'-out' *adj.* complete or wholehearted

all'o'ver *adj.* over the whole surface

al·low (ə lou') *vt.* ⟦see ALLOCATE⟧ 1 to permit; let [*I'm not allowed to go*] 2 to let have [*she allowed herself no sweets*] 3 to acknowledge as valid 4 to provide (a certain amount), as for shrinkage, waste, etc. —**allow for** to leave room, time, etc. for —**al·low'a·ble** *adj.*

al·low'ance (-əns) *n.* 1 an allowing 2 something allowed 3 an amount of money, food, etc. given regularly to a child, soldier, etc. **4** a reduction in price, as for a trade-in —**make allowance(s) for** to excuse because of mitigating factors

al·loy (al′oi; *also, and for v. usually,* ə loi′) ***n.*** ⟦< L *ad-*, to + *ligare*, to bind⟧ **1** a substance that is a mixture of two or more metals **2** something that debases another thing when mixed with it —***vt.*** to make into an alloy

all′-pur′pose ***adj.*** useful in many ways

all right **1** satisfactory; adequate **2** unhurt; safe **3** correct **4** yes; very well **5** [Inf.] certainly

all′-round′ ***adj., adv.*** *var. of* ALL-AROUND

all·spice (ôl′spīs′) ***n.*** a spice, that seems to combine the flavors of several spices, made from the berry of a West Indian tree of the myrtle family

all′-star′ ***adj.*** **1** made up of outstanding or star performers **2** of or characteristic of an all-star event —***n.*** a member of an all-star team

all′-time′ ***adj.*** unsurpassed up to the present time

al·lude (ə lo͞od′) ***vi.*** **-lud′ed, -lud′ing** ⟦L *alludere*, to jest⟧ to refer indirectly (*to*)

al·lure (ə lo͝or′) ***vt., vi.*** **-lured′, -lur′ing** ⟦< OFr *a-*, to + *loirer*, to lure⟧ to tempt with something desirable; attract; entice —***n.*** fascination; charm —**al·lure′ment** ***n.*** —**al·lur·ing** (ə lo͝or′iŋ, a-) ***adj.***

al·lu·sion (ə lo͞o′zhən) ***n.*** **1** an alluding **2** an indirect or casual reference

al·lu′sive (-siv) ***adj.*** **1** containing an allusion **2** full of allusions —**al·lu′sive·ly** ***adv.*** —**al·lu′sive·ness** ***n.***

al·lu·vi·um (ə lo͞o′vē əm) ***n., pl.*** **-vi·ums** or **-vi·a** (-vē ə) ⟦< L *ad-*, to + *luere*, to wash⟧ sand, clay, etc. deposited by moving water —**al·lu′vi·al** ***adj.***

al·ly (ə lī′; *also, and for n. usually,* al′ī) ***vt., vi.*** **-lied′, -ly′ing** ⟦< L *ad-*, to + *ligare*, to bind⟧ **1** to unite or join for a specific purpose **2** to relate by similarity of structure, etc. —***n., pl.*** **-lies** a country or person joined with another for a common purpose

al·ma ma·ter (al′mə mät′ər, äl′-) ⟦L, fostering mother⟧ **1** the college or school that one attended **2** its anthem

al·ma·nac (ôl′mə nak′, al′-) ***n.*** ⟦< *c.* 5th-c. Gr *almenichiaka*, calendar⟧ **1** a calendar with astronomical data, weather forecasts, etc. **2** a book published annually, with statistical information

al·might·y (ôl mīt′ē) ***adj.*** all-powerful —**the Almighty** God

al·mond (ä′mənd, al′-, ôl′-; am′ənd) ***n.*** ⟦< Gr *amygdalē*⟧ **1** the edible, nutlike kernel of a peachlike fruit **2** the tree it grows on **3** the light-tan color of its shell —***adj.*** shaped like an almond; oval and pointed at one or both ends

al·most (ôl′mōst′, ôl mōst′) ***adv.*** very nearly; all but

alms (ämz) ***n., pl.*** **alms** ⟦< Gr *eleos*, mercy⟧ money, food, etc. given to poor people —**alms′giv′er** ***n.***

alms′house′ ***n.*** **1** [Archaic] a poorhouse **2** [Brit.] a privately endowed home for the poor

al·oe (al′ō′) ***n., pl.*** **-oes′** ⟦< Gr *aloē*⟧ an African plant of the lily family

a·loft (ə lôft′) ***adv.*** ⟦ME < *o*, on+ *loft*, loft⟧ **1** high up **2** in the air; flying **3** high above the deck of a ship

a·lo·ha (ä lō′hə, -hä′; ə lō′ə) ***n., interj.*** ⟦Haw, love⟧ **1** hello **2** goodbye

a·lone (ə lōn′) ***adj., adv.*** ⟦ME < *al*, all + *one*, one⟧ **1** apart from anything or anyone else **2** without any other person **3** only **4** without equal —**let alone** **1** to refrain from interfering with: also **leave alone** **2** not to speak of *[we hadn't a dime, let alone a dollar]*

a·long (ə lôŋ′) ***prep.*** ⟦< OE *and-*, over against + *-lang*, long⟧ **1** on or beside the length of **2** in conformity with —***adv.*** **1** lengthwise **2** progressively forward **3** together (*with*) **4** with one *[take me along]* **5** advanced *[well along in years]* —**all along** from the beginning —**be along** [Inf.] to come or arrive —**get along** **1** to advance **2** to manage **3** to survive **4** to be compatible

a·long′shore′ ***adv.*** near or beside the shore

a·long′side′ ***adv.*** at or by the side; side by side —***prep.*** beside —**alongside of** at the side of

a·loof (ə lo͞of′) ***adv.*** ⟦< *a-*, on & Du *loef*, windward side⟧ at a distance but in view —***adj.*** cool and reserved *[an aloof manner]* —**a·loof′ness** ***n.***

a·loud (ə loud′) ***adv.*** **1** loudly **2** with the normal voice; not silently

alp (alp) ***n.*** ⟦after ALPS⟧ a high mountain

al·pac·a (al pak′ə) ***n.*** ⟦< AmInd⟧ **1** a South American llama **2** its silky wool, or cloth woven from it

al·pha (al′fə) ***n.*** **1** the first letter of the Greek alphabet (Α, α) **2** the beginning of anything —***adj.*** of the dominant member of a group

al′pha·bet′ (-bet′) ***n.*** ⟦< Gr *alpha* & *bēta*, first two letters of the Gr alphabet⟧ the letters used in writing a language, esp. as arranged in their usual order —**al′pha·bet′i·cal** ***adj.*** —**al′pha·bet′i·cal·ly** ***adv.***

al·pha·bet·ize (al′fə bə tīz′) ***vt.*** **-ized′, -iz′ing** to arrange in the usual order of the alphabet —**al′pha·bet′i·za′tion** ***n.***

al′pha·nu·mer′ic (-no͞o mer′ik) ***adj.*** having both alphabetical and numerical symbols

alpha particle a positively charged particle given off by certain radioactive substances

alpha ray a stream of alpha particles

alpha wave an electrical brain wave indicating relaxation: also **alpha rhythm**

Al·pine (al′pīn′) ***adj.*** **1** of the Alps **2** [**a-**] of or like high mountains

Alps (alps) mountain system in SC Europe

al·read·y (ôl red′ē) ***adv.*** **1** by or before the given or implied time **2** even now or even then

al·right (ôl rīt′) ***adj., adv., interj.*** *disputed sp. of* ALL RIGHT

Al·sace (al sās′, al′sas′) historical region of NE France —**Al·sa′tian** (-sā′shən) ***adj., n.***

al·so (ôl′sō) ***adv.*** ⟦< OE *eall*, all + *swa*, so⟧ in addition; likewise; too; besides

al′so-ran′ ***n.*** [Inf.] a defeated contestant in a race, election, etc.

alt *abbrev.* **1** alternate **2** altitude **3** alto

al·tar (ôl′tər) ***n.*** ⟦< L *altus*, high⟧ **1** a platform where sacrifices are made to a god, etc. **2** a table, etc. for sacred purposes in a place of worship

altar boy a boy or man who helps a priest at religious services, esp. at Mass

al·ter (ôl′tər) ***vt., vi.*** ⟦< L *alter*, other⟧ to change; make or become different —**al′ter·a′tion** ***n.***

al·ter·ca·tion (ôl′tər kā′shən) ***n.*** ⟦< L *altercari*, to dispute⟧ an angry or heated argument; quarrel

al′ter e′go ⟦L, other I⟧ **1** another aspect of oneself **2** a constant companion

al·ter·nate (ôl′tər nit; *for v.*, -nāt′) ***adj.*** ⟦< L *alternus*, one after the other⟧ **1** succeeding each other **2** every other **3** ALTERNATIVE (*adj.* 1) —***n.*** a substitute —***vt.*** **-nat′ed, -nat′ing** to do or use by turns —***vi.*** **1** to act, happen, etc. by turns **2** to take turns regularly —**al′ter·nate·ly** ***adv.*** —**al′ter·na′tion** ***n.***

alternating current an electric current reversing direction periodically: abbrev. *AC*

al·ter·na·tive (ôl tur′nə tiv) ***adj.*** **1** providing a choice between things **2** of an institution, etc. appealing to unconventional interests *[an alternative school]* —***n.*** **1** a choice between things **2** one of the things to be chosen **3** something left to choose

al·ter·na·tor (ôl′tər nāt′ər) ***n.*** an electric generator producing alternating current

al·though (ôl *th*ō′) ***conj.*** ⟦ME < *al*, even + THOUGH⟧ in spite of the fact that; though: sometimes sp. **al·tho′**

al·tim·e·ter (al tim′ət ər) ***n.*** ⟦< L *altus*, high + -METER⟧ an instrument for measuring altitude

al·ti·tude (al′tə to͞od′) ***n.*** ⟦< L *altus*, high⟧ **1** the height of a thing, esp. above sea level **2** a high place: *usually used in pl.*

al·to (al′tō) ***n.***, *pl.* **-tos** ⟦It < L *altus*, high⟧ **1** the range of a voice between tenor and mezzo-soprano **2** a voice, singer, or instrument with such a range **3** a part for an alto —***adj.*** of or for an alto

al·to·geth·er (ôl′to͞o ge*th*′ər) ***adv.*** **1** completely **2** in all **3** on the whole

al·tru·ism (al′tro͞o iz′əm) ***n.*** ⟦< L *alter*, other⟧ unselfish concern for the welfare of others —**al′tru·ist** ***n.*** —**al′tru·is′tic** ***adj.*** —**al′tru·is′ti·cal·ly** ***adv.***

al·um (al′əm) ***n.*** ⟦< L *alumen*⟧ any of a group of salts of aluminum, etc., used in manufacturing and medicine

al·u·min·i·um (al′yo͞o min′ē əm) ***n.*** [Brit.] *var. of* ALUMINUM

a·lu·mi·num (ə lo͞o′mə nəm) ***n.*** ⟦< L *alumen*, alum⟧ a silvery, lightweight metallic chemical element

a·lum·nus (ə lum′nəs) ***n.***, *pl.* **-ni′** (-nī′) ⟦L, foster son⟧ a person, esp. a boy or man, who has attended or is a graduate of a particular school, college, etc. —**a·lum′na** (-nə), *pl.* **-nae** (-nē), ***fem.n.***

al·ways (ôl′wāz) ***adv.*** ⟦OE *ealne weg*⟧ **1** at all times **2** all the time **3** at any time **4** in every instance

Alz·hei·mer's disease (älts′hī′mərz) ⟦after A. *Alzheimer*, 20th-c. Ger doctor⟧ a degenerative brain disease

am (am) ***vi.*** ⟦OE *eom*⟧ *1st pers. sing., pres. indic., of* BE

Am *abbrev.* **1** America **2** American

AM[1] (ā′em′) ***n.*** amplitude-modulation broadcasting or sound transmission

AM[2] *abbrev.* **1** amplitude modulation **2** ⟦L *ante meridiem*⟧ before noon: used to designate the time from midnight to noon: also **A.M., am,** or **a.m. 3** ⟦L *Artium Magister*⟧ master of arts: also **A.M.**

AMA *abbrev.* American Medical Association

a·mal·gam (ə mal′gəm) ***n.*** ⟦< Gr *malagma*, an emollient⟧ **1** any alloy of mercury with another metal *[a dental filling of silver amalgam]* **2** a mixture; blend

a·mal′ga·mate′ (-gə māt′) ***vt., vi.*** **-mat′ed, -mat′ing** to unite; mix; combine —**a·mal′ga·ma′tion** ***n.***

a·man·dine (ä′mən dēn′) ***adj.*** ⟦Fr⟧ prepared with almonds

a·man·u·en·sis (ə man′yo͞o en′sis) ***n.***, *pl.* **-ses′** (-sēz′) ⟦L < *a-*, from + *manus*, hand + *-ensis*, relating to⟧ a secretary: now a jocular usage

am·a·ranth (am′ə ranth′) ***n.*** ⟦< Gr *amarantos*, unfading⟧ **1** any of a large group of similar plants, some bearing showy flowers **2** [Old Poet.] an imaginary flower that never dies

am·a·ret·to (am′ə ret′ō) ***n.*** ⟦It, rather bitter⟧ [*also* **A-**] a liqueur with an almond flavor

Am·a·ril·lo (am′ə ril′ō) city in NW Texas: pop. 158,000

am·a·ryl·lis (am′ə ril′is) ***n.*** ⟦< Gr *Amaryllis*, name for a shepherdess⟧ a lilylike plant with white, purple, pink, or red flowers

a·mass (ə mas′) ***vt.*** ⟦< Fr < L *massa*, a lump⟧ to pile up; accumulate

am·a·teur (am′ə chər, -tər) ***n.*** ⟦Fr < L *amare*, to love⟧ **1** one who does something for pleasure, not for money; nonprofessional **2** one who is somewhat unskillful —***adj.*** of or done by amateurs —**am′a·teur′ish** (-choor′-) ***adj.*** —**am′a·teur·ism′** ***n.***

am·a·to·ry (am′ə tôr′ē) ***adj.*** ⟦< L *amare*, to love⟧ of or showing love, esp. sexual love

a·maze (ə māz′) ***vt.*** **a·mazed′, a·maz′ing** ⟦OE *āmasian*⟧ to fill with great surprise or wonder; astonish —**a·maze′ment** ***n.*** —**a·maz′ing** ***adj.*** —**a·maz′ing·ly** ***adv.***

Am·a·zon[1] (am′ə zän′, -zən) ***n.*** **1** *Gr. Myth.* any of a race of female warriors

2 [a-] a tall, strong, aggressive woman

Am'a·zon'[2] river in N South America: *c.* 4,000 mi.

am·bas·sa·dor (am bas'ə dər) ***n.*** ⟦< Prov *ambaissador*⟧ the highest-ranking diplomatic representative of one country to another —**am·bas'sa·do'ri·al** (-dôr'ē əl) ***adj.*** —**am·bas'sa·dor·ship'** ***n.***

am·ber (am'bər) ***n.*** ⟦< Ar *'anbar*, ambergris⟧ **1** a brownish-yellow fossil resin used in jewelry, etc. **2** its color —***adj.*** amberlike or amber-colored

am'ber·gris' (-grēs', -gris') ***n.*** ⟦< OFr *ambre gris*, gray amber⟧ a grayish, waxy substance in the intestines of sperm whales, used in perfumes

ambi- ⟦L⟧ *combining form* both *[ambidextrous]*

am·bi·dex·trous (am'bə deks'trəs) ***adj.*** ⟦< earlier *ambidexter* + -OUS⟧ using both hands with equal ease —**am'bi·dex·ter'i·ty** (-deks ter'ə tē) ***n.***

am·bi·ence (am'bē əns, äm'bē äns') ***n.*** ⟦Fr: see fol.⟧ an environment or its distinct atmosphere: also sp. **am'bi·ance** (-əns)

am·bi·ent (am'bē ənt) ***adj.*** ⟦< L *ambi-*, around + *ire*, to go⟧ surrounding; on all sides

am·bi·gu·i·ty (am'bə gyōō'ə tē) ***n.*** **1** a being ambiguous **2** *pl.* **-ties** an ambiguous word, statement, etc.

am·big·u·ous (am big'yōō əs) ***adj.*** ⟦< L *ambi-*, around + *agere*, to do⟧ **1** having two or more meanings **2** not clear; vague —**am·big'u·ous·ly** ***adv.***

am·bi·tion (am bish'ən) ***n.*** ⟦< L *ambitio*, a going around (to solicit votes)⟧ **1** a strong desire for fame, power, etc. **2** the thing so desired

am·bi'tious (-əs) ***adj.*** **1** full of or showing ambition **2** demanding great effort —**am·bi'tious·ly** ***adv.***

am·biv·a·lence (am biv'ə ləns) ***n.*** ⟦AMBI- + VALENCE⟧ simultaneous conflicting feelings —**am·biv'a·lent** ***adj.*** —**am·biv'a·lent·ly** ***adv.***

am·ble (am'bəl) ***vi.*** **-bled**, **-bling** ⟦< L *ambulare*, to walk⟧ **1** to move at an easy gait, as a horse **2** to walk in a leisurely way —***n.*** **1** a horse's ambling gait **2** a leisurely walking pace

am·bro·sia (am brō'zhə) ***n.*** ⟦< Gr *a-*, not + *brotos*, mortal⟧ **1** *Gr. & Rom. Myth.* the food of the gods **2** anything that tastes or smells delicious —**am·bro'sial** ***adj.***

am·bu·lance (am'byə ləns) ***n.*** ⟦< L *ambulare*, to walk⟧ a vehicle equipped for carrying the sick or wounded

am·bu·late (am'byōō lāt', -byə-) ***vi.*** **-lat'ed**, **-lat'ing** to move about; walk —**am'bu·lant** (-lənt) ***adj.*** —**am'bu·la'tion** ***n.***

am'bu·la·to'ry (-lə tôr'ē) ***adj.*** **1** of or for walking **2** able to walk

am·bus·cade (am'bəs kād') ***n.***, ***vt.***, ***vi.*** **-cad'ed**, **-cad'ing** AMBUSH

am·bush (am'boosh') ***n.*** ⟦< ML *in-*, in + *boscus*, woods⟧ **1** a deployment of persons in hiding to make a surprise attack **2** their hiding place **3** a surprise attack —***vt.***, ***vi.*** to attack from ambush

a·me·ba (ə mē'bə) ***n.***, *pl.* **-bas** or **-bae** (-bē) *alt. sp. of* AMOEBA —**a·me'bic** (-bik) ***adj.***

a·mel·io·rate (ə mēl'yə rāt') ***vt.***, ***vi.*** **-rat'ed**, **-rat'ing** ⟦< Fr < L *melior*, better⟧ to make or become better; improve —**a·mel'io·ra'tion** ***n.***

a·men (ā'men', ä'-) ***interj.*** ⟦< Heb *amen*, truly⟧ may it be so!: used after a prayer or to express approval

a·me·na·ble (ə mē'nə bəl, -men'ə-) ***adj.*** ⟦< OFr < L *minare*, to drive (animals)⟧ **1** responsible or answerable **2** able to be controlled; submissive —**a·me'na·bil'i·ty** ***n.*** —**a·me'na·bly** ***adv.***

a·mend (ə mend') ***vt.*** ⟦< L *emendare*⟧ **1** to correct; emend **2** to improve **3** to change or revise (a law, etc.) —***vi.*** to improve one's conduct —**a·mend'a·ble** ***adj.***

a·mend'ment ***n.*** **1** a correction of errors, faults, etc. **2** improvement **3** a revision or change proposed or made in a bill, law, etc.

a·mends (ə mendz') ***pl.n.*** ⟦see AMEND⟧ [*sometimes with sing. v.*] payment made or satisfaction given for injury, loss, etc.

a·men·i·ty (ə men'ə tē, -mēn'-) ***n.***, *pl.* **-ties** ⟦< L *amoenus*, pleasant⟧ **1** pleasantness **2** an attractive feature or convenience **3** [*pl.*] courteous acts

am·ent (am'ənt, ā'mənt) ***n.*** ⟦< L *amentum*, thong⟧ CATKIN

Am·er·a·sian (am'ər ā'zhən) ***n.*** ⟦AMER(ICAN) + ASIAN⟧ a person of both American and Asian descent —***adj.*** both American and Asian *[an Amerasian child]*

a·merce (ə murs') ***vt.*** **a·merced'**, **a·merc'ing** ⟦< OFr *a merci*, at the mercy of⟧ to punish, esp. by imposing a fine —**a·merce'ment** ***n.***

A·mer·i·ca (ə mer'i kə) ⟦associated with *Amerigo* VESPUCCI⟧ **1** North America, South America, and the West Indies, considered together: also **the Americas** **2** North America **3** the United States of America

A·mer'i·can (-kən) ***adj.*** **1** of or in America **2** of the U.S. or its people —***n.*** **1** a person born or living in North or South America **2** a citizen of the U.S.

A·mer·i·can·a (ə mer'i kan'ə, -kä'nə) ***pl.n.*** books, papers, objects, etc. having to do with the U.S., its people, and its history

American Indian a member of any of the indigenous peoples of North or South America or the West Indies

A·mer'i·can·ism' ***n.*** **1** a custom or belief of or originating in the U.S. **2** a word or idiom originating in American English **3** devotion to the U.S., its customs, etc.

A·mer'i·can·ize' (-īz') ***vt.***, ***vi.*** **-ized'**, **-iz'ing** to make or become American in character, manners, etc. —**A·mer'i·can·i·za'tion** ***n.***

American plan a system of hotel operation in which the price charged covers room, service, and meals

American Revolution the war (1775-

83) fought by the American colonies to gain independence from Great Britain

American Samoa group of seven islands in the SW Pacific: an unincorporated territory of the U.S.: 77 sq. mi.; pop. 47,000

Am·er·in·di·an (am′ər in′dē ən) ***n., adj.*** AMERICAN INDIAN —**Am′er·ind′** ***n., adj.***

am·e·thyst (am′i thist) ***n.*** ⟦< Gr *amethystos*, not drunken: the Greeks thought the amethyst prevented intoxication⟧ **1** a purple or violet quartz or corundum, used in jewelry **2** purple or violet

a·mi·a·ble (ā′mē ə bəl) ***adj.*** ⟦< L *amicus*, friend⟧ good-natured; friendly —**a′mi·a·bil′i·ty** ***n.*** —**a′mi·a·bly** ***adv.***

am·i·ca·ble (am′i kə bəl) ***adj.*** ⟦see prec.⟧ friendly; peaceable —**am′i·ca·bil′i·ty** ***n.*** —**am′i·ca·bly** ***adv.***

a·mid (ə mid′) ***prep.*** in the middle of; among: also **a·midst** (ə midst′)

am·ide (am′īd′) ***n.*** any of several organic compounds derived from ammonia

a·mid′ships′ ***adv., adj.*** in or toward the middle of a ship

a·mi·go (ə mē′gō) ***n.***, *pl.* **-gos′** (-gōz′) ⟦Sp⟧ a friend

a·mi·no acid (ə mē′nō) ⟦< AMMONIA⟧ any of the nitrogenous organic acids that form proteins necessary for all life

Am·ish (äm′ish, am′-) ***pl.n.*** ⟦after Jacob *Ammann* (or *Amen*), the founder⟧ the members of a Christian sect that favors plain living in an agrarian society —***adj.*** of this sect

a·miss (ə mis′) ***adv.*** ⟦see A-[1] & MISS[1]⟧ in a wrong way; astray —***adj.*** wrong, faulty, improper, etc. [what is *amiss?*]

am·i·ty (am′i tē) ***n.***, *pl.* **-ties** ⟦< L *amicus*, friend⟧ peaceful relations

am·me·ter (am′mēt′ər) ***n.*** ⟦AM(PERE) + -METER⟧ an instrument for measuring an electric current in amperes

am·mo (am′ō) ***n.*** [Slang] ammunition

am·mo·ni·a (ə mōn′yə) ***n.*** ⟦prob. from a salt found near Egyptian shrine of Jupiter *Ammon*⟧ **1** a colorless, pungent gas, a compound of nitrogen and hydrogen **2** a 10% water solution of this gas

am·mu·ni·tion (am′yoo nish′ən) ***n.*** ⟦< L *munire*, fortify⟧ **1** bullets, gunpowder, bombs, grenades, rockets, etc. **2** any means of attack or defense

am·ne·sia (am nē′zhə) ***n.*** ⟦< Gr *a-*, not + *mnasthai*, to remember⟧ partial or total loss of memory

am·nes·ty (am′nəs tē) ***n.***, *pl.* **-ties** ⟦< Gr *amnēstia*, a forgetting⟧ a pardon, esp. for political offenses —***vt.*** **-tied, -ty·ing** to pardon

am·ni·o·cen·te·sis (am′nē ō′sen tē′sis) ***n.*** ⟦< fol. + Gr *kentēsis*, a pricking⟧ the surgical procedure of extracting amniotic fluid from a pregnant woman to determine the sex of the fetus, detect disease, etc.

am·ni·on (am′nē ən, -än′) ***n.***, *pl.* **-ni·ons** or **-ni·a** (-ə) ⟦Gr, dim. of *amnos*, lamb⟧ the membrane enclosing the embryo of a mammal, reptile, or bird: it is filled with a watery fluid (**amniotic fluid**) —**am′ni·ot′ic** (-ät′ik) ***adj.***

a·moe·ba (ə mē′bə) ***n.***, *pl.* **-bas** or **-bae** (-bē) ⟦< Gr *ameibein*, to change⟧ a one-celled, microscopic organism reproducing by fission —**a·moe′bic** (-bik) ***adj.***

a·mok (ə muk′) ***adj., adv.*** ⟦< Malay *amuk*, attacking furiously⟧ used chiefly in **run amok**, lose control and behave violently

a·mong (ə muŋ′) ***prep.*** ⟦< OE *on*, in + *gemang*, a crowd⟧ **1** surrounded by [*among* friends] **2** in the group of [best *among* books] **3** to or for each or several of [divide it *among* the crowd] **4** by the joint action of Also [Chiefly Brit.] **a·mongst** (ə muŋst′)

A·mon-Re (ä′mən rā′) ***n.*** the ancient Egyptian sun god: also **A′mon-Ra′** (-rä′)

a·mon·til·la·do (ə män′tə lä′dō) ***n.*** ⟦< Sp, after *Montilla*, town in Spain⟧ a pale, dry sherry

a·mor·al (ā môr′əl) ***adj.*** **1** neither moral nor immoral **2** without moral sense —**a′mo·ral′i·ty** ***n.*** —**a·mor′al·ly** ***adv.***

am·o·rous (am′ə rəs) ***adj.*** ⟦< L *amor*, love⟧ **1** fond of making love **2** full of love **3** of sexual love —**am′o·rous·ly** ***adv.***

a·mor·phous (ə môr′fəs) ***adj.*** ⟦< Gr *a-*, without + *morphē*, form⟧ **1** without definite form **2** vague or indefinite **3** *Chem.* not crystalline

am·or·tize (am′ər tīz′, ə môr′-) ***vt.*** **-tized′, -tiz′ing** ⟦< ME < L *ad*, to + *mors*, death⟧ to put money aside at intervals for gradual payment of (a debt, etc.) —**am′or·ti·za′tion** ***n.***

a·mount (ə mount′) ***vi.*** ⟦< OFr *amont*, upward < L *ad*, to + *mons*, mountain⟧ **1** to add up (*to*) **2** to be equal (*to*) in value, etc. —***n.*** **1** a sum total **2** the whole value or effect **3** a quantity

a·mour (ə moor′) ***n.*** ⟦< L *amor*, love⟧ a love affair, esp. an illicit one

a·mour-pro·pre (á moor prô′pr′) ***n.*** ⟦Fr⟧ self-esteem

amp[1] (amp) ***n.*** *short for:* **1** AMPERE **2** AMPLIFIER

amp[2] *abbrev.* **1** amperage **2** ampere(s)

am·per·age (am′pər ij) ***n.*** the strength of an electric current in amperes

am·pere (am′pir′) ***n.*** ⟦< A. M. *Ampère*, 19th-c. Fr physicist⟧ the standard unit for measuring an electric current, equal to one coulomb per second

am·per·sand (am′pər sand′) ***n.*** ⟦< *and per se and*, (the sign) & by itself (is) *and*⟧ a sign (&), meaning *and*

am·phet·a·mine (am fet′ə mēn′, -min) ***n.*** a drug used esp. as a stimulant and to lessen appetite

am·phib·i·an (am fib′ē ən) ***n.*** ⟦see fol.⟧ **1** any amphibious animal, as a frog, or plant **2** any aircraft that can take off from or land on water or land —***adj.*** AMPHIBIOUS

am·phib′i·ous ***adj.*** ⟦Gr *amphibios*, living a double life < *amphi-*, around + *bios*, life⟧ that can live or operate on land and in water

am·phi·the·a·ter or **am·phi·the·a·tre** (am′fə thē′ə tər) ***n.*** ⟦< Gr *amphi-*, around + *theatron*, theater⟧ a round or oval building with rising rows of seats around an open space

am·ple (am′pəl) ***adj.*** **-pler, -plest** ⟦< L *amplus*⟧ **1** large in size, scope, etc. **2** more than enough **3** adequate —**am′ply** ***adv.***

am·pli·fi·er (am′plə fī′ər) ***n.*** one that amplifies; esp., a device for strengthening electrical signals

am′pli·fy′ (-fī′) ***vt.*** **-fied′, -fy′ing** ⟦< L *amplus*, large + *facere*, to make⟧ **1** to make stronger; esp., to strengthen (electrical signals) **2** to develop more fully —**am′pli·fi·ca′tion** ***n.***

am·pli·tude (am′plə to͞od′) ***n.*** ⟦see AMPLE⟧ **1** scope, extent, breadth, etc. **2** abundance **3** range from mean to extreme of a fluctuating quantity, as of an alternating current

amplitude modulation the changing of the amplitude of the transmitting radio wave in accordance with the signal being broadcast: abbrev. *AM*

am·pul (am′po͞ol′) ***n.*** ⟦< L *ampulla*, bottle⟧ a small, sealed, glass or plastic container for a single dose of a hypodermic medicine: also **am′pule′** (-pyo͞ol′) or **am′poule′** (-po͞ol′)

am·pu·tate (am′pyo͞o tāt′) ***vt., vi.*** **-tat′ed, -tat′ing** ⟦< L *am-*, AMBI- + *putare*, to prune⟧ to cut off (an arm, etc.), esp. by surgery —**am′pu·ta′tion** ***n.***

am′pu·tee′ (-tē′) ***n.*** one who has had a limb or limbs amputated

Am·ster·dam (am′stər dam′) constitutional capital of the Netherlands: pop. 724,000

amt *abbrev.* amount

Am·trak (am′trak′) *abbrev.* ⟦*Am(erican) tr(avel) (tr)a(c)k*⟧ a national U.S. passenger railroad system

a·muck (ə muk′) ***n.*** *alt. sp. of* AMOK

am·u·let (am′yo͞o lit) ***n.*** ⟦< L⟧ something worn to protect against evil

a·muse (ə myo͞oz′) ***vt.*** **a·mused′, a·mus′ing** ⟦< Fr < *à*, at + OFr *muser*, to gaze⟧ **1** to keep pleasantly occupied; entertain **2** to make laugh, smile, etc. —**a·mus′ed·ly** ***adv.***

a·muse′ment ***n.*** **1** a being amused **2** something that amuses; entertainment

amusement park an outdoor place with devices for entertainment, as a merry-go-round, roller coaster, etc.

am·yl·ase (am′ə lās′) ***n.*** ⟦< Gr *amylon*, starch⟧ an enzyme that helps change starch into sugar, found in saliva, etc.

an (an; *unstressed*, ən, ′n) ***adj., indefinite article*** ⟦< OE *an*, one⟧ **1** one; one sort of **2** each; any one —***prep.*** per *[*two *an* hour*]* *An* is used before words beginning with a vowel sound *[an* eye, *an* honor*]* See also A²

-an (ən, in, ′n) ⟦< L *-anus*⟧ *suffix* **1** (one) belonging to *[diocesan]* **2** (one) born in or living in *[Mexican]* **3** (one) believing in *[Lutheran]*

a·nach·ro·nism (ə nak′rə niz′əm) ***n.*** ⟦< Gr *ana-*, against + *chronos*, time⟧ **1** anything out of its proper historical time **2** the representation of this —**a·nach′ro·nis′tic** ***adj.***

an·a·con·da (an′ə kän′də) ***n.*** ⟦< Sinhalese *henacandāya*, a snake of Sri Lanka⟧ a long, heavy South American boa living in trees and water

an·aer·o·bic (an′ər ō′bik) ***adj.*** ⟦< Gr *an-*, without + *aēr*, air + *bios*, life⟧ able to live and grow without air or free oxygen, as certain bacteria

an·aes·the·sia (an′əs thē′zhə) ***n.*** ANESTHESIA —**an′aes·thet′ic** (-thet′ik) ***adj., n.***

an·a·gram (an′ə gram′) ***n.*** ⟦< Gr *anagrammatizein*, transpose letters⟧ **1** a word, etc. made by rearranging letters (Ex.: *now — won*) **2** [*pl., with sing. v.*] a word game based on this

An·a·heim (an′ə hīm′) city in SW California: pop. 266,000

a·nal (ā′nəl) ***adj.*** **1** of or near the anus **2** [Inf.] excessively orderly, stingy, etc.

an·al·ge·si·a (an′əl jē′zē ə) ***n.*** ⟦< Gr *an-*, without + *algēsia*, pain⟧ a fully conscious state in which pain is not felt

an′al·ge′sic (-zik) ***adj.*** of or causing analgesia —***n.*** a drug that produces analgesia

an·a·log (an′ə lôg′) ***adj.*** **1** of electronic devices in which the signal corresponds to a physical change **2** using hands, dials, etc. to show numerical amounts, as on a clock: cf. DIGITAL (sense 2) —***n.*** ANALOGUE

a·nal·o·gize (ə nal′ə jīz′) ***vi., vt.*** **-gized′, -giz′ing** to use, or explain by, analogy

a·nal′o·gous (-gəs) ***adj.*** ⟦see ANALOGY⟧ similar in some way —**a·nal′o·gous·ly** ***adv.***

an·a·logue (an′ə lôg′) ***n.*** something analogous

a·nal·o·gy (ə nal′ə jē) ***n.***, *pl.* **-gies** ⟦< Gr *ana-*, according to + *logos*, word, reckoning⟧ **1** similarity in some ways **2** the inference that certain resemblances imply further similarity

a·nal·y·sand (ə nal′ə sand′) ***n.*** a person undergoing psychoanalysis

a·nal′y·sis (-sis) ***n.***, *pl.* **-ses′** (-sēz′) ⟦< Gr *ana-*, up + *lysis*, a loosing⟧ **1** *a)* a breaking up of a whole into its parts to find out their nature, etc. *b)* any detailed examination **2** a statement of the results of this **3** PSYCHOANALYSIS **4** *Chem.* an analysis of compounds or mixtures —**an·a·lyt·ic** (an′ə lit′ik) or **an′a·lyt′i·cal** ***adj.*** —**an′a·lyt′i·cal·ly** ***adv.***

an·a·lyst (an′ə list) ***n.*** **1** one who analyzes **2** a psychoanalyst

an′a·lyze′ (-līz′) ***vt.*** **-lyzed′, -lyz′ing** **1** to make an analysis of; examine in detail **2** to psychoanalyze —**an′a·lyz′a·ble** ***adj.*** —**an′a·lyz′er** ***n.***

an·a·pest (an′ə pest′) ***n.*** ⟦< Gr *ana-*, back + *paiein*, to strike⟧ a metrical foot of two unaccented syllables followed by an accented one

an·ar·chism (an′ər kiz′əm) ***n.*** **1** the theory that all forms of government interfere unjustly with individual liberty **2** resistance to all government —**an′ar·chist′** ***n.*** —**an′ar·chis′tic** ***adj.***

an′ar·chy (-kē) ***n.***, *pl.* **-chies** ⟦< Gr *an-*, without + *archos*, leader⟧ **1** the absence of government **2** political disorder and violence **3** disorder; confusion —**an·ar·chic** (an är′kik) ***adj.*** —**an·ar′chi·cal·ly** ***adv.***

a·nath·e·ma (ə nath′ə mə) ***n.***, *pl.* **-mas** ⟦Gr, thing devoted to evil⟧ **1** a thing or person accursed or damned **2** a thing or person greatly detested **3** a formal curse, as in excommunication

a·nath′e·ma·tize′ (-tīz′) ***vt.***, ***vi.*** **-tized′**, **-tiz′ing** to utter an anathema (against); curse

a·nat·o·mize (ə nat′ə mīz′) ***vt.***, ***vi.*** **-mized′**, **-miz′ing** ⟦see ANATOMY⟧ **1** to dissect (an animal or plant) in order to examine the structure **2** to analyze —**a·nat′o·mist** ***n.***

a·nat′o·my (-mē) ***n.***, *pl.* **-mies** ⟦< Gr *ana-*, up + *temnein*, to cut⟧ **1** dissection of an organism to study its structure **2** the science of the structure of animals or plants **3** the structure of an organism **4** any analysis —**an·a·tom·i·cal** (an′ə täm′i kəl) or **an′a·tom′ic** ***adj.***

-ance (əns) ⟦< L⟧ *suffix* **1** the act or process of ___ing *[discontinuance]* **2** the quality or state of being *[forbearance]* **3** a thing that ___s *[hindrance]* **4** a thing that is ___ed *[utterance]*

an·ces·tor (an′ses′tər) ***n.*** ⟦< L *ante-*, before + *cedere*, go⟧ **1** a person from whom one is descended; forebear **2** a precursor or forerunner —**an·ces·tral** (an ses′trəl) ***adj.*** —**an·ces·tress** (an′ses′ trəs) ***fem.n.***

an′ces′try (-trē) ***n.***, *pl.* **-tries** **1** family descent **2** ancestors collectively

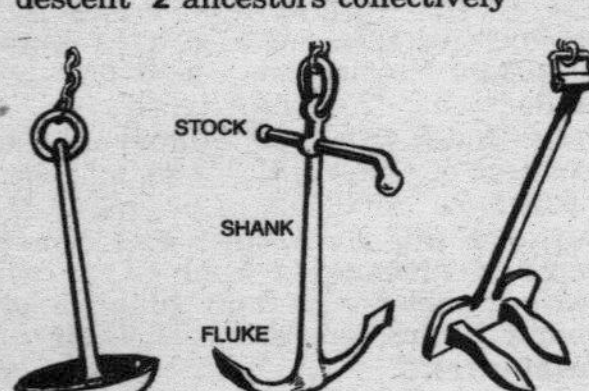

MUSH-ROOM ANCHOR   STOCKED ANCHOR   STOCK-LESS ANCHOR

an·chor (aŋ′kər) ***n.*** ⟦< Gr *ankyra*, an anchor, hook⟧ **1** a heavy object, usually an iron weight with flukes, lowered from a vessel, as by cable, to prevent drifting **2** anything giving stability **3** one who anchors a newscast: also **an′chor·per′son** —***vt.*** **1** to hold secure as by an anchor **2** to be the final contestant on (a relay team, etc.) **3** to serve as coordinator and chief reporter for (a newscast) —***vi.*** **1** to lower an anchor overboard **2** to be or become fixed —**at anchor** kept from drifting by its anchor

an′chor·age (-ij) ***n.*** **1** an anchoring or being anchored **2** a place to anchor

An·chor·age (aŋ′kər ij) seaport in S Alaska: pop. 226,000

an·cho·rite (aŋ′kə rīt′) ***n.*** ⟦< Gr *ana-*, back + *chōrein*, retire⟧ a religious recluse; hermit

an′chor·man′ ***n.***, *pl.* **-men′** a person, often, specif., a man, who anchors a newscast —**an′chor·wom′an**, *pl.* **-wom′en**, ***fem.n.***

an·cho·vy (an′chō′vē) ***n.***, *pl.* **-vies** ⟦< Port *anchova*⟧ a herringlike fish, eaten as a relish

an·cient (ān′chənt) ***adj.*** ⟦< L *ante*, before⟧ **1** of times long past **2** very old —***n.*** an aged person

an·cil·la (an sil′ə) ***n.*** a handbook or manual

an·cil·lar·y (an′sə ler′ē) ***adj.*** ⟦< L *ancilla*, maidservant⟧ **1** subordinate: often with *to* **2** auxiliary

-an·cy (ən sē) *suffix* -ANCE

and (and; *unstressed*, ənd, ən) ***conj.*** ⟦OE⟧ **1** also; in addition **2** plus **3** as a result **4** in contrast; but **5** then; following this **6** [Inf.] to *[try and come today]*

an·dan·te (än dän′tā) ***adj.***, ***adv.*** ⟦It < *andare*, to walk⟧ *Music* moderate in tempo: also written ***an·dan′te***

An·der·sen (an′dər sən), **Hans Christian** (häns, hänz) 1805-75; Dan. writer of fairy tales

An·des (Mountains) (an′dēz′) mountain system of W South America

and·i·ron (and′ī′ərn) ***n.*** ⟦< OFr *andier*⟧ either of a pair of metal supports for logs in a fireplace

and/or (and′ôr′) ***conj.*** either *and* or *or* *[personal and/or real property]*

An·dor·ra (an dôr′ə) country in the E Pyrenees: 175 sq. mi.; pop. 63,000

an·dro·gen (an′drō jən) ***n.*** ⟦< Gr *andros*, of man + -GEN⟧ a type of steroid that acts as a male sex hormone —**an′dro·gen′ic** (-jen′ik) ***adj.***

an·drog·y·nous (an dräj′ə nəs) ***adj.*** ⟦< Gr *andros*, of man + *gynē*, woman⟧ **1** both male and female in one **2** that blends male and female characteristics, roles, etc. **3** not differentiated as to gender *[androgynous clothing]*

an·droid (an′droid′) ***n.*** ⟦< Gr *andros*, of man + -OID⟧ in science fiction, a robot made to resemble a human being

an·ec·dote (an′ik dōt′) ***n.*** ⟦< Gr *anekdotos*, unpublished⟧ a short, entertaining account of some event —**an′ec·dot′al** ***adj.***

a·ne·mi·a (ə nē′mē ə) ***n.*** ⟦< Gr *an-*, without + *haima*, blood⟧ a condition in which the blood is low in red cells or in hemoglobin, resulting in paleness, weakness, etc. —**a·ne′mic** ***adj.***

an·e·mom·e·ter (an′ə mäm′ət ər) ***n.*** ⟦< Gr *anemos*, the wind + -METER⟧ a gauge for determining the force or speed of the wind; wind gauge

a·nem·o·ne (ə nem′ə nē′) ***n.*** ⟦< Gr *anemos*, the wind⟧ **1** a plant with cup-shaped flowers of white, pink, red, or purple **2** SEA ANEMONE

a·nent (ə nent′) ***prep.*** ⟦< OE *on efen*, on even (with)⟧ [Now Rare] concerning; about

aneroid barometer (an′ər oid′) ⟦< Gr *a-*, without + *nēros*, liquid + -OID⟧ a barometer working by the bending of a thin metal disk instead of by the rise or fall of mercury

an·es·the·sia (an′es thē′zhə) ***n.*** ⟦< Gr *an-*, without + *aisthēsis*, feeling⟧ a partial or total loss of the sense of pain, touch, etc., specif. when induced by an anesthetic

an'es·the'si·ol'o·gist (-thē'zē äl'ə jist) ***n.*** a doctor who specializes in giving anesthetics —**an'es·the'si·ol'o·gy** ***n.***

an'es·thet'ic (-thet'ik) ***adj.*** of or producing anesthesia —***n.*** a drug, gas, etc. used to produce anesthesia, as before surgery

an·es·the·tist (ə nes'thə tist') ***n.*** one trained to give anesthetics

an·es'the·tize' (-tīz') ***vt.*** **-tized', -tiz'ing** to cause anesthesia in —**an·es'the·ti·za'tion** ***n.***

an·eu·rysm or **an·eu·rism** (an'yo͞o riz' əm) ***n.*** ⟦< Gr *ana-*, up + *eurys*, broad⟧ a sac formed by an enlargement in a weakened wall of an artery, a vein, or the heart

a·new (ə no͞o') ***adv.*** **1** once more; again **2** in a new manner or form

an·gel (ān'jəl) ***n.*** ⟦< Gr *angelos*, messenger⟧ **1** *Theol. a*) a messenger of God *b*) a supernatural being with greater than human power, etc. **2** an image of a human figure with wings and a halo **3** a person regarded as beautiful, good, innocent, etc. **4** [Inf.] a financial backer, as for a play —**an·gel·ic** (an jel' ik) or **an·gel'i·cal** ***adj.*** —**an·gel'i·cal·ly** ***adv.***

angel dust [Slang] a powerful psychedelic drug

An·ge·le·no (an'jə lē'nō) ***n.***, *pl.* **-nos** ⟦AmSp⟧ a person born or living in Los Angeles

an·gel·fish (ān'jəl fish') ***n.***, *pl.* **-fish'** or (for different species) **-fish'es** a bright-colored tropical fish with spiny fins

angel (food) cake a light, spongy, white cake made with egg whites

an·ger (aŋ'gər) ***n.*** ⟦< ON *angr*, distress⟧ a feeling of displeasure and hostility that a person has because of being injured, mistreated, opposed, etc. —***vt.***, ***vi.*** to make or become angry

an·gi·na (pec·to·ris) (an jī'nə pek'tər is) ⟦L, lit., squeezing of the breast⟧ a condition marked by chest pain, caused by a sudden decrease of blood to the heart

an·gi·o·gram (an'jē ō gram') ***n.*** an X-ray photograph of blood vessels

an'gi·o·plas'ty (-plas'tē) ***n.*** any of various surgical techniques for repairing or replacing damaged blood vessels

an'gi·o·sperm' (-spurm') ***n.*** ⟦< Gr *angos*, vessel + *sperma*, seed⟧ any of a large division of plants having seeds produced within a closed pod or ovary

an·gle¹ (aŋ'gəl) ***n.*** ⟦< Gr *ankylos*, bent⟧ **1** the shape or space made by two straight lines or plane surfaces that meet **2** the measure of this space, expressed in degrees, etc. **3** a sharp corner **4** a point of view; aspect **5** [Inf.] a tricky method for achieving a purpose —***vt.***, ***vi.*** **-gled, -gling 1** to move or bend at an angle **2** [Inf.] to give a specific point of view to (a story, etc.)

an·gle² (aŋ'gəl) ***vi.*** **-gled, -gling** ⟦< OE *angul*, fishhook⟧ **1** to fish with a hook and line **2** to use tricks to get something [to *angle* for a promotion] —**an'gler** ***n.***

An·gle (aŋ'gəl) ***n.*** a member of a Germanic people that settled in E England in the 5th c. A.D.

angle iron a piece of iron or steel bent at a right angle, for joining or reinforcing two beams, etc.

an'gle·worm' ***n.*** an earthworm

An·gli·can (aŋ'gli kən) ***adj.*** ⟦< ML *Anglicus*, of the Angles⟧ of or connected with the Church of England —***n.*** an Anglican church member

An'gli·cize' (-glə sīz') ***vt.***, ***vi.*** **-cized', -ciz'ing** [*also* **a-**] to change to English idiom, pronunciation, customs, etc. —**An'gli·ci·za'tion** ***n.***

An·glo (aŋ'glō) ***n.***, *pl.* **-glos** ⟦AmSp⟧ [*also* **a-**] a white inhabitant of the U.S. who is of non-Hispanic descent

Anglo- *combining form* **1** English **2** Anglican

An'glo-A·mer'i·can (aŋ'glō-) ***adj.*** English and American —***n.*** an American of English birth or ancestry

An'glo-French' ***adj.*** English and French —***n.*** the French spoken in England from the Norman Conquest through the Middle Ages

An'glo-Sax'on ***n.*** **1** a member of the Germanic peoples in England at the time of the Norman Conquest **2** the language of these peoples, OLD ENGLISH **3** an Englishman —***adj.*** **1** of the Anglo-Saxons **2** of the English

An·go·la (aŋ gō'lə, an-) country on the SW coast of Africa: 481,354 sq. mi.; pop. 5,646,000

An·go·ra (aŋ gôr'ə, an-) ***n.*** ⟦former name of ANKARA⟧ **1** a breed of cat, goat, or rabbit with long, silky fur or hair **2** *a*) yarn of Angora rabbit hair *b*) mohair

an·gry (aŋ'grē) ***adj.*** **-gri·er, -gri·est 1** feeling or showing anger **2** wild and stormy —**an'gri·ly** (-grə lē) ***adv.***

ang·strom (aŋ'strəm) ***n.*** ⟦after A. J. *Angström*, 19th-c. Swed physicist⟧ one hundred-millionth of a centimeter: a unit used in measuring the length of light waves

an·guish (aŋ'gwish) ***n.*** ⟦< L *angustia*, tightness⟧ great mental or physical pain; agony —***vi.***, ***vt.*** to feel or cause to feel anguish —**an'guished** ***adj.***

an·gu·lar (aŋ'gyə lər) ***adj.*** **1** having or forming an angle or angles; having sharp corners **2** lean; gaunt **3** without ease or grace; stiff —**an'gu·lar'i·ty** (-lar' ə tē), *pl.* **-ties**, ***n.***

an·i·line (an'ə lin) ***n.*** ⟦< Ar *an-nīl*, the indigo plant⟧ a colorless, poisonous, oily derivative of benzene, used in making dyes, resins, etc.

an·i·mad·vert (an'i məd vurt', -mad'-) ***vi.*** ⟦L *animadvertere*, lit., to turn the mind⟧ to comment adversely (*on* or *upon*) —**an'i·mad·ver'sion** ***n.***

an·i·mal (an'i məl) ***n.*** ⟦L < *anima*, breath, soul⟧ **1** any of a group of living organisms, excluding plants, bacteria, and certain other simple organisms, typically able to move about **2** any such organism other than a human being;

esp., any four-footed creature **3** a brutish or inhuman person —***adj.*** **1** of or like an animal **2** gross, bestial, etc.

an·i·mate (an′i māt′; *for adj.*, -mit) ***vt.*** **-mat′ed, -mat′ing** ⟦see prec.⟧ **1** to give life or motion to **2** to make energetic or spirited **3** to inspire —***adj.*** living —**an′i·ma′tion** ***n.*** —**an′i·ma′tor** ***n.***

an′i·mat′ed ***adj.*** **1** living or lifelike **2** lively **3** designating or of a movie made by photographing a series of drawings so that the figures in them seem to move

an·i·mism (an′i miz′əm) ***n.*** ⟦< L *anima*, soul⟧ the belief that all life is produced by a spiritual force, or that all natural phenomena have souls —**an′i·mis′tic** ***adj.***

an·i·mos·i·ty (an′ə mäs′ə tē) ***n.***, *pl.* **-ties** ⟦see fol.⟧ a feeling of strong dislike or hatred; hostility

an·i·mus (an′ə məs) ***n.*** ⟦L, passion⟧ animosity; hostility

an·i·on (an′ī′ən) ***n.*** ⟦< Gr *anion*, thing going up⟧ a negatively charged ion: in electrolysis, anions move toward the anode

an·ise (an′is) ***n.*** ⟦< Gr *anison*⟧ **1** a dicotyledonous plant related to celery and parsley **2** its fragrant seed, used for flavoring: also **an′i·seed′** (-i sēd′)

an·i·sette (an′i zet′, -set′) ***n.*** ⟦Fr⟧ a sweet, anise-flavored liqueur

An·ka·ra (aŋ′kər ə, äŋ′-) capital of Turkey: pop. 2,235,000

ankh (aŋk) ***n.*** ⟦Egypt, life, soul⟧ a cross with a loop at the top, an ancient Egyptian symbol of life

an·kle (aŋ′kəl) ***n.*** ⟦OE *ancleow*⟧ **1** the joint that connects the foot and the leg **2** the area of the leg between the foot and calf

an·klet (aŋk′lit) ***n.*** **1** an ornament worn around the ankle **2** a short sock

an·nals (an′əlz) ***pl.n.*** ⟦< L *annus*, year⟧ **1** a written account of events year by year **2** historical records; history **3** a journal containing reports of a society, etc. —**an′nal·ist** ***n.***

An·nap·o·lis (ə nap′ə lis) capital of Maryland: pop. 33,000

Ann Ar·bor (an är′bər) city in SE Michigan: pop. 110,000

an·neal (ə nēl′) ***vt.*** ⟦< OE *an-*, on + *æl*, fire⟧ to heat (glass, metals, etc.) and cool to prevent brittleness

an·ne·lid (an′ə lid′) ***n.*** ⟦< L dim. of *anulus*, a ring⟧ any of various wormlike animals, including leeches, having long, segmented bodies

an·nex (ə neks′; *for n.*, an′eks′) ***vt.*** ⟦< L *ad-*, to + *nectere*, to tie⟧ **1** to attach or append, esp. to something larger **2** to incorporate into a country, etc. the territory of (another country, etc.) —***n.*** something annexed; esp., an addition to a building —**an·nex·a·tion** (an′eks ā′shən) ***n.***

an·ni·hi·late (ə nī′ə lāt′) ***vt.*** **-lat′ed, -lat′ing** ⟦< L *ad*, to + *nihil*, nothing⟧ to destroy completely —**an·ni′hi·la′tion** ***n.*** —**an·ni′hi·la′tor** ***n.***

an·ni·ver·sa·ry (an′ə vur′sə rē) ***n.***, *pl.* **-ries** ⟦< L *annus*, year + *vertere*, to turn⟧ the date on which some event occurred in an earlier year

an·no·tate (an′ō tāt′) ***vt.***, ***vi.*** **-tat′ed, -tat′ing** ⟦< L *ad-*, to + *nota*, a sign⟧ to provide explanatory notes for (a text, etc.) —**an′no·ta′tion** ***n.*** —**an′no·ta′tor** ***n.***

an·nounce (ə nouns′) ***vt.*** **-nounced′, -nounc′ing** ⟦< L *ad-*, to + *nuntius*, messenger⟧ **1** to declare publicly **2** to make known the arrival of **3** to be an announcer for —***vi.*** to serve as announcer —**an·nounce′ment** ***n.***

an·nounc′er ***n.*** one who announces; specif., one who introduces radio or TV programs

an·noy (ə noi′) ***vt.*** ⟦< VL *in odio*, in hate⟧ to irritate or bother, as by a repeated action —**an·noy′ance** ***n.*** —**an·noy′ing** ***adj.*** —**an·noy′ing·ly** ***adv.***

an·nu·al (an′yoo əl) ***adj.*** ⟦< L *annus*, year⟧ **1** of or measured by a year **2** yearly **3** living only one year or season —***n.*** **1** a periodical published once a year **2** a plant living only one year or season —**an′nu·al·ly** ***adv.***

an·nu·i·ty (ə noo′ə tē) ***n.***, *pl.* **-ties** ⟦see prec.⟧ **1** an investment yielding periodic payments, esp. yearly **2** such a payment —**an·nu′i·tant** ***n.***

an·nul (ə nul′) ***vt.*** **-nulled′, -nul′ling** ⟦< L *ad-*, to + *nullum*, nothing⟧ **1** to do away with **2** to make no longer legally binding; nullify —**an·nul′ment** ***n.***

an·nu·lar (an′yoo lər) ***adj.*** ⟦< L *anulus*, a ring⟧ like or forming a ring

an·nun·ci·a·tion (ə nun′sē ā′shən) ***n.*** an announcing —**the Annunciation** **1** *Bible* the angel Gabriel's announcement to Mary that she would bear Jesus **2** the church festival commemorating this

an·ode (an′ōd′) ***n.*** ⟦< Gr *anodos*, a way up⟧ **1** the positive electrode in an electrolytic cell **2** the principal electrode for collecting electrons in an electron tube **3** the negative electrode in a battery

an·o·dize (an′ō dīz′) ***vt.*** **-dized′, -diz′ing** to put a protective film on (a metal) by an electrolytic process in which the metal is the anode

an′o·dyne′ (-dīn′) ***adj.*** ⟦< Gr *an-*, without + *odynē*, pain⟧ **1** soothing **2** bland; insipid —***n.*** anything that relieves pain or soothes

a·noint (ə noint′) ***vt.*** ⟦< L *in-*, on + *unguere*, to smear⟧ to put oil on, as in consecrating —**a·noint′ment** ***n.***

a·nom·a·lous (ə näm′ə ləs) ***adj.*** ⟦< Gr *an-*, not + *homos*, the same⟧ **1** abnormal **2** inconsistent or odd

a·nom′a·ly (-lē) ***n.***, *pl.* **-lies** **1** abnormality **2** anything anomalous

an·o·mie or **an·o·my** (an′ə mē) ***n.*** ⟦Fr < Gr *anomia*, lawlessness⟧ lack of purpose, identity, etc.

a·non (ə nän′) ***adv.*** ⟦< OE *on an*, into one⟧ [Archaic] **1** soon **2** at another time

Anon or **anon** *abbrev.* anonymous

a·non·y·mous (ə nän′ə məs) ***adj.*** ⟦< Gr *an-*, without + *onyma*, name⟧ **1** with no name known **2** given, written, etc. by one whose name is withheld or unknown **3** lacking individuality —**an·o·nym·i·ty** (an′ə nim′ə tē) ***n.*** —**a·non′y·mous·ly** ***adv.***

a·noph·e·les (ə näf′ə lēz′) ***n.*** ⟦< Gr *anōphelēs*, harmful⟧ the mosquito that can transmit malaria

an·o·rex·i·a (an′ə reks′ē ə) ***n.*** ⟦< Gr *an-*, without + *orexis*, desire⟧ an eating disorder characterized by obsession with weight loss: in full **anorexia ner·vo·sa** (nər vō′sə) —**an′o·rex′ic** ***adj.***, ***n.***

an·oth·er (ə nuth′ər) ***adj.*** **1** one more; an additional **2** a different —***pron.*** **1** one additional **2** a different one **3** one of the same kind

an·swer (an′sər) ***n.*** ⟦< OE *and-*, against + *swerian*, swear⟧ **1** a reply to a question, letter, etc. **2** any act in response **3** a solution to a problem —***vi.*** **1** to reply **2** to be sufficient **3** to be responsible or liable (*to* a person *for* an action, etc.) **4** to conform (*to*) *[he answers to the description]* —***vt.*** **1** to reply or respond to **2** to serve or fulfill *[to answer the purpose]* **3** to defend oneself against (a charge) **4** to conform to *[she answers the description]* —**answer back** [Inf.] to reply forcefully or insolently —**an′swer·a·ble** ***adj.***

an′swer·ing machine a device for recording telephone messages automatically

answering service a business whose function is to answer telephone calls for its clients

ant (ant) ***n.*** ⟦< OE *æmet(t)e*⟧ any of a family of insects, generally wingless, that live in complex colonies

ant- *prefix* ANTI-

-ant (ənt) ⟦ult. < L⟧ *suffix* **1** that has, shows, or does *[defiant]* **2** one that *[occupant]*

ant·ac·id (ant′as′id) ***adj.*** counteracting acidity, specif. gastric acidity —***n.*** an antacid substance

an·tag·o·nism (an tag′ə niz′əm) ***n.*** ⟦see ANTAGONIZE⟧ opposition or hostility

an·tag′o·nist ***n.*** an adversary; opponent —**an·tag′o·nis′tic** ***adj.*** —**an·tag′o·nis′ti·cal·ly** ***adv.***

an·tag′o·nize′ (-nīz′) ***vt.*** **-nized′**, **-niz′ing** ⟦< Gr *anti-*, against + *agōn*, a contest⟧ to incur the dislike of or make an enemy of

ant·arc·tic (ant ärk′tik, -är′-) ***adj.*** ⟦see ANTI- & ARCTIC⟧ of or near the South Pole or the region around it —**the Antarctic** the region including Antarctica and the Antarctic Ocean

Ant·arc′ti·ca (-ti kə) land area about the South Pole, completely covered by an ice shelf: *c.* 5,400,000 sq. mi.

Antarctic Circle [*also* **a- c-**] an imaginary circle parallel to the equator, *c.* 66°34′ south of it

ant bear a large anteater of Central America and tropical South America

an·te (an′tē) ***n.*** ⟦L, before⟧ *Poker* the stake that each player must put into the pot before receiving cards —***vt.***, ***vi.*** **-ted** or **-teed**, **-te·ing** *Poker* to put in (one's ante): also **ante up**

ante- ⟦see prec.⟧ *prefix* before in time or place

ant′eat′er ***n.*** a mammal with a long snout, that feeds mainly on ants

an·te·bel·lum (an′ti bel′əm) ***adj.*** ⟦L⟧ before the war; specif., before the American Civil War

an·te·ced·ent (an′tə sēd′′nt) ***adj.*** ⟦< L *ante-*, before + *cedere*, go⟧ prior; previous —***n.*** **1** any thing prior to another **2** [*pl.*] one's ancestry, past life, etc. **3** *Gram.* the word or phrase to which a pronoun refers

an·te·cham·ber (an′ti chām′bər) ***n.*** a room leading into a larger or main room

an′te·date′ (-dāt′) ***vt.*** **-dat′ed**, **-dat′ing** **1** to put a date on that is earlier than the actual date **2** to come before in time

an′te·di·lu′vi·an (-də lo͞o′vē ən) ***adj.*** ⟦< ANTE- + L *diluvium*, a flood + -AN⟧ **1** of the time before the biblical Flood **2** very old or old-fashioned

an·te·lope (an′tə lōp′) ***n.*** ⟦< Gr *antholops*, deer⟧ a swift, cud-chewing, horned animal resembling the deer

an·te me·ri·di·em (an′tē mə rid′ē əm) ⟦L⟧ before noon

an·ten·na (an ten′ə) ***n.*** ⟦L, sail yard⟧ **1** *pl.* **-nae** (-ē) or **-nas** either of a pair of feelers on the head of an insect, crab, etc. **2** *pl.* **-nas** *Radio, TV* an arrangement of wires, rods, etc. used in sending and receiving electromagnetic waves

an·te·ri·or (an tir′ē ər) ***adj.*** ⟦< L *ante*, before⟧ **1** at or toward the front **2** previous; earlier

an·te·room (an′tē ro͞om′) ***n.*** a room leading to a larger or main room

an·them (an′thəm) ***n.*** ⟦< Gr *anti-*, over against + *phōnē*, voice⟧ **1** a religious choral song **2** a song of praise or devotion, as to a nation

an·ther (an′thər) ***n.*** ⟦< Gr *anthēros*, blooming⟧ the part of a stamen that produces pollen

ant′hill′ ***n.*** the soil heaped up by ants around their nest opening

an·thol·o·gize (an thäl′ə jīz′) ***vi.*** **-gized′**, **-giz′ing** to make anthologies —***vt.*** to include in an anthology —**an·thol′o·gist** (-jist) or **an·thol′o·giz′er** ***n.***

an·thol′o·gy (-jē) ***n.***, *pl.* **-gies** ⟦< Gr *anthos*, flower + *legein*, gather⟧ a collection of poems, stories, songs, etc.

An·tho·ny (an′thə nē, -tə-), **Mark** *see* ANTONY, Mark

an·thra·cite (an′thrə sīt′) ***n.*** ⟦< Gr *anthrax*, coal⟧ hard coal, which gives much heat and little smoke

an·thrax (an′thraks′) ***n.*** ⟦< Gr, coal, carbuncle⟧ an infectious disease of cattle, sheep, etc. that can be transmitted to humans

anthropo- ⟦< Gr *anthrōpos*, man⟧ *combining form* man, human

an·thro·po·cen·tric (an′thrə pō′sen′trik) ***adj.*** ⟦see ANTHROPO-⟧ centering one's view of everything around humankind

an·thro·poid (an′thrə poid′) ***adj.*** ⟦see ANTHROPO- & -OID⟧ **1** resembling a human **2** apelike —***n.*** any of certain highly developed primates, as the chimpanzee and gorilla

an·thro·pol·o·gy (an′thrə päl′ə jē) ***n.*** ⟦ANTHROPO- + -LOGY⟧ the study of the characteristics, customs, etc. of humanity —**an′thro·po·log′i·cal** (-pə läj′i kəl) ***adj.*** —**an′thro·pol′o·gist** ***n.***

an′thro·po′mor′phism′ (-pō′môr′fiz′ əm) ***n.*** the attributing of human characteristics to gods, objects, etc. —**an′thro·po′mor′phic** ***adj.*** —**an′thro·po′mor′phi·cal·ly** ***adv.*** —**an′thro·po′mor′phize′** (-fīz′), **-phized′**, **-phiz′ing**, ***vt.***, ***vi.***

an·ti (an′tī′, -tē) [Inf.] ***n.***, *pl.* **-tis′** ⟦< fol.⟧ a person opposed to something —***prep.*** opposed to

anti- ⟦< Gr *anti*, against⟧ *prefix* **1** against, hostile to **2** that operates against **3** that prevents, cures, or neutralizes **4** opposite, reverse **5** rivaling

an·ti·air·craft (an′tē er′kraft′) ***adj.*** used against hostile aircraft

an′ti·bal·lis′tic missile (-bə lis′tik) a missile intended to destroy an enemy ballistic missile in flight

an′ti·bi·ot′ic (-bī ät′ik, -bē-) ***n.*** ⟦< ANTI- + Gr *bios*, life⟧ any of certain substances, as penicillin or streptomycin, produced by various microorganisms and capable of destroying or weakening bacteria, etc. —***adj.*** of antibiotics

an·ti·bod·y (an′ti bäd′ē) ***n.***, *pl.* **-bod′ies** a protein produced in the body to neutralize a toxin or other antigen

an·tic (an′tik) ***adj.*** ⟦< L: see ANTIQUE⟧ odd and funny —***n.*** a playful or ludicrous act, trick, etc.: *usually used in pl.*

An·ti·christ (an′ti krīst′) ***n.*** *Bible* the great opponent of Christ: 1 John 2:18

an·tic·i·pate (an tis′ə pāt′) ***vt.*** **-pat′ed**, **-pat′ing** ⟦< L *ante-*, before + *capere*, take⟧ **1** to look forward to **2** to forestall **3** to use or deal with in advance **4** to be ahead of in doing —**an·tic′i·pa′tion** ***n.*** —**an·tic′i·pa·to′ry** (-pə tôr′ē) ***adj.***

an·ti·cli·max (an′ti klī′maks′) ***n.*** **1** a sudden drop from the important to the trivial **2** a descent which is in disappointing contrast to a preceding rise —**an′ti·cli·mac′tic** (-klī mak′tik) ***adj.***

an·ti·cline (an′ti klīn′) ***n.*** ⟦< ANTI- + Gr *klinein*, to lean⟧ *Geol.* a sharply arched fold of stratified rock

an·ti·co·ag·u·lant (an′ti kō ag′yoo lənt) ***n.*** a drug or substance that delays or prevents the clotting of blood

an′ti·de·pres′sant (-dē pres′ənt) ***adj.*** lessening emotional depression —***n.*** an antidepressant drug

an·ti·dote (an′tə dōt′) ***n.*** ⟦< Gr *anti-*, against + *dotos*, given⟧ **1** a remedy to counteract a poison **2** anything that works against an evil or unwanted condition

an·ti·freeze (an′ti frēz′) ***n.*** a substance used, as in the radiator of an automobile, to prevent freezing

an·ti·gen (an′tə jən) ***n.*** ⟦ANTI- + -GEN⟧ any substance to which the body reacts by producing antibodies

An·ti·gua and Bar·bu·da (an tē′gwə ′n bär boo′də) country in the E West Indies, consisting of three small islands: 171 sq. mi.; pop. 66,000

an·ti·he·ro (an′tī hir′ō) ***n.***, *pl.* **-roes** the protagonist of a novel, etc. who lacks the virtues of a traditional hero

an·ti·his·ta·mine (an′ti his′tə mēn′, -min) ***n.*** any of several drugs used to block histamine, as in allergic reactions

an·ti-in·flam·ma·to·ry (an′tē in flam′ə tôr′ē) ***adj.*** reducing inflammation —***n.*** an anti-inflammatory medication, as aspirin

an·ti·knock (an′ti näk′) ***n.*** a substance added to the fuel of internal-combustion engines to reduce noise resulting from too rapid combustion

An·til·les (an til′ēz′) group of islands of the West Indies, including Cuba, Jamaica, etc. (**Greater Antilles**) & the Leeward Islands and Windward Islands (**Lesser Antilles**)

an·ti-lock (an′tē läk′) ***adj.*** designating an automotive braking system that prevents the wheels from locking during a sudden stop

an·ti·log·a·rithm (an′ti lôg′ə rith′əm) ***n.*** the number resulting when a base is raised to a power by a logarithm

an·ti·ma·cas·sar (an′ti mə kas′ər) ***n.*** ⟦ANTI- + *macassar*, a hair oil⟧ a small cover on the back or arms of a chair, sofa, etc. to prevent soiling

an·ti·mat·ter (an′ti mat′ər) ***n.*** a form of matter in which the electrical charge or other property of each particle is the reverse of that in the usual matter of our universe

an·ti·mis·sile (an′tī mis′əl) ***adj.*** designed as a defense against ballistic missiles

an·ti·mo·ny (an′tə mō′nē) ***n.*** ⟦< ML⟧ a silvery-white, nonmetallic chemical element used in alloys to harden them

an·ti·pas·to (an′ti päs′tō, -pas′-) ***n.*** ⟦It < *anti-*, before + *pasto*, food⟧ an appetizer of meats, cheeses, marinated vegetables, etc.

an·tip·a·thy (an tip′ə thē) ***n.***, *pl.* **-thies** ⟦< Gr *anti-*, against + *pathein*, to suffer⟧ **1** strong dislike; aversion **2** the object of such dislike

an·ti·per·son·nel (an′ti pur′sə nel′) ***adj.*** intended to destroy people rather than objects *[antipersonnel* mines*]*

an′ti·per′spi·rant (-pur′spə rənt) ***n.*** a substance applied to the skin to reduce perspiration

an·tiph·o·nal (an tif′ə nəl) ***adj.*** ⟦see ANTHEM⟧ sung or chanted in alternation

an·tip·o·des (an tip′ə dēz′) ***pl.n.*** ⟦< Gr *anti-*, opposite + *pous*, foot⟧ any two places directly opposite each other on the earth —**an·tip′o·dal** ***adj.***

an·ti·quar·i·an (an′ti kwer′ē ən) ***adj.*** **1** of antiques or antiquities **2** of antiquaries **3** dealing in old books —***n.*** an antiquary

an·ti·quar·y (an′ti kwer′ē) ***n.***, *pl.* **-quar′ies** a collector or student of antiquities

an′ti·quate′ (-kwāt′) ***vt.*** **-quat′ed**, **-quat′ing** ⟦see fol.⟧ to make old, out-of-date, or obsolete —**an′ti·quat′ed** ***adj.*** —**an′ti·qua′tion** ***n.***

an·tique (an tēk′) ***adj.*** ⟦< L *antiquus*,

ancient⟧ **1** of ancient times **2** out-of-date **3** of, or in the style of, a former period **4** dealing in antiques —*n.* **1** any ancient relic **2** a piece of furniture, etc. from a former period —*vt.* **-tiqued′**, **-tiqu′ing** to make look antique —*vi.* to shop for antique furniture, etc.

an·tiq·ui·ty (an tik′wə tē) *n., pl.* **-ties** ⟦see prec.⟧ **1** the ancient period of history **2** great age **3** [*pl.*] relics, etc. of the distant past

an·ti-Se·mit·ic (an′tē sə mit′ik) *adj.* **1** having or showing prejudice against Jews **2** discriminating against or persecuting Jews Also **an′ti·se·mit′ic** —**an′ti-Sem′ite′** (-sem′īt′) *n.* —**an′ti-Sem′i·tism′** (-ə tiz′əm) *n.*

an·ti·sep·sis (an′tə sep′sis) *n.* ⟦ANTI- + SEPSIS⟧ **1** a being antiseptic **2** the use of antiseptics

an′ti·sep′tic (-tik) *adj.* **1** preventing infection, decay, etc. by acting against bacteria, etc. **2** using antiseptics **3** sterile —*n.* any antiseptic substance —**an′ti·sep′ti·cal·ly** *adv.*

an·ti·se·rum (an′ti sir′əm) *n., pl.* **-rums** or **-ra** a serum containing antibodies

an′ti·slav′er·y (an′tī-) *adj.* against slavery

an′ti·so′cial *adj.* **1** not sociable; avoiding others **2** harmful to the welfare of people

an′ti·tank′ *adj.* for use against tanks in war

an·tith·e·sis (an tith′ə sis) *n., pl.* **-ses′** (-sēz′) ⟦< Gr *anti-*, against + *tithenai*, to place⟧ **1** a contrast or opposition, as of ideas **2** the exact opposite —**an·ti·thet·i·cal** (an′tə thet′i kəl) *adj.* —**an′ti·thet′i·cal·ly** *adv.*

an·ti·tox·in (an′ti täks′in) *n.* **1** a circulating antibody formed by the body to act against a specific toxin **2** a serum containing an antitoxin, injected into a person to prevent a disease

an·ti·trust (an′tī trust′) *adj.* opposed to or regulating trusts, or business monopolies

an·ti·vi·ral (an′tī vī′rəl) *adj.* capable of checking the growth of a virus

an′ti·viv′i·sec′tion·ist (-viv′ə sek′shən ist) *n.* one opposing vivisection

ant·ler (ant′lər) *n.* ⟦< OFr *antoillier*⟧ the branched, bony growth on the head of any animal of the deer family —**ant′lered** (-lərd) *adj.*

An·to·ny (an′tə nē), **Mark** (or **Marc**) 83?-30 B.C.; Rom. general

an·to·nym (an′tə nim′) *n.* ⟦< Gr *anti-*, opposite + *onyma*, name⟧ a word meaning the opposite of another

Ant·werp (an′twurp′) seaport in N Belgium: pop. 459,000

a·nus (ā′nəs) *n., pl.* **a′nus·es** or **a′ni′** (-nī′) ⟦L⟧ the opening at the lower end of the alimentary canal

an·vil (an′vəl) *n.* ⟦< OE *anfilt*⟧ **1** an iron or steel block on which metal objects are hammered into shape **2** one of three small bones in the middle ear

anx·i·e·ty (aŋ zī′ə tē) *n., pl.* **-ties** ⟦see fol.⟧ **1** worry or uneasiness about what may happen **2** an eager but uneasy desire [*anxiety* to do well]

anx·ious (aŋk′shəs) *adj.* ⟦< L *angere*, to choke⟧ **1** worried **2** causing anxiety **3** eagerly wishing —**anx′ious·ly** *adv.*

an·y (en′ē) *adj.* ⟦OE *ænig*⟧ **1** one, no matter which, of more than two [*any* boy may go] **2** some [has he *any* pain?] **3** without limit [*any* number can play] **4** even one or the least amount of [I haven't *any* dimes] **5** every [*any* child can do it] —*pron.* (*sing. & pl.*) any one or ones —*adv.* to any degree or extent; at all [is he *any* better today?]

an′y·bod′y (-bäd′ē, -bud′ē) *pron.* any person —*n., pl.* **-bod′ies** a person of some importance

an′y·how′ *adv.* ANYWAY

an′y·more′ *adv.* now; nowadays

an′y·one′ *pron.* any person; anybody

any one any single (person or thing)

an′y·place′ *adv.* [Inf.] in, at, or to any place

an′y·thing′ *pron.* any object, event, fact, etc. —*n.* a thing, no matter of what kind —*adv.* in any way —**anything but** not at all

an′y·time′ *adv.* at any time —*conj.* WHENEVER

an′y·way′ *adv.* **1** in any manner **2** nevertheless; anyhow **3** haphazardly

an′y·where′ *adv.* **1** in, at, or to any place **2** [Inf.] at all

A/o or **a/o** *abbrev.* account of

A-OK (ā′ō kā′) *adj.* ⟦A(LL) OK⟧ [Inf.] excellent, fine, in working order, etc.: also **A′-O·kay′**

A one (ā′ wun′) [Inf.] first-class: also **A 1** or **A number 1**

a·or·ta (ā ôr′tə) *n., pl.* **-tas** or **-tae** (-tē) ⟦< Gr *aeirein*, to raise⟧ the main artery of the body, carrying blood from the heart —**a·or′tic** or **a·or′tal** *adj.*

AP *abbrev.* Associated Press

a·pace (ə pās′) *adv.* at a fast pace

A·pach·e (ə pach′ē) *n., pl.* **-es** or **-e** ⟦AmSp⟧ a member of a group of North American Indians of the SW U.S.

a·part (ə pärt′) *adv.* ⟦< L *ad*, to, at + *pars*, part⟧ **1** aside **2** away in place or time **3** in or to pieces —*adj.* separated —**apart from** other than —**tell apart** to distinguish between or among

a·part·heid (ə pär′tāt′, -tīt′) *n.* ⟦Afrik, separateness⟧ the official policy of racial segregation as practiced in South Africa, *c.* 1950-91

a·part′ment *n.* ⟦< It *appartare*, to separate⟧ a room or suite of rooms to live in, esp. one of a number in an **apartment building** (or **house**)

ap·a·thy (ap′ə thē) *n., pl.* **-thies** ⟦< Gr *a-*, without + *pathos*, emotion⟧ **1** lack of emotion **2** lack of interest; indifference; listlessness —**ap′a·thet′ic** (-thet′ik) *adj.* —**ap′a·thet′i·cal·ly** *adv.*

ap·a·tite (ap′ə tīt′) *n.* ⟦< Ger < Gr *apatē*, deceit⟧ a mineral incorporating calcium phosphate and found in rocks, bones, and teeth

a·pat·o·saur·us (ə pat′ə sôr′əs) *n.* a huge, plant-eating dinosaur

APB (ā′pē′bē′) *n.* all-points bulletin

ape (āp) ***n.*** ⟦< OE *apa*⟧ **1** any gibbon or great ape **2** loosely, any monkey **3** a mimic **4** a person who is uncouth, clumsy, etc. —***vt.*** **aped, ap′ing** to mimic —**ape′like′** ***adj.***

Ap·en·nines (ap′ə nīnz′) mountain range of central Italy

a·pe·ri·tif (ə per′ə tēf′) ***n.*** ⟦Fr⟧ an alcoholic drink taken before a meal

ap·er·ture (ap′ər chər) ***n.*** ⟦< L *aperire*, to open⟧ an opening; hole

a·pex (ā′peks′) ***n.***, *pl.* **a′pex′es** or **ap·i·ces** (ap′ə sēz′) ⟦L⟧ **1** the highest point **2** the pointed end; tip **3** the climax

a·pha·sia (ə fā′zhə) ***n.*** ⟦Gr < *a-*, not + *phanai*, to say⟧ loss of the power to use or understand words —**a·pha′sic** (-zik) ***adj., n.***

a·phe·li·on (ə fē′lē ən) ***n.***, *pl.* **-li·ons** or **-li·a** (-ə) ⟦< Gr *apo-*, from + *hēlios*, sun⟧ the point farthest from the sun in the orbit of a planet or comet, or of a manmade satellite

a·phid (ā′fid, af′id) ***n.*** ⟦< ModL *aphis*⟧ an insect that lives on plants by sucking their juices

aph·o·rism (af′ə riz′əm) ***n.*** ⟦< Gr *apo-*, from + *horizein*, to bound⟧ a concise statement of a general truth; maxim; adage —**aph′o·ris′tic** ***adj.*** —**aph′o·ris′ti·cal·ly** ***adv.***

aph·ro·di·si·ac (af′rə dē′zē ak′) ***adj.*** ⟦ult. after fol.⟧ arousing or increasing sexual desire —***n.*** an aphrodisiac drug, etc.

Aph·ro·di·te (af′rə dīt′ē) ***n.*** the Greek goddess of love and beauty

a·pi·ar·y (ā′pē er′ē) ***n.***, *pl.* **-ar′ies** ⟦< L *apis*, bee⟧ a place where bees are kept —**a′pi·a·rist** (-ə rist) ***n.***

a·piece (ə pēs′) ***adv.*** ⟦ME *a pece*⟧ for each one; each

a·plen·ty (ə plen′tē) ***adj., adv.*** [Inf.] in abundance

a·plomb (ə pläm′, -plum′) ***n.*** ⟦Fr: see PLUMB⟧ self-possession; poise

a·poc·a·lypse (ə päk′ə lips′) ***n.*** ⟦< Gr *apokalyptein*, disclose⟧ **1** a revelation of a violent struggle in which evil will be destroyed **2** a disastrous event, esp. the end of the world **3** [**A-**] *Bible* the book of Revelation —**a·poc′a·lyp′tic** (-lip′tik) ***adj.***

A·poc·ry·pha (ə päk′rə fə) ***pl.n.*** ⟦< Gr *apo-*, away + *kryptein*, to hide⟧ fourteen books of the Septuagint rejected in Judaism and Protestantism: eleven are in the Roman Catholic Bible

a·poc′ry·phal (-fəl) ***adj.*** **1** of doubtful authenticity **2** not genuine; spurious

ap·o·gee (ap′ə jē′) ***n.*** ⟦< Gr *apo-*, from + *gē*, earth⟧ the point farthest from the earth in the orbit of the moon or a satellite

a·po·lit·i·cal (ā′pə lit′i kəl) ***adj.*** not concerned with political matters —**a′po·lit′i·cal·ly** ***adv.***

A·pol·lo (ə päl′ō) ***n.*** **1** the Greek and Roman god of music, poetry, prophecy, and medicine **2** *pl.* **-los** a handsome young man

a·pol·o·get·ic (ə päl′ə jet′ik) ***adj.*** showing regret; making an apology —**a·pol′o·get′i·cal·ly** ***adv.***

a·pol·o·gist (ə päl′ə jist) ***n.*** one who defends or attempts to justify a doctrine, faith, action, etc.

a·pol′o·gize′ (-jīz′) ***vi.*** **-gized′, -giz′ing** to make an apology —**a·pol′o·giz′er** ***n.***

a·pol·o·gy (ə päl′ə jē) ***n.***, *pl.* **-gies** ⟦< Gr *apo-*, from + *logos*, speech⟧ **1** a formal defense of some idea, doctrine, etc.: also **ap·o·lo·gi·a** (ap′ə lō′jē ə) **2** an expression of regret for a fault, insult, etc.

ap·o·plex·y (ap′ə plek′sē) ***n.*** ⟦< Gr *apo-*, from + *plēssein*, to strike⟧ [Old-fashioned] STROKE (*n.* 3) —**ap′o·plec′tic** (-plek′tik) ***adj.***

a·pos·ta·sy (ə päs′tə sē) ***n.***, *pl.* **-sies** ⟦< Gr *apo-*, away + *stasis*, a standing⟧ an abandoning of what one has believed in, as a faith or cause

a·pos′tate′ (-tāt′) ***n.*** a person guilty of apostasy

a·pos′ta·tize′ (-tə tīz′) ***vi.*** **-tized′, -tiz′ing** to become an apostate

a pos·te·ri·o·ri (ā′ päs tir′ē ôr′ī′) ⟦L⟧ **1** from effect to cause **2** based on observation or experience

a·pos·tle (ə päs′əl) ***n.*** ⟦< Gr *apo-*, from + *stellein*, send⟧ **1** [*usually* **A-**] any of the disciples of Jesus, esp. the original twelve **2** the leader of a new movement

ap·os·tol·ic (ap′əs täl′ik) ***adj.*** **1** of the Apostles or their teachings, work, etc. **2** [*often* **A-**] of the pope; papal

a·pos·tro·phe (ə päs′trə fē) ***n.*** ⟦< Gr *apo-*, from + *strephein*, to turn⟧ **1** a mark (’) indicating: *a*) omission of a letter or letters from a word (Ex.: *it's* for *it is*) *b*) the possessive case (Ex.: *Mary's* dress) *c*) certain plural forms (Ex.: five *6's*, dot the *i's*) **2** an exclamatory address to a person or thing

a·poth·e·car·y (ə päth′ə ker′ē) ***n.***, *pl.* **-ies** ⟦< Gr *apothēkē*, storehouse⟧ [Old-fashioned] a pharmacist or druggist

ap·o·thegm (ap′ə them′) ***n.*** ⟦< Gr *apo-*, from + *phthengesthai*, to utter⟧ a short, pithy saying

a·poth·e·o·sis (ə päth′ē ō′sis, ap′ə thē′ə sis) ***n.***, *pl.* **-ses′** (-sēz′) ⟦< Gr *apo-*, from + *theos*, god⟧ **1** the deifying of a person **2** the glorification of a person or thing **3** a glorified ideal

Ap·pa·la·chi·a (ap′ə lā′chə, -chē ə; -lach′ə) the highland region of the E U.S. extending from SW Pennsylvania through N Alabama

Ap′pa·la′chi·an Mountains mountain system extending from S Quebec to N Alabama: also **Appalachians**

ap·pall or **ap·pal** (ə pôl′) ***vt.*** **-palled′, -pal′ling** ⟦ult. < L *ad*, to + *pallere*, to be pale⟧ to horrify, dismay, or shock

ap·pa·loo·sa (ap′ə lo͞o′sə) ***n.*** ⟦after *Palouse* Indians of NW U.S.⟧ a Western saddle horse with black and white spots on the rump and loins

ap·pa·ra·tus (ap′ə rat′əs, -rāt′-) ***n.***, *pl.* **-tus** or **-tus·es** ⟦< L *ad-*, to + *parare*, prepare⟧ **1** the instruments, materials, tools, etc. for a specific use **2** any complex device, machine, or system

ap·par·el (ə per′əl) ***n.*** ⟦ult. < L *ad-*, to + *parere*, prepare⟧ clothing; attire —***vt.*** **-eled** or **-elled, -el·ing** or **-el·ling** to clothe; dress

ap·par·ent (ə per′ənt) ***adj.*** ⟦see APPEAR⟧ **1** readily seen; visible **2** evident; obvious **3** appearing real or true —**ap·par′ent·ly** ***adv.***

ap·pa·ri·tion (ap′ə rish′ən) ***n.*** ⟦see APPEAR⟧ **1** anything that appears unexpectedly or in a strange way **2** a ghost; phantom

ap·peal (ə pēl′) ***vt.*** ⟦< L *ad-*, to + *pellere*, to drive⟧ to make an appeal of (a case) —***vi.*** **1** to appeal a law case to a higher court **2** to make an urgent request (*to* a person *for* help, etc.) **3** to be attractive or interesting —***n.*** **1** a call upon some authority for a decision **2** a request for the transference of a case to a higher court for rehearing **3** a request for help, etc. **4** a quality that arouses interest, desire, etc. —**ap·peal′ing** ***adj.***

ap·pear (ə pir′) ***vi.*** ⟦< L *ad-*, to + *perere*, be visible⟧ **1** to come into sight **2** to come into being **3** to become understood or obvious **4** to seem; look **5** to present oneself formally in court **6** to come before the public

ap·pear′ance ***n.*** **1** an appearing **2** the look or outward aspect of a person or thing **3** an outward show; pretense —**keep up appearances** to maintain an outward show of being proper, prosperous, etc.

ap·pease (ə pēz′) ***vt.*** **-peased′**, **-peas′ing** ⟦ult. < L *ad*, to + *pax*, peace⟧ to pacify, quiet, or satisfy, esp. by giving in to the demands of —**ap·pease′ment** ***n.*** —**ap·peas′er** ***n.***

ap·pel·lant (ə pel′ənt) ***n.*** a person who appeals to a higher court

ap·pel′late (-it) ***adj.*** *Law* having to do with appeals *[an appellate court]*

ap·pel·la·tion (ap′ə lā′shən) ***n.*** ⟦see APPEAL⟧ **1** a naming **2** a name or title

ap·pend (ə pend′) ***vt.*** ⟦< L *ad-*, to + *pendere*, hang⟧ to attach or affix; add as a supplement or appendix

ap·pend′age ***n.*** **1** anything appended **2** any external organ or part, as a tail

ap·pen·dec·to·my (ap′ən dek′tə mē) ***n.***, *pl.* **-mies** ⟦see -ECTOMY⟧ the surgical removal of the appendix

ap·pen·di·ci·tis (ə pen′də sīt′is) ***n.*** ⟦see -ITIS⟧ inflammation of the appendix

ap·pen·dix (ə pen′diks) ***n.***, *pl.* **-dix·es** or **-di·ces′** (-də sēz′) ⟦L, appendage⟧ **1** additional material at the end of a book **2** a small, saclike appendage of the large intestine

ap·per·tain (ap′ər tān′) ***vi.*** ⟦< L *ad-*, to + *pertinere*, to reach⟧ to belong as a function, part, etc.; pertain

ap·pe·ten·cy (ap′ə tən sē) ***n.***, *pl.* **-cies** ⟦see fol.⟧ a craving; appetite

ap·pe·tite (ap′ə tīt′) ***n.*** ⟦< L *ad-*, to + *petere*, to desire⟧ **1** a desire for food **2** any strong desire or craving

ap′pe·tiz′er (-tī′zər) ***n.*** a small portion of a tasty food to stimulate the appetite

ap′pe·tiz′ing (-tī′ziŋ) ***adj.*** **1** stimulating the appetite **2** savory; delicious

ap·plaud (ə plôd′) ***vt.***, ***vi.*** ⟦< L *ad-*, to + *plaudere*, clap hands⟧ **1** to show approval (of) by clapping the hands, etc. **2** to approve —**ap·plaud′er** ***n.***

ap·plause (ə plôz′) ***n.*** approval, esp. as shown by clapping hands

ap·ple (ap′əl) ***n.*** ⟦< OE *æppel*, fruit, apple⟧ **1** a firm, round, edible fruit **2** the tree it grows on

apple butter a thick, sweet spread made from apples stewed with spices

ap′ple·jack′ ***n.*** brandy distilled from fermented cider

ap′ple-pie′ ***adj.*** [Inf.] **1** neat and tidy *[apple-pie order]* **2** suggesting wholesomeness

ap′ple·sauce′ ***n.*** a dessert or relish of apples cooked to a pulp in water and sweetened

ap·pli·ance (ə plī′əns) ***n.*** a device or machine, esp. one for household use

ap·pli·ca·ble (ap′li kə bəl) ***adj.*** that can be applied; appropriate —**ap′pli·ca·bil′i·ty** (-bil′ə tē) ***n.***

ap′pli·cant (-kənt) ***n.*** one who applies, as for employment or help

ap·pli·ca·tion (ap′li kā′shən) ***n.*** **1** an applying **2** anything applied, as a remedy **3** a specific use **4** a request, or a form filled out in making one *[an employment application]* **5** continued effort; diligence **6** relevance or practicality **7** a computer program for performing a specific task

ap·pli·ca·tor (ap′li kāt′ər) ***n.*** any device for applying medicine or paint, polish, etc.

ap·plied (ə plīd′) ***adj.*** used in actual practice *[applied science]*

ap·pli·qué (ap′li kā′) ***n.*** ⟦Fr⟧ a decoration made of one material attached to another —***vt.*** **-quéd′**, **-qué′ing** to decorate with appliqué

ap·ply (ə plī′) ***vt.*** **-plied′**, **-ply′ing** ⟦< L *ad-*, to + *plicare*, to fold⟧ **1** to put or spread on *[apply glue]* **2** to put to practical or specific use *[apply your knowledge]* **3** to devote (oneself or one's faculties) diligently —***vi.*** **1** to make a formal request **2** to be suitable or relevant —**ap·pli′er** ***n.***

ap·point (ə point′) ***vt.*** ⟦< L *ad*, to + *punctum*, a point⟧ **1** to set (a date, place, etc.) **2** to name for an office, position, etc. **3** to furnish *[well-appointed]* —**ap·point′ee′** ***n.***

ap·point′ive ***adj.*** of or filled by appointment *[an appointive office]*

ap·point′ment ***n.*** **1** an appointing or being appointed **2** a position filled by appointing **3** an arrangement to meet someone or be somewhere **4** [*pl.*] furniture; equipment

Ap·po·mat·tox Court House (ap′ə mat′əks) former village in central Virginia, where Lee surrendered to Grant (1865)

ap·por·tion (ə pôr′shən) ***vt.*** ⟦see AD- & PORTION⟧ to distribute in shares according to a plan —**ap·por′tion·ment** ***n.***

ap·pose (ə pōz′) ***vt.*** **-posed′**, **-pos′ing** ⟦< L *ad-*, to + *ponere*, put⟧ to put side by side or opposite

ap·po·site (ap′ə zit) ***adj.*** ⟦see prec.⟧ appropriate; apt —**ap′po·site·ly** ***adv.*** —**ap′po·site·ness** ***n.***

ap·po·si·tion (ap′ə zish′ən) ***n.*** **1** an apposing, or the position resulting from this 2 the placing of a word or phrase beside another in explanation ["my niece" is in *apposition* with "Jill" in "Jill, my niece, is here"] —**ap·pos·i·tive** (ə päz'ə tiv) ***adj., n.***

ap·prais·al (ə prāz'əl) ***n.*** **1** an appraising **2** an appraised value

ap·praise (ə prāz') ***vt.*** **-praised', -prais'ing** ⟦< L *ad*, to + *pretium*, price⟧ **1** to set a price for; estimate the value of **2** to judge the quality or worth of —**ap·prais'er** ***n.***

ap·pre·ci·a·ble (ə prē'shə bəl, -shē ə-) ***adj.*** ⟦see prec.⟧ enough to be perceived or estimated; noticeable —**ap·pre'ci·a·bly** ***adv.***

ap·pre·ci·ate (ə prē'shē āt') ***vt.*** **-at'ed, -at'ing** ⟦see APPRAISE⟧ **1** to think well of; esteem **2** to recognize gratefully **3** to estimate the quality of **4** to be fully or sensitively aware of —***vi.*** to rise in value —**ap·pre'ci·a'tor** ***n.*** —**ap·pre'ci·a·to'ry** (-shə tôr'ē, -shē ə-) ***adj.***

ap·pre'ci·a'tion ***n.*** **1** grateful recognition, as of a favor **2** sensitive awareness, as of art **3** a rise in value or price

ap·pre'ci·a·tive (-shə tiv, -shē ə-) ***adj.*** feeling or showing appreciation —**ap·pre'ci·a·tive·ly** ***adv.***

ap·pre·hend (ap'rē hend') ***vt.*** ⟦< L *ad-*, to + *prehendere*, take⟧ **1** to capture or arrest **2** to perceive; understand **3** to fear; dread

ap'pre·hen'sion (-hen'shən) ***n.*** **1** capture or arrest **2** perception or understanding **3** fear; anxiety

ap'pre·hen'sive (-siv) ***adj.*** anxious; uneasy —**ap'pre·hen'sive·ly** ***adv.*** —**ap'pre·hen'sive·ness** ***n.***

ap·pren·tice (ə pren'tis) ***n.*** ⟦see APPREHEND⟧ **1** a person being taught a craft or trade, now usually as a member of a labor union **2** any beginner —***vt.*** **-ticed, -tic·ing** to place or accept as an apprentice —**ap·pren'tice·ship'** ***n.***

ap·prise or **ap·prize** (ə prīz') ***vt.*** **-prised'** or **-prized', -pris'ing** or **-priz'ing** ⟦see APPREHEND⟧ to inform or notify

ap·proach (ə prōch') ***vi.*** ⟦< L *ad-*, to + *propius*, nearer⟧ to come closer —***vt.*** **1** to come nearer to **2** to approximate **3** to make a proposal or request to **4** to begin dealing with —***n.*** **1** a coming closer **2** an approximation **3** an overture (*to* someone): *usually used in pl.* **4** a means of reaching a person or place; access **5** a means of attaining a goal —**ap·proach'a·ble** ***adj.***

ap·pro·ba·tion (ap'rə bā'shən) ***n.*** ⟦see APPROVE⟧ approval

ap·pro·pri·ate (ə prō'prē āt'; *for adj.*, -it) ***vt.*** **-at'ed, -at'ing** ⟦< L *ad-*, to + *proprius*, one's own⟧ **1** to take for one's own use, often improperly **2** to set aside (money, etc.) for a specific use —***adj.*** suitable; fit; proper —**ap·pro'pri·ate·ly** ***adv.*** —**ap·pro'pri·ate·ness** ***n.*** —**ap·pro'pri·a'tor** ***n.***

ap·pro'pri·a'tion ***n.*** **1** an appropriating or being appropriated **2** money set aside for a specific use

ap·prov·al (ə pro͞o'vəl) ***n.*** **1** the act of approving **2** favorable attitude or opinion **3** formal consent —**on approval** for the customer to examine and decide whether to buy or return

ap·prove (ə pro͞ov') ***vt.*** **-proved', -prov'ing** ⟦< L *ad-*, to + *probus*, good⟧ **1** to give one's consent to **2** to consider to be good, satisfactory, etc. —***vi.*** to have a favorable opinion (*of*) —**ap·prov'ing·ly** ***adv.***

ap·prox·i·mate (ə präk'sə mit; *for v.*, -māt') ***adj.*** ⟦< L *ad-*, to + *proximus*, nearest⟧ **1** much like; resembling **2** more or less correct or exact —***vt.*** **-mat'ed, -mat'ing** to come near to; be almost the same as —**ap·prox'i·mate·ly** ***adv.***

ap·prox'i·ma'tion ***n.*** an estimate or guess that is approximately correct

ap·pur·te·nance (ə purt''n əns) ***n.*** ⟦see APPERTAIN⟧ **1** anything added to a more important thing **2** [*pl.*] apparatus or equipment **3** *Law* an incidental right attached to some thing

APR *abbrev.* annual percentage rate

ap·ri·cot (ap'ri kät', ā'pri-) ***n.*** ⟦Fr *abricot* < L *praecoquum*, early matured (fruit)⟧ **1** a small, yellowish-orange, peachlike fruit **2** the tree it grows on

A·pril (ā'prəl) ***n.*** ⟦< L⟧ the fourth month of the year, having 30 days: abbrev. **Apr**

a pri·o·ri (ā' prī ôr'ī) ⟦L⟧ **1** from cause to effect; deductive or deductively **2** based on theory, logic, etc. instead of experience

a·pron (ā'prən) ***n.*** ⟦< L *mappa*, napkin⟧ **1** a garment worn over the front part of the body to protect one's clothes **2** any extending or protecting part **3** a paved area, as where a driveway broadens to meet the road **4** the part of a stage in front of the proscenium arch

ap·ro·pos (ap'rə pō') ***adv.*** ⟦Fr *à propos*, to the purpose⟧ at the right time; opportunely —***adj.*** relevant; apt —***prep.*** with regard to —**apropos of** with regard to

apse (aps) ***n.*** ⟦L *apsis*, an arch⟧ a semicircular or polygonal projection of a church, usually domed or vaulted

apt[1] (apt) ***adj.*** ⟦< L *aptus*⟧ **1** appropriate; fitting [an *apt* remark] **2** tending or inclined; likely [*apt* to rain] **3** quick to learn —**apt'ly** ***adv.*** —**apt'ness** ***n.***

apt[2] *abbrev.* apartment

ap·ti·tude (ap'tə to͞od') ***n.*** ⟦see APT[1]⟧ **1** a natural tendency, ability, or talent **2** quickness to learn

aq·ua (ak'wə, äk'-) ***n.***, *pl.* **-uas** or **-uae'** (-wē') ⟦L⟧ water —***adj.*** ⟦< AQUAMARINE⟧ bluish-green

aq'ua·cul'ture ***n.*** ⟦prec. + CULTURE⟧ the cultivation of water plants and animals for human use

aq'ua·ma·rine' ***n.*** ⟦L *aqua marina*, sea water⟧ bluish green —***adj.*** bluish-green

aq'ua·naut' (-nôt') ***n.*** ⟦AQUA + (ASTRO)NAUT⟧ one trained to use a watertight underwater chamber as a base for undersea experiments

aq'ua·plane' ***n.*** ⟦AQUA + PLANE[1]⟧ a board on which one rides standing up as it is pulled by a motorboat —***vi.*** **-planed', -plan'ing** to ride on such a board as a sport

a·quar·i·um (ə kwer'ē əm) ***n.***, *pl.* **-i·ums**

or **-i·a** (-ə) ⟦< L *aquarius*, of water⟧ **1** a tank, etc. for keeping live water animals and plants **2** a building where such collections are exhibited

A·quar'i·us (-əs) ***n.*** ⟦L, water carrier⟧ the 11th sign of the zodiac

a·quat·ic (ə kwat'ik, -kwät'-) ***adj.*** **1** growing or living in water **2** done in or upon the water *[aquatic* sports*]*

aq·ua·vit (ak'wə vēt', äk'-) ***n.*** ⟦< L *aqua vitae*, water of life⟧ a Scandinavian alcoholic liquor distilled from grain or potatoes and flavored with caraway

aq·ue·duct (ak'wə dukt') ***n.*** ⟦< L *aqua*, water + *ductus*, a leading⟧ **1** a large pipe or conduit for bringing water from a distant source **2** an elevated structure supporting this

a·que·ous (ā'kwē əs, ak'wē-) ***adj.*** of, like, or formed by water

aqueous humor a watery fluid in the space between the cornea and the lens of the eye

aq·ui·fer (ak'wə fər, äk'-) ***n.*** ⟦< L *aqua*, water + *ferre*, carry⟧ an underground layer of porous rock, etc. containing water

aq·ui·line (ak'wə līn', -lin) ***adj.*** ⟦< L *aquila*, eagle⟧ **1** of or like an eagle **2** curved like an eagle's beak *[*an *aquiline* nose*]*

A·qui·nas (ə kwī'nəs), Saint **Thom·as** (täm'əs) (1225?-74); It. theologian & philosopher

Ar *Chem. symbol for* argon

AR Arkansas

Ar·ab (ar'əb, er'-) ***n.*** **1** a person born or living in Arabia **2** a member of a Semitic people orig. living in Arabia, now throughout the Middle East

ar·a·besque (ar'ə besk', er'-) ***n.*** ⟦< It *Arabo*, Arab⟧ an elaborate design consisting of intertwined lines suggesting flowers, foliage, etc.

ARABESQUE

A·ra·bi·a (ə rā'bē ə) peninsula in SW Asia —**A·ra'bi·an** ***adj.***, ***n.***

Arabian camel the one-humped camel ranging from N Africa to India

Arabian Nights, **The** a collection of tales from Arabia, India, Persia, etc.

Arabian Peninsula ARABIA

Ar·a·bic (ar'ə bik, er'-) ***adj.*** **1** of Arabia **2** of the Arabs or their language or culture —***n.*** the Semitic language of the Arabs, spoken in Arabia, Syria, N Africa, etc.

Arabic numerals the figures 1, 2, 3, 4, 5, 6, 7, 8, 9, and the 0 (zero)

ar·a·ble (ar'ə bəl, er'-) ***adj.*** ⟦< L *arare*, to plow⟧ suitable for plowing and farming

a·rach·nid (ə rak'nid) ***n.*** ⟦< Gr *arachnē*, spider⟧ any of a class of arthropods with four pairs of legs, including spiders and scorpions

Ar·a·ma·ic (ar'ə mā'ik, er'-) ***n.*** a Semitic language spoken during biblical times

ar·bi·ter (är'bət ər) ***n.*** ⟦L, a witness or judge⟧ an arbitrator; judge

ar·bi·trage (är'bə träzh') ***n.*** ⟦see prec.⟧ the simultaneous purchase and sale, as of stock, in two financial markets to profit from a price difference

ar·bit·ra·ment (är bi'trə mənt) ***n.*** **1** arbitration **2** an arbitrator's verdict or award

ar·bi·trar·y (är'bə trer'ē) ***adj.*** ⟦see ARBITER⟧ **1** left to one's judgment **2** based on one's preference or whim; capricious **3** absolute; despotic —**ar'bi·trar'i·ly** ***adv.***

ar'bi·trate' (-trāt') ***vt.***, ***vi.*** **-trat'ed**, **-trat'ing** ⟦see ARBITER⟧ **1** to submit (a dispute) to an arbitrator **2** to decide (a dispute) as an arbitrator —**ar'bi·tra'tion** ***n.***

ar'bi·tra'tor ***n.*** a person selected to judge a dispute, as in collective bargaining

ar·bor (är'bər) ***n.*** ⟦< L *herba*, grass, herb⟧ a place shaded by trees or shrubs or by vines on a latticework; bower

ar·bo·re·al (är bôr'ē əl) ***adj.*** ⟦< L *arbor*, tree⟧ **1** of or like a tree **2** living in trees

ar·bo·re·tum (är'bə rēt'əm) ***n.***, *pl.* **-tums** or **-ta** (-ə) ⟦L⟧ a place where many kinds of trees and shrubs are grown for exhibition or study

ar·bor·vi·tae (är'bər vīt'ē) ***n.*** ⟦L, tree of life⟧ any of various cypress trees having sprays of scalelike leaves

ar·bu·tus (är byōōt'əs) ***n.*** ⟦L⟧ **1** a tree or shrub with dark-green leaves and strawberrylike fruit **2** a trailing plant with white or pink flower clusters

arc (ärk) ***n.*** ⟦< L *arcus*, a bow, arch⟧ **1** a bowlike curved line or object **2** the band of incandescent light formed when a current leaps a short gap between electrodes **3** any part of a curve, esp. of a circle —***vi.*** **arced** or **arcked**, **arc'ing** or **arck'ing** to move in a curved course or form an arc

ar·cade (är kād') ***n.*** ⟦see prec.⟧ **1** a covered passageway, esp. one lined with shops **2** a line of arches and their supporting columns **3** a penny arcade or a similar place with coin-operated video games

ar·cane (är kān') ***adj.*** ⟦< L *arcanus*, hidden⟧ secret or esoteric

arch[1] (ärch) ***n.*** ⟦see ARC⟧ **1** a curved structure used as a support over an open space, as in a doorway **2** the form of an arch **3** anything shaped like an arch —***vt.*** to span with or as an arch —***vi.*** to form an arch

arch[2] (ärch) ***adj.*** ⟦< ARCH-⟧ **1** chief; principal **2** gaily mischievous; pert *[*an *arch* look*]*

Arch or **arch** *abbrev.* **1** archaic **2** architecture

arch- ⟦< Gr *archos*, first, ruler⟧ *prefix* main, principal *[archenemy]*

-arch (ärk) ⟦see prec.⟧ *suffix* ruler *[matriarch]*

ar·chae·ol·o·gy (är'kē äl'ə jē) ***n.*** ⟦< Gr *archaios*, ancient + -LOGY⟧ the study of the life of ancient peoples, as by excavation of ancient cities or artifacts: also sp. **ar'che·ol'o·gy** —**ar'chae·o·log'i·cal** (-ə läj'i kəl) ***adj.*** —**ar'chae·o·log'i·cal·ly** ***adv.*** —**ar'chae·ol'o·gist** ***n.***

ar·cha·ic (är kā'ik) ***adj.*** ⟦< Gr *archaios,* ancient⟧ **1** ancient **2** old-fashioned **3** no longer used except in poetry, church ritual, etc.: said as of the word *thou* —**ar·cha'i·cal·ly** ***adv.***

ar·cha·ism (är'kā iz'əm) ***n.*** an archaic word, usage, style, etc. —**ar'cha·is'tic** ***adj.***

arch·an·gel (ärk'ān'jəl) ***n.*** an angel of high rank

arch'bish'op (ärch'-) ***n.*** a bishop of the highest rank

arch'dea'con ***n.*** a church official ranking just below a bishop

arch'di'o·cese ***n.*** the diocese of an archbishop —**arch'di·oc'e·san** ***adj.***

arch'duke' ***masc.n.*** a sovereign prince, esp. of the former Austrian imperial family —**arch'duch'ess** ***fem.n.***

arch'en'e·my ***n.***, *pl.* **-mies** a chief enemy —**the archenemy** Satan

arch·er (är'chər) ***n.*** ⟦< L *arcus,* bow⟧ one who shoots with bow and arrow

arch'er·y ***n.*** the sport of shooting with bow and arrow

ar·che·type (är'kə tīp') ***n.*** ⟦< Gr *archos,* first + *typos,* a mark⟧ **1** an original pattern, or model; prototype **2** a perfect example of a type or group —**ar'che·typ'al** (-tīp'əl) or **ar'che·typ'i·cal** (-tip'i kəl) ***adj.***

ar·chi·e·pis·co·pal (är'kē ē pis'kə pəl) ***adj.*** of or related to an archbishop

Ar·chi·me·des (är'kə mē'dēz') 287?-212 B.C.; Gr. mathematician & inventor

ar·chi·pel·a·go (är'kə pel'ə gō') ***n.***, *pl.* **-goes'** or **-gos'** ⟦< Gr *archi-,* chief + *pelagos,* sea⟧ **1** a sea with many islands **2** a group of many islands

ar·chi·tect (är'kə tekt') ***n.*** ⟦< Gr *archi-,* chief + *tektōn,* carpenter⟧ **1** one who designs buildings and supervises their construction **2** any designer or planner

ar·chi·tec·ton·ics (är'kə tek tän'iks) ***pl.n.*** [*usually with sing. v.*] **1** the science of architecture **2** structural design, as of a symphony —**ar'chi·tec·ton'ic** ***adj.***

ar·chi·tec·ture (är'kə tek'chər) ***n.*** **1** the science or profession of designing and constructing buildings **2** a style of construction **3** design and construction —**ar'chi·tec'tur·al** ***adj.*** —**ar'chi·tec'tur·al·ly** ***adv.***

ar·chi·trave (är'kə trāv') ***n.*** ⟦< L *archi-,* first + *trabs,* a beam⟧ in a classical building, the beam resting directly on the tops of the columns

ar·chive (är'kīv') ***n.*** ⟦< Gr *archeion,* town hall⟧ [*usually pl.*] **1** a place for keeping public records, documentary material, etc. **2** the records, material, etc. kept there —***vt.*** **-chived', -chiv'ing** to keep in or as in archives —**ar·chi·vist** (är'kə vist, -kī'-) ***n.***

arch·way (ärch'wā') ***n.*** a passage under an arch, or the arch itself

-ar·chy (är kē) ⟦< Gr *archein,* to rule⟧ *combining form* rule, government *[monarchy]*

arc·tic (ärk'tik, är'-) ***adj.*** ⟦< Gr *arktikos,* northern⟧ **1** of or near the North Pole **2** very cold —**the Arctic** the region around the North Pole

Arctic Circle [*also* **a- c-**] an imaginary circle parallel to the equator, *c.* 66°34' north of it

Arctic Ocean ocean surrounding the North Pole

-ard (ərd) ⟦< MHG *hart,* bold⟧ *suffix* one who does something to excess *[drunkard]*

ar·dent (är'dənt) ***adj.*** ⟦< L *ardere,* to burn⟧ **1** passionate **2** zealous **3** glowing or burning —**ar'dent·ly** ***adv.***

ar·dor (är'dər) ***n.*** ⟦< L *ardor,* a flame⟧ **1** emotional warmth; passion **2** zeal **3** intense heat Also, Brit. sp., **ar'dour**

ar·du·ous (är'jo͞o əs) ***adj.*** ⟦L *arduus,* steep⟧ **1** difficult to do; laborious **2** using much energy; strenuous —**ar'du·ous·ly** ***adv.***

are (är) ***vi.*** ⟦OE *aron*⟧ *pl. & 2d pers. sing., pres. indic., of* BE

ar·e·a (er'ē ə) ***n.*** ⟦L, vacant place⟧ **1** a part of the earth's surface; region **2** the measure, in square units, of a surface **3** a location having a specific use or character *[play area]* **4** scope or extent

area code a three-digit telephone code assigned to a specific area of the U.S., Canada, etc.

a·re·na (ə rē'nə) ***n.*** ⟦L, sandy place⟧ **1** a place or building for contests, shows, etc. **2** any sphere of struggle *[political arena]*

arena theater a theater having a central stage surrounded by seats

aren't (ärnt) *contr.* are not

Ar·es (er'ēz') ***n.*** *Gr. Myth.* the god of war

ar·gent (är'jənt) ***adj.*** ⟦L *argentum,* silver⟧ [Old Poet.] silvery

Ar·gen·ti·na (är'jən tē'nə) country in S South America: 1,073,518 sq. mi.; pop. 32,616,000 —**Ar'gen·tine'** (-tēn', -tīn') or **Ar'gen·tin'i·an** (-tin'ē ən) ***adj., n.***

ar·gon (är'gän') ***n.*** ⟦Gr, inert⟧ a chemical element; a nonreactive gas found in the air and used in light bulbs, electron tubes, etc.

Ar·go·naut (är'gə nôt') ***n.*** *Gr. Myth.* any of those who sail with Jason to search for the Golden Fleece

ar·go·sy (är'gə sē) ***n.***, *pl.* **-sies** ⟦after *Ragusa,* It name of Dubrovnik in Croatia⟧ [Old Poet.] a large merchant ship or a fleet of such ships

ar·got (är'gō, -gət) ***n.*** ⟦Fr⟧ the specialized vocabulary of a particular group, as of criminals

ar·gue (är'gyo͞o) ***vi.*** **-gued, -gu·ing** ⟦< L *arguere,* prove⟧ **1** to give reasons (*for* or *against*) **2** to quarrel; dispute —***vt.*** **1** to discuss; debate **2** to maintain; contend **3** to persuade by giving reasons —**ar'gu·a·ble** ***adj.***

ar·gu·ment (är'gyo͞o mənt) ***n.*** **1** a reason or reasons offered in arguing **2** an arguing; debate **3** a summary

ar'gu·men·ta'tion (-men tā'shən) ***n.*** the process of arguing; debate

ar'gu·men'ta·tive (-men'tə tiv) ***adj.*** **1**

controversial 2 apt to argue; contentious Also **ar'gu·men'tive**

ar·gyle (är'gīl') ***adj.*** ⟦after *Argyll*, Scotland⟧ knitted or woven in a diamond-shaped pattern *[argyle* socks*]*

a·ri·a (ä'rē ə) ***n.*** ⟦It < L *aer*, air⟧ a song, as in an opera, for solo voice

-ar·i·an (er'ē ən) ⟦< L⟧ *suffix* **1** (one) characterized by *[octogenarian]* **2** (one) believing in or associated with *[Unitarian]*

ar·id (ar'id) ***adj.*** ⟦< L *arere*, be dry⟧ **1** dry and barren **2** uninteresting; dull —**a·rid·i·ty** (ə rid'ə tē) ***n.***

Ar·i·es (er'ēz') ***n.*** ⟦L, ram (male sheep)⟧ the first sign of the zodiac

a·right (ə rīt') ***adv.*** correctly

a·rise (ə rīz') ***vi.*** **a·rose'** (-rōz'), **a·ris'en** (-riz'ən), **a·ris'ing** ⟦< OE *a-*, out + *risan*, to rise⟧ **1** to get up, as from sleeping **2** to ascend **3** to come into being **4** to result *(from)*

ar·is·toc·ra·cy (ar'i stä'krə sē) ***n.***, *pl.* **-cies** ⟦< Gr *aristos*, best + *kratos*, to rule⟧ **1** government by a privileged minority, usually of inherited wealth **2** a country with such government **3** a privileged ruling class

a·ris·to·crat (ə ris'tə krat') ***n.*** **1** a member of the aristocracy **2** one with the tastes, manners, etc. of the upper class —**a·ris'to·crat'ic** ***adj.***

Ar·is·toph·a·nes (ar'i stäf'ə nēz') 450?-388? B.C.; Gr. writer of comedies

Ar·is·tot·le (ar'is tät''l) 384-322 B.C.; Gr. philosopher —**Ar·is·to·te·li·an** (ar'is tə tēl'yən) ***adj.***, ***n.***

a·rith·me·tic (ə rith'mə tik) ***n.*** ⟦< Gr *arithmos*, number⟧ the science or art of computing by positive, real numbers —**ar·ith·met·ic** (ar'ith met'ik) or **ar'ith·met'i·cal** ***adj.*** —**ar'ith·me·ti'cian** (-mə tish'ən) ***n.***

arithmetic mean the average obtained by dividing a sum by the number of its addends

Ar·i·zo·na (ar'ə zō'nə) state of the SW U.S.: 113,956 sq. mi.; pop. 3,665,000; cap. Phoenix: abbrev. *AZ* —**Ar'i·zo'nan** or **Ar'i·zo'ni·an** ***adj.***, ***n.***

ark (ärk) ***n.*** ⟦< L *arcere*, enclose⟧ **1** ARK OF THE COVENANT **2** an enclosure in a synagogue for the scrolls of the Torah **3** *Bible* the boat in which Noah, his family, and two of every kind of creature survived the Flood

Ar·kan·sas (är'kən sô') state of the SC U.S.: 53,187 sq. mi.; pop. 2,351,000; cap. Little Rock: abbrev. *AR* —**Ar·kan'san** (-kan'zən) ***adj.***, ***n.***

ark of the covenant the chest containing the two stone tablets inscribed with the Ten Commandments

Ar·ling·ton (är'liŋ tən) city in NE Texas: pop. 262,000

arm[1] (ärm) ***n.*** ⟦OE *earm*⟧ **1** an upper limb of the human body **2** anything like this in shape, function, position, etc. **3** anything connected to something larger *[arm* of the sea*]* —**with open arms** cordially

arm[2] (ärm) ***n.*** ⟦< L *arma*, weapons⟧ **1** a weapon: *usually used in pl.* **2** any branch of the military forces —***vt.*** to provide with weapons, etc. —***vi.*** to prepare for war or any struggle —**under arms** ready for war —**up in arms** **1** prepared to fight **2** indignant

ar·ma·da (är mä'də) ***n.*** ⟦Sp < L *arma*, weapons⟧ **1** a fleet of warships **2** a fleet of military aircraft

ar·ma·dil·lo (är'mə dil'ō) ***n.***, *pl.* **-los** ⟦Sp: see prec.⟧ a burrowing mammal of tropical America, covered with bony plates

Ar·ma·ged·don (är'mə ged''n) ***n.*** **1** *Bible* the site of the last, decisive battle between the forces of good and evil **2** any great, decisive battle

ar·ma·ment (är'mə mənt) ***n.*** ⟦< L *armare*, to arm⟧ **1** [*often pl.*] all the military forces and equipment of a nation **2** all the military equipment of a warship, tank, etc. **3** an arming or being armed for war

ar·ma·ture (är'mə chər) ***n.*** ⟦< L *armare*, to arm⟧ **1** any protective covering **2** the iron core wound with wire in which electromotive force is produced in a generator or motor

arm'chair' ***n.*** a chair with supports at the sides for one's arms

armed forces all the military, naval, and air forces of a country

Ar·me·ni·a (är mēn'yə, -mē'nē ə) country in W Asia: 11,490 sq. mi.; pop. 3,305,000 —**Ar·me'ni·an** ***adj.***, ***n.***

arm·ful (ärm'fool) ***n.***, *pl.* **-fuls** as much as the arms or one arm can hold

arm'hole' ***n.*** an opening for the arm in a garment

ar·mi·stice (är'mə stis) ***n.*** ⟦< L *arma*, weapons + *stare*, to stand⟧ a truce preliminary to the signing of a peace treaty

Armistice Day Nov. 11, the anniversary of the armistice of WWI in 1918

arm·let (ärm'lət) ***n.*** **1** an ornamental band worn around the upper arm **2** a narrow, deep inlet of the sea

arm'load' ***n.*** an armful

ar·mor (är'mər) ***n.*** ⟦< L *armare*, to arm⟧ any defensive or protective covering —***vt.***, ***vi.*** to put armor on —**ar'mored** ***adj.***

armored car a vehicle covered with armor plate, as a truck for carrying money to or from a bank

ar·mo·ri·al (är môr'ē əl) ***adj.*** of coats of arms

armor plate a protective covering of steel plates

ar·mor·y (är'mər ē) ***n.***, *pl.* **-mor·ies** ⟦see ARMOR⟧ **1** an arsenal **2** a National Guard unit drill hall

arm'pit' ***n.*** the hollow under the arm at the shoulder

arm'rest' ***n.*** a support for the arm, as on the inside of an automobile door

ar·my (är'mē) ***n.***, *pl.* **-mies** ⟦ult. < L *arma*, weapons⟧ **1** a large, organized body of soldiers for waging war, esp. on land **2** a large number of persons, animals, etc. *[*an *army* of ants*]*

Ar·nold (är'nəld), **Ben·e·dict** (ben'ə dikt') 1741-1801; Am. Revolutionary general who became a traitor

a·ro·ma (ə rō'mə) ***n.*** ⟦< Gr *arōma*, spice⟧

a pleasant odor; fragrance

a·ro′ma·ther′a·py *n.* the therapeutic use of aromatic oils from herbs, etc.

ar·o·mat·ic (ar′ə mat′ik) *adj.* of or having an aroma; fragrant or pungent —*n.* an aromatic plant, chemical, etc. —**ar′o·mat′i·cal·ly** *adv.*

a·rose (ə rōz′) *vi. pt. of* ARISE

a·round (ə round′) *adv.* ⟦ME⟧ **1** in a circle **2** in every direction **3** in circumference **4** to the opposite direction **5** [Inf.] nearby *[stay around]* —*prep.* **1** so as to encircle or envelop **2** on the border of **3** in various places in or on **4** about *[around 1890]*

a·rouse (ə rouz′) *vt.* **a·roused′, a·rous′ing** **1** to awaken, as from sleep **2** to stir, as to action **3** to evoke *[to arouse pity]* —**a·rous′al** *n.*

ar·peg·gio (är pej′ō) *n., pl.* **-gios** ⟦It < *arpa*, a harp⟧ a chord whose notes are played in quick succession

ar·raign (ə rān′) *vt.* ⟦< L *ad*, to + *ratio*, reason⟧ **1** to bring before a law court to answer charges **2** to call to account; accuse —**ar·raign′ment** *n.*

ar·range (ə rānj′) *vt.* **-ranged′, -rang′ing** ⟦< OFr *a-*, to + *renger*, to range⟧ **1** to put in the correct order **2** to classify **3** to prepare or plan **4** to arrive at an agreement about **5** *Music* to adapt (a composition) to particular instruments or voices —*vi. Music* to write arrangements, esp. as a profession —**ar·rang′er** *n.*

ar·range′ment *n.* **1** an arranging **2** a result or manner of arranging **3** [*usually pl.*] a plan **4** a settlement **5** *Music a*) an arranging of a composition *b*) the composition as thus arranged

ar·rant (ar′ənt) *adj.* ⟦var. of ERRANT⟧ that is plainly such; out-and-out; notorious

ar·ras (ar′əs) *n.* ⟦after *Arras*, Fr city⟧ a wall hanging, esp. of tapestry

ar·ray (ə rā′) *vt.* ⟦< OFr *areer*⟧ **1** to place in order **2** to dress in finery —*n.* **1** an orderly grouping, esp. of troops **2** an impressive display **3** fine clothes

ar·rears (ə rirz′) *pl.n.* ⟦< L *ad*, to + *retro*, behind⟧ overdue debts —**in arrears** behind in paying a debt, doing one's work, etc.

ar·rest (ə rest′) *vt.* ⟦< L *ad-*, to + *restare*, to stop⟧ **1** to stop or check **2** to seize by authority of the law **3** to catch and keep (one's attention, etc.) —*n.* an arresting or being arrested —**under arrest** in legal custody

ar·rest′ing *adj.* attracting attention; interesting

ar·rhyth·mi·a (ə rith′mē ə) *n.* ⟦< Gr *a-*, without + *rhythmos*, measure⟧ an irregularity in the heart's rhythm —**ar·rhyth′mic** or **ar·rhyth′mi·cal** *adj.*

ar·riv·al (ə rī′vəl) *n.* **1** an arriving **2** a person or thing that arrives

ar·rive (ə rīv′) *vi.* **-rived′, -riv′ing** ⟦< L *ad-*, to + *ripa*, shore⟧ **1** to reach one's destination **2** to come *[the time has arrived]* **3** to attain fame, etc. —**arrive at** to reach by thinking, etc.

ar·ri·ve·der·ci (är rē′ve der′chē) *interj.* ⟦It⟧ goodbye

ar·ro·gant (ar′ə gənt) *adj.* ⟦< L *arrogare*, to claim⟧ full of or due to pride; haughty —**ar′ro·gance** *n.* —**ar′ro·gant·ly** *adv.*

ar′ro·gate′ (-gāt′) *vt.* **-gat′ed, -gat′ing** ⟦< L *ad-*, for + *rogare*, to ask⟧ to claim or seize without right —**ar′ro·ga′tion** *n.*

ar·row (ar′ō) *n.* ⟦OE *arwe*⟧ **1** a pointed shaft for shooting from a bow **2** a sign (←), used to indicate direction

ar′row·head′ *n.* the separable, pointed tip of an arrow

ar′row·root′ *n.* ⟦from use as antidote for poisoned arrows⟧ **1** a tropical plant with starchy roots **2** a starch made from its roots

ar·roy·o (ə roi′ō) *n., pl.* **-os** ⟦Sp < L *arrugia*, mine shaft⟧ [Southwest] **1** a dry gully **2** a rivulet or stream

ar·se·nal (är′sə nəl) *n.* ⟦< Ar *dār aṣṣinā'a*, workshop⟧ **1** a place for making or storing weapons **2** a store or collection

ar·se·nic (är′sə nik′; *for adj.* är sen′ik) *n.* ⟦< Gr *arsenikon*⟧ a very poisonous chemical element, compounds of which are used in insecticides, etc. —*adj.* of or containing arsenic: also **ar·sen′i·cal**

ar·son (är′sən) *n.* ⟦< L *ardere*, to burn⟧ the crime of purposely setting fire to a building or property —**ar′son·ist** *n.*

art[1] (ärt) *n.* ⟦< L *ars*⟧ **1** human creativity **2** skill **3** any specific skill or its application **4** any craft or its principles **5** creative work or its principles **6** any branch of creative work, as painting or sculpture **7** products of this, as paintings or statues **8** *a*) a branch of learning *b*) [*pl.*] LIBERAL ARTS **9** cunning **10** sly trick; wile: *usually used in pl.*

art[2] (ärt) *vi. archaic 2d pers. sing., pres. indic., of* BE: used with *thou*

art[3] *abbrev.* **1** article **2** artificial

art dec·o (dek′ō) a decorative style of the late 1920s and the 1930s, derived from cubism

ar·te·ri·al (är tir′ē əl) *adj.* **1** of or in the arteries **2** of a main road

ar·te·ri·ole (är tir′ē ōl′) *n.* ⟦see ARTERY⟧ any of the small blood vessels between the arteries and capillaries

ar·te·ri·o·scle·ro·sis (är tir′ē ō′sklə rō′sis) *n.* ⟦< Gr *artēria*, artery + SCLEROSIS⟧ an abnormal thickening and hardening of the walls of the arteries

ar·ter·y (ärt′ər ē) *n., pl.* **-ter·ies** ⟦< Gr *aeirein*, to lift⟧ **1** any of the blood vessels that carry blood away from the heart **2** a main route

ar·te·sian well (är tē′zhən) ⟦Fr *artésien*, of Artois (in France)⟧ a deep well in which water is forced up by pressure of underground water draining from higher ground

art film a film characterized by artistic sophistication, realism, etc.

art·ful (ärt′fəl) *adj.* **1** skillful or clever **2** cunning; crafty —**art′ful·ly** *adv.* —**art′ful·ness** *n.*

art house a theater that shows art films, etc.

ar·thri·tis (är thrīt′is) *n.* ⟦Gr < *arthron*,

joint + -ITIS] inflammation of a joint or joints —**ar·thrit·ic** (är thrit′ik) ***adj.***

arthro- [< Gr *arthron*, joint] *combining form* joint, joints

ar·thro·pod (är′thrə päd′) ***n.*** [prec. + -POD] any of a phylum of invertebrates with jointed legs and a segmented body

ar′thro·scope′ (-skōp′) ***n.*** [ARTHRO- + -SCOPE] an endoscope used inside a joint —**ar′thro·scop′ic** (-skäp′ik) ***adj.***

Ar·thur[1] (är′thər) ***n.*** legendary 6th-c. king of Britain —**Ar·thu·ri·an** (är thoor′ ē ən) ***adj.***

Ar·thur[2] (är′thər), **Ches·ter A**(**lan**) (ches′ tər) 1829-86; 21st president of the U.S. (1881-85)

ar·ti·choke (ärt′ə chōk′) ***n.*** [ult. < Ar *al-ḥarshaf*] **1** a thistlelike plant **2** its edible flower head

ar·ti·cle (ärt′i kəl) ***n.*** [< L *artus*, joint] **1** one of the sections of a document **2** a complete piece of writing, as in a newspaper, magazine, etc. **3** a separate item [an *article* of luggage] **4** *Gram.* any one of the words *a, an,* or *the*, used as adjectives

ar·tic·u·late (är tik′yoo lit; *for v.*, -lāt′) ***adj.*** [see prec.] **1** jointed: usually **ar·tic′u·lat′ed** **2** made up of distinct sounds, as speech **3** able to speak **4** expressing oneself clearly —***vt.*** **-lat′ed, -lat′ing** **1** to connect by joints **2** to arrange in connected sequence **3** to utter distinctly **4** to express clearly —***vi.*** **1** to speak distinctly **2** to be jointed or connected —**ar·tic′u·late·ly** ***adv.*** —**ar·tic′u·la′tion** ***n.***

ar·ti·fact (ärt′ə fakt′) ***n.*** any object made by human work

ar·ti·fice (ärt′ə fis) ***n.*** [< L *ars*, art + *facere*, make] **1** skill or ingenuity **2** trickery **3** an artful trick

ar·tif·i·cer (är tif′ə sər) ***n.*** **1** a skilled craftsman **2** an inventor

ar·ti·fi·cial (ärt′ə fish′əl) ***adj.*** [see ARTIFICE] **1** made by human work; not natural **2** simulated [*artificial* teeth] **3** affected [an *artificial* smile] —**ar′ti·fi′ci·al′i·ty** (-fish′ē al′ə tē), *pl.* **-ties**, ***n.*** —**ar′ti·fi′cial·ly** ***adv.***

artificial intelligence **1** the capability of computers to mimic human thought processes **2** the science dealing with this

artificial respiration the maintenance of breathing by artificial means, as by forcing air into the mouth

ar·til·ler·y (är til′ər ē) ***n.*** [< OFr *atillier*, equip] **1** mounted guns, as cannon or missile launchers **2** gunnery —**the artillery** the branch of an army using heavy mounted guns —**ar·til′ler·y·man** (-mən), *pl.* **-men** (-mən), ***n.***

ar·ti·san (ärt′ə zən) ***n.*** [ult. < L *ars*, art] a skilled craftsman

art·ist (ärt′ist) ***n.*** **1** one who is skilled in any of the fine arts **2** one who does anything very well **3** a professional in any of the performing arts

ar·tis·tic (är tis′tik) ***adj.*** **1** of art or artists **2** done skillfully and tastefully **3** sensitive to beauty —**ar·tis′ti·cal·ly** ***adv.***

art·ist·ry (ärt′is trē) ***n.*** artistic quality, ability, or work

art·less (ärt′lis) ***adj.*** **1** lacking skill or art **2** simple; natural **3** without guile; ingenuous; innocent —**art′less·ly** ***adv.***

Arts and Crafts a 19th-c. movement that promoted handwork and craftsmanship

art·y (ärt′ē) ***adj.*** **art′i·er, art′i·est** [Inf.] affectedly artistic —**art′i·ness** ***n.***

ar·um (er′əm) ***n.*** [L] any of a family of plants with flowers enveloped within a hoodlike leaf

Ar·y·an (ar′ē ən) ***n.*** [< Sans *āzya-*, noble] **1** [Obs.] the hypothetical parent language of the Indo-European family **2** a person supposed to be a descendant of the prehistoric peoples that spoke this language: *Aryan* is not a valid ethnological term

as (az) ***adv.*** [< ALSO] **1** equally [just *as* happy at home] **2** for instance [a card game, *as* bridge] **3** when related in a specified way [my view *as* contrasted with yours] —***conj.*** **1** to the same amount or degree that [straight *as* an arrow] **2** in the same manner that [do *as* you are told] **3** while [she wept *as* she spoke] **4** because [*as* you object, we won't go] **5** that the consequence is [so obvious *as* to need no reply] **6** though [tall *as* he was, he couldn't reach it] —***pron.*** **1** a fact that [we are tired, *as* you can see] **2** that: preceded by *such* or *the same* [such books *as* I own] —***prep.*** in the role or function of [he poses *as* a friend] —**as for** (or **to**) concerning — **as if** (or **though**) as it (or one) would if — **as is** [Inf.] just as it is —**as it were** as if it were so

As *Chem. symbol for* arsenic

ASAP *abbrev.* as soon as possible

as·bes·tos (as bes′təs, az-) ***n.*** [< Gr *a-*, not + *sbennynai*, extinguish] a nonconducting, fireproof mineral used, esp. formerly, in electrical insulation, roofing, etc.

as·cend (ə send′) ***vi.*** [< L *ad-*, to + *scandere*, to climb] to move upward; rise —***vt.*** **1** to move upward along; mount **2** to succeed to (a throne)

as·cend·an·cy or **as·cend·en·cy** (ə sen′ dən sē) ***n.*** a position of control; domination

as·cend′ant or **as·cend′ent** (-dənt) ***adj.*** **1** rising **2** in control; dominant — **in the ascendant** at or approaching the height of power, fame, etc.

as·cen′sion (-shən) ***n.*** **1** an ascending **2** [**A-**] the 40th day after Easter, celebrating the Ascension —**the Ascension** *Bible* the bodily ascent of Jesus into heaven

as·cent (ə sent′) ***n.*** **1** an ascending **2** an upward slope

as·cer·tain (as′ər tān′) ***vt.*** [see AD- & CERTAIN] to find out with certainty

as·cet·ic (ə set′ik) ***adj.*** [< Gr *askein*, to train the body] self-denying; austere — ***n.*** [< Gr *awkētēs*, monk] one who leads a life of strict self-denial, esp. for religious purposes —**as·cet′i·cism′** (-ə siz′ əm) ***n.***

ASCII (as′kē) ***n.*** a code that facilitates information exchange among various computers

a·scor·bic acid (ə skôr′bik) ⟦A-[2] + *scorbutic,* of scurvy + -IC⟧ vitamin C

as·cot (as′kət, -kät′) ***n.*** a necktie with very broad ends hanging from the knot

as·cribe (ə skrīb′) ***vt.* -cribed′, -crib′ing** ⟦< L *ad-,* to + *scribere,* write⟧ **1** to assign (something) *to* a supposed cause **2** to regard (something) as belonging *to* or coming from someone **—as·crip·tion** (ə skrip′shən) ***n.***

a·sep·tic (ā sep′tik, ə-) ***adj.*** free from disease-producing bacteria, etc.

a·sex·u·al (ā sek′sho͞o əl) ***adj.*** **1** having no sex or sexual organs **2** without the union of male and female germ cells **3** having little or no sexual activity, desire, character, etc. **—a·sex′u·al·ly *adv.***

ash[1] (ash) ***n.*** ⟦< OE *æsce*⟧ **1** the grayish powder left after something has burned **2** fine, volcanic lava **3** the gray color of wood ash See also ASHES

ash[2] (ash) ***n.*** ⟦< OE *æsc*⟧ **1** a shade tree of the olive family **2** its wood

a·shamed (ə shāmd′) ***adj.*** **1** feeling shame **2** reluctant because fearing shame beforehand **—a·sham·ed·ly** (ə shām′id lē) ***adv.***

ash·en (ash′ən) ***adj.*** **1** of ashes **2** like ashes, esp. in color; pale

ash·es (ash′iz) ***pl.n.*** **1** the grayish powder and small particles left after a thing has burned **2** human remains, esp. the part left after cremation

a·shore (ə shôr′) ***adv., adj.*** **1** to or on the shore **2** to or on land

ash·ram (äsh′rəm) ***n.*** ⟦< Sans *ā,* toward + *śrama,* penance⟧ **1** a secluded place for a Hindu religious community **2** such a community

ash′tray′ ***n.*** a container for smokers' tobacco ashes, etc.: also **ash tray**

Ash Wednesday the first day of Lent: from the putting of ashes on the forehead in penitence

ash′y ***adj.* -i·er, -i·est** **1** of or covered with ashes **2** ashen; pale

A·sia (ā′zhə) largest continent, in the Eastern Hemisphere: *c.* 17,400,000 sq. mi.; pop. *c.* 3,451,000,000 **—A′sian** or less preferred **A·si·at·ic** (ā′zhē at′ik) ***adj., n.***

Asia Minor large peninsula in W Asia, between the Black Sea and the Mediterranean

a·side (ə sīd′) ***adv.*** **1** on or to one side **2** in reserve *[put one aside for me]* **3** apart; notwithstanding *[joking aside]* **—*n.*** words spoken by an actor but supposedly not heard by the other actors **—aside from** **1** with the exception of **2** apart from

as·i·nine (as′ə nīn′) ***adj.*** ⟦< L *asinus,* ass⟧ like an ass; stupid; silly **—as′i·nine′ly *adv.* —as′i·nin′i·ty** (-nin′ə tē) ***n.***

ask (ask) ***vt.*** ⟦OE *āscian*⟧ **1** to use words in seeking the answer to (a question) **2** to inquire of (a person) **3** to request or demand **4** to invite **—*vi.*** **1** to make a request (*for*) **2** to inquire (*about* or *after*) **—ask′er *n.***

a·skance (ə skans′) ***adv.*** ⟦ME⟧ **1** with a sideways glance **2** with suspicion, disapproval, etc.

a·skew (ə skyo͞o′) ***adv.*** to one side; awry **—*adj.*** on one side; awry

asking price the price asked by a seller, esp. as a basis for bargaining

a·slant (ə slant′) ***adv.*** on a slant **—*prep.*** on a slant across **—*adj.*** slanting

a·sleep (ə slēp′) ***adj.*** **1** sleeping **2** inactive; dull **3** numb **4** dead **—*adv.*** into a sleeping condition

a·so·cial (ā sō′shəl) ***adj.*** **1** avoiding contact with others **2** selfish

asp (asp) ***n.*** ⟦< Gr *aspis*⟧ a poisonous snake of Africa, Arabia, etc.

as·par·a·gus (ə spar′ə gəs, -sper′-) ***n.*** ⟦< Gr *asparagos*⟧ **1** a plant of the lily family, with edible shoots **2** these shoots

as·par·tame (as′pər tām′) ***n.*** an artificial, low-calorie sweetener, used in soft drinks, candy, etc.

as·pect (as′pekt′) ***n.*** ⟦< L *ad-,* to + *specere,* to look⟧ **1** the way one appears **2** the appearance of something from a specific position or viewpoint **3** a side facing in a given direction

as·pen (as′pən) ***n.*** ⟦OE *æspe*⟧ a poplar tree whose leaves flutter in the least breeze

as·per·i·ty (ə sper′ə tē) ***n., pl.* -ties** ⟦< L *asper,* rough⟧ **1** roughness or harshness **2** sharpness of temper

as·per·sion (ə spur′zhən) ***n.*** a damaging or disparaging remark; slander

as·phalt (as′fôlt′) ***n.*** ⟦< Gr *asphaltos*⟧ a brown or black tarlike substance mixed with sand or gravel and used for paving, roofing, etc. **—*vt.*** to pave, roof, etc. with asphalt

as·pho·del (as′fə del′) ***n.*** ⟦< Gr *asphodelos*⟧ a plant of the lily family, having white or yellow flowers

as·phyx·i·ate (as fik′sē āt′) ***vt., vi.* -at′ed, -at′ing** ⟦< Gr *a-,* not + *sphyzein,* to throb⟧ **1** to make or become unconscious from lack of oxygen in the blood **2** to suffocate **—as·phyx′i·a′tion *n.***

as·pic (as′pik′) ***n.*** ⟦< OFr *aspe,* asp⟧ a cold jelly of meat juice, tomato juice, etc., served as a garnish or in a mold

as·pi·rant (as′pə rənt, ə spī′-) ***adj.*** aspiring **—*n.*** one who aspires

as·pi·rate (as′pə rāt′; *for n.,* -pər it) ***vt.* -rat′ed, -rat′ing** **1** to begin (a word) with the sound of English (h) **2** to follow (a consonant) with an audible puff of breath **3** to suck in or draw in **4** *Med.* to remove (fluid, etc.) by suction **—*n.*** an aspirated sound

as·pi·ra·tion (as′pə rā′shən) ***n.*** **1** *a)* strong desire or ambition, as for advancement *b)* the thing so desired **2** a drawing in by breathing or suction **3** *Med.* removal of fluid, etc. by suction

as′pi·ra′tor ***n.*** an apparatus using suction to remove air, fluids, etc.

as·pire (ə spīr′) ***vi.* -pired′, -pir′ing** ⟦< L *ad-,* to + *spirare,* breathe⟧ to be ambitious (*to* get or do something); seek (*after*)

as·pi·rin (as′pə rin′, -prin′) ***n.*** ⟦Ger⟧ **1** a white, crystalline powder used for reducing fever, relieving pain, etc. **2** a tablet of this

ass (as) ***n.*** ⟦< L *asinus*⟧ **1** a horselike animal having long ears and a short mane **2** a stupid or silly person

as·sail (ə sāl′) ***vt.*** ⟦< L *ad-*, to + *salire*, to leap⟧ **1** to attack physically and violently **2** to attack with arguments, etc. —**as·sail′a·ble** ***adj.***

as·sail′ant (-ənt) ***n.*** an attacker

as·sas·sin (ə sas′ən) ***n.*** ⟦< Ar *ḥashshāshīn*, hashish users⟧ a murderer who strikes suddenly; now, esp., the murderer of a politically important or prominent person

as·sas′si·nate′ (-āt′) ***vt.*** **-nat′ed, -nat′ing** to murder as an assassin does —**as·sas′si·na′tion** ***n.***

as·sault (ə sôlt′) ***n.*** ⟦< L *ad-*, to + *salire*, to leap⟧ **1** a violent attack **2** *euphemism for* RAPE[1] **3** *Law* an unlawful threat or attempt to harm another physically —***vt.***, ***vi.*** to make an assault (upon)

assault and battery *Law* the carrying out of threatened physical harm

as·say (as′ā, a sā′; *for v.* a sā′) ***n.*** ⟦< OFr *essai*, trial⟧ **1** a testing **2** an analysis of the ingredients of an ore, drug, etc. —***vt.*** **1** to make an assay of; test **2** to try; attempt —***vi.*** to be shown by assay to have a specified proportion of something —**as·say′er** ***n.***

as·sem·blage (ə sem′blij; *for 3, also* ä′ sem bläzh′) ***n.*** **1** an assembling **2** a group of persons or things gathered together **3** *Art* things assembled in a sculptured collage

as·sem·ble (ə sem′bəl) ***vt.***, ***vi.*** **-bled, -bling** ⟦< L *ad-*, to + *simul*, together⟧ **1** to gather into a group; collect **2** to fit or put together the parts of —**as·sem′bler** ***n.***

as·sem′bly (-blē) ***n.***, *pl.* **-blies** **1** an assembling **2** a group of persons gathered together **3** *a)* a legislative body *b)* [A-] the lower house of some state legislatures **4** a fitting together of parts to make a whole

assembly line in many factories, a method whereby each worker performs a specific task in assembling the work as it is passed along

as·sem′bly·man (-mən) ***n.***, *pl.* **-men** a member of a legislative assembly —**as·sem′bly·wom′an**, *pl.* **-wom′en**, ***fem.n.***

as·sent (ə sent′) ***vi.*** ⟦< L *ad-*, to + *sentire*, to feel⟧ to express acceptance; agree (*to*) —***n.*** consent or agreement

as·sert (ə surt′) ***vt.*** ⟦< L *ad-*, to + *serere*, join⟧ **1** to declare; affirm **2** to maintain or defend (rights, etc.) —**assert oneself** to insist on one's rights, or on being recognized —**as·sert′er** or **as·ser′tor** ***n.***

as·ser·tion (ə sur′shən) ***n.*** **1** an asserting **2** a positive statement

as·ser·tive (ə surt′iv) ***adj.*** persistently, forcefully, or boldly positive or confident —**as·ser′tive·ly** ***adv.*** —**as·ser′tive·ness** ***n.***

as·sess (ə ses′) ***vt.*** ⟦< L *ad-*, to + *sedere*, sit⟧ **1** to set an estimated value on (property, etc.) for taxation **2** to set the amount of (a tax, fine, etc.) **3** to impose a tax, etc. on **4** to judge the worth or importance of —**as·sess′ment** ***n.*** —**as·ses′sor** ***n.***

as·set (as′et) ***n.*** ⟦< L *ad*, to + *satis*, enough⟧ **1** anything owned that has value **2** a desirable thing *[charm is an asset]* **3** [*pl.*] the accounting entries showing the resources of a person or business **4** [*pl.*] *Law* property available to pay debts

as·sev·er·ate (ə sev′ə rāt′) ***vt.*** **-at′ed, -at′ing** ⟦< L *ad-*, to + *severus*, earnest⟧ to state positively; assert —**as·sev′er·a′tion** ***n.***

as·sid·u·ous (ə sij′o͞o əs) ***adj.*** ⟦< L *assidere*, to assist⟧ diligent; persevering; careful —**as·si·du·i·ty** (as′ə dyo͞o′ə tē), *pl.* **-ties**, ***n.*** —**as·sid′u·ous·ly** ***adv.*** —**as·sid′u·ous·ness** ***n.***

as·sign (ə sīn′) ***vt.*** ⟦< L *ad-*, to + *signare*, to sign⟧ **1** to set apart or mark for a specific purpose; designate **2** to appoint, as to a duty **3** to give out as a task; allot **4** to ascribe; attribute **5** *Law* to transfer (a right, etc.) —**as·sign′a·ble** ***adj.*** —**as·sign′er** or *Law* **as·sign·or** (ə sīn′ôr′) ***n.***

as·sig·na·tion (as′ig nā′shən) ***n.*** an appointment to meet, esp. one made secretly by lovers, or the meeting itself

as·sign·ment (ə sīn′mənt) ***n.*** **1** an assigning or being assigned **2** anything assigned

as·sim·i·late (ə sim′ə lāt′) ***vt.*** **-lat′ed, -lat′ing** ⟦< L *ad-*, to + *similare*, make similar⟧ **1** to absorb and incorporate **2** to make like or alike: with *to* —***vi.*** **1** to become like or alike **2** to become absorbed and incorporated —**as·sim′i·la′tion** ***n.***

as·sist (ə sist′) ***vt.***, ***vi.*** ⟦< L *ad-*, to + *sistere*, make stand⟧ to help; aid —***n.*** an instance or act of helping —**assist at** to be present at; attend

as·sist·ance (ə sis′təns) ***n.*** help; aid

as·sist′ant (-tənt) ***adj.*** assisting; helping —***n.*** one who assists; helper; aid

assisted living a living arrangement providing assistance to elderly or disabled persons

as·siz·es (ə sīz′iz) ***pl.n.*** ⟦see ASSESS⟧ **1** court sessions held periodically in each county of England **2** the time or place of these

assn *abbrev.* association

assoc *abbrev.* **1** associate(s) **2** association

as·so·ci·ate (ə sō′shē āt′, -sē-; *for n. & adj.*, -it) ***vt.*** **-at′ed, -at′ing** ⟦< L *ad-*, to + *socius*, companion⟧ **1** to connect; combine; join **2** to bring into relationship as partner, etc. **3** to connect in the mind —***vi.*** to join (*with*) as a partner, friend, etc. —***n.*** **1** a friend, partner, coworker, etc. **2** a degree granted by a junior college —***adj.*** **1** joined with others in work, etc. **2** having less than full status

as·so′ci·a′tion ***n.*** **1** an associating or being associated **2** fellowship; partnership **3** an organization, society, etc. **4** a mental connection between ideas, etc.

association football soccer

as·so′ci·a′tive (-shē āt′iv, -sē-; -shə tiv) ***adj.*** **1** of, by, or causing association **2** *Math.* producing the same result regardless of how the elements are grouped

as·so·nance (as′ə nəns) ***n.*** ⟦< L *ad-*, to + *sonare*, to sound⟧ **1** likeness of sound **2** a partial rhyme made by repetition of a vowel sound —**as′so·nant** ***adj.***, ***n.***

as·sort (ə sôrt′) ***vt.*** ⟦ult. < L *ad-*, to + *sors*, lot, fate⟧ to sort or classify

as·sort′ed ***adj.*** **1** various; miscellaneous **2** sorted; classified

as·sort′ment ***n.*** **1** an assorting **2** a miscellaneous collection; variety

asst *abbrev.* assistant

as·suage (ə swāj′) ***vt.*** **-suaged′**, **-suag′ing** ⟦< L *ad-*, to + *suavis*, sweet⟧ **1** to lessen (pain, distress, etc.) **2** to calm (anger, etc.) **3** to satisfy or slake (thirst, etc.)

as·sume (ə so͞om′) ***vt.*** **-sumed′**, **-sum′ing** ⟦< L *ad-*, to + *sumere*, to take⟧ **1** to take on (the appearance, role, etc. of) **2** to seize; usurp **3** to undertake **4** to take for granted; suppose **5** to pretend to have; feign —**as·sum′a·ble** ***adj.***

as·sumed′ ***adj.*** **1** pretended; fictitious **2** taken for granted

as·sump·tion (ə sump′shən) ***n.*** **1** [**A-**] *R.C.Ch.* *a)* the ascent of the Virgin Mary into heaven *b)* a feast on Aug. 15 celebrating this **2** an assuming **3** a supposition —**as·sump′tive** ***adj.***

as·sur·ance (ə shoor′əns) ***n.*** **1** an assuring or being assured **2** a promise, guarantee, etc. **3** self-confidence **4** [Chiefly Brit.] insurance

as·sure (ə shoor′) ***vt.*** **-sured′**, **-sur′ing** ⟦< L *ad-*, to + *securus*, secure⟧ **1** to make (a person) sure of something **2** to give confidence to; reassure **3** to tell or promise confidently **4** to guarantee **5** [Chiefly Brit.] to insure against loss

as·sured′ ***adj.*** **1** made sure; certain **2** confident; sure of oneself —**as·sur·ed·ly** (ə shoor′id lē) ***adv.***

As·syr·i·a (ə sir′ē ə) ancient empire in SW Asia —**As·syr′i·an** ***adj.***, ***n.***

as·ter (as′tər) ***n.*** ⟦< Gr *astēr*, star⟧ any of several plants of the composite family with variously colored daisylike flowers

as·ter·isk (as′tər isk′) ***n.*** ⟦< Gr dim. of *astēr*, star⟧ a starlike sign (*) used in printing to mark footnotes, etc.

a·stern (ə sturn′) ***adv.*** **1** behind a ship or aircraft **2** AFT **3** backward

as·ter·oid (as′tər oid′) ***n.*** ⟦see ASTER & -OID⟧ any of the small planets in orbits mainly between Mars and Jupiter

asth·ma (az′mə) ***n.*** ⟦Gr⟧ a chronic disorder characterized by wheezing, coughing, difficulty in breathing, etc. —**asth·mat·ic** (az mat′ik) ***adj.***, ***n.***

a·stig·ma·tism (ə stig′mə tiz′əm) ***n.*** ⟦< Gr *a-*, without + *stigma*, a mark + -ISM⟧ an irregularity in the lens of the eye, that prevents proper focusing of light rays, causing distortion, poor eyesight, etc. —**as·tig·mat·ic** (as′tig mat′ik) ***adj.***

a·stil·be (ə stil′bē) ***n.*** a plant having spikes of white, pink, or red flowers

a·stir (ə stur′) ***adv.***, ***adj.*** **1** in motion **2** out of bed

as·ton·ish (ə stän′ish) ***vt.*** ⟦< L *ex-*, intens. + *tonare*, to thunder⟧ to fill with sudden wonder; amaze —**as·ton′ish·ing** ***adj.*** —**as·ton′ish·ing·ly** ***adv.*** —**as·ton′ish·ment** ***n.***

as·tound (ə stound′) ***vt.*** ⟦see prec.⟧ to astonish greatly —**as·tound′ing** ***adj.*** —**as·tound′ing·ly** ***adv.***

a·strad·dle (ə strad′'l) ***adv.*** in a straddling position

as·tra·khan (as′trə kən) ***n.*** ⟦after *Astrakhan*, Russ city⟧ loosely curled fur from young lamb pelts, or a wool fabric resembling this

as·tral (as′trəl) ***adj.*** ⟦< Gr *astron*, star⟧ of, from, or like the stars

a·stray (ə strā′) ***adv.***, ***adj.*** ⟦ME < pp. of OFr *estraier*, stray⟧ **1** off the right path **2** in error

a·stride (ə strīd′) ***adv.*** with a leg on either side —***prep.*** **1** with a leg on either side of **2** extending over or across

as·trin·gent (ə strin′jənt) ***adj.*** ⟦< L *ad-*, to + *stringere*, to draw tight⟧ **1** that contracts body tissue and stops secretions **2** harsh; biting —***n.*** an astringent substance —**as·trin′gen·cy** ***n.***

astro- ⟦< Gr *astron*, star⟧ *combining form* star or stars *[astrophysics]*

as·tro·bi·ol·o·gy (as′trō bī äl′ə jē) ***n.*** the branch of biology that investigates the existence of living organisms on planets other than earth

as′tro·dy·nam′ics ***n.*** the branch of dynamics dealing with the motion and gravitation of objects in space

as·trol·o·gy (ə sträl′ə jē) ***n.*** ⟦< Gr *astron*, star + *-logia*, -LOGY⟧ a method or theory based on the assumption that the positions of the moon, sun, and stars affect human affairs and can be used to foretell the future —**as·trol′o·ger** ***n.*** —**as·tro·log·i·cal** (as′trə läj′i kəl) ***adj.***

as·tro·naut (as′trə nôt′) ***n.*** ⟦< Fr < Gr *astron*, star + *nautēs*, sailor⟧ one trained to make flights into outer space —**as′tro·nau′tics** ***n.***

as·tro·nom·i·cal (as′trə näm′i kəl) ***adj.*** **1** of astronomy **2** extremely large: said as of numbers Also **as′tro·nom′ic** —**as′tro·nom′i·cal·ly** ***adv.***

astronomical unit a unit of length based on the mean distance of the earth from the sun, *c.* 149.6 million km (*c.* 93 million mi.)

as·tron·o·my (ə strän′ə mē) ***n.*** ⟦< Gr *astron*, star + *nomos*, law⟧ the science that studies the origin, size, motion, etc. of stars, planets, etc. —**as·tron′o·mer** ***n.***

as·tro·phys·ics (as′trō fiz′iks) ***n.*** the branch of astronomy dealing with the physical properties of the universe —**as′tro·phys′i·cist** (-ə sist) ***n.***

As′tro·Turf′ (-turf′) *trademark for* a grasslike synthetic carpet used in stadiums, etc.

as·tute (ə sto͞ot′) ***adj.*** ⟦< L *astus*, craft, cunning⟧ clever or shrewd; keen —**as·tute′ly** ***adv.*** —**as·tute′ness** ***n.***

a·sun·der (ə sun′dər) ***adv.*** ⟦< OE *on sundran*⟧ **1** into pieces **2** apart in direction or position

a·sy·lum (ə sī′ləm) ***n.*** ⟦< Gr *a-*, without +

sylon, right of seizure⟧ **1** a place of safety; refuge **2** an institution for the care of mentally ill, aged, or poor people: a term now rarely used

a·sym·me·try (ā sim′ə trē) ***n.*** lack of symmetry —**a·sym·met·ri·cal** (ā′sə me′ tri kəl) ***adj.*** —**a′sym·met′ri·cal·ly** ***adv.***

a·symp·to·mat·ic (ā′simp tə ma′tik) ***adj.*** without symptoms

at (at) ***prep.*** ⟦< OE *æt*⟧ **1** on; in; near; by *[at* the office*]* **2** to or toward *[*look *at* her*]* **3** from *[*visible *at* one mile*]* **4** attending *[at* a party*]* **5** busy with *[at* work*]* **6** in the state or manner of *[at* war, *at* a trot*]* **7** because of *[*sad *at* his death*]* **8** with reference to *[*good *at* tennis*]* **9** in the amount, etc. of *[at* five cents each*]* **10** on or near the time or age of *[at* noon, *at* twenty-one*]* **11** attacking, etc. *[*they're *at* him again*]*

at·a·vism (at′ə viz′əm) ***n.*** ⟦< L *at-*, beyond + *avus*, grandfather⟧ resemblance or reversion to a characteristic of a remote ancestor —**at′a·vis′tic** ***adj.***

a·tax·i·a (ə tak′sē ə) ***n.*** ⟦< Gr *a-*, not + *tassein*, arrange⟧ an inability to coordinate one's movements, as in walking —**a·tax′ic** ***adj.***, ***n.***

ate (āt; *Brit, or U.S. dial.*, et) ***vt.***, ***vi.*** *pt. of* EAT

-ate[1] (āt; *for 2*, it) *suffix* **1** to become, cause to become, form, provide with *[maturate, ulcerate]* **2** of or characteristic of, characterized by, having *[passionate]*

-ate[2] (āt, it) *suffix* an office, function, agent, or official *[directorate]*

at·el·ier (at′'l yā′) ***n.*** ⟦Fr⟧ a studio or workshop, esp. of an artist

Ath·a·bas·kan or **Ath·a·bas·can** (ath′ə bas′kən) ***n.*** a family of North American Indian languages, including Navajo —***adj.*** designating or of these languages or the peoples that speak them

a·the·ism (ā′thē iz′əm) ***n.*** ⟦< Gr *a-*, without + *theos*, god⟧ the belief that there is no God —**a′the·ist** ***n.*** —**a′the·is′tic** ***adj.***

A·the·na (ə thē′nə) ***n.*** the Greek goddess of wisdom, skills, and warfare

Ath·ens (ath′ənz) capital of Greece, in the SE part: pop. 772,000 —**A·the·ni·an** (ə thē′nē ən) ***adj.***, ***n.***

ath·er·o·scle·ro·sis (ath′ər ō′sklə rō′sis) ***n.*** ⟦< Gr *athērōma*, grainy tumor + SCLEROSIS⟧ formation of fatty nodules on hardening artery walls

a·thirst (ə thurst′) ***adj.*** **1** [Archaic] thirsty **2** eager; longing (*for*)

ath·lete (ath′lēt′) ***n.*** ⟦< Gr *athlon*, a prize⟧ a person trained in exercises or games requiring strength, skill, stamina, etc.

athlete's foot ringworm of the feet

ath·let·ic (ath let′ik) ***adj.*** **1** of or like athletes or athletics **2** physically strong, active, fit, etc. —**ath·let′i·cal·ly** ***adv.*** —**ath·let′i·cism′** (-ə siz′əm) ***n.***

ath·let′ics ***pl.n.*** [*sometimes with sing. v.*] athletic sports, games, etc.

-a·thon (ə thän′) ⟦< (MAR)ATHON⟧ *suffix* an event marked by length or endurance *[walkathon]*

a·thwart (ə thwôrt′) ***prep.*** **1** across **2** against —***adv.*** crosswise

a·tilt (ə tilt′) ***adj.***, ***adv.*** tilted

-a·tion (ā′shən) ⟦< Fr or L⟧ *suffix* the act, condition, or result of *[alteration]*

-a·tive (ə tiv, āt′iv) ⟦< Fr or L⟧ *suffix* of or relating to, serving to *[informative]*

At·lan·ta (at lan′tə) capital of Georgia: pop. 394,000

At·lan·tic (at lan′tik) ocean touching the Americas to the west and Europe and Africa to the east

Atlantic City city in SE New Jersey: an ocean resort: pop. 38,000

At·lan·tis (at lan′tis) ***n.*** ⟦< Gr⟧ legendary sunken continent in the Atlantic

At·las (at′ləs) ***n.*** **1** *Gr. Myth.* a giant who supports the heavens on his shoulders **2** [**a-**] a book of maps

ATM (ā′tē em′) ***n.*** ⟦*a*(*utomated*) *t*(*eller*) *m*(*achine*)⟧ a computer terminal that allows a bank customer to deposit, withdraw, or transfer funds automatically

at·mos·phere (at′məs fir′) ***n.*** ⟦< Gr *atmos*, vapor + *sphaira*, sphere⟧ **1** the air surrounding the earth **2** a pervading mood or spirit **3** the general tone or effect **4** a unit of pressure equal to 101,325 newtons per sq. m —**at′mos·pher′ic** (-fer′ik, -fir′-) ***adj.*** —**at′mos·pher′i·cal·ly** ***adv.***

at·oll (a′tôl′) ***n.*** ⟦< Malayalam *atolu*⟧ a ring-shaped coral island surrounding a lagoon

at·om (at′əm) ***n.*** ⟦< Gr *a-*, not + *temnein*, to cut⟧ **1** a tiny particle; jot **2** *Chem., Physics* any of the smallest particles of an element that combine with similar particles of other elements to form molecules —**the atom** nuclear energy

atom bomb ATOMIC BOMB

a·tom·ic (ə täm′ik) ***adj.*** **1** of an atom or atoms **2** of or using atomic energy or atomic bombs **3** tiny —**a·tom′i·cal·ly** ***adv.***

atomic bomb an extremely destructive bomb whose power results from a chain reaction of nuclear fission

atomic energy NUCLEAR ENERGY

atomic number *Chem.* a number indicating the number of protons in the nucleus of an atom of an element

atomic weight *Chem.* the weight of one atom of an element based upon the average weight of the element's isotopes

at·om·iz·er (at′əm ī zər) ***n.*** a device used to shoot out a fine spray, as of medicine or perfume

a·to·nal·i·ty (ā′tō nal′ə tē) ***n.*** *Music* the organization of tones without relation to a key —**a·ton·al** (ā tōn′əl) ***adj.*** —**a·ton′al·ly** ***adv.***

a·tone (ə tōn′) ***vi.*** **a·toned′**, **a·ton′ing** ⟦< ME *at one*, in accord⟧ to make amends (*for* wrongdoing, etc.)

a·tone′ment ***n.*** **1** an atoning **2** amends —**the Atonement** *Theol.* the redeeming of humanity by the death of Jesus

a·top (ə täp′) ***adv.*** on or at the top —***prep.*** on the top of

a·top·ic (ā täp′ik) ***adj.*** of allergic reactions, as a type of dermatitis, thought to be inherited

-a·to·ry (ə tôr′ē) ⟦< L⟧ *suffix* -ORY

ATP (ā′tē′pē′) ***n.*** ⟦*a*(*denosine*) *t*(*ri*)*p*(*hosphate*)⟧ an organic compound present in, and vital to, all living cells

a·tri·um (ā′trē əm) ***n.***, *pl.* **a′tri·a** (-ə) or **a′tri·ums** ⟦L⟧ **1** the central court or main room of an ancient Roman house **2** a court or entrance hall, usually of more than one story **3** either of the heart's upper chambers

a·tro·cious (ə trō′shəs) ***adj.*** ⟦< L *atrox*, fierce⟧ **1** very cruel, evil, etc. **2** very bad or unpleasant; offensive —**a·tro′cious·ly *adv.*** —**a·tro′cious·ness *n.***

a·troc·i·ty (ə träs′ə tē) ***n.***, *pl.* **-ties** **1** atrocious behavior **2** an atrocious act **3** [Inf.] a very displeasing thing

at·ro·phy (a′trə fē) ***n.*** ⟦< Gr *a-*, not + *trephein*, to feed⟧ a wasting away or failure to grow, esp. of body tissue, an organ, etc. —***vi.*** **-phied**, **-phy·ing** to undergo atrophy —***vt.*** to cause atrophy in

at·ro·pine (at′rə pēn′, -pin′) ***n.*** ⟦< Gr *Atropos*, one of the Fates + -INE[3]⟧ an alkaloid obtained from belladonna, used to relieve spasms, etc.

at·tach (ə tach′) ***vt.*** ⟦< OFr *estache*, a post, stake⟧ **1** to fasten by sticking, tying, etc. **2** to join: often used reflexively **3** to connect by ties of affection, etc. **4** to add (a signature, etc.) **5** to ascribe **6** *Law* to take (property) by writ —**at·tach′a·ble *adj.***

at·ta·ché (at′ə shā′; *chiefly Brit* ə tash′ā) ***n.*** ⟦Fr: see prec.⟧ a member of an ambassador's diplomatic staff

attaché case a briefcase

at·tach′ment ***n.*** **1** an attaching or being attached **2** anything that attaches; fastening **3** devotion **4** anything attached **5** an accessory for an electrical appliance, etc. **6** *Law* a taking of property into custody

at·tack (ə tak′) ***vt.*** ⟦< It *attaccare*⟧ **1** to use force against in order to harm **2** to speak or write against **3** to undertake vigorously **4** to begin acting upon harmfully —***vi.*** to make an assault —***n.*** **1** an attacking **2** any hostile action, esp. with troops **3** the onset of a disease **4** a beginning of a task, undertaking, etc. —**at·tack′er *n.***

at·tain (ə tān′) ***vt.*** ⟦< L *ad-*, to + *tangere*, to touch⟧ **1** to gain; accomplish; achieve **2** to reach; arrive at —**at·tain′a·bil′i·ty *n.*** —**at·tain′a·ble *adj.***

at·tain′der (-dər) ***n.*** ⟦see prec.⟧ loss of civil rights and property of one sentenced to death or outlawed

at·tar (at′ər) ***n.*** ⟦< Ar *ʿiṭr*, perfume⟧ a perfume made from flower petals, esp. of roses (**attar of roses**)

at·tempt (ə tempt′) ***vt.*** ⟦< L *ad-*, to + *temptare*, to try⟧ to try to do, get, etc. —***n.*** **1** a try; endeavor **2** an attack, as on a person's life

at·tend (ə tend′) ***vt.*** ⟦< L *ad-*, to + *tendere*, to stretch⟧ **1** [Now Rare] to take care of **2** to go with **3** to accompany as a result **4** to be present at —***vi.*** **1** to pay attention **2** to wait (*on* or *upon*) **3** to apply oneself (*to*) **4** to give

the required care (*to*)

at·tend′ance ***n.*** **1** an attending **2** the number of persons attending

at·tend′ant ***adj.*** **1** attending or serving **2** being present **3** accompanying —***n.*** one who attends or serves

at·ten·tion (ə ten′shən) ***n.*** ⟦see ATTEND⟧ **1** mental concentration or readiness **2** notice or observation **3** care or consideration **4** an act of courtesy or devotion: *usually used in pl.* **5** the erect posture of soldiers ready for a command

attention-deficit hyperactivity disorder a mental disorder marked by inability to concentrate, impulsiveness, etc.

at·ten′tive (-tiv) ***adj.*** **1** paying attention **2** courteous, devoted, etc. —**at·ten′tive·ly *adv.*** —**at·ten′tive·ness *n.***

at·ten·u·ate (ə ten′yo͞o āt′) ***vt.*** **-at′ed**, **-at′ing** ⟦< L *ad-*, to + *tenuis*, thin⟧ **1** to make thin **2** to dilute **3** to lessen or weaken —***vi.*** to become thin, weak, etc. —**at·ten′u·a′tion *n.*** —**at·ten′u·a′tor *n.***

at·test (ə test′) ***vt.*** ⟦< L *ad-*, to + *testari*, to bear witness⟧ **1** to declare to be true or genuine **2** to certify, as by oath **3** to serve as proof of —***vi.*** to bear witness (*to*) —**at·tes·ta·tion** (at′əs tā′shən) ***n.***

at·tic (at′ik) ***n.*** ⟦< Gr *Attikos*, of Attica (ancient Gr state): with reference to architectural style⟧ the room or space just below the roof; garret

At·ti·la (at′'l ə, ə til′ə) A.D. 406?-453; king of the Huns: called *Attila the Hun*

at·tire (ə tīr′) ***vt.*** **-tired′**, **-tir′ing** ⟦< OFr *a*, to + *tire*, order, row⟧ to dress, esp. in fine garments; clothe —***n.*** clothes, esp. fine or rich apparel

at·ti·tude (at′ə to͞od′) ***n.*** ⟦ult. < L *aptus*, apt⟧ **1** a bodily posture showing mood, action, etc. **2** a manner showing one's feelings or thoughts **3** one's disposition, opinion, etc. **4** [Slang] a quarrelsome or haughty temperament or manner

at·ti·tu·di·nize (at′ə to͞od′'n īz′) ***vi.*** **-nized′**, **-niz′ing** to pose for effect

Attn or **attn** *abbrev.* attention

at·tor·ney (ə tur′nē) ***n.***, *pl.* **-neys** ⟦< OFr *a-*, to + *torner*, to turn⟧ any person legally empowered to act for another; esp., a lawyer

attorney at law a lawyer

attorney general *pl.* **attorneys general** or **attorney generals** the chief law officer of a government

at·tract (ə trakt′) ***vt.*** ⟦< L *ad-*, to + *trahere*, to draw⟧ **1** to draw to itself or oneself **2** to get the admiration, attention, etc. of; allure —***vi.*** to be attractive —**at·tract′a·ble *adj.***

at·trac·tion (ə trak′shən) ***n.*** **1** an attracting or being attracted **2** power to attract; esp., charm **3** anything that attracts **4** *Physics* the mutual tendency of bodies to draw together

at·trac′tive (-tiv) ***adj.*** that attracts; esp., pleasing, charming, pretty, etc. —**at·trac′tive·ly *adv.*** —**at·trac′tive·ness *n.***

at·trib·ute (ə trib′yo͞ot; *for n.* a′trə byo͞ot′) ***vt.*** **-ut·ed**, **-ut·ing** ⟦< L *ad-*, to +

tribuere, assign⟧ to think of as belonging *to* a certain person or thing —***n.*** a characteristic or quality of a person or thing —**at·trib'ut·a·ble** ***adj.*** —**at·tri·bu·tion** (a'trə byo͞o'shən) ***n.***

at·trib·u·tive (ə trib'yo͞o tiv) ***adj.*** **1** attributing **2** preceding the noun it modifies: said of an adjective —**at·trib'u·tive·ly** ***adv.***

at·tri·tion (ə trish'ən) ***n.*** ⟦< L *ad-*, to + *terere*, to rub⟧ **1** a wearing away by or as by friction **2** a normal loss of personnel, as by retirement

at·tune (ə to͞on') ***vt.*** **-tuned'**, **-tun'ing** **1** to tune **2** to bring into harmony

atty *abbrev.* attorney

ATV (ā'tē'vē') ***n.***, *pl.* **ATVs** ⟦*A*(*ll-*) *T*(*errain*) *V*(*ehicle*)⟧ a small motor vehicle for traveling over rough ground, snow and ice, etc.

a·twit·ter (ə twit'ər) ***adv.***, ***adj.*** twittering

a·typ·i·cal (ā tip'i kəl) ***adj.*** not typical; abnormal —**a·typ'i·cal·ly** ***adv.***

Au ⟦L *aurum*⟧ *Chem. symbol for* gold

au·burn (ô'bərn) ***adj.***, ***n.*** ⟦< L *albus*, white: infl. by ME *brun*, brown⟧ reddish brown

Auck·land (ôk'lənd) seaport in N New Zealand: pop. 910,000

auc·tion (ôk'shən) ***n.*** ⟦< L *augere*, to increase⟧ a public sale of items, one by one, to the highest bidder for each item —***vt.*** to sell at auction —**auction off** to sell at auction —**auc'tion·eer'** ***n.***

au·da·cious (ô dā'shəs) ***adj.*** ⟦< L *audax*, bold⟧ **1** bold; daring **2** too bold; brazen; insolent —**au·da'cious·ly** ***adv.*** —**au·da'cious·ness** ***n.***

au·dac·i·ty (ô das'ə tē) ***n.*** **1** bold courage **2** insolence; impudence **3** *pl.* **-ties** an audacious act or remark

au·di·ble (ô'də bəl) ***adj.*** ⟦< L *audire*, hear⟧ loud enough to be heard —**au'di·bil'i·ty** (-bil'ə tē) ***n.*** —**au'di·bly** ***adv.***

au·di·ence (ô'dē əns) ***n.*** ⟦< L *audire*, hear⟧ **1** those assembled to hear and see something **2** all those reached by a TV or radio program, book, etc. **3** a hearing, esp. a formal interview

au·di·o (ô'dē ō') ***adj.*** ⟦< L *audire*, hear⟧ **1** of frequencies corresponding to audible sound waves **2** of sound reproduction, as of the sound phase of television

au'di·o·book' ***n.*** a recording of a reading of a book, as by the author

au·di·ol·o·gy (ô'dē äl'ə jē) ***n.*** evaluation and treatment of hearing defects —**au'di·ol'o·gist** ***n.***

au'di·om'e·ter (-äm'ət ər) ***n.*** an instrument for measuring the sharpness and range of hearing —**au'di·o·met'ric** (-ō me'trik) ***adj.***

au·di·o·phile (ô'dē ō fīl') ***n.*** a devotee of high-fidelity sound reproduction, as from recordings

au·di·o·vis·u·al (ô'dē ō vizh'o͞o əl) ***adj.*** **1** involving both hearing and sight **2** of teaching aids such as films and recordings

au·dit (ôd'it) ***n.*** ⟦< L *auditus*, a hearing⟧ a formal checking of financial records —***vt.***, ***vi.*** **1** to check (accounts, etc.) **2** to attend (a college class) as a listener receiving no credit

au·di·tion (ô dish'ən) ***n.*** ⟦< L *audire*, hear⟧ a hearing to try out an actor, singer, etc. —***vt.***, ***vi.*** to try out in an audition

au·di·tor (ô'dit ər) ***n.*** **1** a listener **2** one who audits accounts **3** one who audits classes

au·di·to·ri·um (ô'də tôr'ē əm) ***n.*** **1** a room where an audience sits **2** a building or hall for speeches, concerts, etc.

au·di·to·ry (ô'də tôr'ē) ***adj.*** of hearing or the sense of hearing

auf Wie·der·seh·en (ouf vē'dər zā'ən) ⟦Ger⟧ goodbye

au·ger (ô'gər) ***n.*** ⟦< OE *nafu*, hub (of a wheel) + *gar*, a spear⟧ a tool for boring holes in wood

aught (ôt) ***n.*** ⟦< OE *a*, ever + *wiht*, creature⟧ **1** anything whatever **2** ⟦< (N)AUGHT⟧ a zero

aug·ment (ôg ment') ***vt.***, ***vi.*** ⟦< L *augere*, to increase⟧ to make or become greater —**aug'men·ta'tion** ***n.*** —**aug·ment'er** ***n.***

au gra·tin (ō grat''n, -grät'-) ⟦Fr⟧ with a crust of bread crumbs and grated cheese

au·gur (ô'gər) ***n.*** ⟦L, priest at fertility rites⟧ a prophet; soothsayer —***vt.***, ***vi.*** **1** to prophesy **2** to be an omen (of) —**augur ill** (or **well**) to be a bad (or good) omen

au·gu·ry (ô'gyo͞o rē) ***n.*** **1** the practice of divination **2** *pl.* **-ries** an omen; portent

au·gust (ô gust') ***adj.*** ⟦L *augustus*⟧ inspiring awe; imposing —**au·gust'ly** ***adv.*** —**au·gust'ness** ***n.***

Au·gust (ô'gəst) ***n.*** ⟦< L *Augustus*⟧ the eighth month of the year, having 31 days: abbrev. **Aug**

Au·gus·ta (ô gus'tə) capital of Maine: pop. 21,000

Au·gus·tine (ô'gəs tēn', ə gus'tin), Saint (A.D. 354-430); early Christian church father

Au·gus·tus (ô gus'təs) 63 B.C.-A.D. 14; 1st Rom. emperor (27 B.C.-A.D. 14)

au jus (ō zho͞o', ō jo͞os') ⟦Fr⟧ served in its natural juices: said of meat

auk (ôk) ***n.*** ⟦< ON *alka*⟧ a diving bird of northern seas, with webbed feet and short wings used as paddles

auld lang syne (ôld' laŋ' zīn') ⟦Scot, lit., old long since⟧ the good old days

aunt (ant, änt) ***n.*** ⟦< L *amita*⟧ **1** a sister of one's mother or father **2** the wife of one's uncle

au poivre (ō pwäv'rə) ⟦Fr⟧ with crushed black peppercorns and a sauce

au·ra (ô'rə) ***n.***, *pl.* **-ras** or **-rae** (-rē) ⟦< Gr⟧ **1** an invisible emanation **2** a particular quality surrounding a person or thing

au·ral (ô'rəl) ***adj.*** ⟦< L *auris*, ear⟧ of the ear or the sense of hearing

au·re·ole (ô'rē ōl') ***n.*** ⟦< L *aurum*, gold⟧ **1** a halo **2** a corona around the sun

Au·re·o·my·cin (ô'rē ō mī'sin) *trademark for* an antibiotic used to treat infections and viruses

au re·voir (ō'rə vwär') ⟦Fr⟧ goodbye

au·ri·cle (ô'ri kəl) ***n.*** ⟦< L dim. of *auris*,

ear⟧ the outer part of the ear

Au·ro·ra[1] (ô rôr′ə) ***n.***, *pl.* for 2 & 3 **-ras** or **-rae** (-ē) **1** the Rom. goddess of dawn **2** [**a-**] the dawn **3** [**a-**] a luminous band in the night sky

Au·ro·ra[2] (ô rôr′ə) city in central Colorado: pop. 222,000

aurora aus·tra·lis (ô strā′lis) the aurora in the sky of the S Hemisphere

aurora bo·re·al·is (bôr′ē al′is) the aurora in the sky of the N Hemisphere

aus·cul·ta·tion (ôs′kəl tā′shən) ***n.*** ⟦L *auscultare*, to listen⟧ a listening, often with a stethoscope, to sounds in the chest, abdomen, etc. so as to determine the condition of the heart, lungs, etc. —**aus′cul·tate′**, **-tat′ed**, **-tat′ing**, ***vt.***, ***vi.***

aus·pice (ôs′pis) ***n.***, *pl.* **-pi·ces** (-pə siz, -sēz′) ⟦< L *auspicium*, omen⟧ **1** an omen **2** a favorable omen or sign **3** [*pl.*] sponsorship; patronage

aus·pi·cious (ôs pish′əs) ***adj.*** **1** favorable; propitious **2** successful —**aus·pi′cious·ly *adv.*** —**aus·pi′cious·ness *n.***

Aus·sie (ôs′ē) ***adj.***, ***n.*** [Inf.] Australian

Aus·ten (ôs′tən), **Jane** 1775-1817; Eng. novelist

aus·tere (ô stir′) ***adj.*** ⟦< Gr *austēros*, dry⟧ **1** stern; severe **2** showing strict self-control; ascetic **3** very plain; lacking ornament —**aus·tere′ly *adv.***

aus·ter·i·ty (ô ster′ə tē) ***n.***, *pl.* **-ties** **1** sternness **2** an austere practice, act, or manner **3** tightened economy

Aus·tin (ôs′tən) capital of Texas, in the central part: pop. 466,000

aus·tral (ôs′trəl) ***adj.*** ⟦< L *auster*, the south⟧ southern

Aus·tral·ia (ô strāl′yə) **1** island continent between the S Pacific and Indian oceans **2** country comprising this continent & Tasmania: 2,966,150 sq. mi.; pop. 16,849,000 —**Aus·tral′i·an *adj.***, ***n.***

Aus·tri·a (ôs′trē ə) country in central Europe: 32,378 sq. mi.; pop. 7,796,000 —**Aus′tri·an *adj.***, ***n.***

au·then·tic (ô then′tik) ***adj.*** ⟦< Gr *authentikos*, genuine⟧ **1** credible, reliable, etc.: said as of a news report **2** genuine; real —**au·then′ti·cal·ly *adv.*** —**au·then·tic·i·ty** (ô′thən tis′ə tē) ***n.***

au·then′ti·cate′ (-ti kāt′) ***vt.*** **-cat′ed**, **-cat′ing** **1** to make authentic or valid **2** to verify **3** to prove to be genuine —**au·then′ti·ca′tion *n.***

au·thor (ô′thər) ***n.*** ⟦< L *augere*, to increase⟧ **1** one who makes or creates something **2** a writer of books, etc. —***vt.*** to be the author of

au·thor·i·tar·i·an (ə thôr′ə ter′ē ən) ***adj.*** believing in or characterized by absolute obedience to authority —***n.*** an advocate or enforcer of such obedience —**au·thor′i·tar′i·an·ism′ *n.***

au·thor′i·ta′tive (-tāt′iv) ***adj.*** **1** having authority; official **2** based on competent authority; reliable —**au·thor′i·ta′tive·ly *adv.*** —**au·thor′i·ta′tive·ness *n.***

au·thor′i·ty (-tē) ***n.***, *pl.* **-ties** ⟦see AUTHOR⟧ **1** the power or right to command, act, etc. **2** [*pl.*] officials with this power **3** power or influence resulting from knowledge, prestige, etc. **4** a person, writing, etc. cited to support an opinion **5** an expert

au·thor·ize (ô′thər īz′) ***vt.*** **-ized′**, **-iz′ing** **1** to give official approval to **2** to give power or authority to **3** to justify —**au′thor·i·za′tion *n.*** —**au′thor·iz′er *n.***

Authorized Version the revised English translation of the Bible published in England in 1611 with the authorization of King James I

au′thor·ship′ ***n.*** origin or source with regard to author or originator

au·tism (ô′tiz′əm) ***n.*** ⟦AUT(O)- + -ISM⟧ a developmental disorder marked by impaired social interaction, communication difficulties, etc. —**au·tis′tic** (-tis′tik) ***adj.***

au·to (ôt′ō) ***n.***, *pl.* **-tos** an automobile

auto- ⟦< Gr *autos*, self⟧ *combining form* **1** self **2** by oneself or itself **3** automatic

au·to·bi·og·ra·phy (ôt′ō bī ä′grə fē) ***n.***, *pl.* **-phies** the story of one's own life written by oneself —**au′to·bi′o·graph′i·cal** (-bī′ə graf′i kəl) ***adj.*** —**au′to·bi′o·graph′i·cal·ly *adv.***

au·toc·ra·cy (ô tä′krə sē) ***n.*** ⟦see fol.⟧ **1** government in which one person has absolute power **2** *pl.* **-cies** a country with such government

au·to·crat (ôt′ə krat′) ***n.*** ⟦< Gr *autos*, self + *kratos*, power⟧ **1** a ruler with absolute power **2** any domineering person —**au′to·crat′ic *adj.*** —**au′to·crat′i·cal·ly *adv.***

au·to·di·dact (ôt′ō dī′dakt′) ***n.*** ⟦see AUTO- & DIDACTIC⟧ a person who is self-taught

au·to·graph (ôt′ə graf′) ***n.*** ⟦< Gr *autos*, self + *graphein*, write⟧ a person's own signature or handwriting —***vt.*** to write one's signature on or in

au′to·mate′ (-māt′) ***vt.*** **-mat′ed**, **-mat′ing** ⟦< AUTOMATION⟧ to convert to automation or use automation in

au·to·mat·ic (ôt′ə mat′ik) ***adj.*** ⟦Gr *automatos*, self-moving⟧ **1** done unthinkingly, as from habit or by reflex **2** working by itself **3** using automatic equipment **4** capable of firing continuously until the trigger is released —***n.*** **1** an automatic firearm **2** a motor vehicle with a transmission that shifts gears automatically —**au′to·mat′i·cal·ly *adv.***

automatic pilot a gyroscopic instrument that automatically keeps an aircraft, missile, etc. to a predetermined course and position

au′to·ma′tion (-mā′shən) ***n.*** ⟦AUTOMA(TIC) + -TION⟧ a manufacturing system in which many or all of the processes are automatically performed or controlled, as by electronic devices

au·tom·a·tism (ô täm′ə tiz′əm) ***n.*** automatic quality, condition, or action —**au·tom′a·tize′** (-tīz′), **-tized′**, **-tiz′ing**, ***vt.***

au·tom′a·ton′ (-tän′, -tən) ***n.***, *pl.* **-tons′** or **-ta** (-tə) ⟦see AUTOMATIC⟧ **1** any automatic device, esp. a robot **2** a person acting like a robot

au·to·mo·bile (ôt′ə mə bēl′) ***n.*** ⟦Fr: see AUTO- & MOBILE⟧ a four-wheeled passenger car with a built-in engine

au'to·mo'tive (-mōt'iv) ***adj.*** ⟦AUTO- + -MOTIVE⟧ **1** self-moving **2** having to do with automobiles, trucks, etc.

au'to·nom'ic (-näm'ik) ***adj.*** of or controlled by the part of the nervous system regulating motor functions of the heart, lungs, etc.

au·ton·o·mous (ô tän'ə məs) ***adj.*** ⟦< Gr *autos*, self + *nomos*, law⟧ **1** having self-government **2** existing or functioning independently —**au·ton'o·mous·ly** ***adv.*** —**au·ton'o·my** (-mē) ***n.***

au·top·sy (ô'täp'sē) ***n.***, *pl.* **-sies** ⟦< Gr *autos*, self + *opsis*, a sight⟧ examination of a dead body to discover the cause of death

au·tumn (ôt'əm) ***n.*** ⟦< L *autumnus*⟧ the season between summer and winter; fall —**au·tum·nal** (ô tum'nəl) ***adj.***

aux·il·ia·ry (ôg zil'yə rē, -ə rē) ***adj.*** ⟦< L *augere*, to increase⟧ **1** helping **2** subsidiary **3** supplementary —***n.***, *pl.* **-ries** an auxiliary person or thing

auxiliary verb *Gram.* a verb that helps form tenses, moods, voices, etc. of other verbs, as *have, be, do, will, must*

aux·in (ôk'sin) ***n.*** ⟦< Gr *auxein*, to increase⟧ a plant hormone that promotes and controls growth

av *abbrev.* **1** average **2** avoirdupois

Av *abbrev.* **1** Avenue **2** avoirdupois

a·vail (ə vāl') ***vi., vt.*** ⟦< L *ad*, to + *valere*, be strong⟧ to be of use, help, or worth (to) —***n.*** use or help; advantage *[to no avail]* —**avail oneself of** to take advantage of; utilize

a·vail'a·ble ***adj.*** **1** that can be used **2** that can be gotten or had; handy —**a·vail'a·bil'i·ty** ***n.***

av·a·lanche (av'ə lanch') ***n.*** ⟦Fr⟧ **1** a large mass of loosened snow, earth, etc. sliding down a mountain **2** an overwhelming amount coming suddenly

a·vant-garde (ə vänt'gärd', ä'-) ***n.*** ⟦Fr⟧ the leaders in new movements, esp. in the arts; vanguard —***adj.*** of such movements

av·a·rice (av'ə ris) ***n.*** ⟦< L *avere*, to desire⟧ greed for money —**av·a·ri·cious** (av'ə rish'əs) ***adj.*** —**av'a·ri'cious·ly** ***adv.***

a·vast (ə vast') ***interj.*** ⟦< Du *houd vast*, hold fast⟧ *Naut.* stop! cease!

av·a·tar (av'ə tär') ***n.*** ⟦Sans *avatāra*, descent⟧ **1** *Hinduism* a god's coming to earth in bodily form **2** an embodiment, as of a quality in a person

a·vaunt (ə vônt') ***interj.*** ⟦< L *ab*, from + *ante*, before⟧ [Archaic] go away!

avdp *abbrev.* avoirdupois

Ave *abbrev.* Avenue

A·ve Ma·ri·a (ä'vā mə rē'ə) ⟦L⟧ *R.C.Ch.* the prayer beginning with the words "Hail, Mary"

a·venge (ə venj') ***vt.*** **a·venged', a·veng'ing** ⟦< L *ad*, to + *vindicare*, to claim⟧ **1** to get revenge for (an injury, etc.) **2** to take vengeance on behalf of —**a·veng'er** ***n.***

av·e·nue (av'ə no͞o') ***n.*** ⟦< L *ad-*, to + *venire*, come⟧ **1** a street, drive, etc., esp. when broad **2** a way of approach

a·ver (ə vur') ***vt.*** **a·verred', a·ver'ring** ⟦< L *ad-*, to + *verus*, true⟧ to declare to be true; affirm; assert

av·er·age (av'ər ij, av'rij) ***n.*** ⟦< OFr *avarie*, damage to ship or goods; hence, idea of shared losses⟧ **1** the result of dividing the sum of two or more quantities by the number of quantities **2** the usual kind, amount, etc. —***adj.*** **1** constituting an average **2** ordinary; normal —***vt.*** **-aged, -ag·ing** **1** to figure out the average of **2** to do, take, etc. on average *[to average six sales a day]* **3** to divide proportionally —**average out** to arrive at an average eventually —**on (the) average** as an average amount, rate, etc.

a·verse (ə vurs') ***adj.*** ⟦see AVERT⟧ unwilling; opposed (*to*)

a·ver·sion (ə vur'zhən) ***n.*** **1** an intense dislike **2** the object arousing this

a·vert (ə vurt') ***vt.*** ⟦< L *a-*, from + *vertere*, to turn⟧ **1** to turn (the eyes, etc.) away **2** to ward off; prevent

avg *abbrev.* average

a·vi·an (ā'vē ən) ***adj.*** ⟦< L *avis*, bird + -AN⟧ of or having to do with birds

a·vi·ar·y (ā'vē er'ē) ***n.***, *pl.* **-ar'ies** ⟦< L *avis*, bird⟧ a large cage or building for keeping many birds

a·vi·a·tion (ā'vē ā'shən) ***n.*** ⟦see prec.⟧ **1** the art or science of flying airplanes **2** the field of aircraft design, construction, etc.

a'vi·a'tor ***n.*** ⟦Fr *aviateur*⟧ an airplane pilot —**a'vi·a'trix** (-triks), *pl.* **-trix·es** or **-tri·ces'** (-tri sēz'), ***fem.n.***

av·id (av'id) ***adj.*** ⟦< L *avere*, to desire⟧ very eager or greedy —**a·vid·i·ty** (ə vid'ə tē) ***n.*** —**av'id·ly** ***adv.***

a·vi·on·ics (ā'vē än'iks) ***n.*** ⟦AVI(ATION) + (ELECTR)ONICS⟧ electronics as applied in aviation and astronautics

av·o·ca·do (av'ə kä'dō, ä'və-) ***n.***, *pl.* **-dos** ⟦< AmInd⟧ **1** a thick-skinned, pear-shaped tropical fruit with yellow, buttery flesh **2** the tree it grows on **3** a yellowish-green color

av·o·ca·tion (av'ə kā'shən) ***n.*** ⟦< L *a-*, away + *vocare*, to call⟧ something done in addition to one's regular work; hobby —**av'o·ca'tion·al** ***adj.***

a·void (ə void') ***vt.*** ⟦ME < OFr *esvuidier*, to empty⟧ **1** to keep away from; evade; shun **2** to prevent —**a·void'a·ble** ***adj.*** —**a·void'a·bly** ***adv.*** —**a·void'ance** ***n.***

av·oir·du·pois (av'ər də poiz') ***n.*** ⟦< OFr *aveir de peis*, goods of weight⟧ **1** a system of weights in which 16 oz. = 1 lb.: also **avoirdupois weight** **2** [Inf.] weight, esp. of a person

a·vouch (ə vouch') ***vt.*** ⟦see ADVOCATE⟧ **1** to vouch for **2** to affirm **3** to avow

a·vow (ə vou') ***vt.*** ⟦see ADVOCATE⟧ to declare or acknowledge openly —**a·vow'al** ***n.*** —**a·vowed'** ***adj.*** —**a·vow'ed·ly** ***adv.***

a·vun·cu·lar (ə vuŋ'kyo͞o lər) ***adj.*** ⟦< L *avunculus*⟧ of or like an uncle

aw (ô) ***interj.*** a sound of protest, sympathy, etc.

a·wait (ə wāt') ***vt., vi.*** **1** to wait for or expect **2** to be in store for

a·wake (ə wāk') ***vt., vi.*** **a·woke'** or **a·waked'**, **a·waked'** or **a·wok'en**, **a·**

wak′ing ⟦< OE⟧ **1** to rouse from sleep **2** to rouse from inactivity —***adj.*** **1** not asleep **2** active or alert

a·wak·en (ə wā′kən) ***vt.***, ***vi.*** to awake; wake up —**a·wak′en·ing** ***n.***, ***adj.***

a·ward (ə wôrd′) ***vt.*** ⟦< ME < Anglo-Fr *eswarder*⟧ **1** to give, as by legal decision **2** to give (a prize, etc.); grant —***n.*** **1** *Law* a decision, as by a judge **2** something awarded; prize

a·ware (ə wer′) ***adj.*** ⟦< OE *wær*, cautious⟧ knowing; realizing; conscious —**a·ware′ness** ***n.***

a·wash (ə wôsh′) ***adv.***, ***adj.*** **1** at a level where the water washes over the surface **2** flooded

a·way (ə wā′) ***adv.*** ⟦< OE *on weg*⟧ **1** from a place [run *away*] **2** *a*) in another place or direction [*away* from here] *b*) in the proper place [put your tools *away*] **3** off; aside [turn *away*] **4** far [*away* behind] **5** from one's possession [give it *away*] **6** at once [fire *away*] **7** continuously [working *away* all night] —***adj.*** **1** absent **2** at a distance [a mile *away*] —***interj.*** begone! —**away with** go, come, or take away —**do away with** get rid of or kill

awe (ô) ***n.*** ⟦< ON *agi*⟧ a mixed feeling of reverence, fear, and wonder —***vt.*** **awed**, **aw′ing** to fill with awe —**stand** (or **be**) **in awe of** to respect and fear

a·weigh (ə wā′) ***adj.*** just clear of the bottom: said of an anchor

awe·some (ô′səm) ***adj.*** **1** inspiring awe **2** [Slang] wonderful; impressive —**awe′some·ly** ***adv.*** —**awe′some·ness** ***n.***

awe-struck (ô′struk′) ***adj.*** filled with awe: also **awe′strick′en** (-strik′ən)

aw·ful (ô′fəl) ***adj.*** **1** inspiring awe **2** terrifying **3** very bad —***adv.*** [Inf.] very —**aw′ful·ness** ***n.***

aw·ful·ly (ô′fə lē, ô′flē) ***adv.*** **1** in an awful way **2** [Inf.] very

a·while (ə wīl′, -hwīl′) ***adv.*** for a short time

awk·ward (ôk′wərd) ***adj.*** ⟦< ON *ǫfugr*, turned backward⟧ **1** clumsy; bungling **2** hard to handle; unwieldy **3** uncomfortable [an *awkward* pose] **4** embarrassed or embarrassing —**awk′ward·ly** ***adv.*** —**awk′ward·ness** ***n.***

awl (ôl) ***n.*** ⟦< OE *æl*⟧ a small, pointed tool for making holes in wood, leather, etc.

awn (ôn) ***n.*** ⟦< ON *ǫgn*⟧ the bristly fibers on a head of barley, oats, etc.

awn·ing (ôn′iŋ) ***n.*** ⟦< ? MFr *auvent*, a sloping roof⟧ a structure, as of canvas, extended before a window, door, etc. as a protection from the sun or rain

a·woke (ə wōk′) ***vt.***, ***vi.*** *pt. of* AWAKE

a·wok′en ***vt.***, ***vi.*** *alt. pp. of* AWAKE

A·WOL or **a·wol** (ā′wôl′) ***adj.***, ***adv.*** *Mil.* absent without leave

a·wry (ə rī′) ***adv.***, ***adj.*** ⟦see A-[1] & WRY⟧ **1** with a twist to a side; askew **2** wrong; amiss [our plans went *awry*]

ax or **axe** (aks) ***n.***, *pl.* **ax′es** ⟦< OE *æx*⟧ a tool with a long handle and a head with a blade, for chopping wood, etc. —***vt.*** **axed**, **ax′ing** **1** to trim, split, etc. with an ax **2** to get rid of —**give** (or **get**) **the ax** [Inf.] to discharge (or be discharged) from a job —**have an ax to grind** [Inf.] to have an object of one's own to gain or promote

ax·el (ak′səl) ***n.*** ⟦after *Axel* Paulsen (1865-1938), Norw skater⟧ a jump in which a skater turns in the air and lands facing in the opposite direction

ax·i·al (ak′sē əl) ***adj.*** **1** of, like, or forming an axis **2** around, on, or along an axis —**ax′i·al·ly** ***adv.***

ax·i·om (ak′sē əm) ***n.*** ⟦< Gr *axios*, worthy⟧ **1** *a*) a statement universally accepted as true; maxim *b*) a self-evident truth **2** an established principle, scientific law, etc. —**ax′i·o·mat′ic** (-ə mat′ik) ***adj.***

ax·is (ak′sis) ***n.***, *pl.* **ax′es** (-sēz′) ⟦L⟧ **1** a real or imaginary straight line on which an object rotates **2** a central line around which the parts of a thing, system, etc. are evenly arranged —**the Axis** Germany, Italy, and Japan in WWII

ax·le (ak′səl) ***n.*** ⟦< ON *ǫxull*⟧ **1** a rod on or with which a wheel turns **2** *a*) a bar connecting two opposite wheels, as of an automobile *b*) the spindle at either end of such a bar

Ax·min·ster (aks′min′stər) ***n.*** ⟦< English town where first made⟧ varicolored, patterned carpet with a cut pile

ax·o·lotl (ak′sə lät′'l) ***n.*** ⟦< AmInd⟧ a dark salamander of Mexico and the W U.S.

ax·on (ak′sän′) ***n.*** ⟦< Gr *axōn*, axis⟧ that part of a nerve cell through which impulses travel away from the cell body

a·ya·tol·lah (ī′yə tō′lə) ***n.*** ⟦< Ar *āyat*, sign + *Allah*, Allah⟧ a leader of a Muslim sect, serving as teacher, judge, etc.

aye[1] (ā) ***adv.*** ⟦< ON *ei*⟧ [Old Poet.] always; ever: also **ay**

aye[2] (ī) ***adv.*** ⟦prob. < *I*, pers. pron.⟧ yes —***n.*** an affirmative vote or voter Also **ay**

AZ Arizona

a·za·lea (ə zāl′yə) ***n.*** ⟦< Gr *azaleos*, dry: it thrives in dry soil⟧ **1** a shrub of the heath family, with flowers of various colors **2** the flower

Az·er·bai·jan (äz′ər bī jän′, az′-) country in W Asia: formerly a republic of the U.S.S.R.: 33,430 sq. mi.; pop. 7,021,000

az·i·muth (az′ə məth) ***n.*** ⟦< Ar *al*, the + *samt*, way⟧ *Astronomy, Surveying* distance clockwise in degrees from the north point or, in the Southern Hemisphere, south point

A·zores (ā′zôrz′, ə zôrz′) group of Portuguese islands in the N Atlantic, west of Portugal

AZT (ā′zē′tē′) ***n.*** ⟦*az*(*ido*)*t*(*hymidine*)⟧ an antiviral drug used to treat AIDS

Az·tec (az′tek′) ***n.*** **1** a member of an Amerindian people that had an advanced civilization in Mexico before the Spanish conquest in 1519 **2** the language of this people —***adj.*** of the Aztecs, their language, etc.: also **Az′tec·an**

az·ure (azh′ər) ***adj.*** ⟦< Pers *lāzhuward*, lapis lazuli⟧ sky-blue —***n.*** sky blue or any similar blue color

B

b[1] or **B** (bē) ***n.***, *pl.* **b's, B's** the second letter of the English alphabet

b[2] *abbrev.* born

B[1] (bē) ***n.*** **1** a blood type **2** a grade indicating above-average but not outstanding work **3** *Music* the seventh tone in the scale of C major —***adj.*** inferior to the best *[a B movie]*

B[2] *abbrev.* **1** bachelor **2** *Baseball a)* base *b)* baseman **3** *Music* bass Also **b**

B[3] *Chem. symbol for* boron

Ba *Chem. symbol for* barium

BA or **B.A.** *abbrev.* Bachelor of Arts

baa (bä) ***vi., n.*** ⟦echoic⟧ bleat

Ba·al (bā′əl) ***n.*** ⟦< Heb⟧ an ancient fertility god

bab·ble (bab′əl) ***vi.*** **-bled, -bling** ⟦echoic⟧ **1** to talk like a small child; prattle **2** to talk foolishly or too much **3** to murmur, as a brook does when flowing over stones —***vt.*** to say incoherently or foolishly —***n.*** **1** incoherent vocal sounds **2** foolish talk **3** a murmuring sound —**bab′bler** ***n.***

babe (bāb) ***n.*** **1** a baby **2** a naive person: also **babe in the woods** **3** [Slang] a girl or young woman, esp. an attractive one

Ba·bel (bā′bəl, bab′əl) ***n.*** **1** *Bible* a city thwarted in building a tower to heaven when God created a confusion of tongues **2** [*also* **b-**] a confusion of voices, sounds, etc. or the scene of this

ba·boon (ba bo͞on′, bə-) ***n.*** ⟦< OFr *babuin,* ape, fool⟧ a large, fierce, dog-faced, short-tailed monkey of Africa and Arabia

ba·bush·ka (bə bo͞osh′kə) ***n.*** ⟦Russ, grandmother⟧ a woman's scarf worn on the head and tied under the chin

ba·by (bā′bē) ***n.***, *pl.* **-bies** ⟦ME *babi*⟧ **1** a very young child; infant **2** one who acts like an infant **3** a very young animal **4** the youngest or smallest in a group **5** [Slang] darling; honey **6** [Slang] any person or thing —***adj.*** **1** of or for an infant **2** very young **3** small of its kind **4** childish —***vt.*** **-bied, -by·ing** to pamper; coddle —**ba′by·hood′** ***n.*** —**ba′by·ish** ***adj.***

baby beef meat from a prime heifer or steer that is one to two years old

baby boomer a person born during the birthrate increase (the **baby boom**) after 1945

baby carriage a small vehicle, pushed by hand, for wheeling a baby about: also **baby buggy**

baby grand a small grand piano

Bab·y·lon (bab′ə län′) capital of Babylonia: noted for luxury and wickedness

Bab·y·lo·ni·a (bab′ə lō′nē ə) ancient empire in SW Asia —**Bab′y·lo′ni·an** ***adj., n.***

baby's breath a plant with small, delicate, white or pink flowers

baby sitter a person hired to take care of a child or children, as when the parents are away for the evening —**ba′by-sit′, -sat′, -sit′ting,** ***vi., vt.***

baby talk playful talk for amusing a baby or in imitating a baby

bac·ca·lau·re·ate (bak′ə lôr′ē it) ***n.*** ⟦< ML *baccalaris,* young nobleman seeking knighthood⟧ **1** the degree of Bachelor of Arts, Bachelor of Science, etc. **2** a commencement address

bac·cha·nal (bak′ə nal′) ***n.*** a drunken orgy —**bac′cha·na′li·an** (-nā′lē ən) ***adj., n.***

Bac·chus (bak′əs) ***n.*** the Greek and Roman god of wine and revelry

Bach (bäkh), **Jo·hann Se·bas·ti·an** (yō′ hän′ zā bäs′tē än′) 1685-1750; Ger. organist & composer

bach·e·lor (bach′ə lər, bach′lər) ***n.*** ⟦< ML *baccalaris:* see BACCALAUREATE⟧ an unmarried man —**bach′e·lor·hood′** ***n.***

Bachelor of Arts (or **Science,** etc.) **1** a degree given by a college or university to one who has completed a four-year course in the humanities (or in science, etc.): also **bachelor's degree** **2** one who holds this degree

bachelor's button any of several plants with white, pink, or blue flowers, as the cornflower

ba·cil·lus (bə sil′əs) ***n.***, *pl.* **-cil′li′** (-ī′) ⟦< L *bacillum,* little stick⟧ **1** any of a genus of rod-shaped bacteria **2** loosely, any of the bacteria —**bac·il·lar·y** (bas′ə ler′ē, bə sil′ər ē) ***adj.***

back (bak) ***n.*** ⟦< OE *baec*⟧ **1** the rear (or, in some animals, the top) part of the body from the nape of the neck to the end of the spine **2** the backbone **3** a part that supports or fits the back **4** the rear part or reverse of anything **5** *Sports* a player or position behind the front line —***adj.*** **1** at the rear **2** remote **3** of or for the past *[back pay]* **4** backward —***adv.*** **1** at, to, or toward the rear **2** to or toward a former condition, time, etc. **3** in reserve or concealment **4** in return or requital *[pay him back]* —***vt.*** **1** to move backward **2** to support **3** to bet on **4** to provide or be a back for —***vi.*** to go backward —**back and forth** backward and forward —**back down** to withdraw from a position or claim —**(in) back of** behind —**back off** **1** to move back **2** [Inf.] BACK DOWN —**back out (of)** **1** to withdraw from an enterprise **2** to evade keeping a promise, etc. —**back up** **1** to support **2** to move backward: also **back away** **3** to accumulate because of restricted movement *[traffic backed up]* **4** *Comput.* to make a standby copy of (data, etc.) —**go back on** [Inf.] **1** to be disloyal to; betray **2** to fail to keep (one's word, etc.) —**turn one's back on** **1** to turn away from, as in contempt **2** to abandon

back′ache′ ***n.*** an ache or pain in the back

back′bite′ ***vt., vi.*** **-bit′, -bit′ten** or **-bit′,**

-**bit′ing** to slander (someone absent) —**back′bit′er** *n.*

back′board′ *n.* **1** a board at or forming the back of something **2** *Basketball* the board behind the basket

back′bone′ *n.* **1** the spine **2** a main support **3** willpower, courage, etc.

back′break′ing *adj.* very tiring

back′coun′try *n.* a remote, thinly populated area

back′drop′ *n.* **1** a curtain, often scenic, at the back of a stage **2** background or setting

back′er *n.* **1** a patron; sponsor **2** one who bets on a contestant

back′field′ *n.* *Football* the players behind the line

back′fire′ *n.* **1** the burning out of a small area, as in a forest, to check the spread of a big fire **2** premature ignition or an explosion of gases in an internal-combustion engine **3** reverse explosion in a gun —*vi.* -**fired′**, -**fir′ing** **1** to explode as a backfire **2** to go awry or boomerang

back′gam′mon (-gam′ən) *n.* ⟦BACK + ME *gammen,* game⟧ a game for two, with dice governing moves of pieces on a special board

back′ground′ *n.* **1** the distant part of a scene **2** surroundings, sounds, etc. behind or subordinate to something **3** one's training and experience **4** events leading up to something

back′ground′er *n.* a press briefing at which background information is provided

back′hand′ *n.* **1** handwriting that slants up to the left **2** a backhand catch, stroke, etc. —*adj.* **1** done with the back of the hand; specif., done with the back of the hand turned inward, as for a baseball catch, or forward, as for a tennis stroke, and with the arm across the body **2** written in backhand —*adv.* with a backhand —*vt.* to hit, catch, swing, etc. backhand

back′hand′ed *adj.* **1** BACKHAND **2** indirect or sarcastic —*adv.* with a backhand

back′hoe′ (-hō′) *n.* an excavating vehicle with a hinged bucket at the end of a long arm

back′ing *n.* **1** something forming a back for support **2** support given to a person or cause **3** supporters; backers

back′lash′ *n.* sharp reaction or recoil

back′log′ *n.* an accumulation or reserve —*vi., vt.* -**logged′**, -**log′ging** to accumulate as a backlog

back order an order not yet filled

back′pack′ *n.* a knapsack, specif. one attached to a frame and worn as by hikers —*vi., vt.* to hike with, or carry in, a backpack —**back′pack′er** *n.*

back′ped′al *vi.* -**ped′aled** or -**ped′alled**, -**ped′al·ing** or -**ped′al·ling** **1** to pedal backward, as in braking a bicycle **2** to move backward; retreat **3** to retract an earlier opinion

back′rest′ *n.* a support for or at the back

back′-scratch′ing *n.* [Inf.] a reciprocal exchange of favors, etc.

back′side′ *n.* **1** the back part **2** the rump

back′slap′per (-slap′ər) *n.* [Inf.] an effusively friendly person

back′slash′ *n.* a short diagonal line (\): a character found esp. on computer keyboards

back′slide′ *vi.* -**slid′**, -**slid′** or -**slid′den**, -**slid′ing** to regress in morals, etc. —**back′slid′er** *n.*

back′space′ *vi.* -**spaced′**, -**spac′ing** to move a typewriter carriage, cursor, etc. one or more spaces back along the line

back′spin′ *n.* a backward spin given to a ball, etc., making it reverse direction upon hitting a surface

back′splash′ *n.* a washable surface behind a sink, etc. to protect a wall from splashes

back′stage′ *adv., adj.* behind and off the stage, as in the wings or dressing rooms

back′stairs′ *adj.* involving intrigue or scandal; secret: also **back′stair′**

back′stop′ *n.* a fence, screen, etc. to keep balls from going too far, as behind the catcher in baseball

back′stretch′ *n.* the part of a racetrack opposite the homestretch

back′stroke′ *n.* a swimming stroke made while lying face upward

back′swing′ *n.* that part of a player's swing in which the golf club, tennis racket, etc. is swung backward before being swung forward

back talk [Inf.] insolent replies

back′-to-back′ *adj.* [Inf.] one right after another

back′track′ *vi.* **1** to return by the same path **2** to retreat or recant

back′up′ or **back′-up′** *adj.* **1** standing by as an alternate or auxiliary **2** supporting —*n.* a backing up; specif., *a*) an accumulation *b*) a support or help

back′ward *adv.* **1** toward the back **2** with the back foremost **3** in reverse order **4** in a way opposite to usual **5** into the past Also **back′wards** —*adj.* **1** turned toward the rear or in the opposite way **2** shy **3** slow or retarded —**back′ward·ness** *n.*

back′wash′ *n.* **1** water or air moved backward, as by a ship, propeller, etc. **2** a reaction caused by some event

back′wa′ter *n.* **1** water moved or held back by a dam, tide, etc. **2** stagnant water in an inlet, etc. **3** a backward place or condition

back′woods′ *pl.n.* [*occas. with sing. v.*] **1** heavily wooded areas far from centers of population **2** any remote, thinly populated area —*adj.* of or like the backwoods —**back′woods′man** (-mən), *pl.* -**men** (-mən), *n.*

ba·con (bā′kən) *n.* ⟦< OS *baco,* side of bacon⟧ salted and smoked meat from the back or sides of a hog

Ba·con (bā′kən), **Fran·cis** (fran′sis) 1561-1626; Eng. philosopher & writer

bac·te·ri·a (bak tir′ē ə) *pl.n., sing.* -**ri·um** (-əm) or -**ri·a** ⟦< Gr *baktērion,* small staff⟧ microorganisms which have no chlorophyll and multiply by simple division: some bacteria cause diseases, but others are necessary for fermentation, etc. —**bac·te'ri·al** ***adj.***

bac·te'ri·cide' (-tir'ə sīd') ***n.*** an agent that destroys bacteria —**bac·te'ri·cid'al** ***adj.***

bac·te'ri·ol'o·gy (-tir'ē äl'ə jē) ***n.*** the science that deals with bacteria —**bac·te'ri·o·log'i·cal** (-ə läj'ə kəl) ***adj.*** —**bac·te'ri·ol'o·gist** ***n.***

bad[1] (bad) ***adj.*** **worse, worst** ⟦ME⟧ **1** not good; not as it should be **2** inadequate or unfit **3** unfavorable *[bad news]* **4** rotten or spoiled **5** incorrect or faulty **6** *a)* wicked; immoral *b)* misbehaving; mischievous **7** harmful **8** severe **9** ill **10** sorry; distressed *[he feels bad about it]* **11** offensive —***adv.*** [Inf.] badly —***n.*** anything bad —**not bad** [Inf.] fairly good —**bad'ness** ***n.***

bad[2] (bad) ***vt., vi.*** *archaic pt. of* BID

bad blood (mutual) ill will

bade (bad) ***vt., vi.*** *alt. pt. of* BID

bad egg [Slang] a mean or dishonest person: also **bad actor, bad apple,** or **bad lot**

bad faith insincerity; dishonesty

badge (baj) ***n.*** ⟦ME *bage*⟧ **1** an emblem worn to show rank, membership, etc. **2** any distinctive sign, etc.

badg·er (baj'ər) ***n.*** ⟦< ?⟧ **1** a burrowing animal with a broad back and thick, short legs **2** its fur —***vt.*** to nag or torment

bad·i·nage (bad''n äzh') ***n.*** ⟦Fr⟧ playful talk; banter

bad·lands (bad'landz') ***pl.n.*** **1** an area of barren land with dry soil and soft rocks eroded into odd shapes **2** [**B-**] any of several such W U.S. areas

bad'ly ***adv.*** **worse, worst** **1** in a bad manner **2** [Inf.] very much; greatly

bad'man' (-man') ***n.***, *pl.* **-men'** (-men') a cattle thief or desperado of the old West

bad·min·ton (bad'mint''n) ***n.*** ⟦after *Badminton,* Eng estate⟧ a game in which a shuttlecock is batted back and forth with rackets across a net

bad'-mouth' ***vt.*** [Slang] to find fault with; disparage

bad'-tem'pered ***adj.*** irritable

Bae·de·ker (bā'də kər) ***n.*** **1** any of a series of guidebooks to foreign countries, first published in Germany **2** loosely, any guidebook

baf·fle (baf'əl) ***vt.*** **-fled, -fling** ⟦< ?⟧ **1** to perplex completely; bewilder **2** to impede; check —***n.*** a wall or screen to deflect air, sound, etc. —**baf'fle·ment** ***n.*** —**baf'fler** ***n.*** —**baf'fling** ***adj.***

bag (bag) ***n.*** ⟦< ON *baggi*⟧ **1** a nonrigid container of paper, plastic, etc., with an open top **2** a satchel; suitcase, etc. **3** a purse **4** game taken in hunting **5** a baglike shape or part **6** a bagful **7** [Slang] an unattractive woman **8** [Slang] one's special interest **9** *Baseball* a base —***vt.*** **bagged, bag'ging** **1** to put into a bag **2** to capture **3** to kill in hunting **4** [Slang] to obtain —***vi.*** **1** to swell; bulge **2** to hang loosely —**in the bag** [Slang] having its success assured

bag·a·telle (bag'ə tel') ***n.*** ⟦Fr < L *baca,* berry⟧ a trifle

ba·gel (bā'gəl) ***n.*** ⟦Yiddish⟧ a chewy bread roll shaped like a small doughnut

bag'ful' ***n.***, *pl.* **-fuls'** as much as a bag will hold

bag·gage (bag'ij) ***n.*** ⟦< ML *bagga,* chest, bag⟧ **1** the bags, etc. of a traveler; luggage **2** burdensome beliefs, practices, etc.

bag·gie (bag'ē) ***n.*** ⟦< *Baggies,* a trademark for such bags⟧ a small, clear plastic bag for storing food, etc.

bag·gy (bag'ē) ***adj.*** **-gi·er, -gi·est** puffed out or hanging loosely —**bag'gi·ly** ***adv.*** —**bag'gi·ness** ***n.***

Bagh·dad (bag'dad) capital of Iraq: pop. 1,900,000: also sp. **Bag·dad**

bag lady [Slang] a homeless, poor woman who wanders city streets carrying her belongings in shopping bags

BAGPIPE

bag'pipe' ***n.*** [*often pl.*] a wind instrument, now chiefly Scottish, played by forcing air from a bag into reed pipes and fingering the stops

bah (bä, ba) ***interj.*** used to express contempt, scorn, or disgust

Ba·ha·mas (bə hä'məz) country on a group of islands (**Bahama Islands**) in the West Indies: 5,353 sq. mi.; pop. 264,000

Bah·rain (bä rān') country on a group of islands in the Persian Gulf: 266 sq. mi.; pop. 518,000: also sp. **Bah·rein**

bail[1] (bāl) ***n.*** ⟦< L *bajulare,* bear a burden⟧ **1** money deposited with the court to get a prisoner temporarily released **2** such a release —***vt.*** **1** to have (a prisoner) set free by giving bail **2** to help out of financial or other difficulty Often with *out* —**bail'a·ble** ***adj.***

bail[2] (bāl) ***n.*** ⟦ME *baille,* bucket⟧ a bucket for dipping up water from a boat —***vi., vt.*** to dip out (water) from (a boat): usually with *out* —**bail out** **1** to parachute from an aircraft **2** [Inf.] to flee a difficult situation

bail[3] (bāl) ***n.*** ⟦ME *beil*⟧ a hoop-shaped handle for a bucket, etc.

bail·iff (bā'lif) ***n.*** ⟦ME *bailif*⟧ **1** a deputy sheriff **2** a court officer who guards the jurors, keeps order in the court, etc. **3** in England, a district official **4** [Chiefly Brit.] a steward of an estate

bail·i·wick (bā′lə wik′) ***n.*** ⟦ME < *baili,* bailiff + *wik,* village⟧ **1** a bailiff's district **2** one's particular area of activity, authority, interest, etc.

bails·man (bālz′mən) ***n.***, *pl.* **-men** (-mən) a person who gives bail for another

bairn (bern) ***n.*** [Scot.] a child

bait (bāt) ***vt.*** ⟦< ON *beita*⟧ **1** to set dogs on for sport *[to bait bears]* **2** to torment or harass, esp. by verbal attacks **3** to goad or provoke **4** to put food on (a hook or trap) as a lure for game **5** to lure; entice; tempt —***n.*** **1** food, etc. put on a hook or trap as a lure **2** anything used as a lure

bait′-and-switch′ ***adj.*** of or using an unethical sales technique in which a seller lures customers by advertising an often nonexistent bargain item and then tries to switch their attention to more expensive items

baize (bāz) ***n.*** ⟦< L *badius,* brown⟧ a coarse, feltlike woolen cloth

Ba·ja Ca·li·for·nia (bä′hä kä′lē fôr′nyä) state of NW Mexico, south of California: 27,071 sq. mi.; pop. 1,661,000

Baja California Sur state of NW Mexico, south of Baja California: 28,447 sq. mi.; pop. 318,000

bake (bāk) ***vt.*** **baked, bak′ing** ⟦< OE *bacan*⟧ **1** to cook (food) by dry heat, esp. in an oven **2** to dry and harden (pottery, etc.) by heat; fire —***vi.*** **1** to bake bread, etc. **2** to become baked —***n.*** **1** a baking **2** a social affair at which baked food is served

baked beans navy beans baked with salt pork, molasses or brown sugar, etc.

bak·er (bā′kər) ***n.*** one whose work or business is baking bread, etc.

baker's dozen thirteen

Bak·ers·field (bā′kərz fēld′) city in SC California: pop. 175,000

bak′er·y ***n.*** **1** *pl.* **-er·ies** a place where bread, etc. is baked or sold **2** [Dial.] baked goods

baking powder a leavening agent containing baking soda and an acid-forming substance

baking soda sodium bicarbonate, used as a leavening agent and as an antacid

bal·a·lai·ka (bal′ə lī′kə) ***n.*** ⟦Russ⟧ a Russian stringed instrument somewhat like a guitar

bal·ance (bal′əns) ***n.*** ⟦< LL *bilanx,* having two scales⟧ **1** an instrument for weighing, esp. one with two matched hanging scales **2** a state of equilibrium in weight, value, etc. **3** bodily equilibrium **4** mental or emotional stability **5** harmonious proportion of elements in a design, etc. **6** a weight, value, etc. that counteracts another **7** equality of debits and credits, or the difference between them **8** a remainder —***vt.*** **-anced, -anc·ing** **1** to weigh in or as in a balance **2** to compare as to relative value, etc. **3** to counteract; offset **4** to bring into proportion, harmony, etc. **5** to make or be equal to in weight, value, etc. **6** to find the difference between, or to equalize, the debits and credits of (an account) —***vi.*** **1** to be in equilibrium **2** to be equal in weight, value, etc. **3** to have the credits and debits equal —**in the balance** not yet settled

balance sheet a statement showing the financial status of a business

bal·co·ny (bal′kə nē) ***n.***, *pl.* **-nies** ⟦< It *balcone*⟧ **1** a platform projecting from an upper story and enclosed by a railing **2** an upper floor of seats in a theater, etc., often projecting over the main floor

bald (bôld) ***adj.*** ⟦< ME⟧ **1** having a head with white fur, etc. growing on it **2** lacking hair on the head **3** not covered by natural growth **4** having the tread worn off **5** plain or blunt *[bald truth]* —**bald′ly *adv.*** —**bald′ness *n.***

bald eagle a large eagle of North America, with a white-feathered head

bal·der·dash (bôl′dər dash′) ***n.*** ⟦orig. (17th c.), an odd mixture⟧ nonsense

bald·faced (bôld′fāst′) ***adj.*** brazen; shameless *[a baldfaced lie]*

bald′ing ***adj.*** becoming bald

bal·dric (bôl′drik′) ***n.*** ⟦ult. < L *balteus,* belt⟧ a belt worn over one shoulder to support a sword, etc.

bale (bāl) ***n.*** ⟦< OHG *balla,* ball⟧ a large bundle, esp. a standardized quantity of goods, as raw cotton, compressed and bound —***vt.*** **baled, bal′ing** to make into bales —**bal′er *n.***

ba·leen (bə lēn′) ***n.*** ⟦ult. < Gr *phallaina,* whale⟧ the horny, elastic material hanging from the upper jaw of some whales (**baleen whales**)

bale·ful (bāl′fəl) ***adj.*** ⟦< OE *bealu,* evil⟧ deadly; harmful; ominous

Ba·li (bä′lē, bal′ē) island of Indonesia —**Ba′li·nese′**, *pl.* **-nese′**, ***adj.***, ***n.***

balk (bôk) ***n.*** ⟦OE *balca,* ridge⟧ **1** an obstruction, hindrance, etc. **2** *Baseball* an illegal motion by the pitcher entitling base runners to advance one base —***vt.*** to obstruct; foil —***vi.*** **1** to stop and refuse to move or act **2** to hesitate or recoil (*at*)

Balkan Peninsula peninsula in SE Europe, east of Italy

Bal·kans (bôl′kənz) countries of Yugoslavia, Slovenia, Croatia, Bosnia and Herzegovina, Macedonia, Romania, Bulgaria, Albania, Greece, & European Turkey, in SE Europe —**Bal′kan *adj.***

balk·y (bôk′ē) ***adj.*** **-i·er, -i·est** stubbornly resisting

ball[1] (bôl) ***n.*** ⟦ME *bal*⟧ **1** any round object; sphere; globe **2** *a*) a round or egg-shaped object used in various games *b*) any of several such games, esp. baseball **3** a throw or pitch of a ball *[a fast ball]* **4** a missile for a cannon, rifle, etc. **5** a rounded part of the body **6** *Baseball* a pitched ball that is not hit and is not a strike —***vi.***, ***vt.*** to form into a ball —**ball up** [Slang] to muddle or confuse —**be on the ball** [Slang] to be alert; be efficient

ball[2] (bôl) ***n.*** ⟦< Fr < Gr *ballizein,* to dance⟧ **1** a formal social dance **2** [Slang] a good time

bal·lad (bal′əd) ***n.*** ⟦< OFr *ballade,* dancing song⟧ **1** a sentimental song with the same melody for each stanza **2** a narrative song or poem, usually anonymous, with simple words, short stanzas, and a refrain 3 a popular love song —**bal'lad·eer'** *n.* —**bal'lad·ry** *n.*

ball'-and-sock'et joint a joint, as of the hip, formed by a ball in a socket

bal·last (bal'əst) *n.* ⟦< MDu *bal*, bad⟧ **1** anything heavy carried in a ship or vehicle to give stability **2** crushed rock or gravel, used in railroad beds, etc. —*vt.* to furnish with ballast

ball bearing 1 a bearing in which the parts turn on freely rolling metal balls **2** one of these balls

BALL BEARING

bal·le·ri·na (bal'ə rē'nə) *n.* ⟦It⟧ a girl or woman ballet dancer

bal·let (ba lā', bal'ā) *n.* ⟦Fr⟧ **1** an artistic dance form of graceful, precise gestures and movements **2** a play, etc. performed by ballet dancers, or the music for this **3** ballet dancers

ball'game' *n.* **1** a game played with a ball **2** [Inf.] a set of circumstances *[a different ballgame]*

ballistic missile a long-range guided missile designed to fall free as it approaches its target

bal·lis·tics (bə lis'tiks) *n.* the science dealing with the motion and impact of projectiles —**bal·lis'tic** *adj.*

ball joint a ball-and-socket joint used in automotive vehicles to connect the tie rods to the turning wheels

bal·loon (bə lo͞on') *n.* ⟦< Fr < It *palla*, ball⟧ **1** a large, airtight bag that rises when filled with hot air or a gas lighter than air **2** an airship with such a bag **3** an inflatable rubber bag, used as a toy **4** the large final payment on certain loans —*vt.* to inflate —*vi.* to swell; expand —*adj.* like a balloon —**bal·loon'ist** *n.*

bal·lot (bal'ət) *n.* ⟦< It *palla*, ball⟧ **1** a ticket, card, form, etc. by which a vote is registered **2** act or right of voting, as by ballots **3** the total number of votes cast —*vi.* to vote

ball'park' *n.* a baseball stadium

ball'-peen' hammer a hammer with one end of the head rounded and the other end flat

ball'play'er *n.* a baseball player

ball'point' (pen) a writing pen with a small ball bearing instead of a point: also **ball'-point'** *n.*

ball'room' *n.* a large hall for dancing

bal·lute (ba lo͞ot') *n.* ⟦BALL(OON) + (PARACH)UTE⟧ a balloonlike device used to slow down a spacecraft reentering the atmosphere

bal·ly·hoo (bal'ē ho͞o') *n.* ⟦< ?⟧ noisy talk, sensational advertising, etc. —*vt.*, *vi.* **-hooed'**, **-hoo'ing** [Inf.] to promote with ballyhoo

balm (bäm) *n.* ⟦< Gr *balsamon*⟧ **1** a fragrant, healing ointment or oil **2** anything healing or soothing

balm'y *adj.* **-i·er**, **-i·est 1** soothing, mild, etc. **2** [Slang, Chiefly Brit.] crazy

ba·lo·ney (bə lō'nē) *n.* ⟦< *bologna*⟧ **1** bologna **2** [Slang] nonsense

bal·sa (bôl'sə) *n.* ⟦Sp⟧ **1** the wood, very light in weight, of a tropical American tree **2** the tree

bal·sam (bôl'səm) *n.* ⟦see BALM⟧ **1** an aromatic resin obtained from certain trees **2** any of various aromatic, resinous oils or fluids **3** balm **4** any of various trees yielding balsam

bal·sam·ic vinegar (bôl sam'ik) aromatic, dark-brown vinegar used in salad dressings, etc.

Bal·tic Sea (bôl'tik) sea in N Europe, west of Latvia, Lithuania, & Estonia

Bal·ti·more (bôl'tə môr) seaport in N Maryland: pop. 736,000

bal·us·ter (bal'əs tər) *n.* ⟦< Gr *balaustion*, wild pomegranate flower: from the shape⟧ any of the small posts of a railing, as on a staircase

bal·us·trade (bal'əs trād') *n.* a railing having an upper rail supported by balusters

Bal·zac (bȧl zȧk'; *E* bôl'zak), **Ho·no·ré de** (ô nô rā'də) 1799-1850; Fr. novelist

bam·boo (bam bo͞o') *n.* ⟦Malay *bambu*⟧ a treelike tropical grass with woody, jointed, often hollow stems used for furniture, canes, etc.

bam·boo·zle (bam bo͞o'zəl) *vt.* **-zled**, **-zling** ⟦< ?⟧ **1** to trick; cheat; dupe **2** to confuse; puzzle

ban (ban) *vt.* **banned**, **ban'ning** ⟦< OE *bannan*, summon⟧ to prohibit or forbid, esp. officially —*n.* **1** a condemnation by church authorities **2** a curse **3** an official prohibition **4** strong public condemnation

ba·nal (bā'nəl, bə nal') *adj.* ⟦Fr: see prec.⟧ trite; hackneyed —**ba·nal'i·ty**, *pl.* **-ties**, *n.* —**ba'nal·ly** *adv.*

ba·nan·a (bə nan'ə) *n.* ⟦Sp & Port⟧ **1** a tropical plant with large clusters of edible fruit **2** the narrow, curved fruit, having soft pulp and thick, usually yellow skin

band[1] (band) *n.* ⟦ON⟧ **1** something that binds, ties, or encircles, as a strip or ring of wood, rubber, metal, etc. **2** a strip of color or of material **3** a division of an LP phonograph record **4** a range of wavelengths —*vt.* to put a band on or around

band[2] (band) *n.* ⟦< Gothic *bandwa*, a sign⟧ **1** a group of people united for some purpose **2** a group of musicians playing together, esp. upon wind and percussion instruments —*vi.*, *vt.* to unite for some purpose

band·age (ban'dij) *n.* ⟦Fr < *bande*, a strip⟧ a strip of cloth, etc. used to bind or cover an injury —*vt.* **-aged**, **-ag·ing** to put a bandage on

Band-Aid (band'ād') ⟦prec. + AID⟧ *trademark for* a small bandage of gauze and adhesive tape —*n.* [*also* **band-aid**] such a bandage: also **band'aid'**

ban·dan·na or **ban·dan·a** (ban dan'ə) *n.* ⟦Hindi *bāndhnū*, a method of dyeing⟧ a large, colored handkerchief

band'box' *n.* a light, round box to hold hats, etc.

ban·deau (ban dō') *n.*, *pl.* **-deaux'** (-dōz') ⟦Fr⟧ **1** a narrow ribbon **2** a band of material covering the breasts, as a strapless bikini top

ban·dit (ban′dit) ***n.*** ⟦< It⟧ **1** a robber; brigand **2** one who steals, defrauds, etc. —**ban′dit·ry** ***n.***

ban·do·leer or **ban·do·lier** (ban′də lir′) ***n.*** ⟦< Fr⟧ a broad belt with pockets for bullets, etc., worn over one shoulder and across the chest

band saw an endless toothed steel belt on pulleys, powered for sawing

bands·man (bandz′mən) ***n.***, *pl.* **-men** (-mən) a member of a band of musicians

band′stand′ ***n.*** a platform for a band, esp. one for outdoor concerts

band′wag′on ***n.*** a wagon for a band to ride on, as in a parade —**on the bandwagon** [Inf.] on the popular or apparently winning side

band′width′ ***n.*** the transmission rate of information along electronic communications lines

ban·dy[1] (ban′dē) ***vt.*** **-died, -dy·ing** ⟦Fr *bander,* bandy at tennis⟧ **1** to toss or hit back and forth **2** to pass (rumors, etc.) freely **3** to exchange (words), esp. angrily

ban·dy[2] (ban′dē) ***adj.*** ⟦Fr *bandé,* bent⟧ curved outward; bowed

ban′dy·leg′ged (-leg′id, -legd′) ***adj.*** bowlegged

bane (bān) ***n.*** ⟦OE *bana*⟧ **1** ruin, death, harm, or their cause **2** [Obs.] poison —**bane′ful** ***adj.***

bang[1] (baŋ) ***vt.*** ⟦ON *banga,* to pound⟧ to hit, shut, etc. hard and noisily —***vi.*** **1** to make a loud noise **2** to hit noisily or sharply —***n.*** **1** a hard, noisy blow or impact **2** a loud, sudden noise **3** [Inf.] a burst of vigor **4** [Slang] a thrill —***adv.*** **1** hard and noisily **2** abruptly —**bang up** to damage

bang[2] (baŋ) ***n.*** ⟦< prec.: see *adv.,* 2⟧ [*usually pl.*] hair cut to hang straight across the forehead

Bang·kok (baŋ′käk′) seaport & capital of Thailand: pop. 4,697,000

Ban·gla·desh (bäŋ′glə desh′, baŋ′-) country in S Asia, on the Bay of Bengal: 57,295 sq. mi.; pop. 109,887,000

ban·gle (baŋ′gəl) ***n.*** ⟦Hindi *bangrī*⟧ a decorative bracelet or anklet

bang-up (baŋ′up′) ***adj.*** [Inf.] very good; excellent

ban·ish (ban′ish) ***vt.*** ⟦< OFr *banir*⟧ **1** to exile **2** to get rid of —**ban′ish·ment** ***n.***

ban·is·ter (ban′is tər) ***n.*** ⟦< BALUSTER⟧ a handrail, specif. one with balusters

ban·jo (ban′jō′) ***n.***, *pl.* **-jos′** or **-joes′** ⟦of Afr orig.⟧ a musical instrument with a long neck, circular body, and strings that are plucked —**ban′jo·ist** ***n.***

bank[1] (baŋk) ***n.*** ⟦ult. < OHG *bank,* bench⟧ **1** an establishment for receiving or lending money **2** a reserve supply; pool —***vi.*** to do business with a bank —***vt.*** to deposit (money) in a bank —**bank on** [Inf.] to rely on —**bank′a·ble** ***adj.***

bank[2] (baŋk) ***n.*** ⟦< ON *bakki*⟧ **1** a long mound or heap **2** a steep slope **3** a rise of land along a river, etc. **4** a shallow place, as in a sea **5** the lateral, slanting turn of an aircraft —***vt.*** **1** to cover (a fire) with ashes and fuel so that it will burn slowly **2** to pile up so as to form a bank **3** to slope (a curve in a road, etc.) **4** to make (an aircraft) slant laterally on a turn **5** to make (a billiard ball) recoil from a cushion

bank[3] (baŋk) ***n.*** ⟦< OFr *banc,* bench⟧ **1** a row of oars **2** a row or tier, as of keys in a keyboard —***vt.*** to arrange in a row or tier

bank account money deposited in a bank and credited to the depositor

bank′book′ ***n.*** a book recording a bank depositor's deposits and withdrawals; passbook

bank card an encoded plastic card issued by a bank as for use at an ATM

bank′er ***n.*** a person who owns or manages a bank

bank′ing ***n.*** the business of a bank

bank note a promissory note issued by a bank: a form of paper money

bank′roll′ ***n.*** a supply of money —***vt.*** [Inf.] to supply with money; finance

bank·rupt (baŋk′rupt′) ***n.*** ⟦< Fr < It *banca,* bench + *rotta,* broken⟧ a person legally declared unable to pay debts —***adj.*** **1** that is a bankrupt; insolvent **2** lacking in some quality [*morally bankrupt*] —***vt.*** to make bankrupt —**bank′rupt′cy,** *pl.* **-cies,** ***n.***

ban·ner (ban′ər) ***n.*** ⟦ME *banere* < OFr *baniere*⟧ **1** a flag **2** a headline running across a newspaper page —***adj.*** foremost

banns (banz) ***pl.n.*** ⟦see BAN⟧ the proclamation made in church of an intended marriage

ban·quet (baŋ′kwət) ***n.*** ⟦ult. < OHG *bank,* bench⟧ **1** a feast **2** a formal dinner —***vt.*** to honor with a banquet

ban·quette (baŋ ket′) ***n.*** ⟦Fr⟧ **1** a gunners' platform inside a trench, etc. **2** an upholstered bench

ban·shee or **ban·shie** (ban′shē) ***n.*** ⟦< Ir *bean,* woman + *sith,* fairy⟧ *Celt. Folklore* a female spirit whose wailing warns of impending death

ban·tam (ban′təm) ***n.*** ⟦after *Bantam,* former province in Java⟧ **1** any of various small, domestic fowls **2** a small but aggressive person —***adj.*** like a bantam

ban′tam·weight′ ***n.*** a boxer weighing 113 to 118 lb.

ban·ter (ban′tər) ***vt.*** ⟦17th-c. slang⟧ to tease playfully —***vi.*** to exchange banter (*with* someone) —***n.*** playful teasing —**ban′ter·ing·ly** ***adv.***

Ban·tu (ban′to͞o′) ***n.*** ⟦Bantu *ba-ntu,* the men⟧ **1** a large group of languages of S Africa, including Swahili and Zulu **2** *pl.* **-tus′** or **-tu′** a member of a Bantu-speaking people

ban·yan (ban′yən) ***n.*** ⟦ult. < Sans⟧ an Indian fig tree whose branches grow shoots that take root and become new trunks over a wide area

ba·o·bab (bā′ō bab′, bä′-) ***n.*** ⟦< ? Ethiopian native name⟧ a thick-trunked tree of Africa, with edible, gourdlike fruit

bap·tism (bap′tiz′əm) ***n.*** ⟦see BAPTIZE⟧

1 the sacrament of admitting a person into a Christian church by immersing the individual in water or by sprinkling water on the individual 2 an initiating experience —**bap·tis'mal** (-tiz'məl) *adj.*

Bap'tist (-tist) *n.* a member of a Protestant denomination practicing baptism of believers by immersion

bap'tis·ter·y (-tis tər ē, -tis trē) *n., pl.* **-ies** a place, esp. in a church, used for baptizing: also **bap'tis·try**, *pl.* **-tries**

bap·tize (bap tīz', bap'tīz) *vt.* **-tized'**, **-tiz'ing** ⟦< Gr *baptizein,* to immerse⟧ 1 to administer baptism to 2 to initiate 3 to christen

bar (bär) *n.* ⟦< ML *barra*⟧ 1 any long, narrow piece of wood, metal, etc., often used as a barrier, lever, etc. 2 an oblong piece, as of soap 3 anything that obstructs or hinders 4 a band or strip 5 a law court, esp. that part, enclosed by a railing, where the lawyers sit 6 lawyers collectively 7 the legal profession 8 a counter, as for serving alcoholic drinks 9 a place with such a counter 10 *Music a)* a vertical line dividing a staff into measures *b)* a measure —*vt.* **barred**, **bar'ring** 1 to fasten with a bar 2 to obstruct; close 3 to oppose 4 to exclude —*prep.* excluding *[the best, bar none]* —**cross the bar** to die

barb (bärb) *n.* ⟦< L *barba,* beard⟧ 1 a beardlike growth 2 a sharp point projecting backward from the main point of a fishhook, etc. 3 a cutting remark —*vt.* to provide with a barb —**barbed** *adj.*

Bar·ba·dos (bär bā'dōs, -dōz) country on an island in the West Indies: 166 sq. mi.; pop. 263,000

bar·bar·i·an (bär ber'ē ən) *n.* ⟦see BARBAROUS⟧ 1 a member of a people considered primitive, savage, etc. 2 a cruel person —*adj.* uncivilized, cruel, etc. —**bar·bar'i·an·ism'** *n.*

bar·bar'ic (-ber'ik) *adj.* 1 uncivilized; primitive 2 wild, crude, etc.

bar·ba·rism (bär'bə riz'əm) *n.* 1 a nonstandard word or expression 2 the state of being primitive or uncivilized 3 a barbarous act or custom

bar·bar·i·ty (bär ber'ə tē) *n., pl.* **-ties** 1 cruelty; brutality 2 a barbaric taste, manner, etc.

bar·ba·rize (bär'bə rīz') *vt.* **-rized'**, **-riz'ing** to make or become barbarous —**bar'ba·ri·za'tion** *n.*

bar·ba·rous (bär'bə rəs) *adj.* ⟦< Gr *barbaros,* foreign⟧ 1 uncivilized; primitive 2 crude, coarse, etc. 3 cruel; brutal —**bar'ba·rous·ly** *adv.*

bar·be·cue (bär'bə kyōō') *n.* ⟦AmSp *barbacoa*⟧ 1 *a)* a hog, steer, etc. roasted whole over an open fire *b)* any meat broiled over an open fire 2 a party, picnic, etc. featuring this —*vt.* **-cued'**, **-cu'ing** to roast or broil over an open fire, often with a highly seasoned sauce (**barbecue sauce**)

barbed wire wire with barbs at close intervals

bar·bel (bär'bəl) *n.* ⟦< L *barba,* beard⟧ a threadlike growth from the lips or jaws of certain fishes

BARBELL

bar·bell (bär'bel') *n.* ⟦BAR + (DUMB)BELL⟧ a metal bar with weights attached at each end, used for weight lifting: also **bar bell**

bar·ber (bär'bər) *n.* ⟦see BARB⟧ one whose work is cutting hair, shaving beards, etc. —*vt.* to cut the hair of, shave, etc. —*vi.* to work as a barber

bar·ber·ry (bär'ber'ē, -bə rē) *n., pl.* **-ries** ⟦< ML *barberis*⟧ 1 a spiny shrub with sour, red berries 2 the berry

bar·bi·tu·rate (bär bich'ər it, -bich'ə wit) *n.* ⟦< Ger⟧ a salt or ester of a crystalline acid (**bar'bi·tu'ric acid**), used as a sedative

barb'wire' *n.* BARBED WIRE

bar·ca·role or **bar·ca·rolle** (bär'kə rōl') *n.* ⟦< Fr < It⟧ a Venetian gondolier song, or music like this

Bar·ce·lo·na (bär'sə lō'nə) seaport in NE Spain: pop. 1,753,000

bar code UNIVERSAL PRODUCT CODE

bard (bärd) *n.* ⟦Gael & Ir⟧ 1 an ancient Celtic poet 2 a poet

bare (ber) *adj.* **bar'er**, **bar'est** ⟦OE *bær*⟧ 1 not covered or clothed; naked 2 without furnishings; empty 3 simple; plain 4 mere *[bare* needs*]* —*vt.* **bared**, **bar'ing** to make bare; uncover —**lay bare** to uncover; expose —**bare'ness** *n.*

bare'back' *adv., adj.* on a horse with no saddle

bare'-bones' *adj.* simple; basic

bare'faced' *adj.* 1 with the face uncovered 2 open; shameless

bare'foot' *adj., adv.* without shoes and stockings: also **bare'foot'ed**

bare'hand'ed *adj., adv.* 1 with hands uncovered or unprotected 2 without weapons, etc.

bare'head'ed *adj., adv.* wearing no hat or other covering on the head

bare'leg'ged (-leg'id, -legd') *adj., adv.* with the legs bare

bare·ly (ber'lē) *adv.* 1 plainly 2 only just; scarcely 3 scantily

bar·gain (bär'gən) *n.* ⟦< OFr *bargaignier,* haggle⟧ 1 a mutual agreement or contract 2 such an agreement with regard to worth *[a bad bargain]* 3 something sold at a price favorable to the buyer —*vi.* 1 to haggle 2 to make a bargain —**bargain for** (or **on**) to expect; count on —**into** (or **in**) **the bargain** besides —**bar'gain·er** *n.*

bargain counter a store counter for

displaying goods at reduced prices

barge (bärj) ***n.*** ⟦< ML *barga*⟧ **1** a large, flat-bottomed boat for freight on rivers, etc. **2** a large pleasure boat —***vi.*** **barged, barg′ing** **1** to move slowly and clumsily **2** to come or go (*in* or *into*) rudely or abruptly

bar graph a graph in which the lengths of parallel bars are used to compare quantities, etc.

Bar Harbor resort town on an island off E Maine: pop. 4,400

bar·i·tone (bar′ə tōn′) ***n.*** ⟦< Gr *barys*, deep + *tonos*, tone⟧ **1** the range of a male voice between tenor and bass **2** a voice, singer, or instrument with such a range

bar·i·um (ber′ē əm) ***n.*** ⟦< Gr *barys*, heavy⟧ a metallic chemical element

bark[1] (bärk) ***n.*** ⟦< ON *bǫrkr*⟧ the outside covering of trees and woody plants —***vt.*** **1** to remove bark from **2** [Inf.] to scrape; skin (the knees, etc.)

bark[2] (bärk) ***vi.*** ⟦OE *beorcan*⟧ **1** to make the sharp, abrupt cry of a dog or a similar sound **2** to speak sharply; snap —***n.*** the characteristic cry of a dog, or any noise like this —**bark up the wrong tree** to misdirect one's attack, energies, etc.

bark[3] (bärk) ***n.*** ⟦< LL *barca*⟧ **1** [Old Poet.] a boat **2** a sailing vessel with two square-rigged masts forward and a fore-and-aft mast aft

bar′keep′er ***n.*** **1** an owner of a barroom **2** a bartender Also **bar′keep′**

bark′er ***n.*** one who talks loud to attract customers to a sideshow, etc.

bar·ley (bär′lē) ***n.*** ⟦OE *bærlic*⟧ **1** a cereal grass **2** its grain, used in making malt, in soups, etc.

bar′maid′ ***n.*** a waitress who serves alcoholic drinks in a bar

bar mitz·vah (bär mits′və) ⟦< Yiddish < Aram *bar*, son of + Heb *mitsva*, commandment⟧ [*also* **B- M-**] **1** a Jewish boy who has arrived at the age of religious responsibility, thirteen years **2** the ceremony celebrating this event

barn (bärn) ***n.*** ⟦OE *bern*⟧ a farm building for sheltering harvested crops, livestock, machines, etc.

bar·na·cle (bär′nə kəl) ***n.*** ⟦ME *bernacle*⟧ a saltwater shellfish that attaches itself to rocks, ship bottoms, etc.

barn′burn′er ***n.*** [Slang] something dramatic and exciting, as a close contest

barn′storm′ ***vi.***, ***vt.*** to tour (the country, esp. rural areas) giving speeches or lectures, performing exhibitions, etc. —**barn′storm′er** ***n.***

barn′yard′ ***n.*** the ground near a barn —***adj.*** of, like, or fit for a barnyard; specif., earthy or crude

ba·rom·e·ter (bə räm′ət ər) ***n.*** ⟦< Gr *baros*, weight + -METER⟧ **1** an instrument for measuring atmospheric pressure and thus forecasting weather **2** anything that marks change —**bar·o·met·ric** (bar′ə me′trik) ***adj.***

bar·on (bar′ən) ***n.*** ⟦ME⟧ **1** a member of the lowest rank of British nobility **2** a magnate —**bar′on·age** ***n.*** —**bar′on·ess** ***fem.n.*** —**ba·ro·ni·al** (bə rō′nē əl) ***adj.***

bar′on·et (-ət) ***n.*** a man holding the lowest hereditary British title, below a baron —**bar′on·et·cy**, *pl.* **-cies**, ***n.***

ba·roque (bə rōk′) ***adj.*** ⟦Fr < Port *barroco*, imperfect pearl⟧ **1** [*often* **B-**] *a*) very ornate and full of curved lines, as much art and architecture of about 1600-1750 *b*) full of highly embellished melodies, fugues, etc., as much music of that time **2** gaudily ornate

bar·racks (bar′əks) ***pl.n.*** ⟦< Sp *barro*, clay⟧ [*often with sing. v.*] a building or group of buildings for housing soldiers, etc.

bar·ra·cu·da (bar′ə ko͞o′də) ***n.***, *pl.* **-da** or **-das** ⟦AmSp⟧ a fierce, pikelike fish of tropical seas

bar·rage (bə räzh′, -räj′) ***n.*** ⟦Fr < *barrer*, to stop⟧ **1** artillery fire that holds down the enemy while one's army attacks **2** any prolonged attack —***vi.***, ***vt.*** **-raged′**, **-rag′ing** to subject to a barrage

barred (bärd) ***adj.*** **1** having bars or stripes **2** closed off with bars **3** not allowed

bar·rel (bar′əl) ***n.*** ⟦< ML *barillus*⟧ **1** a large, cylindrical container with slightly bulging sides and flat ends **2** a similar cylindrical container **3** the capacity of a standard barrel, used as a measure **4** the straight tube of a gun —***vt.*** **-reled** or **-relled**, **-rel·ing** or **-rel·ling** to put in barrels —***vi.*** [Slang] to go at high speed

bar′rel·ful′ (-fo͝ol′) ***n.*** **1** as much as a barrel will hold **2** [Inf.] a great amount

bar′rel·head′ ***n.*** the flat end of a barrel —**on the barrelhead** when delivered [*to pay cash on the barrelhead*]

barrel organ a mechanical musical instrument played by turning a crank

bar·ren (bar′ən) ***adj.*** ⟦< OFr⟧ **1** that cannot bear offspring; sterile **2** without vegetation **3** unproductive **4** boring; dull **5** devoid (*of*) —**bar′ren·ness** ***n.***

bar·rette (bə ret′) ***n.*** ⟦Fr⟧ a bar or clasp for holding a woman's hair in place

bar·ri·cade (bar′i kād′; *also, esp. for v.*, bar′ə kād′) ***n.*** ⟦Fr < It *barricare*, fortify⟧ a barrier, esp. one put up hastily for defense —***vt.*** **-cad′ed**, **-cad′ing** to block with a barricade

bar·ri·er (bar′ē ər) ***n.*** ⟦< ML *barra*⟧ **1** an obstruction, as a fence **2** anything that blocks or hinders

bar·ring (bär′iŋ) ***prep.*** excepting

bar·ris·ter (bar′is tər) ***n.*** ⟦< *bar* (law court)⟧ in England, a lawyer who pleads cases in court

bar′room′ ***n.*** a room with a bar where alcoholic drinks are sold

bar·row[1] (bar′ō) ***n.*** ⟦< OE *beran*, to bear⟧ a handbarrow or wheelbarrow

bar·row[2] (bar′ō) ***n.*** ⟦< OE *beorg*, hill⟧ a heap of earth or rocks covering a grave

bar′tend′er ***n.*** one who serves alcoholic drinks at a bar

bar·ter (bärt′ər) ***vi.***, ***vt.*** ⟦< OFr *barater*⟧ to trade by exchanging (goods) without money —***n.*** **1** a bartering **2** anything bartered —**bar′ter·er** ***n.***

Bar·tók (bär′tôk′), **Bé·la** (bā′lä) 1881-

1945; Hung. composer

bar·y·on (bar′ē än′) ***n.*** ⟦< Gr *barys,* heavy + (ELECTR)ON⟧ any of certain subatomic particles including the proton and neutron

ba·sal (bā′səl) ***adj.*** **1** of or at the base **2** basic; fundamental

basal metabolism the minimum quantity of energy used by an organism at rest to sustain its life

ba·salt (bə sôlt′, bā′sôlt′) ***n.*** ⟦L *basaltes*⟧ a hard, dark volcanic rock

base[1] (bās) ***n.*** ⟦< Gr *basis*⟧ **1** the thing or part on which something rests **2** the most important element or principal ingredient **3** the part of a word to which affixes are attached **4** a basis **5** any of the four markers a baseball player must consecutively touch to score a run **6** a headquarters or a source of supply **7** *Chem.* a substance that forms a salt when it reacts with an acid —***adj.*** forming a base —***vt.*** **based, bas′ing 1** to make a base for **2** to establish

base[2] (bās) ***adj.*** **bas′er, bas′est** ⟦< VL *bassus,* low⟧ **1** mean; ignoble **2** menial **3** poor in quality **4** of comparatively low worth [*base* metal] —**base′ly** ***adv.*** —**base′ness** ***n.***

base′ball′ ***n.*** **1** a game played with a ball and bat by two opposing teams on a field with four bases forming a diamond **2** the ball used in this game

base′board′ ***n.*** a board or molding at the base of a wall

base hit *Baseball* a play in which the batter hits a fair ball and gets on base without an error or without forcing out a teammate

base′less ***adj.*** having no basis in fact; unfounded —**base′less·ness** ***n.***

base line 1 a line serving as a base **2** *Baseball* the lane between any two consecutive bases **3** *Basketball, Tennis* the line at either end of the court Also **base′line′**

base′man (-mən) ***n.,*** *pl.* **-men** (-mən) *Baseball* an infielder stationed at first, second, or third base

base′ment ***n.*** the story below the main floor

base on balls *Baseball* WALK

base pay the basic rate of pay not counting overtime pay, etc.

base runner *Baseball* a player who is on base or is trying to reach a base

bash (bash) ***vt.*** ⟦echoic⟧ [Inf.] to hit hard —***n.*** [Slang] a party

bash′ful (-fəl) ***adj.*** ⟦(A)BASH + -FUL⟧ easily embarrassed; shy —**bash′ful·ly** ***adv.*** —**bash′ful·ness** ***n.***

bas·ic (bā′sik) ***adj.*** **1** fundamental **2** *Chem.* alkaline —***n.*** a basic principle, factor, etc. —**bas′i·cal·ly** ***adv.***

BASIC (bā′sik) ***n.*** ⟦*B*(*eginner's*) *A*(*ll-purpose*) *S*(*ymbolic*) *I*(*nstruction*) *C*(*ode*)⟧ a simple computer language that uses common words and algebra

bas·il (bā′zəl, baz′əl) ***n.*** ⟦< Gr *basilikon*⟧ a fragrant herb of the mint family, used in cooking

ba·sil·i·ca (bə sil′i kə) ***n.*** ⟦< Gr *basilikē* (*stoa*), royal (portico)⟧ **1** a church with a broad nave, side aisles, and an apse **2** *R.C.Ch.* a church with certain ceremonial rights

ba·sin (bā′sin) ***n.*** ⟦< VL *bacca,* water vessel⟧ **1** a wide, shallow container for liquid **2** its contents **3** a sink **4** any shallow, rounded hollow, often containing water **5** RIVER BASIN

ba·sis (bā′sis) ***n.,*** *pl.* **-ses′** (-sēz′) ⟦< Gr, a base⟧ **1** a base or foundation **2** a principal constituent **3** a fundamental principle or theory

bask (bask) ***vi.*** ⟦ME *basken,* to wallow⟧ **1** to warm oneself pleasantly **2** to enjoy a warm feeling from being in a certain situation

bas·ket (bas′kit) ***n.*** ⟦ME⟧ **1** a container made of interwoven cane, wood strips, etc. **2** its contents **3** *Basketball a*) the goal, a round, open, hanging net *b*) a goal made by shooting the ball through this net

bas′ket·ball′ ***n.*** ⟦invented & named (1891) by James A. Naismith (1861-1939)⟧ **1** a team game played with a bouncy, round ball on a court having a raised basket at each end **2** this ball

basket weave a weave of fabrics resembling the weave used in making baskets

bas′ket·work′ ***n.*** work that is woven like a basket; wickerwork

bas mitz·vah (bäs mits′və) BAT MITZVAH

Basque (bask) ***n.*** **1** a member of a people living in the W Pyrenees **2** the language of this people —***adj.*** of the Basques

bas-re·lief (bä′ri lēf′, bas′-) ***n.*** ⟦Fr < It: see BASS[1] & RELIEF⟧ sculpture in which figures project slightly from a flat background

bass[1] (bās) ***n.*** ⟦< VL *bassus,* low⟧ **1** the range of the lowest male voice **2** a voice, singer, or instrument with such a range; specif., a double bass **3** a part for a bass **4** a low, deep sound —***adj.*** of or for a bass

bass[2] (bas) ***n.,*** *pl.* **bass** or **bass′es** ⟦OE *baers*⟧ a spiny-finned food and game fish of fresh or salt water

bas·set (bas′it) ***n.*** ⟦< OFr *bas,* low⟧ a hunting hound with a long body, short forelegs, and long, drooping ears

bas·si·net (bas′ə net′) ***n.*** ⟦< Fr dim. of *berceau,* a cradle⟧ a basketlike bed for an infant, often hooded and on wheels

bas·so (bas′ō, bäs′-) ***n.,*** *pl.* **-sos** or **-si** (-sē) ⟦< VL *bassus,* low⟧ a bass voice or singer

BASSOON

bas·soon (ba so͞on′, bə-) ***n.*** ⟦< VL *bassus,* low⟧ a double-reed bass woodwind instrument

bast (bast) ***n.*** ⟦OE *bæst*⟧ plant fiber used in ropes, mats, etc.

bas·tard (bas′tərd) ***n.*** ⟦< OFr⟧ an illegitimate child —***adj.*** **1** of illegitimate birth **2** inferior, sham, etc. —**bas′tar·dy** (-tər dē) ***n.***

bas·tard·ize (bas′tər dīz′) ***vt.*** **-ized′, -iz′ing** **1** to make, declare, or show to be a bastard **2** to make corrupt; debase —**bas′tard·i·za′tion** ***n.***

baste[1] (bāst) ***vt.*** **bast′ed, bast′ing** ⟦< Gmc *bastjan,* make with bast⟧ to sew temporarily with long, loose stitches until properly sewed

baste[2] (bāst) ***vt.*** **bast′ed, bast′ing** ⟦< OFr *bassin,* basin⟧ to moisten (meat) with melted butter, drippings, etc. while roasting —**bast′er** ***n.***

baste[3] (bāst) ***vt.*** **bast′ed, bast′ing** ⟦ON *beysta*⟧ **1** to beat soundly **2** to attack with words

bas·tille or **bas·tile** (bas tēl′) ***n.*** ⟦< OFr *bastir,* to build⟧ a prison —**the Bastille** a state prison in Paris destroyed (1789) in the French Revolution

bas·tion (bas′chən, -tē ən) ***n.*** ⟦see BASTILLE⟧ **1** a projection from a fortification **2** any strong defense

bat[1] (bat) ***n.*** ⟦OE *batt*⟧ **1** a stout club **2** a club to hit the ball in baseball, etc. **3** a turn at batting **4** [Inf.] a blow —***vt.*** **bat′ted, bat′ting** to hit, as with a bat —***vi.*** to take a turn at batting

bat[2] (bat) ***n.*** ⟦< Scand⟧ a furry, nocturnal flying mammal with membranous wings

bat[3] (bat) ***vt.*** **bat′ted, bat′ting** ⟦< OFr *battre,* to batter⟧ [Inf.] to wink —**not bat an eye** [Inf.] not show surprise

batch (bach) ***n.*** ⟦OE *bacan,* to bake⟧ **1** the amount (of bread, etc.) in one baking **2** one set, lot, group, etc. **3** an amount of work for processing by a computer in a single run

bate (bāt) ***vt.*** **bat′ed, bat′ing** ⟦< OFr *abattre,* beat down⟧ to abate or lessen —**with bated breath** holding the breath, as in fear

bath (bath) ***n.,*** *pl.* **baths** (ba*th*z, baths) ⟦OE *bæth*⟧ **1** a washing, esp. of the body, in water **2** water, etc. for bathing or for soaking or treating something **3** a bathtub **4** a bathroom **5** a BATHHOUSE (sense 1)

bathe (bā*th*) ***vt.*** **bathed, bath′ing** ⟦OE *bæth*⟧ **1** to put into a liquid **2** to give a bath to **3** to cover as with liquid —***vi.*** **1** to take a bath **2** to soak oneself in something —**bath·er** (bā′*th*ər) ***n.***

bath′house′ ***n.*** **1** a public building for taking baths **2** a building used by bathers for changing clothes

bathing suit a swimsuit

bath′mat′ ***n.*** a mat used in or next to a bathtub

ba·thos (bā′thäs′) ***n.*** ⟦< Gr *bathys,* deep⟧ **1** ANTICLIMAX (sense 1) **2** excessive sentimentality **3** triteness —**ba·thet·ic** (bə thet′ik) ***adj.***

bath′robe′ ***n.*** a loose robe worn to and from the bath, etc.

bath′room′ ***n.*** **1** a room with a bathtub, toilet, etc. **2** a lavatory

bath′tub′ ***n.*** a tub to bathe in

bath·y·scaph (bath′ə skaf′) ***n.*** ⟦< Gr *bathys,* deep + *skaphē,* boat⟧ a deep-sea diving apparatus for reaching great depths without a cable: also **bath′y·scaphe′** (-skaf′, -skāf′)

ba·tik (bə tēk′) ***n.*** ⟦Malay⟧ cloth with a design made by dyeing only the parts not coated with wax

ba·tiste (bə tēst′, ba-) ***n.*** ⟦Fr: after supposed orig. maker, *Baptiste*⟧ a fine, thin cloth of cotton, rayon, etc.

bat mitz·vah (bät mits′və) [*also* **B- M-**] **1** a Jewish girl who has arrived at the age of religious responsibility, 13 years **2** the ceremony celebrating this event

ba·ton (bə tän′, ba-) ***n.*** ⟦Fr⟧ **1** a staff serving as a symbol of office **2** a slender stick used in directing music **3** a metal rod twirled by a drum major **4** a short, light rod used in relay races

Bat·on Rouge (bat′'n ro͞ozh′) capital of Louisiana: pop. 220,000

bat·tal·ion (bə tal′yən) ***n.*** ⟦< VL *battalia,* battle⟧ a tactical military unit forming part of a division

bat·ten[1] (bat′'n) ***n.*** ⟦var. of *baton*⟧ **1** a sawed strip of wood **2** a strip of wood put over a seam between boards as a fastening or covering —***vt.*** to fasten or supply with battens

bat·ten[2] (bat′'n) ***vi., vt.*** ⟦ON *batna,* improve⟧ to fatten; thrive

bat·ten[3] (bat′'n) ***n.*** ⟦< OFr *battre,* to batter⟧ in a loom, the movable frame that presses into place the threads of a woof

bat·ter[1] (bat′ər) ***vt.*** ⟦< L *battuere,* to beat⟧ **1** to strike with blow after blow **2** to injure by pounding, hard wear, or use —***vi.*** to pound noisily and repeatedly

bat·ter[2] (bat′ər) ***n.*** *Baseball, Cricket* the player at bat

bat·ter[3] (bat′ər) ***n.*** ⟦OFr *bature*⟧ a flowing mixture of flour, milk, etc. for making pancakes, etc.

battering ram a heavy beam, etc. for battering down gates, etc.

bat·ter·y (bat′ər ē) ***n.,*** *pl.* **-ies** ⟦< OFr *battre,* to batter⟧ **1** a battering **2** a set of things used together **3** *Baseball* the pitcher and the catcher **4** *Elec.* a cell or group of cells storing an electrical charge and able to furnish a current **5** *Law* any illegal beating of another person: see ASSAULT AND BATTERY **6** *Mil.* a set of heavy guns, rockets, etc.

bat·ting (bat′'n, -iŋ) ***n.*** ⟦OE *batt,* BAT[1]⟧ cotton, wool, or synthetic fiber wadded into sheets

bat·tle (bat′'l) ***n.*** ⟦< L *battuere,* to beat⟧ **1** a large-scale fight between armed forces **2** armed fighting **3** any fight or conflict —***vt., vi.*** **-tled, -tling** to fight —**give** (or **do**) **battle** to fight

bat′tle-ax′ or **bat′tle-axe′** ***n.*** **1** a heavy ax formerly used as a weapon **2** [Slang] a harsh, domineering woman

bat′tle·field′ ***n.*** the site of a battle: also **bat′tle·ground′**

bat′tle·ment (-mənt) ***n.*** ⟦< OFr *batailler,* fortify⟧ a parapet with spaces for shooting, built atop a tower, etc.

battle royal *pl.* **battles royal** **1** a free-for-all **2** a heated dispute

bat′tle·ship′ ***n.*** a large warship with big guns and very heavy armor

bat·ty (bat′ē) ***adj.*** **-ti·er, -ti·est** ⟦< BAT[2]⟧ [Slang] crazy or eccentric

bau·ble (bô′bəl) ***n.*** ⟦< L *bellus,* pretty⟧ a showy trifle; trinket

baud (bôd) ***n.*** ⟦after J. M. E. *Baudot* (1845-1903), Fr inventor⟧ the number of bits per second transmitted in a computer system

baux·ite (bôks′īt′) ***n.*** ⟦Fr, after (*Les*) *Baux,* town in S France⟧ a claylike sedimentary rock, the chief ore of aluminum

Ba·var·i·a (bə ver′ē ə) state of SW Germany —**Ba·var′i·an** ***adj., n.***

bawd (bôd) ***n.*** ⟦< ? OFr *baud,* licentious⟧ [Literary] a person, esp. a woman, who keeps a brothel

bawd·y (bô′dē) ***adj.*** **-i·er, -i·est** indecent; lewd —**bawd′i·ness** ***n.***

bawl (bôl) ***vi., vt.*** ⟦< ML *baulare,* to bark⟧ **1** to shout **2** to weep loudly —***n.*** **1** an outcry **2** a noisy weeping —**bawl out** [Slang] to scold angrily

bay[1] (bā) ***n.*** ⟦< ML *baia*⟧ a wide inlet of a sea or lake, along the shoreline

bay[2] (bā) ***n.*** ⟦< VL *batare,* to gape⟧ **1** an alcove or recess **2** BAY WINDOW

bay[3] (bā) ***vi.*** ⟦< OFr *baiier*⟧ to bark or howl in long, deep tones —***n.*** **1** the sound of baying **2** the situation of a hunted animal forced to turn and fight —**at bay** **1** cornered **2** held off —**bring to bay** to corner

bay[4] (bā) ***n.*** ⟦< L *baca,* berry⟧ **1** LAUREL (*n.* 1) **2** [*pl.*] a laurel wreath

bay[5] (bā) ***adj.*** ⟦< L *badius*⟧ reddish-brown —***n.*** **1** a reddish-brown horse, etc. **2** reddish brown

bay′ber′ry ***n.***, *pl.* **-ries** **1** a shrub with small, wax-coated, berrylike fruit **2** the fruit

bay leaf the dried, aromatic leaf of certain laurel plants, used as a seasoning

bay·o·net (bā′ə net′, bā′ə nət) ***n.*** ⟦< Fr: after *Bayonne,* city in France⟧ a detachable blade put on a rifle muzzle, for stabbing —***vt., vi.*** **-net′ed** or **-net′ted, -net′ing** or **-net′ting** to stab with a bayonet

bay·ou (bī′o͞o′) ***n.*** ⟦< AmInd *bayuk,* small stream⟧ in S U.S., a marshy inlet or outlet of a lake, river, etc.

bay window **1** a window or set of windows jutting out from a wall **2** [Slang] a large protruding belly

ba·zaar (bə zär′) ***n.*** ⟦Pers *bāzār*⟧ **1** a marketplace, esp. in the Middle East **2** a benefit sale for a church, etc.

ba·zoo·ka (bə zo͞o′kə) ***n.*** ⟦< name of a comic horn⟧ a portable weapon for launching armor-piercing rockets

BB (bē′bē′) ***n.***, *pl.* **BB's** ⟦designation of size⟧ a pellet of shot (diameter, .18 in.) fired from an air rifle (**BB gun**) or shotgun

bbl *abbrev.* barrel

BC *abbrev.* **1** before Christ: also **B.C.** **2** British Columbia

B cell any of the lymphatic leukocytes not derived from the thymus, that build antibodies: cf. T CELL

be (bē) ***vi.*** **was** or **were, been, being** ⟦OE *beon*⟧ **1** to exist; live **2** to happen; occur **3** to remain or continue *Note*: *be* is used to link its subject to a predicate complement *[she* is *nice]* or as an auxiliary: (1) with a past participle: *a*) to form the passive voice *[he will* be *sued]* *b*) [Archaic] to form the perfect tense *[Christ* is *risen]* (2) with a present participle to express continuation *[he* is *running]* (3) with a present participle or infinitive to express futurity, possibility, obligation, intention, etc. *[she* is *going soon, he* is *to cut it]* *Be* is conjugated in the present indicative: (I) *am,* (he, she, it) *is,* (we, you, they) *are*; in the past indicative: (I, he, she, it) *was,* (we, you, they) *were*

Be *Chem. symbol for* beryllium

be- ⟦< OE *bi-, be-,* at⟧ *prefix* **1** around *[beset]* **2** completely *[bedeck]* **3** away *[betake]* **4** about *[bemoan]* **5** to make *[besot]* **6** to furnish with, affect by *[becloud]*

beach (bēch) ***n.*** ⟦E dial., pebbles⟧ a sandy shore —***vt., vi.*** to ground (a boat) on a beach

beach′comb′er (-kōm′ər) ***n.*** **1** COMBER (sense 2) **2** one who lives on items found on beaches —**beach′comb′ing** ***n.***

beach′head′ ***n.*** a position gained, specif. by invading an enemy shore

beach′wear′ ***n.*** garments worn at the beach, as swimsuits

bea·con (bē′kən) ***n.*** ⟦< OE *beacen,* a signal⟧ **1** a light for warning or guiding **2** a radio transmitter sending guiding signals for aircraft

bead (bēd) ***n.*** ⟦< OE *bed,* prayer bead⟧ **1** a small ball of glass, etc., pierced for stringing **2** [*pl.*] a rosary **3** [*pl.*] a string of beads **4** any small, round object, as the front sight of a rifle **5** a drop or bubble **6** the rim edge of a rubber tire —***vt.*** to decorate with beads —**draw a bead on** to take careful aim at —**say one's beads** to pray with a rosary —**bead′y, -i·er, -i·est,** ***adj.***

bea·dle (bēd′'l) ***n.*** ⟦ME *bidel*⟧ [Historical] a minor officer in the Church of England, who kept order in church

bea·gle (bē′gəl) ***n.*** ⟦< ? Fr *bee gueule,*

wide throat⟧ a small hound with short legs and drooping ears

beak (bēk) ***n.*** ⟦< L *beccus*⟧ **1** a bird's bill **2** a beaklike part, as the snout of various insects

beak·er (bēk′ər) ***n.*** ⟦< ? Gr *bikos,* vessel with handles⟧ **1** a goblet **2** *Chem.* a glass or metal container with a beaklike lip for pouring

beam (bēm) ***n.*** ⟦ME⟧ **1** a long, thick piece of wood, metal, etc. **2** the crossbar of a balance **3** a ship's breadth at its widest point **4** a shaft of light, etc. **5** a radiant look, smile, etc. **6** a steady radio or radar signal for guiding aircraft or ships **—*vt.*** **1** to give out (shafts of light) **2** to direct (a radio signal, etc.) **—*vi.*** **1** to shine brightly **2** to smile warmly **—on the beam** [Inf.] working well

bean (bēn) ***n.*** ⟦OE *bean*⟧ **1** a plant of the pea family, bearing kidney-shaped seeds **2** the edible, smooth seed of this plant **3** any beanlike seed *[coffee bean]* **4** [Slang] the head or brain **—*vt.*** [Slang] to hit on the head **—full of beans** [Slang] lively **—spill the beans** [Inf.] to tell a secret

bear[1] (ber) ***vt.*** **bore, borne** or **born, bear′ing** ⟦OE *beran*⟧ **1** to carry **2** to have or show **3** to give birth to **4** to produce or yield **5** to support or sustain **6** to withstand or endure **7** to need *[this bears watching]* **8** to carry or conduct (oneself) **9** to give *[to bear witness]* **—*vi.*** **1** to be productive **2** to lie, point, or move in a given direction **3** to have bearing (*on*) **4** to tolerate **—bear down (on)** **1** to exert pressure or effort (on) **2** to approach **—bear out** to confirm **—bear up** to endure **—bear′a·ble *adj.* —bear′er *n.***

bear[2] (ber) ***n.,*** *pl.* **bears** or **bear** ⟦OE *bera*⟧ **1** a large, heavy mammal with shaggy fur and a short tail **2** one who is clumsy, rude, etc. **3** one who sells stocks, etc. hoping to buy them back later at a lower price **4** [Slang] a difficult task **—*adj.*** falling in price **— bear′like′ *adj.***

beard (bird) ***n.*** ⟦OE⟧ **1** the hair on the chin and cheeks of a man **2** any beardlike part **3** an awn **—*vt.*** **1** to defy **2** to provide with a beard **—beard′ed *adj.* — beard′less *adj.***

bear·ing (ber′iŋ) ***n.*** **1** way of carrying and conducting oneself **2** a supporting part **3** a producing or ability to produce **4** endurance **5** [*often pl.*] relative direction or position **6** [*pl.*] awareness of one's situation **7** relevance; relation **8** a part of a machine on which another part revolves, slides, etc.

bear′ish ***adj.*** **1** bearlike; rude, rough, etc. **2** falling, or causing, expecting, etc. a fall, in prices on the stock exchange **—bear′ish·ly *adv.***

bé·ar·naise sauce (bā′är nāz′) a creamy sauce, esp. for meat or fish

bear′skin′ ***n.*** **1** the fur or hide of a bear **2** a rug, coat, etc. made from this

beast (bēst) ***n.*** ⟦< L *bestia*⟧ **1** any large, four-footed animal **2** one who is gross, brutal, etc.

beast′ly ***adj.*** **-li·er, -li·est** **1** of or like a beast; brutal, etc. **2** [Inf.] disagreeable; unpleasant **—beast′li·ness *n.***

beast of burden any animal used for carrying things

beast of prey any animal that hunts and kills other animals for food

beat (bēt) ***vt.*** **beat, beat′en, beat′ing** ⟦OE *beatan*⟧ **1** to hit repeatedly; pound **2** to punish by so hitting; whip, spank, etc. **3** to dash repeatedly against **4** *a)* to form (a path, etc.) by repeated treading or riding *b)* to keep walking on **5** to mix (eggs, etc.) by hard stirring **6** to move (esp. wings) up and down **7** to search through (a forest, etc.) **8** to defeat or outdo **9** to mark (time or rhythm) by tapping, etc. **10** [Inf.] to baffle **11** [Inf.] to cheat or trick **12** [Slang] to escape the penalties of (an indictment, rap, etc.) **—*vi.*** **1** to hit or dash repeatedly **2** to throb, vibrate, etc. **—*n.*** **1** a beating, as of the heart **2** any of a series of movements, blows, etc. **3** a throb **4** a habitual route **5** the unit of musical rhythm **6** BEATNIK **— *adj.*** **1** [Inf.] tired out **2** of a group of young persons, esp. of the 1950s, expressing social disillusionment by unconventional dress, actions, etc. **— beat down** to put or force down **—beat it!** [Slang] go away! **—beat off** to drive back **—beat up (on)** [Slang] to give a beating to **—beat′er *n.***

beat′en ***adj.*** **1** shaped by hammering **2** much traveled *[a beaten path]* **3** crushed in spirit; defeated **4** tired out

be·a·tif·ic (bē′ə tif′ik) ***adj.*** **1** making blessed **2** showing happiness or delight

be·at·i·fy (bē at′ə fī′) ***vt.*** **-fied′, -fy′ing** ⟦< L *beatus,* happy + *facere,* to make⟧ **1** to make blissfully happy **2** *R.C.Ch.* to declare (a deceased person) to be in heaven **—be·at′i·fi·ca′tion *n.***

beat′ing ***n.*** **1** the act of one that beats **2** a whipping **3** a throbbing **4** a defeat

be·at·i·tude (bē at′ə to͞od′) ***n.*** ⟦< L *beatus,* happy⟧ perfect blessedness or happiness **—the Beatitudes** the pronouncements in the Sermon on the Mount

beat·nik (bēt′nik) ***n.*** a member of the beat group

beat′-up′ ***adj.*** [Slang] worn-out, dilapidated, etc.

beau (bō) ***n.,*** *pl.* **beaus** or **beaux** (bōz) ⟦Fr < L *bellus,* pretty⟧ [Old-fashioned] a woman's sweetheart

beau·te·ous (byo͞ot′ē əs) ***adj.*** ⟦ME⟧ beautiful **—beau′te·ous·ly *adv.***

beau·ti·cian (byo͞o tish′ən) ***n.*** one who works in a beauty shop

beau·ti·ful (byo͞ot′ə fəl) ***adj.*** having beauty **—beau′ti·ful·ly *adv.***

beau′ti·fy′ (-fī′) ***vt., vi.*** **-fied′, -fy′ing** to make or become beautiful **—beau′ti·fi·ca′tion *n.* —beau′ti·fi′er *n.***

beau·ty (byo͞ot′ē) ***n.,*** *pl.* **-ties** ⟦< L *bellus,* pretty⟧ **1** the quality of being very pleasing, as in form, color, etc. **2** a thing with this quality **3** good looks **4** a very attractive person, feature, etc.

beauty salon (or **shop, parlor,** etc.) a place where people, esp. women, go for hair styling, manicuring, etc.

bea·ver (bē′vər) ***n.*** ⟦< OE *beofor*⟧ **1** a large amphibious rodent with soft, brown fur, webbed hind feet, and a flat, broad tail **2** its fur

be·calm (bē käm′, bi-) ***vt.*** **1** to make calm **2** to make (a ship) motionless from lack of wind

be·cause (bē kôz′, -kuz′; bi-) ***conj.*** ⟦ME *bi*, by + *cause*⟧ for the reason or cause that —**because of** by reason of

beck (bek) ***n.*** a beckoning gesture —**at the beck and call of** at the service of

beck·on (bek′′n) ***vi.***, ***vt.*** ⟦OE *beacnian*⟧ **1** to summon by a gesture **2** to lure; entice

be·cloud (bē kloud′, bi-) ***vt.*** **1** to cloud over **2** to confuse; muddle

be·come (bē kum′, bi kum′) ***vi.*** **-came′**, **-come′**, **-com′ing** ⟦OE *becuman*⟧ to come or grow to be —***vt.*** to befit; suit *[*modesty *becomes* her*]* —**become of** to happen to

be·com′ing ***adj.*** **1** appropriate; fit **2** suitable to the wearer

bed (bed) ***n.*** ⟦OE⟧ **1** a piece of furniture for sleeping or resting on **2** a plot of soil where plants are raised **3** the bottom of a river, lake, etc. **4** any flat surface used as a foundation **5** a geologic layer; stratum **6** the flat surface of a truck —***vt.*** **bed′ded**, **bed′ding** **1** to put to bed **2** to provide with a sleeping place **3** to embed **4** to plant in a bed of earth **5** to arrange in layers —***vi.*** **1** to go to bed; rest; sleep **2** to stratify

bed′-and-break′fast ***adj.***, ***n.*** (of) a hotel, etc. that provides breakfast as part of the price: also **bed and breakfast**

be·daz·zle (bē daz′əl, bi-) ***vt.*** **-zled**, **-zling** to dazzle thoroughly; bewilder

bed′bug′ ***n.*** a small, wingless, biting insect that infests beds, etc.

bed′clothes′ ***pl.n.*** sheets, blankets, etc. for a bed

bed′cov′er ***n.*** a cover for a bed; bedspread

bed′ding ***n.*** **1** mattresses and bedclothes **2** a bottom layer; base **3** straw, etc. for animals to sleep on

be·deck (bē dek′, bi-) ***vt.*** to adorn

be·dev·il (bē dev′əl, bi-) ***vt.*** **-iled** or **-illed**, **-il·ing** or **-il·ling** to plague or bewilder —**be·dev′il·ment** ***n.***

bed′fel′low ***n.*** **1** a person who shares one's bed **2** an associate, ally, etc.

be·dim (bē dim′, bi-) ***vt.*** **-dimmed′**, **-dim′ming** to make (the eyes or the vision) dim

bed·lam (bed′ləm) ***n.*** ⟦after (the old London mental hospital of St. Mary of) *Bethlehem*⟧ any place or condition of noise and confusion

bed of roses [Inf.] a situation or position of ease and luxury

Bed·ou·in (bed′o͞o in′) ***n.***, *pl.* **-ins** or **-in** ⟦< Ar *badāwīn*, desert dwellers⟧ *[also* **b-**] an Arab of the desert tribes of Arabia, Syria, or N Africa

bed′pan′ ***n.*** a shallow pan for use as a toilet by one confined to bed

be·drag·gle (bē drag′əl, bi-) ***vt.*** **-gled**, **-gling** to make wet, limp, and dirty, as by dragging through mire

bed′rid′den (-rid′′n) ***adj.*** confined to bed by illness, infirmity, etc.

bed′rock′ ***n.*** **1** solid rock beneath the soil, etc. **2** a foundation or bottom

bed′roll′ ***n.*** a portable roll of bedding, as for sleeping outdoors

bed′room′ ***n.*** a room for sleeping

bed′side′ ***n.*** the space beside a bed —***adj.*** near a bed

bed′sore′ ***n.*** a sore on the body of a bedridden person, caused by chafing

bed′spread′ ***n.*** an ornamental spread covering the blanket on a bed

bed′stead′ (-sted′) ***n.*** a framework for supporting the mattress, etc. of a bed

bed′time′ ***n.*** one's usual time for going to bed

bee[1] (bē) ***n.*** ⟦OE *beo*⟧ a broad-bodied, four-winged, hairy insect that gathers pollen and nectar and that can sting

bee[2] (bē) ***n.*** ⟦OE *ben*, compulsory service⟧ a meeting of people to work together or to compete *[*a spelling *bee]*

beech (bēch) ***n.*** ⟦OE *bece*⟧ **1** a tree with smooth, gray bark, hard wood, and edible nuts **2** its wood

beech′nut′ ***n.*** the small, three-cornered, edible nut of the beech tree

beef (bēf) ***n.***, *pl.* for 1 & 5, **beefs**; for 1, also **beeves** ⟦< L *bos*, ox⟧ **1** a full-grown ox, cow, bull, or steer, esp. one bred for meat **2** such animals collectively **3** their meat **4** [Inf.] *a)* human flesh *b)* strength **5** [Slang] a complaint —***vi.*** [Slang] to complain —**beef up** [Inf.] to reinforce

beef′cake′ ***n.*** ⟦BEEF (*n.* 4*a*) + (CHEESE)CAKE⟧ [Inf.] display of the figure of a nude or partly nude, muscular man, as in a photograph

beef′steak′ ***n.*** a thick slice of beef for broiling or frying

beef′y ***adj.*** **-i·er**, **-i·est** brawny —**beef′i·ness** ***n.***

bee′hive′ ***n.*** **1** a shelter for a colony of bees **2** a place of great activity

bee′keep′er ***n.*** one who keeps bees for producing honey —**bee′keep′ing** ***n.***

bee′line′ ***n.*** a straight line or direct route

Be·el·ze·bub (bē el′zə bub′) ***n.*** *Bible* the chief devil; Satan

been (bin; *often* ben) ***vi.*** *pp. of* BE

beep (bēp) ***n.*** ⟦echoic⟧ the brief, high-pitched sound of a horn or electronic signal —***vi.***, ***vt.*** to make or cause to make this sound

beer (bir) ***n.*** ⟦OE *beor*⟧ **1** an alcoholic, fermented drink made from malt and hops **2** a soft drink made from extracts of roots, etc. *[*root *beer]*

bees′wax′ ***n.*** wax secreted by honeybees, used to make their honeycombs: it is used in candles, etc.

beet (bēt) ***n.*** ⟦< L *beta*⟧ **1** a plant with edible leaves and a thick, fleshy, white or red root **2** the edible root, also a source of sugar

Bee·tho·ven (bā′tō′vən), **Lud·wig van** (lo͞ot′viH vän) 1770-1827; Ger. composer

bee·tle[1] (bēt′'l) ***n.*** ⟦OE *bītan,* to bite⟧ an insect with hard front wings that cover the membranous hind wings when these are folded

bee·tle[2] (bēt′'l) ***vi.*** **-tled, -tling** ⟦prob. < fol.⟧ to overhang —***adj.*** overhanging: also **bee′tling**

bee′tle-browed′ (-broud′) ***adj.*** ⟦< ME < ? *bitel,* sharp + *brouwe,* brow⟧ **1** having overhanging or bushy eyebrows **2** frowning

be·fall (bē fôl′, bi-) ***vi., vt.*** **-fell′, -fall′en, -fall′ing** ⟦< OE *be-,* BE- + *feallan,* to fall⟧ to happen or occur (to)

be·fit (bē fit′, bi-) ***vt.*** **-fit′ted, -fit′ting** to be suitable or proper for; be suited to —**be·fit′ting** ***adj.***

be·fog (bē fôg′, -fäg′; bi-) ***vt.*** **-fogged′, -fog′ging 1** to envelop in fog; make foggy **2** to obscure; confuse

be·fore (bē fôr′, bi-) ***adv.*** ⟦OE *be-,* by + *foran,* fore⟧ **1** ahead; in front **2** previously **3** earlier; sooner —***prep.*** **1** ahead of in time, space, order, etc. **2** located in front of **3** in or into the sight, presence, etc. of **4** earlier than; prior to **5** in preference to **6** being considered, judged, or decided by *[*a case *before* the court*]* —***conj.*** **1** earlier than the time that *[*call *before* you go*]* **2** rather than *[*I'd die *before* I'd tell*]*

be·fore′hand′ ***adv., adj.*** ahead of time; in anticipation

be·foul (bē foul′, bi-) ***vt.*** **1** to make filthy **2** to slander

be·friend (bē frend′, bi-) ***vt.*** to act as a friend to

be·fud·dle (bē fud′'l, bi-) ***vt.*** **-dled, -dling** to confuse or stupefy

beg (beg) ***vt., vi.*** **begged, beg′ging** ⟦< Du *beggaert,* religious mendicant⟧ **1** to ask for (alms) **2** to ask earnestly; entreat —**beg off** to ask to be released from —**go begging** to be available but unwanted

be·gan (bē gan′, bi-) ***vi., vt.*** *pt. of* BEGIN

be·get (bē get′, bi-) ***vt.*** **-got′** or [Archaic] **-gat′** (-gat′), **-got′ten** or **-got′, -get′ting** ⟦< OE *begietan,* acquire⟧ **1** to be the father of **2** to produce; cause

beg·gar (beg′ər) ***n.*** **1** one who begs **2** a pauper —***vt.*** **1** to make poor **2** to make (a description, etc.) seem inadequate —**beg′gar·y,** *pl.* **-ies,** ***n.***

beg′gar·ly ***adj.*** very poor, worthless, inadequate, etc.

be·gin (bē gin′, bi-) ***vi., vt.*** **-gan′, -gun′, -gin′ning** ⟦< OE *beginnan*⟧ **1** to start doing, acting, etc. **2** to originate **3** to have a first part or be the first part of

be·gin′ner ***n.*** one just beginning to do or learn something; novice

be·gin′ning ***n.*** **1** a starting **2** the time or place of starting; origin **3** the first part **4** [*usually pl.*] an early stage or example

be·gone (bē gôn′, bi-) ***interj., vi.*** (to) be gone; go away; get out

be·gon·ia (bi gōn′yə) ***n.*** ⟦after M. *Bégon* (1638-1710), Fr patron of science⟧ a tropical plant with showy flowers and ornamental leaves

be·got (bē gät′, bi-) ***vt.*** *pt. & alt. pp. of* BEGET

be·got′ten ***vt.*** *alt. pp. of* BEGET

be·grime (bē grīm′, bi-) ***vt.*** **-grimed′, -grim′ing** to cover with grime; soil

be·grudge (bē gruj′, bi gruj′) ***vt.*** **-grudged′, -grudg′ing 1** to resent another's possession of (something) **2** to give with reluctance —**be·grudg′ing·ly** ***adv.***

be·guile (bē gīl′, bi-) ***vt.*** **-guiled′, -guil′ing 1** to mislead by tricking, etc.; deceive **2** to deprive *of* or cheat *out of* by deceit **3** to pass (time) pleasantly **4** to charm or delight —**be·guile′ment** ***n.*** —**be·guil′er** ***n.***

be·gun (bē gun′, bi-) ***vi., vt.*** *pp. of* BEGIN

be·half (bē haf′, bi-) ***n.*** ⟦OE *be,* by + *healf,* side⟧ support —**in** (or **on**) **behalf of** in the interest of; for

be·have (bē hāv′, bi-) ***vt., vi.*** **-haved′, -hav′ing** ⟦see BE- & HAVE⟧ **1** to conduct (oneself) in a specified way; act **2** to conduct (oneself) properly

be·hav′ior (-yər) ***n.*** way of behaving; conduct or action —**be·hav′ior·al** ***adj.***

behavioral science any of the sciences, as sociology, that study human behavior

be·head (bē hed′, bi-) ***vt.*** to cut off the head of

be·held (bē held′, bi-) ***vt.*** *pt. & pp. of* BEHOLD

be·he·moth (bə hē′məth) ***n.*** ⟦< Heb *behema,* beast⟧ **1** *Bible* some huge animal **2** any huge or powerful animal or thing

be·hest (bē hest′, bi-) ***n.*** ⟦< OE *behæs,* a vow⟧ an order, command, or request

be·hind (bē hīnd′, bi-) ***adv.*** ⟦< OE *behindan*⟧ **1** in or to the rear **2** in a former time, place, etc. **3** in or into arrears **4** slow; late —***prep.*** **1** remaining after **2** in or to the rear of **3** inferior to in position, achievement, etc. **4** later than *[behind* schedule*]* **5** beyond **6** gone by or ended for *[*school was *behind* him now*]* **7** supporting *[behind* their team*]* **8** prompting or instigating *[behind* the plot*]* **9** hidden by *[*what's *behind* this news*]* —***n.*** [Inf.] the buttocks

be·hind′hand′ ***adv., adj.*** behind in payment, time, or progress

be·hold (bē hōld′, bi-) ***vt.*** **-held′, -hold′ing** ⟦< OE *bihealdan*⟧ to look at; see —***interj.*** look! see! —**be·hold′er** ***n.***

be·hold′en ***adj.*** obliged to feel grateful; indebted

be·hoove (bē hōōv′, bi-) ***vt.*** **-hooved′, -hoov′ing** ⟦< OE *behofian,* to need⟧ to be incumbent upon or proper for *[*it *behooves* you to drive carefully*]*

beige (bāzh) ***n., adj.*** ⟦Fr⟧ grayish tan

Bei·jing (bā′jiŋ′, -zhiŋ′) capital of China, in the NE part: pop. 5,531,000

be·ing (bē′iŋ) ***n.*** ⟦see BE⟧ **1** existence; life **2** fundamental nature **3** one that lives or exists **4** personality —**being as** (or **that**) [Inf. or Dial.] since; because —**for the time being** for now

Bei·rut (bā rōōt′) seaport & capital of Lebanon: pop. c. 1,500,000

be·jew·el (bē jōō′əl, bi-) ***vt.*** **-eled** or

-**elled**, -**el·ing** or -**el·ling** to decorate with or as with jewels

be·la·bor (bē lā′bər, bi-) ***vt.*** **1** to beat severely **2** to scold **3** to spend too much time on

Bel·a·rus (bel′ə ro͞os′) country in central Europe: formerly part of the U.S.S.R.: 80,134 sq. mi.; pop. 10,152,000

be·lat·ed (bē lāt′id, bi-) ***adj.*** late or too late —**be·lat′ed·ly** ***adv.***

be·lay (bi lā′) ***vt., vi.*** -**layed′**, -**lay′ing** ⟦< OE *belecgan*, make fast⟧ **1** to make (a rope) secure by winding around a cleat, etc. **2** [Inf.] *Naut.* to hold; stop **3** to secure by a rope

bel can·to (bel′kän′tō) ⟦It⟧ a style of singing with brilliant vocal display

belch (belch) ***vi., vt.*** ⟦OE *bealcian*⟧ **1** to expel (gas) through the mouth from the stomach **2** to throw forth (its contents) violently —***n.*** a belching

be·lea·guer (bē lē′gər, bi-) ***vt.*** ⟦< Du < *be-*, around + *leger*, a camp⟧ **1** to besiege by encircling **2** to beset or harass

Bel·fast (bel′fast) seaport & capital of Northern Ireland: pop. 284,000

bel·fry (bel′frē) ***n.***, *pl.* -**fries** ⟦ult. < OHG⟧ **1** a bell tower **2** the part of a tower that holds the bells

Belg Belgium

Bel·gium (bel′jəm) kingdom in W Europe: 11,778 sq. mi.; pop. 9,979,000 —**Bel′gian** ***adj., n.***

Bel·grade (bel′grād′, -gräd′) capital of Yugoslavia: pop. 1,470,000

be·lie (bē lī′, bi-) ***vt.*** -**lied′**, -**ly′ing** **1** to disguise or misrepresent **2** to leave unfulfilled; disappoint **3** to prove false

be·lief (bə lēf′, bē-) ***n.*** ⟦< OE *geleafa*⟧ **1** conviction that certain things are true **2** religious faith **3** trust or confidence **4** creed or doctrine **5** an opinion; expectation; judgment

be·lieve (bə lēv′, bē-) ***vt.*** -**lieved′**, -**liev′ing** ⟦< OE *geliefan*⟧ **1** to take as true, real, etc. **2** to trust a statement or promise of (a person) **3** to suppose or think —***vi.*** to have trust, faith, or confidence (*in*) —**be·liev′a·ble** ***adj.*** —**be·liev′er** ***n.***

be·lit·tle (bē lit′'l, bi-) ***vt.*** -**tled**, -**tling** to make seem little, less important, etc. —**be·lit′tle·ment** ***n.***

Be·lize (bə lēz′) country in Central America, on the Caribbean: 8,866 sq. mi.; pop. 184,000

bell (bel) ***n.*** ⟦OE *belle*⟧ **1** a hollow, cuplike object, as of metal, which rings when struck **2** the sound of a bell **3** anything shaped like a bell **4** *Naut.* a bell rung to mark the periods of the watch —***vt.*** to attach a bell to —***vi.*** to flare out like a bell

Bell (bel), **Al·ex·an·der Gra·ham** (al′ig zan′dər grā′əm) 1847-1922; U.S. inventor of the telephone, born in Scotland

bel·la·don·na (bel′ə dän′ə) ***n.*** ⟦< It, beautiful lady⟧ **1** a poisonous plant with purplish flowers and black berries **2** ATROPINE

bell′-bot′tom ***adj.*** flared at the ankles, as trousers or slacks: also **bell′-bot′tomed** —***n.*** [*pl.*] bell-bottom trousers

bell′boy′ ***n.*** BELLHOP

belle (bel) ***n.*** ⟦Fr, fem. of *beau*⟧ a pretty woman or girl

belles-let·tres (bel le′tr′, -trə) ***pl.n.*** ⟦Fr⟧ literature as distinguished from technical writings

bell′hop′ ***n.*** one employed by a hotel, club, etc. to carry luggage and do errands

bel·li·cose (bel′i kōs′) ***adj.*** ⟦< L *bellicus*, of war⟧ quarrelsome; warlike —**bel′li·cos′i·ty** (-käs′ə tē) ***n.***

bel·lig·er·ent (bə lij′ər ənt) ***adj.*** ⟦< L *bellum*, war + *gerere*, carry on⟧ **1** at war **2** of war **3** warlike **4** ready to fight or quarrel —***n.*** a belligerent person, group, or nation —**bel·lig′er·ence** ***n.*** —**bel·lig′er·en·cy** ***n.*** —**bel·lig′er·ent·ly** ***adv.***

bell jar a bell-shaped container made of glass, used to keep air, moisture, etc. in or out: also **bell glass**

bel·low (bel′ō) ***vi.*** ⟦< OE *bylgan*⟧ **1** to roar with a reverberating sound, as a bull **2** to cry out loudly, as in anger —***vt.*** to utter loudly or powerfully —***n.*** a bellowing sound

BELLOWS

bel·lows (bel′ōz′) ***n.*** ⟦< ME *beli*, belly⟧ [*with sing. or pl. v.*] **1** a device that forces air out when its sides are pressed together: used in pipe organs, for blowing fires, etc. **2** anything like a bellows

bell pepper a large, sweet red pepper

Bell's palsy ⟦after C. *Bell* (1774-1842), Scot anatomist⟧ a sudden, usually temporary paralysis of the muscles on one side of the face

bell·weth·er (bel′weth′ər) ***n.*** ⟦ME⟧ **1** a male sheep, usually wearing a bell, that leads the flock **2** a leader

bel·ly (bel′ē) ***n.***, *pl.* -**lies** ⟦< OE *belg*, leather bag⟧ **1** the part of the body between the chest and thighs; abdomen **2** the underside of an animal's body **3** the stomach **4** the deep interior, as of a ship —***vt., vi.*** -**lied**, -**ly·ing** to swell out

bel′ly·ache′ ***n.*** pain in the abdomen —***vi.*** -**ached′**, -**ach′ing** [Slang] to complain

bel′ly·but′ton ***n.*** [Inf.] the navel

bel′ly·ful′ (-fo͝ol′) ***n.*** **1** enough or more than enough to eat **2** [Slang] all that one can bear

belly laugh [Inf.] a hearty laugh

be·long (bē lôŋ′, bi-) ***vi.*** ⟦< ME⟧ **1** to have a proper place [*it belongs here*] **2** to be related (*to*) **3** to be a member: with *to* **4** to be owned: with *to*

be·long'ings ***pl.n.*** possessions

be·lov·ed (bi luv'id, -luvd') ***adj.*** ⟦ME *biloven*⟧ dearly loved —***n.*** a dearly loved person

be·low (bi lō') ***adv., adj.*** ⟦see BE- & LOW[1]⟧ **1** in or to a lower place; beneath **2** later (in a book, etc.) **3** in or to hell **4** on earth **5** under in rank, amount, etc. —***prep.*** **1** lower than **2** unworthy of

Bel·shaz·zar (bel shaz'ər) ***n.*** *Bible* the last king of Babylon

belt (belt) ***n.*** ⟦ult. < L *balteus*⟧ **1** a band of leather, etc. worn around the waist **2** any encircling thing like this **3** an endless band for transferring motion, as with pulleys, or conveying things **4** a distinctive area *[the Corn Belt]* **5** [Inf.] a hard blow; punch **6** [Slang] *a)* a gulp, esp. of liquor *b)* a thrill —***vt.*** **1** to encircle or fasten with a belt **2** [Inf.] to hit hard **3** [Inf.] to sing loudly: usually with *out* **4** [Slang] to gulp (liquor): often with *down* —**below the belt** unfair(ly) —**tighten one's belt** to live more thriftily —**under one's belt** [Inf.] as part of one's experience

belt'-tight'en·ing ***n.*** an economizing —***adj.*** involving the cutting of expenses

belt'way' ***n.*** an expressway passing around an urban area

be·moan (bē mōn', bi-) ***vt., vi.*** to lament

be·muse (bē myo͞oz', bi-) ***vt.*** **-mused', -mus'ing** ⟦BE- + MUSE⟧ **1** to confuse or stupefy **2** to preoccupy: usually used in the passive —**be·muse'ment** ***n.***

bench (bench) ***n.*** ⟦OE *benc*⟧ **1** a long, hard seat **2** the place where judges sit in a court **3** [*sometimes* **B-**] *a)* the status of a judge *b)* judges collectively *c)* a law court **4** WORKBENCH **5** a seat on which members of a sports team sit when they are not playing —***vt.*** *Sports* to take (a player) out of a game —**on the bench 1** serving as a judge **2** *Sports* not playing

bench mark a standard in measuring, judging quality, etc.: also **bench'mark'** ***n.***

bench press a weight-lifting exercise, done while one is lying on a bench with the feet on the floor, in which a barbell is pushed upward from the chest —**bench'-press'** ***vt.***

bench warrant an order issued by a judge or court for the arrest of a person

bend[1] (bend) ***vt.*** **bent, bend'ing** ⟦< OE *bendan*, confine with a string⟧ **1** to make curved or crooked **2** to turn, esp. from a straight line **3** to make submit —***vi.*** **1** to turn, esp. from a straight line **2** to yield by curving, as from pressure **3** to curve the body; stoop (*over* or *down*) **4** to give in; yield —***n.*** **1** a bending or being bent **2** a bent part —**bend'a·ble** ***adj.***

bend[2] (bend) ***n.*** ⟦ME < prec.⟧ any of various knots for tying rope

be·neath (bē nēth', bi-) ***adv., adj.*** ⟦OE *beneothan*⟧ in a lower place; underneath —***prep.*** **1** below **2** under; underneath **3** unworthy of *[it is beneath him to cheat]*

ben·e·dic·tion (ben'ə dik'shən) ***n.*** ⟦< L *bene*, well + *dicere*, speak⟧ **1** a blessing **2** an invocation of blessing, esp. at the end of a religious service

ben·e·fac·tion (ben'ə fak'shən) ***n.*** ⟦< L *bene*, well + *facere*, do⟧ **1** the act of helping, esp. by charitable gifts **2** the money or help given

ben·e·fac·tor (ben'ə fak'tər) ***n.*** one who has given help, esp. financially; patron —**ben'e·fac'tress** (-tris) ***fem.n.***

ben·e·fice (ben'ə fis) ***n.*** ⟦< L *beneficium*, a kindness⟧ an endowed church office providing a living for a vicar, rector, etc.

be·nef·i·cence (bə nef'ə səns) ***n.*** ⟦see BENEFACTION⟧ **1** a being kind **2** a charitable act or gift

be·nef'i·cent (-sənt) ***adj.*** showing beneficence; doing or resulting in good —**be·nef'i·cent·ly** ***adv.***

ben·e·fi·cial (ben'ə fish'əl) ***adj.*** producing benefits; advantageous; favorable —**ben'e·fi'cial·ly** ***adv.***

ben'e·fi'ci·ar'y (-fish'ē er'ē, -fish'ər ē) ***n.***, *pl.* **-ar'ies** anyone receiving or to receive benefits, as funds from a will or insurance policy

ben·e·fit (ben'ə fit) ***n.*** ⟦see BENEFACTION⟧ **1** anything contributing to improvement; advantage **2** [*often pl.*] payments made by an insurance company, public agency, etc. as during sickness or retirement, or for death **3** a public performance, bazaar, etc. the proceeds of which are to help some person or cause —***vt.*** **-fit·ed, -fit·ing** to help; aid —***vi.*** to receive advantage; profit

be·nev·o·lence (bə nev'ə ləns) ***n.*** ⟦< L *bene*, well + *volens*, wishing⟧ **1** an inclination to do good; kindliness **2** a kindly, charitable act —**be·nev'o·lent** ***adj.*** —**be·nev'o·lent·ly** ***adv.***

Ben·gal (ben gôl'), **Bay of** part of the Indian Ocean, east of India

be·night·ed (bē nīt'id, bi-) ***adj.*** **1** surrounded by darkness **2** not enlightened; ignorant

be·nign (bi nīn') ***adj.*** ⟦< L *benignus*, good, lit., well-born⟧ **1** good-natured; kindly **2** favorable; beneficial **3** *Med.* not malignant; specif., not cancerous —**be·nign'ly** ***adv.***

be·nig·nant (bi nig'nənt) ***adj.*** ⟦< prec.⟧ **1** kindly or gracious **2** BENIGN (senses 2 & 3)

be·nig'ni·ty (-nə tē) ***n.*** **1** kindliness **2** *pl.* **-ties** a kind act

Be·nin (be nēn') country in WC Africa: 43,484 sq. mi.; pop. 4,855,000

ben·i·son (ben'ə zən, -sən) ***n.*** ⟦OFr < L: see BENEDICTION⟧ [Archaic] a blessing

bent[1] (bent) ***vt., vi. pt. & pp. of*** BEND[1] —***adj.*** **1** curved or crooked **2** strongly determined: with *on* **3** [Slang] *a)* dishonest *b)* eccentric; odd —***n.*** a natural leaning; propensity

bent[2] (bent) ***n.*** ⟦OE *beonot*⟧ a dense, low-growing grass that spreads by runners, used for lawns: also **bent'grass'**

bent'wood' ***adj.*** of furniture made of wood permanently bent into various forms

be·numb (bē num', bi-) ***vt.*** **1** to make

numb **2** to deaden the mind, will, etc. of

ben·zene (ben′zēn, ben zēn′) ***n.*** ⟦ult. < Ar *lubān jāwī*, incense of Java⟧ a clear, flammable, poisonous, aromatic liquid used as a solvent, in plastics, etc.

ben·zo·caine (ben′zō kān′, -zə-) ***n.*** ⟦< BENZENE & COCAINE⟧ a white, odorless powder used in ointments as a local anesthetic and for protection against sunburn

be·queath (bē kwēth′, -kwēth′; bi-) ***vt.*** ⟦< OE *be-*, BE- + *cwethan*, say⟧ **1** to leave (property) to another by one's will **2** to hand down; pass on

be·quest′ (-kwest′) ***n.*** **1** a bequeathing **2** anything bequeathed

be·rate (bē rāt′, bi-) ***vt.*** **-rat′ed, -rat′ing** ⟦BE- + RATE²⟧ to scold severely

Ber·ber (bur′bər) ***n.*** **1** a member of a Muslim people of N Africa **2** the language of this people —***adj.*** of the Berbers

be·reave (bē rēv′, bi-) ***vt.*** **-reaved′** or **-reft′** (-reft′), **-reav′ing** ⟦< OE *be-*, BE- + *reafian*, rob⟧ **1** to deprive: now usually in the pp. *bereft [bereft* of hope*]* **2** to leave forlorn, as by death —**be·reave′ment** ***n.***

be·ret (bə rā′) ***n.*** ⟦< Fr < L *birrus*, a hood⟧ a flat, round cap of felt, wool, etc.

berg (burg) ***n.*** ICEBERG

ber·i·ber·i (ber′ē ber′ē) ***n.*** ⟦Sinhalese, intens. of *beri*, weakness⟧ a disease caused by lack of vitamin B_1 and characterized by nerve disorders, etc.

Ber·ing Sea (ber′iŋ) part of the N Pacific, between Siberia & Alaska

Bering Strait strait joining the Bering Sea with the Arctic Ocean

Berke·ley (burk′lē) city in California, near San Francisco: pop. 103,000

Ber·lin (bər lin′) city & state of E Germany; capital of Germany (1871-1945; 1990-): formerly divided into four sectors of occupation, the eastern sector (*East Berlin*), capital of East Germany, and three western sectors (*West Berlin*), a state of West Germany: pop. 3,305,000

berm (burm) ***n.*** ⟦< MDu *baerm*⟧ **1** a ledge **2** [Dial.] a shoulder, as along the edge of a paved road

Ber·mu·da (bər myo͞o′də) group of British islands in the W Atlantic

Bermuda shorts knee-length pants: also **ber·mu′das** ***pl.n.***

Bern or **Berne** (burn) capital of Switzerland: pop. 134,000

ber·ry (ber′ē) ***n.***, *pl.* **-ries** ⟦OE *berie*⟧ **1** any small, juicy, fleshy fruit, as a strawberry **2** the dry seed of various plants, as a coffee bean —***vi.*** **-ried, -ry·ing** **1** to produce berries **2** to pick berries —**ber′ry·like′** ***adj.***

ber·serk (bər surk′, -zurk′; bə-) ***adj.***, ***adv.*** ⟦ON *berserkr*, warrior⟧ in or into a violent rage or frenzy

berth (burth) ***n.*** ⟦< BEAR¹ + -TH¹⟧ **1** a place where a ship anchors or moors **2** a position, job, etc. **3** a built-in bed, as on a ship or train —***vt.*** to put into or furnish with a berth —***vi.*** to occupy a berth —**give (a) wide berth to** to keep well clear of

ber·yl (ber′əl) ***n.*** ⟦< Gr *bēryllos*⟧ a very hard mineral of which emerald and aquamarine are two varieties

be·ryl·li·um (bə ril′ē əm) ***n.*** ⟦< L *beryllus*, beryl⟧ a hard, silver-white, metallic chemical element used in forming alloys

be·seech (bē sēch′, bi-) ***vt.*** **-sought′** or **-seeched′, -seech′ing** ⟦< OE *be-* + *secan*, seek⟧ **1** to ask (someone) earnestly; entreat **2** to beg for —**be·seech′ing·ly** ***adv.***

be·seem (bē sēm′, bi-) ***vi.*** [Archaic] to be suitable or appropriate (to)

be·set (bē set′, bi-) ***vt.*** **-set′, -set′ting** ⟦< OE *be-* + *settan*, set⟧ **1** to attack from all sides; harass **2** to surround or hem in

be·set′ting ***adj.*** constantly harassing

be·side (bē sīd′, bi-) ***prep.*** ⟦OE *bi sidan*⟧ **1** at the side of; near **2** in comparison with *[beside* yours my share seems small*]* **3** in addition to **4** other than **5** not relevant to *[*that's *beside* the point*]* —**beside oneself** wild or upset, as with fear or rage

be·sides′ (-sīdz′) ***adv.*** **1** in addition **2** except for that mentioned **3** moreover —***prep.*** **1** in addition to **2** other than

be·siege (bē sēj′, bi-) ***vt.*** **-sieged′, -sieg′ing** **1** to hem in with armed forces **2** to crowd around **3** to overwhelm, harass, etc. *[*she was *besieged* with queries*]*

be·smear (bē smir′, bi-) ***vt.*** ⟦OE *bismerian*⟧ to smear over; soil

be·smirch (bē smurch′, bi-) ***vt.*** to soil

be·som (bē′zəm) ***n.*** ⟦OE *besma*⟧ a broom, esp. one made of twigs tied to a handle

be·sot (bē sät′, bi-) ***vt.*** **-sot′ted, -sot′ting** to stupefy, as with liquor —**be·sot′ted** ***adj.***

be·sought (bē sôt′, bi-) ***vt.*** *alt. pt. & alt. pp. of* BESEECH

be·span·gle (bē spaŋ′gəl, bi-) ***vt.*** **-gled, -gling** to cover with or as with spangles

be·spat·ter (bē spat′ər, bi-) ***vt.*** to spatter, as with mud or slander

be·speak (bē spēk′, bi-) ***vt.*** **-spoke′** (-spōk′), **-spo′ken** or **-spoke′, -speak′ing** **1** to speak for in advance; reserve **2** to be indicative of; show

best (best) ***adj.*** ⟦OE *betst*⟧ **1** *superl. of* GOOD **2** most excellent **3** most suitable, desirable, etc. **4** largest *[*the *best* part of a day*]* —***adv.*** **1** *superl. of* WELL² **2** in the most excellent manner **3** in the highest degree —***n.*** **1** the most excellent person, thing, etc. **2** the utmost *[*she did her *best]* —***vt.*** to defeat or outdo —**all for the best** turning out to be good after all —**at best** under the most favorable conditions —**get the best of** **1** to defeat **2** to outwit —**make the best of** to do as well as one can with

bes·tial (bes′chəl, -tyəl; *often* bēs′-) ***adj.*** ⟦< L *bestia*, beast⟧ like a beast; savage, brutal, etc. —**bes·ti·al·i·ty** (bes′chē al′ə tē, -tē-; *often* bēs′-), *pl.* **-ties**, ***n.***

bes·tial·ize (bes′chəl īz′, -tyəl-; *often* bēs′-) ***vt.*** **-ized′, -iz′ing** to make bestial

bes·ti·ar·y (bes′tē er′ē) ***n.***, *pl.* **-ies** ⟦< L *bestia,* beast⟧ a medieval book with fables about real or mythical animals

be·stir (bē stur′, bi-) ***vt.*** **-stirred′, -stir′ring** to stir to action; busy (oneself)

best man the principal attendant of the bridegroom at a wedding

be·stow (bē stō′, bi-) ***vt.*** ⟦see BE- & STOW⟧ to present as a gift: often with *on* or *upon* —**be·stow′al** ***n.***

be·strew (bē strōō′, bi-) ***vt.*** **-strewed′, -strewed′** or **-strewn′, -strew′ing 1** to cover (a surface) *with* something **2** to strew or scatter about a surface

be·stride (bē strīd′, bi-) ***vt.*** **-strode′** (-strōd′), **-strid′den** (-strid′'n), **-strid′ing** to sit on, mount, or stand over with a leg on each side

bet (bet) ***n.*** ⟦prob. < ABET⟧ **1** an agreement in which the person proved wrong about the outcome of something will do or pay what is stipulated **2** the thing or sum thus staked **3** a person or thing with regard to its likelihood of bringing about some result *[*a good *bet* to win the election*]* —***vt., vi.*** **bet** or **bet′ted, bet′ting 1** to declare as in a bet **2** to stake (money, etc.) in a bet with (someone)

be·ta (bāt′ə) ***n.*** the second letter of the Greek alphabet (Β, β)

beta blocker a drug used to control heartbeat, treat hypertension, etc.

beta car·o·tene (kar′ə tēn′) a hydrocarbon found in butter, carrots, etc. and converted by the liver into vitamin A

be·take (bē tāk′, bi-) ***vt.*** **-took′** (-to͝ok′), **-tak′en, -tak′ing** ⟦ME *bitaken*⟧ to go (used reflexively) *[*he *betook* himself to his castle*]*

beta particle an electron or positron ejected from the nucleus of an atom during radioactive disintegration

beta ray a stream of beta particles

be·tel nut (bēt′'l) ⟦Port < Malayalam *veṭṭilai*⟧ the fruit of a palm (**betel palm**), chewed together with lime and the leaves of a pepper plant (**betel pepper**) by some Asians as a mild stimulant

be·think (bē thiŋk′, bi-) [Archaic] ***vt.*** **-thought′** (-thôt′), **-think′ing** ⟦OE *bethencan*⟧ to remind (oneself)

Beth·le·hem (beth′lə hem′) ancient town in Judea: traditionally regarded as Jesus' birthplace

be·tide (bē tīd′, bi-) ***vi., vt.*** **-tid′ed, -tid′ing** ⟦< ME *be-*, BE- + *tiden*, happen⟧ to happen (to); befall

be·times (bē tīmz′, bi-) ***adv.*** [Archaic] **1** early or early enough **2** promptly

be·to·ken (bē tō′kən, bi-) ***vt.*** ⟦ME *betocnen*⟧ **1** to be a token or sign of **2** to show beforehand; presage

be·tray (bē trā′, bi-) ***vt.*** ⟦< L *tradere,* hand over⟧ **1** to help the enemy of (one's country, etc.) **2** to expose treacherously **3** to fail to uphold *[*to *betray* a trust*]* **4** to deceive; specif., to seduce and then desert **5** to reveal unknowingly **6** to disclose (secrets, etc.) —**be·tray′al** ***n.*** —**be·tray′er** ***n.***

be·troth (bē trōth′; -trôth′, bi-) ***vt.*** ⟦< ME: see BE- & TRUTH⟧ to promise in marriage —**be·troth′al** ***n.***

be·trothed′ (-trōthd′, -trôtht′) ***adj.*** engaged to be married —***n.*** the person to whom one is engaged

bet·ta (bet′ə) ***n.*** ⟦ModL⟧ a brightly colored gourami of SE Asia: often an aquarium fish

bet·ter (bet′ər) ***adj.*** ⟦OE *betera*⟧ **1** *compar. of* GOOD **2** more excellent **3** more suitable, desirable, etc. **4** larger *[*the *better* part of a day*]* **5** improved in health —***adv.*** **1** *compar. of* WELL[2] **2** in a more excellent manner **3** in a higher degree **4** more —***n.*** **1** a person superior in authority, etc. **2** a more excellent thing, condition, etc. —***vt.*** **1** to outdo; surpass **2** to improve —**better off** in a better situation —**get** (or **have**) **the better of 1** to outdo **2** to outwit —**had better** ought to

bet′ter·ment (-mənt) ***n.*** a bettering; improvement

bet·tor (bet′ər) ***n.*** one who bets: also **bet′ter**

be·tween (bē twēn′, bi-) ***prep.*** ⟦OE *betweonum*⟧ **1** in the space, time, etc. that separates (two things) **2** connecting *[*a bond *between* friends*]* **3** by the joint action of **4** possessed jointly by **5** from one or the other of *[*choose *between* us*]* **6** involving *Between* is sometimes used of more than two if each part is seen as individually related to each of the others *[*peace *between* nations*]* —***adv.*** in an intermediate space, time, etc. —**between ourselves** as a secret: also **between you and me**

be·twixt (bē twikst′, bi-) ***prep., adv.*** ⟦< OE *be,* by + *twegen,* twain⟧ between: archaic except in **betwixt and between,** in an intermediate position

BeV or **bev** (bev) *abbrev.* one billion (10^9) electron-volts

bev·el (bev′əl) ***n.*** ⟦< ?⟧ **1** a tool for measuring or marking angles, etc. **2** an angle other than a right angle **3** sloping part or surface —***adj.*** beveled —***vt.*** **-eled** or **-elled, -el·ing** or **-el·ling** to cut to an angle other than a right angle —***vi.*** to slope at an angle; slant

bevel gear a gearwheel meshed with another at an angle

bev·er·age (bev′ər ij′, bev′rij) ***n.*** ⟦< L *bibere,* to drink⟧ any liquid for drinking, esp. one other than water

bev·y (bev′ē) ***n.***, *pl.* **-ies** ⟦ME *bevey*⟧ **1** a group, esp. of girls or women **2** a flock: now used chiefly of quail

be·wail (bē wāl′, bi-) ***vt.*** to wail over; lament; mourn

be·ware (bē wer′, bi-) ***vi., vt.*** **-wared′, -war′ing** ⟦prob. < OE *bewarian,* keep watch⟧ to be wary or careful (of)

be·wigged (bē wigd′, bi-) ***adj.*** wearing a wig

be·wil·der (bē wil′dər, bi-) ***vt.*** ⟦ult. < OE *wilde,* wild⟧ to confuse hopelessly; puzzle —**be·wil′der·ing·ly** ***adv.*** —**be·wil′der·ment** ***n.***

be·witch (bē wich′, bi-) ***vt.*** ⟦< OE *wicca,* sorcerer⟧ **1** to cast a spell over **2** to attract and delight greatly —**be·witch′ing** ***adj.***

bey (bā) ***n.*** ⟦Turk⟧ a Turkish title of respect and former title of rank

be·yond (bē änd′) ***prep.*** ⟦< OE *be,* by + *geond*, yonder⟧ **1** farther on than; past **2** later than **3** outside the reach of *[beyond* help*]* **4** more than **—*adv.*** farther away **—the (great) beyond** whatever follows death

bez·el (bez′əl) ***n.*** ⟦< ?⟧ **1** a sloping surface, as the cutting edge of a chisel **2** the slanting faces of the upper part of a cut gem **3** the groove and flange holding a gem, watch crystal, etc. in place

Bhu·tan (bo͞o tän′) kingdom in the Himalayas, SC Asia: 18,000 sq. mi.; pop. 600,000

Bi *Chem. symbol for* bismuth

bi- ⟦L⟧ *prefix* **1** having two **2** doubly **3** happening every two (specified periods) **4** happening twice during every (specified period) **5** using two or both **6** joining or involving two

bi·an·nu·al (bī an′yo͞o əl) ***adj.*** coming twice a year; semiannual **—bi·an′nu·al·ly *adv.***

bi·as (bī′əs) ***n.***, *pl.* **-as·es** ⟦MFr *biais,* a slant⟧ **1** a slanting or diagonal line, cut or sewn in cloth **2** partiality; prejudice **—*adj.*** slanting; diagonal **—*adv.*** diagonally **—*vt.*** **-ased** or **-assed, -as·ing** or **-as·sing** to prejudice **—on the bias** diagonally

bi·ath·lon (bī ath′län′) ***n.*** ⟦BI- + Gr *athlon,* contest⟧ a winter sports event combining cross-country skiing and rifle marksmanship

bib (bib) ***n.*** ⟦< L *bibere,* to drink⟧ **1** a cloth or plastic cover tied under a child's chin at meals **2** the upper front part of an apron

Bib *abbrev.* **1** Bible **2** Biblical

bibb lettuce (bib) ⟦after J. *Bibb* (1789-1884), who developed it⟧ a type of lettuce with loose heads of crisp, dark-green leaves

Bi·ble (bī′bəl) ***n.*** ⟦< Gr *biblos*, papyrus < *Byblos,* Phoenician city that exported papyrus⟧ **1** the sacred book of Christianity; Old Testament and New Testament **2** the Holy Scriptures of Judaism; Old Testament **3** [**b-**] any book regarded as authoritative or official **—bib·li·cal** or **Bib·li·cal** (bib′li kəl) ***adj.***

biblio- ⟦< Gr *biblion,* book⟧ *combining form* book, books *[bibliophile]*

bib·li·og·ra·phy (bib′lē äg′rə fē) ***n.***, *pl.* **-phies** a list of writings on a given subject or by a given author, or of those used by the author of a given work **—bib′li·og′ra·pher *n.* —bib′li·o·graph′ic** (-ə graf′ik) ***adj.***

bib′li·o·phile′ (-ə fīl′) ***n.*** a person who loves or collects books

bib·u·lous (bib′yo͞o ləs) ***adj.*** ⟦< L *bibere,* to drink⟧ addicted to or fond of alcoholic beverages

bi·cam·er·al (bī kam′ər əl) ***adj.*** ⟦< BI- + L *camera*, chamber⟧ having two legislative chambers

bi·car·bon·ate of soda (bī kär′bən it) SODIUM BICARBONATE

bi·cen·ten·ni·al (bī′sen ten′ē əl) ***adj.*** happening once in every 200 years **—*n.*** a 200th anniversary

bi·ceps (bī′seps′) ***n.***, *pl.* **-ceps** or **-ceps′es** ⟦< L < *bis,* two + *caput*, head⟧ a muscle with two points of origin; esp., the large muscle in the front of the upper arm

bick·er (bik′ər) ***vi.*** ⟦ME *bikeren*⟧ to squabble; quarrel **—bick′er·er *n.***

bi·con·cave (bī kän′kāv′) ***adj.*** concave on both surfaces *[a biconcave* lens*]*

bi·con′vex′ (-veks′) ***adj.*** convex on both surfaces *[a biconvex* lens*]*

bi·cus·pid (bī kus′pid) ***adj.*** ⟦< BI- + L *cuspis*, pointed end⟧ having two points **—*n.*** any of eight adult teeth with two-pointed crowns

bi·cy·cle (bī′sik′əl, -si kəl) ***n.*** ⟦Fr: see BI- & CYCLE⟧ a vehicle consisting of a metal frame on two large wheels, with handlebars, foot pedals, and a seat **—*vi.*** **-cled, -cling** to ride or travel on a bicycle **—*vt.*** **1** to carry on or as on a bicycle **2** to travel over by bicycle **—bi′cy′clist *n.***

bid (bid) ***vt.*** **bade** or **bid, bid′den** or **bid, bid′ding** ⟦< OE *biddan*, to urge & *beodan*, to command⟧ **1** to command, ask, or tell **2** to state (an amount) as the price one will pay or accept **3** to express *[*to *bid* farewell*]* **4** *Card Games* to state (a number of tricks) and declare (trump) **—*vi.*** to make a bid **—*n.*** **1** a bidding **2** an amount bid **3** a chance to bid **4** an attempt or try (*for*) **5** [Inf.] an invitation **—bid fair** to seem likely **—bid′der *n.***

bid·dy (bid′ē) ***n.***, *pl.* **-dies** ⟦< ?⟧ **1** a hen **2** [Inf.] an elderly woman regarded as annoying, gossipy, etc.: usually **old biddy**

bide (bīd) ***vi.*** **bode** or **bid′ed, bid′ed, bid′ing** ⟦OE *bidan*⟧ [Now Chiefly Dial.] **1** to stay; continue **2** to dwell **3** to wait **—*vt.*** [Now Chiefly Dial.] to endure or tolerate **—bide one's time** to wait patiently for an opportunity *[*she *bided* her time*]*

bi·det (bē dā′) ***n.*** ⟦Fr⟧ a low, bowl-shaped bathroom fixture, with running water, for bathing the crotch

bi·en·ni·al (bī en′ē əl) ***adj.*** ⟦< L *bi-*, BI- + *annus,* year⟧ **1** happening every two years **2** lasting for two years **—*n.*** **1** a biennial event **2** *Bot.* a plant that lasts two years **—bi·en′ni·al·ly *adv.***

bier (bir) ***n.*** ⟦OE *bær*⟧ a portable framework on which a coffin is placed

bi·fo·cals (bī′fō′kəlz) ***pl.n.*** eyeglasses with lenses having one part ground for close focus and the other for distant focus

bi·fur·cate (bī′fər kāt′) ***vt., vi.*** **-cat′ed, -cat′ing** ⟦< L *bi-*, BI- + *furca*, a fork⟧ to divide into two parts or branches **—bi′fur·ca′tion *n.***

big (big) ***adj.*** **big′ger, big′gest** ⟦ME⟧ **1** of great size; large **2** great in amount or force **3** full-grown **4** elder *[*his *big* sister*]* **5** noticeably pregnant (*with*) **6** loud **7** important *[big* plans*]* **8** famous **9** extravagant *[big* talk*]* **10** noble *[a big* heart*]* **—*adv.*** [Inf.] **1** boastfully **2** impressively **—big′ness *n.***

big·a·my (big′ə mē) ***n.*** ⟦< L *bi-*, BI- + Gr *gamos,* marriage⟧ the crime of marrying a second time when one is already legally married **—big′a·mist *n.* —big′a·**

mous *adj.* —**big'a·mous·ly** *adv.*

big'-bang' theory a theory that the expansion of the universe began with a gigantic explosion (**big bang**) between 12 and 20 billion years ago

Big Dipper, the a dipper-shaped group of bright stars in the northern sky

big game 1 large wild animals hunted for sport, as lions, tigers, moose, etc. 2 the object of any important or dangerous undertaking

big'heart'ed (-här'tid) *adj.* quick to give or forgive; generous —**big'heart'ed·ly** *adv.*

big'horn' *n., pl.* **-horns'** or **-horn'** a Rocky Mountain wild sheep with large horns

bight (bīt) *n.* ⟦OE *byht,* a bend⟧ 1 a slack part in a rope 2 a curve in a coastline 3 a bay formed by such a curve

big'mouth' *n.* [Slang] a person who talks too much, esp. in an opinionated way

big·ot (big'ət) *n.* ⟦Fr < ?⟧ 1 one who holds blindly and intolerantly to a particular creed, opinion, etc. 2 a prejudiced person —**big'ot·ed** *adj.* —**big'ot·ry** *n.*

big shot [Slang] an important or influential person: also **big wheel**

big'-time' *adj., adv.* [Slang] at, of, or to a very great degree, extent, etc.

bike (bīk) *n.* [Inf.] 1 a bicycle 2 a motorcycle —**bik'er** *n.*

bi·ki·ni (bi kē'nē) *n.* ⟦Fr after *Bikini,* Pacific atoll⟧ 1 a very brief two-piece swimsuit for women 2 very brief, legless underpants or swimming trunks

bi·lat·er·al (bī lat'ər əl) *adj.* 1 of, having, or involving two sides, factions, etc. 2 affecting both sides equally; reciprocal [a *bilateral* pact] —**bi·lat'er·al·ly** *adv.*

bile (bīl) *n.* ⟦Fr < L *bilis*⟧ 1 the bitter, greenish fluid secreted by the liver: it aids digestion 2 bad temper; anger

bilge (bilj) *n.* ⟦var. of BULGE⟧ 1 the rounded lower part of a ship's hold 2 stagnant water that collects there: also **bilge water** 3 [Slang] nonsense

bi·lin·gual (bī liŋ'gwəl) *adj.* ⟦< L *bi-,* BI- + *lingua,* tongue⟧ of, in, or able to use two languages —**bi·lin'gual·ism'** *n.*

bil·ious (bil'yəs) *adj.* ⟦< L *bilis,* bile⟧ 1 having or appearing to have some ailment of the bile or liver 2 bad-tempered

bilk (bilk) *vt.* ⟦? < BALK⟧ to cheat or swindle; defraud —**bilk'er** *n.*

bill[1] (bil) *n.* ⟦< ML *bulla,* sealed document⟧ 1 a statement of charges for goods or services; invoice 2 a list, as a menu or theater program 3 a poster or handbill 4 a draft of a proposed law 5 a bill of exchange 6 a piece of paper money 7 *Law* a written declaration of charges or complaints filed —*vt.* 1 to make out a bill of (items) 2 to present a statement of charges to 3 *a*) to advertise by bills *b*) to book (a performer) —**fill the bill** [Inf.] to meet the requirements —**bill'a·ble** *adj.*

bill[2] (bil) *n.* ⟦OE *bile*⟧ 1 the projecting jaws of a bird, usually pointed; beak 2 a beaklike part of the mouth, as that of a turtle —*vi.* to touch bills together —**bill and coo** to kiss, talk softly, etc. in a loving way

bill'board' *n.* a signboard, usually outdoors, for advertising posters

bil·let (bil'it) *n.* ⟦see BILL[1]⟧ 1 *a*) a written order to provide lodging for military personnel *b*) the lodging 2 a position, job, or situation —*vt.* to assign to lodging by billet

bil·let-doux (bē'yā do͞o') *n., pl.* **bil·lets-doux** (bē'yā do͞o') ⟦Fr, sweet letter⟧ a love letter

bill·fold (bil'fōld') *n.* a wallet

bil·liard (bil'yərd) *adj.* of or for billiards

bil'liards (-yərdz) *n.* ⟦< Fr *billard,* orig., a cue⟧ a game played with a cue and three hard balls on a table with raised, cushioned edges

bill·ing (bil'iŋ) *n.* 1 the listing of actors' names on a theater marquee, etc. 2 the order in which the names are listed

bil·lings·gate (bil'iŋz gāt') *n.* ⟦after a London fish market⟧ foul, vulgar, abusive talk

bil·lion (bil'yən) *n.* ⟦Fr < *bi-,* two + (*mi*)*llion*⟧ 1 a thousand millions (1,000,000,000) 2 *former Brit. term for* TRILLION (a million millions) —**bil'lionth** *adj., n.*

bil'lion·aire' (-yə ner') *n.* a person whose wealth comes to at least a billion dollars, pounds, francs, etc.

bill of exchange a written order to pay a certain sum of money to the person named

bill of fare a menu

bill of lading a receipt issued to a shipper by a carrier, describing the goods to be shipped

Bill of Rights the first ten amendments to the U.S. Constitution, which guarantee civil liberties

bill of sale a written statement transferring ownership of something by sale

bil·low (bil'ō) *n.* ⟦ON *bylgja*⟧ 1 a large wave 2 any large swelling mass or surge, as of smoke —*vi.* to surge or swell in a billow —**bil'low·y, -i·er, -i·est,** *adj.*

bil·ly (bil'ē) *n., pl.* **-lies** ⟦ult. < OFr *bille,* tree trunk⟧ a club, esp. a policeman's heavy stick: in full **billy club**

billy goat a male goat

Bi·lox·i (bə luk'sē, -läk'sē) city in SE Mississippi, on the Gulf of Mexico: pop. 46,000

bi·me·tal·lic (bī'mə tal'ik) *adj.* ⟦< Fr *bi-,* BI- + *métallique,* metallic⟧ 1 of, containing, or using two metals 2 of or based on bimetallism

bi·met·al·lism (bī met''l iz'əm) *n.* the use of two metals, esp. gold and silver, as the monetary standard, with fixed values in relation to each other

bi·month·ly (bī munth'lē) *adj., adv.* 1 once every two months 2 [Now Rare] twice a month

bin (bin) *n.* ⟦OE, crib⟧ a box or enclosed space used for storage

bi·na·ry (bī′nə rē) ***adj.*** ⟦< L *bis,* double⟧ **1** made up of two parts; double **2** designating or of a number system in which the base used is two, each number being expressed by using only two digits, specif. 0 and 1 —***n.,*** *pl.* **-ries** something with two parts

bi·na·tion·al (bī nash′ə nəl) ***adj.*** involving two nations or two nationalities

bin·au·ral (bī nôr′əl) ***adj.*** **1** of or involving both ears **2** of or using two sources of sound

bind (bīnd) ***vt.*** **bound, bind′ing** ⟦< OE *bindan*⟧ **1** to tie together, as with rope **2** to hold or restrain **3** to encircle with a belt, etc. **4** to bandage: often with *up* **5** to constipate **6** to reinforce or ornament the edges of by a band, as of tape **7** to fasten together the pages of (a book) and enclose in a cover **8** to obligate by duty, love, etc. **9** to compel, as by oath, legal restraint, or contract —***vi.*** **1** to do the act of binding **2** to be or become tight or stiff **3** to stick together **4** to be obligatory or binding in force —***n.*** **1** anything that binds **2** [Inf.] a difficult or restrictive situation

bind′er ***n.*** **1** one that binds **2** a substance that binds, as tar **3** a cover for holding sheets of paper together

bind′er·y ***n.,*** *pl.* **-er·ies** a place where books are bound

bind′ing ***n.*** a thing that binds, as a band, a tape, the covers and backing of a book, or a cohesive substance —***adj.*** that binds, obligates, etc.

binge (binj) [Inf.] ***n.*** unrestrained activity; spree —***vi.*** **binged, binge′ing** to indulge without restraint

bin·go (biŋ′gō) ***n.*** a game played with cards having rows of numbered squares: the first player with an entire row drawn by lot wins —***interj.*** used to signify sudden success, etc.

bin·na·cle (bin′ə kəl) ***n.*** ⟦ult. < L *habitaculum,* dwelling place⟧ the case holding a ship's compass

bin·oc·u·lar (bī näk′yə lər; *for n.,* bi-) ***adj.*** ⟦< L *bini,* double + *oculus,* eye⟧ using, or for, both eyes —***n.*** [*pl.*] field glasses

bi·no·mi·al (bī nō′mē əl) ***n.*** ⟦< L *bi-,* BI- + Gr *nomos,* law⟧ **1** *Math.* an expression consisting of two terms connected by a plus or minus sign **2** a two-word scientific name of a plant or animal, indicating the genus and species

bi·o (bī′ō) ***n.,*** *pl.* **bios** [Inf.] a biography

bio- ⟦Gr < *bios,* life⟧ *combining form* life, of living things

bi·o·chem·is·try (bī′ō kem′is trē) ***n.*** the study of the chemistry of life processes in plants and animals —**bi′o·chem′ist** ***n.***

bi·o·cide (bī′ō sīd′) ***n.*** ⟦BIO- + -CIDE⟧ a substance that kills microorganisms

bi·o·de·grad·a·ble (bī′ō di grā′də bəl) ***adj.*** ⟦BIO- + *degrad(e),* decompose + -ABLE⟧ capable of being readily decomposed by the action of microbes, as some detergents

bi′o·di·ver′si·ty ***n.*** variety in the living things of a particular area

bi′o·feed′back′ ***n.*** a technique of seeking to control certain emotional states by training oneself, using electronic devices, to modify autonomic body functions, such as heartbeat

biog *abbrev.* **1** biographical **2** biography

bi·og·ra·phy (bī äg′rə fē) ***n.,*** *pl.* **-phies** ⟦< Gr: see BIO- & -GRAPHY⟧ a person's life story written by another —**bi·og′ra·pher** ***n.*** —**bi·o·graph·i·cal** (bī′ə graf′i kəl) ***adj.***

biol *abbrev.* **1** biological **2** biology

biological warfare the use of toxic microorganisms, etc. in war

bi·ol·o·gy (bī äl′ə jē) ***n.*** ⟦see BIO- & -LOGY⟧ the science that deals with the origin, history, characteristics, etc. of plants and animals —**bi·o·log·i·cal** (bī′ə läj′i kəl) ***adj.*** —**bi′o·log′i·cal·ly** ***adv.*** —**bi·ol′o·gist** ***n.***

bi·on·ic (bī än′ik) ***adj.*** ⟦see fol.⟧ **1** of bionics **2** having an artificial body part or parts, as in science fiction, so as to enhance strength, etc.

bi·on′ics ***n.*** ⟦BI(O)- + (ELECTR)ONICS⟧ the science of designing instruments or systems modeled after living organisms

bi·o·phys·ics (bī′ō fiz′iks) ***n.*** the study of biological phenomena in relation to physics —**bi′o·phys′i·cal** ***adj.*** —**bi′o·phys′i·cist** ***n.***

bi·o·pic (bī′ō pik′) ***n.*** [Inf.] a film dramatizing the life of a famous person

bi·op·sy (bī′äp′sē) ***n.,*** *pl.* **-sies** ⟦< BI(O)- + Gr *opsis,* a sight⟧ *Med.* the removal of bits of living tissue for diagnosis

bi·o·rhythm (bī′ō rith′əm) ***n.*** any biological cycle that involves periodic changes in blood pressure, body temperature, etc.

bi·o·tin (bī′ə tin) ***n.*** ⟦< Gr *bios,* life⟧ a factor of the vitamin B group

bi·par·ti·san (bī pär′tə zən) ***adj.*** of, representing, or supported by two parties —**bi·par′ti·san·ship′** ***n.***

bi·par·tite (bī pär′tīt′) ***adj.*** ⟦< L *bi-,* BI- + *partire,* to divide⟧ **1** having two parts **2** involving two

bi·ped (bī′ped′) ***n.*** ⟦< L *bi-,* BI- + *pes,* foot⟧ any two-footed animal —**bi·ped′al** ***adj.***

bi·plane (bī′plān′) ***n.*** an airplane with two sets of wings, one above the other

bi·po·lar (bī pō′lər) ***adj.*** **1** of or involving poles or polarity **2** having alternating periods of mania and mental depression

bi·ra·cial (bī rā′shəl) ***adj.*** consisting of or involving two races

birch (burch) ***n.*** ⟦OE *beorc*⟧ **1** a tree having smooth bark in thin layers, and hard, closegrained wood **2** its wood **3** a bunch of birch twigs used for whipping —***vt.*** to flog

bird (burd) ***n.*** ⟦< OE *bridd,* young bird⟧ a warmblooded vertebrate with feathers and wings —***vi.*** to observe wild birds in their habitat —**birds of a feather** people with the same traits or tastes —**for the birds** [Slang] ridiculous, foolish, etc.

bird′er ***n.*** a bird-watcher

bird′ie ***n.*** *Golf* a score of one stroke under par for a hole

bird′ing ***n.*** bird-watching

bird's′-eye′ ***adj.*** having marks resembling birds' eyes *[bird's-eye* maple*]*

bird's-eye view **1** a view from high above **2** an overall, but cursory, view

bird′-watch′ing ***n.*** a hobby involving observation of wild birds in their habitat —**bird′-watch′er** ***n.***

bi·ret·ta (bə ret′ə) ***n.*** ⟦< LL *birrettum,* small cloak⟧ a square ceremonial hat with three or four vertical projections, worn by Roman Catholic clergy

Bir·ming·ham (bur′miŋ əm; *for 2,* -ham′) **1** city in central England: county district pop. 961,000 **2** city in N Alabama: pop. 265,000

birth (burth) ***n.*** ⟦< ON *byrth*⟧ **1** the act of bringing forth offspring **2** a being born **3** origin or descent **4** the beginning of anything —***vi., vt.*** to give birth (to) —**give birth (to)** **1** to bring forth (offspring) **2** to create

birth′day′ ***n.*** the anniversary of the day of a person's birth

birth′ing ***adj., n.*** (of or for) giving birth

birth′mark′ ***n.*** a skin blemish or mark present at birth

birth′place′ ***n.*** the place of one's birth or of a thing's origin

birth′rate′ ***n.*** the number of births per year per thousand people in a given area, group, etc.: also **birth rate**

birth′right′ ***n.*** any right that a person has by birth

birth′stone′ ***n.*** a gem symbolizing the month of a person's birth

bis·cot·ti (bi skät′ē) ***pl.n.,*** *sing.* **-to** or **-ti** ⟦It, cognate with fol.⟧ hard, bar-shaped cookie made with almonds, etc.

bis·cuit (bis′kit) ***n.,*** *pl.* **-cuits** or **-cuit** ⟦< L *bis,* twice + *coquere,* to cook⟧ **1** [Chiefly Brit.] a cracker or cookie **2** *a)* a quick bread baked in small pieces *b)* any of these pieces

bi·sect (bī sekt′) ***vt.*** ⟦< L *bi-,* BI- + *secare,* to cut⟧ **1** to cut in two **2** *Geom.* to divide into two equal parts —***vi.*** to divide; fork —**bi·sec′tor** (-sekt′ər) ***n.***

bi·sex·u·al (bī sek′sho͞o əl) ***adj.*** of, or sexually attracted to, both sexes —***n.*** one who is bisexual

bish·op (bish′əp) ***n.*** ⟦< Gr *episkopos,* overseer⟧ **1** a high-ranking member of the Christian clergy, governing a diocese or church district **2** a chess piece that can move in a diagonal direction only

bish·op·ric (bish′əp rik) ***n.*** the district, office, or rank of a bishop

Bis·marck[1] (biz′märk′), Prince **Ot·to von** (ät′ō vän) 1815-98; Prussian chancellor (1871-90) who unified Germany

Bis·marck[2] (biz′märk′) capital of North Dakota: pop. 49,000

bis·muth (biz′məth) ***n.*** ⟦< Ger *wismut*⟧ a brittle, grayish-white metallic chemical element used in alloys of low melting point

bi·son (bī′sən) ***n.,*** *pl.* **bi′son** ⟦< L, wild ox⟧ a bovine ruminant having a shaggy mane and a humped back, as the American buffalo

bisque (bisk) ***n.*** ⟦Fr⟧ a thick, creamy soup made as from shellfish or vegetables

bis·tro (bē′strō′) ***n.*** ⟦Fr⟧ a small cafe

bit[1] (bit) ***n.*** ⟦< OE *bite,* a bite⟧ **1** the part of a bridle in the horse's mouth, used as a control **2** anything that curbs or controls **3** a drilling or boring tool for use in a brace, drill press, etc.

bit[2] (bit) ***n.*** ⟦< OE *bita,* a piece⟧ **1** *a)* a small piece or quantity *b)* small extent *[a bit* bored*]* *c)* a short time **2** [Inf.] 12½ cents: now usually in *two bits* —***adj.*** very small *[a bit* role*]* —**bit by bit** gradually —**do one's bit** to do one's share

bit[3] (bit) ***n.*** ⟦*b*(*inary*) (*dig*)*it*⟧ **1** a single digit in a binary number system **2** a unit of information

bitch (bich) ***n.*** ⟦OE *bicce*⟧ **1** the female of the dog, fox, etc. **2** a woman regarded as bad-tempered, malicious, etc. **3** [Slang] anything especially difficult —***vi.*** [Slang] to complain

bitch′y ***adj.*** **-i·er, -i·est** [Slang] bad-tempered or malicious: used esp. of a woman

bite (bīt) ***vt.*** **bit** (bit), **bit·ten** (bit′'n) or **bit, bit′ing** ⟦OE *bītan*⟧ **1** to seize or pierce with or as with the teeth **2** to cut into, as with a sharp weapon **3** to sting, as an insect **4** to cause to smart **5** to eat into; corrode —***vi.*** **1** to press or snap the teeth (*into, at,* etc.) **2** to cause a biting sensation **3** to grip **4** to seize a bait **5** to be caught, as by a trick —***n.*** **1** a biting **2** biting quality; sting **3** a wound or sting from biting **4** *a)* a mouthful *b)* a snack **5** [Inf.] a sum deducted, as by a tax —**bite the bullet** to confront a painful situation bravely: from the patient's biting a bullet during battlefield surgery without an anesthetic

bit·ing (bīt′iŋ) ***adj.*** **1** cutting; sharp **2** sarcastic —**bit′ing·ly** ***adv.***

bit·ter (bit′ər) ***adj.*** ⟦OE *biter,* akin to *bītan,* to bite⟧ **1** having a sharp, often unpleasant taste **2** causing or showing sorrow, pain, etc. **3** sharp and disagreeable; harsh *[a bitter* wind*]* **4** resentful or cynical —**bit′ter·ly** ***adv.*** —**bit′ter·ness** ***n.***

bit·tern (bit′ərn) ***n.*** ⟦< OFr *butor*⟧ a wading bird with a thumping cry

bit′ters ***pl.n.*** a liquor containing bitter herbs, etc. and usually alcohol, used as in some cocktails

bit′ter·sweet′ ***n.*** **1** a woody vine bearing small orange fruits with bright-red fleshy seeds **2** a poisonous vine with purple flowers and red berries **3** pleasure mixed with sadness —***adj.*** **1** both bitter and sweet **2** pleasant and sad

bi·tu·men (bi to͞o′mən) ***n.*** ⟦L < Celt⟧ any of various black mixtures of hydrocarbons obtained in the distillation of petroleum, used for paints, roofing, etc. —**bi·tu′mi·nous** (-mə nəs) ***adj.***

bituminous coal coal that yields pitch or tar when it burns; soft coal

bi·va·lent (bī vā′lənt) ***adj.*** *Chem.* DIVALENT

bi·valve (bī′valv′) ***n.*** any mollusk having a shell made of two valves hinged together, as a clam

biv·ou·ac (biv′wak′) ***n.*** ⟦Fr < OHG *bi-*, by + *wahta,* watchman⟧ a temporary encampment (esp. of soldiers) in the open **—*vi.* -acked′, -ack′ing** to encamp in the open

bi·week·ly (bī wēk′lē) ***adj., adv.*** **1** once every two weeks **2** [Now Rare] semiweekly

bi·zarre (bi zär′) ***adj.*** ⟦Fr < Basque *bizar,* beard⟧ **1** odd; grotesque **2** unexpected; fantastic

bk *abbrev.* **1** bank **2** book

bl *abbrev.* **1** bale(s) **2** barrel(s)

B/L or **b/l** *abbrev.* bill of lading

blab (blab) ***vt., vi.*** **blabbed, blab′bing** ⟦ME *blabben*⟧ **1** to reveal (a secret) **2** to chatter; prattle Also **blab′ber** **—*n.*** gossip

blab′ber·mouth′ ***n.*** [Inf.] one who blabs

black (blak) ***adj.*** ⟦OE *blæc*⟧ **1** opposite to white; of the color of coal **2** [*sometimes* **B-**] of or for the dark-skinned peoples of Africa, etc. or their descendants elsewhere, specif. African-Americans in the U.S. *[black studies]* **3** without light; dark **4** dirty **5** evil; wicked **6** sad; dismal **7** sullen **—*n.*** **1** black color or pigment **2** black clothes, esp. when worn in mourning **3** [*sometimes* **B-**] a member of a black people **4** darkness **—*vt., vi.*** to blacken **—black out** to lose consciousness **—in the black** operating at a profit **—black′ish *adj.* —black′ly *adv.* —black′ness *n.***

black′-and-blue′ ***adj.*** discolored, as by a bruise

black′ball′ ***n.*** a vote against **—*vt.*** **1** to vote against **2** to ostracize

black belt a black belt or sash awarded to an expert of the highest skill in judo or karate

black′ber′ry (-ber′ē, -bər ē) ***n., pl.*** **-ries** **1** the fleshy, purple or black, edible fruit of various brambles of the rose family **2** a bush or vine bearing this fruit

black′bird′ ***n.*** any of various birds the male of which is almost entirely black

black′board′ ***n.*** a smooth, usually dark surface on which to write with chalk

black′en (-ən) ***vi.*** to become black or dark **—*vt.*** **1** to make black; darken **2** to slander; defame

black eye **1** a discoloration of the skin around an eye, resulting from a blow or contusion **2** [Inf.] dishonor, or its cause

black′-eyed′ Su′san (-so͞o′zən) a yellow, daisylike wildflower with a dark center

black·guard (blag′ərd) ***n.*** a scoundrel; villain

black′head′ ***n.*** a dark plug of dried fatty matter in a pore of the skin

black hole **1** an object or region in space with intense gravitation from which light, etc. cannot escape **2** *a*) an emptiness or void *b*) anything endlessly devouring resources, etc.

black′jack′ ***n.*** **1** a small, leather-covered bludgeon with a flexible handle **2** a gambling card game in which a player getting closer to 21 points than the dealer, without exceeding it, wins **—*vt.*** to hit with a blackjack

black light ultraviolet or infrared radiation used for fluorescent effects

black′list′ ***n.*** a list of those who are censured, refused employment, etc. **—*vt.*** to put on a blacklist

black lung (disease) a disease of the lungs caused by the inhalation of coal dust

black magic sorcery

black′mail′ ***n.*** ⟦lit., black rent < ME *male,* rent⟧ **1** payment extorted to prevent disclosure of information that could bring disgrace **2** extortion of such payment **—*vt.*** to get or try to get blackmail from **—black′mail′er *n.***

black mark an unfavorable item in one's record

black market a system for selling goods illegally **—black marketeer** (or **marketer**)

black′out′ ***n.*** **1** an extinguishing of stage lights to end a scene **2** a concealing of lights that might be visible to enemy aircraft at night **3** a temporary loss of electric power **4** temporary unconsciousness **5** suppression, as of news by censorship

black power political and economic power as sought by black Americans in the struggle for civil rights

Black Sea sea between Asia & SE Europe, north of Turkey

black sheep a family or group member regarded as not so respectable as the others

black′smith′ ***n.*** a smith who works in iron and makes and fits horseshoes

black′thorn′ ***n.*** a thorny shrub with purple or black, plumlike fruit; sloe

black′top′ ***n.*** a bituminous mixture, usually asphalt, used as a surface for roads, etc. **—*vt.* -topped′, -top′ping** to cover with blacktop

black widow a black spider with a red mark underneath: the female has a poisonous bite and sometimes eats its mate

blad·der (blad′ər) ***n.*** ⟦OE *blæddre*⟧ **1** a sac that fills with fluid or gas, esp. one that holds urine flowing from the kidneys **2** a thing like this

blade (blād) ***n.*** ⟦OE *blæd,* leaf⟧ **1** *a*) the leaf of a plant, esp. of grass *b*) the flat part of a leaf **2** a broad, flat surface or part, as of an oar or snowplow **3** the cutting part of a tool, knife, etc. **4** a sword or swordsman

Blair (bler), **To·ny** (tō′nē) 1953- ; Brit. prime minister (1997-)

blam·a·ble or **blame·a·ble** (blām′ə bəl) ***adj.*** that deserves blame **—blam′a·bly *adv.***

blame (blām) ***vt.*** **blamed, blam′ing** ⟦see BLASPHEME⟧ **1** to accuse of being at fault; condemn (*for*) **2** to put the responsibility of (an error, etc.) *on* **—*n.*** **1** a blaming **2** responsibility for a fault **—be to blame** to be at fault **—blame′less *adj.* —blame′less·ly *adv.* —blame′less·ness *n.***

blame′wor′thy ***adj.*** deserving to be blamed

blanch (blanch) ***vt.*** ⟦< OFr *blanc,* white⟧ **1** to whiten or bleach **2** to make pale **3** to scald (vegetables, almonds, etc.) —***vi.*** to turn pale

bland (bland) ***adj.*** ⟦L *blandus,* mild⟧ **1** gently agreeable **2** mild; not harsh **3** insipid —**bland′ly** ***adv.*** —**bland′ness** ***n.***

blan·dish (blan′dish) ***vt., vi.*** ⟦< L *blandiri,* to flatter⟧ to flatter; coax; cajole —**blan′dish·ment** ***n.***

blank (blaŋk) ***adj.*** ⟦< OFr *blanc,* white⟧ **1** not written on **2** empty; vacant; plain **3** dazed or vacant *[a blank look]* **4** utter; complete *[a blank denial]* —***n.*** **1** an empty space, esp. one to be filled out in a printed form **2** such a printed form **3** an empty place or time **4** a powder-filled cartridge without a bullet —***vt.*** to hold (an opponent) scoreless —**blank out** to conceal by covering over —**draw a blank** [Inf.] **1** to be unsuccessful **2** to be unable to remember a particular thing —**blank′ly** ***adv.*** —**blank′ness** ***n.***

blank check **1** a bank check not yet filled in **2** a signed check with no amount filled in **3** permission to use an unlimited amount of money, authority, etc.

blan·ket (blaŋk′it) ***n.*** ⟦< OFr dim. of *blanc,* white⟧ **1** a large piece of cloth used for warmth, esp. as a bed cover **2** any covering like this *[a blanket of leaves]* —***adj.*** including many or all items *[blanket insurance]* —***vt.*** **1** to cover; overlie **2** to obscure

blank verse unrhymed verse having five iambic feet per line

blan·quette (blän ket′) ***n.*** ⟦Fr⟧ a stew, as of chicken or veal, in cream sauce

blare (bler) ***vt., vi.*** **blared, blar′ing** ⟦ME *bleren,* to wail⟧ to sound or exclaim loudly —***n.*** a loud, harsh sound

blar·ney (blär′nē) ***n.*** ⟦< *Blarney* stone in Ireland, traditionally kissed to gain skill in flattery⟧ smooth or flattering talk

bla·sé (blä zā′) ***adj.*** ⟦Fr⟧ unexcited or jaded

blas·pheme (blas fēm′) ***vt.*** **-phemed′, -phem′ing** ⟦< Gr *blasphēmein,* to speak evil of⟧ **1** to speak profanely of or to (God or sacred things) **2** to curse —***vi.*** to utter blasphemy —**blas·phem′er** ***n.***

blas′phe·my (-fə mē) ***n.,*** *pl.* **-mies** profane speech, writing, or action concerning God or sacred things —**blas′phe·mous** ***adj.***

blast (blast) ***n.*** ⟦OE *blæst,* puff of wind⟧ **1** a strong rush of air or gas **2** the sound of a sudden rush of air, as through a horn **3** a blight **4** an explosion, as of dynamite **5** an outburst, as of criticism **6** [Slang] an exciting, enjoyable experience —***vi.*** **1** to make a loud, harsh sound **2** to set off explosives, etc. —***vt.*** **1** to wither; ruin **2** to blow up; explode **3** to criticize sharply —**blast off** to take off: said of a rocket, etc. —**(at) full blast** at full speed or capacity

blast furnace a smelting furnace in which a blast of air forced in from below produces the intense heat

blast′off′ or **blast′-off′** ***n.*** the launching of a rocket, spacecraft, etc.

bla·tant (blāt′′nt) ***adj.*** ⟦prob. < L *blaterare,* to babble⟧ **1** disagreeably loud; noisy **2** boldly conspicuous or obtrusive —**bla′tan·cy** ***n.***

blaze[1] (blāz) ***n.*** ⟦OE *blæse*⟧ **1** a bright burst of flame; fire **2** a very bright light **3** a spectacular outburst or display —***vi.*** **blazed, blaz′ing** **1** to burn rapidly or shine brightly **2** to be excited, as with anger

blaze[2] (blāz) ***n.*** ⟦< ON *blesi*⟧ **1** a light-colored spot on an animal's face **2** a mark made on a tree by cutting off bark —***vt.*** **blazed, blaz′ing** to mark (a tree or trail) with blazes

blaze[3] (blāz) ***vt.*** **blazed, blaz′ing** ⟦ME *blasen,* to blow < OE or ON⟧ to proclaim

blaz·er (blā′zər) ***n.*** a light sport coat usually in a solid color and with metal buttons

bla·zon (blā′zən) ***n.*** ⟦OFr *blason,* a shield⟧ a coat of arms —***vt.*** **1** to proclaim **2** to adorn

bldg *abbrev.* building

bleach (blēch) ***vt., vi.*** ⟦OE *blæcan*⟧ to make or become white or colorless —***n.*** a substance for bleaching

bleach′ers ***pl.n.*** benches in tiers, for spectators as at sporting events

bleak (blēk) ***adj.*** ⟦ON *bleikr,* pale⟧ **1** exposed to wind and cold; bare **2** cold; harsh **3** gloomy **4** not hopeful —**bleak′ly** ***adv.*** —**bleak′ness** ***n.***

blear·y (blir′ē) ***adj.*** **-i·er, -i·est** ⟦< ME *blere*⟧ dim or blurred, as the eyes by tears, fatigue, etc.: also **blear**

bleat (blēt) ***vi.*** ⟦OE *blætan*⟧ to make the cry of a sheep, goat, or calf —***n.*** a bleating cry or sound

bleed (blēd) ***vi.*** **bled** (bled), **bleed′ing** ⟦< OE *blod,* blood⟧ **1** to emit or lose blood **2** to feel pain, grief, or sympathy **3** to ooze sap, juice, etc. **4** to show through or run together: said of dyes, stains, etc. —***vt.*** **1** to draw blood from **2** to ooze (sap, juice, etc.) **3** to draw off (liquid, etc.) slowly —**bleed′er** ***n.***

bleep (blēp) ***n., vi.*** ⟦echoic⟧ beep —***vt.*** to censor (something said) in a telecast, etc., as with a beep

blem·ish (blem′ish) ***vt.*** ⟦< OFr *blesmir,* injure⟧ to mar; spoil —***n.*** a flaw, defect, etc., as a spot or scar

blench (blench) ***vt., vi.*** to blanch

blend (blend) ***vt.*** **blend′ed** or **blent, blend′ing** ⟦OE *blendan*⟧ **1** to mix or mingle (varieties of tea, etc.) **2** to mix thoroughly —***vi.*** **1** to mix or merge **2** to pass gradually into each other, as colors **3** to harmonize —***n.*** **1** a blending **2** a mixture of varieties

blend′er ***n.*** an electrical appliance that can chop, whip, mix, or liquefy foods

bless (bles) ***vt.*** **blessed** or **blest, bless′ing** ⟦< OE *bletsian,* consecrate with blood⟧ **1** to make holy **2** to ask divine favor for **3** to endow (*with*) **4** to make happy **5** to glorify **6** to make the sign of the cross over

bless·ed (bles′id, blest) ***adj.*** **1** holy; sacred **2** blissful **3** beatified **4** bringing comfort or joy —**bless′ed·ly** ***adv.*** —**bless′ed·ness** ***n.***

bless'ing *n.* **1** an invocation or benediction **2** a grace said before or after eating **3** good wishes or approval **4** anything that gives happiness

blew (blo͞o) *vi., vt. pt. of* BLOW[1] & BLOW[3]

blight (blīt) *n.* ⟦? < ON *blikja,* turn pale⟧ **1** any insect, disease, etc. that destroys plants **2** anything that destroys, frustrates, etc. —*vt.* **1** to wither **2** to destroy

blimp (blimp) *n.* [Inf.] a nonrigid or semirigid airship

blind (blīnd) *adj.* ⟦OE⟧ **1** without the power of sight **2** of or for sightless persons **3** lacking insight **4** hard to see; hidden **5** closed at one end *[a blind alley]* **6** not controlled by intelligence *[blind destiny]* **7** guided only by instruments *[a blind landing]* —*vt.* **1** to make sightless **2** to dazzle **3** to deprive of insight —*n.* **1** anything that obscures sight or keeps out light, as a window shade **2** a place of concealment **3** a decoy —*adv.* **1** blindly **2** guided only by instruments *[to fly blind]* —**blind'ly** *adv.* —**blind'ness** *n.*

blind date [Inf.] **1** a date with a stranger, arranged by a third person **2** either person involved

blind'ers *pl.n.* bridle flaps for preventing a horse from seeing to the side

blind'fold' *vt.* ⟦< ME *blindfeld,* struck blind⟧ to cover the eyes of, as with a cloth —*n.* a cloth used to cover the eyes —*adj., adv.* **1** with the eyes covered **2** reckless(ly)

blind'side' *vt.* **-sid'ed, -sid'ing** to attack (someone) from an unexpected direction

blink (bliŋk) *vi.* ⟦ME *blenken*⟧ **1** to wink one or more times **2** to flash on and off **3** to ignore (with *at*) —*vt.* **1** to cause (eyes, light, etc.) to blink **2** to evade or avoid —*n.* **1** a blinking **2** a glimmer —**on the blink** [Slang] not working right

blink'er *n.* a flashing warning light

blintz (blints) *n.* ⟦Yiddish *blintze* < Russ *blin,* pancake⟧ a thin pancake rolled with a filling of cottage cheese, fruit, etc.

blip (blip) *n.* ⟦echoic of a brief sound⟧ a luminous image on an oscilloscope

bliss (blis) *n.* ⟦< OE *blithe,* blithe⟧ **1** great happiness **2** spiritual joy —**bliss'ful** *adj.* —**bliss'ful·ly** *adv.* —**bliss'ful·ness** *n.*

blis·ter (blis'tər) *n.* ⟦< ?⟧ **1** a raised patch of skin, filled with watery matter and caused as by a burn **2** anything like a blister —*vt.* **1** to raise blisters on **2** to lash with words —*vi.* to form blisters

blis'ter·ing *adj.* very hot, intense, etc.

blithe (blī*th*, blīth) *adj.* ⟦OE⟧ cheerful; carefree; lighthearted: also **blithe'some** (-səm) —**blithe'ly** *adv.* —**blithe'ness** *n.*

blitz (blits) *n.* ⟦< Ger *blitz,* lightning⟧ a sudden destructive or overwhelming attack —*vt.* to subject to a blitz

bliz·zard (bliz'ərd) *n.* ⟦? < dial. *bliz,* violent blow⟧ a violent snowstorm with very cold winds

bloat (blōt) *vt., vi.* ⟦< ON *blautr,* soft⟧ **1** to swell, as with water or air **2** to puff up, as with pride

blob (bläb) *n.* ⟦echoic⟧ **1** a drop or a small lump or spot **2** something of indefinite shape —*vt.* **blobbed, blob'bing** to splash, as with blobs

bloc (bläk) *n.* ⟦Fr < MDu *block,* log⟧ an alliance of persons, nations, etc.

block (bläk) *n.* ⟦< OFr *bloc* & MDu *block*⟧ **1** a large, solid piece of wood, stone, metal, etc. **2** a heavy stand on which chopping, etc. is done **3** an auctioneer's platform **4** an obstruction or hindrance **5** a pulley in a frame **6** [Now Brit.] a group or row of buildings **7** an area with streets or buildings on four sides **8** a number of things regarded as a unit **9** a toy brick, typically a cube of wood, etc. **10** *Printing* a piece of wood, etc. engraved with a design —*vt.* **1** to obstruct; hinder **2** to mount or mold on a block **3** to sketch roughly: often with *out* —**block'er** *n.*

block·ade (blä kād') *n.* ⟦prec. + -ADE⟧ **1** a shutting off of a place by troops or ships to prevent passage **2** any strategic barrier —*vt.* **-ad'ed, -ad'ing** to subject to a blockade

block and tackle an arrangement of pulley blocks and ropes, used for lifting heavy objects

block'bust'er *n.* a particularly effective person or thing; specif., an expensive film, etc. generating widespread appeal

block'bust'ing *n.* [Inf.] the inducing of owners to sell their homes out of fear that a minority group may move into the neighborhood

block grant a grant of federal funds to a state or local government to fund a block of programs

block'head' *n.* a stupid person

block'house' *n.* **1** [Historical] a wooden, two-story fortified building **2** a reinforced structure for observers, as of missile launchings

blond (bländ) *adj.* ⟦OFr < ? Gmc⟧ **1** having light-colored hair and, often, fair skin **2** light in color Also **blonde** —*n.* a blond person —**blonde** *fem.n.* —**blond'ness** *n.*

blood (blud) *n.* ⟦OE *blod*⟧ **1** the red fluid circulating in the arteries and veins of animals **2** bloodshed **3** the essence of life; life **4** the sap of a plant **5** passion, temperament, etc. **6** parental heritage; lineage **7** kinship **8** people, esp. youthful people *[new blood in a group]* —**bad blood** anger; hatred —**in cold blood 1** with cruelty **2** deliberately

blood bank a supply of blood stored for future use in transfusion

blood count the number of red or white cells in a given volume of blood

blood'cur'dling (-kurd'liŋ) *adj.* frightening; terrifying

blood'ed *adj.* **1** having (a specified kind of) blood *[hot-blooded]* **2** of fine breed

blood'hound' *n.* any of a breed of large tracking dogs with a keen sense of smell

blood'less *adj.* **1** without bloodshed **2** anemic or pale **3** having little energy —**blood'less·ly** *adv.* —**blood'less·ness**

n.

blood'line' *n.* line of descent

blood'mo·bile' (-mō bēl') *n.* a traveling unit for collecting blood from donors for blood banks

blood poisoning *nontechnical term for* SEPTICEMIA

blood pressure the pressure of the blood against the blood-vessel walls

blood relation (or **relative**) a person related by birth

blood'shed' *n.* the shedding of blood; killing

blood'shot' *adj.* tinged with red because small blood vessels are broken: said of eyes

blood'suck'er *n.* an animal that sucks blood, esp. a leech

blood'thirst'y *adj.* murderous; very cruel —**blood'thirst'i·ness** *n.*

blood vessel an artery, vein, or capillary

blood'y *adj.* **-i·er**, **-i·est** **1** of, like, containing, or covered with blood **2** involving bloodshed **3** bloodthirsty **4** [Brit. Slang] cursed; damned —*adv.* [Brit. Slang] very —*vt.* **-ied**, **-y·ing** to stain with blood —**blood'i·ly** *adv.* —**blood'i·ness** *n.*

bloody mar·y (mer'ē) *pl.* **bloody mar'ys** a drink made of vodka and tomato juice

bloom (blo͞om) *n.* ⟦< ON *blomi*, flowers⟧ **1** a flower; blossom **2** the state or time of flowering **3** a period of greatest health, vigor, etc. **4** a youthful, healthy glow **5** the powdery coating on some fruits and leaves —*vi.* **1** to blossom **2** to be in one's prime **3** to glow with health, etc.

bloom'ers *pl.n.* ⟦after Amelia *Bloomer* (1818-94), U.S. feminist⟧ baggy trousers gathered at the knee, once worn by women for athletics

bloom'ing *adj.* **1** blossoming **2** flourishing **3** [Inf.] complete *[a blooming idiot]*

bloop·er (blo͞op'ər) *n.* ⟦*bloop*, echoic + -ER⟧ **1** a stupid mistake **2** *Baseball* a fly that falls just beyond the infield for a hit

blos·som (bläs'əm) *n.* ⟦OE *blostma*⟧ **1** a flower, esp. of a fruit-bearing plant **2** a state or time of flowering —*vi.* **1** to have or open into blossoms **2** to begin to flourish —**blos'som·y** *adj.*

blot (blät) *n.* ⟦ME < ?⟧ **1** a spot or stain, esp. of ink **2** anything that spoils or mars **3** disgrace —*vt.* **blot'ted**, **blot'ting** **1** to spot; stain **2** to disgrace **3** to erase, obscure, or get rid of: often with *out* **4** to dry, as with blotting paper —*vi.* **1** to make blots **2** to become blotted **3** to be absorbent

blotch (bläch) *n.* ⟦? < prec.⟧ **1** a discoloration on the skin **2** any large blot or stain —*vt.* to mark with blotches —**blotch'y**, **-i·er**, **-i·est**, *adj.*

blot·ter (blät'ər) *n.* **1** a piece of blotting paper **2** a book for recording events as they occur *[a police blotter]*

blotting paper a thick, soft, absorbent paper used to dry a surface freshly written on in ink

blouse (blous) *n.* ⟦Fr, workman's smock⟧ **1** a garment like a shirt, worn by women and girls **2** a uniform coat worn by soldiers, etc. —*vi.*, *vt.* **bloused**, **blous'ing** to gather in and drape over loosely

blow[1] (blō) *vi.* **blew**, **blown**, **blow'ing** ⟦OE *blawan*⟧ **1** to move with some force, as the wind **2** to send forth air, as with the mouth **3** to pant **4** to give sound by blowing or being blown **5** to spout water and air, as whales do **6** to be carried by the wind **7** to be stormy **8** to burst suddenly: often with *out* **9** [Slang] to leave —*vt.* **1** to force air from, into, onto, or through **2** to drive or expel by blowing **3** to sound by blowing **4** to form by blown air or gas **5** to burst by an explosion: often with *up* **6** to melt (a fuse, etc.) **7** [Inf.] to spend (money) freely **8** [Slang] to leave **9** [Slang] to bungle **10** [Slang] to reveal *[to blow one's cover]* —*n.* **1** a blowing **2** a blast of air or a gale —**blow over** to pass over or by —**blow up** **1** to enlarge or exaggerate **2** [Inf.] to lose one's temper —**blow'er** *n.*

blow[2] (blō) *n.* ⟦ME *blowe*⟧ **1** a hard hit, as with the fist **2** a sudden attack **3** a sudden calamity; shock —**come to blows** to begin fighting one another

blow[3] (blō) *vi.* **blew**, **blown**, **blow'ing** ⟦OE *blowan*⟧ [Archaic] to bloom

blow'-by-blow' *adj.* told in great detail

blow'-dry' *vt.* **-dried'**, **-dry'ing** to dry (wet hair) with hot air blown from an electric device (**blow'-dry'er**)

blow'fly' *n.*, *pl.* **-flies'** a fly that lays its eggs on meat, in wounds, etc.

blow'gun' *n.* a long tube through which darts, etc. are blown

blow'hard' *n.* [Slang] a loudly boastful person

blow'out' *n.* **1** the bursting of a tire **2** [Slang] a party, banquet, etc.

blow'torch' *n.* a small torch that shoots out a hot flame

blow'up' *n.* **1** an explosion **2** an enlarged photograph **3** [Inf.] an angry outburst

blow'y *adj.* **-i·er**, **-i·est** windy

blowz·y (blou'zē) *adj.* **-i·er**, **-i·est** ⟦< obs. *blouze*, wench⟧ slovenly: also **blows'y**

BLT (bē'el'tē') *n.* a bacon, lettuce, and tomato sandwich

blub·ber[1] (blub'ər) *n.* ⟦ME *blober*, a bubble⟧ the fat of the whale —**blub'ber·y** *adj.*

blub·ber[2] (blub'ər) *vi.* ⟦ME *bloberen*, to bubble⟧ to weep loudly, like a child

bludg·eon (bluj'ən) *n.* ⟦? < earlier Fr *bouge*, club⟧ a short club with a heavy end —*vt.*, *vi.* **1** to strike with a bludgeon **2** to bully or coerce

blue (blo͞o) *adj.* ⟦< ?⟧ **1** of the color of the clear sky **2** livid: said of the skin **3** sad and gloomy **4** puritanical **5** [Inf.] indecent; risqué —*n.* **1** the color of the clear sky **2** any blue pigment —**out of the blue** unexpectedly —**the blue** **1** the sky **2** the sea

blue baby a baby born with bluish skin, esp. because of a heart defect

blue'bell' ***n.*** any of various plants with blue, bell-shaped flowers

blue'ber'ry (-ber'ē, -bər ē) ***n.***, *pl.* **-ries** **1** a shrub bearing small, edible, blue-black berries **2** any of the berries

blue'bird' ***n.*** a small North American songbird with a bluish back

blue blood an aristocrat: also **blue'blood'** ***n.*** —**blue'-blood'ed** ***adj.***

blue cheese a strong cheese containing bluish mold

blue'-chip' ***adj.*** ⟦< high-value *blue chips* of poker⟧ **1** of any high-priced stock with good earnings and a stable price **2** [Inf.] valuable

blue'-col'lar ***adj.*** ⟦< color of work shirts⟧ designating or of industrial workers

blue flu ⟦< *blue* police uniforms⟧ a sick-out, esp. by police officers

blue'gill' ***n.*** a freshwater sunfish of a bluish color

blue'grass' ***n.*** **1** a type of grass with bluish-green horizontal stems **2** fast, bluesy country music

blue'jack'et ***n.*** an enlisted person in the navy

blue jay a common crested bird with a blue upper body and head: sometimes **blue'jay'** ***n.***

blue'jeans' (-jēnz') ***pl.n.*** jeans made of blue denim: also **blue jeans**

blue law a puritanical law, esp. one prohibiting certain activities on Sunday

blue'nose' ***n.*** [Inf.] a puritanical person

blue'-pen'cil ***vt.*** **-ciled** or **-cilled, -cil·ing** or **-cil·ling** to edit or correct with or as with a blue pencil

blue'-plate' special an inexpensive restaurant meal served at a fixed price

blue'point' ***n.*** ⟦after *Blue Point*, Long Island, New York⟧ a small oyster, usually eaten raw

blue'print' ***n.*** **1** a photographic reproduction in white on a blue background, as of architectural plans **2** any detailed plan or outline —***vt.*** to make a blueprint of

blues (blo͞oz) ***pl.n.*** [*with sing. or pl. v.*] **1** [Inf.] a depressed feeling: with *the* **2** black folk music having, usually, slow tempo, melancholy words, etc.: often with *the* —**blues'y, -i·er, -i·est,** ***adj.***

blue'stock'ing ***n.*** a learned or bookish woman

blu·et (blo͞o'it) ***n.*** ⟦< Fr dim. of *bleu*, blue⟧ a small plant having little, pale-blue flowers

blue whale a baleen whale with a blue-gray back: the largest animal

bluff[1] (bluf) ***vt., vi.*** ⟦prob. < Du *bluffen*, to brag, or *verbluffen*, to baffle⟧ to mislead (a person) by a false, bold front —***n.*** **1** a bluffing **2** one who bluffs: also **bluff'er**

bluff[2] (bluf) ***adj.*** ⟦? < Du *blaf*, flat⟧ **1** having a flat, steep front **2** having a rough, frank manner —***n.*** a high, steep bank or cliff

blu·ing (blo͞o'iŋ) ***n.*** a blue rinse used on white fabrics to prevent yellowing

blu'ish (-ish) ***adj.*** somewhat blue: also **blue'ish**

blun·der (blun'dər) ***vi.*** ⟦< ON *blunda*, shut the eyes⟧ **1** to move clumsily **2** to make a foolish mistake —***n.*** a foolish mistake —**blun'der·er** ***n.***

blun'der·buss' (-bus') ***n.*** ⟦< Du *donderbus*, thunder box⟧ [Historical] a short gun with a broad muzzle

blunt (blunt) ***adj.*** ⟦< ?⟧ **1** having a dull edge, etc. **2** plain-spoken —***vt., vi.*** to make or become dull —**blunt'ly** ***adv.*** —**blunt'ness** ***n.***

blur (blur) ***vt., vi.*** **blurred, blur'ring** ⟦< ?⟧ **1** to smear or smudge **2** to make or become indistinct in shape, etc. **3** to dim —***n.*** anything indistinct or hazy —**blur'ry, -ri·er, -ri·est,** ***adj.*** —**blur'ri·ness** ***n.***

blurb (blurb) ***n.*** ⟦a coinage⟧ an advertisement, as on a book jacket, esp. a laudatory one

blurt (blurt) ***vt.*** ⟦prob. echoic⟧ to say impulsively: often with *out*

blush (blush) ***vi.*** ⟦< OE *blyscan*, to shine⟧ **1** to become red in the face, as from embarrassment **2** to be ashamed: usually with *at* or *for* **3** to become rosy —***n.*** **1** a reddening of the face, as from shame **2** a rosy color **3** BLUSHER (sense 2) —***adj.*** rosy —**at first blush** at first sight

blush'er ***n.*** **1** one who blushes readily **2** a red or reddish cosmetic powder, cream, etc. for the cheeks

blush wine a dry, pale-pink wine

blus·ter (blus'tər) ***vi.*** ⟦? < LowG *blüstern*⟧ **1** to blow stormily: said of wind **2** to speak in a noisy, swaggering manner —***n.*** **1** stormy blowing or noisy commotion **2** noisy or swaggering talk —**blus'ter·er** ***n.*** —**blus'ter·y** ***adj.***

Blvd *abbrev.* Boulevard

BM *abbrev.* [Inf.] bowel movement

BO *abbrev.* body odor

bo·a (bō'ə) ***n.*** ⟦L⟧ **1** a tropical snake that suffocates its prey in its coils, as the anaconda **2** a woman's long scarf, as of fur or feathers

boar (bôr) ***n.***, *pl.* **boars** or **boar** ⟦OE *bar*⟧ **1** a mature, uncastrated male pig **2** a wild hog

board (bôrd) ***n.*** ⟦OE *bord*, plank⟧ **1** a long, flat piece of sawed wood **2** a flat piece of wood, etc. for some special use *[bulletin board]* **3** pasteboard **4** meals, esp. as provided regularly for pay **5** a group of administrators; council **6** [*also* **B-**] [*pl.*] *Educ.* a qualifying examination for admission to an academic program —***vt.*** **1** to cover (*up*) with boards **2** to provide with meals, or room and meals, regularly for pay **3** to get on (a ship, train, etc.) —***vi.*** to receive meals, or room and meals, regularly for pay —**on board** **1** on a ship, aircraft, etc. **2** in a group as a member, etc. —**the boards** the stage (of a theater) —**board'er** ***n.***

board'ing·house' ***n.*** a house where meals, or room and meals, can be had for pay: also **boarding house**

board'walk' ***n.*** a walk made of thick boards, esp. one along a beach

boast (bōst) ***vi.*** ⟦< Anglo-Fr⟧ to talk, esp.

about oneself, with too much pride; brag —*vt.* **1** to brag about **2** glory in having or doing (something) —*n.* **1** a boasting **2** anything boasted of —**boast′er** *n.* —**boast′ful** *adj.* —**boast′ful·ly** *adv.*

boat (bōt) *n.* ⟦OE *bat*⟧ **1** a small, open vehicle for traveling on water **2** loosely, a ship **3** a boat-shaped dish —**in the same boat** in the same unfavorable situation —**rock the boat** [Inf.] to disturb the status quo —**boat′man** (-mən), *pl.* **-men** (-mən), *n.*

boat′er *n.* a stiff straw hat with a flat crown and brim

boat′ing *n.* rowing, sailing, etc.

boat·swain (bō′sən) *n.* a ship's petty officer in charge of the deck crew, the rigging, anchors, boats, etc.

bob (bäb) *n.* ⟦ME *bobbe,* hanging cluster; 3 & 4 < the *v.*⟧ **1** any knoblike hanging weight **2** a woman's or child's short haircut **3** a quick, jerky motion **4** a float on a fishing line —*vt.* **bobbed**, **bob′bing** ⟦ME *bobben,* knock against⟧ **1** to make move with a jerky motion **2** to cut (hair, etc.) short —*vi.* to move with a jerky motion —**bob up** to appear suddenly

bob·bin (bäb′in) *n.* ⟦Fr *bobine* < ?⟧ a spool for thread or yarn, used in spinning, machine sewing, etc.

bob·ble (bäb′əl) *n.* [Inf.] *Sports* an awkward fumbling of the ball —*vt.* **-bled**, **-bling** [Inf.] to make a bobble with (a ball)

bob·by (bäb′ē) *n., pl.* **-bies** ⟦after Sir Robert (*Bobby*) Peel (1788-1850), who reorganized the London police force⟧ [Inf., Chiefly Brit.] a British policeman

bobby pin ⟦from use with *bobbed* hair⟧ a small metal hairpin with the sides pressing close together

bobby socks (or **sox**) ⟦< BOB (*vt.* 2)⟧ [Inf.] esp. in the 1940s and 1950s, girls' ankle-length socks

bob′by-sox′er or **bob′by·sox′er** (-säks′ər) *n.* [Inf.] esp. in the 1940s, a girl in her early teens

bob′cat′ *n.* a small North American lynx

bob′sled′ *n.* a long racing sled with a protective shell —*vi.* **-sled′ded**, **-sled′ding** to ride or race on a bobsled

Boc·cac·ci·o (bō käch′ē ō; *It* bô kä′chô), **Gio·van·ni** (jô vän′nē) 1313-75; It. writer

boc·cie, boc·ce, or **boc·ci** (bäch′ē) *n.* ⟦It *bocce,* (wooden) balls⟧ an Italian game similar to lawn bowling

bode[1] (bōd) *vt.* **bod′ed**, **bod′ing** ⟦< OE *boda,* messenger⟧ to be an omen of —**bode ill** (or **well**) to be a bad (or good) omen

bode[2] (bōd) *vi. alt. pt. of* BIDE

bod·ice (bäd′is) *n.* ⟦altered < *bodies,* pl. of *body*⟧ the upper part of a dress

bod·i·ly (bäd′'l ē) *adj.* **1** physical **2** of, in, by, or to the body —*adv.* **1** in person **2** as a single group

bod·kin (bäd′kin) *n.* ⟦ME *bodekin* < ?⟧ [Obs.] a dagger

bod·y (bäd′ē) *n., pl.* **-ies** ⟦OE *bodig,* cask⟧ **1** the whole physical substance of a human being, animal, or plant **2** the trunk of a human being or animal **3** a corpse **4** [Inf.] a person **5** a distinct group of people or things **6** the main part **7** a distinct mass *[a body of water]* **8** density or consistency, as of paint or fabric **9** richness of flavor

bod′y·guard′ *n.* a person or persons assigned to guard someone

body language gestures, unconscious bodily movements, etc. that serve as nonverbal communication

body politic the people who collectively constitute a political unit under a government

body stocking a tightfitting garment, usually of one piece, that covers the torso and, sometimes, the legs

bod′y·suit′ *n.* a one-piece, tightfitting garment that covers the torso, usually worn with slacks, a skirt, etc.: also **body shirt**

Boer (bôr, boor, bō′ər) *n.* ⟦Du *boer,* peasant⟧ a South African of Dutch descent

bog (bäg, bôg) *n.* ⟦< Gael & Ir *bog,* soft, moist⟧ wet, spongy ground; a small marsh —*vt., vi.* **bogged**, **bog′ging** to sink in or as in a bog: often with *down* —**bog′gy** *adj.*

bo·gey (bō′gē; *for 1, usually* boog′ē) *n.* **1** BOGY **2** ⟦after an imaginary Col. *Bogey*⟧ *Golf* one stroke more than par on a hole: also **bo′gie**

bog·gle (bäg′əl) *vi.* **-gled**, **-gling** ⟦< Scot *bogle,* specter⟧ **1** to be startled (*at*) **2** to hesitate (*at*) —*vt.* to confuse (the mind, imagination, etc.)

Bo·go·tá (bō′gə tä′) capital of Colombia: pop. 3,975,000

bo·gus (bō′gəs) *adj.* ⟦< ?⟧ not genuine; false

bo·gy (boog′ē, bō′gē) *n., pl.* **-gies** ⟦< Scot *bogle,* specter⟧ an imaginary evil spirit; goblin: also **bo′gie**

bo·gy·man or **bo·gey·man** (boog′ē man′, bō′gē-) *n., pl.* **-men′** (-men′) BOOGEYMAN

Bo·he·mi·a (bō hē′mē ə) region of Czech Republic: a former kingdom

Bo·he′mi·an (-ən) *n.* **1** CZECH (*n.* 2) **2** a person born or living in Bohemia **3** [*usually* **b-**] one who lives unconventionally —*adj.* **1** of Bohemia or its people, etc. **2** [*usually* **b-**] like a bohemian —**Bo·he′mi·an·ism′** *n.*

bo·ho (bō′hō′) [Slang] *n.* BOHEMIAN (*n.* 3) —*adj.* BOHEMIAN (*adj.* 2)

boil[1] (boil) *vi.* ⟦< L *bulla,* a bubble⟧ **1** to bubble up and vaporize over direct heat **2** to seethe like a boiling liquid **3** to be agitated, as with rage **4** to cook in boiling liquid —*vt.* **1** to heat to the boiling point **2** to cook in boiling liquid —*n.* the act or state of boiling —**boil down** **1** to lessen in quantity by boiling **2** to condense

boil[2] (boil) *n.* ⟦OE *byle*⟧ an inflamed, painful, pus-filled swelling on the skin

boil′er *n.* **1** a container in which things are boiled or heated **2** a tank in which water is turned to steam **3** a tank for heating water and storing it

boiling point **1** the temperature at

which a specified liquid boils **2** the point at which one loses one's temper

Boi·se (boi′zē, -sē) capital of Idaho: pop. 126,000: also **Boise City**

bois·ter·ous (bois′tər əs) ***adj.*** ⟦ME *boistreous,* crude⟧ **1** rough and stormy; turbulent **2** loud and exuberant; rowdy —**bois′ter·ous·ly *adv.***

bok choy (bäk′ choi′) ⟦Chin⟧ a variety of Chinese cabbage

bo·la (bō′lə) ***n.*** ⟦< Sp, a ball⟧ a set of cords with heavy balls at the ends, thrown to entangle cattle

bold (bōld) ***adj.*** ⟦OE *beald*⟧ **1** daring; fearless **2** too free in manner; impudent **3** steep **4** prominent and clear —**bold′ly *adv.*** —**bold′ness *n.***

bold′face′ *n.* a heavy, dark printing type

bold′faced′ *adj.* impudent

bole (bōl) ***n.*** ⟦ON *bolr*⟧ a tree trunk

bo·le·ro (bō ler′ō) ***n.,*** *pl.* **-ros** ⟦Sp < L *bulla,* a bubble⟧ **1** a lively Spanish dance, or the music for it **2** a short, open vest

Bol·í·var (bäl′ə vər), **Si·món** (sī′mən) 1783-1830; South American revolutionary leader

Bo·liv·i·a (bə liv′ē ə) inland country in WC South America: 424,165 sq. mi.; pop. 7,610,000 —**Bo·liv′i·an *adj., n.***

boll (bōl) ***n.*** ⟦ME *bolle,* BOWL[1]⟧ the roundish seed pod of a plant, esp. of cotton or flax

boll weevil a small weevil whose larvae destroy cotton bolls

bo·lo·gna (bə lō′nē) ***n.*** ⟦after *Bologna,* It city⟧ a large smoked sausage of beef, pork, or veal

Bol·she·vik (bōl′shə vik′) ***n.,*** *pl.* **-viks′** or **-vi′ki** (-vē′kē) ⟦Russ < *ból′she,* larger⟧ [*also* **b-**] **1** a member of a faction that seized power in Russia in 1917 **2** a Communist, esp. of the Soviet Union —**Bol′she·vism′ *n.*** —**Bol′she·vist *n., adj.***

bol·ster (bōl′stər) ***n.*** ⟦OE⟧ **1** a long, narrow pillow **2** any bolsterlike object or support —***vt.*** to prop up as with a bolster: often with *up*

bolt[1] (bōlt) ***n.*** ⟦OE⟧ **1** a short, blunt arrow shot from a crossbow **2** a flash of lightning **3** a sudden dash **4** a sliding bar for locking a door, etc. **5** a threaded metal rod used with a nut for joining parts **6** a roll (*of* cloth, paper, etc.) —***vt.*** **1** to say suddenly; blurt (*out*) **2** to swallow (food) hurriedly **3** to fasten as with a bolt **4** to abandon (a party, group, etc.) —***vi.*** **1** to start suddenly; spring away **2** to withdraw support from one's party, etc. —**bolt upright** erect or erectly

bolt[2] (bōlt) ***vt.*** ⟦< OFr *buleter*⟧ to sift (flour, grain, etc.)

bo·lus (bō′ləs) ***n.*** ⟦< Gr *bōlos*⟧ **1** a small, round lump **2** a mass injected into a blood vessel, as a radioactive tracer **3** a large pill

bomb (bäm) ***n.*** ⟦prob. < Gr *bombos,* hollow sound⟧ **1** a container filled as with an explosive or incendiary chemical, for dropping, hurling, etc. **2** a small container with compressed gas in it *[an aerosol bomb]* **3** [Inf.] a complete failure —***vt.*** to attack with bombs —***vi.*** [Inf.] to be a complete failure

bom·bard (bäm bärd′) ***vt.*** ⟦< Fr *bombarde,* mortar⟧ **1** to attack with artillery or bombs **2** to attack with questions, etc. **3** to direct a stream of particles at (atomic nuclei) —**bom·bard′ment *n.***

bom′bar·dier′ (-bər dir′) ***n.*** one who releases the bombs in a bomber

bom·bast (bäm′bast′) ***n.*** ⟦< Pers *pambak,* cotton⟧ grand, pompous language with little real meaning —**bom·bas′tic *adj.*** —**bom·bas′ti·cal·ly *adv.***

Bom·bay (bäm′bā′) seaport in W India: pop. 8,243,000: now officially *Mumbai*

bomb·er (bäm′ər) ***n.*** **1** an airplane for dropping bombs **2** one who bombs

bomb′shell′ *n.* **1** a bomb **2** any sudden, shocking surprise

bo·na fi·de (bō′nə fīd′, bō′nə fī′dē) ⟦L⟧ **1** in good faith; without fraud *[a bona fide offer]* **2** genuine; real *[a bona fide movie star]*

bo·nan·za (bə nan′zə) ***n.*** ⟦Sp, prosperity⟧ **1** a rich vein of ore **2** any source of wealth

Bo·na·parte (bō′nə pärt′), **Na·po·le·on** (nə pō′lē ən) 1769-1821; Fr. military leader & emperor (1804-15)

bon·bon (bän′bän′; *Fr* bōn bōn′) ***n.*** ⟦< Fr *bon,* good⟧ a small piece of candy

bond (bänd) ***n.*** ⟦ult. < Gothic *bindan,* bind⟧ **1** anything that binds, fastens, or unites **2** [*pl.*] shackles **3** a binding agreement **4** an obligation imposed by a contract, promise, etc. **5** the status of goods kept in a warehouse until taxes or duties are paid **6** an interest-bearing certificate issued by a government or business, redeemable on a specified date **7** surety provided against theft, embezzlement, etc. **8** an amount paid for bail, etc. —***vt.*** **1** to join; bind **2** to furnish surety for (someone) **3** to place or hold (goods) in bond

bond·age (bän′dij) ***n.*** ⟦ult. < ON *bua,* inhabit⟧ **1** serfdom or slavery **2** subjection to some force, influence, etc.

bond′ing *n.* the development of a close relationship, esp. between family members

bond′man (-mən) ***n.,*** *pl.* **-men** (-mən) **1** a serf **2** a slave —**bond′wom′an,** *pl.* **-wom′en, *fem.n.***

bond paper ⟦orig. used for bonds, etc.⟧ high-quality writing paper

bonds·man (bändz′mən) ***n.,*** *pl.* **-men** (-mən) **1** BONDMAN **2** one who furnishes bail, etc.

bone (bōn) ***n.*** ⟦< OE *ban*⟧ **1** any of the parts of hard tissue forming the skeleton of most vertebrates **2** this hard tissue **3** a bonelike substance or thing —***vt.*** **boned, bon′ing** to remove the bones from —***vi.*** [Slang] to study hard: usually with *up* —**have a bone to pick** [Inf.] to have cause to quarrel —**make no bones about** [Inf.] admit freely —**boneless *adj.***

bone china translucent china made of white clay to which the ash of burned bones has been added

bone′-dry′ *adj.* [Inf.] very dry
bone meal crushed or ground bones, used as feed, fertilizer, or a nutritional supplement
bon·er (bōn′ər) *n.* [Slang] a blunder
bon·fire (bän′fīr′) *n.* ⟦ME *banefyre,* bone fire, pyre⟧ an outdoor fire
bong (bôŋ, bäŋ) *n.* ⟦echoic⟧ a deep ringing sound, as of a large bell —*vi.* to make this sound

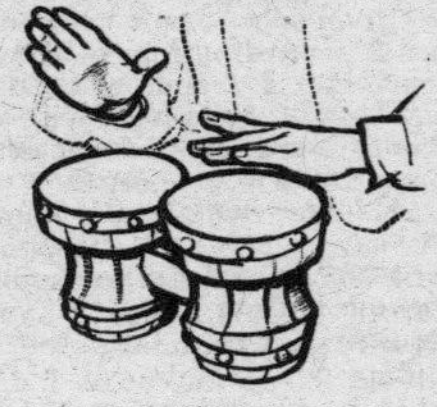

BONGOS

bon·go (bäŋ′gō) *n., pl.* **-gos** ⟦AmSp < ?⟧ either of a pair of small drums of different pitch struck with the fingers: in full **bongo drum**
bo·ni·to (bō nēt′ō, bə-) *n., pl.* **-tos** or **-toes** ⟦Sp⟧ a saltwater food fish similar to a tuna
bon·jour (bōn zhōōr′) *interj., n.* ⟦Fr⟧ good day; hello
bonk·ers (bäŋ′kərz) *adj.* [Slang] crazy
bon mot (bōn′ mō′; *Fr* bōn mō′) *pl.* **bons mots** (bōn′ mōz′; *Fr,* -mō′) ⟦Fr, lit., good word⟧ a clever or witty remark
Bonn (bän) city in W Germany: capital of West Germany (1949-90): pop. 298,000
bon·net (bän′it) *n.* ⟦< OFr *bonet*⟧ [Inf.] any hat worn by a woman or girl
bon·ny or **bon·nie** (bän′ē) *adj.* **-ni·er, -ni·est** ⟦< L *bonus,* good⟧ [Now Chiefly Brit.] **1** handsome or pretty, with a healthy glow **2** pleasant
bo·no·bo (bə nō′bō) *n., pl.* **-bos** a kind of chimpanzee, small with long limbs
bon·sai (bän′sī′) *n., pl.* **-sai′** ⟦Jpn⟧ a tree or shrub grown in a pot and dwarfed by pruning, etc.
bo·nus (bō′nəs) *n., pl.* **-nus·es** ⟦L, good⟧ anything given in addition to the customary or required amount
bon voy·age (bän′ voi äzh′) ⟦Fr⟧ pleasant journey
bon·y (bō′nē) *adj.* **-i·er, -i·est 1** of, like, or having bones **2** thin; emaciated
bony fish any fish with an air bladder, covered gills, and a bony skeleton
boo (bōō) *interj., n., pl.* **boos** a sound made to express disapproval, etc., or to startle someone —*vi., vt.* **booed, boo′ing** to shout "boo" (at)
boo-boo or **boo·boo** (bōō′bōō′) *n., pl.* **-boos′** [Slang] a stupid mistake
boob tube [Slang] TV or a TV set
boo·by (bōō′bē) *n., pl.* **-bies** ⟦prob. < Sp *bobo*⟧ a fool; nitwit: also **boob** (bōōb)
booby trap any scheme or device for tricking a person unexpectedly
boo·dle (bōōd′'l) *n.* ⟦< Du *boedel,* property⟧ [Old Slang] **1** something given as a bribe; graft **2** the loot taken in a robbery
boo·gey·man (boog′ē man′, bō′gē-) *n., pl.* **-men′** (-men′) a frightening imaginary being
book (book) *n.* ⟦OE *boc*⟧ **1** a printed work on sheets of paper bound together, usually between protective covers **2** a main division of a literary work **3** [*usually pl.*] the records or accounts as of a business **4** [*pl.*] studies; lessons **5** *a*) a libretto *b*) the script of a play **6** a booklike package, as of matches —*vt.* **1** to record in a book; list **2** to engage (rooms, etc.) ahead of time **3** to record charges against on a police record —**by the book** according to the rules —**the (Good) Book** the Bible
book′bind′ing *n.* the art, trade, or business of binding books —**book′bind′er** *n.*
book′case′ *n.* a set of shelves or a cabinet for holding books
book′end′ *n.* a support, usually one of a pair, used to keep a row of books upright
book′ie (-ē) *n.* [Slang] a bookmaker
book′ing *n.* an engagement, as for a concert
book′ish (-ish) *adj.* **1** inclined to read and study **2** pedantic
book′keep′ing *n.* the work of keeping a record of business transactions —**book′keep′er** *n.*
book′let (-lit) *n.* a small book
book′mak′er *n.* a person in the business of taking bets, as on horses
book′mark′ *n.* a thing put between the pages of a book to mark a place
book matches safety matches made of paper and fastened into a cardboard holder
book′mo·bile′ (-mō bēl′) *n.* a lending library in a van that visits rural schools, etc.
book′plate′ *n.* a label pasted in a book to identify its owner
book′shelf *n., pl.* **-shelves′** a shelf on which books are kept
book′store′ *n.* a store where books are sold: also **book′shop′**
book′worm′ *n.* **1** an insect larva that feeds on the binding, paste, etc. of books **2** one who reads or studies frequently
boom[1] (bōōm) *vi., vt.* ⟦echoic⟧ to make, or say with, a deep, hollow, resonant sound —*n.* this sound
boom[2] (bōōm) *n.* ⟦Du, a beam⟧ **1** a spar extending from a mast to hold the bottom of a sail outstretched **2** a long beam extending as from an upright for supporting and guiding anything lifted [the *boom* of a derrick] **3** a barrier, as of logs, to prevent floating logs from dispersing —*vi.* to go rapidly along
boom[3] (bōōm) *vi.* ⟦< ? prec. *vi.*⟧ to increase or grow rapidly —*n.* a period of prosperity
boom′box′ *n.* [Slang] a large portable radio and tape player

boom'er ***n.*** *short for* BABY BOOMER

boom·er·ang (bo͞om'ər aŋ') ***n.*** ⟦< Australian native name⟧ **1** a flat, curved stick that can be thrown so that it returns to the thrower **2** a scheme gone awry, to the schemer's harm **—*vi.*** to act as a boomerang

boom'town' ***n.*** a town that has grown very rapidly: also **boom town**

boon[1] (bo͞on) ***n.*** ⟦ON *bon,* a petition⟧ a welcome benefit; blessing

boon[2] (bo͞on) ***adj.*** ⟦< L *bonus,* good⟧ merry; convivial: now only in **boon companion**, a close friend

boon·docks (bo͞on'däks') ***pl.n.*** ⟦< native Philippine name⟧ [Inf.] **1** a jungle or wilderness **2** any remote rural region Used with *the*

boon·dog·gle (bo͞on'dôg'əl, -däg'-) ***n.*** a trifling, pointless project **—*vi.*** **-gled, -gling** to engage in a boondoggle **—boon'dog'gler *n.***

boor (boor) ***n.*** ⟦Du *boer,* a peasant⟧ a rude, awkward, or ill-mannered person **—boor'ish *adj.*** **—boor'ish·ly *adv.***

boost (bo͞ost) ***vt.*** ⟦< ?⟧ **1** to raise as by a push from below **2** to urge others to support **3** to increase **—*n.*** **1** a push upward or forward **2** an increase **—boost'er *n.***

booster shot a later injection of a vaccine, for maintaining immunity

boot[1] (bo͞ot) ***n.*** ⟦OFr *bote*⟧ **1** a covering of leather, rubber, etc. for the foot and part of the leg **2** a kick **—*vt.*** **1** to put boots on **2** to kick **3** [Inf.] to dismiss (a person) **4** to start (a computer): often with *up* **—*vi.*** to start a computer: usually with *up* **—the boot** [Slang] dismissal

boot[2] (bo͞ot) ***n.*, *vt.*, *vi.*** ⟦OE *bot,* advantage⟧ [Archaic] profit **—to boot** besides; in addition

boot'black' ***n.*** one whose work is shining shoes or boots

boot·ee or **boot·ie** (bo͞o tē'; *for 2* bo͞ot'ē) ***n.*** **1** a short boot for women or children **2** a baby's knitted or cloth shoe

booth (bo͞oth) ***n.***, *pl.* **booths** (bo͞oths, bo͞o*th*z) ⟦< ON *bua,* dwell⟧ **1** a stall for selling goods **2** a small enclosure for voting **3** a small structure to house a public telephone, etc. **4** an eating area in a restaurant with a table and benchlike seats

boot'leg' ***vt.*, *vi.*** **-legged', -leg'ging** ⟦< hiding liquor in a boot⟧ to make or sell (liquor, etc.) illegally **—*adj.*** bootlegged; illegal **—*n.*** bootlegged liquor, etc. **—boot'leg'ger *n.***

boot'less ***adj.*** ⟦BOOT[2] + -LESS⟧ useless

boo·ty (bo͞ot'ē) ***n.***, *pl.* **-ties** ⟦LowG *bute*⟧ **1** spoils of war **2** plunder

booze (bo͞oz) ***vi.*** **boozed, booz'ing** ⟦< MDu *busen*⟧ [Inf.] to drink too much liquor **—*n.*** [Inf.] liquor —[Slang] **booz'er *n.***

bop[1] (bäp) ***vt.*** **bopped, bop'ping** [Inf.] to hit; punch

bop[2] (bäp) ***n.*** a style of jazz (*c.* 1945-55) marked by complex rhythms, harmonic experimentation, etc. **—*vi.*** **bopped, bop'ping** [Slang] to walk, esp. in an easy, strutting way

bo·rax (bôr'aks') ***n.*** ⟦< Pers *būrah*⟧ a white crystalline salt used in the manufacture of glass, soaps, etc.

Bor·deaux (bôr dō') ***n.*** ⟦after *Bordeaux,* city and region in SW France⟧ [*also* **b-**] **1** a red or white wine from the Bordeaux region **2** a similar wine made elsewhere

bor·der (bôr'dər) ***n.*** ⟦< OFr *border,* to border⟧ **1** an edge or part near an edge; margin **2** a dividing line between two countries, etc. **3** a narrow strip along an edge **—*vt.*** **1** to provide with a border **2** to extend along the edge of **—*adj.*** of or near a border **—border on** (or **upon**) **1** to be next to **2** to be like; almost be

bor'der·land' ***n.*** **1** land near a border **2** a vague condition

bor'der·line' ***n.*** a boundary **—*adj.*** **1** on a boundary **2** indefinite

bore[1] (bôr) ***vt.*** **bored, bor'ing** ⟦< OE *bor,* auger⟧ **1** to make a hole in with a drill, etc. **2** to make (a well, etc.) as by drilling **3** to weary by being dull **—*vi.*** to bore a hole or passage **—*n.*** **1** a hole made as by boring **2** *a*) the hollow part of a tube or gun barrel *b*) its inside diameter **3** a tiresome, dull person or thing

bore[2] (bôr) ***vt.*, *vi.*** *pt. of* BEAR[1]

bore·dom (bôr'dəm) ***n.*** the condition of being bored or uninterested

bo·ric acid (bôr'ik) a white crystalline compound, used as an antiseptic, in making glass, etc.

born (bôrn) ***vt.*, *vi.*** *alt. pp. of* BEAR[1] **—*adj.*** **1** brought into life **2** natural, as if from birth *[*a *born* athlete*]*

born-a·gain (bôrn'ə gen') ***adj.*** having a new, strong faith or belief

borne (bôrn) ***vt.*, *vi.*** *alt. pp. of* BEAR[1]

Bor·ne·o (bôr'nē ō') large island in the Malay Archipelago

bo·ron (bôr'än') ***n.*** ⟦< BORAX⟧ a nonmetallic chemical element

bor·ough (bur'ō) ***n.*** ⟦OE *burg,* town⟧ **1** a self-governing, incorporated town **2** any of the five administrative units of New York City

bor·row (bär'ō, bôr'-) ***vt.*, *vi.*** ⟦OE *borgian*⟧ **1** to take or receive (something) with the intention of returning it **2** to adopt (an idea, etc.) as one's own **—bor'row·er *n.***

borscht or **borsch** (bôrsh) ***n.*** ⟦Russ *borshch*⟧ a beet soup, served usually with sour cream

bor·zoi (bôr'zoi') ***n.*** ⟦Russ *borzój,* swift⟧ a large dog with a narrow head, long legs, and silky coat

bosh (bäsh) ***n.*, *interj.*** ⟦Turk, empty⟧ [Inf.] nonsense

Bos·ni·a and Her·ze·go·vi·na (bäz'nē ə and hert'sə gō vē'nə) country in SE Europe: 19,741 sq. mi.; pop. 4,366,000 **—Bos'ni·an *adj.*, *n.***

bos·om (booz'əm; *also* bo͞o'zəm) ***n.*** ⟦OE *bosm*⟧ **1** the human breast **2** the breast regarded as the source of feelings **3** the inside; midst *[*in the *bosom* of one's family*]* **4** the part of a garment that covers the breast —*adj.* close; intimate *[a bosom friend]*

bos'om·y *adj.* having large breasts

bo·son (bō'sän) *n.* ⟦after S. N. *Bose* (1894-1974), Indian physicist + -ON⟧ any of certain subatomic particles, including photons and mesons

boss[1] (bôs, bäs) *n.* ⟦Du *baas,* a master⟧ **1** an employer or manager **2** one who controls a political organization —*vt.* **1** to act as boss of **2** [Inf.] to order (a person) about —*adj.* [Slang] excellent

boss[2] (bôs, bäs) *n.* ⟦OFr *boce,* a swelling⟧ a protruding ornament or projecting knob

boss'y *adj.* **-i·er, -i·est** [Inf.] domineering —**boss'i·ness** *n.*

Bos·ton (bôs'tən, bäs'-) seaport & capital of Massachusetts: pop. 574,000 —**Bos·to'ni·an** (-tō'nē ən) *adj., n.*

bo·sun (bō'sən) *n. phonetic sp. of* BOATSWAIN

bot·a·ny (bät''n ē) *n.* ⟦< Gr *botanē,* a plant⟧ the science that deals with plants and plant life —**bo·tan·i·cal** (bə tan'i kəl) or **bo·tan'ic** *adj.* —**bot'a·nist** *n.*

botch (bäch) *vt.* ⟦ME *bocchen,* to repair < ?⟧ to bungle —*n.* a bungled piece of work —**botch'er** *n.*

bot·fly (bät'flī') *n., pl.* **-flies'** a fly resembling a small bumblebee

both (bōth) *adj., pron.* ⟦OE *ba tha,* both these⟧ the two *[both birds sang loudly]* —*conj., adv.* together; equally *[both tired and hungry]*

both·er (bä*th*'ər) *vt., vi.* ⟦prob. < *pother*⟧ **1** to worry; harass **2** to concern (oneself) —*n.* **1** worry; trouble **2** one who gives trouble —**both'er·some** (-səm) *adj.*

Bot·swa·na (bät swä'nə) country in S Africa: 224,607 sq. mi.; pop. 1,327,000

Bot·ti·cel·li (bät'ə chel'ē; *It* bôt'tē chel'ē), **San·dro** (sän'drô) 1445?-1510; It. painter

bot·tle (bät''l) *n.* ⟦< LL *buttis,* a cask⟧ **1** a narrow-necked container for liquids, usually of glass **2** its contents —*vt.* **-tled, -tling** to put into a bottle —**bottle up** to restrain —**hit the bottle** [Slang] to drink much alcoholic liquor —**bot'tler** *n.*

bot'tle·neck' *n.* **1** a narrow passage or road where traffic is slowed or stopped **2** any similar hindrance to movement or progress

bot·tom (bät'əm) *n.* ⟦OE *botm,* ground⟧ **1** the lowest part or place **2** the part on which something rests **3** the side underneath **4** the seat of a chair **5** the ground beneath a body of water **6** basis; cause; source **7** [Inf.] the buttocks —*adj.* lowest; last; basic —**at bottom** fundamentally —**bot'tom·less** *adj.*

bottom line **1** [Inf.] profits or losses, as of a business **2** [Slang] *a)* the basic factor, etc. *b)* the final statement, decision, etc.

bot·u·lism (bäch'ə liz'əm) *n.* ⟦< L *botulus,* sausage⟧ poisoning, often fatal, by the toxin produced by a bacterium sometimes found in foods improperly canned or preserved

bou·doir (bōō dwär', bōō'dwär') *n.* ⟦< Fr, lit., pouting room⟧ a woman's private room

bouf·fant (bōō fänt') *adj.* ⟦< Fr *bouffer,* puff out⟧ puffed out; full

bou·gain·vil·le·a or **bou·gain·vil·lae·a** (bōō'gən vil'ē ə, -vil'yə, -vē'yə) *n.* ⟦ModL⟧ a woody tropical vine having large, showy purple or red bracts

bough (bou) *n.* ⟦OE *bog,* shoulder or arm⟧ a main branch of a tree

bought (bôt) *vt. pt. & pp. of* BUY

bouil·lon (bool'yän', -yən) *n.* ⟦< Fr *bouillir,* to boil⟧ a clear broth

boul·der (bōl'dər) *n.* ⟦< ME *bulderston,* noisy stone⟧ a large rock worn by weather and water

bou·le·vard (bool'ə värd') *n.* ⟦Fr < MDu *bolwerc,* bulwark⟧ a broad street lined with trees, etc.

bounce (bouns) *vi.* **bounced, bounc'ing** ⟦ME *bounsen,* to thump⟧ **1** to spring back, as upon impact; rebound **2** to spring; leap **3** [Slang] to be returned: said of a worthless check —*vt.* **1** to cause (a ball, etc.) to bounce **2** [Slang] to put (a person) out by force **3** [Slang] to fire from a job —*n.* **1** *a)* a bouncing; rebound *b)* a leap or jump **2** capacity for bouncing **3** [Inf.] energy, zest, etc. —**the bounce** [Slang] dismissal —**bounc'y** *adj.*

bounc'er *n.* [Slang] a person hired to remove disorderly people from a nightclub, restaurant, etc.

bounc'ing *adj.* big, healthy, etc.

bound[1] (bound) *vi.* ⟦< OFr *bondir,* to leap⟧ **1** to move with a leap or leaps **2** to bounce; rebound —*vt.* to cause to bound or bounce —*n.* **1** a jump; leap **2** a bounce; rebound

bound[2] (bound) *vt., vi. pt. & pp. of* BIND —*adj.* **1** tied **2** closely connected **3** certain; sure *[bound to lose]* **4** obliged **5** having a binding: said as of a book **6** [Inf.] determined; resolved

bound[3] (bound) *adj.* ⟦< ON *bua,* prepare⟧ going; headed *[bound for home]*

bound[4] (bound) *n.* ⟦< ML *butina,* boundary⟧ **1** a boundary **2** [*pl.*] an area near a boundary —*vt.* **1** to limit **2** to be a limit or boundary to **3** to name the boundaries of —**out of bounds** **1** beyond the boundaries **2** forbidden

bound·a·ry (boun'drē, -də rē) *n., pl.* **-ries** anything marking a limit; bound

bound'en *adj.* ⟦old pp. of BIND⟧ **1** [Archaic] obligated; indebted **2** obligatory *[one's bounden duty]*

bound'er *n.* ⟦< BOUND[1]⟧ [Inf., Chiefly Brit.] a cad

bound'less *adj.* unlimited; vast

boun·te·ous (boun'tē əs) *adj.* ⟦see BOUNTY⟧ **1** generous **2** plentiful —**boun'te·ous·ly** *adv.*

boun'ti·ful (-tə fəl) *adj.* BOUNTEOUS

boun'ty (-tē) *n., pl.* **-ties** ⟦< L *bonus,* good⟧ **1** generosity **2** a generous gift **3** a reward or premium

bou·quet (bō kā'; *for 2, usually* bōō-) *n.* ⟦Fr⟧ **1** a bunch of flowers **2** aroma, as of wine

bour·bon (bur′bən) ***n.*** ⟦after *Bourbon* County, KY⟧ [*sometimes* **B-**] a whiskey distilled from corn mash

bour·geois (boor zhwä′) ***n.***, *pl.* **-geois′** ⟦Fr < OFr *borc*, town⟧ a member of the bourgeoisie —***adj.*** of the bourgeoisie: used variously to mean conventional, smug, materialistic, etc.

bour·geoi·sie (boor′zhwä zē′) ***n.*** [*with sing. or pl. v.*] the social class between the very wealthy and the working class; middle class

bout (bout) ***n.*** ⟦ME *bught*⟧ **1** a struggle or contest **2** a period of some activity, as a spell of illness

bou·tique (bo͞o tēk′; *occas.*, bō-) ***n.*** ⟦Fr < L *apotheca*, storehouse⟧ a small shop where fashionable articles are sold

bou·ton·niere or **bou·ton·nière** (bo͞o′ tə nir′, -tən yer′) ***n.*** ⟦Fr, buttonhole⟧ a flower worn in a buttonhole

bo·vine (bō′vīn′, -vēn′) ***adj.*** ⟦< L *bos*, ox⟧ **1** of an ox, cow, etc. **2** slow, dull, stupid, etc.

bow[1] (bou) ***vi.*** ⟦< OE *bugan*, to bend⟧ **1** to bend down the head or body in respect, agreement, etc. **2** to give in —***vt.*** **1** to bend (the head or body) down in respect, etc. **2** to weigh (*down*) —***n.*** a bending down of the head or body, as in respect or greeting —**take a bow** to acknowledge applause, etc.

bow[2] (bō) ***n.*** ⟦OE *boga*⟧ **1** anything curved *[a rainbow]* **2** a curve; bend **3** a flexible, curved strip of wood with a cord connecting the two ends, for shooting arrows **4** a slender stick strung with horsehairs, as for playing a violin **5** a decorative knot, as a bowknot —***adj.*** curved —***vt.***, ***vi.*** **1** to bend; curve **2** to play (a violin, etc.) with a bow

bow[3] (bou) ***n.*** ⟦< LowG *būg*⟧ the front part of a ship, etc.

bowd·ler·ize (boud′lər īz′) ***vt.*** **-ized′**, **-iz′ing** ⟦after T. *Bowdler* (1754-1825), Eng editor⟧ to expurgate —**bowd′ler·ism′** ***n.*** —**bowd′ler·i·za′tion** ***n.***

bow·el (bou′əl) ***n.*** ⟦< L *botulus*, sausage⟧ **1** an intestine, esp. of a human being **2** [*pl.*] the inner part —**move one's bowels** to defecate

bow·er (bou′ər) ***n.*** ⟦< OE *bur*, dwelling⟧ a place enclosed by boughs or vines; arbor

bow·ie knife (bo͞o′ē, bō′-) ⟦after Col. J. *Bowie* (1799?-1836)⟧ a long single-edged hunting knife

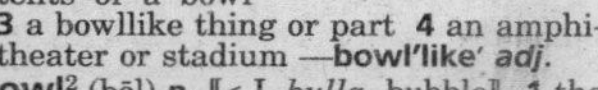

BOWIE KNIFE

bow·knot (bō′ nät′) ***n.*** a decorative knot, usually with two loops and two ends

bowl[1] (bōl) ***n.*** ⟦OE *bolla*⟧ **1** a deep, rounded dish **2** the contents of a bowl **3** a bowllike thing or part **4** an amphitheater or stadium —**bowl′like′** ***adj.***

bowl[2] (bōl) ***n.*** ⟦< L *bulla*, bubble⟧ **1** the wooden ball used in the game of lawn bowling **2** a roll of the ball in bowling —***vi.*** **1** to roll a ball or participate in bowling **2** to move swiftly and smoothly —**bowl over** **1** to knock over **2** [Inf.] to astonish —**bowl′er** ***n.***

bowl·der (bōl′dər) ***n.*** *alt. sp. of* BOULDER

bow·leg (bō′leg′) ***n.*** a leg with outward curvature —**bow′leg′ged** (-leg′id, -legd′) ***adj.***

bowl′ing ***n.*** **1** a game in which a heavy ball is rolled along a wooden lane (**bowling alley**) at ten wooden pins **2** LAWN BOWLING

bowling green a lawn for lawn bowling

bowls (bōlz) ***n.*** LAWN BOWLING

bow·man (bō′mən) ***n.***, *pl.* **-men** (-mən) an archer

bow·sprit (bou′sprit′, bō′-) ***n.*** ⟦prob. < Du⟧ a tapered spar extending forward from the bow of a sailing ship

bow tie (bō) a necktie tied in a bow

box[1] (bäks) ***n.*** ⟦< Gr *pyxos*, BOX[3]⟧ **1** a container, usually rectangular and lidded; case **2** the contents of a box **3** a boxlike thing or space *[a jury box]* **4** a small, enclosed group of seats, as in a theater **5** a booth *[a sentry box]* **6** *Baseball* an area designated for the batter, catcher, etc. —***vt.*** to put into a box —**box in** (or **up**) to shut in or keep in; surround or confine —**in a box** [Inf.] in difficulty —**box′like′** ***adj.*** —**box′y**, **-i·er**, **-i·est**, ***adj.***

box[2] (bäks) ***n.*** ⟦< ?⟧ a blow struck with the hand —***vt.*** **1** to strike with such a blow **2** to engage in boxing with —***vi.*** to fight with the fists

box[3] (bäks) ***n.*** ⟦< Gr *pyxos*⟧ an evergreen shrub with small leathery leaves: also **box′wood′**

box′car′ ***n.*** a fully enclosed railroad freight car

box′er ***n.*** **1** one who boxes; prizefighter **2** a medium-sized dog with a sturdy body and a smooth coat

box′ing ***n.*** the skill or sport of fighting with the fists, esp. in padded leather mittens (**boxing gloves**)

box office **1** a place where admission tickets are sold, as in a theater **2** [Inf.] the power of a show or performer to attract a paying audience

box wrench a wrench with an enclosed head

boy (boi) ***n.*** ⟦ME *boie*⟧ **1** a male child **2** any man: familiar term **3** a male servant: a patronizing term —***interj.*** [Slang] used to express pleasure, surprise, etc.: often **oh, boy!** —**boy′hood′** ***n.*** —**boy′ish** ***adj.***

boy·cott (boi′kät′) ***vt.*** ⟦after Capt. *Boycott,* Irish land agent so treated in 1880⟧ to join together in refusing to deal with, buy, etc. so as to punish or coerce —***n.*** a boycotting

boy′friend′ ***n.*** [Inf.] **1** a sweetheart or escort of a girl or woman **2** a boy who is someone's friend

Boy Scout a member of the **Boy Scouts**, a boys' organization that stresses outdoor life and service to others

boy·sen·ber·ry (boi′zən ber′ē) ***n.***, *pl.*

-ries ⟦after R. *Boysen,* U.S. horticulturist, developer (*c.* 1935)⟧ a berry that is a cross of the raspberry, loganberry, and blackberry

Br[1] *abbrev.* **1** Branch **2** British **3** Brother

Br[2] *Chem. symbol for* bromine

bra (brä) ***n.*** ⟦< BRASSIERE⟧ a woman's undergarment for supporting the breasts

brace (brās) ***vt.*** **braced, brac'ing** ⟦< Gr *brachiōn,* arm⟧ **1** to bind **2** to strengthen by supporting the weight of, etc. **3** to make ready for an impact, shock, etc. **4** to stimulate; invigorate —***n.*** **1** a couple; pair **2** a thing that clasps or connects **3** [*pl.*] [Brit.] suspenders **4** a device for setting up or maintaining tension **5** either of the signs { }, used to connect words, lines, etc. **6** any propping device **7** *a*) a device for supporting a weak part of the body *b*) [*often pl.*] a device worn for straightening teeth **8** a tool for holding a drilling bit —**brace up** to call forth one's courage, etc.

brace and bit a tool for boring, consisting of a removable drill (*bit*) in a rotating handle (*brace*)

brace·let (brās'lit) ***n.*** ⟦< Gr *brachiōn,* arm⟧ an ornamental band or chain worn around the wrist or arm —**brace'let·ed *adj.***

brack·en (brak'ən) ***n.*** ⟦ME *braken*⟧ a large, weedy fern found in meadows, woods, etc.

brack·et (brak'it) ***n.*** ⟦< Fr *brague,* knee pants⟧ **1** a support projecting from a wall, etc. **2** any angle-shaped support **3** either of the signs [ ], used to enclose a word, etc. **4** the part of a classified grouping within certain limits *[high income bracket]* —***vt.*** **1** to support with brackets **2** to enclose within brackets **3** to classify together

brack·ish (brak'ish) ***adj.*** ⟦< MDu *brak*⟧ **1** salty **2** nauseating —**brack'ish·ness *n.***

bract (brakt) ***n.*** ⟦L *bractea,* thin metal plate⟧ a modified leaf growing at the base of a flower or on its stalk

brad (brad) ***n.*** ⟦ON *broddr,* arrow⟧ a thin wire nail with a small head

brae (brā, brē) ***n.*** ⟦ON *bra,* brow⟧ [Scot.] a sloping bank; hillside

brag (brag) ***vt., vi.*** **bragged, brag'ging** ⟦ME *braggen* < ?⟧ to boast —***n.*** boastful talk —**brag'ger *n.***

brag'gart (-ərt) ***n.*** an offensively boastful person —***adj.*** boastful

Brah·ma (brä'mə) ***n.*** Hindu god regarded as the creator of the universe

Brah·man (brä'mən) ***n.,*** *pl.* **-mans** ⟦Hindi < Sans, worship⟧ **1** a member of the Hindu priestly caste **2** a breed of domestic cattle developed from the zebu of India and having a large hump

Brahms (brämz), **Jo·han·nes** (yō hän'əs) 1833-97; Ger. composer

braid (brād) ***vt.*** ⟦< OE *bregdan,* to move quickly⟧ **1** to interweave three or more strands of (hair, straw, etc.) **2** to make by such interweaving —***n.*** **1** a length of hair, etc. formed by braiding **2** a woven band of cloth, etc., used to bind or decorate clothing

Braille (brāl) ***n.*** ⟦after L. *Braille* (1809-52), its Fr inventor⟧ [*also* **b-**] a system of printing for the blind, using raised dots felt with the fingers

brain (brān) ***n.*** ⟦OE *brægen*⟧ **1** the mass of nerve tissue in the cranium of vertebrates **2** [*often pl.*] intelligence **3** [Inf.] an intelligent person —***vt.*** [Slang] to hit hard on the head

brain'child' ***n.*** [Inf.] an idea, plan, etc. produced by a person's own mental labor

brain drain [Inf.] an exhausting of the intellectual or professional resources of a country, region, etc., esp. through emigration

brain'less *adj.* foolish or stupid

brain'storm' *n.* [Inf.] a sudden inspiration, idea, or plan —***vi.*** to engage in brainstorming

brain'storm'ing *n.* the unrestrained offering of ideas by all members of a group to seek solutions to problems

brain'wash' *vt.* [Inf.] to indoctrinate so thoroughly as to effect a radical change of beliefs and attitudes

brain wave a series of rhythmic electric impulses from the nerve centers in the brain

brain'y *adj.* **-i·er, -i·est** [Inf.] having a good mind; intelligent

braise (brāz) ***vt.*** **braised, brais'ing** ⟦< Fr *braise,* live coals⟧ to brown (meat, etc.) and then simmer slowly

brake (brāk) ***n.*** ⟦< ODu *breken,* to break⟧ any device for slowing or stopping a vehicle or machine, as by causing a block, band, etc. (**brake shoe**) to press against a moving part —***vt., vi.*** **braked, brak'ing** to slow down or stop with or as with a brake —**brake'less *adj.***

brake'man (-mən) ***n.,*** *pl.* **-men** (-mən) a railroad worker who operated the brakes on a train, but is now chiefly an assistant to the conductor

bram·ble (bram'bəl) ***n.*** ⟦< OE *brom,* broom (the plant)⟧ a prickly shrub of the rose family, as the raspberry or blackberry —**bram'bly *adj.***

Bramp·ton (bramp'tən) city in SE Ontario, Canada: pop. 268,000

bran (bran) ***n.*** ⟦OFr *bren*⟧ the husk of grains of wheat, rye, etc. separated from the flour

branch (branch) ***n.*** ⟦< LL *branca,* a claw⟧ **1** any woody extension from a tree or shrub; limb **2** a tributary stream **3** any part or extension of a main body or system, as a division of a family or a separately located unit of a business, library, etc. —***vi.*** **1** to put forth branches **2** to come out (*from* the main part) as a branch —**branch off** **1** to separate into branches **2** to diverge —**branch out** to extend one's interests, activities, etc. —**branched** (brancht) ***adj.*** —**branch'like' *adj.***

brand (brand) ***n.*** ⟦OE < *biernan,* to burn⟧ **1** a burning or partially burned stick **2** a mark burned on the skin, formerly used to punish criminals, now used on cattle to show ownership **3** the iron used in branding **4** a stigma **5** *a*) an identifying mark or label on a company's products *b*) the make of a commodity [a *brand* of coffee] *c*) a special kind —*vt.* **1** to mark with a brand **2** to put a stigma on —**brand'er** *n.*

brand'ing *n.* the marketing of products by connecting them with a popular brand name

bran·dish (bran'dish) *vt.* ⟦< OFr *brandir*⟧ to wave menacingly or as a challenge; flourish

brand name the name by which a certain brand or make of commodity is known —**brand'-name'** *adj.*

brand'-new' *adj.* ⟦orig., fresh from the fire: see BRAND⟧ entirely new

bran·dy (bran'dē) *n., pl.* **-dies** ⟦< Du *brandewijn,* distilled wine⟧ an alcoholic liquor distilled from wine or from fermented fruit juice —*vt.* **-died, -dy·ing** to flavor or preserve with brandy

brant (brant) *n.* ⟦< ?⟧ a wild goose of Europe and North America

brash (brash) *adj.* ⟦orig. Brit dial.; < ?⟧ **1** hasty and reckless **2** insolent; impudent

Bra·sí·lia (brä zē'lyä; *E* brə zil'yə) capital of Brazil, in the central part: pop. 1,596,000

brass (bras) *n., pl.* **brass'es** ⟦OE *bræs*⟧ **1** a yellowish metal, an alloy of copper and zinc **2** [*often with pl. v.*] musical instruments made of brass **3** [Inf.] bold impudence **4** [*often with pl. v.*] [Slang] officers or officials of high rank —*adj.* of brass —**brass'y, -i·er, -i·est,** *adj.*

bras·siere or **bras·sière** (brə zir') *n.* ⟦Fr < *bras,* an arm⟧ a bra

brass tacks [Inf.] basic facts: used chiefly in **get** (or **come**) **down to brass tacks**

brat (brat) *n.* ⟦< Gael *bratt,* cloth, rag, ? child's bib⟧ a child, esp. an impudent, unruly child: scornful or playful term

Bra·ti·sla·va (brä'ti slä'və) capital of Slovakia, on the Danube: pop. 448,000

brat·wurst (brät'wurst') *n.* ⟦Ger < OHG, *brato,* lean meat + *wurst,* sausage⟧ highly seasoned, fresh sausage of veal and pork

braun·schwei·ger (broun'shwī'gər) *n.* ⟦after *Braunschweig,* Germany, where orig. made⟧ smoked liver sausage

bra·va·do (brə vä'dō) *n.* ⟦< Sp < *bravo,* brave⟧ pretended courage or feigned defiant confidence

brave (brāv) *adj.* **brav'er, brav'est** ⟦Fr < It *bravo*⟧ **1** not afraid; having courage **2** having a fine appearance —*n.* **1** any brave man **2** a North American Indian warrior —*vt.* **braved, brav'ing 1** to face with courage **2** to defy; dare —**brave'ly** *adv.* —**brave'ness** *n.*

brav·er·y (brāv'ər ē) *n.* courage; valor

bra·vo (brä'vō) *interj.* ⟦It⟧ well done! excellent! —*n., pl.* **-vos** a shout of "bravo!"

bra·vu·ra (brə vyoor'ə) *n.* ⟦It < *bravo,* brave⟧ **1** bold daring; dash **2** a brilliant musical passage or brilliant technique

brawl (brôl) *vi.* ⟦ME *braulen,* to cry out⟧ to quarrel or fight noisily —*n.* a noisy quarrel or fight

brawn (brôn) *n.* ⟦< OFr *braon,* muscle⟧ **1** strong, well-developed muscles **2** muscular strength —**brawn'y, -i·er, -i·est,** *adj.* —**brawn'i·ness** *n.*

bray (brā) *vi.* ⟦< OFr *braire*⟧ to make the loud, harsh cry of a donkey —*n.* the harsh cry of a donkey, or a sound like this

braze (brāz) *vt.* **brazed, braz'ing** ⟦Fr *braser*⟧ to solder with a metal having a high melting point

bra·zen (brā'zən) *adj.* ⟦< OE *bræsen,* brass⟧ **1** of brass **2** like brass in color, etc. **3** shameless; bold; impudent **4** harsh and piercing —**brazen it out** to act in a bold, unashamed way —**bra'zen·ly** *adv.* —**bra'zen·ness** *n.*

bra·zier[1] (brā'zhər) *n.* ⟦see BRAISE⟧ a metal container to hold burning coals

bra·zier[2] (brā'zhər) *n.* ⟦see BRASS⟧ a person who works in brass

Bra·zil (brə zil') country in South America, on the Atlantic: 3,286,485 sq. mi.; pop. 146,155,000 —**Bra·zil'ian** *adj., n.*

Brazil nut the edible, three-sided seed of a tree of South America

breach (brēch) *n.* ⟦< OE *brecan,* to break⟧ **1** a failure to observe a law, promise, etc. **2** an opening made by a breakthrough **3** a break in friendly relations —*vt.* **1** to make a breach in **2** to violate (a contract, etc.) —**breach of promise** a breaking of a promise, esp. to marry

bread (bred) *n.* ⟦OE, crumb⟧ **1** a baked food made of flour or meal mixed with water, etc. **2** livelihood [to earn one's *bread*] —*vt.* to coat with bread crumbs before cooking —**break bread** to eat

breadth (bredth) *n.* ⟦< OE *brad,* broad⟧ **1** width **2** scope; extent **3** lack of restriction

bread·win·ner (bred'win'ər) *n.* one who supports dependents by his or her earnings

break (brāk) *vt.* **broke, bro'ken, break'ing** ⟦OE *brecan*⟧ **1** to split or crack into pieces; smash **2** to cut open the surface of (soil, the skin, etc.) **3** to make unusable by cracking, disrupting, etc. **4** to tame as with force **5** to get rid of (a habit) **6** to demote **7** to make poor, ill, bankrupt, etc. **8** to surpass (a record) **9** to violate (a law, promise, etc.) **10** to disrupt the order of [*break* ranks] **11** to interrupt (a journey, electric circuit, etc.) **12** to reduce the force of by interrupting (a fall, etc.) **13** to bring to an end suddenly or by force **14** to penetrate (silence, darkness, etc.) **15** to disclose **16** to decipher or solve [*break* a code] —*vi.* **1** to split into pieces; come apart **2** to force one's way (*through* obstacles, etc.) **3** to stop associating (*with*) **4** to become unusable **5** to change suddenly [his voice *broke*] **6** to begin suddenly [to *break* into song] **7** to come suddenly into being, notice, etc. [the story *broke*] **8** to stop activity temporarily **9** to suffer a collapse as of spirit —*n.* **1** a breaking **2** a broken place 3 a beginning or appearance *[the break of day]* 4 an interruption of regularity 5 a gap, interval, or rest 6 a sudden change 7 an escape 8 a chance piece of luck —**break down** 1 to go out of working order 2 to have a physical or nervous collapse 3 to analyze —**break in** 1 to enter forcibly 2 to interrupt 3 to train (a beginner) 4 to prepare (something new) by use or wear —**break off** to stop abruptly —**break out** 1 to become covered with pimples, etc. 2 to escape suddenly —**break up** 1 to separate; disperse 2 to stop 3 [Inf.] to laugh or make laugh —**give someone a break** [Inf.] to stop treating someone harshly, critically, etc. —**break'a·ble** ***adj., n.***

break'age ***n.*** 1 a breaking 2 things broken 3 loss due to breaking or the sum allowed for it

break'down' ***n.*** 1 a breaking down 2 a failure of health 3 an analysis

break'er ***n.*** 1 a person or thing that breaks 2 a wave that breaks into foam

break·fast (brek'fəst) ***n.*** the first meal of the day —***vi.*** to eat breakfast

break·front (brāk'frunt') ***adj.*** having a projecting center section in front —***n.*** a breakfront cabinet

break'-in' ***n.*** the act of forcibly entering a building, esp. in order to rob

break'neck' ***adj.*** very fast, reckless, or dangerous *[breakneck speed]*

break'through' ***n.*** 1 the act of forcing a way through against resistance, as in warfare 2 a very important advance or discovery

break'up' ***n.*** 1 a dispersion 2 a disintegration 3 a collapse

break'wa'ter ***n.*** a barrier to break the impact of waves, as before a harbor

breast (brest) ***n.*** ⟦OE *breost*⟧ 1 either of two milk-secreting glands on a woman's body 2 the upper front part of the body 3 the part of a garment, etc. over the breast 4 the breast regarded as the center of emotions —***vt.*** to face firmly; oppose

breast'bone' ***n.*** STERNUM

breast'-feed' ***vt.*** **-fed', -feed'ing** to feed (a baby) milk from the breast

breast'plate' ***n.*** a piece of armor for the breast

breast stroke a swimming stroke in which both arms are brought out sideways from the chest

breast'work' ***n.*** a low wall put up quickly as a defense in battle

breath (breth) ***n.*** ⟦< OE *bræth,* odor⟧ 1 air taken into the lungs and then let out 2 respiration 3 the power to breathe easily 4 life; spirit 5 a fragrant odor 6 a slight breeze 7 a whisper; murmur —**catch one's breath** 1 to gasp 2 [Inf.] to rest or pause —**in the same breath** almost simultaneously —**out of breath** breathless, as from exertion —**take someone's breath away** to thrill someone —**under** (or **below**) **one's breath** in a whisper

breathe (brēth) ***vi., vt.*** **breathed, breath'ing** 1 to take (air) into the lungs and let it out again; inhale and exhale 2 to live 3 to rest —**breathe again** to have a feeling of relief —**breath'a·ble** ***adj.***

breath·er (brē'thər) ***n.*** 1 one who breathes 2 [Inf.] a pause for rest

breath·less (breth'lis) ***adj.*** 1 without breath 2 panting; gasping 3 unable to breathe easily because of emotion —**breath'less·ly** ***adv.***

breath'tak'ing ***adj.*** very exciting

breath'y ***adj.*** **-i·er, -i·est** marked by an audible emission of breath

bred (bred) ***vt., vi.*** *pt. & pp. of* BREED

breech (brēch) ***n.*** ⟦OE *brec*⟧ 1 the buttocks 2 the part of a gun behind the barrel

breech'cloth' ***n.*** LOINCLOTH

breech·es (brich'iz) ***pl.n.*** ⟦see BREECH⟧ 1 trousers reaching to the knees 2 [Inf.] any trousers

breed (brēd) ***vt.*** **bred, breed'ing** ⟦< OE *brod,* fetus⟧ 1 to bring forth (offspring) 2 to be the source of; produce 3 to raise (animals) 4 to rear; train —***vi.*** 1 to be produced; originate 2 to reproduce —***n.*** 1 a stock; strain 2 a sort; type —**breed'er** ***n.***

breed'ing ***n.*** 1 the producing of young 2 good upbringing 3 the producing of plants and animals, esp. for improving the stock

breeze (brēz) ***n.*** ⟦16th-c. nautical term *brise,* prob. < Du⟧ 1 a gentle wind 2 [Inf.] a thing easy to do —***vi.*** **breezed, breez'ing** [Inf.] to move or go quickly

breeze'way' ***n.*** a covered passageway, as between a house and garage

breez'y ***adj.*** **-i·er, -i·est** 1 slightly windy 2 light and lively —**breez'i·ly** ***adv.*** —**breez'i·ness** ***n.***

Bre·men (brem'ən) seaport in NW Germany: pop. 553,000

breth·ren (breth'rən) ***pl.n.*** ⟦ME *bretheren*⟧ brothers: now chiefly religious

bre·vet (brə vet') ***n.*** ⟦< L *brevis,* brief⟧ [Historical] *Mil.* a commission of higher honorary rank without extra pay —***vt.*** **-vet'ted** or **-vet'ed, -vet'ting** or **-vet'ing** to give a brevet to

bre·vi·ar·y (brē'vē er'ē) ***n., pl.*** **-ar'ies** ⟦< L *brevis,* brief⟧ a book of Psalms, prayers, etc. to be recited daily by priests, nuns, etc.

brev·i·ty (brev'ə tē) ***n.*** ⟦< L *brevis,* brief⟧ 1 briefness 2 conciseness

brew (brōō) ***vt.*** ⟦OE *breowan*⟧ 1 to make (beer, etc.) from malt and hops by boiling and fermenting 2 to steep (tea, etc.) 3 to plot —***vi.*** to begin to form —***n.*** a brewed beverage —**brew'er** ***n.***

brew·er·y (brōō'ər ē) ***n., pl.*** **-er·ies** a place where beer, etc. is brewed

bri·ar[1] (brī'ər) ***n.*** BRIER[1]

bri·ar[2] (brī'ər) ***n.*** a tobacco pipe made from the root of the BRIER[2]

bribe (brīb) ***n.*** ⟦< OFr *briber,* to beg⟧ anything given or promised as an inducement, esp. to do something illegal or wrong —***vt.*** **bribed, brib'ing** to offer or give a bribe to —**brib'er·y** ***n.***

bric-a-brac (brik'ə brak') ***n.*** ⟦< Fr *de bric et de brac,* by hook or by crook⟧ 1 small artistic objects used to ornament a room 2 knickknacks

brick (brik) ***n.*** ⟦MDu < *breken,* piece of baked clay⟧ **1** an oblong block of baked clay, used in building, etc. **2** anything shaped like a brick **3** bricks collectively —***adj.*** built or paved with brick —***vt.*** to build or cover with brick

brick'bat' ***n.*** **1** a piece of brick used as a missile **2** an unfavorable remark

brick'lay'er ***n.*** one whose work is building with bricks —**brick'lay'ing** ***n.***

brid·al (brīd''l) ***adj.*** ⟦< OE *bryd ealu,* marriage feast⟧ **1** of a bride **2** of a wedding

bride (brīd) ***n.*** ⟦OE *bryd*⟧ a woman just married or about to be married

bride'groom' ***n.*** ⟦< OE *bryd,* bride + *guma,* man⟧ a man just married or about to be married

brides·maid (brīdz'mād') ***n.*** one of the women who attend the bride at a wedding

bridge[1] (brij) ***n.*** ⟦OE *brycge*⟧ **1** a structure built over a river, etc. to provide a way across **2** a thing that provides connection, contact, etc. **3** the bony upper part of the nose **4** a raised platform on a ship **5** a mounting for false teeth **6** *Music* a connecting passage —***vt.*** **bridged, bridg'ing** to build or be a bridge over —**burn one's bridges (behind one)** to follow a course from which there is no retreat —**bridge'a·ble** ***adj.***

bridge[2] (brij) ***n.*** ⟦< ? Russ⟧ a card game, for two pairs of players, in which they bid for the right to name the trump suit or declare no-trump

bridge'head' ***n.*** a fortified position established by an attacking force on the enemy's side of a bridge, river, etc.

Bridge·port (brij'pôrt') seaport in SW Connecticut: pop. 142,000

bridge'work' ***n.*** a dental bridge or bridges

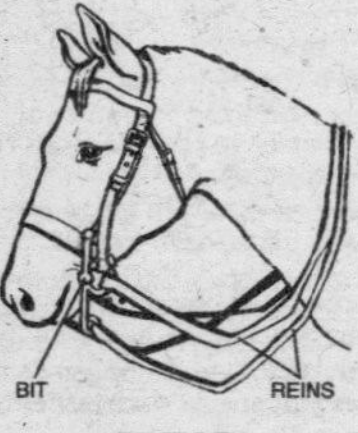

BRIDLE

bri·dle (brīd''l) ***n.*** ⟦< OE *bregdan,* move quickly⟧ **1** a head harness for guiding a horse: it has a bit for the mouth to which the reins are fastened **2** anything that controls or restrains —***vt.*** **bri'dled, bri'dling** **1** to put a bridle on **2** to curb or control —***vi.*** **1** to pull one's head back quickly as an expression of anger, scorn, etc. **2** to take offense (*at*)

bridle path a path for horseback riding

brief (brēf) ***adj.*** ⟦< L *brevis*⟧ **1** short **2** concise —***n.*** **1** a summary, specif. of the main points of a law case **2** [*pl.*] legless undershorts —***vt.*** **1** to summarize **2** to supply with all pertinent information —**brief'ly** ***adv.*** —**brief'ness** ***n.***

brief'case' ***n.*** a flat, flexible case for carrying papers, books, etc.

brief'ing ***n.*** a supplying of pertinent information

bri·er[1] (brī'ər) ***n.*** ⟦OE *brer*⟧ any thorny bush, as a bramble

bri·er[2] (brī'ər) ***n.*** ⟦Fr *bruyère*⟧ a variety of heath, whose root is used for making tobacco pipes

brig[1] (brig) ***n.*** ⟦< BRIGANTINE⟧ a two-masted ship with square sails

brig[2] ***n.*** ⟦< ?⟧ a prison, as on a warship

bri·gade (bri gād') ***n.*** ⟦< OIt *briga,* strife⟧ **1** a military unit composed of two or more battalions with service and administrative units **2** a group of people organized to function as a unit in some work *[a fire brigade]*

brig·a·dier general (brig'ə dir') *U.S. Mil.* a military officer ranking just above a colonel

brig·and (brig'ənd) ***n.*** ⟦see BRIGADE⟧ a bandit, esp. one of a roving band

brig'and·age ***n.*** plundering by brigands

brig·an·tine (brig'ən tēn') ***n.*** ⟦< OIt *brigantino,* pirate vessel⟧ a ship with a square-rigged foremast and a square-rigged topsail on the mainmast

bright (brīt) ***adj.*** ⟦OE *bryht*⟧ **1** shining with light **2** brilliant in color or sound; vivid **3** lively; cheerful **4** mentally quick; smart **5** favorable or hopeful **6** illustrious —**bright'ly** ***adv.*** —**bright'ness** ***n.***

bright'en ***vt., vi.*** to make or become bright or brighter

Brigh·ton (brīt''n) resort city in S England: county district pop. 144,000

bril·liant (bril'yənt) ***adj.*** ⟦< Fr < It *brillare,* to sparkle⟧ **1** shining brightly **2** vivid; intense **3** very splendid **4** very intelligent, talented, etc. —**bril'liance** or **bril'lian·cy** ***n.*** —**bril'liant·ly** ***adv.***

bril·lian·tine (bril'yən tēn') ***n.*** ⟦< Fr⟧ an oily substance for grooming the hair

brim (brim) ***n.*** ⟦ME *brimme*⟧ **1** the topmost edge of a cup, glass, etc. **2** a projecting rim, as of a hat —***vt., vi.*** **brimmed, brim'ming** to fill or be full to the brim —**brim'less** ***adj.***

brim'ful' (-fool') ***adj.*** full to the brim

brim'stone' ***n.*** ⟦< OE *bærnan,* to kindle + *stan,* stone⟧ sulfur

brin·dle (brin'dəl) ***adj.*** BRINDLED —***n.*** **1** a brindled color **2** a brindled animal

brin'dled (-dəld) ***adj.*** ⟦prob. < ME *brennen,* to burn⟧ having a gray or tawny coat streaked or spotted with a darker color

brine (brīn) ***n.*** ⟦OE⟧ **1** water full of salt **2** the ocean —**brin'y, -i·er, -i·est,** ***adj.***

bring (briŋ) ***vt.*** **brought, bring'ing** ⟦OE *bringan*⟧ **1** to carry or lead "here" or to a place where the speaker will be **2** to cause to be, happen, appear, have, etc. **3** to lead to an action or belief **4** to sell for —**bring about** to cause —**bring**

forth to give birth to; produce —**bring off** to accomplish —**bring out 1** to reveal **2** to offer (a play, book, etc.) to the public —**bring up 1** to rear (children) **2** to introduce, as into discussion

brink (briŋk) ***n.*** ⟦< MLowG or Dan, shore⟧ the edge, esp. at the top of a steep place; verge

brink'man·ship' (-mən ship') ***n.*** the policy of pursuing a risky course of action to the brink of disaster: also **brinks'man·ship'**

bri·oche (brē ōsh') ***n.*** ⟦Fr⟧ a light, rich roll made with flour, butter, eggs, and yeast

bri·quette or **bri·quet** (bri ket') ***n.*** ⟦Fr < *brique,* brick⟧ a small block of charcoal, coal dust, etc., used for fuel or kindling

Bris·bane (briz'bān', -bən) seaport in E Australia: pop. 1,455,000

brisk (brisk) ***adj.*** ⟦< ? Fr *brusque,* brusque⟧ **1** quick in manner; energetic **2** keen, bracing, etc. —**brisk'ly *adv.*** —**brisk'ness *n.***

bris·ket (bris'kit) ***n.*** ⟦ME *brusket*⟧ meat cut from the breast of an animal

bris·ling (bris'liŋ) ***n.*** ⟦< Dan *bretling*⟧ SPRAT

bris·tle (bris'əl) ***n.*** ⟦< OE *byrst*⟧ **1** any short, stiff hair **2** such a hair, or a piece like it, in a brush —***vi.* -tled, -tling 1** to be stiff and erect **2** to have the bristles become erect **3** to stiffen with anger **4** to be thickly covered (*with*) —**bris'tly** (-lē), **-tli·er, -tli·est, *adj.***

bris'tle·cone' pine a Rocky Mountain pine tree of the W U.S.

Bris·tol (bris'təl) seaport in SW England: county district pop. 376,000

Brit *abbrev.* British

Brit·ain (brit''n) GREAT BRITAIN

britch·es (brich'iz) ***pl.n.*** [Inf.] BREECHES (sense 2)

Brit·i·cism (brit'ə siz'əm) ***n.*** a word or idiom peculiar to British English

Brit·ish (brit'ish) ***adj.*** of Great Britain or its people, language, etc. —**the British** the people of Great Britain

British Columbia province of SW Canada: 367,671 sq. mi.; pop. 3,725,000; cap. Victoria: abbrev. *BC*

British Commonwealth (of Nations) *former name for* THE COMMONWEALTH

British Isles group of islands including Great Britain, Ireland, etc.

British thermal unit a unit of heat equal to about 252 calories

Brit·on (brit''n) ***n.*** **1** a member of an early Celtic people of S Britain **2** a person born or living in Great Britain, esp. in England

brit·tle (brit''l) ***adj.*** ⟦< OE *breotan,* to break⟧ easily broken or shattered —***n.*** a brittle, crunchy candy with nuts in it —**brit'tle·ness *n.***

broach (brōch) ***n.*** ⟦< ML *brocca,* a spike⟧ a tapering bit for boring holes —***vt.* 1** to make a hole in so as to let out liquid **2** to ream with a broach **3** to start a discussion of

broad (brôd) ***adj.*** ⟦OE *brad*⟧ **1** of large extent from side to side; wide **2** extending about; full *[broad* daylight*]* **3** obvious *[*a *broad* hint*]* **4** tolerant; liberal *[*a *broad* view*]* **5** wide in range *[*a *broad* variety*]* **6** not detailed; general *[*in *broad* outline*]* —**broad'ly *adv.*** —**broad'ness *n.***

broad'band' ***adj.*** designating cable, communication devices, etc. allowing the transmission of much data at high speeds

broad'-based' ***adj.*** comprehensive or extensive

broad'cast' (-kast') ***vt.*, *vi.* -cast'** or **-cast'ed, -cast'ing 1** to scatter or spread widely **2** to transmit by radio or TV —***adj.*** of or for radio or TV broadcasting —***n.*** a radio or TV program —***adv.*** far and wide —**broad'cast'er *n.***

broad'cloth' ***n.*** a fine, smooth woolen, cotton, or silk cloth

broad'en ***vt.*, *vi.*** to widen

broad jump *former name for* LONG JUMP

broad'loom' ***adj.*** woven on a wide loom

broad'-mind'ed ***adj.*** tolerant of unconventional opinions and behavior; liberal —**broad'-mind'ed·ly *adv.*** —**broad'-mind'ed·ness *n.***

broad'side' ***n.*** **1** the firing of all guns on one side of a warship **2** a vigorous attack in words —***adv.*** **1** with the side facing **2** in the side *[*hit *broadside]* **3** indiscriminately

broad'-spec'trum ***adj.*** effective against a wide range of germs

broad'sword' ***n.*** a broad-bladed sword for slashing

Broad·way (brôd'wā') street in New York City, with many theaters, etc.

bro·cade (brō kād') ***n.*** ⟦< Sp < It *broccare,* embroider⟧ a rich cloth with a raised design woven into it —***vt.* -cad'ed, -cad'ing** to weave a raised design into (cloth)

broc·co·li (bräk'ə lē) ***n.*** ⟦It < ML *brocca,* a spike⟧ a plant related to the cauliflower but bearing tender shoots with greenish buds

bro·chette (brō shet') ***n.*** ⟦Fr⟧ a skewer for broiling chunks of meat, etc.

bro·chure (brō shoor') ***n.*** ⟦Fr < *brocher,* to stitch⟧ a pamphlet

bro·gan (brō'gən) ***n.*** ⟦Ir⟧ a heavy work shoe, fitting high on the ankle

brogue[1] (brōg) ***n.*** ⟦< ?⟧ a dialectal pronunciation, esp. that of English by the Irish

brogue[2] (brōg) ***n.*** ⟦< Ir *brōg,* a shoe⟧ a man's heavy oxford shoe

broil (broil) ***vt.*, *vi.*** ⟦< OFr *bruillir*⟧ to cook by exposure to direct heat

broil'er ***n.*** **1** a pan, grill, etc. for broiling **2** a chicken suitable for broiling

broke (brōk) ***vt.*, *vi.*** *pt. of* BREAK —***adj.*** [Inf.] without money; bankrupt

bro·ken (brō'kən) ***vt.*, *vi.*** *pp. of* BREAK —***adj.*** **1** splintered, fractured, etc. **2** not in working order **3** violated *[*a *broken* promise*]* **4** ruined **5** interrupted; discontinuous **6** imperfectly spoken **7** tamed —**bro'ken·ly *adv.*** —**bro'ken·ness *n.***

bro'ken-down' ***adj.*** **1** sick or worn out

2 out of order; useless

bro'ken·heart'ed *adj.* crushed by sorrow, grief, etc.

bro·ker (brō'kər) *n.* ⟦< OFr *brokier,* to tap; orig. sense "wine dealer"⟧ **1** a person hired as an agent in negotiating contracts, buying and selling, etc. **2** STOCKBROKER —*vt., vi.* **1** to act as a broker (for) **2** to negotiate

bro'ker·age *n.* **1** the business or office of a broker **2** a broker's fee

bro·mide (brō'mīd') *n.* **1** a compound of bromine with another element or a radical **2** potassium bromide, used as a sedative **3** a trite saying

bro·mid'ic (-mid'ik) *adj.* trite or dull

bro·mine (brō'mēn') *n.* ⟦< Gr *brōmos,* stench⟧ a chemical element, a reddish-brown, corrosive liquid

bron·chi (bräŋ'kī) *pl.n., sing.* **-chus** (-kəs) ⟦< Gr *bronchos,* windpipe⟧ the two main branches of the windpipe —**bron'chi·al** (-kē əl) *adj.*

bron·chi'tis (-kīt'is) *n.* an inflammation of the bronchial tubes

bron·co (bräŋ'kō) *n., pl.* **-cos** ⟦Sp, rough⟧ a wild or only partly tamed horse or pony of the W U.S.: also **bron'cho** *n., pl.* **-chos**

bron'co·bust'er *n.* [Inf.] a tamer of broncos —**bron'co·bust'ing** *n.*

Bron·të (brän'tē) **1 Char·lotte** (shär'lət) 1816-55; Eng. novelist **2 Em·i·ly** (em'ə lē) 1818-48; Eng. novelist: sister of Charlotte

bron·to·saur (brän'tō sôr', -tə-) *n.* ⟦< Gr *brontē,* thunder + *sauros,* lizard⟧ APATOSAURUS: also **bron'to·saur'us**

Bronx (bräŋks) borough of New York City: pop. 1,204,000: used with *the*

bronze (bränz) *n.* ⟦Fr, prob. ult. < Pers *biriṅǵ,* copper⟧ **1** an alloy of copper and tin **2** a reddish-brown color —*adj.* of or like bronze —*vt.* **bronzed, bronz'ing** ⟦Fr *bronzer* < the *n.*⟧ to make bronze in color

brooch (brōch, brōōch) *n.* ⟦see BROACH⟧ a large ornamental pin with a clasp

brood (brōōd) *n.* ⟦OE *brod*⟧ **1** a group of birds hatched at one time **2** the children in a family —*vi.* **1** to sit on and hatch eggs **2** to worry: often with *on, over,* or *about*

brood'er *n.* **1** one that broods **2** a heated shelter for raising fowl

brood'mare' *n.* a mare kept for breeding

brook[1] (brook) *n.* ⟦< OE *broc*⟧ a small stream

brook[2] (brook) *vt.* ⟦OE *brucan,* to use⟧ to put up with; endure

Brook·lyn (brook'lən) borough of New York City: pop. 2,301,000

broom (brōōm, broom) *n.* ⟦OE *brom,* brushwood⟧ **1** a flowering shrub of the pea family **2** a bundle of fibers or straws fastened to a long handle (**broom'stick'**), used for sweeping

Bros or **bros** *abbrev.* brothers

broth (brôth) *n.* ⟦OE⟧ a thin soup made by boiling meat, etc. in water

broth·el (bräth'əl) *n.* ⟦< OE *broethan,* go to ruin⟧ a house of prostitution

broth·er (bruth'ər) *n., pl.* **-ers** or **breth'ren** ⟦OE *brothor*⟧ **1** a male related to one by having the same parents **2** a friend who is like a brother **3** a fellow member of the same race, church, profession, etc. **4** [*often* **B-**] a lay member of a men's religious order

broth'er·hood' *n.* **1** the state of being brothers **2** an association of men united in some interest, work, etc. **3** a feeling of unity among all people

broth'er-in-law' *n., pl.* **broth'ers-in-law'** **1** the brother of one's spouse **2** the husband of one's sister **3** the husband of the sister of one's spouse

broth'er·ly *adj.* **1** of or like a brother **2** friendly, kind, loyal, etc.

brought (brôt) *vt. pt. & pp. of* BRING

brou·ha·ha (brōō'hä hä') *n.* ⟦Fr⟧ an uproar or commotion

brow (brou) *n.* ⟦OE *bru*⟧ **1** the eyebrow **2** the forehead **3** the edge of a cliff

brow'beat' *vt.* **-beat', -beat'en, -beat'ing** to intimidate with harsh, stern looks and talk; bully

brown (broun) *adj.* ⟦OE *brun*⟧ **1** having the color of chocolate, a mixture of red, black, and yellow **2** tanned; dark-skinned —*n.* brown color —*vt., vi.* to make or become brown —**brown'ish** *adj.*

brown'-bag' *vt., vi.* **-bagged', -bag'ging** to carry (one's lunch) to work or school, as in a brown paper bag

brown·ie (broun'ē) *n.* **1** a small, helpful elf **2** a small square cut from a flat chocolate cake

Brown·ing (broun'iŋ), **Rob·ert** (räb'ərt) 1812-89; Eng. poet

brown'out' *n.* a dimming of lights in a city, as during an electric power shortage

brown rice rice that has not had its brown outer coating removed

brown'stone' *n.* a reddish-brown sandstone, used for building

brown study deep thought; reverie

brown sugar sugar whose crystals retain a brown coating of syrup

browse (brouz) *n.* ⟦< OS *brustian,* to sprout⟧ leaves, shoots, etc. which animals feed on —*vt., vi.* **browsed, brows'ing** **1** to nibble at (leaves, shoots, etc.) **2** to examine (a book, articles for sale, etc.) in a casual way

brows'er *n.* **1** one that browses **2** software for gaining access to the World Wide Web

bru·in (brōō'in) *n.* ⟦Du, brown⟧ a bear

bruise (brōōz) *vt.* **bruised, bruis'ing** ⟦< OE *brysan,* crush⟧ **1** to injure and discolor (body tissue) without breaking the skin **2** to injure the surface of, causing spoilage, denting, etc. **3** to hurt (the feelings, spirit, etc.) —*vi.* to be or become bruised —*n.* a bruised area, as of tissue

bruis'er *n.* [Inf.] a strong, pugnacious man

bruit (brōōt) *vt.* ⟦< OFr, noise, rumor⟧ to spread (*about*) by rumor

brunch (brunch) *n.* a combined breakfast and lunch —*vi.* to eat brunch

Bru·nei (brōō nī′) country on the N coast of Borneo: 2,226 sq. mi.; pop. 261,000

bru·net (brōō net′) ***adj.*** ⟦< OFr, dim. of *brun,* brown⟧ having black or dark-brown hair, often with dark eyes and complexion —***n.*** a brunet person

bru·nette′ (-net′) ***adj.*** BRUNET —***n.*** a brunette woman or girl

Bruns·wick (brunz′wik) city in NC Germany: pop. 258,000

brunt (brunt) ***n.*** ⟦ME *bront*⟧ **1** the shock (of an attack) or impact (of a blow) **2** the hardest part

brush[1] (brush) ***n.*** ⟦< OFr *broce,* bush⟧ **1** BRUSHWOOD **2** sparsely settled country **3** a device for cleaning, painting, etc., having bristles, wires, etc. fastened into a back **4** a brushing **5** a light, grazing stroke **6** a bushy tail, as of a fox —***vt.*** **1** to clean, paint, etc. with a brush **2** to apply, remove, etc. as with a brush **3** to touch or graze in passing —***vi.*** to graze past something —**brush up** to refresh one's memory

brush[2] (brush) ***n.*** ⟦< ME *bruschen,* to rush⟧ a short, quick fight

brush′off′ ***n.*** [Slang] a curt dismissal, esp. in the phrase **give** (or **get**) **the brushoff**

brush′wood′ ***n.*** **1** chopped-off tree branches **2** underbrush

brusque (brusk) ***adj.*** ⟦Fr < ML *bruscus,* brushwood⟧ rough and abrupt in manner or speech; curt: also **brusk** —**brusque′ly** ***adv.*** —**brusque′ness** ***n.***

Brus·sels (brus′əlz) capital of Belgium: pop. 952,000

BRUSSELS SPROUT

Brussels sprout **1** *often* **Brussels sprouts** a plant that bears small cabbagelike heads on an erect stem **2** one of its edible heads

bru·tal (brōōt′'l) ***adj.*** **1** like a brute; very savage, cruel, etc. **2** very harsh —**bru′tal·ly** ***adv.***

bru·tal·i·ty (brōō tal′ə tē) ***n.*** **1** a being brutal **2** *pl.* **-ties** a brutal act

bru·tal·ize (brōōt′'l īz′) ***vt.*** **-ized′**, **-iz′ing** **1** to make brutal **2** to treat in a brutal way —**bru′tal·i·za′tion** ***n.***

brute (brōōt) ***adj.*** ⟦< L *brutus,* irrational⟧ of or like an animal; specif., savage, stupid, etc. —***n.*** **1** an animal **2** a brutal person —**brut′ish** ***adj.*** —**brut′ish·ly** ***adv.***

bs *abbrev.* bill of sale

BS *abbrev.* Bachelor of Science: also **B.S.**

Btu *abbrev.* British thermal unit(s): also **BTU** or **btu**

bu *abbrev.* bushel(s)

bub·ble (bub′əl) ***n.*** ⟦echoic⟧ **1** a film of liquid forming a ball around air or gas **2** a tiny ball of air or gas in a liquid or solid **3** a transparent dome **4** a plausible scheme that proves worthless —***vi.*** **-bled, -bling** **1** to rise in bubbles; boil **2** to make a gurgling sound —**on the bubble** with the outcome uncertain but already being determined —**bub′bly, -bli·er, -bli·est,** ***adj.***

bubble gum a kind of chewing gum that can be blown into large bubbles

bub′ble·head′ ***n.*** a person who is silly, ignorant, etc.

Bubble Wrap *trademark for* plastic packaging material with air bubbles —[**b- w-**] such packaging material

bu·bo (byōō′bō′) ***n.***, *pl.* **-boes′** ⟦< Gr *boubōn,* groin⟧ an inflamed swelling of a lymph node, esp. in the armpit or groin

bu·bon′ic plague (-bän′ik) a contagious disease characterized by buboes, fever, and delirium

buc·ca·neer (buk′ə nir′) ***n.*** ⟦< Fr *boucanier*⟧ a pirate

Bu·chan·an (byōō kan′ən), **James** (jāmz) 1791-1868; 15th president of the U.S. (1857-61)

Bu·cha·rest (bōō′kə rest′) capital of Romania: pop. 1,990,000

buck[1] (buk) ***n.*** ⟦OE *bucca,* male goat⟧ **1** a male deer, goat, etc.: see DOE **2** the act of bucking **3** BUCKSKIN **4** [Inf.] a bold, vigorous young man —***vi.*** **1** to rear upward quickly, as to throw off a rider: said of a horse **2** [Inf.] to resist something as if plunging against it —***vt.*** **1** to dislodge or throw by bucking **2** [Inf.] to resist stubbornly —**buck for** [Slang] to work eagerly for (a promotion, etc.) —**buck up** [Inf.] to cheer up

buck[2] (buk) ***n.*** ⟦< ?⟧ [Slang] a dollar —**pass the buck** [Inf.] to try to shift blame or responsibility onto another person

buck′board′ ***n.*** ⟦BUCK[1], *vi.* + BOARD⟧ an open carriage whose floorboards rest directly on the axles

buck·et (buk′it) ***n.*** ⟦< OE *buc,* pitcher⟧ **1** a cylindrical container with a curved handle, for carrying water, etc.; pail **2** the amount held by a bucket: also **buck′et·ful′**, *pl.* **-fuls′** **3** a thing like a bucket, as a scoop on a steam shovel —**kick the bucket** [Slang] to die

bucket seat a single contoured seat with a movable back, as in sports cars

buck·eye (buk′ī′) ***n.*** ⟦BUCK[1] + EYE < the appearance of the seed⟧ **1** a horse chestnut with large capsules enclosing shiny brown seeds **2** the seed

buck·le[1] (buk′əl) ***n.*** ⟦< L *buccula,* cheek strap of a helmet⟧ a clasp for fastening a strap, belt, etc. —***vt., vi.*** **-led, -ling** to fasten with a buckle —**buckle down** to apply oneself energetically

buck·le[2] (buk′əl) ***vt., vi.*** **-led, -ling** ⟦prob. infl. by OFr *bocler,* to bulge: see prec.⟧ to bend or crumple —***n.*** a bend, bulge, etc.

buck·ler (buk′lər) *n.* ⟦< OFr *bocler*⟧ a small, round shield

buck′-pass′er *n.* [Inf.] one who regularly tries to shift blame or responsibility to someone else —**buck′-pass′ing** *n.*

buck·ram (buk′rəm) *n.* ⟦? < *Bukhara*, city in central Asia⟧ a coarse, stiff cloth used in bookbinding, etc.

buck′saw′ *n.* a wood-cutting saw set in a frame

buck′shot′ *n.* a large lead shot for shooting deer and other large game

buck′skin′ *n.* **1** a soft leather made from the skins of deer or sheep **2** [*pl.*] clothes made of buckskin

buck′tooth′ *n.*, *pl.* **-teeth′** a projecting front tooth —**buck′toothed′** *adj.*

buck′wheat′ *n.* ⟦< OE *boc-*, beech + WHEAT⟧ **1** a plant with beechnut-shaped seeds **2** a dark flour made from the seeds

bu·col·ic (byōō käl′ik) *adj.* ⟦< Gr *boukolos*, herdsman⟧ **1** of shepherds; pastoral **2** of country life; rustic —**bu·col′i·cal·ly** *adv.*

bud (bud) *n.* ⟦ME *budde*⟧ **1** a small swelling on a plant, from which a shoot, leaf, or flower develops **2** an early stage of development —*vi.* **bud′ded**, **bud′ding** **1** to put forth buds **2** to begin to develop —**in** (**the**) **bud** **1** in a budding condition **2** in an early stage —**bud′like′** *adj.*

Bu·da·pest (bōō′də pest′) capital of Hungary: pop. 2,104,000

Bud·dha (bōō′də) religious leader who lived in India 563?-483? B.C.: founder of Buddhism

Bud·dhism (bōō′diz′əm) *n.* a religion of Asia teaching that by right thinking and self-denial one achieves nirvana, a state of blessedness —**Bud′dhist** *n.*, *adj.*

bud·dy (bud′ē) *n.*, *pl.* **-dies** ⟦< ?⟧ [Inf.] a close friend; comrade

budge (buj) *vt.*, *vi.* **budged**, **budg′ing** ⟦< OFr *bouger*, to move⟧ to move even a little

budg·er·i·gar (buj′ər i gär′) *n.* ⟦native name⟧ a greenish-yellow Australian parakeet: also [Inf.] **budg′ie**

budg·et (buj′it) *n.* ⟦< L *bulga*, bag⟧ **1** a plan adjusting expenses to income **2** estimated cost of living, operating, etc. **3** amount allotted for a specific use —*vt.* **1** to put on a budget **2** to plan *[budget your time]* —**budg′et·ar′y** *adj.*

Bue·nos Ai·res (bwā′nəs er′ēz) seaport & capital of Argentina: pop. 2,908,000

buff (buf) *n.* ⟦< Fr < It *bufalo*, buffalo⟧ **1** a soft, brownish-yellow leather **2** a dull brownish yellow **3** [Inf.] a devotee; fan —*adj.* of the color buff —*vt.* to polish or shine, as with soft leather —**in the buff** naked

buf·fa·lo (buf′ə lō′) *n.*, *pl.* **-loes′**, **-lo′**, or **-los′** ⟦It *bufalo* < Gr *bous*, ox⟧ **1** any of various wild oxen, as the water buffalo of India **2** popularly, the American bison —*vt.* **-loed′**, **-lo′ing** [Slang] to baffle, bluff, etc.

Buf·fa·lo (buf′ə lō′) city in W New York, on Lake Erie: pop. 328,000

Buffalo wings ⟦after prec.⟧ [*also* **b- w-**] spicy fried segments of chicken wings

buff·er[1] (buf′ər) *n.* ⟦BUFF, *v.* + -ER⟧ **1** one who buffs **2** something used for buffing

buff·er[2] (buf′ər) *n.* ⟦< OFr *buffe*, a blow⟧ **1** anything that lessens shock, as of collision **2** a temporary storage area in a computer, for data being transferred to another device

buf·fet[1] (buf′it) *n.* ⟦OFr < *buffe*, a blow⟧ a blow or shock —*vt.* **1** to punch; hit **2** to thrust about

buf·fet[2] (bə fā′, bōō-) *n.* ⟦Fr⟧ **1** a sideboard **2** a counter or table at which guests, etc. serve themselves food **3** a meal served on such a table, etc.

buf·foon (bə fōōn′) *n.* ⟦< Fr < It *buffare*, to jest⟧ one who is always clowning and trying to be funny; clown —**buf·foon′er·y** *n.* —**buf·foon′ish** *adj.*

bug (bug) *n.* ⟦prob. < ME *bugge*: see fol.⟧ **1** an insect with sucking mouthparts **2** any small arthropod, as a cockroach **3** a defect, as in a machine **4** [Inf.] a germ or virus **5** [Inf.] a hidden microphone —*vt.* **bugged**, **bug′ging** **1** [Inf.] to hide a microphone in (a room, etc.) **2** [Slang] to annoy, anger, etc.

bug′bear′ *n.* ⟦ME *bugge*, a hobgoblin + BEAR[2]⟧ **1** an imaginary evil being **2** a cause of needless fear Also **bug′a·boo′** (-ə bōō′) *n.*, *pl.* **-boos′**

bug′-eyed′ *adj.* [Slang] with bulging eyes

bug·gy[1] (bug′ē) *n.*, *pl.* **-gies** ⟦< ?⟧ **1** a light one-horse carriage with one seat **2** BABY CARRIAGE

bug·gy[2] (bug′ē) *adj.* **-gi·er**, **-gi·est** infested with bugs

bu·gle (byōō′gəl) *n.* ⟦< L *buculus*, young ox⟧ a brass instrument like a small trumpet, usually without valves —*vi.*, *vt.* **-gled**, **-gling** to signal by blowing a bugle —**bu′gler** *n.*

build (bild) *vt.* **built**, **build′ing** ⟦< OE *bold*, house⟧ **1** to make by putting together materials, parts, etc.; construct **2** to establish; base *[build a theory on facts]* **3** to create or develop: often with *up* —*vi.* **1** to put up buildings **2** to grow or intensify: often with *up* —*n.* the way a thing is built or shaped *[a stocky build]* —**build up** to make more attractive, healthy, etc. —**build′er** *n.*

build′ing *n.* **1** anything that is built; structure **2** the work or business of making houses, etc.

build′up′ or **build′-up′** *n.* [Inf.] **1** praise or favorable publicity **2** a gradual increase or expansion

built (bilt) *vt.*, *vi.* *pt.* & *pp.* *of* BUILD

built′-in′ *adj.* **1** made as part of the structure **2** inherent

built′-up′ *adj.* **1** made higher, stronger, etc. with added parts **2** having many buildings on it

bulb (bulb) *n.* ⟦< Gr *bolbos*⟧ **1** an underground bud with roots and a short, scaly stem, as in a lily or onion **2** a tuber or tuberous root resembling a bulb, as in a crocus **3** anything shaped like a bulb *[an electric light bulb]* —

bul'bous ***adj.***

Bul·gar·i·a (bəl ger'ē ə, bool-) country in SE Europe: 42,855 sq. mi.; pop. 8,473,000 —**Bul·gar'i·an** ***adj., n.***

bulge (bulj) ***n.*** ⟦< L *bulga*, leather bag⟧ an outward swelling; protuberance —***vi., vt.*** **bulged, bulg'ing** to swell or bend outward —**bulg'y, -i·er, -i·est,** ***adj.***

bu·lim·i·a (byōō lē'mē ə) ***n.*** ⟦< Gr *bous*, ox + *limos*, hunger⟧ **1** *Med.* a continuous, abnormal hunger **2** a disorder characterized by eating large quantities of food followed by self-induced vomiting, etc.: also **bulimia nervosa** —**bu·lim'ic** ***adj.***

bulk (bulk) ***n.*** ⟦< ON *bulki*, a heap⟧ **1** size, mass, or volume, esp. if great **2** the main mass; largest part —***vi.*** to have, or to increase in, size or importance —***adj.*** **1** total; aggregate **2** not put up in individual packages —**bulk'y, -i·er, -i·est,** ***adj.***

bulk·head (bulk'hed') ***n.*** ⟦< ON *balkr*, partition + HEAD⟧ **1** an upright partition, as in a ship, that is watertight, fireproof, etc. **2** a retaining wall **3** a boxlike structure over an opening

bull[1] (bool) ***n.*** ⟦< OE *bula*, a steer⟧ **1** the adult male of any bovine animal, as the ox, or of certain other large animals, as the elephant or whale **2** a speculator who buys stocks expecting their prices to rise, or who seeks to bring about such a rise **3** [Slang] insincere talk; nonsense —***adj.*** **1** male **2** rising in price

bull[2] (bool) ***n.*** ⟦< LL *bulla*, a seal⟧ an official document from the pope

bull'dog' ***n.*** a short-haired, heavily built dog with a strong stubborn grip —***adj.*** like a bulldog; stubborn —***vt.*** **-dogged', -dog'ging** to throw (a steer) by holding its horns and twisting its neck

bull'doze' (-dōz') ***vt.*** **-dozed', -doz'ing** ⟦< *bull*, a flogging + DOSE⟧ **1** [Inf.] to force or frighten by threatening; bully **2** to move, make level, etc. with a bulldozer

bull'doz'er ***n.*** a tractor with a large, shovel-like blade, for pushing earth, debris, etc.

bul·let (bool'it) ***n.*** ⟦< L *bulla*, a knob⟧ a small, shaped piece of lead, steel, etc., to be shot from a firearm

bul·le·tin (bool'ə tin) ***n.*** ⟦< LL *bulla*, a seal⟧ **1** a brief statement of the latest news **2** a regular publication, as of an organization

bulletin board a board or wall area on which bulletins, notices, etc. are put up

bul'let·proof' ***adj.*** that bullets cannot pierce —***vt.*** to make bulletproof

bull'fight' ***n.*** a spectacle in which a bull is first provoked in various ways and then killed with the thrust of a sword by a matador —**bull'fight'er** ***n.*** —**bull'fight'ing** ***n.***

bull'frog' ***n.*** a large North American frog with a deep, loud croak

bull'head'ed ***adj.*** blindly stubborn; headstrong —**bull'head'ed·ness** ***n.***

bull'horn' ***n.*** a portable electronic voice amplifier

bul·lion (bool'yən) ***n.*** ⟦< OFr *billon*, small coin⟧ ingots, bars, etc. of gold or silver

bull·ish (bool'ish) ***adj.*** **1** of or like a bull **2** rising, or causing a rise, in prices on the stock exchange **3** optimistic

bull'ock (-ək) ***n.*** ⟦< OE dim. of *bula*, steer⟧ a castrated bull; steer

bull'pen' ***n.*** **1** [Inf.] a temporary detention room in a jail **2** *Baseball a*) a practice area for relief pitchers *b*) the relief pitchers of one team

bull's'-eye' ***n.*** **1** the central mark of a target **2** a direct hit

bul·ly (bool'ē) ***n.***, *pl.* **-lies** ⟦< MHG *buole*, lover; later infl. by BULL[1]⟧ a person who hurts or browbeats those who are weaker —***vt.*** **-lied, -ly·ing** to behave as a bully toward —***adj., interj.*** [Inf.] fine; good

bul·rush (bool'rush') ***n.*** ⟦< ME *bol*, stem + *rusche*, a rush⟧ a tall plant of the sedge family, found in wet places

bul·wark (bool'wərk) ***n.*** ⟦MDu *bolwerc*⟧ **1** a defensive wall; rampart **2** a defense; protection **3** [*usually pl.*] a ship's side above the deck

bum (bum) ***n.*** ⟦prob. < Ger *bummeln*, go slowly⟧ [Inf.] **1** a vagrant **2** a loafer **3** a devotee, as of golf or skiing —***vi.*** **bummed, bum'ming** [Inf.] to live as a bum or by begging —***vt.*** [Slang] to get by begging *[to bum* a cigarette*]* —***adj.*** **bum'mer, bum'mest** [Slang] **1** poor in quality **2** false **3** lame —**bum someone out** [Slang] to annoy, depress, bore, etc. someone —**on the bum** [Inf.] **1** living as a vagrant **2** out of repair

bum·ble (bum'bəl) ***vi.*** **-bled, -bling** to blunder —***vt.*** to bungle or botch —**bum'bler** ***n.***

bum'ble·bee' ***n.*** ⟦< ME *bomben*, to buzz⟧ a large, hairy, yellow-and-black bee

bummed ***adj.*** ⟦< BUM⟧ [Slang] depressed, upset, annoyed, etc.: usually with *out*

bum·mer (bum'ər) ***n.*** [Slang] an unpleasant experience

bump (bump) ***vt., vi.*** ⟦echoic⟧ to collide (with) or hit (against) with a jolt —***n.*** **1** a knock; light jolt **2** a swelling, esp. one caused by a blow —**bump into** [Inf.] to meet unexpectedly —**bump off** [Slang] to murder —**bump'y, -i·er, -i·est,** ***adj.***

bump'er[1] ***n.*** a device to absorb the shock of a collision; esp., either of the bars at the front and rear of a motor vehicle

bump'er[2] ***adj.*** ⟦prob. < obs. *bombard*, liquor jug⟧ unusually abundant *[a bumper* crop*]*

bumper sticker a gummed paper with a printed slogan, witticism, etc., for sticking on a vehicle's bumper

bump·kin (bump'kin) ***n.*** ⟦prob. < MDu *bommekijn*, small cask⟧ an awkward or simple person from the country

bump'tious (-shəs) ***adj.*** ⟦prob. < BUMP⟧ disagreeably conceited or forward —**bump'tious·ly** ***adv.*** —**bump'tious·ness** ***n.***

bun (bun) ***n.*** ⟦prob. < OFr *buigne*, a swelling⟧ **1** a small roll made of bread dough, sometimes sweetened **2** hair worn in a roll or knot

bunch (bunch) ***n.*** ⟦< Fl *boudje,* little bundle⟧ **1** a cluster of similar things growing or grouped together **2** [Inf.] a group of people —***vt.***, ***vi.*** to collect into a bunch —**bunch'y, -i·er, -i·est,** ***adj.***

bun·combe (buŋ'kəm) ***n.*** ⟦after *Buncombe* county, NC⟧ [Inf.] BUNKUM

bun·dle (bun'dəl) ***n.*** ⟦MDu *bondel*⟧ **1** a number of things bound together **2** a package **3** a bunch; collection —***vt.*** **-dled, -dling 1** to make into a bundle **2** to hustle (*away, off, out,* or *into*) —**bundle up** to dress warmly

Bundt (bunt, boont) *trademark for* a deep cake pan with a tube in the center and grooved sides —***adj.*** [*often* **b-**] designating or baked in such a pan

bung (buŋ) ***n.*** ⟦< MDu *bonge*⟧ a stopper for a bunghole

bun·ga·low (buŋ'gə lō') ***n.*** ⟦< Hindi *bānglā,* thatched house⟧ a small house or cottage, usually of one story and an attic

bun·gee cord (bun'jē) elasticized cord used as to secure luggage or to hold persons leaping for sport from great heights

bung·hole (buŋ'hōl') ***n.*** a hole in a barrel or keg for pouring in or drawing out liquid

bun·gle (buŋ'gəl) ***vt.***, ***vi.*** **-gled, -gling** ⟦< ?⟧ to do or make (something) badly or clumsily —***n.*** **1** a bungling **2** a bungled piece of work —**bun'gler** ***n.*** —**bung'ling·ly** ***adv.***

bun·ion (bun'yən) ***n.*** ⟦< OFr: see BUN⟧ an inflamed swelling at the base of the big toe

bunk[1] (buŋk) ***n.*** ⟦prob. < Scand cognate of BENCH⟧ **1** a shelflike bed built against a wall, as in a ship **2** [Inf.] any sleeping place —***vi.*** to sleep in a bunk —***vt.*** to provide a sleeping place for

bunk[2] (buŋk) ***n.*** [Slang] *short for* BUNKUM

bunk'er ***n.*** ⟦Scot < ?⟧ **1** a large bin, as for a ship's fuel **2** an underground fortification **3** a sand trap or other area serving as a hazard on a golf course

bunk'house' ***n.*** a barracks for ranch hands

bun·kum (buŋ'kəm) ***n.*** ⟦respelling of BUNCOMBE⟧ [Inf.] empty, insincere talk

bun·ny (bun'ē) ***n.***, *pl.* **-nies** ⟦dim. of dial. *bun*⟧ a rabbit: a child's term

buns (bunz) ***pl.n.*** [Slang] the human buttocks

Bun·sen burner (bun'sən) ⟦after R. W. *Bunsen,* 19th-c. Ger chemist⟧ a small tubular gas burner that produces a hot, blue flame

bunt (bunt) ***vt.***, ***vi.*** ⟦< ? ME *bounten,* to return⟧ *Baseball* to bat (a pitch) lightly without swinging so that it rolls within the infield —***n.*** a bunted ball

bun·ting[1] (bun'tiŋ) ***n.*** ⟦< ? ME *bonten,* sift⟧ **1** a thin cloth for making flags, etc. **2** decorative flags

bun·ting[2] (bun'tiŋ) ***n.*** ⟦ME⟧ a small, brightly colored, short-billed bird

buoy (bo͞o'ē, boi) ***n.*** ⟦< L *boia,* fetter⟧ **1** a floating object anchored in water to warn of a hazard, etc. **2** a ring-shaped life preserver —***vt.*** ⟦< Sp *boyar,* to float⟧ **1** to mark with a buoy **2** to keep afloat **3** to lift up in spirits

buoy·ant (boi'ənt; *also* bo͞o'yənt) ***adj.*** ⟦< ? Sp *boyar,* to float⟧ **1** having the ability or tendency to float **2** cheerful —**buoy'an·cy** ***n.***

bur (bur) ***n.*** ⟦< Scand⟧ **1** a rough, prickly seed capsule of certain plants **2** a plant with burs **3** BURR[1] & BURR[2]

Bur *abbrev.* Bureau

bur·den[1] (burd''n) ***n.*** ⟦< OE *byrthen*⟧ **1** anything that is carried; load **2** heavy load, as of work, care, or duty **3** the carrying capacity of a ship —***vt.*** to put a burden on; oppress —**bur'den·some** ***adj.***

bur·den[2] (burd''n) ***n.*** ⟦< OFr *bourdon,* a humming⟧ **1** a chorus or refrain of a song **2** a repeated, central idea; theme

bur·dock (bur'däk') ***n.*** ⟦BUR + DOCK[3]⟧ a plant with large leaves and purple-flowered heads with prickles

bu·reau (byoor'ō) ***n.***, *pl.* **-reaus** or **-reaux** (-ōz) ⟦Fr, desk⟧ **1** a chest of drawers, as for clothing **2** an agency **3** a government department

bu·reauc·ra·cy (byoo rä'krə sē) ***n.***, *pl.* **-cies 1** government by departmental officials following an inflexible routine **2** the officials collectively **3** inflexible governmental routine **4** the concentration of authority in administrative bureaus —**bu·reau·crat** (byoor'ə krat') ***n.*** —**bu'reau·crat'ic** ***adj.*** —**bu'reau·crat'i·cal·ly** ***adv.***

bu·reauc'ra·tize' (-tīz') ***vt.***, ***vi.*** **-tized', -tiz'ing** to develop into a bureaucracy —**bu·reauc'ra·ti·za'tion** ***n.***

burg (burg) ***n.*** [Inf.] a quiet or dull town

bur·geon (bur'jən) ***vi.*** ⟦< OFr *burjon,* a bud⟧ **1** to put forth buds, etc. **2** to grow or develop rapidly

bur·ger (bur'gər) ***n.*** [Inf.] a hamburger, cheeseburger, etc.

-bur·ger (bur'gər) *combining form* sandwich of ground meat, etc. *[hamburger]*

burgh (burg; *Scot* bu'rə) ***n.*** ⟦Scot var. of BOROUGH⟧ **1** [Brit.] a borough **2** in Scotland, a chartered town

burgh·er (bur'gər) ***n.*** a citizen of a town

bur·glar (bur'glər) ***n.*** ⟦< OFr *burgeor*⟧ one who commits burglary

bur'glar·ize' ***vt.*** **-ized', -iz'ing** to commit burglary in

bur'gla·ry (-glə rē) ***n.***, *pl.* **-ries** the act of breaking into a building to commit a felony, as theft, or a misdemeanor

bur·gle (bur'gəl) ***vt.***, ***vi.*** **-gled, -gling** [Inf.] to burglarize or commit burglary

bur·go·mas·ter (bur'gō mas'tər, -gə-) ***n.*** ⟦< MDu *burg,* town + *meester,* master⟧ the mayor of a town in the Netherlands, Flanders, Austria, or Germany

Bur·gun·dy (bur'gən dē) ***n.***, *pl.* **-dies** [*often* **b-**] a red or white wine, typically dry, orig. made in Burgundy, a region in E France —**Bur·gun·di·an** (bər gun'dē ən) ***adj.***, ***n.***

bur·i·al (ber'ē əl) ***n.*** the burying of a dead body in a grave, tomb, etc.

Bur·ki·na Fa·so (boor kē'nə fä'sō) country in W Africa: 105,839 sq. mi.; pop. 7,967,000

burl (burl) ***n.*** ⟦< OFr *bourle*, ends of threads⟧ **1** a knot in thread or yarn that makes cloth look nubby **2** a knot on some tree trunks **3** veneer from wood with burls —**burled** ***adj.***

bur·lap (bur′lap′) ***n.*** ⟦< ? ME *borel*⟧ a coarse cloth of jute or hemp

bur·lesque (bər lesk′) ***n.*** ⟦Fr < It *burla*, a jest⟧ **1** any broadly comic or satirical imitation; parody **2** a sort of vaudeville with low comedy, striptease acts, etc. —***vt., vi.*** **-lesqued′**, **-lesqu′ing** to imitate comically

bur·ley (bur′lē) ***n.*** ⟦< ?⟧ [*also* **B-**] a thin-leaved, light-colored tobacco grown in Kentucky, etc.

bur·ly (bur′lē) ***adj.*** **-li·er**, **-li·est** ⟦ME *borlich*, excellent⟧ **1** big and strong **2** hearty in manner

Bur·ma (bur′mə) *former name for* MYANMAR —**Bur·mese** (bər mēz′), *pl.* **-mese′**, ***adj.***, ***n.***

burn (burn) ***vt.*** **burned** or **burnt**, **burn′ing** ⟦< OE *beornan*, to be on fire⟧ **1** to set on fire, as in order to produce heat, light, or power **2** to destroy by fire **3** to injure or damage by fire, acid, etc. **4** to consume as fuel **5** to sunburn **6** to cause (a hole, etc.) as by fire **7** to cause a sensation of heat in **8** to transform (body fat, etc.) into energy **9** [Slang] to cheat or trick [I got *burned* in that deal] —***vi.*** **1** to be on fire **2** to give out light or heat **3** to be destroyed or injured by fire or heat **4** to feel hot **5** to be excited —***n.*** **1** an injury or damage caused by fire, heat, etc. **2** the process or result of burning —**burn down** to burn to the ground —**burn out** to exhaust or become exhausted from overwork, etc. —**burn up** [Slang] to make or become angry —**burn′a·ble** ***adj.***, ***n.***

burn′er ***n.*** the part of a stove, furnace, etc. from which the flame comes

bur·nish (bur′nish) ***vt.***, ***vi.*** ⟦< OFr *brunir*, make brown⟧ to make or become shiny by rubbing —***n.*** a gloss or polish —**bur′nish·er** ***n.***

bur·noose (bər no͞os′) ***n.*** ⟦< Ar *burnus*⟧ a hooded cloak worn by Arabs

burn·out (burn′out′) ***n.*** **1** the point at which a rocket's fuel is burned up and the rocket enters free flight or is jettisoned **2** a state of emotional exhaustion from mental stress

Burns (burnz), **Rob·ert** (rä′bərt) 1759-96; Scot. poet

burnt (burnt) ***vt.***, ***vi.*** *alt. pt. & pp. of* BURN

burp (burp) ***n.***, ***vi.*** ⟦echoic⟧ belch —***vt.*** to cause (a baby) to belch

burr[1] (bur) ***n.*** ⟦var. of BUR⟧ **1** a bur **2** a rough edge left on metal, etc. by cutting or drilling —***vt.*** to form a rough edge on

burr[2] (bur) ***n.*** ⟦prob. echoic⟧ **1** the trilling of *r*, as in Scottish speech **2** a whir

bur·ri·to (bə rē′tō) ***n.***, *pl.* **-tos** ⟦MexSp < Sp, little burro⟧ a Mexican dish consisting of a flour tortilla wrapped around a filling of meat, cheese, fried beans, etc.

bur·ro (bur′ō) ***n.***, *pl.* **-ros** ⟦Sp < LL *burricus*, small horse⟧ a donkey

bur·row (bur′ō) ***n.*** ⟦see BOROUGH⟧ **1** a hole dug in the ground by an animal **2** any similar hole —***vi.*** **1** to make a burrow **2** to live or hide in a burrow **3** to search, as if by digging —***vt.*** **1** to make burrows in **2** to make by burrowing

bur·sa (bur′sə) ***n.***, *pl.* **-sae** (-sē) or **-sas** ⟦< Gr *byrsa*, a hide⟧ *Anat.* a sac or cavity with a lubricating fluid, as between a tendon and bone

bur·sar (bur′sər) ***n.*** ⟦< ML *bursa*, a purse⟧ a treasurer, as of a college

bur·si·tis (bər sīt′is) ***n.*** ⟦< BURSA + -ITIS⟧ inflammation of a bursa

burst (burst) ***vi.*** **burst**, **burst′ing** ⟦OE *berstan*⟧ **1** to come apart suddenly and violently; explode **2** to give sudden vent; break (*into* tears, etc.) **3** to appear, start, etc. suddenly **4** *a*) to be as full or crowded as possible *b*) to be filled (*with* pride, etc.) —***vt.*** to cause to burst —***n.*** **1** a bursting **2** a break or rupture **3** a sudden action or effort; spurt **4** a volley of shots

Bu·run·di (bo͞o ro͞on′dē, -run′-) country in EC Africa, east of Democratic Republic of the Congo: 10,759 sq. mi.; pop. 5,293,000

bur·y (ber′ē) ***vt.*** **-ied**, **-y·ing** ⟦OE *byrgan*⟧ **1** to put (a dead body) into the earth, a tomb, etc. **2** to hide or cover **3** to put away **4** to immerse [to *bury* oneself in work]

bus (bus) ***n.***, *pl.* **bus′es** or **bus′ses** ⟦< (OMNI)BUS⟧ a large motor coach for many passengers, usually following a regular route —***vt.*** **bused** or **bussed**, **bus′ing** or **bus′sing** **1** to transport by bus **2** to clear dirty dishes from —***vi.*** **1** to go by bus **2** to do the work of a busboy

bus′boy′ ***n.*** a restaurant worker who clears tables, brings water, etc.

bus·by (buz′bē) ***n.***, *pl.* **-bies** ⟦prob. < name *Busby*⟧ a tall fur hat worn with a full-dress uniform

bush (bo͝osh) ***n.*** ⟦OE *busc*⟧ **1** a low woody plant with spreading branches; shrub **2** anything like a bush **3** uncleared land —***vi.*** to grow thickly —**beat around the bush** to talk around a subject without getting to the point

Bush (bo͝osh) **1 George** (**Herbert Walker**) 1924- ; 41st president of the U.S. (1989-93) **2 George W**(**alker**) 1946- ; 43d president of the U.S. (2001-): son of George

bushed (bo͝osht) ***adj.*** [Inf.] very tired; exhausted

bush·el (bo͝osh′əl) ***n.*** ⟦< OFr *boisse*, grain measure⟧ a dry measure equal to 4 pecks or 32 quarts

bush·ing (bo͝osh′iŋ) ***n.*** ⟦< MDu *busse*, box⟧ a removable metal lining for reducing friction on moving parts

bush league [Slang] a small or second-rate minor league, etc. —**bush′-league′** ***adj.*** —**bush leaguer**

bush′man (-mən) ***n.***, *pl.* **-men** (-mən) one who lives in the Australian bush

bush′mas′ter ***n.*** a large poisonous snake of Central and South America

bush′whack′ ***vt.***, ***vi.*** to ambush —**bush′whack′er** ***n.***

bush′y ***adj.*** **-i·er, -i·est** thick and spreading out like a bush

bush′y-tailed′ ***adj.*** used mainly in **bright-eyed and bushy-tailed**, alert, eager, etc.

bus·i·ly (biz′ə lē) ***adv.*** in a busy manner

busi·ness (biz′nis) ***n.*** ⟦OE *bisignes*: see BUSY⟧ **1** one's work; occupation **2** a special task, duty, etc. **3** rightful concern *[no one's business but his own]* **4** a matter or activity **5** commerce; trade **6** a commercial or industrial establishment —***adj.*** of or for business —**mean business** [Inf.] to be in earnest

business administration college studies covering finance, management, etc. to prepare for a business career

business agent a representative of a labor union local

business card a small card identifying one's business connection, given to clients, etc.

business college a school of typing, bookkeeping, etc.

busi′ness·like′ ***adj.*** efficient, methodical, systematic, etc.

busi′ness·man′ ***n.***, *pl.* **-men′** (-men′) a man in business, esp. as an owner —**busi′ness·wom′an**, *pl.* **-wom′en, *fem.n.***

business school a school offering graduate courses in business administration

bus·ing or **bus·sing** (bus′iŋ) ***n.*** the transporting of children by bus to a school outside of their neighborhood, esp. so as to desegregate the school

bus·kin (bus′kin) ***n.*** ⟦? < MDu *brosekin*, small boot⟧ **1** a high, laced boot worn in ancient tragedy **2** tragic drama

buss (bus) ***n., vt., vi.*** ⟦prob. of echoic orig.⟧ [Now Chiefly Dial.] kiss

bust[1] (bust) ***n.*** ⟦< It *busto*⟧ **1** a sculpture of a person's head and shoulders **2** a woman's bosom

bust[2] (bust) [Inf.] ***vt., vi.*** ⟦< BURST⟧ **1** to burst or break **2** to make or become bankrupt or demoted **3** to hit **4** to arrest —***n.*** **1** a failure **2** financial collapse **3** a punch **4** a spree **5** an arrest —**bust′ed** ***adj.***

bus·tle[1] (bus′əl) ***vi., vt.*** **-tled, -tling** ⟦< ME *busken*, prepare⟧ to hurry busily —***n.*** busy and noisy activity

bus·tle[2] (bus′əl) ***n.*** ⟦< ?⟧ a padding formerly worn to fill out the upper back of a woman's skirt

bus·y (biz′ē) ***adj.*** **-i·er, -i·est** ⟦OE *bisig*⟧ **1** active; at work **2** full of activity **3** in use, as a telephone **4** too detailed —***vt.*** **bus′ied, bus′y·ing** to make or keep busy —**bus′y·ness** ***n.***

bus′y·bod′y ***n.***, *pl.* **-ies** a meddler in the affairs of others

but (but) ***prep.*** ⟦OE *butan*, without⟧ except; save *[nobody went but me]* —***conj.*** **1** yet; still *[it's good, but not great]* **2** on the contrary *[I am old, but you are young]* **3** unless *[it never rains but it pours]* **4** that *[I don't doubt but you're right]* **5** that . . . not *[I never gamble but I lose]* —***adv.*** **1** only *[if I had but known]* **2** merely *[he is but a child]* —***pron.*** who . . . not; which . . . not *[not a man but felt it]* —**but for** if it were not for

bu·tane (byo͞o′tān′) ***n.*** ⟦ult. < L *butyrum*, butter⟧ a hydrocarbon used as a fuel, etc.

butch (bo͝och) ***adj.*** ⟦< ? fol.⟧ [Slang] masculine: sometimes said of a lesbian —***n.*** [Inf.] BUZZ CUT

butch·er (bo͝och′ər) ***n.*** ⟦< OFr *bouc*, he-goat⟧ **1** one whose work is killing and dressing animals for meat **2** one who cuts meat for sale **3** a brutal killer —***vt.*** **1** to kill or dress (animals) for meat **2** to kill brutally or senselessly **3** to botch —**butch′er·y**, *pl.* **-ies, *n.***

but·ler (but′lər) ***n.*** ⟦< OFr *bouteille*, bottle⟧ a manservant, usually the head servant of a household

butt[1] (but) ***n.*** ⟦< ?⟧ **1** the thick end of anything **2** a stub or stump, as of a cigar **3** a target **4** an object of ridicule **5** [Slang] a cigarette —***vt., vi.*** to join end to end

butt[2] (but) ***vt., vi.*** ⟦< OFr *buter*, thrust against⟧ **1** to ram with the head **2** to project —***n.*** a butting —**butt in** (or **into**) [Inf.] to mix into (another's business, etc.)

butt[3] (but) ***n.*** ⟦< LL *buttis*, cask⟧ a large cask for wine or beer

butte (byo͞ot) ***n.*** ⟦Fr, mound⟧ a steep hill with a flat top, surrounded by a plain

but·ter (but′ər) ***n.*** ⟦< Gr *bous*, cow + *tyros*, cheese⟧ **1** the solid, yellowish, edible fat that results from churning cream **2** any substance somewhat like butter —***vt.*** **1** to spread with butter **2** [Inf.] to flatter: often with *up* —**but′ter·y** ***adj.***

butter bean a light-colored bean, as a lima bean or wax bean

but′ter·cup′ ***n.*** a plant with yellow, cup-shaped flowers

but′ter·fat′ ***n.*** the fatty part of milk, from which butter is made

but′ter·fin′gers ***n.*** [Inf.] one who often fumbles and drops things

but′ter·fly′ ***n.***, *pl.* **-flies′** ⟦OE *buttorfleoge*⟧ an insect with a slender body and four broad, usually brightly colored wings

but′ter·milk′ ***n.*** **1** the liquid left after churning butter from milk **2** a drink made from skim milk

but′ter·nut′ ***n.*** **1** a walnut tree of E North America **2** its edible, oily nut

but′ter·scotch′ ***n.*** **1** a hard, sticky candy made with brown sugar, butter, etc. **2** the flavor of this candy **3** a syrup with this flavor

but·tock (but′ək) ***n.*** ⟦< OE *buttuc*, end⟧ **1** either of the fleshy, rounded parts behind the hips **2** [*pl.*] the rump

but·ton (but′′n) ***n.*** ⟦< OFr *boton*⟧ **1** any small disk or knob used as a fastening, ornament, etc., as on a garment **2** anything small and shaped like a button —***vt., vi.*** to fasten with a button or buttons

but′ton-down′ ***adj.*** **1** designating a collar, as on a shirt, fastened down by small buttons **2** conservative, unimaginative, etc.

but'ton·hole' ***n.*** a slit or loop through which a button is inserted —***vt.*** **-holed', -hol'ing** **1** to make buttonholes in **2** to detain and talk to

but·tress (bu'tris) ***n.*** ⟦see BUTT[2]⟧ **1** a structure built against a wall to support or reinforce it **2** a support or prop —***vt.*** to prop up; bolster

bux·om (buk'səm) ***adj.*** ⟦ME, humble⟧ having a shapely, full-bosomed figure: said of a woman

buy (bī) ***vt.*** **bought, buy'ing** ⟦OE *bycgan*⟧ **1** to get by paying money; purchase **2** to get by an exchange [*buy* victory with human lives] **3** to bribe **4** [Slang] to accept as true [I can't *buy* this excuse] —***n.*** **1** anything bought **2** [Inf.] something worth its price —**buy in** [Slang] to pay money so as to participate —**buy into** [Slang] BUY (*vt.* 4) —**buy off** to bribe —**buy out** to buy all the stock, rights, etc. of —**buy up** to buy all that is available of

buy'back' ***n.*** *Finance* the buying by a corporation of its own stock to reduce the outstanding shares

buy'er ***n.*** **1** one who buys; consumer **2** one whose work is to buy merchandise for a retail store

buy'out' ***n.*** the outright purchase of a business, as by the employees or management

buzz (buz) ***vi.*** ⟦echoic⟧ **1** to hum like a bee **2** to gossip **3** to be filled with noisy activity or talk —***vt.*** **1** to fly an airplane low over (a building, etc.) **2** to signal with a buzzer —***n.*** **1** a sound like a bee's hum **2** [Inf.] BUZZ CUT

buz·zard (buz'ərd) ***n.*** ⟦< L *buteo,* kind of hawk⟧ **1** a kind of hawk that is slow and heavy in flight **2** TURKEY VULTURE

buzz cut [Inf.] a man's very short haircut

buzz'er ***n.*** an electrical device that makes a buzzing sound as a signal

buzz saw a saw with teeth around the edge of a large disk fixed on a motor-driven shaft

bx *abbrev.* box

by (bī) ***prep.*** ⟦OE *be, bi*⟧ **1** near; at [sit *by* the fire] **2** *a*) in or during [to travel *by* day] *b*) not later than [be back *by* noon] **3** *a*) through; via [to Boston *by* Route 6] *b*) past; beyond [he walked right *by* me] **4** toward [east *by* northeast] **5** within a distance of [missed *by* a foot] **6** in behalf of [she did well *by* me] **7** through the agency of [gained *by* fraud] **8** according to [to go *by* the book] **9** at the rate of [getting dark *by* degrees] **10** following in series [marching two *by* two] **11** *a*) in or to the amount of [apples *by* the peck] *b*) and in another dimension [two *by* four] *c*) using (the given number) as multiplier or divisor —***adv.*** **1** close at hand [stand *by*] **2** away; aside [to put money *by*] **3** past [she sped *by*] **4** at the place specified [stop *by* on your way] —**by and by** soon or eventually —**by and large** considering everything —**by the by** incidentally

by- *prefix* **1** near **2** secondary; incidental [*byproduct*]

by-and-by (bī'ən bī') ***n.*** a future time

bye (bī) ***n.*** ⟦var. of BY⟧ the privilege, granted a contestant in a tournament with an uneven number of participants, of not being paired with another contestant in the first round

bye-bye (bī'bī') ***n., interj.*** [Inf.] goodbye

by·gone (bī'gôn') ***adj.*** past; former —***n.*** anything gone or past

by'law' ***n.*** ⟦< ME *bi,* village + *laue,* law⟧ any of a set of rules adopted by an organization or assembly for its own meetings or affairs

by'line' ***n.*** a line identifying the writer of a newspaper or magazine article

by'pass' ***n.*** **1** a way, pipe, channel, etc. between two points that avoids or is auxiliary to the main way **2** a surgical operation to allow fluid to pass around a diseased or blocked part or organ —***vt.*** **1** to detour **2** to furnish with a bypass **3** to ignore

by'path' or **by'-path'** ***n.*** a byway

by'play' ***n.*** action, gestures, etc. going on aside from the main action or conversation

by'prod'uct or **by'-prod'uct** ***n.*** anything produced in the course of making another thing

By·ron (bī'rən), **George Gor·don** (jôrj gôrd''n) 1788-1824; Eng. poet

by'stand'er ***n.*** a person who stands near but does not participate

byte (bīt) ***n.*** ⟦arbitrary formation⟧ a string of binary digits (*bits*), usually eight, operated on as a basic unit by a digital computer

by'way' ***n.*** a secondary road or path, esp. one not much used

by'word' ***n.*** **1** a proverb **2** one well-known for some quality **3** an object of scorn or ridicule **4** a favorite word or phrase

Byz·an·tine Empire (biz'ən tēn', -tīn'; bi zan'tin) empire (A.D. 395-1453) in SE Europe & SW Asia

C

c or **C** (sē) ***n.***, *pl.* **c's, C's** the third letter of the English alphabet

C[1] (sē) ***n.*** **1** a Roman numeral for 100 **2** *Educ.* a grade for average work **3** *Music* the first tone in the scale of C major

C[2] *abbrev.* **1** carat(s) **2** *Baseball* catcher **3** Catholic **4** Celsius (or centigrade) **5** cent(s) **6** *Sports* center **7** centimeter(s) **8** Central **9** century **10** chapter **11** circa: also **ca** **12** College **13** copyright **14** cup(s) **15** cycle(s) Also, except 3, 4, 8, & 12, **c**

C[3] *Chem. symbol for* carbon

Ca *Chem. symbol for* calcium

CA California

cab (kab) ***n.*** ⟦< Fr *cabriole*, a leap⟧ **1** a carriage, esp. one for public hire **2** TAXICAB **3** the place in a truck, crane, etc. where the operator sits —***vi.*** **cabbed, cab′bing** [Inf.] to take or drive a taxicab

ca·bal (kə bäl′) ***n.*** ⟦Fr, intrigue⟧ **1** a small group joined in a secret intrigue **2** an intrigue; plot

cab·a·la (kab′ə lə, kə bä′lə) ***n.*** ⟦< Heb *kabala*, tradition⟧ **1** a Jewish mystical movement **2** any esoteric or secret doctrine

ca·bal·le·ro (kab′ə ler′ō, -əl yer′ō) ***n.***, *pl.* **-ros** ⟦Sp⟧ **1** a Spanish gentleman **2** [Southwest] *a)* a horseman *b)* a lady's escort

ca·ban·a (kə ban′ə, -bä′nə) ***n.*** ⟦Sp < LL *capanna*⟧ **1** a cabin or hut **2** a small bathhouse

cab·a·ret (kab′ə rā′) ***n.*** ⟦Fr, tavern⟧ a cafe with musical entertainment

cab·bage (kab′ij) ***n.*** ⟦OFr *caboche* < ?⟧ a vegetable with thick leaves formed into a round head

cab·by or **cab·bie** (kab′ē) ***n.***, *pl.* **-bies** [Inf.] one who drives a cab

ca·ber·net (kab′ər nā′) ***n.*** [*also* **C-**] a dry red wine; esp., CABERNET SAUVIGNON

cabernet sau·vi·gnon (sō vē nyōn′) [*also* **C- S-**] a fragrant, dry red wine

cab·in (kab′in) ***n.*** ⟦< LL *capanna*, hut⟧ **1** a small, crudely or simply built house; hut **2** a room on a ship or boat **3** the space for passengers, crew, or cargo in an aircraft

cab·i·net (kab′ə nit) ***n.*** ⟦Fr, prob. ult. < L *cavea*, cage⟧ **1** a case with drawers or shelves **2** a case holding a TV, radio, etc. **3** [*often* **C-**] a body of official advisors to a chief executive

cab′i·net·mak′er ***n.*** a maker of fine furniture

cab′i·net·work′ ***n.*** articles made by a cabinetmaker: also **cab′i·net·ry**

cabin fever a condition of increased anxiety caused by being confined or isolated

ca·ble (kā′bəl) ***n.*** ⟦< L *capere*, to take hold⟧ **1** a thick, heavy rope, often of wire strands **2** a bundle of insulated wires to carry an electric current **3** a cablegram **4** CABLE TV —***vt.*** **-bled, -bling** **1** to fasten with a cable **2** to send a cablegram to —***vi.*** to send a cablegram

cable car a car drawn by a moving cable, as up a steep incline

ca′ble·cast′ ***vt.*** **-cast′, -cast′ing** to transmit to receivers by coaxial cable —***n.*** a program that is cablecast

ca′ble·gram′ ***n.*** a message sent by undersea cable

cable TV a TV system in which various antennas receive local and distant signals and transmit them by cable to subscribers' receivers

cab·o·chon (kab′ə shän′) ***n.*** ⟦Fr < *caboche*, head⟧ any precious stone cut in convex shape

ca·bood·le (kə bo͞od′'l) ***n.*** ⟦< BOODLE⟧ [Inf.] lot; group *[the whole caboodle]*

ca·boose (kə bo͞os′) ***n.*** ⟦MDu *kambuis*, cabin house⟧ the car at the rear of a freight train, used by the crew when eating, sleeping, etc.

ca·ca·o (kə kā′ō, -kä′-) ***n.***, *pl.* **-os** ⟦Sp < AmInd (Mexico)⟧ **1** the seed of a tropical American tree from which cocoa and chocolate are made: also **cacao bean** **2** this tree

cache (kash) ***n.*** ⟦Fr < L *cogere*, to collect⟧ **1** a safe place in which stores of food, supplies, etc. are hidden **2** anything so hidden —***vt.*** **cached, cach′ing** to place in a cache

cache·pot (kash′pät, -pō′) ***n.*** ⟦Fr < *cacher*, to hide⟧ a decorative jar for holding potted plants: also **cache pot**

ca·chet (ka shā′) ***n.*** ⟦Fr⟧ **1** a stamp or official seal, as on a document **2** any sign of official approval, authenticity, superior quality, etc. **3** distinction; prestige

cack·le (kak′əl) ***vi.*** **-led, -ling** ⟦echoic⟧ **1** to make the shrill, broken vocal sounds of a hen **2** to laugh or chatter with similar sounds —***n.*** a cackling

ca·coph·o·ny (kə käf′ə nē) ***n.***, *pl.* **-nies** ⟦< Gr *kakos*, bad + *phōnē*, voice⟧ harsh, jarring sound; discord —**ca·coph′o·nous** ***adj.***

cac·tus (kak′təs) ***n.***, *pl.* **-tus·es** or **-ti′** (-tī′) ⟦< Gr *kaktos*, kind of thistle⟧ any of various desert plants with fleshy stems and spinelike leaves

cad (kad) ***n.*** ⟦< CADET⟧ a man whose behavior is not gentlemanly —**cad′dish** ***adj.*** —**cad′dish·ly** ***adv.*** —**cad′dish·ness** ***n.***

ca·dav·er (kə dav′ər) ***n.*** ⟦L, prob. < *cadere*, to fall⟧ a corpse, as for dissection

ca·dav′er·ous ***adj.*** ⟦< L⟧ of or like a cadaver; esp., pale, ghastly, etc.

CAD/CAM (kad′kam′) ***n.*** ⟦*C*(*omputer-*) *A*(*ided*) *D*(*esign*) / *C*(*omputer-*) *A*(*ided*) *M*(*anufacturing*)⟧ design and manufacturing by means of a computer system, as for complex wiring diagrams

cad·die (kad′ē) ***n.*** ⟦Scot form of Fr *cadet*: see CADET⟧ one who attends a golfer, carrying the clubs, etc. —***vi.*** **-died**, **-dy·ing** to act as a caddie

cad·dy[1] (kad′ē) ***n.***, *pl.* **-dies** ⟦< Malay *kātī*, unit of weight⟧ a small container for holding or storing

cad·dy[2] (kad′ē) ***n.***, ***vi.*** CADDIE

-cade (kād) ⟦< (CAVAL)CADE⟧ *suffix* procession, parade *[motorcade]*

ca·dence (kād′'ns) ***n.*** ⟦< L *cadere*, to fall⟧ **1** fall of the voice in speaking **2** any rhythmic flow of sound **3** measured movement, as in marching

ca·den·za (kə den′zə) ***n.*** ⟦It: see prec.⟧ an elaborate passage for the solo instrument in a concerto

ca·det (kə det′) ***n.*** ⟦Fr < L dim. of *caput*, head⟧ **1** a student in training at an armed forces academy **2** any trainee, as a practice teacher

cadge (kaj) ***vt.***, ***vi.*** **cadged**, **cadg′ing** ⟦< ?⟧ to beg or get by begging; sponge —**cadg′er** ***n.***

cad·mi·um (kad′mē əm) ***n.*** ⟦< L *cadmia*, zinc ore (with which it occurs)⟧ a silver-white, metallic chemical element used in alloys, pigments, etc.

ca·dre (ka′drē, -drā; kä′-) ***n.*** ⟦< Fr < L *quadrum*, a square⟧ a nucleus around which an expanded organization, as a military unit, can be built

CADUCEUS

ca·du·ce·us (kə do͞o′sē əs) ***n.***, *pl.* **-ce·i′** (-sē ī′) ⟦L⟧ the winged staff of Mercury: now a symbol of the medical profession

Cae·sar[1] (sē′zər) ***n.*** ⟦after fol.⟧ **1** the title of the Roman emperors from 27 B.C. to A.D. 138 **2** [*often* **c-**] any emperor or dictator

Cae·sar[2] (sē′zər), **Jul·ius** (jo͞ol′yəs) 100?-44 B.C.; Rom. general & dictator (49-44)

Cae·sar·e·an section (sə zer′ē ən) CESAREAN (SECTION)

cae·su·ra (si zyoor′ə, -zhoor′ə) ***n.***, *pl.* **-ras** or **-rae** (-ē) ⟦L < *caedere*, to cut down⟧ a break or pause in a line of verse, usually in the middle

ca·fe or **ca·fé** (kə fā′, ka-) ***n.*** ⟦Fr, coffeehouse⟧ a small restaurant or a barroom, nightclub, etc.

caf·e·te·ri·a (kaf′ə tir′ē ə) ***n.*** ⟦AmSp, coffee store⟧ a self-service restaurant

caf·feine or **caf·fein** (ka fēn′, kaf′ēn′) ***n.*** ⟦Ger *kaffein*⟧ the alkaloid present in coffee, tea, cola nuts, etc.: it is a stimulant

caf·tan (kaf′tən, -tan′) ***n.*** ⟦Turk *qaftān*⟧ **1** a long-sleeved robe, worn in eastern Mediterranean countries **2** a long, loose dress with wide sleeves

cage (kāj) ***n.*** ⟦< L *cavea*, hollow place⟧ **1** a structure of wires, bars, etc., for confining animals **2** any openwork structure or frame —***vt.*** **caged**, **cag′ing** to put or confine, as in a cage

cag·er (kāj′ər) ***n.*** [Slang] a basketball player

ca·gey or **ca·gy** (kā′jē) ***adj.*** **-gi·er**, **-gi·est** ⟦< ?⟧ [Inf.] **1** sly; tricky; cunning **2** cautious —**ca′gi·ly** ***adv.*** —**ca′gi·ness** ***n.***

ca·hoots (kə ho͞ots′) ***pl.n.*** ⟦< ?⟧ [Slang] used chiefly in **in cahoots** (**with**), in league (with): usually applied to questionable dealing, etc.

Cain (kān) ***n.*** *Bible* oldest son of Adam and Eve: he killed his brother Abel —**raise Cain** [Slang] to create a great commotion, cause trouble, etc.

cairn (kern) ***n.*** ⟦Scot⟧ a conical heap of stones built as a monument

Cai·ro (kī′rō) capital of Egypt: pop. 5,084,000

cais·son (kā′sən) ***n.*** ⟦Fr < L *capsa*, box⟧ **1** a two-wheeled wagon with a chest for ammunition **2** a watertight box for underwater construction work

cai·tiff (kāt′if) ***n.*** ⟦< L *captivus*, CAPTIVE⟧ a mean or cowardly person —***adj.*** mean or cowardly

ca·jole (kə jōl′) ***vt.***, ***vi.*** **-joled′**, **-jol′ing** ⟦< Fr⟧ to coax with flattery and insincere talk —**ca·jol′er** ***n.*** —**ca·jol′er·y** ***n.***

Ca·jun or **Ca·jan** (kā′jən) ***n.*** **1** a native of Louisiana of Canadian French ancestry **2** the dialect of Cajuns —***adj.*** of spicy cooking

cake (kāk) ***n.*** ⟦< ON⟧ **1** a small, flat mass of baked or fried dough, batter, hashed food, etc. **2** a mixture of flour, eggs, sugar, etc. baked as in a loaf and often covered with icing **3** a shaped, solid mass, as of soap —***vt.***, ***vi.*** **caked**, **cak′ing** to form into a hard mass or crust —**take the cake** [Inf.] to be the prime example of something: usually used ironically —**cak′y** or **cak′ey**, **-i·er**, **-i·est**, ***adj.***

cal *abbrev.* **1** caliber **2** calorie(s)

cal·a·bash (kal′ə bash′) ***n.*** ⟦< Sp *calabaza*⟧ **1** the gourdlike fruit of a tropical American tree **2** *a*) the bottle-shaped, gourdlike fruit of a tropical vine *b*) a large smoking pipe made from it **3** a gourd

cal·a·boose (kal′ə bo͞os′) ***n.*** ⟦Sp *calabozo*⟧ [Dial. or Old Slang] a prison; jail

ca·la·ma·ri (kä′lə mä′rē) ***n.*** squid cooked as food, esp. as an Italian dish

cal·a·mine (kal′ə mīn′) ***n.*** ⟦Fr < L *cadmia*, zinc ore⟧ a zinc oxide powder used in skin lotions

ca·lam·i·ty (kə lam′ə tē) ***n.***, *pl.* **-ties** ⟦< L *calamitas*⟧ a great misfortune; disaster —**ca·lam′i·tous** ***adj.***

cal·car·e·ous (kal ker′ē əs) ***adj.*** ⟦< L *calx*, lime⟧ of or like limestone, calcium, or lime

cal·ci·fy (kal′sə fī′) ***vt.***, ***vi.*** **-fied′**, **-fy′ing** ⟦< L *calx*, lime + -FY⟧ to change into a hard, stony substance by the deposit of lime or calcium salts —**cal′ci·fi·ca′tion** ***n.***

cal′ci·mine′ (-mīn′) ***n.*** ⟦< L *calx*, lime⟧ a white liquid, used as a wash for plastered surfaces —***vt.*** **-mined′**, **-min′ing** to coat with calcimine

cal·cine (kal′sīn′) ***vt.***, ***vi.*** **-cined′**, **-cin′ing** ⟦< L *calx*, lime⟧ to change to an ashy powder by heat

cal·cite (kal′sīt′) ***n.*** CALCIUM CARBONATE

cal·ci·um (kal′sē əm) ***n.*** ⟦< L *calx*, lime⟧ a soft, silver-white, metallic chemical element found combined in limestone, chalk, etc.

calcium carbonate a white powder or crystalline compound found in limestone, chalk, marble, bones, shells, etc.

cal·cu·late (kal′kyə lāt′) ***vt.*** **-lat′ed**, **-lat′ing** ⟦< L *calculare*, reckon⟧ **1** to determine by using mathematics; compute **2** to determine by reasoning; estimate **3** to plan or intend for a purpose —***vi.*** **1** to compute **2** to rely (*on*) —**cal′cu·la·ble** (-lə bəl) ***adj.***

cal′cu·lat′ed ***adj.*** deliberately planned or carefully considered —**cal′cu·lat′ed·ly** ***adv.***

cal′cu·lat′ing ***adj.*** shrewd or scheming

cal′cu·la′tion ***n.*** **1** a calculating **2** something deduced by calculating **3** careful planning or forethought —**cal′cu·la′tive** ***adj.***

cal′cu·la′tor ***n.*** **1** one who calculates **2** a device for the automatic performance of mathematical operations

cal′cu·lus (-ləs) ***n.***, *pl.* **-li′** (-lī′) or **-lus·es** ⟦L, pebble used in counting⟧ **1** an abnormal stony mass in the body **2** *Math.* a system of calculation or analysis using special symbolic notation

Cal·cut·ta (kal kut′ə) seaport in NE India: pop. 9,194,000: now officially *Kolkata*

cal·de·ra (kal der′ə) ***n.*** ⟦Sp < L *caldarium*, room for hot baths⟧ a broad, craterlike basin of a volcano

cal·dron (kôl′drən) ***n.*** ⟦< L *calidus*, warm, hot⟧ **1** a large kettle or boiler **2** a state of violent agitation

cal·en·dar (kal′ən dər) ***n.*** ⟦< L *kalendarium*, account book⟧ **1** a system of determining the length and divisions of a year **2** a table that shows the days, weeks, and months of a given year **3** a schedule, as of programs

cal·en·der (kal′ən dər) ***n.*** ⟦< Gr *kylindros*, cylinder⟧ a machine with rollers for giving paper, cloth, etc. a smooth or glossy finish

calf[1] (kaf) ***n.***, *pl.* **calves** ⟦< OE *cealf*⟧ **1** a young cow or bull **2** the young of some other large animals, as the elephant or seal **3** CALFSKIN

calf[2] (kaf) ***n.***, *pl.* **calves** ⟦ON *kalfi*⟧ the fleshy back part of the leg below the knee

calf′skin′ ***n.*** soft leather made from the skin of a calf

Cal·ga·ry (kal′gə rē) city in S Alberta, Canada: pop. 768,000

cal·i·ber (kal′ə bər) ***n.*** ⟦Fr & Sp, ult. < Gr *kalopodion*, shoemaker's last⟧ **1** the diameter of a cylindrical body, esp. of a bullet or shell **2** the diameter of the bore of a gun **3** quality or ability Also, esp. Brit., **cal′i·bre**

cal·i·brate (kal′ə brāt′) ***vt.*** **-brat′ed**, **-brat′ing** **1** to determine the caliber of **2** to fix or correct the graduations of (a measuring instrument) —**cal′i·bra′tion** ***n.*** —**cal′i·bra′tor** ***n.***

cal·i·co (kal′i kō′) ***n.***, *pl.* **-coes′** or **-cos′** ⟦after *Calicut*, city in India⟧ a printed cotton fabric —***adj.*** spotted like calico [*a calico cat*]

Cal·i·for·nia (kal′ə fôr′nyə) state of the SW U.S., on the Pacific: 155,973 sq. mi.; pop. 29,760,000; cap. Sacramento: abbrev. *CA* —**Cal′i·for′nian** ***adj.***, ***n.***

cal·i·per (kal′ə pər) ***n.*** ⟦var. of CALIBER⟧ **1** [*usually pl.*] an instrument consisting of a pair of hinged legs, for measuring thickness or diameter **2** a part of a braking system on a bicycle or motor vehicle

ca·liph (kā′lif; *also*, kal′if) ***n.*** ⟦Ar *khalīfa*⟧ supreme ruler: the title taken by Mohammed's successors as heads of Islam —**ca′liph·ate** (-ət, -āt′) ***n.***

cal·is·then·ics (kal′is then′iks) ***pl.n.*** ⟦< Gr *kallos*, beauty + *sthenos*, strength⟧ athletic exercises —**cal′is·then′ic** ***adj.***

calk (kôk) ***vt.*** CAULK —**calk′er** ***n.***

call (kôl) ***vt.*** ⟦< ON *kalla*⟧ **1** to say in a loud tone; shout **2** to summon **3** to give or apply a name to **4** to describe as specified **5** to awaken **6** to telephone **7** to give orders for (a strike, etc.) **8** to stop (a game, etc.) **9** to demand payment of (a loan, etc.) **10** to expose (someone's bluff) by challenging it **11** *Poker* to equal (the preceding bet) or to equal the bet of (the last previous bettor) —***vi.*** **1** to shout **2** to visit for a short while: often with *on* **3** to telephone —***n.*** **1** a calling **2** a loud utterance **3** the distinctive cry of an animal or bird **4** a summons; invitation **5** an act of telephoning **6** CALLING (sense 3) **7** an economic demand, as for a product **8** need [*no call for tears*] **9** a demand for payment **10** a brief visit **11** an option to buy a stock, commodity, etc. at a specified price and time **12** a referee's decision —**call down** [Inf.] to scold —**call for** **1** to demand **2** to come and get —**call off** to cancel (a scheduled event) —**call up** **1** to recall **2** to summon for duty **3** to telephone —**on call** available when summoned —**call′er** ***n.***

cal·la (kal′ə) ***n.*** ⟦< L, a plant (of uncert. kind)⟧ a plant with a large, white leaf around a yellow flower spike: also **calla lily**

call forwarding a telephone service that allows incoming calls to be transferred automatically to another number

call girl a prostitute who is called by telephone to assignations

cal·lig·ra·phy (kə lig′rə fē) ***n.*** ⟦< Gr *kallos*, beauty + *graphein*, write⟧ artistic handwriting —**cal·lig′ra·pher** ***n.*** —**cal·li·graph·ic** (kal′ə graf′ik) ***adj.***

call′-in′ ***adj.*** of a radio or TV program whose audience members telephone to comment, ask questions, etc.

call′ing ***n.*** **1** the act of one that calls **2** one's work or profession **3** an inner urging toward some vocation

calling card **1** a small card with one's name and address on it **2** a credit card for long-distance telephone calls

cal·li·o·pe (kə lī′ə pē′, kal′ē ōp′) ***n.*** ⟦< Gr *kallos*, beauty + *ops*, voice⟧ a keyboard instrument like an organ, having a series of steam whistles

call letters the letters, and sometimes numbers, that identify a radio or TV station

cal·lous (kal′əs) ***adj.*** ⟦< L *callum*, hard skin⟧ **1** hardened: usually **cal′loused** **2** unfeeling —**cal·los·i·ty** (kə läs′ə tē) ***n.*** —**cal′lous·ly** ***adv.*** —**cal′lous·ness** ***n.***

cal·low (kal′ō) ***adj.*** ⟦OE *calu*, bare⟧ immature; inexperienced —**cal′low·ness** ***n.***

cal·lus (kal′əs) ***n.***, *pl.* **-lus·es** ⟦L, var. of *callum*, hard skin⟧ a hardened, thickened place on the skin

call waiting a telephone service that signals an incoming call to a person already talking and allows that person to take that call by putting the first call on hold

calm (käm) ***n.*** ⟦< Gr *kauma*, heat⟧ **1** lack of motion; stillness **2** lack of excitement; tranquillity —***adj.*** **1** still; quiet **2** not excited; tranquil —***vt.***, ***vi.*** to make or become calm: often with *down* —**calm′ly** ***adv.*** —**calm′ness** ***n.***

ca·lor·ic (kə lôr′ik) ***adj.*** of calories —**ca·lor′i·cal·ly** ***adv.***

cal·o·rie (kal′ə rē) ***n.*** ⟦Fr < L *calor*, heat⟧ a unit for measuring heat, esp. for measuring the energy produced by food when oxidized in the body

cal·o·rif·ic (kal′ə rif′ik) ***adj.*** ⟦< L *calor*, heat + *facere*, make⟧ producing heat

cal·u·met (kal′yə met′) ***n.*** ⟦CdnFr < L *calamus*, reed⟧ a long-stemmed ceremonial pipe, smoked by North American Indians as a token of peace

ca·lum·ni·ate (kə lum′nē āt′) ***vt.***, ***vi.*** **-at′ed**, **-at′ing** ⟦see fol.⟧ to slander

cal·um·ny (kal′əm nē) ***n.***, *pl.* **-nies** ⟦< L *calumnia*, slander⟧ a false and malicious statement; slander

Cal·va·ry (kal′və rē) ***n.*** *Bible* the place where Jesus was crucified

calve (kav) ***vi.***, ***vt.*** **calved**, **calv′ing** to give birth to (a calf)

calves (kavz) ***n.*** *pl. of* CALF[1] & CALF[2]

Cal·vin (kal′vin), **John** 1509-64; Fr. Protestant reformer

Cal′vin·ism′ ***n.*** the Christian doctrines of John Calvin and his followers, esp. predestination —**Cal′vin·ist** ***n.***, ***adj.*** —**Cal′vin·is′tic** ***adj.***

ca·lyp·so (kə lip′sō) ***n.*** ⟦< ?⟧ a kind of lively, topical folk song that originated in Trinidad

ca·lyx (kā′liks′; *also* kal′iks′) ***n.***, *pl.* **-lyx′es** or **-ly·ces′** ⟦L, pod⟧ the outer whorl of protective leaves, or sepals, of a flower

cam (kam) ***n.*** ⟦Du *cam*, orig., a comb⟧ a wheel, projection on a wheel, etc. that gives irregular motion, as to a wheel or shaft, or receives such motion from it

ca·ma·ra·de·rie (kam′ə räd′ə rē, käm′-) ***n.*** ⟦Fr⟧ loyalty and warm, friendly feeling among comrades

cam·ber (kam′bər) ***n.*** ⟦OFr < L *camur*, arched⟧ a slight convex curve of a surface, as of a road —***vt.***, ***vi.*** to arch slightly

cam·bi·um (kam′bē əm) ***n.*** ⟦< LL *cambiare*, to change⟧ a layer of cells between the wood and bark in woody plants, which will eventually become more wood and bark —**cam′bi·al** ***adj.***

Cam·bo·di·a (kam bō′dē ə) country in S Indochina: 69,898 sq. mi.; pop. 5,756,000; cap. Phnom Penh —**Cam·bo′di·an** ***adj.***, ***n.***

cam·bric (kām′brik) ***n.*** ⟦after *Cambrai*, Fr city⟧ a fine linen or cotton cloth

Cam·bridge (kām′brij′) **1** city in EC England: county district pop. 92,000 **2** city in E Massachusetts: pop. 96,000

cam·cord·er (kam′kôrd′ər) ***n.*** a small, portable videotape recorder and TV camera

came (kām) ***vi.*** *pt. of* COME

cam·el (kam′əl) ***n.*** ⟦ult. < Heb *gāmāl*⟧ a large, domesticated mammal with a humped back and long neck: because it can store water in its body, it is used in Asian and African deserts

ca·mel·lia (kə mēl′yə, -mē′lē ə) ***n.*** ⟦after G. J. *Kamel* (1661-1706), missionary to the Far East⟧ **1** an Asiatic evergreen tree or shrub with glossy leaves and roselike flowers **2** the flower

Cam·em·bert (cheese) (kam′əm ber′, -bərt) ⟦after *Camembert*, Fr village⟧ a soft, rich, creamy cheese

cam·e·o (kam′ē ō′) ***n.***, *pl.* **-os′** ⟦< It < ML *camaeus*⟧ **1** a gem carved with a figure raised in relief **2** a choice minor role, esp. one played by a notable actor

cam·er·a (kam′ər ə, kam′rə) ***n.*** ⟦L, vault⟧ **1** a device for taking photographs: a closed box containing a sensitized plate or film on which an image is formed when light enters through a lens **2** *TV* the device that receives the image and transforms it into a flow of electrical impulses for transmission —**in camera** in privacy or secrecy

cam′er·a·man′ (-man′) ***n.***, *pl.* **-men′** (-men′) an operator of a film or TV camera

Cam·e·roon (kam′ə ro͞on′) country in WC Africa, on the Atlantic: 183,569 sq. mi.; pop. 10,494,000 —**Cam′e·roon′i·an** ***adj.***, ***n.***

cam·i·sole (kam′i sōl′) ***n.*** ⟦Fr < LL *camisia*, shirt⟧ a woman's sleeveless undergarment for the upper body

cam·o·mile (kam′ə mīl′, -mēl′) ***n.*** ⟦< Gr *chamaimēlon*, earth apple⟧ a plant whose dried, daisylike flower heads are used in a medicinal tea

cam·ou·flage (kam′ə fläzh′, -fläj′) ***n.*** ⟦Fr < *camoufler*, to disguise⟧ **1** a disguising, as of ships or guns, to conceal them from the enemy **2** a disguise; deception

—*vt.*, *vi.* **-flaged′**, **-flag′ing** to disguise (a thing or person) for concealment —**cam′ou·flag′er** *n.*

camp (kamp) *n.* ⟦< L *campus*, field⟧ **1** *a*) a place where temporary tents, huts, etc. are put up, as for soldiers *b*) a group of such tents, etc. **2** the supporters of a particular cause **3** a recreational place in the country for vacationers, esp. children **4** the people living in a camp **5** [Slang] banality, artifice, etc. so extreme as to amuse or have a perversely sophisticated appeal —*vi.* **1** to set up a camp **2** to live or stay in a camp: often with *out* —**break camp** to dismantle a camp and depart

cam·paign (kam pān′) *n.* ⟦Fr < L *campus*, field⟧ **1** a series of military operations with a particular objective **2** a series of planned actions, as to elect a candidate —*vi.* to participate in a campaign —**cam·paign′er** *n.*

cam·pa·ni·le (kam′pə nē′lē) *n.*, *pl.* **-les** or **-li** (-lē) ⟦It < LL *campana*, a bell⟧ a bell tower

camp·er (kam′pər) *n.* **1** a vacationer at a camp **2** a motor vehicle or trailer equipped for camping out

camp′fire′ *n.* **1** an outdoor fire at a camp **2** a social gathering around such a fire

cam·phor (kam′fər) *n.* ⟦< Sans *karpuraḥ*, camphor tree⟧ a crystalline substance with a strong odor, derived from the wood of an E Asian evergreen tree (**camphor tree**): used to repel moths, in medicine as a stimulant, etc. —**cam′phor·at′ed** *adj.*

camp meeting a religious meeting held outdoors or in a tent, etc.

camp′site′ *n.* **1** any site for a camp **2** an area in a park set aside for camping

cam·pus (kam′pəs) *n.*, *pl.* **-pus·es** ⟦L, a field⟧ the grounds, and sometimes buildings, of a school or college —*adj.* of a school or college *[campus* politics*]*

camp′y *adj.* **-i·er**, **-i·est** [Slang] characterized by CAMP (*n.* 5)

cam′shaft′ *n.* a shaft having a cam, or to which a cam is fastened

can[1] (kan; *unstressed* kən) *vi.*, *v.aux.* *pt.* **could** ⟦< OE *cunnan*, to know⟧ **1** know(s) how (to) **2** am, are, or is able (to) **3** am, are, or is likely (to) *[can* that be true?*]* **4** have or has the right (to) **5** [Inf.] am, are, or is permitted (to); may —**can but** can only

can[2] (kan) *n.* ⟦OE *canne*, a cup⟧ **1** a container, usually metal, with a separate cover *[*a garbage *can]* **2** a tinned metal container in which foods, etc. are sealed for preservation **3** the amount a can holds —*vt.* **canned**, **can′ning** **1** to put up in cans or jars for preservation **2** [Slang] to dismiss

Ca·naan (kā′nən) ancient region at the SE end of the Mediterranean: the Biblical Promised Land

Can·a·da (kan′ə də) country in N North America: 3,849,671 sq. mi.; pop. 28,847,000; cap. Ottawa —**Ca·na·di·an** (kə nā′dē ən) *adj.*, *n.*

Canadian bacon cured, smoked pork taken from the loin

Canadian English English as spoken and written in Canada

Ca·na′di·an·ism′ *n.* **1** a custom or belief originating in Canada **2** a word or phrase originating in Canadian English

ca·nal (kə nal′) *n.* ⟦< L *canalis*, channel⟧ **1** an artificial waterway for transportation or irrigation **2** *Anat.* a tubular passage or duct

Canal Zone *former name for* a strip of land on either side of the Panama Canal: leased by the U.S. (1904-79)

ca·na·pé (kan′ə pā′, kan′ə pē) *n.* ⟦Fr⟧ a small piece of bread or a cracker, spread with spiced meat, cheese, etc., served as an appetizer

ca·nard (kə närd′) *n.* ⟦Fr, a duck⟧ a false, esp. malicious, report

ca·nar·y (kə ner′ē) *n.*, *pl.* **-ies** ⟦after *Canary* Islands⟧ **1** a small, yellow finch **2** a light yellow

Canary Islands group of Spanish islands off NW Africa

ca·nas·ta (kə nas′tə) *n.* ⟦Sp, basket⟧ a card game using a double deck

Can·ber·ra (kan′ber′ə, -bə rə) capital of Australia: pop. 328,000

can·can (kan′kan′) *n.* ⟦Fr⟧ a lively dance with much high kicking

can·cel (kan′səl) *vt.* **-celed** or **-celled**, **-cel·ing** or **-cel·ling** ⟦< L *cancellus*, lattice⟧ **1** to mark over with lines, etc., as in deleting written matter or marking a postage stamp, check, etc. as used **2** to make invalid **3** to do away with; abolish **4** to neutralize or balance: often with *out* **5** *Math.* to remove (a common factor, equivalents, etc.) —**can′cel·la′tion** *n.*

can·cer (kan′sər) *n.* ⟦L, crab⟧ **1** [C-] the fourth sign of the zodiac **2** a malignant tumor that can spread **3** anything bad or harmful that spreads —**can′cer·ous** *adj.*

can·de·la·brum (kan′də lä′brəm, -lā′-) *n.*, *pl.* **-bra** (-brə) or **-brums** ⟦L: see CHANDELIER⟧ a large branched candlestick: also **can′de·la′bra**, *pl.* **-bras**

can·did (kan′did) *adj.* ⟦L *candidus*, white, pure, sincere⟧ **1** very honest or frank **2** unposed and informal *[*a *candid* photo*]* —**can′did·ly** *adv.*

can·di·date (kan′də dāt′, -dət) *n.* ⟦L *candidatus*, white-robed, as were Roman office seekers⟧ **1** one seeking an office, award, etc. **2** one seemingly destined to come to a certain end

can·died (kan′dēd′) *adj.* cooked in sugar or syrup until glazed or encrusted

can·dle (kan′dəl) *n.* ⟦< L *candela*⟧ a cylinder of tallow or wax with a wick through it, which gives light when burned —*vt.* **-dled**, **-dling** to examine (eggs) for freshness by placing in front of a light —**can′dler** *n.*

can′dle·stick′ *n.* a cupped or spiked holder for a candle or candles

can′-do′ *adj.* [Inf.] confident of one's ability to accomplish something

can·dor (kan′dər) *n.* ⟦L, openness⟧ unreserved honesty or frankness in expressing oneself: Brit. sp. **can′dour**

can·dy (kan′dē) ***n.**, pl.* **-dies** ⟦< Pers *qand*, cane sugar⟧ a solid confection of sugar or syrup with flavoring, fruit, nuts, etc. —***vt.*** **-died, -dy·ing 1** to cook in sugar, esp. so as to preserve **2** to crystallize into sugar

cane (kān) ***n.*** ⟦< Gr *kanna*⟧ **1** the slender, jointed stem of certain plants, as bamboo **2** a plant with such a stem, as sugar cane **3** WALKING STICK **4** split rattan —***vt.*** **caned, can′ing 1** to flog with a cane **2** to make (chair seats, etc.) with cane —**can′er** ***n.***

cane·brake (kān′brāk′) ***n.*** a dense growth of cane plants

ca·nine (kā′nīn′) ***adj.*** ⟦< L *canis*, dog⟧ **1** of or like a dog **2** of the family of carnivores that includes dogs, wolves, and foxes —***n.*** **1** a dog or other canine animal **2** any of the sharp-pointed teeth next to the incisors: in full **canine tooth**

can·is·ter (kan′is tər) ***n.*** ⟦< Gr *kanastron*, wicker basket⟧ a small box or can for coffee, tea, etc.

can·ker (kaŋ′kər) ***n.*** ⟦< L *cancer*, a crab⟧ an ulcerlike sore, esp. in the mouth —**can′ker·ous** ***adj.***

can·na·bis (kan′ə bis) ***n.*** ⟦L, hemp⟧ **1** HEMP **2** marijuana or any other substance made from the flowering tops of the hemp

canned (kand) ***adj.*** **1** preserved, as in cans **2** [Slang] recorded for reproduction, as on radio or TV

can·nel (coal) (kan′əl) a dense bituminous coal that burns with a steady, bright flame

can·ner·y (kan′ər ē) ***n.**, pl.* **-ies** a factory where foods are canned

can·ni·bal (kan′ə bəl) ***n.*** ⟦Sp *canibal*⟧ **1** a person who eats human flesh **2** an animal that eats its own kind —***adj.*** of or like cannibals —**can′ni·bal·ism′** ***n.*** —**can′ni·bal·is′tic** ***adj.***

can′ni·bal·ize′ (-īz′) ***vt., vi.*** **-ized′, -iz′ing** to strip (old or worn equipment) of parts for use in other units

can·non (kan′ən) ***n.**, pl.* **-nons** or **-non** ⟦< L *canna*, cane⟧ **1** a large, mounted piece of artillery **2** an automatic gun on an aircraft

can′non·ade′ (-ād′) ***n.*** a continuous firing of artillery —***vt., vi.*** **-ad′ed, -ad′ing** to fire artillery (at)

can·not (kan′ät′, kə nät′) can not —**cannot but** have or has no choice but to

can·ny (kan′ē) ***adj.*** **-ni·er, -ni·est** ⟦< CAN[1]⟧ cautious and shrewd —**can′ni·ly** ***adv.*** —**can′ni·ness** ***n.***

ca·noe (kə no͞o′) ***n.*** ⟦< Sp *canoa* < WInd⟧ a light, narrow boat moved by paddles —***vi.*** **-noed′, -noe′ing** to paddle, or go in, a canoe —**ca·noe′ist** ***n.***

ca·no·la (oil) (kə nō′lə) an oil from the seed of the rape plant, used in cooking

can·on (kan′ən) ***n.*** ⟦OE, a rule < L⟧ **1** a law or body of laws of a church **2** *a*) a basic rule or principle *b*) a criterion **3** an official list, as of books of the Bible **4** the complete works, as of an author **5** *Music* a round **6** a clergyman serving in a cathedral

ca·ñon (kan′yən) ***n.*** *alt. sp. of* CANYON

ca·non·i·cal (kə nän′i kəl) ***adj.*** **1** of or according to church law **2** of or belonging to a canon

can·on·ize (kan′ən īz′) ***vt.*** **-ized′, -iz′ing 1** to declare (a deceased person) a saint **2** to glorify —**can′on·i·za′tion** ***n.***

can·o·py (kan′ə pē) ***n.**, pl.* **-pies** ⟦< Gr *kōnōpeion*, couch with mosquito nets⟧ **1** a drapery, etc. fastened above a bed, throne, etc., or held over a person **2** a rooflike projection —***vt.*** **-pied, -py·ing** to place or form a canopy over; cover

cant[1] (kant) ***n.*** ⟦< L *cantus*, song⟧ **1** the secret slang of beggars, thieves, etc.; argot **2** the special vocabulary of those in a certain occupation; jargon **3** insincere talk, esp. when pious —***vi.*** to use cant

cant[2] (kant) ***n.*** ⟦L *cantus*, tire of a wheel⟧ **1** an outside angle **2** a beveled edge **3** a tilt, turn, slant, etc. —***vt., vi.*** to slant; tilt

can't (kant, känt) *contr.* cannot

can·ta·loupe or **can·ta·loup** (kant′ə lōp′) ***n.*** ⟦Fr < It *Cantalupo*, estate near Rome, where first grown in Europe⟧ a muskmelon with a rough rind and juicy, orange flesh

can·tan·ker·ous (kan taŋ′kər əs) ***adj.*** ⟦prob. < ME *contakour*, troublemaker⟧ bad-tempered; quarrelsome —**can·tan′ker·ous·ly** ***adv.*** —**can·tan′ker·ous·ness** ***n.***

can·ta·ta (kän tät′ə, kən-) ***n.*** ⟦It < *cantare*, to sing⟧ a choral composition that sets to music the words of a story to be sung but not acted

can·teen (kan tēn′) ***n.*** ⟦< Fr < It *cantina*, wine cellar⟧ **1** a recreation center for military personnel, teenagers, etc. **2** a place where food is dispensed, as in a disaster area **3** a small flask for carrying water

can·ter (kant′ər) ***n.*** ⟦< *Canterbury gallop*, a riding pace⟧ a moderate gallop —***vi., vt.*** to ride at a canter

can·ti·cle (kan′ti kəl) ***n.*** ⟦< L *cantus*, song⟧ a hymn with words taken from the Bible

can·ti·le·ver (kant″l ē′vər, -ev′ər) ***n.*** ⟦< ?⟧ a bracket or block projecting as a support; esp., a projecting structure anchored at one end to a pier or wall —***vt.*** to support by means of cantilevers —**can′ti·le′vered** ***adj.***

can·to (kan′tō) ***n.**, pl.* **-tos** ⟦It < L *cantus*, song⟧ any of the main divisions of certain long poems

can·ton (kan′tən, -tän′) ***n.*** ⟦Fr < LL *cantus*, corner⟧ any of the states in the Swiss Republic

Can·ton (kan tän′) *a former transliteration of* GUANGZHOU

Can·ton·ese (kan′tə nēz′) ***n.*** **1** *pl.* **-ese′** a person born or living in Canton, China **2** the variety of Chinese spoken in Canton —***adj.*** of Canton

can·ton·ment (kan tän′mənt, -tōn′-) ***n.*** ⟦Fr: see CANTON⟧ temporary quarters for troops

can·tor (kan′tər) ***n.*** ⟦L, singer⟧ a singer of liturgical solos in a synagogue

can·vas (kan′vəs) ***n.*** ⟦< L *cannabis*, hemp⟧ **1** a coarse cloth of hemp, cotton, etc., used for tents, sails, etc. **2** a sail, tent, etc. **3** an oil painting on canvas

can'vas·back' ***n.*** a North American wild duck with a grayish back

can·vass (kan'vəs) ***vt., vi.*** ⟦< *canvas* < ? use of canvas for sifting⟧ to go through (places) or among (people) asking for (votes, opinions, orders, etc.) —***n.*** a canvassing —**can'vass·er *n.***

can·yon (kan'yən) ***n.*** ⟦Sp *cañón*, tube < L *canna*, a reed⟧ a long, narrow valley between high cliffs

cap[1] (kap) ***n.*** ⟦< LL *cappa*, hooded cloak⟧ **1** any closefitting head covering, with or without a visor or brim **2** a caplike part or thing; cover or top —***vt.* capped, cap'ping** **1** to put a cap on **2** to cover the top or end of **3** to equal or excel

cap[2] *abbrev.* **1** capacity **2** capital

ca·pa·ble (kā'pə bəl) ***adj.*** ⟦< L *capere*, to take⟧ having ability; skilled; competent —**capable of 1** having the qualities necessary for **2** able or ready to —**ca'pa·bil'i·ty**, *pl.* **-ties, *n.*** —**ca'pa·bly *adv.***

ca·pa·cious (kə pā'shəs) ***adj.*** ⟦< L *capere*, to take⟧ roomy; spacious —**ca·pa'cious·ly *adv.*** —**ca·pa'cious·ness *n.***

ca·pac·i·tor (kə pas'ə tər) ***n.*** a device for storing an electric charge

ca·pac'i·ty (-tē) ***n.***, *pl.* **-ties** ⟦< L *capere*, take⟧ **1** the ability to contain, absorb, or receive **2** all that can be contained; volume **3** ability **4** maximum output **5** position; function

ca·par·i·son (kə par'i sən, -zən) ***n.*** ⟦< LL *cappa*, cloak⟧ trappings for a horse —***vt.*** to cover (a horse) with trappings

cape[1] (kāp) ***n.*** ⟦see prec.⟧ a sleeveless garment fastened at the neck and hanging over the back and shoulders

cape[2] (kāp) ***n.*** ⟦< L *caput*, head⟧ a piece of land projecting into a body of water

ca·per[1] (kā'pər) ***vi.*** ⟦? < Fr *capriole*, a leap⟧ to skip about in a playful manner —***n.*** **1** a playful leap **2** a prank **3** [Slang] a criminal act, esp. a robbery —**cut a caper** (or **cut capers**) to caper

ca·per[2] (kā'pər) ***n.*** ⟦< Gr *kapparis*⟧ the green flower bud of a Mediterranean bush, pickled and used as a seasoning

cape'skin' ***n.*** ⟦orig. made from the skin of goats from the *Cape* of Good Hope⟧ fine leather made from sheepskin

Cape Town seaport in South Africa: seat of the legislature: pop. 855,000

Cape Verde (vʉrd) country on a group of islands in the Atlantic, west of Senegal: 1,557 sq. mi.; pop. 337,000

cap·il·lar·y (kap'ə ler'ē) ***adj.*** ⟦< L *capillus*, hair⟧ very slender —***n.***, *pl.* **-ies** **1** a tube with a very small bore: also **capillary tube** **2** any of the tiny blood vessels connecting the arteries with the veins

capillary attraction the action by which liquids in contact with solids, as in a capillary tube, rise or fall: also **capillary action**

cap·i·tal (kap'ət 'l) ***adj.*** ⟦< L *caput*, head⟧ **1** punishable by death **2** principal; chief **3** of, or being, the seat of government **4** of capital, or wealth **5** excellent —***n.*** **1** CAPITAL LETTER **2** a city that is the seat of government of a state or nation **3** money or property owned or used in business **4** [*often* **C-**] capitalists collectively **5** the top part of a column

capital gain profit resulting from the sale of capital investments such as stocks

cap'i·tal·ism' ***n.*** an economic system in which the means of production and distribution are privately owned and operated for profit

cap'i·tal·ist ***n.*** **1** an owner of wealth used in business **2** an upholder of capitalism **3** a wealthy person —**cap'i·tal·is'tic *adj.***

cap'i·tal·ize' (-īz') ***vt.* -ized', -iz'ing** **1** to use as or convert into capital **2** to supply capital to or for **3** to begin (a word) with a capital letter —**capitalize on something** to use something to one's advantage —**cap'i·tal·i·za'tion *n.***

capital letter the form of an alphabetical letter used to begin a sentence or proper name, as *A, B,* or *C*

cap'i·tal·ly ***adv.*** very well

capital punishment the penalty of death for a crime

Cap·i·tol (kap'ət 'l) ***n.*** ⟦< L *Capitolium*, temple of Jupiter in Rome⟧ **1** the building in which the U.S. Congress meets in Washington, DC **2** [*usually* **c-**] the building in which a state legislature meets

ca·pit·u·late (kə pich'yoo lāt', -pich'ə lāt') ***vi.* -lat'ed, -lat'ing** ⟦< LL *capitulare*, arrange conditions⟧ **1** to give up (*to* an enemy) on prearranged conditions **2** to stop resisting —**ca·pit'u·la'tion *n.***

cap·let (kap'lit) ***n.*** a solid, elongated medicine tablet, coated for easy swallowing

ca·pon (kā'pän', -pən) ***n.*** ⟦< L *capo*⟧ a castrated rooster fattened for eating

cap·puc·ci·no (kä'pə chē'nō, kap'ə-) ***n.*** ⟦It⟧ espresso coffee mixed with steamed milk and topped with cinnamon, etc.

ca·price (kə prēs') ***n.*** ⟦Fr < It⟧ **1** a sudden, impulsive change in thinking or acting **2** a capricious quality

ca·pri·cious (kə prish'əs) ***adj.*** subject to caprices; erratic —**ca·pri'cious·ly *adv.*** —**ca·pri'cious·ness *n.***

Cap·ri·corn (kap'ri kôrn') ***n.*** ⟦< L *caper*, goat + *cornu*, horn⟧ the tenth sign of the zodiac

cap·size (kap'sīz', kap sīz') ***vt., vi.*** **-sized', -siz'ing** ⟦< ?⟧ to overturn or upset: said esp. of a boat

cap·stan (kap'stən) ***n.*** ⟦? < L *capere*, take⟧ an upright cylinder, as on ships, around which cables are wound for hoisting anchors, etc.

cap·sule (kap'səl, -sool') ***n.*** ⟦Fr < L *capsa*, box⟧ **1** a soluble gelatin container enclosing a dose of medicine **2** a detachable compartment to hold people, instruments, etc. in a rocket: in full **space capsule** **3** *Bot.* a seed vessel —***adj.*** in a concise form —**cap'su·lar *adj.***

cap'sul·ize' (-īz') ***vt.* -ized', -iz'ing** **1** to enclose in a capsule **2** to condense

Capt *abbrev.* Captain

cap·tain (kap′tən) ***n.*** ⟦< L *caput*, head⟧ **1** a chief; leader **2** *U.S. Mil.* an officer ranking just above first lieutenant **3** *U.S. Navy* an officer ranking just above commander **4** *a)* the person in command of a ship *b)* the pilot of an airplane **5** the leader of a team, as in sports **—*vt.*** to be captain of **—cap′tain·cy**, *pl.* **-cies**, ***n.***

cap·tion (kap′shən) ***n.*** ⟦< L *capere*, to take⟧ **1** a heading or title, as of a newspaper article or illustration **2** *Film, TV* a subtitle **—*vt.*** to supply a caption for

cap′tious (-shəs) ***adj.*** ⟦see prec.⟧ **1** made only for the sake of argument or faultfinding *[a captious remark]* **2** quick to find fault **—cap′tious·ly *adv.* —cap′tious·ness *n.***

cap·ti·vate (kap′tə vāt′) ***vt.*** **-vat′ed, -vat′ing** to capture the attention or affection of **—cap′ti·vat′ing·ly *adv.* —cap′ti·va′tion *n.* —cap′ti·va′tor *n.***

cap·tive (kap′tiv) ***n.*** ⟦< L *capere*, to take⟧ a prisoner **—*adj.*** **1** taken or held prisoner **2** obliged to listen *[a captive audience]* **—cap·tiv′i·ty**, *pl.* **-ties**, ***n.***

cap′tor (-tər) ***n.*** one who captures

cap′ture (-chər) ***vt.*** **-tured, -tur·ing** ⟦< L *capere*, to take⟧ **1** to take or seize by force, surprise, etc. **2** to represent in a more permanent form *[to capture her charm on canvas]* **—*n.*** a capturing or being captured

car (kär) ***n.*** ⟦< L *carrus*, chariot⟧ **1** any vehicle on wheels **2** a vehicle that moves on rails, as a streetcar **3** an automobile **4** an elevator cage

Ca·ra·cas (kə räk′əs, -rak′-) capital of Venezuela: pop. 1,825,000

car·a·cul (kar′ə kul′, -kəl) ***n.*** *alt. sp. of* KARAKUL (esp. sense 2)

ca·rafe (kə raf′, -räf′) ***n.*** ⟦Fr⟧ a glass bottle for serving wine, water, or coffee

car·a·mel (kär′məl, kar′ə məl) ***n.*** ⟦Fr⟧ **1** burnt sugar used to color or flavor food **2** a chewy candy made from sugar, milk, etc.

car′a·mel·ize′ (-īz′) ***vt., vi.*** **-ized′, -iz′ing** to turn into CARAMEL (sense 1)

car·a·pace (kar′ə pās′) ***n.*** ⟦Fr < Sp⟧ the upper shell of the turtle, crab, etc.

car·at (kar′ət) ***n.*** ⟦Fr < Gr *keration*, little horn⟧ **1** a unit of weight for precious stones, equal to 200 milligrams **2** KARAT

car·a·van (kar′ə van′) ***n.*** ⟦< Pers *kārwān*⟧ **1** a company of people traveling together for safety, as through a desert **2** VAN[2]

car·a·van·sa·ry (kar′ə van′sə rē) ***n.***, *pl.* **-ries** ⟦< Pers *kārwān*, caravan + *sarāi*, palace⟧ in the Middle East, an inn for caravans

car·a·way (kar′ə wā′) ***n.*** ⟦< Ar *al-karawiyā′*⟧ the spicy seeds of an herb, used to flavor bread, etc.

car·bide (kär′bīd′) ***n.*** a solid compound of a metal with carbon

car·bine (kär′bīn′, -bēn′) ***n.*** ⟦< Fr *scarabée*, beetle⟧ **1** a short-barreled rifle **2** a light, semiautomatic or automatic rifle of relatively limited range

carbo- *combining form* carbon: also **carb-**

car·bo·hy·drate (kär′bō hī′drāt, -bə-) ***n.*** ⟦prec. + HYDRATE⟧ an organic compound composed of carbon, hydrogen, and oxygen, as a sugar or starch

car·bol·ic acid (kär bäl′ik) *see* PHENOL

car·bon (kär′bən) ***n.*** ⟦< L *carbo*, coal⟧ **1** a nonmetallic chemical element found esp. in all organic compounds: diamond and graphite are pure carbon: a radioactive isotope of carbon (**carbon-14**) is used in dating fossils, etc. **2** CARBON PAPER **3** a copy made with carbon paper **—*adj.*** of or like carbon

car′bon·ate (-bə nit; *also, and for v. always*, -nāt′) ***n.*** a salt or ester of carbonic acid **—*vt.*** **-at′ed, -at′ing** to charge with carbon dioxide **—car′bon·a′tion *n.***

carbon black carbon produced by the incomplete burning of oil or gas

carbon copy **1** a copy made with carbon paper **2** anything very much like another

carbon dating a method of establishing the approximate age of fossils, etc. by measuring the amount of carbon-14 in them **—car′bon-date′, -dat′ed, -dat′ing, *vt.***

carbon di·ox·ide (dī äks′īd′) a heavy, colorless, odorless gas: it passes out of the lungs in respiration

car·bon·ic acid (kär bän′ik) a weak acid formed by carbon dioxide in water

car·bon·if·er·ous (kär′bə nif′ər əs) ***adj.*** containing carbon or coal

carbon mon·ox·ide (mə näks′īd′) a colorless, odorless, highly poisonous gas

carbon paper thin paper coated on one side, as with a carbon preparation, used to make copies of letters, etc.

carbon tet·ra·chlo·ride (te′trə klôr′īd′) a nonflammable liquid, used as a solvent for fats and oils, etc.

Car·bo·run·dum (kär′bə run′dəm) ⟦CARB(ON) + (*c*)*orundum*⟧ *trademark for* a hard abrasive, esp. of carbon and silicon **—*n.*** [c-] such a substance

car·boy (kär′boi′) ***n.*** ⟦< Pers *qarābah*⟧ a large bottle enclosed in a protective container, for holding corrosive liquids

car·bun·cle (kär′buŋ′kəl) ***n.*** ⟦< L dim. of *carbo*, coal⟧ a painful bacterial infection deep beneath the skin **—car·bun′cu·lar** (-kyoo͞ lər) ***adj.***

car·bu·ret·or (kär′bə rāt′ər) ***n.*** a device for mixing air with gasoline spray to make an explosive mixture in an internal-combustion engine

car·cass (kär′kəs) ***n.*** ⟦< Fr *carcasse*⟧ **1** the dead body of an animal **2** a framework or shell

car·cin·o·gen (kär sin′ə jən) ***n.*** ⟦< fol. + -GEN⟧ any substance that produces cancer **—car·ci·no·gen·ic** (kär′sə nō jen′ik) ***adj.***

car·ci·no·ma (kär′sə nō′mə) ***n.***, *pl.* **-mas** or **-ma·ta** (-mə tə) ⟦L < Gr *karkinos*, crab⟧ any of several kinds of epithelial cancer

car coat a short overcoat

card[1] (kärd) ***n.*** ⟦< Gr *chartēs*, layer of papyrus⟧ **1** a flat, stiff piece of paper or pasteboard; specif., *a*) any of a pack of playing cards *b*) a card identifying a person, esp. as a member, agent, etc. *c*) a postcard *d*) an illustrated, usually folded card bearing a greeting *e*) any of a series of cards on which information is recorded **2** a small, plug-in circuit board **3** [Inf.] a witty or clowning person —**put** (or **lay**) **one's cards on the table** to reveal something frankly

card[2] (kärd) ***n.*** ⟦< L *carrere*, to card⟧ a metal comb or a machine with wire teeth for combing fibers of wool, cotton, etc. —***vt.*** to use a card on

card′board′ ***n.*** stiff, thick paper or pasteboard, used for cards, boxes, etc.

car·di·ac (kär′dē ak′) ***adj.*** ⟦< Gr *kardia*, heart⟧ of or near the heart

cardiac arrest the complete failure of the heart to pump blood

car·di·gan (kär′di gən) ***n.*** ⟦after 7th Earl of *Cardigan*⟧ a sweater or jacket, usually knitted and collarless, that opens down the front

car·di·nal (kärd′′n əl) ***adj.*** ⟦< L *cardo*, pivot⟧ **1** principal; chief **2** bright-red —***n.*** **1** an official appointed by the pope to his council **2** a bright-red American songbird **3** CARDINAL NUMBER

cardinal number any number used in counting or in showing how many (e.g., two, 40, 627, etc.)

cardio- ⟦< Gr *kardia*, heart⟧ *combining form* of the heart

car·di·o·gram (kär′dē ō gram′, -dē ə-) ***n.*** ELECTROCARDIOGRAM

car′di·o·graph′ (-graf′) ***n.*** ELECTROCARDIOGRAPH

car′di·ol′o·gy (-äl′ə jē) ***n.*** the branch of medicine dealing with the heart —**car′di·ol′o·gist** ***n.***

car·di·o·pul·mo·nar·y (kär′dē ō pool′ mə ner′ē) ***adj.*** of or involving the heart and lungs

car′di·o·vas′cu·lar (-vas′kyə lər) ***adj.*** of the heart and the blood vessels as a unified body system

cards ***pl.n.*** any game played with a deck of playing cards, as poker

card′sharp′ ***n.*** [Inf.] a professional cheater at cards: also **card shark**

care (ker) ***n.*** ⟦< OE *caru*, sorrow⟧ **1** *a*) a troubled state of mind; worry *b*) a cause of such a mental state **2** close attention; heed **3** a liking or regard (*for*) **4** custody; protection **5** a responsibility —***vi.*** **cared**, **car′ing** **1** to feel concern **2** to feel love or a liking (*for*) **3** to look after; provide (*for*) **4** to wish (*for*); want —***vt.*** **1** to feel concern about or interest in **2** to wish —**(in) care of** at the address of —**take care of** **1** to attend to **2** to provide for

ca·reen (kə rēn′) ***vt.***, ***vi.*** ⟦< L *carina*, keel⟧ to lean or cause to lean sideways; tip; tilt; lurch

ca·reer (kə rir′) ***n.*** ⟦< L *carrus*, car⟧ **1** [Archaic] a swift course **2** one's progress through life **3** a profession or occupation —***vi.*** to rush wildly

care′free′ ***adj.*** free from worry

care′ful ***adj.*** **1** cautious; wary **2** accurate; thorough; painstaking —**care′ful·ly** ***adv.*** —**care′ful·ness** ***n.***

care′giv′er ***n.*** one who takes care of a child, invalid, etc.

care′less ***adj.*** **1** carefree; untroubled **2** not paying enough heed; neglectful **3** done or made without enough attention, precision, etc. —**care′less·ly** ***adv.*** —**care′less·ness** ***n.***

ca·ress (kə res′) ***vt.*** ⟦ult. < L *carus*, dear⟧ to touch lovingly or gently —***n.*** an affectionate touch

car·et (kar′it, ker′-) ***n.*** ⟦L, there is lacking⟧ a mark (∧) used to show where something is to be inserted in a written or printed line

care′tak′er ***n.*** **1** a person hired to take care of something or someone **2** one acting as temporary replacement

care′worn′ ***adj.*** worn out by, or showing the effects of, troubles and worry; haggard

car·fare (kär′fer′) ***n.*** the price of a ride on a subway, bus, etc.

car·go (kär′gō) ***n.***, *pl.* **-goes** or **-gos** ⟦< Sp *cargar*, to load⟧ the load carried by a ship, truck, etc.; freight

car′hop′ ***n.*** ⟦CAR + (BELL)HOP⟧ one who serves food at a drive-in restaurant

Car·ib·be·an (Sea) (kar′ə bē′ən, kə rib′ē ən) part of the Atlantic, bounded by the West Indies, Central America, and N South America

car·i·bou (kar′ə bo͞o′) ***n.*** ⟦CdnFr⟧ a large North American reindeer

car·i·ca·ture (kar′i kə chər) ***n.*** ⟦Fr < It *caricare*, exaggerate⟧ **1** the exaggerated imitation of a person, literary style, etc. for satirical effect **2** a picture, etc. in which this is done —***vt.*** **-tured**, **-tur·ing** to depict as in a caricature —**car′i·ca·tur·ist** ***n.***

car·ies (ker′ēz′) ***n.*** ⟦L, decay⟧ decay of bones or, esp., of teeth

car·il·lon (kar′ə län′) ***n.*** ⟦Fr, chime of four bells < L *quattuor*, four⟧ a set of bells tuned to the chromatic scale

ca·ri·tas (kär′ē täs′) ***n.*** love for all people

car·jack·ing (kär′jak′iŋ) ***n.*** the taking of a car and its passengers by force —**car′jack′** ***vt.*** —**car′jack′er** ***n.***

car·mine (kär′min, -mīn′) ***n.*** ⟦ult. < Ar *qirmiz*, crimson⟧ a red or purplish-red color —***adj.*** red or purplish-red

car·nage (kär′nij) ***n.*** ⟦Fr < L *caro*, flesh⟧ extensive slaughter, esp. in battle

car′nal (-nəl) ***adj.*** ⟦< L *caro*, flesh⟧ **1** of the flesh; material; worldly **2** sensual or sexual —**car·nal′i·ty** (-nal′i tē), *pl.* **-ties**, ***n.*** —**car′nal·ly** ***adv.***

car·na·tion (kär nā′shən) ***n.*** ⟦< L *caro*, flesh⟧ **1** a plant of the pink family, widely cultivated for its white, pink, or red flowers **2** its flower

car·nel·ian (kär nēl′yən) ***n.*** ⟦< L *carnis*, of flesh (color)⟧ a red variety of chalcedony, used in jewelry

car·ni·val (kär′nə vəl) ***n.*** ⟦< Fr *carnaval* (or It *carnevale*)⟧ **1** the period of feasting and revelry just before Lent **2** a reveling; festivity **3** an entertainment with sideshows, rides, etc.

car·ni·vore (kär′nə vôr′) ***n.*** a carnivorous animal or plant

car·niv·o·rous (kär niv′ə rəs) ***adj.*** ⟦< L *caro*, flesh + *vorare*, to devour⟧ **1** flesh-eating **2** of the carnivores —**car·niv′o·rous·ness** ***n.***

car·ob (kar′əb) ***n.*** a tree of the E Mediterranean region with sweet pods used in making candy, etc.

car·ol (kar′əl) ***n.*** ⟦< OFr *carole*, kind of dance⟧ a song of joy or praise; esp., a Christmas song —***vi.***, ***vt.*** **-oled** or **-olled**, **-ol·ing** or **-ol·ling** to sing; esp., to sing Christmas carols —**car′ol·er** or **car′ol·ler** ***n.***

car·om (kar′əm) ***n.*** ⟦< Sp *carambola*⟧ **1** *Billiards* a shot in which the cue ball successively hits two balls **2** a hitting and rebounding —***vi.*** **1** to make a carom **2** to hit and rebound

ca·rot·id (kə rät′id) ***adj.*** ⟦Gr *karōtis*⟧ designating or of either of the two main arteries, one on each side of the neck, which convey blood to the head —***n.*** a carotid artery

ca·rouse (kə rouz′) ***vi.*** **-roused′**, **-rous′ing** ⟦< Ger *gar austrinken*, to drink⟧ to engage in a noisy drinking party —***n.*** a noisy drinking party

car·ou·sel (kar′ə sel′) ***n.*** ⟦Fr < It dial. (Naples) *carusiello*, kind of tournament⟧ **1** a merry-go-round **2** a circular baggage conveyor in an airport

carp[1] (kärp) ***n.***, *pl.* **carp** or **carps** ⟦< VL *carpa*⟧ an edible freshwater fish widely cultivated for food

carp[2] (kärp) ***vi.*** ⟦< ON *karpa*, to brag⟧ to find fault in a petty or nagging way —**carp′er** ***n.***

car·pal (kär′pəl) ***adj.*** of the carpus —***n.*** a bone of the carpus

carpal tunnel syndrome a condition of a pinched nerve in the wrist, often caused by repetitive movement

car·pel (kär′pəl) ***n.*** ⟦< Gr *karpos*, fruit⟧ a simple pistil, regarded as a modified leaflike structure

car·pen·ter (kär′pən tər) ***n.*** ⟦< L *carpentum*, a cart⟧ one who builds and repairs wooden things, esp. buildings, ships, etc. —**car′pen·try** (-trē) ***n.***

carpenter ant a large ant that gnaws holes in trees, wooden buildings, etc. for its nest

car·pet (kär′pət) ***n.*** ⟦< L *carpere*, to card⟧ **1** a heavy fabric for covering a floor **2** anything that covers like a carpet —***vt.*** to cover as with a carpet —**on the carpet** being reprimanded

car′pet·bag′ ***n.*** an old-fashioned traveling bag, made of carpeting

car′pet·bag′ger ***n.*** a politician, promoter, etc. from the outside whose influence is resented

car′pet·ing ***n.*** carpets or carpet fabric

car pool a plan by a group to rotate the use of their cars, as for going to work —**car′pool′** ***vi.***, ***vt.***

car·port (kär′pôrt′) ***n.*** an automobile shelter built as a roof extending from the side of a building

car·pus (kär′pəs) ***n.***, *pl.* **-pi′** (-pī′) ⟦< Gr *karpos*, wrist⟧ *Anat.* the wrist, or the wrist bones

car·rel or **car·rell** (kar′əl) ***n.*** ⟦< ML *carula*⟧ a small enclosure in a library, for privacy in studying or reading

car·riage (kar′ij) ***n.*** ⟦ult. < L *carrus*, chariot⟧ **1** a carrying; transportation **2** the manner of carrying oneself; bearing **3** *a*) a horse-drawn passenger vehicle, esp. one with four wheels *b*) a baby carriage **4** a moving part, as on a typewriter, that supports and shifts something

car·ri·er (kar′ē ər) ***n.*** **1** one that carries **2** one in the business of transporting **3** one that transmits disease germs **4** AIRCRAFT CARRIER **5** *a*) a telephone-service company *b*) an insurance company

carrier pigeon *former name for* HOMING PIGEON

car·ri·on (kar′ē ən) ***n.*** ⟦< L *caro*, flesh⟧ the decaying flesh of a dead body

Car·roll (kar′əl), **Lew·is** (lo͞o′is) (pseud. of *C. L. Dodgson*) 1832-98; Eng. writer

car·rot (kar′ət) ***n.*** ⟦< Gr *karōton*⟧ **1** a plant with an edible, fleshy, orange-red root **2** the root

car·rou·sel (kar′ə sel′) ***n.*** *alt. sp. of* CAROUSEL

car·ry (kar′ē) ***vt.*** **-ried**, **-ry·ing** ⟦< L *carrus*, chariot⟧ **1** to hold or support **2** to take from one place to another **3** to keep with one *[to carry an ID]* **4** to transmit *[air carries sounds]* **5** to transfer or extend **6** to have as a quality, consequence, etc. *[to carry a guarantee]* **7** to bear (oneself) in a specified way **8** to win (an election, argument, etc.) **9** *a*) to keep in stock *b*) to keep on one's account books, etc. **10** to publish or broadcast *[to carry a syndicated column, a TV show, etc.]* —***vi.*** to cover a range or distance: said of a voice, missile, etc. —***n.***, *pl.* **-ries** the distance covered by a gun, ball, etc. —**be** (or **get**) **carried away** to become very emotional or enthusiastic —**carry on 1** to engage in **2** to go on (*with*) **3** [Inf.] to behave wildly or childishly —**carry out** (or **through**) **1** to put (plans, etc.) into practice **2** to accomplish —**carry over** to postpone

carrying charge interest paid on the balance owed in installment buying

car′ry-on′ ***adj.*** small enough to fit under an airplane seat or in an overhead compartment —***n.*** a piece of carry-on luggage

car′ry·out′ ***adj.*** designating or of prepared food sold as by a restaurant to be consumed elsewhere

car′ry-o′ver ***n.*** something carried over or left over

car seat a seat in an automobile, specif., a portable seat for securing a small child

car′sick′ ***adj.*** nauseated from riding in an automobile, bus, etc.

Car·son City (kär′sən) capital of Nevada, in the W part: pop. 40,000

cart (kärt) ***n.*** ⟦< ON *kartr*⟧ **1** a small wagon, carriage, etc. **2** a handcart —***vt.***, ***vi.*** to carry as in a cart, truck, etc.; transport

cart·age (kärt′ij) ***n.*** **1** the work of carting **2** the charge for this

carte blanche (kärt′ blänsh′) ⟦Fr, lit., white card⟧ full authority or freedom

car·tel (kär tel′) ***n.*** ⟦< Ger < Fr⟧ an association of businesses in an international monopoly; trust

Car·ter (kärt′ər), **Jim·my** (jim′ē) (legal name *James Earl Carter, Jr.*) 1924- ; 39th president of the U.S. (1977-81)

car·ti·lage (kärt′'l ij) ***n.*** ⟦< L *cartilago*⟧ tough, elastic tissue forming parts of the skeleton; gristle —**car′ti·lag′i·nous** (-aj′ə nəs) ***adj.***

car·tog·ra·phy (kär täg′rə fē) ***n.*** ⟦see CARD¹ & -GRAPHY⟧ the art of making maps or charts —**car·tog′ra·pher *n.***

car·ton (kärt′'n) ***n.*** ⟦Fr < It *carta*, card⟧ a cardboard box or container

car·toon (kär to͞on′) ***n.*** ⟦< Fr: see prec.⟧ **1** a drawing caricaturing a person or event **2** *a*) COMIC STRIP *b*) an animated cartoon —***vi.*** to draw a cartoon —**car·toon′ist *n.***

car·tridge (kär′trij) ***n.*** ⟦< Fr < It *carta*, card⟧ **1** a cylindrical case containing the charge and primer, and usually the projectile, for a firearm **2** a small container, as for camera film or ink for a pen

cart′wheel′ *n.* a handspring performed sideways

carve (kärv) ***vt.* carved, carv′ing** ⟦OE *ceorfan*⟧ **1** to make or shape by or as by cutting **2** to decorate the surface of with cut designs **3** to divide by cutting; slice —***vi.*** **1** to carve statues or designs **2** to carve meat —**carv′er *n.*** —**carv′ing *n.***

car′wash′ *n.* an establishment at which automobiles are washed

car·y·at·id (kar′ē at′id) ***n.***, *pl.* **-ids** or **-i·des′** (-ə dēz′) ⟦< Gr *karyatides*, priestesses at Karyai, in ancient Greece⟧ a supporting column having the form of a draped female figure

ca·sa·ba (kə sä′bə) ***n.*** ⟦after *Kasaba*, town in Asia Minor⟧ a kind of cultivated melon with a hard, yellow rind

Ca·sa·blan·ca (kas′ə blaŋ′kə, kä′sə bläŋ′kə) seaport in NW Morocco: pop. 1,506,000

Ca·sa·no·va (kaz′ə nō′və, kas′ə-) ***n.*** ⟦after G. *Casanova* (1725-98), It adventurer⟧ a man who has many love affairs

cas·cade (kas kād′) ***n.*** ⟦Fr < L *cadere*, to fall⟧ **1** a small, steep waterfall **2** anything resembling this, as a shower of sparks —***vt.*, *vi.* -cad′ed, -cad′ing** to fall or drop in a cascade

cas·car·a (kas ker′ə) ***n.*** ⟦Sp *cáscara*, bark⟧ a thorny tree growing on the Pacific coast of the U.S.

case¹ (kās) ***n.*** ⟦< L *casus*, a chance < *cadere*, to fall⟧ **1** an example or instance *[*a *case* of flu*]* **2** a person being helped, as by a doctor **3** any matter requiring study or investigation **4** *a*) the argument of one side, as in a law court *b*) convincing arguments *[*he has no *case]* **5** a lawsuit **6** *Gram.* the syntactic function of a noun or pronoun *[*nominative, objective, or possessive *case]* —***vt.* cased, cas′ing** [Slang] to look over carefully —**in any case** anyhow —**in case** in the event that; if —**in case of** in the event of —**in no case** never

case² (kās) ***n.*** ⟦< L *capsa*, box⟧ **1** a container, as a box **2** a protective cover *[*a watch *case]* **3** a full box or its contents *[*a *case* of beer*]* **4** a frame, as for a window —***vt.* cased, cas′ing** **1** to put in a container **2** to enclose; encase

case′hard′en (-härd′'n) ***vt.*** *Metallurgy* to form a hard surface on (an iron alloy)

ca·se·in (kā′sē in, -sēn′) ***n.*** ⟦< L *caseus*, cheese⟧ a protein that is one of the chief constituents of milk

case′load′ *n.* the number of cases handled by a court, social agency, etc.

case′ment (-mənt) ***n.*** ⟦ult. < OFr *enchassement*⟧ a window frame that opens on hinges along the side

case′work′ *n.* social work in which guidance is given in cases of personal or family maladjustment —**case′work′er *n.***

cash (kash) ***n.*** ⟦< L *capsa*, box⟧ **1** money that a person actually has; esp., ready money **2** bills and coins **3** money, a check, etc. paid at the time of purchase —***vt.*** to give or get cash for —***adj.*** of or for cash —**cash in** to exchange for cash

cash·ew (kash′o͞o; *also*, kə sho͞o′) ***n.*** ⟦< AmInd (Brazil) *acajú*⟧ **1** a tropical tree bearing kidney-shaped nuts **2** the nut

cash·ier¹ (ka shir′) ***n.*** ⟦Fr⟧ a person handling the cash transactions of a bank or store

cash·ier² (ka shir′) ***vt.*** ⟦< LL *cassare*, destroy⟧ to dismiss in dishonor

cash·mere (kash′mir′, kazh′-) ***n.*** ⟦after *Kashmir*, region in India⟧ **1** a fine carded wool from goats of N India and Tibet **2** a soft, twilled cloth as of this wool

cash register a device, usually with a money drawer, used for registering visibly the amount of a sale

cas·ing (kās′iŋ) ***n.*** **1** the skin of a sausage **2** the outer covering of a pneumatic tire **3** a frame, as for a door

ca·si·no (kə sē′nō) ***n.***, *pl.* **-nos** ⟦It < *casa*, house⟧ **1** a room or building for dancing, gambling, etc. **2** a card game for two to four players

cask (kask) ***n.*** ⟦ult. < L *quassare*, shatter⟧ **1** a barrel of any size, esp. one for liquids **2** its contents

cas·ket (kas′kit) ***n.*** ⟦< NormFr *casse*, box⟧ **1** a small box or chest, as for valuables **2** a coffin

Cas·pi·an (Sea) (kas′pē ən) inland salt sea between Asia and extreme SE Europe

Cas·san·dra (kə san′drə) ***n.*** *Gr. Myth.* a Trojan prophetess of doom whose prophecies are never believed

cas·sa·va (kə sä′və) ***n.*** ⟦< Fr < WInd *casávi*⟧ **1** a tropical American plant with starchy roots **2** a starch made from these roots, used in tapioca

cas·se·role (kas′ə rōl′) ***n.*** ⟦Fr < Gr *kyathos*, a bowl⟧ **1** a baking dish in which food can be cooked and served **2** the food baked in such a dish

cas·sette (kə set′, ka-) ***n.*** ⟦< NormFr *casse*, box⟧ a case with magnetic tape or film in it, for loading a tape recorder,

VCR, camera, etc. quickly

cas·sia (kash′ə, kas′ē ə) ***n.*** ⟦ult. < Heb *qeṣīʿāh*, lit., something scraped off⟧ **1** *a*) the bark of a tree of SE Asia: a source of cinnamon *b*) the tree **2** any of various tropical plants whose leaves yield senna

cas·si·no (kə sē′nō) ***n.*** *alt. sp. of* CASINO

cas·sock (kas′ək) ***n.*** ⟦prob. < Turk *qazaq*, nomad⟧ a long, closefitting vestment worn by clergymen, etc.

cast (kast) ***vt.* cast, cast′ing** ⟦< ON *kasta*⟧ **1** to throw with force; hurl **2** to deposit (a ballot or vote) **3** to direct *[to cast one's eyes]* **4** to project *[to cast light]* **5** to throw off or shed (a skin) **6** to shape (molten metal, etc.) by pouring into a mold **7** to select (an actor) for (a role or play) **8** to calculate **—*vi.*** to throw **—*n.*** **1** a casting; throw **2** *a*) something formed in a mold *b*) a mold or impression **3** a plaster form for immobilizing a broken limb **4** the set of actors in a play, movie, etc. **5** an appearance, as of features **6** a kind; quality **7** a tinge; shade **—cast about** to look (*for*) **—cast aside** (or **away** or **off**) to discard

CASTANETS

cas·ta·nets (kas′tə nets′) ***pl.n.*** ⟦< Sp < L *castanea*, chestnut: from the shape⟧ a pair of small, hollowed pieces of hard wood or ivory, clicked together in the hand in time to music

cast′a·way′ ***n.*** a shipwrecked person **—*adj.*** **1** discarded **2** shipwrecked

caste (kast) ***n.*** ⟦Fr < L *castus*, pure⟧ **1** any of the hereditary Hindu social classes of a formerly segregated system of India **2** any exclusive group **3** rigid class distinction based on birth, wealth, etc. **—lose caste** to lose social status

cast′er ***n.*** **1** a container for vinegar, oil, etc. at the table **2** any of a set of small wheels for supporting and moving furniture

cas·ti·gate (kas′ti gāt′) ***vt.* -gat′ed, -gat′ing** ⟦< L *castigare*⟧ to rebuke severely, esp. by public criticism **—cas′ti·ga′tion *n.* —cas′ti·ga′tor *n.***

cast′ing ***n.*** a thing, esp. of metal, cast in a mold

cast iron a hard, brittle alloy of iron used for casting **—cast′-i′ron *adj.***

cas·tle (kas′əl) ***n.*** ⟦< L *castrum*, fort⟧ **1** a large, fortified building or group of buildings **2** any massive dwelling like this **3** *Chess* ROOK[2]

cast′off′ ***adj.*** discarded; abandoned **—*n.*** a person or thing cast off

cas·tor-oil plant (kas′tər oil′) a tropical plant with large seeds that yield an oil (**castor oil**) used as a cathartic

cas·trate (kas′trāt′) ***vt.* -trat′ed, -trat′ing** ⟦< L *castrare*⟧ to remove the testicles of; emasculate **—cas·tra′tion *n.***

cas·u·al (kazh′o͞o əl) ***adj.*** ⟦< L *casus*, chance⟧ **1** happening by chance; not planned; incidental **2** occasional **3** careless or cursory **4** nonchalant **5** *a*) informal *b*) for informal use **—cas′u·al·ly *adv.* —cas′u·al·ness *n.***

cas·u·al·ty (kazh′o͞o əl tē) ***n.***, *pl.* **-ties** **1** an accident, esp. a fatal one **2** a member of the armed forces killed, wounded, captured, etc. **3** anyone hurt or killed in an accident **4** anything lost, destroyed, etc.

cas·u·ist·ry (kazh′o͞o is trē) ***n.***, *pl.* **-ries** ⟦< L *casus*, CASE[1]⟧ subtle but false reasoning, esp. about moral issues; sophistry **—cas′u·ist *n.***

cat (kat) ***n.*** ⟦OE⟧ **1** a small, soft-furred animal, often kept as a pet or for killing mice **2** any flesh-eating mammal related to this, as the lion, tiger, leopard, etc. **3** a spiteful woman **—let the cat out of the bag** to let a secret be found out

cat·a·clysm (kat′ə kliz′əm) ***n.*** ⟦< Gr *kata-*, down + *klyzein*, to wash⟧ any sudden, violent change, as in war **—cat′a·clys′mic** (-kliz′mik) ***adj.***

cat·a·comb (kat′ə kōm′) ***n.*** ⟦< ? L *cata*, by + *tumba*, tomb⟧ a gallery in an underground burial place: *usually used in pl.*

cat′a·falque′ (-falk′, -fôlk′) ***n.*** ⟦Fr < It *catafalco*, funeral canopy⟧ a wooden framework on which a body in a coffin lies in state

cat′a·lep′sy (-lep′sē) ***n.*** ⟦< Gr *katalēpsis*, a seizing⟧ a condition of muscle rigidity and sudden, temporary loss of consciousness, as in epilepsy **—cat′a·lep′tic *adj., n.***

cat·a·log or **cat·a·logue** (kat′ə lôg′) ***n.*** ⟦< Gr *kata-*, down + *legein*, to count⟧ a complete list, as a card file of the books in a library, a list of articles for sale, etc. **—*vt., vi.* -loged′** or **-logued′**, **-log′ing** or **-logu′ing** to arrange (an item or items) in a catalog **—cat′a·log′er** or **cat′a·logu′er *n.***

ca·tal·pa (kə tal′pə) ***n.*** ⟦< AmInd⟧ a tree with heart-shaped leaves and slender, beanlike pods

ca·tal·y·sis (kə tal′ə sis) ***n.***, *pl.* **-ses′** (-sēz′) ⟦< Gr *katalysis*, dissolution⟧ the speeding up or, sometimes, slowing down of a chemical reaction by adding a substance which itself is not changed thereby

cat·a·lyst (kat′ə list) ***n.*** **1** a substance serving as the agent in catalysis **2** anything bringing about or hastening a result **—cat′a·lyt′ic** (-lit′ik) ***adj.***

catalytic converter a chemical filter connected to the exhaust system of an automotive vehicle, to reduce air pollution

cat·a·ma·ran (kat′ə mə ran′) ***n.*** ⟦Tamil *kaṭṭumaram*⟧ **1** a narrow log raft propelled by sails or paddles **2** a boat like this with two parallel hulls

cat·a·mount (kat′ə mount′) ***n.*** a wildcat, esp. a cougar or lynx

cat·a·pult (kat′ə pult′) ***n.*** ⟦< Gr *kata-*, down + *pallein*, to hurl⟧ **1** an ancient military contrivance for throwing large stones, etc. **2** a device for launching an airplane, missile, etc. as from a deck or ramp —***vt.*** to shoot or launch as from a catapult —***vi.*** to leap

cat·a·ract (kat′ə rakt′) ***n.*** ⟦< Gr *kata-*, down + *rhassein*, to strike or ? *arassein*, to smite⟧ **1** a large waterfall **2** *a)* an eye disease in which the lens becomes opaque, causing partial or total blindness *b)* the opaque area

ca·tas·tro·phe (kə tas′trə fē) ***n.*** ⟦< Gr *kata-*, down + *strephein*, to turn⟧ any great and sudden disaster —**cat·a·stroph·ic** (kat′ə sträf′ik) ***adj.***

cat·a·ton·ic (kat′ə tän′ik) ***adj.*** ⟦< Gr *kata-*, down + *tonos*, tension⟧ of or having a psychiatric condition involving catalepsy —***n.*** a catatonic person

cat′bird′ ***n.*** a slate-gray North American songbird with a call like a cat's

cat′boat′ ***n.*** a sailboat with a single sail on a mast set well forward

cat′call′ ***n.*** a shrill shout or whistle expressing derision, etc. —***vi.*** to make catcalls

catch (kach, kech) ***vt.*** **caught**, **catch′ing** ⟦< L *capere*, to take hold⟧ **1** to seize and hold; capture **2** to take by a trap **3** to deceive **4** to surprise in some act **5** *a)* to get to in time *[*to *catch* a train*]* *b)* to overtake **6** to lay hold of; grab *[*to *catch* a ball*]* **7** to become infected with *[*he *caught* a cold*]* **8** to understand **9** to cause to be entangled or snagged **10** [Inf.] to see, hear, etc. —***vi.*** **1** to become held, fastened, etc. **2** to take hold, as fire **3** to keep hold, as a lock —***n.*** **1** a catching **2** a thing that catches **3** something caught **4** one worth catching, esp. as a spouse **5** a break in the voice **6** [Inf.] a tricky qualification or condition —**catch at** to seize desperately —**catch on** **1** to understand **2** to become popular —**catch up** **1** to seize; snatch **2** to overtake

catch′all′ ***n.*** a container or place for holding all sorts of things

catch′er ***n.*** *Baseball* the player behind home plate, who catches pitched balls

catch′ing ***adj.*** **1** contagious; infectious **2** attractive

catch′phrase′ ***n.*** a phrase that has become popular

catch′up′ (-up′) ***n.*** KETCHUP

catch′y ***adj.*** **-i·er**, **-i·est** **1** attracting attention and easily remembered *[*a *catchy* tune*]* **2** tricky

cat·e·chism (kat′ə kiz′əm) ***n.*** ⟦< Gr *kata-*, thoroughly + *ēchein*, to sound⟧ **1** a handbook of questions and answers for teaching the principles of a religion **2** a close questioning

cat·e·gor·i·cal (kat′ə gôr′i kəl) ***adj.*** **1** positive; explicit: said of a statement, etc. **2** of, as, or in a category —**cat′e·gor′i·cal·ly** ***adv.***

cat·e·go·rize (kat′ə gə rīz′) ***vt.*** **-rized′**, **-riz′ing** to place in a category; classify

cat′e·go′ry (-gôr′ē) ***n.***, *pl.* **-ries** ⟦< Gr *katēgorein*, to assert⟧ a division in a scheme of classification

ca·ter (kāt′ər) ***vi.*** ⟦< L *ad-*, to + *capere*, take hold⟧ **1** to provide food and service, as for parties **2** to seek to gratify another's needs or desires: with *to* —***vt.*** to serve as caterer for (a banquet, etc.) —**ca′ter·er** ***n.***

cat·er·cor·nered (kat′ə kôr′nərd, kat′ ē-) ***adj.*** ⟦< OFr *catre*, four + CORNERED⟧ diagonal —***adv.*** diagonally Also **cat′er-cor′ner**

cat·er·pil·lar (kat′ər pil′ər, kat′ə-) ***n.*** ⟦< L *catta pilosus*, hairy cat⟧ the wormlike larva of a butterfly, moth, etc. —[**C-**] *trademark for* a kind of tractor for rough or muddy ground

cat·er·waul (kat′ər wôl′) ***vi.*** ⟦prob. echoic⟧ to make a shrill sound like that of a cat; wail —***n.*** such a sound

cat′fight′ ***n.*** [Inf.] a fight between two women

cat′fish′ ***n.***, *pl.* **-fish′** or (for different species) **-fish′es** a fish with long, whiskerlike feelers about the mouth

cat′gut′ ***n.*** a tough thread made from dried intestines, as of sheep, and used for surgical sutures, etc.

ca·thar·sis (kə thär′sis) ***n.*** ⟦< Gr *katharos*, pure⟧ a relieving of emotional tensions, as through the arts or psychotherapy

ca·thar′tic (-tik) ***adj.*** purging —***n.*** a medicine for purging the bowels; purgative

ca·the·dral (kə thē′drəl) ***n.*** ⟦< Gr *kata-*, down + *hedra*, a seat⟧ **1** the main church of a bishop's see **2** any large, imposing church

cath·e·ter (kath′ət ər) ***n.*** ⟦< Gr *kata-*, down + *hienai*, to send⟧ a slender tube inserted into a body passage, as into the bladder for drawing off urine —**cath′e·ter·ize′** (-īz′), **-ized′**, **-iz′ing**, ***vt.*** —**cath′e·ter·i·za′tion** ***n.***

cath·ode (kath′ōd′) ***n.*** ⟦< Gr < *kata-*, down + -ODE⟧ **1** the negative electrode in an electrolytic cell **2** the electron emitter in an electron tube **3** the positive terminal of a battery

cathode rays streams of electrons projected from a cathode: they produce X-rays when they strike solids

cath′ode-ray′ tube a vacuum tube in which a stream of electrons can be focused on a fluorescent screen: such tubes are used as picture tubes, etc.

cath·o·lic (kath′ ə lik, kath′lik) ***adj.*** ⟦< Gr *kata-*, completely + *holos*, whole⟧ **1** all-inclusive; universal **2** broad in sympathies, tastes, etc. **3** [**C-**] ROMAN CATHOLIC —***n.*** [**C-**] ROMAN CATHOLIC —**Ca·thol·i·cism** (kə thäl′ə siz′əm) ***n.*** —**cath·o·lic·i·ty** (kath′ə lis′i tē) ***n.***

cat·i·on (kat′ī′ən) ***n.*** ⟦< Gr *kata*, down + *ienai*, to go⟧ a positively charged ion: in electrolysis, cations move toward the cathode

cat·kin (kat′kin) ***n.*** ⟦< Du *katte*, cat⟧ a drooping, scaly spike of small flowers without petals, as on poplars, walnuts, etc.

cat′nap′ ***n.*** a short nap; doze —***vi.*** **-napped′**, **-nap′ping** to doze briefly

cat'nip' *n.* ⟦CAT + dial. *nep*, catnip⟧ an herb of the mint family: cats like its odor

cat-o'-nine-tails (kat'ə nīn'tālz') *n.*, *pl.* **-tails'** a whip made of nine knotted cords attached to a handle

CAT scan (kat) ⟦*c*(*omputerized*) *a*(*xial*) *t*(*omography*)⟧ CT SCAN —**CAT scanner** —**CAT scanning**

cat's cradle a game in which a string looped over the fingers is transferred back and forth on the hands of the players so as to form designs

Cats·kill Mountains (kats'kil') mountain range in SE New York: also **Cats'kills'**

cat's-paw (kats'pô') *n.* a person used to do distasteful or unlawful work

cat·sup (kat'səp) *n.* KETCHUP

cat'tail' *n.* a tall marsh plant with long, brown, fuzzy spikes

cat·tle (kat''l) *pl.n.* ⟦ult. < L *caput*, head⟧ **1** [Archaic] farm animals **2** cows, bulls, steers, or oxen —**cat'tle·man** (-mən), *pl.* **-men** (-mən), *n.*

cat·ty (kat'ē) *adj.* **-ti·er, -ti·est 1** of or like a cat **2** spiteful, mean, malicious, etc. —**cat'ti·ness** *n.*

cat'ty-cor'nered *adj.*, *adv.* CATER-CORNERED: also **cat'ty-cor'ner**

cat'walk' *n.* a narrow, elevated walk

Cau·ca·sian (kô kā'zhən) *adj.* **1** of the Caucasus or its people, etc. **2** CAUCASOID —*n.* **1** a person born or living in the Caucasus **2** CAUCASOID

Cau·ca·soid (kô'kə soid') *adj.* designating or of one of the major geographical varieties of human beings, loosely called the *white race* —*n.* a member of the Caucasoid population

Cau·ca·sus (kô'kə səs) **1** border region between SE Europe & W Asia, between the Black and Caspian seas: often called **the Caucasus 2** mountain range in this region

cau·cus (kô'kəs) *n.* ⟦< ?⟧ **1** a meeting of a party or faction to decide on policy, pick candidates, etc. **2** the group attending such a meeting **3** a faction of politicians —*vi.* **-cused** or **-cussed, -cus·ing** or **-cus·sing** to hold a caucus

cau·dal (kôd''l) *adj.* ⟦< L *cauda*, tail + -AL⟧ of, like, at, or near the tail

caught (kôt) *vt.*, *vi. pt. & pp. of* CATCH

caul (kôl) *n.* the membrane enveloping the head of a child at birth

caul·dron (kôl'drən) *n. alt. sp. of* CALDRON

cau·li·flow·er (kô'lə flou'ər) *n.* ⟦< It *cavolo*, cabbage + *fiore*, flower⟧ **1** a variety of cabbage with a dense white head of fleshy flower stalks **2** the head, eaten as a vegetable

caulk (kôk) *vt.* ⟦< L *calx*, a heel⟧ to stop up (cracks, etc.) of (a boat, etc.) as with a puttylike sealant or oakum —*n.* a soft, puttylike compound used in caulking: also **caulking compound** —**caulk'er** *n.*

caus·al (kôz'əl) *adj.* **1** of, being, or expressing a cause **2** relating to cause and effect —**cau·sal·i·ty** (kô zal'i tē), *pl.* **-ties**, *n.* —**caus'al·ly** *adv.*

cau·sa·tion (kô zā'shən) *n.* **1** a causing **2** a causal agency; anything producing an effect

cause (kôz) *n.* ⟦< L *causa*⟧ **1** anything producing an effect or result **2** a reason or motive for producing an effect **3** any objective or movement that people are interested in and support **4** *Law* a case to be resolved by a court —*vt.* **caused, caus'ing** to be the cause of; bring about —**caus'a·tive** *adj.* —**cause'less** *adj.* —**caus'er** *n.*

cau·se·rie (kō'zə rē') *n.* ⟦Fr⟧ **1** a chat **2** a short, informal piece of writing

cause·way (kôz'wā') *n.* ⟦ult. < L *calx*, lime + WAY⟧ a raised path or road, as across wet ground or shallow water

caus·tic (kôs'tik) *adj.* ⟦< Gr *kaiein*, to burn⟧ **1** that can burn tissue by chemical action; corrosive **2** sarcastic; biting —*n.* a caustic substance —**caus'ti·cal·ly** *adv.* —**caus·tic'i·ty** (-tis'i tē) *n.*

cau·ter·ize (kôt'ər īz') *vt.* **-ized', -iz'ing** ⟦see prec.⟧ to burn with a hot needle, a laser, a caustic substance, etc. so as to destroy dead tissue, etc. —**cau'ter·i·za'tion** *n.*

cau·tion (kô'shən) *n.* ⟦< L *cautio*⟧ **1** a warning **2** wariness; prudence —*vt.* to warn —**cau'tion·ar'y** *adj.*

cau·tious (kô'shəs) *adj.* full of caution; careful to avoid danger —**cau'tious·ly** *adv.* —**cau'tious·ness** *n.*

cav·al·cade (kav'əl kād', kav'əl kād') *n.* ⟦Fr < L *caballus*, horse⟧ a procession, as of horsemen, carriages, etc.

cav·a·lier (kav'ə lir') *n.* ⟦Fr: see prec.⟧ **1** an armed horseman; knight **2** a gallant gentleman, esp. a lady's escort —*adj.* **1** casual or indifferent toward important matters **2** arrogant —**cav'a·lier'ly** *adv.*

cav·al·ry (kav'əl rē) *n.*, *pl.* **-ries** ⟦< Fr: see CAVALCADE⟧ combat troops mounted originally on horses but now often riding in motorized armored vehicles —**cav'al·ry·man** (-mən), *pl.* **-men** (-mən), *n.*

cave (kāv) *n.* ⟦< L *cavus*, hollow⟧ a hollow place inside the earth; cavern —*vi.* **caved, cav'ing** to cave in —**cave in 1** to collapse **2** [Inf.] to give in; yield

ca·ve·at emp·tor (kā'vē at' emp'tôr') ⟦L⟧ let the buyer beware

cave'-in' *n.* **1** a caving in **2** a place where the ground, etc. has caved in

cave man a prehistoric human being of the Stone Age who lived in caves

cav·ern (kav'ərn) *n.* a cave, esp. a large cave —**cav'ern·ous** *adj.*

cav·i·ar or **cav·i·are** (kav'ē är') *n.* ⟦Fr < Pers *khāya*, egg + *-dār*, bearing⟧ the salted eggs of sturgeon, etc. eaten as an appetizer

cav·il (kav'əl) *vi.* **-iled** or **-illed, -il·ing** or **-il·ling** ⟦< L *cavilla*, jeering⟧ to object unnecessarily; quibble —*n.* a trivial objection; quibble —**cav'il·er** or **cav'il·ler** *n.*

cav·i·ty (kav'i tē) *n.*, *pl.* **-ties** ⟦see CAVE⟧ **1** a natural hollow place within the body **2** a hollow place, as one caused by decay in a tooth

ca·vort (kə vôrt') *vi.* ⟦< ?⟧ **1** to prance or caper **2** to romp; frolic

caw (kô) ***n.*** ⟦echoic⟧ the harsh cry of a crow —***vi.*** to make this sound

cay·enne (pepper) (kī en′, kā-) ⟦< AmInd (Brazil) *kynnha*⟧ very hot red pepper made from the dried fruit of a pepper plant

cay·use (kī′yo͞os′, kī yo͞os′) ***n.***, *pl.* **-us′es** or **-use′** ⟦< AmInd tribal name⟧ a small Western horse used by cowboys

CB (sē′bē′) ***adj.*** ⟦*c*(*itizens'*) *b*(*and*)⟧ designating or of shortwave radio frequencies set aside by the FCC for local use by private persons or businesses

cc *abbrev.* **1** carbon copy **2** cubic centimeter(s)

CD (sē′dē′) ***n.*** a compact disc

Cd *Chem. symbol for* cadmium

CDC *abbrev.* Centers for Disease Control and Prevention

Cdn *abbrev.* Canadian

CD-ROM (sē′dē′räm′) ***n.*** a compact disc on which stored data can be accessed

cease (sēs) ***vt.***, ***vi.*** **ceased, ceas′ing** ⟦see CEDE⟧ to end; stop

cease′-fire′ ***n.*** a temporary cessation of warfare; truce

cease′less ***adj.*** unceasing; continual

ce·cum (sē′kəm) ***n.***, *pl.* **-ca** (-kə) ⟦< L *caecus*, blind⟧ the pouch at the beginning of the large intestine

ce·dar (sē′dər) ***n.*** ⟦< Gr *kedros*⟧ **1** a pine tree having fragrant, durable wood **2** its wood —***adj.*** of cedar

cede (sēd) ***vt.*** **ced′ed, ced′ing** ⟦< L *cedere*, to yield⟧ **1** to surrender formally **2** to transfer the title of

ce·dil·la (sə dil′ə) ***n.*** ⟦Sp dim. of *zeda*, a zeta or *z*⟧ a hooklike mark put under *c*, as in some French words (Ex.: *façade*) to show that it has an *s* sound

ceil·ing (sēl′iŋ) ***n.*** ⟦< L *caelum*, heaven⟧ **1** the inside top part of a room, opposite the floor **2** an upper limit *[a price ceiling]* **3** *Aeronautics* cloud cover affecting visibility, or the height of this —**hit the ceiling** [Slang] to lose one's temper

cel·an·dine (sel′ən dīn′, -dēn′) ***n.*** **1** a plant related to the poppy, with yellow flowers **2** a plant of the buttercup family, with yellow flowers

cel·e·brate (sel′ə brāt′) ***vt.*** **-brat′ed, -brat′ing** ⟦< L *celebrare*, to honor⟧ **1** to perform (a ritual, etc.) **2** to commemorate (an anniversary, holiday, etc.) with festivity **3** to honor publicly —***vi.*** to mark a happy occasion with festive activities —**cel′e·brant** (-brənt) ***n.*** —**cel·e·bra′tion** ***n.*** —**cel′e·bra′tor** ***n.***

cel′e·brat′ed ***adj.*** famous; renowned

ce·leb·ri·ty (sə leb′rə tē) ***n.*** **1** fame **2** *pl.* **-ties** a famous person

ce·ler·i·ty (sə ler′i tē) ***n.*** ⟦< L *celer*, swift⟧ swiftness; speed

cel·er·y (sel′ər ē, sel′rē) ***n.*** ⟦< Gr *selinon*, parsley⟧ a plant whose crisp leafstalks are eaten as a vegetable

ce·les·tial (sə les′chəl) ***adj.*** ⟦< L *caelum*, heaven⟧ **1** of or in the sky or universe **2** of heaven; divine **3** of the finest kind

cel·i·ba·cy (sel′ə bə sē) ***n.*** **1** the state of being unmarried **2** sexual abstinence

cel·i·bate (sel′ə bət) ***n.*** ⟦< L *caelebs*⟧ **1** an unmarried person **2** one who abstains from sexual intercourse —***adj.*** of or in a state of celibacy

cell (sel) ***n.*** ⟦< L *cella*⟧ **1** a small room, as in a prison **2** a small hollow, as in a honeycomb **3** a small unit of protoplasm: all plants and animals are made up of one or more cells **4** a container holding an electrolyte, used to generate electricity **5** a small unit of an organization —**celled** ***adj.***

cel·lar (sel′ər) ***n.*** ⟦see prec.⟧ a room or rooms below ground and usually under a building

cel·lo (chel′ō) ***n.***, *pl.* **-los** or **-li** (-ē) ⟦< VIOLONCELLO⟧ an instrument of the violin family, between the viola and double bass in size and pitch —**cel′list** ***n.***

CELLO

cel·lo·phane (sel′ə fān′) ***n.*** ⟦< CELLULOSE⟧ a thin, clear material made from cellulose, used as a wrapping

cell′phone′ ***n.*** *short for* CELLULAR PHONE

cel·lu·lar (sel′yo͞o lər) ***adj.*** of, like, or containing a cell or cells

cellular phone a mobile radio phone used in a communications system of geographically distributed transmitters: also **cellular telephone**

cel·lu·lite (sel′yo͞o līt′) ***n.*** ⟦Fr⟧ fatty deposits on the hips and thighs: a nonmedical term

cel·lu·loid (sel′yo͞o loid′) ***n.*** ⟦fol. + -OID⟧ a tough, flammable plastic substance used, esp. formerly, for making various articles, photographic film, etc.

cel·lu·lose (sel′yo͞o lōs′) ***n.*** ⟦Fr < L *cella*, cell + -OSE[1]⟧ the chief substance in the cell walls of plants, used in making paper, textiles, etc.

cellulose acetate any of several nonflammable thermoplastics, used in making lacquers, etc.

ce·lo·sia (sə lō′shə, -sē ə) ***n.*** an annual garden plant with large clusters of tiny, brilliant red or yellow flowers

Cel·si·us (sel′sē əs) ***adj.*** ⟦after A. *Celsius* (1701-44), Swed astronomer, the inventor⟧ designating or of a thermometer on which 0° is the freezing point and 100° is the boiling point of water

Celt (kelt; *also* selt) ***n.*** ⟦< L⟧ a Celtic-speaking person

Celt′ic ***adj.*** of the Celts, their languages, etc. —***n.*** a subfamily of languages including Gaelic and Welsh

ce·ment (sə ment′) ***n.*** ⟦< L *caementum*, rough stone⟧ **1** a powdered substance of lime and clay, mixed with water and sand to make mortar or with water, sand, and gravel to make concrete: it hardens upon drying **2** CONCRETE **3**

anything that bonds —*vt.* **1** to unite as with cement **2** to cover with cement

cem·e·ter·y (sem′ə ter′ē) *n., pl.* **-ies** ⟦< Gr < *koiman*, to put to sleep⟧ a place for the burial of the dead

cen·o·bite (sen′ə bīt′) *n.* ⟦< Gr < *koinos*, common + *bios*, life⟧ a member of a religious order living in a monastery or convent

cen·o·taph (sen′ə taf′) *n.* ⟦< Gr *kenos*, empty + *taphos*, tomb⟧ a monument honoring a dead person whose remains are elsewhere

Ce·no·zo·ic (sē′nə zō′ik, sen′ə-) *adj.* ⟦*ceno-* (< Gr *kainos*, recent) + ZO(O)- + -IC⟧ designating the geologic era that includes the present, during which the various mammals have developed

cen·ser (sen′sər) *n.* a container in which incense is burned

cen·sor (sen′sər) *n.* ⟦L < *censere*, to judge⟧ an official with the power to examine literature, mail, etc. and remove or prohibit anything considered obscene, objectionable, etc. —*vt.* to subject (a book, etc.) to a censor's examination —**cen′sor·ship′** *n.*

cen·so·ri·ous (sen sôr′ē əs) *adj.* inclined to find fault; harshly critical

cen·sure (sen′shər) *n.* ⟦< L *censor*, censor⟧ strong disapproval; condemnation —*vt.* **-sured, -sur·ing** to condemn as wrong —**cen′sur·a·ble** *adj.*

cen·sus (sen′səs) *n.* ⟦L < *censere*, enroll⟧ an official count of population and gathering of demographic data

cent[1] (sent) *n.* ⟦< L *centum*, hundred⟧ a 100th part of a dollar, or a coin of this value; penny

cent[2] *abbrev.* century; centuries

cen·taur (sen′tôr′) *n.* ⟦< Gr *Kentauros*⟧ *Gr. Myth.* a monster with a man's head, trunk, and arms, and a horse's body and legs

cen·ta·vo (sen tä′vō) *n., pl.* **-vos** ⟦Sp, a hundredth < L *centum*, hundred⟧ a 100th part of the monetary unit of various countries

cen·te·nar·i·an (sen′tə ner′ē ən) *n.* ⟦< fol.⟧ a person at least 100 years old

cen·te·nar·y (sen′tə ner′ē, sen ten′ər ē) *adj.* ⟦< L < *centum*, hundred⟧ **1** of a century **2** of a centennial —*n., pl.* **-ies** CENTENNIAL

cen·ten·ni·al (sen ten′ē əl) *adj.* ⟦< L *centum*, hundred + *annus*, year + -AL⟧ of or lasting 100 years —*n.* a 100th anniversary or its commemoration

cen·ter (sent′ər) *n.* ⟦< Gr *kentron*, sharp point⟧ **1** a point equally distant from all points on the circumference of a circle or surface of a sphere **2** a pivot **3** the approximate middle point or part of anything **4** a focal point of activity **5** [*often* **C-**] a group or position between the left (liberals) and right (conservatives) **6** *Sports* a player whose position is at the center of the line or playing area —*vt.* **1** to place in or near the center **2** to gather to one place —*vi.* to be focused

cen′ter·board′ *n.* a movable board or plate that, when lowered through a slot in the floor of a sailboat, functions like a keel

cen′ter·fold′ *n.* the center facing pages of a magazine, often with an extra fold, showing a photograph, as of a nude woman or man

center of gravity that point in a body or system around which its weight is evenly balanced

cen′ter·piece′ *n.* an ornament for the center of a table

centi- ⟦L⟧ *combining form* **1** one hundred **2** a 100th part of

cen·ti·grade (sen′tə grād′) *adj.* ⟦Fr: see prec. & GRADE⟧ CELSIUS

cen·time (sän′tēm′; *Fr* sän tēm′) *n.* ⟦Fr⟧ a 100th part of a franc

cen·ti·me·ter (sen′tə mēt′ər) *n.* ⟦Fr: see CENTI- & METER[1]⟧ a unit of measure, $\frac{1}{100}$ meter: Brit. sp. **cen′ti·me′tre**

cen·ti·pede (sen′tə pēd′) *n.* ⟦Fr < L *centi-*, CENTI- + *pes*, FOOT⟧ an elongated arthropod with a pair of legs for each body segment

cen·tral (sen′trəl) *adj.* ⟦L *centralis*⟧ **1** in, near, or of the center **2** equally accessible from various points **3** main; basic **4** of a controlling source in a system —**cen·tral′i·ty** (-tral′i tē) *n.* —**cen′tral·ly** *adv.*

Central African Republic country in central Africa: 240,324 sq. mi.; pop. 2,568,000

Central America part of North America between Mexico and South America —**Central American**

central city the crowded, industrial, central area of a large city

cen′tral·ize′ (-īz′) *vt.* **-ized′, -iz′ing** **1** to make central; bring to a center **2** to organize under one control —*vi.* to become centralized —**cen′tral·i·za′tion** *n.* —**cen′tral·iz′er** *n.*

cen·tre (sent′ər) *n., vt., vi.* **-tred, -tring** *Brit. sp. of* CENTER

centri- *combining form* CENTRO-

cen·trif·u·gal (sen trif′ə gəl) *adj.* ⟦< prec. + L *fugere*, to flee + -AL⟧ using or acted on by a force (**centrifugal force**) that tends to make rotating bodies move away from the center of rotation

cen·tri·fuge (sen′trə fyo͞oj′) *n.* a machine using centrifugal force to separate particles of varying density

cen·trip·e·tal (sen trip′ət'l) *adj.* ⟦< CENTRI- + L *petere*, rush at⟧ using or acted on by a force (**centripetal force**) that tends to make rotating bodies move toward the center of rotation

cen·trist (sen′trist) *n.* a person with moderate political opinions —**cen′trism′** *n.*

centro- ⟦< L *centrum*, center⟧ *combining form* center

cen·tu·ri·on (sen to͝or′ē ən) *n.* ⟦see fol.⟧ the commanding officer of an ancient Roman military unit, originally of 100 men

cen·tu·ry (sen′chə rē) *n., pl.* **-ries** ⟦L < *centum*, hundred⟧ a period of 100 years, esp. as reckoned from A.D.1

CEO *abbrev.* chief executive officer

ce·phal·ic (sə fal′ik) *adj.* ⟦< Gr < *kephalē*, head⟧ **1** of the head or skull **2**

in, on, near, or toward the head

cephalo- ⟦see prec.⟧ *combining form* the head, skull, or brain

ce·ram·ic (sə ram′ik) ***adj.*** ⟦Gr < *keramos*, potter's clay⟧ **1** of pottery, porcelain, etc. **2** of ceramics —***n.*** **1** [*pl., with sing v.*] the art or work of making pottery, etc. of baked clay **2** an object made of baked clay: *often used in pl.*

ce·ram·ist (ser′ə mist, sə ram′ist) ***n.*** one who works in ceramics; ceramic artist: also **ce·ram·i·cist** (sə ram′ə sist)

ce·re·al (sir′ē əl) ***adj.*** ⟦< L *Cerealis*, of Ceres, Rom goddess of agriculture⟧ of grain —***n.*** **1** any grain used for food, as wheat, rice, etc. **2** any grass producing such grain **3** food made from grain, as oatmeal

cer·e·bel·lum (ser′ə bel′əm) ***n.***, *pl.* **-lums** or **-la** (-ə) ⟦L, dim. of *cerebrum*⟧ the section of the brain behind and below the cerebrum

cer·e·bral (ser′ə brəl, sə rē′-) ***adj.*** **1** of the brain or cerebrum **2** of, by, or for the intellect

cerebral palsy a muscular disorder resulting from damage to the nervous system, esp. at birth

cer·e·brate (ser′ə brāt′) ***vi.*** **-brat′ed, -brat′ing** ⟦< L *cerebrum*, the brain + -ATE[1]⟧ to think —**cer′e·bra′tion** ***n.***

cer·e·brum (ser′ə brəm, sə rē′brəm) ***n.***, *pl.* **-brums** or **-bra** (-brə) ⟦L⟧ the upper, main part of the brain of vertebrates

cer·e·ment (ser′ə mənt, sir′mənt) ***n.*** ⟦< Gr *kēros*, wax⟧ [*usually pl.*] a shroud for a dead person

cer·e·mo·ni·al (ser′ə mō′nē əl) ***adj.*** of or consisting of ceremony; formal —***n.*** **1** a system of rites **2** a rite or ceremony —**cer′e·mo′ni·al·ly** ***adv.***

cer′e·mo′ni·ous (-nē əs) ***adj.*** **1** full of ceremony **2** very polite or formal —**cer′e·mo′ni·ous·ly** ***adv.***

cer·e·mo·ny (ser′ə mō′nē) ***n.***, *pl.* **-nies** ⟦< L *caerimonia*⟧ **1** a set of formal acts proper to a special occasion, as a religious rite **2** behavior that follows rigid etiquette **3** *a*) formality *b*) empty or meaningless formality —**stand on ceremony** to insist on formality

ce·rise (sə rēz′, -rēs′) ***n.***, ***adj.*** ⟦< OFr *cerise*, cherry⟧ cherry red

cer·met (sur′met′) ***n.*** ⟦CER(AMIC) + MET(AL)⟧ a bonded mixture of ceramic material and a metal

cert *abbrev.* **1** certificate **2** certified

cer·tain (surt′'n) ***adj.*** ⟦< L *certus*, determined⟧ **1** fixed; settled **2** inevitable **3** reliable; dependable **4** sure; positive **5** definite, but unnamed [*a certain* person] **6** some [to a *certain* extent] —**for certain** without doubt

cer′tain·ly ***adv.*** undoubtedly; surely

cer′tain·ty ***n.*** **1** the state or fact of being certain **2** *pl.* **-ties** anything certain

cer·tif·i·cate (sər tif′i kit; *for v.*, -kāt′) ***n.*** ⟦see CERTIFY⟧ a document attesting to a fact, qualification, etc. —***vt.*** **-cat′ed, -cat′ing** to issue a certificate to

certificate of deposit a bank certificate issued for a specified deposit of money that draws interest and requires written notice for withdrawal

certified public accountant a public accountant certified as having passed a state examination

cer·ti·fy (surt′ə fī′) ***vt.*** **-fied′, -fy′ing** ⟦< L *certus*, certain + -FY⟧ **1** to declare (a thing) true, accurate, etc. by formal statement **2** to declare officially insane **3** to guarantee (a check, document, etc.) **4** to issue a certificate or license to —**cer′ti·fi′a·ble** ***adj.*** —**cer′ti·fi·ca′tion** ***n.***

cer·ti·tude (surt′ə to͞od′) ***n.*** sureness; inevitability

ce·ru·le·an (sə ro͞o′lē ən) ***adj.*** ⟦< L < *caelum*, heaven⟧ sky-blue; azure

Cer·van·tes (sər van′tēz′, -vän′-), **Mi·guel de** (mē gel′ *th*e) 1547-1616; Sp. writer

cer·vix (sur′viks) ***n.***, *pl.* **cer·vi·ces** (sər vī′sēz′, sur′və-) or **-vix·es** ⟦L, neck⟧ a necklike part, esp. of the uterus —**cer′vi·cal** (-vi kəl) ***adj.***

ce·sar·e·an (section) (sə zer′ē ən) ⟦from the ancient story that Julius CAESAR was born this way⟧ surgery to deliver a baby by cutting through the mother's abdominal and uterine walls

ce·si·um (sē′zē əm) ***n.*** ⟦ult. < L *caesius*, bluish-gray⟧ a metallic chemical element, used in photoelectric cells, radiation therapy, etc.

ces·sa·tion (se sā′shən) ***n.*** ⟦< L *cessare*, cease⟧ a ceasing or stopping

ces·sion (sesh′ən) ***n.*** ⟦< L *cedere*, to yield⟧ a ceding (of rights, property, etc.) to another

cess·pool (ses′po͞ol′) ***n.*** ⟦< ? It *cesso*, privy⟧ a deep hole in the ground to receive drainage or sewage from the sinks, toilets, etc. of a house

ce·ta·cean (sə tā′shən) ***n.*** ⟦< L *cetus*, whale⟧ any of certain fishlike water mammals, including whales, porpoises, etc. —***adj.*** of the cetaceans

Cey·lon (sə län′, sā-, sē-) *former name for* SRI LANKA —**Cey·lo·nese** (sel′ə nēz′, sā′lə-), *pl.* **-nese′**, ***adj.***, ***n.***

Cé·zanne (sā zan′), **Paul** 1839-1906; Fr. painter

cf ⟦L *confer*⟧ *abbrev.* compare

CFO *abbrev.* chief financial officer

cg or **cgm** *abbrev.* centigram(s)

Ch or **ch** *abbrev.* **1** chapter **2** church

Cha·blis (sha blē′) ***n.*** [*occas.* **c-**] a dry white Burgundy wine, orig. from Chablis, France

Chad (chad) country in NC Africa: 495,755 sq. mi.; pop. 6,288,000

chafe (chāf) ***vt.*** **chafed, chaf′ing** ⟦< L *calefacere*, make warm⟧ **1** to rub so as to make warm **2** to wear away or make sore by rubbing **3** to annoy; irritate —***vi.*** **1** to rub (*on* or *against*) **2** to be annoyed or impatient

chaff (chaf) ***n.*** ⟦OE *ceaf*⟧ **1** threshed or winnowed husks of grain **2** anything worthless **3** teasing; banter —***vt.***, ***vi.*** to tease in a good-natured way

chaf·ing dish (chāf′iŋ) a pan with a heating apparatus beneath it, as to cook food at the table

cha·grin (shə grin′) ***n.*** ⟦Fr⟧ embarrassment and annoyance due to failure, disappointment, etc. —*vt.* **-grined′**, **-grin′ing** to cause to feel chagrin

chain (chān) *n.* ⟦< L *catena*⟧ **1** a flexible series of joined links **2** [*pl.*] *a*) bonds; shackles *b*) captivity **3** a chainlike measuring instrument, as for surveying **4** a series of things connected causally, logically, physically, etc. **5** a number of stores, etc. owned by one company —*vt.* **1** to fasten with chains **2** to restrain, etc.

chain gang a gang of prisoners chained together, as when working

chain reaction **1** a self-sustaining series of chemical or nuclear reactions in which the reaction products keep the process going **2** a series of events, each of which results in the following one

chain saw a portable power saw with an endless chain that carries the cutting teeth

chair (cher) *n.* ⟦< L *cathedra*: see CATHEDRAL⟧ **1** a piece of furniture with a back, for one person to sit on **2** an important or official position **3** a chairman —*vt.* to preside over as chairman

chair′lift′ *n.* seats suspended from a power-driven endless cable, used to carry skiers up a slope

chair′man (-mən) *n.*, *pl.* **-men** (-mən) a person in charge of a meeting, etc.: also **chair′per′son** —**chair′man·ship′** *n.* —**chair′wom′an**, *pl.* **-wom′en**, *fem.n.*

CHAISE LONGUE

chaise (shāz) *n.* ⟦Fr⟧ a lightweight carriage, having two or four wheels

chaise longue (lôŋ; *also* lounj) ⟦Fr, lit., long chair⟧ a couchlike chair with a long seat: also **chaise lounge** (lounj)

chal·ced·o·ny (kal sed′'n ē) *n.* quartz having a waxy luster and, often, colored bands

cha·let (shal ā′, shal′ā) *n.* ⟦Swiss-Fr⟧ **1** a Swiss house with overhanging eaves **2** any similar building

chal·ice (chal′is) *n.* ⟦< L *calix*, cup⟧ **1** a cup; goblet **2** the cup for Communion wine

chalk (chôk) *n.* ⟦< L *calx*, limestone⟧ **1** a soft, whitish limestone **2** a piece of chalk or chalklike substance used for writing on a blackboard —*adj.* made with chalk —*vt.* to mark or rub with chalk —**chalk up** **1** to score, get, or achieve **2** to ascribe —**chalk′i·ness** *n.* —**chalk′y**, **-i·er**, **-i·est**, *adj.*

chalk′board′ *n.* BLACKBOARD

chal·lenge (chal′ənj) *n.* ⟦< L *calumnia*, calumny⟧ **1** a demand for identification **2** a calling into question **3** a call to a duel, contest, etc. **4** anything that calls for special effort —*vt.* **-lenged**, **-leng·ing** to subject to a challenge —*vi.* to make a challenge —**chal′leng·er** *n.*

chal′lenged *adj.* disabled or handicapped

chal·lis (shal′ē) *n.* ⟦< ?⟧ a soft, lightweight fabric of wool, etc.

cham·ber (chām′bər) *n.* ⟦< LL *camera*, a chamber, room⟧ **1** a room, esp. a bedroom **2** [*pl.*] a judge's office near the courtroom **3** an assembly hall **4** a legislative or judicial body **5** a council [*chamber* of commerce] **6** an enclosed space; compartment; specif. the part of a gun holding a cartridge —**cham′bered** *adj.*

cham′ber·lain (-lin) *n.* ⟦< OHG *chamarlinc*⟧ **1** an officer in charge of the household of a ruler or lord; steward **2** [Brit.] a treasurer

cham′ber·maid′ *n.* a woman whose work is taking care of bedrooms, as in a hotel

chamber music music for performance by a small group, as a string quartet

chamber of commerce an association established to further the business interests of its community

cham·bray (sham′brā′) *n.* ⟦var. of *cambric*⟧ a smooth fabric of cotton, etc. with white threads woven across a colored warp

cha·me·le·on (kə mē′lē ən, -mēl′yən) *n.* ⟦< Gr *chamai*, on the ground + *leōn*, LION⟧ any of various lizards that can change the color of their skin

cham·ois (sham′ē) *n.*, *pl.* **-ois** ⟦Fr⟧ **1** a small, goatlike antelope of the mountains of Europe and the Caucasus **2** a soft leather made from the skin of chamois, sheep, deer, etc.: also **cham·my** (sham′ē), *pl.* **-mies**

cham·o·mile (kam′ə mīl′, -mēl′) *n.* *alt. sp. of* CAMOMILE

champ[1] (champ) *vt.* ⟦prob. echoic⟧ to chew hard and noisily; munch —**champ at the bit** to be impatient when held back

champ[2] (champ) *n.* [Inf.] CHAMPION (sense 2)

cham·pagne (sham pān′) *n.* an effervescent white wine, orig. from Champagne, region in NE France

cham·paign (sham pān′) *n.* ⟦< L *campus*, field⟧ flat, open country

cham·pi·on (cham′pē ən) *n.* ⟦< LL *campio*, gladiator⟧ **1** one who fights for another or for a cause; defender **2** a winner of first place in a competition —*adj.* excelling all others —*vt.* to fight for; defend; support —**cham′pi·on·ship′** *n.*

chance (chans) *n.* ⟦< L *cadere*, to fall⟧ **1** the happening of events without apparent cause; luck **2** an unpredictable event **3** a risk or gamble **4** a ticket in a lottery **5** an opportunity **6** [*often pl.*] a possibility or probability —*adj.* accidental —*vi.* **chanced**, **chanc′ing** to have the fortune, good or bad —*vt.* to risk —**by chance** accidentally —**chance on** (or **upon**) to find or meet by chance —(**the**) **chances are** the likelihood is —**on the (off) chance** relying on the (remote) possibility

chan·cel (chan′səl) ***n.*** ⟦< L *cancelli*, lattices⟧ the part of a church around the altar, for the clergy and the choir

chan′cel·ler·y (-sə lər ē) ***n.***, *pl.* **-ies** ⟦< ML *cancellaria*⟧ the rank or position of a chancellor

chan′cel·lor (-sə lər) ***n.*** ⟦< LL *cancellarius*, secretary⟧ **1** a high government official, as, in certain countries, a prime minister **2** in some universities, the president or other executive officer

chan·cer·y (chan′sər ē) ***n.***, *pl.* **-ies** ⟦< ML *cancellaria*⟧ **1** a court of equity **2** an office of public archives **3** *R.C.Ch.* the diocesan office performing secretarial services for the bishop

chan·cre (shaŋ′kər) ***n.*** ⟦Fr: see CANCER⟧ a sore or ulcer of syphilis

chanc·y (chan′sē) ***adj.*** **-i·er**, **-i·est** risky; uncertain —**chanc′i·ness** ***n.***

chan·de·lier (shan′də lir′) ***n.*** ⟦Fr < L *candela*, candle⟧ a lighting fixture hung from a ceiling, with branches for candles, light bulbs, etc.

chan·dler (chand′lər) ***n.*** ⟦< L *candela*, candle⟧ **1** a maker of candles **2** a retailer of supplies, as for ships

Chang (chäŋ) river in central China, flowing into the East China Sea: former transliteration YANGTZE

change (chānj) ***vt.*** **changed**, **chang′ing** ⟦< L *cambire*, to barter⟧ **1** to put or take (a thing) in place of something else *[to change jobs]* **2** to exchange *[to change seats]* **3** to make different; alter —***vi.*** **1** to alter; vary **2** to leave one train, plane, etc. and board another **3** to put on other clothes —***n.*** **1** a substitution, alteration, or variation **2** variety **3** another set of clothes **4** *a)* money returned as the difference between the price and the greater sum presented *b)* coins or bills that together equal a single larger coin or bill *c)* small coins —**change off** to take turns —**ring the changes** to ring a set of bells with all possible variations —**change′a·ble** ***adj.*** —**change′less** ***adj.***

change′ling (-liŋ) ***n.*** a child secretly put in the place of another, as, in folk tales, by fairies

change of life MENOPAUSE: also [Inf.] **the change**

change′o′ver ***n.*** a complete change, as in goods produced

chan·nel (chan′əl) ***n.*** ⟦see CANAL⟧ **1** the bed or deeper part of a river, harbor, etc. **2** a body of water joining two larger ones **3** any means of passage **4** [*pl.*] the official course of transmission of communications **5** a groove or furrow **6** a frequency band assigned to a radio or television station —***vt.*** **-neled** or **-nelled**, **-nel·ing** or **-nel·ling** **1** to make a channel in **2** to send through a channel

Channel Islands group of British islands in the English Channel

chan′nel·ize′ (-īz′) ***vt.*** **-ized′**, **-iz′ing** to provide a channel for

chan·son (shän sôn′) ***n.***, *pl.* ***-sons′*** (-sôn′) ⟦Fr⟧ a song

chant (chant) ***n.*** ⟦< L *cantare*, to sing⟧ **1** a song; esp., a liturgical song with a series of syllables or words sung to each tone **2** a singsong way of speaking —***vi.***, ***vt.*** to sing or say in a chant —**chant′er** ***n.***

chan·teuse (shän tōōz′) ***n.*** ⟦Fr⟧ a woman singer, esp. of popular ballads

chan·tey (shan′tē, chan′tē) ***n.***, *pl.* **-teys** a song formerly sung by sailors while working: also **chan′ty**, *pl.* **-ties**

chan·ti·cleer (chan′ti klir′) ***n.*** ⟦< OFr *chante-cler*, lit., sing loud⟧ a rooster

Cha·nu·kah (khä′noo kä′) ***n.*** HANUKKAH

cha·os (kā′äs′) ***n.*** ⟦< Gr, space⟧ extreme confusion or disorder —**cha·ot·ic** (kā ät′ ik) ***adj.***

chap[1] (chap) ***n.*** ⟦< Brit *chapman*, peddler⟧ [Inf.] a man; fellow

chap[2] (chap) ***vt.***, ***vi.*** **chapped** or **chapt**, **chap′ping** ⟦ME *chappen*, cut⟧ to crack open; split; roughen, as skin —***n.*** a chapped place in the skin

chap[3] *abbrev.* **1** chaplain **2** chapter

chap·ar·ral (shap′ə ral′, chap′-) ***n.*** ⟦Sp < *chaparro*, evergreen oak⟧ [Southwest] a thicket of shrubs, etc.

cha·peau (sha pō′) ***n.***, *pl.* **-peaus′** or **-peaux′** (-pōz′) ⟦Fr⟧ a hat

chap·el (chap′əl) ***n.*** ⟦< ML *cappella*, dim. of *cappa*, cape⟧ **1** a small church **2** a private place of worship, as in a hospital **3** a religious service

chap·er·on or **chap·er·one** (shap′ər ōn′, shap′ər ōn′) ***n.*** ⟦< OFr, hood⟧ one who accompanies young, unmarried people to supervise their behavior, as at dances —***vt.***, ***vi.*** **-oned′**, **-on′ing** to act as chaperon (to)

chap·lain (chap′lən) ***n.*** ⟦see CHAPEL⟧ **1** a clergyman attached to a chapel **2** a clergyman serving in a religious capacity with the armed forces, or in a prison, hospital, etc.

chap·let (chap′lit) ***n.*** ⟦< LL *cappa*, cape⟧ **1** a garland for the head **2** a string of beads, esp. prayer beads

chaps (chaps, shaps) ***pl.n.*** ⟦< MexSp *chaparreras*⟧ leather trousers without a seat, worn over ordinary trousers by cowboys to protect their legs

chap·ter (chap′tər) ***n.*** ⟦< L *caput*, head⟧ **1** a main division, as of a book **2** a local branch of an organization

chapter book a book divided into chapters, intended for very young readers

char (chär) ***vt.***, ***vi.*** **charred**, **char′ring** ⟦< CHARCOAL⟧ **1** to reduce to charcoal by burning **2** to burn slightly; scorch

char·ac·ter (kar′ik tər) ***n.*** ⟦< Gr *charassein*, engrave⟧ **1** any letter, figure, or symbol used in writing and printing **2** a distinctive trait, quality, etc.; characteristic **3** kind or sort **4** behavior typical of a person or group **5** moral strength **6** reputation **7** status; position **8** a person in a play, novel, etc. **9** [Inf.] an eccentric person

char′ac·ter·is′tic (-is′tik) ***adj.*** typical; distinctive —***n.*** a distinguishing trait or quality —**char′ac·ter·is′ti·cal·ly** ***adv.***

char′ac·ter·ize′ (-īz′) ***vt.*** **-ized′**, **-iz′ing** **1** to describe the particular traits of **2** to be a characteristic of —**char′ac·ter·i·**

za′tion *n.*

cha·rade (shə rād′) ***n.*** ⟦Fr < Prov *charrar*, to gossip⟧ **1** [*pl.*] a game in which words to be guessed are pantomimed, often syllable by syllable **2** an obvious pretense or fiction

char·broil or **char-broil** (chär′broil′) ***vt.*** to broil over a charcoal fire

char·coal (chär′kōl′) ***n.*** ⟦ME *char cole*⟧ **1** a dark, porous form of carbon made by partially burning wood or other organic matter in an airless kiln or retort: used for fuel, etc. **2** a very dark gray or brown

chard (chärd) ***n.*** ⟦< L *carduus*, thistle⟧ a kind of beet with edible leaves and stalks

char·don·nay (shär′də nā′) ***n.*** [*also* **C-**] a dry white wine

charge (chärj) ***vt.* charged, charg′ing** ⟦ult. < L *carrus*, wagon⟧ **1** to load or fill (*with* something) **2** to add an electrical charge to (a battery, etc.) **3** to give as a duty, command, etc. to **4** to accuse **5** to make liable for (an error, etc.) **6** to ask as a price **7** to record as a debt **8** to pay for by using a credit card **9** to attack vigorously **—*vi.*** **1** to ask payment (*for*) **2** to attack vigorously **—*n.*** **1** a load or burden **2** the necessary quantity, as of fuel, for a container or device **3** the amount of chemical energy stored in a battery **4** a cartridge or shell, or the amount of gunpowder needed to discharge a gun, etc. **5** responsibility or care (*of*) **6** a person or thing entrusted to someone's care **7** instruction; command **8** accusation; indictment **9** cost **10** a debt, debit, or expense **11** an onslaught **12** the signal for an attack **13** [Slang] a thrill **—in charge (of)** having the responsibility, control, or supervision (of) **—charge′a·ble *adj.***

charge account an arrangement by which a customer may pay for purchases within a specified future period

charge card a thin, flat, plastic card embossed with the owner's name, account number, etc., used when charging purchases

charg′er *n.* **1** a person or thing that charges **2** a horse ridden in battle **3** a device used to charge storage batteries

char·grill (chär′gril′) ***vt.*** to grill (meat) over a charcoal fire, etc.

char·i·ly (cher′ə lē, char′-) ***adv.*** cautiously **—char′i·ness *n.***

char·i·ot (char′ē ət) ***n.*** ⟦see CAR⟧ a horse-drawn, two-wheeled cart used in ancient times for war, racing, etc. **— char′i·ot·eer′** (-ə tir′) ***n.***

cha·ris·ma (kə riz′mə) ***n.*** ⟦< Gr, favor, grace⟧ a special quality in one that inspires devotion or fascination

char·is·mat·ic (kar′iz mat′ik) ***adj.*** **1** of or having charisma **2** designating or of a religious group that stresses direct divine inspiration, manifested as in glossolalia, etc. **—*n.*** a member of a charismatic group

char·i·ta·ble (char′i tə bəl) ***adj.*** **1** generous to the needy **2** of or for charity **3** kind and forgiving; lenient **—char′i·ta·bly *adv.***

char·i·ty (char′i tē) ***n.*, *pl.* -ties** ⟦< L *caritas*, affection⟧ **1** *Christian Theol.* love for one's fellow human beings **2** leniency in judging others **3** *a)* generosity toward the needy *b)* help so given **4** a welfare institution, fund, etc.

char·la·tan (shär′lə tən) ***n.*** ⟦ult. < VL *cerretanus*, seller of papal indulgences⟧ a fraud; quack

Char·le·magne (shär′lə mān′) A.D. 742-814; king of the Franks (768-814): emperor of the Holy Roman Empire (800-814)

Charles·ton[1] (chärls′tən) ***n.*** ⟦< name of the seaport⟧ a lively dance of the 1920s, in 4/4 time

Charles·ton[2] (chärls′tən) capital of West Virginia, in the W part: pop. 57,000

char·ley horse (chär′lē) [Inf.] a cramp in a muscle, esp. a thigh muscle

Char·lotte (shär′lət) city in S North Carolina: pop. 396,000

Char·lotte·town (shär′lət toun′) capital of Prince Edward Island, Canada: pop. 33,000

charm (chärm) ***n.*** ⟦< L *carmen*⟧ **1** an action, object, or words assumed to have magic power **2** a trinket worn on a bracelet, etc. **3** a quality that attracts or delights **4** *Particle Physics* a property of certain quarks **—*vt.*, *vi.*** **1** to act on as if by magic **2** to fascinate; delight **—charm′er *n.* —charm′ing *adj.* — charm′ing·ly *adv.***

char·meuse (shär mo͞oz′, -mo͞os′) ***n.*** ⟦Fr < *charmer*, to bewitch⟧ a smooth fabric of silk or polyester

char·nel (house) (chär′nəl) ⟦< LL *carnale*, graveyard⟧ a building or place where corpses or bones are deposited

Cha·ron (ker′ən) ***n.*** *Gr. Myth.* the ferryman on the river Styx

chart (chärt) ***n.*** ⟦< Gr *chartēs*, layer of papyrus⟧ **1** a map, esp. for use in navigation **2** an information sheet with tables, graphs, etc. **3** a table, graph, etc. **—*vt.*** **1** to make a chart of **2** to plan (a course of action)

char·ter (chärt′ər) ***n.*** ⟦see prec.⟧ **1** a franchise granted by a government **2** a written statement of basic laws or principles; constitution **3** written permission to form a local chapter or lodge of a society **4** the hire or lease of an airplane, bus, etc. **—*vt.*** **1** to grant a charter to **2** to hire for exclusive use

charter member a founder or original member

charter school a publicly-funded alternative school founded on a charter with the government

char·treuse (shär tro͞oz′, -tro͞os′) ***n.*** ⟦Fr⟧ pale, yellowish green

char·wom·an (chär′wo͝om′ən) ***n.*, *pl.* -wom′en** ⟦see CHORE⟧ a cleaning woman

char·y (cher′ē, char′ē) ***adj.* -i·er, -i·est** ⟦< OE *cearig*, sorrowful⟧ **1** careful; cautious **2** sparing

chase[1] (chās) ***vt.* chased, chas′ing** ⟦ult. <

L *capere*, to take] **1** to follow so as to catch **2** to run after; pursue **3** to drive away **4** to hunt —***vi.*** **1** to go in pursuit **2** [Inf.] to rush —***n.*** **1** a chasing; pursuit **2** the hunting of game —**give chase** to pursue

chase[2] (chās) ***vt.*** **chased, chas′ing** [< OFr *enchasser*] to ornament (metal) as by engraving

chas′er ***n.*** **1** one that chases or hunts; pursuer **2** a mild drink, as water, taken after whiskey, etc.

chasm (kaz′əm) ***n.*** [< Gr *chasma*] **1** a deep crack in the earth's surface; abyss **2** any break or gap

chas·sis (chas′ē, shas′ē) ***n.***, *pl.* **-sis′** (-ēz′) [Fr] **1** the frame, wheels, engine, etc. of a motor vehicle, but not the body **2** *a)* a frame, as for the parts of a TV set *b)* the assembled frame and parts

chaste (chāst) ***adj.*** [< L *castus*, pure] **1** not indulging in unlawful sexual activity; virtuous **2** decent; modest **3** simple in style; not ornate —**chaste′ly *adv.***

chas·ten (chās′ən) ***vt.*** [< L *castigare*, punish] **1** to punish so as to correct **2** to restrain or subdue

chas·tise (chas tīz′, chas′tīz′) ***vt.*** **-tised′, -tis′ing** [see prec.] **1** to punish, esp. by beating **2** to scold sharply —**chas·tise′ment *n.*** —**chas·tis′er *n.***

chas·ti·ty (chas′tə tē) ***n.*** a being chaste; specif., *a)* virtuousness *b)* sexual abstinence; celibacy *c)* decency or modesty

chas·u·ble (chaz′ə bəl, chas′-) ***n.*** [< ML *casula*] a sleeveless outer vestment worn by priests at Mass

chat (chat) ***vi.*** **chat′ted, chat′ting** [< CHATTER] **1** to talk in a light, informal manner **2** to hold an electronic conversation by exchanging typed messages on computers —***n.*** light, informal talk

châ·teau (sha tō′) ***n.***, *pl.* **-teaux′** (-tōz′, -tō′) or **-teaus′** [Fr < L *castellum*, castle] **1** a French feudal castle **2** a large country house and estate, esp. in France Also **cha·teau′**

chat·e·laine (shat′'l ān′) ***n.*** [Fr] **1** the mistress of a château **2** a woman's ornamental chain or clasp

Chat·ta·noo·ga (chat′ə nōō′gə) city in SE Tennessee: pop. 152,000

chat·tel (chat′'l) ***n.*** [see CATTLE] a movable item of personal property, as furniture

chat·ter (chat′ər) ***vi.*** [echoic] **1** to make short, rapid, indistinct sounds, as squirrels do **2** to talk much and foolishly **3** to click together rapidly, as teeth do from cold —***n.*** **1** a chattering **2** foolish talk —**chat′ter·er *n.***

chat′ter·box′ ***n.*** an incessant talker

chat·ty (chat′ē) ***adj.*** **-ti·er, -ti·est** fond of chatting —**chat′ti·ness *n.***

Chau·cer (chô′sər), **Geof·frey** (jef′rē) 1340?-1400; Eng. poet

chauf·feur (shō′fər, shō fur′) ***n.*** [Fr, lit., stoker] one hired to drive a private automobile for someone else —***vt.*** to act as chauffeur to

chau·vin·ism (shō′vin iz′əm) ***n.*** [after N. *Chauvin*, fanatical Fr patriot] **1** militant and boastful patriotism; jingoism **2** unreasoning and boastful devotion to one's race, sex, etc. —**chau′vin·ist *n.***, ***adj.*** —**chau′vin·is′tic *adj.*** —**chau′vin·is′ti·cal·ly *adv.***

cheap (chēp) ***adj.*** [ult. < L *caupo*, tradesman] **1** low in price **2** worth more than the price **3** easily gotten [a *cheap* victory] **4** of little value **5** contemptible **6** [Inf.] stingy —***adv.*** at a low cost —**cheap′ly *adv.*** —**cheap′ness *n.***

cheap′en ***vt.***, ***vi.*** to make or become cheap or cheaper

cheap shot [Slang] an unnecessarily rough or mean action or remark

cheap′skate′ ***n.*** [Slang] a stingy person

cheat (chēt) ***n.*** [< L *ex-*, out + *cadere*, to fall] **1** a fraud; swindle **2** a swindler —***vt.*** **1** to defraud; swindle **2** to foil, deprive, or elude [to *cheat* death] —***vi.*** **1** to be dishonest or deceitful **2** [Slang] to be sexually unfaithful: often with *on* —**cheat′er *n.***

check (chek) ***n.*** [< OFr *eschec*, a check in chess] **1** a sudden stop **2** any restraint **3** one that restrains **4** a supervision or test of accuracy, etc. **5** a mark (✓) to show verification **6** an identification ticket, token, etc. [a hat *check*] **7** one's bill at a restaurant or bar **8** a written order to a bank to pay a sum of money **9** a pattern of squares, or one of the squares **10** *Chess* the state of a king that is in danger **11** *Hockey* a bumping of an opponent —***interj.*** [Inf.] agreed! right! —***vt.*** **1** to stop suddenly **2** to restrain; curb; block **3** to test, verify, etc. by examination or comparison: often with *out* **4** to mark with a check (✓): often with *off* **5** to mark with a pattern of squares **6** to deposit temporarily, as in a checkroom **7** to clear (esp. luggage) for shipment **8** *Chess* to place (the opponent's king) in check **9** *Hockey* to bump (an opponent) —***vi.*** **1** to agree with one another, item for item: often with *out* **2** to investigate or verify: often with *on, up on* —**check in** **1** to register at a hotel, etc. **2** [Inf.] to present oneself, as at work —**check out** **1** to pay and leave a hotel, etc. **2** to add up the prices of (items selected) for payment **3** to prove to be accurate, in good condition, etc. —**in check** under control —**check′er *n.***

check′book′ ***n.*** a book of detachable forms for writing bank checks

checked (chekt) ***adj.*** having a pattern of squares

check′er·board′ ***n.*** a square board with 64 squares of two alternating colors, used in checkers and chess

check·ered (chek′ərd) ***adj.*** **1** having a pattern of squares **2** varied [a *checkered* career]

check′ers (-ərz) ***n.*** **1** a game for two played with flat disks on a checkerboard **2** the disks

checking account a bank account against which the depositor can draw checks

check′list′ ***n.*** a list of things, names, etc. to be referred to: also **check list**

check′mate′ ***n.*** [ult. < Pers *šāh māt*, the king is dead] **1** *Chess a)* the move that wins the game by checking the opponent's king so that it cannot be protected *b*) the condition of the king after this move **2** total defeat, frustration, etc. —*vt.* **-mat'ed, -mat'ing 1** *Chess* to place in checkmate **2** to defeat; thwart

check'off' *n.* the withholding of members' dues for the union by the employer

check'out' *n.* **1** the act or place of checking out purchases **2** the time by which one must check out of a hotel, etc.

check'point' *n.* a place on a road, etc. where traffic is inspected

check'room' *n.* a room in which hats, coats, etc. may be left until called for

check'up' *n.* an examination, esp. a medical one

ched·dar (cheese) (ched'ər) ⟦after *Cheddar*, England⟧ [*often* **C-**] a hard, smooth cheese

cheek (chēk) *n.* ⟦OE *ceoke*, jaw⟧ **1** either side of the face below the eye **2** either of two sides of anything **3** [Inf.] sauciness; impudence

cheek'bone' *n.* the bone across the upper cheek, just below the eye

cheek'y *adj.* **-i·er, -i·est** [Inf.] saucy; impudent —**cheek'i·ness** *n.*

cheep (chēp) *n.* ⟦echoic⟧ the short, shrill sound made by a young bird —*vt.*, *vi.* to make, or utter with, this sound —**cheep'er** *n.*

cheer (chir) *n.* ⟦< Gr *kara*, the head⟧ **1** state of mind or of feeling; spirit [be of good *cheer*] **2** gladness; joy **3** festive entertainment **4** encouragement **5** *a*) a glad, excited shout to urge on, greet, etc. *b*) a rallying cry, etc. —*vt.* **1** to gladden; comfort: often with *up* **2** to urge on, greet, or applaud with cheers —*vi.* **1** to become cheerful: usually with *up* **2** to shout cheers

cheer'ful *adj.* **1** full of cheer; joyful **2** bright and attractive **3** willing; ready [a *cheerful* helper] —**cheer'ful·ly** *adv.* —**cheer'ful·ness** *n.*

cheer'i·o' (-ē ō') *interj.* [Brit. Inf.] **1** goodbye **2** good health: used as a toast

cheer'lead' (-lēd') *vi.*, *vt.* to act as a cheerleader (for) —**cheer'lead'ing** *n.*

cheer'lead'er *n.* a leader of cheers, as at football games

cheer'less *adj.* not cheerful; dismal; dreary —**cheer'less·ly** *adv.* —**cheer'less·ness** *n.*

cheers (chirz) *interj.* good health: used as a toast

cheer'y *adj.* **-i·er, -i·est** cheerful; lively; bright —**cheer'i·ly** *adv.* —**cheer'i·ness** *n.*

cheese (chēz) *n.* ⟦OE *cyse*⟧ a solid food made from milk curds

cheese'burg'er *n.* a hamburger topped with melted cheese

cheese'cake' *n.* **1** a cake made with cottage cheese or cream cheese **2** [Inf.] photographic display of the figure, esp. the legs, of a pretty woman

cheese'cloth' *n.* ⟦from its use for wrapping cheese⟧ a thin cotton cloth with a very loose weave

chees'y *adj.* **-i·er, -i·est 1** like cheese **2**

[Slang] inferior; poor

chee·tah (chēt'ə) *n.* ⟦Hindi < Sans *chitraka*, spotted⟧ a swift cat of Africa and S Asia, with long legs and a spotted coat

chef (shef) *n.* ⟦Fr, head, chief⟧ **1** a head cook **2** any cook

Che·khov (chek'ôf), **An·ton** (än tôn') 1860-1904; Russ. writer

chem *abbrev.* **1** chemical(s) **2** chemistry

chem·i·cal (kem'i kəl) *adj.* **1** of, made by, or used in chemistry **2** made with or operated by chemicals **3** of or involving a drug, alcohol, etc. [*chemical* dependency] —*n.* **1** any substance used in or obtained by a chemical process **2** [Slang] a drug, alcoholic beverage, etc. —**chem'i·cal·ly** *adv.*

chemical abuse the habitual use of a mood-altering drug, alcohol, etc. —**chemical abuser**

chemical engineering the science or profession of applying chemistry to industrial uses

chemical warfare warfare by means of poisonous gases, etc.

che·mise (shə mēz') *n.* ⟦< LL *camisia*, tunic⟧ **1** a woman's loose, short slip **2** a straight, loose dress

chem·ist (kem'ist) *n.* ⟦ult. < Ar < ? Gr *cheein*, to pour⟧ **1** a specialist in chemistry **2** [Brit.] a pharmacist, or druggist

chem·is·try (kem'is trē) *n.* ⟦< prec.⟧ **1** the science dealing with the composition and properties of substances, and with the reactions by which substances are produced from or converted into other substances **2** [Inf.] rapport

che·mo (kē'mō) *n.* [Inf.] *short for* CHEMOTHERAPY

chemo- *combining form* of, with, or by chemicals: also, before a vowel, **chem-**

che'mo·ther'a·py (kē'mō-) *n.* the use of drugs to prevent or treat a disease

chem·ur·gy (kem'ər jē) *n.* chemistry dealing with the use of organic, esp. farm, products in industrial manufacture

che·nille (shə nēl') *n.* ⟦Fr, lit., caterpillar⟧ **1** a tufted, velvety yarn **2** a fabric filled or woven with this

cheque (chek) *n.* *Brit. sp. of* CHECK (*n.* 8)

cher·ish (cher'ish) *vt.* ⟦< L *carus*, dear⟧ **1** to feel or show love for **2** to protect; foster **3** to cling to the idea or feeling of

Cher·o·kee (cher'ə kē') *n.*, *pl.* **-kees'** or **-kee'** a member of a North American Indian people now chiefly of Oklahoma and North Carolina

che·root (shə ro͞ot') *n.* ⟦< Tamil⟧ a cigar with both ends cut square

cher·ry (cher'ē) *n.*, *pl.* **-ries** ⟦< Gr *kerasion*⟧ **1** a small, fleshy fruit with a smooth, hard pit **2** the tree that bears this fruit **3** the wood of this tree **4** a bright red color —*adj.* bright-red

chert (churt) *n.* a very dense type of quartz, including jasper and flint

cher·ub (cher'əb) *n.*, *pl.* **-ubs**; for 1 usually **-u·bim'** (-yo͞o bim', -ə bim') *or* **-u·bims** ⟦< Heb *kerūbh*⟧ **1** any of a kind of angel, often represented as a chubby, rosy-faced child with wings **2** a child, etc. having a sweet, innocent face —**che·ru·bic** (chə ro͞o′bik) ***adj.*** —**che·ru′bi·cal·ly** ***adv.***

cher·vil (chur′vəl) ***n.*** ⟦< Gr *chairephyllon*⟧ an herb like parsley, with leaves used to flavor salads, soups, etc.

Ches·a·peake Bay (ches′ə pēk′) arm of the Atlantic, extending into Virginia and Maryland

chess (ches) ***n.*** ⟦< OFr *eschec*, a check in chess⟧ a game played on a chessboard by two players, using a variety of pieces (**chess′men**)

chess′board′ ***n.*** a checkerboard used for chess

chest (chest) ***n.*** ⟦< Gr *kistē*, a box⟧ **1** a box with a lid **2** a cabinet with drawers, as for clothes **3** a cabinet with shelves, as for medicines **4** the part of the body enclosed by the ribs, breastbone, and diaphragm

ches·ter·field (ches′tər fēld′) ***n.*** ⟦after a 19th-c. Earl of *Chesterfield*⟧ a single-breasted topcoat, usually with a velvet collar

chest·nut (ches′nut′) ***n.*** ⟦< Gr *kastaneia*⟧ **1** the edible nut of various trees of the beech family **2** such a tree, or its wood **3** reddish brown **4** a reddish-brown horse **5** [Inf.] an old, stale joke, story, etc. —***adj.*** reddish-brown

chev·i·ot (shev′ē ət; *also* chev′ē ət) ***n.*** ⟦after *Cheviot* Hills, on the Scottish-English border⟧ [*sometimes* **C-**] a rough, twilled wool fabric

chèvre or **che·vre** (shev′rə) ***n.*** a soft cheese made from goat's milk

chev·ron (shev′rən) ***n.*** ⟦< OFr, rafter⟧ a V-shaped bar on the sleeve of a uniform, showing rank

chew (cho͞o) ***vt., vi.*** ⟦ OE *ceowan*⟧ to bite and crush with the teeth —***n.*** **1** a chewing **2** something chewed or for chewing —**chew′er** ***n.*** —**chew′y**, **-i·er**, **-i·est**, ***adj.***

chew′ing gum a gummy substance, as chicle, flavored for chewing

Chey·enne[1] (shī an′, -en′) ***n.***, *pl.* **-ennes′** or **-enne′** a member of a North American Indian people now chiefly of Oklahoma

Chey·enne[2] (shī an′, -en′) capital of Wyoming, in the SE part: pop. 50,000

chg(d) *abbrev.* charge(d)

chi (kī, kē) ***n.*** the 22d letter of the Greek alphabet (Χ, χ)

Chi·an·ti (kē än′tē, -an′-) ***n.*** ⟦It⟧ [*also* **c-**] a dry red wine

chi·a·ro·scu·ro (kē är′ə skoor′ō) ***n.***, *pl.* **-ros** ⟦It < L *clarus*, clear + *obscurus*, dark⟧ **1** light and shade in a painting, etc. treated to suggest depth or for effect **2** a style of painting, etc. emphasizing this **3** a painting in which this is used

chic (shēk) ***n.*** ⟦Fr < medieval LowG *schick*, skill⟧ smart elegance of style —***adj.*** pleasingly stylish

Chi·ca·go (shə kä′gō, -kô′-) city and port in NE Illinois: pop. 2,784,000 (met. area, 6,070,000)

chi·can·er·y (shi kān′ər ē) ***n.***, *pl.* **-ies** ⟦< Fr⟧ **1** trickery **2** a trick

Chi·ca·no (chi kä′nō) ***n.***, *pl.* **-nos** ⟦< AmSp⟧ a U.S. citizen or inhabitant of Mexican descent —***adj.*** of Chicanos —**Chi·ca′na** (-nə), *pl.* **-nas**, ***fem.n.***

chi·chi or **chi-chi** (shē′shē) ***adj.*** ⟦Fr⟧ extremely chic, specif. in a showy way

chick (chik) ***n.*** ⟦ME *chike*⟧ **1** a young chicken or bird **2** [Slang] a young woman

chick·a·dee (chik′ə dē′) ***n.*** ⟦echoic⟧ any of various titmice

chick·en (chik′ən) ***n.*** ⟦< OE *cycen*⟧ **1** a common farm bird raised for its edible eggs or flesh; hen or rooster, esp. a young one **2** its flesh **3** [Slang] a cowardly person —***adj.*** [Slang] cowardly —***vi.*** [Slang] to quit from fear: usually with *out*

chicken feed [Slang] a small sum of money

chick′en-fried′ ***adj.*** coated with seasoned flour or batter and fried

chick′en-heart′ed ***adj.*** cowardly; timid: also **chick′en-liv′ered**

chick′en·pox′ ***n.*** an acute, contagious viral disease, esp. of children, characterized by skin eruptions

chicken wire light, pliable wire fencing

chick′pea′ ***n.*** **1** a bushy annual plant with short, hairy pods **2** its edible seed

chick′weed′ ***n.*** a low-growing plant often found as a weed in lawns, etc.

chic·le (chik′əl) ***n.*** ⟦AmSp⟧ a gumlike substance from a tropical American tree, used in chewing gum

chic·ly (shek′lē) ***adv.*** in a chic way —**chic′ness** ***n.***

chic·o·ry (chik′ə rē) ***n.***, *pl.* **-ries** ⟦< Gr *kichora*⟧ **1** a plant usually with blue flowers: the leaves are used for salad **2** its root, ground for mixing with coffee or for use as a coffee substitute

chide (chīd) ***vt., vi.*** **chid′ed** or **chid** (chid), **chid′ed** or **chid** or **chid·den** (chid′'n), **chid′ing** ⟦OE *cidan*⟧ to reprove mildly —**chid′ing·ly** ***adv.***

chief (chēf) ***n.*** ⟦< L *caput*, head⟧ a leader; head —***adj.*** main; principal

chief′ly ***adv.*** **1** most of all **2** mainly —***adj.*** of or like a chief

chief′tain (-tən) ***n.*** ⟦< L *caput*, head⟧ a chief, esp. of a clan or tribe

chif·fon (shi fän′) ***n.*** ⟦Fr⟧ a sheer, silky fabric —***adj.*** **1** of chiffon **2** made fluffy as with beaten egg whites *[*lemon *chiffon* pie*]*

chif·fo·nier or **chif·fon·nier** (shif′ə nir′) ***n.*** ⟦Fr⟧ a narrow, high chest of drawers, often with a mirror

chig·ger (chig′ər) ***n.*** ⟦of Afr orig.⟧ the tiny, red larva of certain mites, whose bite causes severe itching

chi·gnon (shēn′yän′) ***n.*** ⟦Fr < L *catena*, chain⟧ a coil of hair worn at the back of the neck

Chi·hua·hua[1] (chi wä′wä) ***n.*** ⟦after fol.⟧ a Mexican breed of very small dog with large, pointed ears

Chi·hua·hua[2] (chi wä′wä) state of N Mexico, on the U.S. border: 95,401 sq. mi.; pop. 2,442,000

chil·blain (chil′blān′) ***n.*** ⟦CHIL(L) + *blain* < OE *blegen*, a sore⟧ a painful swelling or sore, esp. on the fingers or toes, caused by exposure to cold

child (chīld) ***n.***, *pl.* **chil′dren** ⟦OE *cild*⟧ **1** an infant **2** a boy or girl before puberty **3** a son or daughter; offspring —**with child** pregnant —**child′hood′** ***n.*** —**child′less** ***adj.***

child′birth′ ***n.*** the act of giving birth to a child

child′ish ***adj.*** of or like a child; specif., immature, silly, etc. —**child′ish·ly** ***adv.*** —**child′ish·ness** ***n.***

child′like′ ***adj.*** of or like a child; specif., innocent, trusting etc.

chil·dren (chil′drən) ***n.*** *pl. of* CHILD

child's play any very simple task

Chi·le (chil′ē) country on the SW coast of South America: 284,520 sq. mi.; pop. 13,232,000 —**Chil·e·an** (chi lā′ən, chil′ē ən) ***adj., n.***

chi·le re·lle·no (chē′le re yā′nō) *pl.* **chi·les re·lle·nos** (chē′les re yā′nōs) a hot, green pepper stuffed with cheese, meat, etc. and fried

chil·i (chil′ē) ***n.***, *pl.* **-ies** or **-is** ⟦MexSp⟧ **1** the very hot, dried pod of red pepper, often ground as a seasoning (**chili powder**) **2** any of certain other peppers used in Mexican cooking **3** a highly spiced dish of beef, chilies or chili powder, and often beans and tomatoes: in full **chil′i con car′ne** (-kän kär′nē) Also **chil′e**

chili dog a hot dog served with chili con carne

chili sauce a spiced sauce of chopped tomatoes, sweet peppers, onions, etc.

chill (chil) ***n.*** ⟦< OE *ciele*⟧ **1** coldness or coolness causing shivers **2** a moderate coldness **3** a sudden fear, etc. **4** unfriendliness —***adj.*** CHILLY —***vi.*** **1** to become cold **2** to shake or shiver **3** [Slang] to relax or calm down: usually with *out* —***vt.*** **1** to make cool or cold **2** to cause a chill in **3** to check (enthusiasm, etc.)

chill factor WINDCHILL FACTOR

chill′y ***adj.*** **-i·er**, **-i·est** **1** moderately cold **2** unfriendly —**chill′i·ness** ***n.***

chime (chīm) ***n.*** ⟦< Gr *kymbalon*, cymbal⟧ **1** [*usually pl.*] *a)* a set of tuned bells or metal tubes *b)* the musical sounds made by these **2** a single bell, as in a clock —***vi.*** **chimed**, **chim′ing** **1** to sound as a chime or bells **2** to agree —***vt.*** to give (the time) by chiming —**chime in** **1** to join in **2** to agree —**chim′er** ***n.***

Chi·me·ra (kī mir′ə, ki-) ***n.*** ⟦< Gr *chimaira*, orig., she-goat⟧ **1** *Gr. Myth.* a monster, with a lion's head, goat's body, and serpent's tail **2** [**c-**] an impossible fancy

chi·mer′i·cal (-mer′i kəl) ***adj.*** **1** imaginary; unreal **2** fanciful

chim·ney (chim′nē) ***n.***, *pl.* **-neys** ⟦ult. < Gr *kaminos*, oven⟧ **1** the passage or structure through which smoke escapes from a fire, usually extending above the roof **2** a glass tube around the flame of a lamp **3** a narrow column of rock

chim·pan·zee (chim′pan zē′, chim pan′zē) ***n.*** ⟦< Bantu⟧ a medium-sized great ape of Africa: also [Inf.] **chimp** (chimp)

chin (chin) ***n.*** ⟦OE *cin*⟧ the part of the face below the lower lip —***vt.*** **chinned**, **chin′ning** to pull (oneself) up, while hanging by the hands from a bar, until the chin is just above the bar

Chin *abbrev.* Chinese

chi·na (chī′nə) ***n.*** ⟦orig. made in China⟧ **1** porcelain or any ceramic ware like porcelain **2** dishes, etc. made of china **3** any earthenware Also **chi′na·ware′**

Chi·na (chī′nə) country in E Asia: 3,696,100 sq. mi.; pop. 1,130,511,000

chin·chil·la (chin chil′ə) ***n.*** ⟦prob. dim. of Sp *chinche*, a small bug⟧ **1** a small rodent of South America **2** its soft, gray fur

chine (chīn) ***n.*** ⟦< OFr *eschine*, spine⟧ a cut of meat from the backbone

Chi·nese (chī nēz′, -nēs′) ***n.*** **1** *pl.* **-nese′** a person born or living in China **2** the standard language of China, any related language of China, or the group consisting of these languages —***adj.*** of China or its people, language, etc.

Chinese checkers a game in which marbles are moved as checkers, on a board with holes arranged in the shape of a six-pointed star

Chinese lantern a paper lantern that can be folded up

chink[1] (chiŋk) ***n.*** ⟦OE *chine*⟧ a crack —***vt.*** to close up the chinks in

chink[2] (chiŋk) ***n.*** ⟦echoic⟧ a sharp, clinking sound —***vi.***, ***vt.*** to make or cause to make this sound

chi·no (chē′nō, shē′-) ***n.***, *pl.* **-nos** ⟦< ?⟧ **1** a strong, twilled cotton, khaki cloth **2** [*pl.*] pants of chino for casual wear

Chi·nook (shə no͝ok′, -no͞ok′; chə-) ***n.***, *pl.* **-nooks′** or **-nook′** ⟦< AmInd name⟧ a member of a North American Indian people of Washington and Oregon

chintz (chints) ***n.*** ⟦< Hindi *chhīnt*⟧ a cotton cloth printed in colored designs and usually glazed

chintz′y (-ē) ***adj.*** **-i·er**, **-i·est** ⟦prec. + -Y[3]⟧ **1** like chintz **2** [Inf.] cheap, stingy, etc.

chin-up ***n.*** PULL-UP

chip (chip) ***vt.*** **chipped**, **chip′ping** ⟦< OE⟧ to break or cut off small pieces from —***vi.*** **1** to break off in small pieces **2** *Golf* to make a short, lofted shot (**chip shot**) —***n.*** **1** a small piece of wood, etc. cut or broken off **2** a place where a small piece has been chipped off **3** a small disk used in gambling games as a counter **4** a thin slice of food *[a potato chip]* **5** INTEGRATED CIRCUIT —**chip in** [Inf.] to contribute (money, etc.) —**chip on one's shoulder** [Inf.] an inclination to fight or quarrel

chip′munk′ (-muŋk′) ***n.*** ⟦< AmInd⟧ a small, striped North American squirrel

chipped beef dried or smoked beef sliced into shavings

chip·per (chip′ər) ***adj.*** ⟦< N Brit Dial.⟧ [Inf.] sprightly; in good spirits

chiro- ⟦< Gr *cheir*, hand⟧ *combining form* hand

chi·rog·ra·phy (kī räg′rə fē) ***n.*** ⟦prec. +

-GRAPHY⟧ handwriting

chi·rop·o·dy (kī räp′ə dē) ***n.*** ⟦CHIRO- + -POD + -Y[4]⟧ PODIATRY —**chi·rop′o·dist *n.***

chi·ro·prac·tic (kī′rō prak′tik) ***n.*** ⟦< CHIRO- + Gr *praktikos*, practical⟧ a method of treating disease by manipulation of the body joints, esp. of the spine —**chi′ro·prac′tor *n.***

chirp (churp) ***vi., vt.*** ⟦echoic⟧ to make, or utter in, short, shrill tones, as some birds do —***n.*** this sound

chir·rup (chir′əp) ***vi.*** ⟦< prec.⟧ to chirp repeatedly —***n.*** a chirruping sound

chis·el (chiz′əl) ***n.*** ⟦< L *caedere*, to cut⟧ a sharp-edged hand tool for cutting or shaping wood, stone, etc. —***vi., vt.* -eled** or **-elled, -el·ing** or **-el·ling 1** to cut or shape with a chisel **2** [Inf.] to swindle or get by swindling —**chis′el·er** or **chis′el·ler *n.***

chit (chit) ***n.*** ⟦< Hindi⟧ a voucher of a small sum owed for drink, food, etc.

chit·chat (chit′chat′) ***n.*** ⟦< CHAT⟧ **1** light, informal talk **2** gossip

chi·tin (kī′tin) ***n.*** ⟦< Gr *chitōn*, tunic⟧ the tough, horny outer covering of insects, crustaceans, etc.

chi·ton (kī′tən) ***n.*** ⟦Gr *chitōn*, tunic⟧ a small marine mollusk with a dorsal shell of eight plates

chit·ter·lings, chit·lins, or **chit·lings** (chit′linz) ***pl.n.*** ⟦< Gmc base⟧ small intestines of pigs, used for food

chiv·al·rous (shiv′əl rəs) ***adj.*** **1** gallant, courteous, etc. like an ideal knight **2** of chivalry Also **chiv′al·ric′** (-rik′, shi val′ rik) —**chiv′al·rous·ly *adv.***

chiv′al·ry (-rē) ***n.*** ⟦< OFr *chevaler*, knight < *cheval*, horse⟧ **1** medieval knighthood **2** the qualities of an ideal knight, as courage, honor, etc.

chives (chīvz) ***pl.n.*** ⟦< L *cepa*, onion⟧ [*sometimes with sing. v.*] an herb with slender, hollow leaves and a mild onion odor, used for flavoring

chla·myd·i·a (klə mid′ē ə) ***n.*** a widespread venereal disease

chlo·ral (hydrate) (klôr′əl) a colorless, crystalline compound used as a sedative

chlo′ride′ (-īd′) ***n.*** a compound of chlorine with another element or radical

chlo′ri·nate′ (-ə nāt′) ***vt.* -nat′ed, -nat′ing** to combine (a substance) with chlorine; esp., to treat (water or sewage) with chlorine for purification —**chlo′ri·na′tion *n.***

chlo′rine′ (-ēn′) ***n.*** ⟦< Gr *chlōros*, pale green⟧ a greenish-yellow, poisonous, gaseous chemical element with a disagreeable odor, used in bleaching, water purification, etc.

chloro- ⟦< Gr *chlōros*, pale green⟧ *combining form* **1** green **2** having chlorine in the molecule

chlo·ro·form (klôr′ə fôrm′) ***n.*** ⟦< Fr: see prec. & FORMIC⟧ a colorless, volatile liquid used as a solvent and, formerly, as an anesthetic —***vt.*** to anesthetize or kill with chloroform

chlo′ro·phyll′ or **chlo′ro·phyl′** (-fil′) ***n.*** ⟦< Fr, ult. < Gr *chlōros*, green + *phyllon*, leaf⟧ the green pigment found in plant cells, essential to photosynthesis

chock (chäk) ***n.*** ⟦NormFr *choque*, a block⟧ a block or wedge placed under a wheel, etc. to prevent motion —***vt.*** to wedge fast as with a chock —***adv.*** as close or tight as can be

chock′-full′ ***adj.*** as full as possible

choc·o·late (chôk′lət, chäk′-; chôk′ə lət, chäk′ə-) ***n.*** ⟦ult. < AmInd (Mexico)⟧ **1** a substance made from roasted and ground cacao seeds **2** a drink or candy made with chocolate **3** reddish brown —***adj.*** **1** made of or flavored with chocolate **2** reddish-brown —**choc′o·lat·y** or **choc′o·lat·ey *adj.***

choice (chois) ***n.*** ⟦< OFr < Gothic *kausjan*, to test⟧ **1** a choosing; selection **2** the right or power to choose **3** a person or thing chosen **4** the best part **5** a variety from which to choose **6** an alternative —***adj.* choic′er, choic′est 1** of special excellence **2** carefully chosen —**of choice** that is preferred

choir (kwīr) ***n.*** ⟦< L < Gr *choros*⟧ **1** a group of singers, esp. in a church **2** the part of a church they occupy

choke (chōk) ***vt.* choked, chok′ing** ⟦< OE *aceocian*⟧ **1** to prevent from breathing by blocking the windpipe; strangle; suffocate **2** to obstruct by clogging **3** to hinder the growth or action of **4** to cut off some air from the carburetor of (a gasoline engine) so as to make a richer gasoline mixture —***vi.*** **1** to be suffocated **2** [Inf.] to be unable to perform because of fear, tension, etc. —***n.*** **1** a choking **2** a sound of choking **3** the valve that chokes a carburetor —**choke back** to hold back (feelings, sobs, etc.) —**choke down** to swallow with difficulty —**choke off** to bring to an end

choke collar a training collar for a dog, that tightens when the dog strains at the leash: also **choke chain**

choke′hold′ ***n.*** **1** a locking one's arms around another's neck **2** absolute control

chok′er ***n.*** a closefitting necklace

chol·er (käl′ər) ***n.*** ⟦< L *cholera*: see fol.⟧ [Now Rare] anger or ill humor

chol·er·a (käl′ər ə) ***n.*** ⟦< Gr *cholē*, bile⟧ any of several severe intestinal diseases

chol′er·ic ***adj.*** easily angered

cho·les·ter·ol (kə les′tər ôl′, -ōl′) ***n.*** ⟦< Gr *cholē*, bile + *stereos*, solid⟧ a crystalline alcohol found esp. in animal fats, blood, nerve tissue, and bile

chomp (chämp) ***vt., vi.*** ⟦var. of CHAMP[1]⟧ **1** to chew hard and noisily **2** to bite down (*on*) repeatedly —**chomp at the bit** to be impatient when held back

Chong·qing (chooŋ′chiŋ′) city in SC China: pop. 2,673,000

choose (cho͞oz) ***vt., vi.* chose, cho′sen, choos′ing** ⟦OE *ceosan*⟧ **1** to take as a choice; select **2** to decide or prefer [*to choose to go*] —**cannot choose but** cannot do otherwise than —**choos′er *n.***

choos′y or **choos′ey** ***adj.* -i·er, -i·est** [Inf.] careful or fussy in choosing

chop (chäp) ***vt.* chopped, chop′ping** ⟦ME *choppen*⟧ **1** to cut by blows with a sharp tool **2** to cut into small bits;

mince —*vi.* to make quick, cutting strokes —*n.* 1 a short, sharp stroke 2 a cut of meat and bone from the rib, loin, or shoulder 3 a short, broken movement of waves

Cho·pin (shō′pan; *Fr* shô pan′), **Fré·dé·ric** (fred′rik; *Fr* frā dā rēk′) 1810-49; Pol. composer, in France after 1831

chop·per (chäp′ər) *n.* 1 one that chops 2 [*pl.*] [Slang] teeth 3 [Inf.] a helicopter

chop′py *adj.* **-pi′er, -pi·est** 1 rough with short, broken waves, as the sea 2 making abrupt starts and stops —**chop′pi·ness** *n.*

chops (chäps) *pl.n.* 1 the jaws 2 the mouth and lower cheeks

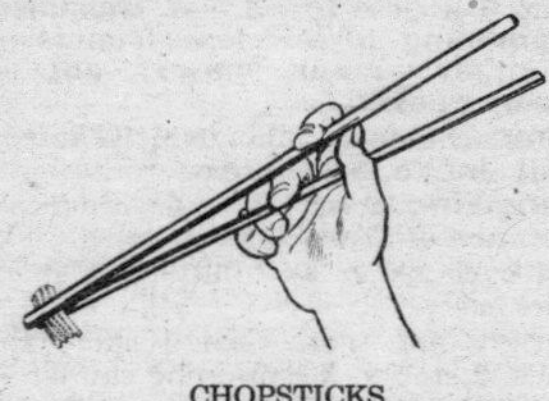

CHOPSTICKS

chop′sticks′ *pl.n.* ⟦Pidgin English⟧ two small sticks held together in one hand and used, mainly in parts of Asia, as an eating utensil

chop su·ey (chäp′ so͞o′ē) ⟦< Chin *tsa-sui,* various pieces⟧ a Chinese-American dish of meat, bean sprouts, etc., served with rice

cho·ral (kôr′əl) *adj.* of, for, or sung by a choir or chorus —**cho′ral·ly** *adv.*

cho·rale or **cho·ral** (kə ral′, -räl′) *n.* 1 a hymn tune 2 a choir or chorus

chord[1] (kôrd) *n.* ⟦altered (infl. by L *chorda*) < CORD⟧ 1 [Archaic] the string of a musical instrument 2 *Geom.* a straight line joining any two points on an arc

chord[2] (kôrd) *n.* ⟦< ME *accord,* accord⟧ *Music* a combination of three or more tones sounded together in harmony

chor·date (kôr′dāt′) *n.* ⟦L *chorda,* CORD + -ATE[1]⟧ any of a phylum of animals having a dorsal nerve cord, including the vertebrates

chore (chôr) *n.* ⟦< OE *cierr,* job⟧ 1 a routine task 2 a hard task

chor·e·o·graph (kôr′ē ə graf′) *vt., vi.* ⟦< fol.⟧ 1 to design or plan the movements of (a dance) 2 to plan (something) in careful detail —**chor′e·og′ra·pher** (-äg′rə fər) *n.*

chor·e·og·ra·phy (kôr′ē äg′rə fē) *n.* ⟦Gr *choreia,* dance + -GRAPHY⟧ 1 dancing, esp. ballet dancing 2 the devising of dances, esp. ballets —**chor′e·o·graph′ic** (-ə graf′ik) *adj.*

chor·is·ter (kôr′is tər) *n.* ⟦see CHORUS⟧ a member of a choir

cho·roid (kôr′oid′) *n.* ⟦Gr < *chorion,* fetal membrane + *-eidēs,* -OID⟧ the dark, middle membrane of the eye

chor·tle (chôrt′'l) *vi.* **-tled, -tling** ⟦prob. < CHUCKLE + SNORT⟧ to make a gleeful chuckling or snorting sound —*n.* such a sound —**chor′tler** *n.*

cho·rus (kôr′əs) *n.* ⟦< Gr *choros*⟧ 1 a group of dancers and singers performing together 2 the part of a drama, song, etc. performed by a chorus 3 a group singing or speaking something together 4 music written for group singing 5 the refrain of a song —*vt., vi.* to sing, speak, or say in unison —**in chorus** in unison

chose (chōz) *vt., vi. pt. & obs. pp. of* CHOOSE

cho·sen (chō′zən) *vt., vi. pp. of* CHOOSE —*adj.* selected

Chou En-lai (jō′en′lī′) 1898-1976; Chin. premier (1949-76): Pinyin *Zhou En-lai*

chow (chou) *n.* ⟦< Chin⟧ 1 any of a breed of medium-sized dog, originally from China: also **chow chow** 2 [Slang] food

chow·der (chou′dər) *n.* ⟦Fr *chaudière,* a pot⟧ a thick soup usually of onions and potatoes and, often, clams and milk

chow′hound′ *n.* [Slang] a glutton

chow mein (chou′ mān′) ⟦Chin *ch'ao,* fry + *mien,* flour⟧ a Chinese-American dish of meat, bean sprouts, etc., served with fried noodles

Chré·tien (krā tyan′), **Jean** (zhän) 1934- ; prime minister of Canada (1993-)

chrism (kriz′əm) *n.* ⟦< Gr *chrisma,* oil⟧ holy oil used as in baptism

Christ (krīst) ⟦< Gr *christos,* the anointed⟧ Jesus of Nazareth, regarded by Christians as the prophesied Messiah

chris·ten (kris′ən) *vt.* 1 to baptize 2 to give a name to, as at baptism 3 [Inf.] to use for the first time —**chris′ten·ing** *n.*

Chris′ten·dom (-dəm) *n.* 1 Christians collectively 2 those parts of the world where most of the inhabitants profess Christianity

Chris·tian (kris′chən) *n.* a believer in Jesus as the prophesied Messiah, or in the religion based on the teachings of Jesus —*adj.* 1 of Jesus Christ 2 of or professing the religion based on his teachings 3 having the qualities taught by Jesus Christ, as love, kindness, humility, etc. 4 of Christians or Christianity

Chris·ti·an·i·ty (kris′chē an′ə tē) *n.* 1 Christians collectively 2 the Christian religion 3 the state of being a Christian

Chris·tian·ize (kris′chən īz′) *vt.* **-ized′, -iz′ing** to make Christian

Christian name the baptismal name or given name, as distinguished from the surname or family name

Christian Science a religion and system of healing: official name **Church of Christ, Scientist**

Chris·tie (kris′tē) *n., pl.* **-ties** ⟦after *Christiania,* former name of Oslo, Norway⟧ *Skiing* a high-speed turn with the skis parallel

Christ·mas (kris′məs) *n.* ⟦see CHRIST & MASS⟧ a holiday on Dec. 25 celebrating the birth of Jesus Christ

chro·mat·ic (krō mat′ik) ***adj.*** ⟦< Gr *chrōma*, color⟧ **1** of or having color or colors **2** *Music* progressing by semitones —**chro·mat′i·cal·ly** ***adv.***

chro·ma·tin (krō′mə tin) ***n.*** ⟦< Gr *chrōma*, color⟧ a substance in cell nuclei containing the genes: it readily absorbs a coloring agent, as for observation under a microscope

chrome (krōm) ***n.*** ⟦Fr: see CHROMIUM⟧ chromium or chromium alloy —***adj.*** designating any of various pigments (**chrome red**, **chrome yellow**) made from chromium compounds —***vt.*** **chromed**, **chrom′ing** to plate with chromium

-chrome (krōm) ⟦< Gr *chrōma*, color⟧ *combining form* **1** color or coloring agent **2** chromium

chro·mi·um (krō′mē əm) ***n.*** ⟦< Gr *chrōma*, color⟧ a hard, metallic chemical element resistant to corrosion

chromo- ⟦< Gr *chrōma*, color⟧ *combining form* color or pigment *[chromosome]* Also **chrom-**

chro·mo·some (krō′mə sōm′) ***n.*** ⟦< prec.⟧ any of the microscopic rod-shaped bodies carrying the genes

chron·ic (krän′ik) ***adj.*** ⟦< Gr *chronos*, time⟧ **1** lasting a long time or recurring: said of a disease **2** having had an ailment for a long time **3** habitual —**chron′i·cal·ly** ***adv.***

chron·i·cle (krän′i kəl) ***n.*** ⟦< Gr *chronika*, annals⟧ a historical record of events in the order in which they happened —***vt.*** **-cled**, **-cling** to tell the history of; recount; record —**chron′i·cler** ***n.***

chrono- ⟦< Gr *chronos*, time⟧ *combining form* time: also **chron-**

chro·nol·o·gy (krə näl′ə jē) ***n.***, *pl.* **-gies** ⟦prec. + -LOGY⟧ **1** the science of measuring time and of dating events **2** the arrangement of events in the order of occurrence —**chron·o·log·i·cal** (krän′ə läj′i kəl) ***adj.*** —**chron′o·log′i·cal·ly** ***adv.***

chro·nom′e·ter (-näm′ət ər) ***n.*** ⟦CHRONO- + -METER⟧ a highly accurate kind of clock or watch

chrys·a·lis (kris′ə lis) ***n.***, *pl.* **chry·sal·i·des** (kri sal′ə dēz′) or **chrys′a·lis·es** ⟦< Gr *chrysallis*⟧ **1** the pupa of a butterfly, encased in a cocoon **2** the cocoon

chrys·an·the·mum (kri san′thə məm) ***n.*** ⟦< Gr *chrysos*, gold + *anthemon*, flower⟧ **1** a late-blooming plant of the composite family, with showy flowers **2** the flower

chub (chub) ***n.***, *pl.* **chub** or **chubs** a small freshwater fish often used as bait

chub·by (chub′ē) ***adj.*** **-bi·er**, **-bi·est** round and plump —**chub′bi·ness** ***n.***

chuck[1] (chuk) ***vt.*** ⟦< ? Fr *choquer*, strike against⟧ **1** to tap playfully, esp. under the chin **2** to throw; toss **3** [Slang] to get rid of —***n.*** a chucking

chuck[2] (chuk) ***n.*** ⟦prob. var. of CHOCK⟧ **1** a cut of beef from around the neck and shoulder blade **2** a clamplike holding device, as on a lathe

chuck′-full′ ***adj.*** *var. of* CHOCK-FULL

chuck′hole′ ***n.*** ⟦see CHOCK & HOLE⟧ a rough hole in pavement

chuck·le (chuk′əl) ***vi.*** **-led**, **-ling** ⟦? < var. of CLUCK⟧ to laugh softly in a low tone —***n.*** a soft, low-toned laugh

chuck wagon a wagon equipped as a kitchen for feeding cowboys, etc.

chuck·wal·la (chuk′wäl′ə) ***n.*** ⟦< AmInd (Mexico)⟧ a large, edible iguana of Mexico and SW U.S.

chug (chug) ***n.*** ⟦echoic⟧ any of a series of puffing or explosive sounds, as of a locomotive —***vi.*** **chugged**, **chug′ging** to make, or move with, such sounds —***vt.*** [Slang] to drink in gulps

chuk·ka (boot) (chuk′ə) an ankle-high bootlike shoe

chum (chum) [Inf.] ***n.*** ⟦prob. < *chamber (mate)*⟧ a close friend —***vi.*** **chummed**, **chum′ming** to be close friends —**chum′my**, **-mi·er**, **-mi·est**, ***adj.*** —**chum′mi·ness** ***n.***

chump (chump) ***n.*** ⟦akin to MHG *kumpf*, dull⟧ [Inf.] a fool or dupe

Chung·king (chooŋ′kiŋ′) *a former transliteration of* CHONGQING

chunk (chuŋk) ***n.*** ⟦< ? CHUCK[2]⟧ a short, thick piece

chunk′y ***adj.*** **-i·er**, **-i·est** **1** short and thick **2** stocky **3** containing chunks —**chunk′i·ness** ***n.***

church (church) ***n.*** ⟦< Gr *kyriakē* (*oikia*), Lord's (house)⟧ **1** a building for public worship, esp. Christian worship **2** religious service **3** [*usually* **C-**] *a)* all Christians *b)* a particular Christian denomination **4** a religious congregation **5** ecclesiastical, as opposed to secular, government

church′go′er (-gō′ər) ***n.*** a person who attends church, esp. regularly

Church·ill (chur′chil), Sir **Win·ston** (win′ stən) 1874-1965; Brit. prime minister (1940-45; 1951-55)

church′man (-mən) ***n.***, *pl.* **-men** (-mən) **1** a clergyman **2** a church member

Church of England the episcopal church of England; Anglican Church: it is an established church headed by the sovereign

church′war′den (-wôrd′n) ***n.*** a lay officer handling certain secular matters in a church

church′yard′ ***n.*** the ground adjoining a church, often used as a cemetery

churl (churl) ***n.*** ⟦OE *ceorl*, peasant⟧ **1** a peasant **2** a surly person; boor —**churl′ish** ***adj.*** —**churl′ish·ness** ***n.***

churn (churn) ***n.*** ⟦OE *cyrne*⟧ a container in which milk or cream is stirred or shaken to form butter —***vt.***, ***vi.*** **1** to stir or shake (milk or cream) in a churn **2** to make (butter) thus **3** to stir up or move vigorously —**churn out** to produce in abundance

chute[1] (sho͞ot) ***n.*** ⟦Fr, a fall⟧ an inclined or vertical trough or passage down which things slide or drop

chute[2] (sho͞ot) ***n.*** [Inf.] *short for* PARACHUTE

chut·ney (chut′nē) ***n.***, *pl.* **-neys** ⟦Hindi *chatnī*⟧ a relish of fruits, spices, herbs, and vinegar

chutz·pah or **chutz·pa** (ho͝ots′pə, kho͝ots′-) ***n.*** ⟦Yiddish < Heb⟧ [Inf.] impudence; brass

chyme (kīm) ***n.*** ⟦< Gr *chymos,* juice⟧ the semifluid mass formed as the stomach digests food: it passes into the small intestine

CIA *abbrev.* Central Intelligence Agency

ci·ca·da (si kā′də) ***n., pl.*** **-das** or **-dae** (-dē) ⟦L⟧ a large, flylike insect with transparent wings: the male makes a loud, shrill sound

cic·a·trix (sik′ə triks′) ***n., pl.*** **cic·a·tri·ces** (sik′ə trī′sēz′) or **cic′a·trix′es** ⟦L⟧ a scar

Cic·e·ro (sis′ə rō′) 106-43 B.C.; Rom. statesman & orator

-cide (sīd) ⟦< L *caedere,* to kill⟧ *suffix* **1** a killer **2** a killing

ci·der (sī′dər) ***n.*** ⟦< Gr *sikera,* an intoxicant⟧ juice pressed from apples, used as a drink or for making vinegar

ci·gar (si gär′) ***n.*** ⟦Sp *cigarro*⟧ a roll of cut tobacco wrapped in a tobacco leaf for smoking

cig·a·rette or **cig·a·ret** (sig′ə ret′, sig′ə ret′) ***n.*** ⟦Fr⟧ a small roll of finely cut tobacco wrapped in thin paper for smoking

cig·a·ril·lo (sig′ə ril′ō) ***n., pl.*** **-los** ⟦Sp, dim. of *cigarro,* cigar⟧ a small, thin cigar

ci·lan·tro (si lan′trō, -län′-) ***n.*** coriander leaves used as an herb

cil·i·a (sil′ē ə) ***pl.n., sing.*** **-i·um** (-ē əm) ⟦< L⟧ small hairlike projections, as those extending from certain plant cells or from around protozoa

ci·met·i·dine (sə met′ə dēn′) ***n.*** a drug that reduces gastric secretion: used to treat peptic ulcers

cinch (sinch) ***n.*** ⟦< Sp < L *cingulum,* girdle⟧ **1** a saddle or pack girth **2** [Slang] a thing easy to do —***vt.*** **1** to fasten (a saddle) on (a horse, etc.) with a cinch **2** [Slang] to make sure of

cin·cho·na (sin kō′nə) ***n.*** ⟦after 17th-c. Peruvian Countess del *Chinchón*⟧ **1** a tropical tree with a bitter bark from which quinine is made **2** this bark

Cin·cin·nat·i (sin′sə nat′ē, -ə) city in SW Ohio: pop. 364,000

cinc·ture (siŋk′chər) ***n.*** ⟦L *cinctura*⟧ a belt or girdle

cin·der (sin′dər) ***n.*** ⟦OE *sinder,* slag⟧ **1** a tiny piece of partly burned coal, wood, etc. **2** [*pl.*] ashes from coal or wood

Cin·der·el·la (sin′dər el′ə) ***n.*** in a fairy tale, a household drudge who eventually marries a prince

cin·e·ma (sin′ə mə) ***n.*** ⟦< Gr *kinēma,* motion⟧ [Chiefly Brit.] a film theater —**the cinema** **1** the making of films **2** films collectively —**cin′e·mat′ic** ***adj.***

cin·e·ma·tog·ra·phy (sin′ə mə täg′rə fē) ***n.*** the art, science, and work of photography in making films —**cin′e·ma·tog′ra·pher** ***n.*** —**cin′e·mat′o·graph′ic** (-mat′ə graf′ik) ***adj.***

cin·na·bar (sin′ə bär′) ***n.*** ⟦< Gr *kinnabari*⟧ mercuric sulfide, a heavy, bright-red mineral

cin·na·mon (sin′ə mən) ***n.*** ⟦< Heb *qinnāmōn*⟧ **1** the yellowish-brown spice made from the dried inner bark of a laurel tree of the East Indies **2** this bark

ci·pher (sī′fər) ***n.*** ⟦< Ar *ṣifr*⟧ **1** the symbol 0; zero **2** a nonentity **3** secret writing based on a key; code **4** the key to such a code

cir·ca (sʉr′kə) ***prep.*** ⟦L⟧ about: used before an approximate date or figure: also written ***cir′ca***

cir·ca·di·an (sər kā′dē ən) ***adj.*** ⟦coined < L *circa,* about + *dies,* day⟧ of the behavioral or physiological rhythms associated with the 24-hour cycle of the earth's rotation

Cir·ce (sʉr′sē) ***n.*** in the *Odyssey,* an enchantress who turns men into swine

cir·cle (sʉr′kəl) ***n.*** ⟦< Gr *kirkos*⟧ **1** a plane figure bounded by a single curved line every point of which is equally distant from the center **2** this curved line **3** anything like a circle, as a ring **4** a complete or recurring series; cycle **5** a group of people with common interests **6** extent, as of influence; scope —***vt.*** **-cled**, **-cling** **1** to form a circle around **2** to move around, as in a circle —***vi.*** to go around in a circle —**cir′cler** ***n.***

cir′clet (-klit) ***n.*** **1** a small circle **2** a circular ornament, as for the head

cir·cuit (sʉr′kit) ***n.*** ⟦< L *circum,* around + *ire,* go⟧ **1** a boundary line or its length **2** a going around something **3** the regular journey through a district of a person at work, as a preacher **4** the district of a U.S. Court of Appeals **5** a chain or association, as of theaters or resorts **6** the path or line of an electric current —***vi.*** to go in a circuit —***vt.*** to make a circuit about —**cir′cuit·al** ***adj.***

circuit breaker a device that automatically interrupts the flow of an electric current

circuit court a court that holds sessions in various places within its district

cir·cu·i·tous (sər kyo͞o′ət əs) ***adj.*** roundabout; indirect —**cir·cu′i·tous·ly** ***adv.*** —**cir·cu′i·tous·ness** ***n.***

cir·cuit·ry (sʉr′kə trē) ***n.*** the system or the elements of an electric circuit

cir·cu·lar (sʉr′kyə lər) ***adj.*** **1** in the shape of a circle; round **2** moving in a circle **3** circuitous —***n.*** an advertisement, etc., intended for many readers —**cir′cu·lar′i·ty** (-ler′ə tē) ***n.***

cir′cu·lar·ize′ (-īz′) ***vt.*** **-ized′**, **-iz′ing** **1** to make circular **2** to send circulars to **3** to canvass —**cir′cu·lar·i·za′tion** ***n.*** —**cir′cu·lar·iz′er** ***n.***

cir·cu·late (sʉr′kyə lāt′) ***vi.*** **-lat′ed**, **-lat′ing** ⟦< L *circulari,* form a circle⟧ **1** to move in a circle or circuit and return, as the blood **2** to go from person to person or from place to place —***vt.*** to make circulate —**cir′cu·lat′or** ***n.*** —**cir′cu·la·to′ry** (-lə tôr′ē) ***adj.***

cir·cu·la·tion (sʉr′kyə lā′shən) ***n.*** **1** a circulating **2** the movement of blood through the arteries and veins **3** the distribution of newspapers, magazines, etc. **4** the average number of copies of a periodical sold in a given period

circum- ⟦< L *circum*⟧ *prefix* around, about, surrounding

cir·cum·cise (sʉr′kəm sīz′) ***vt.*** **-cised′**, **-cis′ing** ⟦< L < *circum,* around + *caedere,* to cut⟧ to cut off all or part of the foreskin of —**cir′cum·ci′sion** (-sizh′ən) ***n.***

cir·cum·fer·ence (sər kum′fər əns, -frəns) ***n.*** ⟦< L *circum,* around + *ferre,* to carry⟧ **1** the line bounding a circle, ball, etc. **2** the length of this line

cir·cum·flex (sur′kəm fleks′) ***n.*** ⟦< L *circum,* around + *flectere,* to bend⟧ a mark (^ or ~) used over a vowel to indicate pronunciation

cir′cum·lo·cu′tion (-lō kyōō′shən) ***n.*** ⟦< L: see CIRCUM- & LOCUTION⟧ a roundabout way of saying something

cir′cum·nav′i·gate′ (-nav′ə-) ***vt.*** **-gat′ed, -gat′ing** ⟦< L: see CIRCUM- & NAVIGATE⟧ to sail or fly around (the earth, etc.) —**cir′cum·nav′i·ga′tion** ***n.***

cir′cum·scribe′ (-skrīb′) ***vt.*** **-scribed′, -scrib′ing** ⟦< L: see CIRCUM- & SCRIBE⟧ **1** to trace a line around; encircle **2** to limit; confine —**cir′cum·scrip′tion** (-skrip′shən) ***n.***

cir′cum·spect′ (-spekt′) ***adj.*** ⟦< L *circumspicere,* look about⟧ cautious; discreet —**cir′cum·spec′tion** ***n.*** —**cir′cum·spect′ly** ***adv.***

cir′cum·stance′ (-stans′) ***n.*** ⟦< L *circum,* around + *stare,* to stand⟧ **1** a fact or event, specif. one accompanying another **2** [*pl.*] conditions affecting a person, esp. financial conditions **3** chance; luck **4** ceremony; show —***vt.*** **-stanced′, -stanc′ing** to place in certain circumstances —**under no circumstances** never —**cir′cum·stanced′** ***adj.***

cir′cum·stan′tial (-stan′shəl) ***adj.*** **1** having to do with, or depending on, circumstances **2** incidental **3** complete in detail —**cir′cum·stan′tial·ly** ***adv.***

circumstantial evidence *Law* indirect evidence of a fact at issue, based on attendant circumstances

cir′cum·vent′ (-vent′) ***vt.*** ⟦< L *circum,* around + *venire,* come⟧ to get the better of or prevent by craft or ingenuity —**cir′cum·ven′tion** ***n.***

cir·cus (sur′kəs) ***n.*** ⟦L, a circle⟧ **1** in ancient Rome, an amphitheater **2** a traveling show of acrobats, trained animals, clowns, etc. **3** [Inf.] a place or event regarded as being frenzied, wildly entertaining, etc.

ci·ré (sē rā′) ***adj.*** ⟦< Fr *cire,* wax⟧ having a smooth, glossy finish

cir·rho·sis (sə rō′sis) ***n.*** ⟦< Gr *kirrhos,* tawny + -OSIS⟧ a degenerative disease, esp. of the liver, marked by excess formation of connective tissue —**cir·rhot′ic** (-rät′ik) ***adj.***

cir·rus (sir′əs) ***n.***, *pl.* **cir′rus** ⟦L, a curl⟧ the type of cloud resembling a wispy filament and found at high altitudes

CIS *abbrev.* Commonwealth of Independent States

cis- ⟦< L *cis,* on this side⟧ *prefix* on this side of

cis·tern (sis′tərn) ***n.*** ⟦< L *cista,* chest⟧ a large tank for storing water, esp. rainwater

cit·a·del (sit′ə del′) ***n.*** ⟦< L *civitas,* city⟧ a fortress

cite (sīt) ***vt.*** **cit′ed, cit′ing** ⟦< L *citare,* summon⟧ **1** to summon before a court of law **2** to quote **3** to mention by way of example, proof, etc. **4** to mention in an official report as meritorious —**ci·ta′tion** ***n.***

cit·i·fied (sit′i fīd′) ***adj.*** having the manners, dress, etc. of city people

cit·i·zen (sit′ə zən) ***n.*** ⟦< L *civis,* townsman⟧ a member of a state or nation who owes allegiance to it by birth or naturalization and is entitled to full civil rights —**cit′i·zen·ship′** ***n.***

cit′i·zen·ry ***n.*** citizens as a group

cit·ric (si′trik) ***adj.*** designating or of an acid obtained from citrus fruits

cit′ron (-trən) ***n.*** ⟦< Fr, lemon⟧ **1** a yellow, thick-skinned, lemonlike fruit **2** its candied rind

cit·ron·el·la (si′trə nel′ə) ***n.*** ⟦see prec.⟧ a sharp-smelling oil used in soap, insect repellents, etc.

cit′rus (-trəs) ***n.*** ⟦L⟧ **1** any of the trees that bear oranges, lemons, limes, etc. **2** any such fruit —***adj.*** of these trees: also **cit′rous**

cit·y (sit′ē) ***n.***, *pl.* **-ies** ⟦< L *civis,* townsman⟧ **1** a population center larger or more important than a town **2** in the U.S., an incorporated municipality with boundaries and powers defined by state charter **3** the people of a city —***adj.*** of, in, or for a city —**cit′y·wide′** ***adj.***

city hall (a building that houses) a municipal government

civ·et (siv′it) ***n.*** ⟦< Ar *zabād*⟧ **1** the musky secretion of a catlike carnivore (**civet cat**) of Africa and S Asia: used in some perfumes **2** the animal, or its fur

civ·ic (siv′ik) ***adj.*** ⟦< L *civis,* townsman⟧ of a city, citizens, or citizenship

civ′ic-mind′ed ***adj.*** having or showing concern for the welfare of one's community

civ′ics (-iks) ***n.*** the study of civic affairs and the duties and rights of citizenship

civ·il (siv′əl) ***adj.*** ⟦see CIVIC⟧ **1** of a citizen or citizens **2** polite **3** of citizens in matters not military or religious **4** having to do with the private rights of individuals —**civ′il·ly** ***adv.***

civil disobedience nonviolent opposition to a law through refusal to comply with it, on grounds of conscience

civil engineering engineering dealing with the construction of highways, bridges, harbors, etc. —**civil engineer**

ci·vil·ian (sə vil′yən) ***n.*** ⟦see CIVIC⟧ a person not in military or naval service —***adj.*** of or for civilians; nonmilitary

ci·vil′i·ty (-ə tē) ***n.*** **1** politeness **2** *pl.* **-ties** a civil, or polite, act

civ·i·li·za·tion (siv′ə lə zā′shən) ***n.*** **1** a civilizing or being civilized **2** the total culture of a people, period, etc. **3** the peoples considered to have attained a high social development

civ′i·lize′ (-līz′) ***vt.*** **-lized′, -liz′ing** ⟦see CIVIC⟧ **1** to bring out of a primitive or savage condition to a higher level of social organization and of cultural and technological development **2** to make refined, sophisticated, etc. —**civ′i·lized′** ***adj.***

civil law the body of law having to do with private rights

civil liberties liberties guaranteed to all

individuals by law, custom, court decisions, etc.; rights, as of speaking or acting as one likes, granted without hindrance except in the interests of the public welfare

civil rights those rights guaranteed to all individuals by the 13th, 14th, 15th, and 19th Amendments to the U.S. Constitution, as the right to vote and the right to equal treatment under the law

civil servant a civil service employee

civil service all those employed in government administration, esp. through competitive public examination

civil war war between different factions of the same nation —**the Civil War** the war between the North (the Union) and the South (the Confederacy) in the U.S. (1861-65)

civ·vies (siv′ēz) ***pl.n.*** [Inf.] civilian clothes: also **civ′ies**

ck *abbrev.* check

cl *abbrev.* centiliter(s)

Cl *Chem. symbol for* chlorine

clack (klak) ***vi., vt.*** ⟦prob. echoic < ON⟧ to make or cause to make a sudden, sharp sound —***n.*** this sound

clad (klad) ***vt.*** *alt. pt. & pp. of* CLOTHE —***adj.*** **1** clothed; dressed **2** having a bonded outer layer of another metal or an alloy *[clad* steel*]*

clad′ding ***n.*** a layer of some metal or alloy bonded to another metal

claim (klām) ***vt.*** ⟦< L *clamare,* cry out⟧ **1** to demand as rightfully belonging to one **2** to require; deserve *[to claim* attention*]* **3** to assert —***n.*** **1** a claiming **2** a right to something **3** something claimed **4** an assertion —**claim′a·ble** ***adj.*** —**claim′ant** or **claim′er** ***n.***

clair·voy·ance (kler voi′əns) ***n.*** ⟦Fr < *clair,* clear + *voyant,* seeing⟧ the supposed ability to perceive things that are not in sight —**clair·voy′ant** ***n., adj.***

clam (klam) ***n.*** ⟦< obs. *clam,* a clamp⟧ any of various hard-shelled, usually edible, bivalve mollusks —***vi.*** **clammed, clam′ming** to dig for clams —**clam up** [Inf.] to keep silent —**clam′mer** ***n.***

clam′bake′ ***n.*** **1** a picnic at which steamed or baked clams are served **2** [Inf.] any large, noisy party

clam·ber (klam′bər) ***vi.*** ⟦ME *clambren*⟧ to climb clumsily, esp. by using both the hands and the feet

clam·my (klam′ē) ***adj.*** **-mi·er, -mi·est** ⟦ME, prob. < OE *clam,* mud⟧ unpleasantly moist, cold, and sticky —**clam′mi·ly** ***adv.*** —**clam′mi·ness** ***n.***

clam·or (klam′ər) ***n.*** ⟦< L *clamare,* cry out⟧ **1** a loud outcry; uproar **2** a loud demand or complaint, as by the public —***vi.*** to make a clamor —**clam′or·ous** ***adj.***

clamp (klamp) ***n.*** ⟦< MDu *klampe*⟧ a device for clasping or fastening things together —***vt.*** to fasten or brace, as with a clamp —**clamp down (on)** to become more strict (with)

clan (klan) ***n.*** ⟦< Gael < L *planta,* offshoot⟧ **1** a group of families claiming descent from a common ancestor **2** a group of people with interests in common —**clans·man** (klanz′mən), *pl.* **-men** (-mən), ***n.***

clan·des·tine (klan des′tin) ***adj.*** ⟦< L *clam,* secret⟧ secret or hidden; furtive —**clan·des′tine·ly** ***adv.***

clang (klaŋ) ***vi., vt.*** ⟦echoic⟧ to make or cause to make a loud, ringing sound, as by striking metal —***n.*** this sound

clang′or (-ər) ***n.*** ⟦L < *clangere,* to sound⟧ a continuous clanging sound

clank (klaŋk) ***n.*** ⟦echoic⟧ a sharp, metallic sound —***vi., vt.*** to make or cause to make this sound

clan·nish (klan′ish) ***adj.*** **1** of a clan **2** tending to associate closely with one's own group only —**clan′nish·ly** ***adv.*** —**clan′nish·ness** ***n.***

clap (klap) ***vi.*** **clapped, clap′ping** ⟦OE *clæppan,* to beat⟧ **1** to make a sudden, explosive sound, as of two flat surfaces struck together **2** to strike the hands together, as in applauding —***vt.*** **1** to strike together briskly **2** to strike with an open hand **3** to put, move, etc. swiftly *[he was clapped* into jail*]* —***n.*** **1** the sound or act of clapping **2** a sharp slap

clap·board (klab′ərd) ***n.*** ⟦transl. of MDu *klapholt* < *klappen,* to fit + *holt,* wood⟧ a thin board with one thicker edge, used as siding —***vt.*** to cover with clapboards

clap′per ***n.*** **1** a person who claps **2** the moving part of a bell, that strikes the side of the bell

clap′trap′ ***n.*** ⟦CLAP + TRAP⟧ insincere, empty talk intended to get applause

claque (klak) ***n.*** ⟦Fr < *claquer,* to clap⟧ **1** a group of people paid to applaud at a play, etc. **2** a group of fawning admirers

clar·et (klar′it) ***n.*** ⟦< OFr (*vin*) *claret,* clear (wine)⟧ a dry red wine

clar·i·fy (klar′ə fī′) ***vt., vi.*** **-fied′, -fy′ing** ⟦< L *clarus,* clear + *facere,* to make⟧ to make or become clear —**clar′i·fi·ca′tion** ***n.***

clar·i·net (klar′ə net′) ***n.*** ⟦< Fr < L *clarus,* clear⟧ a single-reed woodwind instrument played by means of holes and keys —**clar′i·net′ist** or **clar′i·net′tist** ***n.***

clar·i·on (klar′ē ən) ***adj.*** ⟦< L *clarus,* clear⟧ clear, sharp, and ringing *[a clarion* call*]*

clar·i·ty (klar′ə tē) ***n.*** ⟦< L *clarus,* clear⟧ the quality of being clear; clearness

clash (klash) ***vi.*** ⟦echoic⟧ **1** to collide with a loud, harsh, metallic noise **2** to conflict; disagree —***vt.*** to strike with a clashing noise —***n.*** **1** the sound of clashing **2** conflict

clasp (klasp) ***n.*** ⟦ME *claspe*⟧ **1** a fastening, as a hook, to hold things together **2** a holding or grasping; embrace **3** a grip of the hand —***vt.*** **1** to fasten with a clasp **2** to hold or embrace tightly **3** to grip with the hand

class (klas) ***n.*** ⟦< L *classis*⟧ **1** a number of people or things grouped together because of certain likenesses; kind; sort **2** a social or economic rank *[the working class]* **3** *a)* a group of students taught together *b)* a meeting of such a group *c*) a group graduating together **4** grade or quality **5** [Inf.] excellence, as of style or appearance **—*vt.*** to classify **—class′less *adj.***

class action (suit) a legal action that is brought by one or more persons on behalf of themselves and a much larger group

clas·sic (klas′ik) ***adj.*** ⟦< L *classis*, class⟧ **1** being an excellent model of its kind **2** CLASSICAL (senses 2 & 3) **3** balanced, formal, regular, simple, etc. **4** famous as traditional or typical **—*n.*** **1** a literary or artistic work of the highest excellence **2** a creator of such a work **3** [*pl.*] the works of outstanding ancient Greek and Roman authors: usually with *the* **4** a famous traditional or typical event

clas·si·cal (klas′i kəl) ***adj.*** **1** CLASSIC (*adj.* 1 & 3) **2** of the art, literature, etc. of the ancient Greeks and Romans **3** typical of or derived from the artistic standards of the ancient Greeks and Romans **4** well versed in Greek and Roman culture **5** standard and traditional *[classical* economics*]* **6** designating, of, or like music conforming to certain standards of form, complexity, etc. **—clas′si·cal·ly *adv.*** **—class′i·cal′i·ty** (-kal′ə tē) ***n.***

clas′si·cism′ (-ə siz′əm) ***n.*** **1** the aesthetic principles of ancient Greece and Rome **2** adherence to these principles **3** knowledge of classical literature and art **—clas′si·cist *n.***

class·i·fied (klas′ə fīd′) ***adj.*** **1** confidential and available only to authorized persons **2** of classified advertising **—*n.*** [*pl.*] a section of classified advertisements

classified advertising advertising arranged according to subject, under such listings as *help wanted* **—classified advertisement**

clas·si·fy (klas′ə fī′) ***vt.*** **-fied′, -fy′ing** **1** to arrange in classes according to a system **2** to designate (government documents) to be secret or restricted to use by authorized persons only **—clas′si·fi′a·ble *adj.*** **—clas′si·fi·ca′tion *n.*** **—clas′si·fi′er *n.***

class′mate′ ***n.*** a member of the same class at a school or college

class′room′ ***n.*** a room in a school or college in which classes are taught

class′y ***adj.*** **-i·er, -i·est** [Inf.] first-class, esp. in style; elegant **—class′i·ness *n.***

clat·ter (klat′ər) ***vi., vt.*** ⟦ME *clateren*⟧ to make or cause to make a clatter **—*n.*** **1** a rapid succession of loud, sharp noises **2** a tumult; hubbub

clause (klôz) ***n.*** ⟦< L *claudere,* to close⟧ **1** a group of words containing a subject and a finite verb: see DEPENDENT CLAUSE, INDEPENDENT CLAUSE **2** a provision in a document **—claus′al *adj.***

claus·tro·pho·bi·a (klôs′trə fō′bē ə) ***n.*** ⟦< L *claustrum,* enclosed place + -PHOBIA⟧ an abnormal fear of being in an enclosed or confined place **—claus′tro·pho′bic *adj.***

clav·i·chord (klav′i kôrd′) ***n.*** ⟦< L *clavis,* key + *chorda,* string⟧ a stringed musical instrument with a keyboard, predecessor of the piano

clav·i·cle (klav′i kəl) ***n.*** ⟦< L *clavis,* key⟧ a bone connecting the breastbone with the shoulder blade

cla·vier (klə vir′; *for 1, also* klā′vē ər) ***n.*** ⟦Fr < L *clavis,* key⟧ **1** the keyboard of an organ, piano, etc. **2** any stringed keyboard instrument

claw (klô) ***n.*** ⟦OE *clawu*⟧ **1** a sharp, hooked nail on an animal's or bird's foot **2** the pincers of a lobster, etc. **—*vt., vi.*** to scratch, clutch, tear, etc. with or as with claws

clay (klā) ***n.*** ⟦OE *clæg*⟧ **1** a firm, plastic earth, used in making bricks, etc. **2** *a*) earth *b*) the human body **—clay′ey, clay′i·er, clay′i·est, *adj.***

clean (klēn) ***adj.*** ⟦OE *clæne*⟧ **1** *a*) free from dirt and impurities; unsoiled *b*) free from disease, radioactivity, pollutants, etc. **2** morally pure **3** fair; sportsmanlike **4** neat and tidy **5** well-formed **6** clear **7** thorough **—*adv.*** [Inf.] completely **—*vt., vi.*** to make or be made clean **—clean up** **1** to make neat **2** [Inf.] to finish **3** [Slang] to make much profit **—come clean** [Slang] to confess **—clean′ly *adv.*** **—clean′ness *n.***

clean′-cut′ ***adj.*** **1** with a sharp edge or outline **2** well-formed **3** trim, neat, etc.

clean′er ***n.*** a person or thing that cleans; specif., one who dry-cleans clothing

clean·ly (klen′lē) ***adj.*** **-li·er, -li·est** **1** keeping oneself or one's surroundings clean **2** always kept clean **—clean′li·ness *n.***

clean room a room designed to be nearly 100% free of dust, pollen, etc.

cleanse (klenz) ***vt.*** **cleansed, cleans′ing** ⟦OE *clænsian*⟧ to make clean, pure, etc. **—cleans′er *n.***

clean′up′ ***n.*** **1** a cleaning up **2** elimination of crime

clear (klir) ***adj.*** ⟦< L *clarus*⟧ **1** free from clouds; bright **2** transparent **3** easily seen or heard; distinct **4** keen or logical *[*a *clear* mind*]* **5** not obscure; obvious **6** certain; positive **7** free from guilt **8** free from deductions; net **9** free from debt **10** free from obstruction; open **—*adv.*** **1** in a clear way **2** completely **—*vt.*** **1** to make clear **2** to free from impurities, blemishes, etc. **3** to make lucid; clarify **4** to open *[*to *clear* a path*]* **5** to get rid of **6** to prove the innocence of **7** to pass or leap over, by, etc., esp. without touching **8** to be passed or approved by **9** to make as profit **10** *Banking* to pass (a check, etc.) through a clearinghouse **—*vi.*** **1** to become clear **2** *Banking* to pass through a clearinghouse: said as of a check **—clear away** (or **off**) to remove so as to leave a cleared space **—clear out** [Inf.] to depart **—clear up** to make or become clear **—in the clear** **1** free from obstructions **2** [Inf.] guiltless **—clear′ly *adv.*** **—clear′ness *n.***

clear′ance (-əns) ***n.*** the clear space between a moving object and that which it is passing

clear′-cut′ ***adj.*** **1** clearly outlined **2** distinct; definite **3** with all its trees cut down

clear'ing *n.* an area of land cleared of trees

clear'ing·house' *n.* **1** an office maintained by several banks for exchanging checks, balancing accounts, etc. **2** a central office, as for exchanging information

cleat (klēt) *n.* ⟦ME *clete*⟧ a piece of wood or metal fastened to something to strengthen it or give secure footing

cleav·age (klēv'ij) *n.* **1** a cleaving; dividing **2** a cleft; fissure; division

cleave[1] (klēv) *vt., vi.* **cleaved** or **cleft** or **clove**, **cleaved** or **cleft** or **clo'ven**, **cleav'ing** ⟦OE *cleofan*⟧ to divide by a blow; split; sever —**cleav'a·ble** *adj.*

cleave[2] (klēv) *vi.* **cleaved**, **cleav'ing** ⟦OE *cleofian*⟧ **1** to adhere; cling (*to*) **2** to be faithful (*to*)

cleav·er (klēv'ər) *n.* a heavy cutting tool with a broad blade, used by butchers

clef (klef) *n.* ⟦Fr < L *clavis,* key⟧ a symbol used at the beginning of a musical staff to indicate the pitch of the notes

cleft[1] (kleft) *n.* ⟦< OE *cleofan*: see CLEAVE[1]⟧ an opening or hollow made by or as if by cleaving; crack; crevice

cleft[2] (kleft) *vt., vi. alt. pt. & pp. of* CLEAVE[1] —*adj.* split; divided

cleft lip a vertical cleft in the upper lip, often accompanying a CLEFT PALATE

cleft palate a cleft from front to back along the middle of the roof of the mouth, due to incomplete prenatal development

clem·a·tis (klem'ə tis) *n.* ⟦< Gr *klēma,* vine⟧ a vine of the buttercup family, with bright-colored flowers

clem·en·cy (klem'ən sē) *n.* mercy; forbearance

Clem·ens (klem'ənz), **Sam·u·el Lang·horne** (sam'yo͞o əl laŋ'hôrn) (pseud. *Mark Twain*) 1835-1910; U.S. writer & humorist

clem'ent (-ənt) *adj.* ⟦L *clemens*⟧ **1** lenient **2** mild: said as of weather

clench (klench) *vt.* ⟦< OE (*be*)*clencan*, to make cling⟧ **1** to close (the teeth or fist) firmly **2** to grip tightly —*n.* a firm grip

Cle·o·pa·tra (klē'ō pa'trə, klē' ə-) 69?-30 B.C.; queen of Egypt (51-49; 48-30)

clere·sto·ry (klir'stôr'ē) *n., pl.* **-ries** ⟦< ME *cler*, clear + *storie*, story (of a building)⟧ the upper part of a wall, as of a church, having windows for lighting the central space

cler·gy (klur'jē) *n., pl.* **-gies** ⟦see CLERK⟧ ministers, priests, rabbis, etc., collectively

cler'gy·man (-mən) *n., pl.* **-men** (-mən) a member of the clergy; minister, priest, rabbi, etc. —**cler'gy·wom'an**, *pl.* **-wom'en**, *fem.n.*

cler·ic (kler'ik) *n.* a member of the clergy

cler·i·cal (kler'i kəl) *adj.* **1** of the clergy or one of its members **2** of office clerks or their work

cler'i·cal·ism' (-iz'əm) *n.* political power of the clergy —**cler'i·cal·ist** *n.*

clerk (klurk) *n.* ⟦< Gr *klērikos,* a cleric⟧ **1** a lay member of a church with minor duties **2** an office worker who types, files, etc. **3** an official who keeps the records of a court, town, etc. **4** a salesclerk —*vi.* to work as a salesclerk

Cleve·land[1] (klēv'lənd), (**Stephen**) **Gro·ver** (grō'vər) 1837-1908; 22d and 24th president of the U.S. (1885-89; 1893-97)

Cleve·land[2] (klēv'lənd) city and port in NE Ohio: pop. 506,000

clev·er (klev'ər) *adj.* ⟦? < Norw *klöver*⟧ **1** skillful; adroit **2** intelligent; ingenious; smart —**clev'er·ly** *adv.* —**clev'er·ness** *n.*

clev·is (klev'is) *n.* ⟦see CLEAVE[2]⟧ a U-shaped piece of iron with holes for a pin, for attaching one thing to another

clew (klo͞o) *n.* ⟦OE *cliwen*⟧ **1** a ball of thread or yarn **2** *archaic sp. of* CLUE

cli·ché (klē shā') *n.* ⟦Fr < pp. of *clicher,* to stereotype⟧ a trite expression or idea

cli·chéd (klē shād') *adj.* trite; stereotyped

click (klik) *n.* ⟦echoic⟧ a slight, sharp sound like that of a door latch snapping into place —*vi., vt.* to make or cause to make a click

cli·ent (klī'ənt) *n.* ⟦< L *cliens,* follower⟧ **1** a person or company for whom a lawyer, accountant, etc. is acting **2** a customer

cli·en·tele (klī'ən tel') *n.* ⟦< Fr < L *clientela,* patronage⟧ all one's clients or customers, collectively

cliff (klif) *n.* ⟦OE *clif*⟧ a high, steep face of rock

cliff'hang'er or **cliff'-hang'er** *n.* a suspenseful film, story, situation, etc.

cli·mac·ter·ic (klī mak'tər ik, klī'mak ter'ik) *n.* ⟦< Gr *klimax,* ladder⟧ a crucial period in life; esp., menopause —*adj.* crucial

cli·mate (klī'mət) *n.* ⟦< Gr *klima,* region⟧ **1** the prevailing weather conditions of a place **2** a region with reference to its prevailing weather —**cli·mat'ic** (-mat'ik) *adj.*

cli·max (klī'maks') *n.* ⟦L < Gr *klimax,* ladder⟧ **1** the final, culminating element in a series; highest point of interest, excitement, etc. **2** the turning point of action in a drama, etc. **3** an orgasm —*vi., vt.* to reach, or bring to, a climax —**cli·mac'tic** (-mak'tik) *adj.*

climb (klīm) *vi., vt.* **climbed**, **climb'ing** ⟦OE *climban*⟧ **1** to move up by using the feet and, often, the hands **2** to ascend gradually **3** to move (*down, over, along,* etc.) using the hands and feet **4** to grow upward on (a wall, etc.) —*n.* **1** a climbing **2** a thing or place to be climbed —**climb'a·ble** *adj.* —**climb'er** *n.*

clime (klīm) *n.* ⟦see CLIMATE⟧ [Old Poet.] a region, esp. with regard to climate

clinch (klinch) *vt.* ⟦var. of CLENCH⟧ **1** to fasten (a driven nail, etc.) by bending the projecting end **2** to settle (an argument, bargain, etc.) definitely —*vi.* **1** *Boxing* to grip the opponent with the arms so as to hinder punching effectiveness **2** [Slang] to embrace —*n.* a clinching

clinch'er *n.* **1** one that clinches **2** a decisive point, argument, act, etc.

cling (kliŋ) ***vi.*** **clung, cling′ing** ⟦OE *clingan*⟧ **1** to adhere; hold fast, as by embracing **2** to be or stay near **3** to be emotionally attached —**cling′er** ***n.*** —**cling′y, -i·er, -i·est,** ***adj.***

clin·ic (klin′ik) ***n.*** ⟦< Gr *klinē,* bed⟧ **1** the teaching of medicine by treatment of patients in the presence of students **2** a place where medical specialists practice as a group **3** an outpatient department, as in a hospital **4** an intensive session of group instruction, as in a certain skill

clin′i·cal (-i kəl) ***adj.*** **1** of or connected with a clinic or sickbed **2** having to do with the treatment and observation of patients, as distinguished from theoretical study **3** purely scientific —**clin′i·cal·ly** ***adv.***

cli·ni·cian (kli nish′ən) ***n.*** one who practices clinical medicine, psychology, etc.

clink (kliŋk) ***vi., vt.*** ⟦echoic⟧ to make or cause to make a slight, sharp sound, as of glasses striking together —***n.*** **1** such a sound **2** [Inf.] a jail

clink·er (kliŋ′kər) ***n.*** ⟦Du *klinker*⟧ **1** a hard mass of fused stony matter, formed as from burned coal **2** [Slang] a mistake

Clin·ton (klint′′n), **Bill** (bil) (legal name *William Jefferson Clinton;* born *William Jefferson Blythe IV*) 1946- ; 42d president of the U.S. (1993-2001)

clip[1] (klip) ***vt.*** **clipped, clip′ping** ⟦< ON *klippa*⟧ **1** to cut, as with shears **2** to cut short **3** to cut the hair of **4** [Inf.] to hit sharply **5** [Slang] to swindle —***vi.*** to move rapidly —***n.*** **1** a clipping **2** an excerpt from a film, videotape, etc. **3** a rapid pace **4** [Inf.] a quick, sharp blow

clip[2] (klip) ***vi., vt.*** **clipped, clip′ping** ⟦OE *clyppan,* to embrace⟧ to grip tightly; fasten —***n.*** any of various devices that clip, fasten, hold, etc.

clip′board′ ***n.*** a writing board with a hinged clip at the top to hold papers

clip joint [Slang] a nightclub, store, etc. that charges excessive prices

clipped form a shortened form of a word, as *pike* (for *turnpike*) or *fan* (for *fanatic*)

clip·per (klip′ər) ***n.*** **1** [*usually pl.*] a tool for cutting or trimming **2** a sailing ship built for great speed

clip′ping ***n.*** a piece cut out or off, as an item clipped from a newspaper

clique (klik, klēk) ***n.*** ⟦Fr < OFr *cliquer,* make a noise⟧ a small, exclusive circle of people; coterie —**cliqu′ish** ***adj.*** —**cliqu′ish·ly** ***adv.***

clit·o·ris (klit′ər is) ***n., pl.*** **clit′o·ris·es** (-is iz) or **cli·tor·i·des** (kli tôr′i dēz′) ⟦< Gr⟧ a small, sensitive, erectile organ of the vulva

clo·a·ca (klō ā′kə) ***n., pl.*** **-cae** (-sē′, -kē′) or **-cas** ⟦L < *cluere,* to cleanse⟧ a cavity, as in reptiles and birds, into which both the intestinal and the genitourinary tracts empty

cloak (klōk) ***n.*** ⟦< ML *clocca,* bell: from its shape⟧ **1** a loose, usually sleeveless outer garment **2** something that covers or conceals; disguise —***vt.*** **1** to cover with a cloak **2** to conceal

clob·ber (kläb′ər) ***vt.*** ⟦< ?⟧ [Slang] **1** to beat or hit repeatedly **2** to defeat decisively

cloche (klōsh) ***n.*** ⟦Fr, a bell⟧ a woman's closefitting, bell-shaped hat

clock[1] (kläk) ***n.*** ⟦ME *clokke,* orig., clock with bells < ML *clocca,* bell⟧ a device for measuring and indicating time, usually by means of pointers moving over a dial: clocks are not meant to be worn or carried about —***vt.*** to record the time of (a race, etc.) with a stopwatch

clock[2] (kläk) ***n.*** ⟦< ? prec., because of original bell shape⟧ a woven or embroidered ornament on a sock, going up from the ankle

clock radio a radio with a built-in clock that can turn it on or off

clock′wise′ ***adv., adj.*** in the direction in which the hands of a clock rotate

clock′work′ ***n.*** **1** the mechanism of a clock **2** any similar mechanism, with springs and gears —**like clockwork** very regularly

clod (kläd) ***n.*** ⟦OE⟧ **1** a lump, esp. of earth or clay **2** a dull, stupid person —**clod′dish** ***adj.***

clod′hop′per ***n.*** ⟦prec. + HOPPER⟧ **1** a plowman **2** a clumsy, stupid person **3** a coarse, heavy shoe

clog (kläg) ***n.*** ⟦ME *clogge,* lump of wood⟧ **1** anything that hinders or obstructs; hindrance **2** a shoe with a thick, usually wooden, sole —***vt.*** **clogged, clog′ging** **1** to hinder **2** to obstruct (a passage); jam —***vi.*** to become clogged

cloi·son·né (kloi′zə nā′) ***adj.*** ⟦Fr, lit., partitioned⟧ designating enamel work in which the surface decoration is set in hollows formed by thin strips of wire

clois·ter (klois′tər) ***n.*** ⟦< L *claudere,* to close⟧ **1** a monastery or convent **2** monastic life **3** a covered walk along a courtyard wall in a monastery, etc., with an open colonnade —***vt.*** to confine as in a cloister —**clois′tered** ***adj.***

clomp (klämp) ***vi.*** to walk heavily or noisily

clone (klōn) ***n.*** ⟦< Gr *klōn,* a twig⟧ **1** all the descendants derived asexually from a single organism **2** a genetically identical duplicate of an organism, produced by replacing the nucleus of an unfertilized ovum with the nucleus of a body cell from the organism **3** [Inf.] a person or thing very much like another —***vt.*** **cloned, clon′ing** to produce a clone of —**clon′al** ***adj.***

clop (kläp) ***n.*** ⟦echoic⟧ a clattering sound, like hoofbeats —***vi.*** **clopped, clop′ping** to make, or move with, such a sound

close[1] (klōs) ***adj.*** **clos′er, clos′est** ⟦see fol.⟧ **1** confined or confining *[close quarters]* **2** secretive; reserved **3** miserly; stingy **4** warm and stuffy **5** with little space between; near together **6** compact; dense *[close weave]* **7** near to the surface *[a close shave]* **8** intimate; familiar *[a close friend]* **9** strict; careful *[close attention]* **10** nearly alike *[a close resemblance]* **11** nearly equal or even *[a close contest]* —***adv.*** in a close manner —**close′ly** ***adv.*** —

close′ness ***n.***

close[2] (klōz) ***vt.*** **closed, clos′ing** ⟦< L *claudere*, to close⟧ **1** to shut **2** to fill up or stop (an opening) **3** to finish —***vi.*** **1** to undergo shutting **2** to come to an end **3** to come close or together —***n.*** an end or conclusion —**close down** (or **up**) to shut or stop entirely —**close in** to draw near from all directions —**close out** to dispose of (goods) by sale

close call (klōs) [Inf.] a narrow escape from danger: also **close shave**

close-cropped (klōs′kräpt′) ***adj.*** clipped very short *[close-cropped* hair*]*

closed circuit a system for telecasting by cable, etc. only to receivers connected in the circuit —**closed′-cir′cuit** ***adj.***

close·fist·ed (klōs′fis′tid) ***adj.*** stingy

close′fit′ting (-fit′iŋ) ***adj.*** fitting tightly

close′-knit′ (-nit′) ***adj.*** closely united or joined

close·mouthed (klōz′mou*th*d′, -moutht′) ***adj.*** not talking much; taciturn

close′out′ (-out′) ***n.*** a discounted sale of goods no longer carried, or of those of a business being closed down through liquidation

clos·er (klō′zər) ***n.*** a person adept at completing a deal, an assignment, etc. successfully

clos·et (kläz′it) ***n.*** ⟦< L *claudere*, to close⟧ **1** a small room or cupboard for clothes, supplies, etc. **2** a small, private room **3** a state of secrecy —***vt.*** to shut up in a private room for confidential talk

close-up (klōs′up′) ***n.*** a photograph, etc. taken at very close range

clo·sure (klō′zhər) ***n.*** ⟦< L *claudere*, to close⟧ **1** a closing or being closed **2** a finish; end **3** anything that closes **4** CLOTURE

clot (klät) ***n.*** ⟦OE⟧ a soft lump or thickened mass *[*a blood *clot]* —***vt.***, ***vi.*** **clot′ted, clot′ting** to form into a clot or clots; coagulate

cloth (klôth) ***n.***, *pl.* **cloths** (klô*th*z, klôths) ⟦OE *clath*⟧ **1** a woven, knitted, or pressed fabric of fibrous material, as cotton, wool, silk, or synthetic fibers **2** a tablecloth, washcloth, etc. —***adj.*** made of cloth —**the cloth** the clergy collectively

clothe (klō*th*) ***vt.*** **clothed** or **clad, cloth′ing** ⟦see prec.⟧ **1** to provide with or dress in clothes **2** to cover

clothes (klō*th*z, klōz) ***pl.n.*** ⟦OE *clathas*⟧ articles, usually of cloth, for covering, protecting, or adorning the body

clothes′pin′ ***n.*** a small clip for fastening clothes on a line, as for drying

cloth·ier (klō*th*′yər) ***n.*** a dealer in clothes or cloth

cloth·ing (klō′*th*iŋ) ***n.*** **1** clothes; garments **2** a covering

clo·ture (klō′chər) ***n.*** ⟦see CLOSURE⟧ the ending of legislative debate by having the bill put to an immediate vote

cloud (kloud) ***n.*** ⟦OE *clud*, mass of rock⟧ **1** a visible mass of condensed water droplets or ice crystals in the sky **2** a mass of smoke, dust, etc. **3** a crowd; swarm *[*a *cloud* of locusts*]* **4** anything that darkens, obscures, etc. —***vt.*** **1** to darken or obscure as with clouds **2** to make gloomy **3** to sully (a reputation, etc.) —***vi.*** to become cloudy, gloomy, etc. —**under a cloud** under suspicion —**cloud′less** ***adj.*** —**cloud′y, -i·er, -i·est,** ***adj.*** —**cloud′i·ness** ***n.***

cloud′burst′ ***n.*** a sudden, heavy rain

clout (klout) ***n.*** ⟦< OE *clut*, a patch⟧ **1** a blow, as with the hand **2** [Inf.] power, esp. political power —***vt.*** **1** [Inf.] to strike, as with the hand **2** to hit (a ball) hard

clove[1] (klōv) ***n.*** ⟦< L *clavus*, nail: from its shape⟧ **1** the dried flower bud of a tropical evergreen tree, used as a spice **2** the tree

clove[2] (klōv) ***n.*** ⟦OE *clufu*⟧ a segment of a bulb, as of garlic

clove[3] (klōv) ***vt.***, ***vi.*** *alt. pt. of* CLEAVE[1]

clo·ven (klō′vən) ***vt.***, ***vi.*** *alt. pp. of* CLEAVE[1] —***adj.*** divided; split *[*a *cloven* foot*]*

clo·ver (klō′vər) ***n.*** ⟦OE *clafre*⟧ any of various low-growing plants of the pea family, with leaves of three leaflets and small flowers in dense heads

clo′ver·leaf′ ***n.***, *pl.* **-leafs′** a highway interchange with an overpass and curving ramps, allowing traffic to move unhindered in any of four directions

clown (kloun) ***n.*** ⟦< ? Scand⟧ **1** a clumsy or boorish person **2** one who entertains, as in a circus, by antics, jokes, etc. **3** a buffoon —***vi.*** to act as a clown does —**clown′ish** ***adj.***

cloy (kloi) ***vt.*** ⟦< OFr *encloyer*, nail up < L *clavus*, nail⟧ to surfeit with too much of something that is sweet, rich, etc.

cloy′ing ***adj.*** **1** displeasing because of excess *[cloying* sweetness*]* **2** overly sweet or sentimental

club (klub) ***n.*** ⟦< ON *klubba*, cudgel⟧ **1** a heavy stick used as a weapon **2** an implement used to hit the ball in golf **3** *a*) a group of people united for a common purpose *b*) its meeting place **4** *a*) any of a suit of playing cards marked with black figures shaped like leaves of clover (♣) *b*) [*pl.*] this suit —***vt.*** **clubbed, club′bing** to strike as with a club —***vi.*** to unite for a common purpose

club′foot′ ***n.***, *pl.* **-feet′** a congenitally misshapen, often clublike, foot

club′house′ ***n.*** **1** a building used by a club **2** a locker room used by an athletic team

club soda SODA WATER

cluck (kluk) ***vi.*** ⟦echoic⟧ to make a low, sharp, clicking sound, as of a hen calling her chicks —***n.*** this sound

clue (klo͞o) ***n.*** a fact, object, etc. that helps to solve a problem or mystery —***vt.*** **clued, clu′ing** [Inf.] to provide with clues or needed facts: often with *in*

clue′less ***adj.*** [Inf.] **1** stupid **2** uninformed, esp. about a given situation

clump (klump) ***n.*** ⟦< LowG *klump*⟧ **1** a lump; mass **2** a cluster, as of trees **3** the sound of heavy footsteps —***vi.*** **1** to walk heavily **2** to form clumps —

clump'y, **-i·er**, **-i·est**, ***adj.***

clum·sy (klum'zē) ***adj.*** **-si·er**, **-si·est** ⟦ME *clumsid*, numb with cold⟧ **1** lacking grace or skill; awkward **2** awkwardly shaped or made —**clum'si·ly** ***adv.*** —**clum'si·ness** ***n.***

clung (kluŋ) ***vi.*** *pt. & pp. of* CLING

clunk (kluŋk) ***n.*** ⟦echoic⟧ a dull, heavy, hollow sound —***vi.*** to move with a clunk or clunks

clunk'er ***n.*** [Slang] an old machine or automobile in poor repair

clus·ter (klus'tər) ***n.*** ⟦OE *clyster*⟧ a number of persons or things grouped together —***vi.***, ***vt.*** to gather or grow in a cluster

cluster bomb a bomb that explodes in midair and scatters smaller bombs widely

clutch[1] (kluch) ***vt.*** ⟦OE *clyccan*, to clench⟧ to grasp or hold eagerly or tightly —***vi.*** to snatch or seize (*at*) —***n.*** **1** [*usually pl.*] power; control **2** a grasp; grip **3** a device for engaging and disengaging a motor or engine **4** a woman's small purse

clutch[2] (kluch) ***n.*** ⟦< ON *klekja*, to hatch⟧ **1** a nest of eggs **2** a brood of chicks **3** a cluster

clut·ter (klut'ər) ***n.*** ⟦< CLOT⟧ a number of things scattered in disorder; jumble —***vt.*** to put into disorder; jumble: often with *up*

cm *abbrev.* centimeter(s)

Cmdr *abbrev.* Commander

cni·dar·i·an (ni der'ē ən) ***n.*** any of a phylum of invertebrates, as jellyfishes, having stinging cells and a saclike body with only one opening

Co[1] or **co** *abbrev.* **1** company **2** county

Co[2] *Chem. symbol for* cobalt

CO *abbrev.* **1** Colorado **2** Commanding Officer

co- ⟦var. of COM-⟧ *prefix* **1** together **2** equally *[coextensive]* **3** joint or jointly *[copilot]*

C/O or **c/o** *abbrev.* care of

coach (kōch) ***n.*** ⟦after *Kócs*, village in Hungary⟧ **1** a large, covered, four-wheeled carriage **2** a railroad passenger car **3** the lowest-priced class of airline accommodations **4** a bus **5** an instructor or trainer, as of athletes, actors, or singers —***vt.***, ***vi.*** to instruct and train (athletes, actors, etc.)

coach'man (-mən) ***n.***, *pl.* **-men** (-mən) the driver of a coach, or carriage

co·ad·ju·tor (kō aj'ə tər) ***n.*** ⟦< L *co-*, together + *adjuvare*, to help⟧ an assistant, esp. to a bishop

co·ag·u·late (kō ag'yo͞o lāt') ***vt.*** **-lat'ed**, **-lat'ing** ⟦< L *co-*, together + *agere*, to drive⟧ to cause (a liquid) to become somewhat firm; clot —***vi.*** to become coagulated —**co·ag'u·lant** (-lənt) ***n.*** —**co·ag'u·la'tion** ***n.***

coal (kōl) ***n.*** ⟦OE *col*⟧ **1** a black, combustible mineral solid used as fuel **2** a piece (or pieces) of this **3** an ember —***vt.***, ***vi.*** to supply or be supplied with coal —**haul** (or **rake, drag,** or **call**) **over the coals** to criticize sharply

co·a·lesce (kō'ə les') ***vi.*** **-lesced'**, **-lesc'ing** ⟦< L *co-*, together + *alescere*, grow up⟧ to unite into a single body or group —**co'a·les'cence** (-əns) ***n.***

co'a·li'tion (-lish'ən) ***n.*** ⟦see prec.⟧ a combination or alliance, as of factions, esp. a temporary one

coal oil **1** kerosene **2** oil produced from coal, used as a lamp fuel

coal tar a thick, black liquid obtained from the distillation of bituminous coal: used in dyes, medicines, etc.

co-an·chor (kō'aŋ'kər) ***n.*** one of the usually two anchors of a TV or radio newscast

coarse (kôrs) ***adj.*** **coars'er**, **coars'est** ⟦< COURSE in the sense "ordinary or usual order"⟧ **1** of poor quality; common **2** consisting of rather large particles *[coarse sand]* **3** rough; harsh **4** unrefined; vulgar; crude —**coarse'ly** ***adv.*** —**coarse'ness** ***n.***

coars·en (kôr'sən) ***vt.***, ***vi.*** to make or become coarse

coast (kōst) ***n.*** ⟦< L *costa*, rib, side⟧ **1** land alongside the sea; seashore **2** a slide down an incline, as on a sled —***vi.*** **1** to sail near or along a coast **2** to go down an incline, as on a sled **3** to continue in motion on momentum —**coast·al** (kōs'təl) ***adj.***

coast'er ***n.*** **1** a person or thing that coasts **2** a small mat, disk, etc. placed under a glass to protect a table

coaster brake a brake on a bicycle operated by reverse pressure on the pedals

coast guard **1** a governmental force employed to defend a nation's coasts, aid vessels in distress, etc. **2** [**C- G-**] such a branch of the U.S. armed forces

coast'line' ***n.*** the outline of a coast

coat (kōt) ***n.*** ⟦OFr *cote*, a coat⟧ **1** a sleeved outer garment opening down the front **2** the natural covering of an animal or plant **3** a layer of some substance, as paint, over a surface —***vt.*** to cover with a coat or layer

coat'ing ***n.*** a surface coat or layer

coat of arms *pl.* **coats of arms** a group of heraldic emblems, as on a shield, used as the insignia of a family or group

coat'tail' ***n.*** either half of the divided lower back part of a coat

co·au·thor (kō'ô'thər) ***n.*** a joint author; collaborator

coax (kōks) ***vt.***, ***vi.*** ⟦< obs. slang *cokes*, a fool⟧ to urge with or use soft words, flattery, etc. —**coax'er** ***n.*** —**coax'ing·ly** ***adv.***

co·ax·i·al (kō ak'sē əl) ***adj.*** **1** having a common axis **2** designating a double-conductor high-frequency transmission line, as for television

cob (käb) ***n.*** ⟦prob. < LowG⟧ **1** a corncob **2** a short-legged, thickset horse

co·balt (kō'bôlt') ***n.*** ⟦< Ger *kobold*, lit., goblin⟧ a hard, steel-gray, metallic chemical element

cob·ble (käb'əl) ***vt.*** **-bled**, **-bling** ⟦ME < *cobelere*, cobbler⟧ **1** to mend (shoes, etc.) **2** to put together clumsily: often with *up*

cob·bler[1] (käb′lər) ***n.*** ⟦< ?⟧ a kind of deep-dish fruit pie

cob·bler[2] (käb′lər) ***n.*** ⟦ME *cobelere* < ?⟧ one who makes or mends shoes

cob′ble·stone′ ***n.*** a rounded stone formerly much used for paving streets

CO·BOL (kō′bôl′) ***n.*** ⟦*co(mmon) b(usiness) o(riented) l(anguage)*⟧ a computer language using English words, for business applications

co·bra (kō′brə) ***n.*** ⟦< Port⟧ a very poisonous snake of Asia and Africa

cob·web (käb′web′) ***n.*** ⟦ME *coppe,* spider + WEB⟧ **1** a web spun by a spider **2** anything flimsy, gauzy, or ensnaring like this —**cob′web′by *adj.***

co·caine (kō kān′) ***n.*** ⟦< *coca,* tropical shrub from whose leaves it is extracted⟧ a crystalline alkaloid that is habit-forming when used as a stimulant

coc·cus (käk′əs) ***n., pl.*** **coc′ci′** (-sī′) ⟦< Gr *kokkos,* kernel⟧ a spherical bacterium

coc·cyx (käk′siks′) ***n., pl.*** **coc·cy·ges** (käk sī′jēz′) ⟦< Gr *kokkyx,* cuckoo: it is shaped like a cuckoo's beak⟧ a small bone at the base of the spine

co-chair (kō cher′, kō′cher′) ***n.*** one who presides over a meeting, etc. jointly with another —***vt.*** to preside over as cochair

coch·le·a (käk′lē ə) ***n., pl.*** **-ae′** (-ē′) or **-as** ⟦< Gr *kochlias,* snail⟧ the spiral-shaped part of the inner ear —**coch′le·ar *adj.***

cock[1] (käk) ***n.*** ⟦OE *coc*⟧ **1** a rooster or other male bird **2** a faucet or valve **3** *a*) the hammer of a gun *b*) its firing position **4** a jaunty tilt, as of a hat —***vt.*** **1** to tilt jauntily **2** to raise erectly **3** to turn toward **4** to set (a gun) to fire

cock[2] (käk) ***n.*** ⟦ME *cokke*⟧ a small, cone-shaped pile, as of hay

cock·ade (käk ād′) ***n.*** ⟦< OFr *coq,* COCK[1] (*n.* 1)⟧ a rosette, knot of ribbon, etc. worn on the hat as a badge

cock·a·ma·mie (käk′ə mā′mē) ***adj.*** ⟦< *decalcomania*: see DECAL⟧ [Slang] **1** inferior **2** ridiculous

cock′-and-bull′ story an absurd, improbable story

cock·a·too (käk′ə to͞o′) ***n., pl.*** **-toos′** ⟦< Malay *kakatua*⟧ a crested parrot of Australia and the East Indies

cock′a·trice′ (-tris′) ***n.*** ⟦< L *calcare,* to tread⟧ a mythical serpent supposedly able to kill by a look

cocked hat a three-cornered hat with a turned-up brim

cock·er (käk′ər) ***n.*** [Slang] an old man

cock′er·el (-əl) ***n.*** a young rooster, less than a year old

cocker spaniel ⟦< use in hunting woodcock⟧ a small spaniel with long, silky hair and drooping ears

cock′eyed′ ***adj.*** ⟦< COCK[1], *v.* + EYE⟧ **1** cross-eyed **2** [Slang] *a*) awry *b*) silly; foolish *c*) drunk

cock′fight′ ***n.*** a fight between gamecocks, usually wearing metal spurs —**cock′fight′ing *n.***

cock·le (käk′əl) ***n.*** ⟦< Gr *konchē,* mussel⟧ an edible mollusk having two heart-shaped shells —**warm the cockles of someone's heart** to make someone pleased or cheerful

cock·ney (käk′nē) ***n., pl.*** **-neys** ⟦ME *cokenei,* spoiled child, milksop⟧ [*often* **C-**] **1** one born in the East End of London, England, speaking a characteristic dialect **2** this dialect

cock′pit′ ***n.*** **1** an enclosed area for cockfights **2** the space in a small airplane for the crew and passengers, or in a large one for the crew

cock′roach′ ***n.*** ⟦Sp *cucaracha*⟧ an insect with long feelers and a flat, soft body: a household pest

cocks·comb (käks′kōm′) ***n.*** the red, fleshy growth on a rooster's head

cock′sure′ ***adj.*** ⟦COCK[1] + SURE⟧ absolutely sure or self-confident, esp. stubbornly or overbearingly

cock′tail′ ***n.*** ⟦< ?⟧ **1** a mixed alcoholic drink, usually iced **2** an appetizer, as of shrimp or juice

cock′y ***adj.*** **-i·er, -i·est** ⟦< COCK[1] + -Y[2]⟧ [Inf.] jauntily conceited; aggressively self-confident —**cock′i·ly *adv.*** —**cock′i·ness *n.***

co·co (kō′kō′) ***n., pl.*** **-cos′** ⟦Sp < Gr *kokkos,* berry⟧ **1** the coconut palm tree **2** its fruit; coconut

co·coa (kō′kō′) ***n.*** ⟦var. of CACAO⟧ **1** powder made from roasted cacao seeds **2** a drink made of this and sugar, hot milk, etc. **3** a reddish-yellow brown

cocoa butter a yellowish-white fat prepared from cacao seeds

co·co·nut or **co·coa·nut** (kō′kə nut′) ***n.*** the oval fruit of a tropical tree (**coconut palm**), with a hard, brown husk, edible white meat, and a sweet, milky fluid (**coconut milk**) inside

co·coon (kə ko͞on′) ***n.*** ⟦< Fr < ML *coco,* shell⟧ the silky or fibrous case which the larva of certain insects spins about itself for shelter during the pupa stage

cod (käd) ***n., pl.*** **cod** or **cods** ⟦ME⟧ a food fish of northern seas

Cod (käd), **Cape** hook-shaped peninsula in E Massachusetts: 64 mi. long

COD or **cod** *abbrev.* cash, or collect, on delivery

co·da (kō′də) ***n.*** ⟦It < L *cauda,* tail⟧ an added concluding passage, as in music

cod·dle (käd′'l) ***vt.*** **-dled, -dling** ⟦< ?⟧ **1** to cook (esp. eggs in shells) in water not quite boiling **2** to pamper

code (kōd) ***n.*** ⟦< L *codex,* wooden tablet⟧ **1** a systematized body of laws **2** a set of principles, as of ethics **3** a set of signals for sending messages **4** a system of symbols for secret writing, etc. —***vt.*** **cod′ed, cod′ing** to put into code —**cod′er *n.***

co·deine (kō′dēn′) ***n.*** ⟦< Gr *kōdeia,* poppy head⟧ an alkaloid derived from opium: used for pain relief and in cough medicines: also **co′dein′**

co·de·pend·ent or **co-de·pend·ent** (kō′dē pen′dənt) ***adj.*** psychologically influenced by or needing another who is addicted to alcohol, etc. —***n.*** one who is codependent —**co′de·pend′ence** or **co′-de·pend′ence *n.*** —**co′de·pend′en·cy** or **co′-de·pend′en·cy,** *pl.* **-cies, *n.***

co·dex (kō′deks′) ***n.**, pl.* **co·di·ces** (kō′də sēz′, käd′ə-) ⟦L: see CODE⟧ a manuscript volume, esp. of the Scriptures or of a classic text

cod′fish′ ***n.**, pl.* **-fish′** or (for different species) **-fish′es** a cod

codg·er (käj′ər) ***n.*** ⟦prob. var. of CADGER⟧ [Inf.] an elderly fellow, sometimes one who is eccentric

cod·i·cil (käd′i səl) ***n.*** ⟦see CODE⟧ an addition to a will

cod·i·fy (käd′ə fī′) ***vt.*** **-fied′**, **-fy′ing** to arrange (laws, rules, etc.) systematically —**cod′i·fi·ca′tion** ***n.*** —**cod′i·fi′er** ***n.***

cod′-liv′er oil oil from the liver of the cod: it is rich in vitamins A & D

co·ed or **co-ed** (kō′ed′) [Inf.] ***n.*** a young woman attending a coeducational college —***adj.*** **1** coeducational **2** of a coed

co·ed·u·ca·tion (kō′ej′ə kā′shən) ***n.*** an educational system in which students of both sexes attend classes together —**co′ed′u·ca′tion·al** ***adj.***

co·ef·fi·cient (kō′ə fish′ənt) ***n.*** ⟦CO- + EFFICIENT⟧ **1** a factor that contributes to a result **2** a multiplier of a variable or unknown quantity (Ex.: *6* in *6ab*) **3** a number used as a multiplier in measuring some property

coe·len·ter·ate (si len′tər it) ***n.*** ⟦< Gr *koilos,* hollow + *enteron,* intestine⟧ CNIDARIAN

co·e·qual (kō ē′kwəl) ***adj., n.*** equal —**co′e·qual′i·ty** (-ē kwäl′ə tē) ***n.*** —**co·e′qual·ly** ***adv.***

co·erce (kō urs′) ***vt.*** **-erced′**, **-erc′ing** ⟦< L *co-,* together + *arcere,* confine⟧ **1** to restrain by force **2** to compel **3** to enforce —**co·er′cion** (-ur′shən) ***n.*** —**co·er′cive** (-siv) ***adj.***

co·e·val (kō ē′vəl) ***adj., n.*** ⟦< L *co-,* together + *aevum,* age⟧ contemporary

co′ex·ist′ (-ig zist′) ***vi.*** **1** to exist together at the same time or in the same place **2** to live together peacefully, despite differences —**co′ex·ist′ence** ***n.*** —**co′ex·ist′ent** ***adj.***

co′ex·ten′sive (-ik sten′siv) ***adj.*** extending equally in time or space

C of E *abbrev.* Church of England

cof·fee (kôf′ē) ***n.*** ⟦< Ar *qahwa*⟧ **1** a drink made from the roasted, ground, beanlike seeds of a tall tropical shrub of the madder family **2** the seeds, whole or ground, or the shrub **3** light brown

coffee break a brief respite from work when coffee, etc. is taken

cof′fee·cake′ ***n.*** a kind of cake or roll to be eaten as with coffee

cof′fee·house′ ***n.*** a place where coffee is served and people gather for talk, entertainment, etc.

cof′fee·pot′ ***n.*** a container with a spout, for making or serving coffee

coffee shop a small, informal restaurant serving coffee and light refreshments or meals

coffee table a low table, usually in front of a sofa

cof·fer (kôf′ər) ***n.*** ⟦see fol.⟧ **1** a chest for holding money or valuables **2** [*pl.*] a treasury; funds

cof·fin (kôf′in) ***n.*** ⟦< Gr *kophinos,* basket⟧ the case or box in which a dead body is buried

cog (käg) ***n.*** ⟦ME⟧ **1** one of the teeth on the rim of a cogwheel **2** a cogwheel

co·gent (kō′jənt) ***adj.*** ⟦< L *co-,* together + *agere,* to drive⟧ convincingly to the point —**co′gen·cy** ***n.***

cog·i·tate (käj′ə tāt′) ***vi., vt.*** **-tat′ed**, **-tat′ing** ⟦< L⟧ to think deeply (about); ponder —**cog′i·ta′tion** ***n.*** —**cog′i·ta′tive** ***adj.*** —**cog′i·ta′tor** ***n.***

co·gnac (kōn′yak′, kôn′-) ***n.*** ⟦Fr⟧ **1** a brandy from Cognac, France **2** loosely, any brandy

cog·nate (käg′nāt′) ***adj.*** ⟦< L *co-,* together + *gnasci,* to be born⟧ **1** related by family **2** from a common original form, as two words **3** related or similar —***n.*** a cognate person or thing

cog·ni·tion (käg nish′ən) ***n.*** ⟦< L *co-,* together + *gnoscere,* know⟧ **1** the process of knowing, perceiving, etc. **2** an idea, perception, etc. —**cog′ni·tive** (-nə tiv) ***adj.***

cognitive science the study of cognition

cog·ni·za·ble (käg′ni zə bəl) ***adj.*** **1** that can be known or perceived **2** *Law* within the jurisdiction of a court

cog′ni·zance (-zəns) ***n.*** **1** perception or knowledge **2** notice; heed —**cog′ni·zant** ***adj.***

cog·no·men (käg nō′mən) ***n.*** ⟦< L *co-,* with + *nomen,* name⟧ **1** surname **2** any name; esp., a nickname

cog′wheel′ ***n.*** a wheel rimmed with teeth that mesh with those of another wheel, etc., to transmit or receive motion

co·hab·it (kō hab′it) ***vi.*** ⟦< L *co-,* together + *habitare,* dwell⟧ to live together, esp. as if legally married —**co·hab′i·ta′tion** ***n.***

co·heir (kō′er′, kō er′) ***n.*** one who inherits jointly with another or others

co·here (kō hir′) ***vi.*** **-hered′**, **-her′ing** ⟦< L *co-,* together + *haerere,* to stick⟧ **1** to stick together **2** to be connected naturally or logically

co·her′ent (-hir′ənt, -her′-) ***adj.*** **1** sticking together; cohering **2** logically connected and intelligible **3** capable of logical, intelligible speech, thought, etc. —**co·her′ence** ***n.*** —**co·her′ent·ly** ***adv.***

co·he′sion (-hē′zhən) ***n.*** a cohering; tendency to stick together —**co·he′sive** (-hēs′iv) ***adj.***

co·ho (kō′hō′) ***n.**, pl.* **-ho′** or **-hos′** a small Pacific salmon now fished in N U.S. waters

co·hort (kō′hôrt′) ***n.*** ⟦< L *cohors,* enclosure⟧ **1** a band of soldiers **2** any group or band **3** an associate

coif (koif; *for 2 usually* kwäf) ***n.*** **1** ⟦< LL *cofea,* a cap⟧ a closefitting cap **2** ⟦< fol.⟧ a hairstyle

coif·fure (kwä fyoor′) ***n.*** ⟦Fr⟧ **1** a headdress **2** a hairstyle

coil (koil) ***vt., vi.*** ⟦< L *com-,* together + *legere,* gather⟧ to wind into circular or spiral form —***n.*** **1** a series of rings or a spiral, or anything in this form **2** a single turn of a coil **3** *Elec.* a spiral of wire

coin (koin) ***n.*** ⟦< L *cuneus,* a wedge⟧ **1** a piece of stamped metal, issued by a government as money **2** such pieces collectively **—*vt.*** **1** to make (coins) by stamping metal **2** to invent (a new word, phrase, etc.) **—coin′age *n.***

co·in·cide (kō′in sīd′) ***vi.*** **-cid′ed, -cid′ing** ⟦< L *co-,* together + *incidere,* fall upon⟧ **1** to take up the same place in space **2** to occur at the same time **3** to agree exactly

co·in·ci·dence (kō in′sə dəns) ***n.*** **1** a coinciding **2** an accidental, but seemingly planned, occurrence of events, ideas, etc. at the same time **—co·in′ci·dent** or **co·in′ci·den′tal *adj.*** **—co·in′ci·den′tal·ly *adv.***

co·i·tus (kō′it əs) ***n.*** ⟦< L < *co-,* together + *ire,* go⟧ sexual intercourse: also **co·i·tion** (kō ish′ən)

coke[1] (kōk) ***n.*** ⟦< ME *colke,* core⟧ coal from which most of the gases have been removed by heating: used as an industrial fuel

coke[2] (kōk) ***n.*** [Slang] COCAINE

col *abbrev.* column

COL *abbrev.* **1** Colonel **2** cost of living

col- *prefix* COM-: used before *l*

co·la (kō′lə) ***n.*** ⟦< Afr name⟧ **1** an African tree with nuts that yield an extract used in soft drinks and medicine **2** a carbonated soft drink flavored with this extract

col·an·der (kul′ən dər, käl′-) ***n.*** ⟦prob. ult. < L *colum,* strainer⟧ a perforated pan for draining off liquids

cold (kōld) ***adj.*** ⟦OE *cald*⟧ **1** of a temperature much lower than normal, expected, or comfortable **2** not warmed or warmed up **3** unfriendly, indifferent, or depressing **4** devoid of feeling; emotionless **5** *a)* not fresh (said of a hunting scent) *b)* off the track **6** [Inf.] unconscious *[knocked cold]* **7** [Inf.] unlucky or ineffective *[a cold streak in shooting a basketball]* **—*adv.*** [Inf.] **1** completely *[she was stopped cold]* **2** without preparation **—*n.*** **1** lack of heat or warmth **2** cold weather **3** a viral infection of the respiratory tract, causing sneezing, coughing, etc. **—catch** (or **take**) **cold** to become ill with a cold **—have** (or **get**) **cold feet** [Inf.] to be (or become) timid **—in the cold** neglected **—cold′ly *adv.*** **—cold′ness *n.***

cold′blood′ed ***adj.*** **1** having a body temperature that varies with the surrounding air, water, etc., as fish and reptiles **2** cruel or callous

cold cream a creamy preparation for softening and cleansing the skin

cold cuts sliced cold meats and, usually, cheeses

cold front the forward edge of a cold air mass advancing under a warmer mass

cold shoulder [Inf.] a slight; rebuff; snub **—cold′-shoul′der *vt.***

cold sore a sore, caused by a viral infection, consisting of little blisters in or around the mouth during a cold or fever; herpes simplex

cold turkey [Slang] **1** totally and abruptly: said of withdrawal from drugs or tobacco by an addict or user **2** without preparation

cold war an extended period of conflict between nations that does not include direct warfare

cole (kōl) ***n.*** ⟦< L *caulis,* cabbage⟧ any of various plants related to the cabbage; esp., rape

cole′slaw′ (-slô′) ***n.*** ⟦< Du: see prec. & SLAW⟧ a salad of shredded raw cabbage: also **cole slaw**

co·le·us (kō′lē əs) ***n.*** ⟦< Gr *koleos,* a sheath⟧ any of various plants of the mint family with bright-colored leaves

col·ic (käl′ik) ***n.*** ⟦< Gr *kōlon,* colon⟧ **1** acute abdominal pain **2** a condition of infants with frequent crying from discomfort **—col′ick·y *adj.***

col·i·se·um (käl′ə sē′əm) ***n.*** ⟦< L *colosseum*⟧ a large stadium

co·li·tis (kō līt′is) ***n.*** ⟦< COLON[2] + -ITIS⟧ inflammation of the large intestine

coll *abbrev.* **1** collect **2** college

col·lab·o·rate (kə lab′ə rāt′) ***vi.*** **-rat′ed, -rat′ing** ⟦< L *com-,* with + *laborare,* to work⟧ **1** to work together, esp. in some literary or scientific undertaking **2** to cooperate with the enemy **—col·lab′o·ra′tion *n.*** **—col·lab′o·ra′tor *n.***

col·lage (kə läzh′) ***n.*** ⟦Fr, a pasting⟧ an art form in which bits of objects are pasted together on a surface

col·la·gen (käl′ə jən) ***n.*** a fibrous protein in bone and cartilage

col·lapse (kə laps′) ***vi.*** **-lapsed′, -laps′ing** ⟦< L *com-,* together + *labi,* to fall⟧ **1** to fall down or cave in **2** to break down suddenly **3** to fail suddenly in health **4** to fold together compactly **—*vt.*** to make collapse **—*n.*** a collapsing **—col·laps′i·ble *adj.***

col·lar (käl′ər) ***n.*** ⟦< L *collum,* neck⟧ **1** the part of a garment that encircles the neck **2** a band of leather, etc. for an animal's neck **3** anything like a collar **—*vt.*** **1** to put a collar on **2** [Inf.] to seize, as by the collar

col′lar·bone′ ***n.*** CLAVICLE

col·lard (käl′ərd) ***n.*** ⟦< ME⟧ a kind of kale with coarse leaves

col·late (kō′lāt′, kä′-) ***vt.*** **-lat′ed, -lat′ing** ⟦< L *com-,* together + *latus,* brought⟧ **1** to compare (texts, etc.) carefully **2** to put (pages) in proper order **—col·la′tor *n.***

col·lat·er·al (kə lat′ər əl) ***adj.*** ⟦< L *com-,* together + *lateralis,* lateral⟧ **1** parallel or corresponding **2** accompanying or supporting *[collateral evidence]* **3** having the same ancestors but in a different line **4** designating or of security given as a pledge for the repayment of a loan, etc. **—*n.*** **1** a collateral relative **2** collateral security

col·la·tion (kə lā′shən) ***n.*** **1** the act or result of collating **2** a light meal

col·league (käl′ēg′) ***n.*** ⟦< Fr < L *com-,* with + *legare,* appoint as deputy⟧ a fellow worker in the same profession

col·lect (kə lekt′) ***vt.*** ⟦< L *com-,* together + *legere,* gather⟧ **1** to gather together **2** to gather (stamps, etc.) as a hobby **3** to call for and receive (money) for (bills, etc.) **4** to regain control of (oneself) **—*vi.*** to assemble or accumulate **—*adj.*,**

adv. with payment to be made by the receiver *[to telephone someone collect]* **—col·lect'i·ble** or **col·lect'a·ble** ***adj., n.*** **—col·lec'tor** ***n.***

col·lect'ed ***adj.*** **1** gathered together **2** in control of oneself; calm

col·lec'tion ***n.*** **1** a collecting **2** things collected **3** a mass or pile; accumulation **4** money collected

col·lec'tive ***adj.*** **1** formed by collecting **2** of, as, or by a group *[collective effort]* **3** designating a singular noun, as *tribe,* denoting a collection of individuals **—*n.*** **1** any collective enterprise; specif., a collective farm **2** the people who work together in it **3** a collective noun **—col·lec'tive·ly** ***adv.***

collective bargaining negotiation between organized workers and their employer concerning wages, hours, etc.

col·lec'tiv·ism' ***n.*** collective ownership and control **—col·lec'tiv·ist** ***n., adj.*** **— col·lec'tiv·ize', -ized', -iz'ing,** ***vt.*** **—col·lec'ti·vi·za'tion** ***n.***

col·leen (kä lēn') ***n.*** ⟦< Ir *caile,* girl⟧ [Irish] a girl

col·lege (käl'ij) ***n.*** ⟦see COLLEAGUE⟧ **1** a group of individuals with certain powers and duties *[the electoral college]* **2** an institution of higher education that grants degrees **3** any of the schools of a university **4** a school offering specialized instruction *[a business college]* **5** the building or buildings of a college

col·le·gial (kə lē'jəl) ***adj.*** **1** collegiate **2** characterized by consideration and respect among colleagues **—col·le'gi·al'i·ty** (-jē al'ə tē) ***n.***

col·le·gian (kə lē'jən) ***n.*** a college student

col·le'giate (-jit) ***adj.*** of or like a college or college students

col·lide (kə līd') ***vi.*** **-lid'ed, -lid'ing** ⟦< L *com-,* together + *laedere,* to strike⟧ **1** to come into violent contact; crash **2** to conflict; clash

col·lid'er ***n.*** a research device for directing beams of subatomic particles at each other

col·lie (käl'ē) ***n.*** ⟦< ?⟧ a large, long-haired dog, orig. bred as a sheepdog

col·lier (käl'yər) ***n.*** ⟦< ME: see COAL & -IER⟧ [Chiefly Brit.] **1** a coal miner **2** a coal freighter

col'lier·y ***n., pl.*** **-ies** [Chiefly Brit.] a coal mine and its buildings, etc.

col·li·sion (kə lizh'ən) ***n.*** **1** a colliding **2** a clash or conflict

col·lo·cate (käl'ə kāt') ***vt.*** **-cat'ed, -cat'ing** ⟦< L *com-,* together + *locare,* to place⟧ to arrange; esp., to set side by side **—col'lo·ca'tion** ***n.***

col·lo·di·on (kə lō'dē ən) ***n.*** a nitrocellulose solution that dries into a tough, elastic film

col·loid (käl'oid') ***n.*** ⟦< Gr *kolla,* glue + -OID⟧ a substance made up of tiny particles that remain suspended in a medium of different matter **—col·loi'dal** ***adj.***

col·lo·qui·al (kə lō'kwē əl) ***adj.*** ⟦see COLLOQUY⟧ **1** conversational **2** INFORMAL (sense *d*) **—col·lo'qui·al·ism'** ***n.*** **—col·lo'qui·al·ly** ***adv.***

col·lo'qui·um (-əm) ***n., pl.*** **-qui·a** (-ə) or **-qui·ums** ⟦L: see fol.⟧ an organized conference or seminar on some subject

col·lo·quy (käl'ə kwē) ***n., pl.*** **-quies** ⟦< L *com-,* together + *loqui,* speak⟧ a conversation or conference

col·lude (kə lo͞od') ***vi.*** **-lud'ed, -lud'ing** to act in collusion; conspire

col·lu·sion (kə lo͞o'zhən) ***n.*** ⟦< L *com-,* with + *ludere,* to play⟧ a secret agreement for fraudulent or illegal purpose; conspiracy **—col·lu'sive** (-siv) ***adj.*** **—col·lu'sive·ly** ***adv.***

co·logne (kə lōn') ***n.*** ⟦< Fr *eau de cologne,* lit., water of Cologne, city in Germany⟧ a perfumed toilet water made of alcohol and aromatic oils

Co·logne (kə lōn') city in W Germany, on the Rhine: pop. 962,000

Co·lom·bi·a (kə lum'bē ə) country in NW South America: 440,829 sq. mi.; pop. 29,482,000 **—Co·lom'bi·an** ***adj., n.***

co·lon[1] (kō'lən) ***n.*** ⟦< Gr *kōlon,* verse part⟧ a mark of punctuation (:) used before a long quotation, explanation, example, series, etc. and after the salutation of a formal letter

co·lon[2] (kō'lən) ***n., pl.*** **-lons** or **-la** (-lə) ⟦< Gr *kolon*⟧ that part of the large intestine extending from the cecum to the rectum

colo·nel (kur'nəl) ***n.*** ⟦< It *colonna,* (military) column⟧ a military officer ranking just above a lieutenant colonel

co·lo·ni·al (kə lō'nē əl) ***adj.*** **1** of, in, or having a colony **2** [*often* **C-**] of the thirteen British colonies that became the U.S. **—*n.*** an inhabitant of a colony

co·lo'ni·al·ism' ***n.*** the system by which a country maintains foreign colonies, esp. for economic exploitation **—co·lo'ni·al·ist** ***n., adj.***

col·o·nist (käl'ə nist) ***n.*** a settler or inhabitant of a colony

col'o·nize' (-nīz') ***vt., vi.*** **-nized', -niz'ing** **1** to found a colony (in) **2** to settle in a colony **—col'o·ni·za'tion** ***n.*** **—col'o·niz'er** ***n.***

col·on·nade (käl'ə nād') ***n.*** ⟦< L *columna,* column⟧ *Archit.* a row of columns, as along the side of a building

co·lon·os·co·py (kō'lən äs'kə pē) ***n.*** an examination of the inside of the colon using a fiber-optic device

col·o·ny (käl'ə nē) ***n., pl.*** **-nies** ⟦< L *colere,* cultivate⟧ **1** *a)* a group of settlers in a distant land, under the jurisdiction of their native land *b)* the region settled **2** any territory ruled over by a distant state **3** a community of the same nationality or pursuits, as within a city **4** *Biol.* a group living or growing together

col·o·phon (käl'ə fən, -fän') ***n.*** ⟦LL < Gr *kolophōn,* top⟧ a publisher's emblem

col·or (kul'ər) ***n.*** ⟦L⟧ **1** the property of reflecting light of a particular visible wavelength: the *colors* of the spectrum are red, orange, yellow, green, blue, indigo, and violet **2** any coloring matter; dye; pigment **3** color of the face or skin **4** [*pl.*] a colored badge, etc. to identify the wearer **5** [*pl.*] a flag **6** outward appearance **7** vivid quality **—*vt.*** **1** to give color to; paint, dye, etc. **2** to change the color of **3** to alter, as by distorting *[to color a story]* **—*vi.*** **1** to become colored **2** to change color **3** to blush or flush **4** to draw or color pictures with wax crayons **—show one's (true) colors** to reveal one's true self

Col·o·rad·o (käl′ə rad′ō, -rä′dō) Mountain State of the W U.S.: 103,729 sq. mi.; pop. 3,294,000; cap. Denver: abbrev. *CO* **—Col′o·rad′an *adj.*, *n.***

Colorado Springs city in central Colorado: site of the U.S. Air Force Academy: pop. 280,000

col·or·ant (kul′ər ənt) ***n.*** a coloring agent

col′or·a′tion (-ā′shən) ***n.*** a coloring

col·o·ra·tu·ra (kul′ə rə toor′ə) ***n.*** ⟦It⟧ **1** brilliant runs, trills, etc., used to display a singer's skill **2** a soprano capable of singing such music: also **coloratura soprano**

col′or·blind′ *adj.* **1** unable to distinguish certain colors or any colors **2** not influenced by considerations of race **—col′or·blind′ness *n.***

co·lo·rec·tal (kō′lə rek′təl) ***adj.*** of the colon and rectum

col·ored (kul′ərd) ***adj.*** **1** having color **2** *a*) non-Caucasoid *b*) [Old-fashioned] BLACK (*adj.* 2)

col′or·fast′ *adj.* with color not subject to fading or running

col′or·ful *adj.* **1** full of color **2** picturesque, vivid, etc. **—col′or·ful·ly *adv.* —col′or·ful·ness *n.***

col′or·ing *n.* **1** anything applied to impart color; pigment, etc. **2** the way a thing is colored **3** false appearance

col′or·less *adj.* **1** without color **2** lacking interest; dull **—col′or·less·ly *adv.* —col′or·less·ness *n.***

color line the barrier of social, political, and economic restrictions imposed on blacks or other nonwhites: also **color bar**

co·los·sal (kə läs′əl) ***adj.*** enormous in size, degree, etc.; astonishingly great **—co·los′sal·ly *adv.***

co·los·sus (kə läs′əs) ***n.***, *pl.* **-si′** (-ī′) or **-sus·es** ⟦< Gr⟧ **1** a gigantic statue **2** anything huge or important

co·los·to·my (kə läs′tə mē) ***n.***, *pl.* **-mies** a surgical construction of an artificial anal opening from the colon

co·los·trum (kə läs′trəm) ***n.*** ⟦L⟧ fluid secreted by the mammary glands just after a birth

col·our (kul′ər) ***n.***, ***vt.***, ***vi.*** *Brit. sp. of* COLOR

colt (kōlt) ***n.*** ⟦OE⟧ a young male horse, etc.

colt′ish *adj.* of or like a colt; esp., frisky, frolicsome, etc. **—colt′ish·ly *adv.***

Co·lum·bi·a (kə lum′bē ə, -byə) **1** capital of South Carolina: pop. 98,000 **2** river flowing from Canada through Washington, & along the Washington-Oregon border into the Pacific

col·um·bine (käl′əm bīn′) ***n.*** ⟦< L *columbinus,* dovelike⟧ a plant of the buttercup family, having dainty, spurred flowers of various colors

Co·lum·bus[1] (kə lum′bəs), **Chris·to·pher** (kris′tə fər) 1451?-1506; It. explorer: discovered America (1492)

Columbus[2] **1** capital of Ohio, in the central part: pop. 633,000 **2** city in W Georgia: pop. 179,000

col·umn (käl′əm) ***n.*** ⟦< L *columna*⟧ **1** a slender upright structure, usually a supporting member in a building **2** anything like a column *[the spinal column]* **3** a file formation of troops, etc. **4** any of the vertical sections of printed matter on a page **5** a feature article appearing regularly in a newspaper, etc. **—co·lum·nar** (kə lum′nər) ***adj.***

col·um·nist (käl′əm nist′) ***n.*** a writer of a COLUMN (sense 5)

Com *abbrev.* **1** Commissioner **2** Committee

com- ⟦< L *com-*, with⟧ *prefix* with, together: also used as an intensive

co·ma (kō′mə) ***n.*** ⟦< Gr *kōma*, deep sleep⟧ a period of deep, prolonged unconsciousness caused by injury or disease

co·ma·tose (kō′mə tōs′, käm′ə-) ***adj.*** **1** of, like, or in a coma **2** lethargic

comb (kōm) ***n.*** ⟦< OE *camb*⟧ **1** a thin strip of hard rubber, plastic, etc., with teeth, used to arrange or clean the hair **2** any similar tool, as for cleaning and straightening wool, flax, etc. **3** a red, fleshy outgrowth on the head, as of a rooster **4** a honeycomb **—*vt.*** **1** to arrange, etc. with a comb **2** to search thoroughly

com·bat (kəm bat′; *for n. & adj.*, käm′ bat′) ***vi.*** **-bat′ed** or **-bat′ted**, **-bat′ing** or **-bat′ting** ⟦< Fr < L *com-*, with + *battuere,* to fight⟧ to fight, contend, or struggle **—*vt.*** to fight or actively oppose **—*n.*** **1** armed fighting; battle **2** any struggle or conflict **—*adj.*** of or for military combat **—com·bat′ant *adj.*, *n.***

combat fatigue a psychiatric condition involving anxiety, depression, etc., as after prolonged combat in warfare

com·bat′ive *adj.* ready or eager to fight

comb′er *n.* **1** one that combs **2** a large wave that breaks on a beach, etc.

com·bi·na·tion (käm′bə nā′shən) ***n.*** **1** a combining or being combined **2** a thing formed by combining **3** an association of persons, firms, etc. for a common purpose **4** the series of numbers to which a dial is turned on a lock (**combination lock**) to open it

com·bine (kəm bīn′; *for n.* käm′bīn′) ***vt.***, ***vi.*** **-bined′**, **-bin′ing** ⟦< L *com-*, together + *bini*, two by two⟧ to join into one, as by blending; unite **—*n.*** **1** a machine for harvesting and threshing grain **2** an association of persons, corporations, etc. for commercial or political purposes **—com·bin′er *n.***

comb′ings *pl.n.* loose hair, wool, etc. removed in combing

combining form a word form occurring only in compounds and derivatives (Ex.: *cardio-* in *cardiograph*)

com·bo (käm′bō′) ***n.***, *pl.* **-bos′** **1** [Inf.] a combination **2** a small jazz ensemble

com·bust (kəm bust′) ***vi.*** to burn

com·bus·ti·ble (kəm bus′tə bəl) ***adj.*** that can burn; flammable —**com·bus′ti·bil′i·ty** ***n.*** —**com·bus′ti·bly** ***adv.***

com·bus′tion (-chən) ***n.*** ⟦< L *com-*, intens. + *urere*, to burn⟧ the act or process of burning

come (kum) ***vi.*** **came, come, com′ing** ⟦< OE *cuman*⟧ **1** to move from "there" to "here" **2** to arrive or appear **3** to extend; reach **4** to happen **5** to occur mentally *[*the answer *came* to me*]* **6** to occur in a certain order *[*after 8 *comes* 9*]* **7** to be derived or descended **8** to be a native or resident: with *from [*to *come* from Ohio*]* **9** to be caused; result **10** to proceed or progress (*along*) **11** to become *[*to *come* loose*]* **12** to be available *[*it *comes* in four sizes*]* **13** to amount (*to*) —***interj.*** used to express irritation, impatience, etc. —**come about 1** to happen **2** to turn about —**come across** (or **upon**) to meet or find by chance —**come along 1** to appear or arrive **2** to proceed or succeed —**come around** (or **round**) **1** to recover **2** to yield —**come by** to get; gain —**come down with** to contract (a flu, etc.) —**come into 1** to enter into **2** to inherit —**come off 1** to become detached **2** to end up **3** [Inf.] to prove effective, etc. —**come out 1** to be disclosed **2** to make a debut **3** to end up **4** to reveal that one is homosexual —**come out for** to announce endorsement of —**come through 1** to complete something successfully **2** [Inf.] to do or give what is wanted —**come to** to recover consciousness —**come up** to arise, as a point in a discussion —**how come?** [Inf.] why?

come′back′ ***n.*** **1** a return to a previous state or position, as of power **2** a witty answer; retort

co·me·di·an (kə mē′dē ən) ***n.*** **1** an actor who plays comic parts **2** an entertainer who tells jokes —**co·me′di·enne′** (-en′) ***fem.n.***

co·me′dic (-dik) ***adj.*** having to do with comedy

come′down′ ***n.*** a loss of status

com·e·dy (käm′ə dē) ***n.***, *pl.* **-dies** ⟦< Gr *kōmos*, revel + *aeidein*, sing⟧ **1** a humorous play, etc. with a nontragic ending **2** an amusing event

come·ly (kum′lē) ***adj.*** **-li·er, -li·est** ⟦< OE *cymlic*⟧ attractive; fair —**come′li·ness** ***n.***

come′-on′ ***n.*** [Slang] an inducement

co·mes·ti·ble (kə mes′tə bəl) ***n.*** ⟦< L *com-*, intens. + *edere*, to eat⟧ [*usually pl.*] food

com·et (käm′it) ***n.*** ⟦< Gr *komē*, hair⟧ a small, frozen mass of dust and gas revolving around the sun: as it nears the sun it vaporizes, usually forming a long, luminous tail

come·up·pance (kum′up′əns) ***n.*** [Inf.] deserved punishment

com·fit (kum′fit, käm′-) ***n.*** ⟦< L *com-*, with + *facere*, do⟧ a candied fruit, nut, etc.

com·fort (kum′fərt) ***vt.*** ⟦< L *com-*, intens. + *fortis*, strong⟧ to soothe in distress or sorrow; console —***n.*** **1** relief from distress, etc. **2** one that comforts **3** a state of, or thing that provides, ease and quiet enjoyment —**com′fort·ing** ***adj.*** —**com′fort·less** ***adj.***

com·fort·a·ble (kumf′tər bəl, kum′fərt ə bəl) ***adj.*** **1** providing comfort **2** at ease in body or mind **3** [Inf.] sufficient to satisfy *[*a *comfortable* salary*]* —**com′fort·a·bly** ***adv.***

com′fort·er ***n.*** **1** one that comforts **2** a quilted bed covering

comfort station a public toilet or restroom

com·fy (kum′fē) ***adj.*** **-fi·er, -fi·est** [Inf.] comfortable

com·ic (käm′ik) ***adj.*** **1** of comedy **2** amusing; funny —***n.*** **1** a comedian **2** the humorous element in art or life **3** *a*) COMIC STRIP *b*) [*pl.*] a section of comic strips *c*) a comic book

com′i·cal (-i kəl) ***adj.*** causing amusement; humorous; funny —**com′i·cal′i·ty** (-kal′ə tē) ***n.*** —**com′i·cal·ly** ***adv.***

comic strip a series of cartoons telling a humorous or adventurous story, as in a newspaper or in a booklet (**comic book**)

com·ing (kum′iŋ) ***adj.*** **1** approaching; next **2** showing promise of being successful, etc. —***n.*** arrival or approach

com·i·ty (käm′ə tē) ***n.*** ⟦< L *comis*, polite⟧ civility

comm *abbrev.* **1** commission **2** committee

com·ma (käm′ə) ***n.*** ⟦< Gr *komma*, clause⟧ a mark of punctuation (,) used to indicate a slight separation of sentence elements

com·mand (kə mand′) ***vt.*** ⟦< L *com-*, intens. + *mandare*, entrust⟧ **1** to give an order to; direct **2** to have authority over; control **3** to have for use *[*to *command* a fortune*]* **4** to deserve and get *[*to *command* respect*]* **5** to control (a position); overlook —***vi.*** to have authority —***n.*** **1** an order; direction **2** controlling power or position **3** mastery **4** military or naval force, or district, under a specified authority

com·man·dant (käm′ən dant′, -dänt′) ***n.*** a commanding officer, as of a fort

com′man·deer′ (-dir′) ***vt.*** ⟦see COMMAND⟧ **1** to seize (property) for military or government use **2** [Inf.] to take forcibly

com·mand′er ***n.*** **1** one who commands **2** *U.S. Navy* an officer ranking just above a lieutenant commander

commander in chief *pl.* **commanders in chief** the supreme commander of the armed forces of a nation

com·mand′ing ***adj.*** **1** having authority **2** impressive **3** very large

com·mand′ment ***n.*** a command; specif., any of the TEN COMMANDMENTS

com·man·do (kə man′dō) ***n.***, *pl.* **-dos** or **-does** ⟦Afrik < Port⟧ a member of a small military force trained to operate within enemy territory

command post the field headquarters of a military unit, from which operations are directed

com·mem·o·rate (kə mem′ə rāt′) ***vt.*** **-rat′ed, -rat′ing** ⟦< L *com-*, intens. + *memorare*, remind⟧ **1** to honor the memory of, as by a ceremony 2 to serve as a memorial to —**com·mem'o·ra'tion** *n.* —**com·mem'o·ra'tor** *n.*

com·mem'o·ra·tive (-rə tiv, -rāt'iv) *adj.* commemorating —*n.* a stamp or coin marking an event, honoring a person, etc.

com·mence (kə mens') *vi., vt.* **-menced', -menc'ing** ⟦< L *com-,* together + *initiare,* begin⟧ to begin; start

com·mence'ment *n.* 1 a beginning; start 2 the ceremony of conferring degrees or diplomas at a school

com·mend (kə mend') *vt.* ⟦see COMMAND⟧ 1 to put in the care of another; entrust 2 to recommend 3 to praise —**com·mend'a·ble** *adj.* —**com·mend'a·bly** *adv.* —**com·men·da·tion** (käm'ən dā'shən) *n.*

com·mend·a·to·ry (kə men'də tôr'ē) *adj.* praising or recommending

com·men·su·ra·ble (kə men'shoor ə bəl, -sər-) *adj.* ⟦< L *com-,* together + *mensura,* measurement⟧ measurable by the same standard or measure

com·men'su·rate (-shoor it, -sər-) *adj.* ⟦see prec.⟧ 1 equal in measure or size; coextensive 2 proportionate 3 commensurable

com·ment (käm'ent') *n.* ⟦< L *com-,* intens. + *meminisse,* remember⟧ 1 an explanatory or critical note 2 a remark or observation 3 talk; gossip —*vi.* to make a comment or comments

com·men·tar·y (käm'ən ter'ē) *n., pl.* **-ies** a series of explanatory notes or remarks

com'men·tate' (-tāt') *vi.* **-tat'ed, -tat'ing** to perform as a commentator

com'men·ta'tor (-tāt'ər) *n.* one who reports and analyzes events, trends, etc., as on television

com·merce (käm'ərs) *n.* ⟦< L *com-,* together + *merx,* merchandise⟧ trade on a large scale, as between countries

com·mer·cial (kə mur'shəl) *adj.* 1 of commerce or business 2 made or done for profit —*n. Radio, TV* a paid advertisement —**com·mer'cial·ism'** *n.* —**com·mer'cial·ly** *adv.*

com·mer'cial·ize' (-īz') *vt.* **-ized', -iz'ing** to make use of mainly for profit —**com·mer'cial·i·za'tion** *n.*

com·min·gle (kə miŋ'gəl) *vt., vi.* **-gled, -gling** to mingle together

com·mis·er·ate (kə miz'ər āt') *vi.* **-at'ed, -at'ing** ⟦< L *com-,* intens. + *miserari,* to pity⟧ to sympathize (*with*) —**com·mis'er·a'tion** *n.*

com·mis·sar (käm'ə sär') *n.* ⟦Russ *komissar*⟧ the head of any former U.S.S.R. COMMISSARIAT (sense 2): now called *minister*

com'mis·sar'i·at (-ser'ē ət) *n.* ⟦Fr < L: see COMMIT⟧ 1 an army branch providing food and supplies 2 a government department in the U.S.S.R.: now called *ministry*

com'mis·sar'y (-ser'ē) *n., pl.* **-ies** ⟦see COMMIT⟧ 1 a store, as in an army camp, where food and supplies are sold 2 a restaurant in a movie or TV studio

com·mis·sion (kə mish'ən) *n.* ⟦see COMMIT⟧ 1 *a*) an authorization to perform

certain duties or tasks *b*) a document giving such authorization *c*) the authority so granted 2 that which one is authorized to do 3 a group of people appointed to perform specified duties 4 a committing; doing 5 a percentage of money from sales, allotted to an agent, etc. 6 *Mil. a*) an official certificate conferring rank *b*) the rank conferred —*vt.* 1 to give a commission to 2 to authorize 3 to put (a ship or boat) into service —**in** (or **out of**) **commission** in (or not in) working order

commissioned officer an officer in the armed forces holding a commission

com·mis'sion·er *n.* 1 a person authorized to do certain things by a commission or warrant 2 a member of a COMMISSION (*n.* 3) 3 an official in charge of a government bureau, etc. 4 a person selected to regulate and control a professional sport, an amateur league, etc.

com·mit (kə mit') *vt.* **-mit'ted, -mit'ting** ⟦< L *com-,* together + *mittere,* send⟧ 1 to deliver for safekeeping; entrust; consign 2 to put in custody or confinement *[committed to prison]* 3 to do or perpetrate (a crime) 4 to bind, as by a promise; pledge —*vi.* [Inf.] to make a pledge: often with *to* —**com·mit'ment** *n.* —**com·mit'tal** *n.*

com·mit·tee (kə mit'ē) *n.* ⟦see prec.⟧ a group of people chosen to report or act upon a certain matter —**com·mit'tee·man** (-mən), *pl.* **-men,** *n.* —**com·mit'tee·wom'an,** *pl.* **-wom'en,** *fem.n.*

com·mode (kə mōd') *n.* ⟦Fr < L: see COM- & MODE⟧ 1 a chest of drawers 2 a toilet

com·mod·i·fy (kə mäd'ə fī') *vt.* **-fied', -fy'ing** to treat like or make into a mere commodity —**com·mod'i·fi·ca'tion** *n.*

com·mo·di·ous (kə mō'dē əs) *adj.* ⟦see COMMODE⟧ spacious; roomy

com·mod·i·ty (kə mäd'ə tē) *n., pl.* **-ties** ⟦see COMMODE⟧ 1 any useful thing 2 anything bought and sold 3 [*pl.*] basic products, as of agriculture

com·mo·dore (käm'ə dôr') *n.* ⟦see COMMAND⟧ *U.S. Navy* [Historical] an officer ranking just above a captain

com·mon (käm'ən) *adj.* ⟦< L *communis*⟧ 1 belonging to or shared by each or all 2 general; widespread 3 familiar; usual 4 not of the upper classes *[the common people]* 5 vulgar; coarse 6 designating a noun (as *book*) that refers to any of a group —*n.* [*sometimes pl.*] land owned or used by all the inhabitants of a place —**in common** shared by each or all —**com'mon·ly** *adv.*

com'mon·al·ty (-əl tē) *n.* the common people; public: also **com'mon·al'i·ty** (-al'ə tē)

common carrier a person or company that transports people or goods for a fee

common denominator 1 a common multiple of the denominators of two or more fractions 2 a characteristic, etc. held in common

com'mon·er *n.* a person not of the nobility; one of the common people

common law the law based on custom,

usage, and judicial decisions

com'mon-law' marriage *Law* a marriage not solemnized by religious or civil ceremony

common market an association of countries for closer economic union

common multiple *Math.* a multiple of each of two or more quantities

com'mon·place' ***n.*** **1** a platitude **2** anything common or ordinary **—*adj.*** trite or ordinary

common pleas *Law* in some States, a court having jurisdiction over civil and criminal trials

com'mons ***pl.n.*** **1** the common people **2** [C-] HOUSE OF COMMONS **3** [*often with sing. v.*] a room, building, etc. for dining, as at a college

common sense good sense or practical judgment **—com'mon-sense'** ***adj.***

common stock stock in a company without the privileges of preferred stock, but usually giving its owner a vote

com'mon·weal' (-wēl') ***n.*** the public good; general welfare

com'mon·wealth' (-welth') ***n.*** **1** the people of a nation or state **2** a democracy or republic **3** a federation of states **—the Commonwealth** association of independent nations united under the British crown for purposes of consultation and mutual assistance

Commonwealth of Independent States a loose confederation of countries that were part of the U.S.S.R.

com·mo·tion (kə mō'shən) ***n.*** ⟦< L *com-*, together + *movere*, to move⟧ **1** violent motion **2** confusion; bustle

com·mu·nal (kə myōōn'əl, käm'yə nəl) ***adj.*** **1** of a commune **2** of the community; public **3** marked by common ownership of property **—com·mu'nal·ize', -ized', -iz'ing,** ***vt.*** **—com·mu'nal·ly** ***adv.***

com·mune[1] (kə myōōn') ***vi.*** **-muned', -mun'ing** ⟦< OFr *comuner*, to share⟧ **1** to talk together intimately **2** to be in close rapport

com·mune[2] (käm'yōōn') ***n.*** ⟦< L *communis*, common⟧ **1** the smallest administrative district of local government in some European countries **2** a small group of people living communally

com·mu·ni·ca·ble (kə myōō'ni kə bəl) ***adj.*** that can be communicated, as an idea, or transmitted, as a disease **—com·mu'ni·ca·bil'i·ty** ***n.***

com·mu'ni·cant (-kənt) ***n.*** one who receives Holy Communion

com·mu·ni·cate (kə myōō'ni kāt') ***vt.*** **-cat'ed, -cat'ing** ⟦< L *communicare*⟧ **1** to impart; transmit **2** to give (information, etc.) **—*vi.*** **1** to give or exchange information **2** to have a meaningful relationship **3** to be connected, as rooms **—com·mu'ni·ca'tor** ***n.***

com·mu'ni·ca'tion ***n.*** **1** a transmitting **2** *a*) a giving or exchanging of information, etc. *b*) a message, letter, etc. **3** a means of communicating **—com·mu'ni·ca'tive** (-kāt'iv, -kə tiv) ***adj.***

com·mun·ion (kə myōōn'yən) ***n.*** ⟦see COMMON⟧ **1** possession in common **2** a communing **3** a Christian denomination **4** [C-] HOLY COMMUNION

com·mu·ni·qué (kə myōō'ni kā', kə myōō'ni kā') ***n.*** ⟦Fr⟧ an official communication

com·mu·nism (käm'yōō niz'əm, -yə-) ***n.*** ⟦see COMMON⟧ **1** any theory or system of common ownership of property **2** [*often* C-] *a*) socialism as formulated by Marx, Lenin, etc. *b*) any government or political movement supporting this

com'mu·nist (-nist) ***n.*** **1** an advocate or supporter of communism **2** [C-] a member of a Communist Party **—*adj.*** of, like, or supporting communism or communists **—com'mu·nis'tic** ***adj.***

com·mu·ni·ty (kə myōō'nə tē) ***n.***, *pl.* **-ties** ⟦see COMMON⟧ **1** *a*) any group living in the same area or having interests, work, etc. in common *b*) such an area **2** the general public **3** a sharing in common

community college a junior college serving a certain community

community service unpaid work for the community

com·mu·ta·tive (kə myōōt'ə tiv, käm'yə tāt'iv) ***adj.*** **1** involving exchange or replacement **2** *Math.* of an operation in which the order of the elements does not affect the result, as, in addition, 3 + 2 = 2 + 3

com·mute (kə myōōt') ***vt.*** **-mut'ed, -mut'ing** ⟦< L *com-*, intens. + *mutare*, to change⟧ **1** to exchange; substitute **2** to change (an obligation, punishment, etc.) to a less severe one **—*vi.*** to travel as a commuter **—*n.*** [Inf.] the trip of a commuter **—com·mu·ta·tion** (käm'yə tā'shən) ***n.***

com·mut'er ***n.*** a person who travels regularly by train, bus, etc. between two locations that are some distance apart

Com·o·ros (käm'ə rōz') country on a group of islands in the W Indian Ocean: 719 sq. mi.; pop. 347,000

comp *abbrev.* **1** comparative **2** compound

com·pact (kəm pakt', käm'pakt; *for n.* käm'pakt) ***adj.*** ⟦< L *com-*, with, together + *pangere*, to fix⟧ **1** closely and firmly packed **2** taking little space **3** terse; concise **—*vt.*** **1** to pack or join firmly together **2** to make by putting together **—*n.*** **1** a small cosmetic case, usually containing face powder and a mirror **2** a relatively small car **3** an agreement; covenant **—com·pact'ly** ***adv.*** **—com·pact'ness** ***n.***

compact disc (or **disk**) a digital disc on which music, data, etc. has been encoded for playing on a device using a laser beam to read the encoded matter

com·pac·tor (kəm pak'tər, käm'pak'tər) ***n.*** a device that compresses trash into small bundles

com·pan·ion (kəm pan'yən) ***n.*** ⟦< L *com-*, with + *panis*, bread⟧ **1** an associate; comrade **2** a person paid to live or travel with another **3** one of a pair or set **—com·pan'ion·a·ble** ***adj.*** **—com·pan'ion·ship'** ***n.***

com·pan′ion·way′ *n.* a stairway leading from one deck of a ship to another

com·pa·ny (kum′pə nē) *n., pl.* **-nies** ⟦see COMPANION⟧ **1** companionship; society **2** a group of people gathered or associated for some purpose **3** a guest or guests **4** a body of troops **5** a ship's crew —**keep company 1** to associate (*with*) **2** to go together, as a couple intending to marry —**part company** to stop associating (*with*)

com·pa·ra·ble (käm′pə rə bəl, kəm par′ ə bəl) *adj.* **1** that can be compared **2** worthy of comparison —**com′pa·ra·bly** *adv.*

com·par·a·tive (kəm par′ə tiv) *adj.* **1** involving comparison **2** not absolute; relative **3** *Gram.* designating the second degree of comparison of adjectives and adverbs —*n. Gram.* the comparative degree [“finer” is the *comparative* of “fine”] —**com·par′a·tive·ly** *adv.*

com·pare (kəm per′) *vt.* **-pared′**, **-par′ing** ⟦< L *com-*, with + *parare*, make equal⟧ **1** to liken (*to*) **2** to examine for similarities or differences **3** *Gram.* to form the degrees of comparison of —*vi.* **1** to be worth comparing (*with*) **2** to make comparisons —**beyond** (or **past** or **without**) **compare** incomparably good, bad, great, etc.

com·par·i·son (kəm par′ə sən) *n.* **1** a comparing or being compared **2** likeness; similarity **3** *Gram.* change in an adjective or adverb to show the positive, comparative, and superlative degrees —**in comparison with** compared with

com·part·ment (kəm pärt′mənt) *n.* ⟦< L *com-*, intens. + *partire*, divide⟧ **1** any of the divisions into which a space is partitioned off **2** a separate section or category —**com·part·men·tal·ize** (käm′ pärt ment′′l īz′), **-ized′**, **-iz′ing**, *vt.*

com·pass (kum′pəs; *also* käm′-) *vt.* ⟦< L *com-*, together + *passus*, a step⟧ **1** [Archaic] to go around **2** to surround **3** to understand **4** to achieve or contrive —*n.* **1** [*often pl.*] an instrument with two adjustable legs, for drawing circles, for measuring, etc. **2** a boundary **3** an enclosed area **4** range; scope **5** an instrument for showing direction, esp. one with a swinging magnetic needle pointing north

com·pas·sion (kəm pash′ən) *n.* ⟦< L *com-*, together + *pati*, suffer⟧ deep sympathy; pity —**com·pas′sion·ate** *adj.* —**com·pas′sion·ate·ly** *adv.*

com·pat·i·ble (kəm pat′ə bəl) *adj.* ⟦see prec.⟧ **1** getting along or going well together **2** that can be mixed, used, etc. together effectively —**com·pat′i·bil′i·ty** *n.* —**com·pat′i·bly** *adv.*

com·pa·tri·ot (kəm pā′trē ət) *n.* ⟦see COM- & PATRIOT⟧ a person of one's own country

com·peer (käm′pir′, käm pir′) *n.* ⟦see COM- & PAR⟧ **1** an equal; peer **2** a comrade

com·pel (kəm pel′) *vt.* **-pelled′**, **-pel′ling** ⟦< L *com-*, together + *pellere*, to drive⟧ to force or get by force —**com·pel′ling·ly** *adv.*

com·pen·di·um (kəm pen′dē əm) *n., pl.* **-ums** or **-a** (-ə) ⟦< L *com-*, together + *pendere*, weigh⟧ a concise but comprehensive summary

com·pen·sate (käm′pən sāt′) *vt.* **-sat′ed**, **-sat′ing** ⟦< L *com-*, with + *pendere*, weigh⟧ **1** [Now Rare] to make up for; counterbalance **2** to make suitable payment to —*vi.* to make or serve as amends (*for*) —**com′pen·sa′tion** *n.* —**com·pen·sa·to·ry** (kəm pen′sə tôr′ē) *adj.*

com·pete (kəm pēt′) *vi.* **-pet′ed**, **-pet′ing** ⟦< L *com-*, together + *petere*, to desire⟧ to be in rivalry; contend; vie (*in* a contest, etc.)

com·pe·tence (käm′pə təns) *n.* **1** sufficient means for one's needs **2** ability; fitness **3** legal power, jurisdiction, etc. Also **com′pe·ten·cy** (-tən sē)

com′pe·tent (-tənt) *adj.* ⟦see COMPETE⟧ **1** capable; fit **2** sufficient; adequate **3** having legal competence —**com′pe·tent·ly** *adv.*

com·pe·ti·tion (käm′pə tish′ən) *n.* ⟦L *competitio*⟧ **1** a competing; rivalry **2** a contest; match **3** rivalry in business **4** those against whom one competes —**com·pet·i·tive** (kəm pet′ə tiv) *adj.*

com·pet·i·tor (kəm pet′ət ər) *n.* ⟦L⟧ one who competes, as a business rival

com·pile (kəm pīl′) *vt.* **-piled′**, **-pil′ing** ⟦< L *com-*, together + *pilare*, to compress⟧ **1** to collect and assemble (statistics, facts, etc.) **2** to compose (a book, etc.) of materials from various sources —**com·pi·la·tion** (käm′pə lā′shən) *n.*

com·pla·cen·cy (kəm plā′sən sē) *n.* ⟦< L *com-*, intens. + *placere*, to please⟧ contentment; often, specif., self-satisfaction, or smugness: also **com·pla′cence** —**com·pla′cent** *adj.*

com·plain (kəm plān′) *vi.* ⟦< L *com-*, intens. + *plangere*, to strike⟧ **1** to express pain, displeasure, etc. **2** to find fault **3** to make an accusation —**com·plain′er** *n.*

com·plain′ant (-ənt) *n. Law* a plaintiff

com·plaint′ (-plānt′) *n.* **1** a complaining **2** a cause for complaining **3** an ailment **4** *Law* a formal charge or accusation

com·plai·sant (kəm plā′zənt, -sənt) *adj.* ⟦see COMPLACENCY⟧ willing to please; obliging —**com·plai′sant·ly** *adv.* —**com·plai′sance** *n.*

com·plect′ed (-plek′tid) *adj.* COMPLEXIONED

com·ple·ment (käm′plə mənt; *for v.*, -ment′) *n.* ⟦see fol.⟧ **1** that which completes or perfects **2** the amount needed to fill or complete **3** *Math.* the number of degrees that must be added to a given angle to make it equal 90 degrees —*vt.* to make complete —**com′ple·men′ta·ry** (-men′tə rē) *adj.*

com·plete (kəm plēt′) *adj.* ⟦< L *com-*, intens. + *plere*, fill⟧ **1** whole; entire **2** finished **3** thorough; absolute —*vt.* **-plet′ed**, **-plet′ing 1** to finish **2** to make whole or perfect **3** to successfully execute —**com·plete′ly** *adv.* —**com·plete′ness** *n.* —**com·ple′tion** (-plē′shən) *n.*

com·plex (käm pleks′, käm′pleks′ *for n.* käm′pleks′) *adj.* ⟦< L *com-*, with +

plectere, to weave⟧ **1** consisting of two or more related parts **2** complicated —*n.* **1** a complex whole **2** an assemblage of units, as buildings **3** *Psychoanalysis a)* a group of mainly unconscious impulses, etc. strongly influencing behavior *b)* popularly, an exaggerated dislike or fear —**com·plex′i·ty** *n.*

complex fraction a fraction with a fraction in its numerator or denominator, or in both

com·plex·ion (kəm plek′shən) *n.* ⟦see COMPLEX⟧ **1** the color, texture, etc. of the skin, esp. of the face **2** nature; character; aspect

com·plex′ioned *adj.* having a (specified) complexion *[light-complexioned]*

complex sentence a sentence consisting of an independent clause and one or more dependent clauses

com·pli·ance (kəm plī′əns) *n.* **1** a complying; acquiescence **2** a tendency to give in readily to others Also **com·pli′an·cy** —**com·pli′ant** *adj.*

com·pli·cate (käm′pli kāt′) *vt., vi.* **-cat′ed, -cat′ing** ⟦< L *com-,* together + *plicare,* to fold⟧ to make or become intricate, difficult, or involved —**com′pli·ca′tion** *n.*

com′pli·cat′ed *adj.* intricately involved; hard to solve, analyze, etc.

com·plic·i·tous (kəm plis′ə təs) *adj.* having complicity; implicated: also **com·plic′it** (-it)

com·plic′i·ty (-tē) *n., pl.* **-ties** ⟦see COMPLICATE⟧ partnership in wrongdoing

com·pli·ment (käm′plə mənt; *for v.,* -ment′) *n.* ⟦Fr < L: see COMPLETE⟧ **1** a formal act of courtesy **2** something said in praise **3** [*pl.*] respects —*vt.* to pay a compliment to

com′pli·men′ta·ry (-men′tə rē) *adj.* **1** paying or containing a compliment **2** given free as a courtesy

com·ply (kəm plī′) *vi.* **-plied′, -ply′ing** ⟦see COMPLETE⟧ to act in accordance (*with* a request, order, etc.)

com·po·nent (kəm pō′nənt) *adj.* ⟦see COMPOSITE⟧ serving as one of the parts of a whole —*n.* a part, element, or ingredient

com·port (kəm pôrt′) *vt.* ⟦< L *com-,* together + *portare,* carry⟧ to behave (oneself) in a specified manner —*vi.* to accord (*with*) —**com·port′ment** *n.*

com·pose (kəm pōz′) *vt.* **-posed′, -pos′ing** ⟦< OFr *com-,* with + *poser,* to place⟧ **1** to make up; constitute **2** to put in proper form **3** to create (a musical or literary work) **4** to make calm **5** *a)* to set (type) *b)* to produce (printed matter) as by computer, etc. —*vi.* to create musical works, etc. —**com·pos′er** *n.*

com·posed′ *adj.* calm; self-possessed

com·pos·ite (kəm päz′it) *adj.* ⟦< L *com-,* together + *ponere,* to place⟧ **1** compound **2** *Bot.* designating a large family of plants with flower heads composed of dense clusters of small flowers, including the daisy and the chrysanthemum —*n.* a thing of distinct parts —**com·pos′ite·ly** *adv.*

com·po·si·tion (käm′pə zish′ən) *n.* **1** a composing, esp. of literary or musical works **2** the makeup of a person or thing **3** something composed

com·pos·i·tor (kəm päz′ət ər) *n.* one who sets matter for printing, esp. a typesetter

com·post (käm′pōst′) *n.* ⟦see COMPOSITE⟧ a mixture of decomposing vegetable refuse for fertilizing soil —*vt.* to convert (vegetable matter) into compost

com·po·sure (kəm pō′zhər) *n.* ⟦see COMPOSE⟧ calmness; self-possession

com·pote (käm′pōt′) *n.* ⟦Fr: see COMPOSITE⟧ **1** a dish of stewed fruits **2** a long-stemmed dish, as for candy

com·pound[1] (käm pound′, käm′pound′; *for adj. usually & for n. always,* käm′pound′) *vt.* ⟦see COMPOSITE⟧ **1** to mix or combine **2** to make by combining parts **3** to compute (compound interest) **4** to increase or intensify by adding something new —*adj.* made up of two or more parts —*n.* **1** a thing formed by combining parts **2** a substance containing two or more elements chemically combined —**compound a felony** (or **crime**) to agree, for payment, not to inform about or prosecute a felony (or crime)

com·pound[2] (käm′pound′) *n.* ⟦Malay *kampong*⟧ an enclosed area with a building or buildings in it

compound eye an eye made up of numerous simple eyes functioning collectively, as in insects

compound fracture a fracture in which the broken bone pierces the skin

compound interest interest paid on both the principal and the accumulated unpaid interest

compound sentence a sentence consisting of two or more independent, coordinate clauses

com·pre·hend (käm′prē hend′, -pri-) *vt.* ⟦< L *com-,* with + *prehendere,* seize⟧ **1** to grasp mentally; understand **2** to include; take in; comprise —**com′pre·hen′si·ble** (-hen′sə bəl) *adj.* —**com′pre·hen′sion** *n.*

com′pre·hen′sive (-hen′siv) *adj.* wide in scope; inclusive —**com′pre·hen′sive·ly** *adv.* —**com′pre·hen′sive·ness** *n.*

com·press (kəm pres′; *for n.* käm′pres′) *vt.* ⟦< L *com-,* together + *premere,* to press⟧ to press together and make more compact —*n.* a pad of folded cloth, often wet or medicated, applied to the skin —**com·pressed′** *adj.* —**com·pres′sion** *n.*

com·pres′sor (-pres′ər) *n.* a machine, esp. a pump, for compressing air, gas, etc.

com·prise′ (-prīz′) *vt.* **-prised′, -pris′ing** ⟦see COMPREHEND⟧ **1** to consist of **2** to make up; form

com·pro·mise (käm′prə mīz′) *n.* ⟦< L *com-,* together + *promittere,* to promise⟧ **1** a settlement in which each side makes concessions **2** something midway —*vt., vi.* **-mised′, -mis′ing** **1** to adjust by compromise **2** to lay open to suspicion, disrepute, etc. **3** to weaken

comp·trol·ler (kən trō′lər) *n.* ⟦altered (infl. by Fr *compte,* an account) < CONTROLLER⟧ CONTROLLER (sense 1, esp. in government usage)

com·pul·sion (kəm pul′shən) ***n.*** **1** a compelling or being compelled **2** a driving force **3** an irresistible impulse to perform some act —**com·pul′sive** (-siv) ***adj.*** —**com·pul′sive·ly** ***adv.***

com·pul′so·ry (-sə rē) ***adj.*** **1** obligatory; required **2** compelling

com·punc·tion (kəm puŋk′shən) ***n.*** ⟦< L *com-,* intens. + *pungere,* to prick⟧ an uneasy feeling prompted by guilt; remorse

com·pute (kəm pyo͞ot′) ***vt.*** **-put′ed, -put′ing** ⟦< L *com-,* with + *putare,* reckon⟧ to calculate (an amount, etc.) —***vi.*** **1** to calculate an amount, etc. **2** [Inf.] to make sense —**com·pu·ta·tion** (käm′pyo͞o tā′shən) ***n.***

com·put′er ***n.*** an electronic machine that performs rapid, complex calculations or compiles and correlates data —**com·put′er·ize′, -ized′, -iz′ing,** ***vt.*** —**com·put′er·i·za′tion** ***n.***

com·rade (käm′rad′, -rəd) ***n.*** ⟦< Sp *camarada,* chamber mate < L *camera,* room⟧ **1** a friend; close companion **2** an associate —**com′rade·ship′** ***n.***

con[1] (kän) ***adv.*** ⟦< L *contra*⟧ against —***n.*** an opposing reason, vote, etc.

con[2] (kän) ***vt.*** **conned, con′ning** ⟦< OE *cunnan,* know⟧ to study carefully

con[3] (kän) ***adj.*** [Slang] CONFIDENCE [*a con man*] —***vt.*** **conned, con′ning** [Slang] to swindle or trick

con[4] (kän) ***n.*** [Slang] *short for* CONVICT

con- *prefix* COM-: used before *c, d, g, j, n, q, s, t, v,* and sometimes *f*

con·cat·e·na·tion (kən kat′′n ā′shən, kän-) ***n.*** ⟦< L *com-,* together + *catena,* a chain⟧ a connected series, as of events

con·cave (kän kāv′, kän′kāv′) ***adj.*** ⟦< L *com-,* intens. + *cavus,* hollow⟧ hollow and curved like the inside half of a bowl —**con·cav′i·ty** (-kav′ə tē), *pl.* **-ties,** ***n.***

con·ceal (kən sēl′) ***vt.*** ⟦< L *com-,* together + *celare,* to hide⟧ **1** to hide **2** to keep secret —**con·ceal′ment** ***n.***

con·cede (kən sēd′) ***vt.*** **-ced′ed, -ced′ing** ⟦< L *com-,* with + *cedere,* cede⟧ **1** to admit as true, valid, certain, etc. **2** to grant as a right

con·ceit (kən sēt′) ***n.*** ⟦see CONCEIVE⟧ **1** an exaggerated opinion of oneself, one's merits, etc.; vanity **2** a fanciful expression or notion

con·ceit′ed ***adj.*** vain

con·ceiv·a·ble (kən sēv′ə bəl) ***adj.*** that can be understood, imagined, or believed —**con·ceiv′a·bil′i·ty** ***n.*** —**con·ceiv′a·bly** ***adv.***

con·ceive (kən sēv′) ***vt.*** **-ceived′, -ceiv′ing** ⟦< L *com-,* together + *capere,* take⟧ **1** to become pregnant with **2** to form in the mind; imagine **3** to understand —***vi.*** **1** to become pregnant **2** to form an idea (*of*)

con·cen·trate (kän′sən trāt′) ***vt.*** **-trat′ed, -trat′ing** ⟦< L *com-,* together + *centrum,* center + -ATE[1]⟧ **1** to focus (one's thoughts, efforts, etc.) **2** to increase the strength, density, etc. of —***vi.*** to fix one's attention (*on* or *upon*) —***n.*** a concentrated substance —**con′cen·tra′tion** ***n.***

concentration camp a prison camp for political dissidents, ethnic minorities, etc.

con·cen·tric (kən sen′trik) ***adj.*** ⟦< L *com-,* together + *centrum,* center⟧ having a common center: said of circles —**con·cen′tri·cal·ly** ***adv.***

con·cept (kän′sept′) ***n.*** ⟦see CONCEIVE⟧ an idea or thought; abstract notion

con·cep·tion (kən sep′shən) ***n.*** **1** a conceiving or being conceived in the womb **2** the beginning, as of a process **3** the formulation of ideas **4** a concept **5** an original idea or design

con·cep′tu·al (-cho͞o əl) ***adj.*** of conception or concepts —**con·cep′tu·al·ly** ***adv.***

con·cep′tu·al·ize′ (-īz′) ***vt.*** **-ized′, -iz′ing** to form a concept of —**con·cep′tu·al·i·za′tion** ***n.***

con·cern (kən surn′) ***vt.*** ⟦< L *com-,* with + *cernere,* sift⟧ **1** to have a relation to **2** to engage or involve **3** to cause to feel uneasy —***n.*** **1** a matter of interest to one **2** interest in or regard for a person or thing **3** worry; anxiety **4** a business firm —**as concerns** in regard to —**concern oneself** **1** to busy oneself **2** to be worried

con·cerned′ ***adj.*** **1** involved or interested (*in*) **2** uneasy or anxious

con·cern′ing ***prep.*** relating to; about

con·cert (kän′sərt) ***n.*** ⟦< L *com-,* with + *certare,* strive⟧ **1** mutual agreement; concord **2** a performance of music —**in concert** in unison

con·cert·ed (kən surt′id) ***adj.*** mutually arranged or agreed upon; combined —**con·cert′ed·ly** ***adv.***

con·cer·ti·na (kän′sər tē′nə) ***n.*** ⟦< CONCERT⟧ a small accordion

con·cert·ize (kän′sər tīz′) ***vi.*** **-ized′, -iz′ing** to perform as a soloist in concerts, esp. while touring

con′cert·mas′ter ***n.*** the leader of the first violin section of a symphony orchestra, and often the assistant to the conductor

con·cer·to (kən cher′tō) ***n.,*** *pl.* **-tos** or **-ti** (-tē) ⟦It⟧ a musical composition for one or more solo instruments and an orchestra

con·ces·sion (kən sesh′ən) ***n.*** **1** a conceding **2** a thing conceded; acknowledgment **3** a privilege granted by a government, company, etc., as the right to sell food at a park

con·ces′sion·aire′ (-ə ner′) ***n.*** ⟦< Fr⟧ the holder of a CONCESSION (sense 3)

conch (käŋk, känch) ***n.,*** *pl.* **conchs** (käŋks) or **conch·es** (kän′chiz) ⟦< Gr *konchē*⟧ the spiral, one-piece shell of various sea mollusks

con·ci·erge (kän′sē erzh′; *Fr* kōn syerzh′) ***n.*** ⟦Fr < L *conservus,* fellow slave⟧ a custodian or head porter, as of an apartment house or hotel

con·cil·i·ar (kən sil′ē ər) ***adj.*** of, from, or by means of a council

con·cil′i·ate′ (-āt′) ***vt.*** **-at′ed, -at′ing** ⟦see COUNCIL⟧ to win over; make friendly; placate —**con·cil′i·a′tion** ***n.*** —**con·cil′i·a′tor** ***n.*** —**con·cil′i·a·to′ry** (-ə tôr′ē) ***adj.***

con·cise (kən sīs′) ***adj.*** ⟦< L *com-,* intens.

+ *caedere,* to cut⟧ brief and to the point; short and clear —**con·cise'ly** ***adv.*** —**con·cise'ness** ***n.*** —**con·ci'sion** (-sizh'ən) ***n.***

con·clave (kän'klāv') ***n.*** ⟦< L *com-,* with + *clavis,* a key⟧ **1** a private meeting; specif., one held by cardinals to elect a pope **2** any large convention

con·clude (kən klo͞od') ***vt., vi.*** **-clud'ed, -clud'ing** ⟦< L *com-,* together + *claudere,* to shut⟧ **1** to end; finish **2** to deduce **3** to decide; determine **4** to arrange (a treaty, etc.)

con·clu'sion (-klo͞o'zhən) ***n.*** **1** the end **2** a judgment or opinion formed after thought **3** an outcome **4** a concluding (*of* a treaty, etc.) —**in conclusion** lastly; in closing

con·clu'sive (-siv) ***adj.*** final; decisive —**con·clu'sive·ly** ***adv.*** —**con·clu'sive·ness** ***n.***

con·coct (kən käkt') ***vt.*** ⟦< L *com-,* together + *coquere,* to cook⟧ **1** to make by combining ingredients **2** to devise; plan —**con·coc'tion** ***n.***

con·com'i·tant (-käm'ə tənt) ***adj.*** ⟦< L *com-,* together + *comes,* companion⟧ accompanying; attendant —***n.*** a concomitant thing —**con·com'i·tant·ly** ***adv.***

con·cord (kän'kôrd', käŋ'-) ***n.*** ⟦< L *com-,* together + *cor,* heart⟧ **1** agreement; harmony **2** peaceful relations, as between nations

Con·cord (kän'kôrd; *for 2* käŋ'kərd) **1** city in W California: pop. 111,000 **2** capital of New Hampshire: pop. 36,000

con·cord·ance (kən kôrd''ns) ***n.*** **1** agreement **2** an alphabetical list of the words used in a book, with references to the passages in which they occur

con·cord'ant ***adj.*** agreeing

con·cor·dat (kən kôr'dat') ***n.*** ⟦Fr < L: see CONCORD⟧ a formal agreement

Con·cord (grape) (käŋ'kərd) a large, dark-blue grape used esp. for juice and jelly

con·course (kän'kôrs') ***n.*** ⟦see CONCUR⟧ **1** a crowd; throng **2** an open space for crowds, as in a park **3** a broad thoroughfare

con·crete (kän'krēt', kän krēt') ***adj.*** ⟦< L *com-,* together + *crescere,* grow⟧ **1** having a material existence; real; actual **2** specific, not general **3** made of concrete —***n.*** **1** anything concrete **2** a hard building material made of sand and gravel, bonded together with cement —***vt., vi.*** **-cret'ed, -cret'ing** **1** to solidify **2** to cover with concrete —**con·crete'ly** ***adv.*** —**con·crete'ness** ***n.***

con·cre·tion (kən krē'shən) ***n.*** **1** a solidifying **2** a solidified mass

con·cu·bine (käŋ'kyo͞o bīn', käŋ'-) ***n.*** ⟦< L *com-,* with + *cubare,* lie down⟧ in some societies, a secondary wife, of inferior social and legal status

con·cu·pis·cence (kən kyo͞op'ə səns) ***n.*** ⟦< L *com-,* intens. + *cupiscere,* to desire⟧ strong desire, esp. sexual desire; lust —**con·cu'pis·cent** ***adj.***

con·cur (kən kur') ***vi.*** **-curred', -cur'ring** ⟦< L *com-,* together + *currere,* to run⟧ **1** to occur at the same time **2** to act together **3** to agree (*with*) —**con·cur'rence** ***n.***

con·cur'rent ***adj.*** **1** occurring at the same time **2** acting together **3** *Law* having equal authority —**con·cur'rent·ly** ***adv.***

con·cus·sion (kən kush'ən) ***n.*** ⟦< L *com-,* together + *quatere,* to shake⟧ **1** a violent shaking; shock, as from impact **2** a condition of impaired functioning, esp. of the brain, caused by a violent blow —**con·cus'sive** (-kus'iv) ***adj.***

con·demn (kən dem') ***vt.*** ⟦< L *com-,* intens. + *damnare,* to harm⟧ **1** to disapprove of strongly **2** to declare guilty **3** to inflict a penalty upon **4** to doom **5** to appropriate (property) for public use **6** to declare unfit for use —**con·dem·na·tion** (kän'dem nā'shən) ***n.*** —**con·dem·na·to·ry** (kən dem'nə tôr'ē) ***adj.*** —**con·demn'er** ***n.***

con·dense (kən dens') ***vt.*** **-densed', -dens'ing** ⟦< L *com-,* intens. + *densus,* dense⟧ **1** to make more dense or compact **2** to express in fewer words **3** to change to a denser form, as from gas to liquid —***vi.*** to become condensed —**con·den·sa·tion** (kän'dən sā'shən) ***n.***

condensed milk milk made very thick by evaporation, sweetened with sugar, and then canned

con·dens'er ***n.*** one that condenses; specif., *a*) an apparatus for liquefying gases *b*) a lens for concentrating light rays *c*) *Elec.* CAPACITOR

con·de·scend (kän'di send') ***vi.*** ⟦< L *com-,* together + *descendere,* descend⟧ **1** to be gracious about doing a thing regarded as beneath one's dignity **2** to deal with others in a proud or haughty way —**con'de·scend'ing·ly** ***adv.*** —**con'de·scen'sion** (-sen'shən) ***n.***

con·dign (kən dīn', kän'dīn') ***adj.*** ⟦< L *com-,* intens. + *dignus,* worthy⟧ deserved; suitable: said esp. of punishment

con·di·ment (kän'də mənt) ***n.*** ⟦< L *condire,* to pickle⟧ a seasoning or relish, as pepper, mustard, or a sauce

con·di·tion (kən dish'ən) ***n.*** ⟦< L *com-,* together + *dicere,* to speak⟧ **1** anything required for the performance, completion, or existence of something else; provision or prerequisite **2** *a*) state of being *b*) an illness *c*) a healthy state **3** social position; rank —***vt.*** **1** to stipulate **2** to impose a condition on **3** to bring into fit condition **4** to make accustomed (*to*) —**on condition that** provided that; if —**con·di'tion·er** ***n.***

con·di'tion·al ***adj.*** containing, expressing, or dependent on a condition; qualified —***n.*** *Gram.* a word, clause, tense, etc. expressing a condition —**con·di'tion·al·ly** ***adv.***

con·di'tioned ***adj.*** **1** subject to conditions **2** in a desired condition **3** affected by conditioning **4** accustomed (*to*)

con·do (kän'dō) ***n., pl.*** **-dos** or **-does** *short for* CONDOMINIUM (sense 3)

con·dole (kən dōl') ***vi.*** **-doled', -dol'ing** ⟦< L *com-,* with + *dolere,* grieve⟧ to express sympathy; commiserate —**con·do'lence** ***n.***

con·dom (kän'dəm, kun'-) ***n.*** ⟦< It

guanto, a glove⟧ a thin, latex sheath for the penis, used as a prophylactic or contraceptive

con·do·min·i·um (kän′də min′ē əm) ***n.*** ⟦ult. < L *com-,* with + *dominium,* ownership⟧ **1** joint rule by two or more states **2** the territory ruled **3** one of the units in a multiunit dwelling, each separately owned; also, the dwelling as a whole

con·done (kən dōn′) ***vt.*** **-doned′, -don′ing** ⟦< L *com-,* intens. + *donare,* give⟧ to forgive or overlook (an offense) —**con·don′a·ble** ***adj.***

con·dor (kän′dər, -dôr) ***n.*** ⟦< Sp < AmInd (Peru)⟧ **1** a large vulture of the South American Andes, with a bare head and neck **2** a similar vulture of S California

con·duce (kən do͞os′) ***vi.*** **-duced′, -duc′ing** ⟦< L *com-,* together + *ducere,* to lead⟧ to tend or lead (*to* an effect) —**con·du′cive** ***adj.***

con·duct (kän′dukt′; *for v.* kən dukt′) ***n.*** ⟦< L *com-,* together + *ducere,* to lead⟧ **1** management **2** behavior —***vt.*** **1** to lead **2** to manage **3** to direct (an orchestra, etc.) **4** to behave (oneself) **5** to transmit or convey —**con·duc′tion** (-duk′shən) ***n.*** —**con·duc′tive** ***adj.*** —**con′duc·tiv′i·ty** (-duk tiv′ə tē) ***n.***

con·duct·ance (kən duk′təns) ***n.*** the ability to conduct electricity

con·duc′tor ***n.*** **1** the leader of an orchestra, etc. **2** one in charge of the passengers on a train **3** a thing that conducts electricity, heat, etc.

con·du·it (kän′do͞o it) ***n.*** ⟦see CONDUCE⟧ **1** a channel for conveying fluids **2** a tube for electric wires

cone (kōn) ***n.*** ⟦< Gr *kōnos*⟧ **1** a solid with a circle for its base and a curved surface tapering to a point **2** any cone-shaped object **3** the scaly fruit of evergreen trees **4** a light-sensitive cell in the retina

Co·ney Island (kō′nē) beach & amusement park in Brooklyn, New York

con·fab (kän′fab′) ***n.*** ⟦ult. < L *com-,* together + *fabulari,* to converse⟧ [Inf.] a chat

con·fec·tion (kən fek′shən) ***n.*** ⟦< L *com-,* with + *facere,* make⟧ a candy or other sweet, as ice cream

con·fec′tion·er ***n.*** one who makes or sells candy and other confections

con·fec′tion·er′y (-er′ē) ***n.***, *pl.* **-ies** a confectioner's shop; candy store

con·fed·er·a·cy (kən fed′ər ə sē) ***n.***, *pl.* **-cies** a league or alliance —**the Confederacy** the 11 Southern states that seceded from the U.S. in 1860 & 1861: official name, **Confederate States of America**

con·fed′er·ate (-it; *for v.,* -āt′) ***adj.*** ⟦< L *com-,* together + *foedus,* a league⟧ **1** united in an alliance **2** [C-] of the Confederacy —***n.*** **1** an ally; associate **2** an accomplice **3** [C-] a Southern supporter of the Confederacy —***vt.***, ***vi.*** **-at′ed, -at′ing** to unite in a confederacy; ally

con·fed′er·a′tion ***n.*** a league or federation

con·fer (kən fʉr′) ***vt.*** **-ferred′, -fer′ring** ⟦< L *com-,* together + *ferre,* to bear⟧ to give or bestow —***vi.*** to have a conference —**con·fer·ee** (kän′fər ē′) ***n.*** —**con·fer′rer** ***n.***

con·fer·ence (kän′fər əns) ***n.*** **1** a formal meeting for discussion **2** an association of schools, churches, etc.

con·fer·ral (kən fʉr′əl) ***n.*** the bestowing of an honor, degree, or favor: also **con·fer′ment** ***n.***

con·fess (kən fes′) ***vt.***, ***vi.*** ⟦< L *com-,* together + *fateri,* acknowledge⟧ **1** to admit or acknowledge (a fault, crime, belief, etc.) **2** *a*) to tell (one's sins) to God or a priest *b*) to hear the confession of (a person) (said of a priest) —**confess to** to acknowledge

con·fess′ed·ly (-id lē) ***adv.*** admittedly

con·fes·sion (kən fesh′ən) ***n.*** **1** a confessing **2** something confessed **3** *a*) a creed *b*) a church having a creed

con·fes′sion·al ***n.*** an enclosure in a church, where a priest hears confessions

con·fes′sor ***n.*** **1** one who confesses **2** a priest who hears confessions

con·fet·ti (kən fet′ē) ***n.*** ⟦< It, sweetmeats⟧ bits of colored paper scattered about at celebrations

con·fi·dant (kän′fə dant′, -dänt′) ***n.*** a close, trusted friend —**con′fi·dante′** (-dant′, -dänt′) ***fem.n.***

con·fide (kən fīd′) ***vi.*** **-fid′ed, -fid′ing** ⟦< L *com-,* intens. + *fidere,* to trust⟧ to trust (*in* someone), esp. by sharing secrets —***vt.*** **1** to tell about as a secret **2** to entrust

con·fi·dence (kän′fə dəns) ***n.*** **1** trust; reliance **2** assurance **3** belief in one's own abilities **4** the belief that another will keep a secret **5** something told as a secret —***adj.*** swindling or used so as to swindle

confidence game a swindle effected by one (**confidence man**) who first gains the confidence of the victim

con′fi·dent (-dənt) ***adj.*** full of confidence; specif., *a*) certain *b*) sure of oneself —**con′fi·dent·ly** ***adv.***

con′fi·den′tial (-den′shəl) ***adj.*** **1** secret **2** of or showing trust **3** entrusted with private matters —**con′fi·den′ti·al′i·ty** (-shē al′ə tē) ***n.*** —**con′fi·den′tial·ly** ***adv.***

con·fig·u·ra·tion (kən fig′yə rā′shən) ***n.*** ⟦< L *com-,* together + *figurare,* to form⟧ **1** arrangement of parts **2** contour; outline

con·fig′ure (-yər) ***vt.*** **-ured, -ur·ing** to arrange in a certain way

con·fine (kän′fīn′; *for v.* kən fīn′) ***n.*** ⟦< L *com-,* with + *finis,* an end⟧ [*usually pl.*] a boundary or bounded region —***vt.*** **-fined′, -fin′ing** **1** to keep within limits; restrict **2** to keep shut up, as in prison or a sickbed —**con·fine′ment** ***n.***

con·firm (kən fʉrm′) ***vt.*** ⟦< L *com-,* intens. + *firmare,* strengthen⟧ **1** to make firm **2** to give formal approval to **3** to prove the truth of **4** to cause to undergo religious confirmation

con·fir·ma·tion (kän′fər mā′shən) ***n.*** **1** a confirming **2** something that confirms **3** a Christian ceremony admitting a person to full church membership, etc. **4** a Jewish ceremony reaffirming basic beliefs

con·firmed′ ***adj.*** **1** firmly established; habitual **2** corroborated

con·fis·cate (kän′fis kāt′) ***vt.*** **-cat′ed, -cat′ing** ⟦< L *com-*, together + *fiscus*, treasury⟧ **1** to seize (private property) for the public treasury as a penalty **2** to seize by or as by authority; appropriate —**con′fis·ca′tion** ***n.*** —**con′fis·ca′tor** ***n.***

con·fis·ca·to·ry (kən fis′kə tôr′ē) ***adj.*** of or effecting confiscation

con·fla·gra·tion (kän′flə grā′shən) ***n.*** ⟦< L *com-*, intens. + *flagrare*, to burn⟧ a big, destructive fire

con·flict (kən flikt′; *for n.* kän′flikt′) ***vi.*** ⟦< L *com-*, together + *fligere*, to strike⟧ to be antagonistic, incompatible, etc. —***n.*** **1** a fight or war **2** sharp disagreement, as of interests or ideas **3** emotional disturbance due to conflicting impulses, ideas, etc.

con·flict′ed ***adj.*** in emotional conflict

conflict of interest a conflict between one's obligation to the public, as that of a public officeholder, and one's self-interest

con·flic·tu·al (kən flik′chōō əl) ***adj.*** characterized by or having to do with conflict

con·flu·ence (kän′flōō əns) ***n.*** ⟦< L *com-*, together + *fluere*, to flow⟧ **1** a flowing together, esp. of streams **2** the place of this **3** a crowd —**con′flu·ent** ***adj.***

con·form (kən fôrm′) ***vt.*** ⟦< L *com-*, together + *formare*, to form⟧ **1** to make similar **2** to bring into agreement —***vi.*** **1** to be or become similar **2** to be in agreement **3** to act in accordance with accepted rules, customs, etc. —**con·form′ism′** ***n.*** —**con·form′ist** ***n.***

con·for·ma·tion (kän′fôr mā′shən) ***n.*** **1** a symmetrical arrangement of the parts of a thing **2** the shape or outline, as of an animal

con·form·i·ty (kən fôr′mə tē) ***n.***, *pl.* **-ties** **1** agreement; correspondence; similarity **2** conventional behavior

con·found (kən found′; *for 2* kän′-) ***vt.*** ⟦< L *com-*, together + *fundere*, pour⟧ **1** to confuse or bewilder **2** to damn: a mild oath —**con·found′ed** ***adj.***

con·fra·ter·ni·ty (kän′frə tur′nə tē) ***n.***, *pl.* **-ties** ⟦see CON- & FRATERNAL⟧ **1** brotherhood **2** a religious society, usually of laymen

con·frere (kän′frer′, kän frer′) ***n.*** ⟦OFr⟧ a colleague or associate

con·front (kən frunt′) ***vt.*** ⟦< L *com-*, together + *frons*, forehead⟧ **1** to face, esp. boldly or defiantly **2** to bring face to face (*with*) —**con·fron·ta·tion** (kän′frən tā′shən) ***n.*** —**con′fron·ta′tion·al** ***adj.***

Con·fu·cius (kən fyoo′shəs) 551?-479? B.C.; Chin. philosopher —**Con·fu′cian** (-shən) ***adj., n.***

con·fuse (kən fyōōz′) ***vt.*** **-fused′, -fus′ing** ⟦see CONFOUND⟧ **1** to put into disorder **2** to bewilder or embarrass **3** to mistake the identity of —**con·fus′ed·ly** ***adv.***

con·fu′sion (-fyōō′zhən) ***n.*** a confusing or being confused; specif., disorder, bewilderment, etc.

con·fute (kən fyōōt′) ***vt.*** **-fut′ed, -fut′ing** ⟦L *confutare*⟧ to prove to be in error or false —**con·fu·ta·tion** (kän′fyōō tā′shən) ***n.***

Cong *abbrev.* **1** Congregational **2** Congress

con·geal (kən jēl′) ***vt., vi.*** ⟦< L *com-*, together + *gelare*, freeze⟧ **1** to freeze **2** to thicken; coagulate; jell —**con·geal′ment** ***n.***

con·ge·nial (kən jēn′yəl) ***adj.*** ⟦see CON- & GENIAL⟧ **1** kindred; compatible **2** like-minded; friendly **3** suited to one's needs; agreeable —**con·ge′ni·al′i·ty** (-jē′nē al′ə tē) ***n.*** —**con·ge′nial·ly** ***adv.***

con·gen·i·tal (kən jen′ə təl) ***adj.*** ⟦< L *congenitus*, born together with⟧ existing as such at birth —**con·gen′i·tal·ly** ***adv.***

con·ger (eel) (käŋ′gər) ⟦< Gr *gongros*⟧ a large, edible saltwater eel

con·ge·ries (kän′jə rēz′) ***n.***, *pl.* **-ries′** ⟦L: see fol.⟧ a heap or pile of things

con·gest (kən jest′) ***vt.*** ⟦< L *com-*, together + *gerere*, carry⟧ **1** to cause too much blood, mucus, etc. to accumulate in (a part of the body) **2** to fill to excess; overcrowd —**con·ges′tion** ***n.*** —**con·ges′tive** ***adj.***

con·glom·er·ate (kən gläm′ər āt′; *for adj. & n.*, -it) ***vt., vi.*** **-at′ed, -at′ing** ⟦< L *com-*, together + *glomus*, ball⟧ to form into a rounded mass —***adj.*** **1** formed into a rounded mass **2** formed of substances collected into a single mass, esp. of rock fragments or pebbles cemented together by clay, silica, etc. —***n.*** **1** a conglomerate mass **2** a large corporation formed by merging many diverse companies **3** a conglomerate rock —**con·glom′er·a′tion** ***n.***

Con·go (käŋ′gō) **1** river in central Africa, flowing into the Atlantic **2** **Democratic Republic of the Congo** country in central Africa: 905,365 sq. mi.; pop. 29,671,000: formerly *Belgian Congo* (1908-60), *Zaire* (1971-97) **3** **Republic of the Congo** country in WC Africa, west of Democratic Republic of the Congo: 131,978 sq. mi.; pop. 1,909,000: formerly *People's Republic of the Congo* —**Con·go·lese** (käŋ′gə lēz′) ***adj., n.***

con·grat·u·late (kən grach′ə lāt′) ***vt.*** **-lat′ed, -lat′ing** ⟦< L *com-*, together + *gratulari*, to wish joy⟧ to express to (another) one's pleasure at that person's good fortune, etc.; felicitate [*congratulate* the winner] —**con·grat′u·la·to′ry** (-lə tôr′ē) ***adj.***

con·grat′u·la′tion (-lā′shən) ***n.*** **1** a congratulating **2** [*pl.*] expressions of pleasure in another's good fortune, etc.

con·gre·gate (käŋ′grə gāt′) ***vt., vi.*** **-gat′ed, -gat′ing** ⟦< L *com-*, together + *grex*, a flock⟧ to gather into a crowd; assemble

con′gre·ga′tion (-gā′shən) ***n.*** **1** a gathering; assemblage **2** an assembly of people for religious worship **3** its members

con′gre·ga′tion·al ***adj.*** **1** of or like a congregation **2** [**C-**] of a Protestant denomination in which each member church is self-governing

con·gress (käŋ′grəs) ***n.*** ⟦< L *com-*, together + *gradi,* to walk⟧ **1** an association or society **2** an assembly or conference **3** a legislature, esp. of a republic **4** [**C-**] the legislature of the U.S.; the Senate and the House of Representatives —**con·gres·sion·al** (kən gresh′ə nəl) ***adj.*** —**con·gres′sion·al·ly** ***adv.***

con′gress·man (-mən) ***n.***, *pl.* **-men** (-mən) [*often* **C-**] a member of Congress, esp. of the House of Representatives: also **con′gress·per′son** (-pʉr′sən) —**con′gress·wom′an**, *pl.* **-wom′en**, ***fem.n.***

con·gru·ent (käŋ′grōō ənt, kən grōō′ənt) ***adj.*** ⟦< L *congruere,* agree⟧ **1** corresponding; harmonious **2** of geometric figures of the same shape and size —**con′gru·ence** ***n.***

con·gru·ous (käŋ′grōō əs) ***adj.*** **1** congruent **2** fitting; suitable; appropriate —**con·gru·i·ty** (kän grōō′ə tē), *pl.* **-ties**, ***n.*** —**con′gru·ous·ly** ***adv.*** —**con′gru·ous·ness** ***n.***

con·i·cal (kän′i kəl) ***adj.*** **1** of a cone **2** shaped like a cone Also **con′ic** —**con′i·cal·ly** ***adv.***

con·i·fer (kän′ə fər, kō′nə-) ***n.*** ⟦L < *conus,* cone + *ferre,* to bear⟧ any of a class of cone-bearing trees and shrubs, mostly evergreens —**co·nif·er·ous** (kō nif′ər əs, kə-) ***adj.***

conj *abbrev.* **1** conjugation **2** conjunction

con·jec·ture (kən jek′chər) ***n.*** ⟦< L *com-*, together + *jacere,* to throw⟧ **1** an inferring, theorizing, or predicting from incomplete evidence; guesswork **2** a guess —***vt.***, ***vi.*** **-tured**, **-tur·ing** to guess —**con·jec′tur·al** ***adj.*** —**con·jec′tur·al·ly** ***adv.***

con·join (kən join′) ***vt.***, ***vi.*** ⟦< L *com-*, together + *jungere,* join⟧ to join together —**con·joint′** ***adj.***

con·ju·gal (kän′jə gəl) ***adj.*** ⟦< L *conjunx,* spouse⟧ of marriage or the relation between husband and wife —**con′ju·gal·ly** ***adv.***

con·ju·gate (kän′jə gət; *also, and for v. always,* -gāt′) ***adj.*** ⟦< L *com-*, together + *jugare,* join⟧ joined together; coupled —***vt.*** **-gat′ed**, **-gat′ing** *Gram.* to give in order the inflectional forms of (a verb) —**con′ju·ga′tion** ***n.***

con·junc·tion (kən juŋk′shən) ***n.*** ⟦see CONJOIN⟧ **1** a joining together; union; combination **2** coincidence **3** a word used to connect words, phrases, or clauses (Ex.: *and, but, or, if*) —**con·junc′tive** ***adj.***

con·junc·ti·va (kän′jəŋk tī′və) ***n.***, *pl.* **-vas** or **-vae** (-vē) ⟦see CONJOIN⟧ the mucous membrane covering the inner eyelids and the front of the eyeball

con·junc·ti·vi·tis (kən juŋk′tə vīt′is) ***n.*** inflammation of the conjunctiva

con·junc·ture (kən juŋk′chər) ***n.*** ⟦see CONJOIN⟧ a combination of events creating a crisis

con·jure (kun′jər, kän′-; *for vt.* kən joor′) ***vi.*** **-jured**, **-jur·ing** ⟦< L *com-*, together + *jurare,* swear⟧ **1** to summon a demon or spirit by magic **2** to practice magic —***vt.*** to entreat solemnly —**conjure up** to cause to appear as by magic —**con′ju·ra′tion** (-jə rā′shən) ***n.*** —**con′jur·er** or **con′ju·ror** ***n.***

conk (käŋk, kôŋk) ***n.***, ***vt.*** ⟦< CONCH⟧ [Slang] hit on the head —**conk out** [Slang] **1** to fail suddenly: said as of a motor **2** to fall asleep from fatigue

con man [Slang] a confidence man; swindler

con·nect (kə nekt′) ***vt.*** ⟦< L *com-*, together + *nectere,* fasten⟧ **1** to join (two things together, or one thing *with* or *to* another) **2** to show or think of as related —***vi.*** to join —**con·nec′tor** or **con·nect′er** ***n.***

Con·nect·i·cut (kə net′ə kət) New England state of the U.S.: 4,844 sq. mi.; pop. 3,287,000; cap. Hartford: abbrev. *CT*

con·nec·tion (kə nek′shən) ***n.*** **1** a connecting or being connected **2** a thing that connects **3** a relationship; association **4** *a*) a relative, as by marriage *b*) an influential associate, etc.: *usually used in pl.* **5** [*often pl.*] a transferring from one bus, plane, etc. to another

con·nec′tive (-tiv) ***adj.*** connecting —***n.*** that which connects, esp. a connecting word, as a conjunction

connective tissue body tissue, as cartilage, serving to connect and support other tissues

con·nip·tion (kə nip′shən) ***n.*** ⟦pseudo-L⟧ [*often pl.*] [Inf.] a fit of anger, hysteria, etc.; tantrum: also **conniption fit**

con·nive (kə nīv′) ***vi.*** **-nived′**, **-niv′ing** ⟦< L *conivere,* to wink, connive⟧ **1** to pretend not to look (*at* crime, etc.), thus giving tacit consent **2** to cooperate secretly (*with* someone), esp. in wrongdoing; scheme —**con·niv′ance** ***n.*** —**con·niv′er** ***n.***

con·nois·seur (kän′ə sʉr′) ***n.*** ⟦< Fr < L *cognoscere,* know⟧ one who has expert knowledge and keen discrimination, esp. in the fine arts —**con′nois·seur′ship** ***n.***

con·note (kə nōt′) ***vt.*** **-not′ed**, **-not′ing** ⟦< L *com-*, together + *notare,* to mark⟧ to suggest or convey (associations, etc.) in addition to the explicit, or denoted, meaning —**con·no·ta·tion** (kän′ə tā′shən) ***n.*** —**con′no·ta′tive** or **con′no·ta′tion·al** ***adj.***

con·nu·bi·al (kə nōō′bē əl) ***adj.*** ⟦< L *com-*, together + *nubere,* marry⟧ of marriage; conjugal —**con·nu′bi·al·ly** ***adv.***

con·quer (käŋ′kər) ***vt.*** ⟦< L *com-*, intens. + *quaerere,* seek⟧ **1** to get control of as by winning a war **2** to overcome; defeat —***vi.*** to win —**con′quer·a·ble** ***adj.*** —**con′quer·or** ***n.***

con·quest (käŋ′kwest′) ***n.*** **1** a conquering **2** something conquered **3** a winning of someone's affection

con·quis·ta·dor (kän kwis′tə dôr′, -kēs′-) ***n.***, *pl.* **-dors′** or **con·quis′ta·do′res′** (-dôr′ēz′) ⟦Sp, conqueror⟧ any of the 16th-cent. Spanish conquerors of Mexico, Peru, etc.

con·san·guin·e·ous (kän′saŋ gwin′ē əs) ***adj.*** ⟦see CON- & SANGUINE⟧ having the same ancestor —**con′san·guin′i·ty** ***n.***

con·science (kän′shəns) ***n.*** ⟦< L *com-,* with + *scire,* know⟧ a sense of right and wrong, with an urge to do right —**con′science·less *adj.***

con·sci·en·tious (kän′shē en′shəs) ***adj.*** ⟦see prec. & -OUS⟧ **1** governed by one's conscience; scrupulous **2** painstaking —**con′sci·en′tious·ly *adv.*** —**con′sci·en′tious·ness *n.***

conscientious objector one who for reasons of conscience refuses to take part in warfare

con·scious (kän′shəs) ***adj.*** ⟦< L: see CONSCIENCE⟧ **1** having an awareness (*of* or *that*) **2** able to feel and think; awake **3** aware of oneself as a thinking being **4** intentional *[conscious humor]* **5** known to oneself —**con′scious·ly *adv.***

con′scious·ness *n.* **1** the state of being conscious; awareness **2** the totality of one's thoughts and feelings

con·script (kən skript′; *for n.* kän′ skript′) ***vt.*** ⟦ult. < L *com-,* with + *scribere,* write⟧ to enroll for compulsory service in the armed forces; draft —***n.*** a draftee —**con·scrip′tion *n.***

con·se·crate (kän′si krāt′) ***vt.*** **-crat′ed, -crat′ing** ⟦< L *com-,* together + *sacrare,* make holy⟧ **1** to set apart as holy **2** to devote to sacred or serious use —**con′se·cra′tion *n.***

con·sec·u·tive (kən sek′yo͞o tiv) ***adj.*** ⟦see CONSEQUENCE⟧ following in order, without interruption; successive —**con·sec′u·tive·ly *adv.*** —**con·sec′u·tive·ness *n.***

con·sen·sus (kən sen′səs) ***n.*** ⟦see fol.⟧ **1** an opinion held by all or most **2** general agreement, esp. in opinion

con·sent (kən sent′) ***vi.*** ⟦< L *com-,* with + *sentire,* feel⟧ to agree, permit, or assent —***n.*** **1** permission; approval **2** agreement *[by common consent]* —**con·sen′su·al** (-sen′sho͞o əl) ***adj.***

con·se·quence (kän′si kwens′, -kwəns) ***n.*** ⟦< L *com-,* with + *sequi,* follow⟧ **1** a result; effect **2** importance —**take the consequences** to accept the results of one's actions

con′se·quent′ (-kwent′, -kwənt) ***adj.*** following as a result; resulting —**con′se·quent′ly *adv.***

con′se·quen′tial (-kwen′shəl) ***adj.*** **1** consequent **2** important

con·ser·va·tion (kän′sər vā′shən) ***n.*** **1** a conserving; preservation **2** the official care or management of natural resources —**con′ser·va′tion·ist *n.***

con·serv·a·tive (kən sur′və tiv) ***adj.*** **1** tending to conserve **2** tending to preserve established institutions, etc.; opposed to change **3** moderate; cautious —***n.*** a conservative person —**con·serv′a·tism′ *n.*** —**con·serv′a·tive·ly *adv.***

con·serv′a·to′ry (-tôr′ē) ***n.,*** *pl.* **-ries** **1** a greenhouse **2** a music school

con·serve (kən surv′; *for n., usually* kän′surv′) ***vt.*** **-served′, -serv′ing** ⟦< L *com-,* with + *servare,* keep⟧ to keep from being damaged, lost, or wasted; save —***n.*** [*often pl.*] a jam made of two or more fruits

con·sid·er (kən sid′ər) ***vt.*** ⟦< L *considerare,* observe⟧ **1** to think about in order to understand or decide **2** to keep in mind **3** to be thoughtful of (others) **4** to regard as

con·sid′er·a·ble *adj.* **1** worth considering; important **2** much or large —**con·sid′er·a·bly *adv.***

con·sid′er·ate (-it) ***adj.*** having regard for others and their feelings —**con·sid′er·ate·ly *adv.*** —**con·sid′er·ate·ness *n.***

con·sid′er·a′tion (-ā′shən) ***n.*** **1** the act of considering; deliberation **2** thoughtful regard for others **3** something considered in making a decision **4** a recompense; fee **5** something given, as to make a binding contract —**take into consideration** to keep in mind —**under consideration** being thought over or discussed

con·sid′ered *adj.* arrived at after careful thought

con·sid′er·ing *prep.* in view of; taking into account

con·sign (kən sīn′) ***vt.*** ⟦< L *consignare,* to seal⟧ **1** to hand over; deliver **2** to entrust **3** to assign to an inferior place **4** to send (goods to be sold)

con·sign′ment *n.* **1** a consigning or being consigned **2** a shipment of goods sent to a dealer for sale —**on consignment** with payment due after sale of the consignment

con·sist (kən sist′) ***vi.*** ⟦< L *com-,* together + *sistere,* to stand⟧ **1** to be formed or composed (*of*) **2** to be contained or inherent (*in*)

con·sis′ten·cy (-sis′tən sē) ***n.,*** *pl.* **-cies** **1** firmness or thickness, as of a liquid **2** agreement; harmony **3** conformity with previous practice

con·sis′tent (-tənt) ***adj.*** **1** in agreement or harmony; compatible **2** holding to the same principles or practice —**con·sis′tent·ly *adv.***

con·sis′to·ry (-tə rē) ***n.,*** *pl.* **-ries** ⟦see CONSIST⟧ **1** a church council or court **2** its session

con·so·la·tion (kän′sə lā′shən) ***n.*** **1** comfort; solace **2** one that consoles

con·sole[1] (kən sōl′) ***vt.*** **-soled′, -sol′ing** ⟦< L *com-,* with + *solari,* to comfort, solace⟧ to make feel less sad or disappointed; comfort —**con·sol′a·ble *adj.*** —**con·sol′ing·ly *adv.***

con·sole[2] (kän′sōl′) ***n.*** ⟦Fr⟧ **1** the desklike frame containing the keys, stops, etc. of an organ **2** a radio, television, or phonograph cabinet designed to stand on the floor **3** a control panel for operating aircraft, computers, electronic systems, etc. **4** a raised portion between automobile bucket seats

con·sol·i·date (kən säl′ə dāt′) ***vt., vi.*** **-dat′ed, -dat′ing** ⟦< L *com-,* together + *solidus,* solid⟧ **1** to combine into a single whole; unite **2** to make or become strong or stable *[to consolidate one's power]* —**con·sol′i·da′tion *n.*** —**con·sol′i·da′tor *n.***

con·som·mé (kän′sə mā′) ***n.*** ⟦Fr⟧ a clear, strained meat soup

con·so·nance (kän′sə nəns) ***n.*** ⟦< L *com-,* with + *sonus,* sound⟧ **1** harmony of parts or elements **2** musical harmony **3** repetition of consonants

con'so·nant (-nənt) ***adj.*** in harmony or accord **—*n.*** **1** a speech sound made by obstructing the air stream **2** a letter representing such a sound, as *p, t, l,* or *f*

con·sort (kän'sôrt'; *for v.* kən sôrt') ***n.*** ⟦< L *com-*, with + *sors,* a share⟧ a wife or husband, esp. of a reigning king or queen **—*vt.*, *vi.*** to associate

con·sor·ti·um (kən sôrt'ē əm, -sôr'shē əm) ***n.***, *pl.* **-ti·a** (-ə) ⟦see prec.⟧ an international alliance, as of business firms or banks

con·spec·tus (kən spek'təs) ***n.*** ⟦L: see fol.⟧ **1** a general view **2** a summary; digest

con·spic·u·ous (kən spik'yoo əs) ***adj.*** ⟦< L *com-*, intens. + *specere,* see⟧ **1** easy to see **2** outstanding; striking **—con·spic'u·ous·ly *adv.* —con·spic'u·ous·ness *n.***

con·spir·a·cy (kən spir'ə sē) ***n.***, *pl.* **-cies** **1** a conspiring **2** an unlawful plot **3** a conspiring group

con·spire (kən spīr') ***vi.*** **-spired', -spir'ing** ⟦< L *com-*, together + *spirare,* breathe⟧ **1** to plan together secretly, esp. to commit a crime **2** to work together for any purpose or effect **—con·spir'a·tor** (-spir'ət ər) ***n.*** **—con·spir'a·to'ri·al** (-spir'ə tôr'ē əl) ***adj.***

con·sta·ble (kän'stə bəl) ***n.*** ⟦< LL *comes stabuli,* lit., count of the stable⟧ **1** a peace officer in a small town **2** [Chiefly Brit.] a police officer

con·stab·u·lar·y (kən stab'yə ler'ē) ***n.***, *pl.* **-ies** **1** constables, collectively **2** militarized police

con·stant (kän'stənt) ***adj.*** ⟦< L *com-*, together + *stare,* to stand⟧ **1** not changing; faithful, regular, stable, etc. **2** continual; persistent **—*n.*** anything that does not change or vary **—con'stan·cy *n.* —con'stant·ly *adv.***

Con·stan·tine I (kän'stən tēn', -tīn') A.D. 280?-337; first Christian emperor of Rome (306-337)

Con·stan·ti·no·ple (kän'stan tə nō'pəl) *former name* (A.D. 330-1930) *for* ISTANBUL

con·stel·la·tion (kän'stə lā'shən) ***n.*** ⟦< L *com-*, with + *stella,* star⟧ **1** a visible grouping of stars in the sky, usually named for some object, animal, etc. suggested by its outline **2** any brilliant group or gathering

con·ster·na·tion (kän'stər nā'shən) ***n.*** ⟦< L *consternare,* terrify⟧ great fear or shock

con·sti·pate (kän'stə pāt') ***vt.*** **-pat'ed, -pat'ing** ⟦< L *com-*, together + *stipare,* cram⟧ to cause constipation in

con'sti·pa'tion (-pā'shən) ***n.*** infrequent and difficult movement of the bowels

con·stit·u·en·cy (kən stich'oo ən sē) ***n.***, *pl.* **-cies** the voters in a district

con·stit'u·ent (-ənt) ***adj.*** ⟦see fol.⟧ **1** necessary to the whole; component *[a constituent* part*]* **2** that elects **—*n.*** **1** a voter in a district **2** a component

con·sti·tute (kän'stə to͞ot') ***vt.*** **-tut'ed, -tut'ing** ⟦< L *com-*, together + *statuere,* to set⟧ **1** to establish (a law, government, etc.) **2** to set up (an assembly, etc.) in a legal form **3** to appoint **4** to make up; form **—con'sti·tu'tive *adj.***

con'sti·tu'tion (-to͞o'shən) ***n.*** **1** a constituting **2** structure; organization **3** *a)* the system of basic laws and principles of a government, society, etc. *b)* a document stating these laws and principles *c)* [C-] such a document of the U.S.

con'sti·tu'tion·al (-shə nəl) ***adj.*** **1** of or in one's constitution or structure; basic **2** of or in accordance with the constitution of a government, society, etc. **—*n.*** a walk taken for one's health **—con'sti·tu'tion·al'i·ty** (-shə nal'ə tē) ***n.*** **—con'sti·tu'tion·al·ly *adv.***

con·strain (kən strān') ***vt.*** ⟦< L *com-*, together + *stringere,* draw tight⟧ **1** to confine **2** to restrain **3** to compel

con·straint' (-strānt') ***n.*** **1** confinement or restriction **2** force; compulsion **3** forced, unnatural manner **4** something that constrains

con·strict (kən strikt') ***vt.*** ⟦see CONSTRAIN⟧ to make smaller or narrower by squeezing, etc. **—con·stric'tion *n.***

con·stric'tor (-strik'tər) ***n.*** a snake that kills its prey by squeezing

con·struct (kən strukt'; *for n.* kän' strukt') ***vt.*** ⟦< L *com-*, together + *struere,* pile up⟧ to build, devise, etc. **—*n.*** **1** something put together systematically **2** a concept or theory **—con·struc'tor *n.***

con·struc'tion (-struk'shən) ***n.*** **1** a constructing or manner of being constructed **2** a structure **3** an interpretation, as of a statement **4** the arrangement of words in a sentence

construction paper sturdy, colored paper for children's art projects, etc.

con·struc'tive ***adj.*** leading to improvement; positive

con·strue (kən stro͞o') ***vt.*, *vi.*** **-strued', -stru'ing** ⟦see CONSTRUCT⟧ **1** to analyze the construction of (a sentence) **2** to explain; interpret

con·sul (kän'səl) ***n.*** ⟦< L *consulere,* to deliberate⟧ **1** a chief magistrate of ancient Rome **2** a government official appointed to live in a foreign city and look after his or her country's citizens and business there **—con'sul·ar** (-ər) ***adj.***

con'sul·ate (-it) ***n.*** **1** the position, powers, etc. of a consul **2** the office or residence of a consul

con·sult (kən sult') ***vi.*** ⟦< L *consulere,* consider⟧ to talk things over; confer **—*vt.*** **1** to seek advice or information from **2** to consider **—con·sul·ta·tion** (kän'səl tā'shən) ***n.***

con·sult'ant ***n.*** an expert who gives professional or technical advice **—con·sult'an·cy,** *pl.* **-cies, *n.***

con·sume' (-so͞om') ***vt.*** **-sumed', -sum'ing** ⟦< L *com-*, together + *sumere,* to take⟧ **1** to destroy, as by fire **2** to use up or waste (time, money, etc.) **3** to eat or drink up; devour **4** to engross

con·sum'er ***n.*** one that consumes; specif., one who buys goods or services for personal needs only rather than to produce other goods

con·sum'er·ism' ***n.*** a movement for protecting the consumer against defective products, misleading business practices, etc.

con·sum·mate (kän′sə mit, kən sum′it; *for v.* kän′sə māt′) ***adj.*** ⟦< L *com-,* together + *summa,* a sum⟧ perfect; supreme —***vt.*** **-mat′ed, -mat′ing 1** to complete **2** to complete (a marriage) by sexual intercourse —**con′sum·mate·ly** ***adv.*** —**con·sum·ma·tion** (kän′sə mā′shən) ***n.***

con·sump·tion (kən sump′shən) ***n.*** **1** a consuming or being consumed **2** the using up of goods or services **3** the amount consumed **4** [Old-fashioned] tuberculosis of the lungs

cont *abbrev.* continued

con·tact (kän′takt′) ***n.*** ⟦< L *com-,* together + *tangere,* to touch⟧ **1** a touching or meeting **2** the state of being in association (*with*) **3** a connection **4** an influential acquaintance **5** *short for* CONTACT LENS —***vt.*** **1** to come into contact with **2** to get in touch with —***vi.*** to come into contact

contact lens a tiny, thin correctional lens worn directly over the cornea of the eye

con·ta·gion (kən tā′jən) ***n.*** ⟦see CONTACT⟧ **1** the spreading of disease by contact **2** a contagious disease **3** the spreading of an emotion, idea, etc.

con·ta′gious (-jəs) ***adj.*** **1** spread by contact: said of diseases **2** carrying the causative agent of a contagious disease **3** spreading from person to person —**con·ta′gious·ness** ***n.***

con·tain (kən tān′) ***vt.*** ⟦< L *com-,* together + *tenere,* to hold⟧ **1** to have in it; hold **2** to have the capacity for holding **3** to hold back or restrain within fixed limits —**con·tain′ment** ***n.***

con·tain′er ***n.*** a thing for containing something; box, can, etc.

con·tain′er·ize′ ***vt.*** **-ized′, -iz′ing** to pack (cargo) into huge, standardized containers for shipment

con·tam·i·nant (kən tam′ə nənt) ***n.*** a contaminating substance

con·tam′i·nate′ (-nāt′) ***vt.*** **-nat′ed, -nat′ing** ⟦< L *com-,* together + *tangere,* to touch⟧ to make impure, corrupt, etc. by contact; pollute; taint —**con·tam′i·na′tion** ***n.***

contd *abbrev.* continued

con·tem·plate (kän′təm plāt′) ***vt.*** **-plat′ed, -plat′ing** ⟦< L *contemplari,* observe⟧ **1** to look at or think about intently **2** to expect or intend —***vi.*** to muse —**con′tem·pla′tion** (-plā′shən) ***n.*** —**con·tem·pla·tive** (kən tem′plə tiv, kän′təm plāt′iv) ***adj.***

con·tem·po·ra·ne·ous (kən tem′pə rā′nē əs) ***adj.*** ⟦see fol.⟧ happening in the same period —**con·tem′po·ra·ne′i·ty** (-rə nē′ə tē; -nā′-) ***n.*** —**con·tem′po·ra′ne·ous·ly** ***adv.***

con·tem′po·rar′y (-rer′ē) ***adj.*** ⟦< L *com-,* with + *tempus,* time⟧ **1** living or happening in the same period **2** of about the same age **3** of the present time; modern —***n.,*** ***pl.*** **-ies** one living in the same period as another or others

con·tempt (kən tempt′) ***n.*** ⟦< L *com-,* intens. + *temnere,* to scorn⟧ **1** the feeling one has toward somebody or something one considers low, worthless, etc. **2** the condition of being despised **3** a showing disrespect for the dignity of a court (or legislature)

con·tempt′i·ble ***adj.*** deserving of contempt or scorn; despicable —**con·tempt′i·bly** ***adv.***

con·temp·tu·ous (kən temp′cho͞o əs) ***adj.*** full of contempt; scornful —**con·temp′tu·ous·ly** ***adv.*** —**con·temp′tu·ous·ness** ***n.***

con·tend (kən tend′) ***vi.*** ⟦< L *com-,* together + *tendere,* to stretch⟧ **1** to fight or argue **2** to compete —***vt.*** to assert —**con·tend′er** ***n.***

con·tent[1] (kən tent′) ***adj.*** ⟦see CONTAIN⟧ happy with one's lot; satisfied —***vt.*** to satisfy —***n.*** contentment

con·tent[2] (kän′tent′) ***n.*** ⟦see CONTAIN⟧ **1** [*usually pl.*] *a)* what is in a container *b)* what is dealt with in a book, speech, etc. **2** substance or meaning **3** amount contained

con·tent′ed ***adj.*** satisfied —**con·tent′ed·ly** ***adv.*** —**con·tent′ed·ness** ***n.***

con·ten·tion (kən ten′shən) ***n.*** ⟦see CONTEND⟧ **1** strife, dispute, etc. **2** a point argued for —**in** (or **out of**) **contention** having a (or no) chance to win —**con·ten′tious** ***adj.*** —**con·ten′tious·ly** ***adv.*** —**con·ten′tious·ness** ***n.***

con·tent′ment ***n.*** the state or fact of being contented

con·ter·mi·nous (kən tur′mə nəs) ***adj.*** ⟦< L *com-,* together + *terminus,* an end⟧ **1** having a common boundary **2** contained within the same boundaries —**con·ter′mi·nous·ly** ***adv.***

con·test (kən test′; *for n.* kän′test′) ***vt.*** ⟦< L *com-,* together + *testis,* a witness⟧ **1** to dispute (a point, etc.) **2** to fight for (a position, etc.) —***vi.*** to struggle (*with* or *against*) —***n.*** **1** a fight; struggle **2** a competitive game, race, etc. —**con·test′a·ble** ***adj.***

con·test′ant ***n.*** ⟦Fr⟧ a competitor in a game, etc.

con·text (kän′tekst′) ***n.*** ⟦< L *com-,* together + *texere,* to weave⟧ **1** the parts just before and after a passage, that determine its meaning **2** the whole background or environment, as of an event —**con·tex·tu·al** (kən teks′cho͞o əl) ***adj.***

con·tex·tu·al·ize (kən teks′cho͞o əl īz′) ***vt.*** **-ized′, -iz′ing** to put in a context, as for analysis

con·tig·u·ous (kən tig′yo͞o əs) ***adj.*** ⟦see CONTACT⟧ **1** in contact; touching **2** near or next —**con·ti·gu·i·ty** (kän′tə gyo͞o′ə tē) ***n.***

con·ti·nence (känt′'n əns) ***n.*** ⟦see CONTAIN⟧ self-restraint; specif., a refraining from all sexual activity

con′ti·nent (-ənt) ***adj.*** ⟦see CONTAIN⟧ characterized by continence —***n.*** any of the main large land areas of the earth

con′ti·nen′tal (-ent′'l) ***adj.*** **1** of a continent **2** [*sometimes* **C-**] European **3** [**C-**] of the American colonies at the time of the American Revolution

continental breakfast a light breakfast, as of rolls and coffee

continental drift the theory that continents slowly shift position

continental shelf submerged land sloping out gradually from the edge of a continent

con·tin·gen·cy (kən tin′jən sē) ***n.***, *pl.* **-cies** **1** dependence on chance **2** a possible or chance event

con·tin′gent ***adj.*** ⟦see CONTACT⟧ **1** possible **2** accidental **3** dependent (*on* or *upon* an uncertainty) **—*n.*** **1** a quota, as of troops **2** a part of a larger group

con·tin·u·al (kən tin′yo͞o əl) ***adj.*** **1** repeated often **2** continuous **—con·tin′u·al·ly *adv.***

con·tin′u·ance ***n.*** **1** a continuing **2** duration **3** *Law* postponement or adjournment

con·tin′u·a′tion (-ā′shən) ***n.*** **1** a continuing **2** a beginning again; resumption **3** a part added; sequel

con·tin·ue (kən tin′yo͞o) ***vi.*** **-ued, -u·ing** ⟦< L *continuare*, join⟧ **1** to last; endure **2** to go on in a specified course of action or condition **3** to extend **4** to stay **5** to go on again after an interruption **—*vt.*** **1** to go on with **2** to extend **3** to cause to remain, as in office **4** *Law* to postpone

con·ti·nu·i·ty (kän′tə no͞o′ə tē, -nyo͞o′-) ***n.***, *pl.* **-ties** ⟦OFr < L *continuitas*⟧ **1** a continuous state or quality **2** an unbroken, coherent whole **3** the script for a film, radio or TV program, etc.

con·tin·u·ous (kən tin′yo͞o əs) ***adj.*** going on without interruption; unbroken **—con·tin′u·ous·ly *adv.***

con·tin′u·um (-yo͞o əm) ***n.***, *pl.* **-u·a** (-yo͞o ə) or **-u·ums** ⟦L⟧ a continuous whole, quantity, or series

con·tort (kən tôrt′) ***vt.***, ***vi.*** ⟦< L *com-*, together + *torquere*, to twist⟧ to twist or wrench out of shape; distort **—con·tor′tion *n.***

con·tor′tion·ist ***n.*** one who can contort his or her body into unnatural positions

con·tour (kän′toor′) ***n.*** ⟦Fr < L *com-*, intens. + *tornare*, to turn⟧ the outline of a figure, land, etc. **—*vt.*** to shape to the contour of something **—*adj.*** conforming to the shape or contour of something

con·tra (kän′trə) ***prep.*** against

contra- ⟦< L *contra*⟧ *prefix* against, opposite, opposed to

con·tra·band (kän′trə band′) ***n.*** ⟦< Sp < It⟧ smuggled goods **—*adj.*** illegal to import or export

con·tra·cep·tion (kän′trə sep′shən) ***n.*** ⟦CONTRA- + (CON)CEPTION⟧ prevention of the fertilization of an ovum, as by special devices or drugs **—con′tra·cep′tive *adj.*, *n.***

con·tract (kän′trakt′ *for n. & usually for vt. 1 & vi. 1*; kən trakt′ *for v. generally*) ***n.*** ⟦< L *com-*, together + *trahere*, draw⟧ an agreement between two or more people, esp. a written one enforceable by law **—*vt.*** **1** to undertake by contract **2** to get or incur (a disease, debt, etc.) **3** to reduce in size; shrink **—*vi.*** **1** to make a contract **2** to become smaller

con·trac·tile (kən trak′til) ***adj.*** having the power of contracting

con·trac·tion (kən trak′shən) ***n.*** **1** a contracting or being contracted **2** the shortening of a muscle of the uterus during labor **3** the shortened form of a word or phrase (Ex.: *aren't* for *are not*)

con·trac·tor (kän′trak′tər) ***n.*** a builder, etc. who contracts to do work or supply materials

con·trac·tu·al (kən trak′cho͞o əl) ***adj.*** of, or having the nature of, a contract **—con·trac′tu·al·ly *adv.***

con·tra·dict (kän′trə dikt′) ***vt.*** ⟦< L *contra-*, against + *dicere*, speak⟧ **1** to assert the opposite of (something said) **2** to deny the statement of (someone) **3** to be contrary to **—con′tra·dic′tion *n.* —con′tra·dic′to·ry *adj.***

con′tra·dis·tinc′tion (-dis tiŋk′shən) ***n.*** distinction by contrast

con·trail (kän′trāl′) ***n.*** ⟦CON(DENSATION) + TRAIL⟧ a white trail of water vapor in an aircraft's wake

con·tra·in·di·cate (kän′trə in′di kāt′) ***vt.*** **-cat′ed, -cat′ing** to make (as an indicated medical treatment) inadvisable

con·tral·to (kən tral′tō) ***n.***, *pl.* **-tos** ⟦It: see CONTRA- & ALTO⟧ **1** the range of the lowest female voice; alto **2** a voice or singer with such a range

con·trap·tion (kən trap′shən) ***n.*** ⟦< ?⟧ a contrivance or gadget

con·tra·pun·tal (kän′trə punt′'l) ***adj.*** ⟦< It *contrappunto*, counterpoint⟧ of or characterized by counterpoint

con·trar·i·an (kän trer′ē ən) ***n.***, ***adj.*** (one) characterized by thought or action that is contrary to accepted opinion

con·trar·i·wise (kän′trer′ē wīz′) ***adv.*** **1** on the contrary **2** in the opposite way, order, etc.

con·trar·y (kän′trer′ē; *for adj. 4, often* kən trer′ē) ***adj.*** ⟦< L *contra*, against⟧ **1** opposed **2** opposite in nature, order, etc.; altogether different **3** unfavorable **4** always resisting or disagreeing **—*n.***, *pl.* **-ies** the opposite **—on the contrary** as opposed to what has been said **—to the contrary** to the opposite effect **—con′tra·ri′e·ty** (-trə rī′ə tē) ***n.* —con′trar′i·ly *adv.* —con′trar′i·ness *n.***

con·trast (kən trast′; *for n.* kän′trast′) ***vt.*** ⟦< L *contra*, against + *stare*, to stand⟧ to compare so as to point out the differences **—*vi.*** to show differences when compared **—*n.*** **1** a contrasting or being contrasted **2** a striking difference between things being compared **3** a person or thing showing differences when compared with another

con·tra·vene (kän′trə vēn′) ***vt.*** **-vened′, -ven′ing** ⟦< L *contra*, against + *venire*, come⟧ **1** to go against; violate **2** to contradict **—con′tra·ven′tion** (-ven′shən) ***n.***

con·tre·temps (kän′trə tän′) ***n.***, *pl.* **-temps′** (-tän′) ⟦Fr⟧ a confusing, embarrassing, or awkward occurrence

con·trib·ute (kən trib′yo͞ot) ***vt.***, ***vi.*** **-ut·ed, -ut·ing** ⟦< L: see CON- & TRIBUTE⟧ **1** to give jointly with others **2** to write (an article, etc.) as for a magazine **3** to furnish (ideas, etc.) **—contribute to** to be partly responsible for (a result) **—con·trib′u·tor *n.* —con·trib′u·to′ry *adj.***

con·tri·bu·tion (kän′trə byo͞o′shən) ***n.*** **1**

a contributing **2** something contributed, as money

con·trite (kən trīt′) ***adj.*** ⟦< L *com-*, together + *terere*, to rub⟧ having or showing deep sorrow for having done wrong; repentant —**con·trite′ly** ***adv.*** —**con·trite′ness** ***n.*** —**con·tri′tion** (-trish′ən) ***n.***

con·triv·ance (kən trī′vəns) ***n.*** **1** the act, way, or power of contriving **2** something contrived; device, invention, etc.

con·trive (kən trīv′) ***vt.*** **-trived′**, **-triv′ing** ⟦ult. < VL *contropare*, compare⟧ **1** to think up; devise **2** to make inventively **3** to bring about; manage —**con·triv′er** ***n.***

con·trol (kən trōl′) ***vt.*** **-trolled′**, **-trol′ling** ⟦< ML *contrarotulus*, a register⟧ **1** to regulate **2** to verify (an experiment) by comparison **3** to exercise authority over; direct **4** to restrain —***n.*** **1** power to direct or regulate **2** a means of controlling; check **3** an apparatus to regulate a mechanism: *usually used in pl.* —**con·trol′la·ble** ***adj.***

control group the group, in an experiment, that is not given the drug, etc. being tested

controlled substance a drug whose sale is regulated by law

con·trol′ler ***n.*** **1** the person in charge of auditing accounts, as in a business **2** a person or device that controls

control tower an airport tower from which air traffic is directed

con·tro·ver·sial (kän′trə vʉr′shəl) ***adj.*** subject to or stirring up controversy

con′tro·ver′sy (-sē) ***n.***, *pl.* **-sies** ⟦< L *contra*, against + *vertere*, to turn⟧ a conflict of opinion; dispute

con·tro·vert (kän′trə vʉrt′, kän′trə vʉrt′) ***vt.*** **1** to argue against; dispute **2** to argue about; debate —**con′tro·vert′i·ble** ***adj.***

con·tu·ma·cy (kän′tyoo mə sē) ***n.***, *pl.* **-cies** ⟦< L *com-*, intens. + *tumere*, swell up⟧ stubborn resistance to authority —**con′tu·ma′cious** (-mā′shəs) ***adj.***

con·tu·me·ly (kän′too mə lē, -toom lē; kən too′mə lē) ***n.***, *pl.* **-lies** ⟦< L *contumelia*, abuse⟧ **1** humiliating treatment **2** a scornful insult —**con′tu·me′li·ous** (-mē′lē əs) ***adj.***

con·tu·sion (kən tyoo′zhən, -too′-) ***n.*** ⟦< L *com-*, intens. + *tundere*, to beat⟧ a bruise

co·nun·drum (kə nun′drəm) ***n.*** ⟦pseudo-L⟧ **1** a riddle whose answer contains a pun **2** any puzzling problem

con·ur·ba·tion (kän′ər bā′shən) ***n.*** ⟦< CON- + L *urbs*, city + -ATION⟧ a vast urban area around and including a large city

con·va·lesce (kän′və les′) ***vi.*** **-lesced′**, **-lesc′ing** ⟦< L *com-*, intens. + *valere*, be strong⟧ to regain strength and health —**con′va·les′cence** ***n.*** —**con′va·les′cent** ***adj.***, ***n.***

con·vec·tion (kən vek′shən) ***n.*** ⟦< L *com-*, together + *vehere*, carry⟧ **1** a transmitting **2** *a*) movement of parts of a fluid within the fluid because of differences in heat, etc. *b*) heat transference by such movement —**con·vec′tion·al** ***adj.*** —**con·vec′tive** ***adj.***

con·vene (kən vēn′) ***vi.***, ***vt.*** **-vened′**, **-ven′ing** ⟦< L *com-*, together + *venire*, come⟧ to assemble for a meeting —**con·ven′er** ***n.***

con·ven·ience (kən vēn′yəns) ***n.*** ⟦see prec.⟧ **1** the quality of being convenient **2** comfort **3** anything that adds to one's comfort or saves work —**at someone's convenience** at a time or place suitable to someone

con·ven′ient (-yənt) ***adj.*** easy to do, use, or get to; handy —**con·ven′ient·ly** ***adv.***

con·vent (kän′vənt, -vent′) ***n.*** ⟦see CONVENE⟧ **1** the residence of a religious community, esp. of women **2** the community itself

con·ven·ti·cle (kən ven′ti kəl) ***n.*** ⟦see CONVENE⟧ a religious assembly held illegally and secretly

con·ven·tion (kən ven′shən) ***n.*** ⟦see CONVENE⟧ **1** *a*) an assembly, often periodical, of members or delegates *b*) such members or delegates **2** an agreement, as between nations **3** a customary practice **4** customary practices collectively —**con·ven′tion·eer′** ***n.***

con·ven′tion·al ***adj.*** **1** having to do with a convention **2** sanctioned by or following custom or usage; customary **3** formal **4** nonnuclear *[conventional* weapons*]* —**con·ven′tion·al′i·ty** (-nal′ə tē) ***n.*** —**con·ven′tion·al·ly** ***adv.***

con·ven′tion·al·ize′ ***vt.*** **-ized′**, **-iz′ing** to make conventional

con·verge (kən vʉrj′) ***vi.*** **-verged′**, **-verg′ing** ⟦< L *com-*, together + *vergere*, to bend⟧ to come together at a point —**con·ver′gence** ***n.*** —**con·ver′gent** ***adj.***

con·ver·sant (kən vʉr′sənt, kän′vər-) ***adj.*** familiar or acquainted (*with*)

con·ver·sa·tion (kän′vər sā′shən) ***n.*** a conversing; informal talk —**con′ver·sa′tion·al** ***adj.*** —**con′ver·sa′tion·al·ist** ***n.*** —**con′ver·sa′tion·al·ly** ***adv.***

conversation piece something, as an unusual article of furniture, that invites comment

con·verse[1] (kən vʉrs′; *for n.* kän′vʉrs′) ***vi.*** **-versed′**, **-vers′ing** ⟦< L *conversari*, live with⟧ to hold a conversation; talk —***n.*** conversation

con·verse[2] (kän′vʉrs′; *also, for adj.*, kən vʉrs′) ***adj.*** ⟦see CONVERT⟧ reversed in position, order, etc.; opposite; contrary —***n.*** a thing related in a converse way; the opposite —**con·verse′ly** ***adv.***

con·ver·sion (kən vʉr′zhən) ***n.*** a converting or being converted

con·vert (kən vʉrt′; *for n.* kän′vʉrt′) ***vt.*** ⟦< L *com-*, together + *vertere*, to turn⟧ **1** to change; transform **2** to change from one religion, doctrine, etc. to another **3** to exchange for something equal in value —***vi.*** to be converted —***n.*** a person converted, as to a religion —**con·vert′er** ***n.***

con·vert·i·ble (kən vʉrt′ə bəl) ***adj.*** that can be converted —***n.*** an automobile with a folding or removable top

con·vex (kän veks′, kän′veks′) ***adj.*** ⟦< L *com-,* together + *vehere,* bring⟧ curving outward like the surface of a sphere —**con·vex′i·ty** ***n.***

CONVEX LENSES

con·vey (kən vā′) ***vt.*** ⟦< L *com-,* together + *via,* way⟧ **1** to take from one place to another; transport; carry **2** to transmit **3** *Law* to transfer (property, etc.) —**con·vey′a·ble** ***adj.***

con·vey′ance ***n.*** **1** a conveying **2** a means of conveying; esp., a vehicle

con·vey′or (belt) a device, consisting of a continuous moving belt, for conveying things: also **con·vey′er (belt)**

con·vict (kən vikt′; *for n.* kän′vikt′) ***vt.*** ⟦see CONVINCE⟧ to prove or find (a person) guilty —***n.*** a convicted person serving a prison sentence

con·vic·tion (kən vik′shən) ***n.*** **1** a convicting or being convicted **2** a being convinced; strong belief

con·vince (kən vins′) ***vt.*** **-vinced′, -vinc′ing** ⟦< L *com-,* intens. + *vincere,* conquer⟧ to persuade by argument or evidence; make feel sure —**con·vinc′ing** ***adj.*** —**con·vinc′ing·ly** ***adv.***

con·viv·i·al (kən viv′ē əl) ***adj.*** ⟦< L *com-,* together + *vivere,* to live⟧ **1** festive **2** fond of eating, drinking, and good company; sociable —**con·viv′i·al′i·ty** (-al′ə tē) ***n.***

con·vo·ca·tion (kän′vō kā′shən) ***n.*** **1** a convoking **2** an ecclesiastical or academic assembly

con·voke (kən vōk′) ***vt.*** **-voked′, -vok′ing** ⟦< L *com-,* together + *vocare,* to call⟧ to call together; convene

con·vo·lut·ed (kän′və lo͞ot′id) ***adj.*** **1** having convolutions; coiled **2** involved; complicated

con′vo·lu′tion (-lo͞o′shən) ***n.*** ⟦< L *com-,* together + *volvere,* to roll⟧ **1** a twisting, coiling, or winding together **2** a fold, twist, or coil

con·voy (kän′voi′) ***vt.*** ⟦see CONVEY⟧ to escort in order to protect —***n.*** **1** a convoying **2** a protecting escort **3** a group of ships, vehicles, etc. traveling together

con·vulse (kən vuls′) ***vt.*** **-vulsed′, -vuls′ing** ⟦< L *com-,* together + *vellere,* to pluck⟧ **1** to shake violently; agitate **2** to cause to shake with laughter, rage, etc. —**con·vul′sive** ***adj.*** —**con·vul′sive·ly** ***adv.***

con·vul′sion (-vul′shən) ***n.*** **1** a violent, involuntary spasm of the muscles: *often used in pl.* **2** a fit of laughter **3** a violent disturbance

coo (ko͞o) ***vi.*** ⟦echoic⟧ to make the soft, murmuring sound of pigeons or doves —***n.*** this sound

COO *abbrev.* chief operating officer

cook (ko͝ok) ***n.*** ⟦< L *coquere,* to cook⟧ one who prepares food —***vt.*** to prepare (food) by boiling, baking, frying, etc. —***vi.*** **1** to be a cook **2** to undergo cooking —**cook up** [Inf.] to devise; invent —**cook′er** ***n.***

cook′book′ ***n.*** a book containing recipes and other food-preparation information

cook′er·y ***n.*** [Chiefly Brit.] the art or practice of cooking

cook′ie ***n.*** ⟦prob. < Du *koek,* cake⟧ a small, sweet cake, usually flat and either crisp or chewy: also **cook′y,** *pl.* **-ies**

cook′out′ ***n.*** a meal cooked and eaten outdoors

cook′top′ ***n.*** a stove top, with burners, or such a unit installed as on a kitchen counter

cool (ko͞ol) ***adj.*** ⟦OE *col*⟧ **1** moderately cold **2** tending to reduce the effects of heat *[cool* clothes*]* **3** not excited; composed **4** showing dislike or indifference **5** calmly bold **6** [Inf.] without exaggeration *[a cool* $1,000*]* **7** [Slang] very good —***n.*** **1** a cool place, time, etc. *[the cool* of the evening*]* **2** [Slang] cool, dispassionate manner —***vt., vi.*** to make or become cool or colder —**cool′ly** ***adv.*** —**cool′ness** ***n.***

cool′ant ***n.*** a fluid or other substance for cooling engines, etc.

cool′er ***n.*** **1** a container or room for keeping things cool **2** a cold, refreshing drink **3** [Slang] jail: with *the*

Coo·lidge (ko͞o′lij), **(John) Calvin** 1872-1933; 30th president of the U.S. (1923-29)

coo·lie (ko͞o′lē) ***n.*** ⟦Hindi *qulī,* servant⟧ an unskilled native laborer, esp. formerly, in India, China, etc.

coon (ko͞on) ***n.*** *short for* RACCOON

coon′skin′ ***n.*** the skin of a raccoon, used as a fur

coop (ko͞op) ***n.*** ⟦< L *cupa,* cask⟧ a small pen as for poultry —***vt.*** to confine as in a coop: usually with *up*

co-op (kō′äp′) ***n.*** [Inf.] a cooperative

coop·er (ko͞op′ər) ***n.*** ⟦see COOP⟧ one whose work is making or repairing barrels and casks

co·op·er·ate or **co-op·er·ate** (kō äp′ər āt′) ***vi.*** **-at′ed, -at′ing** ⟦< L *co-,* with + *opus,* work⟧ to act or work together with another or others —**co·op′er·a′tion** or **co-op′er·a′tion** ***n.***

co·op′er·a·tive or **co-op′er·a·tive** (-ər ə tiv, -ər āt′iv) ***adj.*** **1** cooperating **2** owned collectively by members who share in its benefits —***n.*** a cooperative store, etc.

co-opt (kō äpt′, kō′äpt′) ***vt.*** ⟦< L < *co-,* with + *optare,* choose⟧ **1** to get (an opponent) to join one's side **2** to take over for one's own purposes

co·or·di·nate or **co-or·di·nate** (kō ôrd′ ′n it; *for v.,* -āt′) ***adj.*** ⟦< L *co-,* with + *ordo,* order⟧ **1** of the same order, importance, etc. *[coordinate* clauses in a sentence*]* **2** of coordination or coordinates —***n.*** **1** a coordinate person or thing **2** [*pl.*] items of clothing, luggage, etc. that form a pleasing ensemble —***vt.*** **-nat′ed, -nat′ing** **1** to make coordinate **2** to bring into proper order or relation; adjust —**co·or′di·na′tor** or **co-or′di·na′tor** ***n.***

coordinating conjunction a conjunction connecting coordinate words, clauses, etc. (Ex.: *and, but, nor*)

co·or′di·na′tion or **co-or′di·na′tion** ***n.***

1 a coordinating or being coordinated 2 harmonious action, as of muscles

coot (ko͞ot) ***n.*** ⟦ME *cote*⟧ **1** a ducklike water bird **2** [Inf.] an eccentric old man

coot·ie (ko͞ot′ē) ***n.*** [Slang] a louse

cop (käp) ***vt.*** **copped, cop′ping** ⟦prob. < L *capere,* take⟧ [Slang] to seize, steal, etc. —***n.*** [Slang] a policeman —**cop out** [Slang] **1** to renege **2** to give up; quit

co·part·ner (kō pärt′nər, kō′pärt′-) ***n.*** an associate

co·pay·ment (kō′pā′mənt) ***n.*** the part of a medical bill, often a fixed fee, not covered by insurance

cope[1] (kōp) ***vi.*** **coped, cop′ing** ⟦< OFr *coper,* to strike⟧ **1** to fight or contend (*with*) successfully **2** to deal with problems, etc.

cope[2] (kōp) ***n.*** ⟦< LL *cappa*⟧ **1** a large, capelike vestment worn by priests **2** any cover like this

Co·pen·hag·en (kō′pən hā′gən, -hä′-) capital of Denmark: pop. 626,000

Co·per·ni·cus (kō pur′ni kəs), **Nic·o·la·us** (nik′ə lā′əs) 1473-1543; Pol. astronomer —**Co·per′ni·can** ***adj.***

cop·i·er (käp′ē ər) ***n.*** **1** one who copies **2** a duplicating machine

co·pi·lot (kō′pī′lət) ***n.*** the assistant pilot of an airplane

cop·ing (kō′piŋ) ***n.*** ⟦< COPE²⟧ the top layer of a masonry wall

co·pi·ous (kō′pē əs) ***adj.*** ⟦< L *copia,* abundance⟧ plentiful; abundant —**co′pi·ous·ly** ***adv.*** —**co′pi·ous·ness** ***n.***

cop′-out′ ***n.*** [Slang] a copping out, as by reneging or quitting

cop·per (käp′ər) ***n.*** ⟦< LL *cuprum*⟧ **1** a reddish-brown, ductile, metallic chemical element **2** a reddish brown —***adj.*** **1** of copper **2** reddish-brown —**cop′per·y** ***adj.***

cop′per·head′ ***n.*** a poisonous North American snake

co·pra (kä′prə, kō′-) ***n.*** ⟦Port < Hindi *khoprā*⟧ dried coconut meat, the source of coconut oil

copse (käps) ***n.*** ⟦< OFr *coper,* to strike⟧ a thicket of small trees or shrubs: also **cop·pice** (käp′is)

cop·ter (käp′tər) ***n.*** *short for* HELICOPTER

cop·u·la (käp′yo͞o lə) ***n.***, *pl.* **-las** ⟦L, a link⟧ LINKING VERB —**cop′u·la′tive** (-lāt′iv) ***adj.***

cop·u·late (käp′yo͞o lāt′) ***vi.*** **-lat′ed, -lat′ing** ⟦< L *co-*, together + *apere*, to join⟧ to have sexual intercourse —**cop′u·la′tion** ***n.***

cop·y (käp′ē) ***n.***, *pl.* **-ies** ⟦< L *copia,* plenty⟧ **1** a thing made just like another; imitation or reproduction **2** any of a number of books, magazines, etc. having the same contents **3** matter to be typeset **4** the words of an advertisement —***vt., vi.*** **cop′ied, cop′y·ing** **1** to make a copy of **2** to imitate **3** [Inf.] to provide (with) a copy —**cop′y·ist** ***n.***

cop′y·cat′ ***n.*** an imitator: chiefly a child's term —***adj.*** done in imitation *[a copycat* crime*]*

cop′y·right′ ***n.*** the exclusive right to the publication, sale, etc. of a literary or artistic work —***vt.*** to protect (a book, etc.) by copyright

cop′y·writ′er ***n.*** a writer of copy, esp. for advertisements

co·quette (kō ket′) ***n.*** ⟦Fr⟧ a girl or woman who flirts —**co·quet′tish** ***adj.***

cor- *prefix* COM-: used before *r*

cor·al (kôr′əl) ***n.*** ⟦< Gr *korallion*⟧ **1** the hard skeleton secreted by certain marine polyps: reefs and atolls of coral occur in tropical seas **2** a piece of coral **3** a yellowish red —***adj.*** of coral

coral snake a small, poisonous snake marked with coral, yellow, and black bands

cor·bel (kôr′bəl) ***n.*** ⟦< L *corvus,* raven⟧ a piece of stone, wood, etc. projecting from a wall and supporting a cornice, arch, etc.

cord (kôrd) ***n.*** ⟦< Gr *chordē*⟧ **1** a thick string **2** a measure of wood cut for fuel (128 cubic feet) **3** a rib on the surface of a fabric **4** ribbed cloth **5** [*pl.*] corduroy trousers **6** *Anat.* any part like a cord **7** *Elec.* a slender cable

cord′age ***n.*** cords and ropes

cor·dial (kôr′jəl) ***adj.*** ⟦< L *cor*, heart⟧ warm; hearty; sincere —***n.*** a liqueur —**cor′di·al′i·ty** (-jē al′ə tē) ***n.*** —**cor′dial·ly** ***adv.***

cor·dil·le·ra (kôr′dil yer′ə, -də ler′ə) ***n.*** ⟦Sp < L *chorda*, a cord⟧ a system or chain of mountains

cord·ite (kôr′dīt′) ***n.*** ⟦< CORD: it is stringy⟧ a smokeless explosive made of nitroglycerin, etc.

cord·less (kôrd′lis) ***adj.*** operated by batteries, as an electric shaver

cor·don (kôr′dən) ***n.*** ⟦see CORD⟧ a line or circle of police, troops, etc. guarding an area —***vt.*** to encircle with a cordon

cor·do·van (kôr′də vən) ***n.*** ⟦after *Córdoba*, Spain⟧ a soft, colored leather

cor·du·roy (kôr′də roi′) ***n.*** ⟦prob. < CORD + obs. *duroy,* a coarse fabric⟧ a heavy, ribbed cotton fabric

core (kôr) ***n.*** ⟦prob. < L *cor,* heart⟧ **1** the central part of an apple, pear, etc. **2** the central part of anything **3** the most important part —***vt.*** **cored, cor′ing** to remove the core of

co·re·spond·ent (kō′ri spän′dənt) ***n.*** ⟦CO- + RESPONDENT⟧ *Law* a person charged with having committed adultery with the wife or husband from whom a divorce is being sought

co·ri·an·der (kôr′ē an′dər) ***n.*** ⟦< Gr *koriandron*⟧ an annual herb with strong-smelling, seedlike fruit used as a flavoring

cork (kôrk) ***n.*** ⟦ult. < L *quercus,* oak⟧ **1** the light, thick, elastic outer bark of an oak tree (**cork oak**) **2** a stopper made of cork, for a bottle, etc. **3** any stopper —***adj.*** of cork —***vt.*** to stop with a cork

cork′board′ ***n.*** a bulletin board made of granulated cork

cork′screw′ ***n.*** a spiral-shaped device for pulling corks out of bottles —***adj.*** spiral —***vi., vt.*** to move in a spiral; twist

corm (kôrm) ***n.*** ⟦< Gr *kormos,* a log⟧ a fleshy, underground stem, as that of the gladiolus

cor·mo·rant (kôr′mə rənt) ***n.*** ⟦< L *corvus,* raven + *marinus,* marine⟧ a large, voracious sea bird

corn[1] (kôrn) ***n.*** ⟦OE⟧ **1** a small, hard seed, esp. of a cereal grass; kernel **2** *a)* an American cereal plant with kernels growing in rows along a woody husk-enclosed core (**corncob**) *b)* the kernels **3** [Brit.] grain, esp. wheat **4** the leading cereal crop in a place **5** [Inf.] ideas, humor, etc. regarded as old-fashioned, trite, etc. —***vt.*** to pickle (meat, etc.) in brine

corn[2] (kôrn) ***n.*** ⟦< L *cornu,* horn⟧ a hard, thick, painful growth of skin, esp. on a toe

corn′ball′ ***adj.*** ⟦CORN[1] (sense 5) + (SCREW)BALL⟧ [Slang] corny

corn bread bread made with cornmeal

cor·ne·a (kôr′nē ə) ***n.*** ⟦< L *cornu,* horn⟧ the transparent outer coat of the eyeball —**cor′ne·al** ***adj.***

cor·ner (kôr′nər) ***n.*** ⟦< L *cornu,* horn⟧ **1** the point or place where lines or surfaces join and form an angle **2** the angle formed **3** any of the angles formed at a street intersection **4** a remote, secluded place **5** a region; quarter **6** a position hard to escape from **7** a monopoly acquired on a stock or commodity so as to raise the price —***vt.*** **1** to force into a CORNER (*n.*6) **2** to get a monopoly on (a stock, etc.) —***vi.*** to turn corners: said of a vehicle —***adj.*** at, on, or for a corner —**cut corners** to cut down expenses, time, etc. —**cor′nered** ***adj.***

cor′ner·back′ ***n.*** *Football* either of two defensive backs positioned outside the linebackers

cor′ner·stone′ ***n.*** **1** a stone laid at a corner of a building, esp. at a ceremony for the beginning of construction **2** the basic part; foundation

cor·net (kôr net′) ***n.*** ⟦< L *cornu,* horn⟧ a brass instrument similar to the trumpet but more compact

corn′flow′er ***n.*** an annual plant with tiny, white, pink, or blue flowers that form a round head

cor·nice (kôr′nis) ***n.*** ⟦< Gr *korōnis,* wreath⟧ **1** a horizontal molding projecting along the top of a wall, etc. **2** a decorative cover for a curtain rod

corn′meal′ ***n.*** meal made from corn

corn′starch′ ***n.*** a powdery starch made from corn, used in cooking

corn syrup a syrup made from cornstarch

cor·nu·co·pi·a (kôr′nə kō′pē ə) ***n.*** ⟦L *cornu copiae,* horn of plenty⟧ **1** a horn-shaped container overflowing with fruits, flowers, etc. **2** an abundance

corn·y (kôr′nē) ***adj.*** **-i·er**, **-i·est** [Inf.] trite, sentimental, etc.

co·rol·la (kə rōl′ə, -räl′ə) ***n.*** ⟦< L, dim. of *corona,* crown⟧ the petals of a flower

cor·ol·lar·y (kôr′ə ler′ē) ***n.***, *pl.* **-ies** ⟦see prec.⟧ **1** a proposition that follows from one already proved **2** a normal result

co·ro·na (kə rō′nə) ***n.***, *pl.* **-nas** or **-nae** (-nē) ⟦L⟧ **1** the layer of ionized gas surrounding the sun **2** a ring of colored light seen around a luminous body, as the sun or moon

cor·o·nar·y (kôr′ə ner′ē) ***adj.*** **1** of or like a crown **2** of the arteries supplying blood to the heart muscle —***n.***, *pl.* **-ies** a thrombosis in a coronary artery: in full **coronary thrombosis**

cor·o·na·tion (kôr′ə nā′shən) ***n.*** the crowning of a sovereign

cor·o·ner (kôr′ə nər) ***n.*** ⟦ME, officer of the crown⟧ a public officer who must determine the cause of any death not obviously due to natural causes

cor·o·net (kôr′ə net′, kôr′ə net′) ***n.*** ⟦< OFr *corone,* crown⟧ **1** a small crown worn by nobility **2** a band of jewels, flowers, etc. for the head

Corp *abbrev.* **1** Corporal **2** Corporation: also **corp**

cor·po·ral[1] (kôr′pə rəl, -prəl) ***n.*** ⟦< L *caput,* head⟧ the lowest-ranking noncommissioned officer, just below a sergeant

cor·po·ral[2] (kôr′pə rəl, -prəl) ***adj.*** ⟦< L *corpus,* body⟧ of the body; bodily

corporal punishment bodily punishment, as flogging

cor·po·rate (kôr′pə rit, -prit) ***adj.*** ⟦< L *corpus,* body⟧ **1** of, like, or being a corporation **2** shared; joint

cor′po·ra′tion (-pə rā′shən) ***n.*** a legal entity, usually a group of people, that has a charter granting it certain legal powers generally given to individuals, as to buy and sell property or to enter into contracts

cor·po·re·al (kôr pôr′ē əl) ***adj.*** ⟦< L *corpus,* body⟧ **1** of or for the body; physical **2** of a material nature; tangible

corps (kôr) ***n.***, *pl.* **corps** (kôrz) ⟦< L *corpus,* body⟧ **1** a body of people associated under common direction **2** *Mil. a)* a specialized branch of the armed forces *b)* a tactical subdivision of an army

corpse (kôrps) ***n.*** ⟦var. of prec.⟧ a dead body, esp. of a person

cor·pu·lence (kôr′pyoo ləns, -pyə-) ***n.*** ⟦< L *corpus,* body⟧ fatness; obesity —**cor′pu·lent** ***adj.***

cor·pus (kôr′pəs) ***n.***, *pl.* **cor′po·ra** (-pə rə) ⟦L⟧ **1** a body, esp. a dead one **2** a complete collection, as of laws

Cor·pus Chris·ti (kôr′pəs kris′tē) city in SE Texas: pop. 257,000

cor·pus·cle (kôr′pus′əl) ***n.*** ⟦< L dim. of *corpus,* body⟧ an unattached body cell, esp. a red or white blood cell —**cor·pus′cu·lar** (-kyoo lər) ***adj.***

corpus de·lic·ti (də lik′tī′) ⟦ModL, lit., body of the crime⟧ **1** the facts constituting a crime **2** loosely, the body of a murder victim

cor·ral (kə ral′) ***n.*** ⟦Sp < L *currere,* to run⟧ an enclosure for horses, cattle, etc.; pen —***vt.*** **-ralled′**, **-ral′ling** **1** to drive into or confine in a corral **2** to surround or capture

cor·rect (kə rekt′) ***vt.*** ⟦< L *com-,* together + *regere,* to rule⟧ **1** to make right **2** to point out or mark the errors of **3** to scold or punish **4** to cure or remove (a fault, etc.) —***adj.*** **1** conforming to an established standard **2** true; accurate; right —**cor·rect′a·ble** *adj.* —**cor·rec′tive** *adj., n.* —**cor·rect′ly** *adv.* —**cor·rect′ness** *n.*

cor·rec′tion (-rek′shən) *n.* **1** a correcting or being corrected **2** a change that corrects a mistake **3** punishment to correct faults **4** *Finance* a temporary reversal in rising stock prices, etc. —**cor·rec′tion·al** *adj.*

cor·re·late (kôr′ə lāt′) *vi., vt.* **-lat′ed, -lat′ing** ⟦see COM- & RELATE⟧ to be in or bring into mutual relation —**cor′re·la′tion** *n.*

cor·rel·a·tive (kə rel′ə tiv) *adj.* **1** having a mutual relationship **2** *Gram.* expressing mutual relation and used in pairs, as the conjunctions *neither* and *nor* —*n.* a correlative word, etc.

cor·re·spond (kôr′ə spänd′) *vi.* ⟦< L *com-,* together + *respondere,* respond⟧ **1** to be in agreement (*with* something) **2** to be similar or equal (*to* something) **3** to communicate by letters —**cor′re·spond′ing·ly** *adv.*

cor′re·spond′ence *n.* **1** agreement; conformity **2** similarity **3** *a*) communication by letters *b*) the letters

cor′re·spond′ent *adj.* corresponding; agreeing; analogous —*n.* **1** a thing that corresponds **2** one who exchanges letters with another **3** one hired by a newspaper, radio network, etc. to furnish news, etc. from a distant place

cor·ri·dor (kôr′ə dər, -dôr′) *n.* ⟦Fr < L *currere,* to run⟧ a long hall

cor·rob·o·rate (kə räb′ə rāt′) *vt.* **-rat′ed, -rat′ing** ⟦< L *com-,* intens. + *robur,* strength⟧ to confirm; support —**cor·rob′o·ra′tion** *n.* —**cor·rob′o·ra′tive** (-ə rāt′iv, -ər ə tiv) *adj.* —**cor·rob′o·ra′tor** *n.*

cor·rode (kə rōd′) *vt., vi.* **-rod′ed, -rod′ing** ⟦< L *com-,* intens. + *rodere,* gnaw⟧ to eat into or wear away gradually, as by rusting or the action of chemicals —**cor·ro′sion** (-rō′zhən) *n.* —**cor·ro′sive** (-rō′siv) *adj., n.* —**cor·ro′sive·ly** *adv.*

cor·ru·gate (kôr′ə gāt′) *vt., vi.* **-gat′ed, -gat′ing** ⟦< L *com-,* intens. + *rugare,* to wrinkle⟧ to shape into parallel grooves and ridges —**cor′ru·ga′tion** *n.*

cor·rupt (kə rupt′) *adj.* ⟦< L *com-,* together + *rumpere,* to break⟧ **1** evil; depraved **2** taking bribes **3** containing alterations, errors, etc. —*vt., vi.* to make or become corrupt —**cor·rupt′i·ble** *adj.* —**cor·rup′tion** *n.* —**cor·rupt′ly** *adv.*

cor·sage (kôr säzh′) *n.* ⟦see CORPS & -AGE⟧ a small bouquet for a woman to wear, as at the waist or shoulder

cor·sair (kôr′ser′) *n.* ⟦< Fr < L *cursus,* course⟧ a pirate or a pirate ship

cor·set (kôr′sit) *n.* ⟦see CORPS⟧ a closefitting undergarment worn, chiefly by women, to give support to or shape the body

cor·tege or **cor·tège** (kôr tezh′, -tāzh′) *n.* ⟦Fr < L *cohors*⟧ **1** a retinue **2** a ceremonial procession

cor·tex (kôr′teks′) *n., pl.* **-ti·ces′** (-tə sēz′) ⟦L, bark of a tree⟧ **1** the outer part of an internal organ; esp., the outer layer of gray matter over most of the brain **2** an outer layer of plant tissue —**cor′ti·cal** (-ti kəl) *adj.*

cor·ti·sone (kôrt′ə sōn′, -zōn′) *n.* ⟦so named by E. C. Kendall (1886-1972), U.S. physician⟧ a hormone used to treat adrenal insufficiency, inflammatory diseases, etc.

co·run·dum (kə run′dəm) *n.* ⟦< Sans *kuruvinda,* ruby⟧ a very hard mineral used for grinding and polishing

cor·us·cate (kôr′ə skāt′) *vi.* **-cat′ed, -cat′ing** ⟦< L *coruscus,* vibrating⟧ to glitter; sparkle —**cor′us·ca′tion** *n.*

cor·vette (kôr vet′) *n.* ⟦Fr⟧ a fast warship smaller than a destroyer and used chiefly for convoy duty

Co·sa Nos·tra (kō′sə nō′strə) *name for* MAFIA, esp. in U.S.

co·sign (kō′sīn′) *vt., vi.* **1** to sign (a promissory note) in addition to the maker, thus becoming responsible if the maker defaults **2** to sign jointly —**co′sign′er** *n.*

co·sig′na·to′ry (-sig′nə tôr′ē) *n., pl.* **-ries** one of two or more joint signers, as of a treaty

cos·met·ic (käz met′ik) *adj.* ⟦< Gr *kosmos,* order⟧ beautifying, or correcting faults in, the face, hair, etc. —*n.* a cosmetic preparation, as lipstick —**cos·met′i·cal·ly** *adv.*

cos′me·tol′o·gy (-mə täl′ə jē) *n.* the work of a beautician —**cos′me·tol′o·gist** *n.*

cos·mic (käz′mik) *adj.* ⟦< Gr *kosmos,* universe⟧ **1** of the cosmos **2** vast

cosmic rays streams of high-energy charged particles from outer space

cos·mog·o·ny (käz mäg′ə nē) *n.* ⟦< Gr *kosmos,* universe + *-gonos,* generation⟧ **1** the study of the origin of the universe **2** *pl.* **-nies** a theory of this

cos·mol′o·gy (-mäl′ə jē) *n.* ⟦< ML⟧ **1** the scientific study of the form, evolution, etc. of the universe **2** the branch of metaphysics dealing with the origin and structure of the universe —**cos′mo·log′i·cal** (-mə läj′ə kəl) *adj.*

cos·mo·naut (käz′mə nôt′) *n.* ⟦Russ *kosmonavt*⟧ a Soviet or Russian astronaut

cos·mo·pol·i·tan (käz′mə päl′ə tən) *adj.* ⟦< Gr *kosmos,* universe + *polis,* city-state⟧ **1** common to or representative of all or many parts of the world **2** not bound by local or national habits or prejudices; at home in all places —*n.* a cosmopolitan person or thing: also **cos·mop′o·lite′** (-mäp′ə līt′)

cos·mos (käz′məs, -mōs′) *n.* ⟦< Gr *kosmos,* universe⟧ **1** the universe considered as an orderly system **2** any complete and orderly system

co·spon·sor (kō′spän′sər) *n.* a joint sponsor, as of a proposed piece of legislation —*vt.* to be a cosponsor of —**co′spon′sor·ship′** *n.*

Cos·sack (käs′ak′, -ək) *n.* a member of any of several groups of peasants that lived in autonomous communal settlements, esp. in the Ukraine, until the late 19th c.

cost (kôst) *vt.* **cost, cost′ing** ⟦< L *com-,* together + *stare,* to stand⟧ **1** to be obtained for (a certain price) **2** to require the expenditure, loss, etc. of —*n.* 1 the amount of money, etc. asked or paid for a thing; price 2 the time, effort, etc. needed to do something 3 loss; sacrifice —**at all costs** by any means required

co·star (kō′stär′; *for v., usually* kō′stär′) *n.* any featured actor or actress given equal billing with another in a movie, play, etc. —*vt., vi.* **-starred′, -star′ring** to present as or be a costar

Cos·ta Ri·ca (käs′tə rē′kə, kôs′-, kōs′-) country in Central America: 19,730 sq. mi.; pop. 2,417,000 —**Cos′ta Ri′can**

cost-ef·fec·tive (kôst′ə fek′tiv) *adj.* producing good results for the amount of money spent; efficient or economical —**cost′-ef·fec′tive·ness** *n.*

cos·tive (käs′tiv, kôs′-) *adj.* ⟦< L *constipare,* to press together⟧ constipated or constipating

cost′ly *adj.* **-li·er, -li·est** ⟦ME⟧ 1 costing much; expensive 2 magnificent —**cost′li·ness** *n.*

cost of living the average cost of the necessities of life, as food, shelter, and clothes

cos·tume (käs′to͞om′, -tyo͞om′) *n.* ⟦< L *consuetudo,* custom⟧ 1 *a*) the style of dress typical of a certain country, period, etc. *b*) a set of such clothes, as worn in a play 2 a set of outer clothes —*vt.* **-tumed′, -tum′ing** to provide with a costume

co·sy (kō′zē) *adj.* **-si·er, -si·est,** *n., pl.* **-sies** *chiefly Brit. sp. of* COZY —**co′si·ly** *adv.* —**co′si·ness** *n.*

cot[1] (kät) *n.* ⟦< Sans *khāṭvā*⟧ a narrow, collapsible bed, as one made of canvas on a folding frame

cot[2] (kät) *n.* ⟦OE⟧ a small shelter

cote (kōt) *n.* ⟦ME⟧ a small shelter for doves, sheep, etc.

co·te·rie (kōt′ər ē) *n.* ⟦Fr⟧ a close circle of friends; clique

co·ter·mi·nous (kō tur′mə nəs) *adj.* CONTERMINOUS

co·til·lion (kō til′yən) *n.* ⟦< OFr *cote,* coat⟧ 1 an intricate, formal group dance 2 a formal ball Also sp. **co·til′lon**

cot·tage (kät′ij) *n.* ⟦ME⟧ 1 a small house 2 a house used for vacations —**cot′tag·er** *n.*

cottage cheese a soft, white cheese made from the curds of sour milk

cot·ter pin (kät′ər) a pin with two stems that can be spread apart to fasten the pin in place

cot·ton (kät′'n) *n.* ⟦< Ar *quṭun*⟧ 1 the soft, white hairs around the seeds of certain plants of the mallow family 2 such a plant or plants 3 thread or cloth made of cotton —**cotton to** [Inf.] to take a liking to —**cot′ton·y** *adj.*

cotton gin ⟦see GIN[2]⟧ a machine for separating cotton from the seeds

cot′ton·mouth′ *n.* WATER MOCCASIN

cot′ton·seed′ *n.* the seed of the cotton plant, yielding an oil (**cottonseed oil**) used in margarine, cooking oil, soap, etc.

cot′ton·tail′ *n.* a common American rabbit with a short, fluffy tail

cot′ton·wood′ *n.* a poplar that has seeds thickly covered with cottony or silky hairs

cot·y·le·don (kät′ə lēd′'n) *n.* ⟦< Gr *kotylē,* cavity⟧ the first leaf or one of the first pair of leaves produced by the embryo of a flowering plant

couch (kouch) *n.* ⟦< OFr *coucher,* lie down⟧ an article of furniture on which one may sit or lie down; sofa —*vt.* 1 to place as on a couch 2 to word in a certain way; phrase; express

cou·gar (ko͞o′gər) *n.* ⟦< AmInd (Brazil)⟧ a large, powerful, tawny cat; mountain lion; puma

cough (kôf) *vi.* ⟦ME *coughen*⟧ to expel air suddenly and noisily from the lungs —*vt.* to expel by coughing —*n.* 1 the act of coughing 2 a condition causing frequent coughing —**cough up** [Slang] to hand over (money, etc.)

cough drop a small medicated tablet for the relief of coughs, etc.

could (ko͝od) *v.aux.* 1 *pt. of* CAN[1] 2 an auxiliary verb generally equivalent to CAN[1], expressing esp. a shade of doubt *[it could be so]*

cou·lomb (ko͞o′läm′, -lōm′) *n.* ⟦after C. A. de *Coulomb* (1736-1806), Fr physicist⟧ a unit of electric charge equal to the charge of 6.281×10^{18} electrons

coun·cil (koun′səl) *n.* ⟦< L *com-,* together + *calere,* to call⟧ 1 a group of people called together for discussion, advice, etc. 2 an administrative, advisory, or legislative body —**coun′cil·man** (-mən), *pl.* **-men** (-mən), *n.* —**coun′cil·per′son** *n.* —**coun′cil·wom′an,** *pl.* **-wom′en,** *fem.n.*

coun′ci·lor (-sə lər) *n.* a member of a council

coun·sel (koun′səl) *n.* ⟦< L *consilium*⟧ 1 advice 2 a lawyer or group of lawyers 3 a consultant —*vt.* **-seled** or **-selled, -sel·ing** or **-sel·ling** 1 to give advice to 2 to recommend (an action, etc.)

coun′se·lor or **coun′sel·lor** (-sə lər) *n.* 1 an advisor 2 a lawyer 3 one in charge of children at a camp

count[1] (kount) *vt.* ⟦< L *computare,* compute⟧ 1 to name or add up, unit by unit, to get a total 2 to take account of; include 3 to believe to be; consider —*vi.* 1 to name numbers or add up items in order 2 to be taken into account; have importance 3 to have a specified value: often with *for* 4 to rely or depend (*on* or *upon*) —*n.* 1 a counting 2 the total number 3 a reckoning 4 *Law* any of the charges in an indictment

count[2] (kount) *n.* ⟦< L *comes,* companion⟧ a European nobleman with a rank equal to that of an English earl

count′down′ *n.* 1 the schedule of operations just before the firing of a rocket, etc. 2 the counting off, in reverse order, of time units in this schedule

coun·te·nance (koun′tə nəns, kount′'n əns) *n.* ⟦< L *continentia,* bearing⟧ 1 facial expression 2 the face 3 approval; support —*vt.* **-nanced, -nanc·ing** to approve or tolerate

count·er[1] (kount′ər) *n.* 1 a person, device, etc. that counts something 2 a small disk for keeping count in games **3** an imitation coin or token **4** a long table, cabinet top, etc. for the displaying of goods, serving of food, etc. —**under the counter** in a secret manner: said of sales, etc. made illegally

coun·ter[2] (kount′ər) ***adv.*** ⟦< L *contra,* against⟧ in opposition; opposite —***adj.*** contrary; opposed —***n.*** the opposite; contrary —***vt., vi.*** to act, do, etc. counter to; oppose

counter- ⟦< L *contra-*, against⟧ *combining form* **1** contrary to *[counterclockwise]* **2** in retaliation *[counterattack]* **3** complementary *[counterpart]*

coun′ter·act′ ***vt.*** to act against; neutralize —**coun′ter·ac′tion** ***n.***

coun′ter·at·tack′ ***n.*** an attack made in opposition to another attack —***vt., vi.*** to attack so as to offset the enemy's attack

coun′ter·bal′ance ***n.*** a weight, force, etc. that balances another —***vt.*** **-anced, -anc·ing** to be a counterbalance to; offset

coun′ter·claim′ ***n.*** an opposing claim —***vt., vi.*** to present as, or make, a counterclaim

coun′ter·clock′wise′ ***adj., adv.*** in a direction opposite to that in which the hands of a clock move

coun′ter·cul′ture ***n.*** a culture with a lifestyle that is opposed to the prevailing culture

coun′ter·es′pi·o·nage′ ***n.*** actions to prevent or thwart enemy espionage

coun′ter·feit′ (-fit′) ***adj.*** ⟦< OFr *contre-*, counter- + *faire*, to make⟧ **1** made in imitation of something genuine so as to deceive; forged **2** sham; pretended —***n.*** an imitation made to deceive; forgery —***vt., vi.*** **1** to make an imitation of (money, etc.), usually to deceive **2** to pretend —**coun′ter·feit′er** ***n.***

count′er·man′ (-man′) ***n.***, *pl.* **-men′** (-men′) a man who serves customers at a counter, as of a lunchroom

coun′ter·mand′ (-mand′) ***vt.*** ⟦< L *contra*, against + *mandare*, to command⟧ to cancel or revoke by a contrary order

coun′ter·mel′o·dy ***n.*** a melody distinct from the principal melody

coun′ter·pane′ (-pān′) ***n.*** ⟦ult. < L *culcita puncta*, embroidered quilt⟧ a bedspread

coun′ter·part′ ***n.*** **1** one that closely resembles another **2** a copy or duplicate

coun′ter·point′ ***n.*** ⟦< It: see COUNTER- & POINT⟧ **1** the technique of combining two or more distinct lines of music that sound simultaneously **2** any melody played or sung against a basic melody **3** a thing set up in contrast with another

coun′ter·poise′ ***n.*** ⟦see COUNTER[2] & POISE⟧ **1** a counterbalance **2** equilibrium —***vt.*** **-poised′, -pois′ing** to counterbalance

coun′ter·pro·duc′tive ***adj.*** having results contrary to those intended

coun′ter·rev′o·lu′tion ***n.*** a political movement against a government set up by a previous revolution —**coun′ter·rev′o·lu′tion·ar′y**, *pl.* **-ies**, ***n., adj.***

coun′ter·sign′ ***n.*** **1** a signature added to a previously signed document, as for confirmation **2** a secret signal to another, as a password —***vt.*** to confirm with one's own signature

coun′ter·sink′ ***vt.*** **-sunk′, -sink′ing** **1** to enlarge the top part of (a hole) so that the head of a bolt, etc. will fit flush with the surface **2** to sink (a bolt, etc.) into such a hole

coun′ter·ten′or ***n.*** **1** the range of the highest male voice, above tenor **2** a voice or singer with such a range

count′er·top′ ***n.*** the upper surface of a COUNTER[1] (sense 4)

coun′ter·weight′ ***n.*** a counterbalance

count·ess (kount′is) ***n.*** **1** the wife or widow of a count or earl **2** a woman of nobility with a rank equal to that of a count or earl

count·less (kount′lis) ***adj.*** too many to count; innumerable; myriad

coun·try (kun′trē) ***n.***, *pl.* **-tries** ⟦< L *contra*, against⟧ **1** an area of land; region **2** the whole land, or the people, of a nation **3** the land of one's birth or citizenship **4** land with farms and small towns **5** *short for* COUNTRY MUSIC

country club a social club with a clubhouse, golf course, etc.

coun′try·man (-mən) ***n.***, *pl.* **-men** (-mən) a person of one's own country

country music popular music that derives from the rural folk music of the S U.S.

coun′try·side′ ***n.*** a rural region

coun′try·wide′ ***adj., adv.*** throughout the entire nation

coun·ty (kount′ē) ***n.***, *pl.* **-ties** ⟦< ML *comitatus*, jurisdiction of a count⟧ a small administrative district of a country, U.S. state, etc.

coup (ko͞o) ***n.***, *pl.* **coups** (ko͞oz) ⟦Fr < L *colaphus*, a blow⟧ **1** a sudden, successful action **2** COUP D'ÉTAT

coup de grâce (ko͞o′ də gräs′) ⟦Fr, stroke of mercy⟧ **1** the blow, shot, etc. that brings death to a sufferer **2** a finishing stroke

coup d'é·tat (ko͞o′ dā tä′) ⟦Fr, stroke of state⟧ the sudden, forcible overthrow as of a ruler or government

coupe (ko͞op) ***n.*** ⟦< Fr *couper*, to cut⟧ a closed, two-door automobile

cou·ple (kup′əl) ***n.*** ⟦< L *copula*⟧ **1** a link **2** a pair of things or persons, as a man and woman who are engaged, married, etc. **3** [Inf.] a few —***vt., vi.*** **-pled, -pling** to link or unite

cou·plet (kup′lit) ***n.*** two successive lines of poetry, esp. two that rhyme

cou·pling (kup′liŋ) ***n.*** **1** a joining together **2** a mechanical device for joining parts together

cou·pon (ko͞o′pän′, kyo͞o′-) ***n.*** ⟦Fr < *couper*, to cut⟧ **1** a detachable printed statement on a bond, specifying the interest due at a given time **2** a certificate entitling one to a specified right, as a discount or gift

cour·age (kur′ij) ***n.*** ⟦< L *cor*, heart⟧ the quality of being brave; valor

cou·ra·geous (kə rā′jəs) ***adj.*** having or

showing courage; brave —**cou·ra'geous·ly** ***adv.***

cou·ri·er (koor'ē ər, kur'-) ***n.*** ⟦< L *currere,* to run⟧ a messenger

course (kôrs) ***n.*** ⟦< L *currere,* to run⟧ **1** an onward movement; progress **2** a way, path, or channel **3** the direction taken **4** a regular manner of procedure or conduct *[our wisest course]* **5** a series of like things in order **6** a part of a meal served at one time **7** *Educ. a)* a complete series of studies, as for a degree *b)* any of the separate units of such a series —***vi.*** **coursed, cours'ing** to run or race —**in due course** in the usual sequence (of events) —**in the course of** during —**of course 1** naturally **2** certainly

cours·er (kôr'sər) ***n.*** a graceful, spirited, or swift horse

court (kôrt) ***n.*** ⟦< L *cohors,* enclosure⟧ **1** a courtyard **2** a short street **3** a space for playing a game, as basketball **4** *a)* the palace, or the family, etc., of a sovereign *b)* a sovereign and councilors, etc. as a governing body *c)* a formal gathering held by a sovereign **5** attention paid to someone in order to get something **6** *Law a)* a judge or judges *b)* a place where trials are held —***vt.*** **1** to pay attention to (a person) so as to get something **2** to seek as a mate; woo **3** to try to get *[to court favor]* —***vi.*** to carry on a courtship

cour·te·ous (kurt'ē əs) ***adj.*** ⟦see prec. & -EOUS⟧ polite and gracious —**cour'te·ous·ly** ***adv.***

cour·te·san (kôrt'ə zən) ***n.*** ⟦see COURT⟧ a prostitute: also **cour'te·zan**

cour·te·sy (kurt'ə sē) ***n.,*** *pl.* **-sies 1** courteous behavior **2** a polite or considerate act or remark —***adj.*** provided free; complimentary

court'house' ***n.*** **1** a building housing law courts **2** a building housing offices of a county government

cour·ti·er (kôrt'ē ər, -yər) ***n.*** an attendant at a royal court

court'ly ***adj.*** **-li·er, -li·est** suitable for a king's court; dignified; elegant —**court'li·ness** ***n.***

court'-mar'tial ***n.,*** *pl.* **courts'-mar'tial;** for 2, now often **court'-mar'tials 1** a court in the armed forces for the trial of persons accused of breaking military law **2** a trial by a court-martial **3** a conviction by a court-martial —***vt.*** **-tialed** or **-tialled, -tial·ing** or **-tial·ling** to try or convict by a court-martial

court reporter one who records exactly what is said in a courtroom during a trial

court'room' ***n.*** *Law* a room in which trials are held

court'ship' ***n.*** the act, process, or period of wooing

court'side' ***n.*** *Sports* the area immediately around a basketball court, tennis court, etc.

court'yard' ***n.*** a space enclosed by walls, adjoining or within a large building

cous·cous (koos'koos') ***n.*** ⟦Fr < Ar *kaskasa,* to grind⟧ a N African dish made with crushed grain, served as with lamb in a spicy sauce

cous·in (kuz'ən) ***n.*** ⟦ult. < L *com-,* with + *soror,* sister⟧ **1** the son or daughter of one's uncle or aunt **2** loosely, any relative by blood or marriage

cous'in·age (-ij) ***n.*** **1** the relationship between cousins **2** a group of cousins or relatives

cou·tu·ri·er (koo'toor ē ā') ***n.*** ⟦Fr⟧ a designer of women's fashions —**cou'tu·ri·ère'** (-ē er') ***fem.n.***

cove (kōv) ***n.*** ⟦OE *cofa,* cave⟧ a small bay or inlet

cov·en (kuv'ən) ***n.*** ⟦see CONVENE⟧ a gathering or meeting, esp. of witches

cov·e·nant (kuv'ə nənt) ***n.*** ⟦see CONVENE⟧ an agreement; compact —***vt.*** to promise by a covenant —***vi.*** to make a covenant

cov·er (kuv'ər) ***vt.*** ⟦< L *co-,* intens. + *operire,* to hide⟧ **1** to place something on or over **2** to extend over **3** to clothe **4** to conceal; hide **5** to shield, protect, or watch (someone or something) **6** to include; deal with *[to cover a subject]* **7** to protect financially *[to cover a loss]* **8** to accept (a bet) **9** to travel over **10** to point a firearm at **11** *Journalism* to gather the details of (a news story) —***vi.*** **1** to spread over a surface, as a liquid does **2** to provide an alibi (*for*) —***n.*** **1** anything that covers, as a lid, top, etc. **2** a shelter for protection **3** a tablecloth and setting **4** COVER CHARGE **5** something used to hide one's real actions, etc. —**cover up** to keep blunders, crimes, etc. from being known —**take cover** to seek shelter —**under cover** in secrecy or concealment

cov'er·age (-ij) ***n.*** **1** the amount, extent, etc. covered by something **2** *Insurance* the risks covered by a policy

cov'er·all' ***n.*** [*usually pl.*] a one-piece outer garment, often worn over regular clothing while working, etc.

cover charge a fixed charge in addition to the cost of food and drink, as at a nightclub or restaurant

cover crop a crop, as clover, grown to prevent erosion and restore soil fertility

covered wagon a large wagon with an arched cover of canvas

cov'er·ing ***n.*** anything that covers

cov'er·let (-lit) ***n.*** ⟦< OFr *covrir,* to cover + *lit,* bed⟧ a bedspread

cover letter an explanatory letter sent with an enclosure or package: also **covering letter**

cover story the article in a magazine that deals with the subject depicted on the cover

cov·ert (kō'vərt, kuv'ərt) ***adj.*** ⟦see COVER⟧ hidden or disguised —***n.*** a protected place, as for game —**cov'ert·ly** ***adv.***

cov'er·up' ***n.*** an attempt to hide blunders, crimes, etc.

cov·et (kuv'it) ***vt., vi.*** ⟦< L *cupiditas,* cupidity⟧ to want intensely (esp., something that another person has)

cov'et·ous ***adj.*** tending to covet; greedy —**cov'et·ous·ly** ***adv.*** —**cov'et·ous·ness** ***n.***

cov·ey (kuv′ē) ***n.**, pl.* **-eys** ⟦< OFr *cover,* to hatch⟧ a small flock of birds, esp. partridges or quail

cow[1] (kou) ***n.*** ⟦OE *cu*⟧ **1** the mature female of domestic cattle, valued for its milk **2** the mature female of certain other mammals, as the whale

cow[2] (kou) ***vt.*** ⟦< ON *kūga,* subdue⟧ to make timid; intimidate

cow·ard (kou′ərd) ***n.*** ⟦ult. < L *cauda,* tail⟧ a person who lacks courage, esp. one who is shamefully afraid

cow′ard·ice′ (-ər dis′) ***n.*** lack of courage

cow′ard·ly ***adj.*** of or like a coward —***adv.*** in the manner of a coward —**cow′ard·li·ness** ***n.***

cow′boy′ ***n.*** a ranch worker who herds cattle: also **cow′hand′** —**cow′girl′** ***fem.n.***

cow·er (kou′ər) ***vi.*** ⟦ME *couren*⟧ to crouch or huddle up, as from fear or cold; shrink; cringe

cow′hide′ ***n.*** **1** the hide of a cow **2** leather from it

cowl (koul) ***n.*** ⟦< L *cucullus,* hood⟧ **1** a monk's hood or a monk's cloak with a hood **2** a hood-shaped part or structure

cow·lick (kou′lik′) ***n.*** ⟦< its looking as if licked by a cow⟧ a tuft of hair that cannot easily be combed flat

cowl·ing (koul′iŋ) ***n.*** ⟦see COWL⟧ a metal covering for an airplane engine, etc.

co-work·er (kō′wur′kər) ***n.*** a fellow worker

cow′poke′ ***n.*** [Inf.] COWBOY

cow pony a horse for herding cattle

cow′pox′ ***n.*** a disease of cows: a vaccine with its virus gives temporary immunity to smallpox

cox·comb (käks′kōm′) ***n.*** ⟦for *cock's comb*⟧ a silly, vain fellow; dandy

cox·swain (käk′sən, -swān′) ***n.*** ⟦< *cock,* small boat + SWAIN⟧ one who steers a boat or racing shell

coy (koi) ***adj.*** ⟦ME, quiet⟧ **1** bashful; shy **2** pretending to be shy —**coy′ly** ***adv.*** —**coy′ness** ***n.***

coy·o·te (kī ōt′ē, kī′ōt′) ***n.*** ⟦< AmInd (Mex)⟧ a small, wolflike animal of North America

coz·en (kuz′ən) ***vt., vi.*** ⟦< ME *cosin,* fraud⟧ to cheat; deceive —**coz′en·age** ***n.***

co·zy (kō′zē) ***adj.*** **-zi·er, -zi·est** ⟦Scot⟧ warm and comfortable; snug —***n.**, pl.* **-zies** a padded cover for a teapot, to keep the tea hot —**cozy up to** [Inf.] to try to ingratiate oneself with —**co′zi·ly** ***adv.*** —**co′zi·ness** ***n.***

CPA *abbrev.* Certified Public Accountant

CPI *abbrev.* consumer price index

CPO *abbrev.* Chief Petty Officer

CPR *abbrev.* cardiopulmonary resuscitation

CPU (sē′pē′yōō′) ***n.*** central processing unit: also **cpu**

Cr *Chem. symbol for* chromium

BLUE CRAB

crab (krab) ***n.*** ⟦OE *crabba*⟧ **1** a crustacean with four pairs of legs and a pair of pincers **2** a peevish person —***vi.*** **crabbed, crab′bing** [Inf.] to complain

crab apple **1** a small, very sour apple **2** a tree bearing crab apples: also **crab tree**

crab·bed (krab′id) ***adj.*** ⟦< CRAB (APPLE)⟧ **1** peevish **2** hard to read or understand, as handwriting —**crab′bed·ness** ***n.***

crab′by ***adj.*** **-bi·er, -bi·est** ⟦see prec.⟧ cross and complaining —**crab′bi·ly** ***adv.*** —**crab′bi·ness** ***n.***

crab grass a weedy grass, with freely rooting stems, that spreads rapidly

crack[1] (krak) ***vi.*** ⟦< OE *cracian,* resound⟧ **1** to make a sudden, sharp noise, as in breaking **2** to break or split, usually without separation of parts **3** to rasp or shift erratically in register: said of the voice **4** [Inf.] to break down as from strain —***vt.*** **1** to cause to make a sharp, sudden noise **2** to cause to break or split **3** to break down (petroleum) into the lighter hydrocarbons of gasoline, etc. **4** to hit hard **5** to solve **6** [Inf.] to break into or force open **7** [Slang] to make (a joke) —***n.*** **1** a sudden, sharp noise **2** a partial break; fracture **3** a chink; crevice **4** a cracking of the voice **5** a sudden, sharp blow **6** [Inf.] an attempt or try **7** [Slang] a joke or gibe —***adj.*** [Inf.] excellent; first-rate —**crack down (on)** to become strict (with) —**cracked up to be** [Inf.] believed to be —**crack up** **1** to crash **2** [Inf.] *a)* to break down physically or mentally *b)* to laugh or cry

crack[2] (krak) ***n.*** [Slang] a highly potent and purified form of cocaine for smoking

crack′down′ ***n.*** a resorting to strict or stricter discipline or punishment

cracked ***adj.*** **1** having a crack or cracks **2** sounding harsh or strident **3** [Inf.] crazy

crack′er ***n.*** **1** a firecracker **2** a thin, crisp wafer

crack′er·jack′ ***adj.*** [Slang] outstanding; excellent —***n.*** [Slang] an excellent person or thing

crack′head′ ***n.*** [Slang] a habitual user of CRACK[2]

crack·le (krak′əl) ***vi.*** **-led, -ling** ⟦ME *crakelen,* to crack⟧ to make a series of slight, sharp, popping sounds —***n.*** **1** a series of such sounds **2** the fine, irregular surface cracks on some pottery, etc.

crack′pot′ ***n.*** [Inf.] a crazy or eccentric person —***adj.*** [Inf.] crazy or eccentric

crack′up′ ***n.*** **1** a crash **2** [Inf.] a physical or mental breakdown

-cra·cy (krə sē) ⟦< Gr *kratos,* rule⟧ *combining form* a (specified) type of government; rule by *[autocracy]*

cra·dle (krād′'l) ***n.*** ⟦OE *cradol*⟧ **1** a baby's small bed, usually on rockers **2** infancy **3** the place of a thing's beginning **4** anything like a cradle **—*vt.* -dled, -dling 1** to place, rock, or hold in or as in a cradle **2** to take care of in infancy

cra′dle·song′ ***n.*** a lullaby

craft (kraft) ***n.*** ⟦OE *cræft,* power⟧ **1** a special skill or art **2** an occupation requiring special skill **3** the members of a skilled trade **4** guile; slyness **5** *pl.* **craft** a boat, ship, or aircraft

crafts·man (krafts′mən) ***n.,*** *pl.* **-men** (-mən) a skilled worker; artisan **—crafts′man·ship′ *n.***

craft′y ***adj.*** **-i·er, -i·est** ⟦ME *crafti,* sly⟧ subtly deceitful; sly **—craft′i·ly *adv.* —craft′i·ness *n.***

crag (krag) ***n.*** ⟦< Celt⟧ a steep, rugged rock rising from a rock mass **—crag′gy, -gi·er, -gi·est, *adj.***

cram (kram) ***vt.*** **crammed, cram′ming** ⟦OE *crammian*⟧ **1** to pack full or too full **2** to stuff; force **3** to feed to excess **—*vi.* 1** to eat too much or too quickly **2** to study a subject in a hurried, intensive way, as for an examination

cramp (kramp) ***n.*** ⟦< OFr *crampe,* bent⟧ **1** a sudden, painful, involuntary contraction of a muscle from chill, strain, etc. **2** [*usually pl.*] abdominal or uterine spasms and pain **—*vt.* 1** to cause a cramp or cramps in **2** ⟦< MDu *krampe,* bent in⟧ to hamper; restrain

cramped ***adj.*** **1** confined or restricted **2** irregular and crowded, as some handwriting

cran·ber·ry (kran′ber′ē, -bər ē) ***n.,*** *pl.* **-ries** ⟦< Du *kranebere*⟧ **1** a firm, sour, edible, red berry, the fruit of an evergreen shrub **2** the shrub

crane (krān) ***n.*** ⟦OE *cran*⟧ **1** a large wading bird with very long legs and neck **2** a machine for lifting or moving heavy weights, using a movable projecting arm or a horizontal traveling beam **—*vt., vi.* craned, cran′ing** to stretch (the neck)

cra·ni·um (krā′nē əm) ***n.,*** *pl.* **-ni·ums** or **-ni·a** (-ə) ⟦< Gr *kranion*⟧ the skull, esp. the part containing the brain **—cra′ni·al *adj.***

crank (kraŋk) ***n.*** ⟦OE *cranc-,* something twisted⟧ **1** a handle or arm bent at right angles and connected to a machine shaft to transmit motion **2** [Inf.] an eccentric or irritable person **—*vt.*** to start or operate by a crank **—crank out** [Inf.] to produce steadily and prolifically

crank′case′ ***n.*** the metal casing that encloses the crankshaft of an internal-combustion engine

crank′shaft′ ***n.*** a shaft with one or more cranks for transmitting motion

crank′y ***adj.*** **-i·er, -i·est 1** apt to operate poorly **2** irritable **3** eccentric **—crank′i·ly *adv.* —crank′i·ness *n.***

cran·ny (kran′ē) ***n.,*** *pl.* **-nies** ⟦< VL *crena,* a notch⟧ a crevice; crack

crap (krap) ***n.*** ⟦< ML *crappa,* chaff⟧ [Slang] **1** nonsense **2** junk; trash **3** excrement: somewhat vulgar **—crap′py, -pi·er, -pi·est, *adj.***

crape (krāp) ***n.*** **1** CREPE (sense 1) **2** a piece of black crepe as a sign of mourning

crap·pie (krap′ē) ***n.*** a small North American sunfish

craps (kraps) ***n.*** ⟦Fr *crabs*⟧ a gambling game played with two dice

crap′shoot′ ***n.*** [Inf.] a very risky undertaking

crap·shoot·er (krap′sho͞ot′ər) ***n.*** a gambler at craps

crash (krash) ***vi.*** ⟦ME⟧ **1** to fall, collide, or break with a loud noise **2** to collapse; fail **3** [Slang] to sleep or get a temporary place to sleep **—*vt.* 1** to cause (a car, airplane, etc.) to crash **2** to force with or as with a crashing noise: with *in, out, through,* etc. **3** [Inf.] to get into (a party, etc.) without an invitation, etc. **—*n.* 1** a loud, sudden noise **2** a crashing **3** a sudden collapse, as of business **—*adj.*** [Inf.] using all possible resources, effort, and speed *[a crash program to build roads]*

crash′-land′ ***vt., vi.*** to bring (an airplane) down in a forced landing, esp. without use of the landing gear **—crash landing**

crash pad [Slang] a place to live or sleep temporarily

crass (kras) ***adj.*** ⟦L *crassus,* thick⟧ **1** tasteless, insensitive, etc. **2** materialistic **—crass′ly *adv.* —crass′ness *n.***

-crat (krat) ⟦< Gr *kratos,* rule⟧ *combining form* member or supporter of (a specified kind of) government

crate (krāt) ***n.*** ⟦L *cratis,* wickerwork⟧ a packing case made of slats of wood **—*vt.* crat′ed, crat′ing** to pack in a crate

cra·ter (krāt′ər) ***n.*** ⟦< Gr *kratēr,* mixing bowl⟧ **1** a bowl-shaped cavity, as at the mouth of a volcano **2** a pit made by an exploding bomb, etc. **—*vt.*** to make craters in **—*vi.*** to form craters

cra·vat (krə vat′) ***n.*** ⟦< Fr⟧ a necktie

crave (krāv) ***vt.*** **craved, crav′ing** ⟦OE *crafian*⟧ **1** to ask for earnestly; beg **2** to desire strongly

cra·ven (krā′vən) ***adj.*** ⟦< L *crepare,* to rattle⟧ cowardly **—*n.*** a coward **—cra′ven·ly *adv.* —cra′ven·ness *n.***

crav′ing ***n.*** an intense and prolonged desire, as for affection or for a food or drug

craw (krô) ***n.*** ⟦ME *craue*⟧ **1** the crop of a bird **2** the stomach

craw·fish (krô′fish′) ***n.,*** *pl.* **-fish′** or (for different species) **-fish′es** crayfish

crawl (krôl) ***vi.*** ⟦< ON *krafla*⟧ **1** to move slowly by dragging the body along the ground **2** to go on hands and knees; creep **3** to move slowly **4** to move or act in a servile manner **5** to swarm (*with* crawling things) **—*n.* 1** a slow movement **2** an overarm swimming stroke

crawl space an unfinished space, as under a floor, allowing access to wiring, plumbing, etc.

crawl'y ***adj.*** **-i·er, -i·est** CREEPY

cray·fish (krā'fish') ***n.***, *pl.* **-fish'** or (for different species) **-fish'es** ⟦< OHG *krebiz*⟧ a freshwater crustacean somewhat like a little lobster

cray·on (krā'ən, -än') ***n.*** ⟦Fr, pencil < L *creta,* chalk⟧ **1** a small stick of chalk, charcoal, or colored wax, used for drawing, coloring, or writing **2** a drawing made with crayons —***vt.*** to draw or color with crayons

craze (krāz) ***vt.***, ***vi.*** **crazed, craz'ing** ⟦ME *crasen,* to crack⟧ to make or become insane —***n.*** a fad

cra·zy (krā'zē) ***adj.*** **-zi·er, -zi·est** ⟦< prec.⟧ **1** unsound of mind; insane **2** [Inf.] foolish; not sensible **3** [Inf.] very enthusiastic or eager —***n.***, *pl.* **-zies** [Slang] a crazy person —**like crazy** [Inf.] with great energy, intensity, etc. —**cra'zi·ly** ***adv.*** —**cra'zi·ness** ***n.***

crazy bone FUNNY BONE

crazy quilt **1** a patchwork quilt with no regular design **2** a hodgepodge

creak (krēk) ***vi.***, ***vt.*** ⟦echoic⟧ to make, cause to make, or move with a harsh, squeaking sound —***n.*** such a sound —**creak'y, -i·er, -i·est,** ***adj.*** —**creak'i·ly** ***adv.*** —**creak'i·ness** ***n.***

cream (krēm) ***n.*** ⟦< OFr⟧ **1** the oily, yellowish part of milk **2** a cosmetic, emulsion, or food with a creamy consistency **3** the best part **4** yellowish white —***adj.*** made of or with cream —***vt.*** **1** to add cream to **2** to beat into a creamy consistency **3** [Slang] *a)* to beat or defeat soundly *b)* to hurt, damage, etc., as by striking with great force —**cream of** creamed purée of —**cream'y, -i·er, -i·est,** ***adj.*** —**cream'·i·ness** ***n.***

cream cheese a soft, white cheese made of cream or of milk and cream

cream'er ***n.*** **1** a pitcher for cream **2** a nondairy substance used in place of cream

cream'·er·y ***n.***, *pl.* **-ies** a place where dairy products are processed or sold

cream of tartar a white substance used in baking powder, etc.

crease (krēs) ***n.*** ⟦< ME *creste,* crest⟧ **1** a line made by folding and pressing **2** a fold or wrinkle —***vt.*** **creased, creas'ing** **1** to make a crease in **2** to wrinkle —***vi.*** to become creased

cre·ate (krē āt') ***vt.*** **-at'ed, -at'ing** ⟦< L *creare*⟧ **1** to cause to come into existence; make; originate **2** to bring about; give rise to; cause

cre·a'tion (-ā'shən) ***n.*** **1** a creating or being created **2** the universe **3** anything created —**the Creation** God's creating of the world

cre·a'tive (-āt'iv) ***adj.*** **1** creating or able to create **2** inventive **3** stimulating the imagination —**cre·a'tive·ly** ***adv.*** —**cre·a'tive·ness** ***n.*** —**cre'a·tiv'i·ty** (-ā tiv'ə tē) ***n.***

cre·a'tor (-āt'ər) ***n.*** ⟦L⟧ one who creates —**the Creator** God

crea·ture (krē'chər) ***n.*** ⟦< L *creatura*⟧ a living being, animal or human

crèche (kresh, krāsh) ***n.*** ⟦Fr⟧ a display of the stable scene of Jesus' birth

cre·dence (krēd''ns) ***n.*** ⟦< L *credere,* believe⟧ belief, esp. in the reports or testimony of another

cre·den·tial (kri den'shəl) ***n.*** ⟦see prec.⟧ [*usually pl.*] a letter or certificate showing one's right to a certain position or authority

cre·den·za (kri den'zə) ***n.*** ⟦It⟧ **1** a type of buffet or sideboard **2** a low office cabinet

credibility gap **1** a disparity between what is said and the facts **2** the inability to have one's truthfulness or honesty accepted

cred·i·ble (kred'ə bəl) ***adj.*** ⟦< L *credere,* believe⟧ that can be believed; reliable —**cred'i·bil'i·ty** ***n.*** —**cred'i·bly** ***adv.***

cred·it (kred'it) ***n.*** ⟦< L *credere,* believe⟧ **1** belief; confidence **2** favorable reputation **3** praise or approval **4** a person or thing bringing approval or honor **5** *a)* acknowledgment of work done *b)* [*pl.*] a list of such acknowledgments in a film, book, etc. **6** a sum available to one, as in a bank account **7** the entry, in an account, of payment on a debt **8** trust in one's ability to meet payments when due **9** the time allowed for payment **10** a completed unit of study in a school —***vt.*** **1** to believe; trust **2** to give credit to or commendation for **3** to give credit in a bank account, etc. —**do credit to** to bring honor to —**on credit** with an agreement to pay later

cred'it·a·ble ***adj.*** deserving some credit or praise —**cred'it·a·bly** ***adv.***

credit card a card entitling one to charge purchases, etc. at certain businesses

cred'i·tor (-it ər) ***n.*** one to whom money is owed

credit union a cooperative association for pooling savings of members and making low-interest loans to them

cred'it·wor'thy ***adj.*** sufficiently sound financially to be granted credit —**cred'it·wor'thi·ness** ***n.***

cre·do (krē'dō', krā'-) ***n.***, *pl.* **-dos'** ⟦L, I believe⟧ a creed

cred·u·lous (krej'oo ləs, -ə ləs) ***adj.*** ⟦< L *credere,* believe⟧ tending to believe too readily —**cre·du·li·ty** (krə dōō'lə tē, -dyōō-) ***n.*** —**cred'u·lous·ly** ***adv.***

creed (krēd) ***n.*** ⟦< L *credo,* I believe⟧ **1** a brief statement of religious belief, esp. one accepted as authoritative by a church **2** any statement of belief, principles, etc.

creek (krēk, krik) ***n.*** ⟦< ON *kriki,* a bend, winding⟧ a small stream —**up the creek** [Slang] in trouble

creel (krēl) ***n.*** ⟦< L *cratis,* wickerwork⟧ a wicker basket for holding fish

creep (krēp) ***vi.*** **crept, creep'ing** ⟦OE *creopan*⟧ **1** to move with the body close to the ground, as on hands and knees **2** to move slowly or stealthily **3** to grow along the ground or a wall, as ivy —***n.*** **1** the act of creeping **2** [Slang] an annoying or disgusting person —**make one's flesh creep** to give one a feeling of fear, disgust, etc. —**the creeps** [Inf.] a feeling of fear, disgust, etc. —**creep'er**

n.

creep'y ***adj.*** **-i·er, -i·est** having or causing a feeling of fear or disgust —**creep'i·ly** ***adv.*** —**creep'i·ness** ***n.***

cre·mains (krē mānz') ***pl.n.*** the ashes remaining after cremation

cre·mate (krē'māt', kri māt') ***vt.*** **-mat'ed, -mat'ing** ⟦< L *cremare*⟧ to burn (a dead body) to ashes —**cre·ma'tion** ***n.***

cre·ma·to·ry (krē'mə tôr'ē, krem'ə-) ***n.***, *pl.* **-ries** a furnace for cremating: also **cre'ma·to'ri·um** (-ē əm), *pl.* **-ri·ums, -ri·a** (-ē ə), or **-ries** —***adj.*** of or for cremation

crème de menthe (krem' də mänt', menth', mint') ⟦Fr, cream of mint⟧ a sweet, mint-flavored liqueur

crème fraîche (krem' fresh') ⟦Fr, fresh cream⟧ slightly fermented high-fat cream, used in sauces, desserts, etc.

cren·el·ate or **cren·el·late** (kren'əl āt') ***vt.*** **-el·at'ed** or **-el·lat'ed, -el·at'ing** or **-el·lat'ing** ⟦< VL *crena*, a notch⟧ to furnish with battlements or with squared notches —**cren'el·a'tion** or **cren'el·la'tion** ***n.***

Cre·ole (krē'ōl') ***n.*** ⟦< Fr < Port *crioulo*, native⟧ **1** a person descended from the original French settlers of Louisiana **2** a person of mixed Creole and black descent **3** [**c-**] a language that develops when different languages remain in contact with each other —***adj.*** [*usually* **c-**] prepared with sautéed tomatoes, green peppers, onions, spices, etc.

cre·o·sote (krē'ə sōt') ***n.*** ⟦< Gr *kreas*, flesh + *sōzein*, to save⟧ an oily liquid distilled from tar and used as a wood preservative, etc.

crepe or **crêpe** (krāp; *for 5, also* krep) ***n.*** ⟦< Fr < L *crispus*, curly⟧ **1** a thin, crinkled cloth of silk, rayon, wool, etc. **2** CRAPE (sense 2) **3** wrinkled soft rubber used for shoe soles: also **crepe rubber** **4** thin, crinkled paper: also **crepe paper** **5** a thin pancake, rolled and filled

crêpes su·zette (krāp' soo̅ zet') ⟦Fr⟧ crêpes rolled in a hot, orange-flavored sauce and served in flaming brandy

crept (krept) ***vi.*** *pt. & pp. of* CREEP

cre·scen·do (kri shen'dō') ***adj.***, ***adv.*** ⟦It < L *crescere*, grow⟧ *Music* with a gradual increase in loudness: also written ***cre·scen'do*** —***n.***, *pl.* **-dos'** a gradual increase in loudness, force, etc.

cres·cent (kres'ənt) ***n.*** ⟦< L *crescere*, grow⟧ **1** a phase of a planet or a moon, when it appears to have one concave edge and one convex edge **2** anything shaped like this —***adj.*** shaped like a crescent

crescent wrench ⟦< *Crescent*, a trademark⟧ a wrench with a crescent-shaped head and an adjustable jaw

cress (kres) ***n.*** ⟦OE *cressa*⟧ a plant with pungent leaves, as watercress, used in salads, etc.

crest (krest) ***n.*** ⟦< L *crista*⟧ **1** any growth on the head of an animal, as a comb or tuft **2** a heraldic device placed on seals, silverware, etc. **3** the top line or surface; summit **4** the highest point, level, degree, etc. —***vi.*** to form or reach a crest —**crest'ed** ***adj.***

crest'fall'en ***adj.*** dejected, disheartened, etc.

Cre·ta·ceous (kri tā'shəs, krē-) ***adj.*** ⟦< L *creta*, chalk⟧ of the latest period of the Mesozoic Era, marked by the dying out of dinosaurs, the rise of mammals and flowering plants, and the formation of oil deposits

Crete (krēt) Greek island in the E Mediterranean —**Cre·tan** (krēt''n) ***adj.***, ***n.***

cre·tonne (krē tän', krē'tän') ***n.*** ⟦Fr, after *Creton*, village in Normandy⟧ a heavy, printed cotton or linen cloth, used for curtains, slipcovers, etc.

cre·vasse (krə vas') ***n.*** ⟦Fr⟧ a deep crack, esp. in a glacier

crev·ice (krev'is) ***n.*** ⟦< L *crepare*, to rattle⟧ a narrow opening caused by a crack or split; fissure

crew[1] (kroo̅) ***n.*** ⟦< L *crescere*, grow⟧ **1** a group of people working together [*a road crew*] **2** a ship's personnel, excluding the officers —**crew'man**, *pl.* **-men** (-mən), ***n.***

crew[2] (kroo̅) ***vi.*** [Chiefly Brit.] *alt. pt. of* CROW[2] (sense 1)

crew cut a man's haircut in which the hair is cropped close to the head

crew·el (kroo̅'əl) ***n.*** ⟦ME *crule*⟧ a loosely twisted, worsted yarn —**crew'el·work'** ***n.***

crib (krib) ***n.*** ⟦OE, ox stall⟧ **1** a rack or box for fodder **2** a small bed with high sides, for a baby **3** an enclosure for storing grain **4** an underwater structure serving as a pier, water intake, etc. **5** [Inf.] a translation or other aid used dishonestly in doing schoolwork —***vt.*** **cribbed, crib'bing** **1** to confine **2** to furnish with a crib **3** [Inf.] to plagiarize —***vi.*** [Inf.] to do schoolwork dishonestly

crib·bage (krib'ij) ***n.*** a card game in which the object is to form combinations for points

crib death SUDDEN INFANT DEATH SYNDROME

crick[1] (krik) ***n.*** ⟦< ON *kriki*, bend⟧ a painful cramp in the neck, back, etc.

crick[2] (krik) ***n.*** [Dial.] CREEK

crick·et[1] (krik'it) ***n.*** ⟦< OFr *criquer*, to creak⟧ a leaping insect similar to a grasshopper

crick·et[2] (krik'it) ***n.*** ⟦OFr *criquet*, a bat⟧ an outdoor game played by two teams of eleven players each, using a ball, bats, and wickets

cried (krīd) ***vi.***, ***vt.*** *pt. & pp. of* CRY

cri·er (krī'ər) ***n.*** **1** one who cries **2** one who shouts out announcements, news, etc.

crime (krīm) ***n.*** ⟦< L *crimen*, offense⟧ **1** an act in violation of a law; specif., a serious violation, as a felony **2** a sin

Cri·me·a (krī mē'ə) peninsula in SW Ukraine, extending into the Black Sea —**Cri·me'an** ***adj.***

crim·i·nal (krim'ə nəl) ***adj.*** **1** having the nature of crime **2** relating to or guilty of crime —***n.*** a person guilty of a crime —**crim'i·nal'i·ty** (-nal'ə tə) ***n.*** —**crim'i·nal·ly** ***adv.***

crim'i·nal·ist (-nəl ist) ***n.*** an expert in the scientific analysis of criminal evidence

crim'i·nol'o·gy (-näl'ə jē) ***n.*** the scientific study of crime and criminals —**crim'i·nol'o·gist *n.***

crimp (krimp) ***vt.*** ⟦< MDu *crimpen,* to wrinkle⟧ **1** to press into narrow folds; pleat **2** to curl (hair) **3** to pinch together —***n.*** **1** a crimping **2** anything crimped —**put a crimp in** [Inf.] to hinder

crim·son (krim'zən, -sən) ***n.*** ⟦< Ar *qirmiz*⟧ deep red —***adj.*** deep-red —***vt., vi.*** to make or become crimson

cringe (krinj) ***vi.*** **cringed, cring'ing** ⟦< OE *cringan,* to fall (in battle)⟧ **1** to draw back, crouch, etc., as when afraid; cower **2** to act timidly servile

crin·kle (kriŋ'kəl) ***vi., vt.*** **-kled, -kling** ⟦see prec.⟧ **1** to wrinkle **2** to rustle or crackle, as crushed paper —**crin'kly, -kli·er, -kli·est,** ***adj.***

crin·o·line (krin'ə lin) ***n.*** ⟦Fr < It < *crino,* horsehair + *lino,* linen⟧ **1** a coarse, stiff cloth used as a lining in garments **2** HOOP SKIRT

crip·ple (krip'əl) ***n.*** ⟦< OE *creopan,* to creep⟧ a disabled person: now somewhat offensive —***vt.*** **-pled, -pling** **1** to lame **2** to disable; impair

cri·sis (krī'sis) ***n., pl.*** **-ses'** (-sēz') ⟦L < Gr *krinein,* to separate⟧ **1** the turning point of a disease for better or worse **2** a decisive or crucial time, etc. **3** a time of great danger, etc.

crisp (krisp) ***adj.*** ⟦< L *crispus,* curly⟧ **1** easily crumbled **2** fresh and firm **3** sharp and clear **4** fresh and invigorating **5** curled and wiry Also **crisp'y, -i·er, -i·est** —**crisp'ly *adv.*** —**crisp'ness *n.***

criss·cross (kris'krôs') ***n.*** ⟦ME *Christcros,* Christ's cross⟧ a mark or pattern made of crossed lines —***adj.*** marked by crossing lines —***vt.*** to mark with crossing lines —***vi.*** to move to and fro —***adv.*** **1** crosswise **2** awry

cri·te·ri·on (krī tir'ē ən) ***n., pl.*** **-ri·a** (-ē ə) or **-ri·ons** ⟦< Gr *kritēs,* judge⟧ a standard, test, etc. by which a thing can be judged

crit·ic (krit'ik) ***n.*** ⟦< Gr *krinein,* discern⟧ **1** one who judges books, music, plays, etc., as for a newspaper **2** one who finds fault

crit'i·cal (-i kəl) ***adj.*** **1** tending to find fault **2** of critics or criticism **3** of or forming a crisis; decisive or dangerous —**crit'i·cal·ly *adv.***

crit'i·cism' (-ə siz'əm) ***n.*** **1** the act of making judgments, esp. of literary or artistic work **2** a review, article, etc. expressing such judgment **3** censure **4** the principles or methods of critics

crit'i·cize' (-ə sīz') ***vi., vt.*** **-cized', -ciz'ing** **1** to analyze and judge as a critic **2** to find fault (with) —**crit'i·ciz'a·ble *adj.*** —**crit'i·ciz'er *n.***

cri·tique (kri tēk') ***n.*** ⟦Fr⟧ a critical analysis or review —***vt., vi.*** **-tiqued', -tiqu'ing** to criticize (a subject, art work, etc.)

crit·ter (krit'ər) ***n.*** *dial. var. of* CREATURE

croak (krōk) ***vi.*** ⟦echoic⟧ **1** to make a deep, hoarse sound, as a frog does **2** [Slang] to die —***vt.*** to utter in deep, hoarse tones —***n.*** a croaking sound

Cro·at (krō'at', -ət) ***n.*** a person born or living in Croatia

Cro·a·tia (krō ā'shə) country in SE Europe: 21,829 sq. mi.; pop. 4,784,000 —**Cro·a'tian *adj., n.***

cro·chet (krō shā') ***n.*** ⟦Fr, small hook⟧ needlework done with one hooked needle —***vi., vt.*** **-cheted'** (-shād'), **-chet'ing** to do, or make by, crochet —**cro·chet'er *n.***

crock (kräk) ***n.*** ⟦OE *crocca*⟧ an earthenware pot or jar —**crock'er·y *n.***

crocked (kräkt) ***adj.*** ⟦< *crock,* to disable⟧ [Slang] drunk

croc·o·dile (kräk'ə dīl') ***n.*** ⟦< Gr *krokodilos,* lizard⟧ a large, lizardlike reptile of tropical streams, having a long, narrow head with massive jaws

cro·cus (krō'kəs) ***n., pl.*** **-cus·es** or **-ci'** (-sī') ⟦< Gr *krokos,* saffron⟧ a spring-blooming plant of the iris family, with a yellow, purple, or white flower

Croe·sus (krē'səs) flourished 6th c. B.C.; king noted for his great wealth

crois·sant (krə sänt'; *Fr* krwȧ sän') ***n.*** ⟦Fr, crescent⟧ a crescent-shaped, flaky bread roll

Cro-Mag·non (krō mag'nən) ***adj.*** ⟦after *Cro-Magnon* cave in France⟧ of a Stone Age type of tall human of the European continent

Crom·well (kräm'wel), **Ol·i·ver** (äl'ə vər) 1599-1658; Eng. revolutionary leader & head (Lord Protector) of England (1653-58)

crone (krōn) ***n.*** ⟦< MDu *kronje,* old ewe⟧ an ugly, withered old woman

cro·ny (krō'nē) ***n., pl.*** **-nies** ⟦< Gr *chronos,* time⟧ a close companion

crook (krook) ***n.*** ⟦< ON *krōkr,* hook⟧ **1** a hooked or curved staff, etc.; hook **2** a bend or curve **3** [Inf.] a swindler or thief —***vt., vi.*** **crooked** (krookt), **crook'ing** to bend or curve

crook·ed (krookt; *for 2 & 3* krook'id) ***adj.*** **1** having a crook **2** not straight; bent **3** dishonest —**crook'ed·ly *adv.*** —**crook'ed·ness *n.***

crook'neck' ***n.*** a squash with a long, curved neck

croon (kro͞on) ***vi., vt.*** ⟦ME *cronen*⟧ **1** to sing or hum in a low, gentle tone **2** to sing (popular songs) softly and sentimentally —***n.*** a low, gentle singing or humming —**croon'er *n.***

crop (kräp) ***n.*** ⟦OE *croppa,* a cluster⟧ **1** a saclike part of a bird's gullet, in which food is stored before digestion **2** any agricultural product, growing or harvested **3** the yield of any product in one season or place **4** a group **5** the handle of a whip **6** a riding whip **7** hair cut close to the head —***vt.*** **cropped, crop'ping** **1** to cut or bite off the tops or ends of **2** to cut (the hair, etc.) short —**crop out** (or **up**) to appear unexpectedly

crop'-dust'ing ***n.*** the spraying of crops with pesticides from an airplane —**crop'-dust' *vi., vt.***

crop'per ***n.*** **1** one that crops **2** a sharecropper —**come a cropper** [Inf.] to come to ruin; fail

cro·quet (krō kā′) ***n.*** ⟦Fr, dial. form of *crochet*, small hook⟧ an outdoor game in which the players use mallets to drive a ball through hoops in the ground

cro·quette (krō ket′) ***n.*** ⟦Fr < *croquer*, to crunch⟧ a small mass of meat, fish, etc. fried in deep fat

cro·sier (krō′zhər) ***n.*** ⟦< OFr *croce*⟧ the staff carried by a bishop or abbot

cross (krôs) ***n.*** ⟦< L *crux*⟧ **1** an upright post with a bar across it, on which the ancient Romans executed people **2** a representation of this as a symbol of the crucifixion of Jesus, hence of Christianity **3** any trouble or affliction **4** any design or mark made by two intersecting lines, bars, etc. **5** a crossing of varieties or breeds —***vt., vi.*** **1** to make the sign of the cross (upon) **2** to place or lie across or crosswise **3** to intersect **4** to draw a line or lines across **5** to go or extend across **6** to meet and pass (each other) **7** to oppose **8** to interbreed (animals or plants) —***adj.*** **1** lying or passing across **2** contrary; opposed **3** cranky; irritable **4** of mixed variety or breed —**cross off** (or **out**) to cancel as by drawing lines across —**cross someone's mind** to come suddenly to someone's mind —**cross someone's path** to meet someone —**cross′ly** ***adv.***

cross′bar′ ***n.*** a bar, line, or stripe placed crosswise

cross′beam′ ***n.*** any transverse beam in a structure

cross′bones′ ***n.*** a representation of two bones placed across each other, under that of a skull, used to symbolize death or danger

cross′bow′ (-bō′) ***n.*** a weapon consisting of a bow set transversely on a grooved wooden stock —**cross′bow′man** (-mən), *pl.* **-men** (-mən), ***n.***

cross′breed′ ***vt., vi.*** **-bred′**, **-breed′ing** HYBRIDIZE —***n.*** HYBRID (sense 1)

cross′-coun′try ***adj., adv.*** across open country or fields *[a cross-country race]*

cross′cut′ saw a saw designed to cut across the grain of wood

cross′-dress′ing ***n.*** the wearing of clothing worn by the opposite sex

cross′-ex·am′ine ***vt., vi.*** **-ined**, **-in·ing** *Law* to question (a witness called by the opposing side) in order to challenge the witness's previous testimony —**cross′-ex·am′i·na′tion** ***n.***

cross′-eye′ ***n.*** an abnormal condition in which the eyes are turned toward each other —**cross′-eyed′** ***adj.***

cross′fire′ ***n.*** **1** lines of fire from two or more positions that cross **2** an energetic exchange, as by opposing forces or of opposing opinions

cross′hatch′ (-hach′) ***vt., vi.*** to shade (a drawing) with two sets of parallel lines that cross each other

cross′ing ***n.*** **1** the act of passing across, interbreeding, etc. **2** an intersection, as of streets **3** a place where a street, etc. may be crossed

cross′piece′ ***n.*** a piece lying across another

cross′-pol′li·nate′ ***vt., vi.*** **-nat′ed**, **-nat′ing** to transfer pollen from the anther of (a flower) to the stigma of (a genetically different flower) —**cross′-pol′li·na′tion** ***n.***

cross′-pur′pose ***n.*** a contrary purpose —**at cross-purposes** having a misunderstanding as to each other's purposes

cross′-ref′er·ence ***n.*** a reference from one part of a book, etc. to another —***vt.*** **-enced**, **-enc·ing** to provide (an index, etc.) with cross-references —**cross′-re·fer′** ***vt., vi.***

cross′road′ ***n.*** **1** a road that crosses another **2** [*usually pl., often with sing. v.*] *a*) the place where roads intersect *b*) any center of activity, etc. *c*) a time of important changes or major decisions

cross section **1** *a*) a cutting through something *b*) a piece so cut off *c*) a representation of this **2** a representative part of a whole —**cross′-sec′tion** ***vt.***

cross′town′ ***adj.*** **1** going across a city *[a crosstown bus]* **2** on the other side of a city *[a crosstown rival]*

cross′walk′ ***n.*** a lane marked off for pedestrians to use in crossing a street

cross′wise′ ***adv.*** so as to cross: also **cross′ways′**

cross′word′ puzzle an arrangement of numbered squares to be filled in with the letters of words, arranged vertically and horizontally, whose synonyms and definitions are given as clues

crotch (kräch) ***n.*** ⟦ME *crucche*, crutch⟧ **1** a forked place, as on a tree **2** the place where the legs fork from the human body or from the upper part of a pair of trousers

crotch·et (kräch′it) ***n.*** ⟦ult. < OFr *croc*, a hook⟧ a peculiar whim or stubborn notion —**crotch′et·y** ***adj.***

crouch (krouch) ***vi.*** ⟦< OFr *croc*, a hook⟧ to stoop low with legs bent —***n.*** a crouching position

croup (kro͞op) ***n.*** ⟦< obs. or dial. *croup*, speak hoarsely⟧ an inflammation of the respiratory passages, with labored breathing, hoarse coughing, etc.

crou·pi·er (kro͞o′pē ā′, -ər) ***n.*** ⟦Fr⟧ one in charge of a gambling table

crou·ton (kro͞o′tän′, kro͞o tän′) ***n.*** ⟦Fr < *croûte*, a crust⟧ a small, crisp piece of toasted bread served in soup or salads

crow[1] (krō) ***n.*** ⟦OE *crawa*⟧ a large, glossy-black bird with a harsh call —**as the crow flies** in a straight, direct line —**eat crow** [Inf.] to admit an error

crow[2] (krō) ***vi.*** **crowed** or, for 1, [Chiefly Brit.] **crew** (kro͞o), **crowed**, **crow′ing** ⟦OE *crawan*⟧ **1** to make the shrill cry of a rooster **2** to boast in triumph **3** to make a sound of pleasure —***n.*** a crowing sound

CROWBAR

crow′bar′ *n.* a long metal bar used as a lever for prying, etc.

crowd (kroud) *vi.* ⟦< OE *crudan*⟧ **1** to push one's way (*into*) **2** to throng —*vt.* **1** to press or push **2** to fill too full; cram —*n.* **1** a large number of people or things grouped closely **2** the common people; the masses **3** [Inf.] a set; clique —**crowd′ed** *adj.*

crow′foot′ *n., pl.* **-foots′** or **-feet′** a plant of the buttercup family, with leaves resembling a crow's foot

crown (kroun) *n.* ⟦< Gr *korōnē*, wreath⟧ **1** a wreath worn on the head in victory **2** a reward; honor **3** a monarch's headdress **4** [*often* **C-**] *a*) the power of a monarch *b*) the monarch **5** a British coin equal to 25 (new) pence: no longer minted **6** the top part, as of the head **7** the highest quality, state, etc. of anything **8** *a*) the part of a tooth outside the gum *b*) an artificial substitute for this —*vt.* **1** to put a crown on **2** to make (a person) a monarch **3** to honor **4** to be the highest part of **5** to complete successfully

crown prince the male heir apparent to a throne —**crown princess**

crow's-foot (krōz′foot′) *n., pl.* **-feet′** any of the wrinkles that often develop at the outer corners of the eyes of adults

crow's′-nest′ (-nest′) *n.* a lookout's platform high on a ship's mast

cro·zier (krō′zhər) *n.* CROSIER

CRT (sē′är′tē′) *n.* a cathode-ray tube

cru·cial (krōō′shəl) *adj.* ⟦< L *crux*, a cross⟧ decisive; critical —**cru′cial·ly** *adv.*

cru·ci·ble (krōō′sə bəl) *n.* ⟦ML *crucibulum*, lamp⟧ **1** a heat-resistant container for melting ores, metals, etc. **2** a severe trial

cru·ci·fix (krōō′sə fiks′) *n.* ⟦see CRUCIFY⟧ a cross with the figure of the crucified Jesus Christ on it

cru′ci·fix′ion (-fik′shən) *n.* **1** a crucifying **2** [**C-**] the crucifying of Jesus, or a representation of this

cru′ci·form′ (-fôrm′) *adj.* cross-shaped

cru′ci·fy′ (-fī′) *vt.* **-fied′**, **-fy′ing** ⟦< L *crux*, a cross + *figere*, fasten⟧ **1** to execute by nailing or binding to a cross and leaving to die **2** to be very cruel to; torment

crude (krōōd) *adj.* **crud′er**, **crud′est** ⟦< L *crudus*, raw⟧ **1** in a raw or natural condition **2** lacking grace, tact, taste, etc. **3** roughly made —**crude′ly** *adv.* —**crude′ness** *n.* —**cru·di·ty** (krōō′də tē) *n.*

cru·di·tés (krōō′də tā′) *pl.n.* ⟦Fr, raw things⟧ raw vegetables cut up and served as hors d'oeuvres, usually with a dip or sauce

cru·el (krōō′əl) *adj.* ⟦see CRUDE⟧ causing pain and suffering; pitiless —**cru′el·ly** *adv.* —**cru′el·ness** *n.* —**cru′el·ty**, *pl.* **-ties**, *n.*

cru·et (krōō′it) *n.* ⟦< OFr *crue*, earthen pot⟧ a small glass bottle, as for holding vinegar or oil for the table

cruise (krōōz) *vi.* **cruised**, **cruis′ing** ⟦< Du *kruisen*, to cross⟧ **1** to sail or ride about from place to place, as for pleasure or in search of something **2** to move at the most efficient speed for sustained travel **3** to operate at a predetermined speed by use of a regulating mechanism (**cruise control**) —*vt.* to sail or journey over or about —*n.* a cruising voyage

cruise missile a long-range, jet-propelled winged missile that can be launched from an airplane, submarine, ship, etc. and guided to its target by remote control

cruis′er *n.* **1** anything that cruises, as a police car **2** a fast warship smaller than a battleship

crul·ler (krul′ər) *n.* ⟦Du < *krullen*, to curl⟧ a kind of twisted doughnut

crumb (krum) *n.* ⟦< OE *cruma*, a bit scraped from bread crust⟧ **1** a small piece broken off, as of bread **2** any bit or scrap [*crumbs* of knowledge] —**crumb·y** (krum′ē), **-i·er**, **-i·est**, *adj.*

crum·ble (krum′bəl) *vt.* **-bled**, **-bling** ⟦< prec.⟧ to break into crumbs —*vi.* to fall to pieces; disintegrate —**crum′bly** (-blē), **-bli·er**, **-bli·est**, *adj.*

crum·my (krum′ē) *adj.* **-mi·er**, **-mi·est** [Slang] **1** dirty, cheap, etc. **2** inferior, worthless, etc.

crum·pet (krum′pit) *n.* ⟦< OE *crump*, twisted⟧ an unsweetened batter cake baked on a griddle

crum·ple (krum′pəl) *vt.* **-pled**, **-pling** ⟦ult. < MDu *crimpen*, to wrinkle⟧ to crush together into wrinkles

crunch (krunch) *vi., vt.* ⟦echoic⟧ **1** to chew, press, grind, etc. with a noisy, crackling sound **2** [Inf.] to process (a large quantity of data) rapidly [*crunching* numbers on a computer] —*n.* **1** the act or sound of crunching **2** [Slang] a showdown or tight situation —**crunch′y**, **-i·er**, **-i·est**, *adj.*

crunch′time′ *n.* [Slang] the tense, crucial phase of some activity

crup·per (krup′ər, kroop′-) *n.* ⟦< OFr *crope*, rump⟧ a leather strap attached to a saddle or harness and passed under a horse's tail

cru·sade (krōō sād′) *n.* ⟦ult. < L *crux*, a cross⟧ **1** [*sometimes* **C-**] any of the Christian military expeditions (11th-13th c.) to recover the Holy Land from the Muslims **2** a vigorous, concerted action for some cause, or against some abuse —*vi.* **-sad′ed**, **-sad′ing** to engage in a crusade —**cru·sad′er** *n.*

cruse (krōōs, krōōz) *n.* ⟦OE⟧ a small container for water, oil, etc.

crush (krush) *vt.* ⟦< OFr *croisir*, to crash, break⟧ **1** to press with force so as to break or put out of shape **2** to grind or pound into small bits **3** to subdue; overwhelm —*vi.* to become crushed —*n.* **1** a crushing; severe pressure **2** a crowded mass of people **3** [Inf.] an infatuation —**crush'er** *n.*

crush'ing *adj.* 1 overwhelming 2 hurtful

crust (krust) *n.* ⟦< L *crusta*⟧ 1 the hard, outer part of bread 2 any dry, hard piece of bread 3 the pastry shell of a pie 4 any hard surface layer 5 [Slang] insolence 6 *Geol.* the solid outer layer of the earth —*vt.*, *vi.* to cover or become covered with a crust —**crust'y**, **-i·er**, **-i·est**, *adj.*

crus·ta·cean (krus tā'shən) *n.* ⟦see prec.⟧ any of a class of arthropods, including shrimps, crabs, and lobsters, that have a hard outer shell

crutch (kruch) *n.* ⟦< OE *crycce*, staff⟧ 1 a device used by lame people as an aid in walking, typically a staff with a crosspiece on top that fits under the armpit 2 any prop or support

crux (kruks) *n.*, *pl.* **crux'es** or **cru·ces** (kro͞o'sēz') ⟦L, a cross⟧ 1 a difficult problem 2 the essential or deciding point

cry (krī) *vi.* **cried**, **cry'ing** ⟦< L *quiritare*, to wail⟧ 1 to utter a loud sound, as in pain or fright 2 to sob and shed tears; weep 3 to plead or clamor (*for*) 4 to show a great need (*for*) 5 to utter its characteristic call: said of an animal —*vt.* to utter loudly; shout —*n.*, *pl.* **cries** 1 a shout 2 a plea 3 a fit of weeping 4 the characteristic call of an animal —**a far cry** a great distance or difference

cry'ba'by *n.*, *pl.* **-bies** one who complains when failing to get his or her own way

cry·o·gen·ics (krī'ō jen'iks, -ə-) *n.* ⟦< Gr *kryos*, cold + -GEN + -ICS⟧ the science that deals with the production of very low temperatures and their effect on the properties of matter —**cry'o·gen'ic** *adj.*

cry'o·sur'ger·y *n.* ⟦< Gr *kryos*, cold + SURGERY⟧ surgery that destroys tissues by freezing them

crypt (kript) *n.* ⟦< Gr *kryptein*, to hide⟧ an underground vault, esp. one under a church, used for burial

cryp·tic (krip'tik) *adj.* 1 hidden or mysterious; baffling 2 obscure and curt in expression —**cryp'ti·cal·ly** *adv.*

crypto- ⟦see CRYPT⟧ *combining form* 1 secret or hidden *[cryptogram]* 2 being such secretly and not publicly *[a crypto-*Fascist*]*

cryp·to·gram (krip'tō gram', -tə-) *n.* ⟦prec. + -GRAM⟧ a message in code or cipher

cryp·tog·ra·phy (krip täg'rə fē) *n.* ⟦CRYPTO- + -GRAPHY⟧ the art of writing or deciphering messages in code —**cryp·tog'ra·pher** *n.*

crys·tal (kris'təl) *n.* ⟦< Gr *krystallos*, crystal, ice < *kryos*, frost⟧ 1 pure quartz 2 *a*) a very clear, brilliant glass *b*) articles of such glass, as goblets 3 anything clear like crystal, as the cover on a watch face 4 a solidified form of a substance having plane faces arranged in a symmetrical, three-dimensional pattern —*adj.* 1 of or made of crystal 2 like crystal; clear

crys'tal·line (-tə lin) *adj.* 1 made of crystal 2 like crystal; clear and transparent

crys'tal·lize' (-tə līz') *vi.*, *vt.* **-lized'**, **-liz'ing** 1 to become or cause to become crystalline 2 to take on or cause to take on a definite form —**crys'tal·li·za'tion** *n.*

cs *abbrev.* case(s)

Cs *Chem. symbol for* cesium

C-sec·tion (sē'sek'shən) *n.* [Inf.] CESAREAN (SECTION)

CST *abbrev.* Central Standard Time

ct *abbrev.* 1 cent 2 court

CT *abbrev.* 1 Central Time 2 Connecticut

CT scan ⟦*c*(*omputerized*) *t*(*omography*)⟧ 1 a diagnostic X-raying of soft tissues, using many single-plane X-rays (*tomograms*) to form the image 2 such an image —**CT scanner** —**CT scanning**

cu *abbrev.* cubic

Cu ⟦L *cuprum*⟧ *Chem. symbol for* copper

cub (kub) *n.* ⟦< ? Old Ir *cuib*, a whelp⟧ 1 a young fox, bear, lion, whale, etc. 2 an inexperienced or immature person

Cu·ba (kyo͞o'bə) country on an island in the West Indies, south of Florida: 42,803 sq. mi.; pop. 9,724,000 —**Cu'ban** *adj.*, *n.*

cub·by·hole (kub'ē hōl') *n.* ⟦< Brit dial. *cub*, little shed + HOLE⟧ a small, enclosed space: also **cub'by**

cube (kyo͞ob) *n.* ⟦< Gr *kybos*⟧ 1 a solid with six equal, square sides 2 the product obtained by multiplying a given number by its square *[*the *cube* of 3 is 27*]* —*vt.* **cubed**, **cub'ing** 1 to obtain the cube of (a number) 2 to cut or shape into cubes —**cub'er** *n.*

cube root the number of which a given number is the cube *[*the *cube root* of 8 is 2*]*

cu·bic (kyo͞o'bik) *adj.* 1 having the shape of a cube: also **cu'bi·cal** (-bi kəl) 2 having the volume of a cube whose length, width, and depth each measure the given unit *[*a *cubic* foot*]*

cu·bi·cle (kyo͞o'bi kəl) *n.* ⟦< L *cubare*, lie down⟧ a small compartment

cub·ism (kyo͞ob'iz'əm) *n.* a school of modern art characterized by the use of cubes and other geometric forms in abstract arrangements —**cub'ist** *n.*, *adj.* —**cu·bis'tic** *adj.*

cu·bit (kyo͞o'bit) *n.* ⟦< L *cubitum*, elbow⟧ an ancient measure of length, about 18 to 22 inches

cuck·old (kuk'əld) *n.* ⟦see fol.⟧ a man whose wife has committed adultery —*vt.* to make a cuckold of —**cuck'old·ry** (-rē) *n.*

cuck·oo (ko͞o'ko͞o') *n.* ⟦< OFr *cucu*, echoic⟧ 1 a gray-brown bird with a long, slender body: many species lay eggs in the nests of other birds 2 its call —*adj.* [Slang] crazy; foolish

cu·cum·ber (kyo͞o'kum'bər) *n.* ⟦< L *cucumis*⟧ a long, green-skinned fruit with firm, white flesh, used in salads or preserved as pickles

cud (kud) *n.* ⟦OE *cudu*⟧ a mouthful of swallowed food regurgitated from the first two parts of the stomach of cattle and other ruminants and chewed again

cud·dle (kud′'l) ***vt.* -dled, -dling** ⟦early Modern Eng, make comfortable⟧ to hold lovingly in one's arms —***vi.*** to lie close and snug; nestle —***n.*** an embrace; hug

cud′dly (-lē) ***adj.* -dli·er, -dli·est** that invites cuddling: also **cud′dle·some**

cudg·el (kuj′əl) ***n.*** ⟦< OE *cycgel*⟧ a short, thick stick or club —***vt.* -eled** or **-elled, -el·ing** or **-el·ling** to beat with a cudgel

cue[1] (kyo͞o) ***n.*** ⟦< *q, Q* (? for L *quando,* when) found in 16th-c. plays⟧ **1** a signal in dialogue, etc. for an actor's entrance or speech **2** any signal to do something **3** a hint —***vt.* cued, cu′ing** or **cue′ing** to give a cue to

cue[2] (kyo͞o) ***n.*** ⟦var. of QUEUE⟧ a long, tapering rod used in billiards and pool to strike the white ball (**cue ball**)

Cuer·na·va·ca (kwer′nə vä′kə) city in SC Mexico: pop. 281,000

cuff (kuf) ***n.*** ⟦< ME *cuffe,* glove⟧ **1** a band or fold at the end of a sleeve **2** a turned-up fold at the bottom of a trouser leg **3** a slap —***vt.*** to slap —**off the cuff** [Slang] in an offhand manner; extemporaneously —**on the cuff** [Slang] on credit

cuff link a pair of linked buttons or any similar small device for fastening a shirt cuff

cui·sine (kwi zēn′, kwē-) ***n.*** ⟦Fr < L *coquere,* to cook⟧ **1** a style of cooking or preparing food **2** the food prepared, as at a restaurant

cuke (kyo͝ok) ***n.*** [Inf.] *short for* CUCUMBER

cul-de-sac (kul′də sak′) ***n., pl.* -sacs′** ⟦Fr, bottom of a sack⟧ a dead-end street

cu·li·nar·y (kyo͞o′lə ner′ē, kul′ə-) ***adj.*** ⟦< L *culina,* kitchen⟧ of cooking

cull (kul) ***vt.*** ⟦< L *colligere,* collect⟧ **1** to pick out and discard **2** to select and gather —***n.*** something rejected as not being up to standard

cul·mi·nate (kul′mə nāt′) ***vi.* -nat′ed, -nat′ing** ⟦< L *culmen,* peak⟧ to reach its highest point or climax —**cul′mi·na′tion *n.***

cu·lotte (ko͞o′lät′) ***n.*** ⟦Fr < L *culus,* posterior⟧ [*often pl.*] a woman's garment consisting of trousers made full in the legs to resemble a skirt

cul·pa·ble (kul′pə bəl) ***adj.*** ⟦< L *culpa,* fault⟧ deserving blame —**cul′pa·bil′i·ty *n.*** —**cul′pa·bly *adv.***

cul·prit (kul′prit) ***n.*** ⟦< Anglo-Fr *culpable,* guilty + *prit,* ready (to prove)⟧ a person guilty of a crime or offense

cult (kult) ***n.*** ⟦< L *cultus,* care, cultivation⟧ **1** a system of religious worship or ritual **2** devoted attachment to a person, principle, etc. **3** a sect —**cult′ism′ *n.*** —**cult′ist *n.***

cul·ti·vate (kul′tə vāt′) ***vt.* -vat′ed, -vat′ing** ⟦< L *colere,* to till⟧ **1** to prepare (land) for growing crops; till **2** to loosen the soil and kill weeds around (plants) **3** to grow (plants) **4** to develop or improve [*cultivate* your mind] **5** to seek to become familiar with —**cul′ti·va·ble** (-və bəl) or **cul′ti·vat′a·ble *adj.*** —**cul′ti·va′tor *n.***

cul′ti·va′tion *n.* **1** the act of cultivating **2** refinement, or culture

cul·ture (kul′chər) ***n.*** ⟦see CULT⟧ **1** cultivation of the soil **2** a growth of bacteria, etc. in a prepared substance **3** improvement of the mind, manners, etc. **4** development by special training or care **5** the skills, arts, etc. of a given people in a given period; civilization —***vt.* -tured, -tur·ing** to cultivate —**cul′tur·al *adj.*** —**cul′tur·al·ly *adv.***

culture shock the alienation, confusion, etc. that may be experienced by someone encountering new surroundings, a different culture, etc.

cul·vert (kul′vərt) ***n.*** ⟦< ?⟧ a drain or conduit under a road or embankment

cum (kum, ko͝om) ***prep.*** ⟦L⟧ with

cum·ber (kum′bər) ***vt.*** ⟦< OFr *combre,* a barrier⟧ to hinder; hamper

cum′ber·some ***adj.*** burdensome; unwieldy: also **cum′brous** (-brəs)

cum·in (kum′in, ko͞o′min) ***n.*** ⟦< Gr *kyminon*⟧ **1** an herb related to parsley and celery **2** its aromatic fruits, used as a seasoning

cum·mer·bund (kum′ər bund′) ***n.*** ⟦< Ar-Pers *kamar,* loins + Pers *band,* band⟧ a wide sash worn as a waistband, esp. with men's formal dress

cu·mu·la·tive (kyo͞o′myə lə tiv′, -lāt′iv) ***adj.*** ⟦< L *cumulus,* a heap⟧ increasing in effect, size, etc. by successive additions

cu·mu·lus (kyo͞o′myə ləs) ***n., pl.* -li′** (-lī′) ⟦L, a heap⟧ a bright, billowy type of cloud with a dark, flat base

cu·ne·i·form (kyo͞o nē′ə fôrm′) ***adj.*** ⟦< L *cuneus,* a wedge + -FORM⟧ **1** wedge-shaped **2** designating the characters in ancient Assyrian and Babylonian inscriptions —***n.*** cuneiform writing

cun·ning (kun′iŋ) ***adj.*** ⟦< ME *cunnen,* know⟧ **1** sly; crafty **2** made with skill **3** pretty and delicate; cute —***n.*** slyness; craftiness —**cun′ning·ly *adv.***

cup (kup) ***n.*** ⟦< L *cupa,* tub⟧ **1** a small, open container for beverages, usually bowl-shaped and with a handle **2** a cup and its contents **3** a cupful **4** anything shaped like a cup —***vt.* cupped, cup′ping** to shape like a cup

cup·board (kub′ərd) ***n.*** a closet or cabinet with shelves for cups, plates, food, etc.

cup′cake′ *n.* a small, round cake, often iced

cup′ful′ *n., pl.* -fuls′ as much as a cup will hold; specif., eight ounces

Cu·pid (kyo͞o′pid) ***n.*** **1** *Rom. Myth.* the god of love **2** [**c-**] a representation of Cupid as a naked, winged boy with bow and arrow

cu·pid·i·ty (kyo͞o pid′ə tē) ***n.*** ⟦< L *cupere,* to desire⟧ strong desire for wealth; avarice

cu·po·la (kyo͞o′pə lə) ***n.*** ⟦It < L *cupa*, a tub⟧ a small dome, etc. on a roof

CUPOLA

cu·pro·nick·el (kyo͞o′prō nik′əl) ***n.*** an alloy of copper and nickel, used as in coins

cur (kʉr) ***n.*** ⟦prob. < ON *kurra*, to growl⟧ **1** a dog of mixed breed; mongrel **2** a contemptible person

cu·rate (kyoor′it) ***n.*** ⟦< L *cura*, care⟧ a member of the clergy who assists a vicar or rector —**cu′ra·cy** (-ə sē), *pl.* **-cies**, ***n.***

cu·ra·tive (kyoor′ət iv) ***adj.*** having the power to cure —***n.*** a remedy

cu·ra·tor (kyo͞o rāt′ər, kyoor′āt′ər) ***n.*** ⟦< L *curare*, take care of⟧ a person in charge of a department or collection in a museum, etc. —**cu·ra·to·ri·al** (kyoor′ə tôr′ē əl) ***adj.*** —**cu·ra′tor·ship** ***n.***

curb (kʉrb) ***n.*** ⟦< L *curvus*, bent⟧ **1** a chain or strap attached to a horse's bit, used to check the horse **2** anything that checks or restrains **3** a stone or concrete edging along a street —***vt.*** to restrain; control

curb service service offered to customers in parked cars, as at some restaurants

curb′side′ ***adj.*** at the curb or on the sidewalk adjacent to the street

curb′stone′ ***n.*** any of the stones or a row of stones, making up a curb

curd (kʉrd) ***n.*** ⟦< ME *crud*, coagulated substance⟧ [*often pl.*] the coagulated part of soured milk, from which cheese is made

cur·dle (kʉrd′'l) ***vt.***, ***vi.*** **-dled**, **-dling** to form into curd; coagulate

cure (kyoor) ***n.*** ⟦< L *cura*, care⟧ **1** a healing or being healed **2** a remedy **3** a method of medical treatment —***vt.*** **cured**, **cur′ing** **1** to restore to health **2** to get rid of (an ailment, evil, etc.) **3** *a*) to preserve (meat), as by salting or smoking *b*) to process (tobacco, leather, etc.), as by drying or aging —**cur′a·ble** ***adj.*** —**cur′er** ***n.***

cu·ré (kyo͞o rā′) ***n.*** ⟦Fr < L *cura*, care⟧ in France, a parish priest

cure′-all′ ***n.*** something supposed to cure all ailments or evils

cu·ret·tage (kyo͞o ret′ij, kyo͞o′rə täzh′) ***n.*** ⟦Fr⟧ the process of cleaning or scraping the walls of a body cavity with a spoonlike instrument

cur·few (kʉr′fyo͞o′) ***n.*** ⟦< OFr *covrefeu*, lit., cover fire: orig. a nightly signal to cover fires and retire⟧ a time in the evening beyond which children, etc. may not appear on the streets or in public places

Cu·ri·a (kyoor′ē ə) ***n.***, *pl.* **-ri·ae′** (-ē′) ⟦L⟧ the official body governing the Roman Catholic Church under the authority of the pope

Cu·rie (kyoo rē′, kyoor′ē), **Ma·rie** (mə rē′) 1867-1934; Pol. chemist in France

cu·ri·o (kyoor′ē ō′) ***n.***, *pl.* **-os′** ⟦contr. of fol.⟧ an unusual or rare article

cu·ri·os·i·ty (kyoor′ē äs′ə tē) ***n.***, *pl.* **-ties** **1** a desire to learn or know **2** inquisitiveness **3** anything curious, rare, etc.

cu·ri·ous (kyoor′ē əs) ***adj.*** ⟦< L *curiosus*, careful⟧ **1** eager to learn or know **2** prying or inquisitive **3** unusual; strange —**cu′ri·ous·ly** ***adv.***

curl (kʉrl) ***vt.*** ⟦< ME *crul*, curly⟧ **1** to twist (esp. hair) into ringlets **2** to cause to bend around —***vi.*** **1** to form curls **2** to form a spiral or curve —***n.*** **1** a ringlet of hair **2** anything with a curled shape —**curl′er** ***n.*** —**curl′y**, **-i·er**, **-i·est**, ***adj.*** —**curl′i·ness** ***n.***

cur·lew (kʉr′lo͞o′, kʉrl′yo͞o′) ***n.*** ⟦echoic⟧ a large, brownish wading bird with long legs

curl·i·cue (kʉr′li kyo͞o′) ***n.*** ⟦< CURLY + CUE[2]⟧ a fancy curve, flourish, etc.

curl·ing (kʉr′liŋ) ***n.*** a game played on ice by two teams, in which a heavy disk of stone or iron is slid toward a target

cur·rant (kʉr′ənt) ***n.*** ⟦ult. < *Corinth*, ancient Gr city⟧ **1** a small, seedless raisin from the Mediterranean region **2** *a*) the sour berry of several species of hardy shrubs, made into jelly or jam *b*) any such shrub

cur·ren·cy (kʉr′ən sē) ***n.***, *pl.* **-cies** ⟦see fol.⟧ **1** circulation **2** the money in circulation in any country; often, specif., paper money **3** general use or acceptance

cur·rent (kʉr′ənt) ***adj.*** ⟦< L *currere*, to run⟧ **1** now going on; of the present time **2** circulating **3** commonly accepted; prevalent —***n.*** **1** a flow of water or air in a definite direction **2** a general tendency or drift, as of opinion **3** the flow or rate of flow of electricity in a conductor —**cur′rent·ly** ***adv.***

cur·ric·u·lum (kə rik′yo͞o ləm, -yə-) ***n.***, *pl.* **-la** (-lə) or **-lums** ⟦L, course for racing⟧ a course of study in a school —**cur·ric′u·lar** ***adj.***

cur·ry[1] (kʉr′ē) ***vt.*** **-ried**, **-ry·ing** ⟦< OFr *correier*, to put in order⟧ **1** to use a currycomb on **2** to prepare (tanned leather) —**curry favor** to try to win favor as by flattery

cur·ry[2] (kʉr′ē) ***n.***, *pl.* **-ries** ⟦Tamil *kari*, sauce⟧ **1** a powder prepared from various spices, or a sauce made with this **2** a stew made with curry —***vt.*** **-ried**, **-ry·ing** to prepare with curry

cur′ry·comb′ ***n.*** a circular comb with teeth or ridges, for rubbing down and cleaning a horse's coat —***vt.*** to use a currycomb on

curse (kʉrs) ***n.*** ⟦OE *curs*⟧ **1** a calling on God or the gods to bring evil on some person or thing **2** a profane or obscene oath **3** evil or injury that seems to come in answer to a curse —***vt.*** **cursed**, **curs′ing** **1** to call evil down on **2** to swear at **3** to afflict —***vi.*** to swear; blaspheme —**be cursed with** to suffer from

curs·ed (kʉr′sid, kʉrst) ***adj.*** **1** under a curse **2** deserving to be cursed; evil;

hateful

cur·sive (kur′siv) ***adj.*** ⟦ult. < L *currere,* to run⟧ designating writing in which the letters are joined

cur·sor (kur′sər) ***n.*** ⟦L, runner⟧ a movable indicator light on a computer video screen, marking the current position at which a character may be entered, changed, etc.

cur·so·ry (kur′sə rē) ***adj.*** ⟦ult. < L *currere,* to run⟧ hastily, often superficially, done —**cur′so·ri·ly** ***adv.*** —**cur′so·ri·ness** ***n.***

curt (kurt) ***adj.*** ⟦L *curtus,* short⟧ brief, esp. to the point of rudeness —**curt′ly** ***adv.*** —**curt′ness** ***n.***

cur·tail (kər tāl′) ***vt.*** ⟦< L *curtus,* short⟧ to cut short; reduce —**cur·tail′ment** ***n.***

cur·tain (kurt′′n) ***n.*** ⟦< LL *cortina*⟧ a piece of cloth, etc. hung at a window, in front of a stage, etc. to decorate or conceal —***vt.*** to provide with or shut off as with a curtain

curtain call **1** a call, usually by applause, for performers to return to the stage **2** such a return

curt·sy (kurt′sē) ***n.***, *pl.* **-sies** ⟦var. of COURTESY⟧ a woman's gesture of greeting, respect, etc. made by bending the knees and lowering the body slightly —***vi.*** **-sied, -sy·ing** to make a curtsy Also sp. **curt′sey**

cur·va·ceous (kər vā′shəs) ***adj.*** ⟦< CURVE⟧ having a full, shapely figure: said of a woman

cur·va·ture (kur′və chər) ***n.*** **1** a curving or being curved **2** a curve

curve (kurv) ***n.*** ⟦< L *curvus,* bent⟧ **1** a line having no straight part; bend with no angles **2** something shaped like, or moving in, a curve —***vt., vi.*** **curved, curv′ing** **1** to form a curve by bending **2** to move in a curve —**curv′y, -i·er, -i·est,** ***adj.***

cush·ion (koosh′ən) ***n.*** ⟦< ML *coxinum*⟧ **1** a pillow or pad **2** a thing like this in shape or use **3** anything that absorbs shock —***vt.*** to provide with a cushion

cush·y (koosh′ē) ***adj.*** **-i·er, -i·est** ⟦< Pers *khūsh,* pleasant⟧ [Slang] easy; comfortable

cusp (kusp) ***n.*** ⟦L *cuspis*⟧ a point or pointed end, as on the chewing surface of a tooth —**on the cusp** at a time of transition

cus·pid (kus′pid) ***n.*** ⟦see prec.⟧ a tooth with one cusp; canine tooth

cus·pi·dor (kus′pə dôr′) ***n.*** ⟦< Port *cuspir,* to spit⟧ a spittoon

cuss (kus) ***n., vt., vi.*** [Inf.] CURSE

cus·tard (kus′tərd) ***n.*** ⟦< L *crusta,* crust⟧ a mixture of eggs, milk, sugar, etc., boiled or baked

cus·to·di·an (kəs tō′dē ən) ***n.*** ⟦< fol.⟧ **1** one who is responsible for the custody or care of something; caretaker **2** a person responsible for the maintenance of a building

cus·to·dy (kus′tə dē) ***n.***, *pl.* **-dies** ⟦< L *custos,* a guard⟧ a guarding or keeping safe; care; guardianship —**in custody** under arrest —**cus·to′di·al** (-tō′dē əl) ***adj.***

cus·tom (kus′təm) ***n.*** ⟦< L *com-,* intens. + *suere,* be accustomed⟧ **1** a usual practice; habit **2** *a)* a social practice carried on by tradition *b)* such practices collectively **3** [*pl.*] duties or taxes imposed on imported goods **4** the regular patronage of a business —***adj.*** **1** made or done to order **2** making things to order

cus′tom·ar′y ***adj.*** in keeping with custom; usual; habitual —**cus′tom·ar′i·ly** ***adv.***

cus′tom-built′ ***adj.*** built to order, to the customer's specifications

cus′tom·er ***n.*** a person who buys, esp. one who buys regularly

cus′tom·house′ ***n.*** an office where customs or duties are paid

cus′tom·ize′ ***vt.*** **-ized′, -iz′ing** to make according to individual specifications

cus′tom-made′ ***adj.*** made to order, to the customer's specifications

cut (kut) ***vt.*** **cut, cut′ting** ⟦ME *cutten*⟧ **1** to make an opening in with a sharp-edged instrument; gash **2** to pierce sharply so as to hurt **3** to have (a new tooth) grow through the gum **4** to divide into parts with a sharp-edged instrument; sever **5** to intersect; divide **6** to hew **7** to mow or reap **8** to reduce; curtail **9** to trim; pare **10** to divide (a pack of cards) **11** to make or do as by cutting **12** to hit (a ball) so that it spins **13** [Inf.] to pretend not to recognize (a person) **14** [Inf.] to stay away from (a school class, etc.) without being excused **15** [Slang] to stop —***vi.*** **1** to pierce, sever, gash, etc. **2** to take cutting *[pine cuts easily]* **3** to go (*across* or *through*) **4** to change direction suddenly **5** to make a sudden shift, as from one scene to another in a film **6** [Inf.] to swing a bat, etc. at a ball —***adj.*** **1** that has been cut **2** made or formed by cutting —***n.*** **1** a cutting or being cut **2** a stroke or opening made by a sharp-edged instrument **3** a piece cut off, as of meat **4** a reduction **5** a passage or channel cut out **6** the style in which a thing is cut **7** an act, remark, etc. that hurts one's feelings **8** a block or plate engraved for printing, or the impression from this **9** [Inf.] an unauthorized absence from school, etc. **10** [Inf.] a share, as of profits —**cut and dried** **1** arranged beforehand **2** lifeless; dull —**cut down** to reduce; lessen —**cut it out** [Inf.] to stop doing what one is doing —**cut off** **1** to sever **2** to stop abruptly; shut off —**cut out** [Inf.] fit or suited —**cut up** **1** to cut into pieces **2** [Slang] to clown, joke, etc.

cu·ta·ne·ous (kyoo tā′nē əs) ***adj.*** ⟦< L *cutis,* skin⟧ of or on the skin

cut′a·way′ ***n.*** a man's formal coat cut so as to curve back to the tails

cut′back′ ***n.*** a reduction or discontinuance, as of production

cute (kyoot) ***adj.*** **cut′er, cut′est** ⟦< ACUTE⟧ [Inf.] **1** clever; shrewd **2** pretty or attractive, esp. in a dainty way —**cute′ly** ***adv.*** —**cute′ness** ***n.***

cute·sy or **cute·sie** (kyoot′sē) ***adj.*** **-si·er, -si·est** [Inf.] cute in an affected way

cut·i·cle (kyoot′i kəl) ***n.*** ⟦< L *cutis,* skin⟧ **1** the outer layer of the skin **2** hardened skin, as at the base and sides of a fingernail

cut·lass (kut′ləs) ***n.*** ⟦< L *culter*, plowshare⟧ a short, thick, curved sword

cut·ler·y (kut′lər ē) ***n.*** ⟦< L *culter*, plowshare⟧ **1** cutting implements, as knives and scissors **2** implements used in preparing and eating food

cut·let (kut′lit) ***n.*** ⟦< L *costa*, rib⟧ **1** a small slice of meat from the ribs or leg **2** a small, flat croquette of chopped meat or fish

cut′off′ ***n.*** a road, etc. that is a shortcut

cut′-rate′ ***adj.*** selling at a lower price

cut·ter (kut′ər) ***n.*** **1** a person or thing that cuts **2** a small, swift boat or ship

cut′throat′ ***n.*** a murderer —***adj.*** **1** murderous **2** merciless; ruthless

cut·ting (kut′iŋ) ***n.*** a shoot cut away from a plant for rooting or grafting —***adj.*** **1** that cuts; sharp **2** chilling or piercing **3** sarcastic; wounding —**cut′ting·ly** ***adv.***

cutting edge the leading or most advanced position; vanguard

cut·tle·fish (kut′'l fish′) ***n.***, *pl.* **-fish′** or (for different species) **-fish′es** ⟦OE *cudele*⟧ a sea mollusk with eight arms and two tentacles and a hard internal shell (**cut′tle·bone′**)

cwt *abbrev.* hundredweight

-cy (sē) ⟦< Gr *-kia*⟧ *suffix* **1** quality, condition, or fact of being *[idiocy]* **2** position, rank, or office of *[captaincy]*

cy·a·nide (sī′ə nīd′) ***n.*** a white, crystalline compound that is extremely poisonous

cy·ber·net·ics (sī′bər net′iks) ***n.*** ⟦< Gr *kybernan*, to steer + -ICS⟧ the comparative study of human control systems, as the brain, and complex electronic systems —**cy′ber·net′ic** ***adj.***

cy·ber·punk (sī′bər puŋk′) ***n.*** ⟦*cyber-* (see prec.) + PUNK[2] (*n.* 2)⟧ science fiction describing a future filled with violence, computers, and drugs

cy′ber·space′ (-spās′) ***n.*** the electronic system of linked computer networks, etc., thought of as an unlimited environment for accessing information, communicating, etc.

cy·cla·men (sī′klə mən) ***n.*** ⟦< Gr⟧ a plant of the primrose family with heart-shaped leaves

cy·cle (sī′kəl) ***n.*** ⟦< Gr *kyklos*, a circle⟧ **1** *a)* a period within which a round of regularly recurring events is completed *b)* a complete set of such events **2** a series of poems or songs on one theme **3** a bicycle, motorcycle, etc. **4** *Elec.* one complete period of the reversal of an alternating current from positive to negative and back again —***vi.*** **-cled**, **-cling** to ride a bicycle, etc.

cy·cli·cal (sik′li kəl) ***adj.*** of, or having the nature of, a cycle; occurring in cycles

cy·clist (sīk′list, sī′kə list) ***n.*** one who rides a bicycle, motorcycle, etc.

cyclo- ⟦< Gr *kyklos*, a circle⟧ *combining form* of a circle or wheel; circular

cy·clom·e·ter (sī kläm′ət ər) ***n.*** ⟦prec. + -METER⟧ an instrument that records the revolutions of a wheel for measuring distance traveled

cy·clone (sī′klōn′) ***n.*** ⟦< Gr *kyklōma*, wheel⟧ a storm with strong winds rotating about a center of low pressure

cyclone fence a heavy-duty fence of interwoven steel links

Cy·clops (sī′kläps′) ***n.***, *pl.* **Cy·clo·pes** (sī klō′pēz′) *Gr. Myth.* any of a race of one-eyed giants

cy·clo·tron (sī′klō trän′, -klə-) ***n.*** a circular apparatus for giving high energy to positive ions, as protons, used in atomic research

cyg·net (sig′net, -nit) ***n.*** ⟦< Gr *kyknos*, swan⟧ a young swan

cyl·in·der (sil′ən dər) ***n.*** ⟦< Gr *kylindein*, to roll⟧ **1** a solid, tubular figure consisting of two equal, parallel, circular bases joined by a smooth, continuous surface **2** anything with this shape; specif., *a)* the turning part of a revolver *b)* the piston chamber of an engine —**cy·lin·dri·cal** (sə lin′dri kəl) ***adj.***

CYMBALS

cym·bal (sim′bəl) ***n.*** ⟦< Gr *kymbē*, hollow of a vessel⟧ *Music* a circular brass plate that makes a sharp, ringing sound when hit —**cym′bal·ist** ***n.***

cyn·ic (sin′ik) ***n.*** ⟦< Gr *kynikos*, doglike⟧ a cynical person

cyn′i·cal (-i kəl) ***adj.*** **1** denying the sincerity of people's motives and actions **2** sarcastic, sneering, etc. —**cyn′i·cal·ly** ***adv.***

cyn′i·cism′ (-ə siz′əm) ***n.*** **1** the attitude or beliefs of a cynic **2** a cynical remark, idea, etc.

cy·no·sure (sī′nə shoor′, sin′ə-) ***n.*** ⟦< Gr *kynosoura*, dog's tail⟧ a center of attention or interest

cy·pher (sī′fər) ***n.***, ***vi.*** *Brit. sp. of* CIPHER

cy·press (sī′prəs) ***n.*** ⟦< Gr *kyparissos*⟧ **1** an evergreen tree with cones and dark foliage **2** its wood

Cy·prus (sī′prəs) country on an island at the E end of the Mediterranean: 3,572 sq. mi.; pop. 714,000 —**Cyp·ri·ot** (sip′rē ət) ***adj.***, ***n.***

cyst (sist) ***n.*** ⟦< Gr *kystis*, sac⟧ a saclike structure in plants or animals, esp. one filled with diseased matter —**cyst′ic** ***adj.***

cystic fibrosis a children's disease marked by fibrosis of the pancreas and by frequent respiratory infections

cy·tol·o·gy (sī täl′ə jē) ***n.*** ⟦< Gr *kytos*, a hollow + -LOGY⟧ the branch of biology dealing with cells —**cy·tol′o·gist** ***n.***

cy·to·plasm (sīt′ō plaz′əm) ***n.*** ⟦< Gr *kytos*, a hollow + *plasma*, something molded⟧ the protoplasm of a cell, outside the nucleus

cy·to·sine (sīt′ō sēn′) ***n.*** ⟦Ger *zytosin*⟧ one of the four bases that combine to form DNA

czar (zär) ***n.*** ⟦Russ < L *Caesar*⟧ **1** the title of any of the former emperors of Russia **2** a person with wide-ranging power —**cza·ri·na** (zä rē′nə) ***fem.n.***

Czech (chek) ***n.*** **1** a member of a Slavic people of central Europe **2** the West Slavic language of the Czechs **3** loosely, a person born or living in Czechoslovakia **4** a person born or living in the Czech Republic —***adj.*** of the Czech Republic, its people, or their language

Czech·o·slo·va·ki·a (chek′ə slō vä′kē ə) former country in central Europe: divided (1993) into Czech Republic and Slovakia —**Czech′o·slo′vak** or **Czech′o·slo·vak′i·an** ***adj., n.***

Czech Republic country in central Europe: formerly the W republic of Czechoslovakia: 30,450 sq. mi.; pop. 10,324,000

D

d[1] or **D** (dē) ***n.***, *pl.* **d's, D's** the fourth letter of the English alphabet

d[2] *abbrev.* **1** day(s) **2** degree **3** diameter **4** died **5** ⟦L *denarii*⟧ penny; pence

D[1] (dē) ***n.*** **1** a Roman numeral for 500 **2** a grade for below-average work **3** *Music* the second tone in the scale of C major

D[2] *abbrev.* **1** December **2** Democrat

-'d *contr.* **1** had or would: a shortened form used in contractions *[I'd seen; they'd see]* **2** *old sp. of* -ED *[foster'd]*

DA or **D.A.** *abbrev.* District Attorney

dab (dab) ***vt., vi.*** **dabbed, dab′bing** ⟦ME *dabben*, to strike⟧ **1** to touch lightly and quickly; pat **2** to put on (paint, etc.) with light, quick strokes —***n.*** **1** a tap; pat **2** a soft or moist bit of something

dab·ble (dab′əl) ***vi.*** **-bled, -bling** ⟦Du *dabbelen*, freq. of MDu *dabben*, to strike, dab⟧ **1** to play, dip, or paddle in water **2** to do something superficially: with *in* or *at*

Dac·ca (dä′kä) *former sp. of* DHAKA

dace (dās) ***n.***, *pl.* **dace** or **daces** a small freshwater fish related to the carp

DACHSHUND

dachs·hund (däks′hoont′) ***n.*** ⟦Ger < *dachs*, badger + *hund*, dog⟧ a small dog with a long body, short legs, and drooping ears

Da·cron (dā′krän′, dak′rän′) *trademark for* a synthetic wrinkle-resistant fabric —***n.*** [*also* **d-**] this fabric

dac·tyl (dak′təl) ***n.*** ⟦< Gr *daktylos*, finger⟧ a metrical foot consisting of one accented syllable followed by two unaccented ones —**dac·tyl′ic** (-til′ik) ***adj.***

dad (dad) ***n.*** ⟦< child's cry *dada*⟧ [Inf.] father: also **dad·dy** (dad′ē), *pl.* **-dies**

daddy long′legs′ an arachnid with long legs

da·do (dā′dō) ***n.***, *pl.* **-does** ⟦< L *datum*, a die⟧ **1** the part of a pedestal between the cap and the base **2** the lower part of a wall if decorated differently from the upper part **3** a rectangular groove cut in a board, used in forming a joint

daf·fo·dil (daf′ə dil′) ***n.*** ⟦< Gr *asphodelos*⟧ a narcissus with long leaves and yellow flowers

daf·fy (daf′ē) ***adj.*** **-fi·er, -fi·est** ⟦< ME *dafte*, daft⟧ [Inf.] crazy; silly —**daf′fi·ness** ***n.***

daft (daft) ***adj.*** ⟦< OE (*ge*)*dæfte*, mild⟧ **1** silly **2** insane

dag·ger (dag′ər) ***n.*** ⟦< Prov *daga*⟧ **1** a weapon with a short, pointed blade, used for stabbing **2** *Printing* a reference mark (†)

da·guerre·o·type (də ger′ō tīp′) ***n.*** ⟦after L. J. M. *Daguerre*, 19th-c. Fr inventor⟧ an early kind of photograph made on a chemically treated plate —***vt.*** **-typed′, -typ′ing** to photograph by this method

dahl·ia (dal′yə, däl′-) ***n.*** ⟦after A. *Dahl*, 18th-c. Swed botanist⟧ a perennial plant with large, showy flowers

dai·li·ness (dā′lē nəs) ***n.*** the ordinary, routine aspects of a way of life

dai·ly (dā′lē) ***adj.*** done, happening, or published every (week)day —***n.***, *pl.* **-lies** a daily newspaper —***adv.*** every day

daily double a bet or betting procedure in which winning depends on choosing both winners in two specified races

dain·ty (dān′tē) ***n.***, *pl.* **-ties** ⟦< OFr *deinté*⟧ a delicacy —***adj.*** **-ti·er, -ti·est** **1** delicious and choice **2** delicately pretty **3** *a*) of refined taste; fastidious *b*) squeamish —**dain′ti·ly** ***adv.*** —**dain′ti·ness** ***n.***

dai·qui·ri (dak′ər ē) ***n.*** ⟦after *Daiquirí*, Cuban village⟧ a cocktail made of rum, sugar, and lime or lemon juice

dair·y (der′ē) ***n.***, *pl.* **-ies** ⟦ME *daie*, dairymaid⟧ **1** a building or room where milk and cream are made into butter and cheese, etc. **2** a farm that produces, or a store that sells, milk and milk products —***adj.*** of milk and milk products —**dair′y·man** (-mən), *pl.* **-men,** ***n.***

dair′y·ing ***n.*** the business of producing

or selling dairy products

da·is (dā′is) ***n.**, pl.* **da′is·es** ⟦< ML *discus,* table⟧ a raised platform, as for a speaker

dai·sy (dā′zē) ***n.**, pl.* **-sies** ⟦< OE *dæges eage,* day's eye⟧ a plant of the composite family, bearing flowers with white rays around a yellow disk

Da·lai La·ma (dä′lī lä′mə) the high priest of Lamaism

dale (dāl) ***n.*** ⟦OE *dæl*⟧ a valley

Dal·las (dal′əs) city in NE Texas: pop. 1,008,000

DALMATIAN

dal·ly (dal′ē) ***vi.*** **-lied, -ly·ing** ⟦< OFr *dalier,* to trifle⟧ **1** to flirt **2** to deal carelessly (*with*); toy **3** to waste time; loiter **—dal·liance** (dal′yəns, -ē əns) ***n.***

Dal·ma·tian (dal mā′shən) ***n.*** a large, short-haired dog with dark spots on a white coat

dam[1] (dam) ***n.*** ⟦ME⟧ a barrier built to hold back flowing water **—*vt.*** **dammed, dam′ming** **1** to build a dam in **2** to keep back or confine

dam[2] (dam) ***n.*** ⟦see DAME⟧ the female parent of any four-legged animal

dam·age (dam′ij) ***n.*** ⟦< L *damnum*⟧ **1** injury or harm resulting in a loss **2** [*pl.*] *Law* money compensating for injury, loss, etc. **—*vt.*** **-aged, -ag·ing** to do damage to **—dam′age·a·ble *adj.***

Da·mas·cus (də mas′kəs) capital of Syria: pop. 1,497,000

dam·ask (dam′əsk) ***n.*** ⟦after prec.⟧ **1** a reversible fabric in figured weave, used for table linen, etc. **2** deep pink or rose **—*adj.*** **1** of or like damask **2** deep-pink or rose

dame (dām) ***n.*** ⟦< L *domina,* lady⟧ **1** [**D-**] in Great Britain, a woman's title of honor **2** [Slang] any woman

damn (dam) ***vt.*** **damned, damn′ing** ⟦< L *damnare,* condemn⟧ **1** to condemn to an unhappy fate **2** *Theol.* to condemn to hell **3** to condemn as bad, inferior, etc. **4** to swear at by saying "damn" **—*n.*** the saying of "damn" as a curse **—*adj., adv.*** [Inf.] *short for* DAMNED **—*interj.*** used to express anger, etc.

dam·na·ble (dam′nə bəl) ***adj.*** **1** deserving damnation **2** deserving to be sworn at **—dam′na·bly *adv.***

dam·na′tion (-nā′shən) ***n.*** a damning or being damned **—*interj.*** used to express anger, etc.

damned (damd) ***adj.*** **1** condemned, as to hell **2** [Inf.] deserving cursing; outrageous **—*adv.*** [Inf.] very

Dam·o·cles (dam′ə klēz′) ***n.*** *Classical Legend* a man whose king seated him under a sword hanging by a hair to show him the perils of a ruler's life

damp (damp) ***n.*** ⟦MDu, vapor⟧ a slight wetness **—*adj.*** somewhat moist or wet; humid **—*vt.*** **1** to bank (a fire): usually with *down* **2** to check or reduce **—damp′ness *n.***

damp′-dry′ ***vt.*** **-dried′, -dry′ing** to dry (laundry) so that some moisture is retained **—*adj.*** designating or of laundry so treated

damp·en (dam′pən) ***vt.*** **1** to make damp; moisten **2** to deaden, depress, or reduce **—damp′en·er *n.***

damp·er (dam′pər) ***n.*** ⟦see DAMP⟧ **1** anything that deadens or depresses **2** a valve in a flue to control the draft **3** a device to check vibration in piano strings

dam·sel (dam′zəl) ***n.*** ⟦see DAME⟧ [Old-fashioned] a girl; maiden

dam′sel·fly′ ***n.**, pl.* **-flies′** a slow-flying, brightly colored dragonfly

dam·son (dam′zən) ***n.*** ⟦ult. < *Damascenus,* of DAMASCUS⟧ a small, purple plum

Dan *abbrev.* Danish

dance (dans) ***vi.*** **danced, danc′ing** ⟦< OFr *danser*⟧ **1** to move the body and feet in rhythm, ordinarily to music **2** to move lightly, rapidly, gaily, etc. **—*vt.*** **1** to perform (a dance) **2** to cause to dance **—*n.*** **1** rhythmic movement, ordinarily to music **2** a particular kind of dance **3** the art of dancing **4** a party for dancing **5** a piece of music for dancing **6** rapid movement **—danc′er *n.***

D and C dilation (of the cervix) and curettage (of the uterus)

dan·de·li·on (dan′də lī′ən) ***n.*** ⟦< OFr *dent,* tooth + *de,* of + *lion,* lion⟧ a common weed with yellow flowers

dan·der (dan′dər) ***n.*** ⟦< ?⟧ **1** tiny, allergenic particles from fur, etc. **2** [Inf.] anger or temper

dan·dle (dan′dəl) ***vt.*** **-dled, -dling** ⟦< ?⟧ to move (a child) up and down on the knee or in the arms

dan·druff (dan′drəf) ***n.*** ⟦< earlier *dandro* + dial. *hurf,* scab⟧ little scales of dead skin on the scalp

dan·dy (dan′dē) ***n.**, pl.* **-dies** ⟦< ?⟧ **1** a man overly attentive to his clothes and appearance **2** [Inf.] something very good **—*adj.*** **-di·er, -di·est** [Inf.] very good; fine

Dane (dān) ***n.*** a person born or living in Denmark

dan·ger (dān′jər) ***n.*** ⟦ult. < L *dominus,* a master⟧ **1** liability to injury, damage, loss, etc.; peril **2** a thing that may cause injury, pain, etc.

dan′ger·ous ***adj.*** full of danger; unsafe; perilous **—dan′ger·ous·ly *adv.***

dan·gle (daŋ′gəl) ***vi.*** **-gled, -gling** ⟦< Scand⟧ to hang loosely so as to swing back and forth **—*vt.*** to cause to dangle **—dan′gler *n.***

Dan·iel (dan′yəl) ***n.*** *Bible* a Hebrew prophet whose faith saved him in the lions' den

Dan·ish (dān′ish) ***adj.*** of Denmark or its people, language, etc. —***n.*** **1** the language of the Danes **2** [*also* **d-**] (a) rich, flaky pastry filled with fruit, cheese, etc.: in full **Danish pastry**

dank (daŋk) ***adj.*** ⟦ME⟧ disagreeably damp —**dank′ly** ***adv.*** —**dank′ness** ***n.***

dan·seuse (dän so͞oz′) ***fem.n.*** ⟦Fr⟧ a female ballet dancer —**dan·seur′** (-sʉr′) ***masc.n.***

Dan·te (Alighieri) (dän′tā, dan′tē) 1265-1321; It. poet

Dan·ube (dan′yo͞ob) river in S Europe, flowing from S Germany into the Black Sea

dap·per (dap′ər) ***adj.*** ⟦MDu, nimble⟧ **1** small and active **2** trim, neat, or dressed stylishly

dap·ple (dap′əl) ***adj.*** ⟦< ON *depill*, a spot⟧ marked with spots; mottled: also **dap′pled** —***vt.*** **-pled**, **-pling** to cover with spots

Dar·da·nelles (där′də nelz′) strait separating the Balkan Peninsula from Asia Minor

dare (der) ***vt.***, ***vi.*** **dared**, **dar′ing** ⟦OE *durran*⟧ **1** to have enough courage for (some act) **2** to challenge (someone) to do something —***n.*** a challenge —**dare say** to think probable —**dar′er** ***n.***

dare′dev′il (-dev′əl) ***adj.*** bold and reckless —***n.*** **1** a bold, reckless person **2** one who performs dangerous stunts

dar′ing ***adj.*** fearless; bold —***n.*** bold courage —**dar′ing·ly** ***adv.***

dark (därk) ***adj.*** ⟦< OE *deorc*⟧ **1** entirely or partly without light **2** *a)* almost black *b)* not light in color **3** hidden; secret **4** gloomy **5** evil; sinister **6** ignorant —***n.*** **1** the state of being dark **2** night or nightfall —**in the dark** uninformed; ignorant —**dark′ly** ***adv.*** —**dark′ness** ***n.***

Dark Ages the Middle Ages, esp. the earlier part

dark·en (där′kən) ***vt.***, ***vi.*** to make or become dark or darker —**dark′en·er** ***n.***

dark horse a little-known contestant thought unlikely to win

dark′room′ ***n.*** a darkened room for developing photographs

dar·ling (där′liŋ) ***n.*** ⟦OE *deorling*⟧ a person much loved by another —***adj.*** **1** very dear; beloved **2** [Inf.] cute or attractive

darn[1] (därn) ***vt.***, ***vi.*** ⟦< Fr dial. *darner*⟧ to mend (cloth) by sewing a network of stitches across the gap —***n.*** a darned place in fabric

darn[2] (därn) ***vt.***, ***n.***, ***adj.***, ***adv.***, ***interj.*** [Inf.] damn: a euphemism —**darned** ***adj.***, ***adv.***

dart (därt) ***n.*** ⟦< OFr⟧ **1** a small, pointed missile for throwing or shooting **2** a sudden movement **3** a short, tapered seam **4** [*pl.*, *with sing. v.*] a game in which darts (see sense 1) are thrown at a target (**dart′board′**) —***vt.***, ***vi.*** to send out or move suddenly and fast

Dar·von (där′vän′) *trademark for* an analgesic drug containing a narcotic painkiller

Dar·win (där′win), **Charles** (**Robert**) (chärlz) 1809-82; Eng. naturalist: originated theory of evolution —**Dar·win′i·an** ***adj.***, ***n.*** —**Dar′win·ism′** ***n.***

dash (dash) ***vt.*** ⟦< Scand⟧ **1** to throw so as to break; smash **2** to throw or thrust (*away*, *down*, etc.) **3** to splash **4** to destroy, frustrate —***vi.*** **1** to strike violently (*against*) **2** to rush —***n.*** **1** a splash **2** a bit of something added [*a dash of salt*] **3** a rush **4** a short, fast race **5** spirit; vigor **6** the mark of punctuation (— or –) used to indicate a break, omission, etc. —**dash off** to do, write, etc. hastily —**dash′er** ***n.***

dash′board′ ***n.*** a panel with controls and gauges, as in an automobile

da·shi·ki (dä shē′kē) ***n.*** a loosefitting, brightly colored robe or tunic, modeled after an African tribal garment

dash′ing ***adj.*** **1** full of dash or spirit; lively **2** showy; striking; stylish —**dash′ing·ly** ***adv.***

das·tard·ly (das′tərd lē) ***adj.*** ⟦< ME *dastard*, a craven⟧ mean, cowardly, etc.

dat *abbrev.* dative

da·ta (dāt′ə, dat′ə) ***pl.n.*** [*now usually with sing. v.*] **1** facts or figures from which conclusions can be drawn **2** information in a form suitable for computer storage, etc.

da′ta·base′ ***n.*** a mass of data, as in a computer, arranged for rapid expansion, updating, and retrieval: also **data base**

data processing the handling of large amounts of information, esp. by a computer —**data processor**

date[1] (dāt) ***n.*** ⟦< L *dare*, give⟧ **1** the time at which a thing happens, was made, etc. **2** the day of the month **3** [*pl.*] a person's birth and death dates **4** *a)* an appointment *b)* a romantic social engagement with a person *c)* this person —***vt.*** **dat′ed**, **dat′ing** **1** to mark (a letter, etc.) with a date **2** to find out or give the date of **3** to make seem old-fashioned **4** to have romantic social engagements with —***vi.*** **1** to belong to a definite period in the past: usually with *from* **2** to have romantic social engagements —**to date** up to now —**dat′er** ***n.***

date[2] (dāt) ***n.*** ⟦< Gr *daktylos*, a date⟧ the sweet, fleshy fruit of a desert palm tree (**date palm**)

date′book′ ***n.*** a notebook for entering appointments, etc.

date′line′ ***n.*** the date and place of writing or issue, as given in a line in a newspaper story, etc.

da·tive (dāt′iv) ***n.*** ⟦< L *dativus*, relating to giving⟧ *Gram.* the case of the indirect object of a verb

da·tum (dāt′əm, dat′-) ***n.*** ⟦L, what is given⟧ *sing. of* DATA

daub (dôb) ***vt.***, ***vi.*** ⟦< L *de-*, intens. + *albus*, white⟧ **1** to cover or smear with sticky, soft matter **2** to paint badly —***n.*** **1** anything daubed on **2** a daubing stroke —**daub′er** ***n.***

daugh·ter (dôt′ər) ***n.*** ⟦< OE *dohtor*⟧ **1** a girl or woman as she is related to either or both parents **2** a female descendant —**daugh′ter·ly** ***adj.***

daugh′ter-in-law′ ***n.***, *pl.* **daugh′ters-in-**

law′ the wife of one's son

Dau·mier (dō myā′), **Ho·no·ré** (ô nô rā′) 1808-79; Fr. painter

daunt (dônt) ***vt.*** ⟦< L *domare,* to tame⟧ to intimidate or dishearten

daunt′less ***adj.*** that cannot be daunted; fearless —**daunt′less·ly** ***adv.*** —**daunt′less·ness** ***n.***

dau·phin (dô′fin) ***n.*** ⟦Fr, dolphin⟧ the eldest son of the king of France: a title used from 1349 to 1830

dav·en·port (dav′ən pôrt′) ***n.*** ⟦< ?⟧ a large couch or sofa

Da·vid (dā′vid) ***n.*** *Bible* the second king of Israel and Judah

da Vin·ci (də vin′chē), **Le·o·nar·do** (lē′ə när′dō) 1452-1519; It. painter, sculptor, architect, & scientist

Da·vis (dā′vis), **Jefferson** 1808-89; president of the Confederacy (1861-65)

da·vit (dā′vit, dav′it) ***n.*** ⟦OFr dim. of *David*⟧ either of a pair of uprights on a ship for lowering or raising a small boat

daw·dle (dôd′'l) ***vi., vt.*** **-dled, -dling** ⟦< ?⟧ to waste (time) in trifling or by being slow —**daw′dler** ***n.***

dawn (dôn) ***vi.*** ⟦< OE *dagian*⟧ **1** to begin to be day **2** to begin to appear, develop, etc. **3** to begin to be understood or felt —***n.*** **1** daybreak **2** the beginning (*of* something)

day (dā) ***n.*** ⟦OE *dæg*⟧ **1** the period of light between sunrise and sunset **2** the time (24 hours) that it takes the earth to rotate once on its axis **3** [*also pl.*] a period; era **4** a time of power, glory, etc. **5** daily work period [an 8-hour *day*] —**day after day** every day: also **day in, day out**

day′bed′ ***n.*** a couch that can also be used as a bed

day′break′ ***n.*** the time in the morning when light first appears

day care daytime care given to children, as at a day-care center, or to the elderly, as at a social agency —**day′-care′** ***adj.***

day′dream′ ***n.*** **1** a pleasant, dreamy series of thoughts **2** a visionary scheme —***vi.*** to have daydreams

day′light′ ***n.*** **1** the light of day **2** dawn **3** understanding

daylight saving time [*often* **D- S- T-**] time that is one hour later than standard time: also **daylight savings time**

Day of Atonement Yom Kippur

day′time′ ***n.*** the time between dawn and sunset

day′-to-day′ ***adj.*** daily; routine

Day·ton (dāt′'n) city in SW Ohio: pop. 182,000

Day·to·na Beach (dā tō′nə) resort city in NE Florida, on the Atlantic: pop. 62,000

day trading rapid buying and selling of stocks on the Internet —**day trader**

daze (dāz) ***vt.*** **dazed, daz′ing** ⟦< ON *dasi,* tired⟧ to stun or bewilder —***n.*** a dazed condition —**daz′ed·ly** ***adv.***

daz·zle (daz′əl) ***vt., vi.*** **-zled, -zling** ⟦freq. of DAZE⟧ **1** to overpower or be overpowered by bright light **2** to surprise or arouse admiration with brilliant qualities, display, etc. —***n.*** a dazzling —**daz′zler** ***n.***

db or **dB** *abbrev.* decibel(s)

DC *abbrev.* **1** direct current: also **dc** **2** District of Columbia

DD or **D.D.** *abbrev.* Doctor of Divinity

DDS or **D.D.S.** *abbrev.* Doctor of Dental Surgery

DDT (dē′dē′tē′) ***n.*** ⟦< its chemical name⟧ a powerful insecticide

de- ⟦< Fr *dé-* or L *de*⟧ *prefix* **1** away from, off *[derail]* **2** down *[degrade]* **3** entirely *[defunct]* **4** reverse the action of *[decode]*

DE Delaware

DEA *abbrev.* Drug Enforcement Administration

dea·con (dē′kən) ***n.*** ⟦< Gr *diakonos,* servant⟧ **1** a cleric ranking just below a priest **2** a church officer who helps the minister —**dea′con·ess** ***fem.n.***

de·ac·ti·vate (dē ak′tə vāt′) ***vt.*** **-vat′ed, -vat′ing** **1** to make (an explosive, chemical, etc.) inactive **2** *Mil.* to demobilize

dead (ded) ***adj.*** ⟦OE⟧ **1** no longer living **2** without life **3** deathlike **4** lacking warmth, interest, brightness, etc. **5** without feeling, motion, or power **6** extinguished or extinct **7** no longer used; obsolete **8** unerring [a *dead* shot] **9** complete [a *dead* stop] **10** precise [*dead* center] **11** [Inf.] very tired —***n.*** the time of most darkness, most cold, etc. [the *dead* of night] —***adv.*** **1** completely **2** directly [*dead* ahead] —**the dead** those who have died

dead′beat′ ***n.*** [Slang] one who tries to evade paying debts

dead′bolt′ ***n.*** a lock for a door, with a bolt that can be moved only by turning the key

dead·en (ded′'n) ***vt.*** **1** to lessen the vigor or intensity of; dull **2** to numb

dead end **1** a street, alley, etc. closed at one end **2** an impasse —**dead′-end′** ***adj.***

dead heat a race in which two or more contestants finish even; tie

dead letter **1** a rule, law, etc. no longer enforced **2** an unclaimed postal letter

dead′line′ ***n.*** the latest time by which something must be done

dead′lock′ ***n.*** a standstill resulting from the action of equal and opposed forces —***vt., vi.*** to bring or come to a deadlock

dead′ly ***adj.*** **-li·er, -li·est** **1** causing or likely to cause death **2** implacable [*deadly* enemies] **3** typical of death [*deadly* pallor] **4** extreme **5** very boring **6** very accurate [*deadly* aim] —***adv.*** extremely —**dead′li·ness** ***n.***

dead′-on′ ***adj.*** [Inf.] completely accurate

dead′pan′ ***adj., adv.*** without expression; blank(ly)

Dead Sea inland body of salt water on the Israeli-Jordanian border

dead′wood′ ***n.*** anything useless or burdensome

deaf (def) ***adj.*** ⟦OE⟧ **1** unable to hear **2** unwilling to respond, as to a plea —**deaf′ness** ***n.***

deaf'en (-ən) ***vt.*** **1** to make deaf **2** to overwhelm with noise —**deaf'en·ing** ***adj.***

deaf'-mute' ***n.*** a person who is deaf and therefore has not learned to speak

deal[1] (dēl) ***vt.*** **dealt** (delt), **deal'ing** ⟦< OE *dǣlan*⟧ **1** to portion out or distribute **2** to give; administer (a blow, etc.) **3** [Slang] to sell (illegal drugs) —***vi.*** **1** to have to do (*with*) *[*science *deals* with facts*]* **2** to conduct oneself *[deal* fairly with others*]* **3** to do business (*with* or *in*) **4** to distribute playing cards to the players —***n.*** **1** the distributing of playing cards **2** a business transaction **3** a bargain or agreement, esp. when secret **4** [Inf.] treatment *[*a fair *deal]* —**deal'er** ***n.***

deal[2] (dēl) ***n.*** ⟦OE *dǣl*, a part⟧ an indefinite amount —**a good** (or **great**) **deal** **1** a large amount **2** very much

deal'er·ship' ***n.*** a franchise to sell a product in a specified area

deal'ing ***n.*** **1** way of acting **2** [*usually pl.*] transactions or relations

dean (dēn) ***n.*** ⟦< LL *decanus*, chief of ten (monks, etc.)⟧ **1** the presiding official of a cathedral **2** a college official in charge of students or faculty **3** the senior or preeminent member of a group

dean's list a list of students at a college who have earned high grades

dear (dir) ***adj.*** ⟦OE *deore*⟧ **1** much loved **2** esteemed: a polite form of address *[Dear* Sir*]* **3** high-priced; costly **4** earnest *[*our *dearest* wish*]* —***n.*** a loved person; darling —**dear'ly** ***adv.*** —**dear'ness** ***n.***

Dear John (letter) [Inf.] a letter, as to a fiancé, breaking off a close relationship

dearth (durth) ***n.*** ⟦ME *derth*⟧ scarcity or lack

death (deth) ***n.*** ⟦OE⟧ **1** the act or fact of dying **2** the state of being dead **3** end or destruction **4** the cause of death —**death'like'** ***adj.***

death'bed' ***n.*** used chiefly in the phrase **on one's deathbed**, during the last hours of one's life

death'blow' ***n.*** **1** a blow that kills **2** a thing fatal (*to* something)

death'less ***adj.*** that cannot die; immortal —**death'less·ly** ***adv.***

death'ly ***adj.*** like or characteristic of death —***adv.*** extremely *[deathly* ill*]*

death'trap' ***n.*** an unsafe building, vehicle, etc.

Death Valley dry, hot desert basin in E California & S Nevada

deb (deb) ***n.*** [Inf.] *short for* DEBUTANTE

de·ba·cle (di bä'kəl) ***n.*** ⟦Fr *débâcler*, break up⟧ **1** a crushing defeat **2** a ruinous collapse

de·bar (dē bär') ***vt.*** **-barred'**, **-bar'ring** ⟦< Anglo-Fr: see DE- & BAR⟧ to keep (a person) *from* some right, etc. —**de·bar'ment** ***n.***

de·bark (dē bärk') ***vt.***, ***vi.*** ⟦< Fr: see DE- & BARK[3]⟧ to unload from or leave a ship or aircraft —**de·bar·ka·tion** (dē'bär kā'shən) ***n.***

de·base (dē bās') ***vt.*** **-based'**, **-bas'ing** ⟦DE- + BASE[2]⟧ to make lower in value, dignity, etc. —**de·base'ment** ***n.***

de·bate (dē bāt') ***vi.***, ***vt.*** **-bat'ed**, **-bat'ing** ⟦< OFr: see DE- & BATTER[1]⟧ **1** to discuss reasons for and against (something) **2** to take part in a debate with (a person) or about (a question) —***n.*** **1** a discussion of opposing reasons **2** a formal contest of skill in reasoned argument —**de·bat'a·ble** ***adj.*** —**de·bat'er** ***n.***

de·bauch (dē bôch') ***vt.*** ⟦< OFr *desbaucher*, seduce⟧ to lead astray morally; corrupt —***n.*** an orgy —**de·bauch'er·y**, *pl.* **-ies**, ***n.***

deb·au·chee (deb'ô shē', di bôch'ē') ***n.*** a dissipated person

de·ben·ture (di ben'chər) ***n.*** ⟦< L: see DEBT⟧ **1** a voucher acknowledging a debt **2** an interest-bearing bond issued without specified security

de·bil·i·tate (dē bil'ə tāt') ***vt.*** **-tat'ed**, **-tat'ing** ⟦< L *debilis*, weak⟧ to make weak

de·bil·i·ty (də bil'ə tē) ***n.***, *pl.* **-ties** ⟦see prec.⟧ weakness; feebleness

deb·it (deb'it) ***n.*** ⟦< L *debere*, owe⟧ **1** an entry in an account of money owed **2** the total of such entries —***vt.*** to enter as a debit

debit card a bank card that allows the cost of purchases to be deducted from a bank account

deb·o·nair (deb'ə ner') ***adj.*** ⟦< OFr *de bon aire*, lit., of good breed⟧ **1** carefree; jaunty **2** urbane Also sp. **deb'o·naire'** —**deb'o·nair'ly** ***adv.***

de·brief (dē brēf') ***vt.*** ⟦DE- + BRIEF⟧ to receive information from (a pilot, emissary, etc.) about a recent mission

de·bris or **dé·bris** (də brē') ***n.*** ⟦Fr < OFr *desbrisier*, break apart⟧ bits and pieces of stone, rubbish, etc.

debt (det) ***n.*** ⟦< L *debere*, owe⟧ **1** something owed to another **2** the condition of owing *[*to be in *debt]*

debt'or (-ər) ***n.*** one who owes a debt

de·bug (dē bug') ***vt.*** **-bugged'**, **-bug'ging** ⟦DE- + BUG⟧ **1** to correct defects in **2** [Inf.] to find and remove hidden electronic listening devices from

de·bunk (dē buŋk') ***vt.*** ⟦DE- + BUNK[2]⟧ to expose the exaggerated or false claims, etc. of

De·bus·sy (də bü sē'; *E* deb'yoo sē'), **Claude** (klōd; *E* klôd) 1862-1918; Fr. composer

de·but or **dé·but** (dā byōō', dā'byōō') ***n.*** ⟦Fr < *débuter*, to lead off⟧ **1** a first public appearance **2** the formal introduction of a young woman into society —***vi.*** to make a debut

deb·u·tante (deb'yoo tänt') ***n.*** ⟦Fr⟧ a young woman making a debut into society

dec *abbrev.* deceased

Dec *abbrev.* December

deca- ⟦< Gr *deka*, ten⟧ *combining form* ten: also **dec-**

dec·ade (dek'ād') ***n.*** ⟦< Gr *deka*, ten⟧ a period of ten years

dec·a·dence (dek'ə dəns, di kād''ns) ***n.*** ⟦< L *de-*, from + *cadere*, to fall⟧ a decline, as in morals, art, etc.; deterioration —**dec′a·dent** *adj., n.*

de·caf (dē′kaf′) *n.* [Inf.] decaffeinated coffee

de·caf·fein·at·ed (dē kaf′ə nāt′id) *adj.* with caffeine removed

de·cal (dē′kal, di kal′) *n.* ⟦< *decalcomania* < Fr < L *calcare*, to tread + Gr *mania*, madness⟧ a picture or design transferred from prepared paper to glass, wood, etc.

Dec·a·logue or **Dec·a·log** (dek′ə lôg′) *n.* ⟦see DECA- & -LOGUE⟧ [*sometimes* **d-**] TEN COMMANDMENTS

de·camp (dē kamp′) *vi.* ⟦< Fr⟧ **1** to break camp **2** to go away suddenly and secretly

de·cant (dē kant′) *vt.* ⟦< Fr < L *de-*, from + *canthus*, tire of a wheel⟧ to pour gently from one container into another

de·cant′er *n.* a decorative glass bottle for serving wine, etc.

de·cap·i·tate (dē kap′ə tāt′) *vt.* **-tat′ed, -tat′ing** ⟦< L *de-*, off + *caput*, head⟧ to behead —**de·cap′i·ta′tion** *n.*

de·cath·lon (di kath′län′) *n.* ⟦DEC(A)- + Gr *athlon*, a prize⟧ an athletic contest in which each contestant takes part in ten TRACK (sense 6*b*) events

de·cay (dē kā′) *vi.* ⟦see DECADENCE⟧ **1** to lose strength, prosperity, etc. gradually; deteriorate **2** to rot **3** to undergo radioactive disintegration —*vt.* to cause to decay —*n.* **1** deterioration **2** a rotting or rottenness

de·cease (dē sēs′) *n.* ⟦< L *de-*, from + *cedere*, go⟧ death

de·ceased (dē sēst′) *adj.* dead —**the deceased** the dead person or persons

de·ce·dent (dē sēd′'nt) *n.* ⟦see DECEASE⟧ *Law* a deceased person

de·ceit (dē sēt′) *n.* **1** a deceiving or lying **2** a dishonest action **3** deceitful quality

de·ceit′ful *adj.* **1** apt to lie or cheat **2** deceptive; false —**de·ceit′ful·ly** *adv.*

de·ceive (dē sēv′) *vt., vi.* **-ceived′, -ceiv′ing** ⟦< L *de-*, from + *capere*, take⟧ to make (a person) believe what is not true; mislead —**de·ceiv′er** *n.* —**de·ceiv′ing·ly** *adv.*

de·cel·er·ate (dē sel′ər āt′) *vt., vi.* **-at′ed, -at′ing** ⟦DE- + (AC)CELERATE⟧ to reduce the speed (of); slow down —**de·cel′er·a′tion** *n.*

De·cem·ber (dē sem′bər) *n.* ⟦< L *decem*, ten: tenth month in Roman calendar⟧ the twelfth and last month of the year, having 31 days

de·cen·cy (dē′sən sē) *n., pl.* **-cies** a being decent; propriety, courtesy, etc.

de·cen·ni·al (dē sen′ē əl) *adj.* ⟦< L *decem*, ten + *annus*, year⟧ **1** happening every ten years **2** lasting ten years

de·cent (dē′sənt) *adj.* ⟦< L *decere*, befit⟧ **1** proper and fitting **2** not obscene **3** respectable **4** adequate [*decent* wages] **5** fair and kind —**de′cent·ly** *adv.*

de·cen·tral·ize (dē sen′trə līz′) *vt.* **-ized′, -iz′ing** to break up a concentration of (governmental authority, industry, etc.) and distribute more widely —**de·cen′tral·i·za′tion** *n.*

de·cep·tion (dē sep′shən) *n.* **1** a deceiving or being deceived **2** an illusion or fraud —**de·cep′tive** *adj.*

deci- ⟦< L *decem*, ten⟧ *combining form* one tenth part of

dec·i·bel (des′ə bəl) *n.* ⟦prec. + *bel*, after BELL⟧ a unit for measuring relative loudness of a sound

de·cide (dē sīd′) *vt.* **-cid′ed, -cid′ing** ⟦< L *de-*, off + *caedere*, to cut⟧ **1** to end (a contest, dispute, etc.) by giving one side the victory **2** to reach a decision about; resolve —*vi.* to reach a decision —**de·cid′a·ble** *adj.*

de·cid′ed *adj.* **1** definite; clear-cut **2** determined —**de·cid′ed·ly** *adv.*

de·cid·u·ous (dē sij′o͞o əs) *adj.* ⟦< L *de-*, off, down + *cadere*, to fall⟧ **1** falling off or out at a certain season or stage of growth, as some leaves or antlers do **2** shedding leaves annually

dec·i·mal (des′ə məl) *adj.* ⟦< L *decem*, ten⟧ of or based on the number 10 —*n.* a fraction with a denominator of 10 or some power of 10, shown by a point (**decimal point**) before the numerator (Ex.: .5 = $\frac{5}{10}$)

dec·i·mate (des′ə māt′) *vt.* **-mat′ed, -mat′ing** ⟦< L *decem*, ten⟧ to destroy or kill a large part of (lit., a tenth part of) —**dec′i·ma′tion** *n.*

de·ci·pher (dē sī′fər) *vt.* ⟦DE- + CIPHER⟧ **1** DECODE **2** to make out the meaning of (illegible writing, etc.)

de·ci·sion (dē sizh′ən) *n.* **1** the act of deciding or settling a dispute or question **2** the act of making up one's mind **3** a judgment or conclusion **4** determination; firmness of mind

de·ci·sive (dē sī′siv) *adj.* **1** that settles a dispute, question, etc.; conclusive **2** critically important; crucial **3** showing firmness —**de·ci′sive·ly** *adv.*

deck[1] (dek) *n.* ⟦prob. < earlier LowG *verdeck*⟧ **1** a floor of a ship **2** any platform, floor, etc., like a ship's deck **3** a pack of playing cards **4** TAPE DECK

deck[2] (dek) *vt.* ⟦MDu *decken*, to cover⟧ to array or adorn: often with *out*

de·claim (dē klām′) *vi., vt.* ⟦< L *de-*, intens. + *clamare*, to cry⟧ to recite or speak in a studied, dramatic, or impassioned way —**dec·la·ma·tion** (dek′lə mā′shən) *n.* —**de·clam·a·to·ry** (dē klam′ə tôr′ē) *adj.*

dec·la·ra·tion (dek′lə rā′shən) *n.* **1** a declaring; announcement **2** a formal statement

de·clar·a·tive (dē kler′ə tiv) *adj.* making a statement or assertion

de·clare (dē kler′) *vt.* **-clared′, -clar′ing** ⟦< L *de-*, intens. + *clarus*, clear⟧ **1** to announce openly or formally **2** to show or reveal **3** to say emphatically —**de·clar′er** *n.*

de·clas·si·fy (dē klas′ə fī′) *vt.* **-fied′, -fy′ing** to make (secret documents, etc.) available to the public —**de·clas′si·fi·ca′tion** *n.*

de·clen·sion (dē klen′shən) *n.* ⟦see fol.⟧ **1** a descent **2** a decline **3** *Gram.* the inflection of nouns, pronouns, or adjectives

de·cline (dē klīn′) *vi.* **-clined′, -clin′ing** ⟦< L *de-*, from + *clinare*, to bend⟧ **1** to bend or slope downward **2** to deteriorate; decay 3 to refuse something —*vt.* 1 to cause to bend or slope downward 2 to refuse politely 3 *Gram.* to give the inflected forms of (a noun, pronoun, or adjective) —*n.* 1 a declining; dropping, failing, decay, etc. 2 a period of decline 3 a downward slope —**dec·li·na·tion** (dek′lə nā′shən) *n.* —**de·clin′er** *n.*

de·cliv·i·ty (dē kliv′ə tē) *n., pl.* **-ties** ⟦< L *de-*, down + *clivus*, a slope⟧ a downward slope

de·code (dē kōd′) *vt.* **-cod′ed**, **-cod′ing** to decipher (a coded message)

dé·col·le·té (dā käl′ə tā′) *adj.* ⟦Fr < L *de*, from + *collum*, neck⟧ cut low so as to bare the neck and shoulders

de·col·o·ni·za·tion (dē käl′ə nə zā′shən) *n.* a freeing or being freed from colonial status —**de·col′o·nize′** (-ə nīz′), **-nized′**, **-niz′ing**, *vt.*, *vi.*

de·com·pose (dē′kəm pōz′) *vt.*, *vi.* **-posed′**, **-pos′ing** ⟦< Fr: see DE- & COMPOSE⟧ 1 to break up into basic parts 2 to rot —**de·com·po·si·tion** (dē käm pə zish′ən) *n.*

de·com·press (dē′kəm pres′) *vt.* to free from pressure, esp. from air pressure —**de′com·pres′sion** *n.*

de·con·gest·ant (dē′kən jes′tənt) *n.* a medication that relieves congestion, as in the nasal passages

de·con·struct (dē′kən strukt′) *vt.* ⟦Fr⟧ 1 to analyze rigorously 2 to take apart; disassemble —**de′con·struc′tion** *n.*

de·con·tam·i·nate (dē′kən tam′ə nāt′) *vt.* **-nat′ed**, **-nat′ing** to rid of a harmful substance, as radioactive material

dé·cor or **de·cor** (dā kôr′) *n.* ⟦Fr⟧ a decorative scheme, as of a room

dec·o·rate (dek′ə rāt′) *vt.* **-rat′ed**, **-rat′ing** ⟦< L *decus*, an ornament⟧ 1 to adorn; ornament 2 to paint or wallpaper 3 to give a medal or similar honor to —**dec·o·ra·tive** (dek′ə rə tiv, -ə rāt′iv) *adj.* —**dec′o·ra′tor** *n.*

dec′o·ra′tion *n.* 1 a decorating 2 an ornament 3 a medal, etc.

Decoration Day MEMORIAL DAY

dec·o·rous (dek′ə rəs, di kôr′əs) *adj.* having or showing decorum, good taste, etc. —**dec′o·rous·ly** *adv.*

de·co·rum (di kôr′əm) *n.* ⟦< L *decorus*, proper⟧ propriety and good taste in behavior, speech, etc.

de·cou·page or **dé·cou·page** (dā′ko͞o päzh′) *n.* ⟦< Fr *dé-*, DE- + *couper*, to cut⟧ the art of decorating a surface with varnished paper cutouts

de·coy (dē koi′; *for n., usually* dē′koi′) *n.* ⟦< Du *de kooi*, the cage⟧ 1 an artificial or trained bird, etc. used to lure game within gun range 2 a thing or person used to lure into danger —*vt.* to lure into danger

de·crease (dē krēs′; *for n., usually* dē′krēs′) *vi., vt.* **-creased′**, **-creas′ing** ⟦< L *de-*, from + *crescere*, grow⟧ to become or make less, smaller, etc.; diminish —*n.* 1 a decreasing 2 amount of decreasing

de·cree (dē krē′) *n.* ⟦< L *de-*, from + *cernere*, to judge⟧ an official order or decision —*vt.* **-creed′**, **-cree′ing** to order or decide by decree

de·crep·it (dē krep′it) *adj.* ⟦< L *de-*, intens. + *crepare*, to creak⟧ broken down or worn out by old age or long use —**de·crep′i·tude′** (-ə to͞od′) *n.*

de·cre·scen·do (dā′krə shen′dō, dē′-) [*also in italics*] *Music adj., adv.* ⟦It < L, DECREASE⟧ gradually decreasing in loudness —*n., pl.* **-dos** a gradual decrease in loudness

de·crim·i·nal·ize (dē krim′ə nəl īz′) *vt.* **-ized′**, **-iz′ing** to eliminate or reduce the penalties for (a crime)

de·cry (dē krī′) *vt.* **-cried′**, **-cry′ing** ⟦< Fr: see DE- & CRY⟧ to speak out against openly; denounce

ded·i·cate (ded′i kāt′) *vt.* **-cat′ed**, **-cat′ing** ⟦< L *de-*, intens. + *dicare*, proclaim⟧ 1 to set apart for, or devote to, a special purpose 2 to address (a book, etc.) to someone as a sign of honor —**ded′i·ca′tion** *n.*

ded′i·cat′ed *adj.* 1 devoted; faithful 2 designating a device, etc. to be used only for a particular purpose

de·duce (dē do͞os′) *vt.* **-duced′**, **-duc′ing** ⟦< L *de-*, down + *ducere*, to lead⟧ to infer or decide by reasoning —**de·duc′i·ble** *adj.*

de·duct (dē dukt′) *vt.* ⟦see prec.⟧ to take away or subtract (a quantity)

de·duct′i·ble (-duk′tə bəl) *adj.* that can be deducted —*n.* an amount stipulated in an insurance policy to be paid by the person insured in the event of a loss, etc., with the insurer paying the remainder

de·duc′tion (-duk′shən) *n.* 1 a deducting; subtraction 2 an amount deducted 3 *a*) reasoning from the general to the specific *b*) a conclusion reached by such reasoning —**de·duc′tive** *adj.*

deed (dēd) *n.* ⟦< OE *ded*⟧ 1 a thing done; act 2 a feat of courage, skill, etc. 3 a legal document which transfers a property —*vt.* to transfer (property) by deed

deem (dēm) *vt.*, *vi.* ⟦< OE *deman*, to judge⟧ to think, believe, or judge

de·em·pha·size (dē em′fə sīz′) *vt.* **-sized′**, **-siz′ing** to lessen the importance of —**de·em′pha·sis** (-sis) *n.*

deep (dēp) *adj.* ⟦OE *deop*⟧ 1 extending far downward, inward, backward, etc. 2 hard to understand; abstruse 3 serious; profound 4 dark and rich [a *deep* red] 5 absorbed by: with *in* [*deep* in thought] 6 great in degree; intense 7 of low pitch [a *deep* voice] 8 large; big —*n.* a deep place —*adv.* far down, far back, etc. —**the deep** [Old Poet.] the ocean —**deep′ly** *adv.* —**deep′ness** *n.*

deep′en *vt.*, *vi.* to make or become deep or deeper

deep′freeze′ *n.* a condition of suspended activity, etc. —*vt.* **-froze′**, **-fro′zen**, **-freez′ing** to subject (foods) to sudden freezing so as to preserve and store

deep′-fry′ *vt.* **-fried′**, **-fry′ing** to fry in a deep pan of boiling fat or oil

deep′-root′ed *adj.* 1 having deep roots 2 firmly fixed

deep′-seat′ed *adj.* 1 buried deep 2 firmly fixed

deep'-six' ***vt.*** ⟦< six fathoms⟧ [Slang] to get rid of, as by throwing overboard

deep space OUTER SPACE

deer (dir) ***n.***, *pl.* **deer** or **deers** ⟦OE *deor*, wild animal⟧ any of various ruminants, including the elk, moose, and reindeer, the male of which grows and sheds antlers annually

de·es·ca·late (dē es'kə lāt') ***vi.***, ***vt.*** **-lat'ed**, **-lat'ing** to reduce in scope, magnitude, etc. —**de-es'ca·la'tion** ***n.***

de·face (dē fās') ***vt.*** **-faced'**, **-fac'ing** ⟦see DE- & FACE⟧ to spoil the look of; mar —**de·face'ment** ***n.***

de fac·to (dē fak'tō) ⟦L⟧ actually existing but not officially approved

de·fal·cate (dē fal'kāt') ***vi.*** **-cat'ed**, **-cat'ing** ⟦< L *de-*, from + *falx*, a sickle⟧ to steal or misuse funds entrusted to one's care; embezzle —**de'fal·ca'tion** ***n.***

de·fame (dē fām') ***vt.*** **-famed'**, **-fam'ing** ⟦< L *dis-*, from + *fama*, fame⟧ to attack the reputation of; slander or libel —**def·a·ma·tion** (def'ə mā'shən) ***n.*** —**de·fam·a·to·ry** (dē fam'ə tôr'ē) ***adj.*** —**de·fam'er** ***n.***

de·fang (dē faŋ') ***vt.*** **1** to remove the fangs of **2** to make harmless —**de·fanged'** ***adj.***

de·fault (dē fôlt') ***n.*** ⟦< L *de-*, away + *fallere*, fail⟧ failure to do or appear as required; specif., failure to pay money due —***vi.***, ***vt.*** **1** to fail to do or pay when required **2** to lose (a contest) by default —**de·fault'er** ***n.***

de·feat (dē fēt') ***vt.*** ⟦< L *dis-*, from + *facere*, do⟧ **1** to win victory over **2** to bring to nothing; frustrate —***n.*** a defeating or being defeated

de·feat'ist ***n.*** one who too readily accepts or expects defeat —**de·feat'ism'** ***n.***

def·e·cate (def'i kāt') ***vi.*** **-cat'ed**, **-cat'ing** ⟦< L *de-*, from + *faex*, dregs⟧ to excrete waste matter from the bowels —**def'e·ca'tion** ***n.***

de·fect (dē'fekt'; *for v.* dē fekt') ***n.*** ⟦< L *de-*, from + *facere*, do⟧ **1** lack of something necessary for completeness **2** an imperfection or weakness; fault —***vi.*** to forsake a party, cause, etc., esp. so as to join the opposition —**de·fec'tion** ***n.*** —**de·fec'tor** ***n.***

de·fec·tive (dē fek'tiv) ***adj.*** having defects; imperfect; faulty

de·fend (dē fend') ***vt.*** ⟦< L *de-*, away + *fendere*, to strike⟧ **1** to guard from attack; protect **2** to support or justify **3** *Law a)* to oppose (an action) *b)* to act as lawyer for (an accused) —**de·fend'er** ***n.***

de·fend·ant (dē fen'dənt, -dant') ***n.*** *Law* the person sued or accused

de·fense (dē fens', dē'fens') ***n.*** **1** a defending against attack **2** something that defends **3** justification by speech or writing **4** *a)* the arguments of a defendant *b)* the defendant and his or her counsel Brit. sp. **defence** —**de·fense'less** ***adj.*** —**de·fen'si·ble** ***adj.***

defense mechanism any thought process used unconsciously to protect oneself against painful feelings

de·fen'sive ***adj.*** **1** defending **2** of or for defense —***n.*** a position of defense —**de·fen'sive·ly** ***adv.***

de·fer[1] (dē fʉr') ***vt.***, ***vi.*** **-ferred'**, **-fer'ring** ⟦see DIFFER⟧ **1** to postpone; delay **2** to postpone the induction of (a person) into compulsory military service —**de·fer'ment** or **de·fer'ral** ***n.***

de·fer[2] (dē fʉr') ***vi.*** **-ferred'**, **-fer'ring** ⟦< L *de-*, down + *ferre*, to BEAR[1]⟧ to yield with courtesy (*to*)

def·er·ence (def'ər əns) ***n.*** **1** a yielding in opinion, judgment, etc. **2** courteous respect

def'er·en'tial (-en'shəl) ***adj.*** showing deference; very respectful

de·fi·ance (dē fī'əns) ***n.*** a defying; open, bold resistance to authority —**de·fi'ant** ***adj.*** —**de·fi'ant·ly** ***adv.***

de·fi·cien·cy (dē fish'ən sē) ***n.*** ⟦< L *de-*, from + *facere*, do⟧ **1** a being deficient **2** *pl.* **-cies** a shortage

deficiency disease a disease caused by a lack of vitamins, minerals, etc. in the diet

de·fi·cient (dē fish'ənt) ***adj.*** ⟦see DEFICIENCY⟧ **1** lacking in some essential; incomplete **2** inadequate in amount

def·i·cit (def'ə sit) ***n.*** ⟦L < *deficere*, to lack⟧ the amount by which a sum of money is less than the required amount, as when there are more expenditures than income

de·file[1] (dē fīl') ***vt.*** **-filed'**, **-fil'ing** ⟦< OFr *defouler*, tread underfoot⟧ **1** to make filthy **2** to profane; sully —**de·file'ment** ***n.*** —**de·fil'er** ***n.***

de·file[2] (dē fīl', dē'fīl') ***vi.*** **-filed'**, **-fil'ing** ⟦< Fr *dé-*, from + *fil*, thread⟧ to march in single file —***n.*** a narrow passage, valley, etc.

de·fine (dē fīn') ***vt.*** **-fined'**, **-fin'ing** ⟦< L *de-*, from + *finis*, boundary⟧ **1** to determine the limits or nature of; describe exactly **2** to state the meaning of (a word, etc.) —**de·fin'er** ***n.***

def·i·nite (def'ə nit) ***adj.*** ⟦see prec.⟧ **1** having exact limits **2** precise in meaning; explicit **3** certain; positive **4** *Gram.* limiting or specifying *[*"the" is the *definite* article*]* —**def'i·nite·ly** ***adv.*** —**def'i·nite·ness** ***n.***

def'i·ni'tion (-nish'ən) ***n.*** **1** a defining or being defined **2** a statement of the meaning of a word **3** clarity of outline, sound, etc.

de·fin·i·tive (dē fin'ə tiv) ***adj.*** **1** conclusive; final **2** most nearly complete **3** serving to define

de·flate (dē flāt') ***vt.***, ***vi.*** **-flat'ed**, **-flat'ing** ⟦DE- + (IN)FLATE⟧ **1** to collapse by letting out air or gas **2** to lessen in size, importance, etc. **3** to cause deflation of (currency, etc.)

de·fla'tion ***n.*** **1** a deflating **2** a reduction in prices resulting from severe economic decline

de·flect (dē flekt') ***vt.***, ***vi.*** ⟦< L *de-*, from + *flectere*, to bend⟧ to turn or make go to one side —**de·flec'tion** ***n.*** —**de·flec'tive** ***adj.*** —**de·flec'tor** ***n.***

De·foe (di fō'), **Daniel** 1660-1731; Eng. writer

de·fog·ger (dē fôg′ər) ***n.*** an apparatus for clearing condensed moisture, as from a car window

de·fo·li·ant (dē fō′lē ənt) ***n.*** a chemical substance that causes leaves to fall from growing plants

de·fo′li·ate′ (-āt′) ***vt.*** **-at′ed, -at′ing** ⟦< L *de-*, from + *folium*, leaf⟧ to strip (trees, etc.) of leaves —**de·fo′li·a′tion** ***n.***

de·form (dē fôrm′) ***vt.*** ⟦< L *de-*, from + *forma*, form⟧ **1** to impair the form of **2** to make ugly —**de·for·ma·tion** (dē′fôr mā′shən, def′ər-) ***n.***

de·formed′ ***adj.*** misshapen

de·form′i·ty ***n.***, *pl.* **-ties** **1** a deformed part, as of the body **2** ugliness or depravity

de·fraud (dē frôd′) ***vt.*** to take property, rights, etc. from by fraud; cheat —**de·fraud′er** ***n.***

de·fray (dē frā′) ***vt.*** ⟦Fr *défrayer*⟧ to pay (the cost or expenses) —**de·fray′a·ble** ***adj.*** —**de·fray′al** ***n.***

de·frost (dē frôst′) ***vt., vi.*** to rid or get rid of frost or ice —**de·frost′er** ***n.***

deft (deft) ***adj.*** ⟦see DAFT⟧ skillful; dexterous —**deft′ly** ***adv.***

de·funct (dē fuŋkt′) ***adj.*** ⟦< L *defungi*, to finish⟧ no longer existing; dead or extinct

de·fuse (dē fyo͞oz′) ***vt.*** **-fused′, -fus′ing** **1** to remove the fuse from (a bomb, etc.) **2** to make harmless, less tense, etc.

de·fy (dē fī′) ***vt.*** **-fied′, -fy′ing** ⟦< LL *dis-*, from + *fidus*, faithful⟧ **1** to resist or oppose boldly or openly **2** to dare to do or prove something

de·gen·er·ate (dē jen′ər it; *for v.*, -āt′) ***adj.*** ⟦< L *de-*, from + *genus*, race⟧ **1** having sunk below a former or normal condition, etc.; deteriorated **2** depraved —***n.*** a degenerate person —***vi.*** **-at′ed, -at′ing** to lose former normal or higher qualities —**de·gen′er·a·cy** (-ə sē) ***n.*** —**de·gen′er·a′tion** ***n.*** —**de·gen′er·a·tive** (-ə tiv, -āt′iv) ***adj.***

de·grad·a·ble (dē grād′ə bəl) ***adj.*** capable of being degraded, esp. of being readily decomposed by chemicals, as some plastics

de·grade (dē grād′) ***vt.*** **-grad′ed, -grad′ing** ⟦< L *de-*, down + *gradus*, a step⟧ **1** to demote **2** to lower in quality, moral character, dignity, etc.; debase, dishonor, etc. —**deg·ra·da·tion** (deg′rə dā′shən) ***n.***

de·gree (di grē′) ***n.*** ⟦see prec.⟧ **1** any of the successive steps in a process **2** social or official rank **3** extent, amount, or intensity **4** a rank given by a college or university to one who has completed a course of study, or to a distinguished person as an honor **5** a grade of comparison of adjectives and adverbs *[the superlative degree]* **6** *Law* the seriousness of a crime *[murder in the first degree]* **7** *Math.* a unit of measure for angles or arcs, one 360th of the circumference of a circle **8** *Physics* a unit of measure for temperature —**to a degree** somewhat

de·greed′ (-grēd′) ***adj.*** having a college or university degree

de·hu·man·ize (dē hyo͞o′mə nīz′) ***vt.*** **-ized′, -iz′ing** to deprive of human qualities; make machinelike —**de·hu′man·i·za′tion** ***n.***

de·hu·mid·i·fy (dē′hyo͞o mid′ə fī′) ***vt.*** **-fied′, -fy′ing** to remove moisture from (air, etc.) —**de′hu·mid′i·fi′er** ***n.***

de·hy·drate (dē hī′drāt′) ***vt.*** **-drat′ed, -drat′ing** to remove water from (a substance, etc.); dry —***vi.*** to lose water —**de′hy·dra′tion** ***n.*** —**de·hy′dra′tor** ***n.***

de-ice (dē īs′) ***vt.*** **-iced′, -ic′ing** to melt ice from —**de-ic′er** ***n.***

de·i·fy (dē′ə fī′) ***vt.*** **-fied′, -fy′ing** ⟦< L *deus*, god + *facere*, make⟧ **1** to make a god of **2** to look upon as a god —**de′i·fi·ca′tion** (-fi kā′shən) ***n.***

deign (dān) ***vi., vt.*** ⟦< L *dignus*, worthy⟧ to condescend (to do or give)

de·ism (dē′iz′əm) ***n.*** ⟦< L *deus*, god⟧ the belief that God exists and created the world but takes no part in its functioning —**de′ist** ***n.***

de·i·ty (dē′ə tē) ***n.*** ⟦< L *deus*, god⟧ **1** the state of being a god **2** *pl.* **-ties** a god or goddess —**the Deity** God

dé·jà vu (dā′zhä vo͞o′) ⟦Fr, already seen⟧ a feeling of having been in a place or experienced something before

de·ject (dē jekt′) ***vt.*** ⟦< L *de-*, down + *jacere*, throw⟧ to dishearten; depress —**de·ject′ed** ***adj.*** —**de·jec′tion** ***n.***

Del·a·ware (del′ə wer′, -war′) state of the E U.S.: 1,955 sq. mi.; pop. 666,000; cap. Dover: abbrev. *DE* —**Del′a·war′e·an** ***adj., n.***

de·lay (dē lā′) ***vt.*** ⟦< OFr *de-*, intens. + *laier*, to leave⟧ **1** to put off; postpone **2** to make late; detain —***vi.*** to linger —***n.*** **1** a delaying or being delayed **2** the time one is delayed

de·lec·ta·ble (dē lek′tə bəl) ***adj.*** ⟦see DELIGHT⟧ delightful or delicious

de·lec·ta·tion (dē′lek tā′shən) ***n.*** ⟦see DELIGHT⟧ delight; enjoyment

del·e·gate (del′ə git; *for v.*, -gāt′) ***n.*** ⟦< L *de-*, from + *legare*, send⟧ a person authorized to act for others; representative —***vt.*** **-gat′ed, -gat′ing** **1** to appoint as a delegate **2** to entrust (authority, etc.) to another

del′e·ga′tion (-gā′shən) ***n.*** **1** a delegating or being delegated **2** a body of delegates

de·lete (dē lēt′) ***vt.*** **-let′ed, -let′ing** ⟦< L *delere*, destroy⟧ to take out (a word, etc.); cross out —**de·le′tion** ***n.***

del·e·te·ri·ous (del′ə tir′ē əs) ***adj.*** ⟦< Gr *dēleisthai*, injure⟧ harmful to health or well-being

delft·ware (delft′wer′) ***n.*** ⟦after *Delft*, city in the Netherlands⟧ glazed earthenware, usually blue and white: also **delft**

Del·hi (del′ē) city in N India: pop. 4,884,000: see also NEW DELHI

del·i (del′ē) ***n.*** *short for* DELICATESSEN

de·lib·er·ate (di lib′ər it; *for v.*, -āt′) ***adj.*** ⟦< L *de-*, intens. + *librare*, weigh⟧ **1** carefully thought out; premeditated **2** not rash or hasty **3** unhurried —***vi., vt.*** **-at′ed, -at′ing** to consider carefully —**de·lib′er·ate·ly** ***adv.*** —**de·lib′er·a′tive** (-āt′iv, -ə tiv) ***adj.***

de·lib′er·a′tion (-ā′shən) ***n.*** **1** a deliberating **2** [*often pl.*] consideration of alternatives **3** carefulness; slowness

del·i·ca·cy (del′i kə sē) ***n.***, *pl.* **-cies** **1** the quality of being delicate; fineness, weakness, sensitivity, etc. **2** a choice food

del′i·cate (-kit) ***adj.*** ⟦< L *delicatus*, delightful⟧ **1** pleasing in its lightness, mildness, etc. **2** beautifully fine in texture, workmanship, etc. **3** slight and subtle **4** easily damaged **5** frail in health **6** *a*) needing careful handling *b*) showing tact, consideration, etc. **7** finely sensitive —**del′i·cate·ly** ***adv.*** —**del′i·cate·ness** ***n.***

del·i·ca·tes·sen (del′i kə tes′ən) ***n.*** ⟦< Ger pl. < Fr *délicatesse*, delicacy⟧ **1** prepared cooked meats, fish, cheeses, salads, etc., collectively **2** a shop where such foods are sold

de·li·cious (di lish′əs) ***adj.*** ⟦see fol.⟧ **1** delightful **2** very pleasing to taste or smell —**de·li′cious·ly** ***adv.*** —**de·li′cious·ness** ***n.***

de·light (di līt′) ***vt.*** ⟦< L *de-*, from + *lacere*, entice⟧ to give great pleasure to —***vi.*** **1** to give great pleasure **2** to be highly pleased; rejoice —***n.*** **1** great pleasure **2** something giving great pleasure —**de·light′ed** ***adj.***

de·light′ful ***adj.*** giving delight; very pleasing —**de·light′ful·ly** ***adv.***

De·li·lah (di lī′lə) ***n.*** *Bible* the mistress and betrayer of Samson

de·lim·it (dē lim′it) ***vt.*** to fix the limits of —**de·lim′i·ta′tion** ***n.***

de·lin·e·ate (di lin′ē āt′) ***vt.*** **-at′ed**, **-at′ing** ⟦< L *de-*, from + *linea*, a line⟧ **1** to draw; sketch **2** to depict in words —**de·lin′e·a′tion** ***n.***

de·lin·quent (di liŋ′kwənt) ***adj.*** ⟦< L *de-*, from + *linquere*, leave⟧ **1** failing to do what duty or law requires **2** overdue, as taxes —***n.*** a delinquent person; esp., a juvenile delinquent —**de·lin′quen·cy**, *pl.* **-cies**, ***n.*** —**de·lin′quent·ly** ***adv.***

del·i·quesce (del′i kwes′) ***vi.*** **-quesced′**, **-quesc′ing** ⟦< L < *de-*, from + *liquere*, be liquid⟧ to become liquid by absorbing moisture from the air —**del′i·ques′cent** ***adj.***

de·lir·i·ous (di lir′ē əs) ***adj.*** **1** in a state of delirium **2** of or caused by delirium **3** wildly excited —**de·lir′i·ous·ly** ***adv.*** —**de·lir′i·ous·ness** ***n.***

de·lir′i·um (-əm) ***n.*** ⟦< L *de-*, from + *lira*, a line⟧ **1** a temporary mental disturbance, as during a fever, marked by confused speech and hallucinations **2** uncontrollably wild excitement

de·liv·er (di liv′ər) ***vt.*** ⟦< L *de-*, intens. + *liber*, free⟧ **1** to set free or rescue **2** to assist at the birth of **3** to make (a speech, etc.) **4** to hand over **5** to distribute (mail, etc.) **6** to strike (a blow) **7** to throw (a ball, etc.) —***vi.*** **1** to make deliveries **2** to produce, etc. something promised

de·liv′er·ance ***n.*** a freeing or being freed; rescue

de·liv′er·y ***n.***, *pl.* **-er·ies** **1** a handing over **2** a distributing, as of mail **3** a giving birth **4** any giving forth **5** the act or manner of delivering a speech, ball, etc. **6** something delivered

dell (del) ***n.*** ⟦OE *dell*⟧ a small, secluded valley or glen, usually wooded

del·phin·i·um (del fin′ē əm) ***n.*** ⟦< Gr *delphin*, dolphin⟧ a tall plant bearing spikes of flowers, usually blue

del·ta (del′tə) ***n.*** **1** the fourth letter of the Greek alphabet (Δ, δ) **2** a deposit of soil, usually triangular, formed at the mouth of a large river

de·lude (di lo͞od′) ***vt.*** **-lud′ed**, **-lud′ing** ⟦< L *de-*, from + *ludere*, to play⟧ to mislead; deceive

del·uge (del′yo͞oj′) ***n.*** ⟦< L *dis*, off + *luere*, to wash⟧ **1** a great flood **2** a heavy rainfall **3** an overwhelming rush of anything —***vt.*** **-uged′**, **-ug′ing** **1** to flood **2** to overwhelm

de·lu·sion (di lo͞o′zhən) ***n.*** **1** a deluding or being deluded **2** a false belief, specif. one that persists psychotically —**de·lu′sive** or **de·lu′sion·al** ***adj.***

de·luxe (di luks′, -lo͝oks′) ***adj.*** ⟦Fr, of luxury⟧ of extra fine quality —***adv.*** in a deluxe manner

delve (delv) ***vi.*** **delved**, **delv′ing** ⟦OE *delfan*⟧ **1** [Now Dial., Chiefly Brit.] to dig **2** to search (*into*) —**delv′er** ***n.***

Dem *abbrev.* **1** Democrat **2** Democratic

de·mag·net·ize (dē mag′nə tīz′) ***vt.*** **-ized′**, **-iz′ing** to remove magnetism or magnetic properties from —**de·mag′net·i·za′tion** ***n.***

dem·a·gogue or **dem·a·gog** (dem′ə gäg′) ***n.*** ⟦< Gr *dēmos*, the people + *agōgos*, leader⟧ one who tries to stir up people's emotions in order to win them over and so gain power —**dem′a·gog′y** (-gä′jē, -gäg′ē) or **dem′a·gogu′er·y** (-gäg′ər ē) ***n.***

de·mand (di mand′) ***vt.*** ⟦< L *de-*, from + *mandare*, entrust⟧ **1** to ask for boldly or urgently **2** to ask for as a right **3** to require; need —***vi.*** to make a demand —***n.*** **1** a demanding **2** a thing demanded **3** a strong request **4** an urgent requirement **5** *Economics* the desire for a commodity together with ability to pay for it; also, the amount people are ready to buy at a certain price —**in demand** wanted or sought —**on demand** when presented for payment

de·mand′ing ***adj.*** making difficult demands on one's patience, energy, etc.

de·mar·ca·tion (dē′mär kā′shən) ***n.*** ⟦< Sp *de-*, from + *marcar*, to mark⟧ **1** the act of setting and marking limits or boundaries **2** a limit or boundary

de·mean[1] (dē mēn′) ***vt.*** ⟦DE- + MEAN[2]⟧ to degrade; humble

de·mean[2] (dē mēn′) ***vt.*** ⟦see fol.⟧ to behave or conduct (oneself)

de·mean·or (di mēn′ər) ***n.*** ⟦< OFr *demener*, to lead⟧ outward behavior; conduct; deportment: Brit. sp. **demeanour**

de·ment·ed (dē ment′id) ***adj.*** ⟦see fol.⟧ mentally deranged; insane

de·men·tia (di men′shə) ***n.*** ⟦< L *de-*, out from + *mens*, the mind⟧ a disorder of the mind impairing perception, memory, etc.

de·mer·it (dē mer′it) ***n.*** ⟦< L *de-*, intens. + *merere*, to deserve, with *de-* taken as negative⟧ **1** a fault; defect **2** a mark recorded against a student, etc. for poor conduct or work

de·mesne (di mān′, -mēn′) ***n.*** ⟦see DOMAIN⟧ a region or domain

De·me·ter (di mēt′ər) ***n.*** *Gr. Myth.* the goddess of agriculture

demi- ⟦< L *dimidius*, half⟧ *prefix* **1** half **2** less than usual in size, power, etc. *[demigod]*

dem·i·god (dem′i gäd′) ***n.*** **1** a minor deity **2** a godlike person

dem′i·john′ (-jän′) ***n.*** ⟦Fr *dame-jeanne*⟧ a large bottle of glass or earthenware in a wicker casing

de·mil·i·ta·rize (dē mil′ə tə rīz′) ***vt.*** **-rized′**, **-riz′ing** to free from organized military control

dem·i·monde (dem′i mänd′) ***n.*** ⟦Fr < *demi-* + *monde*, world⟧ the class of women who have lost social standing because of sexual promiscuity

de·mise (dē mīz′) ***n.*** ⟦< L *de-*, down + *mittere*, send⟧ **1** *Law* a transfer of an estate by lease **2** death **—*vt.*** **-mised′**, **-mis′ing** to transfer (an estate) by lease

dem·i·tasse (dem′i täs′, -tas′) ***n.*** ⟦Fr < *demi-* + *tasse*, cup⟧ a small cup of or for after-dinner coffee

dem·o (dem′ō) ***n.***, *pl.* **-os** **1** a recording made to demonstrate a song, the talent of a performer, etc. **2** a product used in demonstrations

de·mo·bi·lize (dē mō′bə līz′) ***vt.*** **-lized′**, **-liz′ing** to disband (troops) **—de·mo′bi·li·za′tion *n.***

de·moc·ra·cy (di mäk′rə sē) ***n.***, *pl.* **-cies** ⟦< Gr *dēmos*, the people + *kratein*, to rule⟧ **1** government by the people, directly or through representatives **2** a country, etc. with such government **3** equality of rights, opportunity, and treatment

dem·o·crat (dem′ə krat′) ***n.*** **1** one who supports or practices democracy **2** **[D-]** a Democratic Party member

dem′o·crat′ic ***adj.*** **1** of or for democracy **2** of or for all the people **3** not snobbish **4** **[D-]** of the Democratic Party **—dem′o·crat′i·cal·ly *adv.***

Democratic Party one of the two major political parties in the U.S.

de·mod·u·la·tion (dē mä′jə lā′shən) ***n.*** *Radio* the recovery, at the receiver, of a signal that has been modulated on a carrier wave

dem·o·graph·ics (dem′ə graf′iks) ***pl.n.*** demographic characteristics of a population, as age, sex, or income, used for research, etc.

de·mog·ra·phy (di mä′grə fē) ***n.*** ⟦< Gr *dēmos*, the people + -GRAPHY⟧ the statistical study of human populations **—de·mog′ra·pher *n.*** **—dem·o·graph·ic** (dem′ə graf′ik) ***adj.*** **—dem′o·graph′i·cal·ly *adv.***

de·mol·ish (di mäl′ish) ***vt.*** ⟦< L *de-*, down + *moliri*, build⟧ **1** to pull down or smash **2** to destroy; ruin **—dem·o·li·tion** (dem′ə lish′ən) ***n.***

de·mon (dē′mən) ***n.*** ⟦< L *daemon*⟧ **1** a devil; evil spirit **2** one regarded as evil, cruel, etc. **3** one with great energy, skill, etc. **—de·mon·ic** (di män′ik) ***adj.*** **—de·mon′i·cal·ly *adv.***

de·mon·e·tize (dē män′ə tīz′) ***vt.*** **-tized′**, **-tiz′ing** to deprive (esp. currency) of its standard value

de·mon·ize (dē′mən īz′) ***vt.*** **-ized′**, **-iz′ing** **1** to make into a demon **2** to characterize as evil, cruel, etc. **—de′mon·i·za′tion *n.***

de·mon·stra·ble (di män′strə bəl) ***adj.*** that can be demonstrated, or proved **—de·mon′stra·bly *adv.***

dem·on·strate (dem′ən strāt′) ***vt.*** **-strat′ed**, **-strat′ing** ⟦< L *de-*, from + *monstrare*, to show⟧ **1** to show by reasoning; prove **2** to explain by using examples, etc. **3** to show how something works **—*vi.*** to show feelings or views publicly by meetings, etc. **—dem′on·stra′tion *n.*** **—dem′on·stra′tor *n.***

de·mon·stra·tive (di män′strə tiv) ***adj.*** **1** illustrative **2** giving proof (*of*) **3** showing feelings openly **4** *Gram.* pointing out *[*"this" is a *demonstrative* pronoun*]* **—*n.*** *Gram.* a demonstrative pronoun or adjective **—de·mon′stra·tive·ly *adv.***

de·mor·al·ize (dē môr′ə līz′) ***vt.*** **-ized′**, **-iz′ing** **1** to lower the morale of **2** to throw into confusion **—de·mor′al·i·za′tion *n.***

De·mos·the·nes (di mäs′thə nēz′) 384-322 B.C.; Athenian orator

de·mote (dē mōt′) ***vt.*** **-mot′ed**, **-mot′ing** ⟦DE- + (PRO)MOTE⟧ to reduce to a lower rank **—de·mo′tion *n.***

de·mul·cent (dē mul′sənt) ***adj.*** ⟦< L *de-*, down + *mulcere*, to stroke⟧ soothing **—*n.*** a soothing ointment

de·mur (dē mur′, di-) ***vi.*** **-murred′**, **-mur′ring** ⟦< L *de-*, from + *mora*, a delay⟧ to hesitate, as because of doubts; have scruples; object **—*n.*** a demurring: also **de·mur′ral**

de·mure (di myoor′) ***adj.*** ⟦< ME *de-* (prob. intens.) + OFr *mëur*, mature⟧ **1** modest or reserved **2** affectedly modest; coy **—de·mure′ly *adv.***

de·mur·rage (di mur′ij) ***n.*** **1** the compensation payable for delaying a vehicle or vessel carrying freight, as by failure to load or unload **2** the delay itself

de·mur·rer (di mur′ər) ***n.*** ⟦see DEMUR⟧ **1** a plea for dismissal of a lawsuit because statements supporting a claim are defective **2** an objection

den (den) ***n.*** ⟦OE *denn*⟧ **1** the lair of a wild animal **2** a haunt, as of thieves **3** a small, cozy room where a person can be alone to read, work, etc.

de·na·ture (dē nā′chər) ***vt.*** **-tured**, **-tur·ing** **1** to change the nature of **2** to make (alcohol) unfit to drink

den·drite (den′drīt′) ***n.*** ⟦< Gr *dendron*, tree⟧ the part of a nerve cell that carries impulses toward the cell body

Deng Xiao·ping (duŋ′ shou′piŋ′) 1904-97; Chin. Communist leader; held various official titles (1967-89); China's de facto ruler (*c.* 1981-97)

de·ni·al (dē nī′əl) ***n.*** **1** a denying; saying

"no" (to a request, etc.) **2** a contradiction **3** a refusal to believe or accept (a doctrine, etc.) **4** SELF-DENIAL

de·nier[1] (den′yər) ***n.*** ⟦< L *deni*, by tens⟧ a unit of weight for measuring the fineness of threads of silk, nylon, etc.

de·ni·er[2] (dē nī′ər) ***n.*** one who denies

den·i·grate (den′ə grāt′) ***vt.*** **-grat′ed, -grat′ing** ⟦< L < *de-*, entirely + *nigrare*, blacken⟧ to belittle the character of; defame —**den′i·gra′tion** ***n.***

den·im (den′im) ***n.*** ⟦< Fr *(serge) de Nîmes*, (serge) of Nîmes, town in France⟧ a coarse, twilled cotton cloth

den·i·zen (den′ə zən) ***n.*** ⟦< L *de intus*, from within⟧ an inhabitant or frequenter of a particular place

Den·mark (den′märk′) country in Europe, on a peninsula & several islands in the North & Baltic seas: 16,631 sq. mi.; pop. 4,938,000

de·nom·i·nate (dē näm′ə nāt′) ***vt.*** **-nat′ed, -nat′ing** ⟦< L *de-*, intens. + *nominare*, to name⟧ to name; call

de·nom′i·na′tion (-nā′shən) ***n.*** **1** the act of naming **2** a name **3** a class or kind, as of coins, having a specific name or value **4** a particular religious body

de·nom′i·na′tion·al ***adj.*** of, or under the control of, a religious denomination

de·nom′i·na′tor (-nāt′ər) ***n.*** **1** a shared characteristic **2** *Math.* the term below the line in a fraction

de·note (dē nōt′) ***vt.*** **-not′ed, -not′ing** ⟦< L *de-*, down + *notare*, to mark⟧ **1** to indicate **2** to signify; mean —**de·no·ta·tion** (dē′nō tā′shən) ***n.***

de·noue·ment or **dé·noue·ment** (dā′ nōō män′) ***n.*** ⟦Fr⟧ the outcome or unraveling of a plot in a drama, story, etc.

de·nounce (dē nouns′) ***vt.*** **-nounced′, -nounc′ing** ⟦see DENUNCIATION⟧ **1** to accuse publicly; inform against **2** to condemn strongly and usually publicly —**de·nounce′ment** ***n.***

dense (dens) ***adj.*** **dens′er, dens′est** ⟦< L *densus*, compact⟧ **1** packed tightly together **2** difficult to get through, penetrate, etc. **3** stupid —**dense′ly** ***adv.*** —**dense′ness** ***n.***

den·si·ty (den′sə tē) ***n.***, *pl.* **-ties** **1** a dense condition **2** stupidity **3** number per unit, as of area *[population density]* **4** ratio of the mass of an object to its volume

dent (dent) ***n.*** ⟦ME, var. of DINT⟧ **1** a slight hollow made in a surface by a blow **2** a noticeable effect —***vt.***, ***vi.*** to make or receive a dent (in)

den·tal (dent′'l) ***adj.*** ⟦< L *dens*, tooth⟧ of or for the teeth or dentistry

dental floss thread for removing food particles from between the teeth

den·ti·frice (den′tə fris) ***n.*** ⟦< L *dens*, tooth + *fricare*, rub⟧ any preparation for cleaning teeth

den·tin (den′tin) ***n.*** ⟦see DENTAL⟧ the hard tissue under the enamel of a tooth: also **den′tine′** (-tēn′, -tin)

den·tist (den′tist) ***n.*** one whose profession is the care and repair of teeth —**den′tist·ry** ***n.***

den·ti·tion (den tish′ən) ***n.*** the arrangement of teeth in the mouth

den·ture (den′chər) ***n.*** ⟦see DENTAL⟧ [*often pl.*] a set of artificial teeth

de·nu·cle·ar·ize (dē nōō′klē ər īz′) ***vt.*** **-ized′, -iz′ing** to prohibit the possession of nuclear weapons in

de·nude (dē nōōd′) ***vt.*** **-nud′ed, -nud′ing** ⟦< L *de-*, off + *nudare*, to strip⟧ to make bare or naked; strip

de·nun·ci·a·tion (dē nun′sē ā′shən) ***n.*** ⟦< L *de-*, intens. + *nuntiare*, announce⟧ the act of denouncing

Den·ver (den′vər) capital of Colorado: pop. 468,000

de·ny (dē nī′) ***vt.*** **-nied′, -ny′ing** ⟦< L *de-*, intens. + *negare*, to deny⟧ **1** to declare (a statement) untrue **2** to refuse to accept as true or right **3** to repudiate **4** to refuse to grant or give **5** to refuse the request of

de·o·dor·ant (dē ō′dər ənt) ***adj.*** that can counteract undesired odors —***n.*** any deodorant preparation, esp. one for use on the body

de·o′dor·ize′ (-dər īz′) ***vt.*** **-ized′, -iz′ing** to counteract the odor of —**de·o′dor·iz′er** ***n.***

de·part (dē pärt′) ***vi.*** ⟦< L *dis-*, apart + *partire*, divide⟧ **1** to go away; leave or set out **2** to die **3** to deviate *(from)* —***vt.*** to leave

de·part′ed ***adj.*** **1** gone away **2** dead —**the departed** the dead

de·part·ment (dē pärt′mənt) ***n.*** **1** a separate part or division, as of a business **2** a field of activity —**de′part·men′tal** (-ment′'l) ***adj.***

de′part·men′tal·ize′ (-men′t'l īz′) ***vt.*** **-ized′, -iz′ing** to organize into departments —**de′part·men′tal·i·za′tion** ***n.***

department store a large retail store for the sale of many kinds of goods arranged in departments

de·par·ture (dē pär′chər) ***n.*** **1** a departing **2** a starting out, as on a trip **3** a deviation *(from)*

de·pend (dē pend′) ***vi.*** ⟦< L *de-*, down + *pendere*, to hang⟧ **1** to be determined by something else; be contingent *(on)* **2** to have trust; rely *(on)* **3** to rely *(on)* for support or aid

de·pend′a·ble ***adj.*** trustworthy; reliable —**de·pend′a·bil′i·ty** ***n.*** —**de·pend′a·bly** ***adv.***

de·pend′ence ***n.*** **1** a being dependent **2** reliance *(on)* for support or aid **3** reliance; trust **4** DEPENDENCY (sense 4)

de·pend′en·cy ***n.***, *pl.* **-cies** **1** dependence **2** something dependent **3** a territory, as a possession, subordinate to its governing country **4** addiction to alcohol or drugs

de·pend′ent ***adj.*** **1** hanging down **2** determined by something else **3** relying *(on)* for support, etc. **4** subordinate **5** addicted —***n.*** one relying on another for support, etc. Also **de·pend′ant** —**de·pend′ent·ly** ***adv.***

dependent clause *Gram.* a clause that cannot function as a complete sentence by itself

de·pict (dē pikt′) ***vt.*** ⟦< L *de-*, intens. + *pingere*, to paint⟧ **1** to represent by drawing, painting, etc. **2** to describe —**de·pic′tion** ***n.***

de·pil·a·to·ry (di pil′ə tôr′ē) ***adj.*** ⟦< L *de-*, from + *pilus*, hair⟧ serving to remove unwanted hair —***n.***, *pl.* **-ries** a depilatory substance or device

de·plane (dē plān′) ***vi.*** **-planed′**, **-plan′ing** to get out of an airplane after it lands

de·plete (dē plēt′) ***vt.*** **-plet′ed**, **-plet′ing** ⟦< L *de-*, from + *plere*, fill⟧ **1** to use up (funds, etc.) **2** to use up the resources, etc. of —**de·ple′tion** ***n.***

de·plor·a·ble (dē plôr′ə bəl) ***adj.*** regrettable, very bad, wretched, etc.

de·plore (dē plôr′) ***vt.*** **-plored′**, **-plor′ing** ⟦< L *de-*, intens. + *plorare*, weep⟧ **1** to be sorry about **2** to disapprove of

de·ploy (dē ploi′) ***vt.*** ⟦< L *dis-*, apart + *plicare*, to fold⟧ to spread out or position (troops, equipment, etc.) according to a plan —***vi.*** to be deployed —**de·ploy′ment** ***n.***

de·po·lar·ize (dē pō′lər īz′) ***vt.*** **-ized′**, **-iz′ing** to destroy or counteract the polarization of —**de·po′lar·i·za′tion** ***n.***

de·po·lit·i·cize (dē′pə lit′ə sīz′) ***vt.*** **-cized′**, **-ciz′ing** to remove from political influence

de·pon·ent (dē pōn′ənt) ***n.*** ⟦< L *de-*, down + *ponere*, put⟧ *Law* one who makes a deposition

de·pop·u·late (dē päp′yə lāt′) ***vt.*** **-lat′ed**, **-lat′ing** to reduce the population of —**de·pop′u·la′tion** ***n.***

de·port (dē pôrt′) ***vt.*** ⟦< L *de-*, from + *portare*, carry⟧ **1** to conduct (oneself) in a specified way **2** to expel (an alien) —**de′por·ta′tion** ***n.***

de·port′ment ***n.*** conduct; behavior

de·pose (dē pōz′) ***vt.*** **-posed′**, **-pos′ing** ⟦< OFr *de-*, from + *poser*, cease⟧ **1** to remove from office **2** *Law* to take the deposition of

de·pos·it (dē päz′it) ***vt.*** ⟦< L *de-*, down + *ponere*, put⟧ **1** to place (money, etc.) for safekeeping, as in a bank **2** to give as a pledge or partial payment **3** to put or set down **4** to cause (sediment, etc.) to settle —***n.*** **1** something placed for safekeeping, as money in a bank **2** a pledge or partial payment **3** a natural accumulation, as of minerals —**de·pos′i·tor** ***n.***

dep·o·si·tion (dep′ə zish′ən) ***n.*** **1** a deposing or being deposed, as from office **2** something deposited **3** *Law* testimony made under oath that is written down for later use

de·pos·i·to·ry (dē päz′ə tôr′ē) ***n.***, *pl.* **-ries** a place where things are put for safekeeping

de·pot (dē′pō; *military & Brit* dep′ō) ***n.*** ⟦< Fr: see DEPOSIT⟧ **1** a warehouse **2** a railroad or bus station **3** a storage place for military supplies

de·prave (dē prāv′) ***vt.*** **-praved′**, **-prav′ing** ⟦< L *de-*, intens. + *pravus*, crooked⟧ to make morally bad; corrupt —**de·praved′** ***adj.*** —**de·prav′i·ty** (-prav′ə tē), *pl.* **-ties**, ***n.***

dep·re·cate (dep′rə kāt′) ***vt.*** **-cat′ed**, **-cat′ing** ⟦< L *de-*, off + *precari*, pray⟧ **1** to express disapproval of **2** to belittle —**dep′re·ca′tion** ***n.*** —**dep′re·ca·to′ry** (-kə tôr′ē) ***adj.***

de·pre·ci·ate (dē prē′shē āt′) ***vt.***, ***vi.*** **-at′ed**, **-at′ing** ⟦< L *de-*, from + *pretium*, price⟧ **1** to lessen in value or price **2** to belittle —**de·pre′ci·a′tion** ***n.***

dep·re·da·tion (dep′rə dā′shən) ***n.*** ⟦< L *de-*, intens. + *praedari*, to plunder⟧ a robbing or plundering

de·press (dē pres′) ***vt.*** ⟦< L *de-*, down + *premere*, to press⟧ **1** to press down **2** to sadden or discourage **3** to weaken or make less active **4** to lower in value, price, etc. —**de·pressed′** ***adj.***

de·pres′sant ***n.*** a medicine, drug, etc. that lessens nervous activity

de·pres·sion (dē presh′ən) ***n.*** **1** a depressing or being depressed **2** a hollow or low place **3** low spirits; dejection **4** a condition marked by hopelessness, self-doubt, lethargy, etc. **5** a decrease in force, activity, etc. **6** a period of reduced business, much unemployment, etc.

de·pres·sive (dē pres′iv) ***adj.*** **1** tending to depress **2** characterized by psychological depression —***n.*** one suffering from psychological depression

de·pres·sur·ize (dē presh′ər īz′) ***vt.*** **-ized′**, **-iz′ing** to reduce pressure in

de·prive (dē prīv′) ***vt.*** **-prived′**, **-priv′ing** ⟦< L *de-*, intens. + *privare*, to separate⟧ **1** to take away from forcibly **2** to keep from having, etc. —**dep·ri·va·tion** (dep′rə vā′shən) ***n.***

de·pro·gram (dē prō′gram′, -grəm) ***vt.*** **-grammed′** or **-gramed′**, **-gram′ming** or **-gram′ing** to cause to abandon rigidly held beliefs, etc. by undoing the effects of indoctrination

dept *abbrev.* **1** department **2** deputy

depth (depth) ***n.*** ⟦< ME *dep*, deep + -TH[1]⟧ **1** the distance from the top downward, or from front to back **2** deepness **3** intensity **4** profundity of thought **5** [*usually pl.*] the deepest or inmost part —**in depth** comprehensively

dep·u·ta·tion (dep′yoo tā′shən) ***n.*** **1** a deputing **2** a delegation

de·pute (dē pyoot′) ***vt.*** **-put′ed**, **-put′ing** ⟦< L *de-*, from + *putare*, cleanse⟧ **1** to give (authority, etc.) to a deputy **2** to appoint as one's substitute, etc.

dep·u·tize (dep′yoo tīz′) ***vt.*** **-tized′**, **-tiz′ing** to appoint as deputy

dep·u·ty (dep′yoo tē) ***n.***, *pl.* **-ties** a person appointed to act as a substitute or assistant

de·rail (dē rāl′) ***vt.***, ***vi.*** to run off the rails, as a train —**de·rail′ment** ***n.***

de·rail·leur (də rāl′ər) ***n.*** ⟦Fr⟧ a gear-shifting mechanism on a bicycle for shifting the sprocket chain from one size of sprocket wheel to another

de·range (dē rānj′) ***vt.*** **-ranged′**, **-rang′ing** ⟦< OFr *des-*, apart + *rengier*, to range⟧ **1** to upset or disturb **2** to make insane —**de·range′ment** ***n.***

Der·by (dur′bē; *Brit* där′-) ***n.***, *pl.* **-bies** **1** ⟦after an Earl of *Derby*, who founded the race held in England⟧ any of various horse races, as ones held annually in England, Kentucky, etc. **2** [**d-**] any of various contests or races, open to anyone **3** [**d-**] a stiff felt hat with a round crown

de·reg·u·late (dē reg′yə lāt′) ***vt.* -lat′ed, -lat′ing** to remove regulations governing —**de·reg′u·la′tion** ***n.***

der·e·lict (der′ə likt′) ***adj.*** ⟦< L *de-*, intens. + *relinquere*: see RELINQUISH⟧ **1** deserted by the owner; abandoned **2** negligent —***n.*** **1** an abandoned ship on the open sea **2** a destitute and rejected person

der′e·lic′tion (-lik′shən) ***n.*** **1** a forsaking or being forsaken **2** a neglect of, or failure in, duty

de·ride (di rīd′) ***vt.* -rid′ed, -rid′ing** ⟦< L *de-*, down + *ridere*, to laugh⟧ to laugh at in scorn; ridicule —**de·ri′sion** (-rizh′ən) ***n.*** —**de·ri′sive** (-rī′siv) ***adj.*** —**de·ri′sive·ly** ***adv.***

der·i·va·tion (der′ə vā′shən) ***n.*** **1** a deriving or being derived **2** the source or origin of something, specif. of a word

de·riv·a·tive (də riv′ə tiv) ***adj.*** derived; specif., not original or novel —***n.*** something derived

de·rive (di rīv′) ***vt.* -rived′, -riv′ing** ⟦< L *de-*, from + *rivus*, a stream⟧ **1** to get or receive (something) *from* a source **2** to deduce or infer **3** to trace from or to a source —***vi.*** to come (*from*)

der·ma·bra·sion (dur′mə brā′zhən) ***n.*** ⟦DERM(IS) + ABRASION⟧ the surgical procedure of scraping off upper layers of the skin with an abrasive device, to remove acne scars, blemishes, etc.

der·ma·ti·tis (dur′mə tīt′is) ***n.*** ⟦< Gr *derma*, skin + -ITIS⟧ inflammation of the skin

der·ma·tol·o·gy (dur′mə täl′ə jē) ***n.*** ⟦< Gr *derma*, skin + -LOGY⟧ the branch of medicine dealing with the skin —**der′ma·tol′o·gist** ***n.***

der·mis (dur′mis) ***n.*** ⟦see EPIDERMIS⟧ the layer of skin just below the epidermis

der·o·gate (der′ə gāt′) ***vi., vt.* -gat′ed, -gat′ing** ⟦< L *de-*, from + *rogare*, ask⟧ to detract (*from*) or disparage —**der′o·ga′tion** ***n.***

de·rog·a·to·ry (di räg′ə tôr′ē) ***adj.*** ⟦see prec.⟧ disparaging; belittling —**de·rog′a·to′ri·ly** ***adv.***

der·rick (der′ik) ***n.*** ⟦after Thos. *Derrick*, London hangman of the early 17th c.: orig. applied to a gallows⟧ **1** a pivoted beam for lifting and moving heavy objects **2** a tall framework, as over an oil well, to support drilling machinery, etc.

DERRICK (sense 2)

der·ri·ère (der′ē er′) ***n.*** ⟦Fr, back part⟧ the buttocks

der·rin·ger (der′in jər) ***n.*** ⟦after H. *Deringer*, 19th-c. U.S. gunsmith⟧ a small, short-barreled pistol

der·vish (dur′vish) ***n.*** ⟦< Pers *darvēsh*, beggar⟧ a member of any of various Muslim ascetic religious groups

de·sal·i·na·tion (dē′sal′ə nā′shən) ***n.*** ⟦DE- + SALIN(E) + -ATION⟧ the removal of salt, esp. from sea water to make it drinkable —**de′sal′i·nate′, -nat′ed, -nat′ing, *vt.***

Des·cartes (dā kärt′), **Re·né** (rə nā′) 1596-1650; Fr. philosopher

de·scend (dē send′) ***vi.*** ⟦< L *de-*, down + *scandere*, climb⟧ **1** to move down to a lower place **2** to pass from an earlier to a later time, from greater to less, etc. **3** to slope downward **4** to come down (*from* a source) **5** to lower oneself or stoop (*to*) **6** to make a sudden raid (*on* or *upon*) —***vt.*** to move down along

de·scend′ant (-sen′dənt) ***n.*** an offspring of a certain ancestor, family, group, etc.

de·scent′ (-sent′) ***n.*** **1** a coming down or going down **2** ancestry **3** a downward slope **4** a way down **5** a sudden attack (*on* or *upon*) **6** a decline

de·scribe (di skrīb′) ***vt.* -scribed′, -scrib′ing** ⟦< L *de-*, from + *scribere*, write⟧ **1** to tell or write about **2** to trace the outline of —**de·scrib′er** ***n.***

de·scrip·tion (di skrip′shən) ***n.*** **1** the act or technique of describing **2** a statement or passage that describes **3** sort; kind [books of every *description*] **4** a tracing or outlining —**de·scrip′tive** ***adj.***

de·scry (di skrī′) ***vt.* -scried′, -scry′ing** ⟦< OFr *descrier*, proclaim⟧ **1** to catch sight of; discern **2** to detect

des·e·crate (des′i krāt′) ***vt.* -crat′ed, -crat′ing** ⟦DE- (sense 4) + (CON)SECRATE⟧ to violate the sacredness of; profane —**des′e·cra′tion** ***n.***

de·seg·re·gate (dē seg′rə gāt′) ***vt., vi.* -gat′ed, -gat′ing** to abolish racial segregation in (public schools, etc.) —**de·seg′re·ga′tion** ***n.***

de·sen·si·tize (dē sen′sə tīz′) ***vt.* -tized′, -tiz′ing** to make less sensitive, as to an allergen

de·sert[1] (di zurt′) ***vt., vi.*** ⟦< L *de-*, from + *serere*, join⟧ **1** to abandon; forsake **2** to leave (one's military post, etc.) without permission and with no intent to return —**de·sert′er** ***n.*** —**de·ser′tion** (-zur′shən) ***n.***

des·ert[2] (dez′ərt) ***n.*** ⟦see prec.⟧ **1** an uninhabited region; wilderness **2** a dry, barren, sandy region, often one that is hot —***adj.*** wild and uninhabited [a *desert* island]

de·sert[3] (di zurt′) ***n.*** ⟦see fol.⟧ [*often pl.*] deserved reward or punishment [one's just *deserts*]

de·serve (di zurv′) ***vt., vi.* -served′, -serv′ing** ⟦< L *de-*, intens. + *servire*, serve⟧ to be worthy (of); merit —**de·serv′ed·ly** (-zur′vid lē) ***adv.***

des·ic·cate (des′i kāt′) ***vt., vi.* -cat′ed, -cat′ing** ⟦< L *de-*, intens. + *siccus*, dry⟧ to dry out completely —**des′ic·ca′tion** ***n.***

de·sid·er·a·tum (di sid′ə rät′əm) ***n., pl.* -ta** (-ə) ⟦see DESIRE⟧ something needed and wanted

de·sign (di zīn′) ***vt.*** ⟦< L *de-*, out + *signum*, a mark⟧ **1** to sketch an outline for; plan **2** to contrive **3** to intend —***vi.***

to make original plans, etc. —*n.* 1 a plan; scheme 2 purpose; aim 3 a working plan; pattern 4 arrangement of parts, form, color, etc. —**by design** purposely —**de·sign'er** *n.*

des·ig·nate (dez'ig nāt') *vt.* **-nat'ed, -nat'ing** ⟦see prec.⟧ 1 to point out; specify 2 to name 3 to appoint —**des'ig·na'tion** *n.*

designated driver the one in a group who refrains from drinking alcoholic beverages so as to be able to safely transport the others in a motor vehicle

de·sign'ing *adj.* scheming; crafty —*n.* the art of creating designs, etc.

de·sir·a·ble (di zīr'ə bəl) *adj.* 1 worth having 2 arousing desire —**de·sir'a·bil'i·ty** *n.* —**de·sir'a·bly** *adv.*

de·sire (di zīr') *vt.* **-sired', -sir'ing** ⟦< L *desiderare*⟧ 1 to long for; crave 2 to ask for —*vi.* to have a desire —*n.* 1 a wish; craving 2 sexual appetite 3 a request 4 a thing desired —**de·sir'ous** *adj.*

de·sist (di zist', -sist') *vi.* ⟦< L *de-*, from + *stare*, to stand⟧ to cease; stop

desk (desk) *n.* ⟦< ML *desca*, table⟧ a piece of furniture with a flat surface for writing, etc. —*adj.* of, for, or at a desk *[a desk job]*

desk'top' *n., adj.* (equipment, as a microcomputer) for use on a desk or table

desk·top publishing the production of printed matter by means of a microcomputer and special software for laying out text and illustrations

Des Moines (də moin') capital of Iowa: pop. 193,000

des·o·late (des'ə lit; *for v.*, -lāt') *adj.* ⟦< L *de-*, intens. + *solus*, alone⟧ 1 lonely; solitary 2 uninhabited 3 laid waste 4 forlorn —*vt.* **-lat'ed, -lat'ing** 1 to rid of inhabitants 2 to lay waste 3 to make forlorn

des'o·la'tion *n.* 1 a making desolate 2 a desolate condition or place 3 misery 4 loneliness

de·spair (di sper') *vi.* ⟦< L *de-*, without + *sperare*, to hope⟧ to lose hope —*n.* 1 loss of hope 2 a person or thing causing despair

des·patch (di spach') *vt., n.* DISPATCH

des·per·a·do (des'pər ä'dō, -ā'-) *n., pl.* **-does** or **-dos** ⟦< 17th-c. Sp < L *desperare*: see DESPAIR⟧ a dangerous criminal; bold outlaw

des·per·ate (des'pər it) *adj.* 1 rash or violent because of despair 2 having a very great need 3 very serious, dangerous, etc. 4 drastic —**des'per·ate·ly** *adv.*

des·per·a·tion (des'pər ā'shən) *n.* 1 the state of being desperate 2 recklessness resulting from despair

des·pi·ca·ble (di spik'ə bəl) *adj.* deserving scorn; contemptible

de·spise (di spīz') *vt.* **-spised', -spis'ing** ⟦< L *de*, down + *specere*, look at⟧ 1 to scorn 2 to loathe

de·spite (di spīt') *prep.* ⟦see prec.⟧ in spite of; notwithstanding

de·spoil (dē spoil') *vt.* ⟦< L *de-*, intens. + *spoliare*, to strip⟧ to rob; plunder —**de·spo·li·a·tion** (di spō'lē ā'shən) *n.*

de·spond·en·cy (di spän'dən sē) *n.* ⟦< L *de-*, from + *spondere*, to promise⟧ loss of hope; dejection: also **de·spond'ence** —**de·spond'ent** *adj.*

des·pot (des'pət) *n.* ⟦< Gr *despotēs*, a master⟧ 1 an absolute ruler 2 anyone like a tyrant —**des·pot'ic** (-pät'ik) *adj.* —**des'pot·ism'** (-pə tiz'əm) *n.*

des·sert (di zurt') *n.* ⟦< L *de*, from + *servire*, serve⟧ the final course of a meal, typically cake, pie, etc.

des·ti·na·tion (des'tə nā'shən) *n.* the place toward which one is going or sent

des·tine (des'tin) *vt.* **-tined, -tin·ing** ⟦< L *de-*, intens. + *stare*, to stand⟧ 1 to predetermine, as by fate 2 to intend —**destined for** 1 headed for 2 intended for

des·ti·ny (des'tə nē) *n., pl.* **-nies** 1 the seemingly inevitable succession of events 2 (one's) fate

des·ti·tute (des'tə to͞ot') *adj.* ⟦< L *de-*, down + *statuere*, to set⟧ 1 lacking: with *of* 2 totally impoverished —**des'ti·tu'tion** *n.*

de·stroy (di stroi') *vt.* ⟦< L *de-*, down + *struere*, to build⟧ 1 to tear down; demolish 2 to ruin 3 to do away with 4 to kill

de·stroy'er *n.* 1 one that destroys 2 a small, fast warship

de·struct (di strukt', dē'strukt') *vi.* ⟦< fol.⟧ to be automatically destroyed

de·struc·tion (di struk'shən) *n.* 1 a destroying or being destroyed 2 the cause or means of destroying —**de·struc'tive** *adj.* —**de·struc'tive·ly** *adv.* —**de·struc'tive·ness** *n.*

des·ue·tude (des'wi to͞od') *n.* ⟦< L *de-*, from + *suescere*, be accustomed⟧ disuse

des·ul·to·ry (des'əl tôr'ē) *adj.* ⟦< L *de-*, from + *salire*, to leap⟧ 1 aimless; disconnected 2 random

de·tach (dē tach') *vt.* ⟦< Fr: see DE- & ATTACH⟧ 1 to unfasten and remove; disconnect; disengage 2 to send (troops, etc.) on a special mission —**de·tach'a·ble** *adj.*

de·tached' *adj.* 1 not connected 2 aloof; disinterested; impartial

de·tach'ment *n.* 1 a detaching 2 a unit of troops, etc. on a special mission 3 impartiality or aloofness

de·tail (di tāl', dē'tāl') *n.* ⟦< Fr < *dé-*, from + *tailler*, to cut⟧ 1 a dealing with things item by item 2 a minute account *[to go into detail]* 3 a small part; item 4 *a)* one or more soldiers, etc. on special duty *b)* the duty —*vt.* 1 to tell, item by item 2 to assign to special duty —**in detail** with particulars

de·tain (dē tān') *vt.* ⟦< L *de-*, off + *tenere*, to hold⟧ 1 to keep in custody; confine 2 to keep from going on —**de'tain·ee'** (-ē') *n.* —**de·tain'ment** *n.*

de·tect (dē tekt') *vt.* ⟦< L *de-*, from + *tegere*, to cover⟧ to discover (something hidden, not clear, etc.) —**de·tect'a·ble** or **de·tect'i·ble** *adj.* —**de·tec'tion** *n.* —**de·tec'tor** *n.*

de·tec'tive (-tek'tiv) *n.* one whose work is to investigate crimes, uncover evidence, etc.

dé·tente or **de·tente** (dā tänt′) *n.* ⟦Fr⟧ a lessening of tension, esp. between nations

de·ten·tion (dē ten′shən) *n.* **1** a detaining or being detained **2** the punishment of having to stay after school

detention home a place where juvenile offenders are held in custody

de·ter (dē tur′) *vt.* **-terred′**, **-ter′ring** ⟦< L *de-*, from + *terrere*, frighten⟧ to keep or discourage (a person or group) from doing something through fear, doubt, etc. —**de·ter′ment** *n.* —**de·ter′rence** *n.*

de·ter·gent (dē tur′jənt) *adj.* ⟦< L *de-*, off + *tergere*, wipe⟧ cleansing —*n.* cleansing substance that emulsifies dirt and oil

de·te·ri·o·rate (dē tir′ē ə rāt′) *vt.*, *vi.* **-rat′ed**, **-rat′ing** ⟦< L *deterior*, worse⟧ to make or become worse —**de·te′ri·o·ra′tion** *n.*

de·ter·mi·nant (dē tur′mi nənt) *n.* a thing or factor that determines

de·ter′mi·nate (-nit) *adj.* clearly determined; fixed; settled

de·ter′mi·na′tion (-nā′shən) *n.* **1** a determining or being determined **2** a firm intention **3** firmness of purpose

de·ter′mine (-mən) *vt.* **-mined**, **-min·ing** ⟦< L *de-*, from + *terminus*, a limit⟧ **1** to set limits to **2** to settle conclusively **3** to decide or decide upon **4** to affect the nature or quality of **5** to find out exactly —*vi.* to decide —**de·ter′mi·na·ble** *adj.*

de·ter′mined (-mənd) *adj.* **1** having one's mind made up **2** resolute; firm

de·ter′rent *adj.* deterring —*n.* something that deters

de·test (dē test′) *vt.* ⟦< L *detestari*, to curse by the gods⟧ to dislike intensely; hate —**de·test′a·ble** *adj.* —**de′tes·ta′tion** (-tes tā′shən) *n.*

de·thatch (dē thach′) *vt.* to remove the thatch from (a lawn)

de·throne (dē thrōn′) *vt.* **-throned′**, **-thron′ing** to depose (a monarch)

det·o·nate (det′′n āt′) *vi.*, *vt.* **-nat′ed**, **-nat′ing** ⟦< L *de-*, intens. + *tonare*, to thunder⟧ to explode violently —**det′o·na′tion** *n.* —**det′o·na′tor** *n.*

de·tour (dē′toor′) *n.* ⟦< Fr: see DE- & TURN⟧ **1** a roundabout way **2** a substitute route —*vi.*, *vt.* to go or route on a detour

de·tox (dē täks′; *for n.* dē′täks′) [Inf.] *vt.* *short for* DETOXIFY —*n.* *short for* DETOXIFICATION

de·tox·i·fy (dē täk′si fī′) *vt.* **-fied′**, **-fy′ing** ⟦DE- + TOXI(N) + -FY⟧ **1** to remove a poison or poisonous effect from **2** to treat for drug or alcohol addiction —**de·tox′i·fi·ca′tion** *n.*

de·tract (dē trakt′) *vt.* ⟦< L *de-*, from + *trahere*, to draw⟧ to take away —*vi.* to take something desirable (*from*) —**de·trac′tion** *n.*

de·trac′tor (-trak′tər) *n.* one who disparages

det·ri·ment (de′trə mənt) *n.* ⟦< L *de-*, off + *terere*, to rub⟧ **1** damage; injury **2** anything that causes this —**det′ri·men′tal** (-ment′′l) *adj.*

de·tri·tus (dē trīt′əs) *n.* ⟦L, a rubbing away: see prec.⟧ debris, specif. rock fragments

De·troit (di troit′) city & port in SE Michigan: pop. 1,028,000

deuce (do͞os) *n.* ⟦< L *duo*, two⟧ **1** a playing card or side of a die with two spots **2** *Tennis, Badminton, etc.* a tie score after which one side must score twice in a row to win

deu·te·ri·um (do͞o tir′ē əm) *n.* ⟦< Gr *deuteros*, second⟧ a hydrogen isotope used in nuclear reactors

Deu·ter·on·o·my (do͞ot′ər än′ə mē) *n.* ⟦< Gr *deuteros*, second + *nomos*, law⟧ the fifth book of the Pentateuch

deutsche mark (doich′ märk′) the former monetary unit of Germany, superseded in 2002 by the EURO: also written **deutsche′mark′**

de·val·ue (dē val′yo͞o) *vt.* **-ued**, **-u·ing** **1** to lessen the value of **2** to lower the exchange value of (a currency) —**de·val′u·a′tion** *n.*

dev·as·tate (dev′ə stāt′) *vt.* **-tat′ed**, **-tat′ing** ⟦< L *de-*, intens. + *vastus*, empty⟧ **1** to lay waste; ravage; destroy **2** to make helpless; overwhelm —**dev′as·ta′tion** *n.* —**dev′as·ta′tor** *n.*

de·vel·op (di vel′əp) *vt.* ⟦< OFr *des-*, apart + *voloper*, to wrap⟧ **1** to make fuller, bigger, better, etc. **2** to show or work out by degrees **3** to enlarge upon **4** *Photog.* to put (film, etc.) into chemicals to make the picture visible —*vi.* **1** to come into being or activity; occur **2** to become developed —**de·vel′op·er** *n.* —**de·vel′op·ment** *n.* —**de·vel′op·men′tal** (-ment′′l) *adj.*

de·vi·ant (dē′vē ənt) *adj.* deviating, esp. from what is considered normal —*n.* one whose behavior is deviant —**de′vi·ance** or **de′vi·an·cy** *n.*

de·vi·ate (dē′vē āt′; *for adj. & n.*, -it) *vi.* **-at′ed**, **-at′ing** ⟦< L *de-*, from + *via*, road⟧ to turn aside (*from* a course, standard, etc.); diverge —*adj.* DEVIANT —*n.* a deviant, esp. in sexual behavior —**de′vi·a′tion** *n.* —**de′vi·a′tor** *n.*

de·vice (di vīs′) *n.* ⟦see DEVISE⟧ **1** a thing devised; plan, scheme, or trick **2** a mechanical contrivance **3** an ornamental figure or design **4** an emblem, as on a coat of arms —**leave to one's own devices** to allow to do as one wishes

dev·il (dev′əl) *n.* ⟦ult. < Gr *diabolos*, slanderous⟧ **1** *Theol.* *a*) [*often* **D-**] the chief evil spirit; Satan (with *the*) *b*) any evil spirit; demon **2** a very wicked person **3** a person who is mischievous, reckless, unlucky, etc. **4** anything hard to operate, control, etc. —*vt.* **-iled** or **-illed**, **-il·ing** or **-il·ling** **1** to prepare (food) with hot seasoning **2** to annoy; tease —**dev′il·ish** *adj.*

dev′il·fish′ *n.*, *pl.* **-fish′** or (for different species) **-fish′es** MANTA

dev′il-may-care′ *adj.* careless or reckless

dev′il·ment *n.* mischievous action

devil's advocate a person upholding the wrong side for argument's sake

dev'il's-food' cake a rich chocolate cake

dev'il·try (-trē) ***n.***, *pl.* **-tries** reckless mischief

de·vi·ous (dē'vē əs) ***adj.*** ⟦< L *de-*, off + *via*, road⟧ **1** not direct; roundabout or deviating **2** not straightforward; dishonest —**de'vi·ous·ness** ***n.***

de·vise (di vīz') ***vt.***, ***vi.*** **-vised'**, **-vis'ing** ⟦< L *dividere*, to divide⟧ **1** to work out or create (a plan, device, etc.) **2** *Law* to bequeath (real property) by a will —***n.*** *Law* a bequest of property

de·vi·tal·ize (dē vīt''l īz') ***vt.*** **-ized'**, **-iz'ing** to deprive of vitality

de·void (di void') ***adj.*** ⟦see DE- & VOID⟧ completely without; empty (*of*)

de·volve (di välv', -vôlv') ***vt.***, ***vi.*** **-volved'**, **-volv'ing** ⟦< L *de-*, down + *volvere*, to roll⟧ **1** to pass (*on*) to another: said of duties, responsibilities, etc. **2** to degenerate —**dev·o·lu·tion** (dev'ə lo͞o'shən) ***n.***

de·vote (di vōt') ***vt.*** **-vot'ed**, **-vot'ing** ⟦< L *de-*, from + *vovere*, to vow⟧ to set apart for or give up to some purpose, activity, or person; dedicate

de·vot'ed (-id) ***adj.*** very loving, loyal, or faithful —**de·vot'ed·ly** ***adv.***

dev·o·tee (dev'ə tē', -tā') ***n.*** one who is strongly devoted to something

de·vo·tion (di vō'shən) ***n.*** **1** a devoting or being devoted **2** piety **3** religious worship **4** [*often pl.*] one or more prayers, etc. **5** loyalty or deep affection —**de·vo'tion·al** ***adj.***

de·vour (di vour') ***vt.*** ⟦< L *de-*, intens. + *vorare*, swallow whole⟧ **1** to eat hungrily **2** to swallow up **3** to take in greedily, as with the eyes

de·vout (di vout') ***adj.*** ⟦see DEVOTE⟧ **1** very religious; pious **2** earnest; sincere —**de·vout'ly** ***adv.***

dew (do͞o) ***n.*** ⟦OE *deaw*⟧ **1** atmospheric moisture condensed in drops on cool surfaces at night **2** anything refreshing, pure, etc., like dew —**dew'y**, **-i·er**, **-i·est**, ***adj.***

dew'ber'ry ***n.***, *pl.* **-ries** **1** a trailing blackberry plant **2** its fruit

dew'drop' ***n.*** a drop of dew

dew'lap' ***n.*** ⟦see DEW & LAP[1]⟧ loose skin under the throat of cattle, etc.

dew point the temperature at which water vapor in the air starts to condense into liquid

dex·ter·i·ty (deks ter'ə tē) ***n.*** ⟦see fol.⟧ skill in using one's hands, body, or mind

dex·ter·ous (deks'tər əs, -trəs) ***adj.*** ⟦< L *dexter*, right⟧ having or showing dexterity: also **dex'trous**

dex·trose (deks'trōs') ***n.*** a glucose found in plants and animals

Dhak·a (däk'ə, dak'ə) capital of Bangladesh: pop. 3,459,000

dho·ti (dō'tē) ***n.*** ⟦Hindi *dhotī*⟧ a loincloth worn by Hindu men

dhur·rie or **dur·rie** (dur'ē, du'rē) ***n.*** a coarse rug woven in India

di-[1] ⟦Gr *di-* < *dis-*, twice⟧ *prefix* twice, double, twofold

di-[2] *prefix* DIS-

di·a·be·tes (dī'ə bēt'ēz', -is) ***n.*** ⟦< Gr *diabainein*, to pass through⟧ a disease caused by an insulin deficiency and characterized by excess sugar in the blood and urine: also **sugar diabetes** —**di'a·bet'ic** (-bet'ik) ***adj.***, ***n.***

di·a·bol·ic (dī'ə bäl'ik) ***adj.*** ⟦see DEVIL⟧ very wicked or cruel; fiendish: also **di'a·bol'i·cal**

di·a·crit·i·cal mark (dī'ə krit'i kəl) ⟦< Gr *dia-*, across + *krinein*, discern⟧ a mark, as a macron, put on a letter or symbol to show pronunciation, etc.: also **di'a·crit'ic** ***n.***

di·a·dem (dī'ə dem') ***n.*** ⟦< Gr *diadēma*, a band, fillet⟧ **1** a crown **2** an ornamental headband

di·ag·nose (dī'əg nōs') ***vt.***, ***vi.*** **-nosed'**, **-nos'ing** to make a diagnosis (of)

di'ag·no'sis (-nō'sis) ***n.***, *pl.* **-ses'** (-sēz') ⟦< Gr *dia-*, through + *gignoskein*, to know⟧ **1** the act of deciding the nature of a disease, situation, problem, etc. by examination and analysis **2** the resulting decision —**di'ag·nos'tic** (-näs'tik) ***adj.*** —**di'ag·nos·ti'cian** (-tish'ən) ***n.***

di·ag·o·nal (dī ag'ə nəl, -ag'nəl) ***adj.*** ⟦< Gr *dia-*, through + *gōnia*, an angle⟧ **1** extending slantingly between opposite corners **2** slanting; oblique —***n.*** a diagonal line, plane, course, part, etc. —**di·ag'o·nal·ly** ***adv.***

di·a·gram (dī'ə gram') ***n.*** ⟦< Gr *dia-*, across + *graphein*, write⟧ a sketch, plan, graph, etc. that explains something, as by outlining its parts —***vt.*** **-gramed'** or **-grammed'**, **-gram'ing** or **-gram'ming** to make a diagram of

di·al[1] (dī'əl) ***n.*** ⟦< L *dies*, day⟧ **1** the face of a clock, etc. **2** the face of a meter, etc., for indicating, as by a pointer, an amount, direction, etc. **3** a graduated disk, strip, knob, etc., as on a radio or TV for tuning in stations, etc. **4** a rotating disk, or set of numbered push buttons, on a telephone, used to make automatic connections —***vt.***, ***vi.*** **-aled** or **-alled**, **-al·ing** or **-al·ling** **1** to tune in (a radio station, etc.) **2** to call by using a telephone dial

dial[2] *abbrev.* **1** dialect(al) **2** dialectic(al)

di·a·lect (dī'ə lekt') ***n.*** ⟦< Gr *dia*, between + *legein*, to talk⟧ the form of a spoken language peculiar to a region, social group, etc. —**di'a·lec'tal** ***adj.***

di·a·lec·tic (dī'ə lek'tik) ***n.*** **1** [*often pl.*] the practice of examining ideas logically **2** logical argumentation —***adj.*** DIALECTICAL

di'a·lec'ti·cal (-ti kəl) ***adj.*** **1** of or using dialectic **2** of a dialect

di·a·logue (dī'ə lôg', -läg') ***n.*** ⟦see DIALECT⟧ **1** interchange of ideas by open discussion **2** the passages of talk in a play, story, etc. Also sp. **di'a·log'**

di·al·y·sis (dī al'ə sis) ***n.***, *pl.* **-ses'** (-sēz') ⟦< Gr *dia-*, apart + *lyein*, dissolve⟧ the separation of smaller dissolved molecules from the larger molecules in a solution by diffusion through a membrane: used in purifying the blood of those with impaired kidney function

di·am·e·ter (dī am'ət ər) ***n.*** ⟦< Gr *dia-*, through + *metron*, a measure⟧ **1** a line segment passing through the center of a circle, sphere, etc. from one side to the other **2** its length

di·a·met·ri·cal (dī′ə me′tri kəl) ***adj.*** designating an opposite, a difference, etc. that is wholly so; complete

di·a·mond (dī′mənd, dī′ə mənd) ***n.*** ⟦< Gr *adamas*⟧ **1** nearly pure, colorless, crystalline carbon, the hardest mineral known, used for gems or cutting tools **2** a gem or other piece cut from this **3** *a)* a conventionalized figure of a diamond (◇) *b)* any of a suit of playing cards marked with such figures in red **4** *Baseball* the infield or the whole field —***adj.*** **1** of a diamond **2** marking the 60th, or sometimes 75th, year

di′a·mond·back′ ***n.*** a large, poisonous rattlesnake of the S U.S.

Di·an·a (dī an′ə) ***n.*** *Rom. Myth.* the goddess of the moon and of hunting

di·a·pa·son (dī′ə pā′zən) ***n.*** ⟦< Gr *dia*, through + *pas*, all⟧ an organ stop covering the instrument's entire range

di·a·per (dī′pər, dī′ə pər) ***n.*** ⟦< ML *diasprum*, flowered cloth⟧ a soft, absorbent cloth folded and arranged between the legs and around the waist of a baby —***vt.*** to put a diaper on (a baby)

di·aph·a·nous (dī af′ə nəs) ***adj.*** ⟦< Gr *dia-*, through + *phainein*, to show⟧ transparent or translucent

di·a·phragm (dī′ə fram′) ***n.*** ⟦< Gr *dia-*, through + *phragma*, fence⟧ **1** the muscular partition between the chest cavity and abdominal cavity **2** a vibrating disk producing sound waves **3** a vaginal contraceptive device

di·ar·rhe·a (dī′ə rē′ə) ***n.*** ⟦< Gr *dia-*, through + *rhein*, to flow⟧ too frequent and loose bowel movements: chiefly Brit. sp. **di′ar·rhoe′a**

di·a·ry (dī′ə rē) ***n.***, *pl.* **-ries** ⟦< L *dies*, day⟧ a daily written record of the writer's experiences, etc. —**di′a·rist** ***n.***

di·a·stase (dī′ə stās′) ***n.*** ⟦< Gr *dia*, apart + *histanai*, stand⟧ an enzyme in the seed of grains and malt capable of changing starches into dextrose

di·as·to·le (dī as′tə lē′) ***n.*** ⟦< Gr *dia-*, apart + *stellein*, put⟧ the usual rhythmic expansion of the heart —**di·a·stol·ic** (dī′ə stäl′ik) ***adj.***

di·a·ther·my (dī′ə thur′mē) ***n.*** ⟦< Gr *dia-*, through + *thermē*, heat⟧ medical treatment by means of heat produced under the skin, as by radiation

di·a·tom (dī′ə täm′) ***n.*** ⟦< Gr *diatomos*, cut in two⟧ any of various microscopic algae that are an important source of food for marine life

di·a·tom·ic (dī′ə täm′ik) ***adj.*** ⟦DI-[1] + ATOMIC⟧ having two atoms or radicals in the molecule

di·a·ton·ic (dī′ə tän′ik) ***adj.*** ⟦< Gr *dia-*, through + *teinein*, to stretch⟧ *Music* designating or of a scale of eight tones that is either a MAJOR SCALE or a MINOR SCALE

di·a·tribe (dī′ə trīb′) ***n.*** ⟦< Gr *dia-*, through + *tribein*, to rub⟧ a bitter, abusive denunciation

dib·ble (dib′əl) ***n.*** ⟦ME *dibbel*⟧ a pointed tool used for making holes in the soil for seeds, bulbs, etc.

dice (dīs) ***pl.n.***, *sing.* **die** or **dice** ⟦see DIE[2]⟧ small cubes marked on each side with a different number of spots (from one to six), used in games of chance —***vi.*** **diced, dic′ing** to play or gamble with dice —***vt.*** to cut (vegetables, etc.) into small cubes —**no dice** [Inf.] **1** no: used in refusing a request **2** no luck

di·chot·o·my (dī kät′ə mē) ***n.***, *pl.* **-mies** ⟦< Gr *dicha*, in two + *temnein*, to cut⟧ division into two parts or groups

dick (dik) ***n.*** [Slang] a detective

Dick·ens (dik′ənz), **Charles** (chärlz) (pseud. *Boz*) 1812-70; Eng. novelist

dick·er (dik′ər) ***vi.*** ⟦ult. < L *decem*, ten⟧ to bargain or haggle

dick·ey (dik′ē) ***n.***, *pl.* **-eys** ⟦< nickname *Dick*⟧ **1** a detachable shirt front **2** a small bird: also **dickey bird** Also **dick′y**, *pl.* **-ies**

Dick·in·son (dik′in sən), **Em·i·ly** (em′ə lē) 1830-86; U.S. poet

di·cot·y·le·don (dī′kät′ə lēd′′n) ***n.*** a plant with two seed leaves (*cotyledons*): also **di′cot′** —**di′cot′y·le′don·ous** ***adj.***

Dic·ta·phone (dik′tə fōn′) ⟦fol. + -PHONE⟧ *trademark for* a machine that records and plays back speech for typed transcripts, etc. —***n.*** [*sometimes* **d-**] any such machine

dic·tate (dik′tāt′) ***vt.***, ***vi.*** **-tat′ed, -tat′ing** ⟦< L *dicere*, speak⟧ **1** to speak (something) aloud for someone else to write down **2** to command forcefully **3** to give (orders) with authority —***n.*** an authoritative order —**dic·ta′tion** ***n.***

dic′ta′tor ***n.*** one who dictates; esp., a ruler or tyrant with absolute power —**dic′ta·to′ri·al** (-tə tôr′ē əl) ***adj.*** —**dic·ta′tor·ship′** ***n.***

dic·tion (dik′shən) ***n.*** ⟦< L *dicere*, say⟧ **1** manner of expression in words; wording **2** enunciation

dic·tion·ar·y (dik′shə ner′ē) ***n.***, *pl.* **-ar′ies** ⟦see prec.⟧ a book of alphabetically listed words in a language, with definitions, pronunciations, etc.

dic·tum (dik′təm) ***n.***, *pl.* **-tums** or **-ta** (-tə) ⟦< L *dicere*, say⟧ a formal statement of opinion; pronouncement

did (did) ***vt.***, ***vi.*** *pt. of* DO[1]

di·dac·tic (dī dak′tik) ***adj.*** ⟦< Gr *didaskein*, teach⟧ **1** intended for instruction **2** morally instructive

did·dle (did′′l) ***vt.***, ***vi.*** **-dled, -dling** ⟦< ?⟧ [Inf.] **1** to cheat **2** to waste (time) in trifling —**did′dler** ***n.***

di·do (dī′dō) ***n.***, *pl.* **-does** or **-dos** ⟦< ?⟧ [Inf.] a mischievous or foolish action

die[1] (dī) ***vi.*** **died, dy′ing** ⟦< ON *deyja*⟧ **1** to stop living **2** to stop functioning; end **3** to lose force or activity **4** [Inf.] to wish very much [I'm *dying* to go] —**die away** (or **down**) to cease gradually —**die off** to die one by one until all are gone —**die out** to stop existing

die[2] (dī) ***n.***, *pl.* for 2, **dies** (dīz) ⟦< L *dare*, give⟧ **1** *sing. of* DICE **2** a tool for shaping, punching, etc. metal or other material

die′-hard′ or **die′hard′** ***n.*** a person stubbornly resistant to new ideas, reform, etc.

di·e·lec·tric (dī′i lek′trik) ***n.*** ⟦< *dia-*, across + ELECTRIC⟧ a material that does not conduct electricity

di·er·e·sis (dī er′ə sis) ***n.***, *pl.* **-ses′** (-sēz′) ⟦< Gr *dia-*, apart + *hairein*, to take⟧ a mark (¨) placed over the second of two consecutive vowels to show that it is pronounced separately

die·sel (dē′zəl, -səl) ***n.*** ⟦after R. *Diesel* (1858-1913), Ger inventor⟧ [*often* **D-**] an internal-combustion engine that burns oil ignited by heat from air compression: also **diesel engine** (or **motor**) —***vi.*** to continue to run after the ignition is turned off: said of an internal-combustion engine

di·et[1] (dī′ət) ***n.*** ⟦< Gr *diaita*, way of life⟧ **1** what a person or animal usually eats or drinks **2** a special or limited selection of food and drink, chosen or prescribed as to bring about weight loss —***vi.***, ***vt.*** to adhere to or place on a diet —**di′et·er** ***n.*** —**di′e·tar′y** (-ə ter′ē) ***adj.***

di·et[2] (dī′ət) ***n.*** ⟦< ML *dieta*⟧ **1** a formal assembly **2** in some countries, a legislative assembly

di′e·tet′ic (-ə tet′ik) ***adj.*** of or for a particular diet of food and drink

di′e·tet′ics (-iks) ***n.*** the study of the kinds and quantities of food needed for health

di·e·ti·tian (dī′ə tish′ən) ***n.*** an expert in dietetics

dif- *prefix* DIS-: used before *f*

dif·fer (dif′ər) ***vi.*** ⟦< L *dis-*, apart + *ferre*, to bring⟧ **1** to be unlike or not the same **2** to be of opposite or unlike opinions; disagree

dif·fer·ence (dif′ər əns, dif′rəns) ***n.*** **1** a being different **2** the way in which people or things are different **3** a differing in opinion; disagreement **4** a dispute **5** *Math.* the amount by which one quantity is less than another

dif′fer·ent ***adj.*** **1** not alike **2** not the same **3** various **4** unusual —**dif′fer·ent·ly** ***adv.***

dif·fer·en·tial (dif′ər en′shəl) ***adj.*** of, showing, or constituting a difference —***n.*** **1** a differentiating amount, degree, etc. **2** a differential gear

differential gear (or **gearing**) a gear arrangement allowing one axle of an automobile to turn faster than the other

dif′fer·en′ti·ate′ (-shē āt′) ***vt.*** **-at′ed**, **-at′ing** **1** to constitute a difference in or between **2** to make unlike **3** to distinguish between —***vi.*** **1** to become different or differentiated **2** to note a difference —**dif′fer·en′ti·a′tion** ***n.***

dif·fi·cult (dif′i kult′, -kəlt) ***adj.*** **1** hard to do, understand, etc. **2** hard to satisfy, deal with, etc.

dif′fi·cul′ty ***n.***, *pl.* **-ties** ⟦< L *dis-*, not + *facilis*, easy⟧ **1** a being difficult **2** something difficult, as a problem, obstacle, or objection **3** trouble

dif′fi·dent (-dənt) ***adj.*** ⟦< L *dis-*, not + *fidere*, to trust⟧ lacking self-confidence; shy —**dif′fi·dence** ***n.***

dif·frac·tion (di frak′shən) ***n.*** ⟦< L *dis-*, apart + *frangere*, to break⟧ **1** the breaking up of light waves as into the colors of the spectrum **2** a similar breaking up as of sound waves

dif·fuse (di fyo͞os′; *for v.*, -fyo͞oz′) ***adj.*** ⟦< L *dis-*, apart + *fundere*, to pour⟧ **1** spread out; not concentrated **2** using more words than are needed —***vt.***, ***vi.*** **-fused′**, **-fus′ing** to pour in every direction; spread widely —**dif·fuse′ly** ***adv.*** —**dif·fuse′ness** ***n.*** —**dif·fu′sion** ***n.*** —**dif·fu′sive** ***adj.***

dig (dig) ***vt.*** **dug**, **dig′ging** ⟦< OFr < Du *dijk*, dike⟧ **1** to turn up or remove (ground, etc.) with a spade, the hands, etc. **2** to make (a hole, etc.) by digging **3** to get out by digging **4** to find out, as by careful study **5** to jab **6** [Slang] *a*) to understand *b*) to like —***vi.*** **1** to dig the ground **2** to make a way by digging —***n.*** **1** [Inf.] *a*) a poke, nudge, etc. *b*) a taunt **2** an archaeological excavation —**dig′ger** ***n.***

di·gest (dī′jest′; *for v.* di jest′, dī-) ***n.*** ⟦< L *di-*, apart + *gerere*, to carry⟧ an organized collection of condensed information; summary —***vt.*** **1** to summarize **2** to change (food taken into the body) into an absorbable form **3** to absorb mentally —***vi.*** to undergo digestion —**di·gest′i·ble** ***adj.***

di·ges′tion ***n.*** **1** a digesting or being digested **2** the ability to digest —**di·ges′tive** ***adj.***

dig·it (dij′it) ***n.*** ⟦< L *digitus*, a finger⟧ **1** a finger or toe **2** any number from 0 to 9

dig·i·tal (dij′i təl, -it′l) ***adj.*** **1** of or like a digit **2** using a row of digits, rather than numbers on a dial [*a digital watch*] **3** designating, of, or used by a computer that processes data represented by groups of electronic bits **4** designating a recording technique in which sounds or images are converted into electronic bits: the bits are read electronically, as by a laser beam, for reproduction

dig·i·tal·is (dij′i tal′is) ***n.*** ⟦ModL, foxglove: see DIGIT⟧ **1** a plant with long spikes of thimblelike flowers; foxglove **2** a medicine made from the leaves of the purple foxglove, used as a heart stimulant

dig·i·tize (dij′i tīz′) ***vt.*** **-tized′**, **-tiz′ing** to translate (analog data) into digital data

dig·ni·fied (dig′nə fīd′) ***adj.*** having or showing dignity

dig·ni·fy (dig′nə fī′) ***vt.*** **-fied′**, **-fy′ing** ⟦< L *dignus*, worthy + *facere*, make⟧ to give dignity to; exalt

dig′ni·tar′y (-ter′ē) ***n.***, *pl.* **-tar′ies** ⟦< L *dignitas*, dignity⟧ a person holding a high position or office

dig′ni·ty (-tē) ***n.***, *pl.* **-ties** ⟦< L *dignus*, worthy⟧ **1** honorable quality; worthiness **2** high repute or honor, or the degree of this **3** a high position, rank, or title **4** stately appearance or manner **5** self-respect

di·graph (dī′graf′) ***n.*** a combination of two letters to represent one sound (Ex.: *read*, gra*ph*ic)

di·gress (di gres′, dī-) ***vi.*** ⟦< L *dis-*, apart + *gradi*, to go⟧ to wander temporarily from the subject, in talking or writing

—di·gres′sion (-gresh′ən) *n.* —di·gres′sive *adj.*

Di·jon mustard (dē zhän′, dē′zhän′) ⟦after *Dijon*, city in France⟧ a mild mustard paste blended with white wine

dike (dīk) *n.* ⟦OE *dic*, ditch⟧ an embankment or dam made to prevent flooding as by the sea

di·lap·i·dat·ed (də lap′ə dāt′id) *adj.* ⟦< L *dis-*, apart + *lapidare*, throw stones at⟧ falling to pieces; broken down —**di·lap′i·da′tion** *n.*

di·late (dī′lāt′, dī lāt′) *vt.* **-lat′ed, -lat′ing** ⟦< L *dis-*, apart + *latus*, wide⟧ to make wider or larger —*vi.* **1** to become wider or larger **2** to speak or write in detail (*on* or *upon* a subject) —**di·la′tion** or **dil·a·ta·tion** (dil′ə tā′shən) *n.*

dil·a·to·ry (dil′ə tôr′ē) *adj.* ⟦see prec.⟧ **1** causing delay **2** inclined to delay; slow; tardy —**dil′a·to′ri·ness** *n.*

di·lem·ma (di lem′ə) *n.* ⟦< LGr *di-*, two + *lēmma*, proposition⟧ **1** any situation requiring a choice between unpleasant alternatives **2** any serious problem

dil·et·tante (dil′ə tänt′, dil′ə tänt′) *n., pl.* **-tantes′** or **-tan′ti′** (-tī′, -tē) ⟦It < L *delectare*, to delight⟧ one who dabbles in an art, science, etc. in a superficial way —**dil′et·tant′ish** *adj.* —**dil′et·tant′ism′** *n.*

dil·i·gent (dil′ə jənt) *adj.* ⟦< L *di-*, apart + *legere*, choose⟧ **1** persevering and careful in work; hard-working **2** done carefully —**dil′i·gence** *n.* —**dil′i·gent·ly** *adv.*

dill (dil) *n.* ⟦OE *dile*⟧ an herb related to parsley, with bitter seeds and aromatic leaves, used to flavor pickles, soups, etc.

dil·ly (dil′ē) *n., pl.* **-lies** ⟦? < DEL(IGHTFUL) + -Y[2]⟧ [Slang] a remarkable person or thing

dil·ly·dal·ly (dil′ē dal′ē) *vi.* **-lied, -ly·ing** ⟦< DALLY⟧ to waste time by hesitating; loiter or dawdle

di·lute (di lo͞ot′, dī-) *vt.* **-lut′ed, -lut′ing** ⟦< L *dis-*, off + *lavare*, to wash⟧ to thin down or weaken as by mixing with water —*adj.* diluted —**di·lu′tion** *n.*

dim[1] (dim) *adj.* **dim′mer, dim′mest** ⟦OE⟧ **1** not bright, clear, or distinct; dull, obscure, etc. **2** not seeing, hearing, or understanding clearly **3** [Inf.] stupid —*vt., vi.* **dimmed, dim′ming** to make or grow dim —**dim′ly** *adv.* —**dim′ness** *n.*

dim[2] *abbrev.* diminutive

dime (dīm) *n.* ⟦< L *decem*, ten⟧ a U.S. or Canadian 10-cent coin

di·men·sion (də men′shən) *n.* ⟦< L *dis-*, off, from + *metiri*, to measure⟧ **1** any measurable extent, as length, width, or depth **2** [*pl.*] measurements in length, width, and often depth **3** [*often pl.*] extent; scope —**di·men′sion·al** *adj.*

dime store FIVE-AND-TEN-CENT STORE

di·min·ish (də min′ish) *vt., vi.* ⟦< L *diminuere*, reduce⟧ to make or become smaller in size, degree, importance, etc.; lessen —**dim·i·nu·tion** (dim′ə no͞o′shən, -nyo͞o′-) *n.*

di·min·u·en·do (də min′yo͞o en′dō) *adj., adv.* ⟦It: see prec.⟧ *Music* with gradually diminishing volume: also written ***di·min′u·en′do***

di·min·u·tive (də min′yo͞o tiv) *adj.* ⟦see DIMINISH⟧ very small; tiny —*n.* a word having a suffix that expresses smallness, endearment, etc. (Ex.: *piglet*)

dim·i·ty (dim′ə tē) *n., pl.* **-ties** ⟦< Gr *dis-*, two + *mitos*, a thread⟧ a thin, corded or patterned cotton cloth

dim′mer *n.* a device, as a rheostat, for dimming electric lights

dim·ple (dim′pəl) *n.* ⟦ME *dimpel*⟧ a small, natural hollow, as on the cheek or chin —*vi., vt.* **-pled, -pling** to form dimples (in) —**dim′ply** (-plē) *adj.*

dim sum (dim′ sum′, -soom′) ⟦Chin⟧ small dumplings filled with meat, vegetables, etc.; also, a light meal of these together with other foods

dim′wit′ *n.* [Slang] a stupid person; simpleton —**dim′wit′ted** *adj.*

din (din) *n.* ⟦OE *dyne*⟧ a loud, continuous noise; confused uproar —*vt.* **dinned, din′ning** to repeat insistently or noisily —*vi.* to make a din

din-din (din′din′) *n.* [Inf.] dinner

dine (dīn) *vi.* **dined, din′ing** ⟦ult. < L *dis-*, away + *jejunus*, hungry⟧ to eat dinner —*vt.* to provide a dinner for

din·er (dīn′ər) *n.* **1** a person eating dinner **2** a railroad car equipped to serve meals **3** a small restaurant built to look like such a car

di·nette (dī net′) *n.* an alcove or small space used as a dining room

ding (diŋ) *n.* ⟦< Scand⟧ the sound of a bell: also **ding′-dong′** (-dôŋ′)

din·ghy (diŋ′gē) *n., pl.* **-ghies** ⟦Hindi *ḍiṅgī*⟧ any of various small boats, as one carried on a ship

din·gle (diŋ′gəl) *n.* ⟦ME *dingel*, abyss⟧ a small, deep, wooded valley

din·go (diŋ′gō) *n., pl.* **-goes** ⟦native name⟧ the Australian wild dog, usually tawny in color

ding·us (diŋ′əs) *n.* ⟦< Du *ding*, thing⟧ [Inf.] any device; gadget

din·gy (din′jē) *adj.* **-gi·er, -gi·est** ⟦orig. dial. var. < DUNG⟧ **1** not bright or clean; grimy **2** dismal; shabby —**din′gi·ness** *n.*

dining room a room where meals are eaten

dink·y (diŋ′kē) *adj.* **-i·er, -i·est** ⟦< Scot *dink*, trim⟧ [Inf.] small and unimportant

din·ner (din′ər) *n.* ⟦see DINE⟧ **1** the main meal of the day **2** a banquet in honor of a person or event

dinner jacket a tuxedo jacket

din′ner·ware′ *n.* plates, cups, saucers, etc., collectively

di·no·saur (dī′nə sôr′) *n.* ⟦< Gr *deinos*, terrible + *sauros*, lizard⟧ an extinct prehistoric reptile, often huge

dint (dint) *n.* ⟦OE *dynt*⟧ force; exertion: now chiefly in **by dint of**

di·o·cese (dī′ə sis, -sēz′) *n.* ⟦< Gr *dioikein*, to keep house⟧ the district under a bishop's jurisdiction —**di·oc′e·san** (-äs′ə sən) *adj.*

di·ode (dī′ōd′) *n.* ⟦DI-[1] + -ODE⟧ an electron tube used esp. to convert alternating current into direct current

Di·og·e·nes (dī äj′ə nēz′) 412?-323? B.C.; Gr. philosopher

Di·o·ny·sus or **Di·o·ny·sos** (dī′ə nī′səs) ***n.*** *Gr. Myth.* the god of wine and revelry

di·o·ram·a (dī′ə ram′ə) ***n.*** ⟦< Gr *dia-*, through + *horama*, a view⟧ a scenic display, as of three-dimensional figures against a painted background

di·ox·in (dī äk′sin) ***n.*** a highly toxic chemical contaminant found in some herbicides

dip (dip) ***vt.*** **dipped**, **dip′ping** ⟦OE *dyppan*⟧ **1** to immerse briefly **2** to scoop (liquid) up or out **3** to lower (a flag, etc.) and immediately raise again —***vi.*** **1** to plunge into a liquid and quickly come out **2** to sink suddenly **3** to decline slightly **4** to slope down **5** to lower a container, the hand, etc. as into water **6** to read or inquire superficially: with *into* —***n.*** **1** a dipping or being dipped **2** a brief plunge into water, etc. **3** a liquid, sauce, etc. into which something is dipped **4** a portion removed by dipping **5** a downward slope or plunge

diph·the·ri·a (dif thir′ē ə, dip-) ***n.*** ⟦< Gr *diphthera*, leather⟧ an acute infectious disease marked by high fever and difficult breathing

diph·thong (dif′thôŋ; *often* dip′-) ***n.*** ⟦< Gr *di-*, two + *phthongos*, a sound⟧ a sound made by gliding from one vowel to another within one syllable, as the sound (oi) in *oil*

di·plo·ma (də plō′mə) ***n.*** ⟦< Gr *diplōma*, folded letter⟧ a certificate issued by a school, college, etc. indicating graduation or the conferring of a degree

di·plo′ma·cy (-sē) ***n.*** **1** the conducting of relations between nations **2** tact

dip·lo·mat (dip′lə mat′) ***n.*** **1** a representative of a government who conducts relations with another government **2** a tactful person

dip′lo·mat′ic ***adj.*** **1** of diplomacy **2** tactful —**dip′lo·mat′i·cal·ly** ***adv.***

di·pole (dī′pōl′) ***n.*** a kind of radio or TV antenna with a single line separated at the center for connection to the receiver

dip·per (dip′ər) ***n.*** a long-handled cup, etc. for dipping

dip·so·ma·ni·a (dip′sə mā′nē ə) ***n.*** ⟦< Gr *dipsa*, thirst + *mania*, madness⟧ an abnormal craving for alcoholic drink —**dip′so·ma′ni·ac′** (-ak′) ***n.***

dip′stick′ ***n.*** a graduated rod for measuring quantity or depth

dir *abbrev.* director

dire (dīr) ***adj.*** **dir′er**, **dir′est** ⟦L *dirus*⟧ **1** dreadful; terrible: also **dire′ful** **2** urgent *[a dire need]*

di·rect (də rekt′; *also* dī-) ***adj.*** ⟦< L *di-*, apart + *regere*, to rule⟧ **1** not roundabout or interrupted; straight **2** honest; frank *[a direct answer]* **3** with nothing between; immediate **4** in an unbroken line of descent; lineal **5** exact; complete *[the direct opposite]* **6** in the exact words *[a direct quote]* —***vt.*** **1** to manage; guide **2** to order; command **3** to turn or point; aim; head **4** to tell (a person) the way to a place **5** to address (a letter, etc.) **6** *a*) to plan and supervise the action and effects of (a play, film, etc.) *b*) to conduct the performance of (a choir, band, etc.) —***adv.*** directly —**di·rect′ness** ***n.***

direct current an electric current flowing in one direction

di·rec·tion (də rek′shən; *also* dī-) ***n.*** **1** a directing **2** [*usually pl.*] instructions for doing, using, etc. **3** a command **4** the point toward which something faces or the line along which it moves or lies —**di·rec′tion·al** ***adj.***

di·rec′tive (-rek′tiv) ***adj.*** directing —***n.*** a general order issued authoritatively

di·rect′ly ***adv.*** **1** in a direct way or line; straight **2** with nothing or no one between *[directly responsible]* **3** exactly *[directly opposite]* **4** instantly; right away

direct object *Gram.* the word or words denoting the receiver of the action of a transitive verb (Ex.: *me* in "he saw me")

di·rec′tor (-rek′tər) ***n.*** one who directs a school, corporation, etc. or a play, choir, etc. —**di·rec′tor·ship′** ***n.***

di·rec′tor·ate (-it) ***n.*** **1** the position of director **2** a board of directors

di·rec′to·ry (-tə rē) ***n.***, *pl.* **-ries** a book listing the names, addresses, etc. of a specific group of persons

dirge (durj) ***n.*** ⟦< L *dirige* (direct), first word of a prayer⟧ a song, poem, etc. of grief or mourning

dir·i·gi·ble (dir′ə jə bəl, də rij′ə-) ***n.*** ⟦see DIRECT & -IBLE⟧ AIRSHIP

dirk (durk) ***n.*** ⟦< ?⟧ a long dagger

dirn·dl (durn′dəl) ***n.*** ⟦< Ger *dirne*, girl⟧ a full skirt gathered at the waist

dirt (durt) ***n.*** ⟦< ON *drita*, excrement⟧ **1** any unclean matter, as mud or trash; filth **2** earth; soil **3** dirtiness, corruption, etc. **4** obscenity **5** malicious gossip

dirt′-cheap′ ***adj.***, ***adv.*** [Inf.] very inexpensive(ly)

dirt′-poor′ ***adj.*** extremely poor

dirt′y ***adj.*** **-i·er**, **-i·est** **1** not clean **2** obscene **3** contemptible or nasty **4** unfair; dishonest **5** showing anger *[a dirty look]* **6** rough *[dirty weather]* —***vt.***, ***vi.*** **dirt′ied**, **dirt′y·ing** to make or become dirty —**dir′ti·ly** ***adv.*** —**dirt′i·ness** ***n.***

dis (dis) ***vt.*** **dissed**, **dis′sing** [Slang] to insult

dis- ⟦< L⟧ *prefix* separation, negation, reversal *[disbar, disable, disintegrate]*

dis·a·bil·i·ty (dis′ə bil′ə tē) ***n.***, *pl.* **-ties** **1** a disabled condition **2** that which disables, as an illness or physical limitation

dis·a·ble (dis ā′bəl) ***vt.*** **-bled**, **-bling** to make unable or unfit; cripple; incapacitate

dis·a′bled ***adj.*** having a physical or mental disability

dis·a·buse (dis′ə byōōz′) ***vt.*** **-bused′**, **-bus′ing** to rid of false ideas

dis·ad·van·tage (dis′əd vant′ij) ***n.*** **1** an unfavorable situation or circumstance **2** detriment —**dis′ad′van·ta′geous** (-ad′ vən tā′jəs) ***adj.***

dis′ad·van′taged ***adj.*** underprivileged

dis·af·fect (dis′ə fekt′) ***vt.*** to make

unfriendly, discontented, or disloyal —**dis'af·fect'ed** *adj.* —**dis'af·fec'tion** *n.*

dis'af·fil'i·ate' (-ə fil'ē āt') *vt., vi.* **-at'ed, -at'ing** to end an affiliation (with) —**dis'af·fil'i·a'tion** *n.*

dis'a·gree' (-ə grē') *vi.* **-greed', -gree'ing 1** to fail to agree; differ **2** to differ in opinion **3** to give distress: with *with [plums disagree with me]* —**dis'a·gree'ment** *n.*

dis'a·gree'a·ble *adj.* **1** unpleasant; offensive **2** quarrelsome —**dis'a·gree'a·bly** *adv.*

dis·al·low (dis'ə lou') *vt.* to refuse to allow (a claim, etc.); reject

dis'ap·pear' (-ə pir') *vi.* **1** to cease to be seen; vanish **2** to cease existing —**dis'ap·pear'ance** *n.*

dis'ap·point' (-ə point') *vt.* to fail to satisfy the hopes or expectations of —**dis'ap·point'ment** *n.*

dis·ap·pro·ba·tion (dis'ap'rə bā'shən) *n.* disapproval

dis·ap·prove (dis'ə pro͞ov') *vt., vi.* **-proved', -prov'ing 1** to have or express an unfavorable opinion (of) **2** to refuse to approve —**dis'ap·prov'al** *n.* —**dis'ap·prov'ing·ly** *adv.*

dis·arm (dis ärm') *vt.* **1** to take away weapons from **2** to make harmless **3** to make friendly —*vi.* to reduce armed forces and armaments —**dis·ar'ma·ment** (-är'mə mənt) *n.*

dis·ar·range (dis'ə rānj') *vt.* **-ranged', -rang'ing** to undo the order of; make less neat

dis'ar·ray' (-ə rā') *n.* disorder

dis'as·sem'ble (-ə sem'bəl) *vt.* **-bled, -bling** to take apart

dis'as·so'ci·ate' (-ə sō'shē āt', -sē-) *vt.* **-at'ed, -at'ing** to disconnect or separate; dissociate

dis·as·ter (di zas'tər) *n.* ⟦< L *dis-*, away + *astrum*, a star⟧ any happening that causes great harm or damage; calamity —**dis·as'trous** (-trəs) *adj.*

dis·a·vow (dis'ə vou') *vt.* to deny any knowledge of or responsibility for; disclaim —**dis'a·vow'al** *n.*

dis·band (dis band') *vt., vi.* to break up: said as of an organization or its members

dis·bar' (-bär') *vt.* **-barred', -bar'ring** to deprive (a lawyer) of the right to practice law —**dis·bar'ment** *n.*

dis·be·lieve (dis'bə lēv') *vt., vi.* **-lieved', -liev'ing** to refuse to believe —**dis'be·lief'** (-lēf') *n.*

dis·burse (dis burs') *vt.* **-bursed', -burs'ing** ⟦< OFr *desbourser*⟧ to pay out; expend —**dis·burse'ment** *n.* —**dis·burs'er** *n.*

disc (disk) *n.* **1** DISK **2** a phonograph record

dis·card (dis kärd'; *for n.* dis'kärd') *vt.* ⟦< OFr: see DIS- & CARD[1]⟧ **1** *Card Games* to remove (a card or cards) from one's hand **2** to get rid of as no longer useful —*n.* **1** a discarding or being discarded **2** something discarded

disc brake a brake, as on a car, with two friction pads that press on a disc rotating with the wheel

dis·cern (di surn', -zurn') *vt.* ⟦< L *dis-*, apart + *cernere*, to separate⟧ to perceive or recognize clearly —**dis·cern'i·ble** *adj.* —**dis·cern'ment** *n.*

dis·cern'ing *adj.* having good judgment; astute

dis·charge (dis chärj'; *also, and for n.usually,* dis'chärj') *vt.* **-charged', -charg'ing** ⟦< L *dis-*, from + *carrus*, wagon⟧ **1** to release or dismiss **2** to unload (a cargo) **3** to shoot (a gun or projectile) **4** to emit *[to discharge pus]* **5** to pay (a debt) or perform (a duty) **6** *Elec.* to remove stored energy from (a battery, etc.) —*vi.* **1** to get rid of a load, etc. **2** to go off, as a gun —*n.* **1** a discharging or being discharged **2** that which discharges or is discharged

dis·ci·ple (di sī'pəl) *n.* ⟦< L *dis-*, apart + *capere*, to hold⟧ **1** a pupil or follower of any teacher or school **2** an early follower of Jesus, esp. one of the Apostles —**dis·ci'ple·ship'** *n.*

dis·ci·pli·nar·i·an (dis'ə pli ner'ē ən) *n.* a person who believes in or enforces strict discipline

dis·ci·pline (dis'ə plin') *n.* ⟦see DISCIPLE⟧ **1** a branch of learning **2** training that develops self-control, efficiency, etc. **3** strict control to enforce obedience **4** self-control **5** a system of rules, as for a church **6** treatment that corrects or punishes —*vt.* **-plined', -plin'ing 1** to train; control **2** to punish —**dis'ci·pli·nar'y** (-pli ner'ē) *adj.*

disc jockey one who conducts a radio program of recorded music

dis·claim (dis klām') *vt.* **1** to give up any claim to **2** to repudiate; deny

dis·claim'er *n.* a denial or renunciation, as of responsibility

dis·close (dis klōz') *vt.* **-closed', -clos'ing** to reveal —**dis·clo'sure** (-klō'zhər) *n.*

dis·co (dis'kō) *n.* **1** *pl.* **-cos** a place for dancing to recorded music **2** a kind of popular dance music with a strong beat

dis·col·or (dis kul'ər) *vt., vi.* to change in color as by fading, streaking, or staining: Brit. sp. **dis·col'our** —**dis'col·or·a'tion** *n.*

dis·com·fit (dis kum'fit) *vt.* ⟦< L *dis-*, away + *conficere*, prepare⟧ to frustrate or disconcert —**dis·com'fi·ture** (-fi chər) *n.*

dis·com·fort (dis kum'fərt) *n.* **1** lack of comfort; uneasiness **2** anything causing this —*vt.* to cause discomfort to

dis·com·mode (dis'kə mōd') *vt.* **-mod'ed, -mod'ing** ⟦< DIS- + L *commodare*, to make suitable⟧ to cause bother to; inconvenience

dis'com·pose' (-kəm pōz') *vt.* **-posed', -pos'ing** to disturb; fluster —**dis'com·po'sure** (-pō'zhər) *n.*

dis'con·cert' (-kən surt') *vt.* to upset; embarrass

dis'con·nect' (-kə nekt') *vt.* to break the connection of; separate —**dis'con·nec'tion** *n.*

dis'con·nect'ed *adj.* **1** separated **2** incoherent

dis·con·so·late (dis kän'sə lit) *adj.* ⟦see DIS- & CONSOLE[1]⟧ inconsolable; dejected —**dis·con'so·late·ly** *adv.*

dis·con·tent (dis'kən tent') *adj.* ⟦ME⟧ DISCONTENTED —*n.* dissatisfaction with one's situation: also **dis'con·tent'ment** —*vt.* to make discontented

dis'con·tent'ed *adj.* not contented; wanting something more or different

dis·con·tin·ue (dis'kən tin'yo͞o) *vt., vi.* **-ued, -u·ing** to stop; cease; give up —**dis'con·tin'u·ance** or **dis'con·tin'u·a'tion** *n.*

dis'con·tin'u·ous (-yo͞o əs) *adj.* not continuous; having interruptions or gaps

dis·cord (dis'kôrd') *n.* ⟦< L *dis-*, apart + *cor*, heart⟧ **1** disagreement **2** harsh noise **3** a lack of musical harmony —**dis·cord'ant** *adj.*

dis·co·thèque (dis'kə tek') *n.* ⟦Fr⟧ DISCO (sense 1)

dis·count (dis'kount'; *for v., also* dis kount') *n.* ⟦see DIS- & COMPUTE⟧ **1** a reduction from a usual or list price **2** the rate of interest charged on a discounted bill, note, etc.: also called **discount rate** —*vt.* **1** to pay or receive the value of (a bill, promissory note, etc.), minus a deduction for interest **2** to deduct an amount from (a bill, price, etc.) **3** to sell at less than the regular price **4** *a)* to allow for exaggeration, bias, etc. in (a story, etc.) *b)* to disregard **5** to lessen the effect of by anticipating

dis·coun·te·nance (dis kount''n əns) *vt.* **-nanced, -nanc·ing** **1** to make ashamed or embarrassed **2** to refuse approval or support

discount house (or **store**) a retail store that sells goods for less than regular prices

dis·cour·age (di skʉr'ij) *vt.* **-aged, -ag·ing** **1** to deprive of courage or confidence **2** to persuade (a person) to refrain **3** to try to prevent by disapproving —**dis·cour'age·ment** *n.*

dis·course (dis'kôrs'; *also, and for v. usually,* dis kôrs') *n.* ⟦< L *dis-*, from + *currere*, to run⟧ **1** talk; conversation **2** a formal treatment of a subject, in speech or writing —*vi.* **-coursed', -cours'ing** to talk; confer

dis·cour·te·ous (dis kʉr'tē əs) *adj.* impolite; rude; ill-mannered

dis·cour'te·sy (-kʉrt'ə sē) *n.* **1** lack of courtesy **2** *pl.* **-sies** a rude or impolite act or remark

dis·cov·er (di skuv'ər) *vt.* ⟦see DIS- & COVER⟧ **1** to be the first to find out, see, etc. **2** to learn of the existence of —**dis·cov'er·er** *n.*

dis·cov·er·y (di skuv'ər ē) *n., pl.* **-er·ies** **1** a discovering **2** anything discovered

dis·cred·it (dis kred'it) *vt.* **1** to disbelieve **2** to cast doubt on **3** to disgrace —*n.* **1** loss of belief; doubt **2** disgrace —**dis·cred'it·a·ble** *adj.*

dis·creet (di skrēt') *adj.* ⟦see DISCERN⟧ careful about what one says or does; prudent —**dis·creet'ly** *adv.*

dis·crep·an·cy (di skrep'ən sē) *n., pl.* **-cies** ⟦< L *dis-*, from + *crepare*, to rattle⟧ (a) lack of agreement; inconsistency

dis·crete (di skrēt') *adj.* ⟦see DISCERN⟧ separate and distinct; unrelated

dis·cre·tion (di skresh'ən) *n.* **1** the freedom to make decisions **2** the quality of being discreet; prudence —**dis·cre'tion·ar'y** *adj.*

dis·crim·i·nate (di skrim'i nāt') *vi.* **-nat'ed, -nat'ing** ⟦see DISCERN⟧ **1** to distinguish **2** to make distinctions in treatment; show partiality or prejudice —**dis·crim'i·nat'ing** *adj.* —**dis·crim'i·na'tion** *n.*

dis·crim'i·na·to'ry (-nə tôr'ē) *adj.* showing discrimination or bias

dis·cur·sive (di skʉr'siv) *adj.* ⟦see DISCOURSE⟧ wandering from one topic to another; rambling

DISCUS

dis·cus (dis'kəs) *n.* ⟦< Gr *diskos*⟧ a heavy disk, usually of metal and wood, thrown for distance at a track meet

dis·cuss (di skus') *vt.* ⟦< L *dis-*, apart + *quatere*, to shake⟧ to talk or write about; consider the pros and cons of —**dis·cus'sion** (-skush'ən) *n.*

dis·cuss'ant (-ənt) *n.* a participant in an organized discussion

dis·dain (dis dān') *vt.* ⟦< L *dis-*, DIS- + *dignari*, deign⟧ to regard as beneath one's dignity; scorn —*n.* aloof contempt —**dis·dain'ful** *adj.*

dis·ease (di zēz') *n.* ⟦< OFr *des-*, DIS- + *aise*, ease⟧ **1** illness in general **2** a particular destructive process in an organism; specif., an illness **3** any harmful condition, as of society —**dis·eased'** *adj.*

dis·em·bark (dis'im bärk') *vi., vt.* to leave, or unload from, a ship, aircraft, etc. —**dis'em·bar·ka'tion** *n.*

dis'em·bod'y (-im bäd'ē) *vt.* **-bod'ied, -bod'y·ing** to free from bodily existence —**dis'em·bod'i·ment** *n.*

dis'em·bow'el (-im bou'əl) *vt.* **-eled** or **-elled, -el·ing** or **-el·ling** to take out the entrails of

dis'en·chant' (-in chant') *vt.* **1** to free from an enchantment or illusion **2** DISILLUSION (sense 2) —**dis'en·chant'ment** *n.*

dis'en·cum'ber (-in kum'bər) *vt.* to relieve of a burden

dis·en·fran·chise (dis'in fran'chīz') *vt.* **-chised', -chis'ing** to deprive of a right, privilege, etc., esp. the right to vote

dis'en·gage' (-in gāj') *vt., vi.* **-gaged', -gag'ing** to release or get loose from something that engages, holds, entangles, etc.; unfasten —**dis'en·gage'ment** *n.*

dis'en·tan'gle (-in taŋ'gəl) *vt.* **-gled,**

-gling to free from something that entangles, confuses, etc.; extricate; untangle

dis'es·teem' (-i stēm') ***n.*** lack of esteem; disfavor

dis·fa·vor (dis fā'vər) ***n.*** **1** an unfavorable opinion; dislike; disapproval **2** the state of being disliked, etc.

dis·fig'ure (-fig'yər) ***vt.*** **-ured, -ur·ing** to hurt the appearance of; deface —**dis·fig'ure·ment** ***n.***

dis·gorge' (-gôrj') ***vt., vi.*** **-gorged', -gorg'ing** ⟦< OFr: see DIS- & GORGE⟧ **1** to vomit **2** to pour forth (its contents); empty (itself)

dis·grace' (-grās') ***n.*** ⟦< It *dis-*, not + *grazia*, favor⟧ **1** loss of favor or respect; shame; disrepute **2** a person or thing bringing shame —***vt.*** **-graced', -grac'ing** to bring shame or dishonor upon —**dis·grace'ful** ***adj.***

dis·grun'tle (-grunt''l) ***vt.*** **-tled, -tling** ⟦ult. < DIS- + GRUNT⟧ to make peevishly discontented; make sullen

dis·guise' (-gīz') ***vt.*** **-guised', -guis'ing** ⟦< OFr: see DIS- & GUISE⟧ **1** to make appear, sound, etc. so different as to be unrecognizable **2** to hide the real nature of —***n.*** **1** anything that disguises **2** a being disguised

dis·gust' (-gust') ***n.*** ⟦< DIS- + L *gustus*, a taste⟧ a sickening dislike —***vt.*** to cause to feel disgust —**dis·gust'ed** ***adj.*** —**dis·gust'ing** ***adj.***

dish (dish) ***n.*** ⟦see DISCUS⟧ **1** a container, generally shallow and concave, for holding food **2** as much as a dish holds **3** a particular kind of food **4** any dishlike object —***vt.*** to serve in a dish: with *up* or *out* —**dish it out** [Slang] to subject others to criticism, etc.

dis·ha·bille (dis'ə bēl') ***n.*** ⟦< Fr *dés-*, DIS- + *habiller*, to dress⟧ the state of being dressed only partially or in night clothes

dish antenna a radio or TV antenna with a dish-shaped reflector

dis·har·mo·ny (dis här'mə nē) ***n.*** absence of harmony; discord —**dis'har·mo'ni·ous** (-mō'nē əs) ***adj.***

dish'cloth' ***n.*** a cloth for washing dishes, etc.

dis·heart·en (dis härt''n) ***vt.*** to discourage; depress —**dis·heart'en·ing** ***adj.***

di·shev·el (di shev'əl) ***vt.*** **-eled** or **-elled, -el·ing** or **-el·ling** ⟦< OFr *des-*, DIS- + *chevel*, hair⟧ to cause (hair, clothing, etc.) to become disarranged; rumple —**di·shev'el·ment** ***n.***

dis·hon·est (dis än'ist) ***adj.*** not honest; lying, cheating, etc. —**dis·hon'est·ly** ***adv.***

dis·hon'es·ty ***n.*** **1** a being dishonest **2** *pl.* **-ties** a dishonest act

dis·hon·or (dis än'ər) ***n.*** **1** loss of honor or respect; shame; disgrace **2** a cause of dishonor —***vt.*** **1** to insult or disgrace **2** to refuse to pay (a check, etc.) —**dis·hon'or·a·ble** ***adj.***

dish'pan' ***n.*** a pan in which dishes, cups, etc. are washed

dish'rag' ***n.*** DISHCLOTH

dish'wash'er ***n.*** a person or machine that washes dishes, cups, etc.

dis·il·lu·sion (dis'i lo͞o'zhən) ***vt.*** **1** to free from illusion **2** to take away the idealism of and make bitter, etc. —**dis'il·lu'sion·ment** ***n.***

dis·in·clined (dis'in klīnd') ***adj.*** unwilling; reluctant

dis·in·fect (dis'in fekt') ***vt.*** to destroy the harmful bacteria, viruses, etc. in —**dis'in·fect'ant** ***n.***

dis'in'for·ma'tion (-in'fər mā'shən) ***n.*** deliberately false information leaked so as to confuse another nation's intelligence operations

dis·in·gen·u·ous (dis'in jen'yo͞o əs) ***adj.*** not candid or frank; insincere

dis·in·her·it (dis'in her'it) ***vt.*** to deprive of an inheritance

dis·in·te·grate (dis in'tə grāt') ***vt., vi.*** **-grat'ed, -grat'ing** **1** to separate into parts or fragments; break up **2** to undergo nuclear transformation —**dis·in'te·gra'tion** ***n.***

dis·in·ter (dis'in tur') ***vt.*** **-terred', -ter'ring** to remove from a grave, etc.; exhume

dis·in·ter·est·ed (dis in'trəs tid, -int'ər əs tid) ***adj.*** **1** impartial; unbiased **2** uninterested; indifferent

dis'in'ter·me'di·a'tion (-in'tər mē'dē ā'shən) ***n.*** the withdrawal of funds from banks to invest them at higher rates of interest, as in government securities

dis·joint' (-joint') ***vt.*** **1** to put out of joint; dislocate **2** to dismember **3** to destroy the unity, connections, etc. of —**dis·joint'ed** ***adj.***

disk (disk) ***n.*** ⟦L *discus*: see DISCUS⟧ **1** any thin, flat, circular thing **2** DISC **3** a thin, flat, circular plate coated with magnetic particles, for storing computer data **4** a layer of fibrous cartilage between adjacent vertebrae

disk·ette (di sket') ***n.*** FLOPPY DISK

dis·like (dis līk') ***vt.*** **-liked', -lik'ing** to have a feeling of not liking —***n.*** a feeling of not liking

dis·lo·cate (dis'lō kāt') ***vt.*** **-cat'ed, -cat'ing** **1** to displace (a bone) from its proper position **2** to disarrange; disrupt —**dis'lo·ca'tion** ***n.***

dis·lodge (dis läj') ***vt.*** **-lodged', -lodg'ing** to force from a place

dis·loy'al (-loi'əl) ***adj.*** not loyal or faithful —**dis·loy'al·ty** ***n.***

dis·mal (diz'məl) ***adj.*** ⟦< ML *dies mali*, evil days⟧ **1** causing gloom or misery **2** dark and gloomy

dis·man·tle (dis mant''l) ***vt.*** **-tled, -tling** ⟦see DIS- & MANTLE⟧ **1** to strip (a ship, etc.), as of equipment **2** to take apart —**dis·man'tle·ment** ***n.***

dis·may' (-mā') ***vt.*** ⟦< Anglo-Fr⟧ to make startled and discouraged by some problem, etc. difficult to resolve —***n.*** upset and discouragement caused by a problem, etc. difficult to resolve

dis·mem'ber (-mem'bər) ***vt.*** ⟦see DIS- & MEMBER⟧ **1** to cut or tear the limbs from **2** to pull or cut to pieces —**dis·mem'ber·ment** ***n.***

dis·miss' (-mis') ***vt.*** ⟦< L *dis-*, from + *mittere*, send⟧ **1** to cause or allow to leave **2** to discharge from employment, etc. **3** to put aside mentally **4** *Law* to reject (a claim, etc.) —**dis·miss'al** *n.*

dis·mis'sive (-mis'iv) *adj.* condescending in dismissing from consideration

dis·mount' (-mount') *vi.* to get off, as from a horse —*vt.* **1** to remove (a thing) from its mounting **2** to take apart; dismantle

dis·o·be·di·ence (dis'ō bē'dē əns) *n.* refusal to obey; insubordination —**dis'o·be'di·ent** *adj.*

dis'o·bey' (-ō bā') *vt., vi.* to refuse to obey

dis'o·blige' (-ə blīj') *vt.* **-bliged', -blig'ing 1** to refuse to oblige **2** to offend

dis·or'der (-ôr'dər) *n.* **1** a lack of order; confusion **2** a breach of public peace; riot **3** an ailment —*vt.* **1** to throw into disorder **2** to upset the normal functions of

dis·or'der·ly *adj.* **1** untidy **2** violating public peace, safety, etc. —**dis·or'der·li·ness** *n.*

dis·or·gan·ize (dis ôr'gə nīz') *vt.* **-ized', -iz'ing** to break up the order or system of; throw into confusion —**dis·or'gan·i·za'tion** *n.*

dis·o'ri·ent' (-ôr'ē ent') *vt.* ⟦see DIS- & ORIENT, *v.*⟧ **1** to cause to lose one's bearings **2** to confuse mentally —**dis·o'ri·en·ta'tion** *n.*

dis·own' (-ōn') *vt.* to refuse to acknowledge as one's own; repudiate

dis·par·age (di spar'ij) *vt.* **-aged, -ag·ing** ⟦< OFr *des-* (see DIS-) + *parage*, rank⟧ **1** to discredit **2** to belittle —**dis·par'age·ment** *n.*

dis·pa·rate (dis'pə rət) *adj.* ⟦< L *dis-*, not + *par*, equal⟧ distinct or different in kind; unequal —**dis·par·i·ty** (di spar'ə tē), *pl.* **-ties**, *n.*

dis·pas·sion·ate (dis pash'ə nət) *adj.* free from passion or bias; impartial —**dis·pas'sion·ate·ly** *adv.*

dis·patch (di spach'; *for n., also* dis'pach') *vt.* ⟦< L *dis-*, away + *pes*, foot⟧ **1** to send promptly, as on an errand **2** to kill **3** to finish quickly —*n.* **1** a sending off **2** a killing **3** speed; promptness **4** a message **5** a news story sent by a reporter —**dis·patch'er** *n.*

dis·pel (di spel') *vt.* **-pelled', -pel'ling** ⟦< L *dis-*, apart + *pellere*, to drive⟧ to scatter and drive away

dis·pen·sa·ble (di spen'sə bəl) *adj.* **1** that can be dealt out **2** that can be dispensed with; not important

dis·pen'sa·ry (-sə rē) *n., pl.* **-ries** a room or place where medicines and first-aid treatment are available

dis·pen·sa·tion (dis'pən sā'shən) *n.* **1** a dispensing **2** something dispensed **3** an administrative system **4** a release from an obligation **5** *Theol.* the ordering of events under divine authority

dis·pense (di spens') *vt.* **-pensed', -pens'ing** ⟦< L *dis-*, out + *pendere*, weigh⟧ **1** to give out; distribute **2** to prepare and give out (medicines) **3** to administer (the law or justice) —**dis·pense with 1** to get rid of **2** to do without —**dis·pens'er** *n.*

dis·perse' (-spurs') *vt.* **-persed', -pers'ing** ⟦< L *dis-*, out + *spargere*, scatter⟧ **1** to break up and scatter **2** to dispel (mist, etc.) —*vi.* to scatter —**dis·per'sal** *n.* —**dis·per'sion** *n.*

dis·pir·it (di spir'it) *vt.* to depress; discourage —**dis·pir'it·ed** *adj.*

dis·place (dis plās') *vt.* **-placed', -plac'ing 1** to move from its usual place **2** to remove from office; discharge **3** to replace

displaced person one forced from one's country, esp. as a result of war

dis·place'ment *n.* **1** a displacing or being displaced **2** the weight or volume of air, water, or other fluid displaced by a floating object

dis·play (di splā') *vt.* ⟦< L *dis-*, apart + *plicare*, to fold⟧ **1** [Obs.] to spread out; unfold **2** to exhibit —*n.* **1** an exhibition **2** anything displayed

dis·please (dis plēz') *vt., vi.* **-pleased', -pleas'ing** to fail to please; offend

dis·pleas'ure (-plezh'ər) *n.* a being displeased

dis·port (di spôrt') *vi.* ⟦< OFr *des-* (see DIS-) + *porter*, carry⟧ to play; frolic —*vt.* to amuse (oneself)

dis·pos·al (di spō'zəl) *n.* **1** a disposing **2** a device in the drain of a kitchen sink to grind up garbage

dis·pose' (-spōz') *vt.* **-posed', -pos'ing** ⟦see DIS- & POSITION⟧ **1** to arrange **2** to settle (affairs) **3** to make willing; incline —**dispose of 1** to settle **2** to give away or sell **3** to get rid of —**dis·pos'a·ble** *adj.*

dis·po·si·tion (dis'pə zish'ən) *n.* **1** arrangement **2** management of affairs **3** a selling or giving away **4** the authority to settle, etc.; control **5** a tendency **6** one's temperament

dis'pos·sess' (-pə zes') *vt.* to deprive of the possession of land, a house, etc.; oust

dis·praise' (-prāz') *vt.* **-praised', -prais'ing** ⟦< OFr *despreisier*⟧ to blame; censure —*n.* blame

dis'pro·por'tion (-prə pôr'shən) *n.* a lack of proportion —**dis'pro·por'tion·al** or **dis'pro·por'tion·ate** *adj.*

dis·prove' (-pro͞ov') *vt.* **-proved', -proved'** or **-prov'en, -prov'ing** to prove to be false

dis·pu·ta·tion (dis'pyo͞o tā'shən) *n.* **1** a disputing **2** debate

dis'pu·ta'tious (-pyo͞o tā'shəs) *adj.* inclined to dispute; contentious —**dis'pu·ta'tious·ly** *adv.*

dis·pute (di spyo͞ot') *vi.* **-put'ed, -put'ing** ⟦< L *dis-*, apart + *putare*, to think⟧ **1** to argue; debate **2** to quarrel —*vt.* **1** to argue (a question) **2** to doubt **3** to oppose in any way —*n.* **1** a disputing; debate **2** a quarrel —**in dispute** not settled —**dis·put'a·ble** *adj.* —**dis·pu'tant** *adj., n.*

dis·qual·i·fy (dis kwôl'ə fī') *vt.* **-fied', -fy'ing** to make or declare unqualified, unfit, or ineligible —**dis·qual'i·fi·ca'tion** *n.*

dis·qui·et (dis kwī'ət) *vt.* to make uneasy; disturb —*n.* restlessness: also

dis·qui'e·tude' (-ə to͞od')

dis·qui·si·tion (dis'kwi zish'ən) ***n.*** ⟦< L *dis-*, apart + *quaerere*, to seek⟧ a formal discussion; treatise

dis·re·gard (dis'ri gärd') ***vt.*** **1** to pay little or no attention to **2** to treat without due respect —***n.*** **1** lack of attention **2** lack of due regard or respect

dis're·pair' (-ri per') ***n.*** the condition of needing repairs; state of neglect

dis·rep'u·ta·ble (-rep'yo͞o tə bəl) ***adj.*** **1** not reputable **2** not fit to be seen

dis're·pute' (-ri pyo͞ot') ***n.*** lack or loss of repute; bad reputation; disgrace

dis're·spect' (-ri spekt') ***n.*** lack of respect; discourtesy —**dis're·spect'ful** ***adj.***

dis·robe (dis rōb') ***vt.***, ***vi.*** **-robed'**, **-rob'ing** to undress

dis·rupt (dis rupt') ***vt.***, ***vi.*** ⟦< L *dis-*, apart + *rumpere*, to break⟧ **1** to break apart **2** to disturb or interrupt —**dis·rup'tion** ***n.*** —**dis·rup'tive** ***adj.***

dis·sat'is·fy' (-sat'is fī') ***vt.*** **-fied'**, **-fy'ing** to fail to satisfy; displease —**dis·sat'is·fac'tion** ***n.***

dis·sect (di sekt') ***vt.*** ⟦< L *dis-*, apart + *secare*, to cut⟧ **1** to cut apart piece by piece, as a body for purposes of study **2** to examine or analyze closely —**dis·sec'tion** ***n.*** —**dis·sec'tor** ***n.***

dis·sem·ble (di sem'bəl) ***vt.***, ***vi.*** **-bled**, **-bling** ⟦< OFr *dessembler*⟧ to conceal (the truth, one's feelings, motives, etc.) under a false appearance —**dis·sem'blance** ***n.*** —**dis·sem'bler** ***n.***

dis·sem·i·nate (di sem'ə nāt') ***vt.*** **-nat'ed**, **-nat'ing** ⟦< L *dis-*, apart + *seminare*, to sow⟧ to scatter about; spread widely —**dis·sem'i·na'tion** ***n.***

dis·sen·sion (di sen'shən) ***n.*** a dissenting; disagreement or quarreling

dis·sent (di sent') ***vi.*** ⟦< L *dis-*, apart + *sentire*, feel⟧ **1** to disagree **2** to reject doctrines of an established church —***n.*** a dissenting —**dis·sent'er** ***n.***

dis·ser·ta·tion (dis'ər tā'shən) ***n.*** ⟦< L *dis-*, apart + *serere*, join⟧ a formal discourse or treatise, esp. one written to fulfill the requirements for a doctorate from a university

dis·serv·ice (dis sur'vis) ***n.*** harm

dis·sev·er (di sev'ər) ***vt.*** **1** to sever; separate **2** to divide into parts —***vi.*** to separate; disunite

dis·si·dence (dis'ə dəns) ***n.*** ⟦< L *dis-*, apart + *sidere*, sit⟧ disagreement; dissent —**dis'si·dent** (-dənt) ***adj.***, ***n.***

dis·sim·i·lar (dis sim'ə lər) ***adj.*** not similar; different —**dis'sim'i·lar'i·ty** (-lar'ə tē), *pl.* **-ties**, ***n.***

dis·si·mil·i·tude (dis'si mil'ə to͞od') ***n.*** difference

dis·sim·u·late (di sim'yo͞o lāt') ***vt.***, ***vi.*** **-lat'ed**, **-lat'ing** ⟦see DIS- & SIMULATE⟧ to dissemble —**dis·sim'u·la'tion** ***n.*** —**dis·sim'u·la'tor** ***n.***

dis·si·pate (dis'ə pāt') ***vt.*** **-pat'ed**, **-pat'ing** ⟦< L *dis-*, apart + *supare*, to throw⟧ **1** to scatter; disperse **2** to make disappear **3** to waste or squander —***vi.*** **1** to vanish **2** to indulge in pleasure to the point of harming oneself —**dis'si·pa'tion** ***n.***

dis·so·ci·ate (di sō'shē āt') ***vt.*** **-at'ed**, **-at'ing** ⟦< L *dis-*, apart + *sociare*, join⟧ to break the connection between; disunite —**dis·so'ci·a'tion** ***n.***

dis·so·lute (dis'ə lo͞ot') ***adj.*** ⟦see DISSOLVE⟧ dissipated and immoral; profligate —**dis'so·lute'ly** ***adv.*** —**dis'so·lute'ness** ***n.***

dis·so·lu·tion (dis'ə lo͞o'shən) ***n.*** a dissolving or being dissolved; specif., *a*) a breaking up or into parts *b*) a termination *c*) death

dis·solve (di zälv', -zôlv') ***vt.***, ***vi.*** **-solved'**, **-solv'ing** ⟦< L *dis-*, apart + *solvere*, loosen⟧ **1** to make or become liquid; melt **2** to pass or make pass into solution **3** to break up **4** to end as by breaking up; terminate **5** to disappear or make disappear

dis·so·nance (dis'ə nəns) ***n.*** ⟦< L *dis-*, apart + *sonus*, a sound⟧ **1** an inharmonious combination of sounds; discord **2** any lack of harmony or agreement —**dis'so·nant** ***adj.***

dis·suade (di swād') ***vt.*** **-suad'ed**, **-suad'ing** ⟦< L *dis-*, away + *suadere*, to persuade⟧ to turn (a person) aside (*from* a course, etc.) by persuasion or advice —**dis·sua'sion** (-swā'zhən) ***n.***

dist *abbrev.* **1** distance **2** district

dis·taff (dis'taf') ***n.*** ⟦< OE *dis-*, flax + *stæf*, staff⟧ a staff on which flax, wool, etc. is wound for use in spinning —***adj.*** female; specif., of the maternal side of a family

dis·tal (dis'təl) ***adj.*** ⟦DIST(ANT) + -AL⟧ *Anat.* farthest from the point of attachment or origin; terminal —**dis'tal·ly** ***adv.***

dis·tance (dis'təns) ***n.*** ⟦< L *dis-*, apart + *stare*, to stand⟧ **1** a being separated in space or time; remoteness **2** a gap, space, or interval between two points in space or time **3** a remoteness in behavior; reserve **4** a faraway place —***vt.*** **-tanced**, **-tanc·ing** to place at an emotional distance (*from*)

dis'tant (-tənt) ***adj.*** **1** far away in space or time **2** away *[100 miles distant]* **3** far apart in relationship **4** aloof; reserved **5** from or at a distance —**dis'tant·ly** ***adv.***

dis·taste (dis tāst') ***n.*** dislike —**dis·taste'ful** ***adj.***

dis·tem·per (dis tem'pər) ***n.*** ⟦< ML *distemperare*, to disorder⟧ an infectious viral disease of young dogs, horses, etc.

dis·tend (di stend') ***vt.***, ***vi.*** ⟦< L *dis-*, apart + *tendere*, to stretch⟧ **1** to stretch out **2** to expand, as by pressure from within; make or become swollen —**dis·ten'tion** or **dis·ten'sion** ***n.***

dis·till or **dis·til** (di stil') ***vi.***, ***vt.*** **-tilled'**, **-till'ing** ⟦< L *de-*, down + *stillare*, to drop⟧ **1** to fall or let fall in drops **2** to undergo, subject to, or produce by distillation —**dis·till'er** ***n.***

dis·til·late (dis'tə lāt', -lit) ***n.*** a liquid obtained by distilling

dis·til·la·tion (dis'tə lā'shən) ***n.*** **1** the process of heating a mixture and condensing the resulting vapor to produce a more nearly pure substance **2** anything distilled; distillate

dis·till·er·y (di stil′ər ē) ***n.**, pl.* **-ies** a place where alcoholic liquors are distilled

dis·tinct (di stiŋkt′) ***adj.*** ⟦see DISTINGUISH⟧ **1** not alike **2** separate **3** clearly perceived or marked off **4** unmistakable; definite —**dis·tinct′ly** ***adv.***

dis·tinc′tion (-stiŋk′shən) ***n.*** **1** the act of making or keeping distinct **2** difference **3** a quality or feature that differentiates **4** fame; eminence **5** the quality that makes one seem superior **6** a mark of special recognition or honor

dis·tinc′tive ***adj.*** making distinct; characteristic —**dis·tinc′tive·ly** ***adv.*** —**dis·tinc′tive·ness** ***n.***

dis·tin·guish (di stiŋ′gwish) ***vt.*** ⟦< L *dis-*, apart + *-stinguere*, to prick⟧ **1** to perceive or show the difference in **2** to characterize **3** to perceive clearly **4** to classify **5** to make famous —***vi.*** to make a distinction (*between* or *among*) —**dis·tin′guish·a·ble** ***adj.***

dis·tin′guished ***adj.*** celebrated; famous

dis·tort (di stôrt′) ***vt.*** ⟦< L *dis-*, intens. + *torquere*, to twist⟧ **1** to twist out of shape **2** to misrepresent (facts, etc.) **3** to modify so as to reproduce unfaithfully —**dis·tor′tion** ***n.***

dis·tract (di strakt′) ***vt.*** ⟦< L *dis-*, apart + *trahere*, draw⟧ **1** to draw (the mind, etc.) away in another direction; divert **2** to confuse; bewilder —**dis·tract′ed** ***adj.*** —**dis·tract′ing** ***adj.***

dis·trac′tion ***n.*** **1** a distracting or being distracted **2** anything that distracts confusingly or amusingly; diversion **3** great mental distress

dis·trait (di strā′) ***adj.*** ⟦see DISTRACT⟧ absent-minded; inattentive

dis·traught′ (-strôt′) ***adj.*** ⟦var. of prec.⟧ **1** mentally confused; distracted **2** driven mad; crazed

dis·tress (di stres′) ***vt.*** ⟦ult. < L *dis-*, apart + *stringere*, to stretch⟧ to cause misery or suffering to —***n.*** **1** pain, suffering, etc. **2** an affliction **3** a state of danger or trouble —**dis·tressed′** ***adj.***

dis·trib·ute (di strib′yo͞ot) ***vt.*** **-ut·ed**, **-ut·ing** ⟦< L *dis-*, apart + *tribuere*, allot⟧ **1** to give out in shares **2** to spread out **3** to classify **4** to put (things) in various distinct places —**dis′tri·bu′tion** ***n.***

dis·trib′u·tor ***n.*** one that distributes; specif., *a*) a dealer who distributes goods to consumers *b*) a device for distributing electric current to the spark plugs of a gasoline engine

dis·trict (dis′trikt) ***n.*** ⟦< L *dis-*, apart + *stringere*, to stretch⟧ **1** a division of a state, city, etc. made for a specific purpose **2** any region

district attorney the prosecuting attorney for the state or the federal government in a specified district

District of Columbia federal district of the U.S., on the Potomac: 61 sq. mi.; pop. 607,000; coextensive with the city of Washington: abbrev. *DC*

dis·trust (dis trust′) ***n.*** a lack of trust; doubt —***vt.*** to have no trust in; doubt —**dis·trust′ful** ***adj.***

dis·turb (di sturb′) ***vt.*** ⟦< L *dis-*, intens. + *turbare*, to disorder⟧ **1** to break up the quiet or settled order of **2** to make uneasy; upset **3** to interrupt —**dis·turb′er** ***n.***

dis·turb′ance ***n.*** **1** a disturbing or being disturbed **2** anything that disturbs **3** commotion; disorder

dis·u·nite (dis′yo͞o nīt′) ***vt.***, ***vi.*** **-nit′ed**, **-nit′ing** to divide or separate into parts, factions, etc. —**dis·u′ni·ty** ***n.***

dis·use′ (-yo͞os′) ***n.*** lack of use

ditch (dich) ***n.*** ⟦OE *dic*⟧ a long, narrow channel dug into the earth, as for drainage —***vt.*** **1** to make a ditch in **2** [Slang] to get rid of

dith·er (di*th*′ər) ***vi.*** ⟦ME *dideren*⟧ **1** to be nervously excited or confused **2** to be indecisive —***n.*** a nervously excited or confused state

dit·sy (dit′sē) ***adj.*** **-si·er**, **-si·est** ⟦? < DIZZY⟧ [Slang] silly, flighty, eccentric, etc.: also sp. **dit′zy**

dit·to (dit′ō) ***n.**, pl.* **-tos** ⟦It < L *dicere*, to say⟧ **1** the same (as above or before) **2** DITTO MARK

ditto mark a mark (") used in lists or tables to show that the item above is to be repeated

dit·ty (dit′ē) ***n.**, pl.* **-ties** ⟦< L *dicere*, to say⟧ a short, simple song

di·u·ret·ic (dī′yo͞o ret′ik) ***adj.*** ⟦< Gr *dia-*, through + *ourein*, urinate⟧ increasing the flow of urine —***n.*** a diuretic drug or substance

di·ur·nal (dī ur′nəl) ***adj.*** ⟦< L *dies*, day⟧ **1** daily **2** of the daytime —**di·ur′nal·ly** ***adv.***

div *abbrev.* **1** dividend **2** division

di·va (dē′və) ***n.**, pl.* **-vas** or **-ve** (-ve) ⟦It < L, goddess⟧ a leading woman singer

di·va·lent (dī′vā′lənt, dī vā′-) ***adj.*** *Chem.* having two valences or a valence of two

di·van (di van′, dī′van′) ***n.*** ⟦< Pers *dīwān*⟧ a large, low couch or sofa

dive (dīv) ***vi.*** **dived** or **dove**, **dived**, **div′ing** ⟦OE *dyfan*⟧ **1** to plunge headfirst into water **2** to submerge **3** to plunge suddenly into something **4** to make a steep descent, as an airplane —***n.*** **1** a diving **2** any sudden plunge **3** a sharp descent **4** [Inf.] a cheap, disreputable saloon, etc. —**div′er** ***n.***

di·verge (dī vurj′, di-) ***vi.*** **-verged′**, **-verg′ing** ⟦< L *dis-*, apart + *vergere*, to turn⟧ **1** to go or move in different directions; branch off **2** to differ, as in opinion —**di·ver′gence** ***n.*** —**di·ver′gent** ***adj.***

di·vers (dī′vərz) ***adj.*** ⟦see fol.⟧ various

di·verse (də vurs′, dī-) ***adj.*** ⟦< L *dis-*, apart + *vertere*, to turn⟧ **1** different **2** varied —**di·verse′ly** ***adv.***

di·ver·si·fy (də vur′sə fī′) ***vt.*** **-fied′**, **-fy′ing** **1** to make diverse; vary **2** to divide up (investments, etc.) among different companies, etc. —***vi.*** to expand product lines, etc. —**di·ver′si·fi·ca′tion** ***n.***

di·ver·sion (də vur′zhən, dī-) ***n.*** **1** a diverting or turning aside **2** distraction of attention **3** a pastime

di·ver′sion·ar′y ***adj.*** serving to divert or distract *[diversionary* tactics*]*

di·ver·si·ty (də vur′sə tē, dī-) ***n.**, pl.* **-ties** **1** difference **2** variety

di·vert (də vurt′, dī-) ***vt.*** ⟦see DIVERSE⟧ **1** to turn (a person or thing) aside from a course, etc. **2** to distract **3** to amuse

di·ver·tic·u·li·tis (dī′vər tik′yoo līt′is) ***n.*** ⟦< L *de-*, from + *vertere*, to turn + -ITIS⟧ inflammation of a sac (**di′ver·tic′u·lum**) opening out from a tubular organ or main cavity

di·vest (də vest′, dī-) ***vt.*** ⟦< L *dis-*, from + *vestire*, to dress⟧ **1** to strip *of* clothing, etc. **2** to deprive *of* rank, rights, etc. **3** to rid *of* something unwanted

di·vide (də vīd′) ***vt.*** **-vid′ed**, **-vid′ing** ⟦< L *dividere*⟧ **1** to separate into parts; sever **2** to classify **3** to make or keep separate **4** to apportion **5** to cause to disagree **6** *Math.* to separate into equal parts by a divisor **—*vi.*** **1** to be or become separate **2** to disagree **3** to share **4** *Math.* to do division **—*n.*** a boundary; specif., a ridge that divides two drainage areas **—di·vid′er *n.***

div·i·dend (div′ə dend′) ***n.*** **1** the number or quantity to be divided **2** *a)* a sum to be divided among stockholders, etc. *b)* a single share of this **3** a bonus

div·i·na·tion (div′ə nā′shən) ***n.*** ⟦see fol.⟧ **1** the practice of trying to foretell the future **2** a prophecy

di·vine (də vīn′) ***adj.*** ⟦< L *divus*, god⟧ **1** of, like, or from God or a god; holy **2** devoted to God; religious **3** [Inf.] very pleasing, etc. **—*n.*** a member of the clergy **—*vt.*** **-vined′**, **-vin′ing** **1** to prophesy **2** to guess **3** to find out by intuition **—di·vine′ly *adv.***

divining rod a forked stick believed to dip downward when held over an underground supply of water, etc.

di·vin·i·ty (də vin′ə tē) ***n.*** **1** a being divine **2** *pl.* **-ties** a god **3** theology **— the Divinity** God

di·vis·i·ble (də viz′ə bəl) ***adj.*** that can be divided, esp. without leaving a remainder **—di·vis′i·bil′i·ty *n.***

di·vi·sion (də vizh′ən) ***n.*** **1** a dividing or being divided **2** an apportioning **3** a difference of opinion **4** anything that divides **5** a segment, section, department, class, etc. **6** the process of finding how many times a number (the *divisor*) is contained in another (the *dividend*) **7** a major military unit

di·vi·sive (də vī′siv) ***adj.*** causing disagreement or dissension **—di·vi′sive·ly *adv.* —di·vi′sive·ness *n.***

di·vi·sor (də vī′zər) ***n.*** the number by which the dividend is divided

di·vorce (də vôrs′) ***n.*** ⟦< L *dis-*, apart + *vertere*, to turn⟧ **1** legal dissolution of a marriage **2** any complete separation **— *vt.*** **-vorced′**, **-vorc′ing** **1** to dissolve legally a marriage between **2** to dissolve the marriage with (one's spouse) **3** to separate **—di·vorce′ment *n.***

di·vor·cée or **di·vor·cee** (di vôr′sā′, -sē′) ***fem.n.*** ⟦Fr⟧ a divorced woman **—di·vor′cé′** (-sā′, -sē′) ***masc.n.***

div·ot (div′ət) ***n.*** ⟦Scot⟧ *Golf* a lump of turf dislodged in making a stroke

di·vulge (də vulj′) ***vt.*** **-vulged′**, **-vulg′ing** ⟦< L *dis-*, apart + *vulgare*, make public⟧ to make known; reveal

div·vy (div′ē) ***vt.**, **vi.*** **-vied**, **-vy·ing** [Slang] to share; divide (*up*)

Dix·ie (dik′sē) ⟦< *Dixie*, the minstrel song⟧ the Southern states of the U.S.

Dix′ie·land′ ***adj.*** in, of, or like a style of jazz with a ragtime tempo

DIY (dē′ī′wī′) ***n.*** DO-IT-YOURSELF

diz·zy (diz′ē) ***adj.*** **-zi·er**, **-zi·est** ⟦OE *dysig*, foolish⟧ **1** feeling giddy or unsteady **2** causing giddiness **3** confused **4** [Inf.] silly; harebrained **— diz′zi·ly *adv.* —diz′zi·ness *n.***

DJ (dē′jā′) *abbrev.* ***n.*** DISC JOCKEY

djel·la·ba or **djel·la·bah** (jə lä′bə) ***n.*** ⟦< Ar⟧ a long, loose outer garment worn in Arabic countries

Dji·bou·ti (ji boot′ē) country in E Africa: 8,958 sq. mi.; pop. 695,000

DMZ *abbrev.* demilitarized zone

DNA (dē′en′ā′) ***n.*** ⟦< *d(eoxyribo)n(ucleic) a(cid)*⟧ the basic chromosome material, containing and transmitting the hereditary pattern

Dne·pr (nē′pər) river in W Russia, Belarus, & Ukraine, flowing into the Black Sea

do[1] (doo) ***vt.*** **did**, **done**, **do′ing** ⟦OE *don*⟧ **1** to perform (an action, etc.) **2** to complete; finish **3** to cause *[it does* no *harm]* **4** to exert *[do* your *best]* **5** to deal with as is required *[do* the *ironing]* **6** to have as one's occupation; work at **7** to move at a speed of *[to do* 65 *mph]* **8** [Inf.] to serve (a jail term) **9** [Slang] to ingest *[to do drugs]* **—*vi.*** **1** to behave or perform *[do* as you *please]* **2** to be active *[up and doing]* **3** to get along; fare *[he is doing* well after *surgery]* **4** to be adequate *[casual dress will do]* **5** to take place *[anything doing tonight?]* **—*v.aux.*** **1** used to give emphasis *[do* stay a *while]* **2** used to ask a question *[did* you *go?]* **3** used as a substitute verb *[act as I do* (act)*]* **4** used in a negative construction *[do* not *go]* **—do in** **1** [Slang] to kill **2** [Inf.] to tire out **—do over** [Inf.] to redecorate **—do up** to wrap up **—do with** to make use of **—do without** to get along without **—have to do with** to be related to

do[2] (dō) ***n.*** ⟦It⟧ *Music* the first or last tone of the diatonic scale

DOA *abbrev.* dead on arrival

do·a·ble (doo′ə bəl) ***adj.*** that can be done

Do·ber·man (pin·scher) (dō′bər mən pin′chər) ⟦< Ger after L. *Dobermann*, 19th-c. breeder + *pinscher*, terrier⟧ a large dog with a short, dark coat

doc (däk) ***n.*** [Slang] doctor

do·cent (dō′sənt) ***n.*** ⟦< L *docere*, to teach⟧ a lecturer or tour guide, as at a museum

doc·ile (däs′əl) ***adj.*** ⟦see prec.⟧ easy to discipline; submissive **—do·cil·i·ty** (dō sil′ə tē, dä-) ***n.***

dock[1] (däk) ***n.*** ⟦< It *doccia*, canal⟧ **1** an excavated basin for receiving ships **2** a wharf; pier **3** the water between two piers **4** a platform for loading and unloading trucks, etc. **—*vt.*, *vi.*** to bring or come to or into a dock: said of a ship

dock[2] (däk) ***n.*** ⟦< Fl *dok*, a cage⟧ the

place where the accused stands or sits in court

dock[3] (däk) ***n.*** ⟦OE *docce*⟧ a tall, coarse weed of the buckwheat family

dock[4] (däk) ***vt.*** ⟦ME *dok*, tail⟧ **1** to cut off the end of (a tail, etc.); bob **2** to deduct from (wages, etc.)

dock·et (däk′it) ***n.*** ⟦< ?⟧ **1** a list of cases to be tried by a law court **2** an agenda —***vt.*** to enter in a docket

dock′yard′ ***n.*** SHIPYARD

doc·tor (däk′tər) ***n.*** ⟦< L, teacher⟧ **1** one who holds a doctorate **2** a physician or surgeon **3** one licensed to practice any of the healing arts —***vt.*** [Inf.] **1** to try to heal **2** to tamper with

doc′tor·ate (-it) ***n.*** the highest degree awarded by universities —**doc′tor·al** ***adj.***

Doctor of Philosophy the highest doctorate awarded for original research

doc·tri·naire (däk′tri ner′) ***adj.*** ⟦Fr⟧ adhering to a doctrine dogmatically —**doc′tri·nair′ism′** ***n.***

doc·trine (däk′trin) ***n.*** ⟦see DOCTOR⟧ something taught, esp. as the principles of a religion, political party, etc.; tenet or tenets; dogma —**doc′tri·nal** (-tri nəl) ***adj.***

doc·u·dra·ma (däk′yo͞o drä′mə) ***n.*** a TV dramatization of real events

doc·u·ment (däk′yo͞o mənt, -yə-; *for v.*, -ment′) ***n.*** ⟦< L *documentum*, proof⟧ anything printed, written, etc. that contains information or is relied upon to record or prove something —***vt.*** to provide with or support by documents

doc′u·men′ta·ry (-ment′ə rē) ***adj.*** **1** of or supported by documents **2** depicting news events, social conditions, etc. in nonfictional but dramatic form —***n.***, *pl.* **-ries** a documentary film, etc.

doc′u·men·ta′tion (-mən tā′shən, -men-) ***n.*** **1** the supplying of documents **2** the documents thus supplied **3** instructions for using computer hardware or software

dod·der (däd′ər) ***vi.*** ⟦ME *daderen*⟧ **1** to shake or tremble, as from old age **2** to totter —**dod′der·ing** ***adj.***

dodge (däj) ***vi.***, ***vt.*** **dodged**, **dodg′ing** ⟦< ?⟧ **1** to move quickly aside, or avoid by so moving **2** to use tricks or evasions, or evade by so doing —***n.*** **1** a dodging **2** a trick used in evading or cheating —**dodg′er** ***n.***

do·do (dō′dō) ***n.***, *pl.* **-dos** or **-does** ⟦Port *doudo*, lit., stupid⟧ **1** a large, flightless bird, now extinct **2** [Slang] a stupid person

doe (dō) ***n.*** ⟦OE *da*⟧ the female deer, antelope, rabbit, etc.

do·er (do͞o′ər) ***n.*** **1** one who does something **2** one who gets things done

does (duz) ***vt.***, ***vi.*** *3d pers. sing., pres. indic., of* DO[1]

doe′skin′ ***n.*** **1** leather from the skin of a female deer **2** a soft woolen cloth

doff (däf, dôf) ***vt.*** ⟦see DO[1] & OFF⟧ to take off (one's hat, clothes, etc.)

dog (dôg) ***n.*** ⟦OE *docga*⟧ **1** any of various canines, esp. one of a domesticated breed kept as a pet, for hunting, etc. **2** a mean, contemptible fellow **3** [*pl.*] [Slang] feet **4** [Slang] an unattractive person or unsatisfactory thing **5** *Mech.* a device for holding or grappling —***vt.*** **dogged**, **dog′ging** to follow or hunt doggedly —**go to the dogs** [Inf.] to deteriorate

dog days the hot, uncomfortable days in July and August

dog′-ear′ ***n.*** a turned-down corner of a page —**dog′-eared′** ***adj.***

dog′fight′ ***n.*** a violent fight; specif., combat between fighter planes

dog′fish′ ***n.***, *pl.* **-fish′** or (for different species) **-fish′es** any of various small sharks

dog·ged (dôg′id) ***adj.*** persistent; stubborn —**dog′ged·ly** ***adv.***

dog·ger·el (dôg′ər əl) ***n.*** ⟦ME *dogerel*⟧ trivial poetry with a monotonous rhythm

dog·gie bag (dôg′ē) a bag supplied by a restaurant for carrying leftovers, as for one's dog

dog′gone′ ***interj.*** damn! darn! —***adj.*** [Inf.] damned

dog′house′ ***n.*** a structure for sheltering a dog —**in the doghouse** [Slang] in disfavor

do·gie (dō′gē) ***n.*** ⟦< ?⟧ [West] a stray calf

dog·ma (dôg′mə) ***n.*** ⟦< Gr, opinion⟧ a doctrine; tenet, esp. a theological doctrine strictly adhered to

dog·mat′ic (-mat′ik) ***adj.*** **1** of or like dogma **2** asserted without proof **3** stating opinion positively or arrogantly —**dog·mat′i·cal·ly** ***adv.***

dog′ma·tism′ (-mə tiz′əm) ***n.*** dogmatic assertion of opinion —**dog′ma·tist** ***n.***

do′-good′er ***n.*** [Inf.] an idealistic, but impractical person who seeks to correct social ills

dog′-tired′ ***adj.*** very tired; exhausted

dog′trot′ ***n.*** a slow, easy trot

dog′wood′ ***n.*** a small, flowering tree of the E U.S.

doi·ly (doi′lē) ***n.***, *pl.* **-lies** ⟦after a 17th-c. London draper⟧ a small mat, as of lace, put under a vase, etc. as a decoration or to protect a surface

do·ings (do͞o′iŋz) ***pl.n.*** actions or events

do′-it-your·self′ ***n.*** the practice of making or repairing things oneself, instead of hiring another —**do′-it-your·self′er** ***n.***

Dol·by (dōl′bē) ⟦after R. *Dolby*, U.S. recording engineer⟧ *trademark for* an electronic system used to reduce unwanted noise

dol·drums (dōl′drəmz, däl′-) ***pl.n.*** ⟦< ? DULL⟧ **1** *a*) low spirits *b*) sluggishness **2** equatorial ocean regions having little wind

dole (dōl) ***n.*** ⟦OE *dal*, a share⟧ **1** money or food given in charity **2** money paid by a government to the unemployed —***vt.*** **doled**, **dol′ing** to give (*out*) sparingly or as a dole

dole′ful (-fəl) ***adj.*** ⟦< L *dolere*, suffer⟧ sad; mournful —**dole′ful·ly** ***adv.***

doll (däl) ***n.*** ⟦< nickname for *Dorothy*⟧ **1** a child's toy made to resemble a human being **2** [Slang] any attractive or lovable person —*vt., vi.* [Inf.] to dress stylishly or showily: with *up*

dol·lar (däl′ər) ***n.*** ⟦< Ger *thaler*, a coin⟧ **1** the monetary unit of the U.S., equal to 100 cents **2** the monetary unit of various other countries, as of Canada **3** a piece of money worth one dollar

dol·lop (däl′əp) ***n.*** ⟦< ?⟧ **1** a soft mass **2** a quantity, often a small one

dol·ly (däl′ē) ***n.***, *pl.* **-lies** **1** a doll: child's word **2** a low, flat, wheeled frame for moving heavy objects

dol·men (dōl′mən, däl′-) ***n.*** ⟦Fr⟧ a prehistoric monument consisting of a large, flat stone laid across upright stones

do·lo·mite (dō′lə mīt′, däl′ə-) ***n.*** ⟦after D. *Dolomieu*, 18th-c. Fr geologist⟧ **1** a mineral used in making cement, etc. **2** a sedimentary rock used as a building stone

do·lor·ous (dō′lər əs, däl′ər-) ***adj.*** ⟦< L *dolere*, suffer⟧ sorrowful; sad —**do′lor·ous·ly** ***adv.***

dol·phin (däl′fin, dôl′-) ***n.*** ⟦< Gr *delphis*⟧ a highly intelligent toothed whale with a beaklike snout

dolt (dōlt) ***n.*** ⟦prob. < ME *dolte*⟧ a stupid person —**dolt′ish** ***adj.***

-dom (dəm) ⟦OE *dom*, state⟧ *suffix* **1** rank or domain of *[kingdom]* **2** fact or state of being *[martyrdom]* **3** all who are *[officialdom]*

do·main (dō mān′) ***n.*** ⟦< L *dominus*, a lord⟧ **1** territory under one government or ruler **2** field of activity or influence

dome (dōm) ***n.*** ⟦< Gr *dōma*, housetop⟧ **1** a rounded roof or ceiling **2** any dome-shaped structure or object; specif., a sports stadium covered with a dome

do·mes·tic (dō mes′tik, də-) ***adj.*** ⟦< L *domus*, house⟧ **1** of the home or family **2** of or made in one's country **3** tame: said of animals **4** enjoying family life —***n.*** a maid, cook, etc. in the home —**do·mes′ti·cal·ly** ***adv.***

do·mes′ti·cate′ (-ti kāt′) ***vt.*** **-cat′ed, -cat′ing** **1** to accustom to home life **2** to tame or cultivate for human use —**do·mes′ti·ca′tion** ***n.***

do·mes·tic·i·ty (dō′mes tis′ə tē) ***n.*** home life or devotion to it

dom·i·cile (däm′ə sīl′, -sil; *also* dō′mə-) ***n.*** ⟦< L *domus*, home⟧ a home; residence —***vt.*** **-ciled′, -cil′ing** to establish in a domicile

dom·i·nant (däm′ə nənt) ***adj.*** dominating; ruling; prevailing —**dom′i·nance** ***n.*** —**dom′i·nant·ly** ***adv.***

dom′i·nate′ (-nāt′) ***vt., vi.*** **-nat′ed, -nat′ing** ⟦< L *dominus*, a master⟧ **1** to rule or control by superior power **2** to rise above (the surroundings) —**dom′i·na′tion** ***n.***

dom·i·neer (däm′ə nir′) ***vi., vt.*** ⟦< Du: see prec.⟧ to rule (*over*) in a harsh or arrogant way; tyrannize

dom′i·neer′ing ***adj.*** overbearing

Do·min·i·can Republic (dō min′i kən, də-) country in the E part of Hispaniola, in the West Indies: 18,700 sq. mi.; pop. 5,648,000 —**Do·min′i·can** ***adj., n.***

do·min·ion (də min′yən) ***n.*** ⟦see DOMINATE⟧ **1** rule or power to rule **2** a governed territory or country **3** [**D-**] [Historical] a self-governing nation of the Commonwealth

dom·i·no (däm′ə nō′) ***n.***, *pl.* **-noes′** or **-nos′** ⟦Fr & It⟧ **1** a hooded cloak and a mask, worn at masquerades **2** a small mask that covers the area around the eyes **3** *a)* a small, oblong tile marked with dots *b)* [*pl., with sing. v.*] a game played with such tiles

don[1] (dän) ***n.*** ⟦Sp < L *dominus*, master⟧ **1** [**D-**] Sir; Mr.: a Spanish title of respect **2** a Spanish gentleman **3** [Chiefly Brit.] a teacher at a British university **4** a Mafia leader

don[2] (dän) ***vt.*** **donned, don′ning** ⟦contr. of *do on*⟧ to put on (clothes)

Don (dän) river in SC European Russia, flowing into the Black Sea

Do·ña (dô′nyä) ***n.*** ⟦Sp⟧ Lady; Madam: a Spanish title of respect

do·nate (dō′nāt′) ***vt., vi.*** **-nat′ed, -nat′ing** ⟦< L *donum*, gift⟧ to give or contribute —**do·na′tion** ***n.*** —**do′nat′or** (-ər) ***n.***

done (dun) ***vt., vi.*** *pp. of* DO[1] —***adj.*** **1** completed **2** cooked —**done** (**for**) [Inf.] dead, ruined, etc.

Don Juan (dän′ wän′) *Sp. Legend* a dissolute nobleman and seducer of women

don·key (däŋ′kē, dôŋ′-, duŋ′-) ***n.***, *pl.* **-keys** ⟦< ?⟧ **1** a domesticated ass **2** a stupid or foolish person

don·ny·brook (dän′ē brook′) ***n.*** ⟦after a fair formerly held near Dublin⟧ [Inf.] a rowdy fight or free-for-all

do·nor (dō′nər, -nôr′) ***n.*** one who donates

Don Qui·xo·te (dän′kē hōt′ē, dän′ kwik′sət) **1** a satirical novel by Cervantes **2** its chivalrous but unrealistic hero

don't (dōnt) *contr.* do not

do·nut (dō′nut′) ***n.*** *inf. sp. of* DOUGHNUT

doo·dle (do͞od′'l) ***vi.*** **-dled, -dling** ⟦Ger *dudeln*, to trifle⟧ to scribble aimlessly —***n.*** a mark made in doodling —**doo′dler** ***n.***

doo-doo (do͞o′do͞o′) ***n.*** **1** [Inf.] excrement **2** [Slang] trouble

doom (do͞om) ***n.*** ⟦OE *dom*⟧ **1** a judgment; sentence **2** fate **3** ruin or death —***vt.*** **1** to pass judgment on; condemn **2** to destine to a tragic fate

dooms′day′ ***n.*** Judgment Day

doom′y ***adj.*** filled with a sense of doom or disaster

door (dôr) ***n.*** ⟦OE *duru*⟧ **1** a movable structure for opening or closing an entrance **2** a doorway **3** a means of access —**out of doors** outdoors

door′bell′ ***n.*** a bell, etc. at the entrance of a building or room, sounded to alert the occupants of a visitor

door′man′ (-man′, -mən) ***n.***, *pl.* **-men′** (-men′, -mən) one whose work is opening the door of a building, hailing taxicabs, etc.

door′mat′ ***n.*** a mat to wipe the shoes on before entering a house, etc.

door′step′ ***n.*** a step that leads from an outer door to a path, lawn, etc.

door′-to-door′ ***adj., adv.*** from one home to the next, calling on each in turn

door′way′ ***n.*** **1** an opening in a wall that can be closed by a door **2** any means of access

door′yard′ ***n.*** a yard onto which a door of a house opens

do·pa (dō′pə) ***n.*** ⟦< chemical name⟧ an amino acid that is converted by an enzyme in the blood into certain biological chemicals: one isomer (*L-dopa*) is used in treating Parkinson's disease

dope (dōp) ***n.*** ⟦Du *doop,* sauce⟧ **1** any thick liquid used as a lubricant, varnish, filler, etc. **2** [Inf.] a drug or narcotic **3** [Inf.] a stupid person **4** [Slang] information —***vt.*** **doped, dop′ing** to drug

dop′er ***n.*** [Slang] a drug addict

dop·ey or **dop·y** (dō′pē) ***adj.*** **-i·er, -i·est** [Inf.] **1** lethargic **2** stupid

Dor·ic (dôr′ik) ***adj.*** designating or of a classical style of architecture marked by fluted columns with plain capitals

dorm (dôrm) ***n.*** [Inf.] DORMITORY

dor·mant (dôr′mənt) ***adj.*** ⟦< L *dormire,* to sleep⟧ **1** inactive **2** *Biol.* in a resting or torpid state —**dor′man·cy** ***n.***

DORMER

dor·mer (dôr′mər) ***n.*** ⟦see prec.⟧ **1** a window set upright in a structure projecting from a sloping roof: also **dormer window** **2** such a structure

dor·mi·to·ry (dôr′mə tôr′ē) ***n.,*** *pl.* **-ries** ⟦see DORMANT⟧ **1** a room with beds for a number of people **2** a building with rooms for many people to sleep and live in, as at a college

dor·mouse (dôr′mous′) ***n.,*** *pl.* **-mice′** (-mīs′) ⟦ME *dormous*⟧ a small, furry-tailed Old World rodent

dor·sal (dôr′səl) ***adj.*** ⟦< L *dorsum,* the back⟧ of, on, or near the back

do·ry (dôr′ē) ***n.,*** *pl.* **-ries** ⟦< ? AmInd (Central America) *dori,* dugout⟧ a flat-bottomed fishing boat with high sides

dose (dōs) ***n.*** ⟦< Gr *dosis,* a giving⟧ an amount of a medicine to be taken at one time —***vt.*** **dosed, dos′ing** to give doses to —**dos′age** ***n.***

do·sim·e·ter (dō sim′ət ər) ***n.*** a device for measuring exposure to ionizing radiation

dos·si·er (dä′sē ā′) ***n.*** ⟦Fr⟧ a collection of documents about some person or matter

dost (dust) ***vt., vi.*** *archaic 2d pers. sing., pres. indic., of* DO[1]: used with *thou*

Dos·to·ev·ski or **Dos·to·yev·sky** (dôs′ tô yef′skē), **Feo·dor** (fyô′dôr) 1821-81; Russ. novelist

dot (dät) ***n.*** ⟦OE *dott,* head of boil⟧ **1** a tiny speck or mark **2** a small, round spot —***vt.*** **dot′ted, dot′ting** to mark with or as with a dot or dots —**on the dot** [Inf.] at the exact time

dot·age (dōt′ij) ***n.*** ⟦ME < *doten,* DOTE⟧ childish state due to old age

dot′ard (-ərd) ***n.*** one in his or her dotage

dot.com (dät′käm′) ***adj.*** [Inf.] designating or of a company doing business mostly on the Web: also **dot-com**

dote (dōt) ***vi.*** **dot′ed, dot′ing** ⟦ME *doten*⟧ to be excessively fond: with *on* or *upon*

doth (duth) ***vt., vi.*** *archaic 3d pers. sing., pres. indic., of* DO[1]

dot·ing (dōt′iŋ) ***adj.*** foolishly or excessively fond —**dot′ing·ly** ***adv.***

dot′-ma′trix ***adj.*** of or by printing in which characters are formed of closely spaced dots

Dou·ay Bible (do͞o ā′) an English version of the Bible for Roman Catholics: after Douai, France, where the Old Testament was published

dou·ble (dub′əl) ***adj.*** ⟦< L *duplus*⟧ **1** twofold **2** having two layers **3** paired or repeated *[a double consonant]* **4** being of two kinds *[a double standard]* **5** twice as much, as many, etc. **6** made for two —***adv.*** **1** twofold or twice **2** two together —***n.*** **1** anything twice as much, as many, etc. as normal **2** a duplicate; counterpart **3** a fold **4** [*pl.*] a game of tennis, etc. with two players on each side **5** *Baseball* a hit on which the batter reaches second base **6** *Bridge* the doubling of an opponent's bid —***vt.*** **-bled, -bling** **1** to make twice as much or as many **2** to fold **3** to repeat or duplicate **4** *Bridge* to increase the point value or penalty of (an opponent's bid) —***vi.*** **1** to become double **2** to turn sharply backward **3** to serve as a double **4** to serve an additional purpose **5** *Baseball* to hit a double —**double back** to turn back in the direction from which one came —**double up** **1** to clench (one's fist) **2** to bend over, as in pain **3** to share a room, etc. with someone —**on the double** [Inf.] quickly

double agent a spy employed by two rival espionage organizations

dou′ble-bar′reled ***adj.*** **1** having two barrels, as a kind of shotgun **2** having a double purpose or meaning

double bass (bās) the largest, deepest-toned instrument of the violin family

dou′ble-blind′ ***adj.*** designating or of a test of the effects of a drug, treatment, etc. in which neither the subjects nor the researchers know who is receiving the drug, treatment, etc.

double boiler a cooking utensil in which one pan, for food, fits over another, for boiling water

dou′ble-breast′ed ***adj.*** overlapping across the breast, as a coat

dou′ble-cross′ ***vt.*** [Inf.] to betray —**dou′ble-cross′er** ***n.***

double date [Inf.] a social engagement

shared by two couples —**dou'ble-date'**, **-dat'ed**, **-dat'ing**, ***vi.***, ***vt.***

dou'ble-deal'ing ***n.*** duplicity

dou'ble-deck'er ***n.*** **1** any structure or vehicle with an upper deck **2** [Inf.] a sandwich with two layers of filling and three slices of bread

dou'ble-dig'it ***adj.*** amounting to ten percent or more *[double-digit inflation]*

double dipping an unethical receiving of pay from two or more sources

dou·ble-en·ten·dre (dub'əl än tän'drə, dōō'blôn tôn'drə) ***n.*** ⟦< Fr⟧ a term with two meanings, esp. when one is risqué

dou'ble-head'er ***n.*** two games played in succession on the same day

dou'ble-joint'ed ***adj.*** having joints that permit limbs, fingers, etc. to bend at other than the usual angles

dou'ble-knit' ***adj.*** knit with a double stitch that makes the fabric extra thick

double play *Baseball* a play in which two players are put out

dou'ble-reed' ***adj.*** designating or of a woodwind instrument, as the oboe, having two reeds separated by a narrow opening

double standard a system, code, etc. applied unequally; specif., a moral code stricter for women than for men

dou·blet (dub'lit) ***n.*** ⟦< OFr *double*, orig., something folded⟧ **1** a man's closefitting jacket of the 14th-16th c. **2** a pair, or one of a pair

double take a delayed reaction, as a second glance, following unthinking acceptance

double talk **1** ambiguous and deceptive talk **2** meaningless syllables made to sound like talk

dou·bloon (də blōōn') ***n.*** ⟦< Fr < Sp < L *duplus*, double⟧ an obsolete Spanish gold coin

dou·bly (dub'lē) ***adv.*** **1** twice **2** two at a time

doubt (dout) ***vi.*** ⟦< L *dubius*, uncertain⟧ to be uncertain or undecided —***vt.*** **1** to be uncertain about **2** to tend to disbelieve —***n.*** **1** *a)* a wavering of opinion or belief *b)* lack of trust **2** a condition of uncertainty —**beyond** (or **without**) **doubt** certainly —**no doubt** **1** certainly **2** probably —**doubt'er** ***n.*** —**doubt'ing·ly** ***adv.***

doubt'ful ***adj.*** **1** uncertain **2** causing doubt or suspicion **3** feeling doubt —**doubt'ful·ly** ***adv.***

doubt'less ***adv.*** **1** without doubt; certainly **2** probably —**doubt'less·ly** ***adv.***

douche (dōōsh) ***n.*** ⟦Fr < It *doccia*⟧ **1** a jet of liquid applied externally or internally to the body **2** a device for douching —***vt.***, ***vi.*** **douched**, **douch'ing** to apply a douche (to)

dough (dō) ***n.*** ⟦OE *dag*⟧ **1** a mixture of flour, liquid, etc. worked into a soft mass for baking **2** [Slang] money

dough'nut' ***n.*** a small, usually ring-shaped cake, fried in deep fat

dough·ty (dout'ē) ***adj.*** **-ti·er**, **-ti·est** ⟦OE *dohtig*⟧ [Now Rare] valiant; brave

dough·y (dō'ē) ***adj.*** **-i·er**, **-i·est** of or like dough; soft, pasty, etc.

Doug·las fir (dug'ləs) ⟦after D. *Douglas*, 19th-c. Scot botanist in U.S.⟧ a giant North American evergreen tree valued for its wood

dour (dŏŏr, dour) ***adj.*** ⟦< L *durus*, hard⟧ **1** [Scot.] stern; severe **2** sullen; gloomy

douse (dous) ***vt.*** **doused**, **dous'ing** ⟦< ?⟧ **1** to thrust suddenly into liquid **2** to drench **3** [Inf.] to put out (a light or fire) quickly

dove[1] (duv) ***n.*** ⟦ME *douve*⟧ **1** any of the smaller species of pigeon: often used as a symbol of peace **2** an advocate of measures which avoid or end wars

dove[2] (dōv) ***vi.*** *alt. pt. of* DIVE

dove'cote' ***n.*** a cote with compartments for nesting pigeons

Do·ver (dō'vər) capital of Delaware: pop. 28,000

dove·tail (duv'tāl') ***n.*** a projecting part that fits into a corresponding cut-out space to form a joint —***vt.*** to join, piece together, or fasten, as with dovetails —***vi.*** to fit together logically or closely

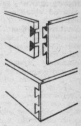

DOVETAIL

dow·a·ger (dou'ə jər) ***n.*** ⟦< L *dotare*, to endow⟧ **1** a widow with a title or property derived from her dead husband **2** an elderly, wealthy woman

dow·dy (dou'dē) ***adj.*** **-di·er**, **-di·est** ⟦< ME *doude*, plain woman⟧ not neat or smart in dress —**dow'di·ness** ***n.***

dow·el (dou'əl) ***n.*** ⟦ME *doule*⟧ a peg of wood, etc., usually fitted into corresponding holes in two pieces to fasten them together —***vt.*** **-eled** or **-elled**, **-el·ing** or **-el·ling** to fasten with dowels

dow·er (dou'ər) ***n.*** ⟦< L *dare*, give⟧ that part of a man's property which his widow inherits for life

down[1] (doun) ***adv.*** ⟦OE *adune*, from the hill⟧ **1** to, in, or on a lower place or level **2** in or to a low or lower condition, amount, etc. **3** southward *[down to Mexico]* **4** from an earlier to a later period **5** out of one's hands *[put it down]* **6** in a serious manner *[get down to work]* **7** completely *[loaded down]* **8** when purchased *[$5 down and $5 a week]* **9** in writing *[take down notes]* —***adj.*** **1** descending **2** in a lower place **3** gone, brought, etc. down **4** dejected; discouraged **5** ill **6** finished *[four down, six to go]* **7** inoperative *[the computer is down]* —***prep.*** down toward, along, through, into, or upon —***vt.*** **1** to put or throw down **2** to swallow quickly —***n.*** **1** a misfortune *[ups and downs]* **2** *Football* one of a series of plays in which a team tries to advance the ball —**down and out** penniless, ill, etc. —**down on** [Inf.] angry or annoyed with —**down with!** do away with!

down[2] (doun) ***n.*** ⟦< ON *dūnn*⟧ **1** soft,

fine feathers **2** soft, fine hair

down[3] (doun) ***n.*** ⟦OE *dun*, hill⟧ an expanse of open, high, grassy land: *usually used in pl.*

down'-and-dirt'y ***adj.*** [Slang] **1** vulgar; coarse **2** unscrupulous **3** fiercely competitive

down'beat' ***n.*** *Music* the first beat of each measure

down'cast' ***adj.*** **1** directed downward **2** unhappy; dejected

Down East [*also* **d- e-**] [Inf.] in or into New England, esp. Maine

down'er ***n.*** [Slang] any depressant or sedative

down'fall' ***n.*** **1** a sudden fall, as from power **2** the cause of this

down'grade' ***n.*** a downward slope —***vt.*** **-grad'ed, -grad'ing** **1** to demote **2** to belittle

down'heart'ed ***adj.*** discouraged

down'hill' ***adv.*** toward the bottom of a hill —***adj.*** **1** going downward **2** without difficulty

Down·ing Street (doun'iŋ) street in London, location of some of the principal government offices of the United Kingdom

down'load' ***vt.***, ***vi.*** to transfer (information) as from a network or main computer to another computer

down payment a partial payment at the time of purchase

down'play' ***vt.*** to play down; minimize

down'pour' ***n.*** a heavy rain

down'right' ***adv.*** utterly —***adj.*** **1** absolute; utter **2** plain; frank

down'scale' ***adj.*** of or for people who are unstylish, not affluent, etc. —***vt.***, ***vi.*** **-scaled', -scal'ing** to make smaller, less, cheaper, etc.

down'size' ***vt.***, ***vi.*** **-sized', -siz'ing** to make or become smaller, as by eliminating employees

down'stage' ***adj.***, ***adv.*** of or toward the front of the stage

down'stairs' ***adv.*** **1** down the stairs **2** on or to a lower floor —***adj.*** on a lower floor —***n.*** a lower floor

down'state' ***adj.***, ***adv.*** in, to, or from the southerly part of a U.S. state

down'stream' ***adv.***, ***adj.*** in the direction of the current of a stream

down'swing' ***n.*** **1** a downward swing, as of a golf club **2** a downward trend: also **down'turn'**

Down (or **Down's**) **syndrome** ⟦after J. *Down*, 19th-c. Brit physician⟧ a congenital condition characterized by mental deficiency, a broad face, etc.

down'time' ***n.*** the time a machine, factory, etc. is not working or functioning

down'-to-earth' ***adj.*** **1** realistic or practical **2** without affectation

down'town' ***adj.***, ***adv.*** in or toward the main business section of a city —***n.*** the downtown section of a city

down'trod'den ***adj.*** oppressed

down'ward (-wərd) ***adv.***, ***adj.*** toward a lower place, position, state, etc.: also **down'wards** ***adv.***

down'y ***adj.*** **-i·er, -i·est** **1** covered with soft, fine feathers or hair **2** soft and fluffy, like down

dow·ry (dou'rē) ***n.***, *pl.* **-ries** ⟦see DOWER⟧ property a woman brings to her husband at marriage

dowse (douz) ***vi.*** **dowsed, dows'ing** ⟦< ?⟧ to use a divining rod —**dows'er** ***n.***

dox·ol·o·gy (däks äl'ə jē) ***n.***, *pl.* **-gies** ⟦< Gr *doxa*, praise + *-logia*, -LOGY⟧ a hymn of praise to God

doz *abbrev.* dozen(s)

doze (dōz) ***vi.*** **dozed, doz'ing** ⟦prob. < Scand⟧ to sleep lightly; nap —***n.*** a light sleep —**doz'er** ***n.***

doz·en (duz'ən) ***n.***, *pl.* **-ens** or **-en** ⟦< L *duo*, two + *decem*, ten⟧ a set of twelve —**doz'enth** ***adj.***

dpt *abbrev.* **1** department **2** deponent

Dr or **Dr.** *abbrev.* **1** Doctor **2** Drive

drab (drab) ***n.*** ⟦< VL *drappus*, cloth⟧ a dull yellowish brown —***adj.*** **drab'ber, drab'best** **1** dull yellowish-brown **2** dull; dreary —**drab'ness** ***n.***

drach·ma (drak'mə) ***n.*** ⟦< Gr *drachmē*⟧ **1** an ancient Greek coin **2** the former monetary unit of modern Greece, superseded in 2002 by the EURO

Drac·u·la (drak'yə lə) ***n.*** the title character in a novel (1897): a Romanian vampire and count

draft (draft) ***n.*** ⟦OE *dragan*, to draw⟧ **1** a drawing or pulling, as of a vehicle or load **2** *a*) a drawing in of a fish net *b*) the amount of fish caught in one draw **3** *a*) a drinking or the amount taken at one drink *b*) [Inf.] a portion of beer, etc. drawn from a cask **4** an inhalation **5** a preliminary or tentative piece of writing **6** a plan or drawing of a work to be done **7** a current of air **8** a device for regulating the current of air in a heating system **9** a written order for payment of money; check **10** *a*) the choosing or taking of persons, esp. for compulsory military service *b*) those so taken **11** the depth of water that a ship needs in order to float —***vt.*** **1** to take, as for military service, by drawing from a group **2** to make a sketch of or plans for —***adj.*** **1** used for pulling loads **2** drawn from a cask *[draft* beer*]* —**draft'er** ***n.***

draft·ee (draf tē') ***n.*** a person drafted, esp. for military service

drafts·man (drafts'mən) ***n.***, *pl.* **-men** (-mən) **1** one who draws plans, as of machinery **2** an artist skillful in drawing —**drafts'man·ship'** ***n.***

draft'y ***adj.*** **-i·er, -i·est** open to drafts of air

drag (drag) ***vt.***, ***vi.*** **dragged, drag'ging** ⟦see DRAW⟧ **1** to pull or be pulled with effort, esp. along the ground **2** to search (a lake bottom, etc.) with a dragnet or the like **3** to draw (something) out over a period of time; move or pass too slowly: often with *on* or *out* —***n.*** **1** a dragging **2** a dragnet, grapnel, etc. **3** anything that hinders **4** [Slang] influence **5** [Slang] clothing of the opposite sex, esp. as worn by a male homosexual **6** [Slang] a puff of a cigarette, etc. **7** [Slang] street *[*the main *drag]* **8** [Slang] a dull person, situation, etc.

drag'gy (-ē) ***adj.*** **-gi·er, -gi·est** dragging; slow-moving, dull, etc.

drag'net' ***n.*** **1** a net dragged along a lake bottom, etc., as for catching fish **2** an organized system or network for catching criminals, etc.

drag·on (drag'ən) ***n.*** ⟦< Gr *drakōn*⟧ a mythical monster, usually shown as a large, winged reptile breathing out fire

drag'on·fly' ***n.***, *pl.* **-flies'** a large, long-bodied insect with transparent, net-veined wings

dra·goon (drə go͞on') ***n.*** ⟦< Fr *dragon*, DRAGON⟧ a heavily armed cavalryman —***vt.*** to force *into* doing something; coerce

drag race a race between cars accelerating from a standstill on a short, straight course (**drag strip**) —**drag'-race', -raced', -rac'ing,** ***vi.***

drain (drān) ***vt.*** ⟦OE *dryge*, dry⟧ **1** to draw off (liquid) gradually **2** to draw liquid from gradually **3** to drink all the liquid from (a cup, etc.) **4** to exhaust (strength, resources, etc.) gradually —***vi.*** **1** to flow off or trickle through gradually **2** to become dry by draining **3** to disappear gradually; fade —***n.*** **1** a channel or pipe for draining **2** a draining **3** that which gradually exhausts strength, etc. —**drain'er** ***n.***

drain'age ***n.*** **1** a draining **2** a system of drains **3** that which is drained off **4** an area drained

drain'pipe' ***n.*** a pipe used to carry off water, sewage, etc.

drake (drāk) ***n.*** ⟦ME⟧ a male duck

dram (dram) ***n.*** ⟦< Gr *drachmē*, handful⟧ **1** a unit of apothecaries' weight equal to 3.89 grams **2** a unit of avoirdupois weight equal to 1.77 grams **3** a small drink of alcoholic liquor

dra·ma (drä'mə, dram'ə) ***n.*** ⟦< Gr⟧ **1** a literary composition to be performed by actors; play, esp. one that is not a comedy **2** the art of writing, acting, or producing plays **3** a series of events suggestive of those of a play **4** dramatic quality

Dram·a·mine (dram'ə mēn') *trademark for* a drug to relieve motion sickness

dra·mat·ic (drə mat'ik) ***adj.*** **1** of drama **2** like a play **3** vivid, striking, etc. —**dra·mat'i·cal·ly** ***adv.***

dra·mat'ics ***pl.n.*** **1** [*usually with sing. v.*] the performing or producing of plays **2** exaggerated emotionalism

dram·a·tist (dram'ə tist, drä'mə-) ***n.*** a playwright

dram'a·tize' (-tīz') ***vt.*** **-tized', -tiz'ing** **1** to make into a drama **2** to regard or show in a dramatic manner —**dram'a·ti·za'tion** ***n.***

drank (draŋk) ***vt.***, ***vi.*** *pt. of* DRINK

drape (drāp) ***vt.*** **draped, drap'ing** ⟦< VL *drappus*, cloth⟧ **1** to cover or hang as with cloth in loose folds **2** to arrange (a garment, etc.) in folds or hangings —***n.*** **1** cloth hanging in loose folds **2** a heavy curtain hanging in loose folds

drap·er (drā'pər) ***n.*** [Brit.] a dealer in cloth and dry goods

drap'er·y ***n.***, *pl.* **-er·ies** **1** [Brit.] DRY GOODS **2** hangings or clothing arranged in loose folds **3** [*pl.*] curtains of heavy material

dras·tic (dras'tik) ***adj.*** ⟦Gr *drastikos*, active⟧ having a strong effect; extreme —**dras'ti·cal·ly** ***adv.***

draught (draft) ***n.***, ***vt.***, ***adj.*** *now chiefly Brit. sp. of* DRAFT

draughts (drafts) ***n.*** [Brit.] the game of checkers

draw (drô) ***vt.*** **drew, drawn, draw'ing** ⟦OE *dragan*⟧ **1** to make move toward one; pull **2** to pull up, down, back, in, or out **3** to need (a specified depth of water) to float in: said of a ship **4** to attract **5** to breathe in **6** to elicit (a reply, etc.) **7** to bring on; provoke **8** to receive [*to draw a salary*] **9** to withdraw (money) held in an account **10** to write (a check or draft) **11** to reach (a conclusion, etc.); deduce **12** to take or get (a playing card, etc.) **13** to stretch **14** to make (lines, pictures, etc.), as with a pencil **15** to make (comparisons, etc.) **16** to cause to flow —***vi.*** **1** to draw something **2** to be drawn **3** to come; move **4** to shrink **5** to allow a draft of air, smoke, etc. to move through **6** to make a demand (*on*) —***n.*** **1** a drawing or being drawn **2** the result of drawing **3** a thing drawn **4** a tie; stalemate **5** a thing that attracts **6** a shallow ravine —**draw out** **1** to extend **2** to take out; extract **3** to get (a person) to talk —**draw up** **1** to arrange in order **2** to draft (a document) **3** to stop

draw'back' ***n.*** anything that prevents or lessens satisfaction; shortcoming

draw'bridge' ***n.*** a bridge that can be raised or drawn aside, as to permit passage of ships

draw·er (drô'ər; *for 2* drôr) ***n.*** **1** one that draws **2** a sliding box in a table, chest, etc.

drawers (drôrz) ***pl.n.*** UNDERPANTS

draw'ing ***n.*** **1** the act of one that draws; specif., the art of making pictures, etc., as with a pencil **2** a picture, etc. thus made **3** a lottery

drawing board a flat board to hold paper, etc. for making drawings —**back to the drawing board** [Inf.] back to the beginning, as to see what went wrong

drawing card an entertainer, show, etc. that draws a large audience

drawing room ⟦< *withdrawing room*: guests withdrew there after dinner⟧ a room where guests are received or entertained; living room

drawl (drôl) ***vt.***, ***vi.*** ⟦prob. < DRAW, *v.*⟧ to speak slowly, prolonging the vowels —***n.*** such a way of speaking

drawn (drôn) ***vt.***, ***vi.*** *pp. of* DRAW —***adj.*** **1** pulled out **2** disemboweled **3** tense; haggard

drawn butter melted butter

draw'string' ***n.*** a string drawn through a hem, as to tighten a garment

dray (drā) ***n.*** ⟦OE *dragan*, to draw⟧ a low cart for carrying heavy loads

dread (dred) ***vt.*** ⟦OE *ondrædan*⟧ to anticipate with fear or distaste —***n.*** **1** intense fear **2** fear mixed with awe **3** reluctance and uneasiness —***adj.***

inspiring dread

dread'ful (-fəl) ***adj.*** **1** awesome or terrible **2** [Inf.] very bad, offensive, etc. —**dread'ful·ly** ***adv.***

dread'locks' ***pl.n.*** hair worn in long, thin braids or uncombed, twisted locks

dread'nought' or **dread'naught'** (-nôt') ***n.*** a large, heavily armored battleship

dream (drēm) ***n.*** ⟦OE, joy, music⟧ **1** a sequence of images, etc. passing through a sleeping person's mind **2** a daydream; reverie **3** a fond hope **4** anything dreamlike —***vi., vt.*** **dreamed** or **dreamt** (dremt), **dream'ing** to have a dream or remote idea (*of*) —**dream up** [Inf.] to devise (a fanciful plan, etc.) —**dream'er** ***n.*** —**dream'less** ***adj.*** —**dream'like'** ***adj.***

dream'land' ***n.*** **1** any lovely but imaginary place **2** sleep

dream world **1** DREAMLAND **2** the realm of fantasy

dream'y ***adj.*** **-i·er, -i·est** **1** filled with dreams **2** fond of daydreaming **3** like something in a dream **4** soothing **5** [Slang] wonderful —**dream'i·ly** ***adv.***

drear·y (drir'ē) ***adj.*** **-i·er, -i·est** ⟦OE *dreorig*, sad⟧ dismal: also [Old Poet.] **drear** —**drear'i·ly** ***adv.*** —**drear'i·ness** ***n.***

dredge[1] (drej) ***n.*** ⟦prob. < MDu⟧ an apparatus for scooping up mud, etc., as in deepening channels —***vt., vi.*** **dredged, dredg'ing** **1** to search for or gather (*up*) as with a dredge **2** to enlarge or clean out with a dredge

dredge[2] (drej) ***vt.*** **dredged, dredg'ing** ⟦ME *dragge*, sweetmeat⟧ to coat (food) with flour, etc.

dregs (dregz) ***pl.n.*** ⟦< ON *dregg*⟧ **1** particles settling at the bottom in a liquid **2** the most worthless part

Drei·ser (drī'sər, -zər), **The·o·dore** (**Herman Albert**) (thē'ə dôr') 1871-1945; U.S. novelist

drench (drench) ***vt.*** ⟦OE *drincan*, to drink⟧ to make wet all over; soak

Dres·den (drez'dən) city in E Germany: pop. 481,000

dress (dres) ***vt.*** **dressed** or **drest, dress'ing** ⟦< L *dirigere*, lay straight⟧ **1** to put clothes on; clothe **2** to trim; adorn **3** to arrange (the hair) in a certain way **4** to align (troops) **5** to apply medicines and bandages to (a wound, etc.) **6** to prepare for use, esp. for cooking *[to dress a fowl]* **7** to smooth or finish (stone, wood, etc.) —***vi.*** **1** to put on clothes **2** to dress formally **3** to line up in rank —***n.*** **1** clothing **2** the usual outer garment of women, generally of one piece with a skirt —***adj.*** **1** of or for dresses **2** for formal wear —**dress down** **1** to scold **2** to wear casual clothes to work, etc. —**dress up** to dress formally, elegantly, etc.

dres·sage (dre säzh') ***n.*** ⟦Fr, training⟧ horsemanship using slight movements to control the horse

dress circle a semicircle of seats in a theater, etc., usually behind and above the orchestra seats

dress code a set of rules governing clothing to be worn, as in a given school or business

dress'er ***n.*** **1** one who dresses (in various senses) **2** a chest of drawers for clothes, usually with a mirror

dress'ing ***n.*** **1** the act of one that dresses **2** bandages, etc. applied to wounds **3** a sauce for salads, etc. **4** a stuffing for roast fowl, etc.

dress'ing-down' ***n.*** a sound scolding

dressing gown a loose robe for one not fully clothed, as when lounging

dress'mak'er ***n.*** one who makes dresses, etc. —**dress'mak'ing** ***n.***

dress rehearsal a final rehearsal, as of a play, with costumes, etc.

dress'y ***adj.*** **-i·er, -i·est** **1** showy or elaborate in dress or appearance **2** stylish, elegant, etc. —**dress'i·ness** ***n.***

drew (dro͞o) ***vt., vi.*** *pt. of* DRAW

drib·ble (drib'əl) ***vi., vt.*** **-bled, -bling** ⟦< DRIP⟧ **1** to flow, or let flow, in drops **2** to drool **3** *Sports* to move (a ball or puck) along by repeated bouncing, kicking, or tapping —***n.*** **1** a dribbling **2** a tiny amount: also **drib'let** (-lit) —**drib'bler** ***n.***

dried (drīd) ***vt., vi.*** *pt. & pp. of* DRY

dri·er (drī'ər) ***n.*** **1** a substance added to paint, etc. to make it dry fast **2** DRYER —***adj.*** *compar. of* DRY

dri'est (-ist) ***adj.*** *superl. of* DRY

drift (drift) ***n.*** ⟦OE *drifan*, to drive⟧ **1** *a)* a being carried along, as by a current *b)* the course of this **2** a trend; tendency **3** general meaning; intent **4** a heap of snow, sand, etc. piled up by wind —***vi.*** **1** to be carried along, as by a current **2** to go along aimlessly **3** to pile up in drifts —***vt.*** to cause to drift —**drift'er** ***n.***

drift'wood' ***n.*** wood drifting in the water or washed ashore

drill[1] (dril) ***n.*** ⟦< Du *drillen*, to bore⟧ **1** a tool for boring holes **2** *a)* systematic military or physical training *b)* the method or practice of teaching by repeated exercises —***vt., vi.*** **1** to bore with a drill (the tool) **2** to train in, or teach by means of, a drill —**drill'er** ***n.***

drill[2] (dril) ***n.*** ⟦< ?⟧ a planting machine for making holes or furrows and dropping seeds into them

drill[3] (dril) ***n.*** ⟦< L *trilix*, three-threaded⟧ a coarse, twilled cotton cloth, used for uniforms, etc.

drill'mas'ter ***n.*** **1** an instructor in military drill **2** one who teaches by drilling

drill press a power-driven machine for drilling holes in metal, etc.

dri·ly (drī'lē) ***adv.*** DRYLY

drink (driŋk) ***vt.*** **drank, drunk, drink'ing** ⟦OE *drincan*⟧ **1** to swallow (liquid) **2** to absorb (liquid) **3** to swallow the contents of —***vi.*** **1** to swallow liquid **2** to drink alcoholic liquor, esp. to excess —***n.*** **1** any liquid for drinking **2** alcoholic liquor —**drink in** to take in eagerly with the senses or mind —**drink to** to drink a toast to —**drink'a·ble** ***adj.*** —**drink'er** ***n.***

drip (drip) ***vi., vt.*** **dripped** or **dript, drip'ping** ⟦OE *dryppan*⟧ to fall, or let fall, in drops —***n.*** **1** a dripping **2** the sound of falling drops of a liquid **3**

[Slang] a dull person —**drip'per** ***n.***

drip'-dry' ***adj.*** designating garments that dry quickly when hung wet and require little or no ironing

drive (drīv) ***vt.*** **drove**, **driv·en** (driv'ən), **driv'ing** ⟦OE *drifan*⟧ **1** to force to go; push forward **2** to force into or from a state or act **3** to force to work, esp. to excess **4** to hit (a ball, etc.) hard **5** to make penetrate **6** *a*) to control the movement of; operate (a car, bus, etc.) *b*) to transport in a car, etc. **7** to push (a bargain, etc.) through **8** to motivate, influence, etc. —***vi.*** **1** to advance violently **2** to try hard, as to reach a goal **3** to drive a blow, ball, etc. **4** to be driven: said of a car, bus, etc. **5** to operate, or go in, a car, etc. —***n.*** **1** a driving **2** a trip in a car, etc. **3** *a*) a road for cars, etc. *b*) a driveway **4** a rounding up of animals **5** an organized effort to gain an objective **6** energy and initiative **7** a strong impulse or urge **8** the propelling mechanism of a machine, etc. **9** a computer device that reads and writes data —**drive at** to mean; intend —**drive in** **1** to force in, as by a blow **2** *Baseball* to cause (a runner) to score or (a run) to be scored

drive'-by' ***n.***, *pl.* **-bys'** a shooting in which the shots are fired from a passing car, etc.

drive'-in' ***n.*** a restaurant, movie theater, bank, etc. designed to serve people seated in their cars

driv·el (driv'əl) ***vi.***, ***vt.*** **-eled** or **-elled**, **-el·ing** or **-el·ling** ⟦OE *dreflian*⟧ **1** to let (saliva) drool **2** to speak or say in a silly, stupid way —***n.*** silly, stupid talk —**driv'el·er** or **driv'el·ler** ***n.***

driv'en (-ən) ***adj.*** acting because of urgency or compulsion

driv·er (drī'vər) ***n.*** a person or thing that drives, as *a*) one who drives a car, etc. *b*) one who herds cattle *c*) a golf club for hitting from the tee

drive shaft a shaft that transmits motion, as to the rear axle of a car

drive'-through' ***n.*** a restaurant, bank, etc. that provides service through a window to a person in a car, etc.: also sp. **drive'-thru'**

drive'train' ***n.*** the system that transmits an engine's power to wheels, a propeller, etc.

drive'way' ***n.*** a path for cars, from a street to a garage, house, etc.

driz·zle (driz'əl) ***vi.***, ***vt.*** **-zled**, **-zling** ⟦prob. < ME⟧ to rain in fine, misty drops —***n.*** a fine, misty rain —**driz'zly** ***adj.***

drogue (drōg) ***n.*** ⟦prob. < Scot *drug*, drag⟧ a funnel-shaped device towed behind an aircraft, etc., as for its drag effect or as a target

droll (drōl) ***adj.*** ⟦< Fr < MDu *drol*, stout fellow⟧ amusing in an odd or wry way —**droll'er·y** (-ər ē), *pl.* **-ies**, ***n.*** —**droll'ness** ***n.*** —**drol'ly** ***adv.***

drom·e·dar·y (dräm'ə der'ē) ***n.***, *pl.* **-ies** ⟦< LL *dromedarius* (*camelus*), running (camel)⟧ an Arabian camel, esp. one for riding

drone[1] (drōn) ***n.*** ⟦OE *dran*⟧ **1** a male bee or ant that does no work **2** an idler; loafer **3** a drudge **4** a pilotless airplane

drone[2] (drōn) ***vi.*** **droned**, **dron'ing** ⟦< prec.⟧ **1** to make a continuous humming sound **2** to talk in a monotonous way —***vt.*** to utter in a monotonous tone —***n.*** a droning sound

drool (dro͞ol) ***vi.*** ⟦< DRIVEL⟧ **1** to let saliva flow from one's mouth **2** to flow from the mouth, as saliva —***n.*** saliva running from the mouth

droop (dro͞op) ***vi.*** ⟦< ON *drūpa*⟧ **1** to sink, hang, or bend down **2** to lose strength or vitality **3** to become dejected —***vt.*** to let hang down —***n.*** a drooping —**droop'y**, **-i·er**, **-i·est**, ***adj.*** —**droop'i·ness** ***n.***

drop (dräp) ***n.*** ⟦OE *dropa*⟧ **1** a bit of liquid rounded in shape by falling, etc. **2** anything like this in shape, etc. **3** a very small quantity **4** a sudden fall, descent, slump, etc. **5** something that drops, as a curtain or trapdoor **6** the distance between a higher and lower level —***vi.*** **dropped**, **drop'ping** **1** to fall in drops **2** to fall; come down **3** to fall exhausted, wounded, or dead **4** to pass into a specified state *[to drop off to sleep]* **5** to come to an end *[let the matter drop]* **6** to become lower —***vt.*** **1** to let or make fall **2** to utter (a hint, etc.) casually **3** to send (a letter) **4** to stop, end, or dismiss **5** to lower or lessen **6** [Inf.] to leave at a specified place: often with *off* **7** to omit or remove **8** [Slang] to lose (money, etc.) —**drop in** (or **over** or **by**) to pay a casual visit —**drop off** [Inf.] to fall asleep —**drop out** to stop participating —**drop'let** (-lit) ***n.***

drop'-dead' [Slang] ***adj.*** spectacular; striking —***adv.*** extremely *[drop-dead handsome]*

drop kick *Rugby, etc.* a kick of a dropped ball just as it hits the ground —**drop'-kick'** ***vt.***, ***vi.*** —**drop'-kick'er** ***n.***

drop'-off' ***n.*** **1** a very steep drop **2** a decline, as in sales or prices

drop'out' ***n.*** one who withdraws from school before graduating

drop'per ***n.*** a small tube with a hollow rubber bulb at one end, used to measure out a liquid in drops

drop·sy (dräp'sē) ***n.*** ⟦< Gr *hydrōps* < *hydōr*, water⟧ *former term for* EDEMA

dross (drôs) ***n.*** ⟦OE *dros*⟧ **1** scum on molten metal **2** refuse; rubbish

drought (drout) ***n.*** ⟦< OE *drugoth*, dryness⟧ **1** prolonged dry weather **2** a prolonged shortage

drove[1] (drōv) ***n.*** ⟦OE *draf*⟧ **1** a number of cattle, sheep, etc. driven or moving along as a group; flock; herd **2** a moving crowd of people: *usually used in pl.*

drove[2] (drōv) ***vt.***, ***vi.*** *pt. of* DRIVE

dro·ver (drō'vər) ***n.*** one who herds droves of animals, esp. to market

drown (droun) ***vi.*** ⟦ME *drounen*⟧ to die by suffocation in water —***vt.*** **1** to kill by such suffocation **2** to flood **3** to be so loud as to overcome (another sound): usually with *out*

drowse (drouz) ***vi.*** **drowsed**, **drows'ing** ⟦< OE *drusian*, become sluggish⟧ to be half asleep; doze —*n.* a doze

drows·y (drou′zē) *adj.* **-i·er, -i·est** being or making sleepy or half asleep —**drows′i·ly** *adv.* —**drows′i·ness** *n.*

drub (drub) *vt.* **drubbed, drub′bing** ⟦< Ar *daraba,* to cudgel⟧ **1** to beat as with a stick **2** to defeat soundly —**drub′ber** *n.* —**drub′bing** *n.*

drudge (druj) *n.* ⟦ME *druggen*⟧ one who does hard or tedious work —*vi.* **drudged, drudg′ing** to do such work —**drudg′er·y**, *pl.* **-ies,** *n.*

drug (drug) *n.* ⟦< OFr *drogue*⟧ **1** any substance used as or in a medicine **2** a narcotic, hallucinogen, etc. —*vt.* **drugged, drug′ging 1** to put a harmful drug in (a drink, etc.) **2** to stupefy as with a drug —**drug on the market** a thing in plentiful supply for which there is little or no demand

drug′gie (-ē) *n.* [Slang] a habitual user of drugs: also **drug′gy**, *pl.* **-gies**

drug′gist (-ist) *n.* **1** a dealer in drugs, medical supplies, etc. **2** a pharmacist **3** a drugstore owner or manager

drug′store′ *n.* a store where drugs, medical supplies, and various items are sold and prescriptions are filled

dru·id (dro͞o′id) *n.* ⟦< Celt⟧ [*often* **D-**] a member of a Celtic religious order in ancient Britain, Ireland, and France —**dru′id·ism′** *n.*

drum (drum) *n.* ⟦< Du *trom*⟧ **1** a percussion instrument consisting of a hollow cylinder with a membrane stretched over the end or ends **2** the sound produced by beating a drum **3** any drumlike cylindrical object **4** the eardrum —*vi.* **drummed, drum′ming 1** to beat a drum **2** to tap continually —*vt.* **1** to play (a rhythm, etc.) as on a drum **2** to instill (ideas, facts, etc.) *into* by continued repetition —**drum out of** to expel from in disgrace —**drum up** to get (business, etc.) by soliciting

drum·lin (drum′lin) *n.* ⟦< Ir⟧ a low, flattened, oval mound or hill formed by a glacier

drum major one who leads a marching band, keeping time with a baton —**drum ma′jor·ette′** (-et′) *fem.*

drum′mer *n.* **1** a drum player **2** [Old Inf.] a traveling salesman

drum′stick′ *n.* **1** a stick for beating a drum **2** the lower half of the leg of a cooked fowl

drunk (druŋk) *vt., vi. pp. of* DRINK —*adj.* **1** overcome by alcoholic liquor; intoxicated **2** overcome by any powerful emotion **3** [Inf.] DRUNKEN (sense 2) Usually used in the predicate —*n.* **1** [Inf.] a drunken person **2** [Slang] a drinking spree

drunk′ard *n.* a person who often gets drunk

drunk′en *adj.* **1** intoxicated **2** caused by or occurring during intoxication Used before a noun —**drunk′en·ly** *adv.* —**drunk′en·ness** *n.*

drupe (dro͞op) *n.* ⟦< Gr *druppa* (*elaa*), olive⟧ any fleshy fruit with an inner stone, as a peach

dry (drī) *adj.* **dri′er, dri′est** ⟦OE *dryge*⟧ **1** not under water [*dry* land] **2** not wet or damp **3** lacking rain or water; arid **4** thirsty **5** not yielding milk **6** solid; not liquid **7** not sweet [*dry* wine] **8** prohibiting alcoholic beverages [a *dry* town] **9** funny in a quiet but sharp way [*dry* wit] **10** unproductive **11** boring; dull —*n., pl.* **drys** [Inf.] a prohibitionist —*vt., vi.* **dried, dry′ing** to make or become dry —**dry up 1** to make or become thoroughly dry **2** to make or become unproductive **3** [Slang] to stop talking —**dry′ly** *adv.* —**dry′ness** *n.*

dry·ad (drī′ad′) *n.* ⟦< Gr *drys,* tree⟧ [*also* **D-**] *Gr. & Rom. Myth.* a tree nymph

dry cell a voltaic cell containing a moist, pastelike electrolyte which cannot spill

dry′-clean′ *vt.* to clean (garments, etc.) with a solvent other than water, as naphtha —**dry cleaner**

dry dock a dock from which the water can be emptied, used for building and repairing ships

dry′er *n.* **1** one that dries; specif., an appliance for drying clothes with heat **2** DRIER

dry farming farming without irrigation, by conserving the soil's moisture, etc.

dry goods cloth, cloth products, etc.

dry ice solidified carbon dioxide: used as a refrigerant

dry run [Inf.] a simulated or practice performance; rehearsal

dry′wall′ *n.* PLASTERBOARD —*vt., vi.* to cover (a wall, etc.) with plasterboard

DSL *abbrev.* digital subscriber line

DST *abbrev.* daylight saving time

Du *abbrev.* Dutch

du·al (do͞o′əl) *adj.* ⟦< L *duo,* two⟧ **1** of two **2** double; twofold —**du′al·ism′** *n.* —**du·al′i·ty** (-al′ə tē) *n.*

dub[1] (dub) *vt.* **dubbed, dub′bing** ⟦< OE *dubbian,* to strike⟧ **1** *a*) to confer a title or rank upon *b*) to name or nickname **2** to smooth by hammering, scraping, etc. —**dub′ber** *n.*

dub[2] (dub) *vt.* **dubbed, dub′bing** ⟦< DOUBLE⟧ to provide with a soundtrack, esp. one with dialogue in another language —**dub in** to insert (dialogue, music, etc.) in the soundtrack —**dub′ber** *n.*

dub·bin (dub′in) *n.* ⟦< DUB[1]⟧ a greasy preparation for waterproofing leather

du·bi·e·ty (do͞o bī′ə tē) *n.* **1** a being dubious **2** *pl.* **-ties** a doubtful thing

du·bi·ous (do͞o′bē əs) *adj.* ⟦< L *dubius,* uncertain⟧ **1** causing doubt **2** skeptical **3** questionable —**du′bi·ous·ly** *adv.*

Dub·lin (dub′lən) capital of Ireland: pop. 478,000

du·cal (do͞o′kəl) *adj.* ⟦< LL *ducalis,* of a leader⟧ of a duke or dukedom

duc·at (duk′ət) *n.* ⟦see DUCHY⟧ any of several former European coins

duch·ess (duch′is) *n.* **1** a duke's wife or widow **2** a woman ruling a duchy

duch′y (-ē) *n., pl.* **-ies** ⟦< L *dux,* leader⟧ the territory ruled by a duke or duchess

duck[1] (duk) *n.* ⟦< OE *duce,* diver⟧ **1** a small waterfowl with a flat bill, a short neck, and webbed feet **2** the flesh of a duck as food

duck[2] (duk) ***vt., vi.*** ⟦ME *douken*⟧ **1** to plunge or dip under water for a moment **2** to lower or bend (the head, body, etc.) suddenly, as to avoid a blow **3** [Inf.] to avoid (an issue, etc.) —***n.*** a ducking

duck[3] (duk) ***n.*** ⟦Du *doek*⟧ a cotton or linen cloth like canvas but lighter in weight

duck'bill' ***n.*** PLATYPUS

duck'ling ***n.*** a young duck

duck'pins' ***n.*** a game like bowling, played with smaller pins and balls

duck'y ***adj.*** **-i·er, -i·est** [Old Slang] pleasing, delightful, etc.

duct (dukt) ***n.*** ⟦< L *ducere*, to lead⟧ a tube, channel, or pipe, as for passage of a liquid —**duct'less** ***adj.***

duc·tile (duk'til) ***adj.*** ⟦see prec.⟧ **1** that can be drawn or hammered thin without breaking: said of metals **2** easily led; tractable —**duc·til'i·ty** (-til'ə tē) ***n.***

ductless gland an endocrine gland

duct tape a very strong, waterproof tape, used to seal ducts, hoses, etc.

duct'work' ***n.*** a system of ducts used to circulate air for heating, cooling, etc.

dud (dud) ***n.*** ⟦prob. < Du *dood*, dead⟧ [Inf.] **1** a bomb, etc. that fails to explode **2** a failure

dude (do͞od) ***n.*** ⟦< ?⟧ **1** a dandy; fop **2** [West Slang] a tourist at a ranch **3** [Slang] any man or boy —***vt., vi.*** **dud'ed, dud'ing** [Slang] to dress up, esp. in showy clothes: usually with *up*

dude ranch a vacation resort on a ranch, with horseback riding, etc.

dud·geon (duj'ən) ***n.*** now chiefly in **in high dudgeon**, very angry, offended, etc.

duds (dudz) ***pl.n.*** ⟦ME *dudde*, cloth, cloak < ?⟧ [Inf.] **1** clothes **2** belongings

due (do͞o, dyo͞o) ***adj.*** ⟦< L *debere*, owe⟧ **1** owed or owing as a debt; payable **2** suitable; proper **3** enough *[due care]* **4** expected or scheduled to arrive —***adv.*** exactly; directly *[due west]* —***n.*** **1** deserved recognition **2** [*pl.*] fees or other charges *[union dues]* —**due to 1** caused by **2** [Inf.] because of —**pay one's dues** [Slang] to earn a right, etc., as by having suffered in struggle

due bill a receipt for money paid, exchangeable for goods or services only

du·el (do͞o'əl) ***n.*** ⟦< medieval L *duellum*⟧ **1** a prearranged fight between two persons armed with deadly weapons **2** any contest like this —***vi., vt.*** **-eled** or **-elled, -el·ing** or **-el·ling** to fight a duel with —**du'el·ist** or **du'el·list, du'el·er** or **du'el·ler** ***n.***

due process (of law) legal proceedings established to protect individual rights and liberties

du·et (do͞o et') ***n.*** ⟦< L *duo*, two⟧ **1** a composition for two voices or instruments **2** the two performers of this

duf·fel (or **duf·fle**) **bag** (duf'əl) ⟦after *Duffel*, town in Belgium⟧ a large cloth bag for carrying clothing, etc.

duff·er (duf'ər) ***n.*** ⟦< thieves' slang *duff*, to fake⟧ [Inf.] **1** a slow-witted or dawdling elderly person **2** a relatively unskilled golfer

dug (dug) ***vt., vi.*** *pt. & pp. of* DIG

dug'out' ***n.*** **1** a boat hollowed out of a log **2** a shelter, as in warfare, dug in the ground **3** *Baseball* a covered shelter, one for each team

DUI (dē'yo͞o'ī') ***n.*** a citation for driving while under the influence of alcohol, drugs, etc.

du jour (do͞o-zhoor') offered on this day *[soup du jour]*

duke[1] (do͞ok) ***n.*** ⟦< L *dux*, leader⟧ **1** a prince ruling an independent duchy **2** a nobleman next in rank to a prince —**duke'dom** ***n.***

duke[2] (do͞ok) ***n.*** [*pl.*] [Slang] the fists or hands —**duke it out** to fight, esp. with the fists

dul·cet (dul'sit) ***adj.*** ⟦< L *dulcis*, sweet⟧ soothing or pleasant to hear

dul·ci·mer (dul'sə mər) ***n.*** ⟦< L *dulce*, sweet + *melos*, song⟧ a musical instrument with metal strings, which are struck with two small hammers or plucked with a plectrum or quill

dull (dul) ***adj.*** ⟦OE *dol*⟧ **1** mentally slow; stupid **2** physically slow; sluggish **3** boring; tedious **4** not sharp; blunt **5** not feeling or felt keenly **6** not vivid or bright *[a dull color]* **7** not distinct; muffled *[a dull thud]* —***vt., vi.*** to make or become dull —**dull'ness** ***n.*** —**dul'ly** ***adv.***

dull'ard (-ərd) ***n.*** a stupid person

Du·luth (də lo͞oth') city & port in NE Minnesota, on Lake Superior: pop. 85,000

du·ly (do͞o'lē) ***adv.*** in due manner; in the proper way, at the right time, etc.

Du·mas (do͞o mä'), **Alexandre** 1802-70; Fr. novelist & playwright

dumb (dum) ***adj.*** ⟦OE⟧ **1** lacking the power of speech; mute **2** silent **3** ⟦Ger *dumm*⟧ [Inf.] stupid —**dumb down** [Inf.] to make or become less intellectually demanding —**dumb'ly** ***adv.*** —**dumb'ness** ***n.***

dumb'bell' ***n.*** **1** a device consisting of round weights joined by a short bar, lifted for muscular exercise **2** [Slang] a stupid person

dumb'found' or **dum'found'** ***vt.*** ⟦DUMB + (CON)FOUND⟧ to make speechless by shocking; amaze

dumb'wait'er ***n.*** a small elevator for sending food, etc. between floors

dum·dum (bullet) (dum'dum') ⟦after *Dumdum*, arsenal in India⟧ a soft-nosed bullet that expands when it hits, causing a large wound

dum·my (dum'ē) ***n.***, *pl.* **-mies** **1** a figure made in human form, as for displaying clothing **2** an imitation; sham **3** [Slang] a stupid person **4** *Bridge* the declarer's partner, whose hand is exposed on the table and played by the declarer —***adj.*** sham

dump (dump) ***vt.*** ⟦prob. < ON⟧ **1** to unload in a heap or mass **2** to throw away (rubbish, etc.) **3** to sell (a commodity) in a large quantity at a low price **4** *Comput. a)* to transfer (data) to another section of storage *b)* to make a printout of (data) —***n.*** **1** a place for dumping rubbish, etc. **2** *Mil.* a temporary storage center in the field **3** an ugly, run-down place —(**down**) **in the dumps** [Inf.] in low spirits —**dump on** [Slang] to treat with contempt

dump'er ***n.*** [Slang] a container for refuse

dump·ling (dump'liŋ) ***n.*** ⟦< ?⟧ **1** a small piece of steamed or boiled dough served with meat or soup **2** a crust of baked dough filled with fruit

Dump·ster (dump'stər) *trademark for* a large metal trash bin, often one emptied by a special truck —***n.*** [*usually* **d-**] such a trash bin

dump'y ***adj.*** **-i·er, -i·est 1** short and thick; squat **2** [Inf.] ugly, run-down, etc.

dun[1] (dun) ***adj., n.*** ⟦OE⟧ dull grayish-brown

dun[2] (dun) ***vt., vi.*** **dunned, dun'ning** ⟦? dial. var. of DIN⟧ to ask (a debtor) repeatedly for payment —***n.*** an insistent demand for payment

dunce (duns) ***n.*** ⟦after John *Duns* Scotus, 13th-c. Scot scholar⟧ a dull, ignorant person

dune (do͞on) ***n.*** ⟦Fr < MDu⟧ a rounded hill or ridge of drifted sand

dung (duŋ) ***n.*** ⟦OE⟧ animal excrement; manure

dun·ga·ree (duŋ'gə rē') ***n.*** ⟦Hindi *dungrī*⟧ **1** a coarse cotton cloth **2** [*pl.*] work trousers or overalls made of this

dun·geon (dun'jən) ***n.*** ⟦< OFr *donjon*⟧ a dark underground cell or prison

dung'hill' ***n.*** a heap of dung

dunk (duŋk) ***vt.*** ⟦Ger *tunken*⟧ **1** to dip (bread, etc.) into coffee, etc. before eating it **2** to immerse briefly

Dun·kirk (dun'kurk') seaport in N France: scene of the evacuation of Allied troops under fire (1940)

du·o (do͞o'ō) ***n.***, *pl.* **du'os** ⟦It⟧ **1** DUET (esp. sense 2) **2** a pair; couple

du·o·de·num (do͞o'ō dē'nəm, do͞o äd''n əm) ***n.***, *pl.* **-na** (-nə) or **-nums** ⟦< L *duodeni*, twelve each: its length is about twelve fingers' breadth⟧ the first section of the small intestine, below the stomach —**du'o·de'nal** ***adj.***

dup *abbrev.* duplicate

dupe (do͞op) ***n.*** ⟦< L *upupa*, stupid bird⟧ a person easily tricked —***vt.*** **duped, dup'ing** to deceive; fool; trick —**dup'er** ***n.***

du·plex (do͞o'pleks') ***adj.*** ⟦L < *duo*, TWO + *-plex*, -fold⟧ double —***n.*** **1** an apartment with rooms on two floors **2** a house consisting of two separate family units

du·pli·cate (do͞o'pli kit; *for v.*, -kāt') ***adj.*** ⟦< L *duplicare*, to double⟧ **1** double **2** corresponding exactly —***n.*** an exact copy —***vt.*** **-cat'ed, -cat'ing 1** to make an exact copy of **2** to make or do again —**du'pli·ca'tion** ***n.***

duplicating machine a machine for making copies of a letter, drawing, etc.

du·plic·i·ty (do͞o plis'ə tē) ***n.***, *pl.* **-ties** ⟦< LL *duplicitas*⟧ hypocritical cunning or deception

du·ra·ble (door'ə bəl) ***adj.*** ⟦< L *durare*, to last⟧ **1** lasting in spite of hard wear or frequent use **2** stable —**du'ra·bil'i·ty** ***n.*** —**du'ra·bly** ***adv.***

du·ra ma·ter (door'ə māt'ər) ⟦< ML, lit., hard mother, transl. of Ar term⟧ the tough, outermost membrane covering the brain and spinal cord

dur·ance (door'əns) ***n.*** ⟦see DURABLE⟧ long imprisonment: mainly in **in durance vile**

du·ra·tion (do͞o rā'shən) ***n.*** ⟦see DURABLE⟧ the time that a thing continues or lasts

du·ress (doo res') ***n.*** ⟦< L *durus*, hard⟧ coercion

Dur·ham (dur'əm) city in NC North Carolina: pop. 137,000

dur·ing (door'iŋ) ***prep.*** ⟦see DURABLE⟧ **1** throughout the entire time of **2** in the course of

durst (durst) ***vt., vi.*** *now chiefly dial. pt. of* DARE

du·rum (door'əm) ***n.*** ⟦< L *durus*, hard⟧ a hard wheat that yields flour for macaroni, spaghetti, etc.

dusk (dusk) ***n.*** ⟦< OE *dox*, dark-colored⟧ **1** the dim part of twilight **2** dusky quality —**dusk'y, -i·er, -i·est,** ***adj.***

dust (dust) ***n.*** ⟦OE⟧ **1** powdery earth or any finely powdered matter **2** earth **3** disintegrated mortal remains **4** anything worthless —***vt.*** **1** to sprinkle with dust, powder, etc. **2** to rid of dust, as by wiping: often with *off* —***vi.*** to remove dust, as from furniture —**bite the dust** [Inf.] to die, esp. in battle —**dust'less** ***adj.***

dust bowl an arid region with eroded topsoil easily blown off by winds

dust'er ***n.*** **1** a person or thing that dusts **2** a lightweight housecoat

dust'pan' ***n.*** a shovel-like pan into which floor dust is swept

dust'y ***adj.*** **-i·er, -i·est 1** covered with or full of dust **2** powdery **3** muted with gray: said of a color —**dust'i·ness** ***n.***

Dutch (duch) ***n.*** the language of the Netherlands —***adj.*** of the Netherlands or its people, language, or culture —**go Dutch** [Inf.] to have each pay his or her own expenses —**in Dutch** [Inf.] in trouble or disfavor —**the Dutch** Dutch people

Dutch door a door with upper and lower halves that can be opened separately

Dutch oven a heavy pot with an arched lid, for pot roasts, etc.

Dutch treat [Inf.] any date, etc. on which each pays his or her own expenses

Dutch uncle [Inf.] one who bluntly and sternly lectures another, often with benevolent intent

du·te·ous (do͞ot'ē əs) ***adj.*** dutiful; obedient —**du'te·ous·ly** ***adv.***

du·ti·a·ble (do͞ot'ē ə bəl) ***adj.*** necessitating payment of a duty or tax

du·ti·ful (do͞ot'i fəl) ***adj.*** showing, or resulting from, a sense of duty; obedient —**du'ti·ful·ly** ***adv.***

du·ty (do͞ot'ē) ***n.***, *pl.* **-ties** ⟦see DUE & -TY⟧ **1** obedience or respect to be shown to one's parents, elders, etc. **2** any action required by one's position or by moral or legal considerations, etc. **3** service, esp. military service *[overseas duty]* **4** a tax, as on imports —**on** (or **off**) **duty** at (or temporarily relieved from) one's work

du·vet (do͞o vā′, dyo͞o-) ***n.*** a comforter, often down-filled, within a slipcover

DVD ***n.*** ⟦< *d(igital) v(ideo) d(isc)*⟧ a digital optical disc for recording images, sounds, or data for reproduction, specif. one on which a film has been recorded

dwarf (dwôrf) ***n.***, *pl.* **dwarfs** or **dwarves** (dwôrvz) ⟦< OE *dweorg*⟧ **1** any abnormally small person, animal, or plant **2** *Folklore* a little being in human form, with magic powers —***vt.*** **1** to stunt the growth of **2** to make seem small in comparison —***vi.*** to become dwarfed —***adj.*** undersized —**dwarf′ish** ***adj.*** —**dwarf′ism′** ***n.***

dweeb (dwēb) ***n.*** [Slang] a person regarded as dull, awkward, unsophisticated, etc.

dwell (dwel) ***vi.*** **dwelt** or **dwelled**, **dwell′ing** ⟦< OE *dwellan*, to hinder⟧ to make one's home; reside —**dwell on** (or **upon**) to think or talk about at length —**dwell′er** ***n.***

dwell′ing (place) ⟦ME: see prec.⟧ a residence; abode

DWI (dē′dub′əl yo͞o′ī′) ***n.*** a citation for driving while intoxicated

dwin·dle (dwin′dəl) ***vi.*** **-dled**, **-dling** ⟦< OE *dwīnan*, waste away⟧ to keep on becoming smaller or less; diminish; shrink

dyb·buk (dib′ək) ***n.*** ⟦Heb *dibbūq*⟧ *Jewish Folklore* the spirit of a dead person that enters the body of a living person

dye (dī) ***n.*** ⟦< OE *deag*⟧ a substance or solution for coloring fabric, hair, etc.; also, the color produced —***vt.*** **dyed**, **dye′ing** to color with dye —**dy′er** ***n.***

dyed′-in-the-wool′ ***adj.*** not changing, as in beliefs

dye′stuff′ ***n.*** any substance constituting or yielding a dye

dy·ing (dī′iŋ) ***vi.*** *prp. of* DIE[1] —***adj.*** **1** about to die or end **2** at death —***n.*** death

dy·nam·ic (dī nam′ik) ***adj.*** ⟦< Gr *dynasthai*, be able⟧ **1** relating to bodies in motion **2** energetic; vigorous —**dy·nam′i·cal·ly** ***adv.***

dy·nam′ics ***n.*** the science dealing with motions produced by given forces —***pl.n.*** the forces operative in any field

dy·na·mite (dī′nə mīt′) ***n.*** ⟦see DYNAMIC⟧ a powerful explosive made with nitroglycerin —***vt.*** **-mit′ed**, **-mit′ing** to blow up with dynamite

dy·na·mo (dī′nə mō′) ***n.***, *pl.* **-mos′** ⟦see DYNAMIC⟧ **1** *former term for* GENERATOR **2** a dynamic person

dy·nas·ty (dī′nəs tē) ***n.***, *pl.* **-ties** ⟦< Gr *dynasteia*, rule⟧ a succession of rulers who are members of the same family —**dy·nas′tic** (-nas′tik) ***adj.***

dys- ⟦Gr⟧ *prefix* bad, ill, difficult, etc.

dys·en·ter·y (dis′ən ter′ē) ***n.*** ⟦< Gr *dys-*, bad + *entera*, bowels⟧ an intestinal inflammation characterized by abdominal pain and bloody diarrhea

dys·func·tion (dis fuŋk′shən) ***n.*** abnormal or impaired functioning —**dys·func′tion·al** ***adj.***

dys·lex·i·a (dis lek′sē ə) ***n.*** ⟦< DYS- + L *lexis*, speech⟧ impairment of the ability to read —**dys·lex′ic** or **dys·lec′tic** ***adj.***, ***n.***

dys·pep·si·a (dis pep′sē ə, -shə) ***n.*** ⟦< Gr *dys-*, bad + *pepsis*, digestion⟧ indigestion —**dys·pep′tic** ***adj.***, ***n.***

dz *abbrev.* dozen(s)

E

e or **E** (ē) ***n.***, *pl.* **e's**, **E's** the fifth letter of the English alphabet

E[1] (ē) ***n.*** **1** *Educ.* a grade for below-average work or, sometimes, excellence **2** *Music* the third tone in the scale of C major

E[2] *abbrev.* **1** east(ern) **2** *Baseball* error(s) **3** *Physics* energy

e- *prefix* EX-

E- or **e-** *prefix* done, etc. electronically on the Internet *[E-commerce]*

each (ēch) ***adj.***, ***pron.*** ⟦OE *ælc*⟧ every one of two or more considered separately —***adv.*** apiece Abbrev. **ea.** —**each other** each one the other or others; one another

ea·ger (ē′gər) ***adj.*** ⟦< L *acer*⟧ keenly desiring; impatient or anxious —**ea′ger·ly** ***adv.*** —**ea′ger·ness** ***n.***

ea·gle (ē′gəl) ***n.*** ⟦< L *aquila*⟧ **1** a large bird of prey, with sharp vision and powerful wings **2** a representation of the eagle, as the U.S. emblem **3** *Golf* a score of two under par on a hole

ea′gle-eyed′ ***adj.*** having keen vision

ea·glet (ē′glit) ***n.*** a young eagle

ear[1] (ir) ***n.*** ⟦OE *ēare*⟧ **1** the part of the body that perceives sound **2** the visible, external part of the ear **3** one's sense of hearing or hearing ability **4** anything like an ear —**be all ears** to listen attentively —**give** (or **lend**) **ear** to give attention; heed —**play by ear** to play (music) without using notation —**play it by ear** [Inf.] to improvise

ear[2] (ir) ***n.*** ⟦< OE *ēar*⟧ the grain-bearing spike of a cereal plant, esp. of corn —***vi.*** to sprout ears

ear′ache′ ***n.*** an ache in the ear

ear′drum′ ***n.*** TYMPANIC MEMBRANE

earl (url) ***n.*** ⟦< OE *eorl*, warrior⟧ a British nobleman ranking above a viscount —**earl′dom** ***n.***

ear′lobe′ ***n.*** the fleshy lower part of the external ear

ear·ly (ur′lē) ***adv.***, ***adj.*** **-li·er**, **-li·est** ⟦< OE *ær*, before + *-lice*, -ly⟧ **1** near the beginning **2** before the expected or usual time **3** in the distant past **4** in the near future —**early on** at an early stage —**ear'li·ness** *n.*

ear'mark' *n.* **1** a mark put on the ear of livestock **2** an identifying mark or feature —*vt.* **1** to put such a mark on **2** to reserve for a special purpose

ear'muffs' (-mufs') *pl.n.* coverings worn over the ears in cold weather

earn (urn) *vt.* ⟦OE *earnian*⟧ **1** to receive (wages, etc.) for one's work **2** to get as deserved **3** to receive (interest, etc.) as from a bank account —**earn'er** *n.*

ear·nest[1] (ur'nist) *adj.* ⟦OE *eornoste*⟧ serious and intense; not joking —**in earnest** **1** serious **2** in a determined manner —**ear'nest·ly** *adv.* —**ear'nest·ness** *n.*

ear·nest[2] (ur'nist) *n.* ⟦ult. < Heb *eravon*⟧ money, etc. given as a pledge in binding a bargain

earn'ings *pl.n.* **1** wages or other recompense **2** profits, interest, etc.

ear'phone' *n.* a receiver for radio, etc., held to, or put into, the ear

ear'ring' *n.* a ring or other small ornament for the lobe of the ear

ear'shot' *n.* the distance within which a sound can be heard

ear'split'ting *adj.* so loud as to hurt the ears; deafening

earth (urth) *n.* ⟦OE *eorthe*⟧ **1** [*often* **E-**] the planet we live on, the third planet from the sun: see PLANET **2** this world, as distinguished from heaven and hell **3** land, as distinguished from sea or sky **4** soil; ground —**down to earth** **1** practical; realistic **2** sincere; without affectation

Earth Day April 22, a day on which environmentalist concerns are acknowledged

earth'en *adj.* made of earth or clay

earth'en·ware' *n.* clay pottery

earth'ling *n.* a human being: now mainly in science fiction

earth'ly *adj.* **1** *a*) terrestrial *b*) worldly **2** conceivable *[*no *earthly* reason*]*

earth'quake' *n.* a trembling of the earth's crust, caused by underground volcanic forces or shifting of rock

earth'ward *adv., adj.* toward the earth: also **earth'wards** *adv.*

earth'work' *n.* an embankment made by piling up earth, esp. as a fortification

earth'worm' *n.* a round, segmented worm that burrows in the soil

earth'y *adj.* **-i·er, -i·est** **1** of or like earth **2** *a*) coarse; unrefined *b*) simple and natural

ease (ēz) *n.* ⟦< L *adjacens*, lying nearby⟧ **1** freedom from pain or trouble; comfort **2** natural manner; poise **3** freedom from difficulty; facility **4** affluence —*vt.* **eased, eas'ing** **1** to free from pain or trouble; comfort **2** to lessen (pain, anxiety, etc.) **3** to facilitate **4** to reduce the strain or pressure of **5** to move by careful shifting, etc. —*vi.* to become less tense, severe, etc.

ea·sel (ē'zəl) *n.* ⟦ult. < L *asinus*, ass⟧ an upright frame or tripod to hold an artist's canvas, etc.

ease·ment (ēz'mənt) *n. Law* a right that one may have in another's land, as the right to pass through

eas·i·ly (ē'zə lē) *adv.* **1** with ease **2** certainly **3** very likely

east (ēst) *n.* ⟦OE⟧ **1** the direction in which sunrise occurs (90° on the compass) **2** a region in or toward this direction —*adj.* **1** in, of, toward, or facing the east **2** from the east *[*an *east* wind*]* —*adv.* in or toward the east —**the East** **1** the eastern part of the U.S. **2** Asia and the nearby islands

East Asia countries of E Asia, including China, Japan, North & South Korea, and Mongolia —**East Asian**

East Berlin *see* BERLIN

East China Sea part of the Pacific Ocean, between China & Japan

Eas·ter (ēs'tər) *n.* ⟦< OE *Eastre*, dawn goddess⟧ an annual Christian festival in the spring, celebrating the resurrection of Jesus

east'er·ly *adj., adv.* **1** in or toward the east **2** from the east

east'ern *adj.* **1** in, of, or toward the east **2** from the east **3** [**E-**] of the East

east'ern·er *n.* a person born or living in the east

Eastern Hemisphere that half of the earth which includes Europe, Africa, Asia, and Australia

Eastern Orthodox Church the Christian church dominant in E Europe, W Asia, and N Africa

East Germany *see* GERMANY

East In·dies (in'dēz') Malay Archipelago; esp., the islands of Indonesia —**East Indian**

east'ward *adv., adj.* toward the east *[*moving *eastward]*: also **east'wards** *adv.*

eas·y (ē'zē) *adj.* **-i·er, -i·est** ⟦see EASE⟧ **1** not difficult **2** free from anxiety, pain, etc. **3** comfortable; restful **4** free from constraint; not stiff **5** not strict or severe **6** *a*) unhurried *b*) gradual —*adv.* [Inf.] easily —**take it easy** [Inf.] **1** to refrain from anger, haste, etc. **2** to relax; rest —**eas'i·ness** *n.*

easy chair a stuffed armchair

eas'y·go'ing *adj.* **1** acting in a relaxed manner **2** not strict; lenient

eat (ēt) *vt.* **ate, eat'en, eat'ing** ⟦OE *etan*⟧ **1** to chew and swallow (food) **2** to consume or ravage: with *away* or *up* **3** to destroy, as acid does; corrode **4** to make by or as by eating *[*acid *eats* holes in cloth*]* **5** [Slang] to worry or bother —*vi.* to eat food; have a meal —**eat'a·ble** *adj.* —**eat'er** *n.*

eat·er·y (ēt'ər ē) *n., pl.* **-ies** [Inf.] a restaurant

eats *pl.n.* [Inf.] food

eaves (ēvz) *pl.n., sing.* **eave** ⟦< OE *efes*, edge⟧ the projecting lower edge or edges of a roof

eaves'drop' *vi.* **-dropped', -drop'ping** ⟦prob. < *eavesdropper*, one who stands under the eaves to listen⟧ to listen secretly to a private conversation —**eaves'drop'per** *n.*

ebb (eb) *n.* ⟦OE *ebba*⟧ **1** the flow of the tide back toward the sea **2** a lessening —*vi.* **1** to recede, as the tide **2** to lessen; decline

eb·on·y (eb′ə nē) ***n.***, *pl.* **-ies** ⟦< Gr *ebenos*⟧ the hard, heavy, dark wood of certain tropical trees **—*adj.*** **1** of ebony **2** like ebony; specif., dark or black

e·bul·lient (i bool′yənt, -bul′-) ***adj.*** ⟦< L *e-*, out + *bullire*, to boil⟧ **1** bubbling; boiling **2** enthusiastic; exuberant **—e·bul′lience *n.***

EC European Community

ec·cen·tric (ək sen′trik) ***adj.*** ⟦< Gr *ek-*, out of + *kentron*, center⟧ **1** not concentric: said of two circles, one inside the other **2** with its axis off center [an *eccentric* wheel] **3** not exactly circular **4** odd, as in conduct; unconventional **—*n.*** **1** a disk set off center on a shaft, for converting circular motion into back-and-forth motion **2** an eccentric person **—ec·cen′tri·cal·ly *adv.*** **—ec·cen·tric·i·ty** (ek′sen tris′ə tē), *pl.* **-ties, *n.***

Ec·cle·si·as·tes (e klē′zē as′tēz′) ***n.*** ⟦< Gr *ek-*, out + *kalein*, to call⟧ a book of the Old Testament

ec·cle′si·as′tic (-tik) ***adj.*** ⟦see prec.⟧ ECCLESIASTICAL **—*n.*** a member of the clergy

ec·cle′si·as′ti·cal (-ti kəl) ***adj.*** of the church or the clergy

ech·e·lon (esh′ə län′) ***n.*** ⟦< Fr < L *scala*, ladder⟧ **1** a steplike formation of ships, troops, or aircraft **2** a subdivision of a military force **3** any of the levels of responsibility in an organization

e·chi·no·derm (ē kī′nō durm′) ***n.*** ⟦< ModL⟧ a marine animal with a hard, spiny skeleton and radial body, as the starfish

ech·o (ek′ō) ***n.***, *pl.* **-oes** ⟦< Gr *ēchō*⟧ **1** the repetition of a sound by reflection of sound waves from a surface **2** a sound so produced **3** any repetition or imitation of the words, ideas, etc. of another **—*vi.*** **-oed, -o·ing** **1** to reverberate **2** to make an echo **—*vt.*** to repeat (another's words, ideas, etc.)

e·cho·ic (e kō′ik) ***adj.*** imitative in sound, as the word *tinkle*

é·clair (ā kler′, i-, ē-) ***n.*** ⟦Fr, lit., lightning⟧ an oblong pastry shell filled with custard, etc.

é·clat (ā klä′, i-, ē-) ***n.*** ⟦Fr < *éclater*, burst (out)⟧ **1** brilliant success **2** striking effect **3** acclaim; fame

ec·lec·tic (ek lek′tik) ***adj.*** ⟦< Gr *ek-*, out + *legein*, choose⟧ selecting or selected from various sources **—*n.*** one who uses eclectic methods **—ec·lec′ti·cal·ly *adv.*** **—ec·lec′ti·cism′** (-tə siz′əm) ***n.***

e·clipse (i klips′, ē-) ***n.*** ⟦< Gr *ek-*, out + *leipein*, leave⟧ **1** the obscuring of the sun when the moon comes between it and the earth (**solar eclipse**), or of the moon when the earth's shadow is cast upon it (**lunar eclipse**) **2** any obscuring of light, or of fame, glory, etc. **—*vt.*** **e·clipsed′, e·clips′ing** **1** to cause an eclipse of **2** to surpass

e·clip·tic (i klip′tik) ***n.*** the sun's apparent annual path, as seen from the orbiting earth

ec·logue (ek′lôg′) ***n.*** ⟦see ECLECTIC⟧ a short pastoral poem

eco- ⟦< Gr *oikos*, house⟧ *combining form* **1** environment or habitat **2** ecology

ec·o·cide (ē′kō sīd′) ***n.*** ⟦prec. + -CIDE⟧ the destruction of the environment, as by pollutants

e·col·o·gy (ē käl′ə jē) ***n.*** ⟦< Gr *oikos*, house + *-logia*, -LOGY⟧ the branch of biology that deals with the relations between living organisms and their environment **—ec′o·log′i·cal *adj.*** **—ec′o·log′i·cal·ly *adv.*** **—e·col′o·gist *n.***

econ *abbrev.* economic(s)

ec·o·nom·ic (ek′ə näm′ik, ē′kə-) ***adj.*** **1** of the management of income, expenditures, etc. **2** of economics **3** of the satisfaction of the material needs of people

ec′o·nom′i·cal ***adj.*** **1** not wasting money, time, etc.; thrifty **2** that uses no more of something than is necessary **—ec′o·nom′i·cal·ly *adv.***

ec′o·nom′ics ***n.*** **1** the science that deals with the production, distribution, and consumption of wealth **2** economic factors

e·con·o·mist (i kän′ə mist, ē-) ***n.*** a specialist in economics

e·con′o·mize′ (-mīz′) ***vi.*** **-mized′, -miz′ing** to reduce waste or expenses **—e·con′o·miz′er *n.***

e·con′o·my (-mē) ***n.***, *pl.* **-mies** ⟦< Gr *oikos*, house + *nomos*, law⟧ **1** the management of the income, expenditures, etc. of a household, government, etc. **2** careful management of wealth, etc.; thrift **3** efficient use of one's materials **4** an instance of thrift **5** a system of producing and distributing wealth **—*adj.*** costing less or less per unit than the standard kind

ec·o·sys·tem (ē′kō sis′təm) ***n.*** ⟦< Gr *oikos*, house + SYSTEM⟧ a community of animals and plants, together with its environment

ec·sta·sy (ek′stə sē) ***n.***, *pl.* **-sies** ⟦< Gr *ek-*, out + *histanai*, to set⟧ a state or feeling of overpowering joy; rapture **—ec·stat·ic** (ek stat′ik) ***adj.*** **—ec·stat′i·cal·ly *adv.***

-ec·to·my (ek′tə mē) ⟦< Gr *ek-*, out + *temnein*, to cut⟧ *combining form* a surgical excision of

Ec·ua·dor (ek′wə dôr′) country on the NW coast of South America: 104,506 sq. mi.; pop. 9,648,000 **—Ec′ua·do′re·an, Ec′ua·do′ri·an,** or **Ec′ua·dor′an *adj., n.***

ec·u·men·i·cal (ek′yoo men′i kəl) ***adj.*** ⟦< Gr *oikoumenē* (*gē*), the inhabited (world)⟧ **1** general, or universal; esp., of the Christian church as a whole **2** furthering religious unity, esp. among Christian churches **—ec′u·men′i·cal·ly *adv.***

ec·u·men·ism (ek′yoo mə niz′əm, e kyoo′-) ***n.*** the ecumenical movement, esp. among Christian churches **—ec′u·men·ist *n.***

ec·ze·ma (ek′zə mə, eg′zə-) ***n.*** ⟦< Gr *ek-*, out + *zein*, to boil⟧ a skin disorder characterized by inflammation, itching, and scaliness

ed *abbrev.* **1** edited (by) **2** *a*) edition *b*) editor *c*) education

-ed ⟦OE⟧ *suffix* **1** forming the past tense or past participle of certain verbs **2** forming adjectives from nouns or verbs

[cultured, bearded]

E·dam (cheese) (ē′dəm, -dam′) ⟦after *Edam*, Netherlands⟧ a mild, yellow cheese

ed·dy (ed′ē) ***n.***, *pl.* **-dies** ⟦prob. < ON *itha*⟧ a little whirlpool or whirlwind —***vi.*** **-died, -dy·ing** to move in an eddy

e·del·weiss (ā′dəl vīs′) ***n.*** ⟦Ger < *edel*, noble + *weiss*, white⟧ a small, flowering plant, esp. of the Alps, with white and woolly leaves

e·de·ma (ē dē′mə) ***n.***, *pl.* **-mas** or **-ma·ta** (-mə tə) ⟦< Gr *oidēma*, swelling⟧ an abnormal accumulation of fluid in body tissues or cavities

E·den (ēd′′n) ***n.*** **1** *Bible* the garden where Adam and Eve first lived; Paradise **2** any delightful place —**E·den′ic** or **e·den·ic** (ē den′ik) ***adj.***

edge (ej) ***n.*** ⟦OE *ecg*⟧ **1** the sharp, cutting part of a blade **2** sharpness; keenness **3** the projecting ledge of a cliff, etc.; brink **4** the part farthest from the middle; border; margin **5** [Inf.] advantage *[he has the edge on me]* —***vt., vi.*** **edged, edg′ing** **1** to form an edge (on) **2** to make (one's way) sideways **3** to move gradually —**on edge** **1** very tense; irritable **2** impatient —**edg′er** ***n.***

edge′ways′ (-wāz′) ***adv.*** with the edge foremost: also **edge′wise′** (-wīz′)

edg′ing ***n.*** a fringe, trimming, etc. for a border

edg·y (ej′ē) ***adj.*** **-i·er, -i·est** **1** irritable; on edge **2** [Inf.] innovative, daring, etc. —**edg′i·ness** ***n.***

ed·i·ble (ed′ə bəl) ***adj.*** ⟦< L *edere*, eat⟧ fit to be eaten —***n.*** anything fit to be eaten: *usually used in pl.* —**ed′i·bil′i·ty** (-bil′ə tē) ***n.***

e·dict (ē′dikt′) ***n.*** ⟦< L *e-*, out + *dicere*, speak⟧ a public order; decree

ed·i·fice (ed′i fis) ***n.*** ⟦see fol.⟧ a building, esp. a large, imposing one

ed·i·fy (ed′i fī′) ***vt.*** **-fied′, -fy′ing** ⟦< L *aedificare*, build⟧ to instruct so as to improve or uplift morally —**ed′i·fi·ca′tion** ***n.*** —**ed′i·fi′er** ***n.***

Ed·in·burgh (ed′′n bur′ə, -ō) capital of Scotland: district pop. 419,000

Ed·i·son (ed′i sən), **Thom·as Alva** (täm′əs al′və) 1847-1931; U.S. inventor

ed·it[1] (ed′it) ***vt.*** ⟦< EDITOR⟧ **1** to prepare (a manuscript) for publication by arranging, revising, etc. **2** to control the policy and publication of (a newspaper, etc.) **3** to prepare (a film, tape, etc.) for presentation by cutting, dubbing, etc. **4** to make changes in (a computer file)

edit[2] *abbrev.* **1** edited (by) **2** edition **3** editor

e·di·tion (i dish′ən) ***n.*** ⟦see fol.⟧ **1** the size or form in which a book is published **2** the total number of copies of a book, etc. published at one time **3** any particular issue of a newspaper

ed·i·tor (ed′it ər) ***n.*** ⟦L < *e-*, out + *dare*, give⟧ **1** one that edits **2** a department head of a newspaper, etc.

ed·i·to·ri·al (ed′i tôr′ē əl) ***adj.*** of or by an editor —***n.*** a statement of opinion in a newspaper, etc., as by an editor, publisher, or owner —**ed′i·to′ri·al·ly** ***adv.***

ed′i·to′ri·al·ize′ (-īz′) ***vi.*** **-ized′, -iz′ing** to express editorial opinions

editor in chief *pl.* **editors in chief** the editor who heads the editorial staff of a publication

Ed·mon·ton (ed′mən tən) capital of Alberta, Canada: pop. 616,000

educ *abbrev.* **1** education **2** educational

ed·u·ca·ble (ej′o͞o kə bəl, ej′ə-) ***adj.*** that can be educated or trained —**ed′u·ca·bil′i·ty** ***n.***

ed′u·cate′ (-kāt′) ***vt.*** **-cat′ed, -cat′ing** ⟦< L *e-*, out + *ducere*, to lead⟧ **1** to develop the knowledge, skill, or character of, esp. by formal schooling; teach **2** to pay for the schooling of —**ed′u·ca′tor** ***n.***

ed′u·cat′ed ***adj.*** **1** having much education **2** based on experience

ed′u·ca′tion (-kā′shən) ***n.*** **1** the process of educating; teaching **2** knowledge, etc. thus developed **3** formal schooling —**ed′u·ca′tion·al** ***adj.***

e·duce (ē do͞os′) ***vt.*** **e·duced′, e·duc′ing** ⟦see EDUCATE⟧ **1** to draw out; elicit **2** to deduce

-ee (ē) ⟦< Anglo-Fr pp. ending⟧ *suffix* **1** the recipient of a (specified) action *[appointee]* **2** one in a (specified) condition *[absentee]*

EEG *abbrev.* electroencephalogram

EEL

eel (ēl) ***n.*** ⟦OE *æl*⟧ a long, slippery, snakelike fish

EEOC *abbrev.* Equal Employment Opportunity Commission

e′er (er, ar) ***adv.*** [Old Poet.] EVER

-eer (ir) ⟦< L *-arius*⟧ *suffix* **1** *a)* one having to do with *[auctioneer]* *b)* one who writes, makes, etc. *[profiteer]* **2** to have to do with *[electioneer]*

ee·rie or **ee·ry** (ir′ē) ***adj.*** **-ri·er, -ri·est** ⟦< OE *earg*, timid⟧ mysterious, uncanny, or weird —**ee′ri·ly** ***adv.*** —**ee′ri·ness** ***n.***

ef- *prefix* EX-: used before *f [efface]*

ef·face (ə fās′, i-) ***vt.*** **-faced′, -fac′ing** ⟦< L *ex-*, out + *facies*, face⟧ **1** to rub out; erase **2** to make (oneself) inconspicuous —**ef·face′ment** ***n.***

ef·fect (e fekt′, i-) ***n.*** ⟦< L *ex-*, out + *facere*, do⟧ **1** anything brought about by a cause; result **2** the power to cause results **3** influence **4** meaning *[spoke to this effect]* **5** an impression made on the mind, or its cause **6** a being operative or in force **7** [*pl.*] belongings; property —***vt.*** to bring about; accomplish —**in effect** **1** actually **2** virtually **3** in operation —**take effect** to become operative

ef·fec′tive ***adj.*** **1** producing a desired effect; efficient **2** in effect; operative **3** impressive —**ef·fec′tive·ly** ***adv.*** —**ef·**

fec′tive·ness ***n.***

ef·fec·tu·al (e fek′cho͞o əl, i-) ***adj.*** **1** producing, or able to produce, the desired effect **2** having legal force; valid —**ef·fec′tu·al·ly** ***adv.***

ef·fec′tu·ate′ (-āt′) ***vt.*** **-at′ed, -at′ing** to bring about; effect

ef·fem·i·nate (e fem′ə nit, i-) ***adj.*** ⟦< L *ex-*, out + *femina*, woman⟧ having qualities attributed to women, as weakness, delicacy, etc.; unmanly —**ef·fem′i·na·cy** ***n.***

ef·fer·ent (ef′ər ənt) ***adj.*** ⟦< L *ex-*, out + *ferre*, to bear⟧ carrying away from a central part, as nerves

ef·fer·vesce (ef′ər ves′) ***vi.*** **-vesced′, -vesc′ing** ⟦< L *ex-*, out + *fervere*, to boil⟧ **1** to give off gas bubbles; bubble **2** to be lively —**ef′fer·ves′cence** ***n.*** —**ef′fer·ves′cent** ***adj.***

ef·fete (e fēt′, i-) ***adj.*** ⟦< L *ex-*, out + *fetus*, productive⟧ **1** no longer able to produce; sterile **2** decadent, soft, too refined, etc. —**ef·fete′ly** ***adv.*** —**ef·fete′ness** ***n.***

ef·fi·ca·cious (ef′i kā′shəs) ***adj.*** ⟦see EFFECT⟧ that produces the desired effect —**ef′fi·ca′cious·ly** ***adv.*** —**ef′fi·ca·cy** (-kə sē) ***n.***

ef·fi′cien·cy ***n.*** **1** a being efficient **2** a small, usually one-room, apartment: in full **efficiency apartment**

ef·fi·cient (e fish′ənt, i-) ***adj.*** ⟦see EFFECT⟧ producing the desired result with a minimum of effort, expense, or waste —**ef·fi′cient·ly** ***adv.***

ef·fi·gy (ef′i jē) ***n.***, *pl.* **-gies** ⟦< L *ex-*, out + *fingere*, to form⟧ a statue or other image; often, a crude representation of a despised person that is hanged or burned to show protest

ef·flu·ent (ef′lo͞o ənt) ***adj.*** ⟦< L *effluere*, flow out⟧ flowing out —***n.*** the outflow of a sewer, septic tank, etc. —**ef′flu·ence** ***n.***

ef·flu·vi·um (e flo͞o′vē əm) ***n.***, *pl.* **-vi·a** (-ə) or **-vi·ums** ⟦see prec.⟧ a disagreeable vapor or odor

ef·fort (ef′ərt) ***n.*** ⟦< L *ex-*, intens. + *fortis*, strong⟧ **1** the use of energy to do something **2** a try; attempt **3** a result of working or trying —**ef′fort·less** ***adj.*** —**ef′fort·less·ly** ***adv.***

ef·fron·ter·y (e frunt′ər ē, i-) ***n.*** ⟦< L *ex-*, from + *frons*, forehead⟧ impudence; audacity

ef·ful·gence (e ful′jəns, i-) ***n.*** ⟦< L *ex-*, forth + *fulgere*, shine⟧ radiance; brilliance —**ef·ful′gent** ***adj.***

ef·fuse (e fyo͞oz′, i-) ***vt., vi.*** **-fused′, -fus′ing** ⟦< L *ex-*, out + *fundere*, pour⟧ **1** to pour out or forth **2** to spread out; diffuse

ef·fu′sion (-fyo͞o′zhən) ***n.*** **1** a pouring forth **2** unrestrained expression in speaking or writing —**ef·fu′sive** ***adj.*** —**ef·fu′sive·ly** ***adv.*** —**ef·fu′sive·ness** ***n.***

e.g. *abbrev.* ⟦L *exempli gratia*⟧ for example

e·gad (ē gad′) ***interj.*** ⟦prob. < *oh God*⟧ [Archaic] used as a softened oath

e·gal·i·tar·i·an (ē gal′ə ter′ē ən) ***adj.*** ⟦< Fr *égalité*, equality⟧ advocating full political, social, and economic equality for all people —***n.*** a person advocating this

egg[1] (eg) ***n.*** ⟦ON⟧ **1** the oval or round body laid by a female bird, fish, etc., containing the germ of a new individual **2** a reproductive cell produced by a female; ovum **3** a hen's egg, raw or cooked

egg[2] (eg) ***vt.*** ⟦< ON *eggja*, give edge to⟧ to urge or incite: with *on*

egg′beat′er ***n.*** a kitchen utensil for beating eggs, whipping cream, etc.

egg foo yong (or **young** or **yung**) (eg′ fo͞o yuŋ′) a Chinese-American dish of beaten eggs cooked with bean sprouts, onions, minced pork or shrimp, etc.

egg′head′ ***n.*** [Slang] an intellectual

egg′nog′ (-näg′) ***n.*** ⟦EGG[1] + *nog*, strong ale⟧ a drink made of beaten eggs, milk, sugar, nutmeg, and, often, whiskey or rum

egg′plant′ ***n.*** **1** a plant with a large, ovoid, purple-skinned fruit eaten as a vegetable **2** the fruit

egg roll a Chinese-American dish, a thin egg pancake wrapped around minced vegetables, meat, etc. and deep-fried

eg·lan·tine (eg′lən tīn′, -tēn′) ***n.*** ⟦< L *aculeus*, a sting⟧ a European rose with sweet-scented leaves and pink flowers

e·go (ē′gō) ***n.***, *pl.* **-gos** ⟦L, I[2]⟧ **1** the self; the individual as self-aware **2** egotism **3** *Psychoanalysis* the part of the psyche that organizes thoughts rationally and governs action

e′go·cen′tric (-sen′trik) ***adj.*** viewing everything in relation to oneself —**e′go·cen′tri·cal·ly** ***adv.*** —**e′go·cen′trism′** ***n.***

e′go·ism′ ***n.*** **1** selfishness; self-interest **2** egotism; conceit —**e′go·ist** ***n.*** —**e′go·is′tic** or **e′go·is′ti·cal** ***adj.***

e′go·tism′ ***n.*** **1** excessive reference to oneself in speaking or writing **2** conceit; vanity —**e′go·tist** ***n.*** —**e′go·tis′tic** or **e′go·tis′ti·cal** ***adj.*** —**e′go·tis′ti·cal·ly** ***adv.***

ego trip [Slang] an experience that gratifies or indulges the ego

e·gre·gious (ē grē′jəs, i-) ***adj.*** ⟦< L *e-*, out + *grex*, a herd⟧ remarkably bad; flagrant *[an egregious error]* —**e·gre′gious·ly** ***adv.*** —**e·gre′gious·ness** ***n.***

e·gress (ē′gres′) ***n.*** ⟦< L *e-*, out + *gradi*, go⟧ a way out; exit

e·gret (ē′gret′, -grit) ***n.*** ⟦< OFr *aigrette*⟧ **1** a kind of heron with long, white plumes **2** AIGRETTE

E·gypt (ē′jipt) country in NE Africa, on the Mediterranean: 386,662 sq. mi.; pop. 48,205,000

E·gyp·tian (ē jip′shən, i-) ***n.*** **1** the language of the ancient Egyptians **2** a person born or living in Egypt —***adj.*** of Egypt or its people, language, etc.

eh (ā, e) ***interj.*** **1** used to express doubt or surprise **2** used to make an inquiry

ei·der (ī′dər) ***n.*** ⟦ult. < ON *æthr*⟧ **1** a large sea duck of northern regions **2** EIDERDOWN

ei′der·down′ ***n.*** the fine, soft down of the eider, used as a stuffing for quilts, pillows, etc.

eight (āt) ***adj., n.*** ⟦< OE *eahta*⟧ one more than seven; 8; VIII —**eighth** (ātth) ***adj., n.***

eight ball a black ball with the number eight on it, used in playing pool —**behind the eight ball** [Slang] in a very unfavorable position

eight·een (ā'tēn') ***adj., n.*** eight more than ten; 18; XVIII —**eight'eenth'** ***adj., n.***

eight'y ***adj., n.***, *pl.* **-ies** eight times ten; 80; LXXX —**the eighties** the numbers or years, as of a century, from 80 through 89 —**eight'i·eth** ***adj., n.***

Ein·stein (īn'stīn'), **Al·bert** (al'bərt) 1879-1955; U.S. physicist, born in Germany: formulated theory of relativity

Eir·e (er'ə) *Ir. name for* IRELAND

Ei·sen·how·er (ī'zen hou'ər), **Dwight David** (dwīt) 1890-1969; U.S. general & 34th president of the U.S. (1953-61)

ei·ther (ē'*th*ər, ī'-) ***adj.*** ⟦OE *æghwæther*⟧ **1** one or the other (of two) **2** each (of two) —***pron.*** one or the other (of two) —***conj.*** a correlative used with *or* to imply a choice of alternatives *[either* go or stay*]* —***adv.*** any more than the other; also *[*if you don't go, I won't *either]*

e·jac·u·late (ē jak'yo͞o lāt', i-) ***vt., vi.*** **-lat'ed, -lat'ing** ⟦see fol.⟧ **1** to eject (esp. semen) **2** to utter suddenly; exclaim —**e·jac'u·la'tion** ***n.***

e·ject (ē jekt', i-) ***vt.*** ⟦< L *e-*, out + *jacere*, to throw⟧ to throw or force out; expel —**e·jec'tion** ***n.***

eke (ēk) ***vt.*** **eked, ek'ing** ⟦< OE *eacan*, to increase⟧ to manage to make (a living) with difficulty: with *out*

EKG *abbrev.* electrocardiogram

e·lab·o·rate (ē lab'ə rit, i-; *for v.*, -rāt') ***adj.*** ⟦< L *e-*, out + *labor*, work⟧ developed in great detail; complicated —***vt.*** **-rat'ed, -rat'ing** to work out in great detail —***vi.*** to add more details: usually with *on* or *upon* —**e·lab'o·rate·ly** ***adv.*** —**e·lab'o·rate·ness** ***n.*** —**e·lab'o·ra'tion** ***n.***

é·lan (ā län', -län') ***n.*** ⟦Fr < *élancer*, to dart⟧ spirited self-assurance; dash

e·lapse (ē laps', i-) ***vi.*** **e·lapsed', e·laps'ing** ⟦< L *e-*, out + *labi*, to glide⟧ to slip by; pass: said of time

e·las·tic (ē las'tik, i-) ***adj.*** ⟦< Gr *elaunein*, set in motion⟧ **1** able to spring back to its original size, shape, etc. after being stretched, squeezed, etc.; flexible **2** able to recover easily, as from dejection; buoyant **3** adaptable —***n.*** an elastic band or fabric —**e'las·tic'i·ty** (-tis'ə tē) ***n.***

e·las'ti·cize' (-tə sīz') ***vt.*** **-cized', -ciz'ing** to make (fabric) elastic

e·late (ē lāt', i-) ***vt.*** **-lat'ed, -lat'ing** ⟦< L *ex-*, out + *ferre*, to bear⟧ to raise the spirits of; make very proud, happy, etc. —**e·la'tion** ***n.***

el·bow (el'bō') ***n.*** ⟦see ELL² & BOW²⟧ **1** the joint between the upper and lower arm; esp., the outer angle made by a bent arm **2** anything bent like an elbow —***vt., vi.*** to shove as with the elbows

elbow grease [Inf.] vigorous physical effort

el'bow·room' ***n.*** ample space or room

eld·er¹ (el'dər) ***adj.*** ⟦< OE *eald*, old⟧ older —***n.*** **1** an older or aged person **2** an older person with some authority, as in a tribe **3** any of certain church officers

el·der² (el'dər) ***n.*** ⟦OE *ellern*⟧ a shrub or tree of the honeysuckle family, with red or purple berries

el'der·ber'ry (-ber'ē) ***n.***, *pl.* **-ries 1** ELDER² **2** its berry, used for making wine, jelly, etc.

eld'er·ly ***adj.*** **1** somewhat old **2** in old age; aged

eld·est (el'dist) ***adj.*** oldest; esp., first-born

El Do·ra·do or **El·do·ra·do** (el'də rä'dō) ***n.***, *pl.* **-dos** ⟦Sp, the gilded⟧ any place supposed to be rich in gold, opportunity, etc.

e·lect (ē lekt', i-) ***adj.*** ⟦< L *e-*, out + *legere*, choose⟧ **1** chosen **2** elected but not yet installed in office: usually used in combination *[*mayor-*elect]* —***vt., vi.*** **1** to select for an office by voting **2** to choose; select —**e·lect'a·ble** ***adj.*** —**e·lect'a·bil'i·ty** ***n.***

e·lec·tion (ē lek'shən, i-) ***n.*** **1** a choosing or choice **2** a choosing or being chosen by vote

e·lec'tion·eer' ***vi.*** to canvass votes in an election

e·lec'tive (-tiv) ***adj.*** **1** *a)* filled by election *[*an *elective* office*]* *b)* chosen by election **2** having the power to choose **3** optional —***n.*** an optional course or subject in a school curriculum

e·lec'tor (-tər) ***n.*** **1** one who elects; specif., a qualified voter **2** a member of the electoral college —**e·lec'tor·al** ***adj.***

electoral college an assembly elected by the voters to perform the formal duty of electing the president and vice president of the U.S.

e·lec'tor·ate (-it) ***n.*** all those qualified to vote in an election

E·lec·tra (ē lek'trə, i-) ***n.*** *Gr. Myth.* a daughter of Agamemnon: she plots the death of her mother

e·lec·tric (ē lek'trik, i-) ***adj.*** ⟦< Gr *ēlektron*, amber: from the effect of friction upon amber⟧ **1** of, charged with, or conducting electricity **2** producing, or produced by, electricity **3** operated by electricity **4** using electronic amplification *[*an *electric* guitar*]* **5** very tense or exciting Also **e·lec'tri·cal** —**e·lec'tri·cal·ly** ***adv.***

electric chair a chair equipped for use in electrocuting persons sentenced to death

e·lec·tri·cian (ē'lek trish'ən, ē lek'-) ***n.*** one whose work is the construction and repair of electric apparatus

e'lec·tric'i·ty (-tris'i tē) ***n.*** **1** a property of certain fundamental particles of all matter, as electrons (negative charges) and protons or positrons (positive charges): electrical charge is generated by friction, induction, or chemical change **2** an electric current **3** electric current as a public utility for lighting, heating, etc.

e·lec·tri·fy (ē lek′trə fī′, i-) ***vt.* -fied′, -fy′ing 1** to charge with electricity **2** to excite; thrill **3** to equip for the use of electricity —**e·lec′tri·fi·ca′tion** ***n.*** —**e·lec′tri·fi′er** ***n.***

electro- *combining form* electric, electricity

e·lec·tro·car·di·o·gram (ē lek′trō kär′dē ə gram′, i-) ***n.*** a tracing showing the variations in electric force which trigger heart contractions

e·lec′tro·car′di·o·graph′ (-graf′) ***n.*** an instrument for making electrocardiograms

e·lec′tro·cute′ (-trə kyo͞ot′) ***vt.* -cut′ed, -cut′ing** ⟦ELECTRO- + (EXE)CUTE⟧ to kill or execute with electricity —**e·lec′tro·cu′tion** ***n.***

e·lec′trode′ (-trōd′) ***n.*** ⟦ELECTR(O)- + -ODE⟧ any terminal by which electricity enters or leaves a battery, etc.

e·lec′tro·en·ceph′a·lo·gram′ (-trō en sef′ə lō gram′) ***n.*** ⟦see ENCEPHALITIS & -GRAM⟧ a tracing of the variations in electric force in the brain

e·lec′tro·en·ceph′a·lo·graph′ (-graf′) ***n.*** an instrument for making electroencephalograms

e′lec·trol′y·sis (-i sis) ***n.*** ⟦ELECTRO- + -LYSIS⟧ **1** the decomposition of an electrolyte by the action of an electric current passing through it **2** the eradication of unwanted hair with an electrified needle

e·lec·tro·lyte (ē lek′trō līt′, i-) ***n.*** ⟦ELECTRO- + -LYTE⟧ any chemical compound that ionizes when molten or in solution and becomes capable of conducting electricity —**e·lec′tro·lyt′ic** (-lit′ik) ***adj.***

e·lec′tro·mag′net (-mag′nit) ***n.*** a soft iron core that becomes a magnet when an electric current flows through a surrounding coil —**e·lec′tro·mag·net′ic** (-net′ik) ***adj.***

electromagnetic wave a wave generated by an oscillating electric charge

e·lec′tro·mo′tive (-mōt′iv) ***adj.*** producing an electric current through differences in potential

e·lec·tron (ē lek′trän′, i-) ***n.*** ⟦see ELECTRIC⟧ a stable, negatively charged elementary particle that forms a part of all atoms

e·lec·tron·ic (ē′lek trän′ik) ***adj.*** **1** of electrons **2** operating, produced, or done by the action of electrons —**e·lec′tron′i·cal·ly** ***adv.***

electronic mail E-MAIL

electronic music music in which the sounds are originated or altered by electronic devices

e′lec·tron′ics ***n.*** the science dealing with the action of electrons, and with the use of electron tubes, transistors, etc.

electron microscope a device that focuses a beam of electrons on a fluorescent screen, etc. to form a greatly enlarged image of an object

electron tube a sealed glass tube with gas or a vacuum inside, used to control the flow of electrons

e·lec·tro·plate (ē lek′trō plāt′, i-) ***vt.* -plat′ed, -plat′ing** to deposit a coating of metal on by electrolysis

e·lec′tro·scope′ (-skōp′) ***n.*** a device for detecting very small charges of electricity or radiation —**e·lec′tro·scop′ic** (-skäp′ik) ***adj.***

e·lec′tro·shock′ therapy a form of SHOCK THERAPY using electricity

e·lec′tro·type′ ***n.*** *Printing* a plate made by electroplating a wax or plastic impression of the surface to be reproduced

el·ee·mos·y·nar·y (el′i mäs′ə ner′ē, el′ē ə-) ***adj.*** ⟦< Gr *eleēmosynē*, pity⟧ of, for, or supported by charity

el·e·gant (el′ə gənt) ***adj.*** ⟦< L *e-*, out + *legere*, choose⟧ **1** having dignified richness and grace, as of manner, design, or dress; tastefully luxurious **2** cleverly apt and simple *[an elegant solution]* **3** [Inf.] excellent —**el′e·gance** ***n.*** —**el′e·gant·ly** ***adv.***

el·e·gi·ac (el ē′jē ak′, el′ə jī′ak′) ***adj.*** **1** of, like, or fit for an elegy **2** sad; mournful

el·e·gy (el′ə jē) ***n.***, *pl.* **-gies** ⟦< Gr *elegos*, a lament⟧ a mournful poem, esp. of lament and praise for the dead

el·e·ment (el′ə mənt) ***n.*** ⟦< L *elementum*⟧ **1** the natural or suitable environment for a person or thing **2** a component part or quality, often one that is basic or essential **3** *Chem.* any substance that cannot be separated into different substances by ordinary chemical methods, but only by radioactive decay or by nuclear reactions: all matter is composed of such substances —**the elements 1** the first principles; rudiments **2** wind, rain, etc.; forces of the atmosphere

el·e·men·tal (el′ə ment′'l) ***adj.*** **1** of or like basic, natural forces; primal **2** ELEMENTARY (sense 2*a*) **3** being an essential part or parts

el′e·men′ta·ry (-ə rē) ***adj.*** **1** ELEMENTAL **2** *a)* of first principles or fundamentals; basic; simple *b)* of the formal instruction of children in basic subjects

elementary particle a subatomic particle that cannot be divided

elementary school a school of the first six (sometimes eight) grades, where basic subjects are taught

el·e·phant (el′ə fənt) ***n.*** ⟦< Gr *elephas*⟧ a huge, thick-skinned mammal with a long, flexible snout, or trunk, and, usually, two ivory tusks

el·e·phan·ti·a·sis (el′ə fən tī′ə sis) ***n.*** a chronic disease causing the enlargement of certain body parts and hardening of the surrounding skin

el·e·phan·tine (el′ə fan′tēn′) ***adj.*** like an elephant; huge, clumsy, etc.

el·e·vate (el′ə vāt′) ***vt.* -vat′ed, -vat′ing** ⟦< L *e-*, out + *levare*, to lift⟧ **1** to lift up; raise **2** to raise in rank **3** to raise to a higher intellectual or moral level **4** to elate; exhilarate

el′e·va′tion (-vā′shən) ***n.*** **1** an elevating or being elevated **2** a high place or position **3** height above the surface of the earth or above sea level

el′e·va′tor (-vāt′ər) ***n.*** **1** one that elevates, or lifts up **2** a suspended cage for hoisting or lowering people or things **3** a tall warehouse for storing and discharging grain: in full **grain elevator**

e·lev·en (ē lev′ən, i-) ***adj., n.*** ⟦OE *endleofan*⟧ one more than ten; 11; XI —**e·lev′enth** (-ənth) ***adj., n.***

elf (elf) ***n., pl.*** **elves** (elvz) ⟦OE *ælf*⟧ *Folklore* a tiny, often mischievous fairy —**elf′in** or **elf′ish** ***adj.***

El Gre·co (el grek′ō) 1541?-1614?; painter in Italy & Spain, born in Crete

e·lic·it (ē lis′it, i-) ***vt.*** ⟦< L *e-*, out + *lacere*, entice⟧ to draw forth; evoke (a response, etc.) —**e·lic′i·ta′tion** ***n.***

e·lide (ē līd′, i-) ***vt.*** **e·lid′ed, e·lid′ing** ⟦< L *e-*, out + *laedere*, to hurt⟧ to leave out; esp., to slur over (a vowel, etc.) in pronunciation —**e·li′sion** (-lizh′ən) ***n.***

el·i·gi·ble (el′i jə bəl) ***adj.*** ⟦see ELECT⟧ fit to be chosen; qualified —**el′i·gi·bil′i·ty** ***n.***

E·li·jah (ē lī′jə, i-) ***n.*** *Bible* a prophet of Israel in the 9th c. B.C.

e·lim·i·nate (ē lim′ə nāt′, i-) ***vt.*** **-nat′ed, -nat′ing** ⟦< L *e-*, out + *limen*, threshold⟧ **1** to remove; get rid of **2** to leave out of consideration; omit **3** to excrete —**e·lim′i·na′tion** ***n.***

El·i·ot (el′ē ət) **1 George** (pseud. of *Mary Ann Evans*) 1819-80; Eng. novelist **2 T**(**homas**) **S**(**tearns**) 1885-1965; Brit. poet, born in the U.S.

e·lite (i lēt′, ā-) ***n.*** ⟦Fr < L: see ELECT⟧ [*also with pl. v.*] the group or part of a group regarded as the best, most powerful, etc.

e·lit′ism′ ***n.*** government or control by an elite —**e·lit′ist** ***adj., n.***

e·lix·ir (i liks′ir) ***n.*** ⟦< Ar *al-iksīr*⟧ **1** a hypothetical substance sought by medieval alchemists to change base metals into gold or (in full **elixir of life**) to prolong life indefinitely **2** *Pharmacy* a sweetened solution used for medicines, etc.

E·liz·a·beth (ē liz′ə bəth, i-) **1 Elizabeth I** 1533-1603; queen of England (1558-1603) **2 Elizabeth II** 1926- ; queen of Great Britain & Northern Ireland (1952-)

E·liz·a·be·than (ē liz′ə bē′thən) ***adj.*** of or characteristic of the time of Elizabeth I's reign —***n.*** an English person, esp. a writer, of that time

elk (elk) ***n.*** ⟦< OE *eolh*⟧ **1** MOOSE: the common term in Europe **2** WAPITI

ell[1] (el) ***n.*** **1** an extension or wing at right angles to the main structure **2** an L-shaped pipe, etc.

ell[2] (el) ***n.*** ⟦< OE *eln*⟧ a former English unit of measure, equal to 45 inches

el·lipse (e lips′, i-) ***n., pl.*** **-lip′ses′** (-sēz′) ⟦< Gr *elleipein*, fall short⟧ *Geom.* a closed curve in the form of a symmetrical oval

el·lip′sis (-lip′sis) ***n., pl.*** **-ses′** (-sēz′) ⟦see prec.⟧ **1** *Gram.* the omission of a word or words understood in the context (Ex.: "if possible" for "if it is possible") **2** a mark (. . .) indicating an omission of words: in full **ellipsis points**

el·lip′ti·cal (-ti kəl) ***adj.*** **1** of, or having the form of, an ellipse **2** of or characterized by ellipsis Also **el·lip′tic** —**el·lip′ti·cal·ly** ***adv.***

elm (elm) ***n.*** ⟦OE⟧ **1** a tall, deciduous shade tree **2** its hard, heavy wood

El Ni·ño (el nēn′yō) a warm inshore current annually flowing south along the coast of Ecuador

el·o·cu·tion (el′ə kyo͞o′shən) ***n.*** ⟦see ELOQUENT⟧ the art of public speaking —**el′o·cu′tion·ar′y** ***adj.*** —**el′o·cu′tion·ist** ***n.***

e·lo·de·a (ē lō′dē ə, el′ə dē′ə) ***n.*** ⟦< Gr *helōdēs*, swampy⟧ a submerged water plant with whorls of short, grasslike leaves

e·lon·gate (ē lôŋ′gāt′, i-) ***vt., vi.*** **-gat′ed, -gat′ing** ⟦< L *e-*, out + *longus*, long⟧ to make or become longer; stretch —**e′lon·ga′tion** ***n.***

e·lope (ē lōp′, i-) ***vi.*** **e·loped′, e·lop′ing** ⟦prob. < OE *a-*, away + *hleapan*, to run⟧ to run away secretly, esp. in order to get married —**e·lope′ment** ***n.***

el·o·quent (el′ə kwənt) ***adj.*** ⟦< L *e-*, out + *loqui*, speak⟧ vivid, forceful, fluent, etc. in speech or writing —**el′o·quence** ***n.*** —**el′o·quent·ly** ***adv.***

El Pas·o (el pas′ō) city in westernmost Texas.: pop. 515,000

El Sal·va·dor (el sal′və dôr′) country in Central America, on the Pacific: 8,124 sq. mi.; pop. 5,048,000

else (els) ***adj.*** ⟦OE *elles*⟧ **1** different; other [*somebody else*] **2** in addition [*is there anything else?*] —***adv.*** **1** differently; otherwise [*where else can I go?*] **2** if not [*study, (or) else you will fail*]

else′where′ ***adv.*** in or to some other place; somewhere else

e·lu·ci·date (ə lo͞o′sə dāt′) ***vt., vi.*** **-dat′ed, -dat′ing** ⟦< L *e-*, out + *lucidus*, clear⟧ to make (something) clear; explain —**e·lu′ci·da′tion** ***n.***

e·lude (ē lo͞od′, i-) ***vt.*** **e·lud′ed, e·lud′ing** ⟦< L *e-*, out + *ludere*, to play⟧ **1** to avoid or escape from by quickness, cunning, etc.; evade **2** to escape the mental grasp of [*his name eludes me*]

e·lu′sive (-lo͞o′siv) ***adj.*** tending to elude; evasive —**e·lu′sive·ly** ***adv.*** —**e·lu′sive·ness** ***n.***

elves (elvz) ***n. pl. of*** ELF

E·lys·i·um (ē lizh′əm, -liz′ē əm; i-) ***n.*** **1** *Gr. Myth.* the dwelling place of virtuous people after death **2** any state of ideal bliss; paradise —**E·ly′si·an** (-lizh′ən, -liz′ē ən) ***adj.***

em (em) ***n.*** ⟦< the letter *M*⟧ *Printing* a unit of measure, as of column width

'em (əm) ***pron.*** [Inf.] them

em- *prefix* EN-: used before *b, m,* or *p*

e·ma·ci·ate (ē mā′shē āt′, -sē-; i-) ***vt.*** **-at′ed, -at′ing** ⟦< L *e-*, out + *macies*, leanness⟧ to cause to become abnormally lean —**e·ma′ci·a′tion** ***n.***

e-mail (ē′māl′) ***n.*** [*also* **E-**] messages sent from one computer terminal to another, as by telephone line

em·a·nate (em′ə nāt′) ***vi.*** **-nat′ed, -nat′ing** ⟦< L *e-*, out + *manare*, to flow⟧ to come forth; issue, as from a source —**em′a·na′tion** ***n.***

e·man·ci·pate (ē man′sə pāt′, i-) ***vt.***

-pat′ed, -pat′ing ⟦< L *e-*, out + *manus*, the hand + *capere*, to take⟧ **1** to set free (a slave, etc.) **2** to free from restraint —**e·man′ci·pa′tion** ***n.*** —**e·man′ci·pa′tor** ***n.***

e·mas·cu·late (ē mas′kyoo͞ lāt′) ***vt.*** **-lat′ed, -lat′ing** ⟦< L *e-*, out + *masculus*, male⟧ **1** to castrate **2** to weaken —**e·mas′cu·la′tion** ***n.***

em·balm (em bäm′, im-) ***vt.*** ⟦see EN- & BALM⟧ to preserve (a dead body) with various chemicals —**em·balm′er** ***n.***

em·bank (em baŋk′, im-) ***vt.*** to protect, support, or enclose with a bank of earth, etc. —**em·bank′ment** ***n.***

em·bar·go (em bär′gō, im-) ***n.***, *pl.* **-goes** ⟦Sp < L *in-*, in + ML *barra*, a bar⟧ **1** a government order prohibiting the entry or departure of commercial ships at its ports **2** any legal restriction of commerce —***vt.*** **-goed, -go·ing** to put an embargo upon

em·bark (em bärk′, im-) ***vt.*** ⟦ult. < L *in-*, in + *barca*, small boat⟧ to put or take (passengers or goods) aboard a ship, aircraft, etc. —***vi.*** **1** to go aboard a ship, aircraft, etc. **2** to begin; start —**em′bar·ka′tion** (-bär kā′shən) ***n.***

em·bar·rass (em bar′əs, im-) ***vt.*** ⟦< It *in-*, in + ML *barra*, a bar⟧ **1** to cause to feel self-conscious **2** to hinder **3** to cause to be in debt —**em·bar′rass·ing** ***adj.*** —**em·bar′rass·ment** ***n.***

em·bas·sy (em′bə sē) ***n.***, *pl.* **-sies** ⟦see AMBASSADOR⟧ **1** the residence or offices of an ambassador **2** an ambassador and his or her staff **3** a group sent on an official mission

em·bat·tled (em bat′'ld) ***adj.*** ⟦< OFr⟧ engaged in battle or conflict

em·bed (em bed′, im-) ***vt.*** **-bed′ded, -bed′ding** to set or fix firmly in earth, in the mind or memory, etc. —**em·bed′ment** ***n.***

em·bel·lish (em bel′ish, im-) ***vt.*** ⟦< OFr *em-*, in + *bel*, beautiful⟧ **1** to adorn **2** to improve (a story, etc.) by adding details, often fictitious —**em·bel′lish·ment** ***n.***

em·ber (em′bər) ***n.*** ⟦OE *æmerge*⟧ **1** a glowing piece of coal, wood, etc. **2** [*pl.*] the smoldering remains of a fire

em·bez·zle (em bez′əl, im-) ***vt.*** **-zled, -zling** ⟦< OFr *en-*, in + *besillier*, destroy⟧ to steal (money, etc. entrusted to one) —**em·bez′zle·ment** ***n.*** —**em·bez′zler** ***n.***

em·bit′ter (-bit′ər) ***vt.*** to make bitter —**em·bit′ter·ment** ***n.***

em·bla′zon (-blā′zən) ***vt.*** ⟦EM- (see EN-) + BLAZON⟧ **1** to decorate (*with* coats of arms, etc.) **2** to display brilliantly **3** to extol —**em·bla′zon·ment** ***n.***

em·blem (em′bləm) ***n.*** ⟦< Gr *en-*, in + *ballein*, throw⟧ a visible symbol of a thing, idea, etc.; sign; badge —**em′blem·at′ic** (-blə mat′ik) ***adj.***

em·bod·y (em bäd′ē, im-) ***vt.*** **-ied, -y·ing** **1** to give bodily form to **2** to give definite form to **3** to bring together into an organized whole; incorporate —**em·bod′i·ment** ***n.***

em·bold′en (-bōl′dən) ***vt.*** to give courage to

em·bo·lism (em′bə liz′əm) ***n.*** ⟦< Gr *en-*, in + *ballein*, to throw⟧ the obstruction of a blood vessel as by a blood clot or air bubble

em·boss (em bôs′, -bäs′; im-) ***vt.*** ⟦see EN- & BOSS²⟧ **1** to decorate with raised designs, patterns, etc. **2** to raise (a design, etc.) in relief —**em·boss′er** ***n.***

em·bou·chure (äm′boo͞ shoor′) ***n.*** ⟦Fr < L *in*, in + *bucca*, cheek⟧ the method of applying the lips and tongue to the mouthpiece of a wind instrument

em·brace (em brās′, im-) ***vt.*** **-braced′, -brac′ing** ⟦< L *im-*, in + *brachium*, an arm⟧ **1** to clasp in the arms lovingly; hug **2** to accept readily **3** to take up or adopt **4** to encircle **5** to include —***vi.*** to clasp each other in the arms —***n.*** an embracing; hug —**em·brace′a·ble** ***adj.***

em·bra·sure (em brā′zhər, im-) ***n.*** ⟦Fr < obs. *embraser*, widen an opening⟧ **1** an opening (for a door, window, etc.) wider on the inside than on the outside **2** an opening in a wall or parapet for a gun, with the sides slanting outward

em·broi·der (em broi′dər, im-) ***vt.***, ***vi.*** ⟦< OFr *en-*, on + *brosder*, embroider⟧ **1** to make (a design, etc.) on (fabric) with needlework **2** to embellish (a story); exaggerate

em·broi′der·y ***n.***, *pl.* **-ies** **1** the art of embroidering **2** embroidered work or fabric **3** embellishment

em·broil (em broil′, im-) ***vt.*** ⟦< OFr *en-*, in + *brouillier*, to dirty⟧ **1** to confuse; muddle **2** to involve in conflict or trouble —**em·broil′ment** ***n.***

em·bry·o (em′brē ō′) ***n.***, *pl.* **-os′** ⟦< Gr *en-*, in + *bryein*, to swell⟧ **1** an animal in the earliest stages of its development in the uterus or egg **2** the rudimentary plant contained in a seed **3** an early stage of something —**em′bry·on′ic** (-än′ik) ***adj.***

em′bry·ol′o·gy (-äl′ə jē) ***n.*** ⟦prec. + -LOGY⟧ the branch of biology dealing with the formation and development of embryos —**em′bry·ol′o·gist** ***n.***

em·cee (em′sē′) ***vi.***, ***vt.*** **-ceed′, -cee′ing** ⟦< MC, sense 1⟧ [Inf.] to act as master of ceremonies (for) —***n.*** [Inf.] a master of ceremonies

e·mend (ē mend′, i-) ***vt.*** ⟦< L *emendare*, to correct⟧ to make scholarly corrections in (a text) —**e·men·da·tion** (ē′men dā′shən, em′ən-) ***n.***

em·er·ald (em′ər əld) ***n.*** ⟦< Gr *smaragdos*⟧ **1** a transparent, bright-green precious stone **2** bright green

e·merge (ē murj′, i-) ***vi.*** **e·merged′, e·merg′ing** ⟦< L *e-*, out + *mergere*, to dip⟧ **1** to rise as from a fluid **2** to become visible or apparent **3** to evolve —**e·mer′gence** ***n.*** —**e·mer′gent** ***adj.***

e·mer·gen·cy (ē mur′jən sē, i-) ***n.***, *pl.* **-cies** ⟦orig. sense, emergence⟧ a sudden, generally unexpected occurrence demanding immediate action —***adj.*** for use in an emergency

emergency room a hospital unit for accident victims and others needing immediate treatment

e·mer·i·tus (ē mer′i təs, i-) ***adj.*** ⟦< L *e-*, out + *mereri*, to serve⟧ retired from active service, usually for age, but retaining one's title *[professor emeritus]*

Em·er·son (em'ər sən), **Ralph Wal·do** (ralf wôl'dō) 1803-82; U.S. writer & philosopher

em·er·y (em'ər ē) ***n.*** ⟦< Gr *smyris*⟧ a dark, coarse variety of corundum used for grinding, polishing, etc.

emery board a small, flat stick coated with powdered emery, used to shape the fingernails

e·met·ic (ē met'ik, i-) ***adj.*** ⟦< Gr *emein,* to vomit⟧ causing vomiting **—*n.*** an emetic substance

-e·mi·a (ē'mē ə) ⟦< Gr *haima,* blood⟧ *combining form* a (specified) condition of the blood *[leukemia]*

em·i·grate (em'i grāt') ***vi.*** **-grat'ed, -grat'ing** ⟦< L *e-,* out + *migrare,* to move⟧ to leave one country or region to settle in another **—em'i·grant** (-grənt) ***adj., n.*** **—em'i·gra'tion *n.***

é·mi·gré or **e·mi·gré** (em'i grā') ***n.*** ⟦Fr⟧ **1** one who emigrates **2** one forced to flee his or her country for political reasons

em·i·nence (em'i nəns) ***n.*** ⟦< L *eminere,* stand out⟧ **1** a high place, thing, etc. **2** superiority in rank, position, etc. **3** [**E-**] a title of a cardinal: preceded by *Your* or *His*

em'i·nent (-nənt) ***adj.*** ⟦< L *eminens*⟧ **1** high; lofty **2** projecting; prominent **3** renowned; distinguished **4** outstanding **—em'i·nent·ly *adv.***

eminent domain the right of a government to take or purchase private property for public use, with just compensation to the owner

e·mir (e mir', ə-) ***n.*** ⟦< Ar *amara,* to command⟧ in Muslim countries, a ruler or prince

em·is·sar·y (em'i ser'ē) ***n., pl.*** **-ies** ⟦see EMIT⟧ a person or agent sent on a specific mission

e·mis·sion (ē mish'ən, i-) ***n.*** **1** an emitting **2** something emitted; discharge

e·mit (ē mit', i-) ***vt.*** **e·mit'ted, e·mit'ting** ⟦< L *e-,* out + *mittere,* send⟧ **1** to send out; give forth; discharge **2** to utter (words, etc.) **—e·mit'ter *n.***

e·mol·li·ent (ē mäl'yənt, i-) ***adj.*** ⟦< L *e-,* out + *mollire,* soften⟧ softening; soothing **—*n.*** something that softens or soothes, as a preparation applied to the skin

e·mol'u·ment (-yōō mənt) ***n.*** ⟦< L *e-,* out + *molere,* to grind⟧ payment received for work; salary, fees, etc.

e·mote (ē mōt', i-) ***vi.*** **e·mot'ed, e·mot'ing** [Inf.] to act in an emotional or theatrical manner

e·mo·tion (ē mō'shən, i-) ***n.*** ⟦< L *e-,* out + *movere,* to move⟧ **1** strong feeling **2** any specific feeling, as love, hate, fear, or anger

e·mo'tion·al ***adj.*** **1** of or showing emotion **2** easily aroused to emotion **3** appealing to the emotions; moving **—e·mo'tion·al·ism' *n.*** **—e·mo'tion·al·ly *adv.***

e·mo'tion·al·ize' ***vt.*** **-ized', -iz'ing** to treat in an emotional way

em·pa·thet·ic (em'pə thet'ik) ***adj.*** of or showing empathy: also **em·path'ic** (-path'ik)

em·pa·thize (em'pə thīz') ***vt.*** **-thized', -thiz'ing** to feel empathy (*with*)

em'pa·thy (-thē) ***n.*** ⟦< Gr *en-,* in + *pathos,* feeling⟧ the ability to share in another's emotions, thoughts, or feelings

em·per·or (em'pər ər) ***n.*** ⟦< L *in-,* in + *parare,* to set in order⟧ the supreme ruler of an empire

em·pha·sis (em'fə sis) ***n., pl.*** **-ses'** (-sēz') ⟦< Gr *en-,* in + *phainein,* to show⟧ **1** force of expression, action, etc. **2** special stress given to a word or phrase in speaking **3** importance; stress

em'pha·size' (-sīz') ***vt.*** **-sized', -siz'ing** to give emphasis to; stress

em·phat·ic (em fat'ik, im-) ***adj.*** **1** felt or done with emphasis **2** using emphasis in speaking, etc. **3** forcible; striking **—em·phat'i·cal·ly *adv.***

em·phy·se·ma (em'fə sē'mə, -zē'-) ***n.*** ⟦< Gr *en-,* in + *physaein,* to blow⟧ a condition of the lungs in which the air sacs become distended and lose elasticity

em·pire (em'pīr') ***n.*** ⟦see EMPEROR⟧ **1** supreme rule **2** government by an emperor or empress **3** a group of states or territories under one ruler **4** an extensive organization under the control of a single person, corporation, etc.

em·pir·i·cal (em pir'i kəl) ***adj.*** ⟦< Gr *en-,* in + *peira,* trial⟧ relying or based on experiment or experience **—em·pir'i·cal·ly *adv.*** **—em·pir'i·cism'** (-siz'əm) ***n.***

em·place·ment (em plās'mənt, im-) ***n.*** the prepared position from which a heavy gun or guns are fired

em·ploy (em ploi', im-) ***vt.*** ⟦< L *in-,* in + *plicare,* to fold⟧ **1** to use **2** to keep busy or occupied **3** to engage the services of; hire **—*n.*** employment

em·ploy'a·ble ***adj.*** that can be employed; specif., physically or mentally fit to be hired for work

em·ploy'ee or **em·ploy'e** (-ē) ***n.*** one hired by another for wages or salary

em·ploy'er ***n.*** one who employs others for wages or salary

em·ploy'ment ***n.*** **1** an employing or being employed **2** work; occupation **3** the number or percentage of persons gainfully employed

em·po·ri·um (em pôr'ē əm) ***n., pl.*** **-ri·ums** or **-ri·a** (-ə) ⟦< Gr *en-,* in + *poros,* way⟧ a large store with a wide variety of things for sale

em·pow·er (em pou'ər, im-) ***vt.*** **1** to give power to; authorize **2** to enable **—em·pow'er·ment *n.***

em·press (em'pris) ***n.*** **1** an emperor's wife **2** a woman ruler of an empire

emp·ty (emp'tē) ***adj.*** **-ti·er, -ti·est** ⟦OE *æmettig*⟧ **1** having nothing or no one in it; unoccupied **2** worthless *[empty pleasure]* **3** insincere *[empty promises]* **—*vt.*** **-tied, -ty·ing** **1** to make empty **2** to remove (the contents) of something **—*vi.*** **1** to become empty **2** to pour out; discharge **—*n., pl.*** **-ties** an empty truck, bottle, etc. **—emp'ti·ly *adv.*** **—emp'ti·ness *n.***

emp'ty-hand'ed ***adj.*** bringing or carrying away nothing

em·py·re·an (em pir′ē ən, em′pī rē′ən) *n.* ⟦< Gr *en-*, in + *pyr*, fire⟧ **1** the highest heaven **2** the sky; firmament

EMT *abbrev.* emergency medical technician

e·mu (ē′myo͞o′) *n.* ⟦< Port *ema*, a crane⟧ a large, flightless Australian bird, somewhat like the ostrich but smaller

em·u·late (em′yo͞o lāt′, -yə-) *vt.* **-lat′ed, -lat′ing** ⟦< L *aemulus*, trying to equal or excel⟧ **1** to try to equal or surpass **2** to imitate (a person or thing admired) **3** to rival successfully —**em′u·la′tion** *n.* —**em′u·la′tive** *adj.* —**em′u·la′tor** *n.*

e·mul·si·fy (ē mul′sə fī′, i-) *vt., vi.* **-fied′, -fy′ing** to form into an emulsion —**e·mul′si·fi·ca′tion** *n.*

e·mul′sion (-shən) *n.* ⟦< L *e-*, out + *mulgere*, to milk⟧ a colloidal suspension of one liquid in another, as photographic film coatings, some medications, etc.

en- ⟦< L *in-*, in⟧ *prefix* **1** to put or get into or on *[enthrone]* **2** to make, cause to be *[endanger]* **3** in or into *[encase]*

-en (ən, ′n) ⟦OE⟧ *suffix* **1** *a)* to become or cause to be *[darken]* *b)* to cause to have *[heighten]* **2** made of *[wooden]* **3** forming plurals *[children]*

en·a·ble (en ā′bəl, in-) *vt.* **-bled, -bling** **1** to make able; provide with means, power, etc. (*to* do something) **2** to support the dysfunctional behavior of, as by compensating for it —**en·a′bler** *n.*

en·act (en akt′, in-) *vt.* **1** to pass (a bill, law, etc.) **2** to represent as in a play —**en·act′ment** *n.*

en·am·el (e nam′əl, i-) *n.* ⟦< OFr *esmail*⟧ **1** a glassy, opaque substance fused to metal, pottery, etc. as an ornamental or protective coating **2** the hard, white coating of teeth **3** paint that dries to a smooth, glossy surface —*vt.* **-eled** or **-elled, -el·ing** or **-el·ling** to coat with enamel —**en·am′el·er** or **en·am′el·ler** *n.*

en·am·or (en am′ər, in-) *vt.* ⟦ult. < L *in-*, in + *amor*, love⟧ to fill with love; charm: now mainly in the passive voice, with *of* *[enamored of her]*

en bloc (en bläk′) ⟦Fr, lit., in a block⟧ in a mass; all together

en bro·chette (än brô shet′) ⟦Fr⟧ broiled on small skewers

en·camp (en kamp′, in-) *vi., vt.* to set up, or put in, a camp —**en·camp′ment** *n.*

en·cap·su·late (en kap′sə lāt′) *vt.* **-lat′ed, -lat′ing** **1** to enclose in a capsule **2** to make concise; condense Also **en·cap′sule** (-səl, -syo͞ol′), **-suled, -sul·ing** —**en·cap′su·la′tion** *n.*

en·case (en kās′, in-) *vt.* **-cased′, -cas′ing** to enclose, as in a case

en cas·se·role (en kas′ə rōl′) ⟦Fr⟧ (baked and served) in a casserole

-ence (əns, ′ns) ⟦< L⟧ *suffix* act, state, or result *[conference]*

en·ceph·a·li·tis (en sef′ə līt′is) *n.* ⟦< Gr *en-*, in + *kephalē*, the head + -ITIS⟧ inflammation of the brain

en·chain (en chān′) *vt.* to bind with chains; fetter

en·chant (en chant′, in-) *vt.* ⟦< L *in-*, intens. + *cantare*, sing⟧ **1** to cast a spell over **2** to charm greatly; delight —**en·chant′er** *n.* —**en·chant′ing** *adj.* —**en·chant′ment** *n.*

en·chi·la·da (en′chi lä′də) *n.* ⟦AmSp⟧ a tortilla rolled with meat inside, served with a chili-flavored sauce

en·cir·cle (en sʉr′kəl, in-) *vt.* **-cled, -cling** **1** to surround **2** to move in a circle around —**en·cir′cle·ment** *n.*

encl *abbrev.* enclosure

en·clave (en′klāv′, än′-) *n.* ⟦< L *in*, in + *clavis*, a key⟧ a territory surrounded by another country's territory

en·close (en klōz′, in-) *vt.* **-closed′, -clos′ing** **1** to shut in all around; surround **2** to insert in an envelope, etc., often along with something else

en·clo′sure (-klō′zhər) *n.* **1** an enclosing or being enclosed **2** something that encloses, as a fence **3** something enclosed, as in an envelope or by a wall

en·code (en kōd′, in-) *vt.* **-cod′ed, -cod′ing** to put (a message, etc.) into code

en·co·mi·um (en kō′mē əm) *n., pl.* **-ums** or **-a** (-ə) ⟦< Gr *en-*, in + *kōmos*, a revel⟧ high praise; eulogy

en·com·pass (en kum′pəs, in-) *vt.* **1** to surround **2** to contain; include

en·core (än′kôr′) *interj.* ⟦Fr⟧ again; once more —*n.* a further performance, etc. in answer to an audience's applause

en·coun·ter (en koun′tər, in-) *vt.* ⟦< L *in*, in + *contra*, against⟧ **1** to meet unexpectedly **2** to meet in conflict **3** to meet with (difficulties, etc.) —*n.* **1** a direct meeting, as in battle **2** a meeting, esp. when unexpected

en·cour·age (en kʉr′ij, in-) *vt.* **-aged, -ag·ing** **1** to give courage, hope, or confidence to **2** to give support to; help —**en·cour′age·ment** *n.*

en·croach (en krōch′, in-) *vi.* ⟦< OFr *en-*, in + *croc*, a hook⟧ to trespass or intrude (*on* or *upon*) —**en·croach′ment** *n.*

en croûte (än kro͞ot′) ⟦Fr⟧ wrapped in pastry and baked: said esp. of meats

en·crust (en krust′) *vt.* to cover as with a crust —*vi.* to form a crust —**en′crus·ta′tion** (-krus tā′shən) *n.*

en·cum·ber (en kum′bər, in-) *vt.* ⟦see EN- & CUMBER⟧ **1** to hold back the motion or action of; hinder **2** to burden —**en·cum′brance** *n.*

-en·cy (ən sē) ⟦L *-entia*⟧ *suffix* -ENCE *[dependency]*

en·cyc·li·cal (en sik′li kəl, in-) *n.* ⟦< Gr *en-*, in + *kyklos*, a circle⟧ a papal document addressed to the bishops

en·cy·clo·pe·di·a or **en·cy·clo·pae·di·a** (en sī′klə pē′dē ə) *n.* ⟦< Gr *enkyklios*, general + *paideia*, education⟧ a book or set of books with alphabetically arranged articles on all branches, or on one field, of knowledge —**en·cy′clo·pe′dic** or **en·cy′clo·pae′dic** *adj.*

en·cyst (en sist′) *vt., vi.* to enclose or become enclosed in a cyst, sac, etc. —**en·cyst′ment** *n.*

end (end) *n.* ⟦OE *ende*⟧ **1** a limit; boundary **2** the last part of anything; finish;

conclusion **3** a ceasing to exist; death or destruction **4** the part at or near an extremity; tip **5** an object; purpose **6** an outcome; result **7** *Football* a player at either end of the line —*vt., vi.* to bring or come to an end; finish; stop —*adj.* at the end; final —**make (both) ends meet** to manage to keep one's expenses within one's income —**put an end to 1** to stop **2** to do away with

en·dan·ger (en dān′jər, in-) *vt.* to expose to danger, harm, etc.; imperil —**en·dan′ger·ment** *n.*

endangered species a species of animal or plant in danger of becoming extinct

en·dear (en dir′, in-) *vt.* to make dear or beloved —**en·dear′ing** *adj.*

en·dear′ment *n.* **1** an endearing **2** a word or act expressing affection

en·deav·or (en dev′ər, in-) *vi.* ⟦< EN- + OFr *deveir*, duty⟧ to make an earnest attempt; try: usually with an infinitive —*n.* an earnest attempt or effort Brit. sp. **en·deav′our**

en·dem·ic (en dem′ik) *adj.* ⟦< Gr *en-*, in + *dēmos*, people⟧ native to, or constantly present in, a particular place, as a plant or disease —**en·dem′i·cal·ly** *adv.*

end′ing *n.* **1** the last part; finish **2** death

en·dive (en′dīv′, än′dēv′) *n.* ⟦< Gr *entybon*⟧ a cultivated plant with curled, narrow leaves used in salads

end′less *adj.* **1** having no end; eternal; infinite **2** lasting too long *[an endless* speech*]* **3** continual *[endless* problems*]* **4** with the ends joined to form a closed unit *[*an *endless* chain*]* —**end′less·ly** *adv.* —**end′less·ness** *n.*

end′most′ *adj.* at the end; farthest

endo- ⟦< Gr *endon*⟧ *combining form* within, inner

en·do·crine (en′dō krin′, -krīn′; -də-) *adj.* ⟦prec. + Gr *krinein*, to separate⟧ designating or of any gland producing a hormone

en·dorse (en dôrs′, in-) *vt.* **-dorsed′**, **-dors′ing** ⟦< L *in*, on + *dorsum*, the back⟧ **1** to write on the back of (a title, check, etc.) to transfer ownership, make a deposit, etc. **2** to sanction, approve, or support **3** to recommend (an advertised product) for a fee —**en·dorse′ment** *n.* —**en·dors′er** *n.*

en·do·scope (en′dō skōp′, -də-) *n.* an instrument for examining visually the inside of a hollow organ or cavity of the body, as the rectum

en·dow (en dou′, in-) *vt.* ⟦< OFr *en-*, in + *dotare*, to endow⟧ **1** to provide with some talent, quality, etc. *[endowed* with courage*]* **2** to give money or property to (a college, etc.) —**en·dow′ment** *n.*

end′point′ *n.* a point of completion or furthest progress

end product the final result of a series of changes, processes, etc.

end table a small table placed at the end of a sofa, etc.

en·due (en dōō′, in-) *vt.* **-dued′**, **-du′ing** ⟦< L *in-*, in + *ducere*, to lead⟧ to provide (*with* qualities)

en·dur·ance (en door′əns, in-) *n.* the ability to last, stand pain, etc.

en·dure (en door′, in-) *vt.* **-dured′**, **-dur′ing** ⟦< L *durus*, hard⟧ **1** to hold up under (pain, etc.) **2** to tolerate —*vi.* **1** to continue; last **2** to bear pain, etc. without flinching —**en·dur′a·ble** *adj.*

end′ways′ (-wāz′) *adv.* **1** upright **2** with the end foremost **3** lengthwise Also **end′wise′** (-wīz′)

-ene (ēn) ⟦after Gr *-enos*, adj. suffix⟧ *Chem. suffix* a certain type of hydrocarbon *[benzene]*

en·e·ma (en′ə mə) *n.* ⟦< Gr *en-*, in + *hienai*, send⟧ the forcing of a liquid, as a purgative, medicine, etc., into the colon through the anus

en·e·my (en′ə mē) *n., pl.* **-mies** ⟦< L *in-*, not + *amicus*, friend⟧ **1** one who hates and wishes to injure another **2** *a)* a nation or force hostile to another *b)* troops, ship, etc. of a hostile nation **3** one hostile to an idea, cause, etc. **4** anything injurious or harmful

en·er·get·ic (en′ər jet′ik) *adj.* having or showing energy; vigorous —**en′er·get′i·cal·ly** *adv.*

en·er·gize (en′ər jīz′) *vt.* **-gized′**, **-giz′ing** to give energy to; activate —**en′er·giz′er** *n.*

en·er·gy (en′ər jē) *n., pl.* **-gies** ⟦< Gr *en-*, in + *ergon*, work⟧ **1** force of expression **2** *a)* inherent power; capacity for action *b)* [*often pl.*] such power, esp. in action **3** a resource, as oil or gas, from which usable energy can be produced **4** *Physics* the capacity for doing work

en·er·vate (en′ər vāt′) *vt.* **-vat′ed**, **-vat′ing** ⟦< L *e-*, out + *nervus*, nerve⟧ to deprive of strength, force, vigor, etc.; devitalize —**en′er·va′tion** *n.*

en·fee·ble (en fē′bəl, in-) *vt.* **-bled**, **-bling** to make feeble

en·fi·lade (en′fə lād′, en′fə lād′) *n.* ⟦Fr⟧ gunfire directed along a line of troops

en·fold (en fōld′, in-) *vt.* **1** to wrap in folds; wrap up **2** to embrace

en·force (en fôrs′, in-) *vt.* **-forced′**, **-forc′ing** **1** to impose by force *[*to *enforce* one's will*]* **2** to compel observance of (a law, etc.) —**en·force′a·ble** *adj.* —**en·force′ment** *n.* —**en·forc′er** *n.*

en·fran·chise (en fran′chīz′, in-) *vt.* **-chised′**, **-chis′ing** **1** to free from slavery **2** to give the right to vote —**en·fran′chise·ment** (-chiz mənt) *n.*

Eng *abbrev.* **1** England **2** English

en·gage (en gāj′, in-) *vt.* **-gaged′**, **-gag′ing** ⟦see EN- & GAGE[1]⟧ **1** to pledge (oneself) **2** to bind by a promise of marriage **3** to hire **4** to involve or occupy **5** to attract and hold (the attention, etc.) **6** to enter into conflict with (the enemy) **7** to mesh (gears, etc.) —*vi.* **1** to pledge oneself **2** to occupy or involve oneself *[*to *engage* in dramatics*]* **3** to enter into conflict **4** to mesh

en·gaged′ *adj.* **1** betrothed **2** occupied; employed **3** involved in combat, as troops **4** in gear; meshed

en·gage′ment *n.* an engaging or being engaged; specif., *a)* a betrothal *b)* an appointment *c)* employment *d)* a conflict; battle

en·gag'ing *adj.* attractive; pleasant; charming —**en·gag'ing·ly** *adv.*

en·gen·der (en jen'dər, in-) *vt.* ⟦< L *in-*, in + *generare*, beget⟧ to bring into being; cause; produce

en·gine (en'jən) *n.* ⟦< L *in-*, in + base of *gignere*, beget⟧ **1** any machine that uses energy to develop mechanical power **2** a railroad locomotive **3** any machine

en·gi·neer (en'jə nir') *n.* **1** one skilled in some branch of engineering **2** one who operates or supervises the operation of engines or technical equipment *[a locomotive engineer]* —*vt.* **1** to plan, construct, etc. as an engineer **2** to manage skillfully

en'gi·neer'ing *n.* **1** the science concerned with putting scientific knowledge to practical uses **2** the planning, designing, construction, or management of machinery, roads, bridges, etc.

Eng·land (iŋ'glənd) division of the United Kingdom in S Great Britain: 50,357 sq. mi.; pop. 46,382,000

Eng·lish (iŋ'glish) *adj.* **1** of England, its people, etc. **2** of the language of England and the U.S. —*n.* **1** the Germanic language of England and the U.S., also spoken in the Commonwealth, etc. **2** [*sometimes* **e-**] a spinning motion given to a ball —**the English** the people of England

English Channel arm of the Atlantic, between England & France

English horn a double-reed woodwind instrument

Eng'lish·man (-mən) *n., pl.* **-men** (-mən) a person born or living in England —**Eng'lish·wom'an**, *pl.* **-wom'en**, *fem.n.*

en·gorge (en gôrj', in-) *vt.* **-gorged'**, **-gorg'ing** ⟦< OFr *en-*, in + *gorge*, gorge⟧ **1** to devour greedily **2** *Med.* to congest (tissue, etc.) with fluid, as blood

en·grave (en grāv', in-) *vt.* **-graved'**, **-grav'ing** ⟦< Fr *en-*, in + *graver*, to incise⟧ **1** to cut or etch letters, designs, etc. in or on (a metal plate, etc.) **2** to print with such a plate **3** to impress deeply —**en·grav'er** *n.*

en·grav'ing *n.* **1** the act or art of one who engraves **2** an engraved plate, drawing, etc. **3** a print made from an engraved surface

en·gross (en grōs', in-) *vt.* ⟦< OFr *engroissier*, become thick⟧ to take the entire attention of; occupy wholly —**en·gross'ing** *adj.*

en·gulf (en gulf', in-) *vt.* to swallow up

en·hance (en hans', in-) *vt.* **-hanced'**, **-hanc'ing** ⟦< L *in-*, in + *altus*, high⟧ to make greater, better, etc.; heighten —**en·hance'ment** *n.*

e·nig·ma (i nig'mə, e-) *n.* ⟦< Gr *ainos*, story⟧ **1** a riddle **2** a perplexing or baffling matter, person, etc. —**en·ig·mat·ic** (en'ig mat'ik) *adj.*

en·jamb·ment or **en·jambe·ment** (en jam'mənt) *n.* ⟦< Fr *enjamber*, to encroach⟧ in poetry, the movement from one line to the next without a pause

en·join (en join', in-) *vt.* ⟦< L *in-*, in + *jungere*, join⟧ **1** to command; order; impose **2** to prohibit, esp. by legal injunction

en·joy (en joi', in-) *vt.* ⟦< OFr *en-*, in + *joir*, rejoice⟧ **1** to get pleasure from; relish **2** to have the use or benefit of —**enjoy oneself** to have a good time —**en·joy'a·ble** *adj.* —**en·joy'ment** *n.*

en·large (en lärj', in-) *vt.* **-larged'**, **-larg'ing** to make larger; expand —*vi.* **1** to become larger; expand **2** to speak or write at greater length: with *on* or *upon* —**en·large'ment** *n.*

en·light·en (en lit''n, in-) *vt.* **1** to free from ignorance, prejudice, etc. **2** to inform —**en·light'en·ment** *n.*

en·list (en list', in-) *vt., vi.* **1** to enroll in some branch of the armed forces **2** to engage in support of a cause or movement —**en·list'ment** *n.*

en·list'ed *adj.* of a person in the armed forces who is not a commissioned officer or warrant officer

en·liv·en (en lī'vən, in-) *vt.* to make active, cheerful, etc.; liven up

en masse (en mas') ⟦Fr, lit., in mass⟧ in a group; as a whole

en·mesh (en mesh', in-) *vt.* to catch as in the meshes of a net; entangle

en·mi·ty (en'mə tē) *n., pl.* **-ties** ⟦see ENEMY⟧ the bitter attitude or feelings of an enemy or enemies; hostility

en·no·ble (e nō'bəl, i-) *vt.* **-bled**, **-bling** to give a noble quality to; dignify —**en·no'ble·ment** *n.*

en·nui (än'wē') *n.* ⟦Fr⟧ weariness and dissatisfaction from lack of interest; boredom

e·nor·mi·ty (ē nôr'mə tē, i-) *n., pl.* **-ties** ⟦< L *enormis*, immense⟧ **1** great wickedness **2** an outrageous act **3** enormous size or extent

e·nor·mous (ē nôr'məs, i-) *adj.* ⟦see prec.⟧ of great size, number, etc.; huge; vast; immense —**e·nor'mous·ly** *adv.*

e·nough (ē nuf', i-) *adj.* ⟦OE *genoh*⟧ as much or as many as necessary; sufficient —*n.* the amount needed —*adv.* **1** sufficiently **2** fully; quite *[oddly enough]* **3** tolerably

e·now (ē nou', i-) *adj., n., adv.* [Archaic] enough

en·plane (en plān', in-) *vi.* **-planed'**, **-plan'ing** to board an airplane

en·quire (en kwīr', in-) *vt., vi.* **-quired'**, **-quir'ing** INQUIRE —**en·quir'y** (-ē), *pl.* **-ies**, *n.*

en·rage (en rāj', in-) *vt.* **-raged'**, **-rag'ing** to put into a rage; infuriate

en·rap·ture (en rap'chər, in-) *vt.* **-tured**, **-tur·ing** to fill with delight

en·rich (en rich', in-) *vt.* to make rich or richer; give greater value, better quality, etc. to —**en·rich'ment** *n.*

en·roll or **en·rol** (en rōl', in-) *vt., vi.* **-rolled'**, **-roll'ing** **1** to record or be recorded in a roll or list **2** to enlist **3** to make or become a member —**en·roll'ment** or **en·rol'ment** *n.*

en route (än ro͞ot', en-) ⟦Fr⟧ on the way

en·sconce (en skäns', in-) *vt.* **-sconced'**, **-sconc'ing** ⟦< Du *schans*, small fort⟧ to place or settle snugly or securely

en·sem·ble (än säm'bəl) *n.* ⟦Fr < L *in-*,

in + *simul*, at the same time⟧ **1** total effect **2** a whole costume of matching parts **3** *a*) a small group of musicians, actors, etc. *b*) the performance of such a group

en·shrine (en shrīn′, in-) ***vt.*** **-shrined′, -shrin′ing 1** to enclose in a shrine **2** to hold as sacred; cherish —**en·shrine′ment** ***n.***

en·shroud (en shroud′, in-) ***vt.*** to cover as if with a shroud; hide; obscure

en·sign (en′sīn′; *also, & for 2 always,* -sən) ***n.*** ⟦see INSIGNIA⟧ **1** a flag or banner **2** *U.S. Navy* a commissioned officer of the lowest rank

en·si·lage (en′sə lij) ***n.*** ⟦ult. < L *in-*, in + Gr *siros,* silo⟧ the preserving of green fodder in a silo

en·slave (en slāv′, in-) ***vt.*** **-slaved′, -slav′ing 1** to make a slave of **2** to subjugate —**en·slave′ment** ***n.***

en·snare (en sner′, in-) ***vt.*** **-snared′, -snar′ing** to catch in or as in a snare

en·sue (en sōō′, in-) ***vi.*** **-sued′, -su′ing** ⟦< L *in-*, in + *sequi*, follow⟧ **1** to come afterward **2** to result

en·sure (en shoor′, in-) ***vt.*** **-sured′, -sur′ing 1** to make sure **2** to protect

-ent (ənt) ⟦< OFr *-ent*, L *-ens*, prp. ending⟧ *suffix* **1** that has, shows, or does *[insistent]* **2** a person or thing that *[superintendent, solvent]*

en·tail (en tāl′, in-) ***vt.*** ⟦< OFr *taillier*, to cut⟧ **1** *Law* to limit the inheritance of (real property) to a specific line of heirs **2** to make necessary; require

en·tan·gle (en taŋ′gəl, in-) ***vt.*** **-gled, -gling 1** to involve in a tangle **2** to involve in difficulty **3** to confuse **4** to complicate —**en·tan′gle·ment** ***n.***

en·tente (än tänt′) ***n.*** ⟦Fr < OFr *entendre*, understand⟧ **1** an understanding or agreement, as between nations **2** the parties to this

en·ter (ent′ər) ***vt.*** ⟦< L *intra*, within⟧ **1** to come or go into **2** to penetrate **3** to insert **4** to write down in a list, etc. **5** to become a member of or participant in **6** to get (a person, etc.) admitted **7** to begin **8** to put on record, formally or before a law court **9** to input (data, etc.) into a computer —***vi.*** **1** to come or go into some place **2** to penetrate —**enter into 1** to take part in **2** to form a part of —**enter on** (or **upon**) to begin; start

en·ter·i·tis (ent′ər īt′is) ***n.*** ⟦< Gr *enteron*, intestine + -ITIS⟧ inflammation of the intestine

en·ter·prise (ent′ər prīz′) ***n.*** ⟦ult. < L *inter*, in + *prehendere*, take⟧ **1** an undertaking, esp. a big, bold, or difficult one **2** energy and initiative

en′ter·pris′ing ***adj.*** showing enterprise; full of energy and initiative

en·ter·tain (ent′ər tān′) ***vt.*** ⟦ult. < L *inter*, between + *tenere*, to hold⟧ **1** to amuse; divert **2** to have as a guest **3** to have in mind; consider —***vi.*** to give hospitality to guests

en′ter·tain′er ***n.*** one who entertains; esp., a popular singer, comedian, etc.

en′ter·tain′ing ***adj.*** interesting and pleasurable; amusing

en′ter·tain′ment ***n.*** **1** an entertaining or being entertained **2** something that entertains; esp., a show or performance

en·thrall or **en·thral** (en thrôl′, in-) ***vt.*** **-thralled′, -thrall′ing** ⟦see EN- & THRALL⟧ to captivate; fascinate

en·throne (en thrōn′, in-) ***vt.*** **-throned′, -thron′ing 1** to place on a throne **2** to exalt

en·thuse (en thōōz′, in-) [Inf.] ***vi.*** **-thused′, -thus′ing** to express enthusiasm —***vt.*** to make enthusiastic

en·thu·si·asm (en thōō′zē az′əm, in-) ***n.*** ⟦< Gr *en-*, in + *theos*, god⟧ intense or eager interest; zeal —**en·thu′si·ast′** (-ast′, -əst) ***n.*** —**en·thu′si·as′tic** ***adj.*** —**en·thu′si·as′ti·cal·ly** ***adv.***

en·tice (en tīs′, in-) ***vt.*** **-ticed′, -tic′ing** ⟦< L *in*, in + *titio*, a burning brand⟧ to tempt with hope of reward or pleasure —**en·tice′ment** ***n.***

en·tire (en tīr′, in-) ***adj.*** ⟦< L *integer*, whole⟧ not lacking any parts; whole; complete; intact —**en·tire′ly** ***adv.***

en·tire′ty (-tē) ***n.***, *pl.* **-ties 1** the state or fact of being entire; wholeness **2** an entire thing; whole

en·ti·tle (en tīt′'l, in-) ***vt.*** **-tled, -tling 1** to give a title or name to **2** to give a right or claim to

en·ti′tle·ment ***n.*** something to which one is entitled, esp. a benefit, as Medicare, provided by certain government programs

en·ti·ty (en′tə tē) ***n.***, *pl.* **-ties** ⟦ult. < L *esse*, to be⟧ **1** existence **2** a thing that has definite existence

en·tomb (en tōōm′, in-) ***vt.*** to place in a tomb; bury —**en·tomb′ment** ***n.***

en·to·mol·o·gy (en′tə mäl′ə jē) ***n.*** ⟦< Gr *entomon*, insect + -LOGY⟧ the branch of zoology that deals with insects —**en′to·mo·log′i·cal** (-mə läj′i kəl) ***adj.*** —**en′to·mol′o·gist** ***n.***

en·tou·rage (än′too räzh′) ***n.*** ⟦Fr < *entourer*, surround⟧ a group of accompanying attendants, etc.; retinue

en·trails (en′trālz, -trəlz) ***pl.n.*** ⟦< L *interaneus*, internal⟧ the inner organs; specif., the intestines

en·trance[1] (en′trəns) ***n.*** **1** the act of entering **2** a place for entering; door, etc. **3** permission or right to enter; admission

en·trance[2] (en trans′, in-) ***vt.*** **-tranced′, -tranc′ing** ⟦see EN- & TRANCE⟧ to fill with delight; enchant

en·trant (en′trənt) ***n.*** one who enters

en·trap (en trap′, in-) ***vt.*** **-trapped′, -trap′ping** to catch in or as in a trap —**en·trap′ment** ***n.***

en·treat (en trēt′, in-) ***vt.***, ***vi.*** ⟦< OFr *en-*, in + *traiter*, to treat⟧ to ask earnestly; beg; implore

en·treat′y ***n.***, *pl.* **-ies** an earnest request; prayer

en·tree or **en·trée** (än′trā′) ***n.*** ⟦Fr < OFr *entrer*, enter⟧ **1** right to enter, use, etc.; access **2** the main course of a meal

en·trench (en trench′, in-) ***vt.*** **1** to surround or fortify with trenches **2** to establish securely

en·tre·pre·neur (än′trə prə nur′) ***n.*** ⟦Fr:

see ENTERPRISE⟧ one who organizes a business undertaking, assuming the risk for the sake of the profit —**en'tre·pre·neur'i·al** ***adj.***

en·tro·py (en'trə pē) ***n.*** ⟦< Gr *entropē*, a turning toward⟧ **1** a thermodynamic measure of the energy unavailable for useful work in a changing system **2** a process of degeneration with increasing uncertainty, chaos, etc., specif., when regarded as the final stage of a social system

en·trust (en trust', in-) ***vt.*** **1** to charge with a trust or duty **2** to turn over for safekeeping

en·try (en'trē) ***n.***, *pl.* **-tries** ⟦< OFr: see ENTER⟧ **1** an entering; entrance **2** a way by which to enter **3** an item or note in a list, journal, etc. **4** one entered in a race, etc.

en'try-lev'el ***adj.*** **1** designating a job with low pay but possible advancement **2** basic; introductory

en·twine (en twīn', in-) ***vt.***, ***vi.*** **-twined', -twin'ing** to twine together or around

e·nu·mer·ate (ē no͞o'mər āt', i-) ***vt.*** **-at'ed, -at'ing** ⟦< L *e-*, out + *numerare*, to count⟧ **1** to count **2** to name one by one —**e·nu'mer·a'tion** ***n.***

e·nun·ci·ate (ē nun'sē āt', i-) ***vt.***, ***vi.*** **-at'ed, -at'ing** ⟦< L *e-*, out + *nuntiare*, announce⟧ **1** to state definitely **2** to announce **3** to pronounce (words), esp. clearly —**e·nun'ci·a'tion** ***n.***

en·u·re·sis (en'yo͞o rē'sis) ***n.*** ⟦ult. < L *in*, in + Gr *ouron*, urine⟧ inability to control urination

en·vel·op (en vel'əp, in-) ***vt.*** ⟦< OFr: see EN- & DEVELOP⟧ **1** to wrap up; cover completely **2** to surround **3** to conceal; hide —**en·vel'op·ment** ***n.***

en·ve·lope (än'və lōp', en'-) ***n.*** **1** a thing that envelops; covering **2** a folded paper container for a letter, etc., usually with a gummed flap

en·ven·om (en ven'əm, in-) ***vt.*** **1** to put venom into **2** to fill with hate

en·vi·a·ble (en'vē ə bəl) ***adj.*** good enough to be envied or desired —**en'vi·a·bly** ***adv.***

en·vi·ous (en'vē əs) ***adj.*** feeling or showing envy —**en'vi·ous·ly** ***adv.***

en·vi·ron·ment (en vī'rən mənt, in-) ***n.*** ⟦see ENVIRONS⟧ **1** surroundings **2** all the conditions, etc. surrounding, and affecting the development of, an organism, food chain, etc. —**en·vi'ron·men'tal** ***adj.***

en·vi'ron·men'tal·ist ***n.*** one working to solve environmental problems, as air and water pollution

en·vi·rons (en vī'rənz, in-) ***pl.n.*** ⟦< OFr *en-*, in + *viron*, a circuit⟧ **1** the districts surrounding a city; suburbs **2** surrounding area; vicinity

en·vis·age (en viz'ij, in-) ***vt.*** **-aged, -ag·ing** ⟦see EN- & VISAGE⟧ to form an image of in the mind; visualize

en·vi·sion (en vizh'ən, in-) ***vt.*** ⟦EN- + VISION⟧ to imagine (something not yet in existence)

en·voy (än'voi', en'-) ***n.*** ⟦< Fr < L *in*, in + *via*, way⟧ **1** a messenger **2** a diplomatic agent just below an ambassador

en·vy (en'vē) ***n.***, *pl.* **-vies** ⟦< L *in-*, in + *videre*, to look⟧ **1** discontent and ill will over another's advantages, possessions, etc. **2** desire for something that another has **3** an object of such feeling —***vt.*** **-vied, -vy·ing** to feel envy toward or because of —**en'vy·ing·ly** ***adv.***

en·zyme (en'zīm') ***n.*** ⟦< Gr *en-*, in + *zymē*, leaven⟧ a protein, formed in plant and animal cells or made synthetically, acting as a catalyst in chemical reactions

e·on (ē'ən, ē'än') ***n.*** ⟦< Gr *aiōn*, an age⟧ an extremely long, indefinite period of time

-e·ous (ē əs) ⟦< L *-eus* + -OUS⟧ *suffix var. of* -OUS *[gaseous]*

EPA *abbrev.* Environmental Protection Agency

ep·au·let or **ep·au·lette** (ep'ə let', ep'ə let') ***n.*** ⟦< Fr dim. of *épaule*, shoulder⟧ a shoulder ornament, esp. on military uniforms

e·pee or **é·pée** (ā pā') ***n.*** ⟦Fr⟧ a fencing sword like a foil, but heavier and more rigid

e·phed·rine (e fe'drin) ***n.*** ⟦< L *ephedra*, the plant horsetail⟧ an alkaloid used to relieve nasal congestion and asthma

e·phem·er·al (e fem'ər əl, i-) ***adj.*** ⟦< Gr *epi-*, upon + *hēmera*, day⟧ **1** lasting one day **2** short-lived; transitory

epi- ⟦< Gr *epi*, at, on⟧ *prefix* on, upon, over, among *[epiglottis]*

ep·ic (ep'ik) ***n.*** ⟦< Gr *epos*, a word, song, epic⟧ a long narrative poem in a dignified style about the deeds of a hero or heroes —***adj.*** of or like an epic; heroic; grand

ep·i·cen·ter (ep'i sent'ər) ***n.*** **1** the area of the earth's surface directly above the place of origin of an earthquake **2** a focal or central point

ep·i·cure (ep'i kyoor') ***n.*** ⟦after *Epicurus*, ancient Gr philosopher⟧ one who enjoys and has a discriminating taste for fine foods and drinks

ep·i·cu·re·an (ep'i kyo͞o rē'ən, ep'i kyoor'ē ən) ***adj.*** fond of sensuous pleasure, esp. that of eating and drinking —***n.*** an epicure

ep·i·dem·ic (ep'ə dem'ik) ***adj.*** ⟦< Fr < Gr *epi-*, among + *dēmos*, people⟧ spreading rapidly among many people in a community, as a disease —***n.*** **1** an epidemic disease **2** the spreading of such a disease **3** a rapid, widespread growth —**ep'i·dem'i·cal·ly** ***adv.***

ep·i·de·mi·ol·o·gy (ep'ə dē'mē äl'ə jē) ***n.*** ⟦prec. + -LOGY⟧ the branch of medicine that studies epidemics

ep·i·der·mis (ep'ə dur'mis) ***n.*** ⟦< Gr *epi-*, upon + *derma*, the skin⟧ the outermost layer of the skin —**ep'i·der'mal** or **ep'i·der'mic** ***adj.***

ep·i·du·ral (ep'ə door'əl) ***adj.*** on or outside the dura mater —***n.*** local anesthesia of the lower body by epidural injection

ep·i·glot·tis (ep'ə glät'is) ***n.*** ⟦see EPI- & GLOTTIS⟧ the thin, lidlike piece of cartilage that covers the windpipe during swallowing

ep·i·gram (ep′ə gram′) ***n.*** ⟦< Gr *epi-*, upon + *graphein*, write⟧ a terse, witty, pointed statement —**ep′i·gram·mat′ic** (-grə mat′ik) ***adj.***

e·pig·ra·phy (ē pig′rə fē, i-) ***n.*** the study of inscriptions, esp. ancient ones

ep·i·lep·sy (ep′ə lep′sē) ***n.*** ⟦< Gr *epi-*, upon + *lambanein*, seize⟧ a recurrent disorder of the nervous system, characterized by seizures that cause convulsions, unconsciousness, etc.

ep′i·lep′tic (-tik) ***adj.*** of or having epilepsy —***n.*** one who has epilepsy

ep·i·logue or **ep·i·log** (ep′ə lôg′) ***n.*** ⟦< Gr *epi-*, upon + *legein*, speak⟧ a closing section added to a novel, play, etc., providing further comment, as a speech by an actor to the audience

E·piph·a·ny (ē pif′ə nē, i-) ***n.***, *pl.* **-nies** ⟦< Gr *epiphainein*, show forth⟧ **1** a Christian feast day (Jan. 6) commemorating the revealing of Jesus as the Christ to the Gentiles **2** [**e-**] *a)* a flash of insight *b)* an experience that brings this about

e·pis·co·pa·cy (ē pis′kə pə sē, i-) ***n.***, *pl.* **-cies** ⟦< Gr *epi-*, upon + *skopein*, to look⟧ **1** church government by bishops **2** EPISCOPATE

e·pis′co·pal (-pəl) ***adj.*** **1** of or governed by bishops **2** [**E-**] designating or of any of various churches governed by bishops

E·pis′co·pa′lian (-pāl′yən) ***adj.*** Episcopal —***n.*** a member of the Protestant Episcopal Church

e·pis′co·pate (-pit, -pāt′) ***n.*** **1** the position, rank, etc. of a bishop **2** bishops collectively

ep·i·sode (ep′ə sōd′) ***n.*** ⟦< Gr *epi-*, upon + *eisodos*, entrance⟧ **1** any part of a novel, poem, etc. that is complete in itself **2** an event or series of events complete in itself —**ep′i·sod′ic** (-säd′ik) ***adj.*** —**ep′i·sod′i·cal·ly** ***adv.***

e·pis·tle (ē pis′əl) ***n.*** ⟦< Gr *epi-*, to + *stellein*, send⟧ **1** a letter **2** [**E-**] any of the letters in the New Testament —**e·pis′to·lar′y** (-tə ler′ē) ***adj.***

ep·i·taph (ep′ə taf′) ***n.*** ⟦< Gr *epi-*, upon + *taphos*, tomb⟧ an inscription on a tomb, etc. in memory of a dead person

ep·i·the·li·um (ep′i thē′lē əm) ***n.***, *pl.* **-li·ums** or **-li·a** (-ə) ⟦< Gr *epi-*, upon + *thēlē*, nipple⟧ cellular tissue covering external body surfaces or lining internal surfaces —**ep′i·the′li·al** (-əl) ***adj.***

ep·i·thet (ep′ə thet′) ***n.*** ⟦< Gr *epi-*, on + *tithenai*, put⟧ a word or phrase characterizing some person or thing

e·pit·o·me (ē pit′ə mē′, i-) ***n.***, *pl.* **-mes′** (-mēz′) ⟦< Gr *epi-*, upon + *temnein*, to cut⟧ **1** an abstract; summary **2** a person or thing that shows the typical qualities of something

e·pit′o·mize′ (-mīz′) ***vt.*** **-mized′**, **-miz′ing** to make or be an epitome of

e plu·ri·bus u·num (ē′ ploor′ē boos′ o͞o′ noom) ⟦L⟧ out of many, one: a motto of the U.S.

ep·och (ep′ək) ***n.*** ⟦< Gr *epi-*, upon + *echein*, to hold⟧ **1** the start of a new period in the history of anything **2** a period of time in terms of noteworthy events, persons, etc. —**ep′och·al** ***adj.***

ep·ox·y (ē päk′sē, i-) ***adj.*** ⟦EP(I)- + OXY(GEN)⟧ designating a resin used in strong, resistant glues, enamels, etc. —***n.***, *pl.* **-ies** an epoxy resin

ep·si·lon (ep′sə län′) ***n.*** ⟦Gr *e psilon*, plain *e*⟧ the fifth letter of the Greek alphabet (Ε, ε)

Ep·som salts (or **salt**) (ep′səm) ⟦after *Epsom*, town in England⟧ a white, crystalline salt, magnesium sulfate, used as a cathartic

Ep·stein-Barr virus (ep′stīn bär′) a herpes-like virus that causes infectious mononucleosis and may cause various forms of cancer

eq·ua·ble (ek′wə bəl) ***adj.*** ⟦see fol.⟧ steady; uniform; even; tranquil —**eq′ua·bil′i·ty** ***n.*** —**eq′ua·bly** ***adv.***

e·qual (ē′kwəl) ***adj.*** ⟦< L *aequus*, even⟧ **1** of the same quantity, size, value, etc. **2** having the same rights, ability, rank, etc. **3** evenly proportioned **4** having the necessary ability, strength, etc.: with *to* —***n.*** any person or thing that is equal —***vt.*** **e′qualed** or **e′qualled**, **e′qual·ing** or **e′qual·ling** **1** to be equal to **2** to do or make something equal to —**e·qual·i·ty** (ē kwôl′ə tē, -kwäl′-), *pl.* **-ties**, ***n.*** —**e′qual·ly** ***adv.***

e·qual·ize (ē′kwəl īz′) ***vt.*** **-ized′**, **-iz′ing** to make equal or uniform —**e′qual·i·za′tion** ***n.*** —**e′qual·iz′er** ***n.***

e′qual-op′por·tu′ni·ty ***adj.*** treating all employees and job applicants equally, without regard to race, sex, etc.

equal sign the sign (=), indicating that the terms on either side of it are equal or equivalent

e·qua·nim·i·ty (ek′wə nim′ə tē, ē′kwə-) ***n.*** ⟦< L *aequus*, even + *animus*, mind⟧ evenness of temper; composure

e·quate (ē kwāt′, i-) ***vt.*** **e·quat′ed**, **e·quat′ing** **1** to make equal **2** to treat, regard, or express as equal —**e·quat′a·ble** ***adj.***

e·qua·tion (ē kwā′zhən, i-) ***n.*** **1** an equating or being equated **2** a statement of equality between two quantities, as shown by the equal sign (=)

e·qua·tor (ē kwāt′ər, i-) ***n.*** an imaginary circle around the earth, equally distant from the North Pole and the South Pole —**e·qua·to·ri·al** (ē′kwə tôr′ē əl, ek′wə-) ***adj.***

Equatorial Guinea country in WC Africa: 10,831 sq. mi.; pop. 304,000

eq·uer·ry (ek′wər ē, ē kwer′ē) ***n.***, *pl.* **-ries** ⟦< Fr⟧ **1** [Historical] an officer in charge of royal horses **2** an officer who attends a person of royalty

e·ques·tri·an (ē kwes′trē ən, i-) ***adj.*** ⟦< L *equus*, horse⟧ **1** of horses or horsemanship **2** on horseback —***n.*** a rider or circus performer on horseback —**e·ques′tri·enne′** (-trē en′) ***fem.n.***

equi- *combining form* equal, equally *[equidistant]*

e·qui·dis·tant (ē′kwi dis′tənt) ***adj.*** equally distant

e′qui·lat′er·al (-lat′ər əl) ***adj.*** ⟦< L *aequus*, even + *latus*, side⟧ having all sides equal

e′qui·lib′ri·um (-lib′rē əm) ***n.***, *pl.* **-ri·ums**

or -**ri·a** (-ə) ⟦< L *aequus*, even + *libra*, a balance⟧ a state of balance between opposing forces

e·quine (ē′kwīn′) ***adj.*** ⟦< L *equus*, horse⟧ of or like a horse

e·qui·nox (ē′kwi näks′, ek′wə näks′) ***n.*** ⟦< L *aequus*, even + *nox*, night⟧ the time when the sun crosses the equator, making night and day of equal length in all parts of the earth —**e′qui·noc′tial** (-näk′shəl) ***adj.***

e·quip (ē kwip′, i-) ***vt.*** **e·quipped′**, **e·quip′ping** ⟦< OFr *esquiper*, embark⟧ to provide with what is needed

eq·ui·page (ek′wi pij) ***n.*** a carriage with horses and liveried servants

e·quip·ment (ē kwip′mənt, i-) ***n.*** **1** an equipping or being equipped **2** whatever one is equipped with; supplies, furnishings, etc.

eq·ui·poise (ek′wi poiz′, ē′kwi-) ***n.*** ⟦EQUI- + POISE⟧ **1** state of equilibrium **2** a counterbalance

eq·ui·ta·ble (ek′wit ə bəl) ***adj.*** ⟦see EQUITY⟧ fair; just —**eq′ui·ta·bly** ***adv.***

eq·ui·ta·tion (ek′wi tā′shən) ***n.*** ⟦< L *equitare*, to ride⟧ the art of riding on horseback

eq·ui·ty (ek′wit ē) ***n.***, *pl.* **-ties** ⟦< L *aequus*, even⟧ **1** fairness; impartiality; justice **2** the value of property beyond the amount owed on it **3** *Finance a*) assets minus liabilities; net worth *b*) [*pl.*] shares of stock **4** *Law* a system of doctrines supplementing common and statute law

e·quiv·a·lent (ē kwiv′ə lənt, i-) ***adj.*** ⟦< L *aequus*, equal + *valere*, be worth⟧ equal in quantity, value, force, meaning, etc. —***n.*** an equivalent thing —**e·quiv′a·lence** ***n.***

e·quiv·o·cal (ē kwiv′ə kəl, i-) ***adj.*** ⟦< L *aequus*, even + *vox*, voice⟧ **1** having two or more meanings; purposely ambiguous **2** uncertain; doubtful **3** suspicious *[equivocal conduct]* —**e·quiv′o·cal·ly** ***adv.*** —**e·quiv′o·cal·ness** ***n.***

e·quiv′o·cate′ (-kāt′) ***vi.*** **-cat′ed**, **-cat′ing** to use equivocal terms in order to deceive, hedge, etc. —**e·quiv′o·ca′tion** ***n.*** —**e·quiv′o·ca′tor** ***n.***

ER *abbrev.* emergency room

-er (ər) ⟦ME⟧ *suffix* **1** *a*) a person or thing having to do with *[hatter]* *b*) a person living in *[New Yorker]* *c*) one that ____s *[roller]* **2** forming the comparative degree *[later]* **3** repeatedly: added to verbs *[flicker]*

e·ra (ir′ə, er′ə) ***n.*** ⟦LL *aera*⟧ **1** a period of time measured from some important event **2** a period of time having some special characteristic

ERA *abbrev.* **1** *Baseball* earned run average: also **era** **2** Equal Rights Amendment

e·rad·i·cate (ē rad′i kāt′, i-) ***vt.*** **-cat′ed**, **-cat′ing** ⟦< L *e-*, out + *radix*, root⟧ to uproot; wipe out; destroy —**e·rad′i·ca′tion** ***n.*** —**e·rad′i·ca′tor** ***n.***

e·rase (ē rās′, i-) ***vt.*** **e·rased′**, **e·ras′ing** ⟦< L *e-*, out + *radere*, scrape⟧ **1** to rub, scrape, or wipe out (esp. writing) **2** to remove (something recorded) from (magnetic tape) **3** to obliterate, as from the mind —**e·ras′a·ble** ***adj.***

e·ras′er ***n.*** a thing that erases; specif., a rubber device for erasing ink or pencil marks, or a pad for removing chalk marks from a blackboard

E·ras·mus (i raz′məs), **Des·i·der·i·us** (des′ə dir′ē əs) 1466?-1536; Du. humanist & theologian

e·ra·sure (ē rā′shər, i-) ***n.*** **1** an erasing **2** an erased word, mark, etc.

ere (er) [Old Poet.] ***prep.*** ⟦OE *ær*⟧ before (in time) —***conj.*** **1** before **2** rather than

e·rect (ē rekt′, i-) ***adj.*** ⟦< L *e-*, up + *regere*, make straight⟧ upright —***vt.*** **1** to construct (a building, etc.) **2** to set in an upright position; raise **3** to set up; assemble —**e·rec′tion** ***n.*** —**e·rect′ly** ***adv.*** —**e·rect′ness** ***n.*** —**e·rec′tor** ***n.***

e·rec·tile (ē rek′til, i-) ***adj.*** that can become erect: used esp. of tissue that becomes rigid when filled with blood

erg (ʉrg) ***n.*** ⟦< Gr *ergon*, work⟧ *Physics* a unit of work or energy

er·go (er′gō) ***adv.*** ⟦L⟧ therefore

er·go·nom·ics (ʉr′gō näm′iks) ***n.*** ⟦ult. < Gr *ergon*, work + (EC)ONOMICS⟧ the science of adapting working conditions to the needs of the worker

Er·ie (ir′ē), **Lake** one of the Great Lakes, between Lake Huron & Lake Ontario

Er·in (er′in) *old poet. name for* IRELAND

Er·i·tre·a (er′ə trē′ə) country in E Africa: 36,171 sq. mi.; pop. 3,525,000 —**Er′i·tre′an** ***adj.***, ***n.***

er·mine (ʉr′min) ***n.*** ⟦prob. < OHG *harmo*, weasel⟧ **1** a weasel whose fur is white in winter **2** its white fur

e·rode (ē rōd′, i-) ***vt.*** **e·rod′ed**, **e·rod′ing** ⟦< L *e-*, out + *rodere*, gnaw⟧ **1** to wear away **2** to form by wearing away gradually —***vi.*** to become eroded

e·rog·e·nous (ē räj′ə nəs, i-) ***adj.*** ⟦< Gr *erōs*, love + -GEN + -OUS⟧ sensitive to sexual stimulation: also **e·ro·to·gen·ic** (er′ə tō′jen′ik)

E·ros (er′äs′, ir′-) ***n.*** **1** *Gr. Myth.* the god of love **2** [**e-**] sexual love or desire

e·ro·sion (ē rō′zhən, i-) ***n.*** an eroding or being eroded —**e·ro′sive** (-siv) ***adj.***

e·rot·ic (ē rät′ik, i-) ***adj.*** ⟦< Gr *erōs*, love⟧ of or arousing sexual feelings or desires; amatory —**e·rot′i·cal·ly** ***adv.***

e·rot′i·ca (-i kə) ***pl.n.*** [*often with sing. v.*] erotic books, pictures, etc.

err (ʉr, er) ***vi.*** ⟦< L *errare*, wander⟧ **1** to be wrong or mistaken **2** to deviate from the established moral code

er·rand (er′ənd) ***n.*** ⟦OE *ærende*, mission⟧ **1** a trip to do a thing, often esp. for someone else **2** the thing to be done

er·rant (er′ənt) ***adj.*** ⟦see ERR⟧ **1** roving or wandering, esp. in search of adventure *[a medieval knight-errant]* **2** erring **3** shifting about *[an errant wind]*

er·rat·ic (i rat′ik) ***adj.*** ⟦< L *errare*, wander⟧ **1** irregular; random **2** eccentric; queer —**er·rat′i·cal·ly** ***adv.***

er·ra·tum (e rät′əm, -rāt′-) ***n.***, *pl.* **-ta** (-ə) ⟦see ERR⟧ an error in a work already printed

er·ro·ne·ous (e rō′nē əs) ***adj.*** containing

error; mistaken; wrong —**er·ro'ne·ous·ly** *adv.*

er·ror (er'ər) *n.* ⟦see ERR⟧ **1** the state of believing what is untrue **2** a wrong belief **3** something incorrectly done; mistake **4** a transgression **5** *Baseball* any misplay in fielding

er·satz (er'zäts', er zäts') *n., adj.* ⟦Ger⟧ substitute or synthetic, and usually inferior

Erse (urs) *adj., n.* ⟦ME *Erish*, var. of *Irisc*, Irish⟧ (of) GAELIC and, sometimes, IRISH (*n.* 1)

erst·while (urst'hwīl') *adv.* [Archaic] formerly —*adj.* former

e·ruct (ē rukt') *vt., vi.* ⟦< L *e-*, out + *ructare*, to belch⟧ to belch —**e'ruc·ta'tion** *n.*

er·u·dite (er'yōō dīt', -ōō-) *adj.* ⟦< L *e-*, out + *rudis*, rude⟧ learned; scholarly —**er'u·dite'ly** *adv.*

er·u·di·tion (er'yōō dish'ən) *n.* learning acquired by reading and study

e·rupt (ē rupt', i-) *vi.* ⟦< L *e-*, out + *rumpere*, to break⟧ **1** to burst forth or out *[lava erupting]* **2** to throw forth lava, water, etc. **3** to break out in a rash —*vt.* to cause to burst forth

e·rup·tion (ē rup'shən, i-) *n.* **1** a bursting forth or out **2** *a)* a breaking out in a rash *b)* a rash

-er·y (ər ē, er'ē) ⟦< LL *-aria*⟧ *suffix* **1** a place to *[tannery]* **2** a place for *[nunnery]* **3** the practice or act of *[midwifery]* **4** the product of *[pottery]* **5** a collection of *[greenery]* **6** the condition of *[drudgery]*

er·y·sip·e·las (er'i sip'ə ləs) *n.* ⟦ult. < Gr *erythros*, red + *-pelas*, skin⟧ a bacterial infection of the skin or mucous membranes

e·ryth·ro·cyte (e rith'rō sīt') *n.* ⟦< Gr *erythros*, red + *kytos*, a hollow⟧ a mature red blood cell that contains hemoglobin, which carries oxygen to the body tissues

-es (iz, əz, z) ⟦< OE⟧ *suffix* **1** forming plurals *[glasses]* **2** forming the 3d person sing., pres. indic., of verbs *[he kisses]*

E·sau (ē'sô') *n. Bible* Isaac's son who sold his birthright to his brother, Jacob

es·ca·late (es'kə lāt') *vi.* **-lat'ed, -lat'ing** **1** to rise as on an escalator **2** to expand step by step **3** to increase rapidly —**es'ca·la'tion** *n.*

es'ca·la'tor (-ər) *n.* ⟦ult. < L *scala*, ladder⟧ a moving stairway on an endless belt

es·ca·pade (es'kə pād') *n.* ⟦Fr: see fol.⟧ a reckless adventure or prank

es·cape (e skāp', i-) *vi.* **-caped', -cap'ing** ⟦< L *ex-*, out of + LL *cappa*, cloak⟧ **1** to get free **2** to avoid an illness, accident, etc. **3** to leak away —*vt.* **1** to get away from **2** to avoid *[to escape death]* **3** to come from involuntarily *[a scream escaped her lips]* **4** to be missed or forgotten by —*n.* **1** an escaping **2** a means of escape **3** a leakage **4** a temporary mental release from reality —*adj.* providing an escape

es·cap·ee (e skāp'ē', es'kā pē') *n.* one who has escaped, as from prison

es·cape'ment *n.* a notched wheel with a detaining catch that controls the action of a mechanical clock or watch

escape velocity the minimum speed required for a particle, space vehicle, etc. to escape permanently from the gravitational field of a planet, star, etc.

es·cap'ism' *n.* a tendency to escape from reality, responsibilities, etc. through the imagination —**es·cap'ist** *adj., n.*

es·car·got (es'kär gō') *n.* ⟦Fr⟧ an edible snail

es·ca·role (es'kə rōl') *n.* ⟦Fr⟧ ENDIVE

es·carp·ment (e skärp'mənt) *n.* ⟦<Fr⟧ a steep slope or cliff

-es·cence (es'əns) ⟦see fol.⟧ *suffix* the process of becoming *[obsolescence]*

-es·cent (es'ənt) ⟦L *-escens*⟧ *suffix* **1** starting to be, being, or becoming *[obsolescent]* **2** giving off light (as specified) *[phosphorescent]*

es·chew (es chōō') *vt.* ⟦< OHG *sciuhan*, to fear⟧ to shun; avoid —**es·chew'al** *n.*

es·cort (es'kôrt'; *for v.* i skôrt') *n.* ⟦< L *ex-*, out + *corrigere*, set right⟧ **1** one or more persons, cars, etc. accompanying another or others to give protection or show honor **2** a man accompanying a woman —*vt.* to go with as an escort

es·cri·toire (es'kri twär') *n.* ⟦OFr < L *scribere*, write⟧ a writing desk

es·crow (es'krō') *n.* ⟦see SCROLL⟧ used chiefly in **in escrow**, put in the care of a third party until certain conditions are fulfilled

es·cutch·eon (e skuch'ən, i-) *n.* ⟦< L *scutum*, shield⟧ a shield on which a coat of arms is displayed

-ese (ēz, ēs) ⟦< L *-ensis*⟧ *suffix* **1** of a country or place *[Javanese]* **2** (in) the language of *[Cantonese]* **3** a person born or living in *[Portuguese]*

Es·ki·mo (es'kə mō') *n.* ⟦prob. < Fr < AmInd⟧ **1** *pl.* **-mos'** or **-mo'** a member of a group of North American peoples in Greenland, N Canada, and Alaska **2** any of the languages of the Eskimos —*adj.* of the Eskimos or their languages, etc.

Eskimo dog any of several large, strong dogs used by the Eskimos to pull sleds

ESL *abbrev.* English as a second language

e·soph·a·gus (i säf'ə gəs) *n., pl.* **-gi'** (-jī') ⟦< Gr *oisophagos*⟧ the tube through which food passes from the pharynx to the stomach

es·o·ter·ic (es'ə ter'ik) *adj.* ⟦< Gr *esōteros*, inner⟧ intended for or understood by only a chosen few

ESP (ē'es'pē') *n.* extrasensory perception

esp. *abbrev.* especially

es·pa·drille (es'pə dril') *n.* ⟦Fr < Sp *esparto*, coarse grass⟧ a casual shoe with a canvas upper and a sole of twisted rope

es·pal·ier (es pal'yər) *n.* ⟦Fr < It *spalla*, shoulder⟧ **1** a lattice on which trees or shrubs are trained to grow flat **2** a plant trained in this way —*vt.* to provide with an espalier

es·pe·cial (e spesh'əl, i-) *adj.* special; particular —**es·pe'cial·ly** *adv.*

Es·pe·ran·to (es′pə rän′tō, -ran′-) ***n.*** an invented international language based on European word roots

es·pi·o·nage (es′pē ə näzh′) ***n.*** ⟦< Fr < It *spia*, spy⟧ the act or practice of spying

es·pla·nade (es′plə nād′, -näd′) ***n.*** ⟦< Fr < It < L *explanare*, to level⟧ a level, open stretch of ground, esp. one serving as a public walk

es·pous·al (e spou′zəl, i-) ***n.*** an espousing (of some cause, idea, etc.); advocacy

es·pouse (e spouz′, i-) ***vt.*** **-poused′, -pous′ing** ⟦see SPOUSE⟧ **1** to marry **2** to advocate (some cause, idea, etc.)

es·pres·so (e spres′ō) ***n.***, *pl.* **-sos** ⟦It⟧ coffee made by forcing steam through finely ground coffee beans

es·prit de corps (e sprē′ də kôr′) ⟦Fr⟧ group spirit; pride, etc. shared by those in the same group

es·py (e spī′, i-) ***vt.*** **-pied′, -py′ing** ⟦see SPY⟧ to catch sight of; spy

-esque (esk) ⟦Fr < It *-esco*⟧ *suffix* **1** in the manner or style of *[Romanesque]* **2** like *[statuesque]*

es·quire (es′kwīr′) ***n.*** ⟦< L *scutum*, a shield⟧ **1** [Historical] a candidate for knighthood; squire **2** in England, a member of the gentry ranking just below a knight **3** [**E-**] a title of courtesy: in the U.S., now specif. used by lawyers: usually abbrev. **Esq** or **Esqr**

-ess (es, is, əs) ⟦< LL *-issa*⟧ *suffix* female *[lioness]*

es·say (e sā′; *for n. 1 usually, & for n. 2 always*, es′ā) ***vt.*** ⟦< LL *ex-*, out of + *agere*, to do⟧ to try; attempt —***n.*** **1** a trying or testing **2** a short literary composition in which the author analyzes or interprets something in a personal way —**es·say′er** ***n.*** —**es′say·ist** ***n.***

es·sence (es′əns) ***n.*** ⟦< L *esse*, to be⟧ **1** the basic nature (of something) **2** *a*) a concentrated substance that keeps the flavor, etc. of that from which it is extracted *b*) perfume

Es·sene (es′ēn′, e sēn′) ***n.*** a member of an ancient Jewish ascetic sect that existed to the middle of the 1st c. A.D.

es·sen·tial (ə sen′shəl, i-) ***adj.*** **1** of or constituting the essence of something; basic **2** absolutely necessary; indispensable —***n.*** something necessary or fundamental —**es·sen′tial·ly** ***adv.***

est *abbrev.* **1** established: also **estab** **2** estimate **3** estimated

EST *abbrev.* Eastern Standard Time

-est (est, ist, əst) ⟦OE⟧ *suffix* forming the superlative degree *[greatest]*

es·tab·lish (ə stab′lish, i-) ***vt.*** ⟦< L *stabilis*, stable⟧ **1** to order, ordain, or enact (a law, etc.) permanently **2** to set up (a nation, business, etc.) **3** to cause to be; bring about **4** to set up in a business, etc. **5** to cause to be accepted **6** to prove; demonstrate

es·tab′lish·ment ***n.*** **1** an establishing or being established **2** a thing established, as a business —**the Establishment** an inner circle thought of as holding decisive power in a nation, institution, etc.

es·tate (ə stāt′, i-) ***n.*** ⟦< OFr *estat*⟧ **1** a condition or stage of life **2** property; possessions **3** a large, individually owned piece of land containing a residence

es·teem (ə stēm′, i-) ***vt.*** ⟦< L *aestimare*, to value⟧ **1** to value highly; respect **2** to consider —***n.*** favorable opinion

es·ter (es′tər) ***n.*** ⟦Ger < *essig*, vinegar + *äther*, ether⟧ an organic compound formed by the reaction of an acid and an alcohol

Es·ther (es′tər) ***n.*** *Bible* the Jewish wife of a Persian king: she saved her people from slaughter

es·thete (es′thēt′) ***n.*** AESTHETE —**es·thet′ics** (-thet′iks) ***pl.n.***

es·ti·ma·ble (es′tə mə bəl) ***adj.*** worthy of esteem

es·ti·mate (es′tə māt′; *for n.*, -mit) ***vt.*** **-mat′ed, -mat′ing** ⟦see ESTEEM⟧ **1** to form an opinion about **2** to calculate approximately (size, cost, etc.) —***n.*** **1** a general calculation; esp., an approximate computation of probable cost **2** an opinion or judgment —**es′ti·ma′tor** ***n.***

es′ti·ma′tion ***n.*** **1** an estimate or judgment **2** esteem; regard

Es·to·ni·a (e stō′nē ə, -stōn′yə) country in N Europe: formerly a republic of the U.S.S.R.: 17,413 sq. mi.; pop. 1,566,000 —**Es·to′ni·an** ***adj.***, ***n.***

es·trange (e strānj′, i-) ***vt.*** **-tranged′, -trang′ing** ⟦< L *extraneus*, strange⟧ to turn (a person) from an affectionate attitude to an indifferent or unfriendly one —**es·trange′ment** ***n.***

es·tro·gen (es′trə jən) ***n.*** ⟦< Gr *oistros*, frenzy + -GEN⟧ any of several female sex hormones or synthetic compounds

es·trous cycle (es′trəs) the regular female reproductive cycle of most placental mammals

es·tu·ar·y (es′tyo͞o er′ē, -cho͞o-) ***n.***, *pl.* **-ies** ⟦< L *aestus*, the tide⟧ the wide mouth of a river into which the tide flows from the sea

ET *abbrev.* Eastern Time

-et (et, it, ət) ⟦< LL *-itus*⟧ *suffix* little *[islet]*

e·ta (āt′ə, ēt′ə) ***n.*** the seventh letter of the Greek alphabet (Η, η)

ETA *abbrev.* estimated time of arrival

é·ta·gère (ā′tä zher′) ***n.*** ⟦Fr⟧ a stand with open shelves, for displaying art objects, ornaments, etc.

et al. *abbrev.* ⟦L *et alii*⟧ and others

et cet·er·a (et set′ər ə, -se′trə) ⟦L⟧ and others; and the like: abbrev. **etc.**

etch (ech) ***vt.*** ⟦< MHG *ezzen*, eat⟧ to make (a drawing, design, etc.) on metal, glass, etc. by the action of an acid —**etch′er** ***n.***

etch′ing ***n.*** **1** the art of an etcher **2** a print made from an etched plate

e·ter·nal (ē tʉr′nəl, i-) ***adj.*** ⟦< L *aeturnus*⟧ **1** without beginning or end; everlasting **2** always the same; unchanging **3** seeming never to stop —**e·ter′nal·ly** ***adv.*** —**e·ter′nal·ness** ***n.***

e·ter·ni·ty (ē tʉr′nə tē, i-) ***n.***, *pl.* **-ties** **1** the state or fact of being eternal **2** infinite or endless time **3** a long period of time that seems endless **4** the endless time after death

eth·ane (eth′ān′) ***n.*** ⟦< fol.⟧ an odorless, colorless, gaseous hydrocarbon, found in natural gas and used as a fuel

e·ther (ē′thər) ***n.*** ⟦< Gr *aithein*, to burn⟧ **1** an imaginary substance once thought to pervade space **2** the upper regions of space **3** a volatile, colorless, highly flammable liquid used as an anesthetic and a solvent

e·the·re·al (ē thir′ē əl, i-) ***adj.*** **1** very light; airy; delicate **2** not earthly; heavenly; celestial —**e·the′re·al·ly *adv.***

eth·ic (eth′ik) ***n.*** ⟦see fol.⟧ a system of moral standards

eth·i·cal (eth′i kəl) ***adj.*** ⟦< Gr *ēthos*, character⟧ **1** having to do with ethics; of or conforming to moral standards **2** conforming to professional standards of conduct —**eth′i·cal·ly *adv.***

eth·ics (eth′iks) ***n.*** **1** the study of standards of conduct and moral judgment **2** [*with sing. or pl. verb*] the system of morals of a particular person, religion, group, etc.

E·thi·o·pi·a (ē′thē ō′pē ə) country in E Africa: 423,940 sq. mi.; pop. 42,019,000 —**E′thi·o′pi·an *adj., n.***

eth·nic (eth′nik) ***adj.*** ⟦< Gr *ethnos*, nation⟧ designating or of a group of people having common customs, characteristics, language, etc. —***n.*** a member of an ethnic group, esp. a minority or nationality group —**eth′ni·cal·ly *adv.***

eth·nic·i·ty (eth nis′ə tē) ***n.*** ethnic classification or affiliation

eth·nol·o·gy (eth näl′ə jē) ***n.*** ⟦< Gr *ethnos*, nation + -LOGY⟧ the branch of anthropology that studies comparatively the cultures of contemporary, or recent, societies or language groups —**eth′no·log′i·cal** (-nə läj′i kəl) ***adj.*** —**eth·nol′o·gist *n.***

e·thos (ē′thäs′) ***n.*** ⟦Gr *ēthos*, character⟧ the characteristic attitudes, habits, etc. of an individual or group

eth·yl (eth′əl) ***n.*** ⟦< ETHER⟧ the hydrocarbon radical that forms the base of ethyl alcohol, ether, etc.

ethyl alcohol ALCOHOL (sense 1)

eth·yl·ene (eth′əl ēn′) ***n.*** ⟦ETHYL + -ENE⟧ a colorless, flammable, gaseous hydrocarbon used to synthesize organic chemicals, esp. polyethylene

ethylene gly·col (glī′kôl′) a colorless, viscous liquid used as an antifreeze, solvent, etc.

e·ti·ol·o·gy (ēt′ē äl′ə jē) ***n., pl.* -gies** ⟦< Gr *aitia*, cause + *logia*, description⟧ **1** the cause assigned, as for a disease **2** the science of causes or origins —**e′ti·o·log′ic** (-ə läj′ik) ***adj.***

et·i·quette (et′i kit) ***n.*** ⟦Fr *étiquette*, lit., ticket⟧ the forms, manners, etc. conventionally acceptable or required in society, a profession, etc.

Et·na (et′nə), **Mount** volcanic mountain in E Sicily

E·to·bi·coke (i tō′bi kō′) city within metropolitan Toronto, Canada: pop. 329,000

E·trus·can (i trus′kən) ***adj.*** of an ancient country (*Etruria*) in what is now central Italy

et seq. *abbrev.* ⟦L *et sequens*⟧ and the following

-ette (et) ⟦Fr: see -ET⟧ *suffix* **1** little *[statuette]* **2** female *[majorette]*

é·tude (ā′to͞od′) ***n.*** ⟦Fr, a study⟧ a musical composition for a solo instrument, designed to give practice in some point of technique

et·y·mol·o·gy (et′ə mäl′ə jē) ***n., pl.* -gies** ⟦< Gr *etymos*, true + *logos*, word⟧ **1** the origin and development of a word **2** the linguistic study of word origins —**et′y·mo·log′i·cal** (-mə läj′i kəl) ***adj.*** —**et′y·mol′o·gist *n.***

EU *abbrev.* European Union

eu- ⟦Fr < Gr⟧ *prefix* good, well *[eulogy, euphony]*

eu·ca·lyp·tus (yo͞o′kə lip′təs) ***n., pl.* -tus·es** or **-ti′** (-tī′) ⟦< Gr *eu-*, well + *kalyptos*, covered⟧ a tall, aromatic, chiefly Australian evergreen tree of the myrtle family

Eu·cha·rist (yo͞o′kə rist) ***n.*** ⟦< Gr *eucharistia*, gratitude⟧ **1** HOLY COMMUNION **2** the consecrated bread and wine used in this —**Eu′cha·ris′tic *adj.***

eu·chre (yo͞o′kər) ***n.*** ⟦< ?⟧ a card game played with thirty-two cards

Eu·clid (yo͞o′klid) flourished 4th c. B.C.; Gr. mathematician: author of a basic work in geometry —**Eu·clid′e·an** (-ē ən) or **Eu·clid′i·an *adj.***

Eu·gene (yo͞o jēn′, yo͞o′jēn) city in W Oregon: pop. 113,000

eu·gen·ics (yo͞o jen′iks) ***n.*** ⟦see EU- & GENESIS⟧ the movement devoted to improving the human species by controlling heredity —**eu·gen′ic *adj.*** —**eu·gen′i·cal·ly *adv.*** —**eu·gen′i·cist** (-ə sist) ***n.***

eu·lo·gize (yo͞o′lə jīz′) ***vt.* -gized′, -giz′ing** ⟦see fol.⟧ to praise highly —**eu′lo·gist** or **eu′lo·giz′er *n.***

eu′lo·gy (-jē) ***n., pl.* -gies** ⟦< Gr *eulegein*, speak well of⟧ **1** speech or writing praising a person or thing; esp., a funeral oration **2** high praise —**eu′lo·gis′tic** (-jis′tik) ***adj.***

eu·nuch (yo͞o′nək) ***n.*** ⟦< Gr *eunouchos*, guardian of the bed⟧ a castrated man

eu·phe·mism (yo͞o′fə miz′əm) ***n.*** ⟦< Gr *eu-*, good + *phēmē*, speech⟧ **1** the use of a less direct word or phrase for one considered offensive **2** a word or phrase so substituted —**eu′phe·mis′tic *adj.*** —**eu′phe·mis′ti·cal·ly *adv.***

eu·pho·ni·ous (yo͞o fō′nē əs) ***adj.*** having a pleasant sound; harmonious —**eu·pho′ni·ous·ly *adv.***

eu·pho·ny (yo͞o′fə nē) ***n., pl.* -nies** ⟦< Gr *eu-*, good + *phōnē*, voice⟧ a pleasant combination of agreeable sounds, as in speech

eu·pho·ri·a (yo͞o fôr′ē ə) ***n.*** ⟦< Gr *eu-*, well + *pherein*, to bear⟧ a feeling of well-being —**eu·phor′ic *adj.***

Eu·phra·tes (yo͞o frāt′ēz) river flowing from EC Turkey through Syria & Iraq into the Persian Gulf: cf. TIGRIS

Eur·a·sia (yoor ā′zhə) land mass made up of Europe & Asia

Eur·a′sian (-zhən) ***adj.*** **1** of Eurasia **2**

of mixed European and Asian descent —*n.* a person of Eurasian descent

eu·re·ka (yoo rē′kə) ***interj.*** ⟦< Gr *heurēka*, I have found⟧ used to express triumphant achievement

Eu·rip·i·des (yoo rip′ə dēz′) 480-406 B.C.; Gr. writer of tragedies

eu·ro (yoor′ō) ***n.*** the basic monetary unit of the European Monetary Union

Eu·rope (yoor′əp) continent between Asia & the Atlantic: *c.* 3,800,000 sq. mi.; pop. *c.* 710,000,000 —**Eu·ro·pe·an** (yoor′ ə pē′ən) ***adj., n.***

European Community an organization of European countries established in 1967 to bring about the political and economic unification of W Europe

European Monetary Union a union of those 12 members of the European Union that use the euro as their only legal currency

European plan a system of hotel operation in which guests are charged for rooms and pay for meals separately

European Union a union of European nations created in 1993 to bring about the gradual unification of Europe

eu·ryth·mics (yoo rith′miks) ***n.*** ⟦< Gr *eu-*, good + *rhythmos,* rhythm⟧ the art of performing bodily movements in rhythm, usually to music

eu·sta·chian tube (yoo stā′shən) ⟦after B. *Eustachio*, 16th-c. It anatomist⟧ [*also* **E- t-**] a slender tube between the middle ear and the pharynx

eu·tha·na·si·a (yoo′thə nā′zhə) ***n.*** ⟦< Gr *eu-*, good + *thanatos*, death⟧ the act of causing death painlessly, so as to end suffering

eu·tha·nize (yoo′thə nīz′) ***vt.*** **-nized′**, **-niz′ing** to put to death by euthanasia

e·vac·u·ate (ē vak′yoo āt′) ***vt.*** **-at′ed**, **-at′ing** ⟦< L *e-*, out + *vacuus*, empty⟧ **1** to make empty **2** to discharge (bodily waste, esp. feces) **3** to withdraw from —***vi.*** to withdraw —**e·vac′u·a′tion** ***n.*** —**e·vac′u·ee′** (-ē′) ***n.***

e·vade (ē vād′, i-) ***vi., vt.*** **e·vad′ed**, **e·vad′ing** ⟦< L *e-*, out, from + *vadere*, go⟧ **1** to avoid or escape (from) by deceit or cleverness **2** to avoid doing or answering directly —**e·vad′er** ***n.***

e·val·u·ate (ē val′yoo āt′, i-) ***vt.*** **-at′ed**, **-at′ing** ⟦ult. < L *valere*, be worth⟧ **1** to find the value or amount of **2** to judge the worth of —**e·val′u·a′tion** ***n.***

ev·a·nes·cent (ev′ə nes′ənt) ***adj.*** ⟦< L *e-*, out + *vanescere*, vanish⟧ tending to fade from sight; fleeting; ephemeral —**ev′a·nes′cence** ***n.***

e·van·gel·i·cal (ē′van jel′i kəl, ev′ən-) ***adj.*** ⟦< Gr *euangelos*, bringing good news⟧ **1** of or according to the Gospels or the New Testament **2** of those Protestant churches that emphasize salvation by faith in Jesus

e·van·ge·list (ē van′jə list) ***n.*** **1** [**E-**] any of the four writers of the Gospels: Matthew, Mark, Luke, or John **2** a revivalist or a preacher who holds large public services in various cities, now often televised —**e·van′ge·lism′** ***n.***

e·van′ge·lize′ (-līz′) ***vt.*** **-lized′**, **-liz′ing** to convert to Christianity —***vi.*** to preach the gospel

e·vap·o·rate (ē vap′ə rāt′) ***vt.*** **-rat′ed**, **-rat′ing** ⟦< L *e-*, out, from + *vaporare*, emit vapor⟧ **1** to change (a liquid or solid) into vapor **2** to remove moisture from (milk, etc.), as by heating, so as to get a concentrated product —***vi.*** **1** to become vapor **2** to give off vapor **3** to disappear like vapor; vanish —**e·vap′o·ra′tion** ***n.*** —**e·vap′o·ra′tor** ***n.***

e·va·sion (ē vā′zhən, i-) ***n.*** **1** an evading; specif., an avoiding of a duty, question, etc. by deceit or cleverness **2** a way of doing this; subterfuge

e·va′sive (-siv) ***adj.*** **1** tending or seeking to evade **2** elusive —**e·va′sive·ly** ***adv.*** —**e·va′sive·ness** ***n.***

eve (ēv) ***n.*** ⟦< OE *æfen*, evening⟧ **1** [Old Poet.] evening **2** [*often* **E-**] the evening or day before a holiday **3** the period just prior to some event

Eve (ēv) ***n.*** *Bible* the first woman, Adam's wife

e·ven (ē′vən) ***adj.*** ⟦OE *efne*⟧ **1** flat; level; smooth **2** not varying; constant *[an even tempo]* **3** calm; tranquil *[an even temper]* **4** in the same plane or line *[even with the rim]* **5** owing and being owed nothing **6** equal in number, quantity, etc. **7** exactly divisible by two **8** exact *[an even mile]* **9** revenged for a wrong, etc. —***adv.*** **1** however improbable; indeed **2** exactly; just *[it happened even as I expected]* **3** still; yet *[he's even better]* —***vt., vi.*** to make or become even —**even if** though —**e′ven·ly** ***adv.*** —**e′ven·ness** ***n.***

e′ven·hand′ed ***adj.*** impartial; fair

eve·ning (ēv′niŋ) ***n.*** ⟦< OE *æfnung*⟧ **1** the last part of the day and early part of night **2** [Dial.] afternoon

even money equal stakes in betting, with no odds

e·vent (ē vent′) ***n.*** ⟦< L *e-*, out + *venire*, come⟧ **1** an occurrence, esp. when important **2** a particular contest in a program of sports **3** any organized activity, celebration, etc. —**in any event** no matter what happens; anyway —**in the event of** in case of —**in the event that** if it should happen that

e′ven-tem′pered ***adj.*** not quickly angered; calm

e·vent′ful ***adj.*** **1** full of outstanding events **2** having an important outcome —**e·vent′ful·ly** ***adv.***

e·ven·tide (ē′vən tīd′) ***n.*** [Archaic] evening

e·ven·tu·al (ē ven′choo əl) ***adj.*** ultimate; final —**e·ven′tu·al·ly** ***adv.***

e·ven′tu·al′i·ty (-al′ə tē) ***n.***, *pl.* **-ties** a possible event or outcome

e·ven′tu·ate′ (-āt′) ***vi.*** **-at′ed**, **-at′ing** to happen in the end; result

ev·er (ev′ər) ***adv.*** ⟦< OE *æfre*⟧ **1** always *[ever the same]* **2** at any time *[do you ever see her?]* **3** at all; by any chance *[how can I ever repay you?]* —**ever so** [Inf.] very

Ev·er·est (ev′ər ist, ev′rist), **Mount** peak of the Himalayas: highest known mountain in the world: 29,035 ft.

ev′er·glade′ ***n.*** marshy land

ev′er·green′ ***adj.*** having green leaves

all year long, as most conifers —*n.* an evergreen plant or tree

ev′er·last′ing *adj.* lasting forever; eternal —*n.* eternity

ev′er·more′ *adv.* [Archaic] forever; constantly

ev·er·y (ev′rē) *adj.* ⟦OE *æfre ælc*, lit., ever each⟧ **1** each, individually and separately **2** the greatest possible *[to make every effort]* **3** each interval *[take a pill every three hours]* —**every now and then** occasionally: also [Inf.] **every so often** —**every other** each alternate, as the first, third, fifth, etc. —**every which way** [Inf.] in complete disorder

ev′er·y·bod′y (-bäd′ē, -bud′ē) *pron.* every person; everyone

ev′er·y·day′ *adj.* **1** daily **2** suitable for ordinary days *[everyday shoes]* **3** usual; common

ev′er·y·one′ *pron.* every person

every one every person or thing of those named *[every one of the boys]*

ev′er·y·thing′ *pron.* every thing; all

ev′er·y·where′ *adv.* in or to every place

e·vict (ē vikt′) *vt.* ⟦< L *e-*, intens. + *vincere*, conquer⟧ to remove (a tenant) by legal procedure —**e·vic′tion** *n.*

ev·i·dence (ev′ə dəns) *n.* **1** something that makes another thing evident; sign **2** a statement of a witness, an object, etc. bearing on or establishing the point in question in a court of law —*vt.* **-denced, -denc·ing** to make evident —**in evidence** plainly seen

ev·i·dent (ev′ə dənt) *adj.* ⟦< L *e-*, from + *videre*, see⟧ easy to see or perceive; clear —**ev′i·dent·ly** *adv.*

e·vil (ē′vəl) *adj.* ⟦OE *yfel*⟧ **1** morally bad or wrong; wicked **2** harmful; injurious **3** unlucky; disastrous —*n.* **1** wickedness; sin **2** anything that causes harm, pain, etc. —**e′vil·ly** *adv.*

e′vil·do′er *n.* one who does evil —**e′vil·do′ing** *n.*

e·vince (ē vins′) *vt.* **e·vinced′, e·vinc′ing** ⟦< L *e-*, intens. + *vincere*, conquer⟧ to show plainly; make clear

e·vis·cer·ate (ē vis′ər āt′) *vt.* **-at′ed, -at′ing** ⟦< L *e-*, out + *viscera*, viscera⟧ **1** to remove the entrails from **2** to deprive of an essential part —**e·vis′cer·a′tion** *n.*

e·voke (ē vōk′) *vt.* **e·voked′, e·vok′ing** ⟦< L *e-*, out, from + *vox*, voice⟧ **1** to call forth **2** to elicit (a reaction, etc.) —**ev·o·ca·tion** (ev′ə kā′shən, ē′vō-) *n.*

ev·o·lu·tion (ev′ə lo͞o′shən) *n.* ⟦see fol.⟧ **1** an unfolding; process of development or change **2** a thing evolved **3** a movement that is part of a series **4** *Biol. a)* the development of a species, organism, etc. from its original to its present state *b)* the theory that all species developed from earlier forms —**ev′o·lu′tion·ar′y** *adj.* —**ev′o·lu′tion·ist** *n.*

e·volve (ē välv′, -vôlv′) *vt., vi.* **e·volved′, e·volv′ing** ⟦< L *e-*, out + *volvere*, to roll⟧ **1** to develop gradually **2** to develop by evolution

ewe (yo͞o) *n.* ⟦OE *eowu*⟧ a female sheep

ew·er (yo͞o′ər) *n.* ⟦< L *aqua*, water⟧ a large, wide-mouthed water pitcher

ex *abbrev.* **1** example **2** exchange

ex- ⟦< OFr or L⟧ *prefix* **1** *a)* from, out *[expel] b)* beyond *c)* thoroughly *d)* upward **2** former, previous *[ex-president]*

ex·ac·er·bate (eg zas′ər bāt′) *vt.* **-bat′ed, -bat′ing** ⟦< L *ex-*, intens. + *acerbus*, bitter⟧ **1** to aggravate (pain, annoyance, etc.) **2** to exasperate; annoy; irritate —**ex·ac′er·ba′tion** *n.*

ex·act (eg zakt′) *adj.* ⟦< L *ex-*, out + *agere*, to do⟧ **1** characterized by or requiring accuracy; methodical; correct **2** without variation; precise —*vt.* **1** to extort **2** to demand; require —**ex·act′ly** *adv.* —**ex·act′ness** *n.*

ex·act′ing *adj.* **1** making severe demands; strict **2** demanding great care, effort, etc.; arduous —**ex·act′ing·ly** *adv.*

ex·ac·tion (eg zak′shən) *n.* **1** an exacting **2** an extortion **3** an exacted fee, tax, etc.

ex·ac′ti·tude′ (-tə to͞od′) *n.* ⟦Fr⟧ the quality of being exact; accuracy

ex·ag·ger·ate (eg zaj′ər āt′) *vt., vi.* **-at′ed, -at′ing** ⟦< L *ex-*, out + *agger*, a heap⟧ to think or tell of (something) as greater than it is; overstate —**ex·ag′ger·a′tion** *n.* —**ex·ag′ger·a′tive** *adj.* —**ex·ag′ger·a′tor** *n.*

ex·alt (eg zôlt′) *vt.* ⟦< L *ex-*, up + *altus*, high⟧ **1** to raise in status, dignity, etc. **2** to praise; glorify **3** to fill with joy, pride, etc.; elate —**ex·al·ta·tion** (eg′zôl tā′shən) *n.*

ex·am·i·na·tion (eg zam′ə nā′shən) *n.* **1** an examining or being examined **2** a set of questions asked in testing: also **ex·am′**

ex·am·ine (eg zam′ən) *vt.* **-ined, -in·ing** ⟦< L *examinare*, weigh⟧ **1** to look at critically or methodically; investigate; inspect **2** to test by questioning —**ex·am′in·er** *n.*

ex·am·ple (eg zam′pəl) *n.* ⟦< L *eximere*, take out⟧ **1** something selected to show the character of the rest; sample **2** a case that serves as a warning **3** a model; pattern **4** an instance that illustrates a principle

ex·as·per·ate (eg zas′pər āt′) *vt.* **-at′ed, -at′ing** ⟦< L *ex-*, out + *asper*, rough⟧ to irritate; anger; vex —**ex·as′per·a′tion** *n.*

ex·ca·vate (eks′kə vāt′) *vt.* **-vat′ed, -vat′ing** ⟦< L *ex-*, out + *cavus*, hollow⟧ **1** to make a hole or cavity in **2** to form (a tunnel, etc.) by hollowing out **3** to unearth **4** to dig out (earth, soil, etc.) —**ex′ca·va′tion** *n.* —**ex′ca·va′tor** *n.*

ex·ceed (ek sēd′) *vt.* ⟦< L *ex-*, out + *cedere*, to go⟧ **1** to go or be beyond (a limit, etc.) **2** to surpass

ex·ceed′ing *adj.* surpassing; extreme —**ex·ceed′ing·ly** *adv.*

ex·cel (ek sel′) *vi., vt.* **-celled′, -cel′ling** ⟦< L *ex-*, out of + *-cellere*, to rise⟧ to be better or greater than (another or others)

ex·cel·lence (ek′sə ləns) *n.* **1** the fact or state of excelling; superiority **2** a particular virtue

ex′cel·len·cy (-lən sē) *n., pl.* **-cies** **1** [E-] a title of honor for certain dignitaries **2**

ex·cel·lent (ek′sə lənt) ***adj.*** ⟦see EXCEL⟧ outstandingly good of its kind; of exceptional merit —**ex′cel·lent·ly** ***adv.***

ex·cel·si·or (eks sel′sē ôr′; *for n.* ek sel′ sē ər) ***interj.*** ⟦see EXCEL⟧ always upward! —***n.*** long, thin wood shavings used for packing

ex·cept (ek sept′) ***vt.*** ⟦< L *ex-*, out + *capere*, to take⟧ to leave out or take out; exclude —***prep.*** leaving out; but —***conj.*** [Inf.] were it not that; only —**except for** if it were not for

ex·cept′ing ***prep., conj.*** EXCEPT

ex·cep′tion ***n.*** **1** an excepting **2** *a*) a case to which a rule does not apply *b*) a person or thing different from others of the same class **3** an objection —**take exception** **1** to object **2** feel offended

ex·cep′tion·a·ble ***adj.*** liable to exception; open to objection

ex·cep′tion·al ***adj.*** **1** unusual; esp., unusually good **2** needing special education, as because mentally gifted or mentally handicapped —**ex·cep′tion·al·ly** ***adv.***

ex·cerpt (ek surpt′; *for n.* ek′surpt′) ***vt.*** ⟦< L *ex-*, out + *carpere*, to pick⟧ to select or quote (passages from a book, etc.); extract —***n.*** a passage selected or quoted; extract

ex·cess (ek ses′; *also, esp. for adj.*, ek′ ses′) ***n.*** ⟦see EXCEED⟧ **1** action that goes beyond a reasonable limit **2** an amount greater than is necessary **3** the amount by which one thing exceeds another —***adj.*** extra; surplus —**in excess of** more than

ex·ces′sive ***adj.*** being too much; immoderate —**ex·ces′sive·ly** ***adv.***

ex·change (eks chānj′) ***vt., vi.*** **-changed′**, **-chang′ing** ⟦see EX- & CHANGE⟧ **1** to give or receive (something) *for* another thing; barter; trade **2** to interchange (similar things) —***n.*** **1** an exchanging; interchange **2** a thing exchanged **3** a place for exchanging *[a stock exchange]* **4** a central office providing telephone service **5** the value of one currency in terms of another —**ex·change′a·ble** ***adj.***

exchange rate the rate at which one currency can be exchanged for another

ex·cheq·uer (eks chek′ər) ***n.*** ⟦ME *escheker*, lit., chessboard < OFr *eschekier*: accounts of revenue were kept on a squared board⟧ **1** a national treasury **2** funds; finances

ex·cise[1] (ek′sīz′) ***n.*** ⟦ult. < L *assidere*, assist (in office)⟧ a tax on various commodities, as liquor or tobacco, within a country: also **excise tax**

ex·cise[2] (ek sīz′) ***vt.*** **-cised′**, **-cis′ing** ⟦< L *ex-*, out + *caedere*, to cut⟧ to remove by cutting out —**ex·ci′sion** (-sizh′ən) ***n.***

ex·cit·a·ble (ek sīt′ə bəl) ***adj.*** easily excited —**ex·cit′a·bil′i·ty** ***n.***

ex·cite (ek sīt′) ***vt.*** **-cit′ed**, **-cit′ing** ⟦< L *ex-*, out + *ciere*, to call⟧ **1** to make active; stir up **2** to arouse; provoke **3** to arouse the feelings of —**ex·ci·ta·tion** (ek′sī tā′shən) ***n.*** —**ex·cit′ed·ly** ***adv.*** —**ex·cit′er** ***n.***

ex·cite′ment ***n.*** **1** an exciting or being excited; agitation **2** that which excites

ex·cit′ing ***adj.*** causing excitement; stirring, thrilling, etc.

ex·claim (ek sklām′) ***vi., vt.*** ⟦< L *ex-*, out + *clamare*, to shout⟧ to cry out; say suddenly and vehemently

ex·cla·ma·tion (ek′sklə mā′shən) ***n.*** **1** an exclaiming **2** something exclaimed; interjection —**ex·clam·a·to·ry** (ek sklam′ə tôr′ē) ***adj.***

exclamation point (or **mark**) a mark (!) used in punctuating to show surprise, strong emotion, etc.

ex·clude (eks klo͞od′) ***vt.*** **-clud′ed**, **-clud′ing** ⟦< L *ex-*, out + *claudere*, to close⟧ **1** to refuse to admit, consider, etc.; reject **2** to put or force out —**ex·clu′sion** (-klo͞o′zhən) ***n.***

ex·clu′sive (-klo͞o′siv) ***adj.*** **1** excluding all others **2** not shared or divided; sole *[an exclusive right]* **3** excluding certain people, as for social or economic reasons —***n.*** something exclusive; specif., a news item distributed by only one news organization —**exclusive of** not including —**ex·clu′sive·ly** ***adv.*** —**ex·clu′sive·ness** ***n.***

ex·com·mu·ni·cate (eks′kə myo͞o′ni kāt′) ***vt.*** **-cat′ed**, **-cat′ing** to exclude from the rights, privileges, etc. of a church —**ex′com·mu′ni·ca′tion** ***n.***

ex·co·ri·ate (eks kôr′ē āt′) ***vt.*** **-at′ed**, **-at′ing** ⟦< L *ex-*, off + *corium*, the skin⟧ to denounce harshly —**ex·co′ri·a′tion** ***n.***

ex·cre·ment (eks′krə mənt) ***n.*** waste matter excreted from the bowels

ex·cres·cence (eks kres′əns) ***n.*** ⟦< L *ex-*, out + *crescere*, grow⟧ an abnormal outgrowth or addition

ex·cre·ta (eks krēt′ə) ***pl.n.*** waste matter excreted from the body

ex·crete (eks krēt′) ***vt., vi.*** **-cret′ed**, **-cret′ing** ⟦< L *ex-*, out of + *cernere*, sift⟧ to eliminate (waste matter) from the body —**ex·cre′tion** ***n.*** —**ex·cre·to·ry** (eks′krə tôr′ē) ***adj.***

ex·cru·ci·at·ing (eks kro͞o′shē āt′iŋ) ***adj.*** **1** intensely painful; agonizing **2** intense or extreme

ex·cul·pate (eks′kəl pāt′) ***vt.*** **-pat′ed**, **-pat′ing** ⟦< L *ex*, out + *culpa*, fault⟧ to free from blame; prove guiltless —**ex′cul·pa′tion** ***n.*** —**ex·cul′pa·to′ry** ***adj.***

ex·cur·sion (eks kur′zhən) ***n.*** ⟦< L *ex-*, out + *currere*, to run⟧ **1** a short trip; jaunt **2** a round trip at reduced rates —***adj.*** for an excursion

ex·cur·sive (eks kur′siv) ***adj.*** rambling; digressive —**ex·cur′sive·ly** ***adv.*** —**ex·cur′sive·ness** ***n.***

ex·cuse (ek skyo͞oz′; *for n.*, -skyo͞os′) ***vt.*** **-cused′**, **-cus′ing** ⟦< L *ex-*, from + *causa*, a charge⟧ **1** to apologize or give reasons for **2** to overlook (an offense or fault) **3** to release from an obligation, etc. **4** to permit to leave **5** to justify —***n.*** **1** a defense of some action; apology **2** something that excuses **3** a pretext —**excuse oneself** **1** to apologize **2** to ask for permission to leave —**ex·cus′a·ble** ***adj.***

exec *abbrev.* **1** executive **2** executor

ex·e·cra·ble (ek′si krə bəl) ***adj.*** ⟦see fol.⟧ **1** detestable **2** very inferior

ex′e·crate′ (-krāt′) ***vt.* -crat′ed, -crat′ing** ⟦< L *execrare,* to curse⟧ **1** to denounce scathingly **2** to loathe; abhor **—ex′e·cra′tion *n.***

ex·e·cute (ek′si kyōōt′) ***vt.* -cut′ed, -cut′ing** ⟦see EXECUTOR⟧ **1** to carry out; do **2** to administer (laws, etc.) **3** to put to death by a legal sentence **4** to create in accordance with a plan, etc. **5** to make valid (a deed, will, etc.)

ex′e·cu′tion *n.* **1** an executing; specif., *a)* a carrying out, performing, etc. *b)* a putting to death by a legal sentence **2** the manner of performing

ex′e·cu′tion·er *n.* one who carries out a court-imposed death penalty

ex·ec·u·tive (eg zek′yōō tiv) ***adj.*** ⟦see fol.⟧ **1** of or capable of carrying out duties, functions, etc. **2** empowered to administer (laws, government affairs, etc.) **—*n.*** **1** the branch of government administering the laws and matters of business of a nation **2** one who administers or manages matters of business of a corporation, etc.

ex·ec·u·tor (eg zek′yōō tər) ***n.*** ⟦< L *ex-,* intens. + *sequi,* to follow⟧ a person appointed to carry out the provisions of a will

ex·e·ge·sis (ek′sə jē′sis) ***n.,*** *pl.* **-ses′** (-sēz′) ⟦< Gr *ex-,* out + *hēgeisthai,* to lead⟧ interpretation of a word, passage, etc., esp. in the Bible

ex·em·plar (eg zem′plər, -plär′) ***n.*** ⟦< L *exemplum,* a pattern⟧ **1** a model; pattern **2** a typical specimen

ex·em·pla·ry (eg zem′plə rē) ***adj.*** ⟦< L *exemplum,* a pattern⟧ serving as a model or example *[an exemplary life]*

ex·em·pli·fy (eg zem′plə fī′) ***vt.* -fied′, -fy′ing** ⟦< L *exemplum,* example + *facere,* to make⟧ to show by example **—ex·em′pli·fi·ca′tion *n.***

ex·empt (eg zempt′) ***vt.*** ⟦< L *ex-,* out + *emere,* to buy⟧ to free from a rule or obligation which applies to others **—*adj.*** freed from a usual rule, duty, etc. **—ex·emp′tion *n.***

ex·er·cise (ek′sər sīz′) ***n.*** ⟦< L *exercere,* put to work⟧ **1** active use or operation **2** performance (of duties, etc.) **3** activity for developing the body or mind **4** a task to be practiced for developing some skill **5** [*pl.*] a program of speeches, etc. **—*vt.* -cised′, -cis′ing** **1** to put into action; use **2** to carry out (duties, etc.); perform **3** to put into use so as to develop or train **4** to exert (influence, etc.) **5** to engage so as to worry, harass, etc. **—*vi.*** to do exercises

ex·ert (eg zurt′) ***vt.*** ⟦< L *exserere,* stretch out⟧ **1** to put into action **2** to apply (oneself) with great effort

ex·er′tion *n.* **1** active use of strength, power, etc. **2** effort

ex·hale (eks hāl′) ***vt., vi.* -haled′, -hal′ing** ⟦< L *ex-,* out + *halare,* breathe⟧ **1** to breathe out (air) **2** to give off (vapor, etc.) **—ex·ha·la·tion** (eks′hə lā′shən) ***n.***

ex·haust (eg zôst′) ***vt.*** ⟦< L *ex-,* out + *haurire,* to draw⟧ **1** to use up **2** to empty completely; drain **3** to tire out **4** to deal with thoroughly **—*n.*** **1** the discharge of used steam, gas, etc. from an engine **2** the pipes through which it is released **3** fumes, etc. given off **—ex·haust′i·ble *adj.***

ex·haus·tion (eg zôs′chən) ***n.*** **1** an exhausting **2** great fatigue

ex·haus′tive *adj.* leaving nothing out **—ex·haus′tive·ly *adv.***

ex·hib·it (eg zib′it) ***vt.*** ⟦< L *ex-,* out + *habere,* to hold⟧ **1** to show; display **2** to present to public view **—*vi.*** to put art objects, etc. on public display **—*n.*** **1** a display **2** a thing exhibited **3** *Law* an object produced as evidence in a court **—ex·hib′i·tor *n.***

ex·hi·bi·tion (ek′sə bish′ən) ***n.*** **1** an exhibiting **2** that which is exhibited **3** a public showing, as of art

ex′hi·bi′tion·ism′ *n.* **1** a tendency to call attention to oneself or show off **2** a tendency to expose oneself sexually **—ex′hi·bi′tion·ist *n.***

ex·hil·a·rate (eg zil′ə rāt′) ***vt.* -rat′ed, -rat′ing** ⟦< L *ex-,* intens. + *hilaris,* glad⟧ **1** to make cheerful or lively **2** to stimulate **—ex·hil′a·ra′tion *n.* —ex·hil′a·ra′tive *adj.***

ex·hort (eg zôrt′) ***vt., vi.*** ⟦< L *ex-,* out + *hortari,* to urge⟧ to urge earnestly; advise strongly **—ex′hor·ta′tion *n.***

ex·hume (eks hyōōm′, eg zyōōm′) ***vt.* -humed′, -hum′ing** ⟦< L *ex-,* out + *humus,* the ground⟧ **1** to dig out of the earth; disinter **2** to bring to light; reveal **—ex′hu·ma′tion *n.***

ex·i·gen·cy (eks′ə jən sē) ***n.,*** *pl.* **-cies** ⟦< L *exigere,* drive out⟧ **1** urgency **2** a situation calling for immediate attention **3** [*pl.*] pressing needs **—ex′i·gent *adj.***

ex·ig·u·ous (eg zig′yōō əs) ***adj.*** ⟦see prec.⟧ scanty; meager

ex·ile (ek′sīl′, eg′zīl′) ***n.*** ⟦< L *exul,* an exile⟧ **1** a prolonged living away from one's country, usually enforced **2** a person in exile **—*vt.* -iled′, -il′ing** to force (a person) into exile; banish

ex·ist (eg zist′) ***vi.*** ⟦< L *ex-,* out + *sistere,* to set, place⟧ **1** to have reality or being; be **2** to occur or be present **3** to continue being; live

ex·ist′ence *n.* **1** the act or fact of being **2** life; living **3** occurrence **—ex·ist′ent *adj.***

ex·is·ten·tial (eg′zis ten′shəl) ***adj.*** **1** of existence **2** of existentialism

ex′is·ten′tial·ism′ *n.* a philosophical movement stressing individual existence and holding that human beings are totally free and responsible for their acts **—ex′is·ten′tial·ist *adj., n.***

ex·it (ek′sit, eg′zit) ***n.*** ⟦< L *ex-,* out + *ire,* to go⟧ **1** an actor's departure from the stage **2** a going out; departure **3** a way out **4** a road leading from an expressway **—*vi.*** to leave a place **—*vt.*** to leave (a building, expressway, etc.)

exo- ⟦< Gr *exō*⟧ *prefix* outside, outer, outer part

ex·o·bi·ol·o·gy (eks′ō bī äl′ə jē) ***n.*** the branch of biology investigating the possibility of extraterrestrial life

ex·o·dus (eks′ə dəs) ***n.*** ⟦< Gr *ex-,* out + *hodos,* way⟧ **1** [**E-**] the departure of the

Israelites from Egypt: with *the* **2** [**E-**] the second book of the Bible, describing this **3** a going out or forth

ex of·fi·ci·o (eks′ ə fish′ē ō′) ⟦L, lit., from office⟧ by virtue of one's position

ex·on·er·ate (eg zän′ər āt′) ***vt.*** **-at′ed, -at′ing** ⟦< L *ex-*, out + *onerare*, to load⟧ to declare or prove blameless **—ex·on′er·a′tion *n.***

ex·or·bi·tant (eg zôr′bi tənt) ***adj.*** ⟦< L *ex-*, out + *orbita*, a track⟧ going beyond what is reasonable, just, etc.; excessive **—ex·or′bi·tance *n.***

ex·or·cise or **ex·or·cize** (eks′ôr sīz′) ***vt.*** **-cised′** or **-cized′**, **-cis′ing** or **-ciz′ing** ⟦< Gr *ex-*, out + *horkos*, an oath⟧ **1** to drive (an evil spirit) out or away by ritual prayers, etc. **2** to free from such a spirit **—ex′or·cism′** (-siz′əm) ***n.*** **—ex′or·cist *n.***

ex·o·skel·e·ton (eks′ō skel′ə tən) ***n.*** any hard, external supporting structure, as the shell of an oyster

ex′o·ther′mic (-thur′mik) ***adj.*** designating or of a chemical change in which heat is liberated

ex·ot·ic (eg zät′ik) ***adj.*** ⟦< Gr *exō*, outside⟧ **1** foreign **2** strangely beautiful, enticing, etc. **—ex·ot′i·cal·ly *adv.***

exp *abbrev.* experience(d)

ex·pand (ek spand′) ***vt., vi.*** ⟦< L *ex-*, out + *pandere*, to spread⟧ **1** to spread out; unfold **2** to increase in size, scope, etc.; enlarge; develop

ex·panse (ek spans′) ***n.*** a large area or unbroken surface; wide extent

ex·pan′si·ble ***adj.*** that can be expanded: also **ex·pand′a·ble**

ex·pan′sion ***n.*** **1** an expanding or being expanded; enlargement **2** an expanded thing or part **3** the degree or extent of expansion

expansion bolt a bolt with an attachment that expands as the bolt is turned

ex·pan′sive ***adj.*** **1** that can expand **2** broad; extensive **3** effusive; demonstrative **—ex·pan′sive·ly *adv.***

ex·pa·ti·ate (eks pā′shē āt′) ***vi.*** **-at′ed, -at′ing** ⟦< L *ex(s)patiari*, wander⟧ to speak or write at length (*on* or *upon*) **—ex·pa′ti·a′tion *n.***

ex·pa·tri·ate (eks pā′trē āt′; *for n.*, -it) ***vt., vi.*** **-at′ed, -at′ing** ⟦< L *ex*, out of + *patria*, fatherland⟧ to exile (a person or oneself) **—*n.*** an expatriated person **—ex·pa′tri·a′tion *n.***

ex·pect (ek spekt′) ***vt.*** ⟦< L *ex-*, out + *spectare*, to look⟧ **1** to look for as likely to occur or appear **2** to look for as proper or necessary **3** [Inf.] to suppose; guess **—be expecting** [Inf.] to be pregnant

ex·pect′an·cy ***n.***, *pl.* **-cies** **1** EXPECTATION **2** that which is expected, esp. on a statistical basis

ex·pect′ant ***adj.*** that expects; expecting **—ex·pect′ant·ly *adv.***

ex·pec·ta·tion (ek′spek tā′shən) ***n.*** **1** an expecting; anticipation **2** a thing looked forward to **3** [*also pl.*] a reason for expecting something

ex·pec·to·rant (ek spek′tə rənt) ***n.*** ⟦see fol.⟧ a medicine that helps to bring up phlegm

ex·pec′to·rate′ (-tə rāt′) ***vt., vi.*** **-rat′ed, -rat′ing** ⟦< L *ex-*, out + *pectus*, breast⟧ to spit **—ex·pec′to·ra′tion *n.***

ex·pe·di·en·cy (ek spē′dē ən sē) ***n.***, *pl.* **-cies** **1** a being expedient; suitability for a given purpose **2** the doing of what is selfish rather than of what is right or just; self-interest **3** an expedient Also **ex·pe′di·ence**

ex·pe′di·ent ***adj.*** ⟦see fol.⟧ **1** useful for effecting a desired result; convenient **2** based on or guided by self-interest **—*n.*** an expedient thing; means to an end

ex·pe·dite (eks′pə dīt′) ***vt.*** **-dit′ed, -dit′ing** ⟦< L *expedire*, lit., to free the foot⟧ **1** to speed up the progress of; facilitate **2** to do quickly

ex′pe·dit′er ***n.*** one employed to expedite urgent or involved projects: also sp. **ex′pe·di′tor**

ex·pe·di·tion (eks′pə dish′ən) ***n.*** ⟦see EXPEDITE⟧ **1** *a)* a voyage, march, etc., as for exploration or battle *b)* those on such a journey **2** efficient speed **—ex′pe·di′tion·ar′y *adj.***

ex′pe·di′tious (-dish′əs) ***adj.*** efficient and speedy; prompt **—ex′pe·di′tious·ly *adv.***

ex·pel (ek spel′) ***vt.*** **-pelled′, -pel′ling** ⟦< L *ex-*, out + *pellere*, to thrust⟧ **1** to drive out by force **2** to dismiss by authority [*expelled* from college] **—ex·pel′la·ble *adj.*** **—ex·pel′ler *n.***

ex·pend (ek spend′) ***vt.*** ⟦< L *ex-*, out + *pendere*, to weigh⟧ **1** to spend **2** to use up

ex·pend′a·ble ***adj.*** **1** that can be expended **2** *Mil.* designating equipment (or personnel) expected to be used up (or sacrificed) in service

ex·pend·i·ture (ek spen′di chər) ***n.*** **1** an expending of money, time, etc. **2** the amount of money, time, etc. expended

ex·pense (ek spens′) ***n.*** ⟦see EXPEND⟧ **1** financial cost; charge **2** any cost or sacrifice **3** [*pl.*] charges met with in doing one's work, etc.

ex·pen′sive ***adj.*** costly; high-priced

ex·pe·ri·ence (ek spir′ē əns) ***n.*** ⟦< L *experiri*, to try⟧ **1** the act of living through an event **2** anything or everything observed or lived through **3** *a)* training and personal participation *b)* knowledge, skill, etc. resulting from this **—*vt.*** **-enced, -enc·ing** to have experience of; undergo

ex·pe′ri·enced ***adj.*** having had or having learned from experience

ex·per·i·ment (ek sper′ə mənt; *also, and for v. usually*, -ment′) ***n.*** ⟦< L *experimentum*, a trial⟧ a test, trial, action, etc. undertaken to discover or demonstrate something **—*vi.*** to make, perform, conduct, etc. experiments **—ex·per′i·men·ta′tion** (-mən tā′shən) ***n.*** **—ex·per′i·ment′er *n.***

ex·per′i·men′tal ***adj.*** **1** based on or used for experiments **2** designed to test **3** tentative **—ex·per′i·men′tal·ly *adv.***

ex·pert (eks′pərt) ***adj.*** ⟦see EXPERIENCE⟧ very skillful **—*n.*** one who is very skillful or well-informed in some special field **—ex′pert·ly *adv.*** **—ex′pert·ness *n.***

ex·per·tise (ek'spər tēz') *n.* ⟦Fr⟧ the skill or knowledge of an expert

ex·pi·ate (eks'pē āt') *vt.* **-at'ed, -at'ing** ⟦< L *ex-*, out + *piare*, to appease⟧ to make amends for (wrongdoing or guilt); atone for —**ex'pi·a'tion** *n.* —**ex'pi·a·to'ry** (-ə tôr'ē) *adj.*

ex·pire (ek spīr') *vi.* **-pired', -pir'ing** ⟦< L *ex-*, out + *spirare*, breathe⟧ **1** to exhale **2** to die **3** to come to an end —**ex·pi·ra·tion** (ek'spə rā'shən) *n.*

ex·plain (ek splān') *vt.* ⟦< L *ex-*, out + *planus*, level⟧ **1** to make plain or understandable **2** to give the meaning of; expound **3** to account for —*vi.* to give an explanation —**ex·plain'a·ble** *adj.*

ex·pla·na·tion (eks'plə nā'shən) *n.* **1** an explaining **2** something that explains; interpretation, meaning, etc.

ex·plan·a·to·ry (ek splan'ə tôr'ē) *adj.* explaining or intended to explain

ex·ple·tive (eks'plə tiv) *n.* ⟦< L *ex-*, out, up + *plere*, to fill⟧ an oath or exclamation

ex·pli·ca·ble (eks'pli kə bəl, ik splik'ə bəl) *adj.* ⟦see fol.⟧ that can be explained

ex·pli·cate (eks'pli kāt') *vt.* **-cat'ed, -cat'ing** ⟦< L *ex-*, out + *plicare*, to fold⟧ to make clear; explain fully

ex·plic·it (eks plis'it) *adj.* ⟦see prec.⟧ **1** clearly stated or shown; definite **2** outspoken —**ex·plic'it·ly** *adv.*

ex·plode (ek splōd') *vt.* **-plod'ed, -plod'ing** ⟦orig., to drive off the stage < L *ex-*, off + *plaudere*, applaud⟧ **1** to expose as false **2** to make burst with a loud noise **3** to cause to change suddenly and violently, as from a solid to an expanding gas —*vi.* to burst forth noisily —**ex·plod'a·ble** *adj.*

ex·ploit (eks'ploit'; *also, and for v. usually*, ek sploit') *n.* ⟦see EXPLICATE⟧ a daring act; bold deed —*vt.* **1** to make use of **2** to make unethical use of for one's own profit —**ex'ploi·ta'tion** *n.* —**ex·ploit'a·tive** *adj.* —**ex·ploit'er** *n.*

ex·plore (ek splôr') *vt., vi.* **-plored', -plor'ing** ⟦< L *ex-*, out + *plorare*, cry out⟧ **1** to examine (something) carefully; investigate **2** to travel in (a little-known region) to learn about it —**ex·plo·ra·tion** (eks'plə rā'shən) *n.* —**ex·plor'a·to'ry** (-ə tôr'ē) *adj.* —**ex·plor'er** *n.*

ex·plo·sion (ek splō'zhən) *n.* **1** an exploding **2** the noise made by exploding **3** a noisy outburst **4** a sudden, widespread increase

ex·plo'sive (-siv) *adj.* **1** of, causing, or like an explosion **2** tending to explode —*n.* a substance that can explode, as gunpowder —**ex·plo'sive·ly** *adv.* —**ex·plo'sive·ness** *n.*

ex·po·nent (ek spōn'ənt; *also, esp. for 3*, eks'pōn'-) *n.* ⟦see EXPOUND⟧ **1** one who expounds or promotes (principles, etc.) **2** a person or thing that is an example or symbol (*of* something) **3** *Algebra* a symbol placed at the upper right of another to show how many times the latter is to be multiplied by itself (Ex.: $b^2 = b \times b$)

ex·po·nen·tial (eks'pō nen'shəl) *adj.* **1** *Math.* of an exponent **2** of or increasing by very large amounts, etc.

ex·port (ek spôrt'; *also, and for n. always*, eks'pôrt') *vt.* ⟦< L *ex-*, out + *portare*, to carry⟧ **1** to send (goods) to another country, esp. for sale **2** to send (ideas, culture, etc.) from one place to another —*n.* **1** something exported **2** an exporting —**ex'por·ta'tion** *n.* —**ex·port'er** *n.*

ex·pose (ek spōz') *vt.* **-posed', -pos'ing** ⟦see EXPOUND⟧ **1** to lay open (*to* danger, attack, etc.) **2** to reveal; exhibit **3** to make (a crime, etc.) known **4** *Photog.* to subject (a sensitized film or plate) to light, etc.

ex·po·sé (eks'pō zā') *n.* ⟦Fr⟧ a public disclosure of a scandal, crime, etc.

ex·po·si·tion (eks'pə zish'ən) *n.* ⟦see EXPOUND⟧ **1** a detailed explanation **2** writing or speaking that explains **3** a large public exhibition or show

ex·pos·i·tor (ek späz'ət ər) *n.* one who expounds or explains

ex·pos'i·to'ry (-ə tôr'ē) *adj.* of or containing exposition; explanatory

ex post fac·to (eks' pōst fak'tō) ⟦L, from (the thing) done afterward⟧ done afterward, but retroactive

ex·pos·tu·late (ek späs'chə lāt') *vi.* **-lat'ed, -lat'ing** ⟦< L *ex-*, intens. + *postulare*, to demand⟧ to reason with a person earnestly, objecting to that person's actions —**ex·pos'tu·la'tion** *n.*

ex·po·sure (ek spō'zhər) *n.* **1** an exposing or being exposed **2** a location, as of a house, in relation to the sun, etc. [*an eastern exposure*] **3** frequent appearance before the public **4** *Photog. a*) the subjection of a sensitized film or plate to light, X-rays, etc. *b*) a section of a film for one picture *c*) the time during which such a section is exposed

ex·pound (ek spound') *vt.* ⟦< L *ex-*, out + *ponere*, to put⟧ **1** to set forth; state in detail **2** to explain

ex·press (ek spres') *vt.* ⟦< L *ex-*, out + *premere*, to press⟧ **1** to squeeze out (juice, etc.) **2** to put into words; state **3** to reveal; show **4** to symbolize; signify **5** to send by express —*adj.* **1** stated; expressed; explicit **2** specific **3** fast, direct, and making few stops [*an express bus*] **4** marked by speed [*an express highway*] **5** having to do with an express train, bus, service, etc. —*adv.* by express —*n.* **1** an express train, bus, etc. **2** *a*) a service for transporting things rapidly *b*) the things sent by express

ex·pres·sion (ek spresh'ən) *n.* **1** a putting into words; stating **2** a manner of expressing, esp. with eloquence **3** a particular word or phrase **4** a showing of feeling, character, etc. **5** a look, intonation, etc. that conveys meaning **6** a mathematical symbol or set of symbols —**ex·pres'sion·less** *adj.*

ex·pres'sion·ism' *n.* [*often* **E-**] a 20th-c. movement in art, literature, etc. seeking to give symbolic, objective expression to inner experience —**ex·pres'sion·ist** *adj., n.* —**ex·pres'sion·is'tic** *adj.*

ex·pres'sive *adj.* **1** that expresses **2** full of meaning or feeling —**ex·**

pres'sive·ly *adv.* —ex·pres'sive·ness *n.*

ex·press'ly *adv.* 1 plainly; definitely 2 especially; particularly

ex·press'way' *n.* a divided highway for high-speed, through traffic, with grade separations at intersections

ex·pro·pri·ate (eks prō'prē āt') *vt.* -at'ed, -at'ing ⟦< L *ex-*, out + *proprius*, one's own⟧ to take (land, etc.) from its owner, esp. for public use —ex·pro'pri·a'tion *n.*

ex·pul·sion (ek spul'shən) *n.* an expelling or being expelled

ex·punge (ek spunj') *vt.* -punged', -pung'ing ⟦< L *ex-*, out + *pungere*, to prick⟧ to blot or strike out; erase

ex·pur·gate (eks'pər gāt') *vt.* -gat'ed, -gat'ing ⟦< L *ex-*, out + *purgare*, cleanse⟧ to remove (passages considered obscene, etc.) from (a book, etc.) —ex'pur·ga'tion *n.*

ex·qui·site (eks'kwi zit, ek skwiz'it) *adj.* ⟦< L *ex-*, out + *quaerere*, to ask⟧ 1 carefully or elaborately done 2 very beautiful, delicate, etc. 3 of highest quality 4 very intense; keen

ext *abbrev.* extension

ex·tant (eks'tənt, ek stant') *adj.* ⟦< L *ex-*, out + *stare*, to stand⟧ still existing; not extinct

ex·tem·po·ra·ne·ous (eks'tem'pə rā'nē əs) *adj.* ⟦see fol.⟧ done or spoken with little preparation; offhand —ex'tem'po·ra'ne·ous·ly *adv.*

ex·tem·po·re (ek stem'pə rē) *adv., adj.* ⟦< L *ex-*, out of + *tempus*, time⟧ with little preparation; offhand

ex·tem'po·rize' (-rīz') *vi., vt.* -rized', -riz'ing to speak, perform, etc. extempore; improvise

ex·tend (ek stend') *vt.* ⟦< L *ex-*, out + *tendere*, to stretch⟧ 1 to make longer; stretch out; prolong 2 to enlarge in area, scope, etc.; expand 3 to stretch forth 4 to offer; grant 5 to make (oneself) work very hard —*vi.* to be extended —ex·tend'ed *adj.* —ex·tend'er *n.* —ex·ten'si·ble (-sten'sə bəl) or ex·tend'i·ble *adj.*

extended care nursing care for a limited time after hospitalization

extended family a nuclear family together with other relatives living with them or nearby

ex·ten'sion (-sten'shən) *n.* 1 an extending or being extended 2 range; extent 3 a part forming a continuation or addition 4 an extra telephone connected to the main line

ex·ten'sive (-siv) *adj.* having great extent; vast; far-reaching; comprehensive —ex·ten'sive·ly *adv.* —ex·ten'sive·ness *n.*

ex·tent (ek stent') *n.* 1 the space, amount, or degree to which a thing extends; size 2 scope; limits 3 an extended space; vast area

ex·ten·u·ate (ek sten'yo͞o āt') *vt.* -at'ed, -at'ing ⟦< L *ex-*, out + *tenuis*, thin⟧ to make (an offense, etc.) seem less serious —ex·ten'u·a'tion *n.*

ex·te·ri·or (ek stir'ē ər) *adj.* ⟦see EXTERNAL⟧ 1 *a*) on the outside; outer *b*) to be used on the outside [*exterior* paint] 2 coming from without —*n.* an outside or outside surface

ex·ter·mi·nate (ek stur'mə nāt') *vt.* -nat'ed, -nat'ing ⟦< L *ex-*, out + *terminus*, boundary⟧ to destroy entirely; wipe out —ex·ter'mi·na'tion *n.*

ex·ter'mi·na'tor (-nāt'ər) *n.* one that exterminates; specif., one whose work is exterminating vermin

ex·ter·nal (ek stur'nəl) *adj.* ⟦< L *externus*⟧ 1 on or of the outside 2 existing apart from the mind; material 3 coming from without 4 superficial 5 foreign —*n.* an outside surface or part —ex·ter'nal·ly *adv.*

ex·tinct (ek stiŋkt') *adj.* ⟦see EXTINGUISH⟧ 1 having died down; extinguished 2 no longer in existence

ex·tinc'tion *n.* 1 an extinguishing 2 a destroying or being destroyed 3 a dying out: said as of a species

ex·tin·guish (ek stiŋ'gwish) *vt.* ⟦< L *ex-*, out + *stinguere*, extinguish⟧ 1 to put out (a fire, etc.) 2 to destroy —ex·tin'guish·er *n.*

ex·tir·pate (eks'tər pāt') *vt.* -pat'ed, -pat'ing ⟦< L *ex-*, out + *stirps*, root⟧ to destroy completely —ex'tir·pa'tion *n.*

ex·tol or **ex·toll** (ek stōl') *vt.* -tolled', -tol'ling ⟦< L *ex-*, up + *tollere*, to raise⟧ to praise highly; laud

ex·tort (ek stôrt') *vt.* ⟦< L *ex-*, out + *torquere*, to twist⟧ to get (money, etc.) from someone by force or threats

ex·tor'tion *n.* 1 an extorting 2 something extorted —ex·tor'tion·ate *adj.* —ex·tor'tion·ist or ex·tor'tion·er *n.*

ex·tra (eks'trə) *adj.* ⟦< L *extra*, more than⟧ more or better than normal, expected, etc.; additional or superior —*n.* an extra person or thing; specif., *a*) a special edition of a newspaper *b*) an extra benefit *c*) an actor hired by the day to play a minor part —*adv.* more than usually; esp., exceptionally

extra- ⟦see EXTERNAL⟧ *prefix* outside, beyond, besides

ex·tract (ek strakt'; *for n.* eks'trakt') *vt.* ⟦< L *ex-*, out + *trahere*, to draw⟧ 1 to draw out by effort 2 to obtain by pressing, distilling, etc. 3 to deduce, derive, or elicit 4 to select or quote (a passage, etc.) —*n.* something extracted; specif., *a*) a concentrate [beef *extract*] *b*) an excerpt

ex·trac'tion *n.* 1 the act or process of extracting 2 origin; descent

ex·tra·cur·ric·u·lar (eks'trə kə rik'yo͞o lər) *adj.* not part of the required curriculum

ex·tra·dite (eks'trə dīt') *vt.* -dit'ed, -dit'ing ⟦< L *ex*, out + *traditio*, a surrender⟧ to turn over (an alleged criminal, etc.) to the jurisdiction of another country, U.S. state, etc. —ex'tra·di'tion (-dish'ən) *n.*

ex·tra·le·gal (eks'trə lē'gəl) *adj.* outside of legal control

ex'tra·mar'i·tal (-mar'ət'l) *adj.* having to do with sexual intercourse with someone other that one's spouse

ex·tra·ne·ous (ek strā'nē əs) *adj.* ⟦L *extraneus*, foreign⟧ 1 coming from outside; foreign 2 not pertinent; irrelevant —**ex·tra'ne·ous·ly** *adv.*

ex·tra·or·di·nar·y (ek strôrd''n er'ē) *adj.* ⟦< L *extra ordinem*, out of order⟧ 1 not ordinary 2 going far beyond the ordinary; unusual; remarkable

ex·trap·o·late (ek strap'ə lāt') *vt.*, *vi.* **-lat'ed, -lat'ing** ⟦see EXTRA- & INTERPOLATE⟧ to estimate (something unknown) on the basis of known facts —**ex·trap'o·la'tion** *n.*

ex·tra·sen·so·ry (eks'trə sen'sə rē) *adj.* apart from, or in addition to, normal sense perception

ex'tra·ter·res'tri·al (-tə res'trē əl) *adj.* being, of, or from outside the earth's limits —*n.* an extraterrestrial being, as in science fiction

ex·trav·a·gant (ek strav'ə gənt) *adj.* ⟦< L *extra*, beyond + *vagari*, to wander⟧ 1 going beyond reasonable limits; excessive 2 costing or spending too much; wasteful —**ex·trav'a·gance** *n.*

ex·trav·a·gan·za (ek strav'ə gan'zə) *n.* ⟦< It *estravaganza*, extravagance⟧ a spectacular theatrical production

ex·treme (ek strēm') *adj.* ⟦< L *exterus*, outer⟧ 1 farthest away; utmost 2 *a*) very great *b*) excessive 3 unconventional or radical, as in politics 4 harsh; drastic —*n.* 1 either of two things that are as different or far as possible from each other 2 an extreme act, state, etc. 3 *Math.* the first or last term of a proportion —**ex·treme'ly** *adv.* —**ex·treme'ness** *n.*

ex·trem'ism' *n.* a going to extremes, esp. in politics —**ex·trem'ist** *adj.*, *n.*

ex·trem·i·ty (ek strem'ə tē) *n.*, *pl.* **-ties** 1 the outermost part; end 2 the greatest degree 3 great need, danger, etc. 4 an extreme measure: *usually used in pl.* 5 [*pl.*] the hands and feet

ex·tri·cate (eks'tri kāt') *vt.* **-cat'ed, -cat'ing** ⟦< L *ex-*, out + *tricae*, vexations⟧ to set free (*from* a net, difficulty, etc.) —**ex'tri·ca'tion** *n.*

ex·trin·sic (eks trin'sik, -zik) *adj.* ⟦< L *exter*, without + *secus*, otherwise⟧ not inherent —**ex·trin'si·cal·ly** *adv.*

ex·tro·vert (eks'trə vurt') *n.* ⟦< L *extra-*, outside + *vertere*, to turn⟧ one who is active and expressive rather than introspective —**ex'tro·ver'sion** (-vur'zhən) *n.* —**ex'tro·vert'ed** *adj.*

ex·trude (ek strōōd') *vt.* **-trud'ed, -trud'ing** ⟦< L *ex-*, out + *trudere*, to thrust⟧ to force out, as through a small opening —*vi.* to be extruded —**ex·tru'sion** *n.*

ex·u·ber·ant (eg zōō'bər ənt) *adj.* ⟦< L *ex-*, intens. + *uberare*, bear abundantly⟧ 1 growing profusely; luxuriant 2 characterized by good health and high spirits —**ex·u'ber·ance** *n.* —**ex·u'ber·ant·ly** *adv.*

ex·ude (eg zōōd') *vt.*, *vi.* **-ud'ed, -ud'ing** ⟦< L *ex-*, out + *sudare*, to sweat⟧ 1 to ooze 2 to seem to radiate *[to exude joy]* —**ex·u·da·tion** (eks'yōō dā'shən, egz'-) *n.*

ex·ult (eg zult') *vi.* ⟦< L *ex-*, intens. + *saltare*, to leap⟧ to rejoice greatly; glory —**ex·ult'ant** *adj.* —**ex·ul·ta·tion** (eg'zəl tā'shən, eks'əl-) *n.*

ex·ur·bi·a (eks ur'bē ə) *n.* ⟦EX- + (SUB)URBIA⟧ the semirural communities beyond the suburbs, typically lived in by upper-income families —**ex·ur'ban** *adj.* —**ex·ur'ban·ite'** *adj.*, *n.*

eye (ī) *n.* ⟦OE *ēage*⟧ 1 the organ of sight in humans and animals 2 *a*) the eyeball *b*) the iris *[brown eyes]* 3 the area around the eye *[a black eye]* 4 [*often pl.*] sight; vision 5 a look; glance 6 attention; observation 7 the power of judging, etc. by eyesight *[a good eye for detail]* 8 [*often pl.*] judgment; opinion *[in the eyes of the law]* 9 a thing like an eye in appearance or function —*vt.* **eyed, eye'ing** or **ey'ing** to look at; observe —**have an eye for** to have a keen appreciation of —**keep an eye on** to look after —**lay** (or **set** or **clap**) **eyes on** to look at —**make eyes at** to look at amorously —**see eye to eye** to agree completely —**with an eye to** paying attention to; considering

eye'ball' *n.* the ball-shaped part of the eye —*vt.* [Inf.] to examine or measure visually

eye'brow' *n.* the bony arch over each eye, or the hair growing on this

eye'-catch'er *n.* something that especially attracts one's attention —**eye'-catch'ing** *adj.*

eye'drops' *pl.n.* liquid medicine for the eyes, applied as with a dropper

eye'ful' (-fool') *n.* [Slang] a person or thing that looks striking or unusual

eye'glass' *n.* 1 a lens to help faulty vision 2 [*pl.*] a pair of such lenses in a frame; glasses

eye'lash' *n.* any of the hairs on the edge of the eyelid

eye'let (-lit) *n.* 1 a small hole for receiving a cord, hook, etc. 2 a metal ring for reinforcing such a hole 3 a small hole edged by stitching in embroidery

eye'lid' *n.* either of the two folds of flesh that cover and uncover the eyeball

eye'-o'pen·er (-ō'pə nər) *n.* a surprising piece of news, sudden realization, etc. —**eye'-o'pen·ing** *adj.*

eye'piece' *n.* in a telescope, microscope, etc., the lens or lenses nearest the viewer's eye

eye'sight' *n.* 1 the power of seeing; sight 2 the range of vision

eye'sore' *n.* an unpleasant sight

eye'strain' *n.* a tired or strained condition of the eye muscles

eye'tooth' *n.*, *pl.* **-teeth'** a canine tooth of the upper jaw

eye'wear' *n.* eyeglasses, sunglasses, etc.

eye'wit'ness *n.* one who sees or has seen something happen, as an accident, etc.

ey·rie or **ey·ry** (er'ē, ir'ē) *n.*, *pl.* **-ries** AERIE

F

f[1] or **F** (ef) ***n.***, *pl.* **f's, F's** the sixth letter of the English alphabet

f[2] *abbrev.* ⟦It⟧ *Music* FORTE[2]

F[1] (ef) ***n.*** **1** *Educ.* a grade for failing work or, sometimes, fair or average work **2** *Music* the fourth tone in the scale of C major

F[2] *abbrev.* **1** Fahrenheit **2** female or feminine **3** folio(s) **4** following **5** franc(s) **6** Friday

F[3] *Chem. symbol for* fluorine

fa (fä) ***n.*** ⟦< ML⟧ *Music* the fourth tone of the diatonic scale

FAA *abbrev.* Federal Aviation Administration

fa·ble (fā′bəl) ***n.*** ⟦< L *fabula*, a story⟧ **1** a fictitious story, usually about animals, meant to teach a moral lesson **2** a myth or legend **3** a falsehood

fa′bled ***adj.*** **1** mythical; legendary **2** unreal; fictitious

fab·ric (fab′rik) ***n.*** ⟦< L *fabrica*, workshop⟧ **1** a framework; structure **2** a material, as cloth, made from fibers, etc. by weaving, felting, etc.

fab·ri·cate (fab′ri kāt′) ***vt.*** **-cat′ed, -cat′ing** ⟦see prec.⟧ **1** to make, build, construct, etc.; manufacture **2** to make up (a story, lie, etc.); invent —**fab′ri·ca′tion** ***n.*** —**fab′ri·ca′tor** ***n.***

fab·u·lous (fab′yo͞o ləs) ***adj.*** ⟦see FABLE⟧ **1** of or like a fable; fictitious **2** incredible; astounding **3** [Inf.] wonderful —**fab′u·lous·ly** ***adv.***

fa·cade or **fa·çade** (fə säd′) ***n.*** ⟦Fr: see fol.⟧ **1** the front or main face of a building **2** an imposing appearance concealing something inferior

face (fās) ***n.*** ⟦< L *facies*⟧ **1** the front of the head **2** the expression of the countenance **3** the main or front surface **4** the surface that is marked, as of a clock, etc., or that is finished, as of fabric, etc. **5** the appearance; outward aspect **6** dignity; self-respect: usually in **lose** (or **save**) **face** —***vt.*** **faced, fac′ing 1** to turn, or have the face turned, toward **2** to confront with boldness, etc. **3** to cover with a new surface —***vi.*** to turn, or have the face turned, in a specified direction —**face to face 1** confronting each other **2** very near to: with *with* —**face up to** to face with courage —**in the face of 1** in the presence of **2** in spite of —**make a face** to grimace —**on the face of it** apparently

-faced (fāst) *combining form* having a (specified kind of) face *[round-faced]*

face′less ***adj.*** without individuality; anonymous

face′-lift′ ***n.*** **1** plastic surgery to remove wrinkles, etc. from the face **2** an altering, cleaning, etc., as of a building's exterior Also **face lift** —***vt.*** to perform a face-lift on

face′-off′ ***n.*** **1** *Hockey* the start or resumption of play when the referee drops the puck between two opposing players **2** [Inf.] a confrontation

face′-sav′ing ***adj.*** preserving one's dignity or self-respect

fac·et (fas′it) ***n.*** ⟦see FACE⟧ **1** any of the polished plane surfaces of a cut gem **2** any of a number of sides or aspects, as of a personality —***vt.*** **-et·ed** or **-et·ted, -et·ing** or **-et·ting** to cut or make facets on

FACETS OF A GEM

fa·ce·tious (fə sē′shəs) ***adj.*** ⟦< L *facetus*, witty⟧ joking, esp. at an inappropriate time —**fa·ce′tious·ly** ***adv.***

face value 1 the value printed on a bill, bond, etc. **2** the seeming value

fa·cial (fā′shəl) ***adj.*** of or for the face —***n.*** a cosmetic treatment, massage, etc. for the skin of the face

facial tissue a sheet of soft tissue paper used as a handkerchief, etc.

fac·ile (fas′il) ***adj.*** ⟦Fr < L *facere*, do⟧ **1** not hard to do **2** working or done easily **3** superficial

fa·cil·i·tate (fə sil′ə tāt′) ***vt.*** **-tat′ed, -tat′ing** ⟦see prec.⟧ to make easy or easier —**fa·cil′i·ta′tion** ***n.*** —**fa·cil′i·ta′tor** ***n.***

fa·cil′i·ty (-tē) ***n.***, *pl.* **-ties 1** ease of doing **2** skill; dexterity **3** [*usually pl.*] the means by which something can be done **4** a building, room, etc. for some activity

fac·ing (fās′iŋ) ***n.*** **1** a lining on the edge of a garment **2** a covering of contrasting material on a building

fac·sim·i·le (fak sim′ə lē) ***n.*** ⟦< L *facere*, make + *simile*, like⟧ an exact reproduction or copy

fact (fakt) ***n.*** ⟦< L *facere*, do⟧ **1** a deed, esp. a criminal deed *[an accessory before (or after) the fact]* **2** a thing that has actually happened or is really true **3** reality; truth **4** something stated to be true —**as a matter of fact** in reality: also **in fact**

fac·tion (fak′shən) ***n.*** ⟦see prec.⟧ **1** a group of people in an organization working in a common cause against the main body **2** dissension —**fac′tion·al** ***adj.*** —**fac′tion·al·ism′** ***n.***

fac′tious (-shəs) ***adj.*** causing dissension or faction

fac·ti·tious (fak tish′əs) ***adj.*** ⟦see FACT⟧ forced or artificial

fac·toid (fak′toid) ***n.*** ⟦FACT + -OID⟧ a trivial or useless fact or statistic

fac·tor (fak′tər) ***n.*** ⟦< L *facere*, do⟧ **1** one who transacts business for another **2** any of the conditions, etc. that bring about a result **3** *Math.* any of the quantities which form a product when multiplied together —***vt.*** *Math.* to resolve into factors —**factor in** (or **into**) to include as a factor

fac·to·ry (fak′tə rē; *often* fak′trē) ***n.***, *pl.*

-ries ⟦see prec.⟧ a building or buildings in which things are manufactured

fac·to·tum (fak tōt′əm) ***n.*** ⟦< L *facere*, do + *totum*, all⟧ a handyman

fac·tu·al (fak′chōō əl) ***adj.*** **1** of or containing facts **2** real; actual

fac·ul·ty (fak′əl tē) ***n.***, *pl.* **-ties** ⟦see FACILE⟧ **1** any natural or specialized power of a living organism **2** special aptitude or skill **3** all the teachers of a school or of one of its departments

fad (fad) ***n.*** ⟦< Brit dial.⟧ a style, etc. that interests many people for a short time; passing fashion —**fad′dish** ***adj.***

fade (fād) ***vi.*** **fad′ed**, **fad′ing** ⟦< OFr *fade*, pale⟧ **1** to lose color, brilliance, etc. **2** to lose freshness or strength **3** to disappear slowly; die out —***vt.*** to cause to fade —**fade in** (or **out**) *Film, Radio, TV* to appear (or disappear) gradually

fa·er·ie or **fa·er·y** (fā′ər ē, fer′ē) ***n.*** [Archaic] **1** fairyland **2** *pl.* **-ies** a fairy

fag (fag) ***vi.***, ***vt.*** **fagged**, **fag′ging** ⟦< ?⟧ to make or become very tired by hard work

fag·ot or **fag·got** (fag′ət) ***n.*** ⟦ult. < Gr *phakelos*, a bundle⟧ a bundle of sticks or twigs, esp. for use as fuel

fag·ot·ing or **fag·got·ing** (fag′ət iŋ) ***n.*** **1** a hemstitch with wide spaces **2** openwork with crisscross or barlike stitches across the open seam

Fahr·en·heit (fer′ən hīt′) ***adj.*** ⟦after G. D. *Fahrenheit* (1686-1736), Ger physicist⟧ designating or of a thermometer on which 32° is the freezing point and 212° is the boiling point of water

fail (fāl) ***vi.*** ⟦< L *fallere*, deceive⟧ **1** to be insufficient; fall short **2** to weaken; die away **3** to stop operating **4** to be negligent in a duty, expectation, etc. **5** to be unsuccessful **6** to become bankrupt **7** *Educ.* to get a grade of failure —***vt.*** **1** to be of no help to; disappoint **2** to leave; abandon **3** to neglect: used with an infinitive **4** *Educ.* to give a grade of failure to or get such a grade in —**without fail** without failing (to occur, do, etc.)

fail′ing ***n.*** **1** a failure **2** a fault —***prep.*** without; lacking

faille (fīl, fāl) ***n.*** ⟦Fr⟧ a soft, ribbed fabric of silk or rayon

fail′-safe′ ***adj.*** of an intricate procedure for preventing a malfunction or accidental operation, as of nuclear weapons

fail·ure (fāl′yər) ***n.*** **1** *a*) a falling short *b*) a weakening *c*) a breakdown in operation *d*) neglect *e*) a not succeeding *f*) a becoming bankrupt **2** one that does not succeed **3** *Educ.* a failing to pass, or a grade showing this

fain (fān) ***adj.***, ***adv.*** ⟦< OE *fægen*, glad⟧ [Archaic] glad(ly); willing(ly)

faint (fānt) ***adj.*** ⟦see FEIGN⟧ **1** weak; feeble **2** timid **3** feeling weak and dizzy **4** dim; indistinct —***n.*** a state of temporary unconsciousness —***vi.*** to fall into a faint —**faint′ly** ***adv.*** —**faint′ness** ***n.***

fair[1] (fer) ***adj.*** ⟦< OE *fæger*⟧ **1** attractive; beautiful **2** unblemished; clean **3** blond *[fair hair]* **4** clear and sunny **5** easy to read *[a fair hand]* **6** just and honest **7** according to the rules **8** moderately large **9** average *[in fair condition]* **10** *Baseball* that is not foul —***adv.*** in a fair manner —**fair′ness** ***n.***

fair[2] (fer) ***n.*** ⟦< L *feriae*, festivals⟧ **1** [Historical] a regular gathering for barter and sale of goods **2** a carnival or bazaar, often for charity **3** a competitive exhibition of farm, household, and manufactured products, with various amusements and educational displays **4** a show or convention with exhibits, vendors, etc. *[a science fair]*

Fair·banks (fer′baŋks′) city in EC Alaska: pop. 31,000

fair game a legitimate object of attack or pursuit

fair′-haired′ ***adj.*** **1** having blond hair **2** [Inf.] favorite

fair′ly ***adv.*** **1** justly; honestly **2** somewhat; moderately

fair shake [Inf.] fair or just treatment

fair′way′ ***n.*** the mowed part of a golf course between a tee and a green

fair·y (fer′ē) ***n.***, *pl.* **-ies** ⟦< OFr *fée*⟧ a tiny, graceful imaginary being in human form, with magic powers —***adj.*** **1** of fairies **2** graceful; delicate

fair′y·land′ ***n.*** **1** the imaginary land where the fairies live **2** a lovely, enchanting place

fairy tale **1** a story about fairies, magic deeds, etc. **2** an unbelievable or untrue story

fait ac·com·pli (fe tà kōn plē′; *E* fāt′ə käm′plē′) ⟦Fr⟧ something done or in effect, making opposition useless

faith (fāth) ***n.*** ⟦< L *fidere*, to trust⟧ **1** unquestioning belief, specif. in God, a religion, etc. **2** a particular religion **3** complete trust or confidence **4** loyalty

faith′ful (-fəl) ***adj.*** **1** loyal **2** conscientious **3** accurate; reliable —**faith′ful·ly** ***adv.*** —**faith′ful·ness** ***n.***

faith′less (-lis) ***adj.*** **1** dishonest or disloyal **2** unreliable —**faith′less·ly** ***adv.*** —**faith′less·ness** ***n.***

fa·ji·ta (fä hē′tä) ***n.*** ⟦AmSp⟧ a dish of grilled strips of beef or chicken, often wrapped in a soft tortilla

fake (fāk) ***vt.***, ***vi.*** **faked**, **fak′ing** ⟦< ?⟧ to make (something) seem real, etc. by deception —***n.*** a fraud; counterfeit —***adj.*** **1** sham; false **2** artificial —**fak′er** ***n.*** —**fak′er·y** ***n.***

fa·kir (fə kir′) ***n.*** ⟦Ar *faqīr*, lit., poor⟧ a Muslim or Hindu itinerant beggar, often one reputed to perform marvels

fa·la·fel (fə läf′əl) ***n.*** ⟦< Ar⟧ a deep-fried patty of ground chickpeas

fal·con (fal′kən, fôl′-, fäl′-) ***n.*** ⟦ult. < L *falx*, sickle⟧ any bird of prey trained to hunt small game —**fal′con·er** ***n.*** —**fal′con·ry** ***n.***

fall (fôl) ***vi.*** **fell**, **fall′en**, **fall′ing** ⟦OE *feallan*⟧ **1** to come down by gravity; drop; descend **2** to come down suddenly from an upright position; tumble or collapse **3** to be wounded or killed in battle **4** to take a downward direction **5** to become lower, less, weaker, etc. **6** to lose power, status, etc. **7** to do wrong; sin **8**

to be captured **9** to take on a sad look *[my face fell]* **10** to take place; occur **11** to come by lot, inheritance, etc. **12** to pass into a specified condition *[to fall ill]* **13** to be directed by chance **14** to be divided (*into*) —***n.*** **1** a dropping; descending **2** a coming down suddenly from an upright position **3** a downward direction or slope **4** a becoming lower or less **5** an overthrow; ruin **6** a loss of status, reputation, etc. **7** a yielding to temptation **8** autumn **9** the amount of what has fallen *[a six-inch fall of snow]* **10** the distance that something falls **11** [*usually pl., often with sing. v.*] water falling over a cliff, etc. **12** a long tress of hair, added to a woman's hairdo —***adj.*** of, in, for, or like autumn —**fall back** to withdraw; retreat —**fall for** [Inf.] **1** to fall in love with **2** to be tricked by —**fall in** to line up in formation —**fall off** to become smaller, worse, etc. —**fall on** (or **upon**) to attack —**fall out** **1** to quarrel **2** to leave one's place in a formation —**fall short** to fail to reach, suffice, etc. —**fall through** to fail —**fall to** **1** to begin **2** to start eating

fal·la·cious (fə lā′shəs) ***adj.*** ⟦see fol.⟧ **1** erroneous **2** misleading or deceptive —**fal·la′cious·ly** ***adv.***

fal·la·cy (fal′ə sē) ***n.***, *pl.* **-cies** ⟦< L *fallere*, deceive⟧ **1** a mistaken idea; error **2** a flaw in reasoning

fall·en (fôl′ən) ***adj.*** that fell; dropped, prostrate, ruined, dead, etc.

fall guy [Slang] one put in a position to take the blame, etc. for a scheme that has miscarried

fal·li·ble (fal′ə bəl) ***adj.*** ⟦< L *fallere*, deceive⟧ liable to be mistaken, deceived, or erroneous —**fal′li·bil′i·ty** or **fal′li·ble·ness** ***n.*** —**fal′li·bly** ***adv.***

fall′ing-out′ ***n.*** a quarrel

falling star METEOR (sense 1)

fall′off′ ***n.*** a decline

fal·lo·pi·an tube (fə lō′pē ən) ⟦after G. *Fallopius*, 16th-c. It anatomist⟧ [*also* **F-t-**] either of two tubes that carry ova to the uterus

fall′out′ ***n.*** **1** the descent to earth of radioactive particles, as after a nuclear explosion **2** these particles **3** an incidental consequence

fal·low (fal′ō) ***adj.*** ⟦< OE *fealh*⟧ **1** left unplanted **2** inactive

false (fôls) ***adj.*** **fals′er**, **fals′est** ⟦< L *fallere*, deceive⟧ **1** not true; incorrect; wrong **2** untruthful; lying **3** unfaithful **4** misleading **5** not real; artificial —***adv.*** in a false manner —**false′ly** ***adv.*** —**false′ness** ***n.***

false′hood′ ***n.*** **1** falsity **2** a lie

fal·set·to (fôl set′ō) ***n.***, *pl.* **-tos** ⟦It, dim. of *falso*, false⟧ an artificial way of singing in which the voice is much higher pitched than normal

fal·si·fy (fôl′sə fī′) ***vt.*** **-fied′**, **-fy′ing** **1** to misrepresent **2** to alter (a record, etc.) fraudulently —**fal′si·fi·ca′tion** ***n.*** —**fal′si·fi′er** ***n.***

fal′si·ty (-tē) ***n.*** **1** the quality of being false **2** *pl.* **-ties** a lie

Fal·staff (fôl′staf′), Sir **John** in Shakespeare's plays, a fat, witty, boastful knight

fal·ter (fôl′tər) ***vi.*** ⟦prob. < ON⟧ **1** to move unsteadily; stumble **2** to stammer **3** to act hesitantly; waver —**fal′ter·ing·ly** ***adv.***

fame (fām) ***n.*** ⟦< L *fama*⟧ **1** reputation, esp. for good **2** the state of being well known —**famed** ***adj.***

fa·mil·ial (fə mil′yəl) ***adj.*** of or common to a family

fa·mil·iar (fə mil′yər) ***adj.*** ⟦see FAMILY⟧ **1** friendly or intimate **2** too friendly; unduly intimate **3** closely acquainted (*with*) **4** common; ordinary —**fa·mil′iar·ly** ***adv.***

fa·mil′i·ar′i·ty (-ē er′ə tē) ***n.***, *pl.* **-ties** **1** intimacy **2** informal behavior **3** undue intimacy **4** close acquaintance (*with* something)

fa·mil′iar·ize′ (-yər īz′) ***vt.*** **-ized′**, **-iz′ing** **1** to make commonly known **2** to make (another or oneself) fully acquainted —**fa·mil′iar·i·za′tion** ***n.***

fam·i·ly (fam′ə lē, fam′lē) ***n.***, *pl.* **-lies** ⟦< L *familia*⟧ **1** parents and their children **2** relatives **3** all those descended from a common ancestor; lineage **4** a group of similar or related things —***adj.*** suitable for a family; specif., wholesome

family planning the regulation, as by birth control methods, of the size, etc. of a family

family practitioner a doctor specializing in the general medical needs of the family

family room a room in a home set apart for relaxation and recreation

family tree a genealogical chart for a given family

fam·ine (fam′in) ***n.*** ⟦< L *fames*, hunger⟧ **1** an acute and general shortage of food **2** any acute shortage

fam′ish (-ish) ***vt.***, ***vi.*** ⟦see prec.⟧ to make or be very hungry

fa·mous (fā′məs) ***adj.*** **1** having fame; renowned **2** [Inf.] excellent; very good

fa′mous·ly ***adv.*** **1** in a way, statement, etc. that has become famous **2** very well

fan[1] (fan) ***n.*** ⟦< L *vannus*, basket for winnowing grain⟧ any device used to set up a current of air for ventilating or cooling —***vt.*** **fanned**, **fan′ning** **1** to move (air) as with a fan **2** to direct air toward as with a fan **3** to stir up; excite **4** to strike (a batter) out —***vi.*** *Baseball* to strike out —**fan out** to spread out

fan[2] (fan) ***n.*** ⟦< FAN(ATIC)⟧ a person enthusiastic about a specified sport, performer, etc.

fa·nat·ic (fə nat′ik) ***n.*** ⟦< L *fanum*, temple⟧ a fanatic person —***adj.*** fanatical —**fa·nat′i·cism′** ***n.***

fa·nat′i·cal ***adj.*** unreasonably enthusiastic; overly zealous —**fa·nat′i·cal·ly** ***adv.***

fan·ci·er (fan′sē ər) ***n.*** a person with a special interest in something, specif. in plant or animal breeding

fan·ci·ful (fan′sə fəl) ***adj.*** **1** full of fancy; imaginative **2** imaginary; not real —**fan′ci·ful·ly** ***adv.***

fan·cy (fan′sē) ***n.***, *pl.* **-cies** ⟦contr. < ME

fantasie, fantasy⟧ **1** imagination when light, playful, etc. **2** a mental image **3** a notion; caprice; whim **4** a liking or fondness —***adj.*** **-ci·er, -ci·est 1** extravagant *[a fancy price]* **2** ornamental; elaborate *[a fancy necktie]* **3** of superior skill or quality —***vt.*** **-cied, -cy·ing 1** to imagine **2** to be fond of **3** to suppose —**fan′ci·ly** ***adv.*** —**fan′ci·ness** ***n.***

fan′cy-free′ ***adj.*** carefree

fan′cy·work′ ***n.*** embroidery, crocheting, and other ornamental needlework

fan·dom (fan′dəm) ***n.*** fans collectively, as of a sport or entertainer

fan·fare (fan′fer′) ⟦Fr, prob. < *fanfaron*, braggart⟧ ***n.*** **1** a loud flourish of trumpets **2** noisy or showy display

fang (faŋ) ***n.*** ⟦OE < *fon*, seize⟧ **1** one of the long, pointed teeth of meat-eating mammals **2** one of the long, hollow teeth through which poisonous snakes inject venom

fan·ta·sia (fan tā′zhə)′ ***n.*** a musical composition having no fixed form

fan·ta·size (fant′ə sīz′) ***vt., vi.*** **-sized′, -siz′ing** to indulge in fantasies or have daydreams (about)

fan·tas·tic (fan tas′tik) ***adj.*** ⟦see fol.⟧ **1** imaginary; unreal **2** grotesque; odd **3** extravagant **4** incredible —**fan·tas′ti·cal·ly** ***adv.***

fan·ta·sy (fant′ə sē) ***n.***, *pl.* **-sies** ⟦< Gr *phainein*, to show⟧ **1** imagination or fancy **2** an illusion or reverie **3** fiction portraying highly IMAGINATIVE (sense 2) characters or settings

fan′ta·sy·land′ ***n.*** any imaginary or unreal place

far (fär) ***adj.*** **far′ther, far′thest** ⟦OE *feorr*⟧ **1** distant in space or time **2** more distant *[the far side]* **3** very different in quality or nature *[far from poor]* —***adv.*** **1** very distant in space, time, or degree **2** to or from a distance in time or position **3** very much *[far better]* —**as far as** to the distance or degree that —**by far** very much; considerably: also **far and away** —(**in**) **so far as** to the extent that —**so far** up to this place, time, or degree

far′a·way′ ***adj.*** **1** distant in time, place, etc. **2** dreamy

farce (färs) ***n.*** ⟦Fr < L *farcire*, to stuff⟧ **1** (an) exaggerated comedy based on broadly humorous situations **2** an absurd or ridiculous action, pretense, etc. —**far·ci·cal** (fär′si kəl) ***adj.***

fare (fer) ***vi.*** **fared, far′ing** ⟦< OE *faran*, go⟧ **1** to happen; result **2** to be in a specified condition *[to fare well]* —***n.*** **1** money paid for transportation **2** a passenger who pays a fare **3** food

Far East EAST ASIA

fare·well (fer wel′; *for adj.* fer′wel′) ***interj.*** goodbye —***n.*** good wishes at parting —***adj.*** parting; final *[a farewell gesture]*

far-fetched (fär′fecht′) ***adj.*** barely believable; strained; unlikely

far′-flung′ (-fluŋ′) ***adj.*** extending over a wide area

fa·ri·na (fə rē′nə) ***n.*** ⟦< L, meal⟧ flour or meal made from cereal grains, potatoes, etc. and eaten as a cooked cereal

far·i·na·ceous (far′ə nā′shəs) ***adj.*** ⟦see prec.⟧ **1** consisting of or made from flour or meal **2** like meal

farm (färm) ***n.*** ⟦< ML *firma*, fixed payment⟧ **1** a piece of land (with house, barns, etc.) on which crops or animals are raised: orig., such land let out to tenants **2** any place where certain things are raised *[a fish farm]* —***vt.*** to cultivate (land) —***vi.*** to work on or operate a farm —**farm out** to send (work) from an office, etc. to workers outside the office

farm′er ***n.*** a person who manages or operates a farm

farm′hand′ ***n.*** a hired farm worker

farm′house′ ***n.*** a house on a farm

farm′ing ***n.*** the business of operating a farm; agriculture

farm′yard′ ***n.*** the yard surrounding or enclosed by farm buildings

far·o (fer′ō) ***n.*** ⟦Fr *pharaon*, pharaoh: from the picture of a Pharaoh on early French faro cards⟧ a gambling game played with cards

far′-off′ ***adj.*** distant; remote

far′-out′ ***adj.*** [Inf.] nonconformist; esp., avant-garde

far·ra·go (fə rā′gō, -rä′-) ***n.***, *pl.* **-goes** ⟦< L *far*, kind of grain⟧ a jumble

far′-reach′ing ***adj.*** having a wide range, extent, influence, or effect

far·ri·er (far′ē ər) ***n.*** ⟦< L *ferrum*, iron⟧ [Chiefly Brit.] a blacksmith

far·row (far′ō) ***n.*** ⟦< OE *fearh*, young pig⟧ a litter of pigs —***vt., vi.*** to give birth to (a litter of pigs)

far·sight·ed (fär′sīt′id; *for* 2, -sīt′əd) ***adj.*** **1** planning ahead; provident: also **far′see′ing 2** seeing distant objects more clearly than near ones —**far′sight′ed·ness** ***n.***

far·ther (fär′*th*ər) ***adj.*** **1** *compar. of* FAR **2** more distant **3** additional; further —***adv.*** **1** *compar. of* FAR **2** at or to a greater distance **3** to a greater degree; further Cf. FURTHER

far·thest (fär′*th*ist) ***adj.*** **1** *superl. of* FAR **2** most distant —***adv.*** **1** *superl. of* FAR **2** at or to the greatest distance or degree

far·thing (fär′*th*iŋ) ***n.*** ⟦OE *feorthing*⟧ a former British coin worth ¼ penny

fas·ci·nate (fas′ə nāt′) ***vt.*** **-nat′ed, -nat′ing** ⟦< L *fascinum*, a charm⟧ to hold the attention of, as by being very interesting or delightful; charm; captivate —**fas′ci·na′tion** ***n.***

fas·cism (fash′iz′əm) ***n.*** ⟦< It < L *fasces*, rods bound about an ax, ancient Roman symbol of authority⟧ [*sometimes* **F-**] a system of government characterized by dictatorship, belligerent nationalism and racism, militarism, etc. —**fas′cist** ***n., adj.***

fash·ion (fash′ən) ***n.*** ⟦< L *factio*, a making⟧ **1** the form or shape of a thing **2**

way; manner **3** the current style of dress, conduct, etc. —***vt.*** **1** to make; form **2** to fit; accommodate (*to*) —**after** (or **in**) **a fashion** to some extent —**fash′ion·er** ***n.***

fash′ion·a·ble ***adj.*** **1** stylish **2** of or used by people who follow fashion —**fash′ion·a·bly** ***adv.***

fast[1] (fast) ***adj.*** ⟦OE *fæst*⟧ **1** firm; firmly fastened **2** loyal; devoted **3** nonfading *[fast* colors*]* **4** swift; quick **5** ahead of time *[a fast* watch*]* **6** wild, promiscuous, or reckless **7** [Inf.] glib **8** *Photog.* allowing very short exposure time —***adv.*** **1** firmly; fixedly **2** thoroughly *[fast* asleep*]* **3** rapidly

fast[2] (fast) ***vi.*** ⟦OE *fæstan*⟧ to abstain from all or certain foods —***n.*** **1** a fasting **2** a period of fasting

fas·ten (fas′ən) ***vt.*** ⟦see FAST[1]⟧ **1** to attach; connect **2** to make secure, as by locking, buttoning, etc. **3** to fix (the attention, etc.) *on* something —***vi.*** to become fastened —**fas′ten·er** ***n.***

fas′ten·ing ***n.*** anything used to fasten; bolt, clasp, hook, etc.

fast′-food′ ***adj.*** designating a business that offers food, as hamburgers, prepared and served quickly

fast forward **1** the setting on a VCR, etc. that allows the user to advance the tape or disc rapidly **2** the act or condition of speeding up and advancing —**fast′-for′ward** ***vi., vt.***

fas·tid·i·ous (fa stid′ē əs) ***adj.*** ⟦< L *fastus*, disdain⟧ **1** not easy to please **2** daintily refined; oversensitive —**fas·tid′i·ous·ly** ***adv.*** —**fas·tid′i·ous·ness** ***n.***

fast′ness ***n.*** **1** a being fast **2** a stronghold

fast′-talk′ ***vt.*** [Inf.] to persuade with smooth, but often deceitful talk

fat (fat) ***adj.*** **fat′ter, fat′test** ⟦< OE *fætt*⟧ **1** containing fat; oily **2** *a)* fleshy; plump *b)* too plump **3** thick; broad **4** fertile *[fat* land*]* **5** profitable *[a fat* job*]* **6** plentiful —***n.*** **1** an oily or greasy material found in animal tissue and plant seeds **2** the richest part of anything **3** superfluous part —**chew the fat** [Slang] to chat —**fat′ly** ***adv.*** —**fat′ness** ***n.***

fa·tal (fāt′'l) ***adj.*** **1** fateful; decisive **2** resulting in death **3** destructive; disastrous —**fa′tal·ly** ***adv.***

fa′tal·ism′ ***n.*** the belief that all events are determined by fate and are hence inevitable —**fa′tal·ist** ***n.*** —**fa′tal·is′tic** ***adj.*** —**fa′tal·is′ti·cal·ly** ***adv.***

fa·tal·i·ty (fā tal′ə tē, fə-) ***n.***, *pl.* **-ties** **1** a deadly effect; deadliness **2** a death caused by a disaster or accident

fat′back′ ***n.*** fat from a hog's back, usually dried and salted in strips

fat cat [Slang] a wealthy, influential donor, esp. to a political campaign

fate (fāt) ***n.*** ⟦< L *fatum*, oracle⟧ **1** the power supposed to determine the outcome of events; destiny **2** one's lot or fortune **3** final outcome **4** death; destruction

fat·ed (fāt′id) ***adj.*** **1** destined **2** doomed

fate′ful (-fəl) ***adj.*** **1** prophetic **2** significant; decisive **3** controlled as if by fate —**fate′ful·ly** ***adv.***

Fates (fāts) ***pl.n.*** *Gr. & Rom. Myth.* the three goddesses who control human destiny and life

fa·ther (fä′*th*ər) ***n.*** ⟦OE *fæder*⟧ **1** a male parent **2** an ancestor **3** an originator, founder, or inventor **4** [*often* **F-**] a Christian priest: used esp. as a title **5** [**F-**] God —***vt.*** to be the father of —**fa′ther·hood′** ***n.*** —**fa′ther·less** ***adj.***

fa′ther-in-law′ ***n.***, *pl.* **fa′thers-in-law′** the father of one's spouse

fa′ther·land′ ***n.*** one's native land

fa′ther·ly ***adj.*** of or like a father; kind, protective, etc. —**fa′ther·li·ness** ***n.***

fath·om (fa*th*′əm) ***n.*** ⟦< OE *fæthm*, the two arms outstretched⟧ a length of 6 feet, used as a nautical unit of depth or length —***vt.*** **1** to measure the depth of **2** to understand thoroughly —**fath′om·a·ble** ***adj.*** —**fath′om·less** ***adj.***

fa·tigue (fə tēg′) ***n.*** ⟦Fr < L *fatigare*, to weary⟧ **1** exhaustion; weariness **2** [*pl.*] soldiers' work clothing **3** the tendency of a metal, etc. to crack under continued stress —***vt., vi.*** **-tigued′, -tigu′ing** to tire out

fat·so (fat′sō) ***n.***, *pl.* **-sos** or **-soes** [Slang] a fat person

fat·ten (fat′'n) ***vt., vi.*** to make or become fat (in various senses)

fat′ty ***adj.*** **-ti·er, -ti·est** **1** of or containing fat **2** like fat; greasy

fatty acid any of a group of organic acids in animal or vegetable fats and oils

fat·u·ous (fach′o͞o əs) ***adj.*** ⟦L *fatuus*⟧ complacently stupid; foolish —**fa·tu·i·ty** (fə to͞o′ə tē) ***n.*** —**fat′u·ous·ly** ***adv.*** —**fat′u·ous·ness** ***n.***

fau·cet (fô′sit) ***n.*** ⟦prob. < OFr *faulser*, to breach⟧ a device with a valve for regulating the flow of a liquid from a pipe, etc.; tap

Faulk·ner (fôk′nər), **Wil·liam** (wil′yəm) 1897-1962; U.S. novelist

fault (fôlt) ***n.*** ⟦< L *fallere*, deceive⟧ **1** something that mars; defect or failing **2** a misdeed or mistake **3** blame for something wrong **4** a fracture in rock strata **5** *Tennis, etc.* an improper serve —**at fault** deserving blame —**find fault** (**with**) to criticize

fault′find′ing ***n., adj.*** criticizing

fault′less ***adj.*** perfect

fault′y ***adj.*** **fault′i·er, fault′i·est** having a fault or faults; defective —**fault′i·ly** ***adv.*** —**fault′i·ness** ***n.***

faun (fôn) ***n.*** ⟦< L *faunus*⟧ any of a class of minor Roman deities, half man and half goat

fau·na (fô′nə) ***n.*** ⟦< LL *Fauna*, Roman goddess⟧ the animals of a specified region or time

Faust (foust) ***n.*** a man in legend and literature who sells his soul to the devil for knowledge and power —**Faus′ti·an** ***adj.***

faux pas (fō pä′) *pl.* **faux pas** (fō päz′) ⟦Fr, lit., false step⟧ a social blunder

fa·vor (fā′vər) ***n.*** ⟦< L *favere*, to favor⟧ **1** friendly regard; approval **2** partiality **3** a kind or obliging act **4** a small gift or token —*vt.* **1** to approve or like **2** to be partial to **3** to support; advocate **4** to make easier; help **5** to do a kindness for **6** to resemble *[to favor* one's mother*]* **7** to use gently *[to favor* a sore leg*]* Brit. sp. **fa'vour** —**in favor of 1** approving **2** to the advantage of —**fa'vor·er** *n.*

fa'vor·a·ble *adj.* **1** approving **2** helpful **3** pleasing —**fa'vor·a·bly** *adv.*

fa·vor·ite (fā'vər it) *n.* **1** a person or thing regarded with special liking **2** a contestant regarded as most likely to win —*adj.* highly regarded; preferred

fa'vor·it·ism' *n.* partiality; bias

fawn[1] (fôn) *vi.* ⟦< OE *fægen*, glad⟧ **1** to show friendliness by licking hands, etc.: said of a dog **2** to try to gain favor by acting humble, flattering, etc. —**fawn'er** *n.* —**fawn'ing·ly** *adv.*

fawn[2] (fôn) *n.* ⟦< L *fetus*, progeny⟧ **1** a deer less than one year old **2** a pale, yellowish brown —*adj.* of this color

fax (faks) *n.* ⟦< FACSIMILE⟧ **1** the electronic sending (as over a telephone line) and reproduction of pictures, print, etc. **2** a reproduction made in this way —*vt.* to send by fax

fay (fā) *n.* ⟦see FATE⟧ a fairy

faze (fāz) *vt.* **fazed, faz'ing** ⟦< OE *fesian*, to drive⟧ to disturb; disconcert

FBI *abbrev.* Federal Bureau of Investigation

FCC *abbrev.* Federal Communications Commission

FDA *abbrev.* Food and Drug Administration

FDIC *abbrev.* Federal Deposit Insurance Corporation

Fe ⟦L *ferrum*⟧ *Chem. symbol for* iron

fe·al·ty (fē'əl tē) *n., pl.* **-ties** ⟦< L *fidelitas*, fidelity⟧ loyalty, esp. as owed to a feudal lord

fear (fir) *n.* ⟦< OE *fær*, sudden attack⟧ **1** anxiety caused by real or possible danger, pain, etc.; fright **2** awe; reverence **3** apprehension; concern **4** a cause for fear —*vt., vi.* **1** to be afraid (of) **2** to be in awe (of) **3** to expect with misgiving *[I fear* it will rain*]* —**fear'less** *adj.* —**fear'less·ly** *adv.*

fear'ful (-fəl) *adj.* **1** causing, feeling, or showing fear **2** [Inf.] very bad, great, etc. —**fear'ful·ly** *adv.* —**fear'ful·ness** *n.*

fear'some *adj.* causing fear; frightful

fea·si·ble (fē'zə bəl) *adj.* ⟦< OFr *faire*, to do⟧ **1** capable of being done; possible **2** likely; probable **3** suitable —**fea'si·bil'i·ty** *n.* —**fea'si·bly** *adv.*

feast (fēst) *n.* ⟦< L *festus*, festal⟧ **1** a religious festival **2** a rich and elaborate meal; banquet —*vi.* to have a feast —*vt.* **1** to entertain at a feast **2** to delight *[to feast* one's eyes on a sight*]*

feat (fēt) *n.* ⟦< L *factum*, a deed⟧ a deed of unusual daring or skill; exploit

feath·er (fe*th*'ər) *n.* ⟦OE *fether*⟧ any of the soft, light growths covering the body of a bird —*vt.* **1** to provide or adorn with feathers **2** to turn (an oar or propeller blade) so that the edge is foremost —**feather in one's cap** a distinctive achievement —**feath'er·y** *adj.*

feath'er·bed'ding *n.* the practice of limiting output or requiring extra, standby workers

feath'er·weight' *n.* **1** a boxer with a maximum weight of 126 pounds **2** any person or thing of light weight or small size

fea·ture (fē'chər) *n.* ⟦< L *facere*, to make⟧ **1** *a)* [*pl.*] facial form or appearance *b)* any of the parts of the face **2** a distinct or outstanding part or quality of something **3** a special attraction, sale item, newspaper article, etc. **4** a film running more than 34 minutes —*vt.* **-tured, -tur·ing** to make a feature of —*vi.* to have a prominent part —**fea'ture·less** *adj.*

fe·brile (fē'brəl, feb'rəl) *adj.* ⟦< L *febris*, FEVER⟧ feverish

Feb·ru·ar·y (feb'ro͞o er'ē, feb'yo͞o-) *n., pl.* **-ies** or **-ys** ⟦< L *Februarius* (*mensis*), orig. month of expiation⟧ the second month of the year, having 28 days (or 29 days in leap years): abbrev. **Feb.**

fe·ces (fē'sēz') *pl.n.* ⟦< L *faeces*, dregs⟧ excrement —**fe'cal** (-kəl) *adj.*

feck·less (fek'lis) *adj.* ⟦Scot < *feck*, effect + -LESS⟧ **1** weak; ineffective **2** irresponsible —**feck'less·ly** *adv.*

fe·cund (fē'kənd, fek'ənd) *adj.* ⟦< L *fecundus*⟧ fertile; productive —**fe·cun·di·ty** (fē kun'də tē) *n.*

fe·cun·date (fē'kən dāt', fek'ən-) *vt.* **-dat'ed, -dat'ing 1** to make fecund **2** to fertilize

fed (fed) *vt., vi. pt. & pp. of* FEED —**fed up** [Inf.] having had enough to become disgusted, bored, etc.

Fed *abbrev.* **1** Federal **2** Federation

fed·a·yeen (fed'ä yēn') *pl.n.* ⟦Ar *fidā'īyīn*, sacrificers⟧ Arab guerrillas

fed·er·al (fed'ər əl) *adj.* ⟦< L *foedus*, a league⟧ **1** designating or of a union of states, etc. in which each member subordinates its power to a central authority **2** *a)* designating or of a central government in such a union *b)* [*often* **F-**] designating or of the central government of the U.S. **3** [**F-**] of or supporting a former U.S. political party (**Federalist Party**) which favored a strong centralized government **4** [**F-**] of or supporting the Union in the Civil War —*n.* [**F-**] a supporter or soldier of the Union in the Civil War —**fed'er·al·ism'** *n.* —**fed'er·al·ist** *adj., n.* —**fed'er·al·ly** *adv.*

fed'er·al·ize' (-īz') *vt.* **-ized', -iz'ing 1** to unite (states, etc.) in a federal union **2** to put under federal authority —**fed'er·al·i·za'tion** *n.*

fed·er·ate (fed'ər āt') *vt., vi.* **-at'ed, -at'ing** to unite in a federation

fed·er·a·tion (fed'ər ā'shən) *n.* ⟦see FEDERAL⟧ **1** a union of states, groups, etc. in which each subordinates its power to that of the central authority **2** a federated organization

fe·do·ra (fə dôr'ə) *n.* ⟦Fr⟧ a soft felt hat worn by men

fee (fē) *n.* ⟦ult < Gmc⟧ a charge for professional services, licenses, etc.

fee·ble (fē'bəl) *adj.* **-bler, -blest** ⟦< L *flere*, weep⟧ **1** weak; infirm *[a feeble* old man*]* **2** without force or effectiveness [a *feeble* attempt] —**fee'ble·ness** ***n.*** —**fee'bly** ***adv.***

feed (fēd) ***vt.* fed, feed'ing** ⟦< OE *foda*, food⟧ **1** to give food to **2** to provide something necessary for the growth, operation, etc. of **3** to gratify [to *feed* one's vanity] —***vi.*** to eat: said esp. of animals —***n.*** **1** food for animals; fodder **2** *a)* the material fed into a machine *b)* the part of the machine supplying this material **3** *Radio, TV* a transmission sent by a network, etc. to individual stations for broadcast —**feed'er** ***n.***

feed'back' ***n.*** **1** the transfer of part of the output back to the input, as of electricity or information **2** a response

feed'stock' ***n.*** raw material for industrial processing

feel (fēl) ***vt.* felt, feel'ing** ⟦OE *felan*⟧ **1** to touch; examine by handling **2** to be aware of through physical sensation **3** to experience (an emotion or condition); be affected by **4** to be aware of **5** to think or believe —***vi.*** **1** to have physical sensation **2** to appear to be to the senses [it *feels* warm] **3** to grope **4** to be aware of being [I *feel* sad] **5** to be moved to sympathy, pity, etc. (*for*) —***n.*** **1** the act of feeling **2** the sense of touch **3** the nature of a thing as perceived through touch **4** an instinctive ability or appreciation [a *feel* for politics] —**feel like** [Inf.] to have a desire for —**feel one's way** to advance cautiously —**feel out** to try cautiously to find out the opinions of (someone) —**feel up to** [Inf.] to feel capable of

feel'er ***n.*** **1** a specialized organ of touch in an animal or insect, as an antenna **2** a cautious remark, offer, etc. made to learn more about something

feel'ing ***n.*** **1** the sense of touch **2** the ability to experience physical sensation **3** an awareness; sensation **4** an emotion **5** [*pl.*] sensibilities [hurt *feelings*] **6** sympathy; pity **7** an opinion or sentiment

fee simple absolute and unrestricted ownership of real property

feet (fēt) ***n.*** *pl. of* FOOT

feign (fān) ***vt., vi.*** ⟦< L *fingere*, to shape⟧ **1** to make up (an excuse, etc.) **2** to pretend; dissemble

feint (fānt) ***n.*** ⟦see prec.⟧ a pretended attack intended to take the opponent off guard, as in boxing —***vi., vt.*** to deliver (such an attack)

feist·y (fīs'tē) ***adj.* -i·er, -i·est** ⟦< Norw *fisa*, to puff + -Y[2]⟧ [Inf. or Dial.] full of spirit; specif., quarrelsome, lively, spunky, etc. —**feist'i·ly** ***adv.*** —**feist'i·ness** ***n.***

feld·spar (feld'spär') ***n.*** ⟦< Ger *feld*, field + *spath*, a mineral⟧ any of several hard, glassy minerals

fe·lic·i·tate (fə lis'i tāt') ***vt.* -tat'ed, -tat'ing** ⟦< L *felix*, happy⟧ to wish happiness to; congratulate —**fe·lic'i·ta'tion** ***n.*** —**fe·lic'i·ta'tor** ***n.***

fe·lic'i·tous (-təs) ***adj.*** ⟦< fol.⟧ used or expressed in a way suitable to the occasion; appropriate

fe·lic'i·ty (-tē) ***n.***, *pl.* **-ties** ⟦< L *felix*, happy⟧ **1** happiness; bliss **2** anything producing happiness **3** apt and pleasing expression in writing, etc.

fe·line (fē'līn) ***adj.*** ⟦< L *feles*, cat⟧ **1** of a cat or the cat family **2** catlike; sly —***n.*** any animal of the cat family

fell[1] (fel) ***vi., vt.*** *pt. of* FALL

fell[2] (fel) ***vt.*** ⟦OE *fellan*⟧ **1** to knock down **2** to cut down (a tree)

fell[3] (fel) ***adj.*** ⟦< ML *fello*⟧ fierce; cruel

fel·low (fel'ō, -ə) ***n.*** ⟦Late OE *feolaga*, partner⟧ **1** an associate **2** one of the same rank; equal **3** one of a pair; mate **4** one holding a fellowship in a college, etc. **5** a member of a learned society **6** [Inf.] a man or boy —***adj.*** **1** having the same position, work, etc. **2** associated [*fellow* workers]

fel'low·ship' ***n.*** **1** companionship **2** a mutual sharing **3** a group of people with the same interests **4** an endowment for the support of a student or scholar doing advanced work

fellow traveler a nonmember who supports the cause of a party

fel·on[1] (fel'ən) ***n.*** ⟦< ML *felo*, villain⟧ a person guilty of a felony; criminal

fel·on[2] (fel'ən) ***n.*** ⟦ME⟧ a painful infection at the end of a finger or toe

fel·o·ny (fel'ə nē) ***n.***, *pl.* **-nies** ⟦< ML *felonia*, treachery⟧ a major crime, as murder, arson, etc. —**fe·lo·ni·ous** (fə lō'nē əs) ***adj.***

felt[1] (felt) ***n.*** ⟦< OE⟧ a fabric of wool, often mixed with fur, hair, cotton, etc., worked together by pressure, etc. —***adj.*** made of felt —***vt.*** to make into felt

felt[2] (felt) ***vt., vi.*** *pt. and pp. of* FEEL

fem *abbrev.* **1** female **2** feminine

fe·male (fē'māl') ***adj.*** ⟦< L *femina*, woman⟧ **1** designating or of the sex that bears offspring **2** of, like, or suitable to women or girls; feminine **3** consisting of women or girls **4** having a hollow part for receiving an inserted part (called *male*): said of electric sockets, etc. —***n.*** a female person, animal, or plant

fem·i·nine (fem'ə nin) ***adj.*** ⟦< L *femina*, woman⟧ **1** of women or girls **2** having qualities characteristic of or suitable to women; gentle, delicate, etc. **3** *Gram.* designating or of the gender of words referring to females or other words with no distinction of sex —**fem'i·nin'i·ty** ***n.***

fem'i·nism' (-niz'əm) ***n.*** the movement to win political, economic, and social equality for women —**fem'i·nist** ***n., adj.*** —**fem'i·nis'tic** ***adj.***

fe·mur (fē'mər) ***n.***, *pl.* **fe'murs** or **fem·o·ra** (fem'ə rə) ⟦< L, thigh⟧ the bone extending from the hip to the knee —**fem'o·ral** ***adj.***

fen (fen) ***n.*** ⟦OE⟧ an area of low, flat, marshy land; swamp; bog

fence (fens) ***n.*** ⟦< ME *defens*, defense⟧ **1** a protective or confining barrier of posts, wire mesh, etc. **2** one who deals in stolen goods —***vt.* fenced, fenc'ing** **1** to enclose, as with a fence: with *in, off*, etc. **2** to keep (*out*) as by a fence **3** to sell (stolen property) to a fence —***vi.*** **1** to practice the art of fencing **2** to avoid giving a direct reply —**on the fence**

uncommitted or undecided —**fenc'er** ***n.***

fenc'ing ***n.*** **1** the art of fighting with a foil or other sword **2** material for making fences **3** a system of fences

fend (fend) ***vt.*** ⟦ME *fenden*, defend⟧ to turn aside; ward (*off*) —***vi.*** —**fend for oneself** to manage by oneself

fend'er ***n.*** anything that fends off or protects something else, as the part of an automobile body over the wheel

fen·nel (fen'əl) ***n.*** ⟦< L *fenum*, hay⟧ a tall herb with aromatic seeds used to flavor foods and medicines

fe·ral (fir'əl, fer'-) ***adj.*** ⟦< L *ferus*, wild⟧ **1** untamed; wild **2** savage; fierce

fer·ment (fur'ment'; *for v.* fər ment') ***n.*** ⟦< L *fervere*, to boil⟧ **1** a substance causing fermentation, as yeast **2** excitement or agitation —***vt.*** **1** to cause fermentation in **2** to excite; agitate —***vi.*** **1** to be in the process of fermentation **2** to be excited or agitated; seethe

fer·men·ta·tion (fur'mən tā'shən) ***n.*** **1** the breakdown of complex molecules in organic compounds, caused by the influence of a ferment *[*bacteria cause milk to curdle by *fermentation]* **2** excitement; agitation

fer·mi·on (fer'mē än', fur'-) ***n.*** ⟦after E. *Fermi*, 20th-c. U.S. nuclear physicist⟧ any of a major subdivision of subatomic particles, including leptons and baryons

FERN

fern (furn) ***n.*** ⟦< OE *fearn*⟧ any of a large group of nonflowering plants having roots, stems, and fronds, and reproducing by spores

fe·ro·cious (fə rō'shəs) ***adj.*** ⟦< L *ferus*, wild⟧ **1** fierce; savage; violently cruel **2** [Inf.] very great *[a ferocious* appetite*]* —**fe·ro'cious·ly** ***adv.*** —**fe·roc·i·ty** (fə räs'ə tē) ***n.***

-fer·ous (fər əs) ⟦< L *ferre*, to bear⟧ *suffix* bearing, yielding

fer·ret (fer'ət) ***n.*** ⟦< L *fur*, thief⟧ a small European polecat, easily tamed for hunting rats, etc. —***vt.*** **1** to force out of hiding with or as if with a ferret **2** to find out by investigation: with *out*

fer·ric (fer'ik) ***adj.*** ⟦< L *ferrum*, iron⟧ of, containing, or derived from iron

Fer·ris wheel (fer'is) ⟦after G. *Ferris* (1859-96), U.S. engineer⟧ a large, upright wheel revolving on a fixed axle and having suspended seats: used as an amusement ride

ferro- ⟦< L *ferrum*, iron⟧ *combining form* **1** iron **2** iron and

fer·rous (fer'əs) ***adj.*** ⟦< L *ferrum*, iron⟧ of, containing, or derived from iron

fer·rule (fer'əl, -o͞ol') ***n.*** ⟦< L *viriae*, bracelets⟧ a metal ring or cap put around the end of a cane, tool handle, etc. to give added strength

fer·ry (fer'ē) ***vt.*** **-ried, -ry·ing** ⟦OE *ferian*⟧ **1** to take (people, cars, etc.) across a river, etc. **2** to deliver (airplanes) by flying them **3** to transport by airplane —***n.***, *pl.* **-ries** **1** a system for carrying people, goods, etc. across a river, etc. by boat **2** a boat used for this: also **fer'ry·boat'**

fer·tile (furt''l) ***adj.*** ⟦< L *ferre*, to bear⟧ **1** producing abundantly; fruitful; prolific **2** able to produce young, seeds, fruit, pollen, spores, etc. **3** fertilized *[*a *fertile* egg*]* —**fer·til·i·ty** (fər til'ə tē) ***n.***

fer'til·ize' (-īz') ***vt.*** **-ized', -iz'ing** **1** to make fertile **2** to spread fertilizer on **3** to make (the female cell or female) fruitful by pollinating, or impregnating, with the male gamete —**fer'til·iz'a·ble** ***adj.*** —**fer'til·i·za'tion** ***n.***

fer'til·iz'er ***n.*** manure, chemicals, etc., used to enrich the soil

fer·ule (fer'əl, -o͞ol') ***n.*** ⟦< L *ferula*, a whip, rod⟧ a flat stick or ruler used for punishing children

fer·vent (fur'vənt) ***adj.*** ⟦< L *fervere*, to glow⟧ showing great warmth of feeling; intensely devoted or earnest —**fer'ven·cy** ***n.*** —**fer'vent·ly** ***adv.***

fer·vid (fur'vid) ***adj.*** ⟦see prec.⟧ impassioned; fervent —**fer'vid·ly** ***adv.***

fer·vor (fur'vər) ***n.*** ⟦see FERVENT⟧ great warmth of emotion; ardor; zeal

-fest (fest) ⟦< Ger *fest*, a feast⟧ *combining form* an occasion of much or many *[songfest]*

fes·tal (fes'təl) ***adj.*** ⟦< L *festum*, feast⟧ of or like a joyous celebration; festive

fes·ter (fes'tər) ***n.*** ⟦< L *fistula*, ulcer⟧ a small sore filled with pus —***vi.*** **1** to form pus **2** to grow more bitter, virulent, etc.

fes·ti·val (fes'tə vəl) ***n.*** ⟦see fol.⟧ **1** a time or day of feasting or celebration **2** a celebration or series of performances

fes·tive (fes'tiv) ***adj.*** ⟦< L *festum*, feast⟧ **1** of or for a feast or festival **2** merry; joyous —**fes'tive·ly** ***adv.*** —**fes'tive·ness** ***n.***

fes·tiv·i·ty (fes tiv'ə tē) ***n.***, *pl.* **-ties** **1** merrymaking; gaiety **2** a festival **3** [*pl.*] things done in celebration

fes·toon (fes to͞on') ***n.*** ⟦< It *festa*, feast⟧ a wreath or garland of flowers, etc. hanging in a loop or curve —***vt.*** to adorn with festoons

fet·a (cheese) (fet'ə) ⟦< ModGr < It *fetta*, a slice⟧ a soft, white cheese, first made in Greece

fe·tal (fēt''l) ***adj.*** of a fetus

fetch (fech) ***vt.*** ⟦OE *feccan*⟧ **1** to go after and bring back; get **2** to cause to come **3** to sell for

fetch'ing ***adj.*** attractive; charming

fete or **fête** (fāt, fet) ***n.*** ⟦Fr *fête*: see FEAST⟧ a festival; entertainment, esp. outdoors —***vt.*** **fet'ed** or **fêt'ed**, **fet'ing** or **fêt'ing** to honor with a fete

fet·id (fet'id) ***adj.*** ⟦< L *foetere*, to stink⟧ having a bad smell; stinking; putrid —**fet'id·ness** ***n.***

fet·ish (fet'ish) ***n.*** ⟦< Port *feitiço*⟧ **1** any object believed to have magic power **2** anything to which one is irrationally devoted **3** any nonsexual object that abnormally excites erotic feelings Also **fet'ich** —**fet'ish·ism'** ***n.*** —**fet'ish·ist** ***n.***

fet·lock (fet'läk') ***n.*** ⟦< ME *fet*, feet⟧ **1** a tuft of hair on the back of a horse's leg above the hoof **2** the joint bearing this tuft

fe·to·scope (fē'tə skōp') ***n.*** **1** an endoscope used to examine a fetus in the womb **2** a special stethoscope used to listen to the fetal heartbeat

fet·ter (fet'ər) ***n.*** ⟦< OE *fot*, foot⟧ **1** a shackle or chain for the feet **2** any check or restraint —***vt.*** **1** to bind with fetters **2** to restrain

fet·tle (fet''l) ***n.*** ⟦ME *fetlen*, make ready⟧ condition; state *[in fine fettle]*

fe·tus (fēt'əs) ***n.***, *pl.* **-tus·es** ⟦L, a bringing forth⟧ the unborn young of an animal, esp. in its later stages and specif., in humans, from about the eighth week after conception until birth

feud (fyo͞od) ***n.*** ⟦< OFr *faide*⟧ a deadly quarrel, esp. between clans or families —***vi.*** to carry on a feud; quarrel

feu·dal (fyo͞od''l) ***adj.*** ⟦ML *feudalis*⟧ of or like feudalism

feu'dal·ism' ***n.*** the economic, political, and social system in medieval Europe, in which land, worked by serfs, was held by vassals in exchange for military and other services they give to overlords —**feu'dal·is'tic** ***adj.***

fe·ver (fē'vər) ***n.*** ⟦< L *febris*⟧ **1** an abnormally increased body temperature **2** any disease marked by a high fever **3** a restless excitement —**fe'ver·ish** ***adj.*** —**fe'ver·ish·ly** ***adv.***

fever blister (or **sore**) COLD SORE

few (fyo͞o) ***adj.*** ⟦OE *feawe*⟧ not many; a small number of —***pron.*** not many; a small number —**few and far between** scarce; rare —**the few** the minority

fey (fā) ***adj.*** ⟦OE *fæge*, fated⟧ strange or unusual; specif., eccentric, whimsical, etc. —**fey'ness** ***n.***

fez (fez) ***n.***, *pl.* **fez'zes** ⟦after *Fez*, city in Morocco⟧ a red, brimless felt hat, shaped like a truncated cone, worn formerly by Turkish men

ff *abbrev.* **1** folios **2** following (pages, etc.)

fi·an·cé (fē'än sā') ***n.*** ⟦Fr < OFr *fiance*, a promise⟧ a man who is engaged to be married

fi·an·cée (fē'än sā') ***n.*** ⟦Fr: see prec.⟧ a woman who is engaged to be married

fi·as·co (fē as'kō) ***n.***, *pl.* **-coes** or **-cos** ⟦Fr < It⟧ a complete, ridiculous failure

fi·at (fē'ät, fī'at') ***n.*** ⟦L, let it be done⟧ **1** a decree; order **2** a sanction; authorization **3** any arbitrary order

fib (fib) ***n.*** ⟦< ? FABLE⟧ a small or trivial lie —***vi.*** **fibbed**, **fib'bing** to tell such a lie —**fib'ber** ***n.***

fi·ber (fī'bər) ***n.*** ⟦< L *fibra*⟧ **1** a threadlike structure that combines with others to form animal or vegetable tissue **2** any substance that can be separated into threadlike parts for weaving, etc. **3** texture **4** character or nature **5** ROUGHAGE —**fi'brous** (-brəs) ***adj.***

fi'ber·board' ***n.*** a building material consisting of fibers of wood, etc. pressed into stiff sheets

Fi'ber·glas' (-glas') *trademark for* finespun filaments of glass made into textiles, insulating material, or molded plastic —***n.*** this substance

fi'ber·glass' (-glas') ***n.*** finespun filaments of glass like Fiberglas

fiber optics **1** the science of transmitting light and images, as around curves, through transparent fibers **2** such fibers —**fi'ber-op'tic** or **fiber optic** ***adj.***

fi·bril·la·tion (fib'ri lā'shən) ***n.*** ⟦< L *fibra*, fiber + -ATION⟧ very rapid contractions of part of the heart muscle, causing irregular heartbeats

fi·brin (fī'brin) ***n.*** a fibrous, insoluble blood protein formed in blood clots

fi·brin·o·gen (fī brin'ə jən) ***n.*** ⟦prec. + -GEN⟧ a protein in the blood from which fibrin is formed

fi·broid (fī'broid') ***adj.*** like or composed of fibrous tissue: said as of a tumor

fi·bro·sis (fī brō'sis) ***n.*** an excessive growth of fibrous connective tissue in an organ, part, etc.

fib·u·la (fib'yo͞o lə) ***n.***, *pl.* **-lae'** (-lē') or **-las** ⟦L, a clasp⟧ the long, thin outer bone of the lower leg —**fib'u·lar** ***adj.***

-fic (fik) ⟦< L *facere*, make⟧ *suffix* making *[terrific]*

FICA (fī'kə) *abbrev.* Federal Insurance Contributions Act

-fi·ca·tion (fi kā'shən) ⟦see -FIC⟧ *suffix* a making *[glorification]*

fich·u (fish'o͞o) ***n.*** ⟦Fr⟧ a triangular lace or muslin cape for women, worn tied in front

fick·le (fik'əl) ***adj.*** ⟦< OE *ficol*, tricky⟧ changeable or unstable; capricious

fic·tion (fik'shən) ***n.*** ⟦< L *fingere*, to form⟧ **1** an imaginary statement, story, etc. **2** *a*) literary narratives, collectively, with imaginary characters or events, specif. novels and short stories *b*) a narrative of this kind —**fic'tion·al** ***adj.***

fic'tion·al·ize' (-shə nəl īz') ***vt.*** **-ized'**, **-iz'ing** to deal with (historical events) in fictional form —**fic'tion·al·i·za'tion** ***n.***

fic·ti·tious (fik tish'əs) ***adj.*** **1** of or like fiction; imaginary **2** false **3** assumed for disguise *[a fictitious name]*

fic·tive (fik'tiv) ***adj.*** **1** of fiction **2** imaginary —**fic'tive·ly** ***adv.***

fi·cus (fī'kəs) ***n.***, *pl.* **fi'cus** ⟦< L, fig tree⟧ any of a genus of tropical shrubs, trees, etc. with glossy, leathery leaves

fid·dle (fid''l) [Inf.] ***n.*** ⟦OE *fithele*⟧ a violin —***vi.*** **-dled**, **-dling** **1** to play a fiddle **2** to tinker (*with*) nervously —**fid'dler** ***n.***

fid'dle·sticks' ***interj.*** nonsense!

fi·del·i·ty (fə del'ə tē) ***n.***, *pl.* **-ties** ⟦< L *fides*, faith⟧ 1 faithful devotion to duty; loyalty 2 accuracy of description, sound reproduction, etc.

fidg·et (fij′it) ***n.*** ⟦< ME < ?⟧ a restless or nervous state: esp. in phrase **the fidgets** —***vi.*** to move about restlessly or nervously —**fidg′et·y** ***adj.***

fi·du·ci·ar·y (fi do͞o′shē er′ē) ***adj.*** ⟦< L *fiducia*, trust⟧ holding or held in trust —***n.***, *pl.* **-ies** TRUSTEE (sense 1)

fie (fī) ***interj.*** [Archaic] for shame!

fief (fēf) ***n.*** ⟦Fr: see FEE⟧ in feudalism, heritable land held by a vassal

fief′dom (-dəm) ***n.*** 1 FIEF 2 anything under a person's complete control

field (fēld) ***n.*** ⟦OE *feld*⟧ 1 a stretch of open land 2 a piece of cleared land for crops or pasture 3 a piece of land used for a particular purpose *[a landing field]* 4 any wide, unbroken expanse *[a field of ice]* 5 *a*) a battlefield *b*) a battle 6 a realm of knowledge or work 7 the background, as on a flag 8 *a*) an area for athletics or games *b*) all the entrants in a contest 9 *Physics* a physical quantity specified at points throughout a region of space —***vt.*** 1 to stop or catch and throw (a baseball, etc.) 2 to put (a player or team) into active play 3 [Inf.] to answer (a question) extemporaneously —**play the field** to not confine one's activities to one object —**field′er** ***n.***

field day an occasion of extraordinary opportunity or highly successful activity

field glasses a small, portable binocular telescope

field goal 1 *Basketball* a shot, made from play, scoring two points or, if from a certain distance, three points 2 *Football* a goal kicked from the field, scoring three points

field guide a handbook for identifying plants, etc., as while hiking

field hand a hired farm laborer

field hockey HOCKEY (sense 2)

field marshal in some armies, an officer of the highest rank

field′-test′ ***vt.*** to test (a device, method, etc.) under operating conditions

fiend (fēnd) ***n.*** ⟦OE *feond*, the one hating⟧ 1 an evil spirit; devil 2 an inhumanly wicked person 3 [Inf.] an addict *[a dope fiend]* —**fiend′ish** ***adj.***

fierce (firs) ***adj.*** **fierc′er**, **fierc′est** ⟦< L *ferus*, wild⟧ 1 savage 2 violent 3 intense *[a fierce embrace]* —**fierce′ly** ***adv.*** —**fierce′ness** ***n.***

fi·er·y (fī′ər ē) ***adj.*** **-er·i·er**, **-er·i·est** 1 like fire; glaring, hot, etc. 2 ardent; spirited 3 excitable 4 inflamed

fi·es·ta (fē es′tə) ***n.*** ⟦Sp < L *festus*, festal⟧ 1 a religious festival 2 any gala celebration; holiday

fife (fīf) ***n.*** ⟦Ger *pfeife*⟧ a small flute used mainly with drums in playing marches

fif·teen (fif′tēn′) ***adj.***, ***n.*** ⟦OE *fiftene*⟧ five more than ten; 15; XV —**fif′teenth′** (-tēnth′) ***adj.***, ***n.***, ***adv.***

fifth (fifth) ***adj.*** ⟦< OE *fif*, five⟧ preceded by four others in a series; 5th —***n.*** 1 the one following the fourth 2 any of the five equal parts of something; $\frac{1}{5}$ 3 a fifth of a gallon —***adv.*** in the fifth place, rank, etc.

Fifth Amendment an amendment to the U.S. Constitution mainly guaranteeing certain protections in criminal cases; specif., the clause protecting persons from being compelled to testify against themselves

fifth column a group of people aiding an enemy from within their own country

fifth wheel a superfluous person or thing

fif·ty (fif′tē) ***adj.***, ***n.***, *pl.* **-ties** ⟦OE *fiftig*⟧ five times ten; 50; L —**the fifties** the numbers or years, as of a century, from 50 through 59 —**fif′ti·eth** (-ith) ***adj.***, ***n.***

fif′ty-fif′ty [Inf.] ***adj.*** equal; even —***adv.*** equally

fig[1] (fig) ***n.*** ⟦< L *ficus*⟧ 1 *a*) a small, sweet, pear-shaped fruit that grows on a tree related to the mulberry *b*) the tree 2 a trifle *[not worth a fig]*

fig[2] *abbrev.* 1 figurative(ly) 2 figure(s)

fight (fīt) ***vi.*** **fought**, **fight′ing** ⟦OE *feohtan*⟧ to take part in a struggle, contest, etc., esp. against a foe or for a cause —***vt.*** 1 to oppose physically or in battle 2 to struggle against 3 to engage in (a war, etc.) 4 to gain (one's way) by struggle —***n.*** 1 any struggle, contest, or quarrel 2 power or readiness to fight

fight′er ***n.*** 1 one that fights 2 a prizefighter 3 a fast, highly maneuverable combat airplane

fig·ment (fig′mənt) ***n.*** ⟦< L *fingere*, to form⟧ something merely imagined

fig·ur·a·tive (fig′yoor ə tiv′) ***adj.*** 1 representing by means of a figure or symbol 2 not in its literal sense; metaphorical 3 using figures of speech —**fig′ur·a·tive′ly** ***adv.***

fig·ure (fig′yər) ***n.*** ⟦< L *fingere*, to form⟧ 1 an outline or shape; form 2 the human form 3 a person thought of in a specified way *[a historical figure]* 4 a likeness of a person or thing 5 an illustration; diagram 6 a design; pattern 7 the symbol for a number 8 [*pl.*] arithmetic 9 a sum of money 10 *Geom.* a surface or space bounded by lines or planes —***vt.*** **-ured**, **-ur·ing** 1 to represent in definite form 2 to imagine 3 to ornament with a design 4 to compute with figures 5 [Inf.] to believe; consider —***vi.*** 1 to appear prominently 2 to do arithmetic —**figure in** to include —**figure on** to rely on —**figure out** 1 to solve 2 to understand —**figure up** to add; total

fig′ure·head′ ***n.*** 1 a carved figure on the bow of a ship 2 one put in a position of leadership, but having no real power or authority

figure of speech an expression, as a metaphor or simile, using words in a nonliteral sense or unusual way

figure skating ice skating with emphasis on tracing patterns on the ice or, now, performing leaps and spins —**figure skater**

fig·u·rine (fig′yo͞o rēn′) ***n.*** ⟦Fr⟧ a small

sculptured or molded figure

Fi·ji (fē′jē) country on a group of islands (**Fiji Islands**) in the SW Pacific: 7,078 sq. mi.; pop. 715,000

fil·a·ment (fil′ə mənt) ***n.*** ⟦< L *filum*, thread⟧ a very slender thread or threadlike part; specif., the fine wire in a light bulb or electron tube

fil·bert (fil′bərt) ***n.*** ⟦ME *filberde*⟧ the edible nut of a hazel tree

filch (filch) ***vt.*** ⟦ME *filchen*⟧ to steal (usually something small or petty)

file[1] (fīl) ***vt.*** **filed**, **fil′ing** ⟦< L *filum*, thread⟧ **1** to put (papers, etc.) in order for future reference **2** to dispatch or register (a news story, application, etc.) **3** to put on public record —***vi.*** **1** to move in a line **2** to make application (*for* divorce, etc.) —***n.*** **1** a container for keeping papers in order **2** an orderly arrangement of papers, etc. **3** a line of persons or things **4** *Comput.* a collection of data stored as a single unit —**file′a·ble** ***adj.*** —**fil′er** ***n.***

file[2] (fīl) ***n.*** ⟦OE *feol*⟧ a steel tool with a rough, ridged surface for smoothing or grinding —***vt.*** **filed**, **fil′ing** to smooth or grind, as with a file

fi·let (fi lā′, fil′ā′) ***n.*** ⟦< OFr: see FILLET⟧ FILLET (*n.* 2) —***vt.*** FILLET

fi·let mi·gnon (fi lā′min yōn′, -yän′) ⟦Fr, lit., tiny fillet⟧ a thick, round cut of lean beef tenderloin

fil·i·al (fil′ē əl, fil′yəl) ***adj.*** ⟦< L *filius*, son⟧ of, suitable to, or due from a son or daughter

fil·i·bus·ter (fil′i bus′tər) ***n.*** ⟦< Sp < MDu *vrijbuiter*, freebooter⟧ **1** the making of long speeches, etc. to obstruct a bill's passage in the Senate **2** a Senator who does this —***vt.***, ***vi.*** to obstruct (a bill) by a filibuster

fil·i·gree (fil′i grē′) ***n.*** ⟦< L *filum*, thread + *granum*, grain⟧ lacelike ornamental work of intertwined wire of gold, silver, etc.—***vt.*** **-greed′**, **-gree′ing** to ornament with filigree

fil·ing (fīl′iŋ) ***n.*** a small piece scraped off with a file: *usually used in pl.*

Fil·i·pi·no (fil′i pē′nō) ***n.***, *pl.* **-nos** ⟦Sp⟧ a person born or living in the Philippines —***adj.*** of the Philippines or its people, etc. —**Fil′i·pi′na** (-nə), *pl.* **-nas**, ***fem.n.***, ***adj.***

fill (fil) ***vt.*** ⟦OE *fyllan*⟧ **1** to put as much as possible into **2** to occupy wholly **3** to put a person into or to occupy (a position, etc.) **4** to supply the things called for in (an order, etc.) **5** to close or plug (holes, etc.) —***vi.*** to become full —***n.*** **1** enough to make full or to satisfy **2** anything that fills —**fill in** **1** to complete by supplying something **2** to supply for completion **3** to be a substitute —**fill out** **1** to make or become larger, etc. **2** to make (a document, etc.) complete by supplying information —**fill up** to make or become completely full —**fill′er** ***n.***

fil·let (fil′it; *for n. 2 & vt., usually* fi lā′, fil′ā′) ***n.*** ⟦OFr *filet* < L *filum*, thread⟧ **1** a thin strip or band **2** a lean, boneless piece of meat or fish —***vt.*** to bone and slice (meat or fish)

fill′-in′ ***n.*** one that fills a vacancy or gap, often temporarily

fill′ing ***n.*** a substance used to fill something, as gold in a tooth cavity

filling station SERVICE STATION

fil·lip (fil′ip) ***n.*** ⟦< FLIP[1]⟧ **1** an outward snap of a finger from the thumb **2** something that stimulates —***vt.*** to strike or toss with a fillip

Fill·more (fil′môr), **Mill·ard** (mil′ərd) 1800-74; 13th president of the U.S. (1850-53)

fil·ly (fil′ē) ***n.***, *pl.* **-lies** ⟦< ON *fylja*⟧ a young female horse

film (film) ***n.*** ⟦OE *filmen*⟧ **1** a fine, thin skin, coating, etc. **2** a flexible cellulose material coated with an emulsion sensitive to light and used in photography **3** a haze or blur **4** a series of still pictures projected on a screen in such rapid succession as to create the illusion of moving persons and objects **5** a play, story, etc. in this form —***vt.***, ***vi.*** **1** to cover or be covered as with a film **2** to photograph or make a film (of)

film′strip′ ***n.*** a length of film with still photographs, often of illustrations, charts, etc., for projection separately

film′y ***adj.*** **-i·er**, **-i·est** **1** gauzy; sheer; thin **2** blurred; hazy —**film′i·ness** ***n.***

fil·ter (fil′tər) ***n.*** ⟦< ML *filtrum*, FELT[1]⟧ **1** a device for straining out solid particles, impurities, etc. from a liquid or gas **2** a device or substance for screening out electric oscillations, light waves, etc. of certain frequencies —***vt.***, ***vi.*** **1** to pass through or as through a filter **2** to remove with a filter —**fil′ter·a·ble** or **fil′tra·ble** (-trə bəl) ***adj.***

filter tip **1** a cigarette tip of cellulose, charcoal, etc. for filtering the smoke **2** a cigarette with such a tip

filth (filth) ***n.*** ⟦OE *fylthe*⟧ **1** foul dirt **2** obscenity —**filth′y**, **-i·er**, **-i·est**, ***adj.*** —**filth′i·ness** ***n.***

fil·trate (fil′trāt′) ***vt.*** **-trat′ed**, **-trat′ing** to filter —***n.*** a filtered liquid —**fil·tra′tion** ***n.***

fin (fin) ***n.*** ⟦OE *finn*⟧ **1** any of several winglike organs on the body of a fish, dolphin, etc., used in swimming **2** anything like a fin in shape or use

fi·na·gle (fə nā′gəl) ***vt.***, ***vi.*** **-gled**, **-gling** ⟦< ?⟧ [Inf.] to get by, or use, craftiness, trickery, etc. —**fi·na′gler** ***n.***

fi·nal (fī′nəl) ***adj.*** ⟦< L *finis*, end⟧ **1** of or coming at the end; last **2** deciding; conclusive —***n.*** **1** anything final **2** [*pl.*] the last of a series of contests **3** a final examination —**fi·nal′i·ty** (-nal′ə tē) ***n.*** —**fi′nal·ly** ***adv.***

fi·na·le (fə nal′ē) ***n.*** ⟦It⟧ the concluding part of a musical work, etc.

fi′nal·ist ***n.*** a contestant in the final, deciding contest of a series

fi′nal·ize′ ***vt.*** **-ized′**, **-iz′ing** ⟦FINAL + -IZE⟧ to make final; complete —**fi′nal·i·za′tion** ***n.***

fi·nance (fī′nans′, fə nans′) ***n.*** ⟦< L *finis*, end⟧ **1** [*pl.*] money resources, income, etc. **2** the science of managing money —***vt.*** **-nanced′**, **-nanc′ing** to supply or get money for —**fi·nan′cial** (-nan′shəl) ***adj.*** —**fi·nan′cial·ly** ***adv.***

fin·an·cier (fin′ən sir′, fī′nən-) ***n.*** ⟦Fr⟧

one skilled in finance

finch (finch) ***n.*** ⟦OE *finc*⟧ any of various small, seed-eating birds, including canaries, goldfinches, etc.

find (fīnd) ***vt.*** **found, find′ing** ⟦OE *findan*⟧ **1** to discover by chance; come upon **2** to get by searching **3** to perceive; learn **4** to recover (something lost) **5** to reach; attain **6** to decide and declare to be —***vi.*** to reach a decision *[*the jury *found* for the accused*]* —***n.*** **1** a finding **2** something found —**find out** to discover; learn —**find′er** ***n.***

find′ing ***n.*** **1** discovery **2** something found **3** [*often pl.*] the verdict of a judge, scholar, etc.

fine[1] (fīn) ***adj.*** ⟦< L *finis*, end⟧ **1** very good; excellent **2** with no impurities; refined **3** in good health **4** clear and bright *[fine* weather*]* **5** not heavy or coarse *[fine* sand*]* **6** very thin or small *[fine* print*]* **7** sharp *[*a *fine* edge*]* **8** subtle; delicate *[*a *fine* distinction*]* **9** elegant —***adv.*** in a fine manner —**fine′ly** ***adv.*** —**fine′ness** ***n.***

fine[2] (fīn) ***n.*** ⟦see prec.⟧ a sum of money paid as a penalty —***vt.*** **fined, fin′ing** to order to pay a fine

fine art any of the art forms that include drawing, painting, sculpture, etc.: *usually used in pl.*

fin·er·y (fīn′ər ē) ***n.***, *pl.* **-ies** elaborate clothes, jewelry, etc.

fines herbes (fēn zerb′) ⟦Fr⟧ a seasoning of chopped herbs, traditionally parsley, chives, tarragon, and chervil

fi·nesse (fə nes′) ***n.*** ⟦see FINE[1]⟧ **1** adroitness; skill **2** the ability to handle difficult situations diplomatically **3** cunning; artfulness —***vt.*** **-nessed′, -ness′ing** **1** to manage or bring about by finesse **2** to evade (a problem, etc.)

fin·ger (fiŋ′gər) ***n.*** ⟦OE⟧ **1** any of the five jointed parts extending from the palm of the hand, esp. any one other than the thumb **2** anything like a finger in shape or use —***vt.*** **1** to touch with the fingers; handle **2** *Music* to play by using the fingers in a certain way —**have** (or **keep**) **one's fingers crossed** to hope for or against something —**put one's finger on** to ascertain exactly

fin′ger·board′ ***n.*** the part of a stringed instrument against which the strings are pressed to produce the desired tones

fin′ger·ling (-liŋ) ***n.*** a small fish

fin′ger·nail′ ***n.*** the horny substance at the upper end of a finger

finger painting a painting done by using the fingers, hand, or arm to spread, on wet paper, paints (**finger paints**) made of starch, glycerin, and pigments —**fin′ger-paint′** ***vi.***, ***vt.***

fin′ger-point′ing ***n.*** the act of assigning blame to others, often so as to deflect blame from oneself

fin′ger·print′ ***n.*** an impression of the lines and whorls on a finger tip, used to identify a person —***vt.*** to take the fingerprints of

fin′ger·tip′ ***n.*** the tip of a finger —**have at one's fingertips** to have available for instant use

fin·i·al (fin′ē əl) ***n.*** ⟦ult. < L *finis*, end⟧ a decorative terminal part at the tip of a spire, lamp, etc.

fin·ick·y (fin′ik ē) ***adj.*** ⟦< FINE[1]⟧ too particular; fussy: also **fin′i·cal** (-i kəl) or **fin′ick·ing**

fin·is (fin′is; *also, as if Fr,* fē nē′) ***n.***, *pl.* **-nis·es** the end; finish

fin·ish (fin′ish) ***vt.*** ⟦< L *finis*, an end⟧ **1** *a)* to bring to an end *b)* to come to the end of **2** to consume all of **3** to give final touches to; perfect **4** to give (wood, etc.) a desired surface effect —***vi.*** to come to an end —***n.*** **1** the last part; end **2** *a)* anything used to finish a surface *b)* the finished effect **3** means or manner of completing or perfecting **4** polished manners, speech, etc. —**finish off** **1** to end **2** to kill or ruin —**finish with** to bring to an end —**fin′ished** ***adj.*** —**fin′ish·er** ***n.***

fi·nite (fī′nīt′) ***adj.*** ⟦< L *finis*, end⟧ having definable limits; not infinite

fink (fiŋk) ***n.*** ⟦Ger, lit., finch⟧ [Slang] **1** an informer **2** a strikebreaker —***vi.*** [Slang] to inform (*on*)

Fin·land (fin′lənd) country in N Europe: 130,547 sq. mi.; pop. 5,078,000

Finn (fin) ***n.*** a person born or living in Finland

fin·nan had·die (fin′ən had′ē) ⟦prob. < *Findhorn* (Scotland) *haddock*⟧ smoked haddock

Finn·ish (fin′ish) ***n.*** the language spoken in Finland —***adj.*** of Finland or its people, language, etc.

fin·ny (fin′ē) ***adj.*** **1** having fins **2** like a fin **3** of or being fish

fiord (fyôrd) ***n.*** ⟦Norw < ON *fjörthr*⟧ a narrow inlet of the sea bordered by steep cliffs

fir (fur) ***n.*** ⟦OE *fyrh*⟧ **1** a cone-bearing evergreen tree of the pine family **2** its wood

fire (fīr) ***n.*** ⟦OE *fyr*⟧ **1** the flame, heat, and light of combustion **2** something burning **3** a destructive burning *[*a forest *fire]* **4** strong feeling **5** a discharge of firearms —***vt.***, ***vi.*** **fired, fir′ing** **1** to start burning; ignite **2** to supply with fuel **3** to bake (bricks, etc.) in a kiln **4** to excite or become excited **5** to shoot (a gun, bullet, etc.) **6** to hurl or direct with force **7** to dismiss from a position; discharge —**catch** (**on**) **fire** to ignite —**on fire** **1** burning **2** greatly excited —**under fire** under attack —**fir′er** ***n.***

fire′arm′ ***n.*** any hand weapon from which a shot is fired by explosive force, as a rifle or pistol

fire′base′ ***n.*** a military base in a combat zone, from which artillery, rockets, etc. are fired

fire′bomb′ ***n.*** an incendiary bomb —***vt.*** to attack or damage with a firebomb

fire′brand′ ***n.*** **1** a piece of burning wood **2** one who stirs up others to rebellion or strife

fire′break′ ***n.*** a strip of forest or prairie land cleared or plowed to stop the spread of fire

fire·brick (fīr′brik′) ***n.*** a highly heat-resistant brick for lining fireplaces, furnaces, etc.

fire'bug' ***n.*** [Inf.] one who deliberately starts destructive fires; pyromaniac

fire'crack'er ***n.*** a roll of paper containing an explosive, set off as a noisemaker at celebrations, etc.

fire'damp' ***n.*** an explosive gas, largely methane, formed in coal mines

fire engine a motor truck with equipment for fighting fires

fire escape an outside stairway for escaping from a burning building

fire'fight' ***n.*** a short, intense exchange of gunfire between small units of soldiers

fire'fight'er ***n.*** a person whose work is putting out fires —**fire'fight'ing** ***n.***

fire'fly' ***n.***, *pl.* **-flies'** a winged beetle whose abdomen glows with a luminescent light

fire'man (-mən) ***n.***, *pl.* **-men** (-mən) **1** FIREFIGHTER **2** a person who tends a fire in a furnace, etc.

fire'place' ***n.*** a place for a fire, esp. an open place built in a wall under a chimney

fire'plug' ***n.*** a street hydrant supplying water for fighting fires

fire'proof' ***adj.*** not easily destroyed by fire —***vt.*** to make fireproof

fire'side' ***n.*** **1** the space around a fireplace **2** home or home life

fire'storm' ***n.*** **1** an intense fire over a large area, as one caused by an atomic explosion with its high winds **2** a strong, often violent, outburst or upheaval

fire tower a tower used as a lookout for forest fires

fire'trap' ***n.*** a building easily set on fire or hard to get out of if on fire

fire'truck' ***n.*** FIRE ENGINE

fire'wa'ter ***n.*** alcoholic beverage: now humorous

fire'wood' ***n.*** wood used as fuel

fire'works' ***pl.n.*** **1** firecrackers, rockets, etc., for noisy effects or brilliant displays: *sometimes used in sing.* **2** a noisy quarrel or display of anger

firing line **1** the line from which gunfire is directed at the enemy **2** the forefront in any kind of activity

firm[1] (fɚrm) ***adj.*** ⟦< L *firmus*⟧ **1** solid; hard **2** not moved easily; fixed **3** unchanging; steady **4** resolute; constant **5** showing determination; strong **6** definite *[a firm contract]* —***vt.***, ***vi.*** to make or become firm —**firm'ly** ***adv.*** —**firm'ness** ***n.***

firm[2] (fɚrm) ***n.*** ⟦< It < L *firmus*: see prec.⟧ a business company

fir·ma·ment (fɚr'mə mənt) ***n.*** ⟦< L *firmare*, strengthen⟧ the sky, viewed poetically as a solid arch or vault

first (fɚrst) ***adj.*** ⟦OE *fyrst*⟧ **1** before all others in a series; 1st **2** earliest **3** foremost, as in rank or quality —***adv.*** **1** before any other person or thing **2** for the first time **3** sooner; preferably —***n.*** **1** any person or thing that is first **2** the beginning **3** a first happening or thing of its kind **4** the winning place, as in a race **5** the slowest forward gear ratio of a motor vehicle transmission

first aid emergency treatment for injury or sudden illness, before regular medical care is available —**first'-aid'** ***adj.***

first'born' ***adj.*** born first in a family; oldest —***n.*** the firstborn child

first'-class' ***adj.*** **1** of the highest class, quality, etc. **2** designating the most expensive accommodations **3** designating or of the most expensive class of ordinary mail —***adv.*** **1** with first-class accommodations **2** as or by first-class mail

first family [*often* **F- F-**] the family of the U.S. president

first'hand' ***adj.***, ***adv.*** from the original producer or source; direct

first lady [*often* **F- L-**] the wife of the U.S. president

first lieutenant a military officer ranking just above a second lieutenant

first'ly ***adv.*** in the first place; first

first person the form of a pronoun or verb that refers to the speaker or writer

first'-rate' ***adj.*** highest in rank, quality, etc. —***adv.*** [Inf.] very well

first'-string' ***adj.*** [Inf.] *Sports* that is the first choice for regular play at a specified position

firth (fɚrth) ***n.*** ⟦< ON *fjörthr*⟧ a narrow inlet or arm of the sea

fis·cal (fis'kəl) ***adj.*** ⟦< L *fiscus*, public chest⟧ **1** relating to the public treasury or revenues **2** financial **3** designating or of government policies of spending and taxation —**fis'cal·ly** ***adv.***

fish (fish) ***n.***, *pl.* **fish** or (for different species) **fish'es** ⟦OE *fisc*⟧ **1** any of a large group of coldblooded vertebrate animals living in water and having fins, gills for breathing, and, usually, scales **2** the flesh of a fish used as food —***vi.*** **1** to catch or try to catch fish **2** to try to get something indirectly: often with *for* —***vt.*** to grope for, find, and bring to view: often with *out*

fish'er ***n.*** **1** the largest marten, having very dark fur **2** this fur

fish'er·man (-mən) ***n.***, *pl.* **-men** (-mən) **1** a person who fishes for sport or for a living **2** a commercial fishing vessel

fish'er·y ***n.***, *pl.* **-ies** **1** the business of catching, selling, etc. fish **2** a place where fish, etc. are caught or bred

fish'hook' ***n.*** a hook, usually barbed, for catching fish

fish'ing ***n.*** the catching of fish for sport or for a living

fish meal ground, dried fish, used as fertilizer or fodder

fish'wife' ***n.***, *pl.* **-wives'** a coarse, scolding woman

fish'y ***adj.*** **-i·er**, **-i·est** **1** like a fish in odor, taste, etc. **2** dull or expressionless *[fishy eyes]* **3** [Inf.] questionable; odd —**fish'i·ly** ***adv.*** —**fish'i·ness** ***n.***

fis·sion (fish'ən, fizh'-) ***n.*** ⟦< L *findere*, to split⟧ **1** a splitting apart; cleavage **2** NUCLEAR FISSION —**fis'sion·a·ble** ***adj.***

fis·sure (fish'ər) ***n.*** ⟦see prec.⟧ a cleft or crack

fist (fist) ***n.*** ⟦OE *fyst*⟧ a hand with the fingers closed tightly into the palm

fist·i·cuffs (fis′ti kufs′) ***pl.n.*** [Old-fashioned] a fight with the fists

fis·tu·la (fis′tyo͞o lə, -chə lə) ***n.***, *pl.* **-las** or **-lae′** (-lē′) ⟦L, a pipe, ulcer⟧ an abnormal passage, as from an abscess to the skin

fit[1] (fit) ***vt.*** **fit′ted** or **fit, fit′ting** ⟦ME *fitten*⟧ **1** to be suitable to **2** to be the proper size, shape, etc. for **3** to adjust so as to fit **4** to equip; outfit —***vi.*** **1** [Archaic] to be suitable or proper **2** to have the proper size or shape —***adj.*** **fit′ter, fit′test 1** suited to some purpose, function, etc. **2** proper; right **3** healthy **4** [Inf.] inclined *[she was fit to scream]* —***n.*** the manner of fitting *[a tight fit]* —**fit′ly *adv.*** —**fit′ness *n.*** —**fit′ter *n.***

fit[2] (fit) ***n.*** ⟦OE *fitt*, conflict⟧ **1** any sudden, uncontrollable attack, as of coughing **2** an outburst, as of anger **3** a seizure involving convulsions, loss of consciousness, etc. —**by fits** (**and starts**) in an irregular way —**have** (or **throw**) **a fit** [Inf.] to become very angry or upset

fit′ful (-fəl) ***adj.*** characterized by intermittent activity; spasmodic —**fit′ful·ly *adv.*** —**fit′ful·ness *n.***

fit′ting *adj.* suitable; proper —***n.*** **1** an adjustment or trying on of clothes, etc. **2** a small part used to join or adapt other parts **3** [*pl.*] fixtures

five (fīv) ***adj., n.*** ⟦OE *fif*⟧ one more than four; 5; V

five′-and-ten′-cent′ store a store that sells a wide variety of inexpensive merchandise: also **five′-and-ten′ *n.***

five′-star′ *adj.* having the highest rating, based on a given set of criteria for excellence

fix (fiks) ***vt.*** **fixed, fix′ing** ⟦< L *figere*, fasten⟧ **1** to fasten firmly **2** to set firmly in the mind **3** to direct (one's eyes) steadily at something **4** to make rigid **5** to make permanent **6** to establish (a date, etc.) definitely **7** to set in order; adjust **8** to repair **9** to prepare (food or meals) **10** [Inf.] to influence the result or action of (a race, jury, etc.), as by bribery **11** [Inf.] to punish —***vi.*** **1** to become fixed **2** [Inf. or Dial.] to prepare or intend —***n.*** **1** the position of a ship, etc. determined from the bearings of two known positions **2** [Inf.] a predicament **3** [Slang] a contest, etc. that has been fixed **4** [Slang] an injection of a narcotic by an addict —**fix up** [Inf.] **1** to repair **2** to arrange; set in order —**fix′a·ble *adj.*** —**fix′er *n.***

fix·a·tion (fik sā′shən) ***n.*** **1** a fixing or being fixed **2** an obsession **3** a remaining at an early stage of psychosexual development

fix·a·tive (fik′sə tiv) ***adj.*** that is able or tends to make permanent, prevent fading, etc. —***n.*** a fixative substance

fixed (fikst) ***adj.*** **1** firmly in place **2** established; settled **3** resolute; unchanging **4** persistent *[a fixed idea]* —**fix·ed·ly** (fiks′id lē) ***adv.***

fix·ings (fik′siŋz′) ***pl.n.*** [Inf.] accessories or trimmings *[turkey and all the fixings]*

fix·i·ty (fik′si tē) ***n.*** the quality or state of being fixed or steady

fix·ture (fiks′chər) ***n.*** ⟦see FIX⟧ **1** anything firmly in place **2** any attached piece of equipment in a house, etc. **3** a person long established in a job, etc.

fizz (fiz) ***n.*** ⟦? akin to fol.⟧ **1** a hissing, sputtering sound **2** an effervescent drink —***vi.*** **1** to make a hissing sound **2** to effervesce

fiz·zle (fiz′əl) ***vi.*** **-zled, -zling** ⟦< ME⟧ **1** FIZZ (*vi.* 1) **2** [Inf.] to fail, esp. after a good start —***n.*** **1** a hissing sound **2** [Inf.] a failure

fl *abbrev.* **1** floor **2** ⟦L *floruit*⟧ (he or she) flourished **3** fluid

FL *abbrev.* Florida

flab (flab) ***n.*** ⟦< FLABBY⟧ [Inf.] sagging flesh

flab·ber·gast (flab′ər gast′) ***vt.*** ⟦18th-c. slang < ?⟧ to dumbfound

flab·by (flab′ē) ***adj.*** **-bi·er, -bi·est** ⟦< FLAP⟧ **1** limp and soft **2** weak —**flab′bi·ly *adv.*** —**flab′bi·ness *n.***

flac·cid (flak′sid, flas′id) ***adj.*** ⟦< L *flaccus*⟧ soft and limp; flabby

flack (flak) ***n.*** ⟦< ?⟧ [Slang] PRESS AGENT —**flack′er·y *n.***

fla·con (flak′ən; *Fr* flȧ kōn′) ***n.***, *pl.* **-cons** (-ənz; -kōn′) ⟦Fr⟧ a small flask with a stopper, as for perfume

flag[1] (flag) ***n.*** ⟦< FLAG[4], in obs. sense "to flutter"⟧ a cloth with colors, patterns, etc., used as a symbol of a nation, state, etc., or as a signal —***vt.*** **flagged, flag′ging 1** to signal with or as with a flag; esp., to signal to stop: often with *down* **2** to mark with a symbol

flag[2] (flag) ***n.*** ⟦< ON *flaga*, slab of stone⟧ FLAGSTONE

flag[3] (flag) ***n.*** ⟦ME *flagge*⟧ any of various irises, or a flower or leaf of one

flag[4] (flag) ***vi.*** **flagged, flag′ging** ⟦prob. < ON *flǫgra*, to flutter⟧ **1** to become limp; droop **2** to grow weak or tired

flag·el·late (flaj′ə lāt′) ***vt.*** **-lat′ed, -lat′ing** ⟦< L *flagellum*, a whip⟧ to whip; flog —**flag′el·la′tion *n.***

fla·gel·lum (flə jel′əm) ***n.***, *pl.* **-la** (-ə) or **-lums** ⟦L, a whip⟧ a whiplike part of some cells, as of bacteria or protozoans, used as for moving about

flag·on (flag′ən) ***n.*** ⟦< LL *flasco*⟧ a container for liquids, with a handle, a narrow neck, a spout, and, often, a lid

flag′pole′ *n.* a pole on which a flag is raised and flown: also **flag′staff′**

fla·grant (flā′grənt) ***adj.*** ⟦< L *flagrare*, to blaze⟧ glaringly bad; outrageous —**fla′gran·cy** (-grən sē) or **fla′grance *n.*** —**fla′grant·ly *adv.***

flag′ship′ *n.* **1** the ship that carries the commander of a fleet or other large naval unit **2** the largest or most important member or part, as of a group

flag′stone′ *n.* a flat paving stone

flail (flāl) ***n.*** ⟦< L *flagellum*, a whip⟧ a farm tool for threshing grain by hand —***vt., vi.*** **1** to thresh with a flail **2** to beat **3** to move (one's arms) like flails

flair (fler) ***n.*** ⟦< L *fragrare*, to smell⟧ **1** a natural talent; aptitude **2** a sense of style; dash

flak (flak) ***n.*** ⟦Ger acronym⟧ **1** the fire of antiaircraft guns **2** [Inf.] strong criticism Also sp. **flack**

flake (flāk) ***n.*** ⟦< Scand⟧ **1** a small, thin mass **2** a piece split off; chip **—*vt.*, *vi.* flaked, flak'ing 1** to form into flakes **2** to peel off in flakes

flak'y ***adj.*** **-i·er, -i·est 1** of or producing flakes **2** [Slang] eccentric

flam·bé (fläm bā') ***adj.*** ⟦Fr⟧ served with a sauce of flaming brandy, rum, etc. —***n.*** a dessert so served

flam·boy·ant (flam boi'ənt) ***adj.*** ⟦Fr < L *flamma*, a flame⟧ **1** flamelike or brilliant **2** too showy or ornate **—flam·boy'ance** or **flam·boy'an·cy *n.* —flam·boy'ant·ly *adv.***

flame (flām) ***n.*** ⟦< L *flamma*⟧ **1** the burning gas of a fire, appearing as a tongue of light **2** the state of burning with a blaze **3** a thing like a flame **4** an intense emotion **5** a sweetheart —***vi.* flamed, flam'ing 1** to burst into flame **2** to grow red or hot **3** to become excited —***vt.*** [Inf.] to attack, as by e-mail

fla·men·co (flə meŋ'kō) ***n.*** ⟦Sp⟧ a Spanish gypsy style of dance or music

flame'out' ***n.*** **1** a failure of combustion in a jet's engine during flight **2** a sudden and complete failure

flame'throw'er ***n.*** a weapon that shoots flaming oil, napalm, etc.

fla·min·go (flə miŋ'gō') ***n.***, *pl.* **-gos'** or **-goes'** ⟦Port⟧ a tropical wading bird with long legs and pink or red feathers

flam·ma·ble (flam'ə bəl) ***adj.*** easily set on fire; that will burn readily or quickly **—flam'ma·bil'i·ty *n.***

Flan·ders (flan'dərz) region in NW Europe, in France & Belgium

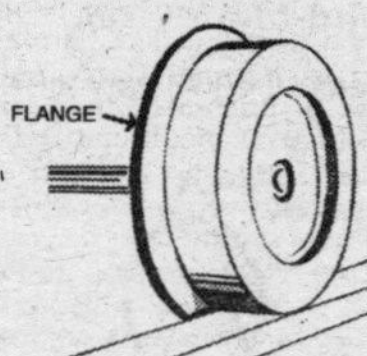

flange (flanj) ***n.*** ⟦< ? ME⟧ a projecting rim on a wheel, etc., that serves to hold it in place, give it strength, etc.

flank (flaŋk) ***n.*** ⟦< OFr *flanc*⟧ **1** the side of an animal between the ribs and the hip **2** the side of anything **3** *Mil.* the right or left side of a formation or force —***vt.* 1** to be at the side of **2** *Mil.* to attack, or pass around, the side of (enemy troops)

flan·nel (flan'əl) ***n.*** ⟦prob. < Welsh *gwlan*, wool⟧ **1** a loosely woven cloth of wool or cotton **2** [*pl.*] trousers, etc. made of this

flan·nel·ette or **flan·nel·et** (flan'əl et') ***n.*** a soft, napped cotton cloth

flap (flap) ***n.*** ⟦ME *flappe*⟧ **1** anything flat and broad hanging loose at one end **2** the motion or sound of a swinging flap **3** [Inf.] a commotion; stir **—*vt.* flapped, flap'ping 1** to slap **2** to move back and forth or up and down

flap'jack' ***n.*** a pancake

flap'per ***n.*** [Inf.] in the 1920s, a bold, unconventional young woman

flare (fler) ***vi.* flared, flar'ing** ⟦ME *fleare* < ?⟧ **1** *a)* to blaze brightly *b)* to burn unsteadily **2** to burst out suddenly, as in anger: often with *up* or *out* **3** to curve outward, as a bell's rim —***n.* 1** a bright, unsteady blaze **2** a brightly flaming light for signaling, etc. **3** an outburst, as of emotion **4** a curving outward

flare'-up' ***n.*** a sudden outburst of flame or of anger, trouble, etc.

flash (flash) ***vi.*** ⟦ME *flashen*, to splash⟧ **1** to send out a sudden, brief light **2** to sparkle **3** to come or pass suddenly —***vt.* 1** to cause to flash **2** to send (news, etc.) swiftly **3** [Inf.] to display or expose briefly —***n.* 1** a sudden, brief light **2** a brief moment **3** a sudden, brief display **4** a brief item of late news **5** a gaudy display —***adj.*** happening swiftly or suddenly **—flash'er *n.***

flash'back' ***n.*** **1** an interruption in the continuity of a story, etc. by the telling or showing of an earlier episode **2** a sudden, vivid recollection of a past event

flash'bulb' ***n.*** a bulb giving a brief, bright light, for taking photographs

flash'cube' ***n.*** a rotating cube with flashbulbs in four sides

flash'-for'ward ***n.*** an interruption in the continuity of a story, etc. by the telling or showing of a future episode

flash'ing ***n.*** sheets of metal used to weatherproof roof joints or edges

flash'light' ***n.*** a portable electric light

flash point the lowest temperature at which vapor, as of an oil, will ignite with a flash

flash'y ***adj.*** **-i·er, -i·est 1** dazzling **2** gaudy; showy **—flash'i·ness *n.***

flask (flask) ***n.*** ⟦< L *flasca*, bottle⟧ **1** any bottle-shaped container used in laboratories, etc. **2** a small, flat container for liquor, etc., to be carried in the pocket

flat[1] (flat) ***adj.* flat'ter, flat'test** ⟦< ON *flatr*⟧ **1** having a smooth, level surface **2** lying spread out **3** broad, even, and thin **4** absolute *[a flat denial]* **5** not fluctuating *[a flat rate]* **6** tasteless; insipid **7** not interesting **8** emptied of air *[a flat tire]* **9** without gloss *[flat paint]* **10** *Music a)* lower in pitch by a half step *b)* below true pitch —***adv.* 1** in a flat manner or position **2** exactly **3** *Music* below true pitch —***n.* 1** anything flat, esp. a surface, part, or expanse **2** a deflated tire **3** *Music a)* a note one half step below another *b)* the symbol (♭) for this **—*vt.* flat'ted, flat'ting** *Music* to make flat —***vi.*** to sing or play below true pitch **—fall flat** to fail in the desired effect **—flat'ly *adv.* —flat'ness *n.* —flat'tish *adj.***

flat[2] (flat) ***n.*** ⟦< Scot dial. *flet*, floor⟧ [Chiefly Brit.] an apartment or suite of rooms

flat'bed' ***n.*** a truck, trailer, etc. having a bed or platform without sides or stakes

flat'boat' ***n.*** a flat-bottomed boat for carrying freight in shallow bodies of water or on rivers

flat′car′ *n.* a railroad freight car without sides or a roof

flat′fish′ *n., pl.* **-fish′** or (for different species) **-fish′es** a fish having both eyes and mouth on the upper side of a very flat body

flat′foot′ *n.* **1** a condition of the foot in which the instep arch is flattened **2** *pl.* **-foots′** or **-feet′** [Slang] a policeman —**flat′-foot′ed** *adj.*

flat′i′ron *n.* an iron for clothes

flat′-out′ *adj.* [Inf.] **1** at full speed, with maximum effort, etc. **2** absolute; thorough

flat·ten (flat′′n) *vt., vi.* to make or become flat or flatter

flat·ter (flat′ər) *vt.* ⟦< OFr *flater*, to smooth⟧ **1** to praise insincerely **2** to try to please, as by praise **3** to make seem more attractive than is so **4** to gratify the vanity of —**flat′ter·er** *n.* —**flat′ter·ing·ly** *adv.* —**flat′ter·y** *n.*

flat′top′ *n.* [Slang] **1** an aircraft carrier **2** a haircut in which the hair on top of the head is cut so as to form a flat surface

flat·u·lent (flach′ə lənt) *adj.* ⟦see fol.⟧ **1** having or producing gas in the stomach or intestines **2** pompous —**flat′u·lence** *n.*

fla·tus (flāt′əs) *n.* ⟦L < *flare*, to blow⟧ intestinal gas

flat′ware′ *n.* knives, forks, and spoons

flat′worm′ *n.* any of various worms with flat bodies, as the tapeworm

Flau·bert (flō ber′), **Gus·tave** (güs tàv′) 1821-80; Fr. novelist

flaunt (flônt) *vi.* ⟦? < dial. *flant*, to strut⟧ to make a gaudy or defiant display —*vt.* **1** to show off proudly or defiantly **2** FLOUT: usage objected to by many —**flaunt′ing·ly** *adv.*

flau·tist (flôt′ist, flout′-) *n.* ⟦< It⟧ *var. of* FLUTIST

fla·vor (flā′vər) *n.* ⟦ult. < L *flare*, to blow⟧ **1** that quality of a substance that is a mixing of its characteristic taste and smell **2** flavoring **3** characteristic quality —*vt.* to give flavor to Brit. sp. **fla′vour** —**fla′vor·ful** *adj.* —**fla′vor·less** *adj.*

fla′vor·ing *n.* an essence, extract, etc. that adds flavor to food or drink

flaw (flô) *n.* ⟦ME, a flake, splinter⟧ **1** a crack, etc. as in a gem **2** a fault, as in reasoning —**flaw′less** *adj.* —**flaw′less·ly** *adv.* —**flaw′less·ness** *n.*

flax (flaks) *n.* ⟦< OE *fleax*⟧ **1** a slender, erect plant with delicate blue flowers: its seed (**flax′seed′**) is used to make linseed oil **2** the fibers of this plant, which are spun into linen thread

flax·en (flak′sən) *adj.* **1** of or made of flax **2** pale-yellow

flay (flā) *vt.* ⟦OE *flean*⟧ **1** to strip off the skin of, as by whipping **2** to criticize harshly

flea (flē) *n.* ⟦OE *fleah*⟧ a small, wingless jumping insect that is a bloodsucking parasite as an adult

flea market an outdoor bazaar dealing mainly in cheap, secondhand goods

fleck (flek) *n.* ⟦ON *flekkr*⟧ a spot, speck, or flake —*vt.* to spot; speckle

fled (fled) *vi., vt. pt. & pp. of* FLEE

fledg·ling (flej′liŋ) *n.* ⟦< ME *flegge*, ready to fly⟧ **1** a young bird just able to fly **2** a young, inexperienced person Also, chiefly Brit., **fledge′ling**

flee (flē) *vi.* **fled**, **flee′ing** ⟦OE *fleon*⟧ **1** to go swiftly or escape, as from danger **2** to pass away swiftly —*vt.* to run away or try to escape from

fleece (flēs) *n.* ⟦OE *fleos*⟧ **1** the wool covering a sheep or similar animal **2** a soft, warm, napped fabric —*vt.* **fleeced**, **fleec′ing** **1** to shear the fleece from **2** to swindle —**fleec′er** *n.*

fleec·y (flēs′ē) *adj.* **-i·er**, **-i·est** of or like fleece; soft and light —**fleec′i·ness** *n.*

fleet[1] (flēt) *n.* ⟦OE *fleot*⟧ **1** a number of warships under one command **2** any group of ships, trucks, etc. under one control

fleet[2] (flēt) *adj.* ⟦< OE *fleotan*, to float⟧ swift; rapid —**fleet′ness** *n.*

fleet′ing *adj.* passing swiftly —**fleet′ing·ly** *adv.* —**fleet′ing·ness** *n.*

Flem·ish (flem′ish) *adj.* of Flanders or its people, language, etc. —*n.* the West Germanic language of Flanders

flesh (flesh) *n.* ⟦OE *flæsc*⟧ **1** the soft substance of the body; esp., the muscular tissue **2** meat **3** the pulpy part of fruits and vegetables **4** the body as distinct from the soul **5** all humankind **6** yellowish pink —**in the flesh** **1** alive **2** in person —**one's (own) flesh and blood** one's close relatives —**flesh′y**, **-i·er**, **-i·est**, *adj.*

flesh′-and-blood′ *adj.* **1** alive **2** actual **3** present; in person

flesh′ly *adj.* **-li·er**, **-li·est** **1** of the body; corporeal **2** sensual

FLEUR-DE-LIS

fleur-de-lis (flur′də lē′) *n., pl.* **fleurs-de-lis** (flur′ də lē′, -lēz′) ⟦< OFr *flor de lis*, lit., flower of the lily⟧ a lilylike emblem: the coat of arms of the former French royal family

flew (flo͞o) *vi., vt. pt. of* FLY[1]

flex (fleks) *vt., vi.* ⟦< L *flectere*, to bend⟧ **1** to bend (an arm, knee, etc.) **2** to shorten and thicken (a muscle) in action

flex·i·ble (flek′sə bəl) *adj.* **1** able to bend without breaking; pliant **2** easily influenced **3** adjustable to change —

flex'i·bil'i·ty *n.*

flex'time' *n.* a system allowing individual employees some flexibility in choosing when they work

flib·ber·ti·gib·bet (flib'ər tē jib'it) *n.* ⟦< ?⟧ a frivolous, flighty person

flick[1] (flik) *n.* ⟦echoic⟧ a light, quick stroke —*vt.* to strike, remove, etc. with a light, quick stroke

flick[2] (flik) *n.* ⟦< fol.⟧ [Slang] a film —**the flicks** [Slang] a showing of a film

flick·er (flik'ər) *vi.* ⟦OE *flicorian*⟧ **1** to move with a quick, light, wavering motion **2** to burn or shine unsteadily —*n.* **1** a flickering **2** a dart of flame or light

fli·er (flī'ər) *n.* **1** a thing that flies **2** an aviator **3** a bus, train, etc. with a fast schedule **4** a widely distributed handbill **5** [Inf.] a reckless gamble

flight[1] (flīt) *n.* ⟦OE *flyht*⟧ **1** the act, manner, or power of flying **2** the distance flown **3** a group of things flying together **4** an airplane scheduled to fly a certain trip **5** a trip by airplane **6** a soaring above the ordinary *[a flight of fancy]* **7** a set of stairs, as between landings

flight[2] (flīt) *n.* ⟦< OE *fleon*, flee⟧ a fleeing from or as from danger

flight attendant an airplane attendant who sees to passengers' comfort and safety

flight'less *adj.* not able to fly

flight'y *adj.* **-i·er, -i·est** **1** given to sudden whims; frivolous **2** easily excited, upset, etc. —**flight'i·ness** *n.*

flim·sy (flim'zē) *adj.* **-si·er, -si·est** ⟦< ?⟧ **1** easily broken or damaged; frail **2** ineffectual *[a flimsy excuse]* —**flim'si·ly** *adv.* —**flim'si·ness** *n.*

flinch (flinch) *vi.* ⟦< OFr *flenchir*⟧ to draw back from a blow or anything difficult or painful —*n.* a flinching

fling (fliŋ) *vt.* **flung, fling'ing** ⟦< ON *flengja*, to whip⟧ **1** to throw, esp. with force; hurl **2** to put abruptly or violently **3** to move (one's limbs, head, etc.) suddenly —*n.* **1** a flinging **2** a brief time of wild pleasures **3** a spirited dance **4** [Inf.] a try **5** [Inf.] a brief love affair

flint (flint) *n.* ⟦OE⟧ a very hard, siliceous rock, usually gray, that produces sparks when struck against steel —**flint'y, -i·er, -i·est,** *adj.*

flip[1] (flip) *vt.* **flipped, flip'ping** ⟦echoic⟧ **1** to toss with a quick jerk; flick **2** to snap (a coin) into the air with the thumb **3** to turn or turn over —*vi.* **1** to move jerkily **2** [Slang] to lose self-control —*n.* a flipping —**flip one's lid** (or **wig**) [Slang] to go berserk

flip[2] (flip) *adj.* **flip'per, flip'pest** [Inf.] flippant

flip chart a series of large paper sheets containing information, charts, etc., fastened loosely for sequential display

flip'pant (-ənt) *adj.* ⟦prob. < FLIP[1]⟧ frivolous and disrespectful; saucy —**flip'pan·cy,** *pl.* **-cies,** *n.* —**flip'pant·ly** *adv.*

flip'per (-ər) *n.* ⟦< FLIP[1]⟧ **1** a broad, flat limb adapted for swimming, as in seals **2** a paddlelike rubber device worn on each foot by skin divers, etc.

flirt (flurt) *vt.* ⟦< ?⟧ to move jerkily *[the bird flirted its tail]* —*vi.* **1** to pay amorous attention to someone, without serious intentions **2** to trifle or toy *[to flirt with an idea]* —*n.* **1** a quick, jerky movement **2** one who flirts with others

flir·ta·tion (flər tā'shən) *n.* a frivolous love affair —**flir·ta'tious** *adj.*

flit (flit) *vi.* **flit'ted, flit'ting** ⟦< ON *flytja*⟧ to pass or fly lightly and rapidly

float (flōt) *n.* ⟦< OE *flota*, a ship⟧ **1** anything that stays on the surface of a liquid, as a raftlike platform for swimmers, a cork on a fishing line, etc. **2** a floating ball, etc. that regulates a valve, as in a water tank **3** a low, flat vehicle decorated for exhibit in a parade **4** a beverage with ice cream floating in it —*vi.* **1** to stay on the surface of a liquid **2** to drift easily on water, in air, etc. **3** to move about aimlessly **4** to fluctuate freely: said of exchange rates —*vt.* **1** to cause to float **2** to put into circulation *[to float a bond issue]* **3** to arrange for (a loan) —**float'er** *n.*

flock (fläk) *n.* ⟦OE *flocc*⟧ **1** a group of certain animals, as sheep, birds, etc., living or feeding together **2** any group, esp. a large one —*vi.* to assemble or travel in a flock or crowd

flock·ing (fläk'iŋ) *n.* ⟦< L *floccus*, tuft of wool⟧ **1** tiny fibers of wool, rayon, etc. applied to a fabric, wallpaper, etc. as a velvetlike surface: also **flock** **2** such a fabric, etc.

floe (flō) *n.* ⟦? < Norw *flo*, layer⟧ ICE FLOE

flog (fläg, flôg) *vt.* **flogged, flog'ging** ⟦? < L *flagellare*, to whip⟧ to beat with a stick, whip, etc. —**flog'ger** *n.*

flood (flud) *n.* ⟦OE *flod*⟧ **1** an overflowing of water on an area normally dry **2** the rising of the tide **3** a great outpouring, as of words —*vt.* **1** to cover or fill, as with a flood **2** to put too much water, fuel, etc. on or in —*vi.* **1** to gush out in a flood **2** to become flooded —**the Flood** *Bible* the great flood in Noah's time

flood'light' *n.* **1** a lamp that casts a broad beam of bright light **2** such a beam of light —*vt.* **-light'ed** or **-lit', -light'ing** to illuminate by a floodlight

flood tide the rising tide

floor (flôr) *n.* ⟦OE *flor*⟧ **1** the inside bottom surface of a room **2** the bottom surface of anything *[the ocean floor]* **3** a story in a building **4** the right to speak in an assembly —*vt.* **1** to furnish with a floor **2** to knock down **3** [Inf.] *a)* to defeat *b)* to flabbergast; astound

floor'board' *n.* **1** a board in a floor **2** the floor of an automobile, etc.

floor exercise any gymnastic exercise done without apparatus

floor'ing *n.* **1** a floor or floors **2** material for making a floor

floor show a show presenting singers, dancers, etc., as in a nightclub

flop (fläp) *vt.* **flopped, flop'ping** ⟦var. of FLAP⟧ to flap or throw noisily and clumsily —*vi.* **1** to move, drop, or flap around loosely or clumsily **2** [Inf.] to fail —*n.* **1** the act or sound of flopping **2** [Inf.] a failure —**flop'py**, **-pi·er**, **-pi·est**, *adj.*

flop'house' *n.* [Inf.] a cheap hotel for indigents

floppy disk a small, flexible computer disk for storing data

flo·ra (flôr'ə) *n.* ⟦L < *flos*, a flower⟧ the plants of a specified region or time

flo'ral (-əl) *adj.* of or like flowers

Flor·ence (flôr'əns) city in central Italy: pop. 403,000 —**Flor'en·tine'** (-ən tēn') *adj.*, *n.*

flo·res·cence (flō res'əns) *n.* ⟦< L *flos*, a flower⟧ a blooming or flowering —**flo·res'cent** *adj.*

flor·id (flôr'id) *adj.* ⟦< L *flos*, a flower⟧ **1** ruddy: said of the complexion **2** gaudy; showy; ornate

Flor·i·da (flôr'ə də, flär'-) Southern state of the SE U.S.: 53,937 sq. mi.; pop. 12,938,000; cap. Tallahassee: abbrev. *FL* —**Flo·rid·i·an** (flô rid'ē ən) or **Flor'i·dan** *adj.*, *n.*

flor·in (flôr'in) *n.* ⟦< L *flos*, a flower⟧ any of various European or South African silver or gold coins

flo·rist (flôr'ist) *n.* ⟦< L *flos*, a flower⟧ one who grows or sells flowers

floss (flôs, fläs) *n.* ⟦ult. < L *floccus*, tuft of wool⟧ **1** the short, downy waste fibers of silk **2** a soft, loosely twisted thread or yarn, as of silk, for embroidery **3** a substance like this **4** DENTAL FLOSS —*vt.*, *vi.* to clean (the teeth) with dental floss —**floss'y**, **-i·er**, **-i·est**, *adj.*

flo·ta·tion (flō tā'shən) *n.* the act or condition of floating

flo·til·la (flō til'ə) *n.* ⟦Sp, dim. of *flota*, a fleet⟧ **1** a small fleet **2** a fleet of boats or small ships

flot·sam (flät'səm) *n.* ⟦< MDu *vloten*, to float⟧ the wreckage of a ship or its cargo floating at sea: used in the phrase **flotsam and jetsam**

flounce[1] (flouns) *vi.* **flounced**, **flounc'ing** ⟦< ? Scand⟧ to move with quick, flinging motions of the body, as in anger —*n.* a flouncing

flounce[2] (flouns) *n.* ⟦< OFr *froncir*, to wrinkle⟧ a wide ruffle sewn to a skirt, sleeve, etc. —**flounc'y**, **-i·er**, **-i·est**, *adj.*

floun·der[1] (floun'dər) *vi.* ⟦< ? FOUNDER⟧ **1** to struggle awkwardly, as in deep mud **2** to speak or act in an awkward, confused manner

floun·der[2] (floun'dər) *n.* ⟦< Scand⟧ any of various flatfishes caught for food, as the halibut

flour (flour) *n.* ⟦orig., flower (i.e., best) of meal⟧ **1** a fine, powdery substance produced by grinding and sifting grain, esp. wheat **2** any finely powdered substance —**flour'y** *adj.*

flour·ish (flur'ish) *vi.* ⟦< L *flos*, a flower⟧ **1** to grow vigorously; thrive **2** to be at the peak of development, etc. —*vt.* to brandish (a sword, etc.) —*n.* **1** anything done in a showy way **2** a brandishing **3** decorative lines in handwriting **4** a musical fanfare

flout (flout) *vt.*, *vi.* ⟦< ? ME *flouten*, play the flute⟧ to mock or scoff —*n.* a scornful act or remark —**flout'er** *n.*

flow (flō) *vi.* ⟦OE *flowan*⟧ **1** to move as a liquid does **2** to move gently and smoothly **3** to pour out **4** to issue; proceed **5** to hang loose *[flowing* hair*]* **6** to be plentiful —*n.* **1** a flowing **2** the rate of flow **3** anything that flows **4** the rising of the tide

flow'chart' *n.* a diagram showing steps in a sequence of operations, as in manufacturing

flow·er (flou'ər) *n.* ⟦< L *flos*⟧ **1** the seed-producing structure of a flowering plant; blossom **2** a plant cultivated for its blossoms **3** the best or finest part —*vi.* **1** to produce blossoms **2** to reach the best stage —**in flower** flowering

flow'er·pot' *n.* a container in which to grow plants

flow'er·y *adj.* **-i·er**, **-i·est** **1** covered or decorated with flowers **2** full of ornate expressions and fine words —**flow'er·i·ness** *n.*

flown (flōn) *vi.*, *vt.* *pp. of* FLY[1]

flu (flo͞o) *n.* **1** *short for* INFLUENZA **2** a respiratory or intestinal infection caused by a virus

flub (flub) [Inf.] *vt.*, *vi.* **flubbed**, **flub'bing** ⟦< ? FL(OP) + (D)UB[1]⟧ to bungle (a job, stroke, etc.) —*n.* a blunder

fluc·tu·ate (fluk'cho͞o āt') *vi.* **-at'ed**, **-at'ing** ⟦< L *fluctus*, a wave⟧ to be continually varying in an irregular way —**fluc'tu·a'tion** *n.*

flue (flo͞o) *n.* ⟦< ? OFr *fluie*, a flowing⟧ a tube or shaft for the passage of smoke, hot air, etc., esp. in a chimney

flu·ent (flo͞o'ənt) *adj.* ⟦< L *fluere*, to flow⟧ **1** flowing or moving smoothly **2** able to write or speak easily, expressively, etc. —**flu'en·cy** *n.* —**flu'ent·ly** *adv.*

fluff (fluf) *n.* ⟦? blend of *flue*, soft mass + PUFF⟧ **1** soft, light down **2** a loose, soft mass, as of hair **3** something trivial —*vt.* **1** to shake or pat until loose or fluffy **2** to bungle (one's lines), as in acting

fluff'y *adj.* **-i·er**, **-i·est** soft and light like fluff; feathery

flu·id (flo͞o'id) *adj.* ⟦< L *fluere*, to flow⟧ **1** that can flow as a liquid or gas does **2** that can change rapidly or easily **3** available for investment or as cash —*n.* a liquid or gas —**flu·id'i·ty** *n.* —**flu'id·ly** *adv.*

fluke[1] (flo͞ok) *n.* ⟦OE *floc*, a flatfish⟧ TREMATODE

fluke[2] (flo͞ok) *n.* ⟦< ?⟧ **1** a pointed end of an anchor, which catches in the ground **2** a barb of a harpoon, etc. **3** a lobe of a whale's tail **4** [Inf.] a stroke of luck

flung (fluŋ) *vt.* *pt. & pp. of* FLING

flunk (fluŋk) *vt.*, *vi.* ⟦< ?⟧ [Inf.] to fail, as in a school assignment

flunk·y (fluŋ'kē) *n.*, *pl.* **-ies** ⟦orig. Scot⟧ **1** a toady **2** a person with menial tasks Also **flunk'ey**

fluo·resce (flô res') *vi.* **-resced'**, **-resc'ing** to produce, show, or undergo fluorescence

fluo·res'cence (-res'əns) *n.* ⟦ult. < L

fluor, flux⟧ **1** the property of producing light when acted upon by radiant energy **2** the production of such light **3** light so produced —**fluo·res'cent** ***adj.***

fluorescent lamp (or **tube**) a glass tube coated on the inside with a fluorescent substance that gives off light (**fluorescent light**) when mercury vapor in the tube is acted upon by a stream of electrons

fluo·ri·date (flôr'ə dāt', floor'-) ***vt.*** **-dat'ed, -dat'ing** to add fluorides to (a supply of drinking water) in order to reduce tooth decay —**fluo'ri·da'tion** ***n.***

fluo·ride (flôr'īd', floor'īd') ***n.*** any of various compounds of fluorine, esp. one put in toothpaste, etc. to prevent tooth decay

fluo'rine' (-ēn') ***n.*** ⟦< L *fluor*, flux⟧ a greenish-yellow, gaseous chemical element

fluo'rite' (-īt') ***n.*** ⟦< L *fluor*, flux⟧ calcium fluoride, a transparent, crystalline mineral: the principal source of fluorine

fluo'ro·car'bon (-kär'bən) ***n.*** any of certain compounds containing carbon, fluorine, and, sometimes, hydrogen

fluo'ro·scope' (-skōp') ***n.*** a machine for examining internal structures by viewing the shadows cast on a fluorescent screen by objects through which X-rays are directed

flur·ry (flur'ē) ***n.***, *pl.* **-ries** ⟦< ?⟧ **1** a sudden gust of wind, rain, or snow **2** a sudden commotion —***vt.*** **-ried, -ry·ing** to confuse; agitate

flush[1] (flush) ***vi.*** ⟦blend of FLASH & ME *flusshen*, fly up suddenly⟧ **1** to flow rapidly **2** to blush or glow **3** to be washed out with a sudden flow of water **4** to start up from cover: said of birds —***vt.*** **1** to wash out with a sudden flow of water **2** to make blush or glow **3** to excite *[flushed* with victory*]* **4** to drive (birds) from cover —***n.*** **1** a rapid flow, as of water **2** a sudden, vigorous growth **3** sudden excitement **4** a blush; glow **5** a sudden feeling of heat, as in a fever —***adj.*** **1** well supplied, esp. with money **2** abundant **3** level or even (*with*) **4** direct; full —***adv.*** **1** so as to be level **2** directly

flush[2] (flush) ***n.*** ⟦< L *fluere*, to flow⟧ a hand of cards all in the same suit

flus·ter (flus'tər) ***vt., vi.*** ⟦prob. < Scand⟧ to make or become confused —***n.*** a being flustered

flute (floot) ***n.*** ⟦< Prov *flaut*⟧ **1** a high-pitched wind instrument consisting of a long, slender tube with finger holes and keys **2** a groove in the shaft of a column, etc. —**flut'ed** ***adj.*** —**flut'ing** ***n.*** —**flut'ist** ***n.***

flut·ter (flut'ər) ***vi.*** ⟦< OE *fleotan*, to float⟧ **1** to flap the wings rapidly, without flying **2** to wave, move, or beat rapidly and irregularly —***vt.*** to cause to flutter —***n.*** **1** a fluttering movement **2** an excited or confused state —**flut'ter·y** ***adj.***

flux (fluks) ***n.*** ⟦< L *fluere*, to flow⟧ **1** a flowing **2** a continual change **3** a substance used to help metals fuse together, as in soldering

fly[1] (flī) ***vi.*** **flew, flown, fly'ing** ⟦OE *fleogan*⟧ **1** to move through the air in an aircraft or by using wings, as a bird does **2** to wave or float in the air **3** to move or pass swiftly **4** to flee **5 flied, fly'ing** *Baseball* to hit a fly —***vt.*** **1** to cause to float in the air **2** to operate (an aircraft) **3** to flee from —***n.***, *pl.* **flies** **1** a flap that conceals the zipper, etc. in a garment **2** a flap serving as the door of a tent **3** *Baseball* a ball batted high in the air **4** [*pl.*] *Theater* the space above a stage —**let fly (at)** **1** to throw (at) **2** to direct a verbal attack (at) —**on the fly** [Inf.] while in a hurry

fly[2] (flī) ***n.***, *pl.* **flies** ⟦OE *fleoge*⟧ **1** any of a large group of insects with two or four wings **2** an artificial fly used as a lure in fishing

fly'a·ble ***adj.*** suitable for flying

fly'by' or **fly'-by'** ***n.***, *pl.* **-bys'** a flight past a designated point or place by an aircraft or spacecraft

fly'-by-night' ***adj.*** financially irresponsible —***n.*** an absconding debtor

fly'-by-wire' ***adj.*** of a system for controlling an airplane or spacecraft electronically, as by computer

fly'-cast' ***vt.*** **-cast', -cast'ing** to fish by casting artificial flies

fly'catch'er ***n.*** a small bird that catches insects in flight

fly'er ***n.*** *alt. sp. of* FLIER

flying buttress a buttress connected with a wall by an arch, serving to resist outward pressure

FLYING BUTTRESS

flying colors used in **with flying colors**, with notable success

fly'ing·fish' ***n.***, *pl.* **-fish'** or (for different species) **-fish'es** a fish with winglike fins used in gliding through the air: also **flying fish**

flying saucer a UFO

fly'leaf' ***n.***, *pl.* **-leaves'** a blank leaf at the beginning or end of a book

fly'pa'per ***n.*** a sticky or poisonous paper set out to catch flies

fly'speck' ***n.*** **1** a speck of fly excrement **2** any tiny spot or petty flaw

fly'way' ***n.*** a route taken regularly by birds migrating to and from breeding grounds

fly'weight' ***n.*** a boxer who weighs 112 pounds or less

fly'wheel' ***n.*** a heavy wheel on a machine, for regulating its speed

FM[1] (ef'em') ***n.*** frequency-modulation broadcasting or sound transmission

FM[2] *abbrev.* frequency modulation

f-num·ber (ef'num'bər) ***n.*** *Photog.* a number indicating the relative aperture of a lens: a higher number means a smaller opening

foal (fōl) ***n.*** ⟦OE *fola*⟧ a young horse, mule, etc.; colt or filly —***vt., vi.*** to give birth to (a foal)

foam (fōm) ***n.*** ⟦OE *fam*⟧ **1** the whitish mass of bubbles formed on or in liquids by agitation, fermentation, etc. **2** something like foam, as frothy saliva **3** a rigid or spongy cellular mass, made from liquid rubber, plastic, etc. —***vi.*** to produce foam —**foam'y, -i·er, -i·est,** ***adj.***

fob (fäb) ***n.*** ⟦prob. < dial. Ger *fuppe*, a pocket⟧ **1** a short ribbon or chain attached to a pocket watch **2** any ornament worn on such a chain, etc.

fo·cal (fō'kəl) ***adj.*** of or at a focus

focal length the distance from the optical center of a lens to the point where the light rays converge

fo'c'sle or **fo'c's'le** (fōk'səl) *contr.* ***n.*** *phonetic sp. of* FORECASTLE

fo·cus (fō'kəs) ***n.,*** *pl.* **-cus·es** or **-ci'** (-sī') ⟦L, hearth⟧ **1** the point where rays of light, heat, etc. come together; specif., the point where rays of reflected or refracted light meet **2** FOCAL LENGTH **3** an adjustment of this to make a clear image *[bring a lens into focus]* **4** any center of activity, attention, etc. —***vt.*** **-cused** or **-cussed, -cus·ing** or **-cus·sing** **1** to bring into focus **2** to adjust the focal length of (the eye, a lens, etc.) so as to produce a clear image **3** to concentrate —**in focus** clear and sharp —**out of focus** blurred

fod·der (fäd'ər) ***n.*** ⟦OE *fodor*⟧ coarse food for cattle, horses, etc., as hay

foe (fō) ***n.*** ⟦OE *fah*, hostile⟧ an enemy

foe·tus (fēt'əs) ***n.*** *alt. sp. of* FETUS

fog (fôg, fäg) ***n.*** ⟦prob. < Scand⟧ **1** a large mass of water vapor condensed to fine particles, at or just above the earth's surface **2** a state of mental confusion —***vt., vi.*** **fogged, fog'ging** to make or become foggy

fog'gy ***adj.*** **-gi·er, -gi·est** **1** full of fog **2** dim; blurred **3** confused —**fog'gi·ness** ***n.***

fog'horn' ***n.*** a horn blown to warn ships in a fog

fo·gy (fō'gē) ***n.,*** *pl.* **-gies** ⟦< ?⟧ one who is old-fashioned: usually with *old*: also **fo'gey,** *pl.* **-geys**

foi·ble (foi'bəl) ***n.*** ⟦< Fr *faible*, feeble⟧ a small weakness in character

foil[1] (foil) ***vt.*** ⟦< OFr *fuler*, trample⟧ to keep from being successful; thwart

foil[2] (foil) ***n.*** ⟦< L *folium*, leaf⟧ **1** a very thin sheet of metal **2** a person or thing that sets off another by contrast **3** ⟦< ?⟧ a long, thin, blunted fencing sword

foist (foist) ***vt.*** ⟦prob. < dial. Du *vuisten*, to hide in the hand⟧ to get (a thing) accepted, sold, etc. by fraud, deception, etc.; palm off: with *on* or *upon*

fol *abbrev.* **1** folio(s) **2** following

fold[1] (fōld) ***vt.*** ⟦OE *faldan*⟧ **1** to double (material) up on itself **2** to draw together and intertwine *[to fold the arms]* **3** to embrace **4** to wrap up; envelop —***vi.*** **1** to be or become folded **2** [Inf.] *a)* to fail, as a business, play, etc. *b)* to fail suddenly; collapse —***n.*** a folded part

fold[2] (fōld) ***n.*** ⟦OE *fald*⟧ **1** a pen for sheep **2** a flock of sheep **3** a group sharing a common faith, goal, etc.

-fold (fōld) ⟦< OE *-feald*⟧ *suffix* **1** having (a specified number of) parts **2** (a specified number of) times as many or as much *[to profit tenfold]*

fold'a·way' ***adj.*** that can be folded together for easy storage

fold'er ***n.*** **1** a sheet of heavy paper folded for holding loose papers **2** a pamphlet or circular of one or more folded, unstitched sheets

fo·li·age (fō'lē ij) ***n.*** ⟦< L *folia*⟧ leaves, as of a plant or tree

fo·lic acid (fō'lik) ⟦< L *folium*, leaf⟧ a substance belonging to the vitamin B complex, used in treating anemia

fo·li·o (fō'lē ō') ***n.,*** *pl.* **-os'** ⟦< L *folium*, leaf⟧ **1** a large sheet of paper folded once **2** a large size of book, about 12 by 15 inches, made of sheets so folded **3** the number of a page in a book

folk (fōk) ***n.,*** *pl.* **folks** or **folk** ⟦OE *folc*⟧ **1** a people or nation **2** [*pl.*] people; persons —***adj.*** of or originating among the common people —**one's** (or **the**) **folks** [Inf.] one's family, esp. one's parents

folk'lore' ***n.*** ⟦prec. + LORE⟧ the traditional beliefs, legends, etc. of a culture

folk song **1** a song made and handed down among the common people **2** a song composed in imitation of this —**folk singer**

folk'sy (-sē) ***adj.*** **-si·er, -si·est** [Inf.] friendly or sociable

fol·li·cle (fäl'i kəl) ***n.*** ⟦< L *follis*, bellows⟧ any small sac, cavity, or gland for excretion or secretion *[a hair follicle]*

fol·low (fäl'ō) ***vt.*** ⟦< OE *folgian*⟧ **1** to come or go after **2** to pursue **3** to go along *[follow the road]* **4** to take up (a trade, etc.) **5** to result from **6** to take as a model; imitate **7** to obey **8** to watch or listen to closely **9** to be interested in developments in *[to follow local politics]* **10** to understand —***vi.*** **1** to come or go after something else in place, time, etc. **2** to result —**follow out** (or **up**) to carry out fully —**follow through** to continue and complete a stroke or action

fol'low·er ***n.*** one that follows; specif., *a)* one who follows another's teachings; disciple *b)* an attendant

fol'low·ing ***adj.*** that follows; next after —***n.*** a group of followers —***prep.*** after *[following dinner they left]*

fol'low-up' ***n.*** a letter, visit, etc. that follows as a review, addition, etc.

fol·ly (fäl'ē) ***n.,*** *pl.* **-lies** ⟦see FOOL⟧ **1** a lack of sense; foolishness **2** a foolish action or belief **3** a foolish and useless but expensive undertaking

fo·ment (fō ment') ***vt.*** ⟦< L *fovere*, keep warm⟧ to stir up (trouble); incite —**fo'men·ta'tion** ***n.***

fond (fänd) ***adj.*** ⟦< ME *fonnen*, be foolish⟧ **1** tender and affectionate; loving or doting **2** cherished *[a fond hope]* —**fond of** having a liking for —**fond'ly** ***adv.*** —**fond'ness** ***n.***

fon·dle (fän'dəl) ***vt.*** **-dled, -dling** ⟦< prec.⟧ to caress or handle lovingly

fon·due or **fon·du** (fän dōō', fän'dōō')

n. ⟦Fr < *fondre*, melt⟧ melted cheese, etc. used as a dip for cubes of bread

font[1] (fänt) **n.** ⟦< L *fons*, spring⟧ **1** a basin to hold baptismal water **2** a container for holy water **3** a source

font[2] (fänt) **n.** ⟦see FOUND[2]⟧ *Printing* a complete assortment of type in one size and style

fon·ta·nel or **fon·ta·nelle** (fänt'n el') **n.** ⟦ME *fontinel*, a hollow⟧ a soft, boneless area in the skull of a baby or young animal, that gradually closes up as bone is formed

food (fo͞od) **n.** ⟦OE *foda*⟧ **1** any substance, esp. a solid, taken in by a plant or animal to enable it to live and grow **2** anything that nourishes

food chain *Ecology* a sequence (as grass, rabbit, fox) of organisms in a community in which each member feeds on the one below it

food poisoning sickness caused by contaminants, as bacteria, in food, or by naturally poisonous foods

food processor an electrical appliance that can blend, purée, slice, grate, chop, etc. foods rapidly

food stamp any of the federal coupons given to qualifying low-income persons for use in buying food

food'stuff' **n.** any substance used as food

fool (fo͞ol) **n.** ⟦< L *follis*, windbag⟧ **1** a silly or stupid person **2** a jester **3** a victim of a trick, etc.; dupe —***vi.*** **1** to act like a fool **2** to joke **3** [Inf.] to meddle (*with*) —***vt.*** to trick; deceive —**fool around** [Inf.] to trifle —**fool'er·y** ***n.***

fool'har'dy ***adj.*** **-di·er, -di·est** foolishly daring; reckless —**fool'har'di·ly** ***adv.*** —**fool'har'di·ness** ***n.***

fool'ish ***adj.*** **1** silly; unwise **2** ridiculous **3** embarrassed —**fool'ish·ly** ***adv.*** —**fool'ish·ness** ***n.***

fool'proof' ***adj.*** so simple, well-designed, etc. as not to be mishandled, damaged, misunderstood, etc. even by a fool

fools·cap (fo͞olz'kap') **n.** ⟦from a watermark of a jester's cap⟧ a size of writing paper, 13 by 16 in. in the U.S.

foot (foot) ***n.***, *pl.* **feet** ⟦OE *fot*⟧ **1** the end part of the leg, on which one stands **2** the base or bottom *[the foot of a page]* **3** the muscular part of a mollusk used in burrowing, moving, etc. **4** a measure of length equal to 12 inches: symbol ′ **5** [*with pl. v.*] [Brit.] infantry **6** a group of syllables serving as a unit of meter in verse —***vt.*** **1** to add (a column of figures): often with *up* **2** [Inf.] to pay (costs, etc.) —**foot it** [Inf.] to dance, walk, etc. —**on foot** walking —**under foot** in the way

foot'age (-ij) **n.** **1** measurement in feet, as of film **2** a length of film that has been shot

foot'-and-mouth' disease a contagious disease of cloven-footed animals, causing blisters in the mouth and around the hoofs

foot'ball' **n.** **1** a game played on a rectangular field with an inflated, oval leather ball by two teams that try to score touchdowns **2** [Brit.] *a)* soccer *b)* rugby **3** the ball used in any of these games

foot'bridge' **n.** a bridge for pedestrians

foot'-can'dle **n.** a unit for measuring illumination

foot'ed ***adj.*** having feet of a specified number or kind *[four-footed]*

foot'fall' **n.** the sound of a footstep

foot'hill' **n.** a low hill at or near the foot of a mountain or mountain range

foot'hold' **n.** **1** a secure place for a foot, as in climbing **2** a secure position

foot'ing **n.** **1** a secure placing of the feet **2** the condition of a surface, as for walking **3** a foothold **4** a secure position **5** a basis for relationship

foot'less (-lis) ***adj.*** **1** without a foot or feet **2** without basis **3** [Inf.] clumsy; inept

foot'lights' ***pl.n.*** a row of lights along the front of a stage floor —**the footlights** the theater or the profession of acting

foot'lock'er **n.** a small trunk, usually kept at the foot of a bed

foot'loose' ***adj.*** free to go wherever, or do whatever, one likes

foot'man (-mən) ***n.***, *pl.* **-men** (-mən) a male servant who assists the butler

foot'note' **n.** **1** a note of comment or reference at the bottom of a page **2** such a note at the end of a chapter or a book **3** an additional comment, etc. —***vt.*** **-not'ed, -not'ing** to add a footnote or footnotes to

foot'path' **n.** a narrow path for use by pedestrians only

foot'-pound' **n.** a unit of energy or work, the amount required to raise one pound a distance of one foot

foot'print' **n.** **1** a mark made by a foot **2** an area, or its shape, which something affects, occupies, etc.

foot'sore' ***adj.*** having sore or tender feet, as from much walking

foot'step' **n.** **1** the distance covered in a step **2** the sound of a step **3** FOOTPRINT (sense 1) —**follow in someone's footsteps** to follow someone's example, etc.

foot'stool' **n.** a low stool for supporting the feet of a seated person

foot'wear' **n.** shoes, boots, etc.

foot'work' **n.** the act or manner of using the feet, as in boxing or dancing

fop (fäp) **n.** ⟦ME *foppe*, a fool⟧ DANDY (*n.* 1) —**fop'per·y**, *pl.* **-ies**, ***n.*** —**fop'pish** ***adj.*** —**fop'pish·ly** ***adv.***

for (fôr, fər) ***prep.*** ⟦OE⟧ **1** in place of *[use a rope for a belt]* **2** in the interest of *[to act for another]* **3** in favor of *[vote for the levy]* **4** in honor of *[a party for her]* **5** in order to be, get, have, keep, find, etc. *[walk for exercise, start for home]* **6** meant to be received by *[flowers for a friend]* **7** suitable to *[a room for sleeping]* **8** with regard to; concerning *[an ear for music]* **9** as being *[to know for a fact]* **10** considering the nature of *[cool for July]* **11** because of *[a cry for pain]* **12** at the price of *[sold for $20,000]* **13** to the length, amount, or duration of —**conj.** because; since —**for all** in spite of

for- ⟦OE⟧ *prefix* away, apart, off *[forbid, forgo]*

for·age (fôr′ij, fär′-) ***n.*** ⟦< OFr *forre,* fodder⟧ **1** food for domestic animals **2** a search for food —***vi.*** **-aged, -ag·ing 1** to search for food **2** to search for something one wants —***vt.*** to take food from; raid —**for′ag·er** ***n.***

for·ay (fôr′ā) ***vt., vi.*** ⟦< OFr *forrer,* to forage⟧ to plunder —***n.*** a raid in order to seize things

for·bear[1] (fôr ber′) ***vt.*** **-bore′, -borne′, -bear′ing** ⟦see FOR- & BEAR[1]⟧ to refrain from (doing, saying, etc.) —***vi.*** **1** to refrain **2** to control oneself under provocation

for′bear[2] ***n.*** *alt. sp. of* FOREBEAR

for·bear′ance ***n.*** **1** the act of forbearing **2** self-restraint

for·bid (fər bid′, fôr-) ***vt.*** **-bade′** (-bad′) or **-bad′, -bid′den, -bid′ding** ⟦see FOR- & BID⟧ **1** to order (a person) not to do (something); prohibit **2** to prevent

for·bid′ding ***adj.*** looking dangerous or disagreeable; repellent —**for·bid′ding·ly** ***adv.***

force (fôrs) ***n.*** ⟦< L *fortis,* strong⟧ **1** strength; power **2** physical coercion against a person or thing **3** the power to control, persuade, etc.; effectiveness **4** military power **5** any group of people organized for some activity *[a sales force]* **6** energy that causes or alters motion **7** *Law* binding power; validity —***vt.*** **forced, forc′ing 1** to make do something by force; compel **2** to break open, into, or through by force **3** to take by force; extort **4** to impose by force: with *on* or *upon* **5** to produce as by force *[to force a smile]* **6** to cause (plants, etc.) to develop faster by artificial means —**in force 1** in full strength **2** in effect; valid —**force′less** ***adj.***

forced (fôrst) ***adj.*** **1** compulsory *[forced labor]* **2** not natural; strained *[a forced smile]* **3** due to necessity *[a forced landing]* **4** at a faster pace *[a forced march]* —**forc·ed·ly** (fôrs′id lē) ***adv.***

force′-feed′ ***vt.*** **-fed′, -feed′ing** to feed as by a tube through the throat to the stomach

force′ful (-fəl) ***adj.*** full of force; powerful, vigorous, effective, etc. —**force′ful·ly** ***adv.*** —**force′ful·ness** ***n.***

for·ceps (fôr′seps′) ***n.***, *pl.* **-ceps′** ⟦L < *formus,* warm + *capere,* to take⟧ small tongs or pincers for grasping, pulling, etc.

for·ci·ble (fôr′sə bəl) ***adj.*** **1** done by force **2** having force —**for′ci·bly** ***adv.***

ford (fôrd) ***n.*** ⟦OE⟧ a shallow place in a stream, etc. where one can cross by wading —***vt.*** to cross at a ford —**ford′a·ble** ***adj.***

Ford (fôrd) **1 Ger·ald R(udolph), Jr.** (jer′əld) 1913- ; 38th president of the U.S. (1974-77) **2 Henry** 1863-1947; U.S. automobile manufacturer

fore (fôr) ***adv., adj.*** ⟦OE⟧ at, in, or toward the front part, as of a ship —***n.*** the front —***interj.*** *Golf* a shout warning that one is about to hit the ball

fore- ⟦OE⟧ *prefix* **1** before in time, place, etc. *[forenoon]* **2** the front part of *[forehead]*

fore-and-aft (fôr′ən aft′) ***adj.*** *Naut.* from the bow to the stern; set lengthwise, as sails

fore′arm′[1] ***n.*** the part of the arm between the elbow and the wrist

fore·arm′[2] ***vt.*** to arm in advance

fore′bear′ (-ber′) ***n.*** ⟦< FORE + BE + -ER⟧ an ancestor

fore·bode′ (-bōd′) ***vt., vi.*** **-bod′ed, -bod′ing** ⟦< OE⟧ **1** to foretell; predict **2** to have a presentiment of (something bad) —**fore·bod′ing** ***n.***

fore′cast′ ***vt.*** **-cast′** or **-cast′ed, -cast′ing 1** to predict **2** to serve as a prediction of —***n.*** a prediction —**fore′cast′er** ***n.***

fore·cas·tle (fōk′səl, fôr′kas′əl) ***n.*** **1** the upper deck of a ship in front of the foremast **2** the front part of a merchant ship, where the crew's quarters are located

fore·close (fôr klōz′) ***vt., vi.*** **-closed′, -clos′ing** ⟦< OFr *fors,* outside + *clore,* CLOSE[2]⟧ to take away the right to redeem (a mortgage) —**fore·clo′sure** (-klō′zhər) ***n.***

fore·doom′ ***vt.*** to doom in advance

fore′fa′ther ***n.*** an ancestor

fore′fin′ger ***n.*** the finger nearest the thumb

fore′foot′ ***n.***, *pl.* **-feet′** either of the front feet of an animal

fore′front′ ***n.*** **1** the extreme front **2** the position of most importance, activity, etc.

fore·go′[1] ***vt., vi.*** **-went′, -gone′, -go′ing** to go before in place, time, etc.; precede

fore·go′[2] ***vt.*** *alt. sp. of* FORGO

fore′go′ing ***adj.*** previously said, written, etc.; preceding

fore·gone′ ***adj.*** **1** previous **2** previously determined; inevitable

fore′ground′ ***n.*** **1** the part of a scene, etc. nearest to the viewer **2** the most noticeable position —***vt.*** to place in the foreground; emphasize

fore′hand′ ***n.*** a stroke, as in tennis, made with the palm of the hand turned forward —***adj.*** done as with a forehand

fore·head (fôr′ed′, -hed′; fär′-) ***n.*** the part of the face between the eyebrows and the line where the hair normally begins

for·eign (fôr′in, fär′-) ***adj.*** ⟦< L *foras,* out-of-doors⟧ **1** situated outside one's own country, locality, etc. **2** of, from, or having to do with other countries **3** not belonging; not characteristic

for′eign-born′ ***adj.*** born in some other country; not native

for′eign·er ***n.*** a person from another country; alien

foreign minister a member of a governmental cabinet in charge of foreign affairs for the country

fore·know (fôr nō′) ***vt.*** **-knew′, -known′, -know′ing** to have knowledge of beforehand —**fore′knowl′edge** (-näl′ij) ***n.***

fore′leg′ ***n.*** either of the front legs of an

animal

fore'lock' *n.* a lock of hair growing just above the forehead

fore'man (-mən) *n., pl.* **-men** (-mən) **1** the chairman of a jury **2** the head of a group of workers

fore'mast' *n.* the mast nearest the bow of a ship

fore'most' *adj.* first in place, time, etc. —*adv.* first

fore'noon' *n.* the time from sunrise to noon; morning

fo·ren·sic (fə ren'sik, -zik) *adj.* ⟦< L *forum*, marketplace⟧ **1** of or suitable for public debate **2** involving the application of scientific, esp. medical, knowledge to legal matters —*n.* [*pl.*] debate or formal argumentation —**fo·ren'si·cal·ly** *adv.*

forensic medicine MEDICAL JURISPRUDENCE

fore'or·dain' *vt.* to ordain beforehand; predestine —**fore'or'di·na'tion** *n.*

fore'run'ner *n.* **1** a herald **2** a sign that tells or warns of something to follow **3** a predecessor; ancestor

fore'sail' (-sāl', -səl) *n.* the lowest sail on the foremast of a square-rigged ship or a schooner

fore·see' *vt.* **-saw', -seen', -see'ing** to see or know beforehand —**fore·see'a·ble** *adj.* —**fore·se'er** *n.*

fore·shad'ow *vt.* to indicate or suggest beforehand; prefigure

FORESHORTENED ARM

fore·short'en *vt.* in drawing, etc., to shorten some lines of (an object) to give the illusion of proper relative size

fore'sight' *n.* **1** *a)* the act of foreseeing *b)* the power to foresee **2** prudent regard or provision for the future

fore'skin' *n.* the fold of skin that covers the end of the penis

for·est (fôr'ist) *n.* ⟦< L *foris*, out-of-doors⟧ a thick growth of trees, etc. covering a large tract of land —*vt.* to plant with trees

fore·stall' *vt.* ⟦< OE *foresteall*, ambush⟧ **1** to prevent by doing something ahead of time **2** to act in advance of; anticipate

for·est·a·tion (fôr'is tā'shən, fär'-) *n.* the planting or care of forests

for'est·ed *adj.* covered with trees and underbrush

for'est·er *n.* one trained in forestry

for'est·ry *n.* the science of planting and taking care of forests

fore·taste (fôr'tāst') *n.* a taste or sample of what can be expected

fore·tell' *vt.* **-told', -tell'ing** to tell or indicate beforehand; predict

fore'thought' *n.* **1** a thinking or planning beforehand **2** foresight

for·ev·er (fôr ev'ər, fər-) *adv.* **1** for always; endlessly **2** at all times; always Also **for·ev'er·more'**

fore·warn (fôr wôrn') *vt.* to warn beforehand

fore'wom'an *n., pl.* **-wom'en** a woman serving as a foreman

fore'word *n.* an introductory statement in a book

for·feit (fôr'fit) *n.* ⟦< OFr *forfaire*, transgress⟧ **1** a fine or penalty for some crime, fault, or neglect **2** the act of forfeiting —*adj.* lost or taken away as a forfeit —*vt.* to lose or be deprived of as a forfeit

for'fei·ture (-fə chər) *n.* **1** the act of forfeiting **2** anything forfeited

for·gath·er (fôr gath'ər) *vi.* to come together; meet; assemble

for·gave (fər gāv', fôr-) *vt., vi. pt. of* FORGIVE

forge[1] (fôrj) *n.* ⟦< L *faber*, workman⟧ **1** a furnace for heating metal to be wrought **2** a place where metal is heated and wrought; smithy —*vt.* **forged, forg'ing 1** to form or shape (metal) by heating and hammering **2** to form; shape **3** to imitate (a signature) fraudulently, counterfeit (a check), etc. —*vi.* **1** to work at a forge **2** to commit forgery —**forg'er** *n.*

forge[2] (fôrj) *vi.* **forged, forg'ing** ⟦prob. < FORCE⟧ to move forward steadily: often with *ahead*

for'ger·y *n., pl.* **-ies 1** the act or crime of imitating or counterfeiting documents, signatures, etc. to deceive **2** anything forged

for·get (fər get', fôr-) *vt., vi.* **-got', -got'ten** or **-got', -get'ting** ⟦OE *forgietan*⟧ **1** to be unable to remember **2** to overlook or neglect (something) —**forget oneself** to act in an improper manner —**for·get'ta·ble** *adj.*

for·get'ful *adj.* **1** apt to forget **2** heedless or negligent —**for·get'ful·ly** *adv.* —**for·get'ful·ness** *n.*

for·get'-me-not' *n.* a marsh plant with small blue, white, or pink flowers

for·give (fər giv', fôr-) *vt., vi.* **-gave', -giv'en, -giv'ing** ⟦OE *forgiefan*⟧ **1** to give up resentment against or the desire to punish; pardon (an offense or offender) **2** to cancel (a debt) —**for·giv'a·ble** *adj.* —**for·give'ness** *n.* —**for·giv'er** *n.*

for·giv'ing *adj.* inclined to forgive —**for·giv'ing·ly** *adv.*

for·go (fôr gō') *vt.* **-went', -gone', -go'ing** ⟦OE *forgan*⟧ to do without; abstain from; give up —**for·go'er** *n.*

for·got (fər gät') *vt., vi. pt. & alt. pp. of* FORGET

for·got'ten *vt., vi. alt. pp. of* FORGET

fork (fôrk) ***n.*** ⟦< L *furca*⟧ **1** an instrument of varying size with prongs at one end, as for eating food, pitching hay, etc. **2** something like a fork in shape, etc. **3** the place where a road, etc. divides into branches **4** any of these branches —***vi.*** to divide into branches —***vt.*** to pick up or pitch with a fork —**fork over** (or **out** or **up**) [Inf.] to pay out; hand over —**fork'ful'**, *pl.* **-fuls'**, ***n.***

fork'lift' ***n.*** **1** a device for lifting heavy objects by means of projecting prongs that are slid under the load **2** a small truck with such a device

for·lorn (fôr lôrn') ***adj.*** ⟦< OE *forleosan*, lose utterly⟧ **1** abandoned **2** wretched; miserable **3** without hope —**for·lorn'ly** ***adv.***

form (fôrm) ***n.*** ⟦< L *forma*⟧ **1** shape; general structure **2** the figure of a person or animal **3** a mold **4** a particular mode, kind, type, etc. *[ice is a form of water, the forms of poetry]* **5** arrangement; style **6** a way of doing something requiring skill **7** a customary or conventional way of acting; ceremony; ritual **8** a printed document with blanks to be filled in **9** condition of mind or body **10** RACING FORM **11** a changed appearance of a word to show inflection, etc. **12** type, etc. locked in a frame for printing **13** what is expected, based on past performances *[according to form]* —***vt.*** **1** to shape; fashion **2** to train; instruct **3** to develop (habits) **4** to make up; constitute **5** to organize into *[to form a club]* —***vi.*** to be formed

-form (fôrm) ⟦< L⟧ *combining form* having the form of *[cuneiform]*

for·mal (fôr'məl) ***adj.*** ⟦< L *formalis*⟧ **1** according to fixed customs, rules, etc. **2** stiff in manner **3** *a)* designed for wear at ceremonies, etc. *b)* requiring clothes of this kind **4** done or made in explicit, definite form *[a formal contract]* **5** designating language usage characterized by expanded vocabulary, complex syntax, etc. **6** designating education in schools, etc. —***n.*** **1** a formal dance **2** a woman's evening dress —**for'mal·ly** ***adv.***

form·al·de·hyde (fôr mal'də hīd') ***n.*** ⟦FORM(IC) + *aldehyde*⟧ a pungent gas used in solution as a disinfectant and preservative

for'mal·ism' ***n.*** strict attention to outward forms and traditions

for·mal·i·ty (fôr mal'ə tē) ***n.***, *pl.* **-ties** **1** *a)* an observing of customs, rules, etc.; propriety *b)* excessive attention to convention; stiffness **2** a formal act; ceremony

for·mal·ize (fôr'mə līz') ***vt.*** **-ized', -iz'ing** **1** to shape **2** to make formal —**for'mal·i·za'tion** ***n.***

for'mal·wear' ***n.*** formal clothes, as tuxedos

for·mat (fôr'mat') ***n.*** ⟦< L *formatus*, formed⟧ **1** the shape, size, and arrangement of a book, etc. **2** the arrangement or plan, as of a TV program **3** a specific way in which computer data is stored, processed, etc. **4** a particular type of audio or video recording and playback system —***vt.*** **-mat'ted, -mat'ting** to arrange according to a format

for·ma·tion (fôr mā'shən) ***n.*** **1** a forming or being formed **2** a thing formed **3** the way in which something is formed; structure **4** an arrangement or positioning, as of troops

form·a·tive (fôr'mə tiv) ***adj.*** helping or involving formation or development

for·mer (fôr'mər) ***adj.*** ⟦ME *formere*⟧ **1** earlier; past *[in former times]* **2** being the first mentioned of two

for'mer·ly ***adv.*** in the past

form'-fit'ting ***adj.*** fitting the body closely: also **form'fit'ting**

for·mic (fôr'mik) ***adj.*** ⟦< L *formica*, ant⟧ designating a colorless acid found in ants, spiders, etc.

For·mi·ca (fôr mī'kə) *trademark for* a laminated, heat-resistant plastic used for counter tops, etc.

for·mi·da·ble (fôr'mə də bəl, fôr mid'ə bəl) ***adj.*** ⟦< L *formidare*, to dread⟧ **1** causing fear, dread, or awe **2** hard to handle

form'less ***adj.*** shapeless; amorphous

form letter a standardized letter, usually one of many, with the date, address, etc. added separately

for·mu·la (fôr'myoo lə, -myə-) ***n.***, *pl.* **-las** or **-lae'** (-lē', -lī') ⟦L < *forma*, form⟧ **1** a fixed form of words, esp. a conventional expression **2** a conventional rule for doing something **3** a prescription or recipe **4** fortified milk for a baby **5** a set of symbols expressing a mathematical rule, fact, etc. **6** *Chem.* an expression of the composition, as of a compound, using symbols and figures

for'mu·late' (-lāt') ***vt.*** **-lat'ed, -lat'ing** **1** to express in a formula **2** to express in a definite way **3** to work out in one's mind; devise —**for'mu·la'tion** ***n.*** —**for'mu·la'tor** ***n.***

for·ni·cate (fôr'ni kāt') ***vi.*** **-cat'ed, -cat'ing** ⟦< L *fornix*, a brothel⟧ to commit fornication —**for'ni·ca'tor** ***n.***

for'ni·ca'tion ***n.*** sexual intercourse between unmarried persons

for·sake (fôr sāk') ***vt.*** **-sook'** (-sook'), **-sak'en, -sak'ing** ⟦< OE *for-*, FOR- + *sacan*, to strive⟧ **1** to give up (a habit, etc.) **2** to leave; abandon

for·sooth (fôr sooth') ***adv.*** ⟦ME *forsoth*⟧ [Archaic] indeed

for·swear (fôr swer') ***vt.*** **-swore', -sworn', -swear'ing** to deny or renounce on oath —***vi.*** to commit perjury

for·syth·i·a (fôr sith'ē ə, fər-) ***n.*** ⟦after W. *Forsyth* (1737-1804), Eng botanist⟧ a shrub with yellow, bell-shaped flowers that bloom in early spring

fort (fôrt) ***n.*** ⟦< L *fortis*, strong⟧ **1** a fortified place for military defense **2** a permanent army post

forte[1] (fôrt; *often* fôr'tā') ***n.*** ⟦< OFr: see prec.⟧ that which one does particularly well

for·te[2] (fôr'tā') ***adj., adv.*** ⟦It < L *fortis*, strong⟧ [*also in italics*] *Music* loud

forth (fôrth) ***adv.*** ⟦OE⟧ **1** forward; onward **2** out into view

Forth (fôrth), **Firth of** long estuary of the

Forth River in SE Scotland

forth′com′ing *adj.* **1** about to appear; approaching **2** ready when needed **3** friendly, outgoing, etc. **4** open; frank

forth′right′ *adj.* direct and frank

forth′with′ (-with′, -with′) *adv.* at once

for·ti·fy (fôrt′ə fī′) *vt.* **-fied′**, **-fy′ing** ⟦< L *fortis*, strong + *facere*, to make⟧ **1** to strengthen physically, emotionally, etc. **2** to strengthen against attack, as with forts **3** to support **4** to add alcohol to (wine, etc.) **5** to add vitamins, etc. to (milk, etc.) —**for′ti·fi·ca′tion** *n.* —**for′ti·fi′er** *n.*

for·tis·si·mo (fôr tis′ə mō′) *adj., adv.* ⟦It, superl. of *forte*, strong⟧ [*also in italics*] *Music* very loud

for·ti·tude (fôrt′ə to͞od′) *n.* ⟦< L *fortis*, strong⟧ patient endurance of trouble, pain, etc.; courage

Fort Knox (näks) military reservation in N Kentucky: site of U.S. gold bullion depository

Fort Lau·der·dale (lô′dər dāl′) city on the SE coast of Florida: pop. 149,000

fort·night (fôrt′nīt′) *n.* ⟦< OE *feowertyn niht*, lit., fourteen nights⟧ [Chiefly Brit.] a period of two weeks —**fort′night′ly** *adj., adv.*

for·tress (fôr′tris) *n.* ⟦< L *fortis*, strong⟧ a fortified place; fort

for·tu·i·tous (fôr to͞o′ə təs) *adj.* ⟦< L *fors*, luck⟧ **1** happening by chance **2** lucky —**for·tu′i·tous·ly** *adv.*

for·tu·nate (fôr′chə nət) *adj.* **1** having good luck **2** coming by good luck; favorable —**for′tu·nate·ly** *adv.*

for·tune (fôr′chən) *n.* ⟦< L *fors*, luck⟧ **1** luck; chance; fate **2** [*also pl.*] one's future lot, good or bad **3** good luck; success **4** wealth; riches

for′tune·tell′er *n.* one who professes to foretell the future of others —**for′tune·tell′ing** *n., adj.*

Fort Wayne (wān) city in NE Indiana: pop. 173,000

Fort Worth (wurth) city in N Texas: pop. 448,000

for·ty (fôrt′ē) *adj., n., pl.* **-ties** ⟦OE *feowertig*⟧ four times ten; 40; XL —**the forties** the numbers or years, as of a century, from 40 through 49 —**for′ti·eth** (-ith) *adj.*

fo·rum (fôr′əm) *n.* ⟦L⟧ **1** the public square of an ancient Roman city **2** an assembly, program, etc. for the discussion of public matters

for·ward (fôr′wərd) *adj.* ⟦OE *foreweard*⟧ **1** at, toward, or of the front **2** advanced **3** onward; advancing **4** prompt; ready **5** bold; presumptuous **6** of or for the future —*adv.* toward the front; ahead —*n. Basketball, Hockey, etc.* a player positioned ahead of the rest of the team, esp. when on the offense —*vt.* **1** to promote **2** to send on

for′wards *adv.* FORWARD

fos·sil (fäs′əl) *n.* ⟦< L *fossilis*, dug up⟧ **1** any hardened remains of a plant or animal of a previous geologic period, preserved in the earth's crust **2** a person with outmoded ideas or ways —*adj.* **1** of or like a fossil **2** dug from the earth [*coal is a fossil fuel*] **3** antiquated

fos′sil·ize′ (-īz′) *vt., vi.* **-ized′**, **-iz′ing** **1** to change into a fossil **2** to make or become out of date, rigid, etc. —**fos′sil·i·za′tion** *n.*

fos·ter (fôs′tər) *vt.* ⟦OE *fostrian*, to nourish⟧ **1** to bring up; rear **2** to help to develop; promote —*adj.* having a specified standing in a family but not by birth or adoption [*a foster brother*]

fought (fôt) *vi., vt. pt. & pp. of* FIGHT

foul (foul) *adj.* ⟦OE *ful*⟧ **1** stinking; loathsome **2** extremely dirty **3** indecent; profane **4** wicked; abominable **5** stormy [*foul weather*] **6** tangled [*a foul rope*] **7** not within the limits or rules set **8** designating lines setting limits on a playing area **9** dishonest **10** [Inf.] unpleasant, disagreeable, etc. —*adv.* in a foul manner —*n. Sports* a hit, blow, move, etc. that is FOUL (*adj.* 7) —*vt.* **1** to make filthy **2** to dishonor **3** to obstruct [*grease fouls drains*] **4** to entangle (a rope, etc.) **5** to make a foul against, as in a game **6** *Baseball* to bat (the ball) foul —*vi.* to be or become fouled —**foul up** [Inf.] to bungle —**foul′ly** *adv.* —**foul′ness** *n.*

fou·lard (fo͞o lärd′) *n.* ⟦Fr⟧ a lightweight printed fabric of silk, etc.

foul′-up′ *n.* [Inf.] a mix-up; botch

found[1] (found) ⟦OE *funden*⟧ *vt., vi. pp. & pt. of* FIND

found[2] (found) *vt.* ⟦< L *fundus*, bottom⟧ **1** to set for support; base **2** to bring into being; set up; establish —**found′er** *n.*

found[3] (found) *vt.* ⟦< L *fundere*, pour⟧ **1** to melt and pour (metal) into a mold **2** to make by founding metal

foun·da·tion (foun dā′shən) *n.* **1** a founding or being founded; establishment **2** *a*) an endowment for an institution *b*) such an institution **3** basis **4** the base of a wall, house, etc. **5** cosmetic over which other makeup is applied

foun·der (foun′dər) *vi.* ⟦< L *fundus*, bottom⟧ **1** to stumble, fall, or go lame **2** to fill with water and sink: said of a ship **3** to break down

found·ling (found′liŋ′) *n.* an infant of unknown parents, found abandoned

found·ry (foun′drē) *n., pl.* **-ries** a place where metal is cast

fount (fount) *n.* ⟦< L *fons*⟧ **1** [Old Poet.] a fountain or spring **2** a source

foun·tain (fount′'n) *n.* ⟦< L *fons*⟧ **1** a natural spring of water **2** a source **3** *a*) an artificial jet or flow of water [*a drinking fountain*] *b*) the basin where this flows **4** a reservoir, as for ink

foun′tain·head′ *n.* the source, as of a stream

fountain pen a pen which is fed ink from its own reservoir or cartridge

four (fôr) *adj., n.* ⟦OE *feower*⟧ one more than three; 4; IV

four′-flush′er (-flush′ər) *n.* ⟦< FLUSH[2]⟧ [Inf.] one who bluffs in an effort to deceive

four′-in-hand′ *n.* a necktie tied in a slipknot with the ends left hanging

four'score' ***adj., n.*** four times twenty; eighty

four'some (-səm) ***n.*** four people

four·square (fôr'skwer') ***adj.*** **1** square **2** unyielding; firm **3** frank; forthright —***adv.*** in a square form or manner

four·teen (fôr'tēn') ***adj., n.*** ⟦OE *feowertyne*⟧ four more than ten; 14; XIV —**four'teenth'** ***adj., n.***

fourth (fôrth) ***adj.*** ⟦OE *feortha*⟧ preceded by three others in a series; 4th —***n.*** **1** the one following the third **2** any of the four equal parts of something; ¼ **3** the fourth forward gear

fourth'-class' ***adj., adv.*** of or in a class of mail consisting of merchandise, printed matter, etc. not included in first-class, second-class, or third-class; parcel post

fourth dimension in the theory of relativity, time added as a dimension to those of length, width, and depth

fourth estate [*often* **F- E-**] journalism or journalists

Fourth of July *see* INDEPENDENCE DAY

4WD *abbrev.* four-wheel-drive (vehicle)

four'-wheel' ***adj.*** **1** having four wheels **2** affecting four wheels *[a four-wheel drive]*

fowl (foul) ***n.*** ⟦OE *fugol*⟧ **1** any bird **2** any of the domestic birds used as food, as the chicken, duck, etc. **3** the flesh of these birds used for food

fox (fäks) ***n.*** ⟦OE⟧ **1** a small, wild animal of the dog family, considered sly and crafty **2** its fur **3** a sly, crafty person —***vt.*** to trick by slyness

fox'glove' ***n.*** DIGITALIS

fox'hole' ***n.*** a hole dug in the ground as a protection against enemy gunfire

fox'hound' ***n.*** a sturdy breed of hound that is trained to hunt foxes

fox terrier a small terrier with a smooth or wiry coat, formerly trained to drive foxes from hiding

fox trot a dance for couples in 4/4 time, or music for it —**fox'-trot'**, **-trot'ted**, **-trot'ting**, ***vi.***

fox'y ***adj.*** **-i·er**, **-i·est** **1** foxlike; crafty; sly **2** [Slang] attractive or sexy: used esp. of women

foy·er (foi'ər; *also* foi'ā', -yā') ***n.*** ⟦Fr < L *focus*, hearth⟧ an entrance hall or lobby, as in a theater or hotel

Fr *abbrev.* **1** Father **2** French

frab·jous (frab'jəs) ***adj.*** ⟦coined by Lewis CARROLL⟧ [Inf.] splendid; fine

fra·cas (frā'kəs) ***n.*** ⟦Fr < It *fracassare*, to smash⟧ a noisy fight; brawl

frac·tion (frak'shən) ***n.*** ⟦< L *frangere*, to break⟧ **1** a small part, amount, etc. **2** *Math. a)* a quotient of two whole numbers, as $\frac{13}{4}$, $\frac{2}{5}$ *b)* any quantity expressed in terms of a numerator and denominator —**frac'tion·al** ***adj.*** —**frac'tion·al·ly** ***adv.***

frac·tious (frak'shəs) ***adj.*** ⟦< ?⟧ **1** hard to manage; unruly; rebellious **2** peevish; irritable; cross —**frac'tious·ly** ***adv.*** —**frac'tious·ness** ***n.***

frac·ture (frak'chər) ***n.*** ⟦< L *frangere*, to break⟧ a breaking or break, esp. in a bone —***vt., vi.*** **-tured**, **-tur·ing** to break, crack, or split

frag·ile (fraj'əl) ***adj.*** ⟦< L *frangere*, to break⟧ easily broken or damaged; delicate —**fra·gil·i·ty** (frə jil'ə tē) ***n.***

frag·ment (frag'mənt; *for v., also*, -ment') ***n.*** ⟦< L *frangere*, to break⟧ **1** a part broken away **2** an incomplete part, as of a novel —***vt., vi.*** to break up —**frag'men·ta'tion** (-mən tā'shən) ***n.***

frag'men·tar'y (-mən ter'ē) ***adj.*** consisting of fragments; not complete

fra·grant (frā'grənt) ***adj.*** ⟦< L *fragrare*, to emit a (sweet) smell⟧ having a pleasant odor; sweet-smelling —**fra'grance** ***n.*** —**fra'grant·ly** ***adv.***

frail (frāl) ***adj.*** ⟦see FRAGILE⟧ **1** easily broken; delicate **2** not robust; weak **3** easily tempted; morally weak —**frail'ly** ***adv.***

frail'ty (-tē) ***n.*** **1** a being frail; esp., moral weakness **2** *pl.* **-ties** a fault arising from such weakness

frame (frām) ***vt.*** **framed**, **fram'ing** ⟦prob. < ON *frami*, profit or benefit⟧ **1** to form according to a pattern; design *[to frame laws]* **2** to construct **3** to put into words *[to frame an excuse]* **4** to enclose (a picture, etc.) in a border **5** [Inf.] to falsify evidence in order to make (an innocent person) appear guilty —***n.*** **1** body structure **2** the framework, as of a house **3** the structural case enclosing a window, door, etc. **4** an ornamental border, as around a picture **5** the way anything is put together; form **6** condition; state *[a good frame of mind]* **7** one exposure in a strip of film **8** *Bowling, etc.* a division of a game —***adj.*** having a wooden framework *[a frame house]* —**fram'er** ***n.***

frame'-up' ***n.*** [Inf.] a secret, deceitful scheme, as a falsifying of evidence to make a person seem guilty

frame'work' ***n.*** **1** a structure to hold together or support something **2** the basic structure, system, etc.

franc (fraŋk) ***n.*** ⟦Fr < L *Francorum rex*, king of the French, phrase on the coin in 1360⟧ **1** the former monetary unit of France, Belgium, and Luxembourg, superseded in 2002 by the EURO **2** the monetary unit of Chad, Mali, etc.

France (frans, fräns) country in W Europe: 210,033 sq. mi.; pop. 56,615,000

fran·chise (fran'chīz') ***n.*** ⟦< OFr *franc*, free⟧ **1** any special right or privilege granted by a government **2** the right to vote; suffrage **3** the right to sell a product or service —***vt.*** **-chised'**, **-chis'ing** to grant a franchise to

Franco- *combining form* French, French and

fran·gi·ble (fran'jə bəl) ***adj.*** ⟦< L *frangere*, to break⟧ breakable; fragile

frank (fraŋk) ***adj.*** ⟦< OFr *franc*, free⟧ free in expressing oneself; candid —***vt.*** to send (mail) free of postage —***n.*** **1** the right to send mail free **2** a mark indicating this right —**frank'ly** ***adv.*** —**frank'ness** ***n.***

Frank (fraŋk) ***n.*** a member of the Germanic peoples whose 9th-c. empire extended over what is now France, Germany, and Italy

Frank·en·stein (fraŋ′kən stīn′) ***n.*** **1** the title character in a novel (1818), creator of a monster that destroys him **2** popularly, the monster **3** anything that becomes dangerous to its creator

Frank·fort (fraŋk′fərt) capital of Kentucky: pop. 26,000

Frank·furt (fraŋk′fərt; *Ger* fräŋk′foort) city in W Germany: pop. 656,000

frank·furt·er (fraŋk′fər tər) ***n.*** ⟦Ger: after prec.⟧ a smoked sausage of beef, beef and pork, etc.; wiener: also [Inf.] **frank**

frank·in·cense (fraŋ′kin sens′) ***n.*** ⟦see FRANK & INCENSE[1]⟧ a gum resin burned as incense

Frank·ish (fraŋ′kish) ***n.*** the West Germanic language of the Franks —***adj.*** of the Franks or their language, etc.

Frank·lin (fraŋk′lin), **Ben·ja·min** (ben′jə mən) 1706-90; Am. statesman, scientist, inventor, & writer

fran·tic (fran′tik) ***adj.*** ⟦< Gr *phrenitis*, delirium⟧ wild with anger, pain, worry, etc. —**fran′ti·cal·ly** ***adv.***

frap·pé (fra pā′) ***n.*** ⟦Fr < *frapper*, to strike⟧ **1** a dessert made of partly frozen fruit juices, etc. **2** a beverage poured over shaved ice **3** [New England] a milkshake Also, esp. for 3, **frappe** (frap)

fra·ter·nal (frə tur′nəl) ***adj.*** ⟦< L *frater*, brother⟧ **1** of brothers; brotherly **2** designating or of a society organized for fellowship **3** designating twins developed from separate ova and thus not identical —**fra·ter′nal·ly** ***adv.***

fra·ter·ni·ty (frə tur′nə tē) ***n.***, *pl.* **-ties** **1** brotherliness **2** a group of men joined together for fellowship, etc., as in college **3** a group of people with the same beliefs, work, etc.

frat·er·nize (frat′ər nīz′) ***vi.*** **-nized′**, **-niz′ing** to associate in a friendly way —**frat′er·ni·za′tion** ***n.***

frat·ri·cide (fra′trə sīd′) ***n.*** ⟦< L *frater*, brother + *caedere*, to kill⟧ **1** the killing of one's own brother or sister **2** one who commits fratricide —**frat′ri·ci′dal** ***adj.***

Frau (frou) ***n.***, *pl.* ***Frau′en*** (-ən) ⟦Ger⟧ **1** Mrs.; Madam: a German title of respect, used to address a married woman and now also a single woman **2** a wife

fraud (frôd) ***n.*** ⟦< L *fraus*⟧ **1** deceit; trickery **2** *Law* intentional deception **3** a trick **4** an impostor or cheat

fraud·u·lent (frô′jə lənt) ***adj.*** **1** based on or using fraud **2** done or obtained by fraud —**fraud′u·lence** ***n.*** —**fraud′u·lent·ly** ***adv.***

fraught (frôt) ***adj.*** ⟦< MDu *vracht*, a load⟧ **1** filled or loaded (*with*) *[a life fraught with hardship]* **2** tense, anxious, etc.

Fräu·lein (froi′līn′; *E* froi′-) ***n.***, *pl.* ***-lein′*** or Eng. **-leins′** ⟦Ger⟧ **1** Miss: a German title of respect **2** an unmarried woman: see note at FRAU

fray[1] (frā) ***n.*** ⟦< AFFRAY⟧ a noisy quarrel or fight; brawl

fray[2] (frā) ***vt.***, ***vi.*** ⟦< L *fricare*, to rub⟧ **1** to make or become worn or ragged **2** to make or become weakened or strained

fraz·zle (fraz′əl) [Inf.] ***vt.***, ***vi.*** **-zled**, **-zling** ⟦< dial. *fazle*⟧ **1** to wear to tatters; fray **2** to make or become exhausted —***n.*** the state of being frazzled

freak (frēk) ***n.*** ⟦< ?⟧ **1** an odd notion; whim **2** an unusual happening **3** any abnormal animal, person, or plant **4** [Slang] *a)* a user of a specified drug *b)* a devotee; buff *[a chess freak]* —***adj.*** oddly different; abnormal —**freak out** [Slang] **1** to have hallucinations, etc., as from a psychedelic drug **2** to make or become very excited, distressed, etc. —**freak′ish** or **freak′y**, **-i·er**, **-i·est**, ***adj.*** —**freak′ish·ly** ***adv.***

freak′out′ ***n.*** [Slang] the act or an instance of freaking out

freck·le (frek′əl) ***n.*** ⟦< Scand⟧ a small, brownish spot on the skin —***vt.***, ***vi.*** **-led**, **-ling** to make or become spotted with freckles —**freck′led** ***adj.***

Fred·er·ick the Great (fred′rik, -ər ik) 1712-86; king of Prussia (1740-86)

Fred·er·ic·ton (fred′ə rik tən) capital of New Brunswick, Canada: pop. 47,000

free (frē) ***adj.*** **fre′er**, **fre′est** ⟦< OE *freo*⟧ **1** not under the control or power of another; having liberty; independent **2** having civil and political liberty **3** able to move in any direction; loose **4** not burdened by obligations, debts, discomforts, etc. **5** not confined to the usual rules *[free verse]* **6** not exact *[a free translation]* **7** generous; profuse *[a free spender]* **8** frank **9** with no charge or cost **10** exempt from taxes, duties, etc. **11** clear of obstructions *[a free road ahead]* **12** not fastened *[a rope's free end]* —***adv.*** **1** without cost **2** in a free manner —***vt.*** **freed**, **free′ing** to make free; specif., *a)* to release from bondage or arbitrary power, obligation, etc. *b)* to clear of obstruction, etc. —**free from** (or **of**) without —**free up** to make available for use *[he freed up funds]* —**make free with** to use freely —**free′ly** ***adv.*** —**free′ness** ***n.***

-free (frē) *combining form* free of or from, exempt from, without

free′base′ ***n.*** a concentrated form of cocaine for smoking —***vt.***, ***vi.*** **-based′**, **-bas′ing** to prepare or use such a form of (cocaine)

free·bie or **free·bee** (frē′bē) ***n.*** [Slang] something given or gotten free of charge, as a theater ticket

free′boot′er (-bōōt′ər) ***n.*** ⟦< Du *vrij*, free + *buit*, plunder⟧ a pirate

freed·man (frēd′mən) ***n.***, *pl.* **-men** (-mən) a man legally freed from slavery

free·dom (frē′dəm) ***n.*** **1** a being free; esp., *a)* independence *b)* civil or political liberty *c)* exemption from an obligation, discomfort, etc. *d)* a being able to act, use, etc. freely *e)* ease of movement *f)* frankness **2** a right or privilege

free fall any unchecked fall, as of a parachutist before the parachute opens

free flight any flight or part of a flight,

as of a rocket, occurring without propulsion —**free'-flight'** *adj.*

free'-for-all' *n.* a disorganized, general fight; brawl —*adj.* open to anyone

free'-form' *adj.* **1** irregular in shape **2** spontaneous, unrestrained, etc.

free'hand' *adj.* drawn by hand without the use of instruments, etc.

free'hold' *n.* an estate in land held for life or with the right to pass it on to heirs —**free'hold'er** *n.*

free·lance or **free-lance** (frē'lans') *n.* a writer, artist, etc. who sells his or her services to individual buyers: also **free'lanc'er** or **free'-lanc'er** —*adj.* of or working as a freelance —*vi.* **-lanced'**, **-lanc'ing** to work as a freelance

free'load'er (-lōd'ər) *n.* [Inf.] a person who habitually imposes on others for free food, etc. —**free'load'** *vi.*

free·man (frē'mən) *n., pl.* **-men** (-mən) **1** a person not in slavery **2** a citizen

Free·ma·son (frē'mā'sən) *n.* a member of an international secret society based on brotherliness and mutual aid —**Free'ma'son·ry** *n.*

free on board delivered (by the seller) aboard the train, ship, etc. at no extra charge to the buyer

free'stone' *n.* a peach, etc. in which the pit does not cling to the pulp

free'think'er *n.* one who forms opinions about religion, morals, etc. independently

Free'town' seaport & capital of Sierra Leone: pop. 470,000

free trade trade carried on without protective tariffs, quotas, etc.

free verse poetry without regular meter, rhyme, etc.

free'way' *n.* a multiple-lane divided highway with fully controlled access

free'will' *adj.* voluntary

freeze (frēz) *vi.* **froze, fro'zen, freez'ing** ⟦OE *freosan*⟧ **1** to be formed into, or become covered with, ice; be solidified by cold **2** to become very cold **3** to be damaged or killed by cold **4** to become motionless **5** to be made speechless by strong emotion **6** to become formal or unfriendly —*vt.* **1** to form into, or cover with, ice; solidify by cold **2** to make very cold **3** to preserve (food) by rapid refrigeration **4** to kill or damage by cold **5** to make motionless **6** to make formal or unfriendly **7** *a*) to fix (prices, etc.) at a given level by authority *b*) to make (funds, etc.) unavailable to the owners —*n.* **1** a freezing or being frozen **2** a period of freezing weather —**freeze out 1** to die out through freezing, as plants do **2** [Inf.] to keep out by a cold manner, competition, etc. —**freeze over** to become covered with ice —**freez'a·ble** *adj.*

freeze'-dry' *vt.* **-dried'**, **-dry'ing** to quick-freeze (food, etc.) and then dry under high vacuum

freez'er *n.* **1** a refrigerator, compartment, etc. for freezing and storing perishable foods **2** a machine for making ice cream

freezing point the temperature at which a liquid freezes: the freezing point of water is 32°F or 0°C

freight (frāt) *n.* ⟦< MDu *vracht*, a load⟧ **1** the transporting of goods by water, land, or air **2** the cost for this **3** the goods transported **4** a railroad train for transporting goods: in full **freight train** —*vt.* **1** to load; burden **2** to send by freight

freight'er *n.* a ship for freight

Fre·mont (frē'mänt) city in W California, on San Francisco Bay: pop. 173,000

French (french) *adj.* of France or its people, language, etc. —*n.* the language of France —**the French** the people of France —**French'man** (-mən), *pl.* **-men** (-mən), *n.*

French bread bread with a crisp crust made with white flour in a long, slender loaf

French cuff a shirt-sleeve cuff turned back on itself and fastened with a cuff link

French doors a pair of doors hinged at the sides to open in the middle

French dressing a creamy, orange-colored salad dressing

French fries [*often* **f- f-**] strips of potato that have been French fried

French fry [*often* **f- f-**] to fry in hot deep fat

French Gui·a·na (gē an'ə, -ä'nə) French administrative division in NE South America

French horn a mellow-toned brass instrument with a long, spiral tube and a flaring bell: in classical music, now usually *horn*

French leave an unauthorized departure

French toast sliced bread dipped in a batter of egg and milk and then fried

fre·net·ic (frə net'ik) *adj.* ⟦see PHRENETIC⟧ frantic; frenzied —**fre·net'i·cal·ly** *adv.*

fren·zy (fren'zē) *n., pl.* **-zies** ⟦< Gr *phrenitis*, madness⟧ wild excitement; delirium

Fre·on (frē'än') *trademark for* any of a series of gaseous compounds of fluorine, carbon, etc.: used as refrigerants, aerosol propellants, etc.

fre·quen·cy (frē'kwən sē) *n., pl.* **-cies 1** frequent occurrence **2** the number of times any event recurs in a given period **3** *Physics* the number of oscillations or cycles per unit of time

frequency modulation the variation of the frequency of a carrier wave in accordance with the signal being broadcast: abbrev. *FM*

fre·quent (frē'kwənt; *for v.* frē kwent') *adj.* ⟦< L *frequens*, crowded⟧ **1** occurring often **2** constant; habitual —*vt.* to go to or be at often —**fre'quent·ly** *adv.*

fres·co (fres'kō) *n., pl.* **-coes** or **-cos** ⟦It, fresh⟧ a painting made with watercolors on wet plaster

fresh[1] (fresh) *adj.* ⟦OE *fersc*⟧ **1** recently made, grown, etc. *[fresh coffee]* **2** not salted, pickled, frozen, etc. **3** not spoiled **4** not tired; lively **5** not worn, soiled, faded, etc. **6** new; recent **7**

inexperienced **8** cool and refreshing *[a fresh spring day]* **9** brisk: said of wind **10** not salt: said of water —**fresh'ly** ***adv.*** —**fresh'ness** ***n.***

fresh[2] (fresh) ***adj.*** ⟦< Ger *frech*, bold⟧ [Slang] bold; saucy; impertinent

fresh'en ***vt., vi.*** to make or become fresh —**freshen up** to bathe, change into fresh clothes, etc. —**fresh'en·er** ***n.***

fresh'man (-mən) ***n.***, *pl.* **-men** (-mən) ⟦FRESH[1] + MAN⟧ **1** a beginner **2** a person in his or her first year in college, Congress, etc.

fresh'wa'ter ***adj.*** **1** of or living in water that is not salty **2** sailing only on inland waters

Fres·no (frez'nō) city in central California: pop. 354,000

fret[1] (fret) ***vt., vi.*** **fret'ted, fret'ting** ⟦OE *fretan*, to devour⟧ **1** to gnaw, wear away, rub, etc. **2** to make or become rough or disturbed *[wind fretting the water]* **3** to irritate or be irritated; worry —***n.*** irritation; worry —**fret'ter** ***n.***

fret[2] (fret) ***n.*** ⟦ME *frette*⟧ a running design of interlacing small bars

fret[3] (fret) ***n.*** ⟦OFr *frette*, a band⟧ any of the ridges on the fingerboard of a banjo, guitar, etc.

fret'ful (-fəl) ***adj.*** irritable; peevish —**fret'ful·ly** ***adv.*** —**fret'ful·ness** ***n.***

fret'work' ***n.*** decorative carving or openwork, as of interlacing lines

Freud (frɔid), **Sig·mund** (sig'mənd) 1856-1939; Austrian physician: founder of psychoanalysis —**Freud'i·an** ***adj., n.***

Freudian slip a mistake made in speaking that, it is thought, inadvertently reveals unconscious motives, desires, etc.

Fri *abbrev.* Friday

fri·a·ble (frī'ə bəl) ***adj.*** ⟦Fr < L *friare*, to rub⟧ easily crumbled

fri·ar (frī'ər) ***n.*** ⟦< L *frater*, brother⟧ *R.C.Ch.* a member of certain religious orders

fric·as·see (frik'ə sē', frik'ə sē') ***n.*** ⟦< Fr *fricasser*, cut up and fry⟧ a dish consisting of meat cut into pieces, stewed or fried, and served in a sauce of its own gravy —***vt.*** **-seed', -see'ing** to prepare in this way

fric·tion (frik'shən) ***n.*** ⟦< L *fricare*, to rub⟧ **1** a rubbing of one object against another **2** conflict, as because of differing opinions **3** *Mech.* the resistance to motion of moving surfaces that touch —**fric'tion·al** ***adj.*** —**fric'tion·less** ***adj.***

Fri·day (frī'dā) ***n.*** ⟦after *Frigg*, Germanic goddess⟧ **1** the sixth day of the week **2** ⟦after the devoted servant of ROBINSON CRUSOE⟧ a faithful helper: usually **man** (or **girl**) **Friday**

fridge (frij) ***n.*** [Inf.] a refrigerator

fried (frīd) ***vt., vi.*** *pt. & pp. of* FRY[1]

fried'cake' ***n.*** a small cake fried in deep fat; doughnut or cruller

friend (frend) ***n.*** ⟦OE *freond*⟧ **1** a person whom one knows well and is fond of **2** an ally, supporter, or sympathizer **3** [**F-**] a member of the Society of Friends; Quaker —**make** (or **be**) **friends with** to become (or be) a friend of —**friend'less** ***adj.***

friend'ly ***adj.*** **-li·er, -li·est** **1** of or like a friend; kindly **2** not hostile; amicable **3** supporting; helping —**friend'li·ly** ***adv.*** —**friend'li·ness** ***n.***

friend'ship' ***n.*** **1** the state of being friends **2** friendly feeling

fries (frīz) ***pl.n.*** [Inf.] *short for* FRENCH FRIES

frieze (frēz) ***n.*** ⟦< ML *frisium*⟧ an ornamental band with designs or carvings, positioned along a wall, around a room, etc.

frig·ate (frig'it) ***n.*** ⟦< It *fregata*⟧ a fast, medium-sized sailing warship of the 18th and early 19th c.

fright (frīt) ***n.*** ⟦OE *fyrhto*⟧ **1** sudden fear; alarm **2** an ugly, startling, etc. person or thing

fright'en ***vt.*** **1** to make suddenly afraid; scare **2** to force (*away, out,* or *off*) by scaring —**fright'en·ing·ly** ***adv.***

fright'ful (-fəl) ***adj.*** **1** causing fright; alarming **2** shocking; terrible **3** [Inf.] *a)* unpleasant; annoying *b)* great *[in a frightful hurry]* —**fright'ful·ly** ***adv.*** —**fright'ful·ness** ***n.***

frig·id (frij'id) ***adj.*** ⟦< L *frigus*, coldness⟧ **1** extremely cold **2** not warm or friendly **3** sexually unresponsive: said of a woman —**fri·gid·i·ty** (fri jid'ə tē) ***n.*** —**frig'id·ly** ***adv.***

Frigid Zone either of two zones (**North Frigid Zone** or **South Frigid Zone**) between the polar circles and the poles

frill (fril) ***n.*** ⟦< ?⟧ **1** any unnecessary ornament **2** a ruffle —**frill'y, -i·er, -i·est,** ***adj.***

fringe (frinj) ***n.*** ⟦< LL *fimbria*⟧ **1** a border of threads, etc. hanging loose or tied in bunches **2** an outer edge; border **3** a marginal or minor part —***vt.*** **fringed, fring'ing** to be or make a fringe for —***adj.*** **1** at the outer edge **2** additional **3** minor

fringe benefit any form of employee compensation other than wages, as insurance or a pension

frip·per·y (frip'ər ē) ***n.***, *pl.* **-ies** ⟦< OFr *frepe*, a rag⟧ **1** cheap, gaudy clothes **2** showy display in dress, manners, etc.

Fris·bee (friz'bē) ⟦< "Mother *Frisbie's*" pie tins⟧ *trademark for* a saucer-shaped plastic disk sailed back and forth in a simple game —***n.*** [*also* **f-**] **1** such a disk **2** the game

fri·sé (frē zā', fri-) ***n.*** ⟦Fr < *friser*, to curl⟧ an upholstery fabric with a thick pile in loops

Fri·sian (frizh'ən) ***n.*** the West Germanic language of an island chain, the Frisian Islands, along the coast of N Netherlands, Germany, & Denmark

frisk (frisk) ***vi.*** ⟦< OHG *frisc*, lively⟧ to move about in a lively way; frolic —***vt.*** [Slang] to search (a person) for weapons, etc. by passing the hands quickly over the person's clothing

frisk·y (fris'kē) ***adj.*** **-i·er, -i·est** lively; frolicsome —**frisk'i·ly** ***adv.*** —**frisk'i·ness** ***n.***

frit·ter[1] (frit'ər) ***vt.*** ⟦< L *frangere*, to break⟧ to waste (money, time, etc.) bit by bit: usually with *away*

frit·ter[2] (frit′ər) ***n.*** ⟦< L *frigere*, to fry⟧ a small cake of fried batter, usually containing corn, fruit, etc.

friv·o·lous (friv′ə ləs) ***adj.*** ⟦< L *frivolus*, silly⟧ **1** of little value; trivial **2** silly and light-minded; giddy —**fri·vol·i·ty** (fri väl′ə tē), *pl.* **-ties**, ***n.*** —**friv′o·lous·ly** ***adv.***

frizz or **friz** (friz) ***vt.***, ***vi.*** **frizzed**, **friz′zing** ⟦Fr *friser*⟧ to form into small, tight curls —***n.*** hair, etc. that is frizzed —**friz′zy**, **-zi·er**, **-zi·est**, ***adj.***

friz·zle[1] (friz′əl) ***vi.***, ***vt.*** **-zled**, **-zling** ⟦< FRY[1]⟧ to sizzle, as in frying

friz·zle[2] (friz′əl) ***n.***, ***vt.***, ***vi.*** **-zled**, **-zling** FRIZZ —**friz′zly** ***adj.***

fro (frō) ***adv.*** ⟦< ON *frā*⟧ backward; back: now only in TO AND FRO (at TO)

frock (fräk) ***n.*** ⟦< OFr *froc*⟧ **1** a robe worn by friars, monks, etc. **2** a dress

frog (frôg, fräg) ***n.*** ⟦OE *frogga*⟧ **1** a tailless, leaping amphibian with long hind legs and webbed feet **2** a fancy loop of braid used to fasten clothing —**frog in one's throat** temporary hoarseness

frog′man′ ***n.***, *pl.* **-men′** (-men′) a person trained and equipped for underwater demolition, exploration, etc.

frol·ic (fräl′ik) ***n.*** ⟦< MDu *vrō*, merry⟧ **1** a lively party or game **2** merriment; fun —***vi.*** **-icked**, **-ick·ing** **1** to make merry; have fun **2** to romp about; gambol —**frol′ick·er** ***n.***

frol′ic·some (-səm) ***adj.*** playful; merry

from (frum) ***prep.*** ⟦OE⟧ **1** beginning at; starting with *[from* noon to midnight*]* **2** out of *[from* her purse*]* **3** originating with *[*a letter *from* me*]* **4** out of the possibility of or use of *[*kept *from* going*]* **5** as not being like *[*to know good *from* evil*]* **6** because of *[*to tremble *from* fear*]*

frond (fränd) ***n.*** ⟦< L *frons*, leafy branch⟧ the leaf of a fern or palm

front (frunt) ***n.*** ⟦< L *frons*, forehead⟧ **1** *a)* outward behavior *[*a bold *front]* *b)* [Inf.] an appearance of social standing, wealth, etc. **2** the part facing forward **3** the first part; beginning **4** a forward or leading position **5** the land bordering a lake, street, etc. **6** the advanced battle area in warfare **7** an area of activity *[*the home *front]* **8** a person or group used to hide another's activity **9** *Meteorol.* the boundary between two differing air masses —***adj.*** at, to, in, on, or of the front —***vt.***, ***vi.*** **1** to face **2** to serve as a front (*for*) —**in front of** before —**fron′tal** ***adj.***

front·age (frunt′ij) ***n.*** **1** the front part of a building **2** the front boundary line of a lot or the length of this line **3** land bordering a street, lake, etc.

fron·tier (frun tir′) ***n.*** ⟦see FRONT⟧ **1** the border between two countries **2** the part of a country which borders an unexplored region **3** any new field of learning, etc. or any part of a field that is not fully investigated —***adj.*** of, on, or near a frontier —**fron·tiers′man** (-tirz′ mən), *pl.* **-men** (-mən), ***n.***

fron·tis·piece (frunt′is pēs′) ***n.*** ⟦ult. < L *frons*, front + *specere*, to look⟧ an illustration facing the title page of a book

front office the management or administration, as of a company

front′-run′ner ***n.*** a leading contestant

front′-wheel′ drive an automotive design in which only the front wheels receive driving power

frost (frôst, fräst) ***n.*** ⟦OE < *freosan*, to freeze⟧ **1** a temperature low enough to cause freezing **2** frozen dew or vapor; rime —***vt.*** **1** to cover with frost **2** to cover with frosting **3** to give a frostlike, opaque surface to (glass) —**frost′y**, **-i·er**, **-i·est**, ***adj.***

Frost (frôst, fräst), **Robert** (**Lee**) (rä′bərt) 1874-1963; U.S. poet

frost′bite′ ***vt.*** **-bit′**, **-bit′ten**, **-bit′ing** to injure the tissues of (a body part) by exposing to intense cold —***n.*** injury caused by such exposure

frost′ing ***n.*** **1** a mixture of sugar, butter, flavoring, etc. for covering a cake; icing **2** a dull finish on glass, metal, etc.

frost line the limit of penetration of soil by frost

froth (frôth, fräth) ***n.*** ⟦< ON *frotha*⟧ **1** foam **2** foaming saliva **3** light, trifling talk, ideas, etc. —***vi.*** to foam —**froth′y**, **-i·er**, **-i·est**, ***adj.***

frou·frou (frōō′frōō′) ***n.*** ⟦Fr⟧ [Inf.] excessive ornateness

fro·ward (frō′wərd, -ərd) ***adj.*** ⟦see FRO & -WARD⟧ not easily controlled; willful; contrary —**fro′ward·ness** ***n.***

frown (froun) ***vi.*** ⟦< OFr *froigne*, sullen face⟧ **1** to contract the brows, as in displeasure **2** to show disapproval: with *on* or *upon* —***n.*** a frowning

frow·zy (frou′zē) ***adj.*** **-zi·er**, **-zi·est** ⟦< ?⟧ dirty and untidy; slovenly —**frow′zi·ly** ***adv.*** —**frow′zi·ness** ***n.***

froze (frōz) ***vi.***, ***vt.*** *pt. of* FREEZE

fro·zen (frō′zən) ***vi.***, ***vt.*** *pp. of* FREEZE —***adj.*** **1** turned into or covered with ice; solidified by cold **2** damaged or killed by freezing **3** preserved by freezing: said as of food **4** made motionless **5** kept at a fixed level **6** not readily convertible into cash *[frozen* assets*]*

frozen custard a food resembling ice cream, but softer and with less butterfat

fruc·ti·fy (fruk′tə fī′) ***vi.***, ***vt.*** **-fied′**, **-fy′ing** ⟦< L *fructificare*⟧ to bear or cause to bear fruit

fruc·tose (fruk′tōs′, frook′-) ***n.*** ⟦< L *fructus*, fruit + -OSE[1]⟧ a sugar found in sweet fruits and in honey

fru·gal (frōō′gəl) ***adj.*** ⟦< L *frugi*, fit for food⟧ **1** not wasteful; thrifty **2** inexpensive or meager —**fru·gal′i·ty** (-gal′ə tē), *pl.* **-ties**, ***n.*** —**fru′gal·ly** ***adv.***

fruit (frōōt) ***n.*** ⟦< L *fructus*⟧ **1** any plant product, as grain or vegetables: *usually used in pl.* **2** *a)* an edible plant structure, often sweet, containing the seeds inside a juicy pulp: many true fruits that are not sweet, as tomatoes, are popularly called *vegetables* *b)* *Bot.* the mature seed-bearing part of a flowering plant **3** the result or product of any action

fruit′cake′ ***n.*** a rich cake containing

nuts, preserved fruit, citron, spices, etc.

fruit fly any of various small flies whose larvae feed on fruits and vegetables

fruit′ful (-fəl) ***adj.*** **1** bearing much fruit **2** productive; prolific **3** profitable

fru·i·tion (fro͞o ish′ən) ***n.*** **1** the bearing of fruit **2** a coming to fulfillment; realization

fruit′less (-lis) ***adj.*** **1** without results; unsuccessful **2** bearing no fruit; sterile; barren **—fruit′less·ly** ***adv.*** **—fruit′less·ness** ***n.***

frump (frump) ***n.*** ⟦prob. < Du *rompelen,* rumple⟧ a dowdy woman **—frump′ish** ***adj.*** **—frump′y, -i·er, -i·est,** ***adj.***

frus·trate (frus′trāt′) ***vt.*** **-trat′ed, -trat′ing** ⟦< L *frustra,* in vain⟧ **1** to cause to have no effect **2** to prevent from achieving a goal or gratifying a desire **—frus·tra′tion** ***n.***

fry[1] (frī) ***vt., vi.*** **fried, fry′ing** ⟦< L *frigere,* to fry⟧ to cook in a pan over direct heat, usually in hot fat **—*n.*,** *pl.* **fries 1** [*pl.*] fried potatoes **2** a social gathering at which food is fried and eaten *[a fish fry]*

fry[2] (frī) ***pl.n.,*** *sing.* **fry** ⟦< OFr *freier,* to rub, spawn⟧ young fish

fry′er ***n.*** **1** a utensil for deep-frying **2** a chicken for frying

FSLIC *abbrev.* Federal Savings and Loan Insurance Corporation

ft *abbrev.* foot; feet

Ft *abbrev.* Fort

FTC *abbrev.* Federal Trade Commission

fuch·sia (fyo͞o′shə) ***n.*** ⟦after L. *Fuchs* (1501-66), Ger botanist⟧ **1** a shrubby plant with pink, red, or purple flowers **2** purplish red

fud·dle (fud′'l) ***vt.*** **-dled, -dling** ⟦< ?⟧ to confuse or stupefy as with alcoholic liquor **—*n.*** a fuddled state

fud·dy-dud·dy (fud′ē dud′ē) ***n.,*** *pl.* **-dies** [Inf.] a fussy or old-fashioned person

fudge (fuj) ***n.*** ⟦< ?⟧ a soft candy made of butter, milk, sugar, chocolate or other flavoring, etc. **—*vi.*** **fudged, fudg′ing 1** to refuse to commit oneself; hedge **2** to be dishonest; cheat

fu·el (fyo͞o′əl, fyo͞ol) ***n.*** ⟦ult. < L *focus,* fireplace⟧ **1** coal, oil, gas, wood, etc., burned to supply heat or power **2** material from which nuclear energy can be obtained **3** anything that intensifies strong feeling **—*vt., vi.*** **fu′eled** or **fu′elled, fu′el·ing** or **fu′el·ling** to supply with or get fuel

fuel injection a system for injecting a fine spray of fuel into the combustion chambers of an engine

fu·gi·tive (fyo͞o′ji tiv) ***adj.*** ⟦< L *fugere,* to flee⟧ **1** fleeing, as from danger or justice **2** fleeting **—*n.*** one who is fleeing from justice, etc. **—fu′gi·tive·ly** ***adv.***

fugue (fyo͞og) ***n.*** ⟦< L *fugere,* to flee⟧ a musical work in which a theme is taken up successively and developed by the various parts or voices in counterpoint

-ful (fəl; *for 2, usually* fo͝ol) ⟦< FULL[1]⟧ *suffix* **1** *a)* full of, having *[joyful]* *b)* having the qualities of or tendency to *[helpful]* **2** the quantity that will fill *[handful]*

ful·crum (fo͝ol′krəm, ful′-) ***n.,*** *pl.* **-crums** or **-cra** (-krə) ⟦L, a support⟧ the support on which a lever turns in raising something

ful·fill (fo͝ol fil′) ***vt.*** **-filled′, -fill′ing** ⟦OE *fullfyllan*⟧ **1** to carry out (a promise, etc.) **2** to do (a duty, etc.); obey **3** to satisfy (a condition) Brit. sp. **ful·fil′, -filled′, -fill′ing —ful·fill′ment** or **ful·fil′ment** ***n.***

full[1] (fo͝ol) ***adj.*** ⟦OE⟧ **1** having in it all there is space for; filled **2** having eaten all that one wants **3** having a great deal or number (*of*) **4** complete *[a full dozen]* **5** having reached the greatest size, extent, etc. *[a full moon]* **6** plump; round *[a full face]* **7** with wide folds; flowing *[a full skirt]* **—*n.*** the greatest amount, extent, etc. **—*adv.*** **1** to the greatest degree; completely **2** directly; exactly **—full′ness** or **ful′ness** ***n.***

full[2] (fo͝ol) ***vt., vi.*** ⟦< L *fullo,* cloth fuller⟧ to shrink and thicken (wool cloth) **—full′er** ***n.***

full′back′ ***n.*** *Football* one of the running backs, used typically for blocking an opponent

full′-blood′ed ***adj.*** **1** of unmixed breed or race **2** vigorous

full′-blown′ ***adj.*** **1** in full bloom **2** fully developed; matured

full′-bore′ ***adv.*** to the greatest degree or extent **—*adj.*** all-out

full′-fledged′ ***adj.*** completely developed or trained; of full status

full moon the moon when it reflects light as a full disk

full′-scale′ ***adj.*** **1** according to the original or standard scale **2** to the utmost degree; all-out

full′-size′ ***adj.*** **1** of the usual or standard size **2** of a large size Also **full′-sized′**

full′-throat′ed ***adj.*** **1** having or producing deep, rich sound **2** complete and unmitigated

full′-time′ ***adj.*** of or engaged in work, study, etc. that takes all of one's regular working hours

full′y ***adv.*** **1** completely; thoroughly **2** at least

ful·mi·nate (ful′mə nāt′) ***vi.*** **-nat′ed, -nat′ing** ⟦< L *fulmen,* lightning⟧ to express strong disapproval **—ful′mi·na′tion** ***n.***

ful·some (fo͝ol′səm) ***adj.*** ⟦see FULL[1] & -SOME[1], but infl. by ME *ful,* foul⟧ disgusting, esp. because excessive

fum·ble (fum′bəl) ***vi., vt.*** **-bled, -bling** ⟦prob. < ON *famla*⟧ **1** to grope (*for*) or handle (a thing) clumsily **2** to lose one's grasp on (a football, etc.) **—*n.*** a fumbling **—fum′bler** ***n.***

fume (fyo͞om) ***n.*** ⟦< L *fumus*⟧ [*often pl.*] a gas, smoke, or vapor, esp. if offensive or suffocating **—*vi.*** **fumed, fum′ing 1** to give off fumes **2** to show anger

fu·mi·gate (fyo͞o′mə gāt′) ***vt.*** **-gat′ed, -gat′ing** ⟦< L *fumus,* smoke + *agere,* do⟧ to expose to fumes, esp. so as to disinfect or kill the vermin in **—fu′mi·ga′tion** ***n.*** **—fu′mi·ga′tor** ***n.***

fum·y (fyo͞om′ē) ***adj.*** **-i·er, -i·est** full of or producing fumes; vaporous

fun (fun) ***n.*** ⟦< ME *fonne*, foolish⟧ **1** *a)* lively, joyous play or playfulness *b)* pleasure **2** a source of amusement —***adj.*** [Inf.] intended for pleasure or amusement —**make fun of** to ridicule

func·tion (fuŋk′shən) ***n.*** ⟦< L *fungi*, to perform⟧ **1** the normal or characteristic action of anything **2** a special duty required in work **3** a formal ceremony or social occasion **4** a thing that depends on and varies with something else —***vi.*** to act in a required manner; work; be used —**func′tion·less** ***adj.***

func′tion·al ***adj.*** **1** of a function **2** performing a function **3** *Med.* affecting a function of some organ without apparent organic changes

functional illiterate a person who cannot read well enough to carry out everyday activities

func′tion·ar′y (-shə ner′ē) ***n.***, *pl.* **-ies** an official performing some function

function word a word, as an article or conjunction, serving mainly to show grammatical relationship

fund (fund) ***n.*** ⟦L *fundus*, bottom⟧ **1** a supply that can be drawn upon; stock **2** *a)* a sum of money set aside for a purpose *b)* [*pl.*] ready money —***vt.*** **1** to put or convert into a long-term debt that bears interest **2** to provide funds for (a project, retirement of a debt, etc.)

fun·da·men·tal (fun′də ment″l) ***adj.*** ⟦see prec.⟧ of or forming a foundation or basis; basic; essential —***n.*** a principle, theory, law, etc. serving as a basis —**fun′da·men′tal·ly** ***adv.***

fun′da·men′tal·ism′ ***n.*** [*sometimes* **F-**] religious beliefs based on a literal interpretation of the Bible —**fun′da·men′tal·ist** ***n., adj.***

fund′rais′er (-rā′zər) ***n.*** **1** one soliciting money for a charity, political party, etc. **2** an event held to obtain such money —**fund′rais′ing** ***n.***

fu·ner·al (fyo͞o′nər əl) ***n.*** ⟦< L *funus*⟧ the ceremonies connected with burial or cremation of a dead person

funeral director one who manages a funeral home

funeral home (or **parlor**) an establishment where the bodies of the dead are prepared for burial or cremation and where funeral services can be held

fu·ne·re·al (fyo͞o nir′ē əl) ***adj.*** suitable for a funeral; sad and solemn; dismal —**fu·ne′re·al·ly** ***adv.***

fun·gi·cide (fun′jə sīd′) ***n.*** ⟦see -CIDE⟧ any substance that kills fungi

fun·gus (fuŋ′gəs) ***n.***, *pl.* **fun·gi** (fun′jī′) or **fun′gus·es** ⟦< L⟧ any of various plants or plantlike organisms, as molds, mildews, mushrooms, etc., that lack chlorophyll, stems, and leaves and reproduce by spores —**fun′gal** or **fun′gous** ***adj.***

fu·nic·u·lar (fyo͞o nik′yo͞o lər) ***n.*** ⟦< L *funiculus*, little rope⟧ a mountain railway with counterbalanced cable cars on parallel sets of rails: also **funicular railway**

funk (fuŋk) ***n.*** ⟦< ? Fl *fonck*, dismay⟧ **1** [Inf.] a state of great fear; panic **2** [Inf.] a depressed mood **3** popular music derived from rhythm and blues

funk·y (fuŋ′kē) ***adj.*** **-i·er**, **-i·est** ⟦orig., earthy⟧ **1** *Jazz* having an earthy style derived from early blues **2** [Slang] unconventional, eccentric, offbeat, etc.

FUNNEL

fun·nel (fun′əl) ***n.*** ⟦ult. < L *fundere*, to pour⟧ **1** a tapering tube with a cone-shaped mouth, for pouring things into small-mouthed containers **2** the smokestack of a steamship —***vi., vt.*** **-neled** or **-nelled**, **-nel·ing** or **-nel·ling** to move or pour as through a funnel

fun·nies (fun′ēz) ***pl.n.*** [Inf.] comic strips

fun·ny (fun′ē) ***adj.*** **-ni·er**, **-ni·est** **1** causing laughter; humorous **2** [Inf.] *a)* strange *b)* tricky —**fun′ni·ly** ***adv.*** —**fun′ni·ness** ***n.***

funny bone a place on the elbow where a sharp impact on a nerve causes a tingling sensation

funny farm [Slang] an institution for the mentally ill

fur (fɥr) ***n.*** ⟦< OFr *fuerre*, sheath⟧ **1** the soft, thick hair covering certain animals **2** a processed skin bearing such hair —***adj.*** of fur —**furred** ***adj.***

fur·be·low (fɥr′bə lō′) ***n.*** ⟦ult. < Fr *falbala*⟧ **1** a flounce or ruffle **2** a showy, useless decorative addition

fur·bish (fɥr′bish) ***vt.*** ⟦< OFr *forbir*⟧ **1** to polish; burnish **2** to renovate

Fu·ries (fyoor′ēz) ***pl.n.*** *Gr. & Rom. Myth.* the three terrible female spirits who punish the perpetrators of unavenged crimes

fu·ri·ous (fyoor′ē əs) ***adj.*** **1** full of fury; very angry **2** very great, intense, wild, etc. —**fu′ri·ous·ly** ***adv.***

furl (fɥrl) ***vt.*** ⟦< L *firmus*, FIRM[1] + *ligare*, to tie⟧ to roll up (a sail, flag, etc.) tightly and make secure

fur·long (fɥr′lôŋ′) ***n.*** ⟦< OE *furh*, a furrow + *lang*, LONG[1]⟧ a measure of distance equal to $\frac{1}{8}$ of a mile

fur·lough (fɥr′lō) ***n.*** ⟦< Du *verlof*⟧ a leave of absence, esp. for military personnel —***vt.*** to grant a furlough to

fur·nace (fɥr′nəs) ***n.*** ⟦< L *fornax*, furnace⟧ an enclosed structure in which heat is produced, as by burning fuel

fur·nish (fɥr′nish) ***vt.*** ⟦< OFr *furnir*⟧ **1** to supply with furniture, etc.; equip **2** to supply; provide

fur′nish·ings ***pl.n.*** **1** the furniture, carpets, etc. as for a house **2** things to wear *[men's furnishings]*

fur·ni·ture (fur′ni chər) ***n.*** ⟦Fr *fourniture*⟧ **1** the things in a room, etc. which equip it for living, as chairs, beds, etc. **2** necessary equipment

fu·ror (fyoor′ôr′) ***n.*** ⟦< L⟧ **1** fury; frenzy **2** *a*) a widespread enthusiasm; craze *b*) a commotion or uproar Also [Chiefly Brit.] **fu′rore′**

fur·ri·er (fur′ē ər) ***n.*** one who processes furs or deals in fur garments

fur·ring (fur′iŋ) ***n.*** thin strips of wood fixed on a wall, floor, etc. before adding boards or plaster

fur·row (fur′ō) ***n.*** ⟦< OE *furh*⟧ **1** a narrow groove made in the ground by a plow **2** anything like this, as a deep wrinkle —***vt.*** to make furrows in —***vi.*** to become wrinkled

fur·ry (fur′ē) ***adj.*** **-ri·er, -ri·est** **1** of or like fur **2** covered with fur —**fur′ri·ness** ***n.***

fur·ther (fur′thər) ***adj.*** ⟦OE *furthor*⟧ **1** *alt. compar. of* FAR **2** additional **3** more distant; farther —***adv.*** **1** *alt. compar. of* FAR **2** to a greater degree or extent **3** in addition **4** at or to a greater distance; farther —***vt.*** to give aid to; promote In sense 3 of the *adj.* and sense 4 of the *adv.*, FARTHER is more commonly used —**fur′ther·ance** ***n.***

fur′ther·more′ ***adv.*** in addition; besides; moreover

fur·thest (fur′thist) ***adj.*** **1** *alt. superl. of* FAR **2** most distant; farthest: also **fur′ther·most′** —***adv.*** **1** *alt. superl. of* FAR **2** at or to the greatest distance or degree

fur·tive (fur′tiv) ***adj.*** ⟦< L *fur*, a thief⟧ done or acting in a stealthy manner; sneaky —**fur′tive·ly** ***adv.*** —**fur′tive·ness** ***n.***

fu·ry (fyoor′ē) ***n.***, *pl.* **-ries** ⟦< L *furere*, to rage⟧ **1** violent anger; wild rage **2** violence; vehemence

furze (furz) ***n.*** ⟦OE *fyrs*⟧ a prickly evergreen shrub native to Europe

fuse[1] (fyo͞oz) ***vt.***, ***vi.*** **fused, fus′ing** ⟦< L *fundere*, to shed⟧ **1** to melt **2** to unite as if by melting together

fuse[2] (fyo͞oz) ***n.*** ⟦< L *fusus*, spindle⟧ **1** a tube or wick filled with combustible material, for setting off an explosive charge **2** *Elec.* a strip of easily melted metal placed in a circuit: it melts and breaks the circuit if the current becomes too strong

fu·see (fyo͞o zē′) ***n.*** ⟦Fr *fusée*, a rocket⟧ a colored flare used as a signal by railroad workers, truck drivers, etc.

fu·se·lage (fyo͞o′sə läzh′, -läj′) ***n.*** ⟦Fr⟧ the body of an airplane, exclusive of the wings, tail assembly, and engines

fu·si·ble (fyo͞o′zə bəl) ***adj.*** that can be fused or easily melted

fu·si·lier or **fu·sil·eer** (fyo͞o′zə lir′) ***n.*** ⟦Fr⟧ [Historical] a soldier armed with a flintlock musket

fu·sil·lade (fyo͞o′sə läd′, -lād′) ***n.*** ⟦Fr < *fusiller*, to shoot⟧ a simultaneous or rapid and continuous discharge of many firearms

fu·sion (fyo͞o′zhən) ***n.*** ⟦L *fusio*⟧ **1** a fusing or melting together **2** a blending; coalition **3** NUCLEAR FUSION **4** a style of popular music blending elements of jazz, rock, etc.

fuss (fus) ***n.*** ⟦prob. echoic⟧ **1** nervous, excited activity; bustle **2** a nervous state **3** a quarrel **4** a showy display of approval, etc. —***vi.*** **1** to bustle about or worry over trifles **2** to whine, as a baby

fuss′budg′et (-buj′it) ***n.*** ⟦prec. + BUDGET⟧ [Inf.] a fussy person: also [Inf., Chiefly Brit.] **fuss′pot′** (-pät′)

fuss′y ***adj.*** **-i·er, -i·est** **1** *a*) worrying over trifles *b*) hard to please *c*) whining, as a baby **2** full of unnecessary details —**fuss′i·ly** ***adv.*** —**fuss′i·ness** ***n.***

fus·tian (fus′chən) ***n.*** ⟦< L *fustis*, wooden stick⟧ pompous, pretentious talk or writing; bombast

fus·ty (fus′tē) ***adj.*** **-ti·er, -ti·est** ⟦< OFr *fust*, a cask⟧ **1** musty; moldy **2** old-fashioned —**fus′ti·ly** ***adv.*** —**fus′ti·ness** ***n.***

fut *abbrev.* future

fu·tile (fyo͞ot′'l) ***adj.*** ⟦< L *futilis*, lit., that easily pours out⟧ useless; vain —**fu′tile·ly** ***adv.*** —**fu·til·i·ty** (fyo͞o til′ə tē), *pl.* **-ties**, ***n.***

fu·ton (fo͞o′tän′) ***n.*** ⟦Sino-Jpn⟧ a thin mattress like a quilt, placed as on the floor or a platform frame for use as a bed

fu·ture (fyo͞o′chər) ***adj.*** ⟦< L *futurus*, about to be⟧ **1** that is to be or come **2** indicating time to come *[the future tense]* —***n.*** **1** the time that is to come **2** what is going to be **3** the chance to succeed, etc. **4** [*usually pl.*] a contract for a commodity bought or sold for delivery at a later date —**fu′tur·is′tic** ***adj.***

fu·tu·ri·ty (fyo͞o toor′ə tē, -tyoor′-) ***n.***, *pl.* **-ties** **1** the future **2** a future condition or event **3** a race for two-year-old horses in which the entries are selected before birth: in full **futurity race**

fu·tur·ol·o·gy (fyo͞o′chər äl′ə jē) ***n.*** ⟦FUTUR(E) + -OLOGY⟧ the study of probable or presumed future conditions as extrapolated from known facts —**fu′tur·ol′o·gist** ***n.***

futz (futs) ***vi.*** ⟦? < Yiddish⟧ [Slang] to trifle or fool (*around*)

fuzz (fuz) ***n.*** ⟦< ?⟧ **1** loose, light particles of down, wool, etc.; fine hairs or fibers —**the fuzz** [Slang] a policeman or the police —**fuzz′y**, **-i·er, -i·est**, ***adj.***

fuzzy logic ⟦< *fuzzy* (*set*), coined (1965) by L. A. Zadeh, U.S. scientist⟧ a type of logic used in computers for processing imprecise or variable data

-fy (fī) ⟦< L *facere*, do⟧ *suffix* **1** to make *[liquefy]* **2** to cause to have *[glorify]* **3** to become *[putrefy]*

FYI *abbrev.* for your information

G

g or **G** (jē) ***n.***, *pl.* **g's, G's** the seventh letter of the English alphabet

G[1] (jē) ***n.*** *Music* the fifth tone in the scale of C major

G[2] *trademark for* a film rating indicating content suitable for persons of all ages

G[3] *abbrev.* **1** game(s) **2** German **3** goal(s) **4** gram(s) **5** guard **6** gulf Also, except for 2 & 6, **g**

Ga *Chem. symbol for* gallium

GA Georgia

gab (gab) ***n., vt.*** **gabbed, gab'bing** ⟦ON *gabba*, to mock⟧ [Inf.] chatter

gab·ar·dine (gab'ər dēn') ***n.*** ⟦< OFr *gaverdine*, kind of cloak⟧ a twilled cloth of wool, cotton, etc., with a fine, diagonal weave: Brit. sp. **gab'er·dine'**

gab·ble (gab'əl) ***vi., vt.*** **-bled, -bling** ⟦< GAB⟧ to talk or utter rapidly or incoherently —***n.*** such talk

gab·by (gab'ē) ***adj.*** **-bi·er, -bi·est** [Inf.] talkative —**gab'bi·ness** ***n.***

gab'fest' (-fest') ***n.*** [Inf.] an informal gathering of people to talk with one another

ga·ble (gā'bəl) ***n.*** ⟦< Gmc⟧ a triangular part of a wall enclosed by the sloping sides of a peaked roof —**ga'bled** ***adj.***

Ga·bon (ga bōn') country on the W coast of Africa: 103,347 sq. mi.; pop. 1,012,000

Ga·bri·el (gā'brē əl) ***n.*** *Bible* one of the archangels, the herald of good news

gad (gad) ***vi.*** **gad'ded, gad'ding** ⟦ME *gadden*, to hurry⟧ to wander about in an idle or restless way —**gad'der** ***n.***

gad'a·bout' ***n.*** one who gads about, looking for fun, etc.

gad'fly' ***n.***, *pl.* **-flies'** ⟦see GOAD & FLY[2]⟧ **1** a large fly that bites livestock **2** one who annoys others, esp. by rousing them from complacency

gadg·et (gaj'it) ***n.*** ⟦< ?⟧ any small mechanical contrivance or device

Gael·ic (gā'lik) ***adj.*** of the Celtic people of Ireland, Scotland, or the Isle of Man —***n.*** **1** the Celtic language of Scotland **2** the language group that includes GAELIC (*n.* 1), IRISH (*n.* 1), etc.

gaff (gaf) ***n.*** ⟦< OProv *gaf* or Sp *gafa*⟧ **1** a large hook on a pole for landing fish **2** a spar supporting a fore-and-aft sail

gaffe (gaf) ***n.*** ⟦Fr⟧ a blunder

gaf·fer (gaf'ər) ***n.*** a person in charge of lighting on the set of a film

gag (gag) ***vt.*** **gagged, gag'ging** ⟦echoic⟧ **1** to cause to retch **2** to keep from speaking, as by stopping up the mouth of —***vi.*** to retch —***n.*** **1** something put into or over the mouth to prevent talking, etc. **2** any restraint of free speech **3** a joke

gage[1] (gāj) ***n.*** ⟦< OFr, a pledge⟧ a glove, etc. thrown down as by a knight as a challenge to fight

gage[2] (gāj) ***n., vt.*** **gaged, gag'ing** *alt. sp. of* GAUGE

gag·gle (gag'əl) ***n.*** ⟦echoic⟧ **1** a flock of geese **2** any group or cluster

gai·e·ty (gā'ə tē) ***n.***, *pl.* **-ties** **1** the quality of being GAY (*adj.* 1); cheerfulness **2** merrymaking

gai·ly (gā'lē) ***adv.*** in a gay manner; specif., *a*) merrily *b*) brightly

gain (gān) ***n.*** ⟦< OFr *gaaigne*⟧ **1** an increase; specif., *a*) [*often pl.*] profit *b*) an increase in advantage **2** acquisition —***vt.*** **1** to earn **2** to win **3** to attract **4** to get as an addition, profit, or advantage **5** to make an increase in **6** to get to; reach —***vi.*** **1** to make progress **2** to increase in weight —**gain on** to draw nearer to (an opponent in a race, etc.)

gain'er ***n.*** **1** a person or thing that gains **2** a fancy dive forward, but with a backward somersault

gain'ful ***adj.*** producing gain; profitable —**gain'ful·ly** ***adv.***

gain·say (gān'sā') ***vt.*** **-said'** (-sed'), **-say'ing** ⟦< OE *gegn*, against + *secgan*, to say⟧ **1** to deny **2** to contradict —**gain'say'er** ***n.***

gait (gāt) ***n.*** ⟦< ON *gata*, path⟧ **1** manner of walking or running **2** any of the various foot movements of a horse, as a trot, pace, canter, etc.

gai·ter (gāt'ər) ***n.*** ⟦< Fr *guêtre*⟧ a cloth or leather covering for the instep, ankle, and lower leg

gal[1] (gal) ***n.*** [Slang] a girl or woman

gal[2] *abbrev.* gallon(s)

ga·la (gā'lə, gal'ə) ***n.*** ⟦ult. < It *gala*⟧ a celebration —***adj.*** festive

gal·a·bi·a or **gal·a·bi·ya** (gal'ə bē'ə, gə lä'bē ə) ***n.*** ⟦< Ar⟧ *var. of* DJELLABA

Gal·a·had (gal'ə had') ***n.*** *Arthurian Legend* the knight who, because of his purity, finds the Holy Grail

gal·ax·y (gal'ək sē) ***n.***, *pl.* **-ies** ⟦< Gr *gala*, milk⟧ **1** [*often* **G-**] MILKY WAY **2** a large, independent system of stars **3** a group of illustrious people —**ga·lac·tic** (gə lak'tik) ***adj.***

gale (gāl) ***n.*** ⟦< ?⟧ **1** a strong wind **2** an outburst *[a gale of laughter]*

ga·le·na (gə lē'nə) ***n.*** ⟦L, lead ore⟧ native lead sulfide, a soft, lead-gray mineral with a metallic luster

Gal·i·lee (gal'ə lē'), **Sea of** lake in NE Israel

Gal·i·le·o (gal'ə lē'ō, -lā'-) 1564-1642; It. astronomer & physicist

gall[1] (gôl) ***n.*** ⟦OE *galla*⟧ **1** BILE (sense 1) **2** something bitter or distasteful **3** bitter feeling **4** impudence

gall[2] (gôl) ***n.*** ⟦see fol.⟧ a sore on the skin caused by chafing —***vt.*** **1** to make sore by rubbing **2** to annoy; vex

gall[3] (gôl) ***n.*** ⟦< L *galla*⟧ a tumor on plant tissue caused by stimulation by fungi, insects, etc.

gal·lant (gal'ənt; *for adj. 3 & n., usually* gə lant', -länt') ***adj.*** ⟦< OFr *galer*, to make merry⟧ **1** stately; imposing **2**

brave and noble 3 polite and attentive to women —*n.* 1 [Now Rare] a high-spirited, stylish man 2 a man attentive and polite to women

gal·lant·ry (gal′ən trē) *n., pl.* **-ries** 1 heroic courage 2 the behavior of a gallant 3 a courteous act or remark

gall·blad·der (gôl′blad′ər) *n.* a membranous sac closely attached to the liver, in which excess gall, or bile, is stored

gal·le·on (gal′ē ən) *n.* ⟦ult. < Gr *galeos,* shark⟧ a large sailing ship of the 15th and 16th c.

gal·le·ri·a (gal′ə rē′ə) *n.* a large arcade or court, sometimes with a glass roof

gal·ler·y (gal′ər ē) *n., pl.* **-ies** ⟦< ML *galeria*⟧ 1 a covered walk or porch open at one side or having the roof supported by pillars 2 a long, narrow, outside balcony 3 *a*) a balcony in a theater, etc.; esp., the highest balcony with the cheapest seats *b*) the people in these seats 4 the spectators at a sports event, etc. 5 a place for exhibiting or selling works of art; specif., a display room in a museum

GALLEY

gal·ley (gal′ē) *n., pl.* **-leys** ⟦< Gr *galeos,* shark⟧ 1 a long, low ship of ancient times, propelled by oars and sails 2 a ship's kitchen 3 *Printing a*) a shallow tray for holding composed type *b*) proof printed from such type (in full, **galley proof**)

Gal·lic (gal′ik) *adj.* 1 of ancient Gaul or its people 2 French

Gal·li·cism (gal′i siz′əm) *n.* ⟦< prec.⟧ [*also* **g-**] a French idiom, custom, etc.

gal·li·um (gal′ē əm) *n.* ⟦named after L *Gallia,* France⟧ a bluish-white, metallic chemical element with a low melting point, used in semiconductors, lasers, etc.

gal·li·vant (gal′ə vant′) *vi.* ⟦arbitrary elaboration of GALLANT⟧ to go about in search of amusement

gal·lon (gal′ən) *n.* ⟦< OFr *jalon*⟧ a liquid measure equal to four quarts

gal·lop (gal′əp) *vi., vt.* ⟦< OFr *galoper*⟧ to go, or cause to go, at a gallop —*n.* the fastest gait of a horse, etc., a succession of leaping strides

gal·lows (gal′ōz) *n., pl.* **-lows** or **-lows·es** ⟦OE *galga*⟧ an upright frame with a crossbeam and a rope, for hanging condemned persons

gall·stone (gôl′stōn′) *n.* a small, solid mass sometimes formed in the gallbladder or bile duct

ga·lore (gə lôr′) *adj.* ⟦Ir *go leōr,* enough⟧ in abundance; plentifully *[to attract crowds galore]*

ga·losh or **ga·loshe** (gə läsh′) *n.* ⟦< OFr *galoche*⟧ a high, warmly lined overshoe of rubber and fabric

gal·van·ic (gal van′ik) *adj.* ⟦after L. *Galvani* (1737-98), It physicist⟧ 1 of or producing direct current from a chemical reaction, as in a battery 2 startling

gal·va·nize (gal′və nīz′) *vt.* **-nized′, -niz′ing** 1 to stimulate as if by electric shock; rouse; stir 2 to plate (metal) with zinc

gal′va·nom′e·ter (-näm′ət ər) *n.* an instrument for detecting and measuring a small electric current

Gam·bi·a (gam′bē ə) country on the W coast of Africa: 4,361 sq. mi.; pop. 1,026,000

gam·bit (gam′bit) *n.* ⟦< Sp *gambito,* a tripping⟧ 1 *Chess* an opening in which a pawn, etc. is sacrificed to get an advantage in position 2 an action intended to gain an advantage

gam·ble (gam′bəl) *vi.* **-bled, -bling** ⟦ME *gamen,* to play⟧ 1 to play games of chance for money, etc. 2 to take a risk for some advantage —*vt.* to risk in gambling; bet —*n.* an undertaking involving risk —**gam′bler** *n.*

gam·bol (gam′bəl) *n.* ⟦< It *gamba,* leg⟧ a gamboling; frolic —*vi.* **-boled** or **-bolled, -bol·ing** or **-bol·ling** to jump and skip about in play; frolic

gam·brel (roof) (gam′brəl) a roof with two slopes on each of its two sides

game[1] (gām) *n.* ⟦OE *gamen*⟧ 1 any form of play; amusement 2 *a*) any specific amusement or sport involving competition under rules *b*) a single contest in such a competition 3 the number of points required for winning 4 a scheme; plan 5 wild birds or animals hunted for sport or food 6 [Inf.] a business or job, esp. one involving risk —*vi.* **gamed, gam′ing** to play cards, etc. for stakes; gamble —*adj.* 1 designating or of wild birds or animals hunted for sport or food 2 *a*) plucky; courageous *b*) enthusiastic; ready (*for* something) —**the game is up** failure is certain —**game′ly** *adv.* —**game′ness** *n.*

game[2] (gām) *adj.* ⟦< ?⟧ lame or injured *[a game leg]*

game′cock′ *n.* a specially bred rooster trained for cockfighting

game′keep′er *n.* a person who takes care of game birds and animals, as on an estate

game plan 1 the strategy planned before a game 2 any long-range strategy

game point 1 the situation when the next point scored could win a game 2 the winning point

games·man·ship (gāmz′mən ship′) *n.* skill in using ploys to gain an advantage

game·ster (gām′stər) *n.* a gambler

gam·ete (gam′ēt, gə mēt′) *n.* ⟦< Gr *gamos,* marriage⟧ a reproductive cell that unites with another to form the cell that develops into a new individual

gam·in (gam′in) ***n.*** ⟦Fr⟧ **1** a neglected child who roams the streets **2** a girl with saucy charm: also **ga·mine** (ga mēn′)

gam·ma (gam′ə) ***n.*** the third letter of the Greek alphabet (Γ, γ)

gamma glob·u·lin (gläb′yoo lin) that fraction of blood serum which contains most antibodies

gamma ray an electromagnetic radiation with a very short wavelength, produced as by the reactions of nuclei

gam·ut (gam′ət) ***n.*** ⟦< Gr letter *gamma*, for the lowest note of the medieval scale⟧ **1** any complete musical scale **2** the entire range or extent, as of emotions

gam·y (gām′ē) ***adj.*** **-i·er, -i·est** **1** having the strong flavor of cooked game **2** slightly tainted **3** risqué **4** coarse or crude —**gam′i·ness** ***n.***

gan·der (gan′dər) ***n.*** ⟦OE *gan(d)ra*⟧ **1** a male goose **2** [Slang] a look: chiefly in **take a gander**

Gan·dhi (gän′dē), **Mo·han·das** (mō hän′ dəs) 1869-1948; Hindu nationalist leader: called *Mahatma Gandhi*

gang (gaŋ) ***n.*** ⟦< OE *gangan*, to go⟧ a group of people working or acting together; specif., a group of criminals or juvenile delinquents —**gang up on** [Inf.] to attack as a group

Gan·ges (gan′jēz) river in N India & Bangladesh

gan·gling (gaŋ′gliŋ) ***adj.*** ⟦< ?⟧ thin, tall, and awkward: also **gan′gly**

gan·gli·on (gaŋ′glē ən) ***n.***, *pl.* **-gli·a** (-ə) or **-gli·ons** ⟦ult. < Gr, tumor⟧ a mass of nerve cells from which nerve impulses are transmitted

gang′plank′ ***n.*** a movable ramp by which to board or leave a ship

gan·grene (gaŋ′grēn′, gaŋ grēn′) ***n.*** ⟦< Gr *gran*, gnaw⟧ decay of body tissue when the blood supply is obstructed —**gan′gre·nous** (-grə nəs) ***adj.***

gang·ster (gaŋ′stər) ***n.*** a member of a gang of criminals —**gang′ster·ism′** ***n.***

gang′way′ ***n.*** ⟦OE *gangweg*⟧ **1** a passageway **2** *a*) an opening in a ship's bulwarks for loading, etc. *b*) GANGPLANK —***interj.*** clear the way!

gant·let (gônt′lit, gänt′-, gant′-) ***n.*** ⟦< Swed *gata*, lane + *lopp*, a run⟧ **1** a former punishment in which the offender ran between two rows of men who struck him **2** a series of troubles Now sp. equally *gauntlet*

gan·try (gan′trē) ***n.***, *pl.* **-tries** ⟦< L *canterius*, beast of burden⟧ **1** a framework, often on wheels, for a traveling crane **2** a wheeled framework with a crane, platforms, etc., for readying a rocket to be launched

GAO *abbrev.* General Accounting Office

gaol (jāl) ***n.*** *Brit. sp. of* JAIL

gap (gap) ***n.*** ⟦< ON *gapa*, to gape⟧ **1** an opening made by breaking or parting **2** a mountain pass or ravine **3** a blank space; lacuna **4** a lag or disparity

gape (gāp) ***vi.*** **gaped, gap′ing** ⟦< ON *gapa*⟧ **1** to open the mouth wide, as in yawning **2** to stare with the mouth open **3** to open wide —***n.*** **1** a gaping **2** a wide opening —**gap′ing·ly** ***adv.***

gar (gär) ***n.***, *pl.* **gar** or **gars** ⟦< OE *gar*, a spear⟧ a freshwater fish with a long, beaklike snout: also **gar′fish′**

ga·rage (gə räzh′, -räj′) ***n.*** ⟦Fr < *garer*, to protect⟧ **1** a shelter for motor vehicles **2** a business place where motor vehicles are stored, repaired, etc.

garage sale a sale of used or unwanted household articles, etc.

garb (gärb) ***n.*** ⟦< It *garbo*, elegance⟧ clothing; style of dress *[clerical garb]* —***vt.*** to clothe

gar·bage (gär′bij) ***n.*** ⟦ME, entrails of fowls⟧ **1** spoiled or waste food **2** any worthless, offensive, etc. matter

gar·ble (gär′bəl) ***vt.*** **-bled, -bling** ⟦< Ar *gharbāl*, a sieve⟧ to distort or confuse (a story, etc.)

gar·çon (gȧr sōn′) ***n.***, *pl.* ***-çons′*** (-sōn′) ⟦Fr⟧ a waiter

gar·den (gärd″n) ***n.*** ⟦< Frankish⟧ **1** a piece of ground for growing vegetables, flowers, etc. **2** an area of fertile land: also **garden spot** **3** [*often pl.*] a public, parklike place, sometimes having displays of animals or plants —***vi.*** to take care of a garden —***adj.*** of, for, or grown in a garden —**gar′den·er** ***n.***

gar·de·ni·a (gär dēn′yə) ***n.*** ⟦after A. *Garden* (1730-91), Am botanist⟧ a plant with fragrant, waxy flowers

gar′den-va·ri′e·ty ***adj.*** ordinary; commonplace

Gar·field (gär′fēld), **James A·bram** (jāmz ā′brəm) 1831-81; 20th president of the U.S. (1881): assassinated

Gar·gan·tu·a (gär gan′choo ə) ***n.*** a giant king in a satire by Rabelais —**gar·gan′tu·an** ***adj.***

gar·gle (gär′gəl) ***vt., vi.*** **-gled, -gling** ⟦< Fr *gargouille*, throat⟧ to rinse (the throat) with a liquid kept in motion by the expulsion of air from the lungs —***n.*** a liquid for gargling

gar·goyle (gär′goil′) ***n.*** ⟦see prec.⟧ a waterspout formed like a fantastic creature, projecting from a building

Gar·i·bal·di (gar′ə bôl′dē), **Giu·sep·pe** (joo zep′pe) 1807-82; It. patriot & general

gar·ish (gar′ish, ger′-) ***adj.*** ⟦prob. < ME *gauren*, to stare⟧ too bright or gaudy; showy —**gar′ish·ly** ***adv.*** —**gar′ish·ness** ***n.***

gar·land (gär′lənd) ***n.*** ⟦< OFr *garlande*⟧ a wreath of flowers, leaves, etc. —***vt.*** to decorate with garlands

Gar·land (gär′lənd) city in NE Texas: pop. 181,000

gar·lic (gär′lik) ***n.*** ⟦< OE *gar*, a spear + *leac*, leek⟧ **1** an herb of the lily family **2** its strong-smelling bulb, used as seasoning —**gar′lick·y** ***adj.***

gar·ment (gär′mənt) ***n.*** ⟦see GARNISH⟧ any article of clothing

gar·ner (gär′nər) ***vt.*** ⟦< L *granum*, grain⟧ **1** to gather and store **2** to get or earn

gar·net (gär′nit) ***n.*** ⟦< ML *granatum*⟧ a hard, glasslike mineral: red varieties are often used as gems

gar·nish (gär′nish) ***vt.*** ⟦< OFr *garnir*, furnish⟧ **1** to decorate **2** to decorate (food) with something that adds color or flavor **3** *Law* to attach (a debtor's property, wages, etc.) so that it can be used to pay the debt **—*n.*** **1** a decoration **2** something used to garnish food, as parsley

gar·nish·ee (gär′ni shē′) ***vt.*** **-eed′**, **-ee′ing** ⟦< prec.⟧ GARNISH (*vt.* 3): now rare in legal usage

gar′nish·ment ***n.*** *Law* a proceeding by which a creditor seeks to attach a debtor's wages, etc.

gar·ret (gar′it) ***n.*** ⟦< OFr *garite*, watchtower⟧ an attic

gar·ri·son (gar′ə sən) ***n.*** ⟦< OFr *garir*, to watch⟧ **1** troops stationed in a fort or fortified place **2** a military post or station **—*vt.*** to station (troops) in (a fortified place) for its defense

gar·rote (gə rät′, -rōt′) ***n.*** ⟦Sp⟧ **1** a cord, thong, etc. used in strangling a person in a surprise attack **2** a strangling in this way **—*vt.*** **-rot′ed** or **-rot′ted**, **-rot′ing** or **-rot′ting** to execute or attack by such strangling Also **ga·rotte′** or **gar·rotte′** **—gar·rot′er** ***n.***

gar·ru·lous (gar′ə ləs) ***adj.*** ⟦< L *garrire*, to chatter⟧ talking much, esp. about unimportant things **—gar·ru·li·ty** (gə ro͞o′lə tē) or **gar′ru·lous·ness** ***n.*** **—gar′ru·lous·ly** ***adv.***

gar·ter (gärt′ər) ***n.*** ⟦< OFr *garet*, the back of the knee⟧ an elastic band or strap for holding a stocking in place

garter belt a belt of elastic fabric with hanging garters, worn by women

garter snake a small, harmless snake common in North America

Gar·y (ger′ē) city in NW Indiana: pop. 117,000

gas (gas) ***n.***, *pl.* **gas′es** or **gas′ses** ⟦coined < Gr *chaos*, space⟧ **1** the fluid form of a substance in which it can expand indefinitely; vapor **2** any mixture of flammable gases used for lighting or heating **3** any gas used as an anesthetic **4** any poisonous substance dispersed in the air, as in war **5** [Inf.] GASOLINE **—*vt.*** **gassed**, **gas′sing** to injure or kill by gas **—gas up** [Inf.] to supply (a vehicle) with gasoline **—gas′e·ous** (-ē əs) ***adj.***

gas chamber a room in which people are put to be killed with poison gas

gash (gash) ***vt.*** ⟦< Gr *charassein*, to cut⟧ to make a long, deep cut in; slash **—*n.*** a long, deep cut

gas·ket (gas′kit) ***n.*** ⟦prob. < OFr *garcete*, small cord⟧ a piece or ring of rubber, metal, etc. used to make a joint leakproof

gas mask a filtering mask worn to prevent the breathing in of poisonous gases

gas·o·hol (gas′ə hôl′) ***n.*** a motor fuel mixture of gasoline and alcohol

gas·o·line (gas′ə lēn′, gas′ə lēn′) ***n.*** ⟦< *gas* + L *oleum*, oil⟧ a volatile, flammable liquid distilled from petroleum, used chiefly as a fuel in internal-combustion engines: also **gas′o·lene′**

gasp (gasp) ***vi.*** ⟦< ON *geispa*, to yawn⟧ to inhale suddenly, as in surprise, or breathe with effort **—*vt.*** to say with gasps **—*n.*** a gasping

gas station SERVICE STATION

gas′sy ***adj.*** **-si·er**, **-si·est** **1** full of gas; esp., flatulent **2** like gas

gas·tric (gas′trik) ***adj.*** ⟦GASTR(O)- + -IC⟧ of, in, or near the stomach

gastric juice the clear, acid digestive fluid produced by glands in the stomach lining

gas·tri·tis (gas trīt′is) ***n.*** ⟦fol. + -ITIS⟧ inflammation of the stomach

gastro- ⟦< Gr *gastēr*⟧ *combining form* stomach (and)

gas·tron·o·my (gas trän′ə mē) ***n.*** ⟦< Gr *gastēr*, stomach + *nomos*, a rule⟧ the art or science of good eating **—gas′tro·nom′ic** (-trə näm′ik) or **gas′tro·nom′i·cal** ***adj.***

gas·tro·pod (gas′trō päd′) ***n.*** ⟦GASTRO- + -POD⟧ a mollusk of the class including snails, slugs, etc.

gate (gāt) ***n.*** ⟦OE⟧ **1** a movable structure controlling passage through an opening in a fence or wall **2** a gateway **3** a movable barrier **4** a structure controlling the flow of water, as in a canal **5** the total amount or number of paid admissions to a performance **—give** (or **get**) **the gate** [Slang] to subject (or be subjected) to dismissal

-gate (gāt) ⟦< (*Water*)*gate*, political scandal, after the *Watergate*, building in Washington, D.C., site of 1972 burglary⟧ *combining form* a scandal marked by charges of corruption on the part of public officials, etc.

gate′-crash′er ***n.*** [Inf.] one who attends a social affair without an invitation or attends a performance without paying

gate′fold′ ***n.*** an oversize page, as in a magazine, bound so it can be unfolded and opened out

gate′way′ ***n.*** **1** an entrance as in a wall, fitted with a gate **2** a means of access

gath·er (ga*th*′ər) ***vt.*** ⟦OE *gad*(*e*)*rian*⟧ **1** to bring together in one place or group **2** to get gradually; accumulate **3** to collect by picking; harvest **4** to infer; conclude **5** to draw (cloth) into folds or puckers **—*vi.*** **1** to assemble **2** to increase **—*n.*** a pucker or fold **—gath′er·er** ***n.***

gath′er·ing ***n.*** **1** a meeting; crowd **2** a gather in cloth

ga·tor or **'ga·tor** (gā′tər) ***n.*** *short for* ALLIGATOR

gauche (gōsh) ***adj.*** ⟦Fr < MFr *gauchir*, become warped⟧ lacking social grace; awkward; tactless

gau·che·rie (gō′shə rē) ***n.*** gauche behavior or a gauche act

gau·cho (gou′chō) ***n.***, *pl.* **-chos** ⟦AmSp⟧ a South American cowboy

gaud·y (gô′dē) ***adj.*** **-i·er**, **-i·est** ⟦< ME *gaude*, trinket⟧ bright and showy, but lacking in good taste **—gaud′i·ly** ***adv.*** **—gaud′i·ness** ***n.***

gauge (gāj) ***n.*** ⟦NormFr⟧ **1** a standard measure or criterion **2** any device for measuring **3** the distance between the rails of a railroad **4** the size of the bore of a shotgun **5** the thickness of sheet metal, wire, etc. —***vt.* gauged, gaug′ing** **1** to measure the size, amount, etc. of **2** to judge

Gaul[1] (gôl) ***n.*** a member of the people of ancient Gaul

Gaul[2] (gôl) ancient division of the Roman Empire, in W Europe

Gaul′ish ***n.*** the Celtic language of ancient Gaul

gaunt (gônt) ***adj.*** ⟦ME *gawnte*⟧ **1** thin and bony; haggard, as from great hunger **2** looking grim or forbidding —**gaunt′ness** ***n.***

gaunt·let[1] (gônt′lit, gänt′-) ***n.*** ⟦< OFr *gant*, glove⟧ **1** a knight's armored glove **2** a long glove with a flaring cuff —**throw down the gauntlet** to challenge, as to combat

gaunt·let[2] (gônt′lit, gänt′-) ***n.*** *see* GANTLET

gauze (gôz) ***n.*** ⟦< Fr *gaze* < Ar *ḳazz*, silk⟧ any very thin, transparent, loosely woven material, as of cotton or silk —**gauz′y, -i·er, -i·est,** ***adj.***

gave (gāv) ***vt., vi.*** *pt. of* GIVE

gav·el (gav′əl) ***n.*** ⟦? < Scot *gable*, fork⟧ a small mallet rapped on the table, as by a presiding officer, to call for attention, etc.

ga·votte (gə vät′) ***n.*** ⟦Fr⟧ a 17th-c. dance like the minuet, but livelier

gawk (gôk) ***vi.*** ⟦prob. < *gowk*, stupid person⟧ to stare stupidly

gawk·y (gô′kē) ***adj.*** **-i·er, -i·est** ⟦see prec.⟧ clumsy; ungainly —**gawk′i·ly** ***adv.*** —**gawk′i·ness** ***n.***

gay (gā) ***adj.*** ⟦OFr *gai*⟧ **1** joyous and lively; merry **2** bright; brilliant *[gay colors]* **3** homosexual —***n.*** a homosexual; esp., a homosexual man

gay·e·ty (gā′ə tē) ***n.,*** *pl.* **-ties** *alt. sp. of* GAIETY

gay·ly (gā′lē) ***adv.*** *alt. sp. of* GAILY

gaze (gāz) ***vi.*** **gazed, gaz′ing** ⟦< Scand⟧ to look steadily; stare —***n.*** a steady look

ga·ze·bo (gə zē′bō, -zā′-) ***n.,*** *pl.* **-bos** or **-boes** ⟦< prec.⟧ a summerhouse, windowed balcony, etc. from which one can gaze at the scenery around it

ga·zelle (gə zel′) ***n.*** ⟦< Ar *ghazāl*⟧ a small, swift antelope of Africa and Asia, with large, lustrous eyes

ga·zette (gə zet′) ***n.*** ⟦Fr < It dial. *gazeta*, a small coin, price of the newspaper⟧ **1** a newspaper: now mainly in newspaper titles **2** in England, an official publication —***vt.*** **-zet′ted, -zet′ting** [Brit.] to publish or announce in a gazette

gaz·et·teer (gaz′ə tir′) ***n.*** a dictionary or index of geographical names

ga·zil·lion (gə zil′yən) ***n.*** [Slang] a very large, indefinite number

gaz·pa·cho (gäs pä′chō, gäz-) ***n.*** ⟦Sp⟧ a cold Spanish soup of chopped raw tomatoes, cucumbers, onions, and peppers, mixed with oil, vinegar, etc.

GB *abbrev.* **1** gigabyte(s) **2** Great Britain

Ge *Chem. symbol for* germanium

gear (gir) ***n.*** ⟦prob. < ON *gervi*, preparation⟧ **1** clothing **2** equipment, esp. for some task **3** *a*) a toothed wheel designed to mesh with another *b*) [*often pl.*] a system of such gears meshed together to pass motion along *c*) a specific adjustment of such a system *d*) a part of a mechanism with a specific function *[the steering gear]* —***vt.*** **1** to connect by or furnish with gears **2** to adapt (one thing) to conform with another *[to gear supply to demand]* —**in** (or **out of**) **gear** **1** (not) connected to the motor **2** (not) in proper working order

gear′shift′ ***n.*** the lever for engaging or disengaging any of several sets of transmission gears to a motor, etc.

gear′wheel′ ***n.*** a toothed wheel in a system of gears; cogwheel

geck·o (gek′ō) ***n.,*** *pl.* **-os** or **-oes** ⟦prob. < Malay⟧ a tropical lizard with suction pads on its feet

GED[1] *trademark for* General Educational Development

GED[2] *abbrev.* general equivalency diploma

gee (jē) ***interj.*** ⟦< JE(SUS)⟧ [Slang] used to express surprise, wonder, etc.

geek (gēk) ***n.*** [Slang] a person considered to be different from others in a negative way, as in being socially awkward —**geek′y, -i·er, -i·est,** ***adj.***

geese (gēs) ***n.*** *pl. of* GOOSE

gee whiz an exclamation used to express surprise, enthusiasm, protest, etc.

gee·zer (gē′zər) ***n.*** ⟦< GUISE⟧ [Slang] an old man

ge·fil·te fish (gə fil′tə) ⟦E Yiddish⟧ chopped, seasoned fish, boiled and served in balls or cakes

Gei·ger counter (gī′gər) ⟦after H. *Geiger* (1882-1945), Ger physicist⟧ an instrument for detecting and counting ionizing particles, as from radioactive ores

gei·sha (gā′shə) ***n.,*** *pl.* **-sha** or **-shas** ⟦Sino-Jpn *gei*, art + *sha*, person⟧ a Japanese woman trained in singing, conversation, etc. to serve as a hired companion to men

gel (jel) ***n.*** ⟦< fol.⟧ **1** a jellylike substance formed from a colloidal solution **2** any of various jellylike preparations for setting hair, brushing teeth, etc. —***vi.*** **gelled, gel′ling** to form a gel

gel·a·tin (jel′ə tin) ***n.*** ⟦< L *gelare*, freeze⟧ a tasteless, odorless substance extracted by boiling bones, horns, etc., or a similar vegetable substance: dissolved and cooled, it forms a jellylike substance used in foods, photographic film, etc.: also **gel′a·tine** (-tēn, -tin) —**ge·lat·i·nous** (jə lat′'n əs) ***adj.***

geld (geld) ***vt.*** **geld′ed** or **gelt, geld′ing** ⟦< ON *geldr*, barren⟧ to castrate (esp. a horse)

geld′ing ***n.*** a castrated horse

gel·id (jel′id) ***adj.*** ⟦< L *gelu*, frost⟧ extremely cold; frozen

gem (jem) ***n.*** ⟦< L *gemma*, a bud⟧ **1** a cut and polished gemstone or a pearl **2** someone or something very precious or valuable

Gem·i·ni (jem′ə nī′, -nē′) ***n.*** ⟦L, twins⟧

the third sign of the zodiac

gem'stone' *n.* any mineral that can be used in a piece of jewelry when cut and polished

ge·müt·lich (gə müt'liH) *adj.* ⟦Ger⟧ agreeable, cheerful, cozy, etc.

gen *abbrev.* general

Gen *abbrev.* **1** General **2** *Bible* Genesis

-gen (jən, jen) ⟦< Gr *-genēs*, born⟧ *suffix* **1** something that produces *[hydrogen]* **2** something produced (in a specified way)

gen·darme (zhän därm') *n.* ⟦Fr < *gens d'armes*, men-at-arms⟧ a French police officer

gen·der (jen'dər) *n.* ⟦< L *genus*, origin⟧ **1** *Gram.* the classification by which words are grouped as masculine, feminine, or neuter **2** the fact of being a male or female human being, esp. as it affects a person's self-image, social relationships, etc.

gen'dered *adj.* affected by issues of GENDER (*n.* 2)

gene (jēn) *n.* ⟦see -GEN⟧ any of the units in the chromosomes by which hereditary characteristics are transmitted

ge·ne·al·o·gy (jē'nē äl'ə jē) *n.*, *pl.* **-gies** ⟦< Gr *genea*, race + *-logia*, -LOGY⟧ **1** a recorded history of a person's ancestry **2** the study of family descent **3** lineage —**ge'ne·a·log'i·cal** (-ə läj'i kəl) *adj.* —**ge'ne·al'o·gist** *n.*

gen·er·a (jen'ər ə) *n. pl. of* GENUS

gen·er·al (jen'ər əl) *adj.* ⟦< L *genus*, class⟧ **1** of, for, or from all; not local, special, or specialized **2** of or for a whole genus, kind, etc. **3** widespread *[general* unrest*]* **4** most common; usual **5** not specific or precise *[*in *general* terms*]* **6** highest in rank *[*attorney *general]* —*n.* a military officer ranking above a colonel, specif. one ranking above a lieutenant general —**in general** **1** usually **2** without specific details —**gen'er·al·ship'** *n.*

general assembly [*often* **G- A-**] **1** the legislative assembly in some U.S. states **2** the deliberative assembly of the United Nations

general delivery delivery of mail at the post office to addressees who call for it

gen·er·al·is·si·mo (jen'ər ə lis'i mō') *n.*, *pl.* **-mos'** ⟦It⟧ in some countries, the commander in chief of the armed forces

gen·er·al·i·ty (jen'ər al'ə tē) *n.*, *pl.* **-ties** **1** the quality of being general **2** a general or vague statement, idea, etc. **3** the main body

gen·er·al·ize (jen'ər əl īz') *vt.* **-ized'**, **-iz'ing** **1** to state in terms of a general law **2** to infer or derive (a general law) from (particular instances) —*vi.* **1** to formulate general principles **2** to talk in generalities

gen'er·al·ly *adv.* **1** widely; popularly **2** usually **3** not specifically

general practitioner a practicing physician who does not specialize in a particular field of medicine

gen·er·ate (jen'ər āt') *vt.* **-at'ed**, **-at'ing** ⟦< L *genus*, race⟧ **1** to produce (offspring); beget **2** to bring into being —**gen'er·a'tive** (-āt'iv, -ə tiv) *adj.*

gen'er·a'tion *n.* **1** the producing of offspring **2** production **3** a single stage in the succession of descent **4** the average period (*c.* 30 years) between human generations **5** all the people born and living at about the same time —**gen'er·a'tion·al** *adj.*

generation gap the differences in attitudes, experiences, etc. between contemporary older and younger generations

Generation X (eks) the generation of persons born in the 1960s and 1970s

gen'er·a'tor *n.* a machine for changing mechanical energy into electrical energy; dynamo

ge·ner·ic (jə ner'ik) *adj.* ⟦< L *genus*, race, kind⟧ **1** of a whole kind, class, or group; inclusive **2** without a brand name —*n.* a product, as a drug, without a brand name: *often used in pl.* —**ge·ner'i·cal·ly** *adv.*

gen·er·ous (jen'ər əs) *adj.* ⟦< L *generosus*, noble⟧ **1** noble-minded; magnanimous **2** willing to give or share; unselfish **3** large; ample —**gen·er·os·i·ty** (jen'ər äs'ə tē) *n.* —**gen'er·ous·ly** *adv.*

gen·e·sis (jen'ə sis) *n.* ⟦Gr⟧ **1** the beginning; origin **2** [**G-**] the first book of the Bible

gene therapy the experimental treatment of diseases with new chemicals or organisms created by the recombining of units of DNA

genetic code the arrangement of chemical substances in DNA or RNA that determines the characteristics of an organism

ge·net·ics (jə net'iks) *n.* ⟦ult. < GENESIS⟧ the branch of biology dealing with heredity and variation in animal and plant species —**ge·net'ic** *adj.* —**ge·net'i·cal·ly** *adv.* —**ge·net'i·cist** (-ə sist) *n.*

Ge·ne·va (jə nē'və) city in SW Switzerland: pop. 174,000

Gen·ghis Khan (geŋ'gis kän', jeŋ'-) 1162?-1227; Mongol conqueror

gen·ial (jēn'yəl) *adj.* ⟦see GENIUS⟧ **1** good for life and growth *[*a *genial* climate*]* **2** cheerful and friendly; amiable —**ge·ni·al·i·ty** (jē'nē al'ə tē) *n.* —**gen'ial·ly** *adv.*

ge·nie (jē'nē) *n.* ⟦< Fr < Ar *jinnī*⟧ JINNI

gen·i·tal (jen'i təl) *adj.* ⟦< L *genere*, beget⟧ of reproduction or the sexual organs

gen'i·tals *pl.n.* ⟦see prec.⟧ the reproductive organs; esp., the external sex organs: also **gen'i·ta'li·a** (-tā'lē ə, -tāl'yə)

gen·i·tive (jen'i tiv) *n.* ⟦< Gr *genos*, genus⟧ *Gram.* a case expressing possession, source, etc., or referring to a part of a whole

gen·i·to·u·ri·nar·y (jen'i tō yoor'ə ner'ē) *adj.* of the genital and urinary organs

gen·i·us (jēn'yəs) *n.* ⟦L, guardian spirit⟧ **1** particular spirit or nature of a nation, place, age, etc. **2** natural ability; strong inclination (*for*) **3** great mental capacity and inventive ability **4** one having such capacity or ability

Gen·o·a (jen′ə wə) seaport in NW Italy: pop. 679,000

gen·o·cide (jen′ə sīd′) ***n.*** ⟦< Gr *genos*, race + -CIDE⟧ the systematic killing of a whole people or nation —**gen′o·ci′dal** ***adj.***

gen·re (zhän′rə) ***n.*** ⟦Fr < L *genus*, a kind⟧ **1** a kind, or type, as of works of literature, art, or popular fiction **2** painting in which everyday subjects are treated realistically

gent (jent) ***n.*** [Inf.] a gentleman

gen·teel (jen tēl′) ***adj.*** ⟦< Fr *gentil*⟧ polite or well-bred; now, esp., affectedly refined, polite, etc. —**gen·teel′ly** ***adv.***

gen·tian (jen′shən) ***n.*** ⟦< L *gentiana*⟧ a plant typically having fringed, blue flowers

gen·tile (jen′tīl′) [*also* **G-**] ***n.*** ⟦< L *gentilis*, of the same clan⟧ any person not a Jew —***adj.*** not Jewish

gen·til·i·ty (jen til′i tē) ***n.*** ⟦see fol.⟧ the quality of being genteel

gen·tle (jent′'l) ***adj.*** **-tler**, **-tlest** ⟦< L *gentilis*, of the same clan⟧ **1** of the upper classes **2** generous; kind **3** tame *[a gentle dog]* **4** kindly; patient **5** not harsh or rough *[a gentle tap]* **6** gradual *[a gentle slope]* —**gen′tle·ness** ***n.*** —**gen′tly** ***adv.***

gen′tle·folk′ ***pl.n.*** people of high social standing: also **gen′tle·folks′**

gen′tle·man (-mən) ***n.***, *pl.* **-men** (-mən) **1** [Obs.] a man of good family and high social standing **2** a courteous, gracious, and honorable man **3** any man: a polite term, esp. as (in pl.) a form of address —**gen′tle·man·ly** ***adj.*** —**gen′tle·wom′an**, *pl.* **-wom′en**, ***fem.n.***

gen·tri·fy (jen′tri fī′) ***vt.*** **-fied′**, **-fy′ing** ⟦< fol. + -FY⟧ **1** to convert (an aging neighborhood) into a more affluent one, as by remodeling homes **2** to raise to a higher status —**gen′tri·fi·ca′tion** ***n.***

gen·try (jen′trē) ***n.*** ⟦see GENTLE⟧ people of high social standing

gen·u·flect (jen′yə flekt′) ***vi.*** ⟦< L *genu*, knee + *flectere*, to bend⟧ to bend the knee, as in worship —**gen′u·flec′tion** ***n.***

gen·u·ine (jen′yo͞o in) ***adj.*** ⟦L *genuinus*, inborn⟧ **1** not counterfeit or artificial; real; true **2** sincere —**gen′u·ine·ly** ***adv.*** —**gen′u·ine·ness** ***n.***

ge·nus (jē′nəs) ***n.***, *pl.* **gen·er·a** (jen′ər ə) or **ge′nus·es** ⟦L, race, kind⟧ **1** a class; kind; sort **2** a category used in classifying plants or animals that are similar in structure

geo- ⟦< Gr *gē*⟧ *combining form* earth, of the earth

ge·o·cen·tric (jē′ō sen′trik) ***adj.*** **1** viewed as from the center of the earth **2** having the earth as a center —**ge′o·cen′tri·cal·ly** ***adv.***

ge·ode (jē′ōd′) ***n.*** ⟦< Gr *geoidēs*, earthlike⟧ a globular stone with a cavity lined with crystals or silica

ge·o·des·ic (jē′ə des′ik) ***adj.*** **1** GEODETIC (sense 1) **2** *a)* designating the shortest line between two points on a curved surface *b)* of the geometry of such lines **3** having a surface formed of straight bars in a grid of polygons *[geodesic dome]*

ge·o·det·ic (jē′ə det′ik) ***adj.*** **1** of or concerned with the measurement of the earth and its surface **2** GEODESIC (sense 2)

ge·og·ra·phy (jē äg′rə fē) ***n.*** ⟦< Gr *gē*, earth + *graphein*, write⟧ **1** the science dealing with the earth's surface, continents, climates, plants, animals, resources, etc. **2** the physical features of a region —**ge·og′ra·pher** ***n.*** —**ge′o·graph′i·cal** (-ə graf′i kəl) or **ge′o·graph′ic** ***adj.*** —**ge′o·graph′i·cal·ly** ***adv.***

ge·ol·o·gy (jē äl′ə jē) ***n.*** ⟦see GEO- & -LOGY⟧ the science dealing with the development of the earth's crust, its rocks and fossils, etc. —**ge′o·log′ic** (-ə läj′ik) or **ge′o·log′i·cal** ***adj.*** —**ge′o·log′i·cal·ly** ***adv.*** —**ge·ol′o·gist** ***n.***

ge·o·mag·net·ic (jē′ō mag net′ik) ***adj.*** of the magnetic properties of the earth —**ge′o·mag′ne·tism′** ***n.***

ge·om·e·try (jē äm′ə trē) ***n.*** ⟦< Gr *gē*, earth + *metrein*, to measure⟧ the branch of mathematics dealing with the properties, measurement, and relationships of points, lines, planes, and solids —**ge′o·met′ric** (-ə me′trik) or **ge′o·met′ri·cal** ***adj.*** —**ge′o·met′ri·cal·ly** ***adv.***

ge·o·phys·ics (jē′ō fiz′iks) ***n.*** the science dealing with the effects of weather, winds, tides, earthquakes, etc. on the earth —**ge′o·phys′i·cal** ***adj.*** —**ge′o·phys′i·cist** ***n.***

George III (jôrj) 1738-1820; king of Great Britain & Ireland (1760-1820)

George′town′ section of Washington, DC

Geor·gia (jôr′jə) **1** Southern state of the SE U.S.: 57,910 sq. mi.; pop. 6,478,000; cap. Atlanta; abbrev *GA* **2** country in W Asia: formerly part of the U.S.S.R.: 26,900 sq. mi.; pop. 5,456,000 —**Geor·gian** (jôr′jən) ***adj.***, ***n.***

ge·o·sta·tion·ar·y (jē′ō stā′shə ner′ē) ***adj.*** designating or of a satellite orbiting the earth at a speed which keeps it always above the same point on the earth's surface: also **ge′o·syn′chro·nous** (-siŋ′krə nəs)

ge′o·syn′cline′ (-sin′klīn′) ***n.*** a very large depression in the earth's surface

ge′o·ther′mal (-thur′məl) ***adj.*** ⟦GEO- + Gr *thermē*, heat⟧ of the heat inside the earth: sometimes **ge′o·ther′mic** (-thur′mik)

Ger *abbrev.* **1** German **2** Germany

ge·ra·ni·um (jə rā′nē əm) ***n.*** ⟦< Gr *geranos*, a crane⟧ **1** a common garden plant with showy red, white, etc. flowers **2** a related wildflower

ger·bil (jur′bəl) ***n.*** ⟦ult. < Ar⟧ a small rodent with long hind legs, often kept as a pet

ger·i·at·rics (jer′ē a′triks) ***n.*** ⟦< Gr *gēras*, old age + -IATRICS⟧ the branch of medicine dealing with the diseases of old age —**ger′i·at′ric** ***adj.***

germ (jurm) ***n.*** ⟦< L *germen*⟧ **1** the rudimentary form from which a new organism is developed; seed; bud **2** any microscopic disease-bearing organism; esp., one of the bacteria **3** an origin *[the germ of an idea]*

Ger·man (jur′mən) ***n.*** **1** a person born

or living in Germany **2** the language of Germany, Austria, etc. —*adj.* of Germany or its people, language, etc.

ger·mane (jər mān′) *adj.* ⟦see GERM⟧ truly relevant; pertinent

Ger·man·ic (jər man′ik) *adj.* designating or of GERMANIC (*n.* 2) —*n.* **1** [Obs.] the original language of the German people **2** the group of languages descended from it, including English

ger·ma·ni·um (jər mā′nē əm) *n.* ⟦< L *Germania*, Germany⟧ a nonmetallic chemical element used in making transistors, etc.

German measles RUBELLA

German shepherd a large dog with a bushy tail and erect ears, originally used to herd sheep, now often used as a guard dog

Ger·ma·ny (jur′mə nē) country in NC Europe: formerly partitioned (1949-90) into the **Federal Republic of Germany**, also called *West Germany*, and the **German Democratic Republic**, also called *East Germany:* 137,822 sq. mi.; pop. 80,975,000

germ cell an ovum or sperm cell

ger·mi·cide (jur′mə sīd′) *n.* ⟦< GERM + -CIDE⟧ any antiseptic, etc. used to destroy germs —**ger′mi·ci′dal** *adj.*

ger·mi·nal (jur′mə nəl) *adj.* **1** of or like germ cells **2** in the first stage of growth

ger′mi·nate′ (-nāt′) *vi.*, *vt.* **-nat′ed**, **-nat′ing** ⟦< L *germen*, a sprout⟧ **1** to sprout or cause to sprout, as from a seed **2** to start developing —**ger′mi·na′tion** *n.*

germ′y *adj.* **-i·er**, **-i·est** full of germs

ger·on·tol·o·gy (jer′ən täl′ə jē) *n.* ⟦< Gr *gerōn*, old man + -LOGY⟧ the study of aging and the problems of the aged —**ger′on·to·log′i·cal** (-tə läj′i kəl) *adj.* —**ger′on·tol′o·gist** *n.*

ger·ry·man·der (jer′ē man′dər) *vt.*, *vi.* ⟦after Elbridge *Gerry*, governor of MA (1812) + (SALA)MANDER (from the shape of the county redistricted then)⟧ to divide (a voting area) unfairly, so as to give one political party an advantage

ger·und (jer′ənd) *n.* ⟦< L *gerere*, carry out⟧ *Gram.* an English verbal noun ending in *-ing*

Ge·sta·po (gə stä′pō) *n.* ⟦< Ger *Ge(heime) Sta(ats)po(lizei)*, secret state police⟧ the terrorist secret police force of Nazi Germany

ges·ta·tion (jes tā′shən) *n.* ⟦< L *gerere*, to bear⟧ the act or period of carrying young in the uterus; pregnancy —**ges′tate′**, **-tat′ed**, **-tat′ing**, *vt.*

ges·tic·u·late (jes tik′yo͞o lāt′) *vi.* **-lat′ed**, **-lat′ing** ⟦see fol.⟧ to make gestures, esp. with the hands —**ges·tic′u·la′tion** *n.*

ges·ture (jes′chər) *n.* ⟦< L *gerere*, to bear⟧ **1** a movement of part of the body to express or emphasize ideas, emotions, etc. **2** any act or remark conveying a state of mind, intention, etc., often made merely for effect —*vi.* **-tured**, **-tur·ing** to make gestures

get (get) *vt.* **got**, **got′ten** or **got**, **get′ting** ⟦< ON *geta*⟧ **1** to come into the state of having; receive, obtain, acquire, etc. **2** to arrive at *[get* home early*]* **3** to go and bring *[get* your books*]* **4** to catch **5** to persuade *[get* him to leave*]* **6** to cause to be *[get* the jar open*]* **7** to prepare *[to get* lunch*]* **8** to manage or contrive *[to get* to do something*]* **9** [Inf.] *a*) to be obliged (with *have* or *has*) *[*he's *got* to pass*]* *b*) to possess (with *have* or *has*) *[*he's *got* red hair*]* *c*) to strike, kill, baffle, defeat, etc. *d*) to understand **10** [Slang] to cause an emotional response in *[*her singing *gets* me*]* —*vi.* **1** to come, go, or arrive *[*when I *get* to work*]* **2** to come to be *[to get* caught*]* *Get* is used as an auxiliary for emphasis in passive constructions *[to get* praised*]* —*n.* the young of an animal —**get anywhere** to have any success —**get around 1** to move from place to place; circulate: also **get about 2** to circumvent **3** to influence as by flattery —**get away 1** to go away **2** to escape —**get away with** [Inf.] to do without being discovered or punished —**get by** [Inf.] to survive; manage —**get it** [Inf.] **1** to understand **2** to be punished —**get off 1** to come off, down, or out of **2** to leave or start **3** to escape or help to escape —**get on 1** to go on or into **2** to put on **3** to proceed **4** to grow older **5** to succeed —**get out 1** to go out or away **2** to take out **3** to be disclosed **4** to publish —**get over 1** to recover from **2** to forget —**get through 1** to finish **2** to manage to survive —**get together 1** to assemble **2** [Inf.] to reach an agreement —**get up 1** to rise (from sleep, etc.) **2** to organize

get′a·way′ *n.* **1** the act of starting, as in a race **2** the act of escaping

get′-go′ *n.* [Inf.] beginning: used chiefly in **from the get-go**

get′-to·geth′er *n.* an informal social gathering or meeting

Get·tys·burg (get′iz burg′) town in S Pennsylvania: site of a crucial Civil War battle (July, 1863)

get′-up′ *n.* [Inf.] costume; dress

GeV *abbrev.* one billion electron-volts

gew·gaw (gyo͞o′gô′) *n.* ⟦ME⟧ a trinket

gey·ser (gī′zər) *n.* ⟦< ON *gjosa*, to gush⟧ a spring from which columns of boiling water and steam gush into the air at intervals

Gha·na (gä′nə) country on the W coast of Africa: 92,099 sq. mi.; pop. 12,296,000

ghast·ly (gast′lē) *adj.* **-li·er**, **-li·est** ⟦< OE *gast*, spirit⟧ **1** horrible; frightful **2** ghostlike; pale **3** [Inf.] very bad —**ghast′li·ness** *n.*

gher·kin (gur′kin) *n.* ⟦< Pers *angārah*, watermelon⟧ an immature, pickled cucumber

ghet·to (get′ō) *n.*, *pl.* **-tos** or **-toes** ⟦It⟧ **1** a section of some European cities to which Jews were once restricted **2** any section of a city in which many members of a minority group live, or to which they are restricted as by social discrimination

ghet′to·ize′ (-īz′) *vt.* **-ized′**, **-iz′ing** **1** to restrict to a ghetto **2** to make into a ghetto

ghost (gōst) *n.* ⟦< OE *gast*⟧ **1** *Folklore* the disembodied spirit of a dead person, appearing as a pale, shadowy apparition **2** a slight trace; shadow *[not a ghost of a chance]* —**give up the ghost** to die —**ghost'ly** ***adj.***

ghost'writ'er ***n.*** one who writes books, articles, etc. for another who professes to be the author —**ghost'write'**, **-wrote'**, **-writ'ten**, **-writ'ing**, ***vt.***, ***vi.***

ghoul (go͞ol) ***n.*** ⟦< Ar *ghāla*, to seize⟧ *Muslim Folklore* an evil spirit that robs graves and feeds on the dead —**ghoul'ish** ***adj.*** —**ghoul'ish·ness** ***n.*** —**ghoul'ish·ly** ***adv.***

GHQ *abbrev.* General Headquarters

GI (jē'ī') ***adj.*** **1** government issue: designating clothing, etc. issued to military personnel **2** [Inf.] of or characteristic of the U.S. armed forces *[a GI haircut]* —***n.***, *pl.* **GI's** or **GIs** [Inf.] a U.S. enlisted soldier

gi·ant (jī'ənt) ***n.*** ⟦< Gr *gigas*⟧ **1** any imaginary being of superhuman size **2** a person or thing of great size, strength, intellect, etc. —***adj.*** like a giant —**gi'ant·ess** ***fem.n.***

gib·ber (jib'ər) ***vi.***, ***vt.*** ⟦echoic⟧ to speak rapidly and incoherently

gib'ber·ish ***n.*** unintelligible or incoherent chatter

gib·bet (jib'it) ***n.*** ⟦< OFr *gibet*⟧ **1** a gallows **2** a structure from which bodies of executed criminals were hung and exposed to public scorn —***vt.*** to hang on a gibbet

gib·bon (gib'ən) ***n.*** ⟦Fr⟧ a small, slender, long-armed ape of India, S China, and the East Indies

Gib·bon (gib'ən), **Ed·ward** (ed'wərd) 1737-94; Eng. historian

gibe (jīb) ***vi.***, ***vt.*** **gibed**, **gib'ing** ⟦< ?⟧ to jeer or taunt —***n.*** a jeer or taunt

gib·let (jib'lit) ***n.*** ⟦< OFr *gibelet*, stew made of game⟧ any of the edible internal parts of a fowl, as the gizzard or heart

Gi·bral·tar (ji brôl'tər) British colony occupying a peninsula consisting mostly of a rocky hill (**Rock of Gibraltar**) at the S tip of Spain

gid·dy (gid'ē) ***adj.*** **-di·er**, **-di·est** ⟦< OE *gydig*, insane⟧ **1** having or causing a whirling, unsteady sensation; dizzy **2** frivolous —**gid'di·ly** ***adv.*** —**gid'di·ness** ***n.***

Gid·e·on (gid'ē ən) ***n.*** *Bible* a judge of Israel and a victorious leader in battle

gift (gift) ***n.*** ⟦< OE *giefan*, give⟧ **1** something given; present **2** the act of giving **3** a natural ability —***vt.*** **1** to present a gift to **2** to present as a gift

gift'ed ***adj.*** **1** having a natural ability; talented **2** of superior intelligence

gig[1] (gig) ***n.*** ⟦ME *gigge*, whirligig⟧ **1** a light, two-wheeled open carriage **2** a long, light ship's boat

gig[2] (gig) ***n.*** ⟦< ?⟧ [Slang] a job, esp. one performing jazz or rock

gi·ga·byte (gig'ə bīt') ***n.*** 2^{30} bytes, or, loosely, one billion bytes

gi·gan·tic (jī gan'tik) ***adj.*** ⟦see GIANT⟧ huge; enormous; immense

gig·gle (gig'əl) ***vi.*** **-gled**, **-gling** ⟦< Du *giggelen*⟧ to laugh with high, quick sounds in a silly or nervous way —***n.*** such a sound —**gig'gly**, **-gli·er**, **-gli·est**, ***adj.***

gig·o·lo (jig'ə lō') ***n.***, *pl.* **-los'** ⟦Fr⟧ a man paid to be a woman's escort

Gi·la monster (hē'lə) ⟦after the *Gila* River, AZ⟧ a stout, poisonous lizard of SW U.S. deserts

gild (gild) ***vt.*** **gild'ed** or **gilt**, **gild'ing** ⟦< OE *gyldan*⟧ **1** to coat with gold leaf or a gold color **2** to make seem more attractive or valuable than it is —**gild'er** ***n.*** —**gild'ing** ***n.***

gill[1] (gil) ***n.*** ⟦ME *gile*⟧ the breathing organ of most water animals, as fish

gill[2] (jil) ***n.*** ⟦< LL *gillo*, cooling vessel⟧ a unit of liquid measure equal to ¼ pint

gilt (gilt) ***vt.*** *alt. pt. & pp. of* GILD —***n.*** gold leaf or color —***adj.*** coated with gilt

gilt'-edged' ***adj.*** of the highest quality *[gilt-edged securities]*: also **gilt'-edge'**

gim·bal (gim'bəl, jim'-) ***n.*** ⟦< L *gemellus*, twin⟧ [*often pl.*] a device consisting of a pivoted ring or rings mounted on a fixed frame, used as to keep a ship's compass level

gim·crack (jim'krak') ***adj.*** ⟦< ME *gibbecrak*, an ornament⟧ showy but cheap and useless —***n.*** a gimcrack thing —**gim'crack'er·y** ***n.***

gim·let (gim'lit) ***n.*** ⟦< MDu *wimmel*⟧ a small tool for making holes

GIMLET

gim·mick (gim'ik) ***n.*** ⟦< ?⟧ [Inf.] **1** a tricky device **2** an attention-getting device or feature, as for promoting a product —**gim'mick·y** ***adj.***

gimp·y (gim'pē) ***adj.*** ⟦prob. < Norw dial. *gimpa*, to rock⟧ [Inf.] lame; limping

gin[1] (jin) ***n.*** ⟦ult. < L *juniperus*, juniper⟧ a distilled alcoholic liquor typically flavored with juniper berries

gin[2] (jin) ***n.*** ⟦< OFr *engin*, engine⟧ **1** a snare, as for game **2** COTTON GIN —***vt.*** **ginned**, **gin'ning** to remove seeds from (cotton) with a gin

gin[3] (jin) ***n.*** GIN RUMMY

gin·ger (jin'jər) ***n.*** ⟦< Gr *zingiberi*⟧ **1** a tropical herb with rhizomes used esp. as a spice **2** this spice **3** [Inf.] vigor; spirit —**gin'ger·y** ***adj.***

ginger ale a carbonated soft drink flavored with ginger

gin'ger·bread' ***n.*** **1** a cake flavored with ginger and molasses **2** showy ornamentation

gin'ger·ly ***adv.*** very carefully —***adj.*** very careful; cautious

gin'ger·snap' ***n.*** a crisp cookie flavored with ginger and molasses

ging·ham (giŋ'əm) ***n.*** ⟦< Malay *ginggang*⟧ a cotton cloth, usually woven in stripes, checks, or plaids

gin·gi·vi·tis (jin'jə vīt'is) ***n.*** ⟦< L *gingiva*, the gum + -ITIS⟧ inflammation of the gums

gink·go (giŋ'kō) ***n.***, *pl.* **-goes** ⟦Jpn *ginkyo*⟧ an Asian tree with fan-shaped leaves: also **ging'ko**

gin rummy (jin) a variety of the card game rummy

gip (jip) ***n., vt., vi.*** *alt. sp. of* GYP

Gip·sy (jip'sē) ***n.*** GYPSY

gi·raffe (jə raf') ***n.*** ⟦< Ar *zarāfa*⟧ a large African ruminant with a very long neck and long legs

gird (gurd) ***vt.*** **gird'ed** or **girt**, **gird'ing** ⟦OE *gyrdan*⟧ **1** to encircle or fasten with a belt **2** to surround **3** to prepare (oneself) for action

gird·er (gur'dər) ***n.*** a large wooden or steel beam for supporting joists, the framework of a building, etc.

gir·dle (gurd''l) ***n.*** ⟦OE *gyrdel*⟧ **1** [Archaic] a belt for the waist **2** anything that encircles **3** a woman's elasticized undergarment for supporting the waist and hips **—*vt.*** **-dled**, **-dling** to encircle or bind, as with a girdle

girl (gurl) ***n.*** ⟦ME *girle*, youngster⟧ **1** a female child **2** a young, unmarried woman **3** a female servant **4** [Inf.] a woman of any age **5** [Inf.] a sweetheart **—girl'hood'** ***n.*** **—girl'ish** ***adj.***

girl'friend' ***n.*** [Inf.] **1** a sweetheart of a boy or man **2** a girl who is someone's friend **3** a woman friend of a woman

Girl Scout a member of the **Girl Scouts of the United States of America**, a girls' organization providing healthful, character-building activities

girt[1] (gurt) ***vt.*** *alt. pt. & pp. of* GIRD

girt[2] (gurt) ***vt.*** to fasten with a girth

girth (gurth) ***n.*** ⟦< ON *gyrtha*, encircle⟧ **1** a band put around the belly of a horse, etc. to hold a saddle or pack **2** the circumference, as of a tree trunk

gist (jist) ***n.*** ⟦< OFr *giste*, point at issue⟧ the essence or main point, as of an article or argument

give (giv) ***vt.*** **gave**, **giv'en**, **giv'ing** ⟦OE *giefan*⟧ **1** to make a gift of **2** to hand over *[to give the porter a bag]* **3** to hand over in or for payment **4** to pass (regards, etc.) along **5** to cause to have *[to give pleasure]* **6** to act as host or sponsor of **7** to produce; supply *[cows give milk]* **8** to devote or sacrifice **9** to concede; yield **10** to offer *[to give advice]* **11** to perform *[to give a concert]* **12** to utter *[to give a reply]* **13** to inflict (punishment, etc.) **—*vi.*** **1** to bend, move, yield, etc. from force or pressure **2** to make gifts, donations, etc. **—*n.*** a bending, moving, etc. under pressure **—give away** **1** to make a gift of **2** to present (the bride) to the bridegroom **3** [Inf.] to reveal or betray **—give forth** (or **off**) to emit **—give in** to yield **—give it to** [Inf.] to beat or scold **—give or take** plus or minus **—give out** **1** to emit **2** to make public **3** to distribute **4** to become worn out, etc. **—give up** **1** to hand over **2** to cease **3** to stop trying **4** to despair of **5** to sacrifice **—giv'er** ***n.***

give'-and-take' ***n.*** **1** mutual concession **2** repartee or banter

give'a·way' ***n.*** **1** an unintentional revelation **2** something given free or sold cheap **3** an instance of giving something away free **4** a radio or television program giving prizes

give'back' ***n.*** a previously negotiated workers' benefit relinquished to management, as for some concession

giv·en (giv'ən) ***vt., vi.*** *pp. of* GIVE **—*adj.*** **1** accustomed (*to*) by habit, etc.; prone (*to*) **2** specified; stated **3** assumed; granted **—*n.*** something assumed or accepted as fact

given name a person's first name

giz·mo (giz'mō) ***n., pl.*** **-mos** ⟦< ?⟧ [Slang] a gadget: also sp. **gis'mo**

giz·zard (giz'ərd) ***n.*** ⟦< L *gigeria*, cooked entrails of poultry⟧ the muscular second stomach of a bird

Gk *abbrev.* Greek

gla·cé (gla sā') ***adj.*** ⟦< L *glacies*, ice⟧ **1** glossy, as silk **2** candied, as fruits **—*vt.*** **-céed'**, **-cé'ing** to glaze (fruits, etc.)

gla·cial (glā'shəl) ***adj.*** of or like ice or glaciers **—gla'cial·ly** ***adv.***

gla·cier (glā'shər) ***n.*** ⟦< L *glacies*, ice⟧ a large mass of ice and snow moving slowly down a mountain or valley

glad (glad) ***adj.*** **glad'der**, **glad'dest** ⟦OE *glæd*⟧ **1** happy **2** causing joy **3** very willing **4** bright **—glad'ly** ***adv.*** **—glad'ness** ***n.***

glad·den (glad''n) ***vt.*** to make glad

glade (glād) ***n.*** ⟦ME⟧ an open space in a forest

glad hand [Inf.] a cordial or effusive welcome **—glad'-hand'er** ***n.***

glad·i·a·tor (glad'ē āt'ər) ***n.*** ⟦L < *gladius*, sword⟧ **1** in ancient Rome, a man, often a slave, who fought in an arena as a public show **2** any person taking part in a fight **—glad'i·a·to'ri·al** (-ə tôr'ē əl) ***adj.***

glad·i·o·lus (glad'ē ō'ləs) ***n., pl.*** **-lus·es** or **-li'** (-lī') ⟦L, small sword⟧ a plant of the iris family with swordlike leaves and tall spikes of funnel-shaped flowers: also **glad'i·o'la** (-lə), *pl.* **-las**

glad·some (glad'səm) ***adj.*** joyful or cheerful **—glad'some·ly** ***adv.***

glam·or·ize (glam'ər īz') ***vt.*** **-ized'**, **-iz'ing** to make glamorous: also sp. **glam'our·ize'** **—glam'or·i·za'tion** ***n.***

glam·our (glam'ər) ***n.*** ⟦Scot var. of *grammar*, magic⟧ **1** seemingly mysterious allure; bewitching charm **2** elegance, luxury, etc. Also sp. **glam'or** **—glam'or·ous** or **glam'our·ous** ***adj.***

glance (glans) ***vi.*** **glanced**, **glanc'ing** ⟦ME *glansen*⟧ **1** to strike a surface obliquely and go off at an angle: with *off* **2** to flash **3** to take a quick look **—*n.*** **1** a glancing off **2** a flash **3** a quick look

gland (gland) ***n.*** ⟦< L *glans*, acorn⟧ any organ or group of cells that produces secretions, as insulin, or excretions, as urine **—glan·du·lar** (glan'jə lər) ***adj.***

glans (glanz) ***n.*** ⟦L, lit., acorn⟧ **1** the head of the penis **2** the tip of the clitoris

glare (gler) ***vi.*** **glared**, **glar'ing** ⟦ME *glaren*⟧ **1** to shine with a steady, dazzling light **2** to stare fiercely **—*n.*** **1** a steady, dazzling light **2** a fierce stare **3** a bright, glassy surface, as of ice

glar'ing ***adj.*** **1** dazzlingly bright **2** too showy **3** staring fiercely **4** flagrant *[a* *glaring* error*]* —**glar′ing·ly** ***adv.***

Glas·gow (glas′kō, glaz′gō) seaport in SC Scotland: district pop. 663,000

glas·nost (gläs′nôst) ***n.*** ⟦Russ, lit., openness⟧ Soviet official policy after 1985 of publicly acknowledging internal problems

glass (glas) ***n.*** ⟦OE *glæs*⟧ **1** a hard, brittle substance, usually transparent, made by fusing silicates with soda, lime, etc. **2** GLASSWARE **3** *a*) a glass article, as a drinking container *b*) [*pl.*] eyeglasses or binoculars **4** the amount held by a drinking glass —***vt.*** to equip with glass panes; glaze —***adj.*** of or made of glass —**glass′ful′** ***n.***

glass ceiling an unofficial policy that prevents women or minorities from advancing within a company, organization, etc.

glass′ware′ ***n.*** articles made of glass

glass′y ***adj.*** **-i·er, -i·est** **1** like glass, as in smoothness **2** expressionless *[*a *glassy* stare*]* —**glass′i·ly** ***adv.*** —**glass′i·ness** ***n.***

glau·co·ma (glô kō′mə) ***n.*** ⟦< Gr *glaukos*, gleaming⟧ any of various eye disorders marked by increased pressure within the eye causing impaired vision, etc.

glaze (glāz) ***vt.*** **glazed**, **glaz′ing** ⟦ME *glasen*⟧ **1** to fit (windows, etc.) with glass **2** to give a hard, glossy finish to (pottery, etc.) **3** to cover (foods) with a coating of sugar syrup, etc. —***vi.*** to become glassy or glossy —***n.*** **1** a glassy finish or coating **2** a thin coating of ice

gla·zier (glā′zhər) ***n.*** one whose work is fitting glass in windows, etc.

gleam (glēm) ***n.*** ⟦OE *glæm*⟧ **1** a flash or beam of light **2** a faint light **3** a reflected brightness, as from a polished surface **4** a faint manifestation, as of hope, understanding, etc. —***vi.*** **1** to shine with a gleam **2** to appear suddenly —**gleam′y** ***adj.***

glean (glēn) ***vt.***, ***vi.*** ⟦< Celt⟧ **1** to collect (grain left by reapers) **2** to collect (facts, etc.) gradually —**glean′ings** ***pl.n.***

glee (glē) ***n.*** ⟦OE *gleo*⟧ lively joy; merriment —**glee′ful** ***adj.***

glee club a group that sings part songs, etc.

glen (glen) ***n.*** ⟦medieval Scot⟧ a narrow, secluded valley

Glen·dale (glen′dāl) city in SW California: pop. 180,000

glen plaid [*also* **G- p-**] a plaid pattern with thin crossbarred stripes

glib (glib) ***adj.*** **glib′ber**, **glib′best** ⟦< or akin to Du *glibberig*, slippery⟧ speaking or spoken smoothly, often too smoothly to be convincing —**glib′ly** ***adv.*** —**glib′ness** ***n.***

glide (glīd) ***vi.*** **glid′ed**, **glid′ing** ⟦OE *glidan*⟧ **1** to move smoothly and easily **2** *Aeronautics* to descend with little or no engine power —***vt.*** to cause to glide —***n.*** **1** a gliding **2** a disk or ball, as of nylon, under a furniture leg to allow easy sliding

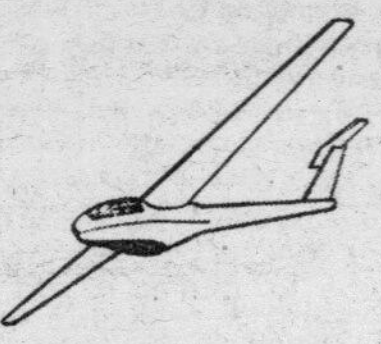

GLIDER

glid·er (glīd′ər) ***n.*** **1** an engineless aircraft carried along by air currents **2** a porch swing suspended in a frame

glim·mer (glim′ər) ***vi.*** ⟦< OE *glæm*, gleam⟧ **1** to give a faint, flickering light **2** to appear faintly —***n.*** **1** a faint, flickering light **2** a faint manifestation —**glim′mer·ing** ***n.***

glimpse (glimps) ***vt.*** **glimpsed**, **glimps′ing** ⟦< OE *glæm*, gleam⟧ to catch a brief, quick view of —***vi.*** to look quickly (*at*) —***n.*** a brief, quick view

glint (glint) ***vi.*** ⟦ME *glenten*⟧ to gleam or glitter —***n.*** a gleam, flash, etc.

glis·san·do (gli sän′dō) ***n.***, *pl.* **-di** (-dē) or **-dos** ⟦as if It < Fr *glisser*, to slide⟧ *Music* a sliding effect achieved by a rapid sounding of tones

glis·ten (glis′ən) ***vi.*** ⟦OE *glisnian*⟧ to shine with reflected light, as a wet surface

glitch (glich) ***n.*** ⟦< Ger *glitsche*, a slip⟧ [Slang] a mishap, error, etc.

glit·ter (glit′ər) ***vi.*** ⟦prob. < ON *glitra*⟧ **1** to shine brightly; sparkle **2** to be brilliant or showy —***n.*** **1** a bright, sparkling light **2** striking or showy brilliance **3** bits of glittering material —**glit′ter·y** ***adj.***

glitz (glits) ***n.*** ⟦< ?⟧ [Inf.] gaudy or glittery showiness —**glitz′y**, **-i·er**, **-i·est**, ***adj.***

gloam·ing (glōm′iŋ) ***n.*** ⟦< OE *glom*⟧ evening dusk; twilight

gloat (glōt) ***vi.*** ⟦prob. < ON *glotta*, grin scornfully⟧ to gaze or think with malicious pleasure: often with *over*

glob (gläb) ***n.*** ⟦prob. < GLOBULE⟧ a rounded mass or lump, as of jelly

glob·al (glō′bəl) ***adj.*** **1** worldwide **2** complete or comprehensive —**glob′al·ly** ***adv.***

glob′al·ism′ (-iz′əm) ***n.*** a policy, outlook, etc. that is worldwide in scope

global warming a slight, continuing rise in atmospheric temperature, usually attributed to an intensifying of the greenhouse effect

globe (glōb) ***n.*** ⟦< L *globus*, a ball⟧ **1** anything spherical or somewhat spherical **2** the earth, or a model of the earth

globe′-trot′ter ***n.*** one who travels widely about the world —**globe′-trot′ting** ***n.***, ***adj.***

glob·u·lar (gläb′yə lər) ***adj.*** **1** spherical **2** made up of globules

glob′ule′ (-yo͞ol′) ***n.*** ⟦< L *globulus*⟧ **1** a tiny ball or globe **2** a drop of liquid

glock·en·spiel (gläk′ən spēl′) ***n.*** ⟦Ger *glocke*, bell + *spiel*, to play⟧ a percussion instrument with tuned metal bars in a frame, played with small hammers

gloom (glo͞om) ***n.*** ⟦prob. < Scand⟧ **1** darkness; dimness **2** deep sadness; dejection —**gloom'y, -i·er, -i·est,** ***adj.***

glop (gläp) ***n.*** ⟦< ? GL(UE) + (SL)OP⟧ [Inf.] any soft, gluey substance —**glop'py** ***adj.***

glo·ri·fy (glôr'ə fī') ***vt.*** **-fied', -fy'ing** ⟦< L *gloria*, glory + *facere*, to make⟧ **1** to give glory to **2** to exalt (God), as in worship **3** to honor; extol **4** to make seem better, greater, etc. than is so —**glo'ri·fi·ca'tion** ***n.***

glo'ri·ous (-ē əs) ***adj.*** **1** having, giving, or deserving glory **2** splendid **3** [Inf.] very delightful or enjoyable —**glo'ri·ous·ly** ***adv.***

glo·ry (glôr'ē) ***n.***, *pl.* **-ries** ⟦< L *gloria*⟧ **1** great honor or fame, or its source **2** adoration **3** great splendor, prosperity, etc. **4** heavenly bliss —***vi.*** **-ried, -ry·ing** to exult (*in*)

gloss[1] (glôs, gläs) ***n.*** ⟦< ? Scand⟧ **1** the shine of a polished surface **2** a deceptive outward show —***vt.*** **1** to give a shiny surface to **2** to hide (an error, etc.) or make seem right or trivial: often with *over* —**gloss'y, -i·er, -i·est,** ***adj.***

gloss[2] (glôs, gläs) ***n.*** ⟦< Gr *glōssa*, tongue⟧ a note of comment or explanation, as in a footnote —***vt.*** to provide glosses for

glos·sa·ry (glôs'ə rē, gläs'-) ***n.***, *pl.* **-ries** ⟦see prec.⟧ a list of difficult terms with explanations, as for a book

glos·so·la·li·a (gläs'ō lā'lē ə, glôs'-) ***n.*** ⟦< Gr *glōssa*, tongue + *lalein*, to speak⟧ an uttering of unintelligible sounds, as in a religious ecstasy

glot·tis (glät'is) ***n.*** ⟦ModL < Gr *glōssa*, tongue⟧ the opening between the vocal cords in the larynx —**glot'tal** ***adj.***

glove (gluv) ***n.*** ⟦OE *glof*⟧ **1** a covering for the hand, with separate sheaths for the fingers and thumb **2** a baseball player's mitt **3** a padded mitten worn by boxers —***vt.*** **gloved, glov'ing** to cover with a glove

glow (glō) ***vi.*** ⟦OE *glowan*⟧ **1** to give off a bright light as a result of great heat **2** to give out a steady light **3** to give out heat **4** to be elated **5** to be bright with color **6** to be ruddy, flushed, etc., as from enthusiasm —***n.*** **1** a light given off, as a result of great heat **2** steady, even light **3** brightness, warmth, ardor, etc. —**glow'ing** ***adj.*** —**glow'ing·ly** ***adv.***

glow·er (glou'ər) ***vi.*** ⟦prob. < ON⟧ to stare with sullen anger; scowl —**glow'er·ing** ***adj.***

glow'worm' (glō'-) ***n.*** a wingless, luminescent female or larva of the firefly

glu·cose (glo͞o'kōs') ***n.*** ⟦Fr < Gr *gleúkos*, sweetness⟧ **1** a crystalline sugar occurring naturally in fruits, honey, etc. **2** a sweet syrup prepared by the hydrolysis of starch

glue (glo͞o) ***n.*** ⟦< LL *glus*⟧ **1** a sticky, viscous liquid made from animal gelatin, used as an adhesive **2** any similar substance —***vt.*** **glued, glu'ing** to make stick as with glue —**glu'ey, -i·er, -i·est,** ***adj.***

glum (glum) ***adj.*** **glum'mer, glum'mest** ⟦prob. < ME *glomen*, look morose⟧ gloomy; sullen —**glum'ly** ***adv.*** —**glum'ness** ***n.***

glut (glut) ***vi.*** **glut'ted, glut'ting** ⟦< L *gluttire*, to swallow⟧ to eat to excess —***vt.*** **1** to feed, fill, etc. to excess **2** to supply (the market) beyond demand —***n.*** **1** a glutting or being glutted **2** a supply greater than the demand

glu·ten (glo͞ot''n) ***n.*** ⟦L, glue⟧ a gray, sticky, nutritious mixture of proteins found in wheat, etc. —**glu'ten·ous** ***adj.***

glu·ti·nous (glo͞ot''n əs) ***adj.*** ⟦see prec.⟧ gluey; sticky —**glu'ti·nous·ly** ***adv.***

glut·ton (glut''n) ***n.*** ⟦see GLUT⟧ **1** one who eats to excess **2** one with a great capacity for something —**glut'ton·ous** ***adj.*** —**glut'ton·ous·ly** ***adv.***

glut'ton·y ***n.***, *pl.* **-ies** the habit or act of eating too much

glyc·er·in (glis'ər in) ***n.*** ⟦< Gr *glykeros*, sweet⟧ *nontechnical term for* GLYCEROL: also **glyc'er·ine**

glyc·er·ol (glis'ər ôl', -ōl') ***n.*** ⟦< prec.⟧ a colorless, syrupy liquid made from fats and oils: used in skin lotions, in making explosives, etc.

gly·co·gen (glī'kə jən) ***n.*** ⟦< Gr *glykys*, sweet + -GEN⟧ a substance in animal tissues that is changed into glucose as the body needs it

GM *abbrev.* General Manager

Gmc *abbrev.* Germanic

gnarl (närl) ***n.*** ⟦< ME *knorre*⟧ a knot on a tree trunk or branch —***vt.*** to make knotted; twist

gnarled ***adj.*** **1** knotty and twisted **2** roughened, hardened, etc.: said as of hands Also **gnarl'y, -i·er, -i·est**

gnash (nash) ***vt.***, ***vi.*** ⟦prob. < ON⟧ to grind (the teeth) together, as in anger —***n.*** a gnashing

gnat (nat) ***n.*** ⟦OE *gnæt*⟧ any of various small, two-winged insects, which often bite

gnaw (nô) ***vt.*** ⟦OE *gnagen*⟧ **1** to bite away bit by bit; consume **2** to harass or vex —***vi.*** **1** to bite repeatedly: with *on, away,* etc. **2** to produce a corroding, tormenting, etc. effect: with *on, at,* etc. —**gnaw'ing** ***n.***

gneiss (nīs) ***n.*** ⟦< OHG *gneisto*, a spark⟧ a granitelike rock formed of layers of quartz, mica, etc.

gnome (nōm) ***n.*** ⟦< Gr *gnōmē*, thought⟧ *Folklore* a dwarf who dwells in the earth and guards its treasures —**gnom'ish** ***adj.***

GNP *abbrev.* gross national product

gnu (no͞o) ***n.*** ⟦< the native name⟧ a large African antelope with an oxlike head and a horselike tail

go (gō) ***vi.*** **went, gone, go'ing** ⟦< OE *gan*⟧ **1** to move along; travel; proceed **2** to work properly; operate */the clock is going/* **3** to act, sound, etc. as specified */the balloon went "pop"/* **4** to turn out; result */the war went badly/* **5** to pass: said of time **6** to pass from person to person **7** to become */to go mad/* **8** to be expressed, sung, etc. */as the saying goes/* **9** to harmonize; agree */blue goes with gold/* **10** to be accepted, valid, etc.

11 to leave; depart 12 to come to an end; fail [his eyesight is *going*] 13 to be allotted (*to*) or sold (*for*) 14 to extend, reach, etc. 15 to be able to pass (*through*), fit (*into*), etc. 16 to belong [socks *go* in that drawer] —*vt.* 1 to travel along [to *go* the wrong way] 2 [Inf.] to furnish (bail) for an arrested person 3 [Inf.] to say [he *goes* "Wow!"] —*n.*, *pl.* **goes** 1 a success [to make a *go* of marriage] 2 [Inf.] animation; energy 3 [Inf.] a try; attempt —**go back on** [Inf.] 1 to betray 2 to break (a promise, etc.) —**go for** 1 to try to get 2 [Inf.] to attack 3 [Inf.] to be attracted by —**go in for** [Inf.] to engage or indulge in —**go into** to be contained in [5 *goes into* 10 twice] —**go off** 1 to depart 2 to explode —**go on** 1 to proceed; continue 2 to happen 3 [Inf.] to chatter —**go out** 1 to be extinguished, become outdated, etc. 2 to attend social affairs, etc. —**go over** 1 to examine thoroughly 2 to do again 3 [Inf.] to be successful —**go through** 1 to endure; experience 2 to look through —**go through with** to pursue to the end —**go together** 1 to match; harmonize 2 [Inf.] to date only each other —**go under** to fail, as in business —**let go** 1 to let escape 2 to release one's hold 3 to dismiss from a job; fire —**let oneself go** to be unrestrained —**on the go** [Inf.] in constant motion or action —**to go** [Inf.] 1 to be taken out: said of food in a restaurant 2 still to be done, etc.

goad (gōd) *n.* ⟦OE *gad*⟧ 1 a sharp-pointed stick used in driving oxen 2 any driving impulse; spur —*vt.* to drive as with a goad; urge on

go′-a·head′ *n.* permission or a signal to proceed: usually with *the*

goal (gōl) *n.* ⟦ME *gol*, boundary⟧ 1 the place at which a race, trip, etc. is ended 2 an end that one strives to attain 3 in some games, *a*) the line or net over or into which the ball or puck must go to score *b*) the score made

goal′keep′er *n.* in some games, a player stationed at a goal to prevent the ball or puck from entering it: also **goal′ie** or **goal′tend′er**

goat (gōt) *n.* ⟦OE *gat*⟧ 1 a cud-chewing mammal with hollow horns, closely related to sheep, antelopes, etc. 2 a lecherous man 3 [Inf.] a scapegoat —**get someone's goat** [Inf.] to annoy someone

goat·ee (gō tē′) *n.* a small, pointed beard on a man's chin

goat′herd′ *n.* one who herds goats

goat′skin′ *n.* the skin of a goat, or leather made from this skin

gob[1] (gäb) *n.* ⟦< OFr *gobe*, mouthful⟧ 1 a soft lump or mass 2 [*pl.*] [Inf.] a large quantity

gob[2] (gäb) *n.* ⟦< ?⟧ [Slang] a sailor in the U.S. Navy

gob·ble[1] (gäb′əl) *n.* ⟦echoic⟧ the throaty sound made by a male turkey —*vi.* **-bled**, **-bling** to make this sound

gob·ble[2] (gäb′əl) *vt.*, *vi.* **-bled**, **-bling** ⟦< OFr *gobet*, mouthful⟧ 1 to eat quickly and greedily 2 to seize eagerly; snatch (*up*)

gob′ble·dy·gook′ (-dē go͝ok′) *n.* ⟦? echoic of turkey cries⟧ [Slang] pompous, wordy talk or writing that is meaningless

gob·bler (gäb′lər) *n.* a male turkey

go′-be·tween′ *n.* one who makes arrangements between each of two sides; intermediary

Go·bi (gō′bē) large desert plateau in E Asia, chiefly in Mongolia

gob·let (gäb′lit) *n.* ⟦< OFr *gobel*⟧ a drinking glass with a base and stem

gob·lin (gäb′lin) *n.* ⟦< ML *gobelinus*⟧ *Folklore* an evil or mischievous spirit

go′-by′ *n.* [Inf.] an intentional disregard or slight

god (gäd, gôd) *n.* ⟦OE⟧ 1 any of various beings conceived of as supernatural and immortal; esp., a male deity 2 an idol 3 a person or thing deified 4 [**G-**] in monotheistic religions, the creator and ruler of the universe; Supreme Being —**god′like′** *adj.*

god′child′ *n.*, *pl.* **-chil′dren** the person a godparent sponsors

god′daugh′ter *n.* a female godchild

god·dess (gäd′is) *n.* 1 a female god 2 a woman of great beauty, charm, etc.

god′fa′ther *n.* 1 a male godparent 2 [*often* **G-**] *a*) [Inf.] the head of a Mafia crime syndicate *b*) [Slang] a very influential or authoritative person

god′head′ *n.* 1 godhood 2 [**G-**] God: usually with *the*

god′hood′ *n.* the state of being a god; divinity

Go·di·va (gə dī′və) *n.* *Eng. Legend* an 11th-c. noblewoman who rode naked through the streets so that her husband would abolish a heavy tax

god′less *adj.* 1 irreligious; atheistic 2 wicked —**god′less·ness** *n.*

god′ly *adj.* **-li·er**, **-li·est** devoted to God; devout —**god′li·ness** *n.*

god′moth′er *n.* a female godparent

god′par′ent *n.* a person who sponsors a child, as at baptism, taking responsibility for its faith

god′send′ *n.* anything unexpected and needed or desired that comes at the opportune moment, as if sent by God

god′son′ *n.* a male godchild

God·win Aus·ten (gäd′win ôs′tən) mountain in the Himalayas: 2d highest mountain in the world: 28,250 ft.: commonly called *K2*

Goe·the (gö′tə; *E* gur′tə), **Jo·hann Wolf·gang von** (yō′hän vôlf′gäŋk fôn) 1749-1832; Ger. poet & dramatist

go·fer or **go-fer** (gō′fər) *n.* ⟦from being asked to *go for* something⟧ [Slang] an employee who performs menial tasks, as running errands

go-get·ter (gō′get′ər) *n.* [Inf.] an enterprising and aggressive person who usually achieves ambitions, goals, etc.

gog·gle (gäg′əl) *vi.* **-gled**, **-gling** ⟦ME *gogelen*⟧ to stare with bulging eyes —*n.* [*pl.*] large spectacles to protect the eyes against dust, wind, sparks, etc. —*adj.* bulging or rolling: said of the eyes

go′-go′ *adj.* ⟦short for *à gogo* < Fr, in

plenty】 **1** of dancing to rock music, as in discothèques **2** of a dancer performing erotic movements to rock music, as in a bar

go·ing (gō′iŋ) ***n.*** **1** a departure **2** the condition of the ground or land as it affects traveling, walking, etc. **3** [Slang] current situation *[tough going in the trial]* **—*adj.*** **1** moving; working **2** conducting its business successfully *[a going concern]* **3** available **4** commonly accepted; current *[the going rate]* **—be going to** will or shall

go′ing-ov′er ***n.*** [Inf.] **1** a thorough inspection **2** a severe scolding or beating

go′ings-on′ ***pl.n.*** [Inf.] actions or events, esp. when disapproved of

goi·ter (goit′ər) ***n.*** 【< L *guttur,* throat】 an enlargement of the thyroid gland, often visible as a swelling in the front of the neck: also [Chiefly Brit.] **goi′tre**

gold (gōld) ***n.*** 【OE】 **1** a heavy, yellow, metallic, highly malleable chemical element: it is a precious metal **2** money; wealth **3** bright yellow

gold′brick′ ***n.*** [Mil. Slang] one who avoids work: also **gold′brick′er —*vi.*** [Mil. Slang] to shirk a duty or avoid work

gol·den (gōl′dən) ***adj.*** **1** made of or containing gold **2** bright-yellow **3** very valuable; excellent **4** flourishing **5** marking the 50th year *[golden anniversary]* **6** favorable *[a golden opportunity]*

golden ag·er (ā′jər) [*also* **G- A-**] [Inf.] an elderly person, specif. one 65 or older and retired

Golden Fleece *Gr. Myth.* the fleece of gold captured by Jason

Golden Gate strait between San Francisco Bay & the Pacific

gold′en·rod′ ***n.*** a North American plant with long, branching stalks bearing clusters of small, yellow flowers

golden rule the precept that one should act toward others as one would want them to act toward oneself

gold′-filled′ ***adj.*** made of a base metal overlaid with gold

gold′finch′ ***n.*** 【OE *goldfinc*】 any of various yellow-and-black finches

gold′fish′ ***n.,*** *pl.* **-fish′** a small, golden-yellow or orange fish, often kept in ponds or aquariums

gold leaf gold beaten into very thin sheets, used for gilding

gold′smith′ ***n.*** an artisan who makes and repairs articles of gold

gold standard a monetary standard in which the basic currency unit equals a specified quantity of gold

golf (gôlf, gälf) ***n.*** 【? < Du *kolf,* a club】 an outdoor game played with a small, hard ball and a set of clubs, the object being to hit the ball into each of a series of 9 or 18 holes with the fewest possible strokes **—*vi.*** to play golf **—golf′er *n.***

golf course (or **links**) a tract of land for playing golf

Go·li·ath (gə lī′əth) ***n.*** *Bible* the Philistine giant killed by David

gol·ly (gäl′ē) ***interj.*** used to express surprise, wonder, etc.: orig. a euphemism for *God*

Go·mor′rah ***n.*** *see* SODOM AND GOMORRAH

-gon (gän, gən) 【< Gr *gōnia,* an angle】 *combining form* a figure having (a specified number of) angles

go·nad (gō′nad′) ***n.*** 【< Gr *gonē,* a seed】 an animal organ or gland that produces reproductive cells; esp., an ovary or testis

gon·do·la (gän′də lə, gän dō′lə) ***n.*** 【It】 **1** a narrow boat used on the canals of Venice **2** a railroad freight car with no top and, often, with low sides **3** a cabin suspended under an airship or balloon

gon′do·lier′ (-lir′) ***n.*** a man who propels a gondola

gone (gôn, gän) ***vi., vt.*** *pp. of* GO **—*adj.*** 【ME *gon* < OE *gan*】 **1** departed **2** ruined **3** lost **4** dead **5** used up; consumed **6** ago; past

gon·er (gôn′ər) ***n.*** a person or thing certain to die, be ruined, etc.

gong (gôŋ, gäŋ) ***n.*** 【Malay *guṅ*】 a slightly convex metallic disk that gives a loud, resonant tone when struck

gon·or·rhe·a or **gon·or·rhoe·a** (gän′ə rē′ə) ***n.*** 【< Gr *gonos,* semen + *rheein,* to flow】 a venereal disease with inflammation of the genital organs

goo (go͞o) ***n.*** [Inf.] **1** anything sticky, or sticky and sweet **2** excessive sentimentality **—goo′ey, -i·er, -i·est, *adj.***

goo·ber (go͞o′bər) ***n.*** 【< Afr *nguba*】 [Chiefly South] a peanut

good (good) ***adj.*** **bet′ter, best** 【OE *gōd*】 **1** effective; efficient **2** beneficial **3** valid; real *[good money]* **4** healthy or sound *[good eyesight, good investments]* **5** honorable *[one's good name]* **6** enjoyable, pleasant, etc. **7** reliable **8** thorough **9** excellent **10** virtuous, devout, kind, dutiful, etc. **11** proper; correct **12** skilled **13** considerable *[a good many]* **14** at least *[waiting a good six hours]* **—*n.*** something good; worth, benefit, etc. **—*adv.*** [Inf. or Dial.] well; fully **—as good as** virtually; nearly **—for good (and all)** permanently **—good and** [Inf.] very or altogether **—good for 1** able to endure or be used for (a period of time) **2** worth **3** able to pay or give **—no good** useless; worthless

good′bye′ or **good′-bye′** (-bī′) ***interj., n.,*** *pl.* **-byes′** 【contr. of *God be with ye*】 farewell: also sp. **good′by′, good′-by′**

good faith good intentions; sincerity

Good Friday the Friday before Easter, commemorating the Crucifixion

good′-heart′ed ***adj.*** kind and generous **—good′-heart′ed·ly *adv.* —good′-heart′ed·ness *n.***

Good Hope, Cape of cape at the SW tip of Africa

good humor a cheerful, agreeable mood **—good′-hu′mored *adj.* —good′-hu′mored·ly *adv.***

good′-look′ing ***adj.*** handsome or beautiful

good′ly ***adj.*** **-li·er, -li·est** **1** of good appearance or quality **2** ample

good′-na′tured *adj.* agreeable; affable —**good′-na′tured·ly** *adv.*

good′ness *n.* the state or quality of being good; virtue, kindness, etc. —*interj.* used to express surprise or wonder: orig. a euphemism for *God*

goods (goodz) *pl.n.* **1** movable personal property **2** merchandise; wares **3** fabric; cloth —**get** (or **have**) **the goods on** [Slang] to discover (or know) something incriminating about

good Sa·mar·i·tan (sə mer′ə tən) one who helps another or others unselfishly: see Luke 10:30-37

good′-sized′ *adj.* ample; fairly big

good′-tem′pered *adj.* amiable

good turn a friendly, helpful act; favor

good′will′ *n.* **1** benevolence **2** willingness **3** the value of a business as a result of patronage, reputation, etc., beyond its tangible assets Also **good will**

good′y *n., pl.* **-ies** [Inf.] something good to eat, as a piece of candy —*interj.* used to express approval or delight: mainly a child's term

good′y-good′y [Inf.] *adj.* affectedly moral or pious —*n.* a goody-goody person

goof (go͞of) [Inf.] *n.* **1** a stupid or silly person **2** a mistake; blunder —*vi.* **1** to err or blunder **2** to waste time, shirk duties, etc.: with *off* or *around* —**goof′y**, **-i·er**, **-i·est**, *adj.*

gook (gook, go͞ok) *n.* ⟦GOO + (GUN)K⟧ [Slang] any sticky or slimy substance

goon (go͞on) *n.* [Slang] **1** a ruffian or thug **2** a grotesque or stupid person

goop (go͞op) *n.* ⟦GOO + (SOU)P⟧ [Slang] any sticky, semiliquid substance

goose (go͞os) *n., pl.* **geese** ⟦< OE *gos*⟧ **1** a long-necked, web-footed waterfowl like a duck but larger **2** its flesh as food **3** a silly person —**cook someone's goose** [Inf.] to spoil someone's chances

goose′ber′ry *n., pl.* **-ries** **1** a small, sour berry **2** the shrub it grows on

goose bumps a momentary roughened condition of the skin, induced by cold, fear, etc.: also **goose flesh** (or **pimples**)

GOP (jē′ō′pē′) *n.* ⟦G(rand) O(ld) P(arty)⟧ *name for* REPUBLICAN PARTY

go·pher (gō′fər) *n.* ⟦< ? Fr *gaufre*, honeycomb: from its burrowing⟧ **1** a burrowing rodent with wide cheek pouches **2** a striped ground squirrel of the prairies of North America

gore[1] (gôr) *n.* ⟦OE *gor*, filth⟧ blood from a wound, esp. when clotted

gore[2] (gôr) *vt.* **gored**, **gor′ing** ⟦< OE *gar*, a spear⟧ **1** to pierce with or as with a horn or tusk **2** to insert gores in —*n.* a tapering piece of cloth inserted in a skirt, sail, etc. to give it fullness

gorge (gôrj) *n.* ⟦< L *gurges*, whirlpool⟧ **1** the throat or gullet **2** the contents of the stomach **3** resentment, disgust, etc. **4** a deep, narrow pass between steep heights —*vi., vt.* **gorged**, **gorg′ing** to eat greedily or swallow gluttonously

gor·geous (gôr′jəs) *adj.* ⟦< OFr *gorgias*⟧ **1** brilliantly showy; magnificent **2** [Inf.] beautiful, delightful, etc. —**gor′geous·ly** *adv.*

go·ril·la (gə ril′ə) *n.* ⟦ult. < name in an ancient W Afr language⟧ the largest, and most powerful, of the great apes, native to Africa

Gor·ki or **Gor′ky** (gôr′kē) *name* (1932-90) *for* NIZHNY NOVGOROD

gor·mand·ize (gôr′mən dīz′) *vi., vt.* **-ized′**, **-iz′ing** ⟦< Fr *gourmandise*, gluttony⟧ to eat like a glutton

go′-round′ *n.* one of a series of actions, encounters, etc., often involving conflict

gorp (gôrp) *n.* a mixture of raisins, nuts, etc. eaten as by hikers for quick energy

gorse (gôrs) *n.* ⟦OE *gorst*⟧ FURZE

gor·y (gôr′ē) *adj.* **-i·er**, **-i·est** **1** covered with gore; bloody **2** with much bloodshed —**gor′i·ness** *n.*

gosh (gäsh, gôsh) *interj.* used to express surprise, wonder, etc.: a euphemism for *God*

gos·ling (gäz′liŋ) *n.* a young goose

gos·pel (gäs′pəl) *n.* ⟦< OE *gōdspel*, good news⟧ **1** [*often* **G-**] the teachings of Jesus and the Apostles **2** [**G-**] any of the first four books of the New Testament **3** anything proclaimed or accepted as the absolute truth: also **gospel truth**

gos·sa·mer (gäs′ə mər) *n.* ⟦ME *gosesomer*, lit., goose summer⟧ **1** a filmy cobweb **2** a very thin, filmy cloth —*adj.* light, thin, and filmy

gos·sip (gäs′əp) *n.* ⟦< Late OE *godsibbe*, godparent⟧ **1** one who chatters idly about others **2** such talk —*vi.* to be a gossip —**gos′sip·y** *adj.*

got (gät) *vt., vi. pt. & alt. pp. of* GET

Goth (gäth, gôth) *n.* a member of a Germanic people that conquered most of the Roman Empire in the 3d, 4th, and 5th c. A.D.

Goth·ic (gäth′ik) *adj.* **1** of the Goths or their language **2** designating or of a style of architecture developed in W Europe between the 12th and 16th c., with pointed arches, steep roofs, etc. **3** [*sometimes* **g-**] uncivilized **4** [*sometimes* **g-**] of a type of fiction that uses remote, gloomy settings and a sinister atmosphere to suggest mystery —*n.* **1** the East Germanic language of the Goths **2** Gothic style, esp. in architecture

got·ten (gät′'n) *vt., vi. alt. pp. of* GET

Gou·da (cheese) (go͞o′də, gou′-) ⟦after *Gouda*, Netherlands⟧ a mild cheese sometimes coated with red wax

gouge (gouj) *n.* ⟦< LL *gulbia*⟧ **1** a chisel for cutting grooves or holes in wood **2** such a groove or hole —*vt.* **gouged**, **goug′ing** **1** to make a groove, etc. in (something) as with a gouge **2** to scoop out **3** [Inf.] to cheat out of money —**goug′er** *n.*

gou·lash (go͞o′läsh′) *n.* ⟦< Hung *gulyás*⟧ a beef or veal stew seasoned with paprika

gou·ra·mi (go͞o rä′mē, goor′ə mē) *n., pl.* **-mies** or **-mi** ⟦Malay *gurami*⟧ any of various freshwater tropical fishes; esp., a food fish of SE Asia

gourd (gôrd, goord) *n.* ⟦< L *cucurbita*⟧ **1**

any trailing or climbing plant of a family that includes the squash, melon, etc. **2** the fruit of one inedible species or its dried, hollowed-out shell, used as a cup, dipper, etc.

gour·mand (goor mänd′) ***n.*** ⟦OFr⟧ one who indulges in good food and drink excessively

gour·met (goor′mā, gôr-) ***n.*** ⟦Fr < OFr, *gormet,* wine taster⟧ one who likes and is an excellent judge of fine food and drink

gout (gout) ***n.*** ⟦< L *gutta*, a drop⟧ a form of arthritis characterized by painful swelling of the joints, esp. in the big toe —**gout′y, -i·er, -i·est,** ***adj.***

gov or **Gov** *abbrev.* **1** government **2** governor

gov·ern (guv′ərn) ***vt., vi.*** ⟦< Gr *kybernan*, to steer⟧ **1** to exercise authority over; rule, control, etc. **2** to influence the action of; guide **3** to determine —**gov′ern·a·ble** ***adj.***

gov′ern·ance (-ər nəns) ***n.*** the action, function, or power of government

gov′ern·ess (-ər nis) ***n.*** a woman employed in a private home to train and teach the children

gov·ern·ment (guv′ərn mənt, -ər mənt) ***n.*** **1** the exercise of authority over a state, organization, etc.; control; rule **2** a system of ruling, political administration, etc. **3** those who conduct the affairs of a state, etc.; administration —**gov′ern·men′tal** ***adj.***

gov·er·nor (guv′ə nər, -ər nər) ***n.*** **1** one who governs; esp., *a*) one appointed to govern a province, etc. *b*) the elected head of any state of the U.S. **2** a mechanical device for automatically controlling the speed of an engine —**gov′er·nor·ship′** ***n.***

governor general *pl.* **governors general** or **governor generals** a governor who has subordinate or deputy governors

govt or **Govt** *abbrev.* government

gown (goun) ***n.*** ⟦< LL *gunna*⟧ **1** a long, loose outer garment; specif., *a*) a nightgown *b*) a long, flowing robe worn by judges, clergymen, scholars, etc. **2** a woman's formal dress

GP or **gp** *abbrev.* general practitioner

gr *abbrev.* **1** grain(s) **2** gross

Gr *abbrev.* **1** Greece **2** Greek

grab (grab) ***vt.*** **grabbed, grab′bing** ⟦prob. < MDu *grabben*⟧ **1** to snatch suddenly **2** to get by unscrupulous methods **3** [Slang] to impress greatly —***n.*** a grabbing —**grab′ber** ***n.***

grab′by ***adj.*** **-bi·er, -bi·est** [Inf.] greedy; avaricious

grace (grās) ***n.*** ⟦< L *gratus*, pleasing⟧ **1** beauty or charm of form, movement, or expression **2** goodwill; favor **3** a delay granted for payment of an obligation **4** a short prayer of thanks for a meal **5** [G-] a title of an archbishop, duke, or duchess **6** the love and favor of God toward human beings —***vt.*** **graced, grac′ing** **1** to decorate **2** to dignify —**in the good** (or **bad**) **graces of** in favor (or disfavor) with

grace′ful ***adj.*** having beauty of form, movement, etc. —**grace′ful·ly** ***adv.*** —**grace′ful·ness** ***n.***

grace′less ***adj.*** **1** lacking any sense of what is proper **2** clumsy or inelegant —**grace′less·ly** ***adv.*** —**grace′less·ness** ***n.***

gra·cious (grā′shəs) ***adj.*** ⟦see GRACE⟧ **1** having or showing kindness, courtesy, charm, etc. **2** compassionate **3** polite to supposed inferiors **4** marked by luxury, ease, etc. *[gracious* living*]* —**gra′cious·ly** ***adv.*** —**gra′cious·ness** ***n.***

grack·le (grak′əl) ***n.*** ⟦L *graculus*, jackdaw⟧ any of several blackbirds somewhat smaller than a crow

grad[1] (grad) ***n.*** [Inf.] a graduate

grad[2] *abbrev.* **1** graduate **2** graduated

gra·da·tion (grā dā′shən) ***n.*** **1** an arranging in grades, or stages **2** a gradual change by stages **3** a step or degree in a graded series

grade (grād) ***n.*** ⟦< L *gradus*⟧ **1** a stage or step in a progression **2** *a*) a degree in a scale of quality, rank, etc. *b*) a group of people of the same rank, merit, etc. **3** *a*) the degree of rise or descent of a sloping surface *b*) such a surface **4** any of the divisions of a school curriculum, usually by years **5** a mark or rating on an examination, etc. —***vt.*** **grad′ed, grad′ing** **1** to classify by grades; sort **2** to give a GRADE (*n.* 5) to **3** to make (ground) level or evenly sloped, as for a road —**make the grade** to succeed

grade crossing the place where a railroad intersects another railroad or a roadway on the same level

grade school ELEMENTARY SCHOOL

grade separation a crossing with an overpass or underpass

gra·di·ent (grā′dē ənt) ***n.*** ⟦< L *gradi*, to step⟧ **1** a slope, as of a road **2** the degree of such slope

grad·u·al (gra′jo͞o əl) ***adj.*** ⟦< L *gradus*, a step⟧ taking place by degrees; developing little by little —**grad′u·al·ly** ***adv.*** —**grad′u·al·ness** ***n.***

grad′u·al·ism′ ***n.*** the principle of promoting gradual rather than rapid change

grad·u·ate (gra′jo͞o it; *for v.*, -āt′) ***n.*** ⟦< L *gradus*, a step⟧ one who has completed a course of study at a school or college —***vt.*** **-at′ed, -at′ing** **1** to give a degree or diploma to upon completion of a course of study **2** [Inf.] to become a graduate of *[to graduate* college*]* **3** to mark with degrees for measuring **4** to classify into grades according to amount, size, etc. —***vi.*** to become a graduate of a school, etc. —***adj.*** **1** having been graduated from a school, etc. **2** of or for degrees above the bachelor's —**grad′u·a′tor** ***n.***

grad′u·a′tion ***n.*** **1** a graduating from a school or college **2** the ceremony connected with this

graf·fi·ti (grə fēt′ē) ***pl.n.***, *sing.* **-to** (-ō) ⟦It < L: see fol.⟧ [*now usually with sing. v.*] inscriptions or drawings on a wall or other public surface

graft (graft) ***n.*** ⟦ult. < Gr *grapheion*, stylus⟧ **1** *a*) a shoot or bud of one plant or tree inserted into another, where it grows permanently *b)* the inserting of such a shoot **2** the transplanting of skin, bone, etc. **3** *a)* the dishonest use of one's position to gain money, etc., as in politics *b)* anything so gained —***vt.***, ***vi.*** to insert (a graft) —**graft'er** ***n.***

gra·ham (grā'əm, gram) ***adj.*** ⟦after S. *Graham*, 19th-c. U.S. dietary reformer⟧ designating or made of whole-wheat flour *[graham* crackers*]*

Grail (grāl) ***n.*** ⟦< ML *gradalis*, cup⟧ *Medieval Legend* the cup used by Jesus at the Last Supper: also **Holy Grail**

grain (grān) ***n.*** ⟦< L *granum*⟧ **1** the small, hard seed of any cereal plant, as wheat or corn **2** cereal plants **3** a tiny, solid particle, as of salt or sand **4** a tiny bit **5** the smallest unit in the system of weights used in the U.S. **6** *a)* the arrangement or direction of fibers, layers, etc. of wood, leather, etc. *b)* the markings or texture due to this **7** disposition; nature

grain'y ***adj.*** **-i·er, -i·est 1** having a clearly defined grain: said as of wood **2** coarsely textured; granular —**grain'i·ness** ***n.***

gram[1] (gram) ***n.*** ⟦< Gr *gramma*, small weight⟧ the basic unit of mass in the metric system, equal to 0.03527 ounce

gram[2] *abbrev.* grammar

-gram (gram) ⟦< Gr *gramma*, writing⟧ *combining form* something written *[telegram]*

gram·mar (gram'ər) ***n.*** ⟦< Gr *gramma*, writing⟧ **1** language study dealing with the forms of words and with their arrangement in sentences **2** a system of rules for speaking and writing a given language **3** one's manner of speaking or writing as judged by such rules —**gram·mar·i·an** (grə mer'ē ən) ***n.*** —**gram·mat'i·cal** (-mat'i kəl) ***adj.*** —**gram·mat'i·cal·ly** ***adv.***

grammar school [Now Rare] ELEMENTARY SCHOOL

gran·a·ry (gran'ə rē, grān'-) ***n.***, *pl.* **-ries** ⟦< L *granum*, grain⟧ a building for storing threshed grain

grand (grand) ***adj.*** ⟦< L *grandis*, large⟧ **1** higher in rank than others *[a grand* duke*]* **2** most important; main *[the grand* ballroom*]* **3** imposing in size, beauty, and extent **4** distinguished; illustrious **5** complete; overall *[the grand* total*]* **6** [Inf.] excellent; delightful —***n.***, *pl.* **grand** [Slang] a thousand dollars —**grand'ly** ***adv.***

grand- *combining form* of the generation older (or younger) than *[grandmother, grandson]*

grand'child' ***n.***, *pl.* **-chil'dren** a child of one's son or daughter

grand'daugh'ter ***n.*** a daughter of one's son or daughter

grande dame (gränd däm') ⟦Fr⟧ a woman, esp. an older one, of great dignity

gran·dee (gran dē') ***n.*** ⟦Sp & Port *grande*: see GRAND⟧ a man of high rank

gran·deur (gran'jər, -joor'; -dyoor') ***n.*** ⟦see GRAND⟧ **1** splendor; magnificence **2** moral or intellectual greatness

grand'fa'ther ***n.*** **1** the father of one's father or mother **2** a forefather —***vt.*** [Inf.] to exempt (a practice, person, etc.) from a new law or regulation

grandfather (or **grandfather's**) **clock** a large clock with a pendulum, in a tall, narrow case

gran·dil·o·quent (gran dil'ə kwənt) ***adj.*** ⟦< L *grandis*, grand + *loqui*, speak⟧ using pompous, bombastic words —**gran·dil'o·quence** ***n.*** —**gran·dil'o·quent·ly** ***adv.***

gran·di·ose (gran'dē ōs') ***adj.*** ⟦< L *grandis*, great⟧ **1** having grandeur; imposing **2** pompous and showy —**gran'di·os'i·ty** (-äs'ə tē) ***n.***

grand jury a jury that investigates accusations and indicts persons for trial if there is sufficient evidence

grand'ma' ***n.*** [Inf.] GRANDMOTHER

grand'mas'ter ***n.*** a chess player of the highest rating

grand'moth'er ***n.*** **1** the mother of one's father or mother **2** a female ancestor

grand opera opera in which the whole text is set to music

grand'pa' ***n.*** [Inf.] GRANDFATHER

grand'par'ent ***n.*** a grandfather or grandmother

grand piano a large piano with strings set horizontally in a wing-shaped case

Grand Rapids city in SW Michigan: pop. 189,000

grand slam **1** *Baseball* a home run hit when there is a runner on each base **2** *Bridge* the winning of all the tricks in a deal

grand'son' ***n.*** a son of one's son or daughter

grand'stand' ***n.*** the main seating structure for spectators at a sporting event

grange (grānj) ***n.*** ⟦< L *granum*, grain⟧ a farm —**the Grange** a fraternal organization, originally of farmers, in the U.S.

gran·ite (gran'it) ***n.*** ⟦< L *granum*, grain⟧ a hard, grainy igneous rock consisting mainly of feldspar and quartz —**gra·nit·ic** (grə nit'ik) ***adj.***

gran·ny or **gran·nie** (gran'ē) ***n.***, *pl.* **-nies** [Inf.] **1** a grandmother **2** an old woman —***adj.*** of a style like that formerly worn by elderly women *[granny* glasses*]*

gran·o·la (grə nō'lə) ***n.*** ⟦< ? L *granum*, grain⟧ a breakfast cereal of rolled oats, wheat germ, sesame seeds, brown sugar or honey, dried fruit or nuts, etc.

grant (grant) ***vt.*** ⟦ult. < L *credere*, believe⟧ **1** to give (what is requested, as permission) **2** to give or transfer by legal procedure **3** to admit as true; concede —***n.*** **1** a granting **2** something granted, as property or a right —**take for granted** to consider as true, already settled, etc. —**grant'er** ***n.***

Grant (grant), **Ulysses S(impson)** 1822-85; 18th president of the U.S. (1869-77): Union commander in the Civil War

grant'-in-aid' ***n.***, *pl.* **grants'-in-aid'** a grant of funds, as by the federal government to a state or by a foundation to a scientist, artist, etc., to support a specific project

grants'man·ship' *n.* skill in acquiring grants-in-aid

gran·u·lar (gran'yə lər) *adj.* **1** containing or consisting of grains **2** like grains or granules —**gran'u·lar'·i·ty** (-ler'ə tē) *n.*

gran'u·late' (-lāt') *vt.*, *vi.* **-lat'ed, -lat'ing** to form into grains or granules —**gran'u·la'tion** *n.*

gran·ule (gran'yool) *n.* ⟦< L *granum*, grain⟧ a small grain or particle

grape (grāp) *n.* ⟦< OFr *graper*, to gather with a hook⟧ **1** a small, round, juicy berry, growing in clusters on a woody vine **2** a grapevine **3** a dark purplish red

grape'fruit' *n.* a large, round, sour citrus fruit with a yellow rind

grape hyacinth a small plant of the lily family, with spikes of small, bell-shaped flowers of blue or white

grape'shot' *n.* a cluster of small iron balls, formerly fired from a cannon

grape'vine' *n.* **1** a woody vine bearing grapes **2** a secret means of spreading information **3** a rumor

graph (graf) *n.* ⟦< *graph*(*ic formula*)⟧ a diagram representing quantitative information and relationships, such as successive changes in a variable quantity —*vt.* to represent by a graph

-graph (graf) ⟦< Gr *graphein*, to write⟧ *combining form* **1** something that writes or records *[telegraph]* **2** something written, etc. *[monograph]*

graph·ic (graf'ik) *adj.* ⟦< Gr *graphein*, to write⟧ **1** described in realistic detail; vivid **2** of those arts (**graphic arts**) that include any form of visual artistic representation, esp. painting, drawing, etching, etc. Also **graph'i·cal** —**graph'i·cal·ly** *adv.*

graph'ics *n.* **1** design as employed in the graphic arts **2** the graphic arts

graph·ite (graf'īt') *n.* ⟦< Gr *graphein*, to write⟧ a soft, black form of carbon used in pencils, electrodes, etc.

graph·ol·o·gy (graf äl'ə jē) *n.* ⟦< Fr: see GRAPHIC & -LOGY⟧ the study of handwriting, esp. as a clue to character —**graph·ol'o·gist** *n.*

-gra·phy (grə fē) ⟦< Gr *graphein*, to write⟧ *combining form* **1** a process or method of writing or graphically representing *[calligraphy]* **2** a descriptive science *[geography]*

grap·nel (grap'nəl) *n.* ⟦< Prov *grapa*, a hook⟧ a small anchor with several curved, pointed arms

grap·ple (grap'əl) *n.* ⟦OFr *grapil*⟧ **1** GRAPNEL **2** a hand-to-hand fight —*vt.* **-pled, -pling** to grip and hold —*vi.* **1** to use a GRAPNEL **2** to wrestle **3** to try to cope (*with*)

grappling iron (or **hook**) GRAPNEL

grasp (grasp) *vt.* ⟦ME *graspen*⟧ **1** to grip, as with the hand **2** to take hold of eagerly; seize **3** to comprehend —*vi.* **1** to try to seize: with *at* **2** to accept eagerly: with *at* —*n.* **1** a grasping; grip **2** control; possession **3** the power to hold or seize **4** comprehension —**grasp'a·ble** *adj.*

grasp'ing *adj.* avaricious; greedy

grass (gras, gräs) *n.* ⟦OE *græs*⟧ **1** a plant with long, narrow leaves, jointed stems, and seedlike fruit, as wheat or rye **2** any of various green plants with narrow leaves, growing densely in meadows, lawns, etc. **3** pasture or lawn **4** [Slang] marijuana —**grass'y, -i·er, -i·est,** *adj.*

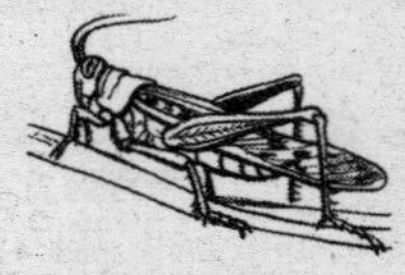

GRASSHOPPER

grass'hop'per *n.* any of various winged, plant-eating insects with powerful hind legs for jumping

grass roots [Inf.] **1** the common people **2** the basic source or support, as of a movement —**grass'-roots'** *adj.*

grass widow a woman divorced or separated from her husband

grate[1] (grāt) *vt.* **grat'ed, grat'ing** ⟦< OFr *grater*⟧ **1** to grind into particles by scraping **2** to rub against (an object) or grind (the teeth) together with a harsh sound **3** to irritate; annoy; fret —*vi.* **1** to rub with or make a rasping sound **2** to be irritating —**grat'er** *n.*

grate[2] (grāt) *n.* ⟦< L *cratis*, a hurdle⟧ **1** GRATING[1] **2** a frame of metal bars for holding fuel in a fireplace, etc. **3** a fireplace

grate·ful (grāt'fəl) *adj.* ⟦obs. *grate*, pleasing (< L *gratus*)⟧ **1** thankful **2** welcome —**grate'ful·ly** *adv.* —**grate'ful·ness** *n.*

grat·i·fy (grat'i fī') *vt.* **-fied', -fy'ing** ⟦< L *gratus*, pleasing + *-ficare*, -FY⟧ **1** to please or satisfy **2** to indulge; humor —**grat'i·fi·ca'tion** *n.* —**grat'i·fy'ing** *adj.*

grat·ing[1] (grāt'iŋ) *n.* a framework of bars set in a window, door, etc.

grat'ing[2] *adj.* **1** rasping **2** irritating

gra·tis (grat'is, grät'-) *adv.*, *adj.* ⟦L < *gratia*, a favor⟧ free of charge

grat·i·tude (grat'i to͞od') *n.* ⟦< L *gratus*, pleasing⟧ thankful appreciation for favors or benefits received

gra·tu·i·tous (grə to͞o'i təs, -tyo͞o'-) *adj.* ⟦< L *gratus*, pleasing⟧ **1** given free of charge **2** uncalled-for —**gra·tu'i·tous·ly** *adv.*

gra·tu'i·ty (-tē) *n.*, *pl.* **-ties** a gift of money for a service; tip

gra·va·men (grə vā'mən) *n.*, *pl.* **-mens** or **gra·vam'i·na** (-vam'i nə) ⟦LL, a burden⟧ *Law* the essential part of a complaint or accusation

grave[1] (grāv) *adj.* **grav'er, grav'est** ⟦< L *gravis*, heavy⟧ **1** important **2** serious *[a grave illness]* **3** solemn or sedate **4** somber; dull —**grave'ly** *adv.* —**grave'ness** *n.*

grave[2] (grāv) *n.* ⟦< OE *grafan*, to dig⟧ **1** *a*) a hole in the ground in which to bury a dead body *b*) any burial place; tomb

2 death —*vt.* **graved, grav′en** or **graved, grav′ing 1** [Archaic] to sculpture or engrave **2** to impress sharply

grave accent (gräv, grāv) a mark (`) showing stress, the quality of a vowel, etc.

grav·el (grav′əl) *n.* ⟦< OFr *grave*, coarse sand⟧ a loose mixture of pebbles and rock fragments coarser than sand

grav′el·ly (-ē) *adj.* **1** full of or like gravel **2** harsh or rasping *[a gravelly voice]*

grav·en (grāv′ən) *vt. alt. pp. of* GRAVE[2]

grave′stone′ *n.* a tombstone

grave′yard′ *n.* a cemetery

graveyard shift [Inf.] work shift at night, esp. one starting at midnight

grav·id (grav′id) *adj.* ⟦< L *gravis*, heavy⟧ pregnant

gra·vim·e·ter (grə vim′ət ər) *n.* ⟦< L *gravis*, heavy + Fr *-mètre*, -METER⟧ **1** a device for determining specific gravity **2** an instrument for measuring the earth's gravitational pull

grav·i·tate (grav′i tāt′) *vi.* **-tat′ed, -tat′ing 1** to move or tend to move in accordance with the force of gravity **2** to be attracted (*toward*)

grav′i·ta′tion *n.* **1** a gravitating **2** *Physics* the force by which every mass attracts and is attracted by every other mass —**grav′i·ta′tion·al** *adj.*

grav·i·ty (grav′i tē) *n., pl.* **-ties** ⟦< L *gravis*, heavy⟧ **1** graveness; seriousness **2** weight *[specific gravity]* **3** *Physics* gravitation; esp., the pull on all bodies in the earth's sphere toward the earth's center

gra·vy (grā′vē) *n., pl.* **-vies** ⟦< ?⟧ **1** the juice given off by meat in cooking **2** a sauce made from this juice **3** [Slang] any benefit beyond what is expected

gray (grā) *n.* ⟦< OE *græg*⟧ a color that is a blend of black and white —*adj.* **1** of this color **2** having hair this color **3** *a*) darkish; dull *b*) dreary; dismal **4** designating a vague, intermediate area —*vt., vi.* to make or become gray —**gray′ish** *adj.* —**gray′ness** *n.*

gray′beard′ *n.* an old man

gray matter 1 grayish nerve tissue of the brain and spinal cord **2** [Inf.] intellectual capacity; brains

graze[1] (grāz) *vt.* **grazed, graz′ing** ⟦< OE *græs*, grass⟧ **1** to put livestock to feed on (growing grass, etc.) **2** to tend (feeding livestock) —*vi.* to feed on growing grass, etc.

graze[2] (grāz) *vt., vi.* **grazed, graz′ing** ⟦prob. < prec.⟧ to scrape or rub lightly in passing —*n.* a grazing

Gr Brit or **Gr Br** Great Britain

grease (grēs; *for v., also* grēz) *n.* ⟦< L *crassus*, fat⟧ **1** melted animal fat **2** any thick, oily substance or lubricant —*vt.* **greased, greas′ing** to smear or lubricate with grease

grease′paint′ *n.* greasy coloring matter used in making up for the stage

greas·y (grē′sē, -zē) *adj.* **-i·er, -i·est 1** soiled with grease **2** containing much grease **3** oily —**greas′i·ness** *n.*

great (grāt) *adj.* ⟦OE⟧ **1** of much more than ordinary size, extent, etc. *[the Great Lakes]* **2** much above the average; esp., *a*) intense *[great pain]* *b*) eminent *[a great writer]* **3** most important; main **4** [Inf.] skillful: often with *at* **5** [Inf.] excellent; fine —*n.* a distinguished person —**great′ly** *adv.* —**great′ness** *n.*

great- *combining form* older (or younger) by one generation *[great-aunt, great-great-grandson]*

great ape any of a family of primates consisting of the gorilla, chimpanzee, and orangutan

Great Britain principal island of the United Kingdom, including England, Scotland, & Wales

Great Dane a very large, muscular dog with a short, smooth coat

great′-grand′child′ *n., pl.* **-chil′dren** a child of any of one's grandchildren

great′-grand′par′ent *n.* a parent of any of one's grandparents

great′heart′ed *adj.* **1** brave; fearless **2** generous; unselfish

Great Lakes chain of five freshwater lakes in EC North America

Great Salt Lake shallow saltwater lake in NW Utah

grebe (grēb) *n.* ⟦Fr *grèbe*⟧ a diving and swimming bird with broadly lobed webbed feet

Gre·cian (grē′shən) *adj., n.* GREEK

Greco- ⟦< L *Graecus*⟧ *combining form* Greek, Greek and *[Greco-Roman]*

Greece (grēs) country in the S Balkan Peninsula, on the Mediterranean: 50,949 sq. mi.; pop. 10,260,000

greed (grēd) *n.* ⟦< fol.⟧ excessive desire, esp. for wealth; avarice

greed·y (grēd′ē) *adj.* **-i·er, -i·est** ⟦OE *grædig*⟧ **1** desiring more than one needs or deserves **2** having too strong a desire for food and drink; gluttonous —**greed′i·ly** *adv.* —**greed′i·ness** *n.*

Greek (grēk) *n.* **1** a person born or living in Greece **2** the language, ancient or modern, of the Greeks —*adj.* of Greece or its people, language, etc.

green (grēn) *adj.* ⟦OE *grene*⟧ **1** of the color of growing grass **2** overspread with green plants or foliage **3** sickly or bilious **4** unripe **5** inexperienced or naive **6** not dried or seasoned **7** [Inf.] jealous —*n.* **1** the color of growing grass **2** [*pl.*] green leafy vegetables, as spinach **3** an area of smooth turf *[a putting green]* —**green′ish** *adj.* —**green′ly** *adv.* —**green′ness** *n.*

green′back′ *n.* any piece of U.S. paper money printed in green ink on the back

Green Bay city & port in Wisconsin: pop 96,000

green bean the edible, immature green pod of the kidney bean

green′belt′ *n.* a beltlike area around a city, reserved for park land or farms

green′er·y *n.* green vegetation; verdure

green′-eyed′ *adj.* very jealous

green′gro′cer *n.* [Brit.] a retail dealer in fresh vegetables and fruit

green′horn′ *n.* **1** an inexperienced person 2 a person easily deceived

green'house' *n.* a heated building, mainly of glass, for growing plants

greenhouse effect the warming of the earth and its lower atmosphere, caused by trapped solar radiation

Green·land (grēn'lənd) self-governing Danish island northeast of North America

green light [Inf.] permission to proceed with some undertaking —**green'light'**, **-light'ed** or **-lit'**, **-light'ing**, *vt.*

green manure a crop, as of clover, plowed under to fertilize the soil

green onion an immature onion with green leaves, often eaten raw; scallion

green pepper the green immature fruit of a red pepper, esp. the bell pepper

green power money as the source of economic power

Greens·bor·o (grēnz'bur'ō) city in NC North Carolina: pop. 184,000

green'sward' *n.* green, grassy turf

green thumb a talent for growing plants

Green·wich (gren'ich; *chiefly Brit*, grin'ij) borough of London, on the prime meridian: pop. 208,000

Green·wich Village (gren'ich) section of New York City: noted as a center for artists, writers, etc.

green'wood' *n.* a forest in leaf

greet (grēt) *vt.* ⟦OE *gretan*⟧ **1** to address with friendliness **2** to meet or receive (a person, event, etc.) in a specified way **3** to come or appear to; meet —**greet'er** *n.*

greet'ing *n.* **1** the act or words of one who greets **2** [*often pl.*] a message of regards

greeting card CARD[1] (*n.* 1d)

gre·gar·i·ous (grə ger'ē əs) *adj.* ⟦< L *grex*, herd⟧ **1** living in herds **2** fond of the company of others; sociable —**gre·gar'i·ous·ly** *adv.* —**gre·gar'i·ous·ness** *n.*

Gre·go·ri·an calendar (grə gôr'ē ən) the calendar now widely used, introduced by Pope Gregory XIII in 1582

Gregorian chant ⟦after Pope Gregory I⟧ a kind of plainsong formerly widely used in the Roman Catholic Church

grem·lin (grem'lin) *n.* ⟦prob. < Dan *gram*, a devil⟧ a small imaginary creature humorously blamed for malfunctions or disruptions

Gre·na·da (grə nā'də) country on an island group in the West Indies: 133 sq. mi.; pop. 95,000

gre·nade (grə nād') *n.* ⟦Fr < OFr, pomegranate⟧ a small bomb detonated by a fuse and usually thrown by hand

gren·a·dier (gren'ə dir') *n.* **1** [Archaic] a soldier who threw grenades **2** a member of a special regiment or corps

gren·a·dine (gren'ə dēn') *n.* ⟦Fr⟧ a red syrup made from pomegranate juice

grew (gro͞o) *vi.*, *vt.* *pt. of* GROW

grey (grā) *n.*, *adj.*, *vt.*, *vi.* *chiefly Brit. sp. of* GRAY

grey'hound' *n.* a tall, slender, swift dog with a narrow head

grid (grid) *n.* ⟦short for GRIDIRON⟧ **1** a framework of parallel bars; grating **2** a metallic plate in a storage battery **3** an electrode, in spiral or gridlike shape, for controlling the flow of electrons in an electron tube

grid·dle (grid''l) *n.* ⟦< L *craticula*, gridiron⟧ a flat, heavy metal pan for cooking pancakes, etc.

grid'dle·cake' *n.* a pancake

grid·i·ron (grid'ī'ərn) *n.* ⟦see GRIDDLE⟧ **1** GRILL (*n.* 1) **2** a football field

grid'lock' *n.* a traffic jam in which no vehicle can move in any direction

grief (grēf) *n.* ⟦see GRIEVE⟧ **1** intense emotional suffering caused as by a loss **2** a cause of such suffering —**come to grief** to fail or be ruined

griev·ance (grēv'əns) *n.* **1** a circumstance thought to be unjust and ground for complaint **2** complaint against a real or imagined wrong

grieve (grēv) *vi.*, *vt.* **grieved**, **griev'ing** ⟦< L *gravis*, heavy⟧ to feel or cause to feel grief

griev·ous (grēv'əs) *adj.* **1** causing grief **2** showing or full of grief **3** severe **4** deplorable; atrocious —**griev'ous·ly** *adv.*

GRIFFIN

grif·fin (grif'in) *n.* ⟦< Gr *gryps*⟧ a mythical monster, part lion and part eagle

grill (gril) *n.* ⟦see GRIDDLE⟧ **1** a unit for broiling meat, etc., consisting of a framework of metal bars or wires **2** a large griddle **3** grilled food **4** a restaurant that specializes in grilled foods —*vt.* **1** to broil **2** to question relentlessly

grille (gril) *n.* ⟦see GRIDDLE⟧ an open grating forming a screen

grim (grim) *adj.* **grim'mer**, **grim'mest** ⟦OE *grimm*⟧ **1** hard and unyielding; stern **2** appearing forbidding, harsh, etc. **3** repellent; ghastly —**grim'ly** *adv.* —**grim'ness** *n.*

gri·mace (gri mās', grim'is) *n.* ⟦Fr⟧ a distortion of the face, as in expressing pain, disgust, etc. —*vi.* **-maced'**, **-mac'ing** to make grimaces

grime (grīm) *n.* ⟦prob. < Fl *grijm*⟧ dirt rubbed into or covering a surface, as of the skin —**grim'y**, **-i·er**, **-i·est**, *adj.* —**grim'i·ness** *n.*

Grimm (grim) **1 Ja·kob (Ludwig Karl)** (yä'kôp) 1785-1863; Ger. philologist **2 Wil·helm (Karl)** (vil'helm) 1786-1859; Ger. philologist: brother of Jakob, with whom he collected fairy tales

grin (grin) *vi.* **grinned**, **grin'ning** ⟦< OE

grennian, bare the teeth⟧ **1** to smile broadly as in amusement **2** to show the teeth in pain, scorn, etc. —*n.* the act or look of grinning

grind (grīnd) *vt.* **ground, grind'ing** ⟦OE *grindan*⟧ **1** to crush or chop into fine particles; pulverize **2** to oppress **3** to sharpen or smooth by friction **4** to rub (the teeth, etc.) together gratingly **5** to operate by turning the crank of —*n.* **1** a grinding **2** long, difficult work or study **3** [Inf.] a student who studies hard —**grind out** to produce by steady or laborious effort

grind·er (grīn'dər) *n.* **1** a person or thing that grinds **2** [*pl.*] [Inf.] the teeth **3** *chiefly New England var. of* HERO SANDWICH

grind'stone' *n.* a revolving stone disk for sharpening tools or polishing things —**keep one's nose to the grindstone** to work hard and steadily

grip (grip) *n.* ⟦< OE *grīpan*, seize⟧ **1** a secure grasp; firm hold **2** the manner of holding a club, bat, etc. **3** the power of grasping firmly **4** mental grasp **5** firm control **6** a handle **7** a small traveling bag —*vt.* **gripped** or **gript, grip'ping** **1** to take firmly and hold fast **2** to get and hold the attention of —*vi.* to get a grip —**come to grips** to struggle (*with*) —**grip'per** *n.*

gripe (grīp) *vt.* **griped, grip'ing** ⟦OE *grīpan*, seize⟧ **1** to cause sharp pain in the bowels of **2** [Slang] to annoy —*vi.* [Slang] to complain —*n.* **1** a sharp pain in the bowels: *usually used in pl.* **2** [Slang] a complaint —**grip'er** *n.*

grippe (grip) *n.* ⟦Fr⟧ *former term for* INFLUENZA

gris-gris (grē'grē') *n., pl.* **gris'-gris'** ⟦of Afr orig.⟧ an amulet, charm, or spell of African origin

gris·ly (griz'lē) *adj.* **-li·er, -li·est** ⟦OE *grislic*⟧ terrifying; ghastly —**gris'li·ness** *n.*

grist (grist) *n.* ⟦OE⟧ grain that is to be or has been ground

gris·tle (gris'əl) *n.* ⟦OE⟧ cartilage, esp. as found in meat —**gris'tly** (-lē) *adj.*

grist'mill' *n.* a mill for grinding grain

grit (grit) *n.* ⟦< OE *greot*⟧ **1** rough particles, as of sand **2** coarse sandstone **3** stubborn courage; pluck —*vt.* **grit'ted, grit'ting** to clench or grind (the teeth) as in determination —*vi.* to make a grating sound —**grit'ty, -ti·er, -ti·est,** *adj.*

grits (grits) *pl.n.* ⟦OE *grytte*⟧ [*often with sing. v.*] coarsely ground grain; esp., hominy

griz·zled (griz'əld) *adj.* ⟦< OFr *gris*, gray⟧ **1** gray or streaked with gray **2** having gray hair

griz'zly (-lē) *adj.* **-zli·er, -zli·est** grayish; grizzled

grizzly (bear) a large, brown bear of W North America

groan (grōn) *vi., vt.* ⟦< OE *granian*⟧ to utter (with) a deep sound expressing pain, distress, etc. —*n.* such a sound

gro·cer (grō'sər) *n.* ⟦< OFr *grossier*⟧ a dealer in food and household supplies

gro'cer·y *n., pl.* **-ies** **1** a grocer's store **2** [*pl.*] the food and supplies sold by a grocer

grog (gräg) *n.* ⟦after Old *Grog*, nickname of an 18th-c. Brit admiral⟧ **1** rum diluted with water **2** any alcoholic liquor

grog'gy *adj.* **-gi·er, -gi·est** ⟦< prec. + -Y²⟧ **1** [Archaic] intoxicated **2** dizzy **3** sluggish or dull —**grog'gi·ly** *adv.* —**grog'gi·ness** *n.*

groin (groin) *n.* ⟦prob. < OE *grynde*, abyss⟧ **1** the fold where the abdomen joins either thigh **2** *Archit.* the sharp, curved edge at the junction of two vaults

grom·met (gräm'it) *n.* ⟦< obs. Fr *gromette*, a curb⟧ **1** a ring of rope **2** a metal eyelet in cloth, etc.

groom (groom) *n.* ⟦ME *grom*, boy⟧ **1** one whose work is tending horses **2** a bridegroom —*vt.* **1** to clean and curry (a horse, etc.) **2** to make neat and tidy **3** to train for a particular purpose

groove (groov) *n.* ⟦< ON *grof*, a pit⟧ **1** a long, narrow furrow cut with a tool **2** any channel or rut **3** a settled routine —*vt.* **grooved, groov'ing** to make a groove in

groov'y *adj.* **-i·er, -i·est** [Slang] very pleasing or attractive

grope (grōp) *vi.* **groped, grop'ing** ⟦< OE *grapian*, to touch⟧ to feel or search about blindly or uncertainly —*vt.* **1** to seek or find (one's way) by groping **2** [Slang] to fondle sexually —**grop'er** *n.* —**grop'ing·ly** *adv.*

gros·beak (grōs'bēk') *n.* ⟦Fr: see GROSS & BEAK⟧ a songbird with a thick, strong, conical bill

gros·grain (grō'grān') *n.* ⟦Fr, lit., coarse grain⟧ a ribbed silk or rayon fabric for ribbons, etc.

gross (grōs) *adj.* ⟦< LL *grossus*, thick⟧ **1** fat and coarse-looking **2** flagrant; very bad **3** lacking in refinement **4** vulgar; coarse **5** with no deductions; total **6** [Slang] disgusting —*n.* **1** *pl.* **gross'es** overall total **2** *pl.* **gross** twelve dozen —*vt., vi.* to earn (a specified total amount) before expenses are deducted —**gross out** [Slang] to disgust —**gross'ly** *adv.*

gross national product the total value of a nation's annual output of goods and services

gro·tesque (grō tesk') *adj.* ⟦< It *grotta*, grotto: from designs found in caves⟧ **1** distorted or fantastic in appearance, shape, etc. **2** ridiculous; absurd —**gro·tesque'ly** *adv.*

grot·to (grät'ō) *n., pl.* **-toes** or **-tos** ⟦< It < L *crypta*, crypt⟧ **1** a cave **2** a cavelike summerhouse, shrine, etc.

grouch (grouch) *vi.* ⟦< ME *grucchen*⟧ to grumble or complain sulkily —*n.* **1** one who grouches **2** a sulky mood —**grouch'y, -i·er, -i·est,** *adj.* —**grouch'i·ly** *adv.* —**grouch'i·ness** *n.*

ground¹ (ground) *n.* ⟦OE *grund*, bottom⟧ **1** the solid surface of the earth **2** soil; earth **3** [*often pl.*] a tract of land [*grounds of an estate*] **4** area, as of discussion **5** [*often pl.*] basis; foundation **6** valid reason or motive: *often used in pl.* **7** the background, as in a design **8**

[*pl.*] sediment [coffee *grounds*] **9** the connection of an electrical conductor with a ground —***adj.*** of, on, or near the ground —***vt.*** **1** to set on the ground **2** to cause to run aground **3** to base; found; establish **4** to instruct in the first principles of **5** *a*) to keep (an aircraft or pilot) from flying *b*) [Inf.] to punish (a teenager) by not permitting him or her to leave home for dates, etc. **6** *Elec.* to connect (a conductor) to a ground —***vi.*** **1** to run ashore **2** *Baseball* to be put out on a grounder: usually with *out* —**break ground** **1** to dig; excavate **2** to plow **3** to start building —**gain** (**or lose**) **ground** to gain (or lose) in achievement, popularity, etc. —**give ground** to retreat; yield —**hold** (or **stand**) **one's ground** to remain firm, not yielding

ground[2] (ground) ***vt.***, ***vi.*** *pt. & pp. of* GRIND

ground control personnel and equipment on the ground, for guiding airplanes and spacecraft in takeoff, landing, etc.

ground cover low, dense-growing plants used for covering bare ground

ground crew a group of workers who maintain and repair aircraft

ground'er ***n.*** *Baseball* a batted ball that travels along the ground: also **ground ball**

ground floor that floor of a building approximately level with the ground; first floor —**in on the ground floor** [Inf.] in at the start (of a business, etc.)

ground glass nontransparent glass with a surface that has been ground to diffuse light

ground'hog' ***n.*** WOODCHUCK: also **ground hog**

ground'less ***adj.*** without reason or cause

ground rule **1** *Baseball* a rule adapted to playing conditions in a specific ballpark **2** any basic rule

ground'swell' ***n.*** **1** a violent rolling of the ocean **2** a wave of popular feeling

ground'wa'ter ***n.*** water found underground

ground'work' ***n.*** a foundation; basis

group (gro͞op) ***n.*** ⟦< It *gruppo*⟧ a number of persons or things gathered or classified together —***vt.***, ***vi.*** to form into a group or groups

grou·per (gro͞o′pər) ***n.*** ⟦Port *garupa*⟧ a large sea bass found in warm seas

group·ie (gro͞o′pē) ***n.*** [Inf.] **1** a female fan of rock groups or other popular personalities, who follows them about **2** a fan; devotee

group therapy (or **psychotherapy**) a form of treatment for a group of patients with similar emotional problems, as by group discussions

grouse[1] (grous) ***n.***, *pl.* **grouse** ⟦< ?⟧ a game bird with a plump body and mottled feathers

grouse[2] (grous) ***vi.*** **groused**, **grous'ing** ⟦< ?⟧ [Inf.] to complain

grout (grout) ***n.*** ⟦ME⟧ a thin mortar used as between tiles

grove (grōv) ***n.*** ⟦< OE *graf*⟧ a group of trees, without undergrowth

grov·el (gräv′əl, gruv′-) ***vi.*** **-eled** or **-elled**, **-el·ing** or **-el·ling** ⟦< ME *grufelinge*, down on one's face⟧ **1** to lie or crawl in a prostrate position, esp. abjectly **2** to behave abjectly —**grov'el·er** or **grov'el·ler** ***n.***

grow (grō) ***vi.*** **grew**, **grown**, **grow'ing** ⟦< OE *growan*⟧ **1** to come into being or be produced naturally **2** to develop or thrive, as a living thing **3** to increase in size, quantity, etc. **4** to become [to *grow* weary] —***vt.*** to cause to or let grow; raise; cultivate —**grow on** [Inf.] to come gradually to seem more likable, attractive, etc. to —**grow up** to mature —**grow'er** ***n.***

growl (groul) ***n.*** ⟦ME *groulen*⟧ a rumbling, menacing sound such as an angry dog makes —***vi.***, ***vt.*** to make, or express by, such a sound

grown (grōn) ***vi.***, ***vt.*** *pp. of* GROW —***adj.*** having completed its growth; mature

grown'-up' ***adj.***, ***n.*** adult: also, for *n.*, **grown'up'**

growth (grōth) ***n.*** **1** a growing or developing **2** *a*) increase in size, etc. *b*) the full extent of this **3** something that grows or has grown **4** a tumor or other abnormal mass of tissue

grub (grub) ***vi.*** **grubbed**, **grub'bing** ⟦ME *grubben*⟧ **1** to dig in the ground **2** to work hard —***vt.*** **1** to clear (ground) of roots **2** to uproot —***n.*** **1** a wormlike larva, esp. of a beetle **2** [Slang] food

grub'by ***adj.*** **-bi·er**, **-bi·est** dirty; untidy —**grub'bi·ness** ***n.***

grub'stake' ***n.*** ⟦GRUB, *n.* 2 + STAKE⟧ [Inf.] **1** money or supplies advanced, as to a prospector **2** money advanced for any enterprise

grudge (gruj) ***vt.*** **grudged**, **grudg'ing** ⟦< OFr *grouchier*⟧ **1** BEGRUDGE **2** to give with reluctance —***n.*** a feeling of resentment or ill will over some grievance —**grudg'ing·ly** ***adv.***

gru·el (gro͞o′əl) ***n.*** ⟦< ML *grutum*, meal⟧ thin porridge made by cooking meal in water or milk

gru'el·ing or **gru'el·ling** ***adj.*** ⟦prp. of obs. v. *gruel*, punish⟧ very trying; exhausting

grue·some (gro͞o′səm) ***adj.*** ⟦< dial. *grue*, to shudder + -SOME[1]⟧ causing horror or disgust; grisly

gruff (gruf) ***adj.*** ⟦< Du *grof*⟧ **1** rough or surly; brusquely rude **2** harsh and throaty; hoarse —**gruff'ly** ***adv.*** —**gruff'ness** ***n.***

grum·ble (grum′bəl) ***vi.*** **-bled**, **-bling** ⟦prob. < Du *grommelen*⟧ **1** to growl **2** to mutter in discontent **3** to rumble —***vt.*** to express by grumbling —***n.*** a grumbling —**grum'bler** ***n.***

grump·y (grum′pē) ***adj.*** **-i·er**, **-i·est** ⟦prob. echoic⟧ grouchy; peevish

grunge (grunj) ***n.*** [Slang] garbage or dirt

grun·gy (grun′jē) ***adj.*** **-gi·er**, **-gi·est** [Slang] dirty, messy, etc.

grun·ion (grun′yən) ***n.*** ⟦prob. < Sp *gruñón*, grumbler⟧ a fish of the California coast: it spawns on sandy beaches

grunt (grunt) ***vi.*, *vt.*** ⟦< OE *grunian*⟧ to utter (with) the deep, hoarse sound of a hog **—*n.* 1** this sound **2** [Slang] one whose job involves routine tasks, strenuous labor, etc.; specif., a U.S. infantryman

Gru·yère (cheese) (groo yer′, grē-) ⟦after *Gruyère*, Switzerland⟧ [*often* **g-**] a light-yellow Swiss cheese, rich in butterfat

Gua·da·la·ja·ra (gwäd″l ə här′ə) city in W Mexico: capital of Jalisco: pop. 1,626,000

Guam (gwäm) island in the W Pacific: an unincorporated territory of the U.S.: 209 sq. mi.; pop. 133,000

Guang·zhou (gwäŋ′jō) seaport in SE China: pop. 3,182,000

gua·nine (gwä′nēn′) ***n.*** ⟦< fol. + -INE[3]⟧ a crystalline base contained in the nucleic acids of all tissue

gua·no (gwä′nō) ***n.***, *pl.* **-nos** ⟦Sp < AmInd (Peru)⟧ manure of seabirds, used as fertilizer

guar *abbrev.* guaranteed

guar·an·tee (gar′ən tē′) ***n.* 1** GUARANTY (sense 1) **2** *a)* a pledge to replace something if it is not as represented *b)* an assurance that something will be done as specified **3** a guarantor **—*vt.* -teed′, -tee′ing 1** to give a guarantee for **2** to promise

guar·an·tor (gar′ən tôr′) ***n.*** one who gives a guaranty or guarantee

guar′an·ty (-tē) ***n.***, *pl.* **-ties** ⟦< OFr *garant*, a warrant⟧ **1** a pledge or security for another's debt or obligation **2** an agreement that secures the existence or maintenance of something **—*vt.* -tied, -ty·ing** GUARANTEE

guard (gärd) ***vt.*** ⟦< OFr *garder*⟧ **1** to watch over and protect; defend **2** to keep from escaping or from trouble **3** to control or restrain **—*vi.* 1** to keep watch (*against*) **2** to act as a guard **—*n.* 1** defense; protection **2** a posture of readiness for defense **3** any device to protect against injury or loss **4** a person or group that guards **5** *Basketball* either of two players who are the main ball handlers **6** *Football* either of two players next to the center **—on (one's) guard** vigilant

guard′ed ***adj.* 1** kept safe **2** cautious [a *guarded* reply] **—guard′ed·ly *adv.***

guard′house′ ***n.*** *Mil.* **1** a building used by a guard when not walking a post **2** a jail for temporary confinement

guard′i·an (-ē ən) ***n.* 1** one who guards or protects; custodian **2** a person legally in charge of the affairs of a minor or of a person of unsound mind **—*adj.*** protecting **—guard′i·an·ship′ *n.***

guard′rail′ ***n.*** a protective railing

Gua·te·ma·la (gwät′ə mä′lə) country in Central America: 42,042 sq. mi.; pop. 6,054,000

gua·va (gwä′və) ***n.*** ⟦< native name⟧ a yellow, pear-shaped tropical American fruit

gua·ya·be·ra (gwä′yä ber′ä) ***n.*** ⟦AmSp⟧ a kind of loosefitting shirt worn with the shirttail outside the trousers

gu·ber·na·to·ri·al (goo′bər nə tôr′ē əl) ***adj.*** ⟦L *gubernator*, governor⟧ of a governor or the office of governor

Guern·sey (gurn′zē) ***n.***, *pl.* **-seys** ⟦after *Guernsey*, one of the Channel Islands⟧ a breed of dairy cattle, usually fawn-colored with white markings

guer·ril·la (gə ril′ə) ***n.*** ⟦Sp, dim. of *guerra*, war⟧ a member of a small defensive force of irregular soldiers, making surprise raids: also sp. **gue·ril′la**

guess (ges) ***vt.*, *vi.*** ⟦ME *gessen*⟧ **1** to form a judgment or estimate of (something) without actual knowledge; surmise **2** to judge correctly by doing this **3** to think or suppose **—*n.* 1** a guessing **2** something guessed; conjecture **—guess′er *n.***

guess′work′ ***n.* 1** a guessing **2** a judgment, result, etc. arrived at by guessing

guest (gest) ***n.*** ⟦< ON *gestr*⟧ **1** a person entertained at the home, club, etc. of another **2** any paying customer of a hotel, restaurant, etc. **—*adj.* 1** for guests **2** performing by special invitation [a *guest* artist]

guff (guf) ***n.*** ⟦echoic⟧ [Slang] **1** nonsense **2** brash or insolent talk

guf·faw (gə fô′) ***n.*** ⟦echoic⟧ a loud, coarse burst of laughter **—*vi.*** to laugh in this way

guid·ance (gīd″ns) ***n.* 1** a guiding; leadership **2** advice or assistance

guide (gīd) ***vt.* guid′ed, guid′ing** ⟦< OFr *guider*⟧ **1** to point out the way for; lead **2** to direct the course of; control **—*n.* 1** one whose work is conducting tours, etc. **2** a controlling device **3** a book of basic instruction

guide′book′ ***n.*** a book containing directions and information for tourists

guided missile a military missile whose course is controlled as by electronic signals

guide′line′ ***n.*** a principle by which to determine a course of action

guild (gild) ***n.*** ⟦< OE *gieldan*, to pay⟧ an association for mutual aid and the promotion of common interests

guil·der (gil′dər) ***n.*** ⟦< MDu *gulden*, golden⟧ the former monetary unit of the Netherlands, superseded in 2002 by the EURO

guile (gīl) ***n.*** ⟦< OFr⟧ slyness and cunning in dealing with others **—guile′ful *adj.* —guile′less *adj.***

guil·lo·tine (gil′ə tēn′, gē′ə-; *for v., usually* gil′ə tēn′, gē′ə-) ***n.*** ⟦Fr: after J. *Guillotin* (1738-1814), Fr physician who advocated its use⟧ an instrument for beheading, having a heavy blade dropped between two grooved uprights **—*vt.* -tined′, -tin′ing** to behead with a guillotine

guilt (gilt) ***n.*** ⟦OE *gylt*, a sin⟧ **1** the state of having done a wrong or committed an offense **2** a feeling of self-reproach from believing that one has done a wrong **—guilt′less *adj.***

guilt′y ***adj.* -i·er, -i·est 1** having guilt **2** legally judged an offender **3** of or showing guilt [a *guilty* look] **—guilt′i·ly *adv.* —guilt′i·ness *n.***

guin·ea (gin′ē) ***n.*** ⟦first coined of gold from *Guinea*⟧ a former English gold coin equal to 21 shillings

Guin·ea (gin′ē) country on the W coast of Africa: 94,926 sq. mi.; pop. 7,300,000

Guin′ea-Bis·sau′ (-bi sou′) country on the W coast of Africa: 13,948 sq. mi.; pop. 777,000

guinea fowl (or **hen**) ⟦orig. imported from *Guinea*⟧ a domestic fowl with a rounded body and speckled feathers

guinea pig ⟦prob. orig. brought to England by ships plying between England, *Guinea*, and South America⟧ **1** a small, plump rodent, often used in biological experiments **2** any subject used in an experiment

guise (gīz) ***n.*** ⟦< OHG *wisa*, manner⟧ **1** manner of dress; garb **2** outward appearance **3** a false appearance; pretense

gui·tar (gi tär′) ***n.*** ⟦ult. < Gr *kithara*, lyre⟧ a musical instrument with usually six strings plucked with the fingers or a plectrum —**gui·tar′ist *n.***

gulch (gulch) ***n.*** ⟦prob. < dial., to swallow greedily⟧ a deep, narrow ravine

gulf (gulf) ***n.*** ⟦ult. < Gr *kolpos*, bosom⟧ **1** a large area of ocean reaching into land **2** a wide, deep chasm **3** a wide gap or separation

Gulf Stream warm ocean current flowing from the Gulf of Mexico northward and then eastward toward Europe

gull[1] (gul) ***n.*** ⟦< Celt⟧ a white and gray water bird with webbed feet

gull[2] (gul) ***n.*** ⟦ME, lit., unfledged bird⟧ a person easily tricked; dupe —***vt.*** to cheat or trick

gul·let (gul′ət) ***n.*** ⟦< L *gula*, throat⟧ **1** the esophagus **2** the throat

gul·li·ble (gul′ə bəl) ***adj.*** easily gulled; credulous —**gul′li·bil′i·ty *n.***

gul·ly (gul′ē) ***n.***, *pl.* **-lies** ⟦see GULLET⟧ a small, narrow ravine

gulp (gulp) ***vt.*** ⟦prob. < Du *gulpen*⟧ to swallow hastily or greedily —***vi.*** to catch the breath as in swallowing —***n.*** a gulping or swallowing

gum[1] (gum) ***n.*** ⟦< LL *gumma*⟧ **1** a sticky substance found in certain trees and plants **2** an adhesive **3** CHEWING GUM —***vt.*** **gummed**, **gum′ming** to coat or unite with gum —**gum up** [Slang] to cause to go awry —**gum′my**, **-mi·er**, **-mi·est**, ***adj.***

gum[2] (gum) ***n.*** ⟦OE *goma*⟧ [*often pl.*] the firm flesh surrounding the base of the teeth —***vt.*** **gummed**, **gum′ming** to chew with toothless gums

gum arabic a gum from certain acacias, used in medicine, candy, etc.

gum·bo (gum′bō) ***n.*** ⟦< Bantu name for okra⟧ a soup thickened with okra

gum′drop′ ***n.*** a small, firm candy made of sweetened gelatin, etc.

gump·tion (gump′shən) ***n.*** ⟦< Scot⟧ [Inf.] courage and initiative

gun (gun) ***n.*** ⟦< ME *gonnilde*, cannon < ON⟧ **1** any weapon with a metal tube from which a projectile is discharged by the force of an explosive **2** any similar device not discharged by an explosive *[an air gun]* **3** anything like a gun in shape or use —***vi.*** **gunned**, **gun′ning** to shoot or hunt with a gun —***vt.*** **1** [Inf.] to shoot (a person) **2** [Slang] to advance the throttle of (an engine) —**gun for** [Slang] to try to get —**jump the gun** [Inf.] to begin before the proper time —**stick to one's guns** [Inf.] to be resolute —**under the gun** [Inf.] in a tense situation, often one involving a deadline

gun′boat′ ***n.*** a small armed ship

gun′fight′ ***n.*** a fight between persons using pistols or revolvers —**gun′fight′er *n.***

gun′fire′ ***n.*** the firing of guns

gung-ho (guŋ′hō′) ***adj.*** ⟦Chin *kung-ho*, lit., work together⟧ [Inf.] enthusiastic

gunk (guŋk) ***n.*** ⟦< ?⟧ [Slang] any viscous or thick, messy substance

gun′man (-mən) ***n.***, *pl.* **-men** (-mən) an armed gangster or hired killer

gun′met′al ***n.*** **1** a bronze with a dark tarnish **2** its dark-gray color

gun′ner ***n.*** **1** a soldier, etc. who helps fire artillery **2** a naval warrant officer in charge of guns, missiles, etc.

gun′ner·y ***n.*** the science of making and using heavy guns and projectiles

gun·ny (gun′ē) ***n.***, *pl.* **-nies** ⟦< Sans *gōnī*, a sack⟧ a coarse fabric of jute or hemp

gun′ny·sack′ ***n.*** a sack made of gunny

gun′play′ ***n.*** an exchange of gunshots, as between gunmen and police

gun′point′ ***n.*** used chiefly in **at gunpoint**, under threat of being shot with a gun at close range

gun′pow′der ***n.*** an explosive powder used in guns, for blasting, etc.

gun′ship′ ***n.*** a heavily armed helicopter used to assault enemy ground forces

gun′shot′ ***n.*** the shooting of a gun

gun′-shy′ ***adj.*** **1** easily frightened at the firing of a gun *[a gun-shy dog]* **2** wary, mistrustful, etc., as because of a previous experience

gun′smith′ ***n.*** one who makes or repairs small guns

gun·wale (gun′əl) ***n.*** ⟦< bulwarks supporting a ship's guns⟧ the upper edge of the side of a ship or boat

gup·py (gup′ē) ***n.***, *pl.* **-pies** ⟦after R. J. L. *Guppy*, of Trinidad⟧ a very small freshwater fish of the West Indies, etc.

gur·gle (gur′gəl) ***vi.*** **-gled**, **-gling** ⟦< L *gurgulio*, gullet⟧ to make a bubbling sound —***n.*** such a sound

gur·ney (gur′nē) ***n.***, *pl.* **-neys** ⟦< ?⟧ a hospital stretcher on wheels

gu·ru (go͞o′ro͞o′; *also* goo ro͞o′) ***n.*** ⟦< Sans *guruḥ*, venerable⟧ in Hinduism, one's personal spiritual advisor or teacher

gush (gush) ***vi.*** ⟦ME *guschen*⟧ **1** to flow out plentifully **2** to have a sudden flow **3** to talk or write effusively —***vt.*** to cause to gush —***n.*** a gushing —**gush′y**, **-i·er**, **-i·est**, ***adj.***

gush′er ***n.*** **1** one who gushes **2** an oil well from which oil spouts forth

gus·set (gus′it) ***n.*** ⟦< OFr *gousset*⟧ a triangular piece inserted in a garment, etc. to make it stronger or roomier

gus·sy or **gus·sie** (gus′ē) ***vt.***, ***vi.*** **-sied**,

-sy·ing ⟦nickname for *Augusta*, a feminine name⟧ [Slang] to dress (*up*) in a fine or showy way

gust (gust) ***n.*** ⟦< ON *gjosa*, to gush⟧ **1** a sudden, strong rush of air **2** a sudden outburst of rain, laughter, etc. **—gust'y, -i·er, -i·est,** ***adj.***

gus·ta·to·ry (gus'tə tôr'ē) ***adj.*** ⟦< L *gustus*, taste⟧ of the sense of taste

gus·to (gus'tō) ***n.*** ⟦see prec.⟧ **1** zest; relish **2** great vigor or liveliness

gut (gut) ***n.*** ⟦< OE *geotan*, to pour⟧ **1** [*pl.*] the entrails **2** the stomach or belly **3** the intestine **4** tough cord made from animal intestines **5** [*pl.*] [Inf.] daring; courage **—*vt.* gut'ted, gut'ting 1** to remove the intestines from **2** to destroy the interior of **—*adj.*** [Slang] **1** basic **2** easy

gut'less ***adj.*** [Inf.] lacking courage

guts·y (gut'sē) ***adj.* -i·er, -i·est** [Inf.] courageous, forceful, etc.

gut·ter (gut'ər) ***n.*** ⟦< L *gutta*, a drop⟧ **1** a channel to carry off water, as along the eaves of a roof or the side of a street **2** a place or condition characterized by squalor **—*vi.*** to flow in a stream

gut·tur·al (gut'ər əl) ***adj.*** ⟦L *guttur*, throat⟧ harsh; rasping: said of vocal sounds

guv (guv) ***n.*** *slang var. of* GOVERNOR

guy[1] (gī) ***n.*** ⟦< OFr *guier*, to guide⟧ a rope, chain, etc. used to steady or guide something **—*vt.*** to guide or steady with a guy

guy[2] (gī) [Inf.] ***n.*** ⟦after *Guy* Fawkes, Eng conspirator⟧ **1** a man or boy **2** any person **—*vt.*** to make fun of; ridicule

Guy·a·na (gī an'ə) country in NE South America: 83,000 sq. mi.; pop. 730,000

guz·zle (guz'əl) ***vi., vt.* -zled, -zling** ⟦< ? OFr *gosier*, throat⟧ to drink greedily or immoderately

gym (jim) ***n.*** [Inf.] **1** *short for* GYMNASIUM **2** PHYSICAL EDUCATION

gym·na·si·um (jim nā'zē əm) ***n., pl.* -si·ums** or **-si·a** (-ə) ⟦< Gr *gymnos*, naked⟧ a room or building equipped for physical training and sports

gym·nas·tics (jim nas'tiks) ***n.*** a sport combining tumbling and acrobatic feats **—gym'nast' *n.* —gym·nas'tic *adj.* —gym·nas'ti·cal·ly *adv.***

gym·no·sperm (jim'nō spurm', -nə-) ***n.*** ⟦< Gr *gymnos*, naked + *sperma*, seed⟧ any of a large division of seed plants, as seed ferns, conifers, etc., having the ovules not enclosed within an ovary

GYN *abbrev.* **1** gynecologic(al) **2** gynecologist **3** gynecology

gy·ne·col·o·gy (gī'nə käl'ə jē) ***n.*** ⟦< Gr *gynē*, woman + -LOGY⟧ the branch of medicine dealing with women's diseases, etc. **—gy'ne·co·log'ic** (-kə läj'ik) or **gy'ne·co·log'i·cal *adj.* —gy'ne·col'o·gist *n.***

gyp (jip) [Inf.] ***n.*** ⟦prob. < GYPSY⟧ **1** a swindle **2** a swindler: also **gyp'per** or **gyp'ster —*vt., vi.* gypped, gyp'ping** to swindle; cheat

gyp·sum (jip'səm) ***n.*** ⟦< Gr *gypsos*⟧ a sulfate of calcium used to make plaster of Paris and cement

Gyp·sy (jip'sē) ***n., pl.* -sies** ⟦< *Egipcien*, Egyptian: orig. thought to be from Egypt⟧ **1** [*also* **g-**] a member of a wandering Caucasoid people, perhaps orig. from India, with dark skin and black hair **2** the language of this people; Romany **3** [**g-**] one who looks or lives like a Gypsy

gypsy moth a moth in the E U.S.: its larvae feed on leaves, damaging trees

gy·rate (jī'rāt') ***vi.* -rat'ed, -rat'ing** ⟦< Gr *gyros*, a circle⟧ to move in a circular or spiral path; whirl **—gy·ra'tion *n.* —gy'ra'tor *n.***

gy·ro (yir'ō, jī'rō') ***n., pl.* -ros** ⟦see prec.⟧ **1** layers of lamb and beef roasted and sliced **2** a pita sandwich of this Also **gy·ros** (yir'ôs)

gyro- ⟦see GYRATE⟧ *combining form* gyrating *[gyroscope]*

gy·ro·scope (jī'rō skōp', -rə-) ***n.*** ⟦prec. + -SCOPE⟧ a wheel mounted in a set of rings so that its axis is free to turn in any direction: when the wheel is spun rapidly, it will keep its original plane of rotation

H

h or **H** (āch) ***n., pl.* h's, H's** the eighth letter of the English alphabet

H[1] or **h** *abbrev.* **1** height **2** high **3** *Baseball* hit(s) **4** hour(s) **5** hundred(s) **6** husband

H[2] *Chem. symbol for* hydrogen

ha (hä) ***interj.*** ⟦echoic⟧ used to express surprise, wonder, anger, triumph, etc.

ha·be·as cor·pus (hā'bē əs kôr'pəs) ⟦L, (that) you have the body⟧ *Law* a writ requiring that a detained person be brought before a court to decide the legality of the detention

hab·er·dash·er (hab'ər dash'ər) ***n.*** ⟦< ME⟧ a dealer in men's hats, shirts, neckties, etc. **—hab'er·dash'er·y *n.***

ha·bil·i·ment (hə bil'ə mənt) ***n.*** ⟦< MFr *habiller*, to clothe⟧ **1** [*usually pl.*] clothing; attire **2** [*pl.*] equipment; trappings

hab·it (hab'it) ***n.*** ⟦< L *habere*, to have⟧ **1** a distinctive costume, as of a nun **2** a thing done often and, hence, easily **3** a usual way of doing **4** an addiction, esp. to narcotics

hab'it·a·ble ***adj.*** fit to be lived in

hab·i·tat (hab'i tat') ***n.*** ⟦L, it inhabits⟧ **1** the region where a plant or animal naturally lives **2** the place where a person is ordinarily found

hab·i·ta·tion (hab'i tā'shən) ***n.*** **1** an inhabiting **2** a dwelling; home

hab'it-form'ing ***adj.*** resulting in the formation of a habit or in addiction

ha·bit·u·al (hə bich'o͞o əl) ***adj.*** **1** done or

acquired by habit **2** steady; inveterate *[a habitual smoker]* **3** much seen, done, or used; usual —**ha·bit'u·al·ly** ***adv.*** —**ha·bit'u·al·ness** ***n.***

ha·bit'u·ate' (-āt') ***vt.*** **-at'ed, -at'ing** to accustom (*to*) —**ha·bit'u·a'tion** ***n.***

ha·bit'u·é' (-ā') ***n.*** ⟦Fr⟧ one who frequents a certain place

ha·ci·en·da (hä'sē en'də) ***n.*** ⟦Sp < L *facere*, do⟧ in Spanish America, a large estate or ranch, or its main house

hack[1] (hak) ***vt.*** ⟦OE *haccian*⟧ to chop or cut crudely, roughly, etc. —***vi.*** **1** to make rough cuts **2** to give harsh, dry coughs —***n.*** **1** a gash **2** a harsh, dry cough

hack[2] (hak) ***n.*** ⟦< HACKNEY⟧ **1** a horse for hire **2** an old, worn-out horse **3** one hired to do routine or dull writing **4** a coach for hire **5** [Inf.] a taxicab —***adj.*** **1** employed as, or done by, a hack *[hack writer]* **2** trite; hackneyed

hack'er ***n.*** **1** an unskilled golfer, etc. **2** a talented amateur user of computers

hack·le (hak'əl) ***n.*** ⟦ME *hechele*⟧ **1** the neck feathers of a rooster, pigeon, etc. **2** [*pl.*] the hairs on a dog's neck and back that bristle

hack·ney (hak'nē) ***n.***, *pl.* **-neys** ⟦after *Hackney*, England⟧ **1** a horse for driving or riding **2** a carriage for hire

hack'neyed' (-nēd') ***adj.*** made trite by overuse

hack'saw' ***n.*** a fine-toothed saw for cutting metal: also **hack saw**

had (had) ***vt.*** *pt. & pp. of* HAVE

had·dock (had'ək) ***n.***, *pl.* **-dock** or **-docks** ⟦ME *hadok*⟧ an Atlantic food fish, related to the cod

Ha·des (hā'dēz') ***n.*** ⟦Gr *Haidēs*⟧ **1** *Gr. Myth.* the home of the dead **2** [*often* **h-**] hell

haft (haft, häft) ***n.*** ⟦OE *hæft*⟧ the handle or hilt of a knife, ax, etc.

hag (hag) ***n.*** ⟦< OE *hægtes*⟧ **1** a witch **2** an ugly, often vicious old woman —**hag'gish** ***adj.***

hag·gard (hag'ərd) ***adj.*** ⟦MFr *hagard*, untamed (hawk)⟧ having a wild, wasted, worn look; gaunt

hag·gle (hag'əl) ***vi.*** **-gled, -gling** ⟦< Scot *hag*, to hack⟧ to argue about terms, price, etc. —***n.*** a haggling —**hag'gler** ***n.***

Hague (hāg), **The** political capital of the Netherlands (cf. AMSTERDAM): pop. 445,000

hah (hä) ***interj.***, ***n.*** HA

hai·ku (hī'ko͞o') ***n.*** ⟦Jpn⟧ **1** a Japanese verse form of three unrhymed lines of 5, 7, and 5 syllables, respectively **2** *pl.* **-ku'** a poem in this form

hail[1] (hāl) ***vt.*** ⟦< ON *heill*, whole, sound⟧ **1** to greet with cheers; acclaim **2** to call out to *[to hail a cab]* —***n.*** a greeting —***interj.*** used to signify tribute, greeting, etc. —**hail from** to be from

hail[2] (hāl) ***n.*** ⟦OE *hægel*⟧ **1** frozen raindrops falling during thunderstorms **2** a shower of or like hail —***vt.***, ***vi.*** to pour down like hail

hail'stone' ***n.*** a pellet of hail

hail'storm' ***n.*** a storm with hail

hair (her, har) ***n.*** ⟦OE *hær*⟧ **1** any of the threadlike outgrowths from the skin **2** a growth of these, as on the human head **3** a very small space, degree, etc. **4** a threadlike growth on a plant —**get in someone's hair** [Slang] to annoy someone —**split hairs** to quibble —**hair'less** ***adj.*** —**hair'like'** ***adj.***

hair'ball' ***n.*** a ball of hair that may form in the stomach of a cow, cat, or other animal that licks its coat

hair'breadth' (-bredth') ***n.*** an extremely small space or amount —***adj.*** very narrow; close Also **hairs'breadth'** or **hair's'-breadth'**

hair'cut' ***n.*** the act of, or a style of, cutting the hair

hair'do' (-do͞o') ***n.***, *pl.* **-dos'** the style in which hair is arranged; coiffure

hair'dress'er ***n.*** one whose work is dressing, or arranging, hair

-haired (herd) having (a specified kind of) hair *[short-haired]*

hair'line' ***n.*** **1** a very thin line **2** the outline of the hair on the head

hair'piece' ***n.*** a toupee or wig

hair'pin' ***n.*** a small, bent piece of wire, etc., for keeping the hair in place —***adj.*** U-shaped *[a hairpin turn in the road]*

hair'-rais'ing ***adj.*** terrifying or shocking

hair'split'ting ***adj.***, ***n.*** making petty distinctions

hair'spring' ***n.*** a slender, hairlike coil spring, as in a watch

hair'y ***adj.*** **-i·er, -i·est** covered with hair —**hair'i·ness** ***n.***

Hai·ti (hāt'ē) country occupying the W portion of the island of Hispaniola, West Indies: 10,700 sq. mi.; pop. 5,054,000 —**Hai·tian** (hā'shən) ***adj.***, ***n.***

hake (hāk) ***n.*** ⟦prob. < ON⟧ a marine food fish related to the cod

hal·berd (hal'bərd) ***n.*** ⟦ult. < MHG *helmbarte*⟧ a combined spear and battle-ax of the 15th-16th c.

hal·cy·on (hal'sē ən) ***adj.*** ⟦< Gr *alkyōn*, kingfisher (fabled calmer of the sea)⟧ tranquil, happy, idyllic, etc. *[halcyon days]*

hale[1] (hāl) ***adj.*** **hal'er, hal'est** ⟦OE *hal*⟧ vigorous and healthy

hale[2] (hāl) ***vt.*** **haled, hal'ing** ⟦< OFr *haler*⟧ to force (a person) to go *[haled him into court]*

half (haf, häf) ***n.***, *pl.* **halves** ⟦OE *healf*⟧ **1** either of the two equal parts of something **2** either of the two equal parts of some games —***adj.*** **1** being a half **2** incomplete; partial —***adv.*** **1** to the extent of a half **2** partly *[half done]* **3** at all: used with *not* *[not half bad]*

half- *combining form* **1** one half *[half-life]* **2** partly *[half-baked]*

half'-and-half' ***n.*** something that is half of one thing and half of another, as a mixture of milk and cream —***adj.*** combining two things equally —***adv.*** in two equal parts

half'back' ***n.*** *Football* one of the running backs, typically smaller and faster than a fullback

half'-breed' ***n.*** one whose parents are of different ethnic types: an offensive term

half brother a brother through one parent only

half dollar a coin of the U.S. or Canada, worth 50 cents

half′heart′ed ***adj.*** with little enthusiasm, determination, interest, etc. —**half′heart′ed·ly** ***adv.***

half′-life′ ***n.*** the constant time period required for the disintegration of half of the atoms in a sample of a radioactive substance: also **half life**

half′-mast′ ***n.*** the position of a flag halfway down its staff, esp. as a sign of mourning

half note *Music* a note having one half the duration of a whole note

half·pen·ny (hāp′nē, hā′pən ē) ***n.***, *pl.* **-pence** (hā′pəns) or **-pen·nies** a former British coin equal to half a penny

half sister a sister through one parent only

half sole a sole (of a shoe or boot) from the arch to the toe

half′track′ ***n.*** an army truck, armored vehicle, etc. with tractor treads instead of rear wheels

half′way′ ***adj.*** **1** midway between two points, etc. **2** partial *[halfway measures]* —***adv.*** **1** to the midway point **2** partially —**meet halfway** to be willing to compromise (with)

halfway house a place for helping people adjust to society after being imprisoned, hospitalized, etc.

half′-wit′ ***n.*** a stupid or silly person; fool —**half′-wit′ted** ***adj.***

hal·i·but (hal′ə bət) ***n.***, *pl.* **-but** or **-buts** ⟦ME *hali*, holy + *butt*, a flounder (so called because eaten on holidays)⟧ a large, edible flounder found in northern seas

Hal·i·fax (hal′ə faks′) capital of Nova Scotia, Canada: pop. 114,000

hal·ite (hal′īt′, hā′līt′) ***n.*** rock salt

hal·i·to·sis (hal′i tō′sis) ***n.*** ⟦< L *halitus*, breath⟧ bad-smelling breath

hall (hôl) ***n.*** ⟦OE *heall*⟧ **1** the main dwelling on an estate **2** a public building with offices, etc. **3** a large room for gatherings, exhibits, etc. **4** a college building **5** a vestibule at the entrance of a building **6** an area onto which rooms open

hal·le·lu·jah or **hal·le·lu·iah** (hal′ə lo͞o′ yə) ***interj.*** ⟦< Heb < *hallelū*, praise (imper.) + *yāh*, Jehovah⟧ used to express praise, thanks, etc., esp. in a hymn or prayer —***n.*** a hymn of praise to God

hall·mark (hôl′märk′) ***n.*** ⟦< the mark stamped on gold and silver articles at Goldsmith's Hall⟧ a mark or symbol of genuineness or high quality

hal·loo (hə lo͞o′) ***n.***, ***interj.*** (a shout or call) used esp. to attract attention —***vi.***, ***vt.*** **-looed′**, **-loo′ing** to call out (to)

hal·low (hal′ō) ***vt.*** ⟦OE *halgian*⟧ to make or regard as holy

hal′lowed (-ōd) ***adj.*** holy or sacred

Hal·low·een or **Hal·low·e′en** (hal′ə wēn′, häl′-) ***n.*** ⟦contr. < *all hallow even*⟧ the evening of Oct. 31, followed by All Saints' Day: now celebrated with masquerading, etc.

hal·lu·ci·nate (hə lo͞o′si nāt′) ***vi.***, ***vt.*** **-nat′ed**, **-nat′ing** ⟦see fol.⟧ to have or cause to have hallucinations

hal·lu·ci·na·tion (hə lo͞o′si nā′shən) ***n.*** ⟦< L *hallucinari*, to wander mentally⟧ **1** the apparent perception of sights, sounds, etc. that are not actually present **2** the thing perceived —**hal·lu′ci·na·to′ry** (-nə tôr′ē) ***adj.***

hal·lu·ci·no·gen (hə lo͞o′si nə jən) ***n.*** a drug or other substance that produces hallucinations —**hal·lu′ci·no·gen′ic** ***adj.***

hall′way′ ***n.*** a passageway; corridor

ha·lo (hā′lō) ***n.***, *pl.* **-los** or **-loes** ⟦< Gr *halōs*, circular threshing floor⟧ **1** a ring of light, as around the sun **2** a symbolic ring of light around the head of a saint, etc., as in pictures

hal·o·gen (hal′ə jən) ***n.*** ⟦< Gr *hals*, salt⟧ any of the five nonmetallic chemical elements fluorine, chlorine, bromine, astatine, and iodine

halt[1] (hôlt) ***n.***, ***vi.***, ***vt.*** ⟦< Ger *halt machen*⟧ stop

halt[2] (hôlt) ***vi.*** ⟦< OE *healt*⟧ **1** [Archaic] to limp **2** to hesitate —***adj.*** lame —**the halt** those who are lame

hal·ter (hôl′tər) ***n.*** ⟦OE *hælftre*⟧ **1** a rope or strap for tying or leading an animal **2** a hangman's noose **3** a woman's upper garment, held up by a loop around the neck

halve (hav, häv) ***vt.*** **halved**, **halv′ing** **1** to divide into two equal parts **2** to reduce to half

halves (havz, hävz) ***n.*** *pl. of* HALF —**by halves** halfway; imperfectly —**go halves** to share expenses equally

hal·yard (hal′yərd) ***n.*** ⟦< ME *halier*: see HALE[2]⟧ a rope or tackle for raising or lowering a flag, sail, etc.

ham (ham) ***n.*** ⟦OE *hamm*⟧ **1** the back of the thigh **2** the upper part of a hog's hind leg, salted, smoked, etc. **3** [Inf.] an amateur radio operator **4** [Slang] an actor who overacts —**ham′my**, **-mi·er**, **-mi·est**, ***adj.***

Ham·burg (ham′bərg) seaport in N Germany: pop. 1,603,000

ham·burg·er (ham′bur′gər) ***n.*** ⟦after *Hamburg*, Germany⟧ **1** ground beef **2** a cooked patty of such meat, often in a sandwich Also **ham′burg** (-bərg)

Ham·il·ton[1] (ham′əl tən), **Alexander** 1755?-1804; Am. statesman

Ham·il·ton[2] (ham′əl tən) city & port in SE Ontario, Canada: pop. 322,000

ham·let (ham′lit) ***n.*** ⟦< OFr *hamelete* < LowG *hamm*, enclosed area⟧ a very small village

Ham·let (ham′lit) ***n.*** the title hero of a tragedy by Shakespeare

ham·mer (ham′ər) ***n.*** ⟦OE *hamor*⟧ **1** a tool for pounding, having a metal head and a handle **2** a thing like this in shape or use, as the part of a gun that strikes the firing pin **3** one of the three small bones in the middle ear —***vt.***, ***vi.*** **1** to strike repeatedly, as with a hammer **2** to drive, force, or shape, as with hammer blows —**hammer (away) at** to keep emphasizing —**ham′mer·er** ***n.***

hammer and sickle the emblem of

Communist parties in some countries

ham'mer·head' *n.* **1** the head of a hammer **2** a shark with a mallet-shaped head having an eye at each end

ham'mer·toe' *n.* a toe that is deformed, with its first joint bent downward

ham·mock (ham'ək) *n.* ⟦Sp *hamaca*, of WInd orig.⟧ a kind of bed of canvas, etc. swung from ropes at both ends

ham·per[1] (ham'pər) *vt.* ⟦ME *hampren*⟧ to hinder; impede; encumber

ham·per[2] (ham'pər) *n.* ⟦< OFr *hanap*, a cup⟧ a large basket, usually covered

ham·ster (ham'stər) *n.* ⟦< OHG *hamustro*⟧ a rodent of Europe and Asia, used in scientific experiments or kept as a pet

ham·string (ham'striŋ') *n.* a tendon at the back of the knee —*vt.* **-strung'**, **-string'ing** **1** to disable by cutting a hamstring **2** to lessen the power of

hand (hand) *n.* ⟦OE⟧ **1** the body part attached to the wrist, used for grasping **2** a side or direction *[at my right hand]* **3** [*pl.*] possession or care *[the land is in my hands]* **4** control *[to strengthen one's hand]* **5** an active part *[take a hand in the work]* **6** a promise to marry **7** skill **8** one having a special skill **9** manner of doing something **10** handwriting **11** applause **12** help *[to lend a hand]* **13** a hired worker *[a farm hand]* **14** a source *[to get news at first hand]* **15** anything like a hand, as a pointer on a clock **16** the breadth of a hand **17** *Card Games a)* the cards held by a player at one time *b)* a round of play —*adj.* of, for, or controlled by the hand —*vt.* **1** to give as with the hand **2** to help or conduct with the hand —**at hand** near —**hand in hand** together —**hand it to** [Slang] to give credit to —**hand over fist** [Inf.] easily and in large amounts —**hands down** easily —**on hand** **1** near **2** available **3** present —**on the one** (or **other**) **hand** from one (or the opposed) point of view

hand'bag' *n.* a woman's purse

hand'ball' *n.* a game in which players bat a small rubber ball against a wall with their hands

hand'bar'row *n.* a frame carried by two people holding handles at the ends

hand'bill' *n.* a small printed notice to be passed out by hand

hand'book' *n.* a compact reference book; manual

hand'breadth' *n.* the breadth of the human palm, about 4 inches

hand'car' *n.* a small, open car, originally hand-powered, used on railroads

hand'cart' *n.* a small cart moved by hand

hand'clasp' *n.* HANDSHAKE

hand'craft' *n.* HANDICRAFT —*vt.* to make skillfully by hand —**hand'craft'ed** *adj.*

hand'cuff' *n.* either of a pair of connected rings for shackling the wrists of a prisoner: *usually used in pl.* —*vt.* to put handcuffs on; manacle

-hand·ed (han'did) *combining form* having or involving (a specified kind or number of) hands *[right-handed, two-handed]*

Han·del (han'dəl), **George Fri·der·ic** (frē'dər ik, -drik) 1685-1759; Eng. composer, born in Germany

hand'ful' *n.*, *pl.* **-fuls'** **1** as much or as many as the hand will hold **2** a few; not many **3** [Inf.] someone or something that is hard to manage

hand'gun' *n.* any firearm that is held and fired with one hand, as a pistol

hand'-held' *adj.* small enough to be held in the hand while being used

hand·i·cap (hand'dē kap') *n.* ⟦< *hand in cap*, former kind of lottery⟧ **1** a competition in which difficulties are imposed on, or advantages given to, the various contestants to equalize their chances **2** such a difficulty or advantage **3** *a)* any hindrance *b)* a physical disability —*vt.* **-capped'**, **-cap'ping** **1** to give a handicap to **2** to hinder —**the handicapped** those who are physically disabled or mentally retarded

hand'i·capped' *adj.* physically disabled

hand'i·cap'per *n.* a person, as a sportswriter, who tries to predict the winners in horse races

hand·i·craft (han'dē kraft') *n.* skill with the hands, or work calling for it

hand'i·work' *n.* **1** HANDWORK **2** anything made or done by a particular person

hand·ker·chief (haŋ'kər chif') *n.* ⟦HAND + KERCHIEF⟧ a small cloth used for wiping the nose, face, etc., or worn for ornament

han·dle (han'dəl) *n.* ⟦OE < *hand*⟧ that part of a tool, etc. by which it is held, lifted, etc. —*vt.* **-dled**, **-dling** **1** to touch, lift, operate, etc. with the hand **2** to manage; control **3** to deal with; treat **4** to sell or deal in —*vi.* to respond to control *[the car handles well]* —**han'dler** *n.*

han'dle·bar' *n.* [*often pl.*] a curved metal bar with handles on the ends, for steering a bicycle, etc.

hand'made' *adj.* made by hand, not by machine

hand'maid'en *n.* [Archaic] a woman or girl servant: also **hand'maid'**

hand'-me-down' *n.* [Inf.] a used garment, etc. passed on to another person

hand'out' *n.* **1** a gift of food, clothing, etc., as to a beggar **2** a leaflet handed out **3** a news release

hand'pick' *vt.* **1** to pick by hand **2** to choose with care or for a purpose

hand'rail' *n.* a rail serving as a guard or support, as along a staircase

hand'set' *n.* a telephone mouthpiece and receiver in a single unit

hand'shake' *n.* a gripping of each other's hand in greeting, agreement, etc.

hands'-off' *adj.* designating or of a policy, etc. of not interfering or intervening

hand·some (han'səm, hand'-) *adj.* ⟦orig., easily handled⟧ **1** large; considerable **2** generous; gracious **3** good-looking, esp. in a manly or impressive way —**hand′some·ness** *n.*

hand′spring′ *n.* an acrobatic feat in which one turns over in midair with one or both hands touching the ground

hand′-to-hand′ *adj.* at close quarters: said of fighting

hand′-to-mouth′ *adj.* needing to consume all that is obtained

hand′work′ *n.* work done or made by hand

hand′-wring′ing or **hand′wring′ing** *n.* expression of distress or anxiety

hand′writ′ing *n.* **1** writing done by hand, with a pen, a pencil, etc. **2** a style of such writing —**hand′writ′ten** *adj.*

hand′y *adj.* **-i·er, -i·est** **1** close at hand; easily reached **2** easily used; convenient **3** clever with the hands; deft —**hand′i·ly** *adv.* —**hand′i·ness** *n.*

hand′y·man′ (-man′) *n., pl.* **-men′** (-men′) a man who does odd jobs

hang (haŋ) *vt.* **hung, hang′ing**; for *vt.* 3 & *vi.* 5, **hanged** is preferred pt. & pp. ⟦OE *hangian*⟧ **1** to attach from above with no support from below; suspend **2** to attach (a door, etc.) so as to permit free motion at the point of attachment **3** to kill by suspending from a rope about the neck **4** to attach (wallpaper, etc.) to walls **5** to let (one's head) droop downward **6** to deadlock (a jury) —*vi.* **1** to be attached above with no support from below **2** to hover in the air **3** to swing freely **4** to fall or drape: said as of cloth **5** to die by hanging **6** to droop; bend —*n.* the way that a thing hangs —**get** (or **have**) **the hang of** **1** to learn (or have) the knack of **2** to understand the meaning or idea of —**hang around** (or **about**) [Inf.] to loiter around —**hang back** (or **off**) to be reluctant, as from shyness —**hang in** (**there**) [Inf.] to persevere —**hang loose** [Slang] to be relaxed, easygoing, etc. —**hang on** **1** to go on; persevere **2** to depend on **3** to listen attentively to —**hang out** [Slang] to spend much time —**hang up** **1** to put on a hanger, hook, etc. **2** to end a telephone call by replacing the receiver **3** to delay

hang·ar (haŋ′ər) *n.* ⟦Fr⟧ a repair shed or shelter for aircraft

hang′dog′ *adj.* abject or ashamed

hang′er *n.* **1** one who hangs things **2** a thing on which something is hung

hang gliding the sport of gliding through the air while hanging suspended by a harness from a large type of kite (**hang glider**)

hang′ing *adj.* that hangs —*n.* **1** a killing by hanging **2** something hung on a wall, etc.

hang′man (-mən) *n., pl.* **-men** (-mən) one who hangs convicted criminals

hang′nail′ *n.* ⟦OE *angnægl*, a corn (on the toe)⟧ a bit of torn skin hanging next to a fingernail

hang′o′ver *n.* headache, nausea, etc. as an aftereffect of drinking much alcoholic liquor

hang′-up′ *n.* [Slang] an emotional or psychological problem, difficulty, etc.

hank (haŋk) *n.* ⟦prob. < Scand⟧ a skein of yarn or thread

han·ker (haŋ′kər) *vi.* ⟦prob. < Du⟧ to long or yearn: used with *for* —**han′ker·ing** *n.*

han·ky-pan·ky (haŋ′kē paŋ′kē) *n.* [Inf.] trickery or deception, as with illicit sex

Ha·noi (ha noi′) capital of Vietnam, in the N part: pop. 2,571,000

HANSOM CAB

han·som (**cab**) (han′səm) ⟦after J. A. *Hansom* (1803-82), Eng inventor⟧ a two-wheeled covered carriage pulled by one horse, with the driver's seat above and behind

Ha·nuk·kah (khä′noo kä′, -kə; hä′-) *n.* ⟦< Heb *chanuka*, lit., dedication⟧ an 8-day Jewish festival commemorating the rededication of the Temple: also **Ha′nu·ka′**

hap (hap) *n.* ⟦< ON *happ*⟧ luck

hap·haz·ard (hap′haz′ərd) *adj.* not planned; random —*adv.* by chance

hap·less (hap′lis) *adj.* unlucky

hap·loid (hap′loid′) *adj. Biol.* having the full number of chromosomes normally occurring in the mature germ cell, or half the number of the usual somatic cell —*n.* a haploid cell or gamete

hap′ly *adv.* [Archaic] by chance; perhaps

hap·pen (hap′ən) *vi.* ⟦ME *happenen*⟧ **1** to take place; occur **2** to be, occur, or come by chance **3** to have the luck or occasion *[I happened to see it]* —**happen on** (or **upon**) to meet or find by chance

hap′pen·ing *n.* occurrence; event

hap′pen·stance′ (-stans′) *n.* [Inf.] a chance or accidental happening

hap·py (hap′ē) *adj.* **-pi·er, -pi·est** ⟦< HAP⟧ **1** lucky; fortunate **2** having, showing, or causing great pleasure or joy **3** suitable and clever; apt —**hap′pi·ly** *adv.* —**hap′pi·ness** *n.*

hap′py-go-luck′y *adj.* easygoing

happy hour a time, as in the late afternoon, when a bar features drinks at reduced prices

har·a-kir·i (här′ə kir′ē) *n.* ⟦Jpn < *hara*, belly + *kiri*, a cutting⟧ ritual suicide by cutting the abdomen

ha·rangue (hə raŋ′) *n.* ⟦< OIt *aringo*, site for public assemblies⟧ a long, blustering speech; tirade —*vi., vt.* **-rangued′, -rangu′ing** to speak or address in a harangue

har·ass (har′əs, hə ras′) *vt.* ⟦< OFr *harer*, to set a dog on⟧ **1** to worry or torment **2** to trouble by repeated raids or attacks —**har'ass·ment** ***n.***

Har·bin (här'bin) city in NE China: pop. 2,519,000

har·bin·ger (här'bin jər) ***n.*** ⟦< OFr *herberge*, a shelter⟧ a forerunner; herald

har·bor (här'bər) ***n.*** ⟦< OE *here*, army + *beorg*, shelter⟧ **1** a shelter **2** a protected inlet for anchoring ships; port —***vt.*** **1** to shelter or house **2** to hold in the mind *[*to *harbor* envy*]* —***vi.*** to take shelter Brit. sp. **har'bour**

hard (härd) ***adj.*** ⟦OE *heard*⟧ **1** firm and unyielding to the touch; solid and compact **2** powerful *[*a *hard* blow*]* **3** difficult to do, understand, or deal with **4** *a*) unfeeling *[*a *hard* heart*]* *b*) unfriendly *[hard* feelings*]* **5** harsh; severe **6** having mineral salts that interfere with lathering **7** energetic *[*a *hard* worker*]* **8** containing much alcohol *[hard* liquor*]* **9** addictive and harmful *[*heroin is a *hard* drug*]* **10** *a*) of currency, not credit (said of money) *b*) readily accepted as foreign exchange *[*a *hard* currency*]* —***adv.*** **1** energetically *[*work *hard]* **2** with strength *[*hit *hard]* **3** with difficulty *[hard*-earned*]* **4** close; near *[*we live *hard* by*]* **5** so as to be solid *[*frozen *hard]* **6** fully *[*turn *hard* right*]* —**hard and fast** invariable; strict —**hard of hearing** partially deaf —**hard up** [Inf.] in great need of money —**hard'ness** ***n.***

hard'back' ***n.*** a hardcover book

hard'ball' ***n.*** BASEBALL

hard'-bit'ten ***adj.*** tough; dogged

hard'-boiled' ***adj.*** **1** boiled until solid: said of an egg **2** [Inf.] unfeeling; tough; callous

hard copy a computer printout, often supplied along with or instead of a video screen display

hard'-core' ***adj.*** absolute; unqualified

hard'cov'er ***adj.***, ***n.*** (designating) any book bound in a stiff cover

hard disk a computer disk with a rigid metal base

hard drive a computer drive for hard disks

hard·en (härd''n) ***vt.***, ***vi.*** to make or become hard —**hard'en·er** ***n.***

hard hat **1** a protective helmet worn by construction workers, miners, etc. **2** [Slang] such a worker

hard'head'ed ***adj.*** **1** shrewd and unsentimental; practical **2** stubborn; dogged

hard'heart'ed ***adj.*** unfeeling; cruel

har·di·hood (här'dē hood') ***n.*** boldness

Har·ding (här'diŋ), **War·ren G(amaliel)** (wôr'ən, wär'-) 1865-1923; 29th president of the U.S. (1921-23)

hard'-line' ***adj.*** aggressive; unyielding, as in politics, etc.

hard'-lin'er (-ər) ***n.*** one who takes a hard-line position

hard·ly (härd'lē) ***adv.*** **1** only just; scarcely **2** probably not; not likely

hard'-nosed' ***adj.*** [Inf.] tough and stubborn or shrewd

hard'-pressed' ***adj.*** confronted with a difficulty

hard·scrab·ble (härd'skrab'əl) ***adj.*** producing or earning only a very small amount; barren *[*a *hardscrabble* farm, life, etc.*]*

hard sell high-pressure salesmanship

hard'ship' ***n.*** a thing hard to bear, as poverty

hard'stand' ***n.*** a paved area for parking aircraft or other vehicles

hard'tack' ***n.*** unleavened bread made in large, hard wafers

hard'top' ***n.*** a motor vehicle having a rigid top

hard'ware' ***n.*** **1** articles made of metal, as tools, nails, or fittings **2** the mechanical, magnetic, and electronic devices of a computer

hard'wood' ***n.*** **1** any tough, heavy timber with a compact texture **2** the wood of any tree with broad, flat leaves, as the oak or maple

har·dy (här'dē) ***adj.*** **-di·er**, **-di·est** ⟦< OFr *hardir*, to make bold⟧ **1** bold and resolute **2** robust; vigorous —**har'di·ly** ***adv.*** —**har'di·ness** ***n.***

hare (her, har) ***n.*** ⟦OE *hara*⟧ a mammal related to and resembling the rabbit

hare'brained' ***adj.*** having or showing little sense, flighty, etc.

Ha·re Krishna (hä'rē) ⟦< Hindi⟧ a member of a cult stressing devotion to Krishna

hare'lip' ***n.*** CLEFT LIP

ha·rem (her'əm, har'-) ***n.*** ⟦Ar *ḥarīm*, lit., prohibited (place)⟧ **1** the part of a Muslim household in which the women live **2** the women in a harem

hark (härk) ***vi.*** ⟦ME *herkien*⟧ to listen carefully: usually in the imperative —**hark back** to go back in thought or speech

hark·en (här'kən) ***vi.*** HEARKEN

Har·le·quin (här'li kwin, -kin) ***n.*** **1** a comic character in pantomime, who wears a mask and diamond-patterned tights of many colors **2** [**h-**] a clown

har·lot (här'lət) ***n.*** ⟦< OFr, rogue⟧ PROSTITUTE —**har'lot·ry** (-lə trē) ***n.***

harm (härm) ***n.*** ⟦OE *hearm*⟧ hurt; injury; damage —***vt.*** to do harm to

harm'ful ***adj.*** causing harm; hurtful —**harm'ful·ly** ***adv.*** —**harm'ful·ness** ***n.***

harm'less ***adj.*** causing no harm —**harm'less·ly** ***adv.*** —**harm'less·ness** ***n.***

har·mon·ic (här män'ik) ***adj.*** of or in harmony —***n.*** *Music* a pure tone making up a composite tone —**har·mon'i·cal·ly** ***adv.***

har·mon'i·ca (-i kə) ***n.*** a small wind instrument with metal reeds that vibrate and produce tones when air is blown or sucked across them

har·mo·ni·ous (här mō'nē əs) ***adj.*** **1** having parts arranged in an orderly or pleasing way **2** having similar ideas, interests, etc. **3** having musical tones combined to give a pleasing effect —**har·mo'ni·ous·ly** ***adv.***

har·mo·nize (här'mə nīz') ***vi.*** **-nized'**, **-niz'ing** **1** to be in harmony **2** to sing in harmony —***vt.*** to make harmonious —**har'mo·ni·za'tion** ***n.*** —**har'mo·niz'er** ***n.***

har·mo·ny (här'mə nē) ***n.***, *pl.* **-nies** ⟦<

Gr *harmos*, a fitting⟧ **1** pleasing arrangement of parts in color, size, etc. **2** agreement in action, ideas, etc.; friendly relations **3** the sounding of two or more tones together in a chord, esp. when satisfying

har·ness (här′nis) ***n.*** ⟦< OFr *harneis*, armor⟧ **1** the combination of leather straps and metal pieces by which a horse, etc. is fastened to a vehicle, etc. **2** anything like this **—*vt.*** **1** to put a harness on **2** to control so as to use the power of

harp (härp) ***n.*** ⟦OE *hearpe*⟧ a musical instrument having strings stretched vertically in an open, triangular frame and played by plucking **—*vi.*** **1** to play a harp **2** to persist in talking or writing tediously (*on* or *upon* something) **—harp′ist *n.***

Har·pers Ferry (här′pərz) town in West Virginia: site of an antislavery raid (1859): pop. 300

har·poon (här po͞on′) ***n.*** ⟦< ON *harpa*, to squeeze⟧ a barbed spear with a line attached to it, used for spearing whales, etc. **—*vt.*** to strike or catch with a harpoon

harp·si·chord (härp′si kôrd′) ***n.*** ⟦< It *arpa*, harp + *corda*, CORD⟧ a pianolike keyboard instrument whose strings are plucked rather than struck **—harp′si·chord′ist *n.***

Har·py (här′pē) ***n.***, *pl.* **-pies** ⟦< Gr *harpazein*, to snatch⟧ **1** *Gr. Myth.* any of several monsters, part woman and part bird **2** [**h-**] *a*) a greedy person *b*) a shrewish woman

har·ri·dan (har′i dən) ***n.*** ⟦prob. < Fr *haridelle*, worn-out horse⟧ a nasty, bad-tempered old woman

har·ri·er (har′ē ər) ***n.*** ⟦< HARE + -IER⟧ **1** a small hound used for hunting hares **2** a cross-country runner

Har·ris·burg (har′is burg′) capital of Pennsylvania, in the S part: pop. 52,000

Har·ri·son (har′ə sən) **1 Ben·ja·min** (ben′jə mən) 1833-1901; 23d president of the U.S. (1889-93): grandson of William Henry **2 William Henry** 1773-1841; 9th president of the U.S. (1841)

har·row (har′ō) ***n.*** ⟦prob. < ON⟧ a heavy frame with spikes or disks, used for breaking up and leveling plowed ground, etc. **—*vt.*** **1** to draw a harrow over (land) **2** to cause mental distress to **—har′row·ing *adj.***

har·ry (har′ē) ***vt.*** **-ried, -ry·ing** ⟦< OE *here*, army⟧ **1** to raid and ravage or rob **2** to torment or worry

harsh (härsh) ***adj.*** ⟦ME *harsk*⟧ **1** unpleasantly rough or sharp to the eye, ear, taste, or touch **2** offensive to the mind or feelings **3** cruel or severe **—harsh′ly *adv.* —harsh′ness *n.***

hart (härt) ***n.*** ⟦OE *heorot*⟧ a full-grown, male European red deer

har·te·beest (här′tə bēst′, härt′bēst′) ***n.*** ⟦obs. Afrik < *harte*, hart + *beest*, beast⟧ a large African antelope with long horns curved backward

Hart·ford (härt′fərd) capital of Connecticut, in the central part: pop. 140,000

har·um-scar·um (her′əm sker′əm) ***adj.*** ⟦< ?⟧ reckless or irresponsible **—*adv.*** in a harum-scarum way

har·vest (här′vist) ***n.*** ⟦OE *hærfest*⟧ **1** the time of the year when grain, fruit, etc. are gathered in **2** a season's crop **3** the gathering in of a crop **4** the outcome of any effort **—*vt.*, *vi.*** to gather in (a crop, etc.) **—har′vest·er *n.***

has (haz; *before "to"* has) ***vt.*** *3d pers. sing., pres. indic., of* HAVE

has′-been′ ***n.*** [Inf.] a person or thing whose popularity is past

hash (hash) ***vt.*** ⟦< Fr *hacher*, to chop⟧ to chop up (meat or vegetables) for cooking **—*n.*** **1** a chopped mixture of cooked meat and vegetables, usually baked **2** a mixture **3** a muddle; mess **4** [Slang] hashish **—hash out** [Inf.] to settle by long discussion **—hash over** [Inf.] to discuss at length

hash·ish (hash′ēsh′, ha shēsh′) ***n.*** ⟦Ar *ḥashīsh*, dried hemp⟧ a narcotic and intoxicant made from hemp

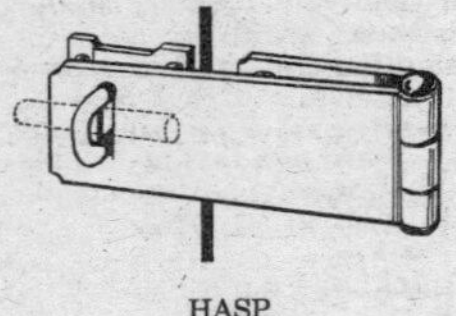

HASP

hasp (hasp, häsp) ***n.*** ⟦OE *hæsp*⟧ a hinged fastening for a door, etc.; esp., a metal piece fitted over a staple and held in place by a pin or padlock

has·sle (has′əl) ***n.*** ⟦< ?⟧ [Inf.] **1** a heated argument; squabble **2** a troublesome situation **—*vi.*** **-sled, -sling** [Inf.] to have a hassle **—*vt.*** [Slang] to annoy, harass, etc.

has·sock (has′ək) ***n.*** ⟦OE *hassuc*, (clump of) coarse grass⟧ a firm cushion used as a footstool or seat

hast (hast) ***vt.*** *archaic 2d pers. sing., pres. indic., of* HAVE: used with *thou*

haste (hāst) ***n.*** ⟦OFr⟧ **1** quickness of motion; rapidity **2** careless or reckless hurrying **—make haste** to hurry

has·ten (hās′ən) ***vt.*** to cause to be or come faster; speed up **—*vi.*** to move or act swiftly; hurry

hast·y (hās′tē) ***adj.*** **-i·er, -i·est** **1** done with haste; hurried **2** done, made, or acting rashly or too quickly **—hast′i·ly *adv.* —hast′i·ness *n.***

hat (hat) ***n.*** ⟦OE *hætt*⟧ a head covering, usually with a brim and a crown **—pass the hat** to take up a collection **—talk through one's hat** [Inf.] to talk nonsense **—throw one's hat into the ring** to enter a contest, esp. one for political office **—under one's hat** [Inf.] strictly confidential

hatch[1] (hach) ***vt.*** ⟦ME *hacchen*⟧ **1** to bring forth (young) from (an egg or eggs) **2** to contrive (a plan, plot, etc.) **—*vi.*** **1** to bring forth young: said of eggs **2** to emerge from the egg

hatch[2] (hach) ***n.*** ⟦OE *hæcc*, grating⟧ **1** HATCHWAY **2** a lid for a hatchway

hatch′back′ *n.* ⟦prec. + BACK⟧ an automobile with a rear section that swings up, giving wide entry to a storage area

hat′check′ *adj.* of or working in a checkroom for hats, coats, etc.

hatch′er·y *n.*, *pl.* **-ies** a place for hatching eggs, esp. of fish or poultry

hatch·et (hach′it) *n.* ⟦< OFr *hache*, an ax⟧ a small ax with a short handle —**bury the hatchet** to make peace

hatchet job [Inf.] a biased, malicious attack on another's character

hatch′way′ *n.* an opening in a ship's deck, or in a floor or roof

hate (hāt) *vt.* **hat′ed, hat′ing** ⟦OE *hatian*⟧ **1** to have strong dislike or ill will for **2** to wish to avoid *[to hate fights]* —*vi.* to feel hatred —*n.* **1** a strong feeling of dislike or ill will; hatred **2** a person or thing hated —**hat′er** *n.*

hate′ful *adj.* **1** causing or deserving hate; loathsome **2** nasty, unpleasant, etc. —**hate′ful·ly** *adv.* —**hate′ful·ness** *n.*

hath (hath) *vt. archaic 3d pers. sing., pres. indic., of* HAVE

ha·tred (hā′trid) *n.* strong dislike or ill will; hate

hat·ter (hat′ər) *n.* one who makes, sells, or cleans hats, esp. men's hats

hau·berk (hô′bərk) *n.* ⟦< Frankish *hals*, neck + *bergan*, to protect⟧ a medieval coat of armor, usually of chain mail

haugh·ty (hôt′ē) *adj.* **-ti·er, -ti·est** ⟦< OFr *haut*, high⟧ having or showing great pride in oneself and contempt for others; arrogant —**haugh′ti·ly** *adv.* —**haugh′ti·ness** *n.*

haul (hôl) *vt.* ⟦< OFr *haler*⟧ **1** to move by pulling; drag **2** to transport by wagon, truck, etc. —*n.* **1** the act of hauling; pull **2** [Inf.] the amount gained, earned, etc. at one time **3** the distance over which something is transported —**haul off** [Inf.] to draw the arm back before hitting —**in** (or **over**) **the long haul** over a long period of time

haunch (hônch, hänch) *n.* ⟦< OFr *hanche* < Gmc⟧ **1** the hip, buttock, and upper thigh together **2** an animal's loin and leg together

haunt (hônt) *vt.* ⟦< OFr *hanter*, to frequent⟧ **1** to visit often or continually **2** to recur repeatedly to *[haunted by memories]* —*n.* a place often visited

haunt′ed *adj.* supposedly frequented by ghosts

haunt′ing *adj.* not easily forgotten

haute cou·ture (ōt′ko͞o to͞or′) ⟦Fr, high sewing⟧ high fashion for women

haute cui·sine (ōt′kwē zēn′) ⟦Fr, high kitchen⟧ **1** the preparation of fine food by skilled chefs **2** food prepared in this way

hau·teur (hō tur′) *n.* ⟦Fr < *haut*, high⟧ disdainful pride; haughtiness

Ha·van·a[1] (hə van′ə) *n.* a cigar made of Cuban tobacco

Havana[2] capital of Cuba: pop. 2,078,000

have (hav; *before "to"* haf) *vt.* **had, hav′ing** ⟦OE *habban*⟧ **1** to hold; own; possess *[to have money, a week has 7 days]* **2** to experience *[have a good time]* **3** to hold mentally *[to have an idea]* **4** to state *[so rumor has it]* **5** to get, take, consume, etc. *[have a drink]* **6** to bear or beget (offspring) **7** to engage in *[to have a fight]* **8** to cause to or cause to be *[have her sing]* **9** to permit; tolerate *[I won't have this noise!]* **10** [Inf.] *a*) to hold at a disadvantage *b*) to deceive; cheat *Have* is used as an auxiliary to express completed action (Ex.: I *had* left) and with infinitives to express obligation or necessity (Ex.: we *have* to go). *Have got* often replaces *have*. *Have* is conjugated in the present indicative: (I) *have*, (he, she, it) *has*, (we, you, they) *have* —*n.* a wealthy person or nation —**have it out** to settle an issue by fighting or discussion —**have on** to be wearing

ha·ven (hā′vən) *n.* ⟦OE *hæfen*⟧ **1** a port **2** any sheltered place; refuge

have-not (hav′nät′) *n.* a person or nation with little or no wealth

hav·er·sack (hav′ər sak′) *n.* ⟦< Ger *habersack*, lit., sack of oats⟧ a canvas bag for rations, etc., worn over one shoulder

hav·oc (hav′ək, -äk′) *n.* ⟦< OFr *havot*⟧ great destruction and devastation —**play havoc with** to devastate; ruin

haw[1] (hô) *n.* ⟦OE *haga*⟧ **1** the berry of the hawthorn **2** HAWTHORN

haw[2] (hô) *vi.* ⟦echoic⟧ *see* HEM AND HAW *under* HEM[2]

Ha·wai·i (hə wä′ē, -wī′ē) **1** state of the U.S., consisting of a group of islands (**Hawaiian Islands**) in the N Pacific: 6,423 sq. mi.; pop. 1,108,000; cap. Honolulu: abbrev. *HI* **2** the largest of these islands —**Ha·wai′ian** (-yən) *adj., n.*

hawk[1] (hôk) *n.* ⟦OE *hafoc*⟧ **1** a bird of prey with short, rounded wings, a long tail, and a hooked beak and claws **2** an advocate of war

hawk[2] (hôk) *vt.* ⟦< HAWKER⟧ to advertise or peddle (goods) in the streets by shouting

hawk[3] (hôk) *vi., vt.* ⟦echoic⟧ to clear the throat (of) audibly

hawk′er *n.* ⟦< Old LowG *hoker*⟧ a peddler or huckster

hawk′-eyed′ (-īd′) *adj.* keen-sighted

haw·ser (hô′zər) *n.* ⟦< OFr *haucier* < L *altus*, high⟧ a large rope used as for mooring a ship

haw·thorn (hô′thôrn′) *n.* ⟦< OE *haga*, hedge + THORN⟧ a thorny shrub or small tree of the rose family, with flowers and small, red fruits

Haw·thorne (hô′thôrn′), **Na·than·iel** (nə than′yəl) 1804-64; U.S. writer

hay (hā) *n.* ⟦< OE *hieg*⟧ grass, clover, etc. cut and dried for fodder —*vi.* to mow and dry grass, etc. for hay —**hit the hay** [Slang] to go to bed to sleep

hay′cock′ *n.* a small, conical heap of hay drying in a field

Hay·dn (hīd′'n), (**Franz**) **Jo·seph** (yō′zef) 1732-1809; Austrian composer

Hayes (hāz), **Ruth·er·ford B**(**irchard**) (ruth′ər fərd) 1822-93; 19th president of the U.S. (1877-81)

hay fever an allergy to pollen, causing

inflammation of the eyes and respiratory tract

hay'loft' *n.* a loft, or upper story, in a barn or stable, for storing hay

hay'mow' (-mou') *n.* **1** a pile of hay in a barn **2** HAYLOFT

hay'stack' *n.* a large heap of hay piled up outdoors

hay'wire' *adj.* [Inf.] **1** out of order; disorganized **2** crazy —**go haywire** [Inf.] **1** to behave erratically **2** to become crazy

haz·ard (haz'ərd) *n.* ⟦< OFr *hasard*, game of dice⟧ **1** risk; danger **2** an obstacle on a golf course —*vt.* to risk

haz'ard·ous *adj.* risky; dangerous

haze[1] (hāz) *n.* ⟦prob. < HAZY⟧ **1** a thin cloud of fog, smoke, etc. in the air **2** a slight vagueness of mind —*vi.*, *vt.* **hazed, haz'ing** to make or become hazy: often with *over*

haze[2] (hāz) *vt.* **hazed, haz'ing** ⟦< ?⟧ to initiate or discipline by forcing to do ridiculous or painful things

ha·zel (hā'zəl) *n.* ⟦OE *hæsel*⟧ **1** a shrub or tree of the birch family, with edible nuts **2** a reddish brown —*adj.* **1** light reddish-brown **2** greenish-gray or greenish-brown: said of eyes

ha'zel·nut' *n.* FILBERT

ha·zy (hā'zē) *adj.* **-zi·er, -zi·est** ⟦prob. < OE *hasu*, dusky⟧ **1** somewhat foggy or smoky **2** somewhat vague —**ha'zi·ly** *adv.* —**ha'zi·ness** *n.*

H-bomb (āch'bäm') *n.* HYDROGEN BOMB

hdqrs *abbrev.* headquarters

HDTV *abbrev.* high-definition television

he (hē) *pron.*, *pl. see* THEY ⟦OE⟧ **1** the man, boy, or male animal previously mentioned **2** anyone *[he* who laughs last laughs best*]* —*n.* a male

He *Chem. symbol for* helium

head (hed) *n.* ⟦OE *heafod*⟧ **1** the part of the body containing the brain, jaws, eyes, ears, nose, mouth, etc. **2** the mind; intelligence **3** *pl.* **head** a unit of counting *[ten head* of cattle*]* **4** the main side of a coin: often **heads** **5** the uppermost part or thing; top **6** the topic or title of a section, chapter, etc. **7** the foremost or projecting part; front **8** the part designed for holding, striking, etc. *[the head* of a nail*]* **9** the part of a tape recorder that records or plays back the magnetic signals on the tape **10** the membrane across the end of a drum, etc. **11** the source of a river, etc. **12** froth, as on beer **13** a position of leadership or honor **14** a leader, ruler, etc. **15** *Bot.* a dense cluster of small flowers **16** [Slang] a person dedicated to, addicted to, etc. some interest, activity, etc. —*adj.* **1** most important; principal **2** at the top or front **3** striking against the front *[head* winds*]* —*vt.* **1** to be the chief of; command **2** to lead; precede **3** to cause to go in a specified direction —*vi.* to set out; travel —**come to a head** **1** to be about to suppurate, as a boil **2** to culminate, or reach a crisis —**go to someone's head** **1** to confuse or intoxicate someone **2** to make someone vain —**head off** to get ahead of and intercept —**head over heels** deeply; completely —**heads up!** [Inf.] look out! —**keep** (or **lose**) **one's head** to keep (or lose) one's poise, self-control, etc. —**on** (or **upon**) **someone's head** as someone's responsibility or misfortune —**over someone's head** **1** too difficult for someone to understand **2** to a higher authority —**turn one's head** to make one vain —**head'less** *adj.*

head'ache' *n.* **1** a continuous pain in the head **2** [Inf.] a cause of worry, annoyance, or trouble

head'board' *n.* a board that forms the head of a bed, etc.

head cold a common cold with congestion of the nasal passages

head'dress' *n.* a decorative head covering

-head·ed (hed'id) *combining form* having a (specified kind or number of) head or heads *[lightheaded*, two-*headed]*

head'er *n.* **1** a pipe, etc. that brings other pipes together, as in an exhaust system **2** in word processing, text repeated at the top of each page **3** [Inf.] a headlong fall or dive

head'first' *adv.* **1** with the head in front; headlong **2** recklessly; rashly —*adj.* with the head first

head'gear' *n.* a hat, cap, etc.

head'ing *n.* **1** something forming the head, top, or front **2** the title, topic, etc., as of a chapter **3** the direction in which a ship, plane, etc. is moving

head'land (-lənd) *n.* a cape or point of land reaching out into the water; promontory

head'light' *n.* a light with a reflector and lens, at the front of a vehicle

head'line' *n.* printed lines at the top of a newspaper article, giving the topic —*vt.* **-lined'**, **-lin'ing** **1** to give (a performer, etc.) featured billing or publicity **2** to be the featured performer, etc. in

head'long' (-lôŋ') *adv.*, *adj.* ⟦ME *hedelinge(s)*⟧ **1** with the head first **2** with uncontrolled speed or force **3** reckless(ly); rash(ly)

head'mas'ter *n.* the male principal of a private school —**head'mis'tress** *fem.n.*

head'-on' *adj.*, *adv.* **1** with the head or front foremost *[a head-on* collision*]* **2** directly *[to meet a problem head-on]*

head'phone' *n.* [*usually pl.*] a listening device for a radio, stereo, etc. worn over the head to position its speakers over the ears

head'quar'ters *pl.n.* [*with sing. or pl. v.*] **1** the main office, or center of operations, of one in command, as in an army **2** the main office in any organization

head'rest' *n.* a support for the head

head'room' *n.* space overhead, as in a doorway, tunnel, etc.

head start an early start or other competitive advantage

head'stone' *n.* a stone marker placed at the head of a grave

head'strong' *adj.* determined to do as one pleases

head'wa'ters *pl.n.* the small streams that are the sources of a river

head'way' ***n.*** **1** forward motion **2** progress or success

head'y ***adj.*** **-i·er, -i·est** **1** intoxicating **2** having, using, etc. good judgment or intelligence

heal (hēl) ***vt., vi.*** ⟦OE *hælan*⟧ **1** to make or become well or healthy again **2** to cure (a disease) or mend, as a wound —**heal'er** ***n.***

health (helth) ***n.*** ⟦OE *hælth*⟧ **1** physical and mental well-being; freedom from disease, etc. **2** condition of body or mind *[poor health]* **3** a wish for one's health and happiness, as in a toast **4** soundness, as of a society or culture

health'care' ***n.*** the prevention and treatment of illness or injury on an ongoing basis

health food food thought to be especially healthful; specif., food grown with natural fertilizers and free of chemical additives

health'ful ***adj.*** helping to produce or maintain health; wholesome

health'y ***adj.*** **-i·er, -i·est** **1** having good health **2** showing or resulting from good health *[a healthy color]* **3** HEALTHFUL —**health'i·ness** ***n.***

heap (hēp) ***n.*** ⟦< OE *heap*, a troop⟧ **1** a pile or mass of jumbled things **2** [*often pl.*] [Inf.] a large amount —***vt.*** **1** to make a heap of **2** to give in large amounts **3** to fill (a plate, etc.) full or to overflowing —***vi.*** to rise in a heap

hear (hir) ***vt.*** **heard** (hurd), **hear'ing** ⟦OE *hieran*⟧ **1** to be aware of (sounds) by the ear **2** to listen to **3** to conduct a hearing of (a law case, etc.) **4** to be informed of; learn —***vi.*** **1** to be able to hear sounds **2** to be told (*of* or *about*) —**hear from** to get a letter, etc. from —**not hear of** to refuse to consider —**hear'er** ***n.***

hear'ing ***n.*** **1** the act or process of perceiving sounds **2** the ability to hear **3** an opportunity to be heard **4** an appearance before a judge, investigative committee, etc. **5** the distance a sound will carry *[within hearing]*

heark·en (härk'ən) ***vi.*** ⟦OE *heorknian*⟧ [Now Literary] to listen carefully; pay heed: with *to*

hear·say (hir'sā') ***n.*** rumor; gossip

hearse (hurs) ***n.*** ⟦< L *hirpex*, a harrow⟧ a vehicle used in a funeral for carrying the corpse

heart (härt) ***n.*** ⟦OE *heorte*⟧ **1** the hollow, muscular organ that circulates the blood by alternate dilation and contraction **2** the central, vital, or main part; core **3** the human heart considered as the center of emotions, personality attributes, etc.; specif., *a)* inmost thought and feeling *b)* love, sympathy, etc. *c)* spirit or courage **4** a conventionalized design of a heart (♥) **5** any of a suit of playing cards marked with such symbols in red —**after someone's own heart** that pleases someone perfectly —**at heart** in one's innermost nature —**by heart** by or from memorization —**set one's heart on** to have a fixed desire for —**take to heart** **1** to consider seriously **2** to be troubled by

heart'ache' ***n.*** sorrow or grief

heart attack any sudden instance of heart failure; esp., a coronary

heart'beat' ***n.*** **1** one full contraction and dilation of the heart **2** a moment; instant

heart'break' ***n.*** overwhelming sorrow, grief, etc. —**heart'break'ing** ***adj.*** —**heart'bro'ken** ***adj.***

heart'break'er ***n.*** one that causes heartbreak

heart'burn' ***n.*** a burning, acid sensation beneath the breastbone

-heart·ed (härt'id) ⟦ME⟧ *combining form* having a (specified kind of) heart *[stouthearted]*

heart·en (härt''n) ***vt.*** to encourage

heart failure the inability of the heart to pump enough blood to supply the body tissues adequately

heart'felt' ***adj.*** sincere; genuine

hearth (härth) ***n.*** ⟦OE *heorth*⟧ **1** the stone or brick floor of a fireplace **2** *a)* the fireside *b)* family life; home

heart'land' ***n.*** a geographically central area having crucial importance

heart'less ***adj.*** unkind; unfeeling —**heart'less·ly** ***adv.*** —**heart'less·ness** ***n.***

heart'-rend'ing ***adj.*** causing much grief or mental anguish

heart'sick' ***adj.*** sick at heart; extremely unhappy or despondent

heart'strings' ***pl.n.*** deepest feelings or affections

heart'-to-heart' ***adj.*** intimate and candid

heart'warm'ing ***adj.*** causing genial feelings

heart'y ***adj.*** **-i·er, -i·est** **1** warm and friendly; cordial **2** strongly felt; unrestrained *[hearty laughter]* **3** strong and healthy **4** nourishing and plentiful *[a hearty meal]* —**heart'i·ly** ***adv.*** —**heart'i·ness** ***n.***

heat (hēt) ***n.*** ⟦OE *hætu*⟧ **1** the quality of being hot; hotness, or the perception of this **2** much hotness **3** hot weather or climate **4** the warming of a house, etc. **5** *a)* strong feeling; ardor, anger, etc. *b)* the period of this **6** a single bout, round, or trial **7** the period of sexual excitement in animals, esp. females **8** [Slang] coercion —***vt., vi.*** **1** to make or become warm or hot **2** to make or become excited

heat'ed ***adj.*** **1** hot **2** vehement or angry —**heat'ed·ly** ***adv.***

heat'er ***n.*** an apparatus for giving heat; stove, furnace, radiator, etc.

heath (hēth) ***n.*** ⟦OE *hæth*⟧ **1** a tract of open wasteland, esp. in the British Isles **2** any of various shrubs that grow on heaths, as heather

hea·then (hē'*th*ən) ***n.***, *pl.* **-thens** or **-then** ⟦OE *hæthen*⟧ **1** anyone not a Jew, Christian, or Muslim **2** a person regarded as irreligious, uncivilized, etc. —***adj.*** **1** pagan **2** irreligious, uncivilized, etc. —**hea'then·ish** ***adj.***

heath·er (he*th*'ər) ***n.*** ⟦ME *haddyr*⟧ a plant of the heath family, esp. common in the British Isles, with small, bell-shaped, purplish-pink flowers

heating pad a pad consisting of an electric heating element covered with fabric, for applying heat to the body

heat lightning lightning without thunder, seen on hot evenings

heat'stroke' ***n.*** a condition of high fever, collapse, etc. resulting from exposure to intense heat

heat wave **1** unusually hot weather **2** a period of such weather

heave (hēv) ***vt.*** **heaved** or (esp. *Naut.*) **hove, heav'ing** ⟦OE *hebban*⟧ **1** to lift, esp. with effort **2** to lift in this way and throw **3** to utter (a sigh, etc.) with effort —***vi.*** **1** to swell up **2** to rise and fall rhythmically **3** *a*) to vomit *b*) to pant; gasp —***n.*** the act or effort of heaving —**heave to** *Naut.* to stop

heave'-ho' (-hō') ***n.*** [Inf.] dismissal, as from a job: chiefly in **give** (or **get**) **the** (**old**) **heave-ho**

heav·en (hev'ən) ***n.*** ⟦OE *heofon*⟧ **1** [*usually pl.*] the visible sky; firmament **2** [*often* **H-**] *Theol. a*) a state or place of complete happiness, etc. attained by the good after death *b*) the abode of God, his angels, and the blessed *c*) God **3** any place of great beauty or state of great happiness —**heav'en·ly** ***adj.***

heav'en·ward ***adv., adj.*** toward heaven: also **heav'en·wards** ***adv.***

heav·y (hev'ē) ***adj.*** **-i·er, -i·est** ⟦OE *hefig*⟧ **1** hard to lift because of great weight **2** of more than the usual, expected, or defined weight **3** larger, greater, or more intense than usual [a *heavy* blow, a *heavy* vote] **4** to an unusual extent [a *heavy* drinker] **5** hard to do [*heavy* work] **6** sorrowful [a *heavy* heart] **7** burdened with sleep [*heavy* eyelids] **8** hard to digest [a *heavy* meal] **9** clinging; penetrating [a *heavy* odor] **10** cloudy; gloomy [a *heavy* sky] **11** designating any large, basic industry that uses massive machinery **12** [Slang] serious and, often, depressing —***adv.*** in a heavy manner —***n.***, *pl.* **-ies** **1** *Theater* a villain **2** [Slang] an important person —**heav'i·ly** ***adv.*** —**heav'i·ness** ***n.***

heav'y-du'ty ***adj.*** made to withstand great strain, bad weather, etc.

heav'y-hand'ed ***adj.*** **1** clumsy or tactless **2** oppressive or tyrannical

heav'y-heart'ed ***adj.*** sad; depressed

heav'y-set' ***adj.*** having a stout or stocky build

heav'y·weight' ***n.*** **1** one weighing more than average; esp., a boxer in the heaviest weight class **2** [Inf.] a very influential or important person

He·bra·ic (hē brā'ik, hi-) ***adj.*** of or characteristic of the Hebrews, their language, or culture; Hebrew

He·brew (hē'brōō') ***n.*** **1** *a*) a member of an ancient Semitic people; Israelite *b*) a Jew **2** *a*) the ancient Semitic language of the Israelites *b*) its modern form, the language of Israel —***adj.*** **1** of Hebrew or the Hebrews **2** JEWISH

Heb·ri·des (heb'rə dēz') group of islands off the W coast of Scotland

heck (hek) ***interj., n.*** [Inf.] *euphemism for* HELL

heck·le (hek'əl) ***vt.*** **-led, -ling** ⟦ME *hechele*⟧ to harass (a speaker) by interrupting with questions or taunts —**heck'ler** ***n.***

hec·tare (hek'ter') ***n.*** ⟦Fr⟧ a metric unit of area, 10,000 square meters

hec·tic (hek'tik) ***adj.*** ⟦< Gr *hektikos*, habitual⟧ **1** feverish; flushed **2** confused, rushed, excited, etc. —**hec'ti·cal·ly** ***adv.***

Hec·tor (hek'tər) ***n.*** in Homer's *Iliad*, a Trojan hero, killed by Achilles —***vt., vi.*** [**h-**] to browbeat; bully

hedge (hej) ***n.*** ⟦OE *hecg*⟧ **1** a dense row of shrubs, etc. forming a boundary **2** any fence or barrier **3** a hedging —***vt.*** **hedged, hedg'ing** **1** to put a hedge around **2** to hinder or guard as with a barrier: often with *in* **3** to try to avoid loss in (a bet, etc.) by making counterbalancing bets, etc. —***vi.*** to avoid giving a direct answer

hedge fund a partnership of investors who pool large sums for speculating in securities

hedge'hog' ***n.*** **1** a small, insect-eating mammal of the Old World, with sharp spines on the back **2** the American porcupine

he·don·ism (hēd''n iz'əm) ***n.*** ⟦< Gr *hēdonē*, pleasure + -ISM⟧ the self-indulgent pursuit of pleasure as a way of life —**he'don·ist** ***n.*** —**he'do·nis'tic** ***adj.***

-he·dron (hē'drən) ⟦< Gr⟧ *combining form* a geometric figure or crystal having (a specified number of) surfaces

heed (hēd) ***vt., vi.*** ⟦OE *hedan*⟧ to pay close attention (to) —***n.*** close attention —**heed'ful** ***adj.*** —**heed'less** ***adj.*** —**heed'less·ly** ***adv.*** —**heed'less·ness** ***n.***

hee·haw (hē'hô') ***n., vi.*** ⟦echoic⟧ bray

heel[1] (hēl) ***n.*** ⟦OE *hela*⟧ **1** the back part of the foot, under the ankle **2** that part of a stocking, shoe, etc. at the heel **3** anything like a heel in location, shape, crushing power, etc. **4** [Inf.] a despicable person —***vt.*** **1** to furnish with a heel **2** to follow closely **3** [Inf.] to provide (a person) with money, etc. —***vi.*** to follow along at the heels of someone —**down at** (**the**) **heel** (or **heels**) shabby; seedy —**kick up one's heels** have fun —**on** (or **upon**) **the heels of** close behind

heel[2] (hēl) ***vi.*** ⟦OE *hieldan*⟧ to lean to one side: said esp. of a ship —***vt.*** to cause (a ship) to heel

heft (heft) [Inf.] ***n.*** ⟦< base of HEAVE⟧ **1** weight; heaviness **2** importance; influence —***vt.*** to try to judge the weight of by lifting

heft'y ***adj.*** **-i·er, -i·est** [Inf.] **1** heavy **2** large and powerful **3** big —**heft'i·ness** ***n.***

he·gem·o·ny (hi jem'ə nē) ***n.***, *pl.* **-nies** ⟦< Gr *hēgeisthai*, to lead⟧ leadership or dominance, esp. that of one state or nation over others

he·gi·ra (hi jī'rə) ***n.*** ⟦< Ar *hijrah*, flight⟧ **1** [*often* **H-**] Mohammed's flight from Mecca in A.D. 622 **2** a journey, esp. one made to escape

Hei·del·berg (hīd''l burg') city in SW Germany: site of a famous university: pop. 140,000

heif·er (hef'ər) ***n.*** ⟦OE *heahfore*⟧ a

young cow that has not borne a calf

height (hīt) ***n.*** ⟦< OE *heah*, high⟧ **1** the topmost point **2** the highest limit; extreme **3** the distance from the bottom to the top **4** elevation above a given level; altitude **5** a relatively great distance above a given level **6** [*often pl.*] an elevation; hill

height′en (-′n) ***vt.***, ***vi.*** **1** to bring or come to a higher position **2** to make or become larger, greater, etc.

Heim·lich maneuver (hīm′lik) ⟦after H. J. *Heimlich*, 20th-c. U.S. surgeon⟧ an emergency technique for dislodging an object stuck in the windpipe, using air forced up the windpipe by applying sharp pressure to the abdomen

hei·nous (hā′nəs) ***adj.*** ⟦< OFr *hair*, to hate⟧ outrageously evil —**hei′nous·ly** ***adv.*** —**hei′nous·ness** ***n.***

heir (er) ***n.*** ⟦< L *heres*⟧ one who inherits or is entitled to inherit another's property, title, etc.

heir apparent *pl.* **heirs apparent** the heir whose right to inherit cannot be denied if the heir outlives the ancestor and the ancestor dies intestate

heir′ess (-is) ***n.*** a female heir, esp. to great wealth

heir′loom′ ***n.*** ⟦see HEIR & LOOM[1]⟧ any treasured possession handed down from generation to generation

heist (hīst) [Slang] ***n.*** ⟦< HOIST⟧ a robbery —***vt.*** to rob or steal

held (held) ***vt.***, ***vi.*** *pt. & pp. of* HOLD[1]

Hel·e·na (hel′ə nə) capital of Montana: pop. 25,000

Helen of Troy *Gr. Legend* the beautiful wife of the king of Sparta: the Trojan War is started because of her abduction by Paris to Troy

hel·i·cal (hel′i kəl) ***adj.*** ⟦< Gr *helix*, spiral⟧ shaped like a helix; spiral

hel·i·cop·ter (hel′i käp′tər) ***n.*** ⟦< Gr *helix*, spiral + *pteron*, wing⟧ a vertical-lift aircraft, capable of hovering or moving in any direction, having a motor-driven, horizontal rotor —***vi.***, ***vt.*** to travel or convey by helicopter

he·li·o·cen·tric (hē′lē ō sen′trik) ***adj.*** ⟦< Gr *hēlios*, the sun + *kentron*, a point⟧ having or regarding the sun as the center

he·li·o·trope (hē′lē ə trōp′) ***n.*** ⟦< Gr *hēlios*, the sun + *trepein*, to turn⟧ **1** a plant with fragrant clusters of small, white or reddish-purple flowers **2** reddish purple —***adj.*** reddish-purple

hel·i·port (hel′i pôrt′) ***n.*** ⟦HELI(COPTER) + (AIR)PORT⟧ an airport for helicopters: also **hel′i·pad′** (-pad′)

he·li·um (hē′lē əm) ***n.*** ⟦< Gr *hēlios*, the sun⟧ a chemical element, a colorless, odorless, very light, nonreactive gas having the lowest known boiling and melting points

he·lix (hē′liks) ***n.***, *pl.* **-lix·es** or **hel·i·ces** (hel′i sēz′) ⟦L & Gr⟧ a spiral

hell (hel) ***n.*** ⟦< OE *helan*, to hide⟧ **1** [*often* **H-**] *Theol.* the state or place of total and final separation from God and so of eternal misery and suffering, arrived at by those who die unrepentant in grave sin **2** any place or condition of evil, pain, etc. —**catch** (or **get**) **hell** [Slang] to receive a severe scolding, punishment, etc.

hell′bent′ or **hell′-bent′** ***adj.*** [Slang] **1** recklessly determined **2** moving fast or recklessly

hell′cat′ ***n.*** an evil, spiteful woman

hel·le·bore (hel′ə bôr′) ***n.*** ⟦< Gr *helleboros*⟧ a plant with buttercuplike flowers, whose rhizomes were once used in medicine

Hel·len·ic (hə len′ik) ***adj.*** **1** Greek **2** of the history, language, or culture of the ancient Greeks —**Hel·len·ism** (hel′ən iz′ əm) ***n.*** —**Hel′len·is′tic** ***adj.***

hell·gram·mite or **hell·gra·mite** (hel′ grəm īt′) ***n.*** ⟦< ?⟧ a dark-brown, aquatic fly larva, often used as fish bait

hel·lion (hel′yən) ***n.*** ⟦< Scot dial. *hallion*, a low fellow⟧ [Inf.] a person fond of deviltry; troublemaker

hell′ish ***adj.*** **1** devilish; fiendish **2** [Inf.] very unpleasant —**hell′ish·ly** ***adv.*** —**hell′ish·ness** ***n.***

hel·lo (he lō′, hel′ō′) ***interj.*** used to express greeting

helm (helm) ***n.*** ⟦OE *helma*⟧ **1** the wheel or tiller by which a ship is steered **2** the control or leadership of an organization, government, etc.

hel·met (hel′mət) ***n.*** ⟦< OFr *helme*⟧ a protective, rigid head covering for use in combat, certain sports, etc.

helms·man (helmz′mən) ***n.***, *pl.* **-men** (-mən) one who steers a ship

hel·ot (hel′ət) ***n.*** ⟦after *Helos*, ancient Greek town⟧ a serf or slave

help (help) ***vt.*** ⟦OE *helpan*⟧ **1** to make things easier or better for; aid; assist **2** to relieve [to *help* a cough] **3** to keep from; avoid [can't *help* crying] **4** to serve or wait on (a customer, etc.) —***vi.*** to give aid; be useful —***n.*** **1** a helping; aid; assistance **2** relief **3** one that helps; esp., a hired person or persons; servant(s), farmhand(s), etc. —***interj.*** used to summon assistance, esp. urgently —**help oneself to** to take without asking —**help out** to help in getting or doing something —**help′er** ***n.***

help′ful ***adj.*** giving help; useful —**help′ful·ly** ***adv.*** —**help′ful·ness** ***n.***

help′ing ***n.*** a portion of food served to one person

help′less ***adj.*** **1** not able to help oneself; weak **2** lacking help or protection **3** incompetent or ineffective —**help′less·ly** ***adv.*** —**help′less·ness** ***n.***

help′mate′ ***n.*** ⟦< fol.⟧ a helpful companion; specif., a wife or husband

help′meet′ ***n.*** ⟦misreading of "an *help meet* for him" (Genesis 2:18)⟧ HELPMATE

Hel·sin·ki (hel′siŋ kē) capital of Finland: pop. 516,000

hel·ter-skel·ter (hel′tər skel′tər) ***adv.*** in haste and confusion —***adj.*** disorderly

helve (helv) ***n.*** ⟦OE *helfe*⟧ the handle of a tool, esp. of an ax

Hel·ve·tian (hel vē′shən) ***adj.***, ***n.*** Swiss

hem[1] (hem) ***n.*** ⟦OE⟧ the border on a garment, etc. made by folding the edge and sewing it down —*vt.* **hemmed, hem′ming** to fold back the edge of and sew down —**hem in 1** to encircle **2** to confine

hem[2] (hem) ***interj., n.*** the sound made in clearing the throat —***vi.*** **hemmed, hem′ming 1** to make this sound, as in trying to get attention **2** to grope about in speech for the right words: usually used in the phrase **hem and haw**

he·ma- *combining form* HEMO-

he′-man′ ***n.*** [Inf.] a strong, virile man

hem·a·tite (hem′ə tīt′, hē′mə-) ***n.*** ⟦< Gr *haimatitēs*, bloodlike⟧ native ferric oxide, an important iron ore

he·ma·tol·o·gy (hē′mə täl′ə jē) ***n.*** ⟦< Gr *haima*, blood + -LOGY⟧ the study of blood and blood diseases —**he′ma·tol′o·gist** ***n.***

he′ma·to′ma (-tō′mə) ***n.**, pl.* **-mas** or **-ma·ta** (-mə tə) ⟦< Gr *haima*, blood + *-ōma*, a mass⟧ a tumorlike collection of blood outside a blood vessel

heme (hēm) ***n.*** ⟦ult. < Gr *haima*, blood⟧ the iron-containing pigment in hemoglobin

hemi- ⟦Gr *hēmi-*⟧ *prefix* half *[hemisphere]*

Hem·ing·way (hem′iŋ wā′), **Er·nest** (ʉr′ nist) 1899-1961; U.S. writer

hem·i·sphere (hem′i sfir′) ***n.*** ⟦< Gr *hēmisphairion*⟧ **1** half of a sphere, globe, celestial body, etc. **2** any of the halves (northern, southern, eastern, or western) of the earth —**hem′i·spher′i·cal** (-sfer′i kəl) or **hem′i·spher′ic** ***adj.***

hem′line′ ***n.*** the bottom edge of a dress, skirt, coat, etc.

hem·lock (hem′läk′) ***n.*** ⟦OE *hemlic*⟧ **1** *a)* a poisonous European plant related to parsley *b)* a poison made from this plant **2** *a)* an evergreen tree of the pine family *b)* the wood of this tree

hemo- ⟦< Gr *haima*⟧ *combining form* blood

he·mo·glo·bin (hē′mə glō′bin) ***n.*** ⟦< prec. + GLOBULE⟧ the red coloring matter of the red blood corpuscles

he·mo·phil·i·a (hē′mə fil′ē ə) ***n.*** ⟦< HEMO- + -PHILE⟧ a hereditary disorder in which the blood fails to clot normally, causing prolonged bleeding from even minor cuts —**he′mo·phil′i·ac′** (-ak′) ***n.***

hem·or·rhage (hem′ər ij′, hem′rij′) ***n.*** ⟦< Gr *haima*, blood + *rhēgnynai*, to break⟧ the escape of large quantities of blood from a blood vessel; heavy bleeding —***vi.*** **-rhaged′, -rhag′ing** (-ij′iŋ) to have a hemorrhage —**hem′or·rhag′ic** (-aj′ik) ***adj.***

hem·or·rhoid (hem′ər oid′, hem′roid′) ***n.*** ⟦< Gr *haima*, blood + *rheein*, to flow⟧ a painful swelling of a vein in the region of the anus, often with bleeding: *usually used in pl.* —**hem′or·rhoi′dal** ***adj.***

he·mo·stat (hē′mō stat′) ***n.*** ⟦see HEMO- & STATIC⟧ anything used to stop bleeding, as a surgical clamp

hemp (hemp) ***n.*** ⟦OE *hænep*⟧ **1** a tall Asiatic plant having tough fiber **2** the fiber, used to make rope, sailcloth, etc. **3** a substance, as marijuana, made from its leaves and flowers

hem′stitch′ ***n.*** an ornamental stitch, used esp. at a hem, made by pulling out several parallel threads and tying the cross threads into small bunches —***vt.*** to put hemstitches on

hen (hen) ***n.*** ⟦OE *henn*⟧ **1** the female of the domesticated chicken **2** the female of various other birds

hence (hens) ***adv.*** ⟦< OE *heonan*, from here⟧ **1** from this place; away *[go hence]* **2** from this time *[a year hence]* **3** as a result; therefore

hence·forth′ ***adv.*** from this time on; after this: also **hence′for′ward**

hench·man (hench′mən) ***n.**, pl.* **-men** (-mən) ⟦< OE *hengest*, stallion + *-man*⟧ a trusted helper or follower

hen·na (hen′ə) ***n.*** ⟦Ar *ḥinnā′*⟧ **1** an Old World plant with tiny, white or red flowers **2** a dye extracted from its leaves, used to tint the hair auburn **3** reddish brown —***adj.*** reddish-brown —***vt.*** **-naed, -na·ing** to tint with henna

hen·peck (hen′pek′) ***vt.*** to nag and domineer over (one's husband) —**hen′pecked′** ***adj.***

Hen·ry VIII (hen′rē) 1491-1547; king of England (1509-47)

hep (hep) ***adj.*** [Slang] *var. of* HIP[2]

hep·a·rin (hep′ə rin) ***n.*** ⟦< Gr *hēpar*, liver⟧ a substance found in the liver, that slows the clotting of blood

he·pat·ic (hi pat′ik) ***adj.*** ⟦< Gr *hēpar*, liver⟧ of or like the liver

hep·a·ti·tis (hep′ə tīt′is) ***n.*** ⟦< Gr *hēpar*, liver + -ITIS⟧ inflammation of the liver

her (hʉr) ***pron.*** ⟦OE *hire*⟧ *objective form of* SHE —***poss. pronominal adj.*** of, belonging to, or done by her

He·ra (hir′ə, her′ə) ***n.*** *Gr. Myth.* the wife of Zeus and queen of the gods

her·ald (her′əld) ***n.*** ⟦< OFr *heralt*⟧ **1** [Historical] an official who made proclamations, carried state messages, etc. **2** one who announces significant news, etc. **3** a forerunner; harbinger —***vt.*** to announce, foretell, etc.

he·ral·dic (hə ral′dik) ***adj.*** of heraldry or heralds

her′ald·ry ***n.*** **1** the study of coats of arms, genealogies, etc. **2** ceremony or pomp

herb (ʉrb, hʉrb) ***n.*** ⟦< L *herba*⟧ **1** any seed plant whose stem withers away annually **2** any plant used as a medicine, seasoning, or flavoring —**her·ba·ceous** (hər bā′shəs, ər-) ***adj.*** —**herb′al** ***adj.***

herb·al·ist (hʉr′bəl ist, ʉr′-) ***n.*** one who grows or deals in herbs

her·bi·cide (hʉr′bə sīd′, ʉr′-) ***n.*** any chemical substance used to destroy plants, esp. weeds —**her′bi·ci′dal** ***adj.***

her·bi·vore (hʉr′bə vôr′) ***n.*** ⟦Fr⟧ a herbivorous animal

her·biv·o·rous (hər biv′ər əs) ***adj.*** ⟦< L *herba*, herb + *vorare*, devour⟧ feeding chiefly on grass or other plants

her·cu·le·an (hər kyōō′lē ən, hʉr′kyōō lē′ən) ***adj.*** [*sometimes* **H-**] **1** having the great size or strength of Hercules **2** calling for great strength, size, or courage

Her·cu·les (hʉr′kyōō lēz′) ***n.*** **1** *Gr. & Rom. Myth.* a hero famous for feats of strength **2** [**h-**] a very large, strong man

herd (hʉrd) ***n.*** ⟦OE *heord*⟧ **1** a number of cattle or other animals feeding or living together **2** *a*) a crowd *b*) the common people; masses (a contemptuous term) —***vt., vi.*** to gather or move as a herd

herds·man (hʉrdz′mən) ***n.***, *pl.* **-men** (-mən) one who keeps or tends a herd

here (hir) ***adv.*** ⟦OE *her*⟧ **1** at or in this place: often used as an intensive *[*John *here* is an actor*]* **2** to or into this place *[*come *here]* **3** at this point; now **4** in earthly life —***n.*** this place —**neither here nor there** irrelevant

here′a·bout′ ***adv.*** in this general vicinity: also **here′a·bouts′**

here·af′ter ***adv.*** **1** from now on; in the future **2** following this —***n.*** **1** the future **2** the state after death

here·by′ ***adv.*** by this means

he·red·i·tar·y (hə red′i ter′ē) ***adj.*** **1** *a*) of, or passed down by, inheritance from an ancestor *b*) having title, etc. by inheritance **2** of, or passed down by, heredity

he·red·i·ty (hə red′i tē) ***n.***, *pl.* **-ties** ⟦< L *heres*, heir⟧ the transmission of characteristics from parent to offspring by means of genes

here·in′ ***adv.*** **1** in here **2** in this writing

here·of′ ***adv.*** of or concerning this

here's (hirz) *contr.* here is

her·e·sy (her′ə sē) ***n.***, *pl.* **-sies** ⟦< Gr *hairesis*, selection, sect⟧ **1** a religious belief opposed to the orthodox doctrines of a church **2** any opinion opposed to official or established views

her′e·tic (-tik) ***n.*** one who professes a heresy; esp., a church member who holds beliefs opposed to church dogma —**he·ret·i·cal** (hə ret′i kəl) ***adj.*** —**he·ret′i·cal·ly** ***adv.***

here′to·fore′ ***adv.*** up until now

here′up·on′ ***adv.*** **1** immediately following this; at once **2** concerning this subject, etc.

here·with′ ***adv.*** **1** along with this **2** by this method or means

her·it·a·ble (her′it ə bəl) ***adj.*** that can be inherited

her·it·age (her′i tij) ***n.*** **1** property that is or can be inherited **2** tradition, etc. handed down from one's ancestors or the past

her·maph·ro·dite (hər maf′rə dīt′) ***n.*** ⟦after *Hermaphroditos*, son of Hermes and Aphrodite, who became united in a single body with a nymph⟧ a person, animal, or plant with the sexual organs of both the male and the female —**her·maph′ro·dit′ic** (-dit′ik) ***adj.***

Her·mes (hʉr′mēz′) ***n.*** *Gr. Myth.* the god who is the messenger of the other gods

her·met·ic (hər met′ik) ***adj.*** ⟦after prec. (reputed founder of alchemy)⟧ airtight: also **her·met′i·cal** —**her·met′i·cal·ly** ***adv.***

her·mit (hʉr′mit) ***n.*** ⟦< Gr *erēmos*, desolate⟧ one who lives alone in a secluded spot; recluse

her′mit·age (-mə tij) ***n.*** a secluded retreat, as the place where a hermit lives

hermit crab a soft-bodied crab that lives in an empty mollusk shell

her·ni·a (hʉr′nē ə) ***n.***, *pl.* **-as** or **-ae′** (-ē′, -ī′) ⟦L⟧ the protrusion of all or part of an organ, esp. the intestine, through a tear in the wall of the surrounding structure; rupture —**her′ni·al** ***adj.***

her′ni·ate′ (-āt′) ***vi.*** **-at′ed, -at′ing** to protrude so as to form a hernia —**her′ni·a′tion** ***n.***

he·ro (hir′ō, hē′rō′) ***n.***, *pl.* **-roes** ⟦< Gr *hērōs*⟧ **1** any person, esp. a man, admired for courage, nobility, etc. **2** the central male character in a novel, play, etc.

He·rod·o·tus (hə räd′ə təs) 484?-425? B.C.; Gr. historian

he·ro·ic (hi rō′ik) ***adj.*** **1** of or like a hero **2** of or about a hero and his deeds **3** daring and risky —***n.*** [*pl.*] heroic behavior, talk, or deeds —**he·ro′i·cal·ly** ***adv.***

her·o·in (her′ō in) ***n.*** ⟦Ger, orig. a trademark⟧ a habit-forming narcotic derived from morphine

GREAT BLUE HERON

her·o·ine (her′ō in) ***n.*** a female hero in life or literature

her′o·ism′ ***n.*** the qualities and actions of a hero or heroine

her·on (her′ən) ***n.*** ⟦< OFr *hairon*⟧ a wading bird with a long neck, long legs, and a long, tapered bill

hero sandwich a long roll sliced and filled with meats, cheeses, vegetables, etc.

her·pes (hʉr′pēz′) ***n.*** ⟦L < Gr *herpein*, to creep⟧ any of several viral diseases causing small blisters on the skin and mucous membranes

herpes sim·plex (sim′pleks′) a recurrent, incurable form of herpes usually affecting the mouth, lips, face, or genitals

herpes zos·ter (zäs′tər) ⟦< HERPES + Gr *zōstēr*, a girdle⟧ a viral infection of certain sensory nerves, causing pain and an eruption of blisters; shingles

her·pe·tol·o·gy (hʉr′pə täl′ə jē) ***n.*** ⟦< Gr *herpeton*, reptile⟧ the branch of zoology having to do with the study of reptiles and amphibians —**her′pe·tol′o·gist** ***n.***

Herr (her) ***n.***, *pl.* ***Her′ren*** (-ən) ⟦Ger⟧ **1** Mr.; Sir: a German title of respect **2** a man; gentleman

her·ring (her′iŋ) ***n.*** ⟦OE *hæring*⟧ a small, silvery food fish of the North Atlantic

her′ring·bone′ ***n.*** **1** the spine of a herring, having numerous thin, parallel bony extensions on each side **2** a pattern with such a design, or anything having such a pattern, as a twill weave

hers (hʉrz) ***pron.*** that or those belonging to her: poss. form of SHE *[hers are better]*

her·self′ (hər-) ***pron.*** a form of SHE, used as an intensive *[she went herself]*, as a reflexive *[she hurt herself]*, or with the meaning "her true self" *[she is not herself today]*

hertz (hʉrts) ***n.***, *pl.* **hertz** ⟦after H. R. *Hertz*, 19th-c. Ger physicist⟧ the international unit of frequency, equal to one cycle per second

Hertz·i·an waves (hert′sē ən, hʉrt′-) ⟦see prec.⟧ [*sometimes* **h- w-**] radio waves or other electromagnetic radiation resulting from the oscillations of electricity in a conductor

he's (hēz) *contr.* **1** he is **2** he has

hes·i·tant (hez′i tənt) ***adj.*** hesitating or undecided; doubtful —**hes′i·tan·cy** ***n.*** —**hes′i·tant·ly** ***adv.***

hes′i·tate′ (-tāt′) ***vi.*** **-tat′ed, -tat′ing** ⟦< L *haerere*, to stick⟧ **1** to stop because of indecision **2** to pause **3** to be reluctant *[I hesitate to ask]* **4** to pause continually in speaking —**hes′i·tat′ing·ly** ***adv.*** —**hes′i·ta′tion** ***n.***

hetero- ⟦Gr *hetero-*⟧ *combining form* other, another, different: also **heter-**

het·er·o·dox (het′ər ə däks′) ***adj.*** ⟦< prec. + Gr *doxa*, opinion⟧ opposed to the usual beliefs, esp. in religion; unorthodox —**het′er·o·dox′y**, *pl.* **-ies**, ***n.***

het·er·o·ge·ne·ous (het′ər ə jē′nē əs) ***adj.*** ⟦< HETERO- + Gr *genos*, a kind⟧ **1** differing in structure, quality, etc.; dissimilar **2** composed of unlike parts

het′er·o·sex′u·al (-sek′sho͞o əl) ***adj.*** **1** of or characterized by sexual desire for those of the opposite sex **2** *Biol.* of different sexes —***n.*** a heterosexual individual —**het′er·o·sex·u·al′i·ty** ***n.***

heu·ris·tic (hyo͞o ris′tik) ***adj.*** ⟦< Gr *heuriskein*, invent⟧ helping to learn, as by a method of education based on following rules to find answers

hew (hyo͞o) ***vt.*** **hewed**, **hewed** or **hewn**, **hew′ing** ⟦OE *heawan*⟧ **1** to chop or cut with an ax, knife, etc.; hack **2** to make or shape in this way —***vi.*** to conform (*to* a line, rule, principle, etc.)

hex (heks) ***n.*** ⟦Pennsylvania Ger *hexe*, witch⟧ a sign, spell, etc. believed to bring bad luck —***vt.*** to cause to have bad luck

hexa- ⟦< Gr *hex*, six⟧ *combining form* six: also **hex-**

hex·a·gon (heks′ə gän′) ***n.*** ⟦< Gr *hex*, six + *gōnia*, an angle⟧ a plane figure with six angles and six sides —**hex·ag·o·nal** (hek sag′ə nəl) ***adj.***

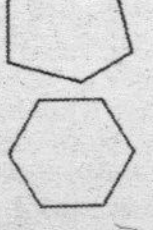

HEXAGONS

hex·am·e·ter (hek sam′ə tər) ***n.*** ⟦see HEXA- & METER¹⟧ a line of verse containing six metrical feet

hey (hā) ***interj.*** used to attract attention, express surprise, etc.

hey·day (hā′dā′) ***n.*** the time of greatest health, vigor, etc.; prime

Hg ⟦L *hydrargyrum*⟧ *Chem. symbol for* mercury

hgt *abbrev.* height

HHS *abbrev.* (Department of) Health and Human Services

hi (hī) ***interj.*** [Inf.] hello

HI Hawaii

Hi·a·le·ah (hī′ə lē′ə) city in SE Florida.: pop. 188,000

hi·a·tus (hī āt′əs) ***n.***, *pl.* **-tus·es** or **-tus** ⟦L < *hiare*, to gape⟧ **1** a gap or break, as where a part is missing **2** any gap or interruption, as in time

hi·ba·chi (hi bä′chē) ***n.***, *pl.* **-chis** ⟦Jpn < *hi*, fire + *bachi*, bowl⟧ a small charcoal-burning grill

hi·ber·nate (hī′bər nāt′) ***vi.*** **-nat′ed, -nat′ing** ⟦< L *hibernus*, wintry⟧ to spend the winter in a dormant state —**hi′ber·na′tion** ***n.***

hi·bis·cus (hī bis′kəs, hi-) ***n.*** ⟦< L⟧ a plant of the mallow family, with large, colorful flowers

hic·cup (hik′up′, -əp) ***n.*** ⟦echoic⟧ a sudden contraction of the diaphragm that causes the glottis to close, producing an abrupt sound —***vi.*** **-cuped′** or **-cupped′**, **-cup′ing** or **-cup′ping** to make a hiccup Also sp. **hic′cough′**

hick (hik) ***n.*** ⟦altered < *Richard*⟧ [Inf.] an awkward, unsophisticated person regarded as typical of rural areas: a contemptuous term

hick·ey (hik′ē) ***n.***, *pl.* **-eys** or **-ies** [Inf.] any device or gadget

hick·o·ry (hik′ə rē, hik′rē) ***n.***, *pl.* **-ries** ⟦< AmInd *pawcohiccora*⟧ **1** a North American tree of the walnut family **2** its hard, tough wood **3** its hard, edible nut: usually **hickory nut**

hid·den (hid′'n) ***vt.***, ***vi.*** ⟦OE *gehydd*⟧ *alt. pp. of* HIDE¹ —***adj.*** concealed; secret

hide¹ (hīd) ***vt.*** **hid** (hid), **hid′den** or **hid**, **hid′ing** ⟦OE *hydan*⟧ **1** to put or keep out of sight; conceal **2** to keep secret **3** to keep from sight by obscuring, etc. —***vi.*** to conceal oneself

hide² (hīd) ***n.*** ⟦OE *hid*⟧ an animal skin or pelt, either raw or tanned

hide′a·way′ ***n.*** [Inf.] a place where one can hide, be secluded, etc.

hide′bound′ ***adj.*** obstinately conservative and narrow-minded

hid·e·ous (hid′ē əs) ***adj.*** ⟦< OFr *hide*, fright⟧ horrible; very ugly; dreadful —**hid′e·ous·ly** ***adv.*** —**hid′e·ous·ness** ***n.***

hide′-out′ ***n.*** [Inf.] a hiding place

hie (hī) ***vi.***, ***vt.*** **hied**, **hie′ing** or **hy′ing** ⟦OE *higian*⟧ to hasten: usually used reflexively

hi·er·ar·chy (hī′ər är′kē) ***n.***, *pl.* **-chies** ⟦< Gr *hieros*, sacred + *archos*, ruler⟧ **1** church government by clergy in graded ranks **2** the highest officials in such a system **3** a group of persons or things arranged in order of rank, grade, etc. —**hi′er·ar′chi·cal** (-ki kəl) ***adj.***

hi·er·o·glyph·ic (hī′ər ō glif′ik, hī′rō-) ***n.*** ⟦< Gr *hieros*, sacred + *glyphein*, to carve⟧ **1** a picture or symbol representing a word, syllable, or sound, used by the ancient Egyptians and others **2** [*usually pl.*] picture writing **3** a symbol, etc. that is hard to understand —*adj.* of or like hieroglyphics

hi·er·o·phant (hī′ər ō fant′) ***n.*** ⟦< Gr *hieros*, sacred + *phainein*, to show⟧ in ancient Greece, a priest of a mystery cult

hi-fi (hī′fī′) ***n.*** a radio, phonograph, etc. having high fidelity —***adj.*** of or having high fidelity of sound reproduction

high (hī) ***adj.*** ⟦OE *heah*⟧ **1** lofty; tall **2** extending upward a (specified) distance **3** reaching to, situated at, or done from a height **4** above others in rank, position, etc.; superior **5** grave [*high* treason] **6** greater in size, amount, degree, etc. than usual [*high* prices] **7** luxurious [*high* living] **8** raised in pitch [a *high* note] **9** slightly tainted: said of meat, esp. game **10** excited [*high* spirits] **11** [Slang] *a*) drunk *b*) under the influence of a drug —***adv.*** in or to a high level, place, degree, etc. —***n.*** **1** a high level, place, etc. **2** an area of high barometric pressure **3** the gear of a motor vehicle, etc. producing the greatest speed **4** [Slang] a condition of euphoria induced as by drugs —**high and low** everywhere —**high on** [Inf.] enthusiastic about —**on high** in heaven

high′ball′ ***n.*** whiskey or brandy mixed with water, soda water, ginger ale, etc.

high′born′ ***adj.*** of noble birth

high′boy′ ***n.*** a high chest of drawers mounted on legs

high′brow′ ***n.*** one having or affecting highly cultivated tastes; intellectual —***adj.*** of or for a highbrow

high′chair′ ***n.*** a baby's chair with long legs and, usually, a tray for food

high′-def′i·ni′tion ***adj.*** designating TV transmission with greater clarity of image and sound than that of standard television

high′-end′ ***adj.*** [Inf.] expensive and of very high quality

high′er-up′ ***n.*** [Inf.] a person of higher rank or position

high′fa·lu′tin (-fə lo͞ot′′n) ***adj.*** [Inf.] pretentious or pompous: also sp. **high′fa·lu′ting**

high fidelity in radio, sound recording, etc., nearly exact reproduction of sound

high′-five′ ***n.*** [Inf.] a slapping of the upraised open hand of another person, as in celebration

high′-flown′ ***adj.*** **1** extravagantly ambitious **2** bombastic

high frequency any radio frequency between 3 and 30 megahertz

High German the group of West Germanic dialects spoken in central and S Germany

high′hand′ed ***adj.*** overbearing —**high′hand′ed·ly** ***adv.*** —**high′hand′ed·ness** ***n.***

high′-hat′ (-hat′; *for v., usually*, -hat′) ***adj.*** [Slang] snobbish —***vt.*** **-hat′ted, -hat′ting** [Slang] to snub

high′land (-lənd) ***n.*** a region with many hills or mountains —**the Highlands** mountainous region occupying most of N Scotland —**High′land·er** ***n.***

high′-lev′el ***adj.*** **1** of or by persons of high office or rank **2** in a high office

high′light′ ***n.*** **1** a part on which light is brightest: also **high light** **2** the most important or interesting part, scene, etc. —***vt.*** **1** to give highlights to **2** to give prominence to; emphasize

high′light′er ***n.*** a pen with a broad felt tip for marking passages as in a textbook

high′ly ***adv.*** **1** very much **2** favorably **3** at a high level, wage, etc.

high′-mind′ed ***adj.*** having high ideals, principles, etc. —**high′-mind′ed·ly** ***adv.***

high′ness ***n.*** **1** height **2** [**H-**] a title used in speaking to or of a member of a royal family

high′-pres′sure ***adj.*** **1** having or withstanding high pressure **2** using forcefully persuasive or insistent methods —***vt.*** **-sured, -sur·ing** [Inf.] to urge with such methods

high′-pro′file′ ***adj.*** well-known, highly publicized, etc.

high′-rise′ ***adj.*** tall and having many stories —***n.*** a high-rise building

high road **1** [Chiefly Brit.] a highway **2** an easy or direct way Also **high′road′** ***n.***

high roller **1** a person who gambles for high stakes **2** a person who spends money freely

high school a secondary school that includes grades 10, 11, 12, and sometimes 9

high seas open ocean waters outside the territorial limits of any nation

high sign a secret signal, given as in warning

high′-spir′it·ed (-spir′i tid) ***adj.*** **1** courageous **2** spirited; fiery **3** lively or merry

high′-strung′ ***adj.*** highly sensitive or nervous and tense

high tech (tek) **1** of specialized, complex technology: in full **high technology** **2** furnishings, fashions, etc. whose design or look suggests industrial use —**high′-tech′** ***adj.***

high′-ten′sion ***adj.*** having or carrying a high voltage

high tide the highest level to which the tide rises

high time time beyond the proper time but before it is too late

high′way′ ***n.*** **1** a public road **2** a main road; thoroughfare

high′way·man (-mən) ***n.***, *pl.* **-men** (-mən) a man who formerly robbed travelers on a highway

high wire a cable stretched high above the ground, on which aerialists perform

hi·jack (hī′jak′) ***vt.*** **1** to steal (goods in transit, etc.) by force **2** to seize control forcibly of (an aircraft, etc.), esp. in order to go to a nonscheduled destination —**hi′jack′er** ***n.***

hike (hīk) ***vi.*** **hiked, hik′ing** ⟦< dial. *heik*⟧ to take a long walk —***vt.*** [Inf.] **1** to pull up; hoist **2** to raise (prices, etc.) —***n.*** **1** a long walk **2** [Inf.] a rise —**hik′er** ***n.***

hi·lar·i·ous (hi ler′ē əs) ***adj.*** ⟦< Gr

hilaros, cheerful⟧ **1** noisily merry **2** very funny —**hi·lar'i·ous·ly** ***adv.*** —**hi·lar'i·ty** (-i tē) ***n.***

hill (hil) ***n.*** ⟦OE *hyll*⟧ **1** a natural raised part of the earth's surface, smaller than a mountain **2** a small pile, heap, or mound

hill'bil'ly ***n.***, *pl.* **-lies** ⟦prec. + *Billy*⟧ [Inf.] one who lives in or comes from the mountains or backwoods of the South, specif. Appalachia: sometimes a contemptuous term

hill'side' ***n.*** the side of a hill

hill'top' ***n.*** the top of a hill

hill'y ***adj.*** **-i·er**, **-i·est** full of hills —**hill'i·ness** ***n.***

hilt (hilt) ***n.*** ⟦OE⟧ the handle of a sword, dagger, tool, etc.

him (him) ***pron.*** ⟦OE⟧ *objective form of* HE

Hi·ma·la·yas (him'ə lā'əz) mountain system of SC Asia, mostly in India & China —**Hi'ma·la'yan** ***adj.***

him·self' ***pron.*** a form of HE, used as an intensive *[*he went *himself]*, as a reflexive *[*he hurt *himself]*, or with the meaning "his true self" *[*he is not *himself* today*]*

hind[1] (hīnd) ***adj.*** ⟦see HINDER[2]⟧ back; rear

hind[2] (hīnd) ***n.*** ⟦OE⟧ the female of the red deer

Hind *abbrev.* **1** Hindi **2** Hindu

hin·der[1] (hin'dər) ***vt.*** ⟦OE *hindrian*⟧ **1** to keep back; stop **2** to impede; thwart

hind·er[2] (hīn'dər) ***adj.*** ⟦OE⟧ [Now Rare] rear

Hin·di (hin'dē) ***n.*** the main (and official) language of India

hind'most' ***adj.*** farthest back; last

hind'quar'ter ***n.*** either of the two hind legs and the adjoining part of a carcass of veal, beef, etc.

hin·drance (hin'drəns) ***n.*** **1** the act of hindering **2** an obstacle

hind'sight' ***n.*** ability to see, after the event, what should have been done

Hin·du (hin'do͞o') ***n.*** a follower of Hinduism —***adj.*** designating or of the Hindus or Hinduism

Hin'du·ism' ***n.*** the principal religion of India

Hin·du·stan (hin'do͞o stan') **1** region in N India **2** the entire Indian subcontinent **3** the republic of India

hinge (hinj) ***n.*** ⟦< ME *hengen*, to hang⟧ **1** a joint on which a door, lid, etc. swings **2** a natural joint, as of the shell of a clam —***vt.*** **hinged**, **hing'ing** to attach by a hinge —***vi.*** to hang as on a hinge; depend

hint (hint) ***n.*** ⟦prob. < OE *hentan*, to grasp⟧ a slight indication; indirect suggestion —***vt.***, ***vi.*** to give a hint (of)

hin·ter·land (hin'tər land') ***n.*** ⟦Ger⟧ **1** the land behind that bordering a coast or river **2** a remote area

hip[1] (hip) ***n.*** ⟦OE *hype*⟧ the part of the body around the joint formed by each thighbone and the pelvis

hip[2] (hip) ***adj.*** **hip'per**, **hip'pest** ⟦< ? HEP⟧ [Slang] **1** sophisticated; aware; fashionable **2** of hippies

hip'-hop' ***n.*** a style of music and dance that originated among inner-city African-American youths in the 1980s

hip·pie (hip'ē) ***n.*** [Slang] a young person of the 1960s and 1970s who, in a state of alienation from conventional society, turned variously to mysticism, psychedelic drugs, etc.

hip·po (hip'ō) ***n.***, *pl.* **-pos** [Inf.] HIPPOPOTAMUS

Hip·poc·ra·tes (hi päk'rə tēz') 460?-377? B.C.; Gr. physician

Hip·po·crat·ic oath (hip'ə krat'ik) the oath, attributed to Hippocrates, generally taken by medical school graduates: it sets forth their ethical code

hip·po·drome (hip'ə drōm') ***n.*** ⟦< Gr *hippos*, horse + *dromos*, course⟧ an arena for circuses, games, etc.

hip·po·pot·a·mus (hip'ə pät'ə məs) ***n.***, *pl.* **-a·mus·es**, **-a·mi'** (-mī'), or **-a·mus** ⟦< Gr *hippos*, a horse + *potamos*, river⟧ a large, plant-eating mammal with a heavy, thick-skinned body and short legs: it lives chiefly in or near African rivers

hip·py (hip'ē) ***n.***, *pl.* **-pies** *alt. sp. of* HIPPIE

hire (hīr) ***n.*** ⟦< OE *hyr*, wages⟧ **1** the amount paid in hiring **2** a hiring —***vt.*** **hired**, **hir'ing** to pay for the services of (a person) or the use of (a thing) —**hire out** to work for pay

hire'ling (-liŋ) ***n.*** one who will follow anyone's orders for pay; mercenary

Hi·ro·shi·ma (hir'ə shē'mə, hi rō'shi mə) seaport in SW Honshu, Japan: largely destroyed (Aug. 6, 1945) by a U.S. atomic bomb, the first ever used in warfare: pop. 1,077,000

hir·sute (hur'so͞ot', hər so͞ot') ***adj.*** ⟦L *hirsutus*⟧ hairy; shaggy

his (hiz) ***pron.*** ⟦OE⟧ that or those belonging to him: poss. form of HE *[his* are better*]* —***poss. pronominal adj.*** of, belonging to, or done by him

His·pan·ic (hi span'ik) ***adj.*** **1** Spanish or Spanish-and-Portuguese **2** of or relating to Hispanics —***n.*** a Spanish-speaking person of Latin American origin who lives in the U.S. For *adj.* 2 and the *n.*, *Latino* and *Latina* are now often preferred

His·pan·io·la (his'pən yō'lə) island in the West Indies, between Cuba & Puerto Rico

hiss (his) ***vi.*** ⟦echoic⟧ **1** to make a sound like that of a prolonged *s* **2** to show disapproval by hissing —***vt.*** to say or indicate by hissing —***n.*** the act or sound of hissing

his·sy fit (his'ē) [Dial.] a fit of anger: usually in **have** (or **throw**) **a hissy fit**: also **his'sy** ***n.***, *pl.* **-sies**

hist[1] (st) ***interj.*** [Inf.] used to attract attention

hist[2] *abbrev.* history

his·ta·mine (his'tə mēn', -min') ***n.*** ⟦< Gr *histos*, web + AMMONIA⟧ an ammonia derivative in all organic matter: it is released in allergic reactions, lowers the blood pressure, etc.

his·tol·o·gy (his täl′ə jē) ***n.*** ⟦< Gr *histos*, web + -LOGY⟧ *Biol.* the microscopic study of tissue structure —**his·tol′o·gist** ***n.***

his·to·ri·an (his tôr′ē ən) ***n.*** a writer of, or authority on, history

his·tor′ic (-ik) ***adj.*** having, or likely to have, lasting importance

his·tor′i·cal (-i kəl) ***adj.*** **1** of or concerned with history **2** based on people or events of the past **3** established by history; factual —**his·tor′i·cal·ly** ***adv.***

historical present the present tense used for the narration of past events

his·to·ric·i·ty (his′tə ris′ə tē) ***n.*** historical authenticity

his·to·ri·og·ra·phy (his tôr′ē äg′rə fē) ***n.*** the study of the techniques of historical research

his·to·ry (his′tə rē, -trē) ***n.***, *pl.* **-ries** ⟦< Gr *histōr*, knowing⟧ **1** an account of what has happened, esp. in the life of a people, country, etc. **2** all recorded past events **3** the branch of knowledge that deals systematically with the past **4** a known or recorded past *[the odd history of his coat]*

his·tri·on·ic (his′trē än′ik) ***adj.*** ⟦< L *histrio*, actor⟧ **1** of acting or actors **2** overacted or overacting; affected

his′tri·on′ics ***pl.n.*** [*sometimes with sing. v.*] **1** dramatics **2** an artificial manner, display of emotion, etc.

hit (hit) ***vt.***, ***vi.*** **hit**, **hit′ting** ⟦< ON *hitta*, meet with⟧ **1** to come against (something) with force; knock **2** to give a blow (to); strike **3** to strike with a missile **4** to affect strongly *[a town hard hit by floods]* **5** to come (upon) by accident or after search **6** to arrive at *[stocks hit a new high]* **7** *Baseball* to get (a hit) —***n.*** **1** a blow that strikes its mark **2** a collision **3** a successful and popular song, book, etc. **4** an instance of finding particular data in a computer search **5** [Slang] a murder **6** [Slang] a dose of a drug, a drink of liquor, etc. **7** *Baseball* BASE HIT —**hit it off** to get along well together —**hit′ter** ***n.***

hit-and-run (hit′'n run′) ***adj.*** hitting a person, car, etc. with a moving vehicle and fleeing the scene immediately: also **hit′-skip′**

hitch (hich) ***vi.*** ⟦ME *hicchen*⟧ **1** to move jerkily **2** to become fastened or caught **3** [Slang] to hitchhike —***vt.*** **1** to move, pull, etc. with jerks **2** to fasten with a hook, knot, etc. —***n.*** **1** a tug; jerk **2** a limp **3** a hindrance; obstacle **4** a fastening or catch **5** [Slang] a period of time served **6** a kind of knot

hitch′hike′ ***vi.*** **-hiked′**, **-hik′ing** to travel by asking for rides from passing drivers —**hitch′hik′er** ***n.***

hith·er (hi*th*′ər) ***adv.*** ⟦< OE *hider*⟧ to this place; here

hith′er·to′ ***adv.*** until this time

Hit·ler (hit′lər), **Ad·olf** (ad′ôlf′, ä′dôlf′) 1889-1945; Nazi dictator of Germany (1933-45), born in Austria —**Hit·ler′i·an** (-lir′ē ən) ***adj.***

hit man [Inf.] a hired murderer

hit′-or-miss′ ***adj.*** haphazard; random

HIV ***n.*** a retrovirus that infects human T cells and causes AIDS

hive (hīv) ***n.*** ⟦< OE *hyfe*⟧ **1** a shelter for a colony of bees; beehive **2** a colony of bees; swarm **3** a crowd of busy people **4** a place of great activity —***vt.*** **hived**, **hiv′ing** to gather (bees) into a hive —***vi.*** to enter a hive

hives (hīvz) ***pl.n.*** ⟦orig. Scot dial.⟧ [*with sing. or pl. v.*] an allergic skin condition characterized by itching, burning, and the formation of smooth patches

HMO ***n.***, *pl.* **HMO's** ⟦*h*(*ealth*) *m*(*aintenance*) *o*(*rganization*)⟧ a healthcare system in which an organization hires medical professionals to provide services for its subscribers

HMS *abbrev.* **1** Her (or His) Majesty's Service **2** Her (or His) Majesty's Ship

hoa·gie or **hoa·gy** (hō′gē) ***n.***, *pl.* **-gies** HERO SANDWICH

hoard (hôrd) ***n.*** ⟦OE *hord*⟧ a supply stored up and hidden —***vi.***, ***vt.*** to accumulate and store away (money, goods, etc.) —**hoard′er** ***n.*** —**hoard′ing** ***n.***

hoar·frost (hôr′frôst′) ***n.*** FROST (sense 2)

hoarse (hôrs) ***adj.*** **hoars′er**, **hoars′est** ⟦OE *has*⟧ **1** harsh and grating in sound **2** having a rough, husky voice —**hoarse′ly** ***adv.*** —**hoarse′ness** ***n.***

hoar·y (hôr′ē) ***adj.*** **-i·er**, **-i·est** ⟦< OE har⟧ **1** white or gray **2** having white or gray hair from old age **3** very old Also **hoar** —**hoar′i·ness** ***n.***

hoax (hōks) ***n.*** ⟦< ? HOCUS-POCUS⟧ a trick or fraud; esp., a practical joke —***vt.*** to deceive with a hoax

hob·ble (häb′əl) ***vi.*** **-bled**, **-bling** ⟦ME *hobelen*⟧ to go unsteadily; limp —***vt.*** **1** to cause to limp **2** to hamper (a horse, etc.) by tying two feet together **3** to hinder —***n.*** **1** a limp **2** a rope, etc. used to hobble a horse

hob·by (häb′ē) ***n.***, *pl.* **-bies** ⟦ME *hobi*⟧ **1** HOBBYHORSE **2** something that one likes to do in one's spare time —**hob′by·ist** ***n.***

hob′by·horse′ ***n.*** **1** a child's toy consisting of a stick with a horse's head **2** ROCKING HORSE **3** an idea with which one is preoccupied

hob·gob·lin (häb′gäb′lin) ***n.*** ⟦*hob*, elf or goblin + GOBLIN⟧ **1** an elf **2** a bugbear

hob′nail′ ***n.*** ⟦*hob*, a peg + NAIL⟧ a short nail with a broad head, put on the soles of heavy shoes to prevent wear or slipping —***vt.*** to put hobnails on

hob′nob′ (-näb′) ***vi.*** **-nobbed′**, **-nob′bing** ⟦< ME *habben*, have + *nabben*, not to have⟧ to be on close terms (*with*)

ho·bo (hō′bō) ***n.***, *pl.* **-bos** or **-boes** **1** a migratory worker **2** a tramp

Ho Chi Minh City (hō′chē′min′) seaport in S Vietnam: formerly (as *Saigon*) capital of South Vietnam (1954-76): pop. 3,420,000

hock[1] (häk) ***n.*** ⟦< OE *hoh*, heel⟧ the joint bending backward in the hind leg of a horse, ox, etc.

hock[2] (häk) ***vt.***, ***n.*** ⟦< Du *hok*, prison⟧ [Slang] PAWN[1] —**in** (or **out of**) **hock** [Slang] in (or out of) debt

hock·ey (häk′ē) ***n.*** ⟦prob. < OFr *hoquet*,

bent stick⟧ **1** a team game played on ice skates, with curved sticks and a hard rubber disk (*puck*) **2** a similar game played on foot on a field, with a small ball; field hockey

hock′shop′ *n.* [Slang] PAWNSHOP

ho·cus-po·cus (hō′kəs pō′kəs) *n.* ⟦imitation L⟧ **1** meaningless words used as a formula by conjurers **2** a magician's trick or tricks **3** trickery

hod (häd) *n.* ⟦prob. < MDu *hodde*⟧ **1** a V-shaped device with a long handle, used for carrying bricks, mortar, etc. on the shoulder **2** a coal scuttle

hodge·podge (häj′päj′) *n.* ⟦< OFr *hochepot*, a stew⟧ a jumbled mixture

Hodg·kin's disease (häj′kinz) ⟦after T. *Hodgkin*, 19th-c. Eng physician⟧ a chronic disease of unknown cause characterized by progressive enlargement of the lymph nodes

GARDEN HOE

hoe (hō) *n.* ⟦< OHG *houwan*, to cut⟧ a tool with a thin, flat blade set across the end of a long handle, used for weeding, loosening soil, etc. —*vt.*, *vi.* **hoed**, **hoe′ing** to cultivate, dig, weed, etc. with a hoe

hoe′cake′ *n.* a thin bread made of cornmeal

hoe′down′ *n.* **1** a lively, rollicking dance **2** a party with such dances

hog (hôg, häg) *n.* ⟦OE *hogg*⟧ **1** any swine, esp. a domesticated adult ready for market **2** [Inf.] a selfish, greedy, gluttonous, or filthy person —*vt.* **hogged**, **hog′ging** [Slang] to take all of or an unfair share of —**go** (**the**) **whole hog** [Slang] to go all the way —**high on** (or **off**) **the hog** [Inf.] in a luxurious or costly way —**hog′gish** *adj.* —**hog′gish·ly** *adv.*

ho·gan (hō′gôn′, -gən) *n.* ⟦< AmInd⟧ a Navajo Indian dwelling, built of earth walls supported by timbers

hogs·head (hôgz′hed′) *n.* **1** a large barrel or cask holding from 63 to 140 gallons **2** a liquid measure, esp. one equal to 63 gallons

hog′tie′ *vt.* **-tied′**, **-ty′ing** or **-tie′ing** **1** to tie the four feet or the hands and feet of **2** [Inf.] to make incapable of effective action

hog′wash′ *n.* **1** refuse fed to hogs; swill **2** insincere talk, writing, etc.

ho-hum (hō′hum′) *interj.* used to show boredom: an utterance suggesting a yawn —*adj.* [Inf.] boring or tiresome

hoi pol·loi (hoi′pə loi′) ⟦Gr, the many⟧ the common people; the masses

hoist (hoist) *vt.* ⟦< Du *hijschen*⟧ to raise aloft; lift, esp. with a pulley, crane, etc. —*n.* **1** a hoisting **2** an apparatus for lifting; elevator; tackle

hoke (hōk) *vt.* **hoked**, **hok′ing** ⟦< fol.⟧ [Slang] to treat in a sentimental or crudely comic way: usually with *up* —**hok′ey** *adj.*

ho·kum (hō′kəm) *n.* ⟦< HOCUS(-POCUS)⟧ [Slang] **1** trite sentiment, crude humor, etc. **2** nonsense or humbug

hold[1] (hōld) *vt.* **held**, **hold′ing** ⟦OE *haldan*⟧ **1** to keep in the hands, arms, etc.; grasp **2** to keep in a certain position or condition **3** to restrain or control; keep back **4** to possess; occupy [to *hold* an office] **5** to guard; defend [*hold* the fort] **6** to carry on (a meeting, etc.) **7** to contain [the jar *holds* a pint] **8** to regard; consider [I *hold* the story to be true] **9** *Law* to decide; decree —*vi.* **1** to go on being firm, loyal, etc. **2** to remain unbroken or unyielding [the rope *held*] **3** to be true or valid [this rule *holds* for any case] **4** to continue [the wind *held* steady] —*n.* **1** a grasping or seizing; grip **2** a thing to hold on by **3** a dominating force [she has a *hold* over him] —**catch** (**get**, **lay**, or **take**) **hold of** to take, seize, acquire, etc. —**hold forth** to preach; lecture —**hold on** [Inf.] stop! wait! —**hold out** **1** to last; endure **2** to stand firm **3** to offer **4** [Inf.] to refuse to give (what is to be given) —**hold over** **1** to postpone **2** to keep for an additional period —**hold up** **1** to prop up **2** to show **3** to last; endure **4** to stop; delay **5** to stop forcibly and rob —**hold′er** *n.*

hold[2] (hōld) *n.* ⟦< HOLE or < MDu *hol*⟧ **1** the interior of a ship below decks, where the cargo is carried **2** the compartment for cargo in an aircraft

hold′ing *n.* **1** land, esp. a farm, rented from another **2** [*pl.*] property owned, as stocks and bonds

hold′o′ver *n.* [Inf.] one staying on from a previous period

hold′up′ *n.* **1** a delay **2** the act of stopping forcibly and robbing

hole (hōl) *n.* ⟦OE *hol*⟧ **1** a hollow place; cavity **2** an animal's burrow; den **3** a small, dingy, squalid place **4** an opening in anything; break; gap; tear **5** *Golf a*) a small cup sunk into a green, into which the ball is to be hit *b*) a section of a course including the tee, fairway, and green —**hole up** [Inf.] **1** to hibernate **2** to shut oneself in **3** to hide out —**in the hole** [Inf.] financially embarrassed or behind

-hol·ic (häl′ik) *combining form* -AHOLIC

hol·i·day (häl′ə dā′) *n.* **1** a religious festival; holy day **2** a day of freedom from labor, often one set aside by law **3** [*often pl.*] [Chiefly Brit.] a vacation —*adj.* of or for a holiday; joyous; gay

ho·li·er-than-thou (hō′lē ər *th*an *th*ou′) *adj.* annoyingly self-righteous

ho·li·ness (hō′lē nis) *n.* **1** a being holy **2** [H-] a title of the pope

ho·lis·tic (hō lis′tik) *adj.* of or dealing with wholes or integrated systems rather than with their parts —**ho·lis′ti·cal·ly** *adv.*

Hol·land (häl′ənd) NETHERLANDS —**Hol′land·er** *n.*

hol·lan·daise sauce (häl′ən dāz′) ⟦Fr, of Holland⟧ a creamy sauce made of butter, egg yolks, lemon juice, etc.

hol·ler (häl′ər) ***vi., vt., n.*** [Inf.] shout or yell

hol·low (häl′ō′) ***adj.*** ⟦OE *holh*⟧ **1** having a cavity inside; not solid **2** shaped like a bowl; concave **3** sunken *[hollow cheeks]* **4** empty or worthless *[hollow praise]* **5** hungry **6** deep-toned and muffled **—*n.*** **1** a hollow place; cavity **2** a valley **—*vt., vi.*** to make or become hollow **—hol′low·ness *n.***

hol·ly (häl′ē) ***n., pl.*** **-lies** ⟦OE *holegn*⟧ an evergreen shrub or tree with stiff, glossy, sharp-pointed leaves and bright-red berries

hol′ly·hock′ (-häk′) ***n.*** ⟦< OE *halig*, holy + *hoc*, mallow⟧ a tall plant of the mallow family, with large, showy flowers

Hol·ly·wood (häl′ē wood′) section of Los Angeles, California, once the site of many U.S. film studios

Holmes (hōmz, hōlmz), **Ol·i·ver Wen·dell** (äl′ə vər wen′dəl) 1841-1935; associate justice, U.S. Supreme Court (1902-32)

hol·o·caust (häl′ə kôst′, hō′lə-) ***n.*** ⟦< Gr *holos*, whole + *kaustos*, burnt⟧ a great destruction of life, esp. by fire **—the Holocaust** [*also* **the h-**] the systematic killing of millions of European Jews by the Nazis

Hol·o·cene (häl′ō sēn′, hō′lə-) ***adj.*** ⟦< Gr *holos*, whole + *kainos*, recent⟧ designating the present epoch of geologic time

hol·o·gram (häl′ə gram′, hō′lə-) ***n.*** a photographic image produced by holography

hol′o·graph′ (-graf′) ***n.*** ⟦< Gr *holos*, whole + *graphein*, to write⟧ a document, letter, etc. in the handwriting of the person under whose name it appears

hol′o·graph′ic (-graf′ik) ***adj.*** **1** of or in the form of a holograph **2** of holography

ho·log·ra·phy (hō läg′rə fē) ***n.*** ⟦< Gr *holos*, whole + -GRAPHY⟧ a method of making three-dimensional photographs using a laser beam

Hol·stein (hōl′stēn′, -stīn′) ***n.*** ⟦after the region of Schleswig-*Holstein*, Germany⟧ a breed of large, black-and-white dairy cattle

hol·ster (hōl′stər) ***n.*** ⟦Du⟧ a pistol case attached to a belt, saddle, etc.

ho·ly (hō′lē) ***adj.*** **-li·er** or **-li·est** ⟦OE *halig*⟧ [*often* **H-**] **1** dedicated to religious use; sacred **2** spiritually pure; sinless **3** deserving deep respect, awe, etc.

Holy Communion a Christian rite in which bread and wine are consecrated and received as the body and blood of Jesus or as symbols of them

Holy Land PALESTINE

Holy Roman Empire empire of WC Europe, from A.D. 962 until 1806

Holy Spirit (or **Ghost**) the third person of the Trinity; spirit of God

hom·age (häm′ij, äm′-) ***n.*** ⟦< L *homo*, man⟧ anything given or done to show reverence, honor, etc.

hom·burg (häm′bərg) ***n.*** ⟦after *Homburg*, Prussia⟧ a man's felt hat with a crown dented front to back and a stiff, curved brim

home (hōm) ***n.*** ⟦OE *hām*⟧ **1** the place where one lives **2** the place where one was born or reared **3** a place thought of as home **4** a household and its affairs **5** an institution for orphans, the aged, etc. **6** the natural environment of an animal, plant, etc. **7** HOME PLATE **—*adj.*** **1** of one's home or country; domestic **2** central *[home office]* **—*adv.*** **1** at, to, or in the direction of home **2** to the point aimed at *[to drive a nail home]* **—at home** **1** in one's home **2** at ease **—bring home to** to impress upon **—home′less *adj.*** **—home′like′ *adj.***

home′boy′ ***masc.n.*** [Slang] **1** a boy or man from one's neighborhood, town, etc. **2** a close male friend **—home′girl′ *fem.n.***

home′-care′ ***adj.*** of medical care, etc. provided in a person's home

home economics the science and art of homemaking, nutrition, etc.

home′land′ ***n.*** the country in which one was born or makes one's home

home′ly ***adj.*** **-li·er, -li·est** **1** suitable for home life; everyday **2** crude **3** plain or unattractive **—home′li·ness *n.***

home′made′ ***adj.*** made, or as if made, at home

home′mak′er ***n.*** one who manages a household

ho·me·op·a·thy (hō′mē äp′ə thē) ***n.*** the treatment of a disease using, in small doses, drugs that produce symptoms like those of the disease **—ho′me·o·path′ic** (-ə path′ik) ***adj.***

home page a website or the initial page of a website

home plate *Baseball* the base that the batter stands beside: it is the last base touched in scoring a run

Ho·mer (hō′mər) semilegendary Gr. epic poet of *c.* 8th c. B.C. **—Ho·mer·ic** (hō mer′ik) ***adj.***

home run *Baseball* a hit that allows the batter to touch all bases and score a run: also [Inf.] **hom′er *n.***

home′sick′ ***adj.*** unhappy at being away from home **—home′sick′ness *n.***

home′spun′ ***n.*** coarse loosely-woven cloth **—*adj.*** **1** spun at home **2** plain; homely

home′stead′ (-sted′) ***n.*** **1** a place where a family makes its home **2** a tract of land granted by the U.S. government to a settler **—home′stead′er *n.***

home′stretch′ ***n.*** **1** the part of a racetrack between the last turn and the finish line **2** the final part of any undertaking

home′ward ***adv., adj.*** toward home *[homeward bound]*: also **home′wards *adv.***

home′work′ ***n.*** **1** work, esp. piecework, done at home **2** lessons to be done outside the classroom **3** preparation for some project: usually in **do one's homework**

home′y ***adj.*** **hom′i·er, hom′i·est** familiar, cozy, etc. **—home′y·ness *n.***

hom·i·cide (häm′ə sīd′) ***n.*** ⟦< L *homo*, a

man + *caedere*, to kill⟧ **1** the killing of one person by another **2** a person who kills another —**hom'i·ci'dal** ***adj.***

hom·i·let·ics (häm'ə let'iks) ***pl.n.*** ⟦see fol.⟧ the art of preparing and delivering sermons

hom·i·ly (häm'ə lē) ***n.***, *pl.* **-lies** ⟦< Gr *homilos*, assembly⟧ **1** a sermon **2** a solemn, moralizing talk or writing

homing pigeon a pigeon trained to find its way home from distant places

hom·i·nid (häm'ə nid) ***n.*** ⟦< L *homo*, a man⟧ a human, extinct or living

hom·i·ny (häm'ə nē) ***n.*** ⟦< AmInd⟧ dry corn hulled and coarsely ground (**hominy grits**): it is boiled for food

homo- ⟦< Gr *homos*⟧ *combining form* same, equal, like

ho·mo·ge·ne·ous (hō'mō jē'nē əs, häm'ō-) ***adj.*** ⟦see prec. & GENUS⟧ **1** the same in structure, quality, etc.; similar **2** composed of similar parts —**ho'mo·ge·ne'i·ty** (-jə nē'ə tē, -nā'-) ***n.***

ho·mog·e·nize (hə mäj'ə nīz') ***vt.*** **-nized'**, **-niz'ing** to make homogeneous, or more uniform throughout; specif., to process (milk) so that fat particles are so finely emulsified that the cream does not separate

hom·o·graph (häm'ə graf', hō'mə-) ***n.*** ⟦HOMO- + -GRAPH⟧ a word with the same spelling as another but with a different meaning and origin

ho·mol·o·gous (hō mäl'ə gəs) ***adj.*** ⟦Gr *homologos*, agreeing⟧ matching in structure, position, etc.

hom·o·nym (häm'ə nim') ***n.*** ⟦< Gr *homos*, same + *onyma*, name⟧ a word with the same pronunciation as another but with a different meaning, origin, and, usually, spelling

ho·mo·pho·bi·a (hō'mə fō'bē ə) ***n.*** ⟦HOMO(SEXUAL) + -PHOBIA⟧ irrational hatred or fear of homosexuals or homosexuality —**ho'mo·pho'bic** (-fō'bik) ***adj.***

Ho·mo sa·pi·ens (hō'mō sā'pē enz') ⟦ModL *homo*, man + *sapiens*, prp. of *sapere*, to know⟧ mankind; human being

ho·mo·sex·u·al (hō'mō sek'sho͞o əl, -mə-) ***adj.*** of or having sexual desire for those of the same sex —***n.*** a homosexual person —**ho'mo·sex'u·al'i·ty** (-al'ə tē) ***n.***

Hon *abbrev.* honorable

Hon·du·ras (hän do͝or'əs) country in Central America: 43,277 sq. mi.; pop. 4,444,000

hone (hōn) ***n.*** ⟦OE *han*, a stone⟧ a hard stone used to sharpen cutting tools —***vt.*** **honed**, **hon'ing** to sharpen, as with a hone

hon·est (än'ist) ***adj.*** ⟦< L *honor*, honor⟧ **1** truthful; trustworthy **2** *a)* sincere or fair *[honest* effort*]* *b)* gained by fair means *[*an *honest* living*]* **3** being what it seems **4** frank and open *[*an *honest* face*]* —**hon'est·ly** ***adv.*** —**hon'es·ty** ***n.***

hon·ey (hun'ē) ***n.***, *pl.* **-eys** ⟦OE *hunig*⟧ **1** a sweet, syrupy substance that bees make as food from the nectar of flowers **2** sweetness **3** darling

hon'ey·comb' ***n.*** the structure of six-sided wax cells made by bees to hold their honey or eggs —***vt.*** to cause to have holes like a honeycomb —***adj.*** of or like a honeycomb: also **hon'ey·combed'**

hon'ey·dew' melon a variety of melon with a smooth, whitish rind and sweet, greenish flesh

hon'ey·lo'cust ***n.*** a North American tree having featherlike foliage and large, twisted pods

hon'ey·moon' ***n.*** the vacation spent together by a newly married couple —***vi.*** to have or spend a honeymoon —**hon'ey·moon'er** ***n.***

hon'ey·suck'le (-suk'əl) ***n.*** a plant with small, fragrant flowers of red, yellow, or white

Hong Kong or **Hong·kong** (häŋ'käŋ', hôŋ'kôŋ') administrative region of China, on the South China Sea: formerly a British colony

honk (hôŋk, häŋk) ***n.*** ⟦echoic⟧ **1** the call of a wild goose **2** a similar sound, as of an automobile horn —***vi.***, ***vt.*** to make or cause to make such a sound

hon·ky-tonk (hôŋ'kē tôŋk') ***n.*** **1** [Old Slang] a cheap, noisy nightclub **2** [Slang] a bar, esp. one where country music if played —***adj.*** designating music played on a piano with a tinkling sound

Hon·o·lu·lu (hän'ə lo͞o'lo͞o) capital of Hawaii: seaport on Oahu: pop. 365,000

hon·or (än'ər) ***n.*** ⟦L⟧ **1** high regard or respect; esp., *a)* glory; fame *b)* good reputation **2** adherence to principles considered right; integrity **3** chastity **4** high rank; distinction **5** [**H-**] a title of certain officials, as judges **6** something done or given as a token of respect **7** a source of respect and fame —***vt.*** **1** to respect greatly **2** to show high regard for **3** to do or give something in honor of **4** to accept and pay *[*to *honor* a check*]* Brit. sp. **hon'our** —**do the honors** to act as host

hon'or·a·ble ***adj.*** **1** worthy of being honored **2** honest; upright **3** bringing honor —**hon'or·a·bly** ***adv.***

hon·o·rar·i·um (än'ə rer'ē əm) ***n.***, *pl.* **-ri·ums** or **-ri·a** (-ə) ⟦L⟧ a payment as to a professional person for services on which no fee is set

hon·or·ar·y (än'ə rer'ē) ***adj.*** **1** given as an honor **2** designating or in an office held as an honor, without service or pay —**hon'or·ar'i·ly** ***adv.***

hon'or·if'ic (-ə rif'ik) ***adj.*** ⟦< L *honor* + *facere*, to make⟧ conferring honor; showing respect

Hon·shu (hän'sho͞o') largest of the islands forming Japan

hood (ho͝od) ***n.*** ⟦OE *hod*⟧ **1** a covering for the head and neck, often part of a coat, etc. **2** anything resembling a hood, as the metal cover over an automobile engine —***vt.*** to cover as with a hood —**hood'ed** ***adj.***

-hood (ho͝od) ⟦OE *had*⟧ *suffix* **1** state or quality *[childhood]* **2** the whole group of *[priesthood]*

hood·lum (ho͝od'ləm, ho͞od'-) ***n.*** ⟦prob. < Ger dial. *hudilump*, wretch⟧ a lawless person, as a member of a gang of criminals

hoo·doo (ho͞o′do͞o′) ***n.***, *pl.* **-doos′** ⟦var. of VOODOO⟧ **1** VOODOO **2** [Inf.] bad luck or its cause

hood′wink′ ***vt.*** ⟦HOOD + WINK⟧ to mislead by trickery; dupe

hoo·ey (ho͞o′ē) ***interj., n.*** ⟦echoic⟧ [Slang] nonsense

hoof (ho͝of, ho͞of) ***n.***, *pl.* **hoofs** or **hooves** (ho͞ovz, ho͝ovz) ⟦OE *hof*⟧ the horny covering on the feet of cattle, horses, etc., or the entire foot —***vt., vi.*** [Inf.] to walk: often with *it* —**hoofed** ***adj.***

hook (ho͝ok) ***n.*** ⟦OE *hoc*⟧ **1** a bent piece of metal, etc. used to catch, hold, or pull something **2** a fishhook **3** something shaped like a hook **4** something moving in a hooklike path, as a punch delivered with the elbow bent —***vt.*** to catch, fasten, throw, etc. with a hook —***vi.*** **1** to curve as a hook does **2** to be fastened or caught by a hook —**by hook or by crook** by any means, honest or dishonest —**hook up** to connect (a radio, etc.) —**off the hook** [Inf.] out of trouble

hook·ah or **hook·a** (ho͝ok′ə, ho͞o′kə) ***n.*** ⟦Ar *ḥuqqa*⟧ a tobacco pipe with a tube for drawing the smoke through a vessel of water to cool it

hooked (ho͝okt) ***adj.*** **1** like a hook **2** made with a hook *[hooked rug]* **3** [Slang] *a)* obsessed with or addicted to (often with *on*) *b)* married

hook′er ***n.*** [Slang] a prostitute

hook′up′ ***n.*** the arrangement and connection of parts, circuits, etc., as in a radio

hook′worm′ ***n.*** a small, parasitic, intestinal roundworm with hooks around the mouth

hook′y ***n.*** [Inf.] used only in **play hooky**, be a truant

hoo·li·gan (ho͞o′li gən) ***n.*** ⟦< ? *Hooligan*, a family name⟧ [Slang] a hoodlum

hoop (ho͞op) ***n.*** ⟦OE *hop*⟧ **1** a circular band for holding together the staves of a barrel, etc. **2** anything like this, as a metal basketball rim —***vt.*** to bind or fasten as with a hoop

hoop·la (ho͞op′lä′) ***n.*** ⟦< ?⟧ [Inf.] **1** great excitement **2** showy publicity

hoop skirt a skirt worn over a framework of hoops

hoo·ray (ho͝o rā′, hə-; ho͞o-) ***interj., n., vi., vt.*** *var. of* HURRAY

hoose·gow (ho͞os′gou′) ***n.*** ⟦< Sp *juzgado*, court of justice⟧ [Slang] a jail

Hoo·sier (ho͞o′zhər) ***n.*** [Inf.] a person born or living in Indiana

hoot (ho͞ot) ***n.*** ⟦echoic⟧ **1** the sound that an owl makes **2** any sound like this, as a shout of scorn **3** [Inf.] an amusing person, thing, etc. —***vi.*** to utter a hoot —***vt.*** to express (scorn) of (someone) by hooting —**hoot′er** ***n.***

hoot·en·an·ny (ho͞ot′′n an′ē) ***n.***, *pl.* **-nies** a meeting of folk singers, as for public entertainment

Hoo·ver (ho͞o′vər), **Her·bert** (**Clark**) (hur′bərt) 1874-1964; 31st president of the U.S. (1929-33)

hop[1] (häp) ***vi.*** **hopped**, **hop′ping** ⟦OE *hoppian*⟧ **1** to make a short leap or leaps on one foot **2** to leap with both, or all, feet at once, as a frog **3** [Inf.] *a)* to go briskly *b)* to take a short trip —***vt.*** **1** to jump over **2** to get aboard —***n.*** **1** a hopping **2** [Inf.] *a)* a dance *b)* a short flight in an airplane

hop[2] (häp) ***n.*** ⟦< MDu *hoppe*⟧ **1** a twining vine with flowers borne in small cones **2** [*pl.*] the dried ripe cones, used for flavoring beer, ale, etc. —**hop up** to stimulate, as by a drug

hope (hōp) ***n.*** ⟦OE *hopa*⟧ **1** a feeling that what is wanted will happen; desire accompanied by expectation **2** the object of this **3** a person or thing on which one may base some hope —***vt.*** **hoped, hop′ing** to want and expect —***vi.*** to have hope (*for*) —**hope′ful** ***adj.*** —**hope′ful·ly** ***adv.*** —**hope′less** ***adj.*** —**hope′less·ly** ***adv.***

hop′head′ ***n.*** [Slang] a drug addict

hop·per (häp′ər) ***n.*** **1** one that hops **2** any hopping insect **3** a box, tank, etc. from which the contents can be emptied slowly and evenly

hop·sack·ing (häp′sak′iŋ) ***n.*** a sturdy fabric resembling coarse material used for bags, that is made into coats, suits, etc. Also **hop′sack′**

hop·scotch (häp′skäch′) ***n.*** a children's game in which a player hops from section to section of a figure drawn on the ground

Hor·ace (hôr′is, här′-) 65-8 B.C.; Rom. poet

horde (hôrd) ***n.*** ⟦ult. < Tatar *urdu*, a camp⟧ a crowd or throng; swarm —***vi.*** **hord′ed, hord′ing** to form or gather in a horde

hore·hound (hôr′hound′) ***n.*** ⟦OE *harhune*⟧ **1** a bitter plant of the mint family **2** medicine or candy made from its juice

ho·ri·zon (hə rī′zən) ***n.*** ⟦< Gr *horos*, boundary⟧ **1** the line where the sky seems to meet the earth **2** [*usually pl.*] the limit of one's experience, interest, etc.

hor·i·zon·tal (hôr′i zänt′′l) ***adj.*** **1** parallel to the plane of the horizon; not vertical **2** flat and even; level —**hor′i·zon′tal·ly** ***adv.***

hor·mone (hôr′mōn′) ***n.*** ⟦< Gr *hormē*, impulse⟧ a substance formed in some organ of the body and carried to another part, where it takes effect —**hor·mo′nal** ***adj.***

horn (hôrn) ***n.*** ⟦OE⟧ **1** a hard, bonelike projection growing on the head of a cow, goat, etc. **2** the substance horns are made of **3** anything like a horn in position, shape, etc. **4** any brass instrument; specif., FRENCH HORN **5** a device sounded to give a warning —***adj.*** made of horn —**horn in** (**on**) to intrude or meddle (in) —**horned** ***adj.*** —**horn′less** ***adj.*** —**horn′like′** ***adj.***

Horn, Cape southernmost point of South America, on an island of Chile

horn·blende (hôrn′blend′) ***n.*** ⟦Ger⟧ a hard, heavy, dark-colored mineral

horned toad a small, scaly, insect-eating lizard with hornlike spines: also **horned lizard**

hor·net (hôr′nit) ***n.*** ⟦OE *hyrnet*⟧ a large, yellow and black wasp

horn of plenty CORNUCOPIA

horn′pipe′ ***n.*** ⟦ME⟧ a lively dance formerly popular with sailors

horn·y (hôr′nē) ***adj.*** **-i·er, -i·est 1** made of horn **2** toughened and calloused *[horny* hands*]* **3** [Slang] easily aroused sexually

ho·rol·o·gy (hō räl′ə jē) ***n.*** ⟦< Gr *hōra*, hour + -LOGY⟧ the science of measuring time or making timepieces

hor·o·scope (hôr′ə skōp′) ***n.*** ⟦< Gr *hōra*, hour + *skopos*, watcher⟧ a chart of the zodiacal signs and positions of planets, etc., esp. at the time of a person's birth, used by an astrologer to make a forecast

hor·ren·dous (hô ren′dəs) ***adj.*** ⟦see HORRID⟧ horrible; frightful

hor·ri·ble (hôr′ə bəl) ***adj.*** ⟦see fol.⟧ **1** causing horror; terrible; dreadful **2** [Inf.] very bad, ugly, unpleasant, etc. —**hor′ri·bly** ***adv.***

hor·rid (hôr′id) ***adj.*** ⟦< L *horrere*, to bristle, shake, be afraid⟧ **1** causing horror; terrible **2** very bad, ugly, unpleasant, etc. —**hor′rid·ly** ***adv.***

hor·rif·ic (hô rif′ik, hə-) ***adj.*** horrifying

hor·ri·fy (hôr′ə fī′) ***vt.*** **-fied′, -fy′ing 1** to cause to feel horror **2** [Inf.] to shock or disgust

hor·ror (hôr′ər) ***n.*** ⟦see HORRID⟧ **1** the strong feeling caused by something frightful or shocking **2** strong dislike **3** something that causes horror

hors de com·bat (ôr də kōn bä′) ⟦Fr, out of combat⟧ disabled

hors d'oeuvre (ôr′ durv′) *pl.* **hors′ d'oeuvres′** ⟦Fr, lit., outside of work⟧ an appetizer, as canapés, served before a meal

horse (hôrs) ***n.*** ⟦OE *hors*⟧ **1** a large, four-legged, solid-hoofed animal with flowing mane and tail, domesticated for drawing loads, carrying riders, etc. **2** a frame with legs to support something —***adj.*** of or on horses —**hold one's horses** [Slang] to curb one's impatience —**horse around** [Slang] to engage in horseplay

horse′back′ ***n.*** the back of a horse —***adv.*** on horseback

horse chestnut 1 a flowering tree with large leaves and glossy brown seeds **2** its seed

horse′feath′ers ***n.***, ***interj.*** [Slang] nonsense

horse′fly′ ***n.***, *pl.* **-flies′** a large fly that sucks the blood of horses, etc.

horse′hair′ ***n.*** **1** hair from the mane or tail of a horse **2** a stiff fabric made from this hair

horse′hide′ ***n.*** **1** the hide of a horse **2** leather made from this

horse′laugh′ ***n.*** a loud, boisterous, usually derisive laugh; guffaw

horse′man (-mən) ***n.***, *pl.* **-men** (-mən) a man skilled in the riding, managing, or care of horses —**horse′man·ship′** ***n.*** —**horse′wom′an**, *pl.* **-wom′en**, ***fem.n.***

horse opera [Slang] WESTERN (*n.*)

horse′play′ ***n.*** rough, boisterous fun

horse′pow′er ***n.***, *pl.* **-pow′er** a unit for measuring the power of engines, etc., equal to 746 watts or 33,000 foot-pounds per minute

horse′rad′ish ***n.*** **1** a plant with a pungent, white, fleshy root **2** a relish made of the grated root

horse sense [Inf.] common sense

horse′shoe′ ***n.*** **1** a flat, U-shaped metal plate nailed to a horse's hoof to protect it **2** anything shaped like this **3** [*pl.*, *with sing. v.*] a game in which players toss horseshoes at two stakes

horseshoe crab a sea arthropod shaped like the base of a horse's foot, with a long, spinelike tail

horse′tail′ ***n.*** a common rushlike plant found in moist areas

horse′whip′ ***n.*** a whip for driving horses —***vt.*** **-whipped′, -whip′ping** to lash with a horsewhip

hors·y (hôr′sē) ***adj.*** **-i·er, -i·est 1** of, like, or suggesting a horse **2** of or like people who are fond of horses, fox-hunting, horse racing, etc. Also **hors′ey**

hor·ta·to·ry (hôr′tə tôr′ē) ***adj.*** ⟦< L *hortari*, incite⟧ exhorting; advising

hor·ti·cul·ture (hôr′tə kul′chər) ***n.*** ⟦< L *hortus*, garden + *cultura*, cultivation⟧ the art or science of growing flowers, fruits, and vegetables —**hor′ti·cul′tur·al** ***adj.***

ho·san·na (hō zan′ə, -zä′nə) ***n.***, ***interj.*** ⟦< Heb *hōshīʿāh nnā*, lit., save, we pray⟧ an exclamation of praise to God

hose (hōz) ***n.***, *pl.* **hose** or, for 2, usually **hos′es** ⟦OE *hosa*⟧ **1** [*pl.*] stockings or socks **2** a flexible tube used to convey fluids —***vt.*** **hosed, hos′ing** to water with a hose: often with *down*

ho·sier·y (hō′zhər ē) ***n.*** stockings

hos·pice (häs′pis) ***n.*** ⟦< L *hospes*, host, guest⟧ **1** a shelter for travelers **2** a homelike facility for the care of terminally ill patients

hos·pi·ta·ble (häs′pit ə bəl, häs pit′-) ***adj.*** ⟦see prec.⟧ friendly and solicitous toward guests, new arrivals, etc. —**hos′pi·ta·bly** ***adv.***

hos·pi·tal (häs′pit′'l) ***n.*** ⟦< L *hospes*, host, guest⟧ an institution providing medical treatment for people who are ill, injured, pregnant, etc.

hos·pi·tal·i·ty (häs′pi tal′ə tē) ***n.***, *pl.* **-ties** the act, practice, or quality of being hospitable

hos·pi·tal·ize (häs′pit'l īz′) ***vt.*** **-ized′, -iz′ing** to put in, or admit to, a hospital —**hos′pi·tal·i·za′tion** ***n.***

host[1] (hōst) ***n.*** ⟦< ML *hostia*⟧ a wafer of the bread used in the Eucharist

host[2] (hōst) ***n.*** ⟦< L *hospes*, host, guest⟧ **1** one who entertains guests, esp. at home **2** a person who keeps an inn or hotel **3** any organism on or in which a parasitic organism lives —***vi.***, ***vt.*** to act as host (to)

host[3] (hōst) ***n.*** ⟦< ML *hostis*, army⟧ **1** an army **2** a great number

hos·tage (häs′tij) ***n.*** ⟦< OFr⟧ a person kept or given as a pledge until certain conditions are met

hos·tel (häs′təl) ***n.*** ⟦< L *hospes*, host,

guest]] an inn: also **hos'tel·ry** (-rē), *pl.* **-ries**

hos'tel·er *n.* a traveler who stops at hostels

host·ess (hōs'tis) *n.* **1** a woman who entertains guests, esp. at home; sometimes, the host's wife **2** a woman employed in a restaurant to supervise serving, seating, etc.

hos·tile (häs'təl) *adj.* [[< L *hostis*, enemy]] **1** of or characteristic of an enemy **2** unfriendly; antagonistic —**hos'tile·ly** *adv.*

hos·til·i·ty (häs til'ə tē) *n., pl.* **-ties** **1** a feeling of enmity, ill will, etc. **2** *a*) an expression of enmity, ill will, etc. *b*) [*pl.*] warfare

hos·tler (häs'lər, äs'-) *n.* [[contr. of HOSTELER]] one who takes care of horses at an inn, stable, etc.

hot (hät) *adj.* **hot'ter, hot'test** [[OE *hat*]] **1** *a*) having a temperature higher than that of the human body *b*) having a relatively high temperature **2** producing a burning sensation *[hot* pepper*]* **3** characterized by strong feeling or intense activity, etc.; specif., *a*) impetuous *[*a *hot* temper*]* *b*) violent *[*a *hot* battle*]* *c*) lustful *d*) very controversial **4** following closely *[*in *hot* pursuit*]* **5** electrically charged *[*a *hot* wire*]* **6** [Inf.] recent; fresh *[hot* news*]* **7** [Slang] *a*) recently stolen or smuggled *b*) excellent; good —**make it hot for** [Inf.] to make things uncomfortable for —**hot'ly** *adv.* —**hot'ness** *n.*

hot air [Slang] empty talk

hot'bed' *n.* **1** a bed of earth covered with glass and heated, as by manure, for forcing plants **2** a place of rapid growth or extensive activity

hot'blood'ed *adj.* easily excited; excitable

hot'box' *n.* an overheated bearing on an axle or shaft

hot cake a pancake —**sell like hot cakes** [Inf.] to be sold rapidly and in large quantities

hot dog [Inf.] a wiener, esp. one served hot in a long, soft roll

ho·tel (hō tel') *n.* [[< OFr *hostel*, hostel]] an establishment providing lodging and, usually, meals for travelers, etc.

ho·tel·ier (hō tel'yər) *n.* [[Fr *hôtelier*]] an owner or manager of a hotel

hot flash the sensation of a wave of heat passing over the body, often experienced by women during menopause

hot'foot' *vi.* [Inf.] to hurry; hasten: with *it*

hot'head'ed *adj.* **1** quick-tempered **2** impetuous —**hot'head'** *n.*

hot'house' *n.* GREENHOUSE

hot line an emergency telephone line between government leaders or to a social agency

hot plate a small portable stove for cooking food

hot potato [Inf.] a troubling problem that no one wants to handle

hot rod [Slang] an automobile, often an old one, rebuilt for great speed —**hot rod'der**

hot seat [Slang] **1** ELECTRIC CHAIR **2** a difficult situation

hot'shot' *n.* [Slang] one seen as an expert or as very aggressive: often used ironically

hot'-tem'pered *adj.* having a fiery temper

Hot·ten·tot (hät''n tät') *n.* **1** a member of a nomadic people of SW Africa **2** the language of this people

hot tub a large wooden tub in which several people can soak in hot water together

hound (hound) *n.* [[OE *hund*, dog]] **1** any of several breeds of hunting dog **2** any dog —*vt.* **1** to hunt or chase with or as with hounds **2** to urge on

hounds·tooth check (houndz'to͞oth') a pattern of irregular broken checks, used in woven material

hour (our) *n.* [[< Gr *hōra*]] **1** one of the twenty-four parts of a day; sixty minutes **2** the time for a particular activity *[*lunch *hour]* **3** [*pl.*] a period fixed for work, etc. *[*office *hours]* **4** the time of day *[*the *hour* is 2:30*]* **5** *Educ.* a credit, equal to one hour spent in class per week —**after hours** after the regular hours for business, school, etc. —**hour after hour** every hour

hour'glass' *n.* an instrument for measuring time by the trickling of sand, etc. from one glass bulb to another

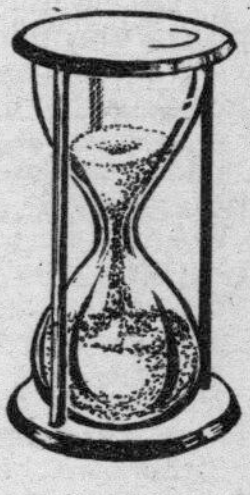

HOURGLASS

hour hand the short hand of a clock or watch, which indicates the hours

hou·ri (ho͞o'rē, hou'-) *n., pl.* **-ris** [[< Ar *ḥūrīyah*, black-eyed woman]] a beautiful nymph of the Muslim Paradise

hour'ly *adj.* **1** happening every hour **2** done during an hour **3** frequent —*adv.* **1** once an hour **2** often

house (hous; *for v.* houz) *n., pl.* **hous·es** (hou'ziz) [[OE *hus*]] **1** a building to live in; specif., a building occupied by one family or person **2** the people who live in a house; household **3** [*often* **H-**] a family as including kin, ancestors, and descendants, esp. a royal family **4** shelter, living or storage space, etc. **5** *a*) a theater *b*) the audience in a theater **6** a business firm **7** [*often* **H-**] a legislative assembly —*adj.* of a salad dressing, wine, etc. at a particular restaurant —*vt.* **housed, hous'ing** **1** to provide a house or lodgings for **2** to cover, shelter, etc. —**keep house** to take care of a home —**on the house** at the expense of the establishment

house'boat' *n.* a large, flat-bottomed boat used as a residence

house'bound' *adj.* confined to one's home, as by illness

house'break'ing *n.* the act of breaking into and entering another's house to commit theft or another felony

house'bro'ken *adj.* trained to live in a house (i.e., to urinate, etc. in a special place or outside): said of a dog, cat, etc.

house'fly' *n., pl.* **-flies'** a two-winged fly found in and around houses

house'guest' *n.* a person who stays overnight in another's home

house'hold' *n.* **1** all those living in one house **2** the home and its affairs —**house'hold'er** *n.*

household word a common saying or thing, familiar to nearly everyone

house'hus'band *n.* a married man whose job is keeping house and taking care of domestic affairs

house'keep'er *n.* one who runs a home, esp. a woman hired to do this

house'maid' *n.* a maid who does housework

House of Commons the lower house of the legislature of Great Britain or Canada

House of Lords the upper house of the legislature of Great Britain

House of Representatives the lower house of the legislature of the U.S. and most of the states of the U.S.

house'plant' *n.* a plant grown indoors, mainly for decoration

house'wares' (-werz') *pl.n.* articles for household use, esp. in the kitchen

house'warm'ing *n.* a party to celebrate moving into a new home

house'wife' *n., pl.* **-wives'** a married woman whose job is keeping house and taking care of domestic affairs

house'work' *n.* the work involved in keeping house; cleaning, cooking, etc.

hous·ing (hou'ziŋ) *n.* **1** the providing of shelter or lodging **2** shelter or lodging **3** houses collectively **4** *Mech.* a frame, box, etc. for containing some part, mechanism, etc.

Hous·ton (hyo͞os'tən) city & port in SE Texas: pop. 1,630,000

hove (hōv) *vt., vi. alt. pt. & pp. of* HEAVE

hov·el (huv'əl, häv'-) *n.* ⟦ME⟧ any small, miserable dwelling; hut

hov·er (huv'ər, häv'-) *vi.* ⟦< ME *hoven,* to stay (suspended)⟧ **1** to flutter in the air near one place **2** to linger close by **3** to waver (*between*)

how (hou) *adv.* ⟦OE *hu*⟧ **1** in what manner or way **2** in what state or condition **3** for what reason **4** to what extent, degree, etc. *How* is also used as an intensive —**how about something** (or **someone**)? [Inf.] what is your opinion, etc. concerning something (or someone)?

how·be·it (hou bē'it) *adv.* [Archaic] however it may be; nevertheless

how·dah (hou'də) *n.* ⟦< Hindi *hauda*⟧ a seat for riding on the back of an elephant or camel

how·ev'er *adv.* **1** in whatever manner **2** to whatever degree **3** nevertheless

how·itz·er (hou'it sər) *n.* ⟦< Czech *houfnice,* orig., a sling⟧ a short cannon, firing shells in a high trajectory

howl (houl) *vi.* ⟦ME *hulen*⟧ **1** to utter the long, wailing cry of wolves, dogs, etc. **2** to utter a similar cry of pain, anger, etc. **3** to shout or laugh in scorn, mirth, etc. —*vt.* **1** to utter with a howl **2** to drive by howling —*n.* **1** the wailing cry of a wolf, dog, etc. **2** any similar sound **3** [Inf.] a joke

howl'er *n.* **1** one that howls **2** [Inf., Chiefly Brit.] a ludicrous blunder

how·so·ev·er (hou'sō ev'ər) *adv.* **1** to whatever degree or extent **2** by whatever means

hoy·den (hoid''n) *n.* ⟦< ? Du⟧ a bold, boisterous girl; tomboy

Hoyle (hoil) *n.* a book of rules for card games, orig. compiled by E. Hoyle (1672-1769) —**according to Hoyle** according to the rules

HP *abbrev.* horsepower: usually written **hp**

HQ or **hq** *abbrev.* headquarters

hr *abbrev.* hour

HR *abbrev.* **1** *Baseball* home run(s) **2** House of Representatives

HRH *abbrev.* Her (or His) Royal Highness

HS *abbrev.* high school

ht *abbrev.* height

HTML *abbrev.* Hypertext Markup Language

Huang (hwäŋ) river in N China, flowing into the Yellow Sea

hua·ra·ches (wə rä'chēz, hə-) *pl.n.* ⟦MexSp⟧ flat sandals with uppers made of straps or woven leather strips

hub (hub) *n.* ⟦< ?⟧ **1** the center part of a wheel **2** a center of activity

hub·bub (hub'bub') *n.* ⟦prob. < Gael exclamation⟧ an uproar; tumult

hub'cap' *n.* a tight cap over the hub of a wheel, esp. on an automobile

hu·bris (hyo͞o'bris) *n.* ⟦Gr *hybris*⟧ arrogance caused by excessive pride

huck·le·ber·ry (huk'əl ber'ē) *n., pl.* **-ries** ⟦prob. ult. < ME *hurtilberye*⟧ **1** a shrub with blue berries **2** this berry

huck·ster (huk'stər) *n.* ⟦< MDu *hoeken,* peddle⟧ **1** a peddler **2** [Inf.] one engaged in advertising —*vt.* to peddle

HUD *abbrev.* (Department of) Housing and Urban Development

hud·dle (hud''l) *vi., vt.* **-dled, -dling** ⟦< ?⟧ **1** to crowd close together **2** to draw (oneself) up —*n.* **1** a confused crowd or heap **2** [Inf.] a private conference **3** *Football* a grouping of a team to get signals before a play

Hud·son (hud'sən) river in E New York

Hudson Bay inland sea in NE Canada; arm of the Atlantic

hue[1] (hyo͞o) *n.* ⟦< OE *heow*⟧ **1** color **2** a particular shade or tint of a color

hue[2] (hyo͞o) *n.* ⟦< OFr *hu,* outcry⟧ a shouting: now only in **hue and cry**

huff (huf) *vi.* to blow; puff —*n.* a state of smoldering anger or resentment —**huff'y, -i·er, -i·est,** *adj.*

hug (hug) *vt.* **hugged, hug'ging** ⟦prob. < ON *hugga,* to comfort⟧ **1** to clasp closely and fondly in the arms; embrace **2** to cling to (a belief, etc.) **3** to keep close to —*vi.* to embrace each other —*n.*

a close embrace

huge (hyo͞oj) ***adj.*** **hug'er, hug'est** ⟦< OFr *ahuge*⟧ very large; gigantic; immense —**huge'ly** ***adv.***

Hu·go (hyo͞o'gō), **Vic·tor** (**Marie**) (vik'tər) 1802-85; Fr. poet, novelist, & playwright

Hu·gue·not (hyo͞o'gə nät') ***n.*** a French Protestant of the 16th or 17th c.

huh (hu, hun) ***interj.*** [Inf.] used to express contempt, surprise, etc., or to ask a question

hu·la (ho͞o'lə) ***n.*** ⟦Haw⟧ a native Hawaiian dance: also **hu'la-hu'la**

hulk (hulk) ***n.*** ⟦< Gr *holkas*, towed ship⟧ **1** the hull of an old, dismantled ship **2** a big, clumsy person or thing

hulk'ing ***adj.*** bulky and clumsy

hull (hul) ***n.*** ⟦OE *hulu*⟧ **1** the outer covering of a seed or fruit, as the husk of grain or shell of a nut **2** the frame or main body of a ship, airship, etc. **3** any outer covering —***vt.*** to take the hulls off (nuts, etc.) —**hull'er** ***n.***

hul·la·ba·loo (hul'ə bə lo͞o') ***n.*** ⟦echoic⟧ noise and confusion; hubbub

hum (hum) ***vi.*** **hummed, hum'ming** ⟦echoic⟧ **1** to make a low, continuous, murmuring sound **2** to sing with closed lips **3** [Inf.] to be full of activity —***vt.*** to sing (a tune) with closed lips —***n.*** a continuous murmur

hu·man (hyo͞o'mən) ***adj.*** ⟦< L *humanus*⟧ of, characteristic of, or having the qualities typical of people, or human beings —***n.*** a person: also **human being** —**hu'man·ness** ***n.***

hu·mane (hyo͞o mān') ***adj.*** ⟦var. of prec.⟧ **1** kind, tender, merciful, etc. **2** civilizing; refining —**hu·mane'ly** ***adv.*** —**hu·mane'ness** ***n.***

hu·man·ism (hyo͞o'mə niz'əm) ***n.*** **1** any system of thought based on the interests and ideals of humanity **2** [**H-**] the intellectual movement that stemmed from the study of the Greek and Latin classics during the Middle Ages —**hu'man·ist** ***n., adj.*** —**hu'man·is'tic** ***adj.*** —**hu'man·is'ti·cal·ly** ***adv.***

hu·man·i·tar·i·an (hyo͞o man'ə ter'ē ən) ***n.*** a person devoted to promoting the welfare of humanity; philanthropist —***adj.*** helping humanity —**hu·man'i·tar'i·an·ism'** ***n.***

hu·man·i·ty (hyo͞o man'ə tē) ***n., pl.*** **-ties** **1** the fact or quality of being human or humane **2** people —**the humanities** literature, philosophy, history, etc., as distinguished from the sciences

hu·man·ize (hyo͞o'mə nīz') ***vt.*** **-ized', -iz'ing** to make or become human or humane —**hu'man·i·za'tion** ***n.*** —**hu'man·iz'er** ***n.***

hu'man·kind' ***n.*** mankind; people

hu'man·ly ***adv.*** **1** in a human manner **2** within human ability or knowledge

hu'man·oid' (-mə noid') ***adj.*** nearly human —***n.*** a nearly human creature

hum·ble (hum'bəl) ***adj.*** **-bler, -blest** ⟦< L *humilis*, low⟧ **1** having or showing a consciousness of one's shortcomings; modest **2** lowly; unpretentious —***vt.*** **-bled, -bling** **1** to lower in condition or rank; abase **2** to lower in pride; make modest —**hum'ble·ness** ***n.*** —**hum'bly** ***adv.***

hum·bug (hum'bug') ***n.*** ⟦< ?⟧ **1** fraud; sham; hoax **2** an impostor —***vt.*** **-bugged', -bug'ging** to dupe; deceive —***interj.*** nonsense!

hum·drum (hum'drum') ***adj.*** ⟦echoic⟧ dull

hu·mer·us (hyo͞o'mər əs) ***n., pl.*** **-mer·i'** (-ī') ⟦L⟧ the bone of the upper arm or forelimb —**hu'mer·al** ***adj.***

hu·mid (hyo͞o'mid) ***adj.*** ⟦< L *umere*, be moist⟧ damp; moist

hu·mid·i·fy (hyo͞o mid'ə fī') ***vt.*** **-fied', -fy'ing** to make humid; dampen —**hu·mid'i·fi'er** ***n.***

hu·mid'i·ty (-ə tē) ***n.*** **1** moistness; dampness **2** the amount of moisture in the air

hu·mi·dor (hyo͞o'mə dôr') ***n.*** a case or jar for keeping tobacco moist

hu·mil·i·ate (hyo͞o mil'ē āt') ***vt.*** **-at'ed, -at'ing** ⟦< L *humilis*, humble⟧ to hurt the pride or dignity of; mortify —**hu·mil'i·a'tion** ***n.***

hu·mil'i·ty (-ə tē) ***n.*** the state or quality of being humble

hum·ming·bird (hum'iŋ burd') ***n.*** a very small, brightly colored bird with narrow wings that vibrate rapidly, often with a humming sound

hum·mock (hum'ək) ***n.*** ⟦< ?⟧ a low, rounded hill; knoll —**hum'mock·y** ***adj.***

hum·mus (hum'əs) ***n.*** ⟦Turk *humus*⟧ a Middle Eastern puree of chickpeas, garlic, etc.

hu·mon·gous (hyo͞o mäŋ'gəs, -muŋ'-) ***adj.*** ⟦? a blend of HUGE + MONSTROUS⟧ [Slang] enormous

hu·mor (hyo͞o'mər) ***n.*** ⟦< L *humor*, fluid: after former belief in four body fluids (*humors*) held responsible for one's disposition⟧ **1** mood; state of mind **2** whim; caprice **3** a comical quality **4** *a*) the ability to appreciate or express what is funny, amusing, etc. *b*) the expression of this —***vt.*** to comply with the mood or whim of; indulge Brit. sp. **hu'mour** —**out of humor** not in a good mood —**hu'mor·ist** ***n.*** —**hu'mor·less** ***adj.***

hu'mor·ous ***adj.*** funny; amusing; comical —**hu'mor·ous·ly** ***adv.***

hump (hump) ***n.*** ⟦prob. < LowG⟧ a rounded, protruding lump, as on a camel's back —***vt.*** to hunch; arch —**over the hump** [Inf.] past the worst or most difficult part

hump'back' ***n.*** **1** a humped, deformed back **2** HUNCHBACK (sense 2) **3** a large whale with long flippers and a raised back —**hump'backed'** ***adj.***

hu·mus (hyo͞o'məs) ***n.*** ⟦L, earth⟧ the dark part of the soil, from partially decayed leaves, etc.

Hun (hun) ***n.*** a member of a warlike Asiatic people that invaded Europe in the 4th and 5th c. A.D.

hunch (hunch) ***vt.*** ⟦< ?⟧ to arch into a hump —***vi.*** to move forward jerkily —***n.*** **1** a hump **2** a feeling not based on known facts; premonition

hunch·back (hunch'bak') ***n.*** **1** HUMP-

BACK (sense 1) **2** a person having a back with a hump —**hunch'backed'** ***adj.***

hun·dred (hun'drəd) ***n., adj.*** ⟦OE⟧ ten times ten; 100; C —**hun'dredth** (-drədth) ***adj., n.***

hun'dred·fold' ***adj., adv.*** (having) a hundred times as much or as many

hun'dred·weight' ***n.*** a unit of weight equal to 100 pounds in the U.S. and 112 pounds in Great Britain

hung (huŋ) ***vt., vi.*** *pt. & pp. of* HANG —**hung over** [Slang] having a hangover —**hung up** (**on**) [Slang] disturbed, frustrated, or obsessed (by)

Hung *abbrev.* **1** Hungarian **2** Hungary

Hun·gar·i·an (huŋ ger'ē ən) ***n.*** **1** the language of Hungary **2** a person born or living in Hungary —***adj.*** of Hungary or its people, language, etc.

Hun·ga·ry (huŋ'gə rē) country in SC Europe: 35,911 sq. mi.; pop. 10,375,000

hun·ger (huŋ'gər) ***n.*** ⟦OE *hungor*⟧ **1** discomfort caused by a need for food **2** starvation **3** a desire for food **4** any strong desire —***vi.*** **1** to be hungry **2** to desire —**hun'gry, -gri·er, -gri·est,** ***adj.*** —**hun'gri·ly** ***adv.***

hunger strike the refusal of a prisoner, demonstrator, etc. to eat until certain demands are met

hung jury a jury unable to reach a verdict

hunk (huŋk) ***n.*** ⟦Fl *hunke*⟧ [Inf.] a large piece

hun·ker (huŋ'kər) ***vi.*** ⟦< dial.⟧ to squat or crouch: often with *down* —***n.*** [*pl.*] haunches or buttocks

hunt (hunt) ***vt., vi.*** ⟦OE *huntian*⟧ **1** to kill or catch (game) for food or sport **2** to try to find; search (for) **3** to chase —***n.*** **1** a hunting **2** a group of people who hunt together **3** a search —**hunt'er** or **hunts'man** (-mən), *pl.* **-men** (-mən), ***n.*** —**hunt'ress** ***fem.n.***

Hun·ting·ton Beach (hun'tiŋ tən) city in SW California: pop. 182,000

Hunts·ville (hunts'vil) city in N Alabama: pop. 160,000

hur·dle (hurd''l) ***n.*** ⟦OE *hyrdel*⟧ **1** a framelike barrier over which horses or runners must leap in a race **2** an obstacle —***vt.*** **-dled, -dling** **1** to jump over **2** to overcome (an obstacle) —**hur'dler** ***n.***

hur·dy-gur·dy (hur'dē gur'dē) ***n.***, *pl.* **-dies** ⟦? echoic⟧ popularly, a barrel organ

hurl (hurl) ***vt.*** ⟦prob. < ON⟧ **1** to throw with force or violence **2** to cast down **3** to utter vehemently —***vi.*** [Inf.] *Baseball* to pitch —**hurl'er** ***n.***

hurl·y-burl·y (hur'lē bur'lē) ***n.***, *pl.* **-burl'ies** a turmoil; uproar

Hu·ron (hyoor'än), **Lake** second largest of the Great Lakes, between Michigan & Canada

hur·rah (hə rä', -rô') ***n., interj., vi., vt.*** HURRAY

hur·ray (hə rā') ***n., interj.*** ⟦echoic⟧ (exclamation) used to express joy, approval, etc. —***vi., vt.*** to shout "hurray" (for); cheer

hur·ri·cane (hur'i kān') ***n.*** ⟦< WInd *huracan*⟧ a violent tropical cyclone

hurricane lamp **1** an oil lamp or candlestick with a glass chimney to protect the flame **2** an electric lamp like this

hur·ry (hur'ē) ***vt.*** **-ried, -ry·ing** ⟦prob. akin to HURL⟧ **1** to move or send with haste **2** to cause to occur or be done more rapidly or too rapidly **3** to urge to act soon or too soon —***vi.*** to move or act with haste —***n.*** **1** rush; urgency **2** eagerness to do, go, etc. quickly —**hur'ried·ly** ***adv.***

hurt (hurt) ***vt.*** **hurt, hurt'ing** ⟦< OFr *hurter*, to hit⟧ **1** to cause pain or injury to **2** to harm **3** to offend —***vi.*** **1** to cause injury, pain, etc. **2** to have pain; be sore —***n.*** **1** a pain or injury **2** harm; damage —***adj.*** injured; damaged

hurt'ful ***adj.*** causing hurt; harmful

hur·tle (hurt''l) ***vi., vt.*** **-tled, -tling** ⟦ME *hurtlen*⟧ to move or throw with great speed or much force

hus·band (huz'bənd) ***n.*** ⟦< ON *hūs*, house + *bondi*, freeholder⟧ a married man —***vt.*** to manage economically; conserve

hus'band·ry ***n.*** **1** thrift **2** farming

hush (hush) ***vt.*** ⟦< ME *huscht*, quiet (adj.)⟧ **1** to make quiet or silent **2** to soothe; lull —***vi.*** to become quiet or silent —***n.*** quiet; silence —***interj.*** used to call for silence

hush'-hush' ***adj.*** [Inf.] very secret

hush puppy a small ball of fried cornmeal dough

husk (husk) ***n.*** ⟦prob. < MDu *huus*, house⟧ **1** the dry outer covering of various fruits or seeds, as of an ear of corn **2** any dry, rough, or useless covering —***vt.*** to remove the husk from

hus·ky[1] (hus'kē) ***n.***, *pl.* **-kies** ⟦< a var. of ESKIMO⟧ [*also* **H-**] a dog of any of several breeds for pulling sleds in the Arctic

husk·y[2] (hus'kē) ***adj.*** **-i·er, -i·est** **1** hoarse; rough **2** ⟦< toughness of a *husk*⟧ big and strong

hus·sar (hoo zär') ***n.*** ⟦< Serb *husar*⟧ a European light-armed cavalryman, usually with a brilliant dress uniform

hus·sy (huz'ē, hus'-) ***n.***, *pl.* **-sies** ⟦< ME *huswife*, housewife⟧ **1** a woman of low morals **2** a bold, saucy girl

hus·tings (hus'tiŋz) ***pl.n.*** ⟦< ON *hūsthing*, house council⟧ [*usually with sing. v.*] the process of, or a place for, political campaigning

hus·tle (hus'əl) ***vt.*** **-tled, -tling** ⟦Du *husselen*, shake up⟧ **1** to push about; jostle **2** to force in a rough, hurried manner —***vi.*** **1** to move hurriedly **2** [Inf.] to work energetically **3** [Slang] to obtain money aggressively or dishonestly —***n.*** **1** a hustling **2** [Inf.] energetic action; drive —**hus'tler** ***n.***

hut (hut) ***n.*** ⟦< OHG *hutta*⟧ a very plain or crude little house or cabin

hutch (huch) ***n.*** ⟦< ML *hutica*, chest⟧ **1** a chest or cupboard **2** a pen or coop for small animals **3** a hut

hutz·pah (hoots'pə) ***n.*** CHUTZPAH

huz·zah or **huz·za** (hə zä') ***n., interj., vi., vt.*** *archaic var. of* HURRAH (see

HURRAY)

HVAC *abbrev.* heating, ventilating, and air conditioning

hwy *abbrev.* highway

hy·a·cinth (hī′ə sinth′) ***n.*** ⟦< Gr *hyakinthos*⟧ a plant of the lily family, with spikes of bell-shaped flowers

hy·brid (hī′brid) ***n.*** ⟦L *hybrida*⟧ **1** the offspring of two animals or plants of different varieties, species, etc. **2** anything of mixed origin —***adj.*** of or like a hybrid —**hy′brid·ism′** ***n.***

hy·brid·ize (hī′bri dīz′) ***vi., vt.*** **-ized′, -iz′ing** to produce or cause to produce hybrids; crossbreed

Hy·der·a·bad (hī′dər ə bad′, -bäd′) city in SC India: pop. 2,546,000

hy·dra (hī′drə) ***n.,*** *pl.* **-dras** or **-drae′** (-drē′) ⟦< Gr, water serpent⟧ a small, freshwater polyp with a soft, tubelike body

hy·dran·ge·a (hī drān′jə, -dran′-; -jē ə) ***n.*** ⟦< HYDR(O)- + Gr *angeion*, vessel⟧ a shrub with large, showy clusters of white, blue, or pink flowers

hy·drant (hī′drənt) ***n.*** ⟦< Gr *hydōr*, water⟧ a large pipe with a valve for drawing water from a water main; fireplug

hy·drate (hī′drāt′) ***n.*** ⟦HYDR(O)- + -ATE[1]⟧ a chemical compound of water and some other substance

hy·drau·lic (hī drô′lik) ***adj.*** ⟦ult. < Gr *hydōr*, water + *aulos*, tube⟧ **1** of hydraulics **2** operated by the movement and force of liquid *[hydraulic brakes]* —**hy·drau′li·cal·ly** ***adv.***

hy·drau′lics ***n.*** the science dealing with the mechanical properties of liquids, as water, in motion and their application in engineering

hydro- ⟦< Gr *hydōr*, WATER⟧ *combining form* **1** water *[hydrometer]* **2** hydrogen

hy·dro·car·bon (hī′drə kär′bən) ***n.*** any compound containing only hydrogen and carbon

hy·dro·chlo·ric acid (hī′drə klôr′ik) a strong, highly corrosive acid that is a water solution of the gas hydrogen chloride

hy·dro·e·lec·tric (hī′drō ē lek′trik) ***adj.*** producing, or relating to the production of, electricity by water power —**hy′dro·e′lec·tric′i·ty** ***n.***

hy·dro·foil (hī′drə foil′) ***n.*** ⟦HYDRO- + (AIR)FOIL⟧ **1** a winglike structure that lifts and carries a watercraft just above the water at high speed **2** such a watercraft

hy·dro·gen (hī′drə jən) ***n.*** ⟦see HYDRO- & -GEN⟧ a flammable, colorless, odorless, gaseous chemical element: the lightest known substance

hy·drog·e·nate (hī dräj′ə nāt′) ***vt.*** **-nat′ed, -nat′ing** to combine with or treat with hydrogen *[vegetable oil is hydrogenated to make a solid fat]*

hydrogen bomb an extremely destructive nuclear bomb in which an atomic bomb explosion starts a nuclear fusion explosion of heavy hydrogen atoms

hydrogen peroxide a colorless liquid used as a bleach or disinfectant

hy·drol·o·gy (hī dräl′ə jē) ***n.*** ⟦see HYDRO- & -LOGY⟧ the study of the earth's waters, their distribution, and the cycle involving evaporation, precipitation, flow, etc.

hy·drol′y·sis (-ə sis) ***n.,*** *pl.* **-ses′** (-sēz′) ⟦HYDRO- + -LYSIS⟧ a chemical reaction in which a substance reacts with water so as to be changed into one or more other substances

hy·drom·e·ter (hī dräm′ət ər) ***n.*** ⟦HYDRO- + -METER⟧ an instrument for measuring the specific gravity of liquids —**hy·drom′e·try** ***n.***

hy·dro·pho·bi·a (hī′drə fō′bē ə) ***n.*** ⟦see HYDRO- & -PHOBIA⟧ **1** an abnormal fear of water **2** ⟦from symptomatic inability to swallow liquids⟧ RABIES

hy·dro·phone (hī′drə fōn′) ***n.*** ⟦HYDRO- + -PHONE⟧ an instrument for registering the distance and direction of sound transmitted through water

hy′dro·plane′ (-plān′) ***n.*** **1** a small, high-speed motorboat with hydrofoils or a flat bottom **2** SEAPLANE

hy′dro·pon′ics (-pän′iks) ***n.*** ⟦< HYDRO- & Gr *ponos*, labor⟧ the science of growing plants in nutrient-rich solutions —**hy′dro·pon′ic** ***adj.***

hy′dro·sphere′ (-sfir′) ***n.*** ⟦HYDRO- + *-sphere*, a layer of the earth's atmosphere⟧ all the water on the surface of the earth, including oceans, etc.

hy′dro·ther′a·py ***n.*** the treatment of disease, etc. by the use of water

hy·drous (hī′drəs) ***adj.*** ⟦HYDR(O)- + -OUS⟧ containing water, esp. in chemical combination

hy·drox·ide (hī dräk′sīd′) ***n.*** ⟦HYDR(O)- + OXIDE⟧ a compound consisting of an element or radical combined with the radical OH

hy·e·na (hī ē′nə) ***n.*** ⟦< Gr *hyaina*⟧ a wolflike, flesh-eating animal of Africa and Asia, with a shrill cry

hy·giene (hī′jēn′) ***n.*** ⟦< Gr *hygiēs*, healthy⟧ **1** the science of maintaining health **2** cleanliness

hy·gi·en·ic (hī jen′ik) ***adj.*** **1** of hygiene or health **2** sanitary —**hy′gi·en′i·cal·ly** ***adv.***

hy·grom·e·ter (hī gräm′ət ər) ***n.*** ⟦< Gr *hygros*, wet + *metron*, a measure⟧ an instrument for measuring humidity

hy·men (hī′mən) ***n.*** ⟦Gr *hymēn*, membrane⟧ the thin mucous membrane that closes part or sometimes all of the opening of the vagina

hy·me·ne·al (hī′mə nē′əl) ***adj.*** ⟦< Gr *Hymēn*, god of marriage⟧ of marriage

hymn (him) ***n.*** ⟦< Gr *hymnos*⟧ a song of praise, esp. in honor of God

hym·nal (him′nəl) ***n.*** a collection of hymns: also **hymn′book′**

hype[1] (hīp) ***vt.*** **hyped, hyp′ing** [Slang] to stimulate, excite, etc. by or as by a drug injection: usually with *up*

hype[2] (hīp) [Inf.] ***n.*** ⟦? < HYPERBOLE⟧ **1** deception **2** excessive promotion —***vt.*** **hyped, hyp′ing** to promote in a sensational way

hy·per (hī′pər) ***adj.*** [Inf.] high-strung; keyed up

hyper- ⟦< Gr *hyper*⟧ *prefix* over, above, excessive

hy·per·ac·tive (hī′per ac′tiv) ***adj.*** abnormally active —**hy′per·ac·tiv′i·ty** ***n.***

hy·per·bo·la (hī pur′bə lə) ***n.***, *pl.* **-las** or **-lae′** (-lē′) ⟦< Gr *hyperbolē*, a throwing beyond, excess⟧ *Geom.* a curve formed by the intersection of a cone with a plane more steeply inclined than its side

hy·per·bo·le (hī pur′bə lē) ***n.*** ⟦see prec.⟧ exaggeration for effect, not meant to be taken literally —**hy·per·bol·ic** (hī′pər bäl′ik) ***adj.***

hy·per·crit·i·cal (hī′pər krit′i kəl) ***adj.*** too critical

hy′per·ex·tend′ (-ek stend′) ***vt.*** to injure (a knee, etc.) by bending it beyond its normal straightened position

hy′per·gly·ce′mi·a (-glī sē′mē ə) ***n.*** ⟦< HYPER- + Gr *glykys*, sweet + -EMIA⟧ an abnormally high amount of sugar in the blood

hy′per·sen′si·tive (-sen′sə tiv) ***adj.*** excessively sensitive —**hy′per·sen′si·tiv′i·ty** ***n.***

hy′per·ten′sion (-ten′shən) ***n.*** abnormally high blood pressure

hy′per·text′ (-tekst′) ***n.*** computer data organized so that related items can be accessed easily

hy′per·thy′roid·ism′ (-thī′roid iz′əm) ***n.*** excessive activity of the thyroid gland, causing nervousness, rapid pulse, etc. —**hy′per·thy′roid′** ***adj.***, ***n.***

hy′per·ven′ti·la′tion (-vent′'l ā′shən) ***n.*** extremely rapid or deep breathing that may cause dizziness, fainting, etc. —**hy′per·ven′ti·late′**, **-lat′ed**, **-lat′ing**, ***vi.***, ***vt.***

hy·phen (hī′fən) ***n.*** ⟦< Gr *hypo-*, under + *hen*, one⟧ a mark (-) used between the parts of a compound word or the syllables of a divided word

hy·phen·ate (hī′fə nāt′) ***vt.*** **-at′ed**, **-at′ing** to connect or write with a hyphen —**hy′phen·a′tion** ***n.***

hyp·no·sis (hip nō′sis) ***n.***, *pl.* **-ses′** (-sēz′) ⟦< Gr *hypnos*, sleep + -OSIS⟧ a trancelike condition usually induced by another person, in which the subject responds to suggestions made by that person

hyp·not′ic (-nät′ik) ***adj.*** **1** causing sleep; soporific **2** of, like, or inducing hypnosis —***n.*** any agent causing sleep —**hyp·not′i·cal·ly** ***adv.***

hyp′no·tism′ (-nə tiz′əm) ***n.*** the act or practice of inducing hypnosis —**hyp′no·tist** ***n.***

hyp′no·tize′ (-tīz′) ***vt.*** **-tized′**, **-tiz′ing** to induce hypnosis in

hy·po (hī′pō) ***n.***, *pl.* **-pos** *short for* HYPODERMIC

hypo- ⟦Gr < *hypo*, under⟧ *prefix* **1** under, beneath *[hypodermic]* **2** less than

hy·po·chon·dri·a (hī′pə kän′drē ə) ***n.*** ⟦LL, pl., abdomen (supposed seat of the condition)⟧ abnormal anxiety over one's health, often with imaginary illnesses —**hy′po·chon′dri·ac′** (-ak′) ***adj.***, ***n.***

hy·poc·ri·sy (hi päk′rə sē) ***n.***, *pl.* **-sies** ⟦< Gr *hypokrisis*, acting a part⟧ a pretending to be what one is not, or to feel what one does not feel; esp., a pretense of virtue, piety, etc.

hyp·o·crite (hip′ə krit′) ***n.*** ⟦see prec.⟧ one who pretends to be pious, virtuous, etc. without really being so —**hyp′o·crit′i·cal** ***adj.***

hy·po·der·mic (hī′pə dur′mik) ***adj.*** ⟦< HYPO- + Gr *derma*, skin⟧ injected under the skin —***n.*** a hypodermic syringe or injection

hypodermic syringe a syringe attached to a hollow needle (**hypodermic needle**) and used for the injection of a medicine or drug under the skin

hy·po·gly·ce·mi·a (hī′pō glī sē′mē ə) ***n.*** ⟦< HYPO- + Gr *glykys*, sweet + -EMIA⟧ an abnormally low amount of sugar in the blood

hy·pot·e·nuse (hī pät′'n o͞os′) ***n.*** ⟦< Gr *hypo-*, under + *teinein*, to stretch⟧ the side of a right-angled triangle located opposite the right angle

hy·po·thal·a·mus (hī′pō thal′ə məs) ***n.***, *pl.* **-mi′** (-mī′) ⟦see HYPO- & THALAMUS⟧ the part of the brain that regulates many basic body functions, as temperature

hy′po·ther′mi·a (-thur′mē ə) ***n.*** ⟦< HYPO- + Gr *thermē*, heat⟧ a subnormal body temperature —**hy′po·ther′mal** ***adj.***

hy·poth·e·sis (hī päth′ə sis) ***n.***, *pl.* **-ses′** (-sēz′) ⟦< Gr *hypo-*, under + *tithenai*, to place⟧ an unproved theory, etc. tentatively accepted to explain certain facts —**hy·poth′e·size′** (-sīz′), **-sized′**, **-siz′ing**, ***vi.***, ***vt.***

hy·po·thet·i·cal (hī′pə thet′i kəl) ***adj.*** based on a hypothesis; assumed; supposed —**hy′po·thet′i·cal·ly** ***adv.***

hy·po·thy·roid·ism (hī′pō thī′roid iz′əm) ***n.*** deficient activity of the thyroid gland, causing sluggishness, puffiness, etc. —**hy′po·thy′roid′** ***adj.***, ***n.***

hys·sop (his′əp) ***n.*** ⟦< Heb *ēzōbh*⟧ a fragrant, blue-flowered herb of the mint family

hys·ter·ec·to·my (his′tər ek′tə mē) ***n.***, *pl.* **-mies** ⟦< Gr *hystera*, uterus + -ECTOMY⟧ surgical removal of all or part of the uterus

hys·te·ri·a (hi ster′ē ə, -stir′-) ***n.*** ⟦< Gr *hystera*, uterus: orig. thought to occur more often in women than in men⟧ **1** a psychiatric condition characterized by excitability, anxiety, the simulation of organic disorders, etc. **2** any outbreak of wild, uncontrolled feeling: also **hys·ter′ics** —**hys·ter′i·cal** or **hys·ter′ic** ***adj.*** —**hys·ter′i·cal·ly** ***adv.***

Hz *abbrev.* hertz

I

i or **I** (ī) ***n.***, *pl.* **i's, I's** the ninth letter of the English alphabet

I[1] (ī) ***n.*** a Roman numeral for 1

I[2] (ī) ***pron.*** ⟦OE *ic*⟧ the person speaking or writing

I[3] *abbrev.* **1** island(s) **2** isle(s)

I[4] *Chem. symbol for* iodine

IA *abbrev.* Iowa

-i·al (ē əl, yəl) ⟦L *-ialis*⟧ *suffix* -AL

i·amb (ī′amb′, -am′) ***n.*** ⟦< Gr *iambos*⟧ a metrical foot of one unaccented syllable followed by one accented one

i·am·bic (ī am′bik) ***adj.*** ⟦< Gr *iambikos*⟧ of or made up of iambs —***n.*** an iamb

-i·at·rics (ē a′triks′) ⟦< Gr *iatros*, physician⟧ *combining form* treatment of disease *[pediatrics]*

-i·a·try (ī′ə trē) ⟦< Gr *iatreia*, healing⟧ *combining form* medical treatment *[psychiatry]*

I·be·ri·a (ī bir′ē ə) peninsula in SW Europe, comprising Spain & Portugal: also **Iberian Peninsula** —**I·be′ri·an** ***adj.***, ***n.***

i·bex (ī′beks′) ***n.***, *pl.* **i′bex′es** or **i·bi·ces** (ī′ bə sēz′) ⟦L⟧ a wild goat of the Old World, with large, backward-curved horns

ibid. *abbrev.* ⟦L *ibidem*⟧ in the same place, i.e., the book, page, etc. just cited: also **ib.**

-i·bil·i·ty (ə bil′ə tē) ⟦L *-ibilitas*⟧ *suffix* -ABILITY

i·bis (ī′bis) ***n.*** ⟦Egypt *hb*⟧ a large wading bird found chiefly in tropical regions

-i·ble (i bəl, ə bəl) ⟦L *-ibilis*⟧ *suffix* -ABLE

Ib·sen (ib′sən), **Hen·rik** (hen′rik) 1828-1906; Norw. playwright

i·bu·pro·fen (ī′byo͞o prō′fən) ***n.*** a drug used to reduce fever and relieve pain, esp. arthritic pain

-ic (ik) ⟦< Gr *-ikos*⟧ *suffix* **1** *a)* of, having to do with *[volcanic]* *b)* like *[angelic]* *c)* produced by *[anaerobic]* *d)* consisting of, containing *[dactylic]* *e)* having, showing *[lethargic]* **2** a person or thing: *a)* having *[paraplegic]* *b)* supporting *[heretic]* *c)* producing *[hypnotic]* Also **-i·cal** (i kəl, ə kəl)

ICBM ***n.*** an intercontinental ballistic missile

ICC *abbrev.* Interstate Commerce Commission

ice (īs) ***n.*** ⟦OE *īs*⟧ **1** water frozen solid by cold **2** a frozen dessert of fruit juice, sugar, etc. **3** [Slang] diamonds —***vt.*** **iced, ic′ing** **1** to change into ice; freeze **2** to cool with ice **3** to cover with icing —***vi.*** to freeze: often with *up* or *over* —**break the ice** to make a start, as in getting acquainted —**cut no ice** [Inf.] to have no influence —**on thin ice** [Inf.] in danger

Ice *abbrev.* **1** Iceland **2** Icelandic

ice′berg′ (-burg′) ***n.*** ⟦prob. < Du *ijsberg*, ice mountain⟧ a great mass of ice broken off from a glacier and floating in the sea

ice′bound′ ***adj.*** held fast or shut in by ice

ice′box′ ***n.*** a refrigerator, esp. one using ice

ice′break′er ***n.*** a sturdy boat for cutting channels through ice

ice′cap′ ***n.*** a mass of glacial ice that spreads slowly from a center

ice cream ⟦orig., *iced cream*⟧ a sweet, frozen food of flavored cream or milk —**ice′-cream′** ***adj.***

ice floe a piece of floating sea ice

ice hockey *see* HOCKEY (sense 1)

Ice·land (īs′lənd) country on an island in the North Atlantic, southeast of Greenland: 39,758 sq. mi.; pop. 229,000 —**Ice′land·er** ***n.***

Ice·lan·dic (īs lan′dik) ***n.*** the Germanic language of Iceland —***adj.*** of Iceland or its people, language, etc.

ice·man (īs′man′, -mən) ***n.***, *pl.* **-men′** (-men′, -mən) one who sells or delivers ice

ice milk a frozen dessert like ice cream, but with less butterfat

ice skate *see* SKATE[1] (*n.* 1) —**ice′-skate′**, **-skat′ed, -skat′ing,** ***vi.***

ich·thy·ol·o·gy (ik′thē äl′ə jē) ***n.*** ⟦< Gr *ichthys*, a fish + -LOGY⟧ the branch of zoology dealing with fish —**ich′thy·ol′o·gist** ***n.***

i·ci·cle (ī′sik′əl, -sə kəl) ***n.*** ⟦< OE īs, ice + *gicel*, piece of ice⟧ a hanging piece of ice, formed by the freezing of dripping water

ic·ing (īs′iŋ) ***n.*** a mixture variously of sugar, butter, flavoring, egg whites, etc. for covering a cake; frosting

ick·y (ik′ē) ***adj.*** **-i·er, -i·est** ⟦< STICKY⟧ [Slang] **1** unpleasantly sticky or sweet **2** disgusting

i·con (ī′kän′) ***n.*** ⟦< Gr *eikōn*, image⟧ **1** *a)* an image; figure *b)* a stylized figure on a computer screen, representing a function **2** *Eastern Orthodox Ch.* a sacred image or picture of Jesus, Mary, etc. **3** one that is revered or that represents an era, etc. —**i·con′ic** ***adj.***

i·con·o·clast (ī kän′ə klast′) ***n.*** ⟦< c. 6th-c. Gr *eikōn*, image + *klaein*, to break⟧ one who attacks widely accepted ideas, beliefs, etc. —**i·con′o·clasm′** ***n.*** —**i·con′o·clas′tic** ***adj.***

-ics (iks) ⟦-IC + -S (pl.)⟧ *suffix* [*usually with sing. v.*] art, science, study *[mathematics]*

ICU *abbrev.* intensive care unit

i·cy (ī′sē) ***adj.*** **i′ci·er, i′ci·est** **1** full of or covered with ice **2** of or like ice; specif., *a)* slippery *b)* very cold **3** cold in manner; unfriendly —**i′ci·ly** ***adv.*** —**i′ci·ness** ***n.***

id (id) ***n.*** ⟦L, it⟧ *Psychoanalysis* that part of the psyche which is the source of psychic energy

ID[1] (ī′dē′) ***n.***, *pl.* **ID's** or **IDs** [Inf.] a document, as a license to drive a car, serving as identification

ID[2] *abbrev.* identification

id. *abbrev.* ⟦L *idem*⟧ the same

I·da·ho (ī′də hō′) Mountain State of the NW U.S.: 82,751 sq. mi.; pop. 1,007,000; cap. Boise: abbrev. **ID** —**I′da·ho′an** ***adj.***, ***n.***

i·de·a (ī dē′ə) ***n.*** ⟦L < Gr, appearance of a thing⟧ **1** a thought; mental conception or image **2** an opinion or belief **3** a plan; scheme **4** meaning or significance

i·de·al (ī dē′əl, -dēl′) ***adj.*** ⟦see prec.⟧ **1** existing as an idea, model, etc. **2** thought of as perfect **3** imaginary —***n.*** **1** a conception of something in its most excellent form **2** a perfect model **3** a noble goal or principle

i·de′al·ism′ ***n.*** **1** behavior or thought based on a conception of things as one thinks they should be **2** a striving to achieve one's ideals —**i·de′al·ist** ***n.*** —**i′de·al·is′tic** ***adj.***

i·de·al·ize (ī dē′əl īz′) ***vt.*** **-ized′, -iz′ing** to regard or show as perfect or more nearly perfect than is true —**i·de′al·i·za′tion** ***n.*** —**i·de′al·iz′er** ***n.***

i·de′al·ly ***adv.*** **1** in an ideal manner; perfectly **2** in theory

i·den·ti·cal (ī den′ti kəl) ***adj.*** ⟦< L *idem*, the same⟧ **1** the very same **2** exactly alike —**i·den′ti·cal·ly** ***adv.***

i·den·ti·fi·ca·tion (ī den′tə fi kā′shən) ***n.*** **1** an identifying or being identified **2** anything by which one can be identified

i·den·ti·fy (ī den′tə fī′) ***vt.*** **-fied′, -fy′ing** **1** to make identical; treat as the same **2** to fix the identity of *[to identify a biological specimen]* **3** to connect or associate closely

i·den·ti·ty (ī den′tə tē) ***n.***, *pl.* **-ties** **1** the state or fact of being the same **2** *a)* the state or fact of being a specific person or thing; individuality *b)* the state of being as described

identity crisis the state of being uncertain about oneself regarding character, goals, etc., esp. in adolescence

id·e·o·gram (id′ē ō gram′, ī′dē-) ***n.*** ⟦see IDEA & -GRAM⟧ a symbol representing an object or idea without expressing the word for it: also **id′e·o·graph′** (-graf′)

i·de·ol·o·gy (ī′dē äl′ə jē, id′ē-) ***n.***, *pl.* **-gies** ⟦see IDEA & -LOGY⟧ the doctrines, etc. on which a particular political or social system is based —**i′de·o·log′i·cal** ***adj.*** —**i′de·ol′o·gist** ***n.***

ides (īdz) ***pl.n.*** ⟦< L *idus*⟧ [*often with sing. v.*] in the ancient Roman calendar, the 15th day of March, May, July, or October, or the 13th of the other months

id·i·o·cy (id′ē ə sē) ***n.*** **1** great foolishness or stupidity **2** *pl.* **-cies** an idiotic act or remark

id·i·om (id′ē əm) ***n.*** ⟦< Gr *idios*, one's own⟧ **1** the language or dialect of a people, region, class, etc. **2** the usual way that the words of a language are joined to express thought **3** a phrase or expression with an unusual syntactic pattern or with a meaning differing from the literal meaning of its parts **4** a characteristic style, as in art or music —**id′i·o·mat′ic** (-ə mat′ik) ***adj.***

id·i·o·path·ic (id′ē ə′path′ik) ***adj.*** ⟦< Gr *idiopatheia*, feeling for oneself alone⟧ of a disease whose cause is unknown

id·i·o·syn·cra·sy (id′ē ō siŋ′krə sē) ***n.***, *pl.* **-sies** ⟦< Gr *idio-*, one's own + *synkrasis*, a mixing⟧ any personal peculiarity, mannerism, etc. —**id′i·o·syn·crat′ic** (-sin krat′ik) ***adj.***

id·i·ot (id′ē ət) ***n.*** ⟦< Gr *idiōtēs*, ignorant person⟧ a very foolish or stupid person —**id′i·ot′ic** (-ät′ik) ***adj.*** —**id′i·ot′i·cal·ly** ***adv.***

i·dle (īd′'l) ***adj.*** **i′dler, i′dlest** ⟦OE *idel*, empty⟧ **1** useless; futile *[an idle wish]* **2** unfounded *[idle rumors]* **3** *a)* unemployed; not busy *b)* inactive; not in use **4** lazy —***vi.*** **i′dled, i′dling** **1** to move slowly or aimlessly **2** to be unemployed or inactive **3** to operate without transmitting power *[the motor idled]* —***vt.*** **1** to waste: usually with *away* **2** to cause (a motor, etc.) to idle —**i′dle·ness** ***n.*** —**i′dler** ***n.*** —**i′dly** ***adv.***

i·dol (īd′'l) ***n.*** ⟦< Gr *eidōlon*, image⟧ **1** an image of a god, used as an object of worship **2** any object of ardent or excessive devotion

i·dol·a·try (ī däl′ə trē) ***n.***, *pl.* **-tries** **1** worship of idols **2** excessive reverence for or devotion to a person or thing —**i·dol′a·ter** ***n.*** —**i·dol′a·trous** ***adj.***

i·dol·ize (īd′'l īz′) ***vt.*** **-ized′, -iz′ing** **1** to make an idol of **2** to love or admire excessively

i·dyll or **i·dyl** (īd′'l; *Brit* id′'l) ***n.*** ⟦< Gr *eidos*, a form⟧ **1** a short poem, etc. describing a simple, peaceful scene of rural life **2** a scene or incident suitable for this —**i·dyl·lic** (ī dil′ik) ***adj.***

IE *abbrev.* Indo-European

-ie (ē) ⟦earlier form of -Y[1]⟧ *suffix* **1** small or little (one, as specified) *[lassie]* **2** *a)* one that is as specified *[softie]* *b)* one connected with *[groupie]*

i.e. *abbrev.* ⟦L *id est*⟧ that is (to say)

-i·er (ē′ər, yər, ir, ər) ⟦< L *-arius*⟧ *suffix* a person concerned with (a specified action or thing) *[bombardier]*

if (if) ***conj.*** ⟦OE *gif*⟧ **1** on condition that; in case that *[if I were you, I would quit]* **2** allowing that *[if she was there, I didn't see her]* **3** whether *[ask him if he knows her]*

if·fy (if′ē) ***adj.*** **-fi·er, -fi·est** [Inf.] not definite; containing doubtful elements

IGLOO

ig·loo (ig′lo͞o′) ***n.***, *pl.* **-loos** ⟦Esk *igdlu*, snow house⟧ an Eskimo hut, usually dome-shaped and built of blocks of packed snow

ig·ne·ous (ig′nē əs) ***adj.*** ⟦< L *ignis*, a fire⟧ **1** of fire **2** produced by volcanic action or intense heat *[igneous rock]*

ig·nite (ig nīt′) ***vt.*** **-nit′ed, -nit′ing** ⟦see prec.⟧ to set fire to —***vi.*** to catch on fire; start burning —**ig·nit′a·ble** or **ig·nit′i·ble** ***adj.***

ig·ni·tion (ig nish′ən) ***n.*** **1** an igniting or being ignited **2** the key-operated switch or system for igniting the explosive mixture in the cylinder of an internal-combustion engine

ig·no·ble (ig nō′bəl) ***adj.*** ⟦< L *in-*, not + *nobilis* (< earlier *gnobilis*, known⟧ not noble; base; mean —**ig·no′bly** ***adv.***

ig·no·min·y (ig′nə min′ē) ***n.*** ⟦< L *in-*, no, not + *nomen*, name⟧ loss of reputation; shame; disgrace —**ig′no·min′i·ous** ***adj.*** —**ig′no·min′i·ous·ly** ***adv.***

ig·no·ra·mus (ig′nə rā′məs, -ram′əs) ***n.***, *pl.* **-mus·es** an ignorant person

ig·no·rant (ig′nə rənt) ***adj.*** ⟦see fol.⟧ **1** lacking knowledge or experience **2** caused by or showing lack of knowledge **3** unaware (*of*) —**ig′no·rance** ***n.*** —**ig′no·rant·ly** ***adv.***

ig·nore (ig nôr′) ***vt.*** **-nored′, -nor′ing** ⟦< L *in-*, not + *gnarus*, knowing⟧ to disregard; pay no attention to

i·gua·na (i gwä′nə) ***n.*** ⟦Sp < WInd⟧ a large tropical American lizard

IL Illinois

il- *prefix* **1** IN-[1] **2** IN-[2] Used before *l*

-ile (il, əl, ′l, īl) *suffix* of or like

Il·i·ad (il′ē əd) ***n.*** ⟦< Gr *Ilios*, Troy⟧ a Greek epic poem, ascribed to Homer, about the Trojan War

ilk (ilk) ***n.*** ⟦< OE *ilca*, same⟧ kind; sort; class: only in **of that** (or **his, her,** etc.) **ilk**

ill (il) ***adj.*** **worse, worst** ⟦< ON *illr*⟧ **1** bad *[ill* repute, *ill* will, *ill* omen*]* **2** not well; sick —***n.*** an evil or a disease —***adv.*** **worse, worst 1** badly **2** scarcely *[*I can *ill* afford it*]* —**ill at ease** uneasy; uncomfortable

ill-ad·vised (il′əd vīzd′) ***adj.*** showing or resulting from poor advice; unwise

ill′-bred′ ***adj.*** rude; impolite

il·le·gal (i lē′gəl) ***adj.*** prohibited by law; against the law —**il·le·gal·i·ty** (il′ē gal′i tē), *pl.* **-ties,** ***n.*** —**il·le′gal·ly** ***adv.***

il·leg·i·ble (i lej′ə bəl) ***adj.*** hard or impossible to read because badly written or printed —**il·leg′i·bly** ***adv.***

il·le·git·i·mate (il′ə jit′ə mət) ***adj.*** **1** born of parents not married to each other **2** not legal or logical —**il′le·git′i·ma·cy** (-mə sē), *pl.* **-cies,** ***n.***

ill-fat·ed (il′fāt′id) ***adj.*** **1** certain to have an evil fate or unlucky end **2** unlucky

ill′-fa′vored ***adj.*** ugly or unpleasant

ill′-got′ten ***adj.*** obtained unlawfully or dishonestly

il·lib·er·al (i lib′ər əl) ***adj.*** **1** narrow-minded **2** not generous

il·lic·it (i lis′it) ***adj.*** ⟦< L *illicitus*, not allowed⟧ unlawful; improper —**il·lic′it·ly** ***adv.*** —**il·lic′it·ness** ***n.***

il·lim·it·a·ble (i lim′i tə bəl) ***adj.*** without limit; immeasurable

Il·li·nois (il′ə noi′) Midwestern state of the U.S.: 55,646 sq. mi.; pop. 11,431,000; cap. Springfield: abbrev. IL —**Il′li·nois′an** ***adj.***, ***n.***

il·liq·uid (i lik′wid) ***adj.*** not readily convertible into cash

il·lit·er·a·cy (i lit′ər ə sē) ***n.*** **1** a being illiterate **2** *pl.* **-cies** a mistake in grammar suggesting this

il·lit·er·ate (i lit′ər it) ***adj.*** uneducated; esp., not knowing how to read or write —***n.*** an illiterate person

ill-man·nered (il′man′ərd) ***adj.*** having bad manners; rude; impolite

ill nature a disagreeable or mean disposition —**ill′-na′tured** ***adj.***

ill′ness ***n.*** the condition of being in poor health; sickness; disease

il·log·i·cal (i läj′i kəl) ***adj.*** not logical or reasonable —**il·log′i·cal·ly** ***adv.***

ill-starred (il′stärd′) ***adj.*** unlucky

ill′-suit′ed ***adj.*** not suited or appropriate

ill′-tem′pered ***adj.*** sullen; irritable

ill′-timed′ ***adj.*** inopportune

ill′-treat′ ***vt.*** to treat unkindly, unfairly, etc. —**ill′-treat′ment** ***n.***

il·lu·mi·nate (i lo͞o′mə nāt′) ***vt.*** **-nat′ed, -nat′ing** ⟦< L *in-*, in + *luminare*, to light⟧ **1** to give light to; light up **2** *a)* to make clear; explain *b)* to inform **3** to decorate with lights **4** to decorate (a page border, etc.) by hand —**il·lu′mi·na·ble** (-nə bəl) ***adj.***

il·lu′mi·na′tion ***n.*** **1** an illuminating **2** the intensity of light per unit of area

il·lu′mine (-mən) ***vt.*** **-mined, -min·ing** to light up

illus *abbrev.* **1** illustrated **2** illustration **3** illustrator

ill-us·age (il′yo͞o′sij) ***n.*** unkind or cruel treatment; abuse: also **ill usage**

ill′-use′ (-yo͞oz′; *for n.*, -yo͞os′) ***vt.*** **-used′, -us′ing** to treat unkindly; abuse —***n.*** ILL-USAGE

il·lu·sion (i lo͞o′zhən) ***n.*** ⟦< L *illudere*, to mock⟧ **1** a false idea or conception **2** an unreal or misleading appearance or image —**il·lu′so·ry** (-sə rē) or **il·lu′sive** (-siv) ***adj.***

il·lus·trate (il′ə strāt′) ***vt.*** **-trat′ed, -trat′ing** ⟦< L *in-*, in + *lustrare*, illuminate⟧ **1** to explain; make clear, as by examples **2** to furnish (books, etc.) with explanatory or decorative pictures, etc. —**il′lus·tra′tor** ***n.***

il′lus·tra′tion (-strā′shən) ***n.*** **1** an illustrating **2** an example, etc. used to help explain **3** a picture, diagram, etc. used to decorate or explain

il·lus·tra·tive (i lus′trə tiv, il′ə strāt′iv) ***adj.*** serving as an illustration or example

il·lus·tri·ous (i lus′trē əs) ***adj.*** ⟦< L *illustris*, clear⟧ distinguished; famous; outstanding —**il·lus′tri·ous·ly** ***adv.*** —**il·lus′tri·ous·ness** ***n.***

ill will hostility; hate; dislike

I'm (īm) *contr.* I am

im- *prefix* **1** IN-[1] **2** IN-[2] Used before *b*, *m*, or *p*

im·age (im′ij) ***n.*** ⟦< L *imago*⟧ **1** a representation of a person or thing; esp., a statue **2** the visual impression of something in a mirror, through a lens, etc. **3** a copy **4** *a)* a mental picture; idea *b)* the concept of a person, product, etc.

held by the general public 5 a metaphor or simile —*vt.* **-aged, -ag·ing 1** to make a representation of **2** to reflect **3** to imagine

im·age·ry (im′ij rē) *n.* **1** mental images **2** figurative language

i·mag·i·na·ble (i maj′i nə bəl) *adj.* that can be imagined

i·mag′i·nar′y (-ner′ē) *adj.* existing only in the imagination; unreal

i·mag′i·na′tion (-nā′shən) *n.* **1** *a)* the act or power of forming mental images of what is not present *b)* the act or power of creating new ideas by combining previous experiences **2** the ability to understand the imaginative creations of others **3** resourcefulness

i·mag′i·na·tive (-nə tiv) *adj.* **1** having, using, or showing imagination **2** of or resulting from imagination —**i·mag′i·na·tive·ly** *adv.*

i·mag·ine (i maj′in) *vt., vi.* **-ined, -in·ing** ⟦< L *imago*, image⟧ **1** to make a mental image (of); conceive in the mind **2** to suppose; think

im′ag·ing *n.* the production of images, esp. by electronic means as in a CAT scan, ultrasound, etc.

i·mam (i mäm′) *n.* [*often* **I-**] a Muslim leader, as of prayer, or ruler: often used as a title

im·bal·ance (im bal′əns) *n.* lack of balance, as in proportion or force

im·be·cile (im′bə sil) *n.* ⟦< L *imbecilis*, feeble⟧ a foolish or stupid person —*adj.* foolish or stupid: also **im′be·cil′ic** (-sil′ik) —**im′be·cil′i·ty** *n.*

im·bed (im bed′) *vt. var. of* EMBED

im·bibe (im bīb′) *vt.* **-bibed′, -bib′ing** ⟦< L *in-*, in + *bibere*, to drink⟧ **1** to drink (esp. alcoholic liquor) **2** to take in with the senses or mind —*vi.* to drink, esp. alcoholic liquor

im·bro·glio (im brōl′yō) *n., pl.* **-glios** ⟦It < *imbrogliare*, embroil⟧ **1** an involved and confusing situation **2** a confused misunderstanding

im·bue (im byo͞o′) *vt.* **-bued′, -bu′ing** ⟦< L *imbuere*, to wet⟧ **1** to dye **2** to permeate (*with* ideas, emotions, etc.)

im·i·tate (im′i tāt′) *vt.* **-tat′ed, -tat′ing** ⟦< L *imitari*⟧ **1** to seek to follow the example of **2** to mimic **3** to reproduce in form, color, etc. **4** to resemble —**im′i·ta′tor** *n.*

im′i·ta′tion (-tā′shən) *n.* **1** an imitating **2** the result of imitating; copy —*adj.* not real; sham *[imitation* leather*]* —**im′i·ta′tive** *adj.*

im·mac·u·late (i mak′yə lit) *adj.* ⟦< L *in-*, not + *macula*, a spot⟧ **1** perfectly clean **2** without a flaw or error **3** pure; innocent; sinless —**im·mac′u·late·ly** *adv.* —**im·mac′u·late·ness** *n.*

im·ma·nent (im′ə nənt) *adj.* ⟦< L *in-*, in + *manere*, remain⟧ **1** operating within; inherent **2** present throughout the universe: said of God —**im′ma·nence** *n.* —**im′ma·nent·ly** *adv.*

im·ma·te·ri·al (im′ə tir′ē əl) *adj.* **1** not consisting of matter **2** not pertinent; unimportant

im·ma·ture (im′ə toor′, -choor′) *adj.* **1** not mature; not completely developed **2** not finished or perfected —**im′ma·tu′ri·ty** *n.*

im·meas·ur·a·ble (i mezh′ər ə bəl) *adj.* that cannot be measured; boundless; vast —**im·meas′ur·a·bly** *adv.*

im·me·di·a·cy (i mē′dē ə sē) *n.* a being immediate; esp., direct relevance to the present time, purpose, etc.

im·me·di·ate (i mē′dē it) *adj.* ⟦see IN-[2] & MEDIATE⟧ **1** not separated in space; closest **2** without delay; instant **3** next in order or relation **4** direct; firsthand —**im·me′di·ate·ly** *adv.*

im·me·mo·ri·al (im′e môr′ē əl) *adj.* extending back beyond memory or record; ancient

im·mense (i mens′) *adj.* ⟦< L *in-*, not + *metiri*, to measure⟧ very large; vast; huge —**im·mense′ly** *adv.* —**im·men′si·ty** *n.*

im·merse (i murs′) *vt.* **-mersed′, -mers′ing** ⟦< L *immergere*⟧ **1** to plunge into or as if into a liquid **2** to baptize by submerging in water **3** to absorb deeply; engross *[immersed* in study*]* —**im·mer′sion** (-mur′zhən, -shən) *n.*

immersion heater an electric coil or rod immersed in water to heat it

im·mi·grant (im′ə grənt) *n.* one who immigrates —*adj.* immigrating

im′mi·grate′ (-grāt′) *vi.* **-grat′ed, -grat′ing** ⟦see IN-[1] & MIGRATE⟧ to come into a new country, etc., esp. to settle there —**im′mi·gra′tion** *n.*

im·mi·nent (im′ə nənt) *adj.* ⟦< L *in-*, on + *minere*, to project⟧ likely to happen without delay; impending

im·mo·bile (i mō′bəl) *adj.* **1** firmly placed; stable **2** motionless —**im′mo·bil′i·ty** *n.* —**im·mo′bi·lize′** (-bə līz′), **-lized′, -liz′ing,** *vt.*

im·mod·er·ate (i mäd′ər it) *adj.* without restraint; unreasonable; excessive

im·mod·est (i mäd′ist) *adj.* **1** indecent **2** not shy; forward —**im·mod′est·ly** *adv.* —**im·mod′es·ty** *n.*

im·mo·late (im′ə lāt′) *vt.* **-lat′ed, -lat′ing** ⟦< L *immolare*, sprinkle with sacrificial meal⟧ to kill as a sacrifice —**im′mo·la′tion** *n.*

im·mor·al (i môr′əl) *adj.* **1** not moral **2** lewd —**im·mor′al·ly** *adv.*

im·mo·ral·i·ty (im′ôr al′i tē) *n.* **1** a being immoral **2** *pl.* **-ties** an immoral act or practice; vice

im·mor·tal (i môrt′'l) *adj.* **1** not mortal; living forever **2** enduring **3** having lasting fame —*n.* an immortal being —**im·mor·tal·i·ty** (im′môr tal′i tē) *n.*

im·mor′tal·ize′ (-īz′) *vt.* **-ized′, -iz′ing** to make immortal, as in fame

im·mov·a·ble (i mo͞ov′ə bəl) *adj.* **1** firmly fixed **2** unyielding; steadfast

im·mune (i myo͞on′) *adj.* ⟦< L *in-*, without + *munia*, duties⟧ **1** exempt from or protected against something disagreeable or harmful **2** not susceptible to some specified disease

im·mu·ni·ty (i myo͞on′ə tē) *n., pl.* **-ties 1** exemption from something burdensome, as a legal obligation **2** resistance to infection or a specified disease

im·mu·nize (im′yo͞o nīz′) ***vt.*** **-nized′**, **-niz′ing** to make immune, as by inoculation —**im′mu·ni·za′tion** ***n.***

im·mu·nol·o·gy (im′yo͞o näl′ə jē) ***n.*** the branch of science dealing with immunity, as to infection or a disease, and with the body mechanisms producing it —**im′mu·nol′o·gist** ***n.***

im·mure (i myoor′) ***vt.*** **-mured′**, **-mur′ing** ⟦< L *in-*, in + *murus*, wall⟧ to shut up within walls; confine

im·mu·ta·ble (i myo͞ot′ə bəl) ***adj.*** unchangeable —**im·mu′ta·bly** ***adv.***

imp (imp) ***n.*** ⟦< Gr *em-*, in + *phyton*, growth⟧ **1** a young demon **2** a mischievous child —**imp′ish** ***adj.***

im·pact (im pakt′; *for n.* im′pakt′) ***vt.*** ⟦< L *impingere*, press firmly together⟧ **1** to force tightly together **2** to affect —***vi.*** **1** to hit with force **2** to have an effect (*on*) —***n.*** **1** a violent contact **2** the power to move feelings, influence thinking, etc.

im·pact′ed ***adj.*** lodged in the jaw: said of a tooth

im·pair (im per′) ***vt.*** ⟦< L *in-*, intens. + *pejor*, worse⟧ to make worse, less, etc. —**im·pair′ment** ***n.***

im·pa·la (im pä′lə) ***n.***, *pl.* **-la** or **-las** a reddish antelope of central and S Africa

im·pale (im pāl′) ***vt.*** **-paled′**, **-pal′ing** ⟦< L *in-*, on + *palus*, a pole⟧ to pierce through with, or fix on, something pointed —**im·pale′ment** ***n.***

im·pal·pa·ble (im pal′pə bəl) ***adj.*** **1** not perceptible to the touch **2** too subtle to be easily understood

im·pan·el (im pan′əl) ***vt.*** **-eled** or **-elled**, **-el·ing** or **-el·ling** to choose (a jury) in a law case —**im·pan′el·ment** ***n.***

im·part (im pärt′) ***vt.*** ⟦see IN-[1] & PART⟧ **1** to give a part of **2** to make known; reveal

im·par·tial (im pär′shəl) ***adj.*** without bias; fair —**im·par′ti·al′i·ty** (-shē al′i tē) ***n.*** —**im·par′tial·ly** ***adv.***

im·pass·a·ble (im pas′ə bəl) ***adj.*** that cannot be passed or traveled over

im·passe (im′pas′, im pas′) ***n.*** ⟦Fr⟧ a situation offering no escape or resolution, as a deadlocked argument

im·pas·sioned (im pash′ənd) ***adj.*** passionate; fiery; ardent

im·pas·sive (im pas′iv) ***adj.*** not feeling or showing emotion; calm —**im·pas·siv·i·ty** (im′pa siv′i tē) ***n.***

im·pas·to (im päs′tō) ***n.*** ⟦It⟧ painting in which the paint is laid thickly on the canvas

im·pa·tient (im pā′shənt) ***adj.*** lacking patience; specif., *a*) annoyed because of delay, opposition, etc. *b*) restlessly eager to do something, etc. —**im·pa′tience** ***n.***

im·peach (im pēch′) ***vt.*** ⟦< L *in-*, in + *pedica*, a fetter⟧ **1** to discredit (a person's honor, etc.) **2** to charge (a public official) with wrongdoing —**im·peach′a·ble** ***adj.*** —**im·peach′ment** ***n.***

im·pec·ca·ble (im pek′ə bəl) ***adj.*** ⟦< L *in-*, not + *peccare*, to sin⟧ without defect or error; flawless —**im·pec′ca·bil′i·ty** ***n.*** —**im·pec′ca·bly** ***adv.***

im·pe·cu·ni·ous (im′pi kyo͞o′nē əs) ***adj.*** ⟦< L *in-*, not + *pecunia*, money⟧ having no money; poor

im·ped·ance (im pēd′'ns) ***n.*** ⟦< fol. + -ANCE⟧ the resistance in an electric circuit to a flow of alternating current

im·pede (im pēd′) ***vt.*** **-ped′ed**, **-ped′ing** ⟦< L *in-*, in + *pes*, foot⟧ to hinder the progress of; obstruct

im·ped·i·ment (im ped′ə mənt) ***n.*** anything that impedes; specif., a speech defect

im·ped′i·men′ta (-men′tə) ***pl.n.*** encumbrances, as baggage or supplies

im·pel (im pel′) ***vt.*** **-pelled′**, **-pel′ling** ⟦< L *in-*, in + *pellere*, to drive⟧ **1** to drive or move forward **2** to force, compel, or urge —**im·pel′ler** ***n.***

im·pend (im pend′) ***vi.*** ⟦< L *in-*, in + *pendere*, hang⟧ to be about to happen; be imminent [*impending* disaster] —**im·pend′ing** ***adj.***

im·pen·e·tra·ble (im pen′i trə bəl) ***adj.*** **1** that cannot be penetrated **2** that cannot be solved or understood

im·pen·i·tent (im pen′ə tənt) ***adj.*** without regret, shame, or remorse

im·per·a·tive (im per′ə tiv) ***adj.*** ⟦< L *imperare*, to command⟧ **1** indicating authority or command **2** necessary; urgent **3** designating or of the mood of a verb that expresses a command, etc. —***n.*** a command

im·per·cep·ti·ble (im′pər sep′tə bəl) ***adj.*** not easily perceived by the senses or the mind; very slight, subtle, etc. —**im′per·cep′ti·bly** ***adv.***

im′per·cep′tive (-tiv) ***adj.*** not perceiving —**im′per·cep′tive·ness** ***n.***

im·per·fect (im pur′fikt) ***adj.*** **1** not complete **2** not perfect **3** designating a verb tense that indicates a past action or state as uncompleted or continuous —**im·per′fect·ly** ***adv.***

im·per·fec·tion (im′pər fek′shən) ***n.*** **1** a being imperfect **2** a defect; fault

im·pe·ri·al (im pir′ē əl) ***adj.*** ⟦< L *imperium*, empire⟧ **1** of an empire, emperor, or empress **2** having supreme authority **3** majestic; august **4** of great size or superior quality —***n.*** a small, pointed chin beard

imperial gallon the standard British gallon, equal to 4.546 liters (about $1\frac{1}{5}$ U.S. gallons)

im·pe′ri·al·ism′ ***n.*** **1** imperial state or authority **2** the policy of forming and maintaining an empire, as by establishing colonies **3** the policy of seeking to dominate the affairs of weaker countries —**im·pe′ri·al·ist** ***n.***, ***adj.*** —**im·pe′ri·al·is′tic** ***adj.***

im·per·il (im per′əl) ***vt.*** **-iled** or **-illed**, **-il·ing** or **-il·ling** to put in peril; endanger

im·pe·ri·ous (im pir′ē əs) ***adj.*** ⟦< L *imperium*, empire⟧ **1** overbearing, arrogant, etc. **2** urgent; imperative —**im·pe′ri·ous·ly** ***adv.***

im·per·ish·a·ble (im per′ish ə bəl) ***adj.*** not perishable; indestructible

im·per·ma·nent (im pur′mə nənt) ***adj.*** not permanent; temporary —**im·per′ma·nent·ly** ***adv.***

im·per·son·al (im pur′sə nəl) ***adj.*** **1** without reference to any particular person **2** not existing as a person *[an impersonal force]* **3** designating or of a verb occurring only in the third person singular, usually with *it* as subject —**im·per′son·al·ly** ***adv.***

im·per·son·ate (im pur′sə nāt′) ***vt.*** **-at′ed, -at′ing** to assume the role of or pretend to be, for purposes of entertainment or fraud —**im·per′son·a′tion** ***n.*** —**im·per′son·a′tor** ***n.***

im·per·ti·nent (im purt′′n ənt) ***adj.*** **1** not pertinent **2** insolent; impudent —**im·per′ti·nence** ***n.***

im·per·turb·a·ble (im′pər tur′bə bəl) ***adj.*** that cannot be disconcerted, disturbed, or excited

im·per·vi·ous (im pur′vē əs) ***adj.*** **1** incapable of being penetrated, as by moisture **2** not affected by: with *to*

im·pe·ti·go (im′pə tī′gō) ***n.*** ⟦see IMPETUS⟧ a contagious skin disease characterized by pustules

im·pet·u·ous (im pech′o͞o əs) ***adj.*** ⟦see fol.⟧ acting or done suddenly with little thought; rash —**im·pet′u·os′i·ty** (-äs′i tē) ***n.*** —**im·pet′u·ous·ly** ***adv.***

im·pe·tus (im′pə təs) ***n.***, *pl.* **-tus·es** ⟦< L *in-*, in + *petere*, rush at⟧ **1** the force with which a body moves against resistance **2** driving force or motive; incentive

im·pi·e·ty (im pī′ə tē) ***n.*** **1** lack of reverence for God **2** *pl.* **-ties** an impious act or remark

im·pinge (im pinj′) ***vi.*** **-pinged′, -ping′ing** ⟦< L *in-*, in + *pangere*, to strike⟧ **1** to strike, hit, etc. (*on* or *upon*) **2** to encroach (*on* or *upon*) —**im·pinge′ment** ***n.***

im·pi·ous (im′pē əs) ***adj.*** not pious; specif., lacking reverence for God

im·plac·a·ble (im plak′ə bəl, -plā′kə-) ***adj.*** not to be placated or appeased; relentless —**im·plac′a·bly** ***adv.***

im·plant (im plant′; *for n.* im′plant′) ***vt.*** **1** to plant firmly **2** to fix firmly in the mind **3** to insert surgically —***n.*** an implanted organ, etc.

im·plau·si·ble (im plô′zə bəl) ***adj.*** not plausible —**im·plau′si·bly** ***adv.***

im·ple·ment (im′plə mənt; *for v.*, -ment′) ***n.*** ⟦< L *in-*, in + *plere*, to fill⟧ something used in a given activity; tool, instrument, etc. —***vt.*** to carry into effect; accomplish —**im′ple·men·ta′tion** (-mən tā′shən) ***n.***

im·pli·cate (im′pli kāt′) ***vt.*** **-cat′ed, -cat′ing** ⟦see IMPLY⟧ to show to be party to a crime, etc. —**im′pli·ca′tive** ***adj.***

im′pli·ca′tion (-kā′shən) ***n.*** **1** an implicating or being implicated **2** an implying or being implied **3** something implied

im·plic·it (im plis′it) ***adj.*** ⟦see IMPLY⟧ **1** suggested though not plainly expressed; implied **2** necessarily involved though not apparent; inherent **3** without reservation or doubt —**im·plic′it·ly** ***adv.***

im·plode (im plōd′) ***vt.***, ***vi.*** **-plod′ed, -plod′ing** ⟦< IN-[1] + (EX)PLODE⟧ to burst or cause to burst inward —**im·plo′sion** (-plō′zhən) ***n.*** —**im·plo′sive** (-plō′siv) ***adj.***

im·plore (im plôr′) ***vt.*** **-plored′, -plor′ing** ⟦< L *in-*, intens. + *plorare*, cry out⟧ **1** to ask earnestly for **2** to beg (a person) to do something —**im·plor′ing·ly** ***adv.***

im·ply (im plī′) ***vt.*** **-plied′, -ply′ing** ⟦< L *in-*, in + *plicare*, to fold⟧ **1** to have as a necessary part, condition, etc. **2** to indicate indirectly; hint; suggest

im·po·lite (im′pə līt′) ***adj.*** not polite; discourteous —**im′po·lite′ly** ***adv.***

im·pol·i·tic (im päl′ə tik′) ***adj.*** not politic; unwise

im·pon·der·a·ble (im pän′dər ə bəl) ***adj.*** that cannot be weighed, measured, explained, etc. —***n.*** anything imponderable

im·port (im pôrt′, *also, and for n. always* im′pôrt′) ***vt.*** ⟦< L *in-*, in + *portare*, carry⟧ **1** to bring in (goods) from another country, especially for sale **2** to mean; signify —***n.*** **1** something imported **2** meaning; signification **3** importance —**im′por·ta′tion** ***n.*** —**im·port′er** ***n.***

im·por·tant (im pôrt′′nt) ***adj.*** ⟦see prec.⟧ **1** meaning a great deal; having much significance or value **2** having, or acting as if having, power, authority, etc. —**im·por′tance** ***n.*** —**im·por′tant·ly** ***adv.***

im·por·tu·nate (im pôr′chə nət) ***adj.*** persistent in asking or demanding

im·por·tune (im′pôr to͞on′) ***vt.***, ***vi.*** **-tuned′, -tun′ing** ⟦< L *importunus*, troublesome⟧ to urge or entreat persistently or repeatedly —**im′por·tu′ni·ty**, *pl.* **-ties**, ***n.***

im·pose (im pōz′) ***vt.*** **-posed′, -pos′ing** ⟦< L *in-*, on + *ponere*, to place⟧ **1** to place (a burden, tax, etc. *on* or *upon*) **2** to force (oneself) on others —**impose on** (or **upon**) **1** to take advantage of **2** to cheat or defraud —**im′po·si′tion** (-pə zish′ən) ***n.***

im·pos′ing ***adj.*** impressive because of great size, strength, dignity, etc. —**im·pos′ing·ly** ***adv.***

im·pos·si·ble (im päs′ə bəl) ***adj.*** **1** not capable of being, being done, or happening **2** not capable of being endured, used, etc. because disagreeable or unsuitable —**im·pos′si·bil′i·ty**, *pl.* **-ties**, ***n.*** —**im·pos′si·bly** ***adv.***

im·post (im′pōst′) ***n.*** ⟦see IMPOSE⟧ a tax; esp., a duty on imported goods

im·pos·tor or **im·post′er** (im päs′tər) ***n.*** ⟦see IMPOSE⟧ one who deceives or cheats others by pretending to be what he or she is not

im·pos′ture (-chər) ***n.*** the act or practice of an impostor; fraud

im·po·tent (im′pə tənt) ***adj.*** **1** lacking physical strength **2** ineffective; powerless **3** unable to engage in sexual intercourse: said of males —**im′po·tence** or **im′po·ten·cy** ***n.*** —**im′po·tent·ly** ***adv.***

im·pound (im pound′) ***vt.*** **1** to shut up (an animal) in a pound **2** to take and hold in legal custody **3** to gather and enclose (water), as for irrigation

im·pov·er·ish (im päv′ər ish) ***vt.*** ⟦< L *in-*, in + *pauper*, poor⟧ **1** to make poor **2** to deprive of strength, resources, etc. —**im·pov′er·ish·ment** ***n.***

im·prac·ti·ca·ble (im prak′ti kə bəl) ***adj.*** not capable of being carried out in practice

im·prac·ti·cal (im prak′ti kəl) ***adj.*** not practical

im·pre·ca·tion (im′pri kā′shən) ***n.*** ⟦< L *in-*, on + *precari*, pray⟧ a curse

im·pre·cise (im′pri sīs′) ***adj.*** not precise; vague —**im′pre·cise′ly** ***adv.*** —**im′pre·ci′sion** (-sizh′ən) ***n.***

im·preg·na·ble (im preg′nə bəl) ***adj.*** **1** that cannot be captured or entered by force **2** unyielding —**im·preg′na·bil′i·ty** ***n.*** —**im·preg′na·bly** ***adv.***

im·preg·nate (im preg′nāt′) ***vt.*** **-nat′ed, -nat′ing** **1** to make pregnant; fertilize **2** to saturate **3** to imbue (*with* ideas, etc.) —**im′preg·na′tion** ***n.***

im·pre·sa·ri·o (im′prə sä′rē ō′) ***n.***, *pl.* **-os** ⟦It⟧ one who manages an opera, organizes concert series, etc.

im·press[1] (im pres′) ***vt.*** ⟦< IN-[1] + PRESS[2]⟧ **1** to force (a person) into military service **2** to seize for public use

im·press[2] (im pres′; *for n.* im′pres′) ***vt.*** ⟦see IMPRINT⟧ **1** to stamp; imprint **2** to affect strongly the mind or emotions of **3** to fix in the memory: with *on* or *upon* —***n.*** **1** an impressing **2** an imprint

im·press′i·ble (-ə bəl) ***adj.*** that can be impressed —**im·press′i·bil′i·ty** ***n.***

im·pres·sion (im presh′ən) ***n.*** **1** an impressing **2** *a*) a mark, imprint, etc. *b*) an effect produced on the mind **3** a vague notion **4** an amusing impersonation; mimicking

im·pres′sion·a·ble ***adj.*** easily impressed or influenced; sensitive

im·pres′sion·ism′ ***n.*** a theory of art, music, etc. whose aim is to capture a brief, immediate impression —**im·pres′sion·ist** ***n.*** —**im·pres′sion·is′tic** ***adj.***

im·pres·sive (im pres′iv) ***adj.*** tending to impress the mind or emotions; eliciting wonder or admiration —**im·pres′sive·ly** ***adv.***

im·pri·ma·tur (im′pri mät′ər) ***n.*** ⟦ModL, lit., let it be printed⟧ **1** permission to publish a book, etc., as granted by a Catholic bishop **2** any sanction or approval

im·print (im print′; *for n.* im′print′) ***vt.*** ⟦< L *in-*, on + *premere*, to press⟧ to mark or fix as by pressing or stamping —***n.*** **1** a mark made by imprinting **2** a lasting effect **3** a note in a book giving facts of its publication

im·pris·on (im priz′ən) ***vt.*** to put in or as in prison —**im·pris′on·ment** ***n.***

im·prob·a·ble (im präb′ə bəl) ***adj.*** not probable; unlikely —**im′prob·a·bil′i·ty**, *pl.* **-ties**, ***n.*** —**im·prob′a·bly** ***adv.***

im·promp·tu (im prämp′to͞o′) ***adj., adv.*** ⟦< L *in promptu*, in readiness⟧ without preparation; offhand

im·prop·er (im präp′ər) ***adj.*** **1** not suitable; unfit **2** incorrect **3** not in good taste —**im·prop′er·ly** ***adv.***

im·pro·pri·e·ty (im′prō prī′ə tē) ***n.***, *pl.* **-ties** **1** a being improper **2** an improper act, word usage, etc.

im·prove (im pro͞ov′) ***vt.*** **-proved′, -prov′ing** ⟦< Anglo-Fr *en-*, in + *prou*, gain⟧ **1** to make better **2** to make (real estate) more valuable by cultivation, construction, etc. —***vi.*** to become better —**improve on** (or **upon**) to do or make better than —**im·prov′a·ble** ***adj.***

im·prove′ment ***n.*** **1** an improving or being improved **2** an addition or change that improves something

im·prov·i·dent (im präv′ə dənt) ***adj.*** lacking foresight or thrift —**im·prov′i·dence** ***n.*** —**im·prov′i·dent·ly** ***adv.***

im·pro·vise (im′prə vīz′) ***vt., vi.*** **-vised′, -vis′ing** ⟦< L *in-*, not + *providere*, foresee⟧ **1** to compose and perform without preparation **2** to make or do with whatever is at hand —**im·prov′i·sa′tion** (-präv′i zā′shən) ***n.*** —**im·prov′i·sa′tion·al** ***adj.***

im·pru·dent (im pro͞od′′nt) ***adj.*** not prudent; rash —**im·pru′dence** ***n.***

im·pu·dent (im′pyo͞o dənt) ***adj.*** ⟦< L *in-*, not + *pudere*, feel shame⟧ shamelessly bold; insolent —**im′pu·dence** ***n.*** —**im′pu·dent·ly** ***adv.***

im·pugn (im pyo͞on′) ***vt.*** ⟦< L *in-*, against + *pugnare*, to fight⟧ to challenge as false or questionable

im·pulse (im′puls′) ***n.*** ⟦see IMPEL⟧ **1** *a*) an impelling force; impetus *b*) the motion or effect caused by such a force **2** *a*) incitement to action by a stimulus *b*) a sudden inclination to act **3** a brief surge in an electric current

im·pul·sion (im pul′shən) ***n.*** **1** an impelling or being impelled **2** IMPULSE (sense 1*a*) **3** IMPULSE (sense 2)

im·pul·sive (im pul′siv) ***adj.*** **1** driving forward **2** likely to act on impulse —**im·pul′sive·ly** ***adv.***

im·pu·ni·ty (im pyo͞o′ni tē) ***n.*** ⟦< L *in-*, without + *poena*, punishment⟧ exemption from punishment, harm, etc.

im·pure (im pyoor′) ***adj.*** **1** unclean; dirty **2** immoral; obscene; **3** mixed with foreign matter; adulterated —**im·pure′ly** ***adv.*** —**im·pure′ness** ***n.***

im·pu′ri·ty (-pyoor′ə tē) ***n.*** **1** a being impure **2** *pl.* **-ties** an impure thing or part

im·pute (im pyo͞ot′) ***vt.*** **-put′ed, -put′ing** ⟦< L *in-*, in, to + *putare*, to think⟧ to attribute (esp. a fault or misconduct) to another —**im′pu·ta′tion** (-pyo͞o tā′shən) ***n.***

in[1] (in) ***prep.*** ⟦OE⟧ **1** contained by *[in* the room*]* **2** wearing *[*dressed *in* furs*]* **3** during *[*done *in* a day*]* **4** at the end of *[*due *in* an hour*]* **5** not beyond *[in* sight*]* **6** employed, enrolled, etc. at *[in* college*]* **7** out of a group of *[*one *in* ten*]* **8** amidst *[in* a storm*]* **9** affected by *[in* trouble*]* **10** with regard to *[*to vary *in* size*]* **11** using *[*speak *in* English*]* **12** because of; for *[*to cry *in* pain*]* **13** into *[*come *in* the house*]* **14** living or located at (*in* Rome) —***adv.*** **1** to the inside *[*he went *in]* **2** to or at a certain place **3** so as to be contained by a certain space, condition, etc. **4** inside one's home, etc. (to stay *in*) —***adj.*** **1** that is in power *[*the *in* group*]* **2** inner; inside **3** gathered, counted, etc. **4** [Inf.] currently smart, popular, etc. —***n.*** **1** one that is in power: *usually used in pl.* **2** [Inf.]

special influence; pull —**have it in for** [Inf.] to hold a grudge against —**ins and outs** all the details and intricacies —**in that** because; since —**in with** associated with

in[2] *abbrev.* inch(es)

IN Indiana

in-[1] ⟦< the prep. IN[1] or L *in*, in⟧ *prefix* in, into, within, on, toward *[inbreed]*

in-[2] ⟦L⟧ *prefix* no, not, without, NON- The following list includes some common compounds formed with *in-*, with no special meanings; they will be understood if "not" or "lack of" is used with the meaning of the base word:

inability
inaccessible
inaccuracy
inaccurate
inaction
inactive
inadequacy
inadequate
inadmissible
inadvisable
inanimate
inapplicable
inappropriate
inapt
inaudible
inauspicious
incapable
incautious
incivility
incombustible
incommensurate
incommunicable
incomprehensible
inconceivable
inconclusive
inconsistency
inconsistent
incorrect
incurable
indecorous
indefinable
indiscernible
indisputable
indistinct
indivisible
inedible
ineffective
ineffectual
inefficacious
inelastic
ineligible
inequality
inequitable
inequity
inexact
inexcusable
inexpensive
infertile
inhospitable
inhumane
injudicious
inopportune
inseparable
insignificance
insignificant
insolvable
insufficient
insurmountable
insusceptible
invariable

-in (in) *combining form* a mass action or gathering of a (specified) type *[pray-in, be-in]*

in ab·sen·ti·a (in ab sen′shə, -shē ə) ⟦L⟧ although not present *[to receive an award in absentia]*

in·ac·ti·vate (in ak′tə vāt′) *vt.* **-vat′ed, -vat′ing** to make inactive —**in·ac′ti·va′tion** *n.*

in·ad·vert·ent (in′ad vurt′'nt, -əd-) *adj.* not on purpose; accidental —**in′ad·vert′ence** *n.* —**in′ad·vert′ent·ly** *adv.*

in·al·ien·a·ble (in āl′yən ə bəl) *adj.* ⟦see ALIEN⟧ that may not be taken away or transferred —**in·al′ien·a·bly** *adv.*

in·am·o·ra·ta (in am′ə rät′ə) *n.* ⟦It⟧ a sweetheart or lover: said of a woman

in·ane (in ān′) *adj.* ⟦L *inanis*, empty⟧ lacking sense; silly —**in·an′i·ty** (-an′i tē) *n.*

in·ar·tic·u·late (in′är tik′yoo lit, -yə-) *adj.* **1** without the articulation of normal speech *[an inarticulate cry]* **2** not able to speak; mute **3** unable to speak clearly or coherently **4** unexpressed or unexpressible

in·as·much as (in′əz much′ az′) **1** since; because **2** to the extent that

in·at·ten·tion (in′ə ten′shən) *n.* failure to pay attention; negligence —**in′at·ten′tive** *adj.*

in·au·gu·ral (in ô′gyə rəl) *adj.* ⟦Fr⟧ **1** of an inauguration **2** first in a series —*n.* **1** a speech made at an inauguration **2** an inauguration

in·au′gu·rate′ (-rāt′) *vt.* **-rat′ed, -rat′ing** ⟦< L *inaugurare*, to practice augury⟧ **1** to induct into office with a formal ceremony **2** to make a formal beginning of **3** to dedicate formally —**in·au′gu·ra′tion** *n.*

in·au·then·tic (in′ô then′tik) *adj.* not authentic

in·board (in′bôrd′) *adv., adj.* **1** inside the hull of a ship or boat **2** close to the fuselage of an aircraft —*n.* a boat with an inboard motor

in·born (in′bôrn′) *adj.* present in the organism at birth; innate

in·bound (in′bound′) *adj.* traveling or going inward —*vt., vi.* *Basketball* to put (the ball) in play from out of bounds

in·bred (in′bred′) *adj.* **1** innate; inborn **2** resulting from inbreeding

in·breed (in′brēd′) *vt.* **-bred′, -breed′ing** to breed by continual mating of individuals of the same or closely related stocks —*vi.* **1** to engage in such breeding **2** to become too refined, effete, etc. —**in′breed′ing** *n.*

inc *abbrev.* **1** incorporated: also **Inc.** **2** increase

In·ca (iŋ′kə) *n.* a member of the highly civilized Indian people that dominated ancient Peru until the Spanish conquest —**In′can** *adj.*

in·cal·cu·la·ble (in kal′kyoo lə bəl) *adj.* **1** that cannot be calculated; too great or too many to be counted **2** unpredictable —**in·cal′cu·la·bly** *adv.*

in·can·des·cent (in′kən des′ənt) *adj.* ⟦< L *in-*, in + *candere*, to shine⟧ **1** glowing with intense heat **2** very bright —**in′can·des′cence** *n.*

incandescent lamp a lamp with a filament in a vacuum heated to incandescence by an electric current

in·can·ta·tion (in′kan tā′shən) *n.* ⟦< L *in-*, intens. + *cantare*, to sing⟧ words chanted in magic spells or rites

in·ca·pac·i·tate (in′kə pas′ə tāt′) *vt.* **-tat′ed, -tat′ing** to make unable or unfit

in′ca·pac′i·ty *n.* lack of capacity, power, or fitness

in·car·cer·ate (in kär′sər āt′) *vt.* **-at′ed, -at′ing** ⟦< L *in*, in + *carcer*, prison⟧ to imprison —**in·car′cer·a′tion** *n.*

in·car·na·dine (in kär′nə dīn′) *vt.* **-dined′, -din′ing** to make red

in·car·nate (in kär′nit; *also, and for v. always,* -nāt′) *adj.* ⟦< L *in-*, in + *caro*, flesh⟧ endowed with a human body; personified —*vt.* **-nat′ed, -nat′ing** **1** to give bodily form to **2** to be the type or embodiment of —**in′car·na′tion** *n.*

in·cen·di·ar·y (in sen′dē er′ē) *adj.* ⟦< L *incendium*, a fire⟧ **1** having to do with the willful destruction of property by fire **2** designed to cause fires, as certain bombs **3** willfully stirring up strife, riot, etc. —*n., pl.* **-ar′ies** **1** one who willfully stirs up strife, riot, etc. **2** an incendiary bomb, etc.

in·cense[1] (in′sens′) ***n.*** ⟦< L *in-*, in + *candere*, to burn⟧ **1** any substance burned to produce a pleasant odor **2** the odor from this

in·cense[2] (in sens′) ***vt.*** **-censed′**, **-cens′ing** ⟦see prec.⟧ to make very angry

in·cen·tive (in sent′iv) ***n.*** ⟦< L *in-*, in, on + *canere*, sing⟧ a stimulus; motive

in·cep·tion (in sep′shən) ***n.*** ⟦see INCIPIENT⟧ the beginning of something; start

in·cer·ti·tude (in surt′ə to͞od′) ***n.*** **1** doubt **2** insecurity

in·ces·sant (in ses′ənt) ***adj.*** ⟦< L *in-*, not + *cessare*, cease⟧ never ceasing; continuing without stopping; constant **—in·ces′sant·ly *adv.***

in·cest (in′sest′) ***n.*** ⟦< L *in-*, not + *castus*, chaste⟧ sexual intercourse between persons too closely related to marry legally **—in·ces·tu·ous** (in ses′tyo͞o əs, -cho͞o-) ***adj.*** **—in·ces′tu·ous·ly *adv.*** **—in·ces′tu·ous·ness *n.***

inch (inch) ***n.*** ⟦< L *uncia*, twelfth part⟧ a measure of length equal to $\frac{1}{12}$ foot: symbol, ″ **—*vt.*, *vi.*** to move very slowly, or by degrees **—every inch** in all respects **—inch by inch** gradually: also **by inches —within an inch of** very close to

in·cho·ate (in kō′it) ***adj.*** ⟦< L *inchoare*, begin⟧ **1** just begun; rudimentary **2** not yet clearly formed

in·ci·dence (in′sə dəns) ***n.*** **1** the degree or range of occurrence or effect **2** [Inf.] an instance

in′ci·dent (-dənt) ***adj.*** ⟦< L *in-*, on + *cadere*, to fall⟧ **1** likely to happen as a result **2** falling upon or affecting *[incident rays]* **—*n.*** **1** an event, esp. a minor one **2** a minor conflict

in′ci·den′tal (-dent′'l) ***adj.*** **1** happening in connection with something more important; casual **2** secondary or minor **—*n.*** **1** something incidental **2** [*pl.*] miscellaneous items

in′ci·den′tal·ly *adv.* **1** in an incidental manner **2** by the way

in·cin·er·ate (in sin′ər āt′) ***vt.*, *vi.*** **-at′ed**, **-at′ing** ⟦< L *in*, in + *cinis*, ashes⟧ to burn to ashes; burn up **—in·cin′er·a′tion *n.***

in·cin′er·a′tor *n.* a furnace for burning trash

in·cip·i·ent (in sip′ē ənt) ***adj.*** ⟦< L *in-*, in + *capere*, to take⟧ just beginning to exist or appear **—in·cip′i·ence *n.***

in·cise (in sīz′) ***vt.*** **-cised′**, **-cis′ing** ⟦< L *in-*, into + *caedere*, to cut⟧ to cut into with a sharp tool; specif., to engrave or carve

in·ci·sion (in sizh′ən) ***n.*** **1** an incising **2** a cut; specif., one made surgically

in·ci·sive (in sī′siv) ***adj.*** **1** cutting into **2** sharp; penetrating **—in·ci′sive·ly *adv.*** **—in·ci′sive·ness *n.***

in·ci·sor (in sī′zər) ***n.*** any of the front cutting teeth between the canines

in·cite (in sīt′) ***vt.*** **-cit′ed**, **-cit′ing** ⟦< L *in-*, on + *citare*, to urge⟧ to urge to action; rouse **—in·cite′ment *n.***

incl *abbrev.* **1** including **2** inclusive

in·clem·ent (in klem′ənt) ***adj.*** ⟦< L *in-*, on + *clemens*, lenient⟧ **1** rough; stormy **2** lacking mercy; harsh **—in·clem′en·cy**, *pl.* **-cies**, ***n.***

in·cli·na·tion (in′klə nā′shən) ***n.*** **1** a bending, leaning, or sloping **2** an inclined surface; slope **3** *a)* a bias; tendency *b)* a preference

INCLINED PLANE

in·cline (in klīn′; *for n., usually* in′klīn′) ***vi.*** **-clined′**, **-clin′ing** ⟦< L *in-*, on + *clinare*, to lean⟧ **1** to lean; slope **2** to have a tendency **3** to have a preference or liking **—*vt.*** **1** to cause to lean, slope, etc. **2** to make willing; influence **—*n.*** a slope; grade

inclined plane a sloping plane surface, esp. one sloping slightly

in·close (in klōz′) ***vt.*** **-closed′**, **-clos′ing** ENCLOSE **—in·clo′sure** (-klō′zhər) ***n.***

in·clude (in klo͞od′) ***vt.*** **-clud′ed**, **-clud′ing** ⟦< L *in-*, in + *claudere*, to close⟧ **1** to have as part of a whole; contain **2** to make part of a whole **3** to take into account **—in·clu′sion** (-klo͞o′zhən) ***n.***

in·clu′sive (-klo͞o′siv) ***adj.*** **1** taking everything into account **2** including the terms or limits mentioned *[*the third to the fifth *inclusive]* **—inclusive of** including **—in·clu′sive·ly *adv.***

in·cog·ni·to (in′käg nē′tō′, in käg′ni tō′) ***adj.*, *adv.*** ⟦It < L *in-*, not + *cognitus*, known⟧ with true identity unrevealed or disguised

in·co·her·ent (in′kō hir′ənt, -her′-) ***adj.*** **1** not logically connected; disjointed **2** characterized by speech, etc. like this **—in′co·her′ence *n.*** **—in′co·her′ent·ly *adv.***

in·come (in′kum′) ***n.*** money, etc. received in a given period, as wages, rent, interest, etc.

in·com·mu·ni·ca·do (in′kə myo͞o′ni kä′dō) ***adj.*, *adv.*** ⟦Sp⟧ not allowed or willing to communicate with others

in·com·pa·ra·ble (in käm′pə rə bəl) ***adj.*** **1** having no basis of comparison **2** beyond comparison; matchless

in·com·pat·i·ble (in′kəm pat′ə bəl) ***adj.*** not compatible; specif., unable to live together harmoniously **—in′com·pat′i·bil′i·ty**, *pl.* **-ties**, ***n.***

in·com·pe·tent (in käm′pə tənt) ***adj.*** without adequate ability, knowledge, fitness, etc. **—*n.*** an incompetent person **—in·com′pe·tence *n.*** **—in·com′pe·tent·ly *adv.***

in·com·plete (in′kəm plēt′) ***adj.*** **1** lacking a part or parts **2** unfinished **—*n.*** *Educ.* a grade, etc. indicating assigned work is not complete

in·con·gru·ous (in käŋ′gro͞o əs) ***adj.*** **1** lacking harmony or agreement of parts, etc. **2** inappropriate **—in′con·gru′i·ty**

(-kän grōō′i tē) ***n.***

in·con·se·quen·tial (in kän′si kwen′ shəl) ***adj.*** unimportant; trivial

in·con·sid·er·a·ble (in′kən sid′ər ə bəl) ***adj.*** trivial; small

in′con·sid′er·ate (-it) ***adj.*** without thought or consideration for others; thoughtless —**in′con·sid′er·ate·ly** ***adv.*** —**in′con·sid′er·ate·ness** or **in′con·sid′er·a′tion** (-ər ā′shən) ***n.***

in·con·sol·a·ble (in′kən sōl′ə bəl) ***adj.*** that cannot be consoled

in·con·spic·u·ous (in′kən spik′yōō əs) ***adj.*** attracting little attention

in·con·stant (in kän′stənt) ***adj.*** not constant; changeable, irregular, etc. —**in·con′stan·cy** ***n.***

in·con·test·a·ble (in′kən tes′tə bəl) ***adj.*** unquestionable; indisputable —**in′con·test′a·bil′i·ty** ***n.*** —**in′con·test′a·bly** ***adv.***

in·con·ti·nent (in känt′′n ənt) ***adj.*** **1** without self-restraint, esp. in sexual activity **2** unable to restrain a natural discharge, as of urine —**in·con′ti·nence** ***n.***

in·con·ven·ience (in′kən vēn′yəns) ***n.*** **1** lack of comfort, ease, etc. **2** anything inconvenient —***vt.*** **-ienced**, **-ienc·ing** to cause inconvenience to

in′con·ven′ient (-yənt) ***adj.*** not favorable to one's comfort; causing bother, etc.

in·cor·po·rate (in kôr′pə rāt′) ***vt.*** **-rat′ed**, **-rat′ing** ⟦see IN-[1] & CORPORATE⟧ **1** to combine; include; embody **2** to bring together into a single whole; merge **3** to form into a corporation —***vi.*** **1** to combine into a single whole **2** to form a corporation —**in·cor′po·ra′tion** ***n.***

in·cor·ri·gi·ble (in kôr′ə jə bəl) ***adj.*** ⟦< LL *incorrigibilis*⟧ that cannot be corrected or reformed, esp. because set in bad habits —**in·cor′ri·gi·bil′i·ty** ***n.*** —**in·cor′ri·gi·bly** ***adv.***

in·cor·rupt·i·ble (in′kə rup′tə bəl) ***adj.*** that cannot be corrupted, esp. morally

in·crease (in krēs′, in′krēs′) ***vi.*** **-creased′**, **-creas′ing** ⟦< L *in-*, in + *crescere*, grow⟧ to become greater in size, amount, degree, etc. —***vt.*** to make greater in size, etc. —***n.*** **1** an increasing or becoming increased **2** the result or amount of an increasing —**on the increase** increasing

in·creas′ing·ly ***adv.*** more and more

in·cred·i·ble (in kred′ə bəl) ***adj.*** **1** not credible **2** seeming too unusual to be possible —**in·cred′i·bly** ***adv.***

in·cred·u·lous (in krej′oo ləs) ***adj.*** **1** unwilling to believe **2** showing doubt or disbelief —**in·cre·du·li·ty** (in′krə dōō′lə tē) ***n.***

in·cre·ment (in′krə mənt, iŋ′-) ***n.*** ⟦< L *incrementum*⟧ **1** an increase **2** amount of increase

in·crim·i·nate (in krim′i nāt′) ***vt.*** **-nat′ed**, **-nat′ing** ⟦< L *in-*, in + *crimen*, offense⟧ **1** to accuse of a crime **2** to involve in, or make appear guilty of, a crime or fault —**in·crim′i·na′tion** ***n.***

in·crust (in krust′) ***vt.***, ***vi.*** ENCRUST —**in·crus·ta·tion** (in′krus tā′shən) ***n.***

in·cu·bate (in′kyōō bāt′, iŋ′-) ***vt.*** **-bat′ed**, **-bat′ing** ⟦< L *in-*, on + *cubare*, to lie⟧ **1** to sit on and hatch (eggs) **2** to heat, etc. so as to hatch or grow, as in an incubator **3** to develop, as by planning —***vi.*** to undergo incubation —**in′cu·ba′tion** ***n.***

in′cu·ba′tor ***n.*** **1** a heated container for hatching eggs **2** any similar device, as for protecting premature babies, growing cell cultures, etc.

in·cu·bus (in′kyə bəs, iŋ′-) ***n.*** ⟦LL⟧ **1** a nightmare **2** an oppressive burden

in·cul·cate (in kul′kāt′, in′kul-) ***vt.*** **-cat′ed**, **-cat′ing** ⟦< L *in-*, in + *calcare*, trample underfoot⟧ to impress upon the mind, as by persistent urging —**in′cul·ca′tion** ***n.***

in·cul·pate (in kul′pāt′, in′kul-) ***vt.*** **-pat′ed**, **-pat′ing** ⟦< L *in*, on + *culpa*, blame⟧ INCRIMINATE

in·cum·ben·cy (in kum′bən sē) ***n.***, *pl.* **-cies** tenure of office

in·cum′bent (-bənt) ***adj.*** ⟦< L *in-*, on + *cubare*, lie down⟧ currently in office —***n.*** one currently in office —**incumbent on** (or **upon**) resting upon as a duty or obligation

in·cum′ber (-bər) ***vt.*** ENCUMBER —**in·cum′brance** (-brəns) ***n.***

in·cu·nab·u·la (in′kyōō nab′yōō lə) ***pl.n.***, *sing.* **-u·lum** (-ləm) ⟦< L *in-*, in + *cunabula*, pl., a cradle⟧ books printed before 1500

in·cur (in kur′) ***vt.*** **-curred′**, **-cur′ring** ⟦< L *in-*, in + *currere*, to run⟧ **1** to acquire (something undesirable) **2** to bring upon oneself

in·cu·ri·ous (in kyoor′ē əs) ***adj.*** not curious; uninterested

in·cur·sion (in kur′zhən) ***n.*** ⟦see INCUR⟧ an invasion or raid

ind *abbrev.* **1** independent **2** index

Ind *abbrev.* **1** India **2** Indian

in·debt·ed (in det′id) ***adj.*** **1** in debt **2** owing gratitude, as for a favor

in·debt′ed·ness ***n.*** **1** a being indebted **2** the amount owed

in·de·cent (in dē′sənt) ***adj.*** not decent; specif., *a*) improper *b*) morally offensive; obscene —**in·de′cen·cy** ***n.*** —**in·de′cent·ly** ***adv.***

in·de·ci·pher·a·ble (in′dē sī′fər ə bəl) ***adj.*** that cannot be deciphered

in·de·ci·sion (in′dē sizh′ən) ***n.*** inability to decide; vacillation

in′de·ci′sive (-sī′siv) ***adj.*** **1** not conclusive or final **2** showing indecision —**in′de·ci′sive·ly** ***adv.*** —**in′de·ci′sive·ness** ***n.***

in·deed (in dēd′) ***adv.*** certainly; truly —***interj.*** used to express surprise, doubt, sarcasm, etc.

in·de·fat·i·ga·ble (in′di fat′i gə bəl) ***adj.*** ⟦< L *in-*, not + *defatigare*, tire out⟧ that cannot be tired out

in·de·fen·si·ble (in′dē fen′sə bəl) ***adj.*** **1** that cannot be defended **2** that cannot be justified

in·def·i·nite (in def′ə nit) ***adj.*** not definite; specif., *a*) having no exact limits *b*) not precise in meaning; vague *c*) blurred; indistinct *d*) uncertain *e*) *Gram.* not limiting or specifying [“a” and "an" are *indefinite* articles*]* —**in·def'i·nite·ly** ***adv.***

in·del·i·ble (in del'ə bəl) ***adj.*** ⟦< L *in-*, not + *delere*, destroy⟧ **1** that cannot be erased, blotted out, etc. **2** leaving an indelible mark

in·del·i·cate (in del'i kit) ***adj.*** lacking propriety or modesty; coarse —**in·del'i·ca·cy**, *pl.* **-cies**, ***n.***

in·dem·ni·fy (in dem'ni fī') ***vt.*** **-fied'**, **-fy'ing** ⟦< L *indemnis*, unhurt + -FY⟧ **1** to insure against loss, damage, etc. **2** to repay for (loss or damage) —**in·dem'ni·fi·ca'tion** ***n.***

in·dem'ni·ty (-tē) ***n.***, *pl.* **-ties** **1** insurance against loss, damage, etc. **2** repayment for loss, damage, etc.

in·dent[1] (in dent') ***vt.*** ⟦< L *in*, in + *dens*, tooth⟧ **1** to notch **2** to space (a line, paragraph, etc.) in from the margin of a page

in·dent[2] (in dent') ***vt.*** ⟦IN-[1] + DENT⟧ to make a dent in

in·den·ta·tion (in'den tā'shən) ***n.*** **1** a being indented **2** a notch, cut, inlet, etc. **3** a dent **4** a spacing in from a margin, or a blank space so made

in·den·ture (in den'chər) ***n.*** **1** a written contract **2** [*often pl.*] a contract binding a person to work for another —***vt.*** **-tured**, **-tur·ing** to bind by indenture

in·de·pend·ence (in'dē pen'dəns) ***n.*** a being independent; freedom from the influence or control of others

In·de·pend·ence (in'dē pen'dəns) city in W Missouri: pop. 112,000

Independence Day the anniversary of the adoption of the Declaration of Independence on July 4, 1776

in'de·pend'ent (-dənt) ***adj.*** **1** free from the influence or control of others; specif., *a*) self-governing *b*) self-reliant *c*) not adhering to any political party *d*) not connected with others *[*an *independent* grocer*]* **2** not depending on another for financial support —***n.*** one who is independent in thinking, action, etc. —**in'de·pend'ent·ly** ***adv.***

independent clause a clause that can function as a complete sentence

in'-depth' ***adj.*** detailed; thorough

in·de·scrib·a·ble (in'di skrīb'ə bəl) ***adj.*** beyond the power of description —**in'de·scrib'a·bly** ***adv.***

in·de·struct·i·ble (in'di struk'tə bəl) ***adj.*** that cannot be destroyed —**in'de·struct'i·bil'i·ty** ***n.***

in·de·ter·mi·nate (in'dē tur'mi nit, -di-) ***adj.*** **1** indefinite; vague **2** doubtful or inconclusive —**in'de·ter'mi·na·cy** (-nə sē) ***n.***

in·dex (in'deks') ***n.***, *pl.* **-dex'es** or **-di·ces'** (-di sēz') ⟦L, indicator⟧ **1** forefinger: in full **index finger** **2** a pointer or indicator **3** an indication *[*an *index* of ability*]* **4** an alphabetical list of names, subjects, etc. indicating pages where found, as in a book **5** a number used to measure change in prices, wages, etc. —***vt.*** to make or be an index of or for

index fund a mutual fund tied to a particular stock-market index

In·di·a (in'dē ə) **1** region in S Asia, south of the Himalayas **2** republic in the central & S part of this region: 1,222,243 sq. mi.; pop. 846,303,000

India ink a black liquid ink

In'di·an ***n.*** **1** a person born or living in India or the East Indies **2** AMERICAN INDIAN —***adj.*** **1** of India, or the East Indies, their people, etc. **2** of the American Indians, their culture, etc.

In·di·an·a (in'dē an'ə) Midwestern state of the U.S.: 35,870 sq. mi.; pop. 5,544,000; cap. Indianapolis: abbrev. *IN* —**In'di·an'an** or **In'di·an'i·an** (-an'ē ən) ***adj.***, ***n.***

In·di·an·ap·o·lis (in'dē ə nap'ə lis) capital of Indiana, in the central part: pop. 742,000

Indian corn CORN[1] (sense 2)

Indian file SINGLE FILE

Indian Ocean ocean south of Asia, between Africa & Australia

Indian summer mild, warm weather following the first frosts of late autumn

India paper **1** a thin, absorbent paper for taking proofs from engraved plates **2** a thin, opaque printing paper, as for Bibles

in·di·cate (in'di kāt') ***vt.*** **-cat'ed**, **-cat'ing** ⟦< L *in-*, in + *dicare*, declare⟧ **1** to direct attention to; point out **2** to be a sign of; signify **3** to show the need for **4** to express briefly or generally —**in'di·ca'tion** ***n.***

in·dic·a·tive (in dik'ə tiv) ***adj.*** **1** giving an indication **2** designating or of the mood of a verb used to express an act, state, etc. as actual, or to ask a question of fact —***n.*** the indicative mood

in·di·ca·tor (in'di kāt'ər) ***n.*** one that indicates; specif., a gauge, dial, etc. that measures

in·dict (in dīt') ***vt.*** ⟦ult. < L *in*, against + *dicere*, speak⟧ to charge with a crime —**in·dict'ment** ***n.***

in·dif·fer·ent (in dif'ər ənt, -dif'rənt) ***adj.*** **1** neutral **2** unconcerned; apathetic **3** of no importance **4** average —**in·dif'fer·ence** ***n.*** —**in·dif'fer·ent·ly** ***adv.***

in·dig·e·nous (in dij'ə nəs) ***adj.*** ⟦< L *indegena*, a native⟧ existing or growing naturally in a region or country; native

in·di·gent (in'di jənt) ***adj.*** ⟦< L *indegere*, to be in need⟧ poor; needy —***n.*** an indigent person —**in'di·gence** ***n.*** —**in'di·gent·ly** ***adv.***

in·di·gest·i·ble (in'di jes'tə bəl) ***adj.*** not easily digested

in'di·ges'tion (-jes'chən) ***n.*** **1** difficulty in digesting food **2** discomfort caused by this

in·dig·nant (in dig'nənt) ***adj.*** ⟦< L *in-*, not + *dignus*, worthy⟧ feeling or expressing anger, esp. at unjust or mean action —**in·dig'nant·ly** ***adv.***

in·dig·na·tion (in'dig nā'shən) ***n.*** righteous anger

in·dig·ni·ty (in dig'nə tē) ***n.***, *pl.* **-ties** an insult or affront to one's dignity or self-respect

in·di·go (in'di gō') ***n.***, *pl.* **-gos'** or **-goes'** ⟦Sp < Gr *Indikos*, Indian⟧ **1** a blue dye obtained from certain plants or made synthetically **2** a deep violet blue —

adj. of this color

in·di·rect (in′də rekt′) ***adj.*** **1** not straight **2** not straight to the point **3** dishonest *[indirect* dealing*]* **4** not immediate; secondary *[*an *indirect* result*]* —**in′di·rect′ly** ***adv.*** —**in′di·rect′ness** ***n.***

indirect object *Gram.* the word or words denoting the person or thing indirectly affected by the action of the verb (Ex.: *him* in "give *him* the ball")

in·dis·creet (in′di skrēt′) ***adj.*** not prudent, as in speech or action; unwise

in′dis·cre′tion (-skresh′ən) ***n.*** **1** lack of discretion; imprudence **2** an indiscreet act or remark

in·dis·crim·i·nate (in′di skrim′i nit) ***adj.*** **1** mixed or random **2** not making careful distinctions —**in′dis·crim′i·nate·ly** ***adv.***

in·dis·pen·sa·ble (in′di spen′sə bəl) ***adj.*** absolutely necessary

in·dis·posed (in′di spōzd′) ***adj.*** **1** slightly ill **2** unwilling; disinclined —**in·dis·po·si·tion** (in′dis pə zish′ən) ***n.***

in·dis·sol·u·ble (in′di säl′yoo bəl) ***adj.*** that cannot be dissolved or destroyed; lasting

in·dite (in dīt′) ***vt.*** **-dit′ed, -dit′ing** ⟦see INDICT⟧ to compose and write

in·di·vid·u·al (in′də vij′oo əl) ***adj.*** ⟦< L < *in-*, not + *dividere*, to divide⟧ **1** existing as a separate thing or being; single **2** of, for, by, or relating to a single person or thing —***n.*** **1** a single thing or being **2** a person

in′di·vid′u·al·ism′ ***n.*** **1** individuality **2** the doctrine that the state exists for the individual **3** the leading of one's life in one's own way —**in′di·vid′u·al·ist** ***n., adj.*** —**in′di·vid′u·al·is′tic** ***adj.***

in′di·vid′u·al′i·ty (-al′ə tē) ***n.***, *pl.* **-ties** **1** the sum of the characteristics that set one person or thing apart **2** the condition of being different from others

in′di·vid′u·al·ize′ (-īz′) ***vt.*** **-ized′, -iz′ing** **1** to make individual **2** to treat as an individual —**in′di·vid′u·al·i·za′tion** ***n.***

in′di·vid′u·al·ly ***adv.*** **1** as individuals; separately **2** distinctively

In·do·chi·na (in′dō chī′nə) **1** large peninsula south of China, including Myanmar, Thailand, etc. **2** E part of this peninsula, consisting of Laos, Cambodia, & Vietnam

in·doc·tri·nate (in däk′trə nāt′) ***vt.*** **-nat′ed, -nat′ing** to instruct in, or imbue with, doctrines, theories, etc. —**in·doc′tri·na′tion** ***n.***

In·do-Eu·ro·pe·an (in′dō yoor′ə pē′ən) ***adj.*** designating a family of languages including most of those of Europe and many of those of Asia

in·do·lent (in′də lənt) ***adj.*** ⟦< L *in-*, not + *dolere*, feel pain⟧ idle; lazy —**in′do·lence** ***n.*** —**in′do·lent·ly** ***adv.***

in·dom·i·ta·ble (in däm′i tə bəl) ***adj.*** ⟦< L *in-*, not + *domitare*, to tame⟧ not easily discouraged or defeated

In·do·ne·sia (in′də nē′zhə) republic in the Malay Archipelago, consisting of Java, Sumatra, & most of Borneo: 741,098 sq. mi.; pop. 179,379,000

In′do·ne′sian ***n.*** **1** a person born or living in Indonesia **2** the official Malay language of Indonesia —***adj.*** of Indonesia, its people, language, etc.

in′door′ ***adj.*** living, belonging, etc. in a building

in′doors′ ***adv.*** in or into a building

in·dorse (in dôrs′) ***vt.*** **-dorsed′, -dors′ing** ENDORSE

in·du·bi·ta·ble (in doo′bi tə bəl) ***adj.*** that cannot be doubted; certain —**in·du′bi·ta·bly** ***adv.***

in·duce (in doos′) ***vt.*** **-duced′, -duc′ing** ⟦< L *in-*, in + *ducere*, to lead⟧ **1** to persuade **2** to bring on or about; cause **3** to draw (a conclusion) from particular facts **4** to bring about (an electric or magnetic effect) in a body by placing it within a field of force —**in·duc′er** ***n.***

in·duce′ment ***n.*** **1** an inducing or being induced **2** a motive; incentive

in·duct (in dukt′) ***vt.*** ⟦see INDUCE⟧ **1** to place formally in an office, a society, etc. **2** to enroll (esp. a draftee) in the armed forces

in·duct′ance ***n.*** the property of an electric circuit by which a varying current in it produces a magnetic field that induces voltages in the same or a nearby circuit

in·duct·ee (in′duk tē′) ***n.*** a person inducted, esp. into the armed forces

in·duc·tion (in duk′shən) ***n.*** **1** an inducting or being inducted **2** reasoning from particular facts to a general conclusion **3** the inducing of an electric or magnetic effect by a field of force —**in·duc′tive** ***adj.***

in·dulge (in dulj′) ***vt.*** **-dulged′, -dulg′ing** ⟦L *indulgere*, be kind to⟧ **1** to satisfy (a desire) **2** to gratify the wishes of; humor —***vi.*** to give way to one's own desires —**in·dulg′er** ***n.***

in·dul·gence (in dul′jəns) ***n.*** **1** an indulging or being indulgent **2** a thing indulged in **3** a favor or privilege **4** *R.C.Ch.* remission of punishment still due for a sin committed but forgiven

in·dul′gent (-jənt) ***adj.*** indulging or inclined to indulge; kind or lenient, often to excess —**in·dul′gent·ly** ***adv.***

in·dus·tri·al (in dus′trē əl) ***adj.*** **1** having to do with industry, its workers, etc. **2** made as for industrial use —**in·dus′tri·al·ly** ***adv.***

industrial arts the mechanical and technical skills used in industry

in·dus′tri·al·ism′ ***n.*** social and economic structure characterized by large industries, machine production, etc.

in·dus′tri·al·ist ***n.*** one who owns or controls an industrial enterprise

in·dus′tri·al·ize′ (-īz′) ***vt., vi.*** **-ized′, -iz′ing** **1** to establish or develop industrialism (in) **2** to organize as an industry —**in·dus′tri·al·i·za′tion** ***n.***

industrial park a planned area for industrial use, usually on the outskirts of a city

Industrial Revolution [*often* **i- r-**] the societal change resulting from the introduction of machinery and large-scale production; esp., this change in

England from *c.* 1760

in·dus·tri·ous (in dus′trē əs) ***adj.*** diligent; hardworking **—in·dus′tri·ous·ly *adv.* —in·dus′tri·ous·ness *n.***

in·dus·try (in′dəs trē) ***n.***, *pl.* **-tries** ⟦< L *industrius*, active⟧ **1** earnest, steady effort **2** *a*) any particular branch of productive, esp. manufacturing, enterprise *b*) manufacturing enterprises collectively **3** any large-scale business activity *[the tourist industry]* **4** the owners and managers of industry

-ine[1] (īn, in, ēn, ən) ⟦< L *-inus*⟧ *suffix* of, having the nature of, like *[aquiline, crystalline]*

-ine[2] (in, ən) ⟦< L *-ina*⟧ *suffix* forming abstract nouns *[discipline, doctrine]*

-ine[3] (ēn, in, īn, ən) ⟦< L *-inus*⟧ *suffix* forming chemical names, as of *a*) halogens *[iodine]* *b*) alkaloids or nitrogenous bases *[morphine]*

in·e·bri·ate (in ē′brē āt′; *for n.*, -it′) ***vt.*** **-at′ed, -at′ing** ⟦< L *in-*, intens. + *ebrius*, drunk⟧ to make drunk **—*n.*** a drunkard **—in·e′bri·a′tion *n.***

in·ed·u·ca·ble (in ej′o͞o kə bəl, -ej′ə-) ***adj.*** thought to be incapable of being educated

in·ef·fa·ble (in ef′ə bəl) ***adj.*** ⟦< L *in-*, not + *effabilis*, utterable⟧ **1** inexpressible **2** too sacred to be spoken

in·ef·fi·cient (in′e fish′ənt) ***adj.*** not producing the desired effect with minimum energy, time, etc. **—in′ef·fi′cien·cy *n.* —in′ef·fi′cient·ly *adv.***

in·el·e·gant (in el′ə gənt) ***adj.*** not elegant; crude **—in·el′e·gant·ly *adv.***

in·e·luc·ta·ble (in′i luk′tə bəl) ***adj.*** ⟦< L *in-*, not + *eluctari*, to struggle⟧ not to be avoided or escaped; inevitable **—in′e·luc′ta·bly *adv.***

in·ept (in ept′) ***adj.*** ⟦< L *in-*, not + *aptus*, apt⟧ **1** unsuitable; unfit **2** foolish **3** awkward; clumsy **—in·ep′ti·tude′** (-ep′tə to͞od′) ***n.*** **—in·ept′ness *n.***

in·ert (in urt′) ***adj.*** ⟦< L *in-*, not + *ars*, skill⟧ **1** without power to move or to resist **2** inactive; dull; slow **3** exhibiting little or no chemical activity *[an inert gas]*

in·er·tia (in ur′shə) ***n.*** ⟦see prec.⟧ **1** *Physics* the tendency of matter to remain at rest or to continue in a fixed direction unless affected by some outside force **2** a disinclination to move or act **—in·er′tial *adj.***

in·es·cap·a·ble (in′e skāp′ə bəl) ***adj.*** that cannot be escaped or avoided

in·es·ti·ma·ble (in es′tə mə bəl) ***adj.*** too great to be properly measured

in·ev·i·ta·ble (in ev′i tə bəl) ***adj.*** ⟦< L *in-*, not + *evitabilis*, avoidable⟧ certain to happen; unavoidable **—in·ev′i·ta·bil′i·ty *n.* —in·ev′i·ta·bly *adv.***

in·ex·haust·i·ble (in′eg zôs′tə bəl) ***adj.*** **1** that cannot be used up or emptied **2** tireless

in·ex·o·ra·ble (in eks′ə rə bəl) ***adj.*** ⟦< L *in-*, not + *exorare*, move by entreaty⟧ **1** that cannot be influenced by persuasion or entreaty; unrelenting **2** that cannot be altered, checked, etc. **—in·ex′o·ra·bly *adv.***

in·ex·pe·ri·ence (in′ek spir′ē əns) ***n.***

lack of experience or of the knowledge or skill resulting from experience **—in′ex·pe′ri·enced *adj.***

in·ex·pert (in ek′spərt, in′ek spurt′) ***adj.*** not expert; unskillful

in·ex·pli·ca·ble (in eks′pli kə bəl) ***adj.*** that cannot be explained or understood

in·ex·press·i·ble (in′eks pres′ə bəl) ***adj.*** that cannot be expressed; indescribable

in·ex·tin·guish·a·ble (in′ek stiŋ′gwish ə bəl) ***adj.*** that cannot be put out or stopped

in ex·tre·mis (in′ eks trē′mis) ⟦L, in extremity⟧ at the point of death

in·ex·tri·ca·ble (in eks′tri kə bəl) ***adj.*** **1** that one cannot extricate oneself from **2** that cannot be untied **3** so complicated as to be unsolvable

in·fal·li·ble (in fal′ə bəl) ***adj.*** ⟦see IN-[2] & FALLIBLE⟧ **1** incapable of error **2** dependable; reliable **—in·fal′li·bil′i·ty *n.* —in·fal′li·bly *adv.***

in·fa·mous (in′fə məs) ***adj.*** **1** having a very bad reputation; notorious **2** causing a bad reputation; scandalous

in′fa·my (-mē) ***n.***, *pl.* **-mies** **1** very bad reputation; disgrace **2** great wickedness **3** an infamous act

in·fan·cy (in′fən sē) ***n.***, *pl.* **-cies** **1** the state or period of being an infant **2** the earliest stage of anything

in·fant (in′fənt) ***n.*** ⟦< L *in-*, not + *fari*, speak⟧ a very young child; baby **—*adj.*** **1** of or for infants **2** in a very early stage

in·fan·ti·cide (in fan′tə sīd′) ***n.*** **1** the murder of a baby **2** a person guilty of this

in·fan·tile (in′fən tīl′) ***adj.*** **1** of infants **2** like an infant; babyish

in·fan·try (in′fən trē) ***n.***, *pl.* **-tries** ⟦< L *infans*, child⟧ **1** that branch of an army consisting of soldiers trained to fight on foot **2** such soldiers collectively **—in′fan·try·man** (-mən), *pl.* **-men**, ***n.***

in·farct (in färkt′) ***n.*** ⟦< L *in-*, in + *farcire*, to stuff⟧ an area of dying or dead tissue resulting from inadequate blood flow to that area: also **in·farc′tion** (-färk′shən)

in·fat·u·at·ed (in fach′o͞o āt′id) ***adj.*** ⟦< L *in-*, intens. + *fatuus*, foolish⟧ completely carried away by foolish love or affection

in·fat′u·a′tion *n.* a being infatuated

in·fect (in fekt′) ***vt.*** ⟦< L *inficere*, to stain⟧ **1** to contaminate or cause to become diseased by contact with a disease-producing organism or matter **2** to imbue with one's feelings, beliefs, etc.

in·fec·tion (in fek′shən) ***n.*** **1** an infecting or being infected **2** an infectious disease

in·fec′tious (-shəs) ***adj.*** **1** likely to cause infection **2** designating a disease that can be communicated by certain bacteria, viruses, etc. **3** tending to affect others, as a laugh **—in·fec′tious·ly *adv.* —in·fec′tious·ness *n.***

in·fe·lic·i·tous (in′fə lis′ə təs) ***adj.*** not felicitous; unfortunate or unsuitable **—in′fe·lic′i·ty**, *pl.* **-ties**, ***n.***

in·fer (in fur′) ***vt.*** **-ferred′, -fer′ring** ⟦< L *in-*, in + *ferre*, to carry⟧ **1** to conclude by reasoning from something known or assumed **2** to imply: still sometimes regarded as a loose usage —**in·fer·ence** (in′fər əns) ***n.***

in·fer·en·tial (in′fər en′shəl) ***adj.*** based on or having to do with inference

in·fe·ri·or (in fir′ē ər) ***adj.*** ⟦< L *inferus*, low⟧ **1** located below or lower down **2** lower in order, status, etc. **3** lower in quality than: with *to* **4** poor in quality —***n.*** an inferior person or thing —**in·fe′ri·or′i·ty** (-ôr′ə tē) ***n.***

in·fer·nal (in fur′nəl) ***adj.*** ⟦< L *inferus*, below⟧ **1** of hell or Hades **2** hellish; fiendish

in·fer·no (in fur′nō) ***n.***, *pl.* **-nos** ⟦see prec.⟧ **1** HELL **2** any place characterized by flames or great heat

in·fest (in fest′) ***vt.*** ⟦< L *infestus*, hostile⟧ **1** to overrun in large numbers, usually so as to be harmful **2** to be parasitic in or on —**in′fes·ta′tion** ***n.*** —**in·fest′er** ***n.***

in·fi·del (in′fə del′) ***n.*** ⟦< L *in-*, not + *fidelis*, faithful⟧ **1** one who does not believe in a particular religion **2** one who has no religion

in·fi·del·i·ty (in′fə del′ə tē) ***n.*** **1** unfaithfulness, esp. in marriage **2** *pl.* **-ties** an unfaithful act

in·field (in′fēld′) ***n.*** **1** the diamond-shaped area enclosed by the four base lines on a baseball field **2** the players (**in′field′ers**) whose field positions are there

in·fight·ing (in′fīt′iŋ) ***n.*** **1** fighting, esp. boxing, at close range **2** personal conflict within a group —**in′fight′er** ***n.***

in·fil·trate (in fil′trāt′, in′fil trāt′) ***vi., vt.*** **-trat′ed, -trat′ing** **1** to filter or pass gradually through or into **2** to penetrate (enemy lines, a region, etc.) gradually or stealthily, so as to attack or to seize control from within —**in′fil·tra′tion** ***n.*** —**in′fil·tra′tor** ***n.***

in·fi·nite (in′fə nit) ***adj.*** ⟦see IN-[2] & FINITE⟧ **1** lacking limits or bounds; endless **2** very great; vast —***n.*** something infinite —**in′fi·nite·ly** ***adv.***

in·fin·i·tes·i·mal (in′fin i tes′i məl) ***adj.*** ⟦< L *infinitus*, infinite⟧ too small to be measured —**in′fin·i·tes′i·mal·ly** ***adv.***

in·fin·i·tive (in fin′i tiv) ***n.*** ⟦see INFINITE⟧ the form of a verb without reference to person, number, or tense: typically with *to*, as in "I want *to go*" —**in·fin′i·ti′val** (-tī′vəl) ***adj.***

in·fin′i·tude′ (-to͞od′, -tyo͞od′) ***n.*** ⟦< L *infinitus*, INFINITE, prob. infl. by MAGNITUDE⟧ **1** a being infinite **2** an infinite quantity

in·fin′i·ty (-tē) ***n.***, *pl.* **-ties** ⟦< L *infinitas*⟧ **1** the quality of being infinite **2** unlimited space, time, etc. **3** an indefinitely large quantity

in·firm (in furm′) ***adj.*** **1** weak; feeble, as from old age **2** not firm; unstable; frail; shaky —**in·firm′ly** ***adv.*** —**in·firm′ness** ***n.***

in·fir·ma·ry (in fur′mə rē) ***n.***, *pl.* **-ries** a school dispensary

in·fir′mi·ty (-mə tē) ***n.***, *pl.* **-ties** (a) physical weakness or defect

in·flame (in flame′) ***vt., vi.*** **-flamed′, -flam′ing** ⟦see IN-[1] & FLAME⟧ **1** to arouse, excite, etc. or become aroused, excited, etc. **2** to undergo or cause to undergo inflammation

in·flam·ma·ble (in flam′ə bəl) ***adj.*** **1** FLAMMABLE **2** easily excited —**in·flam′ma·bil′i·ty** ***n.***

in·flam·ma·tion (in′flə mā′shən) ***n.*** **1** an inflaming or being inflamed **2** redness, pain, heat, and swelling in the body, due to injury, disease, etc.

in·flam·ma·to·ry (in flam′ə tôr′ē) ***adj.*** **1** rousing excitement, anger, etc. **2** *Med.* of or caused by inflammation

in·flate (in flāt′) ***vt.*** **-flat′ed, -flat′ing** ⟦< L *in-*, in + *flare*, to blow⟧ **1** to blow full as with air or gas **2** to puff up with pride **3** to increase beyond what is normal; specif., to cause inflation of (money, credit, etc.) —***vi.*** to become inflated —**in·flat′a·ble** ***adj.***

in·fla′tion ***n.*** **1** an inflating or being inflated **2** *a*) an increase in the amount of money and credit in relation to the supply of goods and services *b*) an excessive or persistent increase in the general price level as a result of this, causing a decline in purchasing power —**in·fla′tion·ar′y** ***adj.***

in·flect (in flekt′) ***vt.*** ⟦< L *in-*, in + *flectere*, to bend⟧ **1** to vary the tone of (the voice) **2** *Gram.* to change the form of (a word) by inflection

in·flec·tion (in flek′shən) ***n.*** **1** a change in the tone of the voice **2** the change of form in a word to indicate number, case, tense, etc. Brit. sp. **in·flex′ion** —**in·flec′tion·al** ***adj.***

in·flex·i·ble (in flek′sə bəl) ***adj.*** not flexible; stiff, rigid, fixed, unyielding, etc. —**in·flex′i·bil′i·ty** ***n.***

in·flict (in flikt′) ***vt.*** ⟦< L *in-*, on + *fligere*, to strike⟧ **1** to cause (pain, wounds, etc.) as by striking **2** to impose (a punishment, etc.) *on* or *upon* —**in·flic′tion** ***n.*** —**in·flic′tive** ***adj.***

in-flight (in′flīt′) ***adj.*** done, shown, etc. while an aircraft is in flight *[in-flight movies]*

in·flo·res·cence (in′flō res′əns, -flô-) ***n.*** *Bot.* **1** the producing of blossoms **2** the arrangement of flowers on a stem **3** a flower cluster **4** flowers collectively

in·flu·ence (in′flo͞o əns) ***n.*** ⟦< L *in-*, in + *fluere*, to flow⟧ **1** power to affect others **2** power to produce effects because of wealth, high position, etc. **3** one that has influence —***vt.*** **-enced, -enc·ing** to have influence or an effect on

in′flu·en′tial (-en′shəl) ***adj.*** exerting influence, esp. great influence

in·flu·en·za (in′flo͞o en′zə) ***n.*** ⟦It, an influence⟧ an acute, contagious viral disease, characterized by inflammation of the respiratory tract, fever, and muscular pain

in·flux (in′fluks′) ***n.*** ⟦see INFLUENCE⟧ a flowing in or streaming in

in·fo (in′fō) ***n.*** [Slang] *short for* INFORMATION (sense 2)

in·fold (in fōld′) ***vt.*** *var. of* ENFOLD

in·fo·mer·cial (in′fō mur′shəl) ***n.*** ⟦INFO(RMATION) + (COM)MERCIAL⟧ a long TV commercial made to resemble a talk show, interview, etc.

in·form (in fôrm′) ***vt.*** ⟦see IN-[1] & FORM⟧ to give knowledge of something to —***vi.*** to give information, esp. in accusing another

in·for·mal (in fôr′məl) ***adj.*** not formal; specif., *a)* not according to fixed customs, rules, etc. *b)* casual, relaxed, etc. *c)* not requiring formal dress *d)* designating or of the words, phrases, etc. characteristic of speech or writing that is casual, ordinary, etc. —**in′for·mal′i·ty** (-mal′ə tē), *pl.* **-ties**, ***n.*** —**in·for′mal·ly** ***adv.***

in·form·ant (in fôr′mənt) ***n.*** a person who gives information; specif., an informer

in·for·ma·tion (in′fər mā′shən) ***n.*** **1** a being informed **2** something told or facts learned; news or knowledge **3** data stored in or retrieved from a computer

information science the science dealing with the collection, storage, and retrieval of information

in·form·a·tive (in fôr′mə tiv) ***adj.*** giving information; instructive

in·formed′ ***adj.*** having or based on knowledge or education

in·form′er ***n.*** one who secretly gives evidence against another

in·fo·tain·ment (in′fō tān′mənt) ***n.*** ⟦INFO(RMATION) + (ENTER)TAINMENT⟧ TV programming of information, as about celebrities, in a dramatic or sensational style

infra- ⟦< L⟧ *prefix* below, beneath

in·frac·tion (in frak′shən) ***n.*** ⟦see INFRINGE⟧ a violation of a law, pact, etc.

in·fra·red (in′frə red′) ***adj.*** designating or of those invisible rays just beyond the red of the visible spectrum: they have a penetrating heating effect

in′fra·son′ic (-sän′ik) ***adj.*** of a frequency of sound below the range audible to the human ear

in′fra·struc′ture (-struk′chər) ***n.*** basic installations and facilities, as roads, power plants, transportation and communication systems, etc.

in·fre·quent (in frē′kwənt) ***adj.*** not frequent; happening seldom; rare; uncommon —**in·fre′quen·cy** or **in·fre′quence** ***n.*** —**in·fre′quent·ly** ***adv.***

in·fringe (in frinj′) ***vt.*** **-fringed′**, **-fring′ing** ⟦< L *in-*, in + *frangere*, to break⟧ to break (a law or pact) —**infringe on** (or **upon**) to encroach on (the rights, etc. of others) —**in·fringe′ment** ***n.***

in·fu·ri·ate (in fyoor′ē āt′) ***vt.*** **-at′ed**, **-at′ing** ⟦< L *in-*, in + *furia*, rage⟧ to make very angry; enrage

in·fuse (in fyo͞oz′) ***vt.*** **-fused′**, **-fus′ing** ⟦< L *in-*, in + *fundere*, pour⟧ **1** to instill or impart (qualities, etc.) **2** to fill; inspire **3** to steep (tea leaves, etc.) to extract the essence —**in·fus′er** ***n.*** —**in·fu′sion** ***n.***

-ing (iŋ) ⟦< OE⟧ *suffix* used to form the present participle or verbal nouns *[talking, painting]*

in·gath·er·ing (in′ga*th*′ər iŋ) ***n.*** a gathering together

in·gen·ious (in jēn′yəs) ***adj.*** ⟦< L *in-*, in + *gignere*, to produce⟧ **1** clever, resourceful, etc. **2** made or done in a clever or original way —**in·gen′ious·ly** ***adv.***

in·gé·nue (an′zhə no͞o′, än′-) ***n.*** ⟦Fr, ingenuous⟧ *Theater* the role of an inexperienced young woman, or an actress in this role

in·ge·nu·i·ty (in′jə no͞o′ə tē, -nyo͞o′-) ***n.*** the quality of being ingenious; cleverness

in·gen·u·ous (in jen′yo͞o əs) ***adj.*** ⟦< L *in-*, in + *gignere*, to produce⟧ **1** frank; open **2** simple; naive —**in·gen′u·ous·ly** ***adv.*** —**in·gen′u·ous·ness** ***n.***

in·gest (in jest′) ***vt.*** ⟦< L *in-*, into + *gerere*, carry⟧ to take (food, etc.) into the body, as by swallowing, inhaling, or absorbing —**in·ges′tion** ***n.***

in·glo·ri·ous (in glôr′ē əs) ***adj.*** shameful; disgraceful

in·got (iŋ′gət) ***n.*** ⟦prob. < OFr *lingo*, tongue⟧ a mass of metal cast into a bar or other convenient shape

in·grained (in′grānd′) ***adj.*** **1** firmly established, as habits **2** inveterate *[an ingrained liar]*

in·grate (in′grāt′) ***n.*** ⟦< L *in-*, not + *gratus*, grateful⟧ an ungrateful person

in·gra·ti·ate (in grā′shē āt′) ***vt.*** **-at′ed**, **-at′ing** ⟦< L *in-*, in + *gratia*, favor⟧ to bring (oneself) into another's favor —**in·gra′ti·a′tion** ***n.***

in·grat·i·tude (in grat′i to͞od′) ***n.*** lack of gratitude; ungratefulness

in·gre·di·ent (in grē′dē ənt) ***n.*** ⟦see fol.⟧ **1** any of the things that a mixture is made of **2** a component

in·gress (in′gres′) ***n.*** ⟦< L *in-*, into + *gradi*, to go⟧ entrance

in·grown (in′grōn′) ***adj.*** grown inward, esp. into the flesh, as a toenail

in·gui·nal (iŋ′gwi nəl) ***adj.*** ⟦< L *inguen*, groin⟧ of or near the groin

in·hab·it (in hab′it) ***vt.*** ⟦< L *in-*, in + *habitare*, dwell⟧ to live in —**in·hab′it·a·ble** ***adj.***

in·hab′it·ant (-i tənt) ***n.*** a person or animal inhabiting a specified place

in·hal·ant (in hāl′ənt) ***n.*** a medicine, etc. to be inhaled

in·ha·la·tor (in′hə lāt′ər) ***n.*** **1** INHALER (*n.* 3) **2** RESPIRATOR (sense 2)

in·hale (in hāl′) ***vt.***, ***vi.*** **-haled′**, **-hal′ing** ⟦< L *in-*, in + *halare*, breathe⟧ to breathe in (air, vapor, etc.) —**in·ha·la·tion** (in′hə lā′shən) ***n.***

in·hal·er (in hāl′ər) ***n.*** **1** one who inhales **2** RESPIRATOR (sense 1) **3** a device used in inhaling medicinal vapors

in·here (in hir′) ***vi.*** **-hered′**, **-her′ing** ⟦< L *in-*, in + *haerere*, to stick⟧ to be inherent

in·her·ent (in hir′ənt, -her′-) ***adj.*** existing in someone or something as a natural and inseparable quality —**in·her′ent·ly** ***adv.***

in·her·it (in her′it) ***vt.***, ***vi.*** ⟦< L *in*, in + *heres*, heir⟧ **1** to receive (property, etc.) as an heir **2** to have (certain characteristics) as by heredity —**in·her′i·tor** ***n.***

in·her·it·ance (in her′i təns) ***n.*** **1** the action of inheriting **2** something inherited

in·hib·it (in hib′it) ***vt.*** ⟦< L *in-*, in, on + *habere*, to hold⟧ to check or repress

in·hi·bi·tion (in′hi bish′ən, in′i-) ***n.*** **1** an inhibiting or being inhibited **2** a mental process that restrains an action, emotion, or thought

in′-house′ ***adj., adv.*** (done) within an organization, company, etc. rather than outside it

in·hu·man (in hyo͞o′mən) ***adj.*** not having worthy human characteristics; heartless, cruel, brutal, etc. —**in′hu·man′i·ty** (-man′ə tē) ***n.***

in·im·i·cal (i nim′i kəl) ***adj.*** ⟦< L *in-*, not + *amicus*, friend⟧ **1** hostile; unfriendly **2** in opposition; adverse

in·im·i·ta·ble (i nim′i tə bəl) ***adj.*** that cannot be imitated or matched

in·iq·ui·ty (i nik′wi tē) ***n.*** ⟦< L *in-*, not + *aequus*, equal⟧ **1** wickedness **2** *pl.* **-ties** a wicked or unjust act —**in·iq′ui·tous** ***adj.***

in·i·tial (i nish′əl) ***adj.*** ⟦< L *in-*, into, in + *ire*, go⟧ of or at the beginning; first —***n.*** the first letter of a name —***vt.*** **-tialed** or **-tialled**, **-tial·ing** or **-tial·ling** to mark with initials —**in·i′tial·ly** ***adv.***

in·i·ti·ate (i nish′ē āt′) ***vt.*** **-at′ed**, **-at′ing** ⟦see prec.⟧ **1** to bring into practice or use **2** to teach the fundamentals of a subject to **3** to admit as a member into a fraternity, club, etc., esp. with a special or secret ceremony —**in·i′ti·a′tion** ***n.*** —**in·i′ti·a·to′ry** (-ə tôr′ē) ***adj.***

in·i·ti·a·tive (i nish′ə tiv, -ē ə tiv) ***n.*** **1** the action of taking the first step or move **2** ability in originating new ideas or methods **3** the introduction of proposed legislation, as by voters' petitions

in·ject (in jekt′) ***vt.*** ⟦< L *in-*, in + *jacere*, to throw⟧ **1** to force (a fluid) into a cavity or chamber; esp., to introduce (a liquid) into a vein, tissue, etc. with a syringe **2** to introduce (a remark, quality, etc.) —**in·jec′tion** ***n.*** —**in·jec′tor** ***n.***

in·junc·tion (in juŋk′shən) ***n.*** ⟦< L *in-*, in + *jungere*, join⟧ **1** a command; order **2** a court order prohibiting or ordering a given action

in·jure (in′jər) ***vt.*** **-jured**, **-jur·ing** ⟦see INJURY⟧ **1** to do harm or damage to; hurt **2** to wrong or offend

in·ju·ri·ous (in joor′ē əs) ***adj.*** injuring or likely to injure; harmful

in·ju·ry (in′jə rē) ***n.***, *pl.* **-ries** ⟦< L *in-*, not + *jus*, right⟧ **1** harm or damage **2** an injurious act

in·jus·tice (in jus′tis) ***n.*** **1** a being unjust **2** an unjust act; wrong

ink (iŋk) ***n.*** ⟦< Gr *en-*, in + *kaiein*, to burn⟧ **1** a colored liquid used for writing, printing, etc. **2** a dark, liquid secretion ejected by cuttlefish, squid, etc. —***vt.*** to cover, mark, or color with ink

ink′blot′ ***n.*** any of the patterns made by blots of ink that are used in the RORSCHACH TEST

ink·ling (iŋk′liŋ′) ***n.*** ⟦ME *ingkiling*⟧ **1** a hint **2** a vague notion

ink′well′ ***n.*** a container for ink

ink′y ***adj.*** **-i·er**, **-i·est** **1** like ink in color; dark; black **2** covered with ink —**ink′i·ness** ***n.***

in·laid (in′lād′, in lād′) ***adj.*** set into a surface or formed, decorated, etc. by inlaying

in·land (in′lənd; *for n. & adv.*, -land′, -lənd) ***adj.*** of or in the interior of a region —***n.*** an inland region —***adv.*** into or toward this region

in-law (in′lô′) ***n.*** ⟦< *mother-* (or *father-*, etc.) *in-law*⟧ [Inf.] a relative by marriage

in·lay (in′lā′, in lā′; *for n.* in′lā′) ***vt.*** **-laid′**, **-lay′ing** **1** to set (pieces of wood, etc.) into a surface, specif. for decoration **2** to decorate thus —***n.***, *pl.* **-lays′** **1** inlaid decoration or material **2** a shaped filling, as of gold, cemented into the cavity of a tooth

in·let (in′let′) ***n.*** a narrow strip of water extending into a body of land

in′-line′ skate a kind of roller skate with its wheels in a line from toe to heel

in·mate (in′māt′) ***n.*** a person confined with others in a prison or mental institution

in·most (in′mōst′) ***adj.*** INNERMOST

inn (in) ***n.*** ⟦OE⟧ **1** a hotel or motel **2** a restaurant or tavern: now usually only in the names of such places

in·nards (in′ərdz) ***pl.n.*** ⟦< INWARDS⟧ [Inf. or Dial.] the inner organs or parts

in·nate (i nāt′, in′āt′) ***adj.*** ⟦< L *in-*, in + *nasci*, be born⟧ inborn; natural

in·ner (in′ər) ***adj.*** **1** farther within **2** of the mind or spirit *[inner* peace*]* **3** more secret

inner circle the small, exclusive, most influential part of a group

inner city the central sections of a large city, esp. when crowded or run-down

inner ear the part of the ear consisting of the semicircular canals, vestibule, and cochlea

in′ner·most′ ***adj.*** **1** farthest within **2** most secret

in′ner·sole′ ***n.*** INSOLE

in′ner·spring′ mattress a mattress with built-in coil springs

in·ning (in′iŋ) ***n.*** ⟦< OE *innung*, getting in⟧ [*pl. for Cricket*] *Baseball, Cricket* **1** a team's turn at bat **2** a numbered round of play in which both teams have a turn at bat

inn′keep′er ***n.*** the owner of an inn

in·no·cent (in′ə sənt) ***adj.*** ⟦< L *in-*, not + *nocere*, to harm⟧ **1** free from sin, evil, etc.; specif., not guilty of a specific crime **2** harmless **3** knowing no evil **4** without guile —***n.*** an innocent person, as a child —**in′no·cence** ***n.*** —**in′no·cent·ly** ***adv.***

in·noc·u·ous (i näk′yo͞o əs) ***adj.*** ⟦see prec.⟧ **1** harmless **2** not controversial or offensive —**in·noc′u·ous·ly** ***adv.*** —**in·noc′u·ous·ness** ***n.***

in·no·va·tion (in′ə vā′shən) ***n.*** ⟦< L *in-*, in + *novus*, new⟧ **1** the process of introducing new methods, devices, etc. **2** a new method, custom, device, etc. —**in′no·vate′**, **-vat′ed**, **-vat′ing**, ***vi., vt.*** —**in′no·va′tive** ***adj.*** —**in′no·va′tor** ***n.***

in·nu·en·do (in'yōō en'dō) ***n.***, *pl.* **-does** or **-dos** ⟦< L *in-*, in + *-nuere*, to nod⟧ a hint or sly remark, usually derogatory; insinuation

in·nu·mer·a·ble (i nōō'mer ə bəl) ***adj.*** too numerous to be counted

in·oc·u·late (i näk'yə lāt') ***vt.*** **-lat'ed, -lat'ing** ⟦< L *in-*, in + *oculus*, eye⟧ to inject a serum, vaccine, etc. into, esp. in order to create immunity —**in·oc'u·la'tion** ***n.***

in·of·fen·sive (in'ə fen'siv) ***adj.*** causing no harm or annoyance; not objectionable —**in'of·fen'sive·ly** ***adv.***

in·op·er·a·ble (in äp'ər ə bəl) ***adj.*** not operable; specif., incapable of being treated by surgery

in·op·er·a·tive (in äp'ər ə tiv, -ər āt'iv) ***adj.*** not working or functioning

in·or·di·nate (in ôrd''n it) ***adj.*** ⟦ult. < L *in-*, not + *ordo*, order⟧ excessive; immoderate —**in·or'di·nate·ly** ***adv.***

in·or·gan·ic (in'ôr gan'ik) ***adj.*** not organic; specif., designating or of matter not animal or vegetable; not living

in·pa·tient (in'pā'shənt) ***n.*** a patient who stays in a hospital, etc. while receiving treatment

in·put (in'poot') ***n.*** **1** what is put in; specif., *a*) power put into a machine, etc. *b*) data or programs entered into a computer **2** opinion; advice —***vt.*** **-put', -put'ting** to enter (data) into a computer —**in'put'ter** ***n.***

in·quest (in'kwest') ***n.*** ⟦see INQUIRE⟧ a judicial inquiry, esp. before a jury, as a coroner's investigation of a death

in·qui·e·tude (in kwī'ə tood') ***n.*** restlessness; uneasiness

in·quire (in kwīr') ***vi.*** **-quired', -quir'ing** ⟦< L *in-*, into + *quaerere*, seek⟧ **1** to ask a question or questions **2** to investigate: usually with *into* —***vt.*** to seek information about —**in·quir'er** ***n.***

in·quir·y (in'kwər ē, in kwīr'ē) ***n.***, *pl.* **-ies** **1** an inquiring; investigation **2** a question

in·qui·si·tion (in'kwə zish'ən) ***n.*** **1** an investigation or inquest **2** [**I-**] *R.C.Ch.* the tribunal established in the 13th c. for suppressing heresy and heretics **3** any relentless questioning or harsh suppression —**in·quis·i·tor** (in kwiz'ə tər) ***n.***

in·quis·i·tive (in kwiz'ə tiv) ***adj.*** **1** inclined to ask many questions **2** unnecessarily curious; prying —**in·quis'i·tive·ness** ***n.***

in re (in rē', -rā') ⟦L⟧ in the matter (of)

-in-res'i·dence *combining form* appointed to work at, and usually residing at, an institution, as a college, for a certain period

in·road (in'rōd') ***n.*** an encroachment: usually used in plural

ins *abbrev.* insurance

in·sane (in sān') ***adj.*** **1** not sane; mentally ill or deranged **2** of or for insane people **3** very foolish, extravagant, etc. —**in·sane'ly** ***adv.*** —**in·san'i·ty** (-san'ə tē) ***n.***

in·sa·ti·a·ble (in sā'shə bəl, -shē ə bəl) ***adj.*** ⟦see IN-[2] & SATIATE⟧ that cannot be satisfied —**in·sa'ti·a·bil'i·ty** ***n.*** —**in·sa'ti·a·bly** ***adv.***

in·scribe (in skrīb') ***vt.*** **-scribed', -scrib'ing** ⟦< L *in-*, in + *scribere*, write⟧ **1** to mark or engrave (words, etc.) on (a surface) **2** *a*) to dedicate (a book, etc.) to someone *b*) to autograph **3** to fix in the mind —**in·scrip'tion** (-skrip'shən) ***n.***

in·scru·ta·ble (in skrōōt'ə bəl) ***adj.*** ⟦< L *in-*, not + *scrutari*, examine⟧ not easily understood; enigmatic —**in·scru'ta·bly** ***adv.***

in·seam (in'sēm') ***n.*** an inner seam; specif., the seam from the crotch to the bottom of a trouser leg

in·sect (in'sekt') ***n.*** ⟦< L *insectum*, lit., notched⟧ any of a large class of small, usually winged, invertebrates, as beetles, flies, or wasps, having three pairs of legs

in·sec·ti·cide (in sek'tə sīd') ***n.*** any substance used to kill insects —**in·sec'ti·ci'dal** ***adj.***

in·sec·ti·vore (in sek'tə vôr') ***n.*** ⟦see fol.⟧ any of various small mammals, as moles and shrews, that are active mainly at night and that feed principally on insects

in·sec·tiv·o·rous (in'sek tiv'ə rəs) ***adj.*** ⟦< INSECT + L *vorare*, devour⟧ feeding chiefly on insects

in·se·cure (in'si kyoor') ***adj.*** **1** not safe from danger **2** feeling anxiety **3** not firm or dependable —**in'se·cure'ly** ***adv.*** —**in'se·cu'ri·ty**, *pl.* **-ties**, ***n.***

in·sem·i·nate (in sem'ə nāt') ***vt.*** **-nat'ed, -nat'ing** ⟦< L *in-*, in + *semen*, seed⟧ **1** to sow seeds in; esp., to impregnate **2** to imbue (with ideas, etc.) —**in·sem'i·na'tion** ***n.***

in·sen·sate (in sen'sāt', -sit) ***adj.*** **1** not feeling sensation **2** foolish **3** cold; insensitive

in·sen·si·ble (in sen'sə bəl) ***adj.*** **1** unable to perceive with the senses **2** unconscious **3** unaware; indifferent **4** so small as to be virtually imperceptible —**in·sen'si·bil'i·ty** ***n.***

in·sen'si·tive (-sə tiv) ***adj.*** **1** not sensitive; not responsive **2** tactless —**in·sen'si·tive·ly** ***adv.*** —**in·sen'si·tiv'i·ty** ***n.***

in·sen·tient (in sen'shənt, -shē ənt) ***adj.*** not sentient; not having life, consciousness, or feeling —**in·sen'tience** ***n.***

in·sert (in surt'; *for n.* in'surt') ***vt.*** ⟦< L *in-*, in + *serere*, join⟧ to put or fit (something) into something else —***n.*** anything inserted or for insertion —**in·ser'tion** ***n.***

in·set (in set'; *for n.* in'set') ***vt.*** **-set', -set'ting** to set in; insert —***n.*** something inserted

in·shore (in'shôr', in shôr') ***adv., adj.*** in, near, or toward the shore

in·side (in'sīd', in'sīd', in sīd') ***n.*** **1** the inner side, surface, or part **2** [*pl.*] [Inf.] the internal organs of the body —***adj.*** **1** internal **2** known only to insiders; secret —***adv.*** **1** on or to the inside; within **2** indoors —***prep.*** in or within —**inside of** within the space or time of —**inside out** **1** reversed **2** [Inf.] thoroughly

in·sid·er (in′sīd′ər, in sīd′ər) ***n.*** **1** one inside a given place or group **2** one having secret or confidential information

in·sid·i·ous (in sid′ē əs) ***adj.*** ⟦< L *insidiae*, an ambush⟧ **1** characterized by treachery or slyness **2** more dangerous than seems evident

in·sight (in′sīt′) ***n.*** **1** the ability to see and understand clearly the inner nature of things, esp. by intuition **2** an instance of such understanding

in·sig·ni·a (in sig′nē ə) ***pl.n.***, *sing.* **in·sig′ne** (-nē) ⟦ult. < L *in-*, in + *signum*, a mark⟧ badges, emblems, or distinguishing marks, as of rank or membership —***sing.n.***, *pl.* **in·sig′ni·as** such a badge, etc.

in·sin·cere (in′sin sir′) ***adj.*** not sincere; deceptive or hypocritical —**in′sin·cere′ly** ***adv.*** —**in′sin·cer′i·ty** (-ser′ə tē), *pl.* **-ties**, ***n.***

in·sin·u·ate (in sin′yo͞o āt′) ***vt.*** **-at′ed**, **-at′ing** ⟦< L *in-*, in + *sinus*, a curve⟧ **1** to introduce or work into gradually, indirectly, etc. **2** to hint or suggest indirectly; imply —**in·sin′u·a′tion** ***n.*** —**in·sin′u·a′tive** ***adj.*** —**in·sin′u·a′tor** ***n.***

in·sip·id (in sip′id) ***adj.*** ⟦< L *in-*, not + *sapidus*, savory⟧ **1** without flavor; tasteless **2** not exciting or interesting; dull

in·sist (in sist′) ***vi.*** ⟦< L *in-*, in, on + *sistere*, to stand⟧ to take and maintain a stand: often with *on* or *upon* —***vt.*** **1** to demand strongly **2** to declare firmly —**in·sist′ing·ly** ***adv.***

in·sist′ent ***adj.*** insisting; persistent —**in·sist′ence** ***n.*** —**in·sist′ent·ly** ***adv.***

in si·tu (in sī′to͞o′) ⟦L⟧ in position; in its original place

in·so·far (in′sō fär′) ***adv.*** to such a degree or extent: usually with *as*

in·sole (in′sōl′) ***n.*** **1** the inside sole of a shoe **2** a removable inside sole put in for comfort

in·so·lent (in′sə lənt) ***adj.*** ⟦< L *in-*, not + *solere*, be accustomed⟧ boldly disrespectful; impudent —**in′so·lence** ***n.***

in·sol·u·ble (in säl′yə bəl) ***adj.*** **1** that cannot be solved **2** that cannot be dissolved —**in·sol′u·bil′i·ty** ***n.***

in·sol·vent (in säl′vənt) ***adj.*** not solvent; unable to pay debts; bankrupt —**in·sol′ven·cy** ***n.***

in·som·ni·a (in säm′nē ə) ***n.*** ⟦< L *in-*, without + *somnus*, sleep⟧ abnormal inability to sleep —**in·som′ni·ac′** (-ak′) ***n.***, ***adj.***

in·so·much (in′sō much′) ***adv.*** **1** to such a degree or extent; so: with *that* **2** inasmuch (*as*)

in·sou·ci·ant (in so͞o′sē ənt) ***adj.*** ⟦Fr < *in-*, not + *soucier*, to care⟧ calm and untroubled; carefree

in·spect (in spekt′) ***vt.*** ⟦< L *in-*, at + *specere*, look at⟧ **1** to look at carefully **2** to examine or review officially —**in·spec′tion** ***n.***

in·spec′tor ***n.*** **1** one who inspects **2** an officer on a police force, ranking next below a superintendent or police chief

in·spi·ra·tion (in′spə rā′shən) ***n.*** **1** an inspiring or being inspired mentally or emotionally **2** *a*) any stimulus to creative thought or action *b*) an inspired idea, action, etc. —**in′spi·ra′tion·al** ***adj.***

in·spire (in spīr′) ***vt.*** **-spired′**, **-spir′ing** ⟦< L *in-*, in, on + *spirare*, breathe⟧ **1** to inhale **2** to stimulate or impel, as to some creative effort **3** to motivate as by divine influence **4** to arouse (a thought or feeling) in (someone) **5** to occasion or cause —***vi.*** **1** to inhale **2** to give inspiration

in·spir·it (in spir′it) ***vt.*** to put spirit into; cheer; hearten

inst *abbrev.* **1** institute **2** institution

in·sta·bil·i·ty (in′stə bil′ə tē) ***n.*** lack of firmness, determination, etc.

in·stall or **in·stal** (in stôl′) ***vt.*** **-stalled′**, **-stall′ing** ⟦< ML *in-*, in + *stallum*, a place⟧ **1** to place in an office, rank, etc., with ceremony **2** to establish in a place **3** to fix in position for use *[to install* new fixtures*]* —**in·stal·la·tion** (in′stə lā′shən) ***n.*** —**in·stall′er** ***n.***

in·stall′ment or **in·stal′ment** ***n.*** **1** an installing or being installed **2** any of the parts of a sum of money to be paid at regular specified times **3** any of several parts, as of a serial

installment plan a credit system by which debts, as for purchased articles, are paid in installments

in·stance (in′stəns) ***n.*** ⟦see fol.⟧ **1** an example; case **2** a step in proceeding; occasion *[*in the first *instance]* —***vt.*** **-stanced**, **-stanc·ing** to give as an example; cite —**at the instance of** at the suggestion or instigation of

in·stant (in′stənt) ***adj.*** ⟦< L *in-*, in, upon + *stare*, to stand⟧ **1** immediate **2** soluble, concentrated, or precooked for quick preparation: said of a food or beverage —***n.*** **1** a moment **2** a particular moment —**the instant** as soon as

in·stan·ta·ne·ous (in′stən tā′nē əs) ***adj.*** done or happening in an instant —**in′stan·ta′ne·ous·ly** ***adv.***

in·stan·ter (in stan′tər) ***adv.*** ⟦L⟧ *Law* immediately

in′stant·ly ***adv.*** immediately

in·state (in stāt′) ***vt.*** **-stat′ed**, **-stat′ing** ⟦IN-[1] + STATE⟧ to put in a particular position, rank, etc.; install

in·stead (in sted′) ***adv.*** ⟦IN[1] + STEAD⟧ in place of the one mentioned —**instead of** in place of

in·step (in′step′) ***n.*** the top surface of the foot, between the ankle and the toes

in·sti·gate (in′stə gāt′) ***vt.*** **-gat′ed**, **-gat′ing** ⟦< L *in-*, on + *-stigare*, to prick⟧ **1** to urge on to some action **2** to foment (rebellion, etc.) —**in′sti·ga′tion** ***n.*** —**in′sti·ga′tor** ***n.***

in·still or **in·stil** (in stil′) ***vt.*** **-stilled′**, **-still′ing** ⟦< L *in-*, in + *stilla*, a drop⟧ **1** to put in drop by drop **2** to put (an idea, etc.) *in* or *into* gradually

in·stinct (in′stiŋkt′) ***n.*** ⟦< L *instinguere*, to impel⟧ **1** (an) inborn tendency to behave in a way characteristic of a species **2** a natural or acquired tendency; knack —**in·stinc′tive** ***adj.*** —**in·stinc′tu·al** ***adj.***

in·sti·tute (in′stə to͞ot′) ***vt.*** **-tut′ed**, **-tut′ing** ⟦< L *in-*, in, on + *statuere*, to cause to set up]] 1 to set up; establish 2 to start; initiate —*n.* something instituted; specif., *a*) an organization for the promotion of art, science, etc. *b*) a school or college specializing in some field —**in′sti·tut′er** or **in′sti·tu′tor** *n.*

in·sti·tu·tion (in′stə to͞o′shən) *n.* **1** an instituting or being instituted **2** an established law, custom, etc. **3** *a*) an organization having a public character, as a school, church, bank, or hospital *b*) the building housing it **4** a person or thing long established in a place —**in′sti·tu′tion·al** *adj.*

in′sti·tu′tion·al·ize′ (-īz′) *vt.* **-ized′**, **-iz′ing** **1** to make into an institution **2** to place in an institution, as for treatment —**in′sti·tu′tion·al·i·za′tion** *n.*

in·struct (in strukt′) *vt.* [[< L *in-*, in + *struere*, pile up]] **1** to teach; educate **2** to inform **3** to order or direct

in·struc′tion (-struk′shən) *n.* **1** an instructing; education **2** something taught **3** any of the steps to be followed, as in operating something: *usually used in pl.* —**in·struc′tion·al** *adj.*

in·struc′tive *adj.* giving knowledge

in·struc′tor *n.* **1** a teacher **2** a college teacher of the lowest rank

in·stru·ment (in′strə mənt) *n.* [[see INSTRUCT]] **1** a thing by means of which something is done **2** a tool or implement **3** any of various devices for indicating, measuring, controlling, etc. **4** any of various devices producing musical sound **5** *Law* a formal document

in′stru·men′tal (-mənt′'l) *adj.* **1** serving as a means; helpful **2** of, performed on, or written for a musical instrument or instruments

in′stru·men′tal·ist *n.* a person who performs on a musical instrument

in′stru·men′tal′i·ty (-men′tal′ə tē) *n.*, *pl.* **-ties** a means; agency

in′stru·men′ta′tion (-tā′shən) *n.* **1** the writing or scoring of music for instruments **2** the use of or an equipping with instruments

instrument flying the flying of an aircraft by the use of instruments only

in·sub·or·di·nate (in′sə bôrd′'n it) *adj.* not submitting to authority; disobedient —**in′sub·or′di·na′tion** *n.*

in·sub·stan·tial (in′səb stan′shəl) *adj.* not substantial; specif., *a*) not real; imaginary *b*) weak or flimsy

in·suf·fer·a·ble (in suf′ər ə bəl) *adj.* intolerable; unbearable

in·su·lar (in′sə lər) *adj.* [[< L *insula*, island]] **1** of or like an island or islanders **2** narrow-minded; illiberal

in′su·late′ (-lāt′) *vt.* **-lat′ed**, **-lat′ing** [[< L *insula*, island]] **1** to set apart; isolate **2** to cover with a nonconducting material in order to prevent the escape of electricity, heat, sound, etc.

in′su·la′tion *n.* **1** an insulating or being insulated **2** material for this

in·su·lin (in′sə lin) *n.* [[< L *insula*, island]] **1** a hormone vital to carbohydrate metabolism, secreted by the islets of Langerhans **2** an extract from the pancreas of sheep, oxen, etc., used in the treatment of diabetes

insulin shock the abnormal condition caused by an excess of insulin: it is characterized by tremors, cold sweat, convulsions, and coma

in·sult (in sult′; *for n.* in′sult′) *vt.* [[< L *in-*, on + *salire*, to leap]] to subject to an act, remark, etc. meant to hurt the feelings or pride —*n.* an insulting act, remark, etc.

in·su·per·a·ble (in so͞o′pər ə bəl) *adj.* [[< L *insuperabilis*]] that cannot be overcome

in·sup·port·a·ble (in′sə pôrt′ə bəl) *adj.* **1** intolerable; unbearable **2** incapable of being upheld, proved, etc.

in·sur·ance (in shoor′əns) *n.* **1** an insuring or being insured against loss **2** a contract (**insurance policy**) purchased to guarantee compensation for a specified loss by fire, death, etc. **3** the amount for which something is insured **4** the business of insuring against loss

in·sure (in shoor′) *vt.* **-sured′**, **-sur′ing** [[ME *ensuren*: see ENSURE]] **1** to take out or issue insurance on **2** ENSURE —**in·sur′a·ble** *adj.*

in·sured′ *n.* a person whose life, property, etc. is insured against loss

in·sur′er *n.* a person or company that insures others against loss

in·sur′gence (-jəns) *n.* a rising in revolt; uprising: also **in·sur′gen·cy**, *pl.* **-cies**

in·sur·gent (in sur′jənt) *adj.* [[< L *in-*, upon + *surgere*, rise]] rising up against established authority —*n.* an insurgent person

in·sur·rec·tion (in′sə rek′shən) *n.* [[see prec.]] a rising up against established authority; rebellion —**in′sur·rec′tion·ist** *n.*

int *abbrev.* **1** interest **2** interjection **3** international

in·tact (in takt′) *adj.* [[< L *in-*, not + *tactus*, touched]] unimpaired or uninjured; kept or left whole

in·ta·glio (in tal′yō′) *n.*, *pl.* **-glios′** [[It < *in-*, in + *tagliare*, to cut]] a design carved or engraved below the surface

in·take (in′tāk′) *n.* **1** a taking in **2** the amount taken in **3** the place in a pipe, etc. where a fluid is taken in

in·tan·gi·ble (in tan′jə bəl) *adj.* **1** that cannot be touched; incorporeal **2** of certain business assets, esp. goodwill, having monetary value but no material being **3** that cannot be easily defined; vague —*n.* something intangible

in·te·ger (in′tə jər) *n.* [[L, whole]] a whole number (e.g., 5, -10) or zero

in·te·gral (in′tə grəl; *often* in teg′rəl) *adj.* [[see prec.]] **1** necessary for completeness; essential **2** made up of parts forming a whole

in′te·grate′ (-grāt′) *vt.*, *vi.* **-grat′ed**, **-grat′ing** [[< L *integer*, whole]] **1** to make or become whole or complete **2** to bring (parts) together into a whole **3** *a*) to remove barriers imposing segregation upon (racial groups) *b*) to abolish segregation in —**in′te·gra′tion** *n.* —**in′te·gra′tive** *adj.*

integrated circuit an electronic circuit with many interconnected circuit elements formed on a single body, or chip, of semiconductor material

in·teg·ri·ty (in teg′rə tē) ***n.*** ⟦see INTEGER⟧ **1** completeness **2** unimpaired condition; soundness **3** honesty, sincerity, etc.

in·teg·u·ment (in teg′yo͞o mənt) ***n.*** ⟦< L *in-*, upon + *tegere*, to cover⟧ an outer covering; skin, shell, rind, etc.

in·tel·lect (in′tə lekt′) ***n.*** ⟦< L *inter-*, between + *legere*, choose⟧ **1** the ability to reason or understand **2** high intelligence **3** a very intelligent person

in·tel·lec·tu·al (in′tə lek′cho͞o əl) ***adj.*** **1** of, involving, or appealing to the intellect **2** requiring intelligence **3** having intellectual interests or tastes **4** showing high intelligence —***n.*** one with intellectual interests or tastes —**in′tel·lec′tu·al·ly *adv.*** —**in′tel·lec′tu·al′i·ty *n.***

in′tel·lec′tu·al·ize′ (-īz′) ***vt.*** **-ized′, -iz′ing** to examine or interpret rationally, often without regard for emotional considerations

intellectual property something produced by the mind, the rights to which may be protected by a copyright, patent, etc.

in·tel·li·gence (in tel′ə jəns) ***n.*** ⟦see INTELLECT⟧ **1** *a*) the ability to learn or understand *b*) the ability to cope with a new situation **2** news or information **3** those engaged in gathering secret, esp. military, information

intelligence quotient *see* IQ

in·tel′li·gent (-jənt) ***adj.*** having or showing intelligence; clever, wise, etc. —**in·tel′li·gent·ly *adv.***

in·tel′li·gent′si·a (-jent′sē ə) ***pl.n.*** ⟦< Russ⟧ [*also with sing. v.*] intellectuals collectively

in·tel·li·gi·ble (in tel′i jə bəl) ***adj.*** that can be understood; clear —**in·tel′li·gi·bil′i·ty *n.*** —**in·tel′li·gi·bly *adv.***

in·tem·per·ate (in tem′pər it, -prit) ***adj.*** **1** not temperate or moderate; excessive **2** drinking too much alcoholic liquor —**in·tem′per·ance *n.***

in·tend (in tend′) ***vt.*** ⟦< L *in-*, at + *tendere*, to stretch⟧ **1** to plan; have in mind as a purpose **2** to mean (something) to be or be used (*for*) **3** to mean; signify

in·tend′ed *n.* [Inf.] one's prospective spouse; fiancé(e)

in·tense (in tens′) ***adj.*** ⟦see INTEND⟧ **1** very strong [*an intense light*] **2** strenuous; earnest [*intense thought*] **3** characterized by much action, strong emotion, etc. —**in·tense′ly *adv.***

in·ten·si·fy (in ten′sə fī′) ***vt., vi.*** **-fied′, -fy′ing** to make or become intense or more intense —**in·ten′si·fi·ca′tion *n.***

in·ten′si·ty *n., pl.* **-ties 1** a being intense **2** great energy or vehemence, as of emotion **3** the amount of force or energy of heat, light, sound, etc.

in·ten′sive *adj.* **1** of or characterized by intensity; thorough **2** designating very attentive care given to critically ill patients **3** *Gram.* giving force or emphasis [*"very" is an intensive adverb*] —***n.*** *Gram.* an intensive word, prefix, etc. —**in·ten′sive·ly *adv.*** —**in·ten′sive·ness *n.***

-in·ten′sive *combining form* intensively using or requiring large amounts of (a specified thing) [*energy-intensive*]

in·tent (in tent′) ***adj.*** ⟦see INTEND⟧ **1** firmly directed; earnest **2** having one's attention or purpose firmly fixed [*intent on going*] —***n.*** **1** an intending **2** something intended; purpose or meaning —**to all intents and purposes** in almost every respect; practically; virtually —**in·tent′ly *adv.*** —**in·tent′ness *n.***

in·ten·tion (in ten′shən) ***n.*** **1** determination to act in a specified way **2** anything intended; purpose

in·ten′tion·al *adj.* done purposely —**in·ten′tion·al·ly *adv.***

in·ter (in tʉr′) ***vt.*** **-terred′, -ter′ring** ⟦< L *in*, in + *terra*, earth⟧ to put (a dead body) into a grave or tomb; bury

inter- ⟦L⟧ *prefix* **1** between or among: the second element of the compound is singular in form [*interstate*] **2** with or on each other (or one another) [*interact*]

in·ter·act (in′tər akt′) ***vi.*** to act on one another —**in′ter·ac′tion *n.***

in′ter·ac′tive (-ak′tiv) ***adj.*** **1** acting on one another **2** designating or of programming or electronic equipment, as for TV, which allows viewers to participate, as by making a response **3** of or involving the continual exchange of information between the computer and the user at a video screen

in·ter·breed (in′tər brēd′, in′tər brēd′) ***vt., vi.*** **-bred′, -breed′ing** HYBRIDIZE

in′ter·cede′ (-sēd′) ***vi.*** **-ced′ed, -ced′ing** ⟦< L *inter-*, between + *cedere*, go⟧ **1** to plead or make a request in behalf of another **2** to mediate; intervene

in′ter·cept′ (-sept′) ***vt.*** ⟦< L *inter-*, between + *capere*, take⟧ **1** to seize or stop in its course [*to intercept a message*] **2** *Math.* to cut off or mark off between two points, lines, etc. —**in′ter·cep′tion *n.***

in′ter·ces′sion (-sesh′ən) ***n.*** an interceding; mediation or prayer in behalf of another —**in′ter·ces′sor** (-ses′ər) ***n.*** —**in′ter·ces′so·ry *adj.***

in·ter·change (in′tər chānj′; *for n.* in′tər chānj′) ***vt.*** **-changed′, -chang′ing 1** to give and take mutually; exchange **2** to put (each of two things) in the other's place **3** to alternate —***n.*** **1** an interchanging **2** a junction which allows movement of traffic between highways on different levels, as a cloverleaf —**in′ter·change′a·ble *adj.***

in′ter·col·le′gi·ate (-kə lē′jit) ***adj.*** between or among colleges and universities

in·ter·com (in′tər käm′) ***n.*** a radio or telephone intercommunication system, as between rooms

in′ter·com·mu′ni·cate′ (-kə myo͞o′ni kāt′) ***vt., vi.*** **-cat′ed, -cat′ing** to communicate with or to one another —**in′ter·com·mu′ni·ca′tion *n.***

in′ter·con·nect′ (-kə nekt′) ***vt., vi.*** to connect or be connected with one another —**in′ter·con·nec′tion *n.***

in′ter·con′ti·nen′tal (-känt′'n ent′'l) ***adj.*** **1** between or among continents **2**

able to travel from one continent to another: said as of a missile

in'ter·cos'tal (-käs'təl, -kôs'-) ***adj.*** between the ribs —***n.*** an intercostal muscle, etc.

in·ter·course (in'tər kôrs') ***n.*** ⟦see INTER- & COURSE⟧ **1** communication or dealings between or among people, countries, etc. **2** SEXUAL INTERCOURSE

in'ter·de·nom'i·na'tion·al (-dē näm'ə nā'shən əl) ***adj.*** between or among religious denominations

in'ter·de'part·men'tal (-dē'pärt ment''l) ***adj.*** between or among departments

in'ter·de·pend'ence (-dē pen'dəns) ***n.*** mutual dependence —**in'ter·de·pend'ent** ***adj.***

in·ter·dict (in'tər dikt'; *for n.* in'tər dikt') ***vt.*** ⟦< L *inter-*, between + *dicere*, speak⟧ **1** to prohibit (an action) **2** to restrain from doing or using something —***n.*** an official prohibition —**in'ter·dic'tion** ***n.***

in'ter·dis'ci·pli·nar'y (-dis'ə pli ner'ē) ***adj.*** involving two or more disciplines, or branches of learning

in·ter·est (in'trist; *for v., also,* -tə rest') ***n.*** ⟦< L *inter-*, between + *esse*, be⟧ **1** a right to, or a share in, something **2** anything in which one has a share **3** [*often pl.*] advantage; benefit **4** [*usually pl.*] those having a common concern or power in some industry, cause, etc. [the steel *interests*] **5** *a)* a feeling of concern, curiosity, etc. about something *b)* the power of causing this feeling *c)* something causing this feeling **6** *a)* money paid for the use of money *b)* the rate of such payment —***vt.*** **1** to involve or excite the interest or attention of **2** to cause to have an interest or take part in —**in the interest(s) of** for the sake of

in'ter·est·ed ***adj.*** **1** having an interest or share **2** influenced by personal interest; biased **3** feeling or showing interest

in'ter·est·ing ***adj.*** exciting curiosity or attention; of interest

in·ter·face (in'tər fās') ***n.*** **1** a plane forming the common boundary between two parts of matter or space **2** a point or means of interaction between two systems, groups, etc. —***vt.***, ***vi.*** **-faced'**, **-fac'ing** to interact with (another system, group, etc.)

in'ter·faith' (-fāth') ***adj.*** between or involving persons adhering to different religions

in·ter·fere (in'tər fir') ***vi.*** **-fered'**, **-fer'ing** ⟦ult. < L *inter-*, between + *ferire*, to strike⟧ **1** to clash; collide **2** *a)* to come in or between; intervene *b)* to meddle **3** to hinder an opposing player in any of various illegal ways —**interfere with** to hinder —**in'ter·fer'ence** ***n.***

in·ter·fer·on (in'tər fir'än') ***n.*** ⟦INTERFER(E) + *-on*, arbitrary suffix⟧ a cellular protein produced in response to infection by a virus and acting to inhibit viral growth

in'ter·gen'er·a'tion·al (-jen'ə rā'shə nəl) ***adj.*** of or involving persons of different generations

in·ter·im (in'tər im) ***n.*** ⟦< L *inter*, between⟧ the period of time between;

meantime —***adj.*** temporary

in·te·ri·or (in tir'ē ər) ***adj.*** ⟦< L *inter*, between⟧ **1** situated within; inner **2** inland **3** private —***n.*** **1** the interior part, as of a building or country **2** the internal, or domestic, affairs of a country

interior decoration the art or business of decorating and furnishing the interiors of houses, offices, etc. —**interior decorator**

in·te'ri·or·ize' (-īz') ***vt.*** **-ized'**, **-iz'ing** to make (a concept, value, etc.) part of one's inner nature

interj *abbrev.* interjection

in·ter·ject (in'tər jekt') ***vt.*** ⟦< L *inter-*, between + *jacere*, to throw⟧ to throw in between; interrupt with; insert

in'ter·jec'tion (-jek'shən) ***n.*** **1** an interjecting **2** something interjected **3** *Gram.* an exclamation or other word(s) inserted into an utterance without grammatical connection to it

in'ter·lace' (-lās') ***vt.***, ***vi.*** **-laced'**, **-lac'ing** to lace or weave together

in'ter·lard' (-lärd') ***vt.*** ⟦see INTER- & LARD⟧ to intersperse; diversify [to *interlard* a talk with quotations]

in·ter·leu·kin (in'tər lo͞o'kin) ***n.*** any of several proteins derived from many cell types and affecting the activity of other cells, as in stimulating the growth of T cells

in'ter·line' (-līn') ***vt.*** **-lined'**, **-lin'ing** to put an inner lining under the ordinary lining of (a garment)

in'ter·lock' (-läk') ***vt.***, ***vi.*** to lock together; join with one another

in·ter·loc·u·to·ry (in'tər läk'yo͞o tôr'ē, -yə-) ***adj.*** *Law* not final [an *interlocutory* divorce decree]

in·ter·lop·er (in'tər lō'pər) ***n.*** ⟦INTER- + *-loper* < Du *lopen*, to run⟧ one who meddles

in·ter·lude (in'tər lo͞od') ***n.*** ⟦< L *inter*, between + *ludus*, a play⟧ **1** anything that fills time between two events, as music between acts of a play **2** intervening time

in'ter·mar'ry (-mar'ē) ***vi.*** **-ried**, **-ry·ing** **1** to become connected by marriage: said of different clans, races, etc. **2** to marry: said of closely related persons —**in'ter·mar'riage** ***n.***

in'ter·me'di·ar'y (-mē'dē er'ē) ***adj.*** **1** acting as a go-between or mediator **2** intermediate —***n.***, *pl.* **-ar'ies** a go-between; mediator

in'ter·me'di·ate (-mē'dē it) ***adj.*** ⟦< L *inter-*, between + *medius*, middle⟧ **1** in the middle; in between **2** of an automobile larger than a compact but smaller than the standard size —***n.*** an intermediate automobile

in·ter·ment (in tʉr'mənt) ***n.*** the act of interring; burial

in·ter·mez·zo (in'tər met'sō') ***n.***, *pl.* **-zos'** or **-zi'** (-sē') ⟦It < L: see INTERMEDIATE⟧ a short piece of music, as between parts of a composition

in·ter·mi·na·ble (in tʉr'mi nə bəl) ***adj.*** lasting, or seeming to last, forever; endless —**in·ter'mi·na·bly** *adv.*

in·ter·min·gle (in'tər miŋ'gəl) *vt., vi.* **-gled, -gling** to mix together; mingle

in·ter·mis·sion (in'tər mish'ən) *n.* ⟦< L *inter-*, between + *mittere*, send⟧ an interval of time between periods of activity, as between acts of a play

in'ter·mit'tent (-mit''nt) *adj.* ⟦see prec.⟧ stopping and starting at intervals; periodic

in·tern (in'turn'; *for vt.* in turn', in'turn') *n.* ⟦< L *internus*, inward⟧ **1** a doctor serving as assistant resident in a hospital generally just after graduation from medical school **2** a student, etc. doing supervised temporary work in a field to gain experience —*vi.* to serve as an intern —*vt.* to detain or confine (foreign persons, etc.), as during a war —**in·tern'ment** *n.* —**in'tern'ship'** *n.*

in·ter·nal (in tur'nəl) *adj.* ⟦< L *internus*⟧ **1** of or on the inside; inner **2** to be taken inside the body *[internal* remedies*]* **3** intrinsic *[internal* evidence*]* **4** domestic *[internal* revenue*]* —**in·ter'nal·ly** *adv.*

in·ter'nal-com·bus'tion engine an engine, as in an automobile, powered by the explosion of a fuel-and-air mixture within the cylinders

in·ter'nal·ize' (-īz') *vt.* **-ized', -iz'ing** to make (others' ideas, etc.) a part of one's thinking —**in·ter'nal·i·za'tion** *n.*

internal medicine the branch of medicine that deals with the diagnosis and nonsurgical treatment of diseases

internal revenue governmental income from taxes on income, profits, etc.

in·ter·na·tion·al (in'tər nash'ə nəl) *adj.* **1** between or among nations **2** concerned with the relations between nations **3** for the use of all nations **4** of or for people in various nations —**in'ter·na'tion·al·ize', -ized', -iz'ing,** *vt.* —**in'ter·na'tion·al·ly** *adv.*

International Phonetic Alphabet a set of phonetic symbols for international use: each symbol represents a single human speech sound

in·ter·ne·cine (in'tər nē'sin) *adj.* ⟦< L *inter-*, between + *necare*, kill⟧ deadly or harmful to both sides of a group in a conflict

In·ter·net (in'tər net') *n.* an extensive computer network linking thousands of smaller networks: also with *the*

in·tern·ist (in'turn'ist, in turn'ist) *n.* a doctor who specializes in INTERNAL MEDICINE

in·ter·of·fice (in'tər ôf'is) *adj.* between or among the offices of an organization

in'ter·per'son·al (-pur'sə nəl) *adj.* between persons *[interpersonal* relationships*]*

in'ter·plan'e·tar'y (-plan'ə ter'ē) *adj.* between planets

in'ter·play' (-plā') *n.* action, effect, or influence on each other or one another

in·ter·po·late (in tur'pə lāt') *vt.* **-lat'ed, -lat'ing** ⟦< L *inter-*, between + *polire*, to polish⟧ **1** to change (a text, etc.) by inserting new material **2** to insert between or among others —**in·ter'po·la'tion** *n.*

in·ter·pose (in'tər pōz') *vt., vi.* **-posed', -pos'ing** **1** to place or come between **2** to intervene (with) **3** to interrupt (with) —**in'ter·po·si'tion** (-pə zish'ən) *n.*

in·ter·pret (in tur'prət) *vt.* ⟦< L *interpres*, agent, broker⟧ **1** to explain or translate **2** to construe *[*to *interpret* a silence as contempt*]* **3** to give one's own conception of (a work of art), as in performance or criticism —*vi.* to explain or translate —**in·ter'pre·ta'tion** *n.* —**in·ter'pret·er** *n.*

in·ter'pre·tive (-prə tiv) *adj.* that interprets; explanatory: also **in·ter'pre·ta'tive** (-tāt'iv)

in·ter·ra·cial (in'tər rā'shəl) *adj.* between, among, or for members of different races: also **in'ter·race'**

in'ter·re·late' (-rē lāt') *vt., vi.* **-lat'ed, -lat'ing** to make or be mutually related —**in'ter·re·lat'ed** *adj.*

in·ter·ro·gate (in ter'ə gāt') *vi., vt.* **-gat'ed, -gat'ing** ⟦< L *inter-*, between + *rogare*, ask⟧ to ask questions (of), esp. formally —**in·ter'ro·ga'tion** *n.* —**in·ter'ro·ga'tor** *n.*

in·ter·rog·a·tive (in'tə räg'ə tiv) *adj.* asking a question: also **in'ter·rog'a·to'ry** (-ə tôr'ē)

in·ter·rupt (in'tə rupt') *vt.* ⟦< L *inter-*, between + *rumpere*, to break⟧ **1** to break into (a discussion, etc.) or to break in upon (a speaker, worker, etc.) **2** to make a break in the continuity of —*vi.* to interrupt an action, talk, etc. —**in'ter·rup'tion** *n.*

in·ter·scho·las·tic (in'tər skə las'tik) *adj.* between or among schools

in·ter·sect (in'tər sekt') *vt.* ⟦< L *inter-*, between + *secare*, to cut⟧ to divide into two parts by passing through or across —*vi.* to cross each other

in'ter·sec'tion (-sek'shən) *n.* **1** an intersecting **2** the place where two lines, roads, etc. meet

in'ter·serv'ice (-sur'vis) *adj.* between or among branches of the armed forces

in'ter·ses'sion (-sesh'ən) *n.* a short session between regular sessions of a college year, for concentrating on specialized projects

in·ter·sperse (in'tər spurs') *vt.* **-spersed', -spers'ing** ⟦< L *inter-*, among + *spargere*, scatter⟧ **1** to put here and there; scatter **2** to vary with things scattered here and there

in'ter·state' (-stāt') *adj.* between or among states, esp. of the U.S. —*n.* one of a network of U.S. highways

in'ter·stel'lar (-stel'ər) *adj.* between or among the stars

in·ter·stice (in tur'stis) *n., pl.* **-sti·ces'** (-stə siz', -sēz') ⟦< L *inter-*, between + *sistere*, to set⟧ a crack; crevice

in'ter·twine' (-twīn') *vt., vi.* **-twined', -twin'ing** to twine together

in'ter·ur'ban (-ur'bən) *adj.* between cities or towns —*n.* an interurban railway, etc.

in·ter·val (in'tər vəl) *n.* ⟦< L *inter-*, between + *vallum*, wall⟧ **1** a space between things; gap **2** the time between events **3** the difference in pitch between two tones —**at intervals** **1** once in a while **2** here and there

in·ter·vene (in′tər vēn′) ***vi.*** **-vened′, -ven′ing** ⟦< L *inter-*, between + *venire*, come⟧ **1** to come or be between **2** to occur between two events, etc. **3** to come between to modify, settle, or hinder some action, etc.

in′ter·ven′tion (-ven′shən) ***n.*** **1** an intervening **2** interference, esp. of one country in the affairs of another

in′ter·view′ (-vyōō′) ***n.*** **1** a meeting of people face to face to confer **2** *a*) a meeting in which a person is asked about personal views, etc., as by a reporter *b*) a published, taped, or filmed account of this —***vt.*** to have an interview with —**in′ter·view·ee′** ***n.*** —**in′ter·view′er** ***n.***

in′ter·weave′ (-wēv′) ***vt., vi.*** **-wove′, -wo′ven, -weav′ing** **1** to weave together **2** to connect closely

in·tes·ta·cy (in tes′tə sē) ***n.*** the fact or state of dying intestate

in·tes·tate (in tes′tāt′, -tit) ***adj.*** ⟦< L *in-*, not + *testari*, make a will⟧ having made no will

in·tes·tine (in tes′tən) ***n.*** ⟦< L *intus*, within⟧ [*usually pl.*] the lower part of the alimentary canal, extending from the stomach to the anus and consisting of the SMALL INTESTINE and the LARGE INTESTINE; bowels —**in·tes′tin·al** ***adj.***

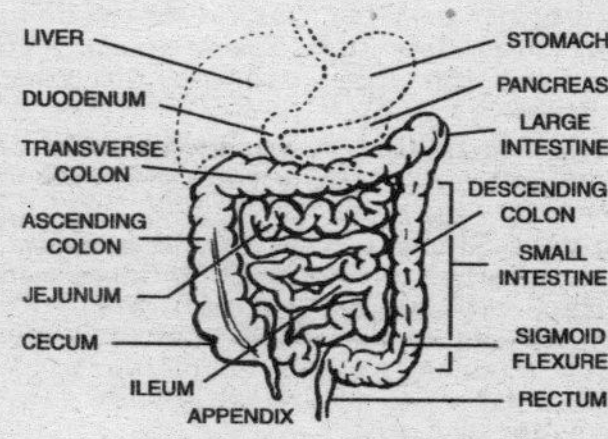

HUMAN INTESTINES

in·ti·mate (in′tə mət; *for vt.*, -māt′) ***adj.*** ⟦< L *intus*, within⟧ **1** most private or personal **2** very close or familiar **3** deep and thorough —***n.*** an intimate friend —***vt.*** **-mat′ed, -mat′ing** to hint or imply —**in′ti·ma·cy** (-mə sē), *pl.* **-cies**, ***n.*** —**in′ti·mate·ly** ***adv.*** —**in′ti·ma′tion** ***n.***

in·tim·i·date (in tim′ə dāt′) ***vt.*** **-dat′ed, -dat′ing** ⟦< L *in-*, in + *timidus*, afraid⟧ to make afraid, as with threats —**in·tim′i·da′tion** ***n.***

intl *abbrev.* international: also **intnl**

in·to (in′tōō) ***prep.*** ⟦OE⟧ **1** from the outside to the inside of *[into* a room*]* **2** continuing to the midst of *[*to talk *into* the night*]* **3** to the form, substance, or condition of *[*divided *into* parts*]* **4** so as to strike *[*to run *into* a wall*]* **5** [Inf.] involved or interested in *[*she's *into* jazz now*]*

in·tol·er·a·ble (in täl′ər ə bəl) ***adj.*** unbearable; too severe, painful, etc. to be endured —**in·tol′er·a·bly** ***adv.***

in·tol′er·ant (-ənt) ***adj.*** unwilling to tolerate others' beliefs, etc. —**intolerant of** not able or willing to tolerate —**in·tol′er·ance** ***n.***

in·to·na·tion (in′tō nā′shən, -tə-) ***n.*** **1** an intoning **2** the quality of producing tones in or out of tune with regard to a given standard of pitch **3** variations in pitch within an utterance

in·tone (in tōn′) ***vt., vi.*** **-toned′, -ton′ing** to speak or recite in a singing tone; chant —**in·ton′er** ***n.***

in to·to (in tō′tō) ⟦L⟧ as a whole

in·tox·i·cate (in täk′si kāt′) ***vt.*** **-cat′ed, -cat′ing** ⟦< L *in-*, in + *toxicum*, poison⟧ **1** to make drunk **2** to excite greatly —**in·tox′i·cant** ***n.*** —**in·tox′i·ca′tion** ***n.***

intra- ⟦L, within⟧ *prefix* within, inside

in·tra·cit·y (in′trə sit′ē) ***adj.*** of or within a large municipality, often, specif. the inner city

in·trac·ta·ble (in trak′tə bəl) ***adj.*** hard to manage; unruly or stubborn

in·tra·der·mal (in′trə dʉr′məl) ***adj.*** within the skin or between the layers of the skin

in′tra·mu′ral (-myoor′əl) ***adj.*** ⟦INTRA- + MURAL⟧ between or among members of the same school, college, etc. *[intramural* athletics*]*

in·tra·net (in′trə net′) ***n.*** a private Internet computer network for one organization, company, etc.

in·tran·si·gent (in tran′sə jənt, -zə-) ***adj.*** ⟦< L *in-*, not + *transigere*, to settle⟧ refusing to compromise —**in·tran′si·gence** ***n.***

in·tran·si·tive (in tran′sə tiv, -zə-) ***adj.*** not transitive; designating a verb that does not require a direct object —**in·tran′si·tive·ly** ***adv.***

in·tra·u·ter·ine (contraceptive) device (in′trə yōōt′ər in) any of various devices, as a plastic loop, inserted in the uterus as a contraceptive

in′tra·ve′nous (-vē′nəs) ***adj.*** ⟦INTRA- + VENOUS⟧ directly into a vein —**in′tra·ve′nous·ly** ***adv.***

in·trench (in trench′) ***vt.*** ENTRENCH

in·trep·id (in trep′id) ***adj.*** ⟦< L *in-*, not + *trepidus*, alarmed⟧ bold; fearless; brave —**in·trep′id·ly** ***adv.***

in·tri·cate (in′tri kit) ***adj.*** ⟦< L *in-*, in + *tricae*, vexations⟧ **1** hard to follow or understand because full of puzzling parts, details, etc. **2** full of elaborate detail —**in′tri·ca·cy** (-kə sē), *pl.* **-cies**, ***n.*** —**in′tri·cate·ly** ***adv.***

in·trigue (in trēg′; *for n., also* in′trēg′) ***vi.*** **-trigued′, -trigu′ing** ⟦see prec.⟧ to plot secretly or underhandedly —***vt.*** to excite the interest or curiosity of —***n.*** **1** a secret or underhanded plotting **2** a secret or underhanded plot or scheme **3** a secret love affair —**in·trigu′er** ***n.*** —**in·trigu′ing** ***adj.*** —**in·trigu′ing·ly** ***adv.***

in·trin·sic (in trin′sik, -zik) ***adj.*** ⟦< L *intra-*, within + *secus*, following⟧ belonging to the real nature of a thing; inherent —**in·trin′si·cal·ly** ***adv.***

intro- ⟦L⟧ *prefix* into, within, inward

in·tro·duce (in′trə dōōs′) ***vt.*** **-duced′, -duc′ing** ⟦< L *intro-*, in + *ducere*, to lead⟧ **1** to put in; insert **2** to bring in as a new feature **3** to bring into use or fashion **4** *a*) to make acquainted; present *[introduce* me to her*]* *b*) to give experience of *[*they *introduced* him to music*]* **5** to bring forward **6** to start; begin *[*to *introduce* a talk with a joke*]*

in′tro·duc′tion (-duk′shən) ***n.*** **1** an introducing or being introduced **2** the preliminary section of a book, speech, etc.; preface

in′tro·duc′to·ry (-duk′tə rē) ***adj.*** serving to introduce; preliminary

in·tro·it (in trō′it, in′troit′) ***n.*** ⟦< L *intro-*, in + *ire*, to go⟧ **1** a psalm or hymn at the opening of a Christian worship service **2** [I-] *R.C.Ch.* the first variable part of the Mass

in·tro·spec·tion (in′trə spek′shən) ***n.*** ⟦< L *intro-*, within + *specere*, to look⟧ a looking into one's own mind, feelings, etc. —**in′tro·spec′tive** ***adj.***

in·tro·vert (in′trə vurt′) ***n.*** ⟦< L *intro-*, within + *vertere*, to turn⟧ one who is introspective rather than being interested in others —**in′tro·ver′sion** (-vur′zhən) ***n.*** —**in′tro·vert′ed** ***adj.***

in·trude (in trōōd′) ***vt.***, ***vi.*** **-trud′ed, -trud′ing** ⟦< L *in-*, in + *trudere*, to push⟧ to force (oneself) upon others unasked —**in·trud′er** ***n.***

in·tru·sion (in trōō′zhən) ***n.*** an intruding —**in·tru′sive** (-siv) ***adj.*** —**in·tru′sive·ly** ***adv.*** —**in·tru′sive·ness** ***n.***

in·trust (in trust′) ***vt.*** ENTRUST

in·tu·bate (in′tōō bāt′) ***vt.*** **-bat′ed, -bat′ing** to insert a tube into (an orifice or hollow organ) to admit air, etc.

in·tu·i·tion (in′tōō ish′ən) ***n.*** ⟦< L *in-*, in + *tueri* to view⟧ the direct knowing of something without the conscious use of reasoning —**in·tu·i·tive** (in tōō′i tiv) ***adj.***

In·u·it (in′ōō it) ***n.*** ⟦Esk⟧ ESKIMO: now the preferred term, esp. in Canada

in·un·date (in′ən dāt′) ***vt.*** **-dat′ed, -dat′ing** ⟦< L *in-*, in + *unda*, a wave⟧ to cover with or as with a flood; deluge —**in′un·da′tion** ***n.***

in·ure (in yoor′) ***vt.*** **-ured′, -ur′ing** ⟦ME *in ure*, in practice⟧ to accustom to pain, trouble, etc.

in u·ter·o (in yōōt′ər ō) ⟦L⟧ in the uterus

in·vade (in vād′) ***vt.*** **-vad′ed, -vad′ing** ⟦< L *in-*, in + *vadere*, to come, go⟧ **1** to enter forcibly or hostilely **2** to intrude upon; violate —**in·vad′er** ***n.***

in·va·lid[1] (in′və lid) ***adj.*** ⟦< L *in-*, not + *validus*, strong⟧ **1** weak and sickly **2** of or for invalids —***n.*** one who is ill or disabled

in·val·id[2] (in val′id) ***adj.*** not valid

in·val′i·date′ (-ə dāt′) ***vt.*** **-dat′ed, -dat′ing** to make invalid; deprive of legal force —**in·val′i·da′tion** ***n.***

in·val·u·a·ble (in val′yōō ə bəl) ***adj.*** too valuable to be measured; priceless —**in·val′u·a·bly** ***adv.***

in·va·sion (in vā′zhən) ***n.*** an invading or being invaded, as by an army

in·va′sive (-siv) ***adj.*** **1** having to do with (an) invasion **2** penetrating into the body

in·vec·tive (in vek′tiv) ***n.*** ⟦see fol.⟧ a violent verbal attack; vituperation

in·veigh (in vā′) ***vi.*** ⟦< L *in-*, in + *vehere*, carry⟧ to make a violent verbal attack; rail *(against)*

in·vei·gle (in vā′gəl) ***vt.*** **-gled, -gling** ⟦< MFr *aveugler*, to blind⟧ to entice or trick into doing or giving something —**in·vei′gler** ***n.***

in·vent (in vent′) ***vt.*** ⟦< L *in-*, in + *venire*, come⟧ **1** to think up *[*to *invent* excuses*]* **2** to think out or produce (a new device, process, etc.); originate —**in·ven′tor** ***n.***

in·ven′tion (-ven′shən) ***n.*** **1** an inventing **2** the power of inventing **3** something invented

in·ven′tive (-tiv) ***adj.*** **1** of invention **2** skilled in inventing —**in·ven′tive·ly** ***adv.*** —**in·ven′tive·ness** ***n.***

in·ven·to·ry (in′vən tôr′ē) ***n.***, *pl.* **-ries** ⟦see INVENT⟧ **1** an itemized list of goods, property, etc., as of a business **2** the store of goods, etc. for such listing; stock —***vt.*** **-ried, -ry·ing** to make an inventory of

in·verse (in vurs′, in′vurs′) ***adj.*** inverted; directly opposite —***n.*** any inverse thing —**in·verse′ly** ***adv.***

in·ver·sion (in vur′zhən) ***n.*** **1** an inverting or being inverted **2** something inverted; reversal **3** *Meteorol.* a temperature reversal in which a layer of warm air traps cooler air near the surface of the earth

in·vert (in vurt′) ***vt.*** ⟦< L *in-*, to + *vertere*, to turn⟧ **1** to turn upside down **2** to reverse the order, position, direction, etc. of

in·ver·te·brate (in vur′tə brit, -brāt′) ***adj.*** not vertebrate; having no backbone —***n.*** any invertebrate animal

in·vest (in vest′) ***vt.*** ⟦< L *in-*, in + *vestis*, clothing⟧ **1** to clothe **2** to install in office with ceremony **3** to furnish with power, authority, etc. **4** to put (money) into business, stocks, etc. in order to get a profit —***vi.*** to invest money —**in·ves′tor** ***n.***

in·ves·ti·gate (in ves′tə gāt′) ***vi.***, ***vt.*** **-gat′ed, -gat′ing** ⟦< L *in-*, in + *vestigare*, to track⟧ to search (into); inquire —**in·ves′ti·ga′tor** ***n.***

in·ves′ti·ga′tion (-gā′shən) ***n.*** an investigating; careful search; systematic inquiry

in·ves′ti·ture (-chər) ***n.*** a formal investing, as with an office

in·vest·ment (in vest′mənt) ***n.*** **1** an investing or being invested **2** *a*) money invested *b*) anything in which money is or may be invested

in·vet·er·ate (in vet′ər it) ***adj.*** ⟦< pp. of L *inveterare*, to age⟧ **1** firmly established **2** habitual —**in·vet′er·a·cy** ***n.***

in·vid·i·ous (in vid′ē əs) ***adj.*** ⟦< L *invidia*, envy⟧ such as to excite ill will; giving offense, as by discriminating unfairly —**in·vid′i·ous·ly** ***adv.*** —**in·vid′i·ous·ness** ***n.***

in·vig·or·ate (in vig′ər āt′) ***vt.*** **-at′ed, -at′ing** to give vigor to; fill with energy —**in·vig′or·a′tion** ***n.***

in·vin·ci·ble (in vin′sə bəl) ***adj.*** ⟦< L *invincibilis*, not easily overcome⟧ that cannot be overcome; unconquerable —

in·vin′ci·bil′i·ty ***n.***

in·vi·o·la·ble (in vī′ə lə bəl) ***adj.*** **1** not to be violated; not to be profaned or injured; sacred **2** indestructible —**in·vi′o·la·bil′i·ty** ***n.***

in·vi′o·late (-lit) ***adj.*** not violated; kept sacred or unbroken

in·vis·i·ble (in viz′ə bəl) ***adj.*** **1** not visible; that cannot be seen **2** out of sight **3** imperceptible —**in·vis′i·bil′i·ty** ***n.*** —**in·vis′i·bly** ***adv.***

in·vi·ta·tion (in′və tā′shən) ***n.*** **1** an inviting **2** a message used in inviting

in′vi·ta′tion·al ***adj.*** only for those invited to take part: said as of an art show

in·vite (in vīt′; *for n.* in′vīt′) ***vt.*** **-vit′ed, -vit′ing** ⟦< L *invitare*⟧ **1** to ask to come somewhere or do something **2** to ask for **3** to give occasion for *[action that invites scandal]* **4** to tempt; entice —***n.*** [Inf.] an invitation —**in′vit·ee′** ***n.***

in·vit′ing ***adj.*** tempting; enticing

in vi·tro (in vē′trō′) ⟦L, in glass⟧ isolated from the living organism and artificially maintained, as in a test tube

in·vo·ca·tion (in′və kā′shən) ***n.*** an invoking of God, the Muses, etc.

in·voice (in′vois′) ***n.*** ⟦prob. < ME *envoie*, message⟧ a list of goods shipped or services rendered, stating prices, etc.; bill —***vt.*** **-voiced′, -voic′ing** to present an invoice for or to

in·voke (in vōk′) ***vt.*** **-voked′, -vok′ing** ⟦< L *in-*, in, on + *vocare*, to call⟧ **1** to call on (God, the Muses, etc.) for blessing, help, etc. **2** to resort to (a law, ruling, etc.) as pertinent **3** to conjure **4** to beg for; implore

in·vol·un·tar·y (in väl′ən ter′ē) ***adj.*** **1** not done by choice **2** not consciously controlled —**in·vol′un·tar′i·ly** ***adv.*** —**in·vol′un·tar′i·ness** ***n.***

in·vo·lu·tion (in′və lo͞o′shən) ***n.*** **1** an involving or being involved **2** a complication; intricacy

in·volve (in välv′, -vôlv′) ***vt.*** **-volved′, -volv′ing** ⟦< L *in-*, in + *volvere*, to roll⟧ **1** to make intricate or complicated **2** to entangle in difficulty, danger, etc.; implicate **3** to affect or include *[the riot involved thousands]* **4** to require *[saving involves thrift]* **5** to make busy; occupy *[involved the class in research]* —**in·volved′** ***adj.*** —**in·volve′ment** ***n.***

in·vul·ner·a·ble (in vul′nər ə bəl) ***adj.*** **1** that cannot be wounded or injured **2** proof against attack —**in·vul′ner·a·bil′i·ty** ***n.***

in·ward (in′wərd) ***adj.*** **1** situated within; internal **2** mental or spiritual **3** directed toward the inside **4** sensitive, subtle, reticent, etc. —***adv.*** **1** toward the inside **2** into the mind or soul Also **in′wards** ***adv.***

in′ward·ly ***adv.*** **1** in or on the inside **2** in the mind or spirit **3** toward the inside

in′-your′-face′ ***adj.*** [Slang] done in a direct, often aggressive way; assertive; daring

I/O *abbrev.* input/output

i·o·dine (ī′ə dīn′, -din) ***n.*** ⟦< Gr *iōdēs*, violetlike⟧ **1** a nonmetallic chemical element, used in medicine, etc. **2** a tincture of iodine, used as an antiseptic

i′o·dize′ (-dīz′) ***vt.*** **-dize′, -diz′ing** to treat with iodine

i·on (ī′ən, -än′) ***n.*** ⟦ult. < Gr *ienai*, to go⟧ an electrically charged atom or group of atoms

-ion (ən) ⟦< L *-io*⟧ *suffix* **1** the act or condition of **2** the result of

I·on·ic (ī än′ik) ***adj.*** designating or of a Greek or Roman style of architecture, distinguished by ornamental scrolls on the capitals

i·on·ize (ī′ən īz′) ***vt., vi.*** **-ized′, -iz′ing** to dissociate into ions, as a salt dissolved in water, or become electrically charged, as a gas under radiation —**i′on·i·za′tion** ***n.*** —**i′on·iz′er** ***n.***

i·on·o·sphere (ī än′ə sfir′) ***n.*** the outer layers of the earth's atmosphere, with some electron and ion content

i·o·ta (ī ōt′ə) ***n.*** **1** the ninth letter of the Greek alphabet (Ι, ι) **2** a very small quantity; jot

IOU (ī′ō′yo͞o′) ***n.***, *pl.* **IOU's** ⟦for *I owe you*⟧ a signed paper bearing the letters *IOU*, acknowledging a specified debt

-i·ous (ē əs, yəs, əs) ⟦see -OUS⟧ *suffix* characterized by *[furious]*

I·o·wa (ī′ə wə) Midwestern state of the U.S.: 55,875 sq. mi.; pop. 2,777,000; cap. Des Moines: abbrev. *IA* —**I′o·wan** ***adj., n.***

ip·e·cac (ip′i kak′) ***n.*** ⟦< AmInd (Brazil) name⟧ an emetic made as from the dried roots of a South American plant

IPO *abbrev.* initial public offering

ip·so fac·to (ip′sō fak′tō) ⟦L⟧ by that very fact

IQ ***n.***, *pl.* **IQ's** ⟦I(NTELLIGENCE) Q(UOTIENT)⟧ a number intended to indicate a person's intelligence, based on a test

I·qa·lu·it (ē kä′lo͞o ēt′) capital of Nunavut, Canada: pop. 4,200

Ir[1] *abbrev.* **1** Ireland **2** Irish

Ir[2] *Chem. symbol for* iridium

ir- *prefix* **1** IN-[1] **2** IN-[2] Used before *r*

IRA (ī′är′ā′; ī′rə) ***n.***, *pl.* **IRA's** ⟦*I*(*ndividual*) *R*(*etirement*) *A*(*ccount*)⟧ a personal retirement plan with taxes on the earnings deferred until funds are withdrawn

I·ran (i ran′, -rän′) country in SW Asia: 634,293 sq. mi.; pop. 49,445,000: former name PERSIA —**I·ra·ni·an** (i rā′nē ən, ī-; -rä′-) ***adj., n.***

I·raq (i räk′, -rak′) country in SW Asia, at the head of the Persian Gulf: 169,235 sq. mi.; pop. 16,335,000 —**I·ra·qi** (i rä′kē, -rak′ē), *pl.* **-qis, *n., adj.***

i·ras·ci·ble (i ras′ə bəl) ***adj.*** ⟦see fol.⟧ easily angered; hot-tempered

i·rate (ī rāt′, ī′rāt′) ***adj.*** ⟦< L *ira*, anger⟧ angry; wrathful; incensed —**i·rate′ly** ***adv.*** —**i·rate′ness** ***n.***

ire (īr) ***n.*** ⟦< L *ira*⟧ anger; wrath

Ire·land (īr′lənd) **1** one of the British Isles, west of Great Britain **2** republic comprising most of this island: 27,137 sq. mi.; pop. 3,560,000

i·ren·ic (ī ren′ik) ***adj.*** ⟦< Gr *eirēnē*, peace⟧ promoting peace

ir·i·des·cent (ir′i des′ənt) ***adj.*** ⟦< Gr *iris*, rainbow⟧ having or showing an interplay of rainbowlike colors —**ir′i·des′cence** ***n.***

i·rid·i·um (ī rid′ē əm) ***n.*** ⟦see fol.⟧ a white metallic chemical element

i·ris (ī′ris) ***n.***, *pl.* **i′ris·es** ⟦Gr, rainbow⟧ **1** the round, pigmented membrane surrounding the pupil of the eye **2** a plant with sword-shaped leaves and a showy flower

I·rish (ī′rish) ***adj.*** of Ireland or its people, language, etc. —***n.*** **1** the Celtic language of Ireland **2** the English dialect of Ireland —**the Irish** the people of Ireland —**I′rish·man** (-mən), *pl.* **-men** (-mən), ***n.*** —**I′rish·wom′an**, *pl.* **-wom′en**, ***fem.n.***

Irish coffee brewed coffee with Irish whiskey, topped with whipped cream

Irish Sea arm of the Atlantic between Ireland & Great Britain

irk (ʉrk) ***vt.*** ⟦ME *irken*, be weary of⟧ to annoy, irritate, tire out, etc.

irk′some (-səm) ***adj.*** that tends to irk; tiresome or annoying

i·ron (ī′ərn) ***n.*** ⟦OE *iren*⟧ **1** a metallic chemical element, the most common of all metals **2** any device of iron; esp., such a device with a flat undersurface, heated for pressing cloth **3** [*pl.*] iron shackles **4** firm strength; power **5** any of certain golf clubs with angled metal heads —***adj.*** **1** of iron **2** like iron; strong; firm —***vt., vi.*** to press with a hot iron —**iron out** to smooth out; eliminate

i′ron·clad′ ***adj.*** **1** covered or protected with iron **2** difficult to change or break *[*an *ironclad* lease*]*

iron curtain **1** [*often* **I- C-**] a barrier of secrecy and censorship seen as isolating the U.S.S.R., etc.: often with *the* **2** any similar barrier

i′ron-fist′ed (-fis′tid) ***adj.*** despotic and brutal

i·ron·ic (ī rän′ik) ***adj.*** **1** meaning the contrary of what is expressed **2** using irony **3** opposite to what is or might be expected Also **i·ron′i·cal** —**i·ron′i·cal·ly** ***adv.***

i·ron·man (ī′ərn man′) ***n.***, *pl.* **-men′** (-men′) [*often* **I-**] a man of great physical strength

i′ron·ware′ ***n.*** things made of iron

i·ro·ny (ī′rə nē, ī′ər nē) ***n.***, *pl.* **-nies** ⟦< Gr *eirōn*, dissembler in speech⟧ **1** expression in which the intended meaning of the words is the direct opposite of their usual sense **2** an event or result that is the opposite of what is expected

Ir·o·quois (ir′ə kwoi′) ***n.***, *pl.* **-quois′** (-kwoi′, -kwoiz′) a member of a confederation of North American Indian peoples that lived in upstate New York —***adj.*** of the Iroquois —**Ir′o·quoi′an** ***n.***, ***adj.***

ir·ra·di·ate (i rā′dē āt′) ***vt.*** **-at′ed, -at′ing** **1** to shine upon; light up **2** to enlighten **3** to radiate **4** to expose to X-rays or other radiant energy —***vi.*** to emit rays; shine —**ir·ra′di·a′tion** ***n.***

ir·ra·tion·al (i rash′ə nəl) ***adj.*** **1** lacking the power to reason **2** senseless; unreasonable; absurd —**ir·ra′tion·al′i·ty** (-ə nal′ə tē), *pl.* **-ties**, ***n.*** —**ir·ra′tion·al·ly** ***adv.***

ir·re·claim·a·ble (ir′i klām′ə bəl) ***adj.*** that cannot be reclaimed

ir·rec·on·cil·a·ble (i rek′ən sīl′ə bəl) ***adj.*** that cannot be brought into agreement; incompatible

ir·re·cov·er·a·ble (ir′i kuv′ər ə bəl) ***adj.*** that cannot be recovered, rectified, or remedied

ir·re·deem·a·ble (ir′i dēm′ə bəl) ***adj.*** **1** that cannot be bought back **2** that cannot be converted into coin: said as of certain paper money **3** that cannot be changed or reformed

ir·ref·u·ta·ble (i ref′yoo tə bəl, ir′i fyoot′ ə bəl) ***adj.*** indisputable —**ir·ref′u·ta·bly** ***adv.***

ir·re·gard·less (ir′i gärd′lis) ***adj.***, ***adv.*** REGARDLESS: a nonstandard or humorous usage

ir·reg·u·lar (i reg′yə lər) ***adj.*** **1** not conforming to an established rule, standard, etc. **2** not straight, even, or uniform **3** *Gram.* not inflected in the usual way —**ir·reg′u·lar′i·ty**, *pl.* **-ties**, ***n.***

ir·rel·e·vant (i rel′ə vənt) ***adj.*** not pertinent; not to the point —**ir·rel′e·vance** ***n.*** —**ir·rel′e·vant·ly** ***adv.***

ir·re·li·gious (ir′i lij′əs) ***adj.*** **1** not religious **2** indifferent or hostile to religion **3** profane; impious —**ir′re·li′gious·ly** ***adv.***

ir·re·me·di·a·ble (ir′i mē′dē ə bəl) ***adj.*** that cannot be remedied or corrected —**ir′re·me′di·a·bly** ***adv.***

ir·rep·a·ra·ble (i rep′ə rə bəl) ***adj.*** that cannot be repaired, mended, etc.

ir·re·place·a·ble (ir′i plās′ə bəl) ***adj.*** that cannot be replaced

ir′re·press′i·ble (-pres′ə bəl) ***adj.*** that cannot be repressed

ir′re·proach′a·ble (-prō′chə bəl) ***adj.*** blameless; faultless

ir′re·sist′i·ble (-zis′tə bəl) ***adj.*** that cannot be resisted; too strong, fascinating, etc. to be withstood —**ir′re·sist′i·bly** ***adv.***

ir·res·o·lute (i rez′ə loot′) ***adj.*** not resolute; wavering; indecisive —**ir·res′o·lu′tion** (-loo′shən) ***n.***

ir·re·spec·tive (ir′i spek′tiv) ***adj.*** regardless (*of*)

ir′re·spon′si·ble (-spän′sə bəl) ***adj.*** **1** not responsible for actions **2** lacking a sense of responsibility —**ir′re·spon′si·bil′i·ty** ***n.***

ir′re·triev′a·ble (-trēv′ə bəl) ***adj.*** that cannot be retrieved —**ir′re·triev′a·bly** ***adv.***

ir·rev·er·ence (i rev′ər əns) ***n.*** lack of reverence; disrespect —**ir·rev′er·ent** ***adj.***

ir·re·vers·i·ble (ir′i vʉr′sə bəl) ***adj.*** that cannot be reversed; esp., that cannot be annulled or turned back

ir·rev·o·ca·ble (i rev′ə kə bəl) ***adj.*** that cannot be revoked or undone —**ir·rev′o·ca·bly** ***adv.***

ir·ri·ga·ble (ir′i gə bəl) ***adj.*** that can be irrigated

ir·ri·gate (ir′ə gāt′) ***vt.*** **-gat′ed, -gat′ing**

⟦< L *in-*, in + *rigare*, to water⟧ **1** to supply (land) with water, as by means of artificial ditches **2** *Med.* to wash out (a cavity, wound, etc.) **—ir'ri·ga'tion** ***n.***

ir·ri·ta·ble (ir'i tə bəl) ***adj.*** **1** easily annoyed or provoked **2** *Med.* excessively sensitive to a stimulus **—ir'ri·ta·bil'i·ty** ***n.*** **—ir'ri·ta·bly** ***adv.***

ir'ri·tant (-tənt) ***adj.*** causing irritation **—*n.*** a thing that irritates

ir'ri·tate' (-tāt') ***vt.*** **-tat'ed, -tat'ing** ⟦< L *irritare*, excite⟧ **1** to provoke to anger; annoy **2** to make inflamed or sore **—ir'ri·ta'tion** ***n.***

ir·rupt (i rupt') ***vi.*** ⟦< L *in-*, in + *rumpere*, to break⟧ to burst suddenly or violently (*into*) **—ir·rup'tion** ***n.*** **—ir·rup'tive** ***adj.***

IRS *abbrev.* Internal Revenue Service

Ir·ving (ʉr'viŋ) city in NW Texas: pop. 155,000

is[1] (iz) ***vi.*** ⟦OE⟧ *3d pers. sing., pres. indic., of* BE

is[2] *abbrev.* **1** island(s) **2** islet(s)

I·saac (ī'zək) ***n.*** *Bible* one of the patriarchs, son of Abraham, and father of Jacob and Esau

I·sa·iah (ī zā'ə) ***n.*** *Bible* **1** a Hebrew prophet of the 8th c. B.C. **2** the book containing his teachings

-ise (īz) *suffix chiefly Brit. sp. of* -IZE

-ish (ish) ⟦< OE *-isc*⟧ *suffix* **1** of (a specified people) *[Irish]* **2** somewhat *[tallish]* **3** [Inf.] approximately *[thirtyish]* **4** like or characteristic of

Ish·tar (ish'tär') ***n.*** the Babylonian and Assyrian goddess of fertility

i·sin·glass (ī'zin glas', -ziŋ-) ***n.*** ⟦prob. < MDu *huizen*, sturgeon + *blas*, bladder⟧ mica, esp. in thin sheets

I·sis (ī'sis) ***n.*** the Egyptian goddess of fertility

isl *abbrev.* **1** island **2** isle

Is·lam (is'läm', iz'-) ***n.*** ⟦Ar *islām*, lit., submission (to God's will)⟧ **1** the Muslim religion, a monotheistic religion founded by Mohammed **2** Muslims collectively or the lands in which they predominate **—Is·lam'ic** (-läm'ik) ***adj.***

Is·lam·a·bad (is läm'ə bäd') capital of Pakistan, in the NE part: pop. 201,000

is·land (ī'lənd) ***n.*** ⟦< OE *igland*, lit., island land: sp. after *isle*⟧ **1** a land mass smaller than a continent and surrounded by water **2** anything like this in position or isolation

is'land·er ***n.*** a person born or living on an island

isle (īl) ***n.*** ⟦< L *insula*⟧ an island, esp. a small island

is·let (ī'lit) ***n.*** a very small island

islets (or **islands**) **of Lang·er·hans** (läŋ'ər häns') ⟦after P. *Langerhans* (1847-88), Ger histologist⟧ endocrine cells in the pancreas that produce the hormone insulin

ism (iz'əm) ***n.*** a doctrine, theory, system, etc. whose name ends in *-ism*

-ism (iz'əm) ⟦< Gr *-ismos*⟧ *suffix* **1** act or result of *[terrorism]* **2** condition, conduct, or qualities of *[patriotism]* **3** theory of *[socialism]* **4** devotion to *[nationalism]* **5** an instance of *[witticism]*

is·n't (iz'ənt) *contr.* is not

ISO *abbrev.* International Standards Organization

iso- ⟦< Gr *isos*⟧ *combining form* equal, similar, identical *[isomorph]*

i·so·bar (ī'sō bär') ***n.*** ⟦< prec. + Gr *baros*, weight⟧ a line on a map connecting points of equal barometric pressure

i·so·late (ī'sə lāt'; *for n., usually*, -lit) ***vt.*** **-lat'ed, -lat'ing** ⟦< It *isola* (< L *insula*), island⟧ to set apart from others; place alone **—*n.*** a person or thing that is isolated **—i'so·lat'ed** ***adj.*** **—i'so·la'tion** ***n.*** **—i'so·la'tor** ***n.***

i'so·la'tion·ist ***n.*** one who opposes the involvement of a country in international alliances, etc. **—*adj.*** of isolationists **—i'so·la'tion·ism'** ***n.***

i·so·mer (ī'sə mər) ***n.*** ⟦< Gr *isos*, equal + *meros*, a part⟧ any of two or more chemical compounds whose molecules contain the same atoms but in different arrangements **—i'so·mer'ic** (-mer'ik) ***adj.***

i'so·met'ric (-met'rik) ***adj.*** ⟦< Gr *isos*, equal + *metron*, measure⟧ **1** equal in measure **2** of isometrics **—*n.*** [*pl.*] exercise in which muscles are briefly tensed in opposition to other muscles or to an immovable object **—i'so·met'ri·cal·ly** ***adv.***

i·sos·ce·les (ī säs'ə lēz') ***adj.*** ⟦< Gr *isos*, equal + *skelos*, leg⟧ designating a triangle with two equal sides

i·so·tope (ī'sə tōp') ***n.*** ⟦< ISO- + Gr *topos*, place⟧ any of two or more forms of an element having the same atomic number but different atomic weights

ISP ***n.***, *pl.* **ISPs** ⟦*I*(*nternet*) *s*(*ervice*) *p*(*rovider*)⟧ a company that provides access to the Internet

Is·ra·el[1] (iz'rē əl) ***n.*** *Bible* Jacob

Is·ra·el[2] (iz'rē əl) **1** ancient land of the Hebrews at the SE end of the Mediterranean **2** kingdom in the N part of this land **3** country between the Mediterranean Sea & Jordan: 8,463 sq. mi.; pop. 4,038,000

Is·rae·li (iz rā'lē) ***n.*** a person born or living in modern Israel **—*adj.*** of modern Israel or its people

Is·ra·el·ite (iz'rē ə līt') ***n.*** any of the people of ancient Israel; Hebrew

is·su·ance (ish'o͞o əns) ***n.*** an issuing; issue

is·sue (ish'o͞o) ***n.*** ⟦< L *ex-*, out + *ire*, go⟧ **1** an outgoing; outflow **2** a result; consequence **3** offspring **4** a point under dispute **5** a sending or giving out **6** all that is put forth at one time *[an issue of bonds, a periodical, etc.]* **—*vi.*** **-sued, -su·ing** **1** to go or flow out; emerge **2** to result (*from*) or end (*in*) **—*vt.*** **1** to give or deal out *[to issue supplies]* **2** to publish **—at issue** in dispute **—take issue** to disagree **—is'su·er** ***n.***

-ist (ist, əst) ⟦< Gr *-istēs*⟧ *suffix* **1** one who does, makes, or practices *[satirist]* **2** one skilled in or occupied with *[druggist, violinist]* **3** an adherent of *[anarchist]*

Is·tan·bul (is'tan bo͞ol', -tän-) seaport in NW Turkey: pop. 5,476,000

isth·mus (is′məs) ***n.***, *pl.* **-mus·es** or **-mi′** (-mī′) ⟦< Gr *isthmos*, a neck⟧ a narrow strip of land having water at each side and connecting two larger bodies of land

it (it) ***pron.***, *pl. see* THEY ⟦< OE *hit*⟧ **1** the animal or thing previously mentioned **2** *it* is also used as: *a)* the subject of an impersonal verb *[it is snowing]* *b)* a subject or object of indefinite sense in various idiomatic constructions *[it's all right, he lords it over us]* **—*n.*** the player, as in tag, who must try to catch another **—with it** [Slang] alert, informed, or hip

It or **Ital** *abbrev.* **1** Italian **2** Italy

IT *abbrev.* information technology

I·tal·ian (i tal′yən) ***adj.*** of Italy or its people, language, etc. **—*n.*** **1** a person born or living in Italy **2** the Romance language of Italy

i·tal·ic (i tal′ik, ī-) ***adj.*** ⟦< its early use in *Italy*⟧ designating a type in which the characters slant upward to the right (Ex.: *this is italic type*) **—*n.*** [*usually pl., sometimes with sing. v.*] italic type or print: abbrev. **ital**

i·tal·i·cize (i tal′ə sīz′, ī-) ***vt.*** **-cized′**, **-ciz′ing** to print in italics

It·a·ly (it′′l ē) country in S Europe: 116,333 sq. mi.; pop. 56,778,000

itch (ich) ***vi.*** ⟦OE *giccan*⟧ **1** to feel a tingling of the skin, with the desire to scratch **2** to have a restless desire **—*vt.*** [Inf.] SCRATCH **—*n.*** **1** an itching **2** a restless desire **—itch′y**, **-i·er**, **-i·est**, ***adj.***

-ite (īt) ⟦< Gr *-itēs*⟧ *suffix* **1** an inhabitant of *[Akronite]* **2** an adherent of *[laborite]* **3** a manufactured product *[dynamite]*

i·tem (īt′əm) ***n.*** ⟦< L *ita*, so, thus⟧ **1** an article; unit; separate thing **2** a bit of news or information

i′tem·ize′ (-īz′) ***vt.*** **-ized′**, **-iz′ing** to specify the items of; set down by items **—i′tem·i·za′tion *n.***

it·er·ate (it′ər āt′) ***vt.*** **-at′ed**, **-at′ing** ⟦< L *iterum*, again⟧ to utter or do again **—it′er·a′tion *n.***

i·tin·er·ant (ī tin′ər ənt) ***adj.*** ⟦< L *iter*, a walk⟧ traveling from place to place **—*n.*** a traveler

i·tin′er·ar′y (-er′ē) ***n.***, *pl.* **-ar′ies** **1** a route **2** a record of a journey **3** a detailed plan for a journey

-i·tis (īt′is) ⟦< Gr *-itis*⟧ *suffix* inflammation of (a specified part or organ) *[neuritis]*

its (its) ***pron.*** that or those belonging to it **—*poss. pronominal adj.*** of, belonging to, or done by it

it's (its) *contr.* **1** it is **2** it has

it·self (it self′) ***pron.*** a form of IT, used as an intensive *[the work itself is easy]*, as a reflexive *[the dog bit itself]*, or with the meaning "its true self" *[the bird is not itself today]*

it·ty-bit·ty (it′ē bit′ē) ***adj.*** ⟦baby talk < *little bit*⟧ [Inf.] very small; tiny: also **it·sy-bit·sy** (it′sē bit′sē)

-i·ty (ə tē, i-) ⟦< L *-itas*⟧ *suffix* state, quality, or instance *[chastity]*

IUD *abbrev.* intrauterine (contraceptive) device

IV[1] ***n.***, *pl.* **IVs** ⟦< I(NTRA)V(ENOUS)⟧ *Med.* **1** a procedure in which a hypodermic needle is inserted into a vein to supply blood, nutrients, etc. **2** the apparatus used for this, including the bag of fluid, tubing, and needle

IV[2] *abbrev.* intravenous(ly)

-ive (iv) ⟦< L *-ivus*⟧ *suffix* **1** of or having the nature of *[sportive]* **2** tending to *[retrospective]*

i·vied (ī′vēd) ***adj.*** covered or overgrown with ivy

i·vo·ry (ī′vər ē, īv′rē) ***n.***, *pl.* **-ries** ⟦ult. < Egypt *ȝbw*⟧ **1** the hard, white substance forming the tusks of elephants, walruses, etc. **2** any substance like ivory **3** creamy white **—*adj.*** **1** of or like ivory **2** creamy-white

Ivory Coast country on the W coast of Africa: 123,855 sq. mi.; pop. 10,813,000

ivory tower a retreat away from reality or action

i·vy (ī′vē) ***n.***, *pl.* **i′vies** ⟦OE *ifig*⟧ **1** a climbing vine with a woody stem and evergreen leaves **2** any of various similar climbing plants

-ize (īz) ⟦< Gr *-izein*⟧ *suffix* **1** to cause to be *[sterilize]* **2** to become (like) *[crystallize]* **3** to combine with *[oxidize]* **4** to engage in *[soliloquize]*

J

j or **J** (jā) ***n.***, *pl.* **j's**, **J's** the tenth letter of the English alphabet

jab (jab) ***vt.***, ***vi.*** **jabbed**, **jab′bing** ⟦< ME *jobben*, to peck⟧ **1** to poke, as with a sharp instrument **2** to punch with short, straight blows **—*n.*** a quick thrust or blow

jab·ber (jab′ər) ***vi.***, ***vt.*** ⟦prob. echoic⟧ to speak or say quickly, incoherently, or foolishly; chatter **—*n.*** chatter **—jab′ber·er *n.***

ja·bot (zha bō′) ***n.*** ⟦Fr, bird's crop⟧ a ruffle or frill down the front of a blouse, etc.

jack (jak) ***n.*** ⟦< the name *Jack*⟧ **1** [*often* **J-**] a man or boy **2** any of various machines used to lift something heavy a short distance *[an automobile jack]* **3** a playing card with a picture of a royal male servant or soldier **4** a small flag flown on a ship's bow to show nationality **5** any of the small, 6-pronged metal pieces tossed and picked up in a game (**jacks**) **6** *Elec.* a plug-in receptacle used to make electrical contact **—*vt.*** to raise by means of a jack: usually with *up* **—jack up** [Inf.] to raise (prices, wages, etc.)

jack- ⟦see prec.⟧ *combining form* **1** male

[jackass] **2** large or strong *[jackknife]* **3** boy; fellow *[jack-in-the-box]*

jack·al (jak′əl) ***n.*** ⟦< Sans⟧ a wild dog of Asia and N Africa

jack·ass (jak′as′) ***n.*** ⟦JACK- + ASS⟧ **1** a male donkey **2** a fool

jack′boot′ (-bo͞ot′) ***n.*** ⟦JACK- + BOOT[1]⟧ a long, heavy military boot that covers the knee

jack′daw′ (-dô′) ***n.*** ⟦JACK- + ME *dawe*, jackdaw⟧ a small European crow

jack·et (jak′it) ***n.*** ⟦< Ar *shakk*⟧ **1** a short coat **2** an outer covering, as the removable paper cover on a book, the metal casing of a bullet, etc.

Jack Frost frost or cold weather personified

jack′ham′mer ***n.*** a portable type of pneumatic hammer, used for breaking up concrete, rock, etc.

jack′-in-the-box′ ***n.***, *pl.* **-box′es** a toy consisting of a box from which a figure on a spring jumps up when the lid is lifted: also **jack′-in-a-box′**

JACK-IN-THE-PULPIT

jack′-in-the-pul′pit (-pool′pit) ***n.***, *pl.* **-pits** a plant with a flower spike partly arched over by a hoodlike covering

jack′knife′ ***n.***, *pl.* **-knives′** **1** a large pocketknife **2** a dive in which the diver keeps knees unbent, touches the feet, and then straightens out —***vi.***, ***vt.*** **-knifed′**, **-knif′ing** to bend or fold at the middle or at a connection

jack′-of-all-trades′ ***n.***, *pl.* **jacks′-** [*often* **J-**] one who can do many kinds of work acceptably

jack-o′-lan·tern (jak′ə lant′ərn) ***n.***, *pl.* **-terns** a hollow pumpkin cut to look like a face and used esp. as a decoration at Halloween

jack′pot′ ***n.*** ⟦*jack*, playing card + *pot*⟧ **1** cumulative stakes, as in poker **2** any large prize, etc.

jack rabbit a large hare of W North America, with long ears and strong hind legs

Jack·son[1] (jak′sən), **An·drew** (an′dro͞o′) 1767-1845; 7th president of the U.S. (1829-37)

Jack·son[2] (jak′sən) capital of Mississippi, in the SW part: pop. 197,000

Jack·son·ville (jak′sən vil′) port in NE Florida: pop. 673,000

Ja·cob (jā′kəb) ***n.*** *Bible* a son of Isaac

jac·quard (jak′ärd, jə kärd′) ***n.*** ⟦after J. M. *Jacquard* (1752-1834), Fr inventor⟧ [*sometimes* **J-**] a fabric with a figured weave

Ja·cuz·zi (jə ko͞o′zē) ⟦< *Jacuzzi*, U.S. developers⟧ *trademark for* a kind of whirlpool bath

jade (jād) ***n.*** ⟦< Sp (*piedra de*) *ijada*, (stone of) the side: supposed to cure pains in the side⟧ **1** a hard, greenish, ornamental gemstone **2** a medium green color

jad·ed (jād′id) ***adj.*** **1** tired; worn-out **2** dulled or satiated —**jad′ed·ly** ***adv.*** —**jad′ed·ness** ***n.***

jade plant a thick-leaved plant native to S Africa and Asia

jag[1] (jag) ***n.*** ⟦ME *jagge*⟧ a sharp, toothlike projection

jag[2] (jag) ***n.*** ⟦< ?⟧ [Slang] a drunken spree

jag·ged (jag′id) ***adj.*** having sharp projecting points; notched or ragged —**jag′ged·ly** ***adv.*** —**jag′ged·ness** ***n.***

jag·uar (jag′wär′) ***n.*** ⟦Port < AmInd (Brazil)⟧ a large, leopardlike cat found from SW U.S. to Argentina

jai a·lai (hī′lī′, hī′ə lī′) ⟦< Basque *jai*, celebration + *alai*, merry⟧ a game like handball, played with a basketlike racket

jail (jāl) ***n.*** ⟦ult. < L *cavea*, cage⟧ a prison, esp. for minor offenders or persons awaiting trial —***vt.*** to put or keep in jail

jail′break′ ***n.*** a breaking out of jail

jail′er or **jail′or** ***n.*** a person in charge of a jail or of prisoners

Ja·kar·ta (jə kär′tə) capital of Indonesia, on Java island: pop. *c.* 6,503,000

ja·la·pe·ño (hä′lə pān′yō) ***n.*** ⟦Mex⟧ a kind of hot pepper, orig. from Mexico

Ja·lis·co (hä lēs′kô) state of W Mexico, on the Pacific: 30,941 sq. mi.; pop. 5,303,000

ja·lop·y (jə läp′ē) ***n.***, *pl.* **-lop′ies** ⟦< ?⟧ [Slang] an old, ramshackle car

jal·ou·sie (jal′ə sē′) ***n.*** ⟦Fr < It *gelosia*, jealousy⟧ a window, shade, or door formed of adjustable horizontal slats of wood, metal, or glass

jam[1] (jam) ***vt.*** **jammed**, **jam′ming** ⟦< ?⟧ **1** to squeeze into a confined space **2** to crush **3** to crowd **4** to crowd into or block (a passageway, etc.) **5** to make stick so that it cannot move or work **6** to make (radio broadcasts, etc.) unintelligible, as by sending out other signals on the same wavelength —***vi.*** **1** *a*) to become stuck fast *b*) to become unworkable because of jammed parts **2** to become squeezed into a confined space **3** [Inf.] *Jazz* to improvise, as in a gathering of musicians (**jam session**) —***n.*** **1** a jamming or being jammed *[a traffic jam]* **2** [Inf.] a difficult situation

jam[2] (jam) ***n.*** ⟦< ? prec.⟧ fruit boiled with sugar to a thick mixture

Ja·mai·ca (jə mā′kə) country on an island in the West Indies, south of Cuba: 4,411 sq. mi.; pop. 2,374,000 —**Ja·mai′can** ***adj.***, ***n.***

jamb (jam) ***n.*** ⟦< LL *gamba*, hoof⟧ a side post of a doorway, window, etc.

jam·bo·ree (jam′bə rē′) ***n.*** ⟦< ?⟧ **1** a noisy party, gathering, etc. **2** a large assembly of Boy Scouts from many places

James (jāmz), **Henry** 1843-1916; U.S. novelist, in England

James·town (jāmz′toun′) former village in Virginia: the 1st permanent English colonial settlement in America (1607)

jam·packed (jam′pakt′) ***adj.*** [Inf.] tightly packed

jan·gle (jaŋ′gəl) ***vi.*** **-gled, -gling** ⟦< OFr *jangler*⟧ to make a harsh, usually metallic sound —***vt.*** **1** to cause to jangle **2** to irritate *[*to *jangle* someone's nerves*]* —***n.*** a jangling —**jan′gler** ***n.***

jan·i·tor (jan′i tər) ***n.*** ⟦L, doorkeeper⟧ one who takes care of a building, doing routine repairs, etc. —**jan′i·to′ri·al** (-i tôr′ē əl) ***adj.***

Jan·u·ar·y (jan′yo͞o er′ē) ***n.***, *pl.* **-ar′ies** ⟦< L < *Janus*, Roman god who was a patron of beginnings and endings⟧ the first month of the year, having 31 days: abbrev. *abbrev.* **Jan.**

ja·pan (jə pan′) ***n.*** ⟦orig. made in Japan⟧ a lacquer giving a hard, glossy finish

Ja·pan (jə pan′) **1** island country in the Pacific, off the E coast of Asia: 145,841 sq. mi.; pop. 123,612,000 **2 Sea of** arm of the Pacific, between Japan & E Asia

Jap·a·nese (jap′ə nēz′) ***adj.*** of Japan or its people, language, etc. —***n.*** **1** *pl.* **-nese′** a person born or living in Japan **2** the language of Japan

Japanese beetle a shiny, green-and-brown beetle, orig. from Japan, damaging to crops

jape (jāp) ***vi.*** **japed, jap′ing** ⟦< OFr *japer*, to howl⟧ **1** to joke **2** to play tricks —***n.*** **1** a joke **2** a trick

jar[1] (jär) ***vi.*** **jarred, jar′ring** ⟦ult. echoic⟧ **1** to make a harsh sound; grate **2** to have an irritating effect (*on* one) **3** to vibrate from an impact **4** to clash; conflict —***vt.*** to jolt —***n.*** **1** a grating sound **2** a vibration due to impact **3** a jolt

jar[2] (jär) ***n.*** ⟦< Ar *jarrah*, earthen container⟧ **1** a container made of glass, earthenware, etc., with a large opening **2** as much as a jar will hold: also **jar′ful′**

jar·di·niere (jär′də nir′) ***n.*** ⟦< Fr < *jardin*, a garden⟧ an ornamental pot or stand for flowers or plants

jar·gon (jär′gən) ***n.*** ⟦< MFr, a chattering⟧ **1** unintelligible talk **2** the specialized vocabulary of those in the same work, way of life, etc.

jas·mine (jaz′min, jas′-) ***n.*** ⟦< Pers *yāsamīn*⟧ any of certain plants of warm regions, with fragrant flowers of yellow, red, or white

Ja·son (jā′sən) ***n.*** *Gr. Myth.* the leader of the Argonauts: cf. ARGONAUT

jas·per (jas′pər) ***n.*** ⟦< Gr *iaspis*⟧ an opaque variety of colored quartz, usually reddish

jaun·dice (jôn′dis) ***n.*** ⟦< L *galbus*, yellow⟧ a diseased condition in which the eyeballs, skin, and urine become abnormally yellowish as a result of increased bile in the blood —***vt.*** **-diced, -dic·ing** **1** to cause to have jaundice **2** to make bitter through envy, etc.

jaunt (jônt) ***vi.*** ⟦< ?⟧ to take a short pleasure trip —***n.*** such a trip

jaun·ty (jôn′tē) ***adj.*** **-ti·er, -ti·est** ⟦< Fr *gentil*, genteel⟧ showing an easy confidence; sprightly or perky —**jaun′ti·ly** ***adv.*** —**jaun′ti·ness** ***n.***

Ja·va[1] (jä′və, jav′ə) ***n.*** **1** a coffee grown on Java **2** [*often* **j-**] [Slang] any coffee

Java[2] (jä′və, jav′ə) large island of Indonesia —**Jav·a·nese** (jä′və nēz′), *pl.* **-nese′**, ***adj.***, ***n.***

jav·e·lin (jav′lin, jav′ə lin) ***n.*** ⟦MFr *javeline*⟧ a light spear, esp. one thrown for distance in an athletic contest

jaw (jô) ***n.*** ⟦< OFr *joue*, cheek⟧ **1** either of the two bony parts that hold the teeth and frame the mouth **2** either of two movable parts that grasp or crush something, as in a vise —***vi.*** [Slang] to talk

jaw′bone′ ***n.*** a bone of a jaw, esp. of the lower jaw —***vt.***, ***vi.*** **-boned′**, **-bon′ing** to try to persuade by using the influence of one's office or position

jaw′break′er ***n.*** **1** a hard, usually round candy **2** [Slang] a word hard to pronounce

jaw′less fish a jawless fish with an eel-like body and a circular sucking mouth, as the lamprey

jay (jā) ***n.*** ⟦< LL *gaius*, jay⟧ any of several birds, usually strikingly colored, as the blue jay

jay′walk′ ***vi.*** to walk across a street without obeying traffic rules and signals —**jay′walk′er** ***n.***

jazz (jaz) ***n.*** ⟦< ?⟧ **1** a kind of syncopated, highly rhythmic music originated by Southern blacks in the late 19th c. **2** [Slang] talk, acts, etc. regarded disparagingly —***vt.*** [Slang] to enliven or embellish: usually with *up*

jazz′y ***adj.*** **-i·er, -i·est** **1** of or like jazz **2** [Slang] lively, flashy, etc.

JD *abbrev.* **1** ⟦L *Jurum Doctor*⟧ Doctor of Laws: also **J.D.** **2** juvenile delinquent: also **jd**

jeal·ous (jel′əs) ***adj.*** ⟦see ZEAL⟧ **1** watchful in guarding *[jealous* of one's rights*]* **2** *a*) resentfully suspicious of rivalry *[*a *jealous* lover*]* *b*) resentfully envious *c*) resulting from such feelings *[*a *jealous* rage*]* —**jeal′ous·ly** ***adv.***

jeal′ous·y ***n.*** **1** the quality or condition of being jealous **2** *pl.* **-ous·ies** a jealous feeling

jean (jēn) ***n.*** ⟦< L *Genua*, Genoa, city in Italy⟧ **1** a durable, twilled cotton cloth **2** [*pl.*] trousers of this or of denim

jeep (jēp) ***n.*** ⟦< creature in comic strip by E. C. Segar (1894-1938)⟧ a small, rugged military vehicle of WWII —[**J-**] *trademark for* a similar vehicle for civilian use

jeer (jir) ***vt.***, ***vi.*** ⟦< ? CHEER⟧ to make fun of (a person or thing) in a rude, sarcastic manner; scoff (at) —***n.*** a jeering remark

Jef·fer·son (jef′ər sən), **Thom·as** (täm′əs) 1743-1826; 3d president of the U.S. (1801-09)

Jefferson City capital of Missouri: pop. 35,000

Je·ho·vah (ji hō′və) ***n.*** ⟦< Heb⟧ God

je·june (ji jo͞on′) ***adj.*** ⟦L *jejunus,* empty⟧ **1** not interesting or satisfying **2** not mature; childish

je·ju·num (jē jo͞o′nəm) ***n.***, *pl.* **-na** (-nə) ⟦< L *jejunus,* empty⟧ the middle part of the small intestine

jell (jel) ***vi., vt.*** ⟦< L *gelare,* freeze⟧ **1** to become, or make into, jelly **2** [Inf.] to crystallize *[plans haven't jelled yet]*

jell·o (jel′ō) ***n.*** ⟦< *Jell-O,* a trademark⟧ a flavored gelatin used as a dessert, etc.

jel·ly (jel′ē) ***n.***, *pl.* **-lies** ⟦< L *gelare,* freeze⟧ **1** a soft, gelatinous food made from cooked fruit syrup or meat juice **2** any substance like this —***vi., vt.*** **-lied, -ly·ing** JELL (sense 1)

jelly bean a small, bean-shaped, gelatinous candy: also **jel′ly·bean′** ***n.***

jel′ly·fish′ ***n.***, *pl.* **-fish′** or (for different species) **-fish′es** **1** a sea animal with an umbrella-shaped, jellylike body and long tentacles **2** [Inf.] a weak-willed person

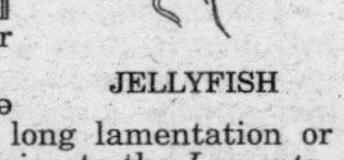
JELLYFISH

jel′ly·roll′ ***n.*** a thin sheet of sponge cake spread with jelly and rolled up

jeop·ard·ize (jep′ər dīz′) ***vt.*** **-ized′, -iz′ing** to put in jeopardy

jeop′ard·y (-dē) ***n.*** ⟦< OFr *jeu parti,* lit., a game with even chances⟧ great danger or risk

jer·e·mi·ad (jer′ə mī′ad′, -əd) ***n.*** a long lamentation or complaint: in allusion to the *Lamentations of Jeremiah*

Jer′e·mi′ah (-ə) ***n.*** *Bible* a Hebrew prophet of the 7th and 6th c. B.C.

Jer·i·cho (jer′i kō′) city in W Jordan: site of an ancient city in Canaan

jerk (jurk) ***n.*** ⟦< ?⟧ **1** a sharp, abrupt pull, twist, etc. **2** a sudden muscular contraction **3** [Slang] a person regarded as disagreeable, contemptible, etc. —***vi., vt.*** **1** to move with a jerk; pull sharply **2** to twitch

jer·kin (jur′kin) ***n.*** ⟦< ?⟧ a short, closefitting jacket, often sleeveless

jerk′wa′ter ***adj.*** [Inf.] small, unimportant, etc. *[a jerkwater town]*

jerk·y[1] (jur′kē) ***adj.*** **jerk′i·er, jerk′i·est** **1** moving by jerks; spasmodic **2** [Slang] foolish, mean, etc. —**jerk′i·ly** ***adv.***

jer·ky[2] (jur′kē) ***n.*** ⟦< Sp *charqui*⟧ meat preserved by being sliced into strips and dried in the sun

jer·ry-built (jer′ē bilt′) ***adj.*** built poorly, of cheap materials

jer·sey (jur′zē) ***n.***, *pl.* **-seys** ⟦after *Jersey,* one of the Channel Islands⟧ **1** [**J-**] any of a breed of reddish-brown dairy cattle, orig. from Jersey **2** a soft, knitted cloth **3** a closefitting, knitted upper garment

Jer·sey City (jur′zē) city in NE New Jersey, across the Hudson from New York City: pop. 229,000

Je·ru·sa·lem (jə ro͞oz′ə ləm) capital of Israel (the country): pop. 591,000

jest (jest) ***n.*** ⟦< L *gerere,* perform⟧ **1** a mocking remark; taunt **2** a joke **3** fun; joking **4** something to be laughed at —***vi.*** **1** to jeer **2** to joke

jest′er ***n.*** one who jests; esp., a man employed to amuse a medieval ruler

Jes·u·it (jezh′o͞o it, jez′-) ***n.*** a member of the Society of Jesus, a Roman Catholic religious order for men, founded in 1534

Je·sus (jē′zəz, -zəs) *c.* 8-4 B.C.-A.D. 29?; founder of the Christian religion: also **Jesus Christ**

jet[1] (jet) ***vt., vi.*** **jet′ted, jet′ting** ⟦< L *jacere,* to throw⟧ **1** to gush out in a stream **2** to travel or convey by jet airplane —***n.*** **1** a stream of liquid or gas suddenly emitted **2** a spout or nozzle for emitting a jet **3** a jet-propelled airplane: in full **jet (air)plane** —***adj.*** driven by jet propulsion

jet[2] (jet) ***n.*** ⟦after *Gagas,* town in Asia Minor⟧ **1** a hard, black mineral like coal, polished and used in jewelry **2** a lustrous black —***adj.*** black like jet

jet lag a disruption of the daily body rhythms, associated with high-speed travel by jet airplane to distant time zones —**jet′-lagged′** ***adj.***

jet′port′ ***n.*** a large airport with long runways, for use by jetliners

jet propulsion propulsion of airplanes, boats, etc. by the forcing of compressed outside air and hot exhaust gases through a jet nozzle —**jet′-pro·pelled′** (-prə peld′) ***adj.***

jet·sam (jet′səm) ***n.*** ⟦var. of JETTISON⟧ cargo thrown overboard to lighten a ship in danger

jet set fashionable people who frequently travel, often by jet, as for pleasure —**jet′-set′ter** ***n.***

Jet Ski *trademark for* a motorcyclelike watercraft propelled by a jet of water —[**j- s-**] any such watercraft

jet stream high-velocity winds moving from west to east, high above the earth

jet·ti·son (jet′ə sən) ***vt.*** ⟦< L *jactare,* to throw⟧ **1** to throw (goods) overboard so as to lighten a ship in danger **2** to discard

jet·ty (jet′ē) ***n.***, *pl.* **-ties** ⟦see JET[1]⟧ **1** a wall built out into the water to restrain currents, protect a harbor, etc. **2** a landing pier

Jew (jo͞o) ***n.*** ⟦< Heb *yehūdī,* citizen of Judah⟧ **1** a person descended, or regarded as descended, from the ancient Hebrews **2** a person whose religion is Judaism

jew·el (jo͞o′əl) ***n.*** ⟦ult. < L *jocus,* a joke⟧ **1** a valuable ring, necklace, etc., esp. one set with gems **2** a precious stone; gem **3** any person or thing that is very precious or valuable **4** a small gem used as a bearing in a watch —***vt.*** **-eled** or **-elled, -el·ing** or **-el·ling** to decorate or set with jewels

jewel box a thin plastic case used to hold a compact disk

jew′el·er or **jew′el·ler** (-ər) ***n.*** ⟦ME *jueler* < OFr *joieleor* < *joel:* see JEWEL⟧

one who makes, repairs, or deals in jewelry, watches, etc.

jew'el·ry *n.* ornaments such as rings, bracelets, etc., collectively

Jew·ish (jōō'ish) *adj.* of or having to do with Jews or Judaism —*n.* loosely, Yiddish —**Jew'ish·ness** *n.*

Jew·ry (jōō'rē) *n.* the Jewish people

jew's-harp or **jews'-harp** (jōōz'härp') *n.* ⟦< Du *jeugdtromp,* child's trumpet⟧ a small, metal musical instrument held between the teeth and plucked to produce twanging tones

Jez·e·bel (jez'ə bel') *n. Bible* a wicked queen of Israel

Ji·ang Ze·min (jē äŋ' zə min') 1926- ; president of China (1993-)

jib (jib) *n.* ⟦Dan *gib*⟧ a triangular sail secured forward of the mast or foremast

jibe[1] (jīb) *vi.* **jibed, jib'ing** ⟦< Du *gijpen*⟧ **1** to shift from one side of a ship to the other, as a fore-and-aft sail **2** to change the course of a ship so that the sails jibe **3** [Inf.] to be in agreement or accord: often with *with*

jibe[2] (jīb) *vi., vt.,* **jibed, jib'ing,** *n.* GIBE

jif·fy (jif'ē) *n., pl.* **-fies** ⟦< ?⟧ [Inf.] a very short time: also **jiff**

jig (jig) *n.* ⟦prob. < MFr *giguer,* to dance⟧ **1** a fast, springy dance in triple time, or music for this **2** a device used to guide a tool —*vi., vt.* **jigged, jig'ging** to dance (a jig) —**in jig time** [Inf.] very quickly —**the jig is up** [Slang] no chance is left

jig·ger (jig'ər) *n.* **1** a small glass, usually of $1\frac{1}{2}$ ounces, used to measure liquor **2** the contents of a jigger

jig·gle (jig'əl) *vt., vi.* **-gled, -gling** ⟦< JIG⟧ to move in quick, slight jerks —*n.* a jiggling

jig·saw (jig'sô') *n.* a saw with a narrow blade set in a frame, for cutting curves, etc.

jigsaw puzzle a puzzle consisting of a picture cut up into irregularly shaped pieces, which must be put together again

jilt (jilt) *vt.* ⟦< *Jill,* sweetheart⟧ to reject or cast off (a previously accepted lover, etc.)

Jim Crow ⟦name of an early black minstrel song⟧ [*also* **j- c-**] [Inf.] discrimination against or segregation of blacks —**Jim'-Crow'** *vt., adj.*

jim·my (jim'ē) *n., pl.* **-mies** ⟦< *James*⟧ a short crowbar, used as by burglars to pry open windows, etc. —*vt.* **-mied, -my·ing** to pry open with or as with a jimmy

jim·son weed (jim'sən) ⟦< *Jamestown weed*⟧ a poisonous weed with white or purplish, trumpet-shaped flowers

jin·gle (jiŋ'gəl) *vi.* **-gled, -gling** ⟦echoic⟧ to make light, ringing sounds, as small bells —*vt.* to cause to jingle —*n.* **1** a jingling sound **2** a catchy verse or song with easy rhythm, simple rhymes, etc.

jin·go·ism (jiŋ'gō iz'əm) *n.* ⟦< phrase *by jingo* in patriotic Brit song⟧ chauvinistic advocacy of an aggressive, warlike foreign policy —**jin'go·ist** *n.* —**jin'go·is'tic** *adj.*

jin·ni (ji nē', jin'ē) *n., pl.* **jinn** ⟦Ar⟧ *Muslim Folklore* a supernatural being that can influence human affairs

jin·rik·i·sha (jin rik'shô') *n.* ⟦Jpn < *jin,* a man + *riki,* power + *sha,* carriage⟧ a small, two-wheeled carriage, pulled by a man, esp. formerly in East Asia: also sp. **jin·rick'sha'** or **jin·rik'sha'**

jinx (jiŋks) [Inf.] *n.* ⟦< Gr *iynx,* the wryneck (bird used in black magic)⟧ a person or thing supposed to bring bad luck —*vt.* to be a jinx to

jit·ney (jit'nē) *n., pl.* **-neys** ⟦< ? Fr *jeton,* a token⟧ a small bus or a car carrying passengers for a low fare

jit·ter·bug (jit'ər bug') *n.* a fast, acrobatic dance for couples, esp. in the 1940s —*vi.* **-bugged', -bug'ging** to do this dance

jit·ters (jit'ərz) *pl.n.* [Inf.] an uneasy, nervous feeling; fidgets: with *the* —**jit'ter·y** *adj.*

jive (jīv) [Slang] *n.* ⟦< JIBE[2]⟧ foolish, exaggerated, or insincere talk —*adj.* insincere, fraudulent, etc.

Joan of Arc (jōn əv ärk), Saint (1412-31); Fr. military heroine: burned at the stake for witchcraft

job (jäb) *n.* ⟦< ?⟧ **1** a piece of work done for pay **2** a task; duty **3** the thing or material being worked on **4** employment; work —*adj.* hired or done by the job —*vt., vi.* **jobbed, job'bing 1** to deal in (goods) as a jobber **2** to let or sublet (work, contracts, etc.) —**job'hold'er** *n.* —**job'less** *adj.*

Job (jōb) *n. Bible* a man who suffered much but kept his faith in God

job action a refusal by a group of employees (esp. a group forbidden by law to strike) to perform their duties in an effort to win certain demands

job·ber (jäb'ər) *n.* **1** one who buys goods in quantity and sells them to dealers; wholesaler **2** one who works by the job or does piecework

job lot an assortment of goods for sale as one quantity

jock (jäk) *n.* **1** *short for: a*) JOCKEY *b*) JOCKSTRAP **2** [Slang] a male athlete

jock·ey (jäk'ē) *n., pl.* **-eys** ⟦< Scot dim. of JACK⟧ one whose work is riding horses in races —*vt., vi.* **-eyed, -ey·ing 1** to cheat; swindle **2** to maneuver for position or advantage

jock·strap (jäk'strap') *n.* ⟦slang *jock,* penis + STRAP⟧ an elastic belt with a pouch for supporting the genitals, worn by male athletes

jo·cose (jō kōs') *adj.* ⟦< L *jocus,* a joke⟧ joking or playful —**jo·cose'ly** *adv.* —**jo·cos'i·ty** (-käs'ə tē), *pl.* **-ties,** or **jo·cose'ness** *n.*

joc·u·lar (jäk'yə lər) *adj.* ⟦< L *jocus,* a joke⟧ joking; full of fun —**joc'u·lar'i·ty** (-lar'ə tē), *pl.* **-ties,** *n.*

joc·und (jäk'ənd) *adj.* ⟦< L *jucundus,* pleasant⟧ cheerful; genial —**joc'und·ly** *adv.*

jodh·purs (jäd'pərz) *pl.n.* ⟦after *Jodhpur,* former state in India⟧ riding breeches made loose and full above the knees and closefitting below

jog[1] (jäg) *vt.* **jogged, jog'ging** ⟦ME *jog-*

gen, to spur (a horse)⟧ **1** to give a little shake to; nudge **2** to rouse (the memory) —***vi.*** to move along at a slow, steady, jolting pace or trot; specif., to engage in jogging as a form of exercise —***n.*** **1** a little shake or nudge **2** a slow, steady, jolting motion or trot **3** a jogging —**jog′ger** ***n.***

jog[2] (jäg) ***n.*** ⟦var. of JAG[1]⟧ **1** a projecting or notched part in a surface or line **2** a sharp change of direction

jog′ging ***n.*** trotting slowly and steadily as a form of exercise

jog·gle (jäg′əl) ***vt., vi.*** **-gled, -gling** ⟦< JOG[1]⟧ to shake or jolt slightly —***n.*** a slight jolt

Jo·han·nes·burg (jō han′is burg′) city in NE South Africa: pop. 713,000

john (jän) ***n.*** [Slang] **1** a toilet **2** [*also* **J-**] a prostitute's customer

John (jän) ***n.*** *Bible* **1** a Christian apostle, the reputed author of the fourth Gospel **2** this book

John Bull *personification of* England or an Englishman

John Doe (dō) a fictitious name used in legal papers for an unknown person

John·son (jän′sən) **1 An·drew** (an′ droo′) 1808-75; 17th president of the U.S. (1865-69) **2 Lyn·don Baines** (lin′ dən bānz′) 1908-73; 36th president of the U.S. (1963-69) **3 Samuel** 1709-84; Eng. lexicographer & writer

John the Baptist *Bible* the forerunner and baptizer of Jesus

join (join) ***vt., vi.*** ⟦< L *jungere*⟧ **1** to bring or come together (with); connect; unite **2** to become a part or member of (a club, etc.) **3** to participate (*in* a conversation, etc.)

join′er ***n.*** a carpenter who finishes interior woodwork

joint (joint) ***n.*** ⟦< L *jungere*⟧ **1** a place where, or way in which, two things are joined **2** any of the parts of a jointed whole **3** a large cut of meat with the bone still in it **4** [Slang] a cheap bar, restaurant, etc., or any house, building, etc. **5** [Slang] a marijuana cigarette —***adj.*** **1** common to two or more *[joint* property*]* **2** sharing with another *[a joint* owner*]* —***vt.*** **1** to connect by or provide with a joint or joints **2** to cut (meat) into joints —**out of joint** **1** dislocated **2** disordered

joint′ly ***adv.*** in common

joist (joist) ***n.*** ⟦< OFr *giste,* a bed⟧ any of the parallel beams that hold up the planks of a floor or the laths of a ceiling

joke (jōk) ***n.*** ⟦L *jocus*⟧ **1** anything said or done to arouse laughter, as a funny anecdote **2** a thing done or said merely in fun **3** a person or thing to be laughed at —***vi.*** **joked, jok′ing** to make jokes —**jok′ing·ly** ***adv.***

jok′er ***n.*** **1** one who jokes: also **joke′ster** **2** a cunningly worded provision, as in a legal document, intended to deceive **3** a playing card with the image of a jester on it **4** [Slang] a contemptibly foolish or inept person

jok′ey ***adj.*** comical or lighthearted: also **jok′y** —**jok′i·ness** ***n.***

jol·li·ty (jäl′ə tē) ***n.*** a being jolly

jol·ly (jäl′ē) ***adj.*** **-li·er, -li·est** ⟦OFr *joli*⟧ **1** full of high spirits and good humor; merry **2** [Inf.] enjoyable —***vt., vi.*** **-lied, -ly·ing** [Inf.] to try to make (a person) feel good, as by coaxing: often with *along* —**jol′li·ly** ***adv.*** —**jol′li·ness** ***n.***

jolt (jōlt) ***vt.*** ⟦< earlier *jot*⟧ **1** to shake up, as with a bumpy ride **2** to shock or surprise —***vi.*** to move along in a bumpy manner —***n.*** **1** a sudden jerk, bump, etc. **2** a shock or surprise

Jo·nah (jō′nə) ***n.*** **1** *Bible* a Hebrew prophet: cast overboard and swallowed by a big fish, he was later cast up unharmed **2** one who brings bad luck

Jones (jōnz), **John Paul** 1747-92; Am. naval officer in the Revolutionary War, born in Scotland

jon·quil (jäŋ′kwil, jän′-) ***n.*** ⟦< L *juncus,* a rush⟧ a species of narcissus with small, yellow flowers

Jon·son (jän′sən), **Ben** (ben) 1572?-1637; Eng. dramatist & poet

Jor·dan (jôrd′'n) **1** river in the Near East, flowing into the Dead Sea **2** country east of Israel: 37,738 sq. mi.; pop. 2,133,000 —**Jor·da·ni·an** (jôr dā′nē ən) ***adj., n.***

Jo·seph (jō′zəf, -səf) ***n.*** *Bible* **1** one of Jacob's sons, who became a high official in Egypt **2** the husband of Mary, mother of Jesus

josh (jäsh) ***vt., vi.*** ⟦< ?⟧ [Inf.] to tease; banter

Josh·u·a (jäsh′yoo ə, -oo-) ***n.*** *Bible* Moses' successor, who led the Israelites into the Promised Land

jos·tle (jäs′əl) ***vt., vi.*** **-tled, -tling** ⟦see JOUST⟧ to push, as in a crowd; shove roughly —***n.*** a jostling

jot (jät) ***n.*** ⟦< Gr *iōta,* the smallest letter⟧ a very small amount —***vt.*** **jot′ted, jot′ting** to make a brief note of: usually with *down* —**jot′ter** ***n.***

joule (jool) ***n.*** ⟦after J. P. *Joule,* 19th-c. Eng physicist⟧ *Physics* a unit of work or energy

jounce (jouns) ***vt., vi.*** **jounced, jounc′ing** ⟦< ?⟧ to jolt or bounce —***n.*** a jolt —**jounc′y** ***adj.***

jour·nal (jur′nəl) ***n.*** ⟦< L *diurnalis,* daily⟧ **1** a daily record of happenings, as a diary **2** a newspaper or periodical **3** *Bookkeeping* a book for recording transactions in the order in which they occur **4** ⟦orig. Scot⟧ the part of an axle or shaft that turns in a bearing

jour′nal·ese′ (-ēz′) ***n.*** a facile style of writing found in many newspapers, magazines, etc.

jour′nal·ism′ ***n.*** the work of gathering news for, or producing, a newspaper, etc. —**jour′nal·ist** ***n.*** —**jour′nal·is′tic** ***adj.***

jour·ney (jur′nē) ***n., pl.*** **-neys** ⟦< OFr *journee;* ult. < L *dies,* day⟧ a traveling from one place to another; trip —***vi.*** **-neyed, -ney·ing** to travel —**jour′ney·er** ***n.***

jour′ney·man (-mən) ***n., pl.*** **-men** (-mən) ⟦ME < *journee,* day's work + *man*⟧ **1** a worker qualified to work at a specified trade **2** any sound, experienced, but not brilliant performer

joust (joust) ***n.*** ⟦ult. < L *juxta,* close to⟧ a combat with lances between two knights on horseback —***vi.*** to engage in a joust

jo·vi·al (jō′vē əl) ***adj.*** ⟦< LL *Jovialis,* of Jupiter: from astrological notion of planet's influence⟧ full of playful good humor —**jo′vi·al′i·ty** (-al′ə tē) ***n.*** —**jo′vi·al·ly** ***adv.***

jowl[1] (joul) ***n.*** ⟦OE *ceafl,* jaw⟧ **1** the lower jaw **2** the cheek, esp. of a hog

jowl[2] (joul) ***n.*** ⟦OE *ceole,* throat⟧ [*usually pl.*] the fleshy hanging part under the jaw —**jowl′y** ***adj.***

joy (joi) ***n.*** ⟦ult. < L *gaudium,* joy⟧ **1** a very glad feeling; happiness; delight **2** anything causing this

Joyce (jois), **James** 1882-1941; Ir. novelist

joy′ful ***adj.*** feeling, expressing, or causing joy; glad —**joy′ful·ly** ***adv.***

joy′ous ***adj.*** joyful; happy —**joy′ous·ly** ***adv.***

joy ride [Inf.] an automobile ride, often at a reckless speed, taken for pleasure, sometimes, specif., in a stolen car —**joy rider** —**joy riding**

joy′stick′ ***n.*** **1** [Slang] the control stick of an airplane **2** a device with a lever for controlling a cursor, etc. as in a video game

JP *abbrev.* Justice of the Peace

Jpn *abbrev.* **1** Japan **2** Japanese

Jr *abbrev.* junior: also **jr**

ju·bi·lant (jo͞o′bə lənt) ***adj.*** ⟦< L *jubilum,* wild shout⟧ joyful and triumphant; elated; rejoicing

ju·bi·la·tion (jo͞o′bə lā′shən) ***n.*** **1** a rejoicing **2** a happy celebration

ju·bi·lee (jo͞o′bə lē′) ***n.*** ⟦< Heb *yōbēl,* a ram's horn (trumpet)⟧ **1** a 50th or 25th anniversary **2** a time of rejoicing **3** jubilation

Ju·dah[1] (jo͞o′də) ***n.*** *Bible* one of Jacob's sons

Ju·dah[2] (jo͞o′də) ancient kingdom in the S part of Palestine

Ju·da·ism (jo͞o′dā iz′əm, -dē-, -də-) ***n.*** the Jewish religion —**Ju·da′ic** (-dā′ik) ***adj.***

Judas (jo͞o′dəs) ***n.*** **1** *Bible* the disciple who betrayed Jesus for money: in full **Judas Is·car·i·ot** (is ker′ē ət) **2** a traitor or betrayer

Ju·de·a (jo͞o dē′ə) ancient region of S Palestine

Judeo- *combining form* Jewish

judge (juj) ***n.*** ⟦< L *jus,* law + *dicere,* say⟧ **1** a public official with authority to hear and decide cases in a court of law **2** a person designated to determine the winner, settle a controversy, etc. **3** a person qualified to decide on the relative worth of anything **4** a governing leader of the Israelites before the time of the kings —***vt., vi.*** **judged, judg′ing** **1** to hear and pass judgment on in a court of law **2** to determine the winner of (a contest) or settle (a controversy) **3** to form an opinion about **4** to criticize or censure **5** to think or suppose —**judge′ship′** ***n.***

judg·ment (juj′mənt) ***n.*** **1** a judging; deciding **2** a legal decision; order given by a judge, etc. **3** an opinion **4** the ability to come to an opinion **5** [**J-**] *short for* LAST JUDGMENT Also sp. **judge′ment**

judg·men′tal (-ment′'l) ***adj.*** making judgments as to value, etc., often, specif., judgments considered to be lacking in tolerance, objectivity, etc.

Judgment Day *Theol.* the time of God's final judgment of all people

ju·di·ca·to·ry (jo͞o′di kə tôr′ē) ***adj.*** ⟦see JUDGE⟧ having to do with administering justice —***n.,*** *pl.* **-ries** a law court, or law courts collectively

ju′di·ca·ture (-chər) ***n.*** **1** the administering of justice **2** jurisdiction **3** judges or courts collectively

ju·di·cial (jo͞o dish′əl) ***adj.*** **1** of judges, courts, or their functions **2** allowed, enforced, etc. by a court **3** befitting a judge **4** fair; impartial

ju·di·ci·ar·y (jo͞o dish′ē er′ē) ***adj.*** of judges or courts —***n.,*** *pl.* **-ar′ies** **1** the part of government that administers justice **2** judges collectively

ju·di′cious (-dish′əs) ***adj.*** having or showing sound judgment —**ju·di′cious·ly** ***adv.***

ju·do (jo͞o′dō) ***n.*** ⟦Jpn < *jū,* soft + *dō,* way⟧ a form of jujitsu

jug (jug) ***n.*** ⟦a pet form of *Judith* or *Joan*⟧ **1** a large container for liquids, with a small opening and a handle **2** [Slang] a jail

jug·ger·naut (jug′ər nôt′) ***n.*** ⟦< Sans *Jagannātha,* lord of the world⟧ a relentless, irresistible force

jug·gle (jug′əl) ***vt.*** **-gled, -gling** ⟦< L *jocus,* a joke⟧ **1** to perform skillful tricks of sleight of hand with (balls, etc.) **2** to catch or hold awkwardly **3** to manipulate so as to deceive —***vi.*** to toss up balls, etc. and keep them in the air —**jug′gler** ***n.***

jug·u·lar (jug′yo͞o lər) ***adj.*** ⟦< L *jugum,* a yoke⟧ of the neck or throat —***n.*** JUGULAR VEIN

jugular vein either of two large veins in the neck carrying blood from the head

juice (jo͞os) ***n.*** ⟦< L *jus,* broth, juice⟧ **1** the liquid part of a plant, fruit, etc. **2** a liquid in or from animal tissue **3** [Inf.] vitality **4** [Slang] *a)* electricity *b)* alcoholic liquor *c)* power or influence —***vt.*** **juiced, juic′ing** to extract juice from —***vi.*** [Slang] to drink alcoholic beverages to excess

juiced (jo͞ost) ***adj.*** [Slang] drunk; intoxicated

juic·er (jo͞o′sər) ***n.*** **1** a device for extracting juice from fruit **2** [Slang] a drunkard

juic·y (jo͞o′sē) ***adj.*** **-i·er, -i·est** **1** full of juice **2** [Inf.] *a)* full of interest *[juicy gossip]* *b)* highly profitable —**juic′i·ness** ***n.***

ju·jit·su (jo͞o jit′so͞o′) ***n.*** ⟦< Jpn *jū,* soft, pliant + *jutsu,* art⟧ a Japanese system of wrestling in which an opponent's strength and weight are used against him or her

ju·ju·be (jo͞o′jo͞o bē′) ***n.*** ⟦< Gr *zizyphon,* name of a fruit⟧ a fruit-flavored, jelly-like lozenge

ju·jut·su (jo͞o jit′so͞o′, -jut′-) ***n.*** JUJITSU

juke·box (jo͝ok′bäks′) ***n.*** ⟦< Am black *juke,* wicked⟧ a coin-operated player for records, CD's, etc. as in a bar

ju·lep (jo͞o′ləp) ***n.*** ⟦< Pers *gul*, rose + *āb,* water⟧ MINT JULEP

ju·li·enne (jo͞o′lē en′) ***adj.*** ⟦Fr⟧ cut into strips: said of vegetables, etc.: also **ju′li·enned′** (-end′)

Ju·li·et (jo͞o′lē et′, jo͞o′lē et′) ***n.*** the heroine of Shakespeare's tragedy *Romeo and Juliet*

Ju·ly (joo lī′) ***n.*** ⟦< L < *Julius* Caesar⟧ the seventh month of the year, having 31 days: abbrev. *abbrev.* **Jul**

jum·ble (jum′bəl) ***vt., vi.*** **-bled, -bling** ⟦? blend of JUMP + TUMBLE⟧ to mix or be mixed in a confused heap —***n.*** a confused mixture or heap

jum·bo (jum′bō) ***n.,*** *pl.* **-bos** ⟦< Am black *jamba,* elephant⟧ a large person, animal, or thing —***adj.*** very large

jump (jump) ***vi.*** ⟦< ?⟧ **1** to spring or leap from the ground, a height, etc. **2** to jerk; bob **3** to move or act eagerly: often with *at* **4** to pass suddenly, as to a new topic **5** to rise suddenly, as prices **6** [Slang] to be lively —***vt.*** **1** *a)* to leap over *b)* to pass over **2** to cause to leap **3** to leap upon **4** to cause (prices, etc.) to rise **5** [Inf.] *a)* to attack suddenly *b)* to react to prematurely **6** [Slang] to leave suddenly *[to jump town]* —***n.*** **1** a jumping **2** a distance jumped **3** a sudden transition **4** a sudden rise, as in prices **5** a sudden, nervous start —**get** (or **have**) **the jump on** [Slang] to get (or have) an advantage over —**jump bail** to forfeit bail by running away

jump·er[1] (jum′pər) ***n.*** **1** one that jumps **2** a short wire to make a temporary electrical connection

jump·er[2] (jum′pər) ***n.*** ⟦< dial. *jump,* short coat⟧ **1** a loose jacket **2** a sleeveless dress for wearing over a blouse, etc.

jumper cables a pair of thick, insulated electrical wires with clamplike terminals, used to jump-start a motor vehicle with a dead battery

jump′-start′ ***vt.*** **1** to start (a motor-vehicle engine) with jumper cables **2** [Inf.] to energize, revive, etc. —***n.*** a starting in such a way

jump′suit′ ***n.*** **1** a coverall worn by paratroops, etc. **2** a lounging outfit like this

jump·y (jum′pē) ***adj.*** **-i·er, -i·est** **1** moving in jumps or jerks **2** easily startled **3** nervous —**jump′i·ly** ***adv.*** —**jump′i·ness** ***n.***

jun·co (juŋ′kō′) ***n.,*** *pl.* **-cos′** ⟦< Sp⟧ a small bird with a gray or black head

junc·tion (juŋk′shən) ***n.*** ⟦< L *jungere,* join⟧ **1** a joining or being joined **2** a place of joining, as of roads —**junc′tion·al** ***adj.***

junc·ture (juŋk′chər) ***n.*** **1** a junction **2** a point of time **3** a crisis

June (jo͞on) ***n.*** ⟦< L *Junius,* of *Juno*⟧ the sixth month of the year, having 30 days: abbrev. *abbrev.* **Jun**

Ju·neau (jo͞o′nō′) capital of Alaska: seaport on the SE coast: pop. 27,000

jun·gle (juŋ′gəl) ***n.*** ⟦< Sans *jaṅgala,* wasteland⟧ **1** land densely covered with trees, vines, etc., as in the tropics **2** [Slang] a situation in which people struggle fiercely for survival

jun·ior (jo͞on′yər) ***adj.*** ⟦L < *juvenis,* young⟧ **1** the younger: written *Jr.* after a son's name if it is the same as his father's **2** of more recent position or lower status *[a junior partner]* **3** of juniors —***n.*** **1** one who is younger, of lower rank, etc. **2** a student in the next-to-last year, as of college

junior college a school offering courses two years beyond high school

junior high school a school usually including grades 7, 8, and 9

ju·ni·per (jo͞o′ni pər) ***n.*** ⟦L *juniperus*⟧ an evergreen shrub or tree with berrylike cones

junk[1] (juŋk) ***n.*** ⟦< ?⟧ **1** old metal, paper, rags, etc. that might be reusable in some way **2** [Inf.] worthless stuff; trash **3** [Slang] heroin —***vt.*** [Inf.] to scrap; discard —**junk′y, -i·er, -i·est,** ***adj.***

JUNK

junk[2] (juŋk) ***n.*** ⟦< Malay *adjong*⟧ a Chinese or Japanese flat-bottomed ship

junk bond [Inf.] a speculative BOND (*n.* 6), often issued to finance the takeover of a corporation

junk·er (juŋ′kər) ***n.*** [Slang] an old, dilapidated car or truck

Jun·ker (yoon′kər) ***n.*** ⟦Ger⟧ [Historical] a Prussian of the militaristic landowning class

jun·ket (juŋ′kit) ***n.*** ⟦ME *joncate,* cream cheese⟧ **1** milk sweetened, flavored, and thickened into curd **2** a picnic **3** an excursion, esp. one by an official at public expense —***vi.*** to go on a junket —**jun′ket·eer′** (-ki tir′) or **jun′ket·er** ***n.***

junk food snack food with chemical additives and little food value

junk·ie or **junk·y** (juŋ′kē) ***n.,*** *pl.* **-ies** ⟦< JUNK[1], *n.* 3⟧ [Slang] **1** a narcotics addict **2** one who is addicted to a specified activity, food, etc.

junk mail advertisements, solicitations, etc. mailed in large quantities

Ju·no (jo͞o′nō) ***n.*** *Gr. Myth.* the wife of Jupiter and queen of the gods

jun·ta (hoon′tə, jun′-) ***n.*** ⟦Sp < L *jungere,* join⟧ a group of political intriguers, esp. military men, in power after a coup d'état

Ju·pi·ter (jo͞o′pit ər) ***n.*** **1** the chief Roman god **2** the largest planet of the solar system: see PLANET

Ju·ras·sic (jo͞o ras′ik) ***adj.*** ⟦< Fr, after *Jura* Mountains, between France and Switzerland⟧ of the geologic period characterized by the dominance of dinosaurs

ju·rid·i·cal (jo͞o rid′i kəl, jo͝o-) ***adj.*** ⟦< L *jus,* law + *dicere,* declare⟧ of judicial proceedings or law

ju·ried (jo͝or′ēd) ***adj.*** of a competition in which the winners are selected by a jury

ju·ris·dic·tion (jo͝or′is dik′shən) ***n.*** ⟦see JURIDICAL⟧ **1** legal authority **2** the range of authority

ju·ris·pru·dence (jo͝or′is pro͞od′'ns) ***n.*** ⟦< L *jus,* law + *prudentia,* a foreseeing⟧ **1** the science or philosophy of law **2** a division of law *[medical jurisprudence]*

ju·rist (jo͝or′ist) ***n.*** ⟦< L *jus,* law⟧ **1** an expert in law or writer on law **2** JUDGE (*n.* 1)

ju·ror (jo͝or′ər, -ôr′) ***n.*** a member of a jury

ju·ry (jo͝or′ē) ***n.***, *pl.* **-ries** ⟦L *jurare,* to swear⟧ **1** a group of people sworn to hear evidence in a law case and to give a decision **2** a committee that decides winners in a contest

just (just) ***adj.*** ⟦< L *jus,* law⟧ **1** right or fair *[a just decision]* **2** righteous *[a just man]* **3** deserved *[just praise]* **4** lawful **5** proper **6** correct or true **7** accurate; exact —***adv.*** **1** exactly *[just one o'clock]* **2** nearly **3** only *[just a taste]* **4** barely *[just missed him]* **5** a very short time ago *[she's just left]* **6** immediately *[just east of here]* **7** [Inf.] really *[just beautiful]* —**just the same** [Inf.] nevertheless —**just′ly** ***adv.*** —**just′ness** ***n.***

jus·tice (jus′tis) ***n.*** **1** a being righteous **2** fairness **3** rightfulness **4** reward or penalty as deserved **5** the use of authority to uphold what is just **6** the administration of law **7** *a*) JUDGE (*n.* 1) *b*) JUSTICE OF THE PEACE —**do justice to** to treat fairly

justice of the peace a local magistrate who decides minor cases, performs marriages, etc.

jus·ti·fy (jus′tə fī′) ***vt.*** **-fied′, -fy′ing** ⟦< L *justus,* just + *facere,* to do⟧ **1** to show to be just, right, etc. **2** *Theol.* to free from blame or guilt **3** to supply grounds for —**jus′ti·fi′a·ble** ***adj.*** —**jus′ti·fi·ca′tion** (-fi kā′shən) ***n.***

Jus·tin·i·an I (jus tin′ē ən) A.D. 483-565; ruler of Byzantine Empire (527-565): codified Roman law

jut (jut) ***vi., vt.*** **jut′ted, jut′ting** ⟦prob. var. of JET[1]⟧ to stick out; project —***n.*** a part that juts

jute (jo͞ot) ***n.*** ⟦< Sans *jūta,* matted hair⟧ **1** a strong fiber used for making burlap, rope, etc. **2** a S Asian plant yielding this fiber

ju·ve·nile (jo͞o′və nīl′, -nəl) ***adj.*** ⟦< L *juvenis,* young⟧ **1** young; immature **2** of or for young persons —***n.*** **1** a young person **2** an actor who plays youthful roles **3** a book for children —**ju′ve·nil′i·ty** (-nil′i tē), *pl.* **-ties,** ***n.***

juvenile delinquency antisocial or illegal behavior by minors, usually 18 years of age or younger —**juvenile delinquent**

jux·ta·pose (juks′tə pōz′) ***vt.*** **-posed′, -pos′ing** ⟦< Fr < L *juxta,* beside + POSE⟧ to put side by side —**jux′ta·po·si′tion** ***n.***

JV *abbrev.* junior varsity

K

k or **K** (kā) ***n.***, *pl.* **k's**, **K's** the eleventh letter of the English alphabet

K[1] ***n.*** **1** *Comput.* KILOBYTE **2** [Inf.] a thousand dollars

K[2] *abbrev.* **1** karat (carat) **2** kilometer **3** kindergarten **4** *Baseball* strikeout **5** *Comput.* the number 1,024, or 2^{10} Also, for 1 & 2, **k**

K[3] ⟦ModL *kalium*⟧ *Chem. symbol for* potassium

Ka·bu·ki (kä bōō′kē) ***n.*** [*also* **k-**] a form of Japanese drama, chiefly in formalized pantomime

kad·dish (käd′ish) ***n.*** ⟦Aram *kadish,* lit., holy⟧ *Judaism* a hymn in praise of God, recited at the daily service or as a mourner's prayer

kaf·fee·klatsch (kä′fā kläch′, kô′fē klach′) ***n.*** ⟦Ger < *kaffee,* coffee + *klatsch,* gossip⟧ [*also* **K-**] an informal gathering to drink coffee and chat

Kai·ser (kī′zər) ***n.*** ⟦ME *caiser,* emperor < L *Caesar*⟧ the title of the former rulers of Austria and Germany

kaiser roll ⟦Ger *kaisersemmel,* kaiser bun⟧ a large, round roll with a hard crust

kale (kāl) ***n.*** ⟦var. of COLE⟧ a hardy cabbage with spreading leaves

ka·lei·do·scope (kə lī′də skōp′) ***n.*** ⟦< Gr *kalos,* beautiful + *eidos,* form + -SCOPE⟧ **1** a small tube containing bits of colored glass reflected by mirrors so that symmetrical patterns appear when the tube is rotated **2** anything that constantly changes —**ka·lei′do·scop′ic** (-skäp′ik) ***adj.***

ka·mi·ka·ze (kä′mə kä′zē) ***adj.*** ⟦Jpn, divine wind⟧ of a suicidal attack by a WWII Japanese airplane pilot

kan·ga·roo (kaŋ′gə rōō′) ***n.*** ⟦< ?⟧ a leaping marsupial of Australia and nearby islands, with short forelegs and strong, large hind legs

kangaroo court [Inf.] an irregular court, usually disregarding normal legal procedure

Kan·sas (kan′zəs) Midwestern state of the U.S.: 81,823 sq. mi.; pop. 2,478,000; cap. Topeka: abbrev. *KS* —**Kan′san *adj.*, *n.***

Kansas City **1** city in W Missouri, on the Missouri River: pop. 435,000 **2** city opposite this, in NE Kansas: pop. 150,000

Kant (känt), **Im·man·u·el** (i man′yōō el′) 1724-1804; Ger. philosopher

ka·o·lin (kā′ə lin) ***n.*** ⟦Fr < Chin name of hill where found⟧ a white clay used in porcelain, etc.

ka·pok (kā′päk′) ***n.*** ⟦Malay⟧ the silky fibers around the seeds of certain tropical trees, used for stuffing mattresses, etc.

kap·pa (kap′ə) ***n.*** the tenth letter of the Greek alphabet (Κ, κ)

ka·put (kə poot′, -pōōt′) ***adj.*** ⟦Ger *kaputt*⟧ [Slang] ruined, destroyed, etc.

Ka·ra·chi (kə rä′chē) seaport in S Pakistan: former capital: pop. 5,076,000

kar·a·kul (kar′ə kul′, -kəl) ***n.*** ⟦ult. < Turkic *qara köl,* dark lake⟧ **1** a sheep native to central Asia **2** the curly black fur from the fleece of its lambs: usually sp. *caracul*

ka·ra·o·ke (kar′ē ō′kē) ***n.*** a form of entertainment in which bar patrons, etc. take turns singing while a special device plays prerecorded music

kar·at (kar′ət) ***n.*** ⟦var. of CARAT⟧ one 24th part (of pure gold)

ka·ra·te (kə rät′ē) ***n.*** ⟦Jpn⟧ a Japanese system of self-defense by sharp, quick blows with the hands and feet

kar·ma (kär′mə) ***n.*** ⟦Sans, act⟧ **1** *Buddhism, Hinduism* the totality of one's acts in each state of one's existence **2** loosely, fate

kart (kärt) ***n.*** ⟦< CART⟧ a small, flat, motorized vehicle, used in racing (**kart′ing**)

ka·ty·did (kāt′ē did′) ***n.*** ⟦echoic of the male's shrill sound⟧ a large, green tree insect

kay·ak (kī′ak′) ***n.*** ⟦Esk⟧ a canoe, originally used by Eskimos, with only a small opening in its shell for the paddler —***vi.*** to go in a kayak —**kay′ak′er *n.***

kay·o (kā′ō′) [Slang] ***vt.* -oed′, -o′ing** ⟦< KO⟧ *Boxing* to knock out —***n.*** *Boxing* a knockout

Ka·zakh·stan (kä′zäk stän′) country in W Asia: formerly a republic of the U.S.S.R.: 1,049,155 sq. mi.; pop. 16,464,000

ka·zoo (kə zōō′) ***n.*** ⟦echoic⟧ a toy musical instrument that makes buzzing tones when hummed into

KB *abbrev.* kilobyte(s)

kc *abbrev.* kilocycle(s)

Keats (kēts), **John** 1795-1821; Eng. poet

ke·bab or **ke·bob** (kə bäb′) ***n.*** ⟦Ar *kabāb*⟧ any of the small pieces of marinated meat used in making shish kebab

keel (kēl) ***n.*** ⟦< ON *kjǫlr*⟧ the chief timber or piece extending along the length of the bottom of a boat or ship —**keel over** **1** to capsize **2** to fall over suddenly —**on an even keel** upright or steady

keen[1] (kēn) ***adj.*** ⟦OE *cene,* wise⟧ **1** having a sharp edge or point *[a keen knife]* **2** cutting *[a keen wind]* **3** very perceptive *[keen eyes]* **4** shrewd **5** eager **6** intense —**keen′ly *adv.*** —**keen′ness *n.***

keen[2] (kēn) ***vt., vi.*** ⟦< Ir *caoinim,* I wail⟧ to make a mournful, wailing sound

keep (kēp) ***vt.* kept, keep′ing** ⟦OE *cœpan,* behold⟧ **1** to celebrate; observe *[to keep the Sabbath]* **2** to fulfill (a promise, etc.) **3** to protect; guard; take care of; tend **4** to preserve **5** to provide for; support **6** to make regular entries in *[to keep a diary]* **7** to maintain in a specified state, position, etc. *[to keep prices down]* **8** to hold for the future; retain **9** to hold and not let go; detain, withhold, restrain, etc. **10** to stay in or on (a course, place, etc.) —*vi.* **1** to stay in a specified state, position, etc. **2** to continue; go on **3** to refrain *[to keep from eating]* **4** to stay fresh; not spoil —*n.* **1** food and shelter; support **2** the inner stronghold of a castle —**for keeps** [Inf.] **1** with the winner keeping what he wins **2** permanently —**keep to oneself** **1** to avoid others **2** to refrain from telling —**keep up** **1** to maintain in good condition **2** to continue **3** to maintain the pace **4** to remain informed about: with *on* or *with*

keep'er *n.* **1** one that keeps; specif., *a*) a guard *b*) a guardian *c*) a custodian **2** [Inf.] something worth keeping

keep'ing *n.* **1** observance (of a rule, holiday, etc.) **2** care; charge —**in keeping with** in conformity or accord with

keep'sake' *n.* something kept, or to be kept, in memory of the giver

keg (keg) *n.* ⟦< ON *kaggi,* keg⟧ **1** a small barrel **2** a unit of weight for nails, equal to 100 lb.

kelp (kelp) *n.* ⟦ME *culp*⟧ a large, coarse, brown seaweed, rich in iodine

Kel·vin (kel'vin) *adj.* ⟦after 1st Baron *Kelvin,* 19th-c. Brit physicist⟧ designating or of a scale of temperature measured from absolute zero (-273.16°C)

ken (ken) *vt.* **kenned, ken'ning** ⟦OE *cennan,* cause to know⟧ [Scot.] to know —*n.* range of knowledge

Ken·ne·dy (ken'ə dē), **John Fitz·ger·ald** (fits jer'əld) 1917-63; 35th president of the U.S. (1961-63): assassinated

ken·nel (ken'əl) *n.* ⟦< L *canis,* dog⟧ **1** a doghouse **2** [*often pl.*] a place where dogs are bred or kept —*vt.* **-neled** or **-nelled, -nel·ing** or **-nel·ling** to keep in a kennel

Ken·tuck·y (kən tuk'ē) EC state of the U.S.: 39,732 sq. mi.; pop. 3,685,000; cap. Frankfort: abbrev. *KY* —**Ken·tuck'i·an** *adj., n.*

Ken·ya (ken'yə, kēn'-) country on the E coast of Africa: 224,961 sq. mi.; pop. 29,295,000

kept (kept) *vt., vi. pt. & pp. of* KEEP —*adj.* maintained so as to be a sexual partner *[a kept woman]*

ker·a·tin (ker'ə tin) *n.* ⟦< Gr *keras,* horn⟧ a tough, fibrous protein, the basic substance of hair, nails, etc.

kerb (kurb) *n. Brit. sp. of* CURB (*n.* 3)

ker·chief (kur'chif) *n.* ⟦< OFr *covrir,* to cover + *chef,* head⟧ **1** a piece of cloth worn over the head or around the neck **2** a handkerchief

ker·nel (kur'nəl) *n.* ⟦< OE *cyrnel*⟧ **1** a grain or seed, as of corn **2** the inner, softer part of a nut, etc. **3** the central, most important part; essence

ker·o·sene (ker'ə sēn') *n.* ⟦Gr *kēros,* wax⟧ a thin oil distilled from petroleum, used as a fuel, solvent, etc.: also **ker'o·sine'**

kes·trel (kes'trəl) *n.* ⟦echoic of its cry⟧ a small European falcon

ketch (kech) *n.* ⟦ME *cache*⟧ a small sailing vessel rigged fore-and-aft

ketch·up (kech'əp) *n.* ⟦? Malay *kēchap,* sauce⟧ a sauce for meat, fish, etc.; esp., a thick sauce (**tomato ketchup**) of tomatoes, onions, spices, etc.

ket·tle (ket''l) *n.* ⟦< L *catinus,* container for food⟧ **1** a metal container for boiling or cooking things **2** a teakettle

ket'tle·drum' *n.* a hemispheric percussion instrument of copper with a parchment top that can be tightened or loosened to change the pitch

KETTLEDRUM

Kev·lar (kev'lär') *trademark for* a tough, light, synthetic fiber used in bulletproof vests, boat hulls, etc.

key[1] (kē) *n., pl.* **keys** ⟦OE *cæge*⟧ **1** a device for moving the bolt of a lock and thus locking or unlocking something **2** any of the buttons, levers, etc. pressed in operating a piano, typewriter, etc. **3** a thing that explains or solves something else, as a code, the legend of a map, etc. **4** an essential person or thing **5** tone or style of expression **6** *Music* a system of related tones based on a keynote and forming a given scale —*adj.* essential; important —*vt.* **keyed, key'ing** **1** to furnish with a key **2** to regulate the tone or pitch of **3** to bring into harmony —**key in** to input (data) by means of a keyboard —**key up** to make tense or excited

key[2] (kē) *n., pl.* **keys** ⟦Sp *cayo*⟧ a reef or low island

key'board' *n.* **1** the row or rows of keys of a piano, typewriter, computer terminal, etc. **2** a musical instrument with a keyboard —*vt., vi.* to write (text) or input (data) by means of a keyboard —**key'board'er** *n.*

key'hole' *n.* an opening (in a lock) into which a key is inserted

key'note' *n.* **1** the lowest, basic note or tone of a musical scale **2** the basic idea or ruling principle —*vt.* **-not'ed, -not'ing** **1** to give the keynote of **2** to give the keynote speech at —**key'not'er** *n.*

keynote speech (or **address**) a speech, as at a convention, setting forth the main line of policy

key'pad' *n.* the keys or push buttons on a computer keyboard, telephone, etc.

key'stone' *n.* **1** the central, topmost stone of an arch **2** the main part or principle

key'stroke' *n.* any of the strokes made in operating a keyboard

Key West island off S Florida, in the Gulf of Mexico

kg *abbrev.* kilogram(s)

kha·ki (kak'ē, kä'kē) *adj.* ⟦< Pers *khāk,* dust⟧ **1** dull yellowish-brown **2** made of khaki (cloth) —*n., pl.* **-kis** **1** a dull yellowish brown **2** strong, twilled cloth of this color **3** [*often pl.*] a khaki uniform or pants

khan (kän, kan) ***n.*** ⟦< Mongolian *qan*, lord⟧ **1** a title of Tatar or Mongol rulers in the Middle Ages **2** a title of various dignitaries in Iran, Afghanistan, etc.

Khar·kov (kär′kôf′) city in NE Ukraine: pop. 1,611,000

Khar·toum (kär to͞om′) capital of Sudan, on the Nile: pop. 476,000

kHz *abbrev.* kilohertz

kib·butz (ki bo͞ots′, -bo͞ots′) ***n.***, *pl.* **kib·but·zim** (kē′bo͞o tsēm′) ⟦ModHeb⟧ an Israeli collective settlement, esp. a collective farm

kib·itz·er (kib′it sər) ***n.*** ⟦Yiddish < Ger *kiebitz*⟧ [Inf.] **1** an onlooker at a card game, etc., esp. one who volunteers advice **2** a giver of unwanted advice or meddler in others' affairs —**kib′itz** ***vi.***

ki·bosh (kī′bäsh′, ki bäsh′) ***n.*** ⟦< ?⟧ used chiefly in **put the kibosh on**, to check, squelch, etc.

kick (kik) ***vi.*** ⟦ME *kiken*⟧ **1** to strike out with the foot **2** to recoil, as a gun **3** [Inf.] to complain **4** *Football* to kick the ball —***vt.*** **1** to strike with the foot **2** to drive, force, etc., as by kicking **3** to score (a goal, etc.) by kicking **4** [Slang] to get rid of (a habit) —***n.*** **1** an act or method of kicking **2** a sudden recoil **3** a complaint **4** [Inf.] an intoxicating effect **5** [*often pl.*] [Inf.] pleasure —**kick in** [Slang] to pay (one's share) —**kick over** to start up, as an automobile engine —**kick′er** ***n.***

kick′back′ ***n.*** [Slang] **1** a giving back of part of money received as payment, often because of coercion or a previous agreement **2** the money so returned

kick′off′ ***n.*** **1** *Football* a kick that puts the ball into play **2** a beginning, as of a campaign

kick′stand′ ***n.*** a pivoted metal bar that can be kicked down to support a bicycle, etc. in an upright position

kick′-start′ ***vt.*** **1** to start (a motorcycle, etc.) with a lever attached to a pedal that one kicks downward **2** [Inf.] to start, energize, revive, etc.

kick′y ***adj.*** **-i·er, -i·est** [Slang] **1** fashionable **2** exciting

kid (kid) ***n.*** ⟦ME *kide*⟧ **1** a young goat **2** leather from the skin of young goats **3** [Inf.] a child —***adj.*** [Inf.] younger [*my kid sister*] —***vt., vi.*** **kid′ded, kid′ding** [Inf.] to tease or fool playfully

kid′die or **kid′dy** (-ē) ***n.***, *pl.* **-dies** ⟦dim. of prec., *n.* 3⟧ [Inf.] a child

kid·nap (kid′nap′) ***vt.*** **-napped′** or **-naped′**, **-nap′ping** or **-nap′ing** ⟦KID, *n.* 3 + dial. *nap*, to snatch⟧ to seize and hold (a person) by force or fraud, as in order to get a ransom —**kid′nap′per** or **kid′nap′er** ***n.***

kid·ney (kid′nē) ***n.***, *pl.* **-neys** ⟦< ?⟧ **1** either of a pair of glandular organs that separate water and waste products from the blood and excrete them as urine **2** an animal's kidney, used as food **3** *a)* disposition *b)* class; kind

kidney bean the kidney-shaped seed of the common garden bean

kidney stone a hard mineral deposit sometimes formed in the kidney

kid′skin′ ***n.*** leather from the skin of young goats

kiel·ba·sa (kēl bä′sə, kil-) ***n.***, *pl.* **-si** (-sē) or **-sas** ⟦Pol⟧ a Polish smoked sausage

Ki·ev (kē′ef′, -ev′) capital of Ukraine, on the Dnepr: pop. 2,587,000

kill (kil) ***vt.*** ⟦< ? OE *cwellan*⟧ **1** to cause the death of; slay **2** to destroy; put an end to **3** to defeat or veto (legislation) **4** to spend (time) on trivial matters **5** to turn off (an engine, etc.) **6** to stop publication of —***n.*** **1** the act of killing **2** an animal or animals killed —**kill′er** ***n.***

killer bee AFRICANIZED BEE

killer whale a large dolphin that hunts in packs and preys on large fish, seals, etc.

kill′ing ***adj.*** **1** causing death; deadly **2** exhausting; fatiguing —***n.*** **1** slaughter; murder **2** [Inf.] a sudden great profit

kill′joy′ ***n.*** one who destroys or lessens other people's enjoyment: also **kill′-joy′**

kiln (kil, kiln) ***n.*** ⟦< L *culina*, cookstove⟧ a furnace or oven for drying, burning, or baking bricks, pottery, etc.

ki·lo (kē′lō, kil′ō) ***n.***, *pl.* **-los** ⟦Fr⟧ **1** KILOGRAM **2** KILOMETER

kilo- ⟦< Gr *chilioi*⟧ *combining form* one thousand

kil·o·byte (kil′ə bīt′) ***n.*** 1,024 bytes, or, loosely, 1,000 bytes

kil′o·cy′cle (-sī′kəl) ***n.*** *former term for* KILOHERTZ

kil′o·gram′ (-gram′) ***n.*** 1,000 grams

kil′o·hertz′ (-herts′, -hurts′) ***n.***, *pl.* **-hertz′** 1,000 hertz

kil′o·li′ter (-lēt′ər) ***n.*** 1,000 liters, or one cubic meter

kil·o·me·ter (kə läm′ət ər, kil′ə mēt′ər) ***n.*** 1,000 meters

kil·o·ton (kil′ə tun′) ***n.*** the explosive force of 1,000 tons of TNT

kil′o·watt′ (-wät′) ***n.*** 1,000 watts

kilt (kilt) ***n.*** ⟦prob. < ON⟧ a knee-length, pleated tartan skirt worn sometimes by men of the Scottish Highlands

kil·ter (kil′tər) ***n.*** ⟦< ?⟧ [Inf.] good condition; proper order: now chiefly in **out of kilter**

ki·mo·no (kə mō′nə) ***n.***, *pl.* **-nos** ⟦Jpn⟧ **1** a robe with wide sleeves and a sash, part of the traditional Japanese costume **2** a woman's dressing gown

kin (kin) ***n.*** ⟦OE *cynn*⟧ relatives; family

-kin (kin) ⟦< MDu *-ken*⟧ *suffix* little [*lambkin*]

kind (kīnd) ***n.*** ⟦OE *cynd*⟧ **1** a natural group or division **2** essential character **3** sort; variety; class —***adj.*** sympathetic, gentle, benevolent, etc. —**in kind** in the same way —**kind of** [Inf.] somewhat; rather —**of a kind** alike

KIMONO

kin·der·gar·ten (kin′dər gärt′'n) ***n.*** ⟦Ger < *kinder*, child + *garten*, garden⟧ a school or class for young children, usually four to six years old, that develops basic skills and social behavior by games, music, handicrafts, etc. —**kin′der·gart′ner** or **kin′der·gar′ten·er** (-gärt′nər) ***n.***

kind′heart′ed ***adj.*** kind

kin·dle (kin′dəl) ***vt.*** **-dled, -dling** ⟦< ON *kynda*⟧ **1** to set on fire; ignite **2** to excite (interest, feelings, etc.) —***vi.*** **1** to catch fire **2** to become excited

kin·dling (kind′liŋ) ***n.*** material, as bits of dry wood, for starting a fire

kind·ly (kīnd′lē) ***adj.*** **-li·er, -li·est** **1** kind; gracious **2** agreeable; pleasant —***adv.*** **1** in a kind, gracious manner **2** agreeably; favorably **3** please *[kindly* shut the door*]* —**kind′li·ness** ***n.***

kind′ness ***n.*** **1** the state, quality, or habit of being kind **2** a kind act

kin·dred (kin′drid) ***n.*** ⟦< OE *cynn,* kin + *ræden,* condition⟧ relatives or family —***adj.*** of like nature; similar *[kindred* spirits*]*

kine (kīn) ***pl.n.*** ⟦< OE *cy,* cows⟧ [Archaic] cows; cattle

ki·net·ic (ki net′ik) ***adj.*** ⟦< Gr *kinein,* to move⟧ of or resulting from motion

kin·folk (kin′fōk′) ***pl.n.*** family; relatives; kin: also **kin′folks′**

king (kiŋ) ***n.*** ⟦< OE *cyning*⟧ **1** a male ruler of a nation **2** a man who is supreme in some field **3** something supreme in its class **4** a playing card with a picture of a king on it **5** *Chess* the chief piece —***adj.*** chief (in size, importance, etc.) —**king′ly** ***adj.***

King (kiŋ), **Mar·tin Luther, Jr.** (märt′'n) 1929-68; U.S. clergyman & leader in the civil rights movement: assassinated

king′dom (-dəm) ***n.*** **1** a country headed by a king or queen; monarchy **2** a realm; domain *[*the *kingdom* of poetry*]* **3** any of three divisions into which all natural objects have been classified *[*the animal, vegetable, and mineral *kingdoms]*

king′fish′er ***n.*** a short-tailed diving bird that feeds chiefly on fish

King James Version AUTHORIZED VERSION

King Lear (lir) the title character of a tragedy by Shakespeare

king′pin′ ***n.*** **1** the pin at the front of a triangle of bowling pins **2** [Inf.] the essential person or thing

king′-size′ ***adj.*** larger than the regular kind: also **king′-sized′**

kink (kiŋk) ***n.*** ⟦< Scand⟧ **1** a short twist, curl, or bend in a rope, wire, hair, etc. **2** a painful cramp in the neck, back, etc. **3** a mental twist; eccentricity —***vi., vt.*** to form or cause to form a kink or kinks

kink′y ***adj.*** **-i·er, -i·est** **1** tightly curled **2** [Slang] weird, eccentric, etc.; specif., sexually abnormal

kin·ship (kin′ship′) ***n.*** **1** family relationship **2** close connection

kins·man (kinz′mən) ***n.,*** *pl.* **-men** (-mən) a relative; esp., a male relative —**kins′wom′an,** *pl.* **-wom′en,** ***n.***

ki·osk (kē′äsk′) ***n.*** ⟦< Pers *kūshk,* palace⟧ a small, open structure used as a newsstand, etc.

kip·per (kip′ər) ***vt.*** ⟦< ?⟧ to cure (herring, salmon, etc.) by salting and drying or smoking —***n.*** a kippered herring, etc.

Kir·i·bati (kir′ə bas′) country on a group of islands in the WC Pacific, on the equator: 277 sq. mi.; pop. 72,000

kirk (kurk) ***n.*** [Scot. or North Eng.] a church

kis·met (kiz′met) ***n.*** ⟦< Ar *qasama,* to divide⟧ fate; destiny

kiss (kis) ***vt., vi.*** ⟦OE *cyssan*⟧ **1** to touch or caress with the lips as an act of affection, greeting, etc. **2** to touch lightly or gently —***n.*** **1** an act of kissing **2** a light, gentle touch **3** any of various candies —**kiss′a·ble** ***adj.***

kit (kit) ***n.*** ⟦ME *kyt,* tub⟧ **1** *a*) personal equipment, esp. as packed for travel *b*) a set of tools *c*) equipment for some particular activity, etc. *d*) a set of parts to be assembled **2** a box, bag, etc. for carrying such parts, equipment, or tools —**the whole kit and caboodle** [Inf.] the whole lot

kitch·en (kich′ən) ***n.*** ⟦ult. < L *coquere,* to cook⟧ a room or place for the preparation and cooking of food

Kitch·e·ner (kich′ə nər) city in SE Ontario, Canada: pop. 178,000

kitch′en·ette′ or **kitch′en·et′** (-et′) ***n.*** a small, compact kitchen

kitch′en·ware′ (-wer′) ***n.*** kitchen utensils

kite (kīt) ***n.*** ⟦< OE *cyta*⟧ **1** any of several long-winged birds of prey **2** a light wooden frame covered with paper or cloth, to be flown in the wind at the end of a string

kith (kith) ***n.*** ⟦< OE *cyth*⟧ friends: now only in **kith and kin** *a*) friends and relatives *b*) relatives

kitsch (kich) ***n.*** ⟦Ger, gaudy trash⟧ pretentious but shallow art or writing —**kitsch′y** ***adj.***

kit·ten (kit′'n) ***n.*** ⟦< OFr dim. of *chat,* cat⟧ a young cat —**kit′ten·ish** ***adj.***

kit·ty[1] (kit′ē) ***n.,*** *pl.* **-ties** **1** a kitten **2** *a pet name for* a cat

kit·ty[2] (kit′ē) ***n.,*** *pl.* **-ties** ⟦prob. < KIT⟧ **1** the stakes in a poker game **2** money pooled for some purpose

kit·ty-cor·nered (kit′ē kôr′nərd) ***adj., adv.*** CATER-CORNERED: also **kit′ty-cor′ner**

ki·wi (kē′wē) ***n.,*** *pl.* **-wis** ⟦echoic of its cry⟧ **1** a flightless bird of New Zealand **2** [*also* **K-**] a hairy, egg-sized fruit with sweet, green pulp

KKK *abbrev.* Ku Klux Klan

Klee·nex (klē′neks′) *trademark for* soft tissue paper used as a handkerchief, etc. —***n.*** [*occas.* **k-**] a piece of such paper

klep·to·ma·ni·a (klep′tō mā′nē ə) ***n.*** ⟦< Gr *kleptēs,* thief + -MANIA⟧ a persistent, abnormal impulse to steal —**klep′to·ma′ni·ac′** ***n., adj.***

klieg light (klēg) ⟦after A. & J. *Kliegl,* who developed it in 1911⟧ a very bright arc light used on motion picture sets

Klon·dike (klän′dīk′) gold-mining region in W Yukon Territory, Canada

klutz (kluts) ***n.*** ⟦< Yiddish *klots,* lit., wooden block⟧ [Slang] a clumsy or stu-

pid person
km *abbrev.* kilometer(s)
knack (nak) ***n.*** ⟦ME *knak,* sharp blow⟧ **1** a clever expedient **2** ability to do something easily
knack·wurst (näk′wurst′) ***n.*** ⟦Ger < *knacken,* to burst + *wurst,* sausage⟧ a thick, highly seasoned sausage
knap·sack (nap′sak′) ***n.*** ⟦< Du *knappen,* eat + *zak,* a sack⟧ a bag of leather, canvas, or nylon for carrying equipment or supplies on the back
knave (nāv) ***n.*** ⟦< OE *cnafa,* boy⟧ **1** a dishonest, deceitful person; rogue **2** JACK (*n.* 3) —**knav′ish *adj.***
knav·er·y (nāv′ər ē) ***n.,*** *pl.* **-ies** rascality; dishonesty
knead (nēd) ***vt.*** ⟦< OE *cnedan*⟧ **1** to work (dough, clay, etc.) into a pliable mass by folding, pressing, and squeezing **2** to massage —**knead′er *n.***
knee (nē) ***n.*** ⟦< OE *cneow*⟧ **1** the joint between the thigh and the lower leg **2** anything shaped like a bent knee —***vt.*** **kneed, knee′ing** to hit or touch with the knee
knee′cap′ *n.* PATELLA
knee′-deep′ *adj.* **1** up to the knees *[knee-deep* mud*]* **2** very much involved
knee′-jerk′ *adj.* ⟦< the reflex when the knee is tapped⟧ [Inf.] characterized by or reacting with an automatic, predictable response
kneel (nēl) ***vi.*** **knelt** or **kneeled, kneel′ing** ⟦< OE *cneow,* knee⟧ to bend or rest on a knee or the knees
kneel′er *n.* a cushion, stool, etc. to kneel on in a church pew
knell (nel) ***vi.*** ⟦< OE *cnyllan*⟧ **1** to ring slowly; toll **2** to sound ominously —***vt.*** to call or announce by or as by a knell —***n.*** **1** the sound of a bell rung slowly, as at a funeral **2** an omen of death, failure, etc.
knelt (nelt) ***vi.*** *alt. pt. and pp. of* KNEEL
knew (no͞o) ***vt., vi.*** *pt. of* KNOW
knick·ers (nik′ərz) ***pl.n.*** ⟦after D. *Knickerbocker*, fictitious Du author of W. Irving's *History of New York*⟧ loose breeches gathered just below the knees: also **knick′er·bock′ers** (-ər bäk′ərz)
knick·knack (nik′nak′) ***n.*** ⟦< KNACK⟧ a small ornamental article
knife (nīf) ***n.,*** *pl.* **knives** ⟦< OE *cnif*⟧ **1** a cutting instrument with a sharp-edged blade set in a handle **2** a cutting blade, as in a machine —***vt.*** **knifed, knif′ing 1** to cut or stab with a knife **2** [Inf.] to injure or defeat by treachery —**under the knife** [Inf.] undergoing surgery
knight (nīt) ***n.*** ⟦< OE *cniht,* boy⟧ **1** in medieval times, a man formally raised to special military rank and pledged to chivalrous conduct **2** in Great Britain, a man who for some achievement is given honorary rank entitling him to use *Sir* before his given name **3** a chess piece shaped like a horse's head —***vt.*** to make (a man) a knight
knight-er·rant (nīt′er′ənt) ***n.,*** *pl.* **knights′-er′rant 1** a medieval knight wandering in search of adventure **2** a chivalrous or quixotic person
knight′hood′ *n.* **1** the rank, status, or vocation of a knight **2** knights collectively
knight′ly *adj.* of, like, or befitting a knight; chivalrous, brave, etc.
knit (nit) ***vt., vi.*** **knit′ted** or **knit, knit′ting** ⟦< OE *cnotta,* a knot⟧ **1** to make (a fabric) by looping yarn or thread together with special needles **2** to join or grow together closely and firmly: said as of a broken bone **3** to draw or become drawn together in wrinkles: said of the brows —**knit′ter *n.***
knit′wear′ *n.* knitted clothing
knob (näb) ***n.*** ⟦ME *knobbe*⟧ **1** a rounded lump or protuberance **2** *a*) a handle, usually round, of a door, drawer, etc. *b*) a similar device used to control a radio, TV, etc.
knob′by *adj.* **-bi·er, -bi·est 1** covered with knobs **2** like a knob
knock (näk) ***vi.*** ⟦< OE *cnocian*⟧ **1** to strike a blow **2** to rap on a door **3** to bump; collide **4** to make a thumping noise: said of an engine, etc. —***vt.*** **1** to hit; strike **2** to make by hitting *[*to *knock* a hole in a wall*]* **3** [Inf.] to find fault with —***n.*** **1** a knocking **2** a hit; rap **3** a thumping noise in an engine, etc., as because of faulty combustion **4** [Inf.] an adverse criticism —**knock about** (or **around**) [Inf.] to wander about —**knock down 1** to hit so as to cause to fall **2** to take apart **3** to indicate the sale of (an article) at an auction —**knock off 1** [Inf.] to stop working **2** [Inf.] to deduct **3** [Slang] to kill, overcome, etc. —**knock out** to make unconscious or exhausted —**knock together** to make or compose hastily
knock′er *n.* one that knocks; esp., a small ring, knob, etc. on a door for use in knocking
knock′-kneed′ (-nēd′) ***adj.*** having legs that bend inward at the knees
knock′out′ *n.* **1** a knocking out or being knocked out **2** [Slang] a very attractive person or thing **3** *Boxing* a victory won when the opponent is unable to continue to fight, as because of having been knocked unconscious
knock·wurst (näk′wurst′) ***n.*** *alt. sp. of* KNACKWURST
knoll (nōl) ***n.*** ⟦OE *cnoll*⟧ a small hill; mound
knot (nät) ***n.*** ⟦< OE *cnotta*⟧ **1** a lump in a thread, etc., formed by a tightened loop or a tangle **2** a fastening made by tying together pieces of string, rope, etc. **3** an ornamental bow of ribbon, etc. **4** a small group or cluster **5** something that ties closely; esp., the bond of marriage **6** a problem; difficulty **7** a hard lump on a tree where a branch grows out, or a cross section of such a lump in a board **8** *Naut.* a unit of speed of one nautical mile (6,076.12 feet) an hour —***vt., vi.*** **knot′ted, knot′ting 1** to make or form a knot (in) **2** to entangle or become entangled —**tie the knot** [Inf.] to get married
knot′hole′ *n.* a hole in a board, etc. where a knot has fallen out
knot′ty *adj.* **-ti·er, -ti·est** ⟦ME⟧ **1** full of

knots *[knotty* pine*]* **2** hard to solve; puzzling *[*a *knotty* problem*]*

know (nō) ***vt.* knew, known, know′ing** ⟦< OE *cnawan*⟧ **1** to be well informed about **2** to be aware of *[*to *know* that one is loved*]* **3** to be acquainted with **4** to recognize or distinguish *[*to *know* right from wrong*]* **—*vi.* 1** to have knowledge **2** to be sure or aware **—in the know** [Inf.] having confidential information

know′-how′ ***n.*** [Inf.] technical skill

know′ing ***adj.*** **1** having knowledge **2** shrewd; clever **3** implying shrewd or secret understanding *[*a *knowing* look*]* **—know′ing·ly *adv.***

know′-it-all′ ***n.*** [Inf.] one claiming to know much about almost everything

knowl·edge (näl′ij) ***n.*** **1** the fact or state of knowing **2** range of information or understanding **3** what is known; learning **4** the body of facts, etc. accumulated by humanity **—to (the best of) one's knowledge** as far as one knows

knowl′edge·a·ble ***adj.*** having knowledge or intelligence **—knowl′edge·a·bly *adv.***

known (nōn) ***vt.*, *vi.*** *pp. of* KNOW **—*adj.*** **1** familiar **2** recognized, proven, etc. *[*a *known* expert*]*

Knox·ville (näks′vil′) city in E Tennessee: pop. 165,000

knuck·le (nuk′əl) ***n.*** ⟦< or akin to MDu & LowG *knokel,* dim. of *knoke,* bone⟧ **1** a joint of the finger; esp., the joint connecting a finger to the rest of the hand **2** the knee or hock joint of an animal, used as food **—knuckle down** to work hard **—knuckle under** to yield; give in

knuck′le·head′ ***n.*** [Inf.] a stupid person

knurl (nurl) ***n.*** ⟦prob. < *knur,* a knot + GNARL⟧ **1** a knot, knob, etc. **2** any of a series of small beads or ridges, as along the edge of a coin **—*vt.*** to make knurls on

KO (kā′ō′) [Slang] ***vt.* KO'd, KO'ing** *Boxing* to knock out **—*n.*,** *pl.* **KO's** *Boxing* a knockout Also **K.O.** or **k.o.**

ko·a·la (kō ä′lə) ***n.*** ⟦< native name⟧ a tree-dwelling Australian marsupial with thick, gray fur

Ko·di·ak (kō′dē ak′) island off the SW coast of Alaska

kohl·ra·bi (kōl rä′bē) ***n.*,** *pl.* **-bies** ⟦< It *cavolo rapa*⟧ a vegetable related to the cabbage, with an edible, turniplike stem

ko·la (kō′lə) ***n.*** COLA (sense 1)

kook (ko͝ok) ***n.*** ⟦prob. < CUCKOO⟧ [Slang] a person regarded as silly, eccentric, etc. **—kook′y** or **kook′ie, -i·er, -i·est,** ***adj.***

kook·a·bur·ra (ko͝ok′ə bur′ə) ***n.*** ⟦< native name⟧ an Australian kingfisher with a harsh cry like loud laughter

ko·peck or **ko·pek** (kō′pek′) ***n.*** ⟦Russ < *kopye,* a lance⟧ a 100th part of a ruble

Ko·ran (kə ran′, kôr′an′) ***n.*** ⟦< Ar *qur'ān,* book⟧ the sacred book of Islam

Ko·re·a (kə rē′ə) peninsula & country northeast of China: divided (1948) into *a)* **Korean People's Democratic Republic** (**North Korea**): 47,399 sq. mi.; pop. 23,030,000 *b)* **Republic of Korea** (**South Korea**): 38,326 sq. mi.; pop. 43,412,000 **—Ko·re′an *adj.*, *n.***

ko·sher (kō′shər) ***adj.*** ⟦< Heb *kāshēr,* proper⟧ *Judaism* clean or fit to eat according to the dietary laws

kow·tow (kou′tou′) ***vi.*** ⟦Chin *k'o-t'ou,* lit., bump head⟧ to show great deference, respect, etc. (*to*)

KP *abbrev.* kitchen police: a detail to assist the cooks in an army kitchen

kraal (kräl) ***n.*** ⟦Afrik⟧ **1** a village of South African native people **2** in South Africa, an enclosure for cattle or sheep

Krem·lin (krem′lin) ***n.*** ⟦< Russ *kryeml'*⟧ **1** the citadel of Moscow, housing many Russian, or, formerly, Soviet, government offices **2** the Russian, or, formerly, Soviet, government

Krish·na (krish′nə) ***n.*** a Hindu god, an incarnation of Vishnu

kro·na (krō′nə) ***n.*,** *pl.* **-nor′** (-nôr′) ⟦ult. < L *corona,* crown⟧ the monetary unit of Sweden

kró·na (krō′nə) ***n.*,** *pl.* **-nur** (-nər) ⟦see prec.⟧ the monetary unit of Iceland

kro·ne (krō′nə) ***n.*,** *pl.* **-ner** (-nər) ⟦see KRONA⟧ the monetary unit of Denmark and Norway

KS Kansas

K2 GODWIN AUSTEN

ku·chen (ko͞o′kən) ***n.*** ⟦Ger, cake⟧ a coffeecake made of yeast dough, often with raisins, nuts, etc.

ku·dos (kyo͞o′däs′, ko͞o′-) ***n.*** ⟦Gr *kydos*⟧ credit for an achievement; glory; fame: often wrongly taken to be the plural (*pron.* -dōz) of an assumed word *"kudo"*

kud·zu (ko͝od′zo͞o′) ***n.*** ⟦Jpn⟧ a fast-growing perennial vine with large, three-part leaves

Ku Klux Klan (ko͞o′ kluks′ klan′) ⟦< Gr *kyklos,* circle⟧ a U.S. secret society that is anti-black, anti-Semitic, anti-Catholic, etc., and uses terrorist methods

kum·quat (kum′kwät′) ***n.*** ⟦< Mandarin *chin-chü,* lit., golden orange⟧ a small, orange-colored, oval fruit with a sour pulp and a sweet rind

kung fu (ko͝oŋ′ fo͞o′, go͝oŋ′-) ⟦< Chin⟧ a Chinese system of self-defense, like karate but with circular movements

Ku·wait (ko͞o wāt′) independent Arab state in E Arabia: 6,880 sq. mi.; pop. 1,697,000 **—Ku·wai′ti** (-wāt′ē) ***adj.*, *n.***

kvetch (kə vech′) ***vi.*** ⟦< Yiddish⟧ [Slang] to complain in a nagging way

kW or **kw** *abbrev.* kilowatt(s)

Kwang·chow (kwäŋ′chō′) *a former transliteration of* GUANGZHOU

Kwan·zaa (kwän′zä) ***n.*** ⟦ult. < Swahili⟧ an African-American cultural festival, Dec. 26 through Jan. 1

KY Kentucky

Kyo·to (kē ōt′ō) city in S Honshu, Japan: pop. 1,473,000

Kyr·gyz·stan (kir′gi stan′) country in south-central Asia: formerly a republic of the U.S.S.R.: 77,180 sq. mi.; pop. 4,463,000

L

l[1] or **L** (el) ***n.***, *pl.* **l's, L's** the 12th letter of the English alphabet

l[2] *abbrev.* **1** latitude **2** left **3** length **4** line **5** liter(s) **6** long **7** loss(es)

L[1] (el) ***n.***, *pl.* **L's 1** an extension forming an L with the main structure **2** a Roman numeral for 50

L[2] *abbrev.* **1** Lake **2** large **3** Latin **4** left **5** length **6** liter(s) **7** longitude **8** ⟦L *libra*, pl. *librae*⟧ pound(s): now usually £

la (lä) ***n.*** ⟦< L⟧ *Music* the sixth tone of the diatonic scale

LA 1 Los Angeles **2** Louisiana

lab (lab) ***n.*** [Inf.] a laboratory

la·bel (lā′bəl) ***n.*** ⟦OFr, a rag⟧ **1** a card, paper, etc. marked and attached to an object to indicate its contents, owner, destination, etc. **2** a term of generalized classification —***vt.*** **-beled** or **-belled, -bel·ing** or **-bel·ling 1** to attach a label to **2** to classify as

la·bi·al (lā′bē əl) ***adj.*** ⟦< L *labium*, lip⟧ **1** of the lips **2** *Phonetics* articulated with one or both lips: said as of (f), (b), and (ü)

la′bi·um (-əm) ***n.***, *pl.* **-bi·a** (-ə) ⟦L, lip⟧ a lip or liplike organ

la·bor (lā′bər) ***n.*** ⟦< L⟧ **1** physical or mental exertion; work **2** a specific task **3** all wage-earning workers **4** labor unions collectively **5** the process of childbirth —***vi.*** **1** to work **2** to work hard **3** to move slowly and with difficulty **4** to be burdened with a liability or limitation (with *under*) **5** to be in childbirth —***vt.*** to develop in too great detail; belabor

lab·o·ra·to·ry (lab′rə tôr′ē) ***n.***, *pl.* **-ries** ⟦see prec.⟧ a room, building, etc. for scientific experimentation or research

Labor Day the first Monday in September, a legal holiday honoring working people

la·bored (lā′bərd) ***adj.*** made or done with great effort; strained

la′bor·er ***n.*** one who labors; esp., a wage-earning worker whose work is largely hard physical labor

la·bo·ri·ous (lə bôr′ē əs) ***adj.*** **1** involving much hard work; difficult **2** LABORED —**la·bo′ri·ous·ly** ***adv.***

labor union an association of workers to promote and protect the welfare, rights, etc. of its members

la·bour (lā′bər) ***n.***, ***vi.***, ***vt.*** *Brit. sp. of* LABOR

Lab·ra·dor (lab′rə dôr′) **1** region along the Atlantic in NE Canada: the mainland part of Newfoundland **2** large peninsula between the Atlantic & Hudson Bay, containing this region & Quebec

Labrador retriever a retriever with a short, dense, black, yellow, or brown coat

la·bur·num (lə bur′nəm) ***n.*** ⟦< L⟧ a small tree or shrub of the pea family, with drooping yellow flowers

lab·y·rinth (lab′ə rinth′) ***n.*** ⟦< Gr *labyrinthos*⟧ a structure containing winding passages hard to follow without losing one's way; maze

lac (lak) ***n.*** ⟦< Sans *lākṣā*⟧ a resinous substance secreted on certain trees in India, etc. by a certain kind of insect: source of shellac

lace (lās) ***n.*** ⟦< L *laqueus*, noose⟧ **1** a string, etc. used to draw together and fasten the parts of a shoe, corset, etc. **2** a fine netting of cotton, silk, etc., woven in ornamental designs —***vt.*** **laced, lac′ing 1** to fasten with a lace **2** to weave together; intertwine **3** to hit hard **4** to add a dash of alcoholic liquor to (a drink)

lac·er·ate (las′ər āt′) ***vt.*** **-at′ed, -at′ing** ⟦< L *lacer*, lacerated⟧ to tear jaggedly; mangle (flesh, etc.) —**lac′er·a′tion** ***n.***

lace′work′ ***n.*** lace, or any openwork decoration like lace

lach·ry·mal (lak′ri məl) ***adj.*** ⟦< L *lacrima*, TEAR[2]⟧ **1** of or producing tears **2** LACRIMAL (sense 1)

lach′ry·mose′ (-mōs′) ***adj.*** ⟦see prec.⟧ shedding, or causing to shed, tears; tearful or sad

lack (lak) ***n.*** ⟦< or akin to medieval LowG *lak*⟧ **1** the fact or state of not having enough or not having any **2** the thing that is needed —***vt.***, ***vi.*** to be deficient in or entirely without (something)

lack·a·dai·si·cal (lak′ə dā′zi kəl) ***adj.*** ⟦< archaic *lackaday*, an exclamation of regret, etc.⟧ showing lack of interest or spirit; listless

lack·ey (lak′ē) ***n.***, *pl.* **-eys** ⟦< Sp *lacayo*⟧ **1** a male servant of low rank, usually in some sort of livery or uniform **2** a servile follower; toady

lack·lus·ter (lak′lus′tər) ***adj.*** **1** lacking brightness; dull **2** lacking vitality; boring Also [Chiefly Brit.] **lack′lus′tre**

la·con·ic (lə kän′ik) ***adj.*** ⟦< Gr *Lakōn*, a Spartan⟧ terse in expression; concise —**la·con′i·cal·ly** ***adv.***

lac·quer (lak′ər) ***n.*** ⟦< Fr < Port *laca*, lac⟧ **1** a coating substance made of shellac, gum resins, etc. dissolved in ethyl alcohol or other solvent that evaporates rapidly **2** a resinous varnish obtained from certain E Asian trees —***vt.*** to coat with lacquer

lac·ri·mal (lak′ri məl) ***adj.*** **1** of or near the glands that secrete tears **2** LACHRYMAL (sense 1)

la·crosse (lə krôs′) ***n.*** ⟦CdnFr, lit., the crutch⟧ a ballgame played by two teams using long-handled, pouched rackets

lac·tate (lak′tāt′) ***vi.*** **-tat′ed, -tat′ing** to secrete milk

lac·ta·tion (lak tā′shən) ***n.*** ⟦< L *lac*, milk⟧ **1** the secretion of milk by a mammary gland **2** the period during which milk is secreted

lac·te·al (lak′tē əl) ***adj.*** ⟦< L *lac*, milk⟧ of or like milk; milky

lac·tic (lak′tik) ***adj.*** ⟦< L *lac*, milk⟧ of or obtained from milk

lactic acid a clear, syrupy acid formed when milk sours

lac·tose (lak′tōs′) ***n.*** ⟦< L *lac*, milk⟧ a sugar found in milk: used in foods

la·cu·na (lə kyōō′nə) ***n.***, *pl.* **-nas** or **-nae** (-nē) ⟦L, a ditch⟧ a blank space; esp., a missing portion in a text, etc.

lac·y (lās′ē) ***adj.*** **-i·er**, **-i·est** of or like lace —**lac′i·ness** ***n.***

lad (lad) ***n.*** ⟦ME *ladde*⟧ a boy; youth

lad·der (lad′ər) ***n.*** ⟦OE *hlæder*⟧ **1** a framework consisting of two sidepieces connected by a series of rungs, for use in climbing up or down **2** any means of climbing

lad·die (lad′ē) ***n.*** [Chiefly Scot.] a young lad

lad·en (lād′'n) ***adj.*** ⟦< OE⟧ **1** loaded **2** burdened

la-di-da (lä′dē dä′) ***adj.*** ⟦imitative⟧ [Inf.] affectedly refined

lad·ing (lād′iŋ) ***n.*** a load; cargo; freight

la·dle (lād′'l) ***n.*** ⟦OE *hlædel*⟧ a long-handled, cuplike spoon —***vt.*** **-dled**, **-dling** to dip out with a ladle

la·dy (lād′ē) ***n.***, *pl.* **-dies** ⟦< OE *hlaf*, loaf + *dæge*, kneader⟧ **1** *a)* a woman of high social position *b)* a woman who is polite, refined, etc. **2** any woman: used (in pl.) to address a group **3** [**L-**] a British title given to women of certain ranks —***adj.*** [Inf.] female

la′dy·bug′ ***n.*** a small, roundish beetle with a spotted back: also **la′dy·bird′**

la′dy·fin′ger ***n.*** a small spongecake shaped somewhat like a finger

la′dy-in-wait′ing ***n.***, *pl.* **la′dies-in-wait′ing** a woman waiting upon a queen or princess

la′dy·like′ ***adj.*** like or suitable for a lady; refined; well-bred

la′dy·love′ ***n.*** a female sweetheart

la′dy·ship′ ***n.*** **1** the rank or position of a lady **2** [*usually* **L-**] a title used in speaking to or of a woman holding the rank of lady

la′dy-slip′per ***n.*** an orchid with flowers that somewhat resemble slippers: also **la′dy's-slip′per**

la·e·trile (lā′ə tril′) ***n.*** any of several compounds obtained chiefly from apricot kernels, claimed by some to be effective in treating cancer

La·fa·yette (lä′fē et′, -fā-), Marquis **de** 1757-1834; Fr. general: served (1777-81) in the American Revolutionary army

lag (lag) ***vi.*** **lagged**, **lag′ging** ⟦< ?⟧ **1** to fall behind or move slowly; loiter **2** to become less intense —***n.*** **1** a falling behind **2** the amount of this

la·ger (beer) (lä′gər) ⟦Ger *lagerbier*, storehouse beer⟧ a beer aged at a low temperature

lag·gard (lag′ərd) ***n.*** ⟦< LAG + -ARD⟧ a slow person, esp. one who falls behind —***adj.*** slow; falling behind

la·gniappe or **la·gnappe** (lan yap′, lan′yap′) ***n.*** ⟦Creole < Fr & Sp⟧ a gratuity

la·goon (lə gōōn′) ***n.*** ⟦< L *lacuna*, pool⟧ **1** a shallow lake or pond, esp. one connected with a larger body of water **2** the water enclosed by a circular coral reef **3** an area of shallow salt water separated from the sea by sand dunes

La·hore (lə hôr′) city in NE Pakistan: pop. 2,953,000

laid (lād) ***vt.***, ***vi.*** *pt. & pp. of* LAY[1]

laid′-back′ ***adj.*** [Slang] relaxed, easygoing, etc.; not frenetic or hurried

lain (lān) ***vi.*** *pp. of* LIE[1]

lair (ler) ***n.*** ⟦OE *leger*⟧ a resting place of a wild animal; den

lais·sez faire (les′ā fer′) ⟦Fr, allow to do⟧ noninterference; specif., absence of government control over industry and business

la·i·ty (lā′i tē) ***n.***, *pl.* **-ties** ⟦< LAY[3]⟧ laymen collectively

lake (lāk) ***n.*** ⟦< L *lacus*⟧ **1** a large inland body of usually fresh water **2** a pool of oil or other liquid

lake′front′ ***n.*** the land along the shore of a lake —***adj.*** near, at, or of the lakefront

lal·ly·gag (lä′lē gag′) ***vi.*** **-gagged′**, **-gag′ging** [Inf.] LOLLYGAG

lam (lam) [Slang] ***n.*** ⟦< ?⟧ headlong flight —***vi.*** **lammed**, **lam′ming** to flee; escape —**on the lam** in flight, as from the police

la·ma (lä′mə) ***n.*** ⟦Tibetan *blama*⟧ a priest or monk in Lamaism

La·ma·ism (lä′mə iz′əm) ***n.*** a form of Buddhism in Tibet and Mongolia

la·ma·ser·y (lä′mə ser′ē) ***n.***, *pl.* **-ies** a monastery of lamas

La·maze (lə mäz′) ***n.*** ⟦after F. *Lamaze*, 20th-c. Fr physician⟧ a training program in natural childbirth, involving the help of the father

lamb (lam) ***n.*** ⟦OE⟧ **1** a young sheep **2** its flesh, used as food **3** a gentle, innocent, or gullible person

lam·baste (lam bāst′, -bast′) ***vt.*** **-bast′ed**, **-bast′ing** ⟦< *lam*, to beat + *baste*, to flog⟧ [Inf.] **1** to beat soundly **2** to scold or denounce severely

lamb·da (lam′də) ***n.*** the 11th letter of the Greek alphabet (Λ, λ)

lam·bent (lam′bənt) ***adj.*** ⟦< L *lambere*, to lick⟧ **1** playing lightly over a surface: said of a flame, etc. **2** glowing softly **3** light and graceful *[lambent wit]* —**lam′ben·cy** ***n.***

lamb′kin ***n.*** a little lamb: sometimes applied to a child, etc. as a term of affection

lame (lām) ***adj.*** ⟦OE *lama*⟧ **1** crippled; esp., having an injury that makes one limp **2** stiff and painful **3** poor; ineffectual *[a lame excuse]* —***vt.*** **lamed**, **lam′ing** to make lame —**lame′ly** ***adv.*** —**lame′ness** ***n.***

la·mé (la mā′, lä-) ***n.*** ⟦< Fr *lame*, metal plate⟧ a cloth interwoven with metal threads, as of gold

lame duck an elected official whose term ends after someone else has been elected to the office

la·mel·la (lə mel′ə) ***n.***, *pl.* **-lae** (-ē) or **-las** ⟦L⟧ a thin plate, scale, or layer

la·ment (lə ment′) ***vi., vt.*** ⟦< L *lamentum*, a wailing⟧ to feel or express deep sorrow (for); mourn —***n.*** **1** a lamenting **2** an elegy, dirge, etc. mourning some loss or death —**lam·en·ta·ble** (lam′ən tə bəl, lə men′-) ***adj.*** —**lam·en·ta·tion** (lam′ən tā′shən) ***n.***

lam·i·na (lam′i nə) ***n.***, *pl.* **-nae′** (-nē′) or **-nas** ⟦L⟧ a thin scale or layer, as of metal, tissue, etc.

lam·i·nate (lam′i nāt′; *for adj. usually*, -nit) ***vt.*** **-nat′ed, -nat′ing** ⟦see prec.⟧ **1** to cover with one or more thin layers **2** to make by building up in layers —***adj.*** LAMINATED —**lam′i·na′tion** ***n.***

lam′i·nat′ed ***adj.*** **1** built in thin sheets or layers **2** covered with a thin protective layer, as of clear plastic

lamp (lamp) ***n.*** ⟦< Gr *lampein*, to shine⟧ **1** a container with a wick for burning oil, etc. to produce light or heat **2** any device for producing light or heat, as an electric light bulb **3** a holder or base for such a device

lamp′black′ ***n.*** fine soot used as a black pigment

lam·poon (lam po͞on′) ***n.*** ⟦< Fr *lampons*, let us drink: used as a refrain⟧ a satirical writing attacking someone —***vt.*** to attack in a lampoon

lamp·post (lam′pōst′) ***n.*** a post supporting a street lamp

lam·prey (lam′prē) ***n.***, *pl.* **-preys** ⟦< ML *lampreda*⟧ an eel-like fish with a jawless, sucking mouth

la·na·i (lə nä′ē, -nī′) ***n.*** ⟦Haw⟧ a veranda or open-sided living room

lance (lans) ***n.*** ⟦< L *lancea*⟧ **1** a long, wooden spear with a sharp metal head **2** *a)* LANCER *b)* LANCET **3** any instrument like a lance —***vt.*** **lanced, lanc′ing** **1** to pierce with a lance **2** to cut open (a boil, etc.) with a lancet

Lan·ce·lot (län′sə lət, -lät′) ***n.*** the most celebrated of the Knights of the Round Table

lanc·er (lans′ər) ***n.*** a cavalry soldier armed with a lance

lan·cet (lan′sit) ***n.*** ⟦< OFr dim. of *lance*, lance⟧ a small, pointed surgical knife, usually two-edged

land (land) ***n.*** ⟦OE⟧ **1** the solid part of the earth's surface **2** a country or nation **3** ground or soil **4** real estate —***vt.*** **1** to put on shore from a ship **2** to bring to a particular place or condition *[*it *landed* him in jail*]* **3** to set (an aircraft) down on land or water **4** to catch *[*to *land* a fish*]* **5** [Inf.] to get or secure *[*to *land* a job*]* **6** [Inf.] to deliver (a blow) —***vi.*** **1** to leave a ship and go on shore **2** to come to a port, etc.: said of a ship **3** to arrive at a specified place **4** to come to rest

land contract a real estate contract in which a buyer makes payments over a specified period until the full price is paid, after which the seller transfers his interest to the buyer

land′ed ***adj.*** owning land *[landed* gentry*]*

land′fall′ ***n.*** **1** a sighting of land from a ship at sea **2** the land sighted

land′fill′ ***n.*** **1** a place used to dispose of garbage, rubbish, etc. by burying it in the ground **2** garbage, etc. so disposed of

land grant a grant of land by the government for a railroad, state college, etc.

land′hold′er ***n.*** an owner of land —**land′hold′ing** ***adj., n.***

land′ing ***n.*** **1** the act of coming to shore **2** a place where a ship or boat is loaded or unloaded **3** a platform at the end of a flight of stairs **4** the act of alighting, as after a flight or jump

landing gear the system of parts on an aircraft or spacecraft used for support or mobility on land or water

land′locked′ ***adj.*** **1** surrounded by land, as a country **2** cut off from the sea and confined to fresh water *[landlocked* salmon*]*

land′lord′ ***n.*** **1** a person who leases land, houses, etc. to others **2** a man who keeps a rooming house, inn, etc. —**land′la′dy**, *pl.* **-dies**, ***fem.n.***

land′lub′ber (-lub′ər) ***n.*** one who has had little experience at sea

land′mark′ ***n.*** **1** an object that marks the boundary of a piece of land **2** any prominent feature of the landscape, distinguishing a locality **3** an important event or turning point

land′mass′ ***n.*** a very large area of land; esp., a continent

land office a government office that handles the sales of public lands

land′-of′fice business [Inf.] a booming business

land′scape′ (-skāp′) ***n.*** ⟦< Du *land*, land + *-schap*, -ship⟧ **1** a picture of natural, inland scenery **2** an expanse of natural scenery —***vt.*** **-scaped′, -scap′ing** to make (a plot of ground) more attractive, as by adding a lawn, trees, bushes, etc. —**land′scap′er** ***n.***

land′slide′ ***n.*** **1** the sliding of a mass of earth or rocks down a slope **2** the mass sliding down **3** an overwhelming victory, esp. in an election

land′ward (-wərd) ***adv., adj.*** toward the land: also **land′wards** ***adv.***

lane (lān) ***n.*** ⟦OE *lanu*⟧ **1** a narrow way, path, road, etc. **2** a path or route designated, for reasons of safety, for ships, aircraft, automobiles, etc. **3** *Bowling* a long, narrow strip of polished wood, along which the balls are rolled

lan·guage (laŋ′gwij) ***n.*** ⟦< L *lingua*, tongue⟧ **1** human speech or the written symbols for speech **2** *a)* any means of communicating *b)* a special set of symbols used in a computer **3** the speech of a particular nation, etc. *[*the French *language]* **4** the particular style of verbal expression characteristic of a person, group, profession, etc.

lan·guid (laŋ′gwid) ***adj.*** ⟦< L *languere*, be weary⟧ **1** without vigor or vitality; weak **2** listless; indifferent **3** slow; dull —**lan′guid·ly** ***adv.***

lan′guish (-gwish) ***vi.*** ⟦see prec.⟧ **1** to become weak; droop **2** to live under distressing conditions *[*to *languish* in poverty*]* **3** to long; pine **4** to put on an air of sentimental tenderness

lan·guor (laŋ′gər) ***n.*** ⟦see LANGUID⟧ lack of vigor or vitality; weakness; listlessness —**lan′guor·ous** ***adj.***

lank (laŋk) ***adj.*** ⟦OE *hlanc*⟧ **1** long and slender **2** straight and limp: said of hair

lank·y (laŋ′kē) ***adj.*** **-i·er**, **-i·est** awkwardly tall and lean

lan·o·lin (lan′ə lin′) ***n.*** ⟦< L *lana*, wool + *oleum*, oil⟧ a fatty substance obtained from wool and used in ointments, cosmetics, etc.

Lan·sing (lan′siŋ) capital of Michigan, in the SC part: pop. 127,000

lan·tern (lan′tərn) ***n.*** ⟦ult. < Gr *lampein*, to shine⟧ a transparent case for holding and shielding a light

lan′tern-jawed′ ***adj.*** having long, thin jaws and sunken cheeks

lan·yard (lan′yərd) ***n.*** ⟦< OFr *lasne*, noose⟧ a short rope used on board ship for holding or fastening something

La·os (lä′ōs′) country in the NW part of Indochina: 91,400 sq. mi.; pop. 3,722,000 —**La·o·tian** (lā ō′shən) ***adj., n.***

lap[1] (lap) ***n.*** ⟦OE *læppa*⟧ **1** the front part, from the waist to the knees, of a sitting person **2** the part of the clothing covering this **3** that in which a person or thing is cared for **4** *a)* an overlapping *b)* a part that overlaps **5** one complete circuit of a racetrack —***vt.*** **lapped**, **lap′ping** **1** to fold (*over* or *on*) **2** to wrap; enfold **3** to overlap **4** to get a lap ahead of (an opponent) in a race —***vi.*** **1** to overlap **2** to extend beyond something in space or time: with *over*

lap[2] (lap) ***vi., vt.*** **lapped**, **lap′ping** ⟦OE *lapian*⟧ **1** to drink (a liquid) by dipping it up with the tongue as a dog does **2** to strike gently with a light splash: said of waves —***n.*** **1** a lapping **2** the sound of lapping

La Paz (lə päz′) city & seat of government of Bolivia: pop. 711,000

lap′board′ ***n.*** a board placed on the lap for use as a table or desk

lap dog any pet dog small enough to be held in the lap: also written **lap′dog′** ***n.***

la·pel (lə pel′) ***n.*** ⟦dim. of LAP[1]⟧ the front part of a coat folded back and forming a continuation of the collar

lap·i·dar·y (lap′ə der′ē) ***n.***, *pl.* **-dar′ies** ⟦< L *lapis*, a stone⟧ one who cuts and polishes precious stones —***adj.*** **1** of the art of a lapidary **2** precise and elegant *[lapidary prose]*

lap·in (lap′in) ***n.*** ⟦Fr, rabbit⟧ rabbit fur, often dyed to resemble other skins

lap·is laz·u·li (lap′is laz′yoo͞ lī′, -lazh′-; -lē′) ⟦< L *lapis*, a stone + ML *lazulus*, azure⟧ an azure, opaque, semiprecious stone

Lap·land (lap′land′) region of N Europe, including the N parts of Norway, Sweden, & Finland

Lapp (lap) ***n.*** ⟦Swed⟧ a member of a people living in Lapland: also **Lap′land′er**

lap·pet (lap′it) ***n.*** ⟦dim. of LAP[1]⟧ a loose flap or fold of a garment or head covering

lapse (laps) ***n.*** ⟦< L *labi*, to slip⟧ **1** a small error **2** *a)* a moral slip *b)* a falling into a lower condition **3** a passing, as of time **4** the termination as of a privilege through failure to meet requirements —***vi.*** **lapsed**, **laps′ing** **1** to fall into a specified state *[he lapsed into silence]* **2** to backslide **3** to elapse **4** to come to an end; stop **5** to become void because of failure to meet requirements

lap′top′ ***n.*** a small, light, portable microcomputer having, in a single unit, a CPU, keyboard, screen, etc., and, usually, a rechargeable battery

lar·board (lär′bərd) ***adj., n.*** ⟦< OE *hladan*, lade + *bord*, side⟧ (of) the port side of a ship

lar·ce·ny (lär′sə nē) ***n.***, *pl.* **-nies** ⟦ult. < L *latro*, robber⟧ the unlawful taking of another's property; theft —**lar′ce·nist** ***n.*** —**lar′ce·nous** ***adj.***

larch (lärch) ***n.*** ⟦< L *larix*⟧ **1** a tree of the pine family that sheds its needles annually **2** its tough wood

lard (lärd) ***n.*** ⟦< L *lardum*⟧ a white, soft solid made by melting the fat of hogs —***vt.*** **1** to put strips of fat pork, bacon, etc. on (meat, etc.) before cooking **2** to embellish *[a talk larded with jokes]*

lard′er ***n.*** **1** a place where food supplies are kept; pantry **2** food supplies; provisions

large (lärj) ***adj.*** **larg′er**, **larg′est** ⟦< L *largus*⟧ **1** of great extent or amount; big, bulky, spacious, etc. **2** bigger than others of its kind **3** operating on a big scale *[a large producer]* —***adv.*** in a large way *[write large]* —**at large** **1** free; not confined **2** taken altogether **3** representing no particular district *[a congressman at large]* —**large′ness** ***n.*** —**larg′ish** ***adj.***

large′heart′ed ***adj.*** generous; kindly

large intestine the relatively large section of the intestines of vertebrates, including the cecum, colon, and rectum

large′ly ***adv.*** for the most part; mainly

large′-scale′ ***adj.*** **1** drawn to a large scale **2** of wide scope; extensive

lar·gess or **lar·gesse** (lär jes′, lär′jis) ***n.*** ⟦see LARGE⟧ **1** generous giving **2** a gift or gifts generously given

lar·go (lär′gō) ***adj., adv.*** ⟦It, slow⟧ *Music* slow and stately: also written ***largo***

lar·i·at (lar′ē ət) ***n.*** ⟦Sp *la reata*, the rope⟧ **1** a rope used for tethering grazing horses, etc. **2** LASSO

lark[1] (lärk) ***n.*** ⟦< OE *læwerce*⟧ any of a large family of chiefly Old World birds, esp. the skylark

lark[2] (lärk) ***vi.*** ⟦? < ON *leika*⟧ to play or frolic —***n.*** a frolic or spree

lark·spur (lärk′spur′) ***n.*** DELPHINIUM

lar·va (lär′və) ***n.***, *pl.* **-vae′** (-vē′) or **-vas** ⟦L, ghost⟧ the early form of any animal that changes structurally when it becomes an adult *[the tadpole is the larva of the frog]* —**lar′val** ***adj.***

lar·yn·gi·tis (lar′in jīt′is) ***n.*** an inflammation of the larynx, often with a temporary loss of voice

lar·ynx (lar′iŋks) ***n.***, *pl.* **lar′ynx·es** or **la·**

ryn·ges (lə rin′jēz′) ⟦< Gr⟧ the structure at the upper end of the trachea, containing the vocal cords

la·sa·gna (lə zän′yə) ***n.*** ⟦It⟧ a dish of wide noodles baked in layers with tomato sauce, ground meat, and cheese

las·civ·i·ous (lə siv′ē əs) ***adj.*** ⟦< L *lascivus*, wanton⟧ **1** characterized by or expressing lust **2** exciting lust

la·ser (lā′zər) ***n.*** ⟦*l(ight) a(mplification by) s(timulated) e(mission of) r(adiation)*⟧ a device containing a substance whose atoms or molecules can be raised to a higher energy state, so that it emits light in an intense, narrow beam

la′ser·disc′ ***n.*** a videodisc for recording audio and video data to be read by a laser beam: also **la′ser·disk′**, **laser disc**, or **laser disk**

lash[1] (lash) ***n.*** ⟦< ?⟧ **1** the flexible striking part of a whip **2** a stroke as with a whip **3** an eyelash **—*vt.*** **1** to strike or drive as with a lash **2** to jerk or swing sharply *[the cat lashed her tail]* **3** to censure or rebuke **—*vi.*** to make strokes as with a whip **—lash out 1** to strike out violently **2** to speak angrily

lash[2] (lash) ***vt.*** ⟦see LACE⟧ to fasten or tie with a rope, etc.

lass (las) ***n.*** ⟦prob. < ON *lǫskr*, weak⟧ a young woman

las·sie (las′ē) ***n.*** [Scot.] a young woman

las·si·tude (las′i to͞od′) ***n.*** ⟦< L *lassus*, faint⟧ weariness; languor

las·so (las′ō) ***n.***, *pl.* **-sos** or **-soes** ⟦< Sp < L *laqueus*, noose⟧ a rope with a sliding noose used to catch cattle, etc. **—*vt.*** **-soed, -so·ing** to catch with a lasso

last[1] (last) ***adj.*** **1** *alt. superl. of* LATE **2** being or coming after all others in place or time; final **3** only remaining **4** most recent *[last month]* **5** least likely *[the last person to suspect]* **6** conclusive *[the last word]* **—*adv.*** **1** after all others **2** most recently **3** finally; in conclusion **—*n.*** the one coming last **—at (long) last** after a long time; finally

last[2] (last) ***vi.*** ⟦OE *læstan*⟧ to remain in existence, use, etc.; endure **—*vt.*** **1** to continue during **2** to be enough for

last[3] (last) ***n.*** ⟦< OE *last*, footstep⟧ a form shaped like the foot, used in making or repairing shoes

last hurrah a final attempt or appearance

last′ing ***adj.*** that lasts a long time **—last′ing·ly *adv.***

Last Judgment *Theol.* the final judgment at the end of the world

last′ly ***adv.*** in conclusion; finally

last straw ⟦< the straw that broke the camel's back⟧ a final trouble that results in a defeat, loss of patience, etc.: with *the*

Las Ve·gas (läs vā′gəs) city in SE Nevada: pop. 258,000

lat *abbrev.* latitude

Lat *abbrev.* Latin

latch (lach) ***n.*** ⟦< OE *læccan*⟧ a fastening for a door, gate, or window; esp., a bar that fits into a notch **—*vt.*, *vi.*** to fasten with a latch **—latch onto** [Inf.] to get or obtain

late (lāt) ***adj.*** **lat′er** or **lat′ter**, **lat′est** or **last** ⟦OE *læt*⟧ **1** happening, coming, etc. after the usual or expected time, or at a time far advanced in a period *[late to class, late Victorian]* **2** recent **3** having recently died **—*adv.*** **lat′er**, **lat′est** or **last 1** after the expected time **2** at or until an advanced time of the day, year, etc. **3** toward the end of a period **4** recently **—of late** recently **—late′ness *n.***

late′ly ***adv.*** recently; not long ago

la·tent (lāt′'nt) ***adj.*** ⟦< L *latere*, lurk⟧ lying hidden and undeveloped in a person or thing **—la′ten·cy *n.***

lat·er·al (lat′ər əl) ***adj.*** ⟦< L *latus*, a side⟧ of, at, from, or toward the side; sideways **—lat′er·al·ly *adv.***

la·tex (lā′teks′) ***n.*** ⟦L, a fluid⟧ **1** a milky liquid in certain plants and trees: used esp. as the basis of rubber **2** a suspension in water of particles of rubber or plastic: used in adhesives, paints, etc.

lath (lath) ***n.***, *pl.* **laths** (la*th*z, laths) ⟦< ME⟧ **1** any of the thin, narrow strips of wood used as a foundation for plaster, etc. **2** any foundation for plaster

lathe (lā*th*) ***n.*** ⟦prob. < MDu *lade*⟧ a machine for shaping wood, metal, etc. by holding and turning it rapidly against the edge of a cutting tool **—*vt.*** **lathed, lath′ing** to shape on a lathe

lath·er (la*th*′ər) ***n.*** ⟦OE *leathor*, soap⟧ **1** the foam formed by soap and water **2** foamy sweat, as on a racehorse **3** [Slang] an excited state **—*vt.*, *vi.*** to cover with or form lather **—lath′er·y *adj.***

Lat·in (lat′'n) ***adj.*** ⟦< *Latium*, ancient country in central Italy⟧ **1** of ancient Rome or its people, language, etc. **2** designating or of the languages derived from Latin, the peoples that speak them, their countries, etc. **—*n.*** **1** a person born or living in ancient Rome **2** the language of ancient Rome **3** a person whose language is derived from Latin, as a Spaniard, Italian, or Latin American

Latin America that part of the Western Hemisphere south of the U.S. where Spanish, Portuguese, & French are the official languages **—Latin American**

La·ti·no (la tē′nō) ***n.***, *pl.* **-nos** ⟦< L *Latinus*, LATIN⟧ a Latin American, esp. one who lives in the U.S. **—*adj.*** of or relating to Latinos Now often preferred to *Hispanic* **—La·ti′na** (-nə) ***fem.n.***

lat·ish (lāt′ish) ***adj.*, *adv.*** somewhat late

lat·i·tude (lat′ə to͞od′) ***n.*** ⟦< L *latus*, wide⟧ **1** freedom from narrow restrictions **2** *a)* distance, measured in degrees, north or south from the equator *b)* a region with reference to this distance

la·trine (lə trēn′) ***n.*** ⟦< L *lavare*, to wash⟧ a toilet for the use of a large number of people, as in an army camp

lat·te (lä′tā) ***n.*** ⟦It⟧ espresso coffee mixed with steamed milk

lat·ter (lat′ər) ***adj.*** ⟦orig. compar. of LATE⟧ **1** *alt. compar. of* LATE **2** *a)* later; more recent *b)* nearer the end or close

3 being the last mentioned of two

lat·tice (lat′is) ***n.*** ⟦< OHG *latta,* lath⟧ an openwork structure of crossed strips of wood, metal, etc. used as a screen, support, etc.

lat′tice·work′ ***n.*** **1** a lattice **2** lattices collectively

Lat·vi·a (lat′vē ə) country in N Europe: formerly a republic of the U.S.S.R.: 24,595 sq. mi.; pop. 2,606,000 —**Lat′vi·an** ***adj., n.***

laud (lôd) ***vt.*** ⟦< L *laus,* glory⟧ to praise; extol

laud′a·ble ***adj.*** praiseworthy; commendable

lau·da·num (lôd′′n əm) ***n.*** ⟦< L *ladanum,* a dark resin⟧ **1** [Archaic] any of various opium preparations **2** a solution of opium in alcohol

laud·a·to·ry (lôd′ə tôr′ē) ***adj.*** expressing praise; commendatory

laugh (laf) ***vi.*** ⟦< OE *hleahhan*⟧ to make the sounds and facial movements that express mirth, ridicule, etc. —***n.*** **1** the act or sound of laughing **2** a cause of laughter **3** [*pl.*] [Inf.] mere diversion or pleasure —**laugh at 1** to be amused by **2** to make fun of

laugh′a·ble ***adj.*** amusing or ridiculous —**laugh′a·bly** ***adv.***

laugh′ing·stock′ ***n.*** an object of ridicule

laugh′ter ***n.*** the action or sound of laughing

launch[1] (lônch) ***vt.*** ⟦< L *lancea,* a lance⟧ **1** to hurl or send forth with some force [to *launch* a rocket] **2** to slide (a new vessel) into the water **3** to set in operation or on some course; start [to *launch* an attack] —***vi.*** **1** to start something new: often with *out* or *forth* **2** to plunge (*into*) —***n.*** a launching —***adj.*** designating or of vehicles, sites, etc. used in launching spacecraft or missiles

launch[2] (lônch) ***n.*** ⟦Sp or Port *lancha*⟧ an open, or partly enclosed, motorboat

launch′pad′ or **launch pad** ***n.*** the platform from which a rocket, guided missile, etc. is launched: also **launching pad**

laun·der (lôn′dər) ***vt.*** ⟦< L *lavare,* to wash⟧ **1** to wash, or wash and iron (clothes, etc.) **2** to exchange or invest (illegally gotten money) so as to conceal its source —**laun′der·er** ***n.*** —**laun′dress** (-dris) ***fem.n.***

laun·dro·mat (lôn′drə mat′) ***n.*** ⟦< *Laundromat,* a former service mark⟧ a self-service laundry: also **laun·der·mat** (lôn′dər mat′)

laun·dry (lôn′drē) ***n.,*** *pl.* **-dries 1** a place for laundering **2** clothes, etc. laundered or to be laundered

laun′dry·man′ (-man′, -mən) ***n.,*** *pl.* **-men′** (-man′, -mən) a man who works in or for a laundry, esp. one who collects and delivers laundry

lau·re·ate (lôr′ē it) ***adj.*** ⟦< L *laurus,* laurel⟧ honored, as with a crown of laurel —***n.*** POET LAUREATE

lau·rel (lôr′əl) ***n.*** ⟦< L *laurus*⟧ **1** an evergreen tree or shrub of S Europe, with large, glossy leaves **2** its foliage, esp. as woven into wreaths once used to crown the victors in contests **3** [*pl.*] fame; honor **4** any of various trees and shrubs resembling the true laurel

la·va (lä′və, lav′ə) ***n.*** ⟦It < L *labi,* to slide⟧ **1** melted rock issuing from a volcano **2** such rock when solidified by cooling

La·val (lə val′) city in SW Quebec, Canada, near Montreal: pop. 330,000

lav·a·liere or **lav·a·lier** (lav′ə lir′, lä′və-) ***n.*** ⟦< Fr⟧ an ornament on a chain, worn around the neck

lav·a·to·ry (lav′ə tôr′ē) ***n.,*** *pl.* **-ries** ⟦< L *lavare,* to wash⟧ a room with a washbowl and a toilet

lave (lāv) ***vt., vi.*** **laved, lav′ing** ⟦< L *lavare*⟧ [Old Poet.] to wash or bathe

lav·en·der (lav′ən dər) ***n.*** ⟦< ML *lavandria*⟧ **1** a fragrant European plant of the mint family with spikes of pale-purplish flowers **2** its dried flowers and leaves, used to perfume clothes, etc. **3** a pale purple —***adj.*** pale-purple

lav·ish (lav′ish) ***adj.*** ⟦< OFr *lavasse,* downpour⟧ **1** very generous; prodigal **2** very abundant —***vt.*** to give or spend generously —**lav′ish·ly** ***adv.***

law (lô) ***n.*** ⟦OE *lagu*⟧ **1** *a*) all the rules of conduct established by the authority or custom of a nation, etc. *b*) any one of such rules **2** obedience to such rules **3** the study of such rules; jurisprudence **4** the seeking of justice in courts under such rules **5** the profession of lawyers, judges, etc. **6** *a*) a sequence of natural events occurring with unvarying uniformity under the same conditions *b*) the stating of such a sequence **7** any rule expected to be observed [the *laws* of health] —**the Law 1** the Mosaic law, or the part of the Jewish Scriptures containing it **2** [**the l-**] [Inf.] a policeman or the police

law′-a·bid′ing ***adj.*** obeying the law

law′break′er ***n.*** a person who violates the law —**law′break′ing** ***adj., n.***

law′ful ***adj.*** **1** in conformity with the law **2** recognized by law [*lawful* debts] —**law′ful·ly** ***adv.***

law′giv′er ***n.*** a lawmaker; legislator

law′less ***adj.*** **1** not regulated by the authority of law **2** not in conformity with law; illegal **3** not obeying the law; unruly —**law′less·ness** ***n.***

law′mak′er ***n.*** one who makes or helps to make laws; esp., a legislator

lawn[1] (lôn) ***n.*** ⟦< OFr *launde,* heath⟧ land covered with grass kept closely mowed, esp. around a house

lawn[2] (lôn) ***n.*** ⟦after *Laon,* city in France⟧ a fine, sheer cloth of linen or cotton

lawn bowling a bowling game played on a smooth lawn with wooden balls

lawn mower a machine for cutting the grass of a lawn

Law·rence (lôr′əns), **D**(avid) **H**(erbert) 1885-1930; Eng. novelist & poet

law′suit′ ***n.*** a suit between private parties in a law court

law·yer (lô′yər) ***n.*** one whose profession is advising others in matters of law or representing them in lawsuits

lax (laks) ***adj.*** ⟦< L *laxus*⟧ **1** loose; slack; not tight **2** not strict or exact —**lax'ly** ***adv.***

lax·a·tive (lak'sə tiv) ***adj.*** ⟦see prec.⟧ making the bowels loose and relieving constipation —***n.*** any laxative medicine

lax·i·ty (lak'si tē) ***n.*** lax quality or condition

lay[1] (lā) ***vt.*** **laid, lay'ing** ⟦< OE *lecgan*⟧ **1** to cause to fall with force; knock down **2** to place or put in a resting position: often with *on* or *in* **3** to put down (bricks, carpeting, etc.) in the correct position or way **4** to place; put; set [to *lay* emphasis on accuracy] **5** to produce (an egg) **6** to allay, suppress, etc. **7** to bet (a specified sum, etc.) **8** to devise [to *lay* plans] **9** to present or assert [to *lay* claim to property] —***n.*** the way or position in which something is situated [the *lay* of the land] —**lay aside** to put away for future use; save: also **lay away** or **lay by** —**lay in** to get and store away —**lay into** [Slang] to attack with blows or words —**lay off** **1** to discharge (an employee), esp. temporarily **2** [Slang] to cease —**lay open** **1** to cut open **2** to expose —**lay out** **1** to spend **2** to arrange according to a plan **3** to spread out (clothes, etc.) ready for wear, etc. —**lay over** to stop a while in a place before going on —**lay up** **1** to store for future use **2** to confine to a sickbed

lay[2] (lā) ***vi.*** *pt. of* LIE[1]

lay[3] (lā) ***adj.*** ⟦< Gr *laos*, the people⟧ **1** of a layman **2** not belonging to a given profession

lay[4] (lā) ***n.*** ⟦ME & OFr *lai*⟧ **1** a short poem, esp. a narrative poem, orig. for singing **2** [Obs.] a song

lay'a·way' ***n.*** a method of buying by making a deposit on something which is delivered only after full payment

lay'er ***n.*** **1** a person or thing that lays **2** a single thickness, fold, etc.

lay·ette (lā et') ***n.*** ⟦< MDu *lade*, chest⟧ a complete outfit of clothes, bedding, etc. for a newborn baby

lay·man (lā'mən) ***n.***, *pl.* **-men** (-mən) a person not a clergyman or one not belonging to a given profession: also **lay'per'son** —**lay'wom'an**, *pl.* **-wom'en**, ***fem.n.***

lay'off' ***n.*** temporary unemployment, or the period of this

lay'out' ***n.*** **1** the manner in which anything is laid out; specif., the makeup of a newspaper, advertisement, etc. **2** the thing laid out

lay'o'ver ***n.*** a stop during a journey

Laz·a·rus (laz'ə rəs) ***n.*** *Bible* a man raised from the dead by Jesus

laze (lāz) ***vi.***, ***vt.*** **lazed, laz'ing** to idle or loaf

la·zy (lā'zē) ***adj.*** **-zi·er, -zi·est** ⟦prob. < medieval LowG or MDu⟧ **1** not eager or willing to work or exert oneself **2** sluggish —***vi.***, ***vt.*** **-zied, -zy·ing** LAZE —**la'zi·ly** ***adv.*** —**la'zi·ness** ***n.***

la'zy·bones' ***n.*** [Inf.] a lazy person

Lazy Su·san (so͞o'zən) a rotating tray for food

lb *symbol* ⟦abbrev. for *libra:* see LIRA⟧ pound; pounds: also, for the plural, **lbs**

l.c. *abbrev.* ⟦L *loco citato*⟧ in the place cited

LCD ***n.*** ⟦*l(iquid-)c(rystal) d(isplay)*⟧ a device for alphanumeric displays, as on digital watches, using a crystalline liquid

LD *abbrev.* **1** learning disability **2** learning-disabled

lea (lē) ***n.*** ⟦OE *leah*⟧ [Old Poet.] a meadow

leach (lēch) ***vt.*** ⟦prob. < OE *leccan*, to water⟧ **1** to wash (some material) with a filtering liquid **2** to extract (a soluble substance) from some material —***vi.*** to dissolve and be washed away

lead[1] (lēd) ***vt.*** **led, lead'ing** ⟦OE *lædan*⟧ **1** to direct, as by going before or along with, by physical contact, pulling a rope, etc.; guide **2** to guide by influence **3** to be the head of (an expedition, orchestra, etc.) **4** to be at the head of [to *lead* one's class] **5** to be ahead of in a contest **6** to live; spend [to *lead* a hard life] —***vi.*** **1** to show the way, as by going before **2** to tend in a certain direction: with *to, from*, etc. **3** to bring as a result: with *to* [hate *led* to war] **4** to be or go first —***n.*** **1** the role or example of a leader **2** first or front place **3** the amount or distance ahead [to hold a safe *lead*] **4** anything that leads, as a clue **5** the leading role in a play, etc. **6** the right of playing first in cards or the card played **7** the most important news story, as in a newspaper or telecast —**lead off** to begin —**lead on** to lure —**lead up to** to prepare the way for

lead[2] (led) ***n.*** ⟦OE⟧ **1** a heavy, soft, bluish-gray metallic chemical element **2** a weight for measuring depth at sea **3** bullets **4** a stick of graphite, used in pencils —***adj.*** of or containing lead —***vt.*** to cover, line, or weight with lead

lead·ed (led'əd) ***adj.*** containing a lead compound: said of gasoline

lead·en (led''n) ***adj.*** **1** of lead **2** heavy **3** sluggish **4** gloomy **5** gray

lead·er (lēd'ər) ***n.*** one that leads; guiding head —**lead'er·ship'** ***n.***

lead·ing (lēd'iŋ) ***adj.*** **1** that leads; guiding **2** principal; chief

leading question a question put in such a way as to suggest the answer sought

lead time (lēd) the period of time between the decision to make a product and the start of production

leaf (lēf) ***n.***, *pl.* **leaves** ⟦OE⟧ **1** any of the flat, thin parts, usually green, growing from the stem of a plant **2** a sheet of paper **3** a very thin sheet of metal **4** a hinged or removable section of a table top —***vi.*** **1** to bear leaves **2** to turn the pages of a book: with *through* —**leaf'less** ***adj.***

leaf'let (-lit) ***n.*** **1** a small or young leaf **2** a separate sheet of printed matter, often folded

leaf'stalk' ***n.*** the part of a leaf supporting the blade and attached to the stem

leaf'y ***adj.*** **-i·er, -i·est** having many or broad leaves [a *leafy* vegetable]

league[1] (lēg) ***n.*** ⟦< L *ligare*, bind⟧ **1** an association of nations, groups, etc. for promoting common interests **2** *Sports* a group of teams organized to play one another —***vt.***, ***vi.*** **leagued**, **leagu'ing** to form into a league

league[2] (lēg) ***n.*** ⟦ult. < OE *leowe*, mile⟧ a measure of distance, about three miles

leak (lēk) ***vi.*** ⟦< ON *leka*, to drip⟧ **1** to let a fluid out or in accidentally **2** to pass in or out of a container thus **3** to become known gradually, by accident, etc. —***vt.*** to allow to leak —***n.*** **1** an accidental crack, etc. that lets something out or in **2** any accidental means of escape **3** leakage **4** a disclosure of confidential information —**leak'y**, **-i·er**, **-i·est**, ***adj.***

leak'age ***n.*** **1** a leaking **2** that which leaks or the amount that leaks

lean[1] (lēn) ***vi.*** **leaned** or [Chiefly Brit.] **leant** (lent), **lean'ing** ⟦OE *hlinian*⟧ **1** to bend or slant from an upright position **2** to bend the body so as to rest part of one's weight on something **3** to rely (*on* or *upon*) **4** to tend (*toward* or *to*) —***vt.*** to cause to lean —**lean'er** ***n.***

lean[2] (lēn) ***adj.*** ⟦OE *hlæne*⟧ **1** with little flesh or fat; thin; spare **2** meager —**lean'ness** ***n.***

lean'ing ***n.*** a tendency; inclination

lean'-to' ***n.***, *pl.* **-tos'** a structure whose sloping roof abuts another building, a wall, etc.

leap (lēp) ***vi.*** **leapt** (lept, lēpt) or **lept** or **leaped**, **leap'ing** ⟦OE *hleapan*⟧ **1** to jump; spring; bound **2** to accept eagerly something offered: with *at* —***vt.*** **1** to pass over by a jump **2** to cause to leap —***n.*** **1** a jump; spring **2** the distance covered in a jump **3** a sudden transition —**leap'er** ***n.***

leap'frog' ***n.*** a game in which each player in turn leaps over the bent backs of the other players —***vt.***, ***vi.*** **-frogged'**, **-frog'ging** to leap or jump in or as in this way; skip (*over*)

leap year every fourth year, containing an extra day in February

learn (lurn) ***vt.***, ***vi.*** **learned** (lurnd) or [Chiefly Brit.] **learnt** (lurnt), **learn'ing** ⟦OE *leornian*⟧ **1** to get knowledge of (a subject) or skill in (an art, trade, etc.) by study, experience, etc. **2** to come to know; hear (*of* or *about*) **3** to memorize —**learn'er** ***n.***

learn·ed (lurn'id; *for 2* lurnd) ***adj.*** **1** having or showing much learning **2** acquired by study, experience, etc.

learn'ing ***n.*** **1** the acquiring of knowledge or skill **2** acquired knowledge or skill

learning disability any of several conditions, believed to involve the nervous system, that interfere with mastering a skill such as reading or writing —**learn'ing-dis·a'bled** ***adj.***

lease (lēs) ***n.*** ⟦< L *laxus*, loose⟧ a contract by which a landlord rents lands, buildings, etc. to a tenant for a specified time —***vt.*** **leased**, **leas'ing** to give or get by a lease —**leas'er** ***n.***

lease'hold' ***n.*** **1** the act of holding by lease **2** land, buildings, etc. held by lease

leash (lēsh) ***n.*** ⟦< L *laxus*, loose⟧ a cord, strap, etc. by which a dog or the like is held in check —***vt.*** to check or control as by a leash

least (lēst) ***adj.*** ⟦OE *læst*⟧ **1** *alt. superl. of* LITTLE **2** smallest or slightest in size, degree, etc. —***adv.*** **1** *superl. of* LITTLE **2** in the smallest degree —***n.*** the smallest in amount, importance, etc. —**at (the) least** **1** at the lowest **2** at any rate —**not in the least** not at all

least'wise' ***adv.*** [Inf.] at least; anyway: also [Chiefly Dial.] **least'ways'**

leath·er (leth'ər) ***n.*** ⟦< OE *lether-*⟧ animal skin prepared for use by removing the hair and tanning —***adj.*** of leather

leath'er·neck' ***n.*** ⟦< former leather-lined uniform collar⟧ [Slang] a U.S. Marine

leath'er·y ***adj.*** like leather; tough and flexible —**leath'er·i·ness** ***n.***

leave[1] (lēv) ***vt.*** **left**, **leav'ing** ⟦OE *læfan*, let remain⟧ **1** to allow to remain *[leave it open]* **2** to have remaining behind or after one **3** to bequeath **4** to go away from **5** to abandon **6** [Chiefly Dial.] to let *[leave us go]* —***vi.*** to go away or set out —**leave off** to stop —**leave out** to omit —**leav'er** ***n.***

leave[2] (lēv) ***n.*** ⟦OE *leaf*⟧ **1** permission **2** *a)* permission to be absent from duty *b)* the period for which this is granted —**take leave of** to say goodbye to —**take one's leave** to depart

leave[3] (lēv) ***vi.*** **leaved**, **leav'ing** to bear leaves; leaf

leav·en (lev'ən) ***n.*** ⟦< L *levare*, raise⟧ **1** LEAVENING (sense 1) **2** LEAVENING (sense 2) —***vt.*** **1** to make (dough) rise **2** to spread through, causing gradual change

leav'en·ing ***n.*** **1** a substance, as baking powder or yeast, used to make dough rise **2** a tempering or modifying quality or thing **3** a causing to be leavened

Leav·en·worth (lev'ən wurth') city in NE Kansas: pop 38,000: site of a federal prison

leave of absence permission to be absent from work or duty, esp. for a long time; also, the period for which this is granted

leaves (lēvz) ***n.*** *pl. of* LEAF

leave'-tak'ing ***n.*** a parting; farewell

leav·ings (lēv'iŋz) ***pl.n.*** leftovers, remnants, refuse, etc.

Leb·a·non (leb'ə nän') country in SW Asia, on the Mediterranean: 4,036 sq. mi.; pop. 2,760,000 —**Leb'a·nese'** (-nēz'), *pl.* **-nese'**, ***adj.***, ***n.***

lech·er (lech'ər) ***n.*** ⟦OFr *lechier*, live debauchedly⟧ a lewd, grossly sensual man —**lech'er·ous** ***adj.*** —**lech'er·y** ***n.***

lec·i·thin (les'i thin) ***n.*** ⟦< Gr *lekithos*, egg yolk⟧ a nitrogenous, fatty compound found in animal and plant cells: used in medicine, foods, etc.

lec·tern (lek'tərn) ***n.*** ⟦< L *legere*, to

read⟧ a reading stand

lec'ture (-chər) ***n.*** ⟦< L *legere*, read⟧ **1** an informative talk to a class, etc. **2** a lengthy scolding **—*vt.*, *vi.*** **-tured, -tur·ing 1** to give a lecture (to) **2** to scold — **lec'tur·er *n.***

led (led) ***vt.*, *vi.*** *pt. & pp. of* LEAD[1]

LED (el'ē'dē') ***n.*** ⟦*l*(*ight-*)*e*(*mitting*) *d*(*iode*)⟧ a semiconductor diode that emits light when voltage is applied: used as in lamps and digital watches

LECTERN

ledge (lej) ***n.*** ⟦ME *legge*⟧ **1** a shelf or shelflike projection **2** a projecting ridge of rocks

ledg·er (lej'ər) ***n.*** ⟦ME *legger*⟧ a book of final entry, in which a record of debits and credits is kept

lee (lē) ***n.*** ⟦OE *hleo*, shelter⟧ **1** shelter **2** *Naut.* the side or direction away from the wind **—*adj.*** of or on the side away from the wind

Lee (lē), **Rob·ert E**(**dward**) (räb'ərt) 1807-70; commander in chief of the Confederate army

leech (lēch) ***n.*** ⟦OE *lǣce*⟧ **1** a bloodsucking worm living in water and used, esp. formerly, to bleed patients **2** one who clings to another for personal advantage **—*vi.*** to cling (*onto*) thus

leek (lēk) ***n.*** ⟦OE *leac*⟧ a vegetable that resembles a thick green onion

leer (lir) ***n.*** ⟦OE *hleor*⟧ a sly, sidelong look showing lust, malicious triumph, etc. **—*vi.*** to look with a leer **—leer'ing·ly *adv.***

leer'y ***adj.*** **-i·er, -i·est** wary; suspicious

lees (lēz) ***pl.n.*** ⟦< ML *lia*⟧ dregs or sediment, as of wine

lee·ward (lē'wərd'; *naut.* lo͞o'ərd) ***adj.*** away from the wind **—*n.*** the side or direction away from the wind **—*adv.*** toward the lee

Lee·ward Islands (lē'wərd) N group of islands in the Lesser Antilles of the West Indies

lee·way (lē'wā') ***n.*** **1** the leeward drift of a ship or aircraft from its course **2** [Inf.] *a*) margin of time, money, etc. *b*) room for freedom of action

left[1] (left) ***adj.*** ⟦< OE *lyft*, weak⟧ **1** of or on the side that is toward the west when one faces north **2** closer to the left side of one who is facing the thing mentioned **—*n.*** **1** the left side **2** [*often* **L-**] *Politics* a liberal or radical position, party, etc.: often with *the* **—*adv.*** on or toward the left hand or side

left[2] (left) ***vt.*, *vi.*** *pt. & pp. of* LEAVE[1]

left'-hand' ***adj.*** **1** on or toward the left **2** of, for, or with the left hand

left'-hand'ed ***adj.*** **1** using the left hand more skillfully than the right **2** done with or made for use with the left hand **3** ambiguous or backhanded [*a left-handed* compliment] **—*adv.*** **1** with the left hand [to write *left-handed*] **2** in such a way that the bat, club, etc. swings rightward

left'ist ***n.*, *adj.*** liberal or radical

left'o'ver ***n.*** **1** something remaining unused, etc. **2** [*usually pl.*] food left from a previous meal **—*adj.*** remaining unused, uneaten, etc.

left wing the more liberal or radical section of a political party, group, etc. **—left'-wing' *adj.*** **—left'-wing'er *n.***

left'y ***n.***, *pl.* **-ies** [Slang] a left-handed person

leg (leg) ***n.*** ⟦ON *leggr*⟧ **1** one of the parts of the body by means of which humans and animals stand and walk **2** the part of a garment covering the leg **3** anything like a leg in shape or use **4** a stage, as of a trip **—*vi.*** **legged, leg'ging** [Inf.] to walk or run: chiefly in the phrase **leg it**

leg·a·cy (leg'ə sē) ***n.***, *pl.* **-cies** ⟦ult. < L *lex*, law⟧ **1** money or property left to someone by a will **2** anything handed down as from an ancestor

le·gal (lē'gəl) ***adj.*** ⟦< L *lex*, law⟧ **1** of or based upon law **2** permitted by law **3** of or for lawyers **—le'gal·ly *adv.***

le'gal·ese' (-ēz') ***n.*** the special language of legal forms, etc., often considered incomprehensible

legal holiday a holiday set by law

le'gal·ism' ***n.*** strict or too strict adherence to the law **—le'gal·is'tic *adj.***

le·gal·i·ty (li gal'i tē) ***n.***, *pl.* **-ties** quality, condition, or instance of being legal or lawful

le·gal·ize (lē'gəl īz') ***vt.*** **-ized', -iz'ing** to make legal or lawful **—le'gal·i·za'tion *n.***

legal pad a pad of lined writing paper, 8 ½ by 13 or 14 inches

legal tender money acceptable by law in payment of an obligation

leg·ate (leg'it) ***n.*** ⟦< L *lex*, law⟧ an envoy or ambassador

leg·a·tee (leg'ə tē') ***n.*** one to whom a legacy is bequeathed

le·ga·tion (li gā'shən) ***n.*** **1** a diplomatic minister and staff collectively **2** the headquarters of such a group

le·ga·to (li gät'ō) ***adj.*, *adv.*** ⟦< L *ligare*, to tie⟧ *Music* in a smooth, even style, with no breaks between notes: also written ***legato***

leg·end (lej'ənd) ***n.*** ⟦< L *legere*, read⟧ **1** a story or body of stories handed down for generations and popularly believed to have a historical basis **2** a notable person or the stories told about his or her exploits **3** an inscription on a coin, etc. **4** a title, key, etc. accompanying an illustration or map

leg·end·ar·y (lej'ən der'ē) ***adj.*** **1** of, based on, or presented in legends **2** famous or remarkable

leg·er·de·main (lej'ər di mān') ***n.*** ⟦< Fr *leger de main*, light of hand⟧ **1** sleight of hand **2** trickery

-leg·ged (leg'id, legd) *combining form* having (a specified number or kind of) legs [short-*legged*]

leg·ging (leg′iŋ, -in) ***n.*** **1** a covering for the lower leg **2** [*pl.*] a child's outer garment with legs **3** [*pl.*] a garment like tights but without feet

leg·gy (leg′ē) ***adj.*** **-gi·er, -gi·est 1** having long legs **2** [Inf.] having long, spindly stems

leg·horn (leg′hôrn′, -ərn) ***n.*** ⟦after *Leghorn*, It seaport⟧ [*sometimes* **L-**] any of a breed of small chicken

leg·i·ble (lej′ə bəl) ***adj.*** ⟦< L *legere*, read⟧ that can be read —**leg′i·bil′i·ty** ***n.*** —**leg′i·bly** ***adv.***

le·gion (lē′jən) ***n.*** ⟦< L *legere*, choose⟧ **1** a large group of soldiers; army **2** a large number; multitude —**le′gion·naire′** (-jə ner′) ***n.***

leg·is·late (lej′is lāt′) ***vi.*** **-lat′ed, -lat′ing** ⟦see fol.⟧ to make or pass a law or laws —***vt.*** to cause to be, go, etc. by making laws —**leg′is·la′tor** ***n.***

leg′is·la′tion ***n.*** ⟦< L *lex*, law + *latio*, a bringing⟧ **1** the making of laws **2** the law or laws made

leg′is·la′tive ***adj.*** **1** of legislation or a legislature **2** having the power to make laws

leg′is·la′ture (-chər) ***n.*** a body of persons given the power to make laws

le·git·i·mate (lə jit′ə mət; *for v.*, -māt′) ***adj.*** ⟦< L *lex*, law⟧ **1** born of parents married to each other **2** lawful **3** *a*) reasonable *b*) justifiable **4** conforming to accepted rules, standards, etc. **5** of stage plays, as distinguished from films, vaudeville, etc. —***vt.*** **-mat′ed, -mat′ing** LEGITIMIZE —**le·git′i·ma·cy** (-mə sē) ***n.*** —**le·git′i·mate·ly** ***adv.***

le·git′i·ma·tize′ (-mə tīz′) ***vt.*** **-tized′, -tiz′ing** LEGITIMIZE

le·git′i·mize′ (-mīz′) ***vt.*** **-mized′, -miz′ing** to make or declare legitimate —**le·git′i·mi·za′tion** ***n.***

leg·man (leg′man′) ***n.***, *pl.* **-men′** (-mən′) **1** a news reporter who transmits information from the scene **2** an assistant who does routine tasks outside the office

leg′room′ ***n.*** adequate space for the legs while seated, as in a car

leg·ume (leg′yo͞om′, li gyo͞om′) ***n.*** ⟦< L *legere*, gather⟧ **1** any of an order of plants having seeds growing in pods, including peas, beans, etc. **2** the pod or seed of such a plant —**le·gu·mi·nous** (lə gyo͞o′mə nəs) ***adj.***

leg′work′ ***n.*** [Inf.] necessary, routine work, typically involving walking, as part of a job

lei (lā, lā′ē) ***n.***, *pl.* **leis** ⟦Haw⟧ in Hawaii, a garland of flowers, generally worn about the neck

Leip·zig (līp′sig) city in E Germany: pop. 494,000

lei·sure (lē′zhər, lezh′ər) ***n.*** ⟦< L *licere*, be permitted⟧ free time during which one may indulge in rest, recreation, etc. —***adj.*** **1** free and unoccupied **2** done or used during one's leisure

lei′sure·ly ***adj.*** without haste; slow —***adv.*** in an unhurried manner

leit·mo·tif or **leit·mo·tiv** (līt′mō tēf′) ***n.*** ⟦Ger *leitmotiv* < *leiten*, to guide + *motiv*, motive⟧ a dominant theme, as in a musical composition

lem·ming (lem′iŋ) ***n.*** ⟦< ON *læmingi*⟧ a small arctic rodent with a short tail

lem·on (lem′ən) ***n.*** ⟦< Pers *līmūn*⟧ **1** a small, sour, yellow citrus fruit **2** the spiny, semitropical tree that it grows on **3** [Slang] something that is defective —***adj.*** yellow

lem′on·ade′ (-ād′) ***n.*** a drink made of lemon juice, sugar, and water

le·mur (lē′mər) ***n.*** ⟦< L *lemures*, ghosts⟧ a small, tree-dwelling primate with large eyes

lend (lend) ***vt.*** **lent, lend′ing** ⟦< OE *læn*, a loan⟧ **1** to let another use or have (a thing) temporarily **2** to let out (money) at interest **3** to give; impart —***vi.*** to make loans —**lend itself** (or **oneself**) **to** to be useful for or adapted to —**lend′er** ***n.***

length (leŋkth) ***n.*** ⟦< OE *lang*, long⟧ **1** the distance from end to end of a thing **2** extent in space or time **3** a long stretch or extent **4** a piece of a certain length —**at length 1** finally **2** for a long time or in great detail

length′en ***vt., vi.*** to make or become longer

length′wise′ ***adv., adj.*** in the direction of the length: also **length′ways′**

length′y ***adj.*** **-i·er, -i·est** long; esp., too long —**length′i·ly** ***adv.***

le·ni·ent (lēn′yənt, lē′nē ənt) ***adj.*** ⟦< L *lenis*, soft⟧ not harsh or severe; merciful —**le′ni·en·cy** or **le′ni·ence** ***n.*** —**le′ni·ent·ly** ***adv.***

Len·in (len′in), **V**(**ladimir**) **I**(**lyich**) 1870-1924; Russ. leader of the Communist revolution of 1917

Len′in·grad′ (-grad′) *name* (1924-91) *for* ST. PETERSBURG (Russia)

len·i·tive (len′ə tiv) ***adj.*** ⟦< L *lenire*, to soften⟧ lessening pain or distress

lens (lenz) ***n.*** ⟦L, lentil: < its shape⟧ **1** a curved piece of glass, plastic, etc. for bringing together or spreading rays of light passing through it: used in optical instruments to form an image **2** a similar transparent part of the eye: it focuses light rays upon the retina **3** any device used to focus microwaves, sound waves, etc.

lent (lent) ***vt., vi.*** *pt. & pp. of* LEND

Lent (lent) ***n.*** ⟦OE *lengten*, the spring⟧ *Christianity* the forty weekdays of fasting and penitence from Ash Wednesday to Easter —**Lent′en** or **lent′en** ***adj.***

len·til (lent′'l) ***n.*** ⟦< L *lens*⟧ **1** a kind of legume, with small, edible seeds **2** this seed

Le·o (lē′ō) ***n.*** ⟦L, lion⟧ the fifth sign of the zodiac

le·o·nine (lē′ə nīn′) ***adj.*** ⟦< L *leo*, lion⟧ of or like a lion

leop·ard (lep′ərd) ***n.*** ⟦< Gr *leōn*, lion + *pardos*, panther⟧ any of various large, ferocious cats, including the jaguar; esp., one with a black-spotted, tawny coat, found in Africa and Asia

le·o·tard (lē′ə tärd′) ***n.*** ⟦after J. *Léotard*, 19th-c. Fr aerial performer⟧ a tightfitting garment for acrobats, dancers, etc.

lep·er (lep′ər) ***n.*** ⟦< Gr *lepros*, scaly⟧ a person having leprosy

lep·re·chaun (lep′rə kôn′, -kän′) ***n.*** ⟦< Old Ir *lu*, little + *corp*, body⟧ *Ir. Folklore* a fairy who can reveal hidden treasure

lep·ro·sy (lep′rə sē) ***n.*** ⟦see LEPER⟧ a progressive infectious disease of the skin, flesh, nerves, etc., characterized by ulcers, white scaly scabs, deformities, etc. —**lep′rous** ***adj.***

lept (lept) ***vi.***, ***vt.*** *alt. pt. of* LEAP

lep·ton (lep′tän′) ***n.*** ⟦< Gr *leptos*, thin⟧ any of certain atomic particles, as the electron or neutrino

les·bi·an (lez′bē ən) ***n.*** ⟦after *Lesbos*, Gr. island home of the poetess Sappho⟧ a homosexual woman —**les′bi·an·ism′** ***n.***

lèse-ma·jest·é (lez′ma′zhes tā′, -maj′is tē) ***n.*** ⟦Fr < L *laesa majestas*, injured majesty⟧ **1** a crime or offense against the sovereign **2** any lack of proper respect as toward one in authority

le·sion (lē′zhən) ***n.*** ⟦< L *laedere*, to harm⟧ an injury of an organ or tissue resulting in impairment of function

Le·sot·ho (le sōō′tōō) country in SE Africa, surrounded by South Africa: 11,720 sq. mi.; pop. 1,578,000

less (les) ***adj.*** ⟦OE *læs(sa)*⟧ **1** *alt. compar. of* LITTLE **2** not so much **3** fewer —***adv.*** **1** *compar. of* LITTLE **2** to a smaller extent —***n.*** a smaller amount —***prep.*** minus —**less and less** decreasingly

-less (lis, ləs) ⟦OE *leas*, free⟧ *suffix* **1** without **2** not able to **3** not able to be ___ed

les·see (les ē′) ***n.*** ⟦see LEASE⟧ one to whom a lease is given; tenant

less′en ***vt.***, ***vi.*** to make or become less; decrease

less′er ***adj.*** **1** *alt. compar. of* LITTLE **2** smaller, less, or less important

les·son (les′ən) ***n.*** ⟦< L *legere*, to read⟧ **1** an exercise for a student to learn **2** something learned for one's safety, etc. **3** [*pl.*] course of instruction **4** a selection from the Bible read as part of a religious service

les·sor (les′ôr′) ***n.*** ⟦see LEASE⟧ one who gives a lease; landlord

lest (lest) ***conj.*** ⟦< OE *thy læs the*, lit., by the less that⟧ for fear that

let[1] (let) ***vt.*** **let, let′ting** ⟦OE *lætan*, leave behind⟧ **1** to leave: now only in **let alone, let be** **2** *a*) to rent *b*) to assign (a contract) **3** to cause to escape *[to let blood]* **4** to allow; permit Also used as an auxiliary in commands or suggestions *[let us go]* —***vi.*** to be rented *[a house to let]* —**let down** **1** to lower **2** to slow up **3** to disappoint —**let off** **1** to give forth **2** to deal leniently with —**let on** [Inf.] **1** to indicate one's awareness **2** to pretend —**let out** **1** to release **2** to rent out **3** to make a garment larger —**let up** **1** to relax **2** to cease

let[2] (let) ***n.*** ⟦< OE *lettan*, make late⟧ *Law* an obstacle: in **without let or hindrance**

-let (lit, lət) ⟦Fr *-el* + *-et*, dim. suffixes⟧ *suffix* small *[piglet]*

let′down′ ***n.*** **1** a slowing up **2** a disappointment

le·thal (lē′thəl) ***adj.*** ⟦< L *letum*, death⟧ causing death; fatal

leth·ar·gy (leth′ər jē) ***n.***, *pl.* **-gies** ⟦< Gr *lēthē*, oblivion + *argos*, idle⟧ **1** an abnormal drowsiness **2** sluggishness, apathy, etc. —**le·thar·gic** (li thär′jik) ***adj.*** —**le·thar′gi·cal·ly** ***adv.***

let's (lets) *contr.* let us

let·ter (let′ər) ***n.*** ⟦< L *littera*⟧ **1** any character in an alphabet **2** a written or printed message, usually sent by mail **3** [*pl.*] *a*) literature *b*) learning; knowledge **4** the literal meaning —***vt.*** to mark with letters —**let′ter·er** ***n.***

letter carrier a postal employee who delivers mail

let′ter·head′ ***n.*** the name, address, etc. as a heading on stationery

let′ter·ing ***n.*** the act of making or inscribing letters, or such letters

let′ter-per′fect ***adj.*** entirely correct

let·tuce (let′əs) ***n.*** ⟦< L *lac*, milk⟧ **1** a plant with crisp, green leaves **2** the leaves, much used for salads

let·up (let′up′) ***n.*** [Inf.] **1** a slackening **2** a stop or pause

leu·ke·mi·a (lōō kē′mē ə) ***n.*** ⟦see fol. & -EMIA⟧ a disease characterized by an abnormal increase in the number of leukocytes: also sp. **leu·kae′mi·a**

leu·ko·cyte (lōō′kō sīt′, -kə-) ***n.*** ⟦< Gr *leukos*, white + *kytos*, hollow⟧ a colorless cell in the blood, etc. that destroys disease-causing organisms; white blood cell

lev·ee (lev′ē) ***n.*** ⟦ult. < L *levare*, to raise⟧ an embankment to prevent a river from flooding bordering land

lev·el (lev′əl) ***n.*** ⟦< L *libra*, a balance⟧ **1** an instrument for determining an even horizontal plane **2** a horizontal plane or line *[sea level]* **3** a horizontal area **4** normal position with reference to height *[water seeks its level]* **5** position in a scale of values *[income level]* —***adj.*** **1** perfectly flat and even **2** not sloping **3** even in height (*with*) **4** equal in importance, advancement, quality, etc. **5** calm or steady —***vt.***, ***vi.*** **-eled** or **-elled**, **-el·ing** or **-el·ling** **1** to make or become level **2** to demolish **3** to aim (a gun, etc.) —**level with** [Slang] to be honest with —**lev′el·er** or **lev′el·ler** ***n.***

lev′el·head′ed ***adj.*** having an even temper and sound judgment

LEVER

lev·er (lev′ər, lē′vər) ***n.*** ⟦< L *levare*, to raise⟧ **1** a bar used as a pry **2** a means to an end **3** a device consisting of a bar turning about a fixed point, using force at a second point to lift a weight at a third

lev′er·age (-ij) ***n.*** **1** the action or mechanical power of a lever **2** means of accomplishing something —***vt.***

-aged, **-ag·ing** *Finance* to speculate in (a business venture) with borrowed funds

le·vi·a·than (lə vī′ə thən) ***n.*** ⟦< Heb *liwyāthān*⟧ **1** *Bible* a sea monster **2** anything huge

Le·vi's (lē′vīz′) ⟦after *Levi* Strauss, U.S. manufacturer⟧ *trademark for* trousers of heavy denim —***pl.n.*** such trousers: also written **Le′vis** or **le′vis**

lev·i·ta·tion (lev′ə tā′shən) ***n.*** ⟦< L *levis*, light⟧ the illusion of raising a body in the air with no support —**lev′i·tate′**, **-tat′ed**, **-tat′ing**, ***vt.***, ***vi.***

Le·vit·i·cus (lə vit′i kəs) ***n.*** the third book of the Pentateuch

Lev·it·town (lev′it toun′) city in SE New York: post-WWII planned community of mass-produced houses: pop. 53,000

lev·i·ty (lev′i tē) ***n.***, *pl.* **-ties** ⟦< L *levis*, light⟧ gaiety, esp. improper gaiety; frivolity

lev·y (lev′ē) ***n.***, *pl.* **lev′ies** ⟦< L *levare*, to raise⟧ **1** an imposing and collecting of a tax, fine, etc. **2** the amount imposed **3** compulsory enlistment for military service **4** a group so enlisted —***vt.*** **-ied**, **-y·ing** **1** to impose (a tax, fine, etc.) **2** to enlist (troops) **3** to wage (war)

lewd (lo͞od) ***adj.*** ⟦OE *læwede*, unlearned⟧ indecent; lustful; obscene —**lewd′ly** ***adv.*** —**lewd′ness** ***n.***

lex·i·cog·ra·phy (lek′sə käg′rə fē) ***n.*** ⟦see fol. & -GRAPHY⟧ the act, art, or work of writing a dictionary —**lex′i·cog′ra·pher** ***n.***

lex·i·con (lek′si kän′) ***n.*** ⟦< Gr *lexis*, word⟧ **1** a dictionary **2** a special vocabulary —**lex′i·cal** ***adj.***

Lex·ing·ton (lek′siŋ tən) city in NC Kentucky: with the county in which it is located, pop. 225,000

lg *abbrev.* large

Li *Chem. symbol for* lithium

li·a·bil·i·ty (lī′ə bil′ə tē) ***n.***, *pl.* **-ties** **1** the state of being liable **2** anything for which a person is liable **3** a debt of a person or business **4** something that works to one's disadvantage

li·a·ble (lī′ə bəl) ***adj.*** ⟦< L *ligare*, bind⟧ **1** legally bound or responsible **2** subject to *[liable* to heart attacks*]* **3** likely *to [liable* to get hurt*]*

li·ai·son (lē ā′zän′, -zən) ***n.*** ⟦< L *ligare*, bind⟧ **1** a linking up, as of units of a military force **2** an illicit love affair

li·ar (lī′ər) ***n.*** one who tells lies

lib (lib) ***n.*** [Inf.] *short for* LIBERATION

li·ba·tion (lī bā′shən) ***n.*** ⟦< L *libare*, pour out⟧ **1** the ritual of pouring out wine or oil in honor of a god **2** this liquid **3** an alcoholic drink

li·bel (lī′bəl) ***n.*** ⟦< L *liber*, book⟧ **1** any written or printed matter tending to injure a person's reputation unjustly **2** the act or crime of publishing such a thing —***vt.*** **-beled** or **-belled**, **-bel·ing** or **-bel·ling** to make a libel against —**li′bel·er** or **li′bel·ler** ***n.*** —**li′bel·ous** or **li′bel·lous** ***adj.***

lib·er·al (lib′ər əl) ***adj.*** ⟦< L *liber*, free⟧ **1** generous **2** ample; abundant **3** not literal or strict **4** tolerant; broad-minded **5** favoring reform or progress —***n.*** one who favors reform or progress —**lib′er·al·ism′** ***n.*** —**lib′er·al·ly** ***adv.*** —**lib′er·al·ness** ***n.***

liberal arts literature, languages, history, etc. as courses or a course of study

lib′er·al′i·ty (-al′i tē) ***n.***, *pl.* **-ties** **1** generosity **2** broad-mindedness

lib′er·al·ize′ (-əl īz′) ***vt.***, ***vi.*** **-ized′**, **-iz′ing** to make or become liberal —**lib′er·al·i·za′tion** ***n.***

lib·er·ate (lib′ər āt′) ***vt.*** **-at′ed**, **-at′ing** ⟦< L *liber*, free⟧ to release from slavery, oppression, enemy occupation, etc. —**lib′er·a′tion** ***n.*** —**lib′er·a′tor** ***n.***

Li·ber·i·a (lī bir′ē ə) country on the W coast of Africa: founded (1821) as settlement for freed U.S. slaves: 38,250 sq. mi.; pop. 2,102,000 —**Li·ber′i·an** ***adj.***, ***n.***

lib·er·tar·i·an (lib′ər ter′ē ən) ***n.*** an advocate of full individual freedom of thought and action

lib·er·tine (lib′ər tēn′) ***n.*** ⟦< L *liber*, free⟧ one who is sexually promiscuous —***adj.*** licentious

lib·er·ty (lib′ər tē) ***n.***, *pl.* **-ties** ⟦< L *liber*, free⟧ **1** freedom from slavery, captivity, etc. **2** a particular right, freedom, etc. **3** a too free or impertinent action or attitude **4** permission given to a sailor to go ashore See also CIVIL LIBERTIES —**at liberty** **1** not confined **2** permitted (to do or say something) **3** not busy or in use —**take liberties** **1** to be too familiar or impertinent **2** to deal inaccurately (*with* facts, data, etc.)

li·bid·i·nous (li bid′′n əs) ***adj.*** ⟦see fol.⟧ lustful; lascivious

li·bi·do (li bē′dō) ***n.*** ⟦< L, pleasure⟧ **1** the sexual urge **2** *Psychoanalysis* psychic energy; specif., that comprising the positive, loving instincts

Li·bra (lē′brə) ***n.*** ⟦L, balance, scales⟧ the seventh sign of the zodiac

li·brar·i·an (lī brer′ē ən) ***n.*** one in charge of a library or trained in library science

li·brar·y (lī′brer′ē) ***n.***, *pl.* **-ies** ⟦< L *liber*, book⟧ **1** a collection of books, etc. **2** a room or building for, or an institution in charge of, such a collection

li·bret·to (li bret′ō) ***n.***, *pl.* **-tos** or **-ti** (-ē) ⟦It < L *liber*, book⟧ the words, or text, of an opera, oratorio, etc. —**li·bret′tist** ***n.***

Lib·y·a (lib′ē ə) country in N Africa, on the Mediterranean: 679,358 sq. mi.; pop. 3,637,000 —**Lib′y·an** ***adj.***, ***n.***

lice (līs) ***n.*** *pl. of* LOUSE

li·cense (lī′səns) ***n.*** ⟦< L *licere*, be permitted⟧ **1** formal or legal permission to do something specified **2** a document, etc. indicating such permission **3** freedom to deviate from rule, practice, etc. *[*poetic *license]* **4** excessive freedom, constituting an abuse of liberty Brit. sp. **li′cence** —***vt.*** **-censed**, **-cens·ing** to permit formally

li·cen·see (lī′səns ē′) ***n.*** a person to whom a license is granted

li·cen·ti·ate (lī sen′shē it, -āt′) ***n.*** a person having a professional license

li·cen·tious (lī sen′shəs) ***adj.*** ⟦see LICENSE⟧ sexually unrestrained; lascivious —**li·cen′tious·ness** ***n.***

li·chen (lī′kən) ***n.*** ⟦< Gr *leichein*, to lick⟧ a plant resembling moss but actually a combination of fungus and algae, growing in patches on rock, wood, soil, etc.

lic·it (lis′it) ***adj.*** ⟦< L *licitus*, permitted⟧ lawful —**lic′it·ly *adv.***

lick (lik) ***vt.*** ⟦OE *liccian*⟧ **1** to pass the tongue over **2** to pass lightly over like a tongue **3** [Inf.] *a*) to thrash *b*) to vanquish —***vi.*** to move lightly, as a flame —***n.*** **1** a licking with the tongue **2** a small quantity **3** *short for* SALT LICK **4** [Inf.] a sharp blow —**lick up** to consume as by licking

lic·o·rice (lik′ə rish) ***n.*** ⟦< Gr *glykys*, sweet + *rhiza*, root⟧ **1** a black flavoring extract made from the root of a European plant **2** candy flavored with this extract or in imitation of it

lid (lid) ***n.*** ⟦OE *hlid*⟧ **1** a movable cover, as for a box, pot, etc. **2** *short for* EYELID **3** [Inf.] a restraint

lid·ded (lid′id) ***adj.*** **1** having a lid **2** having (a specified kind of) eyelids *[*heavy-*lidded]*

lie[1] (lī) ***vi.*** **lay, lain, ly′ing** ⟦OE *licgan*⟧ **1** to be or put oneself in a reclining or horizontal position **2** to rest on a support in a horizontal position **3** to be in a specified condition **4** to be situated *[*Canada *lies* to the north*]* **5** to extend **6** to be or be found —***n.*** the way in which something is situated; lay

lie[2] (lī) ***vi.*** **lied, ly′ing** ⟦OE *leogan*⟧ to make a statement that one knows is false —***vt.*** to bring, put, accomplish, etc. by lying *[*to *lie* his way into office*]* —***n.*** a false statement made with intent to deceive

Lieb·frau·milch (lēb′frou milk′) ***n.*** ⟦Ger⟧ a white wine

Liech·ten·stein (lik′tən stīn′) country between Switzerland & Austria: 62 sq. mi.; pop. 29,000

lie detector a polygraph used on persons suspected of lying

lief (lēf) ***adv.*** ⟦< OE *leof*, dear⟧ willingly; gladly: only in **would** (or **had**) **as lief**

liege (lēj) ***adj.*** ⟦OFr⟧ loyal; faithful —***n.*** *Feudal Law* **1** a lord or sovereign **2** a subject or vassal

li·en (lēn, lē′ən) ***n.*** ⟦Fr < L *ligare*, to bind⟧ a legal claim on another's property as security for the payment of a debt

lieu (lo͞o) ***n.*** ⟦< L *locus*⟧ place: chiefly in **in lieu of**, instead of

Lieut *abbrev.* Lieutenant

lieu·ten·ant (lo͞o ten′ənt) ***n.*** ⟦< Fr *lieu*, place + *tenant*, holding⟧ **1** one who acts for a superior **2** *U.S. Mil.* an officer ranking below a captain: see FIRST LIEUTENANT, SECOND LIEUTENANT **3** *U.S. Navy* an officer ranking just above a lieutenant junior grade —**lieu·ten′an·cy *n.***

lieutenant colonel *U.S. Mil.* an officer ranking just above a major

lieutenant commander *U.S. Navy* an officer ranking just above a lieutenant

lieutenant general *U.S. Mil.* an officer ranking just above a major general

lieutenant governor an elected official of a U.S. state who ranks below and substitutes for the governor

lieutenant junior grade *U.S. Navy* an officer ranking just above an ensign

life (līf) ***n.**, pl.* **lives** ⟦OE *lif*⟧ **1** that property of plants and animals (ending at death) which makes it possible for them to take in food, get energy from it, grow, etc. **2** the state of having this property **3** a human being *[*100 *lives* were lost*]* **4** living things collectively *[*plant *life]* **5** the time a person or thing is alive or exists **6** one's manner of living *[*a *life* of ease*]* **7** the people and activities of a given time, place, etc. *[*military *life]* **8** *a*) one's animate existence *b*) a biography **9** the source of liveliness *[*the *life* of the party*]* **10** vigor; liveliness

life belt a life preserver in belt form

life′blood′ *n.* **1** the blood necessary to life **2** a vital element

life′boat′ *n.* one of the small boats carried by a ship for use in an emergency

life′-form′ *n.* a particular type of organism, often one that is unusual or newly found

life′guard′ *n.* an expert swimmer employed as at a beach to prevent drownings

life insurance insurance for a stipulated sum paid at the death of the insured

LIFE JACKET

life jacket (or **vest**) a life preserver that is like a sleeveless jacket or vest

life′less *adj.* **1** without life; specif., *a*) inanimate *b*) dead **2** dull

life′like′ *adj.* resembling real life or a real person or thing

life′line′ *n.* **1** a rope or line for saving life, as one thrown to a person in the water **2** a very important commercial route

life′long′ *adj.* lasting or not changing during one's whole life

life net a strong net used as by firefighters to catch people jumping from a burning building

life′-or-death′ *adj.* **1** having death as a possible result *[*a *life-or-death* struggle*]* **2** crucial *[*a *life-or-death* business decision*]*

life preserver a buoyant device for saving a person from drowning by keeping the body afloat

lif′er *n.* [Slang] a person sentenced to prison for life

life raft a small, inflatable raft for emergency use at sea

life′sav′er *n.* **1** a lifeguard **2** [Inf.] a help in time of need

life science a science, as botany or zoology, dealing with organisms and their life processes

life′-size′ *adj.* as big as the person or thing represented *[*a *life-size* portrait*]*:

also **life'-sized'**

life'style' ***n.*** an individual's way of living

life'-sup·port' ***adj.*** *Med.* for providing support needed to maintain life *[a life-support* system*]*

life'time' ***n.*** **1** the period of time that someone lives or that a thing lasts **2** a very long time

life'work' ***n.*** the work to which a person's life is devoted

lift (lift) ***vt.*** ⟦< ON *lopt*, air⟧ **1** to bring up to a higher position; raise **2** to raise in rank, condition, etc.; exalt **3** to pay off (a mortgage, debt, etc.) **4** to end (a blockade, etc.) **5** [Slang] to steal **—*vi.*** **1** to exert strength in raising something **2** to rise; go up **—*n.*** **1** a lifting or rising **2** the distance something is lifted **3** lifting power or influence **4** elevation of mood **5** a ride in the direction one is going **6** help of any kind **7** *a)* [Brit.] ELEVATOR *b)* SKI LIFT

lift'off' ***n.*** **1** the initial vertical takeoff of a rocket, helicopter, etc. **2** the time this occurs

lig·a·ment (lig'ə mənt) ***n.*** ⟦< L *ligare*, bind⟧ a band of tissue connecting bones or holding organs in place

lig·a·ture (lig'ə chər) ***n.*** ⟦< L *ligare*, bind⟧ **1** a tying or binding together **2** a tie, bond, etc. **3** two or more letters united, as *æ, th* **4** *Surgery* a thread used to tie up an artery, etc.

light[1] (līt) ***n.*** ⟦OE *leoht*⟧ **1** *a)* the form of radiant energy acting on the retina of the eye to make sight possible *b)* ultraviolet or infrared radiation **2** brightness; illumination **3** h source of light, as the sun, a lamp, etc. **4** daylight **5** a thing used to ignite something **6** a window or windowpane **7** knowledge; enlightenment **8** public view *[*to bring new facts to *light]* **9** aspect *[*viewed in another *light]* **—*adj.*** **1** having light; bright **2** pale in color; fair **—*adv.*** palely *[*a *light* blue color*]* **—*vt.* light'ed** or **lit, light'ing** **1** to ignite *[*to *light* a bonfire*]* **2** to cause to give off light **3** to furnish with light **4** to brighten; animate **—*vi.*** **1** to catch fire **2** to be lighted: usually with *up* **—in the light of** considering **—see the light (of day)** **1** to come into existence **2** to come to public view **3** to understand

light[2] (līt) ***adj.*** ⟦OE *leoht*⟧ **1** having little weight; not heavy, esp. for its size **2** less than usual in weight, amount, force, etc. *[*a *light* blow*]* **3** not serious or profound **4** easy to bear *[*a *light* tax*]* **5** easy to do *[light* work*]* **6** merry; happy **7** dizzy; giddy **8** containing fewer calories **9** moderate *[*a *light* meal*]* **10** moving with ease *[light* on one's feet*]* **11** producing small products *[light* industry*]* **—*adv.*** LIGHTLY **—*vi.* light'ed** or **lit, light'ing** **1** to come to rest after traveling through the air **2** to come or happen (*on* or *upon*) **—light into** [Inf.] to attack **—light out** [Inf.] to depart suddenly **—make light of** to treat as unimportant

light'en[1] ***vt., vi.*** **1** to make or become light or brighter **2** to shine; flash

light'en[2] ***vt., vi.*** **1** to make or become lighter in weight **2** to make or become more cheerful

light'er[1] ***n.*** a person or thing that starts something burning

light'er[2] ***n.*** ⟦< MDu *licht*, LIGHT[2]⟧ a large barge used to load or unload ships anchored in a harbor

light'-fin'gered ***adj.*** **1** skillful at stealing **2** likely to steal

light'-foot'ed ***adj.*** stepping lightly and gracefully

light'head'ed ***adj.*** **1** giddy; dizzy **2** flighty; frivolous

light'heart'ed ***adj.*** free from care; cheerful **—light'heart'ed·ly *adv.* —light'heart'ed·ness *n.***

light heavyweight a boxer with a maximum weight of 175 lb.

light'house' ***n.*** a tower with a very bright light to guide ships at night

light'ing ***n.*** the act or manner of giving light, or illuminating

light'ly ***adv.*** **1** with little weight or pressure; gently **2** to a small degree or amount **3** nimbly; deftly **4** cheerfully **5** with indifference

light meter an instrument to measure intensity of light, used in photography

light'-mind'ed ***adj.*** silly; frivolous

light'ness[1] ***n.*** **1** the amount of light; brightness **2** paleness in color

light'ness[2] ***n.*** **1** a being light, not heavy **2** mildness, nimbleness, cheerfulness, etc.

light'ning (-niŋ) ***n.*** a flash of light in the sky caused by the discharge of atmospheric electricity

lightning bug FIREFLY

lightning rod a metal rod placed high on a building and grounded to divert lightning from the structure

light opera OPERETTA

light'weight' ***n.*** a boxer with a maximum weight of 135 lb. **—*adj.*** light in weight

light'-year' ***n.*** a unit of distance equal to the distance light travels in one year, *c.* 6 trillion miles

lig·nite (lig'nīt') ***n.*** ⟦< L *lignum*, wood⟧ a soft coal, brownish-black in color and retaining the texture of the original wood

lik·a·ble (līk'ə bəl) ***adj.*** pleasant, genial, etc.: also **like'a·ble —lik'a·ble·ness** or **lik'a·bil'i·ty *n.***

like[1] (līk) ***adj.*** ⟦OE *gelic*⟧ having the same characteristics; similar; equal **—*adv.*** [Inf.] likely *[like* as not, he'll go*]* **—*prep.*** **1** similar to **2** similarly to *[*to sing *like* a bird*]* **3** characteristic of *[*not *like* her to cry*]* **4** in the mood for *[*to feel *like* sleeping*]* **5** indicative of *[*it looks *like* rain*]* **6** as for example *[*fruit, *like* pears and plums*]* **—*conj.*** [Inf.] **1** as *[*it's just *like* he said*]* **2** as if *[*it looks *like* he's late*]* **—*n.*** an equal or counterpart *[*I've never met her *like]* **—more like it** [Inf.] closer to being what is wanted **—nothing like** not at all like **—something like** almost like **—the like** others of the same kind **—the like** (or **likes**) **of** [Inf.] any person or thing like

like[2] (līk) ***vi.*** **liked, lik'ing** ⟦OE *lician*⟧ to be inclined [do as you *like]* —***vt.*** **1** to be pleased with; enjoy **2** to wish [I'd *like* to go] —***n.*** [*pl.*] preferences or tastes —**lik'er *n.***

-like (līk) *suffix* like, characteristic of [*homelike*, bull-*like*]

like·li·hood (līk'lē hood') ***n.*** a being likely to happen; probability

like·ly (līk'lē) ***adj.*** **-li·er, -li·est** ⟦OE *geliclic*⟧ **1** credible [a *likely* cause] **2** reasonably to be expected [*likely* to rain] **3** suitable [a *likely* place to swim] —***adv.*** probably [she'll *likely* go]

like'-mind'ed ***adj.*** having the same ideas, plans, tastes, etc. —**like'-mind'ed·ness *n.***

lik·en (līk'ən) ***vt.*** to compare

like'ness *n.* **1** a being like **2** (the same) form **3** a copy, portrait, etc.

like'wise' *adv.* ⟦< *in like wise*⟧ **1** in the same manner **2** also; too

lik·ing (līk'iŋ) ***n.*** **1** fondness; affection **2** preference; taste; pleasure

li·lac (lī'lək, -läk', -lak') ***n.*** ⟦ult. < Pers *līlak*, bluish⟧ **1** a shrub with large clusters of tiny, fragrant flowers **2** pale purple —***adj.*** pale-purple

Lil·li·pu·tian (lil'ə pyōō'shən) ***adj.*** ⟦after *Lilliput*, place in J. Swift's *Gulliver's Travels*⟧ **1** tiny **2** petty

lilt (lilt) ***n.*** ⟦ME *lilten*, to sound⟧ a light, swingy rhythm or tune —**lilt'ing *adj.***

lil·y (lil'ē) ***n.***, *pl.* **lil'ies** ⟦< L *lilium*⟧ **1** a plant grown from a bulb and having typically trumpet-shaped flowers **2** its flower **3** any similar plant, as the waterlily —***adj.*** like a lily, as in whiteness, purity, etc.

lil'y-liv'ered *adj.* cowardly; timid

lily of the valley *pl.* **lilies of the valley** a low plant with a spike of white, bell-shaped flowers

lily pad one of the large, flat, floating leaves of the waterlily

Li·ma (lē'mə) capital of Peru: pop. 5,706,000

li·ma bean (lī'mə) ⟦after *Lima*, Peru⟧ **1** a bean with broad pods **2** its broad, flat, edible seed

limb (lim) ***n.*** ⟦OE lim⟧ **1** an arm, leg, or wing **2** a large branch of a tree —**out on a limb** [Inf.] in a precarious position —**limb'less *adj.***

lim·ber (lim'bər) ***adj.*** ⟦< ? prec.⟧ **1** easily bent; flexible **2** able to bend the body easily; supple —***vt.***, ***vi.*** to make or become limber

lim·bo (lim'bō) ***n.***, *pl. for 2 & 3* **-bos** ⟦< L (*in*) *limbo*, (on) the border⟧ **1** [*usually* **L-**] in some Christian theologies, the abode after death of unbaptized infants, etc. **2** an indefinite state **3** a condition of neglect, oblivion, etc.

Lim·burg·er (cheese) (lim'burg'ər) a semisoft cheese with a strong odor, originally from Limburg, Belgium

lime[1] (līm) ***n.*** ⟦OE *lim*⟧ a white substance, calcium oxide, obtained from limestone, etc. and used in mortar and cement and to neutralize acid soil —***vt.*** **limed, lim'ing** to treat with lime

lime[2] (līm) ***n.*** ⟦< Ar *līmah*⟧ a small, lemon-shaped, greenish-yellow citrus fruit with a juicy, sour pulp

lime'ade' (-ād') ***n.*** a drink made of lime juice, sugar, and water

lime'light' *n.* **1** a brilliant light created by the incandescence of lime, formerly used in theaters **2** a prominent position before the public

lim·er·ick (lim'ər ik) ***n.*** ⟦prob. after *Limerick*, Ir county⟧ a rhymed nonsense poem of five lines

lime'stone' *n.* rock consisting mainly of calcium carbonate

lim·i·nal (lim'i nəl) ***adj.*** at a boundary or transitional point between two conditions, stages, etc.

lim·it (lim'it) ***n.*** ⟦< L *limes*⟧ **1** the point, line, etc. where something ends; boundary **2** [*pl.*] bounds **3** the greatest amount allowed —***vt.*** to set a limit to; restrict —**lim'i·ta'tion *n.*** —**lim'it·er *n.*** —**lim'it·less *adj.***

lim'it·ed *adj.* **1** *a*) restricted *b*) narrow in scope *c*) brief **2** making a restricted number of stops: said of a train, bus, etc.

limn (lim) ***vt.*** **limned, limn·ing** (lim'iŋ, -niŋ) ⟦< L *illuminare*, to illuminate⟧ **1** to paint or draw **2** to describe

lim·nol·o·gy (lim näl'ə jē) ***n.*** ⟦< Gr *limnē*, marsh + -LOGY⟧ the science that deals with the physical, etc. properties and features of fresh waters, esp. lakes, etc.

lim·o (lim'ō) ***n.***, *pl.* **-os** [Inf.] LIMOUSINE

lim·ou·sine (lim'ə zēn') ***n.*** ⟦Fr, lit., cloak⟧ a large, luxurious sedan, esp. one driven by a chauffeur

limp (limp) ***vi.*** ⟦< OE *limpan*⟧ to walk with or as with a lame leg —***n.*** a lameness in walking —***adj.*** lacking firmness; wilted, flexible, etc. —**limp'ly *adv.*** —**limp'ness *n.***

limp·et (lim'pit) ***n.*** ⟦< ML *lempreda*⟧ a mollusk that clings to rocks, etc.

lim·pid (lim'pid) ***adj.*** ⟦< L *limpidus*⟧ perfectly clear; transparent —**lim·pid'i·ty *n.***

lim·y (līm'ē) ***adj.*** **-i·er, -i·est** of, like, or containing lime

lin·age (līn'ij) ***n.*** the number of written or printed lines, as on a page

linch·pin (linch'pin') ***n.*** ⟦OE *lynis*, linchpin⟧ **1** a pin in an axle to keep the wheel from coming off **2** anything holding together the parts of a whole

Lin·coln[1] (liŋ'kən), **Abraham** 1809-65; 16th president of the U.S. (1861-65): assassinated

Lin·coln[2] (liŋ'kən) capital of Nebraska, in the SE part: pop. 192,000

lin·den (lin'dən) ***n.*** ⟦OE⟧ a tree with heart-shaped leaves

line[1] (līn) ***n.*** ⟦< L *linea*, lit., linen thread⟧ **1** a cord, rope, wire, etc. **2** any wire, pipe, etc., or system of these, conducting fluid, electricity, etc. **3** a thin, threadlike mark **4** a border or boundary **5** a limit **6** outline; contour **7** a row of persons or things, as of printed letters across a page **8** a succession of persons or things **9** lineage **10** a transportation system of buses, ships, etc. **11** the course a moving thing takes **12**

a course of conduct, action, explanation, etc. **13** a person's trade or occupation **14** a stock of goods **15** a short letter, note, etc. **16** [*pl.*] all the speeches of a character in a play **17** the forward combat position in warfare **18** *Football* the players in the forward row **19** *Math.* the path of a moving point —***vt.* lined, lin′ing 1** to mark with lines **2** to form a line along —**bring** (or **come**) **into line** to bring (or come) into alignment or conformity —**down the line** completely; entirely —**draw the** (or **a**) **line** to set a limit —**hold the line** to stand firm —**in line for** being considered for —**line up** to form, or bring into, a line —**read between the lines** to discover a hidden meaning in something written, said, or done

line[2] (līn) ***vt.* lined, lin′ing** ⟦< L *linum*, flax⟧ to put, or serve as, a lining in

lin·e·age (lin′ē ij) ***n.*** ⟦see LINE[1]⟧ **1** direct descent from an ancestor **2** ancestry; family

lin·e·al (lin′ē əl) ***adj.*** **1** in the direct line of descent from an ancestor **2** hereditary **3** of lines; linear

lin·e·a·ment (lin′ē ə mənt) ***n.*** ⟦< L *linea*, line⟧ a distinctive feature, esp. of the face: *usually used in pl.*

lin·e·ar (lin′ē ər) ***adj.*** **1** of, made of, or using a line or lines **2** logical and not complex **3** in relation to length only

line·back·er (līn′bak′ər) ***n.*** *Football* a defensive player directly behind the line

line drive a baseball hit in a straight line parallel to the ground

line′man (-mən) ***n.***, *pl.* **-men** (-mən) **1** one who sets up and repairs telephone lines, electric power lines, etc. **2** *Football* a player in the line

lin·en (lin′ən) ***n.*** ⟦< OE *lin*, flax: see LINE[2]⟧ **1** thread or cloth made of flax **2** [*often pl.*] sheets, cloths, etc. of linen, or of cotton, etc.

lin·er (līn′ər) ***n.*** **1** a steamship, airplane, etc. in regular service for a specific line **2** LINE DRIVE **3** a cosmetic applied in a fine line, as along the eyelid

lines·man (līnz′mən) ***n.***, *pl.* **-men** (-mən) **1** *Football* an official who marks the yardage gained or lost **2** *Tennis* an official who decides whether the ball is inside or outside the lines

line′up′ ***n.*** an arrangement of persons or things in or as in a line

-ling (liŋ) ⟦OE⟧ *suffix* **1** small *[duckling]* **2** unimportant or contemptible *[hireling]*

lin·ger (liŋ′gər) ***vi.*** ⟦OE *lengan*, to delay⟧ **1** to continue to stay, esp. through reluctance to leave **2** to loiter —**lin′ger·er *n.*** —**lin′ger·ing *adj.***

lin·ge·rie (län′zhə rā′) ***n.*** ⟦Fr⟧ women's underwear and nightclothes of silk, nylon, etc.

lin·go (liŋ′gō) ***n.***, *pl.* **-goes** ⟦< L *lingua*, tongue⟧ [Inf.] a dialect, jargon, etc. that one is not familiar with

lin·gua fran·ca (liŋ′gwə fraŋ′kə) a hybrid language used for communication by speakers of different languages

lin·gual (liŋ′gwəl) ***adj.*** ⟦see LANGUAGE⟧ of, or pronounced with, the tongue

lin·gui·ne (liŋ gwē′nē) ***n.*** ⟦< It *lingua*, tongue⟧ pasta in thin, flat, narrow strips: also sp. **lin·gui′ni**

lin·guist (liŋ′gwist) ***n.*** ⟦< L *lingua*, tongue⟧ a specialist in linguistics

lin·guis′tics (-gwis′tiks) ***n.*** **1** the science of language **2** the study of the structure, development, etc. of a particular language —**lin·guis′tic *adj.***

lin·i·ment (lin′ə mənt) ***n.*** ⟦< L *linere*, to smear⟧ a soothing medicated liquid for the skin

lin·ing (līn′iŋ) ***n.*** the material covering an inner surface

link (liŋk) ***n.*** ⟦< Scand⟧ **1** any of the loops making up a chain **2** *a*) a section of something like a chain *[a link of sausage]* *b*) an element in a series *[a weak link in the evidence]* **3** anything that connects *[a link with the past]* —***vt.*, *vi.*** to join; connect

link′age ***n.*** **1** a linking **2** a series or system of links

linking verb a verb that functions chiefly as a connection between a subject and a predicate (Ex.: *be, seem, become*)

links (liŋks) ***pl.n.*** ⟦OE *hlinc*, a slope⟧ GOLF COURSE

link′up′ ***n.*** a linking together

Lin·nae·us (li nē′əs), **Car·o·lus** (kar′ə ləs) 1707-78; Swed. botanist

lin·net (lin′it) ***n.*** ⟦< L *linum*, flax: it feeds on flaxseed⟧ a small finch of either an Old World or New World species

li·no·le·um (li nō′lē əm) ***n.*** ⟦< L *linum*, flax + *oleum*, oil⟧ **1** a smooth, washable floor covering, formerly much used, esp. in kitchens **2** any floor covering like linoleum

lin·seed (lin′sēd′) ***n.*** ⟦OE *linsæd*⟧ the seed of flax; flaxseed

linseed oil a yellowish oil extracted from flaxseed, used in oil paints, etc.

lint (lint) ***n.*** ⟦< L *linum*, flax⟧ bits of thread, fluff, etc. from cloth or yarn —**lint′y, -i·er, -i·est, *adj.***

lin·tel (lin′təl) ***n.*** ⟦ult. < L *limen*, threshold⟧ the horizontal crosspiece over a door, window, etc.

li·on (lī′ən) ***n.*** ⟦< Gr *leōn*⟧ **1** a large, powerful cat, found in Africa and SW Asia **2** a person of great courage or strength **3** a celebrity —**li′on·ess *fem.n.***

li′on·heart′ed *adj.* very brave

li·on·ize (lī′ə nīz′) ***vt.* -ized′, -iz′ing** to treat as a celebrity

lip (lip) ***n.*** ⟦OE *lippa*⟧ **1** either of the two fleshy folds forming the edges of the mouth **2** anything like a lip, as the rim of a pitcher **3** [Slang] insolent talk —***adj.*** spoken, but insincere *[lip worship]* —**keep a stiff upper lip** [Inf.] to bear pain or distress bravely

lip·id (lip′id) ***n.*** ⟦< Gr *lipos*, fat⟧ any of a group of organic compounds consisting of the fats and other similar substances: also **lip·ide** (lip′īd′, -id)

lip·o·suc·tion (lip′ō suk′shən) ***n.*** ⟦< LIPID + SUCTION⟧ surgical removal of fatty tissue under the skin by means of suction

lip·py (lip′ē) ***adj.*** **-pi·er, -pi·est** [Slang] impudent; insolent —**lip′pi·ness** ***n.***

lip reading the act or skill of recognizing words by watching a speaker's lips: it is taught esp. to the deaf —**lip′-read′** ***vt., vi.*** —**lip reader**

lip service insincere words of support, etc.

lip′stick′ ***n.*** a small stick of cosmetic paste for coloring the lips

lip′-sync′ or **lip′-synch′** (-siŋk′) ***vt., vi.*** ⟦< *lip sync(hronization)*⟧ to move the lips silently so as to seem to be speaking or singing (something recorded)

liq·ue·fy (lik′wi fī′) ***vt., vi.*** **-fied′, -fy′ing** ⟦< L *liquere*, be liquid + *facere*, make⟧ to change into a liquid —**liq′ue·fac′tion** (-fak′shən) ***n.***

li·queur (li kur′, -ko͝or′) ***n.*** ⟦Fr⟧ a sweet, syrupy, flavored alcoholic liquor

liq·uid (lik′wid) ***adj.*** ⟦< L *liquidus*⟧ **1** readily flowing; fluid **2** clear; limpid **3** flowing smoothly and musically, as verse **4** readily convertible into cash —***n.*** a substance that, unlike a solid, flows readily but, unlike a gas, does not expand indefinitely —**liq·uid′i·ty** ***n.***

liq·ui·date (lik′wi dāt′) ***vt.*** **-dat′ed, -dat′ing** ⟦see prec.⟧ **1** to settle the accounts of (a business) by apportioning assets and debts **2** to pay (a debt) **3** to convert into cash **4** to get rid of, as by killing —**liq′ui·da′tion** ***n.*** —**liq′ui·da′tor** ***n.***

liq′uid·ize′ (-wid īz′) ***vt.*** **-ized′, -iz′ing** to cause to become liquid

liq·ui·fy (lik′wi fī′) ***vt., vi.*** **-fied′, -fy′ing** *alt. sp. of* LIQUEFY

liq·uor (lik′ər) ***n.*** ⟦L⟧ **1** any liquid **2** an alcoholic drink, esp. a distilled drink, as whiskey or rum

li·ra (lir′ə) ***n., pl.*** **li′re** (-ā) or **li′ras** ⟦< L *libra*, a pound⟧ the former monetary unit of Italy, superseded in 2002 by the EURO

Lis·bon (liz′bən) capital of Portugal: pop. 817,000

lisle (līl) ***n.*** ⟦after *Lisle* (now *Lille*), city in France⟧ **1** a fine, hard, extra-strong cotton thread **2** a fabric woven of lisle

lisp (lisp) ***vi.*** ⟦< OE *wlisp*, a lisping⟧ **1** to substitute the sounds (th) and (*th*) for the sounds of *s* and *z*, respectively **2** to speak imperfectly —***vt.*** to utter with a lisp —***n.*** the act or sound of lisping

lis·some or **lis·som** (lis′əm) ***adj.*** ⟦< *lithesome*⟧ lithe, supple, limber, agile, etc.

list[1] (list) ***n.*** ⟦< OE *liste*, border⟧ a series of names, numbers, etc. set forth in order —***vt.*** to enter in a list, directory, etc.

list[2] (list) ***vi.*** ⟦prob. ult. < OE *lust*, desire⟧ to tilt to one side: said of a ship, etc. —***n.*** such a tilting

lis·ten (lis′ən) ***vi.*** ⟦< OE *hlysnan*⟧ **1** to make a conscious effort to hear **2** to give heed; take advice —**lis′ten·er** ***n.***

list′ing ***n.*** **1** the making of a list **2** an entry in a list

list′less (-lis) ***adj.*** ⟦< OE *lust*, desire + -LESS⟧ indifferent because of illness, dejection, etc.; languid —**list′less·ly** ***adv.*** —**list′less·ness** ***n.***

list price retail price as given in a list or catalog

lists (lists) ***pl.n.*** ⟦< ME *liste*, border⟧ a fenced area in which knights jousted

Liszt (list), **Franz** (fränts) 1811-86; Hung. composer & pianist

lit[1] (lit) ***vt., vi.*** *alt. pt. & pp. of* LIGHT[1]

lit[2] *abbrev.* **1** liter(s) **2** literally **3** literary **4** literature

lit·a·ny (lit′'n ē) ***n., pl.*** **-nies** ⟦< Gr *litē*, a request⟧ a series of fixed invocations and responses, used as a prayer

li·tchi (lē′chē′) ***n.*** ⟦< Chin⟧ the raisinlike fruit of a Chinese evergreen tree, enclosed in a papery shell

lite (līt) ***adj.*** *informal sp. of* LIGHT[2] (*adj.* 8)

li·ter (lēt′ər) ***n.*** ⟦< Gr *litra*, a pound⟧ the basic metric unit of volume, equal to 1 cubic decimeter or 61.0237 cubic inches: Brit. sp. **li′tre**

lit·er·a·cy (lit′ər ə sē) ***n.*** the ability to read and write

lit·er·al (lit′ər əl) ***adj.*** ⟦< L *littera*, a letter⟧ **1** following exactly the wording of the original *[a literal translation]* **2** in a basic or strict sense *[the literal meaning]* **3** prosaic; matter-of-fact *[a literal mind]* **4** restricted to the facts *[the literal truth]* —**lit′er·al·ly** ***adv.***

lit·er·ar·y (lit′ər er′ē) ***adj.*** **1** of or having to do with literature or books **2** familiar with or versed in literature

lit·er·ate (lit′ər it) ***adj.*** ⟦< L *littera*, a letter⟧ **1** able to read and write **2** well-educated —***n.*** a literate person

lit·e·ra·ti (lit′ə rät′ē) ***pl.n.*** ⟦It < L *litterati*: see prec.⟧ writers, scholars, etc.

lit·er·a·ture (lit′ər ə chər′) ***n.*** ⟦< L *littera*, a letter⟧ **1** *a)* all writings in prose or verse of an imaginative character *b)* all such writings having permanent value, excellence of form, etc. *c)* all the writings of a particular time, country, etc. *d)* all the writings on a particular subject **2** any printed matter

lithe (līth) ***adj.*** **lith′er, lith′est** ⟦OE *lithe*, soft⟧ bending easily; flexible; supple: also **lithe′some** (-səm)

lith·i·um (lith′ē əm) ***n.*** ⟦< Gr *lithos*, stone⟧ a soft, silver-white, chemical element

lithium carbonate a white, powdery salt, used in making glass, dyes, etc. and in treating manic-depressive disorders

lith·o·graph (lith′ə graf′) ***n.*** a print made by lithography —***vi., vt.*** to make (prints or copies) by this process —**li·thog·ra·pher** (li thäg′rə fər) ***n.***

li·thog·ra·phy (li thäg′rə fē) ***n.*** ⟦< Gr *lithos*, stone + -GRAPHY⟧ printing from a flat stone or metal plate, parts of which have been treated to repel ink —**lith·o·graph·ic** (lith′ə graf′ik) ***adj.***

lith·o·sphere (lith′ō sfir′) ***n.*** ⟦< Gr *lithos*, stone + *sphaira*, sphere⟧ the solid, rocky part of the earth; earth's crust

Lith·u·a·ni·a (lith′o͞o ā′nē ə) country in N

Europe: formerly a republic of the U.S.S.R.: 25,170 sq. mi.; pop. 3,675,000 —**Lith'u·a'ni·an** ***adj., n.***

lit·i·gant (lit'i gənt) ***n.*** ⟦see fol.⟧ a party to a lawsuit

lit'i·gate' (-gāt') ***vt., vi.*** **-gat'ed, -gat'ing** ⟦< L *lis*, dispute + *agere*, do⟧ to contest in a lawsuit —**lit'i·ga'tion** ***n.*** —**lit'i·ga'tor** ***n.***

li·ti·gious (li tij'əs) ***adj.*** ⟦see prec.⟧ **1** *a)* given to carrying on lawsuits *b)* quarrelsome **2** of lawsuits —**li·ti'gious·ness** ***n.***

lit·mus (lit'məs) ***n.*** ⟦< ON *litr*, color + *mosi*, moss⟧ a purple coloring matter obtained from various lichens: paper treated with it (**litmus paper**) turns blue in bases and red in acids

litmus test a test in which a single factor determines the finding

LittD or **Litt.D.** *abbrev.* Doctor of Letters

lit·ter (lit'ər) ***n.*** ⟦< L *lectus*, a couch⟧ **1** a framework enclosing a couch on which a person can be carried **2** a stretcher for carrying the sick or wounded **3** straw, hay, etc. used as bedding for animals **4** granular clay used in an indoor receptacle (**litter box**) to absorb cat waste **5** the young borne at one time by a dog, cat, etc. **6** things lying about in disorder, esp. bits of rubbish —***vt.*** **1** to make untidy **2** to scatter about carelessly

lit'ter·bug' (-bug') ***n.*** [Inf.] one who litters public places with rubbish, etc.

lit·tle (lit''l) ***adj.*** **lit'tler** or **less** or **less'er**, **lit'tlest** or **least** ⟦OE *lytel*⟧ **1** small in size, amount, degree, etc. **2** short in duration; brief **3** small in importance or power *[the rights of the little man]* **4** narrow-minded *[a little mind]* —***adv.*** **less, least 1** slightly; not much **2** not in the least —***n.*** a small amount, degree, etc. —**little by little** gradually — **make** (or **think**) **little of** to consider as not very important —**lit'tle·ness** ***n.***

Little Dipper, the a dipper-shaped group of stars containing the North Star

Little Rock capital of Arkansas: pop. 176,000

lit·to·ral (lit'ə rəl) ***adj.*** ⟦< L *litus*, seashore⟧ of or along the shore

lit·ur·gy (lit'ər jē) ***n.***, *pl.* **-gies** ⟦ult. < Gr *leōs, laos*, people + *ergon*, work⟧ prescribed ritual for public worship —**li·tur·gi·cal** (lə tur'ji kəl) ***adj.***

liv·a·ble (liv'ə bəl) ***adj.*** **1** fit or pleasant to live in *[a livable house]* **2** endurable: said as of a way of life Also sp. **live'a·ble**

live[1] (liv) ***vi.*** **lived, liv'ing** ⟦OE *libban*⟧ **1** to have life **2** *a)* to remain alive *b)* to endure **3** to pass one's life in a specified manner **4** to enjoy life *[to know how to live]* **5** to feed *[to live on fruit]* **6** to reside —***vt.*** **1** to carry out in one's life *[to live one's faith]* **2** to spend; pass *[to live a useful life]* —**live down** to live so as to wipe out the shame of (a misdeed, etc.) —**live up to** to live or act in accordance with (one's ideals, etc.)

live[2] (līv) ***adj.*** ⟦< ALIVE⟧ **1** having life **2** of present interest *[a live issue]* **3** still burning *[a live spark]* **4** unexploded *[a live shell]* **5** carrying electrical current *[a live wire]* **6** *a)* in person *b)* broadcast, recorded, etc. during the actual performance **7** *Sports* in play *[a live ball]*

live·bear·er (līv'ber'ər) ***n.*** any of various small, tropical, American, freshwater fishes, as the guppy and molly

-lived (līvd, livd) *combining form* having (a specified kind of) life *[long-lived]*

live'-in' ***adj.*** living in someone's residence as a domestic, lover, etc.

live·li·hood (līv'lē hood') ***n.*** ⟦< OE *lif*, life + *-lad*, course⟧ means of living or of supporting life

live·long (liv'lôŋ') ***adj.*** ⟦ME *lefe longe*, lit., lief long: *lief* is merely intens.⟧ long in passing; whole *[the livelong day]*

live·ly (līv'lē) ***adj.*** **-li·er, -li·est** ⟦OE *liflic*⟧ **1** full of life; vigorous **2** full of spirit; exciting **3** animated, cheerful, vivacious, etc. **4** vivid; keen **5** bounding back with great resilience *[a lively ball]* —**live'li·ness** ***n.***

liv·en (līv'ən) ***vt., vi.*** to make or become lively; cheer: often with *up*

liv·er (liv'ər) ***n.*** ⟦OE *lifer*⟧ **1** the largest glandular organ in vertebrate animals: it secretes bile and is important in metabolism **2** the liver of cattle, fowl, etc., used as food

Liv·er·pool (liv'ər pōōl') seaport in NW England: county district pop. 452,000

liv·er·wurst (liv'ər wurst') ***n.*** ⟦< Ger *leber*, liver + *wurst*, sausage⟧ a sausage containing ground liver

liv·er·y (liv'ər ē) ***n.***, *pl.* **-er·ies** ⟦ME, gift of clothes to a servant⟧ **1** an identifying uniform as of a servant **2** *a)* the care and feeding of horses for a fee *b)* the keeping of horses or vehicles for hire *c)* a stable for this (usually **livery stable**) **3** a place where boats can be rented

lives (līvz) ***n.*** *pl. of* LIFE

live·stock (līv'stäk') ***n.*** domestic animals raised for use and sale

liv·id (liv'id) ***adj.*** ⟦< L *lividus*⟧ **1** discolored by a bruise; black-and-blue **2** grayish-blue: sometimes taken to mean pale or red *[livid with rage]* **3** very angry; enraged

liv·ing (liv'iŋ) ***adj.*** **1** alive; having life **2** in active operation or use *[a living institution]* **3** of persons alive *[within living memory]* **4** true; lifelike **5** of life *[living conditions]* —***n.*** **1** a being alive **2** livelihood **3** manner of existence —**the living** those that are still alive

living room a room in a home, with sofas, chairs, etc., used for social activities, entertaining guests, etc.

living wage a wage sufficient to maintain a reasonable level of comfort

living will a document directing that the signer's life not be artificially supported during a terminal illness

liz·ard (liz'ərd) ***n.*** ⟦< L *lacerta*⟧ any of various slender, scaly reptiles with four legs and a tail, as the chameleon and iguana

ll *abbrev.* lines

LL *abbrev.* Late Latin

-'ll (əl) *suffix* will or shall: used in contractions *[she'll sing]*

lla·ma (lä'mə) ***n.*** ⟦Sp < AmInd (Peru)⟧ a South American beast of burden related to the camel but smaller

lla·no (lä'nō) ***n.***, *pl.* **-nos** ⟦Sp < L *planus*, plain⟧ any of the level, grassy plains of Spanish America

LLB or **LL.B.** *abbrev.* Bachelor of Laws

LLD or **LL.D.** *abbrev.* Doctor of Laws

lo (lō) ***interj.*** ⟦OE *la*⟧ look! see!

load (lōd) ***n.*** ⟦< OE *lad*, a course, journey⟧ **1** an amount carried at one time **2** something borne with difficulty; burden **3** [*often pl.*] [Inf.] a great amount or number **4** *Finance* an amount added to the price of mutual fund shares to cover costs, etc. —***vt.*** **1** to put (a load) into or upon (a carrier) **2** to burden; oppress **3** to supply in large quantities **4** to put a charge of ammunition into (a firearm) **5** *Comput.* to transfer (a program or data) into main memory from a disk, etc. —**load'er** ***n.*** —**load'ing** ***n.***

load·star (lōd'stär') ***n.*** LODESTAR

load·stone (lōd'stōn') ***n.*** LODESTONE

loaf[1] (lōf) ***n.***, *pl.* **loaves** (lōvz) ⟦OE *hlaf*⟧ **1** a portion of bread baked in one piece **2** any food baked in this shape

loaf[2] (lōf) ***vi.*** ⟦prob. < fol.⟧ to spend time idly; idle, dawdle, etc.

loaf'er ***n.*** ⟦prob. < Ger *landläufer*, a vagabond⟧ one who loafs; idler

Loaf'er *trademark for* a casual shoe like a moccasin —***n.*** [**l-**] a shoe similar to this

loam (lōm) ***n.*** ⟦OE *lam*⟧ a rich soil, esp. one composed of clay, sand, and some organic matter —**loam'y**, **-i·er**, **-i·est**, ***adj.***

loan (lōn) ***n.*** ⟦< ON *lān*⟧ **1** the act of lending **2** something lent, esp. money at interest —***vt.***, ***vi.*** to lend

loan'er ***n.*** **1** one who loans something **2** an automobile, TV, etc. lent in place of one left for repair

loan shark [Inf.] one who lends money at illegal rates of interest

loan'word' ***n.*** a word of one language taken into and used in another

loath (lōth) ***adj.*** ⟦< OE *lath*, hostile⟧ reluctant *[to be loath to depart]*

loathe (lō*th*) ***vt.*** **loathed**, **loath'ing** ⟦< OE *lathian*, be hateful⟧ to feel intense dislike or disgust for; abhor

loath'ing ***n.*** intense dislike, disgust, or hatred; abhorrence

loath'some ***adj.*** causing loathing; disgusting

loaves (lōvz) ***n.*** *pl. of* LOAF[1]

lob (läb) ***vt.***, ***vi.*** **lobbed**, **lob'bing** ⟦< ME *lobbe*, heavy⟧ to toss or hit (a ball) in a high curve —**lob'ber** ***n.***

lob·by (läb'ē) ***n.***, *pl.* **-bies** ⟦LL *lobia*⟧ **1** an entrance hall, as of a hotel or theater **2** a group of lobbyists representing the same interest —***vi.*** **-bied**, **-by·ing** to act as a lobbyist

lob'by·ist ***n.*** a person, acting on behalf of a group, who tries to get legislators to support certain measures

lobe (lōb) ***n.*** ⟦< Gr *lobos*⟧ a rounded projecting part, as the lower part of the ear or any of the divisions of the lung

lo·bot·o·my (lō bät'ə mē) ***n.***, *pl.* **-mies** ⟦< prec. + -TOMY⟧ a surgical incision into a lobe of the brain: now rarely used as a treatment

lob·ster (läb'stər) ***n.*** ⟦< OE *loppe*, spider + *-estre*, -ster⟧ an edible sea crustacean usually with four pairs of legs and a pair of large pincers

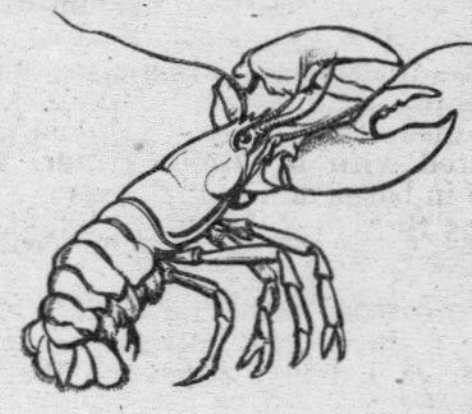

LOBSTER

lobster tail the tail of any of various crustaceans, prepared as food

lo·cal (lō'kəl) ***adj.*** ⟦< L *locus*, a place⟧ **1** of, characteristic of, or confined to a particular place **2** of or for a particular part of the body *[local anesthesia]* **3** making all stops along its run *[a local bus]* —***n.*** **1** a local train, bus, etc. **2** a branch, as of a labor union —**lo'cal·ly** ***adv.***

lo·cale (lō kal') ***n.*** ⟦OFr *local*⟧ a place or locality, esp. with reference to events, etc. associated with it

lo·cal·i·ty (lō kal'ə tē) ***n.***, *pl.* **-ties** a place; district; neighborhood

lo·cal·ize (lō'kəl īz') ***vt.*** **-ized'**, **-iz'ing** to limit, confine, or trace to a particular place —**lo'cal·i·za'tion** ***n.***

lo·cate (lō'kāt', lō kāt') ***vt.*** **-cat'ed**, **-cat'ing** ⟦< L *locus*, a place⟧ **1** to establish in a certain place *[offices located downtown]* **2** to discover the position of **3** to show the position of *[to locate Guam on a map]* —***vi.*** [Inf.] to settle *[she located in Ohio]*

lo·ca'tion ***n.*** **1** a locating or being located **2** position; place —**on location** *Film* in an outdoor setting, away from the studio

loc. cit. *abbrev.* ⟦L *loco citato*⟧ in the place cited

loch (läk, läkh) ***n.*** ⟦< Gael & Old Ir⟧ [Scot.] **1** a lake **2** an arm of the sea

lock[1] (läk) ***n.*** ⟦< OE *loc*, a bolt⟧ **1** a mechanical device for fastening a door, strongbox, etc. as with a key or combination **2** an enclosed part of a canal, etc. equipped with gates for changing the water level to raise or lower boats **3** the mechanism of a firearm that explodes the charge —***vt.*** **1** to fasten with a lock **2** to shut (*up*, *in*, or *out*) by means of a lock **3** to link *[to lock arms]* **4** to jam together so as to make immovable —***vi.*** **1** to become locked **2** to interlock

lock[2] (läk) ***n.*** ⟦OE *loc*⟧ a curl of hair

lock′er ***n.*** **1** a chest, closet, etc. which can be locked **2** a large compartment for freezing and storing foods

lock·et (läk′it) ***n.*** ⟦< OFr *loc*, a latch, lock⟧ a small, hinged case of gold, etc. for holding a picture, lock of hair, etc.: usually worn on a necklace

lock′jaw′ ***n.*** a form of tetanus, in which the jaws become firmly closed

lock′out′ ***n.*** the shutdown of a plant to bring the workers to an agreement

lock′smith′ ***n.*** one whose work is making or repairing locks and making keys

lock′up′ ***n.*** a jail

lo·co (lō′kō) ***adj.*** ⟦Sp, mad⟧ [Slang] crazy; demented

loco disease a nervous disease of horses, cattle, etc. caused by locoweed poison

lo·co·mo·tion (lō′kə mō′shən) ***n.*** ⟦< L *locus*, a place + MOTION⟧ motion, or the power of moving, from one place to another

lo′co·mo′tive (-mōt′iv) ***adj.*** of locomotion **—*n.*** an electric, steam, or diesel engine on wheels, designed to push or pull a railroad train

lo·co·weed (lō′kō wēd′) ***n.*** a plant of W North America that causes the loco disease of cattle, horses, etc.

lo·cus (lō′kəs) ***n.***, *pl.* **lo′ci′** (-sī′) ⟦L⟧ **1** a place **2** *Math.* a line, plane, etc. every point of which satisfies a given condition

lo·cust (lō′kəst) ***n.*** ⟦< L *locusta*⟧ **1** a large grasshopper often traveling in swarms and destroying vegetation **2** SEVENTEEN-YEAR LOCUST **3** a tree of the E or Central U.S., with clusters of fragrant, white flowers

lo·cu·tion (lō kyo͞o′shən) ***n.*** ⟦< L *loqui*, speak⟧ a word, phrase, or expression

lode (lōd) ***n.*** ⟦< OE *lad*, course⟧ a vein, stratum, etc. of metallic ore

lode′star′ ***n.*** a star by which one directs one's course; esp., the North Star

lode′stone′ ***n.*** a strongly magnetic variety of iron ore

lodge (läj) ***n.*** ⟦< OFr *loge*, arbor⟧ **1** *a)* a small house for some special use *[a hunting lodge]* *b)* a resort hotel or motel **2** the local chapter or hall of a fraternal society **—*vt.* lodged, lodg′ing 1** to house temporarily **2** to shoot, thrust, etc. firmly (*in*) **3** to bring (a complaint, etc.) before legal authorities **4** to confer (powers) upon: with *in* **—*vi.* 1** to live (*with* or *in*) as a paying guest **2** to come to rest and stick firmly (*in*)

lodg′er ***n.*** one who lives in a rented room in another's home

lodg′ing ***n.*** **1** a place to live in, esp. temporarily **2** [*pl.*] a room or rooms rented in a private home

loft (lôft, läft) ***n.*** ⟦< ON *lopt*, upper room, air⟧ **1** the space just below the roof of a house, barn, etc. **2** an upper story of a warehouse or factory; specif., a dwelling space, artist's studio, etc. in such an upper story **3** a gallery *[a choir loft]* **4** height given to a ball hit or thrown **—*vt.*** to send (a ball) into a high curve

loft bed a bed on a platform or balcony allowing the use of the floor area below as part of a living room, etc.

loft′y ***adj.*** **-i·er, -i·est 1** very high **2** elevated; noble **3** haughty; arrogant **—loft′i·ness *n.***

log[1] (lôg, läg) ***n.*** ⟦ME *logge*⟧ **1** a section of the trunk or of a large branch of a felled tree **2** a device for measuring the speed of a ship **3** a record of progress, speed, etc., specif. one kept on a ship's voyage or aircraft's flight **—*vt.* logged, log′ging 1** to saw (trees) into logs **2** to record in a log **3** to sail or fly (a specified distance) **—*vi.*** to cut down trees and remove the logs **—log on** (or **off**) to enter the necessary information to begin (or end) a session on a computer terminal

log[2] (lôg, läg) ***n.*** *short for* LOGARITHM

-log (lôg, läg) *combining form* -LOGUE

lo·gan·ber·ry (lō′gən ber′ē) ***n.***, *pl.* **-ries** ⟦after J. H. *Logan*, who developed it (1881)⟧ **1** a hybrid bramble developed from the blackberry and the red raspberry **2** its purplish-red fruit

log·a·rithm (lôg′ə rith əm, läg′-) ***n.*** ⟦< Gr *logos*, ratio + *arithmos*, number⟧ *Math.* the exponent expressing the power to which a fixed number must be raised to produce a given number **—log′a·rith′mic *adj.***

loge (lōzh) ***n.*** ⟦OFr: see LODGE⟧ **1** a theater box or mezzanine section **2** a luxury suite in a stadium or arena

log′ger ***n.*** a person whose work is felling trees for use as lumber, etc.

log′ger·head′ ***n.*** ⟦dial. *logger*, block of wood + HEAD⟧ used chiefly in **at loggerheads**, in sharp disagreement

log·ic (läj′ik) ***n.*** ⟦ult. < Gr *logos*, word⟧ **1** correct reasoning, or the science of this **2** way of reasoning *[bad logic]* **3** what is expected by the working of cause and effect **4** *Comput.* the system of switching functions, circuits, or devices **—lo·gi·cian** (lō jish′ən) ***n.***

log′i·cal (-i kəl) ***adj.*** ⟦ML *logicalis*⟧ **1** based on or using logic **2** expected because of what has gone before **—log′i·cal·ly *adv.***

lo·gis·tics (lō jis′tiks) ***n.*** ⟦< Fr *loger*, to quarter, lodge⟧ the military science of procuring, maintaining, and transporting materiel and personnel **—lo·gis′tic** or **lo·gis′ti·cal *adj.* —lo·gis′ti·cal·ly *adv.***

log′jam′ ***n.*** **1** an obstacle formed by logs jamming together in a stream **2** piled-up work, etc. that obstructs progress **3** a deadlock

log·o (lō′gō) ***n.*** ⟦< Gr *logos*, a word⟧ a distinctive company signature, trademark, etc.: also **log·o·type** (lôg′ə tīp′, läg′-)

log′roll′ing ***n.*** **1** mutual exchange of favors, esp. among legislators **2** the sport of balancing oneself on a floating log while rotating it with one's feet

-logue (lôg, läg) ⟦see LOGIC⟧ *combining form* a (specified kind of) speaking or writing *[Decalogue]*

lo·gy (lō′gē) ***adj.*** **-gi·er, -gi·est** ⟦< ? Du *log*, dull⟧ [Inf.] dull or sluggish

-lo·gy (lə jē) ⟦see LOGIC⟧ *combining form* **1** a (specified kind of) speaking *[eulogy]* **2** the science, doctrine, or theory of *[biology]*

loin (loin) ***n.*** ⟦< L *lumbus*⟧ **1** [*usually pl.*] the lower part of the back between the hipbones and the ribs **2** the front part of the hindquarters of beef, lamb, etc. **3** [*pl.*] the hips and the lower abdomen regarded as the region of strength, etc.

loin'cloth' ***n.*** a cloth worn about the loins, as by some peoples in warm climates

loi·ter (loit'ər) ***vi.*** ⟦< MDu *loteren*⟧ **1** to spend time idly; linger **2** to move slowly and idly —**loi'ter·er *n.***

loll (läl) ***vi.*** ⟦< MDu *lollen*, mumble, doze⟧ **1** to lean or lounge about lazily **2** to hang loosely; droop *[the camel's tongue lolled out]* —***vt.*** to let hang loosely

lol·li·pop or **lol·ly·pop** (läl'ē päp') ***n.*** ⟦prob. < dial. *lolly*, the tongue + *pop*⟧ a piece of hard candy on the end of a stick

lol·ly·gag (läl'ē gag') ***vi.* -gagged', -gag'ging** ⟦var. of *lallygag* < ?⟧ [Inf.] to waste time in trifling or aimless activity

Lon·don (lun'dən) **1** capital of England, the United Kingdom, & the Commonwealth: pop. 7,567,000 **2** city in SE Ontario, Canada: pop. 326,000

lone (lōn) ***adj.*** ⟦< *alone*⟧ **1** by oneself; solitary **2** isolated

lone'ly ***adj.*** **-li·er, -li·est** **1** solitary or isolated **2** unhappy at being alone —**lone'li·ness *n.***

lon·er (lōn'ər) ***n.*** [Inf.] one who prefers to be independent of others, as by living or working alone

lone'some ***adj.*** **1** having or causing a lonely feeling **2** unfrequented

long[1] (lôŋ) ***adj.*** ⟦< OE⟧ **1** measuring much in space or time **2** in length *[six feet long]* **3** of greater than usual length, quantity, etc. *[a long list]* **4** tedious; slow **5** far-reaching *[a long view of the matter]* **6** well-supplied *[long on excuses]* —***adv.*** **1** for a long time **2** from start to finish *[all day long]* **3** at a remote time *[long ago]* —**as** (or **so**) **long as** **1** during the time that **2** seeing that; since **3** provided that —**before long** soon

long[2] (lôŋ) ***vi.*** ⟦< OE *langian*⟧ to feel a strong yearning; wish earnestly

long[3] *abbrev.* longitude

Long Beach seaport in SW California, on the Pacific: pop. 429,000

long distance a telephone service for calls to and from distant places —**long'-dis'tance *adj.*, *adv.***

lon·gev·i·ty (län jev'ə tē, lôn-) ***n.*** ⟦< L *longus*, long + *aevum*, age⟧ long life

long'-faced' ***adj.*** glum

long'hair' ***adj.*** [Inf.] of intellectuals or intellectual tastes

long'hand' ***n.*** ordinary handwriting, as distinguished from shorthand or typed characters

long'ing ***n.*** strong desire; yearning —***adj.*** feeling or showing a yearning

Long Island island in SE New York, in the Atlantic south of Connecticut

lon·gi·tude (län'jə to͞od') ***n.*** ⟦< L *longus*, long⟧ distance east or west of the prime meridian, expressed in degrees or by the difference in time

lon'gi·tu'di·nal (-to͞od''n əl) ***adj.*** **1** of or in length **2** running or placed lengthwise **3** of longitude

long jump *Sports* a jump for distance made with a running start

long'-lived' (-līvd', -livd') ***adj.*** having or tending to have a long life span

long'-range' ***adj.*** **1** having a range of a great distance **2** taking the future into consideration

long·shore·man (lôŋ'shôr'mən) ***n.***, *pl.* **-men** (-mən) ⟦< *alongshore* + MAN⟧ a person who works on a waterfront loading and unloading ships; stevedore

long shot [Inf.] **1** in betting, a choice that is little favored and, hence, carries great odds **2** a venture with only a slight chance of success, but offering great rewards

long'-stand'ing ***adj.*** having continued for a long time

long'-suf'fer·ing ***adj.*** bearing trouble, etc. patiently for a long time

long'-term' ***adj.*** for or extending over a long time

long ton TON (sense 2)

Lon·gueuil (lôŋ gāl') city in S Quebec: suburb of Montreal: pop. 128,000

long'-wind'ed (-win'did) ***adj.*** **1** speaking or writing at great length **2** tiresomely long

look (look) ***vi.*** ⟦< OE *locian*⟧ **1** to direct one's eyes in order to see **2** to search **3** to appear; seem **4** to be facing in a specified direction —***vt.*** **1** to direct one's eyes on **2** to have an appearance befitting *[to look the part]* —***n.*** **1** a looking; glance **2** appearance; aspect **3** [Inf.] *a)* [*usually pl.*] appearance *b)* [*pl.*] personal appearance —***interj.*** **1** see! **2** pay attention! —**look after** to take care of —**look down on** (or **upon**) to regard with contempt —**look for** to expect —**look forward to** to anticipate —**look in** (**on**) to pay a brief visit (to) —**look into** to investigate —**look out** to be careful —**look over** to examine —**look to** **1** to take care of **2** to rely on —**look up** **1** to search for as in a reference book **2** [Inf.] to call on —**look up to** to admire —**look'er *n.***

look'er-on' ***n.***, *pl.* **look'ers-on'** an observer or spectator; onlooker

looking glass a (glass) mirror

look'out' ***n.*** **1** a careful watching **2** a place for keeping watch **3** a person detailed to watch **4** [Inf.] concern

look'-see' ***n.*** [Inf.] a quick look

loom[1] (lo͞om) ***n.*** ⟦< OE (*ge*)*loma*, tool⟧ a machine for weaving thread or yarn into cloth

loom[2] (lo͞om) ***vi.*** ⟦< ?⟧ to come into sight indistinctly, esp. threateningly

loon[1] (lo͞on) ***n.*** ⟦< ON *lomr*⟧ a fish-eating, diving bird, similar to a duck

loon[2] (lo͞on) ***n.*** ⟦< ?⟧ a stupid or crazy person

loon'ie ***n.*** ⟦< LOON[1], depicted on the

reverse] [Cdn.] the Canadian one-dollar coin

loon'y ***adj.*** **-i·er, -i·est** [< LUNATIC] [Slang] crazy; demented

loop (lo͞op) ***n.*** [ME *loup*] **1** the figure made by a line, thread, etc. that curves back to cross itself **2** anything forming this figure **3** an intrauterine contraceptive device **4** a segment of movie film or magnetic tape joined end to end —***vt.*** **1** to make a loop in or of **2** to fasten with a loop —***vi.*** to form a loop or loops

loop'hole' ***n.*** [prob. < MDu *lupen*, to peer + HOLE] **1** a hole in a wall for looking or shooting through **2** a means of evading an obligation, etc.

loop'y ***adj.*** **-i·er, -i·est** [Slang] **1** slightly crazy **2** confused

loose (lo͞os) ***adj.*** **loos'er, loos'est** [< ON *lauss*] **1** not confined or restrained; free **2** not firmly fastened **3** not tight or compact **4** not precise; inexact **5** sexually immoral **6** [Inf.] relaxed —***adv.*** loosely —***vt.*** **loosed, loos'ing** **1** to set free; unbind **2** to make less tight, compact, etc. **3** to relax **4** to release (an arrow, etc.) —**on the loose** not confined; free —**loose'ly** ***adv.*** —**loose'ness** ***n.***

loose cannon an uncontrollable person whose unpredictable words or actions cause embarrassment or harm to others

loose ends unsettled details —**at loose ends** unsettled, idle, etc.

loose'-leaf' ***adj.*** having leaves, or sheets, that can be removed or replaced easily

loos·en (lo͞os'ən) ***vt., vi.*** to make or become loose or looser

loose·strife (lo͞os'strīf') ***n.*** a plant with long spikes of purple flowers

loos·ey-goos·ey (lo͞o'sē go͞o'sē) [Slang] ***adj.*** relaxed; easy —***adv.*** in a loose, relaxed way

loot (lo͞ot) ***n.*** [Hindi *lūt*] **1** goods stolen or taken by force; plunder **2** [Slang] money, gifts, etc. —***vt., vi.*** to plunder

lop[1] (läp) ***vt.*** **lopped, lop'ping** [< OE *loppian*] **1** to trim (a tree, etc.) by cutting off branches, etc. **2** to remove by or as by cutting off: usually with *off*

lop[2] (läp) ***vi.*** **lopped, lop'ping** [prob. akin to LOB] to hang down loosely

lope (lōp) ***vi.*** **loped, lop'ing** [< ON *hlaupa*, to leap] to move with a long, swinging stride —***n.*** such a stride

lop·sid·ed (läp'sīd'id) ***adj.*** noticeably heavier, bigger, or lower on one side

lo·qua·cious (lō kwā'shəs) ***adj.*** [< L *loqui*, speak] very talkative —**lo·qua'cious·ness** ***n.*** —**lo·quac'i·ty** (-kwas'ə tē) ***n.***

lord (lôrd) ***n.*** [< OE *hlaf*, loaf + *weard*, keeper] **1** a ruler; master **2** the head of a feudal estate **3** [**L-**] *a)* God *b)* Jesus Christ **4** in Great Britain, a titled nobleman —**lord it over** to be overbearing toward

lord'ly ***adj.*** **-li·er, -li·est** **1** noble; grand **2** haughty —***adv.*** in the manner of a lord —**lord'li·ness** ***n.***

Lord's Day [*sometimes* **L- d-**] Sunday: with *the*

lord'ship' ***n.*** **1** the rank or authority of a lord **2** rule; dominion **3** the territory of a lord **4** [*often* **L-**] a title used in speaking to or of a lord

Lord's Prayer the prayer beginning *Our Father*: Matt. 6:9-13

lore (lôr) ***n.*** [< OE *lar*] knowledge; learning, esp. of a traditional nature

lor·gnette (lôr nyet') ***n.*** [Fr < OFr *lorgne*, squinting] eyeglasses, or opera glasses, attached to a handle

lo·ris (lō'ris, lôr'is) ***n.*** [ult. < Du *loer*, a clown] a small, slow-moving, large-eyed Asiatic lemur that lives in trees and is active at night

lor·ry (lôr'ē) ***n.***, *pl.* **-ries** [prob. < dial. *lurry*, to pull] [Brit.] a motor truck

Los Al·a·mos (lôs al'ə mōs') town in NC New Mexico: site of nuclear energy facility where the atomic bomb was developed: pop. 11,000

Los An·ge·les (lôs an'jə ləs) city & seaport on the SW coast of California: pop. 3,486,000 (met. area, incl. Long Beach, 8,863,000)

lose (lo͞oz) ***vt.*** **lost, los'ing** [OE *losian*] **1** to become unable to find [to *lose* one's keys] **2** to have taken from one by accident, death, removal, etc. **3** to fail to keep [to *lose* one's temper] **4** to fail to see, hear, or understand **5** to fail to have, get, etc. [to *lose* one's chance] **6** to fail to win **7** to cause the loss of **8** to wander from (one's way, etc.) **9** to squander **10** to go slower by [a watch that *loses* five minutes a day] —***vi.*** to suffer (a) loss —**lose oneself** to become absorbed —**los'er** ***n.***

loss (lôs, läs) ***n.*** [ME *los*] **1** a losing or being lost **2** the damage, trouble, etc. caused by losing **3** the person, thing, or amount lost —**at a loss to** uncertain how to

lost (lôst, läst) ***vt., vi.*** *pt. & pp. of* LOSE —***adj.*** **1** ruined; destroyed **2** not to be found; missing **3** no longer held, seen, heard, etc. **4** not gained or won **5** having wandered astray **6** wasted

lot (lät) ***n.*** [< OE *hlot*] **1** the deciding of a matter by chance, as by drawing counters **2** the decision thus arrived at **3** one's share by lot **4** fortune [her unhappy *lot*] **5** a plot of ground **6** a group of persons or things **7** [*often pl.*] [Inf.] a great number or amount [a *lot* of cars, *lots* of fun] **8** [Inf.] sort [he's a bad *lot*] —**a** (**whole**) **lot** a great deal; very much: somewhat informal — **draw** (or **cast**) **lots** to decide by lot

Lo·thar·i·o (lō ther'ē ō') ***n.***, *pl.* **-i·os'** [after the rake in the play *The Fair Penitent* (1703)] [*often* **l-**] a seducer of women; rake

lo·tion (lō'shən) ***n.*** [< L *lavare*, to wash] a liquid preparation used, as on the skin, for cleansing, healing, etc.

lots ***adv.*** a great deal; very much: somewhat informal

lot·ter·y (lät'ər ē) ***n.***, *pl.* **-ies** [< MDu *lot*, lot] **1** a game of chance in which people buy numbered tickets on prizes, winners being chosen by lot **2** a drawing, event, etc. based on chance

lot·to (lät'ō) ***n.*** [It < MDu: see LOT] a

game resembling bingo

lo·tus (lōt′əs) ***n.*** ⟦< Gr *lōtos*⟧ **1** *Gr. Legend* a plant whose fruit induced forgetfulness **2** any of several tropical water-lilies

lotus position in yoga, an erect sitting position with the legs crossed close to the body

loud (loud) ***adj.*** ⟦< OE *hlud*⟧ **1** strongly audible: said of sound **2** making a loud sound **3** noisy **4** emphatic *[loud denials]* **5** [Inf.] flashy —***adv.*** in a loud manner —**loud′ly *adv.*** —**loud′ness *n.***

loud′mouthed′ (-mouthd′, -moutht′) ***adj.*** talking in a loud, irritating voice

loud′speak′er *n.* SPEAKER (*n.* 2)

Lou·is (lo͞o′ē; *Fr* lwē) **1 Louis XIV** 1638-1715; king of France (1643-1715) **2 Louis XV** 1710-74; king of France (1715-74) **3 Louis XVI** 1754-93; king of France (1774-92): guillotined

Lou·i·si·an·a (lo͞o ē′zē an′ə) Southern state of the U.S.: 43,566 sq. mi.; pop. 4,220,000; cap. Baton Rouge: abbrev. *LA* —**Lou·i′si·an′i·an** or **Lou·i′si·an′an *adj., n.***

Lou·is·ville (lo͞o′ə vəl) city in N Kentucky: pop. 270,000

lounge (lounj) ***vi.*** **lounged, loung′ing** ⟦Scot dial. < ? *lungis*, a laggard⟧ **1** to move, sit, lie, etc. in a relaxed way **2** to spend time in idleness —***n.*** **1** a room with comfortable furniture for lounging **2** a couch or sofa

lounge′wear′ *n.* loose-fitting clothing for casual wear, esp. at home

louse (lous) ***n.***, *pl.* **lice** ⟦< OE *lus*⟧ **1** a small, wingless insect parasitic on humans and other animals **2** any similar insect parasitic on plants **3** *pl.* **lous′es** [Slang] a mean, contemptible person —**louse up** [Slang] to spoil; ruin

lous·y (lou′zē) ***adj.*** **-i·er, -i·est** **1** infested with lice **2** [Slang] *a)* disgusting *b)* poor; inferior **3** well supplied (*with*) —**lous′i·ness *n.***

lout (lout) ***n.*** ⟦prob. < or akin to ME *lutien*, to lurk⟧ a clumsy, stupid fellow —**lout′ish *adj.***

lou·ver (lo͞o′vər) ***n.*** ⟦< MDu *love*, gallery⟧ **1** an opening, window, etc. fitted with a series of sloping slats arranged so as to admit light and air but shed rain **2** any of these slats

love (luv) ***n.*** ⟦< OE *lufu*⟧ **1** strong affection or liking for someone or something **2** a passionate affection of one person for another **3** the object of such affection; a sweetheart or lover **4** *Tennis* a score of zero —***vt., vi.*** to feel love (for) —**fall in love (with)** to begin to feel love (for) —**in love** feeling love —**make love** **1** to woo, embrace, etc. **2** to have sexual intercourse —**lov′a·ble** or **love′a·ble *adj.*** —**love′less *adj.***

love affair a romantic relationship between two people who are not married to each other

love′bird′ *n.* any of various small Old World parrots often kept as cage birds

love handles [Slang] bulges of fat at the sides of the waist

love′lorn′ (-lôrn′) ***adj.*** ⟦LOVE + obs. *lorn*, lost⟧ sad because not loved in return

love′ly *adj.* **-li·er, -li·est** **1** beautiful **2** [Inf.] highly enjoyable —**love′li·ness *n.***

lov·er (luv′ər) ***n.*** **1** a person who greatly enjoys something **2** one who loves; specif., either partner in a sexual relationship, often an illicit one **3** [*pl.*] a couple in love with, or in a sexual relationship with, each other

love seat a small sofa for two people

lov′ing *adj.* feeling or expressing love —**lov′ing·ly *adv.***

loving cup a large drinking cup with two handles, often given as a trophy

low[1] (lō) ***adj.*** ⟦< ON *lagr*⟧ **1** not high or tall **2** below the normal level *[low ground]* **3** shallow **4** less in size, degree, etc. than usual *[low speed]* **5** deep in pitch **6** depressed in spirits **7** not of high rank; humble **8** vulgar; coarse **9** poor; inferior **10** not loud —***adv.*** in or to a low level, degree, etc. —***n.*** **1** a low level, degree, etc. **2** an arrangement of gears giving the lowest speed and greatest power **3** *Meteorol.* an area of low barometric pressure —**lay low** to overcome or kill —**lie low** to keep oneself hidden —**low′ness *n.***

low[2] (lō) ***n., vi.*** ⟦< OE *hlowan*⟧ MOO

low′born′ *adj.* of humble birth

low′boy′ *n.* a chest of drawers mounted on short legs

low′brow′ *n.* one considered to lack cultivated tastes —***adj.*** of or for a lowbrow

Low Countries the Netherlands, Belgium, & Luxembourg

low·down (lō′doun′; *for adj.*, -doun′) ***n.*** [Slang] the true, pertinent facts: with *the* —***adj.*** [Inf.] mean; contemptible

low′-end′ *adj.* [Inf.] **1** inexpensive and low in quality **2** having only the basic features

low·er[1] (lō′ər) ***adj.*** ⟦compar. of LOW[1]⟧ **1** below in place, rank, etc. **2** less in amount, degree, etc. **3** farther south —***vt.*** **1** to let or put down *[lower the window]* **2** to reduce in height, amount, etc. **3** to bring down in respect, etc. —***vi.*** to become lower

low·er[2] (lou′ər) ***vi.*** ⟦ME *louren*⟧ **1** to scowl or frown **2** to appear dark and threatening: said as of the sky —**low′er·ing *adj.*** —**low′er·ing·ly *adv.***

low·er·case (lō′ər kās′) ***n.*** small-letter type used in printing, as distinguished from capital letters —***adj.*** of or in lowercase

low′er·class′man (-klas′mən) ***n.***, *pl.* **-men** (-mən) a student in the freshman or sophomore class of a high school or college

low frequency any radio frequency between 30 and 300 kilohertz

Low German **1** the group of dialects of N Germany **2** the branch of Germanic languages including English, Dutch, Flemish, etc.

low′-grade′ *adj.* of low quality, degree, etc.

low′-key′ *adj.* of low intensity, tone, etc.; subdued: also **low′-keyed′**

low′land (-lənd, -land′) ***n.*** land below the level of the surrounding land —***adj.***

of, in, or from such a region —**the Lowlands** lowland region of SC Scotland

low'life' *n., pl.* **-lifes'** a vulgar or undignified person

low'ly *adj.* **-li·er, -li·est** **1** of low position or rank **2** humble; meek —**low'li·ness** *n.*

low'-mind'ed *adj.* having or showing a coarse, vulgar mind

low'-spir'it·ed *adj.* sad; depressed

low tide the lowest level reached by the ebbing tide

lox[1] (läks) *n.* ⟦< Yiddish < Ger *lachs*, salmon⟧ a kind of smoked salmon

lox[2] (läks) *n.* ⟦*l(iquid) ox(ygen)*⟧ liquid oxygen, esp. when used in rockets: also **LOX**

loy·al (loi'əl) *adj.* ⟦see LEGAL⟧ **1** faithful to one's country, friends, ideals, etc. **2** showing such faithfulness —**loy'al·ly** *adv.* —**loy'al·ty**, *pl.* **-ties**, *n.*

loy'al·ist *n.* one who supports the government during a revolt

loz·enge (läz'ənj) *n.* ⟦< OFr *losenge*⟧ a cough drop, candy, etc., orig. diamond-shaped

LP *n.* ⟦*L(ong) P(laying)*⟧ a phonograph record having microgrooves, for playing at 33⅓ revolutions per minute

LPN *n., pl.* **LPNs** licensed practical nurse

Lr *Chem. symbol for* lawrencium

LSD *n.* ⟦*l(y)s(ergic acid) d(iethylamide)*⟧ a chemical compound used in the study of mental disorders and as a psychedelic drug

Lt *abbrev.* Lieutenant

Ltd or **ltd** *abbrev.* limited

lu·au (lo͞o'ou') *n.* a Hawaiian feast

Lub·bock (lub'ək) city in NW Texas: pop. 186,000

lube (lo͞ob) *n.* **1** a lubricating oil for machinery: also **lube oil** **2** [Inf.] a lubrication

lu·bri·cant (lo͞o'bri kənt) *adj.* reducing friction by providing a smooth film over parts coming into contact —*n.* a lubricant oil, etc.

lu'bri·cate' (-kāt') *vt.* **-cat'ed, -cat'ing** ⟦< L *lubricus*, smooth⟧ **1** to make slippery or smooth **2** to apply a lubricant to (machinery, etc.) —*vi.* to serve as a lubricant —**lu'bri·ca'tion** *n.* —**lu'bri·ca'tor** *n.*

lu·cid (lo͞o'sid) *adj.* ⟦< L *lucere*, to shine⟧ **1** [Old Poet.] shining **2** transparent **3** sane **4** clear; readily understood —**lu·cid'i·ty** *n.* —**lu'cid·ly** *adv.*

Lu·ci·fer (lo͞o'sə fər) *n.* Satan

Lu·cite (lo͞o'sīt') ⟦< L *lux*, light⟧ *trademark for* an acrylic resin that is molded into transparent or translucent sheets, rods, etc.

luck (luk) *n.* ⟦prob. < MDu *gelucke*⟧ **1** the seemingly chance happening of events that affect someone; fortune; lot **2** good fortune —**luck out** [Inf.] to be lucky —**luck'less** *adj.*

luck'y *adj.* **-i·er, -i·est** **1** having good luck **2** resulting fortunately **3** believed to bring good luck —**luck'i·ly** *adv.* —**luck'i·ness** *n.*

lu·cra·tive (lo͞o'krə tiv) *adj.* ⟦< L *lucrum*, riches⟧ producing wealth or profit; profitable

lu·cre (lo͞o'kər) *n.* ⟦< L *lucrum*, riches⟧ riches; money: chiefly humorously derogatory

lu·cu·brate (lo͞o'kə brāt', -kyo͞o-) *vi.* **-brat'ed, -brat'ing** ⟦< L *lucubrare*, to work by candlelight⟧ to work, study, or write laboriously, esp. late at night —**lu'cu·bra'tion** *n.*

lu·di·crous (lo͞o'di krəs) *adj.* ⟦< L *ludus*, a game⟧ causing laughter because absurd or ridiculous —**lu'di·crous·ly** *adv.* —**lu'di·crous·ness** *n.*

luff (luf) *vi.* ⟦< ME *lof*⟧ to turn the bow of a ship toward the wind

lug (lug) *vt.* **lugged, lug'ging** ⟦prob. < Scand⟧ to carry or drag (something heavy) —*n.* **1** an earlike projection by which a thing is held or supported **2** a heavy bolt, used, with a nut (**lug nut**), to secure a wheel to an axle

lug·gage (lug'ij) *n.* ⟦< prec.⟧ suitcases, trunks, etc.; baggage

lu·gu·bri·ous (lə go͞o'brē əs) *adj.* ⟦< L *lugere*, mourn⟧ very sad or mournful, esp. in an exaggerated way —**lu·gu'bri·ous·ly** *adv.* —**lu·gu'bri·ous·ness** *n.*

Luke (lo͝ok) *n. Bible* **1** an early Christian, the reputed author of the third Gospel **2** this Gospel

luke·warm (lo͝ok'wôrm') *adj.* ⟦< ME *luke*, tepid + *warm*, warm⟧ **1** slightly warm **2** lacking enthusiasm —**luke'warm'ly** *adv.* —**luke'warm'ness** *n.*

lull (lul) *vt.* ⟦ME *lullen*⟧ **1** to calm by gentle sound or motion **2** to bring into a specified condition by soothing and reassuring —*vi.* to become calm —*n.* a short period of calm

lull'a·by' (-ə bī') *n., pl.* **-bies'** ⟦< ME, echoic⟧ a song for lulling a baby to sleep

lum·ba·go (lum bā'gō) *n.* ⟦L < *lumbus*, loin⟧ pain in the lower back

lum·bar (lum'bär) *adj.* ⟦< L *lumbus*, loin⟧ of or near the loins

lum·ber[1] (lum'bər) *n.* ⟦< ? pawnbrokers of *Lombardy*, Italy; hence, stored articles⟧ timber sawed into boards, etc. —*vi.* to cut down timber and saw it into lumber —**lum'ber·er** *n.* —**lum'ber·ing** *n.*

lum·ber[2] (lum'bər) *vi.* ⟦< ? Scand⟧ to move heavily and noisily —**lum'ber·ing** *adj.*

lum'ber·jack' (-jak') *n.* LOGGER

lum'ber·man (-mən) *n., pl.* **-men** (-mən) one who deals in lumber

lu·mi·nar·y (lo͞o'mə ner'ē) *n., pl.* **-nar'ies** ⟦< L *lumen*, a light⟧ **1** a body that gives off light, such as the sun **2** a famous or notable person

lu·mi·nes·cence (lo͞o'mə nes'əns) *n.* ⟦< L *lumen*, a light + -ESCENCE⟧ the giving off of light without heat, as in fluorescence or phosphorescence —**lu'mi·nes'cent** *adj.*

lu·mi·nous (lo͞o'mə nəs) *adj.* ⟦< L *lumen*, a light⟧ **1** giving off light; bright **2** clear; readily understood —**lu'mi·nos'i·ty** (-näs'ə tē) *n.*

lum·mox (lum'əks) *n.* ⟦< ?⟧ [Inf.] a clumsy, stupid person

lump[1] (lump) *n.* ⟦ME *lompe*⟧ **1** an

indefinitely shaped mass of something **2** a swelling **3** [*pl.*] [Inf.] hard blows, criticism, etc. —***adj.*** in a lump or lumps —***vt.*** **1** to put together in a lump or lumps **2** to treat or deal with in a mass —***vi.*** to become lumpy —**lump'i·ness** ***n.*** —**lump'y, -i·er, -i·est,** ***adj.***

lump[2] (lump) ***vt.*** ⟦< ?⟧ [Inf.] to have to put up with (something disagreeable) *[like it or lump it]*

lump sum a gross, or total, sum paid at one time

lu·na·cy (lo͞o'nə sē) ***n.*** ⟦< LUNATIC⟧ **1** insanity **2** great folly or a foolish act

lu·nar (lo͞o'nər) ***adj.*** ⟦< L *luna*, the moon⟧ of or like the moon

lu·na·tic (lo͞o'nə tik) ***adj.*** ⟦< L *luna*, the moon⟧ **1** insane or for insane persons **2** utterly foolish —***n.*** an insane person

lunch (lunch) ***n.*** ⟦< ? Sp *lonja*, slice of ham⟧ a light meal; esp., the midday meal between breakfast and dinner —***vi.*** to eat lunch

lunch·eon (lun'chən) ***n.*** a lunch; esp., a formal lunch

lunch·eon·ette (lun'chən et') ***n.*** a place where light lunches are served

luncheon meat meat processed in the form of loaves, sausages, etc. and ready to eat: also [Inf.] **lunch'meat'** ***n.***

lung (luŋ) ***n.*** ⟦OE *lungen*⟧ either of the two spongelike breathing organs in the thorax of vertebrates

lunge (lunj) ***n.*** ⟦< Fr *allonger*, lengthen⟧ **1** a sudden thrust as with a sword **2** a sudden plunge forward —***vi., vt.*** **lunged, lung'ing** to move, or cause to move, with a lunge

lung·fish (luŋ'fish') ***n., pl.*** **-fish'** or (for different species) **-fish'es** any of various fishes having lungs as well as gills

lunk·head (luŋk'hed') ***n.*** ⟦prob. echoic alteration of LUMP[1] + HEAD⟧ [Inf.] a stupid person: also **lunk**

lu·pine (lo͞o'pīn'; *for n.*, -pin) ***adj.*** ⟦< L *lupus*, wolf⟧ of or like a wolf —***n.*** a plant with long spikes of white, rose, yellow, or blue flowers

lu·pus (lo͞o'pəs) ***n.*** ⟦< L, a wolf⟧ any of various diseases with skin lesions

lurch[1] (lurch) ***vi.*** ⟦< ?⟧ **1** to pitch or sway suddenly to one side **2** to stagger —***n.*** a lurching movement

lurch[2] (lurch) ***n.*** ⟦prob. < OFr *lourche*, duped⟧ a difficult situation: only in **leave someone in the lurch**

lure (loor) ***n.*** ⟦< OFr *loirre*⟧ **1** anything that tempts or entices **2** a bait used in fishing —***vt.*** **lured, lur'ing** to attract; tempt; entice

lu·rid (loor'id) ***adj.*** ⟦L *luridus*, ghastly⟧ **1** glowing through a haze: said as of flames enveloped by smoke **2** shocking; sensational —**lu'rid·ly** ***adv.*** —**lu'rid·ness** ***n.***

lurk (lurk) ***vi.*** ⟦ME *lurken*⟧ to stay hidden, ready to attack, spring out, etc.

lus·cious (lush'əs) ***adj.*** ⟦ME *lucius*⟧ **1** highly gratifying to taste or smell; delicious **2** delighting any of the senses —**lus'cious·ness** ***n.***

lush[1] (lush) ***adj.*** ⟦< ? OFr *lasche*, lax⟧ **1** of or showing luxuriant growth **2** rich, abundant, extravagant, etc. —**lush'ness** ***n.***

lush[2] (lush) ***n.*** [Slang] an alcoholic

lust (lust) ***n.*** ⟦OE, pleasure⟧ **1** bodily appetite; esp., excessive sexual desire **2** overwhelming desire *[a lust for power]* —***vi.*** to feel an intense desire —**lust'ful** ***adj.*** —**lust'ful·ly** ***adv.*** —**lust'ful·ness** ***n.***

lus·ter (lus'tər) ***n.*** ⟦< L *lustrare*, illumine⟧ **1** gloss; sheen **2** brightness; radiance **3** brilliant beauty or fame; glory Also [Chiefly Brit.] **lus'tre**

lus'trous (-trəs) ***adj.*** having luster; shining

lust·y (lus'tē) ***adj.*** **-i·er, -i·est** full of vigor; robust —**lust'i·ly** ***adv.*** —**lust'i·ness** ***n.***

lute (lo͞ot') ***n.*** ⟦ult. < Ar *al'ūd*, the wood⟧ an old stringed instrument like the guitar, with a rounded body

lu·te·nist (lo͞ot''n ist) ***n.*** a lute player: also **lu'ta·nist**

Lu·ther (lo͞o'thər), **Mar·tin** (märt''n) 1483-1546; Ger. Reformation leader

Lu'ther·an ***adj.*** of the Protestant denomination founded by Luther —***n.*** a member of a Lutheran Church —**Lu'ther·an·ism'** ***n.***

lut·ist (lo͞ot'ist) ***n.*** LUTENIST

Lux·em·bourg (luk'səm burg') grand duchy in W Europe, north of France: 999 sq. mi.; pop. 401,000

lux·u·ri·ant (lug zhoor'ē ənt) ***adj.*** ⟦see LUXURY⟧ **1** growing with vigor and in abundance **2** having rich ornamentation, etc. —**lux·u'ri·ance** ***n.***

lux·u'ri·ate' (-āt') ***vi.*** **-at'ed, -at'ing** **1** to live in great luxury **2** to revel *(in)* —**lux·u'ri·a'tion** ***n.***

lux·u'ri·ous (-əs) ***adj.*** **1** fond of or indulging in luxury **2** constituting luxury; rich, comfortable, etc. —**lux·u'ri·ous·ly** ***adv.***

lux·u·ry (luk'shə rē, lug'zhə rē) ***n., pl.*** **-ries** ⟦< L *luxus*⟧ **1** the use and enjoyment of the best and most costly things **2** anything contributing to such enjoyment, usually something not necessary —***adj.*** characterized by luxury

Lu·zon (lo͞o zän') main island of the Philippines

-ly[1] (lē) ⟦< OE *-lic*⟧ *suffix* **1** like or characteristic of *[manly]* **2** happening (once) every (specified period of time) *[monthly, hourly]*

-ly[2] (lē) ⟦< OE *-lice*⟧ *suffix* **1** in a (specified) manner or direction, to a (specified) extent, in or at a (specified) time or place *[harshly, inwardly, hourly]* **2** in the (specified) order *[thirdly]*

ly·ce·um (lī sē'əm) ***n.*** ⟦< Gr *Lykeion*, grove at Athens where Aristotle taught⟧ **1** a lecture hall **2** an organization presenting lectures, etc.

Ly·cra (lī'krə) *trademark for* a spandex fabric used in underwear, athletic apparel, etc.

lye (lī) ***n.*** ⟦OE *leag*⟧ any strongly alkaline substance, used in cleaning, making soap, etc.

ly·ing[1] (lī'iŋ) ***vi.*** *prp. of* LIE[1]

ly·ing[2] (lī'iŋ) ***vt., vi.*** *prp. of* LIE[2] —***adj.***

false; not truthful —*n.* the telling of a lie or lies

ly'ing-in' *n.* confinement in childbirth —*adj.* of or for childbirth

lymph (limf) *n.* ⟦L *lympha*, spring water⟧ a clear, yellowish body fluid resembling blood plasma, found in the spaces between cells and in the lymphatic vessels

lym·phat·ic (lim fat'ik) *adj.* containing lymph

lymph node any of the small, compact structures lying in groups along the course of the lymphatic vessels

lym·pho·cyte (lim'fō sīt') *n.* a leukocyte formed in lymphatic tissue, important in the synthesis of antibodies

lymph·oid (lim'foid') *adj.* of or like lymph or the tissue of the lymph nodes

lym·pho·ma (lim fō'mə) *n.* any of a group of diseases resulting from the proliferation of malignant lymphoid cells

lynch (linch) *vt.* ⟦after W. *Lynch*, vigilante in VA in 1780⟧ to murder (an accused person) by mob action and without lawful trial, as by hanging —**lynch'ing** *n.*

lynx (liŋks) *n.* ⟦< Gr *lynx*⟧ a wildcat found throughout the Northern Hemisphere, having a short tail and tufted ears

lynx'-eyed' (-īd') *adj.* keen-sighted

Lyon (lyōn) city in EC France: pop. 415,000

ly·on·naise (lī'ə nāz') *adj.* ⟦Fr⟧ prepared with sliced onions

LYRE

lyre (līr) *n.* ⟦< Gr *lyra*⟧ a small stringed instrument of the harp family, used by the ancient Greeks

lyr·ic (lir'ik) *adj.* ⟦< Gr *lyrikos*⟧ **1** suitable for singing; specif., designating or of poetry expressing the poet's personal emotion **2** of or having a high voice with a light, flexible quality *[a lyric tenor]* —*n.* **1** a lyric poem **2** [*usually pl.*] the words of a song

lyr'i·cal (-i kəl) *adj.* **1** LYRIC **2** expressing rapture or great enthusiasm

lyr'i·cism' (-ə siz'əm) *n.* lyric quality or style

lyr'i·cist (-ə sist) *n.* a writer of lyrics, esp. lyrics for popular songs

ly·ser·gic acid (lī sur'jik) *see* LSD

-ly·sis (lə sis, li-) ⟦< Gr *lysis*, a loosening⟧ *combining form* a loosening, dissolution, dissolving, destruction *[catalysis, electrolysis]*

-lyte (līt) ⟦< Gr *lyein*, dissolve⟧ *combining form* a substance undergoing decomposition *[electrolyte]*

M

m[1] or **M** (em) *n., pl.* **m's, M's** the 13th letter of the English alphabet

m[2] *abbrev.* **1** married **2** masculine **3** medium **4** meter(s) **5** mile(s) **6** minute(s)

M[1] (em) *n.* a Roman numeral for 1,000

M[2] *abbrev.* **1** male **2** married **3** medium **4** Monday **5** Monsieur

ma (mä) *n.* [Inf.] MOTHER (*n.* 1)

MA *abbrev.* **1** Massachusetts **2** ⟦L *Magister Artium*⟧ Master of Arts: also **M.A.**

ma'am (mam, mäm) *contr. n.* [Inf.] madam: used in direct address

ma·ca·bre (mə käb'rə, mə käb') *adj.* ⟦< OFr (*danse*) *Macabré*, (dance) of death⟧ grim and horrible; gruesome

mac·ad·am (mə kad'əm) *n.* ⟦after J. L. *McAdam* (1756-1836), Scot engineer⟧ small broken stones used in making roads, esp. such stones mixed with tar or asphalt

Ma·cao (mə kou') administrative zone of China, near Hong Kong: formerly under Portuguese administration

mac·a·ro·ni (mak'ə rō'nē) *n.* ⟦It *maccaroni*, ult. < Gr *makar*, blessed⟧ pasta in the form of tubes, etc.

mac·a·roon (mak'ə ro͞on') *n.* ⟦see prec.⟧ a small, chewy cookie made with crushed almonds or coconut

ma·caw (mə kô') *n.* ⟦prob. < AmInd (Brazil)⟧ a large, bright-colored parrot of Central and South America

Mac·beth (mək beth') *n.* the title character of a tragedy by Shakespeare

Mac·ca·bees (mak'ə bēz') *n.* a family of Jewish patriots who headed a successful revolt against the Syrians (175-164 B.C.)

mace[1] (mās) *n.* ⟦OFr *masse*⟧ **1** a heavy, spiked war club, used in the Middle Ages **2** a staff used as a symbol of authority by certain officials

mace[2] (mās) *n.* ⟦< ML *macis*⟧ a spice made from the husk of the nutmeg

Mace (mās) ⟦< MACE[1]⟧ *trademark for* a gas, sold in aerosol containers, that temporarily stuns its victims —*n.* [*often* **m-**] such a substance, or a container of it —*vt.* **Maced, Mac'ing** [*often* **m-**] to spray with Mace

Mac·e·do·ni·a (mas′ə dō′nē ə) **1** ancient kingdom in SE Europe **2** country in the Balkan Peninsula: 9,928 sq. mi.; pop. 1,937,000 —**Mac′e·do′ni·an** ***adj.***, ***n.***

mac·er·ate (mas′ər āt′) ***vt.*** **-at′ed, -at′ing** ⟦< L *macerare,* soften⟧ **1** to soften and separate into parts by soaking in liquid **2** to steep (fruit or vegetables), as in wine **3** loosely, to tear, chop, etc. into bits —**mac′er·a′tion** ***n.***

ma·che·te (mə shet′ē, -chet′ē) ***n.*** ⟦Sp < L *marcus,* hammer⟧ a large knife used for cutting sugar cane, underbrush, etc., esp. in Central and South America

Mach·i·a·vel·li·an (mak′ē ə vel′ē ən, mäk′-) ***adj.*** ⟦after N. *Machiavelli* (1469-1527), It statesman⟧ crafty; deceitful

mach·i·na·tion (mak′ə nā′shən) ***n.*** ⟦< L *machinari,* to plot⟧ a plot or scheme, esp. one with evil intent: *usually used in pl.*

ma·chine (mə shēn′) ***n.*** ⟦< Gr *mēchos,* contrivance⟧ **1** a structure consisting of a framework with various moving parts, for doing some kind of work **2** an organization functioning like a machine **3** the controlling group in a political party **4** *Mech.* a device, as the lever, that transmits, or changes the application of, energy —***adj.*** **1** of machines **2** done by machinery —***vt.*** **-chined′, -chin′ing** to make, shape, etc. by machinery

machine gun an automatic gun, firing a rapid stream of bullets

machine language a language entirely in binary digits, used directly by a computer

ma·chin·er·y (mə shēn′ər ē, -shēn′rē) ***n.***, *pl.* **-ies** **1** machines collectively **2** the working parts of a machine **3** the means for keeping something going

ma·chin′ist ***n.*** one who makes, repairs, or operates machinery

ma·chis·mo (mä chēz′mō) ***n.*** ⟦Sp < *macho,* masculine + *-ismo,* -ISM⟧ overly assertive or exaggerated masculinity

Mach number (mäk) ⟦after E. *Mach* (1838-1916), Austrian physicist⟧ [*also* **m- n-**] a number indicating the ratio of an object's speed to the speed of sound in the surrounding medium

ma·cho (mä′chō) ***adj.*** ⟦Sp, masculine⟧ exhibiting or characterized by machismo

mack·er·el (mak′ər əl) ***n.***, *pl.* **-el** or **-els** ⟦< OFr *maquerel*⟧ an edible fish of the North Atlantic

Mack·i·naw (coat) (mak′ə nô′) ⟦after *Mackinac* Island in N Lake Huron⟧ [*also* **m-**] a short, heavy, double-breasted woolen coat, usually plaid

mack·in·tosh (mak′in täsh′) ***n.*** ⟦after C. *Macintosh,* 19th-c. Scot inventor⟧ a raincoat, orig., one made of rubberized cloth

Ma·con (mā′kən) city in central Georgia: pop. 107,000

mac·ra·mé (mak′rə mā′) ***n.*** ⟦Fr, ult. < Ar *miqramah,* a veil⟧ a coarse fringe or lace made as of cord knotted in designs

macro- ⟦< Gr *makros,* long⟧ *combining form* long, large, enlarged

mac·ro·bi·ot·ics (mak′rō bī ät′iks) ***pl.n.*** ⟦< prec. + Gr *bios,* life⟧ [*with sing. v.*] the study of prolonging life, as by special diets —**mac′ro·bi·ot′ic** ***adj.***

mac′ro·cosm′ (-käz′əm) ***n.*** ⟦see MACRO- & COSMOS⟧ **1** the universe **2** any large, complex entity

ma·cron (mā′krən) ***n.*** ⟦< Gr *makros,* long⟧ a mark (¯) placed over a vowel to indicate its pronunciation

mad (mad) ***adj.*** **mad′der, mad′dest** ⟦< OE (*ge*)*mædan,* make mad⟧ **1** insane **2** frantic *[mad* with fear*]* **3** foolish and rash **4** infatuated *[*he's *mad* about her*]* **5** wildly amusing **6** having rabies *[*a *mad* dog*]* **7** angry: often with *at* —**mad′ly** ***adv.*** —**mad′ness** ***n.***

Mad·a·gas·car (mad′ə gas′kər) island country off the SE coast of Africa: 226,658 sq. mi.; pop. 13,469,000

mad·am (mad′əm) ***n.***, *pl.* **mad′ams**; for 1, usually **mes·dames** (mā däm′, -dam′) ⟦Fr *madame,* orig. *ma dame,* my lady⟧ **1** a woman; lady: a polite term of address **2** a woman in charge of a brothel

ma·dame (mə däm′, -dam′; mad′əm; *Fr* må dåm′) ***n.***, *pl.* **mes·dames** (mā däm′, -dam′; *Fr* mā dåm′) ⟦Fr: see prec.⟧ **1** a married woman: French title equivalent to *Mrs.* **2** a distinguished woman: used in English as a title of respect

mad·cap (mad′kap′) ***n.*** ⟦MAD + CAP[1], figurative for head⟧ a reckless, impulsive person —***adj.*** reckless and impulsive

mad·den (mad′′n) ***vt.***, ***vi.*** to make or become insane, angry, or wildly excited —**mad′den·ing** ***adj.*** —**mad′den·ing·ly** ***adv.***

mad·der (mad′ər) ***n.*** ⟦OE *mædere*⟧ **1** any of various related plants, esp. a vine with yellow flowers and a red root **2** a red dye made from this root

made (mād) ***vt.***, ***vi.*** *pt. & pp. of* MAKE

ma·de·moi·selle (mad′ə mə zel′; *Fr* måd mwå zel′) ***n.***, *pl.* **-selles′**; Fr. ***mes·de·moi·selles*** (mād mwå zel′) ⟦Fr < *ma,* my + *demoiselle,* young lady⟧ an unmarried woman or girl: French title equivalent to *Miss*

made′-to-or′der ***adj.*** made to conform to the customer's specifications

made′-up′ ***adj.*** **1** put together **2** invented; false *[*a *made-up* story*]* **3** with cosmetics applied

mad′house′ ***n.*** **1** an insame asylum **2** any place of turmoil, noise, etc.

Mad·i·son[1] (mad′ə sən), **James** 1751-1836; 4th president of the U.S. (1809-17)

Mad·i·son[2] (mad′ə sən) capital of Wisconsin: pop. 191,000

mad′man′ (-man′, -mən) ***n.***, *pl.* **-men′** (-men′, -mən) an insane person —**mad′wom′an**, *pl.* **-wom′en**, ***fem.n.***

Ma·don·na (mə dän′ə) ***n.*** ⟦It < *ma,* my + *donna,* lady⟧ **1** Mary, mother of Jesus **2** a picture or statue of Mary

ma·dras (ma′drəs, mə dras′) ***n.*** ⟦after fol.⟧ a fine, firm cotton cloth, usually striped or plaid

Ma·dras (mə dras′, -dräs′) seaport on

the SE coast of India: pop. 4,289,000: now officially *Chennai*

Ma·drid (mə drid′) capital of Spain, in the central part: pop. 3,159,000

mad·ri·gal (ma′dri gəl) ***n.*** ⟦< It⟧ a part song, without accompaniment, popular in the 15th to 17th c.

mael·strom (māl′strəm) ***n.*** ⟦< Du *malen*, to grind + *stroom*, a stream⟧ **1** a large or violent whirlpool **2** an agitated state of mind, affairs, etc.

ma·es·tro (mīs′trō) ***n.***, *pl.* **-tros** or **-tri** (-trē) ⟦It < L *magister*, master⟧ a master in any art; esp., a great composer or conductor of music

Ma·fi·a (mä′fē ə) ***n.*** ⟦It *maffia*⟧ a secret society engaged in illegal activities

Ma·fi·o·so (mä′fē ō′sō) ***n.***, *pl.* **-si** (-sē) [*also* **m-**] a member of the Mafia

mag·a·zine (mag′ə zēn′) ***n.*** ⟦< Ar *makhzan*, storehouse⟧ **1** a military supply depot **2** a space in which explosives are stored, as in a fort **3** a supply chamber, as in a rifle or camera **4** a periodical publication containing stories, articles, etc.

Ma·gel·lan (mə jel′ən), **Fer·di·nand** (furd′'n and′) 1480?-1521; Port. navigator in the service of Spain

ma·gen·ta (mə jen′tə) ***n.*** ⟦after *Magenta*, town in Italy⟧ **1** a purplish-red dye **2** purplish red —***adj.*** purplish-red

mag·got (mag′ət) ***n.*** ⟦ME *magotte*⟧ a wormlike insect larva, as of the housefly —**mag′got·y *adj.***

Ma·gi (mā′jī′) ***pl.n.***, *sing.* **-gus** (-gəs) ⟦< Old Pers *magus*, magician⟧ the wise men who came bearing gifts to the infant Jesus

mag·ic (maj′ik) ***n.*** ⟦< Gr *magikos*, of the Magi, ancient Persian priests⟧ **1** the use of charms, spells, etc. in seeking or pretending to control events **2** any mysterious power [the *magic* of love] **3** the art of producing illusions by sleight of hand, etc. —***adj.*** **1** of, produced by, or using magic **2** producing extraordinary results, as if by magic —**mag′i·cal *adj.*** —**mag′i·cal·ly *adv.***

magic bullet an invention, discovery, etc. that solves a particular problem; esp., a medicine that can cure a disease

ma·gi·cian (mə jish′ən) ***n.*** ⟦< OFr *magicien*⟧ an expert in magic

mag·is·te·ri·al (maj′is tir′ē əl) ***adj.*** **1** of or suitable for a magistrate or master **2** authoritative —**mag′is·te′ri·al·ly *adv.***

mag·is·trate (maj′is trāt′) ***n.*** ⟦< L *magister*, master⟧ **1** a civil officer empowered to administer the law **2** a minor official, as a justice of the peace

mag·ma (mag′mə) ***n.*** ⟦< Gr *massein*, knead⟧ liquid or molten rock in the earth, which solidifies to produce igneous rock

Mag·na Car·ta or **Mag·na Char·ta** (mag′nə kär′tə) ⟦ML, great charter⟧ the charter, granted in 1215, that guarantees certain civil and political liberties to the English people

mag·nan·i·mous (mag nan′ə məs) ***adj.*** ⟦< L *magnus*, great + *animus*, soul⟧ generous in overlooking injury or insult; rising above pettiness; noble —**mag′na·nim′i·ty** (-nə nim′ə tē) ***n.*** —**mag·nan′i·mous·ly *adv.***

mag·nate (mag′nāt) ***n.*** ⟦< L *magnus*, great⟧ a very influential person, esp. in business

mag·ne·sia (mag nē′zhə, -shə) ***n.*** ⟦ModL, ult. < Gr *Magnēsia*, ancient Gr city⟧ magnesium oxide, a white powder, used as a mild laxative and antacid

mag·ne′si·um (-zē əm) ***n.*** ⟦ModL: see prec.⟧ a lightweight, metallic chemical element

mag·net (mag′nit) ***n.*** ⟦see MAGNESIA⟧ **1** any piece of iron or certain other materials that has the property of attracting similar material **2** one that attracts

MAGNET

mag·net·ic (mag net′ik) ***adj.*** **1** having the properties of a magnet **2** of, producing, or caused by magnetism **3** of the earth's magnetism **4** that can be magnetized **5** powerfully attractive —**mag·net′i·cal·ly *adv.***

magnetic field a physical field arising from an electric charge in motion, producing a force on a moving electric charge

magnetic tape a thin plastic ribbon with a magnetized coating for recording sounds, digital computer data, etc.

mag·net·ism (mag′nə tiz′əm) ***n.*** **1** the property, quality, or condition of being magnetic **2** the force to which this is due **3** personal charm

mag′net·ite′ (-tīt′) ***n.*** ⟦< Ger⟧ black iron oxide, an important iron ore

mag′net·ize′ (-tīz′) ***vt.*** **-ized′**, **-iz′ing** **1** to give magnetic properties to (steel, iron, etc.) **2** to charm (a person) —**mag′net·i·za′tion *n.***

mag·ne·to (mag nēt′ō) ***n.***, *pl.* **-tos** an electric generator, often a small one, in which one or more permanent magnets produce the magnetic field

mag·ne·tom·e·ter (mag′nə täm′ət ər) ***n.*** **1** an instrument for measuring magnetic forces **2** such an instrument used as to detect concealed metal weapons at airports, etc.

magnet school a public school offering new and special courses to attract students from a broad urban area so as to bring about desegregation

mag·nif·i·cent (mag nif′ə sənt) ***adj.*** ⟦< L *magnus*, great + *facere*, do⟧ **1** splendid, stately, or sumptuous, as in form **2** exalted: said of ideas, etc. **3** [Inf.] excellent —**mag·nif′i·cence *n.*** —**mag·nif′i·cent·ly *adv.***

mag·ni·fy (mag′nə fī′) ***vt.*** **-fied′**, **-fy′ing** ⟦see prec.⟧ **1** to exaggerate **2** to increase the apparent size of, esp. with a lens **3** [Archaic] to praise —***vi.*** to have the power of increasing the apparent size of an object —**mag′ni·fi·ca′tion *n.*** —**mag′ni·fi′er *n.***

mag′ni·tude′ (-tood′) ***n.*** ⟦< L *magnus*, great⟧ **1** greatness of size, extent, etc. **2** *a*) size *b*) loudness (of sound) *c*) importance **3** the degree of brightness of a star, etc.

mag·no·li·a (mag nō′lē ə, -nōl′yə) ***n.*** ⟦after P. *Magnol* (1638-1715), Fr botanist⟧ a tree with large, fragrant flowers of white, pink, or purple

mag·num (mag′nəm) ***n.*** ⟦< L *magnus,* great⟧ **1** a wine bottle holding 1.5 liters **2** [*usually* **M-**] a firearm, esp. a revolver, that fires magnum cartridges **—*adj.*** of or pertaining to a cartridge having great explosive force for its size

mag·num o·pus (mag′nəm ō′pəs) ⟦L⟧ a great work; masterpiece

mag·pie (mag′pī′) ***n.*** ⟦< *Mag,* dim. of *Margaret* + *pie*, magpie⟧ **1** a noisy, black-and-white bird related to the jay **2** a person who chatters

Mag·yar (mag′yär′) ***n.*** **1** a member of the main ethnic group of Hungary **2** the language of this people

ma·ha·ra·jah or **ma·ha·ra·ja** (mä′hə rä′jə) ***n.*** ⟦< Sans *mahā,* great + *rājā,* king⟧ [Historical] in India, a prince, specif. the ruler of a native state — **ma′ha·ra′ni** or **ma′ha·ra′nee** (-nē) ***fem.n.***

ma·ha·ri·shi (mä′hə rish′ē) ***n.*** ⟦Hindi < *mahā,* great + *ṛshi,* sage⟧ a Hindu teacher of mysticism

ma·hat·ma (mə hat′mə, -hät′-) ***n.*** ⟦< Sans *mahā,* great + *ātman,* soul⟧ in India, any of a class of wise and holy persons held in special regard

mah-jongg or **mah-jong** (mä′jôŋ′, -zhôŋ′) ***n.*** ⟦< Chin *ma-ch'iao,* sparrow, a figure on one of the tiles⟧ a game of Chinese origin played with small pieces called *tiles*

Mah·ler (mä′lər), **Gus·tav** (goos′täf′) 1860-1911; Austrian composer & conductor

ma·hog·a·ny (mə häg′ə nē, -hôg′-) ***n.***, *pl.* **-nies** ⟦< ?⟧ **1** *a)* a tropical American tree *b)* the reddish-brown wood of this tree **2** reddish brown

Ma·hom·et (mə häm′it) *var. of* MOHAMMED

ma·hout (mə hout′) ***n.*** ⟦< Hindi⟧ in India, an elephant driver or keeper

maid (mād) ***n.*** **1** [Now Chiefly Literary] a girl or young unmarried woman **2** a female servant

maid·en (mād′′n) ***n.*** ⟦OE *mægden*⟧ [Now Rare] a girl or young unmarried woman **—*adj.*** **1** of or for a maiden **2** unmarried or virgin **3** untried **4** first *[a maiden* voyage*]* **—maid′en·hood′ *n.*** — **maid′en·ly *adj.***

maid′en·hair′ (fern) a delicate fern

maid′en·head′ (-hed′) ***n.*** the hymen

maiden name the surname that a married woman had when not yet married

maid of honor an unmarried woman acting as chief attendant to a bride

maid′ser′vant *n.* a female servant

mail[1] (māl) ***n.*** ⟦< OHG *malaha,* wallet⟧ **1** letters, packages, etc. transported and delivered by the post office **2** a postal system **—*adj.*** of mail **—*vt.*** to send by mail **—mail′er *n.***

mail[2] (māl) ***n.*** ⟦< L *macula,* mesh of a net⟧ flexible body armor made of small metal rings, scales, etc.

SUIT OF MAIL

mail′box′ *n.* **1** a box into which mail is put when delivered **2** a box into which mail is put for collection Also **mail box**

mail carrier a person who carries and delivers mail

mail′man′ (-man′, -mən) ***n.***, *pl.* **-men′** (-men′, -mən) a man who is a mail carrier

mail order an order for goods to be sent by mail **—mail′-or′der *adj.***

maim (mām) ***vt.*** ⟦OFr *mahaigner*⟧ to disable; mutilate

main (mān) ***n.*** ⟦OE *mægen,* strength⟧ **1** a principal pipe in a distribution system for water, gas, etc. **2** [Old Poet.] the ocean **—*adj.*** chief in size, importance, etc.; principal **—by main force** (or **strength**) by sheer force (or strength) — **in the main** mostly; chiefly **—with might and main** with all one's strength

main clause *Gram.* INDEPENDENT CLAUSE

main drag [Slang] the principal street of a city or town

Maine (mān) New England state of the U.S.: 30,865 sq. mi.; pop. 1,228,000; cap. Augusta: abbrev. *ME* **—Main·er** (mā′nər) ***n.***

main·frame (mān′frām′) ***n.*** **1** the central processing unit of a large computer **2** a very large computer, to which several terminals may be connected

main′land′ (-land′, -lənd) ***n.*** the principal land mass of a continent, as distinguished from nearby islands — **main′land′er *n.***

main′line′ *n.* the principal road, course, etc. **—*vt.*** **-lined′**, **-lin′ing** [Slang] to inject (a narcotic drug) directly into a large vein

main′ly *adv.* chiefly; principally

main′mast′ (-mast′; *naut.*, -məst) ***n.*** the principal mast of a vessel

main′sail′ (-sāl′; *naut.*, -səl) ***n.*** the principal sail of a vessel, set from the mainmast

main′spring′ *n.* **1** the principal spring in a clock, watch, etc. **2** the chief motive or cause

main′stay′ *n.* **1** the supporting line extending forward from the mainmast **2** a chief support

main′stream′ *n.* a major trend or line of thought, action, etc. **—*vt.*** to cause to undergo mainstreaming

main′stream′ing *n.* the placement of disabled people into regular school classes, workplaces, etc.

main·tain (mān tān′) ***vt.*** ⟦< L *manu tenere,* hold in the hand⟧ **1** to keep or keep up; carry on **2** to keep in continuance or in a certain state, as of repair **3** to affirm or assert **4** to support by providing what is needed —**main·tain'a·ble** *adj.*

main·te·nance (mānt''n əns) ***n.*** a maintaining or being maintained

mai tai (mī' tī') ⟦Tahitian, lit., good⟧ [*often* **M- T-**] a cocktail of rum, fruit juices, etc.

mai·tre d' (māt'ər dē') ⟦< fol.⟧ [Inf.] MAÎTRE D'HÔTEL

maî·tre d'hô·tel (me tr' dô tel') ⟦Fr, master of the house⟧ a supervisor of waiters and waitresses

maize (māz) ***n.*** ⟦< WInd *mahiz*⟧ **1** *chiefly Brit. name for* CORN[1] (*n.* 2) **2** yellow

Maj *abbrev.* Major

ma·jes·tic (mə jes'tik) ***adj.*** grand; stately —**ma·jes'ti·cal·ly** ***adv.***

maj·es·ty (maj'is tē) ***n.***, *pl.* **-ties** ⟦< L *magnus,* great⟧ **1** [**M-**] a title used in speaking to or of a sovereign **2** grandeur

ma·jol·i·ca (mə jäl'i kə) ***n.*** ⟦It⟧ Italian glazed pottery

ma·jor (mā'jər) ***adj.*** ⟦L, compar. of *magnus,* great⟧ **1** greater in size, amount, importance, etc. **2** *Music* designating an interval greater than the corresponding minor by a half tone —***vi.*** *Educ.* to specialize (*in* a field of study) —***n.*** **1** *U.S. Mil.* an officer ranking just above a captain **2** a field of study in which a student specializes

ma'jor-do'mo (-dō'mō) ***n.***, *pl.* **-mos** ⟦< L *major,* greater + *domus,* house⟧ a man in charge of a great household

ma'jor·ette' (-et') ***n.*** a girl or woman with a baton, who leads or accompanies a marching band; drum majorette

major general *pl.* **major generals** *U.S. Mil.* an officer ranking just above a brigadier general

ma·jor·i·ty (mə jôr'ə tē) ***n.***, *pl.* **-ties** ⟦see MAJOR⟧ **1** [*also with pl. v.*] the greater number; more than half of a total **2** the number by which the votes cast for the candidate who receives more than half the votes, exceed the remaining votes **3** full legal age **4** the military rank of a major

major scale a musical scale with semitones between the third and fourth and the seventh and eighth tones, and whole tones in all other positions

make (māk) ***vt.* made, mak'ing** ⟦OE *macian*⟧ **1** to bring into being; build, create, produce, etc. **2** to cause to be or become [*made* king, *made* sad] **3** to prepare for use [*make* the beds] **4** to amount to [two pints *make* a quart] **5** to have the qualities of [to *make* a fine leader] **6** to acquire; earn **7** to cause the success of [that venture *made* her] **8** to regard as the meaning (*of*) [what do you *make* of that?] **9** to execute, do, etc. [to *make* a speech] **10** to cause or force: with an infinitive without *to* [*make* him behave] **11** to arrive at; reach [the ship *made* port] **12** [Inf.] to get on or in [to *make* the team] —***vi.*** **1** to behave as specified [*make* bold] **2** to cause something to be as specified [*make* ready] —***n.*** **1** the way in which something is made; style **2** a type or brand —**make away with** to steal —**make believe** to pretend —**make someone's day** [Slang] to give pleasure that will be the high point of someone's day —**make do** to manage with what is available —**make for** **1** to go toward **2** to help effect —**make good** **1** to repay or replace **2** to fulfill **3** to succeed —**make it** [Inf.] to achieve a certain thing —**make off with** to steal —**make out** **1** to see with difficulty **2** to understand **3** to fill out (a blank form, etc.) **4** to (try to) show or prove to be **5** to succeed; get along **6** [Slang] *a*) to kiss and caress as lovers *b*) to have sexual intercourse —**make over** **1** to change; renovate **2** to transfer the ownership of —**make something of** **1** to treat as of great importance **2** [Inf.] to make an issue of —**make up** **1** to put together **2** to form; constitute **3** to invent **4** to complete by providing what is lacking **5** to compensate (*for*) **6** to become friendly again after a quarrel **7** to put on cosmetics, etc. —**make up one's mind** to come to a decision —**make up to** to try to win over, as by flattering —**mak'er** ***n.***

make'-be·lieve' ***n.*** pretense; feigning —***adj.*** pretended; feigned

make'o'ver ***n.*** **1** a renovation **2** a change in someone's appearance made by altering makeup, hairstyle, etc.

make'shift' ***n.*** a temporary substitute or expedient —***adj.*** that will do as a temporary substitute

make'up' or **make'-up'** ***n.*** **1** the way something is put together; composition **2** nature; disposition **3** the cosmetics, etc. used by an actor **4** cosmetics generally

make'-work' ***adj.*** that serves no other purpose than to give an idle or unemployed person something to do [a *make-work* project]

mal- ⟦< L *malus,* bad⟧ *prefix* bad or badly, wrong, ill

mal·ad·just·ed (mal'ə jus'tid) ***adj.*** poorly adjusted; specif., unable to adjust to the stresses of daily life —**mal'ad·just'ment** ***n.***

mal·a·droit (mal'ə droit') ***adj.*** ⟦Fr: see MAL- & ADROIT⟧ awkward; clumsy; bungling —**mal'a·droit'ly** ***adv.***

mal·a·dy (mal'ə dē) ***n.***, *pl.* **-dies** ⟦< VL *male habitus,* badly kept⟧ a disease; illness

ma·laise (ma lāz') ***n.*** ⟦Fr < *mal,* bad + *aise,* ease⟧ a vague feeling of illness

mal·a·mute (mal'ə myo͞ot') ***n.*** ⟦< *Malemute,* an Eskimo tribe⟧ a strong dog developed as a sled dog by Alaskan Eskimos

mal·a·prop·ism (mal'ə präp'iz'əm) ***n.*** ⟦after Mrs. *Malaprop* in Sheridan's *The Rivals* (1775)⟧ a ludicrous misuse of words that sound alike

ma·lar·i·a (mə ler'ē ə) ***n.*** ⟦It < *mala aria,* bad air⟧ an infectious disease transmitted by the anopheles mosquito, characterized by severe chills and fever —**ma·lar'i·al** ***adj.***

ma·lar·key or **ma·lar·ky** (mə lär′kē) ***n.*** ⟦< ?⟧ [Slang] nonsensical talk

mal·a·thi·on (mal′ə thī′än′) ***n.*** ⟦< chemical names⟧ an organic insecticide

Ma·la·wi (mä′lä wē′) country in SE Africa: 45,747 sq. mi.; pop. 7,983,000

Ma·lay (mā′lā′, mə lā′) ***n.*** **1** the language of a large group of indigenous peoples of the Malay Peninsula and the Malay Archipelago, now the official language of Malaysia and Indonesia **2** a member of any of these peoples —***adj.*** of these peoples or their language or culture

Mal·a·ya·lam (mal′ə yä′ləm) ***n.*** a language of the SW coast of India

Malay Archipelago large group of islands between SE Asia & Australia

Malay Peninsula peninsula in SE Asia

Ma·lay·sia (mə lā′zhə) **1** MALAY ARCHIPELAGO **2** country in SE Asia, mostly on the Malay Peninsula: 127,317 sq. mi.; pop. 17,567,000 —**Ma·lay′sian** ***adj.***, ***n.***

mal·con·tent (mal′kən tent′) ***adj.*** ⟦OFr: see MAL- & CONTENT[1]⟧ dissatisfied or rebellious —***n.*** a malcontent person

Mal·dives (mal′dīvz) country on a group of islands (**Mal′dive Islands**) in the Indian Ocean: 115 sq. mi.; pop. 213,000

male (māl) ***adj.*** ⟦< L *mas*, a male⟧ **1** designating or of the sex that fertilizes the ovum **2** of, like, or suitable for men or boys; masculine **3** having a part shaped to fit into a corresponding hollow part (called *female*): said of electric plugs, etc. —***n.*** a male person, animal, or plant

mal·e·dic·tion (mal′ə dik′shən) ***n.*** ⟦see MAL- & DICTION⟧ a curse

mal′e·fac′tor (-fak′tər) ***n.*** ⟦< L *male*, evil + *facere*, do⟧ an evildoer or criminal —**mal′e·fac′tion** ***n.***

ma·lef·i·cent (mə lef′ə sənt) ***adj.*** ⟦< L: see prec.⟧ harmful; evil —**ma·lef′i·cence** ***n.***

ma·lev·o·lent (mə lev′ə lənt) ***adj.*** ⟦< L *male*, evil + *velle*, to wish⟧ wishing evil or harm to others; malicious —**ma·lev′o·lence** ***n.***

mal·fea·sance (mal fē′zəns) ***n.*** ⟦< Fr *mal*, evil + *faire*, do⟧ wrongdoing, esp. by a public official

mal·for·ma·tion (mal′fôr mā′shən) ***n.*** faulty or abnormal formation of a body or part —**mal·formed′** ***adj.***

mal·func·tion (mal fuŋk′shən) ***vi.*** to fail to function as it should —***n.*** an instance of malfunctioning

Ma·li (mä′lē) country in W Africa: 478,841 sq. mi.; pop. 9,820,000

mal·ice (mal′is) ***n.*** ⟦< L *malus*, bad⟧ **1** active ill will; desire to harm another **2** *Law* evil intent

ma·li·cious (mə lish′əs) ***adj.*** having, showing, or caused by malice; spiteful —**ma·li′cious·ly** ***adv.***

ma·lign (mə līn′) ***vt.*** ⟦< L *male*, ill + *genus*, born⟧ to speak evil of; slander —***adj.*** **1** malicious **2** evil; baleful **3** very harmful

ma·lig′nan·cy (-nən sē) ***n.*** **1** malignant quality **2** *pl.* **-cies** a malignant tumor

ma·lig·nant (mə lig′nənt) ***adj.*** ⟦see MALIGN⟧ **1** having an evil influence **2** wishing evil **3** very harmful **4** causing or likely to cause death; specif., cancerous —**ma·lig′ni·ty** (-nə tē), *pl.* **-ties**, ***n.***

ma·lin·ger (mə liŋ′gər) ***vi.*** ⟦< Fr *malingre*, sickly⟧ to feign illness so as to escape duty —**ma·lin′ger·er** ***n.***

mall (môl) ***n.*** ⟦< *maul*, mallet: from use in a game on outdoor lanes⟧ **1** a shaded walk or public promenade **2** *a*) a shop-lined street for pedestrians only *b*) an enclosed shopping center

mal·lard (mal′ərd) ***n.*** ⟦< OFr *malart*⟧ the common wild duck

mal·le·a·ble (mal′ē ə bəl) ***adj.*** ⟦< L *malleus*, a hammer⟧ **1** that can be hammered, pounded, or pressed into various shapes without breaking **2** adaptable —**mal′le·a·bil′i·ty** ***n.***

mal·let (mal′ət) ***n.*** ⟦< L *malleus*, a hammer⟧ **1** a short-handled hammer with a wooden head, for driving a chisel, etc. **2** any similar, long-handled hammer, as for use in croquet or polo **3** a small hammer for playing a xylophone, etc.

mal·low (mal′ō) ***n.*** ⟦< L *malva*⟧ any of a family of plants, including the hollyhock, cotton, and okra, with large, showy flowers

mal·nour·ished (mal nʉr′isht) ***adj.*** improperly nourished

mal·nu·tri·tion (mal′no͞o trish′ən) ***n.*** faulty or inadequate nutrition or nourishment

mal′oc·clu′sion (-ə klo͞o′zhən) ***n.*** improper meeting of the upper and lower teeth

mal·o′dor·ous (-ō′dər əs) ***adj.*** having a bad odor; stinking

mal·prac′tice (-prak′tis) ***n.*** professional misconduct or improper practice, esp. by a physician

malt (môlt) ***n.*** ⟦OE *mealt*⟧ barley or other grain soaked until it sprouts, then dried in a kiln: used in brewing and distilling —***adj.*** made with malt

Mal·ta (môl′tə) country on a group of islands in the Mediterranean, south of Sicily: 122 sq. mi.; pop. 376,000

malt′ed (milk) a drink made by mixing a preparation of powdered malt and dried milk, with milk, ice cream, etc.

Mal·tese (môl tēz′) ***n.*** **1** the language of Malta, closely related to Arabic **2** *pl.* **Mal·tese′** a person born or living in Malta —***adj.*** of Malta or its people, language, etc.

malt liquor beer, ale, or the like made from malt by fermentation

mal·treat (mal trēt′) ***vt.*** ⟦see MAL- & TREAT⟧ to treat roughly, unkindly, or brutally; abuse —**mal·treat′ment** ***n.***

ma·ma or **mam′ma** (mä′mə, mə mä′) ***n.*** *child's term for* MOTHER

mam·mal (mam′əl) ***n.*** ⟦< L *mamma*, breast⟧ any of a large group of warm-blooded vertebrates the females of which have milk-secreting glands (**mam′ma·ry glands**) for feeding their offspring —**mam·ma·li·an** (mə mā′lē ən) ***adj.***, ***n.***

mam·mo·gram (mam′ə gram′) ***n.*** an X-ray obtained by mammography

mam·mog·ra·phy (mə mäg′rə fē) ***n.*** ⟦< L *mamma*, breast + -GRAPHY⟧ an X-ray technique for detecting breast tumors before they can be seen or felt

mam·mon (mam′ən) ***n.*** ⟦< Aram⟧ [*often* **M-**] riches regarded as an object of worship and greedy pursuit

MAMMOTH

mam·moth (mam′əth) ***n.*** ⟦< Russ *mamont*⟧ an extinct elephant with long tusks and hairy skin —***adj.*** huge; enormous

man (man) ***n.***, *pl.* **men** (men) ⟦OE *mann*⟧ **1** a human being; person **2** the human race; mankind **3** an adult male person **4** an adult male servant, employee, etc. **5** a husband or male lover **6** any of the pieces used in chess, checkers, etc. —***vt.*** **manned, man′ning 1** to furnish with a labor force for work, defense, etc. **2** to take one's station in or at **3** to strengthen; brace [*to man* oneself for an ordeal] —**as a** (or **one**) **man** in unison; unanimously —**to a man** with no exception

Man (man), **Isle of** one of the British Isles, between Northern Ireland & England

-man (mən, man) *combining form* man or person of a (specified) kind, in a (specified) activity, etc.: now often replaced by -PERSON or -WOMAN

man·a·cle (man′ə kəl) ***n.*** ⟦< L *manus*, hand⟧ a handcuff: *usually used in pl.* —***vt.*** **-cled, -cling 1** to put handcuffs on **2** to restrain

man·age (man′ij) ***vt.*** **-aged, -ag·ing** ⟦< L *manus*, hand⟧ **1** to control the movement or behavior of **2** to have charge of; direct [*to manage* a hotel] **3** to succeed in accomplishing —***vi.*** **1** to carry on business **2** to contrive to get along —**man′age·a·ble** ***adj.***

managed care a plan or system for providing medical services at reduced costs to patients who agree to use specified doctors and hospitals

man′age·ment ***n.*** **1** a managing or being managed **2** the persons managing a business, institution, etc.

man′ag·er ***n.*** one who manages; esp., one who manages a business, etc.

man·a·ge·ri·al (man′ə jir′ē əl) ***adj.*** of a manager or management

ma·ña·na (mä nyä′nä) ***n.***, ***adv.*** ⟦Sp⟧ tomorrow or (at) an indefinite future time

Ma·nas·sas (mə nas′əs) city in NE Virginia: site of two Civil War battles: pop. 28,000

man·a·tee (man′ə tē′) ***n.*** ⟦< WInd native name⟧ a large aquatic mammal of tropical waters

Man·ches·ter (man′ches′tər) city & port in NW England: county district pop. 405,000

Man·chu (man chōō′, man′chōō) ***n.*** **1** *pl.* **-chus′** or **-chu′** a member of a Mongolian people of Manchuria that ruled China from 1644 to 1912 **2** the language of this people —***adj.*** of the Manchus, their language, etc.

Man·chu·ri·a (man choor′ē ə) region in NE China —**Man·chu′ri·an** ***adj.***, ***n.***

man·da·rin (man′də rin) ***n.*** ⟦< Sans *mantrin,* counselor⟧ **1** a high official in the Chinese empire **2** [**M-**] the main dialect of Chinese

man·date (man′dāt′) ***n.*** ⟦< L *mandare,* to command⟧ **1** an order or command **2** [Historical] *a*) a League of Nations commission to a country to administer some region *b*) this region **3** the will of voters as expressed in an election —***vt.*** **-dat′ed, -dat′ing** to require as by law

man·da·to·ry (man′də tôr′ē) ***adj.*** authoritatively commanded; obligatory

man·di·ble (man′də bəl) ***n.*** ⟦< L *mandere,* chew⟧ the jaw; specif., *a*) the lower jaw of a vertebrate *b*) either jaw of a beaked animal

man·do·lin (man′də lin′) ***n.*** ⟦< Gr *pandoura,* kind of lute⟧ a lute-like musical instrument with four to six pairs of strings

man·drake (man′drāk′) ***n.*** ⟦< Gr *mandragoras*⟧ a poisonous plant of the nightshade family

man·drill (man′dril) ***n.*** ⟦MAN + *drill,* kind of monkey⟧ a baboon of W Africa: the male has blue and scarlet patches on the face and rump

mane (mān) ***n.*** ⟦OE *manu*⟧ the long hair growing on the neck of the horse, lion, etc. —**maned** ***adj.***

man′-eat′er ***n.*** an animal that eats human flesh —**man′-eat′ing** ***adj.***

ma·neu·ver (mə nōō′vər) ***n.*** ⟦< L *manu operare,* to work by hand⟧ **1** a planned and controlled movement of troops, warships, etc. **2** a skillful change of direction **3** a skillful or shrewd move; stratagem —***vi.***, ***vt.*** **1** to perform or cause to perform a maneuver or maneuvers **2** to manage or plan skillfully **3** to move, get, make, etc. by some scheme —**ma·neu′ver·a·ble** ***adj.***

man·ful (man′fəl) ***adj.*** manly; brave, resolute, etc. —**man′ful·ly** ***adv.***

man·ga·nese (maŋ′gə nēs′, -nēz′) ***n.*** ⟦ult. < ML *magnesia*: see MAGNESIA⟧ a grayish-white, metallic chemical element, used in alloys

mange (mānj) ***n.*** ⟦< OFr *mangeue,* an itch⟧ a skin disease of mammals, causing itching, hair loss, etc.

man·ger (mān′jər) ***n.*** ⟦< L *mandere,* chew⟧ a box or trough to hold fodder for horses or cattle to eat

man·gle[1] (maŋ′gəl) ***vt.*** **-gled, -gling** ⟦prob. < OFr *mehaigner,* maim⟧ **1** to mutilate by roughly cutting, tearing, crushing, etc. **2** to spoil; botch; mar

man·gle[2] (maŋ′gəl) ***n.*** ⟦< Gr *manganon,*

war machine] a machine for pressing and smoothing sheets, etc. between rollers

man·go (maŋ′gō) ***n.***, *pl.* **-goes** or **-gos** [< Tamil *mān-kāy*] **1** the yellow-red, somewhat acid fruit of a tropical tree **2** this tree

man·grove (maŋ′grōv) ***n.*** [< WInd name] a tropical tree of swampy areas, usually with roots that rise out of the water

man·gy (mān′jē) ***adj.*** **-gi·er, -gi·est 1** having mange **2** filthy, low, etc. —**man′gi·ness *n.***

man·han·dle (man′han′dəl) ***vt.*** **-dled, -dling** to handle roughly

Man·hat·tan[1] (man hat′'n) ***n.*** [after fol.] [*often* **m-**] a cocktail made of whiskey and sweet vermouth

Man·hat·tan[2] (man hat′'n) island in SE New York: borough of New York City: pop. 1,488,000

man′hole′ ***n.*** a hole through which one can enter a sewer, conduit, etc.

man′hood′ ***n.*** **1** the state or time of being a man **2** manly qualities; manliness **3** men collectively

man′-hour′ ***n.*** a time unit equal to one hour of work done by one person

man′hunt′ ***n.*** a hunt for a fugitive

ma·ni·a (mā′nē ə) ***n.*** [Gr, madness] **1** wild or violent mental disorder **2** an excessive enthusiasm

-ma·ni·a (mā′nē ə) [see prec.] *combining form* **1** a (specified) type of mental disorder **2** an intense enthusiasm for

ma·ni·ac (mā′nē ak′) ***adj.*** wildly insane —***n.*** a violently insane person —**ma·ni·a·cal** (mə nī′ə kəl) ***adj.***

man·ic (man′ik) ***adj.*** **1** having, characterized by, or like mania **2** [Inf.] very excited, elated, etc. —**man′ic·al·ly *adv.***

man′ic-de·pres′sive (-dē pres′iv) ***adj.*** BIPOLAR (sense 2)

man·i·cure (man′i kyoor′) ***n.*** [< L *manus,* a hand + *cura,* care] a trimming, polishing, etc. of the fingernails —***vt.*** **-cured′, -cur′ing 1** to trim, polish, etc. (fingernails) **2** [Inf.] to trim, clip, etc. meticulously —**man′i·cur′ist *n.***

man·i·fest (man′ə fest′) ***adj.*** [< L *manifestus,* lit., struck by the hand] apparent to the senses or the mind; obvious —***vt.*** to show plainly; reveal —***n.*** an itemized list of a craft's cargo or passengers —**man′i·fest′ly *adv.***

man′i·fes·ta′tion (-fes tā′shən) ***n.*** **1** a manifesting or being manifested **2** something that manifests or is manifested

man′i·fes′to (-fes′tō) ***n.***, *pl.* **-toes** or **-tos** [It < *manifestare,* to manifest] a public declaration of intention by an important person or group

man·i·fold (man′ə fōld′) ***adj.*** [see MANY & -FOLD] **1** having many forms, parts, etc. **2** of many sorts —***n.*** a pipe with several outlets, as for conducting cylinder exhaust from an engine

man·i·kin (man′i kin) ***n.*** [Du *manneken* < *man,* man + *-ken,* -KIN] **1** a little man; dwarf **2** an anatomical model of the human body, used as in art classes **3** MANNEQUIN

Ma·nil·a (mə nil′ə) capital & seaport of the Philippines, in SW Luzon: pop. 1,630,000 (met. area, 7,929,000)

Manila hemp [after prec.] [*often* **m- h-**] a strong fiber from the leafstalks of a Philippine plant, used for making rope, paper, etc.

Manila paper [*often* **m- p-**] a strong, buff-colored paper, orig. made of Manila hemp

man in the street the average person

ma·nip·u·late (mə nip′yoo lāt′, -yə-) ***vt.*** **-lat′ed, -lat′ing** [ult. < L *manus,* a hand + *plere,* to fill] **1** to handle skillfully **2** to manage artfully or shrewdly, often in an unfair way **3** to falsify (figures, etc.) for one's own purposes —**ma·nip′u·la′tion *n.***

Man·i·to·ba (man′ə tō′bə) province of SC Canada: 250,946 sq. mi.; pop. 1,114,000; cap. Winnipeg: abbrev. *MB* —**Man′i·to′ban *adj., n.***

man·kind (man′kind′) ***n.*** **1** the human race **2** all human males

man·ly (man′lē) ***adj.*** **-li·er, -li·est** having the qualities regarded as suitable for a man; virile, brave, etc. —**man′li·ness *n.***

man′-made′ ***adj.*** artificial or synthetic

Mann (tō′mäs), **Thom·as** 1875-1955; Ger. novelist, in the U.S. 1938-52

man·na (man′ə) ***n.*** [< Heb *mān*] **1** *Bible* food miraculously provided for the Israelites in the wilderness **2** anything badly needed that comes unexpectedly

man·ne·quin (man′ə kin) ***n.*** [see MANIKIN] **1** a model of the human body, used as by tailors **2** a woman who models clothes in stores, etc.

man·ner (man′ər) ***n.*** [< L *manus,* a hand] **1** a way in which something is done or happens **2** a way, esp. a usual way, of acting **3** [*pl.*] *a)* ways of social behavior *[bad manners]* *b)* polite ways of social behavior *[to learn manners]* **4** kind; sort

man′nered (-ərd) ***adj.*** **1** having manners of a specified sort *[ill-mannered]* **2** artificial, stylized, etc.

man′ner·ism′ ***n.*** **1** excessive use of some distinctive manner or style in art, literature, etc. **2** a peculiarity of manner in behavior, speech, etc.

man′ner·ly ***adj.*** polite

man·ni·kin (man′ə kin) ***n.*** *alt. sp. of* MANIKIN

man·nish (man′ish) ***adj.*** like a man or man's: used in referring to a woman having characteristics generally attributed to men

ma·noeu·vre (mə noo′vər) ***n., vi., vt.*** **-vred, -vring** *chiefly Brit. sp. of* MANEUVER

man of letters a writer, scholar, editor, etc., esp. in the field of literature

man′-of-war′ ***n.***, *pl.* **men′-of-war′** an armed naval vessel; warship

ma·nom·e·ter (mə näm′ət ər) ***n.*** [Fr < Gr *manos,* rare (as in "thin, sparse") + Fr *-mètre,* -METER] an instrument for measuring the pressure of gases or liquids

man̦ on the street *var. of* MAN IN THE STREET

man·or (man′ər) ***n.*** ⟦< L *manere,* remain, dwell⟧ **1** in England, an estate **2** the main house on an estate —**ma·no·ri·al** (mə nôr′ē əl) ***adj.***

man′pow′er ***n.*** **1** power furnished by human strength **2** the collective strength or availability for work of the people of an area, nation, etc.

man·qué (män kā′) ***adj.*** ⟦Fr < *manquer,* be lacking⟧ unfulfilled; would-be *[a poet manqué]*

MANSARD ROOF

man·sard (roof) (man′särd) ⟦after F. *Mansard,* 17th-c. Fr architect⟧ a roof with two slopes on each of four sides, the lower steeper than the upper

manse (mans) ***n.*** ⟦see MANOR⟧ the residence of a minister; parsonage

man′ser′vant ***n.***, *pl.* **men′ser′vants** a male servant: also **man servant**

-man·ship (mən ship) *combining form* talent or skill (esp. in gaining advantage) in connection with *[grantsmanship]*

man·sion (man′shən) ***n.*** ⟦< L *manere,* remain, dwell⟧ a large, imposing house

man′-sized′ ***adj.*** [Inf.] of a size fit for a man; big: also **man′-size′**

man′slaugh′ter (-slôt′ər) ***n.*** the killing of a human being by another, esp. when unlawful but without malice

man·ta (man′tə) ***n.*** ⟦Sp < LL *mantum,* a cloak⟧ a giant ray, with winglike pectoral fins: also **manta ray**

man·tel (man′təl) ***n.*** ⟦var. of MANTLE⟧ **1** the facing of stone, etc. about a fireplace, including a projecting shelf **2** this shelf Also **man′tel·piece′**

man·til·la (man til′ə, -tē′ə) ***n.*** ⟦Sp: see MANTA⟧ a woman's scarf, as of lace, worn over the hair and shoulders

man·tis (man′tis) ***n.***, *pl.* **-tis·es** or **-tes′** (-tēz′) ⟦< Gr, prophet⟧ an insect with forelegs often held up together as if praying

man·tis·sa (man tis′ə) ***n.*** ⟦L, (useless) addition⟧ the decimal part of a logarithm

man·tle (man′təl) ***n.*** ⟦< L *mantellum*⟧ **1** a loose, sleeveless cloak: sometimes used figuratively to connote authority **2** anything that envelops or conceals **3** a small hood which when placed over a flame gives off incandescent light —***vt.*** **-tled, -tling** to cover as with a mantle —***vi.*** to blush

man′-to-man′ ***adj.*** frank; candid

man·tra (man′trə, män′-) ***n.*** ⟦Sans⟧ a chant of a Vedic hymn, text, etc.

man·u·al (man′yoo əl) ***adj.*** ⟦< L *manus,* a hand⟧ **1** of the hands **2** made, done, or worked by hand **3** involving skill or hard work with the hands —***n.*** **1** a handy book of facts, etc. for use as a guide, reference, etc. **2** prescribed drill in the handling of a weapon —**man′u·al·ly** ***adv.***

man·u·fac·ture (man′yoo fak′chər, -yə-) ***n.*** ⟦< L *manus,* a hand + *facere,* make⟧ **1** the making of goods, esp. by machinery and on a large scale **2** the making of something in any way, esp. when regarded as merely mechanical —***vt.*** **-tured, -tur·ing** **1** to make, esp. by machinery **2** to make up (excuses, etc.); fabricate —**man′u·fac′tur·er** ***n.***

man·u·mit (man′yoo mit′) ***vt.*** **-mit′ted, -mit′ting** ⟦< L *manus,* a hand + *mittere,* send⟧ to free from slavery —**man′u·mis′sion** ***n.***

ma·nure (mə noor′) ***vt.*** **-nured′, -nur′ing** ⟦< OFr *manouvrer,* work with the hands⟧ to put manure on or into —***n.*** animal excrement, etc. used to fertilize soil

man·u·script (man′yoo skript′, -yə-) ***adj.*** ⟦< L *manus,* hand + *scriptus,* written⟧ written by hand or typewritten —***n.*** **1** a written or typewritten document, book, etc., esp. one submitted to a publisher **2** writing as opposed to print

Manx (maŋks) ***n.*** the Celtic language of the Isle of Man, now nearly extinct —***adj.*** of the Isle of Man or its people, etc.

man·y (men′ē) ***adj.*** **more, most** ⟦OE *manig*⟧ numerous —***pl.n.*** a large number (of persons or things) —***pron.*** many persons or things

Ma·o·ri (mä′ō rē, mou′rē) ***n.*** **1** *pl.* **-ris** or **-ri** a member of a Polynesian people native to New Zealand **2** the language of this people —***adj.*** of the Maoris or their language, etc.

Mao Tse-tung (mou′ dzu′dooŋ′) 1893-1976; Chinese Communist leader: Pinyin *Mao Zedong* —**Mao′ism′** ***n.*** —**Mao′ist** ***adj.***, ***n.***

map (map) ***n.*** ⟦< L *mappa,* napkin, cloth⟧ **1** a representation of all or part of the earth's surface, showing countries, bodies of water, cities, etc. **2** a representation of the sky, showing the stars, etc. —***vt.*** **mapped, map′ping** **1** to make a map of **2** to plan

ma·ple (mā′pəl) ***n.*** ⟦OE *mapel*⟧ **1** any of a large group of trees with two-winged fruits, grown for wood, sap, or shade **2** the hard, light-colored wood **3** the flavor of the syrup or sugar made from the sap

mar (mär) ***vt.*** **marred, mar′ring** ⟦OE *mierran,* hinder⟧ to injure or damage so as to make imperfect, etc.; spoil

mar·a·bou (mar′ə boo′) ***n.*** ⟦Fr < Ar *murābit,* hermit⟧ a large-billed African stork

ma·ra·ca (mə rä′kə) ***n.*** ⟦Port *maracá* < native name in Brazil⟧ a percussion instrument that is a dried gourd or a gourd-shaped rattle with pebbles, etc. in it

mar·a·schi·no (mar′ə shē′nō, -skē′-) ***n.*** ⟦It < *marasca,* kind of cherry⟧ a liqueur made from a sour cherry

maraschino cherries cherries in a syrup flavored with maraschino or imitation maraschino

mar·a·thon (mar′ə thän′) ***n.*** ⟦after *Marathon*, plain in ancient Greece⟧ **1** a race on foot, 26 miles and 385 yards in length **2** any contest or endeavor testing endurance —**mar′a·thon′er *n.***

ma·raud (mə rôd′) ***vi., vt.*** ⟦< Fr *maraud*, vagabond⟧ to raid and plunder —**ma·raud′er *n.***

mar·ble (mär′bəl) ***n.*** ⟦< Gr *marmaros*, white stone⟧ **1** a hard limestone, white, colored, or mottled, which takes a high polish **2** a piece of this stone, used in sculpture, etc. **3** anything like marble in hardness, coldness, coloration, etc. **4** *a*) a little ball of stone, glass, etc. *b*) [*pl., with sing. v.*] a children's game played with such balls **5** [*pl.*] [Slang] mental soundness; wits —***adj.*** of or like marble —***vt.* -bled, -bling** to make (book edges) look mottled like marble

mar′bled *adj.* **1** mottled or streaked **2** streaked with fat: said of meat

mar′ble·ize′ (-īz′) ***vt.* -ized′, -iz′ing** to make look like marble

mar′bling *n.* a streaked or mottled appearance like that of marble

march[1] (märch) ***vi.*** ⟦Fr *marcher*⟧ **1** to walk with regular steps, as in military formation **2** to advance steadily —***vt.*** to cause to march —***n.*** **1** a marching **2** a steady advance; progress **3** a regular, steady step **4** the distance covered in marching **5** a piece of music with a beat suitable for marching —**on the march** marching or advancing —**steal a march on** to get an advantage over secretly —**march′er *n.***

march[2] (märch) ***n.*** ⟦< OFr⟧ a border or frontier

March (märch) ***n.*** ⟦< L *Mars*, the god Mars⟧ the third month of the year, having 31 days: abbrev. **Mar.**

March hare a hare in breeding time, proverbially an example of madness

marching orders **1** orders to march, go, or leave **2** notice of dismissal

mar·chion·ess (mär′shən is) ***n.*** **1** the wife or widow of a marquess **2** a lady of the rank of a marquess

Mar·co·ni (mär kō′nē), **Gu·gliel·mo** (g o͞o lyel′mō) 1874-1937; It. physicist: developed wireless telegraphy

Mar·di Gras (mär′dē grä′) ⟦Fr, fat Tuesday⟧ [*sometimes* **M- g-**] the last day before Lent: a day of carnival in New Orleans, etc.

mare[1] (mer) ***n.*** ⟦< OE *mere*⟧ a mature female horse, mule, donkey, etc.

ma·re[2] (mä′rā′) ***n.***, *pl.* **ma·ri·a** (mä′rē ə) ⟦L, sea⟧ a large, dark area on the moon

mare's-nest (merz′nest′) ***n.*** **1** a hoax **2** a jumble; mess

mar·ga·rine (mär′jə rin) ***n.*** ⟦Fr⟧ a spread or cooking fat of vegetable oils processed, often with milk or whey, to the consistency of butter

mar·gin (mär′jən) ***n.*** ⟦< L *margo*⟧ **1** a border; edge **2** the blank border of a printed or written page **3** an amount beyond what is needed **4** provision for increase, error, etc. **5** the amount or degree by which things differ **6** the difference between the cost and the selling price of goods **7** collateral deposited with a broker, either to meet legal requirements or to insure against loss on contracts, as for buying stocks

mar′gin·al *adj.* **1** of, in, or near the margin **2** limited or minimal

mar·gi·na·li·a (mär′jə nā′lē ə) ***pl.n.*** notes written or printed in the margin

mar′gin·al·ize′ *vt.* -ized′, -iz′ing to exclude or ignore

ma·ri·a·chi (mär′ē ä′chē) ***n.***, *pl.* **-chis** ⟦MexSp < Fr *mariage*, marriage: from playing at wedding celebrations⟧ **1** a member of a strolling band of musicians in Mexico **2** such a band **3** its music

Mar·i·an (mer′ē ən, mar′-) ***adj.*** of the Virgin Mary

Ma·rie An·toi·nette (mə rē′ an′twə net′) 1755-93; wife of Louis XVI: queen of France (1774-92): guillotined

mar·i·gold (mar′ə gōld′) ***n.*** ⟦< *Marie* (prob. the Virgin Mary) + GOLD⟧ a plant of the composite family, with red, yellow, or orange flowers

mar·i·jua·na or **mar·i·hua·na** (mar′ə wä′nə) ***n.*** ⟦AmSp⟧ **1** HEMP (*n.* 1) **2** its dried leaves and flowers, smoked for euphoric effects

ma·rim·ba (mə rim′bə) ***n.*** ⟦< native name in Africa⟧ a kind of xylophone with a resonant tube beneath each bar

ma·ri·na (mə rē′nə) ***n.*** ⟦< L *mare*, sea⟧ a small harbor with docks, services, etc. for pleasure craft

mar·i·nade (mar′ə nād′) ***n.*** ⟦Fr < Sp *marinar*, to pickle⟧ a spiced pickling solution for steeping meat, fish, etc., often before cooking —***vt.* -nad′ed, -nad′ing** MARINATE

mar·i·nate (mar′ə nāt′) ***vt.* -nat′ed, -nat′ing** ⟦< It *marinare*, to pickle⟧ to steep in a marinade

ma·rine (mə rēn′) ***adj.*** ⟦< L *mare*, sea⟧ **1** of or found in the sea **2** *a*) maritime; nautical *b*) naval —***n.*** **1** a member of a military force trained for service at sea **2** [*often* **M-**] a member of the MARINE CORPS

Marine Corps a branch of the United States armed forces trained for land, sea, and aerial combat

mar·i·ner (mar′ə nər) ***n.*** a sailor

mar·i·o·nette (mar′ē ə net′, mer′-) ***n.*** ⟦Fr < *Marie*, Mary⟧ a jointed puppet moved by strings or wires

mar·i·tal (mar′ət′l) ***adj.*** ⟦< L *maritus*, a husband⟧ of marriage; matrimonial —**mar′i·tal·ly *adv.***

mar·i·time (mar′ə tīm′) ***adj.*** ⟦< L *mare*, sea⟧ **1** on, near, or living near the sea **2** of sea navigation, shipping, etc.

mar·jo·ram (mär′jə rəm) ***n.*** ⟦prob. ult. < Gr *amarakos*⟧ a fragrant herb of the mint family, used in cooking

mark[1] (märk) ***n.*** ⟦OE *mearc*, boundary⟧ **1** a line, dot, spot, scratch, etc. on a surface **2** a printed or written symbol [*punctuation marks*] **3** a brand or label on an article showing the maker, etc. **4**

an indication of some quality **5** a grade *[a mark of B in Latin]* **6** a standard of quality **7** impression; influence **8** an object of known position, serving as a guide **9** a line, dot, etc. indicating position, as on a graduated scale **10** an object aimed at; target **11** a goal; end; aim —*vt.* **1** to put or make a mark or marks on **2** to identify as by a mark **3** to indicate by a mark **4** to show plainly *[her smile marked her joy]* **5** to set off; characterize **6** to listen to *[mark my words]* **7** to grade; rate —**make one's mark** to achieve fame —**mark down** (or **up**) to mark for sale at a reduced (or an increased) price —**mark time** **1** to keep time while at a halt by lifting the feet as if marching **2** to suspend progress for a time —**mark'er** *n.*

mark[2] (märk) *n.* ⟦< ON *mǫrk*⟧ DEUTSCHE MARK

Mark (märk) *n. Bible* **1** one of the four Evangelists, the reputed author of the second Gospel **2** this Gospel

mark'down' *n.* **1** a selling at a reduced price **2** the amount of reduction in price

marked (märkt) *adj.* **1** having a mark or marks **2** noticeable; obvious —**mark·ed·ly** (märk'id lē) *adv.*

mar·ket (mär'kit) *n.* ⟦ult. < L *merx*, merchandise⟧ **1** a gathering of people for buying and selling things **2** an open space or a building where goods are shown for sale: also **mar'ket·place'** **3** a shop for the sale of provisions *[a meat market]* **4** a region in which goods can be bought and sold *[the European market]* **5** trade; buying and selling **6** demand (for goods, etc.) *[a good market for tea]* —*vt.* **1** to offer for sale **2** to sell —*vi.* to buy provisions —**mar'ket·a·ble** *adj.* —**mar'ket·eer'** (-kə tir') *n.* —**mar'ket·er** *n.*

mar·ket·ing *n.* **1** a buying or selling in a market **2** the total of activities involved in the moving of goods from the producer to the consumer, including selling, advertising, etc.

market share a company's percentage of the total sales of some commodity

Mark·ham (mär'kəm) city in SE Ontario, Canada: pop. 173,000

mark'ing *n.* **1** a mark or marks **2** the characteristic arrangement of marks, as of an animal

marks·man (märks'mən) *n., pl.* **-men** (-mən) a person who shoots, esp. one who shoots well —**marks'man·ship'** *n.*

mark'up' *n.* **1** a selling at an increased price **2** the amount of increase in price

mar·lin (mär'lin) *n., pl.* **-lin** or **-lins** ⟦< fol.: from the shape⟧ a large, slender deep-sea fish

mar·line·spike (mär'lin spīk') *n.* ⟦< Du *marlijn*, small cord + SPIKE[1]⟧ a pointed metal tool for separating the strands of a rope in splicing

mar·ma·lade (mär'mə lād') *n.* ⟦ult. < Gr *meli*, honey + *mēlon*, apple⟧ a jamlike preserve of oranges, etc.

mar·mo·set (mär'mə zet', -set') *n.* ⟦< OFr *marmouset*, grotesque figure⟧ a small monkey of South and Central America

mar·mot (mär'mət) *n.* ⟦prob. < L *mus montanus*, mountain mouse⟧ any of a group of thick-bodied rodents, as the woodchuck

ma·roon[1] (mə ro͞on') *n., adj.* ⟦Fr *marron*, chestnut⟧ dark brownish red

ma·roon[2] (mə ro͞on') *vt.* ⟦< AmSp *cimarrón*, wild⟧ **1** to put (a person) ashore in a lonely place and abandon that person **2** to leave abandoned, helpless, etc.

marque (märk) *n.* ⟦Fr, a sign⟧ a distinctive emblem on an automobile

mar·quee (mär kē') *n.* ⟦< Fr *marquise*, awning⟧ a rooflike projection over an entrance, as to a theater

mar·quess (mär'kwis) *n.* ⟦var. of MARQUIS⟧ **1** a British nobleman ranking above an earl **2** MARQUIS

mar·que·try (mär'kə trē) *n.* ⟦Fr, ult. < *marque*, a mark⟧ decorative inlaid work, as in furniture

mar·quis (mär'kwis) *n.* ⟦< ML *marchisus*, prefect⟧ in some European countries, a nobleman ranking above an earl or count

mar·quise (mär kēz') *n.* **1** the wife or widow of a marquis **2** a lady of the rank of a marquis

mar·qui·sette (mär'ki zet', -kwi-) *n.* ⟦see MARQUEE⟧ a thin, meshlike fabric used for curtains, etc.

mar·riage (mar'ij) *n.* **1** the state of being married **2** the act of marrying; wedding **3** a close union —**mar'riage·a·ble** *adj.*

mar·ried (mar'ēd) *adj.* **1** being husband and wife **2** having a husband or wife **3** of marriage —*n.* a married person

mar·row (mar'ō) *n.* ⟦OE *mearg*⟧ the soft, fatty tissue that fills the cavities of most bones

mar·ry (mar'ē) *vt.* **-ried**, **-ry·ing** ⟦< L *maritus*, husband⟧ **1** to join as husband and wife **2** to take as husband or wife **3** to unite —*vi.* to get married —**marry off** to give in marriage

Mars (märz) *n.* **1** the Roman god of war **2** a planet of the solar system: see PLANET

Mar·seille (mär sā') seaport in SE France: pop. 801,000 Eng. sp. **Mar·seilles'**

marsh (märsh) *n.* ⟦OE *merisc*⟧ a tract of low, wet, soft land; swamp; bog —**marsh'y**, **-i·er**, **-i·est**, *adj.*

mar·shal (mär'shəl) *n.* ⟦< OHG *marah*, horse + *scalh*, servant⟧ **1** in various foreign armies, a general officer of the highest rank **2** an official in charge of ceremonies, parades, etc. **3** in the U.S., *a)* a federal officer appointed to a judicial district with duties like those of a sheriff *b)* the head of some police or fire departments —*vt.* **-shaled** or **-shalled**, **-shal·ing** or **-shal·ling** **1** to arrange (troops, ideas, etc.) in order **2** to guide

Mar·shall (mär'shəl), **John** 1755-1835; U.S. chief justice (1801-35)

Marshall Islands country on a group of islands in the W Pacific: formerly part of a U.S. territory: 70 sq. mi.; pop. 43,000

marsh·mal·low (märsh′mel′ō) ***n.*** ⟦orig. made of the root of a mallow found in marshes⟧ a soft, spongy confection of sugar, gelatin, etc.

mar·su·pi·al (mär so͞o′pē əl) ***adj.*** ⟦< Gr *marsypos*, pouch⟧ of a group of mammals that carry their incompletely developed young in an external abdominal pouch on the mother **—*n.*** such an animal, as a kangaroo or opossum

mart (märt) ***n.*** ⟦MDu *markt*⟧ a market

mar·ten (märt′'n) ***n.*** ⟦< OFr *martre*⟧ **1** a small mammal like a weasel, with soft, thick fur **2** the fur

mar·tial (mär′shəl) ***adj.*** ⟦< L *martialis*, of Mars⟧ **1** of or suitable for war **2** warlike; bold **3** military **—mar′tial·ly *adv.***

martial arts systems of self-defense originating in E Asia, such as karate or kung fu, also engaged in for sport

martial law temporary rule by military authorities over civilians, as during a war

Mar·tian (mär′shən) ***adj.*** of Mars **—*n.*** a being from or living on Mars, as in science fiction

mar·tin (märt′'n) ***n.*** ⟦Fr⟧ any of several birds of the swallow family

mar·ti·net (märt′'n et′) ***n.*** ⟦after *Martinet*, 17th-c. Fr general⟧ a very strict disciplinarian

mar·ti·ni (mär tē′nē) ***n.***, *pl.* **-nis** ⟦< ?⟧ a cocktail made of gin (or vodka) and dry vermouth

mar·tyr (märt′ər) ***n.*** ⟦< Gr *martyr*, a witness⟧ **1** one who chooses to suffer or die for one's faith or principles **2** one who suffers great pain or misery for a long time **—*vt.*** to kill or persecute for a belief **—mar′tyr·dom *n.***

mar·vel (mär′vəl) ***n.*** ⟦< L *mirari*, wonder at⟧ a wonderful thing **—*vi.* -veled** or **-velled**, **-vel·ing** or **-vel·ling** to be filled with wonder **—*vt.*** to wonder at or about: followed by a clause

mar′vel·ous (-və ləs) ***adj.*** **1** causing wonder; extraordinary, etc. **2** fine; splendid Also [Chiefly Brit.] **mar′vel·lous —mar′vel·ous·ly *adv.***

Marx (märks), **Karl** (kärl) 1818-83; Ger. founder of modern socialism

Marx′ism′ ***n.*** the system of thought developed by Karl Marx and Friedrich Engels (1820-95, Ger. socialist leader & writer), serving as a basis for socialism and communism **—Marx′ist** or **Marx′i·an *adj.*, *n.***

Mar·y (mer′ē) ***n.*** *Bible* mother of Jesus

Mar·y·land (mer′ə lənd) state of the E U.S.: 9,775 sq. mi.; pop. 4,781,000; cap. Annapolis: abbrev. *MD* **—Mar′y·land·er** (-lən dər, -lan′-) ***n.***

Mary Mag·da·lene (mag′də lən) *Bible* a repentant woman whom Jesus forgave

mar·zi·pan (mär′zi pan′) ***n.*** ⟦Ger < It *marzapane*⟧ a confection that is a paste of ground almonds, sugar, and egg white, variously shaped

masc or **mas** *abbrev.* masculine

mas·car·a (mas kar′ə) ***n.*** ⟦< It *maschera*, mask⟧ a cosmetic for darkening the eyelashes **—*vt.* -car′aed**, **-car′a·ing** to put mascara on

mas·cot (mas′kät′) ***n.*** ⟦< Prov *masco*, sorcerer⟧ **1** any person, animal, or thing supposed to bring good luck **2** any person, animal, or thing adopted, as by a sports team, as a symbol

mas·cu·line (mas′kyə lin) ***adj.*** ⟦< L *mas*, male⟧ **1** male; of men or boys **2** suitable to or having qualities regarded as typical of men; strong, vigorous, manly, etc. **3** mannish: said of women **4** *Gram.* designating or of the gender of words referring to males as well as to other words to which no sex is attributed **—mas′cu·lin′i·ty *n.***

mash (mash) ***n.*** ⟦< OE *mascwyrt*⟧ **1** crushed malt or meal soaked in hot water for making wort **2** a mixture of watered bran, meal, etc. for feeding horses, etc. **3** any soft mass **—*vt.*** **1** to change into a soft mass by beating, crushing, etc. **2** to crush and injure

mask (mask) ***n.*** ⟦< Fr < It *maschera*⟧ **1** a covering to conceal or protect the face **2** anything that conceals or disguises **3** *a*) a molded likeness of the face *b*) a grotesque representation of a face, worn to amuse or frighten **—*vt.*** to conceal or cover with or as with a mask **—masked *adj.***

mas·o·chism (mas′ə kiz′əm) ***n.*** ⟦after L. von Sacher-*Masoch* (1835-95), Austrian writer⟧ the getting of pleasure, often sexual pleasure, from being hurt or humiliated **—mas′o·chist *n.* —mas′o·chis′tic *adj.* —mas′o·chis′ti·cal·ly *adv.***

ma·son (mā′sən) ***n.*** ⟦< ML *macio*⟧ **1** one whose work is building with stone, brick, etc. **2** [**M-**] FREEMASON

Ma·son-Dix·on line (mā′sən dik′sən) ⟦after C. *Mason* & J. *Dixon*, who surveyed it, 1763-67⟧ boundary line between Pennsylvania & Maryland, regarded as separating the North from the South

Ma·son·ic (mə sän′ik) ***adj.*** [*also* **m-**] of Freemasons or Freemasonry

ma·son·ry (mā′sən rē) ***n.*** **1** a mason's trade **2** *pl.* **-ries** something built, as by a mason, of stone, brick, etc. **3** [*usually* **M-**] FREEMASONRY

masque (mask) ***n.*** ⟦see MASK⟧ **1** MASQUERADE (*n.* 1) **2** a former kind of dramatic entertainment, with lavish costumes, music, etc. **—masqu′er *n.***

mas·quer·ade (mas′kə rād′) ***n.*** ⟦see MASK⟧ **1** a ball or party at which masks and fancy costumes are worn **2** *a*) a disguise *b*) an acting under false pretenses **—*vi.* -ad′ed**, **-ad′ing** **1** to take part in a masquerade **2** to act under false pretenses

mass (mas) ***n.*** ⟦< Gr *maza*, barley cake⟧ **1** a quantity of matter of indefinite shape and size; lump **2** a large quantity or number *[a mass of bruises]* **3** bulk; size **4** the main part **5** *Physics* the quantity of matter in a body as measured by its inertia **—*adj.*** of or for the masses or for a large number **—*vt.*, *vi.*** to gather or form into a mass **—the masses** the common people

Mass (mas) ***n.*** ⟦< L *missa* in the words said by the priest: *ite, missa est* (*contio*), go, (the meeting) is dismissed⟧ [*also* **m-**] *R.C.Ch.* the service that includes the Eucharist

Mas·sa·chu·setts (mas′ə cho͞o′sits) New England state of the U.S.: 7,838 sq. mi.; pop. 6,016,000; cap. Boston: abbrev. *MA*

mas·sa·cre (mas′ə kər) ***n.*** ⟦< OFr *maçacre*, butchery⟧ the indiscriminate, merciless killing of many people or animals —***vt.*** **-cred, -cring** (-kər iŋ, -kriŋ) to kill in large numbers

mas·sage (mə säzh′) ***n.*** ⟦Fr < Ar *massa*, to touch⟧ a rubbing, kneading, etc. of part of the body, as to stimulate circulation or relieve tension —***vt.*** **-saged′, -sag′ing** to give a massage to

mas·seur (mə sur′, -so͞or′) ***masc.n.*** ⟦Fr⟧ a man whose work is giving massages —**mas·seuse** (mə so͞oz′, -so͞os′) ***fem.n.***

mas·sive (mas′iv) ***adj.*** **1** forming or consisting of a large mass; big and solid **2** large and imposing —**mas′sive·ly** ***adv.*** —**mas′sive·ness** ***n.***

mass media those means of communication that reach and influence large numbers of people, as newspapers, radio, and TV

mass noun a noun denoting an abstraction or something that cannot be counted (Ex.: *love, water, news*)

mass number the number of neutrons and protons in the nucleus of an atom

mass production quantity production of goods, esp. by machinery and division of labor —**mass′-pro·duce′, -duced′, -duc′ing,** ***vt.***

mast (mast) ***n.*** ⟦OE *mæst*⟧ **1** a tall vertical spar used to support the sails, yards, radar, etc. on a ship **2** a vertical pole

mas·tec·to·my (mas tek′tə mē) ***n.***, *pl.* **-mies** the surgical removal of all or part of a breast

mas·ter (mas′tər) ***n.*** ⟦< L *magister*⟧ **1** a man who rules others or has control over something; specif., *a*) one who is head of a household *b*) an employer *c*) one who owns a slave or an animal *d*) the captain of a merchant ship **2** *a*) a person very skilled and able in some work, profession, science, etc.; expert *b*) an artist regarded as great **3** [**M-**] a title applied to a boy too young to be addressed as *Mr.* —***adj.*** **1** being a master **2** of a master **3** chief; main; controlling —***vt.*** **1** to become master of **2** to become an expert in (an art, science, etc.)

mas′ter·ful ***adj.*** **1** acting the part of a master; domineering **2** expert; skillful —**mas′ter·ful·ly** ***adv.***

master key a key that will open every one of a set of locks

mas′ter·ly ***adj.*** expert; skillful

mas′ter·mind′ ***n.*** a very clever person, esp. one who plans or runs a project —***vt.*** to be the mastermind of

Master of Arts (or **Science,** etc.) a degree given by a college or university to one who has completed a prescribed course at the first level of graduate study: also **master's (degree)**

master of ceremonies one who supervises or presides over a ceremony, program, etc.

mas′ter·piece′ ***n.*** ⟦< Ger *meisterstück*⟧ **1** a thing made or done with masterly skill **2** the greatest work of a person or group

master sergeant *U.S. Mil.* a noncommissioned officer of high rank

mas′ter·stroke′ ***n.*** a masterly action, move, or achievement

mas′ter·work′ ***n.*** MASTERPIECE

mas′ter·y ***n.***, *pl.* **-ies** **1** rule; control **2** ascendancy or victory **3** expert skill or knowledge

mast′head′ ***n.*** **1** the top part of a ship's mast **2** a box or section in a newspaper or magazine, giving the owner, editors, etc.

mas·ti·cate (mas′ti kāt′) ***vt.*** **-cat′ed, -cat′ing** ⟦ult. < Gr *mastax*, mouth⟧ to chew —**mas′ti·ca′tion** ***n.***

mas·tiff (mas′tif) ***n.*** ⟦< L *mansuetus*, tame⟧ a large, powerful dog with a short, thick coat

mas·to·don (mas′tə dän′) ***n.*** ⟦< Gr *mastos*, breast + *odous*, tooth: from the nipplelike processes on its molar⟧ a large, extinct mammal resembling the elephant but larger

mas·toid (mas′toid′) ***adj.*** ⟦< Gr *mastos*, breast + *-eidēs*, -OID⟧ designating, of, or near a projection of the temporal bone behind the ear —***n.*** the mastoid projection

mas·tur·bate (mas′tər bāt′) ***vi.*** **-bat′ed, -bat′ing** ⟦< L *masturbari*⟧ to manipulate the genitals for sexual gratification —**mas′tur·ba′tion** ***n.***

mat[1] (mat) ***n.*** ⟦< LL *matta*⟧ **1** a flat piece of cloth, rubber, woven straw, etc. used for protection, as on a floor or under a vase **2** a thickly padded floor covering, esp. one used for wrestling, etc. **3** anything densely interwoven or growing in a thick tangle —***vt., vi.*** **mat′ted, mat′ting** **1** to cover as with a mat **2** to form into a thick tangle —**go to the mat** [Inf.] to engage in a struggle or dispute

mat[2] (mat) ***n.*** ⟦< OFr⟧ **1** MATTE **2** a border, as of cardboard, put around a picture —***vt.*** **mat′ted, mat′ting** to frame with a mat

mat[3] (mat) ***n.*** [Inf.] *Printing* a matrix

mat·a·dor (mat′ə dôr′) ***n.*** ⟦< Sp *matar*, to kill⟧ a bullfighter whose specialty is killing the bull

match[1] (mach) ***n.*** ⟦< OFr *mesche*⟧ a slender piece of wood, cardboard, etc. tipped with a substance that catches fire by friction

match[2] (mach) ***n.*** ⟦OE (*ge*)*mæcca*, mate⟧ **1** any person or thing equal or similar to another **2** two persons or things that go well together **3** a contest or game **4** a marriage or mating —***vt.*** **1** to put in opposition (*with*); pit (*against*) **2** to be equal or similar to **3** to make or get a counterpart or equivalent to **4** to fit (one thing) to another —***vi.*** to be equal, similar, suitable, etc.

match′book′ ***n.*** a folder of book matches

match′less ***adj.*** having no equal

match′mak′ing ***n.*** the arranging of marriages, or of boxing matches, etc. —**match′mak′er** ***n.***

match′stick′ ***n.*** a thin strip of wood, cardboard, etc., as or like that of a match

mate (māt) ***n.*** ⟦< MDu⟧ **1** a companion or fellow worker **2** one of a matched pair **3** *a)* a husband or wife *b)* the male or female of paired animals **4** an officer of a merchant ship, ranking below the captain —***vt.***, ***vi.*** **mat′ed**, **mat′ing** **1** to join as a pair **2** to couple in marriage or sexual union

ma·te·ri·al (mə tir′ē əl) ***adj.*** ⟦< L *materia*, matter⟧ **1** of matter; physical *[*a *material* object*]* **2** of the body or bodily needs, comfort, etc.; not spiritual **3** important, pertinent, etc. —***n.*** **1** what a thing is, or may be, made of; elements or parts **2** cloth; fabric **3** [*pl.*] tools, articles, etc. needed to make or do something

ma·te′ri·al·ism′ ***n.*** **1** the doctrine that everything in the world, including thought, can be explained in terms of matter alone **2** the tendency to be more concerned with material than with spiritual or intellectual values —**ma·te′ri·al·ist** ***n.***, ***adj.*** —**ma·te′ri·al·is′tic** ***adj.***

ma·te′ri·al·ize′ (-īz′) ***vt.*** **-ized′**, **-iz′ing** to give material form to —***vi.*** **1** to become fact; be realized **2** to take on bodily form: said of spirits, etc. —**ma·te′ri·al·i·za′tion** ***n.***

ma·te′ri·al·ly ***adv.*** **1** physically **2** to a great extent; substantially

ma·te·ri·el or **ma·té·ri·el** (mə tir′ē el′) ***n.*** ⟦Fr⟧ the necessary materials and tools; specif., military weapons, equipment, etc.

ma·ter·nal (mə tur′nəl) ***adj.*** ⟦< L *mater*, mother⟧ **1** of, like, or from a mother **2** related through the mother's side of the family —**ma·ter′nal·ly** ***adv.***

ma·ter′ni·ty (-nə tē) ***n.*** the state of being a mother; motherhood —***adj.*** **1** for pregnant women **2** for the care of mothers and their newborn babies

math[1] (math) ***n.*** [Inf.] mathematics

math[2] *abbrev.* mathematics

math·e·mat·i·cal (math′ə mat′i kəl) ***adj.*** ⟦< Gr *manthanein*, learn⟧ **1** of, like, or concerned with mathematics **2** very precise, accurate, etc. —**math′e·mat′i·cal·ly** ***adv.***

math·e·mat·ics (math′ə mat′iks) ***n.*** ⟦see prec. & -ICS⟧ the science dealing with quantities, forms, etc. and their relationships, by the use of numbers and symbols —**math′e·ma·ti′cian** (-mə tish′ən) ***n.***

mat·i·nee or **mat·i·née** (mat′'n ā′) ***n.*** ⟦< Fr *matin*, morning⟧ an afternoon performance of a play, etc.

mat·ins (mat′'nz) ***pl.n.*** ⟦< L *matutinus*, of the morning⟧ [*often* **M-**] [*usually with sing. v.*] a church service of morning prayer

Ma·tisse (mȧ tēs′), **Hen·ri** (än rē′) 1869-1954; Fr. painter

matri- ⟦< L *mater*⟧ *combining form* mother: also **matr-**

ma·tri·arch (mā′trē ärk′) ***n.*** ⟦prec. + -ARCH⟧ **1** a woman who rules a family, tribe, etc. **2** a highly respected elderly woman —**ma′tri·ar′chal** (-är′kəl) ***adj.*** —**ma′tri·arch′y**, *pl.* **-ies**, ***n.***

mat·ri·cide (ma′trə sīd′) ***n.*** **1** the murdering of one's mother **2** a person who does this —**mat′ri·ci′dal** ***adj.***

ma·tric·u·late (mə trik′yo͞o lāt′, -yə-) ***vt.***, ***vi.*** **-lat′ed**, **-lat′ing** ⟦< LL: see MATRIX⟧ to enroll, esp. as a student in a college —**ma·tric′u·la′tion** ***n.***

mat·ri·mo·ny (ma′trə mō′nē) ***n.***, *pl.* **-nies** ⟦< L *mater*, mother⟧ **1** the act or rite of marriage **2** married life —**mat′ri·mo′ni·al** ***adj.***

ma·trix (mā′triks′) ***n.***, *pl.* **ma·tri·ces** (mā′trə sēz′, ma′trə-) or **ma′trix′es** ⟦< L *mater*, mother⟧ that within which something originates or develops

ma·tron (mā′trən) ***n.*** ⟦< L *mater*, mother⟧ **1** a wife or widow, esp. one with a mature appearance and manner **2** a woman manager of the domestic arrangements of a hospital, prison, etc. —**ma′tron·ly** ***adj.***

matron of honor a married woman acting as chief attendant to a bride

matte (mat) ***n.*** ⟦var. of MAT[2]⟧ a dull surface or finish —***adj.*** not shiny Also **matt**

mat·ted (mat′id) ***adj.*** closely tangled in a dense mass *[matted* hair*]*

mat·ter (mat′ər) ***n.*** ⟦< L *materia*⟧ **1** what a thing is made of; material **2** whatever occupies space and is perceptible to the senses **3** any specified substance *[*coloring *matter]* **4** material of thought or expression **5** an amount or quantity *[*a *matter* of a few days*]* **6** *a)* a thing or affair *b)* cause or occasion *[*no laughing *matter]* **7** importance *[*it's of no *matter]* **8** trouble; difficulty: with *the [*what's the *matter?]* **9** mail —***vi.*** to be of importance —**as a matter of fact** *see this phrase at* FACT —**no matter** **1** it is not important **2** regardless of

mat′ter-of-fact′ ***adj.*** sticking to facts; literal, unimaginative, etc.

Mat·thew (math′yo͞o′) ***n.*** *Bible* **1** a Christian apostle, reputed author of the first Gospel **2** this Gospel: abbrev. **Matt.**

mat·ting (mat′iŋ) ***n.*** **1** a woven fabric of fiber, as straw, for mats, etc. **2** mats collectively

mat·tock (mat′ək) ***n.*** ⟦OE *mattuc*⟧ a tool like a pickax, for loosening the soil, digging roots, etc.

mat·tress (ma′trəs) ***n.*** ⟦< Ar *maṭraḥ*, cushion⟧ a casing of strong cloth filled with cotton, foam rubber, coiled springs, etc., used on a bed

ma·ture (mə toor′, -choor′) ***adj.*** ⟦< L *maturus*, ripe⟧ **1** full-grown; ripe **2** fully developed, perfected, etc. **3** due: said of a note, bond, etc. —***vt.***, ***vi.*** **-tured′**, **-tur′ing** to make or become mature —**mat·u·ra·tion** (mach′ə rā′shən) ***n.*** —**ma·ture′ly** ***adv.*** —**ma·tu′ri·ty** ***n.***

mat·zo (mät′sə, -sō) ***n.***, *pl.* **mat′zot**, **mat′zoth** (-sōt), or **mat′zos** ⟦Heb *matstsāh*, unleavened⟧ **1** thin, crisp unleavened bread eaten during the Passover

2 a piece of this

maud·lin (môd′lin) ***adj.*** ⟦< ME *Maudeleyne,* (Mary) Magdalene (often represented as weeping)⟧ foolishly, often tearfully, sentimental

maul (môl) ***n.*** ⟦< L *malleus,* a hammer⟧ a heavy hammer for driving stakes, etc. —***vt.*** **1** to bruise or lacerate **2** to handle roughly; manhandle

maun·der (môn′dər) ***vi.*** ⟦< earlier *mander,* to grumble⟧ to talk or move in a confused way

Mau·ri·ta·ni·a (môr′ə tā′nē ə) country in NW Africa, on the Atlantic: 398,000 sq. mi.; pop. 1,864,000

Mau·ri·ti·us (mô rish′ē əs, -rish′əs) island country in the Indian Ocean: 788 sq. mi.; pop. 1,059,000

mau·so·le·um (mô′sə lē′əm, mä′-; -zə-) ***n.,*** *pl.* **-le′ums** or **-le′a** (-ə) ⟦after the tomb of King *Mausolus,* in ancient Asia Minor⟧ **1** a large, imposing tomb **2** a building with spaces for entombing a number of bodies

mauve (mōv, môv) ***n.*** ⟦Fr, mallow⟧ any of several shades of pale purple —***adj.*** of such a color

mav·er·ick (mav′ər ik) ***n.*** ⟦after S. *Maverick,* 19th-c. Texan whose cattle had no brand⟧ **1** an unbranded animal, esp. a lost calf **2** [Inf.] one who takes an independent stand, as in politics

maw (mô) ***n.*** ⟦OE *maga*⟧ **1** [Archaic] the stomach **2** the throat, jaws, or mouth of a voracious animal

mawk·ish (môk′ish) ***adj.*** ⟦< ON *mathkr,* maggot⟧ sentimental in a weak, insipid way —**mawk′ish·ly** ***adv.***

max[1] (maks) [Slang] ***n., adj.*** maximum —**to the max** to the greatest possible degree

max[2] *abbrev.* maximum

maxi- ⟦< MAXI(MUM)⟧ *combining form* maximum, very large, very long

max·il·la (mak sil′ə) ***n.,*** *pl.* **-lae** (-ē) ⟦L⟧ the upper jawbone —**max′il·lar′y** (-sə ler′ē) ***adj.***

max·im (mak′sim) ***n.*** ⟦< LL *maxima* (*propositio*), the greatest (premise)⟧ a concise rule of conduct

max·i·mize (mak′sə mīz′) ***vt.*** **-mized′, -miz′ing** to increase to the maximum

max·i·mum (mak′sə məm) ***n.,*** *pl.* **-mums** or **-ma** (-mə) ⟦< L superl. of *magnus,* great⟧ **1** the greatest quantity, number, etc. possible or permissible **2** the highest degree or point reached —***adj.*** greatest possible, permissible, or reached —**max′i·mal** (-məl) ***adj.***

may (mā) ***v.aux.*** *pt.* **might** ⟦OE *mæg*⟧ used to express *a*) possibility [*it may rain*] *b*) permission [*you may go*] (see also CAN[1]) *c*) contingency [*they died that we may be free*] *d*) a wish or hope [*may he live*]

May (mā) ***n.*** ⟦< L *Maius*⟧ the fifth month of the year, having 31 days

Ma·ya (mä′yə, mī′ə) ***n.*** ⟦Sp < native name⟧ **1** *pl.* **-ya** or **-yas** a member of an American Indian people of Central America that had a highly developed civilization **2** the language of this people —**Ma′yan** ***adj., n.***

may·be (mā′bē) ***adv.*** ⟦ME (for *it may be*)⟧ perhaps

May Day May 1: a traditional spring festival, now also a labor holiday in many countries

may′flow′er ***n.*** **1** an early spring flower, as the trailing arbutus **2** [**M-**] the ship on which the Pilgrims came to America (1620)

may′fly′ ***n.,*** *pl.* **-flies′** ⟦thought to be prevalent in May⟧ a delicate insect with gauzy wings

may·hem (mā′hem, -əm) ***n.*** ⟦see MAIM⟧ **1** *Law* the offense of maiming a person **2** any deliberate destruction

may·o (mā′ō) ***n.*** [Inf.] *short for* MAYONNAISE

may·on·naise (mā′ə nāz′) ***n.*** ⟦after *Mahón,* port on a Sp island⟧ a creamy sauce of egg yolks, oil, vinegar, etc. beaten together

may·or (mā′ər) ***n.*** ⟦< L *major,* greater⟧ the chief administrative official of a city, town, etc. —**may·or·al** (mā′ər əl, mā ôr′əl) ***adj.***

may′or·al·ty ***n.,*** *pl.* **-ties** the office or term of office of a mayor

may·pole (mā′pōl′) ***n.*** [*often* **M-**] a high pole with flowers, streamers, etc., for dancing around on May Day

Ma·za·tlán (mä′sät län′) seaport & resort on the Pacific coast of Mexico: pop. 314,000

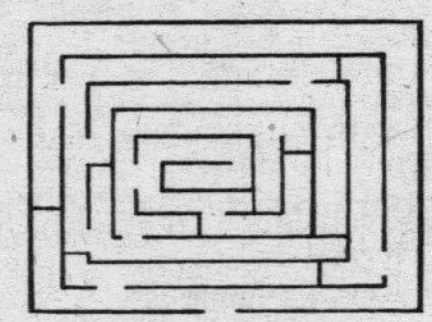

MAZE

maze (māz) ***n.*** ⟦< OE *amasian,* to amaze⟧ **1** a confusing, intricate network of pathways **2** a confused state

maz·el tov (mä′zəl tōv′, -tôf′) ⟦Heb, good luck⟧ used to express congratulations: also **maz′el·tov′** ***interj.***

ma·zur·ka or **ma·zour·ka** (mə zur′kə) ***n.*** ⟦Pol⟧ a lively Polish folk dance in 3/4 or 3/8 time

MB *abbrev.* **1** Manitoba **2** megabyte(s): also **mb**

MBA or **M.B.A.** *abbrev.* Master of Business Administration

MC *abbrev.* **1** Master of Ceremonies **2** Member of Congress

Mc·Kin·ley[1] (mə kin′lē), **William** 1843-1901; 25th president of the U.S. (1897-1901): assassinated

Mc·Kin·ley[2] (mə kin′lē), **Mount** mountain in Alaska: highest peak in North America: 20,320 ft.: popularly called *Denali*

MD *abbrev.* **1** ⟦L *Medicinae Doctor*⟧ Doctor of Medicine: also **M.D.** **2** Maryland

mdse *abbrev.* merchandise

me (mē) ***pron.*** ⟦OE⟧ *objective form of* I[2]

ME Maine

mead[1] (mēd) ***n.*** ⟦OE *meodu*⟧ an alcoholic liquor made of fermented honey and water

mead[2] (mēd) ***n.*** [Old Poet.] *var. of* MEADOW

mead·ow (med′ō) ***n.*** ⟦< OE *mæd*⟧ **1** a grassland where the grass is grown for hay **2** low, level grassland

mea·ger (mē′gər) ***adj.*** ⟦< L *macer*, lean⟧ **1** thin; lean **2** poor; not full or rich; inadequate Brit. sp. **mea′gre** —**mea′ger·ly** ***adv.*** —**mea′ger·ness** ***n.***

meal[1] (mēl) ***n.*** ⟦OE *mæl*⟧ **1** any of the times for eating, as lunch or dinner **2** the food served at such a time

meal[2] (mēl) ***n.*** ⟦OE *melu*⟧ **1** any edible grain, coarsely ground *[cornmeal]* **2** any substance similarly ground —**meal′y, -i·er, -i·est,** ***adj.***

meal·y-mouthed (mēl′ē mouthd′) ***adj.*** not outspoken or blunt; euphemistic

mean[1] (mēn) ***vt.*** **meant** (ment), **mean′ing** ⟦OE *mænan*⟧ **1** to have in mind; intend *[he means to go]* **2** to intend to express *[say what you mean]* **3** to signify; denote *[the German word "ja" means "yes"]* —***vi.*** to have a (specified) degree of importance, effect, etc. *[honors mean little to him]* —**mean well** to have good intentions

mean[2] (mēn) ***adj.*** ⟦OE (*ge*)*mæne*⟧ **1** low in quality or value; paltry **2** poor in appearance; shabby **3** petty **4** stingy **5** pettily bad-tempered, disagreeable, etc. **6** [Slang] *a*) hard to cope with *b*) skillful —**mean′ly** ***adv.*** —**mean′ness** ***n.***

mean[3] (mēn) ***adj.*** ⟦< L *medius*, middle⟧ **1** halfway between extremes **2** average —***n.*** **1** what is between extremes **2** *Math.* a number between the smallest and largest values of a set of quantities; esp., an average

me·an·der (mē an′dər) ***vi.*** ⟦< Gr *Maiandros*, a winding river in Asia Minor⟧ **1** to take a winding course: said of a stream **2** to wander idly —***n.*** an aimless wandering

mean·ie or **mean·y** (mē′nē) ***n.***, *pl.* **-ies** [Inf.] one who is mean, selfish, etc.

mean′ing ***n.*** what is meant; what is intended to be signified, understood, indicated, etc.; import; sense *[the meaning of a word]* —**mean′ing·ful** ***adj.*** —**mean′ing·less** ***adj.***

means (mēnz) ***pl.n.*** ⟦< MEAN[3], *n.*⟧ **1** [*with sing. or pl. v.*] that by which something is done or obtained; agency *[a means of travel]* **2** resources; wealth —**by all means** **1** without fail **2** certainly —**by means of** by using —**by no means** not at all

means test an investigation of a person's financial resources, to determine that person's eligibility for welfare payments, etc.

meant (ment) ***vt.***, ***vi.*** *pt. & pp. of* MEAN[1]

mean′time′ ***adv.*** **1** in or during the intervening time **2** at the same time —***n.*** the intervening time *[in the meantime]* Also **mean′while′**

mea·sles (mē′zəlz) ***n.*** ⟦ME *maseles*⟧ **1** an acute, infectious, communicable viral disease, usually of children, characterized by small, red spots on the skin, high fever, etc. **2** a similar but milder disease; esp., rubella (*German measles*)

mea·sly (mēz′lē) ***adj.*** **-sli·er, -sli·est** [Inf.] contemptibly slight or worthless

meas·ure (mezh′ər) ***n.*** ⟦< L *metiri*, to measure⟧ **1** the extent, dimensions, capacity, etc. of anything **2** a determining of this; measurement **3** *a*) a unit of measurement *b*) any standard of valuation **4** a system of measurement **5** an instrument for measuring **6** a definite quantity measured out **7** a course of action *[reform measures]* **8** a statute; law **9** a rhythmical pattern or unit; specif., the notes and rests between two bars on a musical staff —***vt.*** **-ured, -ur·ing** **1** to find out or estimate the extent, dimensions, etc. of, esp. by a standard **2** to mark off by measuring: often with *off* or *out* **3** to be a measure of —***vi.*** **1** to take measurements **2** to be of a specified dimension, etc. —**beyond measure** exceedingly —**for good measure** as a bonus or something extra —**measure up to** to reach (a standard, etc.) —**meas′ur·a·ble** ***adj.*** —**meas′ur·a·bly** ***adv.*** —**meas′ure·less** ***adj.***

meas′ured ***adj.*** **1** determined or marked off by a standard **2** regular or steady *[measured steps]* **3** careful and guarded: said of speech, etc.

meas′ure·ment ***n.*** **1** a measuring or being measured **2** extent or quantity determined by measuring **3** a system of measuring or of measures

meat (mēt) ***n.*** ⟦OE *mete*⟧ **1** food: now archaic except in **meat and drink** **2** the flesh of animals, esp. of mammals, used as food **3** the edible, inner part *[the meat of a nut]* **4** the substance or essence —**meat′y, -i·er, -i·est,** ***adj.***

meat′-and-po·ta′toes ***adj.*** [Inf.] **1** basic; fundamental **2** ordinary; everyday

meat′pack′ing ***n.*** the process or industry of preparing the meat of animals for market

Mec·ca[1] (mek′ə) ***n.*** ⟦after fol.⟧ [*often* **m-**] any place many people feel drawn to *[a tourist mecca]*

Mecca[2] (mek′ə) city in W Saudi Arabia: birthplace of Mohammed & hence a holy city of Islam: pop. 618,000

me·chan·ic (mə kan′ik) ***n.*** ⟦< Gr *mēchanē*, machine⟧ a worker skilled in using tools, repairing machines, etc.

me·chan′i·cal ***adj.*** **1** having to do with machinery or tools **2** produced or operated by machinery or a mechanism **3** of the science of mechanics **4** machinelike; lacking warmth, spontaneity, etc. —**me·chan′i·cal·ly** ***adv.***

me·chan′ics ***n.*** **1** the science of motion and of the action of forces on bodies **2** knowledge of machinery —***pl.n.*** [*sometimes with sing. v.*] the technical part *[the mechanics of writing]*

mech·a·nism (mek′ə niz′əm) ***n.*** ⟦< Gr *mēchanē*, machine⟧ **1** the working parts of a machine **2** any system of interrelated parts **3** any physical or mental process by which a result is produced —**mech′a·nis′tic** ***adj.***

mech′a·nize′ (-nīz′) ***vt.*** **-nized′, -niz′ing** **1** to make mechanical **2** to equip (an industry) with machinery or (an army, etc.) with motor vehicles, tanks, etc. —**mech′a·ni·za′tion** ***n.***

med *abbrev.* **1** medical **2** medicine **3** medium

med·al (med′'l) ***n.*** ⟦< LL *medialis*, medial⟧ **1** a small, flat piece of inscribed metal commemorating some event or awarded for some distinguished action, merit, etc. **2** a similar piece of metal bearing a religious figure or symbol

med′al·ist ***n.*** one awarded a medal

me·dal·lion (mə dal′yən) ***n.*** ⟦Fr *médaillon*⟧ **1** a large medal **2** a design, portrait, etc. resembling a medal

med·dle (med′'l) ***vi.*** **-dled, -dling** ⟦< L *miscere*, to mix⟧ to interfere in another's affairs —**med′dler** ***n.*** —**med′dle·some** (-səm) ***adj.***

me·di·a (mē′dē ə) ***n.*** *alt. pl. of* MEDIUM: see MEDIUM (*n.* 3) —**the media** [*usually with sing. v.*] all the means of communication such as newspapers, radio, and TV

me·di·al (mē′dē əl) ***adj.*** ⟦< L *medius*⟧ **1** of or in the middle **2** average

me·di·an (mē′dē ən) ***adj.*** **1** middle; intermediate **2** designating the middle number in a series —***n.*** **1** a median number, point, line, etc. **2** the strip of land separating the lanes of opposing traffic of a divided highway: in full **median strip**

me·di·ate (mē′dē āt′) ***vi.*** **-at′ed, -at′ing** ⟦< L *medius*, middle⟧ to be an intermediary —***vt.*** to settle (differences) between persons, nations, etc. by friendly or diplomatic intervention —**me′di·a′tion** ***n.*** —**me′di·a′tor** ***n.***

med·ic (med′ik) ***n.*** [Inf.] **1** a physician or surgeon **2** a medical officer who gives first aid in combat

Med′ic·aid′ (-i kād′) ***n.*** ⟦MEDIC(AL) + AID⟧ [*also* **m-**] a state and federal health program for paying certain medical expenses of persons of low income

med′i·cal (-i kəl) ***adj.*** of or connected with the practice or study of medicine —**med′i·cal·ly** ***adv.***

medical jurisprudence the application of medical knowledge to questions of law

Med·i·care (med′i ker′) ***n.*** ⟦MEDI(CAL) + CARE⟧ [*also* **m-**] a federal health program for paying certain medical expenses of the aged and the needy

med′i·cate′ (-kāt′) ***vt.*** **-cat′ed, -cat′ing** ⟦< L *medicari*, heal⟧ to treat with medicine —**med′i·ca′tion** ***n.***

me·dic·i·nal (mə dis′ən əl) ***adj.*** of, or having the properties of, medicine

med·i·cine (med′i sən) ***n.*** ⟦< L *medicus*, physician⟧ **1** the science and art of treating and preventing disease **2** any substance, as a drug, used in treating disease, relieving pain, etc.

medicine man among North American Indians, etc., a man supposed to have supernatural powers for healing the sick, etc.

me·di·e·val (mē′dē ē′vəl, mi dē′vəl) ***adj.*** ⟦< L *medius*, middle + *aevum*, age⟧ of or characteristic of the Middle Ages

me·di·o·cre (mē′dē ō′kər) ***adj.*** ⟦< L *medius*, middle + *ocris*, peak⟧ **1** ordinary; average **2** inferior —**me′di·oc′ri·ty** (-äk′rə tē), *pl.* **-ties,** ***n.***

med·i·tate (med′ə tāt′) ***vt.*** **-tat′ed, -tat′ing** ⟦< L *meditari*⟧ to plan —***vi.*** to think deeply —**med′i·ta′tion** ***n.*** —**med′i·ta′tive** ***adj.***

Med·i·ter·ra·ne·an (med′ə tə rā′nē ən) ***adj.*** **1** *a*) of the large sea (**Mediterranean Sea**) surrounded by Europe, Africa, & Asia *b*) of the regions near this sea **2** designating furniture made to simulate heavy, ornately carved Renaissance furniture —***n.*** a Mediterranean person

me·di·um (mē′dē əm) ***n.***, *pl.* **-di·ums** or **-di·a** (-ə) ⟦L < *medius*, the middle⟧ **1** an intermediate thing or state **2** an intervening thing through which a force acts **3** *pl. usually* **me′dia** any means, agency, etc.; specif., a means of communication that reaches the general public: a singular form **media** (*pl.* **medias**) is now often used **4** any surrounding substance or environment **5** *pl.* **me′di·ums** one through whom messages are supposedly sent from the dead —***adj.*** intermediate in size, quality, etc.

med·ley (med′lē) ***n.***, *pl.* **-leys** ⟦< L *miscere*, to mix⟧ **1** a mixture of dissimilar things **2** a musical piece made up of various tunes or passages

me·dul·la (mi dul′ə) ***n.***, *pl.* **-las** or **-lae** (-ē) ⟦L, marrow⟧ *Anat.* **1** a widening of the spinal cord forming the lowest part of the brain: in full **medulla ob·lon·ga·ta** (äb′läŋ gät′ə) **2** the inner substance of an organ, as of the kidney

meek (mēk) ***adj.*** ⟦< ON *miukr*, gentle⟧ **1** patient and mild **2** too submissive; spiritless —**meek′ly** ***adv.*** —**meek′ness** ***n.***

meer·schaum (mir′shəm, -shôm′) ***n.*** ⟦Ger, sea foam⟧ **1** a white, claylike, heat-resistant mineral used for tobacco pipes, etc. **2** a pipe made of this

meet[1] (mēt) ***vt.*** **met, meet′ing** ⟦OE *metan*⟧ **1** to come upon; encounter **2** to be present at the arrival of *[to meet a bus]* **3** to come into contact with **4** to be introduced to **5** to contend with; deal with **6** to experience *[to meet disaster]* **7** to be perceived by (the eye, etc.) **8** *a*) to satisfy (a demand, etc.) *b*) to pay (a bill, etc.) —***vi.*** **1** to come together **2** to come into contact, etc. **3** to be introduced **4** to assemble —***n.*** a meeting as for a sporting competition —**meet with** **1** to experience **2** to receive

meet[2] (mēt) ***adj.*** ⟦OE (*ge*)*mæte*, fitting⟧ [Now Rare] suitable; proper

meet′ing ***n.*** **1** a coming together **2** a gathering of people **3** a junction

mega- ⟦Gr < *megas*, great⟧ *combining form* **1** large, great, powerful **2** one million Also **meg-**

meg·a·byte (meg′ə bīt′) ***n.*** ⟦prec. + BYTE⟧ a unit of storage capacity in a computer system, equal to 2^{20} bytes, or, loosely, one million bytes

meg'a·hertz' (-hurts') *n.*, *pl.* **-hertz'** ⟦MEGA- + HERTZ⟧ one million hertz

meg·a·lo·ma·ni·a (meg'ə lō mā'nē ə) *n.* ⟦< Gr *megas*, large + -MANIA⟧ a mental disorder characterized by delusions of grandeur, power, etc. —**meg'a·lo·ma'ni·ac** *adj.*, *n.*

meg·a·lop·o·lis (meg'ə läp'ə lis) *n.* ⟦Gr, great city⟧ a vast, continuously urban area, including any number of cities

meg·a·phone (meg'ə fōn') *n.* ⟦MEGA- + -PHONE⟧ a cone-shaped device for increasing the volume of the voice

meg'a·ton' (-tun') *n.* ⟦MEGA- + TON⟧ the explosive force of a million tons of TNT

Me·kong (mā'käŋ', -kôŋ') river in SE Asia, flowing into the South China Sea

mel·a·mine (mel'ə mēn') *n.* ⟦Ger *melamin*⟧ a white, crystalline compound used in making synthetic resins

mel·an·cho·li·a (mel'ən kō'lē ə) *n.* a mental disorder, often psychotic, characterized by extreme depression

mel'an·chol'y (-käl'ē) *n.*, *pl.* **-ies** ⟦< Gr *melas*, black + *cholē*, bile⟧ sadness and depression of spirits —*adj.* **1** sad and depressed **2** causing sadness —**mel'an·chol'ic** *adj.*

Mel·a·ne·sia (mel'ə nē'zhə) group of islands in the S Pacific —**Mel'a·ne'sian** *adj.*, *n.*

mé·lange (mā lônzh', -lônj') *n.* ⟦Fr < *mêler*, to mix⟧ a mixture; medley

mel·a·nin (mel'ə nin) *n.* ⟦< Gr *melas*, black⟧ a blackish pigment found in skin, hair, etc.

mel'a·no'ma (-nō'mə) *n.*, *pl.* **-mas** or **-ma·ta** (-mə tə) ⟦< Gr *melas*, black + *-ōma*, mass⟧ a skin tumor derived from cells capable of melanin formation

Mel·ba toast (mel'bə) ⟦after N. *Melba* (1861-1931), Australian soprano⟧ [*also* **m- t-**] very crisp, thinly sliced toast

Mel·bourne (mel'bərn) seaport in SE Australia: pop. 2,833,000

meld (meld) *vt.*, *vi.* ⟦< MELT + WELD⟧ to blend; merge

me·lee or **mê·lée** (mā'lā', mā lā') *n.* ⟦Fr⟧ a confused fight or hand-to-hand struggle

mel·io·rate (mēl'yə rāt') *vt.*, *vi.* **-rat'ed**, **-rat'ing** ⟦< L *melior*, better⟧ to make or become better

mel·lif·lu·ous (mə lif'lo͞o əs) *adj.* ⟦< L *mel*, honey + *fluere*, to flow⟧ sounding sweet and smooth: also **mel·lif'lu·ent** —**mel·lif'lu·ence** *n.*

mel·low (mel'ō) *adj.* ⟦ME *melwe*, ripe⟧ **1** full-flavored: said of wine, etc. **2** full, rich, soft, etc.; not harsh: said of sound, light, etc. **3** made gentle, understanding, etc. by age **4** [Inf.] genial, as from drinking liquor —*vt.*, *vi.* to make or become mellow

me·lo·di·ous (mə lō'dē əs) *adj.* **1** producing melody **2** pleasing to hear; tuneful —**me·lo'di·ous·ly** *adv.*

mel·o·dra·ma (mel'ə drä'mə, -dram'ə) *n.* ⟦< Fr < Gr *melos*, song + LL *drama*, drama⟧ a drama with exaggerated conflicts and emotions, stereotyped characters, etc. —**mel'o·dra·mat'ic** (-drə mat'ik) *adj.*

mel'o·dra·mat'ics (-drə mat'iks) *pl.n.* melodramatic behavior

mel·o·dy (mel'ə dē) *n.*, *pl.* **-dies** ⟦< Gr *melos*, song + *aeidein*, sing⟧ **1** pleasing sounds in sequence **2** *Music a*) a tune, song, etc. *b*) the leading part in a harmonic composition —**me·lod·ic** (mə läd'ik) *adj.* —**me·lod'i·cal·ly** *adv.*

mel·on (mel'ən) *n.* ⟦< Gr *mēlon*, apple⟧ the large, juicy, thick-skinned, many-seeded fruit of certain trailing plants, as the watermelon or cantaloupe

melt (melt) *vt.*, *vi.* ⟦OE *m(i)eltan*⟧ **1** to change from a solid to a liquid state, generally by heat **2** to dissolve **3** to disappear or cause to disappear gradually **4** to soften; become gentle, tender, etc.

melt'down' *n.* a dangerous situation in which a nuclear reactor begins to melt its fuel rods

melting pot a country, etc. in which people of various nationalities and races are assimilated

Mel·ville (mel'vil), **Her·man** (hur'mən) 1819-91; U.S. novelist

mem·ber (mem'bər) *n.* ⟦< L *membrum*⟧ **1** a limb or other part of a person, animal, or plant **2** a distinct part of a whole **3** a person belonging to some group, society, etc.

mem'ber·ship' *n.* **1** the state of being a member: with *in* **2** members collectively, as of a group **3** the number of members

mem·brane (mem'brān') *n.* ⟦< L *membrum*, member⟧ a thin, soft layer, esp. of animal or plant tissue, that covers or lines an organ, part, etc. —**mem'bra·nous** (-brə nəs) *adj.*

me·men·to (mə men'tō) *n.*, *pl.* **-tos** or **-toes** ⟦< L *meminisse*, remember⟧ a souvenir

mem·o (mem'ō) *n.*, *pl.* **-os** *short for* MEMORANDUM

mem·oirs (mem'wärz') *pl.n.* ⟦< L *memoria*, memory⟧ **1** an autobiography **2** a record of events based on the writer's personal knowledge

mem·o·ra·bil·i·a (mem'ə rə bil'ē ə, -bil'yə; -bēl'-) *pl.n.* ⟦L⟧ things serving as a record or reminder

mem·o·ra·ble (mem'ə rə bəl) *adj.* worth remembering; notable; remarkable —**mem'o·ra·bly** *adv.*

mem·o·ran·dum (mem'ə ran'dəm) *n.*, *pl.* **-dums** or **-da** (-də) ⟦L⟧ **1** a short note written to remind one of something **2** an informal written communication, as in an office **3** *Law* a short written statement of the terms of an agreement, etc.

me·mo·ri·al (mə môr'ē əl) *adj.* ⟦< L *memoria*, memory⟧ serving to help people remember —*n.* anything meant to help people remember a person or event, as a monument or holiday —**me·mo'ri·al·ize'** (-īz'), **-ized'**, **-iz'ing**, *vt.*

Memorial Day a legal holiday in the U.S. (the last Monday in May in most States) in memory of members of the armed forces killed in war

mem·o·rize (mem'ə rīz') *vt.* **-rized'**, **-riz'ing** to commit to memory —**mem'o·**

ri·za′tion *n.*

mem·o·ry (mem′ə rē, mem′rē) ***n.***, *pl.* **-ries** ⟦< L *memor,* mindful⟧ **1** the power or act of remembering **2** all that one remembers **3** something remembered **4** the period of remembering *[within my memory]* **5** commemoration **6** storage capacity, as of a computer or disk

Mem·phis (mem′fis) city in SW Tennessee: pop. 610,000

men (men) ***n.*** *pl. of* MAN

men·ace (men′əs) ***n.*** ⟦< L *minari,* threaten⟧ **1** a threat **2** [Inf.] one who is a nuisance **—*vt.*, *vi.*** **-aced, -ac·ing** to threaten **—men′ac·ing·ly *adv.***

mé·nage or **me·nage** (mā näzh′, mə-) ***n.*** ⟦Fr < L *mansio,* house⟧ a household

me·nag·er·ie (mə naj′ər ē, -nazh′-) ***n.*** ⟦see prec.⟧ a collection of wild animals kept in cages, etc. for exhibition

mend (mend) ***vt.*** ⟦< ME *amenden,* amend⟧ **1** to repair **2** to make better; reform **—*vi.*** **1** to improve, esp. in health **2** to heal, as a fracture **—*n.*** **1** a mending **2** a mended place **—on the mend** improving, esp. in health **— mend′er *n.***

men·da·cious (men dā′shəs) ***adj.*** ⟦< L *mendax*⟧ not truthful; lying **—men·dac′i·ty** (-das′ə tē), *pl.* **-ties, *n.***

Men·del (men′dəl), **Gre·gor** (grā′gôr) 1822-84; Austrian monk & geneticist

Men·dels·sohn (men′dəl sən, -sōn′), **Fe·lix** (fā′liks) 1809-47; Ger. composer

men·di·cant (men′di kənt) ***adj.*** ⟦< L *mendicus,* needy⟧ begging **—*n.*** **1** a beggar **2** a mendicant friar

men′folk′ (-fōk′) ***pl.n.*** [Inf. or Dial.] men: also **men′folks′**

men·ha·den (men hād′'n) ***n.***, *pl.* **-den** or **-dens** ⟦< AmInd⟧ a common fish of the W Atlantic, used for bait or for making oil and fertilizer

me·ni·al (mē′nē əl) ***adj.*** ⟦< L *mansio,* house⟧ **1** of or fit for servants **2** servile; low **—*n.*** **1** a domestic servant **2** a servile, low person **—me′ni·al·ly *adv.***

me·nin·ges (mə nin′jēz′) ***pl.n.***, *sing.* **me·ninx** (mē′niŋks′) ⟦< Gr *mēninx,* membrane⟧ the three membranes that envelop the brain and the spinal cord **— me·nin′ge·al** (-jē əl) ***adj.***

men·in·gi·tis (men′in jīt′is) ***n.*** ⟦ModL: see prec. & -ITIS⟧ inflammation of the meninges

me·nis·cus (mə nis′kəs) ***n.***, *pl.* **-cus·es** or **-ci′** (-ī′) ⟦< Gr dim. of *mēnē,* the moon⟧ **1** a crescent or crescent-shaped thing **2** the convex or concave upper surface of a column of liquid

Men·non·ite (men′ən īt′) ***n.*** ⟦after *Menno* Simons, 16th-c. Du reformer⟧ a member of an evangelical Christian sect that opposes military service and favors plain living and dress

men·o·pause (men′ə pôz′) ***n.*** ⟦< Gr *mēn,* month + *pauein,* to end⟧ the permanent cessation of menstruation

me·no·rah (mə nō′rə, -nôr′ə) ***n.*** ⟦Heb *menora,* lamp stand⟧ a candelabrum with seven (or nine) branches: a symbol of Judaism

men·ses (men′sēz′) ***pl.n.*** ⟦L, pl. of *mensis,* month⟧ the periodic flow, usually monthly, of blood from the uterus

men·stru·ate (men′stro͞o āt′) ***vi.*** **-at′ed, -at′ing** ⟦< L *mensis,* month⟧ to have a discharge of the menses **—men′strual** (-strəl) ***adj.*** **—men′stru·a′tion *n.***

men·su·ra·tion (men′shə rā′shən) ***n.*** ⟦< L *mensura,* measure⟧ a measuring

-ment (mənt, mint) ⟦< L *-mentum*⟧ *suffix* **1** a result **2** a means of **3** an act **4** a state *[enchantment]*

men·tal (ment′'l) ***adj.*** ⟦< L *mens,* the mind⟧ **1** of, for, by, or in the mind **2** of, having, or related to mental illness **3** for the mentally ill *[a mental hospital]* **—men′tal·ly *adv.***

men′tal·ist *n.* MIND READER

men·tal·i·ty (men tal′i tē) ***n.***, *pl.* **-ties** **1** mental capacity or power **2** mental attitude or outlook

mental reservation a qualification (of a statement) that one makes to oneself but does not express

mental retardation a condition, usually congenital, characterized by subnormal intelligence

men·ta·tion (men tā′shən) ***n.*** ⟦< L *mens,* mind + -ATION⟧ the act or process of using the mind

men·thol (men′thôl′) ***n.*** ⟦Ger < L *mentha,* MINT[2]⟧ a white, crystalline alcohol obtained from oil of peppermint and used in medicine, cosmetics, etc. **— men′tho·lat′ed** (-thə lāt′id) ***adj.***

men·tion (men′shən) ***n.*** ⟦< L *mens,* the mind⟧ **1** a brief reference **2** a citing for honor **—*vt.*** to refer to briefly or incidentally **—make mention of** to mention **— not to mention** without even mentioning

men·tor (men′tər, -tôr′) ***n.*** ⟦after *Mentor,* friend and advisor of Odysseus⟧ **1** a wise advisor **2** a teacher or coach

men·u (men′yo͞o) ***n.***, *pl.* **-us** ⟦Fr, small, detailed⟧ **1** a detailed list of the foods served at a meal or those available at a restaurant **2** a list, as on a computer screen, of the various choices available to the user

me·ow or **me·ou** (mē ou′) ***n.*** ⟦echoic⟧ the characteristic vocal sound made by a cat **—*vi.*** to make such a sound

mer·can·tile (mur′kən tīl′, -til) ***adj.*** ⟦Fr⟧ of or characteristic of merchants or trade

mer·ce·nar·y (mur′sə ner′ē) ***adj.*** ⟦< L *merces,* wages⟧ working or done for payment only **—*n.***, *pl.* **-ies** a soldier hired to serve in a foreign army

mer′cer·ize′ (-īz′) ***vt.*** **-ized′, -iz′ing** ⟦after J. *Mercer* (1791-1866), Eng calico dealer⟧ to treat (cotton thread or fabric) with a sodium hydroxide solution to strengthen it, give it a silky luster, etc.

mer·chan·dise (mur′chən dīz′; *for n., also,* -dīs′) ***n.*** ⟦see fol.⟧ things bought and sold; goods; commodities **—*vt.*, *vi.*** **-dised′, -dis′ing** **1** to buy and sell **2** to promote the sale of (a product) Also, for v., **mer′chan·dize′** (-dīz′), **-dized′, -diz′ing —mer′chan·dis′er** or **mer′chan·diz′er *n.***

mer·chant (mur′chənt) ***n.*** ⟦ult. < L

merx, wares⟧ **1** one whose business is buying and selling goods **2** a retail dealer; storekeeper ***—adj.*** mercantile; commercial

mer′chant·man (-mən) ***n.***, *pl.* **-men** (-mən) a ship used in commerce

merchant marine 1 all of a nation's commercial ships **2** their personnel

mer·ci (mer sē′) ***interj.*** ⟦Fr⟧ thank you

mer·ci·ful (mur′si fəl) ***adj.*** having or showing mercy; compassionate; lenient **—mer′ci·ful·ly *adv.***

mer′ci·less *adj.* without mercy; pitiless **—mer′ci·less·ly *adv.***

mer·cu·ri·al (mər kyoor′ē əl) ***adj.*** **1** of or containing mercury **2** quick, changeable, fickle, etc.

Mer·cu·ry (mur′kyoor ē) ***n.*** **1** *Rom. Myth.* the messenger of the gods **2** a small planet in the solar system: see PLANET **3** [**m-**] a heavy, silver-white metallic chemical element, liquid at ordinary temperatures, used in thermometers, etc. **—mer·cu·ric** (mər kyoor′ik) ***adj.*** **—mer·cu′rous *adj.***

mer·cy (mur′sē) ***n.***, *pl.* **-cies** ⟦< L *merces,* payment⟧ **1** a refraining from harming offenders, enemies, etc. **2** imprisonment rather than death for a capital crime **3** a disposition to forgive or be kind **4** the power to forgive **5** kind or compassionate treatment **6** a lucky thing; blessing **—at the mercy of** completely in the power of

mercy killing EUTHANASIA

mere (mir) ***adj.*** *superl.* **mer′est** ⟦< L *merus,* pure⟧ nothing more or other than *[*a *mere* boy*]*

mere′ly *adv.* only; no more than

mer·e·tri·cious (mer′ə trish′əs) ***adj.*** ⟦< L *meretrix,* a prostitute⟧ **1** attractive in a flashy way **2** superficially plausible; specious

mer·gan·ser (mər gan′sər) ***n.*** ⟦< L *mergus,* diver (bird) + *anser,* goose⟧ a fish-eating, diving duck with a long bill

merge (murj) ***vi., vt.*** **merged, merg′ing** ⟦L *mergere,* to dip⟧ **1** to lose or cause to lose identity by being absorbed or combined **2** to unite; combine

merg·er (mur′jər) ***n.*** a merging; specif., a combining of two or more companies into one

me·rid·i·an (mə rid′ē ən) ***n.*** ⟦< L *meridies,* noon⟧ **1** the highest point of power, etc. **2** *a*) a circle on the earth's surface passing through the geographical poles and any given point *b*) any of the lines of longitude

me·ringue (mə raŋ′) ***n.*** ⟦Fr⟧ egg whites beaten with sugar until stiff: used as a pie covering, etc.

me·ri·no (mə rē′nō) ***n.***, *pl.* **-nos** ⟦Sp⟧ **1** any of a breed of hardy, white-faced sheep with long, fine wool **2** the wool **3** yarn or cloth made of it

mer·it (mer′it) ***n.*** ⟦< L *merere,* deserve⟧ **1** worth; value; excellence **2** something deserving reward, praise, etc. **3** [*pl.*] intrinsic rightness or wrongness ***—vt.*** to deserve

mer·i·to·ri·ous (mer′i tôr′ē əs) ***adj.*** having merit; deserving reward, praise, etc. **—mer′i·to′ri·ous·ly *adv.***

Mer·lin (mur′lin) ***n.*** *Arthurian Legend* a magician and seer, helper of King Arthur

mer·maid (mur′mād′) ***n.*** ⟦< OE *mere,* sea + MAID⟧ an imaginary sea creature with the head and upper body of a woman and the tail of a fish **—mer′man′** (-man′), *pl.* **-men′** (-mən′), ***masc.n.***

mer·ri·ment (mer′i mənt) ***n.*** a merrymaking; gaiety and fun; mirth

mer·ry (mer′ē) ***adj.*** **-ri·er, -ri·est** ⟦< OE *myrge,* pleasing⟧ **1** full of fun; lively **2** festive **—make merry** to be festive and have fun **—mer′ri·ly *adv.*** **—mer′ri·ness *n.***

mer′ry-go-round′ *n.* **1** a circular, revolving platform with forms of animals as seats on it, used at carnivals, etc. **2** a busy series of activities

mer′ry·mak′ing *n.* a having fun; festivity **—mer′ry·mak′er *n.***

me·sa (mā′sə) ***n.*** ⟦Sp < L *mensa,* a table⟧ a small, high plateau with steep sides

Me·sa (mā′sə) city in SC Arizona: pop. 288,000

mes·cal (mes kal′) ***n.*** ⟦< Sp < AmInd(Mex)⟧ a small cactus of N Mexico and the SW U.S.

mes·ca·line (mes′kə lin) ***n.*** ⟦< AmInd(Mex) *mexcalli,* a spineless cactus⟧ a psychedelic drug obtained from the mescal

mes·clun (mes′klən) ***n.*** ⟦Fr⟧ a mixture of salad greens and herbs

mes·dames (mā dăm′; *Fr,* -dȧm′) ***n. pl.*** *of* MADAME, MADAM (sense 1), or MRS.

mes·de·moi·selles (mād mwȧ zel′) ***n.*** *pl. of* MADEMOISELLE

mesh (mesh) ***n.*** ⟦prob. < MDu *mæsche*⟧ **1** any of the open spaces of a net, screen, etc. **2** a net or network **3** a netlike material, as for stockings **4** the engagement of the teeth of gears ***—vt., vi.*** **1** to entangle or become entangled **2** to engage or become engaged: said of gears **3** to interlock

mes·mer·ize (mez′mər īz′, mes′-) ***vt.*** **-ized′, -iz′ing** ⟦after F. A. *Mesmer* (1734-1815), Ger physician⟧ **1** to hypnotize **2** to spellbind **—mes′mer·ism′ *n.*** **—mes′mer·ist *n.***

Mes·o·a·mer·i·ca (mes′ō ə mer′i kə, mez′-) region including parts of modern Mexico and Central America, formerly inhabited by the Maya, the Aztecs, etc.

mes·on (mes′än′, mez′-) ***n.*** ⟦< Gr *mesos,* middle + (ELECTR)ON⟧ any of a group of unstable subatomic particles having a mass between those of an electron and a proton

Mes·o·po·ta·mi·a (mes′ə pə tā′mē ə) ancient country in SW Asia, between the upper Tigris & Euphrates rivers

Mes·o·zo·ic (mes′ə zō′ik, mez′-) ***adj.*** ⟦< Gr *mesos,* middle + ZO(O)- + -IC⟧ designating the geologic era (*c.* 240 to 66 million years ago) characterized by dinosaurs and by the appearance of flowering plants, mammals, birds, etc.

mes·quite or **mes·quit** (me skēt′) ***n.*** ⟦< AmInd(Mex) *mizquitl*⟧ a thorny tree or shrub of Mexico and the SW U.S.

mess (mes) ***n.*** ⟦< L *missus,* course (at a meal)⟧ **1** a portion of food for a meal **2** a group of people who regularly eat together, as in the army **3** the meal they eat **4** a jumble **5** a state of trouble, disorder, or confusion **6** [Inf.] a person in such a state **7** [Inf.] an untidy place **—*vt.*** **1** to make dirty or untidy **2** to muddle; botch Often with *up* **—*vi.*** **1** to eat as one of a mess **2** to make a mess **3** to putter or meddle (*in* or *with*) **—mess′y**, **-i·er**, **-i·est**, ***adj.*** **— mess′i·ly *adv.*** **—mess′i·ness *n.***

mes·sage (mes′ij) ***n.*** ⟦< L *mittere,* send⟧ **1** a communication sent by speech, in writing, etc. **2** the chief idea that an artist, writer, etc. seeks to communicate in a work **—get the message** [Inf.] to understand a hint, etc.

mes·sen·ger (mes′ən jər) ***n.*** one who carries a message or goes on an errand

messenger RNA a single-stranded form of RNA, derived from DNA, that carries the genetic information needed to form proteins

mess hall a room or building where soldiers, etc. regularly have meals

Mes·si·ah (mə sī′ə) ***n.*** ⟦< Heb *māshīaḥ,* anointed⟧ **1** *Judaism* the expected deliverer of the Jews **2** *Christianity* Jesus **3** **[m-]** any expected savior or liberator **—Mes′si·an′ic** or **me·si·an·ic** (mes′ē an′ik) ***adj.***

mes·sieurs (mes′ərz; *Fr* mā syö′) ***n.*** *pl. of* MONSIEUR

Messrs (mes′ərz) *abbrev.* messieurs: now used chiefly as the pl. of MR.

mes·ti·zo (me stē′zō) ***n.,*** *pl.* **-zos** or **-zoes** ⟦Sp < L *miscere,* to mix⟧ a person of mixed parentage, esp. Spanish and American Indian

met[1] (met) ***vt., vi.*** *pt. & pp. of* MEET[1]

met[2] *abbrev.* metropolitan

meta- ⟦< Gr *meta,* after⟧ *prefix* **1** changed *[metathesis]* **2** after, beyond, higher *[metaphysics]*

me·tab·o·lism (mə tab′ə liz′əm) ***n.*** ⟦< Gr *meta,* beyond + *ballein,* throw⟧ the chemical and physical processes continuously going on in living organisms and cells, including the changing of food into living tissue and the changing of living tissue into waste products and energy **—met·a·bol·ic** (met′ə bäl′ik) ***adj.*** **—me·tab′o·lize′** (-līz′), **-lized′**, **-liz′ing**, ***vt., vi.***

met·a·car·pus (met′ə kär′pəs) ***n.,*** *pl.* **-pi′** (-pī′) ⟦< Gr *meta,* over + *karpos,* wrist⟧ the part of the hand between the wrist and the fingers **—met′a·car′pal *adj., n.***

met·al (met′′l) ***n.*** ⟦< Gr *metallon,* a mine⟧ **1** *a)* any of a class of chemical elements, as iron or gold, that have luster, can conduct heat and electricity, etc. *b)* an alloy of such elements, as brass **2** anything consisting of metal **— me·tal·lic** (mə tal′ik) ***adj.***

met·al·lur·gy (met′ə lur′jē) ***n.*** ⟦< Gr *metallon,* metal + *ergon,* work⟧ the science of separating metals from their ores and preparing them for use, by smelting, refining, etc. **—met′al·lur′gi·cal *adj.*** **—met′al·lur′gist *n.***

met·a·mor·phose (met′ə môr′fōz′, -fōs′) ***vt., vi.*** **-phosed′**, **-phos′ing** to change in form; transform

met′a·mor′pho·sis (-môr′fə sis) ***n.,*** *pl.* **-ses′** (-sēz′) ⟦< Gr *meta,* over + *morphē,* form⟧ **1** a change of form, structure, substance, or function; specif., the physical change undergone by some animals during development, as of the tadpole to the frog **2** a marked change of character, appearance, condition, etc. **—met′a·mor′phic *adj.***

met·a·phor (met′ə fôr′) ***n.*** ⟦< Gr *meta,* over + *pherein,* to bear⟧ a figure of speech in which one thing is spoken of as if it were another (Ex.: "all the world's a stage") **—met′a·phor′ic** or **met′a·phor′i·cal *adj.***

met·a·phys·i·cal (met′ə fiz′i kəl) ***adj.*** **1** of, or having the nature of, metaphysics **2** very abstract or subtle **3** supernatural

met′a·phys′ics (-iks) ***n.*** ⟦< Gr *meta (ta) physika,* after (the) *Physics* (of Aristotle)⟧ **1** the branch of philosophy that seeks to explain the nature of being and reality **2** speculative philosophy in general

me·tas·ta·sis (mə tas′tə sis) ***n.,*** *pl.* **-ses′** (-sēz′) ⟦< Gr *meta,* after + *histanai,* to place⟧ the spread of disease from one part of the body to another, esp. the spread of cancer cells by way of the bloodstream **—me·tas′ta·size′** (-sīz′), **-sized′**, **-siz′ing**, ***vi.***

met·a·tar·sus (met′ə tär′səs) ***n.,*** *pl.* **-si′** (-sī′) ⟦< Gr *meta,* over + *tarsos,* flat of the foot⟧ the part of the human foot between the ankle and the toes **—met′a·tar′sal *adj., n.***

me·tath·e·sis (mə tath′ə sis) ***n.,*** *pl.* **-ses′** (-sēz′) ⟦< Gr *meta,* over + *tithenai,* to place⟧ transposition, specif. of sounds in a word

mete (mēt) ***vt.*** **met′ed**, **met′ing** ⟦OE *metan,* to measure⟧ to allot; distribute: usually with *out*

me·tem·psy·cho·sis (mi tem′sī kō′sis) ***n.,*** *pl.* **-ses′** (-sēz′) ⟦< Gr *meta,* over + *en,* in + *psychē,* soul⟧ transmigration of souls

me·te·or (mēt′ē ər, -ôr′) ***n.*** ⟦< Gr *meta,* beyond + *eōra,* a hovering⟧ **1** the streak of light, etc. observed when a meteoroid enters the earth's atmosphere; shooting star **2** loosely, a meteoroid or meteorite

me′te·or′ic (-ôr′ik) ***adj.*** **1** of a meteor **2** like a meteor; momentarily brilliant, swift, etc.

me′te·or·ite′ (-ər īt′) ***n.*** that part of a meteoroid that survives passage through the atmosphere of a planet and falls to its surface

me′te·or·oid′ (-ər oid′) ***n.*** a small, solid body traveling through outer space, seen as a meteor when in the earth's atmosphere

me′te·or·ol′o·gy (-ə räl′ə jē) ***n.*** ⟦see METEOR & -LOGY⟧ the science of the atmosphere and its phenomena; study of weather **—me′te·or·o·log′i·cal** (-ə läj′i kəl) ***adj.*** **—me′te·or·ol′o·gist *n.***

me·ter[1] (mēt′ər) ***n.*** ⟦< Gr *metron,* a measure⟧ **1** rhythm in verse; measured arrangement of syllables according to stress 2 the basic pattern of beats in a piece of music 3 ⟦Fr *mètre*⟧ the basic metric unit of length, equal to 39.3701 inches

me·ter[2] (mēt′ər) ***n.*** ⟦METE + -ER⟧ **1** an apparatus for measuring and recording the quantity of gas, water, etc. passing through it **2** PARKING METER

-me·ter (mēt′ər, mi tər) ⟦< Gr *metron,* a measure⟧ *combining form* a device for measuring *[barometer]*

meth·a·done (meth′ə dōn′) ***n.*** ⟦< its chemical name⟧ a synthetic narcotic drug used in medicine to treat heroin and morphine addicts

meth·ane (meth′ān′) ***n.*** ⟦< METHYL⟧ a colorless, odorless, flammable gas formed by the decomposition of vegetable matter, as in marshes

meth·a·nol (meth′ə nôl′) ***n.*** ⟦< METHAN(E) + (ALCOH)OL⟧ a colorless, flammable, poisonous liquid used as a fuel, solvent, antifreeze, etc.

me·thinks (mē thiŋks′) ***v.impersonal*** *pt.* **-thought′** (-thôt′) ⟦OE *me,* to me + *thyncth,* it seems⟧ [Archaic] it seems to me

meth·od (meth′əd) ***n.*** ⟦< Fr < Gr *meta,* after + *hodos,* a way⟧ **1** a way of doing anything; procedure; process **2** orderliness in doing things or handling ideas

me·thod·i·cal (mə thäd′i kəl) ***adj.*** characterized by method; orderly; systematic —**me·thod′i·cal·ly** ***adv.***

Meth·od·ist (meth′ə dist) ***n.*** a member of a Protestant Christian denomination that developed from the teachings of John Wesley —**Meth′od·ism′** ***n.***

meth·od·ol·o·gy (meth′ə däl′ə jē) ***n.,*** *pl.* **-gies** a system of methods, as in a science

Me·thu·se·lah (mə thoo′zə lə) ***n.*** *Bible* a patriarch who lived 969 years

meth·yl (meth′əl) ***n.*** ⟦< Gr *methy,* wine + *hylē,* wood⟧ a hydrocarbon radical found in methanol

methyl alcohol METHANOL

me·tic·u·lous (mə tik′yoo ləs, -yə-) ***adj.*** ⟦< L *metus,* fear⟧ extremely or excessively careful about details; scrupulous or finicky —**me·tic′u·lous·ly** ***adv.***

mé·tier (mā tyā′) ***n.*** ⟦Fr, a trade⟧ work that one is particularly suited for

me·tre (mēt′ər) ***n.*** *Brit. sp. of* METER[1]

met·ric (me′trik) ***adj.*** **1** METRICAL **2** *a)* of the METER[1] (sense 3) *b)* of the metric system

met·ri·cal (me′tri kəl) ***adj.*** **1** of or composed in meter or verse **2** of or used in measurement —**met′ri·cal·ly** ***adv.***

met·ri·cate (me′tri kāt′) ***vt.*** **-cat′ed, -cat′ing** to change over to the metric system —**met′ri·ca′tion** ***n.***

metric system a decimal system of weights and measures in which the kilogram (2.2046 pounds), the meter (39.3701 inches), and the liter (1,000 cubic centimeters or 1.0567 quarts) are the basic units

met·ro[1] (me′trō) ***adj.*** *short for* METROPOLITAN

met·ro[2] (me′trō) ***n.,*** *pl.* **-ros** ⟦ult. < *metro(politan)*⟧ [*often* **M-**] a subway

met·ro·nome (me′trə nōm′) ***n.*** ⟦< Gr

metron, measure + *nomos,* law⟧ a device that beats time at a desired rate, as for piano practice

me·trop·o·lis (mə träp′ə lis) ***n.*** ⟦< Gr *mētēr,* mother + *polis,* city⟧ **1** the main city of a country, state, etc. **2** any large or important city —**met·ro·pol·i·tan** (me′trə päl′i tən) ***adj.***

met·tle (met′'l) ***n.*** ⟦var. of METAL⟧ spirit; courage; ardor —**on one's mettle** prepared to do one's best

met′tle·some (-səm) ***adj.*** full of mettle; spirited; ardent, brave, etc.

mew (myoo) ***n.*** ⟦echoic⟧ the characteristic vocal sound made by a cat —***vi.*** to make this sound

mewl (myool) ***vi.*** ⟦< prec.⟧ to cry weakly, like a baby; whimper

mews (myooz) ***pl.n.*** ⟦< L *mutare,* to change⟧ [*usually with sing. v.*] [Chiefly Brit.] stables or carriage houses in a court or alley

Mex *abbrev.* **1** Mexican **2** Mexico

Mex·i·ca·li (mek′si kä′lē) city in NW Mexico, on the U.S. border: pop. 602,000

Mex·i·co (mek′si kō′) **1** country in North America, south of the U.S.: 759,529 sq. mi.; pop. 81,250,000 **2 Gulf of** arm of the Atlantic, east of Mexico —**Mex′i·can** ***adj., n.***

Mexico City capital of Mexico: pop. 8,831,000 (met. area, 15,048,000)

mez·za·nine (mez′ə nēn′, mez′ə nēn′) ***n.*** ⟦< It *mezzano,* middle⟧ **1** a low-ceilinged story between two main stories, usually in the form of a balcony over the main floor **2** the first few rows of the balcony in some theaters

mez·zo-so·pra·no (met′sō sə pran′ō) ***n.,*** *pl.* **-nos** or **-ni** (-ē) ⟦It < *mezzo,* medium + SOPRANO⟧ **1** the range of a female voice between soprano and contralto **2** a voice or singer with such a range

MFA or **M.F.A.** *abbrev.* Master of Fine Arts

mfg *abbrev.* manufacturing

mfr *abbrev.* **1** manufacture **2** manufacturer

Mg *Chem. symbol for* magnesium

mg *abbrev.* milligram(s)

Mgr or **mgr** *abbrev.* manager

MHz *abbrev.* megahertz

mi[1] (mē) ***n.*** ⟦ML⟧ *Music* the third tone of the diatonic scale

mi[2] *abbrev.* **1** mile(s) **2** mill(s)

MI *abbrev.* **1** Michigan **2** middle initial

Mi·am·i (mī am′ē) city on the SE coast of Florida: pop. 359,000 —**Mi·am′i·an** ***n.***

mi·as·ma (mī az′mə, mē-) ***n.*** ⟦< Gr *miainein,* pollute⟧ **1** a vapor as from marshes, formerly supposed to poison the air **2** an unwholesome atmosphere or influence

mi·ca (mī′kə) ***n.*** ⟦L, a crumb⟧ a mineral that crystallizes in thin, flexible layers, resistant to heat and electricity

mice (mīs) ***n.*** *pl. of* MOUSE

Mi·chel·an·ge·lo (mī′kəl an′jə lō′, mik′əl-) 1475-1564; It. sculptor, painter, &

architect

Mich·i·gan (mish′i gən) **1** Midwestern state of the U.S.: 58,110 sq. mi.; pop. 9,295,000; cap. Lansing: abbrev. *MI* **2 Lake** one of the Great Lakes, between Michigan & Wisconsin —**Mich′i·gan′der** (-gan′dər) ***n.*** —**Mich′i·ga′ni·an** (-gā′nē ən) or **Mich′i·gan·ite′** ***adj., n.***

Mick·ey Finn (mik′ē fin′) ⟦< ?⟧ [*also* **m- f-**] [Slang] a drink of liquor to which a narcotic, etc. has been added, given to an unsuspecting person: often shortened to **Mick′ey** or **mick′ey** ***n.***, *pl.* **-eys**

micro- ⟦< Gr *mikros,* small⟧ *combining form* **1** little, small *[microcosm]* **2** enlarging *[microscope]* **3** involving microscopes *[microsurgery]* **4** one millionth *[microsecond]* Also **micr-**

mi·crobe (mī′krōb′) ***n.*** ⟦< Gr *mikros,* small + *bios,* life⟧ a microorganism, esp. one causing disease

mi·cro·bi·ol·o·gy (mī′krō bī äl′ə jē) ***n.*** the branch of biology dealing with microorganisms —**mi′cro·bi·ol′o·gist** ***n.***

mi′cro·brew′er·y ***n.***, *pl.* **-er·ies** a small brewery producing high-quality beer for local consumption

mi′cro·chip′ ***n.*** CHIP (*n.* 5)

mi′cro·com·put′er ***n.*** a small, inexpensive computer having a microprocessor and used in the home, etc.

mi′cro·cosm′ (-käz′əm) ***n.*** ⟦see MICRO- & COSMOS⟧ something regarded as a world in miniature

mi′cro·dot′ ***n.*** a copy, as of written or printed matter, photographically reduced to pinhead size, used in espionage, etc.

mi′cro·ec′o·nom′ics ***n.*** a branch of economics dealing with certain specific factors affecting an economy, as the behavior of individual consumers

mi′cro·fiche′ (-fēsh′) ***n.***, *pl.* **-fich′es** or **-fiche′** ⟦Fr < *micro-,* MICRO- + *fiche,* small card⟧ a small sheet of microfilm containing a group of microfilmed pages

mi′cro·film′ ***n.*** film on which documents, etc. are photographed in a reduced size for storage, etc. —***vt., vi.*** to photograph on microfilm

mi′cro·man′age ***vt.*** **-aged**, **-ag·ing** to manage or control closely, often so closely as to be counterproductive

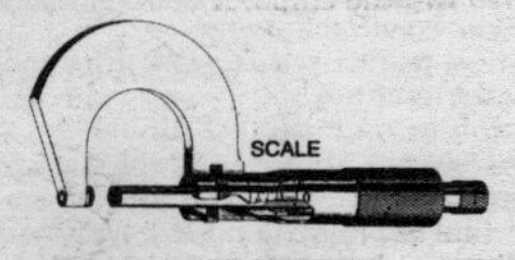

MICROMETER

mi·crom·e·ter (mī kräm′ət ər) ***n.*** ⟦< Fr: see MICRO- & -METER⟧ a tool for measuring very small distances, angles, etc.

mi·cron (mī′krän′) ***n.*** ⟦< Gr *mikros,* small⟧ one millionth of a meter

Mi·cro·ne·sia (mī′krə nē′zhə) country on a group of islands in the Pacific east of the Philippines: 271 sq. mi.; pop. 108,000 —**Mi′cro·ne′sian** ***adj., n.***

mi·cro·or·gan·ism (mī′krō ôr′gə niz′əm) ***n.*** a microscopic animal, plant, bacterium, virus, etc.

mi·cro·phone (mī′krə fōn′) ***n.*** ⟦MICRO- + -PHONE⟧ an instrument for converting sound waves into an electric signal

mi·cro·proc·es·sor (mī′krō prä′ses′ər) ***n.*** a chip that functions to control the operation of a microcomputer

mi·cro·scope (mī′krə skōp′) ***n.*** ⟦see MICRO- & -SCOPE⟧ an instrument consisting of a combination of lenses, for making very small objects, as microorganisms, look larger

mi′cro·scop′ic (-skäp′ik) ***adj.*** **1** so small as to be invisible or obscure except through a microscope; minute **2** of, with, or like a microscope —**mi′cro·scop′i·cal·ly** ***adv.***

mi·cro·sur·ger·y (mī′krō sur′jər ē) ***n.*** surgery performed using a microscope and minute instruments or laser beams

mi′cro·wave′ ***adj.*** **1** designating equipment, etc. using microwaves for radar, communications, etc. **2** designating an oven that cooks quickly using microwaves —***vt.*** **-waved′**, **-wav′ing** to cook in a microwave oven —***n.*** **1** an electromagnetic wave with a frequency of about 300,000 megahertz to 300 megahertz **2** a microwave oven

mid[1] (mid) ***adj.*** ⟦OE *midd-*⟧ middle

mid[2] (mid) ***prep.*** [Old Poet.] amid: also **'mid**

mid- *combining form* middle, middle part of *[mid-May]*

mid′air′ ***n.*** any point in space not in contact with the ground or any other surface

Mi·das (mī′dəs) *Gr. Myth.* a king granted the power to turn everything he touches into gold

mid′course′ ***adj.*** happening in the middle of a flight, journey, or course of action

mid′day′ ***n., adj.*** ⟦OE *middæg*⟧ noon

mid·dle (mid′'l) ***adj.*** ⟦OE *middel*⟧ **1** halfway between two given points, times, etc. **2** intermediate **3** [**M-**] designating a stage in language development intermediate between *Old* and *Modern [Middle* English*]* —***n.*** **1** a middle point, part, time, etc. **2** something intermediate **3** the middle part of the body; waist

middle age the time between youth and old age —**mid′dle-aged′** ***adj.***

Middle Ages the period of European history between ancient and modern times, A.D. 476-*c.* 1450

Middle America the American middle class, seen as being conventional or conservative

mid′dle·brow′ (-brou′) ***n.*** [Inf.] one regarded as having conventional, middle-class tastes or opinions —***adj.*** of or for a middlebrow

middle class the social class between the aristocracy or very wealthy and the lower working class —**mid′dle-class′** ***adj.***

middle ear the part of the ear including the eardrum and the adjacent cavity containing three small bones

Middle East area from Afghanistan to Libya, including Arabia, Cyprus, & Asiatic Turkey —**Middle Eastern**

Middle English the English language between *c.* 1100 and *c.* 1500

mid'dle·man' (-man') ***n.***, *pl.* **-men'** (-men') **1** a trader who buys from a producer and sells at wholesale or retail **2** a go-between

mid'dle·most' ***adj.*** MIDMOST

mid'dle-of-the-road' ***adj.*** avoiding extremes, esp. political extremes

middle school a school with three or four grades, variously including grades 5 through grade 8

mid'dle·weight' ***n.*** a boxer with a maximum weight of 160 pounds

Middle West MIDWEST —**Middle Western**

mid·dling (mid'liŋ) ***adj.*** of middle size, quality, etc.; medium —***adv.*** [Inf.] fairly; moderately

mid·dy (mid'ē) ***n.***, *pl.* **-dies** ⟦< MIDSHIPMAN⟧ a loose blouse with a sailor collar, worn by women and children

Mid·east' MIDDLE EAST —**Mid·east'ern** ***adj.***

midge (mij) ***n.*** ⟦OE *mycg*⟧ a small, gnatlike insect

midg·et (mij'it) ***n.*** **1** a very small person **2** anything very small of its kind —***adj.*** very small of its kind

mid·land (mid'lənd) ***n.*** the middle region of a country; interior —***adj.*** in or of the midland

mid'most' ***adj.*** exactly in the middle, or nearest the middle

mid'night' ***n.*** twelve o'clock at night —***adj.*** **1** of or at midnight **2** like midnight; very dark

mid'point' ***n.*** a point at or close to the middle or center

mid·riff (mid'rif) ***n.*** ⟦< OE *midd-*, MID[1] + *hrif*, belly⟧ **1** DIAPHRAGM (sense 1) **2** the middle part of the torso, between the abdomen and the chest

mid·ship·man (mid'ship'mən) ***n.***, *pl.* **-men** (-mən) a student in training to be a naval officer

mid-size or **mid·size** (mid'sīz') ***adj.*** of a size intermediate between large and small *[a mid-size car]*

midst (midst) ***n.*** the middle; central part —***prep.*** [Old Poet.] in the midst of; amid —**in our** (or **your** or **their**) **midst** among us (or you or them) —**in the midst of** **1** in the middle of **2** during

mid·stream (mid'strēm') ***n.*** the middle of a stream

mid'sum'mer ***n.*** **1** the middle of summer **2** the time of the summer solstice, about June 21

mid'term' ***adj.*** in the middle of the term —***n.*** [Inf.] a midterm examination, as at a college

mid'town' ***adj.*** of or in the central part of a city, esp. a large city —***n.*** a midtown area

mid'way' ***n.*** that part of a fair where sideshows, etc. are located —***adj., adv.*** in the middle of the way or distance; halfway

Mid·west' region of the NC U.S. between the Rocky Mountains & the E border of Ohio & the S borders of Kansas & Missouri —**Mid·west'ern** ***adj.***

mid'wife' (-wīf') ***n.***, *pl.* **-wives'** ⟦< ME *mid*, with + *wif*, woman⟧ a person who helps women in childbirth —**mid'wife'ry** (-wif'rē) ***n.***

mid'win'ter ***n.*** **1** the middle of winter **2** the time of the winter solstice, about Dec. 22

mid'year' ***adj.*** in the middle of the year —***n.*** [Inf.] a midyear examination, as at a college

mien (mēn) ***n.*** ⟦short for DEMEAN[2]⟧ one's appearance, bearing, or manner

miff (mif) ***vt.*** ⟦prob. orig. cry of disgust⟧ [Inf.] to offend

MIG (mig) ***n.*** ⟦after *Mi(koyan)* & *G(urevich)*, its Soviet designers⟧ a high-speed, high-altitude jet fighter plane: also **MiG**

might[1] (mīt) ***v.aux.*** ⟦OE *mihte*⟧ **1** *pt.* of MAY **2** used as an auxiliary generally equivalent to MAY *[it might rain]*

might[2] (mīt) ***n.*** ⟦OE *miht*⟧ strength, power, or vigor

might'y ***adj.*** **-i·er**, **-i·est** **1** powerful; strong **2** remarkably large, etc.; great —***adv.*** [Inf.] very —**might'i·ly** ***adv.*** —**might'i·ness** ***n.***

mi·gnon·ette (min'yə net') ***n.*** ⟦< Fr *mignon*, small⟧ a plant with spikes of small greenish, whitish, or reddish flowers

mi·graine (mī'grān') ***n.*** ⟦< Gr *hēmi-*, half + *kranion*, skull⟧ an intense, periodic headache, usually limited to one side of the head

mi·grant (mī'grənt) ***adj.*** migrating —***n.*** **1** one that migrates **2** a farm laborer who moves from place to place to harvest seasonal crops

mi·grate (mī'grāt') ***vi.*** **-grat'ed**, **-grat'ing** ⟦< L *migrare*⟧ **1** to settle in another country or region **2** to move to another region with the change in seasons, as many birds do —**mi·gra·to·ry** (mī'grə tôr'ē) ***adj.***

mi·gra·tion (mī grā'shən) ***n.*** **1** a migrating **2** a group of people, birds, etc., migrating together

mi·ka·do (mi kä'dō) ***n.***, *pl.* **-dos** ⟦< Jpn *mi*, an honorific title + *kado*, gate⟧ [*often* **M-**] the emperor of Japan: title no longer used

mike (mīk) [Inf.] ***n.*** a microphone —***vt.*** **miked**, **mik'ing** to record, amplify, etc. with a microphone

mil[1] (mil) ***n.*** ⟦L *mille*, thousand⟧ a unit of linear measure, equal to $\frac{1}{1000}$ inch

mil[2] (mil) ***n.*** [Slang] *short for* million

Mi·lan (mi lan', -län') city in NW Italy: pop. 1,602,000

milch (milch) ***adj.*** ⟦ME *milche*⟧ kept for milking *[milch cows]*

mild (mīld) ***adj.*** ⟦OE *milde*⟧ **1** gentle or kind; not severe **2** having a soft, pleasant flavor *[a mild cheese]* —**mild'ly** ***adv.*** —**mild'ness** ***n.***

mil·dew (mil'dōō') ***n.*** ⟦OE *meledeaw*, honeydew⟧ a fungus that attacks some plants or appears on damp cloth, etc. as a whitish coating —*vt., vi.* to affect or be affected with mildew

mile (mīl) *n.* ⟦< L *milia* (*passuum*), thousand (paces)⟧ a unit of linear measure equal to 5,280 feet

mile′age *n.* **1** an allowance per mile for traveling expenses **2** total miles traveled **3** the average number of miles that can be traveled, as per gallon of fuel

mile′post′ *n.* a signpost showing the distance in miles to or from a place

mil′er *n.* one who competes in mile races

mile′stone′ *n.* **1** a stone set up to show the distance in miles to or from a place **2** a significant event in history, in a career, etc.

mi·lieu (mēl yʉ′, -yoo′, -yo͞o′; mil-) *n., pl.* **-lieus′** ⟦Fr < L *medius*, middle + *locus*, a place⟧ environment; esp., social setting

mil·i·tant (mil′i tənt) *adj.* ⟦< L *miles*, soldier⟧ **1** fighting **2** ready to fight, esp. for some cause —*n.* a militant person —**mil′i·tan·cy** *n.* —**mil′i·tant·ly** *adv.*

mil·i·ta·rism (mil′ə tə riz′əm) *n.* **1** military spirit **2** a policy of aggressive military preparedness —**mil′i·ta·rist** *n.* —**mil′i·ta·ris′tic** *adj.*

mil′i·ta·rize′ (-rīz′) *vt.* **-rized′**, **-riz′ing** to equip and prepare for war

mil·i·tar·y (mil′ə ter′ē) *adj.* ⟦< L *miles*, soldier⟧ **1** of, for, or done by soldiers **2** of, for, or fit for war **3** of the army —**the military** the armed forces

military police soldiers assigned to police duties in the army

mil·i·tate (mil′ə tāt′) *vi.* **-tat′ed**, **-tat′ing** ⟦< L *militare*, be a soldier⟧ to operate or work (*against*)

mi·li·tia (mə lish′ə) *n.* ⟦< L *miles*, soldier⟧ **1** an army composed of citizens rather than professional soldiers, called up in time of emergency **2** a group of disaffected citizens organized like an army and opposing federal authority —**mi·li′tia·man** (-mən), *pl.* **-men** (-mən), *n.*

milk (milk) *n.* ⟦OE *meolc*⟧ **1** a white fluid secreted by the mammary glands of female mammals for suckling their young **2** cow's milk, etc., drunk by humans as a food or used to make butter, cheese, etc. **3** any liquid like this, as the liquid in coconuts —*vt.* **1** to squeeze milk from (a cow, goat, etc.) **2** to extract money, ideas, etc. from as if by milking —**milk′er** *n.*

milk glass a nearly opaque whitish glass

milk′maid′ *n.* a girl or woman who milks cows or works in a dairy

milk′man′ (-man′) *n., pl.* **-men′** (-mən′) a man who sells or delivers milk for a dairy

milk of magnesia a milky-white suspension of magnesium hydroxide in water, used as a laxative and antacid

milk′shake′ *n.* a drink made of milk, flavoring, and ice cream, mixed or shaken until frothy

milk′sop′ (-säp′) *n.* a man thought of as timid, ineffectual, effeminate, etc.

milk tooth any of the temporary, first teeth of a child or young animal

milk′weed′ *n.* any of a group of plants with a milky juice

milk′y *adj.* **-i·er**, **-i·est** **1** like milk; esp., white as milk **2** of or containing milk —**milk′i·ness** *n.*

Milky Way the galaxy containing our sun: seen as a broad, faintly luminous band of very distant stars and interstellar gas arching across the night sky

mill¹ (mil) *n.* ⟦< L *mola*, millstone⟧ **1** a building with machinery for grinding grain into flour or meal **2** any of various machines for grinding, crushing, cutting, etc. **3** a factory *[a textile mill]* —*vt.* **1** to grind, form, etc. by or in a mill **2** to raise and ridge the edge of (a coin) —*vi.* to move (*around* or *about*) confusedly —**in the mill** in preparation —**through the mill** [Inf.] through a hard, painful, instructive experience, test, etc.

mill² (mil) *n.* ⟦< L *mille*, thousand⟧ $\frac{1}{10}$ of a cent: unit used in calculating

mill′age *n.* taxation in mills per dollar of valuation

mil·len·ni·um (mi len′ē əm) *n., pl.* **-ni·ums** or **-ni·a** (-ə) ⟦< L *mille*, thousand + *annus*, year⟧ **1** a thousand years **2** *Christian Theol.* the period of a thousand years during which Christ will reign on earth: with *the* **3** any period of great happiness, peace, etc.

mill′er *n.* one who owns or operates a mill, esp. a flour mill

mil·let (mil′it) *n.* ⟦< L *milium*⟧ **1** a cereal grass whose grain is used for food in Europe and Asia **2** any of several similar grasses

milli- ⟦< L *mille*, thousand⟧ *combining form* one thousandth part of *[millimeter]*

mil·li·gram (mil′i gram′) *n.* one thousandth of a gram

mil′li·li′ter (-lēt′ər) *n.* one thousandth of a liter: Brit. sp. **mil′li·li′tre**

mil′li·me′ter (-mēt′ər) *n.* one thousandth of a meter: Brit. sp. **mil′li·me′tre**

mil·li·ner (mil′i nər) *n.* ⟦< *Milaner*, vendor of dress wares from Milan⟧ one who makes or sells women's hats

mil·li·ner·y (mil′i ner′ē) *n.* **1** women's hats, headdresses, etc. **2** the work or business of a milliner

mil·lion (mil′yən) *n.* ⟦< L *mille*, thousand⟧ a thousand thousands; 1,000,000

mil′lion·aire′ (-yə ner′) *n.* a person whose wealth comes to at least a million dollars, pounds, francs, etc.

mil·li·pede (mil′i pēd′) *n.* ⟦< L *mille*, thousand + *pes*, foot⟧ a many-legged arthropod with an elongated body

mill′race′ *n.* the channel in which water runs to turn the wheel driving the machinery in a mill

mill′stone′ *n.* **1** either of a pair of round, flat stones used for grinding grain, etc. **2** a heavy burden

mill′stream′ *n.* the water flowing in a millrace

mill′wright′ *n.* a worker who builds, installs, or repairs the machinery in a mill

milt (milt) *n.* ⟦prob. < Scand⟧ the sex

glands or sperm of male fishes

Mil·ton (milt'ʼn), **John** 1608-74; Eng. poet

Mil·wau·kee (mil wô'kē) city & port in SE Wisconsin, on Lake Michigan: pop. 628,000

mime (mīm) ***n.*** ⟦< Gr *mimos*, imitator⟧ **1** the representation of an action, mood, etc. by gestures, not words **2** a mimic or pantomimist —***vt.* mimed, mim'ing** to mimic or pantomime

mim·e·o·graph (mim'ē ə graf') ***n.*** ⟦< Gr *mimeomai*, I imitate⟧ a machine for making copies of graphic matter by means of an inked stencil —***vt.*** to make (such copies) of

mi·met·ic (mi met'ik, mī-) ***adj.*** ⟦< Gr *mimeisthai*, to imitate⟧ **1** imitative **2** characterized by mimicry

mim·ic (mim'ik) ***adj.*** ⟦< Gr *mimos*, actor⟧ imitative —***n.*** an imitator; esp., an actor skilled in mimicry —***vt.* -icked, -ick·ing** **1** to imitate, often so as to ridicule **2** to copy or resemble closely

mim·ic·ry (mim'ik rē) ***n.***, *pl.* **-ries** the practice or art of, or a way of, mimicking

mi·mo·sa (mi mō'sə) ***n.*** ⟦see MIME⟧ a tree, shrub, or herb growing in warm regions and usually having spikes of white, yellow, or pink flowers

min *abbrev.* **1** minimum **2** minute(s)

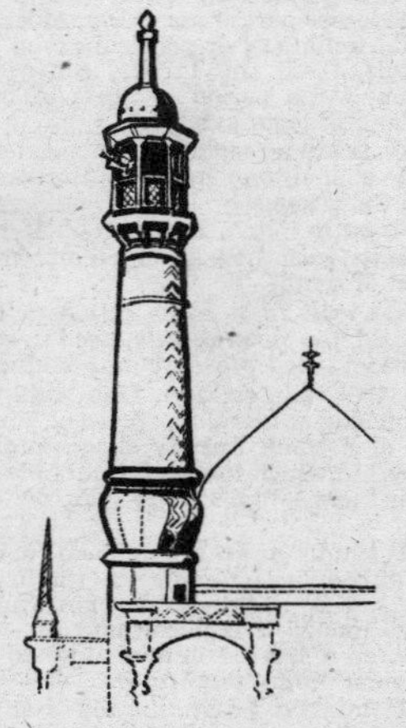

MINARET

min·a·ret (min'ə ret') ***n.*** ⟦< Ar *manāra(t)*, lighthouse⟧ a high, slender tower attached to a mosque

min·a·to·ry (min'ə tôr'ē) ***adj.*** ⟦< L *minari*, threaten⟧ menacing

mince (mins) ***vt.* minced, minc'ing** ⟦< L *minutus*, small⟧ **1** to cut up (meat, etc.) into small pieces **2** to lessen the force of *[to mince no words]* —***vi.*** to speak, act, or walk with an affected daintiness —**minc'ing *adj.***

mince'meat' ***n.*** a mixture of chopped apples, spices, suet, raisins, etc., and sometimes meat, used as a pie filling

mind (mīnd) ***n.*** ⟦< OE *(ge)mynd*⟧ **1** memory *[to bring to mind a story]* **2** opinion *[speak your mind]* **3** the seat of consciousness, in which thinking, feeling, etc. takes place **4** intellect **5** PSYCHE (*n.* 2) **6** reason; sanity —***vt.*** **1** to pay attention to; heed **2** to obey **3** to take care of *[mind the baby]* **4** to be careful about *[mind the stairs]* **5** to care about; object to *[they don't mind the noise]* —***vi.*** **1** to pay attention **2** to be obedient **3** to be careful **4** to care; object —**bear** (or **keep**) **in mind** to remember —**change one's mind** to change one's opinion, purpose, etc. —**have in mind** to intend —**never mind** don't be concerned —**on someone's mind** **1** filling someone's thoughts **2** worrying someone —**out of one's mind** **1** insane **2** frantic (*with* worry, etc.)

mind'-blow'ing ***adj.*** [Slang] **1** causing shock, etc.; overwhelming **2** hard to comprehend

mind'-bog'gling ***adj.*** [Slang] **1** hard to comprehend **2** surprising, overwhelming, etc.

mind'ed ***adj.*** having a (specified kind of) mind: used in compounds *[high-minded]*

mind'ful (-fəl) ***adj.*** having in mind; aware or careful (*of*) —**mind'ful·ly *adv.*** —**mind'ful·ness *n.***

mind'less (-lis) ***adj.*** stupid or foolish

mind reader one who seems or professes to be able to perceive another's thoughts

mind's eye the imagination

mine[1] (mīn) ***pron.*** ⟦OE min⟧ that or those belonging to me: poss. form of I[2] *[this is mine; mine are better]*

mine[2] (mīn) ***n.*** ⟦< Fr⟧ **1** a large excavation made in the earth, from which to extract ores, coal, etc. **2** a deposit of ore, coal, etc. **3** any great source of supply **4** *Mil.* *a)* a tunnel dug under an enemy's fort, etc., in which an explosive is placed *b)* an explosive charge hidden underground or in the sea, for destroying enemy vehicles, ships, etc. —***vt.*, *vi.* mined, min'ing** **1** to dig (ores, etc.) from (the earth) **2** to dig or lay military mines in or under **3** to undermine

min'er ***n.*** one whose work is digging coal, ore, etc. in a mine

min·er·al (min'ər əl) ***n.*** ⟦< ML *minera*, ore⟧ **1** an inorganic substance found naturally in the earth, as metallic ore **2** any substance that is neither vegetable nor animal —***adj.*** of or containing a mineral

mineral jelly PETROLATUM

min·er·al·o·gy (min'ər äl'ə jē) ***n.*** the scientific study of minerals —**min'er·al'o·gist *n.***

mineral oil a colorless, tasteless oil derived from petroleum, used as a laxative

mineral water water impregnated with mineral salts or gases

Mi·ner·va (mi nur'və) ***n.*** *Rom. Myth.* the goddess of wisdom

mi·ne·stro·ne (min′ə strō′nē) ***n.*** ⟦It.: ult. < L *ministrare*, serve⟧ a thick vegetable soup in a meat broth

min·gle (miŋ′gəl) ***vt.*** **-gled**, **-gling** ⟦< OE *mengan*, to mix⟧ to mix together; blend —***vi.*** **1** to become mixed or blended **2** to join or unite with others

mini- ⟦< MINI(ATURE)⟧ *combining form* miniature, very small, very short *[miniskirt]*

min·i·a·ture (min′ē ə chər, min′i chər) ***n.*** ⟦< L *miniare*, to paint red⟧ **1** a small painting, esp. a portrait **2** a copy or model on a very small scale —***adj.*** done on a very small scale

min′i·a·tur·ize′ (-īz′) ***vt.*** **-ized′**, **-iz′ing** to make in a small and compact form —**min′i·a·tur′i·za′tion** ***n.***

min·i·bike (min′ē bīk′) ***n.*** a compact motorcycle, usually used as an off-road vehicle

min′i·cam′ (-kam′) ***n.*** a portable TV camera for telecasting or videotaping news events, etc.

min′i·com·put′er (-kəm pyo͞ot′ər) ***n.*** a computer intermediate in size, power, etc. between a mainframe and a microcomputer

min·i·mal (min′i məl) ***adj.*** **1** smallest or least possible **2** of minimalism —**min′i·mal·ly** ***adv.***

min′i·mal·ism′ ***n.*** a movement in art, music, etc. in which only the simplest design, forms, etc. are used, often repetitiously —**min′i·mal·ist** ***adj.***, ***n.***

min′i·mal·ize′ (-īz′) ***vt.*** **-ized′**, **-iz′ing** to reduce to basic components

min·i·mize (min′i mīz′) ***vt.*** **-mized′**, **-miz′ing** to reduce to or estimate at a minimum

min′i·mum (-məm) ***n.***, *pl.* **-mums** or **-ma** (-mə) ⟦L, least⟧ **1** the smallest quantity, number, etc. possible or permissible **2** the lowest degree or point reached —***adj.*** smallest possible, permissible, or reached

min·ion (min′yən) ***n.*** ⟦Fr *mignon*, darling⟧ **1** a favorite, esp. one who is a servile follower: term of contempt **2** a subordinate official

min·is·cule (min′i skyo͞ol′) ***adj.*** *disputed var. of* MINUSCULE

min·i·se·ries (min′ē sir′ēz) ***n.***, *pl.* **-ries** a TV drama broadcast serially in a limited number of episodes

min·i·skirt (min′ē skurt′) ***n.*** a very short skirt ending well above the knee

min·is·ter (min′is tər) ***n.*** ⟦L, a servant⟧ **1** a person appointed to head a governmental department **2** a diplomat representing his or her government in a foreign nation **3** one authorized to conduct religious services in a church —***vi.*** **1** to serve as a minister in a church **2** to give help (*to*) —**min′is·te′ri·al** (-tir′ē əl) ***adj.*** —**min′is·trant** (-trənt) ***adj.***, ***n.***

min′is·tra′tion (-trā′shən) ***n.*** the act of giving help or care; service

min′is·try (-is trē) ***n.***, *pl.* **-tries** **1** the act of ministering, or serving **2** *a*) the office or function of a religious minister *b*) ministers of religion collectively; clergy **3** *a*) the department under a minister of government *b*) the minister's term of office *c*) the ministers of a government as a group

min·i·van (min′ē van′) ***n.*** a passenger vehicle like a van but smaller, usually with windows all around and removable rear seats: also **min′i-van**

mink (miŋk) ***n.*** ⟦< Scand⟧ **1** a slim, erminelike carnivore living in water part of the time **2** its valuable, white to brown fur

Min·ne·ap·o·lis (min′ē ap′ə lis) city in E Minnesota: pop. 368,000 (met. area, incl. St. Paul, 2,464,000)

Min·ne·so·ta (min′ə sōt′ə) Midwestern state of the U.S.: 79,617 sq. mi.; pop. 4,375,000; cap. St. Paul: abbrev. *MN* —**Min′ne·so′tan** ***adj.***, ***n.***

min·now (min′ō) ***n.*** ⟦< OE *myne*⟧ any of various, usually small, freshwater fishes used commonly as bait

Mi·no·an (mi nō′ən) ***adj.*** ⟦after *Minos*, mythical king of Crete⟧ of an advanced prehistoric culture in Crete from *c.* 3000 to *c.* 1100 B.C.

mi·nor (mī′nər) ***adj.*** ⟦< L⟧ **1** lesser in size, amount, importance, etc. **2** *Music* lower than the corresponding major by a half tone —***vi.*** *Educ.* to have a secondary field of study (*in*) —***n.*** **1** a person under full legal age **2** *Educ.* a secondary field of study

mi·nor·i·ty (mī nôr′ə tē, mi-) ***n.***, *pl.* **-ties** **1** the lesser part or smaller number **2** a racial, religious, or political group that differs from the larger, controlling group **3** the period or state of being under full legal age

minor scale an eight-tone musical scale with a semitone between the second and third tones

Min·o·taur (min′ə tôr′) ***n.*** *Gr. Myth.* a monster with the body of a man and the head of a bull

min·ox·i·dil (min äk′sə dil) ***n.*** a drug that dilates blood vessels, used in treating high blood pressure and baldness

min·strel (min′strəl) ***n.*** ⟦see MINISTER⟧ **1** a medieval traveling singer **2** a member of a comic variety show (**minstrel show**) in which the performers blacken their faces —**min′strel·sy** (-sē), *pl.* **-sies**, ***n.***

mint[1] (mint) ***n.*** ⟦< L < *Moneta*, epithet for Juno, whose temple was the Roman mint⟧ **1** a place where a government coins money **2** a large amount —***adj.*** new, as if freshly minted —***vt.*** to coin (money) —**mint′age** (-ij) ***n.***

mint[2] (mint) ***n.*** ⟦< Gr *mintha*⟧ **1** an aromatic plant whose leaves are used for flavoring **2** a candy flavored with mint

mint julep an iced drink of bourbon, sugar, and mint leaves

min·u·end (min′yo͞o end′) ***n.*** ⟦< L *minuere*, lessen⟧ the number from which another is to be subtracted

min·u·et (min′yo͞o et′) ***n.*** ⟦< Fr < OFr *menu*, small: from the small steps taken⟧ **1** a slow, stately dance **2** the music for this

mi·nus (mī′nəs) ***prep.*** ⟦< L *minor*, less⟧ **1** reduced by subtraction of; less *[four minus two]* **2** [Inf.] without *[minus a toe]* —***adj.*** **1** involving subtraction *[a* *minus* sign*]* **2** negative **3** less than *[*a grade of A *minus]* **—*n.*** a sign (−), indicating subtraction or negative quantity: in full **minus sign**

mi·nus·cule (mi nus′kyo͞ol′, min′i skyo͞ol′) ***adj.*** ⟦L *minusculus*⟧ very small

min·ute[1] (min′it) ***n.*** ⟦see fol.⟧ **1** the sixtieth part of an hour, or of a degree of an arc **2** a moment **3** a specific point in time **4** [*pl.*] an official record of a meeting, etc. **—the minute (that)** just as soon as

mi·nute[2] (mī no͞ot′, -nyo͞ot′) ***adj.*** ⟦< L *minor*, less⟧ **1** very small **2** of little importance **3** of or attentive to tiny details; precise **—mi·nute′ly *adv.***

min′ute hand the longer hand of a clock, indicating the minutes

min′ute·man′ (-man′) ***n.***, *pl.* **-men′** (-men′) [*also* **M-**] a member of the American citizen army at the time of the American Revolution

min′ute steak a small, thin steak that can be cooked quickly

mi·nu·ti·ae (mi no͞o′shə, -nyo͞o′-) ***pl.n.***, *sing.* **-tia** (-shə) ⟦see MINUTE[2]⟧ small or unimportant details

minx (miŋks) ***n.*** ⟦< ?⟧ a pert, saucy girl

mir·a·cle (mir′ə kəl) ***n.*** ⟦< L *mirus*, wonderful⟧ **1** an event or action that apparently contradicts known scientific laws **2** a remarkable thing

mi·rac·u·lous (mi rak′yo͞o ləs, -yə-) ***adj.*** **1** having the nature of, or like, a miracle **2** able to work miracles **—mi·rac′u·lous·ly *adv.*** **—mi·rac′u·lous·ness *n.***

mi·rage (mi räzh′) ***n.*** ⟦< VL *mirare*, look at⟧ an optical illusion, caused by the refraction of light, in which a distant object appears to be nearby, inverted, etc.

mire (mīr) ***n.*** ⟦< ON *myrr*⟧ **1** an area of wet, soggy ground **2** deep mud **—*vt.*** **mired**, **mir′ing** **1** to cause to get stuck as in mire **2** to soil with mud, etc. **—*vi.*** to sink in mud **—mir′y, -i·er, -i·est, *adj.***

mir·ror (mir′ər) ***n.*** ⟦< L *mirare*, look at⟧ **1** a smooth, reflecting surface; esp., a glass coated as with silver on the back **2** anything giving a true representation **—*vt.*** to reflect, as in a mirror

mirth (murth) ***n.*** ⟦< OE *myrig*, pleasant⟧ joyfulness or gaiety, esp. when shown by laughter **—mirth′ful *adj.*** **—mirth′less *adj.***

MIRV (murv) ***n.***, *pl.* **MIRV's** ⟦*m*(*ultiple*) *i*(*ndependently targeted*) *r*(*eentry*) *v*(*ehicle*)⟧ an intercontinental ballistic missile whose several warheads can be launched individually

mis- ⟦< OE *mis-* or OFr *mes-*⟧ *prefix* **1** wrong(ly), bad(ly) **2** no, not

mis·ad·ven·ture (mis′əd ven′chər) ***n.*** a mishap; an instance of bad luck

mis·an·thrope (mis′ən thrōp′) ***n.*** ⟦Gr *misein*, to hate + *anthrōpos*, man⟧ a person who hates or distrusts all people: also **mis·an·thro·pist** (mi san′thrə pist) **—mis′an·throp′ic** (-thräp′ik) ***adj.*** **—mis·an′thro·py *n.***

mis′ap·ply′ ***vt.*** **-plied′**, **-ply′ing** to use badly, improperly, or wastefully

mis′ap·pre·hend′ (-ap rē hend′) ***vt.*** to misunderstand **—mis′ap·pre·hen′sion *n.***

mis′ap·pro′pri·ate′ ***vt.*** **-at′ed**, **-at′ing** to appropriate to a wrong or dishonest use **—mis′ap·pro′pri·a′tion *n.***

mis′be·got′ten ***adj.*** **1** wrongly or unlawfully begotten; illegitimate **2** badly conceived

mis′be·have′ ***vt.***, ***vi.*** **-haved′**, **-hav′ing** to behave (oneself) wrongly **—mis′be·hav′ior *n.***

misc *abbrev.* **1** miscellaneous **2** miscellany

mis·cal′cu·late′ ***vt.***, ***vi.*** **-lat′ed**, **-lat′ing** to calculate incorrectly; miscount or misjudge **—mis′cal·cu·la′tion *n.***

mis·call′ ***vt.*** to call by a wrong name

mis·car·ry (mis kar′ē, mis′kar′ē) ***vi.*** **-ried**, **-ry·ing** **1** to go wrong; fail: said of a plan, etc. **2** to fail to arrive: said of mail, freight, etc. **3** to give birth to a fetus before it has developed enough to live **—mis·car′riage *n.***

mis·cast′ ***vt.*** **-cast′**, **-cast′ing** to cast (an actor or a play) unsuitably

mis·ce·ge·na·tion (mi sej′ə nā′shən) ***n.*** ⟦< L *miscere*, to mix + *genus*, race⟧ marriage or sexual relations between a man and woman of different races

mis·cel·la·ne·ous (mis′ə lā′nē əs) ***adj.*** ⟦< L *miscere*, to mix⟧ consisting of various kinds or qualities

mis·cel·la·ny (mis′ə lā′nē) ***n.***, *pl.* **-nies** a miscellaneous collection, esp. of literary works

mis·chance′ ***n.*** bad luck

mis·chief (mis′chif) ***n.*** ⟦< OFr *mes-*, MIS- + *chief*, end⟧ **1** harm or damage **2** a cause of harm or annoyance **3** *a*) a prank *b*) playful teasing

mis·chie·vous (mis′chə vəs) ***adj.*** **1** causing mischief; specif., *a*) harmful *b*) prankish **2** inclined to annoy with playful tricks **—mis′chie·vous·ly *adv.*** **—mis′chie·vous·ness *n.***

mis·ci·ble (mis′ə bəl) ***adj.*** ⟦< L *miscere*, to mix⟧ that can be mixed

mis·con·ceive (mis′kən sēv′) ***vt.***, ***vi.*** **-ceived′**, **-ceiv′ing** to misunderstand **—mis′con·cep′tion** (-sep′shən) ***n.***

mis·con′duct ***n.*** **1** bad or dishonest management **2** willfully improper behavior

mis·con·strue (mis′kən stro͞o′) ***vt.*** **-strued′**, **-stru′ing** to misinterpret **—mis′con·struc′tion** (-struk′shən) ***n.***

mis·count (mis kount′; *for n.* mis′kount′) ***vt.***, ***vi.*** to count incorrectly **—*n.*** an incorrect count

mis·cre·ant (mis′krē ənt) ***adj.*** ⟦< OFr *mes-*, MIS- + *croire*, believe⟧ villainous **—*n.*** a criminal; villain

mis·deal (mis dēl′; *for n.* mis′dēl′) ***vt.***, ***vi.*** **-dealt′**, **-deal′ing** to deal (playing cards) incorrectly **—*n.*** an incorrect deal

mis·deed′ ***n.*** a wrong or wicked act; crime, sin, etc.

mis·de·mean·or (mis′də mēn′ər) ***n.*** *Law* any minor offense bringing a lesser punishment than a felony

mis′di·rect′ ***vt.*** to direct wrongly or badly **—mis′di·rec′tion *n.***

mis·do′ing ***n.*** wrongdoing

mi·ser (mī′zər) ***n.*** ⟦< L, wretched⟧ a greedy, stingy person who hoards money for its own sake —**mi′ser·ly** ***adj.*** —**mi′ser·li·ness** ***n.***

mis·er·a·ble (miz′ər ə bəl, miz′rə bəl) ***adj.*** **1** in misery **2** causing misery, discomfort, etc. **3** bad; inadequate **4** pitiable —**mis′er·a·bly** ***adv.***

mis·er·y (miz′ər ē) ***n.***, *pl.* **-ies** ⟦see MISER⟧ **1** a condition of great suffering; distress **2** a cause of such suffering; pain, poverty, etc.

mis·file′ ***vt.*** **-filed′**, **-fil′ing** to file (papers, etc.) in the wrong place

mis′fire′ ***vi.*** **-fired′**, **-fir′ing** **1** to fail to go off or ignite properly: said as of a firearm or engine **2** to fail to achieve a desired effect —***n.*** a misfiring

mis·fit (mis fit′; *for n.* mis′fit′) ***vt.***, ***vi.*** **-fit′ted**, **-fit′ting** to fit badly —***n.*** **1** an improper fit **2** a maladjusted person

mis·for′tune ***n.*** **1** ill fortune; trouble **2** a mishap, calamity, etc.

mis·giv′ing ***n.*** a disturbed feeling of fear, doubt, etc.: *usually used in pl.*

mis·gov′ern ***vt.*** to govern badly —**mis′gov′ern·ment** ***n.***

mis·guide′ (-gīd′) ***vt.*** **-guid′ed**, **-guid′ing** to lead into error or misconduct; mislead —**mis·guid′ance** ***n.*** —**mis′guid′ed·ly** ***adv.***

mis·han′dle ***vt.*** **-dled**, **-dling** to handle badly or roughly; abuse or mismanage

mis·hap (mis′hap′) ***n.*** an unlucky or unfortunate accident

mis·hear′ ***vt.***, ***vi.*** **-heard′**, **-hear′ing** to hear wrongly

mish·mash (mish′mash′) ***n.*** a jumble

mis′in·form′ ***vt.*** to supply with false or misleading information —**mis′in′for·ma′tion** ***n.***

mis′in·ter′pret ***vt.*** to interpret wrongly; understand or explain incorrectly —**mis′in·ter′pre·ta′tion** ***n.***

mis·judge′ ***vt.***, ***vi.*** **-judged′**, **-judg′ing** to judge wrongly or unfairly —**mis·judg′ment** ***n.***

mis·la′bel ***vt.*** **-beled** or **-belled**, **-bel·ing** or **-bel·ling** to label incorrectly or improperly

mis·lay′ (-lā′) ***vt.*** **-laid′**, **-lay′ing** to put in a place that is then forgotten

mis·lead′ ***vt.*** **-led′**, **-lead′ing** **1** to lead in a wrong direction **2** to deceive **3** to lead into wrongdoing

mis·man′age ***vt.***, ***vi.*** **-aged**, **-ag·ing** to manage badly or dishonestly —**mis·man′age·ment** ***n.***

mis·match (mis mach′; *for n.* mis′mach′) ***vt.*** to match badly or unsuitably —***n.*** a bad match

mis·name′ ***vt.*** **-named′**, **-nam′ing** to give an inappropriate name to

mis·no·mer (mis nō′mər) ***n.*** ⟦< OFr < *mes-*, MIS- + *nommer*, to name⟧ a wrong name

mi·sog·y·ny (mi säj′ə nē) ***n.*** ⟦< Gr *misein*, to hate + *gynē*, woman⟧ hatred of women —**mi·sog′y·nist** ***n.***

mis·place (mis plās′) ***vt.*** **-placed′**, **-plac′ing** **1** to put in a wrong place **2** to bestow (one's trust, etc.) unwisely **3**

mis·play (mis plā′; *for n.* mis′plā′) ***vt.***, ***vi.*** to play wrongly or badly, as in games or sports —***n.*** a wrong or bad play

mis·print (mis print′; *for n.* mis′print′) ***vt.*** to print incorrectly —***n.*** a printing error

mis·pri′sion (-prizh′ən) ***n.*** ⟦< OFr *mesprendre*, take wrongly⟧ misconduct or neglect of duty by a public official

mis′pro·nounce′ ***vt.***, ***vi.*** **-nounced′**, **-nounc′ing** to pronounce differently from the accepted pronunciations —**mis′pro·nun′ci·a′tion** ***n.***

mis·quote′ ***vt.***, ***vi.*** **-quot′ed**, **-quot′ing** to quote incorrectly —**mis′quo·ta′tion** ***n.***

mis·read′ (-rēd′) ***vt.***, ***vi.*** **-read′** (-red′), **-read′ing** (-rēd′iŋ) to read wrongly, esp. so as to misunderstand

mis′rep·re·sent′ ***vt.*** to represent falsely; give an untrue idea of —**mis′rep·re·sen·ta′tion** ***n.***

mis·rule (mis ro͞ol′) ***vt.*** **-ruled′**, **-rul′ing** to rule badly; misgovern —***n.*** misgovernment

miss[1] (mis) ***vt.*** ⟦OE *missan*⟧ **1** to fail to hit, meet, do, attend, see, hear, etc. **2** to let (a chance, etc.) go by **3** to avoid *[he just missed being hit]* **4** to notice or feel the absence or loss of **5** to lack *[this book is missing a page]* —***vi.*** **1** to fail to hit something **2** to fail to be successful **3** to misfire: said as of an engine —***n.*** a failure to hit, obtain, etc.

miss[2] (mis) ***n.***, *pl.* **miss′es** ⟦< MISTRESS⟧ **1** [**M-**] a title used before the name of an unmarried woman or a girl **2** a young unmarried woman or a girl

mis·sal (mis′əl) ***n.*** ⟦< LL *missa*, Mass⟧ [*often* **M-**] a book of prayers, readings, etc. authorized by the Roman Catholic Church for the celebration of Mass

mis·shape′ ***vt.*** **-shaped′**, **-shap′ing** to shape badly; deform —**mis·shap′en** ***adj.***

mis·sile (mis′əl) ***n.*** ⟦< L *mittere*, send⟧ an object, as a spear, bullet, or rocket, designed to be thrown, fired, or launched toward a target

mis′sile·ry or **mis′sil·ry** (-rē) ***n.*** **1** the science of building and launching guided missiles **2** such missiles

miss·ing (mis′iŋ) ***adj.*** absent; lost

mis·sion (mish′ən) ***n.*** ⟦< L *mittere*, send⟧ **1** a sending out or being sent out to perform a special service **2** *a)* a group of persons sent by a religious body to spread its religion, esp. in a foreign land *b)* its headquarters **3** a diplomatic delegation **4** a group of technicians, specialists, etc. sent to a foreign country **5** the special duty for which one is sent **6** a special task to which one devotes one's life; calling

mis′sion·ar′y (-er′ē) ***adj.*** of religious missions or missionaries —***n.***, *pl.* **-ies** a person sent on a religious mission

Mis·sis·sip·pi (mis′ə sip′ē) **1** river in the central U.S., flowing from NC Minnesota to the Gulf of Mexico **2** Southern state of the U.S.: 47,689 sq. mi.; pop. 2,573,000; cap. Jackson: abbrev. *MS* —**Mis′sis·sip′pi·an** ***adj.***, ***n.***

mis·sive (mis′iv) ***n.*** ⟦< L *mittere*, send⟧ a letter or written message

Mis·sou·ri (mi zoor′ē, -ə) **1** river in the central U.S., flowing from SW Montana into the Mississippi **2** Midwestern state of the U.S.: 68,898 sq. mi.; pop. 5,117,000; cap. Jefferson City: abbrev. *MO* —**Mis·sou′ri·an** ***adj., n.***

mis·spell′ ***vt., vi.*** **-spelled′** or **-spelt′, -spell′ing** to spell incorrectly

mis·spend′ ***vt.*** **-spent′, -spend′ing** to spend improperly or wastefully

mis·state′ ***vt.*** **-stat′ed, -stat′ing** to state incorrectly or falsely —**mis·state′ment** ***n.***

mis′step′ ***n.*** **1** a wrong or awkward step **2** a mistake in conduct

mist (mist) ***n.*** ⟦OE⟧ **1** a large mass of water vapor, less dense than a fog **2** anything that dims or obscures —***vt., vi.*** to make or become misty

mis·take (mi stāk′) ***vt.*** **-took′, -tak′en, -tak′ing** ⟦< ON *mistaka,* take wrongly⟧ to understand or perceive wrongly —***n.*** an idea, answer, act, etc. that is wrong; error or blunder —**mis·tak′a·ble** ***adj.***

mis·tak′en ***adj.*** **1** wrong; having an incorrect understanding **2** incorrect: said of ideas, etc. —**mis·tak′en·ly** ***adv.***

mis·ter[1] (mis′tər) ***n.*** ⟦< MASTER⟧ [**M-**] a title used before the name of a man or his office and usually written *Mr.*

mist′er[2] ***n.*** a bottle for directing a fine spray of water onto a houseplant, etc.

mis·time (mis tīm′) ***vt.*** **-timed′, -tim′ing** to do or say at the wrong time

mis·tle·toe (mis′əl tō′) ***n.*** ⟦< OE *mistel,* mistletoe + *tan,* a twig⟧ a parasitic evergreen plant with yellowish flowers and poisonous, white berries

mis·took (mis took′) ***vt., vi.*** *pt. of* MISTAKE

mis·treat′ ***vt.*** to treat wrongly or badly —**mis·treat′ment** ***n.***

mis·tress (mis′tris) ***n.*** ⟦< OFr, fem. of *maistre,* master⟧ **1** a woman who is head of a household or institution **2** a woman, nation, etc. that has control, power, etc. **3** a woman in a sexual relationship with, and typically supported by, a man without being married to him **4** [**M-**] [Obs.] a title used before the name of a woman: now replaced by *Mrs., Miss,* or *Ms.*

mis′tri′al ***n.*** *Law* a trial made void, as by an error in the proceedings or by the inability of the jury to reach a verdict

mis·trust′ ***n.*** lack of trust or confidence —***vt., vi.*** to have no trust in; doubt —**mis·trust′ful** ***adj.***

mist′y ***adj.*** **-i·er, -i·est** **1** of, like, or covered with mist **2** blurred, as by mist; vague —**mist′i·ly** ***adv.*** —**mist′i·ness** ***n.***

mis′un·der·stand′ ***vt.*** **-stood′, -stand′ing** to fail to understand correctly; misinterpret

mis′un·der·stand′ing ***n.*** **1** a failure to understand **2** a quarrel or disagreement

mis·use (mis yōōz′; *for n.,* -yōōs′) ***vt.*** **-used′, -us′ing** **1** to use improperly **2** to treat badly or harshly —***n.*** incorrect or improper use

mite (mīt) ***n.*** ⟦OE⟧ **1** a tiny arachnid, often parasitic upon animals or plants **2** a very small sum of money **3** a very small creature or object

mi·ter (mīt′ər) ***n.*** ⟦< Gr *mitra,* headband⟧ **1** a tall, ornamented cap worn by bishops and abbots **2** *Carpentry* a joint formed by fitting together two pieces beveled to form a corner: now usually **miter joint**

mit·i·gate (mit′ə gāt′) ***vt., vi.*** **-gat′ed, -gat′ing** ⟦< L *mitis,* soft⟧ **1** to make or become less severe, less painful, etc. **2** ⟦< confusion with MILITATE⟧ to operate or work (*against*): a loose usage —**mit′i·ga′tion** ***n.***

mi·to·sis (mī tō′sis) ***n.*** ⟦< Gr *mitos,* thread⟧ the process by which a cell divides into two with the nucleus of each new cell having the full number of chromosomes —**mi·tot′ic** (-tät′ik) ***adj.***

mitt (mit) ***n.*** ⟦< fol.⟧ **1** a woman's glove covering the hand and forearm, but only part of the fingers **2** [Slang] a hand **3** *a*) *Baseball* a padded glove, worn for protection *b*) a boxing glove

mit·ten (mit′′n) ***n.*** ⟦< OFr *mitaine*⟧ a glove with a thumb but no separately divided fingers

mix (miks) ***vt.*** ⟦< L *miscere*⟧ **1** to blend together in a single mass **2** to make by blending ingredients *[to mix a drink]* **3** to combine *[to mix work and play]* **4** to blend electronically (recorded sounds, etc.) on (a tape, etc.) —***vi.*** **1** to be mixed or blended **2** to get along together —***n.*** **1** a mixture **2** a commercial mixture of ingredients *[a cake mix]* **3** MIXER (*n.* 4) **4** the blend of sounds in a recording, etc. —**mix up** **1** to mix thoroughly **2** to confuse **3** to involve or implicate (*in*): usually used in the passive —**mix′a·ble** ***adj.***

mixed (mikst) ***adj.*** **1** blended **2** made up of different parts, classes, races, etc., or of both sexes **3** confused; muddled

mixed number a number consisting of a whole number and a fraction, as $3\frac{2}{3}$

mixed′-up′ ***adj.*** confused, troubled, etc.

mix′er ***n.*** **1** a person with reference to the ability to get along with others **2** a machine for mixing ingredients together **3** a social dance for helping people meet one another **4** a beverage for mixing with alcoholic beverages

mix·ture (miks′chər) ***n.*** **1** a mixing or being mixed **2** something made by mixing

mix′-up′ ***n.*** a confusion; tangle

miz·zen·mast (miz′ən mast′; *naut.,* -məst) ***n.*** ⟦< L *medius,* middle⟧ the mast third from the bow in a ship

mkt *abbrev.* market

ml *abbrev.* milliliter(s)

Mlle *abbrev.* Mademoiselle

mm *abbrev.* millimeter(s)

MM *abbrev.* Messieurs

Mme *abbrev.* Madame

Mmes *abbrev.* mesdames

Mn *Chem. symbol for* manganese

MN Minnesota

mne·mon·ic (nē män′ik) ***adj.*** ⟦< Gr *mnēmōn,* mindful⟧ of or helping the memory

mo *abbrev.* month

Mo *Chem. symbol for* molybdenum

MO *abbrev.* **1** Missouri **2** ⟦L *modus operandi*⟧ mode of operation

moan (mōn) ***n.*** ⟦prob. < OE *mænan,* complain⟧ a low, mournful sound, as of sorrow or pain —***vi., vt.*** **1** to utter or say with a moan **2** to complain (about)

moat (mōt) ***n.*** ⟦< OFr *mote,* a mound⟧ a deep, broad ditch, often filled with water, around a fortress or castle

mob (mäb) ***n.*** ⟦< L *mobile* (*vulgus*), movable (crowd)⟧ **1** a disorderly, lawless crowd **2** any crowd **3** the masses: contemptuous term **4** [Inf.] a gang of criminals —***vt.*** **mobbed, mob′bing** **1** to crowd around and attack, annoy, etc. **2** to throng; crowd into

mo·bile (mō′bəl, -bīl′; *for n.,* -bēl′) ***adj.*** ⟦< L *movere,* to move⟧ **1** moving or movable **2** movable by means of a motor vehicle *[a mobile* X-ray unit*]* **3** that can change rapidly or easily; adaptable **4** characterized by ease in change of social status —***n.*** a piece of abstract sculpture that aims to depict movement, as by an arrangement of thin forms, rings, etc. suspended and set in motion by air currents —**mo·bil′i·ty** (-bil′ə tē) ***n.***

Mo·bile (mō bēl′) seaport in SW Alabama: pop. 196,000

-mo·bile (mō bēl′) ⟦< (AUTO)MOBILE⟧ *combining form* motorized vehicle *[bookmobile]*

mo·bile home (mō′bəl) a movable dwelling set more or less permanently at a location: cf. MOTOR HOME

mo′bi·lize′ (-bə līz′) ***vt., vi.*** **-lized′, -liz′ing** to make or become organized and ready, as for war —**mo′bi·li·za′tion** ***n.***

mob·ster (mäb′stər) ***n.*** [Slang] a gangster

moc·ca·sin (mäk′ə sən) ***n.*** ⟦< AmInd⟧ **1** a heelless slipper of soft, flexible leather **2** any similar heeled slipper

mo·cha (mō′kə) ***n.*** a choice grade of coffee grown orig. in Arabia —***adj.*** flavored with coffee or coffee and chocolate

mock (mäk) ***vt.*** ⟦< OFr *mocquer*⟧ **1** to ridicule **2** to mimic, as in fun or derision —***vi.*** to express scorn, ridicule, etc. —***adj.*** sham; imitation; pretended —***adv.*** falsely or insincerely

mock′er·y (-ər ē) ***n., pl.*** **-ies** **1** a mocking **2** a person or thing receiving or deserving ridicule **3** a false or derisive imitation

mock′ing·bird′ ***n.*** a bird of the U.S. that imitates the calls of other birds

mock′-up′ ***n.*** ⟦< Fr *maquette*⟧ a model built to scale, often full-sized, for teaching, testing, etc.

mod (mäd) ***adj.*** ⟦< MOD(ERN)⟧ up-to-date, fashionable, stylish, etc.

mode (mōd) ***n.*** ⟦< L *modus*⟧ **1** a manner or way of acting, doing, or being **2** customary usage or current fashion **3** *Gram.* MOOD²

mod·el (mäd′'l) ***n.*** ⟦< L *modus,* a measure⟧ **1** a small representation of a planned or existing object **2** a hypothetical description, often based on an analogy, used in analyzing something **3** a person or thing regarded as a standard of excellence to be imitated **4** a style or design **5** *a)* one who poses for an artist or photographer *b)* one employed to display clothes by wearing them —***adj.*** **1** serving as a model **2** representative of others of the same style, etc. *[a model* home*]* —***vt.*** **-eled** or **-elled, -el·ing** or **-el·ling** **1** *a)* to make a model of *b)* to plan or form after a model **2** to display (clothes) by wearing —***vi.*** to serve as a MODEL (*n.* 5)

mo·dem (mō′dəm) ***n.*** ⟦MO(DULATOR) + DEM(ODULATION)⟧ a device that converts data for transmission, as by telephone, to data-processing equipment

mod·er·ate (mäd′ər it; *for v.,* -āt′) ***adj.*** ⟦< L *moderare,* restrain⟧ **1** within reasonable limits; avoiding extremes **2** mild; calm **3** of medium quality, amount, etc. —***n.*** one holding moderate opinions —***vt., vi.*** **-at′ed, -at′ing** **1** to make or become moderate **2** to preside over (a meeting, etc.) —**mod′er·ate·ly** ***adv.***

mod′er·a′tion ***n.*** **1** a moderating **2** avoidance of extremes **3** calmness

mod′er·a′tor ***n.*** one who presides at an assembly, debate, etc.

mod·ern (mäd′ərn) ***adj.*** ⟦< L *modo,* just now⟧ **1** of the present or recent times; specif., up-to-date **2** [*often* **M-**] designating the most recent form of a language —***n.*** a person living in modern times, having modern ideas, etc. —**mo·der·ni·ty** (mä dur′nə tē) ***n.***

Modern English the English language since about the mid-15th c.

mod′ern·ism′ ***n.*** (a) modern usage, practice, thought, etc. —**mod′ern·ist** ***n., adj.*** —**mod′ern·is′tic** ***adj.***

mod′ern·ize′ ***vt., vi.*** **-ized′, -iz′ing** to make or become modern —**mod′ern·i·za′tion** ***n.***

mod·est (mäd′ist) ***adj.*** ⟦< L *modus,* a measure⟧ **1** not vain or boastful **2** shy or reserved **3** decorous; decent **4** unpretentious —**mod′est·ly** ***adv.*** —**mod′es·ty** ***n.***

mod·i·cum (mäd′i kəm) ***n.*** ⟦< L, moderate⟧ a small amount; bit

mod·i·fy (mäd′ə fī′) ***vt.*** **-fied′, -fy′ing** ⟦< L *modificare,* to limit⟧ **1** to change partially in character, form, etc. **2** to limit slightly **3** *Gram.* to limit in meaning —**mod′i·fi·ca′tion** ***n.*** —**mod′i·fi′er** ***n.***

mod·ish (mōd′ish) ***adj.*** fashionable; stylish —**mo′dish·ly** ***adv.*** —**mod′ish·ness** ***n.***

mod·u·lar (mäj′ə lər) ***adj.*** of modules

mod′u·late′ (-lāt′) ***vt.*** **-lat′ed, -lat′ing** ⟦< L *modus,* a measure⟧ **1** to regulate or adjust **2** to vary the pitch, intensity, etc. of (the voice) **3** *Radio* to vary the frequency of (radio waves, etc.) —**mod′u·la′tion** ***n.*** —**mod′u·la′tor** ***n.***

mod·ule (mäj′o͞ol′) ***n.*** ⟦Fr < L *modus,* a measure⟧ **1** a standard or unit of measurement, as of building materials **2** any of a set of units to be variously fitted together **3** a detachable unit with a specific function, as in a spacecraft

mo·gul (mō′gul′) ***n.*** ⟦Pers *Mughul,* Mongol⟧ a powerful or important person

mo·hair (mō′her′) ***n.*** ⟦< Ar *mukhayyar,* fine cloth⟧ **1** the hair of the Angora goat **2** yarn or fabric made of this

Mo·ham·med (mō ham′id) A.D. 570?-632; Arab prophet: founder of Islam

Mo·ham′med·an ***adj.*** of Mohammed or Islam —***n.*** MUSLIM Term used, esp. formerly, by non-Muslims —**Mo·ham′med·an·ism′** ***n.***

moi·e·ty (moi′ə tē) ***n.,*** *pl.* **-ties** ⟦< L *medius,* middle⟧ **1** a half **2** an indefinite part

moire (mwär, môr) ***n.*** ⟦Fr⟧ a fabric, esp. silk, etc., having a wavy pattern: also **moi·ré** (mwä rā′, mô-)

moist (moist) ***adj.*** ⟦< L *mucus,* mucus⟧ slightly wet; damp —**moist′ly** ***adv.*** —**moist′ness** ***n.***

mois·ten (mois′ən) ***vt., vi.*** to make or become moist

mois′ture (-chər) ***n.*** water or other liquid causing a slight wetness

mois′tur·ize′ (-īz′) ***vt., vi.*** **-ized′, -iz′ing** to make (the skin, air, etc.) moist —**mois′tur·iz′er** ***n.***

Mo·ja·ve Desert (mō hä′vē) desert in SE California: also sp. **Mo·ha′ve Desert**

mo·lar (mō′lər) ***adj.*** ⟦< L *mola,* millstone⟧ designating a tooth or teeth adapted for grinding —***n.*** a molar tooth

MOLARS

mo·las·ses (mə las′iz) ***n.*** ⟦< L *mel,* honey⟧ a thick, dark-brown syrup produced during the refining of sugar

mold[1] (mōld) ***n.*** ⟦< L *modus,* a measure⟧ **1** a hollow form for giving a certain shape to something plastic or molten **2** a frame on which something is modeled **3** a pattern; model **4** something that is formed in or on a mold **5** distinctive character —***vt.*** **1** to make in or on a mold **2** to form; shape

mold[2] (mōld) ***n.*** ⟦ME *moul*⟧ **1** a fungus producing a furry growth on the surface of organic matter **2** this growth —***vi.*** to become moldy

mold[3] (mōld) ***n.*** ⟦OE *molde*⟧ loose, soft soil rich in decayed organic matter

mold·er (mōl′dər) ***vi.*** ⟦< OE *molde,* dust⟧ to crumble into dust

mold·ing (mōl′diŋ) ***n.*** **1** the act of one that molds **2** something molded **3** a shaped strip of wood, etc., as around the upper walls of a room

Mol·do·va (môl dō′və) country in E Europe: formerly a republic of the U.S.S.R.: 13,000 sq. mi.; pop. 4,339,000

mold′y ***adj.*** **-i·er, -i·est** **1** covered or overgrown with mold **2** musty or stale —**mold′i·ness** ***n.***

mole[1] (mōl) ***n.*** ⟦OE *mal*⟧ a small, congenital spot on the human skin, usually dark-colored and raised

mole[2] (mōl) ***n.*** ⟦ME *molle*⟧ **1** a small, burrowing mammal with soft fur **2** a spy in an enemy intelligence agency, etc. who infiltrates long before engaging in spying

mole[3] (mōl) ***n.*** ⟦< L *moles,* a dam⟧ a breakwater

mol·e·cule (mäl′i kyōōl′) ***n.*** ⟦< ModL dim. of L *moles,* a mass⟧ **1** the smallest particle of an element or compound that can exist in the free state and still retain the characteristics of the substance **2** a small particle —**mo·lec·u·lar** (mō lek′yōō lər) ***adj.***

mole′hill′ ***n.*** a small ridge of earth, formed by a burrowing mole

mole′skin′ ***n.*** a napped cotton fabric

mo·lest (mə lest′) ***vt.*** ⟦< L *moles,* a burden⟧ **1** to annoy or to meddle with so as to trouble or harm **2** to make improper sexual advances to **3** to assault or attack (esp. a child) sexually —**mo·les·ta·tion** (mō′les tā′shən) ***n.*** —**mo·lest′er** ***n.***

Mo·lière (mōl yer′) 1622-73; Fr. dramatist

mol·li·fy (mäl′ə fī′) ***vt.*** **-fied′, -fy′ing** ⟦< L *mollis,* soft + *facere,* make⟧ **1** to soothe; appease **2** to make less severe or violent

mol·lusk (mäl′əsk) ***n.*** ⟦< L *mollis,* soft⟧ any of a group of invertebrates, as an oyster or snail, having a soft body, often in a shell

mol·ly (mäl′ē) ***n.,*** *pl.* **-lies** ⟦after F. N. *Mollien* (1758-1850), Fr statesman⟧ any of various brightly colored fishes often kept in aquariums: also **mol′lie**

mol·ly·cod·dle (mäl′ē käd′'l) ***n.*** ⟦< *Molly,* dim. of *Mary* + CODDLE⟧ a man or boy used to being coddled, protected, etc. —***vt.*** **-dled, -dling** to pamper; coddle

molt (mōlt) ***vi.*** ⟦< L *mutare,* to change⟧ to shed hair, skin, horns, etc. prior to replacement by a new growth: said of reptiles, birds, etc.

mol·ten (mōlt′'n) ***vt., vi.*** ⟦ME⟧ *archaic pp. of* MELT —***adj.*** melted by heat

mo·lyb·de·num (mə lib′də nəm) ***n.*** ⟦ult. < Gr *molybdos,* lead⟧ a silvery metallic chemical element, used in alloys

mom (mäm) ***n.*** [Inf.] MOTHER

mo·ment (mō′mənt) ***n.*** ⟦< L *momentum,* movement⟧ **1** an indefinitely brief period of time; instant **2** a definite point in time **3** a brief time of importance **4** importance

mo·men·tar·i·ly (mō′mən ter′ə lē) ***adv.*** **1** for a short time **2** in an instant **3** at any moment

mo·men·tar·y (mō′mən ter′ē) ***adj.*** lasting for only a moment; passing

mo·men·tous (mō men′təs) ***adj.*** of great moment; very important —**mo·men′tous·ness** ***n.***

mo·men·tum (mō men′təm) ***n.,*** *pl.* **-tums** or **-ta** (-tə) ⟦L: see MOMENT⟧ the impetus of a moving object, equal to the product of its mass and its velocity

mom·my (mäm′ē) ***n.,*** *pl.* **-mies** *child's term for* MOTHER

Mon *abbrev.* Monday

Mon·a·co (män′ə kō) country on the Mediterranean: an independent principality & an enclave in SE France: .75 sq. mi.; pop. 30,000

mon·arch (män′ərk, -ärk′) ***n.*** ⟦< Gr *monos,* alone + *archein,* to rule⟧ **1** a hereditary ruler; king, queen, etc. **2** a large butterfly of North America, having black-edged orange wings —**mo·nar·chi·cal** (mə när′ki kəl) ***adj.***

mon′ar·chist (-ər kist) ***n.*** one who favors monarchical government

mon′ar·chy (-kē) ***n.,*** *pl.* **-chies** a government or state headed by a monarch

mon·as·ter·y (män′ə ster′ē) ***n.,*** *pl.* **-ies** ⟦< Gr *monos,* alone⟧ the residence of a group of monks, etc. who have withdrawn from the world for religious reasons

mo·nas·tic (mə nas′tik) ***adj.*** of or like that of a monastery, monk, nun, etc.: also **mo·nas′ti·cal** —**mo·nas′ti·cism′** (-tə siz′əm) ***n.***

mon·au·ral (män ôr′əl) ***adj.*** of sound reproduction in which only one source of sound is used

Mon·day (mun′dā) ***n.*** ⟦OE *monandæg,* moon's day⟧ the second day of the week: abbrev. *Mon*

mon·e·tar·y (män′ə ter′ē) ***adj.*** ⟦< L *moneta,* a MINT[1]⟧ **1** of the coinage or currency of a country **2** of money —**mon′e·tar′i·ly** ***adv.***

mon·ey (mun′ē) ***n.,*** *pl.* **-eys** or **-ies** ⟦< L *moneta,* a MINT[1]⟧ **1** stamped pieces of metal, or any paper notes, authorized by a government as a medium of exchange **2** property; wealth —**in the money** [Slang] **1** among the winners in a race, etc. **2** wealthy —**make money** to gain profits; become wealthy —**put money into** to invest money in

mon′ey·bag′ ***n.*** **1** a bag for money **2** [*pl., with sing. v.*] [Inf.] a rich person

mon·eyed (mun′ēd) ***adj.*** rich; wealthy

mon′ey·mak′er ***n.*** **1** one successful at acquiring money **2** something profitable —**mon′ey·mak′ing** ***adj., n.***

money market the short-term system for lending and borrowing funds, especially by governments and large corporations

money market fund a mutual fund that puts funds into short-term investments, as government treasury bills

money order an order for payment of a specified sum of money, issued for a fee at one post office, bank, etc. and payable at another

mon·ger (muŋ′gər) ***n.*** ⟦< OE *mangere*⟧ [Chiefly Brit.] a dealer or trader: usually in compounds

Mon·gol (mäŋ′gəl) ***n.*** a person born or living in Mongolia —***adj.*** MONGOLIAN

Mon·go·li·a (mäŋ gō′lē ə) **1** region in EC Asia, consisting of the country of Mongolia and a region of China (*Inner Mongolia*) **2** country in EC Asia: 604,250 sq. mi.; pop. 2,096,000

Mon·go·li·an (mäŋ gō′lē ən) ***n.*** **1** MONGOL **2** a family of languages spoken in Mongolia —***adj.*** **1** of Mongolia or its peoples, languages, etc. **2** [Obs.] affected with Down syndrome

Mon·gol·ic (mäŋ gäl′ik) ***adj.*** *var. of* MONGOLIAN

Mon·gol·oid (mäŋ′gəl oid′) ***adj.*** **1** *var. of* MONGOLIAN **2** designating or of one of the major geographical varieties of human beings, including most of the peoples of Asia **3** [*often* **M-**] [Old-fashioned] affected with Down syndrome —***n.*** **1** a member of the Mongoloid population of human beings **2** [*often* **M-**] [Old-fashioned] one affected with Down syndrome

mon·goose (mäŋ′go͞os′) ***n.,*** *pl.* **-goos′es** ⟦< native name in India⟧ a civetlike Old World carnivore that kills snakes, rodents, etc.

mon·grel (mäŋ′grəl) ***n.*** ⟦< OE *mengan,* to mix⟧ an animal or plant, esp. a dog, of mixed breed —***adj.*** of mixed breed, origin, character, etc.

mon·ied (mun′ēd) ***adj.*** MONEYED

mon·i·ker (män′i kər) ***n.*** ⟦< ?⟧ [Slang] a person's name: also **mon′ick·er**

mo·ni·tion (mō nish′ən) ***n.*** ⟦< L *monere,* warn⟧ admonition; warning

mon·i·tor (män′i tər) ***n.*** ⟦< L *monere,* warn⟧ **1** a student chosen to help the teacher **2** any device for regulating the performance of a machine, an aircraft, etc. **3** *Comput.* a video screen for displaying data, images, etc. **4** *Radio, TV* a receiver for checking the quality of transmission —***vt., vi.*** to watch or check on (a person or thing)

monk (muŋk) ***n.*** ⟦< Gr *monos,* alone⟧ a man who is a member of an ascetic religious order

mon·key (muŋ′kē) ***n.,*** *pl.* **-keys** ⟦< ? Fr or Sp *mona,* ape + LowG *-ke,* -KIN⟧ **1** a primate having a flat, hairless face and a long tail **2** loosely, another, similar primate, as a chimpanzee —***vi.*** [Inf.] to play, trifle, or meddle (*around* or *with*)

monkey business [Inf.] foolishness, mischief, or deceit

mon′key·shines′ (-shīnz′) ***pl.n.*** [Inf.] playful tricks or pranks

monkey wrench a wrench with an adjustable jaw —**throw a monkey wrench into** [Inf.] to disrupt the orderly functioning of

monk's cloth a heavy cloth with a basket weave, used for drapes, etc.

mon·o (män′ō) ***adj.*** *short for* MONOPHONIC —***n.*** *short for* MONONUCLEOSIS

mono- ⟦< Gr *monos,* single⟧ *prefix* one, alone, single

mon·o·chrome (män′ə krōm′) ***adj.*** ⟦< MONO- + -CHROME⟧ in one color or shades of one color

mon·o·cle (män′ə kəl) ***n.*** ⟦ult. < Gr *monos,* single + L *oculus,* eye⟧ an eyeglass for one eye only

mon·o·clon·al (män′ō klōn′əl) ***adj.*** of cells derived or cloned from one cell

mon·o·cot·y·le·don (män′ō kät′ə lēd′ ′n) ***n.*** *Bot.* a plant having an embryo with only one cotyledon, or seed leaf: also **mon′o·cot′**

mo·nog·a·my (mə näg′ə mē) ***n.*** ⟦ult. < Gr *monos,* single + *gamos,* marriage⟧ the practice or state of being married to only one person at a time —**mo·nog′a·**

mous *adj.*

mon·o·gram (män′ə gram′) ***n.*** ⟦< Gr *monos*, single + *gramma*, letter⟧ the initials of a name, combined in a single design **—*vt.* -grammed′, -gram′ming** to put a monogram on

mon′o·graph′ (-graf′) ***n.*** ⟦MONO- + -GRAPH⟧ a book or long article, esp. a scholarly one, on a single subject

mon·o·lin·gual (män′ō liŋ′gwəl) ***adj.*** using or knowing only one language

mon·o·lith (män′ə lith′) ***n.*** ⟦< Gr *monos*, single + *lithos*, stone⟧ **1** a single large block of stone, as one made into an obelisk **2** any massive, unyielding structure **—mon′o·lith′ic *adj.***

mon·o·logue or **mon·o·log** (män′ə lôg′) ***n.*** ⟦< Gr *monos*, single + *legein*, speak⟧ **1** a long speech **2** a soliloquy **3** a skit, etc. for one actor only

mon·o·ma·ni·a (män′ō mā′nē ə) ***n.*** an excessive interest in or enthusiasm for some one thing; craze **—mon′o·ma′ni·ac′** (-mā′nē ak′) ***n.*** **—mon′o·ma·ni′a·cal** (-mə nī′ə kəl) ***adj.***

mon·o·nu·cle·o·sis (män′ō no͞o′klē ō′ sis) ***n.*** ⟦MONO- + NUCLE(US) + -OSIS⟧ an acute disease, with fever, swollen lymph nodes, etc.

mon′o·phon′ic (-fän′ik) ***adj.*** of sound reproduction using a single channel to carry sounds

mo·nop·o·list (mə näp′ə list) ***n.*** one who has a monopoly or favors monopoly **—mo·nop′o·lis′tic *adj.***

mo·nop′o·lize′ (-līz′) ***vt.* -lized′, -liz′ing** **1** to get, have, or exploit a monopoly of **2** to get full control of [he *monopolized* the conversation]

mo·nop′o·ly (-lē) ***n.***, *pl.* **-lies** ⟦< Gr *monos*, single + *pōlein*, sell⟧ **1** exclusive control of a commodity or service in a given market **2** such control granted by a government **3** something held as a monopoly **4** a company that has a monopoly

mon·o·rail (män′ə rāl′) ***n.*** **1** a single rail that is a track for cars suspended from it or balanced on it **2** a railway with such a track

mon·o·so·di·um glu·ta·mate (män′ō sō′dē əm glo͞o′tə māt′) a white powder made from vegetable protein, used to intensify flavor in foods

mon·o·syl·la·ble (män′ō sil′ə bəl) ***n.*** a word of one syllable **—mon′o·syl·lab′ic** (-si lab′ik) ***adj.***

mon′o·the·ism′ (-thē iz′əm) ***n.*** ⟦MONO- + THEISM⟧ the belief that there is only one God **—mon′o·the·ist′ *n.*** **—mon′o·the·is′tic *adj.***

mon·o·tone (män′ə tōn′) ***n.*** ⟦see MONO- & TONE⟧ **1** utterance of successive words without change of pitch or key **2** tiresome sameness of style, color, etc. **3** a single, unchanging tone

mo·not·o·nous (mə nät′'n əs) ***adj.*** **1** going on in the same tone **2** having no variety **3** tiresome because unvarying **—mo·not′o·ny *n.***

Mon·roe (mən rō′), **James** (jāmz) 1758-1831; 5th president of the U.S. (1817-25)

mon·sieur (mə syur′; *Fr* mə syö′) ***n.***, *pl.* **mes·sieurs** (mes′ərz; *Fr* mā syö′) ⟦Fr, lit., my lord⟧ **1** a man; gentleman **2** [**M-**] French title, equivalent to *Mr.* or *Sir*

Mon·si·gnor (män sēn′yər) ***n.***, *pl.* **-gnors** ⟦It, lit., my lord⟧ *R.C.Ch.* a title of certain Roman Catholic prelates

mon·soon (män so͞on′) ***n.*** ⟦< Ar *mausim*, a season⟧ **1** a seasonal wind of the Indian Ocean and S Asia **2** the rainy season during which this wind blows from the southwest

mon·ster (män′stər) ***n.*** ⟦< L *monere*, warn⟧ **1** any grotesque imaginary creature **2** a very wicked person **3** any huge animal or thing **—*adj.*** huge

mon·strance (män′strəns) ***n.*** ⟦ult. < L *monstrare*, to show⟧ *R.C.Ch.* a receptacle for displaying the consecrated Host

mon·strous (män′strəs) ***adj.*** **1** huge; enormous **2** greatly malformed **3** horrible; hideous **4** evil **—mon·stros′i·ty** (-sträs′ə tē), *pl.* **-ties, *n.***

mon·tage (män täzh′) ***n.*** ⟦Fr < *monter*, to mount⟧ **1** a composite picture **2** a rapid sequence of film scenes, often superimposed

Mon·taigne (män tān′), **Mi·chel de** (mē shel′ də) 1533-92; Fr. essayist

Mon·tan·a (män tan′ə) Mountain State of the NW U.S.: 145,556 sq. mi.; pop. 799,000; cap. Helena: abbrev. *MT* **—Mon·tan′an *adj.*, *n.***

Mon·te Car·lo (mänt′ə kär′lō) town in Monaco: gambling resort: pop. 13,000

Mon·tes·so·ri method (mänt′ə sôr′ē) ⟦after M. *Montessori* (1870-1952), It educator⟧ a method of teaching young children, emphasizing training of the senses

Mon·te·vi·de·o (mänt′ə və dā′ō) capital & seaport of Uruguay: pop. 1,247,000

Mont·gom·er·y (munt gum′ər ē, -gum′ rē) capital of Alabama: pop. 188,000

month (munth) ***n.*** ⟦OE *monath*⟧ **1** any of the twelve divisions of the calendar year **2** a period of four weeks or 30 days **3** one twelfth of the solar year

month′ly ***adj.*** done, happening, payable, etc. every month **—*n.***, *pl.* **-lies** a periodical published once a month **—*adv.*** once a month; every month

Mon·ti·cel·lo (män′tə sel′ō, -chel′ō) home & burial place of Thomas Jefferson, in central Virginia

Mont·pel·ier (mänt pēl′yər) capital of Vermont: pop. 8,200

Mon·tre·al (män′trē ôl′) city & seaport in SW Quebec, Canada, on an island in the St. Lawrence River: pop. 1,016,000

mon·u·ment (män′yo͞o mənt) ***n.*** ⟦< L *monere*, remind⟧ **1** something set up to keep alive the memory of a person or event, as a tablet or statue **2** a work of enduring significance

mon′u·men′tal (-ment′'l) ***adj.*** **1** of or serving as a monument **2** like a monument; massive, enduring, etc. **3** very great; colossal

moo (mo͞o) ***n.***, *pl.* **moos** ⟦echoic⟧ a cow's vocal sound **—*vi.* mooed, moo′ing** to make this sound

mooch (mo͞och) ***vi.*, *vt.*** ⟦ult. < OFr

muchier, to hide⟧ [Slang] to get (food, money, etc.) by begging, imposition, etc. —**mooch'er** *n.*

mood[1] (mo͞od) *n.* ⟦< OE *mod,* mind⟧ **1** a particular state of mind or feeling **2** a predominant or pervading feeling or spirit

mood[2] (mo͞od) *n.* ⟦< MODE⟧ a characteristic of verbs that indicates whether the action expressed is regarded as a fact, supposition, or command

mood'y *adj.* **-i·er, -i·est 1** changing in mood **2** gloomy —**mood'i·ly** *adv.* —**mood'i·ness** *n.*

moon (mo͞on) *n.* ⟦OE *mona*⟧ [*often* **M-**] **1** the celestial body that revolves around the earth once about every 29½ days **2** anything shaped like the moon (i.e., an orb or crescent) **3** any natural satellite of a planet —*vi.* to behave in an idle or abstracted way

moon'beam' *n.* a ray of moonlight

moon'light' *n.* the light of the moon —*vi.* to engage in moonlighting

moon'light'ing *n.* the holding of a second job along with one's main job

moon'lit' *adj.* lighted by the moon

moon'scape' (-skāp') *n.* ⟦MOON + (LAND)SCAPE⟧ the surface of the moon or a representation of it

moon'shine' *n.* **1** MOONLIGHT **2** [Inf.] whiskey unlawfully distilled —**moon'shin'er** *n.*

moon'shot' *n.* the launching of a spacecraft to the moon

moon'stone' *n.* a feldspar with a pearly luster, used as a gem

moon'struck' *adj.* **1** crazed; lunatic **2** romantically dreamy

moon'walk' *n.* a walking about by an astronaut on the surface of the moon

moor[1] (moor) *n.* ⟦OE *mor*⟧ [Brit.] open wasteland covered with heather and often marshy

moor[2] (moor) *vt.* ⟦< ? MDu *maren,* to tie⟧ **1** to hold (a ship, etc.) in place by cables attached as to a pier **2** to secure —*vi.* to moor a ship, etc.

Moor (moor) *n.* a member of a Muslim people of NW Africa —**Moor'ish** *adj.*

moor'ing *n.* **1** [*often pl.*] the cables, etc. by which a ship is moored **2** [*pl.*] a place where a ship is moored

moose (mo͞os) *n., pl.* **moose** ⟦< AmInd⟧ a large deer of N regions, the male of which has broad, flat antlers

moot (mo͞ot) *adj.* ⟦< OE *mot*, a meeting⟧ **1** debatable **2** resolved and thus not worthy of discussion

mop (mäp) *n.* ⟦earlier *mappe*⟧ **1** a bundle of rags or yarns, a sponge, etc. fastened to the end of a stick, as for washing floors **2** anything suggesting this, as a thick head of hair —*vt.* **mopped, mop'ping** to wash or wipe with a mop —**mop up** [Inf.] **1** to finish **2** to clear remnants of beaten enemy forces from

mope (mōp) *vi.* **moped, mop'ing** ⟦akin to MDu *mopen*⟧ to be gloomy and apathetic —**mop'ey, mop'y,** or **mop'ish** *adj.*

mop·pet (mäp'it) *n.* ⟦< ME *moppe,* rag doll⟧ [Inf.] a little child

MOR *abbrev.* middle-of-the-road: used in radio broadcasting to designate styles of popular music that are not extreme

mo·raine (mə rān') *n.* ⟦Fr⟧ a mass of rocks, sand, etc. left by a glacier

mor·al (môr'əl, mär'-) *adj.* ⟦< L *mos*, pl. *mores*, morals⟧ **1** dealing with, or capable of distinguishing between, right and wrong **2** of, teaching, or in accordance with the principles of right and wrong **3** good in conduct or character; specif., sexually virtuous **4** involving sympathy without action *[moral support]* **5** virtually such because of effects on thoughts or attitudes *[a moral victory]* **6** based on probability *[a moral certainty]* —*n.* **1** a moral lesson taught by a fable, event, etc. **2** [*pl.*] principles or standards with respect to right or wrong in conduct —**mor'al·ly** *adv.*

mo·rale (mə ral') *n.* mental condition related to courage, confidence, enthusiasm, etc.

mor·al·ist (môr'əl ist) *n.* **1** a teacher of or writer on morals **2** one who seeks to impose personal morals on others —**mor'al·is'tic** *adj.*

mo·ral·i·ty (mō ral'i tē, mə-) *n., pl.* **-ties 1** rightness or wrongness, as of an action **2** right or moral conduct **3** moral principles

mor·al·ize (môr'əl īz') *vi.* **-ized', -iz'ing** to think, write, etc. about moral questions, often in a self-righteous or tedious way

mo·rass (mə ras') *n.* ⟦< OFr *maresc*⟧ a bog; marsh; swamp: often used figuratively of a difficult or troublesome situation

mor·a·to·ri·um (môr'ə tôr'ē əm) *n., pl.* **-ri·ums** or **-ri·a** (-ə) ⟦< L *mora,* a delay⟧ **1** a legal authorization to delay payment of money due **2** any authorized delay of a specified activity

mo·ray (eel) (môr'ā) ⟦< Gr *myraina*⟧ a voracious, brilliantly colored eel

mor·bid (môr'bid) *adj.* ⟦< L *morbus,* disease⟧ **1** of or caused by disease; diseased **2** resulting as from a diseased state of mind **3** gruesome *[morbid details]* —**mor·bid'i·ty** *n.* —**mor'bid·ly** *adv.*

mor·dant (môr'dənt) *adj.* ⟦< L *mordere,* to bite⟧ caustic; sarcastic —*n.* a substance that fixes colors in dyeing —**mor'dan·cy** *n.* —**mor'dant·ly** *adv.*

more (môr) *adj.* ⟦OE *mara*⟧ **1** greater in amount, degree, or number: comparative of MUCH or MANY **2** additional *[take more tea]* —*n.* **1** a greater amount or degree **2** [*with pl. v.*] a greater number (*of*) **3** something additional —*adv.* **1** in or to a greater degree or extent **2** in addition

more·o'ver *adv.* in addition to what has been said; besides

mo·res (môr'ēz', -āz') *pl.n.* ⟦L, customs⟧ ways of thinking, behaving, etc. that develop the force of law because most people follow them

morgue (môrg) *n.* ⟦Fr⟧ **1** a place where the bodies of unknown dead persons or those dead of unknown causes are temporarily kept **2** the file of back numbers, photographs, etc. kept as in a newspaper's office

mor·i·bund (môr′i bund′) ***adj.*** ⟦< L *mori,* to die⟧ dying

Mor·mon (môr′mən) ***n.*** a member of the Church of Jesus Christ of Latter-day Saints, founded (1830) in the U.S. —**Mor′mon·ism′** ***n.***

morn (môrn) ***n.*** [Old Poet.] morning

morn·ing (môr′niŋ) ***n.*** ⟦OE *morgen*⟧ the first or early part of the day, from midnight, or esp. dawn, to noon

morning glory a twining vine with trumpet-shaped flowers

morning sickness nausea, vomiting, etc. affecting many women early in pregnancy, occurring usually in the morning

mo·roc·co (mə rä′kō) ***n.*** ⟦< fol.⟧ a fine, soft leather

Mo·roc·co (mə rä′kō) kingdom on the NW coast of Africa: 274,461 sq. mi.; pop. 25,897,000 —**Mo·roc′can** ***adj., n.***

mo·ron (môr′än′) ***n.*** ⟦< Gr *mōros,* foolish⟧ a very foolish or stupid person —**mo·ron′ic** ***adj.***

mo·rose (mə rōs′) ***adj.*** ⟦< L *mōs,* manner⟧ ill-tempered; gloomy, sullen, etc. —**mo·rose′ly** ***adv.***

morph (môrf) ***vt., vi.*** to transform or be transformed as by morphing

mor·pheme (môr′fēm′) ***n.*** ⟦< Gr *morphē,* a form⟧ the smallest meaningful unit in a language, as an affix or base

mor·phine (môr′fēn′) ***n.*** ⟦after *Morpheus,* Gr god of dreams⟧ an alkaloid derived from opium and used in medicine to relieve pain

morph′ing ***n.*** ⟦< (META)MORPH(OSIS) + *-ing*⟧ a film or video process in which persons or objects seem to change form through a continuous series of images created by a computer

mor·phol·o·gy (môr fäl′ə jē) ***n.*** ⟦Ger < Gr *morphē,* form + Ger *-logie,* -LOGY⟧ the study of form and structure, as in biology or linguistics

mor·row (mär′ō, môr′-) ***n.*** ⟦< OE *morgen,* morning⟧ [Archaic] **1** morning **2** the next day

Morse (môrs) ***adj.*** ⟦after S. *Morse,* 19th-c. U.S. inventor⟧ [*often* **m-**] designating or of a code of dots and dashes used in telegraphy

mor·sel (môr′səl) ***n.*** ⟦< L *morsum,* a bite⟧ a small piece or amount, as of food

mor·tal (môrt′'l) ***adj.*** ⟦< L *mors,* death⟧ **1** that must eventually die **2** of a human being seen as a being who must eventually die **3** of death **4** causing physical or spiritual death; deadly; fatal **5** very intense *[mortal* terror*]* —***n.*** a human being —**mor′tal·ly** ***adv.***

mor·tal·i·ty (môr tal′ə tē) ***n.*** **1** the mortal nature of human beings **2** death on a large scale, as from war **3** the ratio of deaths to population

mor·tar (môrt′ər) ***n.*** ⟦< L *mortarium*⟧ **1** a bowl in which substances are pulverized with a pestle **2** a short-barreled cannon which hurls shells in a high trajectory **3** a mixture of cement or lime with sand and water, used to bind bricks or stones

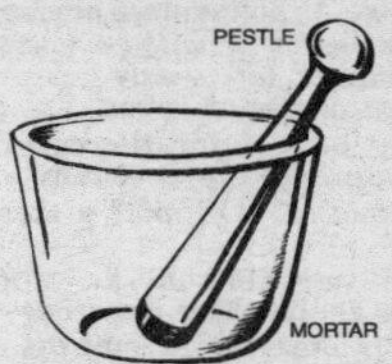

mor′tar·board′ ***n.*** **1** a square board for holding mortar **2** an academic cap with a square, flat top

mort·gage (môr′gij) ***n.*** ⟦< OFr *mort,* dead + *gage,* pledge⟧ **1** the pledging of property to a creditor as security for the payment of a debt **2** the deed by which this is done —***vt.*** **-gaged, -gag·ing 1** to pledge (property) by a mortgage **2** to put an advance claim on *[*to *mortgage* one's future*]* —**mort′ga·gor** or **mort′gag·er** (-gi jər) ***n.***

mort′ga·gee′ (-gə jē′) ***n.*** a person to whom property is mortgaged

mor·ti·cian (môr tish′ən) ***n.*** ⟦< L *mors,* death⟧ FUNERAL DIRECTOR

mor·ti·fy (môrt′ə fī′) ***vt.*** **-fied′, -fy′ing** ⟦< L *mors,* death + *facere,* make⟧ **1** to subdue (physical desires) by self-denial, fasting, etc. **2** to humiliate —**mor′ti·fi·ca′tion** ***n.***

mor·tise (môrt′is) ***n.*** ⟦< Ar *murtazza,* joined⟧ a hole or recess cut, as in a piece of wood, to receive a projecting part (*tenon*) shaped to fit into it

mor·tu·ar·y (môr′cho͞o er′ē) ***n., pl.*** **-ies** a place where dead bodies are kept before burial or cremation; morgue or funeral home

mo·sa·ic (mō zā′ik) ***n.*** ⟦< L *musivus,* artistic⟧ **1** the making of pictures or designs by inlaying small bits of colored stone, etc. in mortar **2** a picture or design so made

Mo·sa·ic (mō zā′ik) ***adj.*** of Moses or the laws, etc. attributed to him

Mos·cow (mäs′kō, -kou′) capital of Russia, in the W part: pop. 8,769,000

Mo·ses (mō′zəz, -zəs) ***n.*** *Bible* the leader and lawgiver who brought the Israelites out of slavery in Egypt

mo·sey (mō′zē) ***vi.*** ⟦prob. < VAMOOSE⟧ [Slang] to stroll or amble along

Mos·lem (mäz′ləm) ***n., adj.*** MUSLIM

mosque (mäsk) ***n.*** ⟦< Ar *masjid,* temple⟧ a Muslim place of worship

mos·qui·to (mə skēt′ō) ***n., pl.*** **-toes** or **-tos** ⟦Sp & Port < L *musca,* a fly⟧ a two-winged insect, the female of which sucks blood from animals, including humans

moss (môs, mäs) ***n.*** ⟦OE *mos,* a swamp⟧ a very small, green plant that grows in velvety clusters on rocks, trees, etc. —**moss′y, -i·er, -i·est,** ***adj.***

moss′back′ ***n.*** [Inf.] an old-fashioned or very conservative person

most (mōst) ***adj.*** ⟦OE *mast*⟧ **1** greatest in amount, degree, or number: superlative of MUCH or MANY **2** in the greatest number of instances *[most* fame is fleeting*]* **—n.** **1** the greatest amount, quantity, or degree **2** [*with pl. v.*] the greatest number (*of*) **—adv.** in or to the greatest degree or extent

most'ly ***adv.*** **1** for the most part **2** chiefly; principally **3** usually

mote (mōt) ***n.*** ⟦OE *mot*⟧ a speck, as of dust

mo·tel (mō tel′) ***n.*** ⟦< MO(TOR) + (HO)TEL⟧ a hotel for motorists

moth (môth) ***n., pl.*** **moths** (môthz, môths) ⟦OE *moththe*⟧ a four-winged, chiefly night-flying insect, similar to the butterfly: the larvae of one kind feed on wool, etc.

moth'ball′ ***n.*** a small ball, as of naphthalene, the fumes of which repel moths from woolens, etc. **—in mothballs** put into storage or reserve

moth·er (mu*th*′ər) ***n.*** ⟦OE *modor*⟧ **1** a female parent **2** the origin or source of something **3** [*often* **M-**] a woman who is the head (**mother superior**) of a religious establishment **—*adj.*** **1** of or like a mother **2** native *[mother* tongue*]* **—*vt.*** **1** to be the mother of **2** to care for as a mother does **—moth'er·hood′** ***n.*** **—moth'er·less** ***adj.***

Mother Goose the imaginary creator of a collection of nursery rhymes

moth'er-in-law′ ***n., pl.*** **moth'ers-in-law′** the mother of one's husband or wife

moth'er·land′ ***n.*** one's native land

moth'er·ly ***adj.*** of or like a mother; protective, nurturing, etc. **—moth'er·li·ness** ***n.***

moth'er-of-pearl′ ***n.*** the hard internal layer of the shell of the pearl oyster, etc., used to make buttons, etc.

mother tongue one's native language

mo·tif (mō tēf′) ***n.*** ⟦Fr: see MOTIVE⟧ **1** *Art, Literature, Music* a main theme for development **2** a repeated figure in a design

mo·tile (mōt′'l) ***adj.*** ⟦< L *movere,* to move⟧ *Biol.* capable of or exhibiting spontaneous motion **—mo·til'i·ty** ***n.***

mo·tion (mō′shən) ***n.*** ⟦< L *movere,* to move⟧ **1** a moving from one place to another; movement **2** a moving of a part of the body; specif., a gesture **3** a proposal formally made in an assembly **—*vi.*** to make a meaningful movement of the hand, etc.; gesture **—*vt.*** to direct by a meaningful gesture **—go through the motions** to do something as from habit, without enthusiasm, enjoyment, etc. **—in motion** moving **—mo'tion·less** ***adj.***

motion picture FILM (*n.* 4)

motion sickness nausea, vomiting, etc. caused by the motion of a car, boat, etc.

mo·ti·vate (mōt′ə vāt′) ***vt.*** **-vat'ed, -vat'ing** to provide with, or affect as, a motive; incite **—mo'ti·va'tion** ***n.*** **—mo'ti·va'tion·al** ***adj.***

mo·tive (mōt′iv) ***n.*** ⟦< L *movere,* to move⟧ **1** an inner drive, impulse, etc. that causes one to act; incentive **2** MOTIF (sense 1)

-mo·tive (mōt′iv) *combining form* moving, of motion *[automotive]*

mot·ley (mät′lē) ***adj.*** ⟦< ?⟧ **1** of many colors **2** of many different or clashing elements

mo·to·cross (mō′tō krôs′) ***n.*** ⟦Fr⟧ a cross-country race for lightweight motorcycles

mo·tor (mōt′ər) ***n.*** ⟦L < *movere,* to move⟧ **1** anything that produces motion **2** an engine; esp., an internal-combustion engine **3** a machine for converting electric energy into mechanical energy **—*adj.*** **1** producing motion **2** of or powered by a motor **3** of, by, or for motor vehicles **4** of or involving muscular movements *[motor* skills*]* **—*vi.*** to travel by automobile

mo'tor·bike′ ***n.*** [Inf.] **1** a motor-driven bicycle **2** a light motorcycle

mo'tor·boat′ ***n.*** a small motor-driven boat

mo'tor·cade′ (-kād′) ***n.*** ⟦MOTOR + -CADE⟧ an automobile procession

mo'tor·car′ ***n.*** [Now Chiefly Brit.] an automobile

mo'tor·cy'cle (-sī′kəl) ***n.*** a two-wheeled vehicle propelled by an internal-combustion engine

motor home a motor vehicle with a truck chassis, outfitted as a traveling home

mo·tor·ist (mōt′ər ist) ***n.*** one who drives an automobile or travels by automobile

mo'tor·ize′ (-īz′) ***vt.*** **-ized′, -iz'ing** to equip with a motor or with motor-driven vehicles

motor vehicle an automotive vehicle, esp. an automobile, truck, or bus

mot·tle (mät′'l) ***vt.*** **-tled, -tling** ⟦< MOTLEY⟧ to mark with blotches, etc. of different colors

mot·to (mät′ō) ***n., pl.*** **-toes** or **-tos** ⟦It, a word⟧ a word or saying that expresses the goals, ideals, etc. of a nation, group, etc.

mould (mōld) ***n., vt., vi.*** *chiefly Brit. sp. of* MOLD[1], MOLD[2], MOLD[3]

mould'ing ***n.*** *chiefly Brit. sp. of* MOLDING

mould'y ***adj.*** *chiefly Brit. sp. of* MOLDY

moult (mōlt) ***vi.*** *chiefly Brit. sp. of* MOLT

mound (mound) ***n.*** ⟦< ? MDu *mond,* protection⟧ a heap or bank of earth, sand, etc. **—*vt.*** to heap up

mount[1] (mount) ***n.*** ⟦< L *mons*⟧ a mountain

mount[2] (mount) ***vi.*** ⟦< L *mons,* mountain⟧ **1** to climb; ascend **2** to climb up on something, as onto a horse **3** to increase in amount **—*vt.*** **1** to go up; ascend *[*to *mount* stairs*]* **2** to get up on (a horse, platform, etc.) **3** to provide with horses *[mounted* police*]* **4** to place or fix (a jewel, picture, etc.) on or in the proper support, backing, etc. **5** to arrange (a dead animal, etc.) for exhibition **6** to place (a gun) into proper position for use **7** to prepare for and undertake (an expedition, etc.) **—*n.*** **1** the act of mounting **2** a horse, etc. for riding **3** the support, setting, etc. on or in which a thing is mounted

moun·tain (mount′'n) ***n.*** ⟦ult. < L *mons*⟧ **1** a natural raised part of the earth, larger than a hill **2** a large pile, amount, etc. —*adj.* of or in the mountains

mountain bike a heavy-duty bicycle with wide tires for use on and off regular road surfaces

moun'tain·eer' (-ir') *n.* **1** one who lives in a mountainous region **2** a mountain climber

mountain goat a long-haired, goatlike antelope of the Rocky Mountains

mountain lion COUGAR

moun'tain·ous *adj.* **1** full of mountains **2** huge

mountain sickness weakness, nausea, etc. caused by thin air at high altitudes

Mountain State any of the eight states of the W U.S. through which the Rocky Mountains pass; Montana, Idaho, Wyoming, Nevada, Utah, Colorado, Arizona, or New Mexico

moun·te·bank (mount'ə baŋk') *n.* ⟦It *montambanco*, lit., mounted on a bench: orig. a person on a bench, or platform, selling quack medicines⟧ a charlatan or quack

mount'ed *adj.* **1** on horseback, a bicycle, etc. **2** on or in a mounting

mount'ing *n.* something serving as a backing, support, setting, etc.

mourn (môrn) *vi., vt.* ⟦OE *murnan*⟧ **1** to feel or express sorrow for (something regrettable) **2** to grieve for (someone who has died) —**mourn'er** *n.*

mourn'ful *adj.* **1** feeling or expressing grief or sorrow **2** causing sorrow

mourn'ing *n.* **1** the expression of grief, esp. at someone's death **2** black clothes, etc., worn as such an expression **3** the period during which one mourns

mouse (mous; *for v., also* mouz) *n., pl.* **mice** ⟦OE *mus*⟧ **1** any of many small rodents, esp. a species that commonly infests buildings **2** a timid person **3** [Slang] a black eye **4** a hand-held device for controlling the video display of a computer —*vi.* **moused, mous'ing** to hunt mice

mousse (mo͞os) *n.* ⟦Fr, foam⟧ **1** a light, chilled dessert made with egg white, whipped cream, etc. **2** an aerosol foam used to keep hair in place, etc. —*vt.* **moussed, mouss'ing** to style (hair) using mousse

mous·tache (mus'tash', məs tash') *n. alt. sp. of* MUSTACHE

mous·y (mous'ē, mouz'-) *adj.* **-i·er, -i·est** of or like a mouse; specif., quiet, timid, drab, etc.: also **mous'ey** —**mous'i·ness** *n.*

mouth (mouth; *for v.* mou*th*) *n., pl.* **mouths** (mou*th*z) ⟦OE *muth*⟧ **1** the opening in the head through which food is taken in and sounds are made **2** any opening regarded as like this [the *mouth* of a jar, river, etc.] —*vt.* **1** to say, esp. insincerely **2** to form (a word) with the mouth silently —**down in** (or **at**) **the mouth** [Inf.] unhappy —**mouth off** [Slang] to talk loudly, impudently, etc.

mouth'ful' *n., pl.* **-fuls'** **1** as much as the mouth can hold **2** as much as is usually taken into the mouth **3** [Slang] a pertinent remark: chiefly in **say a mouthful**

mouth organ HARMONICA

mouth'piece' *n.* **1** a part, as of a musical instrument, held in or to the mouth **2** a person, periodical, etc. which expresses the views as of a group

mouth'wash' *n.* a flavored, often antiseptic liquid for rinsing the mouth

mouth'wa'ter·ing *adj.* appetizing; tasty

mouth'y *adj.* **-i·er, -i·est** talkative, esp. in a bombastic or rude way —**mouth'i·ness** *n.*

mou·ton (mo͞o'tän') *n.* ⟦Fr, sheep⟧ lambskin or sheepskin made to resemble beaver, seal, etc.

mov·a·ble (mo͞o'və bəl) *adj.* that can be moved from one place to another —*n.* **1** something movable **2** *Law* personal property, esp. furniture: *usually used in pl.* Also **move'a·ble**

move (mo͞ov) *vt.* **moved, mov'ing** ⟦< L *movere*⟧ **1** to change the place or position of **2** to set or keep in motion **3** to cause (*to do, say*, etc.) **4** to arouse the emotions, etc. of **5** to propose formally, as in a meeting —*vi.* **1** to change place or position **2** to change one's residence **3** to be active **4** to make progress **5** to take action **6** to be, or be set, in motion **7** to make a formal application (*for*) **8** to evacuate: said of the bowels **9** to be sold: said of goods —*n.* **1** act of moving **2** an action toward some goal **3** a change of residence **4** *Chess, Checkers, etc.* the act of moving a piece, or one's turn to move —**move up** to promote or be promoted —**on the move** [Inf.] moving about from place to place

move'ment *n.* **1** a moving or manner of moving **2** an evacuation (of the bowels) **3** a change in the location of troops, etc. **4** organized action by people working toward a goal **5** the moving parts of a mechanism, as of a clock **6** *Music a*) a principal division of a symphony, etc. *b*) rhythm

mov·er (mo͞o'vər) *n.* one that moves; specif., one whose work is moving furniture, etc. for those changing residence

mov'ie (-vē) *n.* ⟦< *moving picture*⟧ FILM (*n.* 4) —**the movies** **1** the film industry **2** a showing of a film

moving van a large van for transporting belongings, as of a person moving to a new residence

mow[1] (mō) *vt., vi.* **mowed, mowed** or **mown** (mōn), **mow'ing** ⟦OE *mawan*⟧ to cut down (grass, etc.) from (a lawn, etc.) —**mow down** **1** to cause to fall like cut grass **2** to overwhelm (an opponent) —**mow'er** *n.*

mow[2] (mou) *n.* ⟦OE *muga*⟧ a heap of hay, etc., esp. in a barn

Mo·zam·bique (mō'zəm bēk') country in SE Africa: 308,642 sq. mi.; pop. 11,674,000

Mo·zart (mō'tsärt'), **Wolf·gang A·ma·de·us** (vôlf'gäŋk' ä'mä dā'o͝os) 1756-91; Austrian composer

MP *abbrev.* **1** Member of Parliament **2** Military Police

mpg *abbrev.* miles per gallon

mph *abbrev.* miles per hour

Mr. or **Mr** (mis′tər) *abbrev.* mister: used before a man's name or title: pl. *Messrs*

MRI ***n.*** ⟦*m(agnetic) r(esonance) i(maging)*⟧ imaging by means of atomic nuclei in a strong magnetic field, used in medical diagnosis

Mrs. or **Mrs** (mis′iz) *abbrev.* mistress: now used before a married woman's name: pl. *Mmes*

MS *abbrev.* **1** manuscript: also **ms** **2** Master of Science: also **M.S.**, **MSc**, or **M.Sc.** **3** Mississippi **4** multiple sclerosis

Ms. or **Ms** (miz) *abbrev.* a title, free of reference to marital status, used in place of *Miss* or *Mrs.*

MSG *abbrev.* monosodium glutamate

Msgr *abbrev.* Monsignor

MST *abbrev.* Mountain Standard Time

MSW or **M.S.W.** *abbrev.* Master of Social Work

Mt *abbrev.* **1** Mount **2** Mountain

MT *abbrev.* **1** Montana **2** megaton **3** Mountain Time

mtg *abbrev.* **1** meeting **2** mortgage: also **mtge**

MTV *trademark for* Music Television

mu (mo͞o, myo͞o) ***n.*** the 12th letter of the Greek alphabet (Μ, μ)

much (much) ***adj.*** **more, most** ⟦< OE *mycel*⟧ great in quantity, degree, etc. —***adv.*** **more, most** **1** to a great degree or extent *[much* happier*]* **2** nearly *[much* the same*]* —***n.*** **1** a great amount **2** something great or outstanding *[*not *much* to look at*]*

mu·ci·lage (myo͞o′si lij′) ***n.*** ⟦< L *mucere*, be moldy⟧ **1** a thick, sticky substance in certain plants **2** any watery solution of gum, glue, etc. used as an adhesive

muck (muk) ***n.*** ⟦ME *muk*⟧ **1** moist manure **2** black earth with decaying matter, used as fertilizer **3** mud; dirt; filth —**muck′y, -i·er, -i·est,** ***adj.***

muck′rake′ ***vi.*** **-raked′, -rak′ing** ⟦see prec. & RAKE[1]⟧ to search for and publicize real or alleged corruption in politics, etc. —**muck′rak′er** ***n.***

mu·cous (myo͞o′kəs) ***adj.*** **1** of, containing, or secreting mucus **2** slimy

mucous membrane a mucus-secreting lining of certain body cavities

mu·cus (myo͞o′kəs) ***n.*** ⟦L⟧ the thick, slimy substance secreted by the mucous membranes for moistening and protection

mud (mud) ***n.*** ⟦ME⟧ **1** wet, soft, sticky earth **2** defamatory remarks

mud·dle (mud′'l) ***vt.*** **-dled, -dling** ⟦< prec.⟧ **1** to mix up; bungle **2** to confuse mentally; befuddle —***vi.*** to act or think confusedly —***n.*** **1** a mess, jumble, etc. **2** mental confusion

mud′dle-head′ed ***adj.*** confused

mud′dy ***adj.*** **-di·er, -di·est** **1** full of or spattered with mud **2** not clear; cloudy *[muddy* coffee*]* **3** confused, obscure, etc. *[muddy* thinking*]* —***vt.***, ***vi.*** **-died, -dy·ing** to make or become muddy —**mud′di·ness** ***n.***

mud flat low, muddy land that floods at high tide

mud′sling′ing ***n.*** the making of unscrupulous, malicious attacks, as against a political opponent —**mud′sling′er** ***n.***

mu·ez·zin (myo͞o ez′in) ***n.*** ⟦< Ar *adhana*, proclaim⟧ a Muslim crier who calls the people to prayer

muff (muf) ***n.*** ⟦< Fr *moufle*, mitten⟧ **1** a cylindrical covering, as of fur, to warm the hands **2** any bungled action —***vt.*** to bungle; specif., to miss (a catch, etc.)

muf·fin (muf′ən) ***n.*** ⟦< ?⟧ a quick bread baked in a cup-shaped mold

muf·fle (muf′əl) ***vt.*** **-fled, -fling** ⟦prob. < OFr *moufle*, mitten⟧ **1** to wrap or cover so as to keep warm, deaden sound, etc. **2** to deaden (a sound)

muf′fler (-lər) ***n.*** **1** a scarf worn around the throat, as for warmth **2** a device for deadening noise, esp. of a car's exhaust

muf·ti (muf′tē) ***n.***, *pl.* **-tis** ⟦< Ar⟧ ordinary clothes, esp. when worn by one usually wearing a uniform

mug (mug) ***n.*** ⟦prob. < Scand⟧ **1** a cup made of earthenware or metal, with a handle **2** as much as a mug will hold **3** [Slang] the face —***vt.*** **mugged, mug′ging** to assault, usually with intent to rob —***vi.*** [Slang] to grimace, esp. in overacting —**mug′ger** ***n.***

mug·gy (mug′ē) ***adj.*** **-gi·er, -gi·est** ⟦< dial. *mug*, mist⟧ hot, damp, and close —**mug′gi·ness** ***n.***

mug shot a police photograph of the face of a criminal or suspect

Mu·ham·mad (mo͞o ham′əd) *var. of* MOHAMMED

muk·luk (muk′luk′) ***n.*** ⟦Esk *muklok*, a seal⟧ an Eskimo boot of sealskin or reindeer skin

mu·lat·to (mə lät′ō, -lat′ō) ***n.***, *pl.* **-toes** or **-tos** ⟦Sp & Port *mulato*⟧ a person who has one black parent and one white parent

mul·ber·ry (mul′ber′ē, -bər ē) ***n.***, *pl.* **-ries** ⟦< OE *morberie*⟧ **1** a tree with purplish-red, edible, berrylike fruit **2** the fruit

mulch (mulch) ***n.*** ⟦ME *molsh*, soft⟧ leaves, straw, etc., spread around plants to prevent freezing of roots, etc. —***vt.*** to apply mulch to

mulct (mulkt) ***vt.*** ⟦< L *mul(c)ta*, a fine⟧ **1** to fine **2** to take (money, etc.) from (someone) by fraud —***n.*** a fine

mule[1] (myo͞ol) ***n.*** ⟦< L *mulus*⟧ **1** the offspring of a jackass and a female horse **2** [Inf.] a stubborn person **3** [Slang] a drug smuggler

mule[2] (myo͞ol) ***n.*** ⟦< L *mulleus*, red shoe⟧ a lounging slipper that does not cover the heel

mu·le·teer (myo͞o′lə tir′) ***n.*** ⟦OFr *muletier*⟧ a driver of mules: also [Inf.] **mule skin·ner** (skin′ər)

mul′ish ***adj.*** stubborn; obstinate

mull[1] (mul) ***vt.***, ***vi.*** ⟦ME *mullen*, to grind⟧ to ponder (*over*)

mull[2] (mul) ***vt.*** ⟦< ?⟧ to heat, sweeten, and spice (wine, cider, etc.)

mul·let (mul′it) ***n.*** ⟦< L *mullus*⟧ an

edible, spiny-finned fish of fresh and salt waters

mul·li·gan stew (mul′i gən) a stew made of bits of meat and vegetables, esp. as by hobos

mul·li·ga·taw·ny (mul′i gə tô′nē) ***n.*** ⟦Tamil *miḷagutaṇṇir,* lit., pepper water⟧ an East Indian soup of meat, etc., flavored with curry

mul·lion (mul′yən) ***n.*** ⟦prob. < OFr *moien,* median⟧ a vertical dividing bar, as between windowpanes

multi- ⟦L < *multus,* many⟧ *combining form* **1** having many **2** more than two **3** many times more than

mul·ti·cul·tur·al·ism (mul′tē kul′chər əl iz′əm) ***n.*** the practice of giving equal emphasis to the needs and contributions of all cultural groups, esp. traditionally underrepresented minority groups, in a society —**mul′ti·cul′tur·al** ***adj.***

mul′ti·fac′et·ed (-fas′ət id) ***adj.*** having a variety of features, parts, etc. *[a multifaceted* career*]*

mul·ti·far·i·ous (mul′tə far′ē əs) ***adj.*** ⟦< L⟧ having many kinds of parts or elements; diverse

mul·ti·lat·er·al (mul′ti lat′ər əl) ***adj.*** involving more than two parties, nations, etc.

mul′ti·lin′gual ***adj.*** of, in, or capable of using several languages

mul′ti·me′di·a (-mē′dē ə) ***adj.*** combining or using several media, as film and live performance or TV, radio, and printed matter

mul′ti·mil′lion·aire′ ***n.*** one whose wealth amounts to many millions of dollars, pounds, etc.

mul′ti·na′tion·al ***adj.*** **1** of many nations **2** having offices, etc. in many nations —***n.*** a multinational corporation

mul·ti·ple (mul′tə pəl) ***adj.*** ⟦< L *multiplex*⟧ **1** having many parts, elements, etc. **2** shared by or involving many —***n.*** a number which is a product of some specified number and another number

mul′ti·ple-choice′ ***adj.*** listing several answers from which the correct one is to be chosen

multiple sclerosis a disease of the central nervous system, with loss of muscular coordination, etc.

mul·ti·plex (mul′tə pleks′) ***adj.*** ⟦L, multiple⟧ designating a system for sending two or more signals simultaneously over a common circuit, etc. —***n.*** a film-theater complex with three or more screens —**mul′ti·plex′er** or **mul′ti·plex′or** ***n.***

mul′ti·pli·cand′ (-pli kand′) ***n.*** a number to be multiplied by another

mul′ti·pli·ca′tion (-pli kā′shən) ***n.*** a multiplying or being multiplied; specif., the process of finding the quantity obtained by repeated additions of a specified quantity a specified number of times

mul′ti·plic′i·ty (-plis′ə tē) ***n.*** a great number or variety (*of*)

mul′ti·pli′er (-plī′ər) ***n.*** the number by which another is to be multiplied

mul′ti·ply′ (-plī′) ***vt., vi.*** **-plied′, -ply′ing** ⟦see MULTIPLE⟧ **1** to increase in number, degree, etc. **2** to find the product (of) by multiplication

mul·ti·proc·es·sor (mul′ti prä′ses′ər) ***n.*** a computer system capable of processing many programs at once

mul′ti·stage′ ***adj.*** having more than one stage, as a missile, process, etc.

mul·ti·tude (mul′tə to͞od′) ***n.*** ⟦< L *multus,* many⟧ a large number; host

mul′ti·tu′di·nous (-to͞od′′n əs) ***adj.*** very numerous; many

mum[1] (mum) ***n.*** [Inf.] a chrysanthemum

mum[2] (mum) ***adj.*** ⟦ME *momme*⟧ silent; not speaking

mum·ble (mum′bəl) ***vt., vi.*** **-bled, -bling** ⟦ME *momelen*⟧ to speak or say indistinctly; mutter —***n.*** a mumbled utterance —**mum′bler** ***n.***

mum·bo jum·bo (mum′bō jum′bō) ⟦of Afr orig.⟧ meaningless ritual, talk, etc.

mum·mer (mum′ər) ***n.*** ⟦< OFr *momo,* grimace⟧ an actor, esp. one who wears a mask or costume

mum·mi·fy (mum′ə fī′) ***vt., vi.*** **-fied′, -fy′ing** to make into or become (like) a mummy

mum·my (mum′ē) ***n., pl.*** **-mies** ⟦ult. < Pers *mum,* wax⟧ a dead body preserved by embalming, as by the ancient Egyptians

mumps (mumps) ***n.*** ⟦< obs. *mump,* a grimace⟧ an acute communicable disease characterized by swelling of the salivary glands

mun *abbrev.* municipal

munch (munch) ***vt., vi.*** ⟦ME *monchen*⟧ to chew steadily, often with a crunching sound

mun·dane (mun′dān′, mun dān′) ***adj.*** ⟦< L *mundus,* world⟧ **1** of the world; worldly **2** commonplace, ordinary, etc. —**mun′dane′ly** ***adv.***

Mu·nich (myo͞o′nik) city in SE Germany: pop. 1,256,000

mu·nic·i·pal (myo͞o nis′ə pəl) ***adj.*** ⟦< L *municeps,* inhabitant of a free town⟧ of or having to do with a city, town, etc. or its local government

mu·nic′i·pal′i·ty (-pal′ə tē) ***n., pl.*** **-ties** a city, town, etc. having its own incorporated government

mu·nif·i·cent (myo͞o nif′ə sənt) ***adj.*** ⟦< L *munus,* a gift + *facere,* make⟧ very generous; lavish —**mu·nif′i·cence** ***n.***

mu·ni·tions (myo͞o nish′ənz) ***pl.n.*** ⟦< L *munire,* fortify⟧ weapons and ammunition for war

mu·ral (myoor′əl) ***adj.*** ⟦< L *murus,* wall⟧ of, on, or for a wall —***n.*** a picture, esp. a large one, painted directly on a wall —**mu′ral·ist** ***n.***

mur·der (mur′dər) ***n.*** ⟦OE *morthor*⟧ **1** the unlawful and malicious or premeditated killing of a person **2** [Inf.] something very hard, unsafe, etc. to do or deal with —***vt.*** **1** to kill (a person) unlawfully and with malice **2** to spoil, mar, etc., as in performance *[to murder* a song*]* —**mur′der·er** ***n.*** —**mur′der·ess** ***fem.n.***

mur′der·ous *adj.* **1** of or characteristic of murder; brutal **2** capable or guilty of, or intending, murder —**mur′der·ous·ly** *adv.*

murk (murk) *n.* ⟦< ON *myrkr*, dark⟧ darkness; gloom

murk′y *adj.* **-i·er, -i·est** dark or gloomy —**murk′i·ness** *n.*

mur·mur (mur′mər) *n.* ⟦< L⟧ **1** a low, steady sound **2** a mumbled complaint **3** *Med.* an abnormal sound in the body, esp. in the heart —*vi.* to make a murmur —*vt.* to say in a murmur

mus·cat (mus′kət) *n.* ⟦< LL *muscus*, musk⟧ a sweet European grape

mus′ca·tel′ (-kə tel′) *n.* a sweet wine made from the muscat

mus·cle (mus′əl) *n.* ⟦< L *musculus*, lit., little mouse⟧ **1** any body organ consisting of fibrous tissue that can be contracted and expanded to produce bodily movements **2** this tissue **3** muscular strength —*vi.* **-cled, -cling** [Inf.] to force one's way (*in*)

mus′cle-bound′ *adj.* having some of the muscles enlarged and less elastic, as from too much exercise

mus·cu·lar (mus′kyoo lər, -kyə-) *adj.* **1** of, consisting of, or done by muscles **2** having well-developed muscles; strong —**mus′cu·lar′i·ty** (-lar′ə tē) *n.*

muscular dys·tro·phy (dis′trə fē) a chronic disease characterized by a progressive wasting of the muscles

mus·cu·la·ture (mus′kyoo lə chər, -kyə-) *n.* ⟦Fr⟧ the muscular system of a body, limb, etc.

muse (myooz) *vi.* **mused, mus′ing** ⟦< OFr *muser*, ponder⟧ to think deeply; meditate

Muse (myooz) *n.* ⟦< Gr *mousa*⟧ **1** *Gr. Myth.* any of the nine goddesses of literature and of the arts and sciences **2** [**m-**] the spirit thought to inspire a poet or other artist

mu·sette (bag) (myoo zet′) ⟦< OFr, bagpipe⟧ a bag with a shoulder strap, carried as by soldiers

mu·se·um (myoo zē′əm) *n.* ⟦< Gr *mousa*, Muse⟧ a place for preserving and exhibiting artistic or historical objects

mush[1] (mush) *n.* ⟦prob. var. of MASH⟧ **1** a thick porridge of boiled meal **2** any thick, soft mass **3** [Inf.] maudlin sentimentality —**mush′y, -i·er, -i·est,** *adj.*

mush[2] (mush) *interj.* ⟦prob. < Fr *marchons*, let's go⟧ a shout to urge on sled dogs —*vi.* to travel on foot over snow with a dog sled

mush′room′ *n.* ⟦< LL *mussirio*⟧ any of various fleshy fungi, typically with a stalk capped by an umbrellalike top; esp., any edible variety —*adj.* of or like a mushroom —*vi.* to grow or spread rapidly

mu·sic (myoo′zik) *n.* ⟦< Gr *mousikē* (*technē*), art of the Muses⟧ **1** the art of combining tones to form expressive compositions **2** such compositions **3** any rhythmic sequence of pleasing sounds —**face the music** [Inf.] to accept the consequences

mu′si·cal (-zi kəl) *adj.* **1** of or for music **2** melodious or harmonious **3** fond of or skilled in music **4** set to music —*n.* a play or film with a musical score featuring songs and dances —**mu′si·cal·ly** *adv.*

mu·si·cale (myoo′zi kal′) *n.* ⟦Fr⟧ a social affair featuring a musical program

mu·si·cian (myoo zish′ən) *n.* one skilled in music; esp., a performer

mu′si·col′o·gy (-zi käl′ə jē) *n.* the study of the history, forms, etc. of music —**mu′si·col′o·gist** *n.*

musk (musk) *n.* ⟦< Sans *muṣka*, testicle⟧ a strong-smelling animal secretion, used in perfumes —**musk′y, -i·er, -i·est,** *adj.*

mus·kel·lunge (mus′kə lunj′) *n.* ⟦< AmInd⟧ a very large, edible pike of North America: also **mus′kie** (-kē)

mus·ket (mus′kət) *n.* ⟦< L *musca*, a fly⟧ a former kind of firearm with a long barrel and smooth bore

mus·ket·eer (mus′kə tir′) *n.* a soldier armed with a musket

musk′mel′on *n.* any of various sweet, juicy melons, as the cantaloupe

musk ox a hardy ox of arctic North America with a long, coarse coat and a musklike odor

musk′rat′ *n.* **1** an American water rodent with webbed hind feet and a musklike odor **2** its fur

Mus·lim (muz′ləm, mooz′-, moos′-) *n.* ⟦Ar, true believer < *aslama*, to resign oneself (to God)⟧ an adherent of Islam —*adj.* of Islam or the Muslims

mus·lin (muz′lin) *n.* ⟦after *Mosul*, city in Iraq⟧ a strong, plain-woven cotton cloth

muss (mus) *n.* ⟦prob. var. of MESS⟧ [Inf.] a mess; disorder —*vt.* to make messy or disordered: often with *up* —**muss′y, -i·er, -i·est,** *adj.*

mus·sel (mus′əl) *n.* ⟦< OE *muscle*⟧ any of various bivalve mollusks; specif., an edible variety

must (must) *v.aux. pt.* **must** ⟦< OE *moste*⟧ used to express: **1** necessity *[I must go]* **2** probability *[it must be Joe]* **3** certainty *[all men must die]* —*n.* [Inf.] something that must be done, had, etc.

mus·tache (mus′tash′, məs tash′) *n.* ⟦ult. < Gr *mystax*⟧ hair growing on the upper lip; esp., the hair that a man has let grow

mus·tang (mus′taŋ′) *n.* ⟦< L *mixtus*, a mingling⟧ a small wild horse of the SW plains

mus·tard (mus′tərd) *n.* ⟦< OFr⟧ **1** an herb with yellow flowers and round seeds in slender pods **2** a pungent seasoning made from the ground seeds

mustard gas ⟦< its mustardlike odor⟧ an oily liquid used in warfare for its blistering and disabling effects

mus·ter (mus′tər) *vt.* ⟦< L *monstrare*, to show⟧ **1** to assemble (troops, etc.) **2** to collect; summon: often with *up* —*vi.* to assemble, as troops —*n.* **1** a gathering or assembling, as of troops for inspection **2** the persons or things assembled —**muster in** (or **out**) to enlist in (or discharge from) military service —**pass muster** to meet the required standards

mus·ty (mus′tē) *adj.* **-ti·er, -ti·est** ⟦< ? MOIST⟧ **1** having a stale, moldy smell or taste 2 stale or trite; antiquated —**mus′ti·ly** *adv.* —**mus′ti·ness** *n.*

mu·ta·ble (myōōt′ə bəl) *adj.* ⟦< L *mutare,* to change⟧ **1** that can be changed **2** inconstant; fickle —**mu′ta·bil′i·ty** *n.* —**mu′ta·bly** *adv.*

mu·tant (myōōt′'nt) *adj.* of mutation —*n.* an animal or plant with inheritable characteristics that differ from those of the parents; sport

mu·ta·tion (myōō tā′shən) *n.* **1** a change, as in form, nature, etc. **2** a sudden variation in some inheritable characteristic of an animal or plant —**mu′tate′, -tat′ed, -tat′ing,** *vi., vt.*

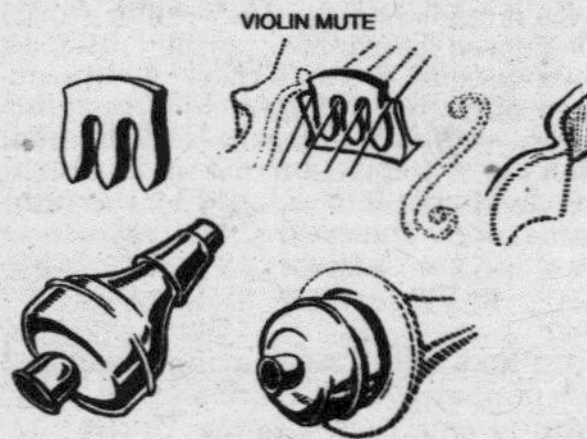

mute (myōōt) *adj.* ⟦< L *mutus*⟧ **1** not speaking; silent **2** unable to speak —*n.* **1** a deaf-mute **2** a device that softens the sound of a musical instrument —*vt.* **mut′ed, mut′ing** to soften the sound of

mu·ti·late (myōōt′'l āt′) *vt.* **-lat′ed, -lat′ing** ⟦< L *mutilus,* maimed⟧ to cut off, damage, or mar an important part of —**mu′ti·la′tion** *n.* —**mu′ti·la′tor** *n.*

mu·ti·ny (myōōt′'n ē) *n., pl.* **-nies** ⟦< L *movere,* to move⟧ revolt against constituted authority; esp., rebellion of soldiers or sailors against their officers —*vi.* **-nied, -ny·ing** to take part in a mutiny —**mu′ti·neer′** *n.* —**mu′ti·nous** *adj.*

mutt (mut) *n.* [Slang] a mongrel dog

mut·ter (mut′ər) *vi., vt.* ⟦ME *moteren*⟧ **1** to speak or say in low, indistinct tones **2** to grumble —*n.* **1** a muttering **2** something muttered

mut·ton (mut′'n) *n.* ⟦< OFr, a ram⟧ the flesh of a sheep, esp. a grown sheep, used as food

mu·tu·al (myōō′chōō əl) *adj.* ⟦< L *mutare,* to exchange⟧ **1** *a*) done, felt, etc. by each of two or more for or toward the other or others *b*) of each other **2** in common *[our mutual friend]* —**mu′tu·al·ly** *adv.*

mutual fund **1** a fund of securities owned jointly by investors who have purchased shares of it **2** a corporation which manages such a fund or funds

muu·muu (mōō′mōō′) *n.* ⟦< Haw⟧ a long, loose dress of Hawaiian style

Mu·zak (myōō′zak′) *trademark for* a system of transmitting recorded background music to stores, etc. —*n.* this music, variously regarded as unobtrusive, bland, etc.

muz·zle (muz′əl) *n.* ⟦< ML *musum*⟧ **1** the mouth, nose, and jaws of a dog, horse, etc. **2** a device put over the mouth of an animal to prevent its biting or eating **3** the front end of the barrel of a firearm —*vt.* **-zled, -zling** **1** to put a muzzle on (an animal) **2** to prevent from talking

MX missile (em′eks′) ⟦< *m*(*issile*), (*e*)*x*(*perimental*)⟧ a U.S. ICBM armed with several nuclear warheads

my (mī) *poss. pronominal adj.* ⟦< OE *min*⟧ of, belonging to, or done by me

Myan·mar (myän′mär′) country in SE Asia: 261,228 sq. mi.; pop. 35,314,000

my·col·o·gy (mī käl′ə jē) *n.* the study of fungi —**my·col′o·gist** *n.*

my·e·li·tis (mī′ə līt′is) *n.* ⟦< Gr *myelos,* marrow + -ITIS⟧ inflammation of the spinal cord or the bone marrow

My·lar (mī′lär′) *trademark for* a strong, thin polyester used for recording tapes, fabrics, etc. —*n.* [*occas.* **m-**] this substance

my·na or **my·nah** (mī′nə) *n.* ⟦Hindi *mainā*⟧ any of various tropical birds of Southeast Asia: some can mimic speech

my·o·pi·a (mī ō′pē ə) *n.* ⟦< Gr *myein,* to close + *ōps,* eye⟧ nearsightedness —**my·op′ic** (-äp′ik) *adj.*

myr·i·ad (mir′ē əd) *n.* ⟦< Gr *myrios,* countless⟧ a great number —*adj.* countless; innumerable

myr·mi·don (mur′mə dän′, -dən) *n.* ⟦after name of a Gr tribe led by Achilles⟧ an unquestioning follower

myrrh (mur) *n.* ⟦< Ar *murr*⟧ a fragrant gum resin of Arabia and E Africa, used in incense, etc.

myr·tle (murt′'l) *n.* ⟦< Gr *myrtos*⟧ **1** an evergreen shrub with white or pink flowers and dark berries **2** any of various other plants, as the periwinkle

my·self (mī self′) *pron.* a form of I, used as an intensive *[I went myself],* as a reflexive *[I hurt myself],* or with the meaning "my true self" *[I am not myself today]*

mys·te·ri·ous (mis tir′ē əs) *adj.* of, containing, implying, or characterized by mystery —**mys·te′ri·ous·ly** *adv.* —**mys·te′ri·ous·ness** *n.*

mys·ter·y (mis′tə rē) *n., pl.* **-ies** ⟦< Gr *mystērion,* secret rite⟧ **1** something unexplained or secret **2** a story involving unknown persons, facts, etc. *[a murder mystery]* **3** secrecy

mys·tic (mis′tik) *adj.* **1** of esoteric rites or doctrines **2** MYSTICAL **3** mysterious —*n.* a believer in mysticism

mys′ti·cal (-ti kəl) *adj.* **1** spiritually significant or symbolic **2** of mystics or mysticism **3** occult —**mys′ti·cal·ly** *adv.*

mys·ti·cism (mis′tə siz′əm) *n.* **1** belief in the possibility of attaining direct communion with God or knowledge of spiritual truths, as by meditation **2** obscure thinking or belief

mys′ti·fy′ (-fī′) *vt.* **-fied′, -fy′ing** to puzzle or perplex —**mys′ti·fi·ca′tion** *n.*

mys·tique (mis tēk′) *n.* ⟦Fr, mystic⟧ a mysterious and fascinating quality

myth (mith) *n.* ⟦< Gr *mythos*⟧ **1** a traditional story serving to explain some phenomenon, custom, etc. **2** mythology **3** any fictitious story, person, or thing —**myth'ic** ***adj.*** —**myth'i·cal** ***adj.***

my·thol·o·gy (mi thäl'ə jē) ***n.***, *pl.* **-gies** **1** the study of myths **2** myths collectively, as of a specific people —**myth·o·log·i·cal** (mith'ə läj'i kəl) ***adj.***

N

n[1] or **N** (en) ***n.***, *pl.* **n's, N's** the 14th letter of the English alphabet

n[2] *abbrev.* **1** name **2** neuter **3** new **4** nominative **5** noun **6** number

N[1] *abbrev.* **1** Navy **2** north **3** northern **4** November

N[2] *Chem. symbol for* nitrogen

Na ⟦L *natrium*⟧ *Chem. symbol for* sodium

NA *abbrev.* North America

NAACP *abbrev.* National Association for the Advancement of Colored People

nab (nab) ***vt.*** **nabbed, nab'bing** ⟦prob. < dial. *nap*, to snatch⟧ [Inf.] **1** to snatch or seize **2** to arrest or catch (a felon or wrongdoer)

na·bob (nā'bäb') ***n.*** ⟦< Ar *nā'ib*, deputy⟧ a very rich or important man

na·cre (nā'kər) ***n.*** ⟦Fr < Ar *naqqārah*, small kettledrum⟧ MOTHER-OF-PEARL

na·dir (nā'dər, -dir') ***n.*** ⟦< Ar *naẓīr*, opposite⟧ **1** the point opposite the zenith and directly below the observer **2** the lowest point

nae (nā) [Scot.] ***adv.*** no; not —***adj.*** no

nag[1] (nag) ***vt.***, ***vi.*** **nagged, nag'ging** ⟦< ON *gnaga*⟧ **1** to annoy by continual scolding, urging, etc. **2** to keep troubling *[nagged* by doubts*]* —***n.*** one who nags: also **nag'ger**

nag[2] (nag) ***n.*** ⟦ME *nagge*⟧ an old or inferior horse

Na·ga·sa·ki (nä'gə sä'kē) seaport in SW Japan: U.S. atomic-bomb target (1945): pop. 438,000

Na·go·ya (nä'gô yä') seaport in S Honshu, Japan: pop. 2,088,000

nai·ad (nā'ad', nī'-) ***n.*** ⟦< Gr *naein*, to flow⟧ [*also* **N-**] *Gr. & Rom. Myth.* a nymph living in a spring, river, etc.

nail (nāl) ***n.*** ⟦< OE *nægl*⟧ **1** the thin, horny growth at the ends of fingers and toes **2** a tapered, pointed piece of metal driven with a hammer, as to join pieces of wood —***vt.*** **1** to fasten, secure, etc. with or as with nails **2** [Inf.] to catch, capture, etc. **3** [Inf.] to hit hard

nail'-bit'er (-bīt'ər) ***n.*** [Inf.] a suspenseful drama, sports event, etc.

Nai·ro·bi (nī rō'bē) capital of Kenya: pop. 1,346,000

na·ive or **na·ïve** (nä ēv') ***adj.*** ⟦Fr < L *nativus*, natural⟧ **1** unaffectedly simple **2** credulous —**na·ive'ly** or **na·ïve'ly** ***adv.*** —**na·ive·té'** or **na·ïve·té'** (-tā') ***n.***

na·ked (nā'kid) ***adj.*** ⟦OE *nacod*⟧ **1** completely unclothed; nude **2** without covering **3** without additions, disguises, etc.; plain *[*the *naked* truth*]* —**na'ked·ly** ***adv.*** —**na'ked·ness** ***n.***

nam·by-pam·by (nam'bē pam'bē) ***adj.*** ⟦18th-c. play on name *Ambrose*⟧ weak, insipid, indecisive, etc. —***n.***, *pl.* **-bies** a namby-pamby person

name (nām) ***n.*** ⟦OE *nama*⟧ **1** a word or phrase by which a person, thing, or class is known; title **2** a word or words considered descriptive; epithet, often an abusive one **3** reputation **4** appearance only, not reality *[*chief in *name* only*]* —***adj.*** well-known —***vt.*** **named, nam'ing** **1** to give a name to **2** to mention by name **3** to identify by the right name *[name* the oceans*]* **4** to appoint to an office, etc. **5** to specify (a date, price, etc.) —**in the name of** by the authority of

name'less ***adj.*** **1** not having a name **2** left unnamed **3** indescribable

name'ly ***adv.*** that is to say; to wit

name'sake' ***n.*** a person with the same name as another, esp. if named after the other

Na·mib·i·a (nə mib'ē ə) country in S Africa: 318,251 sq. mi.; pop. 1,402,000 —**Na·mib'i·an** ***adj.***, ***n.***

Nan·jing (nän'jiŋ') city in E China, on the Chang: pop. 2,091,000

Nan·king (nan'kiŋ', nän'-) *a former transliteration of* NANJING

nan·ny goat (nan'ē) ⟦< fem. name *Nan*⟧ a female goat

na·no·sec·ond (nan'ə sek'ənd) ***n.*** one billionth of a second

nap[1] (nap) ***vi.*** **napped, nap'ping** ⟦OE *hnappian*⟧ to sleep lightly for a short time —***n.*** a brief, light sleep

nap[2] (nap) ***n.*** ⟦ME *noppe*⟧ the downy or hairy surface of cloth or suede formed by short hairs or fibers —**nap'less** ***adj.***

na·palm (nā'päm') ***n.*** ⟦*na*(*phthene*) + *palm*(*itate*)⟧ a jellylike substance used in flame throwers and fire bombs —***vt.*** to attack or burn with napalm

nape (nāp) ***n.*** ⟦ME⟧ the back of the neck

naph·tha (naf'thə, nap'-) ***n.*** ⟦< Pers *neft*, pitch⟧ a flammable liquid distilled from petroleum, used as a fuel, solvent, etc.

naph'tha·lene' (-lēn') ***n.*** ⟦< prec.⟧ a white crystalline hydrocarbon distilled from coal tar, used in moth repellents, dyes, etc.

nap·kin (nap'kin) ***n.*** ⟦< L *mappa*⟧ **1** a small piece of cloth or paper used while eating to protect the clothes and wipe the lips **2** any small cloth, towel, etc.

Na·ples (nā'pəlz) seaport in S Italy: pop. 1,072,000

Na·po·le·on (nə pō'lē ən) *see* BONAPARTE, Napoleon

narc (närk) ***n.*** ⟦< NARC(OTIC)⟧ [Slang] a police agent who enforces laws dealing with narcotics

nar·cis·sism (när'sə siz'əm) ***n.*** ⟦< fol.⟧

self-love; specif., excessive interest in one's own appearance, comfort, etc. —**nar'cis·sist** *n.*, *adj.* —**nar'cis·sis'tic** *adj.*

Nar·cis·sus (när sis'əs) *n.* **1** *Gr. Myth.* a youth who falls in love with his reflection in a pool and changes into the narcissus **2** *pl.* **-cis'sus**, **-cis'sus·es**, or **-cis'si** (-ī) [**n-**] any of various bulb plants whose flowers have six parts and a cuplike or tubelike center

nar·co·sis (när kō'sis) *n.*, *pl.* **-ses'** (-sēz') unconsciousness caused by a narcotic

nar·cot·ic (när kät'ik) *n.* ⟦< Gr *narkē*, numbness⟧ a drug, as morphine, used to relieve pain and induce sleep: narcotics are often addictive —*adj.* of or having to do with narcotics

nar·co·tize (när'kə tīz') *vt.* **-tized'**, **-tiz'ing** to subject to a narcotic —**nar'co·ti·za'tion** *n.*

nark (närk) *n.* [Slang] *alt. sp. of* NARC

nar·rate (nar'āt', na rāt') *vt.*, *vi.* **-rat'ed**, **-rat'ing** ⟦< L *narrare*, tell⟧ to tell (a story), relate (events), etc.

nar·ra·tion (na rā'shən) *n.* **1** a narrating **2** a narrative

nar·ra·tive (nar'ə tiv) *adj.* in story form —*n.* **1** a story; account **2** the art or practice of narrating

nar·row (nar'ō) *adj.* ⟦OE *nearu*⟧ **1** small in width; not wide **2** limited in meaning, size, amount, etc. **3** limited in outlook; not liberal **4** with limited margin *[*a *narrow* escape*]* —*vi.*, *vt.* to decrease or limit in width, extent, etc. —*n.* [*usually pl.*] a narrow passage; strait

nar'row·cast' (-kast') *vt.*, *vi.* **-cast'**, **-cast'ing** to transmit by cable TV to a selected audience —*n.* a narrowcasting

nar'row-mind'ed *adj.* limited in outlook; bigoted; prejudiced —**nar'row-mind'ed·ness** *n.*

nar·whal (när'wəl) *n.* ⟦< ON *nahvalr*, lit., corpse whale⟧ a small arctic whale: the male has a long, spiral tusk

nar·y (ner'ē) *adj.* ⟦< *ne'er a*, never a⟧ [Dial.] not any; no: with *a* or *an [nary* a doubt*]*

NASA (nas'ə) *abbrev.* National Aeronautics and Space Administration

na·sal (nā'zəl) *adj.* ⟦< L *nasus*, nose⟧ **1** of the nose **2** uttered so that the breath passes through the nose

na'sal·ize' (-īz') *vt.*, *vi.* **-ized'**, **-iz'ing** to pronounce or speak with a nasal sound —**na'sal·i·za'tion** *n.*

NASCAR (nas'kär') *trademark for* National Association for Stock Car Auto Racing

nas·cent (nas'ənt, nā'sənt) *adj.* ⟦< L *nasci*, be born⟧ **1** coming into being **2** beginning to form or develop: said of ideas, etc.

Nash·ville (nash'vil) capital of Tennessee: pop. 511,000

nas·tur·tium (nə stur'shəm) *n.* ⟦< L *nasus*, nose + *torquere*, to twist: from its pungent odor⟧ **1** a plant with trumpet-shaped, red, yellow, or orange flowers **2** its flower

nas·ty (nas'tē) *adj.* **-ti·er**, **-ti·est** ⟦< ?⟧ **1** filthy **2** morally offensive **3** very unpleasant **4** mean; malicious —**nas'ti·ly** *adv.* —**nas'ti·ness** *n.*

na·tal (nāt''l) *adj.* ⟦< L *nasci*, be born⟧ of or relating to one's birth

na·tion (nā'shən) *n.* ⟦< L *natus*, born⟧ **1** a stable community of people with a territory, culture, and language in common **2** the people united under a single government; country

na·tion·al (nash'ə nəl) *adj.* of or affecting a nation as a whole —*n.* a citizen —**na'tion·al·ly** *adv.*

National Guard the organized militia forces of the individual U.S. states, part of the U.S. Army when called into active federal service

na'tion·al·ism' *n.* **1** devotion to one's nation; patriotism **2** the advocacy of national independence —**na'tion·al·ist** *n.*, *adj.* —**na'tion·al·is'tic** *adj.*

na'tion·al'i·ty (-nal'ə tē) *n.*, *pl.* **-ties** **1** the status of belonging to a nation by birth or naturalization **2** a national group, esp. of immigrants

na'tion·al·ize' (-nə līz') *vt.* **-ized'**, **-iz'ing** **1** to make national **2** to transfer ownership or control of (land, industries, etc.) to the government —**na'tion·al·i·za'tion** *n.*

na'tion·wide' *adj.* by or throughout the whole nation; national

na·tive (nāt'iv) *adj.* ⟦< L *natus*, born⟧ **1** inborn **2** belonging to a locality or country by birth, production, or growth **3** being, or connected with, the place of one's birth *[*one's *native* land or language*]* **4** as found in nature; natural **5** of or characteristic of the original inhabitants of a place —*n.* **1** a person born in the place indicated **2** an original inhabitant **3** an indigenous plant or animal

Native American AMERICAN INDIAN

na'tive-born' *adj.* of a specified place by birth

na·tiv·i·ty (nə tiv'ə tē) *n.*, *pl.* **-ties** ⟦see NATIVE⟧ birth —**the Nativity** the birth of Jesus

natl *abbrev.* national

NATO (nā'tō) *n.* North Atlantic Treaty Organization

nat·ty (nat'ē) *adj.* **-ti·er**, **-ti·est** ⟦< ? NEAT⟧ trim and stylish —**nat'ti·ly** *adv.*

nat·u·ral (nach'ər əl) *adj.* ⟦< L *naturalis*, by birth⟧ **1** of or dealing with nature **2** produced or existing in nature; not artificial **3** innate; not acquired **4** true to nature; lifelike **5** normal *[*a *natural* result*]* **6** free from affectation; at ease **7** *Music* neither sharped nor flatted —*n.* [Inf.] a person or thing sure to be successful

natural childbirth childbirth without anesthesia but with prior training

natural gas a mixture of gaseous hydrocarbons, chiefly methane, occurring naturally in the earth and used as fuel

natural history the study of the animal, vegetable, and mineral world

nat'u·ral·ism' *n.* **1** action or thought based on natural desires **2** *Literature, Art, etc.* the realistic portrayal of persons or things

nat′u·ral·ist *n.* one who studies animals and plants

nat′u·ral·ize′ (-īz′) *vt.* **-ized′, -iz′ing** to confer citizenship upon (an alien) —**nat′u·ral·i·za′tion** *n.*

nat′u·ral·ly *adv.* **1** in a natural manner **2** by nature; innately **3** of course

natural number any positive integer, as 1, 2, or 3

natural resource a form of wealth supplied by nature, as coal, oil, or water power

natural science the systematized knowledge of nature, including biology, chemistry, physics, etc.

natural selection the evolutionary process by which the most adaptable species survive

na·ture (nā′chər) *n.* ⟦< L *natus*, born⟧ **1** the essential quality of a thing; essence **2** inherent tendencies of a person **3** kind; type **4** *a)* the physical universe *b)* [*sometimes* **N-**] the power, force etc. that seems to regulate this **5** the primitive state of humans **6** natural scenery —**by nature** naturally; inherently

Naug·a·hyde (nôg′ə hīd′) ⟦arbitrary coinage⟧ *trademark for* an imitation leather, used for upholstery, luggage, etc. —*n.* [**n-**] this material

naught (nôt) *n.* ⟦OE *nawiht*⟧ **1** nothing **2** *alt. sp. of* NOUGHT

naugh·ty (nôt′ē) *adj.* **-ti·er, -ti·est** ⟦ME *naugti*⟧ **1** mischievous or disobedient **2** indelicate; improper —**naugh′ti·ly** *adv.* —**naugh′ti·ness** *n.*

Na·u·ru (nä o͞o′ro͞o) country on an island in the W Pacific, south of the equator: 8 sq. mi.; pop. 8,000

nau·sea (nô′shə, -zhə; -sē ə, -zē ə) *n.* ⟦< Gr *nausia*, seasickness⟧ **1** a sick feeling in the stomach, with an impulse to vomit **2** disgust; loathing

nau′se·ate′ (-shē āt′, -zhē-, -sē-, -zē-) *vt.* **-at′ed, -at′ing** to cause to feel nausea

nau·seous (nô′shəs, -zē əs, -sē-) *adj.* **1** causing nausea **2** feeling nausea; nauseated: usage objected to by some

nau·ti·cal (nôt′i kəl) *adj.* ⟦< Gr *naus*, ship⟧ of sailors, ships, or navigation —**nau′ti·cal·ly** *adv.*

nautical mile a unit of linear measure used in navigation, equal to 1.1508 miles or 1,852 meters

nau·ti·lus (nôt′'l əs) *n., pl.* **-lus·es** or **-li′** (-ī′) ⟦< Gr *naus*, a ship⟧ a tropical mollusk with a spiral shell divided into many chambers —[**N-**] *trademark for* a type of mechanical weight-lifting equipment

Nav·a·jo (nav′ə hō′) *n. pl.* **-jos′, -jo′,** or **-joes′** a member of a North American Indian people of the SW U.S.: also sp. **Nav′a·ho′**

na·val (nā′vəl) *adj.* ⟦< L *navis*, a ship⟧ of, having, characteristic of, or for a navy, its ships, etc.

nave (nāv) *n.* ⟦< L *navis*, a ship⟧ the main part of a church, from the chancel to the principal entrance

na·vel (nā′vəl) *n.* ⟦OE *nafela*⟧ the small scar in the abdomen marking the place where the umbilical cord was attached to the fetus

navel orange a seedless orange with a navel-like hollow at its apex

nav·i·ga·ble (nav′i gə bəl) *adj.* **1** wide or deep enough for the passage of ships **2** that can be steered —**nav′i·ga·bil′i·ty** *n.*

nav·i·gate (nav′ə gāt′) *vt., vi.* **-gat′ed, -gat′ing** ⟦< L *navis*, a ship + *agere*, to lead⟧ **1** to steer or direct (a ship or aircraft) **2** to travel through or over (water, air, etc.) in a ship or aircraft **3** [Inf.] to walk or make one's way (on or through)

nav′i·ga′tion (-gā′shən) *n.* **1** the science of locating the position and plotting the course of ships and aircraft **2** traffic by ship

nav′i·ga′tor *n.* one skilled or employed in the navigation of a ship or aircraft

na·vy (nā′vē) *n., pl.* **-vies** ⟦< L *navis*, a ship⟧ **1** all the warships of a nation **2** [*often* **N-**] a nation's entire military sea force, including ships, personnel, stores, etc. **3** NAVY BLUE

navy bean ⟦from use in U.S. *Navy*⟧ a small white variety of kidney bean

navy blue very dark, purplish blue

nay (nā) *adv.* ⟦< ON *ne*, not + *ei*, ever⟧ **1** no: now used only in voice votes **2** not that only, but also [*I permit, nay encourage it*] —*n.* **1** a denial **2** a negative vote or a person voting negatively

nay·say·er (nā′sā′ər) *n.* one who opposes, refuses, or denies, esp. habitually

Na·zi (nät′sē) *adj.* ⟦Ger contr. of the party name⟧ designating or of the German fascist political party which ruled Germany under Hitler (1933-45) —*n.* a member of this party

NB New Brunswick

n.b. *abbrev.* ⟦L *nota bene*⟧ note well: also **NB**

NC North Carolina

NCO *abbrev.* noncommissioned officer

NC-17 *trademark for* a film rating indicating that no one under 17 may be admitted

ND North Dakota

Ne *Chem. symbol for* neon

NE *abbrev.* **1** Nebraska **2** northeast **3** northeastern

Ne·an·der·thal (nē an′dər thôl′) *adj.* ⟦after a Ger valley⟧ **1** designating or of a widespread form of early human being of the Pleistocene Epoch **2** primitive or regressive —*n.* **1** a Neanderthal human being **2** one who is crude, primitive, etc.

neap (nēp) *adj.* ⟦OE *nep-* in *nepflod*, neap tide⟧ designating either of the two lowest high tides in the month —*n.* neap tide

Ne·a·pol·i·tan (nē′ə päl′ə tən) *adj.* of Naples —*n.* a person born or living in Naples

Neapolitan ice cream brick ice cream in layers of different flavors and colors

near (nir) *adv.* ⟦OE compar. of *neah*, nigh⟧ **1** at a short distance in space or time **2** closely; intimately —*adj.* **1** close in distance or time **2** close in relationship; akin **3** close in friendship **4** close in degree *[a near escape]* **5** short or direct *[the near way]* —***prep.*** close to —***vt.**, **vi.*** to draw near (to); approach —**near′ness *n.***

near′by′ ***adj.**, **adv.*** near; close at hand

Near East countries near the E end of the Mediterranean, including those of SW Asia, the Arabian Peninsula, & NE Africa

near′ly ***adv.*** almost; not quite

near miss **1** a result that is nearly but not quite successful **2** a near escape

near′sight′ed ***adj.*** having better vision for near objects than for objects that are distant; myopic —**near′sight′ed·ness *n.***

neat (nēt) ***adj.*** ⟦< L *nitere*, to shine⟧ **1** unmixed; undiluted *[whiskey neat]* **2** clean and tidy **3** skillful and precise **4** well-proportioned **5** cleverly said or done **6** [Slang] nice, pleasing, etc. —**neat′ly *adv.*** —**neat′ness *n.***

neat′en ***vt.*** to make clean, tidy, orderly, etc.: often with *up*

'neath or **neath** (nēth) ***prep.*** [Old Poet.] *short for* BENEATH

neb·bish (neb′ish) ***n.*** ⟦< Yiddish *nebekh*, pity⟧ one who is pitifully inept, shy, dull, etc.

Ne·bras·ka (nə bras′kə) Midwestern state of the U.S.: 76,878 sq. mi.; pop. 1,578,000; cap. Lincoln: abbrev. *NE* —**Ne·bras′kan *adj.**, **n.***

neb·u·la (neb′yə lə) ***n.**, pl.* **-lae′** (-lē′) or **-las** ⟦L, mist⟧ a cloud of interstellar gas or dust, or, formerly, any hazy, distant celestial object, as a star cluster —**neb′u·lar *adj.***

neb′u·lous (-ləs) ***adj.*** unclear; vague

nec·es·sar·i·ly (nes′ə ser′ə lē) ***adv.*** **1** because of necessity **2** as a necessary result

nec′es·sar′y (-ser′ē) ***adj.*** ⟦< L *ne-*, not + *cedere*, give way⟧ **1** essential; indispensable **2** inevitable **3** required —***n.**, pl.* **-sar′ies** something necessary

ne·ces·si·tate (nə ses′ə tāt′) ***vt.*** **-tat′ed, -tat′ing** to make necessary or unavoidable

ne·ces′si·ty (-tē) ***n.**, pl.* **-ties** ⟦see NECESSARY⟧ **1** natural causation; fate **2** great need **3** something that cannot be done without —**of necessity** necessarily

neck (nek) ***n.*** ⟦OE *hnecca*⟧ **1** that part of a human or animal joining the head to the body **2** the part of a garment near the neck **3** a necklike part; specif., *a)* a narrow strip of land *b)* the narrowest part of a bottle, etc. *c)* a strait —***vt.**, **vi.*** [Slang] to hug, kiss, and caress passionately —**neck and neck** very close, as in a race

neck·er·chief (nek′ər chif, -chēf′) ***n.*** ⟦see prec. & KERCHIEF⟧ a handkerchief or scarf worn around the neck

neck′lace (-lis) ***n.*** ⟦NECK + LACE⟧ an ornamental string of beads, chain of gold, etc., worn around the neck

neck′tie′ ***n.*** a band worn around the neck under a collar and tied in front

neck′wear′ ***n.*** articles worn about the neck, as neckties or scarves

ne·crol·o·gy (ne kräl′ə jē) ***n.**, pl.* **-gies**

⟦ult. < Gr *nekros*, corpse + -LOGY⟧ a list of people who have died

nec·ro·man·cy (nek′rə man′sē) ***n.*** ⟦< Gr *nekros*, corpse + *manteia*, divination⟧ **1** divination by alleged communication with the dead **2** black magic; sorcery —**nec′ro·man′cer *n.***

ne·cro·sis (ne krō′sis) ***n.**, pl.* **-ses′** (-sēz′) ⟦< Gr *nekros*, corpse⟧ the death or decay of tissue in a part of the body

nec·tar (nek′tər) ***n.*** ⟦< Gr *nektar*⟧ **1** *Gr. & Rom. Myth.* the drink of the gods **2** any very delicious beverage **3** the sweetish liquid in many flowers, used by bees to make honey

nec·tar·ine (nek′tə rēn′, nek′tə rēn′) ***n.*** ⟦< prec.⟧ a kind of smooth-skinned peach

nee or **née** (nā; *now often* nē) ***adj.*** ⟦Fr⟧ born *[Mrs. Helen Jones, nee Smith]*

need (nēd) ***n.*** ⟦OE *nied*⟧ **1** necessity **2** a lack of something useful, required, or desired *[to have need of a rest]* **3** something required or desired that is lacking *[your daily needs]* **4** *a)* a condition in which help is required *[a friend in need]* *b)* poverty —***vt.*** **1** to have need of; require **2** to be obliged; must *[she needs to be careful]* —***vi.*** to be in need —**have need to** to be required to —**if need be** if it is required

need′ful ***adj.*** necessary; required

nee·dle (nēd′'l) ***n.*** ⟦OE *nædl*⟧ **1** a small, slender, pointed piece of steel with a hole for thread, used for sewing **2** a slender rod of steel, bone, etc. used for crocheting or knitting **3** STYLUS (sense 2*b*) **4** the pointer of a compass, gauge, etc. **5** the thin, short, pointed leaf of the pine, spruce, etc. **6** the sharp, slender metal tube at the end of a hypodermic syringe —***vt.*** **-dled, -dling** [Inf.] **1** to goad; prod **2** to tease —**nee′dler *n.***

nee′dle·point′ ***n.*** **1** embroidery of woolen threads upon canvas **2** lace made on a paper pattern, with a needle: in full **needlepoint lace**

need′less ***adj.*** not needed; unnecessary *[needless cruelty]* —**need′less·ly *adv.***

nee′dle·work′ ***n.*** work done with a needle; embroidery, crocheting, sewing, etc.

need·n't (nēd′'nt) *contr.* need not

needs (nēdz) ***adv.*** ⟦OE *nedes*⟧ of necessity: with *must [he must needs obey]*

need′y ***adj.*** **-i·er, -i·est** very poor —**need′i·ness *n.***

ne'er (ner) ***adv.*** [Old Poet.] never

ne'er′-do-well′ ***n.*** a shiftless, irresponsible person

ne·far·i·ous (nə fer′ē əs) ***adj.*** ⟦< L *ne-*, not + *fas*, lawful⟧ very wicked; villainous —**ne·far′i·ous·ly *adv.*** —**ne·far′i·ous·ness *n.***

ne·gate (ni gāt′) ***vt.*** **-gat′ed, -gat′ing** ⟦< L *negare*, deny⟧ **1** to deny **2** to make ineffective

ne·ga·tion (ni gā′shən) ***n.*** **1** the act or an instance of denying **2** the lack or opposite of something positive

neg·a·tive (neg′ə tiv) ***adj.*** **1** expressing denial or refusal; saying "no" **2** opposite to or lacking in that which is positive *[a negative force]* **3** *Math.* designating a quantity less than zero, or one to be subtracted **4** *Med.* not showing the presence of a condition, infection, etc. **5** *Photog.* reversing the relation of light and shade of the subject **6** *Elec. a)* of, generating, or charged with negative electricity *b)* having an excess of electrons **—*n.*** **1** a negative word, reply, etc. **2** the point of view that opposes the positive **3** the plate in a battery having an excess of electrons flowing out toward the positive **4** an exposed and developed photographic film or plate on which light and shadow are reversed **—in the negative** with a negative answer **—neg'a·tive·ly *adv.*** **—neg'a·tiv'i·ty *n.***

ne·glect (ni glekt') ***vt.*** ⟦< L *neg-*, not + *legere*, gather⟧ **1** to ignore or disregard **2** to fail to attend to properly **3** to leave undone **—*n.*** **1** a neglecting **2** lack of proper care **3** the state of being neglected **—ne·glect'ful *adj.***

neg·li·gee (neg'lə zhā') ***n.*** ⟦< Fr *négliger*, to neglect⟧ a woman's loosely fitting dressing gown

neg·li·gent (neg'lə jənt) ***adj.*** **1** habitually failing to do the required thing; neglectful **2** careless, inattentive, etc. **—neg'li·gence *n.***

neg'li·gi·ble (-jə bəl) ***adj.*** that can be neglected or disregarded; trifling

ne·go·ti·ate (ni gō'shē āt') ***vi.*** **-at'ed, -at'ing** ⟦< L *negotium*, business⟧ to discuss a matter with a view to reaching agreement **—*vt.*** **1** to settle (a business transaction, treaty, etc.) **2** to transfer or sell (bonds, stocks, etc.) **3** to succeed in crossing, passing, etc. **—ne·go'ti·a·ble** (-shē ə bəl, -shə bəl) ***adj.*** **—ne·go'ti·a'tion *n.*** **—ne·go'ti·a'tor *n.***

neg·ri·tude (neg'rə to͞od', nē'grə-) ***n.*** ⟦Fr *négritude*⟧ [*also* **N-**] an awareness and affirmation by black people of their distinctive cultural heritage

Ne·gro (nē'grō) ***n.***, *pl.* **-groes** ⟦Sp & Port *negro*, black⟧ **1** a member of any of the indigenous dark-skinned peoples of Africa **2** a person having some African ancestors; a black person **—*adj.*** of or for Negroes

Ne'groid' (-groid') ***adj.*** designating or of one of the major groups of human beings, including most of the peoples of Africa

Neh·ru (nā'ro͞o), **Ja·wa·har·lal** (jə wä'hər läl') 1889-1964; prime minister of India (1947-64)

neigh (nā) ***vi.*** ⟦OE *hnægan*⟧ to utter the characteristic cry of a horse **—*n.*** this cry; a whinny

neigh·bor (nā'bər) ***n.*** ⟦OE *neah*, nigh + *gebur*, freeholder⟧ **1** one who lives or is situated near another **2** a fellow human being **—*vt.*, *vi.*** to live or be situated near (someone or something) Brit. sp. **neigh'bour** **—neigh'bor·ing *adj.***

neigh'bor·hood' ***n.*** **1** a particular community, district, or area **2** the people living near one another **—in the neighborhood of** [Inf.] **1** near **2** about; approximately

neigh'bor·ly *adj.* like or appropriate to neighbors; friendly, helpful, etc. **—neigh'bor·li·ness *n.***

nei·ther (nē'thər, nī'-) ***adj.*, *pron.*** ⟦OE *na-hwæther*, lit., not whether⟧ not one or the other (of two); not either *[neither boy went; neither of them was invited]* **—*conj.*** not either *[I could neither laugh nor cry]*

nem·a·tode (nem'ə tōd') ***n.*** ⟦ult. < Gr *nēma*, thread⟧ a long, cylindrical, unsegmented worm; roundworm

nem·e·sis (nem'ə sis) ***n.***, *pl.* **-ses'** (-sēz') ⟦< Gr *nemein*, deal out⟧ **1** *a)* just punishment *b)* one who imposes this **2** anyone or anything that seems inevitably to defeat or frustrate someone

neo- ⟦< Gr *neos*⟧ *combining form* [*often* **N-**] **1** new, recent **2** in a new or different way

ne·o·clas·sic (nē'ō klas'ik) ***adj.*** designating or of a revival of classic style and form in art, literature, etc.: also **ne'o·clas'si·cal** **—ne'o·clas'si·cism' *n.***

ne'o·co·lo'ni·al·ism' *n.* exploitation by a foreign power of a region that has ostensibly achieved independence

ne·ol·o·gism (nē äl'ə jiz'əm) ***n.*** ⟦see NEO-, -LOGY, & -ISM⟧ a new word or a new meaning for an established word

ne·on (nē'än') ***n.*** ⟦ult. < Gr *neos*, new⟧ a nonreactive, gaseous chemical element found in small amounts in the earth's atmosphere

ne·o·nate (nē'ō nāt') ***n.*** ⟦ModL < *neo-*, NEO- + L *natus*, born⟧ a newborn infant **—ne'o·na'tal *adj.***

neon lamp a tube containing neon, which glows red when an electric current is sent through it

ne·o·phyte (nē'ō fīt') ***n.*** ⟦< Gr *neos*, new + *phyein*, to produce⟧ **1** a new convert **2** a beginner; novice

ne·o·plasm (nē'ō plaz'əm) ***n.*** ⟦< NEO- + Gr *plassein*, to form⟧ an abnormal growth of tissue, as a tumor

ne'o·prene' (-prēn') ***n.*** a synthetic rubber resistant to oil, heat, etc.

Ne·pal (nə pôl', -päl') country in the Himalayas: 56,827 sq. mi.; pop. 18,462,000 **—Nep·a·lese** (nep'ə lēz') ***adj.*, *n.***

neph·ew (nef'yo͞o) ***n.*** ⟦< L *nepos*⟧ the son of one's brother or sister, or of one's brother-in-law or sister-in-law

ne·phri·tis (nə frīt'əs) ***n.*** ⟦< Gr *nephros*, kidney + -ITIS⟧ a disease of the kidneys, characterized by inflammation

ne·phro·sis (nə frō'sis) ***n.*** ⟦< Gr *nephros*, kidney + -OSIS⟧ a degenerative disease of the kidneys, characterized by edema

ne plus ul·tra (nā plus ul'trə) ⟦L, no more beyond⟧ the ultimate

nep·o·tism (nep'ə tiz'əm) ***n.*** ⟦< L *nepos*, nephew⟧ favoritism shown to relatives, esp. in providing jobs **—nep'o·tis'tic *adj.***

Nep·tune (nep'to͞on') ***n.*** **1** the Roman god of the sea **2** the planet eighth in distance from the sun: see PLANET

nep·tu·ni·um (nep to͞o'nē əm) ***n.*** ⟦after prec.⟧ a radioactive chemical element produced by irradiating uranium atoms

nerd (nurd) ***n.*** [Slang] a person regarded as dull, ineffective, etc. **—nerd'y *adj.***

Ne·ro (nir'ō) A.D. 37-68; emperor of

Rome (54-68)

nerve (nurv) ***n.*** ⟦< L *nervus*⟧ **1** any of the cordlike fibers carrying impulses between body organs and the central nervous system **2** coolness in danger; courage **3** [*pl.*] nervousness **4** [Inf.] impudent boldness —***vt.*** **nerved, nerv′ing** to give strength or courage to —**get on someone's nerves** [Inf.] to make someone irritable or exasperated

nerve center a control center; headquarters

nerve gas a poisonous gas causing paralysis of the respiratory and nervous systems

nerve′less ***adj.*** **1** without strength, vigor, etc.; weak **2** not nervous; cool; controlled —**nerve′less·ly** ***adv.***

nerve′-rack′ing or **nerve′-wrack′ing** (-rak′iŋ) ***adj.*** very trying to one's patience or equanimity

nerv·ous (nur′vəs) ***adj.*** **1** animated **2** of or made up of nerves **3** emotionally tense, restless, etc. **4** fearful — **nerv′ous·ly** ***adv.*** —**nerv′ous·ness** ***n.***

nervous system all the nerve cells and nervous tissues in an organism, including, in the vertebrates, the brain, spinal cord, nerves, etc.

nerv′y ***adj.*** **-i·er, -i·est** **1** bold **2** [Inf.] brazen; impudent

-ness (nis, nəs) ⟦OE *-nes(s)*⟧ *suffix* state, quality, or instance of being *[togetherness, sadness]*

nest (nest) ***n.*** ⟦OE⟧ **1** the structure or place where a bird lays its eggs and shelters its young **2** the place used by insects, fish, etc. for spawning or breeding **3** a cozy place; retreat **4** *a)* a haunt or den *b)* the people who frequent such a place *[a nest of thieves]* **5** a set of things, each fitting within the one next larger —***vi., vt.*** **1** to build or settle in (a nest) **2** to fit (an object) closely within another

nest egg money, etc. put aside as a reserve or to establish a fund

nes·tle (nes′əl) ***vi.*** **-tled, -tling** ⟦OE *nestlian*⟧ **1** to settle down comfortably **2** to press close for comfort or in affection **3** to lie sheltered —***vt.*** to cause to rest snugly

nest·ling (nest′liŋ) ***n.*** a young bird not yet ready to leave the nest

net[1] (net) ***n.*** ⟦OE *nett*⟧ **1** a loose fabric of woven or knotted string, etc., used to snare birds, fish, etc. **2** a trap; snare **3** a loose fabric of woven or knotted threads, etc., esp. one used to hold, protect, etc. *[a hairnet]* **4** [*usually* **N-**] [Inf.] *Comput. short for* INTERNET: with *the* —***vt.*** **net′ted, net′ting** to snare or enclose, as with a net

net[2] (net) ***adj.*** ⟦Fr, clear⟧ remaining after deductions or allowances have been made —***n.*** a net amount, profit, weight, price, etc. —***vt.*** **net′ted, net′ting** to clear as profit, etc.

neth·er (ne*th*′ər) ***adj.*** ⟦OE *neothera*⟧ lower or under *[the nether world]*

Neth·er·lands (ne*th*′ər ləndz) country in W Europe: 16,033 sq. mi.; pop. 15,340,000: usually used with *the* — **Neth′er·land′er** (-land′ər, -lən dər) ***n.***

neth′er·most′ ***adj.*** lowest

net′ting ***n.*** NET[1] (*n.* 1 & 3)

net·tle (net′'l) ***n.*** ⟦OE *netele*⟧ a weed with stinging hairs —***vt.*** **-tled, -tling** to irritate; annoy; vex

net′tle·some (-səm) ***adj.*** that nettles, or irritates

net′work′ ***n.*** **1** an arrangement of parallel wires, etc. crossed at intervals by others so as to leave open spaces **2** anything like this, as a system of interconnected roads, individuals, or computer terminals **3** *Radio, TV* a chain of transmitting stations —***adj.*** broadcast over the stations of a network

net′work′ing ***n.*** **1** the developing of contacts or exchanging of information, as to further a career **2** the interconnection of computer systems

neu·ral (noor′əl) ***adj.*** ⟦NEUR(O)- + -AL⟧ of a nerve, nerves, or the nervous system

neu·ral·gi·a (noo ral′jə) ***n.*** ⟦see NEURO- & -ALGIA⟧ severe pain along a nerve — **neu·ral′gic** (-jik) ***adj.***

neu·ras·the·ni·a (noor′əs thē′nē ə) ***n.*** ⟦< NEURO- + Gr *asthenia*, weakness⟧ a former category of mental disorder, characterized by fatigue, anxiety, etc. —**neu′ras·then′ic** (-then′ik) ***adj., n.***

neu·ri·tis (noo rīt′əs) ***n.*** ⟦fol. + -ITIS⟧ inflammation of a nerve or nerves — **neu·rit′ic** (-rit′ik) ***adj.***

neuro- ⟦< Gr *neuron*, nerve⟧ *combining form* of a nerve or the nervous system: also **neur-**

neu·rol·o·gy (noo räl′ə jē) ***n.*** ⟦prec. + -LOGY⟧ the branch of medicine dealing with the nervous system and its diseases —**neu·ro·log·i·cal** (noor′ə läj′i kəl) ***adj.*** —**neu·rol′o·gist** ***n.***

neu·ro·mus·cu·lar (noor′ō mus′kyoo lər) ***adj.*** of or involving both nerves and muscles

neu·ron (noor′än′) ***n.*** the nerve cell body and all its processes

neu·ro·sis (noo rō′sis) ***n., pl.*** **-ses′** (-sēz′) ⟦NEUR(O)- + -OSIS⟧ any of various mental disorders characterized by anxiety, compulsions, phobias, etc.

neu·ro·sur·ger·y (noor′ō sur′jər ē) ***n.*** the branch of surgery involving the brain or spinal cord —**neu′ro·sur′geon** ***n.***

neu·rot·ic (noo rät′ik) ***adj.*** of, characteristic of, or having a neurosis —***n.*** a neurotic person —**neu·rot′i·cal·ly** ***adv.***

neu·ro·trans·mit·ter (noor′ō trans′mit′ər) ***n.*** a biochemical substance that transmits or inhibits nerve impulses at a synapse

neu·ter (noot′ər) ***adj.*** ⟦< L *ne-*, not + *uter*, either⟧ **1** *Biol. a)* having no sexual organ *b)* having undeveloped sexual organs in the adult **2** *Gram.* designating or of the gender of words that are neither masculine nor feminine — ***vt.*** to castrate or spay (an animal)

neu·tral (noo′trəl) ***adj.*** ⟦see prec.⟧ **1** supporting neither side in a quarrel or war **2** of neither extreme in type, kind, etc.; indefinite **3** having little or no decided color; not vivid —***n.*** **1** a neutral person or nation **2** a neutral color **3** *Mech.* a disengaged position of gears —

neu′tral·ly *adv.*

neu′tral·ism′ (-iz′əm) *n.* a policy of remaining neutral, esp. in international conflicts —**neu′tral·ist** *adj., n.*

neu·tral′i·ty (-tral′ə tē) *n.* **1** a being neutral **2** the status or policy of a neutral nation

neu·tral·ize (nōō′trə līz′) *vt.* **-ized′**, **-iz′ing** to destroy or counteract the effectiveness, force, etc. of —**neu′tral·i·za′tion** *n.* —**neu′tral·iz′er** *n.*

neutral spirits ethyl alcohol of 190 proof or over, used in blended whiskeys, liqueurs, etc.

neu·tri·no (nōō trē′nō) *n., pl.* **-nos** ⟦It, little neutron⟧ any of three leptons having almost no mass

neu·tron (nōō′trän′) *n.* ⟦< NEUTRAL⟧ an elementary particle in the nucleus of an atom, carrying no electrical charge

neutron bomb a small thermonuclear bomb that would release large numbers of neutrons intended to kill enemy soldiers without destroying buildings, etc.

neutron star a collapsed star of extremely high density composed almost entirely of neutrons

Ne·vad·a (nə vad′ə, -väd′ə) Mountain State of the W U.S.: 109,806 sq. mi.; pop. 1,202,000; cap. Carson City: abbrev. *NV* —**Ne·vad′an** *adj., n.*

nev·er (nev′ər) *adv.* ⟦< OE *ne*, not + *æfre*, ever⟧ **1** not ever; at no time **2** not at all; in no case

nev′er·more′ *adv.* never again

nev′er-nev′er land an unreal or unrealistic place or situation

nev′er·the·less′ (-*th*ə les′) *adv.* in spite of that; however

Ne·vis (nē′vis, nev′is) island of the West Indies: see ST. KITTS AND NEVIS

ne·vus (nē′vəs) *n., pl.* **ne′vi′** (-vī′) ⟦< L *naevus*⟧ a birthmark or mole

new (nōō) *adj.* ⟦OE *niwe*⟧ **1** appearing, thought of, developed, made, etc. for the first time **2** different from (the) one in the past *[a new hairdo]* **3** strange; unfamiliar **4** *a)* recently grown; fresh *b)* harvested early *[new potatoes]* **5** unused **6** modern; recent **7** more; additional **8** starting as a repetition of a cycle, series, etc. *[the new moon]* **9** having just reached a position, rank, etc. *[a new arrival]* —*adv.* **1** again **2** recently —**new′ness** *n.*

New Age [*often* **n- a-**] of or pertaining to a cultural movement variously combining belief in reincarnation, astrology, meditation, etc.

New·ark (nōō′ərk) city in NE New Jersey: pop. 275,000

new blood new people as a potential source of new ideas, vigor, etc.

new′born′ *adj.* **1** recently born **2** reborn —*n.* a newborn infant

New Bruns·wick (brunz′wik) province of SE Canada: 28,354 sq. mi.; pop. 738,000; cap. Fredericton: abbrev. *NB*

new′com′er (-kum′ər) *n.* a recent arrival

New Deal the principles and policies adopted by President F. D. Roosevelt in the 1930s to advance economic recovery and social welfare

New Delhi capital of India, adjacent to the old city of Delhi: pop. 301,000

new·el (nōō′əl) *n.* ⟦ult. < L *nux*, nut⟧ **1** the pillar around which the steps of a winding staircase turn **2** the post that supports the handrail of a flight of stairs: also **newel post**

New England the six NE states of the U.S.: Maine, Vermont, New Hampshire, Massachusetts, Rhode Island, and Connecticut —**New Eng′land·er**

new′fan′gled (-faŋ′gəld) *adj.* ⟦ME *newe*, new + *-fangel* < OE *fon*, to take⟧ new; novel: a humorously derogatory term

new′found′ (-found′) *adj.* newly gained or acquired

New·found·land and Labrador (nōō′fənd lənd, -land′) province of Canada, including an island off the E coast & Labrador: 143,501 sq. mi.; pop. 552,000; cap. St. John's: abbrev. *Nfld & Lab*

New Guinea large island in the East Indies, north of Australia

New Hamp·shire (hamp′shir) New England state of the U.S.: 8,993 sq. mi.; pop. 1,109,000; cap. Concord: abbrev. *NH* —**New Hamp′shir·ite′**

New Ha·ven (hā′vən) city in S Connecticut: pop. 130,000

New Jer·sey (jur′zē) state of the E U.S.: 7,417 sq. mi.; pop. 7,730,000; cap. Trenton: abbrev. *NJ* —**New Jer′sey·ite′**

new′ly *adv.* recently; lately

new′ly·wed′ *n.* a recently married person

New Mexico Mountain State of the SW U.S.: 121,335 sq. mi.; pop. 1,515,000; cap. Santa Fe: abbrev. *NM* —**New Mexican**

new moon the moon when it is between the earth and the sun, with its dark side toward the earth: it is followed by a thin crescent phase

New Or·le·ans (ôr′lē ənz, -lənz; ôr lēnz′) city & port in SE Louisiana: pop. 497,000

New·port News (nōō′pôrt′) seaport in SE Virginia: pop. 171,000

news (nōōz) *n.* **1** new information; information previously unknown **2** *a)* recent happenings *b)* reports of these **3** *short for* NEWSCAST —**make news** to do something apt to be reported as news

news′boy′ *n.* a boy who sells or delivers newspapers

news′cast′ *n.* a radio or television news broadcast —**news′cast′er** *n.*

news′deal′er *n.* a retailer of newspapers, magazines, etc.

news′let′ter *n.* a bulletin issued regularly to subscribers, employees, club members, etc., containing news of upcoming events, etc.

news′man′ (-man′, -mən) *n., pl.* **-men′** (-men′, -mən) a newscaster or reporter, esp. a male

news′pa′per *n.* a regular publication, usually daily or weekly, containing news, opinions, advertising, etc.

news′pa′per·man′ (-man′) *n., pl.* **-men′**

(-men′) **1** a person, esp. a man, who works for a newspaper as a reporter, editor, etc. **2** a newspaper owner or publisher —**news′pa′per·wom′an**, *pl.* **-wom′en**, ***fem.n.***

news′print′ ***n.*** a cheap, low-grade paper used chiefly for newspapers

news′stand′ ***n.*** a stand at which newspapers, magazines, etc. are sold

news′wom′an ***n.***, *pl.* **-wom′en** a female newscaster or reporter

news′wor′thy (-wur′*th*ē) ***adj.*** timely and important or interesting

news′y ***adj.*** **-i·er, -i·est** [Inf.] containing much news

newt (no͞ot) ***n.*** ⟦by merging of ME (*a*)*n eute*, a newt⟧ any of various small, amphibious salamanders

New Testament the part of the Bible that contains the life and teachings of Jesus and his followers

new·ton (no͞ot′'n) ***n.*** ⟦after fol.⟧ a unit of force

New·ton (no͞ot′'n), Sir **Isaac** 1642-1727; Eng. mathematician & natural philosopher

New World the Western Hemisphere

New Year's (Day) Jan. 1

New Year's Eve the evening before New Year's Day

New York (yôrk) **1** state of the NE U.S.: 47,224 sq. mi.; pop. 17,990,000; cap. Albany: abbrev. *NY* **2** city & port in SE New York: pop. 7,323,000 (met. area, 8,547,000): often **New York City** —**New York′er**

New Zea·land (zē′lənd) country made up of two large islands in the S Pacific, southeast of Australia: 104,454 sq. mi.; pop. 3,435,000 —**New Zea′land·er**

next (nekst) ***adj.*** ⟦OE *neahst*, superl. of *neah*, nigh⟧ nearest; immediately preceding or following —***adv.*** **1** in the nearest time, place, rank, etc. **2** on the first subsequent occasion

next′-door′ ***adj.*** in or at the next house, building, etc.

nex·us (nek′səs) ***n.***, *pl.* **nex′us·es** or **nex′us** ⟦L⟧ a connection, tie, or link

Nfld & Lab Newfoundland and Labrador

NH New Hampshire

Ni *Chem. symbol for* nickel

ni·a·cin (nī′ə sin) ***n.*** ⟦NI(COTINIC) AC(ID) + *-in*⟧ NICOTINIC ACID

Ni·ag·ara Falls (nī ag′rə) large waterfall on a river (**Niagara**) flowing from Lake Erie into Lake Ontario

nib (nib) ***n.*** ⟦< ME *nebb*, a bird's beak⟧ a point, esp. a pen point

nib·ble (nib′əl) ***vt.***, ***vi.*** **-bled, -bling** ⟦ME *nebyllen*⟧ **1** to eat (food) with quick, small bites **2** to bite (*at*) lightly and intermittently —***n.*** a small bite —**nib′bler** ***n.***

nibs (nibz) ***n.*** ⟦< ?⟧ [Inf.] a self-important person: preceded by *his* or *her*

Nic·a·ra·gua (nik′ə rä′gwə) country in Central America: 50,452 sq. mi.; pop. 4,395,000 —**Nic′a·ra′guan** ***adj.***, ***n.***

nice (nīs) ***adj.*** **nic′er, nic′est** ⟦< L *nescius*, ignorant⟧ **1** fastidious; refined **2** delicate; precise; subtle [a *nice* distinction]

3 calling for care, tact, etc. **4** pleasant, attractive, kind, good, etc.: a generalized term of approval —**nice′ly** ***adv.*** —**nice′ness** ***n.***

ni·ce·ty (nī′sə tē) ***n.***, *pl.* **-ties** **1** precision; accuracy **2** fastidiousness; refinement **3** a subtle or minute detail, distinction, etc.

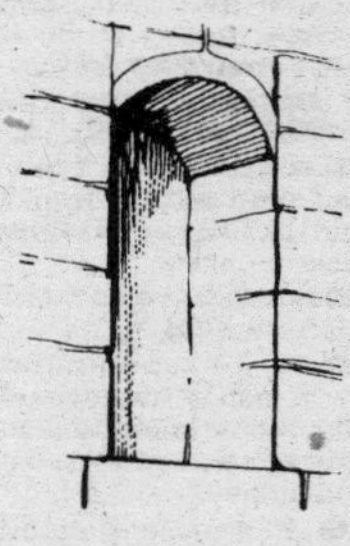

NICHE

niche (nich) ***n.*** ⟦Fr < L *nidus*, a nest⟧ **1** a recess in a wall, for a statue, vase, etc. **2** an especially suitable place or position **3** a specialized business market

nicht wahr? (niHt vär′) ⟦Ger, not true?⟧ isn't that so?

nick (nik) ***n.*** ⟦ME *nyke*⟧ a small cut, chip, etc. made on a surface —***vt.*** **1** to make a nick or nicks in **2** to wound superficially —**in the nick of time** exactly when needed

nick·el (nik′əl) ***n.*** ⟦< Ger *kupfernickel*, copper devil: the copperlike ore contains no copper⟧ **1** a hard, silver-white, metallic chemical element, much used in alloys **2** a U.S. or Canadian coin of nickel and copper, equal to five cents

nick·el·o·de·on (nik′əl ō′dē ən) ***n.*** ⟦prec. + (*mel*)*odeon*, a small keyboard organ⟧ a coin-operated player piano or early type of jukebox

nick·er (nik′ər) ***vi.***, ***n.*** NEIGH

nick·name (nik′nām′) ***n.*** ⟦by merging of ME (*a*)*n ekename*, a surname⟧ **1** a substitute, often descriptive, name given in fun, etc., as "Shorty" **2** a familiar form of a proper name, as "Dick" for "Richard" —***vt.*** **-named′, -nam′ing** to give a nickname to

nic·o·tine (nik′ə tēn′) ***n.*** ⟦Fr, after J. *Nicot*, 16th-c. Fr diplomat who introduced tobacco into France⟧ a toxic alkaloid found in tobacco leaves

nic′o·tin′ic acid (-tin′ik) a white, crystalline substance, a member of the vitamin B complex

niece (nēs) ***n.*** ⟦< L *neptis*⟧ the daughter of one's brother or sister or of one's brother-in-law or sister-in-law

Nie·tzsche (nē′chə), **Fried·rich** (frē′driH) 1844-1900; Ger. philosopher

nif·ty (nif′tē) ***adj.*** **-ti·er, -ti·est** ⟦prob. < *magnificent*⟧ [Slang] attractive, smart, stylish, etc.

Ni·ger (nī′jər) country in WC Africa,

north of Nigeria: 489,191 sq. mi.; pop. 7,250,000

Ni·ger·i·a (nī jir′ē ə) country on the W coast of Africa: 356,669 sq. mi.; pop. 88,515,000 —**Ni·ger′i·an** ***adj., n.***

nig·gard (nig′ərd) ***n.*** ⟦prob. < Scand⟧ a stingy person; miser —**nig′gard·ly** ***adj., adv.*** —**nig′gard·li·ness** ***n.***

nig·gle (nig′əl) ***vi.*** **-gled, -gling** ⟦prob. akin to Norw *nigla*⟧ to be finicky —**nig′gler** ***n.*** —**nig′gling** ***adj., n.***

nigh (nī) ***adv., adj., prep.*** ⟦OE *neah*⟧ [Now Chiefly Dial.] NEAR

night (nīt) ***n.*** ⟦OE *niht*⟧ **1** the period of darkness from sunset to sunrise **2** any period or condition of darkness or gloom

night blindness imperfect vision in the dark or in dim light

night′cap′ ***n.*** **1** a cap worn to bed, esp. formerly **2** [Inf.] an alcoholic drink taken just before going to bed

night′clothes′ ***n.*** clothes to be worn in bed, as pajamas

night′club′ ***n.*** a place of entertainment for eating, drinking, dancing, etc. at night

night crawl′er a large earthworm that comes to the surface at night

night′fall′ ***n.*** the time in the evening when daylight is last visible; dusk

night′gown′ ***n.*** a loose gown worn in bed by women or girls

night′hawk′ ***n.*** **1** any of various usually nocturnal birds that feed on insects **2** NIGHT OWL

night′ie (-ē) ***n.*** [Inf.] NIGHTGOWN

night·in·gale (nīt′′n gāl′) ***n.*** ⟦< OE *niht*, night + *galan*, sing⟧ a small European thrush: the male sings melodiously, esp. at night

Night·in·gale (nīt′′n gāl′), **Florence** 1820-1910; Eng. nurse: regarded as the founder of modern nursing

night life pleasure-seeking activity at night, as in nightclubs

night′ly ***adj.*** done or occurring every night —***adv.*** night after night; every night

night′mare′ (-mer′) ***n.*** ⟦ME < *niht*, night + *mare*, demon⟧ **1** a frightening dream **2** any frightening experience —**night′mar′ish** ***adj.***

night owl a person who works at night or otherwise stays up late

night′shade′ ***n.*** **1** a chiefly tropical plant with five-lobed leaves and flowers of various colors **2** BELLADONNA

night′shirt′ ***n.*** a loose garment like a long shirt, worn in bed

night′spot′ ***n.*** *inf. var. of* NIGHTCLUB

night stand a small bedside table

night′stick′ ***n.*** a policeman's club; billy

night′time′ ***n.*** the time between dusk and dawn

night′wear′ ***n.*** NIGHTCLOTHES

NIH *abbrev.* National Institutes of Health

ni·hil·ism (nī′ə liz′əm, nē′-) ***n.*** ⟦< L *nihil*, nothing⟧ the general rejection of customary beliefs in morality, religion, etc. —**ni′hil·ist** ***n.*** —**ni′hil·is′tic** ***adj.***

Ni·hon (nē′hôn) *Jpn. name for* JAPAN

nil (nil) ***n.*** ⟦L, contr. of *nihil*⟧ nothing

Nile (nīl) river in NE Africa, flowing through Egypt into the Mediterranean

nim·ble (nim′bəl) ***adj.*** **-bler, -blest** ⟦< OE *niman*, to take⟧ **1** quick-witted; alert **2** moving quickly and lightly —**nim′bly** ***adv.***

nim·bus (nim′bəs) ***n., pl.*** **-bi′** (-bī′) or **-bus·es** ⟦L⟧ **1** any rain-producing cloud **2** a halo around the head of a saint, etc., as in a painting

Nim·rod (nim′räd′) ***n.*** *Bible* a mighty hunter

nin·com·poop (nin′kəm po͞op′) ***n.*** ⟦< ?⟧ a stupid, silly person; fool

nine (nīn) ***adj., n.*** ⟦OE *nigon*⟧ one more than eight; 9; IX —**ninth** (nīnth) ***adj., n.***

nine′pins′ ***n.*** a British version of the game of tenpins, played with nine pins

nine′teen′ ***adj., n.*** nine more than ten; 19; XIX —**nine′teenth′** (-tēnth′) ***adj., n.***

nine·ty (nīn′tē) ***adj., n., pl.*** **-ties** nine times ten; 90; XC (or LXXXX) —**the nineties** the numbers or years, as of a century, from 90 through 99 —**nine′ti·eth** (-ith) ***adj., n.***

nin·ny (nin′ē) ***n., pl.*** **-nies** ⟦< (*a*)*n inn*(*ocent*)⟧ a fool; dolt

nip[1] (nip) ***vt.*** **nipped, nip′ping** ⟦prob. < earlier LowG *nippen*⟧ **1** to pinch or bite **2** to sever (shoots, etc.) by clipping **3** to check the growth of **4** to have a painful or injurious effect on because of cold —***n.*** **1** a nipping; pinch; bite **2** a stinging, as in cold air **3** stinging cold; frost —**nip and tuck** so close as to leave the outcome in doubt

nip[2] (nip) ***n.*** ⟦prob. < Du *nippen*, to sip⟧ a small drink of liquor —***vt., vi.*** **nipped, nip′ping** to drink in nips

nip·per (nip′ər) ***n.*** **1** anything that nips **2** [*pl.*] pliers, pincers, etc. **3** the claw of a crab or lobster

nip·ple (nip′əl) ***n.*** ⟦prob. < earlier *neb*, a beak⟧ **1** the small protuberance on a breast or udder through which, in the female, the milk passes; teat **2** the teatlike part in the cap of a baby's bottle

Nip·pon (nip′än′, ni pän′) *var. of* NIHON

Nip·pon·ese (nip′ə nēz′) ***adj., n., pl.*** **-ese′** JAPANESE

nip·py (nip′ē) ***adj.*** **-pi·er, -pi·est** bitingly cold

nir·va·na (nir vä′nə) ***n.*** ⟦< Sans⟧ [*also* **N-**] **1** *Buddhism* the state of perfect blessedness **2** a place or condition of great bliss

ni·sei (nē′sā′) ***n., pl.*** **-sei′** or **-seis′** ⟦Jpn, second generation⟧ [*also* **N-**] a native U.S. or Canadian citizen born of immigrant Japanese parents

nit (nit) ***n.*** ⟦OE *hnitu*⟧ **1** the egg of a louse or similar insect **2** a young louse, etc.

nite (nīt) ***n.*** *inf. sp. of* NIGHT

ni·ter (nīt′ər) ***n.*** ⟦< Gr *nitron*⟧ potassium nitrate or sodium nitrate, used in making explosives, fertilizers, etc.; saltpeter: also [Chiefly Brit.] **ni′tre**

nit-pick·ing (nit′pik′iŋ) ***adj., n.*** stressing petty details; niggling —**nit′-pick′er** ***n.***

ni·trate (nī′trāt′) ***n.*** a salt of nitric acid, as sodium nitrate —***vt.*** **-trat′ed, -trat′ing** to combine with nitric acid or, esp., to make into a nitrate

ni·tric acid (nī′trik) a colorless, corrosive acid containing nitrogen

ni·tro·cel·lu·lose (nī′trō sel′yo͞o lōs′) ***n.*** a substance obtained by treating cellulose with nitric acid, used in making explosives, lacquers, etc.

ni·tro·gen (nī′trə jən) ***n.*** ⟦< Fr: see NITER & -GEN⟧ a colorless, odorless, gaseous chemical element forming nearly four fifths of the atmosphere —**ni·trog′e·nous** (-träj′ə nəs) ***adj.***

ni·tro·glyc·er·in or **ni·tro·glyc·er·ine** (nī′trō glis′ər in) ***n.*** a thick, explosive oil prepared by treating glycerin with nitric and sulfuric acids: used in making dynamite

ni·trous oxide (nī′trəs) a colorless gas containing nitrogen, used as an anesthetic and in aerosols

nit·ty-grit·ty (nit′ē grit′ē) ***n.*** [Slang] the actual, basic facts, issues, etc.

nit′wit′ ***n.*** ⟦? NIT + WIT[1]⟧ a stupid or silly person

nix (niks) [Slang] ***adv.*** ⟦Ger *nichts*⟧ **1** no **2** not at all —***interj.*** **1** stop! **2** I forbid, disagree, etc. —***vt.*** to disapprove of or put a stop to

Nix·on (nik′sən), **Richard M(ilhous)** 1913-94; 37th president of the U.S. (1969-74): resigned

Nizh·ny Nov·go·rod (nēzh′nē nôv′gə rət) city in central European Russia: pop. 1,438,000

NJ New Jersey

NM New Mexico

no[1] (nō) ***adv.*** ⟦< OE *ne a*, not ever⟧ **1** not at all *[no* worse*]* **2** nay; not so: used to deny, refuse, or disagree —***adj.*** not any; not one *[no* errors*]* —***n.***, *pl.* **noes** or **nos** **1** a refusal or denial **2** a negative vote or voter

no[2] *abbrev.* ⟦L *numero*⟧ number

No·ah (nō′ə) ***n.*** *Bible* the patriarch commanded by God to build the ARK (sense 3)

No·bel prizes (nō bel′) ⟦after A. B. *Nobel*, 19th-c. Swed inventor who established them⟧ annual international prizes given for distinction in physics, chemistry, economics, medicine, and literature, and for promoting peace

no·bil·i·ty (nō bil′ə tē) ***n.***, *pl.* **-ties** **1** a being noble **2** high rank in society **3** the class of people of noble rank

no·ble (nō′bəl) ***adj.*** **-bler, -blest** ⟦< L *nobilis*, well-known⟧ **1** having high moral qualities **2** excellent **3** grand; stately **4** of high hereditary rank —***n.*** one having hereditary rank or title —**no′ble·ness** ***n.*** —**no·bly** (nō′blē) ***adv.***

no′ble·man (-mən) ***n.***, *pl.* **-men** (-mən) a member of the nobility; peer

no·blesse o·blige (nō bles′ ō blēzh′) ⟦Fr, nobility obliges⟧ the inferred obligation of people of high rank to behave nobly toward others

no·bod·y (nō′bäd′ē, -bud′ē, -bə dē) ***pron.*** not anybody; no one —***n.***, *pl.* **-ies** a person of no importance

no-brain·er (nō′brān′ər) ***n.*** something so obvious, simple, etc. as to require little thought

noc·tur·nal (näk tʉr′nəl) ***adj.*** ⟦< L *nox*, night⟧ **1** of the night **2** functioning, done, or active during the night —**noc·tur′nal·ly** ***adv.***

noc·turne (näk′tʉrn′) ***n.*** ⟦Fr⟧ a romantic or dreamy musical composition thought appropriate to night

nod (näd) ***vi.*** **nod′ded, nod′ding** ⟦ME *nodden*⟧ **1** to bend the head forward quickly, as in agreement, greeting, etc. **2** to let the head fall forward because of drowsiness —***vt.*** **1** to bend (the head) forward quickly **2** to signify (assent, etc.) by doing this —***n.*** a nodding

node (nōd) ***n.*** ⟦L *nodus*⟧ **1** a knot; knob; swelling **2** that part of a stem from which a leaf starts to grow —**nod·al** (nōd′'l) ***adj.***

nod·ule (näj′o͞ol′) ***n.*** ⟦L *nodulus*⟧ a small knot or rounded lump

No·el or **No·ël** (nō el′) ***n.*** ⟦Fr < L *natalis*, natal⟧ CHRISTMAS

no′-fault′ ***adj.*** **1** designating a form of automobile insurance in which those injured collect damages without blame being fixed **2** designating a form of divorce granted without blame being charged

nog·gin (näg′in) ***n.*** ⟦prob. < Brit dial. *nog*, strong ale⟧ **1** a small cup or mug **2** [Inf.] the head

no′-good′ ***adj.*** [Slang] contemptible

noir (nwär) ***n.*** ⟦Fr, black⟧ a film, novel, etc. pessimistic or cynical in mood and often dealing with urban crime —**noir′ish** ***adj.***

noise (noiz) ***n.*** ⟦< OFr⟧ **1** din of voices; clamor **2** any sound; specif., a loud, disagreeable sound —***vt.*** **noised, nois′ing** to spread (a report, rumor, etc.) *about, around*, etc.

noise′less ***adj.*** with little or no noise; very quiet —**noise′less·ly** ***adv.***

noi·some (noi′səm) ***adj.*** ⟦see ANNOY & -SOME[1]⟧ **1** injurious to health; harmful **2** foul-smelling

nois·y (noiz′ē) ***adj.*** **-i·er, -i·est** **1** making noise **2** full of noise —**nois′i·ly** ***adv.*** —**nois′i·ness** ***n.***

no-load (nō′lōd′) ***adj.*** designating mutual funds charging no commissions on sales

no·mad (nō′mad′) ***n.*** ⟦< Gr *nemein*, to pasture⟧ **1** any of a people having no permanent home, but moving about constantly, as in search of pasture **2** a wanderer —**no·mad′ic** ***adj.***

no man's land the unoccupied region separating opposing armies

nom de plume (näm′ də plo͞om′) ⟦Fr⟧ a pen name

Nome (nōm) city in W Alaska: pop. 3,500

no·men·cla·ture (nō′mən klā′chər) ***n.*** ⟦< L *nomen*, a name + *calare*, to call⟧ the system of names used in a science, etc. or for the parts of a device

-nom·ics (näm′iks) *combining form* economics: also **-om′ics**

nom·i·nal (näm′ə nəl) ***adj.*** ⟦< L *nomen*,

a name⟧ **1** in name only, not in fact *[a nominal leader]* **2** relatively very small —**nom'i·nal·ly** ***adv.***

nom'i·nate' (-nāt') ***vt.*** **-nat'ed, -nat'ing** ⟦< L *nomen*, a name⟧ **1** to appoint to an office or position **2** to name as a candidate for election —**nom'i·na'tion** ***n.***

nom'i·na·tive (-nə tiv) ***n.*** *Gram.* the case of the subject of a verb

nom'i·nee' (-ə nē') ***n.*** a person who is nominated

non- ⟦< L *non*, not⟧ *prefix* not: less emphatic than IN-² and UN-, which often give a word a strong opposite or reverse meaning: the terms in the following list will be understood if "not" is used before the meaning of the base word:

nonabrasive
nonabsorbent
nonactive
nonaddictive
nonadministrative
nonaggression
nonaggressive
nonalcoholic
nonallergenic
nonallergic
nonassignable
nonathletic
nonattendance
nonautomotive
nonavailability
nonbasic
nonbeliever
nonbelligerent
nonbreakable
nonburnable
non-Catholic
nonchargeable
nonclerical
nonclinical
noncollectable
noncombustible
noncommercial
noncommunicable
non-Communist
noncompeting
noncompetitive
noncompliance
noncomplying
nonconducting
nonconforming
nonconsecutive
nonconstructive
noncontagious
noncontributory
noncontroversial
nonconvertible
noncorroding
noncorrosive
noncriminal
noncritical
noncrystalline
noncumulative
nondeductible
nondelivery
nondepartmental
nondepreciating
nondestructive
nondetachable
nondisciplinary
nondramatic
nondrinker
nondrying
noneducational
noneffective
nonenforceable
non-English
nonessential
nonexclusive
nonexempt
nonexistence
nonexistent
nonexplosive
nonfactual
nonfading
nonfat
nonfatal
nonfiction
nonfictional
nonflammable
nonflowering
nonfluctuating
nonflying
nonfreezing
nonfunctional
nongranular
nonhazardous
nonhereditary
nonhuman
nonidentical
noninclusive
nonindependent
nonindustrial
noninfected
noninflationary
nonintellectual
noninterference
nonintoxicating
nonirritating
nonjudicial
nonlegal
nonliterary
nonmagnetic
nonmalignant
nonmember
nonmigratory
nonmilitant
nonmilitary
nonnarcotic
nonnegotiable
nonnumerical
nonobjective
nonobligatory
nonobservance
nonobservant
nonoccurrence
nonofficial
nonoperational
nonoperative
nonpaying
nonpayment
nonperishable
nonphysical
nonpoisonous
nonpolitical
nonporous
nonprejudicial
nonprescriptive
nonproductive
nonprofitable
nonpunishable
nonracial
nonreactive
nonreciprocal
nonrecoverable
nonrecurring
nonredeemable
nonrefillable
nonreligious
nonrenewable
nonresidential
nonresidual
nonresistant
nonreturnable
nonrhythmic
nonrigid
nonsalaried
nonscientific
nonscoring
nonseasonal
nonsecular
nonsensitive
nonsmoker
nonsocial
nonspeaking
nonspecializing
nonspiritual
nonstaining
nonstandard
nonsticking
nonstrategic
nonstriking
nonstructural
nonsuccessive
nonsupporting
nonsustaining
nontaxable
nontechnical
nontheatrical
nonthinking
nontoxic
nontransparent
nontropical
nonuniform
nonuser
nonvenomous
nonverbal
nonvirulent
nonvocal
nonvocational
nonvoter
nonvoting
nonwhite
nonyielding

non·age (nkhankhij, nōkhnij) ***n.***⟦see prec. & AGE⟧ the state of being under full legal age

non·a·ge·nar·i·an (nän'ə jə ner'ē ən) ***n.*** ⟦< L *nonaginta*, ninety⟧ a person between the ages of 90 and 100

non'a·ligned' (-ə līnd') ***adj.*** not aligned with either side in a conflict —**non'a·lign'ment** ***n.***

no'-name' ***adj.*** not famous or distinguished

non'bind'ing (-bīn'diŋ) ***adj.*** not holding one to an obligation, promise, etc.

non'-book' ***n.*** a book produced cheaply and quickly, often in response to a current fad, etc.

nonce (näns) ***n.*** ⟦by merging of ME (*for then*) *ones*, lit., (for the) once⟧ the present use, occasion, or time: chiefly in **for the nonce**

nonce word a word coined and used for a single occasion

non·cha·lant (nän'shə länt') ***adj.*** ⟦Fr, ult. < L *non*, not + *calere*, be warm⟧ casually indifferent —**non'cha·lance'** (-läns') ***n.***

non·com (nän'käm') ***n.*** [Inf.] *short for* NONCOMMISSIONED OFFICER

non·com·bat·ant (nän'kəm bat''nt) ***n.*** **1** a member of the armed forces not engaged in actual combat **2** any civilian in wartime

non·com·mis·sioned officer (nän'kə mish'ənd) an enlisted person of any of various grades in the armed forces: in the U.S. Army, from corporal to sergeant major inclusive

non'com·mit'tal (-kə mit''l) ***adj.*** not committing one to a definite point of view or course of action

non com·pos men·tis (nän' käm'pəs men'tis) ⟦L⟧ *Law* not of sound mind

non'con·duc'tor (-kən duk'tər) ***n.*** a

substance that does not readily transmit sound, heat, or, esp., electricity

non′con·form′ist (-kən fôr′mist) ***n.*** **1** one who does not conform to prevailing beliefs and practices **2** [**N-**] a British Protestant who is not Anglican —**non′con·form′i·ty** ***n.***

non′cus·to′di·al (-kəs tō′dē əl) ***adj.*** without custody, as of one's children after divorce

non·dair·y (nän′der′ē) ***adj.*** containing no milk or milk products

non·de·script (nän′di skript′) ***adj.*** ⟦< L *non*, not + *describere*, describe⟧ **1** belonging to no definite class or type; hard to classify or describe **2** not interesting; colorless

none (nun) ***pron.*** ⟦< OE *ne*, not + *an*, one⟧ **1** no one; not anyone **2** [*with pl. v.*] not any *[there are none on the table]* —***n.*** not any (of); no part *[I want none of it]* —***adv.*** not at all *[none the worse for wear]*

non·en·ti·ty (nän′en′tə tē) ***n.***, *pl.* **-ties** a person or thing of little or no importance

none·the·less (nun′*th*ə les′) ***adv.*** nevertheless: also **none the less**

non·e·vent (nän′ē vent′) ***n.*** [Inf.] an event that is boring or deliberately staged, as for publicity

non′fer′rous (-fer′əs) ***adj.*** **1** not containing iron **2** designating or of metals other than iron

non′in·ter·ven′tion (-in′tər ven′shən) ***n.*** refusal to interfere; esp., a refusal by one nation to interfere in another's affairs

non′in·va′sive (-in vā′siv) ***adj.*** *Med.* not entering the skin or a body cavity

non′judg·men′tal (-juj ment′′l) ***adj.*** objective; tolerant

non′met′al (-met′′l) ***n.*** any chemical element, as oxygen, carbon, nitrogen, fluorine, etc., lacking the characteristics of a metal —**non′me·tal′lic** ***adj.***

no′-no′ ***n.***, *pl.* **-nos′** [Slang] something forbidden or considered unwise to do, say, etc.

no′-non′sense ***adj.*** practical and serious

non·pa·reil (nän′pə rel′) ***adj.*** ⟦Fr < *non*, not + *pareil*, equal⟧ unequaled; unrivaled; peerless

non′par′ti·san (-pärt′ə zən) ***adj.*** not partisan; esp., not connected with any single political party

non′per′son (-pur′sən) ***n.*** a person officially ignored by the government

non·plus (nän plus′) ***vt.*** **-plused′** or **-plussed′**, **-plus′ing** or **-plus′sing** ⟦L *non*, not + *plus*, more⟧ to greatly perplex or bewilder

non′prof′it (-präf′it) ***adj.*** not established or done to earn a profit: said as of a charity

non′res′i·dent (-rez′ə dənt) ***adj.*** not residing in the locality where one works, attends school, etc. —***n.*** a nonresident person

non·re·stric·tive (nän′ri strik′tiv) ***adj.*** *Gram.* designating a clause, phrase, or word felt as not essential to the sense, usually set off by commas (Ex.: John, *who is tall*, is Bill's brother)

non·sched·uled (nän′skej′ōōld) ***adj.*** licensed for commercial air flights as demand warrants rather than on a schedule

non′sec·tar′i·an (-sek ter′ē ən) ***adj.*** not confined to any specific religion

non·sense (nän′sens′) ***n.*** words, actions, etc. that are absurd or meaningless —***interj.*** how absurd!: an exclamation —**non·sen′si·cal** (-sen′si kəl) ***adj.***

non se·qui·tur (nän′ sek′wi tər) ⟦L, it does not follow⟧ **1** *Logic* a conclusion which does not follow from the premises **2** a remark having no bearing on what has just been said

non′skid′ (-skid′) ***adj.*** having a surface made so as to reduce slipping or skidding

non′-start′er (-stärt′ər) ***n.*** [Slang] **1** an expected occurrence, project, etc. that fails to materialize **2** a worthless idea

non′stop′ (-stäp′) ***adj.***, ***adv.*** without a stop

non′sup·port′ (-sə pôrt′) ***n.*** failure to provide for a legal dependent

non′un′ion (-yōōn′yən) ***adj.*** **1** not belonging to a labor union **2** not made or serviced by union workers

non′vi′o·lence (-vī′ə ləns) ***n.*** an abstaining from violence or the use of force, as in efforts to obtain civil rights —**non′vi′o·lent** ***adj.***

noo·dle[1] (nōōd′′l) ***n.*** ⟦< ?⟧ [Slang] the head

noo·dle[2] (nōōd′′l) ***n.*** ⟦Ger *nudel*⟧ a flat, narrow strip of dry dough, usually made with egg and served in soup, etc.

nook (nook) ***n.*** ⟦ME *nok*⟧ **1** a corner or separate part of a room **2** a small, secluded spot

noon (nōōn) ***n.*** ⟦< L *nona* (*hora*), ninth (hour)⟧ twelve o'clock in the daytime; midday —***adj.*** of or at noon Also **noon′time′** or **noon′day′**

no one not anyone; nobody

noose (nōōs) ***n.*** ⟦< L *nodus*, knot⟧ a loop in a rope, etc. formed by a slipknot so that the loop tightens as the rope is pulled

nor (nôr) ***conj.*** ⟦ME < *ne-*, not, + *or*, other⟧ and not; and not either *[I can neither go nor stay]*

Nor·dic (nôr′dik) ***adj.*** ⟦OE *north*, north⟧ of a Caucasoid physical type exemplified by the tall, blond Scandinavians

Nor·folk (nôr′fək) seaport in SE Virginia: pop. 261,000

norm (nôrm) ***n.*** ⟦L *norma*, rule⟧ a standard or model for a group

nor·mal (nôr′məl) ***adj.*** **1** conforming with an accepted standard or norm; natural; usual **2** average in intelligence, etc. —***n.*** **1** anything normal **2** the usual state, amount, etc. —**nor′mal·cy** (-sē) or **nor·mal′i·ty** (-mal′ə tē) ***n.*** —**nor′mal·ize′**, **-ized′**, **-iz′ing**, ***vt.***, ***vi.*** —**nor′mal·i·za′tion** ***n.***

nor′mal·ly ***adv.*** **1** in a normal manner **2** under normal circumstances

Nor·man (nôr′mən) ***n.*** ⟦< OFr⟧ **1** a member of the people of Normandy that conquered England in 1066 **2** a person born or living in Normandy —*adj.* of Normandy or its people, etc.

Nor·man·dy (nôr′mən dē) historical region in NW France, on the English Channel

norm·a·tive (nôr′mə tiv) *adj.* of or establishing a norm

Norse (nôrs) *adj., n.* ⟦prob. < Du *noord,* north⟧ **1** SCANDINAVIAN **2** (of) the Scandinavian group of languages

Norse′man (-mən) *n., pl.* **-men** (-mən) a member of any of the medieval Scandinavian peoples

north (nôrth) *n.* ⟦OE⟧ **1** the direction to the right of one facing the sunset (0° or 360° on the compass) **2** a region in or toward this direction —*adj.* **1** in, of, toward, or facing the north **2** from the north *[a north wind]* —*adv.* in or toward the north —**the North** that part of the U.S. north of Maryland, the Ohio River, and Missouri

North America N continent in the Western Hemisphere: *c.* 9,400,000 sq. mi.; pop. *c.* 449,000,000 —**North American**

North Car·o·li·na (kar′ə lī′nə) state of the SE U.S.: 48,718 sq. mi.; pop. 6,629,000; cap. Raleigh: abbrev. *NC* —**North Car′o·lin′i·an** (-lin′ē ən)

North Da·ko·ta (də kōt′ə) Midwestern state of the U.S.: 68,994 sq. mi.; pop. 639,000; cap. Bismarck: abbrev. *ND* —**North Da·ko′tan**

north′east′ *n.* **1** the direction halfway between north and east **2** a region in or toward this direction —*adj.* **1** in, of, or toward the northeast **2** from the northeast *[a northeast wind]* —*adv.* in or toward the northeast —**north′east′er·ly** *adj., adv.* —**north′east′ern** *adj.* —**north′east′ward** *adj., adv.* —**north′east′wards** *adv.*

north·er·ly (nôr*th*′ər lē) *adj., adv.* **1** toward the north **2** from the north

north·ern (nôr′*th*ərn) *adj.* **1** in, of, or toward the north **2** from the north **3** [**N-**] of the North

north′ern·er *n.* a person born or living in the north

Northern Hemisphere the half of the earth north of the equator

Northern Ireland division of the United Kingdom, in the NE part of the island of Ireland: 5,467 sq. mi.; pop. 1,578,000

northern lights [*also* **N- L-**] the aurora borealis

Northern Ma·ri·an·a Islands (mer′ē an′ə) group of islands in the W Pacific: a commonwealth associated with the U.S.: land area *c.* 179 sq. mi.; pop. 43,000: also **Northern Marianas**

North Pole the northern end of the earth's axis

North Sea arm of the Atlantic, between Great Britain & the N European mainland

North Star POLARIS

north′ward *adv., adj.* toward the north: also **north′wards** *adv.*

north′west′ *n.* **1** the direction halfway between north and west **2** a region in or toward this direction —*adj.* **1** in, of, or toward the northwest **2** from the northwest *[a northwest wind]* —*adv.* in or toward the northwest —**north′west′er·ly** *adj., adv.* —**north′west′ern** *adj.* —**north′west′ward** *adj., adv.* —**north′west′wards** *adv.*

Northwest Territories division of N Canada: 552,909 sq. mi.; pop. 39,000; cap. Yellowknife: abbrev. *NT*

North York (yôrk) city in SE Ontario, Canada: part of metropolitan Toronto: pop. 590,000

Norw *abbrev.* **1** Norway **2** Norwegian

Nor·way (nôr′wā′) country in N Europe: 125,001 sq. mi.; pop. 4,248,000

Nor·we·gian (nôr wē′jən) *n.* **1** the language of Norway **2** a person born or living in Norway —*adj.* of Norway or its people, language, etc.

nose (nōz) *n.* ⟦OE *nosu*⟧ **1** the part of the face above the mouth, having two openings for breathing and smelling; in animals, the snout, muzzle, etc. **2** the sense of smell **3** anything like a nose in shape or position —*vt.* **nosed, nos′ing 1** to nuzzle **2** to push (a way, etc.) with the front forward —*vi.* **1** to pry inquisitively **2** to move forward —**nose out 1** to defeat by a very small margin **2** to discover, as by smelling —**on the nose** [Slang] precisely

nose′bleed′ *n.* a bleeding from the nose

nose cone the cone-shaped foremost part of a rocket or missile

nose dive 1 a swift, steep downward plunge of an airplane, nose first **2** any sudden, sharp drop, as in profits —**nose′-dive′, -dived′, -div′ing,** *vi.*

nose drops medication administered through the nose with a dropper

nose·gay (nōz′gā′) *n.* ⟦NOSE + GAY (obs. sense "bright object")⟧ a small bouquet

nose guard *Football* the defensive lineman directly opposite the offensive center: also **nose tackle**

nosh (näsh) *vt., vi.* ⟦< Yiddish < Ger *nashchen,* to nibble⟧ [Slang] to eat (a snack) —*n.* [Slang] a snack —**nosh′er** *n.*

no′-show′ *n.* one who fails to claim or cancel a reservation

nos·tal·gi·a (nä stal′jə) *n.* ⟦< Gr *nostos,* a return + -ALGIA⟧ a longing for something far away or long ago —**nos·tal′gic** (-jik) *adj.*

nos·tril (näs′trəl) *n.* ⟦< OE *nosu,* nose + *thyrel,* hole⟧ either of the external openings of the nose

nos·trum (näs′trəm) *n.* ⟦L, ours⟧ **1** a quack medicine **2** a panacea

nos·y or **nos·ey** (nō′zē) *adj.* **-i·er, -i·est** [Inf.] prying; inquisitive

not (nät) *adv.* ⟦< ME *nought*⟧ in no manner, to no degree, etc.

no·ta·ble (nōt′ə bəl) *adj.* ⟦< L *notare,* to note⟧ worthy of notice; remarkable; outstanding —*n.* a person of distinction —**no′ta·bly** *adv.*

no·ta·rize (nōt′ə rīz′) *vt.* **-rized′, -riz′ing** to certify or attest (a document) as a notary public

no′ta·ry (-rē) *n., pl.* **-ries** ⟦< L *notare,* to

note⟧ an official authorized to certify or attest documents, take affidavits, etc.: in full **notary public**

no·ta·tion (nō tā′shən) ***n.*** **1** the use of signs or symbols to represent words, quantities, etc. **2** any such system of signs or symbols, as in mathematics or music **3** a brief note or noting

notch (näch) ***n.*** ⟦prob. < ME (*a*)*n oche*, a notch⟧ **1** a V-shaped cut in an edge or surface **2** a narrow pass with steep sides **3** [Inf.] a step; degree **—*vt.*** to cut a notch or notches in

note (nōt) ***n.*** ⟦< L *nota*, a mark⟧ **1** a distinguishing feature *[a note of sadness]* **2** importance, distinction, etc. *[a person of note]* **3** a brief writing to aid the memory; memorandum **4** a comment or explanation; annotation **5** notice; heed *[worthy of note]* **6** a short, informal letter **7** a written acknowledgment of a debt **8** *Music a*) a tone of definite pitch *b*) a symbol for a tone, indicating its duration and pitch **—*vt.*** **not′ed, not′ing** **1** to heed; observe **2** to set down in writing **3** to mention particularly **—compare notes** to exchange views

note′book′ ***n.*** **1** a book in which notes, or memorandums, are kept **2** a small laptop computer

not·ed (nōt′id) ***adj.*** renowned; famous

note′wor′thy ***adj.*** worthy of note; outstanding; remarkable **—note′wor′thi·ness *n.***

noth·ing (nuth′iŋ) ***pron.*** ⟦OE *na thing*⟧ **1** no thing; not anything **2** a person or thing considered of little or no importance **—*n.*** **1** nothingness **2** a thing that does not exist **3** a person or thing considered of little or no importance **4** a zero; cipher **—*adv.*** not at all; in no way **—for nothing** **1** free **2** in vain **3** without reason

noth′ing·ness ***n.*** **1** the condition of not existing **2** insignificance **3** unconsciousness or death

no·tice (nōt′is) ***n.*** ⟦see NOTE⟧ **1** announcement or warning **2** a brief article about a book, play, etc. **3** a sign giving some public information, warning, etc. **4** attention; heed **5** a formal warning of intention to end an agreement or contract at a certain time **—*vt.*** **-ticed, -tic·ing** to observe; pay attention to **—take notice** to pay attention

no′tice·a·ble ***adj.*** readily noticed; conspicuous **—no′tice·a·bly *adv.***

no·ti·fy (nōt′ə fī′) ***vt.*** **-fied′, -fy′ing** ⟦< L *notus*, known + *facere*, make⟧ to give notice to; inform **—no′ti·fi·ca′tion** (-fi kā′shən) ***n.***

no·tion (nō′shən) ***n.*** ⟦see NOTE⟧ **1** a general idea **2** a belief; opinion **3** an inclination; whim **4** [*pl.*] small, useful articles, as needles and thread, sold in a store **—no′tion·al *adj.***

no·to·ri·e·ty (nōt′ə rī′ə tē) ***n.*** a being notorious

no·to·ri·ous (nō tôr′ē əs) ***adj.*** ⟦see NOTE⟧ widely known, esp. unfavorably **—no·to′ri·ous·ly *adv.***

not·with·stand·ing (nät′with stan′diŋ, -with-) ***prep.*** in spite of **—*adv.*** nevertheless **—*conj.*** although

nou·gat (nōō′gət) ***n.*** ⟦< Prov *noga*, nut⟧ a confection of sugar paste with nuts

nought (nôt) ***n.*** ⟦< OE *ne*, not + *awiht*, aught⟧ *Arith.* the figure zero (0)

noun (noun) ***n.*** ⟦< L *nomen*, a name⟧ *Gram.* a word that names or denotes a person, thing, place, action, quality, etc.

nour·ish (nur′ish) ***vt.*** ⟦< L *nutrire*⟧ **1** to provide with substances necessary to life and growth **2** to foster; promote **—nour′ish·ing *adj.***

nour′ish·ment (-mənt) ***n.*** **1** a nourishing or being nourished **2** food

nou·veau riche (nōō′vō rēsh′) *pl.* **nou·veaux riches** (nōō′vō rēsh′) ⟦Fr⟧ a newly rich person, esp. one lacking culture, taste, or social grace

no·va (nō′və) ***n.***, *pl.* **-vas** or **-vae** (-vē) ⟦< L, new⟧ a star that brightens intensely and then gradually dims

No·va Sco·tia (nō′və skō′shə) province of SE Canada: 21,425 sq. mi.; pop. 909,000; cap. Halifax: abbrev. *NS* **—No′va Sco′tian**

nov·el (näv′əl) ***adj.*** ⟦< L dim. of *novus*, new⟧ new and unusual **—*n.*** a relatively long fictional prose narrative

nov′el·ette′ (-et′) ***n.*** a short novel

nov′el·ist ***n.*** one who writes novels

nov′el·ize′ (-īz′) ***vt.*** **-ized′, -iz′ing** to make into or like a novel; specif., to use (a film script) as the basis of a novel

nov′el·ty ***n.***, *pl.* **-ties** **1** the quality of being novel; newness **2** something new, fresh, or unusual **3** a small, often cheap, cleverly made article: *usually used in pl.*

No·vem·ber (nō vem′bər) ***n.*** ⟦< L *novem*, nine: ninth month in Roman year⟧ the 11th month of the year, having 30 days: abbrev. **Nov.**

no·ve·na (nō vē′nə) ***n.*** ⟦< L *novem*, nine⟧ *R.C.Ch.* the offering of special prayers and devotions for nine days

nov·ice (näv′is) ***n.*** ⟦< L *novus*, new⟧ **1** a person on probation in a religious order before taking final vows **2** a person new to something; beginner

no·vi·tiate (nō vish′it) ***n.*** the period or state of being a novice

No·vo·cain (nō′və kān′) ⟦L *nov*(*us*), new + (C)OCAIN(E)⟧ *trademark for* PROCAINE

now (nou) ***adv.*** ⟦OE *nu*⟧ **1** *a*) at the present time *b*) at once **2** at that time; then **3** with things as they are *[now we'll never know]* **—*conj.*** since; seeing that **—*n.*** the present time *[that's all for now]* **—*adj.*** of the present time **—just now** recently **—now and then** (or **again**) occasionally

now′a·days′ (-ə dāz′) ***adv.*** at the present time

no·way (nō′wā′) ***adv.*** by no means; not at all: now often **no way**, used with the force of an interjection

no′where′ ***adv.*** not in, at, or to any place **—nowhere near** not by a wide margin

no-win (nō′win′) ***adj.*** designating or of a situation, policy, etc. that cannot lead to success no matter what measures are taken

no′wise′ (-wīz′) ***adv.*** in no manner; noway

nox·ious (näk′shəs) ***adj.*** ⟦< L *nocere,* to hurt⟧ harmful to health or morals; injurious or unwholesome —**nox′ious·ness** ***n.***

noz·zle (näz′əl) ***n.*** ⟦dim. of *nose*⟧ the spout at the end of a hose, pipe, etc.

Np *Chem. symbol for* neptunium

NR *abbrev.* not rated: said of films

NS Nova Scotia

NT *abbrev.* **1** New Testament **2** Northwest Territories

-n't *suffix* not: used with certain verbs in contractions *[aren't]*

nth (enth) ***adj.*** of the indefinitely large or small quantity represented by *n*

nt wt *abbrev.* net weight

nu (no͞o, nyo͞o) ***n.*** the 13th letter of the Greek alphabet (Ν, ν)

NU Nunavut

nu·ance (no͞o′äns′) ***n.*** ⟦Fr < *nuer,* to shade⟧ a slight variation in tone, color, meaning, etc. —**nu′anced′** ***adj.***

nub (nub) ***n.*** ⟦var. of *knub,* knob⟧ **1** a lump or small piece **2** [Inf.] the main point; gist

nub·bin (nub′in) ***n.*** ⟦dim. of prec.⟧ a small thing

nub·by (nub′ē) ***adj.*** **-bi·er, -bi·est** having a rough, knotted surface *[a nubby fabric]*

nu·bile (no͞o′bəl, -bīl′) ***adj.*** ⟦< L *nubere,* marry⟧ **1** marriageable **2** sexually attractive Said of a young woman

nu·cle·ar (no͞o′klē ər) ***adj.*** **1** of, like, or forming a nucleus **2** of or relating to atomic nuclei *[nuclear energy]* **3** of or operated by the use of nuclear energy *[nuclear weapons]* **4** of or involving nuclear weapons *[nuclear warfare]*

nuclear energy the energy released from an atom in nuclear reactions, esp. in nuclear fission or nuclear fusion

nuclear family a basic social unit consisting of parents and their children living in one household

nuclear fission the splitting of the nuclei of atoms, accompanied by conversion of part of their mass into energy, as in the atomic bomb

nuclear fusion the fusion of lightweight atomic nuclei into a nucleus of heavier mass with a resultant loss in the combined mass, which is converted into energy, as in the hydrogen bomb

nuclear physics the branch of physics dealing with the structure of atomic nuclei, nuclear forces, etc.

nuclear reactor a device for creating a controlled nuclear chain reaction using atomic fuel, as for the production of energy

nuclear winter a hypothetical condition following nuclear war in which sunlight is cut off by clouds of smoke and dust, resulting in very low temperatures, destruction of life forms, etc.

nu·cle·ate (no͞o′klē it; *for v.,* -āt′) ***adj.*** having a nucleus —***vt., vi.*** **-at′ed, -at′ing** to form into a nucleus —**nu′cle·a′tion** ***n.***

nu·cle·ic acid (no͞o klē′ik, -klā′-) any of a group of essential complex organic acids found in all living cells: the two types are DNA and RNA

nucleo- *combining form* **1** nucleus **2** nuclear **3** nucleic acid Also **nucle-**

nu·cle·o·lus (no͞o klē′ə ləs) ***n.,*** *pl.* **-li′** (-lī′) ⟦< LL, dim. of L *nucleus*⟧ a conspicuous, usually spherical, dense body in the nucleus of most cells, consisting of protein and RNA

nu·cle·us (no͞o′klē əs) ***n.,*** *pl.* **-cle·i′** (-ī′) or **-cle·us·es** ⟦< L, kernel⟧ **1** a central thing or part around which others are grouped; core **2** any center of growth or development **3** the central part of an atom **4** the central mass of protoplasm in a cell

nude (no͞od) ***adj.*** ⟦L *nudus*⟧ naked; bare —***n.*** **1** a nude human figure, esp. in a work of art **2** the state of being nude *[in the nude]* —**nu′di·ty** ***n.***

nudge (nuj) ***vt.*** **nudged, nudg′ing** ⟦< ?⟧ to push gently, esp. with the elbow, in order to get the attention of, hint slyly, etc. —***n.*** a gentle push

nud·ism (no͞o′diz′əm) ***n.*** the practice or cult of going nude for hygienic reasons —**nud′ist** ***n., adj.***

nu·ga·to·ry (no͞o′gə tôr′ē) ***adj.*** ⟦< L *nugari,* to trifle⟧ **1** trifling; worthless **2** not operative; invalid

nug·get (nug′ət) ***n.*** ⟦prob. < dial. *nug,* a lump⟧ a lump; esp., a lump of native gold

nui·sance (no͞o′səns) ***n.*** ⟦< L *nocere,* annoy⟧ an act, thing, or person causing trouble, annoyance, etc.

nuke (no͞ok) [Slang] ***n.*** ⟦< NUCLEAR⟧ a nuclear weapon —***vt.*** **nuked, nuk′ing** to attack with nuclear weapons

null (nul) ***adj.*** ⟦< L *nullus,* none⟧ **1** without legal force; invalid: usually in the phrase **null and void** **2** amounting to naught **3** of no value, effect, etc.

nul·li·fy (nul′ə fī′) ***vt.*** **-fied′, -fy′ing** ⟦< L *nullus,* none + *facere,* to make⟧ **1** to make legally null or valueless **2** to cancel out —**nul′li·fi·ca′tion** ***n.***

numb (num) ***adj.*** ⟦< ME *nimen,* to take⟧ deadened; insensible —***vt.*** to make numb —**numb′ly** ***adv.*** —**numb′ness** ***n.***

num·ber (num′bər) ***n.*** ⟦< L *numerus*⟧ **1** a symbol or word showing how many or which one in a series (Ex.: 2, 35, four, ninth) **2** [*pl.*] ARITHMETIC **3** the sum of persons or things; total **4** *a*) [*often pl.*] many *b*) [*pl.*] numerical superiority **5** quantity **6** *a*) a single issue of a periodical *b*) a single song, dance, etc. in a program of entertainment **7** [Inf.] a person or thing singled out **8** *Gram.* the form of a word as indicating either singular or plural —***vt.*** **1** to count; enumerate **2** to give a number to **3** to include as one of a group **4** to limit the number of **5** to have or comprise; total —***vi.*** to be included —**a number of** several or many; some —**beyond** (or **without**) **number** too numerous to be counted —**the numbers** an illegal lottery based on certain numbers published in newspapers: also **numbers game** (or **racket**)

num′ber·less ***adj.*** countless

Num·bers (num′bərz) ***n.*** the fourth book of the Pentateuch in the Bible: abbrev. **Num.**

nu·mer·al (no͞o′mər əl) ***adj.*** ⟦< L *numerus*, number⟧ of or denoting a number or numbers —***n.*** a figure, a letter, or a group of figures or letters, expressing a number

nu′mer·ate (-it) ***adj.*** [Chiefly Brit.] able to understand basic mathematical concepts, etc.

nu′mer·a′tor (-āt′ər) ***n.*** the part of a fraction above the line

nu·mer·i·cal (no͞o mer′i kəl) ***adj.*** **1** of, or having the nature of, number **2** in or by numbers **3** expressed by numbers, not letters —**nu·mer′i·cal·ly *adv.***

nu·mer·ol·o·gy (no͞o′mər äl′ə jē) ***n.*** divination by numbers, as with birth dates

nu·mer·ous (no͞o′mər əs) ***adj.*** **1** consisting of many persons or things **2** very many

nu·mi·nous (no͞o′mə nəs) ***adj.*** ⟦< L *numen*, deity⟧ having a deeply spiritual or mystical effect

nu·mis·mat·ics (no͞o′miz mat′iks, -mis-) ***n.*** ⟦< L *numisma*, a coin⟧ the study or collection of coins, medals, paper money, etc. —**nu·mis′ma·tist** (-mə tist) ***n.***

num·skull (num′skul′) ***n.*** ⟦NUM(B) + SKULL⟧ a dunce

nun (nun) ***n.*** ⟦< LL *nonna*⟧ a woman devoted to a religious life, esp. one living in a convent under vows

Nu·na·vut (no͞o′nə vo͞ot′) territory of N Canada: 770,000 sq. mi.; pop. 25,000; cap. Iqaluit: abbrev. *NU*

nun·ci·o (nun′shō′, -sē ō′) ***n.***, *pl.* **-ci·os′** ⟦< It < L *nuntius*, messenger⟧ a papal ambassador to a foreign state

nun·ner·y (nun′ər ē) ***n.***, *pl.* **-ies** *former term for* CONVENT

nup·tial (nup′shəl, -chəl) ***adj.*** ⟦< L *nubere*, marry⟧ of marriage or a wedding —***n.*** [*pl.*] a wedding

nurse (nurs) ***n.*** ⟦< L *nutrire*, nourish⟧ **1** a woman hired to care for another's children **2** a person trained to care for the sick, assist surgeons, etc. —***vt.*** **nursed, nurs′ing 1** to suckle (an infant) **2** to take care of (a child, invalid, etc.) **3** to nourish, foster, etc. **4** to try to cure [*to nurse a cold*] **5** to use or handle so as to protect or conserve —***vi.*** **1** to feed at the breast; suckle **2** to serve as a nurse

nurse′maid′ ***n.*** a woman hired to care for a child or children

nurs·er·y (nurs′ə rē) ***n.***, *pl.* **-ies 1** a room set aside for children **2** a place where parents may temporarily leave children to be cared for **3** a place where young trees or other plants are raised for transplanting, etc.

nurs′er·y·man (-mən) ***n.***, *pl.* **-men** (-mən) one who owns or works in a tree nursery

nursery rhyme a poem for children

nursery school PRESCHOOL

nursing home a residence providing care for the infirm, chronically ill, disabled, etc.

nur·ture (nur′chər) ***n.*** ⟦< L *nutrire*, nourish⟧ training; rearing —***vt.*** **-tured, -tur·ing 1** to nourish **2** to train, educate, rear, etc. —**nur′tur·er *n.***

nut (nut) ***n.*** ⟦OE *hnutu*⟧ **1** a dry, one-seeded fruit, consisting of a kernel, often edible, in a woody shell, as the walnut **2** the kernel itself **3** loosely, any hard-shell, relatively nonperishable fruit, as the peanut **4** a small metal block with a threaded hole for screwing onto a bolt, etc. **5** [Slang] *a*) a crazy or eccentric person *b*) a devotee; fan

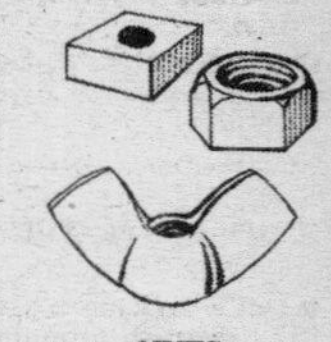
NUTS

nut case [Slang] one who is eccentric or crazy: also **nut′case′ *n.***

nut′crack′er ***n.*** **1** an instrument for cracking nutshells **2** a crowlike bird that feeds on nuts

nut′hatch′ ***n.*** a small nut-eating bird with a sharp beak

nut′meat′ ***n.*** the kernel of a nut

nut′meg′ (-meg′) ***n.*** ⟦< L *nux*, nut + LL *muscus*, musk⟧ the aromatic seed of an East Indian tree, grated and used as a spice

nu·tri·a (no͞o′trē ə) ***n.*** ⟦Sp < L *lutra*, otter⟧ the soft, brown fur of a South American rodent

nu·tri·ent (no͞o′trē ənt) ***adj.*** ⟦< L *nutrire*, nourish⟧ nourishing —***n.*** anything nutritious

nu′tri·ment (-trə mənt) ***n.*** anything that nourishes; food

nu·tri·tion (no͞o trish′ən) ***n.*** ⟦see NUTRIENT⟧ **1** the process by which an organism takes in and assimilates food **2** anything that nourishes; food **3** the study of diet and health —**nu·tri′tion·al *adj.*** —**nu·tri′tion·al·ly *adv.*** —**nu′tri·tive** (-trə tiv) ***adj.***

nu·tri′tious (-trish′əs) ***adj.*** nourishing

nuts (nuts) [Slang] ***adj.*** crazy; foolish —***interj.*** used to express disgust, scorn, refusal, etc.: often in the phrase **nuts to someone** (or **something**) —**be nuts about 1** to be greatly in love with **2** to be very enthusiastic about

nuts and bolts [Inf.] the basic elements or practical aspects of something —**nuts′-and-bolts′ *adj.***

nut′shell′ ***n.*** the shell enclosing the kernel of a nut —**in a nutshell** in concise form; in a few words

nut′ty ***adj.*** **-ti·er, -ti·est 1** containing nuts **2** having a nutlike flavor **3** [Slang] *a*) very enthusiastic *b*) foolish, crazy, etc. —**nut′ti·ness *n.***

nuz·zle (nuz′əl) ***vt.***, ***vi.*** **-zled, -zling** ⟦< ME *nose*, NOSE⟧ **1** to push (against) or rub with the nose, snout, etc. **2** to nestle; snuggle —**nuz′zler *n.***

NV Nevada

NW *abbrev.* **1** northwest **2** northwestern

NY New York

NYC or **N.Y.C.** New York City

ny·lon (nī′län′) ***n.*** ⟦arbitrary coinage⟧ **1** an elastic, very strong synthetic material that is made into fiber, yarn, bristles, etc. **2** [*pl.*] stockings made of this

nymph (nimf) ***n.*** ⟦< Gr *nymphē*⟧ **1** *Gr. & Rom. Myth.* any of a group of minor nature goddesses, living in rivers, trees, etc. **2** a lovely young woman **3** the young of an insect with incomplete metamorphosis

nym·pho·ma·ni·a (nim′fō mā′nē ə) ***n.*** uncontrollable desire by a woman for sexual intercourse —**nym′pho·ma′ni·ac′** ***adj., n.***

O

o or **O** (ō) ***n.***, *pl.* **o's, O's** the 15th letter of the English alphabet

O[1] (ō) ***n.***, *pl.* **O's** **1** the numeral zero **2** a blood type

O[2] (ō) ***interj.*** **1** used in direct address *[O Lord!]* **2** OH

O[3] *abbrev.* **1** Ocean **2** *Physics* ohm **3** Old **4** *Baseball* out(s)

O[4] *Chem. symbol for* oxygen

-o (ō) *suffix* forming slangy words, as slang nouns from adjectives *[weirdo, sicko]*

oaf (ōf) ***n.*** ⟦< ON *alfr,* elf⟧ a stupid, clumsy fellow; lout —**oaf′ish** ***adj.***

O·a·hu (ō ä′ho͞o) chief island of Hawaii

oak (ōk) ***n.*** ⟦OE *ac*⟧ **1** a large hardwood tree with nuts called *acorns* **2** its wood —***adj.*** of oak —**oak′en** ***adj.***

Oak·land (ōk′lənd) seaport in W California: pop. 372,000

Oak Ridge city in E Tennessee: center for atomic research: pop. 27,000

oa·kum (ō′kəm) ***n.*** ⟦< OE *a-*, out + *camb,* a comb⟧ stringy hemp fiber gotten by taking apart old ropes, used as a caulking material

oar (ôr) ***n.*** ⟦OE *ar*⟧ a long pole with a broad blade at one end, used in rowing —**oars·man** (ôrz′mən), *pl.* **-men,** ***n.***

oar′lock′ ***n.*** a device, often U-shaped, for holding an oar in place in rowing

OAS *abbrev.* Organization of American States

o·a·sis (ō ā′sis) ***n.***, *pl.* **-ses′** (-sēz′) ⟦< Gr, fertile spot⟧ a fertile place in a desert, resulting from the presence of water

oat (ōt) ***n.*** ⟦OE *ate*⟧ [*usually pl.*] **1** a hardy cereal grass **2** its edible grain —**oat′en** ***adj.***

oat′cake′ ***n.*** a thin, flat cake made of oatmeal

oath (ōth) ***n.***, *pl.* **oaths** (ō*th*z, ōths) ⟦OE *ath*⟧ **1** a declaration based on an appeal to God that one will speak the truth, keep a promise, etc. **2** a swearword; curse

oat′meal′ ***n.*** **1** oats ground or rolled into meal or flakes **2** a porridge of this

OB *abbrev.* **1** obstetrician **2** obstetrics

ob. *abbrev.* ⟦L *obiit*⟧ he (or she) died

ob- ⟦< L *ob*⟧ *prefix* **1** to, toward, before *[obtrude]* **2** against *[obstinate]* **3** upon, over *[obscure]* **4** completely *[obdurate]*

ob·bli·ga·to (äb′li gät′ō) ***n.***, *pl.* **-tos** or **-ti** (-ē) ⟦see OBLIGE⟧ a musical accompaniment, usually by a solo instrument

ob·du·rate (äb′door it) ***adj.*** ⟦< L *obduratus* < *ob-*, intens. + *durus*, hard⟧ **1** hardhearted **2** stubborn; obstinate —**ob′du·ra·cy** (-ə sē) ***n.***

o·be·di·ent (ō bē′dē ənt) ***adj.*** obeying or willing to obey —**o·be′di·ence** ***n.*** —**o·be′di·ent·ly** ***adv.***

o·bei·sance (ō bā′səns, -bē′-) ***n.*** ⟦< OFr *obeir*, obey⟧ **1** a gesture of respect, as a bow **2** homage; deference —**o·bei′sant** ***adj.***

OBELISK

ob·e·lisk (äb′ə lisk, ō′bə-) ***n.*** ⟦< Gr *obelos*, needle⟧ a tall, four-sided stone pillar tapering to its pyramidal top

o·bese (ō bēs′) ***adj.*** ⟦< L *obesus* < *ob-* (see OB-) + *edere*, to eat⟧ very fat; stout —**o·be′si·ty** (-ə tē) ***n.***

o·bey (ō bā′) ***vt.*** ⟦< L *obedire* < *ob-* (see OB-) + *audire*, hear⟧ **1** to carry out the orders of **2** to carry out (an order, etc.) **3** to be guided by *[to obey one's conscience]* —***vi.*** to be obedient

ob·fus·cate (äb′fəs kāt′, äb fus′kāt′) ***vt.*** **-cat′ed, -cat′ing** ⟦< L *obfuscatus* < *ob-* (see OB-) + *fuscus,* dark⟧ to obscure; confuse —**ob′fus·ca′tion** ***n.***

ob·i·ter dic·tum (äb′i tər dik′təm, ō bi-) *pl.* **ob′i·ter dic′ta** (-tə) an incidental remark

o·bit·u·ar·y (ō bich′o͞o er′ē) ***n.***, *pl.* **-ar′ies** ⟦< L *obire*, to die⟧ a notice of someone's death, usually with a brief biography: also **o·bit** (ō′bit)

obj *abbrev.* **1** object **2** objective

ob·ject (äb′jikt; *for v.* äb jekt′) ***n.*** ⟦< ML *objectum,* thing thrown in the way < L *objectus* < *ob-* (see OB-) + *jacere,* to throw⟧ **1** a thing that can be seen or touched **2** a person or thing to which action, feeling, etc. is directed **3** purpose; goal **4** *Gram.* a noun or other substantive receiving the action of a verb or governed by a preposition —***vt.*** to state by way of objection —***vi.*** to feel or express disapproval or opposition —**ob·jec′tor** ***n.***

ob·jec·tion (əb jek′shən) ***n.*** **1** a feeling or expression of opposition or disapproval **2** a reason for objecting

ob·jec′tion·a·ble ***adj.*** **1** open to objection **2** disagreeable; offensive

ob·jec·tive (əb jek′tiv) ***adj.*** **1** existing as an object or fact, independent of the mind; real **2** determined by the realities of the thing dealt with rather than the thoughts of the writer or speaker **3** without bias or prejudice **4** *Gram.* designating or of the case of an object of a preposition or verb —***n.*** something aimed at —**ob·jec′tive·ly** ***adv.*** —**ob·jec·tiv·i·ty** (äb′jek tiv′ə tē) or **ob·jec′tive·ness** ***n.***

object lesson an actual or practical demonstration or exemplification of some principle

ob·jet d'art (äb′zhā där′) *pl.* **ob′jets d'art′** (-zhā-) ⟦Fr⟧ a small object of artistic value, as a figurine

ob·jur·gate (äb′jər gāt′) ***vt.*** **-gat′ed, -gat′ing** ⟦< L *objurgatus* < *ob-* (see OB-) + *jurgare,* chide⟧ to upbraid sharply; rebuke

ob·late (äb′lāt′) ***adj.*** ⟦ModL *oblatus,* thrust forward⟧ *Geom.* flattened at the poles

ob·la·tion (äb lā′shən) ***n.*** ⟦< L *oblatus,* offered⟧ an offering or sacrifice to God or a god

ob·li·gate (äb′li gāt′) ***vt.*** **-gat′ed, -gat′ing** ⟦see OBLIGE⟧ to bind by a promise, sense of duty, etc.

ob′li·ga′tion (-gā′shən) ***n.*** **1** an obligating or being obligated **2** a binding contract, promise, responsibility, etc. **3** the binding power of a contract, etc. **4** a being indebted for a favor, etc.

ob·lig·a·to·ry (ə blig′ə tôr′ē, äb′lə gə-) ***adj.*** legally or morally binding

o·blige (ə blīj′) ***vt.*** **o·bliged′, o·blig′ing** ⟦< L *obligare* < *ob-* (see OB-) + *ligare,* to bind⟧ **1** to compel by moral, legal, or physical force **2** to make indebted for a favor; do a favor for

o·blig′ing ***adj.*** helpful; accommodating —**o·blig′ing·ly** ***adv.***

ob·lique (ō blēk′) ***adj.*** ⟦< L *obliquus* < *ob-* (see OB-) + *liquis,* awry⟧ **1** slanting **2** indirect or evasive —**ob·lique′ly** ***adv.*** —**ob·liq·ui·ty** (ə blik′wə tē) or **ob·lique′ness** ***n.***

ob·lit·er·ate (ə blit′ər āt′) ***vt.*** **-at′ed, -at′ing** ⟦< L *obliteratus* < *ob-* (see OB-) + *littera,* a letter⟧ **1** to blot out; efface **2** to destroy —**ob·lit′er·a′tion** ***n.***

ob·liv·i·on (ə bliv′ē ən) ***n.*** ⟦< L *oblivisci,* to forget⟧ **1** forgetfulness **2** the condition of being forgotten

ob·liv′i·ous (-əs) ***adj.*** forgetful or indifferent: usually with *to* or *of*

ob·long (äb′lôŋ′) ***adj.*** ⟦< L *oblongus,* rather long < *ob-* (see OB-) + *longus,* long⟧ longer than broad; specif., rectangular and longer in one direction —***n.*** an oblong figure

ob·lo·quy (äb′lə kwē) ***n.,*** *pl.* **-quies** ⟦< L *obloqui* < *ob-* (see OB-) + *loqui,* speak⟧ **1** widespread censure or abuse **2** disgrace resulting from this

ob·nox·ious (əb näk′shəs, äb-) ***adj.*** ⟦< L *obnoxiosus* < *ob-* (see OB-) + *noxa,* harm⟧ very unpleasant; offensive; repugnant —**ob·nox′ious·ly** ***adv.*** —**ob·nox′ious·ness** ***n.***

OBOE

o·boe (ō′bō) ***n.*** ⟦< Fr *haut,* high (pitch) + *bois,* wood⟧ a double-reed woodwind instrument having a high, penetrating tone —**o′bo·ist** ***n.***

obs *abbrev.* obsolete

ob·scene (äb sēn′) ***adj.*** ⟦< L *obscenus,* filthy⟧ **1** offensive to modesty or decency; lewd **2** repulsive —**ob·scen′i·ty** (-sen′ə tē), *pl.* **-ties,** ***n.***

ob·scur·ant·ism (äb′skyoor′ən tiz′əm) ***n.*** **1** opposition to human progress **2** a being deliberately obscure or vague

ob·scure (əb skyoor′) ***adj.*** ⟦< L *obscurus,* covered over⟧ **1** dim; dark **2** not easily seen; faint **3** vague; ambiguous [an *obscure* answer] **4** inconspicuous or hidden **5** not well-known [an *obscure* actor] —***vt.*** **-scured′, -scur′ing** to make obscure —**ob·scure′ly** ***adv.*** —**ob·scu′ri·ty** ***n.***

ob·se·quies (äb′si kwēz′) ***pl.n.*** ⟦< L *obsequium,* compliance, substituted for L *exsequiae,* funeral⟧ funeral rites

ob·se·qui·ous (əb sē′kwē əs) ***adj.*** ⟦< L *obsequi,* to comply with⟧ servile or fawning

ob·serv·ance (əb zurv′əns) ***n.*** **1** the observing of a law, custom, etc. **2** a customary act, rite, etc.

ob·serv′ant (-ənt) ***adj.*** **1** strict in observing a law, custom, etc. **2** paying careful attention **3** perceptive or alert

ob·ser·va·tion (äb′zər vā′shən) ***n.*** **1** *a)* the act or power of noticing *b)* something noticed **2** a being seen **3** a noting and recording of facts, as for research **4** a comment or remark

ob·serv·a·to·ry (əb zurv′ə tôr′ē) ***n.,*** *pl.* **-ries** a building equipped for astronomical research, esp. one with a large telescope

ob·serve′ (-zurv′) ***vt.*** **-served′, -serv′ing**

⟦< L *observare* < *ob-* (see OB-) + *servare,* to keep⟧ **1** to adhere to (a law, custom, etc.) **2** to celebrate (a holiday, etc.) **3** *a)* to notice (something) *b)* to pay special attention to **4** to say; remark **5** to examine scientifically —**ob·serv'a·ble** *adj.* —**ob·serv'er** *n.*

ob·sess (əb ses') *vt.* ⟦< L *obsessus* < *ob-* (see OB-) + *sedere,* sit⟧ to haunt or trouble in mind; preoccupy —*vi.* to be obsessed or preoccupied: usually with *about, over,* or *on* —**ob·ses'sive** *adj.* —**ob·ses'sive·ly** *adv.*

ob·ses'sion (-sesh'ən) *n.* **1** a being obsessed **2** an idea, desire, etc. that obsesses one

ob·sid·i·an (əb sid'ē ən) *n.* ⟦ModL *obsidianus,* ult. after *Obsius,* finder of a similar stone in ancient times⟧ a hard, dark, volcanic glass

ob·so·les·cent (äb'sə les'ənt) *adj.* becoming obsolete —**ob'so·les'cence** *n.*

ob·so·lete (äb'sə lēt') *adj.* ⟦< L *obsoletus* < *ob-* (see OB-) + *exolescere,* to grow out of use⟧ **1** no longer in use **2** out-of-date

ob·sta·cle (äb'stə kəl) *n.* ⟦< L *obstaculum* < *ob-* (see OB-) + *stare,* to stand⟧ anything that stands in the way; obstruction

ob·stet·rics (əb stet'riks) *n.* ⟦< L *obstetrix,* midwife⟧ the branch of medicine concerned with the care and treatment of women during pregnancy and childbirth —**ob·stet'ric** or **ob·stet'ri·cal** *adj.* —**ob·ste·tri·cian** (äb'stə trish'ən) *n.*

ob·sti·nate (äb'stə nət) *adj.* ⟦< L *obstinare,* to resolve on⟧ **1** determined to have one's own way; stubborn **2** hard to treat or cure *[an obstinate fever]* —**ob'sti·na·cy** (-nə sē) *n.* —**ob'sti·nate·ly** *adv.*

ob·strep·er·ous (əb strep'ər əs) *adj.* ⟦< L *obstreperus* < *ob-* (see OB-) + *strepere,* to roar⟧ noisy or unruly, esp. in resisting —**ob·strep'er·ous·ly** *adv.* —**ob·strep'er·ous·ness** *n.*

ob·struct (əb strukt') *vt.* ⟦< L *obstructus* < *ob-* (see OB-) + *struere,* to pile up⟧ **1** to block or stop up (a passage) **2** to hinder (progress, etc.) **3** to cut off from view —**ob·struc'tive** *adj.* —**ob·struc'tive·ly** *adv.* —**ob·struc'tive·ness** *n.*

ob·struc'tion (-struk'shən) *n.* **1** an obstructing **2** anything that obstructs; hindrance

ob·struc'tion·ist *n.* one who obstructs progress —*adj.* that obstructs progress

ob·tain (əb tān') *vt.* ⟦< L *obtinere* < *ob-* (see OB-) + *tenere,* to hold⟧ to get possession of by trying; procure —*vi.* to prevail or be in effect —**ob·tain'a·ble** *adj.* —**ob·tain'ment** *n.*

ob·trude (əb tro͞od', äb-) *vt.* **-trud'ed, -trud'ing** ⟦< L *obtrudere* < *ob-* (see OB-) + *trudere,* to thrust⟧ to force (oneself, one's opinions, etc.) upon others unasked or unwanted —*vi.* to obtrude oneself (*on* or *upon*) —**ob·tru'sion** *n.* —**ob·tru'sive** *adj.* —**ob·tru'sive·ly** *adv.* —**ob·tru'sive·ness** *n.*

ob·tuse (äb to͞os', əb-) *adj.* ⟦< L *obtundere,* to strike upon, blunt⟧ **1** blunt **2** greater than 90° and less than 180° *[an obtuse angle]* **3** slow to understand —**ob·tuse'ly** *adv.* —**ob·tuse'ness** *n.*

ob·verse (äb vurs'; *also, and for n. always,* äb'vurs') *adj.* ⟦< L *obversus* < *ob-* (see OB-) + *vertere,* to turn⟧ **1** turned toward the observer **2** forming a counterpart —*n.* **1** the side, as of a coin or medal, bearing the main design **2** a counterpart

ob·vi·ate (äb'vē āt') *vt.* **-at'ed, -at'ing** ⟦see fol.⟧ to do away with or prevent by effective measures; make unnecessary —**ob'vi·a'tion** *n.*

ob·vi·ous (äb'vē əs) *adj.* ⟦L *obvius,* in the way⟧ easy to see or understand; evident —**ob'vi·ous·ly** *adv.* —**ob'vi·ous·ness** *n.*

oc- *prefix* OB-: used before *c [occur]*

oc·a·ri·na (äk'ə rē'nə) *n.* ⟦It < LL *auca,* goose: from its shape⟧ a small wind instrument with finger holes and a mouthpiece

occas *abbrev.* occasional(ly)

oc·ca·sion (ə kā'zhən, ō-) *n.* ⟦< L *occasio* < *ob-* (see OB-) + *cadere,* to fall⟧ **1** a favorable time; opportunity **2** an event, etc. that makes something else possible **3** *a)* a happening *b)* a particular time **4** a special time or event **5** need arising from circumstances —*vt.* to cause —**on occasion** sometimes

oc·ca'sion·al *adj.* **1** of or for special occasions **2** happening now and then; infrequent —**oc·ca'sion·al·ly** *adv.*

oc·ci·dent (äk'sə dənt, -dent') *n.* ⟦< L *occidere,* to fall: with reference to the setting sun⟧ [Old Poet.] the west —**the Occident** Europe and the Americas —**oc'ci·den'tal** or **Oc'ci·den'tal** *adj., n.*

oc·clude (ə klo͞od') *vt.* **-clud'ed, -clud'ing** ⟦< L *occludere* < *ob-* (see OB-) + *claudere,* to shut⟧ **1** to close or block (a passage) **2** to shut in or out —*vi. Dentistry* to meet with the cusps fitting closely —**oc·clu'sion** (-klo͞o'zhən) *n.* —**oc·clu·sive** (ə klo͞o'siv) *adj.*

oc·cult (ə kult') *adj.* ⟦< L *occulere,* to conceal⟧ **1** hidden **2** secret **3** mysterious **4** of mystic arts, such as magic, astrology, etc.

oc·cu·pan·cy (äk'yo͞o pən sē) *n., pl.* **-cies** an occupying; a taking or keeping in possession

oc'cu·pant (-pənt) *n.* one who occupies

oc·cu·pa·tion (äk'yo͞o pā'shən) *n.* **1** an occupying or being occupied **2** that which occupies one's time; work; profession —**oc'cu·pa'tion·al** *adj.*

oc·cu·py (äk'yo͞o pī') *vt.* **-pied', -py'ing** ⟦< L *occupare* < *ob-* (see OB-) + *capere,* seize⟧ **1** to take possession of by settlement or seizure **2** to hold possession of; specif., *a)* to dwell in *b)* to hold (a position or office) **3** to take up (space, time, etc.) **4** to employ (oneself, one's mind, etc.)

oc·cur (ə kur') *vi.* **-curred', -cur'ring** ⟦< L *occurrere* < *ob-* (see OB-) + *currere,* to run⟧ **1** to be found; exist **2** to come to mind *[an idea occurred to me]* **3** to take place; happen

oc·cur'rence (-əns) *n.* **1** the act or fact of occurring **2** an event; incident

o·cean (ō'shən) *n.* ⟦< Gr *Ōkeanos*⟧ **1** the

body of salt water that covers about 71% of the earth's surface **2** any of its four principal divisions: the Atlantic, Pacific, Indian, or Arctic Ocean **3** a great quantity —**o·ce·an·ic** (ō′shē an′ik) ***adj.***

o′cean·go′ing (-gō′iŋ) ***adj.*** of, or made for, travel on the ocean

O·ce·an·i·a (ō′shē an′ē ə) islands in the Pacific, including Melanesia, Micronesia, & Polynesia —**O′ce·an′i·an** ***adj., n.***

o·cean·og·ra·phy (ō′shə näg′rə fē) ***n.*** the study of the environment in the ocean, its plants and animals, etc. —**o′cean·o′graph′ic** (-nō′graf′ik) ***adj.*** —**o′cean·og′ra·pher** ***n.***

o′cean·ol′o·gy (-näl′ə jē) ***n.*** the study of the sea in all its aspects, including oceanography, undersea exploration, etc.

o·ce·lot (äs′ə lət, -lät′) ***n.*** ⟦Fr < AmInd⟧ a spotted wildcat of North and South America

o·cher or **o·chre** (ō′kər) ***n.*** ⟦< Gr *ōchros,* pale-yellow⟧ **1** a yellow or reddish-brown clay containing iron, used as a pigment **2** its color

o′clock (ə kläk′, ō-) ***adv.*** of or according to the clock *[*nine *o'clock* at night*]*

octa- ⟦< Gr *oktō,* eight⟧ *combining form* eight *[octagon]*

oc·ta·gon (äk′tə gän′) ***n.*** ⟦< Gr: see prec. & -GON⟧ a plane figure with eight angles and eight sides —**oc·tag′o·nal** (-tag′ə nəl) ***adj.***

octane number (or **rating**) (äk′tān′) a number representing the antiknock properties of a gasoline, etc.

oc·tave (äk′tiv, -tāv′) ***n.*** ⟦< L *octavus,* eighth⟧ **1** any group of eight **2** *Music a)* the eighth tone of a diatonic scale, or a tone seven degrees above or below a given tone *b)* the interval of seven degrees between a tone and either of its octaves *c)* the series of tones within this interval, or the keys of an instrument producing such a series

oc·ta·vo (äk tā′vō, -tä′-) ***n.,*** *pl.* **-vos** ⟦< L (*in*) *octavo,* (in) eighth⟧ **1** the page size (usually 6 by 9 in.) of a book made up of printer's sheets folded into eight leaves **2** a book of such pages

oc·tet or **oc·tette** (äk tet′) ***n.*** ⟦OCT(A)- + (DU)ET⟧ **1** a composition for eight voices or instruments **2** the eight performers of this

Oc·to·ber (äk tō′bər) ***n.*** ⟦< L *octo,* eight: eighth month in Roman calendar⟧ the tenth month of the year, having 31 days: abbrev. **Oct.**

oc·to·ge·nar·i·an (äk′tə ji ner′ē ən) ***n.*** ⟦< L *octoginta,* eighty⟧ a person between the ages of 80 and 90

oc·to·pus (äk′tə pəs) ***n.,*** *pl.* **-pus·es** or **-pi′** (-pī′) ⟦< Gr *oktō,* eight + *pous,* foot⟧ a mollusk with a soft body and eight arms covered with suckers

OCTOPUS

oc·u·lar (äk′yoo lər) ***adj.*** ⟦< L *oculus,* eye⟧ **1** of, for, or like the eye **2** by eyesight

oc′u·list (-list) ***n.*** *former term for* OPHTHALMOLOGIST

OD[1] (ō′dē′) [Slang] ***n.,*** *pl.* **ODs** or **OD's** an overdose, esp. of a narcotic —***vi.*** **OD'd** or **ODed, OD'ing** or **ODing** to take an overdose, esp. a fatal overdose of a narcotic

OD[2] or **O.D.** *abbrev.* ⟦L⟧ Doctor of Optometry

o·da·lisque or **o·da·lisk** (ō′də lisk′) ***n.*** ⟦Fr < Turk *ōdalik,* chambermaid⟧ a female slave or concubine in a harem

odd (äd) ***adj.*** ⟦< ON *oddi*⟧ **1** remaining or separated from a pair, set, etc. **2** having a remainder of one when divided by two **3** with a few more: usually in hyphenated compounds *[*sixty-*odd* years ago*]* **4** occasional *[odd* jobs*]* **5** peculiar or eccentric —**odd′ly** ***adv.*** —**odd′ness** ***n.***

odd′ball′ ***adj., n.*** [Slang] strange or eccentric (person)

odd′i·ty (-ə tē) ***n.*** **1** strangeness **2** *pl.* **-ties** an odd person or thing

odds (ädz) ***pl.n.*** **1** difference in favor of one side over the other; advantage **2** an equalizing advantage in betting, based on a bettor's assumed chance of winning and expressed as a ratio *[odds* of 3 to 1*]* —**at odds** quarreling

odds and ends scraps; remnants

odds′mak′er ***n.*** an expert who estimates the odds in betting, etc.

odds′-on′ ***adj.*** having a good chance of winning *[*an *odds-on* favorite*]*

ode (ōd) ***n.*** ⟦< Gr *ōidē,* song⟧ a lyric poem characterized by lofty feeling, elaborate form, and dignified style

-ode (ōd) ⟦< Gr *hodos*⟧ *suffix* way, path *[electrode]*

O·des·sa (ō des′ə) seaport in S Ukraine, on the Black Sea: pop. 1,101,000

O·din (ō′din) ***n.*** *Norse Myth.* the chief deity, god of art, war, and the dead

o·di·ous (ō′dē əs) ***adj.*** ⟦< L *odium,* hatred⟧ disgusting; offensive —**o′di·ous·ly** ***adv.*** —**o′di·ous·ness** ***n.***

o·di·um (ō′dē əm) ***n.*** ⟦< L *odi,* I hate⟧ **1** hatred **2** the disgrace brought on by hateful action

o·dom·e·ter (ō däm′ət ər) ***n.*** ⟦< Gr

hodometros < *hodos,* way + *metron,* a measure⟧ an instrument for measuring the distance traveled by a vehicle

o·dor (ō′dər) ***n.*** ⟦L⟧ a smell; scent; aroma Brit. sp. **o′dour** —**o′dor·less** ***adj.*** —**o′dor·ous** ***adj.***

o·dor·if·er·ous (ō′dər if′ər əs) ***adj.*** ⟦< L *odor,* odor + *ferre,* to bear⟧ giving off an odor, now often, specif., a strong or offensive one

O·dys·se·us (ō dis′ē əs, ō dis′yo͞os′) ***n.*** ⟦Gr⟧ the hero of the *Odyssey,* one of the Greek leaders in the Trojan War

Od·ys·sey (äd′i sē) ***n.*** **1** an ancient Greek epic poem, ascribed to Homer, about the wanderings of Odysseus after the fall of Troy **2** *pl.* **-seys** [**o-**] any extended journey

OE *abbrev.* Old English

Oed·i·pal (ed′i pəl, ē′di-) ***adj.*** [*also* **o-**] of or relating to the Oedipus complex

Oed·i·pus (ed′i pəs, ē′di-) ***n.*** *Gr. Myth.* a king who unwittingly kills his father and marries his mother

Oedipus complex *Psychoanalysis* the unconscious tendency of a child to be attached to the parent of the opposite sex

oe·nol·o·gy (ē näl′ə jē) ***n.*** ⟦< Gr *oinos,* wine + -LOGY⟧ the science or study of wines and winemaking —**oe·nol′o·gist** ***n.***

oe·no·phile (ē′nə fīl′) ***n.*** a connoisseur of wine

o'er (ō′ər, ôr) ***prep., adv.*** [Old Poet.] OVER

oeu·vre (ë′vr′) ***n.,*** *pl.* ***-vres*** (-vr′) ⟦Fr⟧ all the works of a writer, artist, or composer

of (uv) ***prep.*** ⟦OE⟧ **1** from; specif., *a*) coming from *[*men *of* Ohio*]* *b*) resulting from *[*to die *of* fever*]* *c*) at a distance from *[*east *of* the city*]* *d*) by *[*the poems *of* Poe*]* *e*) separated from *[*robbed *of* his money*]* *f*) from the whole constituting *[*one *of* her hats*]* *g*) made from *[*a sheet *of* paper*]* **2** belonging to *[*the pages *of* a book*]* **3** *a*) possessing *[*a man *of* wealth*]* *b*) containing *[*a bag *of* nuts*]* **4** specified as *[*a height *of* six feet*]* **5** characterized by *[*a man *of* honor*]* **6** concerning; about *[*think *of* me*]* **7** during *[of* recent years*]*

of- *prefix* OB-: used before *f [offer]*

off (ôf) ***adv.*** ⟦ME var. of *of*⟧ **1** so as to be away, at a distance, etc. **2** so as to be no longer on, attached, etc. *[*take *off* your hat*]* **3** (a specified distance) away in space or time *[*20 yards *off]* **4** so as to be no longer in operation, etc. *[*turn the motor *off]* **5** so as to be less, etc. *[*5% *off* for cash*]* **6** away from one's work *[*take a week *off]* —***prep.*** **1** (so as to be) no longer (or not) on, attached, etc. *[off* the road*]* **2** from the substance of *[*live *off* the land*]* **3** away from *[*a mile *off* shore*]* **4** branching out from *[*an alley *off* Main Street*]* **5** relieved from *[off* duty*]* **6** not up to the usual standard, etc. of *[off* one's game*]* —***adj.*** **1** not on or attached **2** not in operation **3** on the way *[off* to bed*]* **4** away from work *[*we are *off* today*]* **5** not up to the usual standard, etc. **6** more remote *[*on the *off* chance*]* **7** in (specified) circumstances *[*to be well *off]* **8** wrong *[*his figures are *off]* —***vt.*** [Slang] to kill; murder —***interj.*** go away! —**off and on** now and then

-off (ôf, äf) *combining form* a contest of skill in a (specified) activity or field *[*a chili cook-*off]*

of·fal (ôf′əl) ***n.*** ⟦ME *ofall,* lit., off-fall⟧ **1** [*with sing. or pl. v.*] the entrails, etc. of a butchered animal **2** refuse; garbage

off′beat′ ***n.*** *Music* a beat having a weak accent —***adj.*** [Inf.] unconventional, unusual, strange, etc.

off′-col′or ***adj.*** **1** varying from the standard color **2** improper; risqué

of·fend (ə fend′) ***vi.*** ⟦< L *offendere,* to strike against < *ob-* (see OB-) + *fendere,* to hit⟧ **1** to commit a sin or crime **2** to create resentment, anger, etc. —***vt.*** **1** to hurt the feelings of; insult **2** to be displeasing to (the taste, sense, etc.) —**of·fend′er** ***n.***

of·fense (ə fens′, ô′fens′) ***n.*** **1** a sin or crime **2** a creating of resentment, displeasure, etc. **3** a feeling hurt, angry, etc. **4** something that causes anger, etc. **5** the act of attacking **6** the side that is attacking or seeking to score in any contest Brit. sp. **of·fence′** —**take offense** to become offended

of·fen′sive ***adj.*** **1** attacking or for attack **2** unpleasant; disgusting **3** insulting —***n.*** **1** attitude or position of attack: often with *the* **2** an attack —**of·fen′sive·ly** ***adv.*** —**of·fen′sive·ness** ***n.***

of·fer (ôf′ər, äf′-) ***vt.*** ⟦< L *offerre* < *ob-* (see OB-) + *ferre,* to bear⟧ **1** to present in worship *[*to *offer* prayers*]* **2** to present for acceptance *[*to *offer* help*]* **3** to suggest; propose **4** to show or give signs of *[*to *offer* resistance*]* **5** to bid (a price, etc.) —***n.*** the act of offering or thing offered

of′fer·ing ***n.*** **1** the act of making an offer **2** something offered; specif., *a*) a gift *b*) presentation in worship

of′fer·to′ry (-tôr′ē) ***n.,*** *pl.* **-ries** [*often* **O-**] **1** *a*) the part of a Eucharistic service in which the bread and wine are offered to God *b*) the prayers said, or music used, then **2** *a*) the part of a church service during which money offerings are collected *b*) the collection itself

off′hand′ ***adv.*** without preparation; extemporaneously —***adj.*** **1** said or done offhand **2** casual, curt, etc. Also **off′hand′ed**

off′-hour′ ***adj.*** not for or during rush hour or other busy periods

of·fice (ôf′is, äf′-) ***n.*** ⟦< L *officium*⟧ **1** a service done for another **2** a duty, esp. as a part of one's work **3** a position of authority or trust, as in government **4** *a*) the place where the affairs of a business, etc. are carried on *b*) the people working there **5** [*often* **O-**] a religious service or set of prayers

of′fice·hold′er ***n.*** a government official

of·fi·cer (ôf′i sər, äf′-) ***n.*** **1** anyone holding an office, or position of authority, in a government, business, club, etc. **2** a police officer **3** one holding a position of authority, esp. by commission, in the armed forces

of·fi·cial (ə fish′əl) ***adj.*** **1** of or holding an office, or position of authority **2** authorized or authoritative **3** formal —***n.*** a person holding office —**of·fi′cial·dom** (-dəm) ***n.*** —**of·fi′cial·ly** ***adv.***

of·fi·ci·ate (ə fish′ē āt′) ***vi.*** **-at′ed, -at′ing** **1** to perform the duties of an office **2** to perform the functions of a priest, minister, rabbi, etc. at a religious ceremony

of·fi·cious (ə fish′əs) ***adj.*** ⟦see OFFICE⟧ offering unwanted advice or services; meddlesome, esp. overbearingly so —**of·fi′cious·ly** ***adv.*** —**of·fi′cious·ness** ***n.***

off·ing (ôf′iŋ) ***n.*** ⟦< OFF⟧ used chiefly in **in the offing**, at some indefinite future time

off′-key′ ***adj.*** **1** *Music* flat or sharp **2** not harmonious

off′-lim′its ***adj.*** ruled to be a place that cannot be entered, etc. by a specified group

off′-line′ ***adj.*** designating or of equipment not directly connected to and controlled by the central processing unit of a computer

off′load′ ***vt.***, ***vi.*** UNLOAD (1*a*, 2*b*, 4)

off′-put′ting ***adj.*** [Chiefly Brit.] distracting, annoying, etc.

off′-road′ ***adj.*** designating or of a vehicle for use off regular highways, streets, etc.

off′-sea′son ***n.*** a time of the year when the usual activity is reduced or not carried on

off·set (ôf set′; *for n.* ôf′set′) ***vt.*** **-set′, -set′ting** to balance, compensate for, etc. —***n.*** **1** a thing that offsets another **2** OFFSET PRINTING

offset printing a printing process in which the inked impression is first made on a rubber-covered roller, then transferred to paper

off′shoot′ ***n.*** anything that derives from a main source; specif., a shoot growing from the main stem of a plant

off′shore′ ***adj.*** **1** moving away from the shore **2** at some distance from the shore **3** engaged in outside the U.S. as by U.S. banks or manufacturers *[offshore* investments*]* —***adv.*** **1** away from the shore **2** outside the U.S. *[*to borrow *offshore]*

off′side′ ***adj.*** *Sports* not in the proper position for play: also **off′sides′**

off′spring′ ***n.***, *pl.* **-spring′** or **-springs′** a child or children; progeny; young

off′stage′ ***n.*** the part of the stage not seen by the audience —***adj.*** in or from this —***adv.*** to the offstage

off′-the-wall′ ***adj.*** [Slang] very unusual, unconventional, eccentric, etc.

off′-track′ ***adj.*** designating or of legalized betting on horse races, carried on away from the racetrack

off′-white′ ***adj.*** grayish-white or yellowish-white

off year **1** a year in which a major election does not take place **2** a year of little production

oft (ôft) ***adv.*** ⟦OE⟧ *literary var. of* OFTEN

of·ten (ôf′ən, -tən) ***adv.*** ⟦ME var. of prec.⟧ many times; frequently: also **of′ten·times′**

o·gle (ō′gəl) ***vi.***, ***vt.*** **o′gled, o′gling** ⟦prob. < LowG *oog,* an eye⟧ to keep looking (at) flirtatiously —***n.*** an ogling look —**o′gler** ***n.***

o·gre (ō′gər) ***n.*** ⟦Fr⟧ **1** in fairy tales and folklore, a man-eating giant **2** a hideous, cruel man

oh (ō) ***interj.***, ***n.***, *pl.* **oh's** or **ohs** an exclamation of surprise, fear, pain, etc.

O·hi·o (ō hī′ō) **1** river flowing from W Pennsylvania into the Mississippi **2** Midwestern state of the U.S.: 40,952 sq. mi.; pop. 10,847,000; cap. Columbus: abbrev. **OH** —**O·hi′o·an** ***adj.***, ***n.***

ohm (ōm) ***n.*** ⟦after G. S. *Ohm* (1789-1854), Ger physicist⟧ unit of electrical resistance

ohm′me′ter ***n.*** an instrument for measuring electrical resistance in ohms

o·ho (ō hō′) ***interj.*** used to express surprise or triumph

-o·hol·ic (ə häl′ik) *combining form* -AHOLIC

-oid (ơid) ⟦< Gr *eidos,* a form⟧ *suffix* like or resembling *[crystalloid]*

oil (ơil) ***n.*** ⟦< L *oleum*⟧ **1** any of various greasy, combustible, liquid substances obtained from animal, vegetable, and mineral matter **2** PETROLEUM **3** *a)* OIL COLOR *b)* OIL PAINTING —***vt.*** to lubricate or supply with oil —***adj.*** of, from, or like oil

oil′cloth′ ***n.*** cloth made waterproof by being treated with oil or paint

oil color paint made by grinding a pigment in oil: also **oil paint**

oil′man (-mən) ***n.***, *pl.* **-men** (-mən) an entrepreneur or executive in the petroleum industry

oil painting **1** a picture painted in oil colors **2** the art of painting in oil colors

oil shale shale from which oil can be extracted by distillation

oil′skin′ ***n.*** **1** cloth made waterproof by treatment with oil **2** [*often pl.*] a garment or outfit made of this

oil well a well that supplies petroleum

oil·y (ơil′ē) ***adj.*** **-i·er, -i·est** **1** of, like, or containing oil **2** greasy **3** too suave or smooth; unctuous —**oil′i·ness** ***n.***

oink (ơiŋk) ***n.*** ⟦echoic⟧ the grunt of a pig —***vi.*** to make this sound

oint·ment (ơint′mənt) ***n.*** ⟦< L *unguentum,* a salve⟧ a fatty substance used on the skin for healing or cosmetic purposes; salve

OK or **O.K.** (ō kā′) [Inf.] ***adj.***, ***adv.***, ***interj.*** ⟦< "oll korrect," facetious misspelling of *all correct*⟧ all right; correct —***n.***, *pl.* **OK's** or **O.K.'s** approval —***vt.*** **OK'd** or **O.K.'d, OK'ing** or **O.K.'ing** to approve or endorse Also **o'kay′**

O·kla·ho·ma (ō′klə hō′mə) state of the SC U.S.: 68,679 sq. mi.; pop. 3,146,000; cap. Oklahoma City: abbrev. **OK** —**O′kla·ho′man** ***adj.***, ***n.***

Oklahoma City capital of Oklahoma: pop. 445,000

o·kra (ō′krə) ***n.*** ⟦< WAfr name⟧ **1** a plant with sticky green pods **2** the pods, used in soups, stews, etc.

Ok·to·ber·fest (äk tō′bər fest′) ***n.*** ⟦Ger⟧

a beer-drinking festival held in Germany and elsewhere in the fall

old (ōld) ***adj.*** **old'er** or **eld'er, old'est** or **eld'est** ⟦OE *ald*⟧ **1** having lived or existed for a long time **2** of aged people **3** of a specified age *[*two years *old]* **4** not new **5** worn out by age or use **6** former **7** experienced *[*an *old* hand*]* **8** ancient **9** [*often* **O-**] designating the earliest form of a language *[Old* English*]* **10** designating the earlier or earliest of two or more *[*the *Old* World*]* —***n.*** **1** time long past *[*days of *old]* **2** something old: with *the* —**old'ness** ***n.***

Old Church Sla·von·ic (slə văn'ik) the South Slavic language now used only as a liturgical language by Orthodox Slavs: also called **Old Church Slavic** or **Old Bulgarian**

old country the country, esp. in Europe, from which an immigrant came

old·en (ōl'dən) ***adj.*** [Old Poet.] (of) old

Old English the Germanic language of the Anglo-Saxons, spoken in England from *c.* A.D. 400 to *c.* 1100

old'-fash'ioned ***adj.*** suited to or favoring the styles, ideas, etc. of past times —***n.*** [*also* **Old-Fashioned**] a cocktail made with whiskey, bitters, and bits of fruit

old fogy or **old fogey** *see* FOGY

Old French the French language from *c.* A.D. 800 to *c.* 1550

Old Glory *name for* the flag of the United States

old'-growth' ***adj.*** designating or of a forest having very large, very old trees

old guard ⟦transl. < Fr⟧ [*sometimes* **O-G-**] the conservative element of a group, party, etc.

old hat [Slang] old-fashioned or stale

Old High German the High German language before the 12th c.

old·ie or **old·y** (ōl'dē) ***n.***, *pl.* **-ies** [Inf.] an old joke, saying, song, movie, etc.

old lady [Slang] **1** one's mother **2** one's wife

old'-line' ***adj.*** long-established, traditional, conservative, etc.

Old Low German the Low German language before the 12th c.

old maid **1** a woman, esp. an older woman, who has never married: mildly disparaging **2** a prim, prudish, fussy person

old man [Slang] **1** one's father **2** one's husband **3** [*usually* **O- M-**] any man in authority: with *the*

old master **1** any of the great European painters before the 18th c. **2** a painting by any of these

Old Norse the Germanic language of the Scandinavians before the 14th c.

Old Saxon the Low German dialect of the Saxons before the 10th c.

old school a group of people who cling to traditional or conservative ideas, methods, etc.

old'ster (-stər) ***n.*** [Inf.] an old or elderly person

Old Testament *Christian designation for* the Holy Scriptures of Judaism, the first of the two general divisions of the Christian Bible

old'-time' ***adj.*** **1** of past times **2** of long standing

old'-tim'er ***n.*** [Inf.] a long-time resident, employee, member, etc.

old'-tim'ey (-tīm'ē) ***adj.*** [Inf.] reminiscent of the past, usually in a positive way

old'-world' ***adj.*** of or from the Eastern Hemisphere, esp. Europe

o·lé (ô lā') ***interj., n.*** ⟦Sp⟧ used to express approval, triumph, joy, etc.

o·le·ag·i·nous (ō'lē aj'i nəs) ***adj.*** ⟦< L *olea,* olive tree⟧ oily; unctuous

o·le·an·der (ō'lē an'dər) ***n.*** ⟦ML⟧ a poisonous evergreen shrub with fragrant white, pink, or red flowers and narrow, leathery leaves

o·le·o·mar·ga·rine or **o·le·o·mar·ga·rin** (ō'lē ō mär'jə rin) ***n.*** ⟦< L *oleum,* oil + MARGARINE⟧ *former term for* MARGARINE: also **o'le·o'**

ol·fac·to·ry (äl fak'tə rē, ōl-) ***adj.*** ⟦< L *olere,* have a smell + *facere,* make⟧ of the sense of smell

ol·i·gar·chy (äl'i gär'kē) ***n.***, *pl.* **-chies** ⟦< Gr *oligos,* few + -ARCHY⟧ **1** government in which ruling power belongs to a few persons **2** a state governed in this way **3** the persons ruling such a state —**ol'i·gar'chic** ***adj.***

ol·ive (äl'iv) ***n.*** ⟦< L *oliva*⟧ **1** *a)* an evergreen tree of S Europe and the Near East *b)* its small, oval fruit, eaten green or ripe as a relish or pressed, when ripe, to extract its oil (**olive oil**) **2** the yellowish-green color of the unripe fruit

olive branch the branch of the olive tree, a symbol of peace

O·lym·pi·a (ō lim'pē ə) capital of Washington: pop. 34,000

O·lymp·ic games (ō lim'pik) ⟦< *Olympia,* plain in Greece, site of ancient games⟧ an international athletic competition now held every two years, alternating between summer games and winter games: also **O·lym'pics**

O·lym·pus (ō lim'pəs), **Mount** mountain in N Greece: in Greek mythology, the home of the gods —**O·lym'pi·an** (-pē ən) ***adj., n.***

om (ōm) ***n.*** ⟦Sans⟧ *Hinduism* a word intoned as during meditation

O·ma·ha (ō'mə hô) city in E Nebraska: pop. 336,000

O·man (ō män') country on the SE coast of Arabia: 119,499 sq. mi.; pop. 2,070,000 —**O·man'i** (-ē) ***adj., n.***

om·buds·man (äm'bədz mən) ***n.***, *pl.* **-men** (-mən) ⟦Swed < *ombud,* a deputy⟧ a public official appointed to investigate citizens' complaints

o·me·ga (ō mā'gə) ***n.*** ⟦Gr *ō* + *mega,* great, i.e., long *o*: see OMICRON⟧ the 24th & final letter of the Greek alphabet (Ω, ω)

om·e·let or **om·e·lette** (äm'lət) ***n.*** ⟦< L *lamella,* small plate⟧ eggs beaten and cooked flat in a pan

o·men (ō'mən) ***n.*** ⟦L⟧ a thing or happening supposed to foretell a future event, either good or evil

om·i·cron (äm′i krän′, ō′mi-) ***n.*** ⟦Gr *o mikron,* small *o*: see OMEGA⟧ the 15th letter of the Greek alphabet (O, o)

om·i·nous (äm′ə nəs) ***adj.*** of or serving as an evil omen; threatening —**om′i·nous·ly** ***adv.***

o·mis·sion (ō mish′ən) ***n.*** **1** an omitting **2** something omitted

o·mit (ō mit′) ***vt.*** **o·mit′ted, o·mit′ting** ⟦< L *omittere* < *ob-* (see OB-) + *mittere,* send⟧ **1** to fail to include; leave out **2** to fail to do; neglect

omni- ⟦L < *omnis,* all⟧ *combining form* all, everywhere

om·ni·bus (äm′ni bəs) ***n.***, *pl.* **-bus·es** ⟦< L, for all⟧ **1** BUS **2** a collection of stories, articles, etc., as on one theme —***adj.*** including many things

om·nip·o·tent (äm nip′ə tənt) ***adj.*** ⟦< L *omnis,* all + *potens,* able⟧ having unlimited power or authority; all-powerful —**the Omnipotent** God —**om·nip′o·tence** ***n.***

om·ni·pres·ent (äm′ni prez′ənt) ***adj.*** present in all places at the same time —**om′ni·pres′ence** ***n.***

om·nis·cient (äm nish′ənt) ***adj.*** ⟦< L *omnis,* all + *sciens,* knowing⟧ knowing all things —**the Omniscient** God —**om·nis′cience** ***n.***

om·niv·o·rous (äm niv′ə rəs) ***adj.*** ⟦< L *omnis,* all + *vorare,* devour⟧ **1** eating any sort of food, esp. both animal and vegetable food **2** taking in everything indiscriminately —**om·niv′o·rous·ly** ***adv.*** —**om·niv′o·rous·ness** ***n.***

on (än, ôn) ***prep.*** ⟦OE⟧ **1** in contact with, supported by, or covering **2** in the surface of *[*scars *on* it*]* **3** *a)* near to *[on* my left*]* *b)* having as its location *[*a house *on* Main Street*]* **4** at the time of *[on* Monday*]* **5** connected with *[on* the team*]* **6** engaged in *[on* a trip*]* **7** in a state of *[on* parole*]* **8** as a result of *[*a profit *on* the sale*]* **9** in the direction of *[*light shone *on* us*]* **10** through the use of *[*live *on* bread*]* **11** concerning *[*an essay *on* war*]* **12** onto **13** at the expense of *[*a drink *on* the house*]* **14** [Inf.] using; addicted to *[on* drugs*]* —***adv.*** **1** in a situation of contacting, being supported by, or covering **2** in a direction toward *[*he looked *on]* **3** forward *[*move *on]* **4** without stopping *[*she sang *on]* **5** into action or operation *[*turn *on* the light*]* —***adj.*** **1** in action or operation *[*the TV is *on]* **2** [Slang] performing very well *[*she is really *on* today*]* —**and so on** and more like the preceding —**on and off** intermittently —**on and on** for a long time; continuously —**on to** [Slang] aware of the real nature or meaning of

ON Ontario

once (wuns) ***adv.*** ⟦ME *ones*⟧ **1** one time only **2** at any time; ever **3** formerly *[*a *once* famous woman*]* **4** by one degree *[*a cousin *once* removed*]* —***conj.*** as soon as *[once* he is tired, he will quit*]* —***n.*** one time *[*go this *once]* —**at once 1** immediately **2** at the same time —**once (and) for all** conclusively —**once in a while** now and then

once′-o′ver ***n.*** [Inf.] a quick look

on·co·gene (äŋ′kə jēn′) ***n.*** ⟦< Gr *onkos,* a mass + GENE⟧ a gene that, when activated as by a virus, may cause a normal cell to become cancerous

on·col·o·gy (än käl′ə jē, äŋ-) ***n.*** ⟦< Gr *onkos,* a mass + -LOGY⟧ the branch of medicine dealing with tumors —**on·col′o·gist** ***n.***

on·com·ing (än′kum′iŋ) ***adj.*** coming nearer in position or time

on·co·vi·rus (äŋ′kə vī′rəs) ***n.*** a virus that causes cancer

one (wun) ***adj.*** ⟦OE *an*⟧ **1** being a single thing or unit **2** united *[*with *one* accord*]* **3** a certain but unnamed *[*take *one* path or the other, *one* day last week*]* **4** the same **5** unique; only *[*the *one* solution*]* —***n.*** **1** the first and lowest cardinal number; 1; I **2** a single person or thing —***pron.*** **1** a certain person or thing **2** any person or thing —**at one** in accord —**one another** each one the other or others; each other —**one by one** individually in succession

one′-di·men′sion·al ***adj.*** having one dominant aspect, quality, etc. and hence narrow, limited, etc.

O'Neill (ō nēl′), **Eu·gene** (yo͞o jēn′) 1888-1953; U.S. playwright

one′ness ***n.*** **1** singleness; unity **2** unity of mind, feeling, etc.

one′-on-one′ ***adj.***, ***adv.*** in direct personal confrontation

on·er·ous (än′ər əs) ***adj.*** ⟦< L *onus,* a load⟧ burdensome; oppressive

one′self′ ***pron.*** a person's own self: also **one's self** —**be oneself 1** to function normally **2** to be natural —**by oneself** alone

one′-sid′ed ***adj.*** **1** on, having, or involving only one side **2** unfair **3** unequal *[*a *one-sided* race*]*

one′-stop′ ***adj.*** designating or of a store, bank, etc. that offers a complete range of goods or services

one′time′ ***adj.*** former: also **one′-time′**

one′-track′ ***adj.*** [Inf.] limited in scope

one′-up′ ***adj.*** [Inf.] having an advantage (over another)

one-up′man·ship′ (-up′mən ship′) ***n.*** [Inf.] skill in seizing an advantage over others

one′-way′ ***adj.*** moving, or allowing movement, in one direction only

on′go′ing ***adj.*** going on; progressing

on·ion (un′yən) ***n.*** ⟦< L *unus,* one⟧ **1** a plant of the lily family with an edible bulb **2** this bulb, having a strong, sharp smell and taste

on′ion·skin′ ***n.*** a tough, thin, translucent paper

on′line′ ***adj.*** designating or of equipment directly connected to and controlled by the central processing unit of a computer: also **on′-line′**

on′look′er ***n.*** a spectator

on·ly (ōn′lē) ***adj.*** ⟦< OE *an,* one + *-lic,* -ly⟧ **1** alone of its or their kind; sole **2** alone in superiority; best —***adv.*** **1** and no other; and no more; solely **2** (but) in the end *[*to meet one crisis, *only* to face another*]* **3** as recently as —***conj.*** [Inf.] except that; but —**only too** very;

exceedingly

on·o·mat·o·poe·ia (än′ō mat′ō pē′ə, -mät′-) ***n.*** ⟦< Gr *onoma,* a name + *poiein,* make⟧ the formation of words by imitating sounds (Ex.: *buzz*)

on′rush′ ***n.*** a headlong dash forward

on′set′ ***n.*** **1** an attack **2** a start

on·slaught (än′slôt′) ***n.*** ⟦< Du *slagen,* to strike⟧ a violent attack

on′stream′ or **on′-stream′** ***adv.*** into operation or production *[a new refinery coming onstream]*

On·tar·i·o (än ter′ē ō) **1** province of SC Canada: 412,580 sq. mi.; pop. 10,754,000; cap. Toronto: abbrev. *ON* **2 Lake** smallest of the Great Lakes, between New York & Ontario, Canada —**On·tar′i·an** ***adj., n.***

on·to (än′to͞o) ***prep.*** **1** to a position on **2** [Slang] aware of the real meaning or nature of

on·tog·e·ny (än täj′ə nē) ***n.*** ⟦ult. < Gr *einai,* to be + *-genēs,* born⟧ the life cycle of a single organism

o·nus (ō′nəs) ***n.*** ⟦L⟧ **1** a burden, unpleasant duty, etc. **2** blame

on′ward ***adv.*** toward or at a position ahead; forward: also **on′wards** —***adj.*** advancing

on·yx (än′iks) ***n.*** ⟦< Gr, fingernail⟧ a type of agate with alternate colored layers

oo·dles (o͞od′'lz) ***pl.n.*** ⟦< ?⟧ [Inf.] a great amount; very many

ooze[1] (o͞oz) ***n.*** ⟦OE *wos,* sap⟧ **1** an oozing **2** something that oozes —***vi.*** **oozed, ooz′ing** to flow or leak out slowly —***vt.*** to give forth (a fluid)

ooze[2] (o͞oz) ***n.*** ⟦OE *wase*⟧ soft mud or slime, as at the bottom of a lake

op- *prefix* OB-: used before *p [oppress]*

o·pal (ō′pəl) ***n.*** ⟦< Sans *úpalaḥ,* (precious) stone⟧ an iridescent mineral of various colors: some varieties are semiprecious —**o·pal·es·cent** (ō′pəl es′ənt) ***adj.***

o·paque (ō pāk′) ***adj.*** ⟦< L *opacus,* shady⟧ **1** not transparent **2** dull or dark **3** hard to understand —**o·pac·i·ty** (ō pas′ə tē) or **o·paque′ness** ***n.*** —**o·paque′ly** ***adv.***

op art (äp) a style of abstract painting creating optical effects, as the illusion of movement

op. cit. *abbrev.* ⟦L *opere citato*⟧ in the work cited

OPEC (ō′pek′) ***n.*** Organization of Petroleum Exporting Countries

Op-Ed (äp′ed′) ***adj.*** ⟦*Op(posite) Ed(itorial page)*⟧ designating or on a page in a newspaper featuring a wide variety of columns, letters, etc.

o·pen (ō′pən) ***adj.*** ⟦OE⟧ **1** not closed, covered, clogged, or shut **2** not enclosed *[open* fields*]* **3** spread out; unfolded *[an open* book*]* **4** having gaps, holes, etc. **5** free to be entered, used, etc. *[an open* meeting*]* **6** not decided *[an open* question*]* **7** not closed to new ideas, etc. *[an open* mind*]* **8** generous **9** free from legal or discriminatory restrictions *[open* season, *open* housing*]* **10** not conventional *[open* marriage*]* **11** not already taken *[*the job is *open]* **12** not secret; public **13** frank; candid *[an open* manner*]* —***vt., vi.*** **1** to cause to be, or to become, open **2** to spread out; expand; unfold **3** to begin; start **4** to start operating —**open to 1** willing to receive, discuss, etc. **2** liable to **3** available to —**the open 1** the outdoors **2** public knowledge —**o′pen·er** ***n.*** —**o′pen·ly** ***adv.*** —**o′pen·ness** ***n.***

open air the outdoors —**o′pen-air′** ***adj.***

o′pen-and-shut′ ***adj.*** easily decided

o′pen-end′ed (-en′did) ***adj.*** unlimited

o′pen-eyed′ (-īd′) ***adj.*** with the eyes wide open, as in surprise or watchfulness

o′pen-faced′ ***adj.*** **1** having a frank, honest face **2** designating a sandwich without a top slice of bread Also **o′pen-face′**

o′pen·hand′ed ***adj.*** generous

o′pen-heart′ed ***adj.*** **1** not reserved; frank **2** kindly; generous

o′pen-hearth′ ***adj.*** designating or using a furnace with a wide hearth and low roof, for making steel

o′pen-heart′ surgery surgery on the heart during which the blood is diverted, circulated, and oxygenated by mechanical means

open house 1 an informal reception at one's home **2** a time when an institution is open to visitors

o′pen·ing ***n.*** **1** an open place; hole; gap **2** a clearing **3** a beginning **4** start of operations **5** a favorable chance **6** an unfilled job

o′pen-mind′ed ***adj.*** having a mind open to new ideas; unprejudiced

o′pen·work′ ***n.*** ornamental work, as in cloth, with openings in it

op·er·a[1] (äp′ə rə, äp′rə) ***n.*** ⟦< L, a work⟧ a play having its text set to music and sung to orchestral accompaniment —**op′er·at′ic** (-ə rat′ik) ***adj.***

o·pe·ra[2] (ō′pə rə, äp′ə rə) ***n.*** *pl. of* OPUS

op·er·a·ble (äp′ər ə bəl) ***adj.*** ⟦see OPERATE & -ABLE⟧ **1** able to function **2** that can be treated by surgery

opera glasses a small binocular telescope used in theaters, etc.

op·er·ate (äp′ə rāt′) ***vi.*** **-at′ed, -at′ing** ⟦< L *operari,* to work⟧ **1** to be in action; act; work **2** to have an effect **3** to perform a surgical operation —***vt.*** **1** to put or keep in action **2** to direct; manage

op′er·a′tion (-rā′shən) ***n.*** ⟦< L *operatio*⟧ **1** the act or method of operating **2** a being in action or at work **3** a process or action that is part of a series in some work **4** any surgical procedure to remedy a physical ailment

op′er·a′tion·al ***adj.*** **1** of or having to do with the operation of a device, system, process, etc. **2** *a*) that can be used or operated *b*) in use; operating

op′er·a·tive′ (-rə tiv′, -rāt′iv) ***adj.*** **1** in operation **2** effective **3** connected with physical work or mechanical action

op′er·a′tor (-rāt′ər) ***n.*** **1** one who operates a machine *[a telephone operator]* **2** one engaged in commercial or industrial operations **3** [Slang] a clever, persuasive person

op·er·et·ta (äp'ə ret'ə) ***n.*** ⟦It, dim. of *opera,* OPERA[1]⟧ an amusing opera with spoken dialogue

oph·thal·mic (äf thal'mik) ***adj.*** ⟦< Gr *ophthalmos,* the eye⟧ of or involving the eye

oph·thal·mol·o·gy (äf'thal mäl'ə jē, äp' thə-) ***n.*** ⟦< Gr *ophthalmos,* the eye + -LOGY⟧ the branch of medicine dealing with the eye and its diseases —**oph'thal·mol'o·gist** ***n.***

o·pi·ate (ō'pē it) ***n.*** ⟦ML *opiatum*⟧ **1** a drug containing, or derived from, opium **2** anything that quiets, soothes, or deadens

o·pine (ō pīn') ***vt., vi.*** **o·pined', o·pin'ing** ⟦< L *opinari,* think⟧ to express (an opinion)

o·pin·ion (ə pin'yən) ***n.*** ⟦< L *opinari,* think⟧ **1** a belief based not on certainty but on what seems true or probable **2** an evaluation, estimation, etc. **3** formal expert judgment

o·pin'ion·at'ed (-āt'id) ***adj.*** holding obstinately to one's opinions

o·pi·um (ō'pē əm) ***n.*** ⟦< Gr *opos,* vegetable juice⟧ a narcotic drug prepared from the seed of a certain poppy

o·pos·sum (ə päs'əm) ***n.*** ⟦< AmInd, white beast⟧ a small, nocturnal, tree-dwelling American marsupial that becomes motionless when frightened

op·po·nent (ə pō'nənt) ***n.*** ⟦< L *ob-* (see OB-) + *ponere,* to place⟧ one who opposes, as in a game; adversary

op·por·tune (äp'ər to͞on') ***adj.*** ⟦< L *ob-* (see OB-) + *portus,* PORT[1]⟧ **1** suitable: said of time **2** well-timed

op'por·tun'ism' ***n.*** the adapting of one's actions, thoughts, etc. to circumstances, as in politics, without regard for principles —**op'por·tun'ist** ***n., adj.*** —**op'por·tun·is'tic** (-to͞o nis'tik) ***adj.***

op·por·tu·ni·ty (äp'ər to͞o'nə tē) ***n.,*** *pl.* **-ties** **1** a combination of circumstances favorable for the purpose **2** a good chance, as to advance oneself

op·pose (ə pōz') ***vt.*** **-posed', -pos'ing** ⟦< L *ob-* (see OB-) + *ponere,* to place⟧ **1** to place opposite **2** to contend with; resist —**op·pos'a·ble** ***adj.***

op·po·site (äp'ə zit) ***adj.*** ⟦< L *ob-* (see OB-) + *ponere,* to place⟧ **1** set against; in a contrary direction: often with *to* **2** entirely different; exactly contrary —***n.*** anything opposed —***prep.*** across from —**op'po·site·ly** ***adv.***

opposite number one whose position, rank, etc. parallels another's in a different place or organization

op'po·si'tion (-zish'ən) ***n.*** **1** an opposing **2** resistance, contrast, hostility, etc. **3** *a)* one that opposes *b)* [*often* **O-**] a political party opposing the party in power

op·press (ə pres') ***vt.*** ⟦< L *ob-* (see OB-) + *premere,* to press⟧ **1** to weigh heavily on the mind of; worry **2** to keep down by the cruel or unjust use of authority —**op·pres'sor** ***n.***

op·pres·sion (ə presh'ən) ***n.*** **1** an oppressing or being oppressed **2** a thing that oppresses **3** physical or mental distress

op·pres·sive (ə pres'iv) ***adj.*** **1** causing discomfort **2** tyrannical **3** distressing —**op·pres'sive·ly** ***adv.***

op·pro·bri·ous (ə prō'brē əs) ***adj.*** expressing opprobrium; abusive

op·pro'bri·um (-əm) ***n.*** ⟦< L *ob-* (see OB-) + *probrum,* a disgrace⟧ **1** the disgrace attached to shameful conduct **2** contempt for something regarded as inferior

opt (äpt) ***vi.*** ⟦< L *optare,* to wish⟧ to make a choice: often with *for* —**opt out (of)** to choose not to be or continue in (some activity, organization, etc.)

op·tic (äp'tik) ***adj.*** ⟦< Gr *ōps,* an eye⟧ of the eye or sense of sight

op·ti·cal (äp'ti kəl) ***adj.*** **1** of the sense of sight; visual **2** of optics **3** for aiding vision —**op'ti·cal·ly** ***adv.***

optical disc (or **disk**) any disk on which data, as computer files or music, is stored in the form of microscopic pits to be read by a laser

op·ti·cian (äp tish'ən) ***n.*** one who makes or sells eyeglasses, etc.

op·tics (äp'tiks) ***n.*** the branch of physics dealing with light and vision

op·ti·mism (äp'tə miz'əm) ***n.*** ⟦< L *optimus,* best⟧ **1** the belief that good ultimately prevails over evil **2** the tendency to take the most hopeful view of matters —**op'ti·mist** ***n.*** —**op'ti·mis'tic** ***adj.*** —**op'ti·mis'ti·cal·ly** ***adv.***

op'ti·mum (-məm) ***n.,*** *pl.* **-mums** or **-ma** (-mə) ⟦see prec.⟧ the best or most favorable degree, condition, etc. —***adj.*** most favorable; best: also **op'ti·mal** (-məl)

op·tion (äp'shən) ***n.*** ⟦< L *optare,* to wish⟧ **1** a choosing; choice **2** the right of choosing **3** something that is or can be chosen **4** the right to buy, sell, or lease at a fixed price within a specified time —**op'tion·al** ***adj.***

op·tom·e·try (äp täm'ə trē) ***n.*** ⟦< Gr *optikos,* optic + *metron,* a measure⟧ the profession of testing and examining the eyes and prescribing glasses to correct vision problems —**op·tom'e·trist** ***n.***

op·u·lent (äp'yo͞o lənt, -yə-) ***adj.*** ⟦< L *ops,* riches⟧ **1** very wealthy **2** abundant —**op'u·lence** ***n.***

o·pus (ō'pəs) ***n.,*** *pl.* **o·pe·ra** (ō'pə rə, äp'ə rə) or **o'pus·es** ⟦L, a work⟧ a work; composition; esp., any of the numbered musical works of a composer

or (ôr) ***conj.*** ⟦OE *oththe*⟧ a coordinating conjunction introducing: *a)* an alternative *[* red *or* blue*]* or the last in a series of choices *b)* a synonymous word or phrase *[*oral, *or* spoken*]*

-or (ər, ôr) ⟦< L⟧ *suffix* a person or thing that (does a specified thing) *[inventor]*

OR Oregon

or·a·cle (ôr'ə kəl) ***n.*** ⟦< L *orare,* pray⟧ **1** among the ancient Greeks and Romans, *a)* the place where, or medium by which, deities were consulted *b)* the revelation of a medium or priest **2** *a)* a person of great knowledge *b)* statements of such a person —**o·rac·u·lar** (ō rak'yo͞o lər) ***adj.***

o·ral (ôr'əl) ***adj.*** ⟦< L *os,* the mouth⟧ **1** uttered; spoken **2** of or near the mouth

—**o'ral·ly** ***adv.***

oral history **1** the gathering of personal recollections in tape recorded interviews **2** a historical account based on this

or·ange (ôr'inj, är'-) ***n.*** ⟦< Sans *naranga*⟧ **1** a round, edible, reddish-yellow citrus fruit, with a sweet, juicy pulp **2** the evergreen tree it grows on **3** reddish yellow

or'ange·ade' ***n.*** a drink made of orange juice, water, and sugar

o·rang·u·tan (ô raŋ'oo tan') ***n.*** ⟦< Malay *oraṅ*, man + *utan*, forest⟧ an ape of Borneo and Sumatra with shaggy, reddish-brown hair and very long arms

o·rate (ō rāt', ôr'āt') ***vi.*** **-rat'ed, -rat'ing** to make an oration; speak in a pompous or bombastic way

o·ra·tion (ō rā'shən, ô-) ***n.*** ⟦< L *orare*, speak⟧ a formal speech, esp. one given at a ceremony

or·a·tor (ôr'ət ər, är'-) ***n.*** an eloquent public speaker

or·a·to·ri·o (ôr'ə tôr'ē ō') ***n.***, *pl.* **-os'** ⟦It, small chapel⟧ a long, dramatic musical work, usually on a religious theme, sung but not acted out

or·a·to·ry (ôr'ə tôr'ē, är'-) ***n.***, *pl.* **-ries** ⟦< L *oratoria*⟧ skill in public speaking —**or'a·tor'i·cal** ***adj.***

orb (ôrb) ***n.*** ⟦L *orbis*, a circle⟧ a sphere, esp. a celestial body, as the sun or moon

or·bit (ôr'bit) ***n.*** ⟦< L *orbis*, a circle⟧ **1** the path of a celestial body during its revolution around another **2** the path of an artificial satellite or spacecraft around a celestial body —***vi.***, ***vt.*** to move in, or put into, an orbit —**or'bit·al** ***adj.***

or·chard (ôr'chərd) ***n.*** ⟦OE *ortgeard*⟧ **1** land for growing fruit trees **2** the trees

or·ches·tra (ôr'kis trə, -kes'-) ***n.*** ⟦< Gr *orcheisthai*, to dance⟧ **1** the space in front of a theater stage, where the musicians sit: in full **orchestra pit** **2** the seats on the main floor of a theater **3** *a*) a group of musicians playing together *b*) their instruments —**or·ches'tral** (-kes'trəl) ***adj.***

or'ches·trate' (-trāt') ***vt.***, ***vi.*** **-trat'ed, -trat'ing** **1** to arrange (music) for an orchestra **2** to coordinate or arrange (something) —**or'ches·tra'tion** ***n.***

or·chid (ôr'kid) ***n.*** ⟦< Gr *orchis*, testicle: from the shape of the roots⟧ **1** a perennial plant having flowers with three petals, one of which is lip-shaped **2** this flower **3** pale purple

or·dain (ôr dān') ***vt.*** ⟦< L *ordo*, an order⟧ **1** to decree; establish; enact **2** to invest with the office of minister, priest, or rabbi —**or·dain'ment** ***n.***

or·deal (ôr dēl') ***n.*** ⟦OE *ordal*⟧ any difficult or painful experience

or·der (ôr'dər) ***n.*** ⟦< L *ordo*, straight row⟧ **1** social position **2** a state of peace; orderly conduct **3** arrangement of things or events; series **4** a definite plan; system **5** a military, monastic, or social brotherhood **6** a condition in which everything is in its place and working properly **7** condition in general *[in working order]* **8** an authoritative command, instruction, etc. **9** a class; kind **10** an established method, as of conduct in meetings, etc. **11** *a*) a request to supply something *[an order for books]* *b*) the goods supplied **12** *[usually pl.]* the position of ordained minister, priest, etc. *[to take holy orders]* —***vt.***, ***vi.*** **1** to put or keep (things) in order; arrange **2** to command **3** to request (something to be supplied) —**in** (or **out of**) **order** **1** in (or not in) proper position **2** in (or not in) good condition **3** in (or not in) accordance with the rules —**in order that** so that —**in order to** for the purpose of —**in short order** quickly —**on the order of** similar to —**to order** in accordance with the buyer's specifications

or'der·ly ***adj.*** **1** neat or tidy **2** well-behaved —***n.***, *pl.* **-lies** **1** an enlisted person assigned to perform personal services for an officer **2** a male hospital attendant —**or'der·li·ness** ***n.***

or·di·nal (ôrd''n əl) ***adj.*** ⟦< L *ordo*, order⟧ expressing order in a series —***n.*** any number showing order in a series (e.g., first, tenth): in full **ordinal number**

or·di·nance (ôrd''n əns) ***n.*** ⟦< L *ordo*, an order⟧ a statute or regulation, esp. a municipal one

or·di·nar·i·ly (ôrd''n er'ə lē) ***adv.*** usually; as a rule

or·di·nar·y (ôrd''n er'ē) ***adj.*** ⟦< L *ordo*, an order⟧ **1** customary; usual **2** familiar; unexceptional; common —**out of the ordinary** unusual

or·di·nate (ôrd''n it, -āt') ***n.*** ⟦< L (*linea*) *ordinate* (*applicata*), line applied in ordered manner⟧ *Math.* the vertical distance of a point from a horizontal axis

or·di·na·tion (ôrd''n ā'shən) ***n.*** an ordaining or being ordained to the clergy

ord·nance (ôrd'nəns) ***n.*** ⟦< ORDINANCE⟧ **1** artillery **2** all military weapons, ammunition, etc.

or·dure (ôr'jər) ***n.*** ⟦< L *horridus*, horrid⟧ dung; filth

ore (ôr) ***n.*** ⟦OE *ar*, brass⟧ a natural combination of minerals, esp. one from which a metal or metals can be profitably extracted

o·reg·a·no (ô reg'ə nō, ə-) ***n.*** ⟦< Sp < Gr *origanon*⟧ an herb of the mint family, with fragrant leaves used for seasoning

Or·e·gon (ôr'i gən, -gän') NW coastal state of the U.S.: 97,060 sq. mi.; pop. 2,842,000; cap. Salem: abbrev. *OR* —**Or'e·go'ni·an** (-gō'nē ən) ***adj.***, ***n.***

or·gan (ôr'gən) ***n.*** ⟦< Gr *organon*, an implement⟧ **1** a keyboard musical instrument with sets of graduated pipes through which compressed air is passed, causing sound by vibration **2** in animals and plants, a part adapted to perform a specific function **3** a means for performing some action **4** a means of communicating ideas, as a periodical

or·gan·dy or **or·gan·die** (ôr'gən dē) ***n.***, *pl.* **-dies** ⟦Fr *organdi*⟧ a very sheer, crisp cotton fabric

or·gan·elle (ôr'gə nel') ***n.*** ⟦< L *organum*,

tool + dim. of *-ellus*]] a discrete structure within a cell, as a chloroplast, having specialized functions, a distinctive chemical composition, etc.

or·gan·ic (ôr gan′ik) ***adj.*** **1** of or having to do with a bodily organ **2** inherent; inborn **3** systematically arranged **4** designating or of any chemical compound containing carbon **5** of, like, or derived from living organisms **6** grown with only natural fertilizers —**or·gan′i·cal·ly** ***adv.***

or·gan·ism (ôr′gə niz′əm) ***n.*** any living thing

or′gan·ist ***n.*** an organ player

or·gan·i·za·tion (ôr′gə ni zā′shən) ***n.*** **1** an organizing or being organized **2** any organized group, as a club —**or′gan·i·za′tion·al** ***adj.***

or·gan·ize (ôr′gə nīz′) ***vt.*** **-ized′**, **-iz′ing** **1** to provide with an orderly structure or arrangement **2** to arrange for **3** to institute; establish **4** to persuade to join a cause, group, etc. —***vi.*** to become organized —**or′gan·iz′er** ***n.***

or·gan·za (ôr gan′zə) ***n.*** a thin, stiff fabric of rayon, silk, etc.

or·gasm (ôr′gaz′əm) ***n.*** [[< Gr *organ,* to swell]] the climax of a sexual act

or·gy (ôr′jē) ***n.***, *pl.* **-gies** [[< Gr *orgia,* secret rites]] **1** a wild party, esp. with sexual activity **2** unrestrained indulgence in any activity

o·ri·el (ōr′ē əl, ôr′-) ***n.*** [[< ML *oriolum,* porch]] a bay window resting on a bracket or a corbel

o·ri·ent (ôr′ē ənt; *for v.,* -ent′, -ənt) ***n.*** [[< L *oriri,* arise: used of the rising sun]] [Old Poet.] the east —***vt.*** to adjust (oneself) to a particular situation, with regard to direction or position, etc. —**the Orient** the East, or Asia; esp. the Far East —**o′ri·en·ta′tion** ***n.***

O′ri·en′tal (-ent′'l) ***adj.*** of the Far East or its people, etc. —***n.*** a person born in the Far East or a member of a people of that region Now often regarded as a term of disparagement

or·i·fice (ôr′ə fis, är′-) ***n.*** [[< L *os,* a mouth + *facere,* make]] a mouth of a tube, cavity, etc.; opening

orig *abbrev.* **1** origin **2** original **3** originally

o·ri·ga·mi (ôr′ə gä′mē) ***n.*** [[Jpn]] the Japanese art of folding paper to form flowers, animals, etc.

or·i·gin (ôr′ə jin, är′-) ***n.*** [[< L *oriri,* to rise]] **1** a coming into existence or use; beginning **2** parentage; birth **3** source; root; cause

o·rig·i·nal (ə rij′i nəl) ***adj.*** **1** first; earliest **2** never having been before; new; novel **3** capable of creating something new **4** being that from which copies are made —***n.*** **1** a primary type that has given rise to varieties **2** an original work, as of art or literature —**o·rig′i·nal′i·ty** (-nal′ə tē) ***n.*** —**o·rig′i·nal·ly** ***adv.***

o·rig′i·nate′ (-nāt′) ***vt.*** **-nat′ed**, **-nat′ing** to bring into being; esp., to invent —***vi.*** to begin; start —**o·rig′i·na′tion** ***n.*** —**o·rig′i·na′tor** ***n.***

O-ring (ō′riŋ′) ***n.*** a ring-shaped seal of rubber, plastic, etc., used to prevent leaks

o·ri·ole (ôr′ē ōl′) ***n.*** [[< L *aurum,* gold]] a bright-orange and black American bird that builds a hanging nest

O·ri·on (ō rī′ən) ***n.*** a very bright equatorial constellation

Or·lon (ôr′län′) *trademark for* a synthetic acrylic fiber similar to nylon, or a fabric made from this fiber

or·mo·lu (ôr′mə lo͞o′) ***n.*** [[Fr *or moulu,* ground gold]] a copper and tin alloy used to imitate gold

or·na·ment (ôr′nə mənt; *for v.,* -ment′) ***n.*** [[< L *ornare,* adorn]] **1** anything that adorns; decoration **2** one whose character or talent adds luster to the surroundings, etc. —***vt.*** to decorate —**or′na·men′tal** ***adj.*** —**or′na·men·ta′tion** ***n.***

or·nate (ôr nāt′) ***adj.*** [[< L *ornare,* adorn]] heavily ornamented; showy —**or·nate′ly** ***adv.*** —**or·nate′ness** ***n.***

or·ner·y (ôr′nər ē) ***adj.*** [[< ORDINARY]] [Inf.] **1** mean; nasty **2** obstinate —**or′ner·i·ness** ***n.***

or·ni·thol·o·gy (ôr′nə thäl′ə jē) ***n.*** [[< Gr *ornis,* bird + -LOGY]] the branch of zoology dealing with birds —**or′ni·thol′o·gist** ***n.***

o·ro·tund (ôr′ə tund′) ***adj.*** [[< L *os,* mouth + *rotundas,* round]] **1** resonant: said of the voice **2** bombastic or pompous

or·phan (ôr′fən) ***n.*** [[< Gr *orphanos*]] a child whose parents are dead —***adj.*** **1** being an orphan **2** of or for orphans —***vt.*** to cause to become an orphan

or′phan·age (-ij) ***n.*** an institution that is a home for orphans

Or·phe·us (ôr′fē əs) ***n.*** *Gr. Myth.* a poet-musician with magic musical powers

or·ris (ôr′is, är′-) ***n.*** [[< Gr *iris,* iris]] a European iris, esp. one with a root (**or′ris·root′**) pulverized for perfumery, etc.

ortho- [[< Gr *orthos,* straight]] *combining form* **1** straight *[orthodontics]* **2** proper; correct *[orthography]* Also **orth-**

or·tho·don·tics (ôr′thə dän′tiks) ***n.*** [[< ORTH(O)- + Gr *odōn,* tooth + -ICS]] the branch of dentistry concerned with correcting tooth irregularities: also **or′tho·don′tia** (-dän′shə, -shē ə) —**or′tho·don′tist** ***n.***

or·tho·dox (ôr′thə däks′) ***adj.*** [[< Gr *orthos,* straight + *doxa,* opinion]] conforming to the usual beliefs or established doctrines; approved or conventional —**or′tho·dox′y**, *pl.* **-ies**, ***n.***

or·thog·ra·phy (ôr thäg′rə fē) ***n.***, *pl.* **-phies** [[< Gr: see ORTHO- & -GRAPHY]] **1** correct spelling **2** spelling as a subject for study —**or·tho·graph·ic** (ôr′thə graf′ik) ***adj.***

or·tho·pe·dics or **or·tho·pae·dics** (ôr′thə pē′diks) ***n.*** [[< Gr *orthos,* straight + *paideia,* training of children]] the branch of medicine dealing with deformities, diseases, and injuries of the bones, joints, muscles, etc. —**or′tho·pe′dic** or **or′tho·pae′dic** ***adj.*** —**or′tho·pe′dist** or **or′tho·pae′dist** ***n.***

-o·ry (ôr′ē, ər ē) [[< L *-orius*]] *suffix* **1** of,

having the nature of *[sensory]* 2 a place or thing for *[crematory]*

OS *abbrev.* Old Saxon

O·sa·ka (ō′sä kə) seaport in S Honshu, Japan: pop. 2,648,000

os·cil·late (äs′ə lāt′) ***vi.*** **-lat′ed, -lat′ing** ⟦< L *oscillum,* a swing⟧ **1** to swing to and fro **2** to vacillate **3** *Physics* to vary regularly between high and low values: said as of an electric current —**os′cil·la′tion** ***n.*** —**os′cil·la′tor** ***n.***

os·cil·lo·scope (ə sil′ə skōp′) ***n.*** ⟦< L *oscillare,* to swing + -SCOPE⟧ an instrument that visually displays an electrical wave on a fluorescent screen

os·cu·late (äs′kyo͞o lāt′, -kyə-) ***vt., vi.*** **-lat′ed, -lat′ing** ⟦< L *osculum,* little mouth⟧ to kiss: a facetious usage —**os′cu·la′tion** ***n.***

-ose[1] (ōs) ⟦Fr < (*gluc*)*ose*⟧ *suffix* **1** a carbohydrate *[sucrose]* **2** the product of a protein hydrolysis

-ose[2] (ōs) ⟦L *-osus*⟧ *suffix* full of, like

Osh·kosh (äsh′käsh′) city in E Wisconsin: pop. 55,000

o·sier (ō′zhər) ***n.*** ⟦< ML *auseria,* willow⟧ a willow with branches used for baskets and furniture

-o·sis (ō′sis) ⟦< Gr⟧ *suffix* **1** condition, action *[hypnosis]* **2** an abnormal or diseased condition *[psychosis]*

Os·lo (äz′lō, äs′-) seaport & capital of Norway: pop. 459,000

os·mo·sis (äs mō′sis, äz-) ***n.*** ⟦< Gr *ōsmos,* impulse⟧ **1** the tendency of fluids to pass through a membrane so as to equalize concentrations on both sides **2** the movement of fluids through a membrane **3** an apparently effortless absorption of ideas, feelings, etc. —**os·mot′ic** (-mät′ik) ***adj.***

os·prey (äs′prē, -prā) ***n., pl.*** **-preys** ⟦< L *os,* a bone + *frangere,* to break⟧ a large diving bird that feeds mainly on fish

os·si·fy (äs′ə fī′) ***vt., vi.*** **-fied′, -fy′ing** ⟦< L *os,* a bone + -FY⟧ **1** to change into bone **2** to fix rigidly in a custom, practice, etc. —**os′si·fi·ca′tion** ***n.***

os·ten·si·ble (ä sten′sə bəl) ***adj.*** ⟦< L *ostendere,* to show⟧ apparent; seeming —**os·ten′si·bly** ***adv.***

os·ten·ta·tion (äs′tən tā′shən) ***n.*** ⟦< L *ostendere,* to show⟧ showy display; pretentiousness —**os′ten·ta′tious** ***adj.***

osteo- ⟦< Gr *osteon,* a bone⟧ *combining form* bone or bones

os·te·o·ar·thri·tis (äs′tē ō′är thrīt′is) ***n.*** ⟦prec. + ARTHRITIS⟧ a common form of arthritis marked by cartilage degeneration and bone enlargement

os·te·op·a·thy (äs′tē äp′ə thē) ***n.*** ⟦ModL: see OSTEO- & -PATHY⟧ a school of medicine and surgery that emphasizes the interrelationship of muscles and bones to other body systems —**os·te·o·path** (äs′tē ə path′) ***n.*** —**os′te·o·path′ic** ***adj.***

os·te·o·po·ro·sis (äs′tē ō′pə rō′sis) ***n.*** ⟦OSTEO- + L *porus,* a pore + -OSIS⟧ a bone disorder marked by porous, brittle bones

os·to·my (äs′tə mē) ***n., pl.*** **-mies** any surgery connecting a hollow organ to the outside of the body or to another hollow organ

os·tra·cize (äs′trə sīz′) ***vt.*** **-cized′, -ciz′ing** ⟦< Gr *ostrakon,* a shell or potsherd (cast as a ballot)⟧ to banish from a group, society, etc. —**os′tra·cism′** (-siz′əm) ***n.***

os·trich (äs′trich, ôs′-) ***n.*** ⟦< L *avis,* bird + *struthio,* ostrich⟧ a large, swift-running bird of Africa and SW Asia

OT *abbrev.* **1** Old Testament **2** overtime

O·thel·lo (ō thel′ō) ***n.*** the title character of a tragedy by Shakespeare

oth·er (u*th*′ər) ***adj.*** ⟦OE⟧ **1** being the remaining one or ones *[Bill and the other boys]* **2** different or distinct from that or those referred to or implied *[use your other foot]* **3** additional *[he has no other coat]* —***pron.*** **1** the other one **2** some other one *[do as others do]* —***adv.*** otherwise *[he can't do other than go]* —**the other day** (or **night,** etc.) on a recent day (or night, etc.)

oth′er·wise′ ***adv.*** **1** in another manner; differently *[she believes otherwise]* **2** in all other respects *[he is otherwise intelligent]* **3** in other circumstances **4** if not *[do it now; otherwise, you'll forget it]* —***adj.*** different

oth′er·world′ly ***adj.*** being apart from earthly interests; spiritual

o·ti·ose (ō′shē ōs′) ***adj.*** ⟦< L *otium,* leisure⟧ **1** futile **2** useless

Ot·ta·wa (ät′ə wə, -wä′) capital of Canada, in SE Ontario: pop. 323,000

ot·ter (ät′ər) ***n.*** ⟦OE *oter*⟧ **1** a furry, carnivorous mammal with webbed feet **2** its fur

ot·to·man (ät′ə mən) ***n.*** ⟦Fr *ottomane*⟧ a low, cushioned seat or footstool

ouch (ouch) ***interj.*** used to express sudden pain

ought (ôt) ***v.aux.*** used with infinitives and meaning: **1** to be compelled by obligation, duty, or desirability *[you ought to eat more]* **2** to be expected *[it ought to be over soon]*

oui (wē) ***adv., interj.*** ⟦Fr⟧ yes

Oui·ja (wē′jə, -jē) ⟦< prec. + Ger *ja,* yes⟧ *trademark for* a board with the alphabet and various symbols on it and a sliding pointer: believed by some to convey messages from spirits

ounce (ouns) ***n.*** ⟦< L *uncia,* a twelfth⟧ **1** a unit of weight, $\frac{1}{16}$ pound avoirdupois or $\frac{1}{12}$ pound troy **2** fluid ounce, $\frac{1}{16}$ pint

our (our) ***poss. pronominal adj.*** ⟦OE *ure*⟧ of, belonging to, or done by us

ours (ourz) ***pron.*** that or those belonging to us: poss. form of WE *[that book is ours; ours are better]*

our·selves (our selvz′) ***pron.*** a form of WE, used as an intensive *[we went ourselves]*, as a reflexive *[we saw ourselves in the mirror]*, or with the meaning "our true selves" *[we are not ourselves when we are sick]*

-ous (əs) ⟦< L *-osus*⟧ *suffix* having, full of, characterized by *[beauteous]*

oust (oust) ***vt.*** ⟦< L *ostare,* obstruct⟧ to force out; expel; dispossess

oust′er ***n.*** an ousting or being ousted

out (out) ***adv.*** ⟦OE *ut*⟧ **1** away or

removed from a place, position, etc. **2** into the open air **3** into existence or activity [disease broke *out*] **4** *a*) to a conclusion [argue it *out*] *b*) completely [tired *out*] **5** into sight or notice [the moon came *out*] **6** from existence or activity [fade *out*] **7** aloud [sing *out*] **8** beyond a regular surface, condition, etc. [stand *out*] **9** into disuse [long skirts went *out*] **10** from a group or stock [pick *out*] **11** [Slang] into unconsciousness **12** *Baseball* in a manner that results in an out [to fly *out*] —***adj.*** **1** external: usually in combination [*outpost*] **2** beyond regular limits **3** away from work, etc. **4** in error [*out* in one's estimates] **5** not in use, operation, etc. **6** [Inf.] having suffered a financial loss [*out* twenty dollars] **7** [Inf.] outmoded **8** *Baseball* having failed to get on base —***prep.*** **1** out of **2** along, and away from a central location —***n.*** **1** something that is out **2** [Slang] a way out; excuse **3** *Baseball* the failure of a player to reach base safely —***vi.*** to become known [the truth will *out*] —***vt.*** [Inf.] to identify (a person) publicly as a homosexual —**on the outs** [Inf.] on unfriendly terms —**out for** trying to get or do —**out of 1** from inside of **2** beyond **3** from (material, etc.) [made *out of* stone] **4** because of [*out of* spite] **5** having no [*out of* gas] **6** so as to deprive —**out to** trying to

out- *combining form* **1** at or from a point away, outside, etc. [*outpatient*] **2** going away or forth, outward [*outbound*] **3** better or more than [*outdo*]

out'age ***n.*** an interruption of operation, as of electric power

out'-and-out' ***adj.*** thorough

out'back' ***n.*** any remote, sparsely settled region viewed as uncivilized

out'bid' ***vt.*** **-bid', -bid'ding** to bid or offer more than (someone else)

out'board' ***adj.*** outside the hull of a ship or boat [an *outboard* motor]

out'bound' ***adj.*** outward bound

out'break' ***n.*** a breaking out; sudden occurrence, as of disease or rioting

out'build'ing ***n.*** a structure, as a shed, separate from the main building

out'burst' ***n.*** a sudden release, as of feeling or energy

out'cast' ***adj.*** driven out; rejected —***n.*** a person rejected, as by society

out'class' ***vt.*** to surpass

out'come' ***n.*** result; consequence

out'crop' ***n.*** **1** the emergence of a mineral at the earth's surface **2** the mineral that so emerges

out'cry' ***n., pl.*** **-cries'** **1** a crying out **2** a strong objection

out'dat'ed ***adj.*** no longer current

out'dis'tance ***vt.*** **-tanced, -tanc·ing** to get ahead of, as in a race

out'do' ***vt.*** **-did', -done', -do'ing** to exceed or surpass —**outdo oneself** to do better than one expected to do

out'door' ***adj.*** **1** being or taking place outdoors **2** of or fond of the outdoors

out'doors' ***adv.*** in or into the open; outside —***n.*** any area outside a building

out'er ***adj.*** farther out or away

out'er·most' ***adj.*** farthest out

outer space space beyond the earth's atmosphere or beyond the solar system

out'er·wear' ***n.*** garments, as overcoats, worn over the usual clothing

out'field' ***n.*** *Baseball* **1** the playing area beyond the infield **2** the players (**out'field'ers**) positioned there

out'fit' ***n.*** **1** the equipment used in an activity **2** clothing worn together; ensemble **3** a group associated in an activity —***vt.*** **-fit'ted, -fit'ting** to furnish as with an outfit —**out'fit'ter** ***n.***

out'flank' ***vt.*** to go around and beyond the flank of (enemy troops)

out'fox' ***vt.*** to outsmart

out'go' ***n., pl.*** **-goes'** that which is paid out; expenditure

out'go'ing ***adj.*** **1** *a*) leaving *b*) retiring from office **2** sociable, friendly, etc.

out'grow' ***vt.*** **-grew', -grown', -grow'ing** **1** to grow faster or larger than **2** to lose in becoming mature **3** to grow too large for

out'growth' ***n.*** **1** a growing out or that which grows out **2** a result or development

out'guess' ***vt.*** to outwit in anticipating

out'house' ***n.*** a small outdoor structure used as a toilet, having a seat with a hole over a deep pit

out'ing ***n.*** **1** a pleasure trip **2** an outdoor walk, ride, etc.

out'land'ish (-lan'dish) ***adj.*** very odd or strange; fantastic; bizarre

out'last' ***vt.*** to endure longer than

out'law' ***n.*** a habitual or notorious criminal —***vt.*** to declare illegal

out'lay' ***n.*** **1** a spending (*of* money, etc.) **2** money, etc. spent

out'let' ***n.*** **1** a passage for letting something out **2** a means of expression [an *outlet* for anger] **3** a retail store selling defective or surplus goods at a discount: in full **outlet store** **4** a point in an electric circuit where a plug can be inserted to connect with a power supply

out'line' ***n.*** **1** a line bounding the limits of an object **2** a sketch showing only contours **3** [*also pl.*] a general plan **4** a systematic summary —***vt.*** **-lined', -lin'ing** **1** to draw in outline **2** to give or write the main points of

out'live' ***vt.*** **-lived', -liv'ing** to live or endure longer than; outlast

out'look' ***n.*** **1** the view from a place **2** viewpoint **3** expectation or prospect

out'ly'ing ***adj.*** relatively far out from a certain point; remote

out'ma·neu'ver or **out'ma·noeu'vre** ***vt.*** **-vered** or **-vred, -ver·ing** or **-vring** to outwit by maneuvering

out'match' ***vt.*** to be superior to; outdo

out'mod'ed ***adj.*** no longer in fashion or accepted; obsolete

out'num'ber ***vt.*** to exceed in number

out'-of-date' ***adj.*** no longer in style or use; old-fashioned

out'-of-doors' ***adj.*** OUTDOOR —***adv., n.*** OUTDOORS

out'-of-the-way' ***adj.*** **1** secluded **2**

not common; unusual

out′-of-town′er *n.* a visitor from another town or city

out′pa′tient *n.* a patient treated at a hospital, etc. without becoming an inpatient

out′place′ment *n.* assistance in finding a new job, provided to an employee by the employer

out′play′ *vt.* to play better than

out′post′ *n.* **1** *Mil. a)* a small group stationed at a distance from the main force *b)* the station occupied by such a group *c)* a foreign base **2** a frontier settlement

out′put′ *n.* **1** the work done or amount produced, esp. over a given period **2** information delivered by a computer **3** *Elec.* the useful voltage, current, or power delivered

out′rage′ *n.* ⟦ult. < L *ultra,* beyond⟧ **1** an extremely vicious or violent act **2** a deep insult or offense **3** great anger, etc. aroused by this —*vt.* **-raged′, -rag′ing 1** to commit an outrage upon or against **2** to cause outrage in

out′ra′geous (-rā′jəs) *adj.* **1** involving or doing great injury or wrong **2** very offensive or shocking —**out′ra′geous·ly** *adv.* —**out′ra′geous·ness** *n.*

out′rank′ *vt.* to exceed in rank

ou·tré (o͞o trā′) *adj.* ⟦Fr⟧ **1** exaggerated **2** eccentric; bizarre

out·reach (out′rēch′; *for v., also* out′ rēch′) *vt., vi.* to reach farther (than) —*n.* a reaching out —*adj.* designating or of a program extending assistance, services, etc. to people in the community

out′rid′er *n.* **1** a rider on horseback who accompanies a stagecoach, etc. **2** a cowboy riding a range, as to keep cattle from straying **3** a forerunner

CANOE WITH OUTRIGGER

out′rig′ger (-rig′ər) *n.* **1** a timber rigged out from the side of certain canoes to prevent tipping **2** a canoe of this type

out·right (out′rīt′, out′rīt′) *adj.* **1** without reservation **2** complete —*adv.* **1** entirely **2** openly **3** at once

out′run′ *vt.* **-ran′, -run′, -run′ning 1** to run faster than **2** to exceed

out′sell′ *vt.* **-sold′, -sell′ing** to sell in greater amounts than

out′set′ *n.* a setting out; beginning

out′shine′ *vt.* **-shone′** or **-shined′, -shin′ing 1** to shine brighter or longer than (another) **2** to surpass; excel

out·side (out′sīd′, out′sīd′) *n.* **1** the outer side or part; exterior **2** outward appearance **3** any area not inside —*adj.* **1** of or on the outside; outer **2** extreme *[*an *outside* estimate*]* **3** slight *[*an *outside* chance*]* —*adv.* **1** on or to the outside **2** outdoors —*prep.* **1** on or to the outer side of **2** beyond the limits of —**outside of 1** outside **2** [Inf.] other than

out·sid·er (out′sīd′ər, out′sīd′ər) *n.* one who is not included in a given group

out′size′ *n.* an unusually large size —*adj.* unusually large

out′skirts′ *pl.n.* districts remote from the center, as of a city

out′smart′ *vt.* to overcome by cunning or cleverness; outwit —**outsmart oneself** to have one's efforts at cunning or cleverness result in one's own disadvantage

out′source′ *vt.* **-sourced′, -sourc′ing** to transfer (manufacturing tasks, etc.) to outside contractors, esp. in order to reduce operating costs

out′spo′ken *adj.* **1** unrestrained in speech **2** spoken boldly or candidly

out′spread′ *adj.* spread out; extended

out′stand′ing *adj.* **1** prominent; distinguished **2** unpaid; uncollected **3** issued and sold: said of stocks and bonds

out′sta′tion *n.* a post or station in a remote or unsettled area

out′stretch′ *vt.* to stretch out; extend

out′strip′ *vt.* **-stripped′, -strip′ping 1** to go at a faster pace than **2** to excel; surpass

out′take′ *n.* a filmed scene, defective recording, etc. not used as or in the final version

out′vote′ *vt.* **-vot′ed, -vot′ing** to defeat in a vote

out′ward *adj.* **1** having to do with the outside; outer **2** clearly apparent **3** away from the interior —*adv.* toward the outside: also **out′wards** —**out′ward·ly** *adv.*

out′wear′ *vt.* **-wore′, -worn′, -wear′ing** to outlast

out′weigh′ *vt.* **1** to weigh more than **2** to be more important than

out′wit′ *vt.* **-wit′ted, -wit′ting** to get the better of by cleverness

o·va (ō′və) *n. pl. of* OVUM

o·val (ō′vəl) *adj.* ⟦< L *ovum,* egg⟧ egg-shaped; elliptical —*n.* anything oval

o·va·ry (ō′və rē) *n., pl.* **-ries** ⟦< L *ovum,* egg⟧ **1** a female reproductive gland producing eggs **2** *Bot.* the enlarged, hollow part of the pistil, containing ovules —**o·var·i·an** (ō ver′ē ən) *adj.*

o·vate (ō′vāt′) *adj.* egg-shaped; oval

o·va·tion (ō vā′shən) *n.* ⟦< L *ovare,* celebrate a triumph⟧ enthusiastic applause or an enthusiastic public welcome

ov·en (uv′ən) *n.* ⟦OE *ofen*⟧ a compartment or receptacle for baking, roasting, heating, etc.

ov′en·proof′ *adj.* able to withstand the high temperatures of an oven without being damaged

o·ver (ō′vər) *prep.* ⟦OE *ofer*⟧ **1** *a)* in, at, or to a position above *b)* across and down from *[*to fall *over* a cliff*]* **2** so as to cover [shutters *over* the windows] 3 upon [to cast a spell *over* someone] 4 above in authority, power, etc. 5 on or to the other side of [fly *over* the lake] 6 throughout [*over* the whole city] 7 during [*over* the years] 8 more than [*over* ten cents] 9 in preference to 10 concerning —***adv.*** 1 *a)* above or across *b)* across the brim or edge 2 more [three hours or *over*] 3 from start to finish [think it *over*] 4 *a)* from an upright position [to fall *over*] *b)* upside down [turn the cup *over*] 5 again [do it *over*] 6 at, on, to, or in a specified place [*over* in Spain] 7 from one belief, etc. to another [win him *over*] —***adj.*** 1 upper, outer, superior, excessive, or extra [*overseer*] 2 finished; past 3 having reached the other side 4 [Inf.] as a surplus; extra

over- *combining form* 1 above in position, rank, etc. [*overlord*] 2 passing across or beyond [*overrun*] 3 excessively [*oversell*] The list below includes some common compounds formed with *over-* that can be understood if "too much" or "excessively" is added to the meaning of the base word:

overabundance
overactive
overambitious
overanxious
overbid
overburden
overcautious
overconfident
overcook
overcritical
overcrowd
overdevelop
overeager
overeat
overemphasize
overenthusiastic
overexercise
overexert
overexpose
overextend
overgenerous
overheat
overindulge
overindulgence
overload
overpay
overpopulate
overproduce
overproduction
overrefined
overripe
oversell
oversensitive
overspecialize
overspend
overstimulate
overstock
overstrict
oversupply
overtire

o'ver·a·chieve' ***vi.*** **-chieved', -chiev'ing** 1 to do better, as in school, than expected 2 to drive oneself to reach unreasonable goals —**o'ver·a·chieve'ment** ***n.*** —**o'ver·a·chiev'er** ***n.***

o'ver·act' ***vt., vi.*** to act (a dramatic role) with exaggeration

o·ver·age[1] (ō'vər āj') ***adj.*** over the age fixed as a standard

o·ver·age[2] (ō'vər ij) ***n.*** ⟦OVER + -AGE⟧ a surplus or excess

o·ver·all (ō'vər ôl', ō'vər ôl') ***adj.*** 1 from end to end 2 including everything; total —***adv.*** 1 from end to end 2 in general

o'ver·alls' (-ôlz') ***pl.n.*** loose trousers extending up over the chest, worn, usually over other clothing, to protect against dirt

o'ver·arch'ing ***adj.*** including or linking all that is within its scope [an *overarching* theory]

o'ver·awe' ***vt.*** **-awed', -aw'ing** to overcome or subdue by inspiring awe

o'ver·bal'ance ***vt.*** **-anced, -anc·ing** OUTWEIGH

o'ver·bear'ing ***adj.*** arrogant; domineering

o'ver·bite' ***n.*** a dental condition in which the upper incisors and canines project over the lower ones to an abnormal extent

o'ver·blown' (-blōn') ***adj.*** 1 overdone; excessive 2 pompous or bombastic

o'ver·board' ***adv.*** from a ship into the water —**go overboard** [Inf.] to go to extremes

o'ver·book' ***vt., vi.*** to issue more reservations for (a flight, hotel, etc.) than there are accommodations

o'ver·cast' ***adj.*** cloudy; dark: said of the sky

o·ver·charge (ō'vər chärj'; *also, and for n. always,* ō'vər chärj') ***vt., vi.*** **-charged', -charg'ing** 1 to charge too high a price (to) 2 to overload —***n.*** 1 an excessive charge 2 too full a load

o'ver·cloud' ***vt., vi.*** to make or become cloudy, gloomy, etc.

o'ver·coat' ***n.*** a heavy coat worn over the usual clothing for warmth

o'ver·come' ***vt.*** **-came', -come', -com'ing** 1 to get the better of in competition, etc. 2 to master, prevail over, or surmount —***vi.*** to win

o'ver·de·ter'mine ***vt.*** **-mined, -min·ing** to bring about through many causes or factors

o'ver·do' ***vt.*** **-did', -done', -do'ing** 1 to do too much 2 to exaggerate 3 to overcook —***vi.*** to exhaust oneself by doing too much

o'ver·dose' ***n.*** too large a dose —***vi.*** to take too large an amount of a narcotic, etc.

o'ver·draw' ***vt.*** **-drew', -drawn', -draw'ing** to draw on in excess of the amount credited to the drawer —**o'ver·draft'** ***n.***

o'ver·dress' ***vt., vi.*** to dress too warmly, too showily, or too formally

o'ver·dub' ***n.*** a recording of sounds, music, etc. superimposed on another recording —***vt., vi.*** **-dubbed', -dub'bing** to add (sounds, music, etc.) to (a recording)

o'ver·due' ***adj.*** past the time for payment, arrival, etc.

o'ver·es'ti·mate' ***vt.*** **-mat'ed, -mat'ing** to set too high an estimate on or for

o'ver·flight' ***n.*** the flight of an aircraft over a foreign territory, as in reconnaissance

o·ver·flow (ō'vər flō'; *also, and for n. always,* ō'vər flō') ***vt.*** 1 to flow across; flood 2 to flow over the brim of —***vi.*** 1 to run over 2 to be superabundant —***n.*** 1 an overflowing 2 the amount that overflows 3 an outlet for overflowing liquids

o'ver·grow' ***vt.*** **-grew', -grown', -grow'ing** to overspread with foliage so as to cover —***vi.*** to grow too fast or beyond normal size —**o'ver·grown'** ***adj.*** —**o'ver·growth'** ***n.***

o'ver·hand' ***adj., adv.*** with the hand raised above the elbow or the arm above the shoulder

o·ver·hang (ō'vər haŋ'; *also, and for n. always,* ō'vər haŋ') ***vt., vi.*** **-hung',**

-hang′ing to hang over or project beyond (something) —*n.* the projection of one thing over or beyond another

o·ver·haul (ō′vər hôl′; *also, and for n. always,* ō′vər hôl′) *vt.* **1** *a*) to check thoroughly for needed repairs *b*) to restore (a motor, etc.) to good working order **2** to catch up with —*n.* an overhauling

o·ver·head (ō′vər hed′; *for adv.* ō′vər hed′) *adj.* **1** above the head **2** in the sky **3** on a higher level, with reference to related objects —*n.* the general, continuing costs of a business, as of rent, maintenance, etc. —*adv.* above the head; aloft

o′ver·hear′ *vt.* **-heard′, -hear′ing** to hear (something spoken or a speaker) without the speaker's knowledge or intention

o′ver·joy′ *vt.* to give great joy to; delight —**o′ver·joyed′** *adj.*

o′ver·kill′ *n.* much more of something than is necessary, appropriate, etc.

o′ver·land′ (-land′, -lənd) *adv., adj.* by, on, or across land

o·ver·lap (ō′vər lap′; *also, and for n. always,* ō′vər lap′) *vt., vi.* **-lapped′, -lap′ping** to extend over a part of (something) so as to coincide with this part —*n.* an overlapping part or amount

o′ver·lay′ *vt.* **-laid′, -lay′ing** **1** to lay or spread over **2** to cover, as with a decorative layer

o′ver·lie′ *vt.* **-lay′, -lain′, -ly′ing** to lie on or over

o′ver·look′ *vt.* **1** to look at from above **2** to give a view of from above **3** *a*) to fail to notice *b*) to ignore; neglect **4** to excuse

o′ver·lord′ *n.* person having great authority over others

o′ver·ly *adv.* too or too much

o′ver·mas′ter *vt.* to overcome; subdue

o′ver·much′ *adj., adv., n.* too much

o·ver·night (ō′vər nīt′, ō′vər nīt′) *adv.* **1** during the night **2** suddenly —*adj.* **1** done or going on during the night **2** staying through the night [an *overnight* guest] **3** of or for a brief trip [an *overnight* bag]

o′ver·pass′ *n.* a bridge, etc. over a road, railway, etc.

o′ver·play′ *vt.* to overact, overdo, or overemphasize

o′ver·pow′er *vt.* to get the better of; subdue or overwhelm —**o′ver·pow′er·ing** *adj.*

o′ver·price′ *vt.* **-priced′, -pric′ing** to offer for sale at too high a price

o′ver·pro·tect′ *vt.* to protect more than necessary; specif., to exercise excessive, damaging control over (one's child, etc.) in trying to shield from hurt, disappointment, etc.

o′ver·qual′i·fied′ *adj.* having more knowledge, education, etc. than needed for a particular job

o′ver·rate′ *vt.* **-rat′ed, -rat′ing** to rate or estimate too highly

o′ver·reach′ *vt.* to reach beyond or above —**overreach oneself** to fail because of trying to do too much

o′ver·re·act′ *vi.* to react in an overly emotional way

o′ver·ride′ *vt.* **-rode′, -rid′den, -rid′ing** **1** to prevail over **2** to disregard or nullify

o′ver·rule′ *vt.* **-ruled′, -rul′ing** **1** to set aside or decide against by virtue of higher authority; annul; reverse **2** to prevail over

o′ver·run′ *vt.* **-ran′, -run′, -run′ning** **1** to spread out over so as to cover **2** to swarm over, as vermin do **3** to extend beyond (certain limits)

o′ver·seas′ *adv.* over or beyond the sea —*adj.* **1** foreign **2** over or across the sea

o′ver·see′ *vt.* **-saw′, -seen′, -see′ing** to supervise; superintend —**o′ver·se′er** (-sē′ər) *n.*

o′ver·sexed′ (-sekst′) *adj.* having exceptional sexual drive or interest in sex

o′ver·shad′ow *vt.* **1** *a*) to cast a shadow over *b*) to darken **2** to be more important than by comparison

o′ver·shoe′ *n.* a boot of rubber, etc. worn over the regular shoe to protect against cold or dampness

o′ver·shoot′ *vt.* **-shot′, -shoot′ing** **1** to shoot or pass beyond (a target, mark, etc.) **2** to exceed

o′ver·sight′ *n.* a careless mistake or omission

o′ver·sim′pli·fy′ *vt., vi.* **-fied′, -fy′ing** to simplify to the point of distortion —**o′ver·sim′pli·fi·ca′tion** *n.*

o′ver·size′ *adj.* **1** too large **2** larger than the usual Also **o′ver·sized′**

o′ver·sleep′ *vi.* **-slept′, -sleep′ing** to sleep longer than intended

o′ver·spread′ *vt.* **-spread′, -spread′ing** to spread or cover over

o′ver·state′ *vt.* **-stat′ed, -stat′ing** to exaggerate —**o′ver·state′ment** *n.*

o′ver·stay′ *vt.* to stay beyond the time or limit of

o′ver·step′ *vt.* **-stepped′, -step′ping** to go beyond the limits of

o′ver·strung′ *adj.* high-strung; tense

o′ver·stuff′ *vt.* **1** to stuff with too much of something **2** to upholster with deep stuffing

o·vert (ō vurt′, ō′vurt′) *adj.* ⟦< L *aperire,* to open⟧ not hidden; apparent; open —**o·vert′ly** *adv.*

o′ver·take′ *vt.* **-took′, -tak′en, -tak′ing** **1** to catch up with **2** to come upon suddenly

o′ver·tax′ *vt.* **1** to tax too heavily **2** to make excessive demands on

o′ver-the-count′er *adj.* **1** designating or of securities sold directly to buyers **2** sold legally without prescription: said of some drugs

o′ver-the-top′ *adj.* outrageously or ridiculously excessive

o·ver·throw (ō′vər thrō′; *also & for n.* ō′vər thrō′) *vt.* **-threw′, -thrown′, -throw′ing** **1** to overcome; conquer **2** to throw beyond —*n.* **1** an overthrowing or being overthrown **2** destruction; end

o′ver·time′ *n.* **1** time beyond the established limit, as of working hours **2** pay for work done in such time **—*adj.*, *adv.*** of, for, or during overtime

o'ver·tone' ***n.*** **1** a faint, higher tone accompanying a fundamental tone produced by a musical instrument **2** an implication; nuance: *usually used in pl.*

o·ver·ture (ō'vər chər) ***n.*** ⟦< L *apertura,* opening⟧ **1** an introductory proposal or offer **2** a musical introduction to an opera, etc.

o'ver·turn' ***vt.*** **1** to turn over **2** to conquer **—*vi.*** to tip over; capsize

o'ver·ween'ing (-wēn'iŋ) ***adj.*** ⟦< OE *ofer*, over + *wenan*, to think⟧ **1** arrogant **2** excessive

o·ver·weight (ō'vər wāt', ō'vər wāt') ***adj.*** above the normal or allowed weight

o'ver·whelm' ***vt.*** **1** to pour down upon and bury beneath **2** to crush; overpower **—o'ver·whelm'ing *adj.***

o·ver·work (ō'vər wurk', ō'vər wurk') ***vt.*** to work or use to excess **—*vi.*** to work too hard or too long **—*n.*** severe or burdensome work

o·ver·wrought (ō'vər rôt') ***adj.*** **1** very nervous or excited **2** too elaborate

Ov·id (äv'id) 43 B.C.-A.D. 17?; Rom. poet

o·vi·duct (ō'vi dukt', äv'i-) ***n.*** ⟦< L *ovum*, egg + DUCT⟧ a tube through which the ova pass from an ovary to the uterus

o·vip·a·rous (ō vip'ə rəs) ***adj.*** ⟦< L *ovum*, egg + *parere*, to bear⟧ producing eggs which hatch after leaving the female's body

o·void (ō'void') ***adj.*** ⟦< L *ovum*, egg + -OID⟧ egg-shaped **—*n.*** anything ovoid

ov·u·late (äv'yə lāt') ***vi.*** **-lat'ed, -lat'ing** ⟦< L *ovum*, egg⟧ to produce and discharge ova from the ovary **—ov'u·la'tion *n.***

ov·ule (äv'yōōl', ō'vyōōl') ***n.*** ⟦< L *ovum*, egg⟧ a small egg or seed, esp. one in an early stage of development **—ov'u·lar *adj.***

o·vum (ō'vəm) ***n.***, *pl.* **o·va** (ō'və) ⟦L, egg⟧ a mature female germ cell

ow (ou) ***interj.*** a cry of pain

owe (ō) ***vt.*** **owed, ow'ing** ⟦OE *agan*, to own⟧ **1** to be indebted to the amount of **2** to have the need to do, give, etc., as because of gratitude **3** to be indebted *to* someone for the existence of

ow·ing (ō'iŋ) ***adj.*** ⟦ME *owynge*⟧ due; unpaid **—owing to** because of

owl (oul) ***n.*** ⟦OE *ule*⟧ **1** a predatory night bird having a large, flat face, large eyes, and a short, hooked beak **2** a person of nocturnal habits, solemn appearance, etc. **—owl'ish *adj.***

owl'et (-it) ***n.*** a young or small owl

own (ōn) ***adj.*** ⟦OE *agan*, possess⟧ belonging or relating to oneself or itself [his *own* book] **—*n.*** that which belongs to oneself [that is her *own*] **—*vt.*** **1** to possess; have **2** to admit; acknowledge **—*vi.*** to confess (*to*) **—on one's own** [Inf.] by one's own efforts **—own'er *n.* —own'er·ship' *n.***

ox (äks) ***n.***, *pl.* **ox'en** ⟦OE *oxa*⟧ any of certain cud-chewing, cattlelike mammals, esp. a castrated, domesticated bull used as a draft animal

ox'blood' ***n.*** a deep-red color

ox'bow' (-bō') ***n.*** the U-shaped part of an ox yoke which passes under and around the animal's neck

ox·ford (äks'fərd) ***n.*** ⟦after *Oxford*, England⟧ [*sometimes* **O-**] **1** a low shoe laced over the instep: also **oxford shoe** **2** a cotton or rayon fabric with a basketlike weave: also **oxford cloth**

Ox·ford (äks'fərd) city in SC England; site of Oxford University: county district pop. 110,000

ox·i·dant (äk'si dənt) ***n.*** an oxidizing agent

ox·i·da·tion (äk'si dā'shən) ***n.*** an oxidizing or being oxidized

ox·ide (äk'sīd') ***n.*** ⟦Fr⟧ a compound of oxygen with another element or a radical

ox·i·dize (äk'si dīz') ***vt.*** **-dized', -diz'ing** to unite with oxygen, as in burning or rusting **—*vi.*** to become oxidized **—ox'i·diz'er *n.***

ox·y·a·cet·y·lene (äk'sē ə set''l ēn') ***adj.*** of or using a mixture of oxygen and acetylene, as for producing a hot flame used in welding

ox·y·gen (äk'si jən) ***n.*** ⟦Fr *oxygène*⟧ a colorless, odorless, gaseous chemical element: it is essential to life processes and to combustion

ox'y·gen·ate' (-jə nāt') ***vt.*** **-at'ed, -at'ing** to treat or combine with oxygen **—ox'y·gen·a'tion *n.***

oxygen tent a transparent enclosure filled with oxygen, fitted around a bed patient to aid breathing

ox·y·mo·ron (äk'si môr'än') ***n.***, *pl.* **-mo'ra** (-rə) ⟦< Gr *oxys*, sharp + *mōros*, foolish⟧ a figure of speech in which contradictory ideas or terms are combined (Ex.: thunderous silence)

oys·ter (ois'tər) ***n.*** ⟦< Gr *ostreon*⟧ an edible bivalve mollusk with an irregular shell

oz *symbol* ounce(s)

o·zone (ō'zōn') ***n.*** ⟦Fr < Gr *ozein*, to smell⟧ **1** an unstable, pale-blue form of oxygen with a strong odor, formed by an electrical discharge in air and used as a bleaching agent, water purifier, etc. **2** [Slang] pure, fresh air

ozone layer the layer of ozone within the stratosphere that absorbs much ultraviolet radiation

P

p[1] or **P** (pē) ***n.***, *pl.* **p's, P's** the 16th letter of the English alphabet

p[2] *abbrev.* **1** page **2** participle **3** past **4** per **5** pint

P[1] *abbrev.* petite

P[2] *Chem. symbol for* phosphorus

pa (pä) ***n.*** [Inf.] FATHER

PA *abbrev.* **1** Pennsylvania **2** public address (system)

pab·lum (pab′ləm) ***n.*** ⟦< *Pablum*, trademark for a soft, bland baby food⟧ simplistic or bland writing, ideas, etc.

PAC ***n.***, *pl.* **PAC's** political action committee

pace (pās) ***n.*** ⟦< L *passus*, a step⟧ **1** a step in walking, etc. **2** the length of a step or stride **3** the rate of speed in walking, etc. **4** rate of progress, etc. **5** a gait **6** the gait of a horse in which both legs on the same side are raised together —***vt.*** **paced, pac′ing 1** to walk back and forth across **2** to measure by paces **3** to set the pace for (a runner, etc.) —***vi.*** **1** to walk with regular steps **2** to move at a pace: said of a horse — **put through one's paces** to test one's ability, skills, etc. —**pac′er *n.***

pace′mak′er *n.* **1** one that leads the way: also **pace′set′ter** (-set′ər) **2** an electronic device placed in the body to regulate the heartbeat

pach·y·derm (pak′ə durm′) ***n.*** ⟦< Gr *pachys*, thick + *derma*, skin⟧ a large, thick-skinned, hoofed animal, as the elephant or rhinoceros

pach·y·san·dra (pak′ə san′drə) ***n.*** ⟦< ModL name of genus⟧ a low, hardy evergreen plant often used for a ground cover in the shade

pa·cif·ic (pə sif′ik) ***adj.*** ⟦see PACIFY⟧ **1** making peace **2** of a peaceful nature; tranquil; calm

Pa·cif·ic (pə sif′ik) largest of the earth's oceans, between Asia and the American continents

pac·i·fi·er (pas′ə fī′ər) ***n.*** **1** one that pacifies **2** a nipple or teething ring for babies

pac′i·fism′ (-fiz′əm) ***n.*** opposition to the use of force under any circumstances; specif., refusal to participate in war — **pac′i·fist *n.*, *adj.***

pac·i·fy (pas′ə fī′) ***vt.*** **-fied′, -fy′ing** ⟦< L *pax*, peace + *facere*, make⟧ to make peaceful, calm, nonhostile, etc. —**pac′i·fi·ca′tion *n.***

pack[1] (pak) ***n.*** ⟦< MDu *pak*⟧ **1** a bundle of things tied up for carrying **2** a number of similar persons or things; specif., *a*) a group *[*a *pack* of lies*]* *b*) a package of a standard number *[*a *pack* of cigarettes*]* *c*) a number of wild animals living together —***vt.*** **1** to make a pack of **2** *a*) to put together in a box, trunk, etc. *b*) to fill (a box, etc.) **3** to crowd; cram *[*the hall was *packed]* **4** to fill in tightly, as for prevention of leaks **5** to carry in a pack **6** to send (*off*) *[*to *pack* him off to school*]* **7** [Slang] to carry (a gun, etc.) **8** [Slang] to be able to deliver (a punch, etc.) with force —***vi.*** **1** to make up packs **2** to put one's clothes, etc. into luggage for a trip **3** to crowd together **4** to settle into a compact mass —***adj.*** used for carrying packs, loads, etc. *[*a *pack* animal*]* —**send packing** to dismiss abruptly

pack[2] (pak) ***vt.*** to choose (a jury, etc.) so as to get desired results

pack·age (pak′ij) ***n.*** **1** a wrapped or boxed thing or group of things; parcel **2** a number of items, plans, etc. offered as a unit —***vt.*** **-aged, -ag·ing 1** to make a package of **2** to offer or present in an enticing way —**pack′ag·er *n.***

package store a store where alcoholic beverages are sold by the bottle

pack′et (-it) ***n.*** **1** a small package **2** a boat that travels a regular route carrying passengers, freight, and mail: in full **packet boat**

pack′ing *n.* **1** the act or process of a person or thing that packs **2** any material used to pack

pack′ing·house′ *n.* a plant where meats, etc. are processed and packed for sale

pack rat 1 a North American rat that often hides small articles in its nest **2** [Inf.] one who hoards miscellaneous items

pack′sad′dle *n.* a saddle with fastenings to secure the load carried by a pack animal

pact (pakt) ***n.*** ⟦< L *pax*, peace⟧ an agreement; compact

pad[1] (pad) ***n.*** ⟦echoic⟧ the dull sound of a footstep —***vi.*** **pad′ded, pad′ding** to walk, esp. with a soft step

pad[2] (pad) ***n.*** ⟦? var. of POD⟧ **1** anything soft to protect against friction, pressure, etc.; cushion **2** the cushionlike sole of an animal's paw **3** the floating leaf of a water plant, as the waterlily **4** a number of sheets of paper glued along one edge; tablet **5** [Slang] the place where one lives —***vt.*** **pad′ded, pad′ding 1** to stuff or cover with soft material **2** to lengthen (a speech, etc.) with unnecessary material **3** to fill (an expense account, etc.) with invented or inflated entries

pad′ding *n.* anything used to pad

pad·dle[1] (pad′'l) ***n.*** ⟦ME *padell*, small spade⟧ **1** a short pole with a wide blade at one or both ends, used to propel a canoe, kayak, etc. **2** an implement shaped like this, used to hit a ball, beat something, etc. —***vt.*, *vi.*** **-dled, -dling 1** to propel (a canoe, etc.) with a paddle **2** to beat as with a paddle; spank — **pad′dler *n.***

pad·dle[2] (pad′'l) ***vi.*** **-dled, -dling** ⟦prob. < PAD[1]⟧ to move the hands or feet about in the water, as in playing —**pad′dler *n.***

paddle ball a game like handball

played with a short-handled paddle

paddle wheel a wheel with boards around it for propelling a steamboat

pad·dock (pad′ək) ***n.*** ⟦OE *pearruc,* enclosure⟧ **1** a small enclosure near a stable, in which horses are exercised **2** an enclosure at a racetrack, where horses are saddled

pad·dy (pad′ē) ***n.,*** *pl.* **-dies** ⟦Malay *padi,* rice in the husk⟧ a rice field

pad·lock (pad′läk′) ***n.*** a removable lock with a hinged link to be passed through a staple, chain, or eye —***vt.*** to fasten or close up as with a padlock

PADLOCK

pa·dre (pä′drā′) ***n.*** ⟦< L *pater*⟧ **1** father: the title of a priest in Italy, Spain, etc. **2** [Inf.] a priest or chaplain

pae·an (pē′ən) ***n.*** ⟦< Gr *paian,* hymn⟧ a song of joy, triumph, etc.

pa·gan (pā′gən) ***n.*** ⟦< L *paganus,* peasant⟧ **1** a heathen **2** one who has no religion —***adj.*** of pagans —**pa′gan·ism′** ***n.***

page[1] (pāj) ***n.*** ⟦< L *pangere,* fasten⟧ **1** *a*) one side of a leaf of a book, etc. *b*) an entire leaf in a book, etc. **2** [*often pl.*] a record of events **3** WEB PAGE —***vi.*** **paged, pag′ing** to look (*through*) by turning the pages

page[2] (pāj) ***n.*** ⟦OFr⟧ a boy attendant —***vt.*** **paged, pag′ing** **1** to try to find by calling out the name of **2** to contact with a pager

pag·eant (paj′ənt) ***n.*** ⟦ME *pagent,* stage scene⟧ **1** a spectacular exhibition, parade, etc. **2** an elaborate outdoor drama celebrating a historical event

pag′eant·ry (-ən trē) ***n.,*** *pl.* **-ries** **1** grand spectacle; gorgeous display **2** empty show or display

pag·er (pā′jər) ***n.*** a portable electronic device used to contact people for messages

pag·i·na·tion (paj′ə nā′shən) ***n.*** **1** the numbering of pages **2** the arrangement and number of pages

pa·go·da (pə gō′də) ***n.*** ⟦prob. < Pers *but,* idol + *kadah,* house⟧ in India and the Far East, a temple in the form of a pyramidal tower of several stories

paid (pād) ***vt., vi.*** *pt. & pp. of* PAY —***adj.*** **1** settled by payment **2** with pay *[a paid vacation]*

pail (pāl) ***n.*** ⟦< OE *pægel,* wine vessel⟧ **1** a container, usually with a handle, for holding liquids, etc.; bucket **2** the amount held by a pail: also **pail′ful′**, *pl.* **-fuls′**

pain (pān) ***n.*** ⟦< Gr *poinē,* penalty⟧ **1** physical or mental suffering caused by injury, disease, grief, anxiety, etc. **2** [*pl.*] great care *[take pains with one's work]* —***vt.*** to cause pain to; hurt —**on** (or **under**) **pain of** at the risk of a penalty —**pain′ful** ***adj.*** —**pain′ful·ly** ***adv.*** —**pain′less** ***adj.***

Paine (pān), **Thom·as** (täm′əs) 1737-1809; Am. Revolutionary patriot & writer

pain′kill′er ***n.*** [Inf.] a medicine that relieves pain

pains·tak·ing (pānz′tā′kiŋ) ***adj.*** requiring or showing great care; very careful

paint (pānt) ***vt.*** ⟦< L *pingere*⟧ **1** *a*) to make (a picture, etc.) in colors applied to a surface *b*) to depict with paints **2** to describe vividly **3** to cover or decorate with paint —***vi.*** to paint pictures —***n.*** **1** a mixture of a pigment with oil, water, etc., used as a covering or coloring **2** a dried coat of paint

paint′er ***n.*** **1** an artist who paints pictures **2** one whose work is covering walls, etc. with paint

paint′ing ***n.*** a painted picture

pair (per) ***n.,*** *pl.* **pairs** or **pair** ⟦< L *par,* equal⟧ **1** two corresponding things associated or used together *[a pair of shoes]* **2** a single unit of two corresponding parts *[a pair of pants]* **3** any two persons or animals regarded as a unit —***vi., vt.*** **1** to form a pair (of) **2** to mate

PAISLEY PATTERN

pais·ley (pāz′lē) ***adj.*** ⟦after *Paisley,* Scotland⟧ [*also* **P-**] having an intricate, multicolored pattern of swirls, etc.

pa·ja·mas (pə jä′məz, -jam′əz) ***pl.n.*** ⟦< Pers *pāi,* a leg + *jāma,* garment⟧ a loosely fitting sleeping or lounging suit consisting of jacket (or blouse) and trousers

Pa·ki·stan (pak′i stan′, pä′ki stän′) country in S Asia, west of India: 307,293 sq. mi.; pop. 131,500,000 —**Pak′i·stan′i** (-ē) ***adj., n.***

pal (pal) ***n.*** ⟦Romany, brother, ult. < Sans⟧ [Inf.] a close friend

pal·ace (pal′əs) ***n.*** ⟦< L *Palatium,* one of the Seven Hills of Rome⟧ **1** the official residence of a king, etc. **2** any large, magnificent building

pal·at·a·ble (pal′it ə bəl) ***adj.*** pleasant or acceptable to the taste or mind

pal·ate (pal′it) ***n.*** ⟦< L *palatum*⟧ **1** the roof of the mouth **2** sense of taste —**pal′a·tal** (-it′l) ***adj.***

pa·la·tial (pə lā′shəl) ***adj.*** ⟦see PALACE⟧ **1** of, suitable for, or like a palace **2** magnificent; stately

pal·a·tine (pal′ə tīn′, -tin) ***adj.*** ⟦see PALACE⟧ designating or of a count or earl who ruled in his own territory

Pa·lau (pä lou′) country on a group of islands in the W Pacific: 630 sq. mi.; pop. 15,000

pa·lav·er (pə lav′ər) ***n.*** ⟦Port *palavra*, a word⟧ talk, esp. idle talk —***vi.*** to talk idly

pale[1] (pāl) ***adj.*** **pal′er, pal′est** ⟦< L *pallidus*⟧ **1** of a whitish or colorless complexion **2** faint; dim **3** feeble; weak —***vi.*** **paled, pal′ing** to become pale —**pale′ly** ***adv.*** —**pale′ness** ***n.***

pale[2] (pāl) ***n.*** ⟦< L *palus*, a stake⟧ **1** a pointed stake used in fences **2** a boundary; restriction: now chiefly figurative

pale′face′ ***n.*** a white person: a term allegedly first used by North American Indians

pa·le·on·tol·o·gy (pā′lē ən täl′ə jē) ***n.*** ⟦< Fr⟧ the branch of geology studying prehistoric life by means of fossils —**pa′le·on·tol′o·gist** ***n.***

Pa′le·o·zo′ic (-ə zō′ik) ***adj.*** ⟦< Gr *palaios*, ancient + ZO(O)- + -IC⟧ designating the geologic era (*c.* 570-240 million years ago) characterized by the first fishes, reptiles, and land plants

Pal·es·tine (pal′əs tīn′) historical region in SW Asia at the E end of the Mediterranean, including modern Israel & Jordan

Pal′es·tin′i·an (-tin′ē ən) ***n.*** a person, esp. an Arab, born or living in Palestine —***adj.*** of Palestine or the Palestinians

pal·ette (pal′it) ***n.*** ⟦Fr < L *pala*, a shovel⟧ **1** a thin board on which an artist arranges and mixes paints **2** the colors used as for a painting

pal·frey (pôl′frē) ***n.***, *pl.* **-freys** ⟦ult. < Gr *para*, beside + L *veredus*, post horse⟧ [Archaic] a saddle horse, esp. a gentle one for a woman

pal·i·mo·ny (pal′ə mō′nē) ***n.*** ⟦PAL + (AL)IMONY⟧ an allowance or a property settlement claimed by or granted to one member of an unmarried couple who separate after having lived together

pal·imp·sest (pal′imp sest′) ***n.*** ⟦< Gr *palimpsēstos*, lit., rubbed again⟧ a parchment previously written upon that bears traces of the erased texts

pal·in·drome (pal′in drōm′) ***n.*** ⟦< Gr *palindromos*, running back⟧ a word, phrase, or sentence that reads the same backward or forward (Ex.: madam)

pal·ing (pāl′iŋ) ***n.*** a fence made of pales

pal·i·sade (pal′ə sād′) ***n.*** ⟦< Fr < L *palus*, a stake⟧ **1** any of a row of large, pointed stakes forming a fence as for fortification **2** such a fence **3** [*pl.*] a line of steep cliffs

pall[1] (pôl) ***vi.*** **palled, pall′ing** ⟦ME *pallen*, appall⟧ **1** to become cloying, insipid, boring, etc. **2** to become satiated

pall[2] (pôl) ***n.*** ⟦< L *pallium*, a cover⟧ **1** a cloth covering for a coffin **2** a dark or gloomy covering

pall·bear·er (pôl′ber′ər) ***n.*** ⟦prec. + BEARER⟧ one of the persons who attend or carry the coffin at a funeral

pal·let[1] (pal′it) ***n.*** ⟦see PALETTE⟧ a low, portable platform used for stacking materials, as in a warehouse

pal·let[2] (pal′it) ***n.*** ⟦< L *palea*, chaff⟧ a small bed or a pad filled as with straw and used on the floor

pal·li·ate (pal′ē āt′) ***vt.*** **-at′ed, -at′ing** ⟦< L *pallium*, a cloak⟧ **1** to lessen the severity of without curing; alleviate **2** to make (an offense) appear less serious; excuse —**pal′li·a′tion** ***n.*** —**pal′li·a′tive** (-āt′iv, -ə tiv) ***adj.***, ***n.***

pal·lid (pal′id) ***adj.*** ⟦L *pallidus*, pale⟧ faint in color; pale —**pal′lid·ly** ***adv.***

pal·lor (pal′ər) ***n.*** ⟦< L *pallere*, be pale⟧ unnatural paleness

palm[1] (päm) ***n.*** ⟦< L *palma*: from its handlike leaf⟧ **1** any of a large group of tropical or subtropical trees or shrubs with a branchless trunk and a bunch of large leaves at the top **2** a leaf of such a tree carried as a symbol of victory, etc.

palm[2] (päm) ***n.*** ⟦< L *palma*⟧ the inner surface of the hand between the fingers and wrist —***vt.*** to hide (something) in the palm, as in a sleight-of-hand trick —**palm off** [Inf.] to pass off by fraud

pal·met·to (pal met′ō) ***n.***, *pl.* **-tos** or **-toes** any of certain palms with fan-shaped leaves

palm·is·try (päm′is trē) ***n.*** ⟦prob. < ME *paume*, PALM[2] + *maistrie*, mastery⟧ fortunetelling by interpreting the lines, etc. on the palm of a person's hand —**palm′ist** ***n.***

Palm Springs resort city in SW California: pop. 40,000

Palm Sunday the Sunday before Easter, commemorating Jesus' entry into Jerusalem, when palm branches were strewn before him

palm′top′ ***n.*** a small, portable computer for storing personal information, sending e-mail, etc.

palm·y (päm′ē) ***adj.*** **-i·er, -i·est** **1** of, like, or full of palm trees **2** prosperous *[palmy days]*

pal·o·mi·no (pal′ə mē′nō) ***n.***, *pl.* **-nos** ⟦AmSp < Sp, dove-colored⟧ a golden or cream-colored horse with a white tail

pal·pa·ble (pal′pə bəl) ***adj.*** ⟦< L *palpare*, to touch⟧ **1** that can be touched, felt, etc. **2** easily perceived by the senses; perceptible **3** obvious; plain —**pal′pa·bly** ***adv.***

pal·pi·tate (pal′pə tāt′) ***vi.*** **-tat′ed, -tat′ing** ⟦< L *palpare*, to feel⟧ **1** to beat rapidly, as the heart **2** to throb —**pal′pi·ta′tion** ***n.***

pal·sy (pôl′zē) ***n.***, *pl.* **-sies** ⟦ult. < L *paralysis*, paralysis⟧ paralysis of a muscle, sometimes with involuntary tremors —***vt.*** **-sied, -sy·ing** to affect with or as with palsy

pal·try (pôl′trē) ***adj.*** **-tri·er, -tri·est** ⟦prob. < LowG *palte*, rag⟧ almost worthless; trifling —**pal′tri·ness** ***n.***

pam·pa (pam′pə, päm′-) ***n.*** ⟦AmSp < AmInd *pampa*, plain, field⟧ an extensive, treeless plain of Argentina

pam·per (pam′pər) ***vt.*** ⟦ME *pampren*, to feed too much < LowG⟧ to be overindulgent with; coddle

pam·phlet (pam′flit) ***n.*** ⟦< OFr *Pamphilet*, shortened name of a ML poem⟧ a thin, unbound booklet, often on some topic of current interest —**pam′phlet·eer′** (-flə tir′) ***n.***

pan[1] (pan) ***n.*** ⟦OE *panne*⟧ **1** any broad, shallow container used in cooking, etc. **2** a pan-shaped part or object —***vt.*** **panned**, **pan′ning** **1** [Inf.] to criticize unfavorably **2** *Mining* to wash (gravel) in a pan, as to separate (gold) —***vi.*** *Mining* to wash gravel in a pan, searching for gold —**pan out** [Inf.] to turn out; esp., to succeed

pan[2] (pan) *Film, TV, etc.* ***vt.***, ***vi.*** **panned**, **pan′ning** ⟦< PAN(ORAMA)⟧ to move (a camera) so as to get a panoramic effect —***n.*** the act of panning

Pan (pan) ***n.*** *Gr. Myth.* a god of fields, forests, flocks, and shepherds, represented as having the legs of a goat

pan- ⟦< Gr *pan*, all, every⟧ *combining form* **1** all *[pantheism]* **2** [**P-**] of, comprising, or uniting every *[Pan-*American*]*

pan·a·ce·a (pan′ə sē′ə) ***n.*** ⟦< Gr *pan*, all + *akos*, healing, medicine⟧ a supposed remedy for all ills

pa·nache (pə nash′, -näsh′) ***n.*** ⟦Fr, ult. < L *pinna*, feather⟧ dashing elegance of manner or style

Pan·a·ma (pan′ə mä′, -mô′) country in Central America, a strip of land connecting Central & South America: 29,761 sq. mi.; pop. 2,329,000 —**Pan′a·ma′ni·an** (-mā′nē ən) ***adj.***, ***n.***

Panama Canal ship canal across Panama, connecting the Atlantic & Pacific

Panama (hat) [*also* **p-**] a hand-woven hat made with strawlike strips of the leaves of a tropical plant

Pan′-A·mer′i·can ***adj.*** of North, South, and Central America, collectively

pan·cake (pan′kāk′) ***n.*** a flat cake of batter fried on a griddle or in a pan

pan·chro·mat·ic (pan′krō mat′ik) ***adj.*** sensitive to light of all colors *[panchromatic film]*

pan·cre·as (pan′krē əs, paŋ′-) ***n.*** ⟦< Gr *pan*, all + *kreas*, flesh⟧ a large gland that secretes a digestive juice into the small intestine and produces insulin —**pan′cre·at′ic** (-at′ik) ***adj.***

pan·da (pan′də) ***n.*** ⟦< native name in Nepal⟧ **1** a black-and-white, bearlike mammal of China: in full **giant panda** **2** a reddish, raccoonlike mammal of the Himalayas: in full **lesser panda**

pan·dem·ic (pan dem′ik) ***adj.*** ⟦< Gr *pan*, all + *dēmos*, the people⟧ epidemic over a large region

pan·de·mo·ni·um (pan′də mō′nē əm) ***n.*** ⟦< name of demons' abode in Milton's *Paradise Lost* < Gr *pan*, all + *daimōn*, evil spirit⟧ wild disorder or noise

pan·der (pan′dər) ***n.*** ⟦< L *Pandarus*, lovers' go-between in Chaucer, etc.⟧ **1** a procurer; pimp **2** one who helps others to satisfy their vices, etc. Also **pan′der·er** —***vi.*** to act as a pander (*to*)

P & H *abbrev.* postage and handling

Pan·do·ra (pan dôr′ə) ***n.*** ⟦< Gr *pan*, all + *dōron*, gift⟧ *Gr. Myth.* the first mortal woman: she opens a box, letting all human ills into the world

pane (pān) ***n.*** ⟦< L *pannus*, piece of cloth⟧ a sheet of glass in a frame of a window, etc.

pan·e·gyr·ic (pan′ə jir′ik) ***n.*** ⟦< Gr *panēgyris*, public meeting⟧ **1** a formal speech or piece of writing praising a person or event **2** high praise

pan·el (pan′əl) ***n.*** ⟦see PANE⟧ **1** *a*) a section or division, usually rectangular, forming a part of a wall, door, etc. *b*) a board for instruments or controls **2** a lengthwise strip in a skirt, etc. **3** a list of persons summoned for jury duty **4** a group of persons selected for judging, discussing, etc. —***vt.*** **-eled** or **-elled**, **-el·ing** or **-el·ling** to provide with panels

pan′el·ing or **pan′el·ling** ***n.*** **1** panels collectively **2** sheets of plastic, wood, etc. from which to cut panels

pan′el·ist ***n.*** a member of a PANEL (*n.* 4)

panel truck an enclosed pickup truck

pang (paŋ) ***n.*** ⟦< ?⟧ a sudden, sharp pain, physical or emotional

pan·han·dle[1] (pan′han′dəl) ***n.*** a strip of land projecting like the handle of a pan

pan·han·dle[2] (pan′han′dəl) ***vi.*** **-dled**, **-dling** [Inf.] to beg on the streets —**pan′han′dler** ***n.***

pan·ic (pan′ik) ***n.*** ⟦< Gr *panikos*, of Pan, as inspirer of sudden fear⟧ a sudden, unreasoning fear, often spreading quickly —***vt.*** **-icked**, **-ick·ing** to affect with panic —***vi.*** to show panic —**pan′ick·y** ***adj.***

pan′ic-strick′en ***adj.*** badly frightened: also **pan′ic-struck′**

pan·nier or **pan·ier** (pan′yər, -ē ər) ***n.*** ⟦< L *panis*, bread⟧ a large basket for carrying loads on the back

pa·no·cha (pə nō′chə) ***n.*** ⟦AmSp, ult. < L *panis*, bread⟧ **1** a coarse Mexican sugar **2** *var. of* PENUCHE

pan·o·ply (pan′ə plē) ***n.***, *pl.* **-plies** ⟦< Gr *pan*, all + *hopla*, arms⟧ **1** a complete suit of armor **2** any complete or magnificent covering or array

pan·o·ram·a (pan′ə ram′ə) ***n.*** ⟦< PAN- + Gr *horama*, a view⟧ **1** a wide view in all directions **2** a constantly changing scene —**pan′o·ram′ic** ***adj.***

pan·sy (pan′zē) ***n.***, *pl.* **-sies** ⟦< Fr *penser*, think⟧ a small plant of the violet family, with velvety petals

pant (pant) ***vi.*** ⟦ult. < L *phantasia*, nightmare⟧ **1** to breathe rapidly and heavily, as from running fast **2** to yearn eagerly: with *for* or *after* —***vt.*** to gasp out —***n.*** any of a series of rapid, heavy breaths; gasp

pan·ta·loons (pan′tə lo͞onz′) ***pl.n.*** ⟦< It: ult. after St. *Pantalone*⟧ [Historical] trousers

pan·the·ism (pan′thē iz′əm) ***n.*** ⟦< Gr *pan*, all + *theos*, a god + -ISM⟧ **1** the doctrine that all forces, manifestations, etc. of the universe are God **2** the worship of all gods —**pan′the·ist** ***n.***

pan·the·on (pan′thē än′) ***n.*** ⟦< Gr *pan*, all + *theos*, a god⟧ **1** all the gods of a people **2** [*often* **P-**] a building in which famous dead persons of a nation are entombed or commemorated

pan·ther (pan′thər) ***n.*** ⟦< Gr *panthēr*⟧ **1** a leopard, specif. one that is black **2** COUGAR

pant·ies (pan′tēz) ***pl.n.*** women's or children's short underpants: also **pant′ie** or **pant′y** ***n.***

pan·to·mime (pan′tə mīm′) ***n.*** ⟦ult. < Gr *pan*, all + *mimos,* a mimic⟧ **1** a drama played without words, using only action and gestures **2** action or gestures without words **—*vt.*, *vi.* -mimed′, -mim′ing** to express or act in pantomime — **pan′to·mim′ist** (-mīm′ist) ***n.***

pan·to·then·ic acid (pan′tō then′ik) ⟦< Gr *pantothen*, from every side⟧ a viscous oil, part of the vitamin B complex, occurring widely in animal and plant tissues and thought essential for cell growth

pan·try (pan′trē) ***n.***, *pl.* **-tries** ⟦< L *panis,* bread⟧ a small room off the kitchen, where cooking ingredients and utensils, china, etc. are kept

pants (pants) ***pl.n.*** ⟦< PANTALOONS⟧ **1** trousers **2** drawers or panties

pant′suit′ ***n.*** matched pants and jacket for women: also **pants suit**

pant·y·hose (pan′tē hōz′) ***n.*** women's hose that extend to the waist, forming a one-piece garment

pant′y·waist′ (-wāst′) ***n.*** [Slang] a sissy

pap (pap) ***n.*** ⟦ME⟧ **1** any soft food for babies or invalids **2** any oversimplified or tasteless writing, ideas, etc.

pa·pa (pä′pə, pə pä′) ***n.*** ⟦< baby talk⟧ *child's term for* FATHER

pa·pa·cy (pā′pə sē) ***n.***, *pl.* **-cies** ⟦LL *papa,* pope⟧ **1** the rank of pope **2** the term of office of a pope **3** the governing of the Roman Catholic Church by the pope, its head

pa·pal (pā′pəl) ***adj.*** of or relating to a pope or the papacy

pa·pa·raz·zi (pä′pä rät′tsē) ***pl.n.*** photographers who take candid shots of celebrities

pa·paw (pə pô′, pô′pô′) ***n.*** ⟦< fol.⟧ **1** PAPAYA **2** *a*) a tree of central and S U.S. with an oblong, yellowish, edible fruit *b*) its fruit

pa·pa·ya (pə pī′ə) ***n.*** ⟦Sp < WInd name⟧ **1** a tropical American tree with a large, oblong, yellowish-orange fruit **2** its fruit

pa·per (pā′pər) ***n.*** ⟦ult. < Gr *papyros,* papyrus⟧ **1** a thin, flexible material in sheets, made from rags, wood, etc. and used for writing or printing on, for packaging, etc. **2** a single sheet of this **3** an official document **4** an essay, dissertation, etc. **5** a newspaper **6** wallpaper **7** [*pl.*] credentials **—*adj.*** **1** of, or made of, paper **2** like paper; thin **—*vt.*** to cover with wallpaper **—pa′per·y** ***adj.***

pa′per·back′ ***n.*** a book bound in paper covers

pa′per·boy′ ***n.*** a boy who sells or delivers newspapers **—pa′per·girl′** ***fem.n.***

paper clip a flexible clasp for holding loose sheets of paper together

pa′per·hang′er ***n.*** a person whose work is covering walls with wallpaper

paper tiger a person, nation, etc. that seems to pose a threat but is really powerless

paper trail written records that serve as evidence of a person's actions

pa′per·weight′ ***n.*** any small, heavy object set on papers to keep them from being scattered

pa′per·work′ ***n.*** the keeping of records, etc. incidental to some task

pa·pier-mâ·ché (pā′pər mə shā′) ***n.*** ⟦Fr < *papier*, paper + *mâcher*, to chew⟧ a material made of paper pulp mixed with size, glue, etc., and molded into various objects when moist

pa·pil·la (pə pil′ə) ***n.***, *pl.* **-lae** (-ē) ⟦L < *papula*, pimple⟧ any small nipplelike projection of tissue, as on the surface of the tongue **—pap·il·lar·y** (pap′ə ler′ē) ***adj.***

pa·poose (pə po͞os′, pa-) ***n.*** ⟦< AmInd⟧ a North American Indian baby

pa·pri·ka (pə prē′kə) ***n.*** ⟦Hung, ult. < Gr *peperi*, pepper⟧ a mild or hot, red, powdered condiment ground from the fruit of certain pepper plants

Pap test (pap) ⟦after G. *Papanicolaou*, 20th-c. U.S. anatomist⟧ a test for uterine cancer

Pap·u·a New Guinea (pap′yo͞o ə) country occupying the E half of the island of New Guinea & nearby islands: 178,703 sq. mi.; pop. 3,689,000

pa·py·rus (pə pī′rəs) ***n.***, *pl.* **-ri′** (-rī′) or **-rus·es** ⟦< Gr *papyros*⟧ **1** a tall water plant of Egypt **2** a writing material made from the pith of this plant by the ancients

par (pär) ***n.*** ⟦L, an equal⟧ **1** the established value of a currency in terms of the money of another country **2** an equal status, level, etc.: usually in **on a par (with) 3** the average state, condition, etc. *[work that is above par]* **4** the face value of stocks, etc. **5** *Golf* the number of strokes established as a skillful score for a hole or course **—*adj.*** **1** of or at par **2** average

par *abbrev.* **1** paragraph **2** parish

para- *prefix* **1** beside, beyond *[parapsychology]* **2** helping, accessory *[paramedical]*

par·a·ble (par′ə bəl) ***n.*** ⟦< Gr *parabolē*, analogy < *para-*, beside + *ballein*, to throw⟧ a short, simple story teaching a moral lesson

pa·rab·o·la (pə rab′ə lə) ***n.*** ⟦see prec.⟧ *Geom.* a curve formed by the intersection of a cone with a plane parallel to its side **—par·a·bol·ic** (par′ə bäl′ik) ***adj.***

par·a·chute (par′ə sho͞ot′) ***n.*** ⟦Fr < *para-*, protecting + *chute*, a fall⟧ a cloth contrivance usually shaped like an umbrella when expanded, and used to retard the speed of one dropping from an airplane, etc. **—*vt.*, *vi.* -chut′ed, -chut′ing** to drop by parachute **—par′a·chut′ist** ***n.***

pa·rade (pə rād′) ***n.*** ⟦< L *parare,* prepare⟧ **1** ostentatious display **2** a review of marching troops **3** any organized procession or march, as for display **—*vt.* -rad′ed, -rad′ing 1** to march or walk through, as for display **2** to show off [to *parade* one's knowledge] —*vi.* 1 to march in a parade 2 to walk about ostentatiously

par·a·digm (par′ə dīm′) *n.* ⟦< Gr *para-*, beside + *deigma*, example⟧ 1 an example or model 2 a generally accepted concept that explains a complex idea, set of data, etc. 3 *Gram.* an example of a declension or conjugation, giving all the inflections of a word

Par·a·dise (par′a dīs′) *n.* ⟦< Gr *paradeisos*, garden⟧ 1 the garden of Eden 2 heaven 3 [p-] any place or state of great happiness

par·a·dox (par′ə däks′) *n.* ⟦< Gr *para-*, beyond + *doxa*, opinion⟧ 1 a statement that seems contradictory, etc. but may be true in fact 2 a statement that is self-contradictory and, hence, false —**par′a·dox′i·cal** *adj.* —**par′a·dox′i·cal·ly** *adv.*

par·af·fin (par′ə fin) *n.* ⟦Ger < L *parum*, too little + *affinis*, akin: from its inertness⟧ a white, waxy substance obtained from petroleum and used for making candles, sealing jars, etc.

par·a·gon (par′ə gän′) *n.* ⟦< It *paragone*, touchstone⟧ a model of perfection or excellence

par·a·graph (par′ə graf′) *n.* ⟦< Gr *para-*, beside + *graphein*, write⟧ 1 a distinct section of a piece of writing, begun on a new line and often indented 2 a brief item in a newspaper, etc. —*vt.* to arrange in paragraphs

Par·a·guay (par′ə gwā′, -gwī′) inland country in SC South America: 157,042 sq. mi.; pop. 4,120,000 —**Par′a·guay′an** *adj., n.*

par·a·keet (par′ə kēt′) *n.* ⟦prob. < MFr *perrot*, parrot⟧ a small, slender parrot with a long tail

par·a·le·gal (par′ə lē′gəl) *adj.* designating or of persons trained to aid lawyers but not licensed to practice law —*n.* such a person

par·al·lax (par′ə laks′) *n.* ⟦< Gr *para-*, beyond + *allassein*, to change⟧ the apparent change in the position of an object resulting from a change in the viewer's position

par·al·lel (par′ə lel′) *adj.* ⟦< Gr *para-*, side by side + *allēlos*, one another⟧ 1 extending in the same direction and at the same distance apart, so as never to meet 2 similar or corresponding —*n.* 1 a parallel line, surface, etc. 2 any person or thing similar to another; counterpart 3 any comparison showing likeness 4 any of the imaginary lines parallel to the equator and representing degrees of latitude: in full **parallel of latitude** —*vt.* **-leled′** or **-lelled′**, **-lel′ing** or **-lel′ling** 1 to be parallel with 2 to match; equal —**par′al·lel′ism′** *n.*

par′al·lel′o·gram′ (-ə gram′) *n.* a four-sided plane figure having the opposite sides parallel and equal

parallel parking the parking of vehicles close to and parallel to the curb

pa·ral·y·sis (pə ral′ə sis) *n., pl.* **-ses′** (-sēz′) ⟦< Gr *paralyein*, to loosen or weaken at the side⟧ 1 partial or complete loss of voluntary motion or of sensation in part or all of the body 2 any condition of helpless inactivity —**par·a·lyt·ic** (par′ə lit′ik) *adj., n.*

par·a·lyze (par′ə līz′) *vt.* **-lyzed′**, **-lyz′ing** 1 to cause paralysis in 2 to make ineffective or powerless

par·a·me·ci·um (par′ə mē′sē əm, -shē əm) *n., pl.* **-ci·a** (-ə) ⟦< Gr *paramēkēs*, oval⟧ an elongated protozoan that moves by means of cilia

par·a·med·ic (par′ə med′ik) *n.* a person in paramedical work

par′a·med′i·cal (-med′i kəl) *adj.* ⟦PARA- + MEDICAL⟧ of auxiliary medical personnel, as midwives and nurses' aides

pa·ram·e·ter (pə ram′ət ər) *n.* ⟦< Gr *para-*, beside + *metron*, a measure⟧ 1 any of a set of interdependent variables 2 *a*) a boundary or limit *b*) a characteristic (*usually used in pl.*)

par·a·mil·i·tar·y (par′ə mil′ə ter′ē) *adj.* ⟦PARA- + MILITARY⟧ of forces working along with, or in place of, a regular military organization

par·a·mount (par′ə mount′) *adj.* ⟦< OFr *par*, by + *amont*, uphill⟧ ranking higher than any other; chief

par·a·mour (par′ə moor′) *n.* ⟦< OFr *par amour*, with love⟧ a lover or mistress; esp., the illicit sexual partner of a married man or woman

par·a·noi·a (par′ə noi′ə) *n.* ⟦< Gr *para-*, beside + *nous*, the mind⟧ a mental disorder characterized by delusions, as of grandeur or, esp., persecution —**par′a·noid′** *adj., n.*

par·a·pet (par′ə pet′, -pət) *n.* ⟦< It *parare*, to guard + *petto*, breast⟧ 1 a wall or bank for screening troops from enemy fire 2 a low wall or railing

par·a·pher·na·li·a (par′ə fər nāl′yə, -nā′lē ə) *pl.n.* ⟦< Gr *para-*, beyond + *phernē*, dowry⟧ [*often with sing. v.*] 1 personal belongings 2 equipment

par·a·phrase (par′ə frāz′) *n.* ⟦< Gr *para-*, beside + *phrazein*, say⟧ a rewording of the meaning of something spoken or written —*vt., vi.* **-phrased′**, **-phras′ing** to express (something) in a paraphrase

par·a·ple·gi·a (par′ə plē′jē ə, -jə) *n.* ⟦< Gr *para-*, beside + *plēgē*, a stroke⟧ paralysis of the lower half of the body —**par′a·ple′gic** (-plē′jik) *adj., n.*

par′a·pro·fes′sion·al *n.* ⟦see PARA-⟧ a trained assistant to licensed professionals, as in medicine

par′a·psy·chol′o·gy *n.* ⟦see PARA-⟧ psychology that investigates psychic phenomena, such as telepathy

par′a·sail′ *n.* ⟦< PARACHUTE⟧ a kind of parachute worn by a person who is pulled by a boat, car, etc. fast enough to glide in the air —**par′a·sail′ing** *n.*

par·a·site (par′ə sīt′) *n.* ⟦< Gr *para-*, beside + *sitos*, food⟧ 1 one who lives at others' expense without making any useful return 2 a plant or animal that lives on or in another organism, usually with harmful effects —**par′a·sit′ic** (-sit′ik) *adj.*

par·a·sol (par′ə sôl′) *n.* ⟦< It *parare*, ward off + *sole*, sun⟧ a lightweight umbrella used for protection from the sun's rays

par·a·sym·pa·thet·ic (par'ə sim'pə thet'ik) ***adj.*** ⟦PARA- + SYMPATHETIC⟧ *Physiology* designating the part of the autonomic nervous system whose functions include constricting the pupils of the eyes, slowing the heartbeat, and stimulating some digestive glands

par·a·thi·on (par'ə thī'än') ***n.*** ⟦PARA- + Gr *theion*, sulfur⟧ a highly poisonous insecticide

par'a·thy'roid' (-thī'roid') ***adj.*** ⟦PARA- + THYROID⟧ designating or of the small glands near the thyroid that regulate calcium and phosphorus metabolism

par·a·troops (par'ə tro͞ops') ***pl.n.*** ⟦< PARA(CHUTE) + TROOP⟧ troops trained and equipped to parachute into a combat area —**par'a·troop'er** ***n.***

par·boil (pär'boil') ***vt.*** ⟦< L *per*, through + *bullire*, to boil: infl. by *part*⟧ to boil until partly cooked

par·cel (pär'səl) ***n.*** ⟦ult. < L *pars*, part⟧ **1** a small, wrapped bundle; package **2** a piece (of land) —***vt.*** **-celed** or **-celled**, **-cel·ing** or **-cel·ling** to separate into parts and distribute: with *out*

parcel post a mail service for parcels not over a specified weight and size

parch (pärch) ***vt.*** ⟦< ?⟧ **1** to make hot and dry **2** to make very thirsty —***vi.*** to become very dry, hot, thirsty, etc.

parch·ment (pärch'mənt) ***n.*** ⟦< L (*charta*) *Pergamena*, (paper) of Pergamum, city in Asia Minor⟧ **1** the skin of a sheep, goat, etc. prepared as a surface for writing **2** paper like parchment **3** a manuscript on parchment

par·don (pärd''n) ***vt.*** ⟦< L *per-*, through + *donare*, give⟧ **1** to release from further punishment **2** to forgive (an offense) **3** to excuse (a person) for a fault, etc. —***n.*** **1** forgiveness **2** an official document granting a pardon —**par'don·a·ble** ***adj.***

pare (per) ***vt.*** **pared, par'ing** ⟦< L *parare*, prepare⟧ **1** to cut or trim away (the rind, skin, etc.) of; peel **2** to reduce gradually: often with *down*

par·e·gor·ic (par'ə gôr'ik) ***n.*** ⟦< Gr *parēgoros*, soothing⟧ a tincture of opium, used to relieve diarrhea

par·ent (per'ənt) ***n.*** ⟦< L *parere*, beget⟧ **1** a person in relation to his or her offspring; a mother or father **2** any organism in relation to its offspring **3** a source; origin —***adj.*** of a corporation in relation to a subsidiary that it owns —**pa·ren·tal** (pə rent''l) ***adj.*** —**par'ent·hood'** ***n.***

par'ent·age ***n.*** descent from parents or ancestors; lineage

pa·ren·the·sis (pə ren'thə sis) ***n.***, *pl.* **-ses'** (-sēz') ⟦< Gr *para-*, beside + *entithenai*, to insert⟧ **1** a word, clause, etc. added as an explanation or comment within a sentence **2** either or both of the curved lines, ( ), used to set this off —**par·en·thet·i·cal** (par'ən thet'i kəl) or **par'en·thet'ic** ***adj.***

par'ent·ing ***n.*** the work or skill of a parent in raising a child or children

pa·re·sis (pə rē'sis) ***n.***, *pl.* **-ses'** (-sēz') ⟦Gr < *parienai*, relax⟧ **1** partial paralysis **2** a brain disease caused by syphilis of the central nervous system

par ex·cel·lence (ek'sə läns) ⟦< Fr⟧ in the greatest degree of excellence

par·fait (pär fā') ***n.*** ⟦Fr, lit., perfect⟧ a frozen dessert of cream, eggs, etc., or of layers of ice cream, crushed fruit, etc. in a tall glass

pa·ri·ah (pə rī'ə) ***n.*** ⟦< Tamil *paraiyan*, drummer⟧ **1** a member of one of the lowest social castes in India **2** any outcast

par·i·mu·tu·el (par'ə myo͞o'cho͞o əl) ***n.*** ⟦Fr, lit., a mutual bet⟧ a system of betting on races in which the winning bettors share the net of each pool in proportion to their wagers

par·ing (per'iŋ) ***n.*** a piece pared off

Par·is[1] (par'is) ***n.*** *Gr. Legend* a prince of Troy: see HELEN OF TROY

Par·is[2] (par'is; *Fr* pä'rē') capital of France: pop. 2,166,000 —**Pa·ri·sian** (pə rizh'ən, -rē'zhən) ***adj.***, ***n.***

par·ish (par'ish) ***n.*** ⟦< Gr *paroikia*, diocese⟧ **1** a part of a diocese, under the charge of a priest or minister **2** the congregation of a church **3** a civil division in Louisiana, like a county

pa·rish·ion·er (pə rish'ə nər) ***n.*** a member of a parish

par·i·ty (par'ə tē) ***n.*** ⟦< L *par*, equal⟧ **1** equality in power, value, etc. **2** equality of value at a given ratio between different kinds of money, etc.

park (pärk) ***n.*** ⟦< ML *parricus*⟧ **1** wooded land held as part of an estate or preserve **2** an area of public land, with walks, playgrounds, etc., for recreation **3** the system in an automatic transmission that locks the drive wheels of a motor vehicle —***vt.***, ***vi.*** **1** to leave (a vehicle) in a place temporarily **2** to maneuver (a vehicle) into a space where it can be left temporarily

PARKA

par·ka (pär'kə) ***n.*** ⟦< Russ, fur coat⟧ a heavy jacket with a hood

parking meter a timing device installed near a parking space: drivers pay to park there for a certain length of time by inserting coins in it

Par·kin·son's disease (pär'kin sənz) ⟦after J. *Parkinson* (1755-1824), Eng physician⟧ a degenerative disease of later life, causing a rhythmic tremor and muscular rigidity

park'way' ***n.*** a broad roadway landscaped with trees, bushes, etc.

par·lance (pär'ləns) ***n.*** ⟦< OFr *parler*, speak⟧ language or idiom

par·lay (pär'lā) ***vt.***, ***vi.*** ⟦< It *paro*, a pair⟧ to bet (an original wager plus its winnings) on another race, etc. —***n.*** a parlayed bet

par·ley (pär′lē) ***vi.*** ⟦< Fr *parler,* speak⟧ to confer, esp. with an enemy —***n.,*** *pl.* **-leys** a conference, as to settle a dispute or discuss terms

par·lia·ment (pär′lə mənt) ***n.*** ⟦< OFr *parler,* speak⟧ **1** an official government council **2** [**P-**] the national legislative body of certain countries, esp. Great Britain

par′lia·men·tar′i·an (-men ter′ē ən) ***n.*** one skilled in parliamentary rules or debate

par′lia·men′ta·ry (-ment′ə rē, -men′trē) ***adj.*** **1** of or by a parliament **2** conforming to the rules of a parliament

par·lor (pär′lər) ***n.*** ⟦< OFr *parler,* speak⟧ **1** [Old-fashioned] any living room **2** any of certain kinds of business establishment *[a beauty parlor]*

Parmesan (cheese) (pär′mə zän′, -zhän′) ⟦after *Parma,* It city⟧ a very hard, dry cheese orig. of Italy

par·mi·gia·na (pär′mə zhä′nə, pär′mə zhän′) ***adj.*** prepared with Parmesan cheese

pa·ro·chi·al (pə rō′kē əl) ***adj.*** ⟦see PARISH⟧ **1** of or in a parish or parishes **2** narrow in scope; provincial

parochial school a school supported and run by a church

par·o·dy (par′ə dē) ***n.,*** *pl.* **-dies** ⟦< Gr *para-,* beside + *ōidē,* song⟧ a humorous imitation of a literary or musical work or style —***vt.*** **-died, -dy·ing** to make a parody of

pa·role (pə rōl′) ***n.*** ⟦< LL *parabola,* a speech⟧ the release of a prisoner whose sentence has not expired, on condition of future good behavior —***vt.*** **-roled′, -rol′ing** to release on parole

par·ox·ysm (par′ək siz′əm) ***n.*** ⟦< Gr *para-,* beyond + *oxynein,* sharpen⟧ **1** a sudden attack of a disease **2** a sudden outburst as of laughter

par·quet (pär kā′) ***n.*** ⟦Fr, < MFr *parchet,* dim. of *parc,* park⟧ **1** the main floor of a theater: usually called *orchestra* **2** a flooring of parquetry —***vt.*** **-queted′** (-kād′), **-quet′ing** (-kā′iŋ) to make of parquetry

PARQUET

parquet circle the part of a theater beneath the balcony on the main floor

par·quet·ry (pär′kə trē) ***n.*** inlaid wooden flooring in geometric forms

par·ri·cide (par′ə sīd′) ***n.*** ⟦< L *paricida:* see -CIDE⟧ **1** the act of murdering one's parent, close relative, etc. **2** one who does this

par·rot (par′ət) ***n.*** ⟦Fr dial. *perrot*⟧ **1** a tropical bird with a hooked bill and brightly colored feathers: some parrots can learn to imitate human speech **2** one who parrots what others say —***vt.*** to repeat without understanding

par·ry (par′ē) ***vt.*** **-ried, -ry·ing** ⟦prob. ult. < L *parare,* prepare⟧ **1** to ward off (a blow, etc.) **2** to evade (a question, etc.) —***n.,*** *pl.* **-ries** a parrying

parse (pärs) ***vt., vi.*** **parsed, pars′ing** ⟦< L *pars (orationis),* part (of speech)⟧ to separate (a sentence) into its parts, giving the form and function of each part

par·si·mo·ny (pär′sə mō′nē) ***n.*** ⟦< L *parcere,* to spare⟧ stinginess; extreme frugality —**par′si·mo′ni·ous** ***adj.***

pars·ley (pärs′lē) ***n.*** ⟦< Gr *petros,* stone + *selinon,* celery⟧ a plant with aromatic, often curled leaves used to flavor or garnish some foods

pars·nip (pärs′nip′) ***n.*** ⟦< L *pastinare,* dig up⟧ **1** a plant with a long white root used as a vegetable **2** its root

par·son (pär′sən) ***n.*** ⟦see PERSON⟧ **1** an Anglican minister having a parish **2** [Inf.] any minister

par′son·age ***n.*** the dwelling provided by a church for its minister

part (pärt) ***n.*** ⟦< L *pars*⟧ **1** a portion, division, etc. of a whole *[a part of a book]* **2** an essential, separable element *[automobile parts]* **3** a portion or share; specif., *a)* a share of work *[to do one's part]* *b)* [*usually pl.*] talent; ability *[a man of parts]* *c)* a role in a play *d)* any of the voices or instruments in a musical ensemble, or the score for this **4** [*usually pl.*] a portion of a country **5** a dividing line formed in combing the hair —***vt.*** **1** to break or divide into parts **2** to comb (the hair) so as to leave a part **3** to break or hold apart —***vi.*** **1** to break or divide into parts **2** to separate and go different ways **3** to cease associating **4** to go away; leave: with *from* —***adj.*** partial —**for one's part** as far as one is concerned —**for the most part** mostly —**in part** partly —**part with** to relinquish —**take part** to participate —**take someone's part** to side with someone

par·take (pär tāk′) ***vi.*** **-took′, -tak′en, -tak′ing** ⟦< *part taker*⟧ **1** to participate (*in* an activity) **2** to eat or drink something, esp. with others: usually with *of* —**par·tak′er** ***n.***

part·ed (pärt′id) ***adj.*** separated; divided

par·terre (pär ter′) ***n.*** ⟦Fr < *par,* on + *terre,* earth⟧ **1** a garden with the flower beds and path in a pattern **2** PARQUET CIRCLE

par·the·no·gen·e·sis (pär′thə nō′jen′ə sis) ***n.*** ⟦see fol. & GENESIS⟧ reproduction from an unfertilized ovum, seed, or spore

Par′the·non′ (-nän′) ***n.*** ⟦< Gr *parthenos,* a virgin (i.e., Athena)⟧ the Doric temple of Athena on the Acropolis

par·tial (pär′shəl) ***adj.*** ⟦< L *pars,* a part⟧ **1** favoring one person, faction, etc. more than another; biased **2** not complete —**partial to** fond of —**par′ti·al′i·ty** (-shē al′ə tē) ***n.*** —**par′tial·ly** ***adv.***

par·tic·i·pate (pär tis′ə pāt′) ***vi.*** **-pat′ed, -pat′ing** ⟦< L *pars,* a part + *capere,* to take⟧ to have or take a share with others (*in* some activity) —**par·tic′i·pant** ***adj., n.*** —**par·tic′i·pa′tion** ***n.*** —**par·tic′i·pa′tor** ***n.*** —**par·tic′i·pa·to′ry** (-pə tôr′ē) ***adj.***

par·ti·ci·ple (pärt′i sip′əl) ***n.*** ⟦see prec.⟧ a verbal form having characteristics of both verb and adjective —**par'ti·cip'i·al** (-sip'ē əl) ***adj.***

par·ti·cle (pärt'i kəl) ***n.*** ⟦< L *pars,* a part⟧ **1** a tiny fragment or trace **2** a short, usually invariable part of speech, as an article or preposition **3** *Physics* a subatomic particle that cannot be divided

par·ti·col·ored (pär'ti kul'ərd) ***adj.*** ⟦< Fr *parti,* divided + COLORED⟧ having different colors in different parts

par·tic·u·lar (pär tik'yə lər) ***adj.*** ⟦< L *particula,* particle⟧ **1** of or belonging to a single person, group, or thing **2** regarded separately; specific **3** unusual **4** exacting; fastidious —***n.*** a distinct fact, item, detail, etc. —**in particular** especially —**par·tic'u·lar'i·ty** (-lar'ə tē), *pl.* **-ties,** ***n.***

par·tic'u·lar·ize' (-lər īz') ***vt., vi.*** **-ized', -iz'ing** to give particulars or details (of) —**par·tic'u·lar·i·za'tion** ***n.***

par·tic'u·lar·ly ***adv.*** **1** in detail **2** especially **3** specifically

par·tic'u·late (-lit, -lāt') ***adj.*** of or formed of separate tiny particles

part'ing ***adj.*** **1** dividing; separating **2** departing **3** given, spoken, etc. at parting —***n.*** **1** a breaking or separating **2** a departure

par·ti·san (pärt'ə zən) ***n.*** ⟦< L *pars,* a part⟧ **1** a strong supporter of a faction, party, etc. **2** a guerrilla fighter —***adj.*** of or like a partisan Also sp. **par'ti·zan** —**par'ti·san·ship'** ***n.***

par·ti·tion (pär tish'ən) ***n.*** ⟦< L *partitio*⟧ **1** division into parts **2** something that divides, as a wall separating rooms —***vt.*** **1** to divide into parts; apportion **2** to divide by a partition

part'ly ***adv.*** not fully or completely

part·ner (pärt'nər) ***n.*** ⟦< ME⟧ **1** one who joins in an activity with another or others; specif., one of two or more persons jointly owning a business **2** a spouse **3** either of two persons not married to each other but in an intimate, spouse-like relationship **4** either of two persons dancing together **5** either of two players on the same side or team —**part'ner·ship'** ***n.***

part of speech any of the classes to which a word can be assigned as by form, function, or meaning; noun, verb, adverb, etc.

par·took (pär took') ***vi.*** *pt. of* PARTAKE

par·tridge (pär'trij) ***n.*** ⟦< Gr *perdix*⟧ any of several short-tailed game birds, esp. one with an orange-brown head and grayish neck

part song a song for several voices, usually without accompaniment

part'-time' ***adj.*** designating, of, or engaged in work, study, etc. taking less time than a regular or full schedule

part'-tim'er ***n.*** a part-time employee, student, etc.

par·tu·ri·tion (pär'tōō rish'ən) ***n.*** ⟦< L *parere,* bring forth⟧ childbirth

part'way' ***adv.*** to some degree, but not fully

par·ty (pär'tē) ***n.,*** *pl.* **-ties** ⟦< L *pars,* a part⟧ **1** a group of people working to promote a political platform or group of candidates, a cause, etc. **2** a group acting together to accomplish a task **3** a gathering for social entertainment **4** one concerned in an action, plan, lawsuit, etc. *[a party to the action]* **5** [Inf.] a person —***vi.*** **-tied, -ty·ing** to attend or hold social parties

par'ty·go'er (-gō'ər) ***n.*** a person who attends a party or many parties

party line **1** a single circuit connecting two or more telephone users with the exchange **2** the policies of a political party

par·ve·nu (pär'və nōō') ***n.*** ⟦< L *pervenire,* arrive⟧ a newly rich person who is considered an upstart

Pas·a·de·na (pas'ə dē'nə) city in SW California: pop. 132,000

pas·chal (pas'kəl) ***adj.*** ⟦< LL < Gr < Heb *pesach,* Passover⟧ **1** of Passover **2** of Easter

pa·sha (pə shä', pä'shə) ***n.*** ⟦Turk⟧ [Historical] in Turkey, a title of rank or honor placed after the name

pass (pas) ***vi.*** ⟦< L *passus,* a step⟧ **1** to go or move forward, through, etc. **2** to go or be conveyed from one place, form, condition, etc. to another **3** *a)* to cease *b)* to depart **4** to die: usually with *away* or *on* **5** to go by **6** to elapse *[an hour passed]* **7** to make a way: with *through* or *by* **8** to be accepted without question **9** to be approved, as by a legislature **10** to go through a test, course, etc. successfully **11** to give a judgment, sentence, etc.: with *on* or *upon* **12** *Card Games* to decline a chance to bid —***vt.*** **1** to go by, beyond, over, or through; specif., *a)* to leave behind *b)* to go through (a test, course, etc.) successfully **2** to cause or allow to go, move, or proceed; specif., *a)* to ratify; enact *b)* to spend (time) *c)* to excrete **3** to cause to move from place to place; circulate **4** to give (an opinion or judgment) —***n.*** **1** an act of passing; passage **2** a condition; situation *[a strange pass]* **3** *a)* a ticket, etc. giving permission to come or go freely or without charge *b) Mil.* a brief leave of absence **4** a motion of the hand, as in card tricks or hypnotism, or as if to strike **5** a tentative attempt **6** a narrow passage, etc., esp. between mountains **7** [Inf.] an overly familiar attempt to embrace or kiss **8** *Sports* a transfer of a ball, etc. to another player during play —**come** (or **bring**) **to pass** to (cause to) happen —**pass for** to be accepted as —**pass off** to cause to be accepted through deceit —**pass out** **1** to distribute **2** to faint —**pass over** to disregard; ignore —**pass up** [Inf.] to refuse or let go by —**pass'er** ***n.***

pass'a·ble ***adj.*** **1** that can be passed, traveled over, etc. **2** adequate; fair —**pass'a·bly** ***adv.***

pas·sage (pas'ij) ***n.*** **1** a passing; specif., *a)* migration *b)* transition *c)* the enactment of a law **2** permission or right to pass **3** a voyage **4** a means of passing; road, passageway, etc. **5** an exchange, as of blows or words **6** a portion of a book, musical composition, etc.

pas'sage·way' ***n.*** a narrow way for passage, as a hall or alley

pass'book' *n.* BANKBOOK

pas·sé (pa sā', pä-) *adj.* ⟦Fr, past⟧ out-of-date; old-fashioned

pas·sel (pas'əl) *n.* ⟦< PARCEL⟧ [Inf. or Dial.] a group, esp. a fairly large one

pas·sen·ger (pas'ən jər) *n.* ⟦< OFr *passage*, passage⟧ a person traveling in a train, boat, car, etc.

pass'er·by' *n., pl.* **pass'ers·by'** one who passes by: also **pass'er-by'**, *pl.* **pass'ers-by'**

pass'-fail' *adj. Educ.* designating a grading system recording "pass" or "fail" instead of a letter or number grade

pass'ing *adj.* **1** going by, beyond, etc. **2** fleeting **3** casual *[a passing remark]* **4** satisfying given requirements *[a passing grade]* —*n.* the act of one that passes; specif., death —**in passing** incidentally

pas·sion (pash'ən) *n.* ⟦< L *pati*, endure⟧ **1** any emotion, as hate, love, or fear **2** intense emotional excitement, as rage, enthusiasm, or lust **3** the object of any strong desire **4** [**P-**] the sufferings of Jesus, beginning after the Last Supper and continuing to his death on the Cross

pas'sion·ate (-ə nit) *adj.* **1** having or showing strong feelings **2** hot-tempered **3** ardent; intense **4** sensual —**pas'sion·ate·ly** *adv.*

pas·sive (pas'iv) *adj.* ⟦see PASSION⟧ **1** inactive, but acted upon **2** offering no resistance; submissive **3** *Gram.* denoting the voice of a verb whose subject is the recipient (object) of the action —**pas'sive·ly** *adv.* —**pas·siv·i·ty** (pa siv'ə tē) *n.*

pas'sive-ag·gres'sive *adj. Psychol.* showing disguised resistance to others' expectations, as by procrastination or inefficiency

passive resistance opposition to a government, etc. by refusal to comply or by nonviolent acts such as fasting

pass'key' *n.* **1** *a)* MASTER KEY *b)* SKELETON KEY **2** any private key

Pass·o·ver (pas'ō'vər) *n.* a Jewish holiday commemorating deliverance of the ancient Hebrews from slavery in Egypt

pass'port' *n.* a government document carried by a citizen traveling abroad, certifying identity and citizenship

pass'word' *n.* **1** a secret term used for identification, as in passing a guard **2** any means of gaining entrance

past (past) *vi., vt. rare pp. of* PASS —*adj.* **1** gone by; ended **2** of a former time **3** immediately preceding **4** *Gram.* indicating an action completed, or a condition in existence, at a former time *[the past tense]* —*n.* **1** time gone by **2** the history of a person, group, etc. **3** a personal background that is hidden or questionable —*prep.* beyond in time, space, etc. —*adv.* to and beyond some point

pas·ta (päs'tə) *n.* ⟦It⟧ **1** a flour paste or dough of which spaghetti, etc. is made **2** any food made of this

paste (pāst) *n.* ⟦< Gr *pastē*, porridge⟧ **1** dough for making pastry, etc. **2** any soft, moist, smooth preparation *[toothpaste]* **3** a mixture of flour, water, etc. used as an adhesive **4** the hard, brilliant glass of artificial gems —*vt.* **past'ed, past'ing 1** to make adhere with paste **2** [Slang] to hit

paste'board' *n.* a stiff material made as of layers of paper pasted together

pas·tel (pas tel') *n.* ⟦< LL *pasta*, paste⟧ **1** a crayon of ground coloring matter **2** a picture drawn with such crayons **3** a soft, pale shade of a color —*adj.* soft and pale: said of colors

pas·tern (pas'tərn) *n.* ⟦< L *pastor*, shepherd⟧ the part of the foot of a horse, dog, etc. just above the hoof or toes

Pas·teur (pas tur'), **Louis** 1822-95; Fr. chemist & bacteriologist

pas·teur·ize (pas'chər īz', -tər-) *vt.* **-ized', -iz'ing** ⟦after prec.⟧ to destroy bacteria in (milk, etc.) by heating to a prescribed temperature for a specified time —**pas'teur·i·za'tion** *n.*

pas·tiche (pas tēsh') *n.* ⟦Fr⟧ an artistic composition made up of bits from various sources

pas·time (pas'tīm') *n.* a way of spending spare time; diversion

past master ⟦for *passed master*⟧ a person of long experience in an occupation, art, etc.; expert

pas·tor (pas'tər) *n.* ⟦L, a shepherd⟧ a priest or minister in charge of a congregation —**pas'tor·ate** (-it) *n.*

pas'to·ral (-tə rəl) *adj.* **1** of or relating to a pastor **2** of shepherds **3** of rustic life **4** peaceful; simple

past participle *Gram.* a participle used *a)* to express completed action (Ex.: *gone* in "he has gone") *b)* to form the passive voice (Ex.: *done* in "the deed was done") *c)* as an adjective (Ex.: *fried* in "fried fish")

pas·tra·mi (pə strä'mē) *n.* ⟦E Yiddish, ult. < Turk *basdyrma*, dried meat⟧ highly spiced smoked beef

pas·try (pās'trē) *n., pl.* **-tries** ⟦see PASTE & -ERY⟧ **1** pies, tarts, etc. with crusts baked from flour dough made with shortening **2** broadly, all fancy baked goods

pas·tur·age (pas'chər ij) *n.* PASTURE

pas·ture (pas'chər) *n.* ⟦< L *pascere*, to feed⟧ **1** grass, etc. used as food by grazing animals **2** ground suitable for grazing —*vt.* **-tured, -tur·ing** to put (cattle, etc.) out to graze in a pasture

past·y (pās'tē) *adj.* **-i·er, -i·est** of or like paste in color or texture

pat[1] (pat) *n.* ⟦prob. echoic⟧ **1** a gentle tap or stroke with the hand or a flat object **2** the sound made by this **3** a small lump, as of butter —*vt.* **pat'ted, pat'ting 1** to tap or stroke gently, esp. with the hand **2** to shape or apply by patting —*adj.* **1** exactly suitable **2** so glibly plausible as to seem contrived —**pat on the back 1** a compliment **2** to praise —**stand pat** to refuse to change an opinion, etc.

pat[2] *abbrev.* **1** patent **2** patented

patch (pach) *n.* ⟦ME *pacche*⟧ **1** a piece of material applied to mend a hole or strengthen a weak spot **2** a bandage **3** an area or spot *[patches* of blue sky*]* **4** a small plot of land **5** a scrap; bit **6** an adhesive pad containing a drug or hormone that is absorbed through the skin —*vt.* **1** to put a patch on **2** to produce crudely or hurriedly —**patch up** to settle (differences, a quarrel, etc.)

patch test *Med.* a test for allergy, made by attaching a sample of a substance to the skin and observing the reaction

PATCHWORK QUILT

patch'work' *n.* needlework, as a quilt, made of patches of cloth sewn together at their edges

patch'y *adj.* **-i·er, -i·est** **1** made up of patches **2** not consistent or uniform; irregular —**patch'i·ness** *n.*

pate (pāt) *n.* ⟦< ?⟧ the head, esp. the top of the head: a humorous term

pâ·té (pä tā′) *n.* ⟦Fr⟧ a meat paste or pie

pa·tel·la (pə tel′ə) *n., pl.* **-las** or **-lae** (-ē) ⟦< L *patina,* a pan⟧ a movable bone at the front of the human knee

pat·ent (pat′'nt; *also for adj. 1 & 2,* pāt′-) *adj.* ⟦< L *patere,* be open⟧ **1** obvious; plain **2** of or having to do with patents —*n.* **1** a document granting the exclusive right to produce or sell an invention, etc. for a specified time **2** *a)* the right so granted *b)* the thing protected by such a right —*vt.* to secure a patent for

patent leather (pat′'nt) leather with a hard, glossy finish: formerly patented

patent medicine (pat′'nt) a trademarked medical preparation

pa·ter·nal (pə tur′nəl) *adj.* ⟦< L *pater,* father⟧ **1** of, like, or from a father **2** related through the father's side of the family —**pa·ter′nal·ly** *adv.*

pa·ter′nal·ism′ *n.* the governing or controlling of a country, employees, etc. in a manner suggesting a father's relationship with his children —**pa·ter′nal·is′tic** *adj.*

pa·ter′ni·ty (-nə tē) *n.* **1** the state of being a father **2** male parentage

pa·ter·nos·ter (pät′ər näs′tər) *n.* ⟦L, our father⟧ the Lord's Prayer, esp. in Latin: often **Pater Noster**

path (path) *n.* ⟦OE *pæth*⟧ **1** a way worn by footsteps **2** a walk for the use of people on foot **3** a line of movement **4** a course of conduct, thought, etc. —**path′less** *adj.*

pa·thet·ic (pə thet′ik) *adj.* ⟦see PATHOS⟧ **1** arousing pity, sorrow, etc.; pitiful **2** pitifully unsuccessful, etc. —**pa·thet′i·cal·ly** *adv.*

pathetic fallacy in literature, the attribution of human feelings and characteristics to inanimate things (Ex.: the angry sea)

patho- ⟦< Gr: see PATHOS⟧ *combining form* suffering, disease, feeling: also **path-**

path·o·gen (path′ə jən) *n.* ⟦prec. + -GEN⟧ a microorganism, etc. capable of causing disease —**path′o·gen′ic** (-jen′ik) *adj.*

pa·thol·o·gy (pə thäl′ə jē) *n., pl.* **-gies** ⟦< Gr *pathologia:* see fol. & -LOGY⟧ **1** the branch of medicine that deals with the nature of disease, esp. with structural and functional effects **2** any abnormal variation from a sound condition —**path·o·log·i·cal** (path′ə läj′i kəl) *adj.* —**pa·thol′o·gist** *n.*

pa·thos (pā′thäs′) *n.* ⟦Gr, suffering, disease, feeling⟧ the quality in something which arouses pity, sorrow, sympathy, etc.

path′way′ *n.* PATH

-pa·thy (pə thē) ⟦< Gr: see PATHOS⟧ *combining form* **1** feeling *[telepathy]* **2** (treatment of) disease *[osteopathy]*

pa·tience (pā′shəns) *n.* a being patient; calm endurance

pa′tient (-shənt) *adj.* ⟦< L *pati,* endure⟧ **1** enduring pain, trouble, etc. without complaining **2** calmly tolerating delay, confusion, etc. **3** diligent; persevering —*n.* one receiving medical care —**pa′tient·ly** *adv.*

pat·i·na (pat′'n ə, pə tē′nə) *n.* ⟦Fr < It⟧ a fine greenish crust on bronze or copper, formed by oxidation

pa·ti·o (pat′ē ō′, pät′-) *n., pl.* **-os′** ⟦Sp⟧ **1** a courtyard open to the sky **2** a paved area adjoining a house, for outdoor lounging, dining, etc.

pa·tois (pa′twä′) *n., pl.* **-tois′** (-twäz′) ⟦Fr⟧ a provincial or local dialect

pat pend *abbrev.* patent pending

patri- ⟦< Gr *patēr*⟧ *combining form* father: also **patr-**

pa·tri·arch (pā′trē ärk′) *n.* ⟦< Gr *patēr,* father + *archein,* to rule⟧ **1** the father and head of a family or tribe, as Abraham, Isaac, or Jacob in the Bible **2** a man of great age and dignity **3** [*often* **P-**] a high-ranking bishop, as in the Eastern Orthodox Church —**pa′tri·ar′chal** *adj.*

pa′tri·arch′y (-är′kē) *n., pl.* **-ies** **1** a form of social organization in which the father is head of the family, descent being traced through the male line **2** rule or domination by men

pa·tri·cian (pə trish′ən) *n.* ⟦< L *pater,* father⟧ an aristocrat

pat·ri·cide (pa′trə sīd′) *n.* **1** the murdering of one's father **2** a person who does this —**pat′ri·ci′dal** *adj.*

pat′ri·mo′ny (-mō′nē) *n., pl.* **-nies** ⟦< L *pater,* father⟧ property inherited from one's father or ancestors —**pat′ri·mo′ni·al** *adj.*

pa·tri·ot (pā′trē ət) *n.* ⟦< Gr *patris,* fatherland⟧ one who loves and zealously supports one's own country —

pa'tri·ot'ic (-ät'ik) ***adj.*** —**pa'tri·ot'i·cal·ly** ***adv.*** —**pa'tri·ot·ism'** ***n.***

pa·trol (pə trōl') ***vt., vi.*** **-trolled', -trol'ling** ⟦Fr *patrouiller*⟧ to make a regular, repeated circuit (of) in guarding —***n.*** **1** a patrolling **2** a person or group patrolling

patrol car a police car used to patrol an area

pa·trol'man (-mən) ***n., pl.*** **-men** (-mən) a police officer who patrols a certain area

patrol wagon an enclosed truck used by police to carry prisoners

pa·tron (pā'trən) ***n.*** ⟦< L *pater*, father⟧ **1** a protector; benefactor **2** a person, usually wealthy, who sponsors and supports some person, activity, etc. **3** a regular customer —**pa'tron·ess** ***fem.n.***

pa·tron·age (pā'trə nij, pa'-) ***n.*** **1** support, encouragement, etc. given by a patron **2** *a)* clientele *b)* business; trade **3** *a)* the power to grant political favors *b)* such favors

pa·tron·ize (pā'trə nīz', pa'-) ***vt.*** **-ized', -iz'ing** **1** to sponsor; support **2** to be kind or helpful to, but in a haughty or snobbish way **3** to be a regular customer of

patron saint a saint looked upon as a special guardian

pat·ro·nym·ic (pa'trə nim'ik) ***n.*** ⟦< Gr *patēr*, father + *onyma*, name⟧ a name showing descent from a given person (Ex.: *Johnson*, son of John)

pat·sy (pat'sē) ***n., pl.*** **-sies** [Slang] a person easily imposed upon or victimized

pat·ter[1] (pat'ər) ***vi.*** ⟦< PAT[1]⟧ to make, or move so as to make, a patter —***n.*** a series of quick, light taps *[the patter of rain]*

pat·ter[2] (pat'ər) ***vi.*** ⟦< PATERNOSTER⟧ to speak rapidly or glibly —***n.*** **1** glib, rapid speech, as of salespeople or comedians **2** idle chatter

pat·tern (pat'ərn) ***n.*** ⟦< OFr *patrun*, patron⟧ **1** a person or thing worthy of imitation **2** a model or plan used in making things **3** a design **4** a regular way of acting or doing **5** a predictable route, movement, etc. —***vt.*** to make or do in imitation of a pattern

pat·ty (pat'ē) ***n., pl.*** **-ties** ⟦Fr *pâté*, pie⟧ **1** a small pie **2** a small, flat cake of ground meat, fish, etc.

patty shell a small pastry case for a single portion of creamed fish, etc.

pau·ci·ty (pô'sə tē) ***n.*** ⟦< L *paucus*, few⟧ **1** smallness of number or amount **2** scarcity

Paul (pôl) (original name *Saul*) (died A.D. 67?); the Apostle of Christianity to the Gentiles: author of several Letters in the New Testament: also **Saint Paul**

Paul Bun·yan (bun'yən) *American Folklore* a giant lumberjack who performs superhuman feats

paunch (pônch) ***n.*** ⟦< L *pantex*, belly⟧ a potbelly —**paunch'y** ***adj.***

pau·per (pô'pər) ***n.*** ⟦L⟧ an extremely poor person, esp. one who lives on charity —**pau'per·ize', -ized', -iz'ing,** ***vt.***

pause (pôz) ***n.*** ⟦< Gr *pauein*, to bring to an end⟧ a temporary stop or rest —***vi.*** **paused, paus'ing** to make a pause; stop

pave (pāv) ***vt.*** **paved, pav'ing** ⟦< L *pavire*, to beat⟧ to cover the surface of (a road, etc.), as with concrete —**pave the way (for)** to prepare the way (for)

pave'ment ***n.*** a paved surface, as of concrete; specif., a paved road, etc.

pa·vil·ion (pə vil'yən) ***n.*** ⟦< L *papilio*, tent⟧ **1** a large tent **2** a building, often partly open, for exhibits, etc., as at a fair or park **3** any of a group of related buildings, as of a hospital

Pav·lov (pav'lôv'), **I·van** (i vän') 1849-1936; Russ. physiologist

paw (pô) ***n.*** ⟦< OFr *poue*⟧ **1** the foot of a four-footed animal having claws **2** [Inf.] a hand —***vt., vi.*** **1** to touch, dig, hit, etc. with paws or feet **2** to handle clumsily or roughly

pawl (pôl) ***n.*** ⟦< ?⟧ a device, as a hinged tongue which engages cogs in a wheel, allowing rotation in only one direction

pawn[1] (pôn) ***n.*** ⟦< L *pannus*, cloth⟧ **1** anything given as security, as for a debt **2** the state of being pledged *[a ring in pawn]* —***vt.*** **1** to give as security **2** to wager or risk

pawn[2] (pôn) ***n.*** ⟦< ML *pedo*, foot soldier⟧ **1** a chess piece of the lowest value **2** a person used to advance another's purposes

pawn'bro'ker ***n.*** a person licensed to lend money at interest on personal property left as security

pawn'shop' ***n.*** a pawnbroker's shop

paw·paw (pô'pô') ***n.*** *var. of* PAPAW

pay (pā) ***vt.*** **paid** or [Obs.] (except in PAY OUT) **payed, pay'ing** ⟦< L *pacare*, pacify⟧ **1** to give to (a person) what is due, as for goods or services **2** to give (what is due) in return, as for goods or services **3** to settle (a debt, etc.) **4** *a)* to give (a compliment, etc.) *b)* to make (a visit, etc.) **5** to be profitable to —***vi.*** **1** to give due compensation **2** to be profitable —***n.*** money paid; esp., wages or salary —***adj.*** **1** operated by the insertion of coins *[a pay phone]* **2** designating a service, etc. paid for by fees *[pay TV]* —**in the pay of** employed and paid by —**pay back** **1** to repay **2** to retaliate upon —**pay down** to pay (part of the price) at purchase as an installment —**pay for** to suffer or atone for (a wrong) —**pay off** **1** to pay all that is owed on or to **2** to yield full recompense **3** [Inf.] to succeed —**pay out** to let out (a rope, cable, etc.) —**pay up** to pay in full or on time —**pay'er** ***n.***

pay'a·ble ***adj.*** **1** that can be paid **2** due to be paid (*on* a specified date)

pay'check' ***n.*** a check in payment of wages or salary

pay'day' ***n.*** the day on which salary or wages are paid

pay dirt soil, ore, etc. rich in minerals —**hit (or strike) pay dirt** [Inf.] to discover a source of wealth, success, etc.

pay·ee (pā ē') ***n.*** one to whom a payment is made or owed

pay'load' ***n.*** **1** a cargo **2** a load, as a warhead or satellite, carried by an aircraft, rocket, etc. but not essential to its flight operations

pay'mas'ter ***n.*** the official in charge of paying employees

pay'ment ***n.*** **1** a paying or being paid **2** something that is paid

pay'off' ***n.*** **1** a settlement, reckoning, or payment **2** [Inf.] a bribe **3** [Inf.] a climax or culmination

pay·o·la (pā ō'lə) ***n.*** [Slang] a bribe, as to a disc jockey for unfairly promoting a certain record

pay'out' ***n.*** **1** a paying out; disbursement **2** an amount paid out; dividend

pay'-per-view' ***adj.*** *TV* of a system for paying for single showings of films or programs, as by cable or satellite —***n.*** such a system

pay phone (or **station**) a public telephone, usually coin-operated

pay'roll' ***n.*** **1** a list of employees to be paid, with the amount due to each **2** the total amount needed for this

Pb ⟦L *plumbum*⟧ *Chem. symbol for* lead

PBX ***n.*** ⟦*p*(*rivate*) *b*(*ranch*) (*e*)*x*(*change*)⟧ a telephone system within an organization, having outside lines

PC[1] ***n.***, *pl.* **PCs** or **PC's** PERSONAL COMPUTER

PC[2] *abbrev.* politically correct or political correctness

pct *abbrev.* percent

PCV valve ⟦*p*(*ositive*) *c*(*rankcase*) *v*(*entilation*)⟧ a valve regulating the pollution control system of a motor vehicle

pd *abbrev.* paid

Pd *Chem. symbol for* palladium

PE *abbrev.* **1** physical education **2** Prince Edward Island

pea (pē) ***n.***, *pl.* **peas** ⟦< ME *pese,* a pea, taken as pl.; ult. < Gr *pison*⟧ **1** a climbing plant with green pods **2** its small round seed, used as a vegetable

peace (pēs) ***n.*** ⟦< L *pax*⟧ **1** freedom from war **2** an agreement to end war **3** law and order **4** harmony; concord **5** serenity or quiet —**hold** (or **keep**) **one's peace** to be silent —**peace'a·ble** ***adj.***

peace'ful ***adj.*** **1** not quarrelsome **2** free from disturbance; calm **3** of or in a time of peace —**peace'ful·ly** ***adv.***

peace'mak'er ***n.*** a person who makes peace, as by settling quarrels —**peace'mak'ing** ***n., adj.***

peace officer an officer entrusted with maintaining law and order, as a sheriff

peace pipe a ceremonial pipe smoked by American Indians as part of a peace conference

peace'time' ***n.*** a time of freedom from war —***adj.*** of such a time

peach (pēch) ***n.*** ⟦< L *Persicum* (*malum*), Persian (apple)⟧ **1** a tree with round, juicy, orange-yellow fruit having a fuzzy skin and a rough pit **2** its fruit **3** the color of this fruit **4** [Slang] a well-liked person or thing

pea·cock (pē'käk') ***n.*** ⟦< L *pavo,* peacock⟧ the male of a pheasantlike bird (**pea'fowl'**), with a long, showy tail that can be spread out like a fan —**pea'hen'** ***fem.n.***

pea jacket (pē) ⟦< Du *pijjekker*⟧ a hip-length, double-breasted coat of heavy woolen cloth, worn orig. by seamen

peak (pēk) ***n.*** ⟦var. of Brit dial. *pike,* prob. < ON *pic*⟧ **1** a pointed end or top, as of a cap or roof **2** *a*) the summit of a hill or mountain ending in a point *b*) a mountain with such a summit **3** the highest or utmost point of anything —***adj.*** maximum —***vi.*** to come to a peak

peak·ed (pē'kid) ***adj.*** ⟦< ?⟧ thin and drawn, or weak and pale, as from illness

peal (pēl) ***n.*** ⟦ME *apele,* appeal⟧ **1** the loud ringing of a bell or bells **2** a set of tuned bells **3** a loud, prolonged sound, as of thunder or laughter —***vi., vt.*** to sound in a peal; ring

pea'nut' ***n.*** **1** a vine related to the pea, with underground pods containing edible seeds **2** the pod or any of its seeds **3** [*pl.*] [Slang] a trifling sum of money

peanut butter a food paste or spread made by grinding roasted peanuts

pear (per) ***n.*** ⟦< L *pirum*⟧ **1** a tree with greenish-yellow, brown, or reddish fruit **2** the juicy fruit, round at the base and narrowing toward the stem

pearl (purl) ***n.*** ⟦< L *perna,* sea mussel⟧ **1** a smooth, hard, usually white or bluish-gray object, a roundish growth formed within the shell of some oysters and other mollusks: used as a gem **2** MOTHER-OF-PEARL **3** any person or thing like a pearl in beauty, value, etc. **4** bluish-gray —**pearl'y, -i·er, -iest,** ***adj.***

Pearl Harbor inlet on the S coast of Oahu, Hawaii: site of a U.S. naval base bombed by Japan on Dec. 7, 1941

peas·ant (pez'ənt) ***n.*** ⟦< LL *pagus,* district⟧ **1** a small farmer or farm laborer, as in Europe or Asia **2** a person regarded as boorish, ignorant, etc. —**peas'ant·ry** ***n.***

peat (pēt) ***n.*** ⟦< ML *peta,* piece of turf⟧ partly decayed plant matter from ancient swamps, used for fuel

peat moss peat composed of residues of mosses, used as mulch

peb·ble (peb'əl) ***n.*** ⟦< OE *papol-*(*stan*), pebble (stone), prob. echoic⟧ a small stone worn smooth and round, as by running water —**peb'bly, -bli·er, -bli·est,** ***adj.***

pe·can (pē kän', -kan'; pi-; pē'kän', -kan') ***n.*** ⟦< AmInd⟧ **1** an edible nut with a thin, smooth shell **2** the tree it grows on

pec·ca·dil·lo (pek'ə dil'ō) ***n.***, *pl.* **-loes** or **-los** ⟦< Sp < L *peccare,* to sin⟧ a small fault or offense

pec·ca·ry (pek'ə rē) ***n.***, *pl.* **-ries** ⟦< native name⟧ a piglike animal of North and South America, with sharp tusks

peck[1] (pek) ***vt.*** ⟦ME *picken,* to pick⟧ **1** to strike, as with a beak **2** to make by doing this *[to* peck *a hole]* **3** to pick up with the beak —***vi.*** to make strokes as with a pointed object —***n.*** **1** a stroke so made **2** [Inf.] a quick, casual kiss —**peck at** [Inf.] **1** to eat very little of **2** to criticize constantly

peck[2] (pek) ***n.*** ⟦< OFr *pek*⟧ a unit of dry measure, $\frac{1}{4}$ bushel or eight quarts

pecking order a hierarchy of members of a group, based on status, relative power, etc.

pec·tin (pek′tin) ***n.*** ⟦< Gr *pēktos,* congealed⟧ a carbohydrate, obtained from certain fruits, which yields a gel that is the basis of jellies and jams

pec·to·ral (pek′tə rəl) ***adj.*** ⟦< L *pectus,* breast⟧ of or located in or on the chest or breast

pec·u·la·tion (pek′yoo lā′shən) ***n.*** ⟦ult. < L *peculium,* private property⟧ embezzlement

pe·cu·liar (pi kyool′yər) ***adj.*** ⟦< L *peculium:* see prec.⟧ **1** of only one person, thing, etc.; exclusive **2** special **3** odd; strange —**pe·cu′liar·ly** ***adv.***

pe·cu·li·ar·i·ty (pi kyoo′lē er′ə tē) ***n.*** **1** a being peculiar **2** *pl.* **-ties** something that is peculiar, as a trait

pe·cu·ni·ar·y (pi kyoo′nē er′ē) ***adj.*** ⟦< L *pecunia,* money⟧ of or involving money

ped·a·gogue or **ped·a·gog** (ped′ə gäg′) ***n.*** ⟦< Gr *paidagōgos* < *pais,* child + *agein,* to lead⟧ a teacher, esp. a pedantic one

ped′a·gog′y (-gäj′ē, -gō′jē) ***n.*** the art or science of teaching; esp., instruction in teaching methods —**ped′a·gog′ic** or **ped′a·gog′i·cal** ***adj.***

ped·al (ped′'l) ***adj.*** ⟦< L *pes,* FOOT⟧ of the foot or feet —***n.*** a lever operated by the foot, as on a bicycle or organ —***vt., vi.*** **-aled** or **-alled, -al·ing** or **-al·ling** to operate by pedals; use the pedals of

ped·ant (ped′'nt) ***n.*** ⟦ult. < Gr *paidagōgos:* see PEDAGOGUE⟧ **1** one who emphasizes trivial points of learning **2** a narrow-minded teacher who insists on exact adherence to rules —**pe·dan′tic** ***adj.*** —**ped′ant·ry** ***n.***

ped·dle (ped′'l) ***vt., vi.*** **-dled, -dling** ⟦< ? ME *ped,* basket⟧ to go from place to place selling (small articles) —**ped′dler** ***n.***

-pede (pēd) ⟦< L *pes*⟧ *combining form* foot or feet *[centipede]*

ped·er·as·ty (ped′ər as′tē) ***n.*** ⟦< Gr *paiderastēs,* lover of boys⟧ sodomy between males, esp. between a man and a boy —**ped′er·ast′** ***n.***

ped·es·tal (ped′əs təl) ***n.*** ⟦< It *piè,* foot + *di,* of + *stal,* a rest⟧ a bottom support of a pillar, statue, etc.

pe·des·tri·an (pi des′trē ən) ***adj.*** ⟦< L *pes,* foot⟧ **1** going or done on foot **2** of or for pedestrians **3** ordinary and dull; prosaic —***n.*** one who goes on foot; walker

pe·di·at·rics (pē′dē a′triks) ***n.*** ⟦< Gr *pais,* child + *iatros,* physician⟧ the branch of medicine dealing with the care of infants and children —**pe′di·a·tri′cian** (-ə trish′ən) ***n.*** —**pe′di·at′ric** ***adj.***

ped·i·cab (ped′i kab′) ***n.*** ⟦< L *pes,* foot + CAB⟧ a three-wheeled carriage, esp. formerly in SE Asia, pedaled like a bicycle by the driver

ped·i·cure (ped′i kyoor′) ***n.*** ⟦< L *pes,* FOOT + *cura,* care⟧ a trimming, polishing, etc. of the toenails

ped·i·gree (ped′i grē′) ***n.*** ⟦< MFr *pié de grue,* lit., crane's foot: from lines in genealogical tree⟧ **1** a list of ancestors **2** descent; lineage **3** a known line of descent, esp. of a purebred animal —**ped′i·greed′** ***adj.***

ped·i·ment (ped′i mənt) ***n.*** ⟦< earlier *periment,* prob. < PYRAMID⟧ an ornamental gable or triangular piece on the front of a building, over a doorway, etc.: see PORTICO, illus.

pe·dom·e·ter (pē däm′ət ər, pi-) ***n.*** ⟦< L *pes,* foot + Gr *metron,* a measure⟧ an instrument carried to measure the distance walked

ped·o·phil·i·a (ped′ə fil′ē ə) ***n.*** ⟦< Gr *pais,* child + *philos,* loving⟧ an abnormal condition in which an adult has a sexual desire for children —**pe′do·phile′** ***n.***

pe·dun·cle (pē duŋ′kəl, pē′duŋ′-) ***n.*** ⟦< L *pes,* foot⟧ a stalklike part in some plants, animals, etc.

peek (pēk) ***vi.*** ⟦ME *piken*⟧ to look quickly and furtively —***n.*** such a look

peel (pēl) ***vt.*** ⟦< L *pilare,* make bald⟧ to cut away (the rind, skin, etc.) of —***vi.*** **1** to shed skin, etc. **2** to come off in layers or flakes —***n.*** the rind or skin of fruit —**peel′er** ***n.***

peel′ing ***n.*** a peeled-off strip

peen (pēn) ***n.*** ⟦prob. < Scand⟧ the end of a hammerhead opposite the flat striking surface, usually ball-shaped or wedge-shaped

peep[1] (pēp) ***vi.*** ⟦echoic⟧ to make the short, high-pitched cry of a young bird —***n.*** a peeping sound

peep[2] (pēp) ***vi.*** ⟦ME *pepen*⟧ **1** to look through a small opening or from a place of hiding **2** to appear gradually or partially —***n.*** a brief look; furtive glimpse —**peep′er** ***n.***

peep′hole′ ***n.*** a hole to peep through

peeping Tom ⟦after legendary tailor who peeped at Lady GODIVA⟧ one who gets sexual pleasure from furtively watching others

peer[1] (pir) ***n.*** ⟦< L *par,* an equal⟧ **1** a person or thing of the same rank, ability, etc.; an equal **2** a British noble —**peer′age** (-ij) ***n.*** —**peer′ess** ***fem.n.***

peer[2] (pir) ***vi.*** ⟦< ? APPEAR⟧ **1** to look closely, as in trying to see more clearly **2** to appear partially

peer′less ***adj.*** without equal

peeve (pēv) [Inf.] ***vt.*** **peeved, peev′ing** to make peevish; annoy —***n.*** an annoyance

pee·vish (pē′vish) ***adj.*** ⟦ME *pevische*⟧ irritable; fretful; cross —**pee′vish·ly** ***adv.*** —**pee′vish·ness** ***n.***

pee·wee (pē′wē′) ***n.*** ⟦< ?⟧ [Inf.] an unusually small person or thing

peg (peg) ***n.*** ⟦ME *pegge*⟧ **1** a short piece of wood, metal, etc. used to hold parts together, hang things on, etc. **2** a step or degree **3** [Inf.] a throw —***vt.*** **pegged, peg′ging** **1** to fasten, fix, secure, mark, etc. with pegs **2** [Inf.] to throw —**peg away (at)** to work steadily (at)

Peg·a·sus (peg′ə səs) ***n.*** *Gr. Myth.* a winged horse

peg′board′ ***n.*** a piece of boardlike

material with rows of holes for hooks or pegs to hold displays, tools, etc.

peign·oir (pān wär′, pen-) ***n.*** ⟦Fr⟧ a woman's full, loose dressing gown

Pei·ping (bā′piŋ′) *a former transliteration of* BEIJING

pe·jo·ra·tive (pi jôr′ə tiv) ***adj.*** ⟦< L *pejor*, worse⟧ disparaging or derogatory —**pe·jo′ra·tive·ly** ***adv.***

Pe·king (pē′kiŋ′) *a former transliteration of* BEIJING

Pe·king·ese (pē′kə nēz′) ***n.***, *pl.* **-ese′** a small dog with a long, straight coat, short legs, and a short, wrinkled muzzle: also **Pe′kin·ese′** (-kə nēz′)

pe·koe (pē′kō) ***n.*** ⟦< Chin dial. *pek-ho*, white down (on the leaves used)⟧ a black tea of Sri Lanka and India

pe·lag·ic (pi laj′ik) ***adj.*** ⟦< Gr *pelagos*, sea⟧ of the open sea or ocean

pelf (pelf) ***n.*** ⟦< ? MFr *pelfre*, booty⟧ money or wealth regarded with contempt

pel·i·can (pel′i kən) ***n.*** ⟦< Gr *pelekan*⟧ a large, web-footed water bird with an expandable pouch in the lower bill for scooping up fish

pel·la·gra (pə lā′grə, -lag′rə) ***n.*** ⟦It ult. < L *pellis*, skin + Gr *agra*, seizure⟧ a chronic disease caused by a lack of nicotinic acid in the diet, characterized by skin eruptions and mental disorders

pel·let (pel′it) ***n.*** ⟦< L *pila*, a ball⟧ **1** a little ball, as of clay or medicine **2** a bullet, piece of lead shot, etc.

pell-mell (pel′mel′) ***adv.***, ***adj.*** ⟦< OFr *mesler*, to mix⟧ **1** in a jumble **2** in wild, disorderly haste Also **pell′mell′**

pel·lu·cid (pə lo͞o′sid) ***adj.*** ⟦< L *per*, through + *lucere*, to shine⟧ **1** transparent; clear **2** easy to understand

pelt[1] (pelt) ***vt.*** ⟦ME *pelten*⟧ **1** to throw things at **2** to beat repeatedly —***vi.*** to strike heavily or steadily: said as of hard rain

pelt[2] (pelt) ***n.*** ⟦prob. < OFr *pel*, a skin⟧ the skin of a fur-bearing animal, esp. when stripped from the carcass

pel·vis (pel′vis) ***n.***, *pl.* **-vis·es** or **-ves′** (-vēz′) ⟦L, basin⟧ **1** the basinlike cavity in the posterior part of the trunk in many vertebrates: in humans, it supports the spinal column and rests on the legs **2** the bones forming this cavity —**pel′vic** ***adj.***

pem·mi·can (pem′i kən) ***n.*** ⟦< AmInd⟧ a concentrated food made of dried beef, suet, dried fruit, etc.

pen[1] (pen) ***n.*** ⟦OE *penn*⟧ **1** a small enclosure for domestic animals **2** any small enclosure —***vt.*** **penned** or **pent**, **pen′ning** to enclose as in a pen

pen[2] (pen) ***n.*** ⟦< L *penna*, a feather⟧ a device used in writing, etc. with ink; specif., *a*) a device with a metal point split into two nibs *b*) BALLPOINT (PEN) *c*) FOUNTAIN PEN —***vt.*** **penned**, **pen′ning** to write with or as with a pen

pen[3] (pen) ***n.*** [Slang] a penitentiary

Pen or **pen** *abbrev.* peninsula

pe·nal (pē′nəl) ***adj.*** ⟦< Gr *poinē*, penalty⟧ of, for, constituting, or making a person liable to punishment

pe·nal·ize (pē′nə līz′, pen′ə-) ***vt.*** **-ized′**, **-iz′ing** to impose a penalty on; punish —**pe′nal·i·za′tion** ***n.***

pen·al·ty (pen′əl tē) ***n.***, *pl.* **-ties** **1** a punishment **2** the handicap, etc. imposed on an offender, as a fine

pen·ance (pen′əns) ***n.*** ⟦see PENITENT⟧ voluntary self-punishment to show repentance for wrongdoing, sins, etc.

pence (pens) ***n.*** [Brit.] *pl. of* PENNY

pen·chant (pen′chənt) ***n.*** ⟦Fr < *pencher*, to incline⟧ a strong liking

pen·cil (pen′səl) ***n.*** ⟦< L *penis*, a tail⟧ a rod-shaped instrument with a core of graphite, crayon, etc. that is sharpened to a point for writing, drawing, etc. —***vt.*** **-ciled** or **-cilled**, **-cil·ing** or **-cil·ling** to write, etc. with a pencil

pend (pend) ***vi.*** ⟦< L *pendere*, hang⟧ to await judgment or decision

pend·ant (pen′dənt) ***n.*** ⟦see prec.⟧ a hanging ornamental object, as one on a necklace or earring

pend·ent (pen′dənt) ***adj.*** ⟦see PEND⟧ **1** suspended **2** overhanging **3** undecided; pending

pend′ing ***adj.*** ⟦prp. of PEND, infl. by Fr *pendant*, L *pendens*⟧ **1** not decided **2** impending —***prep.*** until

pen·du·lous (pen′dyo͞o ləs, -jo͞o-) ***adj.*** ⟦see PEND⟧ hanging freely; drooping

pen·du·lum (pen′dyo͞o ləm, -jo͞o-) ***n.*** ⟦see PEND⟧ a weight hung so as to swing freely to and fro: used to regulate clock movements

pen·e·trate (pen′i trāt′) ***vt.***, ***vi.*** **-trat′ed**, **-trat′ing** ⟦< L *penitus*, inward⟧ **1** to enter by or as by piercing **2** to have an effect throughout **3** to affect deeply **4** to understand —**pen′e·tra·ble** (-trə bəl) ***adj.*** —**pen′e·tra′tion** ***n.***

pen·e·trat·ing (pen′i trāt′iŋ) ***adj.*** **1** that penetrates **2** sharp; piercing **3** acute; discerning Also **pen′e·tra′tive** (-trāt′iv)

pen·guin (peŋ′gwin, pen′-) ***n.*** ⟦prob. < Welsh⟧ a flightless bird of the Southern Hemisphere with webbed feet and flippers for swimming

pen·i·cil·lin (pen′i sil′in) ***n.*** ⟦< L *penicillus*, brush⟧ an antibiotic obtained from certain molds or produced synthetically

pen·in·su·la (pə nin′sə lə) ***n.*** ⟦< L *paene*, almost + *insula*, isle⟧ a land area almost surrounded by water —**pen·in′su·lar** ***adj.***

pe·nis (pē′nis) ***n.***, *pl.* **-nis·es** or **-nes′** (-nēz′) ⟦L⟧ the male organ of sexual intercourse —**pe′nile′** (-nīl′) ***adj.***

pen·i·tent (pen′i tənt) ***adj.*** ⟦< L *paenitere*, repent⟧ sorry for having done wrong and willing to atone —***n.*** a penitent person —**pen′i·tence** ***n.*** —**pen′i·ten′tial** (-ten′shəl) ***adj.*** —**pen′i·tent·ly** ***adv.***

pen·i·ten·tia·ry (pen′i ten′shə rē) ***n.***, *pl.* **-ries** a state or federal prison for persons convicted of serious crimes

pen′knife′ ***n.***, *pl.* **-knives′** (-nīvz′) a small pocketknife

pen′light′ or **pen′lite′** ***n.*** a flashlight about the size of a fountain pen

pen′man (-mən) ***n.***, *pl.* **-men** (-mən) one skilled in penmanship

pen′man·ship′ *n.* handwriting as an art or skill

Penn (pen), **William** 1644-1718; Eng. Quaker: founder of Pennsylvania

pen name a pseudonym

pen·nant (pen′ənt) *n.* ⟦< PENNON⟧ **1** any long, narrow flag **2** such a flag symbolizing a championship, esp. in baseball

pen·ne (pen′ā′) *n.* pasta in the form of tubes, cut diagonally on the ends

pen·ni·less (pen′ə lis) *adj.* without even a penny; extremely poor

pen·non (pen′ən) *n.* ⟦< L *penna,* a feather⟧ a flag or pennant

Penn·syl·va·ni·a (pen′səl vān′yə) state of the NE U.S.: 44,820 sq. mi.; pop. 11,882,000; cap. Harrisburg: abbrev. *PA* —**Penn′syl·va′ni·an** *adj., n.*

pen·ny (pen′ē) *n., pl.* **-nies** or **pence** (pens) ⟦< OE *penig*⟧ **1** in the United Kingdom, $\frac{1}{100}$ of a pound **2** a U.S. or Canadian cent

penny arcade a building, as at an amusement park, with coin-operated games, etc.

penny pincher a miserly person —**pen′ny-pinch′ing** *n., adj.*

pen′ny·weight′ *n.* a unit of weight, equal to $\frac{1}{20}$ ounce troy weight

pen′ny-wise′ *adj.* thrifty in small matters —**penny-wise and pound-foolish** thrifty in small matters but wasteful in major ones

pe·nol·o·gy (pē näl′ə jē) *n.* ⟦< Gr *poinē,* punishment + -LOGY⟧ the study of prison management and prison reform

pen pal a person, esp. a stranger in another country, with whom one exchanges letters

pen·sion (pen′shən) *n.* ⟦< L *pensio,* a paying⟧ a regular payment, not wages, as to one who is retired or disabled —*vt.* to grant a pension to

pen′sion·er *n.* one who receives a pension

pen·sive (pen′siv) *adj.* ⟦< L *pensare,* consider⟧ thoughtful or reflective, often in a melancholy way —**pen′sive·ly** *adv.* —**pen′sive·ness** *n.*

pent (pent) *vt. alt. pt. & pp. of* PEN[1] —*adj.* held or kept in; penned: often with *up*

penta- ⟦< Gr *pente,* FIVE⟧ *combining form* five

pen·ta·gon (pen′tə gän′) *n.* ⟦< Gr *penta-,* five + *gōnia,* an angle⟧ a plane figure with five angles and five sides —**the Pentagon** the pentagonal office building of the Defense Department, located near Washington, DC —**pen·tag′o·nal** (-tag′ə nəl) *adj.*

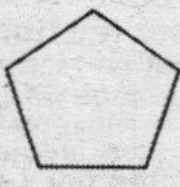

PENTAGON

pen·tam·e·ter (pen tam′ət ər) *n.* ⟦see PENTA- & METER[1]⟧ a line of verse containing five metrical feet; esp., English iambic pentameter (Ex.: "Hĕ jésts| ăt scárs| whŏ név| ĕr félt| ă wóund")

Pen·ta·teuch (pen′tə to͞ok′) *n.* ⟦< Gr *penta-,* five + *teuchos,* book⟧ the first five books of the Bible

pen·tath·lon (pen tath′län′) *n.* ⟦< Gr *penta-,* five + *athlon,* a contest⟧ an athletic contest in which each contestant takes part in five events —**pen·tath′lete′** (-lēt′) *n.*

Pen·te·cost (pen′tə kôst′) *n.* ⟦< Gr *pentēkostē* (*hēmera*), the fiftieth (day)⟧ a Christian festival on the seventh Sunday after Easter

Pen·te·cos·tal (pen′tə kôs′təl) *adj.* **1** of Pentecost **2** designating or of any of various Protestant fundamentalist sects often stressing direct inspiration by the Holy Spirit —**Pen′te·cos′tal·ism′** *n.*

pent·house (pent′hous′) *n.* ⟦ult. < L *appendere,* append⟧ an apartment on the roof or on the top floor of a building

pent-up (pent′up′) *adj.* held in check; curbed *[pent-up* emotion*]*

pe·nu·che or **pe·nu·chi** (pə no͞o′chē) *n.* ⟦var. of PANOCHA⟧ a candy similar to fudge

pe·nul·ti·mate (pē nul′tə mət) *adj.* ⟦< L *paene,* almost + ULTIMATE⟧ next to the last

pe·nu·ri·ous (pe nyoor′ē əs, -noor′-) *adj.* ⟦see fol.⟧ miserly; stingy —**pe·nu′ri·ous·ly** *adv.* —**pe·nu′ri·ous·ness** *n.*

pen·u·ry (pen′yo͞o rē, -yə-) *n.* ⟦< L *penuria,* want⟧ extreme poverty

pe·on (pē′än′) *n.* ⟦< ML *pedo,* foot soldier⟧ **1** in Spanish America, a member of the laboring class **2** in the SW U.S., a person forced into servitude to work off a debt —**pe′on·age** (-ə nij) *n.*

pe·o·ny (pē′ə nē) *n., pl.* **-nies** ⟦< Gr *Paiōn,* Apollo as god of medicine: from its former medicinal use⟧ **1** a plant with large, showy, pink, white, red, or yellow flowers **2** the flower

peo·ple (pē′pəl) *n., pl.* **-ples** ⟦< L *populus,* nation, crowd⟧ all the persons of a racial or ethnic group; nation, race, etc. —***pl.n.*** **1** *pl. of* PERSON (sense 1) **2** the persons of a certain place, group, or class **3** one's family; relatives **4** the populace **5** persons considered indefinitely *[*what will *people* say?*]* **6** human beings —*vt.* **-pled**, **-pling** to populate

Pe·or·i·a (pē ôr′ē ə) city in central Illinois: pop. 114,000

pep (pep) [Inf.] *n.* ⟦< fol.⟧ energy; vigor —*vt.* **pepped**, **pep′ping** to fill with pep; invigorate: with *up* —**pep′py**, **-pi·er**, **-pi·est**, *adj.*

pep·per (pep′ər) *n.* ⟦< Gr *peperi*⟧ **1** *a*) a pungent condiment ground from the dried fruits of an East Indian vine *b*) this vine **2** a plant with red or green, sweet or hot pods —*vt.* **1** to season with ground pepper **2** to pelt with small objects

pep′per·corn′ *n.* the dried berry of the pepper

pepper mill a hand mill used to grind peppercorns

pep′per·mint′ *n.* **1** a plant of the mint family that yields a pungent oil used for flavoring **2** the oil **3** a candy flavored with this oil

pep·per·o·ni (pep′ər ō′nē) *n., pl.* **-nis** or **-ni** ⟦< It *peperoni*⟧ a hard, highly spiced

Italian sausage

pepper shaker a container for ground pepper, with a perforated top

pep'per·y ***adj.*** **1** of, like, or highly seasoned with pepper **2** sharp or fiery, as words **3** hot-tempered

pep·sin (pep'sin) ***n.*** ⟦< Gr *peptein,* to digest⟧ a stomach enzyme, aiding in the digestion of proteins

pep talk a talk, as to an athletic team by its coach, to instill enthusiasm, determination, etc.

pep·tic (pep'tik) ***adj.*** ⟦see PEPSIN⟧ **1** of or aiding digestion **2** caused by digestive secretions *[a peptic* ulcer*]*

per (pur) ***prep.*** ⟦L⟧ **1** through; by; by means of **2** for each *[*fifty cents *per* yard*]* **3** [Inf.] according to

per- ⟦< prec.⟧ *prefix* **1** through, throughout **2** thoroughly

per·ad·ven·ture (pur'əd ven'chər) ***adv.*** ⟦< OFr *par,* by + *aventure,* chance⟧ [Archaic] possibly

per·am·bu·late (pər am'byoo lāt') ***vt., vi.*** **-lat'ed, -lat'ing** ⟦< L *per,* through + *ambulare,* to walk⟧ to walk (through, over, etc.)

per·am'bu·la'tor (-lāt'ər) ***n.*** [Chiefly Brit.] a baby carriage

per an·num (pər an'əm) ⟦L⟧ yearly

per·cale (pər kāl') ***n.*** ⟦Fr < Pers *pargāla,* scrap⟧ fine, closely woven cotton cloth, used for sheets, etc.

per cap·i·ta (pər kap'i tə) ⟦ML, lit., by heads⟧ for each person

per·ceive (pər sēv') ***vt., vi.*** **-ceived', -ceiv'ing** ⟦< L *per,* through + *capere,* take⟧ **1** to understand **2** to become aware (of) through the senses

per·cent (pər sent') ***adv., adj.*** ⟦< L *per centum*⟧ in, to, or for every hundred: symbol, %: also **per cent** —***n.*** [Inf.] percentage

per·cent'age ***n.*** **1** a given part in every hundred **2** part; portion **3** [Inf.] advantage; profit

per·cen·tile (pər sen'tīl', -sent''l) ***n.*** *Statistics* any of 100 divisions of a series, each of equal frequency

per·cep·ti·ble (pər sep'tə bəl) ***adj.*** that can be perceived —**per·cep'ti·bly** ***adv.***

per·cep'tion (-shən) ***n.*** ⟦< L *percipere,* perceive⟧ **1** the mental grasp of objects, etc. through the senses **2** insight or intuition **3** the knowledge, etc. gotten by perceiving —**per·cep'tion·al** ***adj.***

per·cep'tive (-tiv) ***adj.*** **1** of perception **2** able to perceive quickly —**per·cep'tive·ly** ***adv.*** —**per·cep'tive·ness** ***n.***

per·cep'tu·al (-choo əl) ***adj.*** of or involving perception

perch[1] (purch) ***n., pl.*** **-es** ⟦< Gr *perkē*⟧ **1** a small, spiny-finned, freshwater food fish **2** any of various other spiny-finned fishes

perch[2] (purch) ***n.*** ⟦< L *pertica,* pole⟧ **1** a horizontal pole, etc. serving as a roost for birds **2** any high resting place —***vi., vt.*** to rest or place on or as on a perch

per·chance (pər chans') ***adv.*** ⟦< OFr *par,* by + *chance,* chance⟧ [Archaic] **1** by chance **2** perhaps

per·co·late (pur'kə lāt') ***vt.*** **-lat'ed, -lat'ing** ⟦< L *per,* through + *colare,* to strain⟧ to filter (a liquid) through a porous substance —***vi.*** to ooze through a porous substance

per'co·la'tor (-lāt'ər) ***n.*** a coffeepot in which the boiling water bubbles up through a tube and filters back down through the ground coffee

per·cus·sion (pər kush'ən) ***n.*** ⟦< L *per-,* thoroughly + *quatere,* shake⟧ **1** the hitting of one body against another, as the hammer of a firearm against a powder cap (**percussion cap**) **2** the shock, vibration, etc. from this —***adj.*** of a musical instrument producing a tone when struck, as a drum, cymbal, etc.

per·cus'sion·ist ***n.*** a musician who plays percussion instruments

per di·em (pər dē'əm) ⟦L⟧ daily

per·di·tion (pər dish'ən) ***n.*** ⟦< L *perdere,* to lose⟧ *Theol.* **1** the loss of the soul **2** HELL

per·dure (pər door') ***vi.*** **-dured', -dur'ing** ⟦< L *perdurare,* to endure⟧ to remain in existence; last

per·e·gri·nate (per'ə gri nāt') ***vt., vi.*** **-nat'ed, -nat'ing** ⟦see PILGRIM⟧ to travel (along, over, or through) —**per'e·gri·na'tion** ***n.***

per·e·grine (falcon) (per'ə grin) a swift falcon much used in falconry

per·emp·to·ry (pər emp'tə rē) ***adj.*** ⟦< L *perimere,* destroy⟧ **1** *Law* barring further action; final **2** that cannot be denied, delayed, etc., as a command **3** dogmatic; imperious

per·en·ni·al (pə ren'ē əl) ***adj.*** ⟦< L *per-,* through + *annus,* year⟧ **1** continuing for a long time **2** becoming active again and again **3** living more than two years: said of plants —***n.*** a perennial plant

per·fect (pur'fikt; *for v.* pər fekt') ***adj.*** ⟦< L *per-,* through + *facere,* do⟧ **1** complete in all respects; flawless **2** excellent, as in skill or quality **3** completely accurate **4** utter; absolute *[a perfect* fool*]* **5** *Gram.* expressing a state or action completed at the time of speaking —***vt.*** **1** to complete **2** to make perfect or nearly perfect —**per'fect·ly** ***adv.***

per·fec·ta (pər fek'tə) ***n.*** ⟦Sp, perfect⟧ a bet in which one wins if one correctly picks the first and second place finishers in a race

per·fect·i·ble (pər fek'tə bəl) ***adj.*** that can become, or be made, perfect

per·fec·tion (pər fek'shən) ***n.*** **1** the act of perfecting **2** a being perfect **3** a person or thing that is the perfect embodiment of some quality

per·fec'tion·ism' ***n.*** obsessive striving for perfection —**per·fec'tion·ist** ***n., adj.***

per·fi·dy (pur'fə dē) ***n., pl.*** **-dies** ⟦< L *per,* through + *fides,* faith⟧ betrayal of trust; treachery —**per·fid·i·ous** (pər fid'ē əs) ***adj.***

per·fo·rate (pur'fə rāt') ***vt., vi.*** **-rat'ed, -rat'ing** ⟦< L *per,* through + *forare,* to bore⟧ **1** to make a hole or holes through (something), as by boring **2** to pierce with holes in a row —**per'fo·ra'tion** ***n.***

per·force (pər fôrs') ***adv.*** ⟦< OFr: see

PER & FORCE⟧ necessarily

per·form (pər fôrm′) ***vt.*** ⟦< OFr *parfournir*⟧ **1** to do (a task, etc.) **2** to fulfill (a promise, etc.) **3** to render or enact (a piece of music, dramatic role, etc.) —***vi.*** to execute an action or process, esp. in a PERFORMANCE (sense 4) —**per·form′er *n.***

per·form′ance *n.* **1** the act of performing **2** functional effectiveness **3** deed or feat **4** *a)* a formal exhibition or presentation, as a play *b)* one's part in this

performance art an art form combining elements of several art forms, as dance, film, etc., in a presentation of juxtaposed images on various themes

performing arts arts, such as drama, for performance before an audience

per·fume (pər fyo͞om′; *for n. usually* pur′fyo͞om′) ***vt.*** **-fumed′**, **-fum′ing** ⟦< L *per-,* intens. + *fumare,* to smoke⟧ **1** to scent **2** to put perfume on —***n.*** a pleasing odor, or a substance producing this, as a volatile oil extracted from flowers

per·fum′er·y (-fyo͞o′mə rē) ***n.***, *pl.* **-ies** perfumes collectively

per·func·to·ry (pər fuŋk′tə rē) ***adj.*** ⟦< L *per-,* intens. + *fungi,* perform⟧ **1** done without care or interest; superficial **2** indifferent; unconcerned —**per·func′to·ri·ly *adv.***

per·go·la (pur′gə lə) ***n.*** ⟦< L *pergula*⟧ an arbor with a latticework roof

per·haps (pər haps′) ***adv.*** ⟦PER + pl. of *hap,* chance⟧ possibly; maybe

peri- ⟦Gr⟧ *prefix* **1** around; about **2** near

per·i·car·di·um (per′ə kär′dē əm) ***n.***, *pl.* **-di·a** (-ə) ⟦< Gr *peri-,* around + *kardia,* heart⟧ in vertebrates, the thin, closed sac surrounding the heart —**per′i·car′di·al *adj.***

Per·i·cles (per′ə klēz′) 495?-429 B.C.; Athenian statesman & general

per·i·gee (per′ə jē′) ***n.*** ⟦< Gr *peri-,* near + *gē,* earth⟧ the point nearest to the earth in the orbit of the moon or of a man-made satellite

per·i·he·li·on (per′ə hē′lē ən) ***n.***, *pl.* **-li·ons** or **-li·a** (-ə) ⟦< Gr *peri-,* around + *hēlios,* sun⟧ the point nearest the sun in the orbit of a planet, comet, or man-made satellite

per·il (per′əl) ***n.*** ⟦< L *periculum,* danger⟧ **1** exposure to harm or injury **2** something that may cause harm

per′il·ous (-ə ləs) ***adj.*** involving peril or risk; dangerous —**per′il·ous·ly *adv.***

pe·rim·e·ter (pə rim′ə tər) ***n.*** ⟦< Gr *peri-,* around + *metron,* measure⟧ **1** the outer boundary of a figure or area **2** the total length of this

per·i·ne·um (per′ə nē′əm) ***n.***, *pl.* **-ne′a** (-ə) ⟦< Gr *perineon*⟧ the small area between the anus and the genitals

pe·ri·od (pir′ē əd) ***n.*** ⟦< Gr *periodos,* a cycle⟧ **1** the interval between successive occurrences of an event **2** a portion of time characterized by certain processes, etc. *[a period of change]* **3** any of the portions of time into which a game, school day, etc. is divided **4** the menses **5** an end, conclusion **6** *a)* the pause in speaking or a mark of punctuation (.) used at the end of a sentence

b) the dot (.) following many abbreviations —***interj.*** an exclamation used for emphasis

pe·ri·od·ic (pir′ē äd′ik) ***adj.*** **1** appearing or recurring at regular intervals **2** intermittent

pe′ri·od′i·cal *adj.* **1** PERIODIC **2** published at regular intervals, as weekly, etc. **3** of a periodical —***n.*** a periodical publication —**pe′ri·od′i·cal·ly *adv.***

periodic table an arrangement of the chemical elements according to their atomic numbers

pe·ri·od·i·za·tion (pir′ē ə də zā′shən) ***n.*** the dividing, as of history, into chronological periods

per·i·o·don·tal (per′ē ə dänt′'l) ***adj.*** ⟦< PERI- + Gr *odōn,* tooth⟧ occurring around a tooth or affecting the gums

per·i·pa·tet·ic (per′i pə tet′ik) ***adj.*** ⟦< Gr *peri-,* around + *patein,* walk⟧ walking or moving about; itinerant

pe·riph·er·al (pə rif′ər əl) ***adj.*** **1** of or forming a periphery **2** outer; external —***n.*** a piece of equipment used with a computer to increase its range or efficiency, as a disk, etc.

pe·riph·er·y (pə rif′ər ē) ***n.***, *pl.* **-ies** ⟦< Gr *peri-,* around + *pherein,* to bear⟧ **1** an outer boundary, esp. of a rounded object **2** surrounding space

pe·riph·ra·sis (pə rif′rə sis) ***n.***, *pl.* **-ses′** (-sēz′) ⟦< Gr *peri-,* around + *phrazein,* to speak⟧ the use of many words where a few would do —**per·i·phras·tic** (per′ə fras′tik) ***adj.***

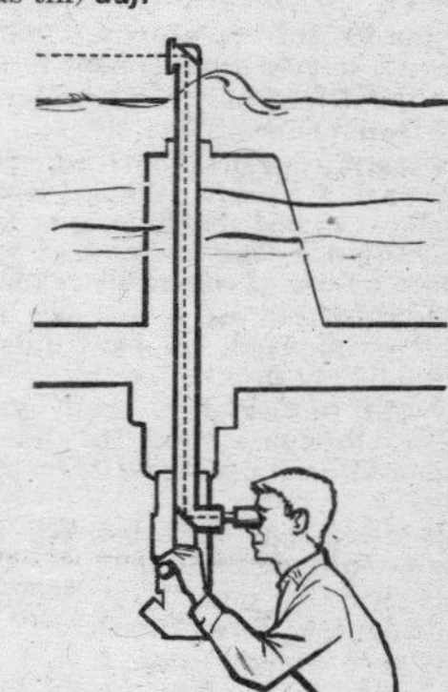

PERISCOPE

per·i·scope (per′ə skōp′) ***n.*** ⟦PERI- + -SCOPE⟧ an optical instrument which allows one to see around or over an obstacle: used on submarines, etc.

per·ish (per′ish) ***vi.*** ⟦< L *per-,* through + *ire,* go⟧ **1** to be destroyed or ruined **2** to die, esp. violently

per·ish·a·ble (per′ish ə bəl) ***adj.*** that may perish; esp., liable to spoil, as some foods —***n.*** something, esp. a food, liable to spoil

per·i·stal·sis (per'ə stal'sis, -stôl'-) ***n.***, *pl.* **-ses'** (-sēz') ⟦< Gr *peri-*, around + *stellein,* to place⟧ the contractions and dilations of the alimentary canal, moving the contents onward —**per'i·stal'tic** ***adj.***

per·i·to·ne·um (per'ə tə nē'əm) ***n.***, *pl.* **-ne'a** (-ə) or **-ne'ums** ⟦< Gr *peri-*, around + *teinein*, to stretch⟧ the serous membrane lining the abdominal cavity

per'i·to·ni'tis (-nīt'is) ***n.*** inflammation of the peritoneum

per·i·wig (per'ə wig') ***n.*** ⟦altered < Fr *perruque*⟧ a wig of a type formerly worn by men

per·i·win·kle[1] (per'ə wiŋ'kəl) ***n.*** ⟦< L *pervincire,* entwine⟧ a creeping plant with blue, white, or pink flowers

per·i·win·kle[2] (per'ə wiŋ'kəl) ***n.*** ⟦OE *pinewincle*⟧ a small saltwater snail with a spherical shell

per·jure (pur'jər) ***vt.*** **-jured**, **-jur·ing** ⟦< L *per,* through + *jurare,* swear⟧ to make (oneself) guilty of perjury —**per'jur·er** ***n.***

per·ju·ry (pur'jə rē) ***n.***, *pl.* **-ries** ⟦< L *perjurus,* false⟧ the willful telling of a lie while under oath

perk[1] (purk) ***vt.*** ⟦ME *perken*⟧ **1** to raise (the head, ears, etc.) briskly **2** to give a smart, fresh, or vivacious look to Often with *up* —***vi.*** to become lively: with *up* —**perk'y**, **-i·er**, **-i·est**, ***adj.***

perk[2] (purk) ***vt.***, ***vi.*** [Inf.] *short for* PERCOLATE

perk[3] (purk) ***n.*** [Inf.] *short for* PERQUISITE

perm (purm) [Inf.] ***n.*** *short for* PERMANENT —***vt.*** to give a permanent to

per·ma·frost (pur'mə frôst') ***n.*** permanently frozen subsoil

per·ma·nent (pur'mə nənt) ***adj.*** ⟦< L *per,* through + *manere,* remain⟧ lasting or intended to last indefinitely or for a long time —***n.*** a long-lasting hair wave produced by use of chemicals or heat

per·me·a·ble (pur'mē ə bəl) ***adj.*** that can be permeated, as by fluids —**per'me·a·bil'i·ty** ***n.***

per'me·ate' (-āt') ***vt.***, ***vi.*** **-at'ed**, **-at'ing** ⟦< L *per,* through + *meare,* to glide⟧ to spread or diffuse; penetrate (*through* or *among*)

per·mis·si·ble (pər mis'ə bəl) ***adj.*** that can be permitted; allowable

per·mis·sion (pər mish'ən) ***n.*** the act of permitting; esp., formal consent

per·mis'sive (-mis'iv) ***adj.*** **1** that permits **2** allowing freedom; lenient —**per·mis'sive·ly** ***adv.*** —**per·mis'sive·ness** ***n.***

per·mit (pər mit'; *for n.* pur'mit', pər mit') ***vt.*** **-mit'ted**, **-mit'ting** ⟦< L *per,* through + *mittere,* send⟧ **1** to allow; consent to **2** to authorize —***vi.*** to give opportunity *[if time permits]* —***n.*** a license

per·mu·ta·tion (pur'myo͞o tā'shən) ***n.*** ⟦< L *per-*, intens. + *mutare,* change⟧ **1** any radical alteration **2** any of the total number of groupings possible within a group

per·ni·cious (pər nish'əs) ***adj.*** ⟦< L < *per,* thoroughly + *necare,* kill⟧ very harmful or destructive —**per·ni'cious·ly** ***adv.***

per·o·ra·tion (per'ə rā'shən) ***n.*** ⟦< L *per,* through + *orare,* speak⟧ the concluding part of a speech

per·ox·ide (pər äk'sīd') ***n.*** ⟦< L *per,* through + OXIDE⟧ any oxide containing the oxygen group linked by a single bond; specif., hydrogen peroxide —***vt.*** **-id'ed**, **-id'ing** to bleach (hair, etc.) with hydrogen peroxide

per·pen·dic·u·lar (pur'pən dik'yo͞o lər, -yə-) ***adj.*** ⟦< L *perpendiculum,* plumb line⟧ **1** at right angles to a given plane or line **2** exactly upright; vertical —***n.*** a line or plane at right angles to another line or plane

per·pe·trate (pur'pə trāt') ***vt.*** **-trat'ed**, **-trat'ing** ⟦< L *per,* thoroughly + *patrare,* to effect⟧ **1** to do (something evil, criminal, etc.) **2** to commit (a blunder, etc.) —**per'pe·tra'tion** ***n.*** —**per'pe·tra'tor** ***n.***

per·pet·u·al (pər pech'o͞o əl) ***adj.*** ⟦< L *perpetuus,* constant⟧ **1** lasting forever or for a long time **2** continuing without interruption; constant —**per·pet'u·al·ly** ***adv.***

per·pet'u·ate' (-āt') ***vt.*** **-at'ed**, **-at'ing** to make perpetual; cause to continue or be remembered —**per·pet'u·a'tion** ***n.***

per·pe·tu·i·ty (pur'pə to͞o'ə tē) ***n.***, *pl.* **-ties** unlimited time; eternity —**in perpetuity** forever

per·plex (pər pleks') ***vt.*** ⟦< L *per,* through + *plectere,* twist⟧ to make (a person) uncertain, doubtful, etc.; confuse —**per·plex'ing** ***adj.*** —**per·plex'i·ty**, *pl.* **-ties**, ***n.***

per·qui·site (pur'kwi zit) ***n.*** ⟦< L *per-*, intens. + *quaerere,* seek⟧ something in addition to regular pay for one's work, as a tip

per se (pur' sā', -sē') ⟦L⟧ by (or in) itself; intrinsically

per·se·cute (pur'si kyo͞ot') ***vt.*** **-cut'ed**, **-cut'ing** ⟦< L *per,* through + *sequi,* follow⟧ to afflict constantly so as to injure or distress, as for reasons of religion, race, etc. —**per'se·cu'tion** ***n.*** —**per'se·cu'tor** ***n.***

per·se·vere (pur'sə vir') ***vi.*** **-vered'**, **-ver'ing** ⟦< L *per-*, intens. + *severus,* severe⟧ to continue a course of action, etc. in spite of difficulty, opposition, etc. —**per'se·ver'ance** ***n.***

Per·sia (pur'zhə) *former name for* IRAN

Per·sian (pur'zhən, -shən) ***adj.*** of Persia or its people, language, etc. —***n.*** **1** person born or living in Persia **2** the language of Iran **3** a variety of domestic cat with a long, thick, glossy coat

Persian Gulf arm of the Indian Ocean, between Iran & Arabia

Persian lamb the pelt of karakul lambs

per·si·flage (pur'sə fläzh') ***n.*** ⟦Fr < L *per,* through + *sifilare,* to hiss⟧ frivolous talk or writing

per·sim·mon (pər sim'ən) ***n.*** ⟦< AmInd⟧ **1** a hardwood tree with plumlike fruit **2** the fruit

per·sist (pər sist', -zist') ***vi.*** ⟦< L *per,* through + *sistere,* cause to stand⟧ **1** to refuse to give up, esp. when faced with opposition **2** to continue insistently **3** to endure; remain

per·sist'ent *adj.* **1** continuing, esp. in the face of opposition, etc. **2** continuing to exist or endure **3** constantly repeated —**per·sist'ence** *n.*

per·snick·e·ty (pər snik'ə tē) *adj.* ⟦< Scot dial.⟧ [Inf.] too particular or precise; fussy

per·son (pur'sən) *n.* ⟦< L *persona*⟧ **1** a human being: now usually pluralized as *people* **2** the human body **3** personality; self **4** *Gram.* any of the three sets of pronouns and corresponding verb forms: see FIRST PERSON, SECOND PERSON, THIRD PERSON **5** *Law* any individual or incorporated group having certain legal rights and responsibilities —**in person** actually present

-per·son (pur'sən) *combining form* person in a (specified) activity: used to avoid the masculine implication of *-man [chairperson]*

per'son·a·ble *adj.* ⟦ME *personabilis*⟧ having a pleasing appearance and personality

per'son·age *n.* a person; esp., an important person; notable

per'son·al (-nəl) *adj.* **1** private; individual **2** done in person **3** involving human beings *[personal* relationships*]* **4** of the body or physical appearance **5** *a)* having to do with the character, conduct, etc. of a person *[a personal* remark*]* *b)* tending to make personal, esp. derogatory, remarks **6** *Gram.* indicating PERSON (sense 4) **7** *Law* of property (**personal property**) that is movable

personal computer MICROCOMPUTER

personal effects personal belongings, esp. those worn or carried

per·son·al·i·ty (pur'sə nal'ə tē) *n.*, *pl.* **-ties 1** distinctive individual qualities of a person, considered collectively **2** such qualities seen as being attractive to others **3** a notable person **4** [*pl.*] offensive remarks aimed at a person

per·son·al·ize (pur'sə nə līz') *vt.* **-ized'**, **-iz'ing 1** to apply to a particular person, esp. to oneself **2** to have marked with one's name, etc.

per'son·al·ly *adv.* **1** in person **2** as a person *[I dislike him personally]* **3** in one's own opinion **4** as though directed at oneself

per·so·na non gra·ta (pər sō'nə nōn grät'ə) ⟦L⟧ an unwelcome person

per·son·i·fy (pər sän'ə fī') *vt.* **-fied'**, **-fy'ing 1** to think of or represent (a thing) as a person **2** to typify; embody —**per·son'i·fi·ca'tion** *n.*

per·son·nel (pur'sə nel') *n.* ⟦Fr⟧ **1** persons employed in any work, enterprise, service, etc. **2** a personnel department or office —*adj.* of or relating to the division within a business, etc. responsible for hiring and training employees, etc.

per·spec·tive (pər spek'tiv) *n.* ⟦< L *per,* through + *specere,* look⟧ **1** the art of picturing objects so as to show relative distance or depth **2** the appearance of objects as determined by their relative distance and positions **3** sense of proportion **4** *a)* a specific point of view in understanding things or events *b)* the ability to see things in a true relationship

per·spi·ca·cious (pur'spi kā'shəs) *adj.* ⟦see prec.⟧ having keen judgment; discerning —**per'spi·ca'cious·ly** *adv.* —**per'spi·cac'i·ty** (-kas'ə tē) *n.*

per·spic·u·ous (pər spik'yoo əs) *adj.* ⟦see PERSPECTIVE⟧ easily understood; lucid —**per·spi·cu·i·ty** (pur'spi kyoo'ə tē) *n.*

per·spi·ra·tion (pur'spə rā'shən) *n.* **1** the action of perspiring **2** sweat

per·spire (pər spīr') *vt.*, *vi.* **-spired'**, **-spir'ing** ⟦< L *per-,* through + *spirare,* breathe⟧ to sweat

per·suade (pər swād') *vt.* **-suad'ed**, **-suad'ing** ⟦< L *per-,* intens. + *suadere,* to urge⟧ to cause to do or believe something by reasoning, urging, etc.; induce or convince —**per·suad'er** *n.*

per·sua·sion (pər swā'zhən) *n.* **1** a persuading or being persuaded **2** power of persuading **3** a strong belief **4** a particular religious belief

per·sua'sive *adj.* having the power, or tending, to persuade —**per·sua'sive·ly** *adv.*

pert (purt) *adj.* ⟦< L *apertus,* open⟧ **1** impudent; saucy **2** chic and jaunty —**pert'ly** *adv.*

per·tain (pər tān') *vi.* ⟦< L *per-,* intens. + *tenere,* hold⟧ **1** to belong; be connected or associated **2** to be appropriate **3** to have reference

per·ti·na·cious (purt''n ā'shəs) *adj.* ⟦< L *per-,* intens. + *tenax,* holding fast⟧ **1** holding firmly to some purpose, belief, etc. **2** hard to get rid of —**per'ti·nac'i·ty** (-as'ə tē) *n.*

per·ti·nent (purt''n ənt) *adj.* ⟦see PERTAIN⟧ having some connection with the matter at hand —**per'ti·nence** *n.*

per·turb (pər turb') *vt.* ⟦< L *per-,* intens. + *turbare,* disturb⟧ to cause to be alarmed, agitated, or upset —**per·tur·ba·tion** (pur'tər bā'shən) *n.*

Pe·ru (pə roo') country in W South America, on the Pacific: 480,041 sq. mi.; pop. 22,048,000 —**Pe·ru'vi·an** (-vē ən) *adj.*, *n.*

pe·ruke (pə rook') *n.* ⟦Fr *perruque*⟧ PERIWIG

pe·ruse (pə rooz') *vt.* **-rused'**, **-rus'ing** ⟦prob. < L *per-,* intens. + ME *usen,* to use⟧ **1** to read carefully; study **2** to read in a leisurely way —**pe·rus'al** *n.*

per·vade (pər vād') *vt.* **-vad'ed**, **-vad'ing** ⟦< L *per,* through + *vadere,* go⟧ to spread or be prevalent throughout —**per·va'sive** (-vā'siv) *adj.*

per·verse (pər vurs') *adj.* ⟦see PERVERT⟧ **1** deviating from what is considered right or good **2** stubbornly contrary **3** obstinately disobedient —**per·verse'ly** *adv.* —**per·verse'ness** or **per·ver'si·ty** *n.*

per·ver·sion (pər vur'zhən) *n.* **1** a perverting or being perverted **2** something perverted **3** any sexual act or practice considered abnormal

per·vert (pər vurt'; *for n.* pur'vurt') *vt.* ⟦< L *per-,* intens. + *vertere,* turn⟧ **1** to lead astray; corrupt **2** to misuse **3** to distort —*n.* one practicing sexual perversion

pe·se·ta (pə sāt′ə) ***n.*** ⟦Sp, dim. of *peso,* peso⟧ the former monetary unit of Spain, superseded in 2002 by the EURO

pes·ky (pes′kē) ***adj.*** **-ki·er, -ki·est** ⟦prob. var. of *pesty*⟧ [Inf.] annoying; troublesome —**pes′ki·ness** ***n.***

pe·so (pā′sō) ***n.,*** *pl.* **-sos** ⟦Sp < L *pensum,* something weighed⟧ the monetary unit of various countries, including Mexico, Colombia, Chile, etc.

pes·si·mism (pes′ə miz′əm) ***n.*** ⟦< L *pejor,* worse⟧ **1** the belief that the evil in life outweighs the good **2** the tendency to expect the worst —**pes′si·mist** ***n.*** —**pes′si·mis′tic** ***adj.*** —**pes′si·mis′ti·cal·ly** ***adv.***

pest (pest) ***n.*** ⟦< L *pestis,* plague⟧ a person or thing that is troublesome, destructive, etc.; specif., a rat, fly, weed, etc.

pes·ter (pes′tər) ***vt.*** ⟦< OFr *empestrer,* entangle⟧ to annoy; vex

pest′hole′ ***n.*** a place infested with an epidemic disease

pes·ti·cide (pes′tə sīd′) ***n.*** any chemical for killing insects, weeds, etc.

pes·tif·er·ous (pes tif′ər əs) ***adj.*** ⟦< L *pestis,* plague + *ferre,* to bear⟧ **1** noxious **2** [Inf.] annoying

pes·ti·lence (pes′tə ləns) ***n.*** **1** a deadly epidemic disease; plague **2** anything regarded as harmful

pes·ti·lent (pes′tə lənt) ***adj.*** ⟦< L *pestis,* plague⟧ **1** likely to cause death **2** dangerous to society *[*the *pestilent* threat of war*]* **3** annoying

pes·tle (pes′əl) ***n.*** ⟦< L *pinsere,* to pound⟧ a tool used to pound or grind substances, esp. in a mortar

pes·to (pes′tō) ***n.*** ⟦see prec.⟧ a sauce for pasta, of ground basil and garlic mixed with olive oil

pet[1] (pet) ***n.*** ⟦orig. Scot dial.⟧ **1** an animal that is domesticated and kept as a companion **2** a person treated with particular indulgence —***adj.*** **1** kept or treated as a pet **2** especially liked **3** particular *[*a *pet* peeve*]* **4** showing fondness *[*a *pet* name*]* —***vt.*** **pet′ted, pet′ting** to stroke or pat gently; caress —***vi.*** [Inf.] to kiss, embrace, etc. as lovers do

pet[2] (pet) ***n.*** ⟦< ?⟧ a sulky mood

pet·al (pet′'l) ***n.*** ⟦< Gr *petalos,* outspread⟧ any of the leaflike parts of a blossom

pe·tard (pi tärd′) ***n.*** ⟦< Fr⟧ used chiefly in **hoist with** (or **by**) **one's own petard,** destroyed by the very thing with which one meant to destroy others

pet·cock (pet′käk′) ***n.*** ⟦< L *pedere,* break wind + *cock,* valve⟧ a small valve for draining pipes, etc.

pe·ter (pēt′ər) ***vi.*** ⟦< ?⟧ [Inf.] to become gradually smaller, weaker, etc. and then disappear: with *out*

Pe·ter (pēt′ər) ***n.*** *Bible* (original name *Simon*) (died A.D. 64?); one of the twelve Apostles, a fisherman: reputed author of two Letters: also **Saint Peter**

Peter I 1672-1725; czar of Russia (1682-1725): called *Peter the Great*

pet·i·ole (pet′ē ōl′) ***n.*** ⟦< L *pes,* FOOT⟧ LEAFSTALK

pe·tite (pə tēt′) ***adj.*** ⟦Fr⟧ small and trim in figure: said of a woman

pe·tit four (pet′ē fôr′) *pl.* **pe·tits fours** or **pe·tit fours** (pet′ē fôrz′) ⟦Fr, lit., small oven⟧ a tiny, frosted cake

pe·ti·tion (pə tish′ən) ***n.*** ⟦< L *petere,* seek⟧ **1** a solemn, earnest request; entreaty **2** a formal document embodying such a request, often signed by many people **3** *Law* a written formal request asking for a specific court action —***vt.*** to address a petition to —***vi.*** to make a petition —**pe·ti′tion·er** ***n.***

pe·tit jury (pet′ē) a group of citizens picked to decide the issues of a trial in court

pet·rel (pe′trəl) ***n.*** ⟦< ?⟧ a small sea bird with long wings

pet·ri·fy (pe′tri fī′) ***vt.*** **-fied′, -fy′ing** ⟦< L *petra,* rock + *facere,* make⟧ **1** to turn into stone **2** to harden or deaden **3** to paralyze, as with fear

petro- ⟦< Gr *petra,* rock⟧ *combining form* **1** rock or stone **2** petroleum **3** of or relating to the petroleum business

pet·ro·chem·i·cal (pe′trō kem′i kəl) ***n.*** a chemical with a petroleum base

pet′ro·dol′lars ***pl.n.*** revenue from the sale of petroleum

pet·rol (pe′trəl) ***n.*** ⟦see PETROLEUM⟧ *Brit. term for* GASOLINE

pet·ro·la·tum (pe′trə lāt′əm) ***n.*** ⟦< fol.⟧ a greasy, jellylike substance derived from petroleum and used in ointments, etc.: also **petroleum jelly**

pe·tro·le·um (pə trō′lē əm) ***n.*** ⟦< L *petra,* rock + *oleum,* oil⟧ an oily, liquid solution of hydrocarbons, occurring naturally in certain rock strata: it yields kerosene, gasoline, etc.

PET (scan) (pet) ⟦*p*(*ositron*) *e*(*mission*) *t*(*omography*), an X-ray technique⟧ a type of X-raying that shows metabolic activity, used to detect abnormalities, esp. of the brain: also **PETT scan**

pet·ti·coat (pet′ē kōt′, pet′i-) ***n.*** ⟦< PETTY + COAT⟧ a woman's underskirt

pet·ti·fog·ger (pet′i fäg′ər, -fôg′-; pet′ē-) ***n.*** ⟦< PETTY + *fogger* < ?⟧ **1** a lawyer who handles petty cases, esp. unethically **2** one who quibbles —**pet′ti·fog′, -fogged′, -fog′ging,** ***vi.***

pet·tish (pet′ish) ***adj.*** ⟦< PET[2]⟧ peevish; petulant —**pet′tish·ly** ***adv.***

pet·ty (pet′ē) ***adj.*** **-ti·er, -ti·est** ⟦< OFr *petit*⟧ **1** relatively unimportant **2** small-minded; mean **3** relatively low in rank —**pet′ti·ness** ***n.***

petty cash a cash fund for incidentals

petty officer *U.S. Navy* a naval enlisted person who is a noncommissioned officer

pet·u·lant (pech′ə lənt) ***adj.*** ⟦< L *petere,* to rush at⟧ impatient or irritable, esp. over a petty annoyance —**pet′u·lance** ***n.*** —**pet′u·lant·ly** ***adv.***

pe·tu·ni·a (pə to͞on′yə) ***n.*** ⟦ult. < AmInd (Brazil)⟧ a plant with showy, funnel-shaped flowers

pew (pyo͞o) ***n.*** ⟦ult. < Gr *pous,* foot⟧ any of the benches with a back that are fixed in rows in a church

pe·wee (pē′wē′) ***n.*** ⟦echoic of its call⟧ a small flycatcher

pew·ter (pyōōt′ər) ***n.*** ⟦OFr *peautre*⟧ **1** an alloy of tin with antimony, copper, lead, etc. **2** articles made of this

pe·yo·te (pā ōt′ē) ***n.*** ⟦AmSp < AmInd (Mexico) *peyotl,* caterpillar⟧ MESCAL: see also MESCALINE

pf or **pfd** *abbrev.* preferred

PFC or **Pfc** *abbrev.* Private First Class

pg *abbrev.* page

PG *trademark for* a film rating indicating parents may find some content unsuitable for children under 17

PG-13 *trademark for* a film rating indicating parents may find some content especially unsuitable for children under 13

pH (pē′āch′) ***n.*** ⟦< Fr *p(ouvoir) h(ydrogène),* lit., hydrogen power⟧ the degree of acidity or alkalinity of a solution

pha·e·ton or **pha·ë·ton** (fā′ə tən) ***n.*** ⟦after *Phaetōn,* son of Helios, Gr sun god⟧ **1** a light, four-wheeled carriage **2** an early type of open automobile

phag·o·cyte (fag′ə sīt′) ***n.*** ⟦< Gr *phagein,* to eat + *kytos,* hollow⟧ any cell, esp. a leukocyte, that destroys foreign matter in the blood and tissues

pha·lan·ger (fə lan′jər) ***n.*** ⟦< Gr *phalanx,* bone between fingers or toes⟧ a small, tree-dwelling Australian marsupial

pha·lanx (fā′laŋks′) ***n.,*** *pl.* **-lanx′es**; also, and for 3 always, **pha·lan·ges** (fə lan′ jēz′) ⟦Gr, line of battle⟧ **1** an ancient close-ranked infantry formation **2** any massed group **3** any of the bones forming the fingers or toes

phal·lo·cen·tric (fal′ō sen′trik) ***adj.*** dominated by attitudes regarded as typically masculine

phal·lus (fal′əs) ***n.,*** *pl.* **-li′** (-ī′) or **-lus·es** ⟦Gr *phallos*⟧ an image of the penis —**phal′lic** ***adj.***

phan·tasm (fan′taz′əm) ***n.*** ⟦< Gr *phantazein,* to show⟧ **1** a figment of the mind **2** a deceptive likeness

phan·tas·ma·go·ri·a (fan taz′mə gôr′ē ə) ***n.*** ⟦< Gr *phantasma,* phantasm + *ageirein,* assemble⟧ a rapid sequence of images, as in a dream

phan·tom (fan′təm) ***n.*** ⟦see PHANTASM⟧ **1** an apparition; specter **2** an illusion —***adj.*** of or like a phantom; illusory

Phar·aoh (far′ō, fā′rō′) ***n.*** [*sometimes* **p-**] the title of the kings of ancient Egypt

Phar·i·see (far′ə sē′) ***n.*** **1** a member of an ancient Jewish group that observed both the written and the oral law **2** ⟦< characterization in NT⟧ [**p-**] a self-righteous, hypocritical person —**phar′i·sa′ic** (-sā′ik) ***adj.***

phar·ma·ceu·ti·cal (fär′mə sōōt′i kəl) ***adj.*** ⟦< Gr *pharmakon,* a drug⟧ of pharmacy or drugs: also **phar′ma·ceu′tic** —***n.*** a drug or medicine

phar′ma·ceu′tics (-iks) ***n.*** PHARMACY (sense 1)

phar·ma·cist (fär′mə sist) ***n.*** one licensed to practice pharmacy; druggist

phar′ma·col′o·gy (-käl′ə jē) ***n.*** ⟦< Gr *pharmakon,* a drug⟧ the science dealing with the effect of drugs on living organisms

phar′ma·co·pe′ia or **phar′ma·co·poe′ia** (-kō pē′ə) ***n.*** ⟦< Gr *pharmakon,* a drug + *poiein,* to make⟧ an official book listing drugs and medicines

phar·ma·cy (fär′mə sē) ***n.,*** *pl.* **-cies** ⟦< Gr *pharmakon,* a drug⟧ **1** the art or profession of preparing drugs and medicines **2** a drugstore

phar·yn·gi·tis (far′in jīt′is) ***n.*** inflammation of the pharynx; sore throat

phar·ynx (far′iŋks) ***n.,*** *pl.* **pha·ryn·ges** (fə rin′jēz′) or **phar′ynx·es** ⟦Gr *pharynx,* throat⟧ the cavity leading from the mouth and nasal passages to the larynx and esophagus —**pha·ryn·ge·al** (fə rin′ jē əl) ***adj.***

phase (fāz) ***n.*** ⟦< Gr *phainesthai,* appear⟧ **1** any stage in a series or cycle of changes, as in the moon's illumination **2** an aspect or side, as of a problem —***vt.*** **phased**, **phas′ing** to introduce or carry out in stages: often with *in* or *into* —**in** (or **out of**) **phase** in (or not in) synchronization —**phase out** to bring or come to an end by stages

phase′out′ ***n.*** a phasing out; gradual termination or withdrawal

PhD or **Ph.D.** *abbrev.* ⟦L *Philosophiae Doctor*⟧ Doctor of Philosophy

pheas·ant (fez′ənt) ***n.*** ⟦< Gr *phasianos,* (bird) of *Phasis,* river in Asia⟧ a large game bird with a long, sweeping tail and brilliant feathers

phe·nac·e·tin (fē nas′ə tin) ***n.*** a white, crystalline powder used to reduce fever, relieve headaches, etc.

phe·no·bar·bi·tal (fē′nə bär′bi tôl′) ***n.*** an odorless, white, crystalline powder used as a sedative

phe·nol (fē′nōl′, -nôl′, -näl′) ***n.*** a white, crystalline compound, corrosive and poisonous, used to make synthetic resins, etc. and, in dilute solution (*carbolic acid*) as an antiseptic

phe·nol·phthal·ein (fē′nōl thal′ēn′, -ē in) ***n.*** a white to pale-yellow, crystalline powder used as a laxative, as an acid-base indicator in chemical analysis, etc.

phe·nom (fē′näm) ***n.*** ⟦< fol.⟧ [Slang] one who is very talented or skilled; specif., a young, very gifted athlete

phe·nom·e·non (fə näm′ə nən, -nän′) ***n.,*** *pl.* **-na** (-nə); also, esp. for 2 and usually for 3, **-nons′** ⟦< Gr *phainesthai,* appear⟧ **1** any observable fact or event that can be scientifically described **2** anything very unusual **3** [Inf.] an extraordinary person; prodigy —**phe·nom′e·nal** ***adj.***

pher·o·mone (fer′ə mōn′) ***n.*** ⟦< Gr *pherein,* carry + (HOR)MONE⟧ a chemical substance secreted by certain animals, as ants, that conveys information to others of the same species

phi (fī, fē) ***n.*** the 21st letter of the Greek alphabet (Φ, φ)

phi·al (fī′əl) ***n.*** ⟦< Gr *phialē,* shallow bowl⟧ a small glass bottle; vial

Phil·a·del·phi·a (fil′ə del′fē ə) city & port in SE Pennsylvania: pop. 1,586,000

Philadelphia lawyer [Inf.] a shrewd or tricky lawyer

phi·lan·der (fi lan′dər, fə-) ***vi.*** ⟦ult. < Gr *philos,* loving + *anēr,* a man⟧ to engage lightly in love affairs: said of a man —**phi·lan′der·er *n.***

phi·lan·thro·py (fə lan′thrə pē) ***n.*** ⟦< Gr *philein,* to love + *anthrōpos,* human being⟧ **1** a desire to help mankind, esp. as shown by gifts to institutions, etc. **2** *pl.* **-pies** a philanthropic gift, institution, etc. —**phil·an·throp·ic** (fil′ən thräp′ ik) ***adj.*** —**phi·lan′thro·pist *n.***

phi·lat·e·ly (fə lat″l ē) ***n.*** ⟦< Fr < Gr *philos,* loving + *ateleia,* exemption from (further) tax (meaning "postage prepaid")⟧ the collection and study of postage stamps, postmarks, etc. —**phi·lat′e·list *n.***

-phile (fīl, fil) ⟦< Gr *philos,* loving⟧ *combining form* one that loves or is attracted to

Phil·har·mon·ic (fil′här män′ik) ***adj.*** ⟦ult. < Gr *philos,* loving + *harmonia,* harmony⟧ designating a group formed to sponsor a symphony orchestra —***n.*** an orchestra so sponsored

phi·lip·pic (fi lip′ik) ***n.*** ⟦< Gr *Philippos,* Philip, Macedonian king denounced by Demosthenes⟧ a bitter verbal attack

Phil·ip·pines (fil′ə pēnz′) country consisting of *c.* 7,100 islands (**Philippine Islands**) in the SW Pacific off the SE coast of Asia: 115,830 sq. mi.; pop. 60,559,000 —**Phil′ip·pine′** (-pēn′) ***adj.***

Phil·is·tine (fil′ə stēn′) ***n.*** **1** a member of a non-Semitic people of SW Palestine in biblical times **2** ⟦< a Ger slang word⟧ [*often* **p-**] a person regarded as smugly conventional, lacking culture, etc.

Phil·lips (fil′ips) ⟦after H. F. *Phillips* (?-1958), its U.S. developer⟧ *trademark for* a screwdriver (**Phillips screwdriver**) with a cross-shaped, pointed tip

philo- ⟦< Gr *philos,* loving⟧ *combining form* loving, liking

phil·o·den·dron (fil′ə den′drən) ***n.*** ⟦< Gr *philos,* loving + *dendron,* tree⟧ a tropical American vine used as a houseplant

phi·lol·o·gy (fi läl′ə jē) ***n.*** ⟦< Gr *philein,* to love + *logos,* word⟧ *former term for* LINGUISTICS —**phil·o·log·i·cal** (fil′ə läj′i kəl) ***adj.*** —**phi·lol′o·gist *n.***

phi·los·o·pher (fə läs′ə fər) ***n.*** ⟦< Gr *philos,* loving + *sophos,* wise⟧ **1** one who is an expert in philosophy **2** one who expounds a system of philosophy **3** one who meets difficulties calmly

phil·o·soph·ic (fil′ə säf′ik) ***adj.*** **1** of philosophy or philosophers **2** sensibly composed or calm Also **phil′o·soph′i·cal**

phi·los·o·phize (fə läs′ə fīz′) ***vi.*** **-phized′, -phiz′ing** **1** to think or reason like a philosopher **2** to moralize, express truisms, etc.

phi·los·o·phy (fə läs′ə fē) ***n.*** ⟦see PHILOSOPHER⟧ **1** the study of the principles underlying conduct, thought, and the nature of the universe **2** the general principles of a field of knowledge **3** *pl.* **-phies** a particular system of principles for the conduct of life

phil·ter (fil′tər) ***n.*** ⟦< Gr *philein,* to love⟧ a magic potion, esp. one thought to arouse sexual love: also [Chiefly Brit.] **phil′tre** (-tər)

phle·bi·tis (flə bīt′is) ***n.*** ⟦< Gr *phleps,* vein + -ITIS⟧ inflammation of a vein

phle·bot·o·my (fli bät′ə mē) ***n.*** ⟦< Gr *pheps,* vein + *temnein,* to cut⟧ the practice of taking blood from the body for therapeutic purposes

phlegm (flem) ***n.*** ⟦< Gr *phlegma,* inflammation⟧ **1** thick mucus discharged from the throat, as during a cold **2** sluggishness or apathy

phleg·mat·ic (fleg mat′ik) ***adj.*** ⟦see prec.⟧ sluggish or unexcited —**phleg·mat′i·cal·ly *adv.***

phlo·em (flō′em′) ***n.*** ⟦< Gr *phloos,* bark⟧ the vascular tissue through which food is distributed in a plant

phlox (fläks) ***n.*** ⟦Gr, lit., a flame⟧ a North American plant with clusters of white, pink, or bluish flowers

-phobe (fōb) ⟦< Gr *phobos,* fear⟧ *combining form* one who fears or hates

pho·bi·a (fō′bē ə) ***n.*** ⟦see prec.⟧ an irrational, excessive, and persistent fear of some thing or situation —**pho′bic *adj.***

-pho·bi·a (fō′bē ə) ⟦Gr *-phobia* < *phobos,* fear⟧ *combining form* fear, dread, hatred

phoe·be (fē′bē) ***n.*** ⟦echoic, with sp. after *Phoebe,* Gr goddess of the moon⟧ an American bird with a grayish or brown back, that catches insects in flight

Phoe·ni·cia (fə nish′ə, -nē′shə) ancient region at the E end of the Mediterranean —**Phoe·ni′cian *adj., n.***

phoe·nix (fē′niks) ⟦< Gr *phoinix*⟧ *Egypt. Myth.* a bird that lives for 500 years and then sets itself on fire, rising renewed from the ashes

Phoe·nix (fē′niks) capital of Arizona: pop. 983,000

phone (fōn) ***n., vt., vi.*** **phoned, phon′ing** *short for* TELEPHONE

-phone (fōn) ⟦< Gr *phōnē,* a sound⟧ *combining form* **1** a device producing or transmitting sound **2** a telephone

phone card CALLING CARD (sense 2)

pho·neme (fō′nēm′) ***n.*** ⟦< Fr < Gr *phōnē,* voice⟧ *Linguistics* a set of related speech sounds with slight variations, that are heard as the same sound by native speakers —**pho·ne·mic** (fō nē′ mik, fə-) ***adj.***

pho·net·ics (fō net′iks, fə-) ***n.*** ⟦< Gr *phōnē,* a sound⟧ the study of the production of speech sounds and their representation in written symbols —**pho·net′ic *adj.*** —**pho·ne·ti·cian** (fō′nə tish′ ən) ***n.***

phon·ics (fän′iks) ***n.*** ⟦< Gr *phōnē,* a sound⟧ a phonetic method of teaching reading —**phon′ic *adj.***

phono- ⟦< Gr *phōnē,* a sound⟧ *combining form* sound, tone, speech [*phonology*]

pho·no·graph (fō′nə graf′) ***n.*** ⟦prec. + -GRAPH⟧ a device for reproducing sound recorded in a spiral groove on a revolving disk —**pho′no·graph′ic *adj.***

pho·nol·o·gy (fō näl′ə jē, fə-) ***n.*** ⟦PHONO- + -LOGY⟧ **1** the study of speech sounds **2** a description of the sounds of a given language —**pho′no·**

log'i·cal (-nō läj'i kəl, -nə-) ***adj.*** —**pho·nol'o·gist** ***n.***

pho·ny (fō'nē) [Inf.] ***adj.*** **-ni·er, -ni·est** ⟦< Brit thieves' argot *fawney,* gilt ring⟧ not genuine; false —***n.***, *pl.* **-nies** something or someone not genuine; fraud; fake Also sp. **pho'ney** —**pho'ni·ness** ***n.***

phoo·ey (fo͞o'ē) ***interj.*** ⟦echoic⟧ used to express scorn, disgust, etc.

phos·phate (fäs'fāt') ***n.*** ⟦Fr⟧ **1** a salt or ester of phosphoric acid **2** a fertilizer containing phosphates

phos·phor (fäs'fər, -fôr') ***n.*** ⟦see PHOSPHORUS⟧ a phosphorescent or fluorescent substance

phos·pho·res·cence (fäs'fə res'əns) ***n.*** **1** the property of giving off a lingering emission of light after exposure to radiant energy such as light **2** a continuing luminescence without noticeable heat —**phos'pho·res'cent** ***adj.***

phos·phor·ic acid (fäs fôr'ik) any of several oxygen acids of phosphorus

phos·pho·rus (fäs'fə rəs) ***n.*** ⟦< Gr *phōs,* a light + *pherein,* to bear⟧ a nonmetallic chemical element, a waxy solid that ignites spontaneously at room temperature

pho·to (fōt'ō) ***n.***, *pl.* **-tos** *short for* PHOTOGRAPH

photo- *combining form* **1** ⟦< Gr *phōs,* a light⟧ of or produced by light **2** ⟦< PHOTOGRAPH⟧ photograph, photography

pho·to·cop·y (fōt'ō käp'ē) ***n.***, *pl.* **-ies** a photographic reproduction, as of a book page, made by a special device (**pho'to·cop'i·er**)

pho'to·e·lec'tric cell any device in which light controls an electric circuit that operates a mechanical device, as for opening doors

pho'to·en·grav'ing ***n.*** **1** a process by which photographs are reproduced on relief printing plates **2** such a plate, or a print made from it —**pho'to·en·grave', -graved', -grav'ing,** ***vt.*** —**pho'to·en·grav'er** ***n.***

photo finish a race finish so close that the winner can be determined only from a photograph of the finish

pho'to·fin'ish·ing ***n.*** the process of developing photographic film, making prints, etc.

pho'to·flash' ***adj.*** designating a flashbulb, etc. electrically synchronized with the camera shutter

pho·to·gen·ic (fōt'ə jen'ik) ***adj.*** ⟦PHOTO- + *-genic,* suitable for⟧ likely to look attractive in photographs

pho·to·graph (fōt'ə graf') ***n.*** a picture made by photography —***vt.*** to take a photograph of —***vi.*** to appear (as specified) in photographs —**pho·tog·ra·pher** (fə täg'rə fər) ***n.***

pho·tog·ra·phy (fə täg'rə fē) ***n.*** ⟦PHOTO- + -GRAPHY⟧ the art or process of producing pictorial images on a surface sensitive to light or other radiant energy, as on film in a camera —**pho·to·graph·ic** (fōt'ə graf'ik) ***adj.***

pho·ton (fō'tän') ***n.*** ⟦PHOT(O)- + (ELECTR)ON⟧ a subatomic particle that is a quantum of electromagnetic energy, including light

pho'to·off'set' ***n.*** offset printing in which the text or pictures are photographically transferred to a metal plate from which inked impressions are made on the roller

pho·to·stat (fōt'ə stat') ***n.*** ⟦< former trademark⟧ **1** a device for making photocopies on special paper **2** a copy so made —***vt.*** **-stat'ed** or **-stat'ted, -stat'ing** or **-stat'ting** to make a photostat of

pho·to·syn·the·sis (fōt'ō sin'thə sis) ***n.*** the production of organic substances, esp. sugars, from carbon dioxide and water by the action of light on the chlorophyll in green plant cells

pho'to·syn'the·size' (-sīz') ***vi.***, ***vt.*** **-sized', -siz'ing** to carry on, or produce by, photosynthesis

phrase (frāz) ***n.*** ⟦< Gr *phrazein,* speak⟧ **1** a short, colorful expression **2** a group of words, not a full sentence or clause, conveying a single thought **3** a short, distinct musical passage —***vt.***, ***vi.*** **phrased, phras'ing** to express in words —**phras·al** (frā'zəl) ***adj.***

phra·se·ol·o·gy (frā'zē äl'ə jē) ***n.***, *pl.* **-gies** choice and pattern of words

phre·net·ic (fri net'ik) ***adj.*** ⟦< Gr *phrenētikos,* mad⟧ *archaic sp. of* FRENETIC

phre·nol·o·gy (fri näl'ə jē, frə-) ***n.*** ⟦< Gr *phrēn,* mind + -LOGY⟧ a system, popular esp. in the 19th c., based on the assumption that character can be analyzed based on the shape of the skull

phy·lac·ter·y (fi lak'tər ē) ***n.***, *pl.* **-ies** ⟦< Gr *phylaktērion,* safeguard⟧ TEFILLIN

phyl·lo (fē'lō, fī'-) ***n.*** ⟦< Gr *phyllon,* leaf⟧ dough in very thin sheets that becomes very flaky when baked

phy·log·e·ny (fī läj'ə nē) ***n.***, *pl.* **-nies** ⟦< Gr *phylon,* tribe + *-geneia,* origin⟧ the origin and evolution of a group or race of animals or plants

phy·lum (fī'ləm) ***n.***, *pl.* **-la** (-lə) ⟦< Gr *phylon,* tribe⟧ a major category in the classification of organisms, esp. animals

phys *abbrev.* **1** physical **2** physician **3** physics

phys·ic (fiz'ik) ***n.*** ⟦< Gr *physis,* nature⟧ a medicine, esp. a laxative

phys·i·cal (fiz'i kəl) ***adj.*** **1** of nature and all matter; material **2** of or according to the laws of nature **3** of, or produced by the forces of, physics **4** of the body as opposed to the mind —***n.*** a general medical examination —**phys'i·cal·ly** ***adv.***

physical anthropology a major division of anthropology that deals with the physical characteristics and evolution of humans

physical education instruction in physical exercise and in the care of the body, including sports, calisthenics, and hygiene

physical science any science dealing with nonliving matter or energy, as physics, chemistry, geology, or astronomy

physical therapy the treatment of disease, injury, etc. by physical means, as by exercise or massage

phy·si·cian (fi zish′ən) ***n.*** ⟦see PHYSIC⟧ a doctor of medicine

phys·ics (fiz′iks) ***n.*** ⟦see PHYSIC⟧ the science dealing with the properties, changes, interactions, etc. of matter and energy —**phys′i·cist** (-ə sist) ***n.***

phys·i·og·no·my (fiz′ē äg′nə mē) ***n.*** ⟦< Gr *physis,* nature + *gnōmōn*, one who knows⟧ facial features and expression

phys′i·ol′o·gy (-äl′ə jē) ***n.*** ⟦< Gr *physis,* nature + -LOGY⟧ the science dealing with the functions and vital processes of living organisms —**phys′i·o·log′i·cal** (-ə läj′i kəl) ***adj.*** —**phys′i·ol′o·gist** ***n.***

phys·i·o·ther·a·py (fiz′ē ō′ther′ə pē) ***n.*** PHYSICAL THERAPY —**phys′i·o·ther′a·pist** ***n.***

phy·sique (fi zēk′) ***n.*** ⟦Fr⟧ the structure or form of the body; build

pi (pī) ***n.*** **1** the 16th letter of the Greek alphabet (Π, π) **2** the symbol (π) designating the ratio of the circumference of a circle to its diameter, about 3.1416

pi·a·nis·si·mo (pē′ə nis′i mō′) ***adj., adv.*** ⟦It⟧ *Music* very soft(ly)

pi·an·ist (pē′ə nist, pē an′ist) ***n.*** one who plays the piano

pi·a·no[1] (pē ä′nō) ***adj., adv.*** ⟦It⟧ *Music* soft(ly)

pi·an·o[2] (pē an′ō) ***n.***, *pl.* **-os** ⟦< fol.⟧ a large, stringed keyboard instrument: each key operates a felt-covered hammer that strikes a corresponding wire or wires

pi·an·o·for·te (pē an′ō fôrt′, pē an′ō fôr′tā) ***n.*** ⟦It < *piano*, soft + *forte*, loud⟧ PIANO[2]

pi·as·ter (pē as′tər) ***n.*** ⟦ult. < L *emplastrum*, plaster⟧ a 100th part of a pound in Egypt, Lebanon, and Syria

pi·az·za (pē ät′sə; *for 2* pē az′ə) ***n.*** **1** in Italy, a public square **2** [Dial.] a large, covered porch

pi·broch (pē′bräk′) ***n.*** ⟦< Gael *piob*, bagpipe⟧ music for the bagpipe, usually of a martial kind

pi·ca (pī′kə) ***n.*** ⟦< ? ML, a directory⟧ a size of printing type, 12 point

pi·can·te (pē kän′tā) ***adj.*** ⟦Sp⟧ designating, prepared with, or served with a hot, spicy sauce

pic·a·resque (pik′ə resk′) ***adj.*** ⟦< Sp *pícaro,* rascal⟧ dealing with sharp-witted vagabonds or rogues and their adventures *[*a *picaresque* novel*]*

Pi·cas·so (pi kä′sō), **Pa·blo** (pä′blō) 1881-1973; Sp. painter & sculptor in France

pic·a·yune (pik′ə yōōn′, pik′ə yōōn′) ***adj.*** ⟦< Fr *picaillon*, small coin⟧ trivial or petty

pic·ca·lil·li (pik′ə lil′ē) ***n.*** ⟦prob. < PICKLE⟧ a relish of chopped vegetables, mustard, vinegar, and hot spices

pic·co·lo (pik′ə lō′) ***n.***, *pl.* **-los** ⟦< It, small⟧ a small flute, pitched an octave above the ordinary flute

pick[1] (pik) ***n.*** ⟦OE *pic,* PIKE[2]⟧ **1** any of several pointed tools or instruments for picking, esp. a heavy one used in breaking up soil, rock, etc. **2** PLECTRUM

pick[2] (pik) ***vt.*** ⟦ME *picken*⟧ **1** to probe, scratch at, etc. so as to remove or clear something from **2** to gather (flowers, berries, etc.) **3** to prepare (a fowl) by removing the feathers **4** to choose; select **5** to provoke (a quarrel or fight) **6** to pluck (the strings) of (a guitar, etc.) **7** to open (a lock) with a wire, etc. instead of a key **8** to steal from (another's pocket, etc.) —***vi.*** **1** to use a pick **2** to select, esp. in a fussy way —***n.*** **1** the act of choosing or the choice made **2** the best —**pick at** to eat small amounts of, esp. fussily —**pick off** **1** to remove by picking **2** to hit with a carefully aimed shot —**pick on** [Inf.] to single out for criticism or abuse; annoy; tease —**pick out** to choose —**pick up** **1** to grasp and lift **2** to get, find, or learn, esp. by chance **3** to stop for and take along **4** to gain (speed) **5** to improve **6** [Inf.] to become acquainted with casually, esp. for sexual activity —**pick′er** ***n.***

pick·ax or **pick·axe** (pik′aks′) ***n.*** ⟦< OFr *picquois*⟧ a pick with a point at one end of the head and a chisel-like edge at the other

pick·er·el (pik′ər əl) ***n.***, *pl.* **-el** or **-els** ⟦ME < *pik*, PIKE[3]⟧ any of various small North American freshwater fishes

pick·et (pik′it) ***n.*** ⟦< Fr *pic,* PIKE[2]⟧ **1** a pointed stake used in a fence, as a hitching post, etc. **2** a soldier or soldiers stationed to guard against surprise attack **3** a person, as a member of a striking labor union, stationed outside a factory, store, etc. to demonstrate opposition, keep workers out, etc. —***vt.*** **1** to hitch (an animal) to a picket **2** to post as a military picket **3** to place pickets, or serve as a picket, at (a factory, etc.)

picket line a line or cordon of people serving as pickets

pick′ings ***pl.n.*** [*occas. sing.*] something picked; specif., *a*) scraps; remains *b*) something gotten by effort, often dishonestly

pick·le (pik′əl) ***n.*** ⟦< MDu *pekel*⟧ **1** any brine, vinegar, etc. used to preserve or marinate food **2** a vegetable, specif. a cucumber, preserved in this **3** [Inf.] an awkward situation —***vt.*** **-led**, **-ling** to treat or preserve in a pickle solution

pick′pock′et ***n.*** a thief who steals from pockets, as in a crowd

pick′up′ ***n.*** **1** a picking up **2** the process or power of increasing in speed **3** a small, open delivery truck **4** [Inf.] a casual acquaintance, esp. one formed for sexual purposes **5** [Inf.] improvement **6** *a*) a device for producing electric currents from the vibrations of a phonograph needle *b*) the pivoted arm holding this device —***adj.*** [Inf.] assembled informally for a single occasion

pick′y ***adj.*** **-i·er**, **-i·est** [Inf.] overly fastidious; fussy

pic·nic (pik′nik) ***n.*** ⟦< Fr⟧ a pleasure outing at which a meal is eaten outdoors —***vi.*** **-nicked**, **-nick·ing** to have a picnic —**pic′nick·er** ***n.***

pi·cot (pē′kō) ***n.***, *pl.* **-cots** ⟦< Fr *pic,* point⟧ any of the small loops forming a fancy edge, as on lace

pic·to·graph (pik′tə graf′) ***n.*** **1** a picture or picturelike symbol used in a system of writing **2** a graph using pictures to convey data

pic·to·ri·al (pik tôr′ē əl) ***adj.*** **1** of, containing, or expressed in pictures **2** suggesting a mental image; vivid —**pic·to′ri·al·ly** ***adv.***

pic·ture (pik′chər) ***n.*** ⟦< L *pingere,* to paint⟧ **1** a likeness of a person, scene, etc. produced by drawing, painting, photography, etc. **2** a perfect likeness or image *[the picture of health]* **3** anything suggestive of a beautiful painting, drawing, etc. **4** a vivid description **5** FILM (*n.* 4) **6** the image on a TV screen —***vt.*** **-tured**, **-tur·ing** **1** to make a picture of **2** to show visibly **3** to describe **4** to imagine —**in** (or **out of**) **the picture** considered (or not considered) as being involved in a situation

pic′ture-per′fect ***adj.*** perfect or flawless

pic′tur·esque′ (-chər esk′) ***adj.*** like or suggesting a picture; beautiful, vivid, quaint, etc.

picture tube a cathode-ray tube in a TV receiver, monitor, etc., that produces visual images on its screen

picture window a large window that seems to frame the outside view

pid·dle (pid′'l) ***vi., vt.*** **-dled**, **-dling** ⟦< ?⟧ to dawdle; trifle

pid·dling (pid′liŋ) ***adj.*** insignificant; trifling

pid·dly (pid′lē) ***adj.*** PIDDLING

pidg·in (pij′in) ***n.*** ⟦supposed Chin pronunciation of *business*⟧ a mixed language for trade purposes, using words from one language and simplified grammar from another: **pidgin English** uses English words and Chinese or Melanesian syntax

pie (pī) ***n.*** ⟦ME⟧ a baked dish as of fruit or of meat, with an under crust or upper crust, or both —(**as**) **easy as pie** [Inf.] extremely easy

pie·bald (pī′bôld′) ***adj.*** ⟦< *pie,* magpie + BALD⟧ covered with patches of two colors —***n.*** a piebald horse, etc.

piece (pēs) ***n.*** ⟦OFr *pece*⟧ **1** a part broken or separated from the whole **2** a section of a whole regarded as complete in itself **3** any single thing, specimen, example, etc. *[a piece of music]* **4** a quantity, as of cloth, manufactured as a unit —***vt.*** **pieced**, **piec′ing** **1** to add pieces to, as in repairing **2** to join (*together*) the pieces of —**go to pieces** **1** to fall apart **2** to lose self-control

pièce de ré·sis·tance (pyes də rā zēs täns′) ⟦Fr, piece of resistance⟧ **1** the principal dish of a meal **2** the main item in a series

piece goods YARD GOODS

piece′meal′ ***adv.*** ⟦< ME *pece,* a piece + *-mele,* part⟧ piece by piece —***adj.*** made or done piecemeal

piece′work′ ***n.*** work paid for at a fixed rate (**piece rate**) per piece of work done

pie chart a graph in the form of a circle divided into sectors in which relative quantities are indicated by the sizes of the sectors

pied (pīd) ***adj.*** ⟦< *pie,* magpie⟧ spotted with various colors

pied-à-terre (pyā tȧ ter′) ***n.***, *pl.* ***pied-à-terre*** ⟦Fr, foot on the ground⟧ a residence, esp. one used only part of the time or temporarily

pie′-eyed′ ***adj.*** [Slang] intoxicated

pier (pir) ***n.*** ⟦< ML *pera*⟧ **1** a structure supporting the spans of a bridge **2** a structure built out over the water and supported by pillars: used as a landing place, pavilion, etc. **3** *Archit.* a heavy column used to support weight

pierce (pirs) ***vt.*** **pierced**, **pierc′ing** ⟦< OFr *percer*⟧ **1** to pass into or through as a pointed instrument does; stab **2** to make a hole in **3** to force a way into; break through **4** to sound sharply through **5** to penetrate with the sight or mind —***vi.*** to penetrate

Pierce (pirs), **Franklin** 1804-69; 14th president of the U.S. (1853-57)

Pierre (pir) capital of South Dakota: pop. 13,000

pi·e·ty (pī′ə tē) ***n.***, *pl.* **-ties** ⟦< L *pius,* pious⟧ **1** devotion to religious duties, etc. **2** devotion to parents, family, etc. **3** a pious act

pif·fle (pif′əl) ***n.*** [Inf.] anything that is regarded as insignificant or nonsensical —**pif·fling** (pif′liŋ) ***adj.***

pig (pig) ***n.*** ⟦ME *pigge*⟧ **1** any swine, esp. the unweaned young of the thick-bodied domesticated species; hog **2** a greedy or filthy person

pi·geon (pij′ən) ***n.*** ⟦< L *pipire,* to chirp⟧ any of various related birds with a small head, a plump body, and short legs

pi′geon·hole′ ***n.*** a small, open compartment, as in a desk, for filing papers —***vt.*** **-holed′**, **-hol′ing** **1** to put in the pigeonhole of a desk, etc. **2** to put aside indefinitely **3** to classify

pi′geon-toed′ (-tōd′) ***adj.*** having the toes or feet turned in

pig·gish (pig′ish) ***adj.*** like a pig; gluttonous or filthy —**pig′gish·ness** ***n.***

pig·gy (pig′ē) ***n.***, *pl.* **-gies** a little pig: also sp. **pig′gie** —***adj.*** **-gi·er**, **-gi·est** PIGGISH

pig′gy·back′ ***adv., adj.*** **1** on the shoulders or back **2** by or of a transportation system in which truck trailers are carried on flatcars **3** carried by or connected with something else as an adjunct —***vt.*** **1** to carry piggyback **2** to place on something in piggyback fashion

pig′head′ed ***adj.*** stubborn

pig iron crude iron, as it comes from the blast furnace

pig·ment (pig′mənt) ***n.*** ⟦< L *pingere,* to paint⟧ **1** coloring matter used to make paints **2** any coloring matter in the tissues of plants or animals

pig·men·ta·tion (pig′mən tā′shən) ***n.*** coloration in plants or animals due to pigment in the tissue

Pig·my (pig′mē) ***n.***, *pl.* **-mies**, ***adj.*** PYGMY

pig′pen′ ***n.*** a pen where pigs are kept: also **pig′sty′** (-stī′), *pl.* **-sties′**

pig′skin′ ***n.*** **1** leather made from the skin of a pig **2** [Inf.] a football

pig′tail′ (-tāl′) ***n.*** a long braid of hair hanging at the back of the head

pike[1] (pīk) ***n.*** a highway: now chiefly in [Inf.] **come down the pike**, to happen or appear

pike[2] (pīk) ***n.*** ⟦Fr *pique*⟧ a weapon, formerly for foot soldiers, consisting of a metal spearhead on a long wooden shaft (**pike′staff′**)

pike[3] (pīk) ***n.***, *pl.* **pike** or **pikes** ⟦ME *pik*⟧ a slender, freshwater bony fish with a narrow, pointed head

pik·er (pīk′ər) ***n.*** ⟦< ? *Pike* County, Missouri⟧ [Slang] a person who does things in a petty or stingy way

pi·laf or **pi·laff** (pē′läf′) ***n.*** ⟦Pers *pilāv*⟧ a dish made of rice boiled in a seasoned liquid

pi·las·ter (pi las′tər) ***n.*** ⟦< L *pila,* a pile⟧ a supporting column projecting partially from a wall

Pi·late (pī′lət), **Pon·tius** (pun′chəs) 1st c. A.D.; Rom. procurator of Judea (26?-36?) who condemned Jesus to be crucified

pil·chard (pil′chərd) ***n.*** ⟦< ?⟧ **1** a small, oily marine fish, the commercial sardine of W Europe **2** any of several related fishes

pile[1] (pīl) ***n.*** ⟦< L *pila,* pillar⟧ **1** a mass of things heaped together **2** a heap of wood, etc. on which a corpse or sacrifice is burned **3** a large building **4** [Inf.] a large amount —***vt.*** **piled**, **pil′ing** **1** to heap up **2** to load **3** to accumulate Often with *up* —***vi.*** **1** to form a pile **2** to move in a mass: with *in, into, out, on, off,* etc.

pile[2] (pīl) ***n.*** ⟦< L *pilus,* hair⟧ a soft, velvety, raised surface of yarn loops, often sheared, as on a rug

pile[3] (pīl) ***n.*** ⟦OE *pil*⟧ a long, heavy beam driven into the ground to support a bridge, dock, etc.

pile driver (or **engine**) a machine for driving piles by raising and dropping a heavy weight on them

piles (pīlz) ***pl.n.*** ⟦< L *pila,* a ball⟧ hemorrhoids

pile′up′ ***n.*** **1** an accumulation of tasks, etc. **2** [Inf.] a collision involving several vehicles

pil·fer (pil′fər) ***vt.***, ***vi.*** ⟦< MFr *pelfre,* booty⟧ to steal (esp. small sums, etc.) —**pil′fer·age** (-ij) ***n.*** —**pil′fer·er** ***n.***

pil·grim (pil′grəm) ***n.*** ⟦< L *peregrinus,* foreigner⟧ **1** a wanderer **2** one who travels to a shrine or holy place as a religious act **3** [**P-**] any of the band of English Puritans who founded Plymouth Colony in 1620

pil′grim·age ***n.*** **1** a journey made by a pilgrim, esp. to a shrine or holy place **2** any long journey

pill (pil) ***n.*** ⟦< L *pila,* a ball⟧ a small ball, tablet, etc. of medicine to be swallowed whole —**the pill** (or **Pill**) [Inf.] any contraceptive drug for women, in the form of a pill

pil·lage (pil′ij) ***n.*** ⟦< MFr *piller,* to rob⟧ **1** a plundering **2** goods stolen or taken by force —***vt.***, ***vi.*** **-laged**, **-lag·ing** to plunder

pil·lar (pil′ər) ***n.*** ⟦< L *pila,* column⟧ **1** a slender, vertical structure used as a support or monument; column **2** a main support of something

pill′box′ ***n.*** **1** a small box for holding pills **2** an enclosed gun emplacement of concrete and steel

pil·lion (pil′yən) ***n.*** ⟦< L *pellis,* a skin⟧ an extra seat behind the saddle on a horse or motorcycle

pil·lo·ry (pil′ə rē) ***n.***, *pl.* **-ries** ⟦< OFr *pilori*⟧ a device consisting of a board with holes for the head and hands, in which petty offenders were formerly locked and exposed to public scorn —***vt.*** **-ried**, **-ry·ing** **1** to punish by placing in a pillory **2** to subject to public scorn or ridicule

pil·low (pil′ō) ***n.*** ⟦OE *pyle*⟧ a cloth case filled with down, foam rubber, etc., used as a support, as for the head in sleeping —***vt.*** to rest as on a pillow

pil′low·case′ ***n.*** a removable covering for a pillow: also **pil′low·slip′**

pi·lot (pī′lət) ***n.*** ⟦< Gr *pēdon,* oar⟧ **1** *a*) [Archaic] HELMSMAN *b*) a person licensed to direct ships into or out of a harbor or through difficult waters **2** a qualified operator of aircraft or spacecraft **3** a guide; leader **4** *a*) pilot light *b*) pilot film (or tape) —***vt.*** **1** to act as a pilot of, on, etc. **2** to guide —***adj.*** serving as a trial unit in testing

pilot film (or **tape**) a film (or videotape) of a single segment of a projected series of TV shows

pi′lot·house′ ***n.*** an enclosure for the helmsman on the upper deck of a ship

pilot light a small gas burner that is kept burning for use in lighting a main burner

Pil·sen·er or **Pil·sner** (pilz′nər) ***n.*** [*often* **P-**] a light lager beer

pi·men·to (pi men′tō) ***n.***, *pl.* **-tos** ⟦< Sp < L *pigmentum,* pigment⟧ a variety of sweet red pepper: also **pi·mien′to** (-myen′-, -men′-)

pimp (pimp) ***n.*** ⟦< ?⟧ a prostitute's agent —***vi.*** to act as a pimp

pim·ple (pim′pəl) ***n.*** ⟦< OE *piplian,* to break out in pimples⟧ a small, usually inflamed swelling of the skin —**pim′ply**, **-pli·er**, **-pli·est**, ***adj.***

pin (pin) ***n.*** ⟦OE *pinn*⟧ **1** a peg, as of wood, or a pointed piece of stiff wire, for fastening things together, etc. **2** anything like a pin **3** an ornament or badge with a pin or clasp for fastening to clothing **4** *Bowling* one of the bottle-shaped wooden objects at which the ball is rolled —***vt.*** **pinned**, **pin′ning** **1** to fasten as with a pin **2** to hold firmly in one position —**pin down** **1** to get (someone) to make a commitment, etc. **2** to determine (a fact, etc.) —**pin something on someone** [Inf.] to lay the blame for something on someone

PIN (pin) ***n.*** ⟦*p*(*ersonal*) *i*(*dentification*) *n*(*umber*)⟧ an identification number, as for use at an ATM

pin·a·fore (pin′ə fôr′) ***n.*** ⟦PIN + archaic *afore,* before⟧ a sleeveless garment worn over a dress

pi·ña·ta (pē nyä′tä) ***n.*** ⟦Sp, ult. < L *pinus,* pine tree⟧ in Mexico, a papier-mâché container hung from the ceiling in a game in which blindfolded children take turns trying to break it open and release the toys, candy, etc. inside

pin'ball' machine a game machine consisting of an inclined board and a rolling ball that hits objects, etc. on it to score points

pince-nez (pans'nā') ***n.*** ⟦Fr, nose-pincher⟧ *pl.* **pince'-nez'** (-nāz'; -nā') eyeglasses kept in place by a spring gripping the bridge of the nose

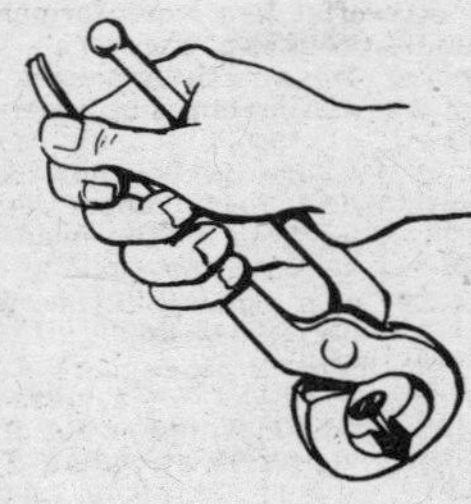

PINCERS

pin·cers (pin'sərz) ***pl.n.*** ⟦< OFr *pincier,* to pinch⟧ **1** a tool formed of two pivoted parts, used in gripping things **2** a grasping claw, as of a crab

pinch (pinch) ***vt.*** ⟦ME *pinchen* < OFr *pincier*⟧ **1** to squeeze between a finger and the thumb or between two edges, surfaces, etc. **2** to press painfully upon (some part of the body) **3** to make cramped, thin, etc., as by hunger or cold **4** [Slang] *a)* to steal *b)* to arrest —***vi.*** **1** to squeeze painfully **2** to be stingy or frugal —***n.*** **1** a squeeze or nip **2** *a)* an amount grasped between finger and thumb *b)* a small amount **3** distress or difficulty **4** an emergency: usually in **in a pinch** —***adj.*** *Baseball* substitute

pinch'-hit' ***vi.*** **-hit', -hit'ting** **1** *Baseball* to bat in place of the batter whose turn it is **2** to substitute in an emergency (*for*) —**pinch hitter**

pin curl a strand of hair kept curled with a bobby pin while it sets

pin'cush'ion ***n.*** a small cushion to stick pins in to keep them handy

pine¹ (pīn) ***n.*** ⟦< L *pinus*⟧ **1** an evergreen tree with cones and needle-shaped leaves **2** its wood

pine² (pīn) ***vi.*** **pined, pin'ing** ⟦< L *poena,* a pain⟧ **1** to waste (*away*) through grief, etc. **2** to yearn

pin·e·al body (pin'ē əl) ⟦< L *pinea,* pine cone⟧ a small, cone-shaped body in the brain that produces a hormone

pine·ap·ple (pīn'ap'əl) ***n.*** ⟦ME *pinappel,* pine cone⟧ **1** a juicy, edible tropical fruit somewhat resembling a pine cone **2** the plant it grows on

pine tar a thick, dark liquid obtained from pine wood, used in disinfectants, paints, etc.

pin'feath'er ***n.*** an undeveloped, emerging feather

ping (piŋ) ***n.*** ⟦echoic⟧ the sound made as by a bullet striking something sharply —***vi., vt.*** to make or cause to make this sound

Ping-Pong (piŋ'pông') ⟦echoic⟧ *trademark for* table-tennis equipment —***n.*** [*often* **ping-pong**] TABLE TENNIS

pin'head' ***n.*** **1** the head of a pin **2** a person regarded as stupid or silly

pin'hole' ***n.*** **1** a tiny hole as from a pin **2** a hole to stick a pin into

pin·ion (pin'yən) ***n.*** ⟦< L *pinna,* feather⟧ **1** a small cogwheel that meshes with a larger gear or with a RACK¹ (*n.* 2) **2** a wing; specif., the outer part of a bird's wing —***vt.*** **1** to bind the wings or arms of **2** to shackle

pink¹ (piŋk) ***n.*** ⟦< ?⟧ **1** any of certain plants with white, pink, or red flowers **2** the flower **3** pale red **4** the highest degree, finest example, etc. —***adj.*** **1** pale-red **2** [Inf.] somewhat leftist: a derogatory term —**in the pink** [Inf.] healthy; fit

pink² (piŋk) ***vt.*** ⟦ME *pynken*⟧ **1** to cut a saw-toothed edge on (cloth, etc.) **2** to prick or stab

pink'eye' ***n.*** a contagious eye infection in which the eyeball and the lining of the eyelid are red and inflamed

pink·ie or **pink·y** (piŋ'kē) ***n.***, *pl.* **-ies** the smallest finger

pink·ing shears (piŋ'kiŋ) shears with notched blades, for pinking edges of cloth

pink slip [Inf.] notice to an employee that he or she is fired

pin money a small sum of money, as for incidental minor expenses

pin·na·cle (pin'ə kəl) ***n.*** ⟦< L *pinna,* feather⟧ **1** a small turret or spire **2** a slender, pointed formation, as a mountain peak **3** the highest point

pin·nate (pin'āt', -it) ***adj.*** ⟦< L *pinna,* feather⟧ *Bot.* with leaflets on each side of a common stem

pi·noch·le or **pi·noc·le** (pē'nuk'əl) ***n.*** ⟦< Fr *binocle,* pince-nez⟧ a card game played with a 48-card deck (two of every card above the eight)

pi·not noir (pē'nō nwär', pē nō'-) [*also* **P- N-**] **1** the main red-wine grape of the Burgundy region **2** a dry red wine made from this grape

pin'point' ***vt.*** to locate precisely —***adj.*** precise

pin'prick' ***n.*** **1** a tiny puncture as by a pin **2** a minor annoyance

pins and needles a tingling feeling as in a numb limb —**on pins and needles** in anxious suspense

pin'set'ter ***n.*** a person or automatic device that sets up bowling pins on the alley: also **pin'spot'ter**

pin'stripe' ***n.*** a pattern of very narrow stripes in suit fabrics, etc.

pint (pīnt) ***n.*** ⟦< ML⟧ a unit of measure equal to $\frac{1}{2}$ quart

pin·to (pin'tō) ***adj.*** ⟦< obs. Sp, spotted⟧ having patches of white and some other color —***n.***, *pl.* **-tos** a pinto horse

pinto bean a kind of mottled kidney

bean grown in the SW U.S.

pin′up′ ***adj.*** **1** that is or can be fastened to a wall **2** [Inf.] designating a sexually attractive person whose picture is often pinned up on walls

pin′wheel′ ***n.*** **1** a small wheel with vanes of paper, etc., pinned to a stick so as to revolve in the wind **2** a revolving fireworks device

Pin·yin (pin yin′) ***n.*** ⟦Chin *pinyin,* lit., phonetic sound⟧ [*also* **p-**] system for transliterating Chinese ideograms into the Latin alphabet

pi·o·neer (pī′ə nir′) ***n.*** ⟦< OFr *peonier,* foot soldier⟧ one who goes before, preparing the way for others, as an early settler —***vi.*** to be a pioneer —***vt.*** to be a pioneer in or of

pi·ous (pī′əs) ***adj.*** ⟦< L *pius*⟧ **1** having or showing religious devotion **2** only seemingly virtuous **3** sacred —**pi′ous·ly** ***adv.***

pip[1] (pip) ***n.*** ⟦< PIPPIN⟧ a small seed, as of an apple

pip[2] (pip) ***n.*** ⟦< ?⟧ any of the figures or spots on playing cards, dice, or dominoes

pip[3] (pip) ***n.*** ⟦< L *pituita,* phlegm⟧ a contagious disease of fowl

pipe (pīp) ***n.*** ⟦< L *pipare,* chirp⟧ **1** a tube of wood, metal, etc. for making musical sounds **2** [*pl.*] the bagpipe **3** a long tube for conveying water, gas, etc. **4** a tube with a small bowl at one end in which tobacco is smoked **5** any tubular part, organ of the body, etc. —***vi.*** **piped, pip′ing 1** to play on a pipe **2** to utter shrill sounds —***vt.*** **1** to play (a tune) on a pipe **2** to utter in a shrill voice **3** to bring, call, etc. by piping **4** to convey (water, gas, etc.) by pipes —**pipe down** [Slang] to stop shouting, talking, etc. —**pip′er** ***n.***

pipe dream [Inf.] a fantastic idea, vain hope or plan, etc.

pipe fitter a mechanic who installs and maintains plumbing pipes, etc.

pipe′line′ ***n.*** **1** a line of pipes for conveying water, gas, oil, etc. **2** any means whereby something is passed on

pipe organ ORGAN (sense 1)

pi·pette or **pi·pet** (pi pet′, pī-) ***n.*** a slender tube for taking up and measuring small amounts of a liquid

pip·ing (pīp′iŋ) ***n.*** **1** music made by pipes **2** a shrill sound **3** a pipelike fold of material for trimming seams, etc. —**piping hot** very hot

pip·it (pip′it) ***n.*** ⟦echoic⟧ a small bird with a slender bill, streaked breast, and the habit of walking rather than hopping

pip·pin (pip′in) ***n.*** ⟦< OFr *pepin,* seed⟧ any of several varieties of apple

pip·squeak (pip′skwēk′) ***n.*** [Inf.] anyone or anything regarded as small or insignificant

pi·quant (pē′kənt) ***adj.*** ⟦Fr < *piquer,* to prick⟧ **1** agreeably pungent to the taste **2** exciting interest; stimulating —**pi′quan·cy** (-kən sē) ***n.***

pique (pēk) ***n.*** ⟦see prec.⟧ resentment at being slighted —***vt.*** **piqued, piqu′ing 1** to arouse such resentment in **2** to stir up; excite

pi·qué or **pi·que** (pē kā′) ***n.*** ⟦see PIQUANT⟧ a cotton fabric with ribbed or corded wales

pi·ra·cy (pī′rə sē) ***n.***, *pl.* **-cies 1** robbery of ships on the high seas **2** the unauthorized use of copyrighted or patented work

pi·ra·nha (pi rä′nə) ***n.*** ⟦< Brazilian Port < AmInd (Brazil) *pirá,* fish + *sainha,* tooth⟧ any of various small, freshwater South American fishes: they hunt in schools, attacking any animals

pi·rate (pī′rət) ***n.*** ⟦< Gr *peirān,* to attack⟧ one who practices piracy —***vt., vi.*** **-rat·ed, -rat·ing 1** to take (something) by piracy **2** to publish, reproduce, etc. (a book, recording, etc.) in violation of a copyright —**pi·rat′i·cal** (-rat′ i kəl) ***adj.***

pi·ro·gi (pi rō′gē) ***n.***, *pl.* **-gi** or **-gies** ⟦Russ⟧ a small pastry turnover filled with meat, cheese, etc.

pir·ou·ette (pir′o͞o et′) ***n.*** ⟦Fr, spinning top⟧ a whirling on one foot or the point of the toe —***vi.*** **-et′ted, -et′ting** to do a pirouette

pis·ca·to·ri·al (pis′kə tôr′ē əl) ***adj.*** ⟦< L *piscator,* fisherman⟧ of fishes or fishing

Pis·ces (pī′sēz′) ***n.*** ⟦ L, pl. of *piscis,* fish⟧ the 12th sign of the zodiac

pis·mire (pis′mīr′, piz′-) ***n.*** ⟦< ME *pisse,* urine + *mire,* ant⟧ [Archaic] an ant

piss·ant (pis′ant′) ***adj., n.*** [Slang] insignificant and contemptible (person)

pis·tach·i·o (pi stash′ē ō) ***n.***, *pl.* **-os′** ⟦< OPers *pistah*⟧ **1** a small tree of the cashew family **2** its edible, greenish seed (**pistachio nut**)

pis·til (pis′təl) ***n.*** ⟦< L *pistillum,* pestle⟧ the seed-bearing organ of a flower —**pis′til·late′** ***adj.***

pis·tol (pis′təl) ***n.*** ⟦< Czech *píšťal*⟧ a small firearm operated with one hand

pis′tol-whip′ ***vt.*** **-whipped′, -whip′ping** to beat with a pistol, esp. about the head

pis·ton (pis′tən) ***n.*** ⟦ult. < L *pinsere,* to pound⟧ the snug-fitting engine part that is forced back and forth within a cylinder by the pressure of combustion, steam, etc. and a reciprocating connecting rod (**piston rod**)

piston ring a split ring fitted into a groove around a piston to seal the cylinder, transfer heat, etc.

pit[1] (pit) ***n.*** ⟦< MDu *pitte*⟧ the hard stone, as of the plum, peach, or cherry, containing the seed —***vt.*** **pit′ted, pit′ting** to remove the pit from

pit[2] (pit) ***n.*** ⟦< L *puteus,* a well⟧ **1** a hole in the ground **2** an abyss **3** hell: used with *the* **4** a pitfall **5** an enclosed area in which animals are kept or made to fight **6** a small hollow in a surface, as a scar left by smallpox **7** the section for the orchestra in front of the stage **8** a work area for mechanics beside an auto-racing track —***vt.*** **pit′ted, pit′ting 1** to make pits or scars in **2** to set in competition (*against*)

pi·ta (pēt′ə) ***n.*** ⟦< Heb < Modern Greek⟧ a round, flat bread of the Middle East:

also **pita bread**

pit·a·pat (pit′ə pat′) ***adv.*** with rapid beating —***n.*** a rapid series of beats or taps

pit bull a short, heavy dog with powerful jaws

pitch[1] (pich) ***n.*** ⟦< L *pix*⟧ a black, sticky substance formed from coal tar, etc. and used for roofing, etc.

pitch[2] (pich) ***vt.*** ⟦ME *picchen*⟧ **1** to set up *[pitch a tent]* **2** *a)* to throw or toss *b)* to throw away **3** to fix at a certain point, degree, key, etc. **4** *Baseball a)* to throw (the ball) to the batter *b)* to act as pitcher for (a game, etc.) —***vi.*** **1** to pitch a ball, etc. **2** to plunge forward or dip downward **3** to rise and fall, as a ship in rough water —***n.*** **1** a throw or toss **2** anything pitched **3** a point or degree **4** the degree of slope **5** [Inf.] a line of talk for persuading **6** *Music, etc.* the highness or lowness of a sound due to vibrations of sound waves —**pitch in** [Inf.] **1** to begin working hard **2** to make a contribution —**pitch into** [Inf.] to attack

pitch′-black′ ***adj.*** very black

pitch′blende′ (-blend′) ***n.*** ⟦< Ger *pech*, PITCH[1] + *blenden*, to blind⟧ a dark mineral, a major source of uranium

pitch′-dark′ ***adj.*** very dark

pitched battle **1** a battle in which troop placement is relatively fixed beforehand **2** a hard-fought battle

pitch′er[1] ***n.*** ⟦< OFr *pichier*⟧ a container, usually with a handle and lip, for holding and pouring liquids

pitch′er[2] ***n.*** ⟦PITCH[2] + -ER⟧ the baseball player who pitches the ball to the batters

pitcher plant a plant with pitcherlike leaves that trap and digest insects

pitch′fork′ ***n.*** a large, long-handled fork for lifting and tossing hay, etc.

pitch′man (-mən) ***n.***, *pl.* **-men** (-mən) **1** a hawker of novelties, as at a carnival **2** [Inf.] any high-pressure salesman

pitch pipe a small pipe that produces a fixed tone used as a standard in tuning instruments, etc.

pit·e·ous (pit′ē əs) ***adj.*** arousing or deserving pity —**pit′e·ous·ly** ***adv.***

pit′fall′ ***n.*** ⟦< PIT[2] + OE *fealle*, a trap⟧ **1** a lightly covered pit for trapping animals **2** an unsuspected danger, etc.

pith (pith) ***n.*** ⟦OE *pitha*⟧ **1** the soft, spongy tissue in the center of certain plant stems **2** the essential part; gist

pith′y ***adj.*** **-i·er, -i·est** **1** of, like, or full of pith **2** terse and full of meaning —**pith′i·ly** ***adv.***

pit·i·ful (pit′i fəl) ***adj.*** **1** arousing or deserving pity **2** contemptible Also **pit·i·a·ble** (pit′ē ə bəl) —**pit′i·ful·ly** ***adv.***

pit′i·less (-lis) ***adj.*** without pity

pi·ton (pē′tän′) ***n.*** ⟦Fr < MFr, a spike⟧ a metal spike with an eye for a rope, driven into rock or ice for support in mountain climbing

pit stop **1** a temporary stop in the PIT[2] (*n.* 8) by a racing car **2** [Slang] *a)* a pause for food, etc. during a journey *b)* a visit to a restroom

pit·tance (pit′'ns) ***n.*** ⟦< OFr *pitance*, food allowed a monk⟧ **1** a meager allowance of money **2** any small amount or share

pit·ter-pat·ter (pit′ər pat′ər) ***n.*** ⟦echoic⟧ a rapid succession of light tapping sounds

Pitts·burgh (pits′burg′) city in SW Pennsylvania: pop. 370,000

pi·tu·i·tar·y (pi to͞o′ə ter′ē) ***adj.*** ⟦< L *pituita*, phlegm⟧ of a small, oval endocrine gland (**pituitary gland**) attached to the brain: it secretes hormones affecting growth, etc.

pit viper any of several poisonous vipers with a heat-sensitive pit on each side of the head

pit·y (pit′ē) ***n.***, *pl.* **-ies** ⟦< L *pietas*, piety⟧ **1** sorrow for another's suffering or misfortune **2** a cause for sorrow or regret —***vt.***, ***vi.*** **-ied, -y·ing** to feel pity (for)

piv·ot (piv′ət) ***n.*** ⟦Fr⟧ **1** a point, shaft, etc. on which something turns **2** a person or thing on which something depends, etc. **3** a pivoting movement —***vt.*** to provide with a pivot —***vi.*** to turn as on a pivot —**piv′ot·al** ***adj.***

pix·el (pik′səl) ***n.*** ⟦< *pic(ture)s* + *el(ement)*⟧ any of the dots that make up an image on a video screen

pix·ie or **pix·y** (pik′sē) ***n.***, *pl.* **-ies** ⟦< Brit dial.⟧ a fairy, elf, etc.

pi·zazz or **piz·zazz** (pi zaz′) ***n.*** [Inf.] **1** vigor **2** style, flair, etc.

piz·za (pēt′sə) ***n.*** ⟦It⟧ an Italian dish made by baking thin dough covered with tomatoes, cheese, etc.

piz·ze·ri·a (pēt′sə rē′ə) ***n.*** ⟦It⟧ a place where pizzas are made and sold

piz·zi·ca·to (pit′si kät′ō) ***adj.*** ⟦It⟧ *Music* plucked: a note to pluck the strings with the finger instead of bowing: also written ***piz′zi·ca′to***

pj's (pē′jāz′) ***pl.n.*** *inf. var. of* PAJAMAS

pk *abbrev.* **1** pack **2** park **3** peck

pkg *abbrev.* package(s)

Pkwy or **Pky** *abbrev.* Parkway

pl *abbrev.* **1** place: also **Pl** **2** plural

plac·ard (plak′ärd; -ərd) ***n.*** ⟦< MDu *placke*, a piece⟧ a notice for display in a public place —***vt.*** to place placards on or in

pla·cate (plā′kāt′) ***vt.*** **-cat′ed, -cat′ing** ⟦< L *placare*⟧ to appease; pacify —**pla·ca′tion** ***n.***

place (plās) ***n.*** ⟦< Gr *plateia*, a street⟧ **1** a court or short street in a city **2** space; room **3** a region **4** *a)* the part of space occupied by a person or thing *b)* situation **5** a city, town, etc. **6** a residence **7** a building or space devoted to a special purpose *[a place of amusement]* **8** a particular point, part, position, etc. *[a sore place on the leg, a place in history]* **9** a step or point in a sequence **10** the proper position, time, etc. **11** a space, seat, etc. reserved or occupied by a person **12** a job or position **13** the duties of any position **14** the second position at the finish of a race —***vt.*** **placed, plac′ing** **1** *a)* to put in a particular place, condition, or relation *b)* to recognize or identify **2** to find employment for **3** to repose (trust) *in* a person or thing **4** to finish in (a specified position) in a race —***vi.*** to finish second or among the first three in a race —**take place** to occur

pla·ce·bo (plə sē′bō) ***n.**, pl.* **-bos** or **-boes** ⟦< L, I shall please⟧ a harmless, unmedicated preparation given as a medicine, as to humor a patient

place mat a small mat serving as an individual table cover for a person at a meal

place′ment ***n.*** **1** a placing or being placed **2** location or arrangement

pla·cen·ta (plə sen′tə) ***n.**, pl.* **-tas** or **-tae** (-tē) ⟦ult. < Gr *plax*, a flat object⟧ the structure in the uterus through which the fetus is nourished: cf. AFTERBIRTH —**pla·cen′tal** ***adj.***

plac·er (plas′ər) ***n.*** ⟦< Sp *placel*⟧ a deposit of gravel or sand containing particles of gold, etc. that can be washed out

place setting the dish, utensils, etc. used for setting one place at a table for a meal

plac·id (plas′id) ***adj.*** ⟦L *placidus*⟧ calm; quiet —**pla·cid·i·ty** (plə sid′ə tē) ***n.*** —**plac′id·ly** ***adv.***

plack·et (plak′it) ***n.*** ⟦< ?⟧ a slit at the waist of a skirt or collar of a shirt, to make it easy to put on and take off

pla·gi·a·rize (plā′jə rīz′) ***vt., vi.*** **-rized′, -riz′ing** ⟦< L *plagiarius*, kidnapper⟧ to take (ideas, writings, etc.) from (another) and pass them off as one's own —**pla′gi·a·rism′** (-riz′əm) ***n.*** —**pla′gi·a·rist** ***n.***

plague (plāg) ***n.*** ⟦< Gr *plēgē*, a misfortune⟧ **1** any affliction or calamity **2** any deadly epidemic disease —***vt.*** **plagued, plagu′ing** **1** to afflict with a plague **2** to vex; torment

plaice (plās) ***n.**, pl.* **plaice** or **plaices** any of various American and European flounders

plaid (plad) ***n.*** ⟦Gael *plaide*, a blanket⟧ **1** cloth with a crossbarred pattern **2** any pattern of this kind —***adj.*** having such a pattern

plain (plān) ***adj.*** ⟦< L *planus*, flat⟧ **1** open; clear *[in plain view]* **2** clearly understood; obvious **3** outspoken; straightforward **4** not luxurious or ornate **5** not complicated; simple **6** homely **7** pure; unmixed **8** common; ordinary *[a plain man]* —***n.*** an extent of level country —***adv.*** clearly —**plain′ly** ***adv.*** —**plain′ness** ***n.***

plain′clothes′ man a detective or police officer who wears civilian clothes while on duty: also **plain′clothes′man**, *pl.* **-men**

plain′song′ ***n.*** a very old, plain kind of church music chanted in unison

plaint (plānt) ***n.*** ⟦< L *plangere*, to lament⟧ a complaint or lament

plain·tiff (plān′tif) ***n.*** ⟦see prec.⟧ one who brings a suit into a court of law

plain′tive (-tiv) ***adj.*** ⟦see PLAINT⟧ expressing sorrow or melancholy; mournful; sad

plait (plāt) ***n.*** ⟦< L *plicare*, to fold⟧ a braid of hair, etc. —***vt.*** to braid

plan (plan) ***n.*** ⟦Fr, plan, foundation⟧ **1** a diagram showing the arrangement of a structure, piece of ground, etc. **2** a scheme for making, doing, or arranging something **3** any outline or sketch —***vt.*** **planned, plan′ning** **1** to make a plan of (a structure, etc.) **2** to devise a scheme for doing, etc. **3** to have in mind as a project or purpose —***vi.*** to make plans —**plan′ner** ***n.***

plane[1] (plān) ***adj.*** ⟦L *planus*⟧ **1** flat; level **2** of or having to do with flat surfaces or points, lines, etc. on them *[plane geometry]* —***n.*** **1** a flat, level surface **2** a level of achievement, etc. **3** *short for* AIRPLANE

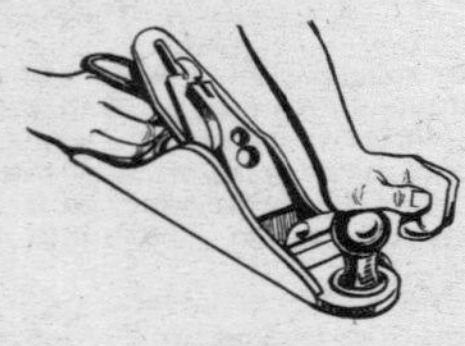

PLANE

plane[2] (plān) ***n.*** ⟦< L *planus*, level⟧ a carpenter's tool for shaving a wood surface to make it smooth or level —***vt.*** **planed, plan′ing** to smooth or level with a plane

plan·et (plan′it) ***n.*** ⟦< Gr *planan*, wander⟧ any celestial body that revolves about a star; esp., one of the sun's nine major planets: Mercury, Venus, Earth, Mars, Jupiter, Saturn, Uranus, Neptune, and Pluto —**plan′e·tar′y** (-ə ter′ē) ***adj.***

plan·e·tar·i·um (plan′ə ter′ē əm) ***n.**, pl.* **-i·ums** or **-i·a** (-ə) **1** a revolving projector used to simulate the past, present, or future motions or positions of the sun, planets, etc. on the inside of a large dome **2** the room or building containing this

plane tree any of various trees with ball-shaped fruits and bark that sheds in large patches; sycamore

plan·gent (plan′jənt) ***adj.*** ⟦< L *plangere*, to beat⟧ loud or resonant, and, often, mournful-sounding

plank (plaŋk) ***n.*** ⟦< LL *planca*⟧ **1** a long, broad, thick board **2** an item in the platform of a political party —***vt.*** **1** to cover with planks **2** to broil and serve (steak, fish, etc.) on a board **3** [Inf.] to set (*down*) with force

plank′ing ***n.*** **1** planks in quantity **2** the planks of a structure

plank·ton (plaŋk′tən) ***n.*** ⟦< Gr *plazesthai*, wander⟧ the microscopic animal and plant life found floating in bodies of water

plant (plant) ***n.*** ⟦< L *planta*, a sprout⟧ **1** any of a group of living organisms, excluding animals, bacteria, and certain other simple organisms, typically having leaves, stems, and roots and the ability to carry on photosynthesis **2** an herb, as distinguished from a tree or shrub **3** the machinery, buildings, etc.

of a factory, etc. —*vt.* **1** to put into the ground to grow **2** to set firmly in position **3** to settle; establish **4** [Slang] to place (a person or thing) in such a way as to trick, trap, etc.

plan·tain[1] (plan′tin) *n.* ⟦< L *plantago*⟧ a plant with basal leaves and spikes of tiny, greenish flowers

plan·tain[2] (plan′tin) *n.* ⟦< Sp *plátano,* banana tree⟧ a hybrid banana plant yielding a fruit that is usually cooked while green

plan·tar (plant′ər) *adj.* ⟦< L *planta,* sole⟧ of or on the sole of the foot

plan·ta·tion (plan tā′shən) *n.* ⟦< L *plantare,* to plant⟧ **1** an estate, as in a warm climate, cultivated by workers living on it **2** a large, cultivated planting of trees

plant·er (plant′ər) *n.* **1** the owner of a plantation **2** one that plants **3** a decorative container for plants

plant′ing *n.* **1** the act of putting seeds, etc. into soil **2** something planted

plant louse APHID

plaque (plak) *n.* ⟦Fr < MDu *placke,* disk⟧ **1** a flat, inscribed piece of wood or metal, used to commemorate an event, etc. **2** a thin film of matter on uncleaned teeth

plash (plash) *vt., vi., n.* ⟦echoic⟧ SPLASH

plas·ma (plaz′mə) *n.* ⟦Ger < Gr, something molded⟧ **1** the fluid part of blood, lymph, or milk **2** a high-temperature, ionized gas that is electrically neutral

plasma membrane a very thin living membrane surrounding a plant or animal cell

plas·ter (plas′tər) *n.* ⟦< Gr *emplassein,* to daub over⟧ **1** a pasty mixture, as of lime, sand, and water, that hardens when it dries, for coating walls, etc. **2** PLASTER OF PARIS **3** a pasty, medicinal preparation spread on cloth and applied to the body —*vt.* **1** to cover as with plaster **2** to apply like a plaster *[to plaster* posters on walls*]* **3** to make lie smooth and flat —**plas′ter·er** *n.*

plas′ter·board′ *n.* thin board consisting of plaster of Paris covered with heavy paper, used in wide sheets for walls, etc.

plaster of Paris ⟦from use of gypsum from *Paris,* France⟧ a thick paste of gypsum and water that sets quickly: used for casts, statuary, etc.

plas·tic (plas′tik) *adj.* ⟦< Gr *plassein,* to form⟧ **1** molding or shaping matter; formative **2** that can be molded or shaped **3** made of plastic —*n.* **1** any of various nonmetallic compounds, synthetically produced, which can be molded and hardened for commercial use **2** [Inf.] a credit card or credit cards, or credit based on their use —**plas·tic′i·ty** (-tis′ə tē) *n.*

plas′ti·cize′ (-tə sīz′) *vt., vi.* **-cized′, -ciz′ing** to make or become plastic

plastic surgery surgery dealing with the repair of deformed or destroyed parts of the body, as by transferring skin, bone, etc. from other parts —**plastic surgeon**

plat (plat) *n.* ⟦var. of PLOT⟧ **1** a small piece of ground **2** a map or plan, as of a subdivision —*vt.* **plat′ted, plat′ting** to make a map or plan of

plate (plāt) *n.* ⟦< Gr *platys,* broad⟧ **1** a smooth, flat, thin piece of metal, etc., specif. one on which an engraving is cut **2** an impression taken from an engraved surface **3** dishes, utensils, etc. of, or plated with, silver or gold **4** a shallow dish **5** the food in a dish; a course **6** a denture, specif. that part of it which fits to the mouth **7** *Baseball short for* HOME PLATE **8** *Photog.* a sheet of glass, metal, etc. coated with a film sensitive to light **9** *Printing* a cast to be printed from —*vt.* **plat′ed, plat′ing** **1** to coat with gold, silver, etc. **2** to cover with metal plates

pla·teau (pla tō′) *n.* ⟦Fr: see prec.⟧ **1** an elevated tract of level land **2** a period of relative stability or little change

plate glass polished, clear glass in thick sheets, for windows, mirrors, etc.

plate·let (plāt′lit) *n.* a small blood cell involved in clotting

plat·en (plat′′n) *n.* ⟦< OFr *plat,* flat⟧ **1** in a printing press, a flat metal plate which presses the paper against the type **2** a typewriter roller on which the keys strike

plate tec·ton·ics (tek tän′iks) *Geol.* the theory that the earth's surface consists of plates whose constant motion explains continental drift, etc.

plat·form (plat′fôrm′) *n.* ⟦Fr *plate-forme,* lit., flat form⟧ **1** a raised horizontal surface, as a stage for speakers, etc. **2** a statement of policy, esp. of a political party

plat·i·num (plat′′n əm) *n.* ⟦< Sp *plata,* silver⟧ a silvery, metallic chemical element, resistant to corrosion: used for jewelry, etc.

plat·i·tude (plat′ə to͞od′) *n.* ⟦Fr < *plat,* flat, after *latitude,* etc.⟧ a commonplace or trite remark

Pla·to (plāt′ō) 427?-347? B.C.; Gr. philosopher

Pla·ton·ic (plə tän′ik) *adj.* **1** of Plato or his philosophy **2** [*usually* **p-**] not sexual but purely spiritual: said of a relationship, etc.

pla·toon (plə to͞on′) *n.* ⟦Fr *peloton,* a ball, group⟧ **1** a military unit composed of two or more squads **2** *Sports* any of the specialized squads making up a team —*vt. Sports* to alternate (players) at a position

plat·ter (plat′ər) *n.* ⟦< OFr *plat,* flat⟧ a large, shallow dish, usually oval, for serving food

plat·y (plat′ē) *n., pl.* **plat′y, plat′ys,** or **plat′ies** ⟦clipped < ModL *Platypoecilus,* genus name⟧ a brightly colored, freshwater fish of Central America: used in aquariums

plat·y·pus (plat′ə pəs) *n., pl.* **-pus·es** or **-pi′** (-pī′) ⟦< Gr *platys,* flat + *pous,* foot⟧ a small, egg-laying water mammal of Australia, with webbed feet and a duck-like bill; duckbill

plau·dit (plô′dit) *n.* ⟦< L *plaudere,* applaud⟧ [*usually pl.*] applause

plau·si·ble (plô′zə bəl) *adj.* ⟦< L

plaudere, applaud⟧ seemingly true, trustworthy, honest, etc. —**plau'si·bil'i·ty** ***n.***

play (plā) ***vi.*** ⟦OE *plegan*⟧ **1** to move lightly, rapidly, etc. *[sunlight played on the water]* **2** to engage in recreation **3** to take part in a game or sport **4** to trifle (*with* a thing or person) **5** to perform on a musical instrument **6** to give out sounds **7** to act in a specified way *[to play dumb]* **8** to act in a drama **9** to impose unscrupulously (*on* another's feelings) —***vt.*** **1** to take part in (a game or sport) **2** to oppose (a person, team, etc.) in a game **3** to do, as in fun *[to play tricks]* **4** to bet on **5** to cause to move, etc.; wield **6** to cause *[to play havoc]* **7** to perform (music, a drama, etc.) **8** to perform on (an instrument) **9** to act the part of *[to play Hamlet]* —***n.*** **1** motion or activity, esp. when free or rapid **2** freedom for motion or action **3** recreation; sport **4** fun; joking **5** the playing of a game **6** a move or act in a game **7** a dramatic composition or performance; drama —**in** (or **out of**) **play** *Sports* in (or not in) the condition for continuing play: said of a ball, etc. —**play down** to attach little importance to —**played out** exhausted —**play up** [Inf.] to give prominence to —**play up to** [Inf.] to try to please by flattery

play'act' ***vi.*** **1** to pretend **2** to behave in an affected or dramatic manner —**play'act'ing** ***n.***

play'back' ***n.*** **1** reproduction of sounds, images, etc. from a recorded disc, tape, etc. **2** the control or device for such reproduction

play'bill' ***n.*** **1** a poster advertising a play **2** a program of a play, listing the cast, etc.

play'boy' ***n.*** a man of means who is given to pleasure-seeking

play'er ***n.*** **1** one who plays a specified game, instrument, etc. **2** an actor

play'ful ***adj.*** **1** fond of play or fun **2** jocular —**play'ful·ly** ***adv.*** —**play'ful·ness** ***n.***

play'go'er (-gō'ər) ***n.*** one who goes to the theater frequently or regularly

play'ground' ***n.*** a place, often near a school, for outdoor recreation

play'house' ***n.*** **1** a theater for live dramatic productions **2** a small house for children to play in

playing cards cards used in playing various games, arranged in four suits

play'mate' ***n.*** a companion in games and recreation

play'off' ***n.*** a contest to break a tie or to decide a championship

play on words a pun or punning

play'pen' ***n.*** a portable enclosure for an infant to play or crawl in safely

play'thing' ***n.*** a toy

play'wright' (-rīt') ***n.*** one who writes plays

pla·za (plä'zə, plaz'ə) ***n.*** ⟦Sp < L *platea*, street⟧ **1** a public square in a city or town **2** a shopping center **3** a service area along a superhighway

plea (plē) ***n.*** ⟦< L *placere*, to please⟧ **1** a statement in defense; excuse **2** a request; appeal **3** *Law* the response of a defendant to criminal charges

plea'-bar'gain ***vi.*** to engage in plea bargaining

plea bargaining pretrial negotiations in which the defendant agrees to plead guilty to a lesser charge if more serious charges are dropped

plead (plēd) ***vi.*** **plead'ed** or **pled** or **plead** (pled), **plead'ing** ⟦see PLEA⟧ **1** to present a plea in a law court **2** to make an appeal; beg —***vt.*** **1** to argue (a law case) **2** to answer (guilty or not guilty) to a charge **3** to offer as an excuse —**plead'er** ***n.***

pleas·ant (plez'ənt) ***adj.*** ⟦< Fr *plaisir*, to please⟧ **1** agreeable to the mind or senses; pleasing **2** having an agreeable manner, look, etc.; amiable —**pleas'ant·ly** ***adv.*** —**pleas'ant·ness** ***n.***

pleas'ant·ry (-ən trē) ***n.***, *pl.* **-ries** **1** a humorous remark **2** a polite social remark *[to exchange pleasantries]*

please (plēz) ***vt.*** **pleased**, **pleas'ing** ⟦< L *placere*⟧ **1** to be agreeable to; satisfy **2** to be the wish of *[it pleased him to go]* —***vi.*** **1** to be agreeable; satisfy **2** to have the wish; like *[to do as one pleases]* *Please* is also used in polite requests *[please sit down]*

pleas'ing ***adj.*** giving pleasure —**pleas'ing·ly** ***adv.***

pleas·ur·a·ble (plezh'ər ə bəl) ***adj.*** pleasant; enjoyable

pleas·ure (plezh'ər) ***n.*** **1** a pleased feeling; delight **2** one's wish, will, or choice **3** a thing that gives delight or satisfaction —**pleas'ure·ful** ***adj.***

pleat (plēt) ***n.*** ⟦ME *pleten*⟧ a flat double fold in cloth, etc. pressed or stitched in place —***vt.*** to lay and press (cloth) in a pleat or pleats

ple·be·ian (pli bē'ən) ***n.*** ⟦< L *plebs*, the common people⟧ **1** one of the common people **2** a vulgar, coarse person —***adj.*** vulgar or common

pleb·i·scite (pleb'ə sīt') ***n.*** ⟦< L *plebs*, the common people + *scitum*, a decree⟧ a direct vote of the people on a political issue, such as independent nationhood or annexation

plec·trum (plek'trəm) ***n.***, *pl.* **-trums** or **-tra** (-trə) ⟦L < Gr *plēssein*, to strike⟧ a thin piece of metal, plastic, etc., for plucking the strings of a guitar, etc.; pick

pled (pled) ***vi.***, ***vt.*** *pt. & pp. of* PLEAD

pledge (plej) ***n.*** ⟦prob < OS *plegan*, to warrant⟧ **1** the condition of being given or held as security for a contract, payment, etc. **2** a person or thing given or held thus as security **3** a promise or agreement **4** something promised —***vt.*** **pledged**, **pledg'ing** **1** to give as security **2** to bind by a promise **3** to promise to give

Pleis·to·cene (plīs'tə sēn') ***adj.*** ⟦< Gr *pleistos*, most + *kainos*, recent⟧ designating an epoch in the Cenozoic Era, characterized by the appearance of modern humans

ple·na·ry (plē'nə rē, plen'ə-) ***adj.*** ⟦< L *plenus*, full⟧ **1** full; complete **2** for attendance by all members *[a plenary* session]

plen·i·po·ten·ti·ar·y (plen′i pō ten′shē er′ē) ***adj.*** ⟦< L *plenus*, full + *potens*, powerful⟧ having or conferring full authority —***n.***, *pl.* **-ar′ies** a diplomat given full authority

plen·i·tude (plen′i to͞od′) ***n.*** ⟦< L *plenus*, full⟧ **1** fullness; completeness **2** abundance; plenty

plen·te·ous (plen′tē əs) ***adj.*** plentiful

plen·ti·ful (plen′ti fəl) ***adj.*** **1** having or yielding plenty **2** abundant —**plen′ti·ful·ly** ***adv.***

plen·ty (plen′tē) ***n.***, *pl.* **-ties** ⟦< L *plenus*, full⟧ **1** prosperity; opulence **2** a sufficient supply **3** a large number —***adv.*** [Inf.] fully; quite

pleth·o·ra (pleth′ə rə) ***n.*** ⟦< Gr *plēthein*, to be full⟧ an overabundance

pleu·ra (plo͝or′ə) ***n.***, *pl.* **-rae** (-ē) ⟦< Gr, rib, side⟧ the thin membrane that covers a lung and lines the chest cavity in mammals

pleu·ri·sy (plo͝or′ə sē) ***n.*** ⟦< Gr *pleura*, rib, side⟧ inflammation of the pleura, characterized by painful breathing

Plex·i·glas (plek′si glas′) *trademark for* a lightweight, transparent thermoplastic substance —***n.*** this material

plex·i·glass (plek′si glas′) ***n.*** a material like Plexiglas

plex·us (plek′səs) ***n.***, *pl.* **-us·es** or **-us** ⟦< L *plectere*, to twine⟧ a network of blood vessels, nerves, etc.

pli·a·ble (plī′ə bəl) ***adj.*** ⟦< L *plicare*, to fold⟧ **1** easily bent; flexible **2** easily influenced or persuaded **3** adaptable —**pli′a·bil′i·ty** ***n.***

pli·ant (plī′ənt) ***adj.*** **1** easily bent; pliable **2** compliant —**pli′an·cy** ***n.***

pli·ers (plī′ərz) ***pl.n.*** ⟦< PLY[1]⟧ small pincers for gripping small objects, bending wire, etc.: often **pair of pliers**

PLIERS

plight[1] (plīt) ***n.*** ⟦< OFr *pleit*, a fold⟧ a distressing situation

plight[2] (plīt) ***vt.*** ⟦< OE *pliht*, a pledge, danger⟧ to pledge, or bind by a pledge

plinth (plinth) ***n.*** ⟦< Gr *plinthos*, a brick⟧ the block at the base of a column, pedestal, etc.

PLO *abbrev.* Palestine Liberation Organization

plod (pläd) ***vi.*** **plod′ded**, **plod′ding** ⟦of echoic orig.⟧ **1** to move heavily and laboriously; trudge **2** to work steadily; drudge —**plod′der** ***n.***

plop (pläp) ***vt.***, ***vi.*** **plopped**, **plop′ping** ⟦echoic⟧ to drop with a sound like that of something flat falling into water —***n.*** such a sound

plot (plät) ***n.*** ⟦OE⟧ **1** a small area of ground **2** a secret, usually evil, scheme **3** the plan of action of a play, novel, etc.: also **plot′line′** —***vt.*** **plot′ted**, **plot′ting** **1** to mark or trace on a chart or map **2** to make secret plans for —***vi.*** to scheme —**plot·ter** ***n.***

plov·er (pluv′ər, plō′vər) ***n.*** ⟦< L *pluvia*, rain⟧ a bird living near the shore, having a short tail and long, pointed wings

plow (plou) ***n.*** ⟦OE *ploh*⟧ **1** a farm implement used to cut and turn up the soil **2** any implement like this, as a snowplow —***vt.*** **1** to cut and turn up (soil) with a plow **2** to make (one's way) through by or as if by plowing —***vi.*** **1** to use a plow **2** to move (*through, into*, etc.) with force **3** to plod **4** to begin work vigorously: with *into* Also, chiefly Brit., **plough** —**plow′man** (-mən), *pl.* **-men**, ***n.***

plow′share′ ***n.*** the cutting blade of a plow

ploy (ploi) ***n.*** ⟦? < (EM)PLOY⟧ an action intended to outwit someone

pluck (pluk) ***vt.*** ⟦OE *pluccian*⟧ **1** to pull off or out; pick **2** to snatch **3** to pull feathers or hair from **4** to pull at (a guitar string, etc.) and release quickly —***vi.*** to pull: often with *at* —***n.*** **1** a pulling; tug **2** courage

pluck′y ***adj.*** **-i·er**, **-i·est** brave; spirited —**pluck′i·ness** ***n.***

plug (plug) ***n.*** ⟦MDu *plugge*⟧ **1** an object used to stop up a hole, etc. **2** a cake of pressed tobacco **3** an electrical device, as with prongs, for making contact or closing a circuit **4** a kind of fishing lure **5** [Inf.] a free boost, advertisement, etc. **6** [Slang] an old, worn-out horse —***vt.*** **plugged**, **plug′ging** **1** to fill (a hole, etc.) with a plug **2** to insert a plug of **3** [Inf.] to advertise with a plug **4** [Slang] to shoot a bullet into —***vi.*** [Inf.] to work doggedly —**plug in** to connect (an electrical device) by inserting a plug into a jack, socket, etc.

plum (plum) ***n.*** ⟦OE *plume*⟧ **1** *a*) a tree bearing a smooth-skinned fruit with a flattened stone *b*) the fruit **2** a raisin [*plum* pudding] **3** the bluish-red color of some plums **4** something desirable

plum·age (plo͞o′mij) ***n.*** ⟦Fr < *plume*, a feather⟧ a bird's feathers

plumb (plum) ***n.*** ⟦< L *plumbum*, LEAD[2]⟧ a lead weight (**plumb bob**) hung at the end of a line (**plumb line**), used to determine how deep water is or whether a wall, etc. is vertical —***adj.*** perfectly vertical —***adv.*** **1** straight down **2** [Inf.] entirely —***vt.*** **1** to test or sound with a plumb **2** to probe or fathom —**out of** (or **off**) **plumb** not vertical

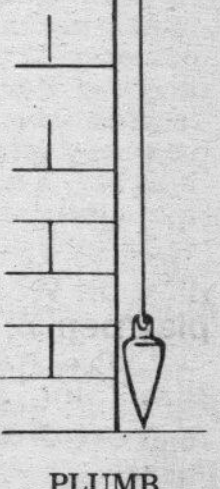

PLUMB

plumb·er (plum′ər) ***n.*** ⟦see prec.⟧ a skilled worker who installs and repairs pipes, fixtures, etc., as of water systems

plumber's helper [Inf.] PLUNGER (sense 2): also **plumber's friend**

plumb·ing (plum′iŋ) ***n.*** **1** the work of a plumber **2** the pipes and fixtures with which a plumber works

plume (plo͞om) ***n.*** ⟦< L *pluma*⟧ **1** a feather, esp. a large, showy one **2** a group of these —***vt.*** **plumed**, **plum′ing**

1 to adorn with plumes 2 to preen —**plum'y, -i·er, -i·est,** ***adj.***

plum·met (plum'it) ***n.*** ⟦see PLUMB⟧ **1** a plumb **2** a thing that weighs heavily —***vi.*** to fall straight downward

plump[1] (plump) ***adj.*** ⟦< MDu *plomp*, bulky⟧ full and rounded in form; chubby —**plump'ness** ***n.***

plump[2] (plump) ***vi., vt.*** ⟦echoic⟧ to drop or bump suddenly or heavily —***n.*** **1** a falling, bumping, etc. **2** the sound of this —***adv.*** **1** suddenly; heavily **2** straight down

plun·der (plun'dər) ***vt., vi.*** ⟦< Ger *plunder*, baggage⟧ **1** to rob or pillage **2** to take (property) by force or fraud —***n.*** **1** a plundering **2** things taken by force or fraud

plunge (plunj) ***vt.*** **plunged, plung'ing** ⟦see PLUMB⟧ to thrust or throw suddenly (*into* a liquid, condition, etc.) —***vi.*** **1** to dive or rush **2** to move violently and rapidly downward or forward **3** [Inf.] to gamble heavily —***n.*** **1** a dive or fall **2** [Inf.] a gamble

plung'er ***n.*** **1** one who plunges **2** a large rubber suction cup used to free clogged drains **3** any cylindrical device that operates with a plunging motion, as a piston

plunk (pluŋk) ***vt.*** ⟦echoic⟧ **1** to strum (a banjo, etc.) **2** to throw or put down heavily —***vi.*** **1** to give out a twanging sound **2** to fall heavily —***n.*** the sound made by plunking —**plunk down** [Inf.] to give in payment

plu·ral (ploor'əl) ***adj.*** ⟦< L *plus*, more⟧ more than one —***n.*** *Gram.* the form of a word designating more than one (Ex.: *hands, men*)

plu'ral·ism' ***n.*** various ethnic, religious, etc. groups existing together in a nation or society —**plu'ral·ist** ***n., adj.*** —**plu'ral·is'tic** ***adj.***

plu·ral·i·ty (ploo ral'ə tē) ***n.***, *pl.* **-ties** **1** a being plural or numerous **2** *a)* the excess of votes in an election that the leading candidate has over the nearest rival *b)* a majority

plu·ral·ize (ploor'ə līz') ***vt., vi.*** **-ized', -iz'ing** to make plural

plus (plus) ***prep.*** ⟦L, more⟧ **1** added to *[2 plus 2]* **2** in addition to —***adj.*** **1** indicating addition **2** positive *[a plus quantity]* **3** somewhat higher than *[a grade of B plus]* **4** involving extra gain *[a plus factor]* **5** [Inf.] and more *[personality plus]* —***n.***, *pl.* **plus'es** or **plus'ses** **1** a sign (**plus sign**, +) indicating addition or positive quantity **2** something added **3** an advantage; benefit

plush (plush) ***n.*** ⟦< L *pilus*, hair⟧ a fabric with a soft, thick pile —***adj.*** [Inf.] luxurious: also **plush'y, -i·er, -i·est**

Plu·tarch (ploo'tärk') A.D. 46?-120?; Gr. biographer & historian

Plu·to (ploot'ō) **1** *Gr. & Rom. Myth.* the god of the lower world **2** the outermost planet: see PLANET

plu·toc·ra·cy (ploo täk'rə sē) ***n.***, *pl.* **-cies** ⟦< Gr *ploutos*, wealth + *kratein*, to rule⟧ **1** government by the wealthy **2** a group of wealthy people who control a government

plu·to·crat (ploot'ə krat') ***n.*** **1** a member of a plutocracy **2** one whose wealth is the source of control or influence —**plu'to·crat'ic** ***adj.***

plu·to·ni·um (ploo tō'nē əm) ***n.*** ⟦after PLUTO (planet)⟧ a radioactive metallic chemical element

plu·vi·al (ploo'vē əl) ***adj.*** ⟦< L *pluvia*, rain⟧ of, or having much, rain

ply[1] (plī) ***vt.*** **plied, ply'ing** ⟦< L *plicare*, to fold⟧ [Now Rare] to twist, fold, etc. —***n.***, *pl.* **plies** **1** a thickness or layer, as of cloth or plywood **2** one of the twisted strands in rope, yarn, etc.

ply[2] (plī) ***vt.*** **plied, ply'ing** ⟦contr. < APPLY⟧ **1** to use (a tool, faculty, etc.), esp. with energy **2** to work at (a trade) **3** to keep supplying, assailing, etc. (*with*) **4** to sail back and forth across —***vi.*** **1** to keep busy (*at*) **2** to travel regularly (*between* places)

Ply·mouth (plim'əth) town in SE Massachusetts: settled by the Pilgrims (1620): pop. 46,000

ply'wood' ***n.*** ⟦PLY[1] + WOOD⟧ a construction material made of thin layers of wood glued together

PM *abbrev.* **1** ⟦L *post meridiem*⟧ after noon: used for the time from noon to midnight: also **P.M.** or **p.m.** or **pm** **2** Postmaster **3** Prime Minister

PMS *abbrev.* ⟦*p(re)m(enstrual) s(yndrome)*⟧ the physical and emotional symptoms that may precede menstruation

pneu·mat·ic (noo mat'ik) ***adj.*** ⟦< Gr *pneuma*, breath⟧ **1** of or containing wind, air, or gases **2** filled with or worked by compressed air

pneu·mo·ni·a (noo mōn'yə) ***n.*** ⟦< Gr *pneumōn*, lung < *pnein*, breathe⟧ inflammation of the lungs caused as by bacteria or viruses

Po (pō) river in N Italy, flowing from the Alps into the Adriatic

PO *abbrev.* **1** Post Office **2** post office box

poach[1] (pōch) ***vt.*** ⟦< MFr *poche*, pocket: the yolk is "pocketed" in the white⟧ to cook (fish, an egg without its shell, etc.) in or over boiling water

poach[2] (pōch) ***vt., vi.*** ⟦< MHG *puchen*, to plunder⟧ **1** to trespass on (private property), esp. to hunt or fish **2** to hunt or catch (game or fish) illegally —**poach'er** ***n.***

pock (päk) ***n.*** ⟦OE *pocc*⟧ **1** a pustule caused by smallpox, etc. **2** POCKMARK —**pocked** ***adj.***

pock·et (päk'it) ***n.*** ⟦< Fr *poque*, a pouch⟧ **1** a little bag or pouch, esp. one sewn into clothing, for carrying small articles **2** a pouchlike cavity or hollow **3** a small area or group *[a pocket of poverty]* —***adj.*** **1** that can be carried in a pocket **2** small —***vt.*** **1** to put into a pocket **2** to envelop; enclose **3** to take (money, etc.) dishonestly **4** to suppress *[to pocket one's pride]* —**pock'et·ful'**, *pl.* **-fuls'**, ***n.***

pock'et·book' ***n.*** **1** a woman's purse or handbag **2** monetary resources

pock'et·knife' ***n.***, *pl.* **-knives'** a knife with a blade or blades that fold into the

pock'mark' *n.* a scar left by a pustule, as of smallpox

pod (päd) *n.* ⟦< ?⟧ a dry fruit or seed vessel, as of peas or beans

-pod (päd) ⟦< Gr *pous*, foot⟧ *combining form* **1** foot **2** (one) having (a specified number or kind of) feet Also **-pode** (pōd)

po·di·a·try (pō dī'ə trē) *n.* ⟦< Gr *pous*, foot + -IATRY⟧ the profession dealing with the care and treatment of the feet —**po·di'a·trist** *n.*

po·di·um (pō'dē əm) *n.* ⟦L < Gr *pous*, foot⟧ **1** a small platform, as for an orchestra conductor **2** LECTERN

Poe (pō), **Ed·gar Al·lan** (ed'gər al'ən) 1809-49; U.S. poet & short-story writer

po·em (pō'əm) *n.* ⟦< Gr *poiein*, to make⟧ an arrangement of words, esp. a rhythmical composition, sometimes rhymed, in a style more imaginative than ordinary speech or prose

po·e·sy (pō'ə sē') *n. old-fashioned var. of* POETRY

po·et (pō'ət) *n.* **1** one who writes poems or verses **2** one who displays imaginative power and beauty of thought, language, etc. —**po'et·ess** *fem.n.*

po·et·as·ter (pō'ə tas'tər) *n.* ⟦< prec. + L *-aster*, dim. suffix⟧ a writer of mediocre verse

po·et·ic (pō et'ik) *adj.* **1** of or for poets or poetry **2** displaying the beauty, imaginative qualities, etc. found in good poetry Also **po·et'i·cal** *adj.* —**po·et'i·cal·ly** *adv.*

poetic justice justice, as in stories, applied in an especially fitting way

poetic license deviation from strict fact or rules, for artistic effect

poet laureate the official poet of a nation, appointed to write poems celebrating national events, etc.

po·et·ry (pō'ə trē) *n.* **1** the art, theory, or structure of poems **2** poems **3** poetic qualities

po·grom (pō'grəm, -gräm') *n.* ⟦< Russ, earlier, riot, storm⟧ an organized massacre, as of Jews in czarist Russia

poi (poi) *n.* ⟦Haw⟧ a Hawaiian food that is a paste of taro root

poign·ant (poin'yənt) *adj.* ⟦< L *pungere*, to prick⟧ **1** pungent **2** *a)* sharply painful to the feelings *b)* emotionally moving **3** sharp, biting, pointed, etc. —**poign'an·cy** *n.*

poin·ci·an·a (poin'sē an'ə) *n.* ⟦after M. de *Poinci*, early governor of the Fr West Indies⟧ a small tropical tree or shrub with showy red, orange, or yellow flowers

poin·set·ti·a (poin set'ə, -set'ē ə) *n.* ⟦after J. R. *Poinsett*, 19th-c. U.S. ambassador to Mexico⟧ a tropical shrub with yellow flowers and petal-like red leaves

point (point) *n.* ⟦< L *pungere*, to prick⟧ **1** a dot in writing, etc. *[a decimal point]* **2** a position or location **3** the exact moment **4** a condition reached *[boiling point]* **5** a detail; item *[point by point]* **6** a distinguishing feature **7** a unit, as of value or game scores **8** a sharp end **9** a projecting piece of land; cape **10** the essential fact or idea *[the point of a joke]* **11** a purpose; object **12** a convincing idea or fact **13** a helpful hint **14** a mark showing direction on a compass **15** *Finance a)* a $1 change in the price of a stock *b)* a unit or amount equal to one percent **16** *Printing* a measuring unit for type, about 1/72 of an inch —*vt.* **1** to sharpen to a point **2** to give (a story, etc.) emphasis: usually with *up* **3** to show: usually with *out [point out the way]* **4** to aim —*vi.* **1** to direct one's finger (*at* or *to*) **2** to call attention (*to*) **3** to be directed (*to* or *toward*) —**at the point of** very close to —**beside the point** irrelevant —**to the point** pertinent; apt

point'-blank' *adj., adv.* ⟦prec. + *blank* (white center of a target)⟧ **1** (aimed) straight at a mark **2** direct(ly); blunt(ly)

point'ed *adj.* **1** having a sharp end **2** sharp; incisive **3** aimed at someone: said as of a remark **4** very evident —**point'ed·ly** *adv.*

poin·telle (poin tel') *n.* a lacy, loosely formed fabric, often of acrylic, used for blouses, sweaters, etc.

point'er *n.* **1** a long, tapered rod for pointing to things **2** an indicator on a meter, etc. **3** a large, muscular hunting dog with a smooth coat **4** [Inf.] a helpful hint or suggestion

poin·til·lism (pwan'tə liz'əm) *n.* ⟦Fr⟧ a style of painting using dots of color that blend together when seen from a distance —**poin'til·list** *n., adj.*

point'less *adj.* **1** without a point **2** without meaning or force; senseless

point man **1** the soldier in the front position in a patrol **2** anyone in the forefront a movement of attacking or supporting a political program, etc.

point of view **1** the way in which something is viewed **2** a mental attitude or opinion

point'y *adj.* **-i·er, -i·est** **1** coming to a sharp point **2** many-pointed

poise (poiz) *n.* ⟦< L *pendere*, weigh⟧ **1** balance; stability **2** ease and dignity of manner **3** carriage, as of the body —*vt., vi.* **poised, pois'ing** to balance or be balanced

poised *adj.* **1** calm; self-assured **2** readied

poi·son (poi'zən) *n.* ⟦< L *potio*, potion⟧ a substance that can cause illness or death when ingested even in small quantities —*vt.* **1** to harm or kill with poison **2** to put poison into **3** to influence wrongfully —*adj.* poisonous

poison ivy a plant having leaves of

three leaflets and ivory-colored berries: it can cause a severe rash if touched

poi'son·ous *adj.* that can injure or kill by or as by poison; toxic —**poi'son·ous·ly** *adv.*

poison pill any defensive measure that makes the takeover of a corporation prohibitively expensive

POISON IVY

poke[1] (pōk) *vt.* **poked, pok'ing** ⟦< MDu *poken*⟧ **1** *a)* to prod, as with a stick *b)* [Slang] to hit **2** to make (a hole, etc.) by poking —*vi.* **1** to jab (*at*) **2** to pry or search (*about* or *around*) **3** to move slowly (*along*) —*n.* **1** a jab; thrust **2** [Slang] a blow with the fist —**poke fun at** to ridicule

poke[2] (pōk) *n.* ⟦OFr⟧ [Dial.] a sack

pok·er[1] (pōk'ər) *n.* ⟦< ? Ger *pochspiel*, lit., game of defiance⟧ a card game in which the players bet on the value of their hands

pok·er[2] (pō'kər) *n.* a rod, usually of iron, for stirring a fire

poker face an expressionless face, as of a poker player trying to conceal the nature of his or her hand

pok·y (pō'kē) *adj.* **-i·er, -i·est** ⟦POKE[1] + -Y[2]⟧ **1** slow, dull, etc. **2** small and uncomfortable *[*a *poky* room*]* Also **pok'ey**

pol (päl) *n.* [Slang] a politician

Pol *abbrev.* **1** Poland **2** Polish

Po·land (pō'lənd) country in EC Europe, on the Baltic Sea: 120,628 sq. mi.; pop. 38,309,000

po·lar (pō'lər) *adj.* **1** of or near the North or South pole **2** of a pole or poles

polar bear a large white bear of coastal arctic regions

Po·la·ris (pō lar'is) *n.* the bright star almost directly above the North Pole

po·lar·i·ty (pō lar'ə tē) *n., pl.* **-ties** **1** the tendency of bodies having opposite magnetic poles to have their ends point to the earth's magnetic poles **2** the tendency to turn, grow, think, etc. in contrary directions, as if because of magnetic repulsion

po·lar·i·za·tion (pō'lə ri zā'shən) *n.* **1** a polarizing or being polarized **2** *Optics* the condition of electromagnetic waves in which the motion of the wave is confined to one plane or one direction

po·lar·ize (pō'lə rīz') *vt.* **-ized', -iz'ing** to give polarity to —*vi.* to acquire polarity; specif., to separate into opposed or antagonistic groups, viewpoints, etc.

Po·lar·oid (pō'lə roid') *trademark for:* **1** a transparent material capable of polarizing light **2** ⟦< *Polaroid* (*Land Camera*)⟧ *a)* a camera that produces a print within seconds *b)* such a print

pole[1] (pōl) *n.* ⟦< L *palus*, a stake⟧ a long, slender piece of wood, metal, etc. —*vt.* **poled, pol'ing** to push along with a pole

pole[2] (pōl) *n.* ⟦< Gr *polos*⟧ **1** either end of any axis, as of the earth's axis **2** either of two opposed forces, parts, etc., as the ends of a magnet or the terminals of a battery

Pole (pōl) *n.* a person born or living in Poland

pole·cat (pōl'kat') *n.* ⟦prob. < OFr *poule*, hen + CAT⟧ **1** a small Old World weasel **2** SKUNK

po·lem·ic (pō lem'ik) *adj.* ⟦< Gr *polemos*, war⟧ of or involving dispute: also **po·lem'i·cal** —*n.* a controversy

po·lem'ics *n.* [*sometimes with pl. v.*] the art or practice of disputation —**po·lem'i·cist** (-i sist) *n.*

pole'star' Polaris, the North Star: usually **Pole Star** —*n.* a guiding principle

pole vault a leap for height by jumping over a bar with the aid of a long pole —**pole'-vault'** *vi.* —**pole'-vault'er** *n.*

po·lice (pə lēs') *n.* ⟦Fr: ult. < Gr *polis*, city⟧ **1** the governmental department (of a city, state, etc.) for keeping order, detecting crime, etc. **2** [*with pl. v.*] the members of such a department —*vt.* **-liced', -lic'ing** **1** to control, protect, etc. with police or a similar force **2** to keep (a military camp, etc.) clean and orderly

po·lice'man (-mən) *n., pl.* **-men** (-mən) a member of a police force —**po·lice'wom'an**, *pl.* **-wom'en**, *fem.n.*

police officer a member of a police force

police state a government that seeks to suppress political opposition by means of police

pol·i·cy[1] (päl'ə sē) *n., pl.* **-cies** ⟦see POLICE⟧ **1** wise management **2** a principle, plan, etc., as of a government

pol·i·cy[2] (päl'ə sē) *n., pl.* **-cies** ⟦< Gr *apodeixis*, proof⟧ a written insurance contract: in full **insurance policy**

pol'i·cy·hold'er *n.* a person to whom an insurance policy is issued

po·li·o·my·e·li·tis (pō'lē ō mī'ə līt'is) *n.* ⟦< Gr *polios*, gray + MYELITIS⟧ an acute infectious disease caused by viral inflammation of the gray matter of the spinal cord, often resulting in muscular paralysis: also **po'li·o'**

pol·ish (päl'ish) *vt.* ⟦< L *polire*⟧ **1** to smooth and brighten, as by rubbing **2** to refine (manners, style, etc.) —*vi.* to take a polish —*n.* **1** a surface gloss **2** elegance, refinement, etc. **3** a substance used to polish —**polish off** [Inf.] to finish (a meal, job, etc.) completely

Pol·ish (pōl'ish) *adj.* of Poland or its people, language, etc. —*n.* the Slavic language of Poland

po·lite (pə līt') *adj.* ⟦< L *polire*, to polish⟧ **1** cultured; refined **2** courteous; mannerly —**po·lite'ly** *adv.* —**po·lite'ness** *n.*

pol·i·tesse (päl'i tes') *n.* ⟦Fr⟧ politeness

pol·i·tic (päl'ə tik') *adj.* ⟦see POLICE⟧ **1** having practical wisdom; prudent **2** expedient: said as of a plan —*vi.* **-ticked', -tick'ing** to campaign in politics

po·lit·i·cal (pə lit′i kəl) ***adj.*** **1** of, concerned with, or engaged in government, politics, etc. **2** of or characteristic of political parties or politicians —**po·lit′i·cal·ly** ***adv.***

politically correct holding orthodox liberal political views: usually used disparagingly to connote dogmatism, etc. —**political correctness**

political science the science of the principles, organization, and methods of government —**political scientist**

pol·i·ti·cian (päl′ə tish′ən) ***n.*** one actively engaged in politics: often used with implications of seeking personal or partisan gain, scheming, etc.

po·lit·i·cize (pə lit′ə sīz′) ***vt.*** **-cized′**, **-ciz′ing** to make political in tone; character, etc.

po·lit·i·co (pə lit′ə kō′) ***n.***, *pl.* **-cos′** ⟦< Sp or It⟧ POLITICIAN

pol·i·tics (päl′ə tiks) ***pl.n.*** [*with sing. or pl. v.*] **1** the science and art of government **2** political affairs **3** political methods, tactics, etc. **4** political opinions, etc. **5** factional scheming for power

pol′i·ty (-ə tē) ***n.***, *pl.* **-ties** ⟦see POLICE⟧ **1** governmental organization **2** a society with a government; state

Polk (pōk), **James K.** 1795-1849; 11th president of the U.S. (1845-49)

pol·ka (pōl′kə) ***n.*** ⟦Czech, Polish dance⟧ **1** a fast dance for couples **2** music for this

pol·ka dot (pō′kə, pōl′kə) any of a regular pattern of small, round dots on cloth

poll (pōl) ***n.*** ⟦ME *pol*⟧ **1** the head **2** a counting, listing, etc. of persons, esp. of voters **3** the number of votes recorded **4** [*pl.*] a place where votes are cast **5** a canvassing of people's opinions on some question —***vt.*** **1** to register the votes of **2** to require each member of (a jury, etc.) to declare individual votes **3** to receive (a specified number of votes) **4** to cast (a vote) **5** to canvass in a POLL (sense 5)

pol·len (päl′ən) ***n.*** ⟦L, dust⟧ the fine, dustlike mass of grains in the anthers of seed plants

pollen count the number of grains of pollen, esp. of ragweed, in a given volume of air at a specified time and place

pol·li·nate (päl′ə nāt′) ***vt.*** **-nat′ed**, **-nat′ing** to transfer pollen to the pistil of (a flower) —**pol′li·na′tion** ***n.*** —**pol′li·na′tor** ***n.***

pol·li·wog (päl′ē wäg′, -wôg′) ***n.*** ⟦< ME: see POLL + WIGGLE⟧ TADPOLE: also **pol′ly·wog′**

poll·ster (pōl′stər) ***n.*** one whose work is taking public-opinion polls

pol·lute (pə lo͞ot′) ***vt.*** **-lut′ed**, **-lut′ing** ⟦< L *polluere*⟧ to make unclean or impure —**pol·lu′tant** ***n.*** —**pol·lu′tion** ***n.***

Pol·ly·an·na (päl′ē an′ə) ***n.*** ⟦after the young heroine of a novel (1913) by E. H. Porter⟧ an excessively optimistic person

po·lo (pō′lō) ***n.*** ⟦ult. < Tibetan *pulu*, ball⟧ a game played on horseback by two teams, using a wooden ball and long-handled mallets

Po·lo (pō′lō), **Mar·co** (mär′kō) 1254-1324; Venetian traveler in E Asia

pol·o·naise (päl′ə nāz′) ***n.*** ⟦Fr (fem.), Polish⟧ a stately Polish dance

pol·ter·geist (pōl′tər gīst′) ***n.*** ⟦Ger < *poltern*, to rumble + *geist*, ghost⟧ a ghost supposed to be responsible for mysterious noisy disturbances

pol·troon (päl tro͞on′) ***n.*** ⟦< It *poltrone*⟧ a thorough coward

poly- ⟦< Gr⟧ *combining form* much, many

pol·y·clin·ic (päl′i klin′ik) ***n.*** ⟦POLY- + CLINIC⟧ a clinic or hospital for the treatment of various kinds of diseases

pol·y·es·ter (päl′ē es′tər) ***n.*** ⟦POLY(MER) + ESTER⟧ a polymeric resin used in making plastics, fibers, etc.

pol·y·eth·yl·ene (päl′ē eth′ə lēn′) ***n.*** ⟦POLY(MER) + ETHYLENE⟧ a thermoplastic resin used in making plastics, films, etc.

po·lyg·a·my (pə lig′ə mē) ***n.*** ⟦< Gr *poly-*, many + *gamos*, marriage⟧ the practice of having two or more spouses at the same time —**po·lyg′a·mist** ***n.*** —**po·lyg′a·mous** ***adj.***

pol·y·glot (päl′i glät′) ***adj.*** ⟦< Gr *poly-*, many + *glōtta*, tongue⟧ **1** knowing several languages **2** written in several languages —***n.*** a polyglot person

pol′y·gon′ (-gän′) ***n.*** ⟦< Gr: see POLY- & -GON⟧ a closed plane figure consisting of straight lines —**po·lyg·o·nal** (pə lig′ə nəl) ***adj.***

pol′y·graph′ (-graf′) ***n.*** ⟦see POLY- & -GRAPH⟧ a device measuring changes in respiration, pulse rate, etc.: see LIE DETECTOR

pol′y·he′dron (-hē′drən) ***n.*** ⟦< Gr: see POLY- & -HEDRON⟧ a solid figure with usually more than six plane surfaces

pol′y·math′ (-ə math′) ***n.*** ⟦< Gr *poly-*, much + *manthanein*, learn⟧ a person of great and varied learning

pol′y·mer (-mər) ***n.*** ⟦Ger < Gr *poly-*, many + *meros*, part⟧ a substance consisting of giant molecules formed from polymerization —**pol′y·mer′ic** (-mer′ik) ***adj.***

po·lym·er·i·za·tion (pō lim′ər ə zā′shən) ***n.*** a chaining together of many simple molecules to form a more complex molecule with different properties —**po·lym′er·ize′** (-īz′), **-ized′**, **-iz′ing**, ***vt.***, ***vi.***

Pol·y·ne·sia (päl′i nē′zhə) group of Pacific islands, east of Micronesia, including Hawaii, etc. —**Pol′y·ne′sian** ***adj.***, ***n.***

pol·y·no·mi·al (päl′i nō′mē əl) ***n.*** ⟦POLY- + (BI)NOMIAL⟧ a mathematical expression containing three or more terms (Ex: $x^3 + 3x + 2$)

pol·yp (päl′ip) ***n.*** ⟦< Gr *poly-*, many + *pous*, foot⟧ **1** a cnidarian with many small tentacles at the top of a tubelike body **2** a growth of mucous membrane in the bladder, rectum, etc.

po·lyph·o·ny (pə lif′ə nē) ***n.*** ⟦< Gr *poly-*, many + *phōnē*, a sound⟧ *Music* a combining of independent, harmonizing melodies, as in a fugue; counterpoint —**pol·y·phon·ic** (päl′i fän′ik) ***adj.*** —**pol′y·**

phon′i·cal·ly *adv.*

pol·y·rhythm (päl′i rith′əm) *n. Music* **1** the simultaneous use of strongly contrasting rhythms **2** such a rhythm: *usually used in pl.* —**pol′y·rhyth′mic** *adj.*

pol′y·sty′rene′ (-stī′rēn′) *n.* ⟦POLY(MER) + *styrene*, an organic compound⟧ a clear polymer used to make containers, etc.

pol·y·syl·lab·ic (päl′i si lab′ik) *adj.* **1** having four or more syllables **2** characterized by polysyllabic words —**pol′y·syl′la·ble** (-sil′ə bəl) *n.*

pol′y·tech′nic (-tek′nik) *n., adj.* ⟦< Gr *poly-*, many + *technē*, art⟧ (school) providing instruction in many scientific and technical subjects

pol′y·the·ism′ (-thē iz′əm) *n.* ⟦< Gr *poly*, many + *theos*, god⟧ belief in more than one god —**pol′y·the·ist** *adj., n.* —**pol′y·the·is′tic** *adj.*

pol·y·un·sat·u·rat·ed (päl′ē un sach′ə rāt′id) *adj.* designating any of certain vegetable and animal fats and oils with a low cholesterol content

pol′y·u·re·thane′ (-yoor′ə thān′) *n.* ⟦POLY- + URETHANE⟧ any of various synthetic polymers, used in cushions, coatings, etc.

pol·y·vi·nyl (päl′i vī′nəl) *adj.* designating or of any of a group of polymerized vinyl compounds

po·made (päm ād′, pō-) *n.* ⟦< It *pomo*, apple (orig. an ingredient)⟧ a perfumed ointment, as for the hair

pome·gran·ate (päm′gran′it, päm′ə-) *n.* ⟦ult. < L *pomum*, fruit + *granum*, seed⟧ **1** a round, red fruit with a hard rind and many seeds **2** the bush or tree it grows on

pom·mel (päm′əl; *for v.* pum′əl) *n.* ⟦< L *pomum*, fruit⟧ **1** the knob on the end of the hilt of some swords and daggers **2** the rounded, upward-projecting part at the front of a saddle —*vt.* **-meled** or **-melled**, **-mel·ing** or **-mel·ling** PUMMEL

pomp (pämp) *n.* ⟦< Gr *pompē*, solemn procession⟧ **1** stately display **2** ostentatious show or display

pom·pa·dour (päm′pə dôr′) *n.* ⟦after Mme. *Pompadour*, mistress of Louis XV⟧ a hairdo in which the hair is brushed up high from the forehead

pom·pa·no (päm′pə nō′) *n., pl.* **-no′** or **-nos′** ⟦< Sp⟧ a food fish of North America and the West Indies

pom·pom (päm′päm′) *n.* ⟦see POMP⟧ an ornamental tuft of silk, etc., used on clothing, etc. or waved as by a cheerleader: also **pom′pon′** (-pän′)

pom·pous (päm′pəs) *adj.* pretentious; self-important —**pom·pos′i·ty** (-päs′ə tē) *n.*

pon·cho (pän′chō) *n., pl.* **-chos** ⟦AmSp < AmInd, woolen cloth⟧ a cloak like a blanket with a hole in the middle for the head, esp. a waterproof one worn as a raincoat

pond (pänd) *n.* ⟦< ME *pounde*, enclosure⟧ a body of water smaller than a lake

pon·der (pän′dər) *vt., vi.* ⟦< L *ponderare*, weigh⟧ to think deeply (about); consider carefully

pon·der·o·sa (pine) (pän′dər ō′sə) ⟦< L *ponderosus*, very heavy⟧ a yellow pine of W North America

pon′der·ous *adj.* **1** very heavy **2** unwieldy **3** labored and dull

pone (pōn) *n.* ⟦< AmInd⟧ [Chiefly South] corn bread in the form of small ovals

pon·gee (pän jē′, pun-) *n.* ⟦< Mandarin Chin dial. *pen-chi*, one's own loom⟧ a soft, thin silk cloth, usually left in its natural light-brown color

pon·iard (pän′yərd) *n.* ⟦ult. < L *pugnus*, fist⟧ a dagger

pon·tiff (pänt′if) *n.* ⟦< L *pontifex*, high priest⟧ **1** a bishop **2** [**P-**] the pope

pon·tif·i·cal (pän tif′i kəl) *adj.* ⟦see prec.⟧ **1** having to do with a bishop, the pope, etc. **2** pompous, dogmatic, etc.

pon·tif′i·cate (-i kit; *for v.*, -kāt′) *n.* the office or term of a pontiff —*vi.* **-cat′ed**, **-cat′ing** **1** to officiate as a pontiff **2** to be pompous or dogmatic

pon·toon (pän to͞on′) *n.* ⟦< L *pons*, a bridge⟧ **1** a flat-bottomed boat **2** any of a row of boats or floating objects used to support a temporary bridge **3** a float on an aircraft's landing gear

po·ny (pō′nē) *n., pl.* **-nies** ⟦prob. < L *pullus*, foal⟧ **1** a horse of any small breed **2** a small liqueur glass **3** [Inf.] a literal translation of a foreign work, used in doing schoolwork

po′ny·tail′ *n.* a hair style in which the hair is tied tightly at the back and hangs down

pooch (po͞och) *n.* ⟦< ?⟧ [Slang] a dog

poo·dle (po͞od′'l) *n.* ⟦Ger *pudel*⟧ a dog with a thick, wiry coat of tight curls in a solid color

pooh (po͞o) *interj.* used to express disdain, disbelief, or impatience

pooh-pooh (po͞o′po͞o′) *vt.* to treat disdainfully; make light of

pool[1] (po͞ol) *n.* ⟦OE *pol*⟧ **1** a small pond **2** a small collection of liquid, as a puddle **3** a tank for swimming

pool[2] (po͞ol) *n.* ⟦< LL *pulla*, hen⟧ **1** a game related to billiards, played on a table with six pockets **2** a combination of resources, funds, supplies, etc. for some common purpose **3** the parties forming such a combination —*vt., vi.* to contribute to a common fund

poop[1] (po͞op) *n.* ⟦< L *puppis*, stern of a ship⟧ a raised deck at the stern of a sailing ship: also **poop deck**

poop[2] (po͞op) *vt.* [Slang] to tire

poop[3] (po͞op) *n.* [Slang] current inside information

poor (poor) *adj.* ⟦< L *pauper*, poor⟧ **1** having little or no means to support oneself; needy **2** lacking in some quality; specif., *a)* inadequate *b)* inferior or worthless *c)* contemptible **3** worthy of pity; unfortunate —**the poor** poor, or needy, people —**poor′ly** *adv.*

poor′house′ *n.* [Historical] a publicly supported institution for paupers

poor′-mouth′ *vi.* [Inf.] to complain about one's lack of money

pop[1] (päp) *n.* ⟦echoic⟧ **1** a sudden, light explosive sound **2** any carbonated, nonalcoholic beverage —*vi.* **popped**,

pop'ping **1** to make, or burst with, a pop **2** to move, go, etc. suddenly **3** to open wide or bulge: said of the eyes **4** *Baseball* to hit the ball high into the infield —***vt.*** **1** to cause to pop, as corn by heating it **2** to put suddenly *[to pop* one's head in*]* **3** [Slang] to swallow (a pill, etc.) —**pop'per** ***n.***

pop[2] (päp) ***n.*** ⟦< PAPA⟧ [Inf.] FATHER

pop[3] (päp) ***adj.*** **1** of music popular with the general public **2** intended for the popular taste, esp. as exploited commercially *[pop* culture*]* **3** of a realistic art style using techniques and subjects adapted from commercial art, comic strips, posters, etc. —***n.*** pop music, etc.

pop *abbrev.* **1** popular **2** popularly **3** population

pop'corn' ***n.*** **1** a variety of corn with hard grains that pop open into a white, puffy mass when heated **2** the popped grains

pope (pōp) ***n.*** ⟦< Gr *pappas*, father⟧ [*often* **P-**] *R.C.Ch.* the bishop of Rome and head of the Church

Pope (pōp), **Alexander** 1688-1744; Eng. poet

pop'gun' ***n.*** a toy gun that shoots a piece of cork, etc. by air compression, with a pop

pop·in·jay (päp'in jā') ***n.*** ⟦< Ar *babghā*, a parrot⟧ a conceited person

pop·lar (päp'lər) ***n.*** ⟦< L *populus*⟧ **1** a tall tree of the willow family having soft wood **2** its wood

pop·lin (päp'lin) ***n.*** ⟦prob. after *Poperinge*, city in Flanders⟧ a sturdy ribbed fabric of cotton, silk, etc.

pop'o'ver ***n.*** a very light, puffy, hollow muffin

pop·py (päp'ē) ***n.***, *pl.* **-pies** ⟦< L *papaver*⟧ **1** a plant with a milky juice and variously colored flowers **2** its flower

pop'py·cock' (-käk') ***n.*** [Inf.] foolish talk; nonsense

poppy seed the small, dark seed of the poppy, used in baking, etc.

pops (päps) ***adj.*** of a symphony orchestra that plays light classical music or arrangements of popular music —***n.*** a pops orchestra, concert, etc.

Pop·si·cle (päp'si kəl) ⟦blend of POP[1] + I(CICLE)⟧ *trademark for* a flavored ice frozen around a stick —***n.*** [*also* **p-**] such a confection

pop-top (päp'täp') ***n.*** a container with a tab or ring pulled or pushed to make an opening in the top

pop·u·lace (päp'yə lis) ***n.*** ⟦< L *populus*⟧ **1** the common people; the masses **2** POPULATION (sense 1*a*)

pop·u·lar (päp'yə lər) ***adj.*** ⟦< L *populus*, the people⟧ **1** of, carried on by, or intended for people generally **2** not expensive *[popular* prices*]* **3** commonly accepted; prevalent **4** liked by many people —**pop'u·lar'i·ty** (-lar'ə tē) ***n.*** —**pop'u·lar·ly** ***adv.***

pop·u·lar·ize (päp'yə lə rīz') ***vt.*** **-ized'**, **-iz'ing** to make popular —**pop'u·lar·i·za'tion** ***n.***

pop'u·late' (-lāt') ***vt.*** **-lat'ed**, **-lat'ing** ⟦< L *populus*, the people⟧ **1** to inhabit **2** to supply with inhabitants

pop'u·la'tion ***n.*** **1** *a*) all the people in a country, region, etc. *b*) the number of these **2** a populating or being populated

population explosion the great and rapid increase in human population in modern times

pop·u·list (päp'yə list) ***n.*** a politician, etc. who claims to represent the common people: often used to suggest demagogy —***adj.*** of a populist —**pop'u·lism'** ***n.***

pop'u·lous (-ləs) ***adj.*** full of people; thickly populated

por·ce·lain (pôr'sə lin) ***n.*** ⟦< It *porcellana*⟧ a hard, white, translucent variety of ceramic ware

porch (pôrch) ***n.*** ⟦< L *porta*, gate⟧ **1** a covered entrance to a building **2** an open or enclosed gallery or room on the outside of a building

por·cine (pôr'sīn', -sin) ***adj.*** ⟦< L *porcus*, hog⟧ of or like pigs or hogs

por·cu·pine (pôr'kyə pīn') ***n.*** ⟦< L *porcus*, pig + *spina*, spine⟧ a rodent having coarse hair mixed with long, stiff, sharp spines

pore[1] (pôr) ***vi.*** **pored**, **por'ing** ⟦ME *poren*⟧ **1** to study carefully: with *over* **2** to ponder: with *over*

pore[2] (pôr) ***n.*** ⟦< Gr *poros*, passage⟧ a tiny opening, as in skin or plant leaves, for absorbing or discharging fluids

pork (pôrk) ***n.*** ⟦< L *porcus*, pig⟧ the flesh of a pig, used as food

pork barrel [Inf.] government appropriations for political patronage

pork'y ***adj.*** **-i·er**, **-i·est** **1** of or like pork **2** fat **3** [Slang] saucy, cocky, etc.

porn (pôrn) ***n.***, ***adj.*** [Slang] *short for* PORNOGRAPHY, PORNOGRAPHIC: also **por·no** (pôr'nō)

por·nog·ra·phy (pôr näg'rə fē) ***n.*** ⟦< Gr *pornē*, a prostitute + *graphein*, write⟧ writings, pictures, etc. intended to arouse sexual desire —**por·nog'ra·pher** ***n.*** —**por'no·graph'ic** (-nə graf'ik) ***adj.***

po·rous (pôr'əs) ***adj.*** full of pores, through which fluids, air, or light may pass —**po·ros·i·ty** (pō räs'ə tē) ***n.***

por·phy·ry (pôr'fə rē) ***n.***, *pl.* **-ries** ⟦< Gr *porphyros*, purple⟧ any igneous rock with large, distinct crystals

por·poise (pôr'pəs) ***n.*** ⟦< L *porcus*, pig + *piscis*, a fish⟧ **1** a small whale with a blunt snout **2** a dolphin

por·ridge (pôr'ij) ***n.*** ⟦< POTTAGE by confusion with VL *porrata*, leek broth⟧ [Chiefly Brit.] a soft food of cereal or meal boiled in water or milk

por'rin·ger (-in jər) ***n.*** ⟦< Fr *potager*, soup dish: infl. by prec.⟧ a small, shallow bowl

port[1] (pôrt) ***n.*** ⟦< L *portus*, haven⟧ **1** a harbor **2** a city with a harbor where ships load and unload cargo

port[2] (pôrt) ***n.*** ⟦after *Oporto*, city in Portugal⟧ a sweet, dark-red wine

port[3] (pôrt) ***vt.*** ⟦< L *portare*, carry⟧ to hold (a rifle, etc.) diagonally in front of one, as for inspection

port[4] (pôrt) ***n.*** ⟦< PORT[1]⟧ the left side of a ship, etc. as one faces forward —***adj.*** of or on this side

port[5] (pôrt) ***n.*** ⟦< L *porta*, door⟧ **1** PORTHOLE **2** an opening, as in a valve face, for the passage of steam, etc. **3** *Comput.* the circuit, outlet, etc. which connects a computer and its peripheral

Port *abbrev.* **1** Portugal **2** Portuguese

port·a·ble (pôr′tə bəl) ***adj.*** ⟦< L *portare*, carry⟧ **1** that can be carried **2** easily carried —***n.*** something portable —**port′a·bil′i·ty** ***n.***

por·tage (pôr′tij, pôr täzh′) ***n.*** ⟦< L *portare*, carry⟧ **1** a carrying of boats and supplies overland between navigable lakes, rivers, etc. **2** any route over which this is done —***vt., vi.*** **-taged**, **-tag·ing** to carry (boats, etc.) over a portage

por·tal (pôrt′'l) ***n.*** ⟦< L *porta*, door⟧ a doorway, gate, or entrance

port·cul·lis (pôrt kul′is) ***n.*** ⟦< MFr *porte*, gate + *coleïce*, sliding⟧ a heavy iron grating lowered to bar the gateway of a castle or fortified town

por·tend (pôr tend′) ***vt.*** ⟦< L *por-*, forth + *tendere*, to stretch⟧ **1** to be an omen of; presage **2** to signify

por·tent (pôr′tent′) ***n.*** **1** something that portends an event **2** significance

por·ten·tous (pôr ten′təs) ***adj.*** **1** portending evil; ominous **2** amazing **3** pompous; self-important —**por·ten′tous·ly** ***adv.***

por·ter[1] (pôr′tər) ***n.*** ⟦< L *porta*, gate⟧ a doorman or gatekeeper

por·ter[2] (pôr′tər) ***n.*** ⟦< L *portare*, carry⟧ **1** one who carries luggage, etc. for hire **2** an employee who sweeps, cleans, etc. in a bank, store, etc. **3** a railroad attendant for passengers as on a sleeper **4** a dark-brown beer

por′ter·house′ ***n.*** ⟦orig. a tavern: see PORTER[2], sense 4⟧ a choice cut of beef next to the sirloin: in full **porterhouse steak**

port·fo·li·o (pôrt fō′lē ō′) ***n.***, *pl.* **-li·os′** ⟦< L *portare*, carry + *folium*, leaf⟧ **1** a flat, portable case, for loose papers; briefcase **2** the office of a minister of state **3** a list of an investor's securities **4** a selection from an artist's, etc. work

port·hole (pôrt′hōl′) ***n.*** an opening in a ship's side to admit light and air

PORTICO

por·ti·co (pôr′ti kō′) ***n.***, *pl.* **-coes′** or **-cos′** ⟦< L *porticus*, porch⟧ a porch or covered walk, consisting of a roof supported by columns

por·tiere or **por·tière** (pôr tyer′) ***n.*** ⟦Fr < *porte*, door⟧ a curtain hung in a doorway

por′tion (-shən) ***n.*** ⟦< L *portio*⟧ **1** a part, esp. that allotted to a person; share **2** one's fate **3** a helping of food —***vt.*** to give out in portions

Port·land (pôrt′lənd) city & port in NW Oregon: pop. 439,000

port·ly (pôrt′lē) ***adj.*** **-li·er**, **-li·est** **1** large and stately **2** stout; corpulent —**port′li·ness** ***n.***

port·man·teau (pôrt man′tō) ***n.***, *pl.* **-teaus** or **-teaux** (-tōz) ⟦< Fr *porter*, carry + *manteau*, cloak⟧ a stiff suitcase that opens into two compartments

portmanteau word a word that is a combination of two other words (Ex.: *smog*, from *smoke* and *fog*)

por·to·bel·lo mushroom (pôr′tə bel′ō) a dark, flavorful mushroom with a broad cap: also **portobello** ***n.***, *pl.* **-los**

port of entry a place where customs officials check people and goods entering a country

Por·to Ri·co (pôr′tə rē′kō) *former var. of* PUERTO RICO —**Por′to Ri′can**

por·trait (pôr′trit, -trāt′) ***n.*** ⟦see PORTRAY⟧ **1** a painting, photograph, etc. of a person, esp. of the face **2** a description, portrayal, etc.

por′trai·ture (-tri chər) ***n.*** the practice or art of portraying

por·tray (pôr trā′) ***vt.*** ⟦< L *pro-*, forth + *trahere*, draw⟧ **1** to make a portrait of **2** to describe graphically **3** to play the part of as in a play or movie —**por·tray′al** ***n.***

Por·tu·gal (pôr′chə gəl) country in SW Europe, on the Atlantic: 35,456 sq. mi.; pop. 9,863,000

Por·tu·guese (pôr′chə gēz′, -gēs′) ***adj.*** of Portugal or its people, language, etc. —***n.*** **1** *pl.* **-guese′** a person born or living in Portugal **2** a Romance language of Portugal and Brazil

por·tu·lac·a (pôr′chə lak′ə) ***n.*** ⟦< L *portula*, small door: from the opening in its seed capsule⟧ a fleshy plant with yellow, pink, or purple flowers

pose (pōz) ***vt.*** **posed**, **pos′ing** ⟦< L *pausare*, to stop⟧ **1** to propose (a question, etc.) **2** to put (a model, etc.) in a certain attitude —***vi.*** **1** to assume a certain attitude, as in modeling for an artist **2** to strike attitudes for effect **3** set oneself up (*as*) [*to pose as an officer*] —***n.*** **1** a bodily attitude, esp. one held for an artist, etc. **2** a way of behaving assumed for effect

Po·sei·don (pō sī′dən) ***n.*** the Greek god of the sea

pos·er (pō′zər) ***n.*** one who poses; esp., a poseur

po·seur (pō zur′) ***n.*** ⟦Fr⟧ one who assumes attitudes or manners merely for effect

posh (päsh) ***adj.*** ⟦< ?⟧ [Inf.] luxurious and fashionable

pos·it (päz′it) ***vt.*** ⟦see fol.⟧ to suppose to be a fact; postulate

po·si·tion (pə zish′ən) ***n.*** ⟦< L *ponere*, to place⟧ **1** the way in which a person or thing is placed or arranged **2** one's attitude or opinion **3** the place where one is; location **4** the usual or proper place **5** rank, esp. high rank **6** a post of employment; job —*vt.* to put into a certain position

pos·i·tive (päz′ə tiv) *adj.* ⟦see prec.⟧ **1** definitely set; explicit *[positive* instructions*]* **2** *a)* having the mind set; confident *b)* overconfident or dogmatic **3** showing agreement; affirmative **4** constructive *[positive* criticism*]* **5** regarded as having real existence *[a positive* good*]* **6** based on facts *[positive* proof*]* **7** *Elec. a)* of the kind of electricity predominating in a glass body after it has been rubbed with silk *b)* charged with positive electricity *c)* having a deficiency of electrons **8** *Gram.* of an adjective or adverb in its uncompared degree **9** *Math.* greater than zero **10** *Med.* showing the presence of a condition, infection, etc. **11** *Photog.* with the light and shade corresponding to those of the subject —*n.* **1** something positive, as a degree, quality, quantity, photographic print, etc. **2** the plate in a battery having an excess of electrons flowing out toward the negative —**pos′i·tive·ly** *adv.*

pos′i·tron′ (-trän′) *n.* ⟦POSI(TIVE) + (ELEC)TRON⟧ the positive antiparticle of an electron, having the same mass and magnitude of charge

poss *abbrev.* **1** possessive **2** possibly

pos·se (päs′ē) *n.* ⟦< L, be able⟧ [Historical] a band of men, usually armed, summoned to assist the sheriff in keeping the peace, etc.

pos·sess (pə zes′) *vt.* ⟦< L *possidere*⟧ **1** to have as belonging to one; own **2** to have as an attribute, quality, etc. **3** to gain control over *[possessed* by an idea*]* —**pos·ses′sor** *n.*

pos·sessed′ *adj.* **1** owned **2** controlled, as if by a demon; crazed

pos·ses′sion (-zesh′ən) *n.* **1** a possessing or being possessed **2** anything possessed **3** [*pl.*] property **4** territory ruled by an outside country

pos·ses′sive (-zes′iv) *adj.* **1** of possession **2** showing or desiring possession, domination, control, influence, etc. **3** *Gram.* designating or of a case, form, or construction expressing possession (Ex: *my, Bill's*) —*n. Gram.* **1** the possessive case **2** a word or phrase in this case —**pos·ses′sive·ness** *n.*

pos·si·ble (päs′ə bəl) *adj.* ⟦< L *posse*, be able⟧ **1** that can be or exist **2** that may or may not happen **3** that can be done, selected, etc. **4** permissible —**pos′si·bil′i·ty** (-bil′ə tē), *pl.* **-ties**, *n.*

pos′si·bly (-blē) *adv.* **1** by any possible means **2** perhaps; maybe

pos·sum (päs′əm) *n.* [Inf.] OPOSSUM —**play possum** to pretend to be asleep, dead, ill, etc.

post[1] (pōst) *n.* ⟦< L *postis*⟧ **1** a piece of wood, metal, etc. set upright to support a building, sign, etc. **2** the starting point of a horse race —*vt.* **1** to put up (a poster, etc.) on (a wall, etc.) **2** to announce by posting notices *[to post* a reward*]* **3** to warn against trespassing on by posted notices **4** to put (a name) on a posted or published list

post[2] (pōst) *n.* ⟦< Fr < It *posto*⟧ **1** the place where a soldier, guard, etc. is stationed **2** a place where troops are garrisoned **3** the place assigned to one **4** a job or duty —*vt.* **1** to assign to a post **2** to put up (a bond, etc.)

post[3] (pōst) *n.* ⟦< Fr < It *posta*⟧ [Chiefly Brit.] (the) mail —*vi.* to travel fast; hasten —*vt.* **1** [Chiefly Brit.] to mail **2** to inform *[keep me posted]*

post- ⟦L < *post*, after⟧ *prefix* **1** after in time, later (than) *[postnatal]* **2** after in space, behind

post·age (pōs′tij) *n.* the amount charged for mailing a letter, etc., esp. as represented by stamps

post·al (pōs′təl) *adj.* ⟦Fr⟧ of mail or post offices

post-bel·lum (pōst bel′əm) *adj.* ⟦L⟧ after the war; specif., after the American Civil War

post′card′ *n.* a card, usually with a picture on one side, for sending short messages by mail

post′date′ *vt.* **-dat′ed, -dat′ing** **1** to assign a later date to than the actual date **2** to be subsequent to

post·er (pōs′tər) *n.* a large advertisement or notice posted publicly

pos·te·ri·or (päs tir′ē ər) *adj.* ⟦L < *post*, after⟧ **1** later; following **2** at the rear; behind —*n.* the buttocks

pos·ter·i·ty (päs ter′ə tē) *n.* ⟦see prec.⟧ **1** all of a person's descendants **2** all succeeding generations

post′grad′u·ate *adj.* of or taking a course of study after graduation, esp. after receipt of the bachelor's degree

post′haste′ *adv.* with great haste

post′hole′ *n.* a hole dug to hold the end of an upright post

post·hu·mous (päs′choo məs, -tyoo-) *adj.* ⟦< L *postumus*, last⟧ **1** published after the author's death **2** arising or continuing after one's death —**post′hu·mous·ly** *adv.*

post′hyp·not′ic *adj.* in the time after a hypnotic trance *[posthypnotic* suggestion*]*

pos·til·ion or **pos·til·lion** (pōs til′yən, päs-) *n.* ⟦Fr < It *posta*, a post⟧ one who rides the leading left-hand horse of a team drawing a carriage

post′in·dus′tri·al *adj.* of a society in which the economy has shifted from heavy industry to service industries, technology, etc.

Post′-it′ *trademark for* small sheets of adhesive-backed paper for attaching notes —*n.* a sheet of this

post·lude (pōst′lo͞od′) *n.* ⟦POST- + (PRE)LUDE⟧ a concluding musical piece

post′man (-mən) *n. pl.* **-men** (-mən) MAIL CARRIER

post′mark′ *n.* a post-office mark stamped on mail, canceling the postage stamp and recording the date and place —*vt.* to stamp with a postmark

post′mas′ter *n.* the manager of a post office

postmaster general *pl.* **postmasters general** the head of a government's postal system

post′me·rid′i·an (-mə rid′ē ən) ***adj.*** ⟦L⟧ after noon

post me·ri·di·em (mə rid′ē əm) ⟦L⟧ after noon: abbrev. *P.M.*, *p.m.*, *PM*, or *pm*

post′mod′ern·ism′ ***n.*** an eclectic cultural and artistic trend in art, etc. of the late 20th c. —**post′mod′ern** ***adj.*** —**post′mod′ern·ist** ***adj.***, ***n.***

post-mor·tem (pōst′môr′təm) ***adj.*** ⟦L⟧ **1** after death **2** of a post-mortem —***n.*** **1** AUTOPSY **2** an evaluation of some event just ended

post·na·sal drip (pōst′nā′zəl) a discharge of mucus from behind the nose onto the pharynx, due to a cold, allergy, etc.

post′na′tal (-nāt′′l) ***adj.*** after birth

post office **1** the governmental department in charge of the mail **2** a place where mail is sorted, postage stamps are sold, etc.

post′op′er·a·tive (-äp′ər ə tiv) ***adj.*** occurring after a surgical operation

post′paid′ ***adj.*** with postage prepaid

post′par′tum (-pär′təm) ***adj.*** ⟦L < *post-*, after + *parere*, to bear⟧ of the time after childbirth

post·pone (pōst pōn′) ***vt.*** **-poned′**, **-pon′ing** ⟦< L *post-*, after + *ponere*, put⟧ to put off until later; delay —**post·pone′ment** ***n.***

post′script′ ***n.*** ⟦< L *post-*, after + *scribere*, write⟧ a note added below the signature in a letter

post time the scheduled starting time of a horse race

pos·tu·late (päs′chə lāt′; *for n.*, -lit) ***vt.*** **-lat′ed**, **-lat′ing** ⟦< L *postulare*, to demand⟧ to assume to be true, real, etc., esp. as a basis for argument —***n.*** something postulated

pos·ture (päs′chər) ***n.*** ⟦MFr < L *ponere*, to place⟧ **1** the position or carriage of the body **2** a position assumed as in posing **3** an official stand or position *[our national posture]* —***vi.*** to pose or assume an attitude merely for effect

post′war′ ***adj.*** after the (or a) war

po·sy (pō′zē) ***n.***, *pl.* **-sies** ⟦< POESY⟧ [Old-fashioned] a flower or bouquet

pot[1] (pät) ***n.*** ⟦OE *pott*⟧ **1** a round vessel for holding liquids, for cooking, etc. **2** a pot with its contents **3** [Inf.] all the money bet at a single time —***vt.*** **pot′ted**, **pot′ting** to put into a pot —**go to pot** to go to ruin —**pot′ful′**, *pl.* **-fuls′**, ***n.***

pot[2] (pät) ***n.*** ⟦< AmSp *potiguaya*⟧ [Slang] MARIJUANA

po·ta·ble (pōt′ə bəl) ***adj.*** ⟦< L *potare*, to drink⟧ drinkable —***n.*** a beverage —**po′ta·bil′i·ty** ***n.***

pot′ash′ ***n.*** ⟦< Du *pot*, POT[1] + *asch*, ASH[1]⟧ any of various potassium compounds used in fertilizers, soaps, etc.

po·tas·si·um (pə tas′ē əm) ***n.*** ⟦see prec.⟧ a soft, silver-white, metallic chemical element

po·ta·to (pə tāt′ō) ***n.***, *pl.* **-toes** ⟦< WInd⟧ **1** the starchy tuber of a widely cultivated plant, eaten as a cooked vegetable **2** this plant

potato chip a very thin slice of potato fried crisp and then salted

pot′bel′lied ***adj.*** **1** having a potbelly **2** having bulging sides *[a potbellied stove]*

pot′bel′ly ***n.***, *pl.* **-lies** a protruding belly

pot′boil′er ***n.*** a piece of writing, etc., done quickly and for money only

pot′-bound′ ***adj.*** having outgrown its container: said of a potted plant

po·tent (pōt′′nt) ***adj.*** ⟦< L *posse*, be able⟧ **1** having authority or power **2** convincing; cogent **3** effective, as a drug **4** able to have sexual intercourse: said of a male —**po′ten·cy** ***n.***

po·ten·tate (pōt′′n tāt′) ***n.*** a person having great power; ruler; monarch

po·ten·tial (pō ten′shəl) ***adj.*** ⟦see POTENT⟧ that can come into being; possible; latent —***n.*** **1** something potential **2** the difference in voltage between two points in an electric circuit or field —**po·ten′ti·al′i·ty** (-shē al′ə tē), *pl.* **-ties**, ***n.*** —**po·ten′tial·ly** ***adv.***

pot′herb′ ***n.*** any herb whose leaves and stems are boiled and eaten or used as a flavoring

pot′hold′er ***n.*** a small pad, or piece of thick cloth, for handling hot pots, etc.

pot′hole′ ***n.*** **1** a deep hole or pit **2** CHUCKHOLE

pot′hook′ ***n.*** an S-shaped hook for hanging a pot over a fire

po·tion (pō′shən) ***n.*** ⟦< L *potare*, to drink⟧ a drink as of medicine, poison, or a supposedly magic substance

pot′luck′ ***n.*** **1** whatever the family meal happens to be *[to take potluck]* **2** a dinner to which everyone brings a dish to share: in full **potluck dinner**

Po·to·mac (pə tō′mək) river in the E U.S., flowing into Chesapeake Bay

pot′pie′ ***n.*** a meat pie made in a deep dish

pot·pour·ri (pō′poo rē′, pät′poo rē′) ***n.*** ⟦Fr < *pot*, a pot + *pourrir*, to rot⟧ **1** a mixture of dried flowers, spices, etc., kept for its fragrance **2** a medley or miscellany; mixture

pot roast a large cut of beef cooked in one piece by braising

pot·sherd (pät′shurd′) ***n.*** ⟦see POT[1] & SHARD⟧ a piece of broken pottery

pot′shot′ ***n.*** **1** an easy or random shot **2** a haphazard try **3** a random attack

pot·tage (pät′ij) ***n.*** ⟦< earlier Fr *pot*, a pot⟧ a kind of thick soup or stew

pot′ter ***n.*** one who makes earthenware pots, dishes, etc.

potter's field a burial ground for paupers or unknown persons

POTTER'S WHEEL

potter's wheel a rotating disk upon which clay is molded into bowls, etc.

pot'ter·y ***n.***, *pl.* **-ies** **1** a potter's workshop **2** the art of a potter; ceramics **3** pots, dishes, etc. made of clay hardened by heat

pot·ty (pät'ē) ***n.***, *pl.* **-ties** **1** a small pot used as a toilet for a child **2** a child's chair for toilet training with such a pot: in full **potty chair** **3** a toilet: a child's word

pouch (pouch) ***n.*** ⟦< earlier Fr *poche*⟧ **1** a small bag or sack *[a tobacco pouch]* **2** a mailbag **3** a saclike structure, as that on the abdomen of the kangaroo, etc. for carrying young —***vi.*** to form a pouch

poul·tice (pōl'tis) ***n.*** ⟦< ML *pultes*, pap⟧ a hot, soft, moist mass applied to a sore part of the body —***vt.*** **-ticed**, **-tic·ing** to apply a poultice to

poul·try (pōl'trē) ***n.*** ⟦< L *pullus*, chicken⟧ domestic fowls; chickens, ducks, etc.

pounce (pouns) ***n.*** ⟦ME *pownce*, talon⟧ a pouncing —***vi.*** **pounced**, **pounc'ing** to swoop down or leap (*on*, *upon*, or *at*) in, or as in, seizing

pound[1] (pound) ***n.***, *pl.* **pounds**; sometimes, after a number, **pound** ⟦< L *pondus*, weight⟧ **1** a unit of weight equal to 16 oz. avoirdupois or 12 oz. troy: abbrev. *lb.* **2** the monetary unit of the United Kingdom: symbol, £ **3** the monetary unit of various other countries, as Egypt and Syria

pound[2] (pound) ***vt.*** ⟦OE *punian*⟧ **1** to beat to a pulp, powder, etc. **2** to hit hard —***vi.*** **1** to deliver repeated, heavy blows (*at* or *on*) **2** to move with heavy steps **3** to throb

pound[3] (pound) ***n.*** ⟦< OE *pund-*⟧ a municipal enclosure for stray animals *[a dog pound]*

pound'cake' ***n.*** a rich cake made (orig. with a pound each) of flour, butter, sugar, etc.

pound sign a symbol (#) on a button on a telephone keypad

pour (pôr) ***vt.*** ⟦ME *pouren*⟧ **1** to cause to flow in a continuous stream **2** to emit, utter, etc. profusely or steadily —***vi.*** **1** to flow freely, continuously, etc. **2** to rain heavily

pout (pout) ***vi.*** ⟦ME *pouten*⟧ **1** to thrust out the lips, as in sullenness **2** to sulk —***n.*** the act of pouting —**pout'er** ***n.***

pov·er·ty (päv'ər tē) ***n.*** ⟦< L *pauper*, poor⟧ **1** the condition or quality of being poor; need **2** deficiency; inadequacy **3** scarcity

pov'er·ty-strick'en ***adj.*** very poor

POW ***n.***, *pl.* **POW's** prisoner of war

pow·der (pou'dər) ***n.*** ⟦< L *pulvis*, dust⟧ **1** any dry substance in the form of fine, dustlike particles, produced by crushing, grinding, etc. **2** a specific kind of powder *[bath powder]* —***vt.*** **1** to sprinkle, etc. with powder **2** to make into powder —**pow'der·y** ***adj.***

powder keg **1** a keg for gunpowder **2** a potential source of violence, war, etc.

powder room a lavatory for women

pow·er (pou'ər) ***n.*** ⟦ult. < L *posse*, be able⟧ **1** ability to do or act **2** vigor; force; strength **3** *a*) authority; influence *b*) legal authority **4** physical force or energy *[electric power]* **5** a person or thing having great influence, force, or authority **6** a nation with influence over other nations **7** the product of the multiplication of a quantity by itself **8** the degree of magnification of a lens —***vt.*** to supply with a source of power —***adj.*** **1** operated by electricity, a fuel engine, etc. *[power tools]* **2** served by an auxiliary system that reduces effort *[power steering]* **3** carrying electricity

pow'er·ful ***adj.*** strong, mighty, influential, etc. —**pow'er·ful·ly** ***adv.***

pow'er·house' ***n.*** **1** a building where electric power is generated **2** [Inf.] a powerful person, team, etc.

pow·er·less (pou'ər lis) ***adj.*** without power; weak, unable, etc. —**pow'er·less·ly** ***adv.***

power of attorney written legal authority for one person to act for another

pow'er·train' ***n.*** DRIVETRAIN

pow·wow (pou'wou') ***n.*** ⟦< AmInd⟧ **1** a conference of or with North American Indians **2** [Inf.] any conference

pox (päks) ***n.*** ⟦for *pocks*: see POCK⟧ **1** a disease characterized by skin eruptions, as smallpox **2** syphilis: with *the*

pp *abbrev.* **1** pages **2** parcel post **3** past participle **4** postpaid **5** prepaid Also, for 4 & 5, **ppd**

PP *abbrev.* parcel post

PPO ***n.***, *pl.* **PPO's** ⟦*p*(*referred*) *p*(*rovider*) *o*(*rganization*)⟧ a healthcare system having certain hospitals, doctors, etc. under contract at a reduced cost

ppr *abbrev.* present participle

P.P.S., p.p.s., PPS, or **pps** *abbrev.* ⟦L *post postscriptum*⟧ an additional postscript

pr *abbrev.* **1** pair(s) **2** price

Pr *abbrev.* Provençal

PR or **P.R.** *abbrev.* **1** public relations **2** Puerto Rico

prac·ti·ca·ble (prak'ti kə bəl) ***adj.*** **1** that can be put into practice; feasible **2** that can be used; useful —**prac'ti·ca·**

bil′i·ty *n.* —prac′ti·ca·bly *adv.*

prac·ti·cal (prak′ti kəl) ***adj.*** **1** of or obtained through practice or action **2** useful **3** concerned with the application of knowledge to useful ends *[practical* science*]* **4** dealing realistically and sensibly with everyday matters **5** that is so in practice, if not in theory, law, etc. —**prac′ti·cal′i·ty** (-kal′ə tē), *pl.* **-ties,** ***n.***

practical joke a trick played on someone in fun —**practical joker**

prac·ti·cal·ly (prak′tik lē, -tik ə lē) ***adv.*** **1** in a practical manner **2** from a practical viewpoint **3** in effect; virtually **4** [Inf.] nearly

practical nurse a nurse with less training than a registered nurse, often one licensed by a U.S. state (**licensed practical nurse**) for specified duties

prac·tice (prak′tis) ***vt.*** **-ticed, -tic·ing** ⟦< Gr *prassein,* do⟧ **1** to do or engage in frequently; make a habit of **2** to do repeatedly so as to become proficient **3** to work at, esp. as a profession —***vi.*** to do something repeatedly so as to become proficient; drill Chiefly Brit. sp. **prac′tise** —***n.*** **1** a practicing; habit, custom, etc. **2** *a)* repeated action to acquire proficiency *b)* proficiency so acquired **3** the actual doing of something **4** *a)* the exercise of a profession *b)* a business based on this

prac′ticed ***adj.*** experienced; skilled

prac·ti·cum (prak′ti kəm) ***n.*** ⟦see PRACTICE⟧ a course involving activities emphasizing the practical application of theory, as on-the-job experience in a field of study

prac·ti·tion·er (prak tish′ə nər) ***n.*** one who practices a profession

Prae·to·ri·an (prē tôr′ē ən) ***adj.*** ⟦< L *praetor,* magistrate⟧ of or belonging to the bodyguard (**Praetorian Guard**) of a Roman emperor

prag·mat·ic (prag mat′ik) ***adj.*** ⟦< Gr *pragma,* thing done⟧ **1** practical **2** testing the validity of all concepts by their practical results —**prag·mat′i·cal·ly** ***adv.*** —**prag′ma·tism′** (-mə tiz′əm) ***n.*** —**prag′ma·tist** ***n.***

Prague (präg) capital of the Czech Republic: pop. 1,217,000

prai·rie (prer′ē) ***n.*** ⟦Fr < L *pratum,* meadow⟧ a large area of level or rolling, grassy land

prairie dog a small, burrowing rodent of North America

prairie schooner a box-shaped covered wagon

praise (prāz) ***vt.*** **praised, prais′ing** ⟦< L *pretium,* worth, price⟧ **1** to express approval or admiration of **2** to glorify (God, etc.), as in song —***n.*** a praising or being praised; commendation

praise′wor′thy ***adj.*** worthy of praise —**praise′wor′thi·ly** ***adv.*** —**praise′wor′thi·ness** ***n.***

pra·line (prä′lēn′, prā′-) ***n.*** ⟦Fr⟧ any of various soft or crisp candies made of nuts, sugar, etc.

prance (prans) ***vi.*** **pranced, pranc′ing** ⟦< ?⟧ **1** to rise up, or move along, on the hind legs, as a horse does **2** to caper or strut —***n.*** a prancing —**pranc′er** ***n.*** —**pranc′ing·ly** ***adv.***

prank (praŋk) ***n.*** ⟦< ?⟧ a mischievous trick —**prank′ster** ***n.***

prate (prāt) ***vi., vt.*** **prat′ed, prat′ing** ⟦< MDu *praten*⟧ to talk much and foolishly; chatter

prat·tle (prat′'l) ***vi., vt.*** **-tled, -tling** ⟦LowG *pratelen*⟧ to prate or babble —***n.*** chatter or babble

prawn (prôn) ***n.*** ⟦< ?⟧ a large shrimp or other similar crustacean

pray (prā) ***vt.*** ⟦< L *prex,* prayer⟧ **1** to implore *[*(I) *pray* (you) tell me*]* **2** to ask for by prayer —***vi.*** to say prayers, as to God

prayer[1] (prer) ***n.*** **1** the act of praying **2** an entreaty; supplication **3** *a)* a humble request, as to God *b)* any set formula for this **4** [*often pl.*] a devotional service chiefly of prayers **5** something prayed for —**prayer′ful** ***adj.*** —**prayer′ful·ly** ***adv.***

pray·er[2] (prā′ər) ***n.*** one who prays

praying mantis MANTIS

pre- ⟦< L *prae,* before⟧ *prefix* before in time, place, rank, etc.

preach (prēch) ***vi.*** ⟦< L *prae-,* before + *dicare,* proclaim⟧ **1** to give a religious sermon **2** to give moral advice, esp. in a tiresome manner —***vt.*** **1** to urge as by preaching **2** to deliver (a sermon) —**preach′ment** ***n.***

preach′er ***n.*** one who preaches; esp., a member of the Protestant clergy

preach′y ***adj.*** **-i·er, -i·est** [Inf.] given to or marked by preaching, or moralizing

pre·am·ble (prē′am′bəl) ***n.*** ⟦< L *prae-,* before + *ambulare,* go⟧ an introduction, esp. one to a constitution, statute, etc., stating its purpose

pre′ap·prove′ (-ə pro͞ov′) ***vt.*** **-proved′, -prov′ing** to authorize before an application is submitted

pre′ar·range′ (-ə rānj′) ***vt.*** **-ranged′, -rang′ing** to arrange beforehand

pre·can·cer·ous (prē kan′sər əs) ***adj.*** likely to become cancerous

pre·car·i·ous (prē ker′ē əs) ***adj.*** ⟦see PRAY⟧ dependent upon circumstances or chance; uncertain; risky —**pre·car′i·ous·ly** ***adv.***

pre·cau·tion (pri kô′shən) ***n.*** ⟦< L *prae-,* before + *cavere,* take care⟧ care taken beforehand, as against danger or failure —**pre·cau′tion·ar′y** ***adj.***

pre·cede (prē sēd′) ***vt., vi.*** **-ced′ed, -ced′ing** ⟦< L *prae-,* before + *cedere,* to go⟧ to be, come, or go before in time, place, rank, etc.

prec·e·dence (pres′ə dəns; prē sēd′'ns) ***n.*** the act, right, or fact of preceding in time, order, rank, etc.

prec·e·dent (pres′ə dənt) ***n.*** an act, statement, etc. that may serve as an example or justification for a later one

pre·ced′ing ***adj.*** that precedes

pre·cept (prē′sept′) ***n.*** ⟦< L *prae-,* before + *capere,* take⟧ a rule of moral conduct; maxim

pre·cep·tor (prē sep′tər) ***n.*** a teacher

pre·cinct (prē′siŋkt′) ***n.*** ⟦< L *prae-,* before + *cingere,* surround⟧ **1** [*usually* *pl.*] an enclosure between buildings, walls, etc. **2** [*pl.*] environs **3** *a*) police district *b*) a subdivision of a voting ward **4** a limited area

pre·ci·os·i·ty (presh′ē äs′ə tē, pres′-) ***n.***, *pl.* **-ties** ⟦see fol.⟧ affectation, esp. in language

pre·cious (presh′əs) ***adj.*** ⟦< L *pretium*, a price⟧ **1** of great price or value; costly **2** beloved; dear **3** very fastidious, affected, etc. —**pre′cious·ly** ***adv.***

precious stone a rare and costly gem: applied to the diamond, emerald, ruby, and sapphire

prec·i·pice (pres′i pis) ***n.*** ⟦< L *prae-*, before + *caput*, a head⟧ a vertical or overhanging rock face

pre·cip·i·tant (prē sip′i tənt) ***adj.*** ⟦see prec.⟧ PRECIPITATE

pre·cip·i·tate (prē sip′ə tāt′; *for adj. & n.*, -tit, -tāt′) ***vt.*** **-tat′ed**, **-tat′ing** ⟦see PRECIPICE⟧ **1** to hurl downward **2** to cause to happen before expected, needed, etc. **3** *Chem.* to separate (a soluble substance) out of a solution —***vi.*** **1** *Chem.* to be precipitated **2** *Meteorol.* to condense and fall as rain, snow, etc. —***adj.*** **1** acting or done hastily or rashly **2** very sudden or abrupt —***n.*** a substance precipitated out of a solution

pre·cip′i·ta′tion (-tā′shən) ***n.*** **1** a headlong fall or rush **2** rash haste; impetuosity **3** a bringing on suddenly **4** *Chem.* a precipitating or being precipitated from a solution **5** *Meteorol.* *a*) rain, snow, etc. *b*) the amount of this

pre·cip′i·tous (-təs) ***adj.*** **1** steep like a precipice **2** rash; impetuous

pré·cis (prā sē′) ***n.***, *pl.* **-cis′** (-sēz′) ⟦Fr: see fol.⟧ a concise abridgment; summary

pre·cise (prē sīs′) ***adj.*** ⟦< L *prae-*, before + *caedere*, to cut⟧ **1** accurately stated; definite **2** minutely exact **3** strict; scrupulous; fastidious —**pre·cise′ly** ***adv.*** —**pre·cise′ness** ***n.***

pre·ci·sion (prē sizh′ən) ***n.*** the quality of being precise; exactness —***adj.*** requiring exactness [*precision* work]

pre·clude (prē klo͞od′) ***vt.*** **-clud′ed**, **-clud′ing** ⟦< L *prae-*, before + *claudere*, to close⟧ to make impossible, esp. in advance; prevent —**pre·clu′sion** (-klo͞o′zhən) ***n.***

pre·co·cious (prē kō′shəs) ***adj.*** ⟦< L *prae-*, before + *coquere*, to cook⟧ matured earlier than usual [a *precocious* child] —**pre·coc′i·ty** (-käs′ə tē) ***n.***

pre·cog·ni·tion (prē′käg nish′ən) ***n.*** ⟦see PRE- & COGNITION⟧ *Parapsychology* the perception of an event, etc. before it occurs, esp. by extrasensory means —**pre·cog′ni·tive** (-nə tiv) ***adj.***

pre-Co·lum·bi·an (prē′kə lum′bē ən) ***adj.*** of any period in the Americas before Columbus's voyages

pre·con·ceive (prē′kən sēv′) ***vt.*** **-ceived′**, **-ceiv′ing** to form (an opinion) in advance —**pre′con·cep′tion** (-sep′shən) ***n.***

pre′con·di′tion (-dish′ən) ***vt.*** to prepare (someone) to behave, react, etc. in a certain way under certain conditions —***n.*** a condition required beforehand if something else is to occur

pre·cur·sor (prē kur′sər, prē′kur′-) ***n.*** ⟦< L *praecurrere*, run ahead⟧ **1** a forerunner **2** a predecessor —**pre·cur′so·ry** ***adj.***

pred·a·to·ry (pred′ə tôr′ē) ***adj.*** ⟦< L *praeda*, a prey⟧ **1** of or living by plundering or robbing **2** preying on other animals —**pred′a·tor** (-tər) ***n.***

pre·de·cease (prē′dē sēs′) ***vt.*** **-ceased′**, **-ceas′ing** to die before (someone else)

pred·e·ces·sor (pred′ə ses′ər) ***n.*** ⟦< L *prae-*, before + *decedere*, go away⟧ a person preceding another, as in office

pre·des·ti·na·tion (prē des′tə nā′shən) ***n.*** **1** *Theol.* the doctrine that *a*) God foreordained everything that would happen *b*) God predestines souls to salvation or to damnation **2** one's destiny

pre·des′tine (-des′tin) ***vt.*** **-tined**, **-tin·ing** to destine beforehand; foreordain

pre′de·ter′mine (-dē tur′min) ***vt.*** **-mined**, **-min·ing** to determine beforehand

pre·dic·a·ment (prē dik′ə mənt) ***n.*** ⟦see PREACH⟧ an unpleasant or embarrassing situation

pred·i·cate (pred′i kāt′; *for n. & adj.*, -kit) ***vt.*** **-cat′ed**, **-cat′ing** ⟦see PREACH⟧ **1** to affirm as a quality or attribute **2** to base (something) *on* or *upon* facts, conditions, etc. —***n.*** *Gram.* the word or words that make a statement about the subject —***adj.*** *Gram.* of a predicate —**pred′i·ca′tion** ***n.***

pre·dict (prē dikt′) ***vt.***, ***vi.*** ⟦< L *prae-*, before + *dicere*, tell⟧ to say in advance (what one believes will happen); foretell —**pre·dict′a·ble** ***adj.*** —**pre·dic′tion** ***n.*** —**pre·dic′tor** ***n.***

pre·di·gest (prē′di jest′, -dī-) ***vt.*** to treat (food) as with enzymes for easier digestion when eaten

pred·i·lec·tion (pred′ə lek′shən, prē′də-) ***n.*** ⟦< L *prae-*, before + *diligere*, prefer⟧ a partiality or preference (*for*)

pre·dis·pose (prē′di spōz′) ***vt.*** **-posed′**, **-pos′ing** to make receptive or susceptible (*to*); incline —**pre′dis·po·si′tion** (-dis pə zish′ən) ***n.***

pre·dom·i·nant (prē däm′ə nənt) ***adj.*** **1** having authority or influence over others; superior **2** most frequent; prevailing —**pre·dom′i·nance** ***n.*** —**pre·dom′i·nant·ly** ***adv.***

pre·dom·i·nate (prē däm′ə nāt′) ***vi.*** **-nat′ed**, **-nat′ing** **1** to have authority or influence (*over* others) **2** to be dominant in amount, number, etc.; prevail

pre·em·i·nent (prē em′ə nənt) ***adj.*** eminent above others; surpassing —**pre·em′i·nence** ***n.*** —**pre·em′i·nent·ly** ***adv.***

pre·empt or **pre-empt′** (prē empt′) ***vt.*** ⟦ult. < L *prae-*, before + *emere*, buy⟧ **1** to gain the right to buy (public land) by settling on it **2** to seize before anyone else can **3** *Radio, TV* to replace (a scheduled program)

pre·emp′tion (-emp′shən) ***n.*** **1** a preempting **2** action taken to check other action beforehand —**pre·emp′tive** ***adj.***

preen (prēn) ***vt.*** ⟦< ME *proinen*, to dress up⟧ **1** to clean and trim (the feathers) with the beak **2** to dress up or adorn (oneself)

pre·ex·ist (prē′eg zist′) ***vt., vi.*** to exist previously or before (another person or thing) —**pre′ex·ist′ence** ***n.***

pref *abbrev.* **1** preface **2** preferred **3** prefix

pre·fab (prē′fab′) ***n.*** [Inf.] a prefabricated building

pre·fab·ri·cate (prē fab′ri kāt′) ***vt.*** **-cat′ed, -cat′ing** to build (a house, etc.) in standardized sections for shipment and quick assembly

pref·ace (pref′is) ***n.*** ⟦< L *prae-*, before + *fari*, speak⟧ an introduction to a book, speech, etc. —***vt.*** **-aced, -ac·ing 1** to furnish with a preface **2** to introduce —**pref′a·to′ry** (-ə tôr′ē) ***adj.***

pre·fect (prē′fekt′) ***n.*** ⟦< L *praeficere*, to set over⟧ any of various administrators —**pre′fec′ture** (-fek′chər) ***n.***

pre·fer (prē fur′, pri-) ***vt.*** **-ferred′, -fer′ring** ⟦< L *prae-*, before + *ferre*, to bear⟧ **1** to put before a court, etc. for consideration **2** to like better

pref·er·a·ble (pref′ər ə bəl) ***adj.*** more desirable —**pref′er·a·bly** ***adv.***

pref′er·ence (-əns) ***n.*** **1** a preferring or being preferred **2** something preferred **3** advantage given to one person, country, etc. over others —**pref′er·en′tial** (-ər en′shəl) ***adj.***

pre·fer·ment (prē fur′mənt) ***n.*** an advancement in rank, etc.; promotion

pre·fig·ure (prē fig′yər) ***vt.*** **-ured, -ur·ing** to suggest beforehand; foreshadow

pre·fix (prē′fiks′; *for v., also* prē fiks′) ***vt.*** ⟦< L *prae-*, before + *figere*, fix⟧ to fix to the beginning of a word, etc.; esp., to add as a prefix —***n.*** a syllable, group of syllables, or word joined to the beginning of another word or a base to alter its meaning

preg·nant (preg′nənt) ***adj.*** ⟦< L *pregnans*⟧ **1** having (an) offspring developing in the uterus; with child **2** mentally fertile; inventive **3** full of meaning, etc. *[a pregnant silence]* **4** filled (*with*); abounding —**preg′nan·cy**, *pl.* **-cies**, ***n.***

pre·hen·sile (prē hen′səl) ***adj.*** ⟦< L *prehendere*, take⟧ adapted for seizing or grasping, esp. by wrapping around something: said as of a monkey's tail

pre·his·tor·ic (prē′his tôr′ik) ***adj.*** of the period before recorded history

pre·ig·ni·tion (prē′ig nish′ən) ***n.*** in an internal-combustion engine, ignition occurring before the intake valve is closed or before the spark plug fires

pre·judge (prē juj′) ***vt.*** **-judged′, -judg′ing** to judge beforehand or without all the evidence —**pre·judg′ment** ***n.***

prej·u·dice (prej′ə dis) ***n.*** ⟦< L *prae-*, before + *judicium*, judgment⟧ **1** a preconceived, usually unfavorable idea **2** an opinion held in disregard of facts that contradict it; bias **3** intolerance or hatred of other races, etc. **4** injury or harm as from some judgment —***vt.*** **-diced, -dic·ing 1** to injure or harm, as by some judgment **2** to cause to have prejudice; bias —**prej′u·di′cial** (-dish′əl) ***adj.***

prel·ate (prel′it) ***n.*** ⟦< L *praelatus*, placed before⟧ a high-ranking member of the clergy, as a bishop —**prel′a·cy**, *pl.* **-cies**, ***n.***

pre·lim·i·nar·y (prē lim′ə ner′ē, pri-) ***adj.*** ⟦< L *prae-*, before + *limen*, threshold⟧ leading up to the main action, discussion, etc.; introductory —***n.***, *pl.* **-ies** [*often pl.*] a preliminary step, procedure, etc.

pre·lit·er·ate (prē lit′ər it) ***adj.*** of a society not having a written language

prel·ude (prel′yōōd′, prā′lōōd′) ***n.*** ⟦< Fr < L *prae-*, before + *ludere*, to play⟧ **1** a preliminary part **2** *Music a)* an introductory instrumental composition, as the overture to an opera *b)* a short, romantic composition

pre·mar·i·tal (prē mar′ət′l) ***adj.*** occurring before marriage

pre·ma·ture (prē′mə toor′, -choor′) ***adj.*** ⟦< L *prae-*, before + *maturus*, ripe⟧ happening, done, arriving, etc. before the proper or usual time; too early —**pre′ma·ture′ly** ***adv.***

pre·med′i·tate′ (-med′ə tāt′) ***vt., vi.*** **-tat′ed, -tat′ing** to think (out) or plan beforehand —**pre·med′i·ta′tion** ***n.***

pre·men·stru·al (prē men′strəl) ***adj.*** occurring before a menstrual period

pre·mier (pri mir′, -myir′) ***adj.*** ⟦Fr < L *primus*, first⟧ first in importance; foremost —***n.*** a chief official; specif., a prime minister —**pre·mier′ship** ***n.***

pre·mière or **pre·miere** (pri mir′, -myer′) ***n.*** ⟦Fr: see prec.⟧ a first performance of a play, movie, etc.

prem·ise (prem′is) ***n.*** ⟦< L *prae-*, before + *mittere*, send⟧ **1** a previous statement serving as a basis for an argument **2** [*pl.*] a piece of real estate —***vt.*** **-ised, -is·ing** to state as a premise

pre·mi·um (prē′mē əm) ***n.***, *pl.* **-ums** ⟦< L *prae-*, before + *emere*, get, buy⟧ **1** a reward or prize, esp. as an inducement to buy **2** an additional amount paid or charged **3** a payment, as for an insurance policy **4** very high value *[to put a premium on wit]* —**at a premium** very valuable because of scarcity

prem·o·ni·tion (prēm′ə nish′ən, prē′ mə-) ***n.*** ⟦< L *prae-*, before + *monere*, warn⟧ **1** a forewarning **2** a foreboding —**pre·mon·i·to·ry** (prē män′i tôr′ē) ***adj.***

pre·na·tal (prē nāt′′l) ***adj.*** before birth

pre·nup·tial (prē nup′shəl) ***adj.*** before a marriage or wedding

pre·oc′cu·pied′ ***adj.*** completely absorbed in one's thoughts; engrossed

pre·oc·cu·py (prē äk′yōō pī′) ***vt.*** **-pied′, -py′ing** ⟦< L *prae-*, before + *occupare*, seize⟧ to wholly occupy the thoughts of; engross —**pre·oc′cu·pa′tion** (-pā′shən) ***n.***

pre·or·dain (prē′ôr dān′) ***vt.*** to ordain or decree beforehand

pre-owned′ ***adj.*** previously owned; used

prep[1] (prep) ***adj.*** *short for* PREPARATORY *[a prep school]* —***vt.*** **prepped, prep′ping** to prepare (a patient) for surgery, etc.

prep[2] *abbrev.* **1** preparatory **2** preposition

pre·pack·age (prē pak′ij) ***vt.*** **-aged, -ag·ing** to package (foods, etc.) in standard units before selling

pre·paid (prē pād′) ***vt.*** *pt. & pp. of* PREPAY

prep·a·ra·tion (prep′ə rā′shən) ***n.*** **1** a preparing or being prepared **2** a preparatory measure **3** something prepared, as a medicine or cosmetic

pre·par·a·to·ry (prē par′ə tôr′ē, prep′ə rə-) ***adj.*** serving to prepare; introductory

preparatory school a private secondary school that prepares students for college

pre·pare (prē par′, pri-) ***vt.*** **-pared′, -par′ing** ⟦< L *prae-*, before + *parare*, get ready⟧ **1** to make ready **2** to equip or furnish **3** to put together *[to prepare dinner]* —***vi.*** **1** to make things ready **2** to make oneself ready

pre·par′ed·ness (-par′id nəs) ***n.*** the state of being prepared, esp. for waging war

pre·pay′ ***vt.*** **-paid′, -pay′ing** to pay or pay for in advance —**pre·pay′ment** ***n.***

pre·pon·der·ate (prē pän′dər āt′, pri-) ***vi.*** **-at′ed, -at′ing** ⟦< L *prae-*, before + *ponderare*, weigh⟧ to be superior in amount, power, etc. —**pre·pon′der·ance** ***n.*** —**pre·pon′der·ant** ***adj.***

prep·o·si·tion (prep′ə zish′ən) ***n.*** ⟦< L *prae-*, before + *ponere*, to place⟧ a word, as *in*, *by*, or *to*, that connects a noun or pronoun to another element of a sentence —**prep′o·si′tion·al** ***adj.***

pre·pos·sess (prē′pə zes′) ***vt.*** to bias, esp. favorably

pre′pos·sess′ing ***adj.*** that impresses favorably

pre·pos·ter·ous (prē päs′tər əs, pri-) ***adj.*** ⟦< L *prae-*, before + *posterus*, following⟧ absurd; ridiculous; laughable

prep·py or **prep·pie** (prep′ē) ***n.***, *pl.* **-pies** a student at or graduate of a preparatory school —***adj.*** **-pi·er, -pi·est** of or like the clothes worn by such students

pre·puce (prē′pyo͞os′) ***n.*** ⟦< L *praeputium*⟧ FORESKIN

pre·re·cord (prē′ri kôrd′) ***vt.*** *Film, Radio, TV* to record (music, a program, etc.) for later use

pre′re·cord′ed ***adj.*** designating or of a magnetic tape, as in a cassette, on which sound, etc. has been recorded before its sale

pre·req·ui·site (prē rek′wə zit, pri-) ***adj.*** required beforehand as a necessary condition —***n.*** something prerequisite

pre·rog·a·tive (prē räg′ə tiv, pri-) ***n.*** ⟦< L *prae-*, before + *rogare*, ask⟧ an exclusive right or privilege

pres *abbrev.* present

Pres *abbrev.* President

pres·age (pres′ij; *for v., usually* prē sāj′, pri-) ***n.*** ⟦< L *prae-*, before + *sagire*, perceive⟧ **1** an omen; portent **2** a foreboding —***vt.*** **-aged′, -ag′ing** to give warning of

pres·by·ter (prez′bi tər) ***n.*** ⟦see PRIEST⟧ **1** in the Presbyterian Church, an elder **2** in the Episcopal Church, a priest

Pres′by·te′ri·an (-tir′ē ən) ***adj.*** designating or of a church of a traditionally Calvinistic Protestant denomination governed by presbyters —***n.*** a member of a Presbyterian church

pre′school′ ***adj.*** of or for a child between infancy and school age —***n.*** a school for very young children, usually those three to five years of age —**pre′school′er** ***n.***

pres·cience (prē′shəns, -shē əns) ***n.*** ⟦< L *prae-*, before + *scire*, know⟧ foreknowledge; foresight —**pres′cient** ***adj.***

pre·scribe (prē skrīb′, pri-) ***vt.*** **-scribed′, -scrib′ing** ⟦< L *prae-*, before + *scribere*, write⟧ **1** to order; direct **2** to order as a medicine or treatment: said as of physicians

pre·script (prē′skript′) ***n.*** a prescribed rule —**pre·scrip′tive** ***adj.***

pre·scrip·tion (prē skrip′shən, pri-) ***n.*** **1** something prescribed **2** *a)* a written direction for the preparation and use of medicine *b)* such a medicine

pres·ence (prez′əns) ***n.*** **1** the fact or state of being present **2** immediate surroundings *[in his presence]* **3** *a)* a person's bearing or appearance *b)* impressive bearing, personality, etc.

presence of mind ability to think and act quickly in an emergency

pres·ent (prez′ənt; *for v.* prē zent′, pri-) ***adj.*** ⟦< L *prae-*, before + *esse*, be⟧ **1** being at the specified place **2** existing or happening now **3** *Gram.* indicating action or state occurring now or action that is always the same *[present tense]* —***n.*** **1** the present time **2** the present tense **3** a gift —***vt.*** **pre·sent′** **1** to introduce (a person) **2** to exhibit; show **3** to offer for consideration **4** to give (a gift, etc.) to a person, etc. —**present arms** to hold a rifle vertically in front of the body

pre·sent·a·ble (prē zent′ə bəl, pri-) ***adj.*** **1** suitable for presentation **2** suitably groomed for meeting people

pres·en·ta·tion (prez′ən tā′shən, prē′zən-) ***n.*** **1** a presenting or being presented **2** something presented

pres′ent-day′ ***adj.*** of the present time

pre·sen·ti·ment (prē zent′ə mənt, pri-) ***n.*** ⟦see PRE- & SENTIMENT⟧ a feeling that something, esp. of an unfortunate nature, is about to take place

pres′ent·ly ***adv.*** **1** soon; shortly **2** at present; now: a usage objected to by some

pre·sent·ment (prē zent′mənt, pri-) ***n.*** presentation

present participle a participle used *a)* to express present or continuing action or existence (Ex.: he is *growing*) *b)* as an adjective (Ex.: a *growing* boy)

pres·er·va·tion·ist (prez′ər vā′shən ist) ***n.*** one who advocates positive measures to preserve historic buildings, wilderness lands, etc.

pre·serv·a·tive (prē zurv′ə tiv, pri-) ***adj.*** preserving —***n.*** anything that preserves *[a preservative added to foods]*

pre·serve (prē zurv′, pri-) ***vt.*** **-served′, -serv′ing** ⟦< L *prae-*, before + *servare*, to keep⟧ **1** to protect from harm, damage, etc. **2** to keep from spoiling **3** to prepare (food), as by canning, for future use **4** to carry on; maintain —***n.*** **1** [*usually pl.*] fruit preserved by cooking with sugar **2** a place where game, fish, etc. are maintained —**pres·er·va·tion** (prez′ər vā′shən) ***n.*** —**pre·serv′er** ***n.***

pre·set (prē set′) ***vt.*** **-set′**, **-set′ting** to set (automatic controls) beforehand

pre·shrink (prē shriŋk′) ***vt.*** **-shrank′** or **-shrunk′**, **-shrunk′** or **-shrunk′en**, **-shrink′ing** to shrink by a special process in manufacture, to minimize further shrinkage in laundering —**pre′shrunk′** ***adj.***

pre·side (prē zīd′, pri-) ***vi.*** **-sid′ed**, **-sid′ing** ⟦< L *prae-*, before + *sedere*, sit⟧ **1** to serve as chairman **2** to have control or authority (*over*)

pres·i·dent (prez′ə dənt) ***n.*** ⟦see prec.⟧ **1** the highest executive officer of a company, club, etc. **2** [*often* **P-**] the chief executive (as in the U.S.), or the nominal head (as in Italy), of a republic —**pres′i·den·cy**, *pl.* **-cies**, ***n.*** —**pres′i·den′tial** (-den′shəl) ***adj.***

press[1] (pres) ***vt.*** ⟦< L *premere*⟧ **1** *a*) to act on with steady force or weight; push against, squeeze, compress, etc. *b*) to push against (a button, key, etc.) as in using an elevator, keyboard, etc. **2** to squeeze (juice, etc.) from **3** to iron (clothes, etc.) **4** to embrace closely **5** to urge persistently; entreat **6** to try to force **7** to emphasize **8** to distress or trouble *[*I'm *pressed* for time*]* **9** to urge on —***vi.*** **1** to exert pressure; apply weight **2** to go forward with determination **3** to crowd —***n.*** **1** pressure, urgency, etc. **2** a crowd **3** a machine for crushing, stamping, etc. **4** *a*) *short for* PRINTING PRESS *b*) a printing establishment *c*) newspapers, magazines, etc., or the persons who write for them *d*) publicity, etc. in newspapers, etc. **5** a closet for storing clothes, etc. —**press′er** ***n.***

press[2] (pres) ***vt.*** ⟦< L *praes*, surety + *stare*, to stand⟧ to force into service, esp. military or naval service

press agent one whose work is to get publicity for a client

press box a place for reporters at sports events, etc.

press conference a group interview granted to media personnel as by a celebrity

press′ing ***adj.*** calling for immediate attention; urgent

press′man (-mən) ***n.***, *pl.* **-men** (-mən) an operator of a printing press

press secretary one whose job is to deal with the news media on behalf of a prominent person

pres·sure (presh′ər) ***n.*** **1** a pressing or being pressed **2** a state of distress **3** a compelling influence *[*social *pressure]* **4** urgent demands; urgency **5** *Physics* force per unit of area exerted upon a surface, etc. —***vt.*** **-sured**, **-sur·ing** to exert pressure on

pressure cooker a container for quick cooking by steam under pressure

pressure group a group trying to influence government through lobbying, propaganda, etc.

pres′sur·ize′ (-īz′) ***vt.*** **-ized′**, **-iz′ing** to keep nearly normal atmosphere pressure inside (an airplane, etc.), as at high altitudes —**pres′sur·i·za′tion** ***n.***

pres·ti·dig·i·ta·tion (pres′tə dij′i tā′shən) ***n.*** ⟦Fr < *preste*, quick + L *digitus*, finger⟧ sleight of hand

pres·tige (pres tēzh′, -tēj′) ***n.*** ⟦< L *praestrigiae*, deceptions⟧ **1** the power to impress or influence **2** reputation based on high achievement, character, etc.

pres·ti′gious (-tij′əs, -tē′jəs) ***adj.*** having or imparting prestige or distinction

pres·to (pres′tō) ***adv.***, ***adj.*** ⟦It, quick⟧ **1** fast or at once **2** *Music* in fast tempo Also written **pres′to**

pre·stressed concrete (prē′strest′) concrete containing tensed steel cables for strength

pre·sume (prē zo͞om′, pri-) ***v.*** **-sumed′**, **-sum′ing** ⟦< L *prae-*, before + *sumere*, take⟧ **1** to dare (to say or do something); venture **2** to take for granted; suppose —***vi.*** to act presumptuously; take liberties —**pre·sum′a·ble** ***adj.*** —**pre·sum′a·bly** ***adv.***

pre·sump·tion (prē zump′shən, pri-) ***n.*** **1** a presuming; specif., *a*) an overstepping of proper bounds *b*) a taking of something for granted **2** the thing presumed **3** a reason for presuming —**pre·sump′tive** ***adj.***

pre·sump′tu·ous (-cho͞o əs) ***adj.*** too bold or forward

pre·sup·pose (prē′sə pōz′) ***vt.*** **-posed′**, **-pos′ing** **1** to suppose or assume beforehand **2** to require or imply as a preceding condition —**pre′sup·po·si′tion** (-sup ə zish′ən) ***n.***

pre·teen (prē′tēn′) ***n.*** a child nearly a teenager

pre·tend (prē tend′, pri-) ***vt.*** ⟦< L *prae-*, before + *tendere*, to stretch⟧ **1** to profess *[*to *pretend* ignorance*]* **2** to feign; simulate *[*to *pretend* anger*]* **3** to make believe *[*to *pretend* to be astronauts*]* —***vi.*** to lay claim (*to*) —**pre·tend′er** ***n.***

pre·tense (prē tens′, pri-; prē′tens′) ***n.*** **1** a claim; pretension **2** a false claim **3** a false show of something **4** a pretending, as at play Brit. sp. **pre·tence′**

pre·ten·sion (prē ten′shən, pri-) ***n.*** **1** a pretext **2** a claim **3** assertion of a claim **4** pretentiousness

pre·ten′tious (-shəs) ***adj.*** **1** making claims to some distinction, importance, etc. **2** affectedly grand; ostentatious —**pre·ten′tious·ly** ***adv.*** —**pre·ten′tious·ness** ***n.***

pret·er·it or **pret·er·ite** (pret′ər it) ***adj.*** ⟦< L *praeter-*, beyond + *ire*, go⟧ *Gram.* expressing past action or state —***n.*** the past tense

pre·term (prē′turm′) ***adj.*** of premature birth

pre·ter·nat·u·ral (prēt′ər nach′ər əl) ***adj.*** ⟦ML *praeternaturalis*⟧ **1** differing from or beyond what is natural; abnormal **2** SUPERNATURAL

pre·test (prē test′) ***vt.***, ***vi.*** to test in advance

pre·text (prē′tekst′) ***n.*** ⟦< L *prae-*, before

+ *texere*, weave⟧ a false reason put forth to hide the real one

Pre·to·ri·a (prē tôr′ē ə) administrative capital of South Africa: pop. 526,000

pret·ti·fy (prit′i fī′) ***vt.*** **-fied′**, **-fy′ing** to make pretty

pret·ty (prit′ē) ***adj.*** **-ti·er**, **-ti·est** ⟦OE *prættig*, crafty⟧ attractive in a dainty, graceful way **—*adv.*** fairly; somewhat **—*vt.*** **-tied**, **-ty·ing** to make pretty: usually with *up* **—pret′ti·ly *adv.*** **—pret′ti·ness *n.***

pret·zel (pret′səl) ***n.*** ⟦< L *brachium*, an arm⟧ a hard, brittle, salted biscuit, often formed in a loose knot

pre·vail (prē vāl′, pri-) ***vi.*** ⟦< L *prae-*, before + *valere*, be strong⟧ **1** to be victorious; triumph: often with *over* or *against* **2** to succeed **3** to be or become more widespread **4** to be prevalent **—prevail on** (or **upon** or **with**) to persuade

pre·vail′ing ***adj.*** **1** superior in strength or influence **2** prevalent

prev·a·lent (prev′ə lənt) ***adj.*** ⟦see PREVAIL⟧ widely existing; generally accepted, used, etc. **—prev′a·lence *n.***

pre·var·i·cate (pri var′i kāt′) ***vi.*** **-cat′ed**, **-cat′ing** ⟦< L *prae-*, before + *varicare*, straddle⟧ **1** to evade the truth **2** to lie **—pre·var′i·ca′tion *n.*** **—pre·var′i·ca′tor *n.***

pre·vent (prē vent′, pri-) ***vt.*** ⟦< L *prae-*, before + *venire*, come⟧ to stop or keep from doing or happening; hinder **—pre·vent′a·ble** or **pre·vent′i·ble *adj.*** **—pre·ven′tion *n.***

pre·ven′tive (-vent′iv) ***adj.*** preventing or serving to prevent **—*n.*** anything that prevents Also **pre·vent′a·tive** (-vent′ə tiv)

pre·view (prē′vyōō′) ***n.*** **1** an advance, restricted showing, as of a movie **2** a showing of scenes from a movie, etc. to advertise it Also sp. **pre′vue′**

pre·vi·ous (prē′vē əs) ***adj.*** ⟦< L *prae-*, before + *via*, a way⟧ occurring before; prior **—previous to** before **—pre′vi·ous·ly *adv.***

pre·war (prē′wôr′) ***adj.*** before a (or the) war

prex·y (prek′sē) ***n.***, *pl.* **-ies** [Slang] the president, esp. of a college, etc.

prey (prā) ***n.*** ⟦< L *prehendere*, seize⟧ **1** an animal hunted for food by another animal **2** a victim **3** the mode of living by preying on other animals *[a bird of prey]* **—*vi.*** **1** to plunder **2** to hunt other animals for food **3** to weigh as an obsession Generally used with *on* or *upon*

pri·ap·ic (prī ap′ik) ***adj.*** ⟦after *Priapos*, Gr god of procreation⟧ overly concerned with masculinity

price (prīs) ***n.*** ⟦< L *pretium*⟧ **1** the amount of money, etc. asked or paid for something; cost **2** value or worth **3** the cost, as in life, labor, etc., of obtaining some benefit **—*vt.*** **priced**, **pric′ing** **1** to fix the price of **2** [Inf.] to find out the price of

price′less ***adj.*** of inestimable value; invaluable

price′y ***adj.*** [Inf.] expensive: also sp. **pri′cy**

prick (prik) ***n.*** ⟦OE *prica*, a point⟧ **1** a tiny puncture made by a sharp point **2** a sharp pain caused as by being pricked **—*vt.*** **1** to make (a hole) in (something) with a sharp point **2** to pain sharply **—prick up one's ears** **1** to raise the ears erect **2** to listen closely

prick·le (prik′əl) ***n.*** ⟦OE *prica*, a point⟧ **1** a small, sharply pointed growth, as a thorn: also **prick′er** **2** a tingling sensation **—*vt.*, *vi.*** **-led**, **-ling** to tingle **—prick′ly**, **-li·er**, **-li·est**, ***adj.***

prickly heat a skin eruption caused by inflammation of the sweat glands

pride (prīd) ***n.*** ⟦< OE *prut*, proud⟧ **1** *a)* an unduly high opinion of oneself *b)* haughtiness; arrogance **2** dignity and self-respect **3** satisfaction in something done, owned, etc. **4** a person or thing in which pride is taken **—pride oneself on** to be proud of **—pride′ful *adj.*** **—pride′ful·ly *adv.***

pri·er (prī′ər) ***n.*** one who pries

priest (prēst) ***n.*** ⟦< Gr *presbys*, old⟧ **1** a person of special rank who performs religious rites in a temple of God or a god **2** *R.C.Ch.* a clergyman ranking next below a bishop **—priest′hood′ *n.*** **—priest′ly**, **-li·er**, **-li·est**, ***adj.***

priest·ess (prēs′tis) ***n.*** a pagan female priest

prig (prig) ***n.*** ⟦< 16th-c. cant⟧ one who smugly affects great propriety or morality **—prig′gish *adj.***

prim (prim) ***adj.*** **prim′mer**, **prim′mest** ⟦< ?⟧ stiffly formal, precise, or moral **—prim′ly *adv.***

pri·ma·cy (prī′mə sē) ***n.***, *pl.* **-cies** ⟦< L *primus*, first⟧ **1** a being first in time, rank, etc.; supremacy **2** the rank or office of a primate

pri·ma don·na (prē′mə dän′ə, prim′ə) *pl.* **pri′ma don′nas** ⟦It, lit., first lady⟧ the principal woman singer in an opera

pri·ma fa·ci·e (prī′mə fā′shə) ⟦L, lit., at first sight⟧ **1** self-evident **2** *Law* designating evidence that establishes a fact unless refuted

pri·mal (prī′məl) ***adj.*** ⟦< L *primus*, first⟧ **1** first in time; original **2** first in importance; chief **3** fundamental; basic *[primal instincts]*

pri·mar·i·ly (prī mer′ə lē) ***adv.*** **1** at first; originally **2** mainly; principally

pri·mar·y (prī′mer′ē) ***adj.*** ⟦< L *primus*, first⟧ **1** first in time or order; original **2** from which others are derived; fundamental *[primary colors]* **3** first in importance; chief **—*n.***, *pl.* **-ries** **1** something first in order, importance, etc. **2** a preliminary election at which candidates are chosen for the final election

primary school **1** ELEMENTARY SCHOOL **2** a school including the first three elementary grades and, sometimes, kindergarten

primary stress (or **accent**) the heaviest stress (′) in pronouncing a word

pri·mate (prī′mit; *for 2*, -māt′) ***n.*** ⟦< L *primus*, first⟧ **1** an archbishop, or the highest-ranking bishop in a province, etc. **2** any of the order of mammals that includes humans, the apes, etc.

prime (prīm) ***adj.*** ⟦< L *primus*, first⟧ **1** first in time; original **2** first in rank or importance; chief; principal **3** first in quality **4** fundamental **5** *Math.* that can be evenly divided by no other whole number than itself and 1 —***n.*** **1** the first or earliest part **2** the best or most vigorous period **3** the best part —***vt.*** **primed, prim′ing** **1** to make ready; prepare **2** to get (a pump) into operation by pouring water into it **3** to undercoat, size, etc. before painting **4** to provide with facts, answers, etc. beforehand

prime meridian the meridian at Greenwich, England, from which longitude is measured east and west

prime minister in some countries, the chief executive of the government

prim·er[1] (prim′ər) ***n.*** ⟦< L *primus*, first⟧ **1** a simple book for teaching reading **2** any elementary textbook

prim·er[2] (prī′mər) ***n.*** a thing that primes; specif., *a*) an explosive cap, etc. used to set off a main charge *b*) a preliminary coat of paint, etc.

prime rate the most favorable interest rate charged on bank loans to large corporations: also **prime interest rate** or **prime lending rate**

prime time *Radio, TV* the hours when the largest audience is available

pri·me·val (prī mē′vəl) ***adj.*** ⟦< L *primus*, first + *aevum*, an age⟧ of the earliest times or ages; primordial

prim·i·tive (prim′i tiv) ***adj.*** ⟦< L *primus*, first⟧ **1** of the earliest times; original **2** crude; simple **3** primary; basic —***n.*** a primitive person or thing

pri·mo·gen·i·ture (prī′mə jen′i chər) ***n.*** ⟦< L *primus*, first + *genitura*, a begetting⟧ the exclusive right of inheritance of the eldest son

pri·mor·di·al (prī môr′dē əl) ***adj.*** ⟦< L *primus*, first + *ordiri*, begin⟧ primitive; fundamental

primp (primp) ***vt., vi.*** ⟦prob. < PRIM⟧ to groom or dress up in a fussy way

prim·rose (prim′rōz′) ***n.*** ⟦altered (after *rose*) < ML *primula*⟧ a plant with tubelike, often yellow flowers

primrose path **1** the path of pleasure, self-indulgence, etc. **2** a course of action that seems easy but that can lead to disaster

prince (prins) ***n.*** ⟦< L *princeps*, chief⟧ **1** a ruler ranking below a king; head of a principality **2** a son of a sovereign **3** any preeminent person

prince consort the husband of a reigning queen

Prince Edward Island island province of SE Canada: 2,185 sq. mi.; pop. 135,000; cap. Charlottetown: abbrev. *PE*

prince′ly ***adj.*** **-li·er, -li·est** **1** of a prince **2** magnificent; generous —**prince′li·ness** ***n.***

prin·cess (prin′sis, -ses′) ***n.*** **1** a daughter of a sovereign **2** the wife of a prince

prin·ci·pal (prin′sə pəl) ***adj.*** ⟦see PRINCE⟧ first in rank, importance, etc. —***n.*** **1** a principal person or thing **2** the head of a school **3** the amount of a loan, on which interest is computed —**prin′ci·pal·ly *adv.***

prin′ci·pal′i·ty (-pal′ə tē) ***n., pl.*** **-ties** the territory ruled by a prince

principal parts the principal inflected forms of a verb: in English, the infinitive, past tense, and past participle (Ex: *drink, drank, drunk*)

prin·ci·ple (prin′sə pəl) ***n.*** ⟦see PRINCE⟧ **1** a fundamental truth, law, etc. upon which others are based **2** *a*) a rule of conduct *b*) adherence to such rules; integrity **3** a basic part **4** *a*) the scientific law explaining a natural action *b*) the method of a thing's operation

prin′ci·pled ***adj.*** having principles, as of conduct

print (print) ***n.*** ⟦< L *premere*, to press⟧ **1** a mark made on a surface by pressing or stamping **2** cloth printed with a design **3** the impression of letters, designs, etc. made by inked type or from a plate, block, etc. **4** a photograph, esp. one made from a negative —***vt., vi.*** **1** to stamp (a mark, letter, etc.) on a surface **2** to produce on (paper, etc.) the impression of inked type, etc. **3** to produce (a book, etc.) **4** to write in letters resembling printed ones **5** to make (a photographic print) —**in** (or **out of**) **print** still (or no longer) being sold by the publisher: said of books, etc. —**print′er** ***n.***

printed circuit an electrical circuit of conductive material, as in fine lines, applied to an insulating sheet

print′ing ***n.*** **1** the act of one that prints **2** something printed **3** all the copies printed at one time

printing press a machine for printing from inked type, plates, or rolls

print′out′ ***n.*** the printed or typewritten output of a computer

pri·or (prī′ər) ***adj.*** ⟦L⟧ **1** earlier; previous **2** preceding in order or importance —***n.*** the head of a priory —**prior to** before in time

pri′or·ess (-is) ***n.*** a woman who heads a priory of nuns

pri·or·i·tize (prī ôr′ə tīz′) ***vt.*** **-tized′, -tiz′ing** to arrange (items) in order of importance

pri·or·i·ty (prī ôr′ə tē) ***n., pl.*** **-ties** **1** a being prior; precedence **2** a prior right to get, buy, or do something **3** something to be given prior attention

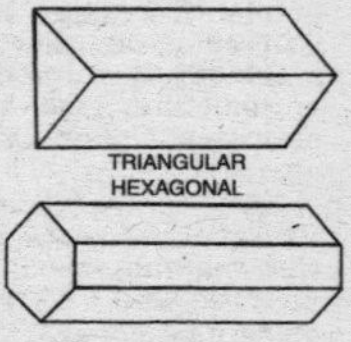

pri·o·ry (prī′ə rē) ***n., pl.*** **-ries** a monastery governed by a prior, or a convent governed by a prioress

TRIANGULAR

HEXAGONAL

PRISMS

prism (priz′əm) ***n.*** ⟦< Gr *prizein*, to saw⟧ **1** *Geom.* a solid figure whose ends are parallel and equal in size and shape, and whose sides are parallelograms **2** a transparent, triangular prism used to disperse light into the spectrum —**pris·mat·ic** (priz mat′ik) ***adj.***

pris·on (priz′ən) ***n.*** ⟦< L *prehendere*,

take] a place of confinement for convicted criminals or persons who are awaiting trial

prison camp 1 a camp with minimum security for holding reliable prisoners 2 a camp for confining prisoners of war

pris'on·er ***n.*** one held captive or confined, esp. in prison

pris·sy (pris'ē) ***adj.*** **-si·er, -si·est** [prob. PR(IM) + (S)ISSY] [Inf.] very prim or prudish —**pris'si·ness** ***n.***

pris·tine (pris'tēn', pris tēn') ***adj.*** [L *pristinus*, former] 1 characteristic of the earliest period 2 unspoiled

prith·ee (pri*th*'ē) ***interj.*** [< *pray thee*] [Archaic] I pray thee; please

pri·va·cy (prī'və sē) ***n.***, *pl.* **-cies** 1 a being private; seclusion 2 secrecy 3 one's private life

pri·vate (prī'vət) ***adj.*** [< L *privus*, separate] 1 of or concerning a particular person or group 2 not open to or controlled by the public *[a private school]* 3 for an individual person *[a private room]* 4 not holding public office *[a private citizen]* 5 secret *[a private matter]* —***n.*** 1 [*pl.*] the genitals: also **private parts** 2 the lowest-ranking enlisted man of either the U.S. Army or Marine Corps —**go private** to restore private corporate ownership by buying back publicly held stock —**in private** not publicly —**pri'vate·ly** ***adv.***

pri·va·teer (prī'və tir') ***n.*** 1 a privately owned ship commissioned in war to capture enemy ships 2 a commander or crew member of a privateer

private eye [Slang] a private detective

pri·va·tion (prī vā'shən) ***n.*** the lack of ordinary necessities or comforts

pri·va·tize (prī'və tīz') ***vt.*** **-tized', -tiz'ing** to turn over (a public property, etc.) to private interests —**pri'va·ti'za'tion** ***n.***

priv·et (priv'it) ***n.*** [< ?] an evergreen shrub used for hedges

priv·i·lege (priv'ə lij, priv'lij) ***n.*** [< L *privus*, separate + *lex*, law] a special right, favor, etc. granted to some person or group —***vt.*** **-leged, -leg·ing** to grant a privilege to

priv·y (priv'ē) ***adj.*** private: now only in such phrases as **privy council**, a body of confidential advisers named by a ruler —***n.***, *pl.* **priv'ies** an outhouse —**privy to** privately informed about

prize[1] (prīz) ***vt.*** **prized, priz'ing** [see PRICE] to value highly; esteem —***n.*** 1 something given to the winner of a contest, etc. 2 anything worth striving for —***adj.*** 1 that has won or is worthy of a prize 2 given as a prize

prize[2] (prīz) ***n.*** [< L *prehendere*, to take] something taken by force, esp. a captured ship —***vt.*** **prized, priz'ing** to pry, as with a lever

prize'fight' ***n.*** a professional boxing match —**prize'fight'er** ***n.***

pro[1] (prō) ***adv.*** [L, for] favorably —***adj.*** favorable —***n.***, *pl.* **pros** 1 a person or vote on the affirmative side 2 an argument in favor of something

pro[2] (prō) ***adj.***, ***n.***, *pl.* **pros** *short for* PROFESSIONAL

pro-[1] [Gr < *pro*, before] *prefix* before in place or time

pro-[2] [L < *pro*, forward] *prefix* 1 moving forward or ahead of *[proclivity]* 2 forth *[produce]* 3 substituting for *[pronoun]* 4 defending, supporting *[prolabor]*

pro-am (prō'am') ***n.*** a sports competition for both amateurs and professionals

prob *abbrev.* 1 probably 2 problem

prob·a·bil·i·ty (präb'ə bil'ə tē) ***n.***, *pl.* **-ties** 1 a being probable; likelihood 2 something probable

prob·a·ble (präb'ə bəl) ***adj.*** [< L *probare*, prove] 1 likely to occur or be 2 reasonably so, but not proved —**prob'a·bly** ***adv.***

pro·bate (prō'bāt') ***n.*** [see PROBE] the act or process of probating —***adj.*** having to do with probating *[probate court]* —***vt.*** **-bat'ed, -bat'ing** to establish officially that (a document, esp. a will) is genuine

pro·ba·tion (prō bā'shən) ***n.*** [see PROBE] 1 a testing, as of one's character, ability, etc. 2 the conditional suspension of a convicted person's sentence —**pro·ba'tion·ar'y** ***adj.***

pro·ba'tion·er ***n.*** a person on probation

probation officer an officer who watches over persons on probation

probe (prōb) ***n.*** [< L *probare*, to test] 1 a surgical instrument for exploring a wound, etc. 2 a searching examination 3 a device, as a spacecraft with instruments, used to get information about an environment —***vt.*** **probed, prob'ing** 1 to explore (a wound, etc.) with a probe 2 to investigate thoroughly —***vi.*** to search

pro·bi·ty (prō'bə tē, präb'ə-) ***n.*** [< L *probus*, good] honesty; integrity

prob·lem (präb'ləm) ***n.*** [< Gr *problēma*] 1 a question proposed for solution 2 a perplexing or difficult matter, person, etc.

prob·lem·at·ic (präb'lə mat'ik) ***adj.*** 1 hard to solve 2 uncertain Also **prob'lem·at'i·cal**

pro·bos·cis (prō bäs'is) ***n.***, *pl.* **-cis·es** [< Gr *pro-*, before + *boskein*, to feed] an elephant's trunk, or any similar long, flexible snout

pro·caine (prō'kān') ***n.*** [PRO-[2] + (CO)CAINE] a synthetic compound used as a local anesthetic

pro·ce·dure (prō sē'jər, prə-) ***n.*** the act or method of proceeding in an action —**pro·ce'dur·al** ***adj.***

pro·ceed (prō sēd', prə-) ***vi.*** [< L *pro-*, forward + *cedere*, go] 1 to go on, esp. after stopping 2 to carry on some action 3 to take legal action (*against*) 4 to come forth or issue (*from*)

pro·ceed'ing ***n.*** 1 a going on with what one has been doing 2 a course of action 3 [*pl.*] a record of the business carried on, as by a learned society 4 [*pl.*] legal action

pro·ceeds (prō'sēdz') ***pl.n.*** the sum derived from a sale, business venture, etc.

proc·ess (prä'ses') ***n.*** [see PROCEED] 1

the course of being done: chiefly in **in process** **2** course (*of* time, etc.) **3** a continuing development involving many changes *[*the *process* of digestion*]* **4** a method of doing something, with all the steps involved **5** *Biol.* a projecting part **6** *Law* a court summons **—*vt.*** to prepare by or subject to a special process **—pro′cess·or *n.***

pro·ces·sion (prō sesh′ən, prə-) ***n.*** ⟦see PROCEED⟧ a number of persons or things moving forward, as in a parade

pro·ces′sion·al *n.* a hymn sung at the beginning of a church service during the entrance of the clergy

pro′-choice′ *adj.* advocating the legal right to obtain an abortion **—pro′-choic′er *n.***

pro·claim (prō klām′) ***vt.*** ⟦< L *pro-*, before + *clamare*, cry out⟧ to announce officially; announce to be

proc·la·ma·tion (präk′lə mā′shən) ***n.*** **1** a proclaiming **2** something that is proclaimed

pro·cliv·i·ty (prō kliv′ə tē) ***n.***, *pl.* **-ties** ⟦< L *pro-*, before + *clivus*, a slope⟧ a tendency or inclination

pro·cras·ti·nate (prō kras′tə nāt′) ***vi.***, ***vt.*** **-nat′ed, -nat′ing** ⟦< L *pro-*, forward + *cras*, tomorrow⟧ to put off doing (something) until later; delay **—pro·cras′ti·na′tion *n.* —pro·cras′ti·na′tor *n.***

pro·cre·ate (prō′krē āt′) ***vt.***, ***vi.*** **-at′ed, -at′ing** ⟦< L *pro-*, before + *creare*, create⟧ to produce (young); beget (offspring) **—pro′cre·a′tion *n.***

proc·tor (präk′tər) ***n.*** ⟦see PROCURE⟧ one who supervises students, as at an examination **—*vt.*** to supervise (an academic examination)

proc·u·ra·tor (präk′yo͞o rāt′ər) ***n.*** ⟦see fol.⟧ in the Roman Empire, the governor of a lesser province

pro·cure (prō kyoor′) ***vt.*** **-cured′, -cur′ing** ⟦< L *pro-*, before + *curare*, attend to⟧ to obtain; get **—pro·cur′a·ble *adj.* —pro·cure′ment *n.***

pro·cur′er *n.* a pimp

prod (präd) ***vt.*** **prod′ded, prod′ding** ⟦< ?⟧ **1** to jab as with a pointed stick **2** to goad into action **—*n.*** **1** a jab or thrust **2** something that prods

prod·i·gal (präd′i gəl) ***adj.*** ⟦< L *pro-*, forth + *agere*, to drive⟧ **1** exceedingly or recklessly wasteful **2** extremely abundant **—*n.*** a spendthrift **—prod′i·gal′i·ty** (-gal′ə tē), *pl.* **-ties, *n.***

pro·di·gious (prō dij′əs, prə-) ***adj.*** ⟦see fol.⟧ **1** wonderful; amazing **2** enormous; huge **—pro·di′gious·ly *adv.***

prod·i·gy (präd′ə jē) ***n.***, *pl.* **-gies** ⟦< L *prodigium*, omen⟧ an extraordinary person, thing, or act; specif., a child of genius

pro·duce (prə do͞os′; *for n.* prō′do͞os′) ***vt.*** **-duced′, -duc′ing** ⟦< L *pro-*, forward + *ducere*, to lead⟧ **1** to bring to view; show *[*to *produce* identification*]* **2** to bring forth; bear **3** to make or manufacture **4** to cause **5** to get (a play, etc.) ready for presentation **—*vi.*** to yield something **—*n.*** something produced; esp., fruit and vegetables **—pro·duc′er *n.***

prod·uct (präd′əkt) ***n.*** **1** something produced by nature, industry, or art **2** result; outgrowth **3** *Math.* the quantity obtained by multiplying two or more quantities together

pro·duc·tion (prə duk′shən) ***n.*** a producing or something produced

pro·duc′tive *adj.* **1** fertile **2** marked by abundant production **3** bringing as a result (with *of*) *[*war is *productive* of misery*]* **—pro·duc′tive·ly *adv.* —pro·duc·tiv·i·ty** (prō′dək tiv′ə tē) or **pro·duc′tive·ness *n.***

prof (präf) ***n.*** [Inf.] *short for* PROFESSOR

Prof *abbrev.* Professor

pro·fane (prō fān′) ***adj.*** ⟦< L *pro-*, before + *fanum*, temple⟧ **1** not connected with religion; secular **2** showing disrespect or contempt for sacred things **—*vt.*** **-faned′, -fan′ing** **1** to treat (sacred things) with irreverence or contempt **2** to debase; defile **—prof·a·na·tion** (präf′ə nā′shən) ***n.* —pro·fane′ly *adv.* —pro·fane′ness *n.***

pro·fan′i·ty (-fan′ə tē) ***n.*** **1** a being profane **2** *pl.* **-ties** profane language; swearing

pro·fess (prō fes′, prə-) ***vt.*** ⟦< L *pro-*, before + *fateri*, avow⟧ **1** to declare openly; affirm **2** to claim to have (some feeling, etc.): often insincerely **3** to declare one's belief in **—pro·fessed′ *adj.***

pro·fes·sion (prō fesh′ən, prə-) ***n.*** **1** a professing, or declaring; avowal **2** an occupation requiring advanced academic training, as medicine, law, etc. **3** all the persons in such an occupation

pro·fes′sion·al *adj.* **1** of or engaged in a profession **2** engaged in some sport or in a specified occupation for pay **—*n.*** a person who is professional **—pro·fes′sion·al·ly *adv.***

pro·fes·sor (prō fes′ər, prə-) ***n.*** a college or university teacher, esp. one of the highest rank **—pro·fes·so·ri·al** (prō′fə sôr′ē əl, prä′-) ***adj.* —pro·fes′sor·ship′ *n.***

prof·fer (präf′ər) ***vt.*** ⟦< OFr: see PRO-[2] & OFFER⟧ to offer (usually something intangible) *[*to *proffer* friendship*]* **—*n.*** an offer

pro·fi·cient (prō fish′ənt, prə-) ***adj.*** ⟦< L *pro-*, forward + *facere*, make⟧ highly competent; skilled **—pro·fi′cien·cy *n.* —pro·fi′cient·ly *adv.***

pro·file (prō′fīl′) ***n.*** ⟦< It *profilare*, to outline⟧ **1** a side view of the face **2** a drawing of this **3** an outline **4** a short, vivid biography **5** a degree of public exposure *[*keeping a low *profile]* **—*vt.*** **1** to draw or write a profile **2** to identify by profiling

pro′fil′ing *n.* the use of a set of characteristics to identify those likely to belong to a certain group, as in detaining suspected criminals

prof·it (präf′it) ***n.*** ⟦see PROFICIENT⟧ **1** advantage; gain **2** [*often pl.*] financial gain; esp. the sum remaining after deducting costs **—*vt.***, ***vi.*** **1** to be of advantage (to) **2** to benefit **—prof′it·a·bil′i·ty *n.* —prof′it·a·ble *adj.* —prof′it·a·bly *adv.* —prof′it·less *adj.***

prof·it·eer (präf′i tir′) ***n.*** one who makes excessive profits by charging exorbitant prices —*vi.* to be a profiteer

pro·fi·te·role (prə fit′ə rōl′) *n.* a small cream puff

prof·li·gate (präf′li git) *adj.* ⟦< L *pro-*, forward + *fligere*, to drive⟧ 1 dissolute 2 recklessly wasteful —**prof′li·ga·cy** (-gə sē) *n.*

pro for·ma (prō fôr′mə) ⟦L⟧ for (the sake of) form; as a matter of form

pro·found (prō found′, prə-) *adj.* ⟦< L *pro-*, forward + *fundus*, bottom⟧ 1 marked by intellectual depth 2 deeply felt *[profound* grief*]* 3 thoroughgoing *[profound* changes*]* —**pro·found′ly** *adv.* —**pro·fun′di·ty** (-fun′də tē), *pl.* **-ties**, *n.*

pro·fuse (prō fyo͞os′, prə-) *adj.* ⟦< L *pro-*, forth + *fundere*, pour⟧ giving or given freely and abundantly —**pro·fuse′ly** *adv.* —**pro·fu′sion** (-fyo͞o′zhən) *n.*

pro·gen·i·tor (prō jen′ə tər) *n.* ⟦< L *pro-*, forth + *gignere*, beget⟧ 1 an ancestor in direct line 2 a precursor

prog·e·ny (präj′ə nē) *n.*, *pl.* **-nies** ⟦see prec.⟧ children; offspring

pro·ges·ter·one (prō jes′tər ōn′) *n.* a female hormone secreted by the ovary or made synthetically

prog·na·thous (präg′nə thəs) *adj.* ⟦PRO-[1] + Gr *gnathos*, jaw⟧ having the jaws projecting beyond the upper face

prog·no·sis (präg nō′sis) *n.*, *pl.* **-no′ses′** (-sēz′) ⟦< Gr *pro-*, before + *gignōskein*, know⟧ a prediction, esp. of the course of a disease

prog′nos′tic (-näs′tik) *adj.* ⟦see prec.⟧ 1 foretelling 2 of a medical prognosis

prog·nos′ti·cate′ (-näs′ti kāt′) *vt.* **-cat′ed**, **-cat′ing** ⟦see PROGNOSIS⟧ to foretell —**prog·nos′ti·ca′tion** *n.* —**prog·nos′ti·ca′tor** *n.*

pro·gram (prō′gram′, -grəm) *n.* ⟦< Gr *pro-*, before + *graphein*, write⟧ 1 a list of the acts, speeches, musical pieces, etc. as of an entertainment 2 a plan or procedure 3 a scheduled radio or TV broadcast 4 a logical sequence of coded instructions specifying the operations to be performed by a computer 5 a series of operations used to control an electronic device —*vt.* **-grammed′** or **-gramed′**, **-gram′ming** or **-gram′ing** 1 to schedule in a program 2 to prepare (a textbook, etc.) for use in programmed instruction 3 to plan a computer program for 4 to furnish (a computer) with a program Also [Chiefly Brit.] **pro′gramme′** —**pro·gram·ma·ble** (prō′ gram′ə bəl, prō gram′-) *adj.*, *n.* —**pro′gram′mer** or **pro′gram′er** *n.*

pro·gram·mat·ic (prō′grə mat′ik) *adj.* of or like a program; often, specif., predictable, mechanical, uninspired, etc.

programmed instruction instruction in which individual students answer questions about a unit of study at their own rate, checking their own answers and advancing only after answering correctly

prog·ress (präg′res; *for v.* prō gres′, prə-) *n.* ⟦< L *pro-*, before + *gradi*, to step⟧ 1 a moving forward or onward 2 development 3 improvement —*vi.* 1 to move forward or onward 2 to move forward toward completion 3 to improve

pro·gres·sion (prō gresh′ən, prə-) *n.* 1 a moving forward 2 a succession, as of events 3 *Math.* a series of numbers, each of which is obtained from its predecessor by the same rule

pro·gres′sive (-gres′iv, prə-) *adj.* 1 moving forward 2 continuing by successive steps 3 of or favoring progress, reform, etc. 4 *Gram.* indicating continuing action or state, as certain verb forms —*n.* one who is progressive —**pro·gres′sive·ly** *adv.*

pro·hib·it (prō hib′it, prə-) *vt.* ⟦< L *pro-*, before + *habere*, have⟧ 1 to forbid by law or an order 2 to prevent; hinder —**pro·hib′i·tive** *adj.*

pro·hi·bi·tion (prō′i bish′ən) *n.* 1 a prohibiting 2 the forbidding by law of the manufacture or sale of alcoholic beverages —**pro′hi·bi′tion·ist** *n.*

proj·ect (prä′jekt′; *for v.* prō jekt′, prə-) *n.* ⟦< L *pro-*, before + *jacere*, to throw⟧ 1 a proposal; scheme 2 an organized undertaking —*vt.* **pro·ject′** 1 to propose (a plan) 2 to throw forward 3 to cause to jut out 4 to cause (a shadow, image, etc.) to fall upon a surface —*vi.* to jut out —**pro·jec′tion** *n.*

pro·jec·tile (prō jek′təl, prə-) *n.* 1 an object designed to be shot forward, as a bullet 2 anything thrown or hurled forward

projection booth a small chamber, as in a theater, from which images on film, slides, etc. are projected

pro·jec′tion·ist *n.* the operator of a film or slide projector

pro·jec′tor *n.* a machine for projecting images onto a screen

pro·lapse (prō laps′, prō′laps′) *n.* ⟦L *pro-*, forward + *labi*, to fall⟧ *Med.* the slipping out of place of an internal organ: said as of the uterus

pro·le·tar·i·at (prō′lə ter′ē ət) *n.* ⟦< L *proletarius*, a citizen of the lowest class⟧ the working class; esp., the industrial working class —**pro′le·tar′i·an** *adj.*, *n.*

pro′-life′ *adj.* opposing the legal right to abortion —**pro′-lif′er** *n.*

pro·lif·er·ate (prō lif′ər āt′, prə-) *vi.* **-at′ed**, **-at′ing** ⟦ult. < L *proles*, offspring + *ferre*, to bear⟧ to increase rapidly —**pro·lif′er·a′tion** *n.*

pro·lif·ic (prō lif′ik, prə-) *adj.* ⟦< L *proles*, offspring + *facere*, make⟧ 1 producing many young or much fruit 2 turning out many products of the mind —**pro·lif′i·cal·ly** *adv.*

pro·lix (prō liks′, prō′liks′) *adj.* ⟦< L *prolixus*, extended⟧ wordy or long-winded —**pro·lix′i·ty** *n.*

pro·logue (prō′lôg′) *n.* ⟦< Gr *pro-*, before + *logos*, discourse⟧ 1 an introduction to a poem, play, etc. 2 any preliminary act, event, etc.

pro·long (prō lôŋ′, prə-) *vt.* ⟦< L *pro-*, forth + *longus*, long⟧ to lengthen in time or space: also **pro·lon′gate′** (-gāt′), **-gat′ed**, **-gat′ing** —**pro·lon·ga·tion** (prō′ lôŋ gā′shən) *n.*

prom (präm) *n.* ⟦< fol.⟧ a dance, as of a particular class in a school

prom·e·nade (präm′ə nād′, -näd′) *n.*

⟦Fr < L *pro-*, forth + *minare*, to herd⟧ **1** a leisurely walk taken for pleasure, display, etc. **2** a public place for walking —***vi.***, ***vt.*** **-nad′ed, -nad′ing** to take a promenade (along or through)

Pro·me·the·us (prō mē′thē əs) ***n.*** *Gr. Myth.* a Titan who steals fire from heaven for the benefit of human beings

prom·i·nent (präm′ə nənt) ***adj.*** ⟦< L *prominere*, to project⟧ **1** sticking out; projecting **2** noticeable; conspicuous **3** widely and favorably known —**prom′i·nence** ***n.*** —**prom′i·nent·ly** ***adv.***

pro·mis·cu·ous (prō mis′kyōō əs, prə-) ***adj.*** ⟦< L *pro-*, forth + *miscere*, to mix⟧ **1** consisting of different elements indiscriminately mingled **2** characterized by a lack of discrimination, esp. in sexual liaisons —**prom·is·cu·i·ty** (präm′is kyōō′ ə tē), *pl.* **-ties**, ***n.*** —**pro·mis′cu·ous·ly** ***adv.***

prom·ise (präm′is) ***n.*** ⟦< L *pro-*, forth + *mittere*, send⟧ **1** an agreement to do or not to do something **2** indication, as of a successful future **3** something promised —***vi.***, ***vt.*** **-ised, -is·ing** **1** to make a promise of (something) **2** to give a basis for expecting (something)

Promised Land *Bible* Canaan, promised by God to Abraham and his descendants: Genesis 17:8

prom·is·so·ry (präm′i sôr′ē) ***adj.*** containing a promise

pro·mo (prō′mō) [Inf.] ***adj.*** of or engaged in the promotion or advertising of a product, etc. —***n.***, *pl.* **-mos** a recorded announcement, radio or TV commercial, etc. used in advertising, etc.

prom·on·to·ry (präm′ən tôr′ē) ***n.***, *pl.* **-ries** ⟦prob. < L *prominere*, to project⟧ a peak of high land that juts out into a body of water; headland

pro·mote (prə ōt′) ***vt.*** **-mot′ed, -mot′ing** ⟦< L *pro-*, forward + *movere*, to move⟧ **1** to raise to a higher position or rank **2** to further the growth, establishment, sales, etc. of —**pro·mo′tion** ***n.*** —**pro·mo′tion·al** ***adj.***

pro·mot′er ***n.*** one who begins, organizes, and furthers an undertaking

prompt (prämpt) ***adj.*** ⟦< L *pro-*, forth + *emere*, take⟧ **1** ready, punctual, etc. **2** done, spoken, etc. without delay —***vt.*** **1** to urge into action **2** to remind (a person) of something he or she has forgotten; specif., to help (an actor, etc.) with a cue **3** to inspire —**prompt′er** ***n.*** —**prompt′ly** ***adv.*** —**prompt′ness** or **promp′ti·tude′** ***n.***

prom·ul·gate (präm′əl gāt′, prō mul′ gāt′) ***vt.*** **-gat′ed, -gat′ing** ⟦< L *promulgare*, publish⟧ **1** to make known officially **2** to make widespread —**prom′ul·ga′tion** ***n.***

pron *abbrev.* **1** pronoun **2** pronunciation

prone (prōn) ***adj.*** ⟦< L *pronus*⟧ **1** lying face downward or prostrate **2** disposed or inclined (*to*) *[prone* to error*]*

prong (prôŋ) ***n.*** ⟦ME *pronge*⟧ **1** any of the pointed ends of a fork; tine **2** any projecting part —**pronged** ***adj.***

prong′horn′ ***n.*** an animal of the W U.S. having curved horns and resembling both the deer and the antelope

pro·noun (prō′noun′) ***n.*** ⟦< L *pro*, for + *nomen*, noun⟧ *Gram.* a word used in place of a noun (Ex.: *I, he, them, ours, which, yourself, anyone*) —**pro·nom′i·nal** (-näm′i nəl) ***adj.***

pro·nounce (prə nouns′, prō-) ***vt.*** **-nounced′, -nounc′ing** ⟦< L *pro-*, before + *nuntiare*, announce⟧ **1** to declare officially, solemnly, etc. **2** to utter or articulate (a sound or word) —**pro·nounce′a·ble** ***adj.***

pro·nounced′ ***adj.*** clearly marked; decided *[a pronounced* change*]*

pro·nounce′ment ***n.*** a formal statement, as of an opinion

pron·to (prän′tō) ***adv.*** ⟦Sp: see PROMPT⟧ [Slang] at once; quickly

pro·nun·ci·a·tion (prə nun′sē ā′shən, prō-) ***n.*** **1** the act or manner of pronouncing words **2** an accepted way of pronouncing a word; also, a rendering of this in symbols

proof (prōōf) ***n.*** ⟦see PROBE⟧ **1** a proving or testing of something **2** evidence that establishes the truth of something **3** the relative strength of an alcoholic liquor **4** *Photog.* a trial print of a negative **5** a sheet printed from set type, for checking errors, etc. —***adj.*** of tested strength in resisting: with *against*

-proof (prōōf) ⟦< prec.⟧ *combining form* **1** impervious to *[waterproof]* **2** protected from *[rustproof]* **3** resistant to *[fireproof]*

proof′read′ (-rēd′) ***vt.***, ***vi.*** to read and mark corrections on (printers' proofs, etc.) —**proof′read′er** ***n.***

prop[1] (präp) ***n.*** ⟦< MDu *proppe*⟧ a support, as a pole, placed under or against something: often used figuratively —***vt.*** **propped, prop′ping** **1** to support with or as with a prop: often with *up* **2** to lean (something) *against* a support

prop[2] (präp) ***n.*** PROPERTY (sense 4)

prop[3] (präp) ***n.*** *short for* PROPELLER

prop[4] *abbrev.* **1** proper(ly) **2** property **3** proposition **4** proprietor

prop·a·gan·da (präp′ə gan′də) ***n.*** ⟦ModL: see fol.⟧ **1** any widespread promotion of particular ideas, doctrines, etc. **2** ideas, etc. so spread —**prop′a·gan′dist** ***n.***, ***adj.*** —**prop′a·gan′dize′** (-dīz′), **-dized′, -diz′ing**, ***vt.***, ***vi.***

prop·a·gate (präp′ə gāt′) ***vt.*** **-gat′ed, -gat′ing** ⟦< L *propago*, slip (of a plant)⟧ **1** to cause (a plant or animal) to reproduce itself **2** to reproduce (itself): said of a plant or animal **3** to spread (ideas, customs, etc.) —***vi.*** to reproduce: said of plants or animals —**prop′a·ga′tion** ***n.***

pro·pane (prō′pān′) ***n.*** a gaseous hydrocarbon obtained from petroleum, used as a fuel

pro·pel (prə pel′, prō-) ***vt.*** **-pelled′, -pel′ling** ⟦< L *pro-*, forward + *pellere*, to drive⟧ to drive onward or forward

pro·pel′lant or **pro·pel′lent** ***n.*** one that propels; specif., the fuel for a rocket

pro·pel′ler ***n.*** a device having two or more blades in a revolving hub, for propelling a ship or aircraft

pro·pen·si·ty (prə pen′sə tē) ***n.***, *pl.* **-ties** ⟦< L *propendere*, hang forward⟧ a natural inclination or tendency

prop·er (präp′ər) ***adj.*** ⟦< L *proprius*, one's own⟧ **1** specially suitable; appropriate; fitting **2** naturally belonging (*to*) **3** conforming to a standard; correct **4** decent; decorous **5** in the most restricted sense *[*Chicago *proper* (i.e., apart from its suburbs)*]* **6** designating a noun that names a specific individual, place, etc. (Ex.: *Bill, Paris*) —**prop′er·ly** ***adv.***

prop·er·ty (präp′ər tē) ***n.***, *pl.* **-ties** ⟦see prec.⟧ **1** ownership **2** something owned, esp. real estate **3** a characteristic or attribute **4** any of the movable articles used in a stage setting —**prop′er·tied** (-tēd) ***adj.***

proph·e·cy (präf′ə sē) ***n.***, *pl.* **-cies** ⟦see PROPHET⟧ **1** prediction of the future, as by divine guidance **2** something predicted

proph′e·sy′ (-sī′) ***vt.***, ***vi.*** **-sied′**, **-sy′ing** **1** to predict as by divine guidance **2** to predict in any way

proph·et (präf′it) ***n.*** ⟦< Gr *pro-*, before + *phanai*, speak⟧ **1** a religious leader regarded as, or claiming to be, divinely inspired **2** one who predicts the future —**proph′et·ess** ***fem.n.***

pro·phet·ic (prə fet′ik, prō-) ***adj.*** **1** of or like a prophet **2** like or containing a prophecy —**pro·phet′i·cal·ly** ***adv.***

pro·phy·lac·tic (prō′fə lak′tik) ***adj.*** ⟦< Gr *pro-*, before + *phylassein*, to guard⟧ preventive or protective; esp., preventing disease —***n.*** **1** a prophylactic medicine, device, etc. **2** a condom

pro′phy·lax′is (-lak′sis) ***n.***, *pl.* **-lax′es′** (-sēz′) **1** prophylactic treatment **2** *Dentistry* a cleaning of the teeth to remove plaque and tartar

pro·pin·qui·ty (prō piŋ′kwə tē) ***n.*** ⟦< L *propinquus*, near⟧ nearness

pro·pi·ti·ate (prō pish′ē āt′, prə-) ***vt.*** **-at′ed**, **-at′ing** ⟦see fol.⟧ to win the good will of; appease —**pro·pi′ti·a′tion** ***n.*** —**pro·pi′ti·a·to′ry** (-ē ə tôr′ē) ***adj.***

pro·pi·tious (prō pish′əs, prə-) ***adj.*** ⟦< L *pro-*, before + *petere*, seek⟧ **1** favorably inclined **2** favorable; auspicious

prop′jet′ ***n.*** TURBOPROP

pro·po·nent (prə pō′nənt, prō-) ***n.*** ⟦see PROPOSE⟧ one who espouses or supports a cause, etc.

pro·por·tion (prə pôr′shən, prō-) ***n.*** ⟦< L *pro*, for + *portio*, a part⟧ **1** the comparative relation in size, amount, etc. between things; ratio **2** a part, share, etc. in its relation to the whole **3** balance or symmetry **4** [*pl.*] dimensions —***vt.*** **1** to put in proper relation with something else **2** to arrange the parts of (a whole) so as to be harmonious —**pro·por′tion·al** or **pro·por′tion·ate** (-shə nit) ***adj.***

pro·pos·al (prə pōz′əl) ***n.*** **1** a proposing **2** a proposed plan, etc. **3** an offer of marriage

pro·pose (prə pōz′) ***vt.*** **-posed′**, **-pos′ing** ⟦< L *pro-*, forth + *ponere*, to place⟧ **1** to put forth for consideration, approval, etc. **2** to plan or intend —***vi.*** to offer marriage

prop·o·si·tion (präp′ə zish′ən) ***n.*** **1** something proposed; plan **2** [Inf.] a proposed deal, as in business **3** [Inf.] an undertaking, etc. to be dealt with **4** a subject to be discussed **5** *Math.* a problem to be solved

pro·pound (prə pound′, prō-) ***vt.*** ⟦see PROPOSE⟧ to put forward for consideration

pro·pri·e·tar·y (prə prī′ə tər ē, prō-) ***adj.*** ⟦see PROPERTY⟧ belonging to a proprietor, as under a patent, trademark, or copyright

pro·pri′e·tor ***n.*** an owner —**pro·pri′e·tor·ship′** ***n.*** —**pro·pri′e·tress** (-tris) ***fem.n.***

pro·pri′e·ty (-tē) ***n.***, *pl.* **-ties** ⟦see PROPER⟧ **1** the quality of being proper, fitting, etc. **2** conformity with accepted standards of behavior

pro·pul·sion (prə pul′shən) ***n.*** ⟦see PROPEL⟧ **1** a propelling or being propelled **2** something that propels —**pro·pul′sive** ***adj.***

pro·rate (prō rāt′, prō′rāt′) ***vt.***, ***vi.*** **-rat′ed**, **-rat′ing** ⟦< L *pro rata*, in proportion⟧ to divide or assess proportionally

pro·sa·ic (prō zā′ik) ***adj.*** ⟦< L *prosa*, prose⟧ commonplace; dull

pro·sce·ni·um (prō sē′nē əm) ***n.***, *pl.* **-ni·ums** or **-ni·a** (-ə) ⟦< Gr *pro-*, before + *skēnē*, tent⟧ in a theater, the plane separating the stage proper from the audience and including the arch (**proscenium arch**) and the curtain within it

pro·scribe (prō skrīb′) ***vt.*** **-scribed′**, **-scrib′ing** ⟦< L < *pro-*, before + *scribere*, write⟧ **1** to outlaw **2** to banish; exile **3** to denounce or forbid the use, etc. of —**pro·scrip′tion** (-skrip′shən) ***n.***

prose (prōz) ***n.*** ⟦< L *prorsus*, straight on⟧ ordinary language; writing that is not poetry

pros·e·cute (präs′ə kyo͞ot′) ***vt.*** **-cut′ed**, **-cut′ing** ⟦< L *pro-*, before + *sequi*, follow⟧ **1** to carry on **2** to conduct legal action against —**pros′e·cu′tion** ***n.*** —**pros′e·cu′tor** ***n.*** —**pros′e·cu·to′ri·al** ***adj.***

pros·e·lyte (präs′ə līt′) ***n.*** ⟦< Gr *prosēlytos*, a stranger⟧ one who has been converted from one religion, sect, etc. to another

pros·e·lyt·ize (präs′ə li tīz′) ***vi.***, ***vt.*** **-ized′**, **-iz′ing** **1** to try to convert (a person), esp. to one's religion **2** to persuade to do or join something —**pros′e·lyt·ism′** (-li tiz′əm) ***n.*** —**pros′e·lyt·iz′er** ***n.***

pro·sim·i·an (prō sim′ē ən) ***n.*** any of various small, arboreal primates

pros·o·dy (präs′ə dē) ***n.*** ⟦< Gr *prosōidia*, accent⟧ versification; study of meter, rhyme, etc.

pros·pect (präs′pekt′) ***n.*** ⟦< L *pro-*, forward + *specere*, to look⟧ **1** a broad view; scene **2** a viewpoint; outlook **3** anticipation **4** *a*) something expected *b*) [*usually pl.*] apparent chance for success **5** a likely customer, candidate, etc. —***vi.*** to explore or search (*for*) —**pros′pec′tor** ***n.***

pro·spec·tive (prə spek′tiv, prä-, prō-) ***adj.*** expected; likely

pro·spec′tus (-spek′təs) ***n.*** ⟦L: see PROS-

PECT⟧ a statement of the features of a new work, enterprise, etc.

pros·per (präs′pər) ***vi.*** ⟦< L *prospere,* fortunately⟧ to succeed; thrive

pros·per·i·ty (präs per′ə tē) ***n.***, *pl.* **-ties** prosperous condition; wealth

pros·per·ous (präs′pər əs) ***adj.*** **1** prospering; successful **2** wealthy —**pros′per·ous·ly** ***adv.***

pros·tate (präs′tāt′) ***adj.*** ⟦< Gr *prostatēs,* one standing before⟧ of or designating a gland surrounding the male urethra at the base of the bladder —***n.*** this gland: in full **prostate gland**

pros·the·sis (präs thē′sis) ***n.***, *pl.* **-ses′** (-sēz′) *Med.* **1** the replacement of a missing part of the body, as a limb, by an artificial substitute **2** such a substitute —**pros·thet′ic** (-thet′ik) ***adj.***

pros·ti·tute (präs′tə to͞ot′) ***n.*** ⟦< L *pro-,* before + *statuere,* cause to stand⟧ one who engages in promiscuous sexual activity for pay —***vt.*** **-tut′ed, -tut′ing** **1** to offer (oneself) as a prostitute **2** to sell (oneself, one's talents, etc.) for base purposes —**pros′ti·tu′tion** ***n.***

pros·trate (präs′trāt′) ***adj.*** ⟦< L *pro-,* before + *sternere,* stretch out⟧ **1** lying face downward **2** lying prone or supine **3** laid low; overcome —***vt.*** **-trat′ed, -trat′ing** **1** to lay flat on the ground **2** to lay low; subjugate —**pros·tra′tion** ***n.***

pros·y (prō′zē) ***adj.*** **-i·er, -i·est** prosaic; commonplace, dull, etc.

pro·tag·o·nist (prō tag′ə nist) ***n.*** ⟦< Gr *prōtos,* first + *agōnistēs,* actor⟧ the main character in a drama, novel, etc.

pro·te·an (prōt′ē ən, prō tē′ən) ***adj.*** ⟦after *Proteus,* Gr god who changes his form⟧ readily taking on different forms

pro·tect (prə tekt′, prō-) ***vt.*** ⟦< L *pro-,* before + *tegere,* to cover⟧ to shield from injury, danger, etc.; defend —**pro·tec′tor** ***n.***

pro·tec′tion ***n.*** **1** a protecting or being protected **2** a person or thing that protects

pro·tec′tive ***adj.*** **1** protecting **2** *Economics* intended to protect domestic industry from foreign competition *[a protective tariff]* —**pro·tec′tive·ly** ***adv.*** —**pro·tec′tive·ness** ***n.***

pro·tec′tor·ate (-tər it) ***n.*** a weak state under the protection and control of a strong state

pro·té·gé (prōt′ə zhā′) ***n.*** ⟦Fr: see PROTECT⟧ a person guided and helped in his or her career by another person

pro·tein (prō′tēn′, prō′tē in) ***n.*** ⟦< Gr *prōtos,* first⟧ any of numerous nitrogenous substances occurring in all living matter and essential to diet

pro tem·po·re (prō tem′pə rē′) ⟦L⟧ for the time (being); temporarily: shortened to **pro tem**

pro·test (prō test′; *also, and for n. always* prō′test′) ***vt.*** ⟦< L *pro-,* forth + *testari,* affirm⟧ **1** to state positively **2** to speak strongly against —***vi.*** to express disapproval; object —***n.*** **1** an objection **2** a formal statement of objection —**prot·es·ta·tion** (prät′es tā′shən) ***n.*** —**pro′test′er** ***n.***

Prot·es·tant (prät′əs tənt) ***n.*** ⟦see prec.⟧ any Christian not belonging to the Roman Catholic Church or the Eastern Orthodox Church —**Prot′es·tant·ism′** ***n.***

proto- ⟦< Gr *prōtos,* first⟧ *combining form* **1** first in time, original **2** first in importance, chief

pro·to·col (prōt′ə kôl′) ***n.*** ⟦< Gr *prōtokollon,* contents page⟧ **1** an original draft of a document, etc. **2** the code of ceremonial forms accepted as correct in official dealings, as between heads of state or diplomatic officials

pro·ton (prō′tän′) ***n.*** ⟦< Gr *prōtos,* first⟧ an elementary particle in the nucleus of all atoms, carrying a unit positive charge of electricity

pro·to·plasm (prōt′ə plaz′əm) ***n.*** ⟦see PROTO- & PLASMA⟧ a semifluid, viscous colloid, the essential living matter of all animal and plant cells —**pro′to·plas′mic** (-plaz′mik) ***adj.***

pro·to·type (prōt′ə tīp′) ***n.*** the first thing or being of its kind; model

pro·to·zo·an (prōt′ə zō′ən) ***n.***, *pl.* **-zo′a** (-ə) ⟦< Gr *prōtos,* first + *zōion,* an animal⟧ any of various microscopic, single-celled animals: also **pro′to·zo′on′** (-än′), *pl.* **-zo′a** (-ə)

pro·tract (prō trakt′, prə-) ***vt.*** ⟦< L *pro-,* forward + *trahere,* draw⟧ to draw out; prolong —**pro·trac′tion** ***n.***

pro·trac·tor (prō′trak′tər) ***n.*** a graduated semicircular instrument for plotting and measuring angles

pro·trude (prō tro͞od′, prə-) ***vt.***, ***vi.*** **-trud′ed, -trud′ing** ⟦< L *pro-,* forth + *trudere,* to thrust⟧ to jut out; project —**pro·tru′sion** (-tro͞o′zhən) ***n.***

pro·tu·ber·ance (prō to͞o′bər əns, prə-) ***n.*** a part or thing that protrudes; bulge —**pro·tu′ber·ant** ***adj.***

proud (proud) ***adj.*** ⟦< LL *prode,* beneficial⟧ **1** having a proper pride in oneself **2** arrogant; haughty **3** feeling or causing great pride or joy **4** caused by pride **5** stately; splendid *[a proud fleet]* —**proud of** highly pleased with —**proud′ly** ***adv.***

proud flesh ⟦from the notion of swelling up⟧ an abnormal growth of flesh around a healing wound

Proust (pro͞ost), **Mar·cel** (mär sel′) 1871-1922; Fr. novelist

prove (pro͞ov) ***vt.*** **proved, proved** or **prov′en, prov′ing** ⟦< L *probare,* to test⟧ **1** to test by experiment, a standard, etc. **2** to establish as true —***vi.*** to be found by experience or trial —**prov′a·bil′i·ty** ***n.*** —**prov′a·ble** ***adj.***

prov·e·nance (präv′ə nəns) ***n.*** ⟦< L *provenire,* come forth⟧ origin; source

Pro·ven·çal (prō′vən säl′) ***n.*** **1** the vernacular of S France, a Romance language **2** the medieval literary language of S France

prov·en·der (präv′ən dər) ***n.*** ⟦< L *praebere,* give⟧ **1** dry food for livestock **2** [Inf.] food

prov·erb (präv′ərb) ***n.*** ⟦< L *pro-,* PRO-[2] + *verbum,* word⟧ a short, traditional saying expressing an obvious truth —**pro·ver·bi·al** (prō vur′bē əl) ***adj.***

Prov′erbs ***n.*** a book of the Bible containing maxims

pro·vide (prə vīd′, prō-) ***vt.*** **-vid′ed, -vid′ing** ⟦< L *pro-*, PRO-[2] + *videre*, see⟧ **1** to make available; supply **2** to furnish (someone) *with* something **3** to stipulate **—*vi.*** **1** to prepare (*for* or *against* a possible situation, etc.) **2** to furnish support (*for*) **—pro·vid′er *n.***

pro·vid′ed or **pro·vid′ing** ***conj.*** on the condition or understanding (*that*)

prov·i·dence (präv′ə dəns) ***n.*** **1** provident management **2** the benevolent guidance of God or nature **3** [**P-**] God

Prov·i·dence (präv′ə dəns) capital of Rhode Island: pop. 161,000

prov′i·dent (-dənt) ***adj.*** ⟦see PROVIDE⟧ **1** providing for the future **2** prudent or economical **—prov′i·dent·ly *adv.***

prov′i·den′tial (-den′shəl) ***adj.*** of, by, or as if decreed by divine providence

prov·ince (präv′ins) ***n.*** ⟦< L *provincia*⟧ **1** an administrative division of a country; specif., of Canada **2** *a*) a district; territory *b*) [*pl.*] the parts of a country removed from the major cities **3** range of duties or work; sphere

pro·vin·cial (prə vin′shəl, prō-) ***adj.*** **1** of a province **2** having the ways, speech, etc. of a certain province **3** countrylike; rustic **4** narrow; limited **—pro·vin′cial·ism′ *n.***

proving ground a place for testing new equipment, new theories, etc.

pro·vi·sion (prə vizh′ən, prō-) ***n.*** **1** a providing or preparing **2** something provided for the future **3** [*pl.*] a stock of food **4** a stipulation; proviso **—*vt.*** to supply with provisions

pro·vi′sion·al ***adj.*** temporary **—pro·vi′sion·al·ly *adv.***

pro·vi·so (prə vī′zō′, prō-) ***n.***, *pl.* **-sos′** or **-soes′** ⟦see PROVIDE⟧ a condition or stipulation, or a clause making one

prov·o·ca·tion (präv′ə kā′shən) ***n.*** **1** a provoking **2** something that provokes; incitement

pro·voc·a·tive (prə väk′ə tiv, prō-) ***adj.*** provoking or tending to provoke, as to action, thought, or feeling **—pro·voc′a·tive·ly *adv.***

pro·voke (prə vōk′, prō-) ***vt.*** **-voked′, -vok′ing** ⟦< L *pro-*, forth + *vocare*, to call⟧ **1** to excite to some action or feeling **2** to anger or irritate **3** to stir up (action or feeling) **4** to evoke **—pro·vok′er *n.*** **—pro·vok′ing *adj.***

pro·vost (prō′vōst′) ***n.*** ⟦< L *praepositus*, chief⟧ a high executive official, as in some colleges

pro·vost guard (prō′vō′) a detail of military police under the command of an officer (**provost marshal**)

prow (prou) ***n.*** ⟦< Gr *prōira*⟧ the forward part of a ship, etc.

prow·ess (prou′is) ***n.*** ⟦< OFr *prouesse*⟧ **1** bravery; valor **2** superior ability, skill, etc.

prowl (proul) ***vi., vt.*** ⟦< ?⟧ to roam about furtively (in), as in search of prey or loot **—*n.*** a prowling **—prowl′er *n.***

prowl car PATROL CAR

prox·im·i·ty (präk sim′ə tē) ***n.*** ⟦< L *prope*, near⟧ nearness

prox·y (präk′sē) ***n.***, *pl.* **-ies** ⟦< ME *procuracie*, function of a procurator⟧ **1** the authority to act for another, as in voting **2** one given such authority

Pro·zac (prō′zak′) *trademark for* a drug used in treating depression, eating disorders, etc.

prude (pro͞od) ***n.*** ⟦Fr < *prudefemme*, excellent woman⟧ one who is overly modest or proper in behavior, dress, etc. **—prud′er·y *n.*** **—prud′ish *adj.*** **—prud′ish·ness *n.***

pru·dent (pro͞o′dənt) ***adj.*** ⟦< L *providens*, provident⟧ **1** exercising sound judgment in practical matters **2** cautious in conduct; not rash **3** managing carefully **—pru′dence *n.*** **—pru·den·tial** (pro͞o den′shəl) ***adj.***

prune[1] (pro͞on) ***n.*** ⟦< Gr *proumnon*, plum⟧ a dried plum

prune[2] (pro͞on) ***vt.*** **pruned, prun′ing** ⟦< OFr *prooignier*⟧ **1** to trim dead or living parts from (a plant) **2** to cut out (unnecessary parts, etc.)

pru·ri·ent (proor′ē ənt) ***adj.*** ⟦< L *prurire*, to itch⟧ tending to excite lust; lewd **—pru′ri·ence *n.***

Prus·sia (prush′ə) former kingdom in N Europe & later the dominant state of the German Empire (1871-1919) **—Prus′sian *adj., n.***

pry[1] (prī) ***n.***, *pl.* **pries** ⟦< PRIZE[2]⟧ a lever or crowbar **—*vt.*** **pried, pry′ing** **1** to raise or move with a pry **2** to obtain with difficulty

pry[2] (prī) ***vi.*** **pried, pry′ing** ⟦< ?⟧ to look closely and inquisitively; snoop

pry′er ***n.*** PRIER

PS *abbrev.* Public School

P.S., p.s., or **PS** *abbrev.* postscript

psalm (säm) ***n.*** ⟦< Gr *psallein*, to pluck (a harp)⟧ **1** a sacred song or poem **2** [*usually* **P-**] any of the songs in praise of God constituting the Book of Psalms **—psalm′ist *n.***

Psalms (sämz) ***n.*** a book of the Bible consisting of 150 psalms

Psal·ter (sôl′tər) ***n.*** ⟦< Gr *psaltērion*, a harp⟧ **1** PSALMS **2** [*also* **p-**] a version of the Book of Psalms for use in religious services

pseu·do (so͞o′dō) ***adj.*** ⟦ME: see fol.⟧ sham; false; spurious

pseudo- ⟦< Gr *pseudein*, deceive⟧ *combining form* sham, counterfeit

pseu·do·nym (so͞o′də nim′) ***n.*** ⟦< Gr *pseudēs*, false + *onyma*, a name⟧ a fictitious name, esp. one assumed by an author; pen name

pshaw (shô) ***n., interj.*** (an exclamation) used to express impatience, disgust, etc.

psi[1] (sī, psē) ***n.*** the 23d letter of the Greek alphabet (Ψ, ψ)

psi[2] *abbrev.* pounds per square inch

psit·ta·co·sis (sit′ə kō′sis) ***n.*** ⟦< Gr *psittakos*, parrot + -OSIS⟧ a disease of birds, esp. parrots, often transmitted to humans

pso·ri·a·sis (sə rī′ə sis) ***n.*** ⟦ult. < Gr *psōra*, an itch⟧ a chronic skin disease characterized by scaly, reddish patches

psst (pst) ***interj.*** [Inf.] used to attract someone's attention quietly

PST *abbrev.* Pacific Standard Time

psych[1] (sīk) ***vt.*** **psyched, psych'ing** ⟦< PSYCHOANALYZE⟧ [Slang] **1** to outwit, overcome, etc. by psychological means: often with *out* **2** to prepare (oneself) psychologically: often with *up*

psych[2] *abbrev.* psychology

psych- *combining form* PSYCHO-

psy·che (sī'kē) ***n.*** ⟦Gr *psychē*⟧ **1** the soul **2** the mind regarded as an entity based ultimately upon physical processes but with its own complex processes **3** [**P-**] *Rom. Folklore* the wife of Cupid

psy·che·del·ic (sī'kə del'ik) ***adj.*** ⟦< prec. + Gr *dēloun*, make manifest⟧ **1** of or causing extreme changes in the conscious mind, as hallucinations **2** of or associated with psychedelic drugs

psy·chi·a·try (sī kī'ə trē) ***n.*** ⟦see PSYCHO- & -IATRY⟧ the branch of medicine dealing with disorders of the mind, including psychoses and neuroses —**psy·chi·at·ric** (sī'kē a'trik) ***adj.*** —**psy'chi'a·trist** ***n.***

psy·chic (sī'kik) ***adj.*** ⟦see PSYCHE⟧ **1** of the psyche, or mind **2** beyond known physical processes **3** apparently sensitive to forces beyond the physical world Also **psy'chi·cal** —***n.*** **1** a person apparently sensitive to nonphysical forces **2** a MEDIUM (*n.* 5) —**psy'chi·cal·ly** ***adv.***

psy·cho (sī'kō) ***adj.***, ***n.*** [Inf.] *short for* PSYCHOTIC, PSYCHOPATHIC, *and* PSYCHOPATH

psycho- ⟦see PSYCHE⟧ *combining form* the mind or mental processes

psy·cho·a·nal·y·sis (sī'kō ə nal'ə sis) ***n.*** a method of treating some mental disorders by analyzing repressed feelings, emotional conflicts, etc. through the use of free association, dream analysis, etc. —**psy'cho·an'a·lyst** (-an'ə list) ***n.*** —**psy'cho·an'a·lyze'** (-līz'), **-lyzed'**, **-lyz'ing**, ***vt.***

psy'cho·bab'ble (-bab'əl) ***n.*** [Inf.] talk or writing that uses psychological terms and concepts in a trite or superficial way

psy'cho·gen'ic (-jen'ik) ***adj.*** ⟦see PSYCHO- & GENESIS⟧ originating in the mind or caused by mental conflicts

psy·chol·o·gy (sī käl'ə jē) ***n.***, *pl.* **-gies** ⟦see PSYCHO- & -LOGY⟧ **1** the science dealing with the mind and with mental and emotional processes **2** the science of human and animal behavior —**psy'cho·log'i·cal** (-kə läj'i kəl) ***adj.*** —**psy·chol'o·gist** ***n.***

psy·cho·neu·ro·sis (sī'kō nōō rō'sis) ***n.***, *pl.* **-ses'** (-sēz') NEUROSIS

psy'cho·path' (-path') ***n.*** ⟦see PSYCHO- & -PATHY⟧ one who has a severe mental disorder and whose behavior is asocial —**psy'cho·path'ic** ***adj.***

psy·cho·sis (sī kō'sis) ***n.***, *pl.* **-ses'** (-sēz') ⟦see PSYCHO- & -OSIS⟧ a mental disorder in which the personality is seriously disorganized and contact with reality is usually impaired —**psy·chot'ic** (-kät'ik) ***adj.***

psy'cho·so·mat'ic (-sō mat'ik) ***adj.*** ⟦PSYCHO- + SOMATIC⟧ designating or of a physical disorder brought on, or made worse, by one's emotional state

psy'cho·ther'a·py (-ther'ə pē) ***n.*** ⟦PSYCHO- + THERAPY⟧ treatment of mental disorders by counseling, psychoanalysis, etc. —**psy'cho·ther'a·pist** ***n.***

pt *abbrev.* **1** part **2** pint(s) **3** point

Pt[1] *abbrev.* **1** Point **2** Port

Pt[2] *Chem. symbol for* platinum

PT *abbrev.* Pacific Time

PTA *abbrev.* Parent-Teacher Association

ptar·mi·gan (tär'mi gən) ***n.*** ⟦< Scot *tarmachan*⟧ a grouse of northern regions

ptero- ⟦< Gr *pteron*, wing⟧ *combining form* feather, wing

pter·o·dac·tyl (ter'ə dak'təl) ***n.*** ⟦see prec. & DACTYL⟧ an extinct flying reptile with wings of skin stretched from the hind limbs to the long digits of each forelimb

Ptol·e·my (täl'ə mē) 2d c. A.D.; Greco-Egyptian astronomer & mathematician

pto·maine (tō'mān') ***n.*** ⟦< Gr *ptōma*, corpse⟧ an alkaloid substance, often poisonous, formed in decaying matter

Pu *Chem. symbol for* plutonium

pub (pub) ***n.*** ⟦< *pub*(*lic house*)⟧ [Inf.] a bar or tavern

pu·ber·ty (pyōō'bər tē) ***n.*** ⟦< L *puber*, adult⟧ the stage of physical development when sexual reproduction first becomes possible —**pu'ber·tal** ***adj.***

pu·bes·cent (pyōō bes'ənt) ***adj.*** ⟦see prec.⟧ reaching or having reached puberty —**pu·bes'cence** ***n.***

pu'bic (-bik) ***adj.*** of or in the region of the genitals

pub·lic (pub'lik) ***adj.*** ⟦ult. < L *populus*, the people⟧ **1** of the people as a whole **2** for the use or benefit of all *[*a *public* park*]* **3** acting officially for the people *[*a *public* prosecutor*]* **4** known by, open to, or available to most or all people *[*to make *public*, a *public* company*]* —***n.*** **1** the people as a whole **2** a specific part of the people *[*the reading *public]* —**in public** openly —**pub'lic·ly** ***adv.***

pub·li·can (pub'li kən) ***n.*** **1** in ancient Rome, a tax collector **2** [Brit.] a saloon proprietor

pub·li·ca·tion (pub'li kā'shən) ***n.*** ⟦see PUBLISH⟧ **1** public notification **2** the printing and distribution of books, magazines, etc. **3** something published, as a periodical or book

public defender an attorney employed at public expense to defend indigent people who are accused of crimes

public domain the condition of being free from copyright or patent

pub·li·cist (pub'lə sist) ***n.*** a person whose business is publicity

pub·lic·i·ty (pub lis'ə tē) ***n.*** **1** *a*) any information or action that brings a person, cause, etc. to public notice *b*) work concerned with such promotional matters **2** notice by the public

pub·li·cize (pub'lə sīz') ***vt.*** **-cized'**, **-ciz'ing** to give publicity to

public relations relations of an organization, etc. with the general public as through publicity

public school **1** in the U.S., an elementary or secondary school maintained by public taxes, free to students, and supervised locally 2 in England, a private boarding school

public servant a government official or a civil-service employee

pub'lic-spir'it·ed ***adj.*** having or showing zeal for the public welfare

public utility an organization supplying water, electricity, transportation, etc. to the public

pub·lish (pub'lish) ***vt.*** ⟦< L *publicare*⟧ **1** to make publicly known; announce **2** to issue (a printed work) for sale —***vi.*** **1** to issue books, newspapers, printed music, etc. to the public **2** to write books, etc. that are published —**pub'lish·er** ***n.***

Puc·ci·ni (po͞o chē'nē), **Gia·co·mo** (jä'kō mō') 1858-1924; It. operatic composer

puck (puk) ***n.*** ⟦< dial. *puck*, to strike⟧ the hard rubber disk used in ice hockey

puck·er (puk'ər) ***vt., vi.*** ⟦< POKE²⟧ to gather into wrinkles or small folds —***n.*** a wrinkle or small fold made by puckering

puck·ish (puk'ish) ***adj.*** ⟦after *Puck*, elf in a Shakespeare play⟧ mischievous

pud·ding (pood'iŋ) ***n.*** ⟦ME *puddyng*, a sausage⟧ a soft, sweet food made of eggs, milk, fruit, etc.

pud·dle (pud''l) ***n.*** ⟦dim. < OE *pudd*, a ditch⟧ a small pool of water, esp. stagnant, spilled, or muddy water

pud'dling (-liŋ) ***n.*** the making of wrought iron from pig iron melted and stirred in an oxidizing atmosphere

pudg·y (puj'ē) ***adj.*** **-i·er, -i·est** ⟦< Scot *pud*, belly⟧ short and fat

pueb·lo (pweb'lō) ***n.***, *pl.* **-los** (-lōz) ⟦Sp < L *populus*, people⟧ an Amerindian communal village, as in the SW U.S., of terraced adobe dwellings

pu·er·ile (pyo͞o'ər əl, pyoor'īl') ***adj.*** ⟦< L *puer*, boy⟧ childish; silly —**pu'er·il'i·ty** ***n.***

Puer·to Ri·co (pwer'tə rē'kō, pôr'-) island in the West Indies: a commonwealth associated with the U.S.: 3,427 sq. mi.; pop. 3,522,000; cap. San Juan —**Puer'to Ri'can** (-kən)

puff (puf) ***n.*** ⟦OE *pyff*⟧ **1** a short, sudden gust or expulsion of air, breath, smoke, etc. **2** a draw at a cigarette, etc. **3** a light pastry filled with whipped cream, etc. **4** a soft pad *[a powder puff]* **5** a book review, etc. giving undue praise —***vi.*** **1** to blow in puffs **2** to breathe rapidly **3** to fill or swell (*out* or *up*) **4** to take puffs at a cigarette, etc. —***vt.*** **1** to blow, smoke, etc. in or with puffs **2** to swell; inflate **3** to praise unduly —**puff'y**, **-i·er, -i·est,** ***adj.*** —**puff'i·ness** ***n.***

puff'ball' ***n.*** a fungus that bursts at the touch and discharges a brown powder

puff'er ***n.*** a small saltwater fish that can expand its body by swallowing water or air

puf·fin (puf'in) ***n.*** ⟦ME *poffin*⟧ a northern sea bird with a brightly colored, triangular beak

puff pastry rich, flaky pastry made of many thin layers of dough

pug (pug) ***n.*** ⟦< ? *Puck*: see PUCK⟧ any of a breed of small, short-haired, snub-nosed dog

pu·gil·ism (pyo͞o'jə iz'əm) ***n.*** ⟦L *pugil*, boxer⟧ the sport of boxing —**pu'gil·ist** ***n.*** —**pu'gil·is'tic** ***adj.***

pug·na·cious (pug nā'shəs) ***adj.*** ⟦< L *pugnare*, to fight⟧ eager and ready to fight; quarrelsome —**pug·na'cious·ly** ***adv.*** —**pug·nac'i·ty** (-nas'ə tē) ***n.***

pug nose a short, thick, turned-up nose —**pug'-nosed'** ***adj.***

puke (pyo͞ok) ***n., vt., vi.*** **puked, puk'ing** ⟦< ?⟧ [Inf.] VOMIT

puk·ka (puk'ə) ***adj.*** ⟦Hindi *pakka*, ripe⟧ **1** [Anglo-Ind.] first-rate **2** genuine; real

pul·chri·tude (pul'krə to͞od') ***n.*** ⟦< L *pulcher*, beautiful⟧ physical beauty

pule (pyo͞ol) ***vi.*** **puled, pul'ing** ⟦echoic⟧ to whimper or whine, as a sick or fretful child does

pull (pool) ***vt.*** ⟦< OE *pullian*, to pluck⟧ **1** to exert force on so as to move toward the source of the force **2** to pluck out *[to pull a tooth]* **3** to rip; tear **4** to strain (a muscle) **5** [Inf.] to carry out; perform *[to pull a raid]* **6** [Inf.] to restrain *[to pull one's punches]* **7** [Inf.] to draw out (a gun, etc.) —***vi.*** **1** to exert force in dragging, tugging, or attracting something **2** to be capable of being pulled **3** to move (*away, ahead*, etc.) —***n.*** **1** the act, force, or result of pulling; a tugging, attracting, etc. **2** a difficult, continuous effort **3** something to be pulled, as a handle **4** [Inf.] *a)* influence *b)* drawing power —**pull for** [Inf.] to cheer on —**pull off** [Inf.] to accomplish —**pull oneself together** to regain one's poise, etc. —**pull out** to depart or withdraw —**pull through** [Inf.] to get over (an illness, etc.) —**pull up** **1** to bring or come to a stop **2** to move ahead —**pull'er** ***n.***

pull'back' ***n.*** a pulling back; esp., a planned military withdrawal

pul·let (pool'it) ***n.*** ⟦ult. < L *pullus*, chicken⟧ a young hen

pul·ley (pool'ē) ***n.***, *pl.* **-leys** ⟦< medieval Gr *polos*, pivot⟧ a small wheel with a grooved rim in which a rope, belt, etc. runs, as to raise weights or transmit power

Pull·man (pool'mən) ***n.*** ⟦after G. M. *Pullman* (1831-97), U.S. inventor⟧ a railroad car with convertible berths for sleeping: also **Pullman car**

pull'out' ***n.*** **1** a pulling out; esp. removal, withdrawal, etc. **2** something to be pulled out, as a magazine insert

pull'o'ver ***adj.*** that is put on by being pulled over the head —***n.*** a pullover sweater, shirt, etc.

pull'-up' or **pull'up'** ***n.*** the act of chinning oneself

pul·mo·nar·y (pul'mə ner'ē) ***adj.*** ⟦< L *pulmo*, lung⟧ of the lungs

pul·mo·tor (pool'mō'tər) ***n.*** ⟦< L *pulmo*, lung + MOTOR⟧ an apparatus for applying artificial respiration

pulp (pulp) ***n.*** ⟦< L *pulpa*, flesh⟧ **1** a soft, moist, sticky mass **2** the soft, juicy part of a fruit or the pith inside a plant stem 3 the soft, sensitive tissue in the center of a tooth 4 ground-up, moistened fibers of wood, rags, etc., used to make paper —**pulp'y**, **-i·er**, **-i·est**, ***adj.***

pul·pit (pool'pit) ***n.*** ⟦< L *pulpitum*, a stage⟧ **1** a raised platform from which a member of the clergy preaches in a church **2** preachers collectively

pul·sar (pul'sär') ***n.*** ⟦< PULSE⟧ any of several celestial objects that emit radio waves at short, regular intervals

pul·sate (pul'sāt') ***vi.*** **-sat'ed**, **-sat'ing** ⟦< L *pulsare*, to beat⟧ **1** to beat or throb rhythmically **2** to vibrate; quiver —**pul·sa'tion** ***n.***

pulse (puls) ***n.*** ⟦< L *pulsus*, a beating⟧ **1** the regular beating in the arteries, caused by the contractions of the heart **2** any regular beat **3** a brief, abnormal burst or surge, as of electric current —***vi.*** **pulsed**, **puls'ing** to pulsate; throb

pul·ver·ize (pul'vər īz') ***vt.***, ***vi.*** **-ized'**, **-iz'ing** ⟦< L *pulvis*, powder⟧ to grind or be ground into powder

pu·ma (pyoo͞'mə) ***n.*** ⟦AmSp⟧ COUGAR

pum·ice (pum'is) ***n.*** ⟦< L *pumex*⟧ a light, porous volcanic rock used for scouring, polishing, etc.

pum·mel (pum'əl) ***vt.*** **-meled** or **-melled**, **-mel·ing** or **-mel·ling** ⟦< POMMEL⟧ to hit with repeated blows, esp. with the fist

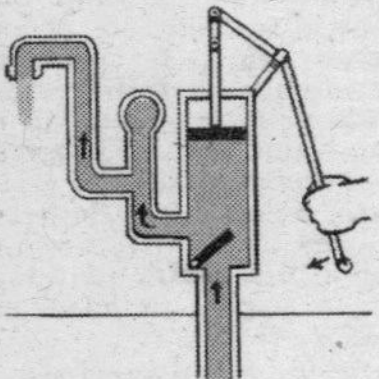

WATER PUMP

pump[1] (pump) ***n.*** ⟦< Sp *bomba*⟧ a machine that forces a liquid or gas into, or draws it out of, something —***vt.*** **1** to move (fluids) with a pump **2** to remove water, etc. from **3** to drive air into with a pump **4** to draw out, move up and down, pour forth, etc. as a pump does **5** [Inf.] to question persistently, or to elicit (information) by this —**pump'er** ***n.***

pump[2] (pump) ***n.*** ⟦prob. < Fr *pompe*, boot⟧ a low-cut shoe without straps or ties

pumped ***adj.*** [Slang] full of confidence, enthusiasm, etc.

pum·per·nick·el (pum'pər nik'əl) ***n.*** ⟦Ger⟧ a coarse, dark rye bread

pump·kin (pump'kin) ***n.*** ⟦< Gr *pepōn*, ripe⟧ a large, round, orange-yellow, edible gourdlike fruit that grows on a vine

pun (pun) ***n.*** ⟦< ? It *puntiglio*, fine point⟧ the humorous use of a word, or of different words sounded alike, so as to play on the various meanings —***vi.*** **punned**, **pun'ning** to make puns

punch[1] (punch) ***n.*** ⟦ult. < L *pungere*, to prick⟧ a tool driven against a surface that is to be stamped, pierced, etc. —***vt.*** **1** to pierce, stamp, etc. with a punch **2** to make (a hole) with or as with a punch

punch[2] (punch) ***vt.*** ⟦ME *punchen*⟧ **1** to prod with a stick **2** to herd (cattle) as by prodding **3** to strike with the fist —***n.*** **1** a thrusting blow with the fist **2** [Inf.] effective force —**punch in** (or **out**) to record with a time clock one's arrival (or departure)

punch[3] (punch) ***n.*** ⟦Hindi *pañca*, five⟧ a sweet drink made with fruit juices, sherbet, etc., often mixed with wine or liquor

punch'-drunk' ***adj.*** confused, unsteady, etc., as from many blows to the head in boxing

punch line the surprise line carrying the point of a joke

punch'y ***adj.*** **-i·er**, **-i·est** [Inf.] **1** forceful; vigorous **2** PUNCH-DRUNK

punc·til·i·ous (puŋk til'ē əs) ***adj.*** ⟦see fol.⟧ **1** very careful about fine points of behavior **2** very exact; scrupulous

punc·tu·al (puŋk'choo͞ əl) ***adj.*** ⟦< L *punctus*, a point⟧ on time; prompt —**punc'tu·al'i·ty** (-al'ə tē) ***n.*** —**punc'tu·al·ly** ***adv.***

punc'tu·ate' (-āt') ***vt.*** **-at'ed**, **-at'ing** ⟦see prec.⟧ **1** to use standardized marks (**punctuation marks**), as the period and comma, in (written matter) to clarify meaning **2** to interrupt *[a speech punctuated with applause]* **3** to emphasize —**punc'tu·a'tion** ***n.***

punc·ture (puŋk'chər) ***n.*** ⟦< L *pungere*, pierce⟧ **1** a piercing **2** a hole made by a sharp point —***vt.***, ***vi.*** **-tured**, **-tur·ing** to pierce or be pierced with or as with a sharp point

pun·dit (pun'dit) ***n.*** ⟦< Sans *paṇḍita*⟧ a person of great learning

pun·gent (pun'jənt) ***adj.*** ⟦< L *pungere*, pierce⟧ **1** producing a sharp sensation of taste and smell **2** sharp, biting, or stimulating *[pungent wit]* —**pun'gen·cy** ***n.*** —**pun'gent·ly** ***adv.***

pun·ish (pun'ish) ***vt.*** ⟦< L *punire*⟧ **1** to cause to undergo pain, loss, etc., as for a crime **2** to impose a penalty for (an offense) —**pun'ish·a·ble** ***adj.***

pun'ish·ment ***n.*** **1** a punishing or being punished **2** the penalty imposed **3** harsh treatment

pu·ni·tive (pyoo͞'ni tiv) ***adj.*** inflicting, or concerned with, punishment —**pu'ni·tive·ly** ***adv.***

punk[1] (puŋk) ***n.*** ⟦prob. < SPUNK⟧ **1** decayed wood used as tinder **2** a fungous substance that smolders when ignited, used to light fireworks, etc.

punk[2] (puŋk) ***n.*** ⟦< ?⟧ **1** [Slang] *a)* a young hoodlum *b)* a young person regarded as inexperienced, insignificant, etc. **2** PUNK ROCK —***adj.*** **1** [Slang] poor; inferior **2** of punk rock

punk rock a loud, fast, and deliberately offensive style of rock music

pun·ster (pun'stər) ***n.*** one who is fond of making puns

punt[1] (punt) ***n.*** ⟦< ? dial. *bunt*, to kick⟧ *Football* a kick in which the ball is dropped and kicked before it hits the ground —***vt., vi.*** to kick (a football) in this way

punt[2] (punt) ***n.*** ⟦< L *ponto*⟧ a flat-bottomed boat with square ends —***vt., vi.*** to propel (a punt) with a long pole

pu·ny (pyo͞o′nē) ***adj.*** **-ni·er, -ni·est** ⟦< OFr *puis*, after + *né*, born⟧ of inferior size, strength, or importance —**pu′ni·ness** ***n.***

pup (pup) ***n.*** **1** a young dog; puppy **2** a young fox, seal, etc.

pu·pa (pyo͞o′pə) ***n., pl.*** **-pae** (-pē) or **-pas** ⟦< L, a doll⟧ an insect in the stage between the last larval form and the adult form

pu·pil[1] (pyo͞o′pəl) ***n.*** ⟦< L *pupillus*, a ward⟧ a person taught under the supervision of a teacher or tutor

pu·pil[2] (pyo͞o′pəl) ***n.*** ⟦< L *pupilla*, figure reflected in the eye⟧ the contractile circular opening, apparently black, in the center of the iris of the eye

pup·pet (pup′ət) ***n.*** ⟦< L *pupa*, a doll⟧ **1** a small figure, as of a person, moved by strings or the hands, as in a performance (**puppet show**) **2** one whose actions, ideas, etc. are controlled by another —**pup′pet·ry** ***n.***

pup′pet·eer′ (-ə tir′) ***n.*** one who operates, designs, etc. puppets

pup·py (pup′ē) ***n., pl.*** **-pies** ⟦< medieval Fr *popee*, a doll⟧ a young dog

pup tent a small, portable tent

pur·blind (pur′blīnd′) ***adj.*** ⟦ME *pur blind*, quite blind⟧ **1** partly blind **2** slow in understanding

pur·chase (pur′chəs) ***vt.*** **-chased, -chas·ing** ⟦< OFr *pour*, for + *chacier*, to chase⟧ to buy —***n.*** **1** anything bought **2** the act of buying **3** a firm hold applied to move something heavy or to keep from slipping —**pur′chas·a·ble** ***adj.*** —**pur′chas·er** ***n.***

pure (pyoor) ***adj.*** **pur′er, pur′est** ⟦< L *purus*⟧ **1** free from anything that adulterates, taints, etc.; unmixed **2** simple; mere **3** utter; absolute **4** faultless **5** blameless **6** virgin or chaste **7** abstract or theoretical *[pure* physics*]* —**pure′ly** ***adv.*** —**pure′ness** ***n.***

pure′bred′ ***adj.*** belonging to a recognized breed with genetic attributes maintained through generations of unmixed descent —***n.*** a purebred animal or plant

pu·rée or **pu·ree** (pyoo rā′) ***n.*** ⟦Fr: see PURE⟧ **1** cooked food pressed through a sieve or whipped in a blender to a soft, smooth consistency **2** a thick soup made with this —***vt.*** **-réed′** or **-reed′, -rée′ing** or **-ree′ing** to make a purée of

pur·ga·tive (pur′gə tiv) ***adj.*** purging —***n.*** a purging substance; cathartic

pur·ga·to·ry (pur′gə tôr′ē) ***n., pl.*** **-ries** ⟦see fol.⟧ *[often* **P-***]* *Theol.* a state or place after death, in some Christian doctrine, for expiating sins by suffering —**pur′ga·to′ri·al** ***adj.***

purge (purj) ***vt.*** **purged, purg′ing** ⟦< L *purus*, clean + *agere*, do⟧ **1** to cleanse of impurities, etc. **2** to cleanse of sin **3** to rid (a nation, party, etc.) of (individuals held to be disloyal) **4** to empty (the bowels) —***n.*** **1** a purging **2** that which purges; esp., a cathartic —**purg′er** ***n.***

pu·ri·fy (pyoor′ə fī′) ***vt.*** **-fied′, -fy′ing** ⟦see PURE & -FY⟧ **1** to rid of impurities, etc. **2** to free from guilt, sin, etc. —***vi.*** to become purified —**pu′ri·fi·ca′tion** ***n.***

Pu·rim (poor′im) ***n.*** ⟦Heb⟧ a Jewish holiday commemorating Esther's deliverance of the Jews from a massacre

pu·rine (pyo͞or′ēn, -in) ***n.*** ⟦Ger *purin*⟧ **1** a colorless, crystalline organic compound, from which is derived a group of compounds including uric acid and caffeine **2** a purine derivative, as adenine

pur·ism (pyoor′iz′əm) ***n.*** strict or excessive observance of precise usage or formal rules in language, style, etc. —**pur′ist** ***n.***

Pu·ri·tan (pyoor′i tən) ***n.*** ⟦see fol.⟧ **1** a member of a group in 16th-17th-c. England and America that wanted to make the Church of England simpler in its forms and stricter about morality **2** [**p-**] a person regarded as excessively strict in morals and religion —**pu′ri·tan′i·cal** (-tan′i kəl) ***adj.*** —**Pu′ri·tan·ism′** or **pu′ri·tan·ism′** ***n.***

pu′ri·ty (-tē) ***n.*** ⟦< LL *puritas*⟧ a being pure; specif., *a)* freedom from adulterating matter *b)* cleanness *c)* freedom from sin; chastity

purl[1] (purl) ***vi.*** ⟦< ? Scand⟧ to move in ripples or with a murmur —***n.*** the sound of purling water

purl[2] (purl) ***vt., vi.*** ⟦earlier *pirl*, prob. ult. < It⟧ to invert (stitches) in knitting

pur·lieu (purl′yo͞o′) ***n.*** ⟦< OFr *pur-*, through + *aler*, go⟧ **1** [*pl.*] environs **2** an outlying part

pur·loin (pər loin′, pur′loin′) ***vt., vi.*** ⟦< OFr *pur-*, for + *loin*, far⟧ to steal

pur·ple (pur′pəl) ***n.*** ⟦ult. < Gr *porphyra*, shellfish yielding a dye⟧ **1** a dark bluish red **2** crimson cloth or clothing, esp. as a former emblem of royalty —***adj.*** **1** bluish-red **2** imperial **3** ornate *[purple* prose*]* **4** profane or obscene

pur·port (pər pôrt′; *for n.* pur′pôrt′) ***vt.*** ⟦< OFr *por-*, forth + *porter*, to bear⟧ **1** to profess or claim as its meaning **2** to give the appearance, often falsely, of being, intending, etc. —***n.*** **1** meaning; sense **2** intention —**pur·port′ed** ***adj.*** —**pur·port′ed·ly** ***adv.***

pur·pose (pur′pəs) ***vt., vi.*** **-posed, -pos·ing** ⟦see PROPOSE⟧ to intend or plan —***n.*** **1** something one intends to get or do; aim **2** determination **3** the object for which something exists or is done —**on purpose** by design; intentionally —**pur′pose·ful** ***adj.*** —**pur′pose·less** ***adj.***

pur′pose·ly ***adv.*** with a definite purpose; intentionally; deliberately

pur′pos·ive ***adj.*** serving or having a purpose

purr (pur) ***n.*** ⟦echoic⟧ a low, vibratory sound made by a cat at ease —***vi., vt.*** to make, or express by, such a sound

purse (purs) ***n.*** ⟦< Gr *byrsa*, a hide⟧ **1** a small bag for carrying money **2** finances; money **3** a sum of money for a present or prize **4** a woman's handbag —***vt.*** **pursed, purs′ing** to draw (the lips) tightly, as in disapproval

purs·er (pur′sər) ***n.*** ⟦ME, purse-bearer⟧

a ship's officer in charge of accounts, tickets, etc.

pur·su·ance (pər so͞o′əns) ***n.*** a pursuing of a project, plan, etc.

pur·su′ant ***adj.*** [Now Rare] pursuing —**pursuant to** in accordance with

pur·sue (pər so͞o′) ***vt.*** **-sued′**, **-su′ing** ⟦< L *pro-*, forth + *sequi*, follow⟧ **1** to follow in order to overtake or capture; chase **2** to follow (a specified course, action, etc.) **3** to strive for **4** to continue to annoy —**pur·su′er** ***n.***

pur·suit′ (-so͞ot′) ***n.*** **1** a pursuing **2** an occupation, interest, etc.

pu·ru·lent (pyoor′ə lənt) ***adj.*** ⟦< L *pus*, pus⟧ of, like, or discharging pus —**pu′ru·lence** ***n.***

pur·vey (pər vā′) ***vt.*** ⟦see PROVIDE⟧ to supply (esp. food) —**pur·vey′or** ***n.***

pur·view (pur′vyo͞o′) ***n.*** ⟦< OFr *pourveü*, provided⟧ scope or extent, as of control or activity

pus (pus) ***n.*** ⟦L⟧ the yellowish-white liquid matter produced by an infection

push (po͝osh) ***vt.*** ⟦< L *pulsare*, to beat⟧ **1** to press against so as to move **2** to press or urge on **3** to urge the use, sale, etc. of —***n.*** **1** a pushing **2** a vigorous effort **3** an advance against opposition **4** [Inf.] aggressiveness; drive

push button a small knob pushed to operate something, as with electricity

push′er ***n.*** **1** one that pushes **2** [Slang] one who sells drugs, esp. narcotics, illegally

push′o′ver ***n.*** [Slang] **1** anything very easy to do **2** one easily persuaded, defeated, etc.

push′-up′ or **push′up′** ***n.*** an exercise in which a prone person, with hands under shoulders, raises the body by pushing down on the palms

push′y ***adj.*** **-i·er**, **-i·est** [Inf.] annoyingly aggressive and persistent —**push′i·ness** ***n.***

pu·sil·lan·i·mous (pyo͞o′si lan′ə məs) ***adj.*** ⟦< L *pusillus*, tiny + *animus*, the mind⟧ timid; cowardly —**pu′sil·la·nim′i·ty** (-si lə nim′ə tē) ***n.***

puss (po͝os) ***n.*** ⟦< ?⟧ a cat: also **puss′y·cat′** or **puss′y**, *pl.* **-ies**

puss′y·foot′ ***vi.*** [Inf.] **1** to move with stealth or caution, like a cat **2** to avoid committing oneself

pussy willow a willow bearing silvery, velvetlike catkins

pus·tule (pus′cho͞ol′) ***n.*** ⟦L *pustula*⟧ a pus-filled blister or pimple

put (po͝ot) ***vt.*** **put**, **put′ting** ⟦< or akin to OE *potian*, to push⟧ **1** *a)* to thrust; drive *b)* to propel with an overhand thrust [to *put* the shot] **2** to cause to be in a certain place, condition, relation, etc.; place; set **3** to impose (a tax, etc.) **4** to attribute; ascribe **5** to express [*put* it plainly] **6** to present for decision [*put* the question] **7** to bet (money) *on* —***n.*** *Finance* an option to sell a stock, etc. —***adj.*** [Inf.] fixed [stay *put*] —**put across** [Inf.] to cause to be understood or accepted —**put aside** (or **by**) to reserve for later use —**put down** **1** to crush; repress **2** to write down **3** [Slang] to belittle or humiliate —**put in for** to apply for —**put it** (or **something**) **over on** [Inf.] to deceive; trick —**put off** **1** to postpone; delay **2** to evade; divert —**put on** **1** to clothe oneself with **2** to pretend **3** to stage (a play) **4** [Slang] to fool; hoax —**put out** **1** to expel; dismiss **2** to extinguish (a fire or light) **3** to inconvenience **4** *Baseball* to retire (a batter or runner) —**put through** **1** to carry out **2** to cause to do or undergo —**put up** **1** to offer **2** to preserve (fruits, etc.) **3** to build **4** to provide lodgings for **5** to provide (money) **6** to arrange (the hair) with curlers, etc. **7** [Inf.] to incite *to* some action —**put up with** to tolerate

pu·ta·tive (pyo͞ot′ə tiv) ***adj.*** ⟦< L *putare*, suppose⟧ generally considered or deemed such; reputed

put′-down′ ***n.*** [Slang] a belittling remark or crushing retort

Pu·tin (po͞o′tən), **Vlad·i·mir** (vlad′ə mir) 1952- ; president of Russia (2000-)

put′-on′ ***n.*** [Slang] a hoax

pu·tre·fy (pyo͞o′trə fī′) ***vt.***, ***vi.*** **-fied′**, **-fy′ing** ⟦see PUTRID & -FY⟧ to make or become putrid; rot —**pu′tre·fac′tion** (-fak′shən) ***n.***

pu·tres·cent (pyo͞o tres′ənt) ***adj.*** putrefying; rotting —**pu·tres′cence** ***n.***

pu·trid (pyo͞o′trid) ***adj.*** ⟦< L *putrere*, to rot⟧ rotten and foul-smelling

putt (put) ***n.*** ⟦< PUT, v.⟧ *Golf* a shot which attempts to roll the ball into the hole —***vt.***, ***vi.*** to hit (the ball) in making a putt

putt·er[1] (put′ər) ***n.*** *Golf* a short, straight-faced club used in putting

put·ter[2] (put′ər) ***vi.*** ⟦< OE *potian*, to push⟧ to busy oneself in an ineffective or aimless way (with *along, around*, etc.) —***vt.*** to fritter (*away*)

put·ty (put′ē) ***n.*** ⟦Fr *potée*, lit., potful⟧ a soft, plastic mixture of powdered chalk and linseed oil, used to fill small cracks, etc. —***vt.*** **-tied**, **-ty·ing** to cement or fill with putty

put′-up′ ***adj.*** [Inf.] planned secretly beforehand

puz·zle (puz′əl) ***vt.*** **-zled**, **-zling** ⟦< ?⟧ to perplex; bewilder —***vi.*** **1** to be perplexed **2** to exercise one's mind, as over a problem —***n.*** **1** something that puzzles **2** a toy or problem for testing skill or ingenuity —**puzzle out** to solve by deep study —**puz′zle·ment** ***n.*** —**puz′zler** ***n.***

PVC ***n.*** ⟦*p*(*oly*)*v*(*inyl*) *c*(*hloride*)⟧ a type of polymer used in packaging materials, plumbing, etc.

Pvt *abbrev. Mil.* Private

PX *service mark for* a general store at an army base

Pyg·my (pig′mē) ***n.***, *pl.* **-mies** ⟦< Gr *pygmaios*, of a forearm's length⟧ **1** a member of any of several groups of African or Asian peoples of small stature **2** [**p-**] a dwarf —***adj.*** **1** of the Pygmies **2** [**p-**] very small

py·ja·mas (pə jä′məz, -jam′əz) ***pl.n.*** *Brit. sp. of* PAJAMAS

py·lon (pī′län′) ***n.*** ⟦Gr *pylōn*, gateway⟧ **1** a gateway, as of an Egyptian temple

2 a towerlike structure supporting electric lines, marking a flight course, etc.

py·lo·rus (pī lôr′əs) ***n.***, *pl.* **-ri** (-rī) ⟦< Gr *pylōros*, gatekeeper⟧ the opening from the stomach into the duodenum —**py·lor′ic *adj.***

py·or·rhe·a (pī′ə rē′ə) ***n.*** ⟦< Gr *pyon*, pus + *rheein*, to flow⟧ a periodontal infection with formation of pus and loosening of teeth —**py′or·rhe′al *adj.***

pyr·a·mid (pir′ə mid) ***n.*** ⟦< Gr *pyramis*⟧ **1** a huge structure with a square base and four triangular sides meeting at the top, as a royal tomb of ancient Egypt **2** *Geom.* a solid figure with a polygonal base, the sides of which form the bases of triangular surfaces meeting at a common vertex —**py·ram·i·dal** (pi ram′i dəl) ***adj.***

pyre (pīr) ***n.*** ⟦< Gr *pyr*, fire⟧ a pile of wood on which a dead body is burned in funeral rites

Pyr·e·nees (pir′ə nēz′) mountain range between France & Spain

py·ret·ic (pī ret′ik) ***adj.*** ⟦< Gr *pyretos*, fever⟧ of, causing, or characterized by fever

Py·rex (pī′reks′) ⟦arbitrary coinage < *pie*⟧ *trademark for* a heat-resistant glassware used for cooking, lab work, etc.

py·rite (pī′rīt′) ***n.***, *pl.* **py·ri·tes** (pi rīt′ēz′, pī′rīts′) ⟦< Gr *pyritēs*, flint⟧ iron sulfide, a lustrous yellow mineral used as a source of sulfur

pyro- ⟦< Gr *pyr*, fire⟧ *combining form* fire, heat

py·ro·ma·ni·a (pī′rə mā′nē ə) ***n.*** ⟦ModL: see prec. & -MANIA⟧ a compulsion to start destructive fires —**py′ro·ma′ni·ac′ *n.*, *adj.***

py·ro·tech·nics (pī′rə tek′niks) ***pl.n.*** ⟦< Gr *pyr*, fire + *technē*, art⟧ **1** a display of fireworks **2** a dazzling display, as of wit

Pyr·rhic victory (pir′ik) ⟦after *Pyrrhus*, Gr king who won such victories over the Romans, 280 and 279 B.C.⟧ a too costly victory

Py·thag·o·ras (pi thag′ə rəs) 6th c. B.C.; Gr. philosopher & mathematician —**Py·thag′o·re′an** (-ə rē′ən) ***adj.*, *n.***

py·thon (pī′thän′, -thən) ***n.*** ⟦< Gr *Pythōn*, a serpent slain by Apollo⟧ a large, nonpoisonous snake of Asia, Africa, and Australia, that squeezes its prey to death

Q

q[1] or **Q** (kyo͞o) ***n.***, *pl.* **q's, Q's** the 17th letter of the English alphabet

q[2] *abbrev.* **1** quart **2** question

Qa·tar (kä tär′) country on a peninsula of E Arabia, on the Persian Gulf: 4,416,000 sq. mi.; pop. 369,000

QC Quebec

Q.E.D. or **q.e.d.** *abbrev.* ⟦L *quod erat demonstrandum*⟧ which was to be demonstrated or proved

qt *abbrev.* quart(s)

q.t. ***n.*** ⟦< *q(uie)t*⟧ [Inf.] quiet: chiefly in **on the q.t.**, secretly: also **Q.T.**

qua (kwā, kwä) ***prep.*** ⟦L < *qui*, who⟧ in the function or character of; as *[*the President *qua* Commander in Chief*]*

quack[1] (kwak) ***vi.*** ⟦echoic⟧ to utter the sound or cry of a duck —***n.*** this sound

quack[2] (kwak) ***n.*** ⟦ult. < MDu *quacken*, to brag⟧ **1** a person who practices medicine fraudulently **2** one who falsely pretends to have knowledge or a skill —***adj.*** fraudulent —**quack′er·y *n.***

quad[1] (kwäd) ***n.*** *short for:* **1** QUADRANGLE **2** QUADRUPLET

quad[2] *abbrev.* **1** quadrangle **2** quadrant **3** quadruplicate

quad·ran·gle (kwä′draŋ′gəl) ***n.*** ⟦see QUADRI- & ANGLE[1]⟧ **1** *Geom.* a plane figure with four angles and four sides **2** an area surrounded on its four sides by buildings —**quad·ran′gu·lar *adj.***

quad·rant (kwä′drənt) ***n.*** ⟦< L *quadrans*, fourth part⟧ **1** an arc of 90° **2** a quarter section of a circle **3** an instrument formerly used in measuring angular elevation and altitude in navigation, etc.

90°

QUADRANT

quad·rat·ic (kwä drat′ik) ***adj.*** *Algebra* involving a quantity or quantities that are squared but none that are raised to a higher power

quad·ren·ni·al (kwä dren′ē əl) ***adj.*** ⟦< L *quadri-* (see fol.) + *annus*, year⟧ **1** happening every four years **2** lasting four years

quadri- ⟦L < *quattuor*, four⟧ *combining form* four, four times

quad·ri·ceps (kwä′dri seps′) ***n.*** ⟦< prec. + L *caput*, the head⟧ a muscle with four points of origin; esp., the large muscle at the front of the thigh

quad·ri·lat·er·al (kwä′dri lat′ər əl) ***adj.*** ⟦see QUADRI- & LATERAL⟧ four-sided —***n.*** *Geom.* a plane figure having four sides and four angles

qua·drille (kwə dril′, kwä-) ***n.*** ⟦Fr: ult. < L *quadra*, a square⟧ a square dance performed by four couples

quad·ri·ple·gi·a (kwä′dri plē′jē ə, -jə) ***n.*** ⟦ModL < QUADRI- + Gr *plēgē*, a stroke⟧ total paralysis of the body from the neck down —**quad′ri·ple′gic** (-plē′jik) ***adj.*, *n.***

quad·ru·ped (kwä′dro͞o ped′) ***n.*** ⟦< L *quadru-*, four + *pes*, foot⟧ an animal, esp. a mammal, with four feet

quad·ru·ple (kwä drōō′pəl) ***adj.*** ⟦< L *quadru-*, four + *-plus*, -fold⟧ **1** consisting of four **2** four times as much or as many —***n.*** an amount four times as much or as many —***vt.***, ***vi.*** **-pled**, **-pling** to make or become four times as much or as many

quad·ru·plet (kwä drōō′plit, -drup′lit) ***n.*** **1** any of four offspring from the same pregnancy **2** a collection or group of four, usually of one kind

quad·ru·pli·cate (kwä drōō′pli kāt′; *for adj. & n.*, -kit, -kāt′) ***vt.*** **-cat′ed**, **-cat′ing** to make four identical copies of —***adj.*** **1** fourfold **2** being the last of four identical copies —***n.*** any one of such copies —**in quadruplicate** in four such copies —**quad·ru′pli·ca′tion** ***n.***

quaff (kwäf, kwaf) ***vt.***, ***vi.*** ⟦prob. < LowG *quassen*, overindulge⟧ to drink deeply and heartily —***n.*** a quaffing

quag·mire (kwag′mīr′) ***n.*** ⟦*quag*, a bog + MIRE⟧ wet, boggy ground

qua·hog or **qua·haug** (kō′hăg′) ***n.*** ⟦AmInd⟧ an edible clam of the E coast of North America

quail[1] (kwāl) ***vi.*** ⟦prob. < L *coagulare*, coagulate⟧ to recoil in fear

quail[2] (kwāl) ***n.*** ⟦< OFr *quaille*⟧ a small, short-tailed bird resembling a partridge

quaint (kwānt) ***adj.*** ⟦< OFr *cointe* < L *cognitus*, known⟧ **1** pleasingly odd or old-fashioned **2** unusual; curious **3** fanciful; whimsical —**quaint′ly** ***adv.*** —**quaint′ness** ***n.***

quake (kwāk) ***vi.*** **quaked**, **quak′ing** ⟦< OE *cwacian*⟧ **1** to tremble or shake **2** to shiver, as from fear or cold —***n.*** **1** a shaking or tremor **2** an earthquake —**quak′y**, **-i·er**, **-i·est**, ***adj.***

Quak·er (kwā′kər) ***n.*** ⟦< founder's admonition to "quake" at the word of the Lord⟧ *name for* a member of the SOCIETY OF FRIENDS

qual·i·fi·ca·tion (kwôl′ə fi kā′shən) ***n.*** **1** a qualifying or being qualified **2** a restriction; limiting condition **3** any skill, etc. that fits one for a job, office, etc.

qual·i·fied (kwôl′ə fīd′) ***adj.*** **1** fit; competent **2** limited; modified

qual′i·fi′er (-fī′ər) ***n.*** **1** one that qualifies **2** an adjective or adverb

qual′i·fy′ (-fī′) ***vt.*** **-fied′**, **-fy′ing** ⟦< L *qualis*, of what kind + *facere*, make⟧ **1** to make fit for a job, etc. **2** to make legally capable **3** to modify; restrict **4** to moderate; soften —***vi.*** to be or become qualified

qual′i·ta′tive (-tāt′iv) ***adj.*** having to do with quality or qualities —**qual′i·ta′tive·ly** ***adv.***

qual′i·ty (-tē) ***n.***, *pl.* **-ties** ⟦< L *qualis*, of what kind⟧ **1** a characteristic element or attribute **2** basic nature; kind **3** the degree of excellence of a thing **4** excellence —***adj.*** of high quality

qualm (kwäm) ***n.*** ⟦OE *cwealm*, disaster⟧ **1** a sudden, brief feeling of sickness, faintness, etc. **2** a doubt; misgiving **3** a twinge of conscience

quan·da·ry (kwän′də rē, -drē) ***n.***, *pl.* **-ries** ⟦prob. < L⟧ a state of uncertainty; dilemma

quan·ti·fy (kwänt′ə fī′) ***vt.*** **-fied′**, **-fy′ing** ⟦< L *quantus*, how much + *facere*, make⟧ **1** to determine or express the quantity of **2** to express as a quantity or number —**quan′ti·fi′er** ***n.***

quan′ti·ta′tive (-tāt′iv) ***adj.*** having to do with quantity

quan′ti·ty (-tē) ***n.***, *pl.* **-ties** ⟦< L *quantus*, how great⟧ **1** an amount; portion **2** any indeterminate bulk or number **3** [*also pl.*] a great amount **4** that property by which a thing can be measured **5** a number or symbol expressing this property

quan·tum (kwän′təm) ***n.***, *pl.* **-ta** (-tə) ⟦L, how much⟧ *Physics* a fixed, elemental unit of energy: the **quantum theory** states that energy is radiated discontinuously in quanta

quantum jump (or **leap**) a sudden, extensive change

quar·an·tine (kwôr′ən tēn) ***n.*** ⟦< L *quadraginta*, forty⟧ **1** the period, orig. 40 days, during which a vessel suspected of carrying contagious disease is detained in port **2** any isolation imposed to keep contagious diseases, etc. from spreading —***vt.*** **-tined′**, **-tin′ing** to place under quarantine

quark (kwôrk) ***n.*** ⟦arbitrary coinage⟧ any of a set of elementary particles that bind together to form protons, neutrons, mesons, etc.

quar·rel (kwôr′əl) ***n.*** ⟦< L *queri*, complain⟧ **1** a cause for dispute **2** a dispute, esp. an angry one —***vi.*** **-reled** or **-relled**, **-rel·ing** or **-rel·ling** **1** to find fault **2** to dispute heatedly **3** to have a breach in friendship —**quar′rel·er** or **quar′rel·ler** ***n.*** —**quar′rel·some** ***adj.***

quar·ry[1] (kwôr′ē) ***n.***, *pl.* **-ries** ⟦< OFr *cuiree*, parts of prey fed to dogs⟧ an animal, etc. being hunted

quar·ry[2] (kwôr′ē) ***n.***, *pl.* **-ries** ⟦< L *quadrare*, to square⟧ a place where stone, slate, etc. is excavated —***vt.*** **-ried**, **-ry·ing** to excavate from a quarry

quart (kwôrt) ***n.*** ⟦< L *quartus*, fourth⟧ **1** $\frac{1}{4}$ gallon in liquid measure **2** $\frac{1}{8}$ peck in dry measure

quar′ter (-ər) ***n.*** ⟦< L *quartus*, fourth⟧ **1** a fourth of something **2** *a*) one fourth of a year *b*) any of the three terms of about eleven weeks each in an academic year **3** one fourth of an hour **4** one fourth of a dollar; 25 cents, or a coin of this value **5** any leg of a four-legged animal, with the adjoining parts **6** a particular district or section **7** [*pl.*] lodgings **8** mercy granted to a surrendering foe **9** a particular source [*news from high quarters*] —***vt.*** **1** to divide into four equal parts **2** to provide lodgings for —***adj.*** constituting a quarter —**at close quarters** close together

quar′ter·back′ ***n.*** *Football* the offensive back who calls the play, passes the ball, etc.

quar′ter·deck′ ***n.*** the after part of the upper deck of a ship, usually for officers

quar′ter·fi′nal ***adj.*** coming just before the semifinals —***n.*** a quarterfinal match, etc.

quarter horse ⟦< its speed in a

quarter-mile sprint⟧ any of a breed of muscular, solid-colored horse

quar'ter·ly ***adj.*** occurring regularly four times a year —***adv.*** once every quarter of the year —***n.***, *pl.* **-lies** a publication issued every three months

quar'ter·mas'ter ***n.*** **1** *Mil.* an officer who provides troops with quarters, clothing, equipment, etc. **2** *Naut.* a petty officer or mate involved in steering and navigating a ship

quarter note *Music* a note having one fourth the duration of a whole note

quar·tet (kwôr tet') ***n.*** ⟦ult. < L *quartus,* fourth⟧ **1** a group of four **2** *Music a)* a composition for four voices or instruments *b)* the four performers of this

quar·to (kwôrt'ō) ***n.***, *pl.* **-tos** ⟦< L (*in*) *quarto,* (in) a fourth⟧ **1** the page size (about 9 by 12 in.) of a book made up of sheets each of which is folded twice to form four leaves, or eight pages **2** a book with pages of this size

quartz (kwôrts) ***n.*** ⟦Ger *quarz*⟧ a crystalline mineral, a form of silica, usually colorless and transparent

quartz crystal *Electronics* a piece of quartz cut and ground so as to vibrate at a particular frequency

qua·sar (kwā'zär') ***n.*** ⟦< *quas*(*i-stell*)*ar* (*radio source*)⟧ a distant celestial object that emits immense quantities of light and radio waves

quash[1] (kwäsh) ***vt.*** ⟦< L *cassus,* empty⟧ *Law* to set aside (an indictment)

quash[2] (kwäsh) ***vt.*** ⟦< L *quatere,* to break⟧ to quell (an uprising)

qua·si (kwā'zī', kwä'zē') ***adv.*** ⟦L⟧ as if; seemingly; in part —***adj.*** seeming Often hyphenated as a prefix [*quasi*-legal]

quat·rain (kwä'trān') ***n.*** ⟦< L *quattuor,* four⟧ a stanza of four lines

qua·ver (kwā'vər) ***vi.*** ⟦ME *cwafien*⟧ **1** to shake or tremble **2** to be tremulous: said of the voice —***n.*** a tremulous quality in a voice or tone

quay (kē) ***n.*** ⟦ult. < Celt⟧ a wharf, usually of concrete or stone

quea·sy (kwē'zē) ***adj.*** **-si·er, -si·est** ⟦ME *qwesye* < Gmc⟧ **1** affected with nausea **2** squeamish; easily nauseated

Que·bec (kwi bek') **1** province of E Canada: 594,860 sq. mi.; pop. 7,139,000: abbrev. *QC* **2** its capital, on the St. Lawrence River: pop. 167,000

queen (kwēn) ***n.*** ⟦< OE *cwen*⟧ **1** the wife of a king **2** a female monarch in her own right **3** a woman noted for her beauty or accomplishments **4** the fully developed, reproductive female in a colony of bees, ants, etc. **5** a playing card with a picture of a queen on it **6** *Chess* the most powerful piece —**queen'ly, -li·er, -li·est,** ***adj.***

Queens (kwēnz) borough of New York City, on W Long Island: pop. 1,952,000

queen'-size' ***adj.*** larger than usual, but smaller than king-size [a *queen-size* bed is 60 by 80 in.]

queer (kwir) ***adj.*** ⟦< ? Ger *quer,* crosswise⟧ **1** different from the usual; strange **2** [Inf.] eccentric —***vt.*** [Slang] to spoil the success of

quell (kwel) ***vt.*** ⟦OE *cwellan,* kill⟧ **1** to subdue **2** to quiet; allay

quench (kwench) ***vt.*** ⟦OE *cwencan*⟧ **1** to extinguish [to *quench* a fire with water] **2** to satisfy [to *quench* one's thirst] **3** to cool (hot steel, etc.) suddenly by plunging into water, etc. —**quench'less** ***adj.***

quer·u·lous (kwer'yoo ləs, -ə-) ***adj.*** ⟦< L *queri,* complain⟧ **1** inclined to find fault **2** full of complaint; peevish —**quer'u·lous·ly** ***adv.***

que·ry (kwir'ē) ***n.***, *pl.* **-ries** ⟦< L *quaerere,* ask⟧ a question; inquiry —***vt.***, ***vi.*** **-ried, -ry·ing** to question

quest (kwest) ***n.*** ⟦see prec.⟧ **1** a seeking **2** a journey in pursuit of a lofty goal —***vi.*** to go in pursuit

ques·tion (kwes'chən) ***n.*** ⟦see QUERY⟧ **1** an asking; inquiry **2** something asked **3** doubt; uncertainty **4** a matter open to discussion **5** a difficult matter [it's not a *question* of money] **6** a point being debated before an assembly —***vt.*** **1** to ask questions of **2** to express doubt about **3** to dispute; challenge —***vi.*** to ask questions —**out of the question** impossible

ques'tion·a·ble ***adj.*** **1** that can be questioned or doubted **2** suspected of being immoral, dishonest, etc. **3** uncertain

question mark a mark of punctuation (?) put after a sentence, word, etc. to indicate a direct question or to express doubt, etc.

ques'tion·naire' (-chə ner') ***n.*** a written or printed set of questions used in gathering information from people

queue (kyoo) ***n.*** ⟦< L *cauda,* tail⟧ **1** a pigtail **2** [Chiefly Brit.] a line, as of persons waiting to be served **3** stored computer data or programs waiting to be processed —***vi.*** **queued, queu'ing** [Chiefly Brit.] to line up in a queue: often with *up*

quib·ble (kwib'əl) ***n.*** ⟦< L *qui,* who⟧ a petty evasion or criticism —***vi.*** **-bled, -bling** to evade the truth of a point under discussion by caviling

quiche (kēsh) ***n.*** a dish consisting of custard baked in a pastry shell with various ingredients, as bacon, cheese, or spinach

quick (kwik) ***adj.*** ⟦< OE *cwicu,* living⟧ **1** *a)* rapid; swift [a *quick* walk] *b)* prompt [a *quick* reply] **2** prompt to understand or learn [a *quick* mind] **3** easily stirred [a *quick* temper] —***adv.*** quickly; rapidly —***n.*** **1** the living: esp. in **the quick and the dead** **2** the sensitive flesh under the nails **3** the deepest feelings [hurt to the *quick*] —**quick'ly** ***adv.*** —**quick'ness** ***n.***

quick bread any bread leavened with baking powder, soda, etc. and baked as soon as the batter is mixed

quick'en ***vt.*** **1** to animate; enliven; revive **2** to cause to move more rapidly —***vi.*** **1** to become enlivened; revive **2** to begin to show signs of life, as a fetus **3** to become more rapid

quick'-freeze' ***vt.*** **-froze', -fro'zen, -freez'ing** to subject (food) to sudden freezing for long storage

quick'ie *n.* [Inf.] anything done or made quickly and, often, cheaply

quick'lime' *n.* unslaked lime

quick'sand' *n.* ⟦< ME: see QUICK & SAND⟧ a loose, deep sand deposit, engulfing heavy objects easily

quick'sil'ver *n.* mercury

quick'-tem'pered *adj.* easily angered

quick'-wit'ted *adj.* mentally nimble

quid (kwid) *n.* ⟦var. of CUD⟧ a piece, as of tobacco, to be chewed

quid pro quo (kwid' prō kwō') ⟦L⟧ one thing in return for another

qui·es·cent (kwī es'ənt) *adj.* ⟦< L *quiescere,* become quiet⟧ still; inactive —**qui·es'cence** *n.*

qui·et (kwī'ət) *adj.* ⟦< L *quies,* rest⟧ **1** still; motionless **2** *a*) not noisy; hushed *b*) not speaking; silent **3** not easily excited **4** not showy **5** not forward; unobtrusive **6** peaceful and relaxing —*n.* **1** calmness, stillness, etc. **2** a quiet or peaceful quality —*vt.* to make quiet —*vi.* to become quiet: usually with *down* —**qui'et·ly** *adv.*

qui·e·tude (kwī'ə to͞od') *n.* a state of being quiet; calmness

qui·e·tus (kwī ēt'əs) *n.* ⟦< ML *quietus* (*est*), (he is) quit⟧ **1** discharge from debt, etc. **2** death

QUILL

quill (kwil) *n.* ⟦prob. < LowG or MDu⟧ **1** a large, stiff feather **2** *a*) the hollow stem of a feather *b*) anything made from this, as a pen **3** a spine of a porcupine or hedgehog

quilt (kwilt) *n.* ⟦< L *culcita,* bed⟧ a bedcover filled with down, cotton, etc. and stitched together in lines or patterns —*vt.* to stitch like a quilt —*vi.* to make a quilt —**quilt'er** *n.*

quince (kwins) *n.* ⟦< Gr *kydōnion*⟧ **1** a yellowish, apple-shaped fruit, used in preserves **2** the tree it grows on

qui·nel·la (kwi nel'ə, kē-) *n.* ⟦< AmSp < L *quinque,* five⟧ a form of betting in horse-racing, in which the bettor, to win, must pick the first two finishers, in whichever order they finish: also **qui·nie·la** (kē nye'lə)

qui·nine (kwī'nīn') *n.* ⟦< *quina,* cinchona bark⟧ a bitter, crystalline alkaloid extracted from cinchona bark, used for treating malaria

quin·tes·sence (kwin tes'əns) *n.* ⟦< ML *quinta essentia*⟧ the pure essence or perfect type

quin·tet or **quin·tette** (kwin tet') *n.* ⟦ult. < L *quintus,* a fifth⟧ **1** a group of five **2** *Music a*) a composition for five voices or instruments *b*) the five performers of this

quin·tu·ple (kwin to͞o'pəl) *adj.* ⟦< L *quintus,* a fifth + *-plex,* -fold⟧ **1** consisting of five **2** five times as much or as many —*vt., vi.* **-pled, -pling** to make or become five times as much or as many

quin·tu·plet (kwin tup'lit, -to͞o'plit) *n.* **1** any of five offspring from the same pregnancy **2** a group of five, usually of one kind

quip (kwip) *n.* ⟦< L *quippe,* indeed⟧ a witty or sarcastic remark or reply —*vi.* **quipped, quip'ping** to utter quips —**quip'ster** *n.*

quire (kwīr) *n.* ⟦< L *quaterni,* four each⟧ a set of 24 or 25 sheets of paper of the same size and stock

quirk (kwurk) *n.* ⟦< ?⟧ **1** a sudden twist or turn **2** a peculiarity —**quirk'i·ness** *n.* —**quirk'y, -i·er, -i·est,** *adj.*

quirt (kwurt) *n.* ⟦AmSp *cuarta*⟧ a riding whip with a braided leather lash and a short handle

quis·ling (kwiz'liŋ) *n.* ⟦after V. *Quisling,* Norw collaborator with the Nazis⟧ a traitor

quit (kwit) *vt.* **quit, quit'ting** ⟦< ML *quittus,* free⟧ **1** to free (oneself) *of* **2** to stop having, using, or doing **3** to depart from **4** to resign from —*vi.* **1** to stop doing something **2** to give up one's job

quit'claim' *n.* a deed relinquishing a claim, as to property

quite (kwīt) *adv.* ⟦see QUIT⟧ **1** completely **2** really; positively **3** very or fairly *[quite* warm*]* —**quite a few** (or **bit,** etc.) [Inf.] more than a few (or bit, etc.)

Qui·to (kē'tō) capital of Ecuador: pop. 1,101,000

quits (kwits) *adj.* ⟦< ML *quittus,* free⟧ on even terms, as by discharge of a debt, retaliation, etc. —**call it quits** [Inf.] **1** to stop working, etc. **2** to end an association

quit·tance (kwit''ns) *n.* ⟦see QUIT⟧ **1** discharge from a debt **2** recompense

quit'ter *n.* [Inf.] one who quits or gives up easily, without trying hard

quiv·er[1] (kwiv'ər) *vi.* ⟦< OE *curifer-,* eager⟧ to shake tremulously; tremble —*n.* a quivering; tremor

quiv·er[2] (kwiv'ər) *n.* ⟦< OFr *coivre*⟧ a case for holding arrows

quix·ot·ic (kwik sät'ik) *adj.* ⟦after DON QUIXOTE⟧ extravagantly chivalrous or foolishly idealistic

quiz (kwiz) *n., pl.* **quiz'zes** ⟦prob. < L *quis,* what⟧ a questioning; esp., a short examination to test knowledge —*vt.* **quizzed, quiz'zing** to ask questions, or test the knowledge, of —**quiz'zer** *n.*

quiz'zi·cal (-i kəl) *adj.* **1** teasing **2** perplexed —**quiz'zi·cal·ly** *adv.*

quoin (koin, kwoin) *n.* ⟦var. of COIN⟧ **1**

the external corner of a building; esp., any of the large stones at such a corner 2 a wedge-shaped block

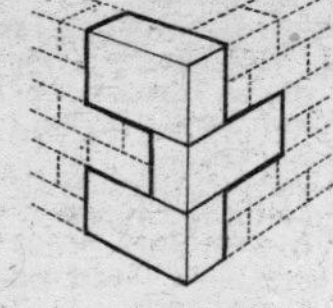
QUOINS

quoit (kwoit) ***n.*** ⟦prob. < OFr *coite,* a cushion⟧ **1** a ring thrown in quoits **2** [*pl.,* with *sing. v.*] a game somewhat like horseshoes, in which rings are thrown at a peg

quon·dam (kwän′dəm) ***adj.*** ⟦L⟧ former

Quon·set hut (kwän′sit) ⟦< *Quonset,* a trademark⟧ a prefabricated, metal shelter like a half cylinder on its flat side

quo·rum (kwôr′əm) ***n.*** ⟦< L *qui,* who⟧ the minimum number of members required to be present before an assembly can transact business

quot *abbrev.* quotation

quo·ta (kwōt′ə) ***n.*** ⟦< L *quota pars,* how large a part⟧ a share or proportion assigned to each of a number

quotation mark either of a pair of punctuation marks (" . . . ") used to enclose a direct quotation

quote (kwōt) ***vt.* quot′ed, quot′ing** ⟦< L *quotus,* of what number⟧ **1** to repeat a passage from or statement of **2** to repeat (a passage, statement, etc.) **3** to state the price of (something) **—*n.*** [Inf.] **1** something quoted **2** QUOTATION MARK **—quot′a·ble *adj.* —quo·ta·tion** (kwō tā′shən) ***n.***

quoth (kwōth) ***vt.*** ⟦< OE *cwethan,* speak⟧ [Archaic] said

quo·tid·i·an (kwō tid′ē ən) ***adj.*** ⟦< L *quotidie*⟧ **1** daily **2** ordinary

quo·tient (kwō′shənt) ***n.*** ⟦< L *quot,* how many⟧ *Math.* the result obtained when one number is divided by another

Qu·ran or **Qu·r′an** (koo rän′) ***n.*** *var. of* KORAN

q.v. *abbrev.* ⟦L *quod vide*⟧ which see

R

r[1] or **R** (är) ***n.,*** *pl.* **r's, R's** the 18th letter of the English alphabet

r[2] *abbrev.* radius

R[1] *trademark for* a film rating indicating that no one under 17 may be admitted unless accompanied by a parent or guardian

R[2] *abbrev.* **1** ⟦L *Rex*⟧ king **2** ⟦L *Regina*⟧ queen **3** Republican **4** right **5** River **6** Road **7** route **8** *Baseball* run(s): also **r**

Ra[1] (rä) ***n.*** *Egypt. Myth.* the sun god and chief deity

Ra[2] *Chem. symbol for* radium

rab·bet (rab′it) ***n.*** ⟦< OFr *rabattre,* beat down⟧ a cut made in a board so that another may be fitted into it **—*vt., vi.*** to cut, or be joined by, a rabbet

rab·bi (rab′ī) ***n.,*** *pl.* **-bis** ⟦< Heb *rabi,* my master⟧ an ordained teacher of the Jewish law

rab·bin·ate (rab′i nit, -nāt′) ***n.*** **1** the position of a rabbi **2** rabbis collectively **—rab·bi·ni·cal** (rə bin′i kəl) ***adj.***

rab·bit (rab′it) ***n.*** ⟦ME *rabette*⟧ a swift, burrowing mammal with soft fur and long ears

rabbit punch *Boxing* a short, sharp blow to the back of the neck

rab·ble (rab′əl) ***n.*** ⟦< ?⟧ a mob

rab′ble-rous′er (-rou′zər) ***n.*** one who tries to arouse people to violent action by appeals to emotions, prejudices, etc.

Ra·be·lais (rab′ə lā′), **Fran·çois** (frän swà′) 1494?-1553; Fr. satirist & humorist

Ra·be·lai·si·an (rab′ə lā′zhən, -zē ən) ***adj.*** ⟦after prec.⟧ broadly and coarsely humorous or satirical

rab·id (rab′id) ***adj.*** ⟦< L *rabere,* to rage⟧ **1** violent; raging **2** fanatic **3** of or having rabies

ra·bies (rā′bēz) ***n.*** ⟦L, madness⟧ an infectious disease characterized by convulsions, etc., transmitted to people by the bite of an infected animal

rac·coon (ra ko͞on′) ***n.*** ⟦< AmInd *aroughcun*⟧ **1** a small, tree-climbing, American mammal, with yellowish-gray fur and a black-ringed tail **2** its fur

race[1] (rās) ***n.*** ⟦< ON *rās,* a running⟧ **1** a competition of speed in running, etc. **2** any similar contest [the *race* for mayor] **3** a swift current of water, or its channel **—*vi.* raced, rac′ing** **1** to take part in a race **2** to go or move swiftly **—*vt.*** **1** to compete with in a race **2** to enter or run (a horse, etc.) in a race **3** to cause to go swiftly **—rac′er *n.***

race[2] (rās) ***n.*** ⟦Fr < It *razza*⟧ **1** any of the different varieties of human beings distinguished by physical traits, blood types, etc. **2** loosely, any geographical population sharing the same habits, ideas, etc. **3** any distinct group of people

race′horse′ ***n.*** a horse bred and trained for racing

ra·ceme (rā sēm′, rə-) ***n.*** ⟦L *racemus,* cluster of grapes⟧ a flower cluster having a central stem along which individual flowers grow on small stalks

race′track′ ***n.*** a course prepared for racing, esp. an oval track for horse races

race′way′ ***n.*** **1** a narrow channel for water **2** a racetrack for harness racing, drag racing, etc.

ra·cial (rā′shəl) ***adj.*** **1** of or characteristic of a RACE[2] **2** between races **—ra′cial·ly *adv.***

rac·i·ness (rā′sē nis) ***n.*** racy quality

racing form a chart, etc. of information about the horse races at a track or tracks

rac·ism (rā′siz′əm) ***n.*** the practice of

racial discrimination, segregation, etc. —**rac'ist** ***n., adj.***

rack[1] (rak) ***n.*** ⟦< LowG *rack*⟧ **1** a framework, etc. for holding or displaying various things *[dish rack]* **2** a toothed bar into which a pinion, etc. meshes **3** an instrument of torture which stretches the victim's limbs —***vt.*** **1** to arrange in or on a rack **2** to torture on a rack **3** to torment —**rack one's brains** to try hard to think of something —**rack up** [Slang] to score or achieve

rack[2] (rak) ***n.*** ⟦var. of WRACK⟧ used only in **go to rack and ruin**, to become ruined

rack[3] (rak) ***n.*** ⟦< ? RACK[1]⟧ the rib section of mutton: in full **rack of lamb**

rack·et[1] (rak'it) ***n.*** ⟦prob. echoic⟧ **1** a noisy confusion **2** *a)* a method or scheme for obtaining money illegally *b)* [Inf.] any dishonest practice

rack·et[2] (rak'it) ***n.*** ⟦< Ar *rāḥa(t)*, palm of the hand⟧ a light bat for tennis, etc., with a network, as of catgut or nylon, in an oval frame attached to a handle: also **rac'quet**

rack·et·eer (rak'ə tir') ***n.*** one who obtains money illegally, as by fraud, extortion, etc. —**rack'et·eer'ing** ***n.***

rac·on·teur (rak'än tur') ***n.*** ⟦Fr < *raconter,* to recount⟧ one skilled at telling stories or anecdotes

rac·quet·ball (rack'it bôl') ***n.*** a game like handball, but played with a short racket

rac·y (rā'sē) ***adj.*** **-i·er**, **-i·est** ⟦RACE[2] + -Y[2]⟧ **1** having the taste or quality of the genuine type *[racy fruit]* **2** lively; spirited **3** pungent **4** risqué

rad (rad) ***n.*** ⟦< RAD(IATION)⟧ a dosage of absorbed radiation

ra·dar (rā'där') ***n.*** ⟦*ra(dio) d(etecting) a(nd) r(anging)*⟧ an apparatus that transmits radio waves to a reflecting object, as an aircraft, to determine its location, speed, etc. by the reflected waves

ra'dar·scope' ***n.*** an oscilloscope that displays reflected radar wave signals

ra·di·al (rā'dē əl) ***adj.*** ⟦< L *radius*, ray⟧ **1** of or like a ray or rays; branching out from a center **2** of a radius

radial (ply) tire an automobile tire with plies of rubberized cords at right angles to the center line of the tread

ra·di·ant (rā'dē ənt) ***adj.*** ⟦< L *radius*, ray⟧ **1** shining brightly **2** showing pleasure, etc.; beaming **3** issuing (from a source) in or as in rays —**ra'di·ance** ***n.*** —**ra'di·ant·ly** ***adv.***

ra·di·ate (rā'dē āt') ***vi.*** **-at'ed**, **-at'ing** ⟦< L *radius,* ray⟧ **1** to send out rays of heat, light, etc. **2** to branch out in lines from a center —***vt.*** **1** to send out (heat, light, etc.) in rays **2** to give forth or spread (happiness, love, etc.)

ra'di·a'tion ***n.*** **1** a radiating **2** the rays sent out **3** energy emitted as nuclear particles, etc.

radiation sickness sickness produced by overexposure to X-rays, radioactive matter, etc.

ra'di·a'tor ***n.*** **1** an apparatus for radiating heat, as into a room **2** a device for circulating coolant, etc., as for a car engine

rad·i·cal (rad'i kəl) ***adj.*** ⟦< L *radix*, root⟧ **1** fundamental; basic **2** favoring basic change, as in the social or economic structure —***n.*** **1** a person holding radical views **2** *Chem.* a group of two or more atoms acting as a single atom **3** *Math.* the sign ($\sqrt{\ }$) used with a quantity to show that its root is to be extracted —**rad'i·cal·ism'** ***n.*** —**rad'i·cal·ly** ***adv.***

ra·dic·chio (rə dē'kyō) ***n.***, *pl.* **-chios** ⟦It⟧ a variety of chicory used in salads

ra·di·i (rā'dē ī') ***n.*** *alt. pl. of* RADIUS

ra·di·o (rā'dē ō') ***n.*** ⟦< *radio(telegraphy)*⟧ **1** the transmission of sounds or signals by electromagnetic waves directly through space to a receiving set **2** *pl.* **-os'** such a set **3** broadcasting by radio as an industry, entertainment, etc. —***adj.*** **1** of, using, used in, or sent by radio **2** of electromagnetic wave frequencies between *c.* 10 kilohertz and *c.* 300,000 megahertz —***vt., vi.*** **-oed'**, **-o'ing** to transmit, or communicate with, by radio

radio- ⟦< L *radius*, ray⟧ *combining form* **1** ray, raylike **2** by radio **3** using radiant energy **4** radioactive *[radiotherapy]*

ra'di·o·ac'tive ***adj.*** giving off radiant energy in the form of particles or rays by the disintegration of atomic nuclei —**ra'di·o·ac·tiv'i·ty** ***n.***

radio astronomy astronomy dealing with radio waves in space in order to obtain information about the universe

ra'di·o·gram' ***n.*** a message sent by radio

ra'di·o·i'so·tope' ***n.*** a radioactive isotope of a chemical element

ra·di·ol·o·gy (rā'dē äl'ə jē) ***n.*** the use of radiant energy, as X-rays, in medical diagnosis and therapy —**ra'di·ol'o·gist** ***n.***

ra'di·o·paque' (-ō pāk') ***adj.*** ⟦RADIO- + (O)PAQUE⟧ not allowing the passage of X-rays, etc.

radio telescope a radio antenna for receiving and measuring radio waves from stars, spacecraft, etc.

ra'di·o·ther'a·py ***n.*** the treatment of disease by the use of X-rays or rays from a radioactive substance

rad·ish (rad'ish) ***n.*** ⟦< L *radix*, root⟧ **1** an annual plant with an edible root **2** the pungent root, eaten raw

ra·di·um (rā'dē əm) ***n.*** ⟦< L *radius,* ray⟧ a radioactive, metallic chemical element found in some uranium, which undergoes spontaneous atomic disintegration

ra·di·us (rā'dē əs) ***n.***, *pl.* **-di·i'** (-ī') or **-us·es** ⟦L, ray⟧ **1** any straight line from the center to the periphery of a circle or sphere **2** the circular area limited by the sweep of such a line *[within a radius of two miles]* **3** the shorter, thicker bone of the forearm

ra·don (rā'dän') ***n.*** ⟦< RADIUM⟧ a radioactive chemical element, a nonreactive gas, formed in the atomic disintegration of radium

RAF *abbrev.* Royal Air Force

raf·fi·a (raf′ē ə) ***n.*** ⟦< native name⟧ **1** a palm tree of Madagascar, with large leaves **2** fiber from its leaves, used as string or for weaving

raff·ish (raf′ish) ***adj.*** ⟦(RIFF)RAFF + -ISH⟧ **1** carelessly unconventional **2** vulgar; low

raf·fle (raf′əl) ***n.*** ⟦ME *rafle*⟧ a lottery in which each participant buys a chance to win a prize —***vt.*** **-fled**, **-fling** to offer as a prize in a raffle: often with *off*

raft[1] (raft) ***n.*** ⟦< ON *raptr,* a log⟧ **1** a flat, buoyant structure of logs, etc. fastened together **2** a flat-bottomed, inflatable boat —***vi.*** to travel on a raft

raft[2] (raft) ***n.*** ⟦< Brit dial. *raff*, rubbish⟧ [Inf.] a large quantity

raf·ter (raf′tər) ***n.*** ⟦OE *ræfter*⟧ any of the beams that slope from the ridge of a roof to the eaves

rag[1] (rag) ***n.*** ⟦< ON *rögg,* tuft of hair⟧ **1** a waste piece of cloth, esp. one old or torn **2** a small piece of cloth for dusting, etc. **3** [*pl.*] old, worn clothes

rag[2] (rag) ***vt.*** **ragged**, **rag′ging** ⟦< ?⟧ [Slang] to tease or scold: often with *on*

rag[3] (rag) ***n.*** a tune in ragtime

ra·ga (rä′gə) ***n.*** ⟦Sans *rāga,* color⟧ any of various melody patterns improvised on by Hindu musicians

rag·a·muf·fin (rag′ə muf′in) ***n.*** ⟦ME *Ragamoffyn,* name of a demon⟧ a poor, ragged child

rag′bag′ ***n.*** **1** a bag for rags **2** a collection of odds and ends

rage (rāj) ***n.*** ⟦< LL *rabia*, madness⟧ **1** a furious, uncontrolled anger **2** a great force, violence, etc. —***vi.*** **raged**, **rag′ing** **1** to show violent anger in action or speech **2** to be forceful, violent, etc. **3** to spread unchecked, as a disease —**(all) the rage** a fad

ragg (rag) ***adj.*** designating or made of sturdy yarn having a speckled pattern

rag·ged (rag′id) ***adj.*** **1** shabby or torn from wear **2** wearing shabby or torn clothes **3** uneven; imperfect **4** shaggy [*ragged* hair] —**run ragged** to tire out; exhaust —**rag′ged·ness** ***n.***

rag′ged·y ***adj.*** tattered

RAGLAN SLEEVES

rag·lan (rag′lən) ***n.*** ⟦after Lord *Raglan,* 19th-c. Brit general⟧ a loose coat with sleeves that continue in one piece to the collar —***adj.*** designating or having such a sleeve

ra·gout (ra go͞o′) ***n.*** ⟦< Fr *ragoûter,* revive the appetite of⟧ a highly seasoned stew of meat and vegetables

rag′time′ ***n.*** ⟦prob. < *ragged time*⟧ **1** a type of American music (*c.* 1890-1920), with strong syncopation in even time **2** its rhythm

rag′weed′ ***n.*** ⟦< its ragged-looking leaves⟧ a weed whose pollen is a common cause of hay fever

rah (rä) ***interj.*** hurrah: used as by cheerleaders

raid (rād) ***n.*** ⟦dial. var. of ROAD⟧ **1** a sudden, hostile attack, esp. by troops or bandits **2** a sudden invasion of a place by police, for discovering violations of the law —***vt.***, ***vi.*** to make a raid (on) —**raid′er** ***n.***

rail[1] (rāl) ***n.*** ⟦< L *regula,* a rule⟧ **1** a bar of wood, metal, etc. placed between posts as a barrier or support **2** any of the parallel metal bars forming a track for a railroad, etc. **3** railroad or railway —***vt.*** to supply with rails or a railing —***adj.*** of a railway or railroad

rail[2] (rāl) ***vi.*** ⟦< LL *ragere,* to bellow⟧ to speak bitterly; complain violently

rail[3] (rāl) ***n.*** ⟦< Fr *raaler,* to screech⟧ a marsh bird with a harsh cry

rail′ing ***n.*** **1** materials for rails **2** a fence, etc. made of rails and posts

rail·ler·y (rā′lər ē) ***n.***, *pl.* **-ies** ⟦see RAIL[2]⟧ light, good-natured ridicule

rail′road′ ***n.*** **1** a track of parallel steel rails for a train **2** a complete system of such tracks, trains, etc. —***vt.*** **1** to transport by railroad **2** [Inf.] to rush through quickly, so as to prevent careful consideration —***vi.*** to work on a railroad —**rail′road′er** ***n.*** —**rail′road′ing** ***n.***

rail′way′ ***n.*** **1** any track with rails for guiding wheels **2** RAILROAD

rai·ment (rā′mənt) ***n.*** ⟦see ARRAY & -MENT⟧ [Archaic] clothing; attire

rain (rān) ***n.*** ⟦OE *regn*⟧ **1** water falling in drops condensed from the atmosphere **2** the falling of such drops **3** a rapid falling of many small objects —***vi.*** **1** to fall: said of rain **2** to fall like rain —***vt.*** **1** to pour down **2** to give in large quantities —**rain out** to cause (an event) to be postponed because of rain —**rain′y**, **-i·er**, **-i·est**, ***adj.***

rain′bow′ (-bō′) ***n.*** ⟦OE *regnboga*⟧ an arc containing the colors of the spectrum, formed in the sky by the refraction, reflection, and dispersion of light in rain or fog

rain check a ticket stub to a ballgame, etc. allowing future admission if the event is rained out

rain′coat′ ***n.*** a water-repellent coat

rain′drop′ ***n.*** a single drop of rain

rain′fall′ ***n.*** **1** a falling of rain **2** the amount of rain over a given area during a given time

rain forest a dense, evergreen forest in a rainy tropical region

rain′storm′ ***n.*** a storm with heavy rain

rain′wa′ter ***n.*** water that is falling or has fallen as rain

raise (rāz) ***vt.*** **raised**, **rais′ing** ⟦< ON *reisa*⟧ **1** to cause to rise; lift **2** to construct; build **3** to increase in size, intensity, amount, degree, etc. [to *raise* prices, *raise* one's voice*]* **4** to provoke; inspire **5** to present for consideration *[raise* a question*]* **6** to collect (an army, money, etc.) **7** to end *[raise* a siege*]* **8** *a*) to cause to grow *b*) to rear (children) —*n.* **1** a raising **2** an increase in salary or in a bet —**raise Cain** (or **hell**, etc.) [Slang] to create a disturbance

rai·sin (rā′zən) *n.* ⟦< L *racemus,* cluster of grapes⟧ a dried sweet grape

rai·son d'être (rā′zōn det′, det′rə) ⟦Fr⟧ reason for being; justification for existence

raj (räj) *n.* ⟦Hindi: see fol.⟧ in India, rule; government —**the Raj** the British government in, or its dominion over, India

ra·jah or **ra·ja** (rä′jə) *n.* ⟦< Sans *rāj,* to rule⟧ a prince in India

rake[1] (rāk) *n.* ⟦OE *raca*⟧ a long-handled tool with teeth at one end, for gathering loose hay, leaves, etc. —*vt.* **raked, rak′ing 1** to gather or smooth with a rake **2** to search through minutely **3** to direct gunfire along (a line of troops, etc.) —**rake in** to gather a great amount of rapidly —**rake up** to uncover facts or gossip about (the past, etc.)

RAKES

rake[2] (rāk) *n.* ⟦contr. of *rakehell*⟧ a dissolute, debauched man

rake[3] (rāk) *vi., vt.* **raked, rak′ing** ⟦< ?⟧ to slant —*n.* a slanting

rake′-off′ *n.* [Slang] a commission or rebate, esp. when illegitimate

rak·ish (rāk′ish) *adj.* ⟦< RAKE[3] + -ISH⟧ **1** having a trim appearance suggesting speed: said of a ship **2** dashing; jaunty —**rak′ish·ly** *adv.*

Ra·legh or **Ra·leigh** (rô′lē, rä′lē), Sir **Wal·ter** (wôl′tər) 1552?-1618; Eng. explorer & poet

Ra·leigh (rô′lē, rä′lē) capital of North Carolina: pop. 212,000

ral·ly[1] (ral′ē) *vt., vi.* **-lied, -ly·ing** ⟦< OFr *re-,* again + *alier,* join⟧ **1** to bring back together in, or come back to, a state of order: said as of troops **2** to bring or come together for a common purpose **3** to recover; revive —*n., pl.* **-lies 1** a rallying or being rallied; esp., a gathering of people for some purpose **2** an organized automobile run designed to test driving skills

ral·ly[2] (ral′ē) *vt., vi.* **-lied, -ly·ing** ⟦see RAIL[2]⟧ to tease or ridicule

ram (ram) *n.* ⟦OE *ramm*⟧ **1** a male sheep **2** BATTERING RAM —*vt.* **rammed, ram′ming 1** to strike against with great force **2** to force into place; press down

RAM (ram) *n.* random-access memory

ram·ble (ram′bəl) *vi.* **-bled, -bling** ⟦< ME *romen*⟧ **1** to roam about; esp., to stroll about idly **2** to talk or write aimlessly **3** to spread in all directions, as a vine does —*n.* a stroll

ram′bler (-blər) *n.* a person or thing that rambles; esp., a climbing rose

ram·bunc·tious (ram buŋk′shəs) *adj.* ⟦altered, (after RAM) < earlier *rambustious*⟧ disorderly, boisterous, unruly, etc. —**ram·bunc′tious·ness** *n.*

ram·e·kin or **ram·e·quin** (ram′ə kin) *n.* ⟦< Fr < MDu⟧ a small individual baking dish

ra·men (rä′mən) *pl.n.* [*sometimes with sing. v.*] Japanese wheat noodles

ram·i·fy (ram′ə fī′) *vt., vi.* **-fied′, -fy′ing** ⟦< L *ramus,* a branch + *facere,* make⟧ to divide or spread out into branches or branchlike divisions —**ram′i·fi·ca′tion** *n.*

ramp (ramp) *n.* ⟦< OFr *ramper,* to climb⟧ **1** a sloping surface, walk, etc. joining different levels **2** a means for boarding a plane, as a movable staircase **3** a sloping runway, as for launching boats

ram·page (ram′pāj′) *vi.* **-paged′, -pag′ing** to rush about wildly; rage —*n.* an outbreak of violent, raging behavior: chiefly in **on the** (or **a**) **rampage**

ramp·ant (ram′pənt) *adj.* ⟦< OFr *ramper,* to climb⟧ growing unchecked; widespread

ram·part (ram′pärt′, -pərt) *n.* ⟦< Fr *re-,* again + *emparer,* fortify⟧ an embankment of earth surmounted by a parapet for defending a fort, etc.

ram′rod′ *n.* a rod for ramming down the charge in a muzzle-loading gun

ram·shack·le (ram′shak′əl) *adj.* ⟦< RANSACK⟧ loose and rickety; likely to fall to pieces

ran (ran) *vi., vt. pt. of* RUN

ranch (ranch) *n.* ⟦< Sp *rancho,* small farm⟧ **1** a large farm, esp. in the W U.S., for raising cattle, horses, or sheep **2** a style of house with all the rooms on one floor: in full **ranch house** —*vi.* to work on or manage a ranch —**ranch′er** *n.*

ranch dressing creamy buttermilk salad dressing

ran·cid (ran′sid) *adj.* ⟦< L *rancere,* to be rank⟧ smelling or tasting of stale fats or oils; spoiled

ran·cor (raŋ′kər) *n.* ⟦< L *rancere,* to be rank⟧ a continuing and bitter hate or ill will: Brit. sp. **ran′cour** —**ran′cor·ous** *adj.* —**ran′cor·ous·ly** *adv.*

rand (rand) *n., pl.* **rand** the monetary unit of South Africa

R & B or **r & b** *abbrev.* rhythm and blues

R & D *abbrev.* research and development

ran·dom (ran′dəm) *adj.* ⟦< OFr *randir,* run violently⟧ purposeless; haphazard —**at random** haphazardly —**ran′dom·ly** *adv.*

ran′dom-ac′cess *adj. Comput.* of a kind of memory that allows data to be directly accessible

ran′dom·ize′ (-īz′) *vt.* **-ized′, -iz′ing** to select or choose (items of a group) in a random order

ran·dy (ran′dē) *adj.* **-di·er, -di·est** [Chiefly Scot.] amorous; lustful

rang (raŋ) *vi., vt. pt. of* RING[1]

range (rānj) *vt.* **ranged, rang′ing** ⟦< OFr

renc, a ring⟧ **1** to arrange in order; set in a row or rows **2** to place (esp. oneself) with others in a cause, etc. **3** to roam through —***vi.*** **1** to extend in a given direction **2** to roam **3** to vary between stated limits —***n.*** **1** a row, line, or series **2** a series of connected mountains **3** the distance that a weapon can fire its projectile **4** *a*) a place for shooting practice *b*) a place for testing rockets in flight **5** extent; scope **6** a large, open area for grazing livestock **7** the limits of possible variations of amount, degree, pitch, etc. *[a wide range of prices]* **8** a cooking stove

rang·er (rān′jər) ***n.*** **1** *a*) a mounted trooper who patrols a region *b*) [*often* **R-**] a soldier trained for raiding and close combat **2** a warden who patrols parks and forests

Ran·goon (ran go͞on′) *former name for* YANGON

rang·y (rān′jē) ***adj.*** **-i·er, -i·est** long-limbed and slender —**rang′i·ness *n.***

rank[1] (raŋk) ***n.*** ⟦< OFr *ranc*⟧ **1** a row, line, or series **2** a social class **3** a high position in society **4** an official grade *[the rank of major]* **5** a relative position in a scale *[a poet of the first rank]* **6** *a*) a row of soldiers, etc. placed side by side *b*) [*pl.*] the army; esp., enlisted soldiers —***vt.*** **1** to place in a rank **2** to assign a position to **3** to outrank —***vi.*** to hold a certain position —**rank and file** **1** enlisted soldiers **2** the common people, as distinguished from leaders

rank[2] (raŋk) ***adj.*** ⟦OE *ranc*, strong⟧ **1** growing vigorously and coarsely *[rank grass]* **2** strong and offensive in smell or taste **3** in bad taste **4** complete; utter *[rank deceit]*

rank′ing ***adj.*** **1** of the highest rank **2** prominent or outstanding

ran·kle (raŋ′kəl) ***vi., vt.*** **-kled, -kling** ⟦ult. < L dim. of *draco*, dragon⟧ **1** [Obs.] to fester **2** to cause, or cause to have, long-lasting anger, rancor, etc.

ran·sack (ran′sak′) ***vt.*** ⟦< ON *rann*, house + *sœkja*, seek⟧ **1** to search thoroughly **2** to plunder

ran·som (ran′səm) ***n.*** ⟦see REDEEM⟧ **1** the redeeming of a captive by paying money or complying with demands **2** the price thus paid or demanded —***vt.*** to obtain the release of (a captive, etc.) by paying the demanded price

rant (rant) ***vi., vt.*** ⟦< obs. Du *ranten*⟧ to talk or say in a loud, wild, extravagant way —***n.*** loud, wild speech

rap (rap) ***vt.*** **rapped, rap′ping** ⟦prob. echoic⟧ **1** to strike quickly and sharply; tap **2** [Slang] to criticize sharply —***vi.*** **1** to knock sharply **2** [Slang] to talk —***n.*** **1** a quick, sharp knock **2** [Slang] blame or punishment **3** [Slang] a chat or serious discussion **4** a kind of popular music in which rhymed verses are chanted over repetitive rhythms

ra·pa·cious (rə pā′shəs) ***adj.*** ⟦< L *rapere*, seize⟧ **1** greedy; voracious **2** predatory —**ra·pa′cious·ly *adv.*** —**ra·pac′i·ty** (-pas′ə tē) ***n.***

rape[1] (rāp) ***n.*** ⟦prob. < L *rapere*, seize⟧ **1** the crime of having sexual intercourse with a person forcibly and without consent **2** the plundering (*of* a city, etc.), as in warfare —***vt.*** **raped, rap′ing** **1** to commit rape on; violate **2** to plunder or destroy —***vi.*** to commit rape —**rap′ist *n.***

rape[2] (rāp) ***n.*** ⟦< L *rapa*, turnip⟧ an annual plant whose leaves are used for fodder

Raph·a·el (rä′fā el′, -fī-) 1483-1520; It. painter & architect

rap·id (rap′id) ***adj.*** ⟦< L *rapere*, to rush⟧ moving or occurring with speed; swift; quick —***n.*** [*usually pl.*] a part of a river where the current is swift —**ra·pid·i·ty** (rə pid′ə tē) ***n.*** —**rap′id·ly *adv.***

rapid transit a system of public transportation in an urban area, using electric trains along an unimpeded right of way

ra·pi·er (rā′pē ər) ***n.*** ⟦Fr *rapière*⟧ a light, sharp-pointed sword used only for thrusting

rap·ine (rap′in) ***n.*** ⟦< L *rapere*, seize⟧ plunder; pillage

rap·pel (ra pel′) ***n.*** ⟦Fr, lit., a recall⟧ a descent by a mountain climber, using a double rope around the body to control the slide downward —***vi.*** **-pelled′, -pel′ling** to make such a descent

rap′per ***n.*** a performer of rap music

rap·port (ra pôr′) ***n.*** ⟦Fr⟧ close relationship; harmony

rap·proche·ment (ra′prōsh män′) ***n.*** ⟦Fr⟧ an establishing of friendly relations

rap·scal·lion (rap skal′yən) ***n.*** ⟦< RASCAL⟧ ROGUE

rap sheet [Slang] one's police record of arrests and convictions

rapt (rapt) ***adj.*** ⟦< L *rapere*, seize⟧ **1** carried away with joy, love, etc. **2** completely engrossed (*in* meditation, study, etc.)

rap·tor (rap′tər, -tôr′) ***n.*** ⟦< L *rapere*, to snatch⟧ a bird, as a hawk, that preys on other animals

rap·ture (rap′chər) ***n.*** the state of being carried away with joy, love, etc.; ecstasy —**rap′tur·ous *adj.*** —**rap′tur·ous·ly *adv.***

ra·ra a·vis (rer′ə ā′vis) *pl.* **ra·rae a·ves** (rer′ē ā′vēz) ⟦L, lit., strange bird⟧ an extraordinary person or thing

rare[1] (rer) ***adj.*** **rar′er, rar′est** ⟦< L *rarus*⟧ **1** not frequently encountered; scarce; unusual **2** unusually good; excellent **3** not dense *[rare atmosphere]* —**rare′ness *n.***

rare[2] (rer) ***adj.*** **rar′er, rar′est** ⟦OE *hrere*⟧ not completely cooked; partly raw: said esp. of meat —**rare′ness *n.***

rare[3] (rer) ***vi.*** **rared, rar′ing** [Inf.] to be eager: used in prp. *[raring to go]*

rare·bit (rer′bit) ***n.*** WELSH RABBIT

rar·e·fy (rer′ə fī′) ***vt., vi.*** **-fied′, -fy′ing** ⟦< L *rarus*, RARE[1] + *facere*, make⟧ to make or become less dense —**rar′e·fac′tion** (-fak′shən) ***n.***

rare·ly (rer′lē) ***adv.*** **1** infrequently; seldom **2** uncommonly

rar·i·ty (rer′ə tē) ***n.*** **1** a being rare; specif., *a*) scarcity *b*) lack of density **2** *pl.* **-ties** something remarkable or valuable because rare

ras·cal (ras′kəl) ***n.*** ⟦< OFr *rascaille*, rabble⟧ **1** a rogue **2** a mischievous child —**ras·cal'i·ty** (-kal'ə tē) ***n.*** —**ras'cal·ly** ***adj., adv.***

rash[1] (rash) ***adj.*** ⟦ME *rasch*⟧ too hasty in acting or speaking; reckless —**rash'ly** ***adv.*** —**rash'ness** ***n.***

rash[2] (rash) ***n.*** ⟦< OFr *rascaille,* rabble⟧ **1** an eruption of spots on the skin **2** a sudden appearance of a large number of instances

rash'er ***n.*** ⟦< L *radere,* to scrape⟧ a thin slice of bacon, etc., or a serving of several such slices

rasp (rasp) ***vt.*** ⟦< OHG *raspon,* to scrape together⟧ **1** to scrape as with a file **2** to grate upon; irritate —***vi.*** **1** to grate **2** to make a rough, grating sound —***n.*** **1** a type of rough file **2** a rough, grating sound —**rasp'y, -i·er, -i·est,** ***adj.***

rasp·ber·ry (raz'ber'ē, -bər-) ***n., pl.*** **-ries** ⟦< earlier *raspis*⟧ **1** a small, juicy, edible reddish fruit of a plant related to the rose **2** this plant **3** [Slang] a sound of derision

rat (rat) ***n.*** ⟦OE *ræt*⟧ **1** a long-tailed rodent, resembling, but larger than, the mouse **2** [Slang] a sneaky, contemptible person; esp., an informer —***vi.*** **rat'ted, rat'ting** [Slang] to inform (*on*) —**smell a rat** to suspect a trick, plot, etc.

ratch·et (rach'it) ***n.*** ⟦< It *rocca,* distaff⟧ **1** a toothed wheel (in full **ratchet wheel**) or bar whose sloping teeth catch a pawl, preventing backward motion **2** such a pawl

rate[1] (rāt) ***n.*** ⟦< L *reri,* reckon⟧ **1** the amount, degree, etc. of anything in relation to units of something else *[rate of pay]* **2** price, esp. per unit —***vt.*** **rat'ed, rat'ing** **1** to appraise **2** to consider **3** [Inf.] to deserve —***vi.*** to have value, status, etc. —**at any rate** **1** in any event **2** anyway

rate[2] (rāt) ***vt., vi.*** **rat'ed, rat'ing** ⟦< L *reputare,* to count⟧ to scold; chide

rath·er (rath'ər) ***adv.*** ⟦OE *hræthe,* quickly⟧ **1** more willingly; preferably **2** with more justice, reason, etc. *[I, rather* than you, should pay*]* **3** more accurately *[*my son, or *rather,* stepson*]* **4** on the contrary **5** somewhat *[rather* hungry*]* —**rather than** instead of

rat'hole' ***n.*** a great waste of money, etc.

raths·kel·ler (rath'skel'ər) ***n.*** ⟦Ger < *rat,* council, town hall + *keller,* cellar⟧ a restaurant, usually below the street level, where beer is served

rat·i·fy (rat'ə fī') ***vt.*** **-fied', -fy'ing** ⟦< L *ratus,* reckoned + *facere,* make⟧ to approve; esp., to give official sanction to —**rat'i·fi·ca'tion** ***n.***

rat·ing (rāt'iŋ) ***n.*** **1** a rank or grade, as of military personnel **2** a placement in a certain rank or class **3** an evaluation; appraisal **4** *Film* a classification, based on content, restricting the age of those who may attend **5** *Radio, TV* the relative popularity of a program according to sample polls

ra·tio (rā'shō, -shē ō') ***n., pl.*** **-tios** ⟦L, a reckoning⟧ a fixed relation in degree, number, etc. between two similar things; proportion

ra·ti·oc·i·nate (rash'ē äs'ə nāt') ***vi.*** **-nat'ed, -nat'ing** ⟦see prec.⟧ to think or argue logically; reason —**ra'ti·oc'i·na'tion** ***n.***

ra·tion (rash'ən, rā'shən) ***n.*** ⟦see RATIO⟧ **1** a fixed portion; share **2** a fixed allowance of food, as a daily allowance for a soldier **3** [*pl.*] food supply —***vt.*** **1** to supply with rations **2** to distribute (food, clothing, etc.) in rations, as in times of scarcity

ra·tion·al (rash'ən əl) ***adj.*** ⟦see RATIO⟧ **1** of or based on reasoning **2** able to reason; reasoning **3** sensible or sane —**ra'tion·al'i·ty** (-ə nal'ə tē) ***n.*** —**ra'tion·al·ly** ***adv.***

ra·tion·ale (rash'ə nal') ***n.*** ⟦< L *rationalis,* rational⟧ **1** the reasons or rational basis for something **2** an explanation of principles

ra'tion·al·ism' ***n.*** the practice of accepting reason as the only authority in determining one's opinions or course of action —**ra'tion·al·ist** ***n., adj.*** —**ra'tion·al·is'tic** ***adj.***

ra'tion·al·ize' ***vt., vi.*** **-ized', -iz'ing** **1** to make or be rational or reasonable **2** to devise plausible explanations for (one's acts, beliefs, etc.), usually in self-deception —**ra'tion·al·i·za'tion** ***n.***

rat·line (rat'lin) ***n.*** ⟦< ?⟧ any of the horizontal ropes which join the shrouds of a ship and serve as a ladder: also sp. **rat'lin**

rat race [Slang] a mad scramble or intense struggle, as in the business world

rat·tan (ra tan') ***n.*** ⟦Malay *rotan*⟧ **1** a tall palm tree with long, slender, tough stems **2** its stem, used in making furniture, etc.

rat·tle (rat''l) ***vi.*** **-tled, -tling** ⟦prob. echoic⟧ **1** to make a series of sharp, short sounds **2** to chatter: often with *on* —***vt.*** **1** to cause to rattle **2** to confuse or upset —***n.*** **1** a series of sharp, short sounds **2** a series of horny rings at the end of a rattlesnake's tail **3** a baby's toy, a percussion instrument, etc. made to rattle when shaken

rat'tle·brain' ***n.*** a frivolous, talkative person —**rat'tle·brained'** ***adj.***

rat'tler ***n.*** a rattlesnake

rat'tle·snake' ***n.*** a poisonous American snake with horny rings at the end of the tail that rattle when shaken

rat'tle·trap' ***n.*** a rickety old car

rat'tling (-liŋ) ***adj.*** **1** that rattles **2** [Inf.] very fast, good, etc. —***adv.*** [Inf.] very *[*a *rattling* good time*]*

rat'trap' ***n.*** **1** a trap for rats **2** [Inf.] a dirty, run-down building

rat·ty (rat'ē) ***adj.*** **-ti·er, -ti·est** [Slang] shabby or run-down

rau·cous (rô'kəs) ***adj.*** ⟦L *raucus*⟧ **1** hoarse **2** loud and rowdy —**rau'cous·ly** ***adv.*** —**rau'cous·ness** ***n.***

raun·chy (rôn'chē) ***adj.*** **-chi·er, -chi·est** ⟦< ?⟧ [Slang] **1** dirty, sloppy, etc. **2** risqué, lustful, etc.

rav·age (rav'ij) ***n.*** ⟦see RAVISH⟧ destruction; ruin —***vt.*** **-aged, -ag·ing** to destroy violently; ruin

rave (rāv) ***vi.*** **raved, rav'ing** ⟦< OFr

raver, roam]] **1** to talk incoherently or wildly **2** to talk with great enthusiasm (*about*) —***n.*** [Inf.] a very enthusiastic commendation

rav·el (rav′əl) ***vt., vi.*** **-eled** or **-elled, -el·ing** or **-el·ling** [[< MDu *ravelen*]] to separate into its parts, esp. threads; fray —***n.*** a raveled part in a fabric

ra·ven (rā′vən) ***n.*** [[OE *hræfn*]] the largest crow, with a straight, sharp beak —***adj.*** black and lustrous

rav·en·ing (rav′ə niŋ) ***adj.*** [[ult. < L *rapere*, seize]] greedily searching for prey *[ravening* wolves*]*

rav·e·nous (rav′ə nəs) ***adj.*** [[< L *rapere*, seize]] **1** greedily hungry **2** rapacious —**rav′e·nous·ly** ***adv.***

ra·vine (rə vēn′) ***n.*** [[Fr, flood]] a long, deep hollow in the earth, esp. one worn by a stream; gorge

rav′ing ***adj.*** **1** that raves; frenzied **2** [Inf.] exciting enthusiastic admiration *[a raving* beauty*]* —***adv.*** so as to cause raving *[raving* mad*]*

ra·vi·o·li (rav′ē ō′lē) ***n., pl.*** **-li** or **-lis** [[It]] small casings of dough filled with meat, cheese, etc.

rav·ish (rav′ish) ***vt.*** [[< L *rapere*, seize]] **1** to seize and carry away forcibly **2** to rape (a woman) **3** to transport with joy or delight —**rav′ish·ment** ***n.***

rav′ish·ing ***adj.*** causing great joy

raw (rô) ***adj.*** [[OE *hreaw*]] **1** not cooked **2** in its natural condition; not processed *[raw* silk*]* **3** inexperienced *[a raw* recruit*]* **4** abraded and sore **5** uncomfortably cold and damp *[a raw* wind*]* **6** brutal, coarse, indecent, etc. **7** [Inf.] harsh or unfair *[a raw* deal*]* —**in the raw** **1** in the natural state **2** naked —**raw′ness** ***n.***

raw bar a place serving uncooked shellfish

raw′boned′ (-bōnd′) ***adj.*** lean; gaunt

raw′hide′ ***n.*** **1** an untanned cattle hide **2** a whip made of this

ray[1] (rā) ***n.*** [[< L *radius*]] **1** any of the thin lines, or beams, of light that appear to come from a bright source **2** any of several lines radiating from a center **3** a tiny amount *[a ray* of hope*]* **4** a beam of radiant energy, radioactive particles, etc.

ray[2] (rā) ***n.*** [[< L *raia*]] a cartilaginous fish with a broad, flat body, widely expanded fins on both sides, and a whiplike tail

ray·on (rā′än) ***n.*** [[< RAY[1]]] **1** a textile fiber made from a cellulose solution **2** a fabric of such fibers

raze (rāz) ***vt.*** **razed, raz′ing** [[< L *radere*, to scrape]] to tear down completely; demolish

ra·zor (rā′zər) ***n.*** [[see prec.]] **1** a sharp-edged cutting instrument for shaving, cutting hair, etc. **2** SHAVER (sense 2)

razor wire sharp-edged wire, as for fences

razz (raz) ***vt.*** [[< RASPBERRY]] [Slang] to tease, ridicule, etc.

raz·zle-daz·zle (raz′əl daz′əl) ***n.*** [Slang] a flashy, deceptive display

razz·ma·tazz (raz′mə taz′) ***n.*** [[prob. < prec.]] [Slang] **1** lively spirit **2** flashy display

RBI or **rbi** ***n., pl.*** **RBIs** or **RBI, rbi's** or **rbi** *Baseball* run batted in

RC *abbrev.* Roman Catholic

rd *abbrev.* **1** rod **2** round

Rd *abbrev.* Road

RD *abbrev.* Rural Delivery

RDA *abbrev.* Recommended Daily (*or* Dietary) Allowance: the amount of protein, vitamins, etc. suggested for various age groups

re[1] (rā) ***n.*** [[It]] *Music* the second tone of the diatonic scale

re[2] (rē, rā) ***prep.*** [[L < *res*, thing]] in the matter of; as regards

re- [[< Fr or L]] *prefix* **1** back **2** again; anew It is sometimes hyphenated, as before a word beginning with *e* or to distinguish between such forms as *re-cover* (to cover again) and RECOVER The words in the following list can be understood if "again" or "anew" is added to the meaning of the base word:

reacquaint
reacquire
readjust
readmit
reaffirm
realign
reappear
reapply
reappoint
reappraise
rearm
reassemble
reassert
reassess
reassign
reawaken
reborn
rebroadcast
rebuild
recharge
recheck
reclassify
recommence
reconquer
reconvene
reconvert
recopy
re-cover
redecorate
rededicate
redesign
redirect
rediscover
redistribute
redivide
redraw
reedit
reeducate
reelect
reembark
reemerge
reemphasize
reenact
reenlist
reenter
reestablish
reevaluate
reexamine
reexplain
refashion
refasten
refinance
reformulate
refuel
refurnish
rehear
reheat
rehire
reinfect
reinsert
reinspect
reinvest
reissue
rekindle
relearn
reload
remake
remarry
rematch
remix
rename
renegotiate
renominate
renumber
reoccupy
reoccur
reopen
reorder
repack
repackage
repaint
rephrase
replay
re-press
reprint
republish
reread
rerelease
reroute
reschedule
resell
reset
resettle
reshuffle
respell
restate
restring
restudy
restyle
resupply
retell
retest

rethink | reuse
retrain | revitalize
retrial | reweigh
reunite | rework
reupholster | rezone

reach (rēch) ***vt.*** ⟦OE *ræcan*⟧ **1** to thrust out (the hand, etc.) **2** to extend to by thrusting out, etc. **3** to obtain and hand over *[reach* me the salt*]* **4** to go as far as; attain **5** to influence; affect **6** to get in touch with, as by telephone —***vi.*** **1** to thrust out the hand, etc. **2** to extend in influence, space, amount, etc. **3** to carry: said of sight, sound, etc. **4** to try to get something —***n.*** **1** a stretching or thrusting out **2** the power of, or the extent covered in, stretching, obtaining, etc. **3** a continuous extent, esp. of water

re·act (rē akt′) ***vi.*** **1** to act in return or reciprocally **2** to act in opposition **3** to act in a reverse way; go back to a former condition, stage, etc. **4** to respond to a stimulus **5** *Chem.* to act with another substance in a chemical change

re·act·ant (rē ak′tənt) ***n.*** any substance involved in a chemical reaction

re·ac·tion (rē ak′shən) ***n.*** **1** a return or opposing action, etc. **2** a response, as to a stimulus or influence **3** a movement back to a former or less advanced condition; extreme conservatism **4** a chemical change

re·ac′tion·ar′y (-shə ner′ē) ***adj.*** of, characterized by, or advocating reaction, esp. in politics —***n.***, *pl.* **-ies** an advocate of reaction, esp. in politics

re·ac·ti·vate (rē ak′tə vāt′) ***vt.***, ***vi.*** **-vat′ed**, **-vat′ing** to make or be made active again; specif., to return (a military unit, ship, etc.) to active status —**re·ac′ti·va′tion** ***n.***

re·ac′tive (-tiv) ***adj.*** **1** tending to react **2** of, from, or showing reaction —**re′ac·tiv′i·ty** ***n.***

re·ac′tor (-tər) ***n.*** NUCLEAR REACTOR

read[1] (rēd) ***vt.*** **read** (red), **read·ing** (rēd′iŋ) ⟦< OE *rædan,* to counsel⟧ **1** to get the meaning of (writing) by interpreting the characters **2** to utter aloud (written matter) **3** to understand or interpret **4** to foretell (the future) **5** [Brit.] to study *[*to *read* law*]* **6** to register: said as of a gauge **7** [Slang] to hear and understand *[*I *read* you*]* **8** *Comput.* to access (data) from (a disk, tape, etc.) —***vi.*** **1** to read something written **2** to learn by reading: with *about* or *of* **3** to contain certain words —**read into** to attribute (a particular meaning) to —**read out of** to expel from (a group) —**read′a·bil′i·ty** ***n.*** —**read′a·ble** ***adj.*** —**read′er** ***n.***

read[2] (red) ***vt.***, ***vi.*** *pt. & pp. of* READ[1] —***adj.*** informed by reading *[*well-*read]*

read·er·ship (rēd′ər ship′) ***n.*** the people who read a certain publication, author, etc.

read·i·ly (red′ə lē) ***adv.*** **1** willingly **2** easily

read·ing (rēd′iŋ) ***n.*** **1** the act of one who reads **2** material to be read **3** the amount measured by a barometer, thermometer, etc. **4** a particular interpretation or performance

read·out (rēd′out′) ***n.*** **1** the retrieving of information from a computer **2** information from a computer, thermostat, etc. displayed visually or recorded, as on tape

read·y (red′ē) ***adj.*** **-i·er**, **-i·est** ⟦OE *ræde*⟧ **1** prepared to act or be used immediately **2** willing **3** likely or liable; apt *[ready* to cry*]* **4** dexterous **5** prompt *[*a *ready* reply*]* **6** available at once *[ready* cash*]* —***vt.*** **-ied**, **-y·ing** to prepare —**at the ready** prepared for immediate use —**read′i·ness** ***n.***

read′y-made′ ***adj.*** made so as to be ready for use or sale at once: also, as applied to clothing, **read′y-to-wear′**

Rea·gan (rā′gən), **Ron·ald** (**Wilson**) (rän′əld) 1911- ; 40th president of the U.S. (1981-89)

re·a·gent (rē ā′jənt) ***n.*** *Chem.* a substance used to detect, measure, or react with another substance

re·al (rē′əl, rēl) ***adj.*** ⟦< L *res,* thing⟧ **1** existing as or in fact; actual; true **2** authentic; genuine **3** *Law* of or relating to permanent, immovable things *[real* property*]* —***adv.*** [Inf.] very —**for real** [Slang] real or really

real estate **1** land, including the buildings, etc. on it **2** the buying and selling of this

re·al·ism (rē′ə liz′əm) ***n.*** **1** a tendency to face facts and be practical **2** the picturing in art and literature of people and things as they really appear to be —**re′al·ist** ***n.*** —**re′al·is′tic** ***adj.*** —**re′al·is′ti·cal·ly** ***adv.***

re·al·i·ty (rē al′ə tē) ***n.***, *pl.* **-ties** **1** the quality or fact of being real **2** a person or thing that is real; fact —**in reality** in fact; actually

re·al·ize (rē′ə līz′) ***vt.*** **-ized′**, **-iz′ing** **1** to make real; achieve **2** to understand fully **3** to convert (assets, rights, etc.) into money **4** to gain; obtain *[*to *realize* a profit*]* **5** to be sold for (a specified sum) —**re′al·i·za′tion** ***n.***

re′al-life′ ***adj.*** actual; not imaginary

re′al·ly ***adv.*** **1** in reality **2** truly —***interj.*** indeed: used to express surprise, doubt, etc.

realm (relm) ***n.*** ⟦see REGAL⟧ **1** a kingdom **2** a region; sphere

Re·al·tor (rē′əl tər, -tôr′) *trademark for* a real estate broker or appraiser who is a member of the National Association of Realtors —***n.*** [**r-**] a real estate agent

re·al·ty (rē′əl tē) ***n.*** REAL ESTATE

ream[1] (rēm) ***n.*** ⟦< Ar *rizma,* a bale⟧ **1** a quantity of paper varying from 480 to 516 sheets **2** [*pl.*] [Inf.] a great amount

ream[2] (rēm) ***vt.*** ⟦OE *reman*⟧ to enlarge (a hole) as with a reamer

ream′er ***n.*** **1** a sharp-edged tool for enlarging or tapering holes **2** a juicer

re·an·i·mate (rē an′ə māt′) ***vt.*** **-mat′ed**, **-mat′ing** to give new life, power, or vigor to —**re·an′i·ma′tion** ***n.***

reap (rēp) ***vt.***, ***vi.*** ⟦OE *ripan*⟧ **1** to cut (grain) with a scythe, reaper, etc. **2** to gather (a harvest) **3** to obtain as the reward of action, etc.

reap′er ***n.*** **1** one who reaps **2** a machine for reaping grain

re·ap·por·tion (rē′ə pôr′shən) ***vt.*** to apportion again; specif., to change the distribution of (a legislature) so that members represent constituents equally —**re′ap·por′tion·ment** ***n.***

rear[1] (rir) ***n.*** ⟦see ARREARS⟧ **1** the back part **2** the position behind or at the back **3** the part of an army, etc. farthest from the enemy **4** [Slang] the buttocks —***adj.*** of, at, or in the rear —**bring up the rear** to come at the end

rear[2] (rir) ***vt.*** ⟦OE *ræran*⟧ **1** to put upright; elevate **2** to build; erect **3** to grow or breed **4** to educate, train, etc. *[to rear a child]* —***vi.*** **1** to rise on the hind legs, as a horse does **2** to rise (*up*), in anger, etc. **3** to rise high

rear admiral a naval officer ranking above a captain

rear-end′ ***vt.*** to crash into, or cause one's vehicle to crash into, the back end of (another vehicle)

rear′most′ ***adj.*** farthest in the rear

re·ar·range (rē′ə rānj′) ***vt.*** **-ranged′, -rang′ing** to arrange again or in a different way

rear′ward ***adj.*** at, in, or toward the rear —***adv.*** toward the rear: also **rear′wards**

rea·son (rē′zən) ***n.*** ⟦< L *ratio,* a reckoning⟧ **1** an explanation of an act, idea, etc. **2** a cause or motive **3** the ability to think, draw conclusions, etc. **4** good sense **5** sanity —***vi., vt.*** **1** to think logically (about); analyze **2** to argue or infer —**stand to reason** to be logical —**rea′son·ing** ***n.***

rea′son·a·ble ***adj.*** **1** able to reason **2** fair; just **3** sensible **4** not excessive —**rea′son·a·bly** ***adv.***

re·as·sure (rē′ə shoor′) ***vt.*** **-sured′, -sur′ing** to restore to confidence —**re′as·sur′ance** ***n.***

re·bate (rē′bāt′) ***vt.*** **-bat′ed, -bat′ing** ⟦< OFr *re-,* RE- + *abattre,* beat down⟧ to give back (part of a payment) —***n.*** a return of part of a payment

Re·bek·ah (ri bek′ə) ***n.*** *Bible* the wife of Isaac: also sp. **Re·bec′ca**

reb·el (reb′əl; *for v.* ri bel′) ***n.*** ⟦< L *re-,* again + *bellare,* wage war⟧ one who resists authority —***adj.*** **1** rebellious **2** of rebels —***vi.*** **re·bel′, -belled′, -bel′ling** **1** to resist authority **2** to feel or show strong aversion

re·bel·lion (ri bel′yən) ***n.*** **1** armed resistance to one's government **2** a defiance of any authority

re·bel′lious (-yəs) ***adj.*** **1** resisting authority **2** opposing control; defiant

re·birth (rē burth′) ***n.*** **1** a new or second birth **2** a reawakening; revival

re·boot (rē bo͞ot′) ***vi., vt.*** *Comput.* to boot again, as to restore normal operation

re·bound (ri bound′; *for n.* rē′bound′) ***vi.*** to spring back, as upon impact —***n.*** a rebounding, or a ball, etc. that rebounds —**on the rebound** **1** after it bounces back **2** just after being jilted

re·buff (ri buf′) ***n.*** ⟦< It *rabbuffare,* disarrange⟧ **1** an abrupt refusal of offered advice, help, etc. **2** any repulse —***vt.*** **1** to snub **2** to check or repulse

re·buke (ri byo͞ok′) ***vt.*** **-buked′, -buk′ing** ⟦< OFr *re-,* back + *buchier,* to beat⟧ to scold in a sharp way; reprimand —***n.*** a reprimand

re·bus (rē′bəs) ***n.*** ⟦L, lit., by things⟧ a puzzle consisting of pictures, etc. combined to suggest words or phrases

re·but (ri but′) ***vt.*** **-but′ted, -but′ting** ⟦< OFr *re-,* back + *buter,* to thrust⟧ to contradict or oppose, esp. in a formal manner by argument, proof, etc. —**re·but′tal** (-'l) ***n.***

rec (rek) ***n.*** *short for* RECREATION: used in compounds, as **rec room**

re·cal·ci·trant (ri kal′si trənt) ***adj.*** ⟦< L *re-,* back + *calcitrare,* to kick⟧ **1** refusing to obey authority, etc. **2** hard to handle —**re·cal′ci·trance** ***n.***

re·call (ri kôl′; *for n.* rē′kôl′) ***vt.*** **1** to call back **2** to remember **3** to take back; revoke —***n.*** **1** a recalling **2** memory **3** the removal of, or right to remove, an official from office by popular vote

re·cant (ri kant′) ***vt., vi.*** ⟦< L *re-,* back + *canere,* sing⟧ to renounce formally (one's beliefs, remarks, etc.) —**re·can·ta·tion** (rē′kan tā′shən) ***n.***

re·cap[1] (rē kap′; *also, and for n. always,* rē′kap′) ***vt.*** **-capped′, -cap′ping** to put a new tread on (a worn tire) —***n.*** such a tire

re·cap[2] (rē′kap′) ***n.*** a recapitulation, or summary —***vt., vi.*** **-capped′, -cap′ping** to recapitulate

re·ca·pit·u·late (rē′kə pich′ə lāt′) ***vi., vt.*** **-lat′ed, -lat′ing** ⟦see RE- & CAPITULATE⟧ to repeat briefly; summarize —**re′ca·pit′u·la′tion** ***n.***

re·cap·ture (rē kap′chər) ***vt.*** **-tured, -tur·ing** **1** to capture again; retake **2** to remember —***n.*** a recapturing

recd or **rec'd** *abbrev.* received

re·cede (ri sēd′) ***vi.*** **-ced′ed, -ced′ing** ⟦see RE- & CEDE⟧ **1** to go, move, or slope backward **2** to diminish

re·ceipt (ri sēt′) ***n.*** ⟦see RECEIVE⟧ **1** *old-fashioned var. of* RECIPE **2** a receiving or being received **3** a written acknowledgment that something has been received **4** [*pl.*] the amount, as of money, received —***vt.*** to write a receipt for (goods, etc.)

re·ceiv·a·ble (ri sē′və bəl) ***adj.*** **1** that can be received **2** due —***n.*** [*pl.*] outstanding bills, loans, etc.

re·ceive (ri sēv′) ***vt.*** **-ceived′, -ceiv′ing** ⟦< L *re-,* back + *capere,* take⟧ **1** to take or get (something given, thrown, sent, etc.) **2** to experience; undergo *[to receive acclaim]* **3** to bear or hold **4** to react to in a specified way **5** to learn *[to receive news]* **6** to let enter **7** to greet (visitors, etc.)

re·ceived′ ***adj.*** accepted; considered as standard

re·ceiv′er ***n.*** one that receives; specif., *a*) a device that converts electrical waves or signals into audible or visual signals *b*) a football player designated to receive a forward pass *c*) one appointed by a court to administer or hold in trust property in bankruptcy or in a lawsuit —**re·ceiv′er·ship′** ***n.***

re·cen·sion (ri sen′shən) ***n.*** ⟦< L *recensere,* revise⟧ a revision of a text based on a critical study of sources

re·cent (rē′sənt) ***adj.*** ⟦< L *recens*⟧ **1** done, made, etc. just before the present; new **2** of a time just before the present —**re′cent·ly *adv.***

re·cep·ta·cle (ri sep′tə kəl) ***n.*** ⟦see RECEIVE⟧ a container

re·cep·tion (ri sep′shən) ***n.*** **1** *a*) a receiving or being received *b*) the manner of this **2** a social function for the receiving of guests **3** *Radio, TV* the receiving of signals, with reference to the quality of reproduction

re·cep′tion·ist ***n.*** an office employee who receives callers, etc.

re·cep′tive ***adj.*** able or ready to accept new ideas, suggestions, etc.

re·cep′tor ***n.*** a nerve ending or group of nerve endings specialized for receiving stimuli

re·cess (rē′ses; *also, & for v. usually,* ri ses′) ***n.*** ⟦< L *recedere,* recede⟧ **1** a hollow place, as in a wall **2** a hidden or inner place **3** a temporary halting as of work, a session, etc. —***vt.*** **1** to place in a recess **2** to halt temporarily —***vi.*** to take a recess

re·ces·sion (ri sesh′ən) ***n.*** **1** a going back; withdrawal **2** a temporary falling off of business activity

re·ces′sion·al ***n.*** a piece of music at the end of a church service played when the clergy, etc. march out

re·ces·sive (ri ses′iv) ***adj.*** **1** tending to recede **2** *Genetics* designating or of that one of any pair of hereditary factors which remains latent —***n.*** *Genetics* a recessive character or characters

re·cher·ché (rə sher′shā, -sher′shā′) ***adj.*** ⟦Fr⟧ **1** rare; choice **2** refined; esp., too refined

re·cid·i·vism (ri sid′ə viz′əm) ***n.*** ⟦< L *re-,* back + *cadere,* to fall⟧ habitual or chronic relapse, esp. into crime

rec·i·pe (res′ə pē′) ***n.*** ⟦L < *recipere,* receive⟧ **1** a list of materials and directions for preparing a dish or drink **2** a way to achieve something

re·cip·i·ent (ri sip′ē ənt) ***n.*** ⟦see RECEIVE⟧ one that receives

re·cip·ro·cal (ri sip′rə kəl) ***adj.*** ⟦< L *reciprocus,* returning⟧ **1** done, given, etc. in return **2** mutual *[reciprocal love]* **3** corresponding but reversed **4** corresponding or complementary —***n.*** **1** a complement, counterpart, etc. **2** *Math.* the quantity resulting from the division of 1 by the given quantity *[the reciprocal of 7 is* $\frac{1}{7}$*]*

re·cip′ro·cate′ (-kāt′) ***vt., vi.*** **-cat′ed, -cat′ing** **1** to give and get reciprocally **2** to do, feel, etc. in return **3** to move alternately back and forth —**re·cip′ro·ca′tion *n.***

rec·i·proc·i·ty (res′ə präs′ə tē) ***n.,*** *pl.* **-ties** **1** reciprocal state **2** mutual exchange; esp., exchange of special privileges between two countries

re·cit·al (ri sīt′'l) ***n.*** **1** a reciting **2** the account, story, etc. told **3** a musical or dance program

rec·i·ta·tion (res′ə tā′shən) ***n.*** **1** a reciting, as of facts, events, etc. **2** *a*) a saying aloud in public of something memorized *b*) a piece so presented **3** a reciting by pupils of answers to questions on a prepared lesson

rec′i·ta·tive′ (-tə tēv′) ***n.*** ⟦< It: see fol.⟧ a type of declamation, as for operatic dialogue, with the rhythms of speech, but in musical tones

re·cite (ri sīt′) ***vt., vi.*** **-cit′ed, -cit′ing** ⟦see RE- & CITE⟧ **1** to say aloud from memory, as a poem, lesson, etc. **2** to tell in detail; relate

reck·less (rek′lis) ***adj.*** ⟦OE *recceleas*⟧ careless; heedless —**reck′less·ly *adv.*** —**reck′less·ness *n.***

reck·on (rek′ən) ***vt.*** ⟦OE *-recenian*⟧ **1** to count; compute **2** to estimate **3** [Inf. or Dial.] to suppose —***vi.*** **1** to count up **2** [Inf.] to rely (*on*) —**reckon with** to take into consideration

reck′on·ing ***n.*** **1** count or computation **2** the settlement of an account

re·claim (ri klām′) ***vt.*** ⟦see RE- & CLAIM⟧ **1** to bring back (a person) from error, vice, etc. **2** to make (wasteland, etc.) usable **3** to recover (useful materials) from waste products —**rec·la·ma·tion** (rek′lə mā′shən) ***n.***

re·cline (ri klīn′) ***vt., vi.*** **-clined′, -clin′ing** ⟦< L *re-,* back + *clinare,* lean⟧ to lie or cause to lie down

re·clin′er ***n.*** an upholstered armchair with an adjustable back and seat for reclining: also **reclining chair**

rec·luse (rek′lo͞os, ri klo͞os′) ***n.*** ⟦< L *re-,* back + *claudere,* shut⟧ one who lives a secluded, solitary life

rec·og·ni·tion (rek′əg nish′ən) ***n.*** **1** a recognizing or being recognized **2** identification of a person or thing as having been known before

re·cog·ni·zance (ri käg′ni zəns, -kän′i-) ***n.*** ⟦< L *re-,* again + *cognoscere,* know⟧ *Law* a bond binding one to some act, as to appear in court

rec·og·nize (rek′əg nīz′) ***vt.*** **-nized′, -niz′ing** ⟦see prec.⟧ **1** to be aware of as someone or something known before **2** to know by some detail, as of appearance **3** to perceive **4** to accept as a fact *[to recognize defeat]* **5** to acknowledge as worthy of approval **6** to acknowledge the status of (a government, etc.) **7** to grant the right to speak in a meeting —**rec′og·niz′a·ble *adj.***

re·coil (ri koil′; *also for n.* rē′koil′) ***vi.*** ⟦< L *re-,* back + *culus,* buttocks⟧ **1** to draw back, as in fear, etc. **2** to spring or kick back, as a gun when fired —***n.*** a recoiling

rec·ol·lect (rek′ə lekt′) ***vt., vi.*** ⟦see RE- & COLLECT⟧ to remember, esp. with some effort —**rec′ol·lec′tion *n.***

re·com·bi·nant DNA (rē käm′bə nənt) DNA formed in the laboratory by splicing together pieces of DNA from different species, as to create new life forms

rec·om·mend (rek′ə mend′) ***vt.*** ⟦see RE- & COMMEND⟧ **1** to entrust **2** to suggest favorably as suited for some position, etc. **3** to make acceptable **4** to advise; counsel —**rec′om·men·da′tion *n.***

re·com·mit (rē′kə mit′) ***vt.*** **-mit′ted,**

-mit′ting **1** to commit again **2** to refer (a question, bill, etc.) back to a committee

rec·om·pense (rek′əm pens′) ***vt.*** **-pensed′, -pens′ing** ⟦see RE- & COMPENSATE⟧ **1** to repay or reward **2** to compensate (a loss, etc.) —***n.*** **1** requital; reward **2** compensation

rec·on·cile (rek′ən sīl′) ***vt.*** **-ciled′, -cil′ing** ⟦see RE- & CONCILIATE⟧ **1** to make friendly again **2** to settle (a quarrel, etc.) **3** to make (ideas, accounts, etc.) consistent **4** to make acquiescent (*to*) —**rec′on·cil′a·ble** ***adj.*** —**rec′on·cil′i·a′tion** (-sil′ē ā′shən) ***n.***

rec·on·dite (rek′ən dīt′) ***adj.*** ⟦< L *re-*, back + *condere,* to hide⟧ beyond ordinary understanding; abstruse

re·con·di·tion (rē′kən dish′ən) ***vt.*** to put back in good condition, as by repairing

re·con·nais·sance (ri kän′ə səns) ***n.*** ⟦Fr: see RECOGNIZANCE⟧ a survey of a region, as in seeking out information about enemy positions

rec·on·noi·ter (rek′ə noit′ər, rē′kə-) ***vt., vi.*** to make a reconnaissance (of): also [Chiefly Brit.] **rec′on·noi′tre, -tred, -tring**

re·con·sid·er (rē′kən sid′ər) ***vt., vi.*** to think over again, esp. with a view to changing a decision

re·con·sti·tute (rē kän′stə to͞ot′) ***vt.*** **-tut′ed, -tut′ing** to constitute again; specif., to restore (a dried or condensed substance) to its full liquid form by adding water

re·con·struct (rē′kən strukt′) ***vt.*** **1** to construct again; rebuild **2** to build up, as from remains, an image of the original

re′con·struc′tion ***n.*** **1** a reconstructing **2** [**R-**] the process or period, after the Civil War, of reestablishing the Southern States in the Union

re·cord (ri kôrd′; *for n. & adj.* rek′ərd) ***vt.*** ⟦< L *recordari,* remember⟧ **1** to write down for future use **2** to register, as on a graph **3** to register (sound or visual images) on a disc, tape, etc. for later reproduction —***n.*** **rec′ord** **1** the condition of being recorded **2** anything written down and preserved; account of events **3** *a*) the known facts about anyone or anything *b*) the recorded crimes of a person **4** a grooved disc for playing on a phonograph **5** the best official performance achieved —***adj.*** **rec′ord** being the best, largest, etc. —**on** (or **off the**) **record** publicly (or confidentially) declared

RECORDER

re·cord′er ***n.*** **1** an official who keeps records **2** a machine or device that records; esp., a TAPE RECORDER **3** an early wind instrument

re·cord′ing ***n.*** **1** that which is recorded, as on a disc or tape **2** a record, disc, etc.

re·count[1] (ri kount′) ***vt.*** ⟦see RE- & COUNT[1]⟧ to tell in detail; narrate

re·count[2] (rē′kount′; *for n.* rē′kount′) ***vt.*** to count again —***n.*** a recounting, as of votes

re·coup (ri ko͞op′) ***vt.*** ⟦< Fr *re-*, again + *couper,* to cut⟧ to make up for or regain *[to recoup* a loss*]*

re·course (rē′kôrs′, ri kôrs′) ***n.*** ⟦see RE- & COURSE⟧ **1** a turning for aid, safety, etc. **2** that to which one turns seeking aid, safety, etc.

re·cov·er (ri kuv′ər) ***vt.*** ⟦< L *recuperare*⟧ **1** to get back (something lost, etc.) **2** to regain (health, etc.) **3** to make up for *[to recover* losses*]* **4** to save (oneself) from a fall, etc. **5** to reclaim (land from the sea, etc.) **6** *Sports* to get control of (a fumbled ball, etc.) —***vi.*** **1** to regain health, balance, or control **2** *Sports* to regain control of a fumbled ball, etc.

re·cov′er·y ***n.***, *pl.* **-ies** a recovering; specif., *a*) a regaining of something lost *b*) a return to health *c*) a retrieval of a capsule, etc. after a spaceflight

recovery room a hospital room where postoperative patients are kept for close observation and care

rec·re·ant (rek′rē ənt) [Archaic] ***adj.*** ⟦< OFr *recreire,* surrender allegiance⟧ **1** cowardly **2** disloyal —***n.*** **1** a coward **2** a traitor

rec·re·a·tion (rek′rē ā′shən) ***n.*** ⟦< L *recreare,* refresh⟧ any form of play, amusement, etc. used to relax or refresh the body or mind —**rec′re·ate′, -at′ed, -at′ing, *vt., vi.*** —**rec′re·a′tion·al** ***adj.***

re·crim·i·nate (ri krim′ə nāt′) ***vi.*** **-nat′ed, -nat′ing** ⟦< L *re-*, back + *crimen,* offense⟧ to answer an accuser by accusing that person in return —**re·crim′i·na′tion** ***n.***

re·cru·desce (rē′kro͞o des′) ***vi.*** **-desced′, -desc′ing** ⟦< L *re-*, again + *crudus,* raw⟧ to break out again after being inactive —**re′cru·des′cence** ***n.*** —**re′cru·des′cent** ***adj.***

re·cruit (ri kro͞ot′) ***vt., vi.*** ⟦< L *re-*, again + *crescere,* grow⟧ **1** to enlist (personnel) into an army or navy **2** to enlist (new members) for an organization —***n.*** **1** a newly enlisted or drafted soldier, etc. **2** a new member of any group —**re·cruit′er** ***n.***

rec·tal (rek′təl) ***adj.*** of, for, or near the rectum

rec·tan·gle (rek′taŋ′gəl) ***n.*** ⟦< L *rectus,* straight + *angulus,* a corner⟧ a four-sided plane figure with four right angles —**rec·tan′gu·lar** (-gyə lər) ***adj.***

rec·ti·fy (rek′tə fī′) ***vt.*** **-fied′, -fy′ing** ⟦< L *rectus,* straight + *facere,* make⟧ **1** to put right; correct **2** *Elec.* to convert (alternating current) to direct current —**rec′ti·fi·ca′tion** ***n.*** —**rec′ti·fi′er** ***n.***

rec·ti·lin·e·ar (rek′tə lin′ē ər) ***adj.*** bounded or formed by straight lines

rec·ti·tude (rek′tə to͞od′) ***n.*** ⟦< L *rectus,* right⟧ strict honesty; uprightness of character

rec·tor (rek′tər) ***n.*** ⟦< L *regere,* to rule⟧ **1** in some churches, a clergyman in charge of a parish 2 the head of certain schools, colleges, etc.

rec·to·ry (rek′tər ē) ***n.***, *pl.* **-ries** the house of a minister or priest

rec·tum (rek′təm) ***n.***, *pl.* **-tums** or **-ta** (-tə) ⟦< L *rectum* (*intestinum*), straight (intestine)⟧ the lowest, or last, segment of the large intestine

re·cum·bent (ri kum′bənt) ***adj.*** ⟦< L *re-*, back + *-cumbere*, lie down⟧ lying down; reclining

re·cu·per·ate (ri ko͞o′pə rāt′) ***vt.***, ***vi.*** **-at′ed**, **-at′ing** ⟦< L *recuperare*, recover⟧ **1** to get well again **2** to recover (losses, etc.) —**re·cu′per·a′tion** ***n.*** —**re·cu′per·a′tive** (-pə rāt′iv, -pə rə tiv) ***adj.***

re·cur (ri kur′) ***vi.*** **-curred′**, **-cur′ring** ⟦< L *re-*, back + *currere*, run⟧ **1** to return in thought, talk, etc. **2** to occur again or at intervals —**re·cur′rence** ***n.*** —**re·cur′rent** ***adj.***

re·cy·cle (rē sī′kəl) ***vt.*** **-cled**, **-cling** **1** to pass through a cycle again **2** to use again and again, as the same water **3** *a*) to process in order to use again [*to recycle* paper] *b*) to gather up and turn in (newspapers, etc.) for such processing

red (red) ***n.*** ⟦OE *read*⟧ **1** the color of blood **2** any red pigment **3** [*often* **R-**] [Inf.] a communist —***adj.*** **red′der**, **red′dest** **1** of the color red **2** [*often* **R-**] communist —**in the red** losing money —**see red** [Inf.] to become angry —**red′dish** ***adj.*** —**red′ness** ***n.***

re·dact (ri dakt′) ***vt.*** ⟦< L *redigere*, get in order⟧ to prepare for publication; edit —**re·dac′tion** ***n.*** —**re·dac′tor** ***n.***

red blood cell (or **corpuscle**) ERYTHROCYTE

red′-blood′ed ***adj.*** high-spirited and strong-willed; vigorous

red′cap′ ***n.*** a baggage porter, as in a railroad station

red carpet a very grand or impressive welcome and entertainment: with *the* —**red′-car′pet** ***adj.***

red′coat′ ***n.*** a British soldier in a uniform with a red coat, as during the American Revolution

Red Cross an international society for the relief of suffering in time of war or disaster

redd (red) ***vt.***, ***vi.*** **redd** or **redd′ed**, **redd′ing** ⟦< OE *hreddan*, take away⟧ [Inf. or Dial.] to put in order; tidy: usually with *up*

red deer a deer of Europe and Asia

red·den (red′′n) ***vt.*** to make red —***vi.*** to become red; esp., to blush

re·deem (ri dēm′) ***vt.*** ⟦< L *re*(*d*)-, back + *emere*, get⟧ **1** to buy or get back; recover **2** to pay off (a mortgage, etc.) **3** to turn in (a coupon, etc.) for a discount, premium, etc. **4** to ransom **5** to deliver from sin **6** to fulfill (a promise) **7** *a*) to make amends or atone for *b*) to restore (oneself) to favor —**re·deem′a·ble** ***adj.*** —**re·deem′er** ***n.*** —**re·demp·tion** (ri demp′shən) ***n.***

re·de·ploy (rē′di ploi′) ***vt.***, ***vi.*** to move (troops, etc.) from one front or area to another —**re′de·ploy′ment** ***n.***

re·de·vel·op (rē′di vel′əp) ***vt.*** **1** to develop again **2** to rebuild or restore —**re′de·vel′op·ment** ***n.***

red′-flag′ ***vt.*** **-flagged′**, **-flag′ging** to mark or otherwise indicate as being risky, etc.

red′-hand′ed ***adv.*** in the very commission of crime or wrongdoing

red′head′ ***n.*** a person with red hair

red herring ⟦< herring drawn across the trace in hunting to divert the hounds⟧ something used to divert attention from the basic issue

red′-hot′ ***adj.*** **1** hot enough to glow **2** very excited, angry, etc. **3** very new

re·dis′trict ***vt.*** to divide anew into districts

red′-let′ter ***adj.*** designating a memorable or joyous day or event

red′lin′ing (-līn′iŋ) ***n.*** ⟦from outlining such areas in red on a map⟧ the refusal by some banks or companies to issue loans or insurance on property in certain neighborhoods

re·do (rē do͞o′) ***vt.*** **-did′**, **-done′**, **-do′ing** **1** to do again **2** to redecorate

red·o·lent (red′′l ənt) ***adj.*** ⟦< L *re*(*d*)-, intens. + *olere*, to smell⟧ **1** sweet-smelling **2** smelling (*of*) **3** suggestive (*of*) —**red′o·lence** ***n.***

re·dou·ble (rē dub′əl) ***vt.***, ***vi.*** **-bled**, **-bling** to make or become twice as much or twice as great

re·doubt (ri dout′) ***n.*** ⟦see REDUCE⟧ **1** a breastwork **2** any stronghold

re·doubt′a·ble ***adj.*** ⟦< L *re-*, intens. + *dubitare*, to doubt⟧ formidable —**re·doubt′a·bly** ***adv.***

re·dound (ri dound′) ***vi.*** ⟦< L *re*(*d*)-, intens. + *undare*, to surge⟧ **1** to have a result (*to* the credit or discredit of) **2** to come back; react (*upon*)

re·dress (ri dres′; *for n., usually* rē′dres′) ***vt.*** ⟦see RE- & DRESS⟧ to compensate for (a wrong, etc.) —***n.*** **1** compensation **2** a redressing

Red Sea sea between NE Africa & W Arabia

red snapper a reddish, edible, deep-water fish

red tape ⟦< tape for tying official papers⟧ rules and details that waste time and effort

red tide sea water discolored by red algae poisonous to marine life

re·duce (ri do͞os′) ***vt.*** **-duced′**, **-duc′ing** ⟦< L *re-*, back + *ducere*, to lead⟧ **1** to lessen, as in size, price, etc. **2** to put into a different form **3** to lower, as in rank or condition —***vi.*** to lose weight, as by dieting

re·duc·tion (ri duk′shən) ***n.*** **1** a reducing or being reduced **2** anything made by reducing **3** the amount by which anything is reduced

re·dun·dant (ri dun′dənt) ***adj.*** ⟦see REDOUND⟧ **1** excess; superfluous **2** wordy **3** unnecessary to the meaning: said of words and affixes —**re·dun′dan·cy** ***n.***

red′wood′ ***n.*** **1** a giant evergreen of the Pacific coast **2** its reddish wood

re·ech·o or **re-ech·o** (rē ek′ō) ***vt.***, ***vi.*** **-oed**, **-o·ing** to echo back or again —***n.***, *pl.* **-oes** the echo of an echo

reed (rēd) ***n.*** ⟦OE *hreod*⟧ **1** a tall, slender grass **2** a rustic musical instrument made from a hollow stem **3** *Music* a thin strip of wood, plastic, etc. placed against the mouthpiece, as of a clarinet, and vibrated by the breath to produce a tone —**reed'y**, **-i·er**, **-i·est**, ***adj.***

reef[1] (rēf) ***n.*** ⟦prob. < ON *rif*, a rib⟧ a ridge of rock, coral, or sand at or near the surface of the water

reef[2] (rēf) ***n.*** ⟦ME *riff*⟧ a part of a sail which can be folded or rolled up and made fast to reduce the area exposed to the wind —***vt.***, ***vi.*** to reduce the size of (a sail) by taking in part of it

reef'er ***n.*** [Slang] a marijuana cigarette

reek (rēk) ***n.*** ⟦OE *rec*⟧ a strong, unpleasant smell —***vi.*** to have a strong, offensive smell

reel[1] (rēl) ***n.*** ⟦OE *hreol*⟧ **1** a spool on which wire, film, fishing line, etc. is wound **2** the quantity of wire, film, etc. usually wound on one reel —***vt.*** to wind on a reel —***vi.*** **1** to sway, stagger, etc. as from drunkenness or dizziness **2** to spin; whirl —**reel in** **1** to wind on a reel **2** to pull in (a fish) by using a reel —**reel off** to tell, write, etc. easily and quickly —**reel out** to unwind from a reel

reel[2] (rēl) ***n.*** ⟦prob. < prec.⟧ a lively dance

re·en·try or **re-en·try** (rē en'trē) ***n.***, *pl.* **-tries** a coming back, as of a space vehicle, into the earth's atmosphere

ref[1] (ref) ***n.***, ***vt.***, ***vi.*** [Inf.] *short for* REFEREE

ref[2] *abbrev.* **1** referee **2** reference **3** reformed **4** refund

re·face (rē fās') ***vt.*** **-faced'**, **-fac'ing** to put a new facing or covering on

re·fec·tion (ri fek'shən) ***n.*** ⟦< L *re-*, again + *facere*, make⟧ a light meal; lunch

re·fec·to·ry (ri fek'tə rē) ***n.***, *pl.* **-ries** a dining hall, as in a monastery

re·fer (ri fur') ***vt.*** **-ferred'**, **-fer'ring** ⟦< L *re-*, back + *ferre*, to bear⟧ **1** to submit (a quarrel, etc.) for settlement **2** to direct *to* someone or something for aid, information, etc. —***vi.*** **1** to relate or apply (*to*) **2** to direct attention (*to*) **3** to turn (*to*) for information, aid, etc. —**re·fer'rer** ***n.***

ref·er·ee (ref'ə rē') ***n.*** **1** one to whom something is referred for decision **2** an official who enforces the rules in certain sports contests —***vt.***, ***vi.*** **-eed'**, **-ee'ing** to act as referee (in)

ref·er·ence (ref'ər əns, ref'rəns) ***n.*** **1** a referring or being referred **2** relation *[in reference to his letter]* **3** *a*) the directing of attention to a person or thing *b*) a mention **4** *a*) an indication, as in a book, of some other source of information *b*) such a source **5** *a*) one who can offer information or recommendation *b*) a statement of character, ability, etc. by such a person

ref·er·en·dum (ref'ə ren'dəm) ***n.***, *pl.* **-dums** or **-da** (-də) ⟦L: see REFER⟧ **1** the submission of a law to a direct vote of the people **2** the vote itself

ref·er·ent (ref'ər ənt) ***n.*** the thing referred to, esp. by a word or expression

re·fer·ral (ri fur'əl) ***n.*** **1** a referring or being referred **2** a person who is referred to another

re·fill (rē fil'; *for n.* rē'fil') ***vt.***, ***vi.*** to fill again —***n.*** **1** a unit to refill a special container **2** a refilling of a medical prescription —**re·fill'a·ble** ***adj.***

re·fine (ri fīn') ***vt.*** **-fined'**, **-fin'ing** ⟦RE- + *fine*, make fine⟧ **1** to free from impurities, etc. **2** to make more polished or elegant

re·fined' ***adj.*** **1** made free from impurities; purified **2** cultivated, elegant, etc. **3** subtle, precise, etc.

re·fine'ment ***n.*** **1** *a*) a refining or being refined *b*) the result of this **2** delicacy or elegance of manners, etc. **3** an improvement **4** a fine distinction; subtlety

re·fin'er·y ***n.***, *pl.* **-er·ies** a plant for purifying materials, as oil, sugar, etc.

re·fin·ish (rē fin'ish) ***vt.*** to change or restore the finish of (furniture, etc.) —**re·fin'ish·er** ***n.***

re·fit (rē fit') ***vt.***, ***vi.*** **-fit'ted**, **-fit'ting** to make or be made fit for use again by repairing, reequipping, etc.

re·flect (ri flekt') ***vt.*** ⟦< L *re-*, back + *flectere*, to bend⟧ **1** to throw back (light, heat, or sound) **2** to give back an image of **3** to bring as a result *[to reflect honor on the city]* —***vi.*** **1** to throw back light, heat, etc. **2** to give back an image **3** to think seriously (*on* or *upon*) **4** to cast blame or discredit (*on* or *upon*) —**re·flec'tive** ***adj.***

re·flec'tion ***n.*** **1** a reflecting or being reflected **2** anything reflected **3** contemplation **4** a thoughtful idea or remark **5** blame; discredit

re·flec'tor ***n.*** a surface, object, etc. that reflects light, sound, heat, etc.

re·flex (rē'fleks') ***adj.*** ⟦see REFLECT⟧ designating or of an involuntary action, as a sneeze, resulting from the direct transmission of a stimulus to a muscle or gland —***n.*** a reflex action

re·flex·ive (ri flek'siv) ***adj.*** **1** designating a grammatical relation in which a verb's subject and object refer to the same person or thing (Ex.: I wash myself) **2** designating a verb, pronoun, etc. in such a relation —**re·flex'ive·ly** ***adv.***

re·for·est (rē fôr'ist) ***vt.***, ***vi.*** to plant new trees on (land once forested) —**re'for·est·a'tion** ***n.***

re·form (ri fôrm') ***vt.*** ⟦see RE- & FORM⟧ **1** to make better as by stopping abuses **2** to cause (a person) to behave better —***vi.*** to become better in behavior —***n.*** a reforming

re-form (rē fôrm') ***vt.***, ***vi.*** to form again

ref·or·ma·tion (ref'ər mā'shən) ***n.*** a reforming or being reformed —**the Reformation** the 16th-c. religious movement that resulted in establishing the Protestant churches

re·form·a·to·ry (ri fôr'mə tôr'ē) ***n.***, *pl.*

-ries an institution to which young offenders are sent to be reformed

ILLUSION CAUSED BY REFRACTION

re·form'er *n.* one who seeks to bring about political or social reform

re·fract (ri frakt') *vt.* ⟦< L *refractus,* turned aside < *re-,* back + *frangere,* to break⟧ to cause (a ray of light, etc.) to undergo refraction

re·frac'tion *n.* the bending of a ray or wave of light, heat, or sound as it passes from one medium to another

re·frac·to·ry (ri frak'tər ē) *adj.* ⟦see REFRACT⟧ hard to manage; stubborn

re·frain[1] (ri frān') *vi.* ⟦< L *re-,* back + *frenare,* to curb⟧ to hold back; keep oneself (*from* doing something)

re·frain[2] (ri frān') *n.* ⟦see REFRACT⟧ a phrase or verse repeated at intervals in a song or poem

re·fresh (ri fresh') *vt.* **1** to make fresh by cooling, wetting, etc. **2** to make (a person) feel cooler, stronger, etc., as by food, sleep, etc. **3** to replenish **4** to stimulate (the memory, etc.)

re·fresh'ing *adj.* **1** that refreshes **2** pleasingly new or different

re·fresh'ment *n.* **1** a refreshing or being refreshed **2** something that refreshes **3** [*pl.*] food or drink or both

re·frig·er·ant (rē frij'ə rənt) *n.* a substance used in refrigeration

re·frig·er·ate (ri frij'ə rāt') *vt.* **-at'ed, -at'ing** ⟦< L *re-,* intens. + *frigus,* cold⟧ to make or keep cool or cold, as for preserving —**re·frig'er·a'tion** *n.*

re·frig'er·a'tor *n.* a box or room in which food, drink, etc. are kept cool

ref·uge (ref'yo͞oj) *n.* ⟦< L *re-,* back + *fugere,* flee⟧ (a) shelter or protection from danger, difficulty, etc.

ref·u·gee (ref'yoo jē', ref'yoo jē') *n.* one who flees from home or country to seek refuge elsewhere

re·ful·gent (ri ful'jənt) *adj.* ⟦< L *re-,* back + *fulgere,* shine⟧ shining; radiant; glowing —**re·ful'gence** *n.*

re·fund (ri fund'; *for n.* rē'fund') *vt., vi.* ⟦< L *re-,* back + *fundere,* pour⟧ to give back (money, etc.); repay —*n.* a refunding or the amount refunded

re·fur·bish (ri fur'bish) *vt.* ⟦RE- + FURBISH⟧ to renovate —**re·fur'bish·ment** *n.*

re·fuse[1] (ri fyo͞oz') *vt., vi.* **-fused', -fus'ing** ⟦< L *re-,* back + *fundere,* pour⟧ **1** to decline to accept **2** to decline (to do something), to grant the request of (someone), etc. —**re·fus'al** *n.*

ref·use[2] (ref'yo͞os, -yo͞oz) *n.* ⟦see prec.⟧ waste; trash; rubbish

re·fute (ri fyo͞ot') *vt.* **-fut'ed, -fut'ing** ⟦L *refutare,* repel⟧ to prove to be false or wrong —**re·fut'a·ble** *adj.* —**ref·u·ta·tion** (ref'yə tā'shən) *n.*

reg *abbrev.* **1** registered **2** regular **3** regulation

re·gain (ri gān') *vt.* **1** to get back; recover **2** to get back to

re·gal (rē'gəl) *adj.* ⟦< L *rex,* king⟧ of, like, or fit for a monarch

re·gale (ri gāl') *vt.* **-galed', -gal'ing** ⟦< Fr *ré-* (see RE-) + OFr *gale,* joy⟧ to amuse or delight as with a story

re·ga·li·a (ri gāl'yə) *pl.n.* ⟦see REGAL⟧ **1** royal insignia **2** the insignia as of a rank or society **3** finery

re·gard (ri gärd') *n.* ⟦see RE- & GUARD⟧ **1** a steady look; gaze **2** consideration; concern **3** respect and affection **4** reference; relation [*in regard to your plan*] **5** [*pl.*] good wishes —*vi.* **1** to look at attentively **2** to consider **3** to hold in affection and respect **4** to concern or involve —**as regards** concerning

re·gard'ing *prep.* concerning; about

re·gard'less *adv.* [Inf.] without regard for objections, etc.; anyway —**regardless of** in spite of

re·gat·ta (ri gät'ə) *n.* ⟦< It⟧ **1** a boat race **2** a series of boat races

re·gen·er·ate (ri jen'ə rit; *for v.,* -rāt') *adj.* ⟦see RE- & GENERATE⟧ **1** spiritually reborn **2** renewed or restored —*vt.* **-at'ed, -at'ing** **1** to cause to be spiritually reborn **2** to cause to be completely reformed **3** to bring into existence again —*vi.* to form again, or be made anew —**re·gen'er·a'tion** *n.* —**re·gen'er·a'tive** (-rāt'iv, -rə tiv) *adj.*

re·gent (rē'jənt) *n.* ⟦< L *regere,* to rule⟧ **1** a person appointed to rule when a monarch is absent, too young, etc. **2** a member of a governing board, as of a university —**re'gen·cy** *n.*

reg·gae (reg'ā) *n.* ⟦< ?⟧ a form of strongly syncopated popular Jamaican music

reg·i·cide (rej'ə sīd') *n.* ⟦< L *regis,* of a king + *-cida* (see -CIDE)⟧ **1** one who kills a monarch **2** the killing of a monarch

re·gime or **ré·gime** (rə zhēm', rā-) *n.* ⟦see fol.⟧ **1** a political system **2** an administration

reg·i·men (rej'ə mən) *n.* ⟦< L *regere,* to rule⟧ a system of diet, exercise, etc. to improve health

reg·i·ment (rej'ə mənt; *for v.,* -ment') *n.* ⟦< L *regere,* to rule⟧ a military unit, smaller than a division —*vt.* **1** to organize systematically **2** to subject to strict discipline and control —**reg'i·men'tal** *adj.* —**reg'i·men·ta'tion** *n.*

Re·gi·na (ri jī'nə) capital of Saskatchewan, Canada: pop. 180,000

re·gion (rē'jən) *n.* ⟦< L *regere,* to rule⟧ **1** a large, indefinite part of the earth's surface **2** a division or part, as of an organism —**re'gion·al** *adj.*

re'gion·al·ism' *n.* **1** regional quality or character in life or literature **2** a word, etc. peculiar to some region

reg·is·ter (rej'is tər) *n.* ⟦< L *regerere,* to record⟧ **1** *a)* a list of names, items, etc. *b)* a book in which this is kept **2** a device for recording [*a cash register*] **3** an opening into a room by which the amount of warm or cold air passing through can be controlled **4** *Music* a part of the range of a voice or instrument —***vt.*** **1** to enter in a list **2** to indicate on or as on a scale **3** to show, as by facial expression *[*to *register* surprise*]* **4** to protect (mail) by paying a fee to have it handled by a special postal service —***vi.*** **1** to enter one's name in a list, as of voters **2** to enroll in a school **3** to make an impression —**reg′is·trant** (-trənt) ***n.***

registered nurse a trained nurse who has passed a state examination

reg·is·trar (rej′i strär′) ***n.*** one who keeps records, as in a college

reg·is·tra·tion (rej′i strā′shən) ***n.*** **1** a registering or being registered **2** an entry in a register **3** the number of persons registered

reg′is·try (-is trē) ***n.***, *pl.* **-tries** **1** a registering **2** an office where registers are kept **3** an official record or list

reg·nant (reg′nənt) ***adj.*** **1** ruling **2** predominant **3** prevalent

re·gress (rē′gres; *for v.* ri gres′) ***n.*** ⟦< L *re-*, back + *gradi,* go⟧ backward movement —***vi.*** to go back —**re·gres′sion** ***n.*** —**re·gres′sive** ***adj.***

re·gret (ri gret′) ***vt.*** **-gret′ted, -gret′ting** ⟦< OFr *regreter*, mourn⟧ to feel sorry about (an event, one's acts, etc.) —***n.*** remorse, esp. over one's acts or omissions —**(one's) regrets** a polite declining of an invitation —**re·gret′ful** ***adj.*** —**re·gret′ta·ble** ***adj.***

re·group′ ***vt.***, ***vi.*** **1** to reassemble or reorganize **2** to collect oneself, as after a setback

reg·u·lar (reg′yə lər) ***adj.*** ⟦< L *regula*, a rule⟧ **1** conforming to a rule, type, etc.; orderly; symmetrical **2** conforming to a fixed principle or procedure **3** customary or established **4** consistent *[*a *regular* customer*]* **5** functioning in a normal way *[*a *regular* pulse*]* **6** properly qualified *[*a *regular* doctor*]* **7** designating or of the standing army of a country **8** [Inf.] *a*) thorough; complete *[*a *regular* nuisance*]* *b*) pleasant, friendly, etc. —***n.*** **1** a regular soldier or a player who is not a substitute **2** [Inf.] one who is regular in attendance **3** *Politics* a loyal party member —**reg′u·lar′i·ty** (-lar′ə tē), *pl.* **-ties**, ***n.*** —**reg′u·lar·ize′**, **-ized′**, **-iz′ing**, ***vt.*** —**reg′u·lar·ly** ***adv.***

reg·u·late (reg′yə lāt′) ***vt.*** **-lat′ed, -lat′ing** ⟦< L *regula,* a rule⟧ **1** to control or direct according to a rule, principle, etc. **2** to adjust to a standard, rate, etc. **3** to adjust for accurate operation —**reg′u·la′tor** ***n.*** —**reg′u·la·to′ry** (-lə tôr′ē) ***adj.***

reg′u·la′tion ***n.*** **1** a regulating or being regulated **2** a rule or law regulating conduct —***adj.*** usual; regular

re·gur·gi·tate (ri gur′jə tāt′) ***vi.***, ***vt.*** **-tat′ed, -tat′ing** ⟦< ML *re-*, back + LL *gurgitare,* to flood⟧ to bring (partly digested food) back up to the mouth —**re·gur′gi·ta′tion** ***n.***

re·hab (rē′hab′) ***n.*** *short for* REHABILITATION —***vt.*** **-habbed′**, **-hab′bing** *short for* REHABILITATE

re·ha·bil·i·tate (rē′hə bil′ə tāt′) ***vt.*** **-tat′ed, -tat′ing** ⟦< L *re-*, back + *habere,* have⟧ **1** to restore to rank, reputation, etc. which one has lost **2** to put back in good condition **3** to bring or restore to a state of health, constructive activity, etc. —**re′ha·bil′i·ta′tion** ***n.*** —**re′ha·bil′i·ta′tive** ***adj.***

re·hash (rē′hash′; *for v., also* rē hash′) ***vt.*** ⟦RE- + HASH⟧ to work up again or go over again —***n.*** a rehashing

re·hearse (ri hurs′) ***vt.***, ***vi.*** **-hearsed′**, **-hears′ing** ⟦< OFr *re-*, again + *hercer,* to harrow⟧ to practice (a play, etc.) for public performance —**re·hears′al** ***n.***

reign (rān) ***n.*** ⟦< L *regere,* to rule⟧ **1** royal power **2** dominance or sway **3** the period of rule, dominance, etc. —***vi.*** **1** to rule as a sovereign **2** to prevail *[*peace *reigns]*

re·im·burse (rē′im burs′) ***vt.*** **-bursed′**, **-burs′ing** ⟦RE- + archaic *imburse,* to pay⟧ to pay back —**re′im·burse′ment** ***n.***

rein (rān) ***n.*** ⟦see RETAIN⟧ **1** a narrow strap of leather attached in pairs to a horse's bit and manipulated to control the animal: *usually used in pl.* **2** [*pl.*] a means of controlling, etc. —**give (free) rein to** to allow to act without restraint

re·in·car·na·tion (rē′in kär nā′shən) ***n.*** ⟦see RE- & INCARNATE⟧ rebirth of the soul in another body —**re′in·car′nate′**, **-nat′ed, -nat′ing**, ***vt.***

REINDEER

rein·deer (rān′dir′) ***n.***, *pl.* **-deer′** ⟦< ON *hreinn,* reindeer + *dȳr*, animal⟧ a large deer found in northern regions and domesticated there as a beast of burden

re·in·force (rē′in fôrs′) ***vt.*** **-forced′**, **-forc′ing** ⟦RE- + var. of ENFORCE⟧ **1** to strengthen (a military force) with more troops, ships, etc. **2** to strengthen, as by patching, propping, or adding new material —**re′in·force′ment** ***n.***

re·in·state (rē′in stāt′) ***vt.*** **-stat′ed**, **-stat′ing** to restore to a former state, position, etc. —**re′in·state′ment** ***n.***

re·it·er·ate (rē it′ə rāt′) ***vt.*** **-at′ed, -at′ing** ⟦< L *re-*, back + *iterare*, repeat⟧ to say or do again or repeatedly —**re·it′er·a′tion** ***n.*** —**re·it′er·a′tive** (-ə rāt′iv, -ər ə tiv) ***adj.***

re·ject (ri jekt′; *for n.* rē′jekt) ***vt.*** ⟦< L *re-*, back + *jacere,* to throw⟧ **1** to refuse to take, agree to, use, believe, etc. **2** to discard —***n.*** a rejected thing or person —**re·jec′tion** ***n.***

re·jig·ger (rē jig′ər) ***vt.*** to adjust or alter the structure, terms, etc. of

re·joice (ri jois′) ***vi.***, ***vt.*** **-joiced′**, **-joic′ing**

⟦< OFr *re-*, again + *joïr*, be glad⟧ to be glad or happy

re·join (rē join′) ***vt.***, ***vi.*** **1** to join again; reunite **2** to answer

re·join·der (ri join′dər) ***n.*** ⟦see RE- & JOIN⟧ an answer, esp. to a reply

re·ju·ve·nate (ri jo͞o′və nāt′) ***vt.*** **-nat′ed, -nat′ing** ⟦< RE- + L *juvenis*, young⟧ to make feel or seem young again —**re·ju′ve·na′tion** ***n.***

rel *abbrev.* **1** relative(ly) **2** religion

re·lapse (ri laps′; *for n., usually* rē′laps) ***vi.*** **-lapsed′, -laps′ing** ⟦see RE- & LAPSE⟧ to slip back into a former state, esp. into illness after apparent recovery —***n.*** a relapsing

re·late (ri lāt′) ***vt.*** **-lat′ed, -lat′ing** ⟦< L *relatus*, brought back⟧ **1** to tell the story of; narrate **2** to connect, as in thought or meaning —***vi.*** to have some connection or relation (*to*)

re·lat′ed ***adj.*** connected by kinship, origin, marriage, etc.

re·la′tion ***n.*** **1** a narrating **2** a narrative; account **3** connection, as in thought or meaning **4** connection by blood or marriage **5** a relative **6** [*pl.*] the connections between or among persons, nations, etc. —**in** (or **with**) **relation to** concerning; regarding —**re·la′tion·ship′** ***n.***

rel·a·tive (rel′ə tiv) ***adj.*** **1** related each to the other **2** pertinent; relevant **3** comparative *[living in relative comfort]* **4** meaningful only in relationship *["cold" is a relative term]* **5** *Gram.* that refers to an antecedent *[a relative pronoun]* —***n.*** one related by blood or marriage —**rel′a·tive·ly** ***adv.***

relative humidity the ratio of the amount of moisture in the air to the maximum amount possible at the given temperature

rel·a·tiv·i·ty (rel′ə tiv′ə tē) ***n.*** **1** a being relative **2** *Physics* the theory of the relative, rather than absolute, character of motion, velocity, mass, etc., and the interdependence of matter, time, and space

re·lax (ri laks′) ***vt.***, ***vi.*** ⟦< L *re-*, back + *laxare*, loosen⟧ **1** to make or become less firm, tense, severe, etc. **2** to rest, as from work —**re·lax′er** ***n.***

re·lax′ant ***adj.*** causing relaxation, esp. of muscles —***n.*** a relaxant drug

re·lax·a·tion (rē′lak sā′shən) ***n.*** **1** a relaxing or being relaxed **2** *a*) rest from work or effort *b*) recreation

re·lay (rē′lā′; *for v., also* ri lā′) ***n.*** ⟦< Fr *re-*, back + *laier*, to leave⟧ **1** a fresh supply of horses, etc., as for a stage of a journey **2** a relief crew of workers **3** a race (in full **relay race**) between teams, each member of which goes a part of the distance —***vt.*** **-layed′, -lay′ing** to get and pass on

re·lease (ri lēs′) ***vt.*** **-leased′, -leas′ing** ⟦see RELAX⟧ **1** to set free from confinement, work, pain, etc. **2** to let go *[to release an arrow]* **3** to permit to be issued, published, etc. —***n.*** **1** a releasing, as from prison **2** a film, news story, etc. released to the public **3** a written surrender of a claim, etc.

rel·e·gate (rel′ə gāt′) ***vt.*** **-gat′ed, -gat′ing** ⟦< L *re-*, away + *legare*, send⟧ **1** to exile or banish (*to*) **2** to consign or assign, esp. to an inferior position **3** to refer or hand over for decision —**rel′e·ga′tion** ***n.***

re·lent (ri lent′) ***vi.*** ⟦< L *re-*, again + *lentus*, pliant⟧ to become less severe, stern, or stubborn; soften

re·lent′less ***adj.*** **1** harsh; pitiless **2** not letting up; persistent —**re·lent′less·ly** ***adv.*** —**re·lent′less·ness** ***n.***

rel·e·vant (rel′ə vənt) ***adj.*** ⟦see RELIEVE⟧ relating to the matter under consideration; pertinent —**rel′e·vance** or **rel′e·van·cy** ***n.***

re·li·a·ble (ri lī′ə bəl) ***adj.*** that can be relied on; dependable —**re·li′a·bil′i·ty** ***n.*** —**re·li′a·bly** ***adv.***

re·li′ance (-əns) ***n.*** **1** a relying **2** trust, dependence, or confidence **3** a thing relied on —**re·li′ant** ***adj.***

rel·ic (rel′ik) ***n.*** ⟦see RELINQUISH⟧ **1** an object, custom, etc. surviving from the past **2** a souvenir **3** [*pl.*] ruins **4** the venerated remains, etc. of a saint

re·lief (ri lēf′) ***n.*** **1** a relieving of pain, anxiety, a burden, etc. **2** anything that lessens tension, or offers a pleasing change **3** aid, esp. by a public agency to the needy **4** release from work or duty, or those bringing it **5** the projection of sculptured forms from a flat surface **6** the differences in height, collectively, of land forms shown as by lines on a map (**relief map**) —***adj.*** *Baseball* designating a pitcher who replaces another during a game —**in relief** carved so as to project from a surface

re·lieve (ri lēv′) ***vt.*** **-lieved′, -liev′ing** ⟦< L *re-*, again + *levare*, to raise⟧ **1** to ease (pain, anxiety, etc.) **2** to free from pain, anxiety, a burden, etc. **3** to give or bring aid to **4** to set free from duty or work by replacing **5** to make less tedious, etc. by providing a pleasing change —**relieve oneself** to urinate or defecate

re·li·gion (ri lij′ən) ***n.*** ⟦< L *religio*, holiness⟧ **1** belief in and worship of God or gods **2** a specific system of belief, worship, etc., often involving a code of ethics

re·li′gi·os′i·ty (-ē äs′ə tē) ***n.*** a being religious, esp. excessively or sentimentally religious

re·li′gious (-əs) ***adj.*** **1** devout; pious **2** of or concerned with religion **3** conscientiously exact; scrupulous —***n.***, *pl.* **-gious** a monk or nun —**re·li′gious·ly** ***adv.***

re·lin·quish (ri liŋ′kwish) ***vt.*** ⟦< L *re-*, from + *linquere*, to leave⟧ **1** to give up (a plan, etc.) or let go (one's grasp, etc.) **2** to renounce or surrender (property, a right, etc.) —**re·lin′quish·ment** ***n.***

rel·ish (rel′ish) ***n.*** ⟦< OFr *relais*, something remaining⟧ **1** an appetizing flavor **2** enjoyment; zest *[to listen with relish]* **3** a food, as pickles or raw vegetables, served with a meal to add flavor **4** a condiment of chopped pickles, spices, etc. for use as on hot dogs —***vt.*** to enjoy; like

re·live (rē liv′) ***vt.*** **-lived′, -liv′ing** to

experience again (a past event) as in the imagination

re·lo·cate (rē lō′kāt′) ***vt., vi.*** **-cat′ed, -cat′ing** to move to a new location —**re′lo·ca′tion *n.***

re·luc·tant (ri luk′tənt) ***adj.*** ⟦< L *re-*, against + *luctari,* to struggle⟧ **1** unwilling; disinclined **2** marked by unwillingness *[a reluctant answer]* —**re·luc′tance *n.*** —**re·luc′tant·ly *adv.***

re·ly (ri lī′) ***vi.*** **-lied′, -ly′ing** ⟦< L *re-*, back + *ligare,* bind⟧ to trust or depend: used with *on* or *upon*

rem (rem) ***n., pl.*** **rem** ⟦*r*(*oentgen*) *e*(*quivalent*), *m*(*an*)⟧ a dose of ionizing radiation with a biological effect equal to one roentgen of X-ray

REM (rem) ***n., pl.*** **REMs** ⟦*r*(*apid*) *e*(*ye*) *m*(*ovement*)⟧ the rapid, jerky movement of the eyeballs during stages of sleep associated with dreaming

re·main (ri mān′) ***vi.*** ⟦< L *re-*, back + *manere,* to stay⟧ **1** to be left over when the rest has been taken away, etc. **2** to stay **3** to continue *[to remain a cynic]* **4** to be left to be done, said, etc.

re·main′der *n.* **1** those remaining **2** what is left when a part is taken away **3** what is left when a smaller number is subtracted from a larger **4** what is left undivided when a number is divided by another that is not one of its factors

re·mains′ *pl.n.* **1** what is left after use, destruction, etc. **2** a dead body

re·mand (ri mand′) ***vt.*** ⟦< L *re-*, back + *mandare,* to order⟧ to send back (a prisoner, etc.) into custody

re·mark (ri märk′) ***vt.*** ⟦< Fr *re-*, again + *marquer,* to mark⟧ **1** to notice or observe **2** to say or write as a comment —***vi.*** to make a comment: with *on* or *upon* —***n.*** a brief comment

re·mark′a·ble *adj.* worthy of notice; extraordinary —**re·mark′a·bly *adv.***

Rem·brandt (rem′brant′) 1606-69; Du. painter & etcher

re·me·di·al (ri mē′dē əl) ***adj.*** **1** providing a remedy **2** for correcting deficiencies: said as of some courses of study

re·me′di·ate′ (-āt′) ***vt.*** **-at′ed, -at′ing** to provide a remedy for

rem·e·dy (rem′ə dē) ***n., pl.*** **-dies** ⟦< L *re-*, again + *mederi,* heal⟧ **1** any medicine or treatment for a disease **2** something to correct a wrong —***vt.*** **-died, -dy·ing** to cure, correct, etc.

re·mem·ber (ri mem′bər) ***vt.*** ⟦< L *re-*, again + *memorare,* bring to mind⟧ **1** to think of again **2** to bring back to mind by an effort; recall **3** to be careful not to forget **4** to mention (a person) to another as sending greetings —***vi.*** to bear something in mind or call something back to mind

re·mem′brance (-brəns) ***n.*** **1** a remembering or being remembered **2** the power to remember **3** a souvenir

re·mind (ri mīnd′) ***vt., vi.*** to put (a person) in mind (*of* something); make remember —**re·mind′er *n.***

rem·i·nisce (rem′ə nis′) ***vi.*** **-nisced′, -nisc′ing** ⟦< fol.⟧ to think, talk, or write about remembered events

rem′i·nis′cence (-əns) ***n.*** ⟦Fr < L *re-*, again + *memini,* remember⟧ **1** a remembering **2** a memory **3** [*pl.*] an account of remembered experiences —**rem′i·nis′cent *adj.***

re·miss (ri mis′) ***adj.*** ⟦see REMIT⟧ careless; negligent —**re·miss′ness *n.***

re·mis·sion (ri mish′ən) ***n.*** ⟦see fol.⟧ **1** forgiveness; pardon **2** release from a debt, tax, etc. **3** an abating of pain, a disease, etc.

re·mit (ri mit′) ***vt.*** **-mit′ted, -mit′ting** ⟦< L *re-*, back + *mittere,* send⟧ **1** to forgive or pardon **2** to refrain from exacting (a payment), inflicting (punishment), etc. **3** to slacken; decrease **4** to send (money) in payment —**re·mit′tance *n.***

rem·nant (rem′nənt) ***n.*** ⟦see REMAIN⟧ what is left over, as a piece of cloth at the end of a bolt

re·mod·el (rē mäd′'l) ***vt.*** **-eled** or **-elled, -el·ing** or **-el·ling** to make over; rebuild

re·mon·strate (ri män′strāt′) ***vt.*** **-strat′ed, -strat′ing** ⟦< L *re-*, again + *monstrare,* to show⟧ to say in protest, objection, etc. —***vi.*** to protest; object —**re·mon′strance** (-strəns) ***n.***

re·morse (ri môrs′) ***n.*** ⟦< L *re-*, again + *mordere,* to bite⟧ a torturing sense of guilt for one's actions —**re·morse′ful *adj.*** —**re·morse′less *adj.***

re·mote (ri mōt′) ***adj.*** **-mot′er, -mot′est** ⟦< L *remotus,* removed⟧ **1** distant in space or time **2** distant in connection, relation, etc. **3** distantly related **4** aloof **5** slight *[a remote chance]* —**re·mote′ly *adv.***

remote control **1** control of aircraft, etc. from a distance, as by radio waves **2** a device to control a TV set, recorder, etc. from a distance

re·move (ri mo͞ov′) ***vt.*** **-moved′, -mov′ing** ⟦see RE- & MOVE⟧ **1** to move (something) from where it is; take away or off **2** to dismiss, as from office **3** to get rid of —***vi.*** to move away, as to another residence —***n.*** a step or degree away —**re·mov′a·ble *adj.*** —**re·mov′al *n.*** —**re·mov′er *n.***

re·mu·ner·ate (ri myo͞o′nə rāt′) ***vt.*** **-at′ed, -at′ing** ⟦< L *re-*, again + *munus,* gift⟧ to pay (a person) for (work, a loss, etc.) —**re·mu′ner·a′tion *n.*** —**re·mu′ner·a′tive *adj.***

ren·ais·sance (ren′ə säns′) ***n.*** ⟦Fr⟧ a rebirth; renascence —**the Renaissance** the great revival of art and learning in Europe in the 14th, 15th, and 16th centuries

Renaissance man (or **woman**) one skilled and knowledgeable in many fields

re·nal (rē′nəl) ***adj.*** ⟦< L *renes,* kidneys⟧ of or near the kidneys

re·nas·cence (ri nas′əns, -nās′-) ***n.*** ⟦< L *renasci*, be born again⟧ [*also* **R-**] RENAISSANCE

rend (rend) ***vt.*** **rent, rend′ing** ⟦OE *rendan*⟧ to tear or split with violence —***vi.*** to tear; split apart

ren·der (ren′dər) ***vt.*** ⟦ult. < L *re*(*d*)-, back + *dare,* give⟧ **1** to submit, as for approval or payment **2** to give in return or pay as due *[render thanks]* **3**

to cause to be **4** to give (aid) or do (a service) **5** to depict, as by drawing **6** to play (music), act (a role), etc. **7** to translate **8** to melt down (fat) **9** to pronounce (a verdict)

ren·dez·vous (rän′dā vo͞o′) ***n.***, *pl.* **-vous′** (-vo͞oz′) ⟦< Fr *rendez-vous,* present yourself⟧ **1** a meeting place **2** an agreement to meet **3** the meeting itself —***vi.***, ***vt.*** **-voused′** (-vo͞od′), **-vous′ing** (-vo͞o′iŋ) to meet or assemble at a certain time or place

ren·di·tion (ren dish′ən) ***n.*** a rendering; performance, translation, etc.

ren·e·gade (ren′ə gād′) ***n.*** ⟦< L *re-,* again + *negare,* deny⟧ one who abandons a party, movement, etc. to join the opposition; turncoat

re·nege (ri nig′) ***vi.*** **-neged′**, **-neg′ing** ⟦see prec.⟧ to go back on a promise

re·new (ri no͞o′) ***vt.*** **1** to make new or fresh again **2** to reestablish; revive **3** to resume **4** to put in a fresh supply of **5** to give or get an extension of *[renew* a lease*]* —**re·new′a·ble** ***adj.*** —**re·new′al** ***n.***

ren·net (ren′it) ***n.*** ⟦< ME *rennen,* coagulate⟧ an extract from the stomach of calves, etc. used to curdle milk

Re·no (rē′nō) city in W Nevada: pop. 134,000

Re·noir (rən wär′, ren′wär′), **Pierre Auguste** (pyer ô güst′) 1841-1919; Fr. painter

re·nounce (ri nouns′) ***vt.*** **-nounced′**, **-nounc′ing** ⟦< L *re-,* back + *nuntiare,* tell⟧ **1** to give up formally (a claim, etc.) **2** to give up (a habit, etc.) **3** to disown —**re·nounce′ment** ***n.***

ren·o·vate (ren′ə vāt′) ***vt.*** **-vat′ed**, **-vat′ing** ⟦< L *re-,* again + *novus,* new⟧ to make as good as new; restore —**ren′o·va′tion** ***n.*** —**ren′o·va′tor** ***n.***

re·nown (ri noun′) ***n.*** ⟦< OFr *re-,* again + *nom(m)er,* to name < L *nominare*⟧ great fame or reputation —**re·nowned′** ***adj.***

rent[1] (rent) ***n.*** ⟦< L *reddita,* paid⟧ a stated payment at fixed intervals for the use of a house, land, etc. —***vt.*** to get or give use of in return for rent —***vi.*** to be let for rent —**for rent** available to be rented —**rent′er** ***n.***

rent[2] (rent) ***vt.***, ***vi.*** *pt. & pp. of* REND —***n.*** a hole or gap made by tearing

rent·al (rent′'l) ***n.*** **1** an amount paid or received as rent **2** a house, car, etc. offered for rent **3** a renting —***adj.*** of or for rent

re·nun·ci·a·tion (ri nun′sē ā′shən) ***n.*** a renouncing, as of a right

re·or·gan·ize (rē ôr′gə nīz′) ***vt.***, ***vi.*** **-ized′**, **-iz′ing** to organize (a business, etc.) anew —**re·or′gan·i·za′tion** ***n.***

rep[1] (rep) ***n.*** ⟦Fr *reps* < Eng *ribs*⟧ a ribbed fabric

rep[2] (rep) ***n.*** a representative

rep[3] *abbrev.* **1** repeat **2** report(ed) **3** reporter

Rep *abbrev.* **1** Representative **2** Republican

re·paid (ri pād′) ***vt.***, ***vi.*** *pt. & pp. of* REPAY

re·pair[1] (ri per′) ***vt.*** ⟦< L *re-,* again + *parare,* prepare⟧ **1** to put back in good condition; fix; renew **2** to make amends for —***n.*** **1** a repairing **2** [*usually pl.*] work done in repairing **3** the state of being repaired *[*kept in *repair]* —**re·pair′a·ble** ***adj.***

re·pair[2] (ri per′) ***vi.*** ⟦< L *re-,* back + *patria,* native land⟧ to go (*to* a place)

re·pair′man (-mən, -man′) ***n.***, *pl.* **-men** (-mən, -men′) one whose work is repairing things

rep·a·ra·tion (rep′ə rā′shən) ***n.*** ⟦see REPAIR[1]⟧ **1** a making of amends **2** [*usually pl.*] compensation, as for war damage

rep·ar·tee (rep′är tē′, -tā′) ***n.*** ⟦< Fr *repartir,* to return a blow quickly⟧ a series of quick, witty retorts; banter

re·past (ri past′) ***n.*** ⟦< OFr *re-,* RE- + *past,* food⟧ food and drink; a meal

re·pa·tri·ate (rē pā′trē āt′) ***vt.***, ***vi.*** **-at′ed**, **-at′ing** ⟦see REPAIR[2]⟧ to return to the country of birth, citizenship, etc. —**re·pa′tri·a′tion** ***n.***

re·pay (ri pā′) ***vt.*** **-paid′**, **-pay′ing** **1** to pay back **2** to make return to for (a favor, etc.) —**re·pay′ment** ***n.***

re·peal (ri pēl′) ***vt.*** ⟦see RE- & APPEAL⟧ to revoke; cancel; annul —***n.*** revocation; abrogation

re·peat (ri pēt′) ***vt.*** ⟦< L *re-,* again + *petere,* to demand⟧ **1** to say again **2** to recite (a poem, etc.) **3** to say (something) as said by someone else **4** to tell to someone else *[*to *repeat* a secret*]* **5** to do or make again —***vi.*** to say or do again —***n.*** **1** a repeating **2** anything said or done again, as a rebroadcast of a television program **3** *Music a*) a passage to be repeated *b*) a symbol for this —**re·peat′er** ***n.***

re·peat′ed ***adj.*** said, made, or done again, or often —**re·peat′ed·ly** ***adv.***

re·pel (ri pel′) ***vt.*** **-pelled′**, **-pel′ling** ⟦< L *re-,* back + *pellere,* to drive⟧ **1** to drive or force back **2** to reject **3** to cause dislike in; disgust **4** to be resistant to (water, dirt, etc.) —**re·pel′lent** ***adj.***, ***n.***

re·pent (ri pent′) ***vi.***, ***vt.*** ⟦< L *re-,* again + *poenitere,* repent⟧ **1** to feel sorry for (an error, sin, etc.) **2** to feel such regret over (an action, intention, etc.) as to change one's mind (about) —**re·pent′ance** ***n.*** —**re·pent′ant** ***adj.***

re·per·cus·sion (rē′pər kush′ən) ***n.*** ⟦see RE- & PERCUSSION⟧ **1** reverberation **2** a far-reaching, often indirect reaction to some event

rep·er·toire (rep′ər twär′) ***n.*** ⟦< Fr < L *reperire,* discover⟧ the stock of plays, songs, etc. that a company, singer, etc. is prepared to perform

rep′er·to′ry (-tôr′ē) ***n.***, *pl.* **-ries** **1** REPERTOIRE **2** the system of alternating several plays throughout a season with a permanent group of actors

rep·e·ti·tion (rep′ə tish′ən) ***n.*** ⟦< L *repetitio*⟧ **1** a repeating **2** something repeated —**rep′e·ti′tious** ***adj.*** —**re·pet·i·tive** (ri pet′ə tiv) ***adj.***

re·pine (ri pīn′) ***vi.*** **-pined′**, **-pin′ing** ⟦RE- + PINE[2]⟧ to feel or express unhappiness or discontent

re·place (ri plās′) *vt.* **-placed′**, **-plac′ing** **1** to put back in a former or the proper place **2** to take the place of **3** to provide an equivalent for —**re·place′a·ble** *adj.* —**re·place′ment** *n.*

re·plen·ish (ri plen′ish) *vt.* ⟦< L *re-*, again + *plenus*, full⟧ **1** to make full or complete again **2** to supply again —**re·plen′ish·ment** *n.*

re·plete (ri plēt′) *adj.* ⟦< L *re-*, again + *plere*, to fill⟧ **1** plentifully supplied **2** stuffed; gorged —**re·ple′tion** *n.*

rep·li·ca (rep′li kə) *n.* ⟦see REPLY⟧ a reproduction or close copy, as of a work of art

rep·li·cate (rep′li kāt′) *vt.* **-cat′ed**, **-cat′ing** ⟦see REPLY⟧ to repeat or duplicate

rep′li·ca′tion *n.* **1** a replicating **2** a reply; answer **3** a copy; reproduction

re·ply (ri plī′) *vi.* **-plied′**, **-ply′ing** ⟦< L *re-*, back + *plicare*, to fold⟧ to answer or respond —*n.*, *pl.* **-plies′** an answer or response

re·port (ri pôrt′) *vt.* ⟦< L *re-*, back + *portare*, carry⟧ **1** to give an account of, as for publication **2** to carry and repeat (a message, etc.) **3** to announce formally **4** to make a charge about (something) or against (someone) to one in authority —*vi.* **1** to make a report **2** to present oneself, as for work —*n.* **1** rumor **2** a statement or account **3** a formal presentation of facts **4** the noise of an explosion —**re·port′ed·ly** *adv.*

re·port·age (ri pôrt′ij, rep′ər täzh′) *n.* **1** the reporting of the news **2** journalistic writings

report card a periodic written report on a student's progress: often used figuratively

re·port′er *n.* one who reports; specif., one who gathers and reports news for a newspaper, etc. —**rep·or·to·ri·al** (rep′ər tôr′ē əl) *adj.*

re·pose[1] (ri pōz′) *vt.* **-posed′**, **-pos′ing** ⟦< L *re-*, again + *pausare*, to rest⟧ to lay or place for rest —*vi.* **1** to lie at rest **2** to rest from work, etc. **3** to lie dead —*n.* **1** *a*) rest *b*) sleep **2** composure **3** calm; peace —**re·pose′ful** *adj.*

re·pose[2] (ri pōz′) *vt.* **-posed′**, **-pos′ing** ⟦see fol.⟧ **1** to place (trust, etc.) *in* someone **2** to place (power, etc.) *in* the control of some person or group

re·pos·i·to·ry (ri päz′ə tôr′ē) *n.*, *pl.* **-ries** ⟦< L *re-*, back + *ponere*, to place⟧ a box, room, etc. in which things may be placed for safekeeping

re·pos·sess (rē′pə zes′) *vt.* to take back, as from a buyer who missed payments —**re′pos·ses′sion** *n.*

rep·re·hend (rep′ri hend′) *vt.* ⟦< L *re-*, back + *prehendere*, take⟧ to rebuke, blame, or censure

rep′re·hen′si·ble (-hen′sə bəl) *adj.* deserving to be reprehended —**rep′re·hen′si·bly** *adv.*

rep·re·sent (rep′ri zent′) *vt.* ⟦< L *re-*, again + *praesentare*, to present⟧ **1** to present to the mind **2** to present a likeness of **3** to describe **4** to stand for; symbolize **5** to be the equivalent of **6** to act (a role) **7** to act in place of, esp. by conferred authority **8** to serve as an example of

rep′re·sen·ta′tion *n.* **1** a representing or being represented, as in a legislative assembly **2** legislative representatives, collectively **3** a likeness, image, picture, etc. **4** [*often pl.*] a statement of facts, arguments, etc. meant to influence action, make protest, etc. —**rep′re·sen·ta′tion·al** *adj.*

rep′re·sent′a·tive *adj.* **1** representing **2** of or based on representation of the people by elected delegates **3** typical —*n.* **1** an example or type **2** one authorized to act for others; delegate, agent, salesman, etc. **3** [**R-**] a member of the lower house of Congress or of a state legislature

re·press (ri pres′) *vt.* ⟦see RE- & PRESS[1]⟧ **1** to hold back; restrain **2** to put down; subdue **3** *Psychiatry* to force (painful ideas, etc.) into the unconscious —**re·pres′sion** *n.* —**re·pres′sive** *adj.*

re·prieve (ri prēv′) *vt.* **-prieved′**, **-priev′ing** ⟦< Fr *reprendre*, take back⟧ **1** to postpone the punishment of, esp. the execution of **2** to give temporary relief to —*n.* a reprieving or being reprieved

rep·ri·mand (rep′rə mand′) *n.* ⟦< L *reprimere*, repress⟧ a severe or formal rebuke —*vt.* to rebuke severely or formally

re·pris·al (ri prī′zəl) *n.* ⟦see REPREHEND⟧ injury done in return for injury received

re·proach (ri prōch′) *vt.* ⟦< L *re-*, back + *prope*, near⟧ to accuse of a fault; rebuke —*n.* **1** shame, disgrace, etc. or a cause of this **2** rebuke or censure —**re·proach′ful** *adj.*

rep·ro·bate (rep′rə bāt′) *adj.* ⟦LL *reprobare*, reprove⟧ unprincipled or depraved —*n.* a reprobate person

re·proc·ess (rē prä′ses) *vt.* to process again so as to reuse; esp., to recover plutonium, etc. from

re·pro·duce (rē′prə do͞os′) *vt.* **-duced′**, **-duc′ing** to produce again; specif., *a*) to produce by propagation *b*) to make a copy of —*vi.* to produce offspring —**re′pro·duc′i·ble** *adj.*

re′pro·duc′tion (-duk′shən) *n.* **1** a reproducing **2** a copy, imitation, etc. **3** the process by which animals and plants produce new individuals —**re′pro·duc′tive** *adj.*

re·proof (ri pro͞of′) *n.* a reproving; rebuke: also **re·prov′al** (-pro͞o′vəl)

re·prove (ri pro͞ov′) *vt.* **-proved′**, **-prov′ing** ⟦see RE- & PROVE⟧ **1** to rebuke **2** to express disapproval of (something done or said)

rep·tile (rep′tīl′) *n.* ⟦< L *repere*, to creep⟧ a coldblooded vertebrate covered as with scales, as a snake, lizard, turtle, or dinosaur —**rep·til·i·an** (rep til′ē ən) *adj.*

re·pub·lic (ri pub′lik) *n.* ⟦< L *res*, thing + *publica*, public (adj.)⟧ a state or government, specif. one headed by a president, in which the power is exercised by officials elected by the voters

re·pub′li·can (-li kən) *adj.* **1** of or like a

republic 2 [R-] of or belonging to the Republican Party —*n.* 1 one who favors a republican form of government 2 [R-] a member of the Republican Party

Republican Party one of the two major political parties in the U.S.

re·pu·di·ate (ri pyo͞o′dē āt′) *vt.* **-at′ed, -at′ing** ⟦< L *repudium,* separation⟧ 1 to refuse to have anything to do with 2 to refuse to accept or support (a belief, treaty, etc.) —**re·pu′di·a′tion** *n.*

re·pug·nant (ri pug′nənt) *adj.* ⟦< L *re-,* back + *pugnare,* fight⟧ 1 contradictory 2 distasteful; offensive —**re·pug′nance** *n.*

re·pulse (ri puls′) *vt.* **-pulsed′, -puls′ing** ⟦see REPEL⟧ 1 to drive back (an attack, etc.) 2 to refuse or reject with discourtesy, etc.; rebuff —*n.* a repelling or being repelled

re·pul·sion (ri pul′shən) *n.* 1 a repelling or being repelled 2 strong dislike 3 *Physics* the mutual action by which bodies tend to repel each other

re·pul′sive (-siv) *adj.* causing strong dislike or aversion; disgusting —**re·pul′sive·ly** *adv.* —**re·pul′sive·ness** *n.*

rep·u·ta·ble (rep′yə tə bəl) *adj.* having a good reputation —**rep′u·ta·bil′i·ty** *n.* —**rep′u·ta·bly** *adv.*

rep·u·ta·tion (rep′yo͞o tā′shən) *n.* ⟦see fol.⟧ 1 estimation in which a person or thing is commonly held 2 favorable estimation 3 fame

re·pute (ri pyo͞ot′) *vt.* **-put′ed, -put′ing** ⟦< L *re-,* again + *putare,* think⟧ to consider or regard [*reputed* to be rich] —*n.* REPUTATION (senses 1 & 3)

re·put′ed *adj.* generally supposed to be such [the *reputed* owner] —**re·put′ed·ly** *adv.*

re·quest (ri kwest′) *n.* ⟦see REQUIRE⟧ 1 an asking for something 2 something asked for 3 the state of being asked for; demand —*vt.* 1 to ask for 2 to ask (a person) to do something

Re·qui·em (rek′wē əm, rā′kwē-) *n.* ⟦< L, rest⟧ [*also* r-] 1 *R.C.Ch.* a Mass for a dead person or persons 2 a musical setting for this

re·quire (ri kwīr′) *vt.* **-quired′, -quir′ing** ⟦< L *re-,* again + *quaerere,* ask⟧ 1 to insist upon; demand 2 to order 3 to need —**re·quire′ment** *n.*

req·ui·site (rek′wə zit) *adj.* ⟦see prec.⟧ required; necessary; indispensable —*n.* something requisite

req·ui·si·tion (rek′wə zish′ən) *n.* 1 a requiring; formal demand 2 a formal written order, as for equipment —*vt.* 1 to demand or take, as by authority 2 to submit a written request for

re·quite (ri kwīt′) *vt.* **-quit′ed, -quit′ing** ⟦RE- + *quite,* obs. var. of QUIT⟧ to repay (someone) for (a benefit, service, etc. or an injury, wrong, etc.) —**re·quit′al** *n.*

re·run (rē′run′) *n.* the showing of a film or TV program after the first run or showing

re′sale′ *n.* a selling of something bought to a third party

re·scind (ri sind′) *vt.* ⟦< L *re-,* back + *scindere,* to cut⟧ to revoke or cancel (a law, etc.) —**re·scis′sion** (-sizh′ən) *n.*

res·cue (res′kyo͞o) *vt.* **-cued, -cu·ing** ⟦ult. < L *re-,* again + *ex-,* off + *quatere,* to shake⟧ to free or save from danger, imprisonment, evil, etc. —*n.* a rescuing; deliverance —**res′cu·er** *n.*

re·search (rē′surch′, ri surch′) *n.* ⟦see RE- & SEARCH⟧ careful, systematic study and investigation in some field of knowledge —*vi., vt.* to do research (on or in) —**re′search′er** *n.*

re·sec·tion (ri sek′shən) *n.* ⟦< L *re-,* back + *secare,* to cut⟧ *Surgery* the removal of part of an organ, bone, etc.

re·sem·blance (ri zem′bləns) *n.* a similarity of appearance; likeness

re·sem′ble (-bəl) *vt.* **-bled, -bling** ⟦ult. < L *re-,* again + *simulare,* feign⟧ to be like or similar to

re·sent (ri zent′) *vt.* ⟦ult. < L *re-,* again + *sentire,* to feel⟧ to feel or show displeasure and hurt or indignation over or toward —**re·sent′ful** *adj.* —**re·sent′ful·ly** *adv.* —**re·sent′ment** *n.*

re·ser·pine (ri sur′pin, -pēn) *n.* ⟦Ger⟧ a crystalline alkaloid used in treating hypertension, mental illness, etc.

res·er·va·tion (rez′ər vā′shən) *n.* 1 a reserving or that which is reserved; specif., *a*) a withholding *b*) public land set aside for a special use, as for American Indians *c*) holding of a hotel room, etc. until called for 2 a limiting condition

re·serve (ri zurv′) *vt.* **-served′, -serv′ing** ⟦< L *re-,* back + *servare,* to keep⟧ 1 to keep back or set apart for later or special use 2 to keep back for oneself —*n.* 1 something kept back or stored up, as for later use 2 the keeping one's thoughts, feelings, etc. to oneself 3 reticence; silence 4 [*pl.*] troops, players, etc. kept out of action for use as replacements 5 land set apart for a special purpose 6 cash, etc. held back to meet future demands —**in reserve** reserved for later use —**without reserve** subject to no limitation

re·served′ *adj.* 1 kept in reserve; set apart 2 self-restrained; reticent

re·serv′ist *n.* a member of a country's military reserves

res·er·voir (rez′ər vwär′, -vwôr′) *n.* ⟦< Fr: see RESERVE⟧ 1 a place where water is collected and stored for use 2 a receptacle for holding a fluid 3 a large supply

re·side (ri zīd′) *vi.* **-sid′ed, -sid′ing** ⟦< L *re-,* back + *sedere,* sit⟧ 1 to dwell for a long time; live (*in* or *at*) 2 to be present or inherent (*in*): said of qualities, etc.

res·i·dence (rez′i dəns) *n.* 1 a residing 2 the place where one resides —**res′i·den′tial** (-den′shəl) *adj.*

res′i·den·cy (-dən sē) *n., pl.* **-cies** 1 RESIDENCE (sense 1) 2 a period of advanced, specialized medical or surgical training at a hospital

res′i·dent (-dənt) *adj.* residing; esp., living in a place while working, etc. —*n.* 1 one who lives in a place, not just a visitor 2 a doctor who is serving a residency

re·sid·u·al (ri zij′o͞o əl) *adj.* of or being a

residue; remaining —*n.* **1** something remaining **2** [*often pl.*] the fee paid for reruns on television, etc.

res·i·due (rez′ə do͞o′) *n.* ⟦< L *residuus,* remaining⟧ that which is left after part is taken away; remainder

re·sid·u·um (ri zij′o͞o əm) *n., pl.* **-u·a** (-ə) RESIDUE

re·sign (ri zīn′) *vt., vi.* ⟦< L *re-,* back + *signare,* to sign⟧ to give up (a claim, position, etc.) —**resign oneself (to)** to become reconciled (to)

res·ig·na·tion (rez′ig nā′shən) *n.* **1** *a)* the act of resigning *b)* formal notice of this **2** patient submission

re·signed (ri zīnd′) *adj.* feeling or showing resignation; submissive —**re·sign′ed·ly** (-zīn′id lē) *adv.*

re·sil·ient (ri zil′yənt) *adj.* ⟦< L *re-,* back + *salire,* to jump⟧ **1** springing back into shape, etc. **2** recovering strength, spirits, etc. quickly —**re·sil′ience** or **re·sil′ien·cy** *n.*

res·in (rez′ən) *n.* ⟦< L *resina*⟧ **1** a substance exuded from various plants and trees and used in varnishes, plastics, etc. **2** ROSIN —**res′in·ous** *adj.*

re·sist (ri zist′) *vt.* ⟦< L *re-,* back + *sistere,* to set⟧ **1** to withstand; fend off **2** to oppose actively; fight against —*vi.* to oppose or withstand something —**re·sist′er** *n.* —**re·sist′i·ble** *adj.*

re·sist′ance *n.* **1** a resisting **2** power to resist, as to ward off disease **3** opposition of some force, thing, etc. to another, as to the flow of an electric current —**re·sist′ant** *adj.*

re·sist′less *adj.* **1** irresistible **2** unable to resist

re·sis′tor *n.* a device used in an electrical circuit to provide resistance

re·sole (rē sōl′) *vt.* **-soled′, -sol′ing** to put a new sole on (a shoe, etc.)

res·o·lute (rez′ə lo͞ot′) *adj.* ⟦see RE- & SOLVE⟧ fixed and firm in purpose; determined —**res′o·lute′ly** *adv.*

res′o·lu′tion *n.* **1** the act or result of resolving something **2** a thing determined upon; decision as to future action **3** a resolute quality of mind **4** a formal statement of opinion or determination by an assembly, etc.

re·solve (ri zälv′, -zôlv′) *vt.* **-solved′, -solv′ing** ⟦see RE- & SOLVE⟧ **1** to break up into separate parts **2** to change: used reflexively **3** to reach as a decision; determine [to *resolve* to go] **4** to solve (a problem) **5** to decide by vote —*n.* **1** firm determination **2** a formal resolution —**re·solv′a·ble** *adj.*

re·solved′ *adj.* determined; resolute

res·o·nant (rez′ə nənt) *adj.* ⟦< L *resonare,* resound⟧ **1** resounding **2** intensifying sound [*resonant* walls] **3** sonorous; vibrant [a *resonant* voice] —**res′o·nance** *n.* —**res′o·nate′** (-nāt′), **-nat′ed, -nat′ing,** *vi., vt.*

res′o·na′tor *n.* a device that produces, or increases sound by, resonance

re·sort (ri zôrt′) *vi.* ⟦< OFr *re-,* again + *sortir,* go out⟧ to have recourse; turn (*to*) for help, etc. [to *resort* to lies] —*n.* **1** a place to which people go often or generally, as on vacation **2** a source of help, support, etc.; recourse —**as a last resort** as the last available means

re·sound (ri zound′) *vi.* ⟦< L *resonare*⟧ **1** to reverberate **2** to make a loud, echoing sound —**re·sound′ing** *adj.* —**re·sound′ing·ly** *adv.*

re·source (rē′sôrs′, ri sôrs′) *n.* ⟦< OFr *re-,* again + *sourdre,* spring up⟧ **1** something that lies ready for use or can be drawn upon for aid **2** [*pl.*] wealth; assets **3** resourcefulness

re·source′ful *adj.* able to deal effectively with problems, etc. —**re·source′ful·ness** *n.*

re·spect (ri spekt′) *vt.* ⟦< L *re-,* back + *specere,* look at⟧ **1** to feel or show honor or esteem for **2** to show consideration for —*n.* **1** honor or esteem **2** consideration or regard **3** [*pl.*] expressions of regard **4** a particular detail **5** reference; relation [with *respect* to the problem] —**re·spect′ful** *adj.* —**re·spect′ful·ly** *adv.*

re·spect′a·ble *adj.* **1** worthy of respect or esteem **2** proper; correct **3** fairly good in quality or size **4** presentable —**re·spect′a·bil′i·ty** *n.*

re·spect′ing *prep.* concerning; about

re·spec′tive *adj.* as relates individually to each one

re·spec′tive·ly *adv.* in regard to each, in the order named

res·pi·ra·tion (res′pə rā′shən) *n.* ⟦< L *re-,* back + *spirare,* breathe⟧ act or process of breathing —**res·pi·ra·to·ry** (res′pər ə tôr′ē, ri spī′rə-) *adj.*

res′pi·ra′tor *n.* **1** a mask, as of gauze, to prevent the inhaling of harmful substances **2** an apparatus to maintain breathing by artificial means

res·pite (res′pit) *n.* ⟦see RESPECT⟧ **1** a delay or postponement **2** temporary relief, as from pain or work; lull

re·splend·ent (ri splen′dənt) *adj.* ⟦< L *re-,* again + *splendere,* to shine⟧ shining brightly; dazzling —**re·splend′ence** *n.* —**re·splend′ent·ly** *adv.*

re·spond (ri spänd′) *vi.* ⟦< L *re-,* back + *spondere,* to pledge⟧ **1** to answer; reply **2** to react **3** to have a favorable reaction

re·spond′ent *adj.* responding —*n. Law* a defendant

re·sponse (ri späns′) *n.* ⟦see RESPOND⟧ **1** something said or done in answer; reply **2** words sung or spoken by the congregation or choir replying to the clergyman **3** any reaction to a stimulus

re·spon·si·bil·i·ty (ri spän′sə bil′ə tē) *n., pl.* **-ties** **1** a being responsible; obligation **2** a thing or person that one is responsible for

re·spon′si·ble (-bəl) *adj.* **1** expected or obliged to account (*for*); answerable (*to*) **2** involving obligation or duties **3** that is the cause of something **4** able to distinguish between right and wrong **5** dependable; reliable —**re·spon′si·bly** *adv.*

re·spon′sive *adj.* reacting readily, as to suggestion or appeal —**re·spon′sive·ness** *n.*

rest[1] (rest) *n.* ⟦OE⟧ **1** sleep or repose **2** ease or inactivity after exertion **3** relief from anything distressing, tiring, etc. **4** absence of motion **5** a resting place **6** a supporting device **7** *Music* a measured interval of silence between tones, or a symbol for this **—*vi.*** **1** to get ease and refreshment by sleeping or by ceasing from work **2** to be at ease **3** to be or become still **4** to lie, sit, or lean **5** to be placed or based (*in, on*, etc.) **6** to be found *[the fault rests with him]* **7** to rely; depend **—*vt.*** **1** to give rest to **2** to put for ease, support, etc. *[rest your head here]* **3** *Law* to stop introducing evidence in (a case) **—lay to rest** to bury

rest[2] (rest) ***n.*** ⟦< L *restare*, remain⟧ **1** what is left **2** [*with pl. v.*] the others **—*vi.*** to go on being *[rest assured]*

res·tau·rant (res′tə ränt′, res′tränt′) ***n.*** ⟦Fr: see RESTORE⟧ a place where meals can be bought and eaten

res·tau·ra·teur (res′tə rə tur′, -toor′) ***n.*** ⟦Fr⟧ one who owns or operates a restaurant: also **res·tau·ran·teur** (res′tə rän′ tur′, -toor′)

rest·ful (rest′fəl) ***adj.*** **1** full of or giving rest **2** quiet; peaceful

rest home a residence that provides care for aged persons or convalescents

res·ti·tu·tion (res′tə to͞o′shən) ***n.*** ⟦< L *re-*, again + *statuere*, set up⟧ **1** a giving back of something that has been lost or taken away; restoration **2** reimbursement, as for loss

res·tive (res′tiv) ***adj.*** ⟦< OFr *rester*, remain⟧ **1** unruly or balky **2** nervous under restraint; restless **—res′tive·ly *adv.*** **—res′tive·ness *n.***

rest′less ***adj.*** **1** unable to relax; uneasy **2** giving no rest; disturbed *[restless sleep]* **3** rarely quiet or still; active **4** discontented **—rest′less·ly *adv.*** **—rest′less·ness *n.***

res·to·ra·tion (res′tə rā′shən) ***n.*** **1** a restoring or being restored **2** something restored, as by rebuilding

re·stor·a·tive (ri stôr′ə tiv) ***adj.*** able to restore health, consciousness, etc. **—*n.*** something that is restorative

re·store (ri stôr′) ***vt.*** **-stored′**, **-stor′ing** ⟦< L *re-*, again + *-staurare*, to erect⟧ **1** to give back (something taken, lost, etc.) **2** to return to a former or normal state, or to a position, rank, use, etc. **3** to bring back to health, strength, etc.

re·strain (ri strān′) ***vt.*** ⟦< L *re-*, back + *stringere*, draw tight⟧ **1** to hold back from action; check; suppress **2** to limit; restrict

re·straint (ri strānt′) ***n.*** **1** a restraining or being restrained **2** a means or instrument of restraining **3** confinement **4** control of emotions, impulses, etc.; reserve

re·strict (ri strikt′) ***vt.*** ⟦see RESTRAIN⟧ to keep within limits; confine **—re·strict′ed *adj.*** **—re·stric′tion *n.***

re·stric′tive ***adj.*** **1** restricting **2** *Gram.* designating a modifier, as a subordinate clause or phrase, that limits the reference of the word it modifies and is not set off by punctuation

rest′room′ ***n.*** a room in a public building, equipped with toilets, washbowls, etc.: also **rest room**

re·struc·ture (rē struk′chər) ***vt.*** **-tured**, **-tur·ing** **1** to plan or provide a new structure or organization for **2** to change the terms of (a loan, etc.)

re·sult (ri zult′) ***vi.*** ⟦< L *resultare*, to rebound⟧ **1** to happen as an effect **2** to end as a consequence (*in* something) **—*n.*** **1** *a*) anything that comes about as an effect *b*) [*pl.*] the desired effect **2** the number, etc. obtained by mathematical calculation **—re·sult′ant *adj.*, *n.***

re·sume (ri zo͞om′) ***vt.*** **-sumed′**, **-sum′ing** ⟦< L *re-*, again + *sumere*, take⟧ **1** to take or occupy again **2** to continue after interruption **—*vi.*** to proceed after interruption **—re·sump′tion** (-zump′shən) ***n.***

ré·su·mé (rez′ə mā′) ***n.*** ⟦Fr: see prec.⟧ a summary, esp. of employment experience: also written **resume** or **resumé**

re·sur·face (rē sur′fis) ***vt.*** **-faced**, **-fac·ing** to put a new surface on **—*vi.*** to come to the surface again

re·sur·gent (ri sur′jənt) ***adj.*** ⟦see fol.⟧ rising or tending to rise again **—re·sur′gence *n.***

res·ur·rec·tion (rez′ə rek′shən) ***n.*** ⟦< L *resurgere*, rise again⟧ **1** a rising from the dead **2** a coming back into notice, use, etc.; revival **—the Resurrection** *Theol.* the rising of Jesus from the dead **—res′ur·rect′ *vt.***

re·sus·ci·tate (ri sus′ə tāt′) ***vt.*, *vi.*** **-tat′ed**, **-tat′ing** ⟦< L *re-*, again + *suscitare*, revive⟧ to revive when apparently dead or in a faint, etc. **—re·sus′ci·ta′tion *n.*** **—re·sus′ci·ta′tor *n.***

ret *abbrev.* **1** retired **2** return(ed)

re·tail (rē′tāl′) ***n.*** ⟦< OFr *re-*, again + *tailler*, to cut⟧ the sale of goods in small quantities directly to the consumer **—*adj.*** of or engaged in such sale **—*adv.*** at a retail price **—*vt.*, *vi.*** to sell or be sold directly to the consumer **—re′tail′er *n.***

re·tain (ri tān′) ***vt.*** ⟦< L *re-*, back + *tenere*, to hold⟧ **1** to keep in possession, use, etc. **2** to hold in **3** to keep in mind **4** to hire by paying a retainer

re·tain′er ***n.*** **1** something that retains **2** a servant, attendant, etc. **3** a fee paid in advance to engage the services of a lawyer, etc.

retaining wall a wall for keeping earth from sliding or water from flooding

re·take (rē tāk′; *for n.* rē′tāk′) ***vt.*** **-took′**, **-tak′en**, **-tak′ing** **1** to take again; recapture **2** to photograph again **—*n.*** a scene, etc. rephotographed

re·tal·i·ate (ri tal′ē āt′) ***vi.*** **-at′ed**, **-at′ing** ⟦< L *re-*, back + *talio*, punishment in kind⟧ to return like for like, esp. injury for injury **—re·tal′i·a′tion *n.*** **—re·tal′i·a·to′ry *adj.***

re·tard (ri tärd′) ***vt.*** ⟦< L *re-*, back + *tardare*, make slow⟧ to hinder, delay, or slow the progress of **—re·tar·da·tion** (rē′tär dā′shən) ***n.***

re·tard′ant ***n.*** something that retards; esp., a substance that delays a chemical reaction **—*adj.*** that retards

re·tard′ed ***adj.*** slowed or delayed in development, esp. mentally

retch (rech) ***vi.*** ⟦OE *hræcan*, clear the

throat⟧ to strain to vomit, esp. without bringing anything up

re·ten·tion (ri ten′shən) ***n.*** **1** a retaining or being retained **2** capacity for retaining **3** a remembering; memory —**re·ten′tive** ***adj.***

ret·i·cent (ret′ə sənt) ***adj.*** ⟦< L *re-*, again + *tacere,* be silent⟧ disinclined to speak; taciturn —**ret′i·cence** ***n.***

ret·i·na (ret′'n ə) ***n.***, *pl.* **-nas** or **-nae′** (-ē′) ⟦prob. < L *rete*, a net⟧ the innermost coat lining the eyeball, containing light-sensitive cells that are directly connected to the brain

ret·i·nue (ret′'n o͞o′) ***n.*** ⟦< OFr, ult. < L: see RETAIN⟧ a group of persons attending a person of rank or importance

re·tire (ri tīr′) ***vi.*** **-tired′**, **-tir′ing** ⟦< Fr *re-*, back + *tirer,* draw⟧ **1** to withdraw to a secluded place **2** to go to bed **3** to retreat, as in battle **4** to give up one's work, business, etc., esp. because of age —***vt.*** **1** to pay off (bonds, etc.) **2** to cause to retire from a position, office, etc. **3** to withdraw from use **4** *Baseball* to put out (a batter, side, etc.) —**re·tir′ee′** ***n.*** —**re·tire′ment** ***n.***

re·tired′ ***adj.*** **1** secluded **2** *a*) no longer working, etc. as because of age *b*) of or for such retired persons

re·tir′ing ***adj.*** reserved; modest; shy

re·tool (rē to͞ol′) ***vt.***, ***vi.*** **1** to adapt (factory machinery) for a different product **2** to reorganize to meet new or different needs or conditions

RETORT

re·tort[1] (ri tôrt′) ***vt.*** ⟦< L *re-*, back + *torquere,* to twist⟧ to say in reply —***vi.*** to make a sharp, witty reply —***n.*** a sharp, witty reply

re·tort[2] (ri tôrt′) ***n.*** ⟦< ML *retorta*: see prec.⟧ a glass container with a long tube, in which substances are distilled

re·touch (rē tuch′) ***vt.*** to touch up details in (a painting, essay, etc.) so as to improve or change it

re·trace (rē trās′) ***vt.*** **-traced′**, **-trac′ing** ⟦see RE- & TRACE[1]⟧ to go back over again *[to retrace one's steps]*

re·tract (ri trakt′) ***vt.***, ***vi.*** ⟦< L *re-*, back + *trahere,* draw⟧ **1** to draw back or in **2** to withdraw (a statement, charge, etc.) —**re·tract′a·ble** or **re·trac′tile** (-trak′təl, -tīl′) ***adj.*** —**re·trac′tion** ***n.***

re·tread (rē tred′; *for n.* rē′tred′) ***vt.***, ***n.*** RECAP[1]

re·treat (ri trēt′) ***n.*** ⟦< L *retrahere:* see RETRACT⟧ **1** a withdrawal, as from danger **2** a safe, quiet place **3** a period of seclusion, esp. for spiritual renewal **4** *a*) the forced withdrawal of troops under attack *b*) a signal for this *c*) a signal, as by bugle, or a ceremony at sunset for lowering the national flag —***vi.*** to withdraw; go back

re·trench (rē trench′) ***vi.*** ⟦< Fr: see RE- & TRENCH⟧ to cut down expenses; economize —**re·trench′ment** ***n.***

ret·ri·bu·tion (re′trə byo͞o′shən) ***n.*** ⟦< L *re-*, back + *tribuere,* to pay⟧ punishment for evil done —**re·trib·u·tive** (ri trib′yoo tiv) ***adj.***

re·trieve (ri trēv′) ***vt.*** **-trieved′**, **-triev′ing** ⟦< OFr *re-*, again + *trouver,* find⟧ **1** to get back; recover **2** to restore **3** to make good (a loss, error, etc.) **4** to access (data) stored in a computer **5** to find and bring back (killed or wounded game): said of dogs —***vi.*** to retrieve game —**re·triev′al** ***n.***

re·triev′er ***n.*** a dog trained to retrieve game

retro- ⟦< L⟧ *combining form* backward, back, behind

ret·ro·ac·tive (re′trō ak′tiv) ***adj.*** having an effect on things that are already past —**ret′ro·ac′tive·ly** ***adv.***

ret·ro·fire (re′trə fīr′) ***vt.*** **-fired′**, **-fir′ing** to ignite (a retrorocket)

ret′ro·fit′ (-fit′) ***n.*** a change in design or equipment, as of an aircraft already in operation, so as to incorporate later improvements —***vt.***, ***vi.*** **-fit′ted**, **-fit′ting** to modify with a retrofit

ret′ro·grade′ (-grād′) ***adj.*** ⟦< L: see RETRO- & GRADE⟧ **1** moving backward **2** going back to a worse condition

ret′ro·gress′ (-gres′) ***vi.*** ⟦< L: see prec.⟧ to move backward, esp. into a worse condition; degenerate —**ret′ro·gres′sion** ***n.*** —**ret′ro·gres′sive** ***adj.***

ret·ro·rock·et or **ret·ro-rock·et** (re′trō räk′it) ***n.*** a small rocket, as on a spacecraft, producing thrust opposite to the direction of flight to reduce speed, as for maneuvering

ret·ro·spect (re′trə spekt′) ***n.*** ⟦< L *retro-*, back + *specere,* to look⟧ contemplation of the past —**ret′ro·spec′tion** ***n.***

ret′ro·spec′tive ***adj.*** looking back on the past —***n.*** a representative show of an artist's lifetime work

ret·si·na (ret sē′nə) ***n.*** ⟦ModGr, prob. < It *resina*, resin⟧ a Greek wine flavored with pine resin

re·turn (ri turn′) ***vi.*** ⟦< OFr: see RE- & TURN⟧ **1** to go or come back **2** to answer; reply —***vt.*** **1** to bring, send, or put back **2** to do in reciprocation *[to return a visit]* **3** to yield (a profit, etc.) **4** to report officially **5** to elect or reelect —***n.*** **1** a coming or going back **2** a bringing, sending, or putting back **3** something returned **4** a recurrence **5** repayment; requital **6** [*often pl.*] yield or profit, as from investments **7** an answer; reply **8** *a*) an official report *[election returns]* *b*) a form for computing income tax —***adj.*** **1** of or for a return *[return postage]* **2** given, done, etc. in return —**in return** as a return; as an equivalent, response, etc. —**re·turn′a·ble** ***adj.***

re·turn′ee′ ***n.*** one who returns, as home from military service

Reu·ben (sandwich) (ro͞o′bən) a sandwich of rye bread, corned beef, sauerkraut, Swiss cheese, etc. served hot

re·u·ni·fy (rē yo͞o′nə fī′) ***vt.***, ***vi.*** **-fied′**, **-fy′ing** to unify again after being divided —**re·u′ni·fi·ca′tion** ***n.***

re·un·ion (rē yo͞on′yən) ***n.*** a coming together again, as after separation

re-up (rē up′) ***vi.*** **-upped′, -up′ping** ⟦RE- + (*sign*) *up*⟧ [Mil. Slang] to reenlist

rev[1] (rev) ***vt.*** **revved, rev′ving** ⟦< REV(OLUTION)⟧ [Inf.] **1** to increase the speed of (an engine) **2** to accelerate, intensify, etc. Usually with *up*

rev[2] *abbrev.* **1** revenue **2** revise(d) **3** revolution

Rev *abbrev.* **1** *Bible* Revelation **2** Reverend

re·vamp (rē vamp′) ***vt.*** to renovate; redo

re·veal (ri vēl′) ***vt.*** ⟦< L *re-,* back + *velum,* veil⟧ **1** to make known (something hidden or secret) **2** to show; exhibit; display

rev·eil·le (rev′ə lē) ***n.*** ⟦< Fr < L *re-,* again + *vigilare,* to watch⟧ a signal on a bugle, drum, etc. in the morning to waken soldiers, etc.

rev·el (rev′əl) ***vi.*** **-eled** or **-elled, -el·ing** or **-el·ling** ⟦< MFr < L *rebellare,* to rebel: see REBEL⟧ **1** to be festive; make merry **2** to take much pleasure (*in*) **—*n.*** merrymaking **—rev′el·er** or **rev′el·ler** ***n.*** **—rev′el·ry,** *pl.* **-ries,** ***n.***

rev·e·la·tion (rev′ə lā′shən) ***n.*** **1** a revealing **2** a striking disclosure **3** *Theol.* God's disclosure to humanity of divine truth, etc. —[**R-**] the last book of the New Testament

re·venge (ri venj′) ***vt.*** **-venged′, -veng′ing** ⟦< OFr: see RE- & VENGEANCE⟧ to inflict harm in return for (an injury, etc.) **—*n.*** **1** the act or result of revenging **2** desire to take vengeance **—re·venge′ful** ***adj.***

rev·e·nue (rev′ə no͞o′) ***n.*** ⟦< MFr, returned⟧ **1** return, as from investment; income **2** the income from taxes, licenses, etc., as of a city or nation

re·ver·ber·ate (ri vur′bə rāt′) ***vi., vt.*** **-at′ed, -at′ing** ⟦< L *re-,* again + *verberare,* to beat⟧ to reecho or cause to reecho **—re·ver′ber·a′tion** ***n.***

re·vere (ri vir′) ***vt.*** **-vered′, -ver′ing** ⟦< L *re-,* again + *vereri,* to fear⟧ to regard with deep respect, love, etc.

Re·vere (ri vir′), **Paul** 1735-1818; Am. silversmith & patriot

rev·er·ence (rev′ə rəns) ***n.*** a feeling of deep respect, love, and awe **—*vt.*** **-enced, -enc·ing** to treat or regard with reverence; venerate **—rev′er·ent** or **rev′er·en′tial** (-ə ren′shəl) ***adj.*** **—rev′er·ent·ly** ***adv.***

rev·er·end (rev′ə rənd) ***adj.*** worthy of reverence: used with *the* as a title of respect for a member of the clergy [the *Reverend* A. B. Smith]

rev·er·ie (rev′ə rē) ***n.*** ⟦< Fr⟧ daydreaming or a daydream

re·vers (ri vir′, -ver′) ***n.,*** *pl.* **-vers′** (-virz′, -verz′) ⟦Fr: see REVERT⟧ a part (of a garment) turned back to show the reverse side, as a lapel: also **re·vere′** (-vir′)

re·verse (ri vurs′) ***adj.*** ⟦see fol.⟧ **1** turned backward; opposite or contrary **2** causing movement in the opposite direction **—*n.*** **1** the opposite or contrary **2** the back of a coin, medal, etc. **3** a change from good fortune to bad **4** a mechanism for reversing, as a gear on a machine **—*vt.*** **-versed′, -vers′ing** **1** to turn backward, in an opposite position or direction, upside down, or inside out **2** to change to the opposite **3** *Law* to revoke or annul (a decision, etc.) **—*vi.*** to go or turn in the opposite direction **—re·ver′sal** (-vur′səl) ***n.*** **—re·vers′i·ble** ***adj.*** **—re·vers′i·bly** ***adv.***

re·vert (ri vurt′) ***vi.*** ⟦< L *re-,* back + *vertere,* to turn⟧ **1** to go back, as to a former practice, state, subject, etc. **2** *Biol.* to return to a former or primitive type **3** *Law* to go back to a former owner or his or her heirs **—re·ver′sion** (-vur′zhən) ***n.*** **—re·vert′i·ble** ***adj.***

re·vet·ment (ri vet′mənt) ***n.*** ⟦< Fr⟧ **1** a facing of stone, cement, etc., as to protect an embankment **2** RETAINING WALL

re·view (ri vyo͞o′) ***n.*** ⟦< L *re-,* again + *videre,* see⟧ **1** a looking at or looking over again **2** a general survey or report **3** a looking back on (past events, etc.) **4** reexamination, as of the decision of a lower court **5** a critical evaluation of a book, play, etc. **6** a formal inspection, as of troops on parade **—*vt.*** **1** to look back on **2** to survey in thought, speech, etc. **3** to inspect (troops, etc.) formally **4** to give a critical evaluation of (a book, etc.) **5** to study again **—re·view′er** ***n.***

re·vile (ri vīl′) ***vt.*** **-viled′, -vil′ing** ⟦< OFr: see RE- & VILE⟧ to use abusive language to or about **—re·vile′ment** ***n.*** **—re·vil′er** ***n.***

re·vise (ri vīz′) ***vt.*** **-vised′, -vis′ing** ⟦< L *re-,* back + *visere,* to survey⟧ **1** to read over carefully and correct, improve, or update **2** to change or amend **—re·vi′sion** (-vizh′ən) ***n.***

Revised Standard Version a 20th-c. version of the Bible

re·vi′sion·ist ***n.*** a person who revises, or favors the revision of, some accepted theory, doctrine, etc. **—*adj.*** of revisionists or their policy or practice **—re·vi′sion·ism′** ***n.***

re·vis·it (rē viz′it) ***vt.*** **1** to visit again **2** to reconsider or reevaluate

re·viv·al (ri vī′vəl) ***n.*** **1** a reviving or being revived **2** a bringing or coming back into use, being, etc. **3** a new presentation of an earlier play, etc. **4** restoration to vigor or activity **5** a meeting led by an evangelist to stir up religious feeling **—re·viv′al·ist** ***n.***

re·vive (ri vīv′) ***vi., vt.*** **-vived′, -viv′ing** ⟦< L *re-,* again + *vivere,* to live⟧ **1** to return to life or consciousness **2** to return to health or vigor **3** to come or bring back into use, attention, popularity, etc.

re·viv·i·fy (ri viv′ə fī′) ***vt.*** **-fied′, -fy′ing** to put new life or vigor into **—*vi.*** to revive **—re·viv′i·fi·ca′tion** ***n.***

re·voke (ri vōk′) ***vt.*** **-voked′, -vok′ing** ⟦< L *re-,* back + *vocare,* to call⟧ to withdraw, repeal, or cancel (a law, etc.) **—rev·o·ca·ble** (rev′ə kə bəl, ri vō′kə-) ***adj.*** **—rev′o·ca′tion** (-kā′shən) ***n.***

re·volt (ri vōlt′) ***n.*** ⟦< Fr: see REVOLVE⟧ a rebelling against the government or any authority **—*vi.*** to rebel against authority **—*vt.*** to disgust **—re·volt′ing** ***adj.*** **—re·volt′ing·ly** ***adv.***

rev·o·lu·tion (rev′ə lo͞o′shən) ***n.*** ⟦see

REVOLVE] 1 the movement of a body in an orbit 2 a turning around an axis; rotation 3 a complete cycle of events 4 a complete change 5 overthrow of a government, social system, etc. —**rev'o·lu'tion·ar'y**, *pl.* **-ies**, ***n., adj.*** —**rev'o·lu'tion·ist** ***n.***

Revolutionary War *see* AMERICAN REVOLUTION

rev'o·lu'tion·ize' (-shə nīz') ***vt.*** **-ized', -iz'ing** to make a fundamental change in

re·volve (ri välv', -vôlv') ***vt.*** **-volved', -volv'ing** [< L *re-*, back + *volvere,* to roll] to turn over in the mind —***vi.*** 1 to move in a circle or orbit 2 to rotate —**re·volv'a·ble** ***adj.***

re·volv'er ***n.*** a handgun with a revolving cylinder containing cartridges

re·vue (ri vyōō') ***n.*** [Fr, review] a musical show with skits, dances, etc., often parodying recent events

re·vul·sion (ri vul'shən) ***n.*** [< L *re-*, back + *vellere,* to pull] extreme disgust; loathing

re·ward (ri wôrd') ***n.*** [< OFr *regarde*: see REGARD] 1 something given in return for something done 2 money offered, as for capturing a criminal —***vt.*** to give a reward to (someone) for (service, etc.)

re·ward'ing ***adj.*** giving a sense of reward or worthwhile return

re·wind (rē wīnd') ***vt.*** **-wound', -wind'ing** to wind again; specif., to wind (film or tape) back on the original reel

re·word' ***vt.*** to change the wording of

re·write' ***vt., vi.*** **-wrote', -writ'ten, -writ'ing** 1 to write again 2 to revise (something written) 3 to write (news turned in) in a form suitable for publication

Rey·kja·vík (rā'kyə vēk', -vik') seaport & capital of Iceland: pop. 103,000

RFD *abbrev.* Rural Free Delivery

rhap·so·dize (rap'sə dīz') ***vi., vt.*** **-dized', -diz'ing** to speak or write in a rhapsodic manner

rhap'so·dy (-sə dē) ***n.,*** *pl.* **-dies** [< Gr *rhaptein,* stitch together + *ōidē,* song] 1 any ecstatic or enthusiastic speech or writing 2 a musical composition of free, irregular form, suggesting improvisation —**rhap·sod'ic** (-säd'ik) or **rhap·sod'i·cal** ***adj.***

rhe·a (rē'ə) ***n.*** [< Gr] a large, flightless South American bird, like an ostrich but smaller

rhe·o·stat (rē'ə stat') ***n.*** [< Gr *rheos,* current + -STAT] a device for varying the resistance of an electric circuit, used as for dimming or brightening electric lights

rhesus (monkey) (rē'səs) [< Gr proper name] a brownish-yellow monkey of India: used in medical research

rhet·o·ric (ret'ə rik) ***n.*** [< Gr *rhētōr,* orator] 1 the art of using words effectively; esp., the art of prose composition 2 showy, elaborate language that is empty or insincere —**rhe·tor·i·cal** (ri tôr'i kəl) ***adj.*** —**rhet'o·ri'cian** (-ə rish'ən) ***n.***

rhetorical question a question asked only for rhetorical effect, no answer being expected

rheum (rōōm) ***n.*** [< Gr *rheuma,* a flow] watery discharge from the eyes, nose, etc., as in a cold

rheumatic fever an acute or chronic disease, usually of children, with fever, swelling of the joints, inflammation of the heart, etc.

rheu·ma·tism (rōō'mə tiz'əm) ***n.*** [see RHEUM] *nontechnical term for* a painful condition of the joints and muscles —**rheu·mat'ic** (-mat'ik) ***adj., n.*** —**rheu'ma·toid'** (-mə toid') ***adj.***

rheumatoid arthritis a chronic disease with painful swelling of joints, often leading to deformity

Rh factor (är'āch') [first discovered in RH(ESUS) monkeys] a group of antigens, usually present in human blood: people who have this factor are **Rh positive**; those who do not are **Rh negative**

Rhine (rīn) river in W Europe, flowing from E Switzerland through Germany & the Netherlands into the North Sea

rhine·stone (rīn'stōn') ***n.*** a bright, colorless artificial gem of hard glass, often cut like a diamond

Rhine wine a light white wine, esp. one produced in the valley of the Rhine

rhi·ni·tis (rī nīt'is) ***n.*** [< Gr *rhis,* nose + -ITIS] inflammation of the nasal mucous membrane

rhi·no (rī'nō) ***n.,*** *pl.* **-nos** or **-no** *short for* RHINOCEROS

rhi·noc·er·os (rī näs'ər əs) ***n.*** [< Gr *rhis,* nose + *keras,* horn] a large, thick-skinned, plant-eating mammal of Africa and Asia, with one or two upright horns on the snout

rhi·zome (rī'zōm') ***n.*** [< Gr *rhiza,* a root] a horizontal stem on or under soil, bearing leaves near its tips and roots from its undersurface

rho (rō) ***n.*** the 17th letter of the Greek alphabet (Ρ, ρ)

Rhode Island (rōd) New England state of the U.S.: 1,045 sq. mi.; pop. 1,003,000; cap. Providence: abbrev. *RI* —**Rhode Islander**

Rhodes (rōdz) large Greek island in the Aegean

rho·do·den·dron (rō'də den'drən) ***n.*** [< Gr *rhodon,* rose + *dendron,* tree] any of various trees or shrubs, mainly evergreen, with showy flowers

rhom·boid (räm'boid') ***n.*** [< Fr: see fol. & -OID] a parallelogram with oblique angles and only the opposite sides equal

rhom·bus (räm'bəs) ***n.,*** *pl.* **-bus·es** or **-bi'** (-bī') [L < Gr *rhombos,* turnable object] an equilateral parallelogram, esp. one with oblique angles

Rhone or **Rhône** (rōn) river flowing through SW Switzerland & France into the Mediterranean

rhu·barb (rōō'bärb') ***n.*** [< Gr *rhēon,* rhubarb + *barbaron,* foreign] 1 a plant with long, thick stalks that are cooked into a sauce, etc. 2 [Slang] a heated argument

rhyme (rīm) ***n.*** [< OFr] 1 a poem or

verse with like recurring sounds, esp. at ends of lines **2** such verse, poetry, or likeness of sounds **3** a word like another in end sound —*vi.* **rhymed, rhym'ing 1** to make (rhyming) verse **2** to form a rhyme /"more" *rhymes* with "door"/ —*vt.* **1** to put into rhyme **2** to use as a rhyme

rhym'er *n.* a maker of rhymes, esp. a rhymester

rhyme'ster *n.* a maker of trivial rhyme

rhythm (rith'əm) *n.* ⟦< Gr *rhythmos,* measure⟧ **1** movement, flow, etc. characterized by regular recurrence of beat, accent, etc. **2** the pattern of this in music, verse, etc. —**rhyth'mic** (-mik) or **rhyth'mi·cal** *adj.* —**rhyth'mi·cal·ly** *adv.*

rhythm and blues the form of American popular music from which rock-and-roll derives

rhythm method a method of seeking birth control by abstaining from intercourse during the woman's probable ovulation period

RI Rhode Island

rib (rib) *n.* ⟦OE⟧ **1** any of the arched bones attached to the spine and enclosing the chest cavity **2** anything like a rib in appearance or function —*vt.* **ribbed, rib'bing 1** to strengthen or form with ribs **2** [Slang] to make fun of; kid

rib·ald (rib'əld) *adj.* ⟦< OHG *riban,* to rub⟧ coarse or vulgar in joking, speaking, etc. —**rib'ald·ry** *n.*

rib·bon (rib'ən) *n.* ⟦< MFr *ruban*⟧ **1** a narrow strip of silk, rayon, etc. used for decoration, tying, etc. **2** [*pl.*] torn shreds **3** an inked strip for printing, as in a typewriter, etc.

rib'bon-cut'ting *n.* a ceremony to officially open a new building, construction site, etc.

rib'-eye' (steak) boneless beefsteak from the rib section

ri·bo·fla·vin (rī'bə flā'vin) *n.* ⟦< *ribose,* a sugar + L *flavus,* yellow⟧ a B vitamin found in milk, eggs, fruits, etc.: see VITAMIN B (COMPLEX)

rice (rīs) *n.* ⟦< Gr *oryza*⟧ **1** an aquatic cereal grass grown widely in warm climates, esp. in East Asia **2** the starchy grains of this grass, used as food —*vt.* **riced, ric'ing** to make ricelike granules from (cooked potatoes, etc.) using a utensil with small holes (**ric'er**)

rich (rich) *adj.* ⟦< OFr⟧ **1** owning much money or property; wealthy **2** well-supplied (*with*); abounding (*in*) **3** valuable or costly **4** full of choice ingredients, as butter, sugar, etc. /*rich* pastries/ **5** *a*) full and mellow (said of sounds) *b*) deep; vivid (said of colors) *c*) very fragrant **6** abundant **7** yielding in abundance, as soil **8** [Inf.] very amusing —**the rich** wealthy people collectively —**rich'ly** *adv.* —**rich'ness** *n.*

Rich·ard I (rich'ərd) 1157-99; king of England (1189-99): called **Richard Coeur de Li·on** (kur' də lē'ən) or **Richard the Li'on-Heart'ed**

rich·es (rich'iz) *pl.n.* ⟦< OFr *richesse*⟧ wealth

Rich·mond (rich'mənd) capital of Virginia: pop. 203,000

Rich·ter scale (rik'tər) ⟦devised by C. *Richter* (1900-85), U.S. geologist⟧ a scale for measuring the magnitude of earthquakes

rick (rik) *n.* ⟦OE *hreac*⟧ a stack of hay, straw, etc.

rick·ets (rik'its) *n.* ⟦< ? Gr *rhachis,* spine⟧ a disease, chiefly of children, characterized by a softening and, often, bending of the bones

rick·et·y (rik'it ē) *adj.* feeble; weak; shaky

rick·shaw or **rick·sha** (rik'shô') *n.* JINRIKISHA

ric·o·chet (rik'ə shā') *n.* ⟦Fr⟧ the oblique rebound of a bullet, etc. after striking a surface at an angle —*vi.* **-cheted'** (-shād'), **-chet'ing** (-shā'iŋ) to make a ricochet

ri·cot·ta (ri kät'ə) *n.* ⟦It < L *recocta,* recooked⟧ a soft cheese made from whey, whole milk, or both

rid (rid) *vt.* **rid** or **rid'ded, rid'ding** ⟦< ON *rythja,* to clear (land)⟧ to free or relieve, as of something undesirable —**get rid of** to give or throw away or to destroy

rid·dance (rid''ns) *n.* a ridding or being rid —**good riddance** an expression of satisfaction at being rid of something

rid·den (rid''n) *vi., vt. pp. of* RIDE —*adj.* dominated: used in compounds /fear-*ridden*/

rid·dle[1] (rid''l) *n.* ⟦OE *rædels*⟧ **1** a puzzling question, etc. requiring some ingenuity to answer **2** any puzzling person or thing

rid·dle[2] (rid''l) *vt.* **-dled, -dling** ⟦< OE *hriddel,* a sieve⟧ **1** to make many holes in **2** to affect every part of /*riddled* with errors/

ride (rīd) *vi.* **rode, rid'den, rid'ing** ⟦OE *ridan*⟧ **1** to be carried along by a horse, in a vehicle, etc. **2** to be supported in motion (*on* or *upon*) /tanks *ride* on treads/ **3** to admit of being ridden /the car *rides* smoothly/ **4** to move or float on water **5** [Inf.] to continue undisturbed /let the matter *ride*/ —*vt.* **1** to sit on or in and control so as to move along **2** to move over, along, or through (a road, area, etc.) by horse, car, etc. **3** to control, dominate, etc. /*ridden* by doubts/ **4** [Inf.] to tease with ridicule, etc. —*n.* **1** a riding **2** a thing to ride at an amusement park

rid'er *n.* **1** one who rides **2** an addition or amendment to a document

rid'er·ship' *n.* the passengers of a particular transportation system

ridge (rij) *n.* ⟦< OE *hrycg,* animal's spine⟧ **1** the long, narrow crest of something **2** a long, narrow elevation of land **3** any raised narrow strip **4** the horizontal line formed by the meeting of two sloping surfaces —*vt., vi.* **ridged, ridg'ing** to mark or be marked with, or form into, ridges

ridge'pole' *n.* the horizontal beam at the ridge of a roof, to which the rafters are attached

rid·i·cule (rid'i kyōōl') *n.* ⟦< L *ridere,* to laugh⟧ **1** the act of making someone the object of scornful laughter **2** words or actions intended to produce such laughter —**vt. -culed′**, **-cul′ing** to make fun of; deride; mock

ri·dic·u·lous (ri dik′yə ləs) ***adj.*** deserving ridicule —**ri·dic′u·lous·ly *adv.*** —**ri·dic′u·lous·ness *n.***

rife (rīf) ***adj.*** ⟦OE *ryfe*⟧ **1** widespread **2** abounding *[rife* with error*]*

riff (rif) ***n.*** ⟦prob. altered < REFRAIN[2]⟧ *Jazz* a constantly repeated musical phrase —***vi.*** *Jazz* to perform a riff

rif·fle (rif′əl) ***n.*** ⟦< ?⟧ **1** a ripple in a stream, produced by a reef, etc. **2** a certain way of shuffling cards —***vt.***, ***vi.*** **-fled**, **-fling** to shuffle (playing cards) by letting a divided deck fall together as the corners are slipped through one's thumbs

riff·raff (rif′raf′) ***n.*** ⟦< OFr⟧ those people regarded as worthless, disreputable, etc.

ri·fle[1] (rī′fəl) ***vt.*** **-fled**, **-fling** ⟦Fr *rifler,* to scrape⟧ to cut spiral grooves within (a gun barrel, etc.) —***n.*** a gun, fired from the shoulder, with a rifled barrel to spin the bullet for greater accuracy

ri·fle[2] (rī′fəl) ***vt.*** **-fled**, **-fling** ⟦< OFr *rifler*⟧ to ransack and rob —**ri′fler *n.***

ri′fle·man (-mən) ***n.***, *pl.* **-men** (-mən) a soldier armed with a rifle

ri·fling (rī′fliŋ) ***n.*** spiral grooves cut within a gun barrel to make the projectile spin

rift (rift) ***n.*** ⟦< Dan, fissure⟧ an opening caused by splitting; cleft —***vt.***, ***vi.*** to burst open; split

rig (rig) ***vt.*** **rigged**, **rig′ging** ⟦< Scand⟧ **1** to fit (a ship, mast, etc.) with (sails, shrouds, etc.) **2** to assemble **3** to equip **4** to arrange dishonestly **5** [Inf.] to dress: with *out* —***n.*** **1** the way sails, etc. are rigged **2** equipment; gear **3** oil-drilling equipment **4** a tractor-trailer

rig·a·ma·role (rig′ə mə rōl′) ***n.*** *var. of* RIGMAROLE

rig′ging ***n.*** the ropes, chains, etc. for a vessel's masts, sails, etc.

right (rīt) ***adj.*** ⟦< OE *riht,* straight⟧ **1** with a straight line or plane perpendicular to a base *[*a *right* angle*]* **2** upright; virtuous **3** correct **4** fitting; suitable **5** designating the side or surface meant to be seen **6** mentally or physically sound **7** *a)* designating or of that side of the body toward the east when one faces north *b)* designating or of the corresponding side of anything *c)* closer to the right side of one who is facing the thing mentioned —***n.*** **1** what is right, just, etc. **2** power, privilege, etc. belonging to one by law, nature, etc. **3** the right side **4** the right hand **5** [*often* **R-**] *Politics* a conservative or reactionary position, party, etc.: often with *the* —***adv.*** **1** straight; directly *[*go *right* home*]* **2** properly; fittingly **3** completely **4** exactly *[right* here*]* **5** according to law, justice, etc. **6** correctly **7** on or toward the right side **8** very: in certain titles *[*the *right* reverend*]* —***interj.*** agreed! OK! —***vt.*** **1** to put upright **2** to correct **3** to put in order —**right away** (or **off**) at once —**right on!** [Slang] that's right! —**right′ly *adv.*** —**right′ness *n.***

right′a·bout′-face′ ***n.*** ABOUT-FACE

right angle an angle of 90 degrees

right·eous (rī′chəs) ***adj.*** **1** acting in a just, upright manner; virtuous **2** morally right or justifiable —**right′eous·ly *adv.*** —**right′eous·ness *n.***

right′ful ***adj.*** **1** fair and just; right **2** having a lawful claim —**right′ful·ly *adv.*** —**right′ful·ness *n.***

right′-hand′ ***adj.*** **1** on or toward the right **2** of, for, or with the right hand **3** most helpful or reliable *[*a *right-hand* man*]*

right′-hand′ed ***adj.*** **1** using the right hand more skillfully than the left **2** done with or made for use with the right hand —***adv.*** **1** with the right hand **2** in such a way that the bat, club, etc. swings leftward —**right′-hand′ed·ness *n.***

right′ist ***n.***, ***adj.*** conservative or reactionary

right′-mind′ed ***adj.*** having sound principles

right of way **1** the right to move first at intersections **2** land over which a road, power line, etc. passes **3** right of passage, as over another's property Also **right′-of-way′**

right′-to-life′ ***adj.*** designating any movement, party, etc. opposed to abortion —**right′-to-lif′er *n.***

right triangle a triangle with a right angle

right wing the more conservative or reactionary section of a political party or group —**right′-wing′ *adj.*** —**right′-wing′er *n.***

rig·id (rij′id) ***adj.*** ⟦< L *rigere,* be stiff⟧ **1** not bending or flexible; stiff **2** not moving; fixed **3** severe; strict **4** having a rigid framework: said of a dirigible —**ri·gid·i·ty** (ri jid′ə tē) or **rig′id·ness *n.*** —**rig′id·ly *adv.***

rig·ma·role (rig′mə rōl′) ***n.*** ⟦< ME *rageman rolle,* long list⟧ **1** nonsense **2** a foolishly complicated procedure

rig·or (rig′ər) ***n.*** ⟦< L *rigere:* see RIGID⟧ **1** severity; strictness **2** hardship Brit. sp. **rig′our** —**rig′or·ous *adj.*** —**rig′or·ous·ly *adv.***

rigor mor·tis (môr′tis) ⟦L, stiffness of death⟧ the stiffening of the muscles after death

rile (rīl) ***vt.*** **riled**, **ril′ing** ⟦var. of ROIL⟧ [Inf. or Dial.] to anger; irritate

rill (ril) ***n.*** ⟦< Du *ril*⟧ a rivulet

rim (rim) ***n.*** ⟦OE *rima*⟧ **1** an edge, border, or margin, esp. of something circular **2** the outer part of a wheel —***vt.*** **rimmed**, **rim′ming** to put a rim or rims on or around —**rim′less *adj.***

rime[1] (rīm) ***n.***, ***vi.***, ***vt.*** **rimed**, **rim′ing** RHYME

rime[2] (rīm) ***n.*** ⟦OE *hrim*⟧ FROST (sense 2)

rind (rīnd) ***n.*** ⟦OE⟧ a hard outer layer or covering

ring[1] (riŋ) ***vi.*** **rang** or [Now Chiefly Dial.] **rung**, **rung**, **ring′ing** ⟦OE *hringan*⟧ **1** to give forth a resonant sound, as a bell **2** to seem *[*to *ring* true*]* **3** to sound a bell, esp. as a summons **4** to resound *[to ring with laughter]* **5** to have a ringing sensation, as the ears —***vt.*** **1** to cause (a bell, etc.) to ring **2** to signal, announce, etc., as by ringing **3** to call by telephone —***n.*** **1** the sound of a bell **2** a characteristic quality *[the ring of truth]* **3** the act of ringing a bell **4** a telephone call —**ring a bell** to stir up a memory

ring[2] (riŋ) ***n.*** ⟦OE *hring*⟧ **1** an ornamental circular band worn on a finger **2** any similar band *[a key ring]* **3** a circular line, mark, figure, or course **4** a group of people or things in a circle **5** a group working to advance its own interests, esp. by dishonest means **6** an enclosed area for contests, exhibitions, etc. *[a circus ring]* **7** prizefighting: with *the* —***vt.*** **ringed, ring'ing** **1** to encircle **2** to form into a ring —**run rings around** **1** to run much faster than **2** to do much better than

ring'er[1] ***n.*** a horseshoe, etc. thrown so that it encircles the peg

ring'er[2] ***n.*** **1** one that rings a bell, etc. **2** [Slang] *a)* a person or thing closely resembling another *b)* a fraudulent substitute in a competition

ring'lead'er ***n.*** one who leads others, esp. in unlawful acts, etc.

ring'let (-lit) ***n.*** a long curl of hair

ring'mas'ter ***n.*** a person who directs the performances in a circus ring

ring'side' ***n.*** **1** the place just outside a boxing or circus ring **2** any place providing a close view

ring'worm' ***n.*** a contagious skin disease caused by a fungus

rink (riŋk) ***n.*** ⟦< OFr *renc,* a rank⟧ **1** an expanse of ice for skating **2** a smooth floor for roller-skating

rinse (rins) ***vt.*** **rinsed, rins'ing** ⟦ult. < L *recens,* fresh⟧ **1** to wash or flush lightly **2** to remove soap, etc. from with clear water —***n.*** **1** a rinsing or the liquid used **2** a solution used to rinse or tint hair

Ri·o de Ja·nei·ro (rē'ō dā' zhə ner'ō) city & seaport in SE Brazil: pop. 5,093,000

Ri·o Gran·de (rē'ō grand', -gran'dē) river flowing from S Colorado into the Gulf of Mexico: the S border of Texas

ri·ot (rī'ət) ***n.*** ⟦< OFr *riote,* dispute⟧ **1** wild or violent disorder, confusion, etc.; esp., a violent public disturbance **2** a brilliant display **3** [Inf.] something very funny —***vi.*** to take part in a riot —**read the riot act to** to command to stop by threatening punishment —**run riot** **1** to act wildly **2** to grow wild in abundance —**ri'ot·er** ***n.*** —**ri'ot·ous** ***adj.***

rip (rip) ***vt.*** **ripped, rip'ping** ⟦ME *rippen*⟧ **1** *a)* to cut or tear apart roughly *b)* to remove in this way (with *off, out,* etc.) *c)* to sever the threads of (a seam) **2** to saw (wood) along the grain —***vi.*** **1** to become ripped **2** [Inf.] to rush; speed —***n.*** a ripped place —**rip into** [Inf.] to attack, esp. verbally —**rip off** [Slang] **1** to steal **2** to cheat or exploit —**rip'per** ***n.***

R.I.P. or **RIP** *abbrev.* may he (she) rest in peace

rip cord a cord, etc. pulled to open a parachute during descent

ripe (rīp) ***adj.*** ⟦OE⟧ **1** ready to be harvested, as grain or fruit **2** of sufficient age, etc. to be used *[ripe cheese]* **3** fully developed; mature **4** fully prepared; ready *[ripe for action]* —**ripe'ly** ***adv.*** —**ripe'ness** ***n.***

rip·en (rī'pən) ***vi., vt.*** to become or make ripe; mature, age, etc.

rip'-off' ***n.*** [Slang] the act or an instance of stealing, cheating, etc.

ri·poste or **ri·post** (ri pōst') ***n.*** ⟦Fr < L *respondere,* to answer⟧ a sharp, swift response; retort

rip·ple (rip'əl) ***vi., vt.*** **-pled, -pling** ⟦prob. < RIP⟧ to have or form little waves on the surface (of) —***n.*** **1** a small wave **2** a rippling

ripple effect the spreading effects caused by a single event

rip'-roar'ing (-rôr'iŋ) ***adj.*** [Slang] boisterous; uproarious

rip'saw' ***n.*** a saw with coarse teeth, for cutting wood along the grain

rip'tide' ***n.*** a current opposing other currents, esp. along a seashore: also **rip tide**

rise (rīz) ***vi.*** **rose, ris·en** (riz'ən), **ris'ing** ⟦< OE *risan*⟧ **1** to stand or sit up after sitting, kneeling, or lying **2** to rebel; revolt **3** to go up; ascend **4** to appear above the horizon, as the sun **5** to attain a higher level, rank, etc. **6** to extend, slant, or move upward **7** to increase in amount, degree, etc. **8** to expand and swell, as dough with yeast **9** to originate; begin **10** *Theol.* to return to life —***n.*** **1** upward movement; ascent **2** an advance in status, rank, etc. **3** a slope upward **4** an increase in degree, amount, etc. **5** beginning; origin —**give rise to** to bring about

ris'er ***n.*** **1** one that rises **2** a vertical piece between the steps in a stairway

ris·i·ble (riz'ə bəl) ***adj.*** ⟦< L *ridere,* to laugh⟧ causing laughter; funny —**ris'i·bil'i·ty,** *pl.* **-ties,** ***n.***

ris'ing ***n.*** an uprising; revolt

risk (risk) ***n.*** ⟦< Fr < It *risco*⟧ the chance of injury, damage, or loss —***vt.*** **1** to expose to risk *[to risk one's life]* **2** to incur the risk of *[to risk a war]* —**risk'y, -i·er, -i·est,** ***adj.***

ris·qué (ris kā') ***adj.*** ⟦Fr < *risquer,* to risk⟧ very close to being improper or indecent; suggestive

Rit·a·lin (rit''l in) *trademark for* a stimulant drug used to treat depression, hyperactivity, etc.

rite (rīt) ***n.*** ⟦L *ritus*⟧ a ceremonial, solemn act, as in religious use

rite of passage a significant event, ceremony, etc. in a person's life

rit·u·al (rich'o͞o əl) ***adj.*** of, like, or done as a rite —***n.*** a set form or system of rites, religious or otherwise —**rit'u·al·ism'** ***n.*** —**rit'u·al·ly** ***adv.***

ri·val (rī'vəl) ***n.*** ⟦< L *rivalis*⟧ one who tries to get or do the same thing as another, or to equal or surpass another; competitor —***adj.*** acting as a rival; competing —***vt.*** **-valed** or **-valled, -val·ing** or

-val·ling **1** to try to equal or surpass **2** to equal in some way —**ri'val·rous** ***adj.*** —**ri'val·ry**, *pl.* **-ries**, ***n.***

riv·en (riv'ən) ***adj.*** torn apart or split

riv·er (riv'ər) ***n.*** ⟦< L *ripa*, a bank⟧ a natural stream of water flowing into an ocean, a lake, etc.

river basin the area drained by a river and its tributaries

riv'er·side' ***n.*** the bank of a river

Riv·er·side (riv'ər sīd') city in S California: pop. 227,000

riv·et (riv'it) ***n.*** ⟦Fr < *river*, to clinch⟧ a metal bolt with a head and a plain end that is flattened after the bolt is passed through parts to be held together —***vt.*** to fasten with or as with rivets —**riv'et·er** ***n.***

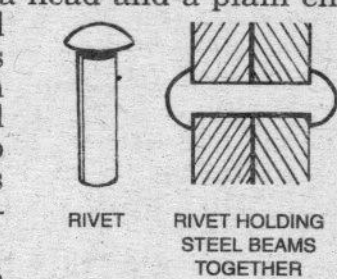

Riv·i·er·a (riv'ē er'ə) strip of the Mediterranean coast of SE France & NW Italy: a resort area

riv·u·let (riv'yo͞o lit) ***n.*** ⟦< L *rivus*, brook⟧ a little stream

rm *abbrev.* **1** ream **2** room

Rn *Chem. symbol for* radon

RN *abbrev.* Registered Nurse

RNA ***n.*** ⟦*r(ibo)n(ucleic) a(cid)*⟧ an essential component of all living matter: one form carries genetic information

roach[1] (rōch) ***n.*** *short for* COCKROACH

roach[2] (rōch) ***n.***, *pl.* **roach** or **roach'es** ⟦< OFr *roche*⟧ a freshwater fish of the carp family

road (rōd) ***n.*** ⟦OE *rad*, a ride⟧ **1** a way made for traveling; highway **2** a way; course *[the road to fortune]* **3** [*often pl.*] a place near shore where ships can ride at anchor —**on the road** traveling, as by a salesman or a touring troupe of actors

road'bed' ***n.*** the foundation laid for railroad tracks, a highway, etc.

road'block' ***n.*** **1** a blockade set up in a road as to prevent movement of vehicles **2** any hindrance

road'kill' ***n.*** [Slang] the body of an animal killed by a passing vehicle

road rage angry or violent behavior by motorists, as caused by stress in traffic

road'run'ner ***n.*** a long-tailed, swift-running desert bird of the SW U.S. and N Mexico: also **road runner**

road'show' ***n.*** a touring theatrical show

road'side' ***n.*** the side of a road —***adj.*** on or at the side of a road

road'way' ***n.*** a road; specif., the part of a road used by vehicles

road'work' ***n.*** distance running or jogging as an exercise, esp. by a boxer

roam (rōm) ***vi.***, ***vt.*** ⟦ME *romen*⟧ to wander aimlessly (over or through) —**roam'er** ***n.***

roan (rōn) ***adj.*** ⟦< OSp *roano*⟧ bay, black, etc. thickly sprinkled with white —***n.*** a roan horse

roar (rôr) ***vi.*** ⟦OE *rarian*⟧ **1** to make a loud, deep, rumbling sound **2** to laugh boisterously —***vt.*** to say loudly —***n.*** a loud, deep, rumbling sound

roast (rōst) ***vt.*** ⟦< OFr *rostir*⟧ **1** to cook (meat, etc.) with little or no moisture, as in an oven or over an open fire **2** to process (coffee, etc.) by exposure to heat **3** to expose to great heat **4** [Inf.] to criticize severely —***vi.*** **1** to undergo roasting **2** to be or become very hot —***n.*** **1** roasted meat **2** a cut of meat for roasting **3** a picnic at which food is roasted —***adj.*** roasted *[roast pork]* —**roast'er** ***n.***

rob (räb) ***vt.*** **robbed**, **rob'bing** ⟦< OFr *rober*⟧ **1** to take money, etc. from unlawfully by force; steal from **2** to deprive *of* something unjustly or injuriously —***vi.*** to be one who robs —**rob'ber** ***n.*** —**rob'ber·y**, *pl.* **-ies**, ***n.***

robe (rōb) ***n.*** ⟦< OFr⟧ **1** a long, loose outer garment **2** such a garment worn to show rank or office, as by a judge **3** a bathrobe or dressing gown **4** a covering or wrap *[a lap robe]* —***vt.***, ***vi.*** **robed**, **rob'ing** to dress in a robe

rob·in (räb'ən) ***n.*** ⟦< OFr dim. of *Robert*⟧ a North American thrush with a dull-red breast

Robin Hood *Eng. Legend* the leader of a band of outlaws who robs the rich to help the poor

Ro·bin·son Cru·soe (rä'bən sən kro͞o'sō') the title hero of Defoe's novel (1719) about a shipwrecked sailor

ro·bot (rō'bät') ***n.*** ⟦< Czech < OSlav *rabu*, servant⟧ **1** a mechanical device operating automatically, in a seemingly human way **2** a person acting like a robot

ro·bot'ics ***n.*** the science or technology of robots, their design, use, etc.

ro·bust (rō bust', rō'bust') ***adj.*** ⟦< L *robur*, oak⟧ strong and healthy —**ro·bust'ly** ***adv.*** —**ro·bust'ness** ***n.***

Roch·es·ter (räch'əs tər) city in W New York: pop. 230,000

rock[1] (räk) ***n.*** ⟦< ML *rocca*⟧ **1** a large mass of stone **2** broken pieces of stone **3** mineral matter formed in masses in the earth's crust **4** anything like a rock; esp., a firm support —**on the rocks** [Inf.] **1** in trouble or near ruin **2** served over ice cubes: said of liquor, etc.

rock[2] (räk) ***vt.***, ***vi.*** ⟦OE *roccian*⟧ **1** to move back and forth or from side to side **2** to sway strongly; shake —***n.*** **1** a rocking motion **2** ROCK-AND-ROLL

rock'a·bil'ly (-ə bil'ē) ***n.*** ⟦ROCK(-AND-ROLL) + *-a-* + (HILL)BILLY⟧ an early form of rock-and-roll with a strong country music influence

rock'-and-roll' ***n.*** a form of popular music that evolved from rhythm and blues, characterized by a strong rhythm with an accent on the offbeat

rock bottom the lowest level

rock'bound' ***adj.*** surrounded or covered by rocks

rock candy large, hard, clear crystals of sugar formed on a string

rock'er ***n.*** **1** either of the curved pieces on which a cradle, etc. rocks **2** a chair mounted on such pieces: also **rocking chair**

rocker panel any panel section below

the doors of an automotive vehicle

rock·et (räk′it) ***n.*** ⟦It *rocchetta,* spool⟧ any device driven forward by gases escaping through a rear vent, as a firework, a projectile weapon, or the propulsion mechanism of a spacecraft —***vi.*** to move in or like a rocket; soar

rock′et·ry (-ə trē) ***n.*** the science of building and launching rockets

rock garden a garden of flowers, etc. in ground studded with rocks

rocking horse a toy horse on rockers or springs, for a child to ride

rock lobster SPINY LOBSTER

rock′-ribbed′ ***adj.*** **1** having rocky ridges **2** firm; unyielding

rock salt common salt in rocklike masses

rock wool a fibrous material made from molten rock, used for insulation

rock·y[1] (räk′ē) ***adj.*** **-i·er, -i·est** **1** full of rocks **2** consisting of rock **3** like a rock; firm, hard, etc. —**rock′i·ness** ***n.***

rock·y[2] (räk′ē) ***adj.*** **-i·er, -i·est** inclined to rock; unsteady —**rock′i·ness** ***n.***

Rocky Mountains mountain system in W North America, extending from New Mexico to N Alaska: also **Rock′ies**

Rocky Mountain sheep BIGHORN

ro·co·co (rə kō′kō) ***n.*** ⟦Fr < *rocaille,* shell work⟧ [*occas.* **R-**] a style of architecture, art, music, etc. marked by profuse and delicate ornamentation, etc. —***adj.*** **1** of or in rococo **2** too elaborate

rod (räd) ***n.*** ⟦< OE *rodd,* straight shoot or stem⟧ **1** a straight stick or bar **2** a stick for beating as punishment **3** a staff carried as a symbol of office; scepter **4** a pole for fishing **5** a measure of length equal to 5½ yards **6** [Slang] a pistol

rode (rōd) ***vi., vt.*** *pt. & archaic pp. of* RIDE

ro·dent (rōd′'nt) ***n.*** ⟦< L *rodere,* gnaw⟧ any of an order of gnawing mammals, as rats or mice

ro·de·o (rō′dē ō′) ***n.,*** *pl.* **-os′** ⟦Sp < L *rotare,* to turn⟧ a public exhibition of the skills of cowboys, with contests in bull riding, lassoing, etc.

Ro·din (rô dan′), **(François) Au·guste (René)** (ô güst′) 1840-1917; Fr. sculptor

roe[1] (rō) ***n.*** ⟦ME *rowe*⟧ fish eggs

roe[2] (rō) ***n.,*** *pl.* **roe** or **roes** ⟦< OE *ra*⟧ a small, agile deer of Europe and Asia

roe′buck′ ***n.*** the male roe deer

roent·gen (rent′gən) ***n.*** ⟦after W. K. *Roentgen* (1845-1923), Ger physicist⟧ the unit for measuring the radiation of X-rays or gamma rays

Rog·er (rä′jər) ***interj.*** ⟦< name of signal flag for *R*⟧ [*also* **r-**] **1** received **2** [Inf.] right! OK!

rogue (rōg) ***n.*** ⟦< ?⟧ **1** a scoundrel **2** a mischievous person —**ro·guer·y** (rō′gər ē), *pl.* **-ies, *n.*** —**ro·guish** (rō′gish) ***adj.***

rogues′ gallery a police collection of photographs of criminals

roil (roil) ***vt.*** ⟦< L *robigo,* rust⟧ **1** to make (a liquid) cloudy, muddy, etc. by stirring up sediment **2** to vex

roist·er (rois′tər) ***vi.*** ⟦see RUSTIC⟧ to revel noisily —**roist′er·er** ***n.***

role (rōl) ***n.*** ⟦Fr⟧ **1** the part played by an actor **2** a function assumed by someone *[an advisory role]* Often **rôle**

role model a person so effective or inspiring as to be a model for others

role′-play′ing ***n.*** *Psychol.* a technique in which participants assume and act out roles so as to practice appropriate behavior, etc.

roll (rōl) ***vi.*** ⟦< L *rota,* a wheel⟧ **1** to move by turning around or over and over **2** to move on wheels **3** to pass *[the years roll by]* **4** to extend in gentle swells **5** to make a loud rising and falling sound *[thunder rolls]* **6** to rock from side to side —***vt.*** **1** to make move by turning around or over and over **2** to make move on wheels **3** to utter with full, flowing sound **4** to pronounce with a trill *[to roll one's r's]* **5** to give a swaying motion to **6** to move around or from side to side *[to roll one's eyes]* **7** to make into a ball or cylinder *[roll up the rug]* **8** to flatten or spread with a roller, etc. —***n.*** **1** a rolling **2** a scroll **3** a list of names **4** something rolled into a cylinder **5** a small portion of bread, etc. **6** a swaying motion **7** a loud, reverberating sound, as of thunder **8** a slight swell on a surface —**on a roll** [Slang] at a high point —**roll back** to reduce (prices) to a previous level —**strike off** (or **from**) **the rolls** to expel from membership

roll′back′ ***n.*** a rolling back, esp. of prices to a previous level

roll call the reading aloud of a roll to find out who is absent

roll·er (rōl′ər) ***n.*** **1** one that rolls **2** a cylinder of metal, wood, etc. on which something is rolled, or one used to crush, smooth, or spread something

roller bearing a bearing in which the shaft turns with rollers in a circular track

Roll′er·blade′ *trademark for* a kind of IN-LINE SKATE —***n.*** [**r-**] any IN-LINE SKATE —**roll′er·blad′ing** ***n.***

roller coaster an amusement ride in which small open cars move on tracks that dip and curve sharply

roller skate SKATE[1] (sense 2) —**roll′er-skate′, -skat′ed, -skat′ing,** ***vi.*** —**roller skater**

rol·lick (räl′ik) ***vi.*** ⟦< ? FROLIC⟧ to play or behave in a lively, carefree way —**rol′lick·ing** ***adj.***

rolling pin a smooth, heavy cylinder of wood, etc. used to roll out dough

roll′-top′ ***adj.*** having a sliding, flexible top of parallel slats *[a roll-top desk]*

Ro·lo·dex (rō′lə deks′) *trademark for* a kind of desktop file holding cards containing names and addresses for ready reference

ro·ly-po·ly (rō′lē pō′lē) ***adj.*** ⟦< ROLL⟧ short and plump; pudgy

Rom *abbrev.* Roman

ROM (räm) ***n.*** ⟦*r(ead-)o(nly) m(emory)*⟧ computer memory whose contents can be read but not altered; also, a memory chip like this

ro·maine (rō mān′) ***n.*** ⟦Fr, ult. < L *Romanus*, Roman⟧ a type of lettuce with long leaves forming a slender head

Ro·man (rō′mən) ***adj.*** **1** of or characteristic of ancient or modern Rome or its people, etc. **2** of the Roman Catholic Church **3** [*usually* **r-**] designating or of the usual upright style of printing types; not italic —***n.*** **1** a person born or living in ancient or modern Rome **2** [*usually* **r-**] roman type or characters

Roman candle a firework consisting of a tube that sends out balls of fire, etc.

Roman Catholic **1** of the Christian church (**Roman Catholic Church**) headed by the pope **2** a member of this church

ro·mance (rō mans′, rō′mans′) ***adj.*** ⟦ult. < L *Romanicus*, Roman⟧ [**R-**] designating or of any of the languages derived from Vulgar Latin, as Italian, Spanish, or French —***n.*** **1** a long poem or tale, orig. written in a Romance dialect, about the adventures of knights **2** a novel of love, adventure, etc. **3** excitement, love, etc. of the kind found in such literature **4** a love affair —***vt.*** **-manced′**, **-manc′ing** to make love to; woo

Roman Empire empire of the ancient Romans (27 B.C.-A.D. 395), including W & S Europe, N Africa, & SW Asia

Ro·ma·ni·a (rō mā′nē ə) country in SE Europe: 91,699 sq. mi.; pop. 22,760,000 —**Ro·ma′ni·an** ***adj.***, ***n.***

Roman numerals Roman letters used as numerals: I = 1, V = 5, X = 10, L = 50, C = 100, D = 500, and M = 1,000

ro·man·tic (rō man′tik) ***adj.*** **1** of, like, or characterized by romance **2** fanciful or fictitious **3** not practical; visionary **4** full of thoughts, feelings, etc. of romance **5** suited for romance **6** [*often* **R-**] of a 19th-c. cultural movement characterized by freedom of form and spirit, emphasis on feeling and originality, etc. —***n.*** a romantic person —**ro·man′ti·cal·ly** ***adv.*** —**ro·man′ti·cism′** (-tə siz′əm) ***n.***

ro·man′ti·cize′ (-tə sīz′) ***vt.*** **-cized′**, **-ciz′ing** to treat or regard romantically —***vi.*** to have romantic ideas, etc.

Rom·a·ny (räm′ə nē, rō′mə-) ***n.*** the language of the Gypsies

Rome (rōm) capital of Italy &, formerly, of the Roman Empire: pop. 2,605,000

Ro·me·o (rō′mē ō′) ***n.*** the hero of Shakespeare's *Romeo and Juliet* (c. 1595)

romp (rämp) ***n.*** ⟦prob. < OFr *ramper*, to climb⟧ boisterous, lively play —***vi.*** to play in a boisterous, lively way

romp′er ***n.*** **1** one who romps **2** [*pl.*] a loose, one-piece outer garment with pants like bloomers, for a small child

Rom·u·lus (räm′yoo ləs) ***n.*** *Rom. Myth.* founder and first king of Rome: he and his twin brother Remus are suckled by a female wolf

rood (ro͞od) ***n.*** ⟦OE *rod*⟧ **1** a crucifix **2** [Brit.] an old unit of area equal to ¼ acre

roof (ro͞of, ro͝of) ***n.***, *pl.* **roofs** ⟦OE *hrof*⟧ **1** the outside top covering of a building **2** anything like this in position or use [the *roof* of the mouth] —***vt.*** to cover with or as with a roof —**roof′less** ***adj.***

roof′er ***n.*** a roof maker or repairer

roof′ing ***n.*** material for roofs

roof′top′ ***n.*** the roof of a building

rook[1] (ro͝ok) ***n.*** ⟦OE *hroc*⟧ a European crow —***vt.***, ***vi.*** to swindle; cheat

rook[2] (ro͝ok) ***n.*** ⟦< Pers *rukh*⟧ a chess piece that can move horizontally or vertically

rook′er·y ***n.***, *pl.* **-ies** a breeding place of rooks, or of seals, penguins, etc.

rook·ie (ro͝ok′ē) ***n.*** [Slang] **1** an inexperienced army recruit **2** [Inf.] any beginner

room (ro͞om, ro͝om) ***n.*** ⟦OE *rum*⟧ **1** space to contain something **2** suitable scope [*room* for doubt] **3** an interior space enclosed or set apart by walls **4** [*pl.*] living quarters **5** the people in a room —***vi.***, ***vt.*** to have or provide with lodgings —**room′ful′** ***n.*** —**room′y**, **-i·er**, **-i·est**, ***adj.*** —**room′i·ness** ***n.***

room and board lodging and meals

room′er ***n.*** one who rents a room or rooms to live in; lodger

room·ette (ro͞o met′) ***n.*** a small room in a railroad sleeping car

rooming house a house with furnished rooms for rent

room′mate′ ***n.*** a person with whom one shares a room or rooms

Roo·se·velt (rō′zə velt′) **1 Franklin Del·a·no** (del′ə nō′) 1882-1945; 32d president of the U.S. (1933-45) **2 Theodore** 1858-1919; 26th president of the U.S. (1901-09)

roost (ro͞ost) ***n.*** ⟦OE *hrost*⟧ **1** a perch on which birds, esp. domestic fowls, can rest **2** a place with perches for birds **3** a place for resting, sleeping, etc. —***vi.*** **1** to perch on a roost **2** to stay or settle down, as for the night

roost′er ***n.*** a male chicken

root[1] (ro͞ot, ro͝ot) ***n.*** ⟦< ON *rot*⟧ **1** the part of a plant, usually underground, that anchors the plant, draws water from the soil, etc. **2** the embedded part of a tooth, a hair, etc. **3** a source or cause **4** a supporting or essential part **5** a quantity that, multiplied by itself a specified number of times, produces a given quantity **6** the basic element of a word or form, without affixes or phonetic changes —***vi.*** to take root —***vt.*** **1** to fix the roots of in the ground **2** to establish; settle —**root up** (or **out**) to pull up by the roots; destroy completely —**take root** **1** to begin growing by putting out roots **2** to become fixed, settled, etc.

root[2] (ro͞ot, ro͝ot) ***vt.*** ⟦< OE *wrot*, snout⟧ to dig (*up* or *out*) with or as with the snout —***vi.*** **1** to search about; rummage **2** [Inf.] to encourage a team, etc.: usually with *for*

root beer a carbonated drink made or flavored with certain plant root extracts

root canal **1** a tubular channel in a tooth's root **2** a treatment involving opening, cleaning, filling, etc. such a channel

root′let (-lit) ***n.*** a little root

rope (rōp) ***n.*** ⟦OE *rap*⟧ **1** a thick, strong

cord made of strands of fiber, etc. twisted together **2** a ropelike string, as of pearls —***vt.* roped, rop′ing** **1** to fasten or tie with a rope **2** to mark off or enclose with a rope **3** to catch with a lasso —**know the ropes** [Inf.] to be well acquainted with a procedure, etc. —**rope in** [Slang] to entice or trick into doing something

Roque·fort (rōk′fərt) ⟦after *Roquefort,* France, where made⟧ *trademark for* a strong French cheese with a bluish mold

Ror·schach test (rôr′shäk′) ⟦after H. *Rorschach* (1884-1922), Swiss psychiatrist⟧ *Psychol.* a personality test in which the subject's interpretations of standard inkblot designs are analyzed

ro·sa·ry (rō′zər ē) ***n.,*** *pl.* **-ries** ⟦ML *rosarium*⟧ *R.C.Ch.* a string of groups of beads, used to keep count in saying prayers

rose[1] (rōz) ***n.*** ⟦< L *rosa* < Gr *rhodon*⟧ **1** a shrub with prickly stems and with flowers of red, pink, white, yellow, etc. **2** its flower **3** pinkish red or purplish red —***adj.*** of this color

rose[2] (rōz) ***vi.*** *pt. of* RISE

ro·sé (rō zā′) ***n.*** ⟦Fr, pink⟧ a pink wine, tinted by the grape skins early in fermentation

ro·se·ate (rō′zē it) ***adj.*** rose-colored

rose′bud′ ***n.*** the bud of a rose

rose′bush′ ***n.*** a shrub that bears roses

rose′-col′ored ***adj.*** **1** pinkish-red or purplish-red **2** optimistic —**through rose-colored glasses** with optimism, esp. undue optimism

rose·mar·y (rōz′mer′ē) ***n.*** ⟦< L *ros marinus,* sea dew⟧ an evergreen herb of the mint family, with fragrant leaves used in perfumes, in cooking, etc.

ro·sette (rō zet′) ***n.*** an ornament or arrangement, as of ribbons, resembling a rose

rose water a preparation of water and attar of roses, used as a perfume

rose window a circular window with a roselike pattern of tracery

ROSE WINDOW

rose′wood′ ***n.*** ⟦< its odor⟧ **1** a hard, reddish wood, used in furniture, etc. **2** a tropical tree yielding this wood

Rosh Ha·sha·na (rōsh′ hə shô′nə, -shä′-) the Jewish New Year

ros·in (räz′ən) ***n.*** ⟦see RESIN⟧ the hard resin left after the distillation of turpentine: it is rubbed on violin bows, used in making varnish, etc.

ros·ter (räs′tər) ***n.*** ⟦< Du *rooster*⟧ a list or roll, as of military personnel

ros·trum (räs′trəm) ***n.,*** *pl.* **-trums** or **-tra** (-trə) ⟦L, beak⟧ a platform for public speaking

ros·y (rō′zē) ***adj.*** **-i·er, -i·est** ⟦ME⟧ **1** rose in color **2** bright, promising, etc. —**ros′i·ly** ***adv.*** —**ros′i·ness** ***n.***

rot (rät) ***vi., vt.*** **rot′ted, rot′ting** ⟦OE *rotian*⟧ to decompose; decay —***n.*** **1** a rotting or something rotten **2** a disease characterized by decay **3** [Slang] nonsense

ro·ta·ry (rōt′ər ē) ***adj.*** ⟦< L *rota,* wheel⟧ **1** turning around a central axis, as a wheel does **2** having rotating parts *[a rotary* press*]* —***n.,*** *pl.* **-ries** **1** a rotary machine **2** TRAFFIC CIRCLE

ro·tate (rō′tāt′) ***vi., vt.*** **-tat′ed, -tat′ing** ⟦< L *rota,* wheel⟧ **1** to turn around an axis **2** to change or cause to change in regular succession —**ro·ta′tion** ***n.*** —**ro′ta′tor** ***n.***

ROTC *abbrev.* Reserve Officers' Training Corps

rote (rōt) ***n.*** ⟦ME⟧ a fixed, mechanical way of doing something —**by rote** by memory alone, without thought

rot·gut (rät′gut′) ***n.*** [Slang] raw, low-grade whiskey or other liquor

ro·tis·ser·ie (rō tis′ər ē) ***n.*** ⟦Fr < earlier Fr *rostir,* to roast⟧ a grill with an electrically turned spit

ro·to·gra·vure (rōt′ə grə vyoor′) ***n.*** ⟦< L *rota,* wheel + Fr *gravure,* engraving⟧ a printing process using a rotary press with cylinders etched from photographic plates

ro·tor (rōt′ər) ***n.*** **1** the rotating part of a motor, etc. **2** a system of rotating airfoils, as on a helicopter

ro·to·till·er (rōt′ə til′ər) ***n.*** a motorized machine with rotary blades, for loosening the earth around growing plants —**ro′to·till′** ***vt.***

rot·ten (rät′′n) ***adj.*** ⟦< ON *rotinn*⟧ **1** decayed; spoiled **2** foul-smelling **3** morally corrupt **4** unsound, as if decayed within **5** [Slang] very bad, unpleasant, etc. —**rot′ten·ness** ***n.***

Rot·ter·dam (rät′ər dam′) seaport in SW Netherlands: pop. 599,000

ro·tund (rō tund′) ***adj.*** ⟦L *rotundus*⟧ plump or stout —**ro·tun′di·ty** or **ro·tund′ness** ***n.***

ro·tun·da (rō tun′də) ***n.*** ⟦see prec.⟧ a round building, hall, or room, esp. one with a dome

rou·é (roo ā′) ***n.*** ⟦Fr < L *rota,* wheel⟧ a dissipated man; rake

rouge (roozh) ***n.*** ⟦Fr, red⟧ **1** a reddish cosmetic powder or paste for adding color to the cheeks **2** a reddish powder for polishing jewelry, etc. —***vt.* rouged, roug′ing** to use cosmetic rouge on

rough (ruf) ***adj.*** ⟦OE *ruh*⟧ **1** not smooth or level; uneven **2** shaggy *[a rough* coat*]* **3** stormy *[rough* weather*]* **4** disorderly *[rough* play*]* **5** harsh or coarse **6** lacking comforts and conveniences **7** not polished or finished; crude **8** approximate *[a rough* guess*]* **9** [Inf.] difficult *[a rough* time*]* —***n.*** **1** rough ground, material, condition, etc. **2** *Golf* any part of the course with grass, etc. left uncut —***adv.*** in a rough way —***vt.*** **1** to roughen: often with *up* **2** to treat roughly: usually with *up* **3** to sketch, shape, etc. roughly: usually with *in* or *out* —**rough it** to live without customary comforts, etc. —**rough'ly** *adv.* —**rough'ness** *n.*

rough'age *n.* rough or coarse food or fodder

rough'en *vt., vi.* to make or become rough

rough'-hew' *vt.* **-hewed', -hewed'** or **-hewn', -hew'ing** **1** to hew (timber, stone, etc.) roughly, or without smoothing **2** to form roughly Also sp. **rough'hew'**

rough'house' [Inf.] *n.* rough, boisterous play, fighting, etc. —*vt., vi.* **-housed', -hous'ing** to treat or act roughly or boisterously

rough'neck' *n.* **1** [Inf.] a rowdy **2** a worker on an oil rig —*vi.* to work as a roughneck

rough'shod' *adj.* shod with horseshoes having metal points —**ride roughshod over** to treat harshly and arrogantly

rou·lette (ro͞o let') *n.* ⟦Fr < L *rota,* wheel⟧ a gambling game played by tossing a small ball into a whirling shallow bowl (**roulette wheel**) with numbered, red or black compartments

round (round) *adj.* ⟦< L *rotundus,* rotund⟧ **1** shaped like a ball, circle, or cylinder **2** plump **3** full; complete *[a round dozen]* **4** expressed by a whole number or in tens, hundreds, etc. —*n.* **1** something round, as the rung of a ladder **2** the part of a beef animal between the rump and the leg **3** a series or succession *[a round of parties]* **4** [*often pl.*] a regular, customary circuit, as by a watchman **5** a single shot from a gun, or from several guns together; also, the ammunition for this **6** a single outburst, as of applause **7** a single period of action, as in boxing **8** a short song which one group begins singing when another reaches the second phrase, etc. —*vt.* **1** to make round **2** to express as a round number: with *off* **3** to finish: with *out* or *off* **4** to go around —*vi.* **1** to turn; reverse direction **2** to become plump: often with *out* —*adv.* **1** AROUND **2** through a recurring period of time *[to work the year round]* **3** for each of several **4** in a roundabout way —*prep.* AROUND —**in the round** **1** in an arena theater **2** in full, rounded form: said of sculpture **3** in full detail —**round about** in or to the opposite direction —**round up** to collect in a herd, group, etc. —**round'ness** *n.*

round'a·bout' *adj.* indirect; circuitous

roun·de·lay (roun'də lā') *n.* ⟦< OFr *rondel,* a short lyrical poem⟧ a simple song in which some phrase, line, etc. is continually repeated

round'house' *n.* a circular building for storing and repairing locomotives

round'ly *adv.* **1** in a round form **2** vigorously **3** fully; completely and thoroughly

round'-shoul'dered *adj.* having the shoulders bent forward

round steak a steak cut from a round of beef

Round Table **1** in legend, the circular table around which King Arthur and his knights sit **2** [**r- t-**] a group gathered for an informal discussion

round'-the-clock' *adj., adv.* throughout the day and night; continuous(ly)

round trip a trip to a place and back again —**round'-trip'** *adj.*

round'-trip'per *n.* [Slang] *Baseball* a home run

round'up' *n.* **1** a driving together of cattle, etc. on the range, as for branding **2** any similar collecting **3** a summary, as of news

round'worm' *n.* NEMATODE

rouse (rouz) *vt., vi.* **roused, rous'ing** ⟦prob. < earlier Fr⟧ **1** to excite or become excited **2** to wake

Rous·seau (ro͞o sō'), **Jean Jacques** (zhän zhäk') 1712-78; Fr. philosopher & writer, born in Switzerland

roust·a·bout (roust'ə bout') *n.* ⟦< ROUSE + ABOUT⟧ an unskilled or transient laborer, as on a wharf or in an oil field

rout[1] (rout) *n.* ⟦< L *rupta,* broken⟧ **1** a disorderly flight **2** an overwhelming defeat —*vt.* **1** to put to flight **2** to defeat overwhelmingly

rout[2] (rout) *vt.* ⟦< ROOT[2]⟧ to force out —**rout out** **1** to gouge out **2** to make (a person) get out

route (ro͞ot, rout) *n.* ⟦< L *rupta (via),* (path) broken through⟧ a road or course for traveling; often, a regular course, as in delivering mail —*vt.* **rout'ed, rout'ing** **1** to send by a certain route **2** to arrange the route for

rou·tine (ro͞o tēn') *n.* ⟦see prec.⟧ a regular procedure, customary or prescribed —*adj.* like or using routine —**rou·tine'ly** *adv.*

rou·tin'ize (-tē'nīz) *vt.* **-ized, -iz·ing** to make routine; reduce to a routine —**rou'tin·i·za'tion** *n.*

rove (rōv) *vi., vt.* **roved, rov'ing** ⟦ME *roven*⟧ to roam —**rov'er** *n.*

row[1] (rō) *n.* ⟦OE *ræw*⟧ **1** a number of people or things in a line **2** a line of seats in a theater, etc. —**in a row** in succession; consecutively

row[2] (rō) *vt., vi.* ⟦OE *rowan*⟧ **1** to propel (a boat) with oars **2** to carry in a rowboat —*n.* a trip by rowboat

row[3] (rou) *n., vi.* ⟦< ? ROUSE⟧ quarrel or brawl

row·boat (rō'bōt') *n.* a small boat made for rowing

row·dy (rou'dē) *n., pl.* **-dies** ⟦< ? ROW[3]⟧ a rough, quarrelsome, and disorderly person —*adj.* **-di·er, -di·est** rough, quarrelsome, etc. —**row'di·ness** *n.* —**row'dy·ism'** *n.*

row·el (rou'əl) *n.* ⟦ult. < L *rota,* wheel⟧ a small wheel with sharp points, at the end of a spur

row house (rō) any of a line of identical houses joined by common walls

roy·al (roi'əl) *adj.* ⟦< L *regalis*⟧ **1** of a king or queen **2** like, or fit for, a king or queen; magnificent, majestic, etc. **3** of a kingdom, its government, etc. —**roy'al·ly** *adv.*

roy'al·ist *n.* one who supports a monarch or a monarchy

roy'al·ty *n., pl.* **-ties** **1** the rank or

power of a king or queen **2** a royal person or persons **3** royal quality **4** a share of the proceeds from a patent, book, etc. paid to the owner, author, etc.

rpm *abbrev.* revolutions per minute

rps *abbrev.* revolutions per second

RR *abbrev.* **1** railroad **2** Rural Route: also **R.R.**

RSV *abbrev.* Revised Standard Version (of the Bible)

R.S.V.P. or **r.s.v.p.** *abbrev.* ⟦Fr, for *répondez s'il vous plaît*⟧ please reply: also **RSVP** or **rsvp**

rte *abbrev.* route

rub (rub) ***vt.* rubbed, rub'bing** ⟦ME *rubben*⟧ **1** to move (one's hand, a cloth, etc.) over (something) with pressure and friction **2** to apply (polish, etc.) in this way **3** to move (things) over each other with pressure and friction **4** to make sore by rubbing **5** to remove by rubbing (*out, off*, etc.) **—*vi.* 1** to move with pressure and friction (*on*, etc.) **2** to rub something **—*n.* 1** a rubbing **2** an obstacle, difficulty, or source of irritation **—rub down 1** to massage **2** to smooth, polish, etc. by rubbing **—rub elbows with** to associate or mingle with: also **rub shoulders with —rub it in** [Slang] to keep reminding someone of his or her mistake **—rub the wrong way** to annoy

ru·ba·to (ro͞o bät'ō) ***adj., adv.*** ⟦It, stolen⟧ *Music* intentionally and temporarily not in strict tempo

rub·ber (rub'ər) ***n.* 1** one that rubs **2** ⟦< orig. use as an eraser⟧ an elastic substance made from the milky sap of various tropical plants or made synthetically **3** something made of this substance; specif., *a)* a low-cut overshoe *b)* [Slang] a condom **—*adj.*** made of rubber **—rub'ber·y *adj.***

rubber band a narrow, continuous band of rubber as for holding small objects together

rubber cement an adhesive of unvulcanized rubber in a solvent that quickly evaporates when exposed to air

rubber check ⟦from the notion that it "bounces": see BOUNCE (*vi.* 3)⟧ [Slang] a check that is worthless because of insufficient funds in the writer's account

rubber game (rub'ər) ⟦< ?⟧ the deciding game in a series

rub'ber·ize' (-īz') ***vt.* -ized', -iz'ing** to coat or impregnate with rubber

rub'ber·neck' ***vi.*** to look at things or gaze about in curiosity by stretching the neck or turning the head, as a sightseer might do

rubber plant 1 any plant yielding latex **2** a house plant with large, glossy leaves

rubber stamp 1 a stamp of rubber, inked for printing dates, signatures, etc. **2** [Inf.] *a)* a person, bureau, etc. that gives routine or automatic approval *b)* such approval **—rub'ber-stamp' *vt.***

rub·bish (rub'ish) ***n.*** ⟦ME *robous*⟧ **1** any material thrown away as worthless; trash **2** nonsense

rub·ble (rub'əl) ***n.*** ⟦ME *robel*⟧ rough, broken pieces of stone, brick, etc.

rub'down' ***n.*** a brisk rubbing of the body, as in massage

rube (ro͞ob) ***n.*** ⟦< name *Reuben*⟧ [Slang] an unsophisticated rustic

ru·bel·la (ro͞o bel'ə) ***n.*** ⟦< L *ruber*, red⟧ an infectious disease causing small red spots on the skin; German measles

Ru·bens (ro͞o'bənz), **Peter Paul** 1577-1640; Fl. painter

ru·bi·cund (ro͞o'bə kund') ***adj.*** ⟦< L *ruber*, red⟧ reddish; ruddy

ru·ble (ro͞o'bəl) ***n.*** ⟦Russ *rubl'*⟧ the monetary unit of Russia, Belarus, & Tajikistan

ru·bric (ro͞o'brik) ***n.*** ⟦< L *ruber*, red⟧ **1** in early books, a section heading, letter, etc., often printed in red **2** any rule, explanatory comment, etc.

ru·by (ro͞o'bē) ***n.**, pl.* **-bies** ⟦ult. < L *rubeus*, reddish⟧ **1** a clear, deep-red precious stone: a variety of corundum **2** deep red **—*adj.*** deep-red

ruck·sack (ruk'sak', ro͝ok'-) ***n.*** ⟦Ger, back sack⟧ a kind of knapsack

ruck·us (ruk'əs) ***n.*** ⟦prob. merging of RUMPUS & *ruction*, uproar⟧ [Inf.] noisy confusion; disturbance

rud·der (rud'ər) ***n.*** ⟦OE *rother*⟧ a broad, flat, movable piece hinged to the rear of a ship or aircraft, used for steering **—rud'der·less *adj.***

rud·dy (rud'ē) ***adj.* -di·er, -di·est** ⟦OE *rudig*⟧ **1** having a healthy red color **2** reddish **—rud'di·ness *n.***

rude (ro͞od) ***adj.* rud'er, rud'est** ⟦< L *rudis*⟧ **1** crude; rough **2** uncouth **3** discourteous **4** unskillful **—rude'ly *adv.* —rude'ness *n.***

ru·di·ment (ro͞o'də mənt) ***n.*** ⟦see RUDE⟧ [*usually pl.*] **1** a first principle as of a subject to be learned **2** a first slight beginning of something **—ru'di·men'ta·ry** (-men'tər ē) ***adj.***

rue[1] (ro͞o) ***vt., vi.* rued, ru'ing** ⟦OE *hreowan*⟧ **1** to feel remorse for (a sin, fault, etc.) **2** to regret (an act, etc.) **—*n.*** [Archaic] sorrow **—rue'ful *adj.* —rue'ful·ly *adv.***

rue[2] (ro͞o) ***n.*** ⟦< Gr *rhytē*⟧ a strong-scented shrub with bitter leaves

RUFF

ruff (ruf) ***n.*** ⟦< RUFFLE⟧ **1** a high, frilled starched collar of the 16th and 17th c. **2** a band of colored or protruding feathers or fur about an animal's neck

ruf·fi·an (ruf'ē ən) ***n.*** ⟦< It *ruffiano*, a

pimp⟧ a rowdy or hoodlum

ruf·fle (ruf′əl) ***vt.*** **-fled, -fling** ⟦< ON or LowG⟧ **1** to disturb the smoothness of **2** to make (feathers, etc.) stand up **3** to disturb or annoy —***vi.*** to become uneven —***n.*** a strip of cloth, lace, etc. gathered along one edge, used as a trimming

rug (rug) ***n.*** ⟦< Scand⟧ a piece of thick fabric used as a floor covering

rug·by (rug′bē) ***n.*** ⟦first played at *Rugby* School in England⟧ a game from which American football developed

rug·ged (rug′id) ***adj.*** ⟦ME⟧ **1** uneven; rough **2** severe; harsh **3** not refined **4** strong; robust —**rug′ged·ly** ***adv.*** —**rug′ged·ness** ***n.***

Ruhr (roor) **1** river in WC Germany, flowing into the Rhine **2** major coal-mining & industrial region along this river: also called **Ruhr Basin**

ru·in (ro͞o′ən) ***n.*** ⟦< L *ruere,* to fall⟧ **1** [*pl.*] the remains of something destroyed, decayed, etc. **2** anything destroyed, etc. **3** downfall, destruction, etc. **4** anything causing this —***vt.*** to bring to ruin; destroy, spoil, bankrupt, etc. —**ru′in·a′tion** ***n.*** —**ru′in·ous** ***adj.***

rule (ro͞ol) ***n.*** ⟦< L *regere,* to rule⟧ **1** an established regulation or guide for conduct, procedure, usage, etc. **2** custom **3** the customary course **4** government; reign **5** RULER (sense 2) —***vt., vi.*** **ruled, rul′ing** **1** to have an influence (over); guide **2** to govern **3** to determine officially **4** to mark lines (on) as with a ruler —**as a rule** usually —**rule out** to exclude

rule of thumb a practical, though imprecise or unscientific, method

rul′er ***n.*** **1** one who governs **2** a strip of wood, etc. with a straight edge, used in drawing lines, measuring length, etc.

rul′ing ***adj.*** that rules —***n.*** an official decision, as of a court

rum (rum) ***n.*** ⟦< ?⟧ **1** an alcoholic liquor distilled from fermented sugar cane, etc. **2** any alcoholic liquor

Ru·ma·ni·a (ro͞o mā′nē ə) *var. of* ROMANIA —**Ru·ma′ni·an** ***adj., n.***

rum·ba (ro͝om′bə, rum′-) ***n.*** ⟦AmSp⟧ a dance of Cuban origin, or music for it —***vi.*** to dance the rumba

rum·ble (rum′bəl) ***vi., vt.*** **-bled, -bling** ⟦ME *romblen*⟧ **1** to make or cause to make a continuous deep, rolling sound **2** to move with such a sound —***n.*** **1** a rumbling sound **2** [Slang] a fight between teenage gangs

ru·mi·nant (ro͞o′mə nənt) ***adj.*** ⟦see RUMINATE⟧ **1** of or belonging to the group of cud-chewing animals **2** meditative —***n.*** any of a group of cud-chewing mammals, as cattle, deer, or camels, having a stomach with three or four chambers

ru′mi·nate′ (-nāt′) ***vi.*** **-nat′ed, -nat′ing** ⟦< L *ruminare*⟧ **1** to chew a cud **2** to meditate —**ru′mi·na′tion** ***n.***

rum·mage (rum′ij) ***n.*** ⟦< Fr *rum,* ship's hold⟧ **1** odds and ends **2** a rummaging —***vt., vi.*** **-maged, -mag·ing** to search through (a place, etc.) thoroughly

rummage sale a sale of contributed miscellaneous articles, as for charity

rum·my (rum′ē) ***n.*** ⟦< ?⟧ a card game in which the object is to match cards into sets and sequences

ru·mor (ro͞o′mər) ***n.*** ⟦L, noise⟧ **1** general talk not based on definite knowledge **2** an unconfirmed report, story, etc. in general circulation —***vt.*** to tell or spread by rumor Brit. sp. **ru′mour**

rump (rump) ***n.*** ⟦< ON *rumpr*⟧ **1** the hind part of an animal, where the legs and back join **2** the buttocks

rum·ple (rum′pəl) ***n.*** ⟦< MDu *rompe*⟧ an uneven crease; wrinkle —***vt., vi.*** **-pled, -pling** to wrinkle; muss

rum·pus (rum′pəs) ***n.*** ⟦< ?⟧ [Inf.] an uproar or commotion

run (run) ***vi.*** **ran, run, run′ning** ⟦< ON & OE⟧ **1** to go by moving the legs faster than in walking **2** to go, move, etc. easily and freely **3** to flee **4** to make a quick trip (*up to, down to,* etc.) **5** to compete in a race, election, etc. **6** to ply between two points: said as of a train **7** to climb or creep, as a vine does **8** to ravel: said as of a stocking **9** to operate: said of a machine **10** to flow **11** to spread over cloth, etc. when moistened, as colors do **12** to discharge pus, etc. **13** to extend in time or space; continue **14** to pass into a specified condition, etc. [to *run* into trouble] **15** to be written, etc. in a specified way **16** to be at a specified size, price, etc. [eggs *run* high] —***vt.*** **1** to follow (a specified course) **2** to perform as by running [to *run* a race] **3** to incur (a risk) **4** to get past [to *run* a blockade] **5** to cause to run, move, compete, etc. **6** to drive into a specified condition, place, etc. **7** to drive (an object) into or against something **8** to make flow in a specified way, place, etc. **9** to manage (a business, etc.) **10** to undergo (a fever, etc.) **11** to publish (a story, etc.) in a newspaper —***n.*** **1** an act or period of running **2** the distance covered in running **3** a trip; journey **4** a route [a delivery *run*] **5** *a*) movement onward, progression, or trend [the *run* of events] *b*) a continuous period [a *run* of good luck] **6** a continuous course of performances, etc., as of a play **7** a continued series of demands, as on a bank **8** a brook **9** a kind or class; esp., the average kind **10** the output during a period of operation **11** an enclosed area for domestic animals **12** freedom to move about at will [the *run* of the house] **13** a large number of fish migrating together **14** a ravel, as in a stocking **15** *Baseball* a scoring point, made by a successful circuit of the bases —**in the long run** in the final outcome —**on the run** running or running away —**run across** to encounter by chance: also **run into** —**run down** **1** to stop operating **2** to run against so as to knock down **3** to pursue and capture or kill **4** to speak of disparagingly —**run out** to come to an end; expire —**run out of** to use up —**run over** **1** to ride over **2** to overflow **3** to examine, rehearse, etc. rapidly —**run through** **1** to use up quickly or recklessly **2** to pierce —**run up** **1** to raise, rise, or accumulate rapidly **2** to sew rapidly

run′a·round′ ***n.*** [Inf.] a series of evasions

run'a·way' *n.* **1** a fugitive **2** a horse, etc. that runs away **—*adj.*** **1** escaping, fleeing, etc. **2** easily won: said as of a race **3** rising rapidly: said as of prices

run'down' *n.* a concise summary

run'-down' *adj.* **1** not wound and therefore not running, as a watch **2** in poor physical condition, as from overwork **3** fallen into disrepair

rune (ro͞on) *n.* ⟦OE *run*⟧ **1** any of the characters of an ancient Germanic alphabet **2** [*often pl.*] writing in these characters

rung[1] (ruŋ) *n.* ⟦OE *hrung,* staff⟧ a rod or bar forming a step of a ladder, a crosspiece on a chair, etc.

rung[2] (ruŋ) *vi., vt. pp. of* RING[1]

run'-in' *n.* [Inf.] a quarrel, fight, etc.

run·nel (run'əl) *n.* ⟦OE *rynel*⟧ a small stream

run'ner *n.* **1** *a*) one that runs, as a racer *b*) a messenger, etc. *c*) a smuggler **2** a long, narrow cloth or rug **3** a ravel, as in hosiery **4** a long, trailing stem, as of a strawberry **5** either of the long, narrow pieces on which a sled, etc. slides

run'ner-up' *n., pl.* **-ners-up'** a person or team that finishes second, etc. in a contest

run'ning *n.* the act of one that runs; racing, managing, etc. **—*adj.*** **1** that runs (in various senses) **2** measured in a straight line **3** continuous [*a running commentary*] **4** current or concurrent **—*adv.*** in succession [*for five days running*] **—in** (or **out of**) **the running** having a (or no) chance to win

running back *Football* an offensive back, responsible primarily for rushing the ball

running lights the lights that a ship or aircraft must display at night

running mate the candidate for the lesser of two closely associated offices, as for the vice-presidency

run'ny *adj.* **-ni·er, -ni·est** **1** flowing, esp. too freely **2** discharging mucus [*a runny nose*]

run'off' *n.* **1** something that runs off, as rain that is not absorbed into the ground **2** a deciding, final contest

run'-of-the-mill' *adj.* ordinary; average

runt (runt) *n.* ⟦< ?⟧ **1** a stunted animal, plant, or (contemptuously) person **2** the smallest animal of a litter **—runt'y, -i·er, -i·est,** *adj.*

run'-through' *n.* a complete rehearsal, from beginning to end

run'way' *n.* a channel, track, etc. in, on, or along which something moves; esp., *a*) a strip of leveled ground for use by airplanes in taking off and landing *b*) a narrow platform extending from a stage into the audience

ru·pee (ro͞o'pē, ro͞o pē') *n.* ⟦< Sans *rūpyaḥ,* wrought silver⟧ the monetary unit of India, Nepal, Pakistan, Sri Lanka, etc.

rup·ture (rup'chər) *n.* ⟦< L *rumpere,* to break⟧ **1** a breaking apart or being broken apart; breach **2** a hernia **—*vt., vi.*** **-tured, -tur·ing** to cause or suffer a rupture

ru·ral (roor'əl) *adj.* ⟦< L *rus,* the country⟧ of, like, or living in the country; rustic **—ru'ral·ism'** *n.*

ruse (ro͞oz) *n.* ⟦< OFr *reuser,* deceive⟧ a stratagem, trick, or artifice

rush[1] (rush) *vi., vt.* ⟦< Fr *ruser,* repel⟧ **1** to move, push, drive, etc. swiftly or impetuously **2** to make a sudden attack (*on*) **3** to pass, go, send, act, do, etc. with unusual haste; hurry **4** *Football* to run with (the ball) on a running play **—*n.*** **1** a rushing **2** an eager movement of many people to get to a place **3** busyness; haste [*the rush of modern life*] **4** a press, as of business, necessitating unusual haste **5** [Slang] a sudden thrill, etc.

rush[2] (rush) *n.* ⟦OE *risc*⟧ a grasslike marsh plant with round stems used in making mats, etc.

rush hour a time of the day when business, traffic, etc. is heavy

rusk (rusk) *n.* ⟦Sp *rosca,* twisted bread roll⟧ **1** sweet, raised bread or cake toasted until browned and crisp **2** a piece of this

Russ *abbrev.* **1** Russia **2** Russian

rus·set (rus'it) *n.* ⟦< L *russus,* reddish⟧ **1** yellowish-brown or reddish brown **2** a winter apple with a mottled skin

Rus·sia (rush'ə) **1** former empire (1547-1917) in E Europe & N Asia: in full **Russian Empire** **2** loosely, the UNION OF SOVIET SOCIALIST REPUBLICS **3** country in E Europe and N Asia, stretching from the Baltic Sea to the Pacific: formerly a republic of the U.S.S.R.: 6,592,844 sq. mi.; pop. 148,022,000

Rus·sian (rush'ən) *adj.* of Russia or its people, language, etc. **—*n.*** **1** a person born or living in Russia **2** the East Slavic language of the Russians

rust (rust) *n.* ⟦OE⟧ **1** the reddish-brown coating on iron or steel caused by oxidation during exposure to air and moisture **2** any stain resembling this **3** a reddish brown **4** a plant disease causing spotted stems and leaves **—*vi., vt.*** **1** to form rust (on) **2** to deteriorate, as through disuse

rus·tic (rus'tik) *adj.* ⟦< L *rus,* the country⟧ **1** rural **2** simple or artless **3** rough or uncouth **—*n.*** a country person **—rus'ti·cal·ly** *adv.*

rus·ti·cate (rus'tə kāt') *vi., vt.* **-cat'ed, -cat'ing** **1** to go or send to live in the country **2** to become or make rustic **—rus'ti·ca'tion** *n.*

rus·tle[1] (rus'əl) *vi., vt.* **-tled, -tling** ⟦ult. echoic⟧ to make or cause to make soft sounds, as of moving leaves, etc. **—*n.*** a series of such sounds

rus·tle[2] (rus'əl) [Inf.] *vi., vt.* **-tled, -tling** ⟦< ?⟧ to steal (cattle, etc.) **—rustle up** to gather together **—rus'tler** *n.*

rust'proof' *vt., adj.* (make) resistant to rust

rust·y (rus'tē) *adj.* **-i·er, -i·est** **1** coated with rust, as a metal **2** *a*) impaired by disuse, neglect, etc. *b*) having lost facility through lack of practice **—rust'i·ly** *adv.* **—rust'i·ness** *n.*

rut[1] (rut) ***n.*** ⟦< ? Fr *route,* route⟧ **1** a groove, track, etc., as made by wheels **2** a fixed, routine course of action, thought, etc. —***vt.*** **rut'ted, rut'ting** to make ruts in —**rut'ty, -ti·er, -ti·est, *adj.***

rut[2] (rut) ***n.*** ⟦< L *rugire,* to roar⟧ the periodic sexual excitement of certain male mammals —***vi.*** **rut'ted, rut'ting** to be in rut —**rut'tish *adj.***

ru·ta·ba·ga (ro͞ot'ə bā'gə) ***n.*** ⟦Swed dial. *rotabagge*⟧ **1** a turniplike plant with a large, yellow root **2** this root

Ruth[1] (ro͞oth) ***n.*** *Bible* a woman devoted to her mother-in-law, for whom she left her own people

Ruth[2] (ro͞o*th*), **Babe** (bāb) (born *George Herman Ruth*) 1895-1948; U.S. baseball player

ruth'less (-lis) ***adj.*** ⟦OE *hreowan,* to rue⟧ without pity or compassion —**ruth'less·ly *adv.*** —**ruth'less·ness *n.***

RV *n.,* *pl.* **RVs** ⟦*R(ecreational) V(ehicle)*⟧ a camper, trailer, motor home, etc. outfitted for living in

Rwan·da (ro͞o än'də) country in EC Africa, east of Democratic Republic of the Congo: 10,169 sq. mi.; pop. 7,165,000

Rwy or **Ry** *abbrev.* Railway

Rx *symbol* PRESCRIPTION (sense 2)

-ry (rē) *suffix* -ERY *[foundry]*

rye (rī) ***n.*** ⟦OE *ryge*⟧ **1** a hardy cereal grass **2** its grain or seeds, used for making flour, etc. **3** whiskey distilled from this grain

S

s[1] or **S** (es) ***n.,*** *pl.* **s's, S's** the 19th letter of the English alphabet —***adj.*** shaped like S

s[2] *abbrev.* **1** second(s) **2** shilling(s)

S[1] *abbrev.* **1** Saturday **2** small **3** south **4** southern **5** Sunday

S[2] *Chem. symbol for* sulfur

-s ⟦alt. of -ES⟧ *suffix* **1** forming the plural of most nouns *[hips]* **2** forming the 3d pers. sing., pres. indic., of certain verbs *[shouts]*

-'s[1] ⟦OE⟧ *suffix* forming the possessive singular of nouns and some pronouns, and the possessive plural of nouns not ending in *s [boy's, men's]*

-'s[2] *suffix* **1** is *[he's a sailor]* **2** has *[she's asked them both]* **3** [Inf.] does *[what's it matter?]* **4** us *[let's go]*

SA South America

Saar (sär, zär) rich coal-mining region in a river valley of SW Germany: also called **Saar Basin**

Sab·bath (sab'əth) ***n.*** ⟦< Heb *shabat,* to rest⟧ **1** the seventh day of the week (Saturday), set aside in Jewish scripture for rest and worship **2** Sunday as the usual Christian day of rest and worship

Sab·bat·i·cal (sə bat'i kəl) ***adj.*** **1** of the Sabbath **2** [**s-**] bringing a period of rest —***n.*** [**s-**] SABBATICAL LEAVE

sabbatical leave ⟦orig. given every seven years⟧ a period of absence with pay, for study, travel, etc., given as to teachers: also **sabbatical year**

sa·ber (sā'bər) ***n.*** ⟦< Hung *szablya*⟧ a heavy cavalry sword with a slightly curved blade: also **sa'bre**

Sa·bin vaccine (sā'bin) ⟦after Dr. A. B. *Sabin* (1906-93), its U.S. developer⟧ a polio vaccine taken orally

sa·ble (sā'bəl) ***n.*** ⟦< Russ *sobol'*⟧ **1** any marten **2** its costly fur pelt —***adj.*** black or dark brown

sa·bot (sa bō', sab'ō) ***n.*** ⟦Fr, ult. < Ar *sabbāṭ,* sandal⟧ a shoe shaped from a single piece of wood

sab·o·tage (sab'ə täzh') ***n.*** ⟦Fr < *sabot,* wooden shoe + -AGE: from damage done to machinery by sabots⟧ deliberate destruction or obstruction, as of railroads, bridges, etc. by enemy agents —***vt., vi.*** **-taged', -tag'ing** to commit sabotage (on) —**sab'o·teur'** (-tur') ***n.***

sa·bra (sä'brə) ***n.*** ⟦Heb *sabra,* a native cactus fruit⟧ [*sometimes* **S-**] a native-born Israeli

sabre saw a portable electric saw with a narrow, oscillating blade

sac (sak) ***n.*** ⟦see SACK[1]⟧ a pouchlike part in a plant or animal

sac·cha·rin (sak'ə rin') ***n.*** ⟦< Gr *sakcharon*⟧ a white, crystalline coal-tar compound used as a sugar substitute

sac'cha·rine' (-rin') ***adj.*** **1** of or like sugar **2** too sweet *[a saccharine voice]*

sac·er·do·tal (sas'ər dōt''l; *occas.* sak'-) ***adj.*** ⟦< L *sacerdos,* priest⟧ of priests or the office of priest

sa·chem (sā'chəm) ***n.*** ⟦AmInd⟧ among some North American Indian tribes, the chief

sa·chet (sa shā') ***n.*** ⟦Fr⟧ a small perfumed packet used to scent clothes

sack[1] (sak) ***n.*** ⟦ult. < Heb *saq*⟧ **1** a bag, esp. a large one of coarse cloth **2** [Slang] dismissal from a job: with *the* **3** *Football* a sacking of a quarterback —***vt.*** **1** to put into sacks **2** [Slang] to fire (a person) **3** *Football* to tackle (a quarterback) behind the line of scrimmage —**hit the sack** [Slang] to go to bed: also **sack out**

sack[2] (sak) ***n.*** ⟦see prec.⟧ the plundering of a city, etc. —***vt.*** to plunder

sack[3] (sak) ***n.*** ⟦< Fr (*vin*)*sec,* dry (wine) < L⟧ a dry, white Spanish wine popular in England during the 16th and 17th c.

sack'cloth' ***n.*** **1** SACKING **2** [Historical] coarse cloth worn as a symbol of mourning

sack'ing ***n.*** a cheap, coarse cloth used for sacks

sac·ra·ment (sak'rə mənt) ***n.*** ⟦< L *sacer,* holy⟧ any of certain Christian rites, as baptism, the Eucharist, etc. —**sac'ra·**

men'tal (-ment'l) ***adj.***

Sac·ra·men·to (sak'rə men'tō) capital of California: pop. 369,000

sa·cred (sā'krid) ***adj.*** ⟦< L *sacer*, holy⟧ **1** consecrated to a god or God; holy **2** having to do with religion **3** venerated; hallowed **4** inviolate —**sa'cred·ly** ***adv.*** —**sa'cred·ness** ***n.***

sac·ri·fice (sak'rə fīs') ***n.*** ⟦< L *sacrificium* < *sacer*, sacred + *facere*, make⟧ **1** an offering, as of a life or object, to a deity **2** a giving up of one thing for the sake of another —***vt., vi.*** **-ficed', -fic'ing** **1** to offer as a sacrifice to a deity **2** to give up one thing for the sake of another **3** to sell at less than the supposed value —**sac'ri·fi'cial** (-fish'əl) ***adj.***

sac·ri·lege (sak'rə lij) ***n.*** ⟦< L *sacer*, sacred + *legere*, take away⟧ desecration of what is sacred —**sac'ri·le'gious** (-lij'əs, -lē'jəs) ***adj.***

sac·ris·tan (sak'ris tən) ***n.*** a person in charge of a sacristy

sac'ris·ty (-tē) ***n.***, *pl.* **-ties** ⟦ult. < L *sacer*, sacred⟧ a room in a church for sacred vessels, etc.

sac·ro·il·i·ac (sak'rō il'ē ak', sā'krō-) ***n.*** ⟦ModL, ult. < L *sacrum*, bone at bottom of spine + *ileum*, flank, groin⟧ the joint between the top part of the hipbone and the fused bottom vertebrae

sac·ro·sanct (sak'rō saŋkt') ***adj.*** ⟦< L *sacer*, sacred + *sanctus*, holy⟧ very sacred, holy, or inviolable

sad (sad) ***adj.*** **sad'der, sad'dest** ⟦OE *sæd*, sated⟧ **1** having or expressing low spirits; unhappy; sorrowful **2** causing dejection, sorrow, etc. **3** [Inf.] very bad; deplorable —**sad'ly** ***adv.*** —**sad'ness** ***n.***

sad'den ***vt.***, ***vi.*** to make or become sad

sad·dle (sad''l) ***n.*** ⟦OE *sadol*⟧ **1** a seat for a rider on a horse, bicycle, etc., usually padded and of leather **2** a cut of lamb, etc., including part of the backbone and the two loins —***vt.*** **-dled, -dling** **1** to put a saddle upon **2** to encumber or burden —**in the saddle** in control

sad'dle·bag' ***n.*** **1** a bag hung behind the saddle of a horse, etc. **2** a bag carried on a bicycle, etc.

saddle horse a horse for riding

saddle shoes white oxford shoes with a contrasting band across the instep

Sad·du·cee (saj'oo sē') ***n.*** a member of an ancient Jewish party that accepted only the written law

sad·ism (sā'diz'əm, sad'iz'əm) ***n.*** ⟦after Marquis de *Sade* (1740-1814), Fr writer⟧ the getting of pleasure from mistreating others —**sad'ist** ***n.*** —**sa·dis'tic** ***adj.*** —**sa·dis'ti·cal·ly** ***adv.***

sad·o·mas·o·chism (sā'dō mas'ə kiz'əm, sad'ō-) ***n.*** the getting of sexual pleasure from sadism or masochism, or both —**sad'o·mas'o·chist** ***n.*** —**sad'o·mas'o·chis'tic** ***adj.***

sa·fa·ri (sə fär'ē) ***n.***, *pl.* **-ris** ⟦< Ar *safar*, to journey⟧ a journey or hunting expedition, esp. in Africa

safe (sāf) ***adj.*** **saf'er, saf'est** ⟦< L *salvus*⟧ **1** *a*) free from damage, danger, etc.; secure *b*) having escaped injury; unharmed **2** *a*) giving protection *b*) trustworthy —***n.*** a locking metal container for valuables —**safe'ly** ***adv.*** —**safe'ness** ***n.***

safe'-con'duct ***n.*** permission to travel safely through enemy regions

safe'-de·pos'it ***adj.*** designating or of a box or vault, as in a bank, for storing valuables: also **safe'ty-de·pos'it**

safe'guard' ***n.*** a protection; precaution —***vt.*** to protect or guard

safe house a house, etc. used as a refuge or hiding place, as by an underground organization

safe'keep'ing ***n.*** protection or custody

safe sex sexual activity incorporating practices, as condom use, that reduce the risk of spreading sexually transmitted diseases

safe·ty (sāf'tē) ***n.***, *pl.* **-ties** **1** a being safe; security **2** any device for preventing an accident **3** *Football a*) a grounding of the ball by the offense behind its own goal line, that scores two points for the defense *b*) a defensive back responsible for covering pass receivers in the middle of the field —***adj.*** giving safety

safety glass shatterproof glass

safety match a match that lights when struck on a prepared surface

safety net **1** a net suspended as beneath aerialists **2** any protection against failure or loss

safety pin a pin bent back on itself and having the point held in a guard

safety razor a razor with a detachable blade held between guards

safety valve **1** an automatic valve that releases steam if the pressure in a boiler, etc. becomes excessive **2** any outlet for the release of strong emotion, etc.

saf·flow·er (saf'lou'ər) ***n.*** ⟦ult. < Ar *aṣfar*, yellow⟧ a thistlelike, annual plant with large, orange flowers and seeds yielding an edible oil

saf·fron (saf'rən) ***n.*** ⟦< Ar *za'farān*⟧ **1** a plant having orange stigmas **2** the dried stigmas, used as a dye and flavoring **3** orange yellow

sag (sag) ***vi.*** **sagged, sag'ging** ⟦prob. < Scand⟧ **1** to sink, esp. in the middle, from weight or pressure **2** to hang down unevenly **3** to weaken through weariness, age, etc. —***n.*** **1** a sagging **2** a sagging place —**sag'gy, -gi·er, -gi·est,** ***adj.***

sa·ga (sä'gə) ***n.*** ⟦ON, a tale⟧ **1** a medieval Scandinavian story relating the legendary history of a family **2** any long story of heroic deeds

sa·ga·cious (sə gā'shəs) ***adj.*** ⟦< L *sagax*, wise⟧ very wise; shrewd —**sa·gac'i·ty** (-gas'ə tē) ***n.***

sage[1] (sāj) ***adj.*** **sag'er, sag'est** ⟦ult. < L *sapere*, know⟧ **1** wise, discerning, etc. **2** showing wisdom —***n.*** a very wise man

sage[2] (sāj) ***n.*** ⟦< L *salvus*, safe: from its reputed healing powers⟧ **1** a plant of the mint family with leaves used for seasoning meats, etc. **2** SAGEBRUSH

sage'brush' ***n.*** a plant with aromatic leaves, in the dry areas of the W U.S.

Sag·it·tar·i·us (saj'ə ter'ē əs) ***n.*** ⟦L,

archer] the ninth sign of the zodiac

sa·go (sā′gō) ***n.***, *pl.* **-gos** an edible starch from a Malayan palm tree, etc.

sa·gua·ro (sə gwär′ō) ***n.***, *pl.* **-ros** [< native name] a giant cactus of the SW U.S. and N Mexico

Sa·ha·ra (sə har′ə) vast desert region extending across N Africa

sa·hib (sä′ib′) ***n.*** [Hindi < Ar] sir; master: title used in colonial India when speaking to or of a European

said (sed) ***vt., vi.*** *pt. & pp. of* SAY **—*adj.*** aforesaid

Sai·gon (sī gän′) *former name for* HO CHI MINH CITY

sail (sāl) ***n.*** [OE *segl*] **1** a sheet, as of canvas, spread to catch the wind, so as to drive a vessel forward **2** sails collectively **3** a trip in a ship or boat **4** anything like a sail **—*vi.*** **1** to be moved forward by means of sails **2** to travel on water **3** to begin a trip by water **4** to manage a sailboat **5** to glide or move smoothly **6** [Inf.] to move quickly **—*vt.*** **1** to move upon (a body of water) in a vessel **2** to manage or navigate (a vessel) **—set** (or **make**) **sail** to begin a trip by water **—under sail** sailing

sail′board′ ***n.*** a board used in windsurfing

sail′boat′ ***n.*** a boat propelled by a sail or sails

sail′cloth′ ***n.*** canvas or other cloth for making sails, tents, etc.

SAILFISH

sail′fish′ ***n.***, *pl.* **-fish′** or (for different species) **-fish′es** a large marine fish with a sail-like dorsal fin

sail′or ***n.*** **1** a person whose work is sailing **2** an enlisted person in the navy

sail′plane′ ***n.*** a light glider

saint (sānt) ***n.*** [< L *sanctus*, holy] **1** a holy person **2** a person who is exceptionally charitable, patient, etc. **3** in certain Christian churches, a person officially recognized for having attained heaven after an exceptionally holy life **—saint′li·ness *n.* —saint′ly, -li·er, -li·est, *adj.***

Saint Ber·nard (bər närd′) a large dog of a breed once used to rescue travelers lost in the snow

Saint Nich·o·las (nik′ə ləs) SANTA CLAUS: also **Saint Nick**

Saint Pat·rick's Day (pa′triks) March 17, observed by the Irish in honor of the patron saint of Ireland

Saint Valentine's Day February 14, observed in honor of a martyr of the 3d c. and as a day for sending valentines

saith (seth) ***vt., vi.*** [Archaic] says

sake[1] (sāk) ***n.*** [OE *sacu*, suit at law] **1** motive; cause *[for the sake of money]* **2** behalf *[for my sake]*

sa·ke[2] (sä′kē) ***n.*** [Jpn] a Japanese alcoholic beverage made from rice: also sp. **sa′ki**

sa·laam (sə läm′) ***n.*** [Ar *salām*, peace] in India and the Near East, a greeting, etc. made by bowing low in respect or obeisance

sal·a·ble (sāl′ə bəl) ***adj.*** that can be sold; marketable: also sp. **sale′a·ble**

sa·la·cious (sə lā′shəs) ***adj.*** [< L *salire*, to leap] **1** lustful **2** obscene **—sa·la′cious·ly *adv.* —sa·la′cious·ness *n.***

sal·ad (sal′əd) ***n.*** [< L *sal*, salt] a dish, usually cold, of fruits, vegetables (esp. lettuce), meat, eggs, etc. usually mixed with salad dressing

salad bar a buffet in a restaurant, at which diners make their own salads

salad dressing oil, vinegar, spices, etc. put on a salad

sa·lade niçoise (sal′əd nē swäz′) a salad of tuna, tomatoes, etc. with a garlic vinaigrette

sal·a·man·der (sal′ə man′dər) ***n.*** [< Gr *salamandra*] **1** a mythological reptile said to live in fire **2** an amphibian with a tail and soft, moist skin

sa·la·mi (sə lä′mē) ***n.*** [It < L *sal*, salt] a spiced, salted sausage

sal·a·ry (sal′ə rē) ***n.***, *pl.* **-ries** [< L *salarium*, orig. part of a soldier's pay for buying salt < *sal*, salt] a fixed payment at regular intervals for work **—sal′a·ried** (-rēd) ***adj.***

sale (sāl) ***n.*** [< ON *sala*] **1** a selling **2** opportunity to sell; market **3** an auction **4** a special offering of goods at reduced prices **5** [*pl.*] receipts in business **6** [*pl.*] the work of, or a department involved in, selling *[a job in sales]* **—for sale** to be sold **—on sale** for sale, esp. at a reduced price

Sa·lem (sā′ləm) capital of Oregon, in the NW part: pop. 108,000

sales·clerk (sālz′klurk′) ***n.*** a person employed to sell goods in a store

sales′girl′ ***n.*** a girl or woman salesclerk

sales′la′dy ***n.***, *pl.* **-dies** [Inf.] a woman employed as a salesclerk

sales′man (-mən) ***n.***, *pl.* **-men** (-mən) **1** a man employed as a salesclerk **2** SALES REPRESENTATIVE

sales′man·ship′ ***n.*** the skill of selling

sales′per′son ***n.***, *pl.* **-peo′ple** a person employed to sell goods or services

sales representative a salesperson, esp. one employed as a traveling agent for a manufacturer, etc.

sales slip a receipt or bill of sale

sales tax a tax on sales

sales′wom′an ***n.***, *pl.* **-wom′en** a woman salesclerk or sales representative

sal·i·cyl·ic acid (sal′ə sil′ik) [< L *salix*,

willow⟧ a crystalline compound used to make aspirin, etc.

sa·lient (sāl′yənt) *adj.* ⟦< L *salire*, to leap⟧ **1** pointing outward; jutting **2** conspicuous; prominent —*n.* a salient angle, part, etc. —**sa′lience** *n.*

sa·line (sā′lēn′, -līn′) *adj.* ⟦< L *sal*, salt⟧ of, like, or containing salt —*n.* a saline solution used in medicine, etc. —**sa·lin·i·ty** (sə lin′ə tē) *n.*

sa·li·va (sə lī′və) *n.* ⟦L⟧ the watery fluid secreted by glands in the mouth: it aids in digestion —**sal·i·var·y** (sal′ə ver′ē) *adj.*

sal·i·vate (sal′ə vāt′) *vi.* **-vat′ed, -vat′ing** ⟦< L *salivare*⟧ to secrete saliva —**sal′i·va′tion** *n.*

sal·low (sal′ō) *adj.* ⟦ME *salou*⟧ of a sickly, pale-yellowish complexion

sal·ly (sal′ē) *n., pl.* **-lies** ⟦< L *salire*, to leap⟧ **1** a sudden rushing forth, as to attack **2** a witty remark; quip **3** an excursion —*vi.* **-lied, -ly·ing** to rush or set (*forth* or *out*) on a sally

salm·on (sam′ən) *n., pl.* **-on** or **-ons** ⟦< L *salmo*⟧ **1** a game and food fish with yellowish pink flesh, that lives in salt water and spawns in fresh water **2** yellowish pink: also **salmon pink**

sal·mo·nel·la (sal′mə nel′ə) *n., pl.* **-nel′lae** (-ē), **-nel′la**, or **-nel′las** ⟦after D. E. *Salmon* (1850-1914), U.S. doctor⟧ any of a genus of bacilli that cause typhoid fever, food poisoning, etc.

sa·lon (sə län′) *n.* ⟦Fr: see fol.⟧ **1** a large reception hall or drawing room **2** a regular gathering of distinguished guests **3** a shop furnished to provide some personal service *[*beauty *salon]*

sa·loon (sə lo͞on′) *n.* ⟦< Fr < It *sala*⟧ **1** any large room or hall for receptions, etc. **2** [Old-fashioned] a place where alcoholic drinks are sold; bar

sal·sa (säl′sə) *n.* ⟦AmSp, sauce < L, salted food⟧ **1** a kind of Latin American dance music usually played at fast tempos **2** a hot sauce made with chilies, tomatoes, etc.

salt (sôlt) *n.* ⟦OE *sealt*⟧ **1** a white, crystalline substance, sodium chloride, found in natural beds, in sea water, etc., and used for seasoning food, etc. **2** a chemical compound derived from an acid by replacing hydrogen with a metal **3** piquancy; esp., pungent wit **4** [*pl.*] mineral salts used as a cathartic or restorative **5** [Inf.] a sailor —*adj.* containing, preserved with, or tasting of salt —*vt.* to sprinkle, season, or preserve with salt —**salt away** [Inf.] to store or save (money, etc.) —**salt of the earth** any person or persons regarded as the finest, etc. —**with a grain of salt** with allowance for exaggeration, etc.; skeptically —**salt′ed** *adj.*

salt′cel′lar (-sel′ər) *n.* ⟦< prec. + Fr *salière*, saltcellar⟧ **1** a small dish for holding salt **2** a saltshaker

salt·ine (sôl tēn′) *n.* ⟦SALT + -INE[3]⟧ a flat, crisp, salted cracker

Salt Lake City capital of Utah: pop. 160,000

salt lick a natural deposit or a block of rock salt which animals lick

salt′pe′ter (-pēt′ər) *n.* ⟦< L *sal*, salt + *petra*, rock⟧ NITER

salt pork pork cured in salt

salt′shak′er *n.* a container for salt, with a perforated top

salt′wa′ter *adj.* of salt water or the sea

salt′y *adj.* **-i·er, -i·est** **1** of or having salt **2** suggesting the sea **3** *a*) sharp; witty *b*) coarse *c*) cross or caustic

sa·lu·bri·ous (sə lo͞o′brē əs) *adj.* ⟦< L *salus*, health⟧ healthful; wholesome

sal·u·tar·y (sal′yo͞o ter′ē) *adj.* ⟦see prec.⟧ **1** healthful **2** beneficial

sal·u·ta·tion (sal′yo͞o tā′shən) *n.* ⟦see fol.⟧ **1** the act of greeting, addressing, etc. **2** a form of greeting, as the "Dear Sir" of a letter

sa·lute (sə lo͞ot′) *vt., vi.* **-lut′ed, -lut′ing** ⟦< L *salus*, health⟧ **1** to greet with friendly words or ceremonial gesture **2** to honor by performing a prescribed act, such as raising the right hand to the head, in military and naval practice **3** to praise; commend —*n.* an act or remark made in saluting

sal·vage (sal′vij) *n.* ⟦see SAVE[1]⟧ **1** *a*) the rescue of a ship and cargo from shipwreck, etc. *b*) compensation paid for such rescue **2** *a*) the rescue of any property from destruction or waste *b*) the property saved —*vt.* **-vaged, -vag·ing** to save or rescue from shipwreck, fire, etc.

sal·va·tion (sal vā′shən) *n.* ⟦< L *salvare*, save⟧ **1** a saving or being saved **2** a person or thing that saves **3** *Theol.* deliverance from sin and from the penalties of sin; redemption

salve (sav) *n.* ⟦OE *sealf*⟧ **1** any soothing or healing ointment for wounds, burns, etc. **2** anything that soothes —*vt.* **salved, salv′ing** to soothe

sal·ver (sal′vər) *n.* ⟦ult. < L *salvare*, save⟧ a tray

sal·vo (sal′vō) *n., pl.* **-vos** or **-voes** ⟦< It < L *salve*, hail!⟧ a discharge of a number of guns, in salute or at a target

SAM (sam) *n.* surface-to-air missile

sam·ba (sam′bə, säm′-) *n.* ⟦Port⟧ a Brazilian dance of African origin, or music for it

same (sām) *adj.* ⟦< ON *samr*⟧ **1** being the very one; identical **2** alike in kind, quality, amount, etc. **3** unchanged *[*to keep the *same* look*]* **4** before-mentioned Usually used with *the* —*pron.* the same person or thing —*adv.* in like manner: usually with *the* —**same′ness** *n.*

sam·iz·dat (säm′iz dät′) *n.* ⟦Russ, self-published⟧ in the U.S.S.R., a system by which writings officially disapproved of were circulated secretly

Sa·mo·a (sə mō′ə) country in the SW Pacific, consisting of two large islands & several small ones: 1,093 sq. mi.; pop. 160,000 —**Sa·mo′an** *adj., n.*

sam·o·var (sam′ə vär′) *n.* a Russian metal urn with a spigot, for heating water in making tea

sam·pan (sam′pan′) *n.* ⟦< Chin dial.⟧ a small boat used in China and Japan, rowed with a scull from the stern

sam·ple (sam′pəl) ***n.*** ⟦see EXAMPLE⟧ **1** a part or item taken as representative of a whole thing, group, etc.; specimen **2** an example —***vt.*** **-pled, -pling** to take (and test) a sample of

sam′pler (-plər) ***n.*** **1** one who samples **2** a collection of representative selections **3** a cloth embroidered with designs, mottoes, etc. in different stitches

Sam·son (sam′sən) ***n.*** *Bible* an Israelite noted for his great strength

Sam·u·el (sam′yo͞o əl) ***n.*** *Bible* a Hebrew leader and prophet

sam·u·rai (sam′ə rī′) ***n.***, *pl.* **-rai′** ⟦Jpn⟧ a member of a military class in feudal Japan

San An·to·ni·o (san′ an tō′nē ō′) city in SC Texas: site of the Alamo: pop. 935,000

san·a·to·ri·um (san′ə tôr′ē əm) ***n.***, *pl.* **-ri·ums** or **-ri·a** (-ə) *chiefly Brit. var. of* SANITARIUM

San Ber·nar·di·no (bur′nər dē′nō, -nə-) city in S California: pop. 164,000

sanc·ti·fy (saŋk′tə fī′) ***vt.*** **-fied′, -fy′ing** ⟦see SAINT & -FY⟧ **1** to set apart as holy; consecrate **2** to make free from sin —**sanc′ti·fi·ca′tion** ***n.***

sanc·ti·mo·ni·ous (saŋk′tə mō′nē əs) ***adj.*** pretending to be pious —**sanc′ti·mo′ni·ous·ly** ***adv.***

sanc′ti·mo′ny ***n.*** ⟦< L *sanctus*, holy⟧ pretended piety

sanc·tion (saŋk′shən) ***n.*** ⟦see SAINT⟧ **1** authorization **2** support; approval **3** a coercive measure, as an official trade boycott against a nation defying international law: *often used in pl.* —***vt.*** **1** to confirm; ratify **2** to authorize; permit

sanc·ti·ty (saŋk′tə tē) ***n.***, *pl.* **-ties** ⟦< L *sanctus*, holy⟧ **1** holiness **2** sacredness

sanc·tu·ar·y (saŋk′cho͞o er′ē) ***n.***, *pl.* **-ies** ⟦< L *sanctus*, sacred⟧ **1** a holy place; specif., *a*) a church, temple, etc. *b*) a particularly holy place within a church or temple **2** a place of refuge or protection

sanc·tum (saŋk′təm) ***n.*** ⟦L⟧ **1** a sacred place **2** a private room where one is not to be disturbed

sand (sand) ***n.*** ⟦OE⟧ **1** loose, gritty grains of eroded rock, as on beaches, in deserts, etc. **2** [*usually pl.*] a tract of sand —***vt.*** **1** to sprinkle with sand **2** to smooth or polish, as with sandpaper —**sand′er** ***n.***

SANDALS

san·dal (san′dəl) ***n.*** ⟦< Gr *sandalon*⟧ **1** a shoe made of a sole fastened to the foot by straps **2** any of various low slippers or shoes

san′dal·wood′ ***n.*** ⟦ult. < Sans⟧ **1** the hard, sweet-smelling wood at the core of certain Asiatic trees **2** such a tree

sand′bag′ ***n.*** a bag filled with sand, used for ballast, protecting levees, etc. —***vt.*** **-bagged′, -bag′ging** **1** to put sandbags in or around **2** [Inf.] to force into doing something

sand′bar′ ***n.*** a ridge of sand, as one formed in a river or along a shore: also **sand bar** or **sand′bank′**

sand′blast′ ***vt.*** to clean with a current of air or steam carrying sand at a high velocity

sand′box′ ***n.*** a box containing sand for children to play in

sand dollar any of various flat, round, disklike echinoderms that live on sandy ocean beds

S & H *abbrev.* shipping and handling

sand′hog′ ***n.*** a laborer in underground or underwater construction

San Di·e·go (san′ dē ā′gō) seaport in S California: pop. 1,111,000

S & L *abbrev.* savings and loan (association)

sand′lot′ ***adj.*** of or having to do with baseball played by amateurs, orig. on a sandy lot

sand′man′ ***n.*** a mythical person supposed to make children sleepy by dusting sand in their eyes

sand′pa′per ***n.*** paper coated on one side with sand, used for smoothing and polishing —***vt.*** to smooth or polish with sandpaper

sand′pip′er (-pī′pər) ***n.*** a small shorebird with a long, soft-tipped bill

sand′stone′ ***n.*** a sedimentary rock composed of sand grains cemented together, as by silica

sand′storm′ ***n.*** a windstorm in which large quantities of sand are blown about in the air

sand trap a hollow filled with sand, serving as a hazard on a golf course

sand·wich (sand′wich′) ***n.*** ⟦after 4th Earl of *Sandwich* (1718-92)⟧ slices of bread with meat, cheese, etc. between them —***vt.*** to place or squeeze between other persons, things, etc.

sand·y (san′dē) ***adj.*** **-i·er, -i·est** **1** of or like sand **2** pale reddish-yellow

sane (sān) ***adj.*** ⟦L *sanus*, healthy⟧ **1** mentally healthy; rational **2** sound; sensible —**sane′ly** ***adv.***

San Fran·cis·co (san′ frən sis′kō) seaport on the coast of central California: pop. 724,000

San Francisco Bay an inlet of the Pacific in WC California: the harbor of San Francisco

sang (saŋ) ***vi.***, ***vt.*** *alt. pt. of* SING[1]

sang-froid (sän frwä′) ***n.*** ⟦Fr, lit., cold blood⟧ cool self-possession or composure

san·gri·a (san grē′ə, saŋ-) ***n.*** ⟦Sp < *sangre*, blood⟧ an iced punch made with red wine, fruit juice, pieces of fruit, etc.

san·gui·nar·y (saŋ′gwi ner′ē) ***adj.*** ⟦see fol.⟧ **1** accompanied by much bloodshed **2** bloodthirsty

san·guine (saŋ′gwin) ***adj.*** ⟦< L *sanguis*, blood⟧ **1** of the color of blood; ruddy **2** cheerful; confident

san·i·tar·i·um (san′ə ter′ē əm) ***n.***, *pl.* **-i·ums** or **-i·a** (-ə) ⟦ModL < L *sanitas*, health⟧ **1** a resort where people go to regain health **2** an institution for the care of invalids or convalescents

san·i·tar·y (san′ə ter′ē) ***adj.*** ⟦< L *sanitas*, health⟧ **1** of or bringing about health and healthful conditions **2** in a clean, healthy condition

sanitary napkin an absorbent pad worn by women during menstruation

san·i·ta·tion (san′ə tā′shən) ***n.*** **1** the science and practice of effecting hygienic conditions **2** drainage and disposal of sewage

san·i·tize (san′ə tīz′) ***vt.*** **-tized′**, **-tiz′ing** **1** to make sanitary **2** to free from anything considered undesirable, damaging, etc.

san·i·ty (san′ə tē) ***n.*** **1** the state of being sane **2** soundness of judgment

San Jo·se (san′ hō zā′) city in WC California: pop. 782,000

San Juan (san′ hwän′) seaport & capital of Puerto Rico: pop. 438,000

sank (saŋk) ***vi., vt.*** *alt. pt. of* SINK

San Ma·ri·no (san′ mə rē′nō) independent country within E Italy: 24 sq. mi.; pop. 24,000

sans (sanz; *Fr* sän) ***prep.*** ⟦Fr < L *sine*⟧ without

San·skrit (san′skrit′) ***n.*** the classical literary language of ancient India: also **San′scrit**

San·ta An·a[1] (san′tə an′ə) hot desert wind from the east or northeast in S California

San·ta An·a[2] (san′tə an′ə) city in SW California: pop. 294,000

San·ta Claus (san′tə klôz′) ⟦< Du *Sant Nikolaas*, St. Nicholas⟧ *Folklore* a fat, white-bearded, jolly old man in a red suit, who distributes gifts at Christmas

San·ta Fe (san′tə fā′) capital of New Mexico: pop. 56,000

San·ti·a·go (sän′tē ä′gō, san′-) capital of Chile: pop. 4,100,000

São Pau·lo (soun pou′lōō) city in SE Brazil: pop. 8,491,000

São To·mé and Prín·ci·pe (tô me′ and prin′sə pē′) country off the W coast of Africa, comprising two islands (**São Tomé** and **Príncipe**): 387 sq. mi.; pop. 120,000

sap[1] (sap) ***n.*** ⟦OE *sæp*⟧ **1** the juice that circulates through a plant, bearing water, food, etc. **2** vigor; energy **3** [Slang] a fool —**sap′less** ***adj.***

sap[2] (sap) ***vt.*** **sapped**, **sap′ping** ⟦< Fr *sappe*, a hoe⟧ **1** to dig beneath; undermine **2** to weaken

sa·pi·ent (sā′pē ənt) ***adj.*** ⟦< L *sapere*, to taste, know⟧ wise —**sa′pi·ence** ***n.***

sap·ling (sap′liŋ) ***n.*** a young tree

sap·phire (saf′īr) ***n.*** ⟦< Sans *śanipriya*⟧ a precious stone of a clear, deep-blue corundum

sap·py (sap′ē) ***adj.*** **-pi·er**, **-pi·est** **1** full of sap; juicy **2** [Slang] foolish; silly —**sap′pi·ness** ***n.***

sap·ro·phyte (sap′rə fīt′) ***n.*** ⟦< Gr *sapros*, rotten + *phyton*, a plant⟧ any plant that lives on dead or decaying organic matter, as some fungi —**sap′ro·phyt′ic** (-fit′ik) ***adj.***

sap′suck′er ***n.*** an American woodpecker that often drills holes in trees for the sap

Sar·a·cen (sar′ə sən) ***n.*** any Arab or any Muslim, esp. at the time of the Crusades

Sar·ah (ser′ə) ***n.*** *Bible* the wife of Abraham and mother of Isaac

Sa·ra·je·vo (sar′ə yā′vō) capital of Bosnia and Herzegovina: pop. 416,000

sa·ran (sə ran′) ***n.*** ⟦arbitrary coinage⟧ a thermoplastic substance used in various fabrics, wrapping material, etc.

sar·casm (sär′kaz′əm) ***n.*** ⟦< Gr *sarkazein*, to tear flesh⟧ **1** a taunting or caustic remark, generally ironic **2** the making of such remarks

sar·cas·tic (sär kas′tik) ***adj.*** **1** of, like, or full of sarcasm **2** using sarcasm —**sar·cas′ti·cal·ly** ***adv.***

sar·co·ma (sär kō′mə) ***n.***, *pl.* **-mas** or **-ma·ta** (-mə tə) ⟦< Gr *sarx*, flesh⟧ a malignant tumor in connective tissue

sar·coph·a·gus (sär käf′ə gəs) ***n.***, *pl.* **-gi′** (-jī′) or **-gus·es** ⟦< Gr *sarx*, flesh + *phagein*, to eat: limestone coffins hastened disintegration⟧ a stone coffin, esp. one exposed to view, as in a tomb

sar·dine (sär dēn′) ***n.*** ⟦< L *sarda*, a fish⟧ any of various small ocean fishes preserved in tightly packed cans for eating

sar·don·ic (sär dän′ik) ***adj.*** ⟦< Gr *sardonios*⟧ scornfully or bitterly sarcastic —**sar·don′i·cal·ly** ***adv.***

sa·ri (sä′rē) ***n.*** ⟦< Sans⟧ the outer garment of a woman of India, Pakistan, etc., consisting of a long cloth wrapped around the body

SARI

sa·rong (sə rôŋ′, -räŋ′) ***n.*** ⟦Malay *sarung*⟧ a garment of men and women in the East Indies, etc., consisting of a cloth worn like a skirt

sar·sa·pa·ril·la (sas′ pə ril′ə) ***n.*** ⟦< Sp *zarza*, bramble + *parra*, vine⟧ **1** a tropical American vine with fragrant roots **2** a carbonated drink flavored with or as with the dried roots

sar·to·ri·al (sär tôr′ ē əl) ***adj.*** ⟦< LL *sartor*, tailor⟧ **1** of tailors or their work **2** of men's dress

SASE *abbrev.* self-addressed, stamped envelope

sash[1] (sash) ***n.*** ⟦Ar *shāsh*, muslin⟧ an ornamental band, ribbon, etc. worn over the shoulder or around the waist

sash[2] (sash) ***n.*** ⟦< Fr *châssis*, a frame⟧ a frame for holding the glass pane of a window or door, esp. a sliding frame

sa·shay (sa shā′) ***vi.*** ⟦< Fr *chassé*, a dance step⟧ [Inf.] **1** to walk or go, esp. casually **2** to move, walk, etc. so as to attract attention

Sas·katch·e·wan (sas kach′ə wän′) province of SC Canada: 251,700 sq. mi.; pop. 990,000; cap. Regina: abbrev. *SK*

sass (sas) [Inf.] ***n.*** ⟦var. of SAUCE⟧ impudent talk —***vt.*** to talk impudently to

sas·sa·fras (sas′ə fras′) ***n.*** ⟦Sp *sasafras*⟧ **1** a small tree having small, bluish fruits **2** its dried root bark, used for flavoring

sass·y (sas′ē) ***adj.*** **-i·er, -i·est** ⟦var. of SAUCY⟧ [Inf.] impudent; saucy

sat (sat) ***vi., vt.*** *pt. & pp. of* SIT

Sat *abbrev.* Saturday

SAT *trademark for* Scholastic Assessment Tests

Sa·tan (sāt′'n) ***n.*** ⟦< Heb *satan*, adversary⟧ the Devil

sa·tan·ic (sā tan′ik, sə-) ***adj.*** like Satan; wicked —**sa·tan′i·cal·ly** ***adv.***

satch·el (sach′əl) ***n.*** ⟦< L *saccus*, a bag⟧ a small bag for carrying clothes, books, etc.

sate (sāt) ***vt.*** **sat′ed, sat′ing** ⟦prob. < L *satiare*, fill full⟧ **1** to satisfy (an appetite, etc.) completely **2** to satiate

sa·teen (sa tēn′) ***n.*** ⟦< SATIN⟧ a cotton cloth made to imitate satin

sat·el·lite (sat′'l īt′) ***n.*** ⟦< L *satelles*, an attendant⟧ **1** *a*) a celestial body revolving around a larger celestial body *b*) a man-made object rocketed into orbit around the earth, moon, etc. **2** a small state dependent on a larger one

sa·ti·ate (sā′shē āt′) ***vt.*** **-at′ed, -at′ing** ⟦< L *satis*, enough⟧ to provide with more than enough, so as to weary or disgust; glut

sa·ti·e·ty (sə tī′ə tē) ***n.*** a being satiated

sat·in (sat′'n) ***n.*** ⟦< Ar *zaitūnī*, of *Zaitūn*, former name of a Chinese seaport⟧ a fabric of silk, nylon, rayon, etc. with a smooth, glossy finish on one side —**sat′in·y** ***adj.***

sat′in·wood′ ***n.*** **1** a smooth wood used in fine furniture **2** any of the trees yielding such a wood

sat·ire (sa′tīr′) ***n.*** ⟦< L *satira*⟧ **1** a literary work in which vices, follies, etc. are held up to ridicule and contempt **2** the use of ridicule, sarcasm, etc. to attack vices, follies, etc. —**sa·tir·i·cal** (sə tir′i kəl) ***adj.*** —**sat·i·rist** (sat′ə rist) ***n.***

sat·i·rize (sat′ə rīz′) ***vt.*** **-rized′, -riz′ing** to attack with satire

sat·is·fac·tion (sat′is fak′shən) ***n.*** **1** a satisfying or being satisfied **2** something that satisfies; specif., *a*) anything that brings pleasure or contentment *b*) settlement of debt

sat′is·fac′to·ry (-tə rē) ***adj.*** good enough to fulfill a need, wish, etc.; satisfying or adequate —**sat′is·fac′to·ri·ly** ***adv.***

sat·is·fy (sat′is fī′) ***vt.*** **-fied′, -fy′ing** ⟦< L *satis*, enough + *facere*, make⟧ **1** to fulfill the needs or desires of; content **2** to fulfill the requirements of **3** to free from doubt; convince **4** *a*) to give what is due to *b*) to discharge (a debt, etc.)

sa·to·ri (sä tôr′ē) ***n.*** ⟦Jpn⟧ spiritual enlightenment: term in Zen Buddhism

sa·trap (sā′trap′, sa′-) ***n.*** ⟦< Pers⟧ a petty tyrant

sat·u·rate (sach′ə rāt′) ***vt.*** **-rat′ed, -rat′ing** ⟦< L *satur*, full⟧ **1** to make thoroughly soaked **2** to cause to be filled, charged, etc. with the most it can absorb —**sat′u·ra′tion** ***n.***

Sat·ur·day (sat′ər dā′) ***n.*** ⟦< OE *Sæterdæg*, Saturn's day⟧ the seventh and last day of the week

Saturday night special ⟦from their use in weekend crimes⟧ [Slang] any small, cheap handgun

Sat·urn (sat′ərn) ***n.*** **1** the Roman god of agriculture **2** the second largest planet of the solar system, with thin, icy rings of particles around its equator: see PLANET

sat·ur·nine (sat′ər nīn′) ***adj.*** ⟦< supposed influence of planet Saturn⟧ sluggish, gloomy, grave, etc.

sat·yr (sāt′ər, sat′-) ***n.*** ⟦< Gr *satyros*⟧ **1** *Gr. Myth.* a lecherous woodland deity represented as a man with a goat's legs, pointed ears, and short horns **2** a lecherous man

sat·y·ri·a·sis (sāt′ə rī′ə sis, sat′-) ***n.*** ⟦< Gr: see prec.⟧ uncontrollable desire by a man for sexual intercourse

sauce (sôs) ***n.*** ⟦< L *sal*, salt⟧ **1** a liquid or soft mixture served with food to add flavor **2** stewed or preserved fruit **3** [Inf.] impudence **4** [Slang] alcoholic liquor: with *the*

sauce′pan′ ***n.*** a small pot with a projecting handle, used for cooking

sau·cer (sô′sər) ***n.*** ⟦see SAUCE⟧ **1** a small, round, shallow dish, esp. one designed to hold a cup **2** anything shaped like a saucer

sau·cy (sô′sē) ***adj.*** **-ci·er, -ci·est** ⟦SAUC(E) + -Y[2]⟧ **1** rude; impudent **2** pert; sprightly —**sau′ci·ly** ***adv.*** —**sau′ci·ness** ***n.***

Sa·u·di Arabia (sou′dē, sô′-) kingdom occupying most of Arabia: 849,400 sq. mi.; pop. 16,900,000

sau·er·bra·ten (sou′ər brät′'n, zou′ər-) ***n.*** ⟦Ger *sauer*, sour + *braten*, roast⟧ beef marinated in vinegar with onions, spices, etc. before cooking

sau·er·kraut (sou′ər krout′) ***n.*** ⟦Ger *sauer*, sour + *kraut*, cabbage⟧ chopped cabbage fermented in brine

Saul (sôl) ***n.*** *Bible* first king of Israel

sau·na (sô′nə, sä′-) ***n.*** ⟦Finnish⟧ a bath involving exposure to hot, dry air

saun·ter (sôn′tər) ***vi.*** ⟦ME *santren*, to muse⟧ to walk about idly; stroll —***n.*** a leisurely walk; stroll

sau·ri·an (sôr′ē ən) ***adj.*** ⟦< Gr *sauros*, lizard⟧ of or like lizards

sau·ro·pod (sôr′ə päd′) ***n.*** ⟦< Gr *sauros*, lizard + -POD⟧ a gigantic dinosaur with a long neck and tail and a small head, as an apatosaurus

sau·sage (sô′sij) ***n.*** ⟦see SAUCE⟧ pork or other meat, chopped fine, seasoned, and often stuffed into a casing

sau·té (sô tā′, sō-) ***vt.*** **-téed′, -té′ing** ⟦Fr < *sauter*, to leap⟧ to fry quickly with a little fat

Sau·ternes (sō turn′) ***n.*** ⟦after *Sauternes*, town in France⟧ [*often* **s-**] any of various white wines, of varying sweetness: also sp. **Sau·terne'**

sav·age (sav'ij) ***adj.*** ⟦< L *silva*, a wood⟧ **1** fierce; untamed *[a savage tiger]* **2** primitive; barbarous **3** cruel; pitiless —***n.*** **1** [Now Rare] a member of a preliterate, often tribal, culture **2** a brutal or crude person —**sav'age·ly** ***adv.*** —**sav'age·ry** ***n.***

sa·van·na or **sa·van·nah** (sə van'ə) ***n.*** ⟦Sp *sabana*⟧ a treeless plain or a grassland with scattered trees

Sa·van·nah (sə van'ə) seaport in SE Georgia: pop. 138,000

sa·vant (sə vänt', -vant'; sav'ənt) ***n.*** ⟦Fr < *savoir*, know⟧ a learned person

save[1] (sāv) ***vt.*** **saved**, **sav'ing** ⟦< L *salvus*, safe⟧ **1** to rescue or preserve from harm or danger **2** to preserve for future use **3** to prevent loss or waste of *[to save time]* **4** to prevent or lessen *[to save expense]* **5** *Theol.* to deliver from sin —***vi.*** **1** to avoid expense, waste, etc. **2** to store (*up*) money or goods —***n.*** *Sports* an action that keeps an opponent from scoring or winning —**sav'er** ***n.***

save[2] (sāv) ***prep., conj.*** ⟦< OFr *sauf*, safe⟧ except; but

sav·ing (sā'viŋ) ***adj.*** that saves; specif., *a*) economizing or economical *b*) redeeming —***n.*** **1** [*often pl., with sing. v.*] any reduction in expense, time, etc. **2** [*pl.*] sums of money saved

sav·ior or **sav·iour** (sāv'yər) ***n.*** ⟦< L *salvare*, to save⟧ **1** one who saves **2** [**S-**] Jesus Christ

sa·voir-faire (sav'wär fer') ***n.*** ⟦Fr, to know (how) to do⟧ ready knowledge of what to do or say in any situation

sa·vor (sā'vər) ***n.*** ⟦< L *sapor*⟧ **1** a particular taste or smell **2** distinctive quality —***vi.*** to have the distinctive taste, smell, or quality (*of*) —***vt.*** to taste with delight Brit. sp. **sa'vour**

sa'vor·y ***adj.*** **-i·er**, **-i·est** **1** pleasing to the taste or smell **2** pleasant, agreeable, etc. Brit. sp. **sa'vour·y**

sav·vy (sav'ē) ***n.*** ⟦< Port *saber*, to know⟧ [Slang] shrewdness or understanding

saw[1] (sô) ***n.*** ⟦OE *sagu*⟧ a cutting tool consisting of a thin metal blade or disk with sharp teeth —***vt.*** to cut or shape with a saw —***vi.*** **1** to cut with or as with a saw **2** to be cut with a saw

saw[2] (sô) ***n.*** ⟦OE *sagu*⟧ a maxim; proverb

saw[3] (sô) ***vt., vi.*** *pt. of* SEE[1]

saw'dust' ***n.*** fine particles of wood formed in sawing wood

sawed'-off' ***adj.*** short or shortened

saw'horse' ***n.*** a rack on which wood is placed while being sawed

saw'mill' ***n.*** a factory where logs are sawed into boards

saw'-toothed' ***adj.*** having notches along the edge like the teeth of a saw: also **saw'tooth'**

saw·yer (sô'yər) ***n.*** one whose work is sawing wood

sax (saks) ***n.*** [Inf.] *short for* SAXOPHONE

Sax·on (sak'sən) ***n.*** **1** a member of an ancient Germanic people, some of whom settled in England **2** an Anglo-Saxon **3** any dialect of the Saxons

sax·o·phone (sak'sə fōn') ***n.*** ⟦Fr, after A. J. *Sax*, 19th-c. Belgian inventor + -PHONE⟧ a single-reed, keyed woodwind instrument with a metal body —**sax'o·phon'ist** (-fōn'ist) ***n.***

say (sā) ***vt.*** **said**, **say'ing** ⟦OE *secgan*⟧ **1** to utter or speak **2** to express in words; state **3** to state positively or as an opinion **4** to indicate or show *[the clock says one]* **5** to recite *[to say one's prayers]* **6** to estimate; assume *[he is, I'd say, forty]* —***n.*** **1** a chance to speak *[I had my say]* **2** authority, as to make a final decision: often with *the* —**that is to say** in other words

say'ing ***n.*** an adage, proverb, or maxim

say'-so' ***n.*** [Inf.] **1** one's word, assurance, etc. **2** right of decision

Sb ⟦L *stibium*⟧ *Chem. symbol for* antimony

sc *abbrev. Printing* small capitals

SC South Carolina

scab (skab) ***n.*** ⟦< ON *skabb*⟧ **1** a crust forming over a sore during healing **2** a worker who replaces a striking worker —***vi.*** **scabbed**, **scab'bing** to become covered with a scab —**scab'by**, **-bi·er**, **-bi·est**, ***adj.*** —**scab'bi·ness** ***n.***

scab·bard (skab'ərd) ***n.*** ⟦< ? OHG *scar*, sword⟧ a sheath for the blade of a sword, dagger, etc.

sca·bies (skā'bēz) ***n.*** ⟦L, the itch⟧ a contagious, itching skin disease caused by a mite

scab·rous (skab'rəs, skā'brəs) ***adj.*** ⟦< L *scabere*, to scratch⟧ **1** scaly or scabby **2** indecent, shocking, etc.

scads (skadz) ***pl.n.*** ⟦< ?⟧ [Inf.] a very large number or amount

scaf·fold (skaf'əld) ***n.*** ⟦< OFr *escafalt*⟧ **1** a temporary framework for supporting workers during the repairing, painting, etc. of a building, etc. **2** a raised platform on which criminals are executed

scaf'fold·ing ***n.*** **1** the materials forming a scaffold **2** a scaffold

scal·a·wag (skal'ə wag') ***n.*** ⟦< ?⟧ [Inf.] a scamp; rascal

scald (skôld) ***vt.*** ⟦< L *ex-*, intens. + *calidus*, hot⟧ **1** to burn with hot liquid or steam **2** to heat almost to the boiling point **3** to use boiling liquid on —***n.*** a burn caused by scalding

scale[1] (skāl) ***n.*** ⟦< L *scala*, ladder⟧ **1** *a*) a series of marks along a line used in measuring *[the scale of a thermometer]* *b*) any instrument so marked **2** the proportion that a map, etc. bears to the thing it represents *[a scale of one inch to a mile]* **3** *a*) a series of degrees classified by size, amount, etc. *[a wage scale]* *b*) any degree in such a series **4** *Music* a series of tones, rising or falling in pitch, according to a system of intervals —***vt.*** **scaled**, **scal'ing** **1** to climb up or over **2** to make according to a scale —**scale back** SCALE DOWN (see phrase below) —**scale down** (or **up**) to reduce (or increase) according to a fixed ratio

scale[2] (skāl) ***n.*** ⟦< OFr *escale*, shell⟧ **1** any of the thin, flat horny plates covering many fishes, reptiles, etc. **2** any thin, platelike layer or piece —***vt.***

scaled, scal′ing to scrape scales from —*vi.* to flake or peel off in scales —**scal′y, -i·er, -i·est,** *adj.*

scale[3] (skāl) *n.* ⟦< ON *skāl,* bowl⟧ **1** either pan of a balance **2** [*often pl.*] *a)* BALANCE (sense 1) *b)* any weighing machine —*vt.* **scaled, scal′ing** to weigh —**turn the scales** to decide or settle

scale insect any of various small insects destructive to plants: the females secrete a waxy scale

sca·lene (skā′lēn′, skā lēn′) *adj.* ⟦< Gr *skalēnos,* uneven⟧ having unequal sides *[a scalene triangle]*

scal·lion (skal′yən) *n.* ⟦< L (*caepa*) *Ascalonia,* (onion of) Ascalon (Philistine city)⟧ any of various onions or onionlike plants, as the shallot, green onion, or leek

scal·lop (skäl′əp, skal′-) *n.* ⟦< OFr *escalope*⟧ **1** *a)* any of various edible mollusks with two curved, hinged shells *b)* one of the shells **2** any of a series of curves, etc. forming an ornamental edge —*vt.* **1** to cut the edge of in scallops **2** to bake until brown, usually with a creamy sauce and bread crumbs

SHELL OF SCALLOP

SCALLOPED BORDER

scalp (skalp) *n.* ⟦< Scand⟧ the skin on the top and back of the head, usually covered with hair —*vt.* **1** to cut or tear the scalp from **2** [Inf.] to buy (theater tickets, etc.) and resell them at higher prices —**scalp′er** *n.*

scal·pel (skal′pəl) *n.* ⟦< L *scalprum,* a knife⟧ a small, sharp, straight knife used in surgery, etc.

scam (skam) *n.* ⟦prob. < *scheme*⟧ [Slang] a swindle or fraud, esp. a CONFIDENCE GAME —*vt.* **scammed, scam′ming** [Slang] to cheat or swindle, as in a confidence game

scamp (skamp) *n.* ⟦< It *scampare,* to flee⟧ a mischievous fellow; rascal

scam·per (skam′pər) *vi.* ⟦see prec.⟧ to run or go quickly —*n.* a scampering

scam·pi (skam′pē) *n., pl.* **-pi** or **-pies** ⟦It⟧ a large, edible shrimp

scan (skan) *vt.* **scanned, scan′ning** ⟦< L *scandere,* to climb⟧ **1** to analyze (verse) by marking the metrical feet **2** to look at closely **3** to glance at quickly **4** to examine the structure or condition of (an internal body organ) with ultrasound, etc. **5** to pass radar beams over (an area) —*vi.* to conform to metrical principles: said of poetry —*n.* the act or an instance of scanning

Scan or **Scand** *abbrev.* Scandinavia(n)

scan·dal (skan′dəl) *n.* ⟦< Gr *skandalon,* a snare⟧ **1** anything that offends moral feelings and leads to disgrace **2** shame, outrage, etc. caused by this **3** disgrace **4** malicious gossip

scan′dal·ize′ (-də līz′) *vt.* **-ized′, -iz′ing** to outrage the moral feelings of by improper conduct

scan′dal·mon′ger (-dəl muŋ′gər, -dəl mäŋ′-) *n.* one who spreads scandal or gossip

scan′dal·ous (-də ləs) *adj.* **1** causing scandal; shameful **2** spreading slander —**scan′dal·ous·ly** *adv.*

Scan·di·na·vi·a (skan′də nā′vē ə) region in N Europe, including Norway, Sweden, & Denmark and, sometimes, Iceland

Scan·di·na·vi·an (skan′də nā′vē ən) *adj.* of Scandinavia or its peoples, languages, etc. —*n.* **1** a person born or living in Scandinavia **2** the subbranch of the Germanic languages spoken by Scandinavians

scan·sion (skan′shən) *n.* ⟦Fr < L *scansio*⟧ the act of scanning, or analyzing, poetry

scant (skant) *adj.* ⟦< ON *skammr,* short⟧ **1** inadequate; meager **2** not quite up to full measure

scant′y *adj.* **-i·er, -i·est 1** barely sufficient **2** insufficient; not enough —**scant′i·ly** *adv.* —**scant′i·ness** *n.*

scape·goat (skāp′gōt′) *n.* ⟦< ESCAPE + GOAT; see Lev. 16:7-26⟧ one who bears the blame for the mistakes of others —*vt.* to make a scapegoat of

scape·grace (skāp′grās′) *n.* ⟦< ESCAPE + GRACE⟧ a rogue; scamp

scap·u·la (skap′yə lə) *n., pl.* **-lae′** (-lē′) or **-las** ⟦< L⟧ either of the two flat bones in the upper back; shoulder blade

scar (skär) *n.* ⟦< Gr *eschara,* orig., fireplace⟧ **1** a mark left after a wound, burn, etc. has healed **2** the lasting mental or emotional effects of suffering —*vt.* **scarred, scar′ring** to mark as with a scar —*vi.* to form a scar in healing

scar·ab (skar′əb) *n.* ⟦< L *scarabaeus*⟧ **1** a large, black beetle **2** a carved image of such a beetle

scarce (skers) *adj.* ⟦ult. < L *excerpere,* pick out⟧ **1** not common; rarely seen **2** not plentiful; hard to get —**make oneself scarce** [Inf.] to go or stay away —**scarce′ness** *n.*

scarce′ly *adv.* **1** hardly; only just **2** probably not or certainly not

scar·ci·ty (sker′sə tē) *n., pl.* **-ties 1** an inadequate supply; dearth **2** rarity; uncommonness

scare (sker) *vt.* **scared, scar′ing** ⟦< ON *skjarr,* timid⟧ to fill with sudden fear —*vi.* to become frightened —*n.* a sudden fear —**scare away** (or **off**) to drive away (or off) by frightening —**scare up** [Inf.] to produce or gather quickly

scare·crow (sker′krō′) *n.* a human figure made with sticks, old clothes, etc., put in a field to scare birds away from crops

scarf (skärf) *n., pl.* **scarves** (skärvz) or sometimes **scarfs** ⟦< OFr *escharpe,* purse hung from the neck⟧ **1** a piece of cloth worn about the neck, head, etc. **2** a long, narrow covering for a table, etc.

scar·i·fy (skar′ə fī′) *vt.* **-fied′, -fy′ing** ⟦< L *scarifare*⟧ to make small cuts in (the skin, etc.) —**scar′i·fi·ca′tion** *n.*

scar·let (skär′lit) ***n.*** ⟦< ML *scarlatum*⟧ very bright red —***adj.*** **1** of this color **2** sinful; specif., whorish

scarlet fever an acute contagious disease characterized by sore throat, fever, and a scarlet rash

scar·y (sker′ē) ***adj.*** **-i·er, -i·est** [Inf.] frightening —**scar′i·ness** ***n.***

scat[1] (skat) ***vi.*** **scat′ted, scat′ting** ⟦? short for SCATTER⟧ [Inf.] to go away: usually in the imperative

scat[2] (skat) ***adj.*** ⟦< ?⟧ *Jazz* using improvised, meaningless syllables in singing —***n.*** such singing —***vi.*** **scat′ted, scat′ting** to sing scat

scath·ing (skā′*th*iŋ) ***adj.*** ⟦< ON *skathi,* harm⟧ harsh or caustic *[scathing remarks]* —**scath′ing·ly** ***adv.***

sca·tol·o·gy (skə täl′ə jē) ***n.*** ⟦< Gr *skōr,* excrement⟧ obsession with excrement or excretion in literature —**scat·o·log·i·cal** (skat′ə läj′i kəl) ***adj.***

scat·ter (skat′ər) ***vt.*** ⟦ME *skateren*⟧ **1** to throw here and there; sprinkle **2** to separate and drive in many directions; disperse —***vi.*** to separate and go off in several directions

scat′ter·brain′ ***n.*** one who is incapable of concentrated thinking

scatter rug a small rug

scav·eng·er (skav′in jər) ***n.*** ⟦< NormFr *escauwer,* to inspect⟧ **1** one who gathers things discarded by others **2** any animal that eats refuse and decaying matter —**scav′enge** (-inj), **-enged, -eng·ing,** ***vt., vi.***

sce·nar·i·o (sə ner′ē ō′; -när′-) ***n.,*** *pl.* **-os′** ⟦see fol.⟧ **1** *a)* an outline of a play, etc. *b)* the script of a film **2** an outline for any planned series of events, real or imagined —**sce·nar′ist** ***n.***

scene (sēn) ***n.*** ⟦< Gr *skēnē,* stage⟧ **1** the place where an event occurs **2** the setting of a play, story, etc. **3** a division of a play, usually part of an act **4** a unit of action in a play, film, etc. **5** SCENERY (sense 1) **6** a display of strong feeling *[to make a scene]* **7** [Inf.] the locale for a specified activity

sce·ner·y (sēn′ə rē) ***n.,*** *pl.* **-ies** **1** painted screens, backdrops, etc., used on the stage to represent places, as in a play, etc. **2** the features of a landscape

sce·nic (sē′nik) ***adj.*** **1** of stage scenery **2** *a)* of natural scenery *b)* having beautiful scenery

scent (sent) ***vt.*** ⟦ult. < L *sentire,* to feel⟧ **1** to smell **2** to get a hint of **3** to fill with an odor; perfume —***n.*** **1** an odor **2** the sense of smell **3** a perfume **4** an odor left by an animal, by which it is tracked —**scent′ed** ***adj.***

scep·ter (sep′tər) ***n.*** ⟦< Gr *skēptron,* staff⟧ a staff held by a ruler as a symbol of sovereignty: chiefly Brit. sp. **scep′tre**

scep·tic (skep′tik) ***n., adj.*** *chiefly Brit. sp. of* SKEPTIC —**scep′ti·cal** ***adj.*** —**scep′ti·cism′** ***n.***

sched·ule (ske′jool; *Brit & often Cdn* shej′ool) ***n.*** ⟦< L *scheda,* a strip of papyrus⟧ **1** a list of details **2** a list of times of recurring events, projected operations, etc.; timetable **3** a timed plan for a project —***vt.*** **-uled, -ul·ing** **1** to place in a schedule **2** to plan for a certain time

sche·mat·ic (skē mat′ik) ***adj.*** of or like a scheme, diagram, etc.

scheme (skēm) ***n.*** ⟦< Gr *schēma,* a form⟧ **1** *a)* a systematic program for attaining some end *b)* a secret plan; plot **2** an orderly combination of things on a definite plan **3** a diagram —***vt., vi.*** **schemed, schem′ing** to devise or plot —**schem′er** ***n.***

scher·zo (sker′tsō) ***n.,*** *pl.* **-zos** or **-zi** (-tsē) ⟦It, a jest⟧ *Music* a lively composition, usually in 3/4 time, as the third movement of a symphony, etc.

schism (siz′əm, skiz′-) ***n.*** ⟦< Gr *schizein,* to cleave⟧ a split, as in a church, because of difference of opinion, doctrine, etc. —**schis·mat′ic** (-mat′ik) ***adj.***

schist (shist) ***n.*** ⟦< Gr *schistos,* easily cleft⟧ a crystalline rock easily split into layers

schiz·o·phre·ni·a (skit′sə frē′nē ə) ***n.*** ⟦< Gr *schizein,* cleave + *phrēn,* the mind⟧ a mental disorder characterized by separation between thought and emotions, by delusions, bizarre behavior, etc. —**schiz′oid** (-soid) or **schiz′o·phren′ic** (-ə fren′ik) ***adj., n.***

schle·miel (shlə mēl′) ***n.*** ⟦Yiddish⟧ [Slang] a bungling person who habitually fails or is easily victimized

schlep or **schlepp** (shlep) [Slang] ***vt.*** **schlepped, schlep′ping** ⟦via Yiddish < LowG *slepen,* to drag⟧ to carry, haul, etc. —***vi.*** to go or move with effort —***n.*** an ineffectual person

schlock (shläk) [Slang] ***n.*** ⟦< ? Ger *schlacke,* dregs⟧ anything cheap or inferior; trash —***adj.*** cheap; inferior: also **schlock′y, -i·er, -i·est**

schmaltz (shmälts, shmôlts) ***n.*** ⟦? via Yiddish < Ger *schmaltz,* rendered fat⟧ [Slang] highly sentimental music, literature, etc.

schnapps (shnäps) ***n.,*** *pl.* **schnapps** ⟦Ger, a nip < Du *snaps,* a gulp⟧ a strong alcoholic liquor: also sp. **schnaps**

schnau·zer (shnou′zər) ***n.*** ⟦Ger < *schnauzen,* to snarl⟧ a sturdily built dog with a wiry coat and bushy eyebrows

schol·ar (skäl′ər) ***n.*** ⟦< L *schola,* a school⟧ **1** a learned person **2** a student or pupil —**schol′ar·ly** ***adj.***

schol′ar·ship′ ***n.*** **1** the quality of knowledge a student shows **2** the systematized knowledge of a scholar **3** a gift of money, etc. as by a foundation, to help a student

scho·las·tic (skə las′tik) ***adj.*** ⟦see fol.⟧ of schools, colleges, students, etc.; educational; academic

school[1] (sko͞ol) ***n.*** ⟦< Gr *scholē,* leisure⟧ **1** a place or institution, with its buildings, etc., for teaching and learning **2** all of its students and teachers **3** a regular session of teaching **4** formal education; schooling **5** a particular division of a university **6** a group following the same beliefs, methods, etc. —***vt.*** **1** to train; teach **2** to discipline or control —***adj.*** of a school or schools

school[2] (sko͞ol) ***n.*** ⟦Du, a crowd⟧ a group of fish, etc. swimming together

school board an elected or appointed group of people in charge of public or private schools

school'book' *n.* a textbook

school'boy' *n.* a boy attending school

school'girl' *n.* a girl attending school

school'house' *n.* a building used as a school

school'ing *n.* training or education; esp., formal instruction at school

school'marm' (-märm', -mäm') *n.* **1** [Old-fashioned] a woman schoolteacher **2** [Inf.] any person who tends to be prudish, pedantic, etc.

school'mas'ter *n.* [Old-fashioned] a man who teaches in a school

school'mate' *n.* a companion or acquaintance at school

school'mis'tress *n.* [Old-fashioned] a woman who teaches in a school

school'room' *n.* a room in which pupils are taught, as in a school

school'teach'er *n.* one who teaches in a school

school'work' *n.* lessons worked on in classes or done as homework

school'yard' *n.* the ground around a school, used as a playground, etc.

school year the part of a year when school is in session, usually September to June

schoon·er (sko͞on'ər) *n.* ⟦< ?⟧ **1** a ship with two or more masts, rigged fore and aft **2** a large beer glass

Schu·bert (sho͞o'bərt), **Franz** (fränts) 1797-1828; Austrian composer

schuss (shoos) *n.* ⟦Ger, lit., shot⟧ a straight run down a hill in skiing —*vi.* to do a schuss

schwa (shwä) *n.* ⟦Ger < Heb *sheva*⟧ **1** the neutral vowel sound of most unstressed syllables in English, as of *e* in *agent* **2** the symbol (ə) for this

sci·at·ic (sī at'ik) *adj.* ⟦see fol.⟧ of or in the hip or its nerves

sci·at·i·ca (sī at'i kə) *n.* ⟦< Gr *ischion*, the hip⟧ any painful condition in the hip or thigh; esp., neuritis of the long nerve (**sciatic nerve**) passing down the back of the thigh

sci·ence (sī'əns) *n.* ⟦< L *scire*, know⟧ **1** systematized knowledge derived from observation, study, etc. **2** a branch of knowledge, esp. one that systematizes facts, principles, and methods, as NATURAL SCIENCE **3** skill or technique

science fiction highly imaginative fiction typically involving some actual or projected scientific phenomenon

sci·en·tif·ic (sī'ən tif'ik) *adj.* **1** of or dealing with science **2** based on, or using, the principles and methods of science; systematic and exact —**sci'en·tif'i·cal·ly** *adv.*

sci'en·tist *n.* a specialist in science, as in biology, chemistry, or physics

sci-fi (sī'fī') *n.* [Inf.] *short for* SCIENCE FICTION

scim·i·tar (sim'ə tər) *n.* ⟦It *scimitarra*⟧ a short, curved sword used chiefly by Turks and Arabs

scin·til·la (sin til'ə) *n.* ⟦L⟧ **1** a spark **2** a particle; the least trace: figurative only

scin·til·late (sint''l āt') *vi.* **-lat'ed, -lat'ing** ⟦< L *scintilla*, a spark⟧ **1** to sparkle or twinkle **2** to be brilliant and witty —**scin'til·la'tion** *n.*

sci·on (sī'ən) *n.* ⟦< OFr *cion*⟧ **1** a shoot or bud of a plant, esp. one for grafting **2** a descendant; heir

scis·sor (siz'ər) *vt.* ⟦< fol.⟧ to cut, cut off, or cut out with scissors —*n.* SCISSORS, esp. in adjectival use

scis·sors (siz'ərz) *n.* ⟦< LL *cisorium*, cutting tool⟧ [*also with pl. v.*] a cutting instrument with two opposing blades pivoted together so that they can work against each other as the instrument is closed on paper, etc.: also called **pair of scissors**

scle·ra (sklir'ə) *n., pl.* **-ras** or **-rae** (-ē) ⟦< Gr *sklēros*, hard⟧ the tough, white membrane covering all of the eyeball except the area covered by the cornea

scle·ro·sis (skli rō'sis) *n., pl.* **-ses** (-sēz') ⟦< Gr *sklēros*, hard⟧ an abnormal hardening of body tissues —**scle·rot'ic** (-rät'ik) *adj.*

scoff (skäf, skôf) *n.* an expression of scorn or derision —*vt., vi.* to mock or jeer (at) —**scoff'er** *n.*

scoff'law' *n.* [Inf.] one who flouts traffic laws, liquor laws, etc.

scold (skōld) *n.* ⟦< ON *skald*, poet (prob. of satirical verses)⟧ a person, esp. a woman, who habitually uses abusive language —*vt., vi.* to find fault (with) angrily; to rebuke —**scold'ing** *adj., n.*

sco·li·o·sis (skō'lē ō'sis) *n.* ⟦< Gr *skolios*, crooked⟧ lateral curvature of the spine

sconce (skäns) *n.* ⟦ult. < L *abscondere*, to hide⟧ a wall bracket for candles

scone (skōn, skän) *n.* ⟦Scot⟧ a light cake resembling a biscuit and often quadrant-shaped

scooch (sko͞och) *vi.* **1** [Inf.] to scrunch (*down, through*, etc.) **2** to slide jerkily

scoop (sko͞op) *n.* ⟦< MDu *schope*, bailing vessel, *schoppe*, a shovel⟧ **1** any of various small, shovel-like utensils, as for taking up flour or ice cream **2** the deep shovel of a dredge, etc. **3** the act or motion of scooping **4** the amount scooped up at one time **5** [Inf.] *a)* the publication or broadcast of a news item before a competitor *b)* such a news item —*vt.* **1** to take up or out with or as with a scoop **2** to hollow (*out*) **3** [Inf.] to publish news before (a competitor)

scoot (sko͞ot) *vi., vt.* ⟦prob. < ON *skjōta*, to shoot⟧ [Inf.] to go or move quickly; hurry (off)

scootch (sko͞och) *vi.* [Inf.] *alt. sp. of* SCOOCH

scoot'er *n.* ⟦< SCOOT⟧ **1** a child's two-wheeled vehicle moved by pushing one foot against the ground **2** a similar, motor-driven vehicle with a seat: in full **motor scooter**

scope (skōp) *n.* ⟦< Gr *skopos*, watcher⟧ **1** the extent of the mind's grasp **2** the range or extent of action, inclusion, inquiry, etc. **3** room or opportunity for freedom of action or thought

-scope (skōp) ⟦< Gr *skopein*, see⟧ *combining form* an instrument, etc. for seeing or observing [telescope, kaleidoscope]

scorch (skôrch) ***vt.*** ⟦< ? Scand⟧ **1** to burn slightly or superficially **2** to parch by intense heat —***vi.*** to become scorched —***n.*** a superficial burn

score (skôr) ***n.*** ⟦< ON *skor*⟧ **1** a scratch, mark, notch, incised line, etc. **2** an account or debt **3** a grievance one seeks to settle **4** a reason or motive **5** the number of points made, as in a game **6** a grade, as on a test **7** *a*) twenty people or things *b*) [*pl.*] very many **8** a copy of a musical composition showing all parts for the instruments or voices **9** [Inf.] the basic facts [to know the *score*] —***vt.*** **scored, scor'ing 1** to mark with notches, cuts, lines, etc. **2** *a*) to make (runs, points, etc.) in a game *b*) to record the score of **3** to achieve [*score* a success] **4** to evaluate, as in testing **5** *Music* to arrange in a score —***vi.*** **1** to make points, as in a game **2** to keep the score of a game **3** to gain an advantage, a success, etc. —**scor'er *n.***

score'board' ***n.*** a large board for posting scores, etc., as in a stadium

score'less ***adj.*** with no points scored

scorn (skôrn) ***n.*** ⟦< OFr *escharnir*, to scorn⟧ extreme, often indignant, contempt —***vt.*** **1** to regard with scorn **2** to refuse or reject with scorn —**scorn'ful *adj.*** —**scorn'ful·ly *adv.***

Scor·pi·o (skôr'pē ō') ***n.*** ⟦L, scorpion⟧ the eighth sign of the zodiac

scor'pi·on (-ən) ***n.*** ⟦< Gr *skorpios*⟧ an arachnid with a long tail ending in a poisonous sting

SCORPION

Scot[1] (skät) ***n.*** a person born or living in Scotland

Scot[2] *abbrev.* **1** Scotland **2** Scottish

scotch (skäch) ***vt.*** ⟦prob. < OFr *coche*, a nick⟧ **1** to maim **2** to put an end to; stifle [to *scotch* a rumor]

Scotch (skäch) ***adj.*** of Scotland: cf. SCOTTISH —***n.*** **1** SCOTTISH **2** [*often* **s-**] whiskey distilled in Scotland from malted barley: in full **Scotch whisky**

Scotch'man (-mən) ***n.***, *pl.* **-men** (-mən) *var. of* SCOTSMAN

Scotch tape ⟦< *Scotch*, a trademark⟧ a thin, transparent adhesive tape

scot-free (skät'frē') ***adv., adj.*** ⟦< earlier *scot*, a tax⟧ without being punished or hurt

Scot·land (skät'lənd) division of the United Kingdom: the N half of Great Britain: 29,794 sq. mi.; pop. 4,962,000

Scotland Yard the London police headquarters, esp. its detective bureau

Scots (skäts) ***adj., n.*** SCOTTISH

Scots'man (-mən) ***n.***, *pl.* **-men** (-mən) a person, esp. a man, born or living in Scotland: in Scotland, *Scotsman* or *Scot* is preferred to *Scotchman* —**Scots'wom'an**, *pl.* **-wom'en, *fem.n.***

Scot·tie or **Scot·ty** (skät'ē) ***n.***, *pl.* **-ties** SCOTTISH TERRIER

Scot·tish (skät'ish) ***adj.*** of Scotland or its people, variety of English, etc.: *Scottish* is formal usage, but with some words, *Scotch* is used (e.g., tweed, whisky), with others, *Scots* (e.g., law) —***n.*** the variety of English spoken in Scotland —**the Scottish** the Scottish people

Scottish terrier a short-legged terrier with a wiry coat

scoun·drel (skoun'drəl) ***n.*** ⟦prob. ult. < L *ab(s)-*, from + *condere*, to hide⟧ a mean, immoral, or wicked person

scour[1] (skour) ***vt., vi.*** ⟦< ? L *ex-*, intens. + *cura*, care⟧ **1** to clean by rubbing hard, as with abrasives **2** to clean or clear out as by a flow of water

scour[2] (skour) ***vt.*** ⟦< L *ex-*, out + *currere*, to run⟧ to pass over quickly, or range over, as in searching [to *scour* a library for a book]

scourge (skurj) ***n.*** ⟦< L *ex*, off + *corrigia*, a whip⟧ **1** a whip **2** any cause of serious affliction —***vt.*** **scourged, scourg'ing 1** to whip or flog **2** to punish or afflict severely

scout (skout) ***n.*** ⟦< L *auscultare*, to listen⟧ **1** a soldier, plane, etc. sent to spy out the enemy's strength, actions, etc. **2** a person sent out to survey a competitor, find new talent, etc. **3** [**S-**] a Boy Scout or Girl Scout —***vt., vi.*** **1** to reconnoiter **2** to go in search of (something)

scout'ing ***n.*** **1** the act of one who scouts **2** [*often* **S-**] the activities of the Boy Scouts or Girl Scouts

scout'mas'ter ***n.*** the adult leader of a troop of Boy Scouts

scow (skou) ***n.*** ⟦Du *schouw*⟧ a large, flat-bottomed boat used for carrying loads, often towed by a tugboat

scowl (skoul) ***vi.*** ⟦prob. < Scand⟧ to look angry, sullen, etc., as by contracting the eyebrows —***n.*** a scowling look —**scowl'er *n.***

scrab·ble (skrab'əl) ***vi.*** **-bled, -bling** ⟦< Du *schrabben*, to scrape⟧ **1** to scratch, scrape, etc. as though looking for something **2** to struggle

scrag·gly (skrag'lē) ***adj.*** **-gli·er, -gli·est** ⟦prob. < ON⟧ uneven, ragged, etc. in growth or form

scram (skram) ***vi.*** **scrammed, scram'ming** ⟦< fol.⟧ [Slang] to get out, esp. in a hurry

scram·ble (skram'bəl) ***vi.*** **-bled, -bling** ⟦< ?⟧ **1** to climb, crawl, etc. hurriedly **2** to scuffle or struggle for something —***vt.*** **1** to mix haphazardly **2** to stir and cook (slightly beaten eggs) **3** to make (transmitted signals) unintelligible without special receiving equipment —***n.*** **1** a hard climb or advance **2** a disorderly struggle, as for something prized

scrap[1] (skrap) ***n.*** ⟦ult. < ON *skrapa*, to scrape⟧ **1** a small piece; fragment **2** discarded material **3** [*pl.*] bits of food —***adj.*** **1** in the form of pieces, leftovers, etc. **2** used and discarded —***vt.*** **scrapped, scrap'ping 1** to make into scrap **2** to discard; junk —**scrap'per *n.***

scrap[2] (skrap) ***n., vi.*** **scrapped, scrap'ping** ⟦< ? SCRAPE⟧ [Inf.] fight or quarrel —**scrap′per** ***n.*** —**scrap′py, -pi·er, -pi·est,** ***adv.***

scrap′book′ ***n.*** a book in which to mount clippings, pictures, etc.

scrape (skrāp) ***vt.*** **scraped, scrap′ing** ⟦< ON *skrapa*⟧ **1** to make smooth or clean by rubbing with a tool or abrasive **2** to remove in this way: with *off, out,* etc. **3** to scratch or abrade **4** to gather slowly and with difficulty *[scrape up some cash]* —***vi.*** **1** to rub against something harshly; grate **2** to manage to get by: with *through, along, by* —***n.*** **1** a scraping **2** a scraped place **3** a grating sound **4** a predicament —**scrap′er** ***n.***

scrap′heap′ (-hēp′) ***n.*** a pile of discarded material, as of scrap iron —**throw** (or **toss, cast,** etc.) **on the scrapheap** to get rid of as useless

scratch (skrach) ***vt.*** ⟦ME *scracchen*⟧ **1** to mark, break, or cut the surface of slightly **2** to tear or dig with the nails or claws **3** to scrape lightly to relieve itching **4** to scrape with a grating noise **5** to write hurriedly or carelessly **6** to strike out (writing, etc.) **7** *Sports* to withdraw (a contestant, etc.) —***vi.*** **1** to use nails or claws in digging, wounding, etc. **2** to scrape —***n.*** **1** a scratching **2** a mark, tear, etc. made by scratching **3** a grating or scraping sound —***adj.*** used for hasty notes, figuring etc. *[scratch paper]* —**from scratch** from nothing; without resources, etc. —**up to scratch** [Inf.] up to standard —**scratch′y, -i·er, -i·est,** ***adj.*** —**scratch′i·ly** ***adv.*** —**scratch′i·ness** ***n.***

scratch′pad′ ***n.*** a pad of paper for jotting notes

scrawl (skrôl) ***vt., vi.*** ⟦< ?⟧ to write or draw hastily, carelessly, etc. —***n.*** sprawling, often illegible handwriting

scraw·ny (skrô′nē) ***adj.*** **-ni·er, -ni·est** ⟦prob. < Scand⟧ very thin; skinny —**scraw′ni·ness** ***n.***

scream (skrēm) ***vi.*** ⟦ME *screamen*⟧ **1** to utter a shrill, piercing cry in fright, pain, etc. **2** to shout, laugh, etc. wildly —***vt.*** to utter with or as with a scream —***n.*** **1** a sharp, piercing cry or sound **2** [Inf.] a very funny person or thing

screech (skrēch) ***vi., vt.*** ⟦< ON *skraekja*⟧ to utter (with) a shrill, high-pitched sound —***n.*** such a sound —**screech′y, -i·er, -i·est,** ***adj.***

screen (skrēn) ***n.*** ⟦< OFr *escren*⟧ **1** a partition, curtain, etc. used to separate, conceal, etc. **2** anything that shields, conceals, etc. **3** a coarse mesh of wire, etc., used as a sieve **4** a frame covered with a mesh *[a window screen]* **5** *a)* a surface on which films, slides, etc. are projected *b)* the film industry *c)* the surface of a TV set, computer, etc. on which images are formed —***vt.*** **1** to conceal or protect, as with a screen **2** to sift through a screen **3** to separate according to skills, etc. **4** to show (a film, etc.) to critics, the public, etc.

screen′play′ ***n.*** the script from which a film is produced

screen′writ′er ***n.*** the writer of a script for a film —**screen′writ′ing** ***n.***

screw (skrōō) ***n.*** ⟦< Fr *escroue,* hole in which the screw turns⟧ **1** a cylindrical or conical piece of metal threaded in an advancing spiral, for fastening things: it penetrates when turned **2** any spiral thing like this **3** anything operating or threaded like a screw —***vt.*** **1** to twist; turn **2** to fasten, tighten, etc. as with a screw **3** to contort —***vi.*** **1** to go together or come apart by being turned like a screw *[the lid screws on]* **2** to twist or turn —**put the screws on** (or **to**) [Inf.] to subject to great pressure; coerce —**screw up** [Inf.] to bungle

screw′ball′ ***n.*** [Slang] an erratic, irrational or unconventional person

screw′driv′er ***n.*** a tool used for turning screws

screw′worm′ ***n.*** the larva of an American blowfly that infests wounds, and the nostrils, navel, etc. of animals

screw·y (skrōō′ē) ***adj.*** **-i·er, -i·est** [Slang] **1** crazy **2** peculiar, eccentric

scrib·ble (skrib′əl) ***vt., vi.*** **-bled, -bling** ⟦< L *scribere,* write⟧ **1** to write carelessly, hastily, etc. **2** to make meaningless or illegible marks (on) —***n.*** scribbled writing —**scrib′bler** ***n.***

scribe (skrīb) ***n.*** ⟦< L *scribere,* write⟧ **1** a person who copied manuscripts before the invention of printing **2** a writer

scrim (skrim) ***n.*** ⟦< ?⟧ **1** a light, sheer, loosely woven cotton or linen cloth **2** such a cloth used as a stage backdrop or semitransparent curtain

scrim·mage (skrim′ij) ***n.*** ⟦< SKIRMISH⟧ **1** *Football* play that follows the snap from center **2** a practice game —***vi.*** **-maged, -mag·ing** to take part in a scrimmage

scrimp (skrimp) ***vt., vi.*** ⟦< ? Scand⟧ to be sparing or frugal (with)

scrim′shaw′ (-shô′) ***n.*** an intricate carving of bone, ivory, etc. done esp. by sailors

scrip (skrip) ***n.*** ⟦< fol.⟧ a certificate of a right to receive something, as money or goods

script (skript) ***n.*** ⟦< L *scribere,* to write⟧ **1** handwriting **2** a copy of the text of a play, film etc.

scrip·ture (skrip′chər) ***n.*** ⟦see prec.⟧ **1** any sacred writing **2** [**S-**] [*often pl.*] the sacred writings of the Jews; Old Testament **3** [**S-**] [*often pl.*] the Christian Bible; Old and New Testaments —**scrip′tur·al** ***adj.***

script′writ′er ***n.*** one who writes scripts for films, TV, etc.

scrod (skräd) ***n.*** ⟦prob. < MDu *schrode,* piece cut off⟧ a young codfish or haddock, esp. one prepared for cooking

scrof·u·la (skräf′yə lə) ***n.*** ⟦< L *scrofa,* a sow⟧ tuberculosis of the lymphatic glands, esp. of the neck —**scrof′u·lous** ***adj.***

scroll (skrōl) ***n.*** ⟦< ME *scrowle*⟧ **1** a roll of parchment, paper, etc., usually with writing on it **2** an ornamental design in coiled or spiral form —***vi.*** to move lines of text, etc. vertically on a video screen

scro·tum (skrōt′əm) ***n., pl.*** **-ta** (-ə) or **-tums** ⟦L⟧ the pouch of skin holding the testicles

scrounge (skrounj) ***vt.*** **scrounged, scroung′ing** ⟦< ?⟧ [Inf.] **1** to get by begging or sponging; mooch **2** to pilfer —*vi.* [Inf.] to seek (*around*) for something —**scroung'er** *n.*

scroung'y *adj.* **-i·er, -i·est** [Slang] shabby, dirty, unkempt, etc. —**scroung'i·ness** *n.*

scrub[1] (skrub) *n.* ⟦ME, var. of *shrubbe,* shrub⟧ **1** a thick growth of stunted trees or bushes **2** any person or thing smaller than the usual, or inferior **3** *Sports* a substitute player —*adj.* small, stunted, inferior, etc. —**scrub'by, -bi·er, -bi·est,** *adj.*

scrub[2] (skrub) *vt., vi.* **scrubbed, scrub'bing** ⟦prob. < Scand⟧ **1** to clean or wash by rubbing hard **2** to rub hard —*n.* a scrubbing —**scrub'ber** *n.*

scrub'wom'an *n., pl.* **-wom'en** CHARWOMAN

scruff (skruf) *n.* ⟦< ON *skrufr,* a tuft of hair⟧ the nape of the neck

scruff·y (skruf'ē) *adj.* **-i·er, -i·est** ⟦< SCURF + -Y[2]⟧ shabby; unkempt

scrump·tious (skrump'shəs) *adj.* ⟦< SUMPTUOUS⟧ [Inf.] very pleasing, etc., esp. to the taste

scrunch (skrunch) *vt., vi.* ⟦< CRUNCH⟧ **1** to crunch, crush, etc. **2** to huddle, squeeze, etc. —*n.* a crunching or crumpling sound

scru·ple (skrōō'pəl) *n.* ⟦< L *scrupulus,* small stone⟧ **1** a very small quantity **2** doubt arising from difficulty in deciding what is right —*vt., vi.* **-pled, -pling** to hesitate (at) from doubt

scru'pu·lous (-pyə ləs) *adj.* **1** having or showing scruples; conscientiously honest **2** careful of details; precise —**scru'pu·los'i·ty** (-läs'ət ē), *pl.* **-ties,** *n.* —**scru'pu·lous·ly** *adv.*

scru·ti·nize (skrōōt''n īz') *vt.* **-nized', -niz'ing** to examine closely

scru·ti·ny (skrōōt''n ē) *n., pl.* **-nies** ⟦< L *scrutari,* examine⟧ **1** a close examination or watch **2** a lengthy, searching look

scu·ba (skōō'bə) *n.* ⟦*s*(*elf-*)*c*(*ontained*) *u*(*nderwater*) *b*(*reathing*) *a*(*pparatus*)⟧ a diver's equipment with compressed-air tanks for breathing underwater

scud (skud) *vi.* **scud'ded, scud'ding** ⟦prob. < ON⟧ to move swiftly —*n.* a scudding

scuff (skuf) *vt., vi.* ⟦prob. < ON *skufa,* to shove⟧ **1** to wear or get a rough place on the surface (of) **2** to drag (the feet) —*n.* **1** a worn or rough spot **2** a flat-heeled house slipper with no back upper part

scuf·fle (skuf'əl) *vi.* **-fled, -fling** ⟦< prec.⟧ **1** to struggle or fight in rough confusion **2** to drag the feet —*n.* **1** a confused fight **2** a shuffling of feet

scull (skul) *n.* ⟦ME *skulle*⟧ **1** an oar worked from side to side over the stern of a boat **2** a light rowboat for racing —*vt., vi.* to propel with a scull

scul·ler·y (skul'ər ē) *n., pl.* **-ies** ⟦< L *scutella,* tray⟧ [Now Rare] a room near the kitchen, where pots, pans, etc. are cleaned and stored

scul·lion (skul'yən) *n.* ⟦ult. < L *scopa,* a broom⟧ [Archaic] a servant doing the rough kitchen work

sculpt (skulpt) *vt., vi.* SCULPTURE

sculp·tor (skulp'tər) *n.* an artist who creates works of sculpture

sculp·ture (skulp'chər) *n.* ⟦< L *sculpere,* to carve⟧ **1** the art of shaping stone, clay, wood, metal, etc. into statues, figures, etc. **2** a work or works of sculpture —*vt., vi.* **-tured, -tur·ing** **1** to cut, carve, chisel, etc. (statues, figures, etc.) **2** to make or form like sculpture —**sculp'tur·al** *adj.*

scum (skum) *n.* ⟦< MDu *schum*⟧ **1** a thin layer of impurities on the top of a liquid **2** refuse **3** [Inf.] a despicable person or persons —*vi.* to become covered with scum —**scum'my, -mi·er, -mi·est,** *adj.*

scup·per (skup'ər) *n.* ⟦< OFr *escopir,* to spit⟧ an opening in a ship's side to allow water to run off the deck

scurf (skurf) *n.* ⟦< ON⟧ **1** little, dry scales shed by the skin, as dandruff **2** any scaly coating —**scurf'y, -i·er, -i·est,** *adj.*

scur·ri·lous (skur'ə ləs) *adj.* ⟦< L *scurra,* buffoon⟧ vulgarly abusive —**scur·ril·i·ty** (skə ril'ə tē), *pl.* **-ties,** *n.* —**scur'ri·lous·ly** *adv.*

scur·ry (skur'ē) *vi.* **-ried, -ry·ing** ⟦< ?⟧ to run hastily; scamper —*n.* a scurrying

scur·vy (skur'vē) *adj.* **-vi·er, -vi·est** ⟦< SCURF⟧ low; mean —*n.* a disease resulting from a deficiency of vitamin C, characterized by weakness, anemia, spongy gums, etc. —**scur'vi·ly** *adv.*

scut·tle[1] (skut''l) *n.* ⟦< L *scutella,* tray⟧ a bucket for carrying coal

scut·tle[2] (skut''l) *vi.* **-tled, -tling** ⟦ME *scutlen*⟧ to scamper —*n.* a scamper

scut·tle[3] (skut''l) *n.* ⟦< Sp *escotilla,* an indentation⟧ an opening fitted with a cover, as in the hull or deck of a ship —*vt.* **-tled, -tling** to cut holes through the lower hull of (a ship, etc.) to sink it

scut·tle·butt (skut''l but') *n.* ⟦< *scuttled butt,* lidded cask⟧ [Inf.] rumor or gossip

scuz·zy (skuz'ē) *adj.* **-zi·er, -zi·est** ⟦< ?⟧ [Slang] dirty, shabby, etc.

scythe (sīth) *n.* ⟦OE *sithe*⟧ a tool with a long, single-edged blade on a long, curved handle, for cutting grass, grain, etc.

SD South Dakota

Se *Chem. symbol for* selenium

SE *abbrev.* **1** southeast **2** southeastern

sea (sē) *n.* ⟦OE *sæ*⟧ **1** the ocean **2** any of various smaller bodies of salt water [the Red *Sea*] **3** a large body of fresh water [*Sea* of Galilee] **4** the condition of the surface of the ocean [a calm *sea*] **5** a heavy wave **6** a very great amount [a *sea* of debt] —**at sea** **1** on the open sea **2** uncertain; bewildered

sea anemone a sea polyp with a gelatinous body and petal-like tentacles

sea bass (bas) a saltwater food fish

sea'bed' *n.* the mineral-rich ocean floor

sea'board' *n.* ⟦SEA + BOARD⟧ land bordering on the sea —*adj.* bordering on the sea

sea'coast' *n.* land bordering on the sea

sea cow a large sea mammal with a cigar-shaped body and a blunt snout, as the manatee

sea′far′er (-fer′ər) ***n.*** a sea traveler; esp., a sailor —**sea′far′ing *adj., n.***

sea′floor′ *n.* the ground along the ocean bottom

sea′food′ *n.* food prepared from or consisting of saltwater fish or shellfish

sea′go′ing *adj.* **1** made for use on the open sea **2** SEAFARING

sea gull GULL[1]

sea horse a small semitropical fish with a head somewhat like that of a horse

seal[1] (sēl) ***n.*** ⟦< L *sigillum*⟧ **1** *a)* a design or initial impressed, often into wax, on a letter or document as a mark of authenticity *b)* a stamp or ring for making such an impression **2** a piece of paper, etc. bearing an impressed design recognized as official **3** something that seals or closes tightly **4** anything that guarantees; pledge **5** an ornamental paper stamp —***vt.*** **1** to mark with a seal, as to authenticate or certify **2** to close or shut tight as with a seal **3** to confirm the genuineness of (a promise, etc.) **4** to decide finally

seal[2] (sēl) ***n.*** ⟦OE *seolh*⟧ **1** a sea mammal with a torpedo-shaped body and four flippers **2** the fur of some seals —***vi.*** to hunt seals —**seal′er *n.***

seal·ant (sēl′ənt) ***n.*** a substance, as a wax or plastic, used for sealing

sea legs the ability to walk without loss of balance on board a ship at sea

sea level the mean level of the sea's surface: used in measuring heights

sea lion a seal of the N Pacific

seal′skin′ *n.* **1** the skin of the seal **2** a garment made of this

seam (sēm) ***n.*** ⟦OE⟧ **1** a line formed where two pieces of material are sewn together **2** a line that marks adjoining edges **3** a mark like this, as a scar or wrinkle **4** a layer of ore, coal, etc. —***vt.*** **1** to join together so as to form a seam **2** to mark with a seamlike line, etc. —**seam′less *adj.***

sea·man (sē′mən) ***n.***, *pl.* **-men** (-mən) **1** a sailor **2** *U.S. Navy* an enlisted person ranking below a petty officer —**sea′man·ship′ *n.***

seam·stress (sēm′stris) ***n.*** a woman whose occupation is sewing

seam′y *adj.* **-i·er, -i·est** unpleasant or sordid *[the seamy side of life]*

sé·ance (sā′äns) ***n.*** ⟦Fr < L *sedere*, to sit⟧ a meeting at which a medium seeks to communicate with the spirits of the dead

sea′plane′ *n.* an airplane designed to land on and take off from water

sea′port′ *n.* a port or harbor used by ocean ships

sear (sir) ***vt.*** ⟦< OE *sear*, dry (adj.)⟧ **1** to wither **2** to burn the surface of **3** to brand

search (surch) ***vt.*** ⟦< LL *circare*, go about⟧ **1** to look through in order to find something **2** to examine (a person) for something concealed **3** to examine carefully; probe —***vi.*** to make a search —***n.*** a searching —**in search of** making a search for —**search′er *n.***

search engine software for locating documents, websites, etc. on a specified topic, etc.

search′ing *adj.* **1** examining thoroughly **2** piercing; penetrating

search′light′ *n.* **1** an apparatus on a swivel that projects a strong beam of light **2** such a beam

search warrant a legal document authorizing a police search

sea′scape′ (-skāp′) ***n.*** ⟦SEA + (LAND)SCAPE⟧ **1** a view of the sea **2** a drawing, painting, etc. of such a scene

sea′shell′ *n.* a saltwater mollusk shell

sea′shore′ *n.* land along the sea

sea′sick′ness *n.* nausea, dizziness, etc. caused by the rolling of a ship or boat —**sea′sick′ *adj.***

sea′side′ *n.* SEASHORE

sea·son (sē′zən) ***n.*** ⟦< VL *satio*, season for sowing⟧ **1** any of the four divisions of the year; spring, summer, fall, or winter **2** the time when something takes place, is popular, is permitted, etc. **3** the suitable time —***vt.*** **1** to make (food) more tasty by adding salt, spices, etc. **2** to add zest to **3** to make more usable, as by aging **4** to make used to; accustom —***vi.*** to become seasoned

sea′son·a·ble *adj.* **1** suitable to the season **2** opportune; timely

sea′son·al *adj.* of or depending on the season —**sea′son·al·ly *adv.***

sea′son·ing *n.* anything that adds zest; esp., salt, spices, etc. added to food

season ticket a ticket or set of tickets for a series of concerts or baseball games

seat (sēt) ***n.*** ⟦ON *sæti*⟧ **1** *a)* a place to sit *b)* a thing to sit on; chair, etc. **2** *a)* the buttocks *b)* the part of a chair, garment, etc. that one sits on **3** the right to sit as a member *[a seat on the council]* **4** the center or the chief location *[the seat of government]* —***vt.*** **1** to set in or on a seat **2** to have seats for *[the car seats six]* **3** to put or fix in a place, position, etc. —**be seated** to sit down: also **take a seat**

seat belt straps across the hips, to protect a seated passenger: also **seat′belt′ *n.***

Se·at·tle (sē at′'l) seaport in WC Washington: pop. 516,000

sea urchin a small sea animal with a round body in a shell covered with sharp spines

sea′ward *adj., adv.* toward the sea: also **sea′wards *adv.***

sea′way′ *n.* an inland waterway to the sea for ocean ships

sea′weed′ *n.* a sea plant, esp. an alga

sea′wor′thy (-wur′thē) ***adj.*** fit to travel on the sea: said of a ship

se·ba·ceous (sə bā′shəs) ***adj.*** ⟦< L *sebum*, tallow⟧ of, like, or secreting fat or a fatty substance *[sebaceous glands]*

seb·or·rhe·a or **seb·or·rhoe·a** (seb′ə rē′ə) ***n.*** ⟦ult. < L *sebum*, tallow + Gr *rheein*, flow⟧ an excessive discharge from the sebaceous glands, causing abnormally oily skin

sec *abbrev.* **1** second(s) **2** secondary **3** secretary **4** section(s)

SEC *abbrev.* Securities and Exchange Commission

se·cede (si sēd′) ***vi.* -ced′ed, -ced′ing** ⟦< L *se-*, apart + *cedere*, to go⟧ to withdraw formally from a group, organization, etc.

se·ces·sion (si sesh′ən) ***n.*** **1** a seceding **2** [*often* **S-**] the withdrawal of the Southern states from the federal Union at the start of the Civil War —**se·ces′sion·ist *n.***

se·clude (si klo͞od′) ***vt.* -clud′ed, -clud′ing** ⟦< L *se-*, apart + *claudere*, to close⟧ to shut off from others; isolate

se·clu·sion (si klo͞o′zhən) ***n.*** a secluding or being secluded; retirement; isolation

sec·ond[1] (sek′ənd) ***adj.*** ⟦< L *sequi*, follow⟧ **1** coming next after the first; 2d or 2nd **2** another of the same kind; other [a *second* chance] **3** next below the first in rank, value, etc. —***n.*** **1** one that is second **2** an article of merchandise not of first quality **3** an aide or assistant, as to a duelist or boxer **4** the gear next after first gear **5** [*pl.*] a second helping of food —***vt.*** **1** to assist **2** to indicate formal support of (a motion) before discussion or a vote —***adv.*** in the second place, group, etc.

sec·ond[2] (sek′ənd) ***n.*** ⟦< ML (*pars minuta*) *secunda*, second (small part): from being a further division⟧ **1** the sixtieth part of a minute of time or of angular measure **2** a moment; instant

sec·ond·ar·y (sek′ən der′ē) ***adj.*** **1** second in order, rank, importance, place, etc.; subordinate; minor **2** derived, not primary; derivative —***n.*, *pl.* -ar′ies** **1** a secondary person or thing **2** *Football* the defensive backfield —**sec′ond·ar′i·ly *adv.***

secondary school a school, esp. a high school, coming after elementary school

secondary stress (or **accent**) a weaker stress (′) than the primary stress of a word

sec′ond-class′ *adj.* **1** of the class, rank, etc. next below the highest, best, etc. **2** of a cheaper mail class, as for periodicals **3** inferior, inadequate, etc. or treated as such —***adv.*** by second-class mail or travel accommodations

sec′ond-guess′ *vt.*, *vi.* [Inf.] to use hindsight in criticizing (someone), remaking (a decision), etc.

sec′ond·hand′ *adj.* **1** not from the original source **2** used before; not new **3** of or dealing in used merchandise

second lieutenant *Mil.* a commissioned officer of the lowest rank

sec′ond·ly *adv.* in the second place

second nature an acquired habit, etc. deeply fixed in one's nature

second person the form of a pronoun or verb that refers to the person(s) spoken to

sec′ond-rate′ *adj.* **1** second in quality, rank, etc. **2** inferior

sec′ond-string′ *adj.* [Inf.] *Sports* that is a substitute player at a specified position —**sec′ond-string′er *n.***

second thought a change in thought after reconsidering —**on second thought** after reconsideration

second wind **1** the return of easy breathing after initial exhaustion, as while running **2** any fresh ability to continue

se·cre·cy (sē′krə sē) ***n.*, *pl.* -cies** **1** a being secret **2** a tendency to keep things secret

se·cret (sē′krit) ***adj.*** ⟦< L *se-*, apart + *cernere*, sift⟧ **1** kept from the knowledge of others **2** beyond general understanding; mysterious **3** concealed from sight; hidden —***n.*** a secret fact, cause, process, etc. —**in secret** secretly —**se′cret·ly *adv.***

sec·re·tar·i·at (sek′rə ter′ē ət) ***n.*** a staff headed by a secretary; specif., an administrative staff, as in a government

sec·re·tar·y (sek′rə ter′ē) ***n.*, *pl.* -tar′ies** ⟦< ML *secretarius*, one entrusted with secrets⟧ **1** one who keeps records, handles correspondence, etc. for an organization or person **2** [*often* **S-**] the head of a government department **3** a writing desk —**sec′re·tar′i·al *adj.***

se·crete (si krēt′) ***vt.* -cret′ed, -cret′ing** ⟦see SECRET⟧ **1** to hide; conceal **2** to form and release (a substance) as a gland, etc. does

se·cre·tion (si krē′shən) ***n.*** **1** a secreting **2** a substance secreted by an animal or plant

se·cre·tive (sē′krə tiv) ***adj.*** concealing one's thoughts, etc.; not frank or open —**se′cre·tive·ly *adv.*** —**se′cre·tive·ness *n.***

se·cre·to·ry (si krēt′ər ē) ***adj.*** having the function of secreting, as a gland

Secret Service a division of the U.S. Treasury Department for uncovering counterfeiters, guarding the President, etc.

sect[1] (sekt) ***n.*** ⟦< L *sequi*, follow⟧ **1** a religious denomination **2** any group of people having a common philosophy, set of beliefs, etc.

sect[2] *abbrev.* section

sec·tar·i·an (sek ter′ē ən) ***adj.*** **1** of or devoted to some sect **2** narrow-minded —***n.*** a sectarian person —**sec·tar′i·an·ism′ *n.***

sec·tion (sek′shən) ***n.*** ⟦< L *secare*, to cut⟧ **1** a cutting or cutting apart **2** a part cut off; portion **3** any distinct part, group, district, etc. **4** a drawing, etc. of a thing as it would appear if cut straight through —***vt.*** to divide into sections

sec′tion·al *adj.* **1** of or characteristic of a given section or district **2** made up of sections —**sec′tion·al·ism′ *n.***

sec·tor (sek′tər) ***n.*** ⟦< L *secare*, to cut⟧ **1** part of a circle bounded by any two radii and the included arc **2** any of the districts into which an area is divided for military operations **3** a distinct part of society or of an economy, group, etc.

sec·u·lar (sek′yə lər) ***adj.*** ⟦< LL *saecularis*, worldly⟧ not religious; not connected with a church —**sec′u·lar·ism′ *n.***

sec′u·lar·ize′ (-lə rīz′) ***vt.* -ized′, -iz′ing** to

change from religious to civil use, control, influence, etc. —**sec'u·lar·i·za'tion** ***n.***

se·cure (si kyoor') ***adj.*** ⟦< L *se-*, free from + *cura*, care⟧ **1** free from fear, care, etc. **2** free from danger, risk, etc.; safe **3** firm, stable, etc. [make the knot *secure*] —***vt.*** **-cured'**, **-cur'ing** **1** to make secure; protect **2** to make certain, as with a pledge **3** to make firm, fast, etc. **4** to obtain or bring about —**se·cure'ly** ***adv.***

se·cu·ri·ty (si kyoor'ə tē) ***n.***, *pl.* **-ties** **1** a feeling secure; freedom from fear, doubt, etc. **2** protection; safeguard **3** something given as a pledge of repayment, etc. **4** [*pl.*] bonds, stocks, etc. **5** a private police force

secy or **sec'y** *abbrev.* secretary

se·dan (si dan') ***n.*** ⟦< ? L *sedere*, to sit⟧ an automobile with two or four doors, a permanent rigid top, and a full-sized rear seat

se·date[1] (si dāt') ***adj.*** ⟦< L *sedare*, to settle⟧ calm or composed; esp., serious and unemotional —**se·date'ly** ***adv.***

se·date[2] (si dāt') ***vt.*** **-dat'ed**, **-dat'ing** to dose with a sedative —**se·da'tion** ***n.***

sed·a·tive (sed'ə tiv) ***adj.*** ⟦see SEDATE[1]⟧ tending to soothe or quiet; lessening excitement, irritation, nervousness, etc. —***n.*** a sedative medicine

sed·en·tar·y (sed''n ter'ē) ***adj.*** ⟦< L *sedere*, to sit⟧ marked by much sitting

Se·der (sā'dər) ***n.***, *pl.* **Se·dar·im** (sə där' im) or **Se'ders** ⟦Heb lit., arrangement⟧ [*also* **s-**] *Judaism* the feast of Passover as observed in the home on the eve of the first (by some also of the second) day of the holiday

sedge (sej) ***n.*** ⟦OE *secg*⟧ a coarse, grasslike plant growing in wet ground

sed·i·ment (sed'ə mənt) ***n.*** ⟦< L *sedere*, sit⟧ **1** matter that settles to the bottom of a liquid **2** *Geol.* matter deposited by water or wind

sed'i·men'ta·ry (-men'tər ē) ***adj.*** **1** of or containing sediment **2** formed by the deposit of sediment, as certain rocks

sed'i·men·ta'tion (-men tā'shən, -mən-) ***n.*** the depositing of sediment

se·di·tion (si dish'ən) ***n.*** ⟦< L *sed-*, apart + *itio*, a going⟧ a stirring up of rebellion against the government —**se·di'tion·ist** ***n.*** —**se·di'tious** ***adj.***

se·duce (si do͞os') ***vt.*** **-duced'**, **-duc'ing** ⟦< L *se-*, apart + *ducere*, to lead⟧ **1** to tempt to wrongdoing **2** to entice into having, esp. for the first time, illicit sexual intercourse —**se·duc'er** ***n.*** —**se·duc'tion** (-duk'shən) ***n.*** —**se·duc'tive** ***adj.*** —**se·duc'tress** (-tris) ***fem.n.***

sed·u·lous (sej'oo ləs) ***adj.*** ⟦L *sedulus*⟧ diligent

se·dum (sē'dəm) ***n.*** ⟦< L⟧ a perennial plant found on rocks or walls, with white, yellow, or pink flowers

see[1] (sē) ***vt.*** **saw**, **seen**, **see'ing** ⟦OE *seon*⟧ **1** to get knowledge of through the eyes; look at **2** to understand **3** to learn; find out **4** to experience **5** to make sure [*see* that he goes] **6** to escort [*see* her to her door] **7** to encounter **8** to call on; consult **9** to receive [too ill to see anyone] —***vi.*** **1** to have the power of sight **2** to understand **3** to think [let me *see*, who's next?] —**see off** to accompany (someone) to the place from which that person is to depart, as on a journey —**see through** **1** to perceive the true nature of **2** to finish **3** to help through difficulty —**see to** to attend to

see[2] (sē) ***n.*** ⟦< L *sedes*, a seat⟧ the official seat or jurisdiction of a bishop

seed (sēd) ***n.***, *pl.* **seeds** or **seed** ⟦OE *sæd*⟧ **1** *a*) the part of a plant, containing the embryo, from which a new plant can grow *b*) such seeds collectively **2** the source of anything **3** [Archaic] descendants; posterity **4** sperm or semen **5** a seeded contestant —***vt.*** **1** to plant with seeds **2** to remove the seeds from **3** to distribute (contestants in a tournament) so that the best teams or players are not matched in early rounds —***vi.*** to produce seeds —**go** (or **run**) **to seed** **1** to shed seeds after flowering **2** to deteriorate, weaken, etc. —**seed'less** ***adj.***

seed'ling (-liŋ) ***n.*** **1** a plant grown from a seed **2** a young tree

seed money money to begin a long-term project

seed vessel any dry, hollow fruit containing seeds: also **seed'case'** ***n.***

seed'y ***adj.*** **-i·er**, **-i·est** **1** full of seed **2** gone to seed **3** shabby, rundown, etc. —**seed'i·ness** ***n.***

seek (sēk) ***vt.*** **sought**, **seek'ing** ⟦OE *secan*⟧ **1** to try to find; search for **2** to try to get **3** to aim at **4** to try; attempt [to *seek* to please] —**seek'er** ***n.***

seem (sēm) ***vi.*** ⟦prob. < ON *sœma*, conform to⟧ **1** to appear to be [to *seem* happy] **2** to give the impression: usually with an infinitive [she *seems* to know]

seem'ing ***adj.*** that seems real, true, etc. without necessarily being so; apparent —**seem'ing·ly** ***adv.***

seem'ly ***adj.*** **-li·er**, **-li·est** suitable, proper, etc. —**seem'li·ness** ***n.***

seen (sēn) ***vt.***, ***vi.*** *pp. of* SEE[1]

seep (sēp) ***vi.*** ⟦OE *sipian*, to soak⟧ to leak through small openings; ooze —**seep'age** ***n.***

seer (sir) ***n.*** one who supposedly foretells the future —**seer'ess** ***fem.n.***

seer·suck·er (sir'suk'ər) ***n.*** ⟦< Pers *shir u shakar*, lit., milk and sugar⟧ a crinkled fabric of linen, cotton, etc.

see·saw (sē'sô') ***n.*** ⟦< SAW[1]⟧ **1** a plank balanced at the middle on which children at play, riding the ends, rise and fall alternately **2** any up-and-down or back-and-forth motion or change —***vt.***, ***vi.*** to move up and down or back and forth

seethe (sēth) ***vi.*** **seethed**, **seeth'ing** **1** to boil, surge, or bubble **2** to be violently agitated

seg·ment (seg'mənt; *for v.*, -ment) ***n.*** ⟦< L *secare*, to cut⟧ any of the parts into which something is or can be separated; section —***vt.***, ***vi.*** to divide into segments —**seg'men·ta'tion** ***n.***

seg·re·gate (seg'rə gāt') ***vt.*** **-gat'ed**,

-gat'ing ⟦< L *se-*, apart + *grex*, a flock⟧ to set apart from others; specif., to impose racial segregation on

seg're·ga'tion ***n.*** the policy of compelling racial groups to live apart and use separate schools, facilities, etc. —**seg're·ga'tion·ist** ***n.***

se·gue (seg'wā, sā'gwā) ***vi.*** **-gued, -gue·ing** ⟦It, (it follows) < L sequi, to follow⟧ to continue without break (*to* or *into* the next part) —***n.*** an immediate transition to the next part

sei·gnior (sān'yər, sān yôr') ***n.*** ⟦< OFr *seignor* < L *senior*⟧ a feudal lord

seine (sān) ***n.*** ⟦< Gr *sagēnē*⟧ a large fishing net weighted along the bottom —***vt., vi.*** **seined, sein'ing** to fish with a seine —**sein'er** ***n.***

Seine (sān; *Fr* sen) river in N France, flowing through Paris

seis·mic (sīz'mik) ***adj.*** ⟦< Gr *seismos*, earthquake⟧ of or caused by an earthquake —**seis'mi·cal·ly** ***adv.***

seis'mo·graph' (-mə graf') ***n.*** ⟦see prec. & -GRAPH⟧ an instrument that records the intensity and duration of earthquakes

seis·mol·o·gy (sīz mäl'ə jē, sīs-) ***n.*** ⟦see SEISMIC & -LOGY⟧ the science dealing with earthquakes —**seis'mo·log'ic** (-mə läj'ik) or **seis'mo·log'i·cal** ***adj.*** —**seis·mol'o·gist** ***n.***

seize (sēz) ***vt.*** **seized, seiz'ing** ⟦< ML *sacire*⟧ **1** *a)* to take legal possession of *b)* to capture; arrest **2** to take forcibly and quickly **3** to grasp suddenly **4** to attack or afflict suddenly *[seized* with pain*]* —***vi.*** to stick or jam: said of a machine: often with *up*

sei·zure (sē'zhər) ***n.*** **1** a seizing or being seized **2** a sudden attack, as of epilepsy

sel·dom (sel'dəm) ***adv.*** ⟦OE *seldan*, strange⟧ rarely; infrequently

se·lect (sə lekt') ***adj.*** ⟦< L *se-*, apart + *legere*, to choose⟧ **1** chosen in preference to others **2** choice; excellent **3** exclusive —***vt., vi.*** to choose or pick out —**se·lec'tor** ***n.***

se·lec'tion (-lek'shən) ***n.*** **1** a selecting or being selected **2** that or those selected

se·lec'tive ***adj.*** **1** of selection **2** careful in choosing; discriminating —**se·lec'tiv'i·ty** ***n.***

selective service compulsory military service set by age, fitness, etc.

se·lect'man (-mən) ***n.***, *pl.* **-men** (-mən) one of a board of governing officers in most New England towns

se·le·ni·um (sə lē'nē əm) ***n.*** ⟦ModL < Gr *selēnē*, the moon⟧ a nonmetallic chemical element, used in photoelectric devices

self (self) ***n.***, *pl.* **selves** ⟦OE⟧ **1** the identity, character, or essential qualities of any person or thing **2** one's own person as distinct from all others **3** one's own welfare or interest —***adj.*** of the same kind, color, material, etc. *[*drapes with a *self* lining*]*

self- *prefix* of, by, in, to, or with oneself or itself The following list includes some common compounds formed with *self-* that do not have special meanings:

self-abasement	**self-induced**
self-advancement	**self-indulgence**
self-appointed	**self-indulgent**
self-awareness	**self-inflicted**
self-complacent	**self-knowledge**
self-deception	**self-love**
self-defeating	**self-pity**
self-delusion	**self-proclaimed**
self-destructive	**self-protection**
self-discipline	**self-reproach**
self-employed	**self-sealing**
self-examination	**self-support**
self-help	**self-supporting**
self-imposed	**self-sustaining**

self'-ad·dressed' ***adj.*** addressed to oneself *[*a *self-addressed* envelope*]*

self'-ad·he'sive ***adj.*** made to stick without moistening

self'-as·ser'tion ***n.*** a demanding to be acknowledged or an insisting upon one's rights, etc.

self'-as·sur'ance ***n.*** confidence in oneself —**self'-as·sured'** ***adj.***

self'-cen'tered ***adj.*** **1** egocentric **2** selfish

self'-con'fi·dence ***n.*** confidence in one's own abilities, etc. —**self'-con'fi·dent** ***adj.***

self'-con'scious ***adj.*** unduly conscious of oneself as an object of notice; specif., ill at ease —**self'-con'scious·ly** ***adv.*** —**self'-con'scious·ness** ***n.***

self'-con·tained' ***adj.*** **1** keeping one's affairs to oneself **2** showing self-control **3** complete within itself

self'-con'tra·dic'tion ***n.*** **1** contradiction of oneself or itself **2** any statement containing elements that contradict each other —**self'-con'tra·dic'to·ry** ***adj.***

self'-con·trol' ***n.*** control of one's own emotions, desires, actions, etc. —**self'-con·trolled'** ***adj.***

self'-de·fense' ***n.*** defense of oneself or of one's rights, beliefs, actions, etc.

self'-de·ni'al ***n.*** denial or sacrifice of one's own desires or pleasures

self'-de·scribed' ***adj.*** described so by the person himself or herself *[*a *self-described* expert*]*

self'-de·struct' ***vi.*** **1** to destroy itself automatically **2** to greatly harm oneself as the result of inherent flaws

self'-de·ter'mi·na'tion ***n.*** **1** a making up one's own mind **2** the right of a people to choose its own form of government —**self'-de·ter'mined** ***adj.***

self'-dis·cov'er·y ***n.*** a becoming aware of one's true potential, character, motives, etc.

self'-ed'u·cat'ed ***adj.*** educated by oneself, with little formal schooling

self'-ef·fac'ing ***adj.*** modest; retiring —**self'-ef·face'ment** ***n.***

self'-es·teem' ***n.*** **1** self-respect **2** undue pride in oneself; conceit

self'-ev'i·dent ***adj.*** evident without need of proof

self'-ex·plan'a·to'ry ***adj.*** explaining itself; obvious

self'-ex·pres'sion ***n.*** expression of one's own personality or emotions, esp. in the arts

self'-ful·fill'ing *adj.* **1** bringing about one's personal goals **2** brought about chiefly as an effect of having been expected or predicted

self'-gov'ern·ment *n.* government of a group by its own members —**self'-gov'ern·ing** *adj.*

self'-im'age *n.* one's conception of oneself and of one's own abilities, worth, etc.

self'-im·por'tant *adj.* having an exaggerated opinion of one's own importance —**self'-im·por'tance** *n.*

self'-in'ter·est *n.* **1** one's own interest or advantage **2** an exaggerated regard for this

self'ish *adj.* having or showing too much concern for one's own interests, etc., with little concern for others —**self'ish·ly** *adv.* —**self'ish·ness** *n.*

self'less *adj.* having or showing devotion to others' welfare; unselfish —**self'less·ly** *adv.* —**self'less·ness** *n.*

self'-made' *adj.* **1** made by oneself or itself **2** successful through one's own efforts

self'-por'trait *n.* a portrait of oneself, done by oneself

self'-pos·ses'sion *n.* full control of one's feelings, actions, etc. —**self'-pos·sessed'** *adj.*

self'-pro·pelled' *adj.* propelled by its own motor or power

self'-re·crim'i·na'tion *n.* a blaming of oneself

self'-reg'u·lat'ing *adj.* regulating oneself or itself, so as to function automatically or without outside control

self'-re·li'ance *n.* reliance on one's own judgment, abilities, etc. —**self'-re·li'ant** *adj.*

self'-re·spect' *n.* proper respect for oneself —**self'-re·spect'ing** *adj.*

self'-re·straint' *n.* restraint imposed on oneself by oneself; self-control

self'-right'eous *adj.* regarding oneself as being morally superior to others; smugly virtuous —**self'-right'eous·ly** *adv.* —**self'-right'eous·ness** *n.*

self'-sac'ri·fice' *n.* sacrifice of oneself or one's own interests for the benefit of others —**self'-sac'ri·fic'ing** *adj.*

self'same' *adj.* identical

self'-sat'is·fied' *adj.* feeling or showing an often smug satisfaction with oneself —**self'-sat'is·fac'tion** *n.*

self'-seek'er *n.* one who seeks mainly to further his or her own interests —**self'-seek'ing** *n., adj.*

self'-serve' *adj.* *short for* SELF-SERVICE

self'-serv'ice *adj.* of or being a store, cafeteria, etc. set up so that customers pay a cashier and serve themselves

self'-serv'ing *adj.* serving one's own selfish interests

self'-styled' *adj.* so called only by oneself

self'-suf·fi'cient *adj.* able to get along without help; independent —**self'-suf·fi'cien·cy** *n.*

self'-taught' *adj.* having taught oneself through one's own efforts

self'-willed' *adj.* stubborn; obstinate

self'-wind'ing (-wīn'diŋ) *adj.* wound automatically, as some wristwatches

sell (sel) *vt.* **sold, sell'ing** ⟦OE *sellan*, to give⟧ **1** to exchange (goods, services, etc.) for money, etc. **2** to offer for sale **3** to promote the sale of —*vi.* **1** to engage in selling **2** to be sold (*for* or *at*) **3** to attract buyers —**sell out 1** to get rid of completely by selling **2** [Inf.] to betray —**sell'er** *n.*

sell'out' *n.* [Inf.] **1** a selling out; betrayal **2** a show, game, etc. for which all seats have been sold

selt·zer (selt'sər) *n.* ⟦< *Niederselters*, Germany⟧ **1** [*often* **S-**] natural, effervescent mineral water **2** any carbonated water, often flavored

sel·vage or **sel·vedge** (sel'vij) *n.* ⟦< SELF + EDGE⟧ a specially woven edge that prevents cloth from raveling

selves (selvz) *n. pl. of* SELF

se·man·tics (sə man'tiks) *pl.n.* ⟦< Gr *sēmainein*, to show⟧ the study of the meanings of words —**se·man'tic** *adj.*

sem·a·phore (sem'ə fôr') *n.* ⟦< Gr *sēma*, sign + *pherein*, to bear⟧ any apparatus or system for signaling, as by lights, flags, etc.

sem·blance (sem'bləns) *n.* ⟦< L *similis*, like⟧ **1** outward appearance **2** a likeness or copy

se·men (sē'mən) *n.* ⟦L, seed⟧ the fluid secreted by the male reproductive organs

se·mes·ter (sə mes'tər) *n.* ⟦< L *sex*, six + *mensis*, month⟧ either of the two terms usually making up a school year

sem·i (sem'ī') *n.* [Inf.] a semitrailer and its attached TRACTOR (sense 2)

semi- ⟦L⟧ *prefix* **1** half **2** partly, not fully **3** twice in a (specified period)

sem·i·an·nu·al (sem'ē an'yo͞o əl) *adj.* happening, coming, etc. every half year

sem'i·au'to·mat'ic *adj.* designating an automatic weapon requiring a trigger pull for each round fired —*n.* a semiautomatic firearm

sem·i·cir·cle (sem'i sur'kəl) *n.* a half circle —**sem'i·cir'cu·lar** (-kyə lər) *adj.*

sem'i·co'lon *n.* a mark of punctuation (;) indicating a degree of separation greater than that marked by the comma

sem'i·con·duc'tor *n.* a substance, as germanium, used as in transistors

sem'i·con'scious *adj.* not fully conscious or awake

sem·i·fi·nal (sem'i fīn'əl; *for n.*, sem'i fīn'əl) *adj.* coming just before the final match, as of a tournament —*n.* a semifinal match, etc.

sem·i·month·ly (sem'i munth'lē) *adj.* done, happening, etc. twice a month —*adv.* twice monthly

sem·i·nal (sem'ə nəl) *adj.* ⟦see SEMEN⟧ **1** of seed or semen **2** that is a source **3** of essential importance; specif., *a)* basic; central *b)* crucial

sem·i·nar (sem'ə när') *n.* ⟦see fol.⟧ **1** a group of supervised students doing research **2** a course for such a group

sem·i·nar·y (sem'ə ner'ē) *n., pl.* **-nar'ies**

⟦< L *seminarium*, nursery⟧ a school where ministers, priests, or rabbis are trained —**sem'i·nar'i·an** ***n.***

Sem·i·nole (sem'ə nōl') ***n.***, *pl.* **-noles'** or **-nole'** a member of a North American Indian people of S Florida & Oklahoma

se·mi·ot·ics (sē'mē ät'iks) ***n.*** ⟦< Gr *sēmeion*, sign⟧ *Philos.* a general theory of signs and symbols; esp., the analysis of signs in language

sem·i·pre·cious (sem'i presh'əs) ***adj.*** designating gems, as the garnet, turquoise, etc., of lower value than precious stones

sem'i·pri'vate ***adj.*** of a hospital room with two, three, or sometimes four beds

sem'i·pro·fes'sion·al ***n.*** a person who engages in a sport for pay but not as a regular occupation: also **sem'i·pro'**

sem'i·skilled' ***adj.*** of or doing manual work requiring only limited training

Sem·ite (sem'īt') ***n.*** ⟦< Heb *Shem*, son of Noah⟧ a member of any of the peoples speaking a Semitic language

Se·mit·ic (sə mit'ik) ***n.*** a major group of African and Asian languages, including Hebrew, Arabic, etc. —***adj.*** designating or of the Semites or their languages, etc.

sem·i·tone (sem'i tōn') ***n.*** *Music* the difference in pitch between any two immediately adjacent keys on the piano

sem'i·trail'er ***n.*** a detachable trailer designed to be attached to a coupling at the rear of a TRACTOR (sense 2)

sem'i·trop'i·cal ***adj.*** partly tropical

sem'i·week'ly ***adj.*** done, happening, etc. twice a week —***adv.*** twice weekly

sem·o·li·na (sem'ə lē'nə) ***n.*** ⟦It⟧ coarse flour from hard wheat

Sen *abbrev.* **1** Senate **2** Senator **3** [*also* **s-**] senior

sen·ate (sen'it) ***n.*** ⟦< L *senex*, old⟧ **1** a legislative assembly **2** [**S-**] the upper house of the U.S. Congress or of most of the U.S. state legislatures

sen·a·tor (sen'ət ər) ***n.*** a member of a senate —**sen·a·to·ri·al** (sen'ə tôr'ē əl) ***adj.***

send (send) ***vt.*** **sent**, **send'ing** ⟦OE *sendan*⟧ **1** to cause to go or be transmitted; dispatch; transmit **2** to cause (a person) to go **3** to impel; drive **4** to cause to happen, come, etc. —**send for** **1** to summon **2** to place an order for —**send'er** ***n.***

send'-off' ***n.*** [Inf.] **1** a farewell demonstration for someone starting out on a trip, career, etc. **2** a start given to someone or something

Sen·e·gal (sen'i gôl') country on the W coast of Africa: 76,124 sq. mi.; pop. 6,982,000

se·nile (sē'nīl') ***adj.*** ⟦< L *senex*, old⟧ **1** of or resulting from old age **2** showing the deterioration accompanying old age, esp. confusion, memory loss, etc. —**se·nil·i·ty** (si nil'ə tē) ***n.***

sen·ior (sēn'yər) ***adj.*** ⟦< L *senex*, old⟧ **1** older: written *Sr.* after a father's name if his son's name is the same **2** of higher rank or longer service **3** of or for seniors —***n.*** **1** one who is older, of higher rank, etc. **2** a student in the last year of high school or college **3** *short for* SENIOR CITIZEN

senior citizen an elderly person, esp. one who is retired

senior high school high school, usually grades 10, 11, and 12

sen·ior·i·ty (sēn yôr'ə tē) ***n.***, *pl.* **-ties** **1** a being senior **2** status, priority, etc. achieved by length of service in a given job

sen·na (sen'ə) ***n.*** ⟦< Ar *sanā*, cassia plant⟧ the dried leaflets of a tropical cassia plant used, esp. formerly, as a laxative

se·ñor (se nyôr') ***n.***, *pl.* ***se·ño'res*** (-nyô'res) ⟦Sp⟧ a man; gentleman: as a title, equivalent to *Mr.* or *Sir*

se·ño·ra (se nyô'rä) ***n.*** ⟦Sp⟧ a married woman: as a title, equivalent to *Mrs.* or *Madam*

se·ño·ri·ta (se'nyô rē'tä) ***n.*** ⟦Sp⟧ an unmarried woman or girl: as a title, equivalent to *Miss*

sen·sa·tion (sen sā'shən) ***n.*** ⟦< L *sensus*, sense⟧ **1** the receiving of sense impressions through hearing, seeing, etc. **2** a conscious sense impression **3** a generalized feeling *[a sensation of joy]* **4** *a*) a feeling of general excitement *b*) the cause of such a feeling

sen·sa'tion·al ***adj.*** **1** arousing intense interest **2** intended to shock, thrill, etc. —**sen·sa'tion·al·ism'** ***n.***

sense (sens) ***n.*** ⟦< L *sentire*, to feel⟧ **1** any faculty of receiving impressions through body organs; sight, touch, taste, smell, or hearing **2** *a*) feeling, perception, etc. through the senses *b*) a generalized feeling or awareness **3** an ability to understand some quality *[a sense of humor]* **4** sound judgment **5** [*pl.*] normal ability to reason *[to come to one's senses]* **6** meaning, as of a word —***vt.*** **sensed**, **sens'ing** **1** to perceive **2** to detect as by sensors —**in a sense** to a limited degree —**make sense** to be intelligible or logical

sense'less ***adj.*** **1** unconscious **2** stupid; foolish **3** meaningless

sen·si·bil·i·ty (sen'sə bil'ə tē) ***n.***, *pl.* **-ties** **1** the ability to respond to stimuli **2** [*often pl.*] (sensitive) awareness or responsiveness

sen'si·ble (-bəl) ***adj.*** **1** that can cause physical sensation **2** easily perceived **3** aware **4** having or showing good sense; wise —**sen'si·bly** ***adv.***

sen'si·tive (-tiv) ***adj.*** **1** keenly susceptible to stimuli **2** tender; raw **3** highly perceptive or responsive **4** easily offended; touchy **5** detecting or reacting to slight changes *[sensitive instruments]* **6** of delicate or secret matters —**sen'si·tiv'i·ty** ***n.***

sen'si·tize' (-tīz') ***vt.*** **-tized'**, **-tiz'ing** to make sensitive

sen·sor (sen'sər) ***n.*** a device to detect, measure, or record physical phenomena, as radiation, heat, etc.

sen·so·ry (sen'sər ē) ***adj.*** of the senses or sensation

sen·su·al (sen'shoo əl) ***adj.*** ⟦< L *sensus*, sense⟧ **1** of the body and the senses as distinguished from the intellect or spirit **2** connected or preoccupied with sexual pleasure —**sen′su·al′i·ty** (-al′ə tē) ***n.*** —**sen′su·al·ly** ***adv.***

sen·su·ous (sen′shoo əs) ***adj.*** **1** of, derived from, or perceived by the senses **2** enjoying sensation

sent (sent) ***vt., vi.*** *pt. & pp. of* SEND

sen·tence (sen′təns) ***n.*** ⟦< L *sententia*, opinion⟧ **1** *a*) a decision as of a court; esp., the determination by a court of a punishment *b*) the punishment **2** a word or group of words, usually containing a subject and predicate, that states, asks, etc. —***vt.*** **-tenced, -tenc·ing** to pronounce punishment upon (a convicted person)

sen·ten·tious (sen ten′shəs) ***adj.*** characterized by pompous moralizing

sen·tient (sen′shənt) ***adj.*** ⟦see SENSE⟧ of or capable of perception; conscious

sen·ti·ment (sen′tə mənt) ***n.*** ⟦see SENSE⟧ **1** a complex combination of feelings and opinions **2** an opinion, etc., often, one colored by emotion: *often used in pl.* **3** tender feelings **4** appeal to the emotions in literature, etc. **5** maudlin emotion

sen·ti·men·tal (sen′tə ment′'l) ***adj.*** **1** having or showing tender or delicate feelings **2** maudlin; mawkish **3** of or resulting from sentiment —**sen′ti·men′tal·ism′** ***n.*** —**sen′ti·men′tal·ist** ***n.*** —**sen′ti·men·tal′i·ty** (-tal′ə tē) ***n.*** —**sen′ti·men′tal·ly** ***adv.***

sen′ti·men′tal·ize′ (-īz′) ***vi., vt.*** **-ized′, -iz′ing** to be sentimental or treat in a sentimental way

sen·ti·nel (sent′'n əl) ***n.*** ⟦< L *sentire*, to sense⟧ a guard or sentry

sen·try (sen′trē) ***n.***, *pl.* **-tries** ⟦< ? obs. *centrinell*, var. of prec.⟧ a sentinel; esp., a soldier posted to guard against danger

Seoul (sōl) capital of South Korea: pop. 8,367,000

se·pal (sē′pəl) ***n.*** ⟦< Gr *skepē*, a covering + *petalon*, petal⟧ any of the leaflike parts of the calyx

sep·a·ra·ble (sep′ə rə bəl) ***adj.*** that can be separated —**sep′a·ra·bly** ***adv.***

sep·a·rate (sep′ə rāt′; *for adj.* sep′ə rit, sep′rit) ***vt.*** **-rat′ed, -rat′ing** ⟦< L *se-*, apart + *parare*, arrange⟧ **1** to set apart into sections, groups, etc.; divide **2** to keep apart by being between —***vi.*** **1** to withdraw **2** to part, become disconnected, etc. **3** to go in different directions **4** to stop living together without a divorce —***adj.*** **1** not joined, united, etc.; severed **2** distinct; individual **3** not shared —**sep′a·rate·ly** ***adv.*** —**sep′a·ra′tor** ***n.***

sep·a·ra·tion (sep′ə rā′shən) ***n.*** **1** a separating or being separated **2** the place this occurs; break; division **3** something that separates

sep′a·ra·tism′ (-rə tiz′əm) ***n.*** advocacy of political, religious, or racial separation —**sep′a·ra·tist** ***n.***

se·pi·a (sē′pē ə) ***n., adj.*** ⟦< Gr *sēpia*, cuttlefish secreting inky fluid⟧ (of) a dark reddish-brown color

sep·sis (sep′sis) ***n.*** ⟦see SEPTIC⟧ a poisoning caused by the absorption of pathogenic microorganisms into the blood

Sep·tem·ber (sep tem′bər) ***n.*** ⟦< L *septem*, seven: seventh month in Roman calendar⟧ the ninth month of the year, having 30 days: abbrev. **Sept.**

sep·tet or **sep·tette** (sep tet′) ***n.*** ⟦< L *septem*, seven⟧ *Music* **1** a composition for seven voices or instruments **2** the seven performers of this

sep·tic (sep′tik) ***adj.*** ⟦< Gr *sēpein*, to make putrid⟧ causing, or resulting from, sepsis or putrefaction

sep·ti·ce·mi·a (sep′tə sē′mē ə) ***n.*** ⟦see prec.⟧ a disease caused by infectious microorganisms in the blood

septic tank an underground tank in which waste matter is putrefied and decomposed by bacteria

sep·tu·a·ge·nar·i·an (sep′too ə jə ner′ē ən) ***n.*** ⟦< L *septuaginta*, seventy⟧ a person between the ages of 70 and 80

Sep·tu·a·gint (sep′too ə jint′) ***n.*** ⟦< L *septuaginta*, seventy: in tradition, done in 70 days⟧ a translation into Greek of the Hebrew Scriptures

sep·tum (sep′təm) ***n.***, *pl.* **-tums** or **-ta** (-tə) ⟦< L *saepire*, enclose, fence⟧ *Biol.* a wall or part that separates, as in the nose or in a fruit

sep·ul·cher (sep′əl kər) ***n.*** ⟦< L *sepelire*, bury⟧ a vault for burial; tomb

se·pul·chral (sə pul′krəl) ***adj.*** **1** of sepulchers, burial, etc. **2** suggestive of the grave or burial; gloomy **3** deep and melancholy: said of sound

seq. *abbrev.* ⟦L *sequentes*⟧ the following

se·quel (sē′kwəl) ***n.*** ⟦< L *sequi*, follow⟧ **1** something that follows; continuation **2** a result; consequence **3** any literary work, film, etc. continuing a story begun in an earlier one

se·quence (sē′kwəns) ***n.*** ⟦< L *sequi*, follow⟧ **1** *a*) the coming of one thing after another; succession *b*) the order in which this occurs **2** a series **3** a resulting event **4** *Film* a succession of scenes forming a single episode

se·quen·tial (si kwen′shəl) ***adj.*** of or occurring in a sequence —**se·quen′tial·ly** ***adv.***

se·ques·ter (si kwes′tər) ***vt.*** ⟦< L *sequester*, trustee⟧ **1** to set off or apart **2** to withdraw; isolate —**se·ques·tra·tion** (sē′kwə strā′shən) ***n.***

se·quin (sē′kwin) ***n.*** ⟦Fr; ult. < Ar *sikka*, a stamp, die⟧ a spangle, esp. one of many sewn on fabric for decoration —**se′quined** or **se′quinned** ***adj.***

se·quoi·a (si kwoi′ə) ***n.*** ⟦after *Sequoyah* (1760?-1843), Indian inventor of Cherokee writing system⟧ REDWOOD (sense 1)

se·ra (sir′ə) ***n.*** *alt. pl. of* SERUM

se·ra·glio (si ral′yō) ***n.***, *pl.* **-glios** ⟦< L *sera*, a lock⟧ HAREM (sense 1)

se·ra·pe (sə rä′pē) ***n.*** ⟦MexSp⟧ a bright-colored wool blanket used as a garment by men in Mexico, etc.

ser·aph (ser′əf) ***n.***, *pl.* **-aphs** or **-a·phim′** (-ə fim′) ⟦< Heb *serafim*, pl.⟧ *Theol.* a heavenly being, or any of the highest order of angels —**se·raph·ic** (sə raf′ik) ***adj.*** —**se·raph′i·cal·ly** ***adv.***

Serb (surb) ***n.*** a person born or living in Serbia; esp., a member of a Slavic people of Serbia and adjacent areas —***adj.*** SERBIAN

Ser·bi·a (sur'bē ə) the major constituent republic of Yugoslavia —**Ser'bi·an** ***adj.***, ***n.***

Ser·bo-Cro·a·tian (sur'bō krō ā'shən) ***n.*** the major Slavic language of Yugoslavia, Bosnia and Herzegovina, and Croatia

ser·e·nade (ser'ə nād') ***n.*** ⟦ult. < L *serenus*, clear⟧ **1** music played or sung at night, esp. by a lover **2** a piece of music like this —***vt.***, ***vi.*** **-nad'ed**, **-nad'ing** to play or sing a serenade (to)

ser·en·dip·i·ty (ser'ən dip'ə tē) ***n.*** ⟦after Pers tale *The Three Princes of Serendip* (Sri Lanka)⟧ a seeming gift for finding good things accidentally —**ser'en·dip'i·tous** ***adj.***

se·rene (sə rēn') ***adj.*** ⟦L *serenus*⟧ **1** clear; unclouded **2** undisturbed; calm —**se·rene'ly** ***adv.*** —**se·ren'i·ty** (-ren'ə tē) or **se·rene'ness** ***n.***

serf (surf) ***n.*** ⟦< L *servus*, a slave⟧ a person in feudal servitude, bound to a master's land and transferred with it to a new owner —**serf'dom** ***n.***

serge (surj) ***n.*** ⟦< L *sericus*, silken⟧ a strong twilled fabric

ser·geant (sär'jənt) ***n.*** ⟦< L *servire*, serve⟧ **1** a noncommissioned officer ranking above a corporal **2** a police officer ranking next below a captain or a lieutenant

ser'geant-at-arms' ***n.***, *pl.* **ser'geants-at-arms'** an officer appointed to keep order, as in a court

sergeant major *pl.* **sergeants major** the highest ranking noncommissioned officer

se·ri·al (sir'ē əl) ***adj.*** ⟦< L *series*, a row, order⟧ appearing in a series of continuous parts at regular intervals —***n.*** a story, etc. presented in serial form —**se'ri·al·i·za'tion** ***n.*** —**se'ri·al·ize'**, **-ized'**, **-iz'ing**, ***vt.***

serial number one of a series of numbers given for identification

se·ries (sir'ēz) ***n.***, *pl.* **-ries** ⟦L < *serere*, join together⟧ a number of similar things or persons arranged in a row or coming one after another

se·ri·ous (sir'ē əs) ***adj.*** ⟦< L *serius*⟧ **1** earnest, grave, sober, etc. **2** not joking; sincere **3** requiring careful consideration **4** weighty **5** dangerous —**se'ri·ous·ly** ***adv.*** —**se'ri·ous·ness** ***n.***

ser·mon (sur'mən) ***n.*** ⟦< L *sermo*, a discourse⟧ **1** a speech on religion or morals, esp. by a member of the clergy **2** any serious talk on behavior, duty, etc., esp. a tedious one —**ser'mon·ize'**, **-ized'**, **-iz'ing**, ***vi.***

se·rous (sir'əs) ***adj.*** **1** of or containing serum **2** thin and watery

ser·pent (sur'pənt) ***n.*** ⟦< L *serpere*, to creep⟧ a snake

ser'pen·tine' (-pən tēn', -tīn') ***adj.*** of or like a serpent; esp., *a*) cunning; treacherous *b*) coiled; winding

ser·rate (ser'āt') ***adj.*** ⟦< L *serra*, a saw⟧ having sawlike notches along the edge: said of some leaves: also **ser'rat'ed** —**ser·ra'tion** ***n.***

ser·ried (ser'ēd) ***adj.*** ⟦< LL *serare*, to lock⟧ placed close together

se·rum (sir'əm) ***n.***, *pl.* **-rums** or **-ra** (-ə) ⟦L, whey⟧ **1** a clear, watery animal fluid, as the yellowish fluid (**blood serum**) separating from a blood clot after coagulation **2** blood serum used as an antitoxin, taken from an animal inoculated for a specific disease

serv·ant (sur'vənt) ***n.*** ⟦ult. < L *servire*, serve⟧ **1** a person employed by another, esp. to do household duties **2** a person devoted to another or to a cause, creed, etc.

serve (surv) ***vt.*** **served**, **serv'ing** ⟦< L *servus*, slave⟧ **1** to work for as a servant **2** to do services for; aid; help **3** to do military or naval service for **4** to spend (a term of imprisonment, etc.) *[to serve ten years]* **5** to provide (customers, etc.) with goods or services **6** to set food, etc. before (a person) **7** to meet the needs of **8** to be used by *[this hospital serves the whole city]* **9** to function for *[if memory serves me well]* **10** to deliver (a summons, etc.) to (someone) **11** to hit (a tennis ball, etc.) in order to start play —***vi.*** **1** to work as a servant **2** to do service *[to serve in the navy]* **3** to carry out the duties of an office **4** to be of service **5** to meet needs **6** to provide guests with food or drink **7** to be favorable: said of weather, etc. —***n.*** a serving of the ball in tennis, etc. —**serve someone right** to be what someone deserves, for doing something wrong

serv'er ***n.*** **1** one who serves **2** a thing for serving, as a tray **3** *Comput.* the central computer in a network, on which shared files, etc. are stored

serv·ice (sur'vis) ***n.*** ⟦< L *servus*, slave⟧ **1** the occupation of a servant **2** *a*) public employment *[diplomatic service]* *b*) a branch of this; specif., the armed forces **3** work done for others *[repair service]* **4** any religious ceremony **5** *a*) benefit; advantage *b*) [*pl.*] friendly help; also, professional aid **6** the act or manner of serving food **7** a set of articles used in serving *[a tea service]* **8** a system of providing people with some utility, as water or gas **9** the act or manner of serving the ball in tennis, etc. —***vt.*** **-iced**, **-ic·ing** **1** to furnish with a service **2** to make fit for service, as by repairing —**at someone's service** **1** ready to serve someone **2** ready for someone's use —**in service** functioning —**of service** helpful

serv'ice·a·ble ***adj.*** **1** that can be of service; useful **2** that will give good service; durable

serv'ice·man' (-man', -mən) ***n.***, *pl.* **-men'** (-men', -mən) **1** a member of the armed forces **2** a person whose work is repairing something *[a TV serviceman]*: also **service man**

service mark a word, etc. used like a trademark by a supplier of a service

service station a place selling gasoline, oil, etc., for motor vehicles

ser·vile (sur'vəl, -vīl') ***adj.*** ⟦< L *servus*,

slave] 1 of slaves 2 like that of slaves or servants 3 humbly submissive —**ser·vil·i·ty** (sər vil′ə tē) ***n.***

ser·vi·tude (sur′və to͞od′) ***n.*** [see SERF] 1 slavery or bondage 2 work imposed to punish a crime

ser·vo (sur′vō) ***n.***, *pl.* **-vos** *short for:* 1 SERVOMECHANISM 2 SERVOMOTOR

ser′vo·mech′a·nism ***n.*** an automatic control system of low power, used to exercise remote but accurate mechanical control

ser′vo·mo′tor ***n.*** a device, as an electric motor, for changing a small force into a large force, as in a servomechanism

ses·a·me (ses′ə mē′) ***n.*** [of Semitic origin] 1 a plant whose edible seeds yield an oil 2 its seeds

ses·qui·cen·ten·ni·al (ses′kwi sen ten′ē əl) ***adj.*** [< L *sesqui-*, more by a half + CENTENNIAL] of a period of 150 years —***n.*** a 150th anniversary

ses·sion (sesh′ən) ***n.*** [< L *sedere*, sit] 1 *a*) the meeting of a court, legislature, etc. *b*) a series of such meetings *c*) the period of these 2 a school term 3 a period of activity of any kind

set (set) ***vt.*** **set, set′ting** [OE *settan*] 1 to cause to sit; seat 2 to put in a specified place, condition, etc. [to *set* books on a shelf, *set* slaves free] 3 to put in a proper condition; fix (a trap for animals), adjust (a clock or dial), arrange (a table for a meal), fix (hair) in a desired style, etc., put (a broken bone, etc.) into normal position, etc. 4 to make settled, rigid, or fixed [pectin *sets* jelly] 5 to mount (gems) 6 to direct; point 7 to appoint; establish; fix (boundaries, the time for an event, a rule, a quota, etc.) 8 to furnish (an example) for others 9 to fit (words *to* music or music *to* words) 10 to arrange (type) for printing —***vi.*** 1 to sit on eggs: said of a fowl 2 to become firm, hard, or fixed [this cement *sets* quickly] 3 to begin to move (*out, forth, off*, etc.) 4 to sink below the horizon [the sun *sets*] —***adj.*** 1 fixed; established [a *set* time] 2 intentional 3 fixed; rigid; firm 4 obstinate 5 ready [get *set*] —***n.*** 1 a setting or being set 2 the way or position in which a thing is set [the *set* of his jaw] 3 direction; tendency 4 the scenery for a play, etc. 5 a group of persons or things classed or belonging together 6 assembled equipment for radio or TV reception, etc. 7 *Tennis* a group of six or more games won by a margin of at least two —**set about** (or **in** or **to**) to begin —**set down** 1 to put in writing 2 to establish (rules, etc.) —**set forth** 1 to publish 2 to state —**set off** 1 to make prominent or enhance by contrast 2 to make explode —**set on** (or **upon**) to attack —**set up** 1 to erect 2 to establish; found

set′back′ ***n.*** a reversal in progress

set′screw′ ***n.*** a screw used in regulating the tension of a spring, etc.

set·tee (se tē′) ***n.*** 1 a seat or bench with a back 2 a small sofa

set′ter ***n.*** a long-haired dog trained to hunt

set′ting ***n.*** 1 the act of one that sets 2 the position of a dial, etc. that has been set 3 a mounting, as of a gem 4 the time, place, etc., as of a story 5 actual physical surroundings

set·tle (set′'l) ***vt.*** **-tled, -tling** [< OE *setl*, a seat] 1 to put in order; arrange [to *settle* one's affairs] 2 to set in place firmly or comfortably 3 to colonize 4 to cause to sink and become more compact 5 to free (the nerves, etc.) from disturbance 6 to decide (doubt) 7 to end (a dispute) 8 to pay (a debt, etc.) —***vi.*** 1 to stop moving and stay in one place 2 to descend, as fog does over a landscape, or gloom over a person 3 to become localized: said as of pain 4 to take up permanent residence 5 to sink [the house *settled*] 6 to become more dense by sinking, as sediment does 7 to become more stable 8 to reach an agreement or decision (*with* or *on*) —**set′tler** ***n.***

set′tle·ment ***n.*** 1 a settling or being settled 2 a new colony 3 a village 4 an agreement

set′-to′ ***n.***, *pl.* **-tos′** [Inf.] 1 a fight 2 an argument

set′up′ ***n.*** 1 *a*) the plan, makeup, or arrangement of equipment, an organization, etc. *b*) the details of a situation, plan, etc. 2 [Inf.] a contest, etc. arranged to result in an easy victory

sev·en (sev′ən) ***adj., n.*** [OE *seofon*] one more than six; 7; VII —**sev′enth** ***adj., n.***

sev′en·teen′ (-tēn′) ***adj., n.*** seven more than ten; 17; XVII —**sev′en·teenth′** (-tēnth′) ***adj., n.***

seventeen-year locust a cicada which lives underground for 13-17 years before emerging as an adult

seventh heaven perfect happiness

sev·en·ty (sev′ən tē) ***adj., n.***, *pl.* **-ties** seven times ten; 70; LXX —**the seventies** the years, from 70 through 79, as of a century —**sev′en·ti·eth** (-ith) ***adj., n.***

sev·er (sev′ər) ***vt., vi.*** [ult. < L *separare*] to separate, divide, or divide off —**sev′er·ance** ***n.***

sev·er·al (sev′ər əl) ***adj.*** [ult. < L *separ*] 1 separate; distinct 2 different; respective 3 more than two but not many; few —***pl.n.*** a small number (*of*) —***pron.*** [*with pl. v.*] a few —**sev′er·al·ly** ***adv.***

se·vere (sə vir′) ***adj.*** **-ver′er, -ver′est** [< L *severus*] 1 harsh or strict, as in treatment 2 serious or grave, as in expression 3 rigidly accurate or demanding 4 extremely plain [a dress with *severe* lines] 5 intense [*severe* pain] 6 rigorous; trying —**se·vere′ly** ***adv.*** —**se·vere′ness** or **se·ver′i·ty** (-ver′ə tē) ***n.***

Se·ville (sə vil′) city in SW Spain: pop. 720,000

Sè·vres (sev′rə; *Fr* se′vr′) ***n.*** [after *Sèvres*, SW suburb of Paris, where made] a type of fine French porcelain

sew (sō) ***vt., vi.*** **sewed, sewn** (sōn) or **sewed, sew′ing** [OE *siwian*] 1 to fasten with stitches made with needle and thread 2 to make, mend, etc. by sewing —**sew up** 1 [Inf.] to get full control of 2 to make sure of success in —**sew′er** ***n.***

sew·age (so͞o′ij) ***n.*** the waste matter carried off by sewers or drains

sew·er (so͞o′ər) ***n.*** ⟦ult. < L *ex*, out + *aqua*, water⟧ a pipe or drain, usually underground, used to carry off water and waste matter

sew′er·age ***n.*** **1** a system of sewers **2** SEWAGE

sew′ing ***n.*** **1** the act of one who sews **2** something to be sewn

sewing machine a machine with a mechanically driven needle used for sewing

sex (seks) ***n.*** ⟦< L *sexus*⟧ **1** either of two divisions, male or female, into which persons, animals, or plants are divided **2** the character of being male or female **3** the attraction between the sexes **4** sexual intercourse —***adj.*** SEXUAL

sex- ⟦< L *sex*, six⟧ *combining form* six

sex·a·ge·nar·i·an (sek′sə ji ner′ē ən) ***n.*** ⟦< L⟧ a person between the ages of 60 and 70

sex appeal the physical charm that attracts members of the opposite sex

sex chromosome a sex-determining chromosome in the germ cells: eggs carry an X chromosome and spermatozoa either an X or a Y chromosome, with a female resulting from an XX pairing and a male from an XY

sex′ism′ ***n.*** discrimination against people, esp. women, on the basis of sex —**sex′ist** ***adj.***, ***n.***

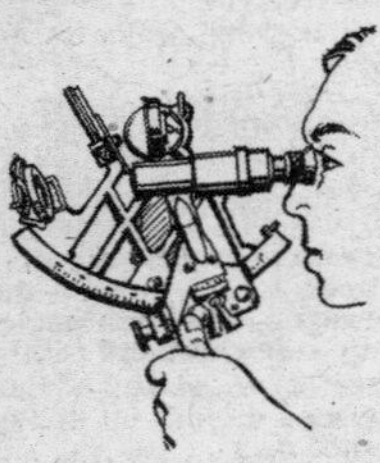

SEXTANT

sex·tant (seks′tənt) ***n.*** ⟦< L *sextans*, a sixth part (of a circle)⟧ an instrument for measuring the angular distance of the sun, a star, etc. from the horizon, as to determine position at sea

sex·tet or **sex·tette** (seks tet′) ***n.*** ⟦ult. < L *sex*, six⟧ **1** a group of six **2** *Music* a composition for six voices or instruments, or its six performers

sex·ton (seks′tən) ***n.*** ⟦ult. < L *sacer*, sacred⟧ a church official who maintains church property

sex·u·al (sek′sho͞o əl) ***adj.*** of or involving sex, the sexes, the sex organs, etc. —**sex′u·al·ly** ***adv.*** —**sex′u·al′i·ty** (-al′ə tē) ***n.***

sexual harassment inappropriate, unwelcome behavior by an employer or colleague that is sexual in nature

sexual intercourse a joining of the sexual organs of a male and a female human being

sex′y ***adj.*** **-i·er, -i·est** **1** [Inf.] exciting or intended to excite sexual desire **2** [Slang] exciting, glamorous, etc. —**sex′i·ly** ***adv.*** —**sex′i·ness** ***n.***

Sey·chelles (sā shel′, -shelz′) country on a group of islands in the Indian Ocean, northeast of Madagascar: 175 sq. mi.; pop. 67,000

sf or **SF** *abbrev.* science fiction

Sgt *abbrev.* Sergeant

sh (sh) ***interj.*** used to ask for silence

shab·by (shab′ē) ***adj.*** **-bi·er, -bi·est** ⟦OE *sceabb*, scab⟧ **1** rundown; dilapidated **2** *a*) ragged; worn *b*) wearing worn clothing **3** mean; shameful *[shabby treatment]* —**shab′bi·ly** ***adv.*** —**shab′bi·ness** ***n.***

shack (shak) ***n.*** ⟦< ?⟧ a small, crudely built house or cabin; shanty

shack·le (shak′əl) ***n.*** ⟦OE *sceacel*⟧ **1** a metal fastening, usually in pairs, for the wrist or ankle of a prisoner; fetter **2** anything that restrains freedom, as of expression **3** a device for fastening or coupling —***vt.*** **-led, -ling** **1** to put shackles on **2** to restrain in freedom of expression or action

shad (shad) ***n.***, *pl.* **shad** or **shads** ⟦OE *sceadd*⟧ an American coastal food fish

shade (shād) ***n.*** ⟦OE *sceadu*⟧ **1** comparative darkness caused by an object cutting off rays of light **2** an area with less light than its surroundings **3** degree of darkness of a color *[shades of blue]* **4** *a*) a small difference *[shades of opinion]* *b*) a slight amount or degree **5** [Chiefly Literary] a ghost **6** a device used to screen from light *[a window shade]* **7** [*pl.*] [Slang] sunglasses —***vt.*** **shad′ed, shad′ing** **1** to screen from light **2** to darken; dim **3** to represent shade in (a painting, etc.) —***vi.*** to change slightly or by degrees —**shades of** *exclamation used to refer to* a reminder of the past

shad′ing ***n.*** **1** a shielding against light **2** shade in a picture **3** a small variation

shad·ow (shad′ō) ***n.*** ⟦< OE *sceadu*, shade⟧ **1** (a) shade cast by a body intercepting light rays **2** gloom or that which causes gloom **3** a shaded area in a picture **4** a ghost **5** a remnant; trace —***vt.*** **1** to throw a shadow upon **2** to follow closely, esp. in secret —**shad′ow·y** ***adj.***

shad′ow·box′ ***vi.*** *Boxing* to spar with an imaginary opponent in training

shad·y (shā′dē) ***adj.*** **-i·er, -i·est** **1** giving shade **2** shaded; full of shade **3** [Inf.] of questionable character —**on the shady side of** beyond (a given age) —**shad′i·ness** ***n.***

shaft (shaft) ***n.*** ⟦OE *sceaft*⟧ **1** an arrow or spear, or its stem **2** anything hurled like a missile *[shafts of wit]* **3** a long, slender part or object, as a pillar, a bar transmitting motion to a mechanical part, or either of the poles between which an animal is harnessed to a vehicle **4** a long, narrow passage sunk into the earth **5** a vertical opening passing through a building, as for an elevator —***vt.*** [Slang] to cheat, trick, exploit, etc.

shag[1] (shag) ***n.*** ⟦< OE *sceacga*, rough hair⟧ a rough, heavy nap, as on some cloth

shag[2] (shag) ***vt.*** **shagged, shag′ging** to chase after and retrieve (baseballs hit in batting practice)

shag′gy ***adj.*** **-gi·er, -gi·est 1** covered with long, coarse hair or wool **2** unkempt, straggly, etc. **3** having a rough nap

shah (shä) ***n.*** ⟦Pers *šāh*⟧ the title of any of the former rulers of Iran

shake (shāk) ***vt., vi.*** **shook, shak′en, shak′ing** ⟦OE *sceacan*⟧ **1** to move quickly up and down, back and forth, etc. **2** to bring, force, mix, etc. by brisk movements **3** to tremble or cause to tremble **4** *a)* to become or cause to become unsteady *b)* to unnerve or become unnerved **5** to clasp (another's hand), as in greeting —***n.*** **1** an act of shaking **2** a wood shingle **3** *short for* MILKSHAKE **4** [*pl.*] [Inf.] a convulsive trembling: usually with *the* —**no great shakes** [Inf.] not outstanding —**shake down 1** to cause to fall by shaking **2** [Slang] to extort money from —**shake off** to get rid of

shake′down′ ***n.*** **1** [Slang] an extortion of money, as by blackmail **2** a thorough search —***adj.*** for testing new equipment, etc. *[a shakedown cruise]*

shake′out′ ***n.*** a drop in economic activity that eliminates unprofitable businesses, etc.

shak′er ***n.*** **1** one that shakes **2** a device used in shaking **3** [**S-**] a member of a religious sect that lived in celibate communities in the U.S.

Shake·speare (shāk′spir), **William** 1564-1616; Eng. poet & dramatist —**Shake·spear′e·an** or **Shake·spear′i·an** ***adj., n.***

shake′-up′ ***n.*** a shaking up; specif., an extensive reorganization

shak′y ***adj.*** **-i·er, -i·est 1** not firm; weak or unsteady **2** *a)* trembling *b)* nervous **3** not reliable; questionable —**shak′i·ness** ***n.***

shale (shāl) ***n.*** ⟦< OE *scealu*, shell⟧ a rock formed of hard clay: it splits easily into thin layers

shale oil oil distilled from a hard shale containing veins of a greasy organic solid

shall (shal) ***v.aux.*** *pt.* **should** ⟦OE *sceal*⟧ **1** used in the first person to indicate simple future time **2** used in the second or third person, esp. in formal speech or writing, to express determination, compulsion, obligation, or necessity See usage note at WILL[2]

shal·lot (shə lät′, shal′ət) ***n.*** ⟦< OFr *eschaloigne*, scallion⟧ **1** a small onion whose clustered bulbs are used for flavoring **2** GREEN ONION

shal·low (shal′ō) ***adj.*** ⟦ME *shalow*⟧ **1** not deep **2** lacking depth of character, intellect, etc. —***n.*** [*usually pl., often with sing. v.*] SHOAL[2] (sense 1)

shalt (shalt) ***v.aux.*** *archaic 2d pers. sing., pres. indic., of* SHALL: used with *thou*

sham (sham) ***n.*** ⟦< ? shame⟧ something false or fake; person or thing that is a fraud —***adj.*** false or fake —***vt., vi.*** **shammed, sham′ming** to pretend; feign

sham·ble (sham′bəl) ***vi.*** **-bled, -bling** ⟦< obs. use in *shamble legs*, bench legs⟧ to walk clumsily; shuffle —***n.*** a shambling walk

sham′bles ***n.*** ⟦ME *schamel*, butcher's bench; ult. < L⟧ **1** a slaughterhouse **2** a scene of great slaughter, destruction, or disorder

shame (shām) ***n.*** ⟦OE *scamu*⟧ **1** a painful feeling of guilt for improper behavior, etc. **2** dishonor or disgrace **3** something regrettable or outrageous —***vt.*** **shamed, sham′ing 1** to cause to feel shame **2** to dishonor or disgrace **3** to force by a sense of shame —**put to shame 1** to cause to feel shame **2** to surpass; outdo —**shame′ful** ***adj.*** —**shame′ful·ly** ***adv.*** —**shame′ful·ness** ***n.***

shame′faced′ ***adj.*** showing shame; ashamed

shame′less ***adj.*** having or showing no shame, modesty, or decency; brazen —**shame′less·ly** ***adv.***

sham·poo (sham po͞o′) ***vt.*** **-pooed′, -poo′ing** ⟦Hindi *chāmpnā*, to press⟧ **1** to wash (the hair) **2** to wash (a rug, sofa, etc.) —***n.*** **1** a shampooing **2** a liquid soap, etc. used for this

sham·rock (sham′räk′) ***n.*** ⟦Ir *seamar*, clover⟧ a plant, esp. a clover, with leaflets in groups of three: the emblem of Ireland

shang·hai (shaŋ′hī′) ***vt.*** ⟦< such kidnapping for crews on the China run⟧ to kidnap, usually by drugging, for service aboard ship

Shang·hai (shaŋ′hī′) seaport in E China: pop. 6,293,000

shank (shaŋk) ***n.*** ⟦OE *scanca*⟧ **1** the part of the leg between the knee and ankle in humans, or a corresponding part in animals **2** the whole leg **3** the part between the handle and the working part of a tool, etc. —**shank of the evening** early evening

shan't (shant) *contr.* shall not

Shan·tung (shan′tuŋ′) ***n.*** ⟦< Chin province⟧ [*sometimes* **s-**] a silk or silky fabric with an uneven surface

shan·ty (shan′tē) ***n.***, *pl.* **-ties** ⟦< CdnFr *chantier*, workshop⟧ a small, shabby dwelling; shack; hut

shape (shāp) ***n.*** ⟦< OE (*ge*)*sceap*, a form⟧ **1** that quality of a thing which depends on the relative position of all the points on its surface; physical form **2** the contour of the body **3** definite or regular form *[to begin to take shape]* **4** good physical condition —***vt.*** **shaped, shap′ing 1** to give definite shape to **2** to arrange, express, etc. (a plan, etc.) in definite form **3** to adapt *[shaped to our needs]* —**shape up** [Inf.] **1** to develop to a definite form, satisfactorily, etc. **2** to behave as required —**take shape** to begin to have definite form —**shape′less** ***adj.*** —**shape′less·ness** ***n.***

shape′ly ***adj.*** **-li·er, -li·est** having a pleasing figure: used esp. of a woman

shard (shärd) ***n.*** ⟦OE *sceard*⟧ a broken piece, esp. of pottery

share[1] (sher) ***n.*** ⟦OE *scearu*⟧ **1** a portion that belongs to an individual **2** any of the equal parts of capital stock of a corporation —*vt.* **shared, shar′ing** **1** to distribute in shares **2** to receive, use, etc. in common with others —*vi.* to have a share (*in*)

share[2] (sher) *n.* ⟦OE *scear*⟧ a plowshare

share′crop′ *vi., vt.* **-cropped′, -crop′ping** to work (land) for a share of the crop, esp. as a tenant farmer —**share′crop′per** *n.*

share′hold′er *n.* a person who owns shares of stock in a corporation

shark[1] (shärk) *n.* ⟦prob. < Ger *schurke,* scoundrel⟧ **1** a swindler **2** [Slang] an expert in an activity

WHITE SHARK

shark[2] (shärk) *n.* ⟦< ?⟧ a large, predatory sea fish with a tough, gray skin

shark′skin′ *n.* a smooth, silky cloth of cotton, wool, rayon, etc.

sharp (shärp) *adj.* ⟦OE *scearp*⟧ **1** having a fine edge or point for cutting or piercing **2** having a point or edge; not rounded **3** not gradual; abrupt **4** clearly defined; distinct *[a sharp contrast]* **5** quick in perception; clever **6** attentive; vigilant **7** crafty; underhanded **8** harsh; severe *[a sharp temper]* **9** violent *[a sharp attack]* **10** brisk; active **11** intense *[a sharp pain]* **12** pungent **13** nippy *[a sharp wind]* **14** [Slang] stylishly dressed **15** *Music* above the true pitch —*adv.* **1** in a sharp manner; specif., *a*) abruptly or briskly *b*) attentively or alertly *c*) *Music* above the true pitch **2** precisely *[one o'clock sharp]* —*n.* **1** [Inf.] an expert or adept **2** *Music a*) a tone one half step above another *b*) the symbol (♯) for such a note —*vt., vi. Music* to make, sing, or play sharp —**sharp′ly** *adv.* —**sharp′ness** *n.*

sharp′en *vt., vi.* to make or become sharp or sharper —**sharp′en·er** *n.*

sharp′er *n.* a swindler or cheat

sharp′-eyed′ *adj.* having keen sight or perception: also **sharp′-sight′ed** *adj.*

sharp·ie (shär′pē) *n.* [Inf.] a shrewd, cunning person, esp. a sharper

sharp′shoot′er *n.* a good marksman

sharp′-tongued′ *adj.* using sharp or harshly critical language

sharp′-wit′ted (-wit′id) *adj.* thinking quickly and effectively

shat·ter (shat′ər) *vt.* ⟦ME *schateren,* scatter⟧ **1** to break or burst into pieces suddenly, as with a blow **2** to damage or be damaged severely

shat′ter·proof′ *adj.* that will resist shattering

shave (shāv) *vt.* **shaved, shaved** or **shav′en, shav′ing** ⟦OE *sceafan*⟧ **1** to cut away thin slices or sections from **2** *a*) to cut off (hair) at the surface of the skin *b*) to cut the hair to the surface of (the face, etc.) *c*) to cut the beard of (a person) **3** to barely touch in passing; graze —*vi.* to cut off a beard with a razor, etc. —*n.* the act or an instance of shaving

shav′er *n.* **1** a person who shaves **2** an instrument used in shaving, esp. one with electrically operated cutters **3** [Inf.] a boy; lad

shav′ing *n.* **1** the act of one who shaves **2** a thin piece of wood, metal, etc. shaved off

Shaw (shô), **George Ber·nard** (bər närd′, bur′nərd) 1856-1950; Brit. dramatist & critic, born in Ireland —**Sha·vi·an** (shā′vē ən) *adj., n.*

shawl (shôl) *n.* ⟦prob. < Pers *shāl*⟧ a cloth worn as a covering for the head or shoulders

shay (shā) *n.* ⟦< CHAISE, assumed as pl.⟧ [Dial.] a light carriage; chaise

she (shē) *pron., pl. see* THEY ⟦< OE *seo*⟧ the woman, girl, or female animal previously mentioned —*n., pl.* **shes** a female

sheaf (shēf) *n., pl.* **sheaves** ⟦OE *sceaf*⟧ **1** a bundle of cut stalks of grain, etc. **2** a collection, as of papers, bound in a bundle

shear (shir) *vt.* **sheared, sheared** or **shorn, shear′ing** ⟦OE *scieran*⟧ **1** to cut with or as with shears **2** to clip (hair) from (the head), (wool) from (sheep), etc. **3** to divest (someone) *of* a power, etc. —*n.* a shearing —**shear′er** *n.*

shears *pl.n.* **1** a large pair of scissors **2** a large cutting tool or machine with opposed blades

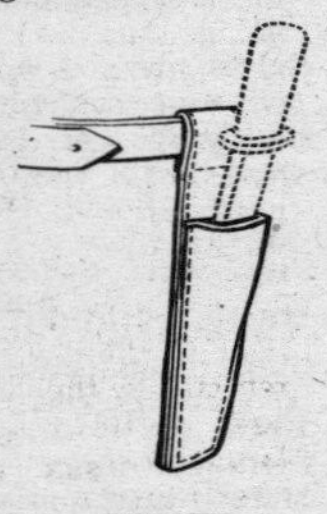

SHEATH

sheath (shēth) *n., pl.* **sheaths** (shē*thz,* shēths) ⟦OE *sceath*⟧ **1** a case for the blade of a knife, sword, etc. **2** a covering resembling this, as the membrane around a muscle **3** a woman's closefitting dress

sheathe (shē*th*) *vt.* **sheathed, sheath′ing** **1** to put into a sheath **2** to enclose in a case or covering

sheath·ing (shē′*th*iŋ) *n.* something that sheathes, as boards, etc. forming the base for roofing or siding

she·bang (shə baŋ′) *n.* [Inf.] an affair, business, contrivance, etc.: chiefly in **the whole shebang**

shed[1] (shed) *n.* ⟦OE *scead*⟧ a small structure for shelter or storage

shed[2] (shed) *vt.* **shed, shed′ding** ⟦< OE *sceadan,* to separate⟧ **1** to pour out; emit **2** to cause to flow *[to shed tears]* **3** to cause to flow off *[oilskin sheds water]* **4** to cast off or lose (a natural growth, as hair, etc.) **5** to get rid of (something unwanted) *[to shed a few* pounds] —*vi.* to shed hair, etc. —**shed blood** to kill violently

sheen (shēn) ***n.*** ⟦< OE *sciene*, beautiful⟧ brightness; luster

sheep (shēp) ***n.***, *pl.* **sheep** ⟦< OE *sceap*⟧ **1** a cud-chewing mammal with heavy wool and edible flesh called *mutton*, closely related to goats, antelope, etc. **2** one who is meek, timid, etc.

sheep′dog′ ***n.*** a dog trained to herd sheep

sheep′fold′ ***n.*** a pen or enclosure for sheep: also, chiefly Brit., **sheep′cote′** (-kōt′) ***n.***

sheep′herd′er ***n.*** a person who herds or takes care of a flock of sheep

sheep′ish ***adj.*** **1** embarrassed or chagrined **2** shy or bashful —**sheep′ish·ly** ***adv.*** —**sheep′ish·ness** ***n.***

sheep′skin′ ***n.*** **1** the skin of a sheep **2** parchment or leather made from it **3** [Inf.] a diploma

sheer[1] (shir) ***vi.***, ***vt.*** ⟦var. of SHEAR⟧ to turn aside or cause to turn aside from a course; swerve

sheer[2] (shir) ***adj.*** ⟦< ON *skærr*, bright⟧ **1** very thin; transparent: said of textiles **2** absolute; utter [*sheer* folly] **3** extremely steep **4** not mixed with anything; pure [*sheer* ice] —***adv.*** very steeply

sheet[1] (shēt) ***n.*** ⟦OE *sceat*⟧ **1** a large piece of cotton, linen, etc., used on a bed **2** *a*) a single piece of paper *b*) [Inf.] a newspaper **3** a broad, continuous surface or expanse, as of flame or ice **4** a broad, thin piece of any material, as glass, plywood, or metal

sheet[2] (shēt) ***n.*** ⟦short for OE *sceatline*⟧ a rope for controlling the set of a sail

sheet′ing ***n.*** **1** cotton or linen material used for making sheets **2** material used to cover or line a surface [copper *sheeting*]

sheet lightning a sheetlike flash of light in the sky, caused by lightning reflected by thunderclouds

sheet metal metal rolled thin in the form of a sheet

sheet music music printed on unbound sheets of paper

sheik or **sheikh** (shēk, shāk) ***n.*** ⟦Ar *shaikh*, lit., old man⟧ the chief of an Arab family, tribe, or village

shek·el (shek′əl) ***n.*** ⟦Heb < *shakal*, weigh⟧ **1** a gold or silver coin of the ancient Hebrews **2** the monetary unit of Israel **3** [*pl.*] [Slang] money

shelf (shelf) ***n.***, *pl.* **shelves** ⟦prob. < MLowG *schelf*⟧ **1** a thin, flat board fixed horizontally to a wall, used for holding things **2** something like a shelf; specif., *a*) a ledge *b*) a sandy reef —**on the shelf** out of use, activity, etc.

shelf life the length of time a packaged food, etc. can be stored without deteriorating

shell (shel) ***n.*** ⟦OE *sciel*⟧ **1** a hard outer covering, as of a turtle, egg, nut, etc. **2** something like a shell in being hollow, empty, a covering, etc. **3** a light, narrow racing boat rowed by a team **4** an explosive artillery projectile **5** a small-arms cartridge —***vt.*** **1** to remove the shell or covering from [to *shell* peas] **2** to bombard with shells from a large gun —**shell out** [Inf.] to pay out (money)

shel·lac or **shel·lack** (shə lak′) ***n.*** ⟦< SHELL & LAC⟧ a thin varnish containing lac and alcohol —***vt.*** **-lacked′**, **-lack′ing** **1** to apply shellac to **2** [Slang] *a*) to beat *b*) to defeat decisively

-shelled (sheld) *combining form* having a (specified kind of) shell

Shel·ley (shel′ē) **1 Mary Woll·stone·craft** (wool′stən kraft′) 1797-1851; Eng. novelist: second wife of Percy **2 Per·cy Bysshe** (pur′sē bish) 1792-1822; Eng. poet

shell′fire′ ***n.*** the firing of artillery shells

shell′fish′ ***n.***, *pl.* **-fish′** or (for different species) **-fish′es** any aquatic animal with a shell, esp. an edible one, as the clam or lobster

shel·ter (shel′tər) ***n.*** ⟦< ? OE *scield*, shield + *truma*, a troop⟧ **1** something that protects, as from the elements, danger, etc. **2** a being covered, protected, etc.; protection **3** a place that provides food and lodging on a temporary basis —***vt.*** to provide shelter for; protect —***vi.*** to find shelter

shelve (shelv) ***vt.*** **shelved**, **shelv′ing** **1** to equip with shelves **2** to put on a shelf **3** to put aside; defer

shelves (shelvz) ***n.*** *pl. of* SHELF

shelv·ing (shel′viŋ) ***n.*** **1** material for shelves **2** shelves collectively

she·nan·i·gan (shi nan′i gən) ***n.*** ⟦altered < ? Ir *sionnachuighim*, I play the fox⟧ [Inf.] a deceitful or mischievous trick: *usually used in pl.*

shep·herd (shep′ərd) ***n.*** ⟦see SHEEP & HERD⟧ **1** one who herds sheep **2** a religious leader **3** GERMAN SHEPHERD —***vt.*** to herd, lead, etc. as a shepherd —**shep′herd·ess** ***fem.n.***

sher·bet (shur′bət) ***n.*** ⟦< Ar *sharba*(*t*), a drink⟧ a frozen dessert like an ice but with gelatin and, often, milk added: also, erroneously, **sher′bert** (-bərt)

sher·iff (sher′if) ***n.*** ⟦< OE *scir*, shire + *gerefa*, chief officer⟧ the chief law-enforcement officer of a county

Sher·pa (shur′pə, sher′-) ***n.*** *pl.* **-pas** or **-pa** a member of a Tibetan people of Nepal, famous as mountain climbers

sher·ry (sher′ē) ***n.***, *pl.* **-ries** ⟦after *Jerez*, Spain⟧ **1** a yellow or brown Spanish fortified wine **2** any similar wine

shib·bo·leth (shib′ə leth′, -ləth) ***n.*** ⟦< Heb *shibolet*, a stream⟧ **1** *Bible* the test word used to distinguish the enemy: Judg. 12:4-6 **2** any phrase, custom, etc. peculiar to a certain party, class, etc.

shied (shīd) ***vi.***, ***vt.*** *pt. & pp. of* SHY[1], SHY[2]

shield (shēld) ***n.*** ⟦OE *scield*⟧ **1** a flat

piece of metal, etc. worn on the forearm to ward off blows, etc. **2** one that guards, protects, etc. **3** anything shaped like a triangular shield with two curved sides —*vt., vi.* to defend; protect

SHIELD

shift (shift) *vt.* ⟦OE *sciftan*, to divide⟧ **1** to move from one person or place to another **2** to replace by another or others **3** to change the arrangement of (gears) —*vi.* **1** to change position, direction, etc. **2** to get along; manage *[to shift for oneself]* —*n.* **1** a shifting; transfer **2** a plan of conduct, esp. for an emergency **3** an evasion; trick **4** a gearshift **5** *a*) a group of people working in relay with another *b*) their regular work period

shift'less *adj.* incapable, inefficient, lazy, etc. —**shift'less·ness** *n.*

shift'y *adj.* **-i·er, -i·est** of a tricky or deceitful nature; evasive —**shift'i·ly** *adv.* —**shift'i·ness** *n.*

Shih Tzu (shēd'zo͞o', shēt'so͞o') *pl.* **Shih Tzus** or **Shih Tzu** ⟦Mandarin *shihtzu*, lion⟧ a small dog with long, silky hair and short legs

shii·ta·ke (shē tä'kē) *n.* ⟦Jpn⟧ an edible Japanese mushroom

shill (shil) [Slang] *n.* a confederate of a gambler, auctioneer, etc. who pretends to bet, bid, etc. so as to lure others —*vi.* to act as a shill

shil·le·lagh or **shil·la·lah** (shi lā'lē, -lə) *n.* ⟦after *Shillelagh*, Ir village⟧ a club or cudgel: used chiefly of or by the Irish

shil·ling (shil'iŋ) *n.* ⟦OE *scylling*⟧ **1** a former British monetary unit and coin, equal to $\frac{1}{20}$ of a pound **2** the basic monetary unit of various countries

shil·ly-shal·ly (shil'ē shal'ē) *vi.* **-lied, -ly·ing** ⟦< *shall I?*⟧ to vacillate, esp. over trifles

shim (shim) *n.* ⟦< ?⟧ a thin wedge of wood, metal, etc. used as for filling space

shim·mer (shim'ər) *vi.* ⟦OE *scymrian*⟧ to shine with an unsteady light; glimmer —*n.* a shimmering light

shim·my (shim'ē) *n.* ⟦< a jazz dance < CHEMISE⟧ a marked vibration or wobble, as in a car's front wheels —*vi.* **-mied, -my·ing** to vibrate or wobble

shin (shin) *n.* ⟦OE *scinu*⟧ the front part of the leg between the knee and the ankle —*vi.* **shinned, shin'ning** to climb a pole, etc. by gripping with hands and legs: also **shin'ny**: with *up* or *down*

shin'bone' *n.* TIBIA

shin·dig (shin'dig') *n.* ⟦< old informal *shindy*, commotion⟧ [Inf.] a dance, party, or other informal gathering

shine (shīn) *vi.* **shone** or, esp. for *vt.* 2, **shined, shin'ing** ⟦OE *scinan*⟧ **1** to emit or reflect light **2** to stand out; excel **3** to exhibit itself clearly *[love shining from her face]* —*vt.* **1** to direct the light of **2** to make shiny by polishing *[to shine shoes]* —*n.* **1** brightness **2** luster; gloss **3** *short for* SHOESHINE

shin·er (shī'nər) *n.* [Slang] BLACK EYE

shin·gle (shiŋ'gəl) *n.* ⟦OE *scindel*⟧ **1** a thin, wedge-shaped piece of wood, slate, etc. laid with others in overlapping rows, as in covering roofs **2** a small signboard, as that of a doctor —*vt.* **-gled, -gling** to cover (a roof, etc.) with shingles

SHINGLES

shin·gles (shiŋ'gəlz) *n.* ⟦< L *cingere*, to gird⟧ *nontechnical name for* HERPES ZOSTER

shin·guard (shin'gärd') *n.* a padded guard worn to protect the shins in some sports

shin'splints' *pl.n.* ⟦< SHIN & *splint*, growth on bone of a horse's leg⟧ *[with sing. or pl. v.]* painful strain of muscles of the lower leg

Shin·to (shin'tō) *n.* ⟦Jpn < Chin *shen*, god + *tō*, *dō*, way⟧ a religion of Japan, emphasizing ancestor worship —**Shin'to·ism'** *n.*

shin·y (shī'nē) *adj.* **-i·er, -i·est** **1** bright; shining **2** highly polished —**shin'i·ness** *n.*

ship (ship) *n.* ⟦OE *scip*⟧ **1** any large vessel for traveling on deep water **2** an aircraft —*vt.* **shipped, ship'ping** **1** to put or take on board a ship **2** to send or transport by any carrier *[to ship coal by rail]* **3** to take in (water) over the side, as in a stormy sea **4** to put (an object) in place on a vessel **5** [Inf.] to send (*away, out*, etc.); get rid of —*vi.* to go aboard, or travel by, ship —**ship'per** *n.*

-ship (ship) ⟦OE *-scipe*⟧ *suffix* **1** the quality or state of being *[friendship]* **2** *a*) the rank or office of *[professorship]* *b*) one having the rank of *[lordship]* **3** skill as *[leadership]* **4** all persons (of a specified group) collectively *[readership]*

ship'board' *n.* used chiefly in **on shipboard**, aboard a ship

ship'build'er *n.* one whose business is building ships —**ship'build'ing** *n.*

ship'mate' *n.* a fellow sailor on the same ship

ship'ment *n.* **1** the shipping of goods **2** goods shipped

ship of the line a warship of the largest class

ship'ping *n.* **1** the act or business of transporting goods **2** ships collectively, as of a nation or port

shipping clerk an employee who

prepares goods for shipment, and keeps records of shipments made

ship'shape' ***adj.*** having everything neatly in place; trim

ship'wreck' ***n.*** **1** the remains of a wrecked ship **2** the loss of a ship through storm, etc. **3** ruin; failure **—*vt.*** to cause to undergo shipwreck

ship'yard' ***n.*** a place where ships are built and repaired

shire (shīr) ***n.*** ⟦OE *scir*, office⟧ in England, a county

shirk (shurk) ***vt., vi.*** ⟦< ?⟧ to neglect or evade (a duty, etc.) **—shirk'er *n.***

shirr (shur) ***vt.*** ⟦< ?⟧ **1** to make shirring in (cloth) **2** to bake (eggs) in buttered dishes

shirr'ing ***n.*** a gathering made in cloth by drawing the material up on parallel rows of short stiches

shirt (shurt) ***n.*** ⟦OE *scyrte*⟧ **1** a garment worn on the upper part of the body, usually with a collar and a buttoned front **2** an undershirt **—keep one's shirt on** [Slang] to remain patient or calm

shirt'tail' ***n.*** the part of a shirt extending below the waist

shirt'waist' ***n.*** **1** [Archaic] a woman's blouse tailored like a shirt **2** a dress with a bodice like this: in full **shirtwaist dress**

shish ke·bab (shish' kə bäb') ⟦< Ar *shīsh*, skewer + *kabāb*, kebab⟧ a dish of kebabs, esp. lamb, stuck on a skewer, often with vegetables, and broiled

shiv (shiv) ***n.*** ⟦prob. < Romany *chiv*, blade⟧ [Slang] a knife

shiv·er[1] (shiv'ər) ***n.*** ⟦ME *schievere*⟧ a fragment **—*vt., vi.*** to break into fragments; shatter

shiv·er[2] (shiv'ər) ***vi.*** ⟦< ? OE *ceafl*, jaw⟧ to shake or tremble, as from fear or cold **—*n.*** a shaking, trembling, etc. **—shiv'er·y *adj.***

shlep or **shlepp** (shlep) ***n., vt., vi.*** **shlepped, shlep'ping** [Slang] *alt. sp. of* SCHLEP

shmaltz (shmôlts, shmälts) ***n.*** [Slang] *alt. sp. of* SCHMALTZ

shoal[1] (shōl) ***n.*** ⟦OE *scolu*⟧ a school of fish

shoal[2] (shōl) ***n.*** ⟦< OE *sceald*, shallow⟧ **1** a shallow place in a river, sea, etc. **2** a sandbar forming a shallow place

shoat (shōt) ***n.*** ⟦ME *schote*⟧ a young, weaned pig

shock[1] (shäk) ***n.*** ⟦< MFr *choquer*, to collide⟧ **1** a sudden, powerful blow, shake, etc. **2** *a*) a sudden emotional disturbance *b*) the cause of this **3** an extreme stimulation of the nerves by the passage of electric current through the body **4** [Inf.] *short for* SHOCK ABSORBER **5** a disorder of the blood circulation produced by hemorrhage, disturbance of heart function, etc. **—*vt.*** **1** to astonish, horrify, etc. **2** to produce electrical shock in **—shock'er *n.***

shock[2] (shäk) ***n.*** ⟦ME *schokke*⟧ a number of grain sheaves stacked together

SHOCKS OF CORN

shock[3] (shäk) ***n.*** ⟦< ? prec.⟧ a thick, bushy mass of hair

shock absorber a device, as on a motor vehicle, that absorbs the force of bumps and jarring

shock'ing ***adj.*** **1** causing great surprise and distress **2** disgusting **—shock'ing·ly *adv.***

shock'proof' ***adj.*** able to absorb shock without being damaged

shock therapy the treatment of certain mental disorders by using electricity or drugs to produce convulsions or coma

shock troops troops trained to lead an attack

shod (shäd) ***vt.*** *alt. pt. & pp. of* SHOE

shod·dy (shäd'ē) ***n., pl.*** **-dies** ⟦< ?⟧ an inferior woolen cloth made from used fabrics **—*adj.*** **-di·er, -di·est** **1** made of inferior material **2** poorly done or made **3** contemptible; low **—shod'di·ly *adv.*** **—shod'di·ness *n.***

shoe (sho͞o) ***n.*** ⟦OE *sceoh*⟧ **1** an outer covering for the foot **2** *short for* HORSESHOE **3** the part of a brake that presses against a wheel **—*vt.*** **shod** or **shoed, shoe'ing** to furnish with shoes **—fill someone's shoes** to take someone's place

shoe'horn' ***n.*** an implement used to help slip the heel of a foot into a shoe **—*vt.*** to force or squeeze into a narrow space

shoe'lace' ***n.*** a length of cord, etc. used for lacing and fastening a shoe

shoe'mak'er ***n.*** one whose business is making or repairing shoes

shoe'shine' ***n.*** the cleaning and polishing of a pair of shoes

shoe'string' ***n.*** **1** a shoelace **2** a small amount of capital *[a business started on a shoestring]* **—*adj.*** **1** like a shoestring; long and narrow **2** of or characterized by a small amount of money **3** at or near the ankles *[a shoestring catch]*

shoe tree a form made of wood, etc. inserted in a shoe to stretch it or preserve its shape

sho·gun (shō'gun') ***n.*** ⟦< Chin *chiang-chun*⟧ any of the hereditary governors of Japan who, until 1867, were absolute rulers **—sho'gun·ate** (-gə nit) ***n.***

shone (shōn) ***vi., vt.*** *alt. pt. & pp. of*

SHINE

shoo (sho͞o) ***interj.*** go away! get out! —***vt.*** **shooed**, **shoo'ing** to drive away, as by crying "shoo"

shoo'-in' ***n.*** [Inf.] one expected to win easily in a race, etc.

shook (shook) ***vt.***, ***vi.*** *pt. and dial. pp. of* SHAKE —**shook up** [Inf.] upset; agitated

shoot (sho͞ot) ***vt.*** **shot**, **shoot'ing** ⟦OE *sceotan*⟧ **1** to move swiftly over, by, etc. *[to shoot the rapids]* **2** to streak or vary (*with* another color, etc.) **3** to thrust or put forth **4** to discharge or fire (a bullet, arrow, etc.) **5** to send forth swiftly or with force **6** to hit, wound, etc. with a bullet, arrow, etc. **7** to photograph **8** *Sports a)* to throw or drive (a ball, etc.) toward the objective *b)* to score (a goal, points, etc.) —***vi.*** **1** to move swiftly **2** to be felt suddenly, as pain **3** to grow rapidly **4** to jut out **5** to send forth a missile; discharge bullets, etc. **6** to use guns, etc. as in hunting —***n.*** **1** a shooting trip, contest, etc. **2** a new growth; sprout —**shoot at** (or **for**) [Inf.] to strive for —**shoot'er** ***n.***

shooting star METEOR (sense 1)

shoot'out' or **shoot'-out'** ***n.*** **1** a battle with handguns, etc., as between police and criminals **2** *Sports* a procedure used to break a tie at the end of a game, esp. in soccer

shop (shäp) ***n.*** ⟦OE *sceoppa*, booth⟧ **1** a place where certain things are offered for sale; esp., a small store **2** a place where a particular kind of work is done —***vi.*** **shopped**, **shop'ping** to visit shops to examine or buy goods —**talk shop** to discuss one's work

shop'keep'er ***n.*** one who owns or operates a shop, or small store

shop'lift' ***vt.***, ***vi.*** to steal (articles) from a store during shopping hours —**shop'lift'er** ***n.***

shoppe (shäp) ***n.*** *alt. sp. of* SHOP (*n.* 1): now used only in shop names

shop'per ***n.*** **1** one who shops **2** one hired by a store to shop for others **3** one hired by a store to compare competitors' prices, etc.

shopping center a complex of stores, restaurants, etc. with a common parking area

shop'talk' ***n.*** **1** the specialized words and idioms of those in the same work **2** talk about work, esp. after hours

shop'worn' ***adj.*** soiled, faded, etc. from having been displayed in a shop

shore[1] (shôr) ***n.*** ⟦ME *schore*⟧ land at the edge of a body of water

shore[2] (shôr) ***n.*** ⟦ME *schore*⟧ a prop, beam, etc. used for support, etc. —***vt.*** **shored**, **shor'ing** to support as with shores; prop (*up*)

shore'bird' ***n.*** a bird that lives or feeds near the shore

shore'line' ***n.*** the edge of a body of water

shore patrol a detail of the U.S. Navy, Coast Guard, or Marine Corps acting as military police on shore

shorn (shôrn) ***vt.***, ***vi.*** *alt. pp. of* SHEAR

short (shôrt) ***adj.*** ⟦OE *scort*⟧ **1** not measuring much from end to end in space or time **2** not great in range or scope **3** not tall **4** brief; concise **5** not retentive *[a short memory]* **6** curt; abrupt **7** less than a sufficient or correct amount **8** crisp or flaky, as pastry rich in shortening **9** designating a sale of securities, etc. which the seller does not yet own but expects to buy later at a lower price —***n.*** **1** something short **2** [*pl.*] *a)* short trousers *b)* a man's undergarment like these **3** *short for a)* SHORTSTOP *b)* SHORT CIRCUIT —***adv.*** **1** abruptly; suddenly **2** briefly; concisely **3** so as to be short in length **4** by surprise *[caught short]* —***vt.***, ***vi.*** **1** to give less than what is needed or usual **2** *short for a)* SHORTCHANGE *b)* SHORT-CIRCUIT —**in short** briefly —**run short** to have less than enough —**short of** **1** less than or lacking **2** without actually resorting to —**short'ness** ***n.***

short'age ***n.*** a deficiency in the amount needed or expected; deficit

short'bread' ***n.*** a rich, crumbly cake or cookie made with much shortening

short'cake' ***n.*** a light biscuit or a sweet cake served with fruit, etc.

short'change' ***vt.***, ***vi.*** **-changed'**, **-chang'ing** [Inf.] **1** to give less money than is due in change **2** to cheat by depriving of something due

short circuit **1** a usually accidental connection between two points in an electric circuit, resulting in excessive current flow that causes damage **2** popularly, a disrupted electric circuit caused by this —**short'-cir'cuit** ***vt.***, ***vi.***

short'com'ing ***n.*** a defect or deficiency

short'cut' ***n.*** **1** a shorter route **2** any way of saving time, effort, etc.

short'en ***vt.***, ***vi.*** to make or become short or shorter

short·en·ing (shôrt''n iŋ, shôrt'niŋ) ***n.*** edible fat used to make pastry, etc. crisp or flaky

short'fall' ***n.*** a falling short, or the amount of the shortage

short'hand' ***n.*** any system of speed writing using symbols for words

short'-hand'ed ***adj.*** short of workers

short'-lived' (-līvd', -livd') ***adj.*** having a short life span or existence

short'ly ***adv.*** **1** briefly **2** soon **3** abruptly and rudely; curtly

short order any food that can be cooked or served quickly when ordered

short'-range' ***adj.*** reaching over a short distance or period of time

short ribs the rib ends from the front half of a side of beef

short shrift very little care or attention —**make short shrift of** to dispose of quickly and impatiently

short'sight'ed ***adj.*** **1** NEARSIGHTED **2** lacking in foresight —**short'sight'ed·ly** ***adv.*** —**short'sight'ed·ness** ***n.***

short'-spo'ken ***adj.*** using few words, esp. to the point of rudeness; curt

short'stop' ***n.*** *Baseball* the infielder usually positioned to the left of second base

short story a piece of prose fiction

shorter than a short novel

short subject a short film, as that shown with a film feature

short'-tem'pered *adj.* easily or quickly angered

short'-term' *adj.* for or extending over a short time

short ton 2,000 pounds: see TON

short'-waist'ed (-wās'tid) *adj.* unusually short between shoulders and waistline

short'wave' *n.* **1** a radio wave 60 meters or less in length: shorter than the waves used in commercial broadcasting **2** a radio or radio band for broadcasting or receiving shortwaves: in full **shortwave radio**

short'-wind'ed (-win'did) *adj.* easily put out of breath by exertion

shot[1] (shät) *n.* ⟦OE *sceot*⟧ **1** the act of shooting **2** range; scope **3** an attempt or try **4** a pointed, critical remark **5** the path of an object thrown, etc. **6** *a)* a projectile for a gun *b)* projectiles collectively **7** small pellets of lead or steel for a shotgun **8** the heavy metal ball used in the shot put **9** a marksman **10** a photograph or a film sequence **11** a hypodermic injection **12** a drink of liquor —**call the shots** [Inf.] to direct or control what is done

shot[2] (shät) *vt., vi. pt. & pp. of* SHOOT —*adj.* [Inf.] ruined or worn out

shot'gun' *n.* **1** a gun for firing a charge of shot at short range **2** *Football* a formation in which the quarterback stands several yards behind the line of scrimmage to receive the ball

shot put a contest in which a heavy metal ball is propelled with an overhand thrust from the shoulder —**shot'-put'ter** *n.* —**shot'-put'ting** *n.*

should (shood) *v.aux.* ⟦OE *sceolde*⟧ **1** *pt. of* SHALL **2** used to express: *a)* obligation, duty, etc. *[you should help] b)* expectation or probability *[he should be here soon] c)* a future condition *[if I should die tomorrow]*

shoul·der (shōl'dər) *n.* ⟦OE *sculdor*⟧ **1** *a)* the joint connecting the arm or forelimb with the body *b)* the part of the body including this joint **2** [*pl.*] the two shoulders and the part of the back between them **3** a shoulderlike projection **4** the land along the edge of a paved road —*vt.* **1** to push along or through, as with the shoulder **2** to carry upon the shoulder **3** to assume the burden of —**straight from the shoulder** without reserve; frankly —**turn** (or **give**) **a cold shoulder to** to snub or shun

shoulder blade SCAPULA

shoulder harness an anchored strap passing across the chest, used with a seat belt, as in a car: also called **shoulder belt**

shout (shout) *n.* ⟦ME *schoute*⟧ a loud cry or call —*vt., vi.* to utter or cry out in a shout —**shout'er** *n.*

shove (shuv) *vt., vi.* **shoved, shov'ing** ⟦OE *scufan*⟧ **1** to push, as along a surface **2** to push roughly —*n.* a push —**shove off 1** to push (a boat) away from shore **2** [Inf.] to leave

shov·el (shuv'əl) *n.* ⟦OE *scofl*⟧ a tool with a broad scoop or blade and a long handle, for lifting and moving loose material —*vt.* **-eled** or **-elled, -el·ing** or **-el·ling 1** to move with a shovel **2** to dig out with a shovel

shov'el·ful' *n., pl.* **-fuls'** as much as a shovel will hold

show (shō) *vt.* **showed, shown** or **showed, show'ing** ⟦< OE *sceawian*⟧ **1** to bring or put in sight **2** to guide; conduct **3** to point out **4** to reveal, as by behavior **5** to prove; demonstrate **6** to bestow (favor, mercy, etc.) —*vi.* **1** to be or become seen; appear **2** to be noticeable **3** to finish third or better in a horse race —*n.* **1** a showing or demonstration **2** pompous display **3** pretense *[sorrow that was mere show]* **4** a public display or exhibition **5** a presentation of entertainment —**show off 1** to make a display of **2** to attract attention to oneself —**show up 1** to expose **2** to be seen **3** to arrive

show'biz' (-biz') *n.* [Inf.] SHOW BUSINESS

show'boat' *n.* **1** a boat with a theater and actors who play river towns **2** [Slang] a showoff —*vi.* [Slang] to show off

show business the theater, films, TV, etc. as a business or industry

show'case' *n.* a glass-enclosed case for displaying things, as in a store —*vt.* **-cased', -cas'ing** to display to good advantage

show'down' *n.* [Inf.] an action that brings matters to a climax or settles them

show·er (shou'ər) *n.* ⟦OE *scur*⟧ **1** a brief fall of rain, etc. **2** a sudden, abundant fall or flow, as of sparks **3** a party at which gifts are presented to the guest of honor **4** a bath in which the body is sprayed from overhead with fine streams of water —*vt.* **1** to spray with water, etc. **2** to pour forth as in a shower —*vi.* **1** to fall or come as a shower **2** to bathe under a shower —**show'er·y** *adj.*

show·ing (shō'iŋ) *n.* **1** a bringing to view or notice; exhibition **2** a performance, appearance, etc. *[a good showing in the contest]*

show·man (shō'mən) *n., pl.* **-men** (-mən) **1** one whose business is producing shows **2** a person skilled at presenting anything in a striking manner —**show'man·ship'** *n.*

shown (shōn) *vt., vi. alt. pp. of* SHOW

show'off' *n.* one who shows off

show of hands a raising of hands, as in voting or volunteering

show'piece' *n.* **1** something displayed or exhibited **2** something that is a fine example of its kind

show'place' *n.* **1** a place displayed to the public for its beauty, etc. **2** any beautiful place

show'room' *n.* a room where merchandise is displayed for advertising or sale

show'time' *n.* the time when a show begins

show window a store window in which

merchandise is displayed

show'y ***adj.*** **-i·er, -i·est 1** of striking appearance **2** attracting attention in a gaudy way —**show'i·ness** ***n.***

shpt *abbrev.* shipment

shrank (shraŋk) ***vt., vi.*** *alt. pt. of* SHRINK

shrap·nel (shrap'nəl) ***n.*** ⟦after Gen. H. *Shrapnel* (1761-1842), its Brit inventor⟧ **1** an artillery shell filled with an explosive charge and small metal balls **2** these balls **3** any fragments scattered by an exploding shell, bomb, etc.

shred (shred) ***n.*** ⟦OE *screade*⟧ **1** a narrow strip cut, torn off, etc. **2** a fragment —***vt.*** **shred'ded** or **shred, shred'ding** to cut or tear into shreds —**shred'da·ble** ***adj.*** —**shred'der** ***n.***

Shreve·port (shrēv'pôrt') city in NW Louisiana: pop. 199,000

shrew (shro͞o) ***n.*** ⟦< OE *screawa*⟧ **1** a small, mouselike mammal with a long snout **2** a nagging, bad-tempered woman —**shrew'ish** ***adj.***

shrewd (shro͞od) ***adj.*** ⟦see prec.⟧ clever or sharp in practical affairs; astute —**shrewd'ly** ***adv.*** —**shrewd'ness** ***n.***

shriek (shrēk) ***vi., vt.*** ⟦ME *schriken*⟧ to make or utter with a loud, piercing cry —***n.*** such a cry

shrift (shrift) ***n.*** ⟦ult. < L *scribere*, write⟧ [Archaic] confession to and absolution by a priest: see also SHORT SHRIFT

shrike (shrīk) ***n.*** ⟦OE *scric*⟧ a shrill-voiced, predatory songbird with a hooked beak

shrill (shril) ***adj.*** ⟦echoic⟧ producing a high, thin, piercing sound —***vi., vt.*** to utter (with) a shrill sound —**shril'ly** ***adv.*** —**shrill'ness** ***n.***

shrimp (shrimp) ***n.*** ⟦OE *scrimman*, to shrink⟧ **1** a small, long-tailed crustacean, valued as food **2** [Inf.] a small or insignificant person

shrine (shrīn) ***n.*** ⟦< L *scrinium*, box⟧ **1** a container holding sacred relics **2** a saint's tomb **3** a place of worship **4** any hallowed place

shrink (shriŋk) ***vi.*** **shrank** or **shrunk, shrunk** or **shrunk'en, shrink'ing** ⟦OE *scrincan*⟧ **1** to contract, as from heat, cold, moisture, etc. **2** to lessen, as in amount **3** to draw back; flinch —***vt.*** to make shrink —**shrink'a·ble** ***adj.***

shrink'age ***n.*** **1** a shrinking **2** the amount of shrinking

shrinking violet a very shy person

shrink'-wrap' (-rap') ***vt.*** **-wrapped', -wrap'ping** to wrap in a plastic material that is then shrunk by heating to fit tightly —***n.*** a wrapping of such material

shrive (shrīv) ***vt.*** **shrived** or **shrove, shriv·en** (shriv'ən) or **shrived, shriv'ing** ⟦OE *scrifan*⟧ [Archaic] to hear the confession of and absolve

shriv·el (shriv'əl) ***vt., vi.*** **-eled** or **-elled, -el·ing** or **-el·ling** ⟦prob. < Scand⟧ to shrink and wrinkle or wither

shroud (shroud) ***n.*** ⟦OE *scrud*⟧ **1** a cloth used to wrap a corpse for burial **2** something that covers, veils, etc. **3** any of the ropes from a ship's side to a masthead —***vt.*** to hide; cover

Shrove Tuesday ⟦see SHRIVE⟧ the last day before Lent

shrub (shrub) ***n.*** ⟦OE *scrybb*, brushwood⟧ a low, woody plant with several stems; bush —**shrub'by** ***adj.***

shrub'ber·y (-ər ē) ***n.*** shrubs collectively

shrug (shrug) ***vt., vi.*** **shrugged, shrug'ging** ⟦ME *schruggen*⟧ to draw up (the shoulders), as in indifference, doubt, etc. —***n.*** the gesture so made —**shrug off** to dismiss or disregard in a carefree way

shrunk (shruŋk) ***vi., vt.*** *alt. pt. & pp. of* SHRINK

shrunk'en ***vi., vt.*** *alt. pp. of* SHRINK —***adj.*** contracted in size; shriveled

shtick (shtik) ***n.*** ⟦Yiddish⟧ **1** a comic scene or gimmick **2** an attention-getting device

shuck (shuk) ***n.*** ⟦< ?⟧ a shell, pod, or husk —***vt.*** to remove shucks from

shucks (shuks) ***interj.*** used to express mild disappointment, embarrassment, etc.

shud·der (shud'ər) ***vi.*** ⟦ME *schoderen*⟧ to shake or tremble, as in horror —***n.*** a shuddering

shuf·fle (shuf'əl) ***vt., vi.*** **-fled, -fling** ⟦prob. < LowG *schuffeln*⟧ **1** to move (the feet) with a dragging gait **2** to mix (playing cards) **3** to mix together in a jumble —***n.*** a shuffling —**shuf'fler** ***n.***

shuf'fle·board' ***n.*** ⟦< earlier *shovel board*⟧ a game in which disks are pushed with a cue toward numbered squares on a diagram

shun (shun) ***vt.*** **shunned, shun'ning** ⟦OE *scunian*⟧ to keep away from; avoid scrupulously

shunt (shunt) ***vt., vi.*** ⟦ME *schunten*⟧ **1** to move or turn to one side **2** to switch from one track to another: said as of a train —***n.*** **1** a shunting **2** a railroad switch **3** a surgically created channel allowing flow from one organ, etc. to another

shush (shush) ***interj.*** ⟦echoic⟧ hush! be quiet! —***vt.*** to say "shush" to

shut (shut) ***vt.*** **shut, shut'ting** ⟦OE *scyttan*⟧ **1** to move (a door, lid, etc.) so as to close (an opening, container, etc.) **2** *a)* to prevent entrance to or exit from *b)* to confine *in* a room, etc. **3** to bring together the parts of (a book, the eyes, etc.) —***vi.*** to be or become shut —***adj.*** closed, fastened, etc. —**shut down** to cease operating —**shut off** to prevent passage of or through —**shut out 1** to deny entrance to **2** to prevent from scoring —**shut up 1** to confine **2** [Inf.] to stop or cause to stop talking

shut'down' ***n.*** a stoppage of work or activity, as in a factory

shut'-eye' ***n.*** [Slang] sleep

shut'-in' ***adj.*** confined indoors by illness —***n.*** an invalid who is shut-in

shut'out' ***n.*** a game in which a team is kept from scoring

shut·ter (shut'ər) ***n.*** **1** a person or thing that shuts **2** a movable cover for a window **3** a device for opening and closing the aperture of a camera lens —***vt.*** to close or furnish with a shutter

shut·tle (shut′'l) ***n.*** ⟦< OE *scytel*, missile⟧ **1** a device that carries thread back and forth, as in weaving **2** *a)* a traveling back and forth over a short route *b)* an airplane, bus, etc. used in a shuttle **—*vt.*, *vi.* -tled, -tling** to move back and forth rapidly

shut′tle·cock′ (-käk′) ***n.*** in badminton, a rounded piece of cork having a flat end stuck with feathers, or a similar plastic device

shy[1] (shī) ***adj.* shy′er** or **shi′er, shy′est** or **shi′est** ⟦OE *sceoh*⟧ **1** easily frightened; timid **2** not at ease with others; bashful **3** distrustful; wary **4** [Slang] lacking **—*vi.* shied, shy′ing 1** to move suddenly as when startled **2** to be or become cautious, etc. **—shy′ly *adv.* —shy′ness *n.***

shy[2] (shī) ***vt.*, *vi.* shied, shy′ing** ⟦< ?⟧ to fling, esp. sideways

shy·ster (shī′stər) ***n.*** ⟦prob. < Ger *scheisser*, one who defecates⟧ [Slang] a lawyer who uses unethical or tricky methods

Si *Chem. symbol for* silicon

Si·am (sī am′) *former name for* THAILAND

Si·a·mese (sī′ə mēz′) ***n.***, *pl.* **-mese′ 1** *former name for* THAI **2** a domestic cat with blue eyes and a light-colored coat **—*adj.*** *former term for* THAI

Siamese twins ⟦after such a pair born in *Siam*⟧ any pair of twins born with bodies joined together

Si·ber·i·a (sī bir′ē ə) region in N Asia, between the Urals & the Pacific: Asian section of Russia **—Si·ber′i·an *adj.*, *n.***

sib·i·lant (sib′ə lənt) ***adj.*** ⟦< L *sibilare*, to hiss⟧ having or making a hissing sound **—*n.*** a sibilant consonant, as (s) or (z)

sib·ling (sib′liŋ) ***n.*** ⟦< OE *sib*, kinsman + -LING⟧ a brother or sister

sib·yl (sib′əl) ***n.*** ⟦< Gr *sibylla*⟧ ancient Greek or Roman prophetess **—sib′yl·line′** (-īn′, -ēn′) ***adj.***

sic (sik) ***vt.* sicced** or **sicked, sic′cing** or **sick′ing** ⟦< SEEK⟧ to incite (a dog) to attack

sic (sik, sēk) ***adv.*** ⟦L⟧ thus; so: used within brackets, [*sic*], to show that a quoted passage, esp. one containing an error, is reproduced accurately

Sic·i·ly (sis′ə lē) island of Italy, off its S tip **—Si·cil·i·an** (si sil′yən) ***adj.*, *n.***

sick[1] (sik) ***adj.*** ⟦OE *seoc*⟧ **1** suffering from disease; ill **2** having nausea **3** of or for sick people *[sick* leave*]* **4** deeply disturbed, as by grief **5** disgusted by an excess *[sick* of excuses*]* **6** [Inf.] sadistic, morbid, etc. *[a sick* joke*]* **—the sick** sick people **—sick′ish *adj.***

sick[2] (sik) ***vt.*** *alt. sp. of* SIC (incite)

sick bay a hospital and dispensary on a ship

sick′bed′ *n.* the bed of a sick person

sick′en *vt.*, *vi.* to make or become ill, disgusted, etc. **—sick′en·ing *adj.***

sick′ie (-ē) ***n.*** [Slang] a sick person, esp. one who is emotionally disturbed, sadistic, etc.

sick·le (sik′əl) ***n.*** ⟦ult. < L *secare*, to cut⟧ a tool having a crescent-shaped blade on a short handle, for cutting tall grasses and weeds

sickle cell anemia an inherited chronic anemia found chiefly among black people, in which defective hemoglobin causes sickle-shaped red blood cells

sick′ly *adj.* -li·er, -li·est 1 in poor health **2** produced by sickness *[a sickly* pallor*]* **3** faint **4** weak

sick′ness *n.* 1 a being sick or diseased **2** a malady **3** nausea

sick′out′ *n.* a staying out of work on the claim of illness, as by a group of employees trying to win demands but forbidden to strike

sick′room′ *n.* the room of a sick person

side (sīd) ***n.*** ⟦OE⟧ **1** the right or left half, as of the body **2** a position beside one **3** *a)* any of the lines or surfaces that bound something *b)* either of the two bounding surfaces of an object that are not the front, back, top, or bottom **4** either of the two surfaces of paper, cloth, etc. **5** an aspect *[his cruel side]* **6** any location, etc. with reference to a central point **7** the position or attitude of one person or faction opposing another **8** one of the parties in a contest, conflict, etc. **9** a line of descent **—*adj.* 1** of, at, or on a side **2** to or from one side *[a side* glance*]* **3** secondary *[a side* issue*]* **—*vi.*** to align oneself (*with* a faction, etc.) **—side by side** together **—take sides** to support a faction

side′arm′ *adj.*, *adv.* with a forward arm motion at or below shoulder level

side arm a weapon worn at the side or waist, as a sword or pistol: *often used in pl.*

side′bar′ *n.* a short article about a sidelight of a major news story and printed alongside it

side′board′ *n.* a piece of furniture for holding linen, china, silverware, etc.

side′burns′ *pl.n.* ⟦< *burnsides*, side whiskers worn by A. E. *Burnside*, Civil War general⟧ the hair growing on the sides of a man's face, just in front of the ears

side′car′ *n.* a small car attached to the side of a motorcycle

side dish any food served along with the main course, usually in a separate dish

side effect an incidental effect, as an unrelated symptom produced by a drug

side′kick′ *n.* [Slang] **1** a close friend **2** a partner; confederate

side′light′ *n.* a bit of incidental knowledge or information

side′line′ *n.* 1 either of two lines marking the side limits of a playing area, as in football **2** a secondary line of merchandise, work, etc.

side′long′ *adv.* toward the side **—*adj.*** directed to the side: said as of a glance

side′man′ (-man′) ***n.***, *pl.* **-men′** (-men′) a band member other than the leader or soloist

side′piece′ *n.* a piece on the side of something

si·de·re·al (sī dir′ē əl) ***adj.*** ⟦< L *sidus*, star⟧ with reference to the stars

side'sad'dle ***n.*** a saddle designed for a rider sitting with both legs on the same side of the animal —***adv.*** on or as if on a sidesaddle

side'show' ***n.*** a small show in connection with the main show, as of a circus

side'slip' ***vi.* -slipped', -slip'ping** to slip or skid sideways —***vt.*** to cause to sideslip —***n.*** a slip or skid to the side

side'split'ting ***adj.*** **1** very hearty: said of laughter **2** very funny

side'step' ***vt., vi.* -stepped', -step'ping** to dodge as by stepping aside

side'swipe' ***vt.* -swiped', -swip'ing** to hit along the side in passing —***n.*** such a glancing blow

side'track' ***vt., vi.*** **1** to switch (a train) to a siding **2** to turn away from the main issue

side'walk' ***n.*** a path for pedestrians, usually paved, along the side of a street

side'wall' ***n.*** the side of a tire between the tread and the wheel rim

side'ways' (-wāz') ***adv., adj.*** **1** toward or from one side **2** with one side forward Also **side'wise'** (-wīz')

sid·ing (sīd'iŋ) ***n.*** **1** a covering, as of overlapping boards, for the outside of a frame building **2** a short railroad track connected with a main track by a switch and used for unloading, etc.

si·dle (sīd''l) ***vi.* -dled, -dling** ⟦< *sideling*, sideways⟧ to move sideways, esp. shyly or stealthily

SIDS (sidz) *abbrev.* SUDDEN INFANT DEATH SYNDROME

siege (sēj) ***n.*** ⟦ult. < L *sedere*, sit⟧ **1** the encirclement of a fortified place by an enemy intending to take it **2** any persistent attempt to gain control, etc. —**lay siege to** to subject to a siege

si·en·na (sē en'ə) ***n.*** ⟦It⟧ yellowish brown or reddish brown

si·er·ra (sē er'ə) ***n.*** ⟦Sp < L *serra*, a saw⟧ a range of hills or mountains with a saw-toothed appearance

Si·er·ra Le·one (sē er'ə lē ōn') country in W Africa, on the Atlantic: 27,925 sq. mi.; pop. 3,518,000

si·es·ta (sē es'tə) ***n.*** ⟦Sp < L *sexta* (*hora*), sixth (hour), noon⟧ a brief nap or rest after the noon meal

sieve (siv) ***n.*** ⟦OE *sife*⟧ a utensil with many small holes for straining liquids, etc.; strainer

sift (sift) ***vt.*** ⟦OE *siftan*⟧ **1** to pass (flour, etc.) through a sieve **2** to examine (evidence, etc.) with care **3** to separate *[to sift fact from fable]* —***vi.*** to pass as through a sieve —**sift'er** ***n.***

sigh (sī) ***vi.*** ⟦< OE *sican*⟧ **1** to take in and let out a long, deep, audible breath, as in sorrow, relief, or longing **2** to feel longing or grief (*for*) —***n.*** the act or sound of sighing

sight (sīt) ***n.*** ⟦< OE *seon*, to see⟧ **1** something seen or worth seeing **2** the act of seeing **3** a device to aid the eyes in aiming a gun, etc. **4** aim or an observation taken, as on a sextant **5** the power or range of seeing; eyesight **6** [Inf.] anything that looks unpleasant, odd, etc. —***vt.*** **1** to observe **2** to glimpse; see **3** to aim at **4** to adjust the sights of —***vi.*** to look carefully *[sight along the line]* —**at** (or **on**) **sight** as soon as seen —**by sight** by appearance —**not by a long sight** **1** not nearly **2** not at all —**out of sight** **1** not in sight **2** far off **3** [Inf.] beyond reach **4** [Slang] excellent; wonderful

sight'ed ***adj.*** **1** having sight; not blind **2** having (a specified kind of) sight *[farsighted]*

sight'ing ***n.*** an observation, as of something rare

sight'less ***adj.*** blind

sight'ly ***adj.* -li·er, -li·est** pleasant to the sight —**sight'li·ness** ***n.***

sight reading the skill of performing written music on first sight —**sight'-read'** ***vt., vi.***

sight'see'ing ***n.*** the visiting of places of interest —**sight'seer** (-sē'ər) ***n.***

sig·ma (sig'mə) ***n.*** the eighteenth letter of the Greek alphabet (Σ, σ, ς)

sign (sīn) ***n.*** ⟦< L *signum*⟧ **1** something that indicates a fact, quality, etc.; token **2** a gesture that conveys information, etc. **3** a mark or symbol having a specific meaning *[a dollar sign ($)]* **4** a placard, etc. bearing information, advertising, etc. **5** any trace or indication —***vt.*** **1** to write (one's name) on (a letter, check, contract, etc.) **2** to engage by written contract —***vi.*** to write one's signature —**sign in** (or **out**) to sign a register on arrival (or departure) —**sign off** to stop broadcasting, as for the day —**sign off on** to approve

sign'age ***n.*** public signs collectively, often, specif., when graphically coordinated

sig·nal (sig'nəl) ***n.*** ⟦< L *signum*, a sign⟧ **1** a sign or event that initiates action *[a bugle signal to attack]* **2** a gesture, device, etc. that conveys command, warning, etc. **3** in radio, etc., the electrical impulses transmitted or received —***adj.*** **1** remarkable; notable **2** used as a signal —***vt., vi.* -naled** or **-nalled, -nal·ing** or **-nal·ling** **1** to make a signal or signals (to) **2** to communicate by signals

sig'nal·ize' (-nə līz') ***vt.* -ized', -iz'ing** to make known or draw attention to

sig'nal·ly ***adv.*** in a signal way; notably

sig·na·to·ry (sig'nə tôr'ē) ***adj.*** having joined in signing something —***n.***, *pl.* **-ries** a signatory person, nation, etc.

sig·na·ture (sig'nə chər) ***n.*** ⟦< L *signare*, to sign⟧ **1** a person's name written by that person **2** *Music* a staff sign showing key or time

sign·board (sīn'bôrd') ***n.*** a board bearing a sign or advertisement

sig·net (sig'nit) ***n.*** ⟦< Fr *signe*, a sign⟧ a seal, as on a ring, used in marking documents as official, etc.

sig·nif·i·cance (sig nif'ə kəns) ***n.*** **1** that which is signified; meaning **2** the quality of being significant; expressiveness **3** importance

sig·nif'i·cant (-kənt) ***adj.*** ⟦< L *significare*, signify⟧ **1** having or expressing a meaning, esp. a special or hidden one **2** full of meaning **3** important —**sig·nif'i·**

cant·ly ***adv.***

sig·ni·fy (sig′nə fī′) ***vt.* -fied′, -fy′ing** ⟦< L *signum*, a sign + *facere*, make⟧ **1** to be an indication of; mean **2** to make known by a sign, words, etc. —***vi.*** to be important —**sig′ni·fi·ca′tion** ***n.***

sign language hand signals and gestures used, as by the deaf, as a language

sign of the cross an outline of a CROSS (sense 2) made symbolically by moving the hand or fingers

sign of the zodiac any of the twelve divisions of the zodiac, each represented by a symbol

si·gnor (sē nyôr′) ***n.***, *pl.* ***-gno′ri*** (-nyô′rē) ⟦It⟧ **1** [**S-**] Mr.: Italian title **2** a man; gentleman

si·gno·ra (sē nyô′rä) ***n.***, *pl.* ***-gno′re*** (-re) ⟦It⟧ **1** [**S-**] Mrs.; Madam: Italian title **2** a married woman

si·gno·ri·na (sē′nyô rē′nä) ***n.***, *pl.* ***-ri′ne*** (-ne) ⟦It⟧ **1** [**S-**] Miss: Italian title **2** an unmarried woman or a girl

sign′post′ ***n.*** **1** a post bearing a sign **2** an obvious clue, symptom, etc.

Sikh (sēk, sik) ***n.*** ⟦Hindi, disciple⟧ a member of a monotheistic religion founded in N India

si·lage (sī′lij) ***n.*** green fodder preserved in a silo

si·lence (sī′ləns) ***n.*** **1** a keeping silent **2** absence of sound **3** an omission of mention —***vt.* -lenced, -lenc·ing** **1** to make silent **2** to put down; repress —***interj.*** be silent!

si′lenc·er ***n.*** **1** one that silences **2** a device to muffle the sound of a gun

si·lent (sī′lənt) ***adj.*** ⟦< L *silere*, be silent⟧ **1** making no vocal sound; mute **2** not talkative **3** still; noiseless **4** not expressed; tacit **5** not active [a *silent* partner] —**si′lent·ly** ***adv.***

sil·hou·ette (sil′ə wet′) ***n.*** ⟦Fr, after E. de *Silhouette*, 18th-c. Fr statesman⟧ **1** a solid, usually black, outline drawing, esp. a profile **2** any dark shape seen against a light background —***vt.* -et′ted, -et′ting** to show in silhouette

SILHOUETTE

sil·i·ca (sil′i kə) ***n.*** ⟦< L *silex*, flint⟧ a hard, glassy mineral found in a variety of forms, as in quartz, opal, or sand —**si·li·ceous** (sə lish′əs) ***adj.***

sil′i·cate (-kit, -kāt′) ***n.*** a salt or ester derived from silica

sil′i·con (-kän′, -kən) ***n.*** ⟦ult. < L *silex*, flint⟧ a nonmetallic chemical element found always in combination

sil′i·cone′ (-kōn′) ***n.*** an organic silicon compound highly resistant to heat, water, etc.

Silicon Valley ⟦after the material used for electronic chips⟧ *name for* an area near San Francisco: a center of high-technology activities

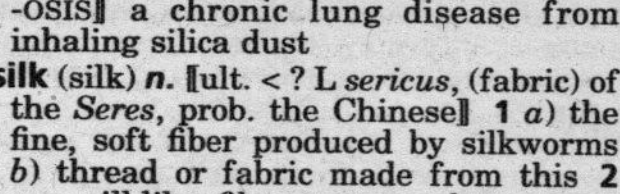

sil′i·co′sis (-kō′sis) ***n.*** ⟦see SILICON & -OSIS⟧ a chronic lung disease from inhaling silica dust

silk (silk) ***n.*** ⟦ult. < ? L *sericus*, (fabric) of the *Seres*, prob. the Chinese⟧ **1** *a*) the fine, soft fiber produced by silkworms *b*) thread or fabric made from this **2** any silklike filament or substance —**silk′en** ***adj.*** —**silk·y** (sil′kē), **-i·er, -i·est,** ***adj.*** —**silk′i·ness** ***n.***

silk-screen process a stencil method of printing a color design through a piece of silk or other fine cloth on which parts of the design not to be printed have been blocked out —**silk′-screen′** ***vt.***

silk′worm′ ***n.*** any of certain moth caterpillars that produce cocoons of silk fiber

sill (sil) ***n.*** **1** a heavy horizontal timber or line of masonry supporting a house wall, etc. **2** a horizontal piece forming the bottom frame of a window or door opening

sil·ly (sil′ē) ***adj.* -li·er, -li·est** ⟦< OE *sælig*, happy⟧ having or showing little sense, judgment, or sobriety; foolish, absurd, etc. —**sil′li·ness** ***n.***

si·lo (sī′lō) ***n.***, *pl.* **-los** ⟦< Gr *siros*⟧ **1** an airtight pit or tower in which green fodder is preserved **2** an underground facility for a long-range ballistic missile

silt (silt) ***n.*** ⟦prob. < Scand⟧ a fine-grained, sandy sediment carried or deposited by water —***vt., vi.*** to fill or choke up with silt

sil·ver (sil′vər) ***n.*** ⟦< OE *seolfer*⟧ **1** a white metallic chemical element that is very ductile and malleable: a precious metal **2** *a*) silver coin *b*) money; riches **3** silverware **4** a lustrous, grayish white —***adj.*** **1** of, containing, or plated with silver **2** silvery **3** marking a 25th anniversary —***vt.*** to cover with or as with silver

sil′ver·fish′ ***n.***, *pl.* **-fish′** a wingless insect with silvery scales and long feelers, found in damp places

silver lining some basis for hope or comfort in the midst of despair

silver nitrate a colorless crystalline salt, used in photography, as an antiseptic, etc.

sil′ver·smith′ ***n.*** an artisan who makes and repairs silver articles

sil′ver-tongued′ (-tuŋd′) ***adj.*** eloquent

sil′ver·ware′ ***n.*** **1** articles, esp. tableware, made of or plated with silver **2** any metal tableware

sil′ver·y ***adj.*** **1** of, like, or containing silver **2** soft and clear in tone

sim·i·an (sim′ē ən) ***adj., n.*** ⟦< L *simia*, an ape⟧ (of or like) an ape or monkey

sim·i·lar (sim′ə lər) ***adj.*** ⟦< L *similis*⟧ nearly but not exactly the same or alike —**sim′i·lar′i·ty** (-ler′ə tē), *pl.* **-ties,** ***n.*** —**sim′i·lar·ly** ***adv.***

sim·i·le (sim′ə lē′) ***n.*** ⟦< L, a likeness⟧ a figure of speech likening one thing to another by the use of *like, as,* etc. (Ex.: tears flowed like wine)

si·mil·i·tude (sə mil′ə to͞od′) ***n.*** ⟦< L *similitudo*⟧ likeness; resemblance

sim·mer (sim′ər) ***vi.*** ⟦echoic⟧ **1** to

remain at or just below the boiling point **2** to be about to break out, as in anger or revolt **—*vt.*** to keep at or just below the boiling point **—*n.*** a simmering

si·mon-pure (sī′mən pyoor′) ***adj.*** ⟦after *Simon Pure*, a character in an 18th-c. play⟧ genuine; authentic

si·mo·ny (sī′mə nē, sim′ə-) ***n.*** ⟦after *Simon* Magus: Acts 8:9-24⟧ the buying or selling of sacraments or benefices

sim·pa·ti·co (sim pät′i kō, -pat′-) ***adj.*** ⟦< It or Sp⟧ compatible or congenial

sim·per (sim′pər) ***vi.*** ⟦early Modern Eng⟧ to smile in a silly or affected way **—*n.*** such a smile

sim·ple (sim′pəl) ***adj.*** **-pler, -plest** ⟦< L *simplus*⟧ **1** having only one or a few parts; uncomplicated **2** easy to do or understand **3** without additions *[*the *simple* facts*]* **4** not ornate or luxurious; plain **5** without guile or deceit **6** without ostentation; natural **7** of low rank or position **8** stupid or foolish **—sim′ple·ness *n.***

simple interest interest computed on principal alone, and not on principal plus interest

sim′ple-mind′ed *adj.* **1** artless; unsophisticated **2** foolish **3** mentally retarded

sim′ple·ton (-tən) ***n.*** a fool

sim·plic·i·ty (sim plis′ə tē) ***n.***, *pl.* **-ties 1** a simple state or quality; freedom from complexity **2** absence of elegance, luxury, etc.; plainness

sim·pli·fy (sim′plə fī′) ***vt.*** **-fied′, -fy′ing** to make simpler or less complex **—sim′pli·fi·ca′tion *n.***

sim·plis·tic (sim plis′tik) ***adj.*** making complex problems unrealistically simple **—sim·plis′ti·cal·ly *adv.***

sim·ply (sim′plē) ***adv.*** **1** in a simple way **2** merely *[simply* trying*]* **3** completely *[simply* furious*]*

sim·u·late (sim′yoo lāt′) ***vt.*** **-lat′ed, -lat′ing** ⟦< L *simulare*⟧ **1** to give a false appearance of; feign **2** to look or act like **—sim′u·la′tion *n.* —sim′u·la′tor *n.***

si·mul·cast (sī′məl kast′) ***vt.*** **-cast′** or **-cast′ed, -cast′ing** to broadcast (a program) simultaneously by radio and television **—*n.*** a program so broadcast

si·mul·ta·ne·ous (sī′məl tā′nē əs) ***adj.*** ⟦< L *simul*, together⟧ occurring, done, etc. at the same time **—si′mul·ta·ne′i·ty** (-tə nē′ə tē, -nā′-) ***n.* —si′mul·ta′ne·ous·ly *adv.***

sin (sin) ***n.*** ⟦OE *synne*⟧ **1** the willful breaking of religious or moral law **2** any offense or fault **—*vi.* sinned, sin′ning** to commit a sin

Si·nai (sī′nī′), **Mount** *Bible* the mountain where Moses received the law from God: Exodus 19

since (sins) ***adv.*** ⟦ult. < OE *sith*, after + *thæt*, that⟧ **1** from then until now *[*I've been here ever *since]* **2** at some time between then and now *[*he has *since* recovered*]* **3** before now; ago *[*long *since* gone*]* **—*prep.* 1** continuously from (then) until now *[since* noon*]* **2** during the period between (then) and now *[*twice *since* May*]* **—*conj.* 1** after the time that *[*two years *since* they met*]* **2** continuously from the time when *[*lonely ever *since* she left*]* **3** because *[since* you're done, let's go*]*

sin·cere (sin sir′) ***adj.*** **-cer′er, -cer′est** ⟦< L *sincerus*, pure⟧ **1** truthful; honest **2** genuine *[sincere* grief*]* **—sin·cere′ly *adv.* —sin·cer′i·ty** (-ser′ə tē) ***n.***

si·ne·cure (sī′nə kyoor′, sin′ə-) ***n.*** ⟦< L *sine*, without + *cura*, care⟧ any position providing an income but requiring little or no work

si·ne di·e (sī′nē dī′ē) ⟦LL, without a day⟧ for an indefinite period

si·ne qua non (sī′nē kwā nän′, sin′ā kwä nōn′) ⟦L, without which not⟧ an indispensable condition or thing

sin·ew (sin′yoo) ***n.*** ⟦OE *seonwe*⟧ **1** a tendon **2** muscular power; strength **—sin′ew·y *adj.***

sin′ful *adj.* wicked; immoral **—sin′ful·ly *adv.***

sing[1] (siŋ) ***vi.*** **sang, sung, sing′ing** ⟦OE *singan*⟧ **1** to produce musical sounds with the voice **2** to use song or verse in praise, etc. *[*of thee I *sing]* **3** to make musical sounds, as a songbird does **4** to hum, buzz, etc., as a bee does **—*vt.* 1** to render (a song, etc.) by singing **2** to extol, etc. in song **3** to bring or put by singing *[*to *sing* a baby to sleep*]* **—*n.*** [Inf.] group singing **—sing′er *n.***

sing[2] *abbrev.* singular

sing′a·long′ *n.* an informal gathering of people to sing songs

Sin·ga·pore (siŋ′ə pôr′) **1** island country off the S tip of the Malay Peninsula: 248 sq. mi.; pop. 2,930,000 **2** its capital, a seaport on the S coast: pop. 2,756,000

singe (sinj) ***vt.*** **singed, singe′ing** ⟦OE *sengan*⟧ **1** to burn superficially **2** to expose (an animal carcass) to flame in removing feathers, etc. **—*n.* 1** a singeing **2** a superficial burn

sin·gle (siŋ′gəl) ***adj.*** ⟦< L *singulus*⟧ **1** *a)* one only *b)* separate and distinct *[*every *single* time*]* **2** solitary **3** of or for one person or family **4** between two persons only *[single* combat*]* **5** unmarried **6** having only one part; not multiple, etc. **7** whole; unbroken *[*a *single* front*]* **—*vt.*** **-gled, -gling** to select from others: usually with *out* **—*vi.*** *Baseball* to hit a single **—*n.* 1** a single person or thing **2** *Baseball* a hit on which the batter reaches first base **3** [*pl.*] *Racket Sports* a match with only one player on each side **—sin′gle·ness *n.***

sin′gle-breast′ed (-bres′tid) ***adj.*** overlapping in front enough to fasten *[*a *single-breasted* coat*]*

single file 1 a single line of people or things, one behind another **2** in such a line

sin′gle-hand′ed *adj., adv.* **1** using only one hand **2** without help **—sin′gle-hand′ed·ly *adv.***

sin′gle-mind′ed *adj.* with only one aim or purpose **—sin′gle-mind′ed·ly *adv.***

sin′gle·ton (-tən) ***n.*** **1** a playing card that is the only one of its suit held by a player **2** a single person or thing

sin′gle-track′ *adj.* ONE-TRACK

sin'gle·tree' (-trē') ***n.*** ⟦< ME *swingle,* rod + *tre,* tree⟧ the crossbar on the hitch of a wagon, etc. to which the traces of a horse's harness are hooked

sin·gly (siŋ'glē) ***adv.*** **1** alone **2** one by one **3** unaided

sing'song' ***n.*** a monotonous rise and fall of tone, as in speaking

sin·gu·lar (siŋ'gyə lər) ***adj.*** ⟦< L *singulus,* single⟧ **1** unique **2** extraordinary; remarkable **3** peculiar; odd **4** *Gram.* designating only one —***n.*** *Gram.* the singular form of a word —**sin'gu·lar'i·ty** (-ler'ə tē) ***n.*** —**sin'gu·lar·ly** ***adv.***

Sin·ha·lese (sin'hə lēz', -lēs') ***adj.*** of Sri Lanka (island country of S Asia) or its principal people, language, etc. —***n.*** **1** *pl.* **-lese'** a member of the Sinhalese people **2** the language of this people

sin·is·ter (sin'is tər) ***adj.*** ⟦< L *sinister,* left-hand (side)⟧ **1** [Archaic] on or to the left-hand side **2** threatening harm, evil, etc. **3** wicked; evil

sink (siŋk) ***vi.*** **sank** or **sunk**, **sunk**, **sink'ing** ⟦OE *sincan*⟧ **1** to go beneath the surface of water, etc. **2** to go down slowly **3** to appear to descend, as the sun does **4** to become lower, as in level, value, or rank **5** to subside: said as of wind or sound **6** to become hollow: said as of the cheeks **7** to pass gradually (*into* sleep, etc.) **8** to approach death —***vt.*** **1** to cause to sink **2** to make (a mine, engraving, etc.) by digging, cutting, etc. **3** to invest **4** to defeat; undo —***n.*** **1** a cesspool or sewer **2** a basin, as in a kitchen, with a drainpipe **3** an area of sunken land —**sink in** [Inf.] to be understood in full —**sink'a·ble** ***adj.***

sink'er ***n.*** **1** one that sinks **2** a lead weight used in fishing

sink'hole' ***n.*** a surface depression resulting when ground collapses

sinking fund a fund built up over time to pay off a future debt, as of a corporation

sin'ner ***n.*** a person who sins

Sino- ⟦< Gr *Sinai*⟧ *combining form* Chinese and

sin tax a tax on something seen as sinful or harmful, as on liquor, tobacco, or gambling

sin·u·ous (sin'yo͞o əs) ***adj.*** ⟦< L *sinus,* a bend⟧ bending or winding in and out; wavy —**sin'u·os'i·ty** (-äs'ə tē) ***n.*** —**sin'u·ous·ly** ***adv.***

si·nus (sī'nəs) ***n.*** ⟦L, a bend⟧ a cavity, hollow, etc.; specif., any of the air cavities in the skull opening into the nasal cavities

si'nus·i'tis (-īt'is) ***n.*** inflammation of the sinuses, esp. those of the skull

Sioux (so͞o) ***n.***, *pl.* **Sioux** (so͞o, so͞oz) a member of a group of Indian tribes of the N U.S. and S Canada —***adj.*** of these tribes

sip (sip) ***vt., vi.*** **sipped**, **sip'ping** ⟦ME *sippen*⟧ to drink a little at a time —***n.*** **1** the act of sipping **2** a quantity sipped —**sip'per** ***n.***

si·phon (sī'fən) ***n.*** ⟦< Gr *siphōn,* tube⟧ a bent tube for carrying liquid out over the edge of a container to a lower level —***vt.*** to draw off through or as through a siphon

SIPHON

sir (sʉr) ***n.*** ⟦ME < *sire,* SIRE⟧ **1** [*sometimes* **S-**] a respectful term of address used to a man: not followed by the name **2** [**S-**] the title used before the name of a knight or baronet

sire (sīr) ***n.*** ⟦< OFr < L *senior,* compar. of *senex,* old⟧ **1** [**S-**] a title of respect used in addressing a king **2** [Old Poet.] a father or forefather **3** the male parent of a four-legged mammal —***vt.*** **sired**, **sir'ing** to beget: said esp. of animals

si·ren (sī'rən) ***n.*** ⟦< Gr *Seirēn*⟧ **1** *Gr. & Rom. Myth.* any of several sea nymphs whose singing lures sailors to their death on rocky coasts **2** a woman considered seductive **3** a warning device producing a loud, wailing sound

sir·loin (sʉr'loin') ***n.*** ⟦< OFr *sur,* over + *loigne,* loin⟧ a choice cut of beef from the loin end in front of the rump

si·roc·co (sə räk'ō) ***n.***, *pl.* **-cos** ⟦It < Ar *sharq,* the east⟧ a hot, oppressive wind blowing from the deserts of N Africa into S Europe

sir·ree or **sir·ee** (sə rē') ***interj.*** ⟦< SIR⟧ used to provide emphasis after *yes* or *no*

sir·up (sʉr'əp, sir'-) ***n.*** *alt. sp. of* SYRUP

sis (sis) ***n.*** [Inf.] *short for* SISTER (senses 1-3)

si·sal (sī'səl, sis'əl) ***n.*** ⟦after *Sisal,* in SE Mexico⟧ a strong fiber obtained from the leaves of an agave

sis·sy (sis'ē) ***n.***, *pl.* **-sies** ⟦dim. of SIS⟧ [Inf.] **1** an effeminate boy or man **2** a timid person —**sis'si·fied'** (-ə fīd') ***adj.***

sis·ter (sis'tər) ***n.*** ⟦< ON *systir*⟧ **1** a woman or girl as she is related to the other children of her parents **2** a half sister or stepsister **3** a female friend who is like a sister **4** a female fellow member of the same race, organization, etc. **5** [*often* **S-**] a nun **6** something of the same kind, model, etc. —**sis'ter·hood'** ***n.*** —**sis'ter·ly** ***adj.***

sis'ter-in-law' ***n.***, *pl.* **sis'ters-in-law'** **1** the sister of one's spouse **2** the wife of one's brother **3** the wife of the brother of one's spouse

Sis·y·phus (sis'ə fəs) *Gr. Myth.* a greedy king doomed in Hades to roll uphill a stone which always rolls down again

sit (sit) ***vi.*** **sat**, **sit'ting** ⟦OE *sittan*⟧ **1** *a)* to rest oneself upon the buttocks, as on a chair *b)* to rest on the haunches with the forelegs braced (said of a dog, etc.) *c)* to perch (said of a bird) **2** to cover and warm eggs for hatching; brood **3** *a)* to occupy a seat as a judge, legislator, etc. *b*) to be in session (said as of court) **4** to pose, as for a portrait **5** to be located **6** to rest or lie as specified *[cares sit lightly on him]* **7** BABY-SIT —*vt.* **1** to cause to sit; seat **2** to keep one's seat on (a horse, etc.) —**sit down** to take a seat —**sit in** to attend: often with *on* —**sit out** to take no part in (a dance, etc.) —**sit up** **1** to sit erect **2** to postpone going to bed **3** [Inf.] to become suddenly alert —**sit'ter** *n.*

si·tar (si tär', si'tär') *n.* ⟦Hindi *sitār*⟧ a lutelike instrument of India with a long, fretted neck

SITAR

sit·com (sit'käm') *n.* [Inf.] *short for* SITUATION COMEDY

sit'-down' (strike) a strike in which the strikers refuse to leave the premises

site (sīt) *n.* ⟦< L *situs*, position⟧ a location or scene

sit'-in' *n.* a method of protest in which demonstrators sit in, and refuse to leave, a public place

sit'ting *n.* **1** the act or position of one that sits **2** a session, as of a court **3** a period of being seated

sitting duck [Inf.] a person or thing especially vulnerable to attack; easy target

sit·u·ate (sich'o͞o āt') *vt.* **-at'ed, -at'ing** ⟦see SITE⟧ to put in a certain place or position; place; locate

sit'u·a'tion *n.* **1** location; position **2** condition with regard to circumstances **3** state of affairs **4** a position of employment

situation comedy a comic TV series made up of episodes involving the same group of characters

sit'-up' or **sit'up'** *n.* an exercise in which a person lying supine rises to a sitting position without using the hands

sitz bath (sits, zits) ⟦< Ger⟧ a therapeutic bath in which only the hips and buttocks are immersed

Si·va (sē'və, shē'-) *n.* Hindu god of destruction and reproduction

six (siks) *adj., n.* ⟦OE *sex*⟧ one more than five; 6; VI —**sixth** *adj., n.*

six'-pack' *n.* a package of six units, as one with six cans of beer

six'-shoot'er *n.* [Inf.] a revolver having a cylinder that holds six cartridges: also **six'-gun'**

six'teen' (-tēn') *adj.* ⟦OE *syxtene*⟧ six more than ten; 16; XVI —**six'teenth'** *adj., n.*

sixth sense intuitive power

six·ty (siks'tē) *adj., n., pl.* **-ties** ⟦OE *sixtig*⟧ six times ten; 60; LX —**the sixties** the numbers or years, as of a century, from 60 through 69 —**six'ti·eth** (-ith) *adj., n.*

siz·a·ble (sī'zə bəl) *adj.* quite large or bulky: also sp. **size'a·ble**

size¹ (sīz) *n.* ⟦ult. < L *sedere*, sit⟧ **1** that quality of a thing which determines how much space it occupies; dimensions or magnitude **2** any of a series of graded classifications of measure into which merchandise is divided —*vt.* **sized, siz'ing** to make or grade according to size —**size up** [Inf.] **1** to make an estimate or judgment of **2** to meet requirements

size² (sīz) *n.* ⟦ME *syse*⟧ a pasty substance used as a glaze or filler on plaster, paper, cloth, etc. —*vt.* **sized, siz'ing** to fill, stiffen, or glaze with size

-sized (sīzd) *combining form* having a (specified) size *[medium-sized]*: also **-size**

siz'ing *n.* **1** SIZE² **2** the act of applying SIZE²

siz·zle (siz'əl) *vi.* **-zled, -zling** ⟦echoic⟧ **1** to make a hissing sound when in contact with heat **2** to be extremely hot —*n.* a sizzling sound

S.J. *abbrev.* Society of Jesus

SK Saskatchewan

skate¹ (skāt) *n.* ⟦< OFr *eschace*, stilt⟧ **1** a metal runner in a frame, fastened to a shoe for gliding on ice **2** a similar frame or shoe with wheels, for gliding on a floor, sidewalk, etc. —*vi.* **skat'ed, skat'ing** to glide or roll on or as on skates —**skat'er** *n.*

skate² (skāt) *n.* ⟦< ON *skata*⟧ any ray fish

skate'board' *n.* a short, oblong board with two wheels at each end, ridden standing up, as down an incline —*vi.* to ride on a skateboard

ske·dad·dle (ski dad''l) *vi.* **-dled, -dling** ⟦< ?⟧ [Inf.] to run away

skeet (skēt) *n.* ⟦< ON *skeyti*, projectile⟧ trapshooting in which the shooter fires from different angles

skein (skān) *n.* ⟦< MFr *escaigne*⟧ a quantity of thread or yarn in a coil

skel·e·ton (skel'ə tən) *n.* ⟦< Gr *skeletos*, dried up⟧ **1** the hard framework of bones of an animal body **2** a supporting framework **3** an outline, as of a book —*adj.* greatly reduced *[a skeleton crew]* —**skel'e·tal** *adj.*

skeleton key a key that can open many simple locks

skep·tic (skep'tik) *n.* ⟦L < Gr *skeptikos*, inquiring⟧ **1** an adherent of skepticism **2** one who habitually questions matters generally accepted **3** one who doubts religious doctrines

skep'ti·cal (-ti kəl) *adj.* doubting; questioning —**skep'ti·cal·ly** *adv.*

skep'ti·cism' (-tə siz'əm) *n.* **1** the doctrine that the truth of all knowledge must always be in question **2** skeptical attitude **3** doubt about religious doctrines

sketch (skech) *n.* ⟦ult. < Gr *schedios,* extempore⟧ **1** a rough drawing or design, done rapidly **2** a brief outline **3** a short, light story, play, etc. —*vt., vi.* make a sketch or sketches (of) —**sketch'y, -i·er, -i·est,** *adj.*

skew (skyo͞o) *vi., vt.* ⟦< OFr *eschiver,* shun < OHG⟧ **1** to slant or set at a slant **2** to distort —*adj.* slanting —*n.* a slant or twist

skew·er (skyo͞o'ər) *n.* ⟦< ON *skifa,* a slice⟧ a long pin used to hold meat together while cooking —*vt.* to fasten or pierce with or as with skewers

ski (skē) *n., pl.* **skis** ⟦Norw < ON *skith,* snowshoe⟧ either of a pair of long runners of wood, etc. fastened to shoes for gliding over snow —*vi.* **skied, ski'ing** to glide on skis —**ski'er** *n.*

skid (skid) *n.* ⟦prob. < ON *skith,* snowshoe⟧ **1** a plank, log, etc., often used as a track upon which to slide a heavy object **2** a low, wooden platform for holding loads **3** a runner on aircraft landing gear **4** a sliding wedge used to brake a wheel **5** the act of skidding —*vt., vi.* **skid'ded, skid'ding** to slide or slip, as a vehicle on ice —**be on** (or **hit**) **the skids** [Slang] to be on the decline, or to fail

skid row ⟦altered < *skid road,* trail to skid logs along⟧ a section of a city frequented by vagrants, derelicts, etc.

skiff (skif) *n.* ⟦< It *schifo*⟧ any light, open boat propelled by oars, motor, or sail

ski lift an endless cable with seats, for carrying skiers up a slope

skill (skil) *n.* ⟦< ON *skil,* distinction⟧ **1** great ability or proficiency **2** *a*) an art, craft, etc., esp. one involving the hands or body *b*) ability in such an art, etc. —**skilled** *adj.* —**skill'ful** or **skil'ful** *adj.*

skil·let (skil'it) *n.* ⟦< ? L *scutra,* dish⟧ a pan for frying

skim (skim) *vt., vi.* **skimmed, skim'ming** ⟦ME *skimen*⟧ **1** to remove (floating matter) from (a liquid) **2** to glance through (a book, etc.) without reading word for word **3** to glide lightly (over)

skim milk milk with the cream removed: also **skimmed milk**

skimp (skimp) *vi., vt.* SCRIMP

skimp'y *adj.* **-i·er, -i·est** [Inf.] barely enough; scanty

skin (skin) *n.* ⟦< ON *skinn*⟧ **1** the outer covering of the animal body **2** a pelt **3** something like skin, as fruit rind, etc. —*vt.* **skinned, skin'ning 1** to remove skin from **2** to injure by scraping (one's knee, etc.) **3** [Inf.] to swindle

skin diving underwater swimming with such gear as a face mask, flippers, scuba equipment, etc. —**skin'-dive', -dived', -div'ing,** *vi.* —**skin diver**

skin'flick' *n.* [Slang] a film emphasizing nudity or explicit sexual activity

skin'flint' *n.* ⟦lit., one who would skin a flint for economy⟧ a miser

-skinned *combining form* having (a specified kind of) skin *[dark-skinned]*

skin'ny *adj.* **-ni·er, -ni·est** without much flesh; very thin —**skin'ni·ness** *n.*

skin'ny-dip' *vi.* **-dipped', -dip'ping** [Inf.] to swim nude —*n.* [Inf.] a swim in the nude

skin'tight' *adj.* tightfitting *[skintight jeans]*

skip (skip) *vi., vt.* **skipped, skip'ping** ⟦ME *skippen*⟧ **1** to move along by hopping on first one foot and then the other **2** to ricochet or bounce **3** to pass from one point to another, omitting or ignoring (what lies between) **4** [Inf.] to leave (town, etc.) hurriedly —*n.* a skipping —**skip it!** [Inf.] it doesn't matter

skip·per (skip'ər) *n.* ⟦< MDu *schip,* a ship⟧ the captain of a ship

skir·mish (skur'mish) *n.* ⟦< It *schermire* < Gmc⟧ **1** a brief fight between small groups, as in a battle **2** any slight, unimportant conflict —*vi.* to take part in a skirmish

skirt (skurt) *n.* ⟦< ON *skyrt,* shirt⟧ **1** that part of a dress, coat, etc. that hangs below the waist **2** a woman's garment that hangs from the waist **3** something like a skirt —*vt., vi.* to be on, or move along, the edge (of)

ski run a slope or course for skiing

skit (skit) *n.* ⟦prob. ult. < ON *skjōta,* to shoot⟧ a short, humorous sketch, as in the theater

ski tow a kind of ski lift for pulling skiers up a slope on their skis

skit·ter (skit'ər) *vi.* ⟦< Scand⟧ to move along quickly and lightly

skit·tish (skit'ish) *adj.* ⟦see SKIT & -ISH⟧ **1** lively; playful **2** easily frightened; jumpy **3** fickle

skiv·vy (skiv'ē) *n., pl.* **-vies** ⟦< ?⟧ [Slang] **1** a man's, esp. a sailor's, short-sleeved undershirt: usually **skivvy shirt 2** [*pl.*] men's underwear

skoal (skōl) *interj.* ⟦< ON *skāl,* a bowl⟧ to your health!: used as a toast

skul·dug·ger·y or **skull·dug·ger·y** (skul dug'ər ē) *n.* ⟦< obs. Scot⟧ [Inf.] sneaky, dishonest behavior; trickery

skulk (skulk) *vi.* ⟦ME *sculken*⟧ to move in a stealthy manner; slink

skull (skul) *n.* ⟦< Scand⟧ **1** the bony framework of the head, enclosing the brain **2** the head; mind

skull'cap' *n.* a light, closefitting, brimless cap, usually worn indoors

skunk (skuŋk) *n.* ⟦< AmInd⟧ **1** a small, bushy-tailed mammal having black fur with white stripes down the back: it ejects a foul-smelling liquid when disturbed or frightened **2** its fur **3** [Inf.] a despicable person

sky (skī) *n., pl.* **skies** ⟦< ON, a cloud⟧ **1** [*often pl.*] the upper atmosphere *[blue skies, a cloudy sky]* **2** the firmament **3** heaven

sky'box' *n.* a private section of seats, often luxurious and usually elevated, in a stadium, etc.

sky'cap' *n.* a porter at an airport terminal

sky diving parachute jumping involving free-fall maneuvers

sky′-high′ *adj.* very high —*adv.* **1** very high **2** in or to pieces

sky′jack′ *vt.* to hijack (an aircraft) —**sky′jack′er** *n.*

sky′lark′ *n.* a Eurasian lark famous for the song it utters as it soars —*vi.* to romp or frolic

sky′light′ *n.* a window in a roof or ceiling

sky′line′ *n.* **1** the visible horizon **2** the outline, as of a city, seen against the sky

sky′rock′et *n.* a fireworks rocket that explodes aloft —*vi., vt.* to rise or cause to rise rapidly

sky′scrap′er *n.* a very tall building

sky′ward *adv., adj.* toward the sky: also **sky′wards** *adv.*

sky′way′ *n.* **1** AIR LANE **2** an elevated highway or walkway

sky′writ′ing *n.* the tracing of words, etc. in the sky by trailing smoke from an airplane —**sky′writ′er** *n.*

slab (slab) *n.* ⟦ME *sclabbe*⟧ a flat, broad, and fairly thick piece

slack[1] (slak) *adj.* ⟦< OE *slæc*⟧ **1** slow; sluggish **2** not busy; dull *[a slack period]* **3** loose; not tight **4** careless *[a slack worker]* —*vt., vi.* to slacken —*n.* **1** a part that hangs loose **2** a lack of tension **3** a dull period; lull —**cut someone some slack** [Slang] to demand less of someone —**slack off** to slacken —**slack′ness** *n.*

slack[2] (slak) *n.* ⟦ME *sleck*⟧ a mixture of small pieces of coal, coal dust, etc. left from screening coal

slack·en (slak′ən) *vt., vi.* **1** to make or become less active, brisk, etc. **2** to loosen or relax, as rope

slack′er *n.* one who shirks

slacks (slaks) *pl.n.* trousers for men or women

slag (slag) *n.* ⟦< earlier LowG *slagge*⟧ the fused refuse separated from metal in smelting

slain (slān) *vt. pp. of* SLAY

slake (slāk) *vt.* **slaked**, **slak′ing** ⟦< OE *slæc*, SLACK[1]⟧ **1** to satisfy (thirst, etc.) **2** to produce a chemical change in (lime) by mixing with water

sla·lom (slä′ləm) *n.* ⟦Norw⟧ a downhill ski race over a zigzag course —*vi.* to take part in a slalom

slam (slam) *vt.* **slammed**, **slam′ming** ⟦prob. < Scand⟧ **1** to shut, hit, throw, or put with force and noise **2** [Inf.] to criticize severely —*n.* **1** a slamming **2** [Inf.] a severe criticism

slam′-bang′ [Inf.] *adv.* **1** swiftly or abruptly and recklessly **2** noisily —*adj.* lively, noisy, etc.

slam′-dunk′ *n.* *Basketball* a forceful shot from directly above the basket

slam·mer (slam′ər) *n.* [Slang] a prison or jail

slan·der (slan′dər) *n.* ⟦see SCANDAL⟧ **1** the utterance of a falsehood that damages another's reputation **2** such a spoken statement —*vt.* to utter a slander about —**slan′der·er** *n.* —**slan′der·ous** *adj.*

slang (slaŋ) *n.* ⟦< ?⟧ highly informal speech that is outside standard usage and consists both of coined words and phrases and of new meanings given to established terms —**slang′y**, **-i·er**, **-i·est**, *adj.*

slant (slant) *vt., vi.* ⟦< Scand⟧ **1** to incline; slope **2** to tell so as to express a particular bias —*n.* **1** an oblique surface, line, etc. **2** a point of view or attitude —*adj.* sloping

slap (slap) *n.* ⟦echoic⟧ **1** a blow with something flat, as the palm of the hand **2** an insult or rebuff —*vt.* **slapped**, **slap′ping** **1** to strike with something flat **2** to put, hit, etc. with force

slap′dash′ *adj., adv.* hurried(ly), careless(ly), haphazard(ly), etc.

slap′-hap′py *adj.* [Slang] **1** dazed, as by blows **2** silly or giddy

slap′stick′ *n.* crude comedy full of horseplay —*adj.* characterized by such comedy

slash (slash) *vt.* ⟦< ? OFr *esclachier*, to break⟧ **1** to cut with sweeping strokes, as of a knife **2** to cut slits in **3** to reduce drastically *[slash prices]* —*vi.* to make a sweeping stroke as with a knife —*n.* **1** a slashing **2** a cut made by slashing **3** a virgule —**slash′er** *n.*

slash′-and-burn′ *adj.* **1** of a method of clearing fields by cutting down and burning vegetation **2** indiscriminately destructive

slash pocket a pocket (in a garment) with a finished diagonal opening

slat (slat) *n.* ⟦< OFr *esclat*, fragment⟧ a narrow strip of wood, metal, etc.

slate (slāt) *n.* ⟦see prec.⟧ **1** a hard, fine-grained rock that cleaves into thin, smooth layers **2** a thin piece of slate or slatelike material, as a roofing tile or writing tablet **3** the bluish-gray color of most slate: also **slate blue** —*vt.* **slat′ed**, **slat′ing** **1** to cover with slate **2** to designate, as for candidacy —**a clean slate** a record showing no marks of discredit, dishonor, etc.

slath·er (sla*th*′ər) *vt.* ⟦< ?⟧ [Inf. or Dial.] to cover or spread on thickly

slat·tern (slat′ərn) *n.* ⟦< dial. *slatter*, to slop⟧ a slovenly or sluttish woman —**slat′tern·ly** *adj.*

slaugh·ter (slôt′ər) *n.* ⟦< ON *slātr*, lit., slain flesh⟧ **1** the killing of animals for food; butchering **2** the brutal killing of a person **3** the killing of many people, as in battle —*vt.* **1** to kill (animals) for food; butcher **2** to kill (people) brutally or in large numbers —**slaugh′ter·er** *n.*

slaugh′ter·house′ *n.* a place where animals are butchered for food

Slav (släv, slav) *n.* a member of a group of peoples of E and SE Europe, including Russians, Serbs, Czechs, Poles, etc. —*adj. var. of* SLAVIC

slave (slāv) *n.* ⟦< Gr *Sklabos*, ult. < OSlav *Slovēne*, first used of captive Slavs⟧ **1** a human being who is owned as property by another **2** one dominated by some influence, etc. **3** one who slaves —*vi.* **slaved**, **slav′ing** to work like a slave; drudge

slave driver **1** one who oversees slaves **2** any merciless taskmaster

slav·er (slav′ər) ***vi.*** ⟦< Scand⟧ to drool

slav·er·y (slā′vər ē) ***n.*** **1** the owning of slaves as a practice **2** the condition of a slave; bondage **3** drudgery; toil

Slav·ic (släv′ik, slav′-) ***adj.*** of the Slavs, their languages, etc. —***n.*** a family of languages, including Russian, Polish, Czech, Bulgarian, etc.

slav·ish (slā′vish) ***adj.*** **1** of or like slaves; servile **2** blindly dependent or imitative —**slav′ish·ly** ***adv.***

slaw (slô) ***n.*** ⟦Du *sla* < Fr *salade*, salad⟧ *short for* COLESLAW

slay (slā) ***vt.*** **slew, slain, slay′ing** ⟦OE *slean*⟧ to kill in a violent way —**slay′er** ***n.***

sleaze (slēz) ***n.*** ⟦< SLEAZY⟧ [Slang] **1** sleaziness **2** someone or something sleazy

slea·zoid (slē′zoid′) [Slang] ***adj.*** SLEAZY (sense 2) —***n.*** a coarse or immoral person

slea·zy (slē′zē) ***adj.*** **-zi·er, -zi·est** ⟦< *silesia*, orig. cloth made in central Europe⟧ **1** flimsy or thin in substance **2** shoddy, shabby, immoral, etc. —**slea′zi·ly** ***adv.*** —**slea′zi·ness** ***n.***

sled (sled) ***n.*** ⟦ME *sledde*⟧ a vehicle on runners for moving over snow, ice, etc. —***vt.***, ***vi.*** **sled′ded, sled′ding** to carry or ride on a sled —**sled′der** ***n.***

sledge[1] (slej) ***n.*** ⟦OE *slecge*⟧ SLEDGE-HAMMER

sledge[2] (slej) ***n.*** ⟦MDu *sleedse*⟧ a sled or sleigh

sledge′ham′mer ***n.*** ⟦see SLEDGE[1]⟧ a long, heavy hammer, usually held with both hands

sleek (slēk) ***adj.*** ⟦var. of SLICK⟧ **1** smooth and shiny; glossy **2** of well-fed or well-groomed appearance **3** suave, elegant, etc. —***vt.*** to make sleek —**sleek′ly** ***adv.*** —**sleek′ness** ***n.***

sleep (slēp) ***n.*** ⟦OE *slæp*⟧ **1** the natural, regularly recurring rest for the body, during which there is little or no conscious thought **2** any state like this —***vi.*** **slept, sleep′ing** to be in a state of or like sleep —**sleep off** to rid oneself of by sleeping —**sleep′less** ***adj.*** —**sleep′less·ness** ***n.***

sleep′er ***n.*** **1** one who sleeps **2** a railroad car with berths for sleeping: also **sleeping car** **3** a beam laid flat to support something **4** something that achieves an unexpected success

sleeping bag a warmly lined, zippered bag for sleeping in outdoors

sleeping sickness an infectious disease, esp. of Africa, transmitted by the tsetse fly and characterized by lethargy, prolonged coma, etc.

sleep′o′ver ***n.*** a spending the night at another's home, as by a group of young people for fun

sleep′walk′ing ***n.*** the act of walking while asleep —**sleep′walk′er** ***n.***

sleep′wear′ ***n.*** NIGHTCLOTHES

sleep′y ***adj.*** **-i·er, -i·est** **1** ready or inclined to sleep; drowsy **2** dull; idle [a *sleepy* town] —**sleep′i·ly** ***adv.*** —**sleep′i·ness** ***n.***

sleet (slēt) ***n.*** ⟦ME *slete*⟧ **1** partly frozen rain **2** the icy coating formed when rain freezes on trees, etc. —***vi.*** to fall as sleet —**sleet′y** ***adj.***

sleeve (slēv) ***n.*** ⟦OE *sliefe*⟧ **1** that part of a garment that covers the arm **2** a tubelike part fitting over or around another part —**up one's sleeve** hidden but ready at hand —**sleeve′less** ***adj.***

sleigh (slā) ***n.*** ⟦Du *slee*⟧ a vehicle on runners, usually horse-drawn, for moving over snow, ice, etc.

sleight of hand (slīt) ⟦< ON *slœgr*, crafty⟧ **1** skill with the hands, esp. in deceiving onlookers, as in magic **2** a trick thus performed

slen·der (slen′dər) ***adj.*** ⟦ME *s(c)lendre* < ?⟧ **1** long and thin **2** slim of figure **3** small in amount, size, force, etc. —**slen′der·ness** ***n.***

slen′der·ize′ ***vt.***, ***vi.*** **-ized′, -iz′ing** to make or become slender

slept (slept) ***vi.***, ***vt.*** *pt. & pp. of* SLEEP

sleuth (slo͞oth) ***n.*** ⟦< ON *slóth*, a trail⟧ [Inf.] a detective

slew[1] (slo͞o) ***n.*** ⟦Ir *sluagh*, a host⟧ [Inf.] a large number or amount

slew[2] (slo͞o) ***vt.*** *pt. of* SLAY

slice (slīs) ***n.*** ⟦< OFr *esclicier*⟧ **1** a relatively thin, broad piece cut from something **2** a part or share —***vt.*** **sliced, slic′ing** **1** to cut into slices **2** to cut off as in a slice or slices: often with *off, from, away,* etc. **3** to hit (a ball) so that it curves to the right if right-handed or the left if left-handed —**slic′er** ***n.***

slick (slik) ***vt.*** ⟦OE *slician*⟧ **1** to make smooth **2** [Inf.] to make smart, neat, etc.: usually with *up* —***adj.*** **1** sleek; smooth **2** slippery **3** adept; clever **4** [Inf.] smooth but superficial, tricky, etc. —***n.*** **1** a smooth area on the water, as from a layer of oil **2** a slippery, oily area on the surface of a road —**slick′ly** ***adv.*** —**slick′ness** ***n.***

slick′er ***n.*** **1** a loose, waterproof coat **2** [Inf.] a tricky person

slide (slīd) ***vi.*** **slid** (slid), **slid′ing** ⟦OE *slidan*⟧ **1** to move along in constant contact with a smooth surface, as on ice **2** to glide **3** to slip [it *slid* from his hand] —***vt.*** **1** to cause to slide **2** to place quietly or deftly (*in* or *into*) —***n.*** **1** a sliding **2** a smooth, often inclined surface for sliding down **3** something that works by sliding **4** a photographic transparency for use with a viewer or projector **5** a small glass plate on which objects are mounted for microscopic study **6** the fall of a mass of rock, snow, etc. down a slope —**let slide** to fail to attend to properly

slide fastener a zipper or a zipperlike device with two grooved plastic edges joined or separated by a sliding tab

slid′er ***n.*** **1** one that slides **2** *Baseball* a fast pitch that curves

sliding scale a schedule, as of fees, wages, etc., that varies with given conditions, as cost of living, etc.

slight (slīt) ***adj.*** ⟦OE *sliht*⟧ **1** *a)* light in build; slender *b)* frail; fragile **2** lacking strength, importance, etc. **3** small in amount or extent —*vt.* **1** to neglect **2** to treat with disrespect **3** to treat as unimportant —*n.* a slighting or being slighted —**slight'ly** *adv.* —**slight'ness** *n.*

slim (slim) *adj.* **slim'mer, slim'mest** ⟦< Du, bad⟧ **1** small in girth; slender **2** small in amount, degree, etc. —*vt., vi.* **slimmed, slim'ming** to make or become slim —**slim'ness** *n.*

slime (slīm) *n.* ⟦OE *slim*⟧ any soft, moist, slippery, often sticky matter —**slim'y, -i·er, -i·est,** *adj.*

sling (sliŋ) *n.* ⟦prob. < ON *slyngua*, to throw⟧ **1** a primitive instrument whirled by hand for throwing stones **2** a cast; throw; fling **3** *a*) a supporting band, etc. as for raising a heavy object *b*) a cloth looped from the neck under an injured arm for support —*vt.* **slung, sling'ing 1** to throw as with a sling **2** to suspend

sling'shot' *n.* a Y-shaped piece of wood, etc. with an elastic band attached to it for shooting stones, etc.

slink (sliŋk) *vi.* **slunk, slink'ing** ⟦OE *slincan*, to creep⟧ to move in a furtive or sneaking way

slink'y *adj.* **-i·er, -i·est 1** furtive; sneaking **2** [Slang] sinuous in movement or line

slip[1] (slip) *vi.* **slipped, slip'ping** ⟦ME *slippen*, ult. < Ger⟧ **1** to go quietly or secretly *[to slip out of a room]* **2** to pass smoothly or easily **3** to escape from one's memory, grasp, etc. **4** to slide, lose footing, etc. **5** to make a mistake; err **6** to become worse —*vt.* **1** to cause to slip **2** to put, pass, etc. deftly or stealthily **3** to escape from (the memory) —*n.* **1** a space between piers for docking ships **2** a woman's undergarment the length of a skirt **3** a pillow case **4** a slipping or falling down **5** an error or mistake —**let slip** to say without intending to —**slip up** to make a mistake

slip[2] (slip) *n.* ⟦< MDu *slippen*, to cut⟧ **1** a stem, root, etc. of a plant, used for planting or grafting **2** a young, slim person **3** a small piece of paper

slip'case' *n.* a boxlike container for a book or books, open at one end

slip'cov'er *n.* a removable, fitted cloth cover for a chair, sofa, etc.

slip'knot' *n.* a knot that will slip along the rope around which it is tied

slip·page (slip'ij) *n.* a slipping, as of one gear past another

slipped disk a ruptured cartilaginous disk between vertebrae

slip·per (slip'ər) *n.* a light, low shoe easily slipped on the foot, esp. one for indoor wear —**slip'pered** *adj.*

slip·per·y (slip'ər ē, slip'rē) *adj.* **-i·er, -i·est 1** liable to cause slipping, as a wet surface **2** tending to slip away, as from a grasp **3** unreliable; deceitful

slip'shod' (-shäd') *adj.* ⟦< obs. *slip-shoe*, a slipper⟧ careless, as in workmanship

slip'-up' *n.* [Inf.] an error: also **slip'up'**

slit (slit) *vt.* **slit, slit'ting** ⟦ME *slitten*⟧ **1** to cut or split open, esp. lengthwise **2** to cut into strips —*n.* a straight, narrow cut, opening, etc.

slith·er (sli*th*'ər) *vi.* ⟦< OE *slidan*, to slide⟧ to slip, slide, or glide along —**slith'er·y** *adj.*

sliv·er (sliv'ər) *n.* ⟦< OE *slifan*, to split⟧ a thin, sharp piece cut or split off; splinter —*vt., vi.* to cut or break into slivers

slob (släb) *n.* ⟦Ir *slab*, mud⟧ [Inf.] a sloppy or coarse person

slob·ber (släb'ər) *vi.* ⟦prob. < LowG *slubberen*, to swig⟧ to drool

sloe (slō) *n.* ⟦OE *sla*⟧ **1** the blackthorn **2** its small, plumlike fruit

sloe'-eyed' *adj.* **1** having large, dark eyes **2** having almond-shaped eyes

sloe gin a liqueur of gin flavored with sloes

slog (släg) *vt., vi.* **slogged, slog'ging** ⟦ME *sluggen*, go slowly⟧ **1** to make (one's way) with great effort; plod **2** to toil (at) —*n.* an arduous trip, task, etc. —**slog'ger** *n.*

slo·gan (slō'gən) *n.* ⟦< Gael *sluagh*, a host + *gairm*, a call: orig., a battle cry⟧ **1** a motto associated with a political party, etc. **2** a catchy phrase used in advertising

sloop (slo͞op) *n.* ⟦< LowG *slupen*, to glide⟧ a sailing vessel having a single mast with a mainsail and a jib

slop (släp) *n.* ⟦OE *sloppe*⟧ **1** watery snow or mud; slush **2** a puddle of spilled liquid **3** unappetizing, watery food **4** [*often pl.*] liquid waste —*vi., vt.* **slopped, slop'ping** to spill or splash

slope (slōp) *n.* ⟦< OE *slupan*, to glide⟧ **1** rising or falling ground **2** any inclined line, surface, etc.; slant **3** the amount or degree of deviation from the horizontal or vertical —*vi.* **sloped, slop'ing** to have an upward or downward inclination; incline; slant —*vt.* to cause to slope

slop·py (släp'ē) *adj.* **-pi·er, -pi·est 1** splashy; slushy **2** *a*) slovenly *b*) slipshod **3** [Inf.] gushingly sentimental —**slop'pi·ness** *n.*

sloppy Joe (jō) ground meat cooked with tomato sauce, spices, etc. and served on a bun

slosh (släsh) *vi.* ⟦var. of SLUSH⟧ **1** to splash through water, mud, etc. **2** to splash about: said of a liquid —*n.* the sound of sloshing liquid —**slosh'y** *adj.*

slot (slät) *n.* ⟦< OFr *esclot*, hollow between the breasts⟧ **1** a narrow opening, as for a coin in a vending machine **2** [Inf.] a position in a group, etc. —*vt.* **slot'ted, slot'ting 1** to make a slot in **2** [Inf.] to place in a series or sequence

sloth (slôth, släth; *also* slōth) *n.* ⟦< OE *slaw*, slow⟧ **1** laziness; idleness **2** a slow-moving, tree-dwelling mammal of tropical America that hangs, back down, from branches —**sloth'ful** *adj.* —**sloth'ful·ness** *n.*

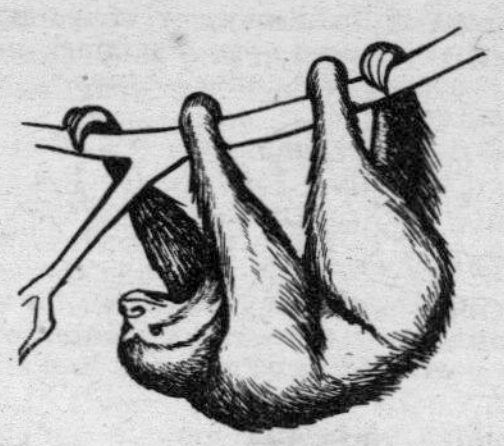

THREE-TOED SLOTH

slot machine a machine, specif. a gambling device, activated by the insertion of a coin in a slot

slouch (slouch) ***n.*** ⟦< ON *slōka*, to droop⟧ **1** a lazy or incompetent person **2** a drooping or slovenly posture —***vi.*** to sit, stand, walk, etc. in a slouch —**slouch'y**, **-i·er**, **-i·est**, ***adj.***

slough[1] (sluf) ***n.*** ⟦ME *slouh*, a skin⟧ a castoff layer or covering, as the skin of a snake —***vt.*** to throw off; discard

slough[2] (slou) ***n.*** ⟦OE *sloh*⟧ **1** a place full of soft, deep mud **2** deep, hopeless dejection

Slo·vak (slō'väk', -vak') ***n.*** **1** a member of a Slavic people living chiefly in Slovakia **2** the language of this people —***adj.*** of the Slovaks

Slo·va·ki·a (slō vä'kē ə) country in central Europe: formerly the E republic of Czechoslovakia: 18,933 sq. mi.; pop. 5,297,000

slov·en (sluv'ən) ***n.*** ⟦prob. < MDu *slof*, lax⟧ a careless, untidy person —**slov'en·ly**, **-li·er**, **-li·est**, ***adj.***

Slo·ve·ni·a (slō vē'nē ə) country in SE Europe: 7,819 sq. mi.; pop. 1,966,000 —**Slo·ve'ni·an** or **Slo'vene'** ***adj.***, ***n.***

slow (slō) ***adj.*** ⟦OE *slaw*⟧ **1** not quick in understanding **2** taking a longer time than is usual **3** marked by low speed, etc.; not fast **4** behind the correct time, as a clock **5** passing tediously; dull —***vt.***, ***vi.*** to make or become slow or slower: often with *up* or *down* —***adv.*** in a slow manner —**slow'ly** ***adv.*** —**slow'ness** ***n.***

slow'down' ***n.*** a slowing down, as of production

slow'-mo'tion ***adj.*** **1** moving slowly **2** designating a film or taped TV sequence showing the action slowed down

slow'poke' (-pōk') ***n.*** [Slang] a person who acts or moves slowly

slow'-wit'ted ***adj.*** mentally slow; dull

SLR ***n.*** ⟦*s*(*ingle*) *l*(*ens*) *r*(*eflex*)⟧ a camera allowing the photographer to see the subject through the same lens that brings the image to the film

slub (slub) ***n.*** ⟦< ?⟧ a soft, thick lump or irregularity in yarn or fabric

sludge (sluj) ***n.*** ⟦var. of *slutch*, mud⟧ any heavy, slimy deposit, sediment, etc.

slue (sloo) ***vt.***, ***vi.*** **slued**, **slu'ing** ⟦< ?⟧ to turn or swing around, as on a pivot

slug[1] (slug) ***n.*** ⟦ME *slugge*, clumsy one⟧ a small mollusk like a shell-less snail

slug[2] (slug) ***n.*** ⟦prob. < prec.⟧ a small piece of metal; specif., a bullet or counterfeit coin

slug[3] (slug) ***n.*** ⟦prob. < Dan *sluge*, to gulp⟧ [Slang] a drink of liquor

slug[4] (slug) [Inf.] ***vt.*** **slugged**, **slug'ging** ⟦< ON *slag*⟧ to hit hard, esp. with the fist or a bat —***n.*** a hard blow or hit —**slug'ger** ***n.***

slug·gard (slug'ərd) ***n.*** ⟦< ME *sluggen*, be lazy⟧ a lazy person

slug'gish (-ish) ***adj.*** ⟦< SLUG[1]⟧ **1** lacking energy or alertness **2** slow or slow-moving **3** not functioning with normal vigor —**slug'gish·ness** ***n.***

sluice (sloos) ***n.*** ⟦< L *excludere*, to shut out⟧ **1** an artificial channel for water, with a gate to regulate the flow **2** such a gate: also **sluice gate** **3** any channel for excess water **4** a sloping trough, as for washing gold ore —***vt.*** **sluiced**, **sluic'ing** **1** to draw off through a sluice **2** to wash with water from a sluice

slum (slum) ***n.*** ⟦< ?⟧ a populous area characterized by poverty, poor housing, etc. —***vi.*** **slummed**, **slum'ming** to visit a slum, etc. for reasons held to be condescending —**slum'my**, **-mi·er**, **-mi·est**, ***adj.***

slum·ber (slum'bər) ***vi.*** ⟦OE *sluma*⟧ **1** to sleep **2** to be inactive —***n.*** **1** sleep **2** an inactive state

slum'lord' ***n.*** [Slang] an absentee landlord who exploits slum property

slump (slump) ***vi.*** ⟦prob. < Ger⟧ **1** to fall or sink suddenly **2** to slouch —***n.*** a decline in activity, prices, performance, etc.

slung (sluŋ) ***vt.*** *pt. & pp. of* SLING

slunk (sluŋk) ***vi.*** *pt. & pp. of* SLINK

slur (slur) ***vt.*** **slurred**, **slur'ring** ⟦prob. < MDu *sleuren*, to drag⟧ **1** to pass over lightly: often with *over* **2** to pronounce indistinctly **3** to disparage **4** *Music* to produce (successive notes) by gliding without a break —***n.*** **1** a slurring **2** an aspersion **3** *Music* a curved line connecting notes to be slurred

slurp (slurp) [Slang] ***vt.***, ***vi.*** ⟦Du *slurpen*, to sip⟧ to drink or eat noisily —***n.*** a loud sipping or sucking sound

slur·ry (slur'ē) ***n.***, *pl.* **-ries** ⟦< MDu *slore*, thin mud⟧ a thin, watery mixture of clay, cement, etc.

slush (slush) ***n.*** ⟦prob. < Scand⟧ **1** partly melted snow or ice **2** soft mud **3** sentimentality; drivel —**slush'y**, **-i·er**, **-i·est**, ***adj.***

slush fund money used for bribery, political pressure, etc.

slut (slut) ***n.*** ⟦ME *slutte*⟧ **1** a dirty, slovenly woman **2** a sexually promiscuous woman: a derogatory term —**slut'tish** ***adj.***

sly (slī) ***adj.*** **sli'er** or **sly'er**, **sli'est** or **sly'est** ⟦< ON *slœgr*⟧ **1** skillful at trickery; crafty **2** cunningly underhanded **3** playfully mischievous —**on the sly** secretly —**sly'ly** or **sli'ly** ***adv.*** —**sly'ness** ***n.***

smack[1] (smak) ***n.*** ⟦OE *smæc*⟧ **1** a slight taste or flavor **2** a small amount; trace —***vi.*** to have a smack (*of*)

smack[2] (smak) ***n.*** ⟦< ?⟧ **1** a sharp noise made by parting the lips suddenly **2** a loud kiss **3** a slap **—*vt.*** **1** to part (the lips) with a smack **2** to slap loudly **—*adv.*** **1** with a smack **2** directly

smack[3] (smak) ***n.*** ⟦prob. < Du *smak*⟧ a fishing boat with a well for keeping fish alive

smack[4] (smak) ***n.*** ⟦< ?⟧ [Slang] heroin

smack'er ***n.*** [Old Slang] a dollar

small (smôl) ***adj.*** ⟦OE *smæl*⟧ **1** comparatively little in size; not big **2** little in quantity, extent, duration, etc. **3** of little importance; trivial **4** young *[small* children*]* **5** mean; petty **6** lowercase **—*n.*** the small part *[*the *small* of the back*]*

small arms firearms of small caliber, as pistols, rifles, etc.

small fry ⟦see FRY[2]⟧ **1** children **2** persons considered insignificant

small intestine the narrow section of the intestines, extending from the stomach to the large intestine

small'-mind'ed ***adj.*** mean, narrow-minded, or selfish

small'pox' ***n.*** an acute, contagious viral disease characterized by fever and pustules

small talk light conversation about common, everyday things; chitchat

small'-time' ***adj.*** [Inf.] minor or petty

smarm·y (smär'mē) ***adj.*** **-i·er, -i·est** ⟦< *smarm*, to smear⟧ [Inf., Chiefly Brit.] flattering in an insincere way

smart (smärt) ***vi.*** ⟦OE *smeortan*⟧ **1** *a)* to cause sharp, stinging pain, as a slap does *b)* to feel such pain **2** to feel mental distress or irritation **—*n.*** **1** a stinging sensation **2** [*pl.*] [Slang] intelligence **—*adj.*** **1** causing sharp pain **2** sharp, as pain **3** brisk; lively *[*a *smart* pace*]* **4** intelligent **5** neat; trim **6** stylish **7** [Inf.] insolent **8** *Comput. a)* working by means of a computer or microchip *b)* programmed in advance **—smart'ly *adv.*** **—smart'ness *n.***

smart al·eck or **smart al·ec** (al'ik) ⟦prec. + *Aleck*, dim. of *Alexander*⟧ [Inf.] an offensively conceited person

smart bomb [Mil. Slang] a guided missile directed to its target by electronic means

smart'en ***vt.***, ***vi.*** to make or become smart or smarter: usually with *up*

smash (smash) ***vt.***, ***vi.*** ⟦prob. < MASH⟧ **1** to break into pieces with noise or violence **2** to hit, collide, or move with force **3** to destroy or be destroyed **—*n.*** **1** a hard, heavy hit **2** a violent, noisy breaking **3** a violent collision **4** a popular success

smash'ing ***adj.*** [Inf.] extraordinary

smash'up' ***n.*** **1** a violent wreck or collision **2** total failure; ruin

smat·ter·ing (smat'ər iŋ) ***n.*** ⟦ME *smateren*, to chatter⟧ **1** a slight knowledge **2** a small number or limited amount

smear (smir) ***vt.*** ⟦< OE *smerian*, to anoint⟧ **1** to cover or soil with something greasy, sticky, etc. **2** to apply (something greasy, etc.) **3** to streak by rubbing **4** to slander **—*vi.*** to be or become smeared **—*n.*** **1** a mark made by smearing **2** slander **—smear'y, -i·er, -i·est, *adj.***

smell (smel) ***vt.*** **smelled** or [Chiefly Brit.] **smelt, smell'ing** ⟦ME *smellen*⟧ **1** to be aware of through the nose; detect the odor of **2** to sense the presence of *[*to *smell* trouble*]* **—*vi.*** **1** to use the sense of smell; sniff **2** to have an odor **3** to stink **—*n.*** **1** the sense by which odors are perceived **2** odor; scent **3** a smelling

smelling salts an ammonia compound sniffed to relieve faintness

smell'y ***adj.*** **-i·er, -i·est** having an unpleasant smell

smelt[1] (smelt) ***n.*** ⟦OE⟧ a small, silvery food fish found esp. in northern seas

smelt[2] (smelt) ***vt.*** ⟦< MDu *smelten*⟧ **1** to melt (ore, etc.) so as to extract the pure metal **2** to refine (metal) in this way

smelt[3] (smelt) ***vt.***, ***vi.*** *chiefly Brit. pt. & pp. of* SMELL

smelt'er ***n.*** **1** one whose work is smelting **2** a place for smelting

smidg·en (smij'ən) ***n.*** ⟦prob. < dial. *smidge*, particle⟧ [Inf.] a small amount; bit: also **smidg'in** or **smidge**

smile (smīl) ***vi.*** **smiled, smil'ing** ⟦ME *smilen*⟧ to show pleasure, amusement, affection, etc. by an upward curving of the mouth **—*vt.*** to express with a smile **—*n.*** the act or expression of smiling **—smil'ing·ly *adv.***

smirch (smurch) ***vt.*** ⟦prob. < OFr *esmorcher*, to hurt⟧ **1** to soil or stain **2** to dishonor **—*n.*** **1** a smudge; smear **2** a stain on reputation, etc.

smirk (smurk) ***vi.*** ⟦< OE *smearcian*, to smile⟧ to smile in a conceited or complacent way **—*n.*** such a smile

smite (smīt) ***vt.*** **smote, smit'ten** or **smote, smit'ing** ⟦OE *smitan*⟧ **1** to strike with powerful effect **2** to affect or impress strongly

smith (smith) ***n.*** **1** one who makes or repairs metal objects **2** *short for* BLACKSMITH

Smith (smith), Captain **John** 1580?-1631; Eng. colonist in America

smith·er·eens (smith'ər ēnz') ***pl.n.*** ⟦Ir *smidirīn*⟧ [Inf.] fragments; bits

smith·y (smith'ē) ***n.***, *pl.* **-ies** the workshop of a smith, esp. a blacksmith

smock (smäk) ***n.*** ⟦OE *smoc*⟧ a loose, shirtlike outer garment worn to protect the clothes

smock'ing ***n.*** decorative stitching used to gather cloth and make it hang in folds

smog (smäg, smôg) ***n.*** ⟦SM(OKE) + (F)OG⟧ a low-lying, perceptible layer of polluted air **—smog'gy, -gi·er, -gi·est, *adj.***

smoke (smōk) ***n.*** ⟦OE *smoca*⟧ **1** the vaporous matter arising from something burning **2** any vapor, etc. like this **3** an act of smoking tobacco, etc. **4** a cigarette, cigar, etc. **—*vi.*** **smoked, smok'ing** **1** to give off smoke **2** *a)* to draw in and exhale the smoke of tobacco, etc. *b)* to be a habitual user of cigarettes, etc. **—*vt.*** **1** to cure (meat, etc.) with smoke **2** to use (a pipe, cigarette, etc.) in smoking **3** to drive out as with smoke —**smoke out** to force out of hiding —**smoke'less** ***adj.*** —**smok'er** ***n.***

smoke detector a warning device that sets off a loud signal when excessive smoke or heat is detected

smoke'house' ***n.*** a building where meats, fish, etc. are cured with smoke

smoke screen **1** a cloud of smoke for hiding troop movements, etc. **2** anything said or done to conceal or mislead

smoke'stack' ***n.*** a pipe for discharging smoke from a factory, etc.

smok·y (smō'kē) ***adj.*** **-i·er, -i·est** **1** giving off smoke **2** of or like smoke **3** filled with smoke —**smok'i·ness** ***n.***

smol·der (smōl'dər) ***vi.*** ⟦ME *smoldren*⟧ **1** to burn and smoke without flame **2** to exist in a suppressed state —***n.*** a smoldering

smooch (smo͞och) ***n., vt., vi.*** [Slang] kiss

smoosh (smo͝osh) ***vt.*** [Inf.] *alt. sp. of* SMUSH

smooth (smo͞oth) ***adj.*** ⟦OE *smoth*⟧ **1** having an even surface, with no roughness **2** without lumps **3** even or gentle in movement *[a smooth voyage]* **4** free from interruptions, obstacles, etc. **5** pleasing to the taste; not harsh or bitter **6** having an easy, flowing rhythm or sound **7** polished or ingratiating, esp. in an insincere way —***vt.*** **1** to make level or even **2** to remove lumps or wrinkles from **3** to free from difficulties, etc.; make easy **4** to make calm; soothe **5** to polish or refine —***adv.*** in a smooth manner —**smooth'ly** ***adv.*** —**smooth'ness** ***n.***

smooth muscle involuntary muscle tissue occurring in the uterus, stomach, blood vessels, etc.

smooth'-spo'ken ***adj.*** speaking in a pleasing, persuasive, or polished manner

smor·gas·bord or **smör·gås·bord** (smôr'gəs bôrd', smur'-) ***n.*** ⟦Swed⟧ a wide variety of appetizers, cheeses, meats, etc., served buffet style

smote (smōt) ***vt., vi.*** *pt. & alt. pp. of* SMITE

smoth·er (smuth'ər) ***vt.*** ⟦< ME *smorther*, dense smoke⟧ **1** to keep from getting air; suffocate **2** to cover over thickly **3** to stifle *[to smother a yawn]* —***vi.*** to be suffocated

smoul·der (smōl'dər) ***vi., n.*** *Brit. sp. of* SMOLDER

smudge (smuj) ***vt., vi.*** **smudged, smudg'ing** ⟦ME *smogen*⟧ to make or become dirty; smear —***n.*** **1** a dirty spot **2** a fire made to produce dense smoke —**smudg'y, -i·er, -i·est,** ***adj.***

smug (smug) ***adj.*** **smug'ger, smug'gest** ⟦prob. < LowG *smuk*, trim, neat⟧ annoyingly self-satisfied; complacent —**smug'ly** ***adv.*** —**smug'ness** ***n.***

smug·gle (smug'əl) ***vt.*** **-gled, -gling** ⟦< LowG *smuggeln*⟧ **1** to bring into or take out of a country secretly or illegally **2** to bring, take, etc. secretly —***vi.*** to practice smuggling —**smug'gler** ***n.***

smush (smo͝osh) ***vt.*** [Inf.] to smash, squeeze, etc.

smut (smut) ***n.*** ⟦< LowG *smutt*⟧ **1** a particle of soot **2** a fungal disease of plants **3** indecent talk, writing, etc. —**smut'ty, -ti·er, -ti·est,** ***adj.***

Sn ⟦L *stannum*⟧ *Chem. symbol for* tin

snack (snak) ***n.*** ⟦< ME *snaken*, to bite⟧ a light meal between regular meals —***vi.*** to eat a snack

snack bar a counter for serving snacks

snag (snag) ***n.*** ⟦< Scand⟧ **1** a sharp point or projection **2** an underwater tree stump or branch **3** a tear, as in cloth, made by a snag, etc. **4** an unexpected or hidden difficulty, etc. —***vt.*** **snagged, snag'ging** **1** to catch, tear, etc. on a snag **2** to impede with a snag

snail (snāl) ***n.*** ⟦OE *snægl*⟧ a slow-moving mollusk having a wormlike body and a spiral protective shell

snake (snāk) ***n.*** ⟦OE *snaca*⟧ **1** a long, scaly, limbless reptile with a tapering tail **2** a treacherous or deceitful person **3** a plumber's tool for clearing pipes —***vi.*** **snaked, snak'ing** to move, twist, etc. like a snake —**snake'like'** ***adj.***

snak·y (snā'kē) ***adj.*** **-i·er, -i·est** **1** of or like a snake or snakes **2** winding; twisting **3** cunningly treacherous or evil

snap (snap) ***vi., vt.*** **snapped, snap'ping** ⟦< MDu *snappen*⟧ **1** to bite or grasp suddenly: with *at* **2** to speak or utter sharply: often with *at* **3** to break suddenly **4** to make or cause to make a sudden, cracking sound **5** to close, fasten, etc. with this sound **6** to move or cause to move suddenly and smartly *[to snap to attention]* **7** to take a snapshot (of) —***n.*** **1** a sudden bite, grasp, etc. **2** a sharp cracking sound *[the snap of a whip]* **3** a short, angry way of speaking **4** a brief period of cold weather **5** a fastening that closes with a click **6** a hard, thin cookie **7** *short for* SNAPSHOT **8** [Inf.] alertness or vigor **9** [Slang] an easy job, problem, etc. —***adj.*** **1** made or done quickly *[a snap decision]* **2** that fastens with a snap **3** [Slang] easy —**snap back** to recover quickly —**snap out of it** to improve or recover quickly —**snap'per** ***n.***

snap bean a green bean or wax bean

snap'drag'on ***n.*** ⟦SNAP + DRAGON: from the mouth-shaped flowers⟧ a plant with saclike, two-lipped flowers

snap'pish ***adj.*** **1** likely to bite **2** irritable

snap'py ***adj.*** **-pi·er, -pi·est** **1** cross; irritable **2** that snaps **3** [Inf.] *a)* brisk or lively *b)* sharply chilly **4** [Inf.] stylish

snap'shot' ***n.*** an informal photograph taken with a hand camera

snare (sner) ***n.*** ⟦< ON *snara*⟧ **1** a trap for small animals **2** anything dangerous, etc. that tempts or attracts **3** a length of wire or gut across the bottom of a drum —***vt.*** **snared, snar'ing** to catch as in a snare; trap

snarl[1] (snärl) ***vi.*** ⟦< earlier *snar*, to growl⟧ **1** to growl, baring the teeth, as a dog does **2** to speak sharply, as in anger —***vt.*** to utter with a snarl —***n.*** a fierce growl —**snarl'ing·ly** ***adv.***

snarl[2] (snärl) ***n., vt., vi.*** ⟦< SNARE⟧ tangle

—**snarl'y, -i·er, -i·est,** ***adj.***

snatch (snach) ***vt.*** ⟦ME *snacchen*⟧ to take suddenly, specif. without right or warning —***vi.*** **1** to try to seize; grab (*at*) **2** to take advantage of a chance, etc. eagerly: with *at* —***n.*** **1** a snatching **2** a brief period **3** a fragment; bit

sneak (snēk) ***vt., vi.*** **sneaked** or [Inf.] **snuck, sneak'ing** ⟦prob. < OE *snican*, to crawl⟧ to move, act, give, put, take, etc. secretly or stealthily —***n.*** **1** one who sneaks **2** a sneaking —***adj.*** without warning *[*a *sneak* attack*]* —**sneak'y, -i·er, -i·est,** ***adj.***

sneak'er ***n.*** a shoe with a canvas upper and a soft rubber sole

sneak preview an advance showing of a film, as for evaluating audience reaction

sneer (snir) ***vi.*** ⟦ME *sneren*⟧ **1** to show scorn as by curling the upper lip **2** to express derision, etc. in speech or writing —***n.*** a sneering

sneeze (snēz) ***vi.*** **sneezed, sneez'ing** ⟦ME *snesen*⟧ to exhale breath from the nose and mouth in an involuntary, explosive action —***n.*** a sneezing

snick·er (snik'ər) ***vi.*** ⟦echoic⟧ to laugh in a sly, partly stifled way —***n.*** a snickering

snide (snīd) ***adj.*** ⟦prob. < Du dial.⟧ slyly malicious or derisive

sniff (snif) ***vi., vt.*** ⟦ME *sniffen*⟧ **1** to draw in (air) forcibly through the nose **2** to express (disdain, etc.) by sniffing **3** to smell by sniffing —***n.*** **1** an act or sound of sniffing **2** something sniffed

snif·fle (snif'əl) ***vi.*** **-fled, -fling** to sniff repeatedly, as in checking mucus running from the nose —***n.*** an act or sound of sniffling —**the sniffles** [Inf.] a head cold

snif·ter (snif'tər) ***n.*** ⟦< *snift*, var. of SNIFF⟧ a goblet tapering to a small opening to concentrate the aroma, as of brandy

snig·ger (snig'ər) ***vi., n.*** ⟦echoic⟧ SNICKER

snip (snip) ***vt., vi.*** **snipped, snip'ping** ⟦Du *snippen*⟧ to cut or cut off in a short, quick stroke, as with scissors —***n.*** **1** a small piece cut off **2** [Inf.] a young or insignificant person

snipe (snīp) ***n.*** ⟦< ON *snipa*⟧ a long-billed wading bird —***vi.*** **sniped, snip'ing** to shoot from a hidden position, as at individuals —**snip'er** ***n.***

snip·pet (snip'it) ***n.*** ⟦dim. of SNIP⟧ a small piece or scrap, specif. of information

snip'py ***adj.*** **-pi·er, -pi·est** [Inf.] insolently curt, sharp, etc.

snit (snit) ***n.*** ⟦< ? prec. + (F)IT[2]⟧ a fit of anger, resentment, etc.: usually **in** (or **into**) **a snit**

snitch (snich) [Slang] ***vt.*** to steal; pilfer —***vi.*** to tattle (*on*) —***n.*** an informer

sniv·el (sniv'əl) ***vi.*** **-eled** or **-elled, -el·ing** or **-el·ling** ⟦ME *snivelen*⟧ **1** to cry and sniffle **2** to complain and whine **3** to make a tearful, often false display of grief, etc. —**sniv'el·er** ***n.***

snob (snäb) ***n.*** ⟦< ?⟧ one who disdains supposed inferiors —**snob'bish** ***adj.*** —**snob'bish·ness** or **snob'ber·y** ***n.***

snood (sno͞od) ***n.*** ⟦OE *snod*⟧ a baglike net worn at the back of a woman's head to hold the hair

snook·er (snook'ər) ***n.*** a variety of the game of pool —***vt.*** [Slang] to deceive

snoop (sno͞op) [Inf.] ***vi.*** ⟦Du *snoepen*, eat on the sly⟧ to pry about in a sneaking way —***n.*** one who snoops: also **snoop'er** —**snoop'y, -i·er, -i·est,** ***adj.***

snoot (sno͞ot) ***n.*** ⟦see SNOUT⟧ [Inf.] the nose

snoot'y ***adj.*** **-i·er, -i·est** [Inf.] haughty; snobbish —**snoot'i·ness** ***n.***

snooze (sno͞oz) ***n., vi.*** ⟦< LowG *snusen*, to snore⟧ **snoozed, snooz'ing** [Inf.] nap; doze —**snooz'er** ***n.***

snore (snôr) ***vi.*** **snored, snor'ing** ⟦see SNARL[1]⟧ to breathe, while asleep, with harsh sounds —***n.*** the act or sound of snoring —**snor'er** ***n.***

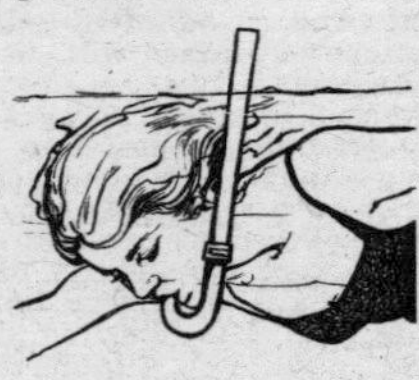

SNORKEL

snor·kel (snôr'kəl) ***n.*** ⟦Ger *schnorchel*, inlet⟧ a breathing tube extending above the water, used in swimming just below the surface —***vi.*** **-keled, -kel·ing** to swim underwater using a snorkel —**snor'kel·er** ***n.***

snort (snôrt) ***vi.*** **1** to force breath audibly through the nostrils **2** to express contempt, etc. by a snort —***vt.*** **1** to express with a snort **2** [Slang] to inhale (a drug) through the nose —***n.*** **1** a snorting **2** [Slang] a quick drink of liquor

snot (snät) ***n.*** ⟦OE (*ge*)*snot*, mucus⟧ [Slang] **1** nasal mucus: considered mildly vulgar **2** an impudent young person —**snot'ty, -ti·er, -ti·est,** ***adj.***

snout (snout) ***n.*** ⟦prob. < MDu *snute*⟧ the projecting nose and jaws of an animal

snow (snō) ***n.*** ⟦OE *snaw*⟧ **1** frozen particles of water vapor that fall to earth as soft, white flakes **2** a falling of snow —***vi.*** to fall as or like snow —***vt.*** **1** to cover or obstruct with snow: with *in, up, under*, etc. **2** [Slang] to deceive or mislead —**snow under** **1** to overwhelm with work, etc. **2** to defeat decisively —**snow'y, -i·er, -i·est,** ***adj.***

snow'ball' ***n.*** a mass of snow packed into a ball —***vi.*** to grow rapidly like a ball of snow rolling downhill

snow'bank' ***n.*** a large mass of snow

Snow'belt' the NE and Midwestern U.S., characterized by cold, snowy winters: also **Snow Belt**

snow'board' ***n.*** a board somewhat like

a small surfboard, for sliding down snowy hills for sport —***vi.*** to use a snowboard —**snow'board'er** ***n.***

snow'bound' ***adj.*** shut in or blocked off by snow

snow'cone' ***n.*** crushed ice mixed with a flavored syrup, served in a paper cone

snow'drift' ***n.*** a heap of snow piled up by the wind

snow'drop' ***n.*** a small plant with small, bell-shaped, white flowers

snow'fall' ***n.*** a fall of snow or the amount of this in a given area or time

snow fence a light fence of lath and wire to control the drifting of snow

snow'flake' ***n.*** a single snow crystal

snow'man' (-man') ***n.***, *pl.* **-men'** (-men') a crude human figure made of snow packed together

snow'mo·bile' ***n.*** a motor vehicle with steerable runners at the front and tractor treads at the rear —***vi.*** **-biled', -bil'ing** to travel by snowmobile

snow'plow' ***n.*** a plowlike machine used to clear snow off a road, etc.

snow'shoe' ***n.*** one of a pair of racket-shaped wooden frames crisscrossed with leather strips, etc., worn on the feet to prevent sinking in deep snow

snow'storm' ***n.*** a storm with a heavy snowfall

snow'suit' ***n.*** a child's heavily lined, hooded garment, for cold weather

snow tire a tire with a deep tread for added traction on snow or ice

snub (snub) ***vt.*** **snubbed, snub'bing** ⟦< ON *snubba*, chide⟧ **1** to treat with scorn, disdain, etc. **2** to check suddenly the movement of (a rope, etc.) —***n.*** scornful treatment —***adj.*** short and turned up: said of a nose

snub'-nosed' ***adj.*** **1** having a snub nose **2** having a short barrel: said of a handgun

snuck (snuk) ***vi., vt.*** [Inf.] *alt. pt. & pp. of* SNEAK

snuff[1] (snuf) ***vt.*** ⟦ME⟧ **1** to trim off the charred end of (a wick) **2** to put out (a candle) —**snuff out 1** to extinguish **2** to destroy —**snuff'er** ***n.***

snuff[2] (snuf) ***vt., vi.*** ⟦< MDu *snuffen*⟧ to sniff or smell —***n.*** **1** a sniff **2** powdered tobacco taken up into the nose or put on the gums —**up to snuff** [Inf.] up to the usual standard

snuff'box' ***n.*** a small box for snuff

snuf·fle (snuf'əl) ***n., vi.*** **-fled, -fling** ⟦< SNUFF[2]⟧ SNIFFLE

snug (snug) ***adj.*** **snug'ger, snug'gest** ⟦prob. < Scand⟧ **1** warm and cozy **2** neat; trim *[a snug cottage]* **3** tight in fit —**snug'ly** ***adv.***

snug'gle (-əl) ***vi., vt.*** **-gled, -gling** ⟦< prec.⟧ to nestle; cuddle

so (sō) ***adv.*** ⟦OE *swa*⟧ **1** as shown or described *[hold the bat just so]* **2** *a)* to such an extent *[why are you so late?]* *b)* very *[they are so happy]* *c)* [Inf.] very much *[she so wants to go]* **3** therefore *[they were tired, and so left]* **4** more or less *[fifty dollars or so]* **5** also; likewise *[I am going, and so are you]* **6** then *[and so to bed]* —***conj.*** **1** in order (*that*) **2** with the result that —***pron.*** that which has been specified or named *[he is a friend and will remain so]* —***interj.*** used to express surprise, triumph, etc. —***adj.*** true *[that's so]* —**and so on** (or **forth**) and the rest; et cetera —**so as** with the purpose or result —**so what?** [Inf.] even if so, what then?

soak (sōk) ***vt.*** ⟦OE *socian*⟧ **1** to make thoroughly wet **2** to take in; absorb: usually with *up* **3** [Inf.] to overcharge —***vi.*** **1** to stay in a liquid for wetting, softening, etc. **2** to penetrate —***n.*** **1** a soaking or being soaked **2** [Slang] a drunkard

so'-and-so' ***n.***, *pl.* **so'-and-sos'** [Inf.] an unspecified person or thing: often used euphemistically

soap (sōp) ***n.*** ⟦OE *sape*⟧ **1** a substance, usually a salt derived from fatty acids, used with water to produce suds for washing **2** [Slang] SOAP OPERA —***vt.*** to lather, etc. with soap —**no soap** [Slang] (it is) not acceptable —**soap'y, -i·er, -i·est,** ***adj.***

soap'box' ***n.*** any improvised platform used in speaking to a street audience

soap opera [Inf.] a radio or television serial melodrama

soap'stone' ***n.*** a soft, impure talc in rock form, used as an insulator, etc.

soap'suds' ***pl.n.*** foamy, soapy water

soar (sôr) ***vi.*** ⟦ult. < L *ex-*, out + *aura*, air⟧ **1** to rise or fly high into the air **2** to glide along high in the air **3** to rise above the usual level

So·a·ve (sə wä'vā, swä'vā) ***n.*** ⟦It⟧ an Italian dry white wine

sob (säb) ***vi.*** **sobbed, sob'bing** ⟦ME *sobben*⟧ to weep aloud with short, gasping breaths —***vt.*** to utter with sobs —***n.*** the act or sound of sobbing

so·ber (sō'bər) ***adj.*** ⟦< L *sobrius*⟧ **1** temperate, esp. in the use of liquor **2** not drunk **3** serious, reasonable, sedate, etc. **4** not flashy; plain —***vt., vi.*** to make or become sober: often with *up* —**so'ber·ly** ***adv.*** —**so'ber·ness** ***n.***

so·bri·e·ty (sə brī'ə tē) ***n.*** a being sober; specif., *a)* temperance, esp. in the use of liquor *b)* seriousness

so·bri·quet (sō'brə kā', -ket') ***n.*** ⟦Fr⟧ **1** a nickname **2** an assumed name

soc *abbrev.* **1** social **2** socialist **3** society

so'-called' ***adj.*** **1** known by this term **2** inaccurately or questionably designated as such *[a so-called liberal]*

soc·cer (säk'ər) ***n.*** ⟦alt. < *(as)soc(iation football)*⟧ a team game played by kicking a round ball

so·cia·ble (sō'shə bəl) ***adj.*** ⟦see fol.⟧ **1** friendly; gregarious **2** characterized by informal conversation and companionship —**so'cia·bil'i·ty** ***n.*** —**so'cia·bly** ***adv.***

so·cial (sō'shəl) ***adj.*** ⟦< L *socius*, companion⟧ **1** of or having to do with human beings, etc. in their living together **2** living with others; gregarious *[man as a social being]* **3** of or having to do with society, esp. fashionable society **4** sociable **5** of or for companionship **6** of or doing welfare work —***n.*** an informal gathering —**so'cial·ly** ***adv.***

social disease any venereal disease

so′cial·ism′ *n.* **1** a theory or system of ownership of the means of production and distribution by society rather than by individuals **2** [*often* **S-**] a political movement for establishing such a system —**so′cial·ist** *n., adj.* —**so′cial·is′tic** *adj.*

so·cial·ite (sō′shə līt′) *n.* a person prominent in fashionable society

so′cial·ize′ (-shə līz′) *vt.* **-ized′, -iz′ing** **1** to make fit for living in a group **2** to subject to governmental ownership or control —*vi.* to take part in social activity —**so′cial·i·za′tion** *n.*

socialized medicine a system supplying complete medical and hospital care to all through public funds

social science a field of study, as economics or anthropology, dealing with the structure, etc. of society —**social scientist**

Social Security [*sometimes* **s- s-**] a federal system of old-age, unemployment, or disability insurance

social studies a course of study including history, geography, etc.

social work any service or activity promoting the welfare of the community and the individual, as through counseling services, etc. —**social worker**

so·ci·e·ty (sə sī′ə tē) *n., pl.* **-ties** ⟦< L *socius*, companion⟧ **1** a group of persons, etc. forming a single community **2** the system of living together in such a group **3** all people, collectively **4** companionship **5** an organized group with some interest in common **6** the wealthy, dominant class —**so·ci′e·tal** (-təl) *adj.*

Society of Friends a Christian denomination that believes in plain worship, pacifism, etc.: see also QUAKER

so·ci·o·e·co·nom·ic (sō′sē ō ē′kə näm′ ik, -shē-; -ek′ə-) *adj.* of or involving both social and economic factors

so·ci·ol·o·gy (sō′sē äl′ə jē, -shē-) *n.* ⟦see SOCIAL & -LOGY⟧ the science of social relations, organization, and change —**so′ci·o·log′i·cal** (-ə lä′ji kəl) *adj.* —**so′ci·ol′o·gist** *n.*

so·ci·o·path (sō′sē ə path′, -shē-) *n.* an aggressively antisocial psychopath

sock[1] (säk) *n., pl.* **socks** or **sox** ⟦< L *soccus*, type of light shoe⟧ a short stocking —**sock away** [Inf.] to set aside (money) as savings

sock[2] (säk) [Slang] *vt.* to hit with force —*n.* a blow

sock·et (säk′it) *n.* ⟦< OFr *soc*, plowshare⟧ a hollow part into which something fits *[an eye socket]*

sock·eye salmon (säk′ī′) a red-fleshed salmon of the N Pacific

Soc·ra·tes (säk′rə tēz′) 470?-399 B.C.; Athenian philosopher & teacher —**So·crat·ic** (sə krat′ik) *adj., n.*

sod (säd) *n.* ⟦prob. < MDu *sode*⟧ **1** a surface layer of earth containing grass with its roots; turf **2** a piece of this —*vt.* **sod′ded, sod′ding** to cover with sod

so·da (sō′də) *n.* ⟦ML⟧ **1** *a)* SODIUM BICARBONATE *b)* SODA WATER *c)* SODA POP **2** a confection of soda water mixed with syrup and having ice cream in it

soda cracker a light, crisp cracker made from flour, water, and leavening, orig. baking soda

soda fountain a counter for making and serving soft drinks, sodas, etc.

soda pop a flavored, carbonated soft drink

soda water **1** water charged under pressure with carbon dioxide gas **2** SODA POP

sod·den (säd′′n) *adj.* **1** soaked through **2** soggy from improper cooking **3** dull or stupefied, as from liquor —**sod′den·ly** *adv.*

so·di·um (sō′dē əm) *n.* ⟦< *soda*⟧ an alkaline, metallic chemical element

sodium bicarbonate a white powder, used in baking powder, as an antacid, etc.

sodium chloride common salt

sodium hydroxide a caustic base used in oil refining, etc.

sodium nitrate a clear, crystalline salt used in explosives, fertilizers, etc.

sodium pen·to·thal (pen′tə thôl′) a yellowish powder injected in solution as a general anesthetic

Sod·om and Go·mor·rah (säd′əm and gə môr′ə) *Bible* two sinful cities destroyed by fire

sod·om·y (säd′ə mē) *n.* ⟦after *Sodom*⟧ any sexual intercourse held to be abnormal —**sod′om·ite′** (-mīt′) *n.*

so·fa (sō′fə) *n.* ⟦< Ar *ṣuffa*, a platform⟧ an upholstered couch with fixed back and arms

sofa bed a sofa that can be opened into a bed

So·fi·a (sō′fē ə, sō fē′ə) capital of Bulgaria: pop. 1,116,000

soft (sôft) *adj.* ⟦OE *softe*, gentle⟧ **1** giving way easily under pressure **2** easily cut, marked, shaped, etc. *[a soft metal]* **3** not as hard as is normal, desirable, etc. *[soft butter]* **4** smooth to the touch **5** easy to digest: said of a diet **6** nonalcoholic: said of drinks **7** having few of the mineral salts that keep soap from lathering **8** mild, as a breeze **9** weak; not vigorous **10** easy *[a soft job]* **11** kind or gentle **12** not bright: said of color or light **13** gentle; low: said of sound —*adv.* gently; quietly —**soft′ly** *adv.* —**soft′ness** *n.*

soft′ball′ *n.* **1** a kind of baseball played with a larger ball **2** this ball

soft′-boiled′ *adj.* boiled a short time to keep the yolk soft: said of an egg

soft coal BITUMINOUS COAL

soft drink a nonalcoholic drink, esp. one that is carbonated

soft·en (sôf′ən) *vt., vi.* to make or become soft or softer —**soft′en·er** *n.*

soft′heart′ed *adj.* **1** full of compassion **2** not strict or severe; lenient

soft landing a landing of a spacecraft without damage to the craft or its contents

soft money money donated to a political party but not for a particular candidate

soft palate the soft, fleshy part at the rear of the roof of the mouth; velum

soft'-ped'al ***vt.*** **-aled** or **-alled**, **-al·ing** or **-al·ling** ⟦from pedal to soften an instrument's tone⟧ [Inf.] to make less emphatic; tone down; play down

soft sell selling that relies on subtle inducement or suggestion

soft soap [Inf.] flattery or smooth talk —**soft'-soap'** ***vt.***

soft'ware' ***n.*** the programs, routines, etc. for a computer

soft'wood' ***n.*** **1** any light, easily cut wood **2** the wood of any tree bearing cones, as the pine

soft'y ***n., pl.*** **soft'ies** [Inf.] one who is too sentimental or trusting

sog·gy (säg'ē, sôg'ē) ***adj.*** **-gi·er**, **-gi·est** ⟦prob. < ON *sea*, a sucking⟧ soaked; moist and heavy —**sog'gi·ness** ***n.***

soil[1] (soil) ***n.*** ⟦< L *solum*⟧ **1** the surface layer of earth, supporting plant life **2** land; country *[native soil]* **3** ground or earth *[barren soil]*

soil[2] (soil) ***vt.*** ⟦ult. < L *sus*, pig⟧ **1** to make dirty; stain **2** to disgrace —***vi.*** to become soiled or dirty —***n.*** a soiled spot; stain

soi·ree or **soi·rée** (swä rā') ***n.*** ⟦< Fr *soir*, evening⟧ an evening party

so·journ (sō'jurn; *also, for v.,* sō jurn') ***vi.*** ⟦< L *sub-*, under + *diurnus*, of a day⟧ to live somewhere temporarily —***n.*** a brief stay; visit

sol (sōl) ***n.*** ⟦< ML⟧ *Music* the fifth tone of the diatonic scale

Sol (säl) ***n.*** ⟦L⟧ **1** *Rom. Myth.* the sun god **2** the sun personified

sol·ace (säl'is) ***n.*** ⟦< L *solacium*⟧ **1** an easing of grief, loneliness, etc. **2** a comfort or consolation —***vt.*** **-aced**, **-ac·ing** to comfort; console

so·lar (sō'lər) ***adj.*** ⟦< L *sol*, the sun⟧ **1** of or having to do with the sun **2** produced by or coming from the sun

solar battery an assembly of cells (**solar cells**) used to convert solar energy into electric power

so·lar·i·um (sō ler'ē əm) ***n., pl.*** **-i·a** (-ē ə) ⟦< L *sol*, sun⟧ a glassed-in porch, etc. to sun oneself

solar plexus a network of nerves in the abdomen behind the stomach

solar system that portion of our galaxy subject to the sun's gravity; esp., the sun and its planets

sold (sōld) ***vt., vi. pt. & pp. of*** SELL

sol·der (säd'ər) ***n.*** ⟦ult. < L *solidus*, solid⟧ a metal alloy heated and used to join or patch metal parts, etc. —***vt., vi.*** to join with solder

sol·dier (sōl'jər) ***n.*** ⟦< LL *solidus*, a coin⟧ **1** a member of an army **2** an enlisted person, as distinguished from an officer **3** one who works for a specified cause —***vi.*** **1** to serve as a soldier **2** to proceed stubbornly (*on*) —**sol'dier·ly** ***adj.***

soldier of fortune a mercenary or any adventurer

sole[1] (sōl) ***n.*** ⟦< L *solum*, a base⟧ **1** the bottom surface of the foot **2** the part of a shoe, etc. corresponding to this —***vt.*** **soled**, **sol'ing** to furnish (a shoe, etc.) with a sole

sole[2] (sōl) ***adj.*** ⟦< L *solus*⟧ without another; single; one and only

sole[3] (sōl) ***n., pl.*** **sole** or **soles** ⟦< L *solea*, SOLE[1]: from its shape⟧ a sea flatfish valued as food

sol·e·cism (säl'ə siz'əm) ***n.*** ⟦< Gr *soloikos*, speaking incorrectly⟧ a violation of the conventional usage, grammar, etc. of a language

sole·ly (sōl'lē) ***adv.*** **1** alone **2** only, exclusively, or merely

sol·emn (säl'əm) ***adj.*** ⟦< L *sollemnis*, annual, hence religious: said of festivals⟧ **1** sacred **2** formal **3** serious; grave; earnest —**sol'emn·ly** ***adv.***

so·lem·ni·ty (sə lem'nə tē) ***n., pl.*** **-ties** **1** solemn ceremony, ritual, etc. **2** seriousness; gravity

sol·em·nize (säl'əm nīz') ***vt.*** **-nized'**, **-niz'ing** **1** to celebrate formally or according to ritual **2** to perform the ceremony of (marriage, etc.)

so·le·noid (sō'lə noid', sä'-) ***n.*** ⟦< Gr *sōlēn*, channel + *eidos*, a form⟧ a coil of wire with a movable iron core, used as an electromagnetic switch

so·lic·it (sə lis'it) ***vt., vi.*** ⟦see SOLICITOUS⟧ **1** to appeal to (persons) for (aid, donations, etc.) **2** to entice or lure —**so·lic'i·ta'tion** ***n.***

so·lic'i·tor ***n.*** **1** one who solicits trade, contributions, etc. **2** in England, a lawyer other than a barrister **3** the law officer for a city, etc.

so·lic·i·tous (sə lis'ə təs) ***adj.*** ⟦< L *sollus*, whole + *ciere*, set in motion⟧ **1** showing care or concern *[solicitous for her welfare]* **2** desirous; eager

so·lic'i·tude' (-to͞od') ***n.*** a being solicitous; care, concern, etc.

sol·id (säl'id) ***adj.*** ⟦< L *solidus*⟧ **1** relatively firm or compact; neither liquid nor gaseous **2** not hollow **3** having three dimensions **4** firm; strong; substantial **5** having no breaks or divisions **6** of one color, material, etc. throughout **7** showing unity; unanimous **8** reliable or dependable —***n.*** **1** a solid substance, not a liquid or gas **2** an object having length, breadth, and thickness —**sol'id·ly** ***adv.*** —**sol'id·ness** ***n.***

sol·i·dar·i·ty (säl'ə dar'ə tē) ***n.*** complete unity, as of opinion or feeling

so·lid·i·fy (sə lid'ə fī') ***vt., vi.*** **-fied'**, **-fy'ing** to make or become solid, hard, etc. —**so·lid'i·fi·ca'tion** ***n.***

so·lid'i·ty (-tē) ***n.*** a being solid

sol'id-state' ***adj.*** **1** of the branch of physics dealing with the structure, properties, etc. of solids **2** equipped with transistors, etc.

so·lil·o·quy (sə lil'ə kwē) ***n., pl.*** **-quies** ⟦< L *solus*, alone + *loqui*, speak⟧ **1** a talking to oneself **2** lines in a drama spoken by a character as if to himself or herself —**so·lil·o·quize** (sə lil'ə kwīz'), **-quized'**, **-quiz'ing**, ***vi., vt.***

sol·i·taire (säl'ə ter') ***n.*** ⟦Fr: see fol.⟧ **1** a diamond or other gem set by itself **2** a card game for one player

sol'i·tar'y (-ter'ē) ***adj.*** ⟦< L *solus*, alone⟧ **1** living or being alone **2** single; only *[a* *solitary* example*]* **3** lonely; remote **4** done in solitude

sol'i·tude' (-to͞od') ***n.*** ⟦see prec.⟧ **1** a being solitary, or alone; seclusion **2** a secluded place

so·lo (sō'lō) ***n.**, pl.* **-los** or **-li** (-lē) ⟦It < L *solus*, alone⟧ **1** a musical piece or passage to be performed by one person **2** any performance by one person alone —***adj.*** for or by a single person —***adv.*** alone —***vi.*** **-loed**, **-lo·ing** to perform a solo —**so'lo·ist** ***n.***

Sol·o·mon (säl'ə mən) ***n.*** *Bible* king of Israel noted for his wisdom

Solomon Islands country on a group of islands in the SW Pacific, east of New Guinea: 10,954 sq. mi.; pop. 286,000

So·lon (sō'lən, -län') 640?-559? B.C.; Athenian statesman & lawgiver

so long [Inf.] GOODBYE

sol·stice (säl'stis, sōl'-) ***n.*** ⟦< L *sol*, sun + *sistere*, to stand⟧ the time of the year when the sun reaches the point farthest north (about June 21) or farthest south (about Dec. 21) of the equator: in the Northern Hemisphere, the **summer solstice** and **winter solstice**, respectively

sol·u·ble (säl'yə bəl) ***adj.*** ⟦see SOLVE⟧ **1** that can be dissolved **2** capable of being solved

sol·ute (säl'yo͞ot') ***n.*** the substance dissolved in a solution

so·lu·tion (sə lo͞o'shən) ***n.*** ⟦see fol.⟧ **1** the solving of a problem **2** an answer, explanation, etc. **3** the dispersion of one substance in another, usually a liquid, so as to form a homogeneous mixture **4** the mixture so produced

solve (sälv, sôlv) ***vt.*** **solved**, **solv'ing** ⟦< L *se-*, apart + *luere*, let go⟧ to find the answer to (a problem, etc.) —**solv'a·ble** ***adj.*** —**solv'er** ***n.***

sol·vent (säl'vənt, sôl'-) ***adj.*** ⟦see prec.⟧ **1** able to pay all one's debts **2** that can dissolve another substance —***n.*** a substance that can dissolve another substance —**sol'ven·cy** ***n.***

So·ma·li·a (sō mä'lē ə) country of E Africa, on the Indian Ocean: 246,201 sq. mi.; pop. 9,200,000

so·mat·ic (sō mat'ik) ***adj.*** ⟦< Gr *sōma*, body⟧ of the body; physical

somatic cell any of the cells that form the tissues and organs of the body: opposed to GERM CELL

som·ber (säm'bər) ***adj.*** ⟦< L *sub*, under + *umbra*, shade⟧ **1** dark and gloomy **2** melancholy **3** solemn Also [Chiefly Brit.] **som'bre** —**som'ber·ly** ***adv.***

som·bre·ro (säm brer'ō) ***n.**, pl.* **-ros** ⟦Sp < *sombra*, shade: see prec.⟧ a broad-brimmed, tall-crowned hat worn in Mexico, the Southwest, etc.

some (sum) ***adj.*** ⟦OE *sum*⟧ **1** certain but not specified or known *[*open *some* evenings*]* **2** of a certain unspecified quantity, degree, etc. *[*have *some* candy*]* **3** about *[some* ten of them*]* **4** [Inf.] remarkable, striking, etc. *[*it was *some* fight*]* —***pron.*** a certain unspecified number, quantity, etc. *[some* of them agree*]* —***adv.*** **1** approximately *[some* ten men*]* **2** [Inf.] to some extent; somewhat *[*slept *some]* **3** [Inf.] to a great extent or at a great rate *[*must run *some* to catch up*]* —**and then some** [Inf.] and more than that

-some[1] (səm) ⟦OE *-sum*⟧ *suffix* tending to (be) *[tiresome]*

-some[2] (sōm) ⟦< Gr *sōma*, body⟧ *combining form* body *[chromosome]*

some·bod·y (sum'bäd'ē, -bud'ē) ***pron.*** a person unknown or not named; some person; someone —***n.**, pl.* **-bod'ies** a person of importance

some'day' ***adv.*** at some future day or time

some'how' ***adv.*** in a way or by a method not known or stated: often in **somehow or other**

some'one' ***pron.*** SOMEBODY

som·er·sault (sum'ər sôlt') ***n.*** ⟦< L *supra*, over + *saltus*, a leap⟧ an acrobatic stunt performed by turning the body one full revolution, heels over head —***vi.*** to perform a somersault

some'thing ***pron.*** **1** a thing not definitely known, understood, etc. *[something* went wrong*]* **2** a definite but unspecified thing *[*have *something* to eat*]* **3** a bit; a little —***n.*** [Inf.] an important or remarkable person or thing —***adv.*** **1** somewhat *[*looks *something* like me*]* **2** [Inf.] really; quite *[*sounds *something* awful*]* —**something else** [Slang] one that is quite remarkable

some'time' ***adv.*** at some unspecified or future time —***adj.*** **1** former **2** occasional

some'times' ***adv.*** occasionally

some'way' ***adv.*** in some way: also **some'ways'**

some'what' ***pron.*** some degree, part, amount, etc. —***adv.*** to some extent or degree; a little

some'where' ***adv.*** **1** in, to, or at some place not known or specified **2** at some time, degree, age, etc. (with *about, around, near, in, between*, etc.)

som·nam·bu·lism (säm nam'byo͞o liz'əm) ***n.*** ⟦< L *somnus*, sleep + *ambulare*, to walk⟧ sleepwalking —**som·nam'bu·list** ***n.***

som·no·lent (säm'nə lənt) ***adj.*** ⟦< L *somnus*, sleep⟧ **1** sleepy **2** inducing drowsiness —**som'no·lence** ***n.***

son (sun) ***n.*** ⟦OE *sunu*⟧ **1** a boy or man as he is related to his parents **2** a male descendant —**the Son** Jesus Christ

so·nar (sō'när') ***n.*** ⟦*so(und) n(avigation) a(nd) r(anging)*⟧ an apparatus that transmits sound waves in water, used to find depths, etc.

so·na·ta (sə nät'ə) ***n.*** ⟦It < L *sonare*, to sound⟧ a musical composition for one or two instruments, usually consisting of several movements

song (sôŋ) ***n.*** ⟦OE *sang*⟧ **1** the act or art of singing **2** a piece of music for singing **3** *a)* [Old Poet.] poetry *b)* a lyric set to music **4** a sound like singing —**for a song** [Inf.] for a small sum; cheap

song'bird' ***n.*** a bird that makes vocal sounds that are like music

song'fest' ***n.*** ⟦SONG + -FEST⟧ an informal gathering of people for singing, esp. folk songs

song'ster (-stər) ***n.*** a singer —**song'stress** (-stris) ***fem.n.***

son·ic (sän'ik) ***adj.*** ⟦< L *sonus*, a sound⟧ of or having to do with sound or the speed of sound

sonic boom the explosive sound of a supersonic jet passing overhead

son'-in-law' ***n.***, *pl.* **sons'-in-law'** the husband of one's daughter

son·net (sän'it) ***n.*** ⟦ult. < L *sonus*, a sound⟧ a poem normally of fourteen lines in any of several rhyme schemes

son·ny (sun'ē) ***n.***, *pl.* **-nies** little son: used as a familiar term of address to a young boy

So·no·ra (sô nô'rä) state of NW Mexico: 71,403 sq. mi.; pop. 1,824,000

so·no·rous (sə nôr'əs, sän'ər əs) ***adj.*** ⟦< L *sonor*, a sound⟧ **1** producing sound; resonant **2** full, deep, or rich in sound —**so·nor'i·ty** (-ə tē), *pl.* **-ties**, ***n.***

soon (so͞on) ***adv.*** ⟦OE *sona*, at once⟧ **1** in a short time *[*will *soon* be there*]* **2** promptly; quickly *[*as *soon* as possible*]* **3** ahead of time; early *[*we left too *soon]* **4** readily; willingly *[*as *soon* go as stay*]* —**sooner or later** inevitably; eventually

soot (soot) ***n.*** ⟦OE *sot*⟧ a black substance consisting chiefly of carbon particles, in the smoke of burning matter —**soot'y**, **-i·er**, **-i·est**, ***adj.***

sooth (so͞oth) ***n.*** ⟦OE *soth*⟧ [Archaic] truth

soothe (so͞o*th*) ***vt.*** **soothed**, **sooth'ing** ⟦OE *sothian*, prove true⟧ **1** to make calm or composed, as by gentleness or flattery **2** to relieve (pain, etc.) —**sooth'er** ***n.*** —**sooth'ing** ***adj.***

sooth·say·er (so͞oth'sā'ər) ***n.*** ⟦ME *sothseyere*, one who speaks the truth⟧ [Historical] a person who professes to predict the future —**sooth'say'ing** ***n.***

sop (säp) ***n.*** ⟦OE *sopp*⟧ **1** a piece of food, as bread, soaked in milk, etc. **2** *a)* something given to appease *b)* a bribe —***vt.***, ***vi.*** **sopped**, **sop'ping** **1** to soak, steep, etc. **2** to take up (liquid) by absorption: usually with *up*

SOP *abbrev.* standard operating procedure

soph·ism (säf'iz'əm) ***n.*** ⟦< Gr *sophos*, clever⟧ a clever and plausible but fallacious argument

soph'ist ***n.*** one who uses clever, specious reasoning —**so·phis·ti·cal** (sə fis'ti kəl) ***adj.***

so·phis·ti·cate (sə fis'tə kāt'; *for n., usually*, -kit) ***vt.*** **-cat'ed**, **-cat'ing** ⟦ult. < Gr *sophistēs*, wise man⟧ to change from a natural or simple state; make worldly-wise —***n.*** a sophisticated person

so·phis'ti·cat'ed ***adj.*** **1** not simple, naive, etc.; worldly-wise or knowledgeable, subtle, etc. **2** for sophisticated people **3** highly complex or developed —**so·phis'ti·ca'tion** ***n.***

soph·ist·ry (säf'is trē) ***n.*** misleading but clever reasoning

Soph·o·cles (säf'ə klēz') 496?-406 B.C.; Gr. writer of tragic dramas

soph·o·more (säf'môr', säf'ə môr') ***n.*** ⟦< obs. *sophumer*, sophism⟧ a student in the second year of college or the tenth grade in high school —***adj.*** of or for sophomores

soph'o·mor'ic ***adj.*** of or like sophomores; seen as opinionated, immature, etc.

-so·phy (sə fē) ⟦< Gr *sophia*, wisdom⟧ *combining form* knowledge

sop·o·rif·ic (säp'ə rif'ik, sō'pə-) ***adj.*** ⟦< L *sopor*, sleep + -FIC⟧ causing sleep —***n.*** a soporific drug, etc.

sop·py (säp'ē) ***adj.*** **-pi·er**, **-pi·est** **1** very wet: also **sop'ping** **2** [Inf.] sentimental

so·pra·no (sə pran'ō, -prä'nō) ***n.***, *pl.* **-nos** or **-ni** ⟦It < *sopra*, above⟧ **1** the range of the highest voice of women or boys **2** a voice, singer, or instrument with such a range **3** a part for a soprano —***adj.*** of or for a soprano

sor·bet (sôr bā', sôr'bət) ***n.*** ⟦Fr < Ar *sharba(t)*, a drink⟧ a tart ice, as of fruit juice

sor·cer·y (sôr'sər ē) ***n.***, *pl.* **-ies** ⟦< L *sors*, lot, chance⟧ **1** in the belief of some, the use of an evil supernatural power over people **2** charm, influence, etc. —**sor'cer·er** ***n.*** —**sor'cer·ess** ***fem.n.***

sor·did (sôr'did) ***adj.*** ⟦< L *sordes*, filth⟧ **1** dirty; filthy **2** squalid; wretched **3** base; ignoble; mean —**sor'did·ly** ***adv.*** —**sor'did·ness** ***n.***

sore (sôr) ***adj.*** **sor'er**, **sor'est** ⟦OE *sar*⟧ **1** giving or feeling pain; painful **2** filled with grief **3** causing irritation *[*a *sore* point*]* **4** [Inf.] angry; offended —***n.*** a sore, usually infected spot on the body —***adv.*** [Archaic] greatly —**sore'ness** ***n.***

sore'head' ***n.*** [Inf.] a person easily angered, made resentful, etc.

sore'ly ***adv.*** **1** grievously; painfully **2** urgently *[sorely* needed*]*

sor·ghum (sôr'gəm) ***n.*** ⟦< It *sorgo*⟧ **1** a cereal grass grown for grain, syrup, fodder, etc. **2** syrup made from its juices

so·ror·i·ty (sə rôr'ə tē) ***n.***, *pl.* **-ties** ⟦< L *soror*, sister⟧ a group of women or girls joined together for fellowship, etc., as in some colleges

sor·rel[1] (sôr'əl, sär'-) ***n.*** ⟦< OFr *surele*⟧ any of various plants with edible sour leaves

sor·rel[2] (sôr'əl, sär'-) ***n.*** ⟦< OFr *sor*, light brown⟧ **1** light reddish brown **2** a horse, etc. of this color

sor·row (sär'ō, sôr'ō) ***n.*** ⟦OE *sorg*⟧ **1** mental suffering caused by loss, disappointment, etc.; grief **2** that which causes such suffering —***vi.*** to grieve —**sor'row·ful** ***adj.*** —**sor'row·ful·ly** ***adv.***

sor·ry (sär'ē, sôr'ē) ***adj.*** **-ri·er**, **-ri·est** ⟦< OE *sar*, sore⟧ **1** full of sorrow, pity, or regret **2** inferior; poor **3** wretched —**sor'ri·ly** ***adv.*** —**sor'ri·ness** ***n.***

sort (sôrt) ***n.*** ⟦< L *sors*, lot, chance⟧ **1** any group of related things; kind; class **2** quality or type —***vt.*** to arrange according to class or kind —**of sorts** of an inferior kind: also **of a sort** —**out of sorts** [Inf.] not in good humor or health —**sort of** [Inf.] somewhat

sor·tie (sôrt'ē) ***n.*** ⟦Fr < *sortir*, go out⟧ **1** a quick raid by forces from a besieged place **2** one mission by a single military plane

SOS (es′ō′es′) ***n.*** a signal of distress, as in wireless telegraphy

so′-so′ ***adv., adj.*** just passably or passable; fair

sot (sät) ***n.*** ⟦< ML *sottus,* a fool⟧ a drunkard —**sot′tish** ***adj.***

sot·to vo·ce (sät′ō vō′chē) ⟦It, under the voice⟧ in a low voice, so as not to be overheard

souf·flé (so͞o flā′) ***n.*** ⟦Fr < L *sufflare,* puff out⟧ a baked food made light and puffy by beaten egg whites added before baking

sough (sou, suf) ***n.*** ⟦OE *swogan,* to sound⟧ a soft sighing or rustling sound —***vi.*** to make a sough

sought (sôt) ***vt., vi.*** *pt. & pp. of* SEEK

soul (sōl) ***n.*** ⟦OE *sawol*⟧ **1** an entity without material reality, regarded as the spiritual part of a person **2** the moral or emotional nature of a person **3** spiritual or emotional warmth, force, etc. **4** vital or essential part, quality, etc. **5** a person *[I didn't see a soul]* **6** the deep spiritual and emotional quality of black American culture; also, the expression of this, as in music —***adj.*** of, for, or like black Americans

soul food [Inf.] food items, as chitterlings, popular orig. in the South, esp. among blacks

soul′ful ***adj.*** full of deep feeling —**soul′ful·ly** ***adv.*** —**soul′ful·ness** ***n.***

soul mate [Inf.] a person, esp. of the opposite sex, with whom one has a deeply personal relationship

sound[1] (sound) ***n.*** ⟦< L *sonus*⟧ **1** that which is heard, resulting from stimulation of auditory nerves by vibrations (**sound waves**) in the air; also the vibrations **2** the distance within which a sound may be heard; earshot **3** the mental impression produced *[the sound of his report]* —***vi.*** **1** to make a sound **2** to seem upon being heard *[to sound troubled]* —***vt.*** **1** to cause to sound **2** to signal, express, etc. **3** to utter distinctly *[to sound one's r's]* —**sound′less** ***adj.***

sound[2] (sound) ***adj.*** ⟦OE *(ge)sund*⟧ **1** free from defect, damage, or decay **2** healthy *[a sound body]* **3** safe; stable *[a sound bank]* **4** based on valid reasoning; sensible **5** thorough; forceful *[a sound defeat]* **6** deep and undisturbed: said of sleep **7** honest, loyal, etc. —***adv.*** deeply *[sound asleep]* —**sound′ly** ***adv.*** —**sound′ness** ***n.***

sound[3] (sound) ***n.*** ⟦< OE & ON *sund*⟧ **1** a wide channel linking two large bodies of water or separating an island from the mainland **2** a long inlet or arm of the sea

sound[4] (sound) ***vt., vi.*** ⟦< L *sub,* under + *unda,* a wave⟧ **1** to measure the depth of (water), esp. with a weighted line **2** to try to find out the opinions of (a person), usually subtly: often with *out* —**sound′ing** ***n.***

sound barrier the large increase of air resistance of some aircraft flying near the speed of sound

sound bite a brief, quotable remark, as by a politician, suitable for use in radio or TV news

sounding board **1** something to increase resonance or reflect sound: often **sound′board′** **2** a person on whom one tests one's ideas, etc.

sound′proof′ ***adj.*** that keeps sound from coming through —***vt.*** to make soundproof

sound′stage′ ***n.*** an enclosed soundproof area for producing films or TV shows

sound′track′ ***n.*** the sound portion of a film

soup (so͞op) ***n.*** ⟦Fr *soupe*⟧ a liquid food made by cooking meat, vegetables, etc. in water, milk, etc. —**soup up** [Slang] to increase the capacity for speed of (an engine, etc.)

soup·çon (so͞op sōn′) ***n.*** ⟦Fr < L *suspicio,* suspicion⟧ **1** a slight trace, as of a flavor **2** a tiny bit

soup·y (so͞o′pē) ***adj.*** **-i·er, -i·est** **1** watery like soup **2** [Inf.] foggy

sour (sour) ***adj.*** ⟦OE *sur*⟧ **1** having the sharp, acid taste of vinegar, etc. **2** made acid or rank by fermentation **3** cross; bad-tempered **4** distasteful or unpleasant —***vt., vi.*** to make or become sour —**sour′ly** ***adv.*** —**sour′ness** ***n.***

source (sôrs) ***n.*** ⟦< L *surgere,* to rise⟧ **1** a spring, etc. from which a stream arises **2** a place or thing from which something originates or develops **3** a person, book, etc. that provides information

sour cream thickened and soured cream

sour·dough (sour′dō′) ***n.*** **1** bread made from fermented dough **2** a lone prospector for gold, etc., as in the W U.S.

sour grapes a scorning of something only because it cannot be had or done

sour′puss′ (-poos′) ***n.*** [Slang] a gloomy or disagreeable person

souse (sous) ***n.*** ⟦< OHG *sulza,* brine⟧ **1** a pickled food, as pigs' feet **2** liquid for pickling; brine **3** a plunging into a liquid **4** [Slang] a drunkard —***vt., vi.*** **soused, sous′ing** **1** to pickle **2** to plunge into a liquid **3** to make or become soaking wet

soused ***adj.*** [Slang] drunk

south (south) ***n.*** ⟦OE *suth*⟧ **1** the direction to the left of one facing the sunset (180° on the compass) **2** a region in or toward this direction —***adj.*** **1** in, of, or toward the south **2** from the south —***adv.*** in or toward the south —**go south** [Inf.] to decline, deteriorate, fail, etc. —**the South** that part of the U.S. south of Pennsylvania and the Ohio River, and generally east of the Mississippi; specif., the states that formed the Confederacy

South Africa country in southernmost Africa: 472,855 sq. mi.; pop. 37,714,000

South America S continent in the Western Hemisphere: *c.* 6,900,000 sq. mi.; pop. *c.* 318,000,000 —**South American**

South Bend city in N Indiana: pop. 106,000

South Car·o·li·na (kar′ə lī′nə) state of the SE U.S.: 30,111 sq. mi.; pop.

3,487,000; cap. Columbia: abbrev. *SC* —**South Car'o·lin'i·an** (-lin'ē ən)

South China Sea arm of the W Pacific, between SE Asia & the Philippines

South Da·ko·ta (də kōt'ə) Midwestern state of the U.S.: 75,898 sq. mi.; pop. 696,000; cap. Pierre: abbrev. *SD* — **South Da·ko'tan**

south'east' *n.* **1** the direction halfway between south and east **2** a region in or toward this direction —*adj.* **1** in, of, or toward the southeast **2** from the southeast —*adv.* in or toward the southeast —**south'east'er·ly** *adj., adv.* —**south'east'ern** *adj.* —**south'east'ward** *adv., adj.* —**south'east'wards** *adv.*

south·er·ly (su*th*'ər lē) *adj., adv.* **1** toward the south **2** from the south

south·ern (su*th*'ərn) *adj.* **1** in, of, or toward the south **2** from the south **3** of the south

south'ern·er *n.* a person born or living in the south

Southern Hemisphere that half of the earth south of the equator

southern lights [*also* **S- L-**] aurora australis

south·paw (south'pô') *n.* [Slang] a left-handed person; esp., a left-handed baseball pitcher

South Pole the southern end of the earth's axis

South Sea Islands the islands in the S Pacific

south'ward *adv., adj.* toward the south: also **south'wards** *adv.*

south'west' *n.* **1** the direction halfway between south and west **2** a region in or toward this direction —*adj.* **1** in, of, or toward the southwest **2** from the southwest *[a southwest* wind*]* —*adv.* toward or in the southwest —**south'west'er·ly** *adj., adv.* —**south'west'ern** *adj.* —**south'west'ward** *adv., adj.* —**south'west'wards** *adv.*

sou·ve·nir (sōō'və nir') *n.* ⟦< Fr < L *subvenire*, come to mind⟧ something kept as a reminder

sov·er·eign (säv'rən, -ər in) *adj.* ⟦< L *super*, above⟧ **1** above all others; chief; supreme **2** supreme in power, rank, etc. **3** independent of all others *[a sovereign* state*]* —*n.* **1** a monarch or ruler **2** a British gold coin worth one pound: no longer minted

sov'er·eign·ty *n.* **1** the status, rule, etc. of a sovereign **2** supreme and independent political authority

so·vi·et (sō'vē et') *n.* ⟦Russ *sovyet*, council⟧ **1** in Russia, Uzbekistan, and, formerly, the Soviet Union, any of the various elected governing councils, local, intermediate, and national **2** any similar council in a socialist governing system —*adj.* [**S-**] of or connected with the Soviet Union

Soviet Union UNION OF SOVIET SOCIALIST REPUBLICS

sow[1] (sou) *n.* ⟦OE *sugu*⟧ an adult female pig

sow[2] (sō) *vt.* **sowed, sown** (sōn) or **sowed, sow'ing** ⟦OE *sawan*⟧ **1** to scatter (seed) for growing **2** to plant seed in (a field, etc.) **3** to spread or scatter —*vi.* to sow seed —**sow'er** *n.*

sox (säks) *n. alt. pl. of* SOCK[1]

soy (soi) *n.* ⟦Jpn⟧ **1** a dark, salty sauce made from fermented soybeans: in full **soy sauce** **2** the soybean plant or its seeds Also [Chiefly Brit.] **soy·a** (soi'ə)

soy'bean' *n.* **1** a plant widely grown for its seeds, which contain much protein and oil **2** its seed

sp *abbrev.* **1** special **2** spelling

Sp *abbrev.* **1** Spain **2** Spanish

spa (spä) *n.* ⟦after *Spa*, resort in Belgium⟧ **1** a health resort having a mineral spring **2** a commercial establishment with exercise rooms, sauna baths, etc.

space (spās) *n.* ⟦< L *spatium*⟧ **1** *a)* the continuous, three-dimensional expanse in which all things are contained *b)* OUTER SPACE **2** *a)* the distance, area, etc. between or within things *b)* room for something *[a parking space]* **3** an interval of time —*vt.* **spaced, spac'ing** to arrange with space or spaces between

space'craft' *n., pl.* **-craft'** any vehicle or satellite for orbiting the earth, for space travel, etc.

spaced'-out' *adj.* [Slang] under or as if under the influence of a drug: also **spaced**

space'flight' *n.* flight in a spacecraft

space heater a small heating unit for a room or other confined area

space'man' (-man', -mən) *n., pl.* **-men'** (-men', -mən) an astronaut or any of the crew of a spaceship

space'port' *n.* a center for assembling, testing, and launching spacecraft

space'ship' *n.* a spacecraft, esp. if manned

space shuttle an airplanelike spacecraft designed to carry personnel and equipment between earth and a space station

space station (or **platform**) a spacecraft in long-term orbit serving as a launch pad, research center, etc.

space'suit' *n.* a garment pressurized for use by astronauts

space'walk' *n.* the act of an astronaut in moving about in space outside a spacecraft

space·y or **spac·y** (spā'sē) *adj.* **-i·er, -i·est** [Slang] **1** SPACED-OUT **2** *a)* eccentric or unconventional *b)* flighty, irresponsible, neurotic, etc. —**spac'i·ness** *n.*

spa·cious (spā'shəs) *adj.* having more than enough space; vast —**spa'cious·ly** *adv.* —**spa'cious·ness** *n.*

Spack·le (spak'əl) ⟦prob. < Ger *spachtel*, spatula⟧ *trademark for* a powder mixed with water to form a paste that dries hard, used to fill holes, cracks, etc. in wallboard, wood, etc. —*n.* [**s-**] this substance —*vt.* **-led, -ling** [**s-**] to fill or cover with spackle

spade[1] (spād) *n.* ⟦OE *spadu*⟧ a flat-bladed, long-handled digging tool, like a shovel —*vt., vi.* **spad'ed, spad'ing** to dig with or as with a spade —**spade'ful** *n.*

spade[2] (spād) *n.* ⟦ult. < Gr *spathē*, flat

blade⟧ **1** any of a suit of playing cards marked with black figures like this ♠ **2** [*pl.*] this suit

spade'work' ***n.*** preparatory work for some main project, esp. when tiresome

spa·dix (spā'diks) ***n.***, *pl.* **-dix·es** or **-di·ces'** (-də sēz') ⟦ult. < Gr⟧ a spike of tiny flowers, usually enclosed in a spathe

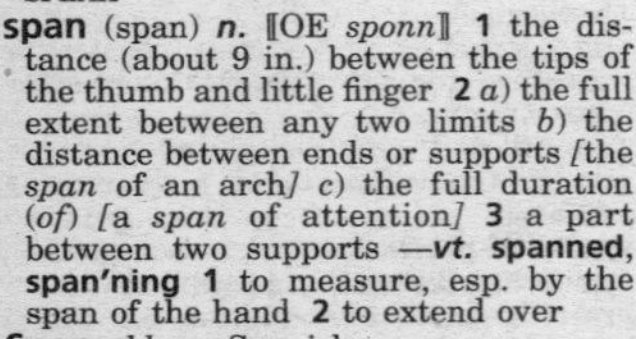

spa·ghet·ti (spə get'ē) ***n.*** ⟦It < *spago,* small cord⟧ pasta in long, thin strings, boiled or steamed

Spain (spān) country in SW Europe: 190,191 sq. mi.; pop. 38,872,000

spake (spāk) ***vi.***, ***vt.*** *archaic pt. of* SPEAK

span (span) ***n.*** ⟦OE *sponn*⟧ **1** the distance (about 9 in.) between the tips of the thumb and little finger **2** *a)* the full extent between any two limits *b)* the distance between ends or supports *[the span of an arch]* *c)* the full duration (*of*) *[a span of attention]* **3** a part between two supports —***vt.*** **spanned, span'ning 1** to measure, esp. by the span of the hand **2** to extend over

Span *abbrev.* Spanish

span·dex (span'deks') ***n.*** ⟦< EXPAND⟧ an elastic synthetic fiber used in girdles, etc.

span·gle (spaŋ'gəl) ***n.*** ⟦< OE *spang,* a clasp⟧ a small piece of bright metal sewn on fabric for decoration —***vt.*** **-gled, -gling** to decorate as with spangles

Span·iard (span'yərd) ***n.*** a person born or living in Spain

span·iel (span'yəl) ***n.*** ⟦< MFr *espagnol,* lit., Spanish⟧ any of several breeds of dog with large, drooping ears and a dense, wavy coat

Span·ish (span'ish) ***adj.*** of Spain or its people, language, etc. —***n.*** the language of Spain and Spanish America —**the Spanish** the people of Spain

Spanish America those countries south of the U.S. in which Spanish is the chief language —**Span'ish-A·mer'i·can** ***adj.***, ***n.***

Spanish moss a rootless plant that grows in long, graceful strands from tree branches in the SE U.S.

spank (spaŋk) ***vt.*** ⟦echoic⟧ to strike with the open hand, etc., esp. on the buttocks, as in punishment —***n.*** a smack given in spanking

spank'ing ***adj.*** **1** swiftly moving **2** brisk: said of a breeze —***adv.*** [Inf.] completely *[spanking new]*

spar¹ (spär) ***n.*** ⟦< ON *sparri* or MDu *sparre*⟧ any pole, as a mast or yard, supporting a sail of a ship

spar² (spär) ***vi.*** **sparred, spar'ring** ⟦prob. < It *parare,* to parry⟧ **1** to box with feinting movements, landing few heavy blows **2** to wrangle

spare (sper) ***vt.*** **spared, spar'ing** ⟦OE *sparian*⟧ **1** to refrain from killing, hurting, etc. **2** to save or free (a person) from something **3** to avoid using or use frugally **4** to part with or give up conveniently *[can you spare a dime?]* —***adj.*** **1** not in regular use; extra **2** free *[spare time]* **3** meager; scanty **4** lean; thin —***n.*** **1** a spare, or extra, thing **2** *Bowling* a knocking down of all the pins with two rolls of the ball —**spare'ly** ***adv.***

spare'ribs' ***pl.n.*** a cut of meat, esp. pork, consisting of the thin end of the ribs

spar'ing ***adj.*** careful; frugal —**spar'ing·ly** ***adv.***

spark (spärk) ***n.*** ⟦OE *spearca*⟧ **1** a glowing bit of matter, esp. one thrown off by a fire **2** any flash or sparkle **3** a particle or trace **4** a brief flash of light accompanying an electric discharge as through air —***vi.*** to make sparks —***vt.*** to stir up; activate

spar·kle (spär'kəl) ***vi.*** **-kled, -kling 1** to throw off sparks **2** to glitter **3** to effervesce or bubble **4** to be brilliant and lively —***n.*** **1** a sparkling **2** brilliance; liveliness —**spar'kler** (-klər) ***n.***

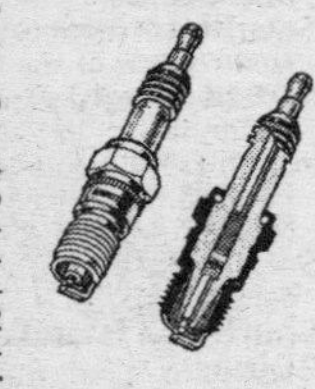
SPARK PLUG

spark plug an electrical device fitted into a cylinder of an engine to ignite the fuel mixture by making sparks

spar·row (spar'ō) ***n.*** ⟦OE *spearwa*⟧ any of numerous small, perching songbirds

sparse (spärs) ***adj.*** ⟦< L *spargere,* scatter⟧ thinly spread; not dense —**sparse'ly** ***adv.*** —**sparse'ness** or **spar'si·ty** (-sə tē) ***n.***

Spar·ta (spärt'ə) ancient city in S Greece: a military power

Spar·tan (spärt''n) ***adj.*** **1** of ancient Sparta or its people or culture **2** like the Spartans; warlike, hardy, disciplined, etc. —***n.*** a Spartan person

spasm (spaz'əm) ***n.*** ⟦< Gr *spasmos*⟧ **1** a sudden, involuntary muscular contraction **2** any sudden, violent, temporary activity, feeling, etc. —***vi.*** to undergo a spasm

spas·mod·ic (spaz mäd'ik) ***adj.*** ⟦see prec. & -OID⟧ of or like spasms; fitful —**spas·mod'i·cal·ly** ***adv.***

spas·tic (spas'tik) ***adj.*** of or characterized by muscular spasms —***n.*** one having spastic paralysis

spat¹ (spat) [Inf.] ***n.*** ⟦prob. echoic⟧ a brief, petty quarrel —***vi.*** **spat'ted, spat'ting** to engage in a spat

spat² (spat) ***n.*** ⟦< *spatterdash,* a legging⟧ a gaiterlike covering for the instep and ankle

spat³ (spat) ***vt.***, ***vi.*** *alt. pt. & pp. of* SPIT²

spate (spāt) ***n.*** ⟦< ?⟧ an unusually large flow, as of words

spathe (spā*th*) ***n.*** ⟦< L *spatha,* a flat blade⟧ a large, leaflike part enclosing a flower cluster

spa·tial (spā′shəl) ***adj.*** ⟦< L *spatium,* space⟧ of, or existing in, space

spat·ter (spat′ər) ***vt., vi.*** ⟦< ?⟧ **1** to scatter or spurt out in drops **2** to splash —***n.*** **1** a spattering **2** a mark caused by spattering

spat·u·la (spach′ə lə) ***n.*** ⟦L < Gr *spathē,* flat blade⟧ an implement with a broad, flat, flexible blade for spreading or blending foods, paints, etc.

spat′u·late′ (-lāt′) ***adj.*** shaped like a spatula

spav·in (spav′in) ***n.*** ⟦< MFr *esparvain*⟧ a disease that lames horses in the hock joint —**spav′ined** ***adj.***

spawn (spôn) ***vt., vi.*** ⟦< L *expandere:* see EXPAND⟧ **1** to produce or deposit (eggs, sperm, or young) **2** to bring forth or produce prolifically —***n.*** **1** the mass of eggs or young produced by fish, mollusks, etc. **2** something produced, esp. in great quantity, as offspring

spay (spā) ***vt.*** ⟦< Gr *spathē,* flat blade⟧ to sterilize (a female animal) by removing the ovaries

speak (spēk) ***vi.*** **spoke, spo′ken, speak′ing** ⟦OE *sp(r)ecan*⟧ **1** to utter words; talk **2** to communicate as by talking **3** to make a request (*for*) **4** to make a speech —***vt.*** **1** to make known as by speaking **2** to use (a given language) in speaking **3** to utter (words) —**so to speak** that is to say — **speak out** (or **up**) to speak clearly or freely — **speak to** to respond to, deal with, etc. — **speak well for** to say or indicate something favorable about

speak′-eas′y (-ē′zē) ***n., pl.*** **-ies** [Old Slang] a place where alcoholic drinks are sold illegally

speak′er ***n.*** **1** one who speaks; esp., *a*) an orator *b*) the presiding officer of various lawmaking bodies *c*) [**S-**] the presiding officer of the U.S. House of Representatives **2** a device for converting electrical signals to audible sound waves

spear (spir) ***n.*** ⟦OE *spere*⟧ **1** a weapon with a long shaft and a sharp point, for thrusting or throwing **2** ⟦var. of SPIRE⟧ a long blade or shoot, as of grass —***vt.*** **1** to pierce or stab with or as with a spear **2** [Inf.] to reach out and catch (a baseball, etc.)

spear′fish′ ***n., pl.*** **-fish′** or (for different species) **-fish′es** any of a group of large food and game fishes of the open seas —***vi.*** to fish with a spear, etc.

spear′head′ ***n.*** **1** the pointed head of a spear **2** the leading person or group, as in an attack —***vt.*** to take the lead in (an attack, etc.)

spear′mint′ ***n.*** ⟦prob. from the shape of its flowers⟧ a fragrant plant of the mint family, used for flavoring

spec[1] (spek) [Inf.] ***n.*** *short for:* **1** SPECIFICATION (sense 1) **2** SPECULATION —**on spec** **1** according to specification(s) **2** as a speculation or gamble

spec[2] *abbrev.* **1** special **2** specifically

spe·cial (spesh′əl) ***adj.*** ⟦< L *species,* kind⟧ **1** distinctive or unique **2** exceptional; unusual **3** highly valued **4** of or for a particular purpose, etc. **5** not general; specific —***n.*** a special thing, as, specif., a sale item —**spe′cial·ly** ***adv.***

special delivery mail delivery by a special messenger, for a special fee

spe′cial·ist ***n.*** one who specializes in a particular field of study, work, etc.

spe′cial·ize′ ***vi.*** **-ized′, -iz′ing** to concentrate on a particular branch of study, work, etc. —**spe′cial·i·za′tion** ***n.***

spe′cial·ty ***n., pl.*** **-ties** **1** a special quality, feature, etc. **2** a special interest, study, etc.

spe·cie (spē′shē, -sē) ***n.*** ⟦< L *species,* kind⟧ coin, rather than paper money

spe·cies (spē′shēz, -sēz) ***n., pl.*** **-cies** ⟦L, appearance, kind⟧ **1** a distinct kind; sort **2** any of the groups of related plants or animals that usually breed only among themselves: similar species form a genus

specif *abbrev.* specifically

spe·cif·ic (spə sif′ik) ***adj.*** ⟦< L *species,* kind + *-ficus,* -FIC⟧ **1** definite; explicit **2** peculiar to or characteristic of something **3** of a particular kind **4** specially indicated as a cure for some disease —***n.*** **1** a specific cure **2** a distinct item or detail; particular —**spe·cif′i·cal·ly** ***adv.***

-spe·cif′ic *combining form* limited or specific to

spec·i·fi·ca·tion (spes′ə fi kā′shən) ***n.*** **1** [*usually pl.*] a statement or enumeration of particulars, as to size, quality, or terms **2** something specified

specific gravity the ratio of the weight or mass of a given volume of a substance to that of an equal volume of another substance (as water) used as a standard

spec·i·fy (spes′ə fī′) ***vt.*** **-fied′, -fy′ing** ⟦< LL *specificus,* specific⟧ **1** to state definitely **2** to include in a set of specifications

spec·i·men (spes′ə mən) ***n.*** ⟦L < *specere,* see⟧ **1** a part or individual used as a sample of a whole or group **2** *Med.* a sample, as of urine, for analysis

spe·cious (spē′shəs) ***adj.*** ⟦< L *species,* appearance⟧ seeming to be good, sound, correct, etc. without really being so —**spe′cious·ly** ***adv.***

speck (spek) ***n.*** ⟦OE *specca*⟧ **1** a small spot, mark, etc. **2** a very small bit —***vt.*** to mark with specks

speck·le (spek′əl) ***n.*** a small speck —***vt.*** **-led, -ling** to mark with speckles

specs (speks) ***pl.n.*** [Inf.] **1** spectacles; eyeglasses **2** specifications

spec·ta·cle (spek′tə kəl) ***n.*** ⟦< L *specere,* see⟧ **1** a remarkable sight **2** a large public show **3** [*pl.*] [Old-fashioned] a pair of eyeglasses

spec·tac·u·lar (spek tak′yə lər) ***adj.*** unusual to a striking degree —***n.*** an elaborate show or display —**spec·tac′u·lar·ly** ***adv.***

spec·ta·tor (spek′tāt′ər) ***n.*** ⟦L < *spectare,* behold⟧ one who watches without taking an active part

spec·ter (spek′tər) ***n.*** ⟦< L *spectare,* behold⟧ a ghost; apparition: Brit. sp. **spec′tre**

spec′tral (-trəl) ***adj.*** **1** of or like a specter 2 of a spectrum

spec·tro·scope (spek′trə skōp′) ***n.*** ⟦< Ger, ult. < L *spectare*, behold⟧ an optical instrument used for forming spectra for study —**spec′tro·scop′ic** (-skäp′ik) ***adj.*** —**spec·tros′co·py** (-träs′kə pē) ***n.***

spec·trum (spek′trəm) ***n.***, *pl.* **-tra** (-trə) or **-trums** ⟦< L: see SPECTER⟧ **1** the series of colored bands separated and arranged in order of their respective wavelengths by the passage of white light through a prism, etc. **2** a continuous range or entire extent

spec·u·late (spek′yə lāt′) ***vi.*** **-lat′ed, -lat′ing** ⟦< L *specere*, see⟧ **1** to ponder; esp., to conjecture **2** to take part in any risky venture (as buying or selling certain stocks, etc.) on the chance of making huge profits —**spec′u·la′tion** ***n.*** —**spec′u·la′tive** (-lāt′iv, -lə tiv) ***adj.*** —**spec′u·la′tor** ***n.***

speech (spēch) ***n.*** ⟦< OE *sprecan*, speak⟧ **1** the act of speaking **2** the power to speak **3** that which is spoken; utterance, remark, etc. **4** a talk given to an audience **5** the language of a certain people

speech′less ***adj.*** **1** incapable of speech **2** silent, as from shock

speed (spēd) ***n.*** ⟦OE *spæd*, success⟧ **1** swiftness; quick motion **2** rate of movement; velocity **3** an arrangement of gears, as for the drive of an engine **4** [Inf.] one's kind of taste, capability, etc. **5** [Slang] any of various amphetamine compounds —***vi.*** **sped** (sped) or **speed′ed, speed′ing** to move rapidly, esp. too rapidly —***vt.*** **1** to help to succeed; aid **2** to cause to speed —**speed up** to increase in speed —**up to speed 1** working, etc. at full speed **2** [Inf.] fully informed —**speed′er** ***n.***

speed′boat′ ***n.*** a fast motorboat

speed·om·e·ter (spi däm′ət ər) ***n.*** a device attached to a motor vehicle, etc. to indicate speed

speed·ster (spēd′stər) ***n.*** a very fast driver, runner, etc.

speed′way′ ***n.*** a track for racing automobiles or motorcycles

speed′y ***adj.*** **-i·er, -i·est 1** rapid; fast; swift **2** without delay; prompt —**speed′i·ly** ***adv.***

spe·le·ol·o·gy (spē′lē äl′ə jē) ***n.*** ⟦< Gr *spēlaion*, a cave⟧ the scientific study and exploration of caves —**spe′le·ol′o·gist** ***n.***

spell[1] (spel) ***n.*** ⟦OE, a saying⟧ **1** a word or formula thought to have some magic power **2** irresistible influence; charm; fascination

spell[2] (spel) ***vt.*** **spelled** or **spelt, spell′ing** ⟦< OFr *espeller*, explain⟧ **1** to name, write, etc. in order the letters of (a word) **2** to make up (a word, etc.): said of specified letters **3** to mean *[red spells danger]* —***vi.*** to spell words —**spell out** to explain in detail

spell[3] (spel) ***vt.*** **spelled, spell′ing** ⟦OE *spelian*⟧ [Inf.] to work in place of (another) for an interval; relieve —***n.*** **1** a period of work, duty, etc. **2** a period of anything *[a spell of brooding]* **3** [Inf.] a fit of illness

spell′bind′ ***vt.*** **-bound′, -bind′ing** to cause to be spellbound; fascinate —**spell′bind′er** ***n.***

spell′bound′ ***adj.*** held by or as by a spell; fascinated

spell′-check′er ***n.*** a word-processing program used to check the spelling of words in a document

spell′down′ ***n.*** SPELLING BEE

spell′er ***n.*** **1** one who spells words **2** a textbook for teaching spelling

spell′ing ***n.*** **1** the act of one who spells words **2** the way a word is spelled; orthography

spelling bee a spelling contest, esp. one in which a contestant is eliminated after misspelling a word

spe·lunk·er (spi luŋ′kər) ***n.*** ⟦< Gr *spēlynx*, a cave⟧ a cave explorer —**spe·lunk′ing** ***n.***

spend (spend) ***vt.*** **spent, spend′ing** ⟦< L *expendere:* see EXPEND⟧ **1** to use up, exhaust, etc. *[his fury was spent]* **2** to pay out (money) **3** to devote (time, labor, etc.) to something **4** to pass (time) —***vi.*** to pay out or use up money, etc. —**spend′a·ble** ***adj.*** —**spend′er** ***n.***

spend′thrift′ ***n.*** one who wastes money —***adj.*** wasteful

spent (spent) ***vt.***, ***vi.*** *pt. & pp. of* SPEND —***adj.*** **1** tired out; exhausted **2** used up; worn out

sperm (spurm) ***n.*** ⟦< Gr *sperma*, seed⟧ **1** the male generative fluid; semen **2** *pl.* **sperm** or **sperms** a male germ cell, esp. a spermatozoon

sper·ma·to·zo·on (spur′mə tə zō′än′, -ən) ***n.***, *pl.* **-zo′a** (-zō′ə) ⟦< Gr *sperma*, seed + *zōion*, animal⟧ the male germ cell, found in semen, which penetrates the egg of the female to fertilize it

sperm·i·cide (spur′mə sīd′) ***n.*** ⟦SPERM + *-i-* + -CIDE⟧ an agent that kills spermatozoa —**sperm′i·cid′al** ***adj.***

sperm whale a large toothed whale found in warm seas: its head contains a valuable lubricating oil (**sperm oil**)

spew (spyōō) ***vt.***, ***vi.*** ⟦OE *spiwan*⟧ **1** to throw up (something) from or as from the stomach; vomit **2** to flow or cause to flow or gush forth —***n.*** something spewed

sp gr *abbrev.* specific gravity

sphere (sfir) ***n.*** ⟦< Gr *sphaira*⟧ **1** any round body having the surface equally distant from the center at all points; globe; ball **2** the place, range, or extent of action, existence, knowledge, experience, etc. —**spher·i·cal** (sfer′i kəl, sfir′-) ***adj.***

sphe·roid (sfir′oid) ***n.*** a body that is almost but not quite a sphere —**sphe·roi′dal** ***adj.***

sphinc·ter (sfiŋk′tər) ***n.*** ⟦< Gr *sphingein*, to draw close⟧ a ring-shaped muscle at a body orifice

sphinx (sfiŋks) ***n.*** ⟦< Gr, strangler⟧ **1** *Gr. Myth.* a winged monster with a lion's body and a woman's head **2** [**S-**] a statue with a lion's body and a man's head, near Cairo, Egypt **3** one who is difficult to know or understand

spice (spīs) ***n.*** ⟦< L *species*, kind⟧ **1** an

aromatic vegetable substance, as nutmeg or pepper, used to season food 2 that which adds zest or interest —*vt.* **spiced**, **spic'ing** 1 to season with spice 2 to add zest to —**spic'y**, **-i·er**, **-i·est**, *adj.*

spick-and-span (spik''n span') *adj.* ⟦< *spike*, nail + ON *spānn*, a chip⟧ 1 new or fresh 2 neat and clean

spic·ule (spik'yōōl') *n.* ⟦< L *spica*, a point⟧ a hard, needlelike part

spi·der (spī'dər) *n.* ⟦< OE *spinnan*, to spin⟧ any of various arachnids that spin webs

spi'der·y *adj.* like a spider

spiel (spēl) *n.* ⟦Ger, play⟧ [Slang] a talk or harangue, as in selling

spiff·y (spif'ē) *adj.* **-i·er**, **-i·est** ⟦< dial. *spiff*, well-dressed person⟧ [Slang] spruce, smart, or dapper

spig·ot (spig'ət) *n.* ⟦ME *spigote*⟧ 1 a plug to stop the vent in a barrel, etc. 2 a faucet

spike[1] (spīk) *n.* ⟦< ON *spīkr* or MDu *spīker*⟧ 1 a long, heavy nail 2 a sharp-pointed projection, as on the sole of a shoe to prevent slipping —*vt.* **spiked**, **spik'ing** 1 to fasten or fit as with spikes 2 to pierce with, or impale on, a spike 3 to thwart (a scheme, etc.) 4 [Slang] to add alcoholic liquor to (a drink) —*vi.* to rise suddenly and rapidly

spike[2] (spīk) *n.* ⟦L *spica*⟧ 1 an ear of grain 2 a long flower cluster

spill (spil) *vt.* **spilled** or **spilt** (spilt), **spill'ing** ⟦OE *spillan*, destroy⟧ 1 to allow or cause, esp. unintentionally, to run, scatter, or flow over from a container 2 to shed (blood) 3 to throw off (a rider, etc.) 4 [Inf.] to let (a secret) become known —*vi.* to be spilled; overflow —*n.* 1 a spilling 2 a fall or tumble —**spill'age** *n.*

spill'way' *n.* a channel to carry off excess water, as around a dam

spin (spin) *vt.* **spun**, **spin'ning** ⟦OE *spinnan*⟧ 1 *a*) to draw out and twist fibers of (wool, cotton, etc.) into thread *b*) to make (thread, etc.) thus 2 to make (a web, cocoon, etc.), as a spider does 3 to draw *out* (a story) to a great length 4 to rotate swiftly —*vi.* 1 to spin thread or yarn 2 to form a web, cocoon, etc. 3 to whirl 4 to seem to be spinning from dizziness 5 to move along swiftly and smoothly —*n.* 1 a spinning or rotating movement 2 a ride in a motor vehicle 3 a descent of an airplane, nose first along a spiral path 4 a particular emphasis or slant given to news, etc. —**spin off** to produce as an outgrowth or secondary development, etc. —**spin'ner** *n.*

spi·na bi·fi·da (spī'nə bif'i də) a congenital defect in which part of the spinal column is exposed, causing paralysis, etc.

spin·ach (spin'ich) *n.* ⟦ult. < Pers *aspanākh*⟧ 1 a plant with dark-green, juicy, edible leaves 2 these leaves

spi·nal (spī'nəl) *adj.* of or having to do with the spine or spinal cord —*n.* a spinal anesthetic

spinal column the series of joined vertebrae forming the axial support for the skeleton; spine; backbone

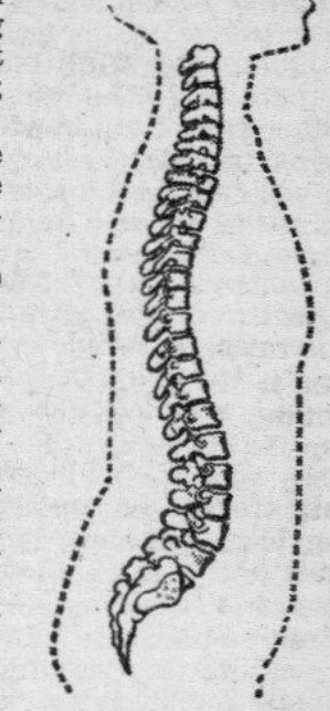

SPINAL COLUMN

spinal cord the thick cord of nerve tissue in the spinal column

spin·dle (spin'dəl) *n.* ⟦< OE *spinnan*, to spin⟧ 1 a slender rod used in spinning for twisting, winding, or holding thread 2 a spindlelike thing 3 any rod or pin that revolves or serves as an axis for a revolving part

spin·dly (spind'lē) *adj.* **-dli·er**, **-dli·est** long or tall and very thin

spin doctor [Slang] a person employed as by a politician to use spin in presenting information in a favorable light

spine (spīn) *n.* ⟦< L *spina*, thorn⟧ 1 *a*) a sharp, stiff projection, as on a cactus *b*) anything like this 2 *a*) SPINAL COLUMN *b*) anything like this, as the back of a book —**spin'y**, **-i·er**, **-i·est**, *adj.*

spine'less *adj.* 1 having no spine or spines 2 lacking courage or willpower

spin·et (spin'it) *n.* ⟦< It *spinetta*⟧ a small upright piano

spine'-tin'gling *adj.* very thrilling, terrifying, etc.

spin·ner·et (spin'ə ret') *n.* the organ in spiders, caterpillars, etc., that spins thread for webs or cocoons

spinning wheel a simple machine for spinning thread with a spindle driven by a large wheel spun as by a treadle

spin·off (spin'ôf') *n.* a secondary benefit, product, development, etc.

spin·ster (spin'stər) *n.* ⟦ME < *spinnen*, to spin⟧ an unmarried woman, esp. an elderly one —**spin'ster·hood'** *n.*

spiny lobster a type of lobster with a spiny shell and no pincers

spi·ra·cle (spir'ə kəl) *n.* ⟦< L < *spirare*, breathe⟧ an opening for breathing, as on the sides of an insect's body or on the top of a whale's head

spi·ral (spī'rəl) *adj.* ⟦< Gr *speira*, a coil⟧ circling around a point in constantly increasing (or decreasing) curves, or in constantly changing planes —*n.* 1 a spiral curve, coil, path, etc. 2 a continuous, widening decrease or increase [*an inflationary spiral*] —*vi.*, *vt.* **-raled** or **-ralled**, **-ral·ing** or **-ral·ling** to move in or form a spiral

spire (spīr) *n.* ⟦OE *spir*⟧ 1 the top part of a pointed, tapering object 2 anything tapering to a point, as a steeple

spi·re·a (spī rē'ə) *n.* ⟦< Gr *speira*, a coil⟧ a plant of the rose family, with dense clusters of small, pink or white flowers:

also sp. **spi·rae'a**

spir·it (spir'it) ***n.*** ⟦< L *spirare,* breathe⟧ **1** *a)* the life principle, esp. in human beings *b)* SOUL (sense 1) **2** [*also* **S-**] life, will, thought, etc., regarded as separate from matter **3** a supernatural being, as a ghost or angel **4** an individual [a brave *spirit]* **5** [*usually pl.*] disposition; mood [high *spirits]* **6** vivacity, courage, etc. **7** enthusiastic loyalty [school *spirit]* **8** real meaning [the *spirit* of the law] **9** a pervading animating principle or characteristic quality [the *spirit* of the times] **10** [*usually pl.*] distilled alcoholic liquor —***vt.*** to carry (*away, off,* etc.) secretly and swiftly —**spir'it·less *adj.***

spir'it·ed *adj.* lively; animated

spir·it·u·al (spir'i cho͞o əl) ***adj.*** **1** of the spirit or the soul **2** of or consisting of spirit; not corporeal **3** of religion; sacred —***n.*** a folk hymn, specif. one originating among S U.S. blacks —**spir'it·u·al'i·ty** (-al'ə tē) ***n.*** —**spir'it·u·al·ly *adv.***

spir'it·u·al·ism' ***n.*** the belief that the dead survive as spirits that can communicate with the living —**spir'it·u·al·ist *n.*** —**spir'it·u·al·is'tic *adj.***

spir·it·u·ous (spir'i cho͞o əs) ***adj.*** of or containing distilled alcohol

spi·ro·chete (spī'rō kēt') ***n.*** ⟦< Gr *speira,* a coil + *chaitē,* hair⟧ any of various spiral-shaped bacteria

spit[1] (spit) ***n.*** ⟦OE *spitu*⟧ **1** a thin, pointed rod on which meat is roasted over a fire, etc. **2** a narrow point of land extending into the water —***vt.*** **spit'ted, spit'ting** to fix as on a spit

spit[2] (spit) ***vt.*** **spit** or **spat, spit'ting** ⟦OE *spittan*⟧ **1** to eject from the mouth **2** to eject explosively —***vi.*** to eject saliva from the mouth —***n.*** **1** a spitting **2** saliva —**spit and image** [Inf.] perfect likeness: also **spitting image**

spit'ball' ***n.*** **1** paper chewed up into a wad for throwing **2** *Baseball* a pitch, now illegal, made to curve by wetting one side of the ball as with spit

spite (spīt) ***n.*** ⟦see DESPITE⟧ ill will; malice —***vt.*** **spit'ed, spit'ing** to vent one's spite upon by hurting, frustrating, etc. —**in spite of** regardless of —**spite'ful *adj.***

spit'fire' ***n.*** a woman or girl easily aroused to violent anger

spit·tle (spit''l) ***n.*** saliva; spit

spit·toon (spi to͞on') ***n.*** a container to spit into

splash (splash) ***vt.*** ⟦echoic⟧ **1** to cause (a liquid) to scatter **2** to dash a liquid, mud, etc. on, so as to wet or soil —***vi.*** to move, strike, etc. with a splash —***n.*** **1** a splashing **2** a spot made by splashing —**make a splash** [Inf.] to attract great attention

splash'down' ***n.*** a spacecraft's soft landing on the sea

splash'y *adj.* **-i·er, -i·est** **1** splashing or apt to splash; wet, muddy, etc. **2** [Inf.] spectacular —**splash'i·ly *adv.*** —**splash'i·ness *n.***

splat[1] (splat) ***n.*** ⟦< SPLIT⟧ a thin slat of wood, as in a chair back

splat[2] (splat) ***n., interj.*** ⟦echoic⟧ (used to suggest) a splattering or wet, slapping sound —***vi.*** **1** to make such a sound **2** to flatten on impact

splat·ter (splat'ər) ***n., vt., vi.*** spatter or splash

splay (splā) ***vt., vi.*** ⟦ME *splaien*⟧ to spread out or apart: often with *out* —***adj.*** spreading outward

splay'foot' ***n., pl.*** **-feet'** a foot that is flat and turned outward —**splay'foot'ed *adj.***

spleen (splēn) ***n.*** ⟦< Gr *splēn*⟧ **1** a large lymphatic organ in the upper left part of the abdomen: it modifies the blood structure **2** malice; spite

splen·did (splen'did) ***adj.*** ⟦< L *splendere,* to shine⟧ **1** shining; brilliant **2** magnificent; gorgeous **3** grand; illustrious **4** [Inf.] very good; fine —**splen'did·ly *adv.***

splen·dor (splen'dər) ***n.*** ⟦see prec.⟧ **1** great luster; brilliance **2** pomp; grandeur Brit. sp. **splen'dour**

sple·net·ic (spli net'ik) ***adj.*** **1** of the spleen **2** bad-tempered; irritable

splice (splīs) ***vt.*** **spliced, splic'ing** ⟦MDu *splissen*⟧ **1** to join (ropes) by weaving together the end strands **2** to join the ends of (timbers) by overlapping **3** to fasten the ends of (wire, film, etc.) together, as by soldering or twisting —***n.*** a joint made by splicing —**splic'er *n.***

splint (splint) ***n.*** ⟦prob. < MDu *splinte*⟧ **1** a thin strip of wood, etc. woven with others to make baskets, etc. **2** a thin, rigid strip of wood, etc. used to hold a broken bone in place

splin·ter (splin'tər) ***vt., vi.*** ⟦see prec.⟧ to break or split into thin, sharp pieces —***n.*** a thin, sharp piece, as of wood, made by splitting, etc.; sliver

split (split) ***vt., vi.*** **split, split'ting** ⟦MDu *splitten*⟧ **1** to separate lengthwise into two or more parts **2** to break or tear apart **3** to divide into shares **4** to disunite **5** *a)* to break (a molecule) into atoms *b)* to produce nuclear fission in (an atom) **6** *Finance* to divide (stock) by converting each share into two for more shares with the same overall value —***n.*** **1** a splitting **2** a break; crack **3** a division in a group, etc. **4** [*often pl.*] the feat of spreading the legs apart on the floor until they lie flat —***adj.*** divided; separated

split'-lev'el *adj.* having floor levels staggered about a half story apart

split pea a green or yellow pea shelled, dried, and split: used esp. for soup

split'ting *adj.* severe, as a headache

splotch (spläch) *n.* ⟦prob. < SPOT + BLOTCH⟧ an irregular spot, splash, or stain —*vt.*, *vi.* to mark or be marked with splotches —**splotch'y**, **-i·er**, **-i·est**, *adj.*

splurge (splurj) [Inf.] *n.* ⟦echoic⟧ a spell of extravagant spending —*vi.* **splurged**, **splurg'ing** to spend money freely

splut·ter (splut'ər) *vi.* ⟦var. of SPUTTER⟧ **1** to make hissing or spitting sounds **2** to speak hurriedly and confusedly —*n.* a spluttering

spoil (spoil) *vt.* **spoiled** or [Brit.] **spoilt**, **spoil'ing** ⟦< L *spolium,* plunder⟧ **1** to damage so as to make useless, etc. **2** to impair the enjoyment, etc. of **3** to cause to expect too much by overindulgence —*vi.* to become spoiled; decay, etc., as food does —*n.* [*usually pl.*] plunder; booty —**spoil'age** *n.* —**spoil'er** *n.*

spoil'sport' *n.* one whose actions ruin the pleasure of others

spoils system the treating of public offices as the booty of a successful political party

Spo·kane (spō kan') city in E Washington: pop. 177,000

spoke[1] (spōk) *n.* ⟦OE *spaca*⟧ any of the braces or bars extending from the hub to the rim of a wheel

spoke[2] (spōk) *vi.*, *vt. pt. & archaic pp. of* SPEAK

spo·ken (spō'kən) *vi.*, *vt. pp. of* SPEAK —*adj.* **1** uttered; oral **2** having a (specified) kind of voice *[soft-spoken]*

spokes·man (spōks'mən) *n.*, *pl.* **-men** (-mən) a person who speaks for another or for a group —**spokes'wom'an**, *pl.* **-wom'en**, *fem.n.*

spokes'per'son *n.* SPOKESMAN: used to avoid the masculine implication of *spokesman*

spo·li·a·tion (spō'lē ā'shən) *n.* ⟦< L *spoliatio*⟧ robbery; plundering

sponge (spunj) *n.* ⟦< Gr *spongia*⟧ **1** a stationary aquatic animal with a porous structure **2** the highly absorbent skeleton of such animals, used for washing surfaces, etc. **3** any substance like this, as a piece of light, porous rubber, etc. —*vt.* **sponged**, **spong'ing** **1** to dampen, wipe, absorb, etc. as with a sponge **2** [Inf.] to get as by begging, imposition, etc. —*vi.* [Inf.] to live as a parasite upon other people —**spong'er** *n.* —**spon'gy**, **-gi·er**, **-gi·est**, *adj.*

sponge bath a bath taken by using a wet sponge or cloth without getting into water

sponge'cake' *n.* a light, spongy cake without shortening: also **sponge cake**

spon·sor (spän'sər) *n.* ⟦L < *spondere,* promise solemnly⟧ **1** one who assumes responsibility for something; proponent, underwriter, endorser, etc. **2** a godparent **3** a business firm, etc. that pays for a radio or TV program advertising its product —*vt.* to act as sponsor for —**spon'sor·ship'** *n.*

spon·ta·ne·i·ty (spän'tə nē'ə tē, -nā'-) *n.* **1** a being spontaneous **2** *pl.* **-ties** spontaneous behavior, action, etc.

spon·ta·ne·ous (spän tā'nē əs) *adj.* ⟦< L *sponte,* of free will⟧ **1** acting or resulting from a natural feeling or impulse, without constraint, effort, etc. **2** occurring through internal causes

spontaneous combustion the process of catching fire through heat generated by internal chemical action

spoof (spo͞of) *n.* **1** a hoax or joke **2** a light satire —*vt.*, *vi.* **1** to fool; deceive **2** to satirize playfully

spook (spo͝ok) [Inf.] *n.* ⟦Du⟧ a ghost —*vt.*, *vi.* to frighten or become frightened

spook'y *adj.* **-i·er**, **-i·est** [Inf.] **1** weird; eerie **2** easily frightened; nervous, jumpy, etc.

spool (spo͞ol) *n.* ⟦< MDu *spoele*⟧ **1** a cylinder on which thread, wire, etc. is wound **2** the material wound on a spool

spoon (spo͞on) *n.* ⟦< OE *spon,* a chip⟧ **1** a utensil consisting of a small, shallow bowl and a handle, used for eating, stirring, etc. **2** something shaped like a spoon, as a shiny, curved fishing lure —*vt.* to take up with a spoon —**spoon'ful'**, *pl.* **-fuls'**, *n.*

spoon'bill' *n.* a wading bird whose flat bill is spoon-shaped at the tip

spoon·er·ism (spo͞on'ər iz'əm) *n.* ⟦after Rev. W. A. *Spooner* (1844-1930), of England, who made such slips⟧ an unintentional interchange of the initial sounds of words (Ex.: "a well-boiled icicle" for "a well-oiled bicycle")

spoon'-feed' *vt.* **-fed'**, **-feed'ing** **1** to feed with a spoon **2** to pamper; coddle

spoor (spoor) *n.* ⟦Afrik⟧ the track or trail of a wild animal

spo·rad·ic (spə rad'ik) *adj.* ⟦< Gr *sporas,* scattered⟧ happening or appearing in isolated instances *[sporadic storms]* —**spo·rad'i·cal·ly** *adv.*

spore (spôr) *n.* ⟦< Gr *spora,* a seed⟧ a small reproductive body produced by algae, ferns, etc. and capable of giving rise to a new individual

sport (spôrt) *n.* ⟦< DISPORT⟧ **1** any recreational activity; specif., a game, competition, etc. requiring bodily exertion **2** fun or play **3** [Inf.] a sportsmanlike person **4** [Inf.] a showy, flashy fellow **5** *Biol.* a plant or animal markedly different from the normal type —*vt.* [Inf.] to display *[to sport a loud tie]* —*vi.* to play —*adj.* **1** of or for sports **2** suitable for casual wear *[a sport coat]* Also, for adj., **sports** —**in** (or **for**) **sport** in jest —**make sport of** to mock or ridicule

sport'ing *adj.* **1** of or interested in sports **2** sportsmanlike; fair **3** of games, races, etc. involving gambling or betting

spor·tive (spôrt'iv) *adj.* **1** full of sport or fun **2** done in fun —**spor'tive·ly** *adv.*

sports car a small car characterized by above-average speed and handling

sports'cast' *n.* a broadcast of sports news on radio or TV —**sports'cast'er** *n.*

sports'man (-mən) *n.*, *pl.* **-men** (-mən) **1** a man who takes part in sports, esp. hunting, fishing, etc. **2** one who plays fair and can lose without complaint or win without gloating —**sports'man·like'** *adj.* —**sports'man·ship'** *n.*

sport utility vehicle a vehicle like a station wagon, but with a small-truck chassis and, usually, four-wheel drive

sport'y *adj.* **-i·er, -i·est** [Inf.] **1** sporting or sportsmanlike **2** flashy or showy —**sport'i·ness** *n.*

spot (spät) *n.* ⟦prob. < MDu *spotte*⟧ **1** *a*) a small area differing in color, etc. from the surrounding area *b*) a stain, speck, etc. **2** a flaw or defect **3** a locality; place —*vt.* **spot'ted, spot'ting 1** to mark with spots **2** to stain; blemish **3** to place; locate **4** to see; recognize **5** [Inf.] to allow as a handicap *[to spot* an opponent points*]* —*vi.* **1** to become marked with spots **2** to make a stain —*adj.* **1** ready *[spot* cash*]* **2** made at random *[a spot* survey*]* —**hit the spot** [Inf.] to satisfy a craving or need —**in a (bad) spot** [Slang] in trouble —**on the spot** [Slang] in a bad or demanding situation —**spot'less** *adj.* —**spot'less·ly** *adv.* —**spot'ted** *adj.*

spot'-check' *vt.* to check or examine at random or by sampling —*n.* such a checking

spot'light' *n.* **1** *a*) a strong beam of light focused on a particular person, thing, etc. *b*) a lamp used to project such a beam **2** public notice or prominence —*vt.* to light or draw attention to, by or as by a spotlight

spot'ty *adj.* **-ti·er, -ti·est 1** having, occurring in, or marked with spots **2** not uniform or consistent —**spot'ti·ly** *adv.*

spouse (spous) *n.* ⟦< L *sponsus,* betrothed⟧ (one's) husband or wife —**spous·al** (spou'zəl) *adj.*

spout (spout) *n.* ⟦< ME *spouten,* to spout⟧ **1** a lip, orifice, or projecting tube by which a liquid is poured or discharged **2** a stream, etc. as of liquid from a spout —*vt., vi.* **1** to shoot out (liquid, etc.) as from a spout **2** to speak or utter (words, etc.) in a loud, pompous manner

sprain (sprān) *vt.* ⟦< ? L *ex-,* out + *premere,* to press⟧ to wrench a ligament or muscle of (a joint) without dislocating the bones —*n.* an injury resulting from this

sprang (spraŋ) *vi., vt. alt. pt. of* SPRING

sprat (sprat) *n.* ⟦OE *sprott*⟧ a small European herring

sprawl (sprôl) *vi.* ⟦< OE *spreawlian,* move convulsively⟧ **1** to sit or lie with the limbs in a relaxed or awkward position **2** to spread out awkwardly or unevenly —*n.* **1** a sprawling movement or position **2** the uncontrolled spread of real-estate development into areas around a city

spray[1] (sprā) *n.* ⟦prob. < MDu *spraeien*⟧ **1** a mist of fine liquid particles **2** *a*) a jet of such particles, as from a spray gun *b*) a device for spraying **3** something likened to a spray —*vt., vi.* **1** to direct a spray (on) **2** to shoot out in a spray —**spray'er** *n.*

spray[2] (sprā) *n.* ⟦ME⟧ a small branch of a tree or plant, with leaves, flowers, etc.

spray can a can from which gas under pressure sprays out the contents

spray gun a device that shoots out a spray of liquid, as paint or insecticide

spread (spred) *vt., vi.* **spread, spread'ing** ⟦OE *sprædan*⟧ **1** to open or stretch out; unfold **2** to move (the fingers, wings, etc.) apart **3** to distribute or be distributed over an area or surface **4** to extend in time **5** to make or be made widely known, felt, etc. **6** to set (a table) for a meal **7** to push or be pushed apart —*n.* **1** the act or extent of spreading **2** an expanse **3** a cloth cover for a table, bed, etc. **4** jam, butter, etc. used on bread **5** [Inf.] a meal with many different foods —**spread'er** *n.*

spread'-ea'gle *adj.* having the figure of an eagle with wings and legs spread —*vt.* **-gled, -gling** to stretch out in this form, as for a flogging

spread'sheet' *n.* a computer program that organizes numerical data into rows and columns on a video screen

spree (sprē) *n.* ⟦< earlier *spray*⟧ **1** a noisy frolic **2** a period of drunkenness **3** a period of uninhibited activity *[a* shopping *spree]*

sprig (sprig) *n.* ⟦ME *sprigge*⟧ a little twig or spray

spright·ly (sprīt'lē) *adj.* **-li·er, -li·est** ⟦< *spright,* var. of SPRITE⟧ full of energy and spirit; lively —*adv.* in a sprightly manner —**spright'li·ness** *n.*

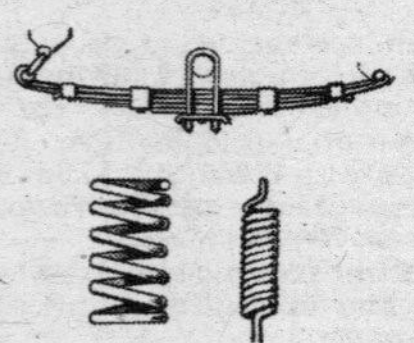

SPRINGS

spring (spriŋ) *vi.* **sprang** or **sprung, sprung, spring'ing** ⟦OE *springan*⟧ **1** to leap; bound **2** to come, appear, etc. suddenly **3** to bounce **4** to arise as from some source; grow or develop **5** to become warped, split, etc. Often followed by *up* —*vt.* **1** to cause (a trap, etc.) to snap shut **2** to cause to warp, split, etc. **3** to make known suddenly **4** [Slang] to get (someone) released from jail —*n.* **1** a leap, or the distance so covered **2** elasticity; resilience **3** a device, as a coil of wire, that returns to its original form after being forced out of shape **4** a flow of water from the ground **5** a source or origin **6** *a*) the season of the year following winter, when plants begin to grow *b*) any period of beginning —*adj.* **1** of, for, appearing in, or planted in the spring **2** having, or supported on, springs **3** coming from a spring *[spring* water*]* —**spring a leak** to begin unexpectedly to leak —**spring for** [Inf.] to bear the cost of for someone else

spring'board' *n.* a springy board used

as a takeoff in leaping or diving

spring fever the laziness or restlessness that many people feel in the early days of spring

Spring·field (spriŋ′fēld′) **1** city in SW Missouri: pop. 140,000 **2** capital of Illinois: pop. 105,000

spring′time′ *n.* the season of spring

spring′y *adj.* **-i·er, -i·est** having spring; elastic, resilient, etc. —**spring′i·ness** *n.*

sprin·kle (spriŋ′kəl) *vt., vi.* **-kled, -kling** ⟦ME *sprinklen*⟧ **1** to scatter or fall in drops or particles **2** to scatter drops or particles (upon) **3** to rain lightly —*n.* **1** a sprinkling **2** a light rain —**sprin′kler** *n.*

sprin′kling (-kliŋ) *n.* a small number or amount, esp. when scattered thinly

sprint (sprint) *vi., n.* ⟦ME *sprenten*⟧ run or race at full speed for a short distance —**sprint′er** *n.*

sprite (sprīt) *n.* ⟦< L *spiritus,* spirit⟧ *Folklore* an imaginary being, as an elf

spritz (sprits, shprits) *vt., vi., n.* ⟦< Ger *spritzen* & Yiddish *shprits*⟧ squirt or spray

spritz′er *n.* a drink consisting of white wine and soda water

sprock·et (spräk′it) *n.* ⟦< ?⟧ **1** any of the teeth, as on the rim of a wheel, arranged to fit the links of a chain **2** a wheel fitted with such teeth: in full **sprocket wheel**

sprout (sprout) *vi.* ⟦OE *sprutan*⟧ to begin to grow; give off shoots —*vt.* to cause to sprout or grow —*n.* **1** a young growth on a plant; shoot **2** a new growth from a bud, etc. **3** a new growth from a seed of alfalfa, etc., used as in salads

spruce[1] (sprōōs) *n.* ⟦ME *Spruce,* Prussia⟧ **1** an evergreen tree with slender needles **2** its wood

spruce[2] (sprōōs) *adj.* **spruc′er, spruc′est** ⟦< *Spruce leather* (see prec.)⟧ neat and trim in a smart way —*vt., vi.* **spruced, spruc′ing** to make (oneself) spruce: usually with *up*

sprung (spruŋ) *vi., vt. pp. & alt. pt. of* SPRING

spry (sprī) *adj.* **spri′er** or **spry′er, spri′est** or **spry′est** ⟦< Scand⟧ full of life; active, esp. though elderly —**spry′ly** *adv.* —**spry′ness** *n.*

spud (spud) *n.* [Inf.] a potato

spume (spyōōm) *n.* ⟦< L *spuma*⟧ foam, froth, or scum —*vi.* **spumed, spum′ing** to foam; froth

spu·mo·ni (spə mō′nē) *n.* ⟦It < L *spuma,* foam⟧ Italian ice cream in variously flavored and colored layers

spun (spun) *vt., vi. pt. & pp. of* SPIN

spunk (spuŋk) *n.* ⟦Ir *sponc,* tinder⟧ [Inf.] courage; spirit —**spunk′y, -i·er, -i·est,** *adj.*

spur (spur) *n.* ⟦OE *spura*⟧ **1** a pointed device worn on the heel by a rider, used to urge a horse forward **2** anything that urges; stimulus **3** any spurlike projection **4** a short railroad track connected with the main track —*vt.* **spurred, spur′ring 1** to prick with spurs **2** to urge or incite —**on the spur of the moment** abruptly and impulsively

spurge (spurj) *n.* ⟦< earlier Fr *espurger,* to purge⟧ any of a group of plants with milky juice and tiny flowers

spu·ri·ous (spyoor′ē əs, spur′-) *adj.* ⟦L *spurius,* illegitimate⟧ not genuine; false —**spu′ri·ous·ly** *adv.* —**spu′ri·ous·ness** *n.*

spurn (spurn) *vt.* ⟦OE *spurnan*⟧ to reject with contempt; scorn

spurt (spurt) *vt.* ⟦prob. < OE *sprutan,* to sprout⟧ to expel in a stream or jet —*vi.* **1** to gush forth in a stream or jet **2** to show a sudden, brief burst of energy, etc. —*n.* **1** a sudden shooting forth; jet **2** a sudden, brief burst of energy, etc.

sput·nik (spoot′nik, sput′-) *n.* ⟦Russ, lit., co-traveler⟧ any of a series of man-made satellites launched by the U.S.S.R. starting in 1957

sput·ter (sput′ər) *vi., vt.* ⟦< MDu *spotten,* to spit⟧ **1** to spit out (bits, drops, etc.) explosively, as when talking excitedly **2** to speak or utter in a confused, explosive way **3** to make sharp, sizzling sounds, as frying fat does —*n.* a sputtering

spu·tum (spyōōt′əm) *n., pl.* **-ta** (-ə) ⟦< L *spuere,* to spit⟧ saliva, usually mixed with mucus, ejected from the mouth

spy (spī) *vt.* **spied, spy′ing** ⟦< OHG *spehōn,* examine⟧ **1** to watch closely and secretly: often with *out* **2** to catch sight of; see —*vi.* to watch closely and secretly; act as a spy —*n., pl.* **spies 1** one who keeps close and secret watch on others **2** one employed by a government to get secret information about another government

spy′glass′ *n.* a small telescope

sq *abbrev.* **1** sequence **2** squadron **3** square

sqq. *abbrev.* ⟦L *sequentes; sequentia*⟧ the following ones; what follows

squab (skwäb) *n.* ⟦prob. < Scand⟧ a nestling pigeon

squab·ble (skwäb′əl) *vi.* **-bled, -bling** ⟦< Scand⟧ to quarrel noisily over a small matter; wrangle —*n.* a noisy, petty quarrel —**squab′bler** *n.*

squad (skwäd) *n.* ⟦< Sp *escuadra* or It *squadra,* a square⟧ **1** a small group of soldiers, often a subdivision of a platoon **2** any small group of people working together

squad car PATROL CAR

squad′ron (-rən) *n.* ⟦< It *squadra,* a square⟧ a unit of warships, military aircraft, etc.

squal·id (skwäl′id, skwôl′id) *adj.* ⟦< L *squalere,* be foul⟧ **1** foul or unclean **2** wretched

squall[1] (skwôl) *n.* ⟦< Scand⟧ a brief, violent windstorm, usually with rain or snow —**squall′y, -i·er, -i·est,** *adj.*

squall[2] (skwôl) *vi., vt.* ⟦< ON *skvala*⟧ to cry or scream loudly and harshly —*n.* a harsh cry or loud scream

squal·or (skwäl′ər, skwôl′ər) *n.* a being squalid; filth and wretchedness

squa·mous (skwā′məs) *adj.* ⟦< L *squama,* a scale⟧ like, formed of, or covered with scales

squan·der (skwän′dər) ***vt.*** ⟦prob. < dial. *squander,* to scatter⟧ to spend or use wastefully or extravagantly

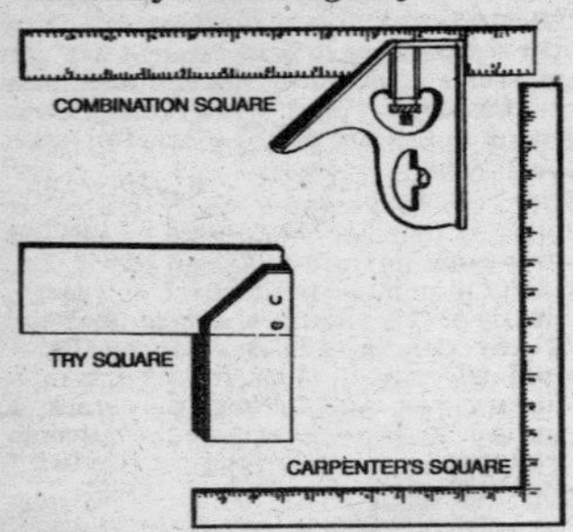

square (skwer) ***n.*** ⟦< L *ex,* out + *quadrare,* to square⟧ **1** *a*) a plane figure having four equal sides and four right angles *b*) anything of or approximating this shape **2** an open area bounded by several streets, used as a park, etc. **3** an instrument for drawing or testing right angles **4** the product of a number multiplied by itself **5** [Slang] a person who is SQUARE (*adj.* 10) —***vt.*** **squared**, **squar′ing** **1** to make square **2** to make straight, even, right-angled, etc. **3** to settle; adjust *[to square accounts]* **4** to make conform *[to square a statement with the facts]* **5** to multiply (a quantity) by itself —***vi.*** to fit; agree; accord (*with*) —***adj.*** **squar′er**, **squar′est** **1** having four equal sides and four right angles **2** forming a right angle **3** straight, level, even, etc. **4** leaving no balance; even **5** just; fair **6** direct; straightforward **7** designating a unit of surface measure in the form of a square *[a square foot]* **8** sturdy and somewhat rectangular *[a square jaw]* **9** [Inf.] substantial *[a square meal]* **10** [Slang] old-fashioned, unsophisticated, etc. —***adv.*** in a square manner —**square off** to assume a posture of attack or self-defense —**square oneself** [Inf.] to make amends —**square′ly** ***adv.*** —**square′ness** ***n.*** —**squar′ish** ***adj.***

square dance a dance with various steps, in which couples are grouped in a given form, as a square —**square′-dance′**, **-danced′**, **-danc′ing**, ***vi.***

square′-rigged′ ***adj.*** rigged with square sails as the principal sails

square root the number or quantity which when squared will produce a given number or quantity *[3 is the square root of 9]*

squash[1] (skwôsh, skwäsh) ***vt.*** ⟦< L *ex-,* intens. + *quatere,* to shake⟧ **1** to crush into a soft or flat mass; press **2** to suppress; quash —***vi.*** **1** to be squashed **2** to make a sound of squashing —***n.*** **1** the act or sound of squashing **2** a game played in a walled court with rackets and a rubber ball —**squash′y**, **-i·er**, **-i·est**, ***adj.***

squash[2] (skwôsh, skwäsh) ***n.*** ⟦< AmInd⟧ the fleshy fruit of various plants of the gourd family, eaten as a vegetable

squat (skwät) ***vi.*** **squat′ted**, **squat′ting** ⟦ult. < L *ex-,* intens. + *cogere,* to force⟧ **1** to crouch so as to sit on the heels with knees bent and weight resting on the balls of the feet **2** to crouch close to the ground **3** to settle on land without right or title **4** to settle on public land in order to get title to it —***adj.*** **-ter**, **-test** short and heavy or thick: also **squat′ty**, **-ti·er**, **-ti·est** —***n.*** the act or position of squatting —**squat′ness** ***n.*** —**squat′ter** ***n.***

squaw (skwô) ***n.*** ⟦< AmInd⟧ [Now Rare] a North American Indian woman or wife: term now considered offensive

squawk (skwôk) ***vi.*** ⟦echoic⟧ **1** to utter a loud, harsh cry **2** [Inf.] to complain loudly —***n.*** **1** a loud, harsh cry **2** [Inf.] a loud complaint

squeak (skwēk) ***vi.*** ⟦ME *squeken*⟧ to make or utter a sharp, high-pitched sound or cry —***vt.*** to say in a squeak —***n.*** a thin, sharp sound or cry —**narrow** (or **close**) **squeak** [Inf.] a narrow escape —**squeak through** (or **by**, etc.) [Inf.] to succeed, survive, etc. with difficulty —**squeak′y**, **-i·er**, **-i·est**, ***adj.***

squeak′er ***n.*** [Inf.] a narrow escape, victory, etc.

squeal (skwēl) ***vi.*** ⟦ME *squelen*⟧ **1** to utter or make a long, shrill cry or sound **2** [Slang] to act as an informer —***vt.*** to utter in a squeal —***n.*** a squealing —**squeal′er** ***n.***

squeam·ish (skwē′mish) ***adj.*** ⟦ME *squaimous*⟧ **1** easily nauseated **2** easily shocked **3** fastidious —**squeam′ish·ly** ***adv.*** —**squeam′ish·ness** ***n.***

squee·gee (skwē′jē) ***n.*** ⟦prob. < fol.⟧ a rubber-edged tool for scraping water from a flat surface

SQUEEGEE

squeeze (skwēz) ***vt.*** **squeezed**, **squeez′ing** ⟦< OE *cwysan*⟧ **1** to press hard, esp. from two or more sides **2** to extract (juice, etc.) from (fruit, etc.) **3** to force (*into, out,* etc.) by pressing **4** to embrace closely; hug —***vi.*** **1** to yield to pressure **2** to exert pressure **3** to force one's way by pushing (*in, out,* etc.) —***n.*** **1** a squeezing or being squeezed **2** a close embrace; hug **3** the state of being closely pressed or packed; crush **4** a period of scarcity, hardship, etc.

squeeze bottle a plastic bottle that is squeezed to eject its contents

squelch (skwelch) [Inf.] ***n.*** ⟦prob. echoic⟧ a crushing retort, rebuke, etc. —***vt.*** to suppress or silence completely

squib (skwib) ***n.*** ⟦prob. echoic⟧ **1** a firecracker that burns with a hissing noise before exploding **2** a short, witty attack in words; lampoon **3** a short news item

squid (skwid) ***n.*** ⟦prob. < *squit,* dial. for SQUIRT⟧ a long, slender sea mollusk with eight arms and two long tentacles

SQUID

squig·gle (skwig′əl) ***n.*** ⟦SQU(IRM) + (W)IGGLE⟧ a short, wavy line or illegible scrawl —***vt.***, ***vi.*** **-gled, -gling** to write as, or make, a squiggle or squiggles

squint (skwint) ***vi.*** ⟦< (*a*)*squint,* with a squint < ME *on skwyn,* sideways⟧ **1** to peer with the eyes partly closed **2** to be cross-eyed —***n.*** **1** a squinting **2** a being cross-eyed **3** [Inf.] a quick look

squire (skwīr) ***n.*** ⟦see ESQUIRE⟧ **1** in England, the owner of a large, rural estate **2** a man escorting a woman —***vt.*** **squired, squir′ing** to escort

squirm (skwʉrm) ***vi.*** ⟦prob. echoic, infl. by WORM⟧ **1** to twist and turn the body; wriggle **2** to show or feel shame or embarrassment —***n.*** a squirming —**squirm′y, -i·er, -i·est,** ***adj.***

squir·rel (skwʉr′əl, skwʉrl) ***n.*** ⟦< Gr *skia,* shadow + *oura,* tail⟧ **1** a small, tree-dwelling rodent with heavy fur and a long, bushy tail **2** its fur

squirt (skwʉrt) ***vt.*** ⟦prob. < LowG *swirtjen*⟧ **1** to shoot out (a liquid) in a jet; spurt **2** to wet with liquid so shot out —***n.*** **1** a jet of liquid **2** [Inf.] a small or young person, esp. an impudent one

squish (skwish) ***vi.*** ⟦echoic var. of SQUASH[1]⟧ to make a soft, splashing sound when squeezed, etc. —***vt.*** [Inf.] to squash —***n.*** **1** a squishing sound **2** [Inf.] a squashing —**squish′y, -i·er, -i·est,** ***adj.***

Sr[1] *abbrev.* **1** Senior **2** Sister

Sr[2] *Chem. symbol for* strontium

Sri Lan·ka (srē läŋ′kə) country coextensive with an island off the SE tip of India: 25,332 sq. mi.; pop. 14,847,000 —**Sri Lan′kan**

SRO *abbrev.* **1** single room occupancy **2** standing room only

SS *abbrev.* **1** Social Security **2** steamship

SST *abbrev.* supersonic transport

St *abbrev.* **1** Saint **2** Strait **3** Street

stab (stab) ***n.*** ⟦prob. < ME *stubbe,* stub⟧ **1** a wound made by stabbing **2** a thrust, as with a knife **3** a sudden, sharp pain —***vt.***, ***vi.*** **stabbed, stab′bing 1** to pierce or wound as with a knife **2** to thrust (a knife, etc.) into something **3** to pain sharply —**make** (or **take**) **a stab at** [Inf.] to make an attempt at

sta·bil·i·ty (stə bil′ə tē) ***n.*** **1** a being stable; steadiness **2** firmness of character, purpose, etc. **3** permanence

sta·bi·lize (stā′bə līz′) ***vt.*** **-lized′, -liz′ing 1** to make stable **2** to keep from changing **3** to give stability to (a plane or ship) —***vi.*** to become stabilized —**sta′bi·li·za′tion** ***n.*** —**sta′bi·liz′er** ***n.***

sta·ble[1] (stā′bəl) ***adj.*** **-bler, -blest** ⟦< L *stare,* to stand⟧ **1** not likely to give way; firm; fixed **2** firm in character, purpose, etc.; steadfast **3** not likely to change; lasting

sta·ble[2] (stā′bəl) ***n.*** ⟦see prec.⟧ **1** a building in which horses or cattle are sheltered and fed **2** all the racehorses belonging to one owner —***vt.***, ***vi.*** **-bled, -bling** to lodge, keep, or be kept in or as in a stable

stac·ca·to (stə kät′ō) ***adj.***, ***adv.*** ⟦It < *distaccare,* detach⟧ *Music* with distinct breaks between successive tones

stack (stak) ***n.*** ⟦< ON *stakkr*⟧ **1** a large, neatly arranged pile of straw, hay, etc. **2** any orderly pile **3** SMOKESTACK **4** [*pl.*] a series of bookshelves, as in a library —***vt.*** **1** to arrange in a stack **2** to rig so as to predetermine the outcome —**stack up** to stand in comparison (*with* or *against*)

sta·di·um (stā′dē əm) ***n.*** ⟦< Gr *stadion,* ancient unit of length, *c.* 607 feet⟧ a large structure as for sports events, with tiers of seats for spectators

staff (staf) ***n.***, *pl.* **staffs**; also, for 1 & 4, **staves** ⟦OE *stæf*⟧ **1** a stick or rod used as a support, a symbol of authority, etc. **2** a group of people assisting a leader **3** a specific group of workers *[a teaching staff]* **4** *Music* the horizontal lines on and between which notes are written —***vt.*** to provide with a staff, as of workers

staff′er ***n.*** a member of a staff, as of a newspaper

stag (stag) ***n.*** ⟦OE *stagga*⟧ a full-grown male deer —***adj.*** for men only *[a stag dinner]*

stage (stāj) ***n.*** ⟦< L *stare,* to stand⟧ **1** a platform **2** *a*) an area or platform on which plays, etc. are presented *b*) the theater, or acting as a profession (with *the*) **3** the scene of an event **4** a stopping place, or the distance between stops, on a journey **5** *short for* STAGECOACH **6** a period or level in a process of development *[the larval stage]* **7** any of the propulsion units used in sequence to launch a missile, spacecraft, etc. —***vt.*** **staged, stag′ing 1** to present as on a stage **2** to plan and carry out *[to stage an attack]*

stage′coach′ ***n.*** a horse-drawn public coach that, formerly, traveled a regular route

stage′hand′ ***n.*** one who sets up scenery, furniture, lights, etc. for a stage play

stage′-struck′ ***adj.*** having an intense desire to become an actor or actress

stag·ger (stag′ər) ***vi.*** ⟦< ON *stakra,* totter⟧ to totter, reel, etc. as from a blow or fatigue —***vt.*** **1** to cause to stagger, as with a blow **2** to affect strongly with astonishment, grief, etc. **3** to set or arrange alternately, as on either side of a line; make zigzag **4** to arrange so as to come at different times *[to stagger employees' vacations]* —***n.*** **1** a staggering **2** [*pl., with sing. or pl. v.*] a nervous disease of horses, etc. causing this

stag·nant (stag′nənt) ***adj.*** ⟦see fol.⟧ **1** not flowing or moving **2** foul from lack of movement: said of water **3** dull; sluggish

stag'nate' (-nāt') ***vi., vt.* -nat'ed, -nat'ing** ⟦< L *stagnare*⟧ to become or make stagnant —**stag·na'tion *n.***

staid (stād) ***vi., vt.*** *archaic pt. & pp. of* STAY[3] —***adj.*** sober; sedate —**staid'ly *adv.***

stain (stān) ***vt.*** ⟦ult. < L *dis-*, from + *tingere*, to tinge⟧ **1** to spoil by discoloring or spotting **2** to disgrace; dishonor **3** to color (wood, etc.) with a dye —***n.*** **1** a color or spot resulting from staining **2** a moral blemish **3** a dye for staining wood, etc.

stain'less steel steel alloyed with chromium, etc., virtually immune to rust and corrosion

stair (ster) ***n.*** ⟦OE *stæger*⟧ **1** [*usually pl.*] a stairway **2** a single step, as of a stairway

stair'case' ***n.*** a stairway in a building, usually with a handrail

stair'way' ***n.*** a means of access, as from one level of a building to another, consisting of a series of stairs

stair'well' ***n.*** a vertical shaft (in a building) containing a staircase

stake (stāk) ***n.*** ⟦OE *staca*⟧ **1** a pointed length of wood or metal for driving into the ground **2** the post to which a person was tied for execution by burning **3** [*often pl.*] money risked, as in a wager or business venture **4** [*often pl.*] the winner's prize in a race, etc. —***vt.*** **staked, stak'ing** **1** to mark the boundaries of [*to stake out a claim*] **2** to fasten to a stake or stakes **3** to gamble **4** [Inf.] to furnish with money or resources —**at stake** being risked —**pull up stakes** [Inf.] to change one's residence, etc. —**stake out** to put under police surveillance

stake'out' ***n.*** **1** the putting of a suspect or a place under police surveillance **2** an area under such surveillance

sta·lac·tite (stə lak'tīt) ***n.*** ⟦< Gr *stalaktos*, trickling⟧ an icicle-shaped mineral deposit hanging from a cave roof

sta·lag (shtä'läk; *E* stä'läg) ***n.*** ⟦Ger⟧ a German prisoner-of-war camp, esp. in WWII

sta·lag·mite (stə lag'mīt') ***n.*** ⟦< Gr *stalagmos*, a dropping⟧ a cone-shaped mineral deposit built up on a cave floor by dripping water

stale (stāl) ***adj.*** **stal'er, stal'est** ⟦prob. < OFr *estale*, quiet⟧ **1** no longer fresh; flat, dry, etc. **2** trite [*a stale joke*] **3** out of condition, bored, etc.

stale'mate' ***n.*** ⟦< OFr *estal*, fixed location⟧ **1** *Chess* any situation in which a player cannot move: it results in a draw **2** any deadlock —***vt.*** **-mat'ed, -mat'ing** to bring into a stalemate

Sta·lin (stä'lin), **Joseph** 1879-1953; Soviet premier (1941-53) —**Sta'lin·ism'** ***n.*** —**Sta'lin·ist *adj., n.***

stalk[1] (stôk) ***vi., vt.*** ⟦OE *stealcian*⟧ **1** to walk (through) in a stiff, haughty manner **2** to advance grimly **3** *a*) to pursue (game, etc.) stealthily *b*) to pursue (a person) in a persistent, harassing, obsessive way —***n.*** **1** a slow, stiff, haughty stride **2** a stalking

stalk[2] (stôk) ***n.*** ⟦ME *stalke*⟧ **1** any stem or stemlike part **2** the main stem of a plant

stall[1] (stôl) ***n.*** ⟦OE *steall*⟧ **1** a section for one animal in a stable **2** *a*) a booth, etc. as at a market *b*) a pew in a church **3** the state of being in a stop or standstill, as a result of some malfunction —***vt., vi.*** **1** to keep or be kept in a stall **2** to bring or be brought to a standstill, esp. unintentionally

stall[2] (stôl) ***vi., vt.*** ⟦< *stall*, a decoy⟧ to act evasively so as to deceive or delay —***n.*** any action used in stalling

stal·lion (stal'yən) ***n.*** ⟦< OFr *estalon*⟧ an uncastrated male horse

stal·wart (stôl'wərt) ***adj.*** ⟦< OE *stathol*, foundation + *wyrthe*, worth⟧ **1** strong; sturdy **2** brave; valiant **3** resolute; firm —***n.*** a stalwart person

sta·men (stā'mən) ***n.*** ⟦< L, thread⟧ the pollen-bearing organ in a flower

Stam·ford (stam'fərd) city in SW Connecticut: pop. 108,000

stam·i·na (stam'ə nə) ***n.*** ⟦L, pl. of STAMEN⟧ resistance to fatigue, illness, hardship, etc.; endurance

stam·mer (stam'ər) ***vt., vi.*** ⟦OE *stamerian*⟧ to speak or say with involuntary pauses and rapid repetitions of some sounds —***n.*** a stammering —**stam'mer·er *n.***

stamp (stamp) ***vt.*** ⟦ME *stampen*⟧ **1** to bring (the foot) down forcibly **2** to crush or pound with the foot **3** to imprint or cut out (a design, etc.) **4** to cut (*out*) by pressing with a die **5** to put a stamp on —***vi.*** **1** to bring the foot down forcibly **2** to walk with loud, heavy steps, as in anger —***n.*** **1** a stamping **2** *a*) a machine, tool, or die for stamping *b*) a mark or form made by stamping **3** any of various seals, gummed pieces of paper, etc. used to show that a fee, as for postage, has been paid **4** any similar stamp **5** class; kind —**stamp out** **1** to crush by treading on forcibly **2** to suppress, or put down —**stamp'er *n.***

stam·pede (stam pēd') ***n.*** ⟦< Sp *estampar*, to stamp⟧ a sudden, headlong rush or flight, as of a herd of cattle —***vi.*** **-ped'ed, -ped'ing** to move, or take part, in a stampede

stamping ground [Inf.] a favorite gathering place: *also used in pl.*

stance (stans) ***n.*** ⟦< L *stare*, to stand⟧ **1** the way one stands, esp. the placement of the feet **2** the attitude taken in a given situation

stanch ***vt., vi., adj.*** *see* STAUNCH

stan·chion (stan'chən) ***n.*** ⟦see STANCE⟧ **1** an upright post or support **2** a device for confining a cow, fitted loosely around the neck

stand (stand) ***vi.*** **stood, stand'ing** ⟦OE *standan*⟧ **1** to be in, or assume, an upright position on the feet **2** to be supported on a base, pedestal, etc. **3** to take or be in a (specified) position, attitude, etc. **4** to have a (specified) height when standing **5** to be placed or situated **6** to gather and remain: said as of water **7** to remain unchanged **8** to make resistance **9** *a*) to halt *b*) to be stationary —*vt.* **1** to place upright **2** to endure **3** to withstand **4** to undergo *[to stand trial]* —*n.* **1** a standing; esp., a halt or stop **2** a position; station **3** a view, opinion, etc. **4** a structure to stand or sit on **5** a place of business, esp. a stall, etc. where goods are sold **6** a rack, small table, etc. for holding things **7** a growth of trees, etc. —**stand a chance** to have a chance (*of* winning, surviving, etc.) —**stand by 1** to be ready if needed **2** to aid —**stand for 1** to represent; mean **2** [Inf.] to tolerate —**stand on 1** to be founded on **2** to insist upon —**stand out 1** to project **2** to be distinct, prominent, etc. —**stand up 1** to rise to a standing position **2** to prove valid, durable, etc. **3** [Slang] to fail to keep a date with —**take the stand** to testify in court

stand·ard (stan′dərd) *n.* ⟦< OFr *estendard*⟧ **1** a flag or banner used as an emblem of a military unit, etc. **2** something established for use as a rule or basis of comparison in measuring **3** an upright support —*adj.* **1** used as, or conforming to, a standard, rule, model, etc. **2** generally accepted as reliable or authoritative **3** typical; ordinary

stand′ard-bear′er *n.* **1** one who carries the flag **2** the leader of a movement, political party, etc.

stand′ard·ize′ *vt.* **-ized′**, **-iz′ing** to make standard or uniform —**stand′ard·i·za′tion** *n.*

standard time the time in any of the 24 time zones, each an hour apart, into which the earth is divided, based on distance east or west of Greenwich, England

stand′by′ *n.*, *pl.* **-bys′** a person or thing that is dependable or is a possible substitute

stand·ee (stan dē′) *n.* one who stands, as in a theater or bus

stand′-in′ *n.* a temporary substitute, as for an actor at rehearsals

stand′ing *n.* **1** status or reputation *[in good standing]* **2** duration *[a rule of long standing]* —*adj.* **1** upright or erect **2** from a standing position *[a standing jump]* **3** stagnant: said as of water **4** lasting; permanent *[a standing order]*

stand′off′ *n.* a tie in a game or contest

stand′off′ish *adj.* reserved; aloof

stand′out′ *n.* [Inf.] a person or thing outstanding in performance or quality

stand′pipe′ *n.* a high vertical pipe or cylindrical tank, as in a town's water-supply system, for storing water at a desired pressure

stand′point′ *n.* point of view

stand′still′ *n.* a stop or halt

stand′-up′ *adj.* **1** in a standing position **2** designating a comedian who tells jokes, etc., as in a nightclub

stank (staŋk) *vi. alt. pt. of* STINK

stan·za (stan′zə) *n.* ⟦It: ult. < L *stare*, to stand⟧ a group of lines of verse forming a division of a poem or song

staph (staf) *n. short for* STAPHYLOCOCCUS

staph·y·lo·coc·cus (staf′ə lō käk′əs) *n.*, *pl.* **-coc′ci′** (-käk′sī′) ⟦< Gr *staphylē*, bunch of grapes + *kokkos*, kernel⟧ any of certain spherical bacteria, a common source of infection

sta·ple[1] (stā′pəl) *n.* ⟦< MDu *stapel*, mart⟧ **1** a chief commodity made or grown in a particular place **2** a chief part or element in anything **3** a regularly stocked item of trade, as flour, salt, etc. **4** the fiber of cotton, wool, etc. —*adj.* **1** regularly stocked, produced, or used **2** most important; principal

sta·ple[2] (stā′pəl) *n.* ⟦OE *stapol*, a post⟧ a U-shaped piece of metal with sharp ends, driven into wood, etc. as to fasten something, or through papers as a binding —*vt.* **-pled**, **-pling** to fasten or bind with a staple or staples —**sta′pler** *n.*

star (stär) *n.* ⟦OE *steorra*⟧ **1** any of the luminous celestial objects seen as points of light in the sky; esp., any far-off, self-luminous one **2** such an object regarded as influencing one's fate: *often used in pl.* **3** a conventionalized figure with five or six points, or anything like this **4** ASTERISK **5** one who excels, as in a sport **6** a leading actor or actress —*vt.* **starred**, **star′ring 1** to mark with stars as a decoration, etc. **2** to feature (an actor or actress) in a leading role —*vi.* **1** to perform brilliantly **2** to perform as a star, as in films —*adj.* **1** having great skill; outstanding **2** of a star

star·board (stär′bərd, -bôrd′) *n.* ⟦< OE *steoran*, to steer (rudder formerly on right side) + *bord*, side (of ship)⟧ the right-hand side of a ship, etc. as one faces forward —*adj.* of or on this side

starch (stärch) *n.* ⟦< OE *stearc*, stiff⟧ **1** a white, tasteless, odorless food substance found in potatoes, cereals, etc. **2** a powdered form of this, used in laundering for stiffening cloth, etc. —*vt.* to stiffen as with starch —**starch′y**, **-i·er**, **-i·est**, *adj.*

star′-crossed′ *adj.* ⟦see STAR, *n.* 2⟧ ill-fated

star·dom (stär′dəm) *n.* the status of a star, as of films

stare (ster) *vi.* **stared**, **star′ing** ⟦OE *starian*⟧ to gaze steadily and intently —*vt.* to look fixedly at —*n.* a steady, intent look —**star′er** *n.*

STARFISH

star′fish′ *n.*, *pl.* **-fish′** or (for different species) **-fish′es** a small, star-shaped sea animal

star′gaze′ *vi.* **-gazed′**, **-gaz′ing 1** to gaze at the stars **2** to indulge in dreamy thought —**star′gaz′er** *n.*

stark (stärk) *adj.* ⟦OE *stearc*⟧ **1** rigorous; severe **2** sharply outlined **3** bleak; desolate **4** sheer; downright —*adv.* utterly; wholly

star′less ***adj.*** with no stars visible

star·let (stär′lit) ***n.*** a young actress being promoted as a future star

star′light′ ***n.*** light given by the stars —**star′lit′** ***adj.***

star·ling (stär′liŋ) ***n.*** ⟦OE *stær*⟧ any of an Old World family of birds; esp., the **common starling** with iridescent plumage, introduced into the U.S.

Star of David a six-pointed star, Judaic symbol

star′ry ***adj.*** **-ri·er, -ri·est 1** shining; bright **2** lighted by or full of stars

star′ry-eyed′ ***adj.*** **1** with sparkling eyes **2** overly optimistic

Stars and Stripes *name for* the U.S. flag

star′-span′gled ***adj.*** studded with stars

Star-Spangled Banner the U.S. national anthem

star′-struck′ or **star′struck′** ***adj.*** fascinated by celebrities, esp. by stars of movies, etc.

start (stärt) ***vi.*** ⟦OE *styrtan*⟧ **1** to make a sudden or involuntary move **2** to go into action or motion; begin; commence **3** to spring into being, activity, etc. —***vt.*** **1** to flush (game) **2** to displace, loosen, etc. [to *start* a seam] **3** *a*) to begin to play, do, etc. *b*) to set into motion, action, etc. **4** to cause to be an entrant in a race, etc. **5** to play in (a game) at the beginning —***n.*** **1** a sudden, startled reaction or movement **2** a starting, or beginning **3** *a*) a place or time of beginning *b*) a lead or other advantage **4** an opportunity of beginning a career —**start out** (or **off**) to start a journey, project, etc. —**start′er** ***n.***

star·tle (stärt′'l) ***vt.*** **-tled, -tling** ⟦< ME *sterten*, to start⟧ to surprise, frighten, or alarm suddenly; esp., to cause to start —***vi.*** to be startled

start′-up′ ***adj., n.*** (of) a new business venture

starve (stärv) ***vi.*** **starved, starv′ing** ⟦< OE *steorfan*, to die⟧ **1** to die from lack of food **2** to suffer from hunger **3** to suffer great need: with *for* —***vt.*** **1** to cause to starve **2** to force by starvation —**star·va·tion** (stär vā′shən) ***n.***

starve′ling (-liŋ) ***n.*** a person or animal that is weak from lack of food

Star Wars ⟦from a film title⟧ [Inf.] a proposed defense system of space-based weapons for destroying missiles

stash (stash) [Inf.] ***vt.*** ⟦< ?⟧ to put or hide away (money, etc.) —***n.*** **1** a place for hiding things **2** something hidden away

-stat (stat) *combining form* a device or agent that keeps something (specified) stable *[thermostat]*

state (stāt) ***n.*** ⟦< L *stare*, to stand⟧ **1** a set of circumstances, etc. characterizing a person or thing; condition **2** condition as regards structure, form, etc. **3** rich display; pomp **4** [*sometimes* **S-**] a body of people politically organized under one government; nation **5** [*often* **S-**] any of the political units forming a federal government, as in the U.S. **6** civil government [church and *state*] —***adj.*** **1** formal; ceremonial **2** [*sometimes* **S-**] of the government or of a state —***vt.*** **stat′ed, stat′ing 1** to establish by specifying **2** *a*) to set forth in words *b*) to express nonverbally —**in a state** [Inf.] in an excited condition —**lie in state** to be displayed formally before burial —**the States** the United States

state′hood′ ***n.*** the condition of being a state

state′house′ ***n.*** [*often* **S-**] the official legislative meeting place of each U.S. state

state′less ***adj.*** having no state or nationality

state′ly ***adj.*** **-li·er, -li·est 1** imposing; majestic **2** slow, dignified, etc. —**state′li·ness** ***n.***

state′ment ***n.*** **1** *a*) a stating *b*) a declaration, assertion, etc. **2** *a*) a financial account *b*) a bill; invoice

Stat·en Island (stat′'n) island borough of New York City: pop. 379,000

state of the art the current level of sophistication, as of technology —**state′-of-the-art′** ***adj.***

state′room′ ***n.*** a private room on a ship or train

state′side′ [Inf.] ***adj.*** of or in the U.S. (as viewed from abroad) —***adv.*** in or to the U.S.

states·man (stāts′mən) ***n., pl.*** **-men** (-mən) one who is wise or experienced in the business of government —**states′man·ship′** ***n.***

stat·ic (stat′ik) ***adj.*** ⟦< Gr *statikos*, causing to stand⟧ **1** of masses, forces, etc. at rest or in equilibrium **2** at rest; inactive **3** of or producing stationary electrical charges, as from friction **4** of or having to do with static —***n.*** **1** noise in radio or TV reception, caused by atmospheric electrical discharges **2** [Slang] adverse criticism —**stat′i·cal·ly** ***adv.***

sta·tion (stā′shən) ***n.*** ⟦< L *stare*, to stand⟧ **1** the place where a person or thing stands or is located; esp., an assigned post **2** a building, etc. at which a service, etc. is provided [police *station*] **3** a regular stopping place, as on a railroad **4** social standing **5** *a*) a place equipped for radio or TV transmission *b*) its assigned frequency or channel —***vt.*** to assign to a station

sta·tion·ar·y (stā′shə ner′ē) ***adj.*** **1** not moving; fixed **2** unchanging

station break a pause in radio or TV programs for station identification

sta·tion·er (stā′shə nər) ***n.*** ⟦< ML *stationarius*, shopkeeper⟧ a dealer in office supplies, etc.

sta′tion·er′y (-ner′ē) ***n.*** writing materials; specif., paper and envelopes

station wagon an automobile with extra space for cargo or seating and a rear door for loading

sta·tis·tics (stə tis′tiks) ***pl.n.*** ⟦< L *status*, standing⟧ numerical data assembled and classified so as to present significant information —***n.*** the science of compiling such data —**sta·tis′ti·cal** ***adj.*** —**stat·is·ti·cian** (stat′is tish′ən) ***n.***

stats (stats) ***pl.n.*** [Inf.] *short for* STATISTICS

stat·u·ar·y (stach′o͞o er′ē) ***n.*** statues collectively

stat·ue (stach′ōō) ***n.*** ⟦< L *statuere,* to set⟧ a figure, as of a person, or an abstract form carved in stone, cast in bronze, etc.

stat′u·esque′ (-esk′) ***adj.*** tall and stately

stat′u·ette′ (-et′) ***n.*** a small statue

stat·ure (stach′ər) ***n.*** ⟦< L *statura*⟧ **1** standing height, esp. of a person **2** level of attainment *[moral stature]*

sta·tus (stat′əs, stāt′-) ***n.,*** *pl.* **-tus·es** ⟦L, standing⟧ **1** legal condition *[the status of a minor]* **2** *a*) position; rank *b*) prestige **3** state, as of affairs

status quo (kwō′) ⟦L, the state in which⟧ the existing state of affairs

status symbol a possession regarded as a mark of high social status

stat·ute (stach′ōōt) ***n.*** ⟦see STATUE⟧ **1** an established rule **2** a law passed by a legislative body

statute of limitations a statute limiting the time for legal action

stat·u·to·ry (stach′ōō tôr′ē) ***adj.*** **1** fixed or authorized by statute **2** punishable by statute

St. Au·gus·tine (ô′gəs tēn′) seaport in NE Florida: oldest city (founded 1565) in the U.S.: pop. 12,000

staunch (stônch, stänch) ***vt.*** ⟦< L *stare,* to stand⟧ to check the flow of (blood, etc.) from (a cut, etc.) —***vi.*** to stop flowing —***adj.*** **1** seaworthy **2** steadfast; loyal **3** strong; solid Also, esp. for v., **stanch** (stänch, stanch) —**staunch′ly** ***adv.***

stave (stāv) ***n.*** ⟦< *staves,* pl. of STAFF⟧ **1** any of the shaped strips of wood forming the wall of a barrel, bucket, etc. **2** a stick or staff **3** a stanza —***vt.*** **staved** or **stove, stav′ing** to smash or break (*in*) —**stave off** to hold off or put off

staves (stāvz) ***n.*** **1** *alt. pl. of* STAFF **2** *pl. of* STAVE

stay[1] (stā) ***n.*** ⟦OE *stæg*⟧ a heavy rope or cable, used as a brace or support

stay[2] (stā) ***n.*** ⟦Fr *estaie*⟧ **1** a support or prop **2** a strip of stiffening material used in a corset, shirt collar, etc. —***vt.*** to support, or prop up

stay[3] (stā) ***vi.*** **stayed, stay′ing** ⟦< L *stare,* to stand⟧ **1** to continue in the place or condition specified; remain **2** to live; dwell **3** to stop; halt **4** to pause; delay **5** [Inf.] to continue; last —***vt.*** **1** to stop or check **2** to hinder or detain **3** to postpone (legal action) **4** to satisfy (thirst, etc.) for a time **5** *a*) to remain to the end of *b*) to be able to last through —***n.*** **1** *a*) a stopping or being stopped *b*) a halt or pause **2** a postponement in legal action **3** the action of remaining, or the time spent, in a place —**stay put** [Inf.] to remain in place or unchanged

staying power endurance

St. Cath·ar·ines (kath′ər inz) city in SE Ontario, Canada: pop. 131,000

St. Chris·to·pher (kris′tə fər) St. Kitts: see ST. KITTS AND NEVIS

STD *abbrev.* sexually transmitted disease

Ste ⟦Fr *Sainte*⟧ *abbrev.* **1** Saint (female) **2** Suite

stead (sted) ***n.*** ⟦OE *stede*⟧ the place of a person or thing as filled by a substitute —**stand someone in good stead** to give someone good service

stead′fast′ ***adj.*** ⟦OE *stedefæste*⟧ **1** firm; fixed **2** constant —**stead′fast′ly** ***adv.***

stead′y ***adj.*** **-i·er, -i·est** ⟦STEAD + -Y[2]⟧ **1** firm; stable; not shaky **2** constant, regular, or uniform *[a steady gaze]* **3** constant in behavior, loyalty, etc. **4** habitual or regular; by habit *[a steady customer]* **5** calm and controlled *[steady nerves]* **6** sober; reliable —***vt., vi.*** **-ied, -y·ing** to make or become steady —***n.*** [Inf.] a person one dates regularly —***adv.*** in a steady manner —**go steady** [Inf.] to date someone (or each other) exclusively —**stead′i·ly** ***adv.*** —**stead′i·ness** ***n.***

steak (stāk) ***n.*** ⟦< ON *steikja,* to roast on a spit⟧ a slice of beef, fish, etc. for broiling or frying

steal (stēl) ***vt.*** **stole, stol′en, steal′ing** ⟦OE *stælan*⟧ **1** to take (another's property, etc.) dishonestly or unlawfully, esp. in a secret manner **2** to take (a look, etc.) slyly **3** to gain insidiously or artfully *[he stole her heart]* **4** to move, put, etc. stealthily (*in, from,* etc.) **5** *Baseball* to gain (a base), as by running to it from another base while the pitch is being delivered —***vi.*** **1** to be a thief **2** to move, etc. stealthily —***n.*** [Inf.] an extraordinary bargain

stealth (stelth) ***n.*** ⟦< ME *stelen,* to steal⟧ secret or furtive action —***adj.*** of or using technology that prevents detection by enemy radar —**stealth′y** ***adj.*** —**stealth′i·ly** ***adv.***

steam (stēm) ***n.*** ⟦OE⟧ **1** water as converted into a vapor by being heated to the boiling point **2** the power of steam under pressure **3** condensed water vapor **4** [Inf.] vigor; energy —***adj.*** using, conveying, or operated by, steam —***vi.*** **1** to give off steam **2** to become covered or coated with condensed steam: usually with *up* **3** to move by steam power —***vt.*** to cook, remove, etc. with steam —**steam′y, -i·er, -i·est,** ***adj.***

steam′boat′ ***n.*** a small steamship

steam engine an engine using steam under pressure to supply mechanical energy

steam′er ***n.*** **1** something operated by steam, as a steamship **2** a container for cooking, cleaning, etc. with steam

steam′fit′ter ***n.*** one whose work is installing boilers, pipes, etc. in steam-pressure systems

steam′roll′er ***n.*** a construction machine or vehicle with a heavy roller —***vt., vi.*** to move, crush, override, etc. as (with) a steamroller: also **steam′roll′**

steam′ship′ ***n.*** a ship driven by steam power

steam shovel a large, mechanically operated digger

steed (stēd) ***n.*** ⟦OE *steda*⟧ a horse for riding

steel (stēl) ***n.*** ⟦OE *stiele*⟧ **1** a hard, tough alloy of iron with carbon **2** a thing of steel **3** great strength or hardness —*adj.* of or like steel —*vt.* to make hard, tough, etc. —**steel'y, -i·er, -i·est,** *adj.*

steel wool long, thin shavings of steel in a pad, used for scouring, polishing, etc.

steel'yard' *n.* ⟦STEEL + obs. *yard,* rod⟧ a scale consisting of a metal arm suspended from above

steep[1] (stēp) *adj.* ⟦OE *steap,* lofty⟧ **1** having a sharp rise or slope; precipitous **2** [Inf.] excessive; extreme —**steep'ly** *adv.* —**steep'ness** *n.*

steep[2] (stēp) *vt.* ⟦ME *stepen*⟧ to soak, saturate, imbue, etc.

stee·ple (stē'pəl) *n.* ⟦OE *stepel*⟧ **1** a tower rising above the main structure, as of a church **2** a spire

stee'ple·chase' *n.* a horse race run over a course obstructed with ditches, hedges, etc.

stee'ple·jack' *n.* one who builds or repairs steeples, smokestacks, etc.

steer[1] (stir) *vt., vi.* ⟦OE *stieran*⟧ **1** to guide (a ship, etc.) with a rudder **2** to direct the course of (an automobile, etc.) **3** to follow (a course) —**steer clear of** to avoid —**steer'a·ble** *adj.*

steer[2] (stir) *n.* ⟦OE *steor*⟧ a castrated male ox, esp. one raised for beef

steer·age (stir'ij) *n.* **1** a steering **2** [Historical] a section in a ship for the passengers paying the lowest fare

steg·o·sau·rus (steg'ə sôr'əs) *n., pl.* **-ri** (-ī) ⟦< Gr *stegos,* roof + *sauros,* lizard⟧ a large dinosaur with pointed, bony plates along the backbone

stein (stīn) *n.* ⟦Ger⟧ a beer mug

stein'bok' (-bäk') *n.* ⟦Ger⟧ an African antelope

stel·lar (stel'ər) *adj.* ⟦< L *stella,* a star⟧ **1** of a star **2** excellent **3** leading; chief *[a stellar role]*

stem[1] (stem) *n.* ⟦OE *stemn*⟧ **1** the main stalk of a plant **2** any stalk or part supporting leaves, flowers, or fruit **3** a stemlike part, as of a pipe, goblet, etc. **4** the prow of a ship; bow **5** the part of a word to which inflectional endings are added —*vt.* **stemmed, stem'ming** to make headway against *[to stem the tide]* —*vi.* to derive

stem[2] (stem) *vt.* **stemmed, stem'ming** ⟦< ON *stemma*⟧ to stop or check by or as if by damming up

stem'ware' *n.* goblets, wineglasses, etc. having stems

stench (stench) *n.* ⟦< OE *stincan,* to stink⟧ an offensive smell; stink

sten·cil (sten'səl) *vt.* **-ciled** or **-cilled, -cil·ing** or **-cil·ling** ⟦ult. < L *scintilla,* a spark⟧ to make or mark with a stencil —*n.* **1** a thin sheet, as of paper, cut through so that when ink, etc. is applied, designs, letters, etc. form on the surface beneath **2** a design, etc. so made

ste·nog·ra·phy (stə näg'rə fē) *n.* shorthand writing, as of dictation, testimony, etc., for later transcription —**ste·nog'ra·pher** *n.* —**sten·o·graph·ic** (sten'ə graf'ik) *adj.*

stent (stent) *n.* ⟦after C.R. *Stent,* Brit dentist⟧ a surgical device used to hold tissue in place, as inside a blood vessel to keep the vessel open

sten·to·ri·an (sten tôr'ē ən) *adj.* ⟦after *Stentor,* Gr herald in the *Iliad*⟧ very loud

step (step) *n.* ⟦OE *stepe*⟧ **1** a single movement of the foot, as in walking **2** the distance covered by such a movement **3** a short distance **4** a manner of stepping **5** the sound of stepping **6** a rest for the foot in climbing, as a stair **7** a degree; level; stage **8** any of a series of acts, processes, etc. —*vi.* **stepped, step'ping** **1** to move by executing a step **2** to walk a short distance **3** to move briskly (*along*) **4** to enter (*into* a situation, etc.) **5** to press the foot down (*on*) —*vt.* to measure by taking steps: with *off* —**in** (or **out of**) **step** conforming (or not conforming) to a rhythm, a regular procedure, etc. —**step by step** **1** gradually **2** by noting each stage in a process —**step down** to resign —**step up** **1** to advance **2** to increase, as in rate —**take steps** to do the things needed —**step'per** *n.*

step'broth'er *n.* one's stepparent's son by a former marriage

step'child' *n., pl.* **-chil'dren** ⟦< OE *steop-,* orphaned + *cild,* child⟧ one's spouse's child (**step'daugh'ter** or **step'son'**) by a former marriage

step'-down' *n.* a decrease, as in amount, intensity, etc.

step'lad'der *n.* a four-legged ladder with broad, flat steps

step'par'ent *n.* the person (**step'fa'ther** or **step'moth'er**) who has married one's parent after the death of or divorce from the other parent

steppe (step) *n.* ⟦Russ *styep'*⟧ any of the great plains of SE Europe and Asia, having few trees

step'ping·stone' *n.* **1** a stone to step on, as in crossing a stream **2** a means of bettering oneself

step'sis'ter *n.* one's stepparent's daughter by a former marriage

step'-up' *n.* an increase, as in amount, intensity, etc.

-ster (stər) ⟦OE *-estre*⟧ *suffix* one who is, does, creates, or is associated with (something specified) *[trickster, gangster]*

ster·e·o (ster'ē ō') *n., pl.* **-os'** a stereophonic device, system, effect, etc. —*adj. short for* STEREOPHONIC

stereo- ⟦< Gr *stereos,* solid⟧ *combining form* solid, firm, three-dimensional *[stereoscope]*

ster·e·o·phon·ic (ster'ē ə fän'ik) *adj.* designating or of sound reproduction using two or more channels to carry a blend of sounds from separate sources through separate speakers

ster'e·o·scop'ic (-skäp'ik) *adj.* appearing three-dimensional

ster'e·o·type' (-tīp') *n.* ⟦see STEREO- & -TYPE⟧ **1** a printing plate cast from a mold, as a page of set type **2** a fixed or conventional notion or conception —*vt.* **-typed', -typ'ing** to make a stereotype of —**ster'e·o·typed'** *adj.*

ster′e·o·typ′i·cal (-tip′i kəl) ***adj.*** **1** stereotyped **2** hackneyed

ster·ile (ster′əl) ***adj.*** ⟦L *sterilis*⟧ **1** incapable of producing offspring, fruit, etc.; barren **2** free from living microorganisms —**ste·ril·i·ty** (stə ril′ ə tē) ***n.***

ster′i·lize′ (-ə līz′) ***vt.*** **-lized′**, **-liz′ing** to make sterile; specif., *a*) to make incapable of reproduction *b*) to make free of germs, etc. —**ster′i·li·za′tion** ***n.*** —**ster′i·liz′er** ***n.***

ster·ling (stur′liŋ) ***n.*** ⟦ME *sterlinge,* Norman coin⟧ **1** sterling silver **2** British money —***adj.*** **1** of silver that is at least 92.5 percent pure **2** of British money **3** made of sterling silver **4** excellent *[a sterling* reputation*]*

stern[1] (sturn) ***adj.*** ⟦OE *styrne*⟧ **1** severe; strict *[stern* measures*]* **2** grim *[a stern* face*]* **3** relentless or firm —**stern′ly** ***adv.*** —**stern′ness** ***n.***

stern[2] (sturn) ***n.*** ⟦< ON *styra,* to steer⟧ the rear end of a ship, etc.

ster·num (stur′nəm) ***n.***, *pl.* **-nums** or **-na** (-nə) ⟦< Gr *sternon*⟧ the flat, bony structure to which most of the ribs are attached in the front of the chest; breastbone

ster·oid (stir′oid′, ster′oid′) ***n.*** ⟦< (CHOLE)STER(OL) + -OID⟧ any of a group of compounds including the bile acids, sex hormones, etc. —**ste·roi′dal** ***adj.***

stet (stet) ***v.*** *imper.* ⟦L⟧ let it stand: printer's term indicating that matter marked for deletion or change is to remain —***vt.*** **stet′ted, stet′ting** to mark with "stet"

steth·o·scope (steth′ə skōp′) ***n.*** ⟦< Gr *stēthos,* chest + -SCOPE⟧ *Med.* an instrument used to examine the heart, lungs, etc. by listening to the sounds they make

ste·ve·dore (stē′və dôr′) ***n.*** ⟦ult. < L *stipare,* cram⟧ LONGSHOREMAN

Ste·ven·son (stē′vən sən), **Rob·ert Lou·is** (rä′bərt lo͞o′is) 1850-94; Scot. writer

stew (sto͞o) ***vt., vi.*** ⟦ult. < L *ex-,* out + Gr *typhos,* steam⟧ **1** to cook by simmering or boiling slowly **2** to worry —***n.*** **1** a dish, esp. of meat and vegetables, cooked by stewing **2** a state of worry

stew·ard (sto͞o′ərd) ***n.*** ⟦< OE *stig,* hall + *weard,* keeper⟧ **1** a person put in charge of a large estate **2** an administrator, as of finances and property **3** one responsible for the food and drink, etc. in a club, etc. **4** an attendant, as on a ship or airplane **5** a union representative —**stew′ard·ship′** ***n.***

stew′ard·ess (-ər dis) ***n.*** a woman flight attendant

stick (stik) ***n.*** ⟦OE *sticca*⟧ **1** a twig or small branch broken or cut off **2** a long, slender piece of wood, as a club, cane, etc. **3** any sticklike piece *[a stick* of gum*]* —***vt.*** **stuck, stick′ing** **1** to pierce, as with a pointed instrument **2** to pierce with (a knife, pin, etc.) **3** to thrust (*in, into, out,* etc.) **4** to attach as by gluing, pinning, etc. **5** to obstruct, detain, etc. *[the wheels were stuck]* **6** [Inf.] to place; put; set **7** [Inf.] to puzzle; baffle **8** [Slang] *a*) to impose a burden, etc. upon *b*) to defraud —***vi.*** **1** to be fixed by a pointed end, as a nail **2** to adhere; cling; remain **3** to persevere *[to stick* at a job*]* **4** to remain firm and resolute *[he stuck* with us*]* **5** to become embedded, jammed, etc. **6** to become stopped or delayed **7** to hesitate; scruple *[he'll stick* at nothing*]* **8** to protrude or project (*out, up,* etc.) —**stick by** to remain loyal to —**stick up for** [Inf.] to uphold; defend —**the sticks** [Inf.] the rural districts

stick′er ***n.*** a person or thing that sticks; specif., a gummed label

stick′-in-the-mud′ ***n.*** [Inf.] one who resists change, new ideas, etc.

stick·le·back (stik′əl bak′) ***n.*** a small, bony-plated fish with sharp dorsal spines: the male builds a nest for the female's eggs

stick·ler (stik′lər) ***n.*** ⟦prob. < ME *stightlen,* to order⟧ **1** one who insists on a certain way of doing things *[a stickler* for discipline*]* **2** [Inf.] something difficult to solve

stick′pin′ ***n.*** an ornamental pin worn in a necktie, on a lapel, etc.

stick shift a gearshift, as on a car, operated manually

stick′um (-əm) ***n.*** ⟦STICK + *'em,* short for THEM⟧ [Inf.] any sticky, or adhesive, substance

stick′up′ ***n.*** *slang term for* HOLDUP (sense 2)

stick′y ***adj.*** **-i·er, -i·est** **1** that sticks; adhesive **2** [Inf.] hot and humid **3** [Inf.] troublesome —**stick′i·ness** ***n.***

stiff (stif) ***adj.*** ⟦OE *stif*⟧ **1** hard to bend or move; rigid; firm **2** sore or limited in movement: said of joints and muscles **3** not fluid; thick **4** strong; powerful *[a stiff* wind*]* **5** harsh *[stiff* punishment*]* **6** difficult *[a stiff* climb*]* **7** very formal or awkward **8** [Inf.] excessive *[a stiff* price*]* —***vt.*** **stiffed, stiff′ing** [Slang] to cheat —**stiff′ly** ***adv.*** —**stiff′ness** ***n.***

stiff′-arm′ ***vt.*** to push (someone) away with one's arm out straight

stiff′en ***vt., vi.*** to make or become stiff or stiffer —**stiff′en·er** ***n.***

stiff′-necked′ (-nekt′) ***adj.*** stubborn

sti·fle (stī′fəl) ***vt.*** **-fled, -fling** ⟦< Fr *estouffer*⟧ **1** to suffocate; smother **2** to suppress; hold back; stop *[to stifle* a sob*]* —***vi.*** to die or suffer from lack of air —**sti′fling·ly** ***adv.***

stig·ma (stig′mə) ***n.***, *pl.* **-mas** or **stig·ma′ta** (-mät′ə) ⟦< Gr, lit., a puncture made with a sharp instrument⟧ **1** a mark of disgrace or reproach **2** a spot on the skin, esp. one that bleeds **3** the upper tip of the pistil of a flower, on which pollen falls and develops —**stig·mat′ic** (-mat′ik) ***adj.***

stig′ma·tize′ (-tīz′) ***vt.*** **-tized′, -tiz′ing** to mark or characterize as disgraceful

stile (stīl) ***n.*** ⟦< OE *stigan,* to climb⟧ a set of steps for climbing over a fence or wall

sti·let·to (sti let′ō) ***n.***, *pl.* **-tos** or **-toes** ⟦It < L *stilus,* pointed tool⟧ a small dagger with a slender blade

still[1] (stil) ***adj.*** ⟦OE *stille*⟧ **1** noiseless; silent **2** stationary **3** tranquil; calm **4** designating or of a single photograph taken from a film —*n.* **1** silence; quiet **2** a still photograph —*adv.* **1** at or up to the time indicated **2** even; yet *[still colder]* **3** nevertheless; yet *[rich but still unhappy]* —*conj.* nevertheless; yet —*vt., vi.* to make or become still — **still'ness** *n.*

still[2] (stil) *n.* ⟦< obs. *still,* to distill⟧ an apparatus used for distilling liquids, esp. alcoholic liquors

still'birth' *n.* **1** the birth of a stillborn fetus **2** such a fetus

still'born' *adj.* **1** dead when delivered from the uterus **2** unsuccessful from the start

still life *pl.* **still lifes** a picture of inanimate objects, as fruit, flowers, etc.

stilt (stilt) *n.* ⟦ME *stilte*⟧ **1** either of a pair of poles, each with a footrest, used for walking high off the ground **2** any of a number of long posts used to hold a building, etc. above ground or out of water **3** a bird with a long, slender bill and long legs

stilt·ed (stil'tid) *adj.* pompous, affected, etc.

stim·u·lant (stim'yə lənt) *n.* anything, as a drug, that stimulates

stim'u·late' (-lāt') *vt.* **-lat'ed, -lat'ing** ⟦see fol.⟧ to rouse or excite to activity or increased activity —**stim'u·la'tion** *n.*

stim'u·lus (-ləs) *n., pl.* **-li'** (-lī') ⟦L, a goad⟧ **1** an incentive **2** any action or agent that causes an activity in an organism, organ, etc.

sting (stiŋ) *vt.* **stung, sting'ing** ⟦OE *stingan*⟧ **1** to prick or wound with a sting **2** to cause sudden, pricking pain to **3** to make unhappy **4** to stimulate suddenly and sharply **5** [Slang] to cheat —*vi.* to cause or feel sharp, smarting pain —*n.* **1** a stinging **2** a pain or wound resulting from stinging **3** a sharp-pointed organ, as in insects and plants, that pricks, wounds, etc. **4** [Slang] *a*) a swindling, as in a confidence game *b*) a scheme by police, etc. for entrapping lawbreakers

sting'er *n.* one that stings, specif., a STING (*n.* 3)

sting'ray' *n.* a large ray with one or more poisonous spines that can inflict painful wounds

stin·gy (stin'jē) *adj.* **-gi·er, -gi·est** ⟦< dial. form of STING⟧ **1** giving or spending grudgingly; miserly **2** less than needed; scanty —**stin'gi·ly** *adv.* — **stin'gi·ness** *n.*

stink (stiŋk) *vi.* **stank** or **stunk, stunk, stink'ing** ⟦OE *stincan*⟧ to give off a strong, unpleasant smell —*n.* a strong, unpleasant smell; stench —**stink'er** *n.* —**stink'y, -i·er, -i·est,** *adj.*

stint (stint) *vt.* ⟦< OE *styntan,* to blunt⟧ to restrict to a certain quantity, often small —*vi.* to be sparing in giving or using —*n.* **1** restriction; limit **2** an assigned task or period of work — **stint'er** *n.*

sti·pend (stī'pənd) *n.* ⟦< L *stips,* coin + *pendere,* to pay⟧ a regular or fixed payment, as a salary

stip·ple (stip'əl) *vt.* **-pled, -pling** ⟦< Du *stippel,* a speckle⟧ to paint, draw, or engrave in small dots

stip·u·late (stip'yə lāt') *vt.* **-lat'ed, -lat'ing** ⟦< L *stipulari,* to bargain⟧ **1** to arrange definitely **2** to specify as an essential condition of an agreement — **stip'u·la'tion** *n.*

stir[1] (stur) *vt., vi.* **stirred, stir'ring** ⟦OE *styrian*⟧ **1** to move, esp. slightly **2** to make or be active **3** to mix (a liquid, etc.) as by agitating with a spoon **4** to excite the feelings (of) **5** to incite: often with *up* —*n.* **1** a stirring **2** movement; activity **3** excitement; tumult —**stir'rer** *n.*

stir[2] (stur) *n.* ⟦19th-c. thieves' slang⟧ [Slang] a prison

stir'-cra'zy *adj.* [Slang] anxious, tense, etc. from long, close confinement, specif. in prison

stir'-fry' *vt.* **-fried', -fry'ing** to fry (diced or sliced vegetables, meat, etc.) quickly in a wok while stirring constantly

stir'ring *adj.* **1** active; busy **2** rousing; exciting

stir·rup (stur'əp) *n.* ⟦OE *stigrap*⟧ **1** a flat-bottomed ring hung from a saddle and used as a footrest **2** one of the three small bones in the middle ear

stitch (stich) *n.* ⟦OE *stice,* a puncture⟧ **1** *a*) a single complete in-and-out movement of a needle in sewing, etc. *b*) a suture **2** a loop, knot, etc. made by stitching **3** a particular kind of stitch or style of stitching **4** a sudden, sharp pain **5** a bit or piece —*vi., vt.* to make stitches (in); sew —**in stitches** in a state of uproarious laughter

stitch'er·y (-ər ē) *n.* ornamental needlework

St. John's seaport & capital of Newfoundland: pop. 102,000

St. Kitts and Nevis (kits) country in the Leeward Islands, consisting of two islands, St. Kitts & Nevis: *c.* 101 sq. mi.; pop. 41,000

St. Lawrence river flowing from Lake Ontario into the Atlantic: the main section of an inland waterway (**St. Lawrence Seaway**) connecting the Great Lakes with the Atlantic

St. Lou·is (lo͞o'is, lo͞o'ē) city & port in E Missouri, on the Mississippi: pop. 397,000

St. Lu·ci·a (lo͞o'shē ə, lo͞o sē'ə) island country of the West Indies: 238 sq. mi.; pop. 133,000

stoat (stōt) *n.* ⟦ME *stote*⟧ a large European ermine, esp. in its brown summer coat

stock (stäk) *n.* ⟦OE *stocc*⟧ **1** the trunk of a tree **2** *a*) descent; lineage *b*) a strain, race, etc. of animals or plants **3** a supporting or main part of an implement, etc., as the wooden handle to which the barrel of a rifle is attached **4** [*pl.*] a wooden frame with holes for confining the ankles or wrists, formerly used for punishment **5** raw material **6** water in which meat, fish, etc. has been boiled, used in soups **7** livestock **8** a supply of goods on hand in a store, etc. **9** (a certificate for) a share or shares of corporate ownership **10** a stock company or its repertoire —*vt.* **1** to furnish (a farm, shop, etc.) with stock **2** to keep a supply of, as for sale or for future use —***vi.*** to put in a stock, or supply: with *up* —***adj.*** **1** kept in stock *[stock* sizes*]* **2** common or trite *[*a *stock* excuse*]* **3** that deals with stock **4** relating to a stock company —**in** (or **out of**) **stock** (not) available for sale or use —**take stock 1** to inventory the stock on hand **2** to make an appraisal — **take** (or **put**) **stock in** to have faith in

stock·ade (stä kād′) ***n.*** ⟦< Prov *estaca,* a stake⟧ **1** a barrier of stakes driven into the ground side by side, for defense **2** an enclosure, as a fort, made with such stakes **3** an enclosure for military prisoners

stock′bro′ker ***n.*** one who acts as an agent in buying and selling stocks, bonds, etc.

stock car a standard automobile, modified for racing

stock company a theatrical company presenting a repertoire of plays

stock exchange 1 a place where stocks and bonds are bought and sold **2** an association of stockbrokers Also **stock market**

stock′hold′er ***n.*** one owning stock in a given company

Stock·holm (stäk′hōm′, -hōlm′) seaport & capital of Sweden: pop. 704,000

stock′ing ***n.*** ⟦< obs. sense of *stock*⟧ a closefitting covering, usually knitted, for the foot and leg

stocking cap a long, tapered knitted cap, often with a tassel at the end

stock′pile′ ***n.*** a reserve supply of goods, raw material, etc. —***vt., vi.*** **-piled′, -pil′ing** to accumulate a stockpile (of)

stock′-still′ ***adj.*** motionless

Stock·ton (stäk′tən) city in central California: pop. 211,000

stock′y ***adj.*** **-i·er, -i·est** heavily built; short and thickset —**stock′i·ness** ***n.***

stock′yard′ ***n.*** an enclosure where cattle, hogs, etc. are kept before slaughtering

stodg·y (stä′jē) ***adj.*** **-i·er, -i·est** ⟦< *stodge,* heavy food⟧ **1** dull; uninteresting **2** old-fashioned; conventional —**stodg′i·ness** ***n.***

sto·gie or **sto·gy** (stō′gē) ***n.,*** *pl.* **-gies** ⟦after *Conestoga* Valley, PA⟧ a cigar, esp. one that is long, thin, and, usually, inexpensive

Sto·ic (stō′ik) ***n.*** ⟦< Gr *stoa,* a colonnade: where first Stoics met⟧ **1** a member of an ancient Greek school of philosophy **2** [**s-**] a stoical person —***adj.*** [**s-**] STOICAL —**sto′i·cism′** (-i siz′əm) ***n.***

sto′i·cal (-i kəl) ***adj.*** showing indifference to joy, grief, pleasure, or pain; impassive —**sto′i·cal·ly** ***adv.***

stoke (stōk) ***vt., vi.*** **stoked, stok′ing** ⟦< Du *stoken,* to poke⟧ **1** to stir up and feed fuel to (a fire) **2** to tend (a furnace, boiler, etc.) —**stok′er** ***n.***

STOL *abbrev.* short takeoff and landing

stole[1] (stōl) ***n.*** ⟦< Gr *stolē,* garment⟧ **1** a long strip of cloth worn about the neck by members of the clergy at various rites **2** a woman's long scarf of cloth or fur worn around the shoulders

stole[2] (stōl) ***vt., vi.*** *pt. of* STEAL

stol·en (stō′lən) ***vt., vi.*** *pp. of* STEAL

stol·id (stäl′id) ***adj.*** ⟦L *stolidus,* slow⟧ having or showing little or no emotion; unexcitable —**sto·lid·i·ty** (stə lid′ə tē) ***n.*** —**stol′id·ly** ***adv.***

sto·lon (stō′län′) ***n.*** ⟦< L *stolo,* a shoot⟧ a creeping stem lying above the soil surface and bearing leaves, as in the strawberry

stom·ach (stum′ək) ***n.*** ⟦ult. < Gr *stoma,* mouth⟧ **1** the saclike digestive organ into which food passes from the esophagus **2** the abdomen, or belly **3** appetite for food **4** desire or inclination —***vt.*** **1** to be able to eat or digest **2** to tolerate; bear

stom′ach·ache′ ***n.*** pain in the stomach or abdomen

stom′ach·er ***n.*** an ornamented piece of cloth formerly worn over the chest and abdomen, esp. by women

stomp (stämp) ***vt., vi.*** *var. of* STAMP (*vt.* 1, 2; *vi.* 1, 2)

stomping ground [Inf.] STAMPING GROUND: *also used in pl.*

stone (stōn) ***n.*** ⟦OE *stan*⟧ **1** the hard, solid, nonmetallic mineral matter of which rock is composed **2** a piece of rock **3** the seed of certain fruits **4** *short for* PRECIOUS STONE **5** *pl.* **stone** [Brit.] 14 pounds avoirdupois **6** an abnormal stony mass formed in the kidney, gall bladder, etc. —***vt.*** **stoned, ston′ing 1** to pelt or kill with stones **2** to remove the stone from (a peach, etc.) —***adv.*** completely

stone- ⟦< prec.⟧ *combining form* completely *[stone-*blind*]*

Stone Age the period in human culture when stone tools were used

stoned ***adj.*** [Slang] drunk or under the influence of a drug

stone's throw a short distance

stone′wall′ ***vi.*** [Inf.] to behave in an obstructive manner, as by withholding information, etc.

stone′ware′ ***n.*** a dense, opaque, glazed or unglazed pottery

ston′y ***adj.*** **-i·er, -i·est 1** full of stones **2** of or like stone; specif., unfeeling; pitiless —**ston′i·ness** ***n.***

stood (stood) ***vi., vt.*** *pt. & pp. of* STAND

stooge (stōōj) ***n.*** ⟦< ?⟧ [Inf.] **1** an actor who serves as the victim of a comedian's jokes, pranks, etc. **2** anyone who acts as a foil or underling

stool (stōōl) ***n.*** ⟦OE *stol*⟧ **1** a single seat having no back or arms **2** feces

stool pigeon [Inf.] a spy or informer, esp. for the police

stoop[1] (stōōp) ***vi.*** ⟦OE *stupian*⟧ **1** to bend the body forward **2** to carry the head and shoulders habitually bent forward **3** to degrade oneself —***n.*** the act or position of stooping

stoop[2] (stōōp) ***n.*** ⟦Du *stoep*⟧ a small porch at the door of a house

stop (stäp) ***vt.*** **stopped, stop′ping** ⟦< L *stuppa,* a kind of stuffing material⟧ **1** to close by filling, shutting off, etc. **2** to cause to cease motion, activity, etc. **3** to block; intercept; prevent **4** to cease; desist from *[stop* talking*]* **—*vi.*** **1** to cease moving, etc.; halt **2** to leave off doing something **3** to cease operating **4** to become clogged **5** to tarry or stay **—*n.*** **1** a stopping or being stopped **2** a finish; end **3** a stay or sojourn **4** a place stopped at, as on a bus route **5** an obstruction, plug, etc. **6** a finger hole in a wind instrument, closed to produce a desired tone **7** a pull, lever, etc. for controlling a set of organ pipes **—stop off** to stop for a while en route to a place **—stop over** to visit for a while: also **stop in** (or **by**)

stop'cock' ***n.*** a cock or valve to stop or regulate the flow of a fluid

stop'gap' ***n.*** a person or thing serving as a temporary substitute

stop'light' ***n.*** a traffic light, esp. when red to signal vehicles to stop

stop'o'ver ***n.*** a brief stop or stay at a place in the course of a journey

stop'page ***n.*** **1** a stopping or being stopped **2** an obstructed condition; block

stop'per ***n.*** something inserted to close an opening; plug

stop'watch' ***n.*** a watch that can be started and stopped instantly, as for timing races

stor·age (stôr'ij) ***n.*** **1** a storing or being stored **2** a place for, or the cost of, storing goods **3** computer memory

storage battery a battery for producing electric current, with cells that can be recharged

store (stôr) ***vt.*** **stored, stor'ing** ⟦< L *instaurare,* restore⟧ **1** to put aside for use when needed **2** to furnish with a supply **3** to put, as in a warehouse, for safekeeping **—*n.*** **1** a supply (*of* something) for use when needed; stock **2** [*pl.*] supplies, esp. of food, clothing, etc. **3** a retail establishment where goods are offered for sale **—in store** set aside for the future; in reserve **—set** (or **put** or **lay**) **store by** to value

store'front' ***n.*** a front room on the ground floor of a building, designed for use as a retail store

store'house' ***n.*** a place where things are stored; esp., a warehouse

store'keep'er ***n.*** **1** a person in charge of military or naval stores **2** a retail merchant

store'room' ***n.*** a room where things are stored

sto·rey (stôr'ē) ***n.***, *pl.* **-reys** *Brit., etc. sp. of* STORY[2]

sto·ried (stôr'ēd) ***adj.*** famous in story or history

stork (stôrk) ***n.*** ⟦OE *storc*⟧ a large, long-legged wading bird with a long neck and bill

storm (stôrm) ***n.*** ⟦OE⟧ **1** a strong wind, with rain, snow, thunder, etc. **2** any heavy fall of snow, rain, etc. **3** a strong emotional outburst **4** any strong disturbance **5** a sudden, strong attack on a fortified place **—*vi.*** **1** to blow rain, snow, etc. violently **2** to rage; rant **3** to rush violently *[to storm* into a room*]* **—*vt.*** to attack vigorously

storm door (or **window**) a door (or window) placed outside the regular one as added protection

storm'y ***adj.*** **-i·er, -i·est** **1** of or characterized by storms **2** violent, raging, etc. **—storm'i·ly *adv.*** **—storm'i·ness *n.***

sto·ry[1] (stôr'ē) ***n.***, *pl.* **-ries** ⟦< Gr *historia,* narrative⟧ **1** the telling of an event or events; account; narration **2** a fictional prose narrative shorter than a novel **3** the plot of a novel, play, etc. **4** [Inf.] a falsehood **5** a news report

sto·ry[2] (stôr'ē) ***n.***, *pl.* **-ries** ⟦< prec.⟧ a horizontal division of a building, from a floor to the ceiling above it

sto'ry·board' ***n.*** a large board on which sketches, etc. for shots or scenes of a film are arranged in sequence **—*vt.*** to make a storyboard of (a shot or scene) for (a film)

sto'ry·book' ***n.*** a book of stories, esp. one for children

sto'ry·tell'er ***n.*** one who narrates stories **—sto'ry·tell'ing *n.***

stoup (sto͞op) ***n.*** ⟦< ON *staup,* cup⟧ a font for holy water

stout (stout) ***adj.*** ⟦< OFr *estout,* bold⟧ **1** courageous **2** strong; sturdy; firm **3** powerful; forceful **4** fat; thickset **—*n.*** a heavy, dark-brown beer **—stout'ly *adv.*** **—stout'ness *n.***

stout'heart'ed ***adj.*** courageous; brave

stove[1] (stōv) ***n.*** ⟦< MDu, heated room⟧ an apparatus for heating, cooking, etc.

stove[2] (stōv) ***vt., vi.*** *alt. pt. & pp. of* STAVE

stove'pipe' ***n.*** a metal pipe used to carry off smoke from a stove

stow (stō) ***vt.*** ⟦< OE *stowe,* a place⟧ to pack in an orderly way **—stow away** **1** to put or hide away **2** to be a stowaway **—stow'age *n.***

stow'a·way' ***n.*** one who hides aboard a ship, airplane, etc. as to get free passage

St. Paul capital of Minnesota: pop. 272,000

St. Pe·ters·burg (pēt'ərz burg') **1** seaport in NW Russia: pop. 4,456,000 **2** city in WC Florida: pop. 240,000

strad·dle (strad''l) ***vt.*** **-dled, -dling** ⟦< STRIDE⟧ **1** to stand or sit astride of **2** to take or appear to take both sides of (an issue) **—*n.*** a straddling **—strad'dler *n.***

strafe (strāf) ***vt.*** **strafed, straf'ing** ⟦< Ger *Gott strafe England* (God punish England)⟧ to attack with machine-gun fire from low-flying aircraft

strag·gle (strag'əl) ***vi.*** **-gled, -gling** ⟦prob. < ME *straken,* roam⟧ **1** to wander from the main group **2** to be scattered over a wide area; ramble **3** to hang in an unkempt way, as hair **—strag'gler *n.*** **—strag'gly *adj.***

straight (strāt) ***adj.*** ⟦< ME *strecchen,* to stretch⟧ **1** having the same direction throughout its length; not crooked, bent, etc. **2** direct; undeviating, etc. **3** in order; properly arranged, etc. **4** honest; sincere **5** undiluted **6** [Slang] normal or conventional **7** [Slang] heterosexual **—*adv.*** **1** in a straight line **2**

upright; erectly **3** without detour, delay, etc. —*n.* *Poker* a hand of five cards in sequence —**straight away** (or **off**) without delay —**straight'ness** *n.*

straight arrow [Inf.] one who is proper, righteous, conscientious, etc. and often regarded as stodgy, dull, etc. —**straight'-ar'row** *adj.*

straight·a·way (strāt'ə wā'; *for adv.*, strāt'ə wā') *n.* a straight section of a racetrack, highway, etc. —*adv.* without delay

straight'edge' *n.* a strip of wood, etc. having a perfectly straight edge, used in drawing straight lines, etc.

straight'en *vt.*, *vi.* to make or become straight —**straighten out** **1** to make or become less confused, easier to deal with, etc. **2** to reform —**straight'en·er** *n.*

straight face a facial expression showing no amusement or other emotion —**straight'-faced'** *adj.*

straight'for'ward *adj.* **1** moving or leading straight ahead; direct **2** honest; frank —*adv.* in a straightforward manner: also **straight'for'wards**

straight man an actor whose remarks a comedian answers with a quip

straight shooter [Inf.] a person who is honest, sincere, etc.

straight ticket a ballot cast for candidates of only one party

straight time **1** the standard number of working hours, as per week **2** the rate of pay for these hours

straight'way' *adv.* [Now Chiefly Literary] at once

strain[1] (strān) *vt.* ⟦< L *stringere*⟧ **1** to stretch tight **2** to exert to the utmost **3** to injure by overexertion *[to strain a muscle]* **4** to stretch beyond normal limits **5** to pass through a screen, sieve, etc.; filter —*vi.* **1** to strive hard **2** to filter, ooze, etc. —*n.* **1** a straining or being strained **2** great effort, exertion, etc. **3** a bodily injury from overexertion **4** stress or force **5** a great demand on one's emotions, resources, etc.

strain[2] (strān) *n.* ⟦< OE *strynan*, to produce⟧ **1** ancestry; lineage **2** race; stock; line **3** a line of individuals differentiated from its species or race **4** an inherited tendency **5** a musical tune

strained *adj.* not natural or relaxed

strain'er *n.* a device for straining, sifting, or filtering; sieve, filter, etc.

strait (strāt) *adj.* ⟦< L *stringere*, draw tight⟧ [Archaic] narrow or strict —*n.* **1** [*often pl.*] a narrow waterway connecting two large bodies of water **2** [*usually pl.*] difficulty; distress

strait'en *vt.* to bring into difficulties: usually in **in straitened circumstances**, lacking enough money

strait'jack'et *n.* a coatlike device for restraining violent persons

strait'-laced' *adj.* narrowly strict in behavior or moral views

strand[1] (strand) *n.* ⟦OE⟧ shore, esp. ocean shore —*vt.*, *vi.* **1** to run or drive aground, as a ship **2** to put or be put into a helpless position *[stranded abroad with no money]*

strand[2] (strand) *n.* ⟦ME *stronde*⟧ **1** any one of the threads, wires, etc. that are twisted together to form a string, cable, etc. **2** a ropelike length of anything *[a strand of pearls]*

strange (strānj) *adj.* **strang'er**, **strang'est** ⟦< L *extraneus*, foreign⟧ **1** not previously known, seen, etc.; unfamiliar **2** unusual; extraordinary **3** peculiar; odd —**strange'ly** *adv.* —**strange'ness** *n.*

stran·ger (strān'jər) *n.* **1** a newcomer **2** a person not known to one

stran·gle (straŋ'gəl) *vt.*, *vi.* **-gled**, **-gling** ⟦< Gr *strangos*, twisted⟧ **1** to choke to death **2** to suppress, stifle, or repress —**stran'gler** *n.*

stran'gle·hold' *n.* **1** an illegal wrestling hold that chokes an opponent **2** a force or action that suppresses freedom

stran·gu·late (straŋ'gyə lāt') *vt.* **-lat'ed**, **-lat'ing** **1** STRANGLE **2** *Med.* to block (a tube, etc.) by constricting —**stran'gu·la'tion** *n.*

strap (strap) *n.* ⟦dial. form of STROP⟧ a narrow strip of leather, etc., as for securing things —*vt.* **strapped**, **strap'ping** to fasten with a strap

strap'less *adj.* having no shoulder straps

strapped *adj.* [Inf.] in great need of money

strap'ping *adj.* [Inf.] tall and well-built; robust

stra·ta (strāt'ə, strat'ə) *n.* *alt. pl. of* STRATUM

strat·a·gem (strat'ə jəm) *n.* ⟦< Gr *stratos*, army + *agein*, to lead⟧ **1** a trick, plan, etc. for deceiving an enemy in war **2** any tricky scheme

strat·e·gy (strat'ə jē) *n.*, *pl.* **-gies** **1** the science of planning and directing military operations **2** skill in managing or planning **3** a stratagem, plan, etc. —**stra·te·gic** (strə tē'jik) *adj.* —**stra·te'gi·cal·ly** *adv.* —**strat'e·gist** *n.*

strat·i·fy (strat'ə fī') *vt.*, *vi.* **-fied'**, **-fy'ing** ⟦< L *stratum*, layer + *facere*, make⟧ to form in layers or strata —**strat'i·fi·ca'tion** *n.*

strat'o·sphere' (-ə sfir') *n.* ⟦< ModL *stratum*, stratum + Fr *sphère*, sphere⟧ **1** the atmospheric zone at an altitude of *c.* 20 to 50 km **2** an extremely high point, level, etc. —**strat'o·spher'ic** (-sfer'ik, -sfir'-) *adj.*

stra·tum (strāt'əm, strat'-) *n.*, *pl.* **-ta** (-ə) or **-tums** ⟦ModL < L *stratus*, a spreading⟧ **1** a horizontal layer of matter, as of sedimentary rock **2** any of the socioeconomic groups of a society

stra'tus (-əs) *n.*, *pl.* **-ti** (-ī) ⟦see prec.⟧ a uniform, low, gray cloud layer

Strauss (strous), **Jo·hann** (yō'hän') 1825-99; Austrian composer, esp. of waltzes

Stra·vin·sky (strə vin'skē), **I·gor** (ē'gôr) 1882-1971; Russ. composer & conductor, in the U.S. after 1940

straw (strô) *n.* ⟦OE *streaw*⟧ **1** hollow stalks of grain after threshing **2** a single one of these **3** a tube used for sucking beverages **4** a trifle —***adj.*** **1** straw-colored; yellowish **2** made of straw

straw'ber'ry (-ber'ē, -bər ē) ***n.***, *pl.* **-ries** ⟦prob. from the strawlike particles on the fruit⟧ **1** the small, red, fleshy fruit of a vinelike plant of the rose family **2** this plant

straw boss [Inf.] one having subordinate authority

straw vote (or **poll**) an unofficial vote taken to determine general group opinion

stray (strā) ***vi.*** ⟦< LL *strata*, street⟧ **1** to wander from a given place, course, etc. **2** to deviate (*from* what is right) —***n.*** one that strays; esp., a lost domestic animal —***adj.*** **1** having strayed; lost **2** isolated or incidental *[*a few *stray* words*]*

streak (strēk) ***n.*** ⟦< OE *strica*⟧ **1** a long, thin mark or stripe **2** a layer, as of fat in meat **3** a tendency in behavior, etc. *[*a nervous *streak]* **4** a period, as of luck —***vt.*** to make streaks on or in —***vi.*** **1** to become streaked **2** to go fast **3** to dash naked in public as a prank —**streak'er** ***n.*** —**streak'y, -i·er, -i·est,** ***adj.***

stream (strēm) ***n.*** ⟦OE⟧ **1** a current of water; specif., a small river **2** a steady flow, as of air, light, etc. **3** a continuous series *[*a *stream* of cars*]* —***vi.*** **1** to flow as in a stream **2** to move swiftly

stream'er ***n.*** **1** a long, narrow flag **2** any long, narrow strip hanging loose at one end

stream'line' ***vt.*** **-lined', -lin'ing** to make streamlined —***adj.*** STREAMLINED

stream'lined' ***adj.*** **1** having a contour designed to offer the least resistance in moving through air, water, etc. **2** efficient, trim, simplified, etc.

street (strēt) ***n.*** ⟦< L *strata* (*via*), paved (road)⟧ **1** a public road in a town or city, esp. a paved one **2** such a road with its sidewalks, buildings, etc. **3** the people living, working, etc. along a given street

street'car' ***n.*** a car on rails for public transportation along certain streets

street'light' ***n.*** a lamp on a post for lighting a street: also **street'lamp'**

street'-smart' ***adj.*** [Inf.] STREETWISE

street smarts [Inf.] cunning or shrewdness needed to live in an urban environment characterized by poverty, crime, etc.

street'walk'er ***n.*** a prostitute

street'wise' ***adj.*** [Inf.] experienced in dealing with the people in urban poverty areas where vice and crime are common

strength (streŋkth) ***n.*** ⟦OE *strengthu*⟧ **1** the state or quality of being strong; force; power **2** toughness; durability **3** the power to resist attack **4** potency or concentration, as of drugs, etc. **5** intensity, as of sound, etc. **6** force of an army, etc., as measured in numbers — **on the strength of** based or relying on

strength'en ***vt.***, ***vi.*** to make or become stronger —**strength'en·er** ***n.***

stren·u·ous (stren'yo͞o əs) ***adj.*** ⟦L *strenuus*⟧ requiring or characterized by great effort or energy —**stren'u·ous·ly** ***adv.*** —**stren'u·ous·ness** ***n.***

strep (strep) ***n.*** *short for:* **1** STREPTOCOCCUS **2** STREP THROAT

strep throat (strep) a sore throat caused by a streptococcus, with inflammation and fever

strep·to·coc·cus (strep'tə käk'əs) ***n.***, *pl.* **-coc'ci'** (-käk'sī') ⟦< Gr *streptos*, twisted + COCCUS⟧ any of various spherical bacteria that occur in chains: some cause serious diseases

strep'to·my'cin (-mī'sin) ***n.*** ⟦< Gr *streptos*, bent + *mykēs*, fungus⟧ an antibiotic drug used in treating various diseases

stress (stres) ***n.*** ⟦< L *strictus*, strict⟧ **1** strain; specif., force that strains or deforms **2** emphasis; importance **3** *a*) mental or physical tension *b*) urgency, pressure, etc. causing this **4** the relative force of utterance given a syllable or word; accent —***vt.*** **1** to put stress or pressure on **2** to accent **3** to emphasize

stressed'-out' ***adj.*** tired, nervous, etc. as from overwork, mental pressure, etc.

stress fracture a leg fracture caused by repetitive stress, as in marathon running

stretch (strech) ***vt.*** ⟦OE *streccan*⟧ **1** to reach out; extend **2** to draw out to full extent or to greater size **3** to cause to extend too far; strain **4** to strain in interpretation, scope, etc. —***vi.*** **1** *a*) to spread out to full extent or beyond normal limits *b*) to extend over a given distance or time **2** *a*) to extend the body or limbs to full length *b*) to lie down (usually with *out*) **3** to become stretched —***n.*** **1** a stretching or being stretched **2** an unbroken period *[*a ten-day *stretch]* **3** an unbroken length, tract, etc. **4** *short for* HOMESTRETCH **5** an action that exceeds someone's normal powers —***adj.*** **1** made of elasticized fabric so as to stretch easily **2** designating a vehicle built extra long to enlarge seating capacity *[*a *stretch* limousine*]* —**stretch'a·ble** ***adj.*** — **stretch'y, -i·er, -i·est,** ***adj.***

stretch'er ***n.*** **1** one that stretches **2** a canvas-covered frame for carrying the sick or injured

strew (stro͞o) ***vt.*** **strewed, strewed** or **strewn, strew'ing** ⟦OE *streawian*⟧ **1** to spread here and there; scatter **2** to cover as by scattering

stri·at·ed (strī'āt'id) ***adj.*** ⟦< L *striare*, to groove⟧ marked with parallel lines, bands, furrows, etc.

strick·en (strik'ən) ***vt.***, ***vi.*** *alt. pp. of* STRIKE —***adj.*** **1** struck or wounded **2** afflicted, as by something painful

strict (strikt) ***adj.*** ⟦< L *stringere*, draw tight⟧ **1** exact or precise **2** *a*) enforcing rules carefully *b*) closely enforced — **strict'ly** ***adv.*** —**strict'ness** ***n.***

stric·ture (strik'chər) ***n.*** ⟦see prec.⟧ **1** adverse criticism **2** a limiting; restriction **3** an abnormal narrowing of a passage in the body

stride (strīd) ***vi.*** **strode, strid'den, strid'ing** ⟦OE *stridan*⟧ **1** to walk with long steps **2** to take a single, long step (esp. *over* something) —***n.*** **1** a long step

2 the distance covered by such a step 3 [*usually pl.*] progress [to make *strides*]

stri·dent (strīd′'nt) ***adj.*** ⟦< L *stridere,* to rasp⟧ harsh-sounding; shrill; grating —**stri′dent·ly *adv.***

strife (strīf) ***n.*** ⟦< OFr *estrif*⟧ 1 contention 2 fighting or quarreling; struggle

strike (strīk) ***vt.*** **struck, struck** or, esp. for *vt.* 7 & 10, **strick′en, strik′ing** ⟦OE *strican,* to go, advance⟧ 1 to hit with the hand, a tool, etc. 2 to make by stamping, etc. [to *strike* coins] 3 to announce (time), as with a bell: said of clocks, etc. 4 to ignite (a match) or produce (a light, etc.) by friction 5 to collide with or cause to collide [he *struck* his head on a beam] 6 to attack 7 to afflict, as with disease, pain, etc. 8 to come upon; notice, find, etc. 9 to affect as if by contact, etc.; occur to [an idea *struck* me] 10 to remove (*from* a list, record, etc.) 11 to make (a bargain, truce, etc.) 12 to lower (a sail, flag, etc.) 13 to assume (an attitude, pose, etc.) —***vi.*** 1 to hit (*at*) 2 to attack 3 to make sounds as by being struck: said of a bell, clock, etc. 4 to collide; hit (*against, on,* or *upon*) 5 to seize bait: said of a fish 6 to come suddenly (*on* or *upon*) 7 to refuse to continue to work until certain demands are met 8 to proceed, esp. in a new direction —***n.*** 1 the act of striking; specif., a military attack 2 a refusal by employees to go on working, in an attempt to gain better working conditions, etc. 3 the discovery of a rich deposit of oil, etc. 4 *Baseball* a pitched ball missed, or fouled off, by the batter or called a good pitch by the umpire 5 *Bowling* a knocking down of all the pins on the first roll —**strike out** 1 to erase 2 to start out 3 *Baseball* to put out, or be put out, on three strikes —**strike up** to begin —**strik′er *n.***

strike′out′ *n.* *Baseball* an out made by a batter charged with three strikes

strik′ing *adj.* very impressive, attractive, etc.

string (striŋ) ***n.*** ⟦OE *streng*⟧ 1 a thin line of fiber, leather, etc. used for tying, pulling, etc. 2 a group of like things on a string [a *string* of pearls] 3 a row, series, etc. of like things [a *string* of houses] 4 *a*) a slender cord of wire, gut, etc. bowed, plucked, or struck to make a musical sound *b*) [*pl.*] all the stringed instruments of an orchestra 5 a fiber of a plant 6 [Inf.] a condition attached to a plan, offer, etc.: *usually used in pl.* —***vt.*** **strung, string′ing** 1 to provide with strings 2 to thread on a string 3 to tie, hang, etc. with a string 4 to remove the strings from (beans, etc.) 5 to arrange in a row 6 to extend [*string* a cable] —**pull strings** to get someone to use influence in one's behalf, often secretly —**string′y, -i·er, -i·est, *adj.***

string bean SNAP BEAN

stringed instrument (striŋd) a musical instrument with vibrating strings, as a violin or guitar

strin·gent (strin′jənt) ***adj.*** ⟦see STRICT⟧ strict; severe —**strin′gen·cy *n.***

string′er *n.* 1 a long horizontal piece in a structure 2 a part-time, local correspondent for a newspaper, magazine, etc.

strip[1] (strip) ***vt.*** **stripped, strip′ping** ⟦OE *stripan*⟧ 1 to remove (the clothing, etc.) from (a person) 2 to dispossess of (honors, titles, etc.) 3 to plunder; rob 4 to take off (a covering, etc.) from (a person or thing) 5 to make bare by taking away removable parts, etc. 6 to break the thread of (a nut, bolt, etc.) or the teeth of (a gear) —***vi.*** to take off all clothing

strip[2] (strip) ***n.*** ⟦< STRIPE⟧ 1 a long, narrow piece, as of land, tape, etc. 2 *short for* AIRSTRIP

strip cropping crop planting in alternate rows to lessen erosion, as on a hillside

stripe (strīp) ***n.*** ⟦< MDu *strīp*⟧ 1 a long, narrow band differing from the surrounding area 2 a strip of cloth on a uniform to show rank, years served, etc. 3 kind; sort [a man of his *stripe*] —***vt.*** **striped, strip′ing** to mark with stripes

strip·ling (strip′liŋ) ***n.*** a grown boy

strip mall a shopping center of connected storefronts with a parking area in front

strip mining mining, esp. for coal, by laying bare a mineral deposit near the surface of the earth

stripped′-down′ *adj.* reduced to essentials

strip′-search′ *vt.* to search (a person) by requiring removal of the clothes —***n.*** such a search Also **strip search**

strip′tease′ *n.* an entertainment in which the performer undresses slowly, usually to musical accompaniment

strive (strīv) ***vi.*** **strove** or **strived, striv·en** (striv′ ən) or **strived, striv′ing** ⟦< OFr *estrif,* effort⟧ 1 to make great efforts; try very hard 2 to struggle

strobe (light) (strōb) ⟦< Gr *strobus,* a twisting around⟧ an electronic tube emitting rapid, brief, and brilliant flashes of light

strode (strōd) ***vi., vt.*** *pt. of* STRIDE

stroke (strōk) ***n.*** ⟦ME⟧ 1 a blow of an ax, whip, etc. 2 a sudden action or event [a *stroke* of luck] 3 an interruption of normal blood flow to the brain, as from a hemorrhage, blood clot, etc., causing paralysis, etc. 4 a single strong effort 5 the sound of striking, as of a clock 6 *a*) a single movement, as with a tool, racket, etc. *b*) any of a series of repeated motions made in rowing, swimming, etc. 7 a mark made by a pen, etc. —***vt.*** **stroked, strok′ing** to draw one's hand, a tool, etc. gently over the surface of

stroll (strōl) ***vi.*** ⟦prob. < Ger *strolch,* vagabond⟧ 1 to walk about leisurely; saunter 2 to wander —***vt.*** to stroll along or through —***n.*** a leisurely walk

stroll′er *n.* 1 one who strolls 2 a light, chairlike baby carriage

strong (strôŋ) ***adj.*** ⟦OE *strang*⟧ 1 *a*) physically powerful *b*) healthy; hearty 2 morally or intellectually powerful [a *strong* will] 3 firm; durable 4 powerful in wealth, numbers, etc. 5 of a specified number *[troops 6,000 strong]* **6** having a powerful effect **7** intense in degree or quality **8** forceful; vigorous, etc. —**strong'ly** ***adv.***

strong'-arm' [Inf.] ***adj.*** using physical force —***vt.*** to use force upon

strong'box' ***n.*** a heavily made box or safe for storing valuables

strong'hold' ***n.*** a place having strong defenses; fortress

strong'-mind'ed ***adj.*** unyielding; determined: also **strong'-willed'**

stron·ti·um (strän'shəm, -shē əm; stränt'ē əm) ***n.*** ⟦ult. after *Strontian,* Scotland, where first found⟧ a metallic chemical element resembling calcium in properties

strop (sträp) ***n.*** ⟦OE⟧ a leather band for sharpening razors —***vt.*** **stropped, strop'ping** to sharpen on a strop

stro·phe (strō'fē) ***n.*** ⟦Gr *strophē,* a turning⟧ a stanza of a poem

strove (strōv) ***vi.*** *alt. pt. of* STRIVE

struck (struk) ***vt., vi.*** *pt. & pp. of* STRIKE

struc·ture (struk'chər) ***n.*** ⟦< L *struere,* arrange⟧ **1** something built or constructed, as a building or dam **2** the arrangement of all the parts of a whole **3** something composed of related parts —***vt.*** **-tured, -tur·ing** to put together systematically —**struc'tur·al** ***adj.***

stru·del (strōōd''l) ***n.*** ⟦Ger⟧ a pastry made of a thin sheet of dough filled with apples, etc., rolled up, and baked

strug·gle (strug'əl) ***vi.*** **-gled, -gling** ⟦ME *strogelen*⟧ **1** to fight violently with an opponent **2** to make great efforts; strive; labor —***n.*** **1** great effort **2** conflict; strife

strum (strum) ***vt., vi.*** **strummed, strum'ming** ⟦echoic⟧ to play (a guitar, etc.) with long strokes across the strings, often casually

strum·pet (strum'pit) ***n.*** ⟦ME⟧ a prostitute

strung (struŋ) ***vt., vi.*** *pt. & alt. pp. of* STRING

strut (strut) ***vi.*** **strut'ted, strut'ting** ⟦OE *strutian,* stand rigid⟧ to walk in a swaggering manner —***n.*** **1** a swaggering walk **2** a brace fitted into a framework to stabilize the structure

strych·nine (strik'nin, -nēn', -nīn') ***n.*** ⟦< Gr *strychnos,* nightshade⟧ a colorless, highly poisonous, crystalline alkaloid

stub (stub) ***n.*** ⟦OE *stybb*⟧ **1** a tree or plant stump **2** a short piece left over *[a pencil stub]* **3** any short or blunt projection **4** the part of a ticket, bank check, etc. kept as a record —***vt.*** **stubbed, stub'bing** **1** to strike (one's toe, etc.) against something **2** to put out (a cigarette, etc.) by pressing the end against a surface: often with *out*

stub·ble (stub'əl) ***n.*** ⟦< L *stipula,* a stalk⟧ **1** short stumps of grain, corn, etc., left after harvesting **2** any short, bristly growth, as of a beard

stub·born (stub'ərn) ***adj.*** ⟦ME *stoburn*⟧ **1** refusing to yield or comply; obstinate **2** done in an obstinate or persistent way **3** hard to handle or deal with —**stub'born·ly** ***adv.*** —**stub'born·ness** ***n.***

stub·by (stub'ē) ***adj.*** **-bi·er, -bi·est** **1** covered with stubs or stubble **2** short and dense **3** short and thickset

stuc·co (stuk'ō) ***n.***, *pl.* **-coes** or **-cos** ⟦It⟧ plaster or cement for surfacing walls, etc. —***vt.*** **-coed, -co·ing** to cover with stucco

stuck (stuk) ***vt., vi.*** *pt. & pp. of* STICK

stuck'-up' ***adj.*** [Inf.] snobbish; conceited

stud[1] (stud) ***n.*** ⟦OE *studu,* a post⟧ **1** any of a series of small knobs, etc. used to ornament a surface **2** a small, button-like device for fastening a shirt front, etc. **3** an upright piece in the wall of a building, to which panels, laths, etc. are nailed —***vt.*** **stud'ded, stud'ding** **1** to set or decorate with studs, etc. **2** to be set thickly on *[rocks stud the hill]*

stud[2] (stud) ***n.*** ⟦OE⟧ a male animal, esp. a horse (**stud'horse'**), kept for breeding

stud'book' ***n.*** a register of purebred animals, esp. racehorses: also **stud book**

stud'ding ***n.*** studs, esp. for walls

stu·dent (stōōd''nt) ***n.*** ⟦< L *studere,* to study⟧ **1** one who studies, or investigates **2** one who is enrolled for study at a school, college, etc.

stud·ied (stud'ēd) ***adj.*** **1** prepared by careful study **2** deliberate

stu·di·o (stōō'dē ō') ***n.***, *pl.* **-os'** ⟦It⟧ **1** a place where an artist, etc. works or where music or dancing lessons, etc. are given **2** a place where films, radio or TV programs, etc. are produced

studio apartment a one-room apartment with a kitchen area and a bathroom

studio couch a couch that can be opened into a full-sized bed

stu·di·ous (stōō'dē əs) ***adj.*** ⟦< L *studiosus*⟧ **1** fond of study **2** zealous or attentive

stud·y (stud'ē) ***n.***, *pl.* **-ies** ⟦< L *studere,* to study⟧ **1** the acquiring of knowledge, as by reading or investigating **2** careful examination of a subject, event, etc. **3** a branch of learning **4** [*pl.*] formal education; schooling **5** an essay, thesis, etc. containing the results of an investigation **6** an earnest effort **7** deep thought **8** a room for study, etc. —***vt.*** **-ied, -y·ing** **1** to try to learn or understand by reading, thinking, etc. **2** to investigate carefully **3** to read (a book, etc.) intently **4** to take a course in, as at a school —***vi.*** **1** to study something **2** to be a student **3** to meditate

stuff (stuf) ***n.*** ⟦< OFr *estoffe*⟧ **1** the material out of which anything is made **2** essence; character **3** matter of an unspecified kind **4** cloth, esp. woolen cloth **5** objects; things **6** worthless objects; junk **7** [Inf.] ability, skill, etc. —***vt.*** **1** to fill or pack; specif., *a)* to fill the skin of (a dead animal) in taxidermy *b)* to fill (a turkey, etc.) with seasoning, bread crumbs, etc. before roasting **2** to fill too full; cram **3** to plug; block —***vi.*** to eat too much

stuffed shirt [Slang] a pompous, pretentious person

stuff'ing ***n.*** something used to stuff, as padding in cushions or a seasoned mixture for stuffing fowl

stuff'y *adj.* **-i·er, -i·est 1** poorly ventilated; close **2** having the nasal passages stopped up, as from a cold **3** [Inf.] dull, conventional, or pompous —**stuff'i·ness** *n.*

stul·ti·fy (stul'tə fī') *vt.* **-fied', -fy'ing** ⟦< L *stultus,* foolish + *facere,* make⟧ **1** to make seem foolish, stupid, etc. **2** to make worthless, etc.

stum·ble (stum'bəl) *vi.* **-bled, -bling** ⟦ME *stumblen*⟧ **1** to trip in walking, running, etc. **2** to walk unsteadily **3** to speak, act, etc. in a blundering way **4** to do wrong **5** to come by chance —*n.* a stumbling —**stum'bler** *n.*

stumbling block a difficulty or obstacle

stump (stump) *n.* ⟦ME *stumpfe*⟧ **1** the end of a tree or plant left in the ground after the upper part has been cut off **2** the part of a limb, tooth, etc. left after the rest has been removed **3** the place where a political speech is made —*vt.* **1** to travel over (a district), making political speeches **2** [Inf.] to puzzle or perplex —*vi.* **1** to walk with a heavy step **2** to travel about, making political speeches —**stump'y, -i·er, -i·est,** *adj.*

stun (stun) *vt.* **stunned, stun'ning** ⟦ult. < L *ex-,* intens. + *tonare,* to thunder⟧ **1** to make unconscious, as by a blow **2** to daze; shock

stung (stuŋ) *vt., vi. pt. & pp. of* STING

stunk (stuŋk) *vi. pp. & alt. pt. of* STINK

stun·ning (stun'iŋ) *adj.* [Inf.] remarkably attractive, excellent, etc.

stunt[1] (stunt) *vt.* ⟦< OE, stupid⟧ **1** to check the growth or development of **2** to hinder (growth, etc.)

stunt[2] (stunt) *n.* ⟦< ?⟧ something done to show one's skill or daring, get attention, etc. —*vi.* to do a stunt

stu·pe·fy (sto͞o'pə fī') *vt.* ⟦< L *stupere,* be stunned + *facere,* make⟧ **1** to produce stupor in; stun **2** to astound; bewilder —**stu'pe·fac'tion** (-fak'shən) *n.*

stu·pen·dous (sto͞o pen'dəs) *adj.* ⟦< L *stupere,* be stunned⟧ **1** astonishing **2** astonishingly great

stu·pid (sto͞o'pid) *adj.* ⟦see prec.⟧ **1** lacking normal intelligence **2** foolish; silly *[a stupid idea]* **3** dull and boring —**stu·pid'i·ty,** *pl.* **-ties,** *n.*

stu·por (sto͞o'pər) *n.* ⟦see STUPENDOUS⟧ a state in which the mind and senses are dulled; loss of sensibility

stur·dy (stur'dē) *adj.* **-di·er, -di·est** ⟦< OFr *estourdi,* hard to control⟧ **1** firm; resolute **2** strong; vigorous **3** strongly constructed —**stur'di·ly** *adv.* —**stur'di·ness** *n.*

stur·geon (stur'jən) *n.* ⟦< OFr *esturjon*⟧ a large food fish valuable as a source of caviar

stut·ter (stut'ər) *vt., vi., n.* ⟦< ME *stutten*⟧ STAMMER

Stutt·gart (stoot'gärt'; *Ger* shto͞ot'gärt') city in SW Germany: pop. 592,000

St. Vin·cent and the Gren·a·dines (sānt vin'sənt and *th*ə gren'ə dēnz') country consisting of the island of St. Vincent and the N Grenadines, in the West Indies: 150 sq. mi.; pop. 106,000

sty[1] (stī) *n., pl.* **sties** ⟦< OE *sti,* hall, enclosure⟧ **1** a pen for pigs **2** any foul place

sty[2] or **stye** (stī) *n., pl.* **sties** or **styes** ⟦ult. < OE *stigan,* to rise⟧ a small, inflamed swelling on the rim of an eyelid

Styg·i·an (stij'ē ən, stij'ən) *adj.* **1** of the Styx **2** [*also* **s-**] *a)* infernal *b)* dark or gloomy

style (stīl) *n.* ⟦< L *stilus,* pointed writing tool⟧ **1** a stylus **2** *a)* manner of expression in language *b)* characteristic manner of expression, design, etc. in any art, period, etc. *c)* excellence of artistic expression **3** *a)* fashion *b)* something stylish —*vt.* **styled, styl'ing 1** to name; call **2** to design the style of **3** to arrange (hair) by cutting, etc.

styl·ish (stī'lish) *adj.* conforming to current style, as in dress; fashionable

styl'ist (-list) *n.* **1** a writer, etc. whose work has style and distinction **2** a person who styles hair —**sty·lis'tic** *adj.* —**sty·lis'ti·cal·ly** *adv.*

styl'ize' (-līz') *vt.* **-ized', -iz'ing** to design or represent according to a style rather than nature

sty·lus (stī'ləs) *n., pl.* **-lus·es** or **-li** (-lī) ⟦L, for *stilus,* pointed instrument⟧ **1** a sharp, pointed marking device **2** *a)* a sharp, pointed device for cutting the grooves of a phonograph record *b)* the short, pointed piece moving in such grooves, that transmits vibrations

sty·mie (stī'mē) *n.* ⟦prob. < Scot, person partially blind⟧ *Golf* a situation in which a ball to be putted has another ball between it and the hole —*vt.* **-mied, -mie·ing** to block; impede

sty'my *n. pl.* **-mies,** *vt.* **-mied, -my·ing** *alt. sp. of* STYMIE

styp·tic pencil (stip'tik) a piece of astringent, used to stop minor bleeding

Sty·ro·foam (stī'rə fōm') *trademark for* a rigid, lightweight, spongelike polystyrene —*n.* [*also* **s-**] this substance

Styx (stiks) *n. Gr. Myth.* the river crossed by dead souls entering Hades

sua·sion (swā'zhən) *n.* ⟦< L *suadere,* to persuade⟧ PERSUASION: now chiefly in **moral suasion,** a persuading by appealing to one's sense of morality

suave (swäv) *adj.* ⟦< L *suavis,* sweet⟧ smoothly gracious or polite; polished —**suave'ly** *adv.* —**suav'i·ty** *n.*

sub[1] (sub) *n. short for:* **1** SUBMARINE **2** SUBSTITUTE **3** SUBMARINE SANDWICH —*vi.* **subbed, sub'bing** [Inf.] to be a substitute (*for* someone)

sub[2] *abbrev.* **1** substitute(s) **2** suburb(an)

sub- ⟦< L *sub,* under⟧ *prefix* **1** under *[submarine]* **2** lower than; inferior to *[subhead]* **3** to a lesser degree than *[subhuman]*

sub·a·tom·ic (sub'ə täm'ik) *adj.* of the inner part of or a particle smaller than an atom

sub'branch' *n.* a division of a branch

sub'com·mit'tee *n.* a small committee chosen from a main committee

sub·com'pact' *n.* an automobile model

smaller than a compact

sub·con'scious ***adj.*** occurring with little or no conscious perception on the part of the individual: said of mental processes and reactions —**the subconscious** subconscious mental activity —**sub·con'scious·ly** ***adv.***

sub'con'ti·nent ***n.*** a large land mass smaller than a continent

sub'con'tract' ***n.*** a secondary contract undertaking some or all obligations of another contract —***vt., vi.*** to make a subcontract (for) —**sub'con'trac'tor** ***n.***

sub'cul'ture ***n.*** **1** a distinctive social group within a larger social group **2** its cultural patterns

sub'cu·ta'ne·ous ***adj.*** beneath the skin

sub'dea'con ***n.*** a cleric ranking below a deacon

sub'dis'trict ***n.*** a subdivision of a district

sub'di·vide' ***vt., vi.*** **-vid'ed, -vid'ing 1** to divide further **2** to divide (land) into small parcels —**sub'di·vi'sion** ***n.***

sub·due (səb dōō') ***vt.*** **-dued', -du'ing** ⟦< L *subducere*, take away⟧ **1** to conquer **2** to overcome; control **3** to make less intense; diminish

sub'fam'i·ly ***n.***, *pl.* **-lies** a main subdivision of a family, as of plants or of languages

sub'head' ***n.*** a subordinate heading or title, as of a magazine article

subj *abbrev.* **1** subject **2** subjunctive

sub·ject (sub'jikt, -jekt'; *for v.* səb jekt') ***adj.*** ⟦< L *sub-*, under + *jacere*, to throw⟧ **1** under the authority or control of another **2** having a tendency *[subject* to anger*]* **3** exposed *[subject* to censure*]* **4** contingent upon: with *to [subject* to approval*]* —***n.*** **1** one under the authority or control of another **2** one made to undergo a treatment, experiment, etc. **3** something dealt with in discussion, study, etc.; theme **4** a course of study in a school or college **5** *Gram.* the noun, etc. in a sentence about which something is said —***vt.*** **1** to bring under the authority or control of **2** to cause to undergo something *[*to *subject* someone to questioning*]* —**sub·jec'tion** ***n.***

sub·jec·tive (səb jek'tiv) ***adj.*** of or resulting from the feelings of the person thinking; not objective; personal —**sub·jec·tiv·i·ty** (sub'jek tiv'ə tē) ***n.***

sub·join (səb join') ***vt.*** ⟦see SUB- & JOIN⟧ to append

sub·ju·gate (sub'jə gāt') ***vt.*** **-gat'ed, -gat'ing** ⟦< L *sub-*, under + *jugum*, a yoke⟧ to bring under control; conquer —**sub'ju·ga'tion** ***n.***

sub·junc·tive (səb juŋk'tiv) ***adj.*** ⟦< L *subjungere*, subjoin⟧ designating or of the mood of a verb that is used to express supposition, desire, possibility, etc., rather than to state an actual fact

sub·lease (sub'lēs'; *for v.* sub lēs') ***n.*** a lease granted by a lessee —***vt.*** **-leased', -leas'ing** to grant or hold a sublease of

sub·let (sub let') ***vt.*** **-let', -let'ting 1** to let to another (property which one is renting) **2** to let out (work) to a subcontractor

sub·li·mate (sub'lə māt') ***vt.*** **-mat'ed, -mat'ing 1** to change (a solid) to a gas, or (a gas) to a solid, without becoming a liquid **2** to express (unacceptable impulses) in acceptable forms, often unconsciously —**sub'li·ma'tion** ***n.***

sub·lime (sə blīm') ***adj.*** ⟦< L *sub-*, up to + *limen*, lintel⟧ **1** noble; exalted **2** inspiring awe or admiration —***vt.*** **-limed', -lim'ing** SUBLIMATE (*vt.* 1) —**sub·lim·i·ty** (sə blim'ə tē) ***n.***

sub·lim·i·nal (sub lim'ə nəl) ***adj.*** ⟦< SUB- + L *limen*, threshold + -AL⟧ below the threshold of consciousness

sub'ma·chine' gun a portable automatic firearm

sub·mar·gin·al (sub mär'jə nəl) ***adj.*** below minimum requirements or standards

sub·ma·rine (sub'mə rēn', sub'mə rēn') ***adj.*** being, living, etc. underwater —***n.*** a ship, esp. a warship, that can operate under water

submarine sandwich HERO SANDWICH

sub·merge (səb murj') ***vt., vi.*** **-merged', -merg'ing** ⟦< L *sub-*, under + *mergere*, to plunge⟧ to place or sink beneath the surface, as of water —**sub·mer'gence** (-mur'jəns) ***n.***

sub·merse' (-murs') ***vt.*** **-mersed', -mers'ing** SUBMERGE —**sub·mers'i·ble** ***adj.*** —**sub·mer'sion** ***n.***

sub·mis·sion (səb mish'ən) ***n.*** **1** a submitting or surrendering **2** obedience; resignation **3** *a)* the submitting of something to another *b)* the thing submitted, as a manuscript —**sub·mis'sive** ***adj.***

sub·mit' (-mit') ***vt.*** **-mit'ted, -mit'ting** ⟦< L *sub-*, down + *mittere*, send⟧ **1** to present to others for consideration, etc. **2** to yield to the control or power of another **3** to offer as an opinion —***vi.*** to yield; give in

sub·nor·mal (sub nôr'məl) ***adj.*** below normal, esp. in intelligence

sub·or'bit·al (-ôr'bit'l) ***adj.*** designating a flight in which a rocket, spacecraft, etc. follows a trajectory of less than one orbit

sub·or·di·nate (sə bôrd''n it; *for v.*, -bôr' də nāt') ***adj.*** ⟦< L *sub-*, under + *ordinare*, to order⟧ **1** below another in rank, importance, etc. **2** under the authority of another **3** *Gram.* having the function of a noun, adjective, or adverb within a sentence *[*a *subordinate* clause*]* —***n.*** one that is subordinate —***vt.*** **-nat'ed, -nat'ing** to place in a subordinate position —**sub·or'di·na'tion** ***n.***

subordinate clause *Gram.* DEPENDENT CLAUSE

sub·orn (sə bôrn') ***vt.*** ⟦< L *sub-*, under + *ornare*, furnish⟧ to induce (another) to commit perjury —**sub·or·na·tion** (sub'ôr nā'shən) ***n.***

sub'plot' ***n.*** a secondary plot in a play, novel, etc.

sub·poe·na (sə pē'nə) ***n.*** ⟦< L *sub poena*, under penalty⟧ a written legal order directing a person to appear in court to testify, etc. —***vt.*** **-naed, -na·ing** to summon with such an order Also **sub·pe'na**

sub ro·sa (sub rō'zə) ⟦L, under the rose,

ancient symbol of secrecy⟧ secretly; privately

sub·scribe (səb skrīb′) ***vt., vi.*** **-scribed′, -scrib′ing** ⟦< L *sub-*, under + *scribere*, write⟧ **1** to sign (one's name) at the end of a document, etc. **2** to give support or consent (to) **3** to promise to contribute (money) **4** to agree to receive and pay for a periodical, service, etc. (with *to*) —**sub·scrib′er** ***n.***

sub·script (sub′skript′) ***n.*** ⟦see prec.⟧ a figure, letter, or symbol written below and to the side of another

sub·scrip·tion (səb skrip′shən) ***n.*** **1** a subscribing **2** money subscribed **3** a formal agreement to receive and pay for a periodical, etc.

sub·se·quent (sub′si kwənt) ***adj.*** ⟦< L *sub-*, after + *sequi*, follow⟧ coming after; following —**subsequent to** after —**sub′se·quent·ly** ***adv.***

sub·ser·vi·ent (səb sʉr′vē ənt) ***adj.*** ⟦< L *sub-*, under + *servire*, to serve⟧ **1** that is of service, esp. in a subordinate capacity **2** submissive —**sub·ser′vi·ence** ***n.***

sub·set (sub′set′) ***n.*** a mathematical set containing some or all of the elements of a given set

sub·side (səb sīd′) ***vi.*** **-sid′ed, -sid′ing** ⟦< L *sub-*, under + *sidere*, to settle⟧ **1** to sink to the bottom or to a lower level **2** to become less active, intense, etc. —**sub·sid′ence** ***n.***

sub·sid·i·ar·y (səb sid′ē er′ē) ***adj.*** ⟦see SUBSIDY⟧ **1** giving aid, service, etc.; auxiliary **2** being in a subordinate relationship —***n.***, *pl.* **-ies** one that is subsidiary; specif., a company controlled by another company

sub·si·dize (sub′sə dīz′) ***vt.*** **-dized′, -diz′ing** to support with a subsidy —**sub′si·di·za′tion** ***n.***

sub·si·dy (sub′sə dē) ***n.***, *pl.* **-dies** ⟦< L *subsidium*, auxiliary forces⟧ a grant of money, as from a government to a private enterprise

sub·sist (səb sist′) ***vi.*** ⟦< L *sub-*, under + *sistere*, to stand⟧ **1** to continue to be or exist **2** to continue to live; remain alive (*on* or *by*)

sub·sist′ence ***n.*** **1** existence **2** the act of providing sustenance **3** means of support or livelihood, esp. the barest means

sub·soil (sub′soil′) ***n.*** the layer of soil beneath the topsoil

sub·son·ic (sub sän′ik) ***adj.*** designating, of, or moving at a speed less than that of sound

sub·stance (sub′stəns) ***n.*** ⟦< L *substare*, be present⟧ **1** the real or essential part of anything; essence **2** the physical matter of which a thing consists **3** *a*) solid or substantial quality *b*) consistency; body **4** the real meaning; gist **5** wealth **6** a drug: see CONTROLLED SUBSTANCE

sub·stand′ard ***adj.*** below standard

sub·stan·tial (səb stan′shəl) ***adj.*** **1** having substance **2** real; true **3** strong; solid **4** ample; large **5** important **6** wealthy **7** with regard to essential elements —**sub·stan′tial·ly** ***adv.***

sub·stan′ti·ate′ (-shē āt′) ***vt.*** **-at′ed, -at′ing** ⟦see SUBSTANCE⟧ to show to be true or real by giving evidence —**sub·stan′ti·a′tion** ***n.***

sub·stan·tive (sub′stən tiv) ***adj.*** ⟦see SUBSTANCE⟧ of or dealing with essentials —***n.*** *Gram.* a noun or any other word or group of words used as a noun

sub′sta′tion ***n.*** a small post-office station, as in a store

sub·sti·tute (sub′stə to͞ot′) ***n.*** ⟦< L *sub-*, under + *statuere*, put⟧ a person or thing serving or used in place of another —***vt., vi.*** **-tut′ed, -tut′ing** to put, use, or serve in place of (another) —**sub′sti·tu′tion** ***n.***

sub·stra·tum (sub′strāt′əm, -strat′-) ***n.***, *pl.* **-ta** (-ə) or **-tums** a part, substance, etc. which lies beneath and supports another

sub′struc′ture ***n.*** a part or structure that is a support, base, etc.

sub·sume (sub so͞om′) ***vt.*** **-sumed′, -sum′ing** ⟦< L *sub-*, under + *sumere*, take⟧ to include within a larger class

sub′teen′ ***n.*** a child nearly a teenager

sub′ten′ant ***n.*** a person who rents from a tenant —**sub·ten′an·cy** ***n.***

sub·ter·fuge (sub′tər fyo͞oj′) ***n.*** ⟦< L *subter*, secretly + *fugere*, flee⟧ any plan or action used to hide or evade something

sub·ter·ra·ne·an (sub′tə rā′nē ən) ***adj.*** ⟦< L *sub-*, under + *terra*, earth⟧ **1** underground **2** secret; hidden

sub·text (sub′tekst′) ***n.*** an underlying meaning, theme, etc.

sub′ti′tle ***n.*** **1** a secondary or explanatory title **2** one or more lines of translated dialogue, etc. at the bottom of a film or video image —***vt.*** **-ti′tled, -ti′tling** to add a subtitle or subtitles to

sub·tle (sut′'l) ***adj.*** **-tler** (-lər, -'l ər), **-tlest** ⟦< L *subtilis*, fine, thin⟧ **1** thin; not dense **2** mentally keen **3** delicately skillful **4** crafty **5** not obvious —**sub′tle·ty**, *pl.* **-ties**, ***n.*** —**sub′tly** ***adv.***

sub′to′tal ***n.*** a total that is part of a complete total —***vt., vi.*** **-taled** or **-talled, -tal·ing** or **-tal·ling** to add up so as to form a subtotal

sub·tract (səb trakt′) ***vt., vi.*** ⟦< L *sub-*, under + *trahere*, to draw⟧ to take away or deduct (one quantity from another) —**sub·trac′tion** ***n.***

sub·tra·hend (sub′trə hend′) ***n.*** a quantity to be subtracted from another (the *minuend*)

sub·trop·i·cal (sub trä′pi kəl) ***adj.*** **1** of regions bordering on the tropics **2** characteristic of such regions Also **sub·trop′ic**

sub·urb (sub′ərb) ***n.*** ⟦< L *sub-*, near + *urbs*, town⟧ a district, town, etc. on the outskirts of a city —**sub·ur·ban** (sə bʉr′bən) ***adj.***

sub·ur·ban·ite (sə bʉr′bən īt′) ***n.*** a person living in a suburb

sub·ur′bi·a (-bē ə) ***n.*** the suburbs or suburbanites collectively

sub·ven·tion (səb ven′shən) ***n.*** ⟦< LL *subventio*, aid⟧ a subsidy

sub·ver·sive (səb vʉr′siv) ***adj.*** tending

to subvert —*n.* a person seen as being subversive

sub·vert (səb vurt′) *vt.* ⟦< L *sub-*, under + *vertere,* to turn⟧ **1** to overthrow or destroy (something established) **2** to corrupt, as in morals —**sub·ver′sion** (-vur′zhən) *n.*

sub′way′ *n.* an underground, electric metropolitan railway

suc- *prefix* SUB-: used before *c [succumb]*

suc·ceed (sək sēd′) *vi.* ⟦< L *sub-*, under + *cedere,* go⟧ **1** to follow, as into office **2** to be successful —*vt.* to come after; follow

suc·cess (sək ses′) *n.* **1** a favorable result **2** the gaining of wealth, fame, etc. **3** a successful person or thing

suc·cess′ful *adj.* **1** turning out as was hoped for **2** having gained wealth, fame, etc. —**suc·cess′ful·ly** *adv.*

suc·ces·sion (sək sesh′ən) *n.* **1** *a*) the act of succeeding another, as to an office *b*) the right to do this **2** a number of persons or things coming one after another

suc·ces′sive (-ses′iv) *adj.* coming one after another —**suc·ces′sive·ly** *adv.*

suc·ces′sor *n.* one that succeeds another, as to an office

suc·cinct (sək siŋkt′) *adj.* ⟦< L *sub-*, under + *cingere,* gird⟧ clear and brief; terse —**suc·cinct′ly** *adv.* —**suc·cinct′ness** *n.*

suc·cor (suk′ər) *vt.* ⟦< L *sub-*, under + *currere,* to run⟧ to help in time of need or distress —*n.* aid; relief

suc·co·tash (suk′ə tash′) *n.* ⟦< AmInd⟧ a dish of lima beans and corn kernels cooked together

suc·cu·lent (suk′yo͞o lənt) *adj.* ⟦< L *sucus,* juice⟧ full of juice —**suc′cu·lence** or **suc′cu·len·cy** *n.*

suc·cumb (sə kum′) *vi.* ⟦< L *sub-*, under + *cumbere,* to lie⟧ **1** to give way (*to*); yield **2** to die

such (such) *adj.* ⟦OE *swilc*⟧ **1** *a*) of the kind mentioned *b*) of the same or a similar kind **2** whatever *[at such time as you go]* **3** so extreme, so much, etc. *[such an honor]* —*adv.* to so great a degree *[such good news]* —*pron.* **1** such a person or thing **2** the person or thing mentioned *[such was her nature]* —**as such 1** as being what is indicated **2** in itself —**such as** for example

such and such (being) something particular but not named or specified *[such and such a place]*

such′like′ *adj.* of such a kind —*pron.* persons or things of such a kind

suck (suk) *vt.* ⟦< OE *sucan*⟧ **1** to draw (liquid) into the mouth **2** to take in by or as by sucking **3** to suck liquid from (fruit, etc.) **4** to hold (ice, etc.) in the mouth and lick so as to dissolve **5** to place (the thumb, etc.) in the mouth and draw on —*vi.* to suck something —*n.* the act of sucking

suck′er *n.* **1** one that sucks **2** a freshwater bony fish with a mouth adapted for sucking **3** a part used for sucking or for holding fast by suction **4** LOLLIPOP **5** [Slang] one easily cheated **6** *Bot.* a subordinate shoot on the root or stem of a plant

suck·le (suk′əl) *vt.* **-led, -ling** ⟦ME *sokelen*⟧ **1** to cause to suck at the breast or udder; nurse **2** to bring up; rear —*vi.* to suck at the breast or udder

suck′ling *n.* an unweaned child or young animal

su·crose (so͞o′krōs′) *n.* ⟦< Fr *sucre,* sugar + -OSE[1]⟧ a sugar extracted from sugar cane or sugar beets

suc·tion (suk′shən) *n.* ⟦< L *sugere,* to suck⟧ **1** a sucking **2** the production of a vacuum in a cavity or over a surface so that external atmospheric pressure forces fluid in or causes something to adhere to the surface

Su·dan (so͞o dan′) country in NE Africa: 967,500 sq. mi.; pop. 20,564,000: often preceded by *the* —**Su·da·nese** (so͞o′də nēz′), *pl.* **-nese′**, *adj.*, *n.*

sud·den (sud′'n) *adj.* ⟦< L *sub-*, under + *ire,* go⟧ **1** *a*) happening or coming unexpectedly *b*) sharp or abrupt **2** quick or hasty —**all of a sudden** unexpectedly —**sud′den·ly** *adv.* —**sud′den·ness** *n.*

sudden death *Sports* an extra period added to a tied game: the game ends when one side scores

sudden infant death syndrome the sudden death of an apparently healthy infant, possibly caused by a breathing problem

suds (sudz) *pl.n.* ⟦prob. < MDu *sudse,* marsh water⟧ **1** soapy, frothy water **2** foam —**suds′y, -i·er, -i·est,** *adj.*

sue (so͞o) *vt., vi.* **sued, su′ing** ⟦< L *sequi,* follow⟧ **1** to appeal (to); petition **2** to prosecute in a court in seeking justice, etc.

suede or **suède** (swād) *n.* ⟦< Fr *gants de Suède,* Swedish gloves⟧ **1** tanned leather with the flesh side buffed into a nap **2** a kind of cloth like this

su·et (so͞o′it) *n.* ⟦ult. < L *sebum,* tallow⟧ the hard fat of cattle and sheep: used in cooking, etc.

Su·ez Canal (so͞o ez′) ship canal joining the Mediterranean & Red seas

suf or **suff** *abbrev.* suffix

suf- *prefix* SUB-: used before *f*

suf·fer (suf′ər) *vt., vi.* ⟦< L *sub-*, under + *ferre,* to bear⟧ **1** to undergo (pain, injury, grief, etc.) **2** to experience (any process) **3** to permit; tolerate —**suf′fer·er** *n.*

suf·fer·ance (suf′ər əns, suf′rəns) *n.* **1** the capacity to endure pain, etc. **2** consent, permission, etc. implied by failure to prohibit

suf′fer·ing (-ər iŋ, -riŋ) *n.* **1** the bearing of pain, distress, etc. **2** something suffered

suf·fice (sə fīs′) *vi.* **-ficed′, -fic′ing** ⟦< L *sub-*, under + *facere,* make⟧ to be enough or adequate

suf·fi·cient (sə fish′ənt) *adj.* as much as is needed; enough —**suf·fi′cien·cy** *n.* —**suf·fi′cient·ly** *adv.*

suf·fix (suf′iks) *n.* ⟦< L *sub-*, under + *figere,* fix⟧ a syllable or syllables joined to the end of a word to alter its meaning, etc. (Ex.: *-ness* in *darkness*)

suf·fo·cate (suf′ə kāt′) *vt.* **-cat′ed,**

-cat′ing ⟦< L *sub-*, under + *fauces*, throat⟧ **1** to kill by cutting off the supply of air for breathing **2** to smother, suppress, etc. —***vi.*** **1** to die by being suffocated **2** to choke; stifle —**suf′fo·ca′tion** ***n.***

suf·frage (suf′rij) ***n.*** ⟦< L *suffragium*, a ballot⟧ **1** a vote or voting **2** the right to vote; franchise

suf·fra·gette (suf′rə jet′) ***n.*** ⟦< prec. + -ETTE⟧ a woman who advocates female suffrage: term objected to by some, who prefer *suffragist*

suf′fra·gist ***n.*** one who believes in extending the right to vote, esp. to women

suf·fuse (sə fyo͞oz′) ***vt.*** **-fused′**, **-fus′ing** ⟦< L *sub-*, under + *fundere*, pour⟧ to overspread so as to fill with a glow, etc. —**suf·fu′sion** ***n.***

sug- *prefix* SUB-: used before *g*

sug·ar (sho͝og′ər) ***n.*** ⟦< Sans *śárkarâ*⟧ any of a class of sweet, soluble carbohydrates, as sucrose or glucose; specif., sucrose used as a food and sweetening agent —***vt.*** to sweeten, etc. with sugar —***vi.*** to form sugar —**sug′ar·less** ***adj.*** —**sug′ar·y** ***adj.***

sugar beet a beet having a white root with a high sugar content

sugar cane a very tall tropical grass cultivated as the main source of sugar

sug′ar·coat′ ***vt.*** **1** to coat with sugar **2** to make (something disagreeable) seem more pleasant

sug′ar·plum′ ***n.*** a round piece of sugary candy

sug·gest (səg jest′) ***vt.*** ⟦< L *sub-*, under + *gerere*, carry⟧ **1** to bring to the mind for consideration **2** to call to mind by association of ideas **3** to propose as a possibility **4** to show indirectly; imply

sug·gest′i·ble ***adj.*** readily influenced by suggestion —**sug·gest′i·bil′i·ty** ***n.***

sug·ges′tion (-jes′chən) ***n.*** **1** a suggesting or being suggested **2** something suggested **3** a hint or trace

sug·ges′tive ***adj.*** **1** that tends to suggest ideas **2** tending to suggest something considered improper or indecent —**sug·ges′tive·ly** ***adv.***

su·i·cide (so͞o′ə sīd′) ***n.*** ⟦L *sui*, of oneself + -CIDE⟧ **1** the act of killing oneself intentionally **2** one who commits suicide —**su′i·ci′dal** ***adj.***

su·i ge·ne·ris (so͞o′ē jen′ər is) ⟦L, of his (or her or its) own kind⟧ without equal; unique

suit (so͞ot) ***n.*** ⟦< L *sequi*, follow⟧ **1** a set of clothes; esp., a coat and trousers (or skirt) **2** any of the four sets of playing cards **3** action to secure justice in a court of law **4** an act of suing, pleading, etc. **5** courtship —***vt.*** **1** to be appropriate to **2** to make right or appropriate; fit **3** to please; satisfy [nothing *suits* him] —**follow suit** to follow the example set —**suit oneself** to act according to one's own wishes —**suit up** to put on an athletic uniform, spacesuit, etc. in preparation for a particular activity

suit′a·ble ***adj.*** that suits a given purpose, etc.; appropriate —**suit′a·bil′i·ty** ***n.*** —**suit′a·bly** ***adv.***

suit′case′ ***n.*** a travel case for clothes, etc.

suite (swēt; *for 3, also* so͞ot) ***n.*** ⟦Fr: see SUIT⟧ **1** a group of attendants; staff **2** a set of connected rooms, as an apartment **3** a set of matched furniture for a given room

suit′ing ***n.*** cloth for making suits

suit′or ***n.*** a man courting a woman

su·ki·ya·ki (so͞o′kē yä′kē) ***n.*** ⟦Jpn⟧ a Japanese dish of thinly sliced meat and vegetables, cooked quickly with soy sauce, sake, etc.

Suk·kot or **Suk·koth** (so͝ok′ōt, so͝ok′ōs) ***n.*** ⟦Heb, lit., tabernacles⟧ a Jewish fall festival commemorating the wandering of the Hebrews during the Exodus

sul·fa (sul′fə) ***adj.*** of a family of drugs used in combating certain bacterial infections

sul·fate (sul′fāt′) ***n.*** a salt or ester of sulfuric acid

sul′fide′ (-fīd′) ***n.*** a compound of sulfur with another element or a radical

sul·fur (sul′fər) ***n.*** ⟦< L *sulphur*⟧ a pale-yellow, nonmetallic chemical element: it burns with a blue flame and a stifling odor

sul·fu·ric (sul fyo͝or′ik) ***adj.*** of or containing sulfur

sulfuric acid an oily, colorless, corrosive liquid used in making dyes, explosives, fertilizers, etc.

sul·fu·rous (sul′fər əs, sul fyo͝or′əs) ***adj.*** **1** of or containing sulfur **2** like burning sulfur in odor, color, etc.

sulk (sulk) ***vi.*** ⟦< fol.⟧ to be sulky —***n.*** a sulky mood: also **the sulks**

sulk·y (sul′kē) ***adj.*** **-i·er**, **-i·est** ⟦prob. < OE *-seolcan*, become slack⟧ showing resentment by petulant withdrawal —***n.***, *pl.* **-ies** a light, two-wheeled carriage for one person —**sulk′i·ly** ***adv.*** —**sulk′i·ness** ***n.***

sul·len (sul′ən) ***adj.*** ⟦< L *solus*, alone⟧ **1** showing resentment and ill humor by morose, unsociable withdrawal **2** gloomy; sad —**sul′len·ly** ***adv.*** —**sul′len·ness** ***n.***

sul·ly (sul′ē) ***vt.*** **-lied**, **-ly·ing** ⟦prob. < OFr *soillier*⟧ to soil, tarnish, etc., esp. by disgracing

sul·phur (sul′fər) ***n.*** *chiefly Brit. sp. of* SULFUR

sul·tan (sult′'n) ***n.*** ⟦Fr < Ar *sulṭān*⟧ a Muslim ruler

sul·tan·a (sul tan′ə) ***n.*** **1** a sultan's wife, mother, sister, or daughter **2** a small, white, seedless grape used for raisins

sul·tan·ate (sult′'n it, -āt′) ***n.*** a sultan's authority, office, or domain

sul·try (sul′trē) ***adj.*** **-tri·er**, **-tri·est** ⟦< SWELTER⟧ **1** oppressively hot and moist **2** suggesting or showing passion, lust, etc.

sum (sum) ***n.*** ⟦< L *summus*, highest⟧ **1** an amount of money **2** gist; summary **3** the result obtained by adding quantities; total —**sum up** to summarize

su·mac or **su·mach** (so͞o′mak′, sho͞o′-) ***n.*** ⟦< Ar *summāq*⟧ any of numerous poisonous and nonpoisonous trees and shrubs of the cashew family

Su·ma·tra (so͞o mä′trə) large island of Indonesia

sum·ma·rize (sum′ə rīz′) ***vt.*** **-rized′, -riz′ing** to make or be a summary of

sum′ma·ry (-rē) ***adj.*** ⟦< L *summa*, a sum⟧ **1** summarizing; concise **2** prompt and without formality **3** hasty and arbitrary —***n.***, *pl.* **-ries** a brief statement covering the main points; digest —**sum·mar·i·ly** (sə mer′ə lē) ***adv.***

sum·ma·tion (sə mā′shən) ***n.*** a final summary of arguments, as in a trial

sum·mer (sum′ər) ***n.*** ⟦< OE *sumor*⟧ the warmest season of the year, following spring —***adj.*** of or typical of summer —***vi.*** to pass the summer —**sum′mer·y** ***adj.***

sum′mer·house′ ***n.*** a small, open structure in a garden, park, etc.

summer sausage a type of hard, dried or smoked sausage

sum′mer·time′ ***n.*** the summer season

sum·mit (sum′it) ***n.*** ⟦< L *summus*, highest⟧ the highest or utmost point; top; apex —***adj.*** of the heads of state *[a summit conference]*

sum·mit·ry (sum′i trē) ***n.***, *pl.* **-ries** the use of conferences between heads of state to resolve problems of diplomacy

sum·mon (sum′ən) ***vt.*** ⟦< L *sub-*, under + *monere*, warn⟧ **1** to call together; order to meet **2** to call or send for with authority **3** to rouse *[summon up one's strength]* —**sum′mon·er** ***n.***

sum′mons (-ənz) ***n.***, *pl.* **-mons·es** ⟦see prec.⟧ **1** an order or command to come, attend, etc. **2** *Law* an official order to appear in court

su·mo (wrestling) (so͞o′mō) ⟦Jpn *sumō*, compete⟧ [*sometimes* **S- w-**] Japanese wrestling by large, extremely heavy men

sump (sump) ***n.*** ⟦ME *sompe*, swamp⟧ a pit, cistern, cesspool, etc. for draining, collecting, or storing liquids

sump·tu·ous (sump′cho͞o əs) ***adj.*** ⟦< L *sumptus*, expense⟧ **1** costly; lavish **2** magnificent

sun (sun) ***n.*** ⟦OE *sunne*⟧ **1** the gaseous, self-luminous central star of the solar system **2** the heat or light of the sun **3** any star that is the center of a planetary system —***vt.***, ***vi.*** **sunned, sun′ning** to expose (oneself) to direct sunlight

Sun *abbrev.* Sunday

sun′bathe′ ***vi.*** **-bathed′, -bath′ing** to expose the body to direct sunlight —**sun bath** —**sun′bath′er** ***n.***

sun′beam′ ***n.*** a beam of sunlight

Sun′belt′ in the U.S., the S and SW states having a sunny climate and an expanding economy: also **Sun Belt**

sun′block′ ***n.*** SUNSCREEN

sun′bon′net ***n.*** a bonnet for shading the face and neck from the sun

sun′burn′ ***n.*** an inflammation of the skin from exposure to the sun's rays or to a sunlamp —***vi.***, ***vt.*** **-burned′** or **-burnt′, -burn′ing** to get or cause to get a sunburn

sun′burst′ ***n.*** **1** sudden sunlight **2** a decorative device representing the sun with spreading rays

sun·dae (sun′dā, -dē) ***n.*** ⟦prob. < fol.⟧ a serving of ice cream covered with a syrup, fruit, nuts, etc.

Sun·day (sun′dā) ***n.*** ⟦OE *sunnandæg*, sun day⟧ the first day of the week: it is the Sabbath for most Christians: abbrev. **Sun**

sun·der (sun′dər) ***vt.***, ***vi.*** ⟦< OE *sundor*, asunder⟧ to break apart; split

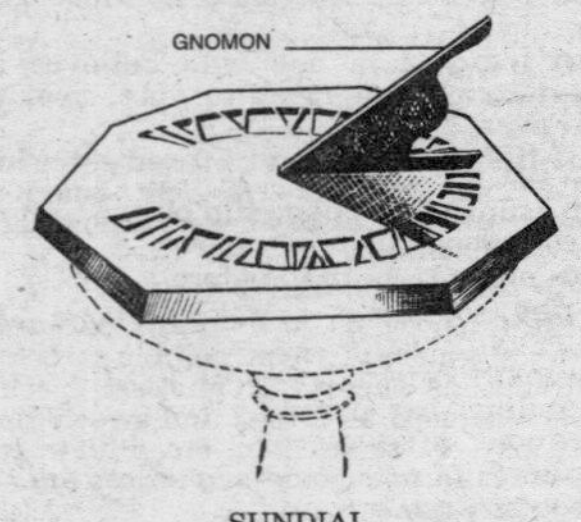

SUNDIAL

sun′di′al ***n.*** an instrument that shows time by the shadow of a pointer cast by the sun onto a dial

sun′down′ ***n.*** SUNSET

sun′dries (-drēz) ***pl.n.*** sundry items

sun′dry (-drē) ***adj.*** ⟦< OE *sundor*, apart⟧ miscellaneous

sun′fish′ ***n.***, *pl.* **-fish′** or (for different species) **-fish′es** **1** any of a family of North American freshwater fishes **2** a large, sluggish ocean fish

sun′flow′er ***n.*** a tall plant having large, yellow, daisylike flowers

sung (suŋ) ***vi.***, ***vt.*** *pp. & rare pt. of* SING[1]

sun′glass′es ***pl.n.*** eyeglasses with tinted lenses to shade the eyes

sunk (suŋk) ***vi.***, ***vt.*** *pp. & alt. pt. of* SINK

sunk′en (-ən) ***adj.*** **1** submerged **2** below the general level *[a sunken patio]* **3** deeply set; hollow *[sunken cheeks]*

sun′lamp′ ***n.*** an ultraviolet-ray lamp, used for tanning the body, etc.

sun′light′ ***n.*** the light of the sun

sun′lit′ ***adj.*** lighted by the sun

sun′ny (-ē) ***adj.*** **-ni·er, -ni·est** **1** full of sunshine **2** bright; cheerful —**sun′ni·ness** ***n.***

sunny side **1** the sunlit side **2** the brighter aspect —**sunny side up** fried upturned and with unbroken yolk *[two eggs sunny side up]*

sun′rise′ ***n.*** **1** the daily appearance of the sun above the E horizon **2** the varying time of this

sun′roof′ ***n.*** a panel in a car roof, that opens to let in light and air: also **sun roof**

sun′room′ ***n.*** a room with large windows to let in sunlight

sun′screen′ ***n.*** a chemical used in lotions, creams, etc. to block certain ultraviolet rays of the sun and reduce the danger of sunburn

sun′set′ ***n.*** **1** the daily disappearance of

the sun below the W horizon **2** the varying time of this

sun'shine' ***n.*** **1** the shining of the sun **2** the light and heat from the sun **3** a sunny place **4** cheerfulness, happiness, etc. —**sun'shin'y** ***adj.***

sun'spot' ***n.*** any of the temporarily cooler regions appearing cyclically as dark spots on the sun

sun'stroke' ***n.*** a form of heatstroke caused by excessive exposure to the sun

sun'suit' ***n.*** short pants with a bib and shoulder straps, worn by babies and young children

sun'tan' ***n.*** a darkened condition of the skin resulting from exposure to the sun

sun'up' ***n.*** SUNRISE

sup (sup) ***vi.*** **supped**, **sup'ping** ⟦< OFr *soupe,* soup⟧ to have supper

sup- *prefix* SUB-: used before *p*

su·per (sōō'pər) ***n.*** ⟦< fol.⟧ *short for:* **1** SUPERNUMERARY (sense 2) **2** SUPERINTENDENT (sense 2) —***adj.*** **1** [Inf.] outstanding; exceptionally fine **2** great, extreme, or excessive

super- ⟦L < *super,* above⟧ *prefix* **1** over, above *[superstructure]* **2** *a)* surpassing *[superabundant]* *b)* greater or better than others of its kind *[supermarket]* **3** additional *[supertax]*

su'per·a·bun'dant ***adj.*** being more than enough —**su'per·a·bun'dance** ***n.***

su·per·an·nu·at·ed (sōō'pər an'yōō āt' id) ***adj.*** ⟦< L *super,* above + *annus*, year⟧ **1** too old for service **2** retired, esp. with a pension, because of old age **3** obsolete; old-fashioned

su·perb (sə purb', sōō-) ***adj.*** ⟦see SUPER-⟧ **1** noble or majestic **2** rich or magnificent **3** extremely fine; excellent —**su·perb'ly** ***adv.***

su'per·car'go ***n.***, *pl.* **-goes** or **-gos** an officer on a merchant ship in charge of the cargo

su'per·charge' ***vt.*** **-charged'**, **-charg'ing** to increase the power of (an engine), as with a device (**su'per·charg'er**) that forces extra air and fuel into the cylinders

su·per·cil·i·ous (sōō'pər sil'ē əs) ***adj.*** ⟦< L *super-*, above + *cilium,* eyelid, hence (in allusion to raised eyebrows) haughtiness⟧ disdainful or contemptuous; haughty

su'per·con'duc·tiv'i·ty ***n.*** *Physics* the lack of resistance to electrical current in certain metals, etc. when cooled to low temperatures

su'per·con·duc'tor ***n.*** any material that exhibits superconductivity

su'per·e'go ***n.***, *pl.* **-gos** *Psychoanalysis* that part of the psyche that enforces moral standards

su'per·er'o·ga'tion (-er'ə gā'shən) ***n.*** ⟦< L *super-*, above + *erogare*, pay out⟧ a doing more than is needed or expected —**su'per·e·rog'a·to'ry** (-i räg'ə tôr'ē) ***adj.***

su'per·fi'cial (-fish'əl) ***adj.*** ⟦< L *super-*, above + *facies*, face⟧ **1** of or being on the surface **2** concerned with and understanding only the obvious; shallow **3** quick and cursory **4** seeming such only at first glance —**su'per·fi'ci·al'i·ty** (-fish'ē al'ə tē), *pl.* **-ties**, ***n.*** —**su'per·fi'cial·ly** ***adv.***

su·per·flu·ous (sə pur'flōō əs, sōō-) ***adj.*** ⟦< L *super-*, above + *fluere*, to flow⟧ excessive or unnecessary —**su·per·flu·i·ty** (sōō'pər flōō'ə tē), *pl.* **-ties**, ***n.***

su'per·he'ro ***n.***, *pl.* **-roes** a nearly invincible hero, as in comic books

su'per·high'way' ***n.*** EXPRESSWAY

su'per·hu'man ***adj.*** **1** having a nature above that of man; divine **2** greater than that of a normal human being

su'per·im·pose' ***vt.*** **-posed'**, **-pos'ing** to put, lay, or stack on top of something else

su·per·in·tend (sōō'pər in tend') ***vt.*** to act as superintendent of; supervise; manage —**su'per·in·tend'ence** or **su'per·in·tend'en·cy** ***n.***

su'per·in·tend'ent (-ten'dənt) ***n.*** ⟦< LL *superintendere,* superintend⟧ **1** a person in charge of a department, institution, etc.; director **2** a person responsible for the maintenance of a building

su·pe·ri·or (sə pir'ē ər) ***adj.*** ⟦see SUPER-⟧ **1** higher in space, order, rank, etc. **2** greater in quality or value than: with *to* **3** above average in quality; excellent **4** refusing to give in to or be affected by: with *to* **5** showing a feeling of being better than others; haughty —***n.*** **1** a superior person or thing **2** the head of a religious community —**su·pe'ri·or'i·ty** (-ôr'ə tē) ***n.***

Su·pe·ri·or (sə pir'ē ər), **Lake** largest of the Great Lakes, between Michigan & Ontario, Canada

superl *abbrev.* superlative

su·per·la·tive (sə pur'lə tiv, sōō-) ***adj.*** ⟦< L *super-*, above + *latus,* pp. of *ferre,* to bear, carry⟧ **1** superior to all others; supreme **2** *Gram.* designating the extreme degree of comparison of adjectives and adverbs —***n.*** **1** the highest degree; peak **2** *Gram.* the superlative degree *[*"finest" is the *superlative* of "fine"*]* —**su·per'la·tive·ly** ***adv.***

su'per·ma·jor'i·ty ***n.*** the quantity of votes, above a mere majority, required to pass certain bills, etc.

su'per·man' (-man') ***n.***, *pl.* **-men'** (-men') an apparently superhuman man

su'per·mar'ket ***n.*** a large, self-service, retail food store or market

su·per·nal (sōō purn'əl) ***adj.*** ⟦< L *supernus,* upper⟧ celestial or divine

su'per·nat'u·ral ***adj.*** not explainable by the known forces or laws of nature; specif., of or involving God, ghosts, spirits, etc.

su'per·no'va ***n.***, *pl.* **-vas** or **-vae** (-vē) a rare, extremely bright nova

su·per·nu·mer·ar·y (sōō'pər nōō'mə rer' ē) ***n.***, *pl.* **-ies** ⟦< L *super*, above + *numerus*, number⟧ **1** an extra person or thing **2** *Theater* a person with a small, nonspeaking part

su'per·pose' ***vt.*** **-posed'**, **-pos'ing** ⟦see SUPER- & POSE⟧ to place on or above something else —**su'per·pos'a·ble** ***adj.*** —**su'per·po·si'tion** ***n.***

su'per·pow'er ***n.*** an extremely powerful, influential nation

su'per·sat'u·rate' *vt.* **-rat'ed, -rat'ing** to make more highly concentrated than in normal saturation —**su'per·sat'u·ra'tion** *n.*

su'per·script' *n.* ⟦see SUPER- & SCRIPT⟧ a figure, letter, or symbol written above and to the side of another

su·per·sede (sōō'pər sēd') *vt.* **-sed'ed, -sed'ing** ⟦< L *supersedere,* sit over⟧ to replace or succeed

su'per·son'ic *adj.* ⟦SUPER- + SONIC⟧ **1** designating, of, or moving at a speed greater than that of sound **2** ULTRASONIC

su'per·star' *n.* a star performer, as in sports or entertainment

su·per·sti·tion (sōō'pər stish'ən) *n.* ⟦< L *superstitio,* lit., a standing (in awe) over⟧ **1** any belief that is inconsistent with known facts or rational thought, esp. such a belief in omens, the supernatural, etc. **2** any action or practice based on such a belief —**su'per·sti'tious** *adj.*

su'per·store' *n.* a very large retail store with a wide variety of goods

su'per·struc'ture *n.* **1** a structure built on top of another **2** that part of a building above the foundation **3** that part of a ship above the main deck

su'per·tank'er *n.* an extremely large tanker, of 300,000 tons or more

su·per·vene (sōō'pər vēn') *vi.* **-vened', -ven'ing** ⟦< L *super-,* over + *venire,* come⟧ to come or happen as something extraneous or unexpected

su·per·vise (sōō'pər vīz') *vt., vi.* **-vised', -vis'ing** ⟦< L *super-,* over + *videre,* see⟧ to oversee or direct (work, workers, etc.) —**su'per·vi'sion** (-vizh'ən) *n.* —**su'per·vi'sor** *n.* —**su'per·vi'so·ry** *adj.*

su·pine (sōō pīn') *adj.* ⟦L *supinus*⟧ **1** lying on the back, face upward **2** inactive; sluggish; listless

supp or **suppl** *abbrev.* **1** supplement **2** supplementary

sup·per (sup'ər) *n.* ⟦see SUP⟧ an evening meal

supper club an expensive nightclub

sup·plant (sə plant') *vt.* ⟦< L *sub-,* under + *planta,* sole of the foot⟧ **1** to take the place of, esp. by force or plotting **2** to remove in order to replace with something else

sup·ple (sup'əl) *adj.* **-pler, -plest** ⟦< L *supplex,* submissive⟧ **1** easily bent; flexible **2** lithe; limber **3** adaptable

sup·ple·ment (sup'lə mənt; *for v.,* -ment') *n.* ⟦see SUPPLY⟧ **1** something added, esp. to make up for a lack **2** a section of additional material in a book, newspaper, etc. —*vt.* to provide a supplement to —**sup'ple·men'tal** or **sup'ple·men'ta·ry** *adj.*

sup·pli·ant (sup'lē ənt) *n.* one who supplicates —*adj.* supplicating

sup'pli·cant (-lə kənt) *adj., n.* SUPPLIANT

sup·pli·cate (sup'lə kāt') *vt., vi.* **-cat'ed, -cat'ing** ⟦< L *sub-,* under + *plicare,* to fold⟧ **1** to ask for (something) humbly **2** to make a humble request (of) —**sup'pli·ca'tion** *n.*

sup·ply (sə plī') *vt.* **-plied', -ply'ing** ⟦< L *sub-,* under + *plere,* fill⟧ **1** to furnish or provide (what is needed) to (someone) **2** to compensate for (a deficiency, etc.); make good —*n., pl.* **-plies' 1** the amount available for use or sale; stock **2** [*pl.*] needed materials, provisions, etc. —**sup·pli'er** *n.*

sup·ply'-side' *adj.* designating or of an economic theory that an increase in money for investment, as supplied by lowering taxes, will stimulate economic growth

sup·port (sə pôrt') *vt.* ⟦< L *sub-,* under + *portare,* carry⟧ **1** to carry the weight of; hold up **2** to encourage; help **3** to advocate; uphold **4** to maintain (a person, institution, etc.) with money or subsistence **5** to help prove, vindicate, etc. **6** to bear; endure **7** to keep up; maintain **8** to have a role subordinate to (a star) in a play —*n.* **1** a supporting or being supported **2** a person or thing that supports **3** a means of maintaining a livelihood —**sup·port'a·ble** *adj.* —**sup·port'er** *n.*

sup·port'ive *adj.* giving support or help

sup·pose (sə pōz') *vt.* **-posed', -pos'ing** ⟦< L *sub-,* under + *ponere,* put⟧ **1** to assume to be true, as for argument's sake **2** to believe, think, etc. **3** to consider as a possibility *[suppose* I go*]* **4** to expect *[*I'm *supposed* to sing*]* —*vi.* to conjecture —**sup·posed'** *adj.* —**sup·pos'ed·ly** *adv.*

sup·po·si·tion (sup'ə zish'ən) *n.* **1** a supposing **2** something supposed

sup·pos·i·to·ry (sə päz'ə tôr'ē) *n., pl.* **-ries** ⟦see SUPPOSE⟧ a small piece of medicated substance placed in the rectum or vagina, where it melts

sup·press (sə pres') *vt.* ⟦< L *sub-,* under + *premere,* to press⟧ **1** to put down by force; quell **2** to keep from being known, published, etc. **3** to keep back; restrain —**sup·pres'sion** (-presh'ən) *n.*

sup·pres'sant (-ənt) *n.* a drug, etc. that tends to suppress an action, condition, etc.

sup·pu·rate (sup'yōō rāt') *vi.* **-rat'ed, -rat'ing** ⟦< L *sub-,* under + *pus,* pus⟧ to form or discharge pus

supra- ⟦< L *supra,* above⟧ *prefix* above, over, beyond

su·pra·na·tion·al (sōō'prə nash'ə nəl) *adj.* of, for, or above all or a number of nations

su·prem·a·cist (sə prem'ə sist, sōō-) *n.* one who believes in the supremacy of a particular group

su·prem'a·cy (-sē) *n., pl.* **-cies** supreme condition or power

su·preme' (-prēm') *adj.* ⟦< L *superus,* that is above⟧ **1** highest in rank, power, etc. **2** highest in quality, achievement, etc. **3** highest in degree **4** final; ultimate —**su·preme'ly** *adv.*

Supreme Being God

Supreme Court 1 the highest U.S. federal court **2** the highest court in most U.S. states

Supreme Soviet 1 a part of the legislature of Russia **2** formerly, the parliament of the U.S.S.R.

Supt *abbrev.* Superintendent

sur- ⟦< L *super*, over⟧ *prefix* over, upon, above, beyond

sur·cease (sur′sēs′) ***n.*** ⟦< L *supersedere*, refrain from⟧ an end, or cessation

sur·charge (sur′chärj′) ***vt.* -charged′, -charg′ing** ⟦see SUR- & CHARGE⟧ **1** to overcharge **2** to mark (a postage stamp) with a surcharge —***n.*** **1** an additional charge **2** a new valuation printed over the original valuation on a postage stamp

sur·cin·gle (sur′siŋ′gəl) ***n.*** ⟦< OFr *sur-*, over + L *cingulum*, a belt⟧ a strap passed around a horse's body to bind on a saddle, pack, etc.

sure (shoor) ***adj.* sur′er, sur′est** ⟦< L *securus*⟧ **1** that will not fail *[a sure method]* **2** that cannot be doubted or questioned **3** having no doubt; confident *[sure of the facts]* **4** that can be counted on to be or happen *[a sure defeat]* **5** certain (to do, be, etc.) *[sure to lose]* —***adv.*** [Inf.] certainly; indeed —**for sure** certain(ly) —**sure enough** [Inf.] without doubt —**sure′ness *n.***

sure′fire′ or **sure′-fire′** ***adj.*** [Inf.] sure to be successful or as expected

sure′-foot′ed ***adj.*** not likely to stumble, slip, fall, or err —**sure′-foot′ed·ness *n.***

sure′ly ***adv.*** **1** with confidence **2** without a doubt; certainly

sur·e·ty (shoor′ə tē, shoor′tē) ***n.***, *pl.* **-ties** **1** something that gives assurance, as against loss, etc. **2** one who takes responsibility for another

surf (surf) ***n.*** ⟦prob. var. of SOUGH⟧ the waves of the sea breaking on the shore or a reef —***vi.*** to engage in surfing —***vt.*** [Inf.] to browse a succession of (TV channels, websites, etc.) on (a TV, computer network, etc.) —**surf′er *n.***

sur·face (sur′fis) ***n.*** ⟦< Fr *sur-*, over + *face*, a face⟧ **1** *a)* the exterior of an object *b)* any of the faces of a solid **2** superficial features or outward appearance —***adj.*** **1** of, on, or at the surface **2** external; superficial —***vt.* -faced, -fac·ing** to give a surface to, as in paving —***vi.*** **1** to rise to the surface of the water **2** to become known

surf′board′ ***n.*** a long, narrow board used in the sport of surfing

surf′-cast′ ***vi.* -cast′, -cast′ing** to fish by casting into the surf from or near the shore

sur·feit (sur′fit) ***n.*** ⟦< OFr *sorfaire*, overdo⟧ **1** too great an amount **2** overindulgence, esp. in food or drink **3** disgust, nausea, etc. resulting from excess —***vt.*** to feed or supply to excess

surf·ing (sur′fiŋ) ***n.*** the sport of riding in toward shore on the crest of a wave, esp. on a surfboard

surge (surj) ***n.*** ⟦< L *surgere*, to rise⟧ **1** a large wave of water, or its motion **2** a sudden, strong increase, as of power —***vi.* surged, surg′ing** **1** to move in or as in a surge **2** to increase suddenly

sur·geon (sur′jən) ***n.*** a doctor who specializes in surgery

sur·ger·y (sur′jər ē) ***n.***, *pl.* **-ger·ies** ⟦< Gr *cheir*, the hand + *ergein*, to work⟧ **1** the treatment of disease, injury, etc. by manual or instrumental operations **2** a

room used for this

sur′gi·cal (-ji kəl) ***adj.*** **1** of surgeons or surgery **2** very accurate, precisely targeted, etc. —**sur′gi·cal·ly *adv.***

sur·gi·cen·ter (sur′jə sent′ər) ***n.*** ⟦< *Surgicenter*, a service mark⟧ a facility for performing minor surgery on outpatients

Su·ri·name (soor′i näm′) country in NE South America: 63,251 sq. mi.; pop. 355,000: formerly **Su′ri·nam′**

sur·ly (sur′lē) ***adj.* -li·er, -li·est** ⟦earlier *sirly*, imperious < *sir*, sir⟧ bad-tempered; sullenly rude

sur·mise (sər mīz′) ***n.*** ⟦OFr *sur-*, upon + *mettre*, put⟧ a conjecture —***vt.*, *vi.*** **-mised′, -mis′ing** to guess

sur·mount (sər mount′) ***vt.*** ⟦SUR- & MOUNT[2]⟧ **1** to overcome (a difficulty) **2** to be at the top of; rise above **3** to climb up and across (a height, etc.) —**sur·mount′a·ble *adj.***

sur·name (sur′nām′) ***n.*** ⟦< OFr *sur-* (see SUR-) + *nom*, name⟧ the family name, or last name

sur·pass (sər pas′) ***vt.*** ⟦< Fr *sur-* (see SUR-) + *passer*, to pass⟧ **1** to excel or be superior to **2** to go beyond the limit, capacity, etc. of

SURPLICE

sur·plice (sur′plis) ***n.*** ⟦< L *super-*, above + *pelliceum*, fur robe⟧ a loose, white outer ecclesiastical vestment

sur·plus (sur′plus′) ***n.*** ⟦< OFr *sur-*, above (see SUR-) + L *plus*, more⟧ a quantity over and above what is needed or used —***adj.*** excess; extra

sur·prise (sər prīz′) ***vt.* -prised′, -pris′ing** ⟦< OFr *sur-* (see SUR-) + *prendre*, to take⟧ **1** to come upon suddenly or unexpectedly; take unawares **2** to amaze; astonish —***n.*** **1** a being surprised **2** something that surprises

sur·re·al (sə rē′əl) ***adj.*** **1** of or like surrealism **2** bizarre; fantastic

sur·re′al·ism′ ***n.*** ⟦see SUR- & REAL⟧ a modern movement in the arts in which the workings of the unconscious are depicted —**sur·re′al·is′tic *adj.*** —**sur·re′al·ist *adj.*, *n.***

sur·ren·der (sə ren′dər) ***vt.*** ⟦< Fr *sur-*, up + *rendre*, render⟧ **1** to give up possession of; yield to another on compulsion **2** to give up or abandon —***vi.*** to give oneself up, esp. as a prisoner —***n.*** the act of surrendering

sur·rep·ti·tious (sur'əp tish'əs) ***adj.*** ⟦< L *sub-*, under + *rapere,* seize⟧ done, gotten, acting, etc. in a stealthy way

sur·rey (sur'ē) ***n.,*** *pl.* **-reys** ⟦after *Surrey,* county in England⟧ a light, four-wheeled carriage with two seats and a flat top

sur·ro·gate (sur'ə git, -gāt') ***n.*** ⟦< L *sub-*, in place of + *rogare,* ask⟧ **1** a deputy or substitute **2** in some U.S. states, a probate court judge **3** a woman who bears a child for another woman, who will raise it —**sur'ro·ga·cy**, *pl.* **-cies**, ***n.***

sur·round (sə round') ***vt.*** ⟦< L *super-*, over + *undare,* to rise⟧ to encircle on all or nearly all sides

sur·round'ings ***pl.n.*** the things, conditions, etc. around a person or thing

sur·tax (sur'taks') ***n.*** an extra tax on top of the regular tax

sur·veil·lance (sər vā'ləns) ***n.*** ⟦Fr < *sur-* (see SUR-) + *veiller,* to watch⟧ close watch kept over someone, esp. a suspect

sur·vey (sər vā'; *for n.* sur'vā') ***vt.*** ⟦< OFr *sur-* (see SUR-) + *veoir,* see⟧ **1** to examine or consider in detail or comprehensively **2** to determine the location, form, or boundaries of (a tract of land) —***n.,*** *pl.* **-veys** **1** a detailed study, as by gathering information and analyzing it **2** a general view **3** *a)* the process of surveying a tract of land *b)* a written description of this —**sur·vey'or** ***n.***

sur·vey'ing ***n.*** the science or work of making land surveys

sur·viv·al·ist (sər vī'vəl ist) ***n.*** one who takes measures, as storing food and weapons, to ensure survival after an economic collapse, nuclear war, etc.

sur·vive (sər vīv') ***vt.*** **-vived', -viv'ing** ⟦< L *super-*, above + *vivere,* to live⟧ to remain alive or in existence after —***vi.*** to continue living or existing —**sur·viv'al** ***n.***

sur·vi'vor (-ər) ***n.*** **1** one that survives **2** someone regarded as capable of surviving changing conditions, misfortune, etc.

sus·cep·ti·ble (sə sep'tə bəl) ***adj.*** ⟦< L *sus-*, under + *capere,* take⟧ easily affected emotionally —**susceptible of** admitting; allowing *[*testimony *susceptible of* error*]* —**susceptible to** easily influenced or affected by —**sus·cep'ti·bil'i·ty** ***n.***

su·shi (so͞o'shē) ***n.*** ⟦Jpn⟧ a dish consisting of small cakes of cold rice garnished with raw or cooked fish, vegetables, etc.

sus·pect (sə spekt'; *for adj. & n.* sus'pekt') ***vt.*** ⟦< L *sus-*, under + *spicere,* to look⟧ **1** to believe to be guilty on little or no evidence **2** to believe to be bad, wrong, etc.; distrust **3** to guess; surmise —***adj.*** suspected —***n.*** one suspected of a crime, etc.

sus·pend (sə spend') ***vt.*** ⟦< L *sus-*, under + *pendere,* hang⟧ **1** to exclude as a penalty from an office, school, etc., for a time **2** to stop temporarily **3** to hold back (judgment, etc.) **4** to hang by a support from above **5** to hold in place as though hanging *[*dust particles *suspended* in the air*]*

suspended animation a temporary cessation of the vital functions, resembling death

sus·pend'ers ***pl.n.*** a pair of straps passed over the shoulders to hold up trousers

sus·pense (sə spens') ***n.*** ⟦< L *suspendere,* suspend⟧ **1** a state of uncertainty **2** the growing excitement felt while awaiting a climax of a novel, play, etc. —**sus·pense'ful** ***adj.***

sus·pen·sion (sə spen'shən) ***n.*** **1** a suspending or being suspended **2** the system of springs, etc. supporting a vehicle upon its undercarriage or axles **3** a substance whose particles are dispersed through a fluid but not dissolved in it

suspension bridge a bridge suspended from cables anchored at either end and supported by towers at intervals

sus·pi·cion (sə spish'ən) ***n.*** ⟦< L *suspicere,* suspect⟧ **1** a suspecting **2** the feeling or state of mind of one who suspects **3** a very small amount; trace —***vt.*** [Inf. or Dial.] to suspect

sus·pi'cious ***adj.*** **1** arousing suspicion **2** showing or feeling suspicion —**sus·pi'cious·ly** ***adv.***

sus·tain (sə stān') ***vt.*** ⟦< L *sus-*, under + *tenere,* to hold⟧ **1** to keep in existence; maintain or prolong **2** to provide sustenance for **3** to carry the weight of; support **4** to endure; withstand **5** to comfort or encourage **6** to suffer (an injury, loss, etc.) **7** to uphold the validity of **8** to confirm; corroborate

sus·te·nance (sus'tə nəns) ***n.*** **1** a sustaining **2** means of livelihood **3** nourishment; food

sut·ler (sut'lər) ***n.*** ⟦< 16th-c. Du *soeteler*⟧ [Historical] a person following an army to sell things to its soldiers

su·ture (so͞o'chər) ***n.*** ⟦< L *suere,* sew⟧ **1** the line of junction of two parts, esp. of bones of the skull **2** *a)* the stitching together of the two edges of a wound or incision *b)* the thread, etc. used or any of the stitches so made

SUV *abbrev.* SPORT UTILITY VEHICLE

su·ze·rain (so͞o'zə rin', -rān') ***n.*** ⟦Fr < L *sursum,* above⟧ **1** a feudal lord **2** a state in relation to another over which it has some political control

svelte (svelt) ***adj.*** ⟦Fr⟧ **1** slender; lithe **2** suave

Sw *abbrev.* **1** Sweden **2** Swedish

SW *abbrev.* **1** southwest **2** southwestern

swab (swäb) ***n.*** ⟦< Du *zwabben,* do dirty work⟧ **1** a yarn mop **2** a small piece of cotton, etc. used to medicate or cleanse a bodily orifice or a wound —***vt.*** **swabbed, swab'bing** to use a swab on

swad·dle (swäd''l) ***vt.*** **-dled, -dling** ⟦prob. < OE *swathian,* swathe⟧ to wrap (a newborn baby) in a blanket or, formerly, in long, narrow bands of cloth (**swaddling clothes**)

swag (swag) ***vt.*** **swagged, swag'ging** ⟦see SWAGGER⟧ to hang in a swag —***n.*** **1** a valance, garland, etc. hanging decoratively in a curve **2** [Slang] loot

swage (swāj) ***n.*** a tool for bending or shaping metal

swag·ger (swag′ər) ***vi.*** ⟦prob. < Norw *svagga,* sway⟧ **1** to walk with a bold, arrogant stride **2** to boast or brag loudly —***n.*** swaggering walk or manner

Swa·hi·li (swä hē′lē) ***n.*** ⟦< Ar *sawāḥil,* the coasts⟧ a Bantu language of E Africa

swain (swān) ***n.*** ⟦< ON *sveinn,* boy⟧ [Archaic] **1** a country youth **2** a lover

swal·low[1] (swä′lō) ***n.*** ⟦OE *swealwe*⟧ a small, swift-flying bird with long, pointed wings and a forked tail

swal·low[2] (swä′lō) ***vt.*** ⟦OE *swelgan*⟧ **1** to pass (food, etc.) from the mouth into the stomach **2** to take in; absorb: often with *up* **3** to retract (words said) **4** to put up with *[to swallow* insults*]* **5** to suppress *[to swallow* one's pride*]* **6** [Inf.] to accept as true without question —***vi.*** to perform the actions of swallowing something, esp. as a result of emotion —***n.*** **1** a swallowing **2** the amount swallowed at one time

swam (swam) ***vi., vt.*** *pt. of* SWIM[1] & SWIM[2]

swa·mi (swä′mē) ***n.,*** *pl.* **-mis** ⟦< Sans *svāmin,* lord⟧ **1** lord; master: title of respect for a Hindu religious teacher **2** a learned man; pundit

swamp (swämp, swômp) ***n.*** ⟦prob. < LowG⟧ a piece of wet, spongy land; marsh; bog —***vt.*** **1** to plunge or sink in a swamp, water, etc. **2** to flood as with water **3** to overwhelm *[swamped* by debts*]* **4** to sink (a boat) by filling with water —**swamp′y, -i·er, -i·est,** ***adj.***

swan (swän, swôn) ***n.*** ⟦OE⟧ a large waterfowl, usually white, with a long, graceful neck

swank (swaŋk) [Inf.] ***n.*** ⟦akin to OE *swancor,* pliant⟧ ostentatious display —***adj.*** ostentatiously stylish

swank′y ***adj.*** **-i·er, -i·est** [Inf.] ostentatiously stylish

swan's′-down′ ***n.*** **1** the soft down of the swan, used for trimming clothes, etc. **2** a soft, thick flannel Also sp. **swans′down′**

swan song ⟦after the song sung, in ancient fable, by a dying swan⟧ the last act, final creative work, etc. of a person

swap (swäp, swôp) [Inf.] ***vt., vi.*** **swapped, swap′ping,** ***n.*** ⟦ME *swappen,* to strike⟧ trade; barter

sward (swôrd) ***n.*** ⟦< OE *sweard,* a skin⟧ grass-covered soil; turf

swarm (swôrm) ***n.*** ⟦OE *swearm*⟧ **1** a large number of bees, led by a queen, leaving a hive to start a new colony **2** a colony of bees in a hive **3** a moving mass, crowd, or throng —***vi.*** **1** to fly off in a swarm: said of bees **2** to move, be present, etc. in large numbers **3** to be crowded

swarth·y (swôr′thē, -thē) ***adj.*** **-i·er, -i·est** ⟦< OE *sweart*⟧ having a dark complexion

swash′buck′ler (-buk′lər) ***n.*** ⟦< *swash,* to swagger + *buckler,* a shield⟧ a blustering, swaggering fighting man —**swash′buck′ling** ***n., adj.***

swas·ti·ka (swäs′ti kə) ***n.*** ⟦< Sans *svasti,* well-being⟧ **1** an ancient design and mystic symbol in the form of a cross with four equal arms, each bent in a right angle **2** this design with the arms bent clockwise, used as an emblem of Nazism and anti-Semitism

swat (swät) ***vt.*** **swat′ted, swat′ting** ⟦echoic⟧ to hit with a quick, sharp blow —***n.*** a quick, sharp blow —**swat′ter** ***n.***

SWAT (swät) ***n.*** ⟦S(*pecial*) W(*eapons*) *a*(*nd*) *T*(*actics*)⟧ a special police unit trained to deal with violence, riots, terrorism, etc.: in full **SWAT team**

swatch (swäch) ***n.*** ⟦orig., a cloth tag or label⟧ a sample piece of cloth, etc.

swath (swäth, swôth) ***n.*** ⟦OE *swathu,* a track⟧ **1** the width covered with one cut of a scythe or other mowing device **2** a strip, row, etc. that has been mowed

swathe (swāth, swāth) ***vt.*** **swathed, swath′ing** ⟦OE *swathian*⟧ **1** to wrap up in a long strip of cloth **2** to envelop; enclose

sway (swā) ***vi.*** ⟦< ON *sveigja,* to turn, bend⟧ **1** to swing or move from side to side or to and fro **2** to lean or go to one side —***vt.*** **1** to cause to sway **2** to influence —***n.*** **1** a swaying or being swayed **2** influence *[the sway* of passion*]* —**hold sway** to reign or prevail

sway′backed′ (-bakt′) ***adj.*** having a sagging spine: said as of some horses

Swa·zi·land (swä′zē land′) country in SE Africa: 6,705 sq. mi.; pop. 681,000

swear (swer) ***vi.*** **swore, sworn, swear′ing** ⟦OE *swerian*⟧ **1** to make a solemn declaration with an appeal to God to confirm it **2** to make a solemn promise; vow **3** to use profane language; curse —***vt.*** to declare, pledge, or vow on oath —**swear in** to administer an oath to (a person taking office, a witness, etc.) —**swear off** to renounce —**swear out** to obtain (a warrant for arrest) by making a charge under oath —**swear′er** ***n.***

swear′word′ ***n.*** a profane word or phrase

sweat (swet) ***vi., vt.*** **sweat** or **sweat′ed, sweat′ing** ⟦< OE *swat,* sweat⟧ **1** to give forth or cause to give forth a salty moisture through the pores of the skin; perspire **2** to give forth or condense (moisture) on its surface **3** to work hard enough to cause sweating —***n.*** **1** the salty liquid given forth in perspiration **2** moisture collected in droplets on a surface **3** a sweating or being sweated **4** a condition of eagerness, anxiety, etc. **5** [*pl.*] clothes worn for exercising, etc.; specif., a sweat suit —**sweat out** [Inf.] **1** to get rid of by sweating *[to sweat out* a cold*]* **2** to wait anxiously for or through —**sweat′y, -i·er, -i·est,** ***adj.***

sweat′er ***n.*** a knitted or crocheted outer garment for the upper body

sweat shirt a heavy, long-sleeved pullover of cotton jersey worn to absorb sweat during or after exercise, sometimes with matching loose trousers (**sweat pants**) in an ensemble (**sweat suit**)

sweat'shop' ***n.*** a shop where employees work long hours at low wages under poor conditions

Swed *abbrev.* **1** Sweden **2** Swedish

Swede (swēd) ***n.*** a person born or living in Sweden

Swe·den (swēd''n) country in N Europe: 173,732 sq. mi.; pop. 8,587,000

Swed·ish (swē'dish) ***adj.*** of Sweden or its people, language, etc. —***n.*** the Germanic language of Sweden

sweep (swēp) ***vt.* swept, sweep'ing** ⟦OE *swapan*⟧ **1** to clean (a floor, etc.) as by brushing with a broom **2** to remove (dirt, etc.) as with a broom **3** to strip, carry away, or destroy with a forceful movement **4** to touch in moving across *[*hands *sweeping* the keyboard*]* **5** to pass swiftly over or across **6** *a)* to win all the games of (a series, etc.) *b)* to win overwhelmingly —***vi.*** **1** to clean a floor, etc. as with a broom **2** to move steadily with speed or grace **3** to extend in a long curve or line *[*a road *sweeping* up the hill*]* —***n.*** **1** the act of sweeping **2** a steady sweeping movement **3** range or scope **4** extent, as of land; stretch **5** a line, curve, etc. that seems to flow or move **6** one whose work is sweeping *[*a chimney *sweep]* —**sweep'er** ***n.*** —**sweep'ing** ***adj.*** —**sweep'ing·ly** ***adv.***

sweep'ings ***pl.n.*** things swept up, as litter from a floor

sweep'stakes' ***n.***, *pl.* **-stakes'** a lottery in which each participant puts up money in a common fund that is given as the prize to the winner or winners, as determined by the result of a horse race or other contest: also **sweep'stake'**

sweet (swēt) ***adj.*** ⟦OE *swete*⟧ **1** having a taste of, or like that of, sugar **2** *a)* having an agreeable taste, smell, sound, etc. *b)* gratifying *c)* friendly, kind, etc. **3** *a)* not rancid or sour *b)* not salty or salted —***n.*** [*pl.*] sweet foods —**sweet'ish** ***adj.*** —**sweet'ly** ***adv.*** —**sweet'ness** ***n.***

sweet'bread' (-bred') ***n.*** the thymus or sometimes the pancreas of a calf, lamb, etc., when used as food: *usually used in pl.*

sweet'bri'er or **sweet'bri'ar** (-brī'ər) ***n.*** EGLANTINE

sweet corn a variety of Indian corn eaten unripe as a table vegetable

sweet'en ***vt.*** **1** to make sweet **2** to make pleasant or agreeable **3** [Inf.] to increase the value of (collateral, an offer, etc.)

sweet'en·er ***n.*** a sweetening agent, esp. a synthetic one, as saccharin

sweet'heart' ***n.*** a loved one; lover

sweetheart contract a contract arranged by collusion between union officials and an employer with terms disadvantageous to union members

sweet'meat' ***n.*** a candy

sweet pea a climbing plant with butterfly-shaped flowers

sweet pepper **1** a red pepper plant producing a large, mild fruit **2** the fruit

sweet potato **1** a tropical plant with a fleshy, brownish root used as a vegetable **2** its root

sweet'-talk' ***vt.*, *vi.*** [Inf.] to talk in a flattering way (to)

sweet tooth [Inf.] a fondness or craving for sweets

swell (swel) ***vi.*, *vt.* swelled, swelled** or **swol'len, swell'ing** ⟦OE *swellan*⟧ **1** to expand as a result of pressure from within **2** to curve out; bulge **3** to fill (*with* pride, etc.) **4** to increase in size, force, intensity, loudness, etc. —***n.*** **1** a part that swells; specif., a large, rolling wave **2** an increase in size, amount, degree, etc. **3** a crescendo —***adj.*** [Slang] excellent

swell'head' ***n.*** [Inf.] a conceited person —**swell'head'ed** ***adj.***

swell'ing ***n.*** **1** an increase in size, volume, etc. **2** a swollen part

swel·ter (swel'tər) ***vi.*** ⟦< OE *sweltan,* to die, faint⟧ to feel uncomfortably hot; sweat, feel weak, etc. from great heat

swel'ter·ing ***adj.*** very hot; sultry

swept (swept) ***vt.*, *vi.*** *pt. & pp. of* SWEEP

swept'back' ***adj.*** having a backward slant: said of the wings of an aircraft

swerve (swurv) ***vi.*, *vt.* swerved, swerv'ing** ⟦< OE *sweorfan,* to scour⟧ to turn aside from a straight line, course, etc. —***n.*** a swerving

swift (swift) ***adj.*** ⟦OE⟧ **1** moving with great speed; fast **2** coming, acting, etc. quickly —***n.*** a swift-flying, swallowlike bird —**swift'ly** ***adv.*** —**swift'ness** ***n.***

Swift (swift), **Jon·a·than** (jän'ə thən) 1667-1745; Eng. satirist, born in Ireland

swig (swig) [Inf.] ***vt.*, *vi.* swigged, swig'ging** ⟦< ?⟧ to drink in gulps —***n.*** a big gulp, as of liquor

swill (swil) ***vt.*, *vi.*** ⟦OE *swilian*⟧ **1** to drink greedily **2** to feed swill to (pigs, etc.) —***n.*** **1** liquid garbage fed to pigs **2** garbage

swim[1] (swim) ***vi.* swam, swum, swim'ming** ⟦OE *swimman*⟧ **1** to move through water by moving arms, legs, fins, etc. **2** to move along smoothly **3** to float on or in a liquid **4** to overflow *[*eyes *swimming* with tears*]* —***vt.*** to swim in or across —***n.*** the act of swimming —***adj.*** [Inf.] of or for swimming *[swim* trunks*]* —**in the swim** active in what is popular at the moment —**swim'mer** ***n.***

swim[2] (swim) ***n.*** ⟦OE *swima*⟧ a dizzy spell —***vi.* swam, swum, swim'ming** **1** to be dizzy **2** to seem to whirl *[*the room *swam* before me*]*

swimming hole a deep place in a river, creek, etc. used for swimming

swim'ming·ly ***adv.*** easily and with success

swim'suit' ***n.*** a garment worn for swimming

swin·dle (swin'dəl) ***vt.*, *vi.* -dled, -dling** ⟦< Ger *schwindeln*⟧ to defraud (another) of money or property; cheat —***n.*** an act of swindling; trick; fraud —**swin'dler** ***n.***

swine (swīn) ***n.*, *pl.* swine** ⟦OE *swin*⟧ **1** a pig or hog: usually used collectively **2**

a vicious, contemptible person

swing (swiŋ) ***vi.*** **swung, swing'ing** ⟦OE *swingan*⟧ **1** to sway or move backward and forward **2** to walk, trot, etc. with relaxed movements **3** to strike (*at*) **4** to turn, as on a hinge **5** to move in a curve **6** to hang; be suspended **7** [Slang] *a)* to be ultra-fashionable, esp. in seeking pleasure *b)* to engage in casual sexual relations —***vt.*** **1** to move, lift, etc. with a sweeping motion **2** to cause to move backward and forward **3** to cause to turn, as on a hinge **4** to cause to move in a curve *[swing* the car around*]* **5** [Inf.] to cause to come about successfully *[*to *swing* an election*]* —***n.*** **1** a swinging **2** the arc through which something swings **3** the manner of swinging a golf club, etc. **4** a relaxed motion, as in walking **5** a sweeping blow **6** the course of some activity, etc. **7** rhythm, as of music **8** a seat hanging from ropes, etc. on which one can swing **9** a trip or tour **10** jazz (*c.* 1935-45) characterized by large bands and written arrangements —***adj.*** having decisive power, as in determining an election *[*the *swing* vote*]*

swing'er ***n.*** [Slang] a sophisticated, uninhibited, pleasure-seeking person

swing shift [Inf.] the evening work shift, commonly from 4:00 P.M. to midnight

swipe (swīp) ***n.*** ⟦prob. var. of SWEEP⟧ [Inf.] **1** a hard, sweeping blow **2** a sweeping motion —***vt.*** **swiped, swip'ing** **1** [Inf.] to hit with a swipe **2** [Inf.] to pass across or through with a sweeping motion **3** [Slang] to steal

swirl (swurl) ***vi., vt.*** ⟦ME (Scot) *swyrl*⟧ to move or cause to move with a whirling motion —***n.*** **1** a whirl; eddy **2** a twist; curl —**swirl'y** ***adj.***

swish (swish) ***vi.*** ⟦echoic⟧ **1** to move with a sharp, hissing sound: said as of a cane swung through the air **2** to move with a light, brushing sound: said as of skirts in walking —***vt.*** **1** to cause to swish **2** to move (liquid), esp. in the mouth, with a hissing or gurgling sound —***n.*** a swishing sound or movement

Swiss (swis) ***adj.*** of Switzerland or its people, etc. —***n.***, *pl.* **Swiss** a person born or living in Switzerland

Swiss chard CHARD

Swiss (cheese) a hard, pale-yellow cheese with many large holes

Swiss steak a thick cut of round steak pounded with flour and braised with vegetables

switch (swich) ***n.*** ⟦Early Modern Eng *swits*⟧ **1** a thin, flexible stick used for whipping **2** a separate tress of hair, used as part of a coiffure **3** a device used to open, close, or divert an electric circuit **4** a device used to transfer a train from one track to another **5** a shift; change —***vt.*** **1** to whip as with a switch **2** to jerk sharply *[*the cow *switched* its tail*]* **3** to shift; change **4** to turn (an electric light, etc.) *on* or *off* **5** to transfer (a train, etc.) to another track **6** [Inf.] to change or exchange —***vi.*** to shift —**switch'er** ***n.***

switch'back' ***n.*** a road or railroad following a zigzag course up a steep grade

switch'blade' (knife) a large jackknife that snaps open when a release button is pressed

switch'board' ***n.*** a panel for controlling a system of electric circuits, as in a telephone exchange

switch'-hit'ter ***n.*** a baseball player who can bat right-handed and left-handed

Swit·zer·land (swit'sər lənd) country in WC Europe: 15,880 sq. mi.; pop. 6,366,000

swiv·el (swiv'əl) ***n.*** ⟦< OE *swifan,* to revolve⟧ a coupling device that allows free turning of the parts attached to it —***vi., vt.*** **-eled** or **-elled, -el·ing** or **-el·ling** to turn or cause to turn on or as on a swivel or pivot

swiz·zle stick (swiz'əl) ⟦< ?⟧ a small rod for stirring mixed drinks

swob (swäb) ***n., vt.*** **swobbed, swob'bing** *alt. sp. of* SWAB

swol·len (swōl'ən) ***vi., vt.*** *alt. pp. of* SWELL —***adj.*** blown up; distended; bulging

swoon (swo͞on) ***vi., n.*** ⟦< OE *geswogen,* unconscious⟧ FAINT

swoop (swo͞op) ***vi.*** ⟦< OE *swapan,* sweep along⟧ to pounce or sweep (*down* or *upon*), as a bird does in hunting —***n.*** the act of swooping

swop (swäp) ***vt., vi.*** **swopped, swop'ping,** ***n.*** [Chiefly Brit.] *alt. sp. of* SWAP

sword (sôrd) ***n.*** ⟦OE *sweord*⟧ a hand weapon with a long, sharp-pointed blade set in a hilt —**at swords' points** ready to quarrel or fight

SWORDFISH

sword'fish' ***n.***, *pl.* **-fish'** a large marine food fish with an upper jawbone extending in a swordlike point

sword'play' ***n.*** the act or skill of using a sword, as in fencing

swords·man (sôrdz'mən) ***n.***, *pl.* **-men** one skilled in using a sword

swore (swôr) ***vi., vt.*** *pt. of* SWEAR

sworn (swôrn) ***vi., vt.*** *pp. of* SWEAR —***adj.*** bound, pledged, etc. by or as by an oath

swum (swum) ***vi., vt.*** *pp. of* SWIM[1] & SWIM[2]

swung (swuŋ) ***vi., vt.*** *pp. & pt. of* SWING

syb·a·rite (sib'ə rīt') ***n.*** ⟦after *Sybaris,* ancient Gr city in Italy⟧ anyone very fond of luxury and pleasure —**syb'a·rit'ic** (-rit'ik) ***adj.***

syc·a·more (sik'ə môr') ***n.*** ⟦< Gr *sykomoros,* a fig tree mentioned in the Bible⟧ **1** a maple tree of Europe and Asia **2** an American tree with bark that sheds in patches

syc·o·phant (sik'ə fənt) ***n.*** ⟦< Gr *sykophantēs,* informer⟧ one who seeks favor by flattering people of wealth or influence —**syc'o·phan·cy** ***n.***

Syd·ney (sid'nē) seaport in SE Australia: pop. 3,365,000

syl·lab·i·cate (si lab′i kāt′) ***vt.* -cat′ed, -cat′ing** SYLLABIFY —**syl·lab′i·ca′tion *n.***

syl·lab·i·fy (si lab′ə fī′) ***vt.* -fied′, -fy′ing** ⟦ult. < L *syllaba,* syllable + *facere,* make⟧ to form or divide into syllables —**syl·lab′i·fi·ca′tion *n.***

syl·la·ble (sil′ə bəl) ***n.*** ⟦< Gr *syn-,* together + *lambanein,* to hold⟧ **1** a word or part of a word pronounced with a single, uninterrupted sounding of the voice **2** one or more letters written to represent a spoken syllable —**syl·lab·ic** (si lab′ik) ***adj.***

syl·la·bus (sil′ə bəs) ***n.,*** *pl.* **-bus·es** or **-bi′** (-bī′) ⟦ult. < Gr *sittybos,* strip of leather⟧ a summary or outline, esp. of a course of study

syl·lo·gism (sil′ə jiz′əm) ***n.*** ⟦< Gr *syn-,* together + *logizesthai,* to reason⟧ a form of reasoning in which two premises are made and a logical conclusion is drawn from them

sylph (silf) ***n.*** ⟦Mod L *sylphus,* a spirit⟧ **1** an imaginary being supposed to inhabit the air **2** a slender, graceful woman or girl —**sylph′like′ *adj.***

syl·van (sil′vən) ***adj.*** ⟦< L *silva,* forest⟧ **1** of, characteristic of, or living in the woods or forest **2** covered with trees; wooded

sym·bi·o·sis (sim′bī ō′sis, -bē-) ***n.*** ⟦< Gr *symbioun,* to live together⟧ the living together of two kinds of organisms to their mutual advantage —**sym′bi·ot′ic** (-ät′ik) ***adj.***

sym·bol (sim′bəl) ***n.*** ⟦< Gr *syn-,* together + *ballein,* to throw⟧ **1** an object used to represent something abstract *[the dove is a peace symbol]* **2** a mark, letter, etc. standing for an object, quality, quantity, process, etc., as in music or chemistry —**sym·bol′ic** (-bäl′ik) or **sym·bol′i·cal *adj.*** —**sym·bol′i·cal·ly *adv.***

sym′bol·ism′ *n.* **1** representation by symbols **2** a system of symbols **3** symbolic meaning

sym′bol·ize′ *vt.* -ized′, -iz′ing **1** to be a symbol of; stand for **2** to represent by a symbol or symbols

sym·me·try (sim′ə trē) ***n.,*** *pl.* **-tries** ⟦< Gr *syn-,* together + *metron,* a measure⟧ **1** correspondence of opposite parts in size, shape, and position **2** balance or beauty of form resulting from this —**sym·met·ri·cal** (si me′tri kəl) ***adj.*** —**sym·met′ri·cal·ly *adv.***

sym·pa·thet·ic (sim′pə thet′ik) ***adj.*** **1** of, feeling, or showing sympathy **2** in agreement with one's tastes, mood, etc. **3** *Physiology* designating the part of the autonomic nervous system involved esp. in communicating the involuntary response to alarm, as by speeding the heart rate —**sym′pa·thet′i·cal·ly *adv.***

sym′pa·thize′ (-thīz′) ***vi.* -thized′, -thiz′ing** **1** to share the feelings or ideas of another **2** to feel or express sympathy —**sym′pa·thiz′er *n.***

sym′pa·thy (-thē) ***n.,*** *pl.* **-thies** ⟦< Gr *syn-,* together + *pathos,* feeling⟧ **1** sameness of feeling **2** mutual liking or understanding **3** *a)* ability to share another's ideas, emotions, etc. *b)* pity or compassion for another's trouble or suffering

sym·pho·ny (sim′fə nē) ***n.,*** *pl.* **-nies** ⟦< Gr *syn-,* together + *phōnē,* a sound⟧ **1** harmony of sounds, color, etc. **2** an extended musical composition in several movements, for full orchestra **3** SYMPHONY ORCHESTRA **4** [Inf.] a concert by a symphony orchestra —**sym·phon′ic** (-fän′ik) ***adj.***

symphony orchestra a large orchestra for playing symphonic works

sym·po·si·um (sim pō′zē əm) ***n.,*** *pl.* **-si·ums** or **-si·a** (-ə) ⟦< Gr *syn-,* together + *posis,* a drinking⟧ **1** a conference to discuss a topic **2** a published group of opinions on a topic

symp·tom (simp′təm) ***n.*** ⟦< Gr *syn-,* together + *piptein,* to fall⟧ any circumstance or condition that indicates the existence of something, as a particular disease —**symp′to·mat′ic** (-tə mat′ik) ***adj.***

syn *abbrev.* synonym

syn- ⟦Gr⟧ *prefix* with, together, at the same time

syn·a·gogue (sin′ə gäg′, -gôg′) ***n.*** ⟦< Gr *syn-,* together + *agein,* do⟧ **1** an assembly of Jews for worship and religious study **2** a building or place for such assembly —**syn′a·gog′al *adj.***

syn·apse (sin′aps′) ***n.*** ⟦< Gr *syn-,* together + *apsis,* a joining⟧ the space between nerve cells through which nerve impulses are transmitted

sync or **synch** (siŋk) ***vi., vt.* synced** or **synched, sync′ing** or **synch′ing** *short for* SYNCHRONIZE —***n.*** *short for* SYNCHRONIZATION —**in** (or **out of**) **sync** in (or out of) synchronization or harmony (*with*)

syn·chro·nize (siŋ′krə nīz′) ***vi.* -nized′, -niz′ing** ⟦< Gr *syn-,* together + *chronos,* time⟧ to move or occur at the same time or rate —***vt.*** to cause to agree in time or rate of speed —**syn′chro·ni·za′tion *n.***

syn′chro·nous *adj.* happening at the same time or at the same rate

syn·co·pate (siŋ′kə pāt′) ***vt.* -pat′ed, -pat′ing** ⟦< Gr *syn-,* together + *koptein,* to cut⟧ *Music* to begin a tone on an unaccented beat and continue it through the next accented beat —**syn′co·pa′tion *n.***

syn·di·cate (sin′də kit; *for v.,* -kāt′) ***n.*** ⟦< Gr *syn-,* together + *dikē,* justice⟧ **1** an association of individuals or corporations formed to carry out a project requiring much capital **2** any group, as of criminals, organized for some undertaking **3** an organization selling articles or features to many newspapers, etc. —***vt.* -cat′ed, -cat′ing** **1** to manage as or form into a syndicate **2** *a)* to sell (an article, etc.) through a syndicate *b)* to sell (a program, etc.) to a number of radio or TV stations —***vi.*** to form a syndicate —**syn′di·ca′tion *n.***

syn·drome (sin′drōm′) ***n.*** ⟦< Gr *syn-,* with + *dramein,* to run⟧ a set of symptoms characterizing a disease or condition

syn·er·gism (sin′ər jiz′əm) ***n.*** ⟦< Gr *syn-,* together + *ergon,* work⟧ an interaction of several things that results in a greater effect than the sum of the things' individual effects: said esp. of drugs —**syn′er·gis′tic** ***adj.***

syn·fu·el (sin′fyo͞o′əl) ***n.*** ⟦SYN(THETIC) + FUEL⟧ a fuel, as oil or gas made from coal, used as a substitute for petroleum or natural gas

syn·od (sin′əd) ***n.*** ⟦< Gr *syn-*, together + *hodos*, way⟧ **1** an ecclesiastical council **2** a high governing body in certain Christian churches

syn·o·nym (sin′ə nim) ***n.*** ⟦< Gr *syn-*, together + *onyma*, a name⟧ a word having the same or nearly the same meaning as another in the same language —**syn·on·y·mous** (si nän′ə məs) ***adj.***

syn·op·sis (si näp′sis) ***n.***, *pl.* **-ses′** (-sēz′) ⟦< Gr *syn-*, together + *opsis*, a seeing⟧ a brief, general review or condensation; summary

syn·tax (sin′taks′) ***n.*** ⟦< Gr *syn-*, together + *tassein*, arrange⟧ the arrangement of and relationships among words, phrases, and clauses forming sentences —**syn·tac′tic** (-tak′tik) or **syn·tac′ti·cal** ***adj.***

syn·the·sis (sin′thə sis) ***n.***, *pl.* **-ses′** (-sēz′) ⟦< Gr *syn-*, together + *tithenai*, to place⟧ the combining of parts or elements so as to form a whole, a compound, etc. —**syn′the·size′** (-sīz′), **-sized′**, **-siz′ing**, ***vt.***

syn′the·siz′er ***n.*** an electronic device producing sounds unobtainable from ordinary musical instruments or imitating instruments and voices

syn·thet′ic (-thet′ik) ***adj.*** **1** of or involving synthesis **2** produced by chemical synthesis, rather than of natural origin **3** not real; artificial —***n.*** something synthetic —**syn·thet′i·cal·ly** ***adv.***

syph·i·lis (sif′ə lis) ***n.*** ⟦after *Syphilus*, hero of a L poem (1530)⟧ a sexually transmitted disease caused by a spirochete —**syph′i·lit′ic** ***adj., n.***

Syr·i·a (sir′ē ə) country in SW Asia, at the E end of the Mediterranean: 71,498 sq. mi.; pop. 9,046,000 —**Syr′i·an** ***adj., n.***

sy·ringe (sə rinj′, sir′inj) ***n.*** ⟦< Gr *syrinx*, a pipe⟧ **1** a device consisting of a tube with a rubber bulb or piston at one end, for drawing in a liquid and then ejecting it in a stream: used to inject fluids into body cavities, etc. **2** HYPODERMIC SYRINGE —***vt.*** **-ringed′**, **-ring′ing** to cleanse, inject, etc. by using a syringe

syr·up (sur′əp, sir′-) ***n.*** ⟦< OFr *sirop* < ML *sirupus* < Ar *sharāb*, a drink⟧ any thick, sweet liquid; specif., a solution of sugar and water boiled together

syr′up·y ***adj.*** **1** like syrup **2** overly sentimental

sys·tem (sis′təm) ***n.*** ⟦< Gr *syn-*, together + *histanai*, to set⟧ **1** a set or arrangement of things related so as to form a whole *[a solar system, a school system]* **2** a set of facts, rules, etc. arranged to show a logical plan linking them **3** a method or plan **4** an established, orderly way of doing something **5** the body, or a number of bodily organs, functioning as a unit

sys′tem·at′ic (-tə mat′ik) ***adj.*** **1** constituting or based on a system **2** according to a system; orderly —**sys′tem·at′i·cal·ly** ***adv.***

sys′tem·a·tize′ (-tə mə tīz′) ***vt.*** **-tized′**, **-tiz′ing** to arrange according to a system; make systematic —**sys′tem·a·ti·za′tion** ***n.***

sys·tem·ic (sis tem′ik) ***adj.*** of or affecting the body as a whole

sys·to·le (sis′tə lē′) ***n.*** ⟦< Gr *syn-*, together + *stellein*, to set up⟧ the usual rhythmic contraction of the heart —**sys·tol′ic** (-täl′ik) ***adj.***

T

t[1] or **T** (tē) ***n.***, *pl.* **t's, T's** the 20th letter of the English alphabet —**to a T** to perfection; exactly

t[2] *abbrev.* **1** teaspoon(s) **2** temperature **3** tense **4** ton(s) **5** transitive

T *abbrev.* **1** tablespoon(s) **2** temperature **3** Thursday **4** Tuesday

't- *prefix* it: used chiefly in poetry *['twas]*

tab[1] (tab) ***n.*** ⟦< ?⟧ **1** a small, flat loop or strap fastened to something **2** a projecting piece as of a file folder, used in filing

tab[2] (tab) ***n.*** ⟦prob. < TABULATION⟧ [Inf.] **1** a bill, as for expenses **2** total cost —**keep tabs** (or **a tab**) **on** [Inf.] to keep a check on

Ta·bas·co (tə bas′kō) *trademark for* a very hot sauce made from a tropical American hot red pepper

tab·bou·leh (tə bo͞o′lē, -le) ***n.*** ⟦Ar⟧ a salad of coarsely ground wheat with chopped parsley, tomatoes, scallions, etc.

tab·by (tab′ē) ***n.***, *pl.* **-bies** ⟦ult. < Ar⟧ a domestic cat, esp. a female

tab·er·nac·le (tab′ər nak′əl) ***n.*** ⟦< L *taberna*, hut⟧ **1** a large place of worship **2** [**T-**] the portable sanctuary carried by the Jews during the Exodus

tab·la (täb′lä) ***n.*** ⟦< Ar *ṭabla*, a drum⟧ a set of two small drums whose pitch can be varied, used esp. in India and played with the hands

ta·ble (tā′bəl) ***n.*** ⟦< L *tabula*, a board⟧ **1** [Obs.] a thin slab of metal, stone, etc. **2** *a)* a piece of furniture having a flat top set on legs *b)* such a table set with food *c)* food served *d)* the people seated at a table **3** *a)* a systematic list of details, contents, etc. *b)* an orderly arrangement of facts, figures, etc. **4** any flat, horizontal surface, piece, etc. —***vt.*** **-bled**, **-bling** to postpone indefinitely the consideration of (a legislative bill, etc.) —**at table** at a meal —**turn the tables** to reverse a situation

tab·leau (tab′lō′, ta blō′) ***n.***, *pl.* **-leaux′** (-lōz′) or **-leaus′** ⟦Fr < OFr, dim. of *table*⟧ a striking, dramatic scene or picture

ta'ble·cloth' *n.* a cloth for covering a table, esp. at meals

ta·ble d'hôte (tä'bəl dōt') ⟦Fr, table of the host⟧ a complete meal served at a restaurant for a set price

ta'ble-hop' *vi.* **-hopped', -hop'ping** to leave one's table, as at a restaurant, and visit at other tables

ta'ble·land' *n.* a plateau

ta'ble·spoon' *n.* **1** a large spoon for serving or for eating soup **2** a measuring spoon holding ½ fluid ounce —**ta'ble·spoon'ful**, *pl.* **-fuls**, *n.*

tab·let (tab'lit) *n.* ⟦see TABLE⟧ **1** a thin, flat piece of stone, metal, etc. with an inscription **2** a writing pad of paper sheets glued together at one edge **3** a small, flat piece of compressed material, as of medicine

table tennis a game somewhat like tennis, played on a table with a small, hollow celluloid ball

ta'ble·ware' (-wer') *n.* dishes, glassware, silverware, etc. for use at a meal

tab·loid (tab'loid') *n.* ⟦TABL(ET) + -OID⟧ a newspaper, usually half size, with many pictures and short, often sensational, news stories

ta·boo (tə bo͞o', ta-) *n.* ⟦< a Polynesian language⟧ **1** among some Polynesian peoples, a sacred prohibition making certain people or things untouchable, etc. **2** any conventional social restriction —*adj.* prohibited by taboo —*vt.* **-booed', -boo'ing** **1** to put under taboo **2** to prohibit or forbid Also **ta·bu'**

ta·bou·li (tə bo͞o'lē) *n. var. of* TABBOULEH

tab·u·lar (tab'yə lər) *adj.* ⟦see TABLE⟧ **1** flat **2** of, arranged in, or computed from a table or list

tab'u·late' (-lāt') *vt.* **-lat'ed, -lat'ing** to put (facts, statistics, etc.) in a table —**tab'u·la'tion** *n.* —**tab'u·la'tor** *n.*

ta·chom·e·ter (ta käm'ət ər) *n.* ⟦< Gr *tachos,* speed + -METER⟧ a device that measures the rate of rotation of a revolving shaft

tach·y·car·di·a (tak'i kär'dē ə) *n.* ⟦< Gr *tachys,* swift + *kardia,* heart⟧ an abnormally fast heartbeat

tac·it (tas'it) *adj.* ⟦< L *tacere,* be silent⟧ **1** unspoken **2** not expressed openly, but implied or understood —**tac'it·ly** *adv.* —**tac'it·ness** *n.*

tac·i·turn (tas'ə turn') *adj.* ⟦see prec.⟧ almost always silent; not liking to talk —**tac'i·tur'ni·ty** *n.*

tack (tak) *n.* ⟦< MDu *tacke,* twig, point⟧ **1** a short nail or pin with a sharp point and a large, flat head **2** a temporary stitch **3** a course of action **4** *a)* the direction a ship goes in relation to the position of the sails *b)* a change of a ship's direction —*vt.* **1** to fasten with tacks **2** to attach or add **3** to change the course of (a ship) —*vi.* to change course suddenly

tack·le (tak'əl) *n.* ⟦< MDu *takel*⟧ **1** equipment; gear **2** a system of ropes and pulleys for moving weights **3** a tackling, as in football **4** *Football* a lineman next to the end —*vt.* **tack'led, tack'ling** **1** to take hold of; seize **2** to try to do; undertake **3** *Football* to throw (the ball carrier) to the ground —**tack'ler** *n.*

tack·y (tak'ē) *adj.* **-i·er, -i·est** **1** sticky: said as of drying varnish **2** dowdy or shabby **3** in poor taste —**tack'i·ness** *n.*

ta·co (tä'kō) *n., pl.* **-cos** ⟦Sp, light lunch⟧ a fried tortilla filled with chopped meat, lettuce, etc.

Ta·co·ma (tə kō'mə) seaport in W Washington: pop. 177,000

tact (takt) *n.* ⟦< L *tangere,* to touch⟧ delicate perception of the right thing to say or do without offending —**tact'ful** *adj.* —**tact'less** *adj.*

tac·tics (tak'tiks) *pl.n.* ⟦< Gr *tassein,* arrange⟧ **1** [*with sing. v.*] the science of maneuvering military and naval forces **2** any skillful methods to gain an end —**tac'ti·cal** *adj.* —**tac·ti'cian** (-tish'ən) *n.*

tac·tile (tak'təl) *adj.* ⟦< L *tangere,* to touch⟧ of, having, or perceived by the sense of touch

tad (tad) *n.* ⟦prob. < TADPOLE⟧ a small amount or degree: often used adverbially *[a tad tired]*

tad·pole (tad'pōl') *n.* ⟦ME *tadde,* toad + *poll,* head⟧ the larva of a frog or toad, having gills and a tail and living in water

taf·fe·ta (taf'i tə) *n.* ⟦< Pers *tāftan,* to weave⟧ a fine, stiff fabric of silk, nylon, etc., with a sheen

taff·rail (taf'rāl') *n.* ⟦< Du⟧ the rail around the stern of a ship

taf·fy (taf'ē) *n.* ⟦< ?⟧ a chewy candy made of sugar or molasses

Taft (taft), **Wil·liam How·ard** (wil'yəm hou'ərd) 1857-1930; 27th president of the U.S. (1909-13): chief justice of the U.S. (1921-30)

tag (tag) *n.* ⟦prob. < Scand⟧ **1** a hanging end or part **2** a hard-tipped end on a cord or lace **3** a card, etc. attached as a label **4** an epithet **5** ending for a story, etc. **6** TAG LINE **7** a children's game in which one player chases the others with the object of touching one of them —*vt.* **tagged, tag'ging** **1** to provide with a tag; label **2** to choose or select **3** to touch in playing tag **4** [Inf.] to strike or hit hard —*vi.* [Inf.] to follow closely: with *along, after,* etc. —**tag'ger** *n.*

Ta·ga·log (tä gä'lôg') *n.* **1** *pl.* **-logs'** or **-log'** a member of the ethnic group native to the Manila region in the Philippines **2** the language of this group, an official language of the Republic of the Philippines

tag line the last line or lines of a speech, etc.

Ta·hi·ti (tə hēt'ē) French island in the S Pacific —**Ta·hi'ti·an** (-hēsh'ən) *adj., n.*

Tai (tī) *n.* **1** a group of languages spoken in central and SE Asia **2** a member of a group of peoples of SE Asia that speak these languages —*adj.* of these languages or peoples

tai chi (tī' jē', tī chē') ⟦Mandarin⟧ a Chinese exercise system consisting of a series of slow, relaxed movements: in full **t'ai chi ch'uan** (chwän)

tai·ga (tī'gə) *n.* ⟦Russ⟧ a type of plant community in the far north, having scattered trees

tail (tāl) ***n.*** ⟦OE *tægel*⟧ **1** the rear end of an animal's body, esp. when a distinct appendage **2** anything like an animal's tail in form or position **3** the hind, bottom, last, or inferior part of anything **4** [*often pl.*] the reverse side of a coin **5** [*pl.*] full-dress attire for men **6** [Inf.] one that follows another, esp. in surveillance **—*adj.*** **1** at the rear or end **2** from the rear *[*a *tail* wind*]* **—*vt.*** [Slang] to follow stealthily **—*vi.*** [Inf.] to follow close behind **—turn tail** to run from danger or difficulty

tail′back′ ***n.*** *Football* the offensive back farthest from the line

tail′bone′ ***n.*** COCCYX

tail end **1** the rear of anything **2** the concluding part

tail fin **1** a fin that forms the tail of a fish, etc. **2** a finlike projection at the rear of a rocket, car, etc.

tail′gate′ ***n.*** the hinged or removable gate at the back of a wagon, truck, etc. **—*vi., vt.*** **-gat′ed, -gat′ing** to drive too closely behind (another vehicle) **—tail′gat′er *n.***

tail′ings ***pl.n.*** waste or refuse left in various processes of milling, mining, etc.

tail′light′ ***n.*** a light, usually red, at the rear of a vehicle to warn vehicles coming from behind

tai·lor (tā′lər) ***n.*** ⟦< VL *taliare,* to cut⟧ one who makes, repairs, or alters clothes **—*vt.*** **1** to make by tailor's work **2** to form, alter, etc. for a certain purpose

tail′pipe′ ***n.*** the exhaust pipe coming from the muffler of a motor vehicle

tail′spin′ ***n.*** SPIN (*n. 3*)

taint (tānt) ***vt.*** ⟦< ?⟧ **1** to affect with something injurious, unpleasant, etc.; infect, spoil, etc. **2** to make morally corrupt **—*n.*** a trace of contamination, corruption, etc.

Tai·pei (tī′pā′) capital of Taiwan: pop. 2,108,000

Tai·wan (tī′wän′) island province of China, off the SE coast: together with nearby islands it forms the *Republic of China*: 13,970 sq. mi.; pop. 21,000,000

Ta·jik·i·stan (tä jik′i stan′) country in WC Asia: formerly a republic of the U.S.S.R.: 55,240 sq. mi.; pop. 5,093,000

take (tāk) ***vt.*** **took, tak′en, tak′ing** ⟦< ON *taka*⟧ **1** to get possession of; capture, seize, etc. **2** to get hold of **3** to capture the fancy of; charm **4** to obtain, acquire, assume, etc. **5** to use, consume, etc. **6** to buy, rent, subscribe to, etc. **7** to join with (one side in a disagreement, etc.) **8** to choose; select **9** to travel by *[*to *take* a bus*]* **10** to deal with; consider **11** to occupy *[take* a chair*]* **12** to require; demand *[*it *takes* money*]* **13** to derive (a name, quality, etc.) from **14** to excerpt; extract **15** to study **16** to write down *[take* notes*]* **17** to make by photographing **18** to win (a prize, etc.) **19** to undergo *[take* punishment*]* **20** to occupy oneself in; enjoy *[take* a nap*]* **21** to accept (an offer, bet, etc.) **22** to react to *[take* a joke in earnest*]* **23** to contract (a disease, etc.) **24** to understand **25** to suppose; presume **26** to feel *[take* pity*]* **27** to lead, escort, etc. **28** to carry **29** to remove, as by stealing **30** to subtract **31** [Slang] to cheat; trick **32** *Gram.* to be used with *[*the verb "hit" *takes* an object*]* **—*vi.*** **1** to take root: said of a plant **2** to catch *[*the fire *took]* **3** to gain favor, success, etc. **4** to be effective *[*the vaccination *took]* **5** [Inf. or Dial.] to become (sick) **—*n.*** **1** a taking **2** *a*) the amount taken *b*) [Slang] receipts or profit **—on the take** [Slang] taking bribes, etc. **—take after** to be, act, or look like **—take back** to retract (something said, etc.) **—take down** to put in writing; record **—take for** **1** to regard as **2** to mistake for **—take in** **1** to admit; receive **2** to make smaller **3** to understand **4** to cheat; trick **—take off** **1** to leave the ground, etc. in flight **2** [Inf.] to start **3** [Inf.] to imitate in a burlesque manner: with *on* **—take on** **1** to acquire; assume **2** to employ **3** to undertake (a task, etc.) **—take over** to assume control or possession of **—take to** **1** to become fond of **2** to go to or withdraw to *[*to *take to* the hills*]* **—take up** **1** to make tighter or shorter **2** to become interested in (an occupation, study, etc.) **—tak′er *n.***

take′off′ ***n.*** **1** the act or place of leaving the ground, as in jumping or flight **2** [Inf.] a mocking imitation; caricature

take′out′ ***n.*** prepared food bought to be taken away **—*adj.*** designating or of such food

take′o′ver ***n.*** **1** the usurpation of power in a nation, organization, etc. **2** the assumption of management in acquiring a corporation

tak·ing (tāk′iŋ) ***adj.*** attractive; winning **—*n.*** **1** the act of one that takes **2** [*pl.*] earnings; profits

talc (talk) ***n.*** ⟦< Ar *ṭalq*⟧ **1** a soft mineral used to make talcum powder, etc. **2** *short for* TALCUM (POWDER)

tal·cum (powder) (tal′kəm) a powder for the body made of purified talc

tale (tāl) ***n.*** ⟦OE *talu*⟧ **1** a story; narrative **2** idle or malicious gossip **3** a fiction; lie

tale′bear′er (-ber′ər) ***n.*** a gossip

tal·ent (tal′ənt) ***n.*** ⟦< Gr *talanton,* a weight⟧ **1** an ancient unit of weight or money **2** any natural ability or power **3** a superior ability in an art, etc. **4** people, or a person, with talent **—tal′ent·ed *adj.***

tal·is·man (tal′is mən, -iz-) ***n.,*** *pl.* **-mans** ⟦< 5th-c. medieval Gr *telesma,* religious rite⟧ **1** a ring, stone, etc. bearing engraved figures thought to bring good luck, avert evil, etc. **2** a charm

talk (tôk) ***vi.*** ⟦prob. < OE *talian,* reckon⟧ **1** to put ideas into words; speak **2** to express ideas by speech substitutes *[talk* by signs*]* **3** to chatter; gossip **4** to confer; consult **5** to confess or inform on someone **—*vt.*** **1** to use in speaking *[*to *talk* French*]* **2** to discuss **3** to put into a specified condition, etc. by talking **—*n.*** **1** the act of talking **2** conversation **3** a speech **4** a conference **5** gossip **6** the subject of conversation, gossip, etc. 7 speech; dialect —**talk back** to answer impertinently —**talk down to** to talk patronizingly to, as by simple speech —**talk up** to promote in discussion —**talk'er** ***n.***

talk'a·tive (-ə tiv) ***adj.*** talking a great deal; loquacious

talking book a recording of a reading of a book, etc. for use esp. by the blind

talk·ing-to (tôk'iŋ to͞o') ***n.*** [Inf.] a scolding

talk show *Radio, TV* a program in which a host talks with guest celebrities, experts, etc.

talk'y ***adj.*** **-i·er, -i·est** 1 talkative 2 containing too much talk, or dialogue

tall (tôl) ***adj.*** ⟦< OE (*ge*)*tæl,* swift⟧ 1 higher in stature than the average 2 having a specified height 3 [Inf.] exaggerated *[a tall tale]* 4 [Inf.] large *[a tall drink]* —***adv.*** in an upright, dignified manner *[to stand tall]* —**tall'ness** ***n.***

Tal·la·has·see (tal'ə has'ē) capital of Florida: pop. 125,000

tal·low (tal'ō) ***n.*** ⟦prob. < LowG *talg*⟧ the solid fat of cattle, sheep, etc., used in candles, soaps, etc.

tal·ly (tal'ē) ***n.***, *pl.* **-lies** ⟦< L *talea,* a stick (notched to keep accounts)⟧ 1 anything used as a record for an account or score 2 an account, score, etc. 3 a tag or label —***vt.*** **-lied, -ly·ing** 1 to put on or as on a tally 2 to add (*up*) —***vi.*** 1 to score a point 2 to agree; correspond

tal·ly·ho (tal'ē hō') ***interj.*** the cry of a hunter on sighting the fox

Tal·mud (täl'mood, tal'məd) ***n.*** ⟦Heb, learning⟧ the body of early Jewish civil and religious law

tal·on (tal'ən) ***n.*** ⟦< L *talus,* an ankle⟧ the claw of a bird of prey

tam (tam) ***n.*** *short for* TAM-O'-SHANTER

ta·ma·le (tə mä'lē) ***n.*** ⟦< MexSp⟧ spicy minced meat wrapped in a dough of corn meal

tam·a·rack (tam'ə rak') ***n.*** ⟦< AmInd⟧ 1 an American larch tree usually found in swamps 2 its wood

tam·a·rind (tam'ə rind') ***n.*** ⟦< Ar *tamr hindī,* date of India⟧ 1 a tropical tree with yellow flowers and brown pods 2 its sharp-tasting, edible fruit

tam·bou·rine (tam'bə rēn') ***n.*** ⟦prob. < Ar *ṭanbūr,* stringed instrument⟧ a shallow, single-headed hand drum with jingling metal disks in the rim: played by shaking, hitting, etc.

tame (tām) ***adj.*** **tam'er, tam'est** ⟦OE *tam*⟧ 1 changed from a wild state and trained for human use 2 gentle; docile 3 without spirit or force; dull —***vt.*** **tamed, tam'ing** 1 to make tame 2 to make gentle; subdue —**tam'a·ble** or **tame'a·ble** ***adj.*** —**tame'ly** ***adv.*** —**tame'ness** ***n.*** —**tam'er** ***n.***

Tam·il (tam'əl) ***n.*** the language of the Tamils, a people of S India and N Sri Lanka

tam-o'-shan·ter (tam'ə shan'tər) ***n.*** ⟦< title character of Robert Burns's poem⟧ a Scottish cap with a round, flat top

TAM-O'-SHANTER

tamp (tamp) ***vt.*** ⟦< ? Fr *tampon,* a plug⟧ to pack firmly or pound (*down*) by a series of blows or taps

Tam·pa (tam'pə) seaport in WC Florida, on the Gulf of Mexico: pop. 280,000

tam·per (tam'pər) ***vi.*** ⟦< TEMPER⟧ 1 to make secret, illegal arrangements (*with*) 2 to interfere (*with*) or meddle (*with*)

tam·pon (tam'pän') ***n.*** ⟦Fr⟧ a plug of cotton, etc. put into a body cavity, etc., as to stop bleeding

tan (tan) ***n.*** ⟦< ML *tanum,* a bark used to tan hides⟧ 1 a yellowish-brown color 2 a darkening of the skin as by exposure to the sun, etc. —***adj.*** **tan'ner, tan'nest** yellowish-brown —***vt.*** **tanned, tan'ning** 1 to change (hide) into leather by soaking in tannin 2 to produce a suntan in 3 [Inf.] to whip severely —***vi.*** to become tanned

tan·a·ger (tan'ə jər) ***n.*** ⟦< AmInd (Brazil) *tangara*⟧ any of various small, American songbirds: the males usually are brightly colored

tan·bark (tan'bark') ***n.*** any bark containing tannin, used to tan hides, etc.

tan·dem (tan'dəm) ***adv.*** ⟦< punning use of L *tandem,* at length⟧ one behind another; in single file —***n.*** teamwork between two persons, etc. *[to work in tandem]*

tang (taŋ) ***n.*** ⟦< ON *tangi,* a sting⟧ 1 a prong on a file, etc., that fits into the handle 2 a strong, penetrating taste or odor —**tang'y, -i·er, -i·est,** ***adj.***

tan·ge·lo (tan'jə lō') ***n.***, *pl.* **-los'** ⟦TANG(ERINE) + (*pom*)*elo,* grapefruit⟧ a fruit produced by crossing a tangerine with a grapefruit

tan·gent (tan'jənt) ***adj.*** ⟦< L *tangere,* to touch⟧ 1 touching 2 *Geom.* touching a curved surface at one point but not intersecting it —***n.*** a tangent line, curve, or surface —**go off at** (or **on**) **a tangent** to change suddenly to another line of action, etc. —**tan·gen'tial** (-jen' shəl) ***adj.***

tan·ge·rine (tan'jə rēn') ***n.*** ⟦after *Tangier,* city in N Africa⟧ a small, loose-skinned, reddish-yellow orange with easily separated segments

tan·gi·ble (tan'jə bəl) ***adj.*** ⟦< L *tangere,* to touch⟧ 1 that can be touched or felt 2 definite; objective —***n.*** [*pl.*] assets having real substance and able to be appraised for value —**tan'gi·bil'i·ty** ***n.***

tan·gle (taŋ'gəl) ***vt.*** **-gled, -gling** ⟦< ? Swed⟧ 1 to catch as in a snare; trap 2 to make a snarl of; intertwine —***vi.*** 1 to become tangled 2 [Inf.] to argue —***n.*** 1 an intertwined, confused mass 2 a confused condition or state

tan·go (taŋ'gō) ***n.***, *pl.* **-gos** ⟦AmSp⟧ 1 a

South American dance for couples with long gliding steps and dips 2 music for this dance in 2/4 or 4/4 time —*vi.* to dance the tango

tank (taŋk) *n.* ⟦in sense 1 < Sans⟧ 1 any large container for liquid or gas 2 an armored combat vehicle with tractor treads —*vi.* [Slang] to fail

tank·ard (taŋ′kərd) *n.* ⟦< OFr *tanquart*⟧ a large drinking cup with a handle

tank·er (taŋ′kər) *n.* 1 a ship equipped to transport oil or other liquids 2 a plane designed to carry liquids, as for refueling another plane in flight 3 a truck, etc. equipped to transport liquids or dry commodities in bulk

tank top ⟦orig. worn in swimming tanks⟧ a sleeveless casual shirt with shoulder straps

tank truck a motor truck built to transport gasoline, oil, etc.

tan·ner (tan′ər) *n.* a person whose work is making leather by tanning hides

tan′ner·y *n., pl.* **-ner·ies** a place where leather is made by tanning hides

tan·nic acid (tan′ik) a yellowish, astringent substance used in tanning hides, dyeing, etc.

tan′nin (-in) *n.* ⟦< *tan*, TAN + *-in*, -INE³⟧ any of a group of compounds, as tannic acid, that convert hide into leather

tan·sy (tan′zē) *n., pl.* **-sies** ⟦< LL *tanacetum*⟧ a plant with a strong smell and small, yellow flowers

tan·ta·lize (tan′tə līz′) *vt.* **-lized′**, **-liz′ing** ⟦after *Tantalus*, in Gr myth, a king doomed in Hades to stand in water that always recedes when he wishes to drink and under fruit he cannot reach⟧ to promise or show something desirable and then withhold it; tease

tan·ta·mount (tant′ə mount′) *adj.* ⟦< OFr *tant*, so much + *amont*, upward⟧ equal (*to*) in value, effect, etc.

tan·tra (tun′trə, tän′-) *n.* ⟦Sans⟧ [*often* **T-**] a form of yoga teaching attainment of ecstasy —**tan′tric** *adj.*

tan·trum (tan′trəm) *n.* ⟦< ?⟧ a violent, willful outburst of rage, etc.

Tan·za·ni·a (tan′zə nē′ə) country in E Africa: 364,881 sq. mi.; pop. 23,174,000 —**Tan′za·ni′an** *adj., n.*

Tao·ism (dou′iz′əm, tou′-) *n.* ⟦Chin *tao*, the way⟧ a Chinese religion and philosophy advocating simplicity, selflessness, etc. —**Tao′ist** *n., adj.*

tap¹ (tap) *vt., vi.* **tapped**, **tap′ping** ⟦echoic⟧ 1 to strike lightly 2 to make or do by tapping [to *tap* a message] 3 to choose, as for membership in a club —*n.* a light, rapid blow

tap² (tap) *n.* ⟦OE *tæppa*⟧ 1 a faucet or spigot 2 a plug, cork, etc. for stopping a hole in a cask, etc. 3 a tool used to cut threads inside a nut, pipe, etc. 4 the act or an instance of wiretapping 5 *Elec.* a place in a circuit where a connection can be made —*vt.* **tapped**, **tap′ping** 1 to put a tap or spigot on 2 to make a hole in, or pull the plug from, for drawing off liquid 3 to draw off (liquid) 4 to make use of [to *tap* new resources] 5 to make a connection with (a pipe, circuit, etc.); specif., to wiretap

tap dance a dance done with sharp, loud taps of the foot, toe, or heel at each step —**tap′-dance′**, **-danced′**, **-danc′ing**, *vi.* —**tap′-danc′er** *n.*

tape (tāp) *n.* ⟦OE *tæppe*, a fillet⟧ 1 a strong, narrow strip of cloth, paper, etc. used for binding, tying, etc. 2 *short for* MAGNETIC TAPE 3 *short for* TAPE MEASURE —*vt.* **taped**, **tap′ing** 1 to bind, tie, etc. with tape 2 to record on magnetic tape

tape deck a component of an audio system, that records and plays back magnetic tapes

tape measure a tape with marks in inches, feet, etc. for measuring

ta·per (tā′pər) *n.* ⟦OE *tapur*⟧ 1 a slender candle 2 a gradual decrease in width or thickness —*vt., vi.* 1 to decrease gradually in width or thickness 2 to lessen; diminish Often with *off*

tape recorder a device for recording on magnetic tape and for playing back what has been recorded

tap·es·try (tap′əs trē) *n., pl.* **-tries** ⟦< Gr *tapes*, a carpet⟧ a heavy woven cloth with decorative designs and pictures, used as a wall hanging, etc.

tape′worm′ *n.* a long, tapelike flatworm that lives as a parasite in the intestines

tap·i·o·ca (tap′ē ō′kə) *n.* ⟦< AmInd (Brazil)⟧ a starchy substance from cassava roots, used for puddings, etc.

ta·pir (tā′pər) *n.* ⟦< AmInd (Brazil)⟧ a large, hoglike mammal of tropical America and the Malay Peninsula

tapped out [Slang] 1 having no money; broke 2 exhausted or depleted

tap′room′ *n.* BARROOM

tap′root′ *n.* ⟦TAP² + ROOT¹⟧ a main root, growing downward, from which small branch roots spread out

taps (taps) *n.* ⟦< TAP¹, because orig. a drum signal⟧ [*with sing. or pl. v.*] a bugle call to put out lights in retiring for the night

tar¹ (tär) *n.* ⟦OE *teru*⟧ a thick, sticky, black liquid formed when hot coal, wood, etc. decomposes in the absence of air —*vt.* **tarred**, **tar′ring** to cover or smear with tar —**tar′ry**, **-ri·er**, **-ri·est**, *adj.*

tar² (tär) *n.* ⟦< TAR(PAULIN)⟧ [Inf.] a sailor

ta·ran·tu·la (tə ran′cho͞o lə) *n.* ⟦after *Taranto*, city in S Italy⟧ any of several large, hairy, somewhat poisonous spiders of S Europe and tropical America

HAIRY TARANTULA

tar·dy (tär′dē) ***adj.*** **-di·er, -di·est** ⟦< L *tardus*, slow⟧ **1** slow in moving, acting, etc. **2** late, delayed, etc. —**tar′di·ly** ***adv.*** —**tar′di·ness** ***n.***

tare[1] (ter) ***n.*** ⟦ME⟧ **1** any of various vetches **2** *Bible* an undesirable weed

tare[2] (ter) ***n.*** ⟦< Ar *ṭaraḥa*, to reject⟧ the weight of a container, etc. deducted from the total weight to determine the weight of the contents or load

tar·get (tär′git) ***n.*** ⟦< medieval Fr *targe*, a shield⟧ **1** a board, etc. marked as with concentric circles, aimed at in archery, rifle practice, etc. **2** any object that is shot at **3** an objective; goal **4** an object of attack, criticism, etc. —***vt.*** to establish as a target, goal, etc.

tar·iff (tar′if) ***n.*** ⟦< Ar *ta'rīf*, information⟧ **1** a list or system of taxes upon exports or, esp., imports **2** such a tax, or its rate **3** a list or scale of prices, charges, etc. **4** [Inf.] any bill, charge, etc.

tar·mac (tär′mak′) ***n.*** ⟦ult. < TAR[1] + MAC(ADAM)⟧ [Chiefly Brit.] an airport runway or apron

tar·nish (tär′nish) ***vt.*** ⟦< Fr *ternir*, make dim⟧ **1** to dull the luster of **2** to sully or mar —***vi.*** **1** to lose luster **2** to become sullied —***n.*** **1** dullness **2** a stain —**tar′nish·a·ble** ***adj.***

ta·ro (ter′ō, tär′ō) ***n.***, *pl.* **-ros** ⟦< a Polynesian language⟧ a tropical Asiatic plant with a starchy, edible root

tar·ot (tar′ō, -ət; ta rō′) ***n.*** ⟦Fr < Ar *ṭaraḥa*, to reject⟧ [*often* **T-**] any of a set of 22 cards with pictures, used in fortunetelling

tarp (tärp) ***n.*** [Inf.] *short for* TARPAULIN

tar·pau·lin (tär pô′lin, tär′pə-) ***n.*** ⟦< TAR[1] + PALL[2], a covering⟧ **1** canvas coated with a waterproofing compound **2** a sheet of this

tar·pon (tär′pən) ***n.*** ⟦< ?⟧ a large, silvery game fish of the W Atlantic

tar·ra·gon (tar′ə gän′) ***n.*** ⟦< Sp < Ar < Gr *drakōn*, a dragon⟧ an Old World plant with fragrant leaves used for seasoning

tar·ry (tar′ē) ***vi.*** **-ried, -ry·ing** ⟦< OE *tergan*, to vex & prob. OFr *targer*, to delay⟧ **1** to delay; linger **2** to stay for a time **3** to wait

tart[1] (tärt) ***adj.*** ⟦OE *teart*⟧ **1** sharp in taste; sour; acid **2** sharp in meaning; cutting *[a tart answer]* —**tart′ly** ***adv.*** —**tart′ness** ***n.***

tart[2] (tärt) ***n.*** ⟦< OFr *tarte*⟧ a small pastry shell filled with jam, jelly, etc.

tart[3] (tärt) ***n.*** ⟦< prec., orig., slang term of endearment⟧ [Inf.] a prostitute

tar·tan (tärt′'n) ***n.*** ⟦prob. < medieval Fr *tiretaine*, a cloth of mixed fibers⟧ a woolen cloth in any of various woven plaid patterns, worn esp. in the Scottish Highlands

tar·tar (tärt′ər) ***n.*** ⟦< medieval Gr *tartaron*⟧ **1** cream of tartar, esp. the crude form present in grape juice and forming a crustlike deposit in wine casks **2** a hard deposit on the teeth

Tar·tar (tärt′ər) ***n.*** TATAR

tar·tar sauce (tärt′ər) ⟦Fr⟧ a sauce of mayonnaise with chopped pickles, olives, capers, etc.: also **tar′tare sauce**

task (task) ***n.*** ⟦ult. < L *taxare*, to rate⟧ **1** a piece of work to be done **2** any difficult undertaking —***vt.*** to burden; strain —**take to task** to scold

task force a group, esp. a military unit, assigned a specific task

task′mas′ter ***n.*** one who assigns tasks to others, esp. when severe

Tas·ma·ni·a (taz mā′nē ə) island of Australia, off its SE coast —**Tas·ma′ni·an** ***adj., n.***

tas·sel (tas′əl) ***n.*** ⟦OFr, knob⟧ **1** an ornamental tuft of threads, etc. hanging loosely from a knob **2** something resembling this, as a tuft of corn silk

taste (tāst) ***vt.*** **tast′ed, tast′ing** ⟦< OFr *taster*⟧ **1** to test the flavor of by putting a little in one's mouth **2** to detect the flavor of by the sense of taste **3** to eat or drink a small amount of **4** to experience *[to taste success]* —***vi.*** to have a specific flavor —***n.*** **1** the sense by which flavor is perceived through the taste buds on the tongue **2** the quality so perceived; flavor **3** a small amount tasted as a sample **4** a bit; trace **5** the ability to appreciate what is beautiful, appropriate, etc. **6** a specific preference **7** a liking; inclination —**in bad** (or **good**) **taste** in a style showing a bad (or good) sense of beauty, fitness, etc. —**taste′less** ***adj.*** —**tast′er** ***n.***

taste bud any of the cells, esp. in the tongue, that are the organs of taste

taste′ful ***adj.*** having or showing good TASTE (*n.* 5) —**taste′ful·ly** ***adv.***

tast·y (tās′tē) ***adj.*** **-i·er, -i·est** that tastes good; flavorful —**tast′i·ness** ***n.***

tat (tat) ***vt.*** **tat′ted, tat′ting** to make by tatting —***vi.*** to do tatting

ta·ta·mi (tə tä′mē) ***n.***, *pl.* **-mi** or **-mis** ⟦Jpn⟧ a floor mat of rice straw, used traditionally in Japanese homes for sitting on

Ta·tar (tät′ər) ***n.*** **1** a member of any of the E Asian peoples that invaded W Asia and E Europe in the Middle Ages **2** a Turkic language

tat·ter (tat′ər) ***n.*** ⟦< ON *töturr*, rags⟧ **1** a torn and hanging piece, as of a garment **2** [*pl.*] torn, ragged clothes —***vt., vi.*** to make or become ragged —**tat′tered** ***adj.***

tat′ter·de·mal′ion (-di māl′yən) ***n.*** ⟦< prec. + ?⟧ a person in torn, ragged clothes

tat·ting (tat′iŋ) ***n.*** ⟦prob. < Brit dial. *tat*,

to tangle⟧ **1** a fine lace made by looping and knotting thread **2** the act or process of making this

tat·tle (tat′'l) ***vi.*** **-tled, -tling** ⟦prob. < MDu *tatelen*⟧ **1** to talk idly **2** to reveal others' secrets **—*vt.*** to reveal (a secret) by gossiping **—tat′tler *n.***

tat′tle·tale′ *n.* an informer; a gossip

tat·too[1] (ta to͞o′) ***vt.*** **-tooed′, -too′ing** ⟦< a Polynesian language⟧ to make (permanent designs) on (the skin) by puncturing and inserting indelible color **—*n., pl.*** **-toos′** a tattooed design

tat·too[2] (ta to͞o′) ***n., pl.*** **-toos′** ⟦< Du *tap toe*, tap to (shut): a signal for closing barrooms⟧ **1** a signal on a drum or bugle, summoning military personnel to their quarters at night **2** a drumming, rapping, etc.

tau (tou, tô) ***n.*** the 19th letter of the Greek alphabet (Τ, τ)

taught (tôt) ***vt., vi. pt. & pp. of*** TEACH

taunt (tônt, tänt) ***vt.*** ⟦< ? Fr *tant pour tant*, tit for tat⟧ to reproach scornfully or sarcastically; mock **—*n.*** a scornful or jeering remark

taupe (tōp) ***n.*** ⟦Fr < L *talpa*, mole⟧ a dark, brownish gray

Tau·rus (tôr′əs) ***n.*** ⟦L, a bull⟧ the second sign of the zodiac

taut (tôt) ***adj.*** ⟦ME *toght*, tight⟧ **1** tightly stretched, as a rope **2** tense *[a taut smile]* **3** trim, tidy, etc. **—taut′ly *adv.* —taut′ness *n.***

tau·tol·o·gy (tô täl′ə jē) ***n., pl.*** **-gies** ⟦< Gr < *to auto*, the same + -LOGY⟧ needless repetition of an idea in a different word, phrase, etc.; redundancy **—tau′to·log′i·cal *adj.***

tav·ern (tav′ərn) ***n.*** ⟦< L *taberna*⟧ **1** a saloon; bar **2** an inn

taw·dry (tô′drē) ***adj.*** **-dri·er, -dri·est** ⟦after *St. Audrey laces,* sold at St. Audrey's fair in Norwich, England⟧ cheap and showy; gaudy

taw·ny (tô′nē) ***adj.*** **-ni·er, -ni·est** ⟦< OFr *tanner*, to tan⟧ brownish-yellow; tan **—taw′ni·ness *n.***

tax (taks) ***vt.*** ⟦< L *taxare*, appraise⟧ **1** to require to pay a tax **2** to assess a tax on (income, purchases, etc.) **3** to put a strain on **4** to accuse; charge **—*n.*** **1** a compulsory payment of a percentage of income, property value, etc. for the support of a government **2** a heavy demand; burden **—tax′a·ble *adj.* —tax·a′tion *n.***

tax·i (tak′sē) ***n., pl.*** **-is** *short for* TAXICAB **—*vi.*** **-ied, -i·ing** or **-y·ing** **1** to go in a taxicab **2** to move along the ground or on the water as after landing: said of an airplane

tax′i·cab′ *n.* ⟦< *taxi*(*meter*) *cab*⟧ an automobile in which passengers are carried for a fare

tax·i·der·my (tak′si dur′mē) ***n.*** ⟦< Gr *taxis*, arrangement + *derma*, skin⟧ the art of preparing, stuffing, etc. the skins of animals to make them appear lifelike **—tax′i·der′mist *n.***

tax·i·me·ter (tak′sē mēt′ər) ***n.*** ⟦< Fr, ult. < ML *taxa*, tax + *-meter*, -METER⟧ an automatic device in taxicabs that registers the fare due

tax·on·o·my (tak sän′ə mē) ***n., pl.*** **-mies** ⟦< Gr *taxis*, arrangement + *nomos*, law⟧ classification, esp. of animals and plants **—tax·on′o·mist *n.***

tax′pay′er *n.* one who pays a tax

tax shelter an investment made to reduce one's income tax

tax·us (tak′səs) ***n.*** ⟦ModL⟧ YEW (*n.* 1)

Tay·lor (tā′lər), **Zach·a·ry** (zak′ə rē) 1784-1850; U.S. general: 12th president of the U.S. (1849-50)

TB (tē′bē′) ***n.*** tuberculosis

TBA, t.b.a., or **tba** *abbrev.* to be announced

T-ball (tē′bôl′) ***n.*** a baseball game for young children in which the ball is placed on and struck from a tall TEE (*n.* 1)

T-bone steak (tē′bōn′) a beefsteak with a T-shaped bone, containing some tenderloin

tbs or **tbsp** *abbrev.* **1** tablespoon(s) **2** tablespoonful(s)

T cell any of the lymphocytes affected by the thymus, that regulate immunity, reject foreign tissue, etc.: cf. B CELL

Tchai·kov·sky (chī kôf′skē), **Peter** 1840-93; Russ. composer

TD *abbrev.* touchdown: sometimes **td**

tea (tē) ***n.*** ⟦< Chin dial. *t'e*⟧ **1** an evergreen plant grown in Asia **2** its dried leaves, used to make a beverage **3** the beverage made by soaking such leaves in boiling water **4** a tealike beverage made from other plants or from a meat extract **5** [Chiefly Brit.] a meal in the late afternoon at which tea is the drink **6** an afternoon party at which tea, etc. is served

tea·ber·ry (tē′ber′ē) ***n., pl.*** **-ries** **1** WINTERGREEN (sense 1) **2** the berry of the wintergreen

teach (tēch) ***vt.*** **taught, teach′ing** ⟦OE *tæcan*⟧ **1** to show or help (a person) to learn (*how*) to do something **2** to give lessons to (a student, etc.) **3** to give lessons in (a subject) **4** to provide with knowledge, insight, etc. **—*vi.*** to give lessons or instruction **—teach′a·ble *adj.***

teach′er *n.* one who teaches, esp. as a profession

teach′ing *n.* **1** the profession of a teacher **2** something taught; precept, doctrine, etc.: *usually used in pl.*

tea′cup′ *n.* a cup for drinking tea, etc. **—tea′cup·ful′,** *pl.* **-fuls′, *n.***

teak (tēk) ***n.*** ⟦< Malayalam *tēkka*⟧ **1** a tall tree of SE Asia, with hard, yellowish-brown wood **2** its wood: also **teak′wood′**

tea′ket′tle *n.* a kettle with a spout, for boiling water to make tea, etc.

teal (tēl) ***n.*** ⟦ME *tele*⟧ **1** a small, short-necked, freshwater wild duck **2** a dark grayish or greenish blue: also **teal blue**

team (tēm) ***n.*** ⟦OE, offspring⟧ **1** two or more horses, oxen, etc. harnessed to the same plow, etc. **2** a group of people working or playing together **—*vi.*** to join in cooperative activity: often with *up* **—*adj.*** of or done by a team

team′mate′ *n.* one on the same team

team'ster (-stər) ***n.*** one whose work is hauling loads with a team or truck

team'work' ***n.*** joint action by a group of people

tea'pot' ***n.*** a pot with a spout and handle, for brewing and pouring tea

tear[1] (ter) ***vt.*** **tore, torn, tear'ing** ⟦OE *teran,* rend⟧ **1** to pull apart into pieces by force; rip **2** to make by tearing *[to tear* a hole*]* **3** to lacerate **4** to disrupt; split *[*ranks *torn* by dissensions*]* **5** to divide with doubt, etc. **6** to pull with force: with *up, out, away, off,* etc. —***vi.*** **1** to be torn **2** to move with force or speed —***n.*** **1** a tearing **2** a torn place; rent —**tear down 1** to wreck **2** to dismantle

tear[2] (tir) ***n.*** ⟦OE *tēar*⟧ a drop of the salty fluid which flows from the eye, as in weeping —**in tears** crying; weeping —**tear'ful** ***adj.*** —**tear'ful·ly** ***adv.*** —**tear'y, -i·er, -i·est,** ***adj.***

tear·drop (tir'dräp') ***n.*** a tear

tear gas (tir) a liquid or gas that causes irritation of the eyes, used as by the police to disperse rioters —**tear'-gas', -gassed', -gas'sing,** ***vt.***

tear·jerk·er (tir'jur'kər) ***n.*** [Slang] a sad, overly sentimental film, play, etc.

tea'room' ***n.*** a restaurant that serves tea, coffee, light lunches, etc.

tease (tēz) ***vt.*** **teased, teas'ing** ⟦OE *tæsan*⟧ **1** *a)* to card or comb (flax, wool, etc.) *b)* to fluff (the hair) by combing toward the scalp **2** to annoy by mocking, poking fun, etc. **3** to beg; importune **4** to tantalize —***vi.*** to indulge in teasing —***n.*** one who teases

tea·sel (tē'zəl) ***n.*** ⟦see prec.⟧ a bristly plant with prickly flowers

teas·er (tē'zər) ***n.*** **1** a person or thing that teases **2** a puzzling problem

tea'spoon' ***n.*** **1** a spoon for stirring tea, etc. **2** a spoon for measuring $\frac{1}{3}$ tablespoon —**tea'spoon·ful',** *pl.* **-fuls',** ***n.***

teat (tēt) ***n.*** ⟦< OFr *tete*⟧ the nipple on a breast or udder

tech *abbrev.* **1** technical(ly) **2** technology

tech·ie (tek'ē) ***n.*** [Inf.] an expert in computer technology

tech·ni·cal (tek'ni kəl) ***adj.*** ⟦< Gr *technē,* an art⟧ **1** dealing with the industrial or mechanical arts or the applied sciences **2** of a specific science, art, craft, etc. **3** of, in or showing technique **4** concerned with minute details —**tech'ni·cal·ly** ***adv.***

tech'ni·cal'i·ty (-kal'ə tē) ***n.,*** *pl.* **-ties 1** the state or quality of being technical **2** a technical point, detail, etc. **3** a minute point, detail, etc. brought to bear upon a main issue

tech·ni·cian (tek nish'ən) ***n.*** one skilled in the technique of some art, craft, or science

Tech·ni·col·or (tek'ni kul'ər) *trademark for* a process of making color movies —***n.*** [**t-**] this process

tech·nique (tek nēk') ***n.*** ⟦Fr⟧ **1** the method of procedure in artistic work, scientific activity, etc. **2** the degree of expertness in following this

tech·noc·ra·cy (tek näk'rə sē) ***n.*** ⟦< Gr *technē,* an art + -CRACY⟧ government by scientists and engineers —**tech'no·crat'** (-nə krat') ***n.***

tech·nol·o·gy (tek näl'ə jē) ***n.*** ⟦Gr *technologia,* systematic treatment⟧ **1** the science of the practical or industrial arts **2** applied science —**tech'no·log'i·cal** (-nə läj'i kəl) ***adj.***

tech·no·phile (tek'nə fīl') ***n.*** one who is enthusiastic about advanced technology

tech'no·pho'bi·a ***n.*** dislike or fear of advanced technology —**tech'no·phobe'** ***n.***

ted·dy bear (ted'ē) ⟦after *Teddy* (Theodore) Roosevelt⟧ a child's stuffed toy made to look like a bear cub

te·di·ous (tē'dē əs) ***adj.*** full of tedium; long and dull —**te'di·ous·ly** ***adv.***

te'di·um (-əm) ***n.*** ⟦< L *taedet,* it offends⟧ the condition or quality of being tiresome, boring, etc.

tee (tē) ***n.*** ⟦prob. < Scot dial. *teaz*⟧ *Golf* **1** a small peg from which the ball is driven **2** the place from which a player makes the first stroke on each hole —***vt., vi.*** **teed, tee'ing** to place (a ball) on a tee —**tee off 1** to play a golf ball from a tee **2** [Slang] to make angry or disgusted

teem (tēm) ***vi.*** ⟦< OE *team,* progeny⟧ to be prolific; abound; swarm

teen (tēn) ***n.*** ⟦OE *tien,* ten⟧ **1** [*pl.*] the years from 13 through 19, as of a person's age **2** TEENAGER

teen·age (tēn'āj') ***adj.*** **1** in one's teens **2** of or for people in their teens —**teen'ag'er** ***n.***

tee·ny (tē'nē) ***adj.*** **-ni·er, -ni·est** *inf. var. of* TINY: also **teen·sy** (tēn'zē, -sē), **-si·er, -si·est**

tee·ny-wee·ny (tē'nē wē'nē) ***adj.*** [Inf.] tiny: also **teen·sy-ween·sy** (tēn'zē wēn'zē, tēn'sē wēn'sē)

tee·pee (tē'pē) ***n.*** *alt. sp. of* TEPEE

tee shirt *var. of* T-SHIRT

tee·ter (tēt'ər) ***vi.*** ⟦< ON *titra,* to tremble⟧ to totter, wobble, etc.

tee'ter-tot'ter (-tôt'ər, -tät'-) ***n., vi.*** SEESAW

teeth (tēth) ***n.*** *pl. of* TOOTH —**in the teeth of 1** directly against **2** defying

teethe (tēth) ***vi.*** **teethed, teeth'ing** to grow teeth; cut one's teeth

tee·to·tal·er or **tee·to·tal·ler** (tē tōt''lər) ***n.*** ⟦< doubling of initial *t* in *total*⟧ one who practices total abstinence from alcoholic liquor

te·fil·lin (tə fil'in) ***n.*** either of two small, leather cases holding Scripture texts, worn in prayer on the forehead and arm by orthodox Jewish men

Tef·lon (tef'län') *trademark for* a tough polymer, used for nonsticking coatings as for cookware —***n.*** [**t-**] this substance

Teh·ran (te rän') capital of Iran: pop. 6,043,000: also **Te·he·ran'**

tek·tite (tek'tīt') ***n.*** ⟦< Gr *tēktos,* molten⟧ a small, dark, glassy body thought to have originated as a meteorite: also sp. **tec'tite'**

tel *abbrev.* **1** telegram **2** telephone

Tel A·viv (tel′ ə vēv′) seaport in W Israel: pop. 356,000

tele- *combining form* **1** ⟦< Gr *tēle*, far off⟧ at, over, etc. a distance *[telegraph]* **2** ⟦< TELE(VISION)⟧ of, in, or by television *[telecast]*

tel·e·cast (tel′ə kast′) ***vt., vi.*** **-cast′** or **-cast′ed, -cast′ing** to broadcast by television —***n.*** a television broadcast —**tel′e·cast′er** ***n.***

tel′e·com·mu′ni·ca′tion ***n.*** [*also pl., with sing. or pl. v.*] communication by electronic or electrical means, as through radio, TV, computers, etc.: also **tel′e·com′** (-käm′)

tel′e·com·mute′ ***vi.*** to do office work at home using a computer

tel′e·con′fer·ence ***n.*** a conference of persons in different locations, as by telephone, TV, etc.

tel′e·gram′ ***n.*** a message transmitted by telegraph

tel′e·graph′ ***n.*** ⟦see TELE- & -GRAPH⟧ an apparatus or system that transmits messages by electrical impulses sent by wire or radio —***vt., vi.*** to send (a message) to (a person) by telegraph —**tel′e·graph′ic** ***adj.***

te·leg·ra·phy (tə leg′rə fē) ***n.*** the operation of telegraph apparatus —**te·leg′ra·pher** ***n.***

tel·e·ki·ne·sis (tel′ə ki nē′sis) ***n.*** ⟦see TELE- & KINETIC⟧ *Parapsychology* the causing of an object to move by psychic, rather than physical, force

tel′e·mar′ket·ing ***n.*** the use of the telephone in selling, market research, promotion, etc. —**tel′e·mar′ket·er** ***n.***

tel·e·me·ter (tel′ə mēt′ər, tə lem′ət ər) ***n.*** a device for measuring and transmitting data about radiation, temperature, etc. from a remote point —**te·lem′e·try** ***n.***

te·lep·a·thy (tə lep′ə thē) ***n.*** ⟦TELE- + -PATHY⟧ *Parapsychology* extrasensory communication between minds —**tel·e·path·ic** (tel′ə path′ik) ***adj.***

tel·e·phone (tel′ə fōn′) ***n.*** ⟦TELE- + -PHONE⟧ an instrument or system for conveying speech or computerized information over distances, usually by converting sound into electrical impulses sent through a wire —***vt., vi.*** **-phoned′, -phon′ing** to convey (a message) to (a person) by telephone —**tel′e·phon′ic** (-fän′ik) ***adj.***

te·leph·o·ny (tə lef′ə nē) ***n.*** the making or operation of telephones

tel·e·pho·to (tel′ə fōt′ō) ***adj.*** designating or of a camera lens that produces a large image of a distant object

tel′e·proc′ess·ing ***n.*** computerized data processing, over communication lines

tel′e·promp′ter (-prämp′tər) ***n.*** ⟦< *TelePrompTer*, a former trademark⟧ an electronic device that unrolls a speech, script, etc. line by line, as an aid to a speaker, etc. on TV

tel·e·scope (tel′ə skōp′) ***n.*** ⟦see TELE- & -SCOPE⟧ an optical instrument for making distant objects appear nearer and larger —***vi., vt.*** **-scoped′, -scop′ing** to slide one into another like the tubes of a collapsible telescope —**tel′e·scop′ic** (-skäp′ik) ***adj.***

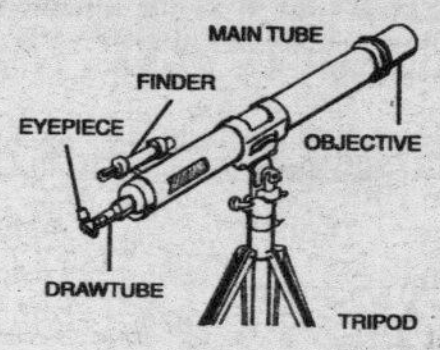

REFRACTING TELESCOPE

tel′e·thon′ (-thän′) ***n.*** ⟦TELE(VISION) + (MARA)THON⟧ a campaign, as on a lengthy telecast, seeking donations

Tel·e·type (tel′ə tīp′) ***n.*** *trademark for* a former kind of telegraphic apparatus for transmitting typed messages —**tel′e·type′writ′er** ***n.***

tel·e·vise (tel′ə vīz′) ***vt., vi.*** **-vised′, -vis′ing** to transmit by television

tel′e·vi′sion (-vizh′ən) ***n.*** **1** the process of transmitting images by converting light rays into electrical signals: the receiver reconverts the signals to reproduce the images on a screen **2** television broadcasting **3** a television receiving set **4** a television program or programs

tel·ex (tel′eks′) ***n.*** ⟦TEL(ETYPEWRITER) + EX(CHANGE)⟧ **1** a teletypewriter which sends messages over telephone lines **2** a message sent in this way —***vt.*** to send by telex

tell (tel) ***vt.*** **told, tell′ing** ⟦OE *tellan*, calculate⟧ **1** to count; reckon *[to tell time]* **2** to narrate; relate *[to tell a story]* **3** to express in words; say *[to tell the truth]* **4** to reveal; disclose **5** to recognize; distinguish *[to tell twins apart]* **6** to inform *[tell me later]* **7** to order *[tell him to go]* —***vi.*** **1** to give an account or evidence (*of* something) **2** to be effective *[each blow told]* —**tell off** [Inf.] to rebuke severely —**tell on 1** to have an adverse effect on **2** [Inf.] to inform against

tell′er ***n.*** **1** one who tells (a story, etc.) **2** a bank clerk who pays out or receives money

tell′ing ***adj.*** **1** forceful; striking **2** that reveals much —**tell′ing·ly** ***adv.***

tell′tale′ ***adj.*** revealing what is meant to be kept secret or hidden

tel·ly (tel′ē) ***n.***, *pl.* **-lies** *Brit. inf. term for* TELEVISION

tem·blor (tem′blôr′, -blər) ***n.*** ⟦Sp < *temblar*, to tremble⟧ EARTHQUAKE

te·mer·i·ty (tə mer′ə tē) ***n.*** ⟦< L *temere*, rashly⟧ foolish or rash boldness

temp[1] (temp) ***n.*** [Inf.] one who works at a place on a temporary basis

temp[2] *abbrev.* **1** temperature **2** temporary

tem·per (tem′pər) ***vt.*** ⟦< L *temperare*, regulate⟧ **1** to moderate, as by mingling with something else *[to temper blame with praise]* **2** to bring to the proper condition by some treatment *[to temper steel]* **3** to toughen —***n.*** **1** the degree of hardness and resiliency of a metal **2** frame of mind; disposition **3** calmness of mind: in **lose** (or **keep**) **one's temper 4** a tendency to become angry **5** anger; rage

tem·per·a (tem′pər ə) ***n.*** ⟦It: see prec.⟧ a process of painting with pigments mixed with size, casein, or egg

tem·per·a·ment (tem′pər ə mənt, -prə mənt) ***n.*** ⟦see TEMPER⟧ **1** one's natural disposition; nature **2** a nature that is excitable, moody, etc. —**tem′per·a·men′tal** ***adj.***

tem·per·ance (tem′pər əns, -prəns) ***n.*** **1** self-restraint in conduct, indulgence of the appetites, etc.; moderation **2** moderation in drinking alcoholic liquors or total abstinence from them

tem·per·ate (tem′pər it, -prit) ***adj.*** ⟦see TEMPER⟧ **1** moderate, as in one's appetites, behavior, etc. **2** neither very hot nor very cold: said of climate, etc.

Temperate Zone either of the two zones of the earth (**North Temperate Zone** and **South Temperate Zone**) between the tropics and the polar circles

tem·per·a·ture (tem′pər ə chər, -prə chər) ***n.*** ⟦< L *temperatus,* temperate⟧ **1** the degree of hotness or coldness of anything **2** an excess of body heat over the normal; fever

tem·pered (tem′pərd) ***adj.*** **1** having been given the desired TEMPER (*n.* 1) **2** having a (specified) TEMPER (*n.* 2)

tem·pest (tem′pist) ***n.*** ⟦< L *tempus,* time⟧ a violent storm with high winds, esp. one accompanied by rain, hail, etc.

tem·pes·tu·ous (tem pes′cho͞o əs) ***adj.*** of or like a tempest; violent

tem·plate (tem′plit) ***n.*** ⟦< L *templum,* small timber⟧ a pattern, as a thin metal plate, for making an exact copy

tem·ple[1] (tem′pəl) ***n.*** ⟦< L *templum*⟧ **1** a building for the worship of God or gods **2** a large building for some special purpose *[a temple of art]*

tem·ple[2] (tem′pəl) ***n.*** ⟦< L *tempus*⟧ **1** the flat surface alongside the forehead, in front of each ear **2** either of the sidepieces of a pair of glasses

tem·po (tem′pō) ***n.***, *pl.* **-pos** or **-pi** (-pē) ⟦It < L *tempus,* time⟧ **1** the speed at which a musical composition is performed **2** rate of activity

tem·po·ral[1] (tem′pə rəl) ***adj.*** ⟦< L *tempus,* time⟧ **1** worldly; not spiritual **2** secular **3** of or limited by time

tem·po·ral[2] (tem′pə rəl) ***adj.*** of or near the temples (of the head)

tem′po·rar′y (-rer′ē) ***adj.*** ⟦< L *tempus,* time⟧ lasting only a while; not permanent —**tem′po·rar′i·ly** ***adv.***

tem′po·rize′ (-rīz′) ***vi.*** **-rized′**, **-riz′ing** to give temporary compliance, evade decision, etc., so as to gain time or avoid argument

tempt (tempt) ***vt.*** ⟦< L *temptare,* to test⟧ **1** to induce or entice, as to something immoral **2** to be inviting to; attract **3** to provoke or risk provoking (fate, etc.) **4** to incline strongly *[to be tempted to accept]* —**temp·ta·tion** (temp tā′shən) ***n.***

tempt·ress (temp′tris) ***n.*** a woman who tempts, esp. sexually

tem·pu·ra (tem′po͝o rä′, tem po͝or′ə) ***n.*** ⟦Jpn⟧ a Japanese dish of deep-fried shrimp, fish, vegetables, etc.

ten (ten) ***adj., n.*** ⟦OE⟧ one more than nine; 10; X

ten·a·ble (ten′ə bəl) ***adj.*** ⟦< L *tenere,* to hold⟧ that can be defended or believed —**ten′a·bil′i·ty** ***n.***

te·na·cious (tə nā′shəs) ***adj.*** ⟦< L *tenere,* to hold⟧ **1** holding firmly *[a tenacious grip]* **2** retentive *[a tenacious memory]* **3** strongly cohesive or adhesive **4** persistent; stubborn *[tenacious courage]* —**te·na′cious·ly** ***adv.*** —**te·nac·i·ty** (tə nas′ə tē) ***n.***

ten·ant (ten′ənt) ***n.*** ⟦see prec.⟧ **1** one who pays rent to occupy land, a building, etc. **2** an occupant —***vt.*** to hold as a tenant; occupy —**ten′an·cy**, *pl.* **-cies**, ***n.***

tenant farmer one who farms land owned by another and pays rent

Ten Commandments *Bible* the ten laws of moral and religious conduct given to Moses by God: Exodus 20:2-17

tend[1] (tend) ***vt.*** ⟦see ATTEND⟧ **1** to take care of **2** to manage or operate

tend[2] (tend) ***vi.*** ⟦< L *tendere,* to stretch⟧ **1** to be inclined, disposed, etc. (*to*) **2** to be directed (*to* or *toward*)

tend·en·cy (ten′dən sē) ***n.***, *pl.* **-cies** ⟦see prec.⟧ **1** an inclination to move or act in a particular direction or way **2** a course toward some object

ten·den·tious (ten den′shəs) ***adj.*** ⟦< Ger *tendenz,* TENDENCY⟧ advancing a definite point of view *[tendentious writings]* —**ten·den′tious·ly** ***adv.***

ten·der[1] (ten′dər) ***adj.*** ⟦< L *tener,* soft⟧ **1** soft and easily chewed, broken, cut, etc. **2** physically weak **3** immature **4** that requires careful handling **5** gentle or light **6** acutely sensitive, as to pain **7** sensitive to emotions, others' feelings, etc. —**ten′der·ly** ***adv.*** —**ten′der·ness** ***n.***

ten·der[2] (ten′dər) ***vt.*** ⟦see TEND[2]⟧ to offer formally —***n.*** **1** a formal offer **2** money, etc. offered in payment

tend·er[3] (ten′dər) ***n.*** **1** one who tends something **2** a small ship for supplying a larger one **3** a railroad car attached behind, and carrying fuel and water for, a steam locomotive

ten′der·foot′ ***n.***, *pl.* **-foots′** or **-feet′** **1** a newcomer to ranching in the West, unused to hardships **2** any novice

ten′der·heart′ed ***adj.*** quick to feel pity or compassion

ten·der·ize (ten′dər īz′) ***vt.*** **-ized′**, **-iz′ing** to make (meat) tender

ten′der·loin′ ***n.*** the tenderest part of a loin of beef, pork, etc.

ten·di·ni·tis (ten′də nīt′is) ***n.*** inflammation of a tendon

ten·don (ten′dən) ***n.*** ⟦< Gr *teinein,* to stretch⟧ any of the inelastic cords of tough, connective tissue by which muscles are attached to bones, etc.

ten·dril (ten′drəl) ***n.*** ⟦prob. ult. < L *tener,* delicate⟧ a threadlike, clinging part of a climbing plant

ten·e·ment (ten′ə mənt) ***n.*** ⟦< L *tenere,* to hold⟧ a building divided into tene-ments; now specif., one that is rundown, overcrowded, etc.: in full **tenement house**

ten·et (ten′it) ***n.*** ⟦L, he holds⟧ a principle, doctrine, or belief held as a truth, as by some group

Ten·nes·see (ten′ə sē′) state of the EC U.S.: 41,220 sq. mi.; pop. 4,877,000; cap. Nashville: abbrev. *TN* —**Ten′nes·se′an** ***adj., n.***

ten·nis (ten′is) ***n.*** ⟦prob. < OFr *tener,* hold (imperative)⟧ a game in which players in a marked area (**tennis court**) hit a ball back and forth with rackets over a net

tennis elbow inflammation of the elbow tendons, caused by strain

tennis shoe a sneaker

Ten·ny·son (ten′i sən), **Al·fred** (al′frəd) 1809-92; Eng. poet: called *Alfred, Lord Tennyson*

ten·on (ten′ən) ***n.*** ⟦ult. < L *tenere,* to hold⟧ a projecting part cut on the end of a piece of wood for insertion into a mortise to make a joint

ten·or (ten′ər) ***n.*** ⟦< L *tenere,* to hold⟧ **1** general tendency **2** general meaning; drift **3** *a)* the range of the highest regular adult male voice *b)* a voice, singer, or instrument with such a range *c)* a part for a tenor —***adj.*** of or for a tenor

ten′pins′ ***n.*** the game of bowling in which ten pins are used

tense[1] (tens) ***adj.*** **tens′er, tens′est** ⟦< L *tendere,* to stretch⟧ **1** stretched tight; taut **2** feeling or showing tension —***vt., vi.*** **tensed, tens′ing** to make or become tense

tense[2] (tens) ***n.*** ⟦< L *tempus,* time⟧ any of the forms of a verb that show the time of its action or existence

ten·sile (ten′səl) ***adj.*** **1** of, undergoing, or exerting tension **2** capable of being stretched

ten·sion (ten′shən) ***n.*** **1** a tensing or being tensed **2** mental or nervous strain **3** a state of strained relations due to mutual hostility **4** VOLTAGE **5** stress on a material produced by the pull of forces causing extension

tent (tent) ***n.*** ⟦< L *tendere,* to stretch⟧ a portable shelter made of canvas, etc. stretched over poles —***vi., vt.*** to lodge in a tent or tents

ten·ta·cle (ten′tə kəl) ***n.*** ⟦< L *tentare,* to touch⟧ a long, slender, flexible growth on the head of some invertebrates, used to grasp, feel, etc.

ten·ta·tive (ten′tə tiv) ***adj.*** ⟦< L *tentare,* to try⟧ **1** made, done, etc. provisionally; not final **2** indicating timidity or uncertainty —**ten′ta·tive·ly** ***adv.***

ten·ter·hook (ten′tər ho͝ok′) ***n.*** ⟦< L *tendere,* to stretch + HOOK⟧ a kind of hooked nail —**on tenterhooks** in anxious suspense

tenth (tenth) ***adj.*** ⟦OE *teogotha*⟧ preceded by nine others in a series; 10th —***n.*** **1** the one following the ninth **2** any of the ten equal parts of something; $\frac{1}{10}$

ten·u·ous (ten′yo͞o əs) ***adj.*** ⟦< L *tenuis,* thin⟧ **1** slender or fine, as a fiber **2** rare, as air at high altitudes **3** flimsy *[tenuous* evidence*]*

ten·ure (ten′yər) ***n.*** ⟦< medieval Fr < *tenir,* to hold⟧ **1** the act or right of holding property, an office, etc. **2** the length of time, or the conditions under which, something is held **3** the status of holding one's position on a permanent basis, granted to teachers, etc.

TEPEE

te·pee (tē′pē) ***n.*** ⟦< AmInd *tʰípi,* dwelling⟧ a cone-shaped tent used by some North American Indians

tep·id (tep′id) ***adj.*** ⟦< L *tepidus*⟧ **1** lukewarm **2** lacking enthusiasm

te·qui·la (tə kē′lə) ***n.*** ⟦< AmInd (Mexico) *Tuiquila,* region in Mexico⟧ an alcoholic liquor of Mexico, distilled from an agave mash

ter·cen·te·nar·y (tur′sen ten′ər ē, tər sen′tə ner′ē) ***adj., n.,*** *pl.* **-ies** ⟦L *ter,* three times + CENTENARY⟧ TRICENTENNIAL

term (turm) ***n.*** ⟦< L *terminus,* a limit⟧ **1** a set date, as for payment, etc. **2** a set period of time *[*school *term, term* of office*]* **3** [*pl.*] conditions of a contract, etc. **4** [*pl.*] mutual relationship between persons *[*on speaking *terms]* **5** a word or phrase, esp. as used in some science, art, etc. **6** [*pl.*] words; speech *[*unkind *terms]* **7** *Math. a)* either quantity of a fraction or a ratio *b)* each quantity in a series or algebraic expression —***vt.*** to call by a term; name —**bring** (or **come**) **to terms** to force into (or arrive at) an agreement

ter·mi·na·ble (tur′mi nə bəl) ***adj.*** that can be, or is, terminated

ter·mi·nal (tur′mə nəl) ***adj.*** ⟦L *terminalis*⟧ **1** of, at, or forming the end or extremity **2** concluding; final **3** close to causing death *[terminal* cancer*]* **4** of or at the end of a transportation line —***n.*** **1** an end; extremity **2** a connective point on an electric circuit **3** either end of a transportation line, or a main station on it **4** a device, usually with a keyboard and video display, for putting data in, or getting it from, a computer

ter·mi·nate (tur′mə nāt′) ***vt.*** **-nat′ed, -nat′ing** ⟦< L *terminus,* a limit⟧ **1** to form the end of **2** to put an end to; stop **3** to dismiss from employment; fire —***vi.*** **1** to come to an end **2** to have its end (*in* something) —**ter′mi·na′tion** ***n.***

ter·mi·nol·o·gy (tur′mə näl′ə jē) ***n., pl.*** **-gies** the terms used in a specific science, art, etc.

term insurance life insurance that

expires after a specified period

ter·mi·nus (tur′mə nəs) ***n.***, *pl.* **-ni′** (-nī′) or **-nus·es** ⟦L, a limit⟧ **1** a limit **2** an end; extremity or goal **3** [Chiefly Brit.] either end of a transportation line

ter·mite (tur′mīt′) ***n.*** ⟦< L *tarmes,* wood-boring worm⟧ a social insect that is very destructive to wooden structures

tern (turn) ***n.*** ⟦< ON *therna*⟧ a gull-like seabird with webbed feet and a straight bill

ter·race (ter′əs) ***n.*** ⟦< L *terra,* earth⟧ **1** a raised, flat mound of earth with sloping sides, esp. one in a series on a hillside **2** an unroofed, paved area, between a house and lawn **3** a row of houses on ground above street level **4** a small, usually roofed balcony, as outside an apartment —***vt.*** **-raced**, **-rac·ing** to form into a terrace or terraces

ter·ra cot·ta (ter′ə kät′ə) ⟦It, lit., baked earth⟧ a hard, brown-red earthenware, or its color

ter·ra fir·ma (ter′ə fur′mə) ⟦L⟧ firm earth

ter·rain (tə rān′) ***n.*** ⟦< L *terra,* earth⟧ a tract of ground, as with regard to its features

ter·ra·pin (ter′ə pin) ***n.*** ⟦< Algonquian⟧ **1** any of various terrestrial, freshwater or tidewater turtles **2** its edible flesh

ter·rar·i·um (tə rer′ē əm) ***n.***, *pl.* **-i·ums** or **-i·a** (-ə) ⟦< L *terra,* earth + *-arium,* as in *aquarium*⟧ an enclosure, as of glass, in which small plants are grown or small land animals are kept

ter·raz·zo (tə raz′ō, tə rät′sō) ***n.*** ⟦It⟧ flooring of small chips of marble set in cement and polished

ter·res·tri·al (tə res′trē əl) ***adj.*** ⟦< L *terra,* earth⟧ **1** worldly; mundane **2** of the earth **3** consisting of land, not water **4** living on land

ter·ri·ble (ter′ə bəl) ***adj.*** ⟦< L *terrere,* frighten⟧ **1** causing terror; dreadful **2** extreme; intense **3** [Inf.] very unpleasant, etc. —**ter′ri·bly** ***adv.***

ter·ri·er (ter′ē ər) ***n.*** ⟦< medieval Fr (*chien*) *terrier,* hunting (dog)⟧ any of several breeds of small and typically aggressive dog

ter·rif·ic (tə rif′ik) ***adj.*** ⟦< L *terrere,* frighten⟧ **1** causing great fear **2** [Inf.] *a*) very great, intense, etc. *b*) unusually fine, admirable, etc.

ter·ri·fy (ter′ə fī′) ***vt.*** **-fied′**, **-fy′ing** to fill with terror; frighten greatly

ter·ri·to·ry (ter′ə tôr′ē) ***n.***, *pl.* **-ries** ⟦< L *terra,* earth⟧ **1** an area under the jurisdiction of a nation, ruler, etc. **2** a part of a country or empire that does not have full status **3** any large tract of land **4** an assigned area **5** a sphere of action, thought, etc. —**ter′ri·to′ri·al** ***adj.***

ter·ror (ter′ər) ***n.*** ⟦< L *terrere,* frighten⟧ **1** intense fear **2** *a*) one that causes intense fear *b*) the quality of causing such fear **3** [Inf.] one who is very annoying or unmanageable, esp. a child

ter′ror·ism′ ***n.*** the use of force or threats to intimidate, etc., esp. as a political policy —**ter′ror·ist** ***n.***, ***adj.***

ter′ror·ize′ (-īz′) ***vt.*** **-ized′**, **-iz′ing** **1** to terrify **2** to coerce, make submit, etc. by filling with terror

ter·ry (ter′ē) ***n.*** ⟦prob. < Fr *tirer,* to draw⟧ cloth having a pile of uncut loops, esp. cotton cloth used for toweling: also **terry cloth**

terse (turs) ***adj.*** **ters′er**, **ters′est** ⟦L *tersus,* wiped off⟧ free of superfluous words; concise; succinct —**terse′ly** ***adv.*** —**terse′ness** ***n.***

ter·ti·ar·y (tur′shē er′ē) ***adj.*** ⟦< L *tertius,* third⟧ third in order

tes·sel·late (tes′ə lāt′) ***vt.*** **-lat′ed**, **-lat′ing** ⟦< L *tessella,* little square stone⟧ to lay out in a mosaic pattern of small, square blocks

test (test) ***n.*** ⟦< OFr, assaying cup⟧ **1** *a*) an examination or trial, as of something's value *b*) the method or a criterion used in this **2** an event, etc. that tries one's qualities **3** a set of questions, etc. for determining one's knowledge, etc. **4** *Chem.* a trial or reaction for identifying a substance —***vt.*** to subject to a test; try —***vi.*** to be rated by a test

tes·ta·ment (tes′tə mənt) ***n.*** ⟦< L *testis,* a witness⟧ **1** [**T-**] either of the two parts of the Bible, the *Old Testament* and the *New Testament* **2** *a*) a testimonial *b*) an affirmation of beliefs **3** *Law* a will —**tes′ta·men′ta·ry** (-men′tə rē) ***adj.***

tes·tate (tes′tāt′) ***adj.*** ⟦< L *testari,* make a will⟧ having left a legally valid will

tes·ta·tor (tes′tāt′ər, tes tāt′-) ***n.*** one who has made a will

tes·ti·cle (tes′ti kəl) ***n.*** ⟦< L *testis*⟧ either of two male sex glands

tes·ti·fy (tes′tə fī′) ***vi.*** **-fied′**, **-fy′ing** ⟦< L *testis,* a witness + *facere,* to make⟧ **1** to give evidence, esp. under oath in court **2** to serve as evidence —***vt.*** to affirm; declare, esp. under oath in court

tes·ti·mo·ni·al (tes′tə mō′nē əl) ***n.*** **1** a statement recommending a person or thing **2** something given or done to show gratitude or appreciation

tes·ti·mo·ny (tes′tə mō′nē) ***n.***, *pl.* **-nies** ⟦< L *testis,* a witness⟧ **1** a statement made under oath to establish a fact **2** any declaration **3** any form of evidence; proof

tes·tis (tes′tis) ***n.***, *pl.* **-tes′** (-tēz′) ⟦L⟧ TESTICLE

tes·tos·ter·one (tes täs′tər ōn′) ***n.*** ⟦see TESTICLE⟧ a male sex hormone

test tube a tube of thin, transparent glass closed at one end, used in chemical experiments, etc.

tes·ty (tes′tē) ***adj.*** **-ti·er**, **-ti·est** ⟦< L *testa,* the head⟧ irritable; touchy

tet·a·nus (tet′′n əs, tet′nəs) ***n.*** ⟦< Gr *tetanos,* spasm⟧ an acute infectious disease, often fatal, caused by a toxin and characterized by spasmodic contractions and rigidity of muscles

tête-à-tête (tāt′ə tāt′) ***n.*** ⟦Fr, lit., head-to-head⟧ a private conversation between two people

teth·er (te*th*′ər) ***n.*** ⟦< ON *tjōthr*⟧ **1** a rope or chain fastened to an animal to keep it from roaming **2** the limit of one's abilities, resources, etc. —***vt.*** to fasten with a tether

tet·ra (te′trə) ***n.*** ⟦< ModL⟧ a brightly colored, tropical American fish

tetra- ⟦Gr < *tettares,* four⟧ *combining form* four

tet·ra·cy·cline (te′trə sī′klin) ***n.*** a yellow, crystalline compound, used as an antibiotic

tet·ra·he·dron (te′trə hē′drən) ***n.***, *pl.* **-drons** or **-dra** (-drə) ⟦see TETRA- & -HEDRON⟧ a solid figure with four triangular faces

te·tram·e·ter (te tram′ət ər) ***n.*** ⟦see TETRA- & METER[1]⟧ **1** a line of verse containing four metrical feet **2** verse consisting of tetrameters

Teu·ton·ic (to͞o tän′ik) ***adj.*** designating or of a group of N European peoples, esp. the Germans —**Teu·ton** (to͞ot′′n) ***n.***

Tex·as (tek′səs) state of the SW U.S.: 261,914 sq. mi.; pop. 16,987,000; cap. Austin: abbrev. *TX* —**Tex′an** ***adj., n.***

text (tekst) ***n.*** ⟦< L *texere,* to weave⟧ **1** the actual words of an author, as distinguished from notes, etc. **2** any form in which a written work exists **3** the principal matter on a printed page, as distinguished from notes, headings, etc. **4** *a)* a Biblical passage used as the topic of a sermon, etc. *b)* any topic or subject **5** *short for* TEXTBOOK —**tex·tu·al** (teks′cho͞o əl) ***adj.***

text′book′ ***n.*** a book giving instructions in a subject of study —***adj.*** so typical as to be a classic example or model of its kind

tex·tile (teks′tīl′, -təl) ***adj.*** ⟦see TEXT⟧ **1** having to do with weaving **2** that has been or can be woven —***n.*** **1** a woven or knitted fabric; cloth **2** raw material suitable for this

tex·ture (teks′chər) ***n.*** ⟦< L *texere,* to weave⟧ **1** the character of a fabric, determined by the arrangement, size, etc. of its threads **2** the arrangement of the constituent parts of anything —**tex′tur·al** ***adj.***

tex′tured ***adj.*** having an uneven surface; not smooth *[textured* wallpaper*]*

-th[1] ⟦OE⟧ *suffix* **1** the act of ___ing *[growth]* **2** the state or quality of being or having *[wealth]*

-th[2] ⟦< OE⟧ *suffix* forming ordinal numerals *[fourth, ninth]*

Th *Chem. symbol for* thorium

Thai (tī) ***n.*** **1** *pl.* **Thais** or **Thai** a person born or living in Thailand **2** the language of Thailand **3** *alt. sp. of* TAI —***adj.*** of Thailand or its people, culture, etc.

Thai·land (tī′land′) country in SE Asia: 198,114 sq. mi.; pop. 54,532,000

thal·a·mus (thal′ə məs) ***n.***, *pl.* **-mi′** (-mī′) ⟦< Gr *thalamos,* inner chamber⟧ a mass of gray matter at the base of the brain, involved in the transmission of certain sensations

thal·lo·phyte (thal′ə fīt′) ***n.*** ⟦< Gr *thallos,* young shoot + *phyton,* a plant⟧ any of a large group of plants lacking true roots, leaves, or stems, as the fungi, the lichens, and most algae

Thames (temz) river in S England, flowing through London into the North Sea

than (*th*an) ***conj.*** ⟦OE *thenne*⟧ introducing the second element in a comparison *[*A is taller *than* B*]*

thank (thaŋk) ***vt.*** ⟦OE *thancian*⟧ **1** to express gratitude to, as by saying "thank you" **2** to blame: an ironic use —**thank you** *short for* I thank you

thank′ful ***adj.*** feeling or expressing thanks —**thank′ful·ly** ***adv.***

thank′less ***adj.*** **1** not feeling or expressing thanks; ungrateful **2** unappreciated

thanks (thaŋks) ***pl.n.*** an expression of gratitude —***interj.*** I thank you —**thanks to** **1** let thanks be given to **2** on account of; because of

thanks′giv′ing ***n.*** **1** a formal public expression of thanks to God **2** [**T-**] an annual U.S. holiday observed on the fourth Thursday of November

that (*th*at) ***pron.***, *pl.* **those** ⟦OE *thæt*⟧ **1** the person or thing mentioned *[that* is John*]* **2** the farther one or the other one *[*this is better than *that]* **3** who, whom, or which *[*the road *that* we took*]* **4** where *[*the place *that* I saw her*]* **5** when *[*the year *that* I was born*]* —***adj.***, *pl.* **those** **1** designating the one mentioned *[that* man is John*]* **2** designating the farther one or the other one *[*this house is larger than *that* one*]* —***conj.*** subordinating conjunction used to introduce: *a)* a noun clause *[that* she's gone is obvious*]* *b)* an adverbial clause expressing purpose *[*they died *that* we might live*]*, result *[*I ran so fast *that* I won*]*, or cause *[*I'm glad *that* I won*]* *c)* an elliptical sentence expressing surprise, desire, etc. *[*oh, *that* she were here!*]* —***adv.*** to that extent *[*I can't see *that* far*]* —**at that** [Inf.] **1** at that point: also **with that** **2** even so —**that is** **1** to be specific **2** in other words

thatch (thach) ***n.*** ⟦OE *thæc*⟧ **1** a roof of straw, rushes, etc. **2** material for such a roof: also **thatch′ing** **3** a layer of tangled, partly decayed leaves, stems, etc. lying on top of the soil —***vt.*** to cover as with thatch

thaw (thô) ***vi.*** ⟦OE *thawian*⟧ **1** *a)* to melt (said of ice, snow, etc.) *b)* to pass to an unfrozen state (said of frozen foods) **2** to become warmer so that snow, etc. melts **3** to lose one's coldness of manner —***vt.*** to cause to thaw —***n.*** **1** a thawing **2** a spell of weather warm enough to allow thawing

THC ***n.*** ⟦*t(etra)h(ydro)c(annabinol)*⟧ the principal and most active chemical in marijuana

ThD or **Th.D.** *abbrev.* ⟦L *Theologiae Doctor*⟧ Doctor of Theology

the (*th*ə; *before vowels th*ē, *th*i) ***adj., definite article*** ⟦< OE *se* with *th-* from other forms⟧ *the* (as opposed to *a, an*) refers to: **1** a particular person, thing, or group *[the* story ended; *the* President*]* **2** a person or thing considered generically *[the* cow is a domestic animal; *the* poor*]* —***adv.*** **1** that much *[the* better to see you with*]* **2** by how much . . . by that much *[the* sooner *the* better*]*

the·a·ter or **the·a·tre** (thē′ə tər) ***n.*** ⟦< Gr *theasthai,* to view⟧ **1** a place, esp. a building, where plays, operas, films, etc. are presented **2** any similar place with banked rows of seats **3** any place where events occur **4** *a*) the dramatic art *b*) the theatrical world

the·at·ri·cal (thē a′tri kəl) ***adj.*** **1** having to do with the theater **2** dramatic; esp. (in disparagement), melodramatic —**the·at′ri·cal·ly** ***adv.***

thee (*th*ē) ***pron.*** ⟦OE *the*⟧ [Archaic] *objective form of* THOU

theft (theft) ***n.*** ⟦OE *thiefth*⟧ the act or an instance of stealing; larceny

their (*th*er) ***poss. pronominal adj.*** ⟦< ON *theirra*⟧ of, belonging to, or done by them

theirs (*th*erz) ***pron.*** that or those belonging to them: poss. form of THEY *[*that book is *theirs*; *theirs* are better*]*

the·ism (thē′iz′əm) ***n.*** ⟦< Gr *theos,* god⟧ **1** belief in a god or gods **2** MONOTHEISM —**the′ist** ***n., adj.*** —**the·is′tic** ***adj.***

them (*th*em) ***pron.*** ⟦< ON *theim*⟧ *objective form of* THEY

theme (thēm) ***n.*** ⟦< Gr *thema,* what is laid down⟧ **1** a topic, as of an essay **2** a short essay **3** a short melody used as the subject of a musical composition **4** a recurring or identifying song in a film, musical, radio or TV series, etc.: in full **theme song** —**the·mat·ic** (thē mat′ik) ***adj.***

them·selves (*th*em selvz′) ***pron.*** a form of THEY, used as an intensive *[*they went *themselves]*, as a reflexive *[*they hurt *themselves]*, or with the meaning "their true selves" *[*they are not *themselves* when they are sick*]*

then (*th*en) ***adv.*** ⟦see THAN⟧ **1** at that time *[*he was young *then]* **2** next in time or order *[*he took his hat and *then* left*]* **3** in that case; accordingly *[*if she read it, *then* she knows*]* **4** besides; moreover *[*he likes to walk, and *then* it's good exercise*]* **5** at another time *[*now it's warm, *then* freezing*]* —***adj.*** being such at that time *[*the *then* director*]* —***n.*** that time *[*by *then*, they were gone*]*

thence (*th*ens) ***adv.*** ⟦OE *thanan*⟧ **1** from that place **2** from that time; thenceforth

thence′forth′ ***adv.*** from that time onward; thereafter: also **thence·for′ward**

the·oc·ra·cy (thē äk′rə sē) ***n.,*** *pl.* **-cies** ⟦< Gr *theos*, god + *kratos*, rule, power⟧ **1** government by a person or persons claiming divine authority **2** a country with this form of government

the·o·lo·gi·an (thē′ə lō′jən) ***n.*** a student of or specialist in theology

the·ol·o·gy (thē äl′ə jē) ***n.*** ⟦< Gr *theos*, god + *logos*, word⟧ the study of God and of religious doctrines and matters of divinity —**the′o·log′i·cal** (-ə läj′i kəl) ***adj.***

the·o·rem (thē′ə rəm, thir′əm) ***n.*** ⟦< Gr *theōrein,* to view⟧ **1** a proposition that can be proved from accepted premises; law or principle **2** *Math., Physics* a proposition embodying something to be proved

the·o·ret·i·cal (thē′ə ret′i kəl) ***adj.*** **1** limited to or based on theory; hypothetical **2** tending to theorize; speculative Also **the′o·ret′ic** —**the′o·ret′i·cal·ly** ***adv.***

the·o·rize (thē′ə rīz′) ***vi.*** **-rized′**, **-riz′ing** to form a theory or theories; speculate —**the′o·re·ti′cian** (-rə tish′ən) or **the′o·rist** (-rist) ***n.***

the·o·ry (thē′ə rē, thir′ē) ***n.,*** *pl.* **-ries** ⟦< Gr *theōrein*, to view⟧ **1** a speculative plan **2** a formulation of underlying principles of certain observed phenomena that has been verified to some degree **3** the principles of an art or science, rather than its practice **4** a conjecture or guess

the·os·o·phy (thē äs′ə fē) ***n.*** ⟦< Gr *theos*, god + *sophia*, wisdom⟧ [*also* **T-**] an eclectic set of occult beliefs, held to be based on mystical insight —**the′o·soph′ic** (-ə säf′ik) or **the′o·soph′i·cal** ***adj.*** —**the·os′o·phist** ***n.***

ther·a·peu·tic (ther′ə pyōōt′ik) ***adj.*** ⟦< Gr *therapeuein*, to nurse⟧ serving to cure or heal or to preserve health

ther′a·peu′tics ***n.*** the branch of medicine that deals with the treatment of diseases; therapy

ther′a·py (-pē) ***n.,*** *pl.* **-pies** ⟦see THERAPEUTIC⟧ **1** the treatment of any physical or mental disorder by medical or physical means, usually excluding surgery **2** *short for* PSYCHOTHERAPY —**ther′a·pist** ***n.***

there (*th*er) ***adv.*** ⟦OE *ther*⟧ **1** at, in, or to that place **2** at that point; then *[there* I paused*]* **3** in that respect *[there* you are wrong*]* *There* is also used in impersonal constructions in which the real subject follows the verb *[there* is little time*]* —***n.*** that place —***interj.*** used to express defiance, satisfaction, sympathy, etc. —(**not**) **all there** [Inf.] (not) mentally sound

there′a·bouts′ (-ə bouts′) ***adv.*** **1** near that place **2** near that time, number, degree, etc. Also **there′a·bout′**

there·af′ter ***adv.*** from then on

there·at′ ***adv.*** **1** at that place; there **2** at that time **3** for that reason

there·by′ ***adv.*** **1** by that means **2** connected with that

there·for′ ***adv.*** for this; for that; for it

there′fore′ (-fôr′) ***adv.*** for this or that reason; hence

there·in′ ***adv.*** **1** in or into that place **2** in that matter, detail, etc.

there·of′ ***adv.*** **1** of that **2** from that as a cause, reason, etc.

there·on′ ***adv.*** **1** on that or it **2** THEREUPON

there·to′ ***adv.*** to that place, thing, etc.: also **there·un·to** (*th*er un′tōō, *th*er′un tōō′)

there′to·fore′ ***adv.*** until that time

there′up·on′ ***adv.*** **1** immediately following that **2** as a consequence of that **3** on that subject, etc.

there·with′ ***adv.*** **1** along with that **2** immediately thereafter

ther·mal (thur′məl) ***adj.*** ⟦< Gr *thermē*, heat⟧ **1** having to do with heat **2** designating a loosely knitted material with air spaces for insulation —***n.*** *Meteorol.* a rising column of warm air

thermal pollution the harmful discharge of heated liquid or air into lakes, rivers, etc.

thermo- ⟦< Gr *thermē,* heat⟧ *combining form* heat

ther·mo·dy·nam·ics (thur′mō dī nam′iks) ***n.*** the branch of physics dealing with the transformation of heat to and from other forms of energy —**ther′mo·dy·nam′ic *adj.***

ther·mom·e·ter (thər mäm′ət ər) ***n.*** ⟦see THERMO- & -METER⟧ an instrument for measuring temperatures, as a graduated glass tube in which mercury, etc. rises or falls as it expands or contracts with changes in temperature

ther·mo·nu·cle·ar (thur′mō nōō′klē ər) ***adj.*** *Physics* **1** designating a reaction in which isotopes of a light element fuse, at extremely high heat, into heavier nuclei **2** of or using the heat energy released in nuclear fusion

ther·mo·plas·tic (thur′mə plas′tik) ***adj.*** soft and moldable when subjected to heat: said of certain plastics —***n.*** a thermoplastic substance

Ther·mos (thur′məs) ⟦< Gr *thermos,* hot⟧ *trademark for* a vacuum-insulated container for keeping liquids at almost their original temperature —***n.*** [*usually* **t-**] such a container

ther·mo·stat (thur′mə stat′) ***n.*** ⟦THERMO- + -STAT⟧ an apparatus for regulating temperature, esp. one that automatically controls a heating or cooling unit

the·sau·rus (thi sô′rəs) ***n.***, *pl.* **-ri′** (-rī′) or **-rus·es** ⟦< Gr *thēsauros,* a treasure⟧ a book of synonyms and antonyms

these (*th*ēz) ***pron., adj.*** *pl. of* THIS

The·seus (thē′sōōs′, thē′sē əs) ***n.*** *Gr. Legend* the king of Athens who kills the Minotaur

the·sis (thē′sis) ***n.***, *pl.* **-ses′** (-sēz′) ⟦< Gr *tithenai,* to put⟧ **1** a proposition to be defended in argument **2** a long research paper, esp. one written by a candidate for a master's degree

Thes·pi·an (thes′pē ən) ***adj.*** ⟦after *Thespis,* ancient Gr poet⟧ [*often* **t-**] having to do with the drama; dramatic —***n.*** [*often* **t-**] an actor or actress

the·ta (thāt′ə, thēt′-) ***n.*** the eighth letter of the Greek alphabet (Θ, θ, ϑ)

thews (thyōōz) ***pl.n.***, *sing.* **thew** ⟦< OE *theaw,* habit⟧ muscles or sinews

they (*th*ā) ***pron.***, *sing.* **he, she,** or **it** ⟦< ON *thei-r*⟧ **1** the persons, animals, or things previously mentioned **2** people generally *[they* say it's so*]*

thi·a·mine (thī′ə min, -mēn′) ***n.*** ⟦ult. < Gr *theion,* brimstone + (VIT)AMIN⟧ a white, crystalline B vitamin, found in cereals, egg yolk, liver, etc.; vitamin B_1: also **thi′a·min** (-min)

thick (thik) ***adj.*** ⟦OE *thicce*⟧ **1** of relatively great extent from side to side **2** as measured between opposite surfaces *[one inch thick]* **3** close and abundant *[thick hair]* **4** viscous **5** dense *[thick smoke]* **6** husky; blurred *[thick speech]* **7** [Inf.] stupid **8** [Inf.] close in friendship —***n.*** the thickest part —**thick′ly *adv.*** —**thick′ness *n.***

thick′en ***vt., vi.*** **1** to make or become thick or thicker **2** to make or become more complex —**thick′en·ing *n.***

thick·et (thik′it) ***n.*** ⟦see THICK⟧ a thick growth of shrubs or small trees

thick′set′ ***adj.*** **1** planted thickly or closely **2** thick in body; stocky

thick′-skinned′ ***adj.*** insensitive, as to insult

thief (thēf) ***n.***, *pl.* **thieves** (thēvz) ⟦OE *theof*⟧ one who steals

thieve (thēv) ***vt., vi.*** **thieved, thiev′ing** to steal —**thiev′ish *adj.***

thiev′er·y (-ər ē) ***n.***, *pl.* **-ies** the act or an instance of stealing; theft

thigh (thī) ***n.*** ⟦OE *theoh*⟧ that part of the leg between the knee and the hip

thigh′bone′ ***n.*** FEMUR

thim·ble (thim′bəl) ***n.*** ⟦< OE *thuma,* a thumb⟧ a small cap worn to protect the finger that pushes the needle in sewing —**thim′ble·ful′**, *pl.* **-fuls′**, ***n.***

thin (thin) ***adj.*** **thin′ner, thin′nest** ⟦OE *thynne*⟧ **1** of relatively little extent from side to side **2** lean; slender **3** not dense or compact *[thin hair]* **4** very fluid or watery *[thin soup]* **5** high-pitched and weak *[a thin voice]* **6** sheer: said as of fabric **7** flimsy or unconvincing *[a thin excuse]* **8** lacking substance, depth, etc.; weak —***vt., vi.*** **thinned, thin′ning** to make or become thin or thinner —**thin′ly *adv.*** —**thin′ness *n.***

thine (*th*īn) [Archaic] ***pron.*** ⟦OE *thin*⟧ that or those belonging to thee: poss. form of THOU —***poss. pronominal adj.*** thy: used esp. before a vowel

thing (thiŋ) ***n.*** ⟦OE, council⟧ **1** any matter, affair, or concern **2** a happening, act, incident, event, etc. **3** *a)* a tangible object *b)* an inanimate object **4** an item, detail, etc. **5** *a)* [*pl.*] personal belongings *b)* a garment **6** [Inf.] a person *[poor thing]* **7** [Inf.] a point of contention; issue **8** [Inf.] an irrational liking, fear, etc. **9** [Inf.] what one wants to do or is adept at *[to do one's own thing]* —**see things** [Inf.] to have hallucinations

think (thiŋk) ***vt.*** **thought, think′ing** ⟦OE *thencan*⟧ **1** to form or have in the mind *[thinking good thoughts]* **2** to judge; consider *[many think her charming]* **3** to believe *[I think I can come]* —***vi.*** **1** to use the mind; reason **2** to have an opinion, etc.: with *of* or *about* **3** to remember or consider: with *of* or *about* **4** to conceive (*of*) —**think up** to invent, plan, etc. by thinking —**think′er *n.***

think tank a group or center organized to do intensive research and problem-solving

thin·ner (thin′ər) ***n.*** a substance added to paint, shellac, etc. to thin it

thin′-skinned′ ***adj.*** sensitive, as to insult

Thin·su·late (thin′sə lāt′) *trademark for* thermal insulation made of synthetic fibers, for lining clothing

third (thurd) ***adj.*** ⟦OE *thridda*⟧ preceded by two others in a series; 3d or 3rd —***adv.*** in the third place, etc.: also **third′ly** —***n.*** **1** the one following the second **2**

any of the three equal parts of something; $\frac{1}{3}$ **3** the third forward gear of a transmission, providing more speed than second

third'-class' ***adj.*** **1** of the class, rank, etc. next below the second **2** of a low-cost mail class, as for advertisements —***adv.*** by third-class mail or travel accommodations

third degree [Inf.] cruel treatment and questioning to force a confession: with *the*

third dimension **1** *a)* depth *b)* solidity **2** the quality of seeming real

third person the form of a pronoun or verb that refers to the person or thing spoken of

third'-rate' ***adj.*** **1** third in quality or other rating **2** inferior; very poor

Third World [*also* **t- w-**] the economically underdeveloped countries of the world

thirst (thurst) ***n.*** ⟦OE *thurst*⟧ **1** the discomfort caused by a need for water **2** a strong desire; craving —***vi.*** **1** to feel thirst **2** to have a strong desire or craving —**thirst'y, -i·er, -i·est,** ***adj.*** —**thirst'i·ly** ***adv.***

thir·teen (thur'tēn') ***adj., n.*** ⟦OE *threotyne*⟧ three more than ten; 13; XIII —**thir'teenth'** ***adj., n.***

thir·ty (thurt'ē) ***adj., n., pl.*** **-ties** ⟦OE *thritig*⟧ three times ten; 30; XXX —**the thirties** the numbers or years, as of a century, from 30 through 39 —**thir'ti·eth** (-ith) ***adj., n.***

this (*th*is) ***pron., pl.*** **these** ⟦OE *thes*⟧ **1** the person or thing mentioned *[this* is John*]* **2** the nearer one or another one *[this* is older than that*]* **3** something about to be presented *[*listen to *this]* —***adj., pl.*** **these** **1** designating the person or thing mentioned *[this* man is John*]* **2** designating the nearer one or another one *[this* desk is older than that one*]* **3** designating something about to be presented *[*hear *this* news*]* —***adv.*** to this extent *[*it was *this* big*]*

THISTLE

this·tle (this'əl) ***n.*** ⟦OE *thistel*⟧ a plant with prickly leaves and white, purple, etc. flowers

this'tle·down' ***n.*** the down growing from the flowers of a thistle

thith·er (*th*i*th*'ər, thi*th*'-) ***adv.*** ⟦OE *thider*⟧ to or toward that place; there

tho or **tho'** (*th*ō) ***conj., adv.*** *phonetic sp. of* THOUGH

thole (thōl) ***n.*** ⟦OE *thol*⟧ one of a pair of pins set as an oarlock into the gunwale of a boat: also **thole'pin'**

-thon (thän) *suffix* -ATHON: used after a vowel *[radiothon]*

thong (thôŋ) ***n.*** ⟦OE *thwang*⟧ a narrow strip of leather, etc. used as a lace, strap, etc.

Thor (thôr) ***n.*** *Norse Myth.* the god of thunder, war, and strength

tho·rax (thôr'aks') ***n., pl.*** **-rax'es** or **-ra·ces'** (-ə sēz') ⟦< Gr⟧ **1** the part of the body between the neck and the abdomen; chest **2** the middle segment of an insect's body —**tho·rac·ic** (thō ras'ik, thô-) ***adj.***

Tho·reau (thôr'ō, thə rō'), **Henry David** 1817-62; U.S. writer

tho·ri·um (thôr'ē əm) ***n.*** ⟦< THOR⟧ a rare, grayish, radioactive, metallic chemical element, used as a nuclear fuel

thorn (thôrn) ***n.*** ⟦OE⟧ **1** *a)* a very short, hard, leafless stem with a sharp point *b)* any small tree or shrub bearing thorns **2** a source of constant trouble or irritation —**thorn'y, -i·er, -i·est,** ***adj.***

thor·ough (thur'ō) ***adj.*** ⟦var. of THROUGH⟧ **1** omitting nothing; complete **2** absolute *[*a *thorough* rascal*]* **3** very exact, accurate, or painstaking —**thor'ough·ly** ***adv.*** —**thor'ough·ness** ***n.***

thor·ough·bred (thur'ō bred', thur'ə-) ***adj.*** of pure stock; pedigreed —***n.*** [**T-**] any of a breed of light horse developed primarily for racing

thor'ough·fare' (-fer') ***n.*** a public street open at both ends, esp. a main highway

thor'ough·go'ing ***adj.*** very thorough

those (*th*ōz) ***pron., adj. pl. of*** THAT

thou (*th*ou) ***pron., pl.*** **you** or **ye** ⟦OE *thu*⟧ [Archaic] you: in poetic or religious use

though (*th*ō) ***conj.*** ⟦OE *theah*⟧ **1** in spite of the fact that *[though* it rained, he went*]* **2** and yet *[*they can win, *though* no one thinks so*]* **3** even if *[though* he may fail, he will have tried*]* —***adv.*** however; nevertheless *[*she sings well, *though]*

thought¹ (thôt) ***n.*** ⟦OE *thoht*⟧ **1** the act or process of thinking **2** the power of reasoning **3** an idea, concept, etc. **4** attention; consideration **5** mental concentration *[*deep in *thought]*

thought² (thôt) ***vt., vi. pt. & pp. of*** THINK

thought'ful ***adj.*** **1** full of thought; meditative **2** considerate of others —**thought'ful·ly** ***adv.*** —**thought'ful·ness** ***n.***

thought'less ***adj.*** **1** not stopping to think; careless **2** ill-considered; rash **3** inconsiderate —**thought'less·ly** ***adv.*** —**thought'less·ness** ***n.***

thou·sand (thou'zənd) ***n., adj.*** ⟦OE *thusend*⟧ ten hundred; 1,000; M —**thou'sandth** (-zəndth) ***adj., n.***

thrall (thrôl) ***n.*** ⟦< ON *thræll*⟧ **1** [Now Chiefly Literary] a slave **2** the condition of being dominated or enslaved, esp. psychologically: now used chiefly in **hold in thrall** —**thrall'dom** or **thral'dom** (-dəm) ***n.***

thrash (thrash) ***vt., vi.*** ⟦OE *therscan*⟧ **1** THRESH **2** to beat; flog **3** to toss about violently **4** to defeat overwhelmingly —**thrash out** to settle by detailed discussion

thrash'er ***n.*** ⟦E dial. *thresher*⟧ a thrushlike American songbird

thread (thred) ***n.*** ⟦OE *thræd*⟧ **1** a fine, stringlike length of spun cotton, silk, nylon, etc. used in sewing **2** any thin line, vein, etc. **3** something like a thread in its length, sequence, etc. *[the thread of a story]* **4** the spiral ridge of a screw, nut, etc. —***vt.*** **1** to put a thread through (a needle, etc.) **2** to make (one's way) by twisting, weaving, etc. **3** to fashion a THREAD (sense 4) on or in (a screw, pipe, etc.)

thread'bare' ***adj.*** **1** worn down so that the threads show *[a threadbare rug]* **2** wearing worn clothes; shabby **3** stale; trite

threat (thret) ***n.*** ⟦OE *threat,* pressure⟧ **1** an expression of intention to hurt, destroy, punish, etc. **2** an indication of, or a source of, imminent danger, harm, etc.

threat'en ***vt., vi.*** **1** to make threats, as of injury (against) **2** to indicate the likely occurrence of (something dangerous, unpleasant, etc.) **3** to be a source of danger (to)

three (thrē) ***adj., n.*** ⟦OE *threo*⟧ one more than two; 3; III

three'-deck'er (-dek'ər) ***n.*** anything having three levels, layers, etc.

three'-di·men'sion·al ***adj.*** having or seeming to have depth or thickness

three'fold' ***adj.*** **1** having three parts **2** having three times as much or as many —***adv.*** three times as much or as many

three R's reading, writing, and arithmetic, regarded as the fundamentals of an education: with *the*

three·score (thrē'skôr') ***adj., n.*** sixty

thren·o·dy (thren'ə dē) ***n.,*** *pl.* **-dies** ⟦< Gr *thrēnos,* lamentation + *ōidē,* song⟧ a song of lamentation; dirge

thresh (thresh) ***vt., vi.*** ⟦ME *threschen*: see THRASH⟧ **1** to beat out (grain) from (husks), as with a flail **2** THRASH —**thresh'er** ***n.***

thresh·old (thresh'ōld', -hōld') ***n.*** ⟦OE *therscwold*⟧ **1** a length of wood, stone, etc. along the bottom of a doorway **2** the beginning point

threw (thro͞o) ***vt., vi.*** *pt. of* THROW

thrice (thrīs) ***adv.*** ⟦OE *thriwa*⟧ **1** three times **2** threefold

thrift (thrift) ***n.*** ⟦< ON *thrifa,* to grasp⟧ economy; frugality —**thrift'less** ***adj.*** —**thrift'y, -i·er, -i·est,** ***adj.*** —**thrift'i·ly** ***adv.*** —**thrift'i·ness** ***n.***

thrift shop a store where castoff clothes, etc. are sold to raise money for charity

thrill (thril) ***vi., vt.*** ⟦< OE *thurh,* through⟧ **1** to feel or cause to feel emotional excitement **2** to quiver or cause to quiver —***n.*** a thrilling or being thrilled —**thrill'er** ***n.***

thrive (thrīv) ***vi.*** **thrived** or **throve, thrived** or **thriv·en** (thriv'ən), **thriv'ing** ⟦< ON *thrifa,* to grasp⟧ **1** to prosper or flourish; be successful **2** to grow vigorously or luxuriantly

throat (thrōt) ***n.*** ⟦OE *throte*⟧ **1** the front part of the neck **2** the upper part of the passage from the mouth and nose to the stomach and lungs **3** any narrow passage

throat'y ***adj.*** **-i·er, -i·est** **1** produced in the throat: said of some sounds **2** husky; hoarse

throb (thräb) ***vi.*** **throbbed, throb'bing** ⟦ME *throbben*⟧ **1** to beat, pulsate, vibrate, etc., esp. strongly or fast **2** to feel excitement —***n.*** **1** a throbbing **2** a strong beat or pulsation

throe (thrō) ***n.*** ⟦prob. < OE *thrawu,* pain⟧ a spasm or pang of pain: *usually used in pl. [*the *throes* of childbirth, death *throes]* —**in the throes of** in the act of struggling with (a problem, task, etc.)

throm·bose (thräm'bōs', -bōz') ***vt., vi.*** **-bosed', -bos'ing** to clot or become clotted with a thrombus

throm·bo·sis (thräm bō'sis) ***n.*** ⟦< Gr *thrombos,* a clot⟧ coagulation of the blood in the heart or a blood vessel, forming a clot

throm·bus (thräm'bəs) ***n.*** **-bi'** (-bī') ⟦see prec.⟧ the clot attached at the site of thrombosis

throne (thrōn) ***n.*** ⟦< Gr *thronos,* a seat⟧ **1** the chair on which a king, cardinal, etc. sits on formal occasions **2** the power or rank of a king, etc.

throng (thrôŋ) ***n.*** ⟦OE *thringan,* to crowd⟧ **1** a crowd **2** any great number of things considered together —***vi.*** to gather together in a throng —***vt.*** to crowd into

throt·tle (thrät''l) ***n.*** ⟦prob. dim. of THROAT⟧ the valve, or its control lever or pedal, that regulates the amount of fuel vapor entering an engine —***vt.*** **-tled, -tling** **1** to choke; strangle **2** to censor or suppress **3** to slow by means of a throttle

through (thro͞o) ***prep.*** ⟦OE *thurh*⟧ **1** in one side and out the other side of **2** in the midst of; among **3** by way of **4** around *[touring through* France*]* **5** *a)* from the beginning to the end of *b)* up to and including **6** by means of **7** as a result of *[done through error]* —***adv.*** **1** in one side and out the other **2** from the beginning to the end **3** completely to the end *[to see something through]* **4** completely *[soaked through]*: also **through and through** —***adj.*** **1** extending from one place to another *[a through street]* **2** traveling to the destination without stops *[a through train]* **3** finished *[through with the job]*

through·out' ***prep.*** all the way through —***adv.*** in every part; everywhere

through'way' ***n.*** *alt. sp. of* THRUWAY: see EXPRESSWAY

throve (thrōv) ***vi.*** *alt. pt. of* THRIVE

throw (thrō) ***vt.*** **threw, thrown, throw'ing** ⟦OE *thrawan,* to twist⟧ **1** to send through the air by a rapid motion of the arm, etc. **2** to cause to fall; upset **3** to send rapidly *[to throw troops into battle]* **4** to put suddenly into a specified state, etc. *[throw into confusion]* **5**

to move (a switch, etc.) so as to connect, disconnect, etc. **6** to direct, cast, etc. *[throw a glance]* **7** [Inf.] to lose (a game, etc.) deliberately **8** [Inf.] to give (a party, etc.) **9** [Inf.] to confuse or disconcert *[the question threw him]* **10** [Inf.] to have (a tantrum, etc.) ***—vi.*** to cast or hurl something ***—n.*** **1** the act of one who throws **2** the distance something is or can be thrown *[a stone's throw]* **3** a spread for a bed, etc. **—throw away** **1** to discard **2** to waste **—throw in** to add on free or add to others **—throw off** **1** to rid oneself of **2** to mislead or confuse **3** to expel, emit, etc. **—throw oneself at** to try very hard to win the love of **—throw out** **1** to discard **2** to reject or remove **—throw over** **1** to give up; abandon **2** to jilt **—throw together** to assemble hurriedly **—throw up** to vomit **—throw'er** ***n.***

throw'a·way' ***n.*** a leaflet, handbill, etc. given out on the streets, from house to house, etc. ***—adj.*** for discarding after use

throw'back' ***n.*** (a) reversion to an earlier or more primitive type

throw rug SCATTER RUG

thru (thro͞o) ***prep., adv., adj.*** *informal sp. of* THROUGH

thrush (thrush) ***n.*** ⟦OE *thrysce*⟧ any of a family of songbirds, including the robin

thrust (thrust) ***vt., vi.*** **thrust, thrust'ing** ⟦< ON *thrysta*⟧ **1** to push with sudden force **2** to stab **3** to force or impose ***—n.*** **1** a sudden, forceful push **2** a stab **3** continuous pressure, as of a rafter against a wall **4** *a)* the driving force of a propeller *b)* the forward force produced by a jet or rocket engine **5** forward movement **6** the basic meaning; point

thru·way (thro͞o'wā') ***n.*** EXPRESSWAY

Thu·cyd·i·des (tho͞o sid'i dēz') 460?-400? B.C.; Athenian historian

thud (thud) ***vi.*** **thud'ded, thud'ding** ⟦prob. < OE *thyddan*, to strike⟧ to hit or fall with a dull sound ***—n.*** a dull sound, as of an object dropping on a soft surface

thug (thug) ***n.*** ⟦Hindi *ṭhag*, swindler⟧ a brutal hoodlum, gangster, etc. **—thug'gish** ***adj.***

thumb (thum) ***n.*** ⟦OE *thuma*⟧ the short, thick digit of the hand ***—vt.*** **1** to handle, soil, etc. as with the thumb **2** [Inf.] to solicit or get (a ride) in hitchhiking by signaling with the thumb **—all thumbs** clumsy **—under someone's thumb** under someone's influence

thumb'nail' ***n.*** the nail of the thumb ***—adj.*** very small, brief, or concise

thumb'screw' ***n.*** **1** a screw that can be turned by the thumb and forefinger **2** a former instrument of torture for squeezing the thumbs

thumb'tack' ***n.*** a tack with a wide, flat head that can be pressed into a board, etc. with the thumb

thump (thump) ***n.*** ⟦echoic⟧ **1** a blow with something heavy and blunt **2** the dull sound made by such a blow ***—vt.*** to strike with a thump ***—vi.*** **1** to hit or fall with a thump **2** to make a dull, heavy sound

thump'ing ***adj.*** **1** that thumps **2** [Inf.] very large; whopping

thun·der (thun'dər) ***n.*** ⟦OE *thunor*⟧ **1** the sound following a flash of lightning **2** any similar sound ***—vi.*** to produce thunder or a sound like this ***—vt.*** to say very loudly **—thun'der·ous** ***adj.***

thun'der·bolt' ***n.*** **1** a flash of lightning and the accompanying thunder **2** something sudden and shocking, as bad news

thun'der·clap' ***n.*** a clap, or loud crash, of thunder

thun'der·cloud' ***n.*** a storm cloud charged with electricity and producing lightning and thunder

thun'der·head' ***n.*** a round mass of cumulus clouds appearing before a thunderstorm

thun'der·show'er ***n.*** a shower accompanied by thunder and lightning

thun'der·storm' ***n.*** a storm accompanied by thunder and lightning

thun'der·struck' ***adj.*** struck with amazement, terror, etc.: also **thun'der·strick'en** (-strik'ən)

Thurs·day (thurz'dā) ***n.*** ⟦< ON *Thorsdagr*, Thor's day⟧ the fifth day of the week: abbrev. **Thur** or **Thurs**

thus (*th*us) ***adv.*** ⟦OE⟧ **1** in this or that manner **2** to this or that degree or extent **3** therefore **4** for example

thwack (thwak) ***vt., n.*** ⟦prob. echoic⟧ WHACK

thwart (thwôrt) ***n.*** ⟦< ON *thvert*, transverse⟧ a seat across a boat ***—vt.*** to obstruct, frustrate, or defeat (a person, plans, etc.)

thy (*th*ī) ***poss. pronominal adj.*** ⟦< ME *thin*⟧ *archaic or poet. var. of* YOUR

thyme (tīm) ***n.*** ⟦< Gr *thymon*⟧ an herb of the mint family, with leaves used for seasoning

thy·mo·sin (thī'mə sin) ***n.*** ⟦< Gr *thymos*, thymus⟧ a hormone secreted by the thymus that stimulates the immune system

thy·mus (thī'məs) ***n.*** ⟦Gr *thymos*⟧ an endocrine gland situated near the throat: also **thymus gland**

thy·roid (thī'roid') ***adj.*** ⟦< Gr *thyreos*, large shield⟧ designating or of a large endocrine gland near the trachea, secreting a hormone that regulates growth ***—n.*** **1** the thyroid gland **2** an animal extract of this gland, used in treating goiter

thy·self (*th*ī self') ***pron.*** [Archaic] *reflexive or intensive form of* THOU

ti (tē) ***n.*** *Music* the seventh tone of the diatonic scale

Ti *Chem. symbol for* titanium

Ti·a Jua·na (tē'ə wä'nə) *former name for* TIJUANA

Tian·jin (tyen'jin') seaport in NE China: pop. 5,152,000

ti·ar·a (tē er'ə, -ar'-, -är'-) ***n.*** ⟦< Gr⟧ **1** the pope's triple crown **2** a woman's crownlike headdress

Ti·ber (tī'bər) river in central Italy, flowing through Rome

Ti·bet (ti bet′) plateau region of SW China, north of the Himalayas —**Ti·bet′an** ***adj., n.***

tib·i·a (tib′ē ə) ***n.***, *pl.* **-i·ae′** (-ē ē′) or **-i·as** ⟦L⟧ the inner and thicker of the bones of the lower leg

tic (tik) ***n.*** ⟦Fr < ?⟧ any involuntary, regularly repeated, spasmodic contraction of a muscle

tick[1] (tik) ***n.*** ⟦prob. echoic⟧ **1** a light clicking sound, as of a clock **2** a mark made to check off items —***vi.*** to make a tick or ticks —***vt.*** to record, mark, or check by ticks —**tick off** [Slang] to make angry

tick[2] (tik) ***n.*** ⟦OE *ticia*⟧ a wingless, bloodsucking mite that infests humans, cattle, etc.

tick[3] (tik) ***n.*** ⟦< ? L *theca*, a cover⟧ the cloth case of a mattress or pillow

ticked (tikt) ***adj.*** ⟦< TICK OFF⟧ [Slang] angry

tick′er ***n.*** **1** one that ticks **2** a telegraphic device for recording stock market quotations, etc. on a paper tape (**ticker tape**) **3** [Slang] the heart

tick·et (tik′it) ***n.*** ⟦< obs. Fr *etiquet*, etiquette⟧ **1** a printed card, etc. that gives one a right, as to attend a theater **2** a license or certificate **3** a label on merchandise giving size, price, etc. **4** the list of candidates nominated by a political party **5** [Inf.] a summons to court for a traffic violation —***vt.*** **1** to label with a ticket **2** to give a ticket to

tick′ing ***n.*** strong cloth, often striped, used for casings of pillows, etc.

tick·le (tik′əl) ***vt.*** **-led**, **-ling** ⟦ME *tikelen*⟧ **1** to please, gratify, delight, etc. **2** to stroke lightly so as to cause involuntary twitching, laughter, etc. —***vi.*** to have or cause an itching or tingling sensation —***n.*** a sensation of being tickled

tick·ler (tik′lər) ***n.*** a pad, file, etc. for noting matters to be remembered

tick′lish (-lish) ***adj.*** **1** sensitive to tickling **2** needing careful handling; precarious; delicate

tick-tack-toe or **tic-tac-toe** (tik′tak tō′) ***n.*** a game for two, each marking X (or O) in turn in a nine-square block so as to complete any one row before the other can

tick·tock (tik′täk′) ***n.*** the sound made by a clock or watch

tid·al (tīd′'l) ***adj.*** of, having, or caused by, a tide or tides

tidal wave **1** *nontechnical term for* a tsunami or a similar huge wave caused by strong winds **2** any widespread movement, feeling, etc.

tid·bit (tid′bit′) ***n.*** ⟦dial. *tid*, small object⟧ a choice bit of food, gossip, etc.

tid·dly·winks (tid′lē wiŋks′) ***n.*** ⟦< ?⟧ a game in which little disks are snapped into a cup by pressing their edges with a larger disk

tide (tīd) ***n.*** ⟦OE *tid*, time⟧ **1** a period of time: now only in combination *[Eastertide]* **2** the alternate rise and fall, about twice a day, of the surface of oceans, seas, etc., caused by the attraction of the moon and sun **3** something that rises and falls like the tide **4** a stream, trend, etc. —***vi.*** **tid′ed**, **tid′ing** to help along temporarily: with *over*

tide′land′ ***n.*** **1** land uncovered at low tide **2** [*pl.*] loosely, land under the sea within territorial waters of a country

tide′wa′ter ***n.*** **1** water that is affected by the tide **2** land that is affected by the tide —***adj.*** of or along a tidewater

ti·dings (tī′diŋz) ***pl.n.*** ⟦OE *tidung*⟧ news; information

ti·dy (tī′dē) ***adj.*** **-di·er**, **-di·est** ⟦<OE *tid*, time⟧ **1** neat in appearance, arrangement, etc.; orderly **2** [Inf.] rather large *[a tidy sum]* —***vt., vi.*** **-died**, **-dy·ing** to make tidy: often with *up* —**ti′di·ness** ***n.***

tie (tī) ***vt.*** **tied**, **ty′ing** or **tie′ing** ⟦< OE *teag*, a rope⟧ **1** to bind, as with string, rope, etc. **2** to knot the laces, etc. of **3** to make (a knot) in **4** to bind in any way **5** to equal the score of, as in a contest —***vi.*** to make an equal score, as in a contest —***n.*** **1** a string, cord, etc. used to tie things **2** something that connects, binds, etc. **3** a necktie **4** a beam, rod, etc. that holds parts together **5** any of the crossbeams to which the rails of a railroad are fastened **6** *a*) an equality of scores, etc. *b*) a contest in which this occurs —***adj.*** that has been made equal *[a tie score]* —**tie down** to confine; restrict —**tie up** **1** to wrap up and tie **2** to moor to a dock **3** to obstruct; hinder **4** to cause to be already in use, committed, etc.

tie′back′ ***n.*** a band or ribbon used to tie curtains, etc. to one side

tie′break′er ***n.*** an additional game, period of play, etc. used to establish a winner from among those tied at the end of a contest

tie clasp a decorative clasp for fastening a necktie to the shirt: also **tie clip**

tie′-dye′ ***n.*** a method of dyeing designs on cloth by tying bunches of it so that the dye affects only exposed parts —***vt.*** **-dyed′**, **-dye′ing** to dye in this way

tie′-in′ ***n.*** a connection or relationship

Tien·tsin (tyen′tsin′) *a former transliteration of* TIANJIN

tier (tir) ***n.*** ⟦< OFr *tire*, order⟧ any of a series of rows arranged one above or behind another

tie rod a rod connecting certain parts in the steering linkage of a motor vehicle

tie tack or **tie tac** a decorative pin fitted into a snap to fasten a necktie to a shirt

tie-up (tī′up′) ***n.*** **1** a temporary stoppage of production, traffic, etc. **2** connection or relation

tiff (tif) ***n.*** ⟦< ?⟧ a slight quarrel; spat

Tif·fa·ny (tif′ə nē) ***adj.*** ⟦after L. C. *Tiffany* (1848-1933), U.S. designer⟧ of a style in stained glass

ti·ger (tī′gər) ***n.*** ⟦< Gr *tigris*⟧ **1** a large, fierce Asian cat, having a tawny coat striped with black **2** one who is dynamic, fierce, etc.

TIGER

tight (tīt) ***adj.*** ⟦< OE *-thight*, strong⟧ **1** so compact in structure that water, air, etc. cannot pass through **2** drawn, packed, etc. closely together **3** fixed securely; firm **4** fully stretched; taut **5** fitting so closely as to be uncomfortable **6** difficult: esp. in **a tight corner** (or **squeeze**, etc.), a difficult situation **7** showing tension, etc. *[a tight smile]* **8** almost tied *[a tight race]* **9** sharp; abrupt *[a tight turn in the road]* **10** difficult to get; scarce **11** [Inf.] stingy **12** [Slang] drunk **13** [Slang] very familiar —***adv.*** **1** securely **2** [Inf.] soundly *[sleep tight]* —**sit tight** to keep one's opinion or position and wait —**tight'ly** ***adv.*** —**tight'ness** ***n.***

tight'en ***vt.***, ***vi.*** to make or become tight or tighter —**tight'en·er** ***n.***

tight'fist'ed ***adj.*** stingy

tight'fit'ting ***adj.*** fitting very tight

tight'-lipped' ***adj.*** secretive

tight'rope' ***n.*** a tightly stretched rope on which acrobats perform

tights ***pl.n.*** a tightly fitting garment for the lower half of the body, as worn by acrobats or dancers

tight ship [Inf.] an organization as efficient as a well-run ship

tight'wad' ***n.*** ⟦TIGHT + *wad*, roll of money⟧ [Slang] a stingy person

ti·gress (tī'gris) ***n.*** a female tiger

Ti·gris (tī'gris) river flowing from EC Turkey to a juncture with the Euphrates in SE Iraq

Ti·jua·na (tē'ə wä'nə) city in Baja California, NW Mexico, on the U.S. border: official pop. 747,000; actual pop. between 1,000,000 and 2,000,000

til·de (til'də) ***n.*** ⟦Sp < L *titulus*, a sign⟧ a diacritical mark (~)

tile (tīl) ***n.*** ⟦< L *tegula*⟧ **1** a thin piece of stone, fired clay, etc. used for roofing, flooring, etc. **2** a similar piece of plastic, etc. **3** a drain of earthenware pipe —***vt.*** **tiled, til'ing** to cover with tiles

til'ing ***n.*** tiles collectively

till[1] (til) ***prep.***, ***conj.*** ⟦OE *til*⟧ UNTIL

till[2] (til) ***vt.***, ***vi.*** ⟦< OE *tilian*, lit., strive for⟧ to prepare (land) for raising crops, as by plowing

till[3] (til) ***n.*** ⟦< ? ME *tillen*, to draw⟧ a drawer for keeping money

till'age ***n.*** **1** the tilling of land **2** land that is tilled

till·er (til'ər) ***n.*** ⟦< ML *telarium*, a weaver's beam⟧ a bar or handle for turning a boat's rudder

tilt (tilt) ***vt.*** ⟦ME *tilten*, totter⟧ to cause to slant; tip —***vi.*** **1** to slope; incline **2** to charge (*at* an opponent) **3** to take part in a tilt —***n.*** **1** a medieval contest in which two horsemen fight with lances **2** any spirited contest **3** a slope —**(at) full tilt** at full speed

tilt'-top' ***adj.*** of a table with a hinged top that can be tipped vertically

tim·bale (tim'bəl) ***n.*** ⟦Fr⟧ **1** chicken, lobster, etc. in a cream sauce, baked in a drum-shaped mold **2** a pastry shell, filled with a cooked food

tim·ber (tim'bər) ***n.*** ⟦OE⟧ **1** wood for building houses, ships, etc. **2** a wooden beam used in building **3** trees collectively —**tim'bered** ***adj.***

tim'ber·line' ***n.*** the line above or beyond which trees do not grow, as on mountains

tim·bre (tam'bər, tim'-) ***n.*** ⟦< OFr, kind of drum⟧ the quality of sound that distinguishes one voice or musical instrument from another

time (tīm) ***n.*** ⟦OE *tima*⟧ **1** every moment there has ever been or ever will be **2** a system of measuring duration *[standard time]* **3** the period during which something exists, happens, etc. **4** [*often pl.*] a period of history; age, era, etc. **5** [*usually pl.*] prevailing conditions *[times are good]* **6** a set period or term, as of work, confinement, etc. **7** standard rate of pay **8** rate of speed in marching, driving, etc. **9** a precise or designated instant, moment, day, etc. **10** an occasion or repeated occasion *[the fifth time it's been on TV]* **11** *Music a*) rhythm as determined by the grouping of beats into measures *b*) tempo **12** *Sports* TIMEOUT —***vt.*** **timed, tim'ing** **1** to arrange the time of so as to be suitable, opportune, etc. **2** to adjust, set, etc. so as to coincide in time *[time our watches]* **3** to calculate the pace, speed, etc. of —***adj.*** **1** having to do with time **2** set to explode, open, etc. at a given time *[a time bomb]* **3** having to do with paying in installments —**ahead of time** early —**at the same time** however —**at times** occasionally —**do time** [Inf.] to serve a prison term —**for the time being** temporarily —**from time to time** now and then —**in time** **1** eventually **2** before it is too late **3** keeping the set tempo, pace, etc. —**make time** to travel, work, etc. rapidly —**on time** **1** at the appointed time **2** for or by payment by installments —**time after time** again and again: also **time and again**

time clock a clock with a mechanism for recording the time an employee begins and ends a work period

time exposure a photograph taken by exposure of a film or plate for a relatively long period

time frame a given period of time

time'-hon'ored ***adj.*** honored because of long existence or usage

time'keep'er ***n.*** one who keeps account of hours worked by employees or of the elapsed time in races, games, etc.

time'-lapse' ***adj.*** of filming a slow process by exposing single frames at long intervals: the film is projected at regular speed, showing the process greatly speeded up

time'less ***adj.*** **1** eternal **2** always valid or true

time'line' ***n.*** a chronological chart or list of events, dates, plans, etc.

time'ly ***adj.*** **-li·er, -li·est** well-timed; opportune —**time'li·ness** ***n.***

time machine in science fiction, a device for conveying a person into the past or the future

time'out' ***n.*** *Sports* any temporary suspension of play

time'piece' ***n.*** any device for measuring and recording time, as a clock or watch

tim·er (tīm'ər) ***n.*** a device for controlling the timing of some mechanism

time'-re·lease' ***adj.*** releasing active ingredients gradually

times (tīmz) ***prep.*** multiplied by

time sharing **1** a system for simultaneous computer use at many remote sites **2** a system for sharing ownership of a vacation home, etc., with each joint purchaser occupying the unit at a specific time each year: also **time share**

time sheet a sheet on which are recorded the hours an employee works

time'ta'ble ***n.*** a schedule of the times of arrival and departure of airplanes, trains, buses, etc.

time'-test'ed ***adj.*** having value proved by long use or experience

time warp displacement from one point in time to another, as in science fiction

time'worn' ***adj.*** **1** worn out by long use **2** hackneyed; trite

time zone *see* STANDARD TIME

tim·id (tim'id) ***adj.*** ⟦< L *timere*, to fear⟧ lacking self-confidence; shy; fearful; hesitant —**ti·mid·i·ty** (tə mid'ə tē) ***n.*** —**tim'id·ly** ***adv.***

tim·ing (tīm'iŋ) ***n.*** the regulation of pace or speed as it affects performance

tim·or·ous (tim'ər es) ***adj.*** ⟦< L *timor*, fear⟧ full of fear; timid; afraid

tim·o·thy (tim'ə thē) ***n.*** ⟦after a *Timothy* Hanson, *c.* 1720⟧ a perennial grass with dense spikes, grown for hay

tim·pa·ni (tim'pə nē) ***pl.n.***, *sing.* **-no'** (-nō') ⟦It: see TYMPANUM⟧ [*often with sing. v.*] kettledrums; esp., a set of them played by one performer —**tim'pa·nist** ***n.***

tin (tin) ***n.*** ⟦OE⟧ **1** a soft, silver-white, metallic chemical element **2** TIN PLATE **3** *a)* a pan, box, etc. made of tin plate *b)* [Chiefly Brit.] CAN² (*n.* 2, 3) Variously used to connote cheapness, etc. of something —***vt.*** **tinned, tin'ning** **1** to plate with tin **2** [Chiefly Brit.] CAN² (*vt.* 1)

tin can CAN² (*n.* 2)

tinc·ture (tiŋk'chər) ***n.*** ⟦< L *tingere*, to dye⟧ **1** a light color; tinge **2** a slight trace **3** a dilute solution of a medicinal substance in alcohol —***vt.*** **-tured, -tur·ing** to tinge

tin·der (tin'dər) ***n.*** ⟦OE *tynder*⟧ any dry, easily flammable material

tin'der·box' ***n.*** **1** [Obs.] a box to hold tinder **2** a highly flammable building, etc. **3** a potential source of war, rebellion, etc.

tine (tīn) ***n.*** ⟦OE *tind*⟧ a slender, projecting point; prong [*fork tines*]

tin'foil' ***n.*** **1** tin in thin sheets **2** aluminum in thin sheets, used for wrapping food, etc.

tinge (tinj) ***n.*** ⟦see TINT⟧ **1** a slight coloring; tint **2** a slight trace, flavor, etc. —***vt.*** **tinged, tinge'ing** or **ting'ing** to give a tinge to

tin·gle (tiŋ'gəl) ***vi.*** **-gled, -gling** ⟦var. of TINKLE⟧ to have a prickling or stinging feeling, as from cold, excitement, etc. —***n.*** this feeling —**tin'gly** ***adj.***

tin·ker (tiŋk'ər) ***n.*** ⟦ME *tinkere*⟧ **1** one who mends pots, pans, etc. **2** a bungler —***vi.*** **1** to attempt clumsily to mend something **2** to putter

tin·kle (tiŋk'əl) ***vi.*** **-kled, -kling** ⟦echoic⟧ to make a series of light sounds as of a tiny bell —***vt.*** to cause to tinkle —***n.*** a tinkling sound

tin·ny (tin'ē) ***adj.*** **-ni·er, -ni·est** **1** of or like tin **2** not well-made **3** high-pitched and lacking resonance [*tinny music*] —**tin'ni·ness** ***n.***

tin plate thin sheets of iron or steel plated with tin

tin·sel (tin'səl) ***n.*** ⟦< L *scintilla*, a spark⟧ **1** thin strips of tin, metal foil, etc., as for decoration **2** something of little worth that glitters

tin'smith' ***n.*** one who works in tin or tin plate

tint (tint) ***n.*** ⟦< L *tingere*, to dye⟧ **1** a pale color **2** a gradation of a color; shade **3** a hair dye —***vt.*** to give a tint to

tin·tin·nab·u·la·tion (tin'ti nab'yoo lā'shən) ***n.*** ⟦< L *tintinnabulum*, little bell⟧ the ringing sound of bells

tin·type (tin'tīp') ***n.*** an old kind of photograph taken directly as a positive print on a treated plate of tin or iron

ti·ny (tī'nē) ***adj.*** **-ni·er, -ni·est** ⟦< ME *tine*, *n.*, a little⟧ very small

-tion (shən) ⟦< Fr < L⟧ *suffix* **1** the act of ___ing **2** the state of being ___ed **3** the thing that is ___ed

-tious (shəs) *suffix* of, having, or characterized by

tip¹ (tip) ***n.*** ⟦ME *tippe*⟧ **1** the point or end of something **2** something attached to the end, as a cap, etc. —***vt.*** **tipped, tip'ping** **1** to form a tip on **2** to cover the tip of

tip² (tip) ***vt.*** **tipped, tip'ping** ⟦< ?⟧ **1** to strike lightly and sharply **2** to give a gratuity to (a waiter, etc.) **3** [Inf.] to give secret information to: often with *off* —***vi.*** to give a tip or tips —***n.*** **1** a light, sharp blow **2** a piece of confidential information **3** a hint, warning, etc. **4** a gratuity —**tip one's hand** [Slang] to reveal a secret, one's plans, etc., often without meaning to —**tip'per** ***n.***

tip³ (tip) ***vt.***, ***vi.*** **tipped, tip'ping** ⟦ME *tipen*⟧ **1** to overturn or upset: often with *over* **2** to tilt or slant —***n.*** a tilt; slant

tip'-off' ***n.*** a tip; confidential disclosure, hint, or warning

tip·ple (tip'əl) ***vi.***, ***vt.*** **-pled, -pling** ⟦< ?⟧ to drink (alcoholic liquor) habitually —**tip'pler** ***n.***

tip·ster (tip′stər) ***n.*** [Inf.] one who sells tips, as on horse races or the stock market

tip·sy (tip′sē) ***adj.*** **-si·er**, **-si·est** **1** that tips easily; not steady **2** somewhat drunk —**tip′si·ly** ***adv.***

tip′toe′ ***vi.*** **-toed′**, **-toe′ing** to walk carefully, with the heels raised —**on tiptoe** **1** standing with the heels raised **2** excited, alert, etc. **3** silently and stealthily

tip′top′ ***n.*** ⟦TIP[1] + TOP[1]⟧ the highest point —***adj.***, ***adv.*** **1** at the highest point **2** [Inf.] at the highest point of excellence, health, etc.

ti·rade (tī′rād′) ***n.*** ⟦< It *tirare*, to fire⟧ a long, vehement speech or denunciation; harangue

tire[1] (tīr) ***vt.***, ***vi.*** **tired**, **tir′ing** ⟦OE *tiorian*⟧ to make or become weary, exhausted, bored, etc.

tire[2] (tīr) ***n.*** ⟦ME *tyre*⟧ **1** a hoop of iron or rubber around the wheel of a vehicle **2** an inflatable, vulcanized rubber or synthetic casing sealed to a wheel rim by air pressure

tired (tīrd) ***adj.*** **1** weary **2** hackneyed —**tired′ly** ***adv.*** —**tired′ness** ***n.***

tire iron a crowbar with a built-in wrench, for changing automobile tires

tire′less ***adj.*** persistent, unwavering, etc. —**tire′less·ly** ***adv.*** —**tire′less·ness** ***n.***

tire′some (-səm) ***adj.*** **1** tiring; boring **2** annoying —**tire′some·ly** ***adv.*** —**tire′some·ness** ***n.***

Ti·rol (ti rōl′, -räl′) E Alpine region in W Austria & N Italy —**Ti·ro·le·an** (ti rō′lē ən, tī-) ***adj.***, ***n.***

′tis (tiz) *contr.* [Old Poet.] it is

tis·sue (tish′o͞o) ***n.*** ⟦< L *texere*, to weave⟧ **1** light, thin cloth **2** an interwoven mass; mesh; web **3** a piece of soft, absorbent paper, used as a disposable handkerchief, etc. **4** TISSUE PAPER **5** the substance of an organic body, consisting of cells and intercellular material

tissue paper very thin wrapping paper

tit[1] (tit) ***n.*** a titmouse

tit[2] (tit) ***n.*** ⟦OE⟧ **1** NIPPLE (sense 1) **2** a breast: in this sense now vulgar

ti·tan (tīt′′n) ***n.*** ⟦< Gr *Titan*, a giant deity⟧ any person or thing of great size or power

ti·tan·ic (tī tan′ik) ***adj.*** of great size, strength, or power

ti·ta·ni·um (tī tā′nē əm) ***n.*** ⟦see TITAN⟧ a silvery or dark-gray, metallic chemical element used in manufacturing

tit for tat ⟦var. of earlier *tip for tap*⟧ this for that: phrase indicating retribution

tithe (tīth) ***n.*** ⟦OE *teothe*, a tenth⟧ a tenth of one's income paid to a church —***vi.*** **tithed**, **tith′ing** to pay a tithe

ti·tian (tish′ən) ***n.*** ⟦after *Titian* (1490?-1576), Venetian painter⟧ reddish gold

tit·il·late (tit′′l āt′) ***vt.*** **-lat′ed**, **-lat′ing** ⟦< L *titillare*, tickle⟧ to excite pleasurably —**tit′il·la′tion** ***n.***

ti·tle (tīt′l) ***n.*** ⟦< L *titulus*⟧ **1** the name of a book, poem, picture, etc. **2** an epithet **3** an appellation indicating one's rank, profession, etc. **4** a claim **5** *Film, TV* a subtitle, credit, etc. **6** *Law a*) a right to ownership, esp. of real estate *b*) a deed **7** *Sports, etc.* a championship —***vt.*** **-tled**, **-tling** to give a title to

ti′tled ***adj.*** having a title, esp. of nobility

ti′tle·hold′er ***n.*** the holder of a title; specif., the champion in some sport

title role (or **character**) the character in a play, film, etc. whose name is used as or in its title

ti·tlist (tīt′′l ist) ***n.*** a champion in some sport

tit·mouse (tit′mous′) ***n.***, *pl.* **-mice′** (-mīs′) ⟦ME *titemose*⟧ a small bird with ashy-gray feathers

tit·ter (tit′ər) ***vi.*** ⟦echoic⟧ to laugh in a half-suppressed way; giggle —***n.*** a tittering

tit·tle (tit′′l) ***n.*** ⟦ME *title*⟧ a very small particle; jot

tit·u·lar (tich′ə lər, tit′yə-) ***adj.*** ⟦see TITLE⟧ **1** of a title **2** having a title **3** in name only *[a titular sovereign]*

tiz·zy (tiz′ē) ***n.***, *pl.* **-zies** ⟦< ?⟧ [Inf.] a state of frenzied excitement

tko or **TKO** ***n.*** *Boxing* a technical knockout

TLC *abbrev.* tender, loving care

TM *abbrev.* trademark

tn *abbrev.* ton(s)

TN Tennessee

TNT ***n.*** ⟦*t*(*ri*)*n*(*itro*)*t*(*oluene*)⟧ a high explosive used for blasting, etc.

to (to͞o, too, tə) ***prep.*** ⟦OE⟧ **1** toward *[turn to the left]* **2** so as to reach *[she went to Boston]* **3** as far as *[wet to the skin]* **4** into a condition of *[a rise to fame]* **5** *a*) on, onto, against, at, etc. *[tied to a post]* *b*) in front of *[face to face]* **6** *a*) until *[from noon to night]* *b*) before *[the time is ten to six]* **7** for the purpose of *[come to dinner]* **8** in regard to *[open to attack]* **9** with the result of producing *[torn to bits]* **10** along with *[add this to the rest]* **11** belonging with *[a key to the house]* **12** as compared with *[a score of 10 to 0]* **13** in agreement with *[not to my taste]* **14** constituting *[four quarts to a gallon]* **15** with (a specified person or thing) as the recipient of the action *[give it to me]* **16** in honor of *[a toast to you]* **17** by *[known to me]* *To* is also a sign of the infinitive (Ex.: I want *to* stay) —***adv.*** **1** forward *[wrong side to]* **2** shut; closed *[pull the door to]* **3** into a state of consciousness *[the boxer came to]* **4** at hand *[we were close to when it happened]* —**to and fro** first in one direction and then in the opposite

toad (tōd) ***n.*** ⟦OE *tadde*⟧ a froglike amphibian that lives on moist land

toad′stool′ (-sto͞ol′) ***n.*** a mushroom; esp., any poisonous mushroom

toad·y (tō′dē) ***n.***, *pl.* **-ies** ⟦short for *toad-eater*, quack doctor's assistant⟧ a servile flatterer —***vt.***, ***vi.*** **-ied**, **-y·ing** to be a toady (to)

toast[1] (tōst) ***vt.*** ⟦< L *torrere*, parch⟧ **1** to brown the surface of (bread, cheese, etc.) by heating **2** to warm thoroughly —***vi.*** to become toasted —***n.*** sliced bread made brown and crisp by heat —**toast′er** ***n.***

toast[2] (tōst) ***n.*** ⟦from the use of toasted spiced bread to flavor the wine⟧ **1** a drink, or a proposal to drink, in honor of some person, etc. **2** someone greatly admired or acclaimed *[*the *toast* of Broadway*]* —***vt.***, ***vi.*** to propose or drink a toast (to)

toast′mas′ter ***n.*** the person at a banquet who proposes toasts, introduces after-dinner speakers, etc.

toast′y ***adj.*** **-i·er, -i·est** warm and comfortable or cozy

to·bac·co (tə bak′ō) ***n.***, *pl.* **-cos** ⟦Sp *tabaco* < ?⟧ **1** a plant with large leaves that are prepared for smoking, chewing, etc. **2** cigars, cigarettes, etc.

to·bac·co·nist (tə bak′ə nist) ***n.*** [Chiefly Brit.] a dealer in tobacco

to·bog·gan (tə bäg′ən) ***n.*** ⟦< AmInd⟧ a long, flat sled without runners, for coasting downhill —***vi.*** **1** to coast on a toboggan **2** to decline rapidly

toc·ca·ta (tə kät′ə) ***n.*** a musical work in free style for the organ, piano, etc., often a prelude to a fugue

toc·sin (täk′sin) ***n.*** ⟦Fr < Prov *toc*, a stroke + *senh*, a bell⟧ an alarm bell or its sound

to·day (tə dā′) ***adv.*** ⟦OE *to dæg*⟧ **1** on or during the present day **2** in the present time —***n.*** **1** the present day **2** the present time

tod·dle (täd′'l) ***vi.*** **-dled, -dling** ⟦? < *totter*⟧ to walk with short, uncertain steps

tod′dler ***n.*** a very young child, esp. one just learning to walk

tod·dy (täd′ē) ***n.***, *pl.* **-dies** ⟦< Hindi⟧ a drink of whiskey, etc. mixed with hot water, sugar, etc.: also **hot toddy**

to-do (tə do͞o′) ***n.***, *pl.* **-dos′** [Inf.] a commotion; fuss

toe (tō) ***n.*** ⟦OE *ta*⟧ **1** *a)* any of the digits of the foot *b)* the forepart of the foot **2** anything like a toe in location, shape, or use —***vt.*** **toed, toe′ing** to touch, kick, etc. with the toes —***vi.*** to stand, walk, etc. with the toes in a specified position *[*he *toes* in*]* —**on one's toes** [Inf.] alert —**toe the line** (or **mark**) to follow orders, rules, etc. strictly

toed (tōd) ***adj.*** having (a specified kind or number of) toes: usually in compounds *[*two-*toed]*

toe dance a dance performed on the tips of the toes, as in ballet —**toe′-dance′, -danced′, -danc′ing,** ***vi.*** —**toe′-danc′er** ***n.***

toe′hold′ ***n.*** **1** a small space to support the toe in climbing, etc. **2** a slight footing or advantage

toe′less ***adj.*** having the toe open or uncovered *[*a *toeless* shoe*]*

toe′nail′ ***n.*** the nail of a toe

tof·fee or **tof·fy** (tôf′ē, täf′ē) ***n.*** ⟦< TAFFY⟧ a hard, chewy candy, a kind of taffy

to·fu (tō′fo͞o) ***n.*** ⟦Jpn⟧ a cheeselike food made from soybeans

to·ga (tō′gə) ***n.***, *pl.* **-gas** or **-gae** (-jē, -gē) ⟦L < *tegere*, to cover⟧ in ancient Rome, a loose outer garment worn in public by citizens

to·geth·er (tə geth′ər) ***adv.*** ⟦< OE *to*, to + *gædre*, together⟧ **1** in or into one group, place, etc. *[*we ate *together]* **2** in or into contact, union, etc. *[*the cars skidded *together]* **3** considered collectively *[*he lost more than all of us *together]* **4** at the same time *[*gunshots fired *together]* **5** in succession *[*sulking for three days *together]* **6** in or into agreement, cooperation, etc. *[*to get *together* on a deal*]* —***adj.*** **1** with one another; not apart **2** [Slang] having a harmoniously organized personality

ROMAN TOGA

to·geth′er·ness ***n.*** the spending of much time together, as by family members, resulting in a more unified relationship

tog·gle switch (täg′əl) a switch consisting of a lever moved back and forth to open or close an electric circuit

To·go (tō′gō) country on the W coast of Africa: 21,925 sq. mi.; pop. 2,701,000

togs (tägz, tôgz) ***pl.n.*** ⟦ult. < L *toga*, toga⟧ [Inf.] clothes

toil (toil) ***vi.*** ⟦< L *tudiculare*, to stir about⟧ **1** to work hard and continuously **2** to proceed laboriously —***n.*** hard, tiring work —**toil′er** ***n.***

toi·let (toi′lit) ***n.*** ⟦< OFr *toile*, cloth < L *tela*, a web⟧ **1** TOILETTE **2** (a room with) a bowl-shaped fixture for defecation or urination

toilet paper (or **tissue**) soft paper for cleaning oneself after evacuation

toi′let·ry (-lə trē) ***n.***, *pl.* **-ries** soap, lotion, etc. used in grooming oneself

toi·lette (twä let′, toi-) ***n.*** ⟦Fr⟧ **1** the process of grooming oneself **2** dress; attire

toilet water a lightly scented liquid containing alcohol, applied to the skin after bathing, etc.

toils (toilz) ***pl.n.*** ⟦< L *tela*, web⟧ any snare suggestive of a net

toil·some (toil′səm) ***adj.*** laborious

toke (tōk) [Slang] ***n.*** ⟦? < fol.⟧ a puff on a cigarette, esp. one of marijuana or hashish —***vi.*** **toked, tok′ing** to take such a puff

to·ken (tō′kən) ***n.*** ⟦OE *tacn*⟧ **1** a sign, indication, symbol, etc. *[*a *token* of one's affection*]* **2** a keepsake **3** a metal disk to be used in place of currency, as for transportation fares —***adj.*** **1** symbolic **2** merely simulated; slight *[token* resistance*]* —**by the same token** for the same reason

to′ken·ism′ ***n.*** the making of small,

often merely formal concessions to a demand, etc.; specif., token integration of blacks, as in jobs

To·ky·o (tō′kē ō′) capital of Japan, on S Honshu: pop. 8,352,000

told (tōld) ***vt., vi.*** *pt. & pp. of* TELL —**all told** all things considered

tole (tōl) ***n.*** ⟦Fr *tôle*, sheet iron⟧ a type of lacquered or enameled metalware, usually dark-green, ivory, or black, used for lamps, trays, etc.

To·le·do (tə lē′dō) city & port in NW Ohio: pop. 333,000

tol·er·a·ble (täl′ər ə bəl) ***adj.*** **1** endurable **2** fairly good; passable —**tol′er·a·bly** ***adv.***

tol′er·ance (-əns) ***n.*** **1** a being tolerant of others' views, beliefs, practices, etc. **2** the amount of variation allowed from a standard **3** *Med.* the (developed) ability to resist the effects of a drug, etc.

tol′er·ant (-ənt) ***adj.*** having or showing tolerance of others' beliefs, etc.

tol′er·ate′ (-āt′) ***vt.*** **-at′ed, -at′ing** ⟦< L *tolerare*, to bear⟧ **1** to allow **2** to respect (others' beliefs, practices, etc.) without sharing them **3** to bear (someone or something disliked); put up with **4** *Med.* to have tolerance for —**tol′er·a′tion** ***n.***

toll[1] (tōl) ***n.*** ⟦ult. < Gr *telos*, tax⟧ **1** a tax or charge for a privilege, as for the use of a turnpike **2** a charge for service, as for a long-distance telephone call **3** the number lost, etc. *[the tornado took a heavy toll of lives]*

toll[2] (tōl) ***vt.*** ⟦ME *tollen*, to pull⟧ **1** to ring (a church bell, etc.) with slow, regular strokes **2** to announce, summon, etc. by this —***vi.*** to ring slowly: said of a bell —***n.*** the sound of a bell tolling

toll′booth′ ***n.*** a booth at which a toll is collected, as before entering a toll road

toll′gate′ ***n.*** a gate for stopping travel at a point where a toll is collected

toll road a road on which a toll must be paid: also **toll′way′** (-wā′) ***n.***

Tol·stoy or **Tol·stoi** (tōl′stoi′), Count **Le·o** (lē′ō) 1828-1910; Russ. novelist

tol·u·ene (täl′yo͞o ēn′) ***n.*** ⟦Sp *tolu*, after *Tolú*, seaport in Colombia + (BENZ)ENE⟧ a colorless, poisonous liquid obtained from coal tar or petroleum and used in making dyes, explosives, etc.

tom (täm) ***adj.*** ⟦after the name *Tom*⟧ male *[a tomcat, a tom turkey]*

tom·a·hawk (täm′ə hôk′) ***n.*** ⟦< AmInd⟧ a light ax used by North American Indians as a tool and a weapon

to·ma·to (tə māt′ō, -mät′ō) ***n., pl.*** **-toes** ⟦< AmInd (Mexico)⟧ **1** a red or yellowish fruit with a juicy pulp, used as a vegetable **2** the plant it grows on

tomb (to͞om) ***n.*** ⟦< Gr *tymbos*⟧ a vault or grave for the dead

tom·boy (täm′boi′) ***n.*** a girl who behaves like an active boy

tomb·stone (to͞om′stōn′) ***n.*** a stone or monument marking a tomb or grave

tom·cat (täm′kat′) ***n.*** a male cat

tome (tōm) ***n.*** ⟦< Gr *tomos*, piece cut off⟧ a book, esp. a large one

tom·fool·er·y (täm′fo͞ol′ər ē) ***n., pl.*** **-ies** foolish behavior; silliness

tom·my gun (täm′ē) [*sometimes* **T- g-**] a submachine gun

to·mog·ra·phy (tə mäg′rə fē) ***n.*** ⟦< Gr *temnein*, to cut + -GRAPHY⟧ an X-ray process for producing an image of a single plane of an object, used in medical diagnosis

to·mor·row (tə mär′ō, -môr′-) ***adv.*** ⟦OE *to morgen*⟧ on the day after today —***n.*** the day after today

tom·tit (täm tit′, täm′tit′) ***n.*** [Chiefly Brit.] a titmouse or other small bird

tom-tom (täm′täm′) ***n.*** ⟦Hindi *ṭamṭam*⟧ a simple kind of drum, usually beaten with the hands

-to·my (tə mē) ⟦< Gr < *tomē*, a cutting⟧ *combining form* a surgical operation

ton (tun) ***n.*** ⟦var. of TUN⟧ **1** a unit of weight equal to 2,000 pounds **2** in Great Britain, a unit of weight equal to 2,240 pounds

ton·al (tō′nəl) ***adj.*** of a tone —**ton′al·ly** ***adv.***

to·nal·i·ty (tō nal′ə tē) ***n., pl.*** **-ties** *Music* **1** KEY[1] (*n.* 6) **2** tonal character, as determined by the relationship of the tones to the keynote

tone (tōn) ***n.*** ⟦< Gr *teinein*, to stretch⟧ **1** a vocal or musical sound, or its quality as to pitch, intensity, etc. **2** a manner of expression showing a certain attitude *[a friendly tone]* **3** style, character, spirit, etc. **4** elegance **5** a quality of color; shade **6** normal, healthy condition of a muscle, organ, etc. **7** *Music a)* a sound of distinct pitch *b)* any of the full intervals of a diatonic scale —***vt.*** **toned, ton′ing** to give a tone to —**tone down** (or **up**) to give a less (or more) intense tone to —**tone′less** ***adj.***

tone′arm′ ***n.*** the pivoted arm beside a phonograph turntable, holding the stylus

tone′-deaf′ ***adj.*** not able to distinguish differences in musical pitch

ton·er (tō′nər) ***n.*** **1** the black or colored powder used to form images in xerography **2** a facial cleanser

tone row (or **series**) see TWELVE-TONE

tong (tôŋ, täŋ) ***n.*** ⟦Mandarin *t'ang*, meeting place⟧ a Chinese association, society, etc.

Ton·ga (täŋ′gə) kingdom on a group of islands (**Tonga Islands**) in the SW Pacific, east of Fiji: 289 sq. mi.; pop. 95,000 —**Ton′gan** ***n.***

tongs (tôŋz, täŋz) ***pl.n.*** ⟦OE *tange*⟧ [*sometimes with sing. v.*] a device for seizing or lifting objects, having two long arms pivoted or hinged together

tongue (tuŋ) ***n.*** ⟦OE *tunge*⟧ **1** the movable, muscular structure in the mouth, used in eating, tasting, and (in humans) speaking **2** talk; speech **3** the act, power, or manner of speaking **4** a language or dialect **5** something like a tongue in shape, position, use, etc., as the flap under the laces of a shoe —**hold one's tongue** to keep from speaking —**speak in tongues** to utter unintelligible sounds, as while in a religious trance —(**with**) **tongue in cheek** in a humorously ironic or insincere way —**tongue'less** *adj.*

tongue'-and-groove' joint a kind of joint in which a projection on one board fits into a groove in another

tongue'-lash'ing *n.* [Inf.] a harsh scolding or reproving; reprimand

tongue'-tied' *adj.* speechless from amazement, embarrassment, etc.

tongue twister a phrase or sentence hard to say fast (Ex: six sick sheiks)

ton·ic (tän'ik) *adj.* ⟦see TONE⟧ **1** of or producing good muscular tone **2** *Music* designating or based on a keynote —*n.* **1** anything that invigorates, as a drug or medicine **2** a quinine-flavored beverage served with gin, vodka, etc. **3** *Music* a keynote

to·night (tə nīt') *adv.* ⟦OE *to niht*⟧ on or during the present or coming night —*n.* the present or coming night

ton·nage (tun'ij) *n.* **1** the total amount of shipping of a country or port, calculated in tons **2** the carrying capacity of a ship, calculated in tons

ton·sil (tän'səl) *n.* ⟦L *tonsillae*, pl.⟧ either of a pair of oval masses of tissue at the back of the mouth

ton·sil·lec·to·my (tän'sə lek'tə mē) *n.*, *pl.* **-mies** ⟦prec. + -ECTOMY⟧ the surgical removal of the tonsils

ton'sil·li'tis (-līt'is) *n.* ⟦ModL < L *tonsillae*, tonsils + -ITIS⟧ inflammation of the tonsils

ton·so·ri·al (tän sôr'ē əl) *adj.* ⟦see fol.⟧ of a barber or barbering: often humorous *[a tonsorial artist]*

ton·sure (tän'shər) *n.* ⟦< L *tondere*, to clip⟧ **1** a shaving off of part of the hair of the head, done as a sign of entrance into the clerical or monastic state **2** the head area so shaved

to·nus (tō'nəs) *n.* ⟦ModL, ult. < Gr *teinein*, to stretch⟧ the slight, continuous contraction characteristic of a normal relaxed muscle

ton·y (tō'nē) *adj.* **-i·er, -i·est** [Slang] very elegant

too (to͞o) *adv.* ⟦stressed form of TO⟧ **1** in addition; also **2** more than enough *[the hat is too big]* **3** extremely; very *[it was just too delicious!]*

took (to͝ok) *vt.*, *vi. pt. of* TAKE

tool (to͞ol) *n.* ⟦OE *tol*⟧ **1** any hand implement, instrument, etc. used for some work **2** any similar instrument that is the working part of a machine, as a drill **3** anything that serves as a means **4** a stooge —*vt.* to impress designs on (leather, etc.) with a tool —*vi.* to install the tools, equipment, etc. needed: often with *up*

toot (to͞ot) *vi.*, *vt.* ⟦echoic⟧ to sound (a horn, whistle, etc.) in short blasts —*n.* a short blast of a horn, whistle, etc.

tooth (to͞oth) *n.*, *pl.* **teeth** (tēth) ⟦OE *toth*⟧ **1** any of the hard, bonelike structures in the jaws, used for biting, chewing, etc. **2** a toothlike part, as on a saw, comb, gearwheel, etc.; tine, prong, cog, etc. **3** [*pl.*] effective means of enforcement *[a law with teeth]* —**tooth and nail** with all one's strength —**toothed** *adj.* —**tooth'less** *adj.*

tooth'ache' *n.* pain in a tooth

tooth'brush' *n.* a small brush for cleaning the teeth

tooth'paste' *n.* a paste used for brushing the teeth

tooth'pick' *n.* a very small, pointed stick for getting bits of food free from between the teeth

tooth powder a powder used like toothpaste

tooth'some (-səm) *adj.* tasty; savory

tooth'y *adj.* **-i·er, -i·est** having or exposing teeth that show prominently —**tooth'i·ly** *adv.*

top[1] (täp) *n.* ⟦OE⟧ **1** the head or crown **2** the highest point or surface of anything **3** the part of a plant above ground **4** the uppermost part or covering, as a lid, cap, etc. **5** the highest degree *[at the top of his voice]* **6** the highest rank *[the top of the class]* —*adj.* of, at, or being the top; highest or foremost —*vt.* **topped, top'ping 1** to take off the top of (a plant, etc.) **2** to provide with a top **3** to be a top for **4** to reach the top of **5** to exceed in amount, etc. **6** to surpass; outdo —**blow one's top** [Slang] to lose one's temper —**on top** successful —**on top of 1** resting upon **2** besides **3** controlling successfully —**top off** to complete by adding a finishing touch —**top'per** *n.*

top[2] (täp) *n.* ⟦OE⟧ a cone-shaped toy with a point upon which it is spun

to·paz (tō'paz') *n.* ⟦< Gr *topazos*⟧ any of various yellow gems, esp. a variety of aluminum silicate

top brass [Slang] important officials

top'coat' *n.* a lightweight overcoat

top'-drawer' (-drôr') *adj.* of first importance

top'-dress'ing *n.* material applied to a surface, as fertilizer on land

To·pe·ka (tə pē'kə) capital of Kansas: pop. 120,000

top·er (tō'pər) *n.* ⟦< archaic *tope*, to drink (much liquor)⟧ a drunkard

top'-flight' *adj.* [Inf.] first-rate

top hat a man's tall, black, cylindrical silk hat, worn in formal dress

top'-heav'y *adj.* too heavy at the top, so as to be unstable

top·ic (täp'ik) *n.* ⟦ult. < Gr *topos*, place⟧ the subject of an essay, speech, discussion, etc.

top'i·cal *adj.* dealing with topics of the day; of current or local interest

top'knot' *n.* a tuft of hair or feathers on the top of the head

top'less *adj.* without a top: said as of a costume exposing the breasts

top-lev·el (täp'lev'əl) *adj.* of or by persons of the highest office or rank

top'mast' *n.* the second mast above the deck of a sailing ship, supported by the lower mast

top'most' *adj.* at the very top

top'-notch' *adj.* [Inf.] first-rate; excellent

to·pog·ra·phy (tə päg'rə fē) *n.*, *pl.* **-phies** ⟦see TOPIC & -GRAPHY⟧ **1** the science of representing surface features of a region on maps and charts **2** these surface features —**top·o·graph·ic** (täp′ə graf′ik) or **top′o·graph′i·cal** *adj.*

top·ping (täp′iŋ) *n.* something put on top of something else, as a sauce on food

top·ple (täp′əl) *vi.* **-pled**, **-pling** ⟦< TOP[1]⟧ to fall top forward; fall (*over*) because top-heavy, etc. —*vt.* to cause to topple; overturn

top·sail (täp′sāl′; *naut.*, -səl) *n.* in a square-rigged vessel, the square sail next above the lowest sail on a mast

top′-se′cret *adj.* designating or of the most secret information

top·side (täp′sīd′) *adv.* on or to an upper deck or the main deck of a ship

top′soil′ *n.* the upper layer of soil, usually richer than the subsoil

top·sy-tur·vy (täp′sē tur′vē) *adv.*, *adj.* ⟦prob. < *top*, highest part + ME *terven*, to roll⟧ **1** upside down; in a reversed condition **2** in disorder

toque (tōk) *n.* ⟦Fr⟧ a woman's small, round, usually brimless hat

To·rah or **To·ra** (tō′rə, tôr′ə) [*occas.* **t-**] *n.* ⟦< Heb, law⟧ **1** the body of Jewish religious literature **2** the Pentateuch

torch (tôrch) *n.* ⟦see TORQUE⟧ **1** a portable flaming light **2** a device for producing a very hot flame, as in welding **3** [Brit.] a flashlight —*vt.* [Slang] to set fire to, as in arson

torch′bear′er *n.* **1** one who carries a torch **2** *a*) one who brings enlightenment, truth, etc. *b*) an inspirational leader, as in some movement

torch′light′ *n.* the light of a torch or torches —*adj.* done by torchlight

torch song a sentimental song of unrequited love —**torch singer**

tore (tôr) *vt.*, *vi. pt. of* TEAR[1]

tor·e·a·dor (tôr′ē ə dôr′) *n.* ⟦Sp < L *taurus*, a bull⟧ a bullfighter

tor·ment (tôr′ment′; *for v.* tôr ment′) *n.* ⟦OFr < L: see TORQUE⟧ **1** great pain or anguish **2** a source of pain, anxiety, etc. —*vt.* **1** to cause great physical pain or mental anguish in **2** to annoy; harass —**tor·ment′ing·ly** *adv.* —**tor·men′tor** or **tor·ment′er** *n.*

torn (tôrn) *vt.*, *vi. pp. of* TEAR[1]

tor·na·do (tôr nā′dō) *n.*, *pl.* **-does** or **-dos** ⟦< Sp < L *tonare*, to thunder⟧ a violently whirling column of air seen as a funnel-shaped cloud that usually destroys everything in its narrow path

To·ron·to (tə ränt′ō) capital of Ontario, Canada: pop. 654,000 (met. area, 4,264,000)

tor·pe·do (tôr pē′dō) *n.*, *pl.* **-does** ⟦< L: see fol.⟧ **1** a large, cigar-shaped, self-propelled underwater projectile containing explosives **2** any of various explosive devices —*vt.* **-doed**, **-do·ing** to attack, destroy, etc. as with a torpedo

tor·pid (tôr′pid) *adj.* ⟦< L *torpere*, be numb⟧ **1** dormant or inactive **2** dull; sluggish

tor′por (-pər) *n.* ⟦L⟧ **1** a torpid state; sluggishness; stupor **2** dullness; apathy

torque (tôrk) *n.* ⟦< L *torquere*, to twist⟧ **1** *Physics* a measure of the tendency of a force to cause rotation **2** popularly, the force that acts to produce rotation, as in an automotive vehicle

tor·rent (tôr′ənt, tär′-) *n.* ⟦< L *torrens*, rushing⟧ **1** a swift, violent stream, esp. of water **2** a flood or rush of words, mail, etc. —**tor·ren·tial** (tô ren′shəl) *adj.*

tor·rid (tôr′id, tär′-) *adj.* ⟦< L *torrere*, to dry⟧ **1** subjected to intense heat, esp. of the sun; parched **2** very hot; scorching **3** passionate; ardent

Torrid Zone the area of the earth's surface between the Tropic of Cancer & the Tropic of Capricorn and divided by the equator

tor·sion (tôr′shən) *n.* ⟦see TORQUE⟧ **1** a twisting or being twisted **2** the stress produced in a rod, wire, etc. by twisting along a longitudinal axis

tor·so (tôr′sō) *n.*, *pl.* **-sos** or **-si** (-sē) ⟦< Gr *thyrsos*, a stem⟧ the trunk of the human body

tort (tôrt) *n.* ⟦< L *torquere*, to twist⟧ *Law* a wrongful act or damage (not involving a breach of contract), for which a civil action can be brought

torte (tôrt; *Ger* tôr′tə) *n.*, *pl.* **tortes** or Ger. ***tor·ten*** (tôr′tən) ⟦Ger < It < LL *torta*, a twisted bread⟧ a rich cake, as one made of eggs, finely chopped nuts, crumbs, etc.

tor·tel·li·ni (tôrt′ə lē′nē) *n.* ⟦It⟧ pasta in tiny ring-shaped pieces, filled with meat, etc.

tor·til·la (tôr tē′ə) *n.* ⟦Sp, dim. of *torta*, a cake⟧ a flat cake of unleavened cornmeal, or of flour

tor·toise (tôrt′əs) *n.* ⟦< ? *c.* 4th-c. Gr *tartarouchos*, evil demon⟧ a turtle, esp. one that lives on land

tor′toise·shell′ *n.* **1** the hard, mottled, yellow-and-brown shell of some turtles **2** a synthetic substance resembling this

tor·to·ni (tôr tō′nē) *n.* ⟦prob. alt. < It *tortone*, lit., big pastry tart⟧ an ice cream made with heavy cream, maraschino cherries, almonds, etc.

tor·tu·ous (tôr′choo əs) *adj.* ⟦see TORQUE⟧ **1** full of twists, turns, etc.; crooked **2** deceitful or tricky

tor·ture (tôr′chər) *n.* ⟦see TORQUE⟧ **1** the inflicting of severe pain, as to elicit information or force a confession **2** any severe physical or mental pain; agony —*vt.* **-tured**, **-tur·ing** **1** to subject to torture **2** to twist or distort (meaning, etc.) —**tor′tur·er** *n.*

To·ry (tôr′ē) *n.*, *pl.* **-ries** ⟦Ir *tōruidhe*, robber⟧ **1** after 1689, a member of the major conservative party of England **2** in the American Revolution, one loyal to Great Britain **3** [*often* **t-**] any extreme conservative

toss (tôs, täs) *vt.* ⟦prob. < Scand⟧ **1** to throw about [*waves tossed the boat*] **2** to throw lightly from the hand **3** to jerk upward [*to toss one's head*] —*vi.* **1** to be thrown about **2** to fling oneself about in sleep, etc. —*n.* a tossing or being tossed

toss′up′ *n.* **1** the flipping of a coin to decide something **2** an even chance

tot[1] (tät) ***n.*** ⟦prob. < ON⟧ **1** a young child **2** [Chiefly Brit.] a small drink of alcoholic liquor

tot[2] (tät) ***vt.***, ***vi.*** **tot′ted**, **tot′ting** [Inf., Chiefly Brit.] to total: with *up*

to·tal (tōt′'l) ***adj.*** ⟦< L *totus*, all⟧ **1** constituting a whole **2** complete; utter *[a total loss]* **—*n.*** the whole amount; sum **—*vt.*** **-taled** or **-talled**, **-tal·ing** or **-tal·ling** **1** to find the total of **2** to add up to **3** [Slang] to demolish **—to′tal·ly *adv.***

to·tal·i·tar·i·an (tō tal′ə ter′ē ən) ***adj.*** ⟦prec. + (AUTHOR)ITARIAN⟧ designating or of a government in which one political group maintains complete control, esp. under a dictator **—*n.*** one who favors such a government **—to·tal′i·tar′i·an·ism′ *n.***

to·tal·i·ty (tō tal′ə tē) ***n.***, *pl.* **-ties** the total amount or sum

to·tal·i·za·tor (tōt′'l i zāt′ər) ***n.*** a machine for registering bets and computing the odds and payoffs, as at a horse race: also **to′tal·iz′er** (-ī′zər) ***n.***

tote (tōt) ***vt.*** **tot′ed**, **tot′ing** ⟦< ?⟧ [Inf.] to carry or haul **—*n.*** **1** a small piece of luggage **2** a large, open handbag: in full **tote bag**

to·tem (tōt′əm) ***n.*** ⟦< Algonquian⟧ **1** among some peoples, an animal or natural object taken as the symbol of a family or clan **2** an image of this

TOTEM POLE

totem pole a pole carved and painted with totems by Indian tribes of NW North America

tot·ter (tät′ər) ***vi.*** ⟦prob. < Scand⟧ **1** to rock as if about to fall **2** to be unsteady on one's feet; stagger

tou·can (to͞o′kan′) ***n.*** ⟦< AmInd (Brazil)⟧ a brightly colored bird of tropical America, with a very large beak

touch (tuch) ***vt.*** ⟦< OFr *tochier*⟧ **1** to put the hand, etc. on, so as to feel **2** to bring (something), or come, into contact with (something else) **3** to border on **4** to strike lightly **5** to give a light tint, aspect, etc. to *[touched with pink]* **6** to handle; use **7** to come up to; reach **8** to compare with; equal **9** to affect; concern **10** to arouse sympathy, gratitude, etc. in **11** [Slang] to seek a loan or gift of money from **—*vi.*** **1** to touch a person or thing **2** to be or come in contact **3** to verge (*on* or *upon*) **4** to pertain; bear (*on* or *upon*) **5** to treat in passing: with *on* or *upon* **—*n.*** **1** a touching or being touched; specif., a light tap **2** the sense by which physical objects are felt **3** a special quality or skill **4** a subtle change or addition in a painting, story, etc. **5** a trace, tinge, etc. **6** a slight attack *[a touch of the flu]* **7** contact or communication *[keep in touch]* **8** [Slang] the act of seeking or getting a loan or gift of money **9** *Music* the manner of striking the keys of a piano, etc. **—touch down** to land: said of an aircraft or spacecraft **—touch up** to improve by minor changes

touch′-and-go′ *adj.* uncertain, risky, etc.

touch′down′ *n.* **1** the moment at which an aircraft or spacecraft lands **2** *Football* a play, scoring six points, in which a player carries, catches, or recovers the ball past the opponent's goal line

tou·ché (to͞o shā′) ***interj.*** ⟦Fr⟧ touched: said when one's opponent in fencing scores a point, or as to acknowledge a clever retort

touched (tucht) ***adj.*** **1** emotionally affected; moved **2** slightly demented

touch′ing *adj.* arousing tender emotions; moving

touch′stone′ *n.* **1** a stone formerly used to test the purity of gold or silver **2** any test of genuineness

touch′-type′ *vi.* **-typed′**, **-typ′ing** to type without looking at the keyboard by regularly touching a given key with a specific finger

touch′y *adj.* **-i·er**, **-i·est** **1** easily offended; oversensitive; irritable **2** very risky or precarious

touch′y-feel′y (-fē′lē) ***adj.*** [Inf.] having or showing too much affection, compassion, etc.

tough (tuf) ***adj.*** ⟦OE *toh*⟧ **1** that will bend, etc. without tearing or breaking **2** not easily cut or chewed *[tough steak]* **3** strong; hardy **4** stubborn **5** brutal or rough **6** very difficult; laborious **—*n.*** a tough person; thug

tough′en *vt.*, ***vi.*** to make or become tough or tougher **—tough′en·er *n.***

tou·pee (to͞o pā′) ***n.*** ⟦< Fr < OFr *toup*, tuft of hair⟧ a man's small wig

tour (to͝or) ***n.*** ⟦< OFr *tourner*, to turn⟧ **1** a turn, period, etc., as of military duty **2** a long trip, as for sightseeing **3** any trip, as for inspection, for giving performances, etc. **—*vt.***, ***vi.*** to go on a tour (through)

tour de force (to͝or′ də fôrs′) *pl.* **tours de force** (to͝or′) ⟦Fr⟧ an unusually skillful or ingenious creation or performance, sometimes a merely clever one

Tou·rette's syndrome (to͞o rets′) ⟦after G. de la *Tourette*, 19th-c. Fr doctor⟧ a nervous disorder characterized by involuntary movements, obscene utterances, etc.

tour′ism′ *n.* tourist travel

tour′ist *n.* one who tours, esp. for pleasure **—*adj.*** of or for tourists

tour·ma·line (to͝or′mə lin, -lēn′) ***n.*** ⟦Fr⟧ a crystalline mineral used as a gemstone, etc.

tour·na·ment (to͝or′nə mənt, tʉr′-) ***n.*** ⟦< OFr *tourner*, to turn⟧ **1** in the Middle Ages, a contest between knights on horseback who tried to unseat one another with lances **2** a series of contests in competition for a championship Also **tour′ney** (-nē) ***n.***, *pl.* **-neys**

tour′ni·quet (toor′ni kit, tur′-) ***n.*** ⟦Fr < L *tunica*, tunic⟧ a device for compressing a blood vessel to stop bleeding, as a bandage twisted about a limb and released at intervals

tou·sle (tou′zəl) ***vt.*** **-sled, -sling** ⟦< ME *tusen*, to pull⟧ to disorder, dishevel, muss, etc.

tout (tout) [Inf.] ***vi., vt.*** ⟦OE *totian*, to peep⟧ **1** to praise highly **2** to sell betting tips on (racehorses) —***n.*** one who touts

tow (tō) ***vt.*** ⟦OE *togian*⟧ to pull, as by a rope or chain —***n.*** **1** a towing or being towed **2** something towed **3** TOWLINE —**in tow** **1** being towed **2** in one's company or charge

toward (tôrd, twôrd) ***prep.*** ⟦see TO & -WARD⟧ **1** in the direction of **2** facing **3** along a likely course to *[steps toward peace]* **4** concerning **5** just before *[toward noon]* **6** for *[save toward a car]* Also **towards**

tow·el (tou′əl) ***n.*** ⟦< OFr *toaille*⟧ a piece of cloth or paper for wiping or drying things —***vt.*** **-eled** or **-elled, -el·ing** or **-el·ling** to wipe or dry with a towel —**throw** (or **toss,** etc.) **in the towel** [Inf.] to admit defeat

tow′el·ing or **tow′el·ling** ***n.*** material for making towels

tow·er (tou′ər) ***n.*** ⟦< L *turris*⟧ **1** a high structure, often part of a building **2** such a structure used as a fortress, etc. —***vi.*** to rise high like a tower —**tow′er·ing** ***adj.***

tow·head (tō′hed′) ***n.*** ⟦< *tow*, fibers of flax, etc.⟧ a person with pale-yellow hair —**tow′head′ed** ***adj.***

tow·hee (tō′hē, -ē) ***n.*** ⟦echoic⟧ any of various small North American sparrows

tow·line (tō′līn′) ***n.*** a rope, etc. used for towing

town (toun) ***n.*** ⟦OE *tun*⟧ **1** a concentration of houses, etc. somewhat larger than a village **2** a city **3** a township **4** the business center of a city **5** the people of a town —**on the town** [Inf.] out for a good time

town crier one who, formerly, cried public announcements through the streets of a village or town

town hall a building in a town, housing the offices of officials, etc.

town house a two-story or three-story dwelling, a unit in a complex of such dwellings

town meeting a meeting of the voters of a town, as in New England

town′ship ***n.*** a division of a county, constituting a unit of local government

towns′peo′ple ***pl.n.*** the people of a town: also **towns′folk′**

tow·path (tō′path′) ***n.*** a path along a canal, used by men or animals towing freight-carrying boats

tow′rope′ ***n.*** a rope used in towing

tox·e·mi·a (täk sē′mē ə) ***n.*** ⟦see fol. & -EMIA⟧ a condition in which the blood contains poisonous substances, esp. toxins produced by pathogenic bacteria

tox·ic (täk′sik) ***adj.*** ⟦< Gr *toxicon*, a poison⟧ **1** of, affected by, or caused by a toxin **2** poisonous

tox·i·col·o·gy (täk′si käl′ə jē) ***n.*** ⟦see prec. & -LOGY⟧ the science of poisons and their effects, antidotes, etc. —**tox′i·col′o·gist** ***n.***

tox·in (täk′sin) ***n.*** ⟦< TOXIC⟧ **1** any of various poisons produced by microorganisms and causing certain diseases **2** any poison secreted by plants or animals

toy (toi) ***n.*** ⟦< ? MDu *toi*, finery⟧ **1** a trifle **2** a plaything for children —***adj.*** **1** like a plaything in size, use, etc. **2** made as a toy —***vi.*** to trifle (*with* a thing, an idea, etc.)

tr *abbrev.* **1** translated **2** translation **3** translator **4** transpose

trace[1] (trās) ***n.*** ⟦< L *trahere*, to draw⟧ **1** a mark, track, sign, etc. left by a person, animal, or thing **2** a barely perceptible amount —***vt.*** **traced, trac′ing** **1** to follow the trail of; track **2** *a)* to follow the development or history of *b)* to determine (a source, etc.) by this procedure **3** to draw, outline, etc. **4** to copy (a drawing, etc.) by following its lines on a superimposed transparent sheet —**trace′a·ble** ***adj.*** —**trac′er** ***n.***

trace[2] (trās) ***n.*** ⟦see TRAIT⟧ either of two straps, etc. connecting a draft animal's harness to the vehicle drawn

trace element a chemical element, as copper, zinc, etc., essential in nutrition, but only in minute amounts

trac·er·y (trās′ər ē) ***n.***, *pl.* **-ies** ⟦< TRACE[1] + -ERY⟧ ornamental work of interlacing or branching lines

tra·che·a (trā′kē ə) ***n.***, *pl.* **-che·ae′** (-ē′) or **-che·as** ⟦< Gr *tracheia* (*arteria*), rough (windpipe)⟧ the passage that conveys air from the larynx to the bronchi; windpipe —**tra′che·al** ***adj.***

tra·che·ot·o·my (trā′kē ät′ə mē) ***n.***, *pl.* **-mies** ⟦see prec. & -TOMY⟧ an incision of the trachea to aid breathing in an emergency

trac·ing (trās′iŋ) ***n.*** something traced; specif., *a)* a copy of a drawing, etc. *b)* a traced line made by a recording instrument

track (trak) ***n.*** ⟦< Fr *trac*⟧ **1** a mark left in passing, as a footprint, wheel rut, etc. **2** a path or trail **3** a sequence of ideas, events, etc. **4** a path or circuit laid out for racing, etc. **5** a pair of parallel metal rails on which trains, etc. run **6** *a)* sports performed on a track, as running, hurdling, etc. *b)* these sports along with other contests in jumping, throwing, etc. **7** *a)* a band on a phonograph record, compact disc, etc. *b)* any of the separate, parallel recording surfaces along a magnetic tape —***vt.*** **1** to follow the track of **2** to trace by means of evidence, etc. **3** to plot the path of, as with radar **4** to leave tracks of (mud, etc.) on: often with *up* —**in one's tracks** where one is at the moment —**keep** (or **lose**) **track of** to stay (or fail to stay) informed about —**track′less** ***adj.***

track lighting a method of lighting a room with spotlights inserted along a narrow, wired track

track record [Inf.] the record of the performance of a person, etc. as in some activity

tract[1] (trakt) ***n.*** ⟦< L *trahere*, to draw⟧ **1** a continuous expanse of land **2** a system of organs having some special function *[the digestive tract]*

tract[2] (trakt) ***n.*** ⟦< LL *tractatus*, treatise⟧ a propagandizing pamphlet

trac·ta·ble (trak′tə bəl) ***adj.*** ⟦< L *trahere*, to draw⟧ easily managed; docile; compliant

tract house a house built to a design that is used many times throughout a housing development

trac·tion (trak′shən) ***n.*** ⟦< L *trahere*, to draw⟧ **1** *a*) a pulling or drawing *b*) a being pulled or drawn *c*) the kind of power used for pulling *[electric traction]* **2** the power, as of tires on pavement, to hold to a surface without slipping

trac·tor (trak′tər) ***n.*** ⟦see prec.⟧ **1** a powerful, motor-driven vehicle for pulling farm machinery, etc. **2** a truck with a driver's cab and no body, for hauling large trailers

trac′tor-trail′er ***n.*** a TRACTOR (sense 2) combined with a trailer or semitrailer, used for transporting goods

trade (trād) ***n.*** ⟦< LowG, a track⟧ **1** occupation; esp., skilled work **2** all the persons in a particular business **3** buying and selling; commerce **4** customers **5** an exchange; swap **—*vi.*** **trad′ed, trad′ing** **1** to carry on a business **2** to have business dealings (*with*) **3** to make an exchange (*with*) **4** [Inf.] to be a customer (*at* a certain store) **—*vt.*** to exchange; barter **—trade on** (or **upon**) to take advantage of

trade′-in′ ***n.*** a thing given or taken as part payment for something else

trade journal (or **magazine**) a magazine devoted to a specific trade or industry

trade′mark′ ***n.*** **1** a symbol, word, etc. used by a manufacturer or dealer to distinguish a product: usually protected by law **2** [Inf.] a distinctive, identifying feature or characteristic

trade name **1** the name by which a commodity is commonly known by those who deal in it **2** a name used as a trademark **3** the business name of a company

trade′-off′ ***n.*** an exchange in which one benefit is given up for another considered more desirable: also **trade′off′**

trad′er ***n.*** **1** one who trades; merchant **2** a ship used in trade

trades·man (trādz′mən) ***n.***, *pl.* **-men** (-mən) [Chiefly Brit.] a storekeeper **—trades′wom′an**, *pl.* **-wom′en**, ***fem.n.***

trade union LABOR UNION

trade wind a wind that blows toward the equator from either side of it

trading post a store in an outpost, settlement, etc., where trading is done

tra·di·tion (trə dish′ən) ***n.*** ⟦< L *tradere*, deliver⟧ **1** the handing down orally of beliefs, customs, etc. from generation to generation **2** a story, belief, custom, etc. handed down in this way

tra·di′tion·al ***adj.*** of, handed down by, or conforming to tradition

tra·di′tion·al·ism′ ***n.*** adherence to tradition; sometimes, specif., excessive devotion to tradition **—tra·di′tion·al·ist** ***n.***

tra·duce (trə dōōs′, -dyōōs′) ***vt.*** **-duced′, -duc′ing** ⟦< L *trans*, across + *ducere*, to lead⟧ to slander

traf·fic (traf′ik) ***n.*** ⟦< It *traffico* < L *trans*, across +It *ficcare*, bring⟧ **1** buying and selling; trade **2** dealings (*with* someone) **3** the movement or number of automobiles, pedestrians, etc. along a street, etc. **4** the business done by a transportation company **—*adj.*** of or having to do with traffic **—*vi.*** **-ficked, -fick·ing** **1** to carry on traffic (*in* a commodity) **2** to have dealings (*with* someone)

traffic circle a circular road at the intersection of several streets: vehicles move on it in one direction only

traffic light (or **signal**) a set of signal lights at a street intersection for regulating traffic

tra·ge·di·an (trə jē′dē ən) ***n.*** **1** a writer of tragedy **2** an actor in tragedies

trag·e·dy (traj′ə dē) ***n.***, *pl.* **-dies** ⟦< Gr *tragos*, goat + *ōidē*, song⟧ **1** a serious play with an unhappy ending **2** a very sad or tragic event; disaster

trag·ic (traj′ik) ***adj.*** **1** of or like a tragedy **2** disastrous, fatal, etc. **—trag′i·cal·ly** ***adv.***

trail (trāl) ***vt.*** ⟦< L *trahere*, to draw⟧ **1** to drag or let drag behind one **2** to follow the tracks of; track **3** to hunt by tracking **4** to follow behind **—*vi.*** **1** to drag along on the ground, etc. **2** to grow along the ground, etc., as some plants do **3** to flow behind: said as of smoke **4** to follow or lag behind; straggle **5** to grow weaker, dimmer, etc.: with *off* or *away* **—*n.*** **1** something that trails behind **2** a mark, scent, etc. left by a person, animal, or thing that has passed **3** a beaten path

trail bike a small motorcycle for off-road riding

trail′blaz′er ***n.*** **1** one who blazes a trail **2** a pioneer in any field

trail′er ***n.*** **1** one that trails **2** *a*) a wagon, van, etc. designed to be pulled by an automobile, truck, etc. *b*) such a vehicle designed to be lived in

trailer park an area, usually with piped water, electricity, etc., for trailers, esp. mobile homes

trail mix GORP

train (trān) ***n.*** ⟦< L *trahere*, to pull⟧ **1** something that drags along behind, as a trailing skirt **2** a group of followers; retinue **3** a procession; caravan **4** any connected order; sequence *[a train of thought]* **5** a line of connected railroad cars pulled by a locomotive **—*vt.*** **1** to guide the growth of (a plant) **2** to guide the mental, moral, etc. development of; rear **3** to instruct so as to make proficient **4** to make fit for an athletic contest, etc. **5** to aim (a gun, etc.) **—*vi.*** to undergo training —**train·ee** (trān ē′) ***n.*** —**train′er** ***n.***

traipse (trāps) ***vi.***, ***vt.*** **traipsed, traips′ing** ⟦< ?⟧ [Inf. or Dial.] to walk, wander, or tramp

trait (trāt) ***n.*** ⟦< L *trahere*, to draw⟧ a distinguishing quality or characteristic

trai·tor (trāt′ər) ***n.*** ⟦< L *tradere*, betray⟧ one who betrays one's country, cause, friends, etc. —**trai′tor·ous** ***adj.***

tra·jec·to·ry (trə jek′tə rē) ***n.***, *pl.* **-ries** ⟦ult. < L *trans*, across + *jacere*, to throw⟧ the curved path of something hurtling through space

tram (tram) ***n.*** ⟦prob. < LowG *traam*, a beam⟧ [Brit.] a streetcar

tram·mel (tram′əl) ***n.*** ⟦< L *tres*, three + *macula*, a mesh⟧ [*usually pl.*] something that confines or restrains —***vt.*** **-meled** or **-melled, -mel·ing** or **-mel·ling** to confine, restrain, etc.

tramp (tramp) ***vi.*** ⟦ME *trampen*⟧ **1** to walk or step heavily **2** to travel about on foot —***vt.*** **1** to step on heavily **2** to walk through —***n.*** **1** a vagrant; hobo **2** the sound of heavy steps **3** a journey on foot; hike **4** a freight ship with no schedule, that picks up cargo, etc. as it goes along **5** [Slang] a sexually promiscuous woman

tram·ple (tram′pəl) ***vi.*** **-pled, -pling** ⟦see prec.⟧ to tread heavily —***vt.*** to crush, destroy, etc. by or as by treading heavily on

tram·po·line (tram′pə lēn′, -lin) ***n.*** ⟦< It⟧ a sheet of strong canvas stretched tightly on a frame with springs, used in acrobatic tumbling and jumping

trance (trans) ***n.*** ⟦< L *transire*, go across, die⟧ **1** a state of altered consciousness, resembling sleep, as in hypnosis **2** a daze; stupor **3** a state of great mental abstraction

tran·quil (traŋ′kwəl) ***adj.*** **-quil·er** or **-quil·ler, -quil·est** or **-quil·lest** ⟦L *tranquillus*⟧ calm, serene, placid, etc. —**tran·quil′li·ty** or **tran·quil′i·ty** (-kwil′ə tē) ***n.*** —**tran′quil·ly** ***adv.***

tran′quil·ize′ or **tran′quil·lize′** (-kwə līz′) ***vt.***, ***vi.*** **-ized′** or **-lized′, -iz′ing** or **-liz′ing** to make or become tranquil

tran′quil·iz′er or **tran′quil·liz′er** ***n.*** a drug used as a calming agent in treating various emotional disturbances, etc.

trans *abbrev.* **1** translated **2** translation **3** translator **4** transportation

trans- ⟦L < *trans*, across⟧ *prefix* over, across, beyond, through

trans·act (tran zakt′, -sakt′) ***vt.*** ⟦< L *trans-*, over + *agere*, to drive⟧ to carry on or complete (business, etc.)

trans·ac′tion ***n.*** **1** a transacting **2** something transacted; specif., *a*) a business deal *b*) [*pl.*] a record of the proceedings of a society, etc.

trans·at·lan·tic (trans′at lan′tik, tranz′-) ***adj.*** **1** crossing the Atlantic **2** on the other side of the Atlantic

trans·ceiv·er (tran sē′vər) ***n.*** a radio transmitter and receiver in a single housing

tran·scend (tran send′) ***vt.*** ⟦< L *trans-*, over + *scandere*, climb⟧ **1** to go beyond the limits of; exceed **2** to surpass; excel —**tran·scend′ent** ***adj.***

tran·scen·den·tal (tran′sen dent′'l) ***adj.*** **1** supernatural **2** abstract —**tran′scen·den′tal·ly** ***adv.***

tran′scen·den′tal·ism′ ***n.*** [*often* **T-**] a philosophy based on a search for reality through spiritual intuition

trans·con·ti·nen·tal (trans′kän tə nent′'l, tranz′-) ***adj.*** **1** that crosses a continent **2** on the other side of a continent

tran·scribe (tran skrīb′) ***vt.*** **-scribed′, -scrib′ing** **1** to write out or type out in full (shorthand notes, etc.) **2** to represent (speech sounds) in symbols

tran·script (tran′skript′) ***n.*** **1** a written, typewritten, or printed copy **2** a copy, esp. an official copy, as of a student's record

tran·scrip′tion (-skrip′shən) ***n.*** **1** a transcribing **2** a transcript; copy **3** an arrangement of a piece of music for an instrument or voice other than that for which it was written

trans·duc·er (trans do͞os′ər, tranz-) ***n.*** ⟦< L *trans-*, over + *ducere*, to lead⟧ a device that transmits energy from one system to another, sometimes converting the energy to a different form

tran·sept (tran′sept′) ***n.*** ⟦< L *trans-*, across + *septum*, enclosure⟧ the part of a cross-shaped church at right angles to the nave, or either of its arms

trans·fer (trans′fər) ***vt.*** **-ferred, -fer·ring** ⟦< L *trans-*, across + *ferre*, to bear⟧ **1** to carry, send, etc. to another person or place **2** to make over (property, etc.) to another **3** to convey (a picture, etc.) from one surface to another —***vi.*** **1** to transfer oneself or be transferred **2** to change as to another school or another bus —***n.*** **1** a transferring or being transferred **2** one that is transferred **3** a ticket entitling the bearer to change to another bus, etc. —**trans·fer′ral** (-fur′-) ***n.***

trans·fer·ence (trans′fər əns, trans fur′-) ***n.*** a transferring or being transferred

trans·fig·ure (trans fig′yər) ***vt.*** **-ured, -ur·ing** ⟦< L *trans-*, across + *figura*, figure⟧ **1** to change the form or appearance of **2** to transform so as to glorify —**trans·fig′u·ra′tion** ***n.***

trans·fix (trans fiks′) ***vt.*** ⟦< L *trans-*, through + *figere*, to fix⟧ **1** to pierce through; impale **2** to make motionless, as if impaled

trans·form (trans fôrm′) ***vt.*** ⟦< L *trans-*, over + *forma*, a form⟧ **1** to change the form or appearance of **2** to change the condition, nature, or function of —**trans′for·ma′tion** ***n.***

trans·form′er ***n.*** a device for changing electrical energy to a different voltage

trans·fuse′ (-fyo͞oz′) ***vt.*** **-fused′, -fus′ing** ⟦< L *trans-*, across + *fundere*, pour⟧ **1** to instill; imbue **2** to transfer (blood, etc.) into a blood vessel —**trans·fu′sion** ***n.***

trans·gress (trans gres′, tranz-) ***vt.***, ***vi.*** ⟦< L *trans-*, over + *gradi*, to step⟧ **1** to break (a law, command, etc.); sin (against) **2** to go beyond (a limit, etc.)

—**trans·gres'sion** (-gresh'ən) ***n.*** —**trans·gres'sor** ***n.***

tran·sient (tran'shənt, -zē ənt) ***adj.*** ⟦< L *trans-*, over + *ire*, to go⟧ **1** passing away with time; temporary **2** passing quickly; fleeting **3** staying only a short time —***n.*** a transient person —**tran'sience** or **tran'sien·cy** ***n.***

tran·sis·tor (tran zis'tər, -sis'-) ***n.*** ⟦TRAN(SFER) + (RE)SISTOR⟧ a compact electronic device, composed of semiconductor material, that controls current flow —**tran·sis'tor·ize'**, **-ized'**, **-iz'ing**, ***vt.***

trans·it (tran'sit, -zit) ***n.*** ⟦< L *trans-*, over + *ire*, to go⟧ **1** passage through or across **2** *a)* a carrying through or across; conveyance *b)* a system of urban public transportation **3** a surveying instrument for measuring horizontal angles

tran·si·tion (tran zish'ən) ***n.*** a passing from one condition, place, etc. to another —**tran·si'tion·al** ***adj.***

tran·si·tive (tran'sə tiv, -zə-) ***adj.*** designating a verb that takes a direct object

tran·si·to·ry (tran'sə tôr'ē, -zə-) ***adj.*** not enduring; temporary; fleeting

transl *abbrev.* **1** translated **2** translation

trans·late (trans lāt', tranz-) ***vt.*** **-lat'ed**, **-lat'ing** ⟦< L *translatus*, transferred⟧ **1** to move from one place or condition to another **2** to put into the words of a different language **3** to put into different words —**trans·la'tor** ***n.***

trans·la'tion ***n.*** **1** a translating **2** writing or speech translated into another language

trans·lit·er·ate (trans lit'ər āt', tranz-) ***vt.*** **-at'ed**, **-at'ing** ⟦< TRANS- + L *litera*, letter⟧ to write (words, etc.) in the characters of another alphabet —**trans·lit'er·a'tion** ***n.***

trans·lu'cent (-lo͞o'sənt) ***adj.*** ⟦< L *trans-*, through + *lucere*, to shine⟧ letting light pass through, but not transparent

trans·mi'grate' (-mī'grāt') ***vi.*** **-grat'ed**, **-grat'ing** ⟦see TRANS- & MIGRATE⟧ to pass into another body at death: said of the soul, as in Hindu religious belief —**trans'mi·gra'tion** ***n.***

trans·mis'sion (-mish'ən) ***n.*** **1** a transmitting **2** something transmitted **3** the part of a motor vehicle that transmits power to the wheels

trans·mit' (-mit') ***vt.*** **-mit'ted**, **-mit'ting** ⟦< L *trans-*, over + *mittere*, send⟧ **1** to cause to go to another person or place; transfer **2** to hand down by heredity, inheritance, etc. **3** *a)* to pass (light, heat, etc.) through some medium *b)* to conduct [water *transmits* sound] **4** to convey (force, movement, etc.) to **5** to send out (radio or television broadcasts) —**trans·mis'si·ble** (-mis'ə bəl) ***adj.*** —**trans·mit'ta·ble** ***adj.*** —**trans·mit'tal** ***n.***

trans·mit'ter ***n.*** the apparatus that transmits signals in telephony, radio, etc.

trans·mute' (-myo͞ot') ***vt.***, ***vi.*** **-mut'ed**, **-mut'ing** ⟦< L *trans-*, over + *mutare*, to change⟧ to change from one form, nature, substance, etc. into another; transform —**trans'mu·ta'tion** ***n.***

trans·na'tion·al (-nash'ə nəl) ***adj.*** transcending the limits, interests, etc. of a single nation

trans'o'ce·an'ic (-ō'shē an'ik) ***adj.*** crossing the ocean

tran·som (tran'səm) ***n.*** ⟦prob. < L *transtrum*, crossbeam⟧ **1** a horizontal crossbar, as across the top of a door or window **2** a small window just above a door or window

trans·pa·cif·ic (trans'pə sif'ik) ***adj.*** **1** crossing the Pacific **2** on the other side of the Pacific

trans·par·en·cy (trans per'ən sē) ***n.***, *pl.* **-cies** a transparent film or slide having an image that can be projected on a screen

trans·par'ent ***adj.*** ⟦< L *trans-*, through + *parere*, appear⟧ **1** transmitting light rays so that objects on the other side can be seen clearly **2** so fine in texture as to be seen through **3** easily understood or detected; clear; obvious —**trans·par'ent·ly** ***adv.***

tran·spire (tran spīr') ***vi.*** **-spired'**, **-spir'ing** ⟦< L *trans-*, through + *spirare*, breathe⟧ **1** to give off vapor, moisture, etc., as through pores **2** to become known **3** to happen

trans·plant (trans plant'; *also, and for n. always,* trans'plant') ***vt.*** **1** to remove from one place and plant, resettle, etc. in another **2** *Surgery* to transfer (tissue or an organ) from one to another; graft —***n.*** a transplanting or something transplanted, as a body organ or a seedling —**trans'plan·ta'tion** (-plan tā'shən) ***n.***

tran·spon·der (tran spän'dər) ***n.*** ⟦< TRAN(SMITTER) & RESPOND⟧ a transceiver that automatically transmits signals

trans·port (trans pôrt'; *for n.* trans' pôrt') ***vt.*** ⟦< L *trans-*, over + *portare*, carry⟧ **1** to carry from one place to another **2** to carry away with emotion —***n.*** **1** a transporting; transportation **2** strong emotion, esp. joy **3** a vehicle for transporting

trans'por·ta'tion (-pər tā'shən) ***n.*** **1** a transporting or being transported **2** a means of conveyance **3** fare or a ticket for being transported

trans·pose (trans pōz') ***vt.***, ***vi.*** **-posed'**, **-pos'ing** ⟦see TRANS- & POSE⟧ **1** to change the usual order or position of; interchange **2** to rewrite or play (a musical composition) in a different key —**trans'po·si'tion** (-pə zish'ən) ***n.***

trans·sex·u·al (trans sek'sho͞o əl) ***n.*** a person who identifies with the opposite sex, sometimes so strongly as to undergo sex-change surgery

trans·ship (trans ship') ***vt.***, ***vi.*** **-shipped'**, **-ship'ping** to transfer from one ship, train, truck, etc. to another for further shipment —**trans·ship'ment** ***n.***

trans·verse (trans vurs', tranz-; *also, and for n. usually,* trans'vurs', tranz'-) ***adj.*** ⟦< L *trans-*, across + *vertere*, to turn⟧ situated across; crosswise —***n.*** a transverse part, etc.

trans·ves·tite (trans ves'tīt', tranz-) ***n.***

⟦< TRANS- + L *vestire*, to dress⟧ a person who gets sexual pleasure from dressing in the clothes of the opposite sex

trap (trap) ***n.*** ⟦< OE *træppe*⟧ **1** a device for catching animals, as one that snaps shut tightly when stepped on **2** any stratagem designed to catch or trick **3** a device, as in a drainpipe, for preventing the escape of gas, etc. —***vt.* trapped, trap'ping** to catch in or as in a trap —***vi.*** to trap animals, esp. for their furs —**trap'per *n.***

trap'door' ***n.*** a hinged or sliding door in a roof, ceiling, or floor

tra·peze (tra pēz') ***n.*** ⟦see fol.⟧ a short horizontal bar, hung high by two ropes, on which gymnasts, etc. swing

tra·pe·zi·um (trə pē'zē əm) ***n.***, *pl.* **-zi·ums** or **-zi·a** (-ə) ⟦< Gr *trapeza*, table⟧ a plane figure with four sides, no two of which are parallel

trap·e·zoid (trap'i zoid') ***n.*** ⟦see prec.⟧ a plane figure with four sides, only two of which are parallel —**trap'e·zoi'dal *adj.***

trap'pings ***pl.n.*** ⟦< OFr *drap*, cloth⟧ **1** an ornamental covering for a horse **2** adornments

trap'shoot'ing ***n.*** the sport of shooting at clay disks sprung into the air from throwing devices

trash (trash) ***n.*** ⟦prob. < Scand⟧ **1** broken, discarded, or worthless things; rubbish **2** a person or people regarded as disreputable, etc. —***vt.*** [Slang] **1** to destroy (property) as by vandalism **2** to criticize or insult (a person, etc.) sharply or maliciously —**trash'y, -i·er, -i·est, *adj.***

trau·ma (trô'mə, trä'-) ***n.***, *pl.* **-mas** or **-ma·ta** (-mə tə) ⟦Gr⟧ **1** a bodily injury or shock **2** an emotional shock, often having a lasting psychic effect —**trau·mat·ic** (trô mat'ik) ***adj.***

trau'ma·tize' (-tīz') ***vt.* -tized', -tiz'ing** to subject to a physical or mental trauma

trav·ail (trə vāl', trav'āl') ***n.*** ⟦< L *tri-*, three + *palus*, stake: referring to a torture device⟧ **1** very hard work **2** intense pain; agony

trav·el (trav'əl) ***vi.* -eled** or **-elled, -el·ing** or **-el·ling** ⟦var. of prec.⟧ **1** to go from one place to another **2** to move, pass, or be transmitted —***vt.*** to make a journey over or through —***n.*** **1** a traveling **2** [pl.] trips, journeys, etc. —**trav'el·er** or **trav'el·ler *n.***

traveler's check a check, issued by a bank, etc., sold to a traveler who signs it at issuance and again when cashing it

trav·e·logue or **trav·e·log** (trav'ə lôg') ***n.*** **1** an illustrated lecture on travels **2** a short film about a place, esp. one that is foreign, unusual, etc.

tra·verse (trə vurs'; *for n. & adj.* trav'ərs) ***vt.* -versed', -vers'ing** ⟦< L *trans-*, across + *vertere*, to turn⟧ to pass over, across, or through —***n.* trav'erse** **1** something that traverses or crosses, as a crossbar **2** a traversing —***adj.* trav'erse** **1** extending across **2** designating or of draperies drawn by pulling a cord at the side

trav·es·ty (trav'is tē) ***n.***, *pl.* **-ties** ⟦< L *trans-*, over + *vestire*, to dress⟧ **1** a farcical imitation in ridicule **2** a ridiculous representation [a *travesty* of justice] —***vt.* -tied, -ty·ing** to make a travesty of

trawl (trôl) ***n.*** ⟦< ? MDu *traghel*, dragnet⟧ **1** a large dragnet for fishing **2** a long line supported by buoys, from which fishing lines are hung —***vi.*, *vt.*** to fish or catch with a trawl

trawl'er ***n.*** a boat used in trawling

tray (trā) ***n.*** ⟦< OE *treg*, wooden board⟧ a flat receptacle with raised edges, for holding or carrying things

treach·er·ous (trech'ər əs) ***adj.*** **1** characterized by treachery; disloyal **2** untrustworthy or insecure —**treach'er·ous·ly *adv.***

treach·er·y (trech'ər ē) ***n.***, *pl.* **-ies** ⟦< OFr *trichier*, to cheat⟧ **1** betrayal of trust; disloyalty **2** treason

trea·cle (trē'kəl) ***n.*** ⟦< Gr (*antidotos*) *thēriakē*, (remedy) for venom⟧ [Brit.] **1** molasses **2** anything very sweet or cloying —**trea'cly** (-klē) ***adj.***

tread (tred) ***vt.* trod, trod'den** or **trod, tread'ing** ⟦OE *tredan*⟧ **1** to walk on, in, along, etc. **2** to do or follow by walking, dancing, etc. **3** to press or beat with the feet —***vi.*** **1** to walk **2** to set one's foot (*on, across,* etc.) **3** to trample (*on* or *upon*) —***n.*** **1** the manner or sound of treading **2** something for treading or moving on, as a shoe sole or surface of a stair **3** the thick outer layer of an automotive tire —**tread water** *pt. & pp. usually* **tread'ed** to stay upright in swimming by moving the legs and arms back and forth

trea·dle (tred''l) ***n.*** ⟦< OE *tredan*, to tread⟧ a lever moved by the foot as to turn a wheel

tread'mill' ***n.*** **1** a mill wheel turned by an animal treading an endless belt **2** any monotonous work in which one seems to make no progress **3** an exercise machine with an endless belt on which one walks or runs

treas *abbrev.* **1** treasurer **2** treasury

trea·son (trē'zən) ***n.*** ⟦< L *trans-*, over + *dare*, give⟧ betrayal of one's country to an enemy —**trea'son·a·ble** or **trea'son·ous *adj.***

treas·ure (trezh'ər) ***n.*** ⟦< Gr *thēsauros*⟧ **1** accumulated wealth, as money or jewels **2** any person or thing considered valuable —***vt.* -ured, -ur·ing** **1** to save up for future use **2** to value greatly

treas·ur·er (trezh'ər ər) ***n.*** one in charge of a treasury, as of a government or club

treas'ure-trove' (-trōv') ***n.*** ⟦*trove* < OFr *trover*, find⟧ **1** treasure found hidden, the original owner of which is unknown **2** a valuable source or collection

treas·ur·y (trezh'ər ē) ***n.***, *pl.* **-ies** **1** a place where treasure or funds are kept **2** the funds or revenues of a state, corporation, etc. **3** [T-] the department of government in charge of revenue, taxation, and public finances

treat (trēt) ***vi.*** ⟦ult. < L *trahere*, to draw⟧ **1** to discuss terms (*with*) **2** to speak or write (*of*) —***vt.*** **1** to deal with (a subject) in writing, music, etc. in a specified manner **2** to act toward (someone or something) in a specified manner **3** to pay for the food, etc. of (another) **4** to subject to some process, chemical, etc. **5** to give medical care to —*n.* **1** a meal, drink, etc. paid for by another **2** anything that gives great pleasure

trea·tise (trēt′is) *n.* ⟦see prec.⟧ a formal article or book on some subject

treat·ment (trēt′mənt) *n.* **1** act, manner, method, etc. of treating **2** medical or surgical care

trea·ty (trēt′ē) *n., pl.* **-ties** ⟦< L *trahere,* to draw⟧ a formal agreement between two or more nations

tre·ble (treb′əl) *adj.* ⟦< L *triplus,* triple⟧ **1** threefold; triple **2** of, for, or performing the treble —*n.* **1** the highest part in musical harmony; soprano **2** a high-pitched voice or sound —*vt., vi.* **-bled, -bling** to make or become threefold

tree (trē) *n.* ⟦OE *trēow*⟧ **1** a large, woody perennial plant with one main trunk and many branches **2** *a*) anything resembling a tree *b*) FAMILY TREE —*vt.* **treed, tree′ing** to chase up a tree —**tree′less** *adj.* —**tree′like′** *adj.*

tre·foil (trē′foil′) *n.* ⟦< L *tri-,* three + *folium,* leaf⟧ **1** a plant with leaves divided into three leaflets, as the clover **2** a design, etc. shaped like such a leaf

trek (trek) *vi.* **trekked, trek′king** ⟦Afrik < Du *trekken,* to pull⟧ **1** to travel slowly or laboriously **2** [Inf.] to go on foot —*n.* **1** a journey **2** a migration

trel·lis (trel′is) *n.* ⟦< L *trilix,* triple-twilled⟧ a lattice on which vines are trained

trem·a·tode (trem′ə tōd′, trē′mə-) *n.* ⟦< Gr *trēmatōdēs,* perforated⟧ a parasitic flatworm with muscular suckers; fluke

trem·ble (trem′bəl) *vi.* **-bled, -bling** ⟦< L *tremere*⟧ **1** to shake or shiver from cold, fear, etc. **2** to feel great anxiety **3** to quiver, vibrate, etc. —*n.* **1** a trembling **2** [*sometimes pl.*] a fit of trembling

tre·men·dous (tri men′dəs) *adj.* ⟦< L *tremere,* to tremble⟧ **1** very large; great **2** [Inf.] wonderful, amazing, etc. —**tre·men′dous·ly** *adv.*

trem·o·lo (trem′ə lō′) *n., pl.* **-los′** ⟦It⟧ *Music* a tremulous effect produced by rapid reiteration of the same tone

trem·or (trem′ər) *n.* ⟦< L *tremere,* to tremble⟧ **1** a trembling, shaking, etc. **2** a trembling sensation

trem·u·lous (trem′yo͞o ləs) *adj.* ⟦< L *tremere,* to tremble⟧ **1** trembling; quivering **2** fearful; timid

trench (trench) *vt.* ⟦< OFr *trenchier,* to cut⟧ to dig a ditch or ditches in —*n.* **1** a deep furrow **2** a long, narrow ditch dug by soldiers for cover, with earth heaped up in front

trench·ant (tren′chənt) *adj.* ⟦see prec.⟧ **1** sharp; incisive *[trenchant* words*]* **2** forceful; effective *[*a *trenchant* argument*]* —**trench′ant·ly** *adv.*

trench coat a belted raincoat in a military style

trench′er *n.* ⟦see TRENCH⟧ [Archaic] a wooden platter for meat

trench′er·man (-mən) *n., pl.* **-men** (-mən) an eater; esp., one who eats much

trench foot a diseased condition of the feet from prolonged exposure to wet and cold

trench mouth an infectious disease of the mucous membranes of the mouth and throat

trend (trend) *vi.* ⟦OE *trendan*⟧ to have a general direction or tendency —*n.* **1** a general tendency or course; drift **2** a current style

trend·y (tren′dē) *adj.* **-i·er, -i·est** [Inf.] of or in the latest style, or trend

Tren·ton (trent′'n) capital of New Jersey: pop. 89,000

trep·i·da·tion (trep′ə dā′shən) *n.* ⟦< L *trepidus,* disturbed⟧ fearful uncertainty; anxiety

tres·pass (tres′pəs, -pas′) *vi.* ⟦< L *trans-,* across + *passus,* a step⟧ **1** to go beyond the limits of what is considered right; do wrong; transgress **2** to enter another's property without permission or right —*n.* a trespassing; specif., a moral offense —**tres′pass·er** *n.*

tress (tres) *n.* ⟦< OFr *tresse,* braid of hair⟧ **1** a lock of human hair **2** [*pl.*] a woman's or girl's hair, esp. when long

tres·tle (tres′əl) *n.* ⟦< L *transtrum,* a beam⟧ **1** a horizontal beam fastened to two pairs of spreading legs, used as a support **2** a framework of uprights and crosspieces, supporting a bridge, etc.

trey (trā) *n.* ⟦< L *tres,* three⟧ a playing card with three spots

tri- ⟦< Fr, L, or Gr⟧ *prefix* **1** having or involving three **2** three times, into three **3** every third

tri·ad (trī′ad′) *n.* ⟦< Gr *treis,* three⟧ a group of three

tri·age (trē äzh′, trē′äzh′) *n.* ⟦< Fr *trier,* sift⟧ a system of establishing the order in which acts are to be carried out in an emergency, esp. acts of medical assistance —*vt.* **-aged′, -ag′ing** to prioritize (patients, problems, etc.)

tri·al (trī′əl) *n.* ⟦see TRY⟧ **1** the act or process of trying, testing, etc.; test; probation **2** a hardship, suffering, etc. **3** a source of annoyance **4** a hearing and deciding of a case in a court of law **5** an attempt; effort —*adj.* **1** of a trial **2** for the purpose of trying, testing, etc. —**on trial** in the process of being tried

trial and error the process of making repeated trials, tests, and adjustments until the right result is found

trial balloon something said or done to test public opinion on an issue

tri·an·gle (trī′aŋ′gəl) *n.* ⟦see TRI- & ANGLE[1]⟧ **1** a plane figure having three angles and three sides **2** anything with three sides or three corners **3** a situation involving three persons *[*a love *triangle]* —**tri·an′gu·lar** (-gyo͞o lər) *adj.*

tri·an′gu·late′ (-gyə lāt′) *vt.* **-lat′ed, -lat′ing** to divide (an area) into triangles in order to determine distance or relative positions —**tri·an′gu·la′tion** *n.*

tri·ath·lon (trī ath′län′, -lən) *n.* ⟦TRI- + Gr *athlon,* a contest⟧ an endurance race combining events in swimming, bicycling, and running

tribe (trīb) ***n.*** ⟦< L *tribus*⟧ **1** a group of persons or clans descended from a common ancestor and living under a leader or chief **2** a natural group of related plants or animals —**trib'al** ***adj.*** —**trib'al·ly** ***adv.*** —**tribes'man** (-mən), *pl.* **-men**, ***n.***

trib·u·la·tion (trib'yə lā'shən) ***n.*** ⟦< L *tribulare,* to press⟧ great misery or distress, or the cause of it

tri·bu·nal (trī byōō'nəl, tri-) ***n.*** ⟦see fol.⟧ **1** a seat for a judge in a court **2** a court of justice

trib·une (trib'yōōn'; *for 2, often* tri byōōn') ***n.*** ⟦< L *tribus,* tribe⟧ **1** in ancient Rome, a magistrate appointed to protect the rights of plebeians **2** a champion of the people: often used in newspaper names

trib·u·tar·y (trib'yōō ter'ē) ***adj.*** **1** paying tribute **2** subject *[*a *tributary* nation*]* **3** flowing into a larger one *[*a *tributary* stream*]* —***n.***, *pl.* **-ies** **1** a tributary nation **2** a tributary river

trib·ute (trib'yōōt) ***n.*** ⟦< L *tribuere,* allot⟧ **1** money paid regularly by one nation to another as acknowledgment of subjugation, for protection, etc. **2** any forced payment **3** something given, done, or said to show gratitude, honor, or praise

trice (trīs) ***n.*** ⟦< MDu *trisen,* to pull⟧ an instant; moment: now only in **in a trice**

tri·cen·ten·ni·al (trī'sen ten'ē əl) ***adj.*** happening once every 300 years —***n.*** a 300th anniversary

tri·ceps (trī'seps') ***n.***, *pl.* **-ceps'** or **-ceps'es** ⟦L < *tri-,* three + *caput,* head⟧ a muscle with three points of origin, esp. the muscle on the back of the upper arm

tri·cer·a·tops (trī ser'ə täps') ***n.*** ⟦< TRI- + Gr *keras,* horn + *ōps,* eye⟧ a plant-eating dinosaur having a bony crest over the neck and three horns

tri·chi·na (tri kī'nə) ***n.***, *pl.* **-nae** (-nē) ⟦< Gr *trichinos,* hairy⟧ a very small worm that causes trichinosis

trich·i·no·sis (trik'i nō'sis) ***n.*** ⟦< Gr *trichinos,* hairy⟧ a disease caused by intestinal worms, and acquired by eating insufficiently cooked pork from an infested hog

trick (trik) ***n.*** ⟦< OFr *trichier,* to cheat⟧ **1** something designed to deceive, cheat, etc. **2** a practical joke; prank **3** a clever act intended to amuse **4** any feat requiring skill **5** a personal mannerism **6** a round of duty; shift **7** *Card Games* the cards won in a single round —***vt.*** to deceive or swindle —***adj.*** apt to malfunction *[*a *trick* knee*]* —**do** (or **turn**) **the trick** [Inf.] to produce the desired result —**not miss a trick** [Inf.] to be very alert —**trick'er·y**, *pl.* **-ies**, ***n.***

trick·le (trik'əl) ***vi.*** **-led**, **-ling** ⟦ME *triklen* < ?⟧ **1** to flow slowly in a thin stream or fall in drops **2** to move slowly *[*the crowd *trickled* away*]* —***n.*** a slow, small flow

trick'le·down' ***adj.*** of an economic theory holding that government aid to the largest businesses will ultimately benefit the poor

trick'-or-treat'er ***n.*** a person in costume who goes from door to door on Halloween asking for candy

trick'ster (-stər) ***n.*** a person who tricks; cheat

trick'y ***adj.*** **-i·er**, **-i·est** **1** given to or characterized by trickery **2** like a trick in deceptiveness or intricacy

tri·col·or (trī'kul'ər) ***n.*** a flag having three colors in large areas; esp., the flag of France

tri·cy·cle (trī'sə kəl) ***n.*** ⟦Fr: see TRI- & CYCLE⟧ a child's three-wheeled vehicle operated by pedals

tri·dent (trīd''nt) ***n.*** ⟦< L *tri-,* three + *dens,* tooth⟧ a three-pronged spear

tried (trīd) ***vt.***, ***vi.*** *pt. & pp. of* TRY —***adj.*** **1** tested; proved **2** trustworthy

tri·en·ni·al (trī en'ē əl) ***adj.*** ⟦< L *tri-,* three + *annus,* year⟧ **1** happening every three years **2** lasting three years —**tri·en'ni·al·ly** ***adv.***

Tri·este (trē est') seaport in NE Italy: pop. 228,000

tri·fle (trī'fəl) ***n.*** ⟦< OFr *truffe,* deception⟧ **1** something of little value or importance **2** a small amount of money —***vi.*** **-fled**, **-fling** **1** to talk or act jokingly **2** to toy (*with*) —***vt.*** to waste *[*to *trifle* the hours away*]* —**tri'fler** ***n.***

tri'fling (-fliŋ) ***adj.*** **1** frivolous; shallow **2** of little importance; trivial

tri·fo·cals (trī'fō'kəlz) ***pl.n.*** eyeglasses like bifocals, but with a third area in the lens ground for viewing objects at an intermediate distance

trig (trig) ***n.*** *short for* TRIGONOMETRY

trig·ger (trig'ər) ***n.*** ⟦< Du *trekken,* to pull⟧ a lever pulled to release a catch, etc., esp. one pressed to activate the firing mechanism on a firearm —***vt.*** to initiate (an action)

trig'ger-hap'py ***adj.*** **1** tending to resort to force rashly or irresponsibly **2** ready to start a war for the slightest cause

tri·glyc·er·ide (trī glis'ər īd') ***n.*** ⟦TRI- + Gr *glykeros,* sweet⟧ an ester derived from glycerol: the chief component of fats and oils

trig·o·nom·e·try (trig'ə näm'ə trē) ***n.*** ⟦< Gr *trigōnon,* triangle + *-metria,* measurement⟧ the branch of mathematics analyzing, and making calculations from, relations between the sides of right triangles with reference to their angles —**trig'o·no·met'ric** (-nə me'trik) ***adj.***

trill (tril) ***n.*** ⟦ult. echoic⟧ **1** a rapid alternation of a musical tone with a slightly higher tone **2** a warble **3** a rapid vibration of the tongue or uvula —***vt.***, ***vi.*** to sound, speak, or play with a trill

tril·lion (tril'yən) ***n.*** **1** 1 followed by 12 zeros **2** [Brit.] 1 followed by 18 zeros —**tril'lionth** ***adj.***, ***n.***

tril·li·um (tril'ē əm) ***n.*** ⟦ModL < L *tri-,* three⟧ a woodland plant having a single flower with three petals and three sepals

TRILLIUM

tril·o·gy (tril'ə jē) ***n.***, *pl.* **-gies** ⟦see TRI- & -LOGY⟧ a set of three related plays, novels, etc.

trim (trim) ***vt.*** **trimmed, trim'ming** ⟦< OE *trymman,* make firm⟧ **1** to put in proper order; make neat or tidy *[to trim hair]* **2** to clip, lop, cut, etc. **3** to decorate, as by adding ornaments, etc. **4** *a)* to balance (a ship) by ballasting, etc. *b)* to put (sails) in order for sailing **5** to balance (a flying aircraft) **6** [Inf.] to beat, punish, defeat, cheat, etc. **—*vi.*** to adjust according to expediency **—*n.*** **1** order; arrangement **2** good condition **3** a trimming, as by clipping **4** decorative parts or borders **—*adj.*** **trim'mer, trim'mest** **1** orderly; neat **2** well-proportioned **3** in good condition **—trim'ly *adv.*** **—trim'mer *n.*** **—trim'ness *n.***

tri·ma·ran (trī'mə ran') ***n.*** a boat like a catamaran, but with three parallel hulls

tri·mes·ter (trī mes'tər, trī'mes'-) ***n.*** ⟦< L *tri-,* three + *mensis,* month⟧ **1** a three-month period, as of pregnancy **2** in some colleges, any of the three periods of the academic year

trim·ming (trim'iŋ) ***n.*** **1** decoration; ornament **2** [*pl.*] *a)* the side dishes of a meal *b)* parts trimmed off **3** [Inf.] a beating, defeat, cheating, etc.

Trin·i·dad and To·ba·go (trin'i dad' and tə bā'gō) island country in the West Indies: 1,980 sq. mi.; pop. 1,260,000

trin·i·ty (trin'i tē) ***n.***, *pl.* **-ties** ⟦< L *trinitas*⟧ a set of three **—the Trinity** *Christian Theol.* the union of Father, Son, and Holy Spirit in one Godhead

trin·ket (triŋ'kit) ***n.*** ⟦ME *trenket*⟧ **1** a small, cheap ornament, piece of jewelry, etc. **2** a trifle or toy

tri·o (trē'ō) ***n.***, *pl.* **-os** ⟦< L *tres,* three⟧ **1** a group of three **2** *Music a)* a composition for three voices or three instruments *b)* the three performers of such a composition

trip (trip) ***vi.***, ***vt.*** **tripped, trip'ping** ⟦< OFr *treper*⟧ **1** to move or perform with light, rapid steps; skip **2** to stumble or cause to stumble **3** to make or cause to make a mistake **4** to run past or release (a spring, wheel, etc.) **—*n.*** **1** a light, quick tread **2** a journey, jaunt, etc. **3** a stumble or a causing to stumble **4** [Slang] *a)* an experience induced by a psychedelic drug, esp. LSD *b)* an experience that is pleasing, exciting, etc. **—trip up** to catch in a lie, error, etc. **—trip'per *n.***

tri·par·tite (trī pär'tīt') ***adj.*** ⟦< L *tri-,* three + *partire,* to part⟧ **1** having three parts **2** made between three parties, as an agreement

tripe (trīp) ***n.*** ⟦prob. ult. < Ar *tharb,* layer of fat lining the intestines⟧ **1** part of the stomach of an ox, etc., used as food **2** [Slang] anything worthless, etc.; nonsense

trip'ham'mer ***n.*** a heavy, power-driven hammer, alternately raised and allowed to fall by a tripping device: also **trip hammer**

tri·ple (trip'əl) ***adj.*** ⟦< L *triplus*⟧ **1** consisting of three; threefold **2** three times as much or as many **—*n.*** **1** an amount three times as much or as many **2** *Baseball* a hit on which the batter reaches third base **—*vt.***, ***vi.*** **tri'pled, tri'pling** **1** to make or become three times as much or as many **2** *Baseball* to hit a triple **—tri'ply *adv.***

tri·plet (trip'lit) ***n.*** **1** a group of three, as three successive lines of poetry **2** any of three offspring from the same pregnancy

trip·li·cate (trip'li kit; *for v.,* -kāt') ***adj.*** ⟦< L *triplex*⟧ **1** threefold **2** being the last of three identical copies **—*n.*** any one of such copies **—*vt.*** **-cat'ed, -cat'ing** to make three identical copies of **—in triplicate** in three identical copies

tri·pod (trī'päd') ***n.*** ⟦< Gr *tri-,* three + *pous,* foot⟧ a three-legged caldron, stool, support, etc.

trip·tych (trip'tik) ***n.*** ⟦< Gr *tri-,* three + *ptychē,* a fold⟧ a set of three hinged panels with pictures, etc., commonly placed above and behind an altar

tri·sect (trī sekt', trī'sekt') ***vt.*** ⟦< TRI- + L *secare,* to cut⟧ to cut or divide into three equal parts

tri-state (trī'stāt') ***adj.*** of an area consisting of all or parts of three contiguous states

trite (trīt) ***adj.*** **trit'er, trit'est** ⟦< L *terere,* wear out⟧ worn out by constant use; stale **—trite'ness *n.***

trit·i·um (trit'ē əm) ***n.*** a radioactive isotope of hydrogen having an atomic weight of 3

Tri·ton (trīt''n) ***n.*** a Greek sea god having the tail of a fish and the head and upper body of a man

tri·umph (trī'əmf) ***n.*** ⟦< L *triumphus*⟧ **1** a victory; success **2** exultation or joy over a victory, etc. **—*vi.*** **1** to gain victory or success **2** to rejoice over victory, etc. **—tri·um'phal** (-um'fəl) ***adj.***

tri·um'phal·ism' ***n.*** an arrogant confidence in a set of beliefs **—tri·um'phal·ist *adj.*, *n.***

tri·um'phant (-fənt) ***adj.*** **1** successful; victorious **2** rejoicing for victory **—tri·um'phant·ly *adv.***

tri·um·vir (trī um'vir') ***n.***, *pl.* **-virs'** or **-vi·ri'** (-vi rī') ⟦L: see fol.⟧ in ancient Rome, any of three administrators sharing authority

tri·um·vi·rate (trī um'və rit) ***n.*** ⟦< L *trium virum,* of three men⟧ government by three persons or parties

tri·va·lent (trī vā′lənt) ***adj.*** *Chem.* having three valences or a valence of three

triv·et (triv′it) ***n.*** ⟦< L *tripes*, tripod⟧ **1** a three-legged stand for holding pots, etc. near a fire **2** a short-legged stand for hot dishes to rest on

triv·i·a (triv′ē ə) ***pl.n.*** [*usually with sing. v.*] unimportant matters

triv·i·al (triv′ē əl) ***adj.*** ⟦< L *trivialis*, commonplace⟧ unimportant; insignificant —**triv′i·al′i·ty** (-al′ə tē) ***n.***

triv′i·al·ize′ (-īz′) ***vt.*** **-ized′**, **-iz′ing** to regard or treat as trivial; make seem unimportant

-trix (triks) ⟦L⟧ *suffix* forming feminine nouns of agency

tro·chee (trō′kē) ***n.*** ⟦< Gr *trechein*, to run⟧ a metrical foot of one accented syllable followed by one unaccented syllable —**tro·cha′ic** (-kā′ik) ***adj.***

trod (träd) ***vt.***, ***vi.*** *pt. & alt. pp. of* TREAD

trod·den (träd′'n) ***vt.***, ***vi.*** *alt. pp. of* TREAD

trog·lo·dyte (träg′lə dīt′) ***n.*** ⟦< Gr *trōglē*, hole + *dyein*, enter⟧ **1** any of the prehistoric people who lived in caves **2** a recluse

troi·ka (troi′kə) ***n.*** ⟦Russ⟧ **1** a vehicle drawn by three horses abreast **2** an association of three in authority

Tro·jan (trō′jən) ***adj.*** of ancient Troy or its people or culture —***n.*** **1** a person born or living in ancient Troy **2** a strong, hard-working, determined person

Trojan horse **1** *Gr. Legend* a huge, hollow wooden horse with Greek soldiers inside: it is brought into Troy, the soldiers creep out and open the gates, and the Greek army destroys the city **2** one that subverts a nation, etc. from within

troll[1] (trōl) ***vt.***, ***vi.*** ⟦ME *trollen*, to roll⟧ **1** to sing the parts of (a round, etc.) in succession **2** to sing in a full voice **3** to fish (in) with a baited line trailed behind a slowly moving boat —**troll′er** ***n.***

troll[2] (trōl) ***n.*** ⟦ON⟧ *Scand. Folklore* a supernatural being, as a giant or dwarf, living in a cave

trol·ley (trä′lē) ***n.***, *pl.* **-leys** ⟦< TROLL[1]⟧ **1** a wheeled basket, etc. that runs suspended from an overhead track **2** a grooved wheel at the end of a pole, for transmitting electric current from an overhead wire to a streetcar, etc. **3** a trolley car

trolley bus an electric bus powered by trolleys

trolley car an electric streetcar that gets its power from a trolley

trol·lop (trä′ləp) ***n.*** ⟦prob. < Ger *trolle*, wench⟧ a prostitute

trom·bone (träm bōn′) ***n.*** ⟦It < *tromba*, a trumpet⟧ a large brass instrument, usually with a slide, or movable section —**trom·bon′ist** ***n.***

TROMBONE

troop (tro͞op) ***n.*** ⟦< ML *troppus*, flock⟧ **1** a group of persons or animals **2** [*pl.*] soldiers **3** a subdivision of a cavalry regiment **4** a unit of Boy Scouts or Girl Scouts —***vi.*** **1** to gather or go together in a group **2** to walk or go

troop′er ***n.*** ⟦prec. + -ER⟧ **1** a soldier in the mounted cavalry **2** a mounted police officer **3** in the U.S., a state police officer

trope (trōp) ***n.*** ⟦< Gr *tropos*, a turning⟧ figurative language or a word used in a figurative sense

tro·phy (trō′fē) ***n.***, *pl.* **-phies** ⟦< Gr *tropaion*⟧ a memorial of victory in war, sports competition, etc.; prize

trop·ic (träp′ik) ***n.*** ⟦< Gr *tropikos*, of a turn (of the sun at the solstices)⟧ **1** either of two parallels of latitude, one, the **Tropic of Cancer**, *c.* 23° 26′ north, and the other, the **Tropic of Capricorn**, *c.* 23° 26′ south **2** [*also* **T-**] [*pl.*] the region between these latitudes —***adj.*** of the tropics; tropical

trop′i·cal (-i kəl) ***adj.*** **1** of, in, characteristic of, or suitable for the tropics **2** very hot; sultry; torrid

tro·pism (trō′piz′əm) ***n.*** ⟦< Gr *tropē*, a turn⟧ the tendency of a plant or animal to grow or turn toward, or away from, a stimulus, as light

tro·po·sphere (trō′pə sfir′, träp′ə-) ***n.*** ⟦Fr < Gr *tropos*, a turning + Fr *sphère*, sphere⟧ the atmospheric zone characterized by water vapor, weather, and decreasing temperatures with increasing altitude

trot (trät) ***vt.***, ***vi.*** **trot′ted**, **trot′ting** ⟦< OHG *trottōn*, to tread⟧ **1** to move, ride, go, etc. at a trot **2** to hurry; run —***n.*** **1** a gait, as of a horse, in which a front leg and the opposite hind leg are lifted at the same time **2** a jogging gait of a person —**trot′ter** ***n.***

troth (trôth, trōth) ***n.*** ⟦ME *trouthe*⟧ [Archaic] **1** faithfulness; loyalty **2** truth **3** a promise, esp. to marry

trou·ba·dour (tro͞o′bə dôr′) ***n.*** ⟦Fr < Prov *trobar*, compose⟧ **1** any of a class of lyric poets and poet-musicians in S France and N Spain and Italy in the 11th to 13th c. **2** a minstrel or singer

trou·ble (trub′əl) ***vt.*** **-bled**, **-bling** ⟦< L *turba*, crowd⟧ **1** to disturb or agitate **2** to worry; harass **3** to cause inconvenience to [don't *trouble* yourself] —***vi.*** to take pains; bother —*n.* **1** a state of mental distress; worry **2** a misfortune; calamity **3** a person, event, etc. causing annoyance, distress, etc. **4** public disturbance **5** effort; bother *[*take the *trouble* to listen*]*

trou'ble·mak'er *n.* one who incites others to quarrel, rebel, etc.

trou'ble·shoot'er *n.* one whose work is to locate and fix breakdowns, eliminate the source of trouble in work flow, etc. —**trou'ble·shoot'ing** *n.*

trou'ble·some (-səm) *adj.* characterized by or causing trouble

trough (trôf, träf) *n.* ⟦OE *trog*⟧ **1** a long, narrow, open container, esp. one to hold water or food for animals **2** a channel or gutter for carrying off rainwater **3** a long, narrow hollow, as between waves **4** a low in an economic cycle **5** a long, narrow area of low barometric pressure

trounce (trouns) *vt.* **trounced, trounc'ing** ⟦< ?⟧ **1** to beat; flog **2** [Inf.] to defeat —**trounc'er** *n.*

troupe (tro͞op) *n.* ⟦Fr⟧ a group of actors, singers, etc. —*vi.* **trouped, troup'ing** to travel as a member of a troupe

troup'er *n.* **1** a troupe member **2** [Inf.] one who is steady, dependable, etc., during trying times

trou·sers (trou'zərz) *pl.n.* ⟦< Gael *triubhas*⟧ a two-legged outer garment, esp. for men and boys, extending from the waist to the ankles

trous·seau (tro͞o sō', tro͞o'sō) *n., pl.* **-seaux'** (-sōz') or **-seaus'** ⟦Fr < OFr *trousse,* a bundle⟧ a bride's clothes, linens, etc.

trout (trout) *n., pl.* **trout** or **trouts** ⟦< Gr *trōgein,* gnaw⟧ a food and game fish, related to the salmon, found chiefly in fresh water

trow (trō, trou) *vi., vt.* ⟦< OE *treow,* faith⟧ [Archaic] to believe

trow·el (trou'əl) *n.* ⟦< L *trua,* ladle⟧ **1** a flat hand tool for smoothing plaster or applying mortar **2** a scooplike tool for loosening soil, etc. —*vt.* **-eled** or **-elled, -el·ing** or **-el·ling** to spread, smooth, dig, etc. with a trowel

troy (troi) *adj.* ⟦after *Troyes,* city in France, where first used⟧ of or by a system of weights (**troy weight**) for gold, silver, gems, etc.

Troy (troi) ancient city in NW Asia Minor

tru·ant (tro͞o'ənt) *n.* ⟦< OFr, beggar⟧ **1** a pupil who stays away from school without permission **2** one who neglects duties —*adj.* **1** that is a truant **2** errant; straying —**tru'an·cy,** *pl.* **-cies,** *n.*

truce (tro͞os) *n.* ⟦< OE *treow,* faith⟧ **1** a temporary cessation of warfare by agreement between the belligerents **2** respite from conflict, trouble, etc.

truck[1] (truk) *n.* ⟦< Gr *trochos,* wheel⟧ **1** a two-wheeled barrow or low, wheeled frame for carrying heavy articles **2** an automotive vehicle for hauling loads **3** a swiveling, wheeled frame under each end of a railroad car, etc. —*vt.* to carry on a truck —*vi.* to drive a truck —**truck'er** *n.*

truck[2] (truk) *vt., vi.* ⟦< Fr *troquer*⟧ to exchange; barter —*n.* **1** small articles of little value **2** vegetables raised for market **3** [Inf.] dealings **4** [Inf.] trash; rubbish

truck farm a farm where vegetables are grown to be marketed

truck·le (truk'əl) *n.* ⟦< Gr *trochos,* wheel⟧ TRUNDLE BED: in full **truckle bed** —*vi.* **-led, -ling** to be servile; submit (*to*)

truc·u·lent (truk'yo͞o lənt, -yə-) *adj.* ⟦< L *trux*⟧ **1** fierce; cruel; savage **2** pugnacious —**truc'u·lence** *n.* —**truc'u·lent·ly** *adv.*

trudge (truj) *vi.* **trudged, trudg'ing** ⟦< ?⟧ to walk, esp. wearily or laboriously —*n.* a wearying walk

true (tro͞o) *adj.* **tru'er, tru'est** ⟦OE *treowe*⟧ **1** faithful; loyal **2** in accordance with fact; not false **3** conforming to standard, etc.; correct **4** rightful; lawful **5** accurately fitted, shaped, etc. **6** real; genuine —*adv.* **1** truly **2** *Biol.* without variation from type —*vt.* **trued, tru'ing** or **true'ing** to fit, place, or shape accurately: often with *up* —*n.* that which is true: with *the*

true believer a dedicated follower or disciple, esp. one who follows without doubts or questions

true bill a bill of indictment endorsed by a grand jury

true'-blue' *adj.* very loyal; staunch

truf·fle (truf'əl) *n.* ⟦ult. < L *tuber,* knob⟧ a fleshy, edible underground fungus

tru·ism (tro͞o'iz'əm) *n.* a statement the truth of which is obvious

tru'ly *adv.* **1** in a true manner; accurately, genuinely, etc. **2** really; indeed **3** sincerely

Tru·man (tro͞o'mən), **Har·ry S** (har'ē) 1884-1972; 33d president of the U.S. (1945-53)

trump (trump) *n.* ⟦< TRIUMPH⟧ **1** any playing card of a suit ranked higher than any other suit for a given hand **2** such a suit **3** any advantage held in reserve —*vt., vi.* to play a trump on (a trick, etc.) —**trump up** to devise fraudulently

trump·er·y (trump'ər ē) *n., pl.* **-ies** ⟦< Fr *tromper,* deceive⟧ **1** something showy but worthless **2** nonsense

trum·pet (trum'pit) *n.* ⟦< OFr *trompe*⟧ **1** a brass instrument consisting of a looped tube with a flared bell and three valves **2** a trumpetlike device for channeling sound, as an early kind of hearing aid **3** a sound like that of a trumpet —*vi.* to make the sound of a trumpet —*vt.* to proclaim loudly —**trum'pet·er** *n.*

trun·cate (truŋ'kāt') *vt.* **-cat'ed, -cat'ing** ⟦< L *truncus,* stem⟧ to cut off a part of —**trun·ca'tion** *n.*

trun·cheon (trun'chən) *n.* ⟦< L *truncus,* stem⟧ [Chiefly Brit.] a policeman's stick or billy

trun·dle (trun'dəl) *vt., vi.* **-dled, -dling** ⟦< OE *trendan,* to roll⟧ to roll along —**trun'dler** *n.*

trundle bed a low bed on small wheels, that can be rolled under another bed when not in use

trunk (truŋk) ***n.*** ⟦< L *truncus*⟧ **1** the main stem of a tree **2** a human or animal body, not including the head and limbs **3** a long snout, as of an elephant **4** a large, reinforced box to hold clothes, etc. in travel **5** [*pl.*] shorts worn by men for athletics **6** a compartment in a car, usually in the rear, for luggage, etc.

trunk line a main line of a railroad, telephone system, etc.

truss (trus) ***vt.*** ⟦< OFr *trousser*⟧ **1** to tie, bind, or bundle: often with *up* **2** to support with a truss **—*n.*** **1** a bundle or pack **2** a framework for supporting a roof, bridge, etc. **3** a padded device for giving support in cases of rupture or hernia

trust (trust) ***n.*** ⟦< ON *traust*⟧ **1** *a)* firm belief in the honesty, reliability, etc. of another; faith *b)* the one trusted **2** confident expectation, hope, etc. **3** responsibility resulting from confidence placed in one **4** care; custody **5** something entrusted to one **6** faith in a buyer's ability to pay; credit **7** a combination of corporations to establish a monopoly **8** *Law a)* the fact of having nominal ownership of property to keep, use, or administer for another *b)* such property **—*vi.*** to be confident **—*vt.*** **1** to have confidence in **2** to commit (something) *to* a person's care **3** to allow to do something without misgivings **4** to believe **5** to hope; expect **6** to grant business credit to **—*adj.*** **1** relating to a trust **2** acting as trustee **—in trust** entrusted to another's care

trust·ee (trus tē′) ***n.*** **1** one to whom another's property or its management is entrusted **2** a member of a board managing the affairs of a college, hospital, etc. **—trust·ee′ship *n.***

trust′ful ***adj.*** full of trust; ready to confide; trusting **—trust′ful·ly *adv.* —trust′ful·ness *n.***

trust fund money, securities, etc. held in trust

trust′ing ***adj.*** that trusts; trustful

trust territory a territory placed under the administrative authority of a country by the United Nations

trust′wor′thy ***adj.*** **-thi·er, -thi·est** worthy of trust; reliable **—trust′wor′thi·ness *n.***

trust′y ***adj.*** **-i·er, -i·est** dependable; trustworthy **—*n.*,** *pl.* **-ies** a convict granted special privileges as a trustworthy person

truth (tro͞oth) ***n.*,** *pl.* **truths** (tro͞o*th*z, tro͞oths) ⟦OE *treowth*⟧ **1** a being true; specif., *a)* sincerity; honesty *b)* conformity with fact *c)* reality; actual existence *d)* correctness; accuracy **2** that which is true **3** an established fact **—in truth** truly

truth′ful ***adj.*** **1** telling the truth; honest **2** corresponding with fact or reality **—truth′ful·ly *adv.* —truth′ful·ness *n.***

try (trī) ***vt.*** **tried, try′ing** ⟦< OFr *trier*⟧ **1** to melt out or render (fat, etc.) **2** to conduct the trial of in a law court **3** to put to the proof; test **4** to subject to trials, etc.; afflict **5** to experiment with *[to try a recipe]* **6** to attempt; endeavor **—*vi.*** to make an effort, attempt, etc. **—*n.*,** *pl.* **tries** an attempt; effort; trial **—try on** to test the fit of (something to wear) by putting it on **—try out** **1** to test by putting into use **2** to test one's fitness, as for a place on a team

try′ing ***adj.*** that tries one's patience; annoying; irksome **—try′ing·ly *adv.***

try′out′ ***n.*** [Inf.] a test to determine fitness, etc.

tryst (trist) ***n.*** ⟦< OFr *triste*, hunting station⟧ **1** an appointment to meet, esp. one made by lovers **2** an appointed meeting or meeting place

tsar (tsär, zär) ***n.*** *alt. sp. of* CZAR (sense 1) **—tsa·ri·na** (tsä rē′nə, zä-) ***fem.n.***

tset·se fly (tset′sē, tsēt′-) ⟦< Bantu name⟧ a small fly of central and S Africa: one kind carries sleeping sickness

T′-shirt′ ***n.*** a collarless pullover knit shirt with short sleeves: also **t′-shirt′**

tsp *abbrev.* teaspoon(s) or teaspoonful(s)

T square a T-shaped ruler for drawing parallel lines

tsu·na·mi (tso͞o nä′mē) ***n.*,** *pl.* **-mis** or **-mi** ⟦Jpn < *tsu*, a harbor + *nami*, a wave⟧ a huge sea wave caused by an undersea earthquake, volcanic eruption, etc.

tub (tub) ***n.*** ⟦< MDu *tubbe*⟧ **1** a round, wooden container, usually with staves and hoops **2** any large, open container, as of metal **3** a bathtub

TUBA

tu·ba (to͞o′bə) ***n.*** ⟦L, trumpet⟧ a large, low-pitched brass musical instrument

tub·al (to͞o′bəl) ***adj.*** of or in a tube, esp. a fallopian tube *[a tubal pregnancy]*

tub·by (tub′ē) ***adj.*** **-bi·er, -bi·est** **1** shaped like a tub **2** fat and short

tube (to͞ob) ***n.*** ⟦< L *tubus*, pipe⟧ **1** a slender pipe of metal, glass, etc. for conveying fluids **2** a tubelike part, organ, etc. **3** a pliable cylinder with a screw cap, for holding paste, etc. **4** *short for*: *a)* ELECTRON TUBE *b)* VACUUM TUBE **5** [Brit.] a subway **—the tube** [Inf.] television **—tube′less *adj.***

tu·ber (to͞o′bər) ***n.*** ⟦L, lit., a swelling⟧ a short, thick part of an underground stem, as a potato **—tu′ber·ous *adj.***

tu′ber·cle (-kəl) ***n.*** ⟦see prec.⟧ **1** a small, rounded projection, as on a bone or a plant root **2** any abnormal hard nodule or swelling; specif., the typical lesion of tuberculosis

tu·ber·cu·lin (to͞o bur′kyə lin) ***n.*** a solution injected into the skin as a test for

tu·ber'cu·lo'sis (-lō'sis) ***n.*** ⟦see TUBERCLE & -OSIS⟧ an infectious disease characterized by the formation of tubercles in body tissue; specif., tuberculosis of the lungs —**tu·ber'cu·lar** or **tu·ber'cu·lous** ***adj.***

tube sock a stretchable sock in the form of a long tube with no shaped heel

tube top a tight-fitting, one-piece, sleeveless and strapless women's garment for the upper body

tub·ing (to͞o'biŋ) ***n.*** **1** a series or system of tubes **2** material in the form of a tube **3** a piece of tube

tu·bu·lar (to͞o'byə lər) ***adj.*** ⟦< L *tubus*, pipe⟧ **1** of or like a tube **2** made with a tube or tubes

tu'bule' (-byo͞ol') ***n.*** a small tube

tuck (tuk) ***vt.*** ⟦< MDu *tucken*⟧ **1** to pull or gather (*up*) in a fold or folds **2** to sew a fold or folds in (a garment) **3** to fold the edges of (a sheet, etc.) under or in, to make secure **4** to press snugly into a small space —***n.*** **1** a sewed fold in a garment **2** [Inf.] cosmetic plastic surgery to remove fat

tuck·er (tuk'ər) ***vt.*** ⟦prob. < prec., in obs. sense "to punish, rebuke"⟧ [Inf.] to tire (*out*); weary

Tuc·son (to͞o'sän') city in S Arizona: pop. 405,000

-tude (to͞od, tyo͞od) ⟦< L *-tudo*⟧ ***suffix*** state, quality, or instance of being

Tues·day (to͞oz'dā) ***n.*** ⟦OE *Tiwes dæg*, day of the god of war *Tiu*⟧ the third day of the week: abbrev. **Tue, Tues**

tuft (tuft) ***n.*** ⟦< OFr *tufe*⟧ **1** a bunch of hairs, grass, etc. growing closely together **2** any cluster, as the fluffy ball forming the end of a cluster of threads drawn through a mattress —***vt.*** **1** to provide with tufts **2** to secure the padding of (a mattress, etc.) with tufts —**tuft'ed** ***adj.*** —**tuft'er** ***n.***

tug (tug) ***vi.***, ***vt.*** **tugged, tug'ging** ⟦prob. < ON *toga*, to pull⟧ **1** to pull hard; drag; haul **2** to tow with a tugboat —***n.*** **1** a hard pull **2** a tugboat

tug·boat (tug'bōt') ***n.*** a sturdy, powerful boat for towing or pushing ships, barges, etc.

tug of war **1** a contest in which two teams pull at opposite ends of a rope **2** a power struggle

tu·i·tion (to͞o ish'ən) ***n.*** ⟦< L *tueri*, protect⟧ the charge for instruction, as at a college

tu·la·re·mi·a (to͞o'lə rē'mē ə) ***n.*** ⟦after *Tulare* County, CA⟧ an infectious disease of rodents, esp. rabbits, transmissible to humans

tu·lip (to͞o'lip) ***n.*** ⟦< Turk *tülbend*, turban: from its shape⟧ **1** a bulb plant with a large, cup-shaped flower **2** the flower

tulle (to͞ol) ***n.*** ⟦after *Tulle*, city in France⟧ a fine netting of silk, rayon, nylon, etc., used as for veils and scarves

Tul·sa (tul'sə) city in NE Oklahoma: pop. 367,000

tum·ble (tum'bəl) ***vi.*** **-bled, -bling** ⟦< OE *tumbian*, to jump⟧ **1** to do somersaults or similar acrobatic feats **2** to fall suddenly or helplessly **3** to toss or roll about **4** to move in a hasty, disorderly manner —***vt.*** **1** to cause to tumble **2** to put into disorder; disarrange —***n.*** **1** a fall **2** disorder

tum'ble·down' ***adj.*** dilapidated

tum'bler (-blər) ***n.*** **1** an acrobat who does somersaults, etc. **2** a drinking glass **3** a part of a lock whose position must be changed by a key in order to release the bolt

tum'ble·weed' ***n.*** a plant that breaks off near the ground in autumn and is blown about by the wind

tum·brel or **tum·bril** (tum'brəl) ***n.*** ⟦< Fr *tomber*, to fall⟧ a cart that can be tilted for emptying

tu·mes·cence (to͞o mes'əns) ***n.*** ⟦see fol.⟧ **1** a swelling; distention **2** a swollen or distended part —**tu·mes'cent** ***adj.***

tu·mid (to͞o'mid) ***adj.*** ⟦< L *tumere*, to swell⟧ **1** swollen; bulging **2** inflated or pompous —**tu·mid'i·ty** ***n.***

tum·my (tum'ē) ***n.***, *pl.* **-mies** [Inf.] the stomach or abdomen

tu·mor (to͞o'mər) ***n.*** ⟦L, a swelling⟧ an abnormal growth of new tissue, independent of its surrounding structures; neoplasm: Brit. sp. **tu'mour**

tu·mult (to͞o'mult') ***n.*** ⟦< L *tumere*, to swell⟧ **1** noisy commotion **2** confusion; disturbance

tu·mul·tu·ous (to͞o mul'cho͞o əs) ***adj.*** full of tumult, uproar, etc.

tun (tun) ***n.*** ⟦OE *tunne*⟧ a large cask

tu·na (to͞o'nə) ***n.***, *pl.* **-na** or **-nas** ⟦AmSp⟧ **1** a large, edible ocean fish, as the albacore **2** the flesh of the tuna, canned for food: also **tuna fish**

tun·dra (tun'drə) ***n.*** ⟦Russ⟧ a vast, treeless arctic plain

tune (to͞on) ***n.*** ⟦ME, var. of *tone*, tone⟧ **1** a rhythmic succession of musical tones; melody **2** *a*) correct musical pitch *b*) agreement; concord: now used chiefly in the phrases **in tune** and **out of tune** —***vt.*** **tuned, tun'ing** **1** to adjust (a musical instrument) to some standard of pitch **2** to adapt to some condition, mood, etc. **3** to adjust (a motor, circuit, etc.) for proper performance —**to the tune of** [Inf.] to the sum, price, or extent of —**tune in** to adjust a radio or TV receiver so as to receive (a station, etc.) —**tun'er** ***n.***

tune'ful ***adj.*** full of music; melodious

tune'less ***adj.*** **1** not melodious **2** not producing music —**tune'less·ly** ***adv.*** —**tune'less·ness** ***n.***

tune'up' or **tune'-up'** ***n.*** an adjusting, as of an engine, to the proper condition

tung·sten (tuŋ'stən) ***n.*** ⟦Swed < *tung*, heavy + *sten*, stone⟧ a hard, heavy metallic chemical element, used in steel, etc.

tu·nic (to͞o'nik, tyo͞o'-) ***n.*** ⟦L *tunica*⟧ **1** a loose, gownlike garment worn by men and women in ancient Greece and Rome **2** a blouselike garment extending to the hips, often belted

tuning fork a two-pronged steel instrument which when struck sounds a certain fixed tone in perfect pitch

Tu·nis (to͞o′nis) seaport & capital of Tunisia: pop. 674,000

Tu·ni·si·a (to͞o nē′zhə) country in N Africa, on the Mediterranean: 63,378 sq. mi.; pop. 6,966,000 —**Tu·ni′si·an** ***adj., n.***

tun·nel (tun′əl) ***n.*** ⟦< Fr *tonnelle*, a vault⟧ **1** an underground passageway, as for autos, etc. **2** any tunnel-like passage, as in a mine —***vt., vi.*** **-neled** or **-nelled**, **-nel·ing** or **-nel·ling** to make a tunnel (through or under) —**tun′nel·er** or **tun′nel·ler** ***n.***

tunnel vision a narrow outlook, as on a particular problem

tun·ny (tun′ē) ***n.***, *pl.* **-nies** TUNA (sense 1)

TURBAN

tur·ban (tʉr′bən) ***n.*** ⟦< Pers *dulbänd*⟧ **1** a headdress worn by men in parts of Asia, consisting of cloth wound in folds about the head **2** any similar headdress

tur·bid (tʉr′bid) ***adj.*** ⟦< L *turba*, a crowd⟧ **1** muddy or cloudy from stirring sediment **2** thick, dense, or dark, as clouds **3** confused

tur·bine (tʉr′bin, -bīn′) ***n.*** ⟦< L *turbo*, a whirl⟧ an engine driven as by the pressure of steam, water, or air against the curved vanes of a wheel

tur·bo·charge (tʉr′bō chärj′) ***vt.*** **-charged′**, **-charg′ing** to increase the power of (an engine) by the use of a type of compressor (**tur′bo·charg′er**) driven by a turbine powered by exhaust gases

tur′bo·fan′ (-fan′) ***n.*** a turbojet engine developing extra thrust from air that bypasses the combustion chamber and is accelerated by a fan: in full **turbofan engine**

tur′bo·jet′ (-jet′) ***n.*** **1** a jet engine in which the energy of the jet spins a turbine which drives the air compressor: in full **turbojet engine** **2** an aircraft with such an engine

tur′bo·prop′ (-präp′) ***n.*** **1** a turbojet engine whose turbine shaft drives a propeller: in full **turboprop engine** **2** an aircraft with such an engine

tur·bot (tʉr′bət) ***n.***, *pl.* **-bot** or **-bots** ⟦< OFr *tourbout*⟧ any of various flounders highly regarded as food

tur·bu·lent (tʉr′byə lənt) ***adj.*** ⟦< L *turba*, a crowd⟧ **1** wild or disorderly **2** full of violent motion —**tur′bu·lence** ***n.*** —**tur′bu·lent·ly** ***adv.***

tu·reen (too rēn′) ***n.*** ⟦< Fr *terrine*, earthen vessel⟧ a large, deep dish with a lid, for soups, etc.

turf (tʉrf) ***n.*** ⟦OE⟧ **1** *a)* a top layer of earth containing grass with its roots; sod *b)* [Chiefly Brit.] a piece of this **2** peat **3** a track for horse racing; also, horse racing: usually with *the* **4** [Slang] *a)* an area seen by a street gang as its territory to be defended *b)* one's own territory —***vt.*** to cover with turf —**turf′y** ***adj.***

tur·gid (tʉr′jid) ***adj.*** ⟦< L *turgere*, to swell⟧ **1** swollen; distended **2** bombastic; pompous —**tur·gid′i·ty** or **tur′gid·ness** ***n.*** —**tur′gid·ly** ***adv.***

Tu·rin (toor′in) city in NW Italy: pop. 953,000

Turk[1] (tʉrk) ***n.*** a person born or living in Turkey

Turk[2] *abbrev.* **1** Turkey **2** Turkish

tur·key (tʉr′kē) ***n.*** ⟦< similarity to a fowl formerly imported through *Turkey*⟧ **1** a large North American bird with a spreading tail **2** its flesh, used as food

Tur·key (tʉr′kē) country occupying Asia Minor & a SE part of the Balkan Peninsula: 300,947 sq. mi.; pop. 56,473,000

turkey vulture a dark-colored vulture of temperate and tropical America: also **turkey buzzard**

TURKEY VULTURE

Turk·ic (tʉr′kik) ***adj.*** designating or of a family of languages including Turkish, Tatar, etc.

Turk·ish (tʉr′kish) ***adj.*** of Turkey or its people, language, etc. —***n.*** the language of Turkey

Turkish bath a bathhouse with steam rooms, showers, massage, etc.

Turk·men·i·stan (tərk men′i stan′) country in central Asia: formerly a republic of the U.S.S.R.: 186,400 sq. mi.; pop. 3,523,000

tur·mer·ic (tʉr′mər ik) ***n.*** ⟦< ML *terra merita*, deserved earth⟧ an East Indian plant whose powdered root is used as a yellow dye or a seasoning

tur·moil (tʉr′moil′) ***n.*** ⟦< ?⟧ tumult; commotion

turn (tʉrn) ***vt.*** ⟦ult. < Gr *tornos*, a lathe⟧ **1** to rotate (a wheel, etc.) **2** to move around or partly around *[turn* the key*]* **3** to give form to, as in a lathe **4** to change the position or direction of **5** to reverse the position or sides of **6** to wrench *[turn* one's ankle*]* **7** to upset (the stomach) **8** to deflect; divert **9** to cause to change actions, beliefs, aims, etc. **10** to go around (a corner, etc.) **11** to reach or pass (a certain age, amount, etc.) **12** to drive, set, let go, etc. *[turn* the dog loose*]* **13** to direct, point, aim, etc. **14** to change *[*to *turn* cream into butter*]* **15** to make sour **16** to affect in some way —***vi.*** **1** to rotate or revolve; pivot **2** to move around or partly around **3** to reel; whirl **4** to become upset: said of the stomach **5** to change or reverse course, direction, etc., or one's feelings, allegiance, etc. **6** to refer (*to*) **7** to apply (*to*) for help **8** to shift one's attention *[*he *turned* to music*]* **9** to make a sudden attack (*on*) **10** to be contingent or depend (*on* or *upon*) **11** to become *[*to *turn* cold*]* **12** to change to another form *[*the rain *turned* to snow*]* **13** to become rancid, sour, etc. —***n.*** **1** a turning around; rotation; revolution **2** a single twist, winding, etc. **3** a change or reversal of course or direction **4** a short walk, ride, etc. **5** a bend; curve *[*a *turn* in the road*]* **6** a change in trend, events, etc. **7** a sudden shock or fright **8** an action or deed *[*a good *turn]* **9** the right, duty, or chance to do something in regular order *[*my *turn* to go*]* **10** a distinctive form, detail, etc. *[*an odd *turn* of speech*]* **11** natural inclination *[*a curious *turn* of mind*]* —**in** (or **out of**) **turn** (not) in proper sequence —**turn down** to reject (a request, etc.) —**turn in** **1** to deliver; hand in **2** [Inf.] to go to bed —**turn off** **1** to stop the flow of (water, gas, etc.) **2** to make (an electrical device) stop functioning **3** [Slang] to cause to be bored, depressed, etc. —**turn on** **1** to start the flow of **2** to make (an electrical device) start functioning **3** [Slang] to make or become elated, enthusiastic, etc. —**turn out** **1** to put out (a light, etc.) **2** to dismiss **3** to come out or assemble **4** to produce **5** to result **6** to prove to be **7** [Inf.] to get out of bed —**turn over** **1** to ponder **2** to hand over; transfer —**turn up** to happen, appear, arrive, etc. —**turn'er** ***n.***

turn'a·bout' ***n.*** a shift or reversal of position, allegiance, opinion, etc.

turn'a·round' ***n.*** **1** TURNABOUT **2** a wide area, as in a driveway, for turning a vehicle around

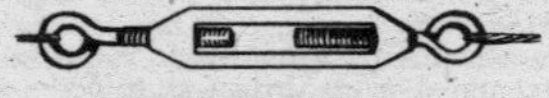

TURNBUCKLE

turn'buck'le (-buk'əl) ***n.*** an adjustable coupling for two rods, etc., consisting of a metal sleeve with opposite internal threads at each end

turn'coat' ***n.*** a renegade; traitor

turn'ing ***n.*** **1** the action of one that turns **2** a place where a road, etc. turns

turning point a point in time when a decisive change occurs

tur·nip (tur'nip) ***n.*** ⟦prob. < Fr *tour*, round + ME *nepe*, turnip⟧ **1** a plant related to cabbage and broccoli, with a light-colored, roundish, edible root **2** the root

turn'key' ***n.***, *pl.* **-keys'** a jailer

turn'off' ***n.*** **1** a turning off **2** a place to turn off, as a road ramp **3** [Slang] someone or something regarded as being boring, distasteful, etc.

turn'-on' ***n.*** [Slang] someone or something regarded as being interesting, exciting, etc.

turn'out' ***n.*** **1** a gathering of people, as for a meeting **2** a wider part of a narrow road, enabling vehicles to pass each other

turn'o'ver ***n.*** **1** a small pie with half the crust folded back over the other half **2** *a*) the number of times a stock of goods is sold and replaced in a given period *b*) the amount of business done during a given period **3** the rate of replacement of workers

turn'pike' (-pīk') ***n.*** ⟦ME *turnpyke*, a spiked road barrier⟧ a toll road, esp. one that is an expressway

turn'stile' (-stīl') ***n.*** a device, as a post with revolving horizontal bars, placed in an entrance to allow the passage of persons one at a time

turn'ta'ble ***n.*** a circular rotating platform, as for supporting a phonograph record being played

tur·pen·tine (tur'pən tīn') ***n.*** ⟦< Gr *terebinthos*, tree yielding this substance⟧ a colorless, volatile oil distilled from a substance extracted from various coniferous trees: used in paints, etc.

tur·pi·tude (tur'pi to͞od') ***n.*** ⟦< L *turpis*, vile⟧ baseness; vileness

tur·quoise (tur'koiz', -kwoiz') ***n.*** ⟦< OFr *turqueis*, Turkish⟧ **1** a greenish-blue semiprecious stone **2** its color

tur·ret (tur'it) ***n.*** ⟦see TOWER⟧ **1** a small tower projecting from a building, usually at a corner **2** a dome or revolving structure for guns, as on a warship, tank, or airplane **3** a rotating attachment for a lathe, etc. holding cutting tools

tur·tle (turt''l) ***n.*** ⟦< Fr *tortue*, tortoise⟧ any of various land or water reptiles having a soft body encased in a tough shell —**turn turtle** to turn upside down

tur'tle·dove' ***n.*** ⟦< L echoic *turtur*⟧ a wild dove with a plaintive call

tur'tle·neck' ***n.*** **1** a high, snug, turned-down collar, as on a pullover sweater **2** a sweater, etc. with such a collar

tusk (tusk) ***n.*** ⟦OE *tucs*⟧ a very long, large, pointed tooth projecting outside the mouth

tus·sle (tus'əl) ***vi.*** **-sled, -sling,** ***n.*** ⟦< ME *tusen*, to pull⟧ struggle; scuffle

tus·sock (tus'ək) ***n.*** ⟦< ?⟧ a thick tuft or clump of grass, sedge, etc.

tu·te·lage (to͞ot''l ij) ***n.*** ⟦< L *tutela*, protection⟧ **1** guardianship; care, protection, etc. **2** instruction —**tu'te·lar'y** (-er'ē) ***adj.***

tu·tor (to͞ot'ər) ***n.*** ⟦< L *tueri*, to guard⟧ a private teacher —***vt.***, ***vi.*** to act as a tutor (to); teach —**tu·to·ri·al** (to͞o tôr'ē əl, tyo͞o-) ***adj.***, ***n.***

tut·ti-frut·ti (to͞ot'ē fro͞ot'ē) ***n.*** ⟦It, all fruits⟧ ice cream, etc. made with mixed fruits

TUTU

tu·tu (to͞o′to͞o′) ***n.*** ⟦Fr⟧ a very short, full, projecting skirt worn by ballerinas

Tu·va·lu (to͞o′və lo͞o′) country on a group of islands in the WC Pacific, north of Fiji: 10 sq. mi.; pop. 10,000

tux (tuks) ***n.***, *pl.* **tux′es** *short for* TUXEDO

tux·e·do (tuk sē′dō) ***n.***, *pl.* **-dos** ⟦after a country club near *Tuxedo* Lake, NY⟧ a man's semiformal suit with a tailless jacket

TV ***n.*** **1** television **2** *pl.* **TVs** or **TV's** a television receiving set

TVA *abbrev.* Tennessee Valley Authority

TV dinner a frozen, precooked dinner packaged in a divided tray for heating and serving

twad·dle (twäd′'l) ***n.*** ⟦prob. var. of TATTLE⟧ foolish, empty talk or writing; nonsense

twain (twān) ***adj.***, ***n.*** ⟦OE *twegen*, two⟧ *archaic var. of* TWO

Twain (twān), **Mark** *pseud. for* Samuel Langhorne CLEMENS

twang (twaŋ) ***n.*** ⟦echoic⟧ **1** a sharp, vibrating sound, as of a plucked string **2** a sharply nasal way of speaking —***vi.***, ***vt.*** to make or cause to make a twang —**twang′y**, **-i·er**, **-i·est**, ***adj.***

'twas (twuz, twäz) *contr.* [Old Poet.] it was

tweak (twēk) ***vt.*** ⟦OE *twiccan*, to twitch⟧ **1** to give a twisting pinch to (someone's nose, ear, etc.) **2** to adjust slightly —***n.*** such a pinch

tweed (twēd) ***n.*** ⟦< misreading of *tweel*, Scot form of TWILL⟧ **1** a rough wool fabric in a weave of two or more colors **2** [*pl.*] clothes of tweed

tweed′y ***adj.*** **-i·er**, **-i·est** **1** of, like, or wearing tweeds **2** having an informal style, a fondness for the outdoors, etc.

'tween (twēn) *contr.* ***prep.*** ⟦ME *twene*⟧ [Old Poet.] between

tweet (twēt) ***interj.***, ***n.*** ⟦echoic⟧ (used to signify or imitate) the thin, chirping sound of a small bird —***vi.*** to make this sound

tweet′er ***n.*** a small, high-fidelity speaker for reproducing high-frequency sounds

tweeze (twēz) ***vt.*** **tweezed**, **tweez′ing** to pluck with tweezers

tweez·ers (twē′zərz) ***pl.n.*** ⟦< obs. *tweeze*, surgical set⟧ [*also with sing. v.*] a small tool having two arms joined at one end, for plucking out hairs, etc.

twelfth (twelfth) ***adj.*** ⟦OE *twelfta*⟧ preceded by eleven others; 12th —***n.*** **1** the one following the eleventh **2** any of the twelve equal parts of something; $\frac{1}{12}$

Twelfth Day Epiphany, the twelfth day after Christmas: **Twelfth Night** is the evening before, or of, Epiphany

twelve (twelv) ***adj.***, ***n.*** ⟦OE *twelf*⟧ two more than ten; 12; XII

12-step or **twelve-step** (twelv′step′) ***adj.*** designating or of any rehabilitation program modeled on that of AA

twelve′-tone′ ***adj.*** *Music* of composition in which the twelve tones of the chromatic scale are fixed in some arbitrary succession (*tone row*)

twen·ty (twent′ē) ***adj.***, ***n.***, *pl.* **-ties** ⟦OE *twegentig*⟧ two times ten; 20; XX —**the twenties** the numbers or years, as of a century, from 20 through 29 —**twen′ti·eth** (-ith) ***adj.***, ***n.***

twen′ty-one′ ***n.*** BLACKJACK (*n.* 2)

twen′ty-twen′ty (or **20/20**) **vision** normal visual ability, i.e., seeing clearly at 20 feet what the normal eye sees at 20 feet

twerp (twurp) ***n.*** ⟦ult. < ? Dan *tver*, perverse⟧ [Slang] a person regarded as insignificant, contemptible, etc.

twice (twīs) ***adv.*** ⟦OE *twiga*⟧ **1** two times **2** two times as much or as many

twid·dle (twid′'l) ***vt.***, ***vi.*** **-dled**, **-dling** ⟦prob. < TW(IST) + (*d*)*iddle*, move back and forth rapidly⟧ to twirl or play with (something) lightly or idly —**twiddle one's thumbs** to be idle

twig (twig) ***n.*** ⟦OE *twigge*⟧ a small branch of a tree or shrub

twi·light (twī′līt′) ***n.*** ⟦ME⟧ **1** the subdued light just after sunset **2** the period from sunset to dark **3** a gradual decline —***adj.*** of twilight

twi·lit (twī′lit) ***adj.*** in the subdued light of twilight

twill (twil) ***n.*** ⟦OE *twilic*, woven of double thread⟧ a kind of cloth woven in parallel diagonal lines —**twilled** ***adj.***

twin (twin) ***adj.*** ⟦OE *twinn*, double⟧ **1** consisting of, or being one of a pair of, two similar things **2** being a twin or twins —***n.*** **1** either of two offspring from the same pregnancy **2** either of two persons or things that are very much alike

twin bed either of a pair of single beds

twine (twīn) ***n.*** ⟦OE *twin*⟧ strong thread, string, etc. of strands twisted together —***vt.***, ***vi.*** **twined**, **twin′ing** **1** to twist together **2** to wind (around)

twinge (twinj) ***vt.***, ***vi.*** **twinged**, **twing′ing** ⟦OE *twengan*, to squeeze⟧ to (cause to) have a sudden, sharp pain, qualm, etc. —***n.*** such a pain, etc.

twi-night or **twi·night** (twī′nīt′) ***adj.*** ⟦TWI(LIGHT) + NIGHT⟧ *Baseball* designating a double-header starting in late afternoon and going into evening

twin·kle (twiŋ′kəl) ***vi.*** **-kled**, **-kling** ⟦OE *twinclian*⟧ **1** to shine with quick, intermittent gleams **2** to light up, as with amusement: said of the eyes **3** to move to and fro quickly: said as of a dancer's feet —*n.* **1** a glint in the eye **2** a gleam; sparkle

twin'kling *n.* an instant

twin'-size' *adj.* of or being the standard size of a twin bed: also **twin'-sized'**

twirl (twurl) *vt., vi.* ⟦prob. < Scand⟧ **1** to rotate rapidly; spin **2** to whirl in a circle —*n.* **1** a twirling **2** a twist, coil, etc. —**twirl'er** *n.*

twist (twist) *vt.* ⟦< OE *-twist*, a rope⟧ **1** to wind (strands, etc.) around one another **2** to wind (rope, etc.) around something **3** to give spiral shape to **4** *a)* to subject to torsion *b)* to wrench; sprain **5** to contort or distort **6** to confuse **7** to pervert the meaning of **8** to cause to rotate **9** to break (*off*) by turning the end —*vi.* **1** to undergo twisting **2** to spiral, twine, etc. (*around* or *about*) **3** to revolve or rotate **4** to wind, as a path does **5** to squirm; writhe —*n.* **1** something twisted **2** a twisting or being twisted **3** stress produced by twisting **4** a contortion **5** a wrench or sprain **6** a turn; bend **7** distortion, as of meaning **8** an unexpected or different direction, method, slant, etc.

twist'er *n.* **1** a person or thing that twists **2** [Inf.] a tornado or cyclone

twist'-tie' *n.* a short wire covered with paper or plastic, twisted to tie closed a plastic bag, etc.

twit[1] (twit) *vt.* **twit'ted, twit'ting** ⟦< OE *æt*, at + *witan*, accuse⟧ to reproach, taunt, etc.

twit[2] (twit) *n.* ⟦< ?⟧ [Inf.] a foolish, contemptible person

twitch (twich) *vt., vi.* ⟦< OE *twiccian*, to pluck⟧ to pull (at) or move with a quick, slight jerk —*n.* **1** a twitching **2** a sudden, quick motion, esp. a spasmodic one

twitch'y *adj.* **-i·er, -i·est** [Inf.] nervous; jittery

twit·ter (twit'ər) *vi.* ⟦ME *twiteren*⟧ **1** to chirp rapidly **2** *a)* to chatter *b)* to giggle **3** to tremble with excitement —*n.* **1** a twittering **2** a condition of trembling excitement

'twixt (twikst) *prep.* [Old Poet.] betwixt; between

two (too͞) *adj., n.* ⟦OE *twa*⟧ one more than one; 2; II —**in two** in two parts

two'-bit' *adj.* [Slang] cheap, inferior, etc.

two bits [Inf.] twenty-five cents

two'-by-four' *n.* a piece of lumber two inches thick and four inches wide when untrimmed ($1\frac{1}{2}$ by $3\frac{1}{2}$ inches trimmed)

two'-edged' *adj.* **1** having two cutting edges **2** that can be taken two ways *[*a *two-edged* remark*]*

two'-faced' *adj.* **1** having two faces, surfaces, etc. **2** deceitful; hypocritical

two·fer (too͞'fər) *n.* ⟦altered < *two for*⟧ [Inf.] a pair, as of theater tickets, sold for the price of one

two'-fist'ed *adj.* [Inf.] **1** able to use both fists **2** vigorous; virile

two'fold' *adj.* **1** having two parts **2** having twice as much or as many —*adv.* twice as much or as many

two'-hand'ed *adj.* **1** requiring the use of both hands **2** operated, played, etc. by two persons

two·pence (tup'əns) *n.* two pence

two'-ply' *adj.* having two layers, strands, etc.

two'some (-səm) *n.* two people; a couple

two'-time' *vt.* **-timed', -tim'ing** [Slang] to be unfaithful to —**two'-tim'er** *n.*

two'-tone' *adj.* of or having two colors

two'-way' *adj.* **1** allowing passage in either direction **2** involving two or used in two ways

Twp *abbrev.* township

TX Texas

-ty (tē, ti) ⟦< L *-tas*⟧ *suffix* quality of, condition of

ty·coon (tī ko͞on') *n.* ⟦< Jpn < Chin *tai*, great + *kuan*, official⟧ a wealthy, powerful industrialist, financier, etc.

ty·ing (tī'iŋ) *vt., vi. prp. of* TIE

tyke (tīk) *n.* ⟦< ON *tik*, a bitch⟧ [Inf.] a small child

Ty·ler (tī'lər), **John** 1790-1862; 10th president of the U.S. (1841-45)

tym·pa·ni (tim'pə nē) *pl.n., sing.* **-no'** (-nō') *alt. sp. of* TIMPANI —**tym'pa·nist** *n.*

tym·pan·ic membrane (tim pan'ik) a thin membrane inside the ear that vibrates when struck by sound waves

tym·pa·num (tim'pə nəm) *n., pl.* **-nums** or **-na** (-nə) ⟦L, a drum⟧ **1** MIDDLE EAR **2** TYMPANIC MEMBRANE

type (tīp) *n.* ⟦< Gr *typos*, a mark⟧ **1** the characteristic form, plan, style, etc. of a class or group **2** a class, group, etc. with characteristics in common **3** a person, animal, or thing representative of a class **4** a perfect example; model **5** *a)* a piece of metal or wood with a raised letter, etc. in reverse on its top, used in printing *b)* such pieces collectively *c)* a printed or photographically reproduced character or characters —*vt.* **typed, typ'ing 1** to classify **2** to write using the keyboard of a typewriter or computer —*vi.* to use the keyboard of a typewriter or computer

-type (tīp) *combining form* **1** type, representative form, example *[stereotype]* **2** print, printing type

type'cast' *vt.* **-cast', -cast'ing** to cast (an actor) repeatedly in the same type of part

type'script' *n.* typewritten matter

type'set' *vt.* **-set', -set'ting** to set in type; compose

type'set'ter *n.* **1** a person who sets type **2** a machine for setting type

type'write' *vt., vi.* **-wrote', -writ'ten, -writ'ing** to write with a typewriter: now usually *type*

type'writ'er *n.* a writing machine with a keyboard, for reproducing letters resembling printed ones

ty·phoid (tī'foid') *n.* ⟦TYPH(US) + -OID⟧ an acute infectious disease caused by a bacillus and acquired by ingesting contaminated food or water: characterized by fever, intestinal disorders, etc.: in full **typhoid fever**

ty·phoon (tī fo͞on') *n.* ⟦< Chin *tai-fung*,

great wind⟧ a violent tropical cyclone originating in the W Pacific

ty·phus (tī′fəs) ***n.*** ⟦< Gr *typhos*, fever⟧ an acute infectious disease caused by certain bacteria, transmitted by fleas, lice, etc., and characterized by fever, skin rash, etc.: in full **typhus fever**

typ·i·cal (tip′i kəl) ***adj.*** **1** serving as a type **2** having the distinguishing characteristics of a class, group, etc.; representative **3** belonging to a type; characteristic —**typ′i·cal·ly** ***adv.***

typ·i·fy (tip′i fī′) ***vt.*** **-fied′**, **-fy′ing** to have the characteristics of; be typical of; exemplify —**typ′i·fi·ca′tion** ***n.***

typ·ist (tīp′ist) ***n.*** a person who operates a typewriter

ty·po (tī′pō) ***n.***, *pl.* **-pos** [Inf.] an error made in setting type or in typing

ty·pog·ra·phy (tī päg′rə fē) ***n.*** ⟦see TYPE & -GRAPHY⟧ **1** setting, and printing with, type **2** the arrangement, style, etc. of matter printed from type —**ty·pog′ra·pher** ***n.*** —**ty′po·graph′i·cal** (-pə graf′i kəl) ***adj.*** —**ty′po·graph′i·cal·ly** ***adv.***

ty·ran·ni·cal (tə ran′i kəl, tī-) ***adj.*** **1** of or suited to a tyrant **2** harsh, cruel, unjust, etc. Also **ty·ran′nic** —**ty·ran′ni·cal·ly** ***adv.***

tyr·an·nize (tir′ə nīz′) ***vi.*** **-nized′**, **-niz′ing** **1** to govern as a tyrant **2** to govern or use authority harshly or cruelly —***vt.*** to treat tyrannically; oppress

TYRANNOSAUR

ty·ran·no·saur (tə ran′ə sôr′) ***n.*** ⟦< Gr *tyrannos*, tyrant + *sauros*, lizard⟧ a huge, two-footed, flesh-eating dinosaur: also **ty·ran′no·saur′us** (-əs)

tyr·an·ny (tir′ə nē) ***n.***, *pl.* **-nies** **1** the authority, government, etc. of a tyrant **2** cruel and unjust use of power **3** a tyrannical act —**tyr′an·nous** ***adj.***

ty·rant (tī′rənt) ***n.*** ⟦< Gr *tyrannos*⟧ **1** an absolute ruler **2** a cruel, oppressive ruler, master, etc.

ty·ro (tī′rō) ***n.***, *pl.* **-ros** ⟦< L *tiro*, young soldier⟧ a beginner in learning something; novice

Ty·rol (ti rōl′, -räl′) *alt. sp. of* TIROL

tzar (tsär, zär) ***n.*** *var. of* CZAR —**tza·ri·na** (tsä rē′nə, zä-) ***fem.n.***

U

u¹ or **U** (yōō) ***n.***, *pl.* **u's, U's** the 21st letter of the English alphabet

u² *abbrev.* unit(s)

U¹ *abbrev.* **1** Union **2** United **3** University

U² *Chem. symbol for* uranium

UAW *abbrev.* United Automobile Workers (of America)

u·biq·ui·tous (yōō bik′wə təs) ***adj.*** ⟦< L *ubique*, everywhere⟧ (seemingly) present everywhere at the same time —**u·biq′ui·ty** ***n.***

U′-boat′ ***n.*** ⟦< Ger *Unterseeboot*, undersea boat⟧ a German submarine

U bolt a U-shaped bolt with threads and a nut at each end

ud·der (ud′ər) ***n.*** ⟦OE *udr*⟧ a baglike, milk-secreting organ with two or more teats, as in cows

UFO ***n.***, *pl.* **UFOs** or **UFO's** an unidentified flying object

u·fol·o·gy (yōō fäl′ə jē) ***n.*** the study of UFOs, esp. when regarded as spacecraft from another planet —**u·fol′o·gist** ***n.***

U·gan·da (yōō gan′də, -gän′-) country in EC Africa: 93,065 sq. mi.; pop. 16,583,000 —**U·gan′dan** ***adj.***, ***n.***

ugh (ookh, oo, ug, *etc.*) ***interj.*** used to express disgust, horror, etc.

ug·ly (ug′lē) ***adj.*** **-li·er**, **-li·est** ⟦< ON *uggr*, fear⟧ **1** unpleasing to look at **2** bad, disgusting, etc. *[an ugly lie]* **3** ominous *[ugly storm clouds]* **4** [Inf.] cross; quarrelsome *[an ugly mood]* —**ug′li·ness** ***n.***

uh (u, un) ***interj.*** **1** HUH **2** used when hesitating in speaking

UHF or **uhf** *abbrev.* ultrahigh frequency

UK United Kingdom

u·kase (yōō′kās′, -kāz′) ***n.*** ⟦Russ *ukaz*, edict⟧ an official decree

U·kraine (yōō krān′) country in SE Europe: formerly a republic of the U.S.S.R.: 231,990 sq. mi.; pop. 51,452,000 —**U·krain′i·an** ***n.***, ***adj.***

u·ku·le·le (yōō′kə lā′lē) ***n.*** ⟦Haw, leaping flea⟧ a small, four-stringed, guitarlike musical instrument

UL *trademark for* Underwriters Laboratories

ul·cer (ul′sər) ***n.*** ⟦L *ulcus*⟧ **1** an open sore, often one discharging pus, on the skin or some mucous membrane **2** any corrupt condition —**ul′cer·ous** ***adj.***

ul′cer·ate′ (-āt′) ***vt.***, ***vi.*** **-at′ed**, **-at′ing** to make or become ulcerous —**ul′cer·a′tion** ***n.***

ul·na (ul′nə) ***n.***, *pl.* **-nae** (-nē) or **-nas** ⟦L, the elbow⟧ the larger of the two bones of the forearm —**ul′nar** ***adj.***

ul·ster (ul′stər) ***n.*** ⟦after *Ulster*, in N Ireland⟧ a long, loose, heavy overcoat

ult *abbrev.* ultimate(ly)

ul·te·ri·or (ul tir′ē ər) ***adj.*** ⟦L: see ULTRA-⟧ **1** lying beyond or on the farther side **2** beyond what is expressed or implied; undisclosed

ul·ti·mate (ul′tə mit) ***adj.*** ⟦< L *ultimus,* last⟧ **1** beyond which it is impossible to go **2** final; conclusive **3** basic **4** greatest possible —***n.*** a final point or result —**ul′ti·mate·ly** ***adv.***

ul·ti·ma·tum (ul′tə māt′əm) ***n.,*** *pl.* **-tums** or **-ta** (-ə) ⟦see prec.⟧ a final offer or demand, as in negotiations

ul·tra (ul′trə) ***adj.*** ⟦< fol.⟧ going beyond the usual limit; extreme

ultra- ⟦L < *ultra,* beyond⟧ *prefix* **1** beyond *[ultrasonic]* **2** extremely *[ultraconservative]*

ul·tra·con·serv·a·tive (ul′trə kən sur′ və tiv) ***adj.*** extremely conservative

ul·tra·high frequency (ul′trə hī′) any radio frequency between 300 and 3,000 megahertz

ul′tra·ma·rine′ (-mə rēn′) ***adj.*** deep-blue —***n.*** deep blue

ul′tra·son′ic (-sän′ik) ***adj.*** above the range of sound audible to the human ear —**ul′tra·son′i·cal·ly** ***adv.***

ul′tra·sound′ (-sound′) ***n.*** ultrasonic waves, used in medical diagnosis and therapy, etc.

ul′tra·vi′o·let (-vī′ə lit) ***adj.*** of or designating those rays that are just beyond the violet end of the visible spectrum

ul·u·late (yōōl′yoo lāt′, ul′-) ***vi.*** **-lat′ed, -lat′ing** ⟦< L *ululare,* to howl⟧ to howl, hoot, or wail loudly —**ul′u·la′tion** ***n.***

U·lys·ses (yoo lis′ēz′) ***n.*** ⟦ML⟧ ODYSSEUS

um·bel (um′bəl) ***n.*** ⟦L *umbella,* parasol: see UMBRELLA⟧ a cluster of flowers with stalks of similar length springing from the same point

um·ber (um′bər) ***n.*** ⟦< It *(terra d')ombra,* (earth of) shade⟧ **1** a kind of earth used as a yellowish-brown or reddish-brown pigment **2** a yellowish-brown or reddish-brown color

um·bil·i·cal (um bil′i kəl) ***adj.*** ⟦< L *umbilicus,* navel⟧ of a cordlike structure (**umbilical cord**) connecting a fetus's navel to the placenta, for conveying nourishment to, and removing waste from, the fetus

um·bil·i·cus (um bil′i kəs) ***n.,*** *pl.* **-ci′** (-sī′) ⟦L⟧ NAVEL

um·bra (um′brə) ***n.,*** *pl.* **-brae** (-brē) or **-bras** ⟦L, a shade⟧ **1** shade or a shadow **2** the dark cone of shadow from a planet or satellite on the side opposite the sun

um·brage (um′brij) ***n.*** ⟦< L *umbra,* a shade⟧ **1** [Obs.] shade **2** offense or resentment

um·brel·la (um brel′ə) ***n.*** ⟦< L *umbra,* a shade⟧ **1** a screen, usually of cloth on a folding frame, carried for protection against rain or sun **2** any comprehensive, protective alliance, strategy, device, etc.

u·mi·ak (ōō′mē ak′) ***n.*** ⟦Esk⟧ a large, open boat made of skins on a wooden frame, used by Eskimos

um·laut (oom′lout) ***n.*** ⟦Ger < *um,* about + *laut,* a sound⟧ *Linguistics* **1** a vowel changed in sound by its assimilation to another vowel **2** the mark (¨) placed over such a vowel

ump (ump) ***n., vt., vi.*** *short for* UMPIRE

um·pire (um′pīr′) ***n.*** ⟦< Fr *nomper,* uneven, hence a third person⟧ **1** a person chosen to judge a dispute **2** an official who administers the rules in certain sports —***vt., vi.*** **-pired′, -pir′ing** to act as umpire (in or of)

ump·teen (ump′tēn′) ***adj.*** [Slang] very many —**ump′teenth′** ***adj.***

UN *abbrev.* United Nations

un- *prefix* **1** ⟦OE⟧ not, lack of, the opposite of *[unconcern]* **2** ⟦OE *un-, on-*⟧ back: indicating a reversal of action *[unfold]* The following list includes some common compounds formed with *un-* (either sense) that do not have special meanings:

unabashed
unable
unabridged
unaccented
unacceptable
unaccompanied
unacquainted
unadorned
unadulterated
unafraid
unaided
unaltered
unambiguous
unannounced
unanswered
unashamed
unasked
unassailable
unassisted
unattainable
unattractive
unauthorized
unavailable
unavoidable
unbearable
unbeaten
unbiased
unbleached
unblemished
unbound
unbreakable
unbroken
unbuckle
unbutton
uncap
unceasing
uncensored
unchallenged
unchanged
unchanging
unchecked
uncivilized
unclassified
unclean
unclear
uncomplaining
uncompleted
unconcealed
unconfirmed
unconnected
uncontaminated
uncontrollable
uncontrolled
uncontroversial
unconventional
unconvinced
uncooked
uncooperative
uncoordinated
uncultivated
undamaged
undefeated
undemocratic
undependable
undeserved
undesirable
undeveloped
undigested
undiminished
undisciplined
undisclosed
undiscovered
undisguised
undisputed
undisturbed
undivided
uneducated
unemotional
unending
unenlightened
unenviable
unethical
uneventful
unexpired
unexplained
unexplored
unexpressed
unexpurgated
unfair
unfashionable
unfasten
unfavorable
unfit
unflattering
unfocused
unforeseen
unforgivable
unforgotten
unfulfilled
unfurnished
ungrammatical
ungrateful
unhampered
unhandy
unharmed
unhealthful
unheeded
unhesitating
unhitch
unhook
unhurried
unhurt

unidentified
unimaginable
unimaginative
unimpaired
unimportant
unimproved
unincorporated
uninformed
uninhabited
uninjured
uninspired
uninsured
unintelligent
unintelligible
unintentional
uninteresting
uninterrupted
uninvited
uninviting
unjustifiable
unjustified
unknowing
unlace
unlatch
unleavened
unlicensed
unlined
unlisted
unloved
unmanageable
unmannerly
unmarked
unmarried
unmatched
unmerited
unmoved
unnamed
unnoticed
unobserved
unobstructed
unobtainable
unobtrusive
unoccupied
unofficial
unopened
unopposed
unorthodox
unpaid
unpalatable
unpardonable
unpaved
unpin
unplanned
unpolished
unpolluted
unpredictable
unprejudiced
unpremeditated
unprepared
unpretentious
unprofitable
unpromising
unprotected
unproved
unproven
unprovoked
unpunished
unquenchable
unquestioned
unquestioning
unreadable
unrealistic
unrealized
unrecognized
unrecorded
unrefined
unregulated
unrelated
unreliable
unrelieved
unrepentant
unresponsive
unrestricted
unsafe
unsanitary
unsatisfactory
unsatisfied
unsaturated
unscientific
unseasoned
unseeing
unseen
unsegmented
unselfish
unshackle
unshakable
unshaken
unshaven
unsociable
unsold
unsolicited
unsought
unspoiled
unspoken
unsuccessful
unsuitable
unsullied
unsupervised
unsure
unsurpassed
unsuspecting
unsweetened
unsympathetic
untainted
untamed
untarnished
untasted
untenable
untiring
untouched
untrained
untried
untroubled
untrue
untrustworthy
unvarying
unverified
unwanted
unwarranted
unwavering
unwed
unworkable
unyielding
unzip

un·ac·count·a·ble (un'ə kount'ə bəl) ***adj.*** **1** that cannot be explained; strange **2** not responsible

un'ac·cus'tomed ***adj.*** **1** not accustomed (*to*) **2** not usual; strange

un'ad·vised' ***adj.*** **1** without counsel or advice **2** indiscreet; rash

un'af·fect'ed ***adj.*** **1** not affected or influenced **2** without affectation; simple; sincere

un'-A·mer'i·can ***adj.*** regarded as not properly American; esp., regarded as opposed to the U.S., its institutions, etc.

u·nan·i·mous (yo͞o nan'ə məs) ***adj.*** ⟦< L *unus*, one + *animus*, the mind⟧ agreeing completely; without dissent —**u·nan·im·i·ty** (yo͞o'nə nim'ə tē) ***n.*** —**u·nan'i·mous·ly** ***adv.***

un'ap·proach'a·ble ***adj.*** **1** not to be approached; inaccessible; aloof **2** having no equal; unmatched

un·armed' ***adj.*** having no weapons

un'as·sum'ing ***adj.*** not forward; modest

un'at·tached' ***adj.*** **1** not attached **2** not engaged or married

un'at·tend'ed ***adj.*** **1** not waited on **2** not accompanied (*by*) **3** neglected

un'a·vail'ing (-ə vāl'iŋ) ***adj.*** futile; useless

un'a·ware' ***adj.*** not aware or conscious —***adv.*** UNAWARES

un'a·wares' ***adv.*** **1** unintentionally **2** unexpectedly

un·backed' ***adj.*** not backed, supported, etc.

un·bal'anced ***adj.*** **1** not in balance **2** *a*) mentally deranged *b*) erratic or unstable

un·bar' ***vt.*** **-barred'**, **-bar'ring** to remove the bar or bars from; open

un'be·com'ing ***adj.*** not appropriate or suited to one's appearance, character, etc.; unattractive, indecorous, etc.

un·be·known (un'bē nōn') ***adj.*** without one's knowledge; unknown: usually with *to*: also **un'be·knownst'** (-nōnst')

un'be·lief' ***n.*** lack of belief, esp. in religion

un'be·liev'a·ble ***adj.*** beyond belief; astounding; incredible

un'be·liev'er ***n.*** **1** one who does not believe **2** one who does not accept any, or any particular, religious belief

un·bend' ***vt.***, ***vi.*** **-bent'** or **-bend'ed**, **-bend'ing** **1** to relax, as from formality **2** to straighten

un·bend'ing ***adj.*** **1** rigid; stiff **2** firm; resolute **3** aloof; austere

un·bid'den ***adj.*** **1** not commanded **2** not invited

un·blush'ing ***adj.*** **1** not blushing **2** shameless —**un·blush'ing·ly** ***adv.***

un·bolt' ***vt.***, ***vi.*** to withdraw the bolt or bolts of (a door, etc.); open

un·born' ***adj.*** **1** not born **2** still in the mother's uterus **3** yet to be

un·bos'om (-bo͝oz'əm) ***vt.***, ***vi.*** to tell or reveal (feelings, secrets, etc.) —**unbosom oneself** to reveal one's feelings, secrets, etc.

un·bound'ed ***adj.*** **1** without bounds or limits **2** not restrained

un'bowed' (-boud') ***adj.*** not yielding or giving in

un·bri'dled ***adj.*** **1** having no bridle on: said of a horse, etc. **2** uncontrolled

un·bur'den ***vt.*** **1** to free from a burden **2** to relieve (oneself, one's mind, etc.) by disclosing (guilt, etc.)

un'but'toned ***adj.*** **1** with buttons unfastened **2** free and easy; casual

un·called'-for' ***adj.*** **1** not needed **2** unnecessary and out of place

un·can·ny (un kan'ē) ***adj.*** **1** mysterious and eerie; weird **2** so good, acute, etc. as to seem preternatural —**un·can'ni·ly** ***adv.***

un·cared'-for' ***adj.*** not cared for or looked after; neglected

un'cer·e·mo'ni·ous ***adj.*** **1** not ceremonious; informal **2** curt; abrupt

un·cer'tain ***adj.*** **1** *a)* not surely or certainly known *b)* not sure or certain in knowledge; doubtful **2** vague **3** not dependable or reliable **4** varying —**un·cer'tain·ty,** *pl.* **-ties,** ***n.***

un·char'i·ta·ble ***adj.*** harsh or severe, as in opinion —**un·char'i·ta·bly** ***adv.***

un·chart'ed ***adj.*** not marked on a chart or map; unexplored or unknown

un·chris'tian ***adj.*** **1** not Christian **2** [Inf.] outrageous; dreadful

un·ci·al (un'shē əl, -shəl) ***adj.*** ⟦L *uncialis,* inch-high⟧ designating or of the large, rounded letters of Greek and Latin manuscripts between A.D. 300 and 900 —***n.*** uncial script or an uncial letter

un·cir'cum·cised' ***adj.*** **1** not circumcised; specif., not Jewish; gentile **2** [Archaic] heathen

un·clasp' ***vt.*** **1** to unfasten the clasp of **2** to release from a clasp or grasp

un·cle (uŋ'kəl) ***n.*** ⟦< L *avunculus*⟧ **1** the brother of one's father or mother **2** the husband of one's aunt

Uncle Sam ⟦< abbrev. *U.S.*⟧ [Inf.] the U.S. (government or people), personified as a tall man with whiskers, dressed in red, white, and blue

Uncle Tom ⟦after main character in novel *Uncle Tom's Cabin* (1852)⟧ [Inf.] a black person regarded as servile toward whites: a term of contempt

un·cloak' ***vt.*** to reveal; expose

un·clothe' ***vt.*** **-clothed'** or **-clad', -cloth'ing** to undress, uncover, etc.

un·coil' ***vt., vi.*** to unwind

un·com'fort·a·ble ***adj.*** **1** feeling discomfort **2** causing discomfort **3** ill at ease —**un·com'fort·a·bly** ***adv.***

un'com·mit'ted ***adj.*** **1** not committed or pledged **2** not taking a stand

un·com'mon ***adj.*** **1** rare; not common or usual **2** strange; remarkable

un'com·mu'ni·ca'tive ***adj.*** not communicative; reserved; taciturn

un·com'pro·mis'ing ***adj.*** not yielding; firm; inflexible

un'con·cern' ***n.*** **1** apathy; indifference **2** lack of concern, or worry

un'con·cerned' ***adj.*** **1** indifferent **2** not solicitous or anxious —**un'con·cern'ed·ly** ***adv.***

un'con·di'tion·al ***adj.*** without conditions or reservations; absolute

un·con·scion·a·ble (un kän'shən ə bəl) ***adj.*** **1** not guided or restrained by conscience **2** unreasonable or excessive **3** not fair or just —**un·con'scion·a·bly** ***adv.***

un·con'scious ***adj.*** **1** deprived of consciousness **2** not aware (*of*) **3** not doing or done on purpose *[an unconscious habit]* —**the unconscious** *Psychoanalysis* the sum of all thoughts, impulses, etc. of which the individual is not conscious but which influence the emotions and behavior —**un·con'scious·ly** ***adv.***

un'con·sti·tu'tion·al ***adj.*** not in accordance with a constitution, specif. the U.S. constitution

un·cool' ***adj.*** [Slang] **1** unsophisticated **2** unfashionable, unacceptable, etc.

un·cork' ***vt.*** to pull the cork out of

un·count'ed ***adj.*** **1** not counted **2** inconceivably numerous

un·cou'ple ***vt.*** **-pled, -pling** to unfasten (things coupled together)

un·couth (un ko͞oth') ***adj.*** ⟦OE < *un-,* not + *cunnan,* know⟧ **1** awkward; ungainly **2** not cultured; crude

un·cov'er ***vt.*** **1** to disclose **2** to remove the cover from **3** to remove the hat, etc. from (the head) —***vi.*** to bare the head, as in respect

unc·tion (uŋk'shən) ***n.*** ⟦< L *ungere,* anoint⟧ **1** *a)* the act of anointing, as for medical or religious purposes *b)* the oil, ointment, etc. used for this **2** anything that soothes or comforts

unc·tu·ous (uŋk'cho͞o əs) ***adj.*** ⟦see prec.⟧ **1** oily or greasy **2** characterized by a smooth but insincere show of deep or earnest feeling

un·cut' ***adj.*** not cut; specif., *a)* not ground to shape (said of a gem) *b)* not abridged or shortened

un·daunt'ed ***adj.*** not daunted; not hesitating because of fear or discouragement

un'de·ceive' ***vt.*** **-ceived', -ceiv'ing** to cause to be no longer deceived or misled

un'de·cid'ed ***adj.*** **1** not decided **2** not having come to a decision

un'de·mon'stra·tive ***adj.*** not demonstrative; not showing feelings openly; reserved

un'de·ni'a·ble ***adj.*** that cannot be denied; indisputable —**un'de·ni'a·bly** ***adv.***

un·der (un'dər) ***prep.*** ⟦OE⟧ **1** in, at, or to a position down from; below **2** beneath the surface of **3** below and to the other side of *[drive under the bridge]* **4** covered by *[a vest under his coat]* **5** *a)* lower in rank, position, amount, etc. than *b)* lower than the required degree of *[under age]* **6** subject to the control, limitations, etc. of *[under oath]* **7** undergoing *[under repair]* **8** with the disguise of *[under an alias]* **9** in (the designated category) **10** during the rule of *[under Elizabeth I]* **11** being the subject of *[under discussion]* **12** because of *[under the circumstances]* **13** authorized by —***adv.*** **1** in or to a lower position or state **2** so as to be covered, concealed, etc. —***adj.*** lower in position, authority, amount, etc.

under- *prefix* **1** in, on, to, or from a lower place; beneath *[undertow]* **2** in a subordinate position *[undersecretary]* **3** too little; insufficiently *[underdeveloped]*

un·der·a·chieve (un'dər ə chēv') ***vi.***

-chieved′, -chiev′ing to fail to do as well in school as might be expected from intelligence tests —un′der·a·chiev′er *n.*

un′der·act′ *vt., vi.* to act (a theatrical role) with insufficient emphasis or too great restraint

un′der·age′ *adj.* below the age required by law

un′der·arm′ *adj.* **1** of, for, in, or used on the area under the arm, or the armpit **2** UNDERHAND (sense 1) —*adv.* UNDERHAND

un′der·bel′ly *n.* **1** the lower, posterior part of an animal's belly **2** any vulnerable area, point, etc.

un′der·bid′ *vt., vi.* -bid′, -bid′ding **1** to bid lower than (another person) **2** to bid less than the worth of (a thing, as one's hand in bridge)

un′der·brush′ *n.* small trees, shrubs, etc. growing in woods or forests

un′der·car′riage *n.* a supporting frame, as of an automobile

un′der·charge′ *vt., vi.* -charged′, -charg′ing **1** to charge too low a price (to) **2** to provide with too small or low a charge

un′der·class′ *n.* the socioeconomic class with incomes below subsistence level, including esp. the underprivileged

un′der·class′man (-mən) *n., pl.* -men (-mən) a freshman or sophomore in high school or college

un′der·clothes′ *pl.n.* UNDERWEAR: also **un′der·cloth′ing** *sing.n.*

un′der·coat′ *n.* **1** a tarlike coating applied to the underside of a motor vehicle to retard rust, etc. **2** a coat of paint, etc. applied before the final coat Also **un′der·coat′ing** —*vt.* to apply an undercoat to

un′der·cov′er *adj.* acting or carried out in secret

un′der·cur′rent *n.* **1** a current flowing beneath the surface **2** an underlying tendency, opinion, etc.

un′der·cut′ *vt.* -cut′, -cut′ting **1** to make a cut below or under **2** to undersell or work for lower wages than **3** to weaken or undermine

un′der·de·vel′oped *adj.* inadequately developed, esp. economically and industrially

un′der·dog′ *n.* **1** a person or team that is losing or expected to lose **2** a person at a disadvantage because of injustice, prejudice, etc.

un′der·done′ *adj.* not cooked enough

un′der·em·ployed′ *adj.* **1** working less than full time **2** working at low-skilled, poorly paid jobs when capable of doing more highly skilled work

un′der·es′ti·mate′ *vt.* -mat′ed, -mat′ing to set too low an estimate on or for —**un′der·es′ti·ma′tion** *n.*

un′der·ex·pose′ *vt.* -posed′, -pos′ing to expose (photographic film, etc.) to inadequate light or for too short a time

un′der·foot′ *adv., adj.* **1** under the foot or feet **2** in the way

un′der·gar′ment *n.* a piece of underwear

un′der·go′ *vt.* -went′, -gone′, -go′ing to experience; go through

un′der·grad′u·ate *n.* a college student who has not yet earned a degree

un′der·ground′ *adj.* **1** under the earth's surface **2** secret; hidden **3** of newspapers, movies, etc. that are unconventional, radical, etc. —*adv.* **1** under the earth's surface **2** in or into secrecy —*n.* **1** the region under the earth's surface **2** a secret movement in a country to oppose the government or enemy occupation forces **3** [Brit.] a subway

un′der·growth′ *n.* UNDERBRUSH

un′der·hand′ *adj.* **1** done with the hand below the level of the elbow or shoulder **2** UNDERHANDED —*adv.* with an underhand motion

un′der·hand′ed *adj.* sly, deceitful, etc. —**un′der·hand′ed·ly** *adv.*

un′der·lie′ *vt.* -lay′, -lain′, -ly′ing **1** to lie beneath **2** to be the basis for; form the foundation of

un′der·line′ *vt.* -lined′, -lin′ing **1** to draw a line beneath **2** to stress

un·der·ling (un′dər liŋ) *n.* ⟦OE: see UNDER- & -LING⟧ a person in a subordinate position; inferior: usually a contemptuous term

un′der·ly′ing *adj.* **1** lying under **2** fundamental; basic

un′der·mine′ *vt.* -mined′, -min′ing **1** to dig beneath, so as to form a tunnel or mine **2** to wear away and weaken the supports of **3** to injure or weaken, esp. by subtle or insidious means

un′der·most′ *adj., adv.* lowest in place, position, rank, etc.

un·der·neath (un′dər nēth′) *adv., prep.* ⟦< OE *under,* UNDER + *neothan,* below⟧ under; below

un′der·nour′ished *adj.* not getting the food needed for health and growth

un′der·pants′ *pl.n.* an undergarment, long or short, for the lower part of the body

un′der·pass′ *n.* a passage under something; esp., a passageway under a railway

un′der·per·form′ *vi.* to be less successful than expected or needed —*vt.* to produce a smaller return than: said of stocks, etc.

un′der·pin′ning (-pin′iŋ) *n.* **1** a support or prop **2** [*pl.*] [Inf.] the legs

un′der·play′ *vt., vi.* **1** UNDERACT **2** to make seem less important

un′der·priv′i·leged *adj.* deprived of a decent standard of living and economic security through poverty, discrimination, etc.

un′der·pro·duce′ *vt., vi.* -duced′, -duc′ing to produce less than is needed or wanted

un′der·rate′ *vt.* -rat′ed, -rat′ing to rate or estimate too low

un′der·score′ *vt.* -scored′, -scor′ing UNDERLINE

un′der·sea′ *adj., adv.* beneath the surface of the sea: also **un′der·seas′** *adv.*

un′der·sec′re·tar′y *n., pl.* -ies an assistant secretary

un'der·sell' *vt.* **-sold', -sell'ing** **1** to sell at a lower price than **2** to publicize or promote in a restrained or inadequate manner

un'der·shirt' *n.* a collarless undergarment worn under an outer shirt

un'der·shorts' *pl.n.* short underpants worn by men and boys

un'der·shot' *adj.* **1** with the lower part extending past the upper [an *undershot* jaw] **2** driven by water flowing along the lower part [an *undershot* water wheel]

un'der·side' *n.* the side or surface that is underneath

un'der·signed' *adj.* whose name is signed at the end —**the undersigned** the person or persons having signed at the end

un'der·skirt' *n.* a skirt worn under another

un'der·staffed' *adj.* having fewer workers on the staff than are needed

un'der·stand' *vt.* **-stood', -stand'ing** ⟦< OE *understandan,* lit., to stand among⟧ **1** to perceive the meaning of **2** to assume from what is heard, etc.; infer **3** to take as meant; interpret **4** to take as a fact **5** to know the nature, character, etc. of **6** to have a sympathetic rapport with —*vi.* **1** to have understanding, comprehension, etc. **2** to be informed; believe —**un'der·stand'a·ble** *adj.* —**un'der·stand'a·bly** *adv.*

un'der·stand'ing *n.* **1** comprehension **2** the power to think and learn; intelligence **3** a specific interpretation **4** mutual agreement, esp. one that settles differences —*adj.* that understands; sympathetic

un'der·state' *vt.* **-stat'ed, -stat'ing** **1** to state too weakly **2** to state in a restrained style —**un'der·state'ment** *n.*

un'der·stud'y *n., pl.* **-ies** an actor prepared to substitute for another —*vt., vi.* **-ied, -y·ing** to learn (a part) as an understudy (to)

un'der·take' *vt.* **-took', -tak'en, -tak'ing** **1** to take upon oneself (a task, etc.) **2** to promise; guarantee

un'der·tak'er *n.* FUNERAL DIRECTOR: a somewhat old-fashioned usage

un'der·tak'ing *n.* **1** something undertaken; task; enterprise **2** a promise; guarantee

un'der-the-count'er *adj.* [Inf.] done secretly in an unlawful way: also **un'der-the-ta'ble**

un'der·things' *pl.n.* women's or girls' underwear

un'der·tone' *n.* **1** a low tone of voice **2** a subdued color **3** an underlying quality, factor, etc.

un'der·tow' *n.* a current of water moving beneath the surface water and in a different direction

un'der·wa'ter *adj.* being, done, etc. beneath the surface of the water

un'der·way' *adj.* **1** moving; making progress **2** *Naut.* not anchored or moored or aground

un'der·wear' *n.* clothing worn under one's outer clothes, usually next to the skin, as undershirts

un·der·weight (un'dər wāt', un'dər wāt') *adj.* below the normal, desirable, or allowed weight

un'der·world' *n.* **1** the mythical world of the dead; Hades **2** criminals regarded as a group

un'der·write' *vt.* **-wrote', -writ'ten, -writ'ing** **1** to agree to market (an issue of securities), guaranteeing to buy any part remaining unsubscribed **2** to agree to pay the cost of or cover the losses of (an undertaking, etc.) **3** to sign one's name to (an insurance policy), thus assuming liability —**un'der·writ'er** *n.*

un·dies (un'dēz') *pl.n.* [Inf.] women's or girls' underwear

un·do' *vt.* **-did', -done', -do'ing** **1** to untie, open, etc. **2** to do away with; cancel **3** to bring to ruin

un·doc'u·ment'ed *adj.* not having a proper visa for U.S. residence [an *undocumented* alien]

un·do'ing *n.* **1** an annulling **2** a bringing to ruin **3** the cause of ruin

un·done' *adj.* **1** not done; not performed, accomplished, etc. **2** ruined **3** emotionally upset

un·doubt'ed *adj.* not doubted or disputed; certain —**un·doubt'ed·ly** *adv.*

un·dreamed' *adj.* not even dreamed (*of*) or imagined: also **un·dreamt'** (-dremt')

un·dress' *vt.* to take off the clothing of —*vi.* to take off one's clothes

un·due' *adj.* **1** not appropriate; improper **2** excessive; immoderate

un·du·lant (un'jə lənt, -dyə-) *adj.* undulating

un'du·late' (-lāt') *vi., vt.* ⟦< L *unda,* a wave⟧ **1** to move or cause to move in waves **2** to have or cause to have a wavy form or surface —**un'du·la'tion** *n.*

un·du'ly *adv.* **1** improperly **2** excessively

un·dy'ing *adj.* immortal or eternal

un·earned' *adj.* not earned by work or service; specif., obtained as a return on an investment [*unearned* income]

un·earth' *vt.* **1** to dig up from the earth **2** to bring to light; disclose

un·earth'ly *adj.* **1** supernatural **2** weird; mysterious **3** [Inf.] fantastic, outlandish, etc.

un·eas'y *adj.* **-i·er, -i·est** **1** having, showing, or allowing no ease of body or mind; uncomfortable **2** awkward; constrained **3** anxious; apprehensive —**un·eas'i·ly** *adv.* —**un·eas'i·ness** *n.*

un'em·ploy'a·ble *adj.* not employable, specif. because of severe physical or mental handicaps, outmoded skills, etc.

un'em·ployed' *adj.* **1** not employed; without work **2** not being used —**un'em·ploy'ment** *n.*

un·e'qual *adj.* **1** not equal, as in size, strength, ability, or value **2** not balanced, even, regular, etc. **3** not adequate (*to*)

un·e'qualed or **un·e'qualled** *adj.* not equaled; unmatched; unrivaled

un'e·quiv'o·cal *adj.* not equivocal; plain; clear

un·err·ing (un ~~ur~~′iŋ, -er′-) *adj.* **1** free from error **2** not missing or failing; sure; exact

UNESCO (yoo͞ nes′kō) *n.* United Nations Educational, Scientific, and Cultural Organization

un·e′ven *adj.* **1** not even, level, smooth, regular, etc. **2** unequal **3** *Math.* odd —**un·e′ven·ly** *adv.*

un′ex·am′pled *adj.* having no parallel or precedent; unprecedented

un′ex·cep′tion·a·ble *adj.* not exceptionable; without fault; beyond criticism

un′ex·cep′tion·al *adj.* ordinary

un′ex·pect′ed *adj.* not expected; unforeseen —**un′ex·pect′ed·ly** *adv.*

un·fail′ing *adj.* **1** not failing **2** never ceasing or falling short; inexhaustible **3** always reliable

un·faith′ful *adj.* **1** lacking or breaking faith or loyalty **2** not true, accurate, etc. **3** adulterous —**un·faith′ful·ness** *n.*

un′fa·mil′iar *adj.* **1** not well-known; strange **2** not acquainted (*with*) —**un′fa·mil′i·ar′i·ty** *n.*

un·feel′ing *adj.* **1** incapable of feeling; insensible **2** hardhearted; cruel —**un·feel′ing·ly** *adv.*

un·feigned (un fānd′) *adj.* genuine

un·fin′ished *adj.* **1** not finished; incomplete **2** not painted, varnished, etc.

un·flap′pa·ble (-flap′ə bəl) *adj.* ⟦< UN- + FLAP, *n.* 3 + -ABLE⟧ [Inf.] not easily excited; imperturbable

un·flinch′ing *adj.* steadfast; firm

un·fold′ *vt.* **1** to open and spread out (something folded) **2** to lay open to view; reveal, explain, etc. —*vi.* **1** to become unfolded **2** to develop fully

un′for·get′ta·ble *adj.* so important, beautiful, shocking, etc. as never to be forgotten

un′for·giv′ing *adj.* not willing or not able to forgive

un·for′tu·nate *adj.* **1** having or bringing bad luck; unlucky **2** not suitable or successful —*n.* an unfortunate person —**un·for′tu·nate·ly** *adv.*

un·found′ed *adj.* not founded on fact or truth

un·friend′ly *adj.* -li·er, -li·est **1** not friendly or kind **2** not favorable —**un·friend′li·ness** *n.*

un·frock′ *vt.* to deprive of the rank of priest or minister

un·furl′ *vt., vi.* to open or spread out from a furled state

un·gain·ly (un gān′lē) *adj.* ⟦< ME *un-*, not + ON *gegn,* ready⟧ awkward; clumsy

un·god′ly *adj.* **1** not godly or religious **2** [Inf.] outrageous —**un·god′li·ness** *n.*

un·gov′ern·a·ble *adj.* that cannot be governed or controlled; unruly

un·gra′cious *adj.* **1** not gracious; rude **2** unpleasant; unattractive

un·guard′ed *adj.* **1** unprotected **2** without guile or cunning **3** careless; imprudent

un·guent (uŋ′gwənt) *n.* ⟦< L *unguere,* anoint⟧ a salve or ointment

un·gu·late (uŋ′gyoo͞ lit, -lāt′) *adj.* ⟦< L *unguis,* a nail⟧ having hoofs —*n.* a mammal having hoofs

un·hand′ *vt.* to release from the hand or hands; let go of

un·hap′py *adj.* **-pi·er, -pi·est 1** unfortunate **2** sad; wretched **3** not suitable —**un·hap′pi·ly** *adv.* —**un·hap′pi·ness** *n.*

un·health′y *adj.* **-i·er, -i·est 1** sickly; not well **2** harmful to health **3** harmful to morals **4** dangerous or risky —**un·health′i·ness** *n.*

un·heard′ *adj.* **1** not perceived by the ear **2** not given a hearing

un·heard′-of′ *adj.* **1** not heard of before; unprecedented or unknown **2** unacceptable or outrageous

un·hinge′ *vt.* **-hinged′, -hing′ing 1** to remove from the hinges **2** to unbalance (the mind) of (someone)

un·ho′ly *adj.* **-li·er, -li·est 1** not sacred, hallowed, etc. **2** wicked; profane **3** [Inf.] outrageous

un·horse′ *vt.* **-horsed′, -hors′ing** to throw (a rider) from a horse

uni- ⟦L < *unus,* one⟧ *prefix* one; having only one

u·ni·bod·y (yoo͞′nə bäd′ē) *adj.* designating automobile construction in which roof, floor, panels, etc. are welded together into a single unit

u′ni·cam′er·al (-kam′ər əl) *adj.* ⟦< UNI- + L *camera,* chamber⟧ of or having a single legislative chamber

UNICEF (yoo͞′nə sef′) *n.* United Nations Children's Fund: formerly, *United Nations International Children's Emergency Fund*

UNICORN

u·ni·corn (yoo͞′nə kôrn′) *n.* ⟦< L *unus,* one + *cornu,* horn⟧ a mythical horselike animal with a single horn growing from its forehead

u·ni·cy·cle (yoo͞′nə sī′kəl) *n.* ⟦UNI- + (BI)CYCLE⟧ a one-wheeled vehicle straddled by the rider who pushes its pedals —**u′ni·cy′clist** *n.*

u·ni·form (yoo͞′nə fôrm′) *adj.* ⟦< L *unus,* one + *-formis,* -FORM⟧ **1** not varying in form, rate, degree, etc. **2** like others of the same class —*n.* the distinctive clothes of a particular group, as of soldiers —*vt.* to supply with a uniform —**u′ni·form′i·ty** *n.* —**u′ni·form′ly** *adv.*

u·ni·fy (yoo͞′nə fī′) *vt., vi.* **-fied′, -fy′ing** ⟦see UNI- & -FY⟧ to become or make united —**u′ni·fi·ca′tion** *n.*

u·ni·lat·er·al (yoo͞′nə lat′ər əl) *adj.* **1** of, occurring on, or affecting one side only **2** involving only one of several parties;

not reciprocal

un·im·peach·a·ble (un'im pēch'ə bəl) ***adj.*** that cannot be doubted or discredited; irreproachable

un'in·hib'it·ed ***adj.*** without inhibition; esp., free of the usual social or psychological restraints on one's behavior

un·in'ter·est·ed ***adj.*** not interested; indifferent

un·ion (yōōn'yən) ***n.*** ⟦< L *unus,* one⟧ **1** a uniting or being united; combination **2** a grouping together of nations, etc. for some specific purpose **3** marriage **4** something united **5** *short for* LABOR UNION **6** a design symbolizing political union, used as in a flag **7** a device for joining parts, as of a machine —**the Union 1** the United States **2** the North in the Civil War

un'ion·ize' (-īz') ***vt., vi.* -ized', -iz'ing** to organize into a labor union —**un'ion·i·za'tion *n.***

union jack 1 a flag, esp. a national flag, consisting only of a UNION (sense 6) **2** [**U- J-**] the flag of the United Kingdom

Union of Soviet Socialist Republics former country in E Europe & N Asia: formed as a union of 15 constituent republics, it was disbanded in 1991

u·nique (yōō nēk') ***adj.*** ⟦< L *unus,* one⟧ **1** one and only; sole **2** without like or equal **3** very unusual: a usage still objected to by some

u·ni·sex (yōō'nə seks') ***adj.*** of or involving a fashion, as in haircuts, that is not differentiated for the sexes

u·ni·son (yōō'nə sən, -zən) ***n.*** ⟦< L *unus,* one + *sonus,* a sound⟧ **1** a musical interval consisting of two identical pitches **2** agreement —**in unison** with all the voices or instruments performing the same part

u·nit (yōō'nit) ***n.*** ⟦< UNITY⟧ **1** the smallest whole number; one **2** a standard basic quantity, measure, etc. **3** a single person or group, esp. as a part of a whole **4** a distinct part or object with a specific purpose

U·ni·tar·i·an (yōō'nə ter'ē ən) ***n.*** a member of a religious denomination accepting the moral teachings of Jesus, but holding that God is a single being

u·ni·tar·y (yōō'nə ter'ē) ***adj.*** **1** of a unit or units **2** of or based on unity

u·nite (yōō nīt') ***vt., vi.* -nit'ed, -nit'ing** ⟦< L *unus,* one⟧ **1** to put or join together so as to make one; combine **2** to bring or come together in common cause, action, etc.

United Arab E·mir·ates (em'ər əts) country in E Arabia, on the Persian Gulf: 32,300 sq. mi.; pop. 1,622,000

United Arab Republic *former name for* Egypt (1961-71)

United Kingdom country in W Europe, consisting of Great Britain & Northern Ireland: 93,636 sq. mi.; pop. 55,734,000

United Nations an international organization of nations for world peace and security: formed in 1945 and having, in 2001, a membership of 189

United States of America country including 49 states in North America, and Hawaii: 3,787,318 sq. mi.; pop. 248,710,000; cap. Washington, DC: also called **United States**

u·nit·ize (yōō'nə tīz') ***vt.* -ized', -iz'ing** to make into a single unit

unit pricing a system of showing prices, as of foods, in terms of standard units

u·ni·ty (yōō'nə tē) ***n., pl.* -ties** ⟦< L *unus,* one⟧ **1** a being united; oneness **2** a single, separate thing **3** harmony; agreement **4** a complex that is a union of related parts **5** a harmonious, unified arrangement of parts in an artistic work **6** continuity of purpose, action, etc. **7** *Math.* any quantity, etc. identified as a unit, or 1

univ *abbrev.* university

u·ni·va·lent (yōō'nə vā'lənt) ***adj.*** *Chem.* **1** having one valence **2** having a valence of one

u·ni·valve (yōō'nə valv') ***n.*** a mollusk with a one-piece shell, as a snail

u·ni·ver·sal (yōō'nə vur'səl) ***adj.*** **1** of the universe; present everywhere **2** of, for, or including all or the whole **3** used, or intended to be used, for all kinds, sizes, etc. or by all people —**u'ni·ver·sal'i·ty** (-vər sal'ə tē) ***n.***

u'ni·ver'sal·ize' ***vt.* -ized', -iz'ing** to make universal

universal joint (or **coupling**) a joint or coupling that permits a swing of limited angle in any direction, esp. one for transmitting rotary motion from one shaft to another not in line with it

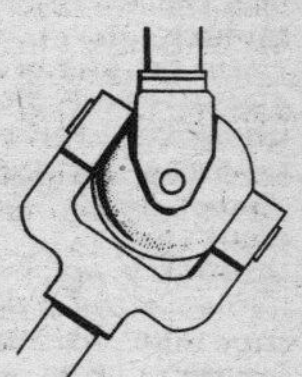

UNIVERSAL JOINT

u'ni·ver'sal·ly ***adv.*** **1** in every instance **2** in every part or place

Universal Product Code a patterned series of vertical bars printed on consumer products: it can be read by computerized scanners for pricing, etc.

u·ni·verse (yōō'nə vurs') ***n.*** ⟦< L *unus,* one + *vertere,* to turn⟧ **1** the totality of all things that exist **2** the world

u·ni·ver·si·ty (yōō'nə vur'sə tē) ***n., pl.* -ties** ⟦see prec.⟧ **1** an educational institution offering bachelor's and advanced degrees **2** the grounds, buildings, etc. of a university

un·just (un just') ***adj.*** not just or right; unfair —**un·just'ly *adv.***

un·kempt' (-kempt') ***adj.*** ⟦UN- + *kempt* < dial. *kemben,* to comb⟧ **1** tangled, disheveled, etc. **2** not tidy; slovenly

un·kind' ***adj.*** not kind; specif., *a)* not considerate of others *b)* harsh, severe, cruel, etc. —**un·kind'ness *n.***

un·kind'ly ***adj.*** UNKIND —***adv.*** in an unkind way

un·known' ***adj.*** not known; specif., *a)* unfamiliar (*to*) *b)* not identified, etc. —***n.*** an unknown person or thing

un·law'ful ***adj.*** **1** against the law; illegal **2** immoral —**un·law'ful·ly *adv.*** —**un·law'ful·ness *n.***

un·lead'ed *adj.* not containing lead compounds: said of gasoline

un·learn' *vt.*, *vi.* to forget or try to forget (something learned)

un·learn'ed (-lur'nid; *for 2*, -lurnd') *adj.* 1 not having much learning; uneducated 2 not learned or memorized *[unlearned* lessons*]*

un·leash' *vt.* to release from or as from a leash

un·less (un les') *conj.* ⟦< ME *on lesse that*, at less than⟧ except if; except that

un·let'tered *adj.* 1 ignorant; uneducated 2 illiterate

un·like' *adj.* not alike; different —*prep.* 1 not like; different from 2 not characteristic of

un·like'ly *adj.* 1 not likely; improbable 2 not likely to succeed —**un·like'li·hood'** *n.*

un·lim'ber *vt.*, *vi.* to get ready for use or action

un·lim'it·ed *adj.* 1 without limits or restrictions 2 vast; immeasurable

un·load' *vt.*, *vi.* 1 *a)* to remove (a load) *b)* to take a load from 2 *a)* to tell (one's troubles, etc.) without restraint *b)* to relieve of something that troubles 3 to remove the charge from (a gun) 4 to get rid of

un·lock' *vt.* 1 *a)* to open (a lock) *b)* to open the lock of (a door, etc.) 2 to let loose; release 3 to reveal

un·looked'-for' *adj.* not expected

un·loose' *vt.* **-loosed'**, **-loos'ing** to set loose; loosen, release, etc.: also **un·loos'en**

un·luck'y *adj.* **-i·er**, **-i·est** having or bringing bad luck; unfortunate

un·make' *vt.* **-made'**, **-mak'ing** 1 to cause to be as before; undo 2 to ruin; destroy 3 to depose from a position or rank

un·man' *vt.* **-manned'**, **-man'ning** to deprive of manly courage, nerve, etc.

un·man'ly *adj.* **-li·er**, **-li·est** not manly; specif., *a)* cowardly, weak, etc. *b)* effeminate; womanish

un·manned' *adj.* without people aboard and operating by remote control

un·mask' *vi.*, *vt.* 1 to remove a mask or disguise (from) 2 to disclose the true nature or character (of)

un·mean'ing *adj.* lacking in meaning or sense

un·men'tion·a·ble *adj.* not fit to be mentioned

un·mer'ci·ful *adj.* having or showing no mercy; cruel; pitiless

un'mis·tak'a·ble *adj.* that cannot be mistaken or misinterpreted; clear —**un'mis·tak'a·bly** *adv.*

un·mit'i·gat'ed *adj.* 1 not lessened or eased 2 out-and-out; absolute

un·mor'al *adj.* AMORAL

un·nat'u·ral *adj.* 1 contrary to nature; abnormal 2 artificial 3 very cruel —**un·nat'u·ral·ly** *adv.*

un·nec'es·sar'y *adj.* not necessary; needless —**un·nec'es·sar'i·ly** *adv.*

un·nerve' *vt.* **-nerved'**, **-nerv'ing** to cause to lose one's self-confidence, courage, etc.

un·num'bered *adj.* 1 not counted 2 innumerable 3 having no identifying number

un·or'gan·ized' *adj.* not organized; specif., not belonging to a labor union

un·pack' *vt.*, *vi.* 1 to remove (the contents of a trunk, suitcase, etc.) 2 to take things out of (a trunk, etc.)

un·par'al·leled' *adj.* that has no parallel, equal, or counterpart

un·pleas'ant *adj.* offensive; disagreeable —**un·pleas'ant·ly** *adv.* —**un·pleas'ant·ness** *n.*

un·plumbed' *adj.* not fully understood

un·pop'u·lar *adj.* not liked by the public or by the majority —**un'pop·u·lar'i·ty** (-lar'ə tē) *n.*

un·prac'ticed *adj.* 1 not habitually or repeatedly done, etc. 2 not skilled or experienced

un·prec'e·dent'ed *adj.* having no precedent or parallel; unheard-of

un·prin'ci·pled *adj.* lacking moral principles; unscrupulous

un·print'a·ble *adj.* not fit to be printed, as because of obscenity

un'pro·fes'sion·al *adj.* not professional; esp., violating the ethical code of a given profession

un·qual'i·fied' *adj.* 1 lacking the necessary qualifications 2 not limited; absolute

un·ques'tion·a·ble *adj.* not to be questioned, doubted, or disputed; certain —**un·ques'tion·a·bly** *adv.*

un'quote' *interj.* I end the quotation

un·rav'el *vt.* **-eled** or **-elled**, **-el·ing** or **-el·ling** 1 to separate the threads of (something woven, tangled, etc.) 2 to make clear; solve —*vi.* to become unraveled

un·read' (-red') *adj.* 1 not read, as a book 2 having read little or nothing

un·re'al *adj.* not real or actual; imaginary, fanciful, false, etc.

un·rea'son·a·ble *adj.* 1 not reasonable or rational 2 excessive; immoderate —**un·rea'son·a·bly** *adv.*

un·rea'son·ing *adj.* not reasoning or reasoned; irrational

un're·con·struct'ed *adj.* holding to an earlier, outmoded practice or point of view

un're·gen'er·ate *adj.* stubbornly defiant

un're·lent'ing *adj.* 1 inflexible; relentless 2 without mercy; cruel 3 not relaxing in effort, speed, etc.

un're·mit'ting *adj.* not stopping, relaxing, etc.; incessant; persistent

un're·quit'ed *adj.* not reciprocated

un're·served' *adj.* not reserved; specif., *a)* frank or open in speech *b)* not restricted; unlimited —**un're·serv'ed·ly** *adv.*

un·rest' *n.* restlessness; specif., angry discontent verging on revolt

un·ripe' *adj.* not ripe or mature; green

un·ri'valed or **un·ri'valled** *adj.* having no rival, equal, or competitor

un·roll' *vt.* 1 to open (something rolled

up) 2 to display —*vi.* to become unrolled

un·ruf′fled *adj.* not ruffled or disturbed; calm; smooth; serene

un·ruly (un ro͞o′lē) *adj.* **-i·er, -i·est** hard to control, restrain, or keep in order —**un·rul′i·ness** *n.*

un·sad′dle *vt.* **-dled, -dling** to take the saddle off (a horse, etc.)

un·said′ *adj.* not expressed

un·sa′vor·y *adj.* **1** unpleasant to taste or smell **2** morally offensive

un·scathed′ (-skāthd′) *adj.* ⟦< *un-* + ON *skathi,* harm⟧ unharmed

un·schooled′ *adj.* not educated or trained, esp. by formal schooling

un·scram′ble *vt.* **-bled, -bling** to cause to be no longer scrambled, mixed up, or unintelligible

un·screw′ *vt.* to detach or loosen by removing screws, or by turning

un·script′ed *adj.* without or not in a prepared script

un·scru′pu·lous *adj.* not restrained by ideas of right and wrong; unprincipled

un·seal′ *vt.* **1** to break the seal of **2** to open

un·sea′son·a·ble *adj.* **1** not usual for the season **2** at the wrong time

un·seat′ *vt.* **1** to dislodge from a seat **2** to remove from office

un·seem′ly *adj.* not seemly; not decent or proper; unbecoming

un·set′tle *vt., vi.* **-tled, -tling** to make or become unstable; disturb or displace

un·set′tled *adj.* **1** not settled; not fixed, orderly, stable, calm, decided, etc. **2** not paid **3** having no settlers

un·sheathe′ (-shēth′) *vt.* **-sheathed′, -sheath′ing** to remove (a sword, etc.) from a sheath

un·sight′ly *adj.* not sightly or pleasant to look at; ugly —**un·sight′li·ness** *n.*

un·skilled′ *adj.* having or requiring no special skill or training

un·skill′ful *adj.* having little or no skill; awkward

un·snap′ *vt.* **-snapped′, -snap′ping** to undo the snaps of, so as to loosen or detach

un·snarl′ *vt.* to untangle

un′so·phis′ti·cat′ed *adj.* not sophisticated; simple, ingenuous, etc.

un·sound′ *adj.* not sound; specif., *a*) not healthy, safe, firm, etc. *b*) not reliable, sensible, etc.

un·spar′ing *adj.* **1** not sparing; lavish **2** not merciful; severe

un·speak′a·ble *adj.* **1** that cannot be spoken **2** so bad, foul, evil, etc. as to defy description or be unfit for discussion *[unspeakable* depravity*]* —**un·speak′a·bly** *adv.*

un·sta′ble *adj.* not stable; specif., *a*) easily upset *b*) changeable *c*) unreliable *d*) emotionally or psychologically unsettled *e*) *Chem.* tending to decompose

un·stead′y *adj.* not steady; specif., *a*) not firm; shaky *b*) changeable; inconstant *c*) erratic in habits, purpose, etc.

un·stop′ *vt.* **-stopped′, -stop′ping 1** to remove the stopper from **2** to clear (a pipe, etc.) of an obstruction

un·struc′tured *adj.* not formally organized; loose, free, open, etc.

un·strung′ *adj.* **1** nervous or upset **2** with the strings loosened or detached, as a bow or racket

un·stuck′ *adj.* loosened or freed from being stuck

un·stud′ied *adj.* not gotten by study or conscious effort; spontaneous; natural

un′sub·stan′tial *adj.* **1** having no material substance **2** not solid; flimsy **3** unreal; visionary

un·sung′ *adj.* not honored or celebrated, as in song or poetry

un·tan′gle *vt.* **-gled, -gling 1** to free from a snarl or tangle **2** to free from confusion; put in order

un·taught′ *adj.* **1** not taught; uneducated **2** acquired without being taught

un·think′a·ble *adj.* **1** that cannot be imagined; inconceivable **2** so foul, etc. as to be unfit to be considered *[unthinkable* war crimes*]*

un·think′ing *adj.* **1** thoughtless; heedless **2** unable to think

un·ti′dy *adj.* **-di·er, -di·est** not neat; messy

un·tie′ *vt.* **-tied′, -ty′ing** or **-tie′ing 1** to unfasten (a thing tied or knotted) **2** to free, as from restraint

un·til (un til′) *prep.* ⟦ME *untill*⟧ **1** up to the time of *[until* death*]* **2** before *[*not *until* tomorrow*]* —*conj.* **1** up to the time when or that *[until* you leave*]* **2** to the point, degree, etc. that *[*cook *until* it is done*]* **3** before *[*not *until* I die*]*

un·time′ly *adj., adv.* **1** before the proper time; premature(ly) **2** at the wrong time —**un·time′li·ness** *n.*

un·to (un′to͞o, -too) *prep.* ⟦ME⟧ *old poet. var. of:* **1** TO **2** UNTIL

un·told′ *adj.* **1** not told or revealed **2** too many to be counted **3** indescribably great *[untold* misery*]*

un·touch′a·ble *adj.* that cannot or should not be touched —*n.* in India, a member of the lowest castes (now called *Scheduled castes*)

un·to·ward (un tō′ərd, -tôrd′) *adj.* **1** improper, unseemly, etc. **2** not favorable; adverse

un·trav′eled or **un·trav′elled** *adj.* **1** not used or frequented by travelers **2** not having done much traveling

un·truth′ *n.* **1** falsity **2** a falsehood; lie —**un·truth′ful** *adj.*

un·tu′tored *adj.* uneducated

un·twist′ *vt., vi.* to loosen or separate, as something twisted together; unwind

un·used′ *adj.* **1** not in use **2** never used before **3** unaccustomed (*to*)

un·u′su·al *adj.* not usual or common; rare —**un·u′su·al·ly** *adv.*

un·ut′ter·a·ble *adj.* inexpressible

un·var′nished *adj.* **1** not varnished **2** plain; simple; unadorned

un·veil′ *vt.* to reveal as by removing a veil from —*vi.* to take off one's veil

un·voiced′ *adj.* not expressed; not spoken

un·war′y ***adj.*** not wary or cautious

un′wea′ried (-wir′ēd) ***adj.*** ⟦ME *unweried* (see UN- & WEARY)⟧ never wearying; tireless; indefatigable

un·well′ ***adj.*** not well; sick

un·whole′some ***adj.*** **1** harmful to body or mind **2** of unsound health or unhealthy appearance **3** morally harmful —**un·whole′some·ness** ***n.***

un·wield′y ***adj.*** hard to wield, manage, etc., as because of large size

un·will′ing ***adj.*** **1** not willing; reluctant **2** done, said, etc. reluctantly —**un·will′ing·ly** ***adv.***

un·wind′ (-wīnd′) ***vt.*** **-wound′**, **-wind′ing** **1** to wind off or undo (something wound) **2** to untangle (something involved) —***vi.*** **1** to become unwound **2** to become relaxed

un·wise′ ***adj.*** having or showing a lack of wisdom or sound judgment

un·wit′ting ***adj.*** **1** not knowing; unaware **2** unintentional

un·wont′ed ***adj.*** not common, usual, or habitual

un·wor′thy ***adj.*** **-thi·er**, **-thi·est** **1** lacking merit or value; worthless **2** not deserving (*of*) **3** not fit or becoming: usually with *of* —**un·wor′thi·ness** ***n.***

un·wrap′ ***vt.*** **-wrapped′**, **-wrap′ping** to take off the wrapping of

un·writ′ten ***adj.*** **1** not in writing **2** operating only through custom or tradition *[an unwritten rule]*

up[1] (up) ***adv.*** ⟦OE⟧ **1** to, in, or on a higher place or level **2** to a later period **3** to or into a higher condition, amount, etc. **4** *a)* in or into a standing or upright position *b)* out of bed **5** in or into action, view, consideration, etc. **6** aside; away *[lay up wealth]* **7** so as to be even with in time, degree, etc. **8** completely; thoroughly *[eat up the cake]* **9** *Baseball* to one's turn at batting **10** used with verbs: *a)* to form idioms with meanings different from the simple verb *[look up this word]* *b)* as an intensive *[dress up]* —***prep.*** up to, toward, along, through, into, or upon —***adj.*** **1** directed toward a higher position **2** in a higher place or position **3** advanced in amount, degree, etc. *[rents are up]* **4** in a standing or upright position **5** in an active or excited state **6** at an end; over *[time's up]* **7** available for use, as a computer **8** [Inf.] going on *[what's up]* **9** *Baseball* at bat —***n.*** **1** an upward slope **2** an upward movement, etc. —***vi.*** **upped**, **up′ping** [Inf.] to get up; rise —***vt.*** [Inf.] **1** to put up, lift up, etc. **2** to cause to rise *[to up prices]* —**on the up and up** [Slang] honest —**up against** [Inf.] confronted with —**up on** (or **in**) [Inf.] well-informed concerning —**ups and downs** good periods and bad periods —**up to** **1** doing or scheming **2** capable of (doing, etc.) **3** as many as **4** as far as **5** dependent upon —**up with!** give or restore power, favor, etc. to!

up[2] (up) ***adv.*** ⟦phonetic respelling of *ap(iece)*⟧ apiece *[a score of ten up]*

up- *combining form* up

up′-and-com′ing ***adj.*** **1** enterprising, promising, etc. **2** gaining in prominence

up′beat′ ***n.*** *Music* an unaccented beat, esp. when on the last note of a bar —***adj.*** [Inf.] cheerful; optimistic

up·braid (up brād′) ***vt.*** ⟦< OE *up-*, up + *bregdan*, to pull⟧ to rebuke severely; censure; scold

up′bring′ing ***n.*** the training and education received while growing up

UPC *abbrev.* Universal Product Code

up′chuck′ ***vi.***, ***vt.***, ***n.*** [Slang] VOMIT

up′com′ing ***adj.*** coming soon

up′coun′try ***adj.***, ***adv.*** in or toward the interior of a country

up·date (up dāt′; *also, and for n. always,* up′dāt′) ***vt.*** **-dat′ed**, **-dat′ing** to make up-to-date; make conform to the most recent facts, methods, etc. —***n.*** **1** an updating **2** an updated report, etc.

up·end′ ***vt.***, ***vi.*** **1** to set, turn, or stand on end **2** to topple

up′front′ [Inf.] ***adj.*** **1** forthright **2** in advance *[upfront money]* —***adv.*** in advance Also **up′-front′**

up·grade (up′grād′; *also, and for v. usually,* up grād′) ***n.*** **1** an upward slope **2** an improvement —***adj.***, ***adv.*** uphill; upward —***vt.***, ***vi.*** **-grad′ed**, **-grad′ing** to raise or improve in value, grade, rank, quality, etc.

up·heav·al (up hē′vəl) ***n.*** **1** a heaving up **2** a sudden, violent change

up′hill′ ***adv.*** **1** toward the top of a hill; upward **2** with difficulty —***adj.*** **1** going or sloping up **2** laborious; tiring

up·hold′ ***vt.*** **-held′**, **-hold′ing** **1** to hold up **2** to keep from falling; support **3** to confirm; sustain

up·hol·ster (up hōl′stər) ***vt.*** ⟦ult. < ME *upholder*, tradesman⟧ to fit out (furniture, etc.) with coverings, padding, springs, etc. —**up·hol′ster·er** ***n.***

up·hol′ster·y ***n.***, *pl.* **-ies** **1** the material used in upholstering **2** the work of an upholsterer

up′keep′ ***n.*** **1** maintenance **2** state of repair **3** the cost of maintenance

up′land (-lənd, -land′) ***n.*** land elevated above other land —***adj.*** of or situated in upland

up·lift (up lift′; *also, and for n. always,* up′lift′) ***vt.*** **1** to lift up **2** to raise to a higher moral, social, or cultural level —***n.*** **1** a lifting up **2** a movement for moral, social, or cultural betterment

up′load′ ***vt.***, ***vi.*** to transfer (information) as from a personal computer to a main computer

up′-mark′et ***adj.*** UPSCALE

up·on (ə pän′, ə pôn′) ***prep.*** on, or up and on: used interchangeably with *on* —***adv.*** on

up·per (up′ər) ***adj.*** **1** higher in place **2** higher in rank, etc. **3** farther north —***n.*** **1** the part of a shoe above the sole **2** [Slang] any drug that is a stimulant —**on one's uppers** [Inf.] in need

up·per·case (up′ər kās′) ***n.*** capital-letter type used in printing, as distinguished from small letters —***adj.*** of or in uppercase

upper class the rich or aristocratic social class —**up′per-class′** ***adj.***

up′per·class′man (-mən) ***n., pl.*** **-men** (-mən) a junior or senior in high school or college

up′per·cut′ ***n.*** *Boxing* a short, swinging blow directed upward

upper hand the position of advantage or control

up′per·most′ ***adj.*** highest in place, authority, etc. —***adv.*** in the highest place, rank, etc.

Upper Vol·ta (väl′tə) *former name for* BURKINA FASO

up·pi·ty (up′ə tē) ***adj.*** [Inf.] haughty, arrogant, snobbish, etc.

up·raise′ ***vt.*** **-raised′**, **-rais′ing** to raise up; lift

up·rear′ ***vt.*** to lift up —***vi.*** to rise up

up·right (up′rīt′; *for adj. and adv., also* up rīt′) ***adj.*** **1** standing, pointing, etc. straight up; erect **2** honest and just —***adv.*** in an upright position or direction —***n.*** something in an upright position

upright piano a piano with a vertical, rectangular body

up′ris′ing ***n.*** a revolt

up′riv′er ***adv., adj.*** in the direction against the current of a river

up·roar (up′rôr′) ***n.*** ⟦Du *oproer,* a stirring up⟧ **1** violent disturbance; tumult **2** loud, confused noise

up·roar·i·ous (up rôr′ē əs) ***adj.*** **1** making an uproar **2** boisterous **3** causing loud laughter

up·root′ ***vt.*** **1** to tear up by the roots **2** to destroy or remove utterly

UPS *service mark for* United Parcel Service

up′scale′ ***adj.*** of or for people who are affluent, stylish, etc.

up·set (up set′; *for n.,* up′set′) ***vt.*** **-set′**, **-set′ting** **1** *a*) to tip over; overturn *b*) to defeat unexpectedly **2** *a*) to disturb the functioning of [to *upset* a schedule] *b*) to disturb emotionally or physically —***vi.*** to become overturned or upset —***n.*** **1** an upsetting **2** an unexpected victory or defeat **3** a disturbance —***adj.*** **1** tipped over **2** overthrown or defeated **3** disturbed or disordered

up′shot′ ***n.*** ⟦orig., final shot in an archery match⟧ the conclusion; result

up′side′[1] ***prep.*** [Chiefly Dial.] on or against the side of [struck *upside* the head]

up′side′[2] ***n.*** **1** the upper side or part **2** appreciation or gain, as on an investment

upside down **1** with the top side or part underneath or turned over; inverted **2** in disorder —**up′side′-down′** ***adj.***

up·si·lon (o͞op′sə län′, up′-) ***n.*** the twentieth letter of the Greek alphabet (Υ, υ)

up·stage (up′stāj′; *for v.,* up stāj′) ***adv., adj.*** toward or at the rear of a stage —***vt.*** **-staged′**, **-stag′ing** to draw attention away from another, as by moving upstage

up′stairs′ ***adv.*** **1** up the stairs **2** on or to an upper floor or higher level **3** [Inf.] in the mind —***adj.*** on an upper floor —***n.*** an upper floor

up′stand′ing ***adj.*** **1** erect **2** upright in character; honorable

up′start′ ***n.*** one who has recently come into wealth, power, etc., esp. one who is presumptuous, aggressive, etc. —***adj.*** of or like an upstart

up′state′ ***adj., adv.*** in, to, or from the northerly part of a U.S. state

up′stream′ ***adv., adj.*** in the direction against the current of a stream

up′surge′ ***n.*** a surge upward

up′swing′ ***n.*** a swing, trend, or movement upward

up′take′ ***n.*** a taking up —**quick** (or **slow**) **on the uptake** [Inf.] quick (or slow) to comprehend

up′tight′ ***adj.*** [Slang] very tense, nervous, etc.: also **up-tight**

up′-to-date′ ***adj.*** **1** extending to the present time **2** keeping up with what is most recent

up′town′ ***adj., adv.*** in or toward the residential part of a city —***n.*** the uptown section of a city

up·turn′ (-turn′; *for n.,* up′turn′) ***vt., vi.*** to turn up or over —***n.*** an upward turn or trend —**up′turned′** ***adj.***

up′ward ***adv., adj.*** toward a higher place, position, etc.: also **up′wards** ***adv.*** —**upwards** (or **upward**) **of** more than —**up′ward·ly** ***adv.***

upward mobility movement to a higher social and economic status

up′wind′ ***adv., adj.*** in the direction from which the wind is blowing or usually blows

Ur (o͝or, ur) ancient city on the Euphrates River

u·ra·cil (yo͝or′ə sil′) ***n.*** a colorless, crystalline base that is a constituent of RNA

U·ral Mountains (yo͝or′əl) mountain system in Russia, regarded as the boundary between Europe & Asia: also **Urals**

u·ra·ni·um (yo͞o rā′nē əm) ***n.*** ⟦after fol.⟧ a very hard, heavy, silver-colored, radioactive, metallic chemical element: used in work on atomic energy

U·ra·nus (yo͝or′ə nəs, yo͞o rā′nəs) ***n.*** ⟦< Gr *Ouranos,* heaven⟧ the planet seventh in distance from the sun: see PLANET

ur·ban (ur′bən) ***adj.*** ⟦< L *urbs,* city⟧ **1** of, in, or constituting a city **2** characteristic of cities

ur·bane (ur bān′) ***adj.*** ⟦see prec.⟧ polite in a smooth, polished way; refined —**ur·ban′i·ty** (-ban′ə tē) ***n.***

ur·ban·ize (ur′bə nīz′) ***vt.*** **-ized′**, **-iz′ing** to change from rural to urban —**ur′ban·i·za′tion** ***n.***

urban legend (or **myth**) a widely circulating secondhand report of a purportedly true incident

urban renewal rehabilitation of deteriorated urban areas, as by slum clearance and housing construction

urban sprawl the spread of urban congestion into surrounding areas

ur·chin (ur′chin) ***n.*** ⟦< L *ericius,* hedgehog⟧ a small child; esp., a mischievous boy

-ure (ər) ⟦Fr < L *-ura*⟧ *suffix* **1** act, process, or result *[exposure]* **2** agent of **3** state of being ___ed *[composure]* **4** office, rank, or collective body *[legislature]*

u·re·a (yoo rē′ə) ***n.*** ⟦< Gr *ouron*, urine⟧ a soluble, crystalline solid found in urine or made synthetically

u·re·mi·a (yoo rē′mē ə) ***n.*** ⟦< Gr *ouron*, urine + *haima*, blood⟧ a toxic condition caused by the presence in the blood of waste products normally eliminated in the urine —**u·re′mic** ***adj.***

u·re·ter (yoo rēt′ər) ***n.*** ⟦< Gr *ourein*, urinate⟧ a tube carrying urine from a kidney to the bladder

u·re·thane (yoor′ə thān′) ***n.*** ⟦< Fr⟧ a white, crystalline compound used as a hypnotic and sedative, a solvent, etc.

u·re·thra (yoo rē′thrə) ***n.***, *pl.* **-thrae** (-thrē′) or **-thras** ⟦< Gr *ouron*, urine⟧ the duct through which urine is discharged from the bladder: in males, also the duct for semen

urge (urj) ***vt.*** **urged, urg′ing** ⟦L *urgere*, press hard⟧ **1** *a)* to press upon the attention; advocate *b)* to plead with; ask earnestly **2** to incite; provoke **3** to drive or force onward —***n.*** **1** an urging **2** an impulse

ur·gent (ur′jənt) ***adj.*** ⟦see prec.⟧ **1** calling for haste, immediate action, etc. **2** insistent —**ur′gen·cy**, *pl.* **-cies**, ***n.*** —**ur′gent·ly** ***adv.***

-ur·gy (ur′jē) ⟦< Gr *ergon*, work⟧ *combining form* a working with or by means of (something specified) *[chemurgy]*

u·ric (yoor′ik) ***adj.*** of, in, or from urine

u·ri·nal (yoor′ə nəl) ***n.*** **1** a receptacle or fixture for urinating **2** a place for urinating

u·ri·nal·y·sis (yoor′ə nal′ə sis) ***n.***, *pl.* **-ses′** (-sēz′) chemical or microscopic analysis of urine

u·ri·nar·y (yoor′ə ner′ē) ***adj.*** **1** of urine **2** of the organs that secrete and discharge urine

u·ri·nate (yoor′ə nāt′) ***vi.*** **-nat′ed, -nat′ing** to discharge urine from the body —**u′ri·na′tion** ***n.***

u·rine (yoor′in) ***n.*** ⟦< L *urina*⟧ the yellowish liquid, containing waste products, secreted by the kidneys and discharged through the urethra

URL ***n.*** ⟦*u(niform) r(esource) l(ocator)*⟧ an address on the World Wide Web

urn (urn) ***n.*** ⟦< L *urna*⟧ **1** *a)* a vase with a pedestal *b)* such a vase used to hold ashes after cremation **2** a metal container with a faucet, for making or serving hot coffee, tea, etc.

URN

u·ro·gen·i·tal (yoor′ō jen′i təl) ***adj.*** of the urinary and genital organs

u·rol·o·gy (yoo räl′ə jē) ***n.*** ⟦< Gr *ouron*, urine + -LOGY⟧ the branch of medicine dealing with the urinary and genital organs and their diseases —**u·rol′o·gist** ***n.***

Ur·sa Major (ur′sə) ⟦L, lit., Great Bear⟧ a prominent N constellation

Ursa Minor ⟦L, lit., Little Bear⟧ a N constellation, containing Polaris

ur·sine (ur′sīn′, -sin) ***adj.*** ⟦< L *ursus*, a bear⟧ of or like a bear

ur·ti·car·i·a (urt′i ker′ē ə) ***n.*** ⟦< L *urtica*, a nettle⟧ HIVES

U·ru·guay (yoor′ə gwā′, oor′-; -gwī′) country in SE South America: 68,037 sq. mi.; pop. 2,940,000 —**Ur′u·guay′an** ***adj., n.***

us (us) ***pron.*** ⟦OE⟧ *objective form of* WE

US or **U.S.** United States

USA *abbrev.* **1** United States of America: also **U.S.A.** **2** United States Army

us·a·ble or **use·a·ble** (yōō′zə bəl) ***adj.*** that can be used; fit for use —**us′a·bil′i·ty** (-bil′ə tē) or **use′a·bil′i·ty** ***n.***

USAF *abbrev.* United States Air Force

us·age (yōō′sij) ***n.*** **1** the act, way, or extent of using; treatment **2** established practice; custom; habit **3** the way in which a word, phrase, etc. is used to express a particular idea

USCG *abbrev.* United States Coast Guard

USDA *abbrev.* United States Department of Agriculture

use (yōōz; *for n.*, yōōs) ***vt.*** **used, us′ing** ⟦< L *uti*⟧ **1** to put into action or service **2** to exercise *[use your judgment]* **3** to deal with; treat *[to use a friend badly]* **4** to consume, expend: often with *up* **5** to consume habitually *[to use drugs]* **6** to exploit (someone) —***n.*** **1** a using or being used **2** the ability to use **3** the right to use **4** the need or opportunity to use **5** a way of using **6** usefulness **7** the purpose for which something is used **8** function —**used to** (yōōs′tə, -tōō) **1** did at one time *[I used to live here]* **2** accustomed to

used (yōōzd) ***vt.*** *pt. & pp. of* USE —***adj.*** not new; secondhand

use·ful (yōōs′fəl) ***adj.*** that can be used; serviceable; helpful —**use′ful·ly** ***adv.*** —**use′ful·ness** ***n.***

use′less (-lis) ***adj.*** **1** having no use **2** to no purpose —**use′less·ly** ***adv.*** —**use′less·ness** ***n.***

us·er (yōō′zər) ***n.*** one that uses something; specif., one who uses drugs habitually, a computer, etc.

us′er-friend′ly ***adj.*** easy to use or understand: said esp. of computer hardware, programs, etc.

ush·er (ush′ər) ***n.*** ⟦< L *ostiarius*, doorkeeper⟧ **1** one who shows people to their seats in a theater, church, etc. **2** a bridegroom's attendant —***vt.*** **1** to escort (others) to seats, etc. **2** to be a forerunner of: often with *in*

USMC *abbrev.* United States Marine Corps

USN *abbrev.* United States Navy

USO *abbrev.* United Service Organizations

USP *abbrev.* United States Pharmacopoeia

USPS *abbrev.* United States Postal Serv-

USS *abbrev.* United States Ship

USSR or **U.S.S.R.** Union of Soviet Socialist Republics

u·su·al (yōō′zhə wəl) ***adj.*** ⟦see USE⟧ such as is most often seen, used, etc.; common; customary —**u′su·al·ly *adv.***

u·surp (yōō surp′, -zurp′) ***vt., vi.*** ⟦< L *usus,* a use + *rapere,* to seize⟧ to take (power, a position, etc.) by force —**u·sur·pa·tion** (yōō′zər pā′shən, -sər-) ***n.*** —**u·surp′er *n.***

u·su·ry (yōō′zhə rē) ***n., pl.*** **-ries** ⟦see USE⟧ **1** the lending of money at an excessive rate of interest **2** an excessive interest rate —**u′su·rer *n.*** —**u·su·ri·ous** (yōō zhoor′ē əs) ***adj.***

U·tah (yōō′tô′, -tä′) Mountain State of the W U.S.: 82,168 sq. mi.; pop. 1,723,000; cap. Salt Lake City: abbrev. UT —**U′tah′an** or (local usage) **U·tahn** (yōō′tôn′, -tän′) ***adj., n.***

u·ten·sil (yōō ten′səl) ***n.*** ⟦< L *uti,* to use⟧ an implement or container, esp. one for use in a kitchen

u·ter·us (yōōt′ə rəs) ***n., pl.*** **-ter·i′** (-ī′) ⟦L⟧ a hollow organ of female mammals in which the embryo and fetus are developed; womb —**u′ter·ine** (-rin, -rīn′) ***adj.***

u·til·i·tar·i·an (yōō til′ə ter′ē ən) ***adj.*** **1** of or having to do with utility **2** stressing usefulness over beauty or other considerations

u·til′i·tar′i·an·ism′ ***n.*** **1** the doctrine that worth or value is determined solely by utility **2** the doctrine that the purpose of all action should be to bring about the greatest happiness of the greatest number

u·til·i·ty (yōō til′ə tē) ***n., pl.*** **-ties** ⟦< L *uti,* to use⟧ **1** usefulness **2** something useful, as the service to the public of gas, water, etc. **3** a company providing such a service

utility room a room containing laundry appliances, heating equipment, etc.

u·ti·lize (yōōt′′l īz′) ***vt.*** **-lized′, -liz′ing** to put to profitable use; make use of —**u′ti·li·za′tion *n.***

ut·most (ut′mōst′) ***adj.*** ⟦< OE superl. of *ut,* out⟧ **1** farthest **2** of the greatest degree, amount, etc. —***n.*** the most that is possible

U·to·pi·a (yōō tō′pē ə) ***n.*** ⟦< Gr *ou,* not + *topos,* a place⟧ **1** an imaginary island with a perfect political and social system, described in *Utopia* (1516) by Sir Thomas More, Eng. statesman **2** [*often* **u-**] *a*) any idealized place of perfection *b*) any visionary scheme for a perfect society —**U·to′pi·an** or **u·to′pi·an *adj., n.***

ut·ter[1] (ut′ər) ***adj.*** ⟦< OE compar. of *ut,* out⟧ **1** complete; total **2** unqualified; absolute; unconditional —**ut′ter·ly *adv.***

ut·ter[2] (ut′ər) ***vt.*** ⟦< ME *utter,* outward⟧ to speak or express audibly (sounds, words, etc.)

ut′ter·ance *n.* **1** an uttering **2** the power or style of speaking **3** that which is uttered

ut′ter·most′ *adj., n.* UTMOST

U′-turn′ *n.* **1** a turn by a car made so as to head in the opposite direction **2** a reversal of opinion, strategy, etc.

UV or **uv** *abbrev.* ultraviolet

u·vu·la (yōō′vyə lə) ***n., pl.*** **-las** or **-lae′** (-lē′) ⟦< L *uva,* grape⟧ the small, fleshy part hanging down from the soft palate above the back of the tongue —**u′vu·lar *adj.***

ux·o·ri·ous (uk sôr′ē əs, -zôr′-) ***adj.*** ⟦< L < *uxor,* wife⟧ dotingly fond of or submissive to one's wife

Uz·bek·i·stan (ooz bek′i stan′) country in central Asia: formerly a republic of the U.S.S.R.: 172,741 sq. mi.; pop. 19,810,000

U·zi (ōō′zē) *trademark for* a small submachine gun

V

v[1] or **V** (vē) ***n., pl.*** **v's, V's** the 22d letter of the English alphabet

v[2] *abbrev.* **1** ⟦L *vide*⟧ see **2** velocity **3** verb **4** versus **5** volt(s) **6** volume

V[1] (vē) ***n.*** a Roman numeral for 5

V[2] *abbrev.* **1** velocity **2** volt(s) **3** volume

V[3] *Chem. symbol for* vanadium

VA *abbrev.* **1** Veterans Administration **2** Virginia

va·can·cy (vā′kən sē) ***n., pl.*** **-cies** **1** a being vacant **2** empty or vacant space **3** an unoccupied position, office, quarters, etc.

va·cant (vā′kənt) ***adj.*** ⟦< L *vacare,* be empty⟧ **1** having nothing in it **2** not held, occupied, etc., as a seat or house **3** free from work; leisure *[vacant* time*]* **4** without thought, interest, etc.

va′cate′ (-kāt′) ***vt.*** **-cat′ed, -cat′ing** **1** to cause (an office, house, etc.) to be vacant **2** *Law* to make void; annul

va·ca·tion (vā kā′shən, və-) ***n.*** ⟦< L *vacatio*⟧ a period of rest from work, study, etc. —***vi.*** to take one's vacation —**va·ca′tion·er** or **va·ca′tion·ist *n.***

vac·ci·nate (vak′sə nāt′) ***vt., vi.*** **-nat′ed, -nat′ing** to inoculate with a vaccine to prevent disease —**vac′ci·na′tion *n.***

vac·cine (vak sēn′) ***n.*** ⟦< L *vacca,* cow: from use of cowpox virus in smallpox vaccine⟧ any preparation introduced into the body to produce immunity to a specific disease

vac·il·late (vas′ə lāt′) ***vi.*** **-lat′ed, -lat′ing** ⟦< L *vacillare*⟧ **1** to sway to and fro; waver **2** to fluctuate **3** to show indecision —**vac′il·la′tion *n.***

va·cu·i·ty (va kyōō′ə tē) ***n., pl.*** **-ties** ⟦< L *vacuus,* empty⟧ **1** emptiness **2** an empty space **3** emptiness of mind **4** something senseless or silly

vac·u·ous (vak′yōō əs) ***adj.*** ⟦L *vacuus*⟧ **1** empty **2** stupid; senseless —**vac′u·**

ous·ly *adv.*

vac·uum (vak′yo͞om) *n., pl.* **-ums** or **-u·a** (-yo͞o ə) ⟦L⟧ **1** space with nothing at all in it **2** a space from which most of the air or gas has been taken **3** any void —*adj.* **1** of or used to make a vacuum **2** having or working by a vacuum —*vt., vi.* to clean with a vacuum cleaner

vacuum cleaner a machine for cleaning carpets, floors, etc. by suction

vac′uum-packed′ *adj.* packed in an airtight container to maintain freshness

vacuum tube an electron tube from which most of the air has been evacuated, containing one or more grids, used as an amplifier, etc.

vag·a·bond (vag′ə bänd′) *adj.* ⟦< L *vagari,* wander⟧ **1** wandering **2** living a drifting or irresponsible life; shiftless —*n.* **1** one who wanders from place to place **2** a wandering beggar **3** an idle or shiftless person —**vag′a·bond′age** *n.*

va·gar·y (vā′gə rē, və ger′ē) *n., pl.* **-ies** ⟦see prec.⟧ **1** an odd or eccentric action **2** a whimsical or freakish notion; caprice —**va·gar′i·ous** *adj.*

va·gi·na (və jī′nə) *n., pl.* **-nas** or **-nae** (-nē) ⟦L, sheath⟧ in female mammals, the canal from the vulva to the uterus —**vag·i·nal** (vaj′ə nəl) *adj.*

va·grant (vā′grənt) *n.* ⟦prob. < OFr *walcrer,* wander⟧ one who wanders from place to place supporting oneself by begging, etc. —*adj.* **1** nomadic **2** of or like a vagrant **3** wayward, erratic, etc. —**va′gran·cy,** *pl.* **-cies,** *n.*

vague (vāg) *adj.* **va′guer, va′guest** ⟦< L *vagus,* wandering⟧ **1** indefinite in shape or form **2** not sharp, certain, or precise in thought or expression —**vague′ly** *adv.* —**vague′ness** *n.*

vain (vān) *adj.* ⟦< L *vanus,* empty⟧ **1** having no real value; worthless *[vain pomp]* **2** without effect; futile *[a vain endeavor]* **3** having an excessively high regard for one's self, looks, etc.; conceited —**in vain 1** fruitlessly **2** profanely

vain′glo′ry (-glôr′ē) *n.* ⟦< L *vana gloria,* empty boasting⟧ excessive vanity —**vain′glo′ri·ous** *adj.*

val *abbrev.* **1** valuation **2** value

val·ance (val′əns, vā′ləns) *n.* ⟦ME < ?⟧ a short curtain forming a border, esp. across the top of a window

vale (vāl) *n.* [Old Poet.] VALLEY

val·e·dic·to·ri·an (val′ə dik tôr′ē ən) *n.* the student, usually the one with the highest grades, who delivers the valedictory at graduation

val′e·dic′to·ry (-tər ē) *n., pl.* **-ries** ⟦< L *vale,* farewell + *dicere,* to say⟧ a farewell speech, esp. at graduation

va·lence (vā′ləns) *n.* ⟦< L *valere,* be strong⟧ *Chem.* the combining capacity of an element or radical as measured by the number of hydrogen or chlorine atoms which one radical or atom of the element will combine with or replace: also **va′len·cy,** *pl.* **-cies**

Va·len·ci·a (və len′shē ə, -shə) seaport in E Spain: pop. 763,000

val·en·tine (val′ən tīn′) *n.* **1** a sweetheart chosen or greeted on Saint Valentine's Day **2** a greeting card or gift sent on this day

val·et (va lā′; *also, but now rarely* val′it) *n.* ⟦Fr, a groom⟧ **1** a personal manservant who takes care of a man's clothes, helps him dress, etc. **2** an employee, as of a hotel, who cleans or presses clothes, etc.

val·e·tu·di·nar·i·an (val′ə to͞o′də ner′ē ən) *n.* ⟦< L *valetudo,* state of health, sickness⟧ **1** a person in poor health **2** one who worries about one's health

Val·hal·la (val hal′ə, väl häl′ə) *n. Norse Myth.* the great hall where Odin feasts the souls of heroes slain in battle

val·iant (val′yənt) *adj.* ⟦< L *valere,* be strong⟧ brave; courageous —**val′iance** *n.* —**val′iant·ly** *adv.*

val·id (val′id) *adj.* ⟦< L *valere,* be strong⟧ **1** having legal force **2** based on evidence or sound reasoning —**val′id·ly** *adv.* —**val′id·ness** *n.*

val·i·date (val′ə dāt′) *vt.* **-dat′ed, -dat′ing 1** to make legally valid **2** to prove to be valid

va·lid·i·ty (və lid′ə tē) *n., pl.* **-ties** the quality or fact of being valid

va·lise (və lēs′) *n.* ⟦Fr < L *valesium* < ?⟧ [Old-fashioned] a piece of hand luggage

Val·i·um (val′ē əm) *trademark for* a tranquilizing drug

Val·kyr·ie (val kir′ē, val′ki rē) *n. Norse Myth.* any of the maidens of Odin who conduct the souls of heroes slain in battle to Valhalla

val·ley (val′ē) *n., pl.* **-leys** ⟦< L *vallis*⟧ **1** low land lying between hills or mountains **2** the land drained by a river system **3** any valleylike dip

Valley Forge village in SE Pennsylvania: scene of Washington's winter encampment (1777-78)

val·or (val′ər) *n.* ⟦< L *valere,* be strong⟧ courage or bravery: Brit. sp. **val′our** —**val′or·ous** *adj.*

Val·pa·rai·so (val′pə rā′zō, -rī′sō) seaport in central Chile: pop. 277,000

val·u·a·ble (val′yə bəl, -yo͞o ə bəl) *adj.* **1** having value, esp. great monetary value **2** highly important, esteemed, etc. —*n.* an article of value: *usually used in pl.*

val·u·a·tion (val′yo͞o ā′shən) *n.* **1** the determining of the value of anything **2** determined or estimated value

val·ue (val′yo͞o) *n.* ⟦< L *valere* be worth⟧ **1** the worth of a thing in money or goods **2** estimated worth **3** purchasing power **4** that quality of a thing which makes it more or less desirable, useful, etc. **5** a thing or quality having intrinsic worth **6** [*pl.*] beliefs or standards **7** relative duration, intensity, etc. —*vt.* **val′ued, val′u·ing 1** to estimate the value of; appraise **2** to place a certain estimate of worth on *[to value health above wealth]* **3** to think highly of —**val′ue·less** *adj.*

val′ue-add′ed tax a tax based and paid on products, etc. at each stage of production or distribution, and included in the cost to the consumer

val′ued *adj.* highly thought of

value judgment an estimate made of the worth, goodness, etc. of a person, action, etc., esp. when such a judgment is not called for or desired

valve (valv) ***n.*** ⟦< L *valva,* leaf of a folding door⟧ **1** *Anat.* a membranous structure which permits body fluids to flow in one direction only, or opens and closes a tube, etc. **2** any device in a pipe, etc. that regulates the flow by means of a flap, lid, etc. **3** *Music* a device, as in the trumpet, that changes the tube length so as to change the pitch **4** *Zoology* one of the parts making up the shell of a mollusk, clam, etc.

va·moose (va mo͞os′) ***vi., vt.* -moosed′, -moos′ing** ⟦< Sp *vamos,* let us go⟧ [Old Slang] to leave quickly

vamp (vamp) ***n.*** ⟦< OFr *avant,* before + *pié,* foot⟧ **1** the part of a boot or shoe covering the instep **2** *Music* a simple, improvised introduction or interlude —***vi.*** *Music* to play a vamp

vam·pire (vam′pīr′) ***n.*** ⟦< Slavic⟧ **1** in folklore, a reanimated corpse that sucks the blood of sleeping persons **2** one who preys ruthlessly on others

vampire bat a tropical American bat that lives on the blood of animals

van[1] (van) ***n.*** *short for* VANGUARD

van[2] (van) ***n.*** ⟦< CARAVAN⟧ a large, closed truck used as for moving, or a small one used for deliveries, fitted out as an RV, etc.

va·na·di·um (və nā′dē əm) ***n.*** ⟦< ON *Vanadis,* goddess of love⟧ a ductile, metallic chemical element used in steel alloys, etc.

Van Al·len radiation belt (van al′ən) ⟦after J. *Van Allen* (1914-), U.S. physicist⟧ a broad belt of radiation encircling the earth at varying levels

Van Bu·ren (van byoor′ən), **Mar·tin** (märt″n) 1782-1862; 8th president of the U.S. (1837-41)

Van·cou·ver (van ko͞o′vər) seaport in SW British Columbia, Canada: pop. 514,000

Van·dal (van′dəl) ***n.*** **1** a member of a Germanic people that sacked Rome (A.D. 455) **2** [v-] one who maliciously destroys property

van·dal·ize (van′də līz′) ***vt.* -ized′, -iz′ing** to destroy or damage (property) maliciously —**van′dal·ism′** ***n.***

Van·dyke (beard) (van dīk′) a closely trimmed, pointed beard

vane (vān) ***n.*** ⟦< OE *fana,* a flag⟧ **1** a free-swinging piece of metal, etc. that shows which way the wind is blowing; weather vane **2** any of the flat pieces set around an axle and rotated about it by moving air, water, etc. or rotated to move the air or water

van Gogh (van gō′, -gôkh′), **Vin·cent** (vin′sənt) 1853-90; Du. painter

van·guard (van′gärd′) ***n.*** ⟦< OFr *avant,* before + *garde,* guard⟧ **1** the part of an army which goes ahead of the main body **2** the leading position or persons in a movement

va·nil·la (və nil′ə) ***n.*** ⟦< Sp *vaina,* pod⟧ **1** a climbing orchid with podlike capsules (**vanilla beans**) **2** a flavoring made from these capsules —***adj.*** **1** of or flavored with vanilla **2** ⟦in allusion to the commonness of *vanilla* ice cream⟧ [Inf.] bland, plain, or basic

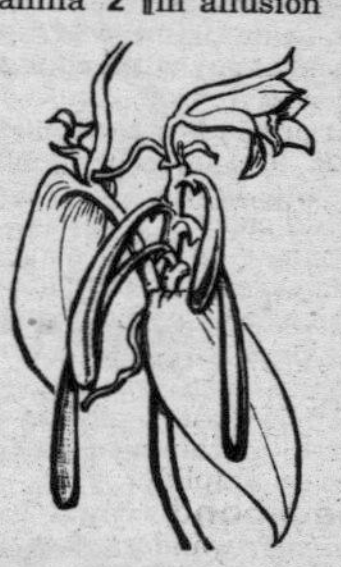

VANILLA PLANT WITH BEANS

van·ish (van′ish) ***vi.*** ⟦see EVANESCENT⟧ **1** to pass suddenly from sight; disappear **2** to cease to exist

van·i·ty (van′ə tē) ***n., pl.* -ties** ⟦< L *vanus,* vain⟧ **1** anything that is vain or futile **2** worthlessness or futility **3** a being vain, or too proud of oneself **4** a small table with a mirror for use while putting on cosmetics, etc. **5** a bathroom cabinet containing a washbowl

vanity case a woman's small traveling case for carrying cosmetics, toilet articles, etc.

van·quish (vaŋ′kwish, van′-) ***vt.*** ⟦< L *vincere*⟧ to conquer or defeat

van·tage (van′tij) ***n.*** ⟦see ADVANTAGE⟧ **1** a favorable position **2** a position allowing a clear view, understanding, etc.: also **vantage point**

Va·nua·tu (van′wä to͞o′) country on a group of islands in the SW Pacific, west of Fiji: 4,706 sq. mi.; pop. 143,000

vap·id (vap′id) ***adj.*** ⟦L *vapidus*⟧ tasteless; dull —**va·pid·i·ty** (va pid′ə tē) or **vap′id·ness** ***n.***

va·por (vā′pər) ***n.*** ⟦L⟧ **1** *a)* visible particles of moisture floating in the air, as fog or steam *b)* smoke, fumes, etc. **2** the gaseous form of any substance normally a liquid or solid Brit. sp. **va′pour**

va′por·ize′ (-pə rīz′) ***vt., vi.* -ized′, -iz′ing** to change into vapor —**va′por·i·za′tion** ***n.*** —**va′por·iz′er** ***n.***

va·por·ous (vā′pər əs) ***adj.*** **1** forming or full of vapor; foggy; misty **2** like vapor

vapor trail CONTRAIL

va·que·ro (vä ker′ō) ***n., pl.* -ros** ⟦Sp < *vaca,* cow⟧ [Southwest] a man who herds cattle; cowboy

var *abbrev.* **1** variant(s) **2** various

var·i·a·ble (ver′ē ə bəl, var′-) ***adj.*** **1** apt to change or vary; changeable, inconstant, etc. **2** that can be changed or varied —***n.*** anything changeable; a thing that varies —**var′i·a·bil′i·ty** ***n.***

var′i·ance (-əns) ***n.*** **1** a varying or being variant **2** degree of change or difference; discrepancy **3** official permission to bypass regulations —**at variance** not in agreement or accord

var′i·ant (-ənt) ***adj.*** varying; different in some way from others of the same kind —***n.*** anything variant, as a different spelling of the same word

var′i·a′tion (-ā′shən) ***n.*** **1** a varying; change in form, extent, etc. **2** the degree of such change **3** a thing somewhat different from another of the same kind **4** *Music* the repetition of a theme with changes in rhythm, key, etc.

var·i·col·ored (ver′i kul′ərd, var′-) ***adj.*** of several or many colors

var·i·cose (var′ə kōs′) ***adj.*** ⟦< L *varix*, enlarged vein⟧ abnormally and irregularly swollen *[varicose* veins*]*

var·ied (ver′ēd, var′-) ***adj.*** **1** of different kinds; various **2** changed; altered

var·i·e·gat·ed (ver′ē ə gāt′id, var′-) ***adj.*** ⟦< L *varius*, various⟧ **1** marked with different colors in spots, streaks, etc. **2** having variety; varied

va·ri·e·tal (və rī′ə təl) ***adj.*** **1** of or being a variety **2** designating a wine named after the kind of grape from which it is made —***n.*** a varietal wine

va·ri′e·ty (-tē) ***n.***, *pl.* **-ties** **1** a being various or varied **2** a different form of some thing, condition, etc.; kind **3** a collection of different things

variety store a retail store selling many small, inexpensive items

var·i·ous (ver′ē əs, var′-) ***adj.*** ⟦L *varius*, diverse⟧ **1** differing one from another; of several kinds **2** several or many —**var′i·ous·ly *adv.***

var·let (vär′lit) ***n.*** ⟦OFr, a page⟧ [Archaic] a scoundrel; knave

var·mint or **var·ment** (vär′mənt) ***n.*** ⟦var. of VERMIN⟧ [Inf. or Dial.] a person or animal regarded as objectionable

var·nish (vär′nish) ***n.*** ⟦< ML *veronix*, resin⟧ **1** a preparation of resinous substances dissolved in oil, alcohol, etc., used to give a hard, glossy surface to wood, metal, etc. **2** this surface **3** a surface smoothness, as of manner —***vt.*** **1** to cover with varnish **2** to make superficially attractive

var·si·ty (vär′sə tē) ***n.***, *pl.* **-ties** ⟦< UNIVERSITY⟧ the main team representing a university, school, etc., as in a sport

var·y (ver′ē, var′ē) ***vt.*** **var′ied, var′y·ing** ⟦< L *varius*, various⟧ **1** to change; alter **2** to make different from one another **3** to give variety to *[*to *vary* one's reading*]* —***vi.*** **1** to undergo change **2** to be different **3** to deviate or depart (*from*)

vas·cu·lar (vas′kyə lər) ***adj.*** ⟦< L *vas*, vessel⟧ of or having vessels or ducts for conveying blood, sap, etc.

vase (vās, vāz) ***n.*** ⟦< L *vas*, vessel⟧ an open container used for decoration, displaying flowers, etc.

vas·ec·to·my (va sek′tə mē) ***n.***, *pl.* **-mies** ⟦< L *vas*, vessel + -ECTOMY⟧ the surgical removal or tying of the duct carrying sperm from the testicle

Vas·e·line (vas′ə lēn′) ⟦< Ger *was*(*ser*), water + Gr *el*(*aion*), oil⟧ *trademark for* petrolatum —***n.*** [v-] petrolatum

vas·o·mo·tor (vas′ō mōt′ər, vā′zō-) ***adj.*** ⟦< L *vas*, vessel + MOTOR⟧ regulating the diameter of blood vessels: said of a nerve, drug, etc.

vas·sal (vas′əl) ***n.*** ⟦< ML *vassus*, servant⟧ **1** under feudalism, one who held land, owing fealty to an overlord **2** a subordinate, servant, slave, etc. —**vas′sal·age** (-ij) ***n.***

vast (vast) ***adj.*** ⟦L *vastus*⟧ very great in size, degree, etc. —**vast′ly *adv.*** —**vast′ness *n.***

vat (vat) ***n.*** ⟦< OE *fæt*, cask⟧ a large container for holding liquids

VAT (vē′ā′tē′, vat) *abbrev.* value-added tax

Vat·i·can (vat′i kən) ***n.*** **1** the papal palace in Vatican City **2** the papal government

Vatican City independent papal state, an enclave in Rome (Italy), including the Vatican: 108 acres or 0.17 sq. mi.; pop. *c.* 1,000

vaude·ville (vôd′vil) ***n.*** ⟦Fr, after *Vau-de-Vire*, a valley in Normandy, famous for convivial songs⟧ a stage show consisting of various acts

GROINED VAULT

vault[1] (vôlt) ***n.*** ⟦< L *volvere*, to roll⟧ **1** an arched roof or ceiling **2** an arched chamber or space **3** a cellar room used for storage **4** a burial chamber **5** a room for the safekeeping of valuables, as in a bank —***vt.*** to cover with, or build as, a vault —***vi.*** to curve like a vault

vault[2] (vôlt) ***vi.***, ***vt.*** ⟦< earlier It *voltare*⟧ to jump over (a barrier), esp. with the hands supported on the barrier or holding a long pole —***n.*** a vaulting —**vault′er *n.***

vault′ing ***adj.*** **1** leaping **2** unduly confident *[vaulting* ambition*]* **3** used in vaulting

vaunt (vônt) ***vi.***, ***n.*** ⟦< L *vanus*, vain⟧ boast —**vaunt′ed *adj.***

VCR ***n.*** VIDEOCASSETTE RECORDER

VD *abbrev.* venereal disease

VDT ***n.*** a video display terminal

-'ve (v, əv) *suffix* have: used in contractions *[we've* seen it*]*

veal (vēl) ***n.*** ⟦< L *vitulus*, calf⟧ the flesh of a young calf, used as food

vec·tor (vek′tər) ***n.*** ⟦< L *vehere*, to carry⟧ **1** an animal that transmits a disease-producing organism **2** *Math. a*) an expression that denotes magnitude and direction, as velocity *b*) a line segment representing such an expression **3** the compass heading of an aircraft, etc.

Ve·da (vā′də, vē′-) ***n.*** ⟦Sans *veda*, knowledge⟧ any of four ancient sacred books of Hinduism —**Ve′dic *adj.***

Veep (vēp) ***n.*** [*sometimes* **v-**] [Inf.] a vice-president

veer (vir) ***vi.***, ***vt.*** ⟦< Fr *virer*, turn around⟧ to change in direction; shift; turn —***n.*** a change of direction

veg·e·ta·ble (vej′tə bəl, vej′ə tə-) ***adj.*** ⟦see VEGETATE⟧ **1** of plants in general **2** of, from, or like edible vegetables —***n.*** **1** any plant, as distinguished from animal or inorganic matter **2** a plant eaten whole or in part, raw or cooked **3** a person thought of as like a vegetable, as a person in a coma

veg·e·tar·i·an (vej′ə ter′ē ən) ***n.*** one who eats no meat —***adj.*** **1** of vegetarians **2** consisting only of vegetables

veg·e·tate (vej′ə tāt′) ***vi.*** **-tat′ed, -tat′ing** ⟦< L *vegere,* quicken⟧ **1** to grow as plants **2** to lead a dull, inactive life —**veg′e·ta′tive** ***adj.***

veg′e·ta′tion (-tā′shən) ***n.*** **1** a vegetating **2** plant life in general

veg·gie (vej′ē) [Slang] ***n.*** **1** a vegetable **2** a vegetarian —***adj.*** vegetarian Also **veg′ie**

ve·he·ment (vē′ə mənt) ***adj.*** ⟦< L *vehere,* carry⟧ **1** violent; impetuous **2** full of intense or strong passion —**ve′he·mence** or **ve′he·men·cy** ***n.*** —**ve′he·ment·ly** ***adv.***

ve·hi·cle (vē′ə kəl) ***n.*** ⟦< L *vehere,* to carry⟧ **1** any device for carrying or conveying persons or objects **2** a means of expressing thoughts, etc. —**ve·hic′u·lar** (-hik′yoo lər) ***adj.***

veil (vāl) ***n.*** ⟦< L *velum,* cloth⟧ **1** a piece of light fabric, as of net, worn, esp. by women, over the face or head **2** anything used to conceal, cover, separate, etc. *[a veil of silence]* **3** a part of a nun's headdress —***vt.*** **1** to cover with a veil **2** to hide or disguise —**take the veil** to become a nun

veiled (vāld) ***adj.*** **1** wearing a veil **2** concealed, hidden, etc. **3** not openly expressed

vein (vān) ***n.*** ⟦< L *vena*⟧ **1** any blood vessel carrying blood to the heart **2** any of the ribs of an insect's wing or of a leaf blade **3** a body of minerals occupying a fissure in rock **4** a lode **5** a streak of a different color, etc., as in marble **6** a distinctive quality in one's character, speech, etc. **7** a mood —***vt.*** to mark as with veins

Vel·cro (vel′krō) *trademark for* a nylon material for fastenings, made up of matching strips with tiny hooks and adhesive pile, that can be easily pressed together or pulled apart —***n.*** [*occas.* **v-**] this material

veld or **veldt** (velt) ***n.*** ⟦Afrik < MDu *veld,* field⟧ in S & E Africa, open, grassy country, with few bushes or trees

vel·lum (vel′əm) ***n.*** ⟦< L *vitulus,* calf⟧ **1** a fine parchment prepared from calfskin, lambskin, etc. used for writing on or for binding books **2** a strong paper made to resemble this

ve·loc·i·ty (və läs′ə tē) ***n.,*** *pl.* **-ties** ⟦< L *velox,* swift⟧ **1** quickness of motion; swiftness **2** rate of change of position, in relation to time; speed

ve·lour or **ve·lours** (və loor′) ***n.,*** *pl.* **-lours′** (-loorz′, -loor′) ⟦Fr < L *villus,* shaggy hair⟧ a fabric with a soft nap like velvet

ve·lum (vē′ləm) ***n.,*** *pl.* **-la** (-lə) ⟦L, a veil⟧ SOFT PALATE

vel·vet (vel′vət) ***n.*** ⟦< L *villus,* shaggy hair⟧ **1** a rich fabric of silk, rayon, etc. with a soft, thick pile **2** anything like velvet in texture —***adj.*** **1** made of velvet **2** like velvet —**vel′vet·y** ***adj.***

vel′vet·een′ (-və tēn′) ***n.*** a cotton cloth with a short, thick pile like velvet

ve·nal (vē′nəl) ***adj.*** ⟦L *venalis,* for sale⟧ open to, or characterized by, bribery or corruption —**ve·nal·i·ty** (vi nal′ə tē) ***n.***

vend (vend) ***vt., vi.*** ⟦< L *venum dare,* offer for sale⟧ to sell (goods) —**ven′dor** or **vend′er** ***n.***

ven·det·ta (ven det′ə) ***n.*** ⟦It < L *vindicta,* vengeance⟧ a bitter feud, as between families

vending machine a coin-operated machine for selling small articles, refreshments, etc.

ve·neer (və nir′) ***vt.*** ⟦< Fr *fournir,* furnish⟧ to cover with a thin layer of more costly material; esp., to cover (wood) with wood of finer quality —***n.*** **1** a thin surface layer, as of fine wood, laid over a base of common material **2** superficial appearance *[a veneer of culture]*

ven·er·a·ble (ven′ər ə bəl) ***adj.*** worthy of respect because of age, dignity, etc. —**ven′er·a·bil′i·ty** ***n.***

ven·er·ate (ven′ər āt′) ***vt.*** **-at′ed, -at′ing** ⟦< L *venerari,* to worship⟧ to look upon with feelings of deep respect; revere —**ven′er·a′tion** ***n.***

ve·ne·re·al (və nir′ē əl) ***adj.*** ⟦< L *venus,* love⟧ **1** of sexual intercourse **2** transmitted by sexual intercourse *[venereal disease]*

Ve·ne·tian (və nē′shən) ***adj.*** of Venice or its people or culture —***n.*** a person born or living in Venice

Venetian blind [*also* **v- b-**] a window blind of thin, horizontal slats that can be set at any angle

Ven·e·zue·la (ven′ə zwā′lə) country in N South America: 352,143 sq. mi.; pop. 19,405,000 —**Ven′e·zue′lan** ***adj., n.***

venge·ance (ven′jəns) ***n.*** ⟦< L *vindicare,* avenge⟧ the return of an injury for an injury, as in retribution; revenge —**with a vengeance** **1** with great force or fury **2** excessively

venge·ful (venj′fəl) ***adj.*** seeking vengeance; vindictive —**venge′ful·ly** ***adv.***

ve·nial (vēn′yəl, vē′nē əl) ***adj.*** ⟦< L *venia,* a grace⟧ that may be forgiven; pardonable *[a venial sin]*

Ven·ice (ven′is) seaport in N Italy built on more than 100 small islands: pop. 306,000

ve·ni·re·man (və nī′rē mən) ***n.,*** *pl.* **-men** (-mən) ⟦< ML *venire facias,* cause to come⟧ one of a group of people from among whom a jury will be selected

ven·i·son (ven′i sən, -zən) ***n.*** ⟦< L *venari,* to hunt⟧ the flesh of a deer, used as food

ven·om (ven′əm) ***n.*** ⟦< L *venenum,* a poison⟧ **1** the poison secreted by some snakes, spiders, etc. **2** malice

ven′om·ous ***adj.*** **1** full of venom; poisonous **2** spiteful; malicious

ve·nous (vē′nəs) ***adj.*** ⟦L *venosus*⟧ **1** of veins **2** designating blood carried in veins

vent[1] (vent) ***n.*** ⟦< L *ventus,* wind⟧ **1** expression; release *[giving vent to emotion]* **2** a small opening to permit passage or escape, as of a gas —*vt.* **1** to make a vent in or for **2** to express; let out

vent[2] (vent) ***n.*** ⟦< L *findere,* to split⟧ a vertical slit in a garment

ven·ti·late (vent''l āt') ***vt.*** **-lat'ed, -lat'ing** ⟦< L *ventus,* wind⟧ **1** to circulate fresh air in (a room, etc.) **2** to provide with an opening for the escape of air, gas, etc. —**ven'ti·la'tion** ***n.***

ven'ti·la'tor ***n.*** an opening or a device used to bring in fresh air and drive out foul air

ven·tral (ven'trəl) ***adj.*** ⟦< L *venter,* belly⟧ of, near, or on the belly

ven·tri·cle (ven'tri kəl) ***n.*** ⟦see prec.⟧ either of the two lower chambers of the heart —**ven·tric'u·lar** (-trik'yə lər) ***adj.***

ven·tril·o·quism (ven tril'ə kwiz'əm) ***n.*** ⟦< L *venter,* belly + *loqui,* speak⟧ the art of speaking so that the voice seems to come from a source other than the speaker —**ven·tril'o·quist** ***n.***

ven·ture (ven'chər) ***n.*** ⟦see ADVENTURE⟧ **1** a risky undertaking, as in business **2** something on which a risk is taken —***vt.*** **-tured, -tur·ing** **1** to expose to danger or chance of loss **2** to express at the risk of criticism *[to venture an opinion]* —***vi.*** to do or go at some risk

ven'ture·some (-səm) ***adj.*** **1** inclined to venture; daring **2** risky; hazardous Also **ven'tur·ous** (-əs)

ven·ue (ven'yo͞o') ***n.*** ⟦< L *venire,* come⟧ **1** *Law a)* the locality in which a cause of action or a crime occurs *b)* the locality in which a jury is drawn and a case is tried **2** the scene of a large gathering for some event

Ve·nus (vē'nəs) ***n.*** **1** the Roman goddess of love and beauty **2** the brightest planet in the solar system: see PLANET

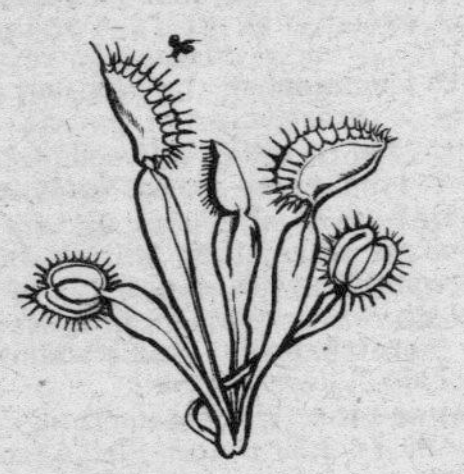

VENUS' FLYTRAP

Venus' fly·trap (flī'trap') a swamp plant with hinged leaves that snap shut, trapping insects

Ve·nu·si·an (vi no͞o'shən) ***adj.*** of the planet Venus —***n.*** an imaginary inhabitant of Venus

ve·ra·cious (və rā'shəs) ***adj.*** ⟦< L *verus,* true⟧ **1** habitually truthful; honest **2** true; accurate

ve·rac·i·ty (və ras'ə tē) ***n.*** **1** honesty **2** accuracy **3** truth

Ver·a·cruz (ver'ə kro͞oz') state of Mexico, on the E coast: 28,114 sq. mi; pop. 6,228,000

ve·ran·da or **ve·ran·dah** (və ran'də) ***n.*** ⟦< Port *varanda,* balcony⟧ an open porch or portico, usually roofed, along the outside of a building

verb (vurb) ***n.*** ⟦L *verbum,* a word⟧ a word expressing action, existence, or occurrence

ver·bal (vur'bəl) ***adj.*** **1** of, in, or by means of words **2** in speech; oral **3** of, like, or derived from a verb —**ver'bal·ly** ***adv.***

ver'bal·ize' ***vi.*** **-ized', -iz'ing** to use words for communication —***vt.*** to express in words —**ver'ba·li·za'tion** ***n.***

verbal noun *Gram.* a noun derived from a verb (Ex.: *swimming* is fun)

ver·ba·tim (vər bāt'əm) ***adv., adj.*** ⟦< L *verbum,* a word⟧ word for word

ver·be·na (vər bē'nə) ***n.*** ⟦L, foliage⟧ an ornamental plant with spikes or clusters of showy red, white, or purplish flowers

ver·bi·age (vur'bē ij') ***n.*** ⟦Fr < L *verbum,* a word⟧ an excess of words; wordiness

ver·bose (vər bōs') ***adj.*** ⟦< L *verbum,* a word⟧ using too many words; wordy —**ver·bos'i·ty** (-bäs'ə tē) ***n.***

ver·dant (vur'dənt) ***adj.*** ⟦prob. VERD(URE) + -ANT⟧ **1** green **2** covered with green vegetation

Ver·di (ver'dē), **Giu·sep·pe** (jo͞o zep'pe) 1813-1901; It. operatic composer

ver·dict (vur'dikt) ***n.*** ⟦< L *vere,* truly + *dictum,* a thing said⟧ **1** the formal finding of a judge or jury **2** any decision or judgment

ver·di·gris (vur'di grēs', -gris) ***n.*** ⟦< OFr *vert de Grece,* lit., green of Greece⟧ a greenish coating that forms on brass, bronze, or copper

ver·dure (vur'jər) ***n.*** ⟦< OFr *verd,* green⟧ **1** the fresh-green color of growing things **2** green vegetation

verge[1] (vurj) ***n.*** ⟦< L *virga,* rod⟧ the edge, brink, or margin (*of* something) —***vi.*** **verged, verg'ing** to be on the verge: usually with *on* or *upon*

verge[2] (vurj) ***vi.*** **verged, verg'ing** ⟦L *vergere,* to bend, turn⟧ **1** to tend or incline (*to* or *toward*) **2** to change or pass gradually (*into*)

verg·er (vur'jər) ***n.*** ⟦ME, ult. < L *virga,* rod⟧ a church caretaker or usher

Ver·gil (vur'jəl) *alt. sp. of* VIRGIL

ver·i·fy (ver'ə fī') ***vt.*** **-fied', -fy'ing** ⟦< L *verus,* true + *-ficare,* -FY⟧ **1** to prove to be true by demonstration, evidence, etc.; confirm **2** to test the accuracy of —**ver'i·fi'a·ble** ***adj.*** —**ver'i·fi·ca'tion** ***n.***

ver·i·ly (ver'ə lē) ***adv.*** [Archaic] truly

ver·i·si·mil·i·tude (ver'ə si mil'ə to͞od') ***n.*** ⟦< L *verus,* true + *similis,* like⟧ the appearance of being true or real

ver·i·ta·ble (ver'i tə bəl) ***adj.*** ⟦see fol.⟧ true; actual

ver·i·ty (ver'ə tē) ***n.*** ⟦< L *verus,* true⟧ **1** truth; reality **2** *pl.* **-ties** a principle, belief, etc. taken to be fundamentally true; a truth

ver·mi·cel·li (vur'mə sel'ē, -chel'ē) ***n.*** ⟦It < L *vermis,* a worm⟧ pasta like thin spaghetti

ver·mic·u·lite (vər mik'yə līt') ***n.*** ⟦< L

vermis, a worm⟧ a hydrous silicate mineral that expands when heated, used as in insulation

ver·mi·form (vʉr′mə fôrm′) ***adj.*** ⟦< L *vermis,* a worm + -FORM⟧ shaped like a worm

vermiform appendix the appendix extending from the cecum of the large intestine

ver·mil·ion (vər mil′yən) ***n.*** ⟦< L *vermis,* a worm⟧ **1** a bright-red pigment **2** a bright red or scarlet

ver·min (vʉr′mən) ***n.,*** *pl.* **-min** ⟦< L *vermis,* a worm⟧ **1** [*pl.*] various destructive insects or small animals regarded as pests, as rats **2** a vile person

Ver·mont (vər mänt′) New England state of the U.S.: 9,249 sq. mi.; pop. 563,000; cap. Montpelier: abbrev. *VT* —**Ver·mont′er** ***n.***

ver·mouth (vər mo͞oth′) ***n.*** ⟦< Ger *wermut,* wormwood⟧ a white fortified wine flavored with herbs, used in cocktails and as an aperitif

ver·nac·u·lar (vər nak′yə lər) ***adj.*** ⟦< L *vernaculus,* indigenous⟧ **1** of, in, or using the native language of a place **2** native to a country —***n.*** **1** the native language or dialect of a country or place **2** the common, everyday language of a people **3** the jargon of a profession or trade

ver·nal (vʉr′nəl) ***adj.*** ⟦< L *ver,* spring⟧ **1** of or in the spring **2** springlike **3** youthful

ver·ni·er (vʉr′nē ər) ***n.*** ⟦after P. *Vernier,* 17th-c. Fr mathematician⟧ a short graduated scale sliding along a longer graduated instrument to indicate parts of divisions: also **vernier scale**

Ver·sailles (vər sī′) city in NC France, near Paris: site of a palace built by Louis XIV: pop. 88,000

ver·sa·tile (vʉr′sə təl) ***adj.*** ⟦< L *vertere,* to turn⟧ competent in many things —**ver′sa·til′i·ty** (-til′ə tē) ***n.***

verse (vʉrs) ***n.*** ⟦< L *vertere,* to turn⟧ **1** a single line of poetry **2** poetry **3** a particular form of poetry **4** a poem **5** a stanza **6** *Bible* any of the short divisions of a chapter

versed (vʉrst) ***adj.*** ⟦< L *versari,* be busy⟧ skilled or learned (*in* a subject)

ver·si·fy (vʉr′sə fī′) ***vi.*** **-fied′, -fy′ing** ⟦< L *versus,* a verse + *facere,* make⟧ to compose verses —***vt.*** **1** to tell about in verse **2** to put into verse form —**ver′si·fi·ca′tion** ***n.*** —**ver′si·fi′er** ***n.***

ver·sion (vʉr′zhən) ***n.*** ⟦see VERSE⟧ **1** a translation, esp. of the Bible **2** an account showing one point of view **3** a particular form of something

ver·sus (vʉr′səs) ***prep.*** ⟦ML < L, toward⟧ **1** against **2** in contrast with

ver·te·bra (vʉr′tə brə) ***n.,*** *pl.* **-brae′** (-brē′, -brā′) or **-bras** ⟦L < *vertere,* to turn⟧ any of the single bones of the spinal column —**ver′te·bral** ***adj.***

ver′te·brate (-brit, -brāt′) ***adj.*** **1** having a backbone, or spinal column **2** of the vertebrates —***n.*** any of a large division of animals having a spinal column, as mammals, birds, etc.

ver·tex (vʉr′teks′) ***n.,*** *pl.* **-tex′es** or **-ti·ces′** (-tə sēz′) ⟦L⟧ **1** the highest point; top **2** *Geom.* the point of intersection of the two sides of an angle

ver·ti·cal (vʉr′ti kəl) ***adj.*** **1** of or at the vertex **2** upright, straight up or down, etc. —***n.*** a vertical line, plane, etc. —**ver′ti·cal·ly** ***adv.***

ver·tig·i·nous (vər tij′ə nəs) ***adj.*** of, having, or causing vertigo

ver·ti·go (vʉr′ti gō′) ***n.*** ⟦L < *vertere,* to turn⟧ a sensation of dizziness

verve (vʉrv) ***n.*** ⟦Fr < OFr, manner of speech⟧ vigor; energy; enthusiasm

ver·y (ver′ē) ***adj.*** ⟦< L *verus,* true⟧ **1** complete; absolute *[*the *very* opposite*]* **2** same *[*the *very* hat I lost*]* **3** being just what is needed **4** actual *[*caught in the *very* act*]*: often an intensive *[*the *very* rafters shook*]* —***adv.*** **1** extremely **2** truly; really *[*the *very* same man*]*

very high frequency any radio frequency between 30 and 300 megahertz

very low frequency any radio frequency between 10 and 30 kilohertz

ves·i·cant (ves′i kənt) ***adj.*** ⟦< L *vesica,* a blister⟧ causing blisters —***n.*** a vesicant agent, as mustard gas used in warfare to blister skin and lungs

ves′i·cle (-kəl) ***n.*** ⟦< L *vesica,* bladder⟧ a small, membranous cavity, sac, or cyst —**ve·sic·u·lar** (və sik′yə lər) or **ve·sic′u·late** (-lit) ***adj.***

ves·pers (ves′pərz) ***n.*** ⟦ult. < L *vespera,* evening⟧ [*often* **V-**] [*usually with sing v.*] an evening prayer or service

Ves·puc·ci (ves po͞ot′chē), **A·me·ri·go** (ä′me rē′gô) (L. name *Americus Vespucius*) 1454-1512; It. navigator & explorer

ves·sel (ves′əl) ***n.*** ⟦< L *vas*⟧ **1** a utensil for holding something, as a bowl, kettle, etc. **2** a boat or ship **3** a tube or duct of the body, containing a fluid

vest (vest) ***n.*** ⟦< L *vestis,* garment⟧ a short, sleeveless garment, esp. one worn under a suit coat by men —***vt.*** **1** to dress, as in clerical robes **2** to place (authority, etc.) in someone **3** to put (a person) in control of, as power, etc. —***vi.*** to pass to a person; become vested (*in* a person), as property

ves·tal (ves′təl) ***adj.*** ⟦< L *Vesta,* goddess of the hearth⟧ chaste; pure —***n.*** a virgin priestess of the Roman goddess Vesta: in full **vestal virgin**

vest·ed (ves′tid) ***adj.*** ⟦pp. of VEST⟧ *Law* fixed; settled; absolute *[*a *vested* right*]*

vested interest **1** an established right, as to some future benefit **2** [*pl.*] groups pursuing selfish goals and exerting controlling influence

ves·ti·bule (ves′tə byo͞ol′) ***n.*** ⟦L *vestibulum*⟧ a small entrance hall, as to a building

ves·tige (ves′tij) ***n.*** ⟦< L *vestigium,* footprint⟧ **1** a trace, mark, or sign, esp. of something that has passed away **2** *Biol.* a degenerate part, more fully developed in an earlier stage —**ves·tig′i·al** (-tij′ē əl, -tij′əl) ***adj.***

vest′ing ***n.*** the retention by an employee of all or part of pension rights

vest·ment (vest′mənt) ***n.*** ⟦< L *vestire,*

clothe⟧ a garment or robe, esp. one worn by a the clergy

vest′-pock′et ***adj.*** very small, or unusually small

ves·try (ves′trē) ***n.***, *pl.* **-tries** ⟦< L *vestis,* garment⟧ **1** a room in a church where vestments, etc. are kept **2** a room in a church, used as a chapel **3** a group of church members managing the temporal affairs of the church

Ve·su·vi·us (və so͞o′vē əs) active volcano in S Italy, near Naples

vet[1] (vet) ***vt.*** to evaluate thoroughly or expertly

vet[2] *abbrev.* **1** veteran **2** veterinarian **3** veterinary

vetch (vech) ***n.*** ⟦< L *vicia*⟧ a leafy, climbing or trailing plant of the pea family, grown for fodder

vet·er·an (vet′ər ən, ve′trən) ***adj.*** ⟦< L *vetus,* old⟧ **1** old and experienced **2** of veterans —***n.*** **1** one who has served in the armed forces **2** one who has served long in some position

Veterans Day a legal holiday in the U.S. honoring all veterans of the armed forces: observed on ARMISTICE DAY

vet·er·i·nar·i·an (vet′ər ə ner′ē ən) ***n.*** one who practices veterinary medicine or surgery

vet′er·i·nar′y (-ē) ***adj.*** ⟦< L *veterina,* beasts of burden⟧ designating or of the branch of medicine dealing with animals —***n.***, *pl.* **-ies** VETERINARIAN

ve·to (vē′tō) ***n.***, *pl.* **-toes** ⟦L, I forbid⟧ **1** *a)* an order prohibiting some act *b)* the power to prohibit action **2** *a)* the power of one branch of government to reject bills passed by another *b)* the exercise of this power —***vt.*** **-toed, -to·ing** **1** to prevent (a bill) from becoming law by a veto **2** to forbid

vex (veks) ***vt.*** ⟦< L *vexare,* agitate⟧ **1** to disturb; annoy, esp. in a petty way **2** to distress; afflict

vex·a·tion (vek sā′shən) ***n.*** **1** a vexing or being vexed **2** something that vexes —**vex·a′tious** ***adj.***

VHF or **vhf** *abbrev.* very high frequency

VHS ⟦*v(ideo) h(ome) s(ystem)*⟧ *trademark for* an electronic system for recording video and audio information on videocassettes

vi *abbrev.* intransitive verb

VI *abbrev.* Virgin Islands: also **V.I.**

vi·a (vī′ə, vē′ə) ***prep.*** ⟦L, way⟧ by way of

vi·a·ble (vī′ə bəl) ***adj.*** ⟦< L *vita,* life⟧ **1** sufficiently developed to be able to live outside the uterus **2** workable *[viable ideas]* —**vi′a·bil′i·ty** ***n.***

vi·a·duct (vī′ə dukt′) ***n.*** ⟦< VIA + (AQUE)DUCT⟧ a bridge consisting of a series of short spans, supported on piers or towers

Vi·ag·ra (vī ag′rə) *trademark for* a compound used to treat erectile dysfunction of the penis

vi·al (vī′əl) ***n.*** ⟦< OFr *fiole*⟧ a small vessel or bottle for liquids

vi·and (vī′ənd) ***n.*** ⟦< L *vivere,* to live⟧ an article of food

vibes (vībz) ***pl.n.*** **1** VIBRAPHONE **2** [Slang] qualities thought of as being like vibrations which produce an emotional reaction in others

vi·brant (vī′brənt) ***adj.*** **1** quivering or vibrating **2** produced by vibration **3** vigorous, vivacious, etc. —**vi′bran·cy** ***n.*** —**vi′brant·ly** ***adv.***

vi·bra·phone (vī′brə fōn′) ***n.*** a musical instrument like the marimba, with electrically operated resonators —**vi′bra·phon′ist** ***n.***

vi·brate (vī′brāt′) ***vt.*** **-brat′ed, -brat′ing** ⟦< L *vibrare*⟧ to set in to-and-fro motion —***vi.*** **1** to swing back and forth; oscillate **2** to move rapidly back and forth; quiver **3** to resound **4** to be emotionally stirred —**vi·bra′tion** ***n.*** —**vi′bra′tor** ***n.***

vi·bra·to (vi brät′ō) ***n.***, *pl.* **-tos** ⟦It⟧ a pulsating effect produced by rapid alternation of a given tone with a barely perceptible variation in pitch

vi·bra·to·ry (vī′brə tôr′ē) ***adj.*** **1** of, like, or causing vibration **2** vibrating or capable of vibrating

vi·bur·num (vī bur′nəm) ***n.*** ⟦L, wayfaring tree⟧ a shrub or small tree with white flowers

vic·ar (vik′ər) ***n.*** ⟦< L *vicis,* a change⟧ **1** *Anglican Ch.* a parish priest receiving a stipend **2** *R.C.Ch.* a church officer acting as a deputy of a bishop

vic′ar·age ***n.*** **1** the residence of a vicar **2** the position or duties of a vicar

vi·car·i·ous (vī ker′ē əs) ***adj.*** ⟦< L *vicarius,* substituted⟧ **1** endured or performed by one person in place of another **2** shared in by imagined participation in another's experience *[a vicarious thrill]* —**vi·car′i·ous·ly** ***adv.***

vice[1] (vīs) ***n.*** ⟦< L *vitium*⟧ **1** *a)* an evil action or habit *b)* evil conduct *c)* prostitution **2** a trivial fault or failing

vi·ce[2] (vī′sē) ***prep.*** ⟦L < *vicis,* a change⟧ in the place of

vice- ⟦see prec.⟧ *prefix* a subordinate; deputy *[vice-president]*

vice·ge·rent (vīs′jir′ənt) ***n.*** ⟦< VICE- + L *gerere,* to direct⟧ a deputy

vice′-pres′i·dent ***n.*** an officer next in rank below a president, acting during the president's absence or incapacity: for the U.S. official, usually **Vice President** —**vice′-pres′i·den·cy** ***n.***

vice·roy (vīs′roi′) ***n.*** ⟦MFr < *vice-* (see VICE-) + *roy,* king⟧ a person ruling a region as the deputy of a sovereign

vi·ce ver·sa (vī′sə vur′sə, vīs′ vur′sə) ⟦L⟧ the relation being reversed

vi·chys·soise (vē′shē swäz′, vish′ē-) ***n.*** a thick, cold soup of potatoes, leeks, and cream

vi·cin·i·ty (və sin′ə tē) ***n.***, *pl.* **-ties** ⟦< L *vicus,* village⟧ **1** nearness; proximity **2** the surrounding area

vi·cious (vish′əs) ***adj.*** ⟦< L *vitium,* vice⟧ **1** characterized by vice; evil or depraved **2** faulty; flawed **3** unruly *[a vicious horse]* **4** malicious; spiteful *[a vicious rumor]* **5** very intense, forceful, etc. *[a vicious blow]* —**vi′cious·ly** ***adv.*** —**vi′cious·ness** ***n.***

vicious circle a situation in which the solution of one problem gives rise to another, eventually bringing back the first problem: also **vicious cycle**

vi·cis·si·tudes (vi sis′ə to͞odz′) ***pl.n.*** ⟦< L *vicis*, a turn⟧ unpredictable changes in life; ups and downs

Vicks·burg (viks′burg′) city in W Mississippi: besieged & captured by Grant in the Civil War (1863): pop. 21,000

vic·tim (vik′təm) ***n.*** ⟦L *victima*⟧ **1** someone or something killed, destroyed, sacrificed, etc. **2** one who suffers some loss, esp. by being swindled

vic′tim·ize′ (-īz′) ***vt.*** **-ized′**, **-iz′ing** to make a victim of

vic·tor (vik′tər) ***n.*** ⟦< L *vincere*, conquer⟧ the winner in a battle, struggle, etc.

Vic·to·ri·a[1] (vik tôr′ē ə) 1819-1901; queen of Great Britain & Ireland (1837-1901)

Vic·to·ri·a[2] (vik tôr′ē ə) capital of British Columbia, Canada: pop. 74,000

Vic·to′ri·an ***adj.*** **1** of or characteristic of the period of the reign of Queen Victoria **2** showing the respectability, prudery, etc. attributed to the Victorians — ***n.*** a person of that time —**Vic·to′ri·an·ism′** ***n.***

vic·to·ri·ous (vik tôr′ē əs) ***adj.*** **1** having won a victory; triumphant **2** of or bringing about victory

vic·to·ry (vik′tər ē, -trē) ***n.***, *pl.* **-ries** ⟦< L *vincere*, conquer⟧ the winning of a battle, war, or any struggle

vict·uals (vit′′lz) ***pl.n.*** ⟦< L *victus*, food⟧ [Inf. or Dial.] articles of food

vi·cu·ña (vī kyo͞o′nyə, -nə) ***n.*** ⟦Sp⟧ **1** a small llama of South America **2** its soft, shaggy wool

vi·de (vī′dē) ***v.*** ⟦L⟧ see; refer to (a certain page, etc.)

vid·e·o (vid′ē ō′) ***adj.*** ⟦L, I see⟧ **1** of television **2** of the picture portion of a telecast **3** of data display on a computer — ***n.***, *pl.* **-os′** **1** TELEVISION **2** *short for* VIDEOCASSETTE, VIDEOTAPE, etc.

vid′e·o·cas·sette′ ***n.*** a cassette of videotape

videocassette recorder a device for recording on and playing back videocassettes: also **vid′e·o·re·cord′er** ***n.***

vid′e·o·con′fer·enc·ing ***n.*** the holding of a conference at several locations by TV

vid′e·o·disc′ ***n.*** a disc on which images and sounds can be recorded for reproduction on a TV set: also **vid′e·o·disk′**

video game any of various games involving images, controlled by players, on a TV screen, computer monitor, etc.

vid′e·o·tape′ ***n.*** a magnetic tape on which images and sounds can be recorded for reproduction on TV —***vt.*** **-taped′**, **-tap′ing** to record on videotape

vie (vī) ***vi.*** **vied**, **vy′ing** ⟦< L *invitare*, invite⟧ to struggle for superiority (*with* someone); compete

Vi·en·na (vē en′ə) capital of Austria: pop. 1,516,000 —**Vi·en·nese** (vē′ə nēz′), *pl.* **-nese′**, ***adj.***, ***n.***

Vi·et·nam (vē′et näm′, -nam′) country on the E coast of Indochina: partitioned into two republics (**North Vietnam** & **South Vietnam**) in 1954, and reunified in 1976 as **Socialist Republic of Vietnam**: 127,246 sq. mi.; pop. 64,412,000 —**Vi′et·nam·ese′** (-nə mēz′), *pl.* **-ese′**, ***adj.***, ***n.***

view (vyo͞o) ***n.*** ⟦< L *videre*, to see⟧ **1** a seeing or looking, as in inspection **2** range of vision **3** mental survey *[a correct view of a situation]* **4** a scene or prospect *[a room with a view]* **5** manner of regarding something; opinion — ***vt.*** **1** to inspect; scrutinize **2** to see; behold **3** to survey mentally; consider —**in view 1** in sight **2** under consideration **3** as a goal or hope —**in view of** because of —**on view** displayed publicly —**with a view to** with the purpose or hope of

view′er ***n.*** **1** one who views something **2** an optical device for individual viewing of slides

view′find′er ***n.*** a camera device for viewing what will appear in the photograph

view′point′ ***n.*** the mental position from which things are viewed and judged; point of view

vig·il (vij′əl) ***n.*** ⟦< L, awake⟧ **1** *a*) a watchful staying awake *b*) a watch kept **2** the eve of a church festival

vig·i·lant (vij′ə lənt) ***adj.*** ⟦< L *vigil*, awake⟧ staying watchful and alert to danger or trouble —**vig′i·lance** ***n.***

vig·i·lan·te (vij′ə lan′tē) ***n.*** ⟦Sp, watchman⟧ one who acts outside the law to punish or avenge a crime —**vig′i·lan′tism′** ***n.*** —**vig′i·lan′tist** ***adj.***

vi·gnette (vin yet′) ***n.*** ⟦Fr < *vigne*, vine⟧ **1** an ornamental design used on a page of a book, etc. **2** a picture shading off gradually at the edges **3** a short literary sketch, scene in a film, etc.

vig·or (vig′ər) ***n.*** ⟦< L *vigere*, be strong⟧ active force or strength; vitality; energy: Brit. sp. **vig′our** —**vig′or·ous** ***adj.*** —**vig′or·ous·ly** ***adv.***

vik·ing (vī′kiŋ) ***n.*** ⟦ON *vikingr*⟧ [*also* **V-**] any of the Scandinavian pirates of the 8th to the 10th c.

vile (vīl) ***adj.*** ⟦< L *vilis*, cheap, base⟧ **1** morally evil; wicked **2** disgusting **3** degrading; mean **4** very bad *[vile weather]* —**vile′ness** ***n.***

vil·i·fy (vil′ə fī′) ***vt***, **-fied′**, **-fy′ing** ⟦see prec. & -FY⟧ to use abusive language about or of; defame —**vil′i·fi·ca′tion** ***n.***

vil·la (vil′ə) ***n.*** ⟦It < L, a farm⟧ a country house or estate, esp. a large one

vil·lage (vil′ij) ***n.*** ⟦see prec.⟧ **1** a community smaller than a town **2** the people of a village, collectively —**vil′lag·er** ***n.***

vil·lain (vil′ən) ***n.*** ⟦< VL *villanus*, a farm servant⟧ a wicked or evil person, or such a character in a play, etc. — **vil′lain·ess** ***fem.n.*** —**vil′lain·ous** ***adj.***

vil′lain·y ***n.***, *pl.* **-ies** **1** wickedness; evil **2** a villainous act

vil·lein (vil′ən) ***n.*** ⟦see VILLAIN⟧ a feudal serf who had become a freeman, except to his lord

vim (vim) ***n.*** ⟦prob. echoic⟧ vigor

vin (van; *E* vin) ***n.*** ⟦Fr⟧ wine

vin·ai·grette (vin′ə gret′) ***n.*** ⟦Fr <

vinaigre, vinegar⟧ a salad dressing of vinegar, oil, etc.

Vinci, Leonardo da *see* DA VINCI, Leonardo

vin·di·cate (vin′də kāt′) ***vt.*** **-cat′ed, -cat′ing** ⟦< L *vis,* force + *dicere,* say⟧ **1** to clear from criticism, blame, etc. **2** to defend against opposition **3** to justify —**vin′di·ca′tion** ***n.*** —**vin′di·ca′tor** ***n.***

vin·dic·tive (vin dik′tiv) ***adj.*** ⟦see prec.⟧ **1** revengeful in spirit **2** said or done in revenge —**vin·dic′tive·ly** ***adv.*** —**vin·dic′tive·ness** ***n.***

vine (vīn) ***n.*** ⟦< L *vinum,* wine⟧ **1** *a*) a plant with a long, thin stem that grows along the ground or climbs a support *b*) the stem of such a plant **2** a grapevine

vin·e·gar (vin′ə gər) ***n.*** ⟦< medieval Fr *vin,* wine + *aigre,* sour⟧ a sour liquid made by fermenting cider, wine, etc. and used as a condiment and preservative —**vin′e·gar·y** ***adj.***

vine·yard (vin′yərd) ***n.*** land devoted to cultivating grapevines

vi·no (vē′nô) ***n.*** ⟦It & Sp⟧ wine

vin ro·sé (rô zā′; *E* rō zā′) ⟦Fr⟧ ROSÉ

vin·tage (vin′tij) ***n.*** ⟦< L *vinum,* wine + *demere,* remove⟧ **1** the grape crop of a single season **2** the wine of a particular region and year **3** the model of a particular period *[a car of prewar vintage]* —***adj.*** **1** of a particular vintage: said of wine **2** representative of the best *[vintage* Hemingway*]* **3** of a past period *[vintage* clothes*]*

vint·ner (vint′nər) ***n.*** ⟦< ME < L *vinum,* wine⟧ one who sells or makes wine

vi·nyl (vī′nəl) ***n.*** ⟦< L *vinum,* wine⟧ any of various compounds polymerized to form resins and plastics (**vinyl plastics**)

vi·ol (vī′əl) ***n.*** ⟦< VL *vitula,* a fiddle⟧ any of an early family of stringed instruments, usually having six strings, frets, and a flat back

vi·o·la (vē ō′lə, vī-) ***n.*** ⟦It⟧ a stringed instrument of the violin family, slightly larger than a violin

vi·o·la·ble (vī′ə lə bəl) ***adj.*** that can be, or is likely to be, violated

vi·o·late (vī′ə lāt′) ***vt.*** **-lat′ed, -lat′ing** ⟦< L *violare,* use violence⟧ **1** to fail to obey or keep (a law, etc.) **2** to rape **3** to desecrate (something sacred) **4** to break in upon; disturb —**vi′o·la′tor** ***n.***

vi′o·la′tion (-lā′shən) ***n.*** a violating or being violated; specif., *a*) infringement, as of a law *b*) rape *c*) desecration of something sacred *d*) disturbance

vi′o·lence (-ləns) ***n.*** ⟦< L *violentus,* violent⟧ **1** physical force used so as to injure **2** powerful force, as of a hurricane **3** harm done by violating rights, etc. **4** a violent act or deed

vi′o·lent ***adj.*** **1** acting with or having great physical force **2** caused by violence **3** furious *[violent* language*]* **4** extreme; intense *[a violent* storm*]* —**vi′o·lent·ly** ***adv.***

vi·o·let (vī′ə lit) ***n.*** ⟦< L *viola*⟧ **1** a plant with white, blue, purple, or yellow flowers **2** a bluish-purple color —***adj.*** bluish-purple

vi·o·lin (vī′ə lin′) ***n.*** ⟦< VIOLA⟧ any of the modern family of four-stringed musical instruments played with a bow; specif., the smallest and highest-pitched one of this family —**vi′o·lin′ist** ***n.***

vi·ol·ist (vī′əl ist; *for 2* vē ō′list) ***n.*** **1** a viol player **2** a viola player

vi·o·lon·cel·lo (vē′ə län chel′ō, vī′ə lən-) ***n.***, *pl.* **-los** CELLO

VIP (vē′ī′pē′) ***n.*** ⟦*v*(*ery*) *i*(*mportant*) *p*(*erson*)⟧ a high-ranking official or important guest

vi·per (vī′pər) ***n.*** ⟦OFr < L *vipera*⟧ **1** a venomous snake **2** a malicious or treacherous person —**vi′per·ous** ***adj.***

vi·ral (vī′rəl) ***adj.*** of or caused by a virus

vir·e·o (vir′ē ō′) ***n.***, *pl.* **-os′** ⟦L, a type of finch⟧ a small American songbird, with olive-green or gray feathers

Vir·gil (vur′jəl) 70-19 B.C.; Rom. poet: author of the *Aeneid*

vir·gin (vur′jən) ***n.*** ⟦< L *virgo,* a maiden⟧ one, esp. a young woman, who has never had sexual intercourse —***adj.*** **1** being a virgin **2** chaste; modest **3** untouched, unused, pure, etc. *[virgin* land*]* —**the Virgin** Mary, the mother of Jesus

vir′gin·al ***adj.*** VIRGIN

Vir·gin·ia (vər jin′yə) state of the S U.S.: 39,598 sq. mi.; pop. 6,187,000; cap. Richmond: abbrev. *VA* —**Vir·gin′i·an** ***adj., n.***

Virginia Beach city in SE Virginia, on the Atlantic: pop. 393,000

Virginia creeper WOODBINE (sense 2)

Virginia reel an American variety of reel danced by couples in two parallel rows

Virgin Islands group of islands in the West Indies, divided between those forming a British territory & those constituting a U.S. territory (**Virgin Islands of the United States**): U.S. part, 134 sq. mi., pop. 102,000

vir·gin·i·ty (vər jin′ə tē) ***n.*** a being a virgin

Virgin Mary Mary, the mother of Jesus

Vir·go (vur′gō′) ***n.*** ⟦L, virgin⟧ the sixth sign of the zodiac

vir·gule (vur′gyōōl′) ***n.*** ⟦< L *virgula,* small rod⟧ a diagonal line (/) used in dates or fractions (3/8) and also standing for "or", "per", etc.

vir·ile (vir′əl) ***adj.*** ⟦< L *vir,* a man⟧ **1** of or characteristic of a man; masculine **2** having manly strength or vigor **3** sexually potent —**vi·ril·i·ty** (və ril′ə tē) ***n.***

vi·rol·o·gy (vī räl′ə jē) ***n.*** ⟦< VIR(US) + -O- + -LOGY⟧ the study of viruses and virus diseases —**vi·rol′o·gist** ***n.***

vir·tu·al (vur′chōō əl) ***adj.*** being so in effect, although not in actual fact or name —**vir′tu·al·ly** ***adv.***

virtual reality computer simulation of three-dimensional images, with which one may seemingly interact using special electronic devices

vir·tue (vur′chōō) ***n.*** ⟦< L *virtus,* worth⟧ **1** general moral excellence **2** a specific moral quality regarded as good **3** chastity **4** *a*) excellence in general *b*) a good quality **5** efficacy, as of a medicine —**by** (or **in**) **virtue of** because of

vir·tu·o·so (vur'choo ō'sō) ***n.**, pl.* **-sos** or **-si** (-sē) ⟦It, skilled⟧ one with great skill in a fine art —**vir'tu·os'i·ty** (-äs'ə tē) ***n.***

vir·tu·ous (vur'choo əs) ***adj.*** **1** having, or characterized by, moral virtue **2** chaste: said of a woman —**vir'tu·ous·ly** ***adv.***

vir·u·lent (vir'yoo lənt, -oo-) ***adj.*** ⟦see fol.⟧ **1** *a)* extremely poisonous *b)* full of hate **2** *Med. a)* violent and rapid in its course *b)* highly infectious —**vir'u·lence** ***n.***

vi·rus (vī'rəs) ***n.*** ⟦L, a poison⟧ **1** a microscopic infectious agent causing various diseases **2** any harmful influence **3** unauthorized, disruptive, spreadable computer program instructions

vi·sa (vē'zə, -sə) ***n.*** ⟦< L *videre,* see⟧ an endorsement on a passport, granting entry into a country

vis·age (viz'ij) ***n.*** ⟦see prec.⟧ **1** the face; countenance **2** aspect; look

vis-à-vis (vē'zə vē') ***adj., adv.*** ⟦Fr⟧ face to face; opposite —***prep.*** **1** opposite to **2** in relation to

vis·cer·a (vis'ər ə) ***pl.n.**, sing.* **vis'cus** (-kəs) ⟦L⟧ the internal organs of the body, as the heart, lungs, intestines, etc.

vis'cer·al ***adj.*** **1** of the viscera **2** intuitive, emotional, etc. rather than intellectual

vis·cid (vis'id) ***adj.*** ⟦< LL *viscidus,* sticky⟧ thick, syrupy, and sticky

vis·cose (vis'kōs') ***n.*** ⟦see VISCID⟧ a syruplike solution of cellulose, used in making rayon and cellophane

vis·cos·i·ty (vis käs'ə tē) ***n.**, pl.* **-ties** **1** a viscous quality **2** *Physics* the resistance of a fluid to flowing freely

vis·count (vī'kount') ***n.*** ⟦see VICE- & COUNT[2]⟧ a nobleman next below an earl or count and above a baron —**vis'count'ess** ***fem.n.***

vis·cous (vis'kəs) ***adj.*** ⟦see VISCID⟧ **1** syrupy; viscid **2** *Physics* having viscosity

vise (vīs) ***n.*** ⟦< L *vitis,* vine, lit., that which winds⟧ a device having two jaws closed by a screw, used for holding firmly an object being worked on

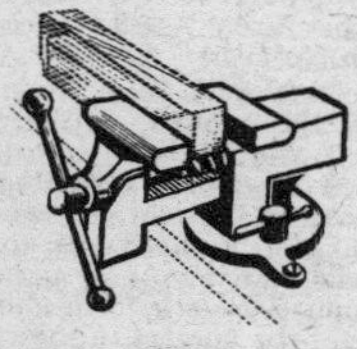

VISE

Vish·nu (vish'noo) ***n.*** a Hindu god, often in human incarnation

vis·i·bil·i·ty (viz'ə bil'ə tē) ***n.**, pl.* **-ties** **1** a being visible **2** *a)* the relative possibility of being seen under the prevailing conditions of distance, light, etc. *[red has good visibility] b)* range of vision

vis·i·ble (viz'ə bəl) ***adj.*** ⟦< L *videre,* to see⟧ **1** that can be seen **2** apparent —**vis'i·bly** ***adv.***

vi·sion (vizh'ən) ***n.*** ⟦see prec.⟧ **1** the power of seeing **2** something seen in a dream, trance, etc., or supernaturally revealed **3** a mental image **4** the ability to perceive or foresee something, as through mental acuteness **5** something or someone of great beauty

vi'sion·ar'y (-er'ē) ***adj.*** **1** seen in a vision **2** not realistic; impractical *[a visionary scheme]* —***n.**, pl.* **-ies** **1** one who sees visions **2** one whose ideas, etc. are impractical

vis·it (viz'it) ***vt.*** ⟦< L *videre,* to see⟧ **1** to go or come to see **2** to stay with as a guest **3** to afflict or trouble —***vi.*** **1** to make a social call **2** [Inf.] to chat —***n.*** **1** a social call **2** a stay as a guest

vis'it·ant ***n.*** a visitor

vis·it·a·tion (viz'ə tā'shən) ***n.*** **1** an official visit, as to inspect **2** a reward or punishment, as sent by God **3** the legal right to visit one's children, as after divorce **4** the visiting of a family in mourning

vis'i·tor ***n.*** a person making a visit

vi·sor (vī'zər) ***n.*** ⟦< OFr *vis,* a face⟧ **1** a part of a helmet that protects the face, often one that can be raised and lowered **2** a projecting brim, as of a cap, for shading the eyes

vis·ta (vis'tə) ***n.*** ⟦< L *videre,* to see⟧ **1** a view, esp. one seen through a long passage **2** a mental view of events

vis·u·al (vizh'oo əl) ***adj.*** ⟦< L *videre,* to see⟧ **1** of or used in seeing **2** based on the use of sight **3** that can be seen; visible

vis'u·al·ize' ***vt., vi.*** **-ized', -iz'ing** to form a mental image of (something not present to the sight) —**vis'u·al·i·za'tion** ***n.***

vi·ta (vīt'ə, vēt'ə) ***n.*** ⟦< *curriculum vitae* < L, course of life⟧ a summary of one's personal history and professional qualifications, as that submitted by a job applicant; résumé

vi·tal (vīt''l) ***adj.*** ⟦< L *vita,* life⟧ **1** of or concerned with life **2** essential to life *[vital organs]* **3** fatal *[a vital wound]* **4** *a)* essential; indispensable *b)* very important **5** full of life; energetic —***n.*** [*pl.*] **1** the vital organs, as the heart, brain, etc. **2** any essential parts —**vi'tal·ly** ***adv.***

vi·tal·i·ty (vī tal'ə tē) ***n.**, pl.* **-ties** **1** power to live **2** power to endure **3** mental or physical vigor

vi·tal·ize (vīt''l īz') ***vt.*** **-ized', -iz'ing** to make vital; give life or vigor to

vital signs the pulse, respiration, and body temperature

vital statistics data on births, deaths, marriages, etc.

vi·ta·min (vīt'ə min) ***n.*** ⟦< L *vita,* life⟧ any of certain complex substances found variously in foods and essential to good health

vitamin A a fat-soluble alcohol found in fish-liver oil, egg yolk, carrots, etc.: a deficiency of this results in imperfect vision in the dark

vitamin B (complex) a group of unrelated water-soluble substances including *a)* **vitamin B₁** (see THIAMINE) *b)* **vitamin B₂** (see RIBOFLAVIN) *c)* NICOTINIC ACID *d)* **vitamin B₁₂**, a vitamin containing cobalt, used in treating anemia

vitamin C a compound occurring in citrus fruits, tomatoes, etc.: a deficiency of this results in scurvy

vitamin D any of several fat-soluble vitamins found in fish-liver oils, milk, etc.: a deficiency of this results in rickets

vitamin E a substance occurring in wheat germ, etc., vital to the reproductive processes in some animals

vitamin K a substance occurring in green vegetables, fish meal, etc., that clots blood

vi·ti·ate (vish′ē āt′) ***vt.*** **-at′ed, -at′ing** ⟦< L *vitium,* a vice⟧ **1** to spoil; corrupt; pervert **2** to invalidate (a contract, etc.) **—vi′ti·a′tion *n.***

vit·re·ous (vi′trē əs) ***adj.*** ⟦< L *vitrum,* glass⟧ **1** of or like glass **2** derived from or made of glass

vitreous humor (or **body**) the transparent, jellylike substance filling the eyeball between the retina and the lens

vit·ri·fy (vi′trə fī′) ***vt., vi.*** **-fied′, -fy′ing** ⟦< L *vitrum,* glass + Fr *-fier,* -FY⟧ to change into glass or a glasslike substance by heat

vit·rine (vi trēn′, vi′trēn′) ***n.*** ⟦see VITREOUS⟧ a glass-paneled cabinet or display case

vit·ri·ol (vi′trē ôl′) ***n.*** ⟦< L *vitreus,* glassy⟧ **1** *a)* any of several sulfates of metals, as of copper (*blue vitriol*) or iron (*green vitriol*) *b)* SULFURIC ACID **2** caustic remarks **—vit′ri·ol′ic** (-äl′ik) ***adj.***

vi·tu·per·ate (vī to͞o′pər āt′, vi-) ***vt.*** **-at′ed, -at′ing** ⟦< L *vitium,* a fault, + *parare,* prepare⟧ to speak abusively to or about **—vi·tu′per·a′tion *n.* —vi·tu′per·a′tive *adj.***

vi·va (vē′vä) ***v.impersonal*** ⟦It & Sp⟧ long live (someone specified)!

vi·va·ce (vē vä′chā) ***adj., adv.*** ⟦It⟧ *Music* in a lively, spirited manner: also written ***vivace***

vi·va·cious (vī vā′shəs, vi-) ***adj.*** ⟦< L *vivere,* to live⟧ full of animation; lively **—vi·va′cious·ly *adv.* —vi·vac′i·ty** (-vas′ə tē) or **vi·va′cious·ness *n.***

vive (vēv) ***v.impersonal*** ⟦Fr⟧ long live (someone specified)!

viv·id (viv′id) ***adj.*** ⟦< L *vivere,* to live⟧ **1** full of life **2** intense: said as of colors **3** active; daring *[a vivid imagination]* **—viv′id·ly *adv.* —viv′id·ness *n.***

viv·i·fy (viv′ə fī′) ***vt.*** **-fied′, -fy′ing** ⟦< L *vivus,* alive + *facere,* make⟧ to give life to

vi·vip·a·rous (vī vip′ər əs) ***adj.*** ⟦< L *vivus,* alive + *parere,* produce⟧ bearing living young, instead of laying eggs

viv·i·sec·tion (viv′ə sek′shən) ***n.*** ⟦< L *vivus,* alive + SECTION⟧ surgery performed on a living animal in medical research **—viv′i·sec′tion·ist *n.***

vix·en (vik′sən) ***n.*** ⟦OE *fyxe,* female fox⟧ **1** a female fox **2** a shrewish or malicious woman

Vi·yel·la (vī yəl′ə) ⟦arbitrary coinage⟧ *trademark for* a fabric like flannel, a blend of lamb's wool and cotton

viz. or **viz** *abbrev.* ⟦< L *videlicet*⟧ that is; namely

vi·zier (vi zir′, viz′yər) ***n.*** ⟦< Ar *wazara,* bear a burden⟧ a high government official in the Turkish empire (*c.* 1300-1918): also sp. **vi·zir′**

viz·or (vī′zər) ***n.*** *alt. sp. of* VISOR

VLF or **vlf** *abbrev.* very low frequency

vo·cab·u·lar·y (vō kab′yə ler′ē) ***n., pl.*** **-ies** ⟦ult. < L *vocare,* to call⟧ **1** a list of words, etc. as in a dictionary or glossary **2** all the words used in a language or by a person, group, etc.

vo·cal (vō′kəl) ***adj.*** ⟦< L *vox,* voice⟧ **1** of or produced by the voice **2** sung **3** capable of making oral sounds **4** speaking freely **—vo′cal·ly *adv.***

vocal cords membranous folds in the larynx that vibrate to produce voice sounds

vo·cal·ic (vō kal′ik) ***adj.*** of, like, or involving a vowel or vowels

vo·cal·ist (vō′kəl ist) ***n.*** a singer

vo′cal·ize′ *vt., vi.* **-ized′, -iz′ing** to speak or sing

vo·ca·tion (vō kā′shən) ***n.*** ⟦< L *vocare,* to call⟧ **1** the career to which one feels one is called **2** any trade or occupation

vo·ca′tion·al *adj.* **1** of a vocation **2** designating or of training, etc. for an occupation or trade

voc·a·tive (väk′ə tiv) ***n.*** ⟦see VOCATION⟧ *Gram.* a case indicating the person or thing addressed

vo·cif·er·ate (vō sif′ər āt′) ***vt., vi.*** **-at′ed, -at′ing** ⟦< L *vox,* voice + *ferre,* to bear⟧ to shout loudly; clamor **—vo·cif′er·a′tion *n.***

vo·cif·er·ous (vō sif′ər əs) ***adj.*** noisy; clamorous

vod·ka (väd′kə) ***n.*** ⟦Russ < *voda,* water⟧ a colorless alcoholic liquor distilled from rye, wheat, etc.

vo-ed (vō′ed′) ***adj., n.*** [Inf.] (of) vocational education

vogue (vōg) ***n.*** ⟦Fr⟧ **1** the current fashion **2** popularity **—*adj.*** in vogue: also **vogu·ish** (vō′gish)

voice (vois) ***n.*** ⟦< L *vox*⟧ **1** sound made through the mouth, esp. by human beings **2** the ability to make such sounds **3** anything regarded as like vocal utterance **4** an expressed wish, opinion, etc. **5** the right to express one's wish, etc.; vote **6** utterance or expression **7** a verb form showing the relation of the subject to the action: see ACTIVE (*adj.* 4), PASSIVE (*adj.* 3) **8** singing ability **—*vt.*** **voiced, voic′ing** to give utterance or expression to **—with one voice** unanimously **—voice′less *adj.***

voice box LARYNX

voice mail **1** an electronic system whereby voice messages can be recorded, stored, and then delivered **2** such messages

voice′-o′ver *n.* the voice of an unseen announcer or narrator, as on TV

void (void) ***adj.*** ⟦< L *vacare,* be empty⟧ **1**

containing nothing **2** devoid (*of*) *[void of common sense]* **3** ineffective; useless **4** of no legal force —***n.*** **1** an empty space **2** a feeling of emptiness —***vt.*** **1** to empty **2** to make void; annul —**void′a·ble** ***adj.***

voi·là (vwȧ lȧ′) ***interj.*** ⟦Fr⟧ behold; there it is

voile (voil) ***n.*** ⟦Fr, a veil⟧ a thin fabric, as of cotton

vol *abbrev.* volume

vol·a·tile (väl′ə təl) ***adj.*** ⟦< L *volare,* to fly⟧ **1** evaporating quickly **2** *a)* unstable; explosive *b)* fickle —**vol′a·til′i·ty** (-til′ə tē) ***n.*** —**vol′a·til·ize′** (-īz′), **-ized′**, **-iz′ing**, ***vt., vi.***

vol·can·ic (väl kan′ik, vôl-) ***adj.*** **1** of or caused by a volcano **2** like a volcano; violently explosive

vol·ca·no (väl kā′nō, vôl-) ***n.***, *pl.* **-noes** or **-nos** ⟦< L *Volcanus,* Vulcan⟧ **1** a vent in the earth's crust through which molten rock, ashes, etc. are ejected **2** a cone-shaped mountain of this material built up around the vent

vole (vōl) ***n.*** ⟦< earlier *vole mouse* < Scand, as in ON *vǫllr,* meadow⟧ any of various small rodents with a stout body and short tail

Vol·ga (väl′gə, vōl′-) river in European Russia, flowing into the Caspian Sea

vo·li·tion (vō lish′ən) ***n.*** ⟦ult. < L *velle,* be willing⟧ the act or power of using the will —**vo·li′tion·al** ***adj.***

vol·ley (väl′ē) ***n.***, *pl.* **-leys** ⟦< L *volare,* to fly⟧ **1** *a)* the simultaneous discharge of a number of weapons *b)* the bullets, etc., so discharged **2** a burst of words or acts **3** *Sports a)* a returning of a ball, etc. before it touches the ground *b)* an extended exchange of shots, as in tennis —***vt., vi.*** **-leyed**, **-ley·ing** **1** to discharge or be discharged as in a volley **2** *Sports* to return (the ball, etc.) as a volley

vol′ley·ball′ ***n.*** **1** a team game played by hitting a large, light, inflated ball back and forth over a net with the hands **2** this ball

volt (vōlt) ***n.*** ⟦after A. *Volta* (1745-1827), It physicist⟧ the basic unit of electromotive force

volt·age (vōl′tij) ***n.*** electromotive force expressed in volts

vol·ta·ic (väl tā′ik) ***adj.*** of or by electricity produced by chemical action

Vol·taire (vōl ter′) 1694-1778; Fr. writer & philosopher

volt′me′ter ***n.*** an instrument for measuring voltage

vol·u·ble (väl′yə bəl) ***adj.*** ⟦< L *volvere,* to roll⟧ characterized by a great flow of words; talkative —**vol′u·bil′i·ty** ***n.*** —**vol′u·bly** ***adv.***

vol·ume (väl′yo͞om) ***n.*** ⟦< L *volumen,* a scroll⟧ **1** *a)* a book *b)* one of a set of books **2** the amount of space occupied in three dimensions **3** *a)* a quantity, bulk, or amount *b)* a large quantity **4** the loudness of sound

vo·lu·mi·nous (və lo͞om′ə nəs) ***adj.*** **1** producing or consisting of enough to fill volumes **2** large; bulky; full —**vo·lu′mi·nous·ly** ***adv.***

vol·un·ta·rism (väl′ən tər iz′əm) ***n.*** (system of) voluntary participation in a course of action

vol′un·tar′y (-ter′ē) ***adj.*** ⟦< L *voluntas,* free will⟧ **1** brought about by one's own free choice **2** acting of one's own accord **3** intentional **4** controlled by one's mind or will —**vol′un·tar′i·ly** ***adv.***

vol·un·teer (väl′ən tir′) ***n.*** one who chooses freely to do something, as entering military service —***adj.*** **1** serving as a volunteer **2** of a volunteer or volunteers —***vt.*** to offer or give of one's own free will —***vi.*** to offer to enter into any service of one's own free will

vo·lup·tu·ar·y (və lup′cho͞o er′ē) ***n.***, *pl.* **-ar′ies** ⟦< L *voluptas,* pleasure⟧ one devoted to sensual pleasures

vo·lup′tu·ous (-cho͞o əs) ***adj.*** full of, producing, or fond of sensual pleasures —**vo·lup′tu·ous·ness** ***n.***

vo·lute (və lo͞ot′) ***n.*** ⟦< L *volvere,* to roll⟧ a spiral or whorl

vom·it (väm′it) ***n.*** ⟦< L *vomere,* to vomit⟧ matter ejected from the stomach through the mouth —***vt., vi.*** **1** to eject (the contents of the stomach) through the mouth; throw up **2** to discharge or be discharged with force —**vom′i·tous** (-ə təs) ***adj.***

voo·doo (vo͞o′do͞o′) ***n.***, *pl.* **-doos′** ⟦of WAfr orig.⟧ a religion of the West Indies, based on a belief in magic, charms, etc. —***adj.*** of or resembling voodoo

vo·ra·cious (vô rā′shəs) ***adj.*** ⟦< L *vorare,* devour⟧ **1** greedy in eating; ravenous **2** very eager *[a voracious reader]* —**vo·rac′i·ty** (-ras′ə tē) ***n.***

vor·tex (vôr′teks′) ***n.***, *pl.* **-tex′es** or **-ti·ces′** (-tə sēz′) ⟦< L *vertere,* to turn⟧ **1** a whirlpool **2** a whirlwind **3** anything like a whirlwind, etc. in effect

vo·ta·ry (vōt′ə rē) ***n.***, *pl.* **-ries** ⟦< L *vovere,* to vow⟧ **1** one bound by a vow, esp. by religious vows, as a monk or nun **2** one devoted to a cause, study, etc.

vote (vōt) ***n.*** ⟦< L *votum,* a vow⟧ **1** a decision on a proposal, etc., or a choice between candidates for office **2** *a)* the expression of such a decision or choice *b)* the ballot, etc. by which it is expressed **3** the right to vote **4** votes collectively —***vi.*** **vot′ed**, **vot′ing** to give or cast a vote —***vt.*** to decide or enact by vote —**vot′er** ***n.***

vo·tive (vōt′iv) ***adj.*** ⟦see prec.⟧ designed to fulfill a promise, express devotion, etc.

vouch (vouch) ***vi.*** ⟦< L *vocare,* to call⟧ to give, or serve as, assurance, a guarantee, etc. (*for*) *[to vouch for someone's honesty]*

vouch′er ***n.*** **1** one who vouches **2** a paper serving as evidence or proof; specif., a receipt

vouch·safe (vouch sāf′) ***vt.*** **-safed′**, **-saf′ing** ⟦< ME *vouchen safe,* vouch as safe⟧ to be kind enough to give or grant

vow (vou) ***n.*** ⟦< L *votum*⟧ **1** a solemn promise, esp. one made to God **2** a promise of love and fidelity *[marriage* *vows]* —**vt.** to promise or declare solemnly —**vi.** to make a vow —**take vows** to enter a religious order

vow·el (vou′əl) **n.** ⟦< L *vocalis,* vocal⟧ **1** a speech sound in which the air passes in a continuous stream through the open mouth **2** a letter representing such a sound, as *a, e, i, o,* or *u*

voy·age (voi′ij) **n.** ⟦< L *via,* way⟧ a relatively long journey by ship or spacecraft —**vi. -aged, -ag·ing** to make a voyage —**voy′ag·er n.**

voy·eur (voi ʉr′, vwä yʉr′) **n.** ⟦< L *videre,* see⟧ one who has an exaggerated interest in viewing sexual objects or activities —**voy·eur′ism′ n.** —**voy′eur·is′tic adj.**

VP *abbrev.* Vice-President

vs. or **vs** *abbrev.* versus

vt *abbrev.* transitive verb

VT Vermont

Vul·can (vul′kən) **n.** the Roman god of fire and of metalworking

vul·can·ize (vul′kən īz′) **vt. -ized′, -iz′ing** to treat (crude rubber) with sulfur under heat to make it stronger and more elastic —**vul′can·i·za′tion n.**

Vulg *abbrev.* Vulgate

vul·gar (vul′gər) **adj.** ⟦< L *vulgus,* common people⟧ **1** of people in general; popular **2** vernacular **3** lacking culture, taste, etc.; crude; boorish **4** indecent or obscene —**vul′gar·ly adv.**

vul·gar′i·an (-ger′ē ən) **n.** a rich person with coarse, showy tastes

vul′gar·ism′ (-gər iz′əm) **n.** **1** a word, phrase, etc. used widely but regarded as nonstandard, coarse, or obscene **2** vulgarity

vul·gar′i·ty (-ger′ə tē) **n.** **1** a being vulgar **2** *pl.* **-ties** a vulgar act, habit, usage in speech, etc.

vul′gar·ize′ (-gər īz′) **vt. -ized′, -iz′ing** **1** to popularize **2** to make vulgar, coarse, obscene, etc. —**vul′gar·i·za′tion n.**

Vulgar Latin the everyday Latin spoken by ancient Romans as distinguished from standard written Latin

Vul·gate (vul′gāt′) **n.** ⟦ML *vulgata (editio),* popular (edition)⟧ a Latin version of the Bible, used in the Roman Catholic Church

vul·ner·a·ble (vul′nər ə bəl) **adj.** ⟦< L *vulnus,* a wound⟧ **1** that can be wounded or injured **2** open to, or easily hurt by, criticism or attack **3** affected by a specified influence, temptation, etc. —**vul′ner·a·bil′i·ty n.** —**vul′ner·a·bly adv.**

vul·pine (vul′pīn) **adj.** ⟦< L *vulpes,* a fox⟧ of or like a fox; cunning

vul·ture (vul′chər) **n.** ⟦< L, akin to *vellere,* to tear⟧ **1** a large bird that lives chiefly on carrion **2** a greedy, ruthless person

vul·va (vul′və) **n.,** *pl.* **-vae** (-vē) or **-vas** ⟦L, womb⟧ the external genital organs of the female

vy·ing (vī′iŋ) **adj.** that vies; competing

W

w[1] or **W** (dub′əl yo͞o′) **n.,** *pl.* **w's, W's** the 23d letter of the English alphabet

w[2] *abbrev.* **1** waist **2** watt(s) **3** week(s) **4** weight **5** west(ern) **6** wide **7** width **8** wife **9** with **10** win(s)

W[1] *abbrev.* **1** watt(s) **2** Wednesday **3** west(ern) **4** win(s)

W[2] ⟦*w*(*olfram*), alt. name of tungsten⟧ *Chem. symbol for* tungsten

WA Washington (state)

Wac (wak) **n.** a member of the Women's Army Corps (**WAC**)

wack·o (wak′ō) [Slang] **adj.** *var. of* WACKY —**n.,** *pl.* **-os** one who is wacko

wack·y (wak′ē) **adj. -i·er, -i·est** ⟦< ?⟧ [Slang] erratic, eccentric, or irrational —**wack′i·ness n.**

wad (wäd) **n.** ⟦ML *wadda,* wadding⟧ **1** a small, soft mass, as of cotton or paper **2** a lump or small, firm mass —**vt. wad′ded, wad′ding** **1** to compress, or roll up, into a wad **2** to plug or stuff with a wad or wadding

wad′ding n. any soft material for use in padding, packing, etc.

wad·dle (wäd′əl) **vi. -dled, -dling** ⟦< fol.⟧ to walk with short steps, swaying from side to side, as a duck does —**n.** a waddling gait

wade (wād) **vi. wad′ed, wad′ing** ⟦OE *waden,* go⟧ **1** to walk through any resisting substance, as water, mud, etc. **2** to proceed with difficulty *[to wade through a dull book]* **3** [Inf.] to attack with vigor: with *in* or *into* —**vt.** to cross by wading

wad′er n. **1** one that wades **2** [*pl.*] *a)* high waterproof boots *b)* waterproof overalls with bootlike parts for the feet

wa·di (wä′dē) **n.,** *pl.* **-dis** or **-dies** ⟦Ar *wādī*⟧ in Arabia, N Africa, etc., a ravine or watercourse that is usually dry

wading bird any long-legged bird that wades the shallows and marshes for food

wa·fer (wā′fər) **n.** ⟦< MDu *wafel*⟧ **1** a thin, flat, crisp cracker or cookie **2** any disklike thing resembling this

waf·fle[1] (wä′fəl) **n.** ⟦see prec.⟧ a crisp batter cake baked in a waffle iron

waf·fle[2] (wä′fəl) **vi. -fled, -fling** ⟦< echoic *waff,* to yelp⟧ to speak or write in a wordy or vague way

waffle iron a utensil with two flat, studded plates pressed together to bake a waffle

waft (wäft, waft) **vt., vi.** ⟦< Du *wachter,* watcher⟧ to carry (sounds, odors, etc.) lightly through the air or over water or to move in this way —**n.** **1** an odor, sound, etc. carried through the air **2** a gust of wind **3** a wafting movement

wag[1] (wag) ***vt.***, ***vi.*** **wagged**, **wag′ging** ⟦ME *waggen*⟧ to move rapidly back and forth, up and down, etc. —***n.*** a wagging

wag[2] (wag) ***n.*** ⟦prob. < obs. *waghalter*, joker⟧ a comical person; wit —**wag′ger·y**, *pl.* **-ies**, ***n.***

wage (wāj) ***vt.*** **waged**, **wag′ing** ⟦< OFr *gage*, a pledge⟧ to engage in or carry on (a war, etc.) —***n.*** **1** [*often pl.*] money paid for work done **2** [*usually pl.*] what is given in return

wa·ger (wā′jər) ***n.*** ⟦see prec.⟧ a bet —***vt.***, ***vi.*** to bet

wag·gish (wag′ish) ***adj.*** **1** of or like a wag; roguishly merry **2** playful; jesting

wag·gle (wag′əl) ***vt.***, ***vi.*** **-gled**, **-gling** ⟦< WAG[1]⟧ to wag, esp. with short, quick movements —***n.*** a waggling —**wag′gly** ***adj.***

Wag·ner (väg′nər), **Rich·ard** (riH′ärt) 1813-83; Ger. composer

wag·on (wag′ən) ***n.*** ⟦Du *wagen*⟧ **1** a four-wheeled vehicle, esp. one for hauling heavy loads **2** *short for* STATION WAGON —**on** (or **off**) **the wagon** [Slang] no longer (or once again) drinking alcohol

waif (wāf) ***n.*** ⟦< NormFr⟧ a homeless person, esp. a child

wail (wāl) ***vi.*** ⟦< ON *væ*, woe⟧ to make a long, loud, sad cry, as in grief or pain —***n.*** such a cry

wain (wān) ***n.*** ⟦OE *wægn*⟧ [Old Poet.] a wagon

wain·scot (wān′skät′, -skət) ***n.*** ⟦< MDu *wagenschot*⟧ a wood paneling on the walls of a room, sometimes on the lower part only —***vt.*** **-scot′ed** or **-scot′ted**, **-scot′ing** or **-scot′ting** to line (a wall) with wood, etc.

wain′scot′ing or **wain′scot′ting** ***n.*** **1** WAINSCOT **2** material used to wainscot

wain·wright (wān′rīt′) ***n.*** ⟦WAIN + WRIGHT⟧ one who builds or repairs wagons

waist (wāst) ***n.*** ⟦< OE *weaxan*, grow⟧ **1** the part of the body between the ribs and the hips **2** the part of a garment that covers the body from the shoulders to the waistline **3** the narrow part of any object that is wider at the ends

waist′band′ ***n.*** a band encircling the waist, as on slacks or a skirt

waist·coat (wes′kət, wāst′kōt′) ***n.*** [Brit.] a man's vest

waist′line′ ***n.*** (the circumference of) the narrowest part of the waist

wait (wāt) ***vi.*** ⟦< NormFr *waitier*⟧ **1** to remain (until something expected happens) **2** to be ready **3** to remain undone *[it can wait]* **4** to serve food at a meal: with *at* or *on* —***vt.*** **1** to await **2** [Inf.] to delay serving (a meal) —***n.*** an act or period of waiting —**lie in wait** (**for**) to wait so as to catch after planning a trap (*for*) —**wait on** (or **upon**) **1** to act as a servant to **2** to serve (a customer) —**wait table** to serve food to people at a table —**wait up** to delay going to bed until someone arrives, etc.

wait′er ***n.*** one who waits; esp., a man who waits on tables, as in a restaurant

wait′ing ***adj.*** **1** that waits **2** of or for a wait —***n.*** the act of one that waits —**in waiting** in attendance, as on a king

waiting game a scheme by which one wins out over another by delaying action until one has an advantage

waiting list a list of applicants, in the order of their application

waiting room a room in which people wait, as in a bus station or doctor's office

wait′per′son ***n.*** a waiter or waitress

wait·ress (wā′tris) ***n.*** a woman who waits on tables, as in a restaurant

waive (wāv) ***vt.*** **waived**, **waiv′ing** ⟦< ON *veifa*, fluctuate⟧ **1** to give up or forgo (a right, etc.) **2** to postpone; defer

waiv·er (wā′vər) ***n.*** *Law* a waiving of a right, claim, etc.

wake[1] (wāk) ***vi.*** **woke** or **waked**, **waked** or **wok′en**, **wak′ing** ⟦< OE *wacian*, be awake & *wacan*, arise⟧ **1** to come out of sleep; awake: often with *up* **2** to stay awake **3** to become active: often with *up* **4** to become alert (*to* a realization, etc.) —***vt.*** **1** to cause to wake: often with *up* **2** to arouse (passions, etc.) —***n.*** a time set aside for viewing a corpse before burial

wake[2] (wāk) ***n.*** ⟦< ON *vök*, hole⟧ **1** the track left in water by a moving ship **2** the track or course of anything —**in the wake of** following closely

wake′ful ***adj.*** **1** alert; watchful **2** unable to sleep —**wake′ful·ness** ***n.***

wak·en (wā′kən) ***vi.***, ***vt.*** to awake

Wal·dorf salad (wôl′dôrf′) ⟦after the old *Waldorf*-Astoria Hotel in New York City⟧ a salad made of diced raw apples, celery, and walnuts, with mayonnaise

wale (wāl) ***n.*** ⟦OE *walu*, weal⟧ **1** a welt raised by a whip, etc. **2** a ridge on the surface of cloth, as corduroy

Wales (wālz) division of the United Kingdom: a peninsula of WC Great Britain: 8,018 sq. mi.; pop. 2,812,000

walk (wôk) ***vi.*** ⟦OE *wealcan*, to roll⟧ **1** to go on foot at a moderate pace **2** to follow a certain course *[walk in the ways of peace]* **3** *Baseball* to go to first base after the pitching of four balls (see BALL[1], *n.* 6) —***vt.*** **1** to go over, along, etc. on foot **2** to cause (a dog, etc.) to walk, as for exercise **3** to accompany on a walk or stroll *[to walk a friend home]* **4** *Baseball* to advance (a batter) to first base by pitching four balls (see BALL[1], *n.* 6) —***n.*** **1** the act of walking **2** a stroll or hike **3** a distance walked *[an hour's walk]* **4** a sphere of activity, occupation, etc. *[people from all walks of life]* **5** a path for walking **6** *Baseball* the walking of a batter —**walk** (**all**) **over** [Inf.] to domineer over —**walk away** (or **off**) **with** **1** to steal **2** to win easily —**walk out** to go on strike —**walk out on** [Inf.] to desert; abandon

walk′a·way′ ***n.*** an easily won victory

walk′er ***n.*** **1** one that walks **2** a tubular frame with wheels used by babies who are learning to walk **3** a framework used as a support in walking, as by the lame

walk·ie-talk·ie (wôk′ē tôk′ē) ***n.*** a compact, portable radio transmitter and receiver

walking stick a stick for carrying when walking; cane

Walk·man (wôk′mən, -man′) *trademark for* a portable, pocket-size radio or tape player with headphones

walk′-on′ ***n.*** a minor role in which the actor has few or no lines

walk′out′ ***n.*** a labor strike

walk′-up′ ***n.*** **1** an upstairs apartment or office in a building without an elevator **2** the building

walk′way′ ***n.*** a path, passage, etc. for pedestrians, esp. one that is sheltered

wall (wôl) ***n.*** ⟦< L *vallus*, palisade⟧ **1** an upright structure of wood, stone, etc., serving to enclose, divide, or protect **2** something like a wall in appearance or function **—*vt.*** **1** to enclose, divide, etc. with or as with a wall **2** to close up (an opening) with a wall: usually with *up* —**drive** (or **push**) **to the wall** to place in a desperate position —**off the wall** [Slang] **1** insane; crazy **2** very eccentric

wal·la·by (wä′lə bē) ***n.***, *pl.* **-bies** ⟦< Australian native name *wolabā*⟧ a marsupial of Australia, etc., like a small kangaroo

wall·board (wôl′bôrd′) ***n.*** fibrous material in thin slabs for making or covering walls and ceilings

wall′cov′er·ing ***n.*** decorative fabric or material, as wallpaper, for covering the walls of a room

wal·let (wô′lit) ***n.*** ⟦ME *walet*⟧ a flat case or folder, as of leather, for carrying money, cards, etc.

wall′eye′ ***n.*** ⟦< ON *vagl*, a beam + *eygr*, eye⟧ **1** an eye that turns outward, showing much white **2** a fish with large, glossy eyes, esp. a North American freshwater perch: in full **wall′eyed′ pike**

wall′flow′er ***n.*** [Inf.] a person who merely looks on at a dance, etc. as from shyness

Wal·loon (wä lo͞on′) ***n.*** ⟦< OHG *walh*, foreigner⟧ **1** a member of a chiefly Celtic people in S Belgium **2** the French dialect of this people

wal·lop (wä′ləp) [Inf.] ***vt.*** ⟦< OFr *galoper*, to gallop⟧ **1** to beat or defeat soundly **2** to strike hard **—*n.*** **1** a hard blow **2** a thrill

wal·low (wä′lō) ***vi.*** ⟦OE *wealwian*, roll around⟧ **1** to roll about, as in mud **2** to indulge oneself fully (*in* a specified thing) **—*n.*** **1** a wallowing **2** a muddy or dusty place

wall′pa′per ***n.*** decorative paper for covering the walls of a room **—*vt.*** to hang wallpaper on or in

Wall Street **1** street in New York City; financial center of the U.S. **2** U.S. financiers and their power, policies, etc. **3** the U.S. securities market

wall′-to-wall′ ***adj.*** **1** covering a floor completely **2** [Inf.] *a*) pervasive *b*) comprehensive

wal·nut (wôl′nut′) ***n.*** ⟦< OE *wealh*, foreign + *hnutu*, nut⟧ **1** a shade tree valued for its nuts and wood **2** its edible nut **3** its wood

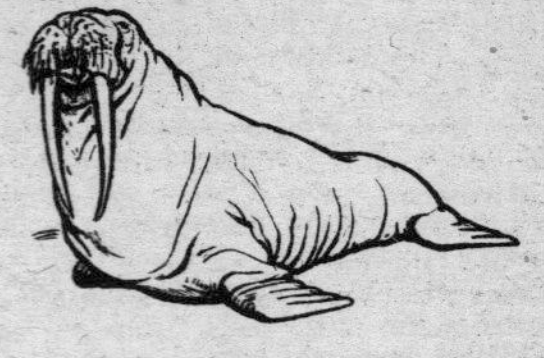

WALRUS

wal·rus (wôl′rəs) ***n.*** ⟦< Dan *hvalros*⟧ a massive arctic sea mammal somewhat like a seal, having two tusks projecting from the upper jaw

waltz (wôlts) ***n.*** ⟦< Ger *walzen*, dance about⟧ **1** a ballroom dance for couples, in 3/4 time **2** music for this **—*vi.*** **1** to dance a waltz **2** to move lightly

wam·pum (wäm′pəm) ***n.*** ⟦< AmInd⟧ small beads made of shells and used by North American Indians as money, for ornament, etc.

wan (wän) ***adj.*** **wan′ner, wan′nest** ⟦OE *wann*, dark⟧ **1** sickly pale **2** feeble or weak *[a wan smile]*

wand (wänd) ***n.*** ⟦< ON *vǫndr*⟧ **1** a staff symbolizing authority **2** a rod regarded as having magical powers **3** any of various rod-shaped devices, as one for reading bar codes

wan·der (wän′dər) ***vi.*** ⟦OE *wandrian*⟧ **1** to roam aimlessly; ramble **2** to stray (*from* a path, etc.) **3** to go astray in mind or purpose **4** to meander, as a river **—*vt.*** to roam in or over —**wan′der·er** ***n.***

wan′der·lust′ ***n.*** ⟦Ger⟧ an urge to wander or travel

wane (wān) ***vi.*** **waned, wan′ing** ⟦OE *wanian*, to decrease⟧ **1** to grow gradually less in extent: said of the visible face of the moon **2** to grow dim **3** to decline in power, etc. **4** to approach the end **—*n.*** a waning

wan·gle (waŋ′gəl) [Inf.] ***vt.***, ***vi.*** **-gled, -gling** ⟦< ? WAGGLE⟧ to get or cause (something) by persuasion, tricks, etc.

wan·na·be (wä′nə bē′) ***n.*** [Slang] one who wants to be like someone else or attain some status: also **wan′na-be′**

want (wänt, wônt) ***vt.*** ⟦< ON *vanta*⟧ **1** to lack **2** to wish for; desire **3** to wish to see or apprehend *[wanted by the police]* **4** [Chiefly Brit.] to require **—*vi.*** to have a need or lack: usually with *for* **—*n.*** **1** a shortage; lack **2** poverty **3** a craving **4** something needed

want ad [Inf.] an advertisement for something wanted, as a job

want′ing ***adj.*** **1** lacking **2** not up to standard **—*prep.*** without or minus —**wanting in** deficient in

wan·ton (wänt′′n) ***adj.*** ⟦< OE *wan*, lacking + *teon*, educate⟧ **1** sexually unrestrained **2** [Old Poet.] playful **3** unprovoked or malicious **4** recklessly ignoring justice, decency, etc. **—*n.*** a wanton person; esp., a sexually unrestrained woman

wap·i·ti (wä′pə tē) ***n.*** ⟦< AmInd⟧ a large North American deer with widely branching antlers; elk

war (wôr) ***n.*** ⟦< NormFr *werre*⟧ **1** open armed conflict as between nations **2** any active hostility or struggle **3** military operations as a science **—*adj.*** of, in, or from war **—*vi.* warred, war′ring 1** to carry on war **2** to contend; strive **—at war** in a state of active armed conflict

war·ble (wôr′bəl) ***vt., vi.* -bled, -bling** ⟦< NormFr *werbler*⟧ to sing (a song, etc.) melodiously, with trills, quavers, etc., as a bird does **—*n.*** a warbling

war·bler (wôr′blər) ***n.*** **1** one that warbles **2** a small, often brightly colored songbird

war crime a violation of laws or norms of humane behavior, committed during war

ward (wôrd) ***vt.*** ⟦OE *weardian,* to guard⟧ to turn aside; fend (*off*) **—*n.* 1** a being under guard **2** one under the care of a guardian or court **3** a division of a jail, hospital, etc. **4** a division of a city or town, for purposes of voting, etc.

-ward (wərd) ⟦OE *-weard*⟧ *suffix* in a (specified) direction *[inward]*: also **-wards** (wərdz)

war·den (wôrd′′n) ***n.*** ⟦< NormFr *wardein*⟧ **1** one who guards, or has charge of, something *[game warden]* **2** the chief official of a prison

ward′er ***n.*** a watchman

ward heeler a follower of a politician, who solicits votes, etc.: often used with mild contempt

ward·robe (wôr′drōb′) ***n.*** **1** a closet, cabinet, etc. for holding clothes **2** one's supply of clothes

ward′room′ ***n.*** in a warship, a room used for eating, etc. by commissioned officers

ware (wer) ***n.*** ⟦OE *waru*⟧ **1** anything for sale: *usually used in pl.* **2** pottery

ware′house′ ***n.*** a building where goods are stored **—*vt.* -housed′, -hous′ing** to store in a warehouse

war·fare (wôr′fer′) ***n.*** (armed) conflict

war′head′ ***n.*** the front part of a torpedo, etc., containing the explosive

war′horse′ ***n.*** [Inf.] one who has been through many struggles; veteran

war·i·ly (wer′ə lē) ***adv.*** cautiously **—war′i·ness** (-ē nis) ***n.***

war′like′ ***adj.*** **1** fond of or ready for war **2** of war **3** threatening war

war·lock (wôr′läk′) ***n.*** ⟦OE *wærloga,* liar⟧ a man who practices black magic

war′lord′ ***n.*** **1** a high military officer in a warlike nation **2** a local ruler or bandit leader

warm (wôrm) ***adj.*** ⟦OE *wearm*⟧ **1** *a)* having or giving off a moderate degree of heat *b)* hot *[a warm night]* **2** that keeps body heat in *[a warm hat]* **3** ardent; enthusiastic **4** lively, vigorous, etc. **5** quick to anger **6** *a)* genial; cordial *[a warm welcome]* *b)* sympathetic or loving **7** newly made; fresh, as a trail **8** [Inf.] close to discovering something **—*vt., vi.*** to make or become warm **—warm up** to practice or exercise, as before going into a game, contest, etc. **—warm′er *n.* —warm′ish *adj.* —warm′ly *adv.***

warm′blood′ed ***adj.*** having a body temperature that is relatively constant and usually higher than that of the surroundings

warmed′-o′ver ***adj.*** **1** reheated **2** presented again, without significant change, as ideas

warm front the forward edge of a warm air mass advancing into a colder mass

warm′heart′ed ***adj.*** kind, sympathetic, friendly, loving, etc.

war′mon′ger (-muŋ′gər, -mäŋ′-) ***n.*** one who tries to cause war **—war′mon′ger·ing *adj., n.***

warmth (wôrmth) ***n.*** **1** *a)* the state of having heat *b)* mild heat **2** *a)* enthusiasm, ardor, etc. *b)* affectionate feelings

warm′-up′ ***n.*** the act of warming up

warn (wôrn) ***vt., vi.*** ⟦OE *wearnian*⟧ **1** to tell of a danger, coming evil, etc. **2** to caution about certain acts **3** to notify in advance; inform

warn′ing ***n.*** **1** the act of one that warns **2** something that serves to warn **—*adj.*** that warns

warp (wôrp) ***n.*** ⟦OE *weorpan,* to throw⟧ **1** *a)* a distortion, as a twist or bend, in wood *b)* any similar distortion **2** a mental quirk, bias, etc. **3** *Weaving* the threads running lengthwise in the loom **—*vt.* 1** to bend or twist out of shape **2** to distort, pervert, etc.: said of the mind, character, etc. **—*vi.*** to become bent or twisted

war′path′ ***n.*** the path taken by American Indians on a warlike expedition **—on the warpath 1** ready for war **2** actively angry; ready to fight

warp speed ⟦< (TIME) WARP + SPEED⟧ [Slang] in science fiction, a very high rate of speed

war·rant (wôr′ənt, wär′-) ***n.*** ⟦< NormFr *warant*⟧ **1** *a)* authorization, as by law *b)* justification for some act, belief, etc. **2** something serving as a guarantee of some event or result **3** *Law* a writ authorizing an arrest, search, etc. **—*vt.* 1** to authorize **2** to serve as justification for (an act, belief, etc.) **3** to guarantee

warrant officer a military officer ranking above a noncommissioned officer but below a commissioned officer

war·ran·ty (wôr′ən tē, wär′-) ***n., pl.* -ties** an assurance by a seller that goods will be repaired or replaced if not as represented; guarantee

war·ren (wôr′ən, wär′-) ***n.*** ⟦< NormFr *warir,* to preserve⟧ **1** an area in which rabbits breed or are numerous **2** any crowded building or buildings

war·rior (wôr′yər, -ē ər) ***n.*** ⟦see WAR⟧ a person experienced in conflict, esp. war; soldier

War·saw (wôr′sô′) capital of Poland: pop. 1,651,000

war′ship′ ***n.*** any combat ship, as a battleship

wart (wôrt) ***n.*** ⟦OE *wearte*⟧ **1** a small, usually hard, tumorous growth on the skin, caused by a virus **2** a small protuberance, as on a plant —**wart'y, -i·er, -i·est,** ***adj.***

wart hog a wild African hog with large tusks, and warts below the eyes

war·y (wer'ē) ***adj.*** **-i·er, -i·est** ⟦OE *wær*, aware⟧ on one's guard; cautious —**wary of** careful of

was (wuz, wäz) ***vi.*** ⟦OE *wæs*⟧ *1st & 3d pers. sing., pt., of* BE

wash (wôsh, wäsh) ***vt.*** ⟦OE *wæscan*⟧ **1** to clean with water or other liquid **2** to purify **3** to wet or moisten **4** to flow over, past, or against: said of a sea, waves, etc. **5** to soak (*out*), flush (*off*), or carry (*away*) with water **6** to erode; wear (*out* or *away*) by flowing over *[*the flood *washed* out the road*]* —***vi.*** **1** to wash oneself **2** to wash clothes **3** to undergo washing **4** to be removed by washing: usually with *out* or *away* **5** to be worn or carried (*out* or *away*) by the action of water *[*the bridge had *washed* out*]* **6** [Inf.] to withstand examination *[*that excuse won't *wash]* —***n.*** **1** a washing **2** a quantity of clothes, etc. washed, or to be washed **3** the rush or surge of water **4** the eddy of water or air caused by a propeller, etc. **5** silt, mud, etc. carried and dropped by running water **6** a liquid for cosmetic or medicinal use *[mouthwash]* **7** in the W U.S., the dry bed of a stream **8** [Inf.] a situation in which contrasted elements offset each other —***adj.*** that can be washed without damage; washable —**wash down** to follow (food, etc.) with a drink —**wash'a·ble** ***adj., n.***

wash'-and-wear' ***adj.*** of fabrics that need little or no ironing after washing

wash'board' ***n.*** a ridged board for scrubbing dirt out of clothes

wash'bowl' ***n.*** a bowl, esp. a bathroom fixture, for use in washing one's hands, etc.: also **wash'ba'sin**

wash'cloth' ***n.*** a small cloth used in washing the body: also **wash'rag'**

washed'-out' ***adj.*** **1** faded **2** [Inf.] tired; spiritless; pale and wan

washed'-up' ***adj.*** **1** [Inf.] tired; exhausted **2** [Slang] finished; done for; having failed

wash'er ***n.*** **1** one who washes **2** a flat ring of metal, rubber, etc., used with a nut, faucet valve, bolt, etc. **3** a machine for washing

wash'er·wom'an ***n., pl.*** **-wom'en** a woman whose work is washing clothes

wash'ing ***n.*** clothes, etc. to be washed

washing machine a clothes WASHER (*n.* 3)

Wash·ing·ton[1] (wôsh'iŋ tən, wäsh'-), **George** 1732-99; 1st president of the U.S. (1789-97)

Wash'ing·ton[2] **1** NW coastal state of the U.S.: 66,582 sq. mi.; pop. 4,867,000; cap. Olympia: abbrev. *WA* **2** capital of the U.S., coextensive with the District of Columbia: pop. 607,000: also called **Washington, DC** —**Wash'ing·to'ni·an** (-tō'nē ən) ***adj., n.***

wash'out' ***n.*** **1** the washing away of soil, etc. by water **2** [Slang] a failure

wash'room' ***n.*** **1** a room for washing **2** RESTROOM

wash'stand' ***n.*** a table or plumbing fixture with a washbowl, etc.

wash'tub' ***n.*** a tub, often with faucets and a drain, for washing clothes, etc.

wash'y ***adj.*** **-i·er, -i·est** feeble; insipid

wasp (wäsp, wôsp) ***n.*** ⟦OE *wæsp*⟧ a winged insect with a slender body and, in the females and workers, a painful sting

WASP or **Wasp** (wäsp, wôsp) ***n.*** a white Anglo-Saxon Protestant

wasp'ish ***adj.*** bad-tempered; snappish

was·sail (wäs'əl, -āl') ***n.*** ⟦< ON *ves heill*, be hearty⟧ **1** a toast formerly used to drink to the health of a person **2** the spiced ale, etc. with which such toasts were drunk **3** a drinking party —***vi., vt.*** to drink a wassail (to)

wast·age (wās'tij) ***n.*** **1** loss by use, decay, etc. **2** anything wasted

waste (wāst) ***vt.*** **wast'ed, wast'ing** ⟦< L *vastare*⟧ **1** to devastate; ruin **2** to wear away **3** to make weak or emaciated *[wasted* by age*]* **4** to use up needlessly; squander **5** to fail to take advantage of **6** [Slang] to kill —***vi.*** **1** to lose strength, etc., as by disease **2** to be used up or worn down gradually —***adj.*** **1** uncultivated or uninhabited; desolate **2** left over or superfluous **3** excreted from the body **4** used for waste —***n.*** **1** uncultivated or uninhabited land **2** a devastated area **3** a wasting or being wasted **4** discarded material, as ashes **5** excretions from the body, as urine —**go to waste** to be wasted —**lay waste (to)** to destroy —**wast'er** ***n.***

waste'bas'ket ***n.*** a container for wastepaper, etc.: also **wastepaper basket**

wast·ed (wās'təd) ***adj.*** [Slang] **1** intoxicated by a drug **2** drunk

waste'ful ***adj.*** using more than is necessary —**waste'ful·ly** ***adv.*** —**waste'ful·ness** ***n.***

waste'land' ***n.*** **1** barren land **2** an unproductive activity, endeavor, etc.

waste'pa'per ***n.*** paper thrown away after use: also **waste paper**

waste'wa'ter ***n.*** water discharged as sewage

wast·rel (wās'trəl) ***n.*** one who wastes; esp., a spendthrift

watch (wäch, wôch) ***n.*** ⟦OE *wæcce*⟧ **1** a keeping awake, esp. in order to guard **2** close observation for a time **3** a guard, or the period of duty of a guard **4** a small timepiece carried in the pocket or worn on the wrist **5** *a)* any of the periods of duty (usually four hours) on shipboard *b)* the crew on duty during such a period —***vi.*** **1** to stay awake, esp. at night; keep vigil **2** to be on the alert **3** to look or observe **4** to be looking or waiting attentively: with *for* —***vt.*** **1** to guard or tend **2** to observe carefully **3** to wait and look for —**watch oneself** to be careful —**watch out** to be alert or careful —**watch over** to protect from harm —**watch'er** ***n.***

watch'band' ***n.*** a band of leather,

metal, etc. to hold a watch on the wrist

watch'dog' *n.* **1** a dog kept to guard property **2** one that keeps watch in order to prevent waste, unethical practices, etc.

watch'ful *adj.* watching closely; vigilant; alert —**watch'ful·ly** *adv.* —**watch'ful·ness** *n.*

watch'man (-mən) *n., pl.* **-men** (-mən) a person hired to guard property

watch'tow'er *n.* a high tower from which watch is kept, as for forest fires

watch'word' *n.* **1** a password **2** a slogan or cry

wa·ter (wôt'ər, wät'-) *n.* ⟦OE *wæter*⟧ **1** the colorless liquid of rivers, lakes, etc., which falls as rain **2** water with reference to its depth, surface, or level *[above water]* **3** a body secretion, as urine **4** a wavy, lustrous finish given to linen, silk, metal, etc. —*vt.* **1** to give (animals) water to drink **2** to supply (crops, etc.) with water **3** to moisten, soak, or dilute with water **4** to give a wavy luster to (silk, etc.) —*vi.* **1** to fill with tears: said of the eyes **2** to secrete saliva *[his mouth watered]* **3** to take on a supply of water **4** to drink water —*adj.* of, for, in, on, near, from, or by water —**hold water** to remain sound, logical, etc. —**water down** to weaken the intensity or effectiveness of

water bed a heavy vinyl bag filled with water and used as a bed or mattress: also **wa'ter·bed'** *n.*

water buffalo a slow, powerful buffalo of S Asia used as a draft animal

water chestnut **1** a Chinese sedge with a nutlike tuber **2** this tuber

water closet TOILET (*n.* 2)

wa'ter·col'or *n.* **1** a pigment mixed with water for use as a paint **2** a painting done with such paints **3** the art of painting with watercolors

wa'ter-cooled' *adj.* cooled by water circulated around or through it

wa'ter·course' *n.* **1** a stream, river, etc. **2** a channel for water, as a canal

wa'ter·craft' *n., pl.* **-craft'** a boat, ship, or other water vehicle

wa'ter·cress' *n.* a white-flowered water plant: its leaves are used in salads, etc.

wa'ter·fall' *n.* a steep fall of water, as of a stream, from a height

wa'ter·fowl' *n.* a water bird, esp. one that swims

wa'ter·front' *n.* land or docks at the edge of a stream, harbor, etc.

water hole a pond or pool

WATERLILY

wa'ter·lil'y *n., pl.* **-lil'ies** **1** a water plant with large, flat, floating leaves and showy flowers **2** the flower

wa'ter·line' *n.* the line to which the surface of the water comes on the side of a ship or boat

wa'ter·logged' (-lôgd') *adj.* soaked or filled with water so as to be heavy and sluggish

Wa·ter·loo[1] (wôt'ər lo͞o', wät'-) *n.* ⟦after fol.⟧ any disastrous or decisive defeat

Wa'ter·loo'[2] town in central Belgium: scene of Napoleon's final defeat (1815)

water main a main pipe in a system of water pipes

wa'ter·mark' *n.* **1** a mark showing the limit to which water has risen **2** a mark in paper, produced by pressure of a design, as in the mold —*vt.* to mark (paper) with a watermark

wa'ter·mel'on *n.* a large, green melon with sweet, juicy, red pulp

water moccasin a large, poisonous water snake of the SE U.S.

water pipe **1** a pipe for water **2** a smoking pipe using water, as a hookah

water polo a water game played with a ball by two teams of swimmers

water power the power of running or falling water, used to drive machinery, etc.: also **wa'ter·pow'er** *n.*

wa'ter·proof' *adj.* that keeps out water, as by being treated with rubber, etc. —*vt.* to make waterproof

water rat any of various rodents living on the banks of streams and ponds

wa'ter-re·pel'lent *adj.* that repels water but is not fully waterproof

wa'ter·shed' *n.* **1** a ridge dividing the areas drained by different river systems **2** the area drained by a river system

wa'ter·side' *n.* land at the edge of a body of water —*adj.* of, at, or on the waterside

wa'ter-ski' *vi.* **-skied'**, **-ski'ing** to be towed on skilike boards (**water skis**) by a line attached to a speedboat —**wa'ter-ski'er** *n.*

wa'ter·spout' *n.* **1** a pipe for spouting water **2** a whirling funnel-shaped column of air full of spray occurring over water in tropical areas

water table the level below which the ground is saturated with water

wa'ter·tight' *adj.* **1** so snugly put together that no water can get in or through **2** that cannot be misconstrued, nullified, etc.; flawless

water tower an elevated tank for water storage

wa'ter·way' *n.* **1** a channel through which water runs **2** any body of water suitable for boats, ships, etc., as a canal or river

water wheel a wheel turned by running water, as for power

water wings an inflated device to keep one afloat as while learning to swim

wa'ter·works' *pl.n.* [*often with sing. v.*] a system of reservoirs, pumps, etc. supplying water to a city

wa'ter·y *adj.* **1** of or like water **2** full

of water **3** thin; diluted **4** tearful **5** weak —**wa'ter·i·ness** ***n.***

WATS (wäts) ***n.*** ⟦*w*(*ide*) *a*(*rea*) *t*(*elecommunications*) *s*(*ervice*)⟧ a long-distance telephone service using a network at special rates

watt (wät) ***n.*** ⟦after James *Watt* (1736-1819), Scot inventor of steam engine⟧ a unit of electrical power, equal to the power developed in a circuit by a current of one ampere flowing through a potential difference of one volt; $\frac{1}{746}$ horsepower

watt'age ***n.*** amount of electrical power, expressed in watts

wat·tle (wät''l) ***n.*** ⟦OE *watul*⟧ **1** a woven work of sticks intertwined with twigs or branches **2** a fleshy flap of skin hanging from the throat of certain birds or lizards —***vt.*** **-tled, -tling 1** to intertwine (sticks, twigs, etc.) **2** to build of or with wattle

wave (wāv) ***vi.*** **waved, wav'ing** ⟦OE *wafian*⟧ **1** to move or sway to and fro **2** to signal by moving a hand, arm, etc. to and fro **3** to have the form of a series of curves —***vt.*** **1** to cause to wave **2** to brandish (a weapon) **3** *a*) to move or swing (something) as a signal *b*) to signal (something) to (someone) by doing this **4** to give an undulating form to (hair, etc.) —***n.*** **1** a ridge or swell moving along the surface of the ocean, etc. **2** an undulation or curve, as in the hair **3** a motion to and fro, as with the hand in signaling **4** a thing like a wave in action or effect; specif., an upsurge *[a crime wave]* **5** *Physics* a periodic motion or disturbance, as in the propagation of sound or light

Wave (wāv) ***n.*** ⟦< *W*(*omen*) *A*(*ppointed for*) *V*(*oluntary*) *E*(*mergency*) *S*(*ervice*)⟧ a member of the women's branch of the U.S. Navy (**WAVES**)

wave'length' ***n.*** **1** *Physics* the distance measured along a wave from any given point to the next similar point **2** [Inf.] chiefly in the phrase **on the same wavelength**, in accord

wave'let (-lit) ***n.*** a little wave

wa·ver (wā'vər) ***vi.*** ⟦< ME *waven*, to wave⟧ **1** to sway to and fro **2** to show indecision; vacillate **3** to falter, flicker, tremble, etc. —***n.*** a wavering

wav·y (wā'vē) ***adj.*** **-i·er, -i·est 1** having or like waves **2** moving in a wavelike motion —**wav'i·ness** ***n.***

wax[1] (waks) ***n.*** ⟦OE *weax*⟧ **1** a plastic, dull-yellow substance secreted by bees; beeswax **2** any plastic substance like this; specif., *a*) paraffin *b*) a substance exuded by the ears —***vt.*** to rub, polish, cover, or treat with wax

wax[2] (waks) ***vi.*** **waxed, wax'ing** ⟦OE *weaxan*, grow⟧ **1** to increase in strength, size, etc. **2** to become gradually full: said of the moon **3** [Literary] to become; grow *[to wax angry]*

wax bean a variety of the common garden bean with long, edible, yellow pods

wax·en (wak'sən) ***adj.*** **1** made of wax **2** pale

wax museum an exhibition of wax figures, as of famous persons

wax myrtle an evergreen shrub with grayish-white, wax-coated berries

wax paper a paper made moistureproof by a wax coating: also **waxed paper**

wax'wing' ***n.*** a fruit-eating bird with brown or gray silky plumage and scarlet waxlike tips on the wings

wax'works' ***n.*** an exhibition of wax figures

wax'y ***adj.*** **-i·er, -i·est** of, full of, or like wax —**wax'i·ness** ***n.***

way (wā) ***n.*** ⟦ME < OE *weg*⟧ **1** a road, street, path, etc. **2** space for passing **3** a route or course **4** course of life or conduct *[avoid evil ways]* **5** a method of doing something **6** a manner of living, acting, etc. *[the way of the world]* **7** distance *[a long way off]* **8** direction of movement or action **9** movement forward **10** respect; specific point *[right in some ways]* **11** wish; will *[get one's own way]* **12** [Inf.] *a*) a condition *[he's in a bad way]* *b*) a locality *[out our way]* **13** [*pl.*] a timber framework on which a ship is built —***adv.*** [Inf.] away; far *[way behind]* —**by the way** incidentally —**by way of 1** passing through **2** as a method, etc. of —**give way 1** to yield **2** to break down —**lead the way** to be a guide or example —**make way 1** to clear a passage **2** to make progress —**under way** moving; advancing

way'far'er (-fer'ər) ***n.*** a traveler, esp. on foot —**way'far'ing** ***adj.***, ***n.***

way·lay (wā'lā') ***vt.*** **-laid', -lay'ing 1** to lie in wait for and attack **2** to wait for and accost (a person) on the way

way'-out' ***adj.*** [Inf.] very unusual or unconventional

-ways (wāz) ⟦ME < *way* (see WAY)⟧ *suffix* in a (specified) direction, position, or manner *[sideways]*

ways and means methods of raising money; specif., such methods, including legislation, in government

way'side' ***n.*** the edge of a road

way'ward ***adj.*** ⟦see AWAY & -WARD⟧ **1** headstrong, willful, disobedient, etc. **2** unpredictable; erratic —**way'ward·ly** ***adv.*** —**way'ward·ness** ***n.***

we (wē) ***pron.***, *sing.* **I** ⟦OE⟧ **1** the persons speaking or writing **2** I: used by a monarch, editor, etc. when speaking for others

weak (wēk) ***adj.*** ⟦< ON *veikr*⟧ **1** lacking physical strength; feeble **2** lacking moral strength or willpower **3** lacking mental power **4** lacking power, authority, force, etc. **5** easily torn, broken, etc. *[a weak railing]* **6** lacking intensity, etc. *[a weak voice]* **7** diluted *[weak tea]* **8** unconvincing *[a weak argument]*

weak'en ***vt.***, ***vi.*** to make or become weak or weaker

weak'-kneed' (-nēd') ***adj.*** lacking in courage, determination, resistance, etc.

weak'ling ***n.*** one that is low in physical or moral strength

weak'ly ***adj.*** **-li·er, -li·est** sickly; feeble —***adv.*** in a weak manner

weak'ness ***n.*** **1** state of being weak **2** a weak point **3** an immoderate fondness (*for* something)

weal[1] (wēl) ***n.*** ⟦< WALE⟧ a mark raised on the skin, as by a blow; welt

weal[2] (wēl) ***n.*** ⟦< OE *wela*, wealth, well-being⟧ well-being; welfare *[the public weal]*

wealth (welth) ***n.*** ⟦< prec.⟧ **1** much money or property; riches **2** a large amount *[a wealth of ideas]* **3** valuable products, contents, etc. **4** everything having value in money

wealth·y (wel′thē) ***adj.*** **-i·er, -i·est** having wealth; rich —**wealth′i·ness *n.***

wean (wēn) ***vt.*** ⟦OE *wenian*, to accustom, train⟧ **1** to accustom (a child or young animal) to take food other than by suckling **2** to withdraw (a person) by degrees (*from* a habit, etc.)

weap·on (wep′ən) ***n.*** ⟦OE *wæpen*⟧ **1** any instrument used to injure or kill **2** any means of attack or defense —**weap′on·less *adj.***

weap′on·ry *n.* weapons collectively

wear (wer) ***vt.*** **wore, worn, wear′ing** ⟦OE *werian*⟧ **1** to have (clothing, etc.) on the body **2** to show in one's appearance *[to wear a smile]* **3** to impair or diminish by use, friction, etc.: often with *away* **4** to make by rubbing, flowing, etc. *[to wear a hole in the rug]* **5** to tire or exhaust —***vi.*** **1** to become impaired or diminished, as by use **2** to hold up in use *[that suit wears well]* **3** to have an irritating effect (*on*) —***n.*** **1** a wearing or being worn **2** things worn; clothes *[women's wear]* **3** impairment or loss, as from use, friction, etc. —**wear off** to diminish by degrees —**wear′a·ble *adj.*** —**wear′er *n.***

wear and tear loss and damage resulting from use

wea·ri·some (wir′i səm) ***adj.*** causing weariness; tiresome or tedious —**wea′ri·some·ly *adv.***

wea·ry (wir′ē) ***adj.*** **-ri·er, -ri·est** ⟦OE *werig*⟧ **1** tired; worn out **2** without further patience, zeal, etc. **3** tiring —***vt., vi.*** **-ried, -ry·ing** to make or become weary —**wea′ri·ly *adv.*** —**wea′ri·ness *n.***

wea·sel (wē′zəl) ***n.*** ⟦OE *wesle*⟧ **1** an agile flesh-eating mammal with a long, slender body and short legs **2** a sly, cunning person —***vi.*** [Inf.] to avoid a commitment: with *out* —**wea′sel·ly *adj.***

weath·er (we*th*′ər) ***n.*** ⟦OE *weder*⟧ **1** the condition of the atmosphere with regard to temperature, moisture, etc. **2** storm, rain, etc. —***vt.*** **1** to expose to the action of weather **2** to pass through safely *[to weather a storm]* **3** *Naut.* to pass to the windward of —***vi.*** to become worn, etc. by exposure to the weather —**under the weather** [Inf.] ill

weath′er-beat′en *adj.* showing the effect of exposure to sun, rain, etc.

weath′er·cock′ *n.* a weather vane in the shape of a rooster

weath′er·ing *n.* the effects of the forces of weather on rock surfaces

weath′er·ize′ *vt.* **-ized′, -iz′ing** to weatherstrip, insulate, etc. (a building) —**weath′er·i·za′tion *n.***

weath′er·man′ (-man′) ***n.***, *pl.* **-men′** (-men′) one whose work is forecasting the weather, or, esp., reporting it, as on

TV

weath′er·proof′ *adj.* that can be exposed to wind, snow, etc. without being damaged —***vt.*** to make weatherproof

weath′er·strip′ *n.* a thin strip of metal, felt, etc. covering the joint between a door or window and the casing, to keep out drafts, etc.: also **weath′er·strip′ping** —***vt.*** **-stripped′, weath′er·strip′ping** to provide with weatherstrips

weather vane a vane for showing which way the wind is blowing

weave (wēv) ***vt.*** **wove** or, chiefly for *vt.* 5 & *vi.* 2, **weaved, wo′ven** or **wove** or, chiefly for *vt.* 5 & *vi.* 2, **weaved, weav′ing** ⟦OE *wefan*⟧ **1** to make (a fabric, basket, etc.) by interlacing (threads, straw, etc.), as on a loom **2** to construct in the mind **3** to twist (something) into or through **4** to spin (a web), as spiders do **5** to make (one's way) by moving from side to side or in and out —***vi.*** **1** to do weaving **2** to move from side to side or in and out —***n.*** a method or pattern of weaving —**weav′er *n.***

web (web) ***n.*** ⟦OE *webb*⟧ **1** any woven fabric **2** the network spun by a spider, etc. **3** a carefully woven trap **4** a network **5** a membrane joining the digits of various water birds, etc. **6** [*usually* **W-**] *Comput.* WORLD WIDE WEB: usually with *the* —***vt.*** **webbed, web′bing** to join by, or cover as with, a web

web′bing *n.* a strong fabric woven in strips and used for belts, etc.

web′foot′ *n.*, *pl.* **-feet′** a foot with the toes webbed —**web′-foot′ed *adj.***

Web page a single file on the World Wide Web, providing text, pictures, etc.

web′site′ *n.* [*occas.* **W-**] a location on the World Wide Web, consisting of one or more Web pages: also **web** (or **Web**) **site**

Web·ster (web′stər), **No·ah** (nō′ə) 1758-1843; U.S. lexicographer

wed (wed) ***vt., vi.*** **wed′ded, wed′ded** or **wed, wed′ding** ⟦OE *weddian*⟧ **1** to marry **2** to unite or join

Wed *abbrev.* Wednesday

wed·ded (wed′id) ***adj.*** **1** married **2** of marriage **3** devoted *[wedded to one's work]* **4** joined

wed′ding *n.* **1** the marriage ceremony **2** a marriage anniversary **3** a joining together

WEDGE

wedge (wej) ***n.*** ⟦OE *wecg*⟧ **1** a piece of wood, metal, etc. tapering to a thin edge: used to split wood, lift a weight, etc. 2 anything shaped like a wedge 3 any act serving to open the way for change, etc. —*vt.* **wedged, wedg'ing** 1 to force apart, or fix in place, with a wedge 2 to crowd together or pack (*in*) —*vi.* to push or be forced as or like a wedge

wedg'ie (-ē) *n.* a shoe having a wedge-shaped piece under the heel, which forms a solid, flat sole

wed'lock' *n.* ⟦OE *wedlac*⟧ the state of being married

Wednes·day (wenz'dā) *n.* ⟦< *Woden*, Germanic god⟧ the fourth day of the week

wee (wē) *adj.* **we'er, we'est** ⟦OE *wege*⟧ 1 very small; tiny 2 very early *[wee* hours of the morning*]*

weed (wēd) *n.* ⟦OE *weod*⟧ any undesired, uncultivated plant, esp. one that crowds out desired plants —*vt., vi.* 1 to remove weeds from (a garden, etc.) 2 to remove as useless, harmful, etc.: often with *out* —**weed'er** *n.* —**weed'less** *adj.*

weeds (wēdz) *pl.n.* ⟦< OE *wæde*, garment⟧ black mourning clothes, esp. those worn by a widow

weed'y *adj.* **-i·er, -i·est** 1 full of weeds 2 of or like a weed

week (wēk) *n.* ⟦OE *wicu*⟧ 1 a period of seven days, esp. one from Sunday through Saturday 2 the hours or days of work in this period

week'day' *n.* any day of the week except Sunday and, often, Saturday

week'end' or **week'-end'** *n.* the period from Friday night or Saturday to Monday morning: also **week end** —*vi.* to spend the weekend

week'ly *adj.* 1 done, happening, etc. once every week 2 of a week, or of each week —*adv.* once a week; every week —*n., pl.* **-lies** a periodical published once a week

ween (wēn) *vi., vt.* ⟦OE *wenan*⟧ [Archaic] to think

weep (wēp) *vi., vt.* **wept, weep'ing** ⟦OE *wepan*⟧ 1 to shed (tears) 2 to mourn (*for*) 3 to drip or exude (water, etc.) —**weep'er** *n.*

weep'ing *n.* the act of one who weeps —*adj.* 1 that weeps 2 having graceful, drooping branches

weeping willow an ornamental willow tree with drooping branches

weep'y *adj.* **-i·er, -i·est** (inclined to) weeping

wee·vil (wē'vəl) *n.* ⟦OE *wifel*⟧ a beetle whose larvae feed on grain, cotton, etc.

weft (weft) *n.* ⟦< OE *wefan*, to weave⟧ *Weaving* the yarns carried back and forth across the warp

weigh (wā) *vt.* ⟦OE *wegan*, carry⟧ 1 to determine the weight of 2 to have (a specified) weight 3 to consider and choose carefully *[weigh* one's words*]* —*vi.* 1 to have significance, importance, etc. 2 to be a burden —**weigh anchor** to hoist a ship's anchor —**weigh down** to burden or bear down on

weight (wāt) *n.* ⟦OE *wiht*⟧ 1 a quantity weighing a definite amount 2 *a*) heaviness *b*) *Physics* the force of gravity acting on a body 3 amount of heaviness 4 *a*) any unit of heaviness *b*) any system of such units *c*) a piece having a specific amount of heaviness, placed on a balance or scale in weighing 5 any mass of material used for its heaviness *[a paperweight]* 6 a burden, as of sorrow 7 importance or consequence 8 influence; power —*vt.* 1 to add weight to 2 to burden

weight'less *adj.* having little or no apparent weight: said as of an astronaut floating freely in an orbiting space vehicle —**weight'less·ness** *n.*

weight lifting the athletic exercise or sport of lifting barbells —**weight lift'er**

weight'y *adj.* **-i·er, -i·est** 1 very heavy 2 burdensome 3 significant; important —**weight'i·ness** *n.*

weir (wir) *n.* ⟦OE *wer*⟧ 1 a low dam built to back up water, as for a mill 2 a fence, as of brushwood, in a stream, etc., for catching fish

weird (wird) *adj.* ⟦< OE *wyrd*, fate⟧ 1 of or about ghosts, etc.; mysterious, eerie, etc. 2 strange; bizarre —**weird'ly** *adv.* —**weird'ness** *n.*

weird·o (wir'dō) *n., pl.* **-os** [Slang] one that is weird, bizarre, etc.: also **weird'ie** (-dē)

wel·come (wel'kəm) *adj.* ⟦OE *wilcuma*, welcome guest⟧ 1 gladly received *[a welcome* guest*]* 2 freely permitted *[he* is *welcome* to use my car*]* —*n.* a welcoming —*vt.* **-comed, -com·ing** to greet or receive with pleasure, etc. —**you're welcome** you're under no obligation

weld (weld) *vt.* ⟦< obs. *well*⟧ 1 to unite (pieces of metal, etc.) by heating until fused or until soft enough to hammer together 2 to unite closely —*vi.* to be welded —*n.* 1 a welding 2 a joint formed by welding —**weld'a·ble** *adj.* —**weld'er** *n.*

wel·fare (wel'fer') *n.* ⟦ME: see WELL[2] & FARE⟧ 1 a condition of health, happiness, prosperity, etc.; well-being 2 *a*) the organized efforts of government agencies granting aid to the poor, the unemployed, etc. *b*) such aid —**on welfare** receiving government aid because of poverty, etc.

wel·kin (wel'kin) *n.* ⟦< OE *wolcen*, a cloud⟧ [Archaic] the vault of the sky

well[1] (wel) *n.* ⟦OE *wella*⟧ 1 a natural spring and pool 2 a hole sunk into the earth to get water, oil, etc. 3 a source of abundant supply 4 a shaft, etc. resembling a well 5 a container for a liquid, as an inkwell —*vi., vt.* to flow or gush from or as from a well

well[2] (wel) *adv.* **bet'ter, best** ⟦OE *wel*⟧ 1 in a satisfactory, proper, or excellent manner *[treat her well;* you sing *well]* 2 prosperously *[to live well]* 3 with good reason *[one may well* ask*]* 4 to a considerable degree *[well* advanced*]* 5 thoroughly *[stir it well]* 6 with certainty; definitely 7 familiarly *[I know her well]* —*adj.* 1 suitable, proper, etc. 2 in good health 3 favorable; comfortable —*interj.* used variously to express surprise, agreement, etc. —**as well** 1 in addition 2 equally —**as well as** in addition to

well-ad·vised (wel′əd vīzd′) ***adj.*** showing or resulting from careful consideration or sound advice; prudent

well′-ap·point′ed ***adj.*** excellently furnished

well′-bal′anced ***adj.*** **1** precisely adjusted or regulated **2** sane, sensible, etc.

well′-be·haved′ ***adj.*** displaying good manners

well′-be′ing ***n.*** the state of being well, happy, or prosperous; welfare

well′-born′ ***adj.*** born into a family of high social position

well′-bred′ ***adj.*** showing good breeding; courteous and considerate

well′-dis·posed′ ***adj.*** friendly (*toward* a person) or receptive (*to* an idea, etc.)

well′-done′ ***adj.*** **1** performed with skill **2** thoroughly cooked: said esp. of meat

well′-fed′ ***adj.*** plump or fat

well′-fixed′ ***adj.*** [Inf.] wealthy

well′-found′ed ***adj.*** based on facts, good evidence, or sound judgment

well′-groomed′ ***adj.*** clean and neat

well′-ground′ed ***adj.*** having a thorough basic knowledge of a subject

well′head′ ***n.*** **1** a source; fountainhead **2** the top of a well, as an oil or gas well

well′-heeled′ ***adj.*** [Slang] rich; prosperous

well′-in·formed′ ***adj.*** having considerable knowledge of a subject or of many subjects

Wel·ling·ton (wel′iŋ tən) capital of New Zealand: pop. 149,000

well′-in·ten′tioned ***adj.*** having or showing good or kindly intentions

well′-knit′ ***adj.*** sturdy in body build

well′-known′ ***adj.*** **1** widely known; famous **2** thoroughly known

well′-made′ ***adj.*** skillfully and soundly put together

well′-man′nered ***adj.*** polite; courteous

well′-mean′ing ***adj.*** **1** having good intentions **2** said or done with good intentions, but often not wisely or effectually: also **well′-meant′**

well′-nigh′ ***adv.*** very nearly; almost

well′-off′ ***adj.*** **1** in a fortunate condition **2** prosperous

well′-pre·served′ ***adj.*** in good condition or looking good, in spite of age

well′-read′ (-red′) ***adj.*** having read much

well′-round′ed ***adj.*** **1** well-planned for proper balance **2** showing diverse talents **3** shapely

well′-spo′ken ***adj.*** **1** speaking easily, graciously, etc. **2** properly or aptly spoken

well′spring′ ***n.*** **1** the source of a stream, etc. **2** a source of abundant supply

well′-tak′en ***adj.*** apt and sound or cogent

well′-thought′-of′ ***adj.*** having a good reputation

well′-timed′ ***adj.*** timely; opportune

well′-to-do′ ***adj.*** prosperous; wealthy

well′-turned′ ***adj.*** **1** gracefully shaped **2** expressed or worded well [*a well-turned* phrase]

well′-wish′er ***n.*** one who wishes well to another or to a cause, etc.

well′-worn′ ***adj.*** much worn or used

welsh (welsh) ***vi.*** [Slang] to fail to pay a debt, fulfill an obligation, etc.: often with *on* —**welsh′er** ***n.***

Welsh (welsh) ***n.*** ⟦OE *Wealh*, foreigner⟧ the Celtic language of Wales —***adj.*** of Wales or its people, language, etc. —**the Welsh** the people of Wales —**Welsh′man** (-mən), *pl.* **-men**, ***n.***

Welsh rabbit a dish of melted cheese served on crackers or toast: also **Welsh rarebit**

welt (welt) ***n.*** ⟦ME *welte*⟧ **1** a strip of leather in the seam between the sole and upper of a shoe **2** a ridge raised on the skin as by a blow

wel·ter (wel′tər) ***vi.*** ⟦< MDu *welteren*⟧ to roll about or wallow —***n.*** a confusion; turmoil

wel·ter·weight (wel′tər wāt′) ***n.*** ⟦prob. < *welt*, to beat⟧ a boxer with a maximum weight of 147 pounds

wen (wen) ***n.*** ⟦OE *wenn*⟧ a benign skin tumor

wench (wench) ***n.*** ⟦OE *wencel*, child⟧ a young woman: derogatory or jocular term

wend (wend) ***vt.*** **wend′ed**, **wend′ing** ⟦OE *wendan*, to turn⟧ to go on (one's way)

went (went) ***vi.***, ***vt.*** *pt. of* GO

wept (wept) ***vi.***, ***vt.*** *pt. & pp. of* WEEP

were (wur) ***vi.*** ⟦OE *wæron*⟧ *pl. & 2d pers. sing., past indic., and the past subjunctive, of* BE

we're (wir) *contr.* we are

were·wolf (wer′woolf′, wir′-) ***n.***, *pl.* **-wolves′** ⟦OE *wer*, man + *wulf*, wolf⟧ *Folklore* a person changed into a wolf: also sp. **wer′wolf′**, *pl.* **-wolves′**

Wes·ley (wes′lē, wez′-), **John** 1703-91; Eng. clergyman; founder of Methodism —**Wes′ley·an** ***adj.***, ***n.***

west (west) ***n.*** ⟦OE⟧ **1** the direction in which sunset occurs (270° on the compass) **2** a region in or toward this direction —***adj.*** **1** in, of, toward, or facing the west **2** from the west [*a west wind*] —***adv.*** in or toward the west —**the West** **1** the western part of the U.S. **2** Europe and the Western Hemisphere

West Berlin *see* BERLIN

west′er·ly ***adj.***, ***adv.*** **1** toward the west **2** from the west

west′ern ***adj.*** ⟦OE *westerne*⟧ **1** in, of, or toward the west **2** from the west **3** [**W-**] of the West —***n.*** a movie, book, etc. about life in the western U.S., esp. during the frontier period

west′ern·er ***n.*** a person born or living in the west

Western Hemisphere that half of the earth which includes North & South America

west′ern·ize′ ***vt.*** **-ized′**, **-iz′ing** to make Western in habits, ideas, etc.

Western Samoa *former name for* SAMOA

West Germany *see* GERMANY

West In·dies (in′dēz′) large group of islands in the Atlantic between North America & South America —**West Indian**

West Point military reservation in SE New York: site of the U.S. Military Academy

West Virginia state of the E U.S.: 24,232 sq. mi.; pop. 1,793,000; cap. Charleston: abbrev. *WV* —**West Virginian**

west′ward ***adv., adj.*** toward the west: also **west′wards** ***adv.***

wet (wet) ***adj.*** **wet′ter, wet′test** ⟦OE *wæt*⟧ **1** covered or saturated with water or other liquid **2** rainy; misty **3** not yet dry *[wet paint]* —***n.*** **1** water or other liquid; moisture **2** rain or rainy weather —***vt., vi.*** **wet** or **wet′ted, wet′ting** to make or become wet —**all wet** [Slang] wrong

wet′back′ ***n.*** [Inf.] a Mexican who illegally enters the U.S. to work: term of derision or contempt

wet blanket a person or thing whose presence or influence lessens the enthusiasm of others

wet′land′ ***n.*** [*usually pl.*] **1** swamps or marshes **2** an area of swamps, etc. preserved for wildlife

wet nurse a woman hired to suckle another's child —**wet′-nurse′, -nursed′, -nurs′ing,** ***vt.***

wet suit a closefitting suit of rubber worn by skin divers for warmth: also **wet′suit′** ***n.***

whack (hwak) ***vt., vi.*** ⟦echoic⟧ to strike or slap with a sharp, resounding blow —***n.*** **1** a sharp, resounding blow **2** the sound of this —**have** (or **take**) **a whack at** [Inf.] **1** to aim a blow at **2** to make an attempt at —**out of whack** [Inf.] not in proper working condition —**whack′er** ***n.***

whale[1] (hwāl) ***n.*** ⟦OE *hwæl*⟧ a large, warmblooded sea mammal that breathes air —***vi.*** **whaled, whal′ing** to hunt whales —**a whale of a** [Inf.] an exceptionally large, fine, etc. example of a (class or group)

whale[2] (hwāl) ***vt.*** **whaled, whal′ing** ⟦prob. < WALE⟧ [Inf.] to beat, whip, etc.

whale′bone′ ***n.*** BALEEN

whal′er ***n.*** **1** a whaling ship **2** one whose work is whaling

wham (hwam) ***interj.*** used to suggest the sound of a heavy blow, explosion, etc. —***n.*** a heavy blow, etc. —***vt., vi.*** **whammed, wham′ming** to strike, explode, etc. loudly

wham′my ***n.***, *pl.* **-mies** [Slang] a jinx

wharf (hwôrf) ***n.***, *pl.* **wharves** or **wharfs** ⟦OE *hwerf,* a dam⟧ a structure on a shore, at which ships are loaded or unloaded; dock

what (hwut, hwät) ***pron.*** ⟦OE *hwæt,* neuter of *wha,* who⟧ **1** which thing, event, etc. *[what is that object?]* **2** that or those which *[to know what one wants]* —***adj.*** **1** which or which kind of: used interrogatively or relatively **2** as much, or as many, as *[take what men you need]* **3** how great, surprising, etc. *[what nonsense!]* —***adv.*** **1** in what way? how? *[what does it matter?]* **2** how greatly, etc. *[what tragic news!]* —***interj.*** used to express surprise, anger, etc. —**what about** what do you think, feel, etc. concerning? —**what for?** why? —**what with** because of *[what with the bad weather, we'll be late]*

what·ev′er ***pron.*** what: an emphatic variant; specif., *a*) which thing, event, etc.? *b*) anything that *[say whatever you like]* *c*) no matter what *[whatever you do, don't hurry]* —***adj.*** **1** of any kind *[I have no plans whatever]* **2** being who it may be *[whatever man said that, it is not true]*

what′not′ ***n.*** a set of open shelves, as for bric-a-brac

what's (hwuts) *contr.* **1** what is **2** what has **3** [Inf.] what does *[what's he want?]*

what·so·ev·er (hwut′sō ev′ər) ***pron., adj.*** whatever: an emphatic form

wheal[1] (hwēl) ***n.*** ⟦ME *whele*⟧ a small, itching elevation of the skin, as from an insect bite

wheal[2] (hwēl) ***n.*** WEAL[1]

wheat (hwēt) ***n.*** ⟦OE *hwæte*⟧ a cereal grass having spikes containing grains used in making flour, cereals, etc.

wheat germ the highly nutritious embryo of the wheat kernel, milled out as a flake

whee·dle (hwēd′'l) ***vt., vi.*** **-dled, -dling** ⟦< ?⟧ to influence or persuade (a person), or get (something), by flattery, coaxing, etc.

wheel (hwēl) ***n.*** ⟦OE *hweol*⟧ **1** a circular disk or frame turning on a central axis **2** anything like a wheel in shape, movement, etc. **3** the steering wheel of a motor vehicle **4** [*pl.*] [Slang] an automobile **5** [*usually pl.*] the moving forces *[the wheels of progress]* **6** a turning movement **7** [Slang] an important person —***vt., vi.*** **1** to move on or in (a wheeled vehicle) **2** to turn, revolve, etc. **3** to turn so as to change direction —**at** (or **behind**) **the wheel** steering a motor vehicle, ship, etc.

wheel′bar′row ***n.*** a kind of cart for carrying small loads, having a wheel in front and two shafts with handles in back for raising the vehicle off its two back legs and moving it

wheel′base′ ***n.*** the length of a motor vehicle between the centers of the front and rear wheels

wheel′chair′ ***n.*** a chair mounted on large wheels, for persons unable to walk

wheeled (hwēld) ***adj.*** having wheels

wheel·er-deal·er (hwēl′ər dēl′ər) ***n.*** [Slang] one who is aggressive in a showy way, as in arranging business deals

wheel′house′ ***n.*** PILOTHOUSE

wheel′wright′ ***n.*** one who makes and repairs wheels and wheeled vehicles

wheeze (hwēz) ***vi.*** **wheezed, wheez′ing** ⟦< ON *hvæsa,* to hiss⟧ to breathe hard with a whistling, breathy sound, as in asthma —***n.*** a wheezing —**wheez′y, -i·er, -i·est,** ***adj.***

WHELK

whelk (hwelk) ***n.*** ⟦OE *wioluc*⟧ a kind of large marine snail

whelm (hwelm) ***vt.*** ⟦ME *welmen*⟧ **1** to submerge **2** to overpower or crush

whelp (hwelp) ***n.*** ⟦OE *hwelp*⟧ a young dog, etc. —***vt.***, ***vi.*** to give birth to (young): said of some animals

when (hwen) ***adv.*** ⟦OE *hwænne*⟧ **1** at what time? *[when* did they leave?*]* **2** on what occasion? —***conj.*** **1** at what time *[*tell me *when* to go*]* **2** at the time that *[when* we were young*]* **3** at which *[*a time *when* people must work*]* **4** as soon as *[*we will eat *when* he comes*]* **5** although **6** if —***pron.*** what or which time —***n.*** the time (*of* an event)

whence (hwens) ***adv.*** ⟦ME *whennes*⟧ from what place, cause, etc.? *[whence* do you come?*]*

when·ev′er ***adv.*** [Inf.] when: an emphatic form —***conj.*** at whatever time *[*go *whenever* you can*]*

where (hwer) ***adv.*** ⟦OE *hwær*⟧ **1** in or at what place? *[where* is it?*]* **2** to or toward what place? *[where* did he go?*]* **3** in what respect? *[where* is he to blame?*]* **4** from what place or source? *[where* did he learn it?*]* —***conj.*** **1** at what place *[*I see *where* it is*]* **2** at which place *[*I went home, *where* I ate dinner*]* **3** wherever **4** to the place to which *[*we go *where* you go*]* —***pron.*** **1** the place at which *[*it's a mile to *where* I live*]* **2** what place *[where* are you from?*]* —***n.*** the place (*of* an event)

where′a·bouts′ (-ə bouts′) ***adv.*** near or at what place? —***n.*** [*now usually with pl. v.*] the place where one is

where·as′ ***conj.*** **1** in view of the fact that **2** while on the contrary *[*I'm slim, *whereas* he is fat*]*

where·at′ ***conj.*** [Archaic] at which point

where·by′ ***conj.*** by which

where′fore′ (-fôr′) ***adv.*** [Archaic] for what reason? why? —***conj.*** [Archaic] **1** for which **2** because of which —***n.*** the reason; cause

where·in′ ***conj.*** in which

where·of′ ***adv.***, ***conj.*** of what, which, or whom *[*the things *whereof* he spoke*]*

where·on′ ***conj.*** [Archaic] on which

where′up·on′ ***conj.*** at which

wher·ev·er (hwer ev′ər) ***adv.*** [Inf.] where: an emphatic form —***conj.*** in, at, or to whatever place or situation *[*go *wherever* you like*]*

where·with′ ***conj.*** [Archaic] with which

where′with·al′ (-*th* ôl′) ***n.*** the necessary means, esp. money: usually with *the*

wher·ry (hwer′ē) ***n.***, *pl.* **-ries** ⟦ME *whery*⟧ a light rowboat

whet (hwet) ***vt.*** **whet′ted, whet′ting** ⟦< OE *hwæt*, keen⟧ **1** to sharpen by rubbing or grinding (the edge of a knife or tool) **2** to stimulate

wheth·er (hweth′ər) ***conj.*** ⟦OE *hwæther*⟧ **1** if it be the case that *[*ask *whether* she sings*]* **2** in case; in either case that: introducing alternatives *[whether* it rains or snows*]*

whet·stone (hwet′stōn′) ***n.*** an abrasive stone for sharpening knives, etc.

whew (hyo͞o) ***interj.*** ⟦echoic⟧ used to express relief, surprise, dismay, etc.

whey (hwā) ***n.*** ⟦OE *hwæg*⟧ the watery part of milk, that separates from the curds

which (hwich) ***pron.*** ⟦OE *hwylc*⟧ **1** what one (or ones) of several? *[which* do you want?*]* **2** the one (or ones) that *[*he knows *which* he wants*]* **3** that *[*the boat *which* sank*]* —***adj.*** what one or ones *[which* man (or men) left?*]*

which·ev′er ***pron.***, ***adj.*** **1** any one *[*take *whichever* (desk) you like*]* **2** no matter which *[whichever* (desk) he chooses, they won't be pleased*]*

whiff (hwif) ***n.*** ⟦echoic⟧ **1** a light puff or gust of air, etc. **2** a slight odor

whif·fle·tree (hwif′əl trē′) ***n.*** *var. of* WHIPPLETREE

Whig (hwig) ***n.*** ⟦< *whiggamore* (derisive term for Scot Presbyterians)⟧ **1** a member of a former English political party that championed reform **2** a supporter of the American Revolution **3** a member of a U.S. political party (*c.* 1834-56)

while (hwīl) ***n.*** ⟦OE *hwil*⟧ a period of time *[*a short *while]* —***conj.*** **1** during the time that *[*I read *while* I eat*]* **2** although; whereas *[while* not poor, she's not rich*]* —***vt.*** **whiled, whil′ing** to spend (time) in a pleasant way: often with *away*

whi·lom (hwī′ləm) ***adj.*** ⟦< OE⟧ former

whilst (hwīlst) ***conj.*** [Chiefly Brit.] WHILE

whim (hwim) ***n.*** a sudden, passing idea or desire

whim·per (hwim′pər) ***vi.***, ***vt.*** ⟦? akin to WHINE⟧ to cry or utter with low, whining, broken sounds —***n.*** a whimpering sound or cry

whim·si·cal (hwim′zi kəl) ***adj.*** **1** full of whims or whimsy **2** oddly out of the ordinary —**whim′si·cal′i·ty** (-kal′ə tē) ***n.*** —**whim′si·cal·ly** ***adv.***

whim·sy (hwim′zē) ***n.***, *pl.* **-sies** ⟦< ?⟧ **1** a sudden, odd notion **2** quaint or fanciful humor Also sp. **whim′sey**, *pl.* **-seys**

whine (hwīn) ***vi.*** **whined, whin′ing** ⟦OE *hwinan*⟧ **1** *a*) to utter a high-pitched, nasal sound, as in complaint *b*) to make a prolonged sound like this **2** to complain in a childish way —***n.*** **1** a whining **2** a complaint uttered in a whining tone —**whin′y, -i·er, -i·est,** ***adj.***

whin·ny (hwin′ē) ***vi.*** **-nied, -ny·ing** ⟦prob. echoic⟧ to neigh in a low, gentle way: said of a horse —***n.***, *pl.* **-nies** a whinnying

whip (hwip) ***vt.*** **whipped** or **whipt**, **whip'ping** ⟦< MDu *wippen*, to swing⟧ **1** to move, pull, throw, etc. suddenly *[to whip out a knife]* **2** to strike, as with a strap; lash **3** to wind (cord, etc.) around (a rope, etc.) so as to prevent fraying **4** to beat into a froth *[to whip cream]* **5** [Inf.] to defeat —***vi.*** **1** to move quickly and suddenly **2** to flap about —***n.*** **1** a flexible instrument for striking or flogging **2** a blow, etc. as with a whip **3** an officer of a political party in a legislature who maintains disclipine, etc. **4** a whipping motion —**whip up 1** to rouse (interest, etc.) **2** [Inf.] to prepare quickly

whip'cord' ***n.*** **1** a hard, twisted or braided cord **2** a strong, diagonally ribbed worsted cloth

whip hand control or advantage

whip'lash' ***n.*** **1** the lash of a whip **2** a sudden, severe jolting of the neck, as in an automobile accident

whip'per·snap'per ***n.*** an insignificant person who appears presumptuous

whip·pet (hwip'it) ***n.*** ⟦< WHIP⟧ a swift dog resembling a small greyhound, used in racing

whip·ple·tree (hwip'əl trē') ***n.*** ⟦< WHIP + TREE⟧ SINGLETREE

whip·poor·will (hwip'ər wil') ***n.*** ⟦echoic⟧ a dark-colored bird of E North America, active at night

whip'py ***adj.*** springy; flexible

whir or **whirr** (hwʉr) ***vi., vt.*** **whirred**, **whir'ring** ⟦ME *quirren*⟧ to fly, revolve, vibrate, etc. with a whizzing or buzzing sound —***n.*** such a sound

whirl (hwʉrl) ***vi.*** ⟦< ON *hvirfla*⟧ **1** to move rapidly in a circle or orbit **2** to rotate or spin fast **3** to seem to spin *[my head is whirling]* —***vt.*** to cause to rotate, revolve, or spin rapidly —***n.*** **1** a whirling motion **2** a confused or giddy condition —**give it a whirl** [Inf.] to make an attempt

whirl·i·gig (hwʉr'li gig') ***n.*** a child's toy that whirls or spins, as a pinwheel

whirl'pool' ***n.*** **1** water in violent, whirling motion, tending to draw floating objects into its center **2** a bath in which an agitating device propels a current of warm water with a swirling motion: in full **whirlpool bath**

whirl'wind' ***n.*** **1** a forward-moving current of air whirling violently in a vertical spiral **2** anything like a whirlwind —***adj.*** impetuous; speedy

whisk (hwisk) ***n.*** ⟦< ON *visk*, a brush⟧ **1** a brushing with a quick, light, sweeping motion **2** such a motion **3** a kitchen utensil of wire loops in a handle, for whipping cream, etc. —***vt.*** to move, carry, brush (*away, off, out,* etc.) with a quick, sweeping motion —***vi.*** to move quickly or nimbly

whisk broom a small, short-handled broom for brushing clothes, etc.

whisk·er (hwis'kər) ***n.*** **1** [*pl.*] the hair growing on a man's face, esp. on the cheeks **2** any of the long, bristly hairs on the upper lip of a cat, rat, etc. **3** a very small amount or margin

whis·key (hwis'kē) ***n.***, *pl.* **-keys** or **-kies** ⟦< Ir *uisce*, water + *beathadh*, life⟧ a strong alcoholic liquor distilled from the fermented mash of grain: also sp. **whis·ky**, *pl.* **-kies**: in general, U.S. and Irish usage favors *whiskey*, and Brit. and Cdn. usage favors *whisky*

whis·per (hwis'pər) ***vi., vt.*** ⟦< OE *hwisprian*⟧ **1** to speak or say very softly, esp. without vibrating the vocal cords **2** to talk or tell furtively, as in gossiping **3** to make a rustling sound —***n.*** **1** a whispering **2** something whispered **3** a soft, rustling sound

whist (hwist) ***n.*** ⟦< earlier *whisk*⟧ a card game that is the forerunner of bridge

whis·tle (hwis'əl) ***vi.*** **-tled**, **-tling** ⟦OE *hwistlian*⟧ **1** to make a clear, shrill sound as by blowing through puckered lips **2** to move with a shrill sound, as the wind does **3** *a*) to blow a whistle *b*) to have its whistle blown *[the train whistled]* —***vt.*** **1** to produce (a tune, etc.) by whistling **2** to signal, etc. by whistling —***n.*** **1** a device for making whistling sounds **2** a whistling —**whis'tler** ***n.***

whis'tle-blow'er ***n.*** one who informs on a wrongdoer

whis'tle-stop' ***n.*** **1** a small town **2** a brief stop in a small town on a tour

whit (hwit) ***n.*** ⟦< OE *wiht*, wight⟧ the least bit; jot

white (hwīt) ***adj.*** **whit'er**, **whit'est** ⟦OE *hwit*⟧ **1** having the color of pure snow or milk; opposite to black **2** of a light or pale color **3** pale; wan **4** lacking color **5** pure; innocent **6** [*sometimes* **W-**] having a light-colored skin; Caucasoid —***n.*** **1** *a*) white color *b*) a white pigment **2** a white or light-colored part, as the albumen of an egg or the white part of the eyeball **3** [*sometimes* **W-**] a person with a light-colored skin —**white'ness** ***n.***

white blood cell (or **corpuscle**) LEUKOCYTE

white'-bread' ***adj.*** [Inf.] **1** of or like the white middle class, its values, etc. **2** bland, conventional, etc.

white'cap' ***n.*** a wave with its crest broken into white foam

white'-col'lar ***adj.*** designating or of office or professional workers

white-collar crime fraud, embezzlement, etc., committed by a person in business, government, or a profession

white elephant **1** an albino elephant **2** something of little use, but expensive to maintain **3** any object no longer wanted by its owner, but possibly useful to another

white'fish' ***n.***, *pl.* **-fish'** or (for different species) **-fish'es** a white or silvery, edible fish, found in cool lakes of the Northern Hemisphere

white flag a white banner or cloth hoisted as a signal of truce or surrender

white gold a gold alloy that looks like platinum

white goods **1** household linens, as sheets and towels **2** large household appliances, as refrigerators and stoves

white heat **1** a temperature at which material glows white **2** a state of intense emotion, excitement, etc. —

white'-hot' ***adj.***

White'horse' capital of the Yukon Territory, Canada: pop. 19,000

White House, the **1** official residence of the President of the U.S. in Washington, DC **2** the executive branch of the U.S. government

white lead a poisonous, white powder, lead carbonate, used in paint

white lie a lie about a trivial matter, often told to spare someone's feelings

white metal any of various light-colored alloys, esp. one containing much lead or tin, as pewter

whit·en (hwīt''n) ***vt., vi.*** to make or become white or whiter —**whit'en·er** ***n.*** —**whit'en·ing** ***n.***

white'-out' ***n.*** ⟦< *Wite-Out*, a trademark⟧ a quick-drying, white fluid that is brushed on to cover printed errors and allow for corrections

white paper **1** an official government report **2** any in-depth, authoritative report

white sale a sale of household linens

white slave a woman forced into prostitution for the profit of others —**white slavery**

white'wall' ***adj.*** designating or of a tire with a circular white band on the side —***n.*** such a tire

white'wash' ***n.*** **1** a mixture of lime, chalk, water, etc., as for whitening walls, etc. **2** a concealing of faults in order to exonerate —***vt.*** **1** to cover with whitewash **2** to conceal the faults of **3** [Inf.] *Sports* to defeat (an opponent) soundly

white'-wa'ter ***adj.*** of or having to do with recreational kayaking, rafting, etc. on rivers with rapids, fast currents, etc. (**white water**)

whith·er (hwi*th*'ər) [Now Rare] ***adv.*** ⟦OE *hwider*⟧ to what place, condition, result, etc.? —***conj.*** **1** to which place, result, etc. **2** wherever

whit·ing[1] (hwīt'iŋ) ***n.*** ⟦< MDu *wit*, white⟧ any of various unrelated food fishes of North America, Europe, etc.

whit·ing[2] (hwīt'iŋ) ***n.*** ⟦ME *hwiting*⟧ powdered chalk used in paints, etc.

whit'ish ***adj.*** somewhat white

Whit·man (hwit'mən), **Walt(er)** 1819-92; U.S. poet

Whit·ney (hwit'nē), **Mount** mountain in EC California: 14,495 ft.

Whit·sun·day (hwit'sun'dā) ***n.*** ⟦OE *Hwita Sunnandæg*, lit., white Sunday⟧ PENTECOST

whit·tle (hwit''l) ***vt.* -tled, -tling** ⟦< OE *thwitan*, to cut⟧ **1** *a)* to cut thin shavings from (wood) with a knife *b)* to carve (an object) thus **2** to reduce gradually —***vi.*** to whittle wood

whiz or **whizz** (hwiz) ***vi.* whizzed, whiz'zing** ⟦echoic⟧ **1** to move swiftly with a buzzing or hissing sound **2** to make this sound —***n.*** **1** this sound **2** [Slang] an expert *[a whiz* at football*]*

who (ho͞o) ***pron.*** ⟦OE *hwa*⟧ **1** what or which person or persons *[who* is he? I asked *who* he was*]* **2** the person or persons that, or a person that *[*a man *who* knows*]*

WHO *abbrev.* World Health Organization

whoa (hwō) ***interj.*** stop!: used esp. in directing a horse to stand still

who·dun·it (ho͞o dun'it) ***n.*** ⟦< WHO + DONE + IT⟧ [Inf.] a mystery novel, play, etc.

who·ev'er ***pron.*** **1** any person that **2** no matter who *[whoever* said it, it's not so*]* **3** who?: an emphatic usage *[whoever* told you that?*]*

whole (hōl) ***adj.*** ⟦OE *hal*⟧ **1** healthy; not diseased or injured **2** not broken, damaged, etc.; intact **3** containing all the parts; complete **4** not divided up; in a single unit **5** not a fraction —***n.*** **1** the entire amount **2** a thing complete in itself —**on the whole** in general —**whole'ness** ***n.***

whole'heart'ed ***adj.*** with all one's energy, enthusiasm, etc.; sincere

whole'-hog' ***adj., adv.*** [Slang] without reservation; complete(ly)

whole milk milk from which no butterfat, etc. has been removed

whole note *Music* a note having four times the duration of a quarter note

whole'sale' ***n.*** the selling of goods in large quantities and at lower prices, esp. to retailers —***adj.*** **1** of or having to do with such selling **2** extensive or indiscriminate *[wholesale* criticism*]* —***adv.*** **1** at wholesale prices **2** extensively or indiscriminately —***vt., vi.* -saled', -sal'ing** to sell wholesale —**whole'sal'er** ***n.***

whole'some ***adj.*** ⟦ME *holsom*⟧ **1** promoting good health or well-being; healthful **2** improving the mind or character **3** healthy; sound —**whole'some·ness** ***n.***

whole tone *Music* an interval consisting of two adjacent semitones: also **whole step**

whole'-wheat' ***adj.*** ground from whole kernels of wheat or made of flour so ground

whol·ly (hōl'lē) ***adv.*** to the whole amount or extent; totally; entirely

whom (ho͞om) ***pron.*** *objective case of* WHO

whom·ev'er (-ev'ər) ***pron.*** *objective case of* WHOEVER

whoop (hwo͞op, wo͞op, ho͞op) ***n.*** ⟦< ? OFr *houper*, cry out⟧ **1** a loud shout, cry, etc., as of joy **2** the convulsive intake of air following a fit of coughing in whooping cough —***vt., vi.*** to utter (with) a whoop or whoops

whoop·ing cough (ho͞o'piŋ, hwo͞o'-) an acute infectious disease, esp. of children, with coughing fits that end in a whoop

whop·per (hwäp'ər, wäp'ər) ***n.*** ⟦< inf. *whop*, to beat⟧ [Inf.] **1** anything extraordinarily large **2** a great lie

whop'ping ***adj.*** [Inf.] extraordinarily large

whore (hôr) ***n.*** ⟦OE *hore*⟧ a prostitute —**whor'ish** ***adj.***

who're (ho͞o'ər) *contr.* who are

whorl (hwôrl, hwurl) ***n.*** ⟦ME *whorwyl*⟧

anything with a coiled or spiral appearance, as any of the circular ridges that form the patterns of a fingerprint —**whorled** ***adj.***

who's (ho͞oz) *contr.* **1** who is **2** who has

whose (ho͞oz) ***pron.*** ⟦OE *hwæs*⟧ that or those belonging to whom —***poss. pronominal adj.*** of, belonging to, or done by whom or which

who·so·ev·er (ho͞o'sō ev'ər) ***pron.*** whoever

why (hwī, wī) ***adv.*** ⟦OE *hwæt*, what⟧ for what reason, cause, or purpose? *[why eat?]* —***conj.*** **1** because of which *[*no reason *why* you shouldn't go*]* **2** the reason for which *[*that is *why* he went*]* —***n.,*** *pl.* **whys** the reason; cause —***interj.*** an exclamation of surprise, impatience, etc.

WI Wisconsin

Wich·i·ta (wich'ə tô') city in S Kansas: pop. 304,000

wick (wik) ***n.*** ⟦OE *weoca*⟧ a piece of cord, etc., as in a candle or oil lamp, that absorbs the fuel and, when lighted, burns

wick·ed (wik'id) ***adj.*** ⟦ME < *wikke*, evil⟧ **1** morally bad; evil **2** generally bad, unpleasant, etc. *[*a *wicked* storm*]* **3** mischievous **4** [Slang] showing great skill —**wick'ed·ly** ***adv.*** —**wick'ed·ness** ***n.***

wick·er (wik'ər) ***n.*** ⟦< Scand⟧ **1** a thin, flexible twig **2** *a)* such twigs or long, woody strips woven together, as in making baskets *b)* WICKERWORK (sense 1) —***adj.*** made of wicker

wick'er·work' ***n.*** **1** things made of wicker **2** WICKER (*n.* 2*a*)

wick·et (wik'it) ***n.*** ⟦ME *wiket*⟧ **1** a small door or gate, esp. one in or near a larger one **2** a small window, as in a box office **3** *Croquet* any of the small wire arches through which balls are hit

wide (wīd) ***adj.*** **wid'er, wid'est** ⟦OE *wid*⟧ **1** extending over a large area, esp. from side to side **2** of a specified extent from side to side **3** of great extent *[*a *wide* variety*]* **4** open fully *[*eyes *wide* with fear*]* **5** far from the point, etc. aimed at: usually with *of [wide* of the target*]* —***adv.*** **1** over a relatively large area **2** to a large or full extent *[wide* open*]* **3** so as to miss the point, etc. aimed at; astray —**wide'ly** ***adv.*** —**wide'ness** ***n.***

-wide (wīd) *combining form* existing or extending throughout *[statewide]*

wide'-an'gle ***adj.*** designating or of a camera lens having a wider than ordinary angle of view

wide'-a·wake' ***adj.*** **1** completely awake **2** alert

wide'-eyed' ***adj.*** **1** with the eyes opened widely, as in surprise or fear **2** naive or unsophisticated

wid·en (wīd''n) ***vt., vi.*** to make or become wider

wide'-o'pen ***adj.*** **1** opened wide **2** having no or few legal restrictions against prostitution, gambling, etc. *[*a *wide-open* city*]*

wide'spread' ***adj.*** occurring over a wide area

widg·eon (wij'ən) ***n.*** *alt. sp. of* WIGEON

wid·ow (wid'ō) ***n.*** ⟦OE *widewe*⟧ a woman whose husband has died and who has not remarried —***vt.*** to cause to become a widow —**wid'ow·hood'** ***n.***

wid'ow·er ***n.*** a man whose wife has died and who has not remarried

width (width) ***n.*** **1** distance from side to side **2** a piece of a certain width *[*two *widths* of cloth*]*

wield (wēld) ***vt.*** ⟦OE *wealdan*⟧ **1** to handle (a tool, etc.), esp. with skill **2** to exercise (power, influence, etc.)

wie·ner (wē'nər) ***n.*** ⟦< Ger *Wiener wurst*, Vienna sausage⟧ a smoked link sausage; frankfurter: also [Inf.] **wie'nie** (-nē)

wife (wīf) ***n.,*** *pl.* **wives** ⟦OE *wif*, woman⟧ a married woman —**wife'less** ***adj.*** —**wife'ly** ***adj.***

wig (wig) ***n.*** ⟦< PERIWIG⟧ a covering of real or synthetic hair worn as to hide baldness —***vt.*** **wigged, wig'ging** **1** to furnish with a wig **2** [Slang] *a)* to annoy, upset, etc. *b)* to make excited, crazy, etc. (often with *out*) —***vi.*** [Slang] to be or become upset, excited, etc.: often with *out*

wi·geon (wij'ən) ***n.*** ⟦prob. < L *vipio*, small crane⟧ any of certain wild, freshwater ducks

wig·gle (wig'əl) ***vt., vi.*** **-gled, -gling** ⟦ME *wigelen*⟧ to move or cause to move with short, jerky motions from side to side —***n.*** a wiggling —**wig'gler** ***n.*** —**wig'gly, -gli·er, -gli·est,** ***adj.***

wight (wīt) ***n.*** ⟦OE *wiht*⟧ [Archaic] a human being

wig·let (wig'lit) ***n.*** a small wig

wig·wag (wig'wag') ***vt., vi.*** **-wagged', -wag'ging** ⟦< obs. *wig*, to move + WAG[1]⟧ **1** to move back and forth; wag **2** to send (a message) by a visible code —***n.*** the sending of messages in this way

wig·wam (wig'wäm') ***n.*** ⟦< Algonquian⟧ a North American Indian dwelling of a dome-shaped framework of poles covered with mats or bark

wild (wīld) ***adj.*** ⟦OE *wilde*⟧ **1** living or growing in its original, natural state **2** not lived in or cultivated; waste **3** not civilized; savage **4** not easily controlled *[*a *wild* child*]* **5** lacking social or moral restraint; dissolute *[*a *wild* time*]* **6** turbulent; stormy **7** enthusiastic *[wild* about golf*]* **8** fantastically impractical; reckless **9** missing the target *[*a *wild* shot*]* **10** *Card Games* having any desired value: said of a card —***adv.*** in a wild manner —***n.*** [*usually pl.*] a wilderness or wasteland —**wild'ly** ***adv.*** —**wild'ness** ***n.***

wild'cat' ***n.*** **1** any fierce, medium-sized, undomesticated cat, as the bobcat, ocelot, etc. **2** an oil well in a previously unproductive area —***adj.*** **1** unsound or risky **2** illegal or unauthorized *[*a *wildcat* strike*]* —***vi.*** **-cat'ted, -cat'ting** to drill for oil in a previously unproductive area

wil·de·beest (wil'də bēst', vil'-) ***n.*** ⟦Afrik⟧ GNU

wil·der·ness (wil'dər nis) ***n.*** ⟦< OE *wilde*, wild + *deor*, animal⟧ an uncultivated region

wild'-eyed' *adj.* **1** staring in a wild or demented way **2** very foolish or impractical

wild'fire' *n.* a fire that spreads widely and rapidly

wild'flow'er *n.* **1** any flowering plant growing wild in fields, etc. **2** its flower Also **wild flower**

wild'fowl' *n., pl.* **-fowls'** or **-fowl'** a wild bird, esp. a game bird: also **wild fowl**

wild'-goose' chase a futile search or pursuit

wild'life' *n.* wild animals and birds

wild oats a wild grass common in the W U.S. —**sow one's wild oats** to be promiscuous or dissolute in one's youth

wild rice **1** an aquatic grass of the U.S. and Canada **2** its edible grain

Wild West [*also* **w- W-**] the western U.S. in its early frontier period of lawlessness

wile (wīl) *n.* ⟦< OE *wigle*, magic⟧ **1** a sly trick; stratagem **2** a beguiling trick: *usually used in pl.* —*vt.* **wiled, wil'ing** to beguile; lure —**wile away** to while away (time, etc.)

wil·ful (wil'fəl) *adj. alt. sp. of* WILLFUL

Wilkes-Bar·re (wilks'bar'ē) city in NE Pennsylvania: pop. 48,000

will[1] (wil) *n.* ⟦OE *willa*⟧ **1** the power of making a reasoned choice or of controlling one's own actions **2** determination **3** attitude toward others [a man of good *will*] **4** *a*) a particular desire, choice, etc. of someone *b*) mandate [the *will* of the people] **5** a legal document directing the disposal of one's property after death —*vt.* **1** to desire; want [to *will* to live] **2** to control by the power of the will **3** to bequeath by a will —*vi.* to wish, desire, or choose —**at will** when one wishes

will[2] (wil) *v.aux. pt.* **would** ⟦OE *willan*, to desire⟧ **1** used to indicate simple future time [when *will* she arrive?] **2** used to express determination, obligation, etc. [you *will* listen to me] **3** used in polite questions [*will* you have some wine?] **4** used to express habit, expectation, etc. [they *will* talk for hours] **5** used to express possibility

USAGE—the distinction between WILL[2] (for second and third person subjects) and SHALL (for the first person) in expressing simple future time or determination, etc. is today virtually nonexistent in North American English; WILL[2] and SHALL and their respective past tenses WOULD and SHOULD are usually interchangeable, with WILL[2] (and WOULD) being the preferred form in all persons

will'ful (-fəl) *adj.* **1** said or done deliberately **2** doing as one pleases —**will'ful·ly** *adv.* —**will'ful·ness** *n.*

Wil·liam I (wil'yəm) 1027?-87; duke of Normandy who invaded England: king of England (1066-87): called *William the Conqueror*

Wil·liams·burg (wil'yəmz burg') city in SE Virginia, restored to its 18th-c. look: pop. 12,000

wil·lies (wil'ēz) *pl.n.* ⟦< ?⟧ [Slang] a nervous feeling; jitters: with *the*

will'ing *adj.* **1** favorably disposed; consenting [*willing* to play] **2** acting, giving, etc. or done, given, etc. readily and cheerfully —**will'ing·ly** *adv.* —**will'ing·ness** *n.*

wil·li·waw or **wil'ly·waw'** (wil'i wô') *n.* **1** a violent, cold wind blowing from mountain passes toward the coast **2** confusion; turmoil

will-o'-the-wisp (wil'ə *th*ə wisp') *n.* a delusive hope or goal

wil·low (wil'ō) *n.* ⟦OE *welig*⟧ **1** a tree with narrow leaves, and flexible twigs used in weaving baskets, etc. **2** its wood

wil'low·y *adj.* like a willow; slender, lithe, etc.

will'pow'er *n.* strength of will, mind, or determination; self-control

wil·ly-nil·ly (wil'ē nil'ē) *adv., adj.* ⟦contr. < *will I, nill I*: *nill* < OE *nyllan*, be unwilling⟧ **1** (happening) whether one wishes it or not **2** in a disordered way; helter-skelter

Wil·son (wil'sən), **(Thomas) Wood·row** (wood'rō) 1856-1924; 28th president of the U.S. (1913-21)

wilt (wilt) *vi.* ⟦< obs. *welk*, to wither⟧ **1** to become limp, as from heat or lack of water; droop: said of plants **2** to become weak or faint; lose strength or courage —*vt.* to cause to wilt

Wil·ton (carpet or **rug)** (wilt''n) ⟦after *Wilton*, England⟧ a kind of carpet with a velvety pile of cut loops

wil·y (wī'lē) *adj.* **-i·er, -i·est** full of wiles; crafty; sly —**wil'i·ness** *n.*

wimp (wimp) *n.* ⟦< ?⟧ [Slang] a weak, ineffectual, or insipid person —**wimp'ish** *adj.* —**wimp'y, -i·er, -i·est,** *adj.*

wim·ple (wim'pəl) *n.* ⟦OE *wimpel*⟧ a nun's head covering that leaves only the face exposed

win (win) *vi.* **won, win'ning** ⟦< OE *winnan*, to fight⟧ **1** *a*) to gain a victory *b*) to finish first in a race, etc. **2** to succeed in reaching a specified condition or place; get [to *win* back to health] —*vt.* **1** to get by labor, struggle, etc. **2** to be victorious in (a contest, etc.) **3** to get to with effort [they *won* the camp by noon] **4** to prevail upon; persuade: often with *over* **5** to gain (the sympathy, favor, etc.) of (someone) **6** to persuade to marry one —*n.* a victory

wince (wins) *vi.* **winced, winc'ing** ⟦< OFr *guenchir*⟧ to shrink or draw back slightly, usually with a grimace, as in pain —*n.* a wincing

winch (winch) *n.* ⟦OE *wince*⟧ **1** a crank with a handle for transmitting motion **2** a machine for hoisting, etc. using a cylinder upon which is wound the rope, etc. attached to an object

Win·ches·ter (win'ches'tər) ⟦after O. F. *Winchester* (1810-80), the manufacturer⟧ *trademark for* a type of repeating rifle

wind[1] (wīnd) *vt.* **wound** or [Rare] **wind'ed, wind'ing** ⟦OE *windan*⟧ **1** to turn [to *wind* a crank] **2** to coil into a ball or around something else; twine **3**

to cover by entwining 4 *a*) to make (one's way) in a twisting course *b*) to cause to move in a twisting course 5 to tighten the spring of (a clock, etc.) as by turning a stem: often with *up* —*vi.* 1 to move or go in a curving or sinuous manner 2 to take a devious course 3 to coil (*about* or *around* something) —*n.* a turn; twist —**wind down** 1 to bring or come to an end 2 to become relaxed; unwind —**wind up** 1 to wind into a ball, etc. 2 to bring to an end; settle 3 to make very tense, excited, etc. 4 *Baseball* to perform a WINDUP (sense 2) —**wind'er** *n.*

wind² (wind) *n.* ⟦OE⟧ 1 air in motion 2 a strong current of air; gale 3 air bearing a scent, as in hunting 4 air regarded as bearing information, etc. *[a rumor in the wind]* 5 breath or the power of breathing 6 empty talk 7 [*pl.*] the wind instruments of an orchestra —*vt.* 1 to get the scent of 2 to put out of breath —**break wind** to expel gas from the bowels —**get wind of** to hear of —**in the wind** happening or about to happen

wind·bag (wind'bag') *n.* [Inf.] one who talks much but says little of importance

wind'break' *n.* a hedge, fence, etc. serving as a protection from wind

Wind'break'er *trademark for* a warm jacket with closefitting waistband and cuffs

wind'burn' *n.* a reddened, sore skin condition, caused by overexposure to the wind

wind'chill' factor an estimated measure of the cooling effect of air and wind on exposed skin

wind chimes (or **bells**) a cluster of small chimes or pendants hung so that they strike one another and tinkle when blown by the wind

wind·ed (win'did) *adj.* out of breath

wind·fall (wind'fôl') *n.* an unexpected gain, stroke of good luck, etc.

wind farm a network of modern, high-speed windmills for generating electricity

wind·ing sheet (wīn'diŋ) a shroud

wind instrument (wind) a musical instrument sounded by blowing air through it, as a flute

wind·jam·mer (wind'jam'ər) *n.* a large sailing ship or one of its crew

wind·lass (wind'ləs) *n.* ⟦< ON *vinda*, to WIND¹ + *ass*, a beam⟧ a winch, esp. one worked by a crank

WINDLASS

wind'mill' *n.* 1 a mill operated by the wind's rotation of large vanes radiating from a shaft 2 a device like this, as one to harness wind power

win·dow (win'dō) *n.* ⟦< ON *vindr*, WIND² + *auga*, an eye⟧ 1 an opening in a building, vehicle, etc. for letting in light, air, etc. usually having a pane of glass in a movable frame 2 a windowpane 3 an opening resembling a window 4 the interval during which something can be done

window box a long, narrow box on or outside a window ledge, for growing plants

window dressing 1 the display of goods in a store window 2 that which is meant to make something seem better than it really is —**win'dow-dress'** *vt.* —**window dresser**

win'dow·pane' *n.* a pane of glass in a window

win'dow-shop' *vi.* **-shopped'**, **-shop'ping** to look at goods in store windows without entering to buy

win'dow·sill' *n.* the sill of a window

wind·pipe (wind'pīp') *n.* TRACHEA

wind'row' (-rō') *n.* a row of hay, etc. raked together to dry

wind shear a sudden change in wind direction, esp., dangerous vertical wind shifts

wind'shield' *n.* in automobiles, etc., a glass screen, in front, to protect from wind, etc.

wind'sock' *n.* a long, cloth cone flown at an airfield to show wind direction: also **wind sleeve**

Wind·sor (win'zər) port in SE Ontario, Canada: pop. 198,000

Windsor knot a double slipknot in a four-in-hand necktie

wind'storm' *n.* a storm with a strong wind but little or no rain, hail, etc.

wind'surf' *vi.* to ride for sport on a kind of surfboard with a pivoting sail —**wind'surf'ing** *n.*

wind tunnel a tunnel-like chamber through which air is forced, for testing the effects of wind pressure on aircraft, motor vehicles, etc.

wind·up (wīnd'up') *n.* 1 a conclusion; end 2 *Baseball* the motion of the pitcher leading up to throwing the ball

wind·ward (wind'wərd) *n.* the direction from which the wind blows —*adv.* toward the wind —*adj.* 1 moving windward 2 on the side from which the wind blows

Windward Islands S group of islands in the West Indies, south of the Leeward Islands

wind·y (win'dē) *adj.* **-i·er**, **-i·est** 1 with much wind *[a windy city]* 2 stormy, blustery, etc. 3 long-winded, pompous, etc. —**wind'i·ness** *n.*

wine (wīn) *n.* ⟦< L *vinum*⟧ the fermented juice of grapes, etc., used as an alcoholic beverage —*vt.*, *vi.* **wined**, **win'ing** usually in the phrase **wine and dine**, to entertain lavishly

wine'-col'ored *adj.* dark purplish-red

win·er·y (wīn'ər ē) *n.*, *pl.* **-ies** an establishment where wine is made

wing (wiŋ) *n.* ⟦ON *vaengr*⟧ 1 either of the paired organs of flight of a bird, bat, insect, etc. 2 something like a wing in use, position, etc., esp., *a*) a (or the) main lateral supporting surface of an airplane *b*) a subordinate, projecting part of a building *c*) either side of the stage out of sight of the audience 3 the section of an army, fleet, etc. to the right (or left) of the center 4 a section, as of a political party, with reference to its radicalism or conservatism 5 a unit in an air force —*vt.* 1 to provide with wings 2 *a*) to send swiftly as on wings *b*) to make (one's way) by flying *c*) to pass through or over, as by flying 3 to wound in the wing, arm, etc. —*vi.* to fly —**on the wing** (while) flying —**take wing** to fly away —**under one's wing** under one's protection, etc. —**wing it** [Inf.] to improvise in acting, etc. —**winged** (wiŋd; *poet.* wiŋ′id) *adj.* —**wing′less** *adj.*

wing′ding′ (-diŋ′) *n.* ⟦< ?⟧ [Slang] an event, party, etc. that is very festive, lively, etc.

wing′span′ *n.* 1 the distance between the tips of an airplane's wings 2 WINGSPREAD (sense 1)

wing′spread′ *n.* 1 the distance between the tips of fully spread wings 2 WINGSPAN

wink (wiŋk) *vi.* ⟦OE *wincian*⟧ 1 to close the eyelids and open them again quickly 2 to close and open one eyelid quickly, as a signal, etc. 3 to twinkle —*vt.* to make (an eye) wink —*n.* 1 a winking 2 an instant 3 a signal given by winking 4 a twinkle —**wink at** to pretend not to see

win·ner (win′ər) *n.* one that wins

win·ning (win′iŋ) *adj.* 1 victorious 2 attractive; charming —*n.* 1 a victory 2 [*pl.*] money won

Win·ni·peg (win′ə peg′) capital of Manitoba, Canada: pop. 618,000

win·now (win′ō) *vt.*, *vi.* ⟦< OE *wind*, WIND[2]⟧ 1 to blow (chaff) from (grain) 2 to scatter 3 to sift out

win·o (wī′nō) *n.*, *pl.* **-os** [Slang] an alcoholic who drinks cheap wine

win·some (win′səm) *adj.* ⟦OE *wynsum*, pleasant⟧ sweetly attractive; charming —**win′some·ly** *adv.*

Win·ston-Sa·lem (win′stən sā′ləm) city in NC North Carolina: pop. 143,000

win·ter (win′tər) *n.* ⟦OE⟧ 1 the coldest season of the year, following autumn 2 a period of decline, distress, etc. —*adj.* of, during, or for winter —*vi.* to pass the winter —*vt.* to keep, feed, etc. during winter

win′ter·green′ *n.* 1 an evergreen plant with white flowers and red berries 2 an aromatic oil (**oil of wintergreen**) made from its leaves and used as a flavoring 3 the flavor

win′ter·ize′ *vt.* **-ized′**, **-iz′ing** to put into condition for winter

win′ter·kill′ *vt.*, *vi.* to kill or die by exposure to winter cold or excessive snow and ice —*n.* the process or an instance of winterkilling

win′ter·time′ *n.* the winter season

win·try (win′trē) *adj.* **-tri·er**, **-tri·est** of or like winter; cold, bleak, etc. *[a wintry day]*

win′-win′ *adj.* designating or of a situation from which all possible outcomes are satisfactory

win·y (wī′nē) *adj.* **-i·er**, **-i·est** like wine in taste, smell, color, etc.

wipe (wīp) *vt.* **wiped**, **wip′ing** ⟦OE *wipian*⟧ 1 to clean or dry by rubbing with a cloth, etc. 2 to rub (a cloth, etc.) over something 3 to apply or remove by wiping —*n.* a wiping —**wipe out** 1 to remove; erase 2 to kill off 3 to destroy —**wip′er** *n.*

wiped′-out′ *adj.* [Slang] exhausted

wire (wīr) *n.* ⟦OE *wir*⟧ 1 metal drawn into a long thread 2 a length of this 3 a telegram 4 the finish line of a horse race —*adj.* made of wire —*vt.* **wired**, **wir′ing** 1 to furnish, connect, etc. with wire 2 to telegraph —*vi.* to telegraph

wired (wīrd) *adj.* [Slang] 1 provided with concealed electronic listening or recording equipment 2 extremely excited, nervous, etc.

wire′hair′ *n.* a fox terrier with a wiry coat: also called **wire′-haired′ terrier**

wire′less (-lis) *adj.* operating by electromagnetic waves, not with conducting wire —*n.* 1 wireless telegraphy or telephony 2 [Chiefly Brit.] *old-fashioned term for* RADIO

wire service an agency sending news electronically to subscribing newspapers, etc.

wire′tap′ *vi.*, *vt.* **-tapped′**, **-tap′ping** to tap (a telephone wire, etc.) to get information secretly —*n.* 1 a wiretapping 2 a device for wiretapping

wir′ing *n.* a system of wires, as to provide a house with electricity

wir·y (wīr′ē) *adj.* **-i·er**, **-i·est** 1 of wire 2 like wire; stiff 3 lean and strong —**wir′i·ness** *n.*

Wis·con·sin (wis kän′sən) Midwestern state of the U.S.: 56,154 sq. mi.; pop. 4,892,000; cap. Madison: abbrev. *WI* —**Wis·con′sin·ite′** *n.*

wis·dom (wiz′dəm) *n.* ⟦OE: see WISE[1] & -DOM⟧ 1 the quality of being wise; good judgment 2 learning; knowledge

wisdom tooth the back tooth on each side of each jaw

wise[1] (wīz) *adj.* **wis′er**, **wis′est** ⟦OE *wis*⟧ 1 having or showing good judgment 2 informed *[none the wiser]* 3 learned 4 shrewd; cunning 5 [Slang] conceited, impudent, fresh, etc. —**wise′ly** *adv.*

wise[2] (wīz) *n.* ⟦OE⟧ way; manner

-wise (wīz) ⟦< prec.⟧ *suffix* 1 in a (specified) direction, position, or manner *[lengthwise]* 2 in a manner characteristic of *[clockwise]* 3 with regard to *[budgetwise]*

wise·a·cre (wīz′ā′kər) *n.* ⟦ult. < OHG *wizzago*, prophet⟧ one who makes annoyingly conceited claims to knowledge

wise′crack′ [Slang] *n.* a flippant or facetious remark —*vi.* to make wisecracks

wish (wish) *vt.* ⟦OE *wyscan*⟧ 1 to have a longing for; want 2 to express a desire concerning *[I wish you well]* 3 to request *[I wish you to go]* —*vi.* 1 to long; yearn 2 to make a wish —*n.* 1 a wishing 2 something wished for 3 a polite request, almost an order 4 [*pl.*] expressed desire for a person's health, etc. [best *wishes*] —**wish'er** *n.*

wish'bone' *n.* the forked bone in front of a bird's breastbone

wish'ful (-fəl) *adj.* having or showing a wish; desirous —**wish'ful·ly** *adv.*

wish·y-wash·y (wish'ē wôsh'ē) *adj.* [Inf.] 1 weak; feeble 2 vacillating; indecisive

wisp (wisp) *n.* ⟦prob. < Scand⟧ 1 a small bundle, as of straw 2 a thin or filmy piece, strand, etc. [a *wisp* of smoke] 3 something delicate, frail, etc. —**wisp'y, -i·er, -i·est,** *adj.*

wis·te·ri·a (wis tir'ē ə) *n.* ⟦after C. *Wistar* (1761-1818), U.S. anatomist⟧ a twining vine with showy clusters of flowers: also **wis·tar'i·a** (-ter'-)

wist·ful (wist'fəl) *adj.* ⟦< earlier *wistly*, attentive⟧ showing or expressing vague yearnings —**wist'ful·ly** *adv.* —**wist'ful·ness** *n.*

wit[1] (wit) *n.* ⟦OE⟧ 1 [*pl.*] powers of thinking; mental faculties 2 good sense 3 *a*) the ability to make clever remarks in a sharp, amusing way *b*) one characterized by wit

wit[2] (wit) *vt., vi.* **wist** (wist), **wit'ting** ⟦OE *witan*⟧ [Archaic] to know —**to wit** that is to say; namely

witch (wich) *n.* ⟦OE *wicce*⟧ 1 a woman thought to have supernatural power as by a compact with evil spirits 2 an ugly, old shrew 3 [Inf.] a fascinating woman or girl

witch'craft' *n.* the power or practices of witches

witch doctor in certain primitive societies, one thought able to cure sickness, ward off evil, etc. by using magic or incantations

witch'er·y (-ər ē) *n., pl.* **-ies** 1 witchcraft; sorcery 2 bewitching charm

witch hazel ⟦< OE *wice*⟧ 1 a shrub with yellow flowers 2 a lotion made from its leaves and bark, used on inflammations, etc.

witch hunt ⟦so named in allusion to persecutions of persons alleged to be witches⟧ a highly publicized investigation carried out ostensibly to uncover disloyalty, etc., relying upon little evidence

with (with, with) *prep.* ⟦OE⟧ 1 in opposition to [to argue *with* a friend] 2 *a*) alongside of; near to *b*) in the company of *c*) into; among [mix blue *with* yellow] 3 as a member of [to play *with* a string quartet] 4 concerning [happy *with* his lot] 5 compared to 6 as well as [she rides *with* the best] 7 in the opinion of [it's OK *with* me] 8 as a result of [faint *with* hunger] 9 by means of 10 having received [*with* your consent, I'll go] 11 having as a possession, attribute, etc. 12 in the keeping, care, etc. of [leave it *with* me] 13 in spite of 14 at the same time as 15 in proportion to [wages that vary *with* skill] 16 to; onto [join one end *with* the other] 17 from [to part *with* one's gains] —**with that** after, or as a consequence of, that

with- *combining form* 1 away, back [*withdraw*] 2 against, from [*withhold*]

with·al (with ôl', with-) *adv.* 1 besides 2 despite that

with·draw' *vt.* **-drew', -drawn', -draw'ing** 1 to take back; remove 2 to retract or recall (a statement, etc.) —*vi.* 1 to move back; go away; retreat 2 to remove oneself (*from* an organization, activity, etc.)

with·draw'al *n.* 1 the act of withdrawing 2 the process of giving up a narcotic drug, typically accompanied by distressing physical and mental effects (**withdrawal symptoms**)

with·drawn' *vt., vi. pp. of* WITHDRAW —*adj.* shy, reserved, etc.

withe (with, with) *n.* ⟦< OE *withthe*⟧ a tough, flexible twig of willow, osier, etc., used for binding

with·er (with'ər) *vi.* ⟦< ME *wederen*, to weather⟧ 1 to dry up; wilt, as plants 2 to become wasted or decayed 3 to weaken; languish —*vt.* 1 to cause to wither 2 to cause to feel abashed

with·ers (with'ərz) *pl.n.* ⟦< OE *wither*, against⟧ the part of a horse's back between the shoulder blades

with·hold (with hōld', with-) *vt.* **-held', -hold'ing** 1 *a*) to hold back; restrain *b*) to deduct (taxes, etc.) from wages 2 to refrain from granting

withholding tax the amount of income tax withheld, as payment in advance, from an employee's pay

with·in (with in', with-) *adv.* ⟦OE *withinnan*⟧ 1 on or into the inside 2 indoors 3 inside the body, mind, etc. —*prep.* 1 in the inner part of 2 not beyond 3 inside the limits of —*n.* the inside

with'-it (-it) *adj.* [Slang] 1 sophisticated, up-to-date, etc. 2 fashionable; stylish

with·out' *adv.* ⟦OE *withutan*⟧ 1 on the outside 2 out-of-doors —*prep.* 1 [Now Rare] at, on, or to the outside of 2 lacking 3 free from 4 with avoidance of [to pass by *without* speaking]

with·stand' (-stand') *vt., vi.* **-stood', -stand'ing** to oppose, resist, or endure, esp. successfully

wit·less (wit'lis) *adj.* lacking wit; foolish —**wit'less·ly** *adv.*

wit·ness (wit'nis) *n.* ⟦< OE *witan*, know⟧ 1 evidence; testimony 2 one who saw, or can give a firsthand account of, something 3 one who testifies in court 4 one who observes, and attests to, a signing, etc. —*vt.* 1 to testify to 2 to serve as evidence of 3 to act as witness of 4 to be present at —**bear witness** to testify

wit·ti·cism (wit'ə siz'əm) *n.* ⟦< WITTY⟧ a witty remark

wit·ting (wit'iŋ) *adj.* ⟦ME *wytting*⟧ intentional

wit·ty (wit'ē) *adj.* **-ti·er, -ti·est** ⟦OE *wittig*⟧ having or showing wit; cleverly amusing —**wit'ti·ly** *adv.* —**wit'ti·ness** *n.*

wive (wīv) *vi., vt.* **wived, wiv'ing** ⟦OE

wifian⟧ [Archaic] to marry (a woman)

wives (wīvz) ***n. pl. of*** WIFE

wiz·ard (wiz′ərd) ***n.*** ⟦ME *wisard*⟧ **1** a magician; sorcerer **2** [Inf.] one very skilled at a specified activity

wiz′ard·ry ***n.*** magic; sorcery

wiz·ened (wiz′ənd) ***adj.*** ⟦< OE *wisnian*, wither⟧ dried up; withered

wk *abbrev.* **1** week **2** work

wkly. *abbrev.* weekly

w/o *abbrev.* without

wob·ble (wäb′əl) ***vi.*** **-bled, -bling** ⟦prob. < LowG *wabbeln*⟧ **1** to move unsteadily from side to side **2** to shake **3** to vacillate —***vt.*** to cause to wobble —***n.*** wobbling motion —**wob′bly, -bli·er, -bli·est,** ***adj.*** —**wob′bli·ness** ***n.***

woe (wō) ***n.*** ⟦OE *wa*⟧ **1** great sorrow; grief **2** trouble —***interj.*** alas!

woe′be·gone′ (-bē gôn′, -bi-) ***adj.*** of woeful appearance; looking sad or wretched

woe′ful (-fəl) ***adj.*** **1** full of woe; sad **2** causing woe **3** pitiful; wretched —**woe′ful·ly** ***adv.***

wok (wäk, wôk) ***n.*** ⟦Chin⟧ a bowl-shaped cooking pan used for frying, steaming, etc.

woke (wōk) ***vi., vt. alt. pt. of*** WAKE[1]

wok·en (wō′kən) ***vi., vt. alt. pp. of*** WAKE[1]

wolf (woolf) ***n., pl.*** **wolves** (woolvz) ⟦OE *wulf*⟧ **1** a wild, flesh-eating, doglike mammal of the Northern Hemisphere **2** *a*) a cruel or greedy person *b*) [Slang] a man who flirts with many women —***vt.*** to eat greedily: often with *down* —**cry wolf** to give a false alarm —**wolf′ish** ***adj.***

wolf′hound′ ***n.*** a breed of large dog, once used for hunting wolves

wol·ver·ine (wool′vər ēn′) ***n.*** ⟦< WOLF⟧ a stocky, flesh-eating mammal of N North America and N Eurasia

wolves (woolvz) ***n. pl. of*** WOLF

wom·an (woom′ən) ***n., pl.*** **wom·en** (wim′ən) ⟦< OE *wif*, a female + *mann*, human being⟧ **1** *a*) an adult female human being *b*) women collectively **2** a female servant **3** womanly qualities

-wom·an (woom′ən) *combining form* woman of a (specified) kind, in a (specified) activity, etc.: sometimes used to avoid the masculine implications of -MAN

wom′an·hood′ ***n.*** **1** the state of being a woman **2** womanly qualities **3** women collectively

wom′an·ish ***adj.*** like or characteristic of a woman

wom′an·ize′ ***vt.*** **-ized′, -iz′ing** to make effeminate —***vi.*** to be sexually promiscuous with women —**wom′an·iz′er** ***n.***

wom′an·kind′ ***n.*** women in general

wom′an·ly ***adj.*** **1** womanish **2** characteristic of or fit for a woman —**wom′an·li·ness** ***n.***

womb (wōōm) ***n.*** ⟦OE *wamb*⟧ UTERUS

wom·bat (wäm′bat′) ***n.*** ⟦< native name⟧ a burrowing marsupial resembling a small bear, found in Australia, etc.

wom·en (wim′in) ***n. pl. of*** WOMAN

wom′en·folk′ ***pl.n.*** [Inf. or Dial.] women or womankind: also **wom′en·folks′**

won (wun) ***vi., vt. pt. & pp. of*** WIN

won·der (wun′dər) ***n.*** ⟦OE *wundor*⟧ **1** a person, thing, or event causing astonishment and admiration; marvel **2** the feeling aroused by something strange, unexpected, etc. —***vi.*** **1** to be filled with wonder; marvel **2** to have curiosity, sometimes mingled with doubt —***vt.*** to have curiosity or doubt about *[he wondered what happened]*

won′der·ful ***adj.*** **1** that causes wonder; marvelous **2** excellent, fine, etc. —**won′der·ful·ly** ***adv.***

won′der·land′ ***n.*** any place, real or imaginary, full of wonders

won′der·ment ***n.*** amazement

won·drous (wun′drəs) ***adj.*** wonderful: now chiefly literary —***adv.*** [Archaic] surprisingly

wont (wônt, wōnt) ***adj.*** ⟦< OE *wunian*, dwell⟧ accustomed *[she was wont to rise early]* —***n.*** usual practice; habit

won't (wōnt) *contr.* will not

wont·ed (wôn′tid, wōn′-) ***adj.*** customary

won ton (wän′ tän′) ⟦Cantonese⟧ Chinese dumplings of noodle dough filled with chopped meat, etc., often served in a soup (**won′-ton′ soup**)

woo (wōō) ***vt.*** ⟦OE *wogian*⟧ **1** to seek the love of, usually in order to propose marriage **2** to seek *[to woo fame]* —***vi.*** to woo a person —**woo′er** ***n.***

wood (wood) ***n.*** ⟦OE *wudu*⟧ **1** [*usually pl., with sing. or pl. v.*] a thick growth of trees; forest **2** the hard, fibrous substance beneath the bark of trees and shrubs **3** lumber or timber **4** *Golf* any of certain clubs, originally with wooden heads —***adj.*** **1** made of wood; wooden **2** growing or living in woods —**out of the woods** [Inf.] out of difficulty, danger, etc.

wood alcohol METHANOL

wood′bine′ (-bīn′) ***n.*** ⟦< OE *wudu*, wood + *binde*, to bind⟧ **1** a climbing honeysuckle **2** a climbing vine with dark-blue berries

wood′carv′ing ***n.*** **1** the art of carving wood by hand **2** an object so made —**wood′carv′er** ***n.***

wood′chuck′ ***n.*** ⟦< AmInd name⟧ a burrowing and hibernating marmot of North America

WOODCHUCK

wood′cock′ ***n.*** a small game bird with short legs and a long bill

wood′craft′ ***n.*** **1** matters relating to

the woods, as camping, hunting, etc. **2** WOODWORKING

wood'cut' *n.* **1** a wooden block engraved with a design, etc. **2** a print from this

wood'cut'ter *n.* one who fells trees, cuts wood, etc. —**wood'cut'ting** *n.*

wood'ed *adj.* covered with trees

wood'en *adj.* **1** made of wood **2** stiff, lifeless, etc. **3** dull; insensitive —**wood'en·ly** *adv.*

wood'land (-lənd, -land') *n.* land covered with woods —*adj.* of the woods

wood'lot' *n.* a piece of land where trees are raised, as for firewood, lumber, etc.

wood'peck'er (-pek'ər) *n.* a climbing bird with a strong, pointed bill used to peck holes in bark to get insects

wood'pile' *n.* a pile of wood, esp. of firewood

wood screw a screw with a sharp point, for use in wood

wood'shed' *n.* a shed for storing firewood

woods·man (woodz'mən) *n., pl.* **-men** (-mən) **1** one who lives or works in the woods **2** one skilled in woodcraft

wood'sy (-zē) *adj.* **-si·er, -si·est** of or like the woods —**wood'si·ness** *n.*

wood·wind (wood'wind') *n.* any of a family of wind instruments made, esp. orig., of wood, as the flute, clarinet, or oboe

wood'work' *n.* **1** work done in wood **2** the wooden moldings, doors, etc. of a house

wood'work'ing *n.* the art or work of making things of wood

wood'y *adj.* **-i·er, -i·est** **1** covered with trees **2** consisting of or forming wood **3** like wood —**wood'i·ness** *n.*

woof[1] (wo͞of) *n.* ⟦ult. < OE *wefan,* to weave⟧ WEFT

woof[2] (woof) *n.* ⟦echoic⟧ the gruff barking sound of a dog —*vi.* to make this sound

woof·er (woof'ər) *n.* a large, high-fidelity speaker for reproducing low-frequency sounds

wool (wool) *n.* ⟦OE *wull*⟧ **1** the soft, curly hair of sheep or of some other animals, as the goat **2** woolen yarn, cloth, clothing, etc. **3** anything that looks or feels like wool

wool'en *adj.* **1** made of wool **2** relating to wool or woolen cloth —*n.* [*pl.*] woolen goods Also [Chiefly Brit.] **wool'len**

Woolf (woolf), **Virginia** 1882-1941; Eng. novelist & critic

wool'gath'er·ing (-ga*th*'ər iŋ) *n.* aimless daydreaming or speculation

wool·ly (wool'ē) *adj.* **-li·er, -li·est** **1** of or like wool **2** bearing or covered with wool **3** rough and uncivilized: used chiefly in **wild and woolly** **4** confused [*woolly* ideas] Also sp. **wool'y**

wooz·y (wo͞o'zē, wooz'ē) *adj.* **-i·er, -i·est** [Inf.] dizzy or befuddled, as from drink or a blow —**wooz'i·ness** *n.*

word (wurd) *n.* ⟦OE⟧ **1** *a*) a speech sound, or series of such sounds, having meaning as a unit of language *b*) the written or printed representation of this **2** a brief remark [a *word* of advice] **3** a promise or assurance [he gave his *word*] **4** news; information **5** *a*) a password *b*) a command, order, etc. **6** [*usually pl.*] *a*) speech *b*) lyrics **7** [*pl.*] a quarrel —*vt.* to put into words; phrase —**in a word** briefly —**in so many words** exactly and plainly —**the Word** the Bible —**word for word** in precisely the same words

word'age *n.* **1** words **2** wordiness

word'ing *n.* choice of words; diction

word of honor solemn promise

word of mouth speech, as opposed to writing

word'play' *n.* **1** repartee **2** punning

word processor a computerized device consisting of a keyboard, video screen, printer, etc., used to generate, edit, store, or duplicate documents, as letters or reports —**word processing**

Words·worth (wurdz'wərth), **William** 1770-1850; Eng. poet

word·y (wur'dē) *adj.* **-i·er, -i·est** containing or using too many words; verbose —**word'i·ness** *n.*

wore (wôr) *vt., vi. pt. of* WEAR

work (wurk) *n.* ⟦OE *weorc*⟧ **1** effort exerted to do or make something; labor; toil **2** employment; occupation **3** something one is making or doing; task **4** something made or done; specif., *a*) an act; deed (*usually used in pl.*) [good *works*] *b*) [*pl.*] collected writings *c*) [*pl.*] engineering structures, as bridges, dams, etc. **5** [*pl., with sing. v.*] a place where work is done, as a factory **6** workmanship —*adj.* of, for, or used in work —*vi.* **worked** or **wrought, work'ing** **1** to do work; labor; toil **2** to be employed **3** to function or operate, esp. effectively **4** to ferment **5** to move, proceed, etc. slowly and with difficulty **6** to come or become, as by repeated movement [the door *worked* loose] —*vt.* **1** to cause; bring about [his idea *worked* wonders] **2** to mold; shape **3** to solve (a mathematical problem, etc.) **4** to manipulate; knead **5** to bring into a specified condition, as by moving back and forth [to *work* a nail loose] **6** to cultivate (soil) **7** to operate; use **8** to cause to work [to *work* a crew hard] **9** to make (one's way, etc.) by effort **10** to provoke; rouse [to *work* oneself into a rage] **11** [Slang] to proceed ingratiatingly through (a crowd, etc.) —**at work** working —**in the works** in the process of being planned or done —**out of work** unemployed —**the works** **1** the working parts (*of* a watch, etc.) **2** [Inf.] everything: also **the whole works** —**work off** to get rid of —**work on** **1** to influence **2** to try to persuade —**work out** **1** to solve **2** to result **3** to develop **4** to have a workout —**work up** **1** to advance **2** to develop **3** to excite

work·a·ble (wur'kə bəl) *adj.* **1** that can be worked **2** practicable; feasible

work'a·day' (-dā') *adj.* **1** of workdays; everyday **2** ordinary

work'a·hol'ic (-hôl'ik) *n.* ⟦WORK + -AHOLIC⟧ a person having an irrational need to work

work'bench' *n.* a table at which work is done, as by a carpenter

work'book' *n.* a book of questions, exercises, etc. for use by students

work'day' *n.* **1** a day on which work is ordinarily done **2** the part of a day during which work is done

work'er *n.* **1** one who works for a living **2** one who works for a cause, etc. **3** a sterile ant, bee, etc. that does work for the colony

work·fare (wʉrk'fer') *n.* ⟦WORK + (WEL)FARE⟧ a government program requiring employable recipients of welfare to register for work, training, etc.

work'force' *n.* the total number of available workers

work'horse' *n.* **1** a horse used for working **2** a reliable worker with a heavy workload

work'house' *n.* a prison where petty offenders are confined and made to work

work'ing *adj.* **1** that works **2** of, for, or used in work **3** sufficient to get work done **4** on which further work may be based [a *working* hypothesis] —*n.* the act of one that works

working class the social class consisting of industrial and manual workers

work'ing·man' (-man') *n., pl.* **-men'** (-men') a worker, esp. an industrial worker

work'load' *n.* the amount of work assigned for completion within a given time period

work'man (-mən) *n., pl.* **-men** (-mən) **1** WORKINGMAN **2** a craftsman

work'man·like' *adj.* capable; competent

work'man·ship' *n.* skill of a workman or the quality of the work done

work'out' *n.* a session of physical exercises or any strenuous work

work'place' *n.* the office, factory, etc. where one works

work sheet a paper sheet with working notes, etc., or with problems, etc. to be worked on by students

work'shop' *n.* **1** a room or building where work is done **2** a seminar for specified intensive study, work, etc.

work'sta'tion *n.* **1** a person's work area, including furniture, etc. and, often, a microcomputer **2** a terminal or personal computer connected to a network

work'ta'ble *n.* a table at which work is done

work'-up' *n.* a complete medical study of a patient, including tests

work'week' *n.* the total number of hours or days worked in a week

world (wʉrld) *n.* ⟦OE *werold*⟧ **1** *a)* the earth *b)* the universe **2** *a)* mankind *b)* people generally; the public **3** *a)* [*also* **W-**] some part of the earth [the Old *World*] *b)* any sphere or domain [the animal *world*] **4** individual experience, outlook, etc. [her *world* is narrow] **5** secular life and interests, or people concerned with these **6** [*often pl.*] a large amount [a *world* of good] —**bring into the world** **1** to give birth to **2** to assist in the delivery of (a baby) —**for all the world** exactly

world'-class' *adj.* of the highest class, as in international competition

world'ly *adj.* **-li·er, -li·est** **1** of this world; secular **2** devoted to the affairs, pleasures, etc. of this world **3** worldly-wise —**world'li·ness** *n.*

world'ly-wise' *adj.* wise in the ways or affairs of the world; sophisticated

world'-shak'ing *adj.* of great significance, effect, or influence; momentous

world'view' *n.* a comprehensive, esp. personal, philosophy of the world and of human life

World War I the war (1914-18) involving Great Britain, France, Russia, the U.S., etc. on one side and Germany, Austria-Hungary, etc. on the other

World War II the war (1939-45) involving Great Britain, France, the Soviet Union, the U.S., etc. on one side and Germany, Italy, Japan, etc. on the other

world'-wea'ry *adj.* bored with living

world'wide' *adj., adv.* (extending) throughout the world

World Wide Web a group of Internet sources giving access to text, images, sound, etc.

worm (wʉrm) *n.* ⟦< OE *wyrm,* serpent⟧ **1** a long, slender, soft-bodied animal **2** an abject or contemptible person **3** something spiral in shape, etc., as the thread of a screw **4** [*pl.*] any disease caused by parasitic worms in the intestines, etc. —*vi.* to proceed like a worm, in a winding or devious manner —*vt.* **1** to bring about, get, make, etc. in a winding or devious manner **2** to purge of intestinal worms —**worm'y, -i·er, -i·est,** *adj.*

worm gear a gear consisting of a rotating screw meshed with a toothed wheel

worm'wood' (-wood') *n.* ⟦< OE *wermod*⟧ a strong-smelling plant that yields a bitter-tasting oil formerly used in making absinthe

worn (wôrn) *vt., vi. pp. of* WEAR —*adj.* **1** damaged by use or wear **2** showing the effects of worry or anxiety

worn'-out' *adj.* **1** used until no longer effective, usable, etc. **2** exhausted; tired out

wor·ri·ment (wʉr'ē mənt) *n.* (a) worry

wor'ri·some (-səm) *adj.* causing worry

wor·ry (wʉr'ē) *vt.* **-ried, -ry·ing** ⟦< OE *wyrgan,* to strangle⟧ **1** to treat roughly, as with continual biting [a dog *worrying* a bone] **2** to annoy, bother, etc. **3** to make troubled or uneasy —*vi.* **1** to bite or tear (*at* an object) **2** to be anxious, troubled, etc. —*n., pl.* **-ries** **1** a troubled state of mind; anxiety **2** a cause of this —**wor'ri·er** *n.*

wor'ry·wart' (-wôrt') *n.* ⟦prec. + WART⟧ [Inf.] one who tends to worry, esp. over trivial matters

worse (wʉrs) *adj.* ⟦OE *wiersa*⟧ **1** *compar. of* BAD[1] & ILL **2** *a)* bad, evil, harmful, etc. in a greater degree *b)* of inferior quality **3** in poorer health; more ill **4** in a less satisfactory condition —*adv.* **1** *compar. of* BADLY & ILL **2**

in a worse manner 3 to a worse extent —*n.* that which is worse —**worse off** in worse circumstances

wor·sen (wur′sən) ***vt.***, ***vi.*** to make or become worse

wor·ship (wur′ship) ***n.*** ⟦< OE *weorthscipe*⟧ 1 a service or rite showing reverence for a deity 2 intense love or admiration 3 [**W-**] [Chiefly Brit.] a title of honor: used in addressing magistrates, etc. —***vt.*** **-shiped** or **-shipped**, **-ship·ing** or **-ship·ping** 1 to show religious reverence for 2 to have intense love or admiration for —***vi.*** to engage in worship —**wor′ship·er** or **wor′ship·per** ***n.***

wor′ship·ful (-fəl) ***adj.*** feeling or offering great devotion or respect

worst (wurst) ***adj.*** ⟦OE *wyrsta*⟧ 1 *superl. of* BAD[1] & ILL 2 *a)* bad, evil, harmful, etc. in the highest degree *b)* of the lowest quality 3 in the least satisfactory condition —***adv.*** 1 *superl. of* BADLY & ILL 2 in the worst manner 3 to the worst extent —***n.*** that which is worst —***vt.*** to defeat —**at worst** under the worst circumstances —**if (the) worst comes to (the) worst** if the worst possible thing happens —**(in) the worst way** [Slang] very much; greatly

wor·sted (woos′tid, wur′stid) ***n.*** ⟦after *Worstead,* England⟧ 1 a smooth, firmly twisted wool thread or yarn 2 fabric made from this

wort (wurt) ***n.*** ⟦OE *wyrt-*⟧ a liquid, produced from malt, that can be fermented to make beer, etc.

worth (wurth) ***n.*** ⟦OE *weorth*⟧ 1 material value, esp. as expressed in terms of money 2 importance, value, merit, etc. 3 the quantity to be had for a given sum *[a dollar's worth]* —***prep.*** 1 deserving or worthy of 2 equal in value to 3 having wealth amounting to

worth′less ***adj.*** without worth or merit; useless —**worth′less·ness** ***n.***

worth′while′ ***adj.*** worth the time or effort spent

wor·thy (wur′*th*ē) ***adj.*** **-thi·er**, **-thi·est** 1 having worth, value, or merit 2 meriting —***n.***, *pl.* **-thies** a person of outstanding worth, etc. —**wor′thi·ly** ***adv.*** —**wor′thi·ness** ***n.***

would (wood) ***v.aux.*** ⟦OE *wolde*⟧ 1 *pt. of* WILL[2] 2 used to express a supposition or condition *[he would write if he knew you would answer]* 3 used to make a polite request *[would you please open the window?]* —***vt.*** [Old Poet.] I wish *[would that she were here]* See usage note at WILL[2]

would′-be′ ***adj.*** 1 wishing or pretending to be 2 intended to be

wound[1] (woond) ***n.*** ⟦OE *wund*⟧ 1 an injury in which tissue is cut, torn, etc. 2 any hurt to the feelings, honor, etc. —***vt.***, ***vi.*** to inflict a wound (on or upon); injure

wound[2] (wound) ***vt.***, ***vi.*** *pt. & pp. of* WIND[1]

wove (wōv) ***vt.***, ***vi.*** *pt. & alt. pp. of* WEAVE

wo·ven (wō′vən) ***vt.***, ***vi.*** *alt. pp. of* WEAVE

wow (wou) ***interj.*** used to express surprise, pleasure, etc. —***vt.*** [Slang] to arouse enthusiasm in

wpm *abbrev.* words per minute

wrack (rak) ***n.*** ⟦< MDu *wrak,* a wreck⟧ *alt. sp. of* RACK[2]

wraith (rāth) ***n.*** ⟦Scot⟧ a ghost

wran·gle (raŋ′gəl) ***vi.*** **-gled**, **-gling** ⟦< OE *wringan,* to press⟧ to argue; quarrel, esp. noisily —***n.*** a noisy dispute —**wran′gler** ***n.***

wran′gler (-glər) ***n.*** ⟦< AmSp *caballerango,* a groom⟧ a cowboy who herds livestock, esp. saddle horses —**wran′gle**, **-gled**, **-gling**, ***vt.***

wrap (rap) ***vt.*** **wrapped**, **wrap′ping** ⟦ME *wrappen*⟧ 1 to wind or fold (a covering) around something 2 to enclose and fasten in paper, etc. —***vi.*** to twine, coil, etc.: usually with *over, around,* etc. —***n.*** 1 an outer covering or garment 2 [*pl.*] secrecy; censorship *[to keep plans under wraps]* 3 *Film* the completion of the filming of a scene, etc. —**wrapped up in** engrossed in or involved in —**wrap up** [Inf.] to conclude; settle

wrap′per ***n.*** 1 one that wraps 2 that in which something is wrapped 3 a woman's dressing gown

wrap′ping ***n.*** [*often pl.*] the material in which something is wrapped

wrap′-up′ ***n.*** [Inf.] a concluding, summarizing statement, report, etc.

wrath (rath) ***n.*** ⟦OE, angry⟧ intense anger; rage; fury —**wrath′ful** ***adj.***

wreak (rēk) ***vt.*** ⟦OE *wrecan,* to revenge⟧ 1 to give vent to (one's anger, etc.) 2 to inflict (vengeance, etc.)

wreath (rēth) ***n.***, *pl.* **wreaths** (rē*th*z, rēths) ⟦OE *writha*⟧ 1 a twisted ring of leaves, flowers, etc. 2 something like this in shape *[wreaths of smoke]*

wreathe (rē*th*) ***vt.*** **wreathed**, **wreath′ing** 1 to form into a wreath 2 to coil or twist around; encircle 3 to decorate with wreaths

wreck (rek) ***n.*** ⟦< ON *vrek,* driftwood⟧ 1 a shipwreck 2 the remains of something destroyed 3 a run-down person 4 a wrecking or being wrecked —***vt.*** 1 to destroy or damage badly 2 to tear down (a building, etc.) 3 to overthrow or thwart

wreck′age ***n.*** 1 a wrecking or being wrecked 2 the remains of something wrecked

wreck′er ***n.*** 1 one who wrecks 2 one that salvages or removes wrecks

wren (ren) ***n.*** ⟦OE *wrenna*⟧ a small songbird with a stubby, erect tail

wrench (rench) ***n.*** ⟦OE *wrenc,* a trick⟧ 1 a sudden, sharp twist or pull 2 an injury caused by a twist, as to the back 3 a sudden feeling of grief, etc. 4 a tool for turning nuts, bolts, pipes, etc. —***vt.***

1 to twist or jerk violently 2 to injure with a twist 3 to distort (a meaning, etc.)

WRENCHES

wrest (rest) ***vt.*** ⟦OE *wræstan*⟧ **1** to pull or force away violently with a twisting motion **2** to take by force

wres·tle (res′əl; *often* ras′-) ***vi., vt.*** **-tled, -tling** ⟦see prec.⟧ **1** to struggle hand to hand with (an opponent) in an attempt to throw him or her **2** to contend (*with*) —***n.*** a wrestling —**wres′tler** ***n.***

wres′tling ***n.*** a sport in which the opponents wrestle, or struggle hand to hand

wretch (rech) ***n.*** ⟦OE *wrecca*, an outcast⟧ **1** a miserable or unhappy person **2** a despised person

wretch′ed ***adj.*** **1** very unhappy; miserable **2** distressing; dismal **3** poor in quality **4** contemptible —**wretch′ed·ly** ***adv.*** —**wretch′ed·ness** ***n.***

wrig·gle (rig′əl) ***vi.*** **-gled, -gling** ⟦medieval Low G *wriggeln*⟧ **1** to twist and turn; squirm **2** to move along with a twisting motion **3** to make one's way by shifty means —***n.*** a wriggling —**wrig′gler** ***n.*** —**wrig′gly, -gli·er, -gli·est,** ***adj.***

wright (rīt) ***n.*** ⟦< OE *wyrcan*, to work⟧ one who makes or constructs: chiefly in compounds *[shipwright]*

wring (riŋ) ***vt.*** **wrung, wring′ing** ⟦OE *wringan*⟧ **1** *a)* to squeeze, press, or twist *b)* to force out (water, etc.) by this means (usually with *out*) **2** to clasp and twist (the hands) in distress **3** to clasp (another's hand) forcefully in greeting **4** to extract by force, threats, etc. —***n.*** a wringing

wring′er ***n.*** a machine with rollers to squeeze water from wet clothes

wrin·kle[1] (riŋ′kəl) ***n.*** ⟦ME *wrinkel*⟧ **1** a small furrow in a normally smooth surface **2** a crease in the skin —***vt., vi.*** **-kled, -kling** to form wrinkles (in); pucker; crease —**wrin′kly, -kli·er, -kli·est,** ***adj.***

wrin·kle[2] (riŋ′kəl) ***n.*** ⟦< OE *wrenc*, a trick⟧ [Inf.] a clever innovation

wrist (rist) ***n.*** ⟦OE⟧ the joint between the hand and forearm —**a slap** (or **tap**) **on the wrist** a token punishment

wrist′band′ ***n.*** a band that goes around the wrist, as on a cuff

wrist′watch′ ***n.*** a watch worn on a strap or band around the wrist

writ (rit) ***n.*** ⟦OE < *writan*, write⟧ a formal legal document ordering or prohibiting some action

write (rīt) ***vt.*** **wrote, writ′ten, writ′ing** ⟦OE *writan*⟧ **1** to form (words, letters, etc.) on a surface, as with a pen **2** to compose (literary or musical material) **3** to communicate (with) in writing *[she wrote (me) that she was ill]* **4** to cover with writing *[to write three pages]* **5** to fill in (a bank check, etc.) **6** to show clearly *[anger was written on his face]* **7** *Comput.* to record (information) on a disk, etc. —***vi.*** to produce writing —**write off 1** to remove from accounts (bad debts, etc.) **2** to drop from consideration **3** to amortize —**write out 1** to put into writing **2** to write in full —**write up** to write an account of

write′-in′ ***n.*** **1** a candidate whose name is not on the ballot, but is written in by a voter **2** a vote of this kind

write′-off′ ***n.*** a cancelled debt, amortized expense, etc.

writ′er ***n.*** one who writes, esp. as an occupation; author

write′-up′ ***n.*** [Inf.] a written report

writhe (rīth) ***vi.*** **writhed, writh′ing** ⟦OE *writhan*, to twist⟧ **1** to twist or turn; squirm *[to writhe in agony]* **2** to suffer great emotional distress

writ·ing (rīt′iŋ) ***n.*** **1** the act of one who writes **2** something written **3** written form **4** *short for* HANDWRITING

writ·ten (rit′'n) ***vt., vi.*** *pp. of* WRITE

wrong (rôŋ) ***adj.*** ⟦< ON *rangr*, twisted⟧ **1** not in accordance with justice, law, morality, etc. **2** not suitable or appropriate **3** *a)* contrary to fact, etc.; incorrect *b)* mistaken **4** not functioning properly **5** not meant to be seen *[the wrong side of a fabric]* —***adv.*** in a wrong manner, direction, etc. —***n.*** an unjust, immoral, or illegal act —***vt.*** to treat badly or unjustly —**wrong′ly** ***adv.*** —**wrong′ness** ***n.***

wrong′do′ing ***n.*** any wrong act or behavior —**wrong′do′er** ***n.***

wrong′ful ***adj.*** **1** unjust or injurious **2** unlawful —**wrong′ful·ly** ***adv.***

wrong′head′ed ***adj.*** stubborn or perverse —**wrong′head′ed·ly** ***adv.*** —**wrong′head′ed·ness** ***n.***

wrote (rōt) ***vt., vi.*** *pt. of* WRITE

wroth (rôth) ***adj.*** ⟦OE *wrath*⟧ angry

wrought (rôt) ***vi., vt.*** *alt. pt. & pp. of* WORK —***adj.*** **1** formed; made **2** shaped by hammering, etc.: said of metals

wrought iron tough, ductile iron containing very little carbon —**wrought′-i′ron** ***adj.***

wrought′-up′ ***adj.*** very disturbed

wrung (ruŋ) ***vt.*** *pt. & pp. of* WRING

wry (rī) ***adj.*** **wri′er** or **wry′er, wri′est** or **wry′est** ⟦< OE *wrigian*, to turn⟧ **1** distorted in a grimace *[a wry face]* **2** ironic, dry, etc. *[wry humor]* —**wry′ly** ***adv.*** —**wry′ness** ***n.***

wt *abbrev.* weight

Wu·han (wōō′hän′) city in EC China: pop. 3,288,000

wuss (woos) ***n.*** [Slang] a person who is regarded as weak, ineffectual, etc.; wimp: also **wuss′y**, *pl.* **wuss′ies**

WV West Virginia

WWI *abbrev.* World War I

WWII *abbrev.* World War II

WWW or **www** *abbrev.* World Wide Web

Wy·o·ming (wī ō′miŋ) Mountain State of the W U.S.: 97,105 sq. mi.; pop. 454,000; cap. Cheyenne: abbrev. **WY** —**Wy·o′ming·ite′** ***n.***

X

x[1] or **X** (eks) ***n.***, *pl.* **x's, X's** **1** the 24th letter of the English alphabet **2** *Math.* an unknown quantity

x[2] *abbrev.* extra: also **X**

x[3] (eks) *symbol* **1** by (in indicating dimensions) *[3 ft. x 4 ft.]* **2** *Optics* the power of magnification **3** *Math.* times *[2 x 3 = 6]*

X (eks) ***n.*** **1** the Roman numeral 10 **2** a film rating meaning that no one under seventeen is to be admitted

X chromosome *see* SEX CHROMOSOME

Xe *Chem. symbol for* xenon

xe·non (zē′nän′) ***n.*** a colorless, nonreactive, gaseous chemical element

xen·o·pho·bi·a (zen′ə fō′bē ə) ***n.*** ⟦< Gr *xenos*, foreign + -PHOBIA⟧ fear or hatred of strangers or foreigners —**xen′o·phobe′** (-fōb′) ***n.*** —**xen′o·pho′bic** (-fō′bik) ***adj.***

xe·rog·ra·phy (zir äg′rə fē) ***n.*** ⟦< Gr *xēros*, dry + -GRAPHY⟧ a process for copying printed material, etc. by the action of light on an electrically charged surface

Xe·rox (zir′äks′) *trademark for* a device for copying by xerography —***vt., vi.*** [*usually* **x-**] to reproduce by xerography —***n.*** [*usually* **x-**] a copy so made

Xer·xes I (zurk′sēz′) 519?-465 B.C.; king of Persia (486-465)

xi (zī, sī) ***n.*** the 14th letter of the Greek alphabet (Ξ, ξ)

XL *abbrev.* extra large

X·mas (eks′məs) ***n.*** *inf. var. of* CHRISTMAS

X-rat·ed (eks′rāt′əd) ***adj.*** designating or like a film with a rating of X; explicit, obscene, etc.

X-ray (eks′rā′) ***n.*** **1** a type of electromagnetic wave of very short wavelength, that can penetrate solid substances: used to study internal body structures and treat various disorders **2** a photograph made by means of X-rays —***adj.*** of or by X-rays —***vt.*** to examine, treat, or photograph with X-rays Also **X ray, x-ray,** or **x ray**

XS *abbrev.* extra small

xy·lem (zī′ləm) ***n.*** ⟦< Gr *xylon*, wood⟧ the woody vascular tissue of a plant

xy·lo·phone (zī′lə fōn′) ***n.*** ⟦< Gr *xylon*, wood + -PHONE⟧ a musical percussion instrument consisting of a series of graduated wooden bars that are struck with small, wooden mallets —**xy′lo·phon′ist** (-fō′nist, zī läf′ə nist) ***n.***

Y

y or **Y** (wī) ***n.***, *pl.* **y's, Y's** the 25th letter of the English alphabet

Y *Chem. symbol for* yttrium

-y[1] (ē, i) ⟦ME⟧ *suffix* little one, dear *[kitty, daddy]*

-y[2] (ē, i) ⟦OE *-ig*⟧ *suffix* **1** full of, like *[dirty]* **2** somewhat *[yellowy]* **3** tending to *[sticky]*

-y[3] (ē, i) ⟦< L *-ia*⟧ *suffix* **1** quality or condition *[jealousy]* **2** a (specified) kind of shop, goods, or group *[bakery]*

-y[4] (ē, i) ⟦< L *-ium*⟧ *suffix* action of *[inquiry]*

yacht (yät) ***n.*** ⟦Du *jacht*⟧ a small vessel for pleasure cruises, racing, etc.

yacht′ing (-iŋ) ***n.*** the sport of sailing a yacht —**yachts′man** (-mən), *pl.* **-men** (-mən), ***n.***

ya·hoo (yä′ho͞o′) ***n.*** ⟦after a race of people in Swift's novel *Gulliver's Travels*⟧ a person regarded as vulgar, uneducated, etc.

Yah·weh or **Yah·we** (yä′we, -wā) ***n.*** ⟦< Heb⟧ God

yak[1] (yak) ***n.*** ⟦< Tibet *g-yag*⟧ a long-haired wild ox of Tibet and central Asia

yak[2] (yak) [Slang] ***vi.*** **yakked, yak′king** ⟦echoic⟧ to talk much or idly —***n.*** a yakking

yam (yam) ***n.*** ⟦< WAfr native name⟧ **1** the edible, starchy, tuberous root of a tropical climbing plant **2** an orange-colored variety of sweet potato

yam·mer (yam′ər) ***vi.*** ⟦< OE *geomerian*, to lament⟧ **1** to shout, yell, etc. **2** to talk loudly or continuously —**yam′mer·er** ***n.***

yang (yäŋ, yaŋ) ***n.*** ⟦Chin⟧ in Chinese philosophy, the masculine force or principle in the universe: cf. YIN

Yan·gon (yan gôn′) capital of Myanmar: pop. 2,513,000

Yang·tze (yaŋk′sē) *a former transliteration of* CHANG

yank (yaŋk) ***n., vt., vi.*** ⟦< ?⟧ [Inf.] jerk

Yank (yaŋk) ***n.*** [Slang] a Yankee; esp., a U.S. soldier in WWI and WWII

Yan·kee (yaŋ′kē) ***n.*** ⟦< ? Du *Jan Kees*, a disparaging nickname⟧ **1** a New Englander **2** a person born or living in the northern U.S. **3** a citizen of the U.S. —***adj.*** of or like Yankees

yap (yap) ***vi.*** **yapped, yap′ping** ⟦echoic⟧ **1** to make a sharp, shrill bark **2** [Slang] to talk noisily and stupidly —***n.*** **1** a sharp, shrill bark **2** [Slang] *a)* jabber *b)* the mouth

yard[1] (yärd) ***n.*** ⟦OE *gierd*, rod⟧ **1** a measure of length, 3 feet or 36 inches **2** *Naut.* a slender rod or spar fastened across a mast to support a sail

yard[2] (yärd) ***n.*** ⟦OE *geard*, enclosure⟧ **1** the ground around or next to a building

2 an enclosed place for a particular purpose *[shipyard]*

yard'age ***n.*** 1 measurement in yards 2 the extent so measured

yard'arm' ***n.*** *Naut.* either half of a yard supporting a square sail, etc.

yard goods textiles made in standard widths, usually sold by the yard

yard·man (yärd'man', -mən) ***n.***, *pl.* **-men'** (-men', -mən) a person who works in a yard

yard'stick' ***n.*** 1 a graduated measuring stick one yard long 2 any standard used in judging, etc.

yar·mul·ke (yär'məl kə, yä'-) ***n.*** ⟦Yiddish < Pol⟧ a skullcap traditionally worn by Jewish men, as at prayer: also **yar'mel·ke**

yarn (yärn) ***n.*** ⟦OE *gearn*⟧ 1 fibers of wool, cotton, etc. spun into strands for weaving, knitting, etc. 2 [Inf.] a tale or story

yat·ter (yat'ər) [Slang] ***vi.*** ⟦prob. < YA(K)[2] + (CHA)TTER⟧ to talk idly about trivial things —***n.*** idle talk; chatter

yaw (yô) ***vi.*** ⟦ON *jaga*, to sway⟧ 1 to swing back and forth across its course, as a ship does when pushed by high waves 2 to rotate or oscillate about the vertical axis: said of a spacecraft, etc. —***n.*** a yawing

yawl (yôl) ***n.*** ⟦< Du *jol*⟧ a small, two-masted sailboat rigged fore-and-aft

yawn (yôn) ***vi.*** ⟦ME *yanen*⟧ 1 to open the mouth wide involuntarily and inhale, as when one is sleepy or bored 2 to open wide —***n.*** a yawning

yaws (yôz) ***n.*** ⟦of WInd origin⟧ an infectious skin disease of the tropics

yay (yā) ***adv.*** 1 YEA (*adv.* 1) 2 [Inf.] this; so: often with a gesture indicating size —***interj.*** YEA

Y chromosome *see* SEX CHROMOSOME

y·clept or **y-clept** (ē klept') ***vt.*** ⟦<OE *clipian*, to call⟧ [Archaic] called; named: also sp. **y·cleped'**

yd *abbrev.* yard(s): also, for the plural, **yds**

ye[1] (*th*ə, *th*i, *th*ē; *now often erroneously or facetiously* yē) ***adj., definite article*** *archaic var. of* THE

ye[2] (yē) ***pron.*** ⟦OE *ge*⟧ [Archaic] YOU

yea (yā) ***adv.*** ⟦OE *gea*⟧ 1 yes 2 indeed; truly —***n.*** 1 an affirmative vote 2 a person voting in the affirmative —***interj.*** [Inf.] hurrah: a shout used in cheering for a team

yeah (ya, ye) ***adv.*** [Inf.] yes

year (yir) ***n.*** ⟦OE *gear*⟧ 1 a period of 365 days (366 days in leap year), divided into 12 months beginning Jan. 1 2 the period (365 days, 5 hours, 48 minutes, and 46 seconds) of one revolution of the earth around the sun: also **solar year** 3 a period of 12 calendar months reckoned from any date 4 an annual period of less than 365 days *[a school year]* 5 [*pl.*] *a)* age *[old for his years]* *b)* a long time *[years ago]* —**year after year** every year

year'book' ***n.*** an annual book; specif., *a)* a book giving data of the preceding year *b)* a publication of the graduating class of a school or college

year'ling ***n.*** an animal in its second year

year'ly ***adj.*** 1 done, happening, appearing, etc. once a year, or every year *[a yearly event]* 2 of a year, or of each year —***adv.*** every year

yearn (yurn) ***vi.*** ⟦< OE *georn*, eager⟧ to be filled with longing or desire —**yearn'ing** ***n.***

year'-round' ***adj.*** open, in use, operating, etc. throughout the year

yea'say'er ***n.*** one having a positive attitude toward life

yeast (yēst) ***n.*** ⟦OE *gist*⟧ 1 a moist, yellowish mass of certain fungi that cause fermentation: used in making beer, etc., and as leavening in baking 2 yeast dried in flakes or granules or compressed into cakes 3 ferment; agitation

yeast'y ***adj.*** **-i·er**, **-i·est** 1 of, like, or containing yeast 2 in a ferment; restless

yegg (yeg) ***n.*** ⟦< ?⟧ [Old Slang] a burglar, etc.

yell (yel) ***vi.***, ***vt.*** ⟦OE *giellan*⟧ to cry out loudly; scream —***n.*** 1 a loud outcry 2 a rhythmic cheer in unison

yel·low (yel'ō) ***adj.*** ⟦OE *geolu*⟧ 1 of the color of ripe lemons 2 having a somewhat yellow skin 3 [Inf.] cowardly 4 sensational: said as of a newspaper —***n.*** 1 a yellow color 2 an egg yolk —***vi.*** to become yellow —**yel'low·ish** ***adj.***

yellow fever an infectious tropical disease caused by a virus transmitted by the bite of a certain mosquito

yellow jacket a wasp or hornet having bright-yellow markings

Yel'low·knife' capital of Northwest Territories, Canada: pop. 17,000

Yellow River HUANG

Yellow Sea arm of the East China Sea, between China & Korea

yelp (yelp) ***vi.*** ⟦OE *gielpan*, to boast⟧ to utter a short, sharp cry or bark, as a dog does —***n.*** a short, sharp cry or bark

Yel·tsin (yelt'sin), **Bor·is** (bôr'is) 1931- ; president of Russia (1990-99)

Yem·en (yem'ən) country in S Arabia, formed (1990) by the merger of the **Yemen Arab Republic** and a country directly east of it, the **People's Democratic Republic of Yemen**: 214,287 sq. mi.; pop. 13,000,000 —**Yem'en·ite'** or **Yem'e·ni** (-ə nē) ***adj.***, ***n.***

yen[1] (yen) ***n.***, *pl.* **yen** ⟦Jpn⟧ the monetary unit of Japan

yen[2] (yen) ***n.*** ⟦prob. < Chin *yan*, opium⟧ [Inf.] a strong longing or desire

yeo·man (yō'mən) ***n.***, *pl.* **-men** (-mən) ⟦ME *yeman*⟧ 1 [Brit. Historical] a freeholder of a class below the gentry 2 *U.S. Navy* a petty officer assigned to clerical duty

yeo'man·ry ***n.*** yeomen collectively

yes (yes) ***adv.*** ⟦OE *gese*⟧ 1 aye; yea; it is so: expressing agreement, consent, etc. 2 not only that, but more *[ready, yes, eager to help]* —***n.***, *pl.* **yes'es** an act of saying *yes*; an affirmative reply, vote, etc. —***vt.***, ***vi.*** **yessed**, **yes'sing** to say *yes* (to)

ye·shi·va (yə shē'və; *Heb* ye shē vä') ***n.***, *pl.* **-vas** or Heb. **-vot'** (-vōt') ⟦Heb, lit., act of sitting] a Jewish school combining religious and secular studies

yes man [Slang] one who is always approving what is said by a superior

yes·ter·day (yes′tər dā′) ***n.*** [OE *geostran,* yesterday + *dæg,* day] **1** the day before today **2** a recent day or time —***adv.*** **1** on the day before today **2** recently

yes′ter·year′ (-yir′) ***n., adv.*** **1** last year **2** (in) past years

yet (yet) ***adv.*** [OE *giet*] **1** up to now; thus far [he hasn't gone *yet*] **2** at the present time; now [we can't go just *yet*] **3** still [there is *yet* a chance] **4** in addition; even [he was *yet* more kind] **5** nevertheless [she's kind, *yet* shy] —***conj.*** but [she seems well, *yet* she is ill] —**as yet** up to now

yew (yo͞o) ***n.*** [OE *iw*] **1** an evergreen tree with flattened needle leaves **2** its wood

Yid·dish (yid′ish) ***n.*** [< Ger *jüdisch,* < L *Judaeus,* Jew] a language derived from medieval High German, written in the Hebrew alphabet and spoken esp. by East European Jews

yield (yēld) ***vt.*** [OE *gieldan,* to pay] **1** to produce as a crop, result, profit, etc. **2** to surrender **3** to concede —***vi.*** **1** to produce **2** to surrender **3** to give way to physical force **4** to lose precedence, etc.: often with *to* —***n.*** the amount yielded

yield′ing ***adj.*** **1** flexible **2** submissive

yin (yin) ***n.*** [Chin] in Chinese philosophy, the feminine force or principle in the universe: cf. YANG

yip (yip) ***n.*** [echoic] [Inf.] a yelp, or bark —***vi.*** **yipped, yip′ping** [Inf.] to yelp, or bark

YMCA *abbrev.* Young Men's Christian Association

yo (yō) ***interj.*** [Inf.] used as to gain attention, greet someone, emphasize a remark, etc.

yo·del (yōd′'l) ***vt., vi.*** **-deled** or **-delled, -del·ing** or **-del·ling** [Ger *jodeln*] to sing with abrupt alternating changes to the falsetto —***n.*** a yodeling

yo·ga (yō′gə) ***n.*** [Sans, union] a mystic and ascetic Hindu discipline for achieving union with the supreme spirit through meditation, prescribed postures, controlled breathing, etc.

yo·gi (yō′gē) ***n.,*** *pl.* **-gis** one who practices yoga: also **yo′gin** (-gin)

yo·gurt (yō′gərt) ***n.*** [Turk *yoğurt*] a thick, somewhat solid food made from fermented milk: also **yo′ghurt**

yoke (yōk) ***n.*** [OE *geoc*] **1** a wooden frame for harnessing together a pair of oxen, etc. **2** such a pair harnessed together **3** bondage; servitude **4** anything like a yoke, as something that binds or unites, or a part of a garment fitted to the shoulders or hips as a support for the gathered parts below —***vt.*** **yoked, yok′ing** **1** to harness (an animal) to (a plow, etc.) **2** to join together

yo·kel (yō′kəl) ***n.*** a person living in a rural area; bumpkin: a contemptuous term

Yo·ko·ha·ma (yō′kə hä′mə) seaport in S Honshu, Japan: pop. 2,774,000

yolk (yōk) ***n.*** [OE *geolca*] the yellow, principal substance of an egg

Yom Kip·pur (yäm′ ki po͝or′) the Day of Atonement: a major Jewish holiday and a day of fasting

yon (yän) ***adj., adv.*** [OE *geon*] [Now Chiefly Dial.] yonder

yon·der (yän′dər) ***adj., adv.*** [ME] (being) at or in that (specified or relatively distant) place; over there

Yon·kers (yäŋ′kərz) city in SE New York: pop. 188,000

yoo-hoo (yo͞o′ho͞o′) ***interj., n.*** (a shout or call) used to attract someone's attention

yore (yôr) ***adv.*** [OE *geara*] [Obs.] long ago —**of yore** formerly

you (yo͞o) ***pron.,*** *pl.* **you** [OE *eow* < *ge,* YE²] **1** the person or persons spoken to **2** a person or people generally; one [*you* can never tell!]

young (yuŋ) ***adj.*** **young′er** (-gər), **young′est** (-gəst) [OE *geong*] **1** being in an early period of life or growth **2** youthful; fresh; vigorous **3** in an early stage **4** inexperienced; immature —***n.*** **1** young people: often with *the* **2** young offspring —**with young** pregnant —**young′ish** ***adj.***

young adult an age group, from about 12 to about 18 years of age, used as a reader category as in libraries

young blood **1** young people; youth **2** youthful strength, vigor, etc.

young′ster ***n.*** a child or youth

your (yo͝or; *often* yôr) ***poss. pronominal adj.*** [OE *eower*] of, belonging to, or done by you: also used before some titles [*Your* Honor]

you're (yo͝or, yo͞or) *contr.* you are

yours (yo͝orz; *often* yôrz) ***pron.*** that or those belonging to you: possessive form of YOU [that book is *yours*; *yours* are better]

your·self (yo͝or self′, yər-) ***pron.,*** *pl.* **-selves′** (-selvz′) a form of YOU, used as an intensive [you said so *yourself*], as a reflexive [you hurt *yourself*], or with the meaning "your true self" [you are not *yourself* today]

yours truly **1** a phrase used in ending a letter **2** [Inf.] I or me

youth (yo͞oth) ***n.,*** *pl.* **youths** (yo͞o*th*z, yo͞oths) [OE *geoguthe*] **1** the state or quality of being young **2** the period of adolescence **3** an early stage of growth or existence **4** young people collectively **5** a young person; esp., a young man

youth′ful ***adj.*** **1** young; not yet old or mature **2** of, like, or fit for youth **3** fresh; vigorous **4** new; early —**youth′ful·ly** ***adv.*** —**youth′ful·ness** ***n.***

yowl (youl) ***vi., n.*** [< ON *gaula*] howl or wail

yo-yo (yō′yō′) ***n.,*** *pl.* **yo′-yos′** [< ?] **1** a spool-like toy reeled up and let down by a string **2** [Slang] a person regarded as stupid, inept, etc. —***vi.*** [Inf.] to move up and down; fluctuate

yr *abbrev.* **1** year(s) **2** your

yrs *abbrev.* **1** years **2** yours

YT Yukon Territory

yt·tri·um (i'trē əm) ***n.*** a rare, silvery, metallic chemical element: used in color TV tubes, etc.

Yu·ca·tán or **Yu·ca·tan** (yo͞o'kə tan') state of Mexico, on a peninsula separating the Gulf of Mexico from the Caribbean: 15,189 sq. mi.; pop. 1,363,000

yuc·ca (yuk'ə) ***n.*** ⟦< AmSp *yuca*⟧ **1** a desert plant with stiff leaves and white flowers **2** its flower

yuck[1] (yuk) ***n.***, ***vi.*** *alt. sp. of* YUK

yuck[2] (yuk) [Slang] ***n.*** something unpleasant, disgusting, etc. **—*interj.*** used to express distaste, disgust, etc. —**yuck'y, -i·er, -i·est,** ***adj.***

Yu·go·slav·i·a (yo͞o'gō slä'vē ə, -gə-) country in the NW Balkan Peninsula: four republics separated from it in 1991: 39,449 sq. mi.; pop. 10,394,000 —**Yu'go·slav'** or **Yu'go·sla'vi·an** ***adj.***, ***n.***

yuk (yuk) ***n.*** ⟦echoic⟧ [Slang] a loud laugh of amusement, or something causing such a laugh **—*vi.*** **yukked, yuk'king** [Slang] to laugh loudly

Yu·kon (yo͞o'kän') territory of NW Canada, east of Alaska: 186,661 sq. mi.; pop. 31,000; cap. Whitehorse: abbrev. *YT*: usually used with *the*: in full **Yukon Territory**

yule (yo͞ol) ***n.*** ⟦OE *geol*⟧ [*often* **Y-**] Christmas or the Christmas season

yule'tide' (-tīd') ***n.*** [*often* **Y-**] the Christmas season

yum·my (yum'ē) ***adj.*** **-mi·er, -mi·est** [Inf.] very tasty; delectable

yup (yup) ***adv.*** [Slang] yes: an affirmative reply

yup·pie (yup'ē) ***n.*** ⟦< *y*(*oung*) *u*(*rban*) *p*(*rofessional*)⟧ [Inf.] a young professional regarded as affluent, ambitious, materialistic, etc.

YWCA *abbrev.* Young Women's Christian Association

Z

z or **Z** (zē; *Brit* zed) ***n.***, *pl.* **z's, Z's** the 26th and last letter of the English alphabet

zaf·tig (zäf'tig) ***adj.*** ⟦< Yiddish *zaft*, juice⟧ [Slang] having a full, shapely figure: said of a woman

Za·ire or **Za·ïre** (zä ir') **1** CONGO (River) **2** *former name for Democratic Republic of the Congo*: see CONGO

Zam·bi·a (zam'bē ə) country in S Africa: 290,586 sq. mi.; pop. 7,818,000

Zam·bo·ni (zam bō'nē) *trademark for* a machine like a tractor, used to smooth the ice in a rink

za·ny (zā'nē) ***n.***, *pl.* **-nies** ⟦< It dial. *zanni*, < *Giovanni*, John⟧ a silly or foolish person **—*adj.*** **-ni·er, -ni·est** foolish or crazy —**za'ni·ness** ***n.***

Zan·zi·bar (zan'zə bär') island off the E coast of Africa: part of Tanzania

zap (zap) ***vt.***, ***vi.*** **zapped, zap'ping** ⟦echoic⟧ [Slang] to move, strike, stun, kill, etc. suddenly and with great speed and force **—*interj.*** used to signify sudden, swift action or change

zeal (zēl) ***n.*** ⟦< Gr *zēlos*⟧ strong interest or devotion; intense enthusiasm; fervor

zeal·ot (zel'ət) ***n.*** one who shows zeal, esp. fanatic zeal

zeal·ous (zel'əs) ***adj.*** of or showing zeal; fervent —**zeal'ous·ly** ***adv.*** —**zeal'ous·ness** ***n.***

ze·bra (zē'brə) ***n.*** ⟦Port⟧ an African mammal related to the horse and having dark stripes on a white or tawny body

ze·bu (zē'byo͞o') ***n.*** ⟦Fr *zébu* < ?⟧ a domesticated ox of Asia and Africa

zed (zed) ***n.*** ⟦< Gr *zēta*⟧ [Brit.] the letter Z, z

zeit·geist (tsīt'gīst') ***n.*** ⟦Ger, time spirit⟧ the trend of thought and feeling in a period

Zen (zen) ***n.*** ⟦Jpn ult. < Sans *dhyāna*, thinking⟧ a variety of Buddhism in which enlightenment is sought through introspection and intuition

ze·nith (zē'nith) ***n.*** ⟦ult. < L *semita*, path⟧ **1** the point in the sky directly overhead **2** the highest point

zeph·yr (zef'ər) ***n.*** ⟦< Gr *zephyros*⟧ a breeze

zep·pe·lin (zep'ə lin, zep'lin) ***n.*** ⟦after Count F. von *Zeppelin* (1838-1917), its Ger designer⟧ [*often* **Z-**] a type of rigid airship designed around 1900

ze·ro (zir'ō, zē'rō) ***n.***, *pl.* **-ros** or **-roes** ⟦< Ar *ṣifr*, cipher⟧ **1** the symbol 0, representing the absence of any quantity or magnitude; cipher; naught **2** the point, marked 0, from which quantities are reckoned on a graduated scale **3** nothing **4** the lowest point **—*adj.*** of or at zero —**zero in on** to concentrate attention on; focus on

zero hour **1** the time set for beginning an attack, etc. **2** any crucial moment

zero (population) growth a condition of equilibrium in a given population, in which the birthrate equals the death rate

ze'ro-sum' (-sum') ***adj.*** of or being a situation in which a gain for one must result in a loss for another or others

zest (zest) ***n.*** ⟦Fr *zeste*, orange peel⟧ **1** a thin piece of orange or lemon peel used as flavoring **2** stimulating quality **3** keen enjoyment [*a zest for life*] —**zest'ful** ***adj.***

ze·ta (zāt'ə) ***n.*** the sixth letter of the Greek alphabet (Z, ζ)

Zeus (zo͞os, zyo͞os) ***n.*** *Gr. Myth.* the chief deity

zig·gu·rat (zig'o͝o rat') ***n.*** ⟦< Assyrian *ziqqurratu*⟧ an ancient Assyrian or Babylonian temple tower in the form of a terraced pyramid

zig·zag (zig'zag') ***n.*** ⟦Fr⟧ **1** a series of short, sharp angles in alternate directions **2** a design, path, etc. in this form —*adj.* having the form of a zigzag —*adv.* in a zigzag course —*vt.*, *vi.* **-zagged′**, **-zag′ging** to form or move in a zigzag

zilch (zilch) *n.* ⟦nonsense syllable⟧ [Slang] nothing; zero

zil·lion (zil′yən) *n.* ⟦< MILLION⟧ [Inf.] a very large, indefinite number

Zim·ba·bwe (zim bäb′wā′) country in S Africa, north of South Africa: 150,872 sq. mi.; pop. 10,402,000

zinc (ziŋk) *n.* ⟦Ger *zink*⟧ a bluish-white, metallic chemical element, used in alloys, as a protective coating for iron, etc.

zinc oxide a white powder used in making rubber articles, cosmetics, ointments, etc.

zin·fan·del (zin′fən del′) *n.* ⟦< ?⟧ a dry red wine made chiefly in California

zing (ziŋ) *n.* ⟦echoic⟧ [Slang] **1** a shrill, high-pitched sound, as of something moving fast **2** zest, vigor, etc.

zing′er *n.* [Slang] **1** a clever, witty remark **2** a sharp, usually critical remark

zin·ni·a (zin′ē ə, zin′yə) *n.* ⟦after J. G. *Zinn* (1727-59), Ger botanist⟧ a plant having colorful composite flowers

Zi·on[1] (zī′ən) *n.* ⟦< fol.⟧ **1** the Jewish people **2** heaven

Zi·on[2] (zī′ən) **1** a hill in Jerusalem, site of Solomon's Temple **2** Jerusalem **3** Israel

Zi′on·ism′ *n.* a movement formerly for reestablishing, now for supporting, the state of Israel —**Zi′on·ist** *n.*, *adj.*

zip (zip) *n.* ⟦echoic⟧ **1** a short, sharp hissing or whizzing sound **2** [Inf.] energy; vigor —*vi.* **zipped**, **zip′ping 1** to make, or move with, a zip **2** [Inf.] to move with speed —*vt.* to fasten with a zipper

ZIP Code (zip) ⟦*Z*(*one*) *I*(*mprovement*) *P*(*lan*)⟧ *trademark for* a system of code numbers assigned by the postal service: each code designates a delivery area —[*usually* **zip c-**] such a code number, containing five or nine digits

zip·per (zip′ər) *n.* a device used to fasten and unfasten two edges of material, as on clothing: it consists of two rows of interlocking tabs worked by a sliding part

zip′py *adj.* **-pi·er**, **-pi·est** [Inf.] full of energy; brisk

zir·con (zur′kän′) *n.* ⟦ult. < Pers *zar*, gold⟧ a crystalline silicate mineral, used as a gem

zir·co·ni·um (zər kō′nē əm) *n.* a ductile, metallic chemical element used in alloys, ceramics, etc.

zit (zit) *n.* [Slang] a pimple, esp. one on the face

zith·er (zith′ər, zith′-) *n.* ⟦< Gr *kithara*, lute⟧ any of various musical instruments with strings stretched across a flat soundboard and plucked, bowed, struck with mallets, etc., as the dulcimer

Zn *Chem. symbol for* zinc

zo·di·ac (zō′dē ak′) *n.* ⟦< Gr *zōdiakos* (*kyklos*), (circle) of animals⟧ **1** an imaginary belt across the sky extending on either side of the apparent path of the sun and divided into twelve equal parts, or signs, named for constellations **2** a diagram representing this —**zo·di′a·cal** (-dī′ə kəl) *adj.*

zom·bie (zäm′bē) *n.* ⟦of Afr orig.⟧ **1** in folklore, an animated corpse **2** [Slang] a person who is listless, machine-like, etc. Also **zom′bi**

zone (zōn) *n.* ⟦Fr < Gr *zōnē*⟧ **1** an encircling band, stripe, etc. **2** any of the five great latitudinal divisions of the earth's surface: see TORRID ZONE, TEMPERATE ZONE, and FRIGID ZONE **3** any area with reference to a specified use or restriction [a canal *zone*, war *zone*] —*vt.* **zoned**, **zon′ing** to mark off into zones —**in the** (or **a**) **zone** [Inf.] in a state producing high achievement, seemingly beyond explanation —**zon′al** *adj.*

zonked (zôŋkt, zäŋkt) *adj.* [Slang] **1** highly intoxicated or under the influence of a drug **2** exhausted

zoo (zo͞o) *n.* ⟦< *zoo*(*logical garden*)⟧ **1** a place where wild animals are kept for public showing **2** [Slang] a place of confusion, disorder, etc.

zoo- ⟦< Gr *zōion*, animal⟧ *combining form* animal(s) [*zoology*]

zo·ol·o·gy (zō äl′ə jē) *n.* ⟦ModL *zoologia*: see prec. & -LOGY⟧ the science that deals with animals and animal life —**zo′o·log′i·cal** (-ə läj′i kəl) *adj.* —**zo·ol′o·gist** *n.*

zoom (zo͞om) *vi.* ⟦echoic⟧ **1** to make a loud, low-pitched, buzzing sound **2** to climb in an airplane suddenly and sharply **3** to move speedily upward or forward **4** to focus with a zoom lens —*vt.* to cause to zoom —*n.* a zooming

zoom lens a system of lenses, as in a film or TV camera, that can be rapidly adjusted for close-up or distant shots while keeping the image in focus

zo·o·phyte (zō′ə fīt′) *n.* ⟦ult. < Gr *zōion*, an animal + *phyton*, a plant⟧ any animal, as a coral or sponge, that looks and grows somewhat like a plant —**zo′o·phyt′ic** (-fit′ik) *adj.*

Zo·ro·as·ter (zō′rō as′tər) *c.* 6th or 7th c. B.C.; Pers. founder of Zoroastrianism

Zo·ro·as·tri·an·ism (zō′rō as′trē ən iz′əm) *n.* the religion of the ancient Persians before Islam

Zr *Chem. symbol for* zirconium

zuc·chi·ni (zo͞o kē′nē) *n.*, *pl.* **-ni** or **-nis** ⟦It⟧ a summer squash that looks like a cucumber

Zu·lu (zo͞o′lo͞o) *n.* **1** *pl.* **-lus** or **-lu** a member of a people living in South Africa **2** the language of this people —*adj.* of the Zulus or their language, etc.

Zu·ni (zo͞o′nē) *n.* **1** *pl.* **-nis** or **-ni** a member of a pueblo-dwelling North American Indian people of W New Mexico **2** the language of this people Also, formerly, **Zu·ñi** (zo͞on′yē)

Zur·ich (zoor′ik) city in N Switzerland: pop. 353,000

zwie·back (swē′bak′, swī′-) *n.* ⟦Ger < *zwie-*, twice + *backen*, to bake⟧ a kind of biscuit that is sliced and toasted after baking

zy·de·co (zī′də kō′) ***n.*** ⟦< ?⟧ a heavily syncopated dance music of S Louisiana, containing elements of blues, white Cajun music, etc.

zy·gote (zī′gōt′) ***n.*** ⟦< Gr *zygon,* a yoke⟧ a cell formed by the union of male and female gametes

zymo- ⟦< Gr *zymē*, a leaven⟧ *combining form* fermentation: also **zym-**

zy·mur·gy (zī′mər jē) ***n.*** ⟦prec. + -URGY⟧ the chemistry of fermentation, as applied in brewing, etc.

GHTS AND MEASURES

near

inches	=	1 foot
3 feet	=	1 yard
5.5 yards	=	1 rod
40 rods	=	1 furlong
8 furlongs	=	1 mile

Liquid

16 ounces	=	1 pint
2 pints	=	1 quart
4 quarts	=	1 gallon
31.5 gallons	=	1 barrel
2 barrels	=	1 hogshead

Metric Equivalents

1 inch	=	2.5400 centimeters
1 foot	=	0.3048 meter
1 yard	=	0.9144 meter
1 mile	=	1.6093 kilometers
1 centimeter	=	0.3937 inch
1 meter	=	39.3701 inches
1 kilometer	=	0.6214 mile
1 quart (dry)	=	1.1012 liters
1 quart (liquid)	=	0.9464 liter
1 gallon	=	3.7854 liters
1 liter	=	0.9081 dry quart
1 liter	=	1.0567 liquid quarts

Square

144 sq. inches	=	1 sq. foot
9 sq. feet	=	1 sq. yard
30.25 sq. yards	=	1 sq. rod
160 sq. rods	=	1 acre
640 acres	=	1 sq. mile

Circular

60 seconds	=	1 minute
60 minutes	=	1 degree
360 degrees	=	1 circle

Metric Equivalents

1 sq. inch	=	6.4516 sq. centimeters
1 sq. foot	=	929.0304 sq. centimeters
1 sq. mile	=	2.590 sq. kilometers
1 sq. centimeter	=	0.155 sq. inch
1 sq. meter	=	1.196 sq. yards
1 sq. kilometer	=	0.3861 sq. mile

Cubic

1,728 cu. inches	=	1 cu. foot
27 cu. feet	=	1 cu. yard
128 cu. feet	=	1 cord (wood)

Dry

2 pints	=	1 quart
8 quarts	=	1 peck
4 pecks	=	1 bushel

Metric Equivalents

1 cu. inch	=	16.3871 cu. centimeters
1 cu. inch	=	16.3871 milliliters
1 cu. foot	=	0.0283 cu. meter
1 cu. foot	=	28.3169 liters
1 cu. meter	=	35.3147 cu. feet
1 ounce (avdp.)	=	28.3495 grams
1 pound	=	0.4536 kilogram
1 gram	=	0.0353 ounce
1 kilogram	=	2.2046 pounds
1 ton (2,000 pounds)	=	907.1847 kilograms

Temperature Conversion Formulas

$$°F = 32 + (1.8 \times °C)$$

$$°C = \frac{°F - 32}{1.8}$$

THE INTERNATIONAL SYSTEM OF UNITS (SI)

Any prefix can be combined with any unit; e.g. milli- + ampere = milliampere (m + A = mA); kilo- + gram = kilogram (k + g = kg); mega- + hertz = megahertz (M + Hz = MHz).

SI base units and prefixes

unit	symbol	quantity
ampere	A	electric current
candela	cd	luminous intensity
kelvin	K	thermodynamic temperature
kilogram	kg	mass
meter	m	length
mole	mol	amount of substance
second	s	time

prefix	symbol	multiplier*
yotta-	Y	$\times 10^{24}$
zetta-	Z	$\times 10^{21}$
exa-	E	$\times 10^{18}$
peta-	P	$\times 10^{15}$
tera-	T	$\times 10^{12}$
giga-	G	$\times 10^{9}$
mega-	M	$\times 10^{6}$
kilo-	k	$\times 10^{3}$
hecto-	h	$\times 10^{2}$
deka-; deca-	da	$\times 10$
deci-	d	$\times 10^{-1}$
centi-	c	$\times 10^{-2}$
milli-	m	$\times 10^{-3}$
micro-	µ	$\times 10^{-6}$
nano-	n	$\times 10^{-9}$
pico-	p	$\times 10^{-12}$
femto-	f	$\times 10^{-15}$
atto-	a	$\times 10^{-18}$
zepto-	z	$\times 10^{-21}$
yocto-	y	$\times 10^{-24}$

* $10^2 = 10 \times 10 = 100$; $10^3 = 10 \times 10 \times 10 = 1{,}000$; $10^{-1} = 1/10^1 = 0.1$; $10^{-2} = 1/10^2 = 0.01$
So, 2 km = 2×10^3 meters = 2,000 meters; 2 mm = 2×10^{-3} meter = 0.002 meter.

Common SI derived units with special names

name	symbol	quantity
coulomb	C	electric charge
degree Celsius	°C	temperature (0°C = 273.16 K)
hertz	Hz	frequency
joule	J	energy; work
newton	N	force
ohm	Ω	electric resistance
pascal	Pa	pressure; stress
volt	V	electric potential; EMF
watt	W	power

Other common units used with the SI

name	symbol	quantity
hectare	ha	area (=10,000 m^2 or 2.471 acres)
knot	kn; kt	speed (navigation) (= 1 NM per hour or 1.1508 mph)
liter	l; L	volume; capacity (= 1,000 cm^3)
metric ton	t	mass (= 1,000 kg)
nautical mile (U.S.)	NM	distance (navigation) (= 1.1508 statute miles)
standard atmosphere	atm	atmospheric pressure (= 101,325 Pa)

PRONUNCIATION KEY

Vowel Sounds

Symbol	*Key Words*
a	at, cap, parrot
ā	ape, play, sail
ä	cot, father, heart
e	ten, wealth, merry
ē	even, feet, money
i	is, stick, mirror
ī	ice, high, sky
ō	go, open, tone
ô	all, law, horn
oo	could, look, pull
yoo	cure, furious
o͞o	boot, crew, tune
yo͞o	cute, few, use
oi	boy, oil, royal
ou	cow, out, sour
u	mud, ton, blood, trouble
ʉ	her, sir, word
ə	ago, agent, collect, focus
’l	cattle, paddle
’n	sudden, sweeten

Consonant Sounds

Symbol	*Key Words*
b	bed, table, rob
d	dog, middle, sad
f	for, phone, cough
g	get, wiggle, dog
h	hat, hope, ahead
hw	which, white
j	joy, badge, agent
k	kill, cat, quiet
l	let, yellow, ball
m	meet, number, time
n	net, candle, ton
p	put, sample, escape
r	red, wrong, born
s	sit, castle, office
t	top, letter, cat
v	voice, every, love
w	wet, always, quart
y	yes, canyon, onion
z	zoo, misery, rise
ch	chew, nature, punch
sh	shell, machine, bush
th	thin, nothing, truth
th	then, other, bathe
zh	beige, measure, seizure
ŋ	ring, anger, drink

Symbols for foreign sounds are explained in the Guide to Pronunciation, p. ix.